THE COMPLETE WORKS
OF
WILLIAM SHAKESPEARE

THE COMPLETE WORKS
OF
WILLIAM SHAKESPEARE

EDITED BY ARTHUR HENRY BULLEN

WITH PORTRAIT AND ILLUSTRATIONS
BY SIR JOHN GILBERT, R.A.

This edition first published in 2005 by
CRW Publishing Limited, 69 Gloucester Crescent, London, NW1 7EG

ISBN 1 904633 92 7

Text and arrangement of this edition © CRW Publishing Limited, 2005

2 4 6 8 10 9 7 5 3 1

Designed and typeset in Scala Sans and Scala Serif by Bookcraft Limited,
Stroud, Gloucestershire, UK

Printed and bound in China by Imago

CONTENTS

William Shakespeare by John Aubrey	vi
Shakespeare's Life	vi
Select Bibliography	viii
Sir John Gilbert, Illustrator & Painter	viii
The Shakespeare Head Press	viii
Dedications from the First Folio	ix

THE PLAYS

The First Part of King Henry The Sixth (1591–2)	1
The Second Part of King Henry The Sixth (1590–1)	17
The Third Part of King Henry The Sixth (1590–1)	35
King Richard The Third (1592–3)	53
Titus Andronicus (1593–4)	75
The Comedy of Errors (1592–3)	91
The Two Gentlemen of Verona (1594–5)	105
Love's Labour's Lost (1594–5)	121
Romeo and Juliet (1594–5)	139
A Midsummer Night's Dream (1595–6)	161
King John (1596–7)	177
The Taming of The Shrew (1593–4)	193
King Richard The Second (1595–6)	211
The Merchant of Venice (1596–7)	227
The First Part of King Henry The Fourth (1597–8)	243
The Second Part of King Henry The Fourth (1597–8)	263
King Henry The Fifth (1598–9)	285
Much Ado About Nothing (1598–9)	303
The Merry Wives of Windsor (1600–1)	321
Julius Cæsar (1599–1600)	339
As You Like It (1599–1600)	357
Twelfth Night; or, What You Will (1599–1600)	375
Hamlet, Prince of Denmark (1600–1)	393
Troilus and Cressida (1601–2)	419
All's Well That Ends Well (1602–3)	441
Measure for Measure (1604–5)	459
Othello, The Moor of Venice (1604–5)	477
Macbeth (1605–6)	499
King Lear (1605–6)	515
Antony and Cleopatra (1606–7)	537
Coriolanus (1606–7)	559
Timon of Athens (1606–8)	581
Pericles, Prince of Tyre (1608–9)	597
Cymbeline (1609–10)	613
The Winter's Tale (1610–11)	635
The Tempest (1611–12)	655
King Henry The Eighth (1612–13)	669

POEMS AND SONNETS

Venus and Adonis (1593)	689
Lucrece (1594)	695
Sonnets (1595–)	704
A Lover's Complaint	714
The Passionate Pilgrim	716
Sonnets to Sundry Notes of Music	718
The Phœnix and Turtle (1601)	719
Scene from Sir Thomas More (1596)	719
Glossary	721

In this volume the Plays are arranged in the chronological order of their composition. Naturally, no claim to finality is made in a subject so beset with difficulties, but the sequence may be taken as fairly representing the general results of recent research. The time-honoured division into Comedies, Histories and Tragedies, dating from the First Folio and since universally followed, has been abandoned, in the belief that there were room and need for an edition that should enable readers to approach the body of the plays, not as a static monument of achievement, but as a vital and growing organism revealing the evolution of the poet's personality and genius. The text used for this edition is that prepared by the late Arthur Henry Bullen for the Stratford Town Edition, to print which he founded the Shakespeare Head Press in 1904.

WILLIAM SHAKESPEARE
1564–1616

by John Aubrey (1626–97)

Mr William Shakespeare was born at Stratford upon Avon in the county of Warwick. His father was a butcher, and I have been told heretofore by some of the neighbours, that when he was a boy he exercised his father's trade, but when he killed a calf he would do it in a high style, and make a speech. There was at that time another butcher's son in this town that was held not at all inferior to him for a natural wit, his acquaintance and coaetanean [contemporary], but he died young.

This William being inclined naturally to poetry and acting, came to London, I guess, about 18; and was an actor at one of the playhouses, and did act exceedingly well (now B. Jonson was never a good actor, but an excellent instructor).

He began early to make essays at dramatic poetry, which at that time was very low; and his plays took well. He was a handsome, well-shaped man: very good company, and of a very ready and pleasant smooth wit.

The humour of the constable in *Midsummer Night's Dream*, he happened to take at Grendon in Bucks—I think it was midsummer night that he happened to lie there—which is on the road from London to Stratford, and there was living that constable about 1642, when I first came to Oxford: Mr Josias Howe is of that parish, and knew him. Ben Jonson and he did gather humours of men daily wherever they came. One time as he was at the tavern at Stratford upon Avon, one Combes, an old rich usurer, was to be buried, he makes there this extemporary epitaph,

> Ten in the hundred the Devil allows,
> But Combes will have twelve, he swears and vows:
> If any one asks who lies in the tomb,
> 'Hoh!' quoth the Devil, ''tis my John o Combe.'

He was wont to go to his native country once a year. I think I have been told that he left £2 or 300 per annum there and thereabout to a sister.

I have heard Sir William Davenant and Mr Thomas Shadwell (who is counted the best comedian writer of comedies we have now) say that he had a most prodigious wit, and did admire his natural parts beyond all other dramatical writers. He was wont to say (B. Jonson's *Underwoods*) that he 'never blotted out a line in his life'; said Ben Jonson, 'I wish he had blotted out a thousand.'

His comedies will remain wit as long as the English tongue is understood, for that he handles *mores homimum* [the ways of men]. Now our present writers reflect so much upon particular persons and coxcombities, that twenty years hence they will not be understood.

Though, as Ben Jonson says of him, that he had but little Latin and less Greek, he understood Latin pretty well, for he had been in his younger years a schoolmaster in the country.

This account of William Shakespeare's life was written by John Aubrey (1626–97), an English antiquarian, about 65 years after the poet's death in his collection of short biographies entitled Brief Lives *in which he chronicled the great and the good of the previous century. He used information furnished by William Beeston, son of Christopher Beeston, who was one of Shakespeare's theatrical colleagues.*

For more detailed biographies, see the Select Bibliography.

SHAKESPEARE'S LIFE

PLAYER AND PLAYWRIGHT

It has generally been supposed that Shakespeare threw in his lot with one or other of the companies which at that period were touring the country, sometimes taking in Stratford on their way. They enjoyed the real or nominal patronage of the noblemen, gentlemen, or towns whose names they bore; for as their 'servants' the players were made secure from the penalties of vagabondage to which, without such protection, their 'masterless' condition might have made them liable, and also from the growing hostility of the Puritans to the drama. There is, however, no evidence to show what company, if any, young Shakespeare joined. The Earl of Leicester's men, who had visited Stratford in 1572–3, were there again in 1576–7; the year before, the boy's imagination may have been stirred by report of sight of the great pageant prepared for the Queen's visit to Kenilworth in July. Within the years 1586–8 they visited Stratford again and also Coventry in the same county. The Queen's men were at Coventry in 1585–6 and at Stratford the next year. A very great number of lesser companies were also active at this period, many of them kept for their own amusement by private gentlemen of position.[1] If reliance could be put on the story of his taking charge of horses at the playhouse door, it would have been either the Theatre or the Curtain, both of them in Shoreditch, since these were the only London theatres to be reached on horseback. James Burbage, who became a Queen's man in 1583, was the builder and chief owner of the Theatre, and had an interest also in the Curtain. Both playhouses were used on occasion by various companies. There is no record connecting Shakespeare's name with any of them, nor indeed any allusion to him, whether as player or playwright, earlier than the year 1592.

In that year died Robert Greene, poet and playwright, leaving for publication his *Groats-worth of Witte, bought with a Million of Repentance*, in which, as he puts it, 'ere I die I will by my repentaunce indevour to do all men good.' In it he warned 'those Gentlemen his Quondam acquaintance, that spend their wits in making plaies' to 'looke backe with sorrow on your time past.' Especially he warned them against the players who performed their plays—'those Puppets that spake from our mouths, those Anticks garnisht in our colours':

> Yes trust them not: for there is an upstart Crow, beautified with our feathers, that with his *Tygers hart wrapt in a Players hyde*, supposes he is as well able to bombast out a blanke verse as the best of you: and beeing an absolute *Johannes fac totum*, is in his owne conceit the onely Shake-scene in a countrey. O that I might intreat your rare wits to be imploied in more profitable courses: & let those Apes imitate your past excellence, and never more acquaint them with your admired inventions.

All this, with its parody of the line in 3 *Henry VI*, I. iv, in which Richard Duke of York apostrophizes Queen Margaret: 'O tiger's heart, wrapt in a woman's hide,' is Greene's legacy of bitter resentment against the companies that have forsaken him 'to whome they all have beene beholding,' and are likely to forsake his fellow-playwrights too; for they now have in their own body a Shake-scene to write their plays.

Greene's Groats-worth had been prepared for the press by Henry Chettle, who in his own *Kind-Harts Dreame*, published in 1592, made apologetic allusion to his part in editing Greene's book, and for the attack on 'his Quondam acquaintance,' 'which [says Chettle] is offensively by one or two of them taken; ... With neither of them that take offence was I acquainted, and with one of them I care not if I never be.' But to the other, 'whome ... I did not so much spare, as since I wish I had,' he pays this tribute:

> my selfe have seene his demeanor no lesse civill than he exelent in the qualitie he professes: Besides, divers of worship have reported his uprightnes of dealing, which argues his honesty, and his facetious grace in writing, that aprooves his Art.

It is generally accepted that Shakespeare was the actor playwright whom Greene attacked, and that Chettle's graceful apology and noble tribute were also made to him. If so, he was writing plays or at any rate refurbishing the dramatic work of other men—it is uncertain how much of 3 *Henry VI* was written by him—at least as early as 1592. That play, it is believed, was acted in 1591, by what company is not known.

If Shakespeare was ever one of Leicester's men, he may have been among those who, after the earl's death in 1588, went to Lord Strange's company, known successively down to 1603 as the Earl of Derby's, the Lord Hunsdon's[2] and the Lord Chamberlain's. Shakespeare was in that company at Christmas, 1594—we do not know how long before—for in the accounts of the Treasurer of the Chamber covering that date we have the earliest record of him as an actor:

> To William Kempe, William Shakespeare and Richarde Burbage, servauntes to the Lord

---

1 For instance, Alexander Hoghton, of Lea in Lancashire, in his will, proved 12th September, 1581, bids his reversionary legatee, Sir Thomas Hesketh, 'to be ffrendlye unto ffoke Gyllome and Willm Shakeshafte now dwelling with me': from the context it is clear that they are players. He leaves annuities to them and to others of his 'servants', some thirty in all. *Cf.* O. Baker, *In Shakespeare's Warwickshire*, pp. 297–302, who points out that the name of the poet's grandfather, Richard Shakespeare of

Snitterfield, is written 'Shakeschafte' in certain records. He suggests that the 'Shakeshafte' of Hoghton's will may have been the poet, who perhaps with his annuity in his pocket went back to Stratford to marry Anne Hathaway. The text of Hoghton's will is printed in the second portion of *Lancashire and Cheshire Wills*, edited by G.J. Piccope (Chetham Society, LI). Besides Gyllome and Shakeshafte three other names known in Stratford or Warwickshire—Dugdale, Cottham and Banester—are

found among the 'pensioned servants', but their particular owners have not been traced in the Stratford Register. There are records of some four-score companies, greater or less, which were performing in the years 1570–90. See J.T. Lawrence, *English Dramatic Companies*.

2 First of George Carey, 1st Lord Hunsdon, and after his death in 1596 of Henry Carey, 2nd Lord, who became Lord Chamberlain in 1597.

Chamberleyne, upon the Councelle's warrant dated at Whitehall xv^to Marcij 1594, for twoe severall comedies or enterludes shewed by them before her majestie in Christmas tyme laste paste viz upon St. Stephen's daye and Innocentes daye xiij^li vj^s viij^d, and by waye of her majesties Rewarde vj^li xiij^s, iiij^d, in all, xx^li.3

By that date, therefore, Shakespeare was ranked as one of the three leading men in the Chamberlain's company. In the same year there appeared *The First part of the Contention betwixt the two famous Houses of Yorke and Lancaster, with the death of the good Duke Humphrey ...* , which was reprinted in the following year with the additional note that it 'was sundrie times acted by the ... Earle of Pembrooke his servants.' This is an imperfect and probably surreptitious version of the plays printed in the Folio of 1623 as the *Second* and *Third Parts of King Henry VI*, from the latter of which Greene parodied the line about the 'Tygers hart'. However much it may owe to other hands than Shakespeare's, the quarto of 1594 was the first appearance in print of any of the plays which now form the Shakespeare canon.

THE DATES OF THE PLAYS

External evidence bearing within very wide limits on the periods at which the plays were written is found for some of them in the mention made by contemporary authors and especially by Francis Meres, in allusions made in the plays to dated events or to contemporary writers, in the records of performances at Court or elsewhere, and—for those printed in quarto—in the dates of their registration by the Stationers' Company or of their printing. All these with the internal evidence of language, imagery, metre, line-endings, rhyme, and what-not that scholars have sedulously gathered, have helped to some measure of agreement as to their order and dates.4

Besides their chronology, many of the plays present problems of the authorship of particular passages and even of large parts of the received text. We know from *Henslowe's Diary* that two, three, or even four playwrights sometimes joined in the writing of a single play. No less than five different hands have been recognized in the manuscript play *Sir Thomas More*,5 and high authorities on Elizabethan handwriting, supported on literary grounds by that great scholar, the late R.W. Chambers, believe one of them to be Shakespeare's. The book of a play delivered to a company of players would invariably need considerable alteration before it could be presented on the stage, and some adaptation would be needed for each new production. It is not rash to assume that in Shakespeare's company that task would have been his, and that his career as a playwright began with the fitting of other men's work to the varying capacity and limitations of the available cast in strength and talent. Most scholars suspect that large portions at least of the trilogy of *King Henry VI*, generally regarded as the earliest of the plays that bear Shakespeare's name, were not his work. It has been supposed that in many more of the plays, especially those of early date, there was either collaboration or adaptation.

THE POEMS

Shakespeare's literary and dramatic career through the rest of Elizabeth's reign is to be traced chiefly in the output of his poems and plays and in the recorded movements and performances of the Chamberlain's men. *Venus and Adonis* and *The Rape of Lucrece*, printed under his own name in the years 1593 and 1594, respectively, were the first of his works to see the light. The dedication of the *Venus*, 'the first heir of my invention', to the Earl of Southampton is apologetic and self-depreciatory, showing some misgiving as to the favour which it might receive.6 That of *Lucrece* to the same nobleman shows, on the other hand, the poet's sense of security in Southampton's present and continued patronage.7

The two poems immediately won wide recognition for the author. Four months after the registration of *Lucrece* allusion is made to it in some prefatory verses to a poetic morality written by Henry Willoughby, entitled *Willobie His Avisa*, which was registered in September of that same year, 1594:

> Yet Tarquyne pluckt his glistering grape,
> And Shake-speare, paints poore Lucrece rape.

This is the earliest direct mention of Shakespeare found in English literature. Of even greater—indeed intriguing—interest to the biographer are the account given in the book of one W.S. and the part allotted to him in the poem. *Willobie His Avisa* contains the author's story, real or fictitious, of his passionate infatuation for the beautiful wife of a country inn-keeper, a woman of unassailable virtue. The love-sick swain consults W.S.:

> On his advise I will depend,
> Where I shall winne, or be denyde,
>   And looke what counsel he shall give,
>   That will I do, where dye or live.

W.S. assures him cynically:

> She is no Saynt, She is no Nonne,
> I thinke in tyme she may be wonne.

And, with his tongue in his cheek, he proceeds to tell him how.

In a prose interlude Willoughby or his editor describes the intensity of H.W.'s passion and explains how he came to betray

> the secresy of his disease unto his familiar frend W.S. who not long before had tryed the curtesy of the like passion, and was now newly recovered of the like infection; yet finding his frend let bloud in the same vaine, he took pleasure for a tyme to see him bleed, and in steed of stopping the issue, he inlargeth the wound, with the sharpe rasor of a willing conceit, perswading him that he thought it a matter very easy to be compassed, & no doubt with payne, diligence & some cost in time to be obtayned. Thus this miserable comforter comforting his frend with an impossibilitie, eyther for that he now would secretly laugh at his frends folly, that had given occasion not long before unto others to laugh at his owne, or because he would see whether an other could play his part better then himselfe, & in vewing a far off the course of this loving Comedy, he determined to see whether it would sort to a happier end for this new actor, then it did for the old player.

Henry Willoughby was the son of Henry Willoughby, esquire, of West Knoyle, Wilts, and matriculated from St. John's College, Oxford, in 1591 at the age of sixteen. The prefatory verses, in which is found the allusion to Shakespeare and his *Lucrece*, are signed *Vigilantius Dormitanus*, which two names the detective ingenuity of Dr. Leslie Hotson finds to stand punningly for Edward *Napper*, of Holywell, Oxford, and Robert *Wake*man, the son of a Worcestershire parson. Both Napper and Wakeman had entered Balliol in 1590, the one aged twelve, the other fourteen. Here we have three young Oxford versifiers, in whose book there are found mention of Shakespeare and of his recent poem, and an account of one W.S., an 'old player', who, having become freed from amours of his own, is thought competent to give counsel to a novice in the *ars amandi*.

That W.S. is William Shakespeare received startling confirmation a few years ago when Professor Hotson proved that Henry Willoughby was allied by marriage and friendship with 'Thomas Russell esquire', whom in 1616 Shakespeare made the overseer of his will, leaving him a legacy of five pounds. He was the second son of Sir Thomas Russell of Strensham, a Worcestershire knight of great possessions, who also owned property at Alderminister and Broad Campden—places all less than twenty miles from Stratford. He matriculated from The Queen's College, Oxford, in 1588. In 1594, then, we find Shakespeare associated with four young Oxford men whom Hotson shows to be linked through Russell in a chain of relationships, whether of kindred, friendship or testamentary trust, not only with one another, but with the Earls of Southampton and Bedford, Sir Charles Blount, the Berkeleys of Bruton, the Sheldons of Beoley, and many more of rank and standing.8

Venus and Adonis was reprinted some ten times within the eight years that followed its publication, and there were three new editions of *Lucrece* before the end of the century. Trading on Shakespeare's well-established reputation, William Jaggard published *The Passionate Pilgrim*9 in 1599 under Shakespeare's name; but it is doubtful whether any of the poems in the book were written by him except the two first, which are versions of the Sonnets 139 and 145, and those numbered 3, 5, and 7, being the poetical love-letters written by Berowne, Longaville and Dumaine in *Love's Labour's Lost*.10 The lovely lines on *The Phœnix and Turtle* were first printed in 1601 over Shakespeare's name as one of 'Divers Poeticall Essaies' appended to Robert Chester's *Love's Martyr*. The other 'Essaies' were written respectively by 'Ignoto', John Marston, George Chapman and Ben Jonson, perhaps as a tribute to Lucy, Countess of Bedford.11

The first mention of the Sonnets, as well as of many of the plays, is found in *Palladis Tamia: Wits Treasury*, printed in 1598. Its author, Francis Meres, rector and schoolmaster at Wing, Rutland, makes comparisons between English writers of his day and some of the classical writers of Greece and Rome:

> As the soule of *Euphorbus* was thought to live in *Pythagoras*: so the sweete wittie soule of *Ovid* lives in mellifluous & hony-tongued *Shakespeare*, witnes his *Venus and Adonis*, his *Lucrece*, his sugred Sonnets among his private friends, & c.

The Sonnets were not printed till 1609, and Meres's allusion may refer only to some of them. Cautious and conservative Shakespearean scholars incline to the period 1593–6 as that in which most of them were written. Some, however, believe Sonnet 107 to allude to the death of Elizabeth and the accession of James in 1603. The dedication by Thomas Thorpe, the stationer for whom they were printed, to their 'Onlie Begetter ... Mr. W.H.' has provoked many volumes of futile conjecture about the identity of Mr. W.H. and about Thorpe's precise meaning. A host of commentators have sought in these Sonnets revelations of Shakespeare's life and character, losing sight the while of their rich poetical content. But one would indeed like to know the identity of the 'lovely boy', to whom most of them seem to be addressed, and whose reluctance to marry is the theme of the first seventeen. Most recent scholars believe him to be Southampton rather than William Herbert, Earl of Pembroke, at one time thought to be the 'Mr. W.H.' of the dedication. It is safer to believe that evidence by which he may be identified is still wanting, so also for the identity of the poet or poets whose rivalry in affection for the youth is indicated in Sonnets 82–87. Spenser, Daniel, Drayton and George Chapman are some of those who have been suggested. *A Lover's Complaint* was printed in the same quarto as the Sonnets.

---

3 R.O., Pipe Office Declared Accounts, in Gray, *Shakespeare's Marriage*, p. 155.
4 Those shown in the table of contents in the present edition are suggested by Sir Edmund Chambers in his *William Shakespeare* after an exhaustive study of the evidence.

5 See p. 1252.
6 See p. 1195.
7 See p. 1207.
8 Leslie Hotson, *I, William Shakespeare, do appoint Thomas Russell, esquire ...* (1937), pp. 33–70.

9 See p. 1247.
10 *Love's Labour's Lost*, IV. ii. 110–23, iii. 58–71, 99–118.
11 See B.H. Newdigate, *The Phœnix and Turtle* (1937), where the 'Essaies' are printed in full.

SELECT BIBLIOGRAPHY

There are many guides to the individual plays and to the Sonnets. Perhaps the best starting point for these is the *Cambridge Student Guides* published by the Cambridge University Press.

Bibliographies

Berman, R.A., *A Reader's Guide to Shakespeare's Plays*, 1965, revised 1973.
Manaway, J.G. and Roberts, J.A., *A Select Bibliography of Shakespeare*, 1975.
Wells, S., *Shakespeare: Select Bibliographical Guides*, 1973.

Biographies

Bentley, G.E., *Shakespeare: A Biographical Handbook*, 1961.
Chambers, E.K., *William Shakespeare*, 1930.
Fraser, R., *Young Shakespeare*, 1988.

Fraser, R., *Shakespeare: The Later Years*, 1993.
Honan, P., *Shakespeare: A Life*, 1999.
Honigman, E.A.J., *Shakespeare: The Lost Years*, 1985.
Quennell, P., *Shakespeare: A Biography*, 1963.
Shoenbaum, S., *A Documentary Life*, 1975.

General Introductions

Dobson, M. and Wells, S., *The Oxford Companion to Shakespeare*, 2001.
Nicoll, A., *Shakespeare: An Introduction*, 1952.
Wells, S., *Shakespeare: A Dramatic Life*, 1994.
Wells, S., *Shakespeare For All Time*, 2003.
Wells, S. and Taylor, G., *Shakespeare: A Textual Companion*, 1988.

Plays

Honigman, E.A.J., *Shakespeare's Seven Tragedies*, 1976.
Hotson, L., *The First Night of Twelfth Night*, 1954.

Knight, G.W., *The Mutual Flame: On Shakespeare's Sonnets and The Phoenix and the Turtle*, 1955.
Lawrence, W.W., *Shakespeare's Problem Comedies*, 1931.
Muir, K., *Shakespeare's Tragic Sequence*, 1972.
Richmond, H.M., *Shakespeare's Political Plays*, 1967.
Tillyard, E.M.W., *Shakespeare's History Plays*, 1944.
Tillyard, E.M.W., *Shakespeare's Last Plays*, 1948.
Tillyard, E.M.W., *Shakespeare's Problem Plays*, 1950.
Wilson, J.D., *What Happens in Hamlet?*, 1935.
Wilson, J.D., *The Fortunes of Falstaff*, 1943.

Stagecraft

Gurr, A., *The Shakespearean Stage*, 1970.
Hotson, L., *Shakespeare's Wooden O*, 1959.
Styan, J.L., *Shakespeare's Stagecraft*, 1967.
Wells, S. and Stanton, S., *The Cambridge Companion to Shakespeare on Stage*, 2002.

SIR JOHN GILBERT, ILLUSTRATOR & PAINTER 1817–97

John Gilbert was born in Blackheath near London, one of six children of George Felix Gilbert, a retired militiaman and a land and estate agent. At sixteen, John was placed in an estate agent's office in Charlotte Row, but it seems that he spent much of his time sketching the colourful spectacle of city life as it unfolded before him. So undistinguished an estate agent was he that after two years Gilbert's parents allowed him to pursue his career as an artist. He failed to enter classes at the Royal Academy, and he was largely self-taught apart from a few lessons from the still-life painter, George Lance.

Gilbert's first exhibited work was a watercolour of *The Arrest of Lord Hastings* at the Society of British Artists. This set the tone for much of his work, which tended to be of an historical or literary nature. He continued to exhibit at the SBA and showed oil paintings at the British Institution—about sixty in all.

He also exhibited at the Royal Academy from 1837 to 1851, when he stopped on the grounds that his works were badly hung. He became closely associated with the Old Watercolour Society, of which he became an associate in 1852 and a full member in 1854. He exhibited nearly 300 works in the Society's gallery, including many depictions of the characters in Don Quixote and Shakespeare. He was elected President in 1871 and knighted in 1872.

He began sending his paintings to the Royal Academy once more in 1867, and was elected an associate RA in 1872 and a full academician in 1876. He continued to paint historical themes, longing for acclaim in this field—he was described as 'the Sir Walter Scott of painting'—but he made a small fortune in book illustration and pictorial journalism. He supplied illustrations to numerous periodicals, including *Punch*, *The London Journal* and, above all, to

The Illustrated London News, to whom he supplied approximately 30,000 illustrations over thirty years.

But it was his association with Shakespeare that earned him his greatest fame. He was engaged by Howard Staunton to illustrate his majestic three-volume edition, published in 1860. Gilbert's 829 designs, most of which are reproduced in this edition, were engraved by the Dalziel brothers; they frequently depict scenes never before illustrated and stand as his best memorial. His main interest was narrative, and this explains his great success as an illustrator. His naturalistic, sketchy and spirited designs sprang from his fertility and quickness of hand. The fact that he could compose and draw directly onto the wood-block—with no preliminary sketches—give his work a spontaneity that is unequalled. He died in Blackheath on 5 October 1897, where he had lived all his life, and his estate was valued at over £230,000.

THE SHAKESPEARE HEAD PRESS

The Shakespeare Head Press, Stratford-upon-Avon, was founded in 1904 by the publisher and Elizabethan scholar Arthur Henry Bullen and his business partner, Frank Sidgwick. Bullen had been inspired by a dream to print and publish an edition of Shakespeare's works in the playwright and poet's native town.

In May 1904, for £30 *per annum*, Bullen and Sidgwick acquired the lease of 21 Chapel Street, Stratford, which was next door but one to the site of New Place, to which William Shakespeare had retired. Here they installed a Crown Broadside Mitre Press, a Double Crown Wharfedale Press (which did the bulk of the printing) and a Demy Albion, which was one of the three once used at the Kelmscott Press by William Morris. They were powered by a two horsepower Crossley, Otto type K gas engine.

Meanwhile, back in London, Bullen started on the

editing and preparation of what he styled The Stratford Town Shakespeare. Planned as a ten-volume set, limited to 1,000 copies on paper and twelve on vellum, the first volume was published in November 1904. Three more volumes were published in 1905, five in 1906 and the final volume in 1907. The handsome quarto volumes were printed in Caslon Old Face type on specially made paper, watermarked with the arms of Shakespeare.

Arthur Waugh of Chapman & Hall was of the opinion that Bullen was 'first and foremost a man; then a man of letters, and last of all a publisher'. This is all too accurate an assessment; Bullen was a hopeless businessman and The Shakespeare Head Press incurred huge losses whilst continuing to publish both modern poetry (W.B. Yeats) and obscure antiquarian

texts. At his death, Bullen's estate consisted of £1.10 cash, sale of his clothes £10, and his library £287. He was buried at Luddington near Stratford, and his grave is inscribed with his name, dates and 'Scholar and gentleman'.

The Press was acquired by the distinguished Oxford bookseller Basil Blackwell, and this saw a revival in the fortunes of the Shakespeare Head Press. Over the next couple of decades beautifully produced editions flowed from the Press, including the works of Defoe, Chaucer, the Brontës and Fielding as well as editions of North's Plutarch, Froissart's Chronicles and Edmund Spencer. In 1934, using the text of The Stratford Town Shakespeare, the Press published *The Works of William Shakespeare Gathered Into One Volume*, and this is the text used in this edition.

DEDICATIONS FROM THE FIRST FOLIO

To the Most Noble and Incomparable Pair
of Brethren,
WILLIAM
EARL OF PEMBROKE, &C., LORD
CHAMBERLAIN TO THE KING'S MOST
EXCELLENT MAJESTY,
AND PHILIP
EARL OF MONTGOMERY, &C.,
GENTLEMAN OF HIS MAJESTY'S BED-
CHAMBER; BOTH KNIGHTS OF THE
MOST NOBLE ORDER OF THE GARTER,
AND OUR SINGULAR GOOD LORDS.

Right Honourable,

Whilst we study to be thankful in our particular for the many favours we have received from your L.L., we are fallen upon the ill fortune, to mingle two the most diverse things that can be, fear and rashness; rashness in the enterprise, and fear of the success. For when we value the places your H.H. sustain, we cannot but know their dignity greater than to descend to the reading of these trifles; and while we name them trifles, we have deprived ourselves of the defence of our dedication. But since your L.L. have been pleased to think these trifles something heretofore, and have prosecuted both them and their author living with so much favour, we hope that (they outliving him, and he not having the fate, common with some, to be executor to his own writings) you will use the like indulgence toward them you have done unto their parent. There is a great difference whether any book choose his patrons, or find them: this hath done both. For so much were your L.L. likings of the several parts when they were acted, as before they were publish'd, the volume ask'd to be yours. We have but collected them, and done an office to the dead, to procure his orphans guardians; without ambition either of self-profit or fame; only to keep the memory of so worthy a friend and fellow alive as was our SHAKESPEARE, by humble offer of his plays to your most noble patronage. Wherein, as we have justly observed no man to come near your L.L. but with a kind of religious address, it hath been the height of our care, who are the presenters, to make the present worthy of your H.H. by the perfection. But there we must also crave our abilities to be consider'd, my Lords. We cannot go beyond our own powers. Country hands reach forth milk, cream, fruits, or what they have; and many nations, we have heard, that had not gums and incense, obtain'd their requests with a leaven'd cake. It was no fault to approach their gods by what means they could: and the most, though meanest, of things are made more precious when they are dedicated to temples. In that name, therefore, we most humbly consecrate to your H.H. these remains of your servant SHAKESPEARE, that what delight is in them may be ever your L.L., the reputation his, and the faults ours, if any be committed by a pair so careful to show their gratitude both to the living and the dead as is

Your Lordships' most bounden,
JOHN HEMINGE, HENRY CONDELL

TO THE GREAT VARIETY OF READERS

From the most able to him that can but spell: there you are number'd. We had rather you were weigh'd: especially when the fate of all books depends upon your capacities; and not of your heads alone, but of your purses. Well, it is now public; and you will stand for your privileges, we know,—to read and censure. Do so, but buy it first. That doth best commend a book, the stationer says. Then how odd soever your brains be or your wisdoms, make your license the same, and spare not. Judge your six-pen'orth, your shillings-worth, your five-shillings-worth at a time, or higher, so you rise to the just rates, and welcome. But, whatever you do, buy. Censure will not drive a trade, or make the jack go. And though you be a magistrate of wit, and sit on the stage at *Black-friars* or the *Cock-pit*, to arraign plays daily, know, these plays have had their trial already, and stood out all appeals, and do now come forth quitted rather by a decree of court than any purchased letters of commendation.

It had been a thing, we confess, worthy to have been wish'd, that the author himself had lived to have set forth and overseen his own writings. But, since it hath been ordain'd otherwise, and he by death departed from that right, we pray you do not envy his friends the office of their care and pain, to have collected and publish'd them; and so to have publish'd them as where before you were abused with divers stolen and surreptitious copies, maim'd and deform'd by the frauds and stealths of injurious impostors, that exposed them, even those are now offer'd to your view cured and perfect of their limbs, and all the rest absolute in their numbers as he conceived them; who, as he was a happy imitator of Nature, was a most gentle expresser of it: his mind and hand went together; and what he thought, he utter'd with that easiness, that we have scarce received from him a blot in his papers. But it is not our province, who only gather his works and give them you, to praise him. It is yours that read him: and there we hope, to your divers capacities, you will find enough both to draw and hold you; for his wit can no more lie hid than it could be lost. Read him, therefore; and again and again: and if then you do not like him, surely you are in some manifest danger not to understand him. And so we leave you to other of his friends, whom if you need, can be your guides: if you need them not, you can lead yourselves and others. And such readers we wish him.

JOHN HEMINGE, HENRY CONDELL

To the memory of the deceased author MASTER W. SHAKESPEARE

Shakespeare, at length thy pious fellows give
The world thy works; thy works, by which outlive
Thy tomb thy name must: when that stone is rent,
And time dissolves thy Stratford monument,
Here we alive shall view thee still; this book,
When brass and marble fade, shall make thee look
Fresh to all ages; when posterity
Shall loathe what's new, think all is prodigy
That is not Shakespeare's, every line, each verse,
Here shall revive, redeem thee from thy hearse.
Nor fire, nor cank'ring age,—as Naso said
Of his, thy wit fraught book shall once invade:
Nor shall I e'er believe or think thee dead,
Though miss'd, until our bankrout stage be sped—
Impossible—with some new strain t'out-do
Passions of Juliet and her Romeo;
Or till I hear a scene more nobly take,
Than when thy half-sword-parleying Romans spake:
Till these, till any of thy volume's rest,
Shall with more fire, more feeling be exprest,
Be sure, our Shakespeare, thou canst never die,
But, crown'd with laurel, live eternally.

L. DIGGES

To the memory of MASTER W. SHAKESPEARE

We wonder'd, Shakespeare, that thou went'st so soon
From the world's stage to the grave's tiring-room:
We thought thee dead; but this thy printed worth
Tells thy spectators that thou went'st but forth
To enter with applause. An actor's art
Can die, and live to act a second part:
That's but an exit of mortality,
This a re-entrance to a plaudite.

I.M.

THE NAMES OF THE PRINCIPAL ACTORS IN ALL THESE PLAYS

William Shakespeare
Richard Burbadge
John Heminge
Augustine Phillips
William Kempt
Thomas Poope
George Bryan
Henry Condell
William Slye
Richard Cowly
John Lowine
Samuel Crosse
Alexander Cooke
Samuel Gilburne
Robert Armin
William Ostler
Nathan Field
John Underwood
Nicholas Tooley
William Ecclestone
Joseph Taylor
Robert Benfield
Robert Goughe
Richard Robinson
John Shancke
John Rice

To the memory of my beloved, the author, MASTER WILLIAM SHAKESPEARE AND WHAT HE HATH LEFT US

To draw no envy, Shakespeare, on thy name,
Am I thus ample to thy book and fame;
While I confess thy writings to be such
As neither man nor Muse can praise too much:
'Tis true, and all men's suffrage: but these ways
Were not the paths I meant unto thy praise;
For seeliest ignorance on these may light,
Which, when it sounds at best, but echoes right;
Or blind affection, which doth ne'er advance
The truth, but gropes, and urgeth all by chance;
Or crafty malice might pretend this praise,
And think to ruin where it seem'd to raise:
These are as some infamous bawd or whore
Should praise a matron: what could hurt her more?
But thou art proof against them; and, indeed,
Above the ill fortune of them or the need.
I, therefore, will begin. Soul of the age,
The applause, delight, the wonder of our stage,
My Shakespeare, rise! I will not lodge thee by
Chaucer or Spenser, or bid Beaumont lie
A little further, to make thee a room:
Thou art a monument without a tomb,
And art alive still, while thy book doth live,
And we have wits to read, and praise to give.
That I not mix thee so, my brain excuses,—
I mean, with great but disproportion'd Muses;
For if I thought my judgement were of years,
I should commit thee surely with thy peers,
And tell how far thou didst our Lyly outshine,
Or sporting Kyd, or Marlowe's mighty line:
And though thou hadst small Latin and less Greek,

From thence to honour thee I would not seek
For names; but call forth thundering Aeschylus,
Euripides, and Sophocles to us,
Pacuvius, Accius, him of Cordova, dead,
To life again, to hear thy buskin tread
And shake a stage; or when thy socks were on,
Leave thee alone for the comparison
Of all that insolent Greece or haughty Rome
Sent forth, or since did from their ashes come.
Triumph, my Britain! thou hast one to show,
To whom all scenes of Europe homage owe.
He was not of an age, but for all time!
And all the Muses still were in their prime,
When, like Apollo, he came forth to warm
Our ears, or like a Mercury to charm.
Nature herself was proud of his designs,
And joy'd to wear the dressing of his lines;
Which were so richly spun, and woven so fit,
As since she will vouchsafe no other wit:
The merry Greek, tart Aristophanes,
Neat Terence, witty Plautus, now not please;
But antiquated and deserted lie,
As they were not of Nature's family.
Yet must I not give Nature all; thy art,
My gentle Shakespeare, must enjoy a part:
For though the poet's matter nature be,
His art doth give the fashion; and that he
Who casts to write a living line, must sweat,—
Such as thine are,—and strike the second heat
Upon the Muses' anvil; turn the same,
And himself with it, that he thinks to frame;
Or, for the laurel, he may gain a scorn,—
For a good poet's made, as well as born:
And such wert thou. Look how the father's face
Lives in his issue; even so the race
Of Shakespeare's mind and manners brightly shines

In his well-turned and true-filed lines;
In each of which he seems to shake a lance,
As brandish'd at the eyes of ignorance.
Sweet Swan of Avon, what a sight it were
To see thee in our waters yet appear,
And make those flights upon the banks of Thames,
That so did take Eliza and our James!
But stay, I see thee in the hemisphere
Advanced, and made a constellation there:
Shine forth, thou star of poets, and with rage
Or influence chide or cheer the drooping stage;
Which, since thy flight from hence, hath mourn'd like
    night,
And despairs day, but for thy volume's light.

BEN. JONSON

Upon the lines and life of the famous scenic poet MASTER WILLIAM SHAKESPEARE

Those hands which you so clapp'd, go now and wring,
You Britons brave; for done are Shakespeare's days;
His days are done that made the dainty plays,
Which made the Globe of heaven and earth to ring:
Dried is that vein, dried is the Thespian spring,
Turn'd all to tears, and Phœbus clouds his rays:
That corpse, that coffin, now bestick those bays,
Which crown'd him poet first, then poets' king.
If tragedies might any prologue have,
All those he made would scarce make one to this;
Where Fame, now that he gone is to the grave—
Death's public tiring-house—the Nuntius is:
For, though his line of life went soon about,
The life yet of his lines shall never out.

HUGH HOLLAND

THE FIRST PART OF KING HENRY THE SIXTH

DRAMATIS PERSONAE

KING HENRY THE SIXTH.
DUKE OF GLOSTER, *uncle to the King, and Protector.*
DUKE OF BEDFORD, *uncle to the King, and Regent of France.*
THOMAS BEAUFORT, *Duke of Exeter, great-uncle to the King.*
HENRY BEAUFORT, *great-uncle to the King, Bishop of Winchester, and afterwards Cardinal.*
JOHN BEAUFORT, *Earl of Somerset, afterwards Duke.*
RICHARD PLANTAGENET, *son of Richard late Earl of Cambridge, afterwards Duke of York.*
EARL OF WARWICK.
EARL OF SALISBURY.
EARL OF SUFFOLK.
LORD TALBOT, *afterwards Earl of Shrewsbury.*
JOHN TALBOT, *his son.*

EDMUND MORTIMER, *Earl of March.*
SIR JOHN FASTOLFE.
SIR WILLIAM LUCY.
SIR WILLIAM GLANSDALE.
SIR THOMAS GARGRAVE.
MAYOR OF LONDON.
WOODVILLE, *Lieutenant of the Tower.*
VERNON, *of the White-Rose or York faction.*
BASSET, *of the Red-Rose or Lancaster faction.*
A LAWYER. — MORTIMER'S KEEPERS.

CHARLES, *Dauphin, and afterwards King, of France.*
REIGNIER, *Duke of Anjou, and titular King of Naples.*
DUKE OF BURGUNDY.
DUKE OF ALENÇON.
BASTARD OF ORLEANS.

GOVERNOR OF PARIS.
MASTER-GUNNER OF ORLEANS, *and his* SON.
GENERAL *of the French forces in Bourdeaux.*
A FRENCH SERGEANT. A PORTER.
AN OLD SHEPHERD, *father to Joan la Pucelle.*

MARGARET, *daughter to Reignier, afterwards married to King Henry.*
COUNTESS OF AUVERGNE.
JOAN LA PUCELLE, *commonly called Joan of Arc.*

LORDS, WARDERS OF THE TOWER, HERALDS, OFFICERS, SOLDIERS, MESSENGERS *and* ATTENDANTS.
FIENDS *appearing to La Pucelle.*

SCENE — *Partly in England, and partly in France.*

ACT I

SCENE I

Westminster Abbey.

Dead march. Enter the Funeral of KING HENRY THE FIFTH, *attended on by the* DUKE OF BEDFORD, *Regent of France; the* DUKE OF GLOSTER, *Protector; the* DUKE OF EXETER, *the* EARL OF WARWICK, *the* BISHOP OF WINCHESTER, HERALDS, *etc.*

BEDFORD
Hung be the heavens with black, yield day to night!
Comets, importing change of times and states,
Brandish your crystal tresses in the sky,
And with them scourge the bad revolting stars
That have consented unto Henry's death!
Henry the Fifth, too famous to live long!
England ne'er lost a king of so much worth.

GLOSTER
England ne'er had a king until his time.
Virtue he had, deserving to command:
His brandish't sword did blind men with his beams;
His arms spread wider than a dragon's wings;
His sparkling eyes, replete with wrathful fire,
More dazzled and drove back his enemies
Than mid-day sun fierce bent against their faces.
What should I say? his deeds exceed all speech:
He ne'er lift up his hand, but conquered.

EXETER
We mourn in black: why mourn we not in blood?
Henry is dead, and never shall revive:
Upon a wooden coffin we attend;
And death's dishonourable victory
We with our stately presence glorify,
Like captives bound to a triumphant car.
What! shall we curse the planets of mishap
That plotted thus our glory's overthrow?
Or shall we think the subtle-witted French
Conjurers and sorcerers, that, afraid of him,
By magic verses have contriv'd his end?

WINCHESTER
He was a king blest of the King of kings.
Unto the French the dreadful judgement-day
So dreadful will not be as was his sight.
The battles of the Lord of hosts he fought:
The church's prayers made him so prosperous.

GLOSTER
The church! where is it? Had not churchmen pray'd,
His thread of life had not so soon decay'd:
None do you like but an effeminate prince,
Whom, like a schoolboy, you may overawe.

WINCHESTER
Gloster, whate'er we like, thou art Protector,
And lookest to command the prince and realm.
Thy wife is proud; she holdeth thee in awe,
More than God or religious churchmen may.

GLOSTER
Name not religion, for thou lovest the flesh;
And ne'er throughout the year to church thou go'st,
Except it be to pray against thy foes.

BEDFORD
Cease, cease these jars, and rest your minds in peace!
Let's to the altar: — heralds, wait on us: —
Instead of gold, we'll offer up our arms;
Since arms avail not, now that Henry's dead. —

GLOSTER I will not slay thee, but I'll drive thee back.

Posterity, await for wretched years,
When at their mothers' moist eyes babes shall suck;
Our isle be made a marish of salt tears,
And none but women left to wail the dead. —
Henry the Fifth! thy ghost I invocate;
Prosper this realm, keep it from civil broils!
Combat with adverse planets in the heavens!
A far more glorious star thy soul will make
Than Julius Cæsar or bright —

Enter a MESSENGER.

MESSENGER
My honourable lords, health to you all!
Sad tidings bring I to you out of France,
Of loss, of slaughter, and discomfiture:
Guienne, Champagne, Rheims, Rouen, Orleans,
Paris, Guysors, Poictiers, are all quite lost.

BEDFORD
What say'st thou, man! before dead Henry's corse
Speak softly, or the loss of those great towns
Will make him burst his lead, and rise from death.

GLOSTER
Is Paris lost? is Rouen yielded up?
If Henry were recall'd to life again,
These news would cause him once more yield
the ghost.

EXETER
How were they lost? what treachery was used?

MESSENGER
No treachery; but want of men and money.
Amongst the soldiers this is muttered,
That here you maintain several factions;
And, whilst a field should be dispatch'd and fought
You are disputing of your generals:
One would have lingering wars, with little cost;
Another would fly swift, but wanteth wings;

A third thinks, without expense at all,
By guileful fair words peace may be obtain'd.
Awake, awake, English nobility!
Let not sloth dim your honours new-begot:
Cropt are the flower-de-luces in your arms;
Of England's coat one half is cut away.

EXETER
Were our tears wanting to this funeral,
These tidings would call forth their flowing tides.

BEDFORD
Me they concern; Regent I am of France. —
Give me my steeled coat! I'll fight for France.
Away with these disgraceful wailing robes!
Wounds will I lend the French, instead of eyes,
To weep their intermissive miseries.

Enter a SECOND MESSENGER.

SECOND MESSENGER
Lords, view these letters, full of bad mischance.
France is revolted from the English quite,
Except some petty towns of no import:
The Dauphin Charles is crowned king in Rheims;
The Bastard of Orleans with him is join'd;
Reignier, Duke of Anjou, doth take his part;
The Duke of Alençon flieth to his side.

EXETER
The Dauphin crowned king! all fly to him!
O, whither shall we fly from this reproach?

GLOSTER
We will not fly, but to our enemies' throats: —
Bedford, if thou be slack, I'll fight it out.

BEDFORD
Gloster, why doubt'st thou of my forwardness?
An army have I muster'd in my thoughts,
Wherewith already France is overrun.

Enter a THIRD MESSENGER.

THIRD MESSENGER
My gracious lords, to add to your laments,
Wherewith you now bedew King Henry's hearse,
I must inform you of a dismal fight
Betwixt the stout Lord Talbot and the French.

WINCHESTER
What! wherein Talbot overcame? is't so?

THIRD MESSENGER
O, no; wherein Lord Talbot was o'erthrown:
The circumstance I'll tell you more at large.
The tenth of August last, this dreadful lord,
Retiring from the siege of Orleans,
Having full scarce six thousand in his troop,
By three-and-twenty thousand of the French
Was round encompassed and set upon.
No leisure had he to enrank his men;
He wanted pikes to set before his archers;
Instead whereof, sharp stakes, pluck'd
out of hedges,
They pitched in the ground confusedly,
To keep the horsemen off from breaking in.
More than three hours the fight continued;
Where valiant Talbot, above human thought,
Enacted wonders with his sword and lance,
Hundreds he sent to hell, and none durst stand him;
Here, there, and every where, enraged he flew:
The French exclaim'd, the devil was in arms;
All the whole army stood agazed on him;
His soldiers, spying his undaunted spirit,
'A Talbot! a Talbot!' cried out amain,
And rusht into the bowels of the battle.
Here had the conquest fully been seal'd up,
If Sir John Fastolfe had not play'd the coward:
He, being in the vaward, — placed behind,
With purpose to relieve and follow them, —
Cowardly fled, not having struck one stroke.
Hence grew the general wrack and massacre;
Enclosed were they with their enemies:
A base Walloon, to win the Dauphin's grace,
Thrust Talbot with a spear into the back;
Whom all France, with their chief assembled strength,
Durst not presume to look once in the face.

BEDFORD
Is Talbot slain? then I will slay myself,
For living idly here in pomp and ease,
Whilst such a worthy leader, wanting aid,
Unto his dastard foemen is betray'd.

THIRD MESSENGER
O, no, he lives; but is took prisoner,
And Lord Scales with him, and Lord Hungerford:
Most of the rest slaughter'd or took likewise.

BEDFORD
His ransom there is none but I shall pay:
I'll hale the Dauphin headlong from his throne, —
His crown shall be the ransom of my friend;
Four of their lords I'll change for one of ours. —
Farewell, my masters; to my task will I;
Bonfires in France forthwith I am to make,
To keep our great Saint George's feast withal:
Ten thousand soldiers with me I will take,
Whose bloody deeds shall make all Europe quake.

THIRD MESSENGER
So you had need; for Orleans is besieged;
The English army is grown weak and faint:
The Earl of Salisbury craveth supply,
And hardly keeps his men from mutiny,
Since they, so few, watch such a multitude.

EXETER
Remember, lords, your oaths to Henry sworn,
Either to quell the Dauphin utterly,
Or bring him in obedience to your yoke.

BEDFORD
I do remember it; and here take my leave,
To go about my preparation. *[Exit.*

GLOSTER
I'll to the Tower, with all the haste I can,
To view th'artillery and munition;
And then I will proclaim young Henry king. *[Exit.*

EXETER
To Eltham will I, where the young king is,
Being ordain'd his special governor;
And for his safety there I'll best devise. *[Exit.*

WINCHESTER
Each hath his place and function to attend:
I am left out; for me nothing remains.
But long I will not be Jack-out-of-office:
The king from Eltham I intend to steal,
And sit at chiefest stern of public weal. *[Exit.*

SCENE II

France. Before Orleans.

Sound a flourish. Enter CHARLES, ALENÇON *and*
REIGNIER, *marching with drum and* SOLDIERS.

CHARLES
Mars his true moving, even as in the heavens,
So in the earth, to this day is not known:
Late did he shine upon the English side;
Now we are victors, upon us he smiles.
What towns of any moment but we have?
At pleasure here we lie, near Orleans;
Otherwhiles the famish'd English, like pale ghosts,
Faintly besiege us one hour in a month.

ALENÇON
They want their porridge and their fat bull-beeves:
Either they must be dieted like mules,
And have their provender tied to their mouths,
Or piteous they will look, like drowned mice.

REIGNIER
Let's raise the siege: why lie we idly here?
Talbot is taken, whom we wont to fear:
Remaineth none but mad-brain'd Salisbury;
And he may well in fretting spend his gall, —
Nor men nor money hath he to make war.

CHARLES
Sound, sound alarum! we will rush on them.
Now for the honour of the forlorn French! —
Him I forgive my death that killeth me
When he sees me go back one foot or fly. *[Exeunt.*

Here alarum; they are beaten back by the English with
great loss. Enter CHARLES, ALENÇON,
REIGNIER, *and others.*

CHARLES
Who ever saw the like? what men have I! —
Dogs! cowards! dastards! — I would ne'er have fled,
But that they left me midst my enemies.

REIGNIER
Salisbury is a desperate homicide;
He fighteth as one weary of his life.
The other lords, like lions wanting food,
Do rush upon us as their hungry prey.

ALENÇON
Froissart, a countryman of ours, records,
England all Olivers and Rowlands bred
During the time Edward the Third did reign.
More truly now may this be verified;
For none but Samsons and Goliases
It sendeth forth to skirmish. One to ten!
Lean raw-boned rascals! who would e'er suppose
They had such courage and audacity?

CHARLES
Let's leave this town; for they are hare-brain'd slaves,
And hunger will enforce them be more eager:
Of old I know them; rather with their teeth
The walls they'll tear down than forsake the siege.

REIGNIER
I think, by some odd gimmers or device,
Their arms are set like clocks, still to strike on;
Else ne'er could they hold out so as they do.
By my consent, we'll even let them alone.

ALENÇON
Be it so.

Enter the BASTARD OF ORLEANS.

BASTARD
Where's the Prince Dauphin? I have news for him.

CHARLES
Bastard of Orleans, thrice welcome to us.

BASTARD
Methinks your looks are sad, your cheer appall'd:
Hath the late overthrow wrought this offence?
Be not dismay'd, for succour is at hand:
A holy maid hither with me I bring,
Which, by a vision sent to her from heaven,
Ordained is to raise this tedious siege,
And drive the English forth the bounds of France.
The spirit of deep prophecy she hath,
Exceeding the nine sibyls of old Rome:
What's past and what's to come she can descry.
Speak, shall I call her in? Believe my words,
For they are certain and unfallible.

CHARLES
Go, call her in. *[Exit* BASTARD.*]* But first, to try her skill,
Reignier, stand thou as Dauphin in my place:
Question her proudly; let thy looks be stern:
By this means shall we sound what skill she hath.
[Retires.

Enter the BASTARD OF ORLEANS,
with JOAN LA PUCELLE.

REIGNIER
Fair maid, is't thou wilt do these wondrous feats?

LA PUCELLE
Reignier, is't thou that thinkest to beguile me?
Where is the Dauphin? — Come, come from behind;
I know thee well, though never seen before.
Be not amaz'd, there's nothing hid from me:
In private will I talk with thee apart. —
Stand back, you lords, and give us leave awhile.

REIGNIER
She takes upon her bravely at first dash.

LA PUCELLE
Dauphin, I am by birth a shepherd's daughter,
My wit untrain'd in any kind of art.
Heaven and our Lady gracious hath it pleased
To shine on my contemptible estate:
Lo, whilst I waited on my tender lambs,
And to sun's parching heat display'd my cheeks,
God's mother deigned to appear to me,
And, in a vision full of majesty,
Will'd me to leave my base vocation,
And free my country from calamity:
Her aid she promis'd, and assured success:
In complete glory she reveal'd herself;
And, whereas I was black and swart before,
With those clear rays which she infused on me
That beauty am I blest with which you see.
Ask me what question thou canst possible,
And I will answer unpremeditated:
My courage try by combat, if thou darest,
And thou shalt find that I exceed my sex.
Resolve on this, — thou shalt be fortunate,
If thou receive me for thy warlike mate.

CHARLES
Thou hast astonish'd me with thy high terms:
Only this proof I'll of thy valour make, —
In single combat thou shalt buckle with me;
And if thou vanquishest, thy words are true;
Otherwise I renounce all confidence.

LA PUCELLE
I am prepared: here is my keen-edg'd sword,
Deck'd with five flower-de-luces on each side;
The which at Touraine, in Saint Katharine's
churchyard,
Out of a deal of old iron I chose forth.

CHARLES
Then come, o' God's name; I fear no woman.

LA PUCELLE
And, while I live, I'll ne'er fly from a man.
[Here they fight and JOAN LA PUCELLE *overcomes.*

CHARLES
Stay, stay thy hands! thou art an Amazon,
And fightest with the sword of Deborah.

LA PUCELLE
Christ's mother helps me, else I were too weak.

CHARLES
Whoe'er helps thee, 'tis thou that must help me:
Impatiently I burn with thy desire;
My heart and hands thou hast at once subdued.
Excellent Pucelle, if thy name be so,
Let me thy servant, and not sovereign, be:
'Tis the French Dauphin sueth to thee thus.

LA PUCELLE
I must not yield to any rites of love,
For my profession's sacred from above:
When I have chased all thy foes from hence,
Then will I think upon a recompense.

CHARLES
Meantime look gracious on thy prostrate thrall.

REIGNIER
My lord, methinks, is very long in talk.

ALENÇON
Doubtless he shrives this woman to her smock;
Else ne'er could he so long protract his speech.

REIGNIER
Shall we disturb him, since he keeps no mean?

ALENÇON
He may mean more than we poor men do know:
These women are shrewd tempters with their tongues.

REIGNIER
My lord, where are you? what devise you on?
Shall we give over Orleans, or no?

LA PUCELLE
Why, no, I say, distrustful recreants!
Fight till the last gasp; I will be your guard.

CHARLES
What she says, I'll confirm: we'll fight it out.

LA PUCELLE
Assign'd am I to be the English scourge.

This night the siege assuredly I'll raise:
Expect Saint Martin's summer, halcyon days,
Since I have entered into these wars.
Glory is like a circle in the water,
Which never ceaseth to enlarge itself,
Till, by broad spreading, it disperse to naught.
With Henry's death the English circle ends;
Dispersed are the glories it included.
Now am I like that proud-insulting ship
Which Cæsar and his fortune bare at once.

CHARLES
Was Mahomet inspired with a dove?
Thou with an eagle art inspired, then.
Helen, the mother of great Constantine,
Nor yet Saint Philip's daughters, were like thee.
Bright star of Venus, fall'n down on the earth,
How may I ever worship thee enough?

ALENÇON
Leave off delays, and let us raise the siege.

REIGNIER
Woman, do what thou canst to save our honours;
Drive them from Orleans, and be immortalised.

CHARLES
Presently we'll try: — come, let's away about it: —
No prophet will I trust, if she prove false. [*Exeunt.*

SCENE III

London. Before the Tower.
Enter the DUKE OF GLOSTER, with his
SERVING-MEN *in blue coats.*

GLOSTER
I am come to survey the Tower this day:
Since Henry's death, I fear, there is conveyance. —
Where be these warders, that they wait not here?
Open the gates; 'tis Gloster that calls. [*Servants knock.*

FIRST WARDER [*within*].
Who's there that knocks so imperiously?

FIRST SERVING-MAN
It is the noble Duke of Gloster.

SECOND WARDER [*within*].
Whoe'er he be, you may not be let in.

FIRST SERVING-MAN
Villains, answer you so the lord Protector?

FIRST WARDER [*within*].
The Lord protect him! so we answer him:
We do no otherwise than we are will'd.

GLOSTER
Who willed you? or whose will stands but mine?
There's none Protector of the realm but I. —
Break up the gates, I'll be your warrantise:
Shall I be flouted thus by dunghill grooms?
[GLOSTER'S *men rush at the Tower-gates, and*
WOODVILLE, *the Lieutenant, speaks within.*

WOODVILLE
What noise is this? what traitors have we here?

GLOSTER
Lieutenant, is it you whose voice I hear?
Open the gates; here's Gloster that would enter.

WOODVILLE
Have patience, noble duke; I may not open;
The Cardinal of Winchester forbids:
From him I have express commandement
That thou nor none of thine shall be let in.

GLOSTER
Faint-hearted Woodville, prizest him 'fore me, —
Arrogant Winchester, that haughty prelate,
Whom Henry, our late sovereign, ne'er could brook?
Thou art no friend to God or to the king:
Open the gates, or I'll shut thee out shortly.

SERVING-MEN
Open the gates unto the lord Protector:
Or we'll burst them open, if that you come not quickly.
Enter to the PROTECTOR *at the Tower-gates*
WINCHESTER, *and his* MEN *in tawny coats.*

WINCHESTER
How now, ambitious Humphrey! what means this?

GLOSTER
Peel'd priest, dost thou command me to be shut out?

WINCHESTER
I do, thou most usurping proditor,
And not Protector, of the king or realm.

GLOSTER
Stand back, thou manifest conspirator,
Thou that contrivedst to murder our dead lord;
Thou that givest whores indulgences to sin:
I'll canvass thee in thy broad cardinal's hat,
If thou proceed in this thy insolence.

WINCHESTER
Nay, stand thou back; I will not budge a foot:

This be Damascus, be thou cursed Cain,
To slay thy brother Abel, if thou wilt.

GLOSTER
I will not slay thee, but I'll drive thee back:
Thy scarlet robes as a child's bearing-cloth
I'll use to carry thee out of this place.

WINCHESTER
Do what thou darest; I beard thee to thy face.

GLOSTER
What! am I dared, and bearded to my face? —
Draw, men, for all this privileged place;
Blue-coats to tawny-coats. — Priest, beware your beard;
I mean to tug it, and to cuff you soundly:
Under my feet I'll stamp thy cardinal's hat;
In spite of Pope or dignities of church,
Here by the cheeks I'll drag thee up and down.

WINCHESTER
Gloster, thou wilt answer this before the Pope.

GLOSTER
Winchester goose! I cry, a rope! a rope! —
Now beat them hence; why do you let them stay? —
Thee I'll chase hence, thou wolf in sheep's array. —
Out, tawny-coats! — out, scarlet hypocrite!
Here GLOSTER'S *men beat out the* CARDINAL'S *men,*
and enter in the hurly-burly the MAYOR OF LONDON
and his OFFICERS.

MAYOR OF LONDON
Fie, lords! that you, being supreme magistrates,
Thus contumeliously should break the peace!

GLOSTER
Peace, mayor! thou know'st little of my wrongs:
Here's Beaufort, that regards nor God nor king,
Hath here distrain'd the Tower to his use.

WINCHESTER
Here's Gloster, a foe to citizens;
One that still motions war, and never peace,
O'ercharging your free purses with large fines;
That seeks to overthrow religion,
Because he is Protector of the realm;
And would have armour here out of the Tower,
To crown himself king, and suppress the prince.

GLOSTER
I will not answer thee with words, but blows.
[*Here they skirmish again.*

MAYOR OF LONDON
Naught rests for me, in this tumultuous strife,
But to make open proclamation: —
Come, officer; as loud as e'er thou canst.

OFFICER [*cries*]
All manner of men assembled here in arms this day
against God's peace and the king's, we charge and
command you, in his highness' name, to repair to
your several dwelling-places; and not to wear,
handle, or use any sword, weapon, or dagger,
henceforward, upon pain of death.

GLOSTER
Cardinal, I'll be no breaker of the law:
But we shall meet, and break our minds at large.

WINCHESTER
Gloster, we'll meet; to thy cost, be sure:
Thy heart-blood I will have for this day's work.

MAYOR OF LONDON
I'll call for clubs, if you will not away: —
This cardinal's more haughty than the devil.

GLOSTER
Mayor, farewell: thou dost but what thou mayst.

WINCHESTER
Abominable Gloster! guard thy head;
For I intend to have it ere long.
[*Exeunt, severally,* GLOSTER *and* WINCHESTER
with their SERVING-MEN.

MAYOR OF LONDON
See the coast clear'd, and then we will depart. —
Good God, these nobles should such stomachs bear!
I myself fight not once in forty year. [*Exeunt.*

SCENE IV

France. Before Orleans.

Enter, on the walls, the MASTER-GUNNER OF
ORLEANS, *and his* BOY.

MASTER-GUNNER
Sirrah, thou know'st how Orleans is besieg'd,
And how the English have the suburbs won.

BOY
Father, I know; and oft have shot at them,
Howe'er unfortunate I miss'd my aim.

MASTER-GUNNER
But now thou shalt not. Be thou rul'd by me:

Chief master-gunner am I of this town;
Something I must do to procure me grace.
The prince's espials have informed me
How the English, in the suburbs close intrench'd,
Wont, through a secret grate of iron bars
In yonder tower, to overpeer the city;
And thence discover how with most advantage
They may vex us with shot or with assault.
To intercept this inconvenience,
A piece of ordnance 'gainst it I have plac'd;
And even these three days have I watch'd, if I
Could see them.
Now do thou watch, for I can stay no longer.
If thou spy'st any, run and bring me word;
And thou shalt find me at the governor's. [*Exit.*

BOY
Father, I warrant you; take you no care;
I'll never trouble you, if I may spy them. [*Exit.*
Enter SALISBURY *and* TALBOT *on the turrets, with*
SIR WILLIAM GLANSDALE, SIR THOMAS
GARGRAVE, *and others.*

SALISBURY
Talbot, my life, my joy, again return'd!
How wert thou handled being prisoner,
Or by what means got'st thou to be releas'd,
Discourse, I prithee, on this turret's top.

TALBOT
The Duke of Bedford had a prisoner
Called the brave Lord Ponton de Santrailles;
For him was I exchang'd and ransomed.
But with a baser man-of-arms by far,
Once, in contempt, they would have barter'd me:
Which I, disdaining, scorn'd; and craved death
Rather than I would be so vile-esteem'd.
In fine, redeem'd I was as I desired.
But, O, the treacherous Fastolfe wounds my heart!
Whom with my bare fists I would execute,
If I now had him brought into my power.

SALISBURY
Yet tell'st thou not how thou wert entertain'd.

TALBOT
With scoffs, and scorns, and contumelious taunts.
In open market-place produc'd they me,
To be a public spectacle to all:
Here, said they, is the terror of the French,
The scarecrow that affrights our children so.
Then broke I from the officers that led me,
And with my nails digg'd stones out of the ground,
To hurl at the beholders of my shame:
My grisly countenance made others fly;
None durst come near for fear of sudden death.
In iron walls they deem'd me not secure;
So great fear of my name 'mongst them was spread,
That they suppos'd I could rend bars of steel,
And spurn in pieces posts of adamant:
Wherefore a guard of chosen shot I had,
That walk'd about me every minute-while;
And if I did but stir out of my bed,
Ready they were to shoot me to the heart.
Enter the BOY *with a linstock.*

SALISBURY
I grieve to hear what torments you endur'd;
But we will be reveng'd sufficiently.
Now it is supper-time in Orleans:
Here, through this grate, I count each one,
And view the Frenchmen how they fortify:
Let us look in; the sight will much delight thee. —
Sir Thomas Gargrave and Sir William Glansdale,
Let me have your express opinions
Where is best place to make our battery next.

GARGRAVE
I think, at the north gate; for there stand lords.

GLANSDALE
And I, here, at the bulwark of the bridge.

TALBOT
For aught I see, this city must be famish'd,
Or with light skirmishes enfeebled.
[*Here they shoot.* SALISBURY *and* SIR THOMAS
GARGRAVE *fall down.*

SALISBURY
O Lord, have mercy on us, wretched sinners!

GARGRAVE
O Lord, have mercy on me, woeful man!

TALBOT
What chance is this that suddenly hath cross'd us?
Speak, Salisbury; at least, if thou canst speak:
How farest thou, mirror of all martial men?
One of thy eyes and thy cheek's side struck off! —
Accursed tower! accursed fatal hand
That hath contriv'd this woeful tragedy!

In thirteen battles Salisbury o'ercame;
Henry the Fifth he first train'd to the wars;
Whilst any trump did sound, or drum struck up,
His sword did ne'er leave striking in the field. —
Yet livest thou, Salisbury? though thy speech doth fail,
One eye thou hast, to look to heaven for grace:
The sun with one eye vieweth all the world. —
Heaven, be thou gracious to none alive,
If Salisbury wants mercy at thy hands! —
Bear hence his body; I will help to bury it. —
Sir Thomas Gargrave, hast thou any life?
Speak unto Talbot; nay, look up to him. —
Salisbury, cheer thy spirit with this comfort;
Thou shalt not die whiles —
He beckons with his hand, and smiles on me,
As who should say, 'When I am dead and gone,
Remember to avenge me on the French.' —
Plantagenet, I will; and, like thee, Nero,
Play on the lute, beholding the towns burn:
Wretched shall France be only in my name.
                    [*Here an alarum, and it thunders and lightens.*
What stir is this? what tumult's in the heavens?
Whence cometh this alarum and this noise?
                    Enter a MESSENGER.

MESSENGER
My lord, my lord, the French have gather'd head:
The Dauphin, with one Joan la Pucelle join'd, —
A holy prophetess new risen up, —
Is come with a great power to raise the siege.
                    [*Here* SALISBURY *lifteth himself up and groans.*

TALBOT
Hear, hear how dying Salisbury doth groan!
It irks his heart he cannot be reveng'd. —
Frenchmen, I'll be a Salisbury to you: —
Pucelle or puzzel, dolphin or dogfish,
Your hearts I'll stamp out with my horse's heels,
And make a quagmire of your mingled brains. —
Convey me Salisbury into his tent:
And then try what these dastard Frenchmen dare.
                    [*Alarum. Exeunt.*

SCENE V
The same.

Here an alarum again: and TALBOT *pursueth the* DAUPHIN, *and driveth him: then enter* JOAN LA PUCELLE, *driving Englishmen before her, and exit after them: then enter* TALBOT.

TALBOT
Where is my strength, my valour, and my force?
Our English troops retire, I cannot stay them;
A woman clad in armour chaseth them.
Here, here she comes.
                    Enter LA PUCELLE.
                         I'll have a bout with thee;
Devil or devil's dam, I'll conjure thee:
Blood will I draw on thee, — thou art a witch, —
And straightway give thy soul to him thou servest.

LA PUCELLE
Come, come, 'tis only I that must disgrace thee.
                    [*They fight.*

TALBOT
Heavens, can you suffer hell so to prevail?
My breast I'll burst with straining of my courage,
And from my shoulders crack my arms asunder,
But I will chastise this high-minded strumpet.
                    [*They fight again.*

LA PUCELLE
Talbot, farewell; thy hour is not yet come:
I must go victual Orleans forthwith.
        [*A short alarum: then enter the town, with* SOLDIERS.
O'ertake me, if thou canst; I scorn thy strength.
Go, go cheer up thy hungry-starved men;
Help Salisbury to make his testament:
This day is ours, as many more shall be. [*Exit.*

TALBOT
My thoughts are whirled like a potter's wheel;
I know not where I am, nor what I do;
A witch by fear, not force, like Hannibal,
Drives back our troops, and conquers as she lists:
So bees with smoke, and doves with noisome stench,
Are from their hives and houses driven away.
They call'd us, for our fierceness, English dogs;
Now, like to whelps, we crying run away.
                    [*A short alarum.*
Hark, countrymen! either renew the fight,
Or tear the lions out of England's coat;
Renounce your soil, give sheep in lions' stead:
Sheep run not half so timorous from the wolf,
Or horse or oxen from the leopard,
As you fly from your oft-subdued slaves.

                    [*Alarum. Here another skirmish.*
It will not be: — retire into your trenches:
You all consented unto Salisbury's death,
For none would strike a stroke in his revenge. —
Pucelle is enter'd into Orleans,
In spite of us or aught that we could do.
O, would I were to die with Salisbury!
The shame hereof will make me hide my head.
                    [*Exit* TALBOT. *Alarum, retreat.*

SCENE VI
The same.
Flourish. Enter, on the walls, LA PUCELLE, CHARLES, REIGNIER, ALENÇON, *and* SOLDIERS.

LA PUCELLE
Advance our waving colours on the walls;
Rescued is Orleans from the English: —
Thus Joan la Pucelle hath perform'd her word.

CHARLES
Divinest creature, Astræa's daughter,
How shall I honour thee for this success?
Thy promises are like Adonis' gardens,
That one day bloom'd, and fruitful were the next. —
France, triumph in thy glorious prophetess! —
Recover'd is the town of Orleans:
More blessed hap did ne'er befall our state.

REIGNIER
Why ring not out the bells aloud throughout the town?
Dauphin, command the citizens make bonfires,
And feast and banquet in the open streets,
To celebrate the joy that God hath given us.

ALENÇON
All France will be replete with mirth and joy,
When they shall hear how we have play'd the men.

CHARLES
'Tis Joan, not we, by whom the day is won;
For which I will divide my crown with her;
And all the priests and friars in my realm
Shall in procession sing her endless praise.
A statelier pyramis to her I'll rear
Than Rhodope's or Memphis ever was:
In memory of her when she is dead,
Her ashes, in an urn more precious
Than the rich-jewell'd coffer of Darius,
Transported shall be at high festivals
Before the kings and queens of France.
No longer on Saint Denis will we cry,
But Joan la Pucelle shall be France's saint.
Come in, and let us banquet royally,
After this golden day of victory. [*Flourish. Exeunt.*

ACT II
SCENE I
France. Before Orleans.
Enter a SERGEANT *of a band, with two* SENTINELS.

SERGEANT
Sirs, take your places, and be vigilant:
If any noise or soldier you perceive
Near to the walls, by some apparent sign
Let us have knowledge at the court-of-guard.

FIRST SENTINEL
Sergeant, you shall. [*Exit* SERGEANT.] Thus are poor
     servitors —
When others sleep upon their quiet beds —
Constrain'd to watch in darkness, rain, and cold.
Enter TALBOT, BEDFORD, BURGUNDY, *and* FORCES,
     with scaling-ladders, their drums beating a dead march.

TALBOT
Lord regent, and redoubted Burgundy, —
By whose approach the regions of Artois,
Wallon, and Picardy are friends to us, —
This happy night the Frenchmen are secure,
Having all day carous'd and banqueted:
Embrace we, then, this opportunity,
As fitting best to quittance their deceit,
Contriv'd by art and baleful sorcery.

BEDFORD
Coward of France! — how much he wrongs his fame,
Despairing of his own arm's fortitude,
To join with witches and the help of hell!

BURGUNDY
Traitors have never other company. —
But what's that Pucelle, whom they term so pure?

TALBOT
A maid, they say.

BEDFORD
                    A maid! and be so martial!

BURGUNDY
Pray God she prove not masculine ere long;
If underneath the standard of the French
She carry armour, as she hath begun.

TALBOT
Well, let them practise and converse with spirits:
God is our fortress, in whose conquering name
Let us resolve to scale their flinty bulwarks.

BEDFORD
Ascend, brave Talbot; we will follow thee.

TALBOT
Not all together: better far, I guess,
That we do make our entrance several ways;
That, if it chance the one of us do fail,
The other yet may rise against their force.

BEDFORD
Agreed: I'll to yond corner.

BURGUNDY
                    And I to this.

TALBOT
And here will Talbot mount, or make his grave. —
Now, Salisbury, for thee, and for the right
Of English Henry, shall this night appear
How much in duty I am bound to both.
                    [*Cry*, St. George! A Talbot!

SENTINEL
Arm! arm! the enemy doth make assault!
*The French leap o'er the walls in their shirts. Enter, several
     ways, the* BASTARD OF ORLEANS, ALENÇON, *and*
     REIGNIER, *half ready and half unready.*

ALENÇON
How now, my lords! what, all unready so?

BASTARD
Unready! ay, and glad we scaped so well.

REIGNIER
'Twas time, I trow, to wake and leave our beds,
Hearing alarums at our chamber-doors.

ALENÇON
Of all exploits since first I follow'd arms,
Ne'er heard I of a warlike enterprise
More venturous or desperate than this.

BASTARD
I think this Talbot be a fiend of hell.

REIGNIER
If not of hell, the heavens, sure, favour him.

ALENÇON
Here cometh Charles: I marvel how he sped.

BASTARD
Tut, holy Joan was his defensive guard.
                    Enter CHARLES *and* LA PUCELLE.

CHARLES
Is this thy cunning, thou deceitful dame?
Didst thou at first, to flatter us withal,
Make us partakers of a little gain,
That now our loss might be ten times so much?

LA PUCELLE
Wherefore is Charles impatient with his friend?
At all times will you have my power alike?
Sleeping or waking, must I still prevail,
Or will you blame and lay the fault on me?
Improvident soldiers! had your watch been good,
This sudden mischief never could have fall'n.

CHARLES
Duke of Alençon, this was your default,
That, being captain of the watch to-night,
Did look no better to that weighty charge.

ALENÇON
Had all your quarters been as safely kept
As that whereof I had the government,
We had not been thus shamefully surprised.

BASTARD
Mine was secure.

REIGNIER
                    And so was mine, my lord.

CHARLES
And, for myself, most part of all this night,
Within her quarter and mine own precinct
I was employ'd in passing to and fro,
About relieving of the sentinels:
Then how or which way should they first break in?

LA PUCELLE
Question, my lords, no further of the case,
How or which way: 'tis sure they found some place
But weakly guarded, where the breach was made.
And now there rests no other shift but this, —
To gather our soldiers, scatter'd and dispersed,
And lay new platforms to endamage them.
Alarums. Enter an English SOLDIER, *crying,* A Talbot!
     a Talbot! *They fly, leaving their clothes behind.*

SOLDIER
I'll be so bold to take what they have left.
The cry of Talbot serves me for a sword;
For I have loaden me with many spoils,
Using no other weapon but his name.   [*Exit.*

SCENE II

Orleans. Within the town.

Enter TALBOT, BEDFORD, BURGUNDY, *a*
CAPTAIN, *and others.*

BEDFORD
The day begins to break, and night is fled,
Whose pitchy mantle over-veil'd the earth.
Here sound retreat, and cease our hot pursuit.
    [*Retreat sounded.*

TALBOT
Bring forth the body of old Salisbury,
And here advance it in the market-place,
The middle centre of this cursed town.
Now have I paid my vow unto his soul;
For every drop of blood was drawn from him,
There hath at least five Frenchmen died to-night.
And that hereafter ages may behold
What ruin happen'd in revenge of him,
Within their chiefest temple I'll erect
A tomb, wherein his corpse shall be interr'd:
Upon the which, that every one may read,
Shall be engrav#d the sack of Orleans,
The treacherous manner of his mournful death,
And what a terror he had been to France.
But, lords, in all our bloody massacre,
I muse we met not with the Dauphin's grace,
His new-come champion, virtuous Joan of Arc,
Nor any of his false confederates.

BEDFORD
'Tis thought, Lord Talbot, when the fight began,
Rous'd on the sudden from their drowsy beds,
They did, amongst the troops of armed men,
Leap o'er the walls for refuge in the field.

BURGUNDY
Myself — as far as I could well discern
For smoke and dusky vapours of the night —
Am sure I scared the Dauphin and his trull,
When arm in arm they both came swiftly running,
Like to a pair of loving turtle-doves,
That could not live asunder day or night.
After that things are set in order here,
We'll follow them with all the power we have.
    Enter a MESSENGER.

MESSENGER
All hail, my lords! Which of this princely train
Call ye the warlike Talbot, for his acts
So much applauded through the realm of France?

TALBOT
Here is the Talbot: who would speak with him?

MESSENGER
The virtuous lady, Countess of Auvergne,
With modesty admiring thy renown,
By me entreats, great lord, thou wouldst vouchsafe
To visit her poor castle where she lies,
That she may boast she hath beheld the man
Whose glory fills the world with loud report.

BURGUNDY
Is it even so? Nay, then, I see our wars
Will turn unto a peaceful comic sport,
When ladies crave to be encounter'd
  with. —
You may not, my lord, despise her gentle
  suit.

TALBOT
Ne'er trust me, then; for when a world of
  men
Could not prevail with all their oratory,
Yet hath a woman's kindness over-ruled: —
And therefore tell her I return great
  thanks,
And in submission will attend on her. —
Will not your honours bear me company?

BEDFORD
No, truly; it is more than manners will:
And I have heard it said, unbidden guests
Are often welcomest when they are gone.

TALBOT
Well then, alone, since there's no remedy,
I mean to prove this lady's courtesy. —
Come hither, captain. [*Whispers.*] You
  perceive my mind?

CAPTAIN
I do, my lord, and mean accordingly.
    [*Exeunt.*

SCENE III

Auvergne. Court of the Castle.

Enter the COUNTESS *and her* PORTER.

COUNTESS
Porter, remember what I gave in charge;
And when you've done so, bring the keys to me.

PORTER
Madam, I will.   [*Exit.*

COUNTESS
The plot is laid: if all things fall out right,
I shall as famous be by this exploit
As Scythian Tomyris by Cyrus' death.
Great is the rumour of this dreadful knight,
And his achievements of no less account:
Fain would mine eyes be witness with mine ears,
To give their censure of these rare reports.
    Enter MESSENGER *and* TALBOT.

MESSENGER
Madam,
According as your ladyship desired,
By message crav'd, so is Lord Talbot come.

COUNTESS
And he is welcome. What! is this the man?

MESSENGER
Madam, it is.

COUNTESS
    Is this the scourge of France?
Is this the Talbot, so much fear'd abroad,
That with his name the mothers still their babes?
I see report is fabulous and false:
I thought I should have seen some Hercules,
A second Hector, for his grim aspect
And large proportion of his strong-knit limbs.
Alas, this is a child, a silly dwarf!
It cannot be this weak and writhled shrimp
Should strike such terror to his enemies.

TALBOT
Madam, I have been bold to trouble you;
But since your ladyship is not at leisure,
I'll sort some other time to visit you.   [*Going.*

COUNTESS
What means he now? — Go ask him whither he goes.

MESSENGER
Stay, my Lord Talbot; for my lady craves
To know the cause of your abrupt departure.

TALBOT
Marry, for that she's in a wrong belief,
I go to certify her Talbot's here.
    Enter PORTER *with keys.*

COUNTESS
If thou be he, then art thou prisoner.

TALBOT
Prisoner! to whom?

COUNTESS
    To me, blood-thirsty lord;
And for that cause I train'd thee to my house.
Long time thy shadow hath been thrall to me,
For in my gallery thy picture hangs:
But now the substance shall endure the like;
And I will chain these legs and arms of thine,

VERNON Then, for the truth and plainness of the case, I pluck
this pale and maiden blossom here.

That hast by tyranny, these many years,
Wasted our country, slain our citizens,
And sent our sons and husbands captivate.

TALBOT
Ha, ha, ha!

COUNTESS
Laughest thou, wretch? thy mirth shall turn to moan.

TALBOT
I laugh to see your ladyship so fond
To think that you have aught but Talbot's shadow
Whereon to practise your severity.

COUNTESS
Why, art not thou the man?

TALBOT
    I am, indeed.

COUNTESS
Then have I substance too.

TALBOT
No, no, I am but shadow of myself;
You are deceived, my substance is not here;
For what you see is but the smallest part
And least proportion of humanity:
I tell you, madam, were the whole frame here,
It is of such a spacious lofty pitch,
Your roof were not sufficient to contain't.

COUNTESS
This is a riddling merchant for the nonce;
He will be here, and yet he is not here:
How can these contrarieties agree?

TALBOT
That will I show you presently.
    [*Winds his horn. Drums strike up: a peal of ordnance.*
        Enter SOLDIERS.
How say you, madam? are you now persuaded
That Talbot is but shadow of himself?
These are his substance, sinews, arms, and strength,
With which he yoketh your rebellious necks,
Razeth your cities, and subverts your towns,
And in a moment makes them desolate.

COUNTESS
Victorious Talbot! pardon my abuse:
I find thou art no less than fame hath bruited,
And more than may be gather'd by thy shape.
Let my presumption not provoke thy wrath;
For I am sorry that with reverence
I did not entertain thee as thou art.

TALBOT
Be not dismay'd, fair lady; nor misconster
The mind of Talbot, as you did mistake
The outward composition of his body.
What you have done hath not offended me:
Nor other satisfaction do I crave,
But only, with your patience, that we may
Taste of your wine, and see what cates you have;
For soldiers' stomachs always serve them well.

COUNTESS
With all my heart; and think me honoured
To feast so great a warrior in my house.   [*Exeunt.*

SCENE IV

London. The Temple-garden.

Enter the EARLS OF SOMERSET, SUFFOLK, *and*
WARWICK; RICHARD PLANTAGENET, VERNON,
and a LAWYER.

PLANTAGENET
Great lords and gentlemen, what means this silence?
Dare no man answer in a case of truth?

SUFFOLK
Within the Temple-hall we were too loud;
The garden here is more convenient.

PLANTAGENET
Then say at once if I maintain'd the truth;
Or else was wrangling Somerset in th'error?

SUFFOLK
Faith, I have been a truant in the law,
And never yet could frame my will to it;
And therefore frame the law unto my will.

SOMERSET
Judge you, my Lord of Warwick, then, between us.

WARWICK
Between two hawks, which flies the higher pitch;
Between two dogs, which hath the deeper mouth;
Between two blades, which bears the better temper;
Between two horses, which doth bear him best;
Between two girls, which hath the merriest eye; —
I have, perhaps, some shallow spirit of judgement:
But in these nice sharp quillets of the law,
Good faith, I am no wiser than a daw.

PLANTAGENET
Tut, tut, here is a mannerly forbearance:
The truth appears so naked on my side,
That any purblind eye may find it out.
SOMERSET
And on my side it is so well apparell'd,
So clear, so shining, and so evident,
That it will glimmer through a blind man's eye.
PLANTAGENET
Since you are tongue-tied and so loth to speak,
In dumb significants proclaim your thoughts:
Let him that is a true-born gentleman,
And stands upon the honour of his birth,
If he suppose that I have pleaded truth,
From off this brier pluck a white rose with me.
SOMERSET
Let him that is no coward nor no flatterer,
But dare maintain the party of the truth,
Pluck a red rose from off this thorn with me.
WARWICK
I love no colours; and, without all colour
Of base-insinuating flattery,
I pluck this white rose with Plantagenet.
SUFFOLK
I pluck this red rose with young Somerset;
And say withal, I think he held the right.
VERNON
Stay, lords and gentlemen, and pluck no more,
Till you conclude that he, upon whose side
The fewest roses are cropt from the tree,
Shall yield the other in the right opinion.
SOMERSET
Good Master Vernon, it is well objected:
If I have fewest, I subscribe in silence.
PLANTAGENET
And I.
VERNON
Then, for the truth and plainness of the case,
I pluck this pale and maiden blossom here,
Giving my verdict on the white rose side.
SOMERSET
Prick not your finger as you pluck it off,
Lest, bleeding, you do paint the white rose red,
And fall on my side so, against your will.
VERNON
If I, my lord, for my opinion bleed,
Opinion shall be surgeon to my hurt,
And keep me on the side where still I am.
SOMERSET
Well, well, come on: who else?
LAWYER [to SOMERSET].
Unless my study and my books be false,
The argument you held was wrong in you;
In sign whereof I pluck a white rose too.
PLANTAGENET
Now, Somerset, where is your argument?
SOMERSET
Here in my scabbard; meditating that
Shall dye your white rose in a bloody red.
PLANTAGENET
Meantime your cheeks do counterfeit our roses;
For pale they look with fear, as witnessing
The truth on our side.
SOMERSET
                No, Plantagenet,
'Tis not for fear, but anger, that thy cheeks
Blush for pure shame to counterfeit our roses,
And yet thy tongue will not confess thy error.
PLANTAGENET
Hath not thy rose a canker, Somerset?
SOMERSET
Hath not thy rose a thorn, Plantagenet?
PLANTAGENET
Ay, sharp and piercing, to maintain his truth;
Whiles thy consuming canker eats his falsehood.
SOMERSET
Well, I'll find friends to wear my bleeding roses,
That shall maintain what I have said is true,
Where false Plantagenet dare not be seen.
PLANTAGENET
Now, by this maiden blossom in my hand,
I scorn thee and thy faction, peevish boy.
SUFFOLK
Turn not thy scorns this way, Plantagenet.
PLANTAGENET
Proud Pole, I will; and scorn both him and thee.
SUFFOLK
I'll turn my part thereof into thy throat.
SOMERSET
Away, away, good William de la Pole!
We grace the yeoman by conversing with him.

WARWICK
Now, by God's will, thou wrong'st him, Somerset;
His grandfather was Lionel Duke of Clarence,
Third son to the third Edward King of England:
Spring crestless yeomen from so deep a root?
PLANTAGENET
He bears him on the place's privilege,
Or durst not, for his craven heart, say thus.
SOMERSET
By Him that made me, I'll maintain my words
On any plot of ground in Christendom.
Was not thy father, Richard Earl of Cambridge,
For treason executed in our late king's days?
And, by his treason, stand'st not thou attainted,
Corrupted, and exempt from ancient gentry?
His trespass yet lives guilty in thy blood;
And, till thou be restored, thou art a yeoman.
PLANTAGENET
My father was attached, not attainted;
Condemn'd to die for treason, but no traitor;
And that I'll prove on better men than Somerset,
Were growing time once ripen'd to my will.
For your partaker Pole, and you yourself,
I'll note you in my book of memory,
To scourge you for this apprehension:
Look to it well, and say you are well warn'd.
SOMERSET
Ah, thou shalt find us ready for thee still;
And know us, by these colours, for thy foes, —
For these my friends, in spite of thee, shall wear.
PLANTAGENET
And, by my soul, this pale and angry rose,
As cognisance of my blood-drinking hate,
Will I for ever, and my faction, wear,
Until it wither with me to my grave,
Or flourish to the height of my degree.
SUFFOLK
Go forward, and be chok'd with thy ambition!
And so, farewell, until I meet thee next.   [Exit.
SOMERSET
Have with thee, Pole. — Farewell, ambitious Richard.
                                              [Exit.
PLANTAGENET
How I am brav'd and must perforce endure it!
WARWICK
This blot, that they object against your house,
Shall be wip'd out in the next parliament,
Call'd for the truce of Winchester and Gloster:
And if thou be not then created York,
I will not live to be accounted Warwick.
Meantime, in signal of my love to thee,
Against proud Somerset and William Pole,
Will I upon thy party wear this rose:
And here I prophesy, — this brawl to-day,
Grown to this faction, in the Temple-garden,
Shall send, between the red rose and the white,
A thousand souls to death and deadly night.
PLANTAGENET
Good Master Vernon, I am bound to you,
That you on my behalf would pluck a flower.
VERNON
In your behalf still will I wear the same.
LAWYER
And so will I.
PLANTAGENET
Thanks, gentle sir.
Come, let us four to dinner: I dare say
This quarrel will drink blood another day.   [Exeunt.

SCENE V

The Tower of London.

Enter MORTIMER, *brought in a chair, and* GAOLERS.

MORTIMER
Kind keepers of my weak decaying age,
Let dying Mortimer here rest himself. —
Even like a man new-haled from the rack,
So fare my limbs with long imprisonment;
And these grey locks, the pursuivants of death,
Nestor-like aged, in an age of care,
Argue the end of Edmund Mortimer:
These eyes — like lamps whose wasting oil is spent —
Wax dim, as drawing to their exigent:
Weak shoulders, overborne with burdening grief;
And pithless arms, like to a wither'd vine
That droops his sapless branches to the ground:
Yet are these feet — whose strengthless stay is numb,
Unable to support this lump of clay —
Swift-winged with desire to get a grave,
As witting I no other comfort have. —
But tell me, keeper, will my nephew come?

FIRST GAOLER
Richard Plantagenet, my lord, will come:
We sent unto the Temple, unto his chamber;
And answer was return'd that he will come.
MORTIMER
Enough: my soul shall then be satisfied. —
Poor gentleman! his wrong doth equal mine.
Since Henry Monmouth first began to reign,
Before whose glory I was great in arms,
This loathsome sequestration have I had;
And even since then hath Richard been obscured,
Deprived of honour and inheritance.
But now, the arbitrator of despairs,
Just death, kind umpire of men's miseries,
With sweet enlargement doth dismiss me hence:
I would his troubles likewise were expired,
That so he might recover what was lost.
          Enter RICHARD PLANTAGENET.
FIRST GAOLER
My lord, your loving nephew now is come.
MORTIMER
Richard Plantagenet, my friend, is he come?
PLANTAGENET
Ay, noble uncle, thus ignobly used,
Your nephew, late-despised Richard, comes.
MORTIMER
Direct mine arms I may embrace his neck,
And in his bosom spend my latter gasp:
O, tell me when my lips do touch his cheeks,
That I may kindly give one fainting kiss. —
And now declare, sweet stem from York's great stock,
Why didst thou say, of late thou wert despised?
PLANTAGENET
First, lean thine aged back against mine arm;
And, in that ease, I'll tell thee my disease.
This day, in argument upon a case,
Some words there grew 'twixt Somerset and me;
Among which terms he used his lavish tongue,
And did upbraid me with my father's death:
Which obloquy set bars before my tongue,
Else with the like I had requited him.
Therefore, good uncle, for my father's sake,
In honour of a true Plantagenet,
And for alliance sake, declare the cause
My father, Earl of Cambridge, lost his head.
MORTIMER
That cause, fair nephew, that imprison'd me,
And hath detain'd me all my flowering youth
Within a loathsome dungeon, there to pine,
Was cursed instrument of his decease.
PLANTAGENET
Discover more at large what cause that was;
For I am ignorant, and cannot guess.
MORTIMER
I will, if that my fading breath permit,
And death approach not ere my tale be done.
Henry the Fourth, grandfather to this king,
Deposed his nephew Richard, — Edward's son,
The first-begotten and the lawful heir
Of Edward king, the third of that descent:
During whose reign, the Percies of the north,
Finding his usurpation most unjust,
Endeavour'd my advancement to the throne:
The reason mov'd these warlike lords to this
Was, for that — young King Richard thus removed,
Leaving no heir begotten of his body —
I was the next by birth and parentage;
For by my mother I derived am
From Lionel Duke of Clarence, the third son
To King Edward the Third; whereas he
From John of Gaunt doth bring his pedigree,
Being but fourth of that heroic line.
But mark: as, in this haughty-great attempt,
They laboured to plant the rightful heir,
I lost my liberty, and they their lives.
Long after this, when Henry the Fifth,
Succeeding his father Bolingbroke, did reign,
Thy father, Earl of Cambridge, then deriv'd
From famous Edmund Langley, Duke of York,
Marrying my sister, that thy mother was,
Again, in pity of my hard distress,
Levied an army, weening to redeem
And have install'd me in the diadem:
But, as the rest, so fell that noble earl,
And was beheaded. Thus the Mortimers,
In whom the title rested, were suppress'd.
PLANTAGENET
Of which, my lord, your honour is the last.
MORTIMER
True; and thou seest that I no issue have,
And that my fainting words do warrant death:

Thou art my heir; the rest I wish thee gather:
But yet be wary in thy studious care.

PLANTAGENET
Thy grave admonishments prevail with me:
But yet, methinks, my father's execution
Was nothing less than bloody tyranny.

MORTIMER
With silence, nephew, be thou politic:
Strong-fixed is the house of Lancaster,
And, like a mountain, not to be removed.
But now thy uncle is removing hence;
As princes do their courts, when they are cloy'd
With long continuance in a settled place.

PLANTAGENET
O, uncle, would some part of my young years
Might but redeem the passage of your age!

MORTIMER
Thou dost, then, wrong me, — as that slaughterer doth
Which giveth many wounds when one will kill.
Mourn not, except thou sorrow for my good;
Only, give order for my funeral:
And so, farewell; and fair be all thy hopes,
And prosperous be thy life in peace and war! *[Dies.*

PLANTAGENET
And peace, no war, befall thy parting soul!
In prison hast thou spent a pilgrimage,
And like a hermit overpass'd thy days. —
Well, I will lock his counsel in my breast;
And what I do imagine, let that rest. —
Keepers, convey him hence; and I myself
Will see his burial better than his life.
[Exeunt GAOLERS, *bearing out the body of* MORTIMER.
Here dies the dusky torch of Mortimer,
Chok'd with ambition of the meaner sort: —
And for those wrongs, those bitter injuries,
Which Somerset hath offer'd to my house,
I doubt not but with honour to redress;
And therefore haste I to the parliament,
Either to be restored to my blood,
Or make my ill th'advantage of my good. *[Exit.*

ACT III

SCENE I

London. The Parliament House.

Flourish. Enter KING HENRY, EXETER, GLOSTER,
WARWICK, SOMERSET, *and* SUFFOLK; *the*
BISHOP OF WINCHESTER, RICHARD
PLANTAGENET, *and others.* GLOSTER *offers to put up
a bill;* WINCHESTER *snatches it, and tears it.*

WINCHESTER
Com'st thou with deep-premeditated lines,
With written pamphlets studiously devis'd,
Humphrey of Gloster? If thou canst accuse,
Or aught intend'st to lay unto my charge,
Do it without invention, suddenly;
As I with sudden and extemporal speech
Purpose to answer what thou canst object.

GLOSTER
Presumptuous priest! this place commands my patience,
Or thou shouldst find thou hast dishonour'd me.
Think not, although in writing I preferr'd
The manner of thy vile outrageous crimes,
That therefore I have forg'd, or am not able
Verbatim to rehearse the method of my pen:
No, prelate; such is thy audacious wickedness,
Thy lewd, pestiferous, and dissentious pranks,
As very infants prattle of thy pride.
Thou art a most pernicious usurer;
Froward by nature, enemy to peace;
Lascivious, wanton, more than well beseems
A man of thy profession and degree;
And for thy treachery, what's more manifest, —
In that thou laid'st a trap to take my life,
As well at London-bridge as at the Tower?
Beside, I fear me, if thy thoughts were sifted,
The king, thy sovereign, is not quite exempt
From envious malice of thy swelling heart.

WINCHESTER
Gloster, I do defy thee. — Lords, vouchsafe
To give me hearing what I shall reply.
If I were covetous, ambitious, or perverse,
As he will have me, how am I so poor?
Or how haps it I seek not to advance
Or raise myself, but keep my wonted calling?
And for dissension, who preferreth peace
More than I do, — except I be provok'd?
No, my good lords, it is not that offends;

It is not that that hath incens'd the duke:
It is, because no one should sway but he;
No one but he should be about the king;
And that engenders thunder in his breast,
And makes him roar these accusations forth.
But he shall know I am as good —

GLOSTER
As good!
Thou bastard of my grandfather! —

WINCHESTER
Ay, lordly sir; for what are you, I pray,
But one imperious in another's throne?

GLOSTER
Am I not lord Protector, saucy priest?

WINCHESTER
And am not I a prelate of the church?

GLOSTER
Yes, as an outlaw in a castle keeps,
And useth it to patronage his theft.

WINCHESTER
Unreverent Gloster!

GLOSTER
Thou art reverent
Touching thy spiritual function, not thy life.

WINCHESTER
This Rome shall remedy.

WARWICK
Roam thither, then.

SOMERSET
My lord, it were your duty to forbear.

WARWICK
Ay, see the bishop be not overborne.

SOMERSET
Methinks my lord should be religious,
And know the office that belongs to such.

WARWICK
Methinks his lordship should be humbler;
It fitteth not a prelate so to plead.

SOMERSET
Yes, when his holy state is touch'd so near.

WARWICK
State holy or unhallow'd, what of that?
Is not his Grace Protector to the king?

PLANTAGENET *[aside].*
Plantagenet, I see, must hold his tongue,
Lest it be said, 'Speak, sirrah, when you should;
Must your bold verdict enter talk with lords?'
Else would I have a fling at Winchester.

KING HENRY
Uncles of Gloster and of Winchester,
The special watchmen of our English weal,
I would prevail, if prayers might prevail,
To join your hearts in love and amity.
O, what a scandal is it to our crown,
That two such noble peers as ye should jar!
Believe me, lords, my tender years can tell
Civil dissension is a viperous worm
That gnaws the bowels of the commonwealth.
[A noise within, 'Down with the tawny-coats!'
What tumult's this?

WARWICK
An uproar, I dare warrant,
Begun through malice of the bishop's men.
[A noise again within, 'Stones! stones!'
Enter MAYOR.

MAYOR
O, my good lords, — and virtuous Henry, —
Pity the city of London, pity us!
The bishop and the Duke of Gloster's men,
Forbidden late to carry any weapon,
Have fill'd their pockets full of pebble-stones,
And, banding themselves in contrary parts,
Do pelt so fast at one another's pate,
That many have their giddy brains knock'd out:
Our windows are broke down in every street,
And we, for fear, compell'd to shut our shops.
Enter SERVING-MEN, *in skirmish, with bloody pates.*

KING HENRY
We charge you, on allegiance to ourself,
To hold your slaughtering hands and keep the peace. —
Pray, uncle Gloster, mitigate this strife.

FIRST SERVING-MAN
Nay, if we be forbidden stones, we'll fall to it with our teeth.

SECOND SERVING-MAN
Do what ye dare, we are as resolute. *[Skirmish again.*

GLOSTER
You of my household, leave this peevish broil,
And set this unaccustom'd fight aside.

GLOSTER Presumptuous priest! this place commands
 my patience.

THIRD SERVING-MAN
My lord, we know your Grace to be a man
Just and upright; and, for your royal birth,
Inferior to none but to his majesty:
And, ere that we will suffer such a prince,
So kind a father of the commonweal,
To be disgraced by an inkhorn mate,
We, and our wives, and children, all will fight,
And have our bodies slaughter'd by thy foes.

FIRST SERVING-MAN
Ay, and the very parings of our nails
Shall pitch a field when we are dead. *[Begin again.*

GLOSTER
Stay, stay, I say!
And if you love me, as you say you do,
Let me persuade you to forbear awhile.

KING HENRY
O, how this discord doth afflict my soul! —
Can you, my Lord of Winchester, behold
My sighs and tears, and will not once relent?
Who should be pitiful, if you be not?
Or who should study to prefer a peace,
If holy churchmen take delight in broils?

WARWICK
Yield, my lord Protector; yield, Winchester;
Except you mean, with obstinate repulse,
To slay your sovereign, and destroy the realm.
You see what mischief, and what murder too,
Hath been enacted through your enmity;
Then be at peace, except ye thirst for blood.

WINCHESTER
He shall submit, or I will never yield.

GLOSTER
Compassion on the king commands me stoop;
Or I would see his heart out, ere the priest
Should ever get that privilege of me.

WARWICK
Behold, my Lord of Winchester, the duke
Hath banish'd moody discontented fury,
As by his smoothed brows it doth appear:
Why look you still so stern and tragical?

GLOSTER
Here, Winchester, I offer thee my hand.

KING HENRY
Fie, uncle Beaufort! I have heard you preach
That malice was a great and grievous sin;
And will not you maintain the thing you teach,
But prove a chief offender in the same?

WARWICK
Sweet king! — the bishop hath a kindly gird. —

For shame, my Lord of Winchester, relent!
What, shall a child instruct you what to do?
WINCHESTER
Well, Duke of Gloster, I will yield to thee,
Love for thy love, and hand for hand I give.
GLOSTER [aside].
Ay, but, I fear me, with a hollow heart.
See here, my friends and loving countrymen;
This token serveth for a flag of truce
Betwixt ourselves and all our followers:
So help me God, as I dissemble not!
WINCHESTER [aside].
So help me God, as I intend it not!
KING HENRY
O loving uncle, kind Duke of Gloster,
How joyful am I made by this contract! —
Away, my masters! trouble us no more;
But join in friendship, as your lords have done.
FIRST SERVING-MAN
Content: I'll to the surgeon's.
SECOND SERVING-MAN
                              And so will I.
THIRD SERVING-MAN
And I will see what physic the tavern affords.
                [Exeunt SERVING-MEN, MAYOR, etc.
WARWICK
Accept this scroll, most gracious sovereign,
Which in the right of Richard Plantagenet
We do exhibit to your majesty.
GLOSTER
Well urg'd, my Lord of Warwick: — for, sweet prince,
And if your Grace mark every circumstance,
You have great reason to do Richard right;
Especially for those occasions
At Eltham-place I told your majesty.
KING HENRY
And those occasions, uncle, were of force:
Therefore, my loving lords, our pleasure is,
That Richard be restored to his blood.
WARWICK
Let Richard be restored to his blood;
So shall his father's wrongs be recompens'd.
WINCHESTER
As will the rest, so willeth Winchester.
KING HENRY
If Richard will be true, not that alone,
But all the whole inheritance I give
That doth belong unto the house of York,
From whence you spring by lineal descent.
PLANTAGENET
Thy humble servant vows obedience
And humble service till the point of death.
KING HENRY
Stoop, then, and set your knee against my foot;
And, in reguerdon of that duty done,
I girt thee with the valiant sword of York:
Rise, Richard, like a true Plantagenet,
And rise created princely Duke of York.
PLANTAGENET
And so thrive Richard as thy foes may fall!
And as my duty springs, so perish they
That grudge one thought against your majesty!
ALL
Welcome, high prince, the mighty Duke of York!
SOMERSET [aside].
Perish, base prince, ignoble Duke of York!
GLOSTER
Now will it best avail your majesty
To cross the seas, and to be crown'd in France:
The presence of a king engenders love
Amongst his subjects and his loyal friends,
As it disanimates his enemies.
KING HENRY
When Gloster says the word, King Henry goes;
For friendly counsel cuts off many foes.
GLOSTER
Your ships already are in readiness.
                [Sennet. Flourish. Exeunt all but EXETER.
EXETER
Ay, we may march in England or in France,
Not seeing what is likely to ensue.
This late dissension grown betwixt the peers
Burns under feigned ashes of forg'd love,
And will at last break out into a flame:
As fester'd members rot but by degree,
Till bones and flesh and sinews fall away,
So will this base and envious discord breed.
And now I fear that fatal prophecy
Which in the time of Henry nam'd the Fifth

Was in the mouth of every sucking babe, —
That Henry born at Monmouth should win all,
And Henry born at Windsor should lose all:
Which is so plain, that Exeter doth wish
His days may finish ere that hapless time.[Exit.

SCENE II

France. Before Rouen.

Enter LA PUCELLE *disguised, with four*
SOLDIERS, *with sacks upon their backs.*

LA PUCELLE
These are the city-gates, the gates of Rouen,
Through which our policy must make a
    breach:
Take heed, be wary how you place your
    words;
Talk like the vulgar sort of market-men
That come to gather money for their corn.
If we have entrance, — as I hope we shall, —
And that we find the slothful watch but
    weak,
I'll by a sign give notice to our friends,
That Charles the Dauphin may encounter
    them.
FIRST SOLDIER
Our sacks shall be a mean to sack the city,
And we be lords and rulers over Rouen;
Therefore we'll knock.   [Knocks.
WATCHMAN [within].
Qui va là?
LA PUCELLE
Paysans, pauvres gens de France, —
Poor market-folks, that come to sell their corn.
WATCHMAN [opening the gates].
Enter, go in; the market-bell is rung.
LA PUCELLE
Now, Rouen, I'll shake thy bulwarks to the ground.
          [LA PUCELLE, etc., enter the town.
Enter CHARLES, *the* BASTARD OF ORLEANS,
ALENÇON, REIGNIER, *and* FORCES.

CHARLES
Saint Denis bless this happy stratagem!
And once again we'll sleep secure in Rouen.
BASTARD
Here enter'd Pucelle and her practisants;
Now she is there, how will she specify
Where is the best and safest passage in?
REIGNIER
By thrusting out a torch from yonder tower;
Which, once discern'd, shows that her meaning is, —
No way to that, for weakness, which she enter'd.

Enter LA PUCELLE *on the top,*
thrusting out a torch burning.

LA PUCELLE
Behold, this is the happy wedding-torch
That joineth Rouen unto her countrymen,
But burning fatal to the Talbotites.   [Exit.
BASTARD
See, noble Charles, the beacon of our friend;
The burning torch in yonder turret stands.
CHARLES
Now shine it like a comet of revenge,
A prophet to the fall of all our foes!
REIGNIER
Defer no time, delays have dangerous ends;
Enter, and cry 'The Dauphin!' presently,
And then do execution on the watch.
                [Alarum. They enter.

An alarum. Enter TALBOT *in an excursion.*

TALBOT
France, thou shalt rue this treason with thy tears,
If Talbot but survive thy treachery. —
Pucelle, that witch, that damned sorceress,
Hath wrought this hellish mischief unawares,
That hardly we escap'd the pride of France.   [Exit.
An alarum: excursions. BEDFORD *brought in sick in a
chair. Enter* TALBOT *and* BURGUNDY *without:
within* LA PUCELLE, CHARLES, *the* BASTARD OF
ORLEANS, ALENÇON, *and* REIGNIER, *on the walls.*

LA PUCELLE
Good morrow, gallants! want ye corn for bread?
I think the Duke of Burgundy will fast,
Before he'll buy again at such a rate:
'Twas full of darnel; — do you like the taste?
BURGUNDY
Scoff on, vile fiend and shameless courtezan!

FIRST SERVING-MAN Nay, if we be forbidden stones, we'll fall
to it with our teeth.

I trust ere long to choke thee with thine own,
And make thee curse the harvest of that corn.
CHARLES
Your Grace may starve, perhaps, before that time.
BEDFORD
O, let no words, but deeds, revenge this treason!
LA PUCELLE
What will you do, good greybeard? break a lance,
And run a tilt at death within a chair?
TALBOT
Foul fiend of France, and hag of all despite,
Encompass'd with thy lustful paramours!
Becomes it thee to taunt his valiant age,
And twit with cowardice a man half dead?
Damsel, I'll have a bout with you again,
Or else let Talbot perish with his shame.
LA PUCELLE
Are ye so hot, sir? — yet, Pucelle, hold thy peace;
If Talbot do but thunder, rain will follow.
          [TALBOT and the rest whisper together in council.
God speed the parliament! who shall be the speaker?
TALBOT
Dare ye come forth and meet us in the field?
LA PUCELLE
Belike your lordship takes us, then, for fools,
To try if that our own be ours or no.
TALBOT
I speak not to that railing Hecate,
But unto thee, Alençon, and the rest;
Will ye, like soldiers, come and fight it out?
ALENÇON
Signior, no.
TALBOT
Signior, hang! — base muleters of France!
Like peasant foot-boys do they keep the walls,
And dare not take up arms like gentlemen.
LA PUCELLE
Away, captains! let's get us from the walls;
For Talbot means no goodness by his looks. —
God b' wi' you, my lord! we came but to tell you
That we are here.
          [Exeunt LA PUCELLE, etc., from the walls.
TALBOT
And there will we be too, ere it be long,
Or else reproach be Talbot's greatest fame! —
Vow, Burgundy, by honour of thy house —
Prick'd on by public wrongs sustain'd in France —
Either to get the town again or die;
And I, — as sure as English Henry lives,
And as his father here was conqueror, —
As sure as in the late-betrayed town
Great Cœur-de-lion's heart was buried, —
So sure I swear to get the town or die.
BURGUNDY
My vows are equal partners with thy vows.

TALBOT

But, ere we go, regard this dying prince,
The valiant Duke of Bedford. — Come, my lord,
We will bestow you in some better place,
Fitter for sickness and for crazy age.

BEDFORD

Lord Talbot, do not so dishonour me:
Here will I sit before the walls of Rouen,
And will be partner of your weal or woe.

BURGUNDY

Courageous Bedford, let us now persuade you.

BEDFORD

Not to be gone from hence; for once I read,
That stout Pendragon, in his litter, sick,
Came to the field, and vanquished his foes:
Methinks I should revive the soldiers' hearts,
Because I ever found them as myself.

TALBOT

Undaunted spirit in a dying breast! —
Then be it so: — heavens keep old Bedford safe! —
And now no more ado, brave Burgundy,
But gather we our forces out of hand,
And set upon our boasting enemy.

[*Exeunt all but* BEDFORD *and* ATTENDANTS.

An alarum: excursions. Enter SIR JOHN FASTOLFE
and a CAPTAIN.

CAPTAIN

Whither away, Sir John Fastolfe, in such haste?

FASTOLFE

Whither away! to save myself by flight:
We are like to have the overthrow again.

CAPTAIN

What! will you fly, and leave Lord Talbot?

FASTOLFE

Ay,
All the Talbots in the world, to save my life. [*Exit.*

CAPTAIN

Cowardly knight! ill fortune follow thee! [*Exit.*

Retreat: excursions. LA PUCELLE, ALENÇON,
and CHARLES *fly.*

BEDFORD

Now, quiet soul, depart when heaven please,
For I have seen our enemies' overthrow.
What is the trust or strength of foolish man?
They that of late were daring with their scoffs,
Are glad and fain by flight to save themselves.

[BEDFORD *dies and is carried in by two in his chair.*

An alarum. Enter TALBOT, BURGUNDY, *and the rest.*

TALBOT

Lost and recover'd in a day again!
This is a double honour, Burgundy:
Yet heavens have glory for this victory!

BURGUNDY

Warlike and martial Talbot, Burgundy
Enshrines thee in his heart, and there erects
Thy noble deeds, as valour's monuments.

TALBOT

Thanks, gentle duke. But where is Pucelle now?
I think her old familiar is asleep:
Now where's the Bastard's braves, and Charles his
    gleeks?
What, all amort? Rouen hangs her head for grief,
That such a valiant company are fled.
Now will we take some order in the town,
Placing therein some expert officers;
And then depart to Paris to the king,
For there young Henry with his nobles lie.

BURGUNDY

What wills Lord Talbot pleaseth Burgundy.

TALBOT

But yet, before we go, let's not forget
The noble Duke of Bedford late deceased,
But see his exequies fulfill'd in Rouen:
A braver soldier never couched lance,
A gentler heart did never sway in court:
But kings and mightiest potentates must die,
For that's the end of human misery. [*Exeunt.*

SCENE III

The plains near Rouen.

Enter CHARLES, *the* BASTARD OF ORLEANS,
ALENÇON, LA PUCELLE, *and* FORCES.

LA PUCELLE

Dismay not, princes, at this accident,
Nor grieve that Rouen is so recovered:
Care is no cure, but rather corrosive,
For things that are not to be remedied.

LA PUCELLE Your honours shall perceive how I will work.

Let frantic Talbot triumph for a while,
And like a peacock sweep along his tail;
We'll pull his plumes, and take away his train,
If Dauphin and the rest will be but ruled.

CHARLES

We have been guided by thee hitherto,
And of thy cunning had no diffidence:
One sudden foil shall never breed distrust.

BASTARD

Search out thy wit for secret policies,
And we will make thee famous through the world.

ALENÇON

We'll set thy statue in some holy place,
And have thee reverenc'd like a blessed saint:
Employ thee, then, sweet virgin, for our good.

LA PUCELLE

Then thus it must be; this doth Joan devise:
By fair persuasions, mix'd with sugar'd words,
We will entice the Duke of Burgundy
To leave the Talbot and to follow us.

CHARLES

Ay, marry, sweeting, if we could do that,
France were no place for Henry's warriors;
Nor should that nation boast it so with us,
But be extirped from our provinces.

ALENÇON

For ever should they be expuls'd from France,
And not have title of an earldom here.

LA PUCELLE

Your honours shall perceive how I will work
To bring this matter to the wished end.

[*Drum sounds afar off.*

Hark! by the sound of drum you may perceive
Their powers are marching unto Paris-ward.

*Here sound an English march. Enter, and pass over at a
distance,* TALBOT *and his* FORCES.

There goes the Talbot, with his colours spread,
And all the troops of English after him.

French march. Enter the DUKE OF BURGUNDY
and his FORCES.

Now in the rearward comes the duke and his:
Fortune in favour makes him lag behind.
Summon a parley; we will talk with him.

[*Trumpets sound a parley.*

CHARLES

A parley with the Duke of Burgundy!

BURGUNDY

Who craves a parley with the Burgundy?

LA PUCELLE

The princely Charles of France, thy countryman.

BURGUNDY

What say'st thou, Charles? for I am marching hence.

CHARLES

Speak, Pucelle, and enchant him with thy words.

LA PUCELLE

Brave Burgundy, undoubted hope of France!
Stay, let thy humble handmaid speak to thee.

BURGUNDY

Speak on; but be not over-tedious.

LA PUCELLE

Look on thy country, look on fertile France,
And see the cities and the towns defac'd
By wasting ruin of the cruel foe!
As looks the mother on her lowly babe
When death doth close his tender dying eyes,
See, see the pining malady of France;
Behold the wounds, the most unnatural wounds,
Which thou thyself hast given her woeful breast!
O, turn thy edged sword another way;
Strike those that hurt, and hurt not those that help!
One drop of blood drawn from thy country's bosom
Should grieve thee more than streams of foreign gore:
Return thee, therefore, with a flood of tears,
And wash away thy country's stained spots.

BURGUNDY [*aside*].

Either she hath bewitch'd me with her words,
Or nature makes me suddenly relent.

LA PUCELLE

Besides, all French and France exclaim on thee,
Doubting thy birth and lawful progeny,
Who join'st thou with, but with a lordly nation,
That will not trust thee but for profit's sake?
When Talbot hath set footing once in France,
And fashion'd thee that instrument of ill,
Who then but English Henry will be lord,
And thou be thrust out like a fugitive?
Call we to mind, — and mark but this for proof, —
Was not the Duke of Orleans thy foe?
And was he not in England prisoner?
But when they heard he was thine enemy,
They set him free, without his ransom paid,
In spite of Burgundy and all his friends.
See, then, thou fight'st against thy countrymen,
And join'st with them will be thy slaughter-men.
Come, come, return; return, thou wandering lord;
Charles and the rest will take thee in their arms.

BURGUNDY [*aside*].
I'm vanquished; these haughty words of hers
Have batter'd me like roaring cannon-shot,
And made me almost yield upon my knees. —
Forgive me, country, and sweet countrymen!
And, lords, accept this hearty kind embrace:
My forces and my power of men are yours: —
So, farewell, Talbot; I'll no longer trust thee.

LA PUCELLE [*aside*].
Done like a Frenchman: turn, and turn again!

CHARLES
Welcome, brave duke! thy friendship makes us fresh.

BASTARD
And doth beget new courage in our breasts.

ALENÇON
Pucelle hath bravely play'd her part in this,
And doth deserve a coronet of gold.

CHARLES
Now let us on, my lords, and join our powers;
And seek how we may prejudice the foe. [*Exeunt.*

SCENE IV

Paris. The palace.

Enter the KING, GLOSTER, WINCHESTER, YORK,
SUFFOLK, SOMERSET, WARWICK, EXETER,
VERNON, BASSET, *etc. To them,*
with his SOLDIERS, TALBOT.

TALBOT
My gracious prince, — and honourable peers, —
Hearing of your arrival in this realm,
I have awhile given truce unto my wars,
To do my duty to my sovereign:
In sign whereof, this arm — that hath reclaim'd
To your obedience fifty fortresses,
Twelve cities, and seven walled towns of strength,
Beside five hundred prisoners of esteem —
Lets fall his sword before your highness' feet,
[*Kneeling.*
And with submissive loyalty of heart
Ascribes the glory of his conquest got
First to my God, and next unto your Grace.

KING HENRY
Is this the Lord Talbot, uncle Gloster,
That hath so long been resident in France?

GLOSTER
Yes, if it please your majesty, my liege.

KING HENRY
Welcome, brave captain and victorious lord!
When I was young, — as yet I am not old, —
I do remember how my father said
A stouter champion never handled sword.
Long since we were resolved of your truth,
Your faithful service, and your toil in war;
Yet never have you tasted our reward,
Or been reguerdon'd with so much as thanks,
Because till now we never saw your face:
Therefore, stand up; and, for these good deserts,
We here create you Earl of Shrewsbury;
And in our coronation take your place.

[*Sennet. Flourish. Exeunt all except*
VERNON *and* BASSET.

VERNON
Now, sir, to you, that were so hot at sea,
Disgracing of these colours that I wear
In honour of my noble Lord of York, —
Darest thou maintain the former words thou spakest?

BASSET
Yes, sir; as well as you dare patronage
The envious barking of your saucy tongue
Against my lord the Duke of Somerset.

VERNON
Sirrah, thy lord I honour as he is.

BASSET
Why, what is he? as good a man as York.

VERNON
Hark ye; not so: in witness, take ye that. [*Strikes him.*

BASSET
Villain, thou know'st the law of arms is such,
That whoso draws a sword, 'tis present death,
Or else this blow should broach thy dearest blood.
But I'll unto his majesty, and crave
I may have liberty to venge this wrong;
When thou shalt see I'll meet thee to thy cost.

VERNON
Well, miscreant, I'll be there as soon as you;
And, after, meet you sooner than you would. [*Exeunt.*

ACT IV

SCENE I

Paris. A room of state in the palace.

Enter the KING, GLOSTER, EXETER, YORK,
SUFFOLK, SOMERSET, WINCHESTER,
WARWICK, TALBOT, *the*
GOVERNOR OF PARIS, *and others.*

GLOSTER
Lord bishop, set the crown upon his head.

WINCHESTER
God save King Henry, of that name the sixth!

GLOSTER
Now, governor of Paris, take your oath, —
[GOVERNOR *kneels.*
That you elect no other king but him;
Esteem none friends but such as are his friends,
And none your foes but such as shall pretend
Malicious practices against his state:
This shall ye do, so help you righteous God!
[*Exeunt* GOVERNOR *and his* TRAIN.

Enter SIR JOHN FASTOLFE.

FASTOLFE
My gracious sovereign, as I rode from Calais,
To haste unto your coronation,
A letter was deliver'd to my hands,
Writ to your Grace from th'Duke of Burgundy.

TALBOT
Shame to the Duke of Burgundy and thee!
I vow'd, base knight, when I did meet thee next,
To tear the garter from thy craven's leg, —
[*Plucks it off.*
Which I have done, — because unworthily
Thou wast installed in that high degree. —
Pardon me, princely Henry, and the rest:
This dastard, at the battle of Patay,
When but in all I was six thousand strong,
And that the French were almost ten to one, —
Before we met, or that a stroke was given,
Like to a trusty squire, did run away:
In which assault we lost twelve hundred men;
Myself, and divers gentlemen beside,
Were there surprised and taken prisoners.
Then judge, great lords, if I have done amiss;
Or whether that such cowards ought to wear
This ornament of knighthood, yea or no.

GLOSTER
To say the truth, this fact was infamous,
And ill beseeming any common man,
Much more a knight, a captain, and a leader.

TALBOT
When first this order was ordain'd, my lords,
Knights of the Garter were of noble birth,
Valiant and virtuous, full of haughty courage,
Such as were grown to credit by the wars;
Not fearing death, nor shrinking for distress,

But always resolute in most extremes.
He, then, that is not furnish'd in this sort
Doth but usurp the sacred name of knight,
Profaning this most honourable order,
And should — if I were worthy to be judge —
Be quite degraded, like a hedge-born swain
That doth presume to boast of gentle blood.

KING HENRY
Stain to thy countrymen, thou hear'st thy doom!
Be packing, therefore, thou that wast a knight:
Henceforth we banish thee, on pain of death.

[*Exit* FASTOLFE.

And now, my lord Protector, view the letter
Sent from our uncle Duke of Burgundy.

GLOSTER
What means his Grace, that he hath chang'd his style?
No more but, plain and bluntly, 'To the king'?
Hath he forgot he is his sovereign?
Or doth this churlish superscription
Pretend some alteration in good will?
What's here? — [*Reads.*] 'I have, upon especial cause, —
Mov'd with compassion of my country's wrack,
Together with the pitiful complaints
Of such as your oppression feeds upon, —
Forsaken your pernicious faction,
And join'd with Charles, the rightful King of France.'
O monstrous treachery! can this be so, —
That in alliance, amity, and oaths,
There should be found such false dissembling guile?

KING HENRY
What! doth my uncle Burgundy revolt?

GLOSTER
He doth, my lord; and is become your foe.

KING HENRY
Is that the worst this letter doth contain?

GLOSTER
It is the worst, and all, my lord, he writes.

KING HENRY
Why, then, Lord Talbot there shall talk with him,
And give him chastisement for this abuse. —
How say you, my lord? are you not content?

TALBOT
Content, my liege! yes, but that I am prevented,
I should have begg'd I might have been employ'd.

KING HENRY
Then gather strength, and march unto him straight:
Let him perceive how ill we brook his treason,
And what offence it is to flout his friends.

TALBOT
I go, my lord; in heart desiring still
You may behold confusion of your foes. [*Exit.*

Enter VERNON AND BASSET.

VERNON
Grant me the combat, gracious sovereign!

BASSET
And me, my lord, grant me the combat too!

KING HENRY And now, my lord Protector, view the letter.

YORK
This is my servant: hear him, noble prince!

SOMERSET
And this is mine: sweet Henry, favour him!

KING HENRY
Be patient, lords; and give them leave to speak. —
Say, gentlemen, what makes you thus exclaim?
And wherefore crave you combat? or with whom?

VERNON
With him, my lord; for he hath done me wrong.

BASSET
And I with him; for he hath done me wrong.

KING HENRY
What is that wrong whereof you both complain?
First let me know, and then I'll answer you.

BASSET
Crossing the sea from England into France,
This fellow here, with envious carping tongue,
Upbraided me about the rose I wear;
Saying, the sanguine colour of the leaves
Did represent my master's blushing cheeks,
When stubbornly he did repugn the truth
About a certain question in the law
Argu'd betwixt the Duke of York and him;
With other vile and ignominious terms;
In confutation of which rude reproach,
And in defence of my lord's worthiness,
I crave the benefit of law of arms.

VERNON
And that is my petition, noble lord:
For though he seem with forged quaint conceit
To set a gloss upon his bold intent,
Yet know, my lord, I was provok'd by him;
And he first took exceptions at this badge,
Pronouncing that the paleness of this flower
Bewray'd the faintness of my master's heart.

YORK
Will not this malice, Somerset, be left?

SOMERSET
Your private grudge, my Lord of York, will out,
Though ne'er so cunningly you smother it.

KING HENRY
Good Lord, what madness rules in brain-sick men,
When for so slight and frivolous a cause
Such factious emulations shall arise! —
Good cousins both, of York and Somerset,
Quiet yourselves, I pray, and be at peace.

YORK
Let this dissension first be tried by fight,
And then your highness shall command a peace.

SOMERSET
The quarrel toucheth none but us alone;
Betwixt ourselves let us decide it, then.

YORK
There is my pledge; accept it, Somerset.

VERNON
Nay, let it rest where it began at first.

BASSET
Confirm it so, mine honourable lord.

GLOSTER
Confirm it so! Confounded be your strife!
And perish ye, with your audacious prate!
Presumptuous vassals, are you not asham'd
With this immodest clamorous outrage
To trouble and disturb the king and us? —
And you, my lords, — methinks you do not well
To bear with their perverse objections;
Much less to take occasion from their mouths
To raise a mutiny betwixt yourselves:
Let me persuade you take a better course.

EXETER
It grieves his highness: — good my lords, be friends.

KING HENRY
Come hither, you that would be combatants:
Henceforth I charge you, as you love our favour,
Quite to forget this quarrel and the cause. —
And you, my lords, remember where we are;
In France, amongst a fickle wavering nation:
If they perceive dissension in our looks,
And that within ourselves we disagree,
How will their grudging stomachs be provok'd
To wilful disobedience, and rebel!
Beside, what infamy will there arise,
When foreign princes shall be certified
That for a toy, a thing of no regard,
King Henry's peers and chief nobility
Destroy'd themselves, and lost the realm of France!
O, think upon the conquest of my father;
My tender years; and let us not forgo
That for a trifle that was bought with blood!

Let me be umpire in this doubtful strife.
I see no reason, if I wear this rose,
                    [*Putting on a red rose.*
That any one should therefore be suspicious
I more incline to Somerset than York:
Both are my kinsmen, and I love them both:
As well they may upbraid me with my crown,
Because, forsooth, the King of Scots is crown'd.
But your discretions better can persuade
Than I am able to instruct or teach:
And therefore, as we hither came in peace,
So let us still continue peace and love. —
Cousin of York, we institute your Grace
To be our regent in these parts of France: —
And, good my Lord of Somerset, unite
Your troops of horsemen with his bands of foot: —
And, like true subjects, sons of your progenitors,
Go cheerfully together, and digest
Your angry choler on your enemies.
Ourself, my lord Protector, and the rest,
After some respite, will return to Calais;
From thence to England; where I hope ere long
To be presented, by your victories,
With Charles, Alençon, and that traitorous rout.
    [*Flourish. Exeunt* KING, GLOSTER, SOMERSET,
            WINCHESTER, SUFFOLK, *and* BASSET.

WARWICK
My Lord of York, I promise you, the king
Prettily, methought, did play the orator.

YORK
And so he did; but yet I like it not,
In that he wears the badge of Somerset.

WARWICK
Tush, that was but his fancy, blame him not;
I dare presume, sweet prince, he thought no harm.

YORK
An if I wist he did, — but let it rest;
Other affairs must now be managed.
        [*Exeunt* YORK, WARWICK, *and* VERNON.

EXETER
Well didst thou, Richard, to suppress thy voice;
For, had the passions of thy heart burst out,
I fear we should have seen decipher'd there
More rancorous spite, more furious raging broils,
Than yet can be imagin'd or supposed.
But howsoe'er, no simple man that sees
This jarring discord of nobility,
This shouldering of each other in the court,
This factious bandying of their favourites,
But that he doth presage some ill event.
'Tis much when sceptres are in children's hands;
But more when envy breeds unkind division;
There comes the ruin, there begins confusion.   [*Exit.*

SCENE II

Before Bourdeaux.

Enter TALBOT, *with trump and drum.*

TALBOT
Go to the gates of Bourdeaux, trumpeter;
Summon their general unto the wall.
Trumpet sounds. Enter GENERAL *and others aloft.*
English John Talbot, captains, calls you forth,
Servant in arms to Harry King of England;
And thus he would, — Open your city-gates;
Be humble to us: call my sovereign yours,
And do him homage as obedient subjects;
And I'll withdraw me and my bloody power:
But, if you frown upon this proffer'd peace,
You tempt the fury of my three attendants,
Lean famine, quartering steel, and climbing fire;
Who, in a moment, even with the earth
Shall lay your stately and air-braving towers,
If you forsake the offer of our love.

GENERAL
Thou ominous and fearful owl of death,
Our nation's terror, and their bloody scourge!
The period of thy tyranny approacheth.
On us thou canst not enter but by death;
For, I protest, we are well fortified,
And strong enough to issue out and fight:
If thou retire, the Dauphin, well appointed,
Stands with the snares of war to tangle thee:
On either hand there are squadrons pitch'd,
To wall thee from the liberty of flight;
And no way canst thou turn thee for redress,
But death doth front thee with apparent spoil,
And pale destruction meets thee in the face.
Ten thousand French have ta'en the sacrament
To rive their dangerous artillery
Upon no Christian soul but English Talbot.

Lo, there thou stand'st, a breathing valiant man,
Of an invincible unconquer'd spirit!
This is the latest glory of thy praise
That I, thy enemy, due thee withal;
For ere the glass, that now begins to run,
Finish the process of his sandy hour,
These eyes, that see thee now well-coloured,
Shall see thee wither'd, bloody, pale, and dead.
                        [*Drum afar off.*
Hark! hark! the Dauphin's drum, a warning bell,
Sings heavy music to thy timorous soul;
And mine shall ring thy dire departure out.
                [*Exeunt* GENERAL, *etc.*

TALBOT
He fables not; I hear the enemy: —
Out, some light horsemen, and peruse their wings. —
O, negligent and heedless discipline!
How are we park'd and bounded in a pale, —
A little herd of England's timorous deer,
Maz'd with a yelping kennel of French curs!
If we be English deer, be, then, in blood;
Not rascal-like, to fall down with a pinch,
But rather, moody-mad and desperate stags,
Turn on the bloody hounds with heads of steel,
And make the cowards stand aloof at bay:
Sell every man his life as dear as mine,
And they shall find dear deer of us, my friends. —
God and Saint George, Talbot and England's right,
Prosper our colours in this dangerous fight!   [*Exeunt.*

SCENE III

Plains in Gascony.

Enter a MESSENGER *that meets* YORK. *Enter* YORK
with trumpet and many SOLDIERS.

YORK
Are not the speedy scouts return'd again,
That dogg'd the mighty army of the Dauphin?

MESSENGER
They are return'd, my lord; and give it out
That he is march'd to Bourdeaux with his power,
To fight with Talbot: as he march'd along,
By your espials were discovered
Two mightier troops than that the Dauphin led;
Which join'd with him, and made their march for
    Bourdeaux.

YORK
A plague upon that villain Somerset,
That thus delays my promised supply
Of horsemen, that were levied for this siege!
Renowned Talbot doth expect my aid;
And I am louted by a traitor villain,
And cannot help the noble chevalier:
God comfort him in this necessity!
If he miscarry, farewell wars in France.

Enter SIR WILLIAM LUCY.

LUCY
Thou princely leader of our English strength,
Never so needful on the earth of France,
Spur to the rescue of the noble Talbot,
Who now is girdled with a waist of iron,
And hemm'd about with grim destruction:
To Bourdeaux, warlike duke! to Bourdeaux, York!
Else, farewell Talbot, France, and England's honour.

YORK
O God, that Somerset — who in proud heart
Doth stop my cornets — were in Talbot's place!
So should we save a valiant gentleman
By forfeiting a traitor and a coward.
Mad ire and wrathful fury makes me weep,
That thus we die, while remiss traitors sleep.

LUCY
O, send some succour to the distress'd lord!

YORK
He dies, we lose; I break my warlike word;
We mourn, France smiles; we lose, they daily get;
All long of this vile traitor Somerset.

LUCY
Then God take mercy on brave Talbot's soul;
And on his son young John, who two hours since
I met in travel toward his warlike father!
This seven years did not Talbot see his son;
And now they meet where both their lives are done.

YORK
Alas, what joy shall noble Talbot have
To bid his young son welcome to his grave?
Away! vexation almost stops my breath,
That sunder'd friends greet in the hour of death. —
Lucy, farewell: no more my fortune can,
But curse the cause I cannot aid the man.

Maine, Blois, Poictiers, and Tours, are won away,
Long all of Somerset and his delay.   [*Exit with* FORCES.

LUCY
Thus, while the vulture of sedition
Feeds in the bosom of such great commanders,
Sleeping neglection doth betray to loss
The conquest of our scarce-cold conqueror,
That ever-living man of memory,
Henry the Fifth: — whiles they each other cross,
Lives, honours, lands, and all, hurry to loss.   [*Exit.*

SCENE IV

Other plains in Gascony.

Enter SOMERSET, *with his* ARMY; *an* OFFICER *of*
TALBOT'S *with him.*

SOMERSET
It is too late: I cannot send them now:
This expedition was by York and Talbot
Too rashly plotted; all our general force
Might with a sally of the very town
Be buckled with: the over-daring Talbot
Hath sullied all his gloss of former honour
By this unheedful, desperate, wild adventure:
York set him on to fight and die in shame,
That, Talbot dead, great York might bear the name.

OFFICER
Here is Sir William Lucy, who with me
Set from our o'er-match'd forces forth for aid.

Enter SIR WILLIAM LUCY.

SOMERSET
How now, Sir William! whither were you sent?

LUCY
Whither, my lord? from bought and sold Lord Talbot;
Who, ring'd about with bold adversity,
Cries out for noble York and Somerset,
To beat assailing death from his weak legions:
And whiles the honourable captain there
Drops bloody sweat from his war-wearied limbs,
And, in advantage lingering, looks for rescue,
You, his false hopes, the trust of England's honour,
Keep off aloof with worthless emulation.
Let not your private discord keep away
The levied succours that should lend him aid,
While he, renowned noble gentleman,
Yields up his life unto a world of odds:
Orleans the Bastard, Charles, Burgundy,
Alençon, Reignier, compass him about,
And Talbot perisheth by your default.

SOMERSET
York set him on, York should have sent him aid.

LUCY
And York as fast upon your Grace exclaims;
Swearing that you withhold his levied host,
Collected for this expedition.

SOMERSET
York lies; he might have sent and had the horse;
I owe him little duty, and less love:
And take foul scorn to fawn on him by sending.

LUCY
The fraud of England, not the force of France,
Hath now entrapp'd the noble-minded Talbot:
Never to England shall he bear his life;
But dies, betray'd to fortune by your strife.

SOMERSET
Come, go; I will dispatch the horsemen straight;
Within six hours they will be at his aid.

LUCY
Too late comes rescue; he is ta'en or slain:
For fly he could not, if he would have fled;
And fly would Talbot never, though he might.

SOMERSET
If he be dead, brave Talbot, then, adieu!

LUCY
His fame lives in the world, his shame in you.   [*Exeunt.*

SCENE V

The English camp near Bourdeaux.

Enter TALBOT *and* JOHN *his son.*

TALBOT
O young John Talbot! I did send for thee
To tutor thee in stratagems of war,
That Talbot's name might be in thee revived
When sapless age and weak unable limbs
Should bring thy father to his drooping chair.
But, — O malignant and ill-boding stars! —
Now thou art come unto a feast of death,
A terrible and unavoided danger:

Therefore, dear boy, mount on my swiftest horse;
And I'll direct thee how thou shalt escape
By sudden flight: come, dally not, be gone.

JOHN TALBOT
Is my name Talbot? and am I your son?
And shall I fly? O, if you love my mother,
Dishonour not her honourable name,
To make a bastard and a slave of me!
The world will say, he is not Talbot's blood,
That basely fled when noble Talbot stood.

TALBOT
Fly, to revenge my death, if I be slain.

JOHN TALBOT
He that flies so will ne'er return again.

TALBOT
If we both stay, we both are sure to die.

JOHN TALBOT
Then let me stay; and, father, do you fly:
Your loss is great, so your regard should be;
My worth unknown, no loss is known in me.
Upon my death the French can little boast;
In yours they will, in you all hopes are lost.
Flight cannot stain the honour you have won;
But mine it will, that no exploit have done:
You fled for vantage, every one will swear;
But, if I bow, they'll say it was for fear.
There is no hope that ever I will stay,
If, the first hour, I shrink and run away.
Here, on my knee, I beg mortality,
Rather than life preserv'd with infamy.

TALBOT
Shall all thy mother's hopes lie in one tomb?

JOHN TALBOT
Ay, rather than I'll shame my mother's womb.

TALBOT
Upon my blessing, I command thee go.

JOHN TALBOT
To fight I will, but not to fly the foe.

TALBOT
Part of thy father may be saved in thee.

JOHN TALBOT
No part of him but will be shamed in me.

TALBOT
Thou never hadst renown, nor canst not lose it.

JOHN TALBOT
Yes, your renowned name: shall flight abuse it?

TALBOT
Thy father's charge shall clear thee from that stain.

JOHN TALBOT
You cannot witness for me, being slain.
If death be so apparent, then both fly.

TALBOT
And leave my followers here, to fight and die?
My age was never tainted with such shame.

JOHN TALBOT
And shall my youth be guilty of such blame?
No more can I be sever'd from your side
Than can yourself yourself in twain divide:
Stay, go, do what you will, the like do I;
For live I will not, if my father die.

TALBOT
Then here I take my leave of thee, fair son,
Born to eclipse thy life this afternoon.
Come, side by side together live and die;
And soul with soul from France to heaven fly.   [*Exeunt.*

SCENE VI

A field of battle.

Alarum: excursions, wherein TALBOT'S SON *is
hemm'd about, and* TALBOT *rescues him.*

TALBOT
Saint George and victory! fight, soldiers, fight:
The regent hath with Talbot broke his word,
And left us to the rage of France his sword.
Where is John Talbot? — Pause, and take thy breath;
I gave thee life, and rescued thee from death.

JOHN TALBOT
O, twice my father, twice am I thy son!
The life thou gavest me first was lost and done,
Till with thy warlike sword, despite of fate,
To my determined time thou gavest new date.

TALBOT
When from the Dauphin's crest thy sword struck fire,
It warm'd thy father's heart with proud desire
Of bold-fac'd victory. Then leaden age,
Quicken'd with youthful spleen and warlike rage,
Beat down Alençon, Orleans, Burgundy,
And from the pride of Gallia rescued thee.

The ireful bastard Orleans — that drew blood
From thee, my boy, and had the maidenhood
Of thy first fight — I soon encountered,
And, interchanging blows, I quickly shed
Some of his bastard blood; and, in disgrace,
Bespoke him thus, — 'Contaminated, base,
And misbegotten blood I spill of thine,
Mean and right poor, for that pure blood of mine
Which thou didst force from Talbot, my brave boy:' —
Here, purposing the Bastard to destroy,
Came in strong rescue. Speak, thy father's care, —
Art thou not weary, John? how dost thou fare?
Wilt thou yet leave the battle, boy, and fly,
Now thou art seal'd the son of chivalry?
Fly, to revenge my death when I am dead:
The help of one stands me in little stead.
O, too much folly is it, well I wot,
To hazard all our lives in one small boat!
If I to-day die not with Frenchmen's rage,
To-morrow I shall die with mickle age:
By me they nothing gain, an if I stay, —
'Tis but the shortening of my life one day:
In thee thy mother dies, our household's name,
My death's revenge, thy youth, and England's fame:
All these, and more, we hazard by thy stay;
All these are saved, if thou wilt fly away.

JOHN TALBOT
The sword of Orleans hath not made me smart;
These words of yours draw life-blood from my heart:
On that advantage, bought with such a shame, —
To save a paltry life, and slay bright fame, —
Before young Talbot from old Talbot fly,
The coward horse that bears me fall and die!
And like me to the peasant boys of France,
To be shame's scorn and subject of mischance!
Surely, by all the glory you have won,
An if I fly, I am not Talbot's son:
Then talk no more of flight, it is no boot;
If son to Talbot, die at Talbot's foot.

TALBOT
Then follow thou thy desperate sire of Crete,
Thou Icarus; thy life to me is sweet:
If thou wilt fight, fight by thy father's side;
And, commendable prov'd, let's die in pride.   [*Exeunt.*

SCENE VII

Another part of the field.

Alarum: excursions. Enter old TALBOT *led by a* SERVANT.

TALBOT
Where is my other life? — mine own is gone; —
O, where's young Talbot? where is valiant John? —
Triumphant death, smear'd with captivity,
Young Talbot's valour makes me smile at thee: —
When he perceiv'd me shrink and on my knee,
His bloody sword he brandish'd over me,
And, like a hungry lion, did commence
Rough deeds of rage and stern impatience;
But when my angry guardant stood alone,
Tendering my ruin, and assail'd of none,
Dizzy-eyed fury and great rage of heart
Suddenly made him from my side to start
Into the clustering battle of the French;
And in that sea of blood my boy did drench
His over-mounting spirit; and there died
My Icarus, my blossom, in his pride.

SERVANT
O my dear lord, lo, where your son is borne!

Enter SOLDIERS, *with* JOHN TALBOT *borne.*

TALBOT
Thou antic death, which laugh'st us here to scorn,
Anon, from thy insulting tyranny,
Coupled in bonds of perpetuity,
Two Talbots, winged through the lither sky,
In thy despite, shall scape mortality. —
O thou whose wounds become hard-favour'd death,
Speak to thy father, ere thou yield thy breath!
Brave death by speaking, whether he will or no;
Imagine him a Frenchman and thy foe. —
Poor boy! he smiles, methinks, as who should say,
Had death been French, then death had died to-day. —
Come, come, and lay him in his father's arms:
My spirit can no longer bear these harms.
Soldiers, adieu! I have what I would have,
Now my old arms are young John Talbot's grave.   [*Dies.*

Enter CHARLES, ALENÇON, BURGUNDY,
BASTARD, LA PUCELLE, *and* FORCES.

CHARLES
Had York and Somerset brought rescue in,
We should have found a bloody day of this.

BASTARD
How the young whelp of Talbot's, raging-wood,
Did flesh his puny sword in Frenchmen's blood!
LA PUCELLE
Once I encounter'd him, and thus I said,
'Thou maiden youth, be vanquish'd by a maid':
But, with a proud majestical high scorn,
He answer'd thus, 'Young Talbot was not born
To be the pillage of a giglot wench':
So, rushing in the bowels of the French,
He left me proudly, as unworthy fight.
BURGUNDY
Doubtless he would have made a noble knight:
See, where he lies inhearsed in the arms
Of the most bloody nurser of his harms!
BASTARD
Hew them to pieces, hack their bones asunder,
Whose life was England's glory, Gallia's wonder.
CHARLES
O, no, forbear! for that which we have fled
During the life, let us not wrong it dead.

Enter SIR WILLIAM LUCY, *attended; a French*
HERALD *preceding.*

LUCY
Herald, conduct me to the Dauphin's tent,
To know who hath obtain'd the glory of the day.
CHARLES
On what submissive message art thou sent?
LUCY
Submission, Dauphin! 'tis a mere French word;
We English warriors wot not what it means.
I come to know what prisoners thou hast ta'en,
And to survey the bodies of the dead.
CHARLES
For prisoners ask'st thou? hell our prison is.
But tell me whom thou seek'st.
LUCY
Where is the great Alcides of the field,
Valiant Lord Talbot, Earl of Shrewsbury, —
Created, for his rare success in arms,
Great Earl of Washford, Waterford, and Valence;
Lord Talbot of Goodrig and Urchinfield,
Lord Strange of Blackmere, Lord Verdun of Alton,
Lord Cromwell of Wingfield, Lord Furnival of Sheffield,
The thrice-victorious Lord of Falconbridge,
Knight of the noble order of Saint George,
Worthy Saint Michael, and the Golden Fleece;
Great Marshal to Henry the Sixth
Of all his wars within the realm of France?
LA PUCELLE
Here is a silly-stately style indeed!
The Turk, that two-and-fifty kingdoms hath,
Writes not so tedious a style as this. —
Him that thou magnifiest with all these titles,
Stinking and fly-blown, lies here at our feet.
LUCY
Is Talbot slain, — the Frenchmen's only scourge,

Your kingdom's terror and black Nemesis?
O, were mine eyeballs into bullets turn'd,
That I, in rage, might shoot them at your faces!
O, that I could but call these dead to life!
It were enough to fright the realm of France:
Were but his picture left amongst you here,
It would amaze the proudest of you all.
Give me their bodies, that I may bear them hence,
And give them burial as beseems their worth.
LA PUCELLE
I think this upstart is old Talbot's ghost,
He speaks with such a proud-commanding spirit.
For God's sake, let him have 'em; to keep them here,
They would but stink, and putrefy the air.
CHARLES
Go, take their bodies hence.
LUCY
I'll bear them hence: but from their ashes shall be
  rear'd
A phœnix that shall make all France afeard.
CHARLES
So we be rid of them, do with 'em what thou wilt. —
And now to Paris, in this conquering vein:
All will be ours, now bloody Talbot's slain.   [*Exeunt.*

ACT V

SCENE I

London. The palace.

Enter KING, GLOSTER, *and* EXETER.

KING HENRY
Have you perus'd the letters from the Pope,
The emperor, and the Earl of Armagnac?
GLOSTER
I have, my lord: and their intent is this, —
They humbly sue unto your excellence
To have a godly peace concluded of
Between the realms of England and of France.
KING HENRY
How doth your Grace affect their motion?
GLOSTER
Well, my good lord; and as the only means
To stop effusion of our Christian blood,
And stablish quietness on every side.
KING HENRY
Ay, marry, uncle; for I always thought
It was both impious and unnatural
That such immanity and bloody strife
Should reign among professors of one faith.
GLOSTER
Beside, my lord, the sooner to effect
And surer bind this knot of amity,
The Earl of Armagnac — near kin to Charles,
A man of great authority in France —
Proffers his only daughter to your Grace

In marriage, with a large and sumptuous dowry.
KING HENRY
Marriage, uncle! alas, my years are young!
And fitter is my study and my books
Than wanton dalliance with a paramour.
Yet, call th'ambassador; and, as you please,
So let them have their answers, every one:
I shall be well content with any choice
Tends to God's glory and my country's weal.

Enter a LEGATE *and two* AMBASSADORS, *with*
WINCHESTER *in a Cardinal's habit.*

EXETER [*aside*].
What! is my Lord of Winchester install'd,
And call'd unto a cardinal's degree?
Then I perceive that will be verified
Henry the Fifth did sometime prophesy, —
'If once he come to be a cardinal,
He'll make his cap co-equal with the crown.'
KING HENRY
My lords ambassadors, your several suits
Have been consider'd and debated on.
Your purpose is both good and reasonable;
And therefore are we certainly resolv'd
To draw conditions of a friendly peace;
Which by my Lord of Winchester we mean
Shall be transported presently to France.
GLOSTER
And for the proffer of my lord your master,
I have inform'd his highness so at large,
As, liking of the lady's virtuous gifts,
Her beauty, and the value of her dower,
He doth intend she shall be England's queen.
KING HENRY [*to the* AMBASSADORS].
In argument and proof of which contract,
Bear her this jewel, pledge of my affection. —
And so, my lord Protector, see them guarded,
And safely brought to Dover; where, inshipt,
Commit them to the fortune of the sea.

[*Exeunt* KING, GLOSTER,
EXETER, *and* AMBASSADORS.

CARDINAL
Stay, my lord legate: you shall first receive
The sum of money which I promised
Should be deliver'd to his holiness
For clothing me in these grave ornaments.
LEGATE
I will attend upon your lordship's leisure.
CARDINAL [*aside*].
Now Winchester will not submit, I trow,
Or be inferior to the proudest peer.
Humphrey of Gloster, thou shalt well perceive
That neither in birth or for authority
The bishop will be overborne by thee:
I'll either make thee stoop and bend thy knee,
Or sack this country with a mutiny.   [*Exeunt.*

SCENE II

France. Plains in Anjou.

Enter CHARLES, BURGUNDY, ALENÇON,
BASTARD, LA PUCELLE, *and* FORCES.

CHARLES
These news, my lords, may cheer our drooping
  spirits:
'Tis said the stout ParFisians do revolt,
And turn again unto the warlike French.
ALENÇON
Then march to Paris, royal Charles of France,
And keep not back your powers in dalliance.
LA PUCELLE
Peace be amongst them, if they turn to us;
Else, ruin combat with their palaces!

Enter a MESSENGER.

MESSENGER
Success unto our valiant general,
And happiness to his accomplices!
CHARLES
What tidings send our scouts? I prithee, speak.
MESSENGER
The English army, that divided was
Into two parties, is now conjoin'd in one,
And means to give you battle presently.
CHARLES
Somewhat too sudden, sirs, the warning is;
But we will presently provide for them.
BURGUNDY
I trust the ghost of Talbot is not there:
Now he is gone, my lord, you need not fear.

KING HENRY Have you perus'd the letters from the Pope?

LA PUCELLE
Of all base passions, fear is most accurst: —
Command the conquest, Charles, it shall be thine;
Let Henry fret, and all the world repine.

CHARLES
Then on, my lords; and France be fortunate!　　[*Exeunt.*

SCENE III

Before Angiers.

Alarum: excursions. Enter LA PUCELLE.

LA PUCELLE
The regent conquers, and the Frenchmen fly. —
Now help, ye charming spells and periapts;
And ye choice spirits that admonish me,
And give me signs of future accidents, —
You speedy helpers, that are substitutes

CARDINAL　I'll either make thee stoop and bend thy
　　knee, or sack this country with a mutiny.

Under the lordly monarch of the north,
Appear, and aid me in this enterprise!　　[*Thunder.*
　　Enter FIENDS.
This speedy and quick appearance argues proof
Of your accustom'd diligence to me.
Now, ye familiar spirits, that are cull'd
Out of the powerful legions under earth,
Help me this once, that France may get the field.
　　　　　　　　[*They walk, and speak not.*
O, hold me not with silence over-long!
Where I was wont to feed you with my blood,
I'll lop a member off, and give it you,
In earnest of a further benefit,
So you do condescend to help me now.
　　　　　　　　[*They hang their heads.*
No hope to have redress? — My body shall
Pay recompense, if you will grant my suit.
　　　　　　　　[*They shake their heads.*
Cannot my body nor blood-sacrifice
Entreat you to your wonted furtherance?
Then take my soul, — my body, soul, and all,
Before that England give the French the foil.
　　　　　　　　[*They depart.*
See, they forsake me! Now the time is come,
That France must vail her lofty-plumed crest,
And let her head fall into England's lap.
My ancient incantations are too weak,
And hell too strong for me to buckle with:
Now, France, thy glory droopeth to the dust.　　[*Exit.*
　　Excursions. LA PUCELLE *and* YORK *fight hand to*
　　hand: LA PUCELLE *is taken. The French fly.*

YORK
Damsel of France, I think I have you fast:
Unchain your spirits now with spelling charms,
And try if they can gain your liberty. —
A goodly prize, fit for the devil's grace!
See, how the ugly witch doth bend her brows,
As if, with Circe, she would change my shape!

LA PUCELLE
Changed to a worser shape thou canst not be.

YORK
O, Charles the Dauphin is a proper man;
No shape but his can please your dainty eye.

LA PUCELLE
A plaguing mischief light on Charles and thee!
And may ye both be suddenly surpris'd
By bloody hands, in sleeping on your beds!

YORK
Fell banning hag, enchantress, hold thy tongue!

LA PUCELLE
I prithee, give me leave to curse awhile.

YORK
Curse, miscreant, when thou comest to the stake. [*Exeunt.*
　Alarum. Enter SUFFOLK, *with* MARGARET *in his hand.*

SUFFOLK
Be what thou wilt, thou art my prisoner.　[*Gazes on her.*
O fairest beauty, do not fear nor fly!
For I will touch thee but with reverent hands,
And lay them gently on thy tender side.
I kiss these fingers for eternal peace.　[*Kissing her hand.*
Who art thou? say, that I may honour thee.

MARGARET
Margaret my name, and daughter to a king,
The King of Naples, — whosoe'er thou art.

SUFFOLK
An earl I am, and Suffolk am I call'd.
Be not offended, nature's miracle,
Thou art allotted to be ta'en by me:
So doth the swan her downy cygnets save,
Keeping them prisoner underneath her wings.
Yet, if this servile usage once offend,
Go, and be free again as Suffolk's friend.　[*She is going.*
O, stay! — [*aside*] I have no power to let her pass;
My hand would free her, but my heart says no.
As plays the sun upon the glassy streams,
Twinkling another counterfeited beam,
So seems this gorgeous beauty to mine eyes.
Fain would I woo her, yet I dare not speak:
I'll call for pen and ink, and write my mind: —
Fie, de la Pole! disable not thyself;
Hast not a tongue? is she not here thy prisoner?
Wilt thou be daunted at a woman's sight?
Ay, beauty's princely majesty is such,
Confounds the tongue, and makes the senses rough.

MARGARET
Say, Earl of Suffolk, — if thy name be so, —
What ransom must I pay before I pass?
For I perceive I am thy prisoner.

SUFFOLK [*aside*].
How canst thou tell she will deny thy suit
Before thou make a trial of her love?

MARGARET
Why speak'st thou not? what ransom must I pay?

SUFFOLK [*aside*].
She's beautiful, and therefore to be woo'd;
She is a woman, therefore to be won.

MARGARET
Wilt thou accept of ransom — yea or no?

SUFFOLK [*aside*].
Fond man, remember that thou hast a wife;
Then how can Margaret be thy paramour?

MARGARET
I were best to leave him, for he will not hear.

SUFFOLK [*aside*].
There all is marr'd; there lies a cooling-card.

MARGARET
He talks at random; sure, the man is mad.

SUFFOLK [*aside*].
And yet a dispensation may be had.

MARGARET
And yet I would that you would answer me.

SUFFOLK [*aside*].
I'll win this Lady Margaret. For whom?
Why, for my king: tush, that's a wooden thing!

MARGARET
He talks of wood: it is some carpenter.

SUFFOLK [*aside*].
Yet so my fancy may be satisfied,
And peace established between these realms.
But there remains a scruple in that too;
For though her father be the King of Naples,
Duke of Anjou and Maine, yet is he poor,
And our nobility will scorn the match.

MARGARET
Hear ye, captain, — are you not at leisure?

SUFFOLK
It shall be so, disdain they ne'er so much:
Henry is youthful, and will quickly yield. —
Madam, I have a secret to reveal.

MARGARET [*aside*].
What though I be enthrall'd? he seems a knight,
And will not any way dishonour me.

SUFFOLK
Lady, vouchsafe to listen what I say.

MARGARET [*aside*].
Perhaps I shall be rescued by the French;
And then I need not crave his courtesy.

SUFFOLK
Sweet madam, give me hearing in a cause —

MARGARET [*aside*].
Tush, women have been captivate ere now.

SUFFOLK
I prithee, lady, wherefore talk you so?

MARGARET
I cry you mercy, 'tis but *quid* for *quo*.

SUFFOLK
Say, gentle princess, would you not suppose
Your bondage happy, to be made a queen?

MARGARET
To be a queen in bondage is more vile
Than is a slave in base servility;
For princes should be free.

SUFFOLK
　　　　　　　　And so shall you,
If happy England's royal king be free.

MARGARET
Why, what concerns his freedom unto me?

SUFFOLK
I'll undertake to make thee Henry's queen;
To put a golden sceptre in thy hand,
And set a precious crown upon thy head,
If thou wilt consent to be my —

MARGARET
　　　　　　　　What?

SUFFOLK
His love.

MARGARET
I am unworthy to be Henry's wife.

SUFFOLK
No, gentle madam; I unworthy am
To woo so fair a dame to be his wife,
And have no portion in the choice myself.
How say you, madam, — are ye so content?

MARGARET
An if my father please, I am content.

SUFFOLK
Then call our captains and our colours forth! —
　　　　　　　[*Troops come forward.*
And, madam, at your father's castle-walls
We'll crave a parley, to confer with him.
　　A parley sounded. Enter REIGNIER *on the walls.*
See, Reignier, see, thy daughter prisoner!

REIGNIER
To whom?

SUFFOLK
　　　　To me.

REIGNIER
　　　　　　Suffolk, what remedy?
I am a soldier, and unapt to weep
Or to exclaim on fortune's fickleness.

SUFFOLK
Yes, there is remedy enough, my lord:
Consent — and, for thy honour, give consent —
Thy daughter shall be wedded to my king;
Whom I with pain have woo'd and won thereto;
And this her easy-held imprisonment
Hath gain'd thy daughter princely liberty.

REIGNIER
Speaks Suffolk as he thinks?

SUFFOLK
　　　　　　　Fair Margaret knows
That Suffolk doth not flatter, face, or feign.

REIGNIER
Upon thy princely warrant, I descend
To give thee answer of thy just demand.

SUFFOLK
And here I will expect thy coming.
　　　　　　[*Exit* REIGNIER *from the walls.*
　　Trumpets sound. Enter REIGNIER, *below.*

REIGNIER
Welcome, brave earl, into our territories:
Command in Anjou what your honour pleases.

SUFFOLK
Thanks, Reignier, happy for so sweet a child,
Fit to be made companion with a king:
What answer makes your Grace unto my suit?

REIGNIER
Since thou dost deign to woo her little worth
To be the princely bride of such a lord;
Upon condition I may quietly
Enjoy mine own, the counties Maine and Anjou,
Free from oppression or the stroke of war,
My daughter shall be Henry's, if he please.

SUFFOLK
That is her ransom, — I deliver her;
And those two counties I will undertake
Your Grace shall well and quietly enjoy.

REIGNIER
And I again, in Henry's royal name,
As deputy unto that gracious king,
Give thee her hand, for sign of plighted faith.

SUFFOLK
Reignier of France, I give thee kingly thanks,
Because this is in traffic of a king: —
[aside] And yet, methinks, I could be well content
To be mine own attorney in this case. —
I'll over, then, to England with this news,
And make this marriage to be solemnis'd.
So, farewell, Reignier: set this diamond safe
In golden palaces, as it becomes.

REIGNIER
I do embrace thee, as I would embrace
The Christian prince King Henry, were he here.

MARGARET
Farewell, my lord: good wishes, praise, and prayers
Shall Suffolk ever have of Margaret.   [Going.

SUFFOLK
Farewell, sweet madam: but, hark you, Margaret, —
No princely commendations to my king?

MARGARET
Such commendations as becomes a maid,
A virgin, and his servant, say to him.

SUFFOLK
Words sweetly plac'd and modestly directed.
But, madam, I must trouble you again, —
No loving token to his majesty?

MARGARET
Yes, my good lord, — a pure unspotted heart,
Never yet taint with love, I send the king.

SUFFOLK
And this withal.   [Kisses her.

MARGARET
That for thyself: — I will not so presume
To send such peevish tokens to a king.
                          [Exeunt REIGNIER and MARGARET.

SUFFOLK
O, wert thou for myself! — But, Suffolk, stay;
Thou mayst not wander in that labyrinth;
There Minotaurs and ugly treasons lurk.
Solicit Henry with her wondrous praise:
Bethink thee on her virtues that surmount,
And natural graces that extinguish art;
Repeat their semblance often on the seas,
That, when thou comest to kneel at Henry's feet,
Thou mayst bereave him of his wits with wonder. [Exit.

SCENE IV

Camp of the DUKE OF YORK in Anjou.
Enter YORK, WARWICK, and others.

YORK
Bring forth that sorceress condemn'd to burn.
    Enter LA PUCELLE, guarded, and a SHEPHERD.

SHEPHERD
Ah, Joan, this kills thy father's heart outright!
Have I sought every country far and near,
And, now it is my chance to find thee out,
Must I behold thy timeless-cruel death?
Ah, Joan, sweet daughter Joan, I'll die with thee!

LA PUCELLE
Decrepit miser! base ignoble wretch!
I am descended of a gentler blood:
Thou art no father nor no friend of mine.

SHEPHERD
Out, out! — My lords, an please you, 'tis not so;
I did beget her, all the parish knows:
Her mother liveth yet, can testify
She was the first fruit of my bachelorship.

WARWICK
Graceless! wilt thou deny thy parentage?

YORK
This argues what her kind of life hath been, —
Wicked and vile; and so her death concludes.

SHEPHERD
Fie, Joan, that thou wilt be so obstacle!
God knows thou art a collop of my flesh;
And for thy sake have I shed many a tear:
Deny me not, I prithee, gentle Joan.

LA PUCELLE
Peasant, avaunt! — You have suborn'd this man,
Of purpose to obscure my noble birth.

SHEPHERD
'Tis true, I gave a noble to the priest
The morn that I was wedded to her mother. —
Kneel down and take my blessing, good my girl.
Wilt thou not stoop? Now cursed be the time
Of thy nativity! I would the milk
Thy mother gave thee when thou suck'dst her breast
Had been a little ratsbane for thy sake!
Or else, when thou didst keep my lambs a-field,
I wish some ravenous wolf had eaten thee!
Dost thou deny thy father, cursed drab?
O, burn her, burn her! hanging is too good.   [Exit.

YORK
Take her away; for she hath liv'd too long,
To fill the world with vicious qualities.

LA PUCELLE
First, let me tell you whom you have condemn'd:
Not one begotten of a shepherd swain,
But issued from the progeny of kings;
Virtuous and holy; chosen from above,
By inspiration of celestial grace,
To work exceeding miracles on earth.
I never had to do with wicked spirits:
But you, — that are polluted with your lusts,
Stain'd with the guiltless blood of innocents,
Corrupt and tainted with a thousand vices, —
Because you want the grace that others have,
You judge it straight a thing impossible
To compass wonders but by help of devils.
No, misconceived! Joan of Arc hath been
A virgin from her tender infancy,
Chaste and immaculate in very thought;
Whose maiden blood, thus rigorously effused,
Will cry for vengeance at the gates of heaven.

YORK
Ay, ay: — away with her to execution!

WARWICK
And hark ye, sirs; because she is a maid,
Spare for no fagots, let there be enow:
Place barrels of pitch upon the fatal stake,
That so her torture may be shortened.

LA PUCELLE
Will nothing turn your unrelenting hearts? —
Then, Joan, discover thine infirmity,
That warranteth by law to be thy privilege. —
I am with child, ye bloody homicides:
Murder not, then, the fruit within my womb,
Although ye hale me to a violent death.

YORK
Now heaven forfend! the holy maid with
    child!

WARWICK
The greatest miracle that e'er ye wrought:
Is all your strict preciseness come to this?

YORK
She and the Dauphin have been juggling:
I did imagine what would be her refuge.

WARWICK
Well, go to; we'll have no bastards live;
Especially since Charles must father it.

LA PUCELLE
You are deceived; my child is none of his;
It was Alençon that enjoy'd my love.

YORK
Alençon! that notorious Machiavel!
It dies, an if it had a thousand lives.

LA PUCELLE
O, give me leave, I have deluded you:
'Twas neither Charles, nor yet the duke I
    named,
But Reignier, king of Naples, that prevail'd.

WARWICK
A married man! that's most intolerable.

YORK
Why, here's a girl! I think she knows not
    well,
There were so many, whom she may
    accuse.

WARWICK
It's sign she hath been liberal and free.

YORK
And yet, forsooth, she is a virgin pure. —
Strumpet, thy words condemn thy brat and thee:
Use no entreaty, for it is in vain.

LA PUCELLE
Then lead me hence — with whom I leave my curse;
May never glorious sun reflex his beams
Upon the country where you make abode;
But darkness and the gloomy shade of death
Environ you, till mischief and despair
Drive you to break your necks or hang yourselves!
                                        [Exit, guarded.

YORK
Break thou in pieces, and consume to ashes,
Thou foul accursed minister of hell!

    Enter CARDINAL BEAUFORT, attended.

BEAUFORT
Lord regent, I do greet your excellence
With letters of commission from the king.
For know, my lords, the states of Christendom,
Mov'd with remorse of these outrageous broils,
Have earnestly implored a general peace
Betwixt our nation and the aspiring French;
And here at hand the Dauphin and his train
Approacheth, to confer about some matter.

YORK
Is all our travail turn'd to this effect?
After the slaughter of so many peers,
So many captains, gentlemen, and soldiers,
That in this quarrel have been overthrown,
And sold their bodies for their country's benefit,
Shall we at last conclude effeminate peace?
Have we not lost most part of all the towns,
By treason, falsehood, and by treachery,
Our great progenitors had conquered? —
O, Warwick, Warwick! I foresee with grief
The utter loss of all the realm of France.

WARWICK
Be patient, York: if we conclude a peace,
It shall be with such strict and severe covenants
As little shall the Frenchmen gain thereby.

    Enter CHARLES, ALENÇON, BASTARD, REIGNIER,
                    and others.

CHARLES
Since, lords of England, it is thus agreed
That peaceful truce shall be proclaim'd in France,
We come to be informed by yourselves
What the conditions of that league must be.

YORK
Speak, Winchester; for boiling choler chokes
The hollow passage of my prison'd voice,
By sight of these our baleful enemies.

BEAUFORT
Charles, and the rest, it is enacted thus:
That, in regard King Henry gives consent,

SHEPHERD Must I behold thy timeless-cruel death?

Of mere compassion and of lenity,
To ease your country of distressful war,
And suffer you to breathe in fruitful peace, —
You shall become true liegemen to his crown:
And, Charles, upon condition thou wilt swear
To pay him tribute, and submit thyself,
Thou shalt be plac'd as viceroy under him,
And still enjoy thy regal dignity.

ALENÇON
Must he be, then, as shadow of himself?
Adorn his temples with a coronet,
And yet, in substance and authority,
Retain but privilege of a private man?
This proffer is absurd and reasonless.

CHARLES
'Tis known already that I am possess'd
With more than half the Gallian territories,
And therein reverenc'd for their lawful king:
Shall I, for lucre of the rest unvanquish'd,
Detract so much from that prerogative,
As to be call'd but viceroy of the whole?
No, lord ambassador; I'll rather keep
That which I have than, coveting for more,
Be cast from possibility of all.

YORK
Insulting Charles! hast thou by secret means
Used intercession to obtain a league,
And, now the matter grows to compromise,
Stand'st thou aloof upon comparison?
Either accept the title thou usurp'st,
Of benefit proceeding from our king,
And not of any challenge of desert,
Or we will plague thee with incessant wars.

REIGNIER [*aside to* CHARLES].
My lord, you do not well in obstinacy
To cavil in the course of this contract:
If once it be neglected, ten to one
We shall not find like opportunity.

ALENÇON [*aside to* CHARLES].
To say the truth, it is your policy
To save your subjects from such massacre
And ruthless slaughters as are daily seen
By our proceeding in hostility;
And therefore take this compact of a truce,
Although you break it when your pleasure
    serves.

WARWICK
How say'st thou, Charles? shall our condition
    stand?

CHARLES
It shall;
Only reserv'd, you claim no interest
In any of our towns of garrison.

YORK
Then swear allegiance to his majesty;
As thou art knight, never to disobey
Nor be rebellious to the crown of England, —
Thou, nor thy nobles, to the crown of England.
So, now dismiss your army when ye please;
Hang up your ensigns, let your drums be still,
For here we entertain a solemn peace. [*Exeunt.*

SCENE V

London. The royal palace.

Enter SUFFOLK *in conference with the* KING;
GLOSTER *and* EXETER.

KING HENRY
Your wondrous rare description, noble earl,
Of beauteous Margaret hath astonish'd me:
Her virtues, graced with external gifts,
Do breed love's settled passions in my heart:
And like as rigour of tempestuous gusts
Provokes the mightiest hulk against the tide,
So am I driven, by breath of her renown,
Either to suffer shipwrack, or arrive
Where I may have fruition of her love.

SUFFOLK
Tush, my good lord, — this superficial tale
Is but a preface of her worthy praise;
The chief perfections of that lovely dame —
Had I sufficient skill to utter them —
Would make a volume of enticing lines,
Able to ravish any dull conceit:
And, which is more, she is not so divine,
So full-replete with choice of all delights,
But, with as humble lowliness of mind,
She is content to be at your command;
Command, I mean, of virtuous chaste intents,
To love and honour Henry as her lord.

KING HENRY
And otherwise will Henry ne'er presume.
Therefore, my lord Protector, give consent
That Margaret may be England's royal queen.

GLOSTER
So should I give consent to flatter sin.
You know, my lord, your highness is betroth'd
Unto another lady of esteem:
How shall we, then, dispense with that contract,
And not deface your honour with reproach?

SUFFOLK
As doth a ruler with unlawful oaths;
Or one that, at a triumph having vow'd
To try his strength, forsaketh yet the lists
By reason of his adversary's odds:
A poor earl's daughter is unequal odds,
And therefore may be broke without offence.

GLOSTER
Why, what, I pray, is Margaret more than that?
Her father is no better than an earl,
Although in glorious titles he excel.

SUFFOLK
Yes, my lord, her father is a king,
The King of Naples and Jerusalem;
And of such great authority in France,
As his alliance will confirm our peace,
And keep the Frenchmen in allegiance.

GLOSTER
And so the Earl of Armagnac may do,
Because he is near kinsman unto Charles.

EXETER
Beside, his wealth doth warrant a liberal dower,
Where Reignier sooner will receive than give.

SUFFOLK
A dower, my lords! disgrace not so your king,

That he should be so abject, base, and poor,
To choose for wealth and not for perfect love.
Henry is able to enrich his queen,
And not to seek a queen to make him rich:
So worthless peasants bargain for their wives,
As market-men for oxen, sheep, or horse.
Marriage is a matter of more worth
Than to be dealt in by attorneyship;
Not whom we will, but whom his Grace affects,
Must be companion of his nuptial bed:
And therefore, lords, since he affects her most,
It most of all these reasons bindeth us,
In our opinions she should be preferr'd.
For what is wedlock forced but a hell,
An age of discord and continual strife?
Whereas the contrary bringeth bliss,
And is a pattern of celestial peace.
Whom should we match with Henry, being a king,
But Margaret, that is daughter of a king?
Her peerless feature, joined with her birth,
Approves her fit for none but for a king:
Her valiant courage and undaunted spirit —
More than in women commonly is seen —
Will answer our hope in issue of a king;
For Henry, son unto a conqueror,
Is likely to beget more conquerors,
If with a lady of so high resolve
As is fair Margaret he be link'd in love.
Then yield, my lords; and here conclude with me
That Margaret shall be queen, and none but she.

KING HENRY
Whether it be through force of your report,
My noble Lord of Suffolk, or for that
My tender youth was never yet attaint
With any passion of inflaming love,
I cannot tell; but this I am assured,
I feel such sharp dissension in my breast,
Such fierce alarums both of hope and fear,
As I am sick with working of my thoughts.
Take, therefore, shipping; post, my lord, to France;
Agree to any covenants; and procure
That Lady Margaret do vouchsafe to come
To cross the seas to England, and be crown'd
King Henry's faithful and anointed queen:
For your expenses and sufficient charge,
Among the people gather up a tenth.
Be gone, I say; for, till you do return,
I rest perplexed with a thousand cares. —
And you, good uncle, banish all offence:
If you do censure me by what you were,
Not what you are, I know it will excuse
This sudden execution of my will.
And so, conduct me where, from company,
I may revolve and ruminate my grief. [*Exit.*

GLOSTER
Ay, grief, I fear me, both at first and last.
        [*Exeunt* GLOSTER *and* EXETER.

SUFFOLK
Thus Suffolk hath prevail'd; and thus he goes,
As did the youthful Paris once to Greece,
With hope to find the like event in love,
But prosper better than the Trojan did.
Margaret shall now be queen, and rule the king;
But I will rule both her, the king, and realm. [*Exit.*

THE SECOND PART OF KING HENRY THE SIXTH

DRAMATIS PERSONAE

KING HENRY THE SIXTH.
HUMPHREY, *Duke of Gloster, his uncle.*
CARDINAL BEAUFORT, *Bishop of Winchester, great-uncle to the King.*
RICHARD PLANTAGENET, *Duke of York.*
EDWARD *and* RICHARD, *his sons.*
DUKE OF SOMERSET.
DUKE OF SUFFOLK.
DUKE OF BUCKINGHAM.
LORD CLIFFORD.
YOUNG CLIFFORD, *his son.*
EARL OF SALISBURY.
EARL OF WARWICK.
LORD SCALES.
LORD SAY.

SIR HUMPHREY STAFFORD, *and* WILLIAM STAFFORD, *his brother.*
SIR JOHN STANLEY.
VAUX.
MATTHEW GOUGH.
A SEA-CAPTAIN, MASTER, *and* MASTER'S-MATE, *and* WALTER WHITMORE.
TWO GENTLEMEN, *prisoners with Suffolk.*
ALEXANDER IDEN, *a Kentish gentleman.*
JOHN HUME *and* JOHN SOUTHWELL, *two priests.*
ROGER BOLINGBROKE, *a conjurer.*
THOMAS HORNER, *an armorer.* PETER, *his man.*
CLERK OF CHATHAM.
MAYOR OF SAINT ALBAN'S.
SAUNDER SIMPCOX, *an impostor.*
JACK CADE, *a rebel.*

GEORGE BEVIS, JOHN HOLLAND, DICK *the butcher,* SMITH *the weaver,* MICHAEL, *etc., his followers.*
TWO MURDERERS.
MARGARET, *Queen to King Henry.*
ELEANOR, *Duchess of Gloster.*
MARGERY JOURDAIN, *a witch.*
WIFE *to Simpcox.*

LORDS, LADIES, *and* ATTENDANTS, PETITIONERS, ALDERMEN, *a* HERALD, *a* BEADLE, SHERIFF, *and* OFFICERS, CITIZENS, PRENTICES, FALCONERS, GUARDS, SOLDIERS, MESSENGERS, *etc.*
A SPIRIT.

SCENE — *In various parts of England.*

ACT I

SCENE I

London. A room of state in the palace.

Flourish of trumpets: then hautboys. Enter the KING, DUKE OF GLOSTER, SALISBURY, WARWICK, and CARDINAL BEAUFORT, on the one side; the QUEEN, SUFFOLK, YORK, SOMERSET, and BUCKINGHAM, on the other.

SUFFOLK
As by your high imperial majesty
I had in charge at my depart for France,
As procurator to your excellence,
To marry Princess Margaret for your Grace;
So, in the famous ancient city Tours,
In presence of the Kings of France and Sicil,
The Dukes of Orleans, Calaber, Bretagne, and Alençon,
Seven earls, twelve barons, and twenty reverend bishops,
I have perform'd my task, and was espoused:
And humbly now, upon my bended knee,
In sight of England and her lordly peers,
Deliver up my title in the queen
To your most gracious hands, that are the substance
Of that great shadow I did represent;
The happiest gift that ever marquess gave,
The fairest queen that ever king received.

KING HENRY
Suffolk, arise. — Welcome, Queen Margaret:
I can express no kinder sign of love
Than this kind kiss. — O Lord, that lends me life,
Lend me a heart replete with thankfulness!
For thou hast given me, in this beauteous face,
A world of earthly blessings to my soul,
If sympathy of love unite our thoughts.

QUEEN MARGARET
Great King of England, and my gracious lord, —
The mutual conference that my mind hath had,
By day, by night, waking and in my dreams,
In courtly company or at my beads,
With you, mine alder-liefest sovereign,
Makes me the bolder to salute my king
With ruder terms, such as my wit affords
And over-joy of heart doth minister.

KING HENRY
Her sight did ravish; but her grace in speech,
Her words yclad with wisdom's majesty,
Makes me from wondering fall to weeping joys;
Such is the fulness of my heart's content. —
Lords, with one cheerful voice welcome my love.

ALL [*kneeling*].
Long live Queen Margaret, England's happiness!
[*Flourish.*

QUEEN MARGARET
We thank you all.

SUFFOLK
My Lord Protector, so it please your Grace,
Here are the articles of contracted peace
Between our sovereign and the French king Charles.
For eighteen months concluded by consent.

GLOSTER [*reads*].
Imprimis, It is agreed between the French king Charles,
and William de la Pole, marquess of Suffolk,
ambassador for Henry King of England, — that the

said Henry shall espouse the Lady Margaret, daughter unto Reignier King of Naples, Sicilia, and Jerusalem; and crown her Queen of England ere the thirtieth of May next ensuing. *Item,* that the duchy of Anjou and the county of Maine shall be released and deliver'd to the king her father —
[*Lets the paper fall.*

KING HENRY
Uncle, how now!

GLOSTER
Pardon me, gracious lord;
Some sudden qualm hath struck me at the heart,
And dimm'd mine eyes, that I can read no further.

KING HENRY
Uncle of Winchester, I pray, read on.

BEAUFORT [*reads*].
Item, It is further agreed between them, that the duchies of Anjou and Maine shall be released and deliver'd over to the king her father; and she sent over of the King of England's own proper cost and charges, without having any dowry.

KING HENRY
They please us well. — Lord marquess, kneel down:
We here create thee the first Duke of Suffolk,
And girt thee with the sword. — Cousin of York,
We here discharge your Grace from being regent
I' th' parts of France, till term of eighteen months
Be full expired. — Thanks, uncle Winchester,
Gloster, York, Buckingham, Somerset, Salisbury, and Warwick;
We thank you all for this great favour done,
In entertainment to my princely queen.
Come, let us in; and with all speed provide
To see her coronation be perform'd.
[*Exeunt KING, QUEEN, and SUFFOLK.*

GLOSTER
Brave peers of England, pillars of the state,
To you Duke Humphrey must unload his grief, —
Your grief, the common grief of all the land.
What! did my brother Henry spend his youth,
His valour, coin, and people in the wars?
Did he so often lodge in open field
In winter's cold and summer's parching heat,
To conquer France, his true inheritance?
And did my brother Bedford toil his wits,
To keep by policy what Henry got?
Have you yourselves, Somerset, Buckingham,
Brave York, Salisbury, and victorious Warwick,
Received deep scars in France and Normandy?
Or hath mine uncle Beaufort and myself,
With all the learned council of the realm,
Studied so long, sat in the council-house
Early and late, debating to and fro
How France and Frenchmen might be kept in awe?
And was his highness in his infancy

KING HENRY *Suffolk, arise. — Welcome, Queen Margaret.*

Crowned in Paris in despite of foes?
And shall these labours and these honours die?
Shall Henry's conquest, Bedford's vigilance,
Your deeds of war, and all our counsel die?
O peers of England, shameful is this league!
Fatal this marriage! cancelling your fame,
Blotting your name from books of memory,
Razing the characters of your renown,
Defacing monuments of conquer'd France,
Undoing all, as all had never been!

BEAUFORT
Nephew, what means this passionate discourse,
This peroration with such circumstance?
For France, 'tis ours; and we will keep it still.

GLOSTER
Ay, uncle, we will keep it, if we can;
But now it is impossible we should:
Suffolk, the new-made duke that rules the roast,
Hath given the duchies of Anjou and Maine
Unto the poor King Reignier, whose large style
Agrees not with the leanness of his purse.

SALISBURY
Now, by the death of him that died for all,
These counties were the keys of Normandy: —
But wherefore weeps Warwick, my valiant son?

WARWICK
For grief that they are past recovery:
For, were there hope to conquer them again,
My sword should shed hot blood, mine eyes no tears.
Anjou and Maine! myself did win them both;
Those provinces these arms of mine did conquer:
And are the cities, that I got with wounds,
Deliver'd up again with peaceful words?
Mort Dieu!

YORK
For Suffolk's duke, may he be suffocate,
That dims the honour of this warlike isle!
France should have torn and rent my very heart,
Before I would have yielded to this league.
I never read but England's kings have had
Large sums of gold and dowries with their wives;
And our King Henry gives away his own,
To match with her that brings no vantages.

GLOSTER
A proper jest, and never heard before,
That Suffolk should demand a whole fifteenth
For costs and charges in transporting her!
She should have stay'd in France, and starv'd in France,
Before —

BEAUFORT
My Lord of Gloster, now ye grow too hot:
It was the pleasure of my lord the king.

GLOSTER
My Lord of Winchester, I know your mind;
'Tis not my speeches that you do mislike,
But 'tis my presence that doth trouble ye.
Rancour will out: proud prelate, in thy face
I see thy fury: if I longer stay,
We shall begin our ancient bickerings. —
Lordings, farewell: and say, when I am gone,
I prophesied — France will be lost ere long. [*Exit.*

BEAUFORT
So, there goes our Protector in a rage.
'Tis known to you he is mine enemy;
Nay, more, an enemy unto you all;
And no great friend, I fear me, to the king.
Consider, lords, he is the next of blood,
And heir-apparent to the English crown:
Had Henry got an empire by his marriage,
And all the wealthy kingdoms of the west,
There's reason he should be displeas'd at it.
Look to it, lords; let not his smoothing words
Bewitch your hearts; be wise and circumspect.
What though the common people favour him,
Calling him 'Humphrey, the good Duke of Gloster';
Clapping their hands, and crying with loud voice,
'Jesu maintain your royal excellence!'
With 'God preserve the good Duke Humphrey!'
I fear me, lords, for all this flattering gloss,
He will be found a dangerous Protector.

BUCKINGHAM
Why should he, then, protect our sovereign,
He being of age to govern of himself? —
Cousin of Somerset, join you with me,
And all together, with the Duke of Suffolk,
We'll quickly hoise Duke Humphrey from his seat.

BEAUFORT
This weighty business will not brook delay;
I'll to the Duke of Suffolk presently. [*Exit.*

SOMERSET
Cousin of Buckingham, though Humphrey's pride
And greatness of his place be grief to us,
Yet let us watch the haughty cardinal:
His insolence is more intolerable
Than all the princes in the land beside:
If Gloster be displac'd, he'll be Protector.

BUCKINGHAM
Or thou or I, Somerset, will be Protector,
Despite Duke Humphrey or the cardinal.
[*Exeunt* BUCKINGHAM *and* SOMERSET.

SALISBURY
Pride went before, ambition follows him.
While these do labour for their own preferment,
Behoves it us to labour for the realm.
I never saw but Humphrey Duke of Gloster
Did bear him like a noble gentleman.
Oft have I seen the haughty cardinal —
More like a soldier than a man o'th'church,
As stout and proud as he were lord of all —
Swear like a ruffian, and demean himself
Unlike the ruler of a commonweal. —
Warwick, my son, the comfort of my age,

Thy deeds, thy plainness, and thy housekeeping,
Have won the greatest favour of the commons,
Excepting none but good Duke Humphrey: —
And, brother York, thy acts in Ireland,
In bringing them to civil discipline;
Thy late exploits done in the heart of France,
When thou wert regent for our sovereign,
Have made thee fear'd and honour'd of the people: —
Join we together, for the public good,
In what we can, to bridle and suppress
The pride of Suffolk and the cardinal,
With Somerset's and Buckingham's ambition;
And, as we may, cherish Duke Humphrey's deeds,
While they do tend the profit of the land.

WARWICK
So God help Warwick, as he loves the land,
And common profit of his country!

YORK [*aside*].
And so says York, for he hath greatest cause.

SALISBURY
Then let's make haste away, and look unto the main.

WARWICK
Unto the main! O father, Maine is lost, —
That Maine which by main force Warwick did win,
And would have kept so long as breath did last!
Main chance, father, you meant; but I meant Maine, —
Which I will win from France, or else be slain.
[*Exeunt* WARWICK *and* SALISBURY.

YORK
Anjou and Maine are given to the French;
Paris is lost; the state of Normandy
Stands on a tickle point, now they are gone:
Suffolk concluded on the articles;
The peers agreed; and Henry was well pleased
To change two dukedoms for a duke's fair daughter.
I cannot blame them all: what is't to them?
'Tis thine they give away, and not their own.
Pirates may make cheap pennyworths of their pillage,
And purchase friends, and give to courtezans,
Still revelling, like lords, till all be gone;
While as the silly owner of the goods
Weeps over them, and wrings his hapless hands,
And shakes his head, and trembling stands aloof,
While all is shared, and all is borne away,
Ready to starve, and dare not touch his own:
So York must sit, and fret, and bite his tongue,
While his own lands are bargain'd for and sold.
Methinks the realms of England, France, and Ireland
Bear that proportion to my flesh and blood
As did the fatal brand Althæa burn'd
Unto the prince's heart of Calydon.
Anjou and Maine, both given unto the French!
Cold news for me; for I had hope of France,
Even as I have of fertile England's soil.
A day will come when York shall claim his own;
And therefore I will take the Nevils' parts,
And make a show of love to proud Duke Humphrey,
And, when I spy advantage, claim the crown,
For that's the golden mark I seek to hit:
Nor shall proud Lancaster usurp my right,
Nor hold the sceptre in his childish fist,
Nor wear the diadem upon his head,
Whose church-like humours fits not for a crown.
Then, York, be still awhile, till time do serve:
Watch thou and wake, when others be asleep,
To pry into the secrets of the state;
Till Henry, surfeiting in joys of love,
With his new bride and England's dear-bought queen,
And Humphrey with the peers be fall'n at jars:
Then will I raise aloft the milk-white rose,
With whose sweet smell the air shall be perfumed;
And in my standard bear the arms of York,
To grapple with the house of Lancaster;
And, force perforce, I'll make him yield the crown,
Whose bookish rule hath pull'd fair England down.
[*Exit.*

SCENE II

The same. The DUKE OF GLOSTER'S *house.*

Enter DUKE HUMPHREY *and his wife* ELEANOR.

DUCHESS OF GLOSTER
Why droops my lord, like over-ripen'd corn
Hanging the head at Ceres' plenteous load?
Why doth the great Duke Humphrey knit his brows,
As frowning at the favours of the world?
Why are thine eyes fix'd to the sullen earth,
Gazing on that which seems to dim thy sight?
What seest thou there? King Henry's diadem,
Enchased with all the honours of the world?
If so, gaze on, and grovel on thy face,

Until thy head be circled with the same.
Put forth thy hand, reach at the glorious gold: —
What, is't too short? I'll lengthen it with mine;
And, having both together heav'd it up,
We'll both together lift our heads to heaven,
And never more abase our sight so low
As to vouchsafe one glance unto the ground.

GLOSTER
O Nell, sweet Nell, if thou dost love thy lord,
Banish the canker of ambitious thoughts!
And may that thought, when I imagine ill
Against my king and nephew, virtuous Henry,
Be my last breathing in this mortal world!
My troublous dream this night doth make me sad.

DUCHESS OF GLOSTER
What dream'd my lord? tell me, and I'll requite it
With sweet rehearsal of my morning's dream.

GLOSTER
Methought this staff, mine office-badge in court,
Was broke in twain; by whom I have forgot,
But, as I think, 'twas by the cardinal;
And on the pieces of the broken wand
Were plac'd the heads of Edmund Duke of Somerset,
And William de la Pole, first duke of Suffolk.
This was my dream: what it doth bode, God knows.

DUCHESS OF GLOSTER
Tut, this was nothing but an argument
That he that breaks a stick of Gloster's grove
Shall lose his head for his presumption.
But list to me, my Humphrey, my sweet duke:
Methought I sat in seat of majesty
In the cathedral church of Westminster,
And in that chair where kings and queens are crown'd;
Where Henry and Dame Margaret kneel'd to me,
And on my head did set the diadem.

GLOSTER
Nay, Eleanor, then must I chide outright:
Presumptuous dame, ill-nurtured Eleanor!
Art thou not second woman in the realm,
And the Protector's wife, belov'd of him?
Hast thou not worldly pleasure at command,
Above the reach or compass of thy thought?
And wilt thou still be hammering treachery,
To tumble down thy husband and thyself
From top of honour to disgrace's feet?
Away from me, and let me hear no more!

DUCHESS OF GLOSTER
What, what, my lord! are you so choleric
With Eleanor, for telling but her dream?
Next time I'll keep my dreams unto myself,
And not be check'd.

GLOSTER
Nay, be not angry, I am pleased again.
Enter a MESSENGER.

MESSENGER
My lord Protector, 'tis his highness' pleasure
You do prepare to ride unto Saint Alban's,
Whereas the king and queen do mean to hawk.

GLOSTER
I go. — Come, Nell, — thou wilt ride with us, I'm sure.

DUCHESS OF GLOSTER
Yes, my good lord, I'll follow presently.
[*Exeunt* GLOSTER *and* MESSENGER.
Follow I must; I cannot go before,
While Gloster bears this base and humble mind.
Were I a man, a duke, and next of blood,
I would remove these tedious stumbling-blocks,
And smooth my way upon their headless necks;
And, being a woman, I will not be slack
To play my part in Fortune's pageant. —
Where are you there, Sir John? nay, fear not, man,
We are alone; here's none but thee and I.
Enter HUME.

HUME
Jesus preserve your royal majesty!

DUCHESS OF GLOSTER
What say'st thou? majesty! I am but grace.

HUME
But, by the grace of God, and Hume's advice,
Your Grace's title shall be multiplied.

DUCHESS OF GLOSTER
What say'st thou, man? hast thou as yet conferr'd
With Margery Jourdain, the cunning witch,
With Roger Bolingbroke, the conjurer?
And will they undertake to do me good?

HUME
This they have promised, — to show your highness
A spirit raised from depth of under-ground,
That shall make answer to such questions

As by your Grace shall be propounded him.

DUCHESS OF GLOSTER
It is enough; I'll think upon the questions:
When from Saint Alban's we do make return,
We'll see these things effected to the full.
Here, Hume, take this reward; make merry, man,
With thy confederates in this weighty cause.   [*Exit.*

HUME
Hume must make merry with the duchess' gold;
Marry, and shall. But, how now, Sir John Hume!
Seal up your lips, and give no words but mum:
The business asketh silent secrecy.
Dame Eleanor gives gold to bring the witch:
Gold cannot come amiss, were she a devil.
Yet have I gold flies from another coast: —
I dare not say, from the rich cardinal,
And from the great and new-made Duke of Suffolk;
Yet I do find it so: for, to be plain,
They, knowing Dame Eleanor's aspiring humour,
Have hired me to undermine the duchess,
And buzz these conjurations in her brain.
They say, — A crafty knave does need no broker;
Yet am I Suffolk and the cardinal's broker.
Hume, if you take not heed, you shall go near
To call them both a pair of crafty knaves.
Well, so it stands; and thus, I fear, at last
Hume's knavery will be the duchess' wrack,
And her attainture will be Humphrey's fall:
Sort how it will, I shall have gold for all.   [*Exit.*

SCENE III

The same. The palace.

Enter PETER, *and other* PETITIONERS.

FIRST PETITIONER
My masters, let's stand close: my lord Protector will
come this way by and by, and then we may deliver
our supplications in the quill.

SECOND PETITIONER
Marry, the Lord protect him, for he's a good man! Jesu
bless him!

PETER
Here 'a comes, methinks, and the queen with him.
I'll be the first, sure.

Enter SUFFOLK *and* QUEEN.

SECOND PETITIONER
Come back, fool; this is the Duke of Suffolk, and not
my lord Protector.

SUFFOLK
How now, fellow! wouldst any thing with me?

FIRST PETITIONER
I pray, my lord, pardon me; I took ye for my lord
Protector.

QUEEN MARGARET
For my lord Protector! Are your supplications to his
lordship? Let me see them: — what is thine?

FIRST PETITIONER
Mine is, an't please your Grace, against John
Goodman, my lord cardinal's man, for keeping my
house, and lands, and wife and all, from me.

SUFFOLK
Thy wife too! that's some wrong, indeed. — What's
yours? — What's here! [*reads*] 'Against the Duke of
Suffolk, for enclosing the commons of Melford.' —
How now, sir knave!

SECOND PETITIONER
Alas, sir, I am but a poor petitioner of our whole
township.

PETER [*presenting his petition*].
Against my master, Thomas Horner, for saying that
the Duke of York was rightful heir to the crown.

QUEEN MARGARET
What say'st thou? did the Duke of York say he was
rightful heir to the crown?

PETER
That my master was? no, forsooth: my master said that
he was; and that the king was an usurper.

SUFFOLK
Who is there? [*Enter* SERVANT.] — Take this fellow in,
and send for his master with a pursuivant presently.
— We'll hear more of your matter before the king.
[*Exit* SERVANT *with* PETER.

QUEEN MARGARET
And as for you, that love to be protected
Under the wings of our Protector's Grace,
Begin your suits anew, and sue to him.
[*Tears the supplications.*
Away, base cullions! — Suffolk, let them go.

ALL
Come, let's be gone.   [*Exeunt* PETITIONERS.

QUEEN MARGARET
My Lord of Suffolk, say, is this the guise,
Is this the fashion in the court of England?
Is this the government of Britain's isle,
And this the royalty of Albion's king?
What, shall King Henry be a pupil still,
Under the surly Gloster's governance?
Am I a queen in title and in style,
And must be made a subject to a duke?
I tell thee, Pole, when in the city Tours
Thou rann'st a tilt in honour of my love,
And stolest away the ladies' hearts of France,
I thought King Henry had resembled thee
In courage, courtship, and proportion:
But all his mind is bent to holiness,
To number *Ave-Maries* on his beads:
His champions are the prophets and apostles;
His weapons, holy saws of sacred writ;
His study is his tilt-yard, and his loves
Are brazen images of canonis'd saints.
I would the college of the cardinals
Would choose him Pope, and carry him to Rome,
And set the triple crown upon his head: —
That were a state fit for his holiness.

SUFFOLK
Madam, be patient: as I was cause
Your highness came to England, so will I
In England work your Grace's full content.

QUEEN MARGARET
Beside the haught Protector, have we Beaufort
The imperious churchman, Somerset, Buckingham,
And grumbling York; and not the least of these
But can do more in England than the king.

SUFFOLK
And he of these that can do most of all
Cannot do more in England than the Nevils:
Salisbury and Warwick are no simple peers.

QUEEN MARGARET
Not all these lords do vex me half so much
As that proud dame, the lord Protector's wife.
She sweeps it through the court with troops of ladies,
More like an empress than Duke Humphrey's wife:
Strangers in court do take her for the queen:
She bears a duke's revenues on her back,
And in her heart she scorns our poverty:
Shall I not live to be avenged on her?
Contemptuous base-born callet as she is,
She vaunted 'mongst her minions t'other day,
The very train of her worst wearing gown
Was better worth than all my father's lands,
Till Suffolk gave two dukedoms for his daughter.

SUFFOLK
Madam, myself have limed a bush for her,
And placed a quire of such enticing birds,
That she will light to listen to the lays,
And never mount to trouble you again.
So, let her rest: and, madam, list to me;
For I am bold to counsel you in this.
Although we fancy not the cardinal,
Yet must we join with him and with the lords,
Till we have brought Duke Humphrey in disgrace.
As for the Duke of York, — this late complaint
Will make but little for his benefit.
So, one by one, we'll weed them all at last,
And you yourself shall steer the happy helm.

Sound a sennet. Enter the KING, DUKE HUMPHREY,
CARDINAL BEAUFORT, BUCKINGHAM, YORK,
SOMERSET, SALISBURY, WARWICK, *and the*
DUCHESS OF GLOSTER.

KING HENRY
For my part, noble lords, I care not which;
Or Somerset or York, all's one to me.

YORK
If York have ill demean'd himself in France,
Then let him be denay'd the regentship.

SOMERSET
If Somerset be unworthy of the place,
Let York be regent; I will yield to him.

WARWICK
Whether your Grace be worthy, yea or no,
Dispute not that: York is the worthier.

CARDINAL BEAUFORT
Ambitious Warwick, let thy betters speak.

WARWICK
The cardinal's not my better in the field.

BUCKINGHAM
All in this presence are thy betters, Warwick.

WARWICK
Warwick may live to be the best of all.

SALISBURY
Peace, son! — and show some reason, Buckingham,
Why Somerset should be preferr'd in this.

QUEEN MARGARET
Because the king, forsooth, will have it so.

GLOSTER
Madam, the king is old enough himself
To give his censure: these are no women's matters.

QUEEN MARGARET
If he be old enough, what needs your Grace
To be Protector of his excellence?

GLOSTER
Madam, I am Protector of the realm;
And, at his pleasure, will resign my place.

SUFFOLK
Resign it, then, and leave thine insolence.
Since thou wert king, — as who is king but thou? —
The commonwealth hath daily run to wrack;
The Dauphin hath prevail'd beyond the seas;
And all the peers and nobles of the realm
Have been as bondmen to thy sovereignty.

CARDINAL BEAUFORT
The commons hast thou rack'd; the clergy's bags
Are lank and lean with thy extortions.

SOMERSET
Thy sumptuous buildings, and thy wife's attire,
Have cost a mass of public treasury.

BUCKINGHAM
Thy cruelty in execution
Upon offenders hath exceeded law,
And left thee to the mercy of the law.

QUEEN MARGARET
Thy sale of offices and towns in France —
If they were known, as the suspect is great —
Would make thee quickly hop without thy head.
[*Exit* GLOSTER. *The* QUEEN *drops her fan.*
Give me my fan: what, minion! can ye not?
[*She gives the* DUCHESS *a box on the ear.*
I cry you mercy, madam; was it you?

DUCHESS OF GLOSTER
Was't I! yea, I it was, proud Frenchwoman:
Could I come near your beauty with my nails,
I'ld set my ten commandments in your face.

KING HENRY
Sweet aunt, be quiet; 'twas against her will.

DUCHESS OF GLOSTER
Against her will! good king, look to't in time;
She'll hamper thee, and dandle thee like a baby:
Though in this place most master wear no breeches,
She shall not strike Dame Eleanor unrevenged.   [*Exit.*

BUCKINGHAM
Lord cardinal, I will follow Eleanor,
And listen after Humphrey, how he proceeds:
She's tickled now; her fury needs no spurs,
She'll gallop fast enough to her destruction.   [*Exit.*

Enter GLOSTER.

GLOSTER
Now, lords, my choler being over-blown
With walking once about the quadrangle,
I come to talk of commonwealth affairs.
As for your spiteful false objections,
Prove them, and I lie open to the law:
But God in mercy so deal with my soul,
As I in duty love my king and country!
But, to the matter that we have in hand: —
I say, my sovereign, York is meetest man
To be your regent in the realm of France.

SUFFOLK
Before we make election, give me leave
To show some reason, of no little force,
That York is most unmeet of any man.

YORK
I'll tell thee, Suffolk, why I am unmeet:
First, for I cannot flatter thee in pride;
Next, if I be appointed for the place,
My Lord of Somerset will keep me here,
Without discharge, money, or furniture,
Till France be won into the Dauphin's hands:
Last time, I danc'd attendance on his will
Till Paris was besieged, famish'd, and lost.

WARWICK
That can I witness; and a fouler fact
Did never traitor in the land commit.

SUFFOLK
Peace, headstrong Warwick!

WARWICK
Image of pride, why should I hold my peace?

Enter HORNER, *the Armourer, and his man* PETER,
guarded.

SUFFOLK
Because here is a man accus'd of treason:
Pray God the Duke of York excuse himself!

YORK
Doth any one accuse York for a traitor?

KING HENRY
What mean'st thou, Suffolk? tell me, what are these?

SUFFOLK
Please it your majesty, this is the man
That doth accuse his master of high treason:
His words were these, — that Richard Duke of York
Was rightful heir unto the English crown,
And that your majesty was an usurper.

KING HENRY
Say, man, were these thy words?

HORNER
An't shall please your majesty, I never said nor thought
    any such matter: God is my witness, I am falsely
    accused by the villain.

PETER [*holding up his hands*].
By these ten bones, my lords, he did speak them to me
    in the garret one night, as we were scouring my Lord
    of York's armour.

YORK
Base dunghill villain and mechanical,
I'll have thy head for this thy traitor's speech. —
I do beseech your royal majesty,
Let him have all the rigour of the law.

HORNER
Alas, my lord, hang me, if ever I spake the words. My
accuser is my prentice; and when I did correct him for
his fault the other day, he did vow upon his knees he
would be even with me: I have good witness of this;
therefore, I beseech your majesty, do not cast away an
honest man for a villain's accusation.

KING HENRY
Uncle, what shall we say to this in law?

GLOSTER
This is my doom, my lord, if I may judge:
Let Somerset be regent o'er the French,
Because in York this breeds suspicion;
And let these have a day appointed them
For single combat in convenient place,
For he hath witness of his servant's malice:
This is the law, and this Duke Humphrey's doom.

KING HENRY
Then be it so. — My Lord of Somerset,
We make your Grace regent over the French.

SOMERSET
I humbly thank your royal majesty.

HORNER
And I accept the combat willingly.

PETER
Alas, my lord, I cannot fight; for God's sake, pity my
case! The spite of man prevaileth against me. O Lord,
have mercy upon me! I shall never be able to fight a
blow: O Lord, my heart!

GLOSTER
Sirrah, or you must fight, or else be hang'd.

KING HENRY
Away with them to prison; and the day
Of combat shall be the last of the next month. —
Come, Somerset, we'll see thee sent away.   [*Exeunt.*

SCENE IV

The same. GLOSTER'S *garden.*

Enter MARGERY JOURDAIN, HUME,
SOUTHWELL, *and* BOLINGBROKE.

HUME
Come, my masters; the duchess, I tell you, expects
    performance of your promises.

BOLINGBROKE
Master Hume, we are therefore provided: will her
    ladyship behold and hear our exorcisms?

HUME
Ay, what else? fear you not her courage.

BOLINGBROKE
I have heard her reported to be a woman of an
invincible spirit: but it shall be convenient, Master
Hume, that you be by her aloft, while we be busy below;
and so, I pray you, go in God's name, and leave us. [*Exit
HUME.*] Mother Jourdain, be you prostrate, and grovel
on the earth; — John Southwell, read you; — and let us
to our work.

BOLINGBROKE False fiend, avoid!

Enter DUCHESS *aloft;* HUME *following.*

DUCHESS OF GLOSTER
Well said, my masters; and welcome all. To this gear, —
    the sooner the better.

BOLINGBROKE
Patience, good lady; wizards know their times:
Deep night, dark night, the silent of the night,
The time of night when Troy was set on fire;
The time when screech-owls cry, and ban-dogs howl,
And spirits walk, and ghosts break up their graves, —
That time best fits the work we have in hand.
Madam, sit you, and fear not: whom we raise,
We will make fast within a hallow'd verge.
    [*Here do the ceremonies belonging, and make the circle;*
    BOLINGBROKE *or* SOUTHWELL *reads,* Conjuro te,
    etc. It thunders and lightens terribly; then the SPIRIT
                                                    riseth.

SPIRIT
Adsum.

JOURDAIN
Asmath,
By the eternal God, whose name and power
Thou tremblest at, answer that I shall ask;
For, till thou speak, thou shalt not pass from hence.

SPIRIT
Ask what thou wilt: — that I had said and done!

BOLINGBROKE [*reading out of a paper*].
'First of the king: what shall of him become?'

SPIRIT
The duke yet lives that Henry shall depose;
But him outlive, and die a violent death.
    [*As the* SPIRIT *speaks,* SOUTHWELL *writes the answer.*

BOLINGBROKE
'What fates await the Duke of Suffolk?'

SPIRIT
By water shall he die, and take his end.

BOLINGBROKE
'What shall befall the Duke of Somerset?'

SPIRIT
Let him shun castles;
Safer shall he be upon the sandy plains
Than where castles mounted stand. —
Have done, for more I hardly can endure.

BOLINGBROKE
Descend to darkness and the burning lake!
False fiend, avoid!
    [*Thunder and lightning. Exit* SPIRIT.
    Enter the DUKE OF YORK *and the* DUKE OF
    BUCKINGHAM, *with their* GUARD, *and break in.*

YORK
Lay hands upon these traitors and their trash. —
Beldam, I think we watch'd you at an inch. —
What, madam, are you there? the king and
    commonweal
Are deeply indebted for this piece of pains:
My lord Protector will, I doubt it not,
See you well guerdon'd for these good deserts.

DUCHESS OF GLOSTER
Not half so bad as thine to England's king,
Injurious duke, that threatest where's no cause.

BUCKINGHAM
True, madam, none at all: — what call you this? —
                                [*Showing her the papers.*
Away with them! let them be clapp'd up close,
And kept asunder. — You, madam, shall with us. —
Stafford, take her to thee.
We'll see your trinkets here all forthcoming. —
Away!

    [*Exeunt, above,* DUCHESS *and* HUME, *guarded.*
    Exeunt, below, SOUTHWELL, BOLINGBROKE, *etc.,*
                                                guarded.

YORK
Lord Buckingham, methinks you watch'd her well:

A pretty plot, well chosen to build upon!
Now, pray, my lord, let's see the devil's writ.
What have we here? *[Reads.*
'The duke yet lives that Henry shall depose;
But him outlive, and die a violent death.'
Why, this is just
Aio te, Æacida, Romanos vincere posse.
Well, to the rest:
'Tell me what fate awaits the Duke of Suffolk?
By water shall he die, and take his end. —
What shall betide the Duke of Somerset?
Let him shun castles;
Safer shall he be upon the sandy plains
Than where castles mounted stand.'
Come, come, my lords;
These oracles are hardly attain'd,
And hardly understood.
The king is now in progress towards Saint Alban's,
With him the husband of this lovely lady:
Thither goes these news, as fast as horse can carry
    them, —
A sorry breakfast for my lord Protector.

BUCKINGHAM
Your Grace shall give me leave, my Lord of York,
To be the post, in hope of his reward.

YORK
At your pleasure, my good lord. — Who's within
    there, ho!

Enter a SERVANT.

Invite my Lords of Salisbury and Warwick
To sup with me to-morrow night. — Away! *[Exeunt.*

ACT II

SCENE I

Saint Alban's.

Enter the KING, QUEEN, GLOSTER,
CARDINAL BEAUFORT, *and* SUFFOLK,
with FALCONERS *hallooing.*

QUEEN MARGARET
Believe me, lords, for flying at the brook,
I saw not better sport these seven years' day:
Yet, by your leave, the wind was very high;
And, ten to one, old Joan had not gone out.

KING HENRY
But what a point, my lord, your falcon made,
And what a pitch she flew above the rest! —
To see how God in all His creatures works!
Yea, man and birds are fain of climbing high.

SUFFOLK
No marvel, an it like your majesty,
My lord Protector's hawks do tower so well;
They know their master loves to be aloft,
And bears his thoughts above his falcon's pitch.

GLOSTER
My lord, 'tis but a base ignoble mind
That mounts no higher than a bird can soar.

CARDINAL BEAUFORT
I thought as much: he would be above the clouds.

GLOSTER
Ay, my lord cardinal, — how think you by that?
Were it not good your Grace could fly to heaven?

KING HENRY
The treasury of everlasting joy!

CARDINAL BEAUFORT
Thy heaven is on earth; thine eyes and thoughts
Beat on a crown, the treasure of thy heart;
Pernicious Protector, dangerous peer,
That smooth'st it so with king and commonweal!

GLOSTER
What, cardinal, is your priesthood grown peremptory?
Tantæne animis cœlestibus iræ?
Churchmen so hot? good uncle, hide such malice;
With such holiness can you not do it?

SUFFOLK
No malice, sir; no more than well becomes
So good a quarrel and so bad a peer.

GLOSTER
As who, my lord?

SUFFOLK
                Why, as you, my lord,
An't like your lordly lord-Protectorship.

GLOSTER
Why, Suffolk, England knows thine insolence.

QUEEN MARGARET
And thy ambition, Gloster.

KING HENRY
                I prithee, peace,
Good queen, and whet not on these furious peers;
For blessed are the peacemakers on earth.

CARDINAL BEAUFORT
Let me be blessed for the peace I make,
Against this proud Protector, with my sword!

GLOSTER [*aside to* CARDINAL].
Faith, holy uncle, would 'twere come to that!

CARDINAL BEAUFORT [*aside to* GLOSTER].
Marry, when thou darest.

GLOSTER [*aside to* CARDINAL].
Make up no factious numbers for the matter;
In thine own person answer thy abuse.

CARDINAL BEAUFORT [*aside to* GLOSTER].
Ay, where thou darest not peep: an if thou darest,
This evening on the east side of the grove.

KING HENRY
How now, my lords!

CARDINAL BEAUFORT
                Believe me, cousin Gloster,
Had not your man put up the fowl so suddenly,
We had had more sport. — [*aside to* GLOSTER]
                Come with thy two-hand sword.

GLOSTER
True, uncle.

CARDINAL BEAUFORT [*aside to* GLOSTER].
Are ye advis'd? — the east side of the grove?

GLOSTER [*aside to* CARDINAL].
Cardinal, I am with you.

KING HENRY
Why, how now, uncle Gloster!

GLOSTER
Talking of hawking; nothing else, my lord. —
[*aside to* CARDINAL] Now, by God's mother, priest, I'll
    shave your crown for this,
Or all my fence shall fail.

CARDINAL BEAUFORT [*aside to* GLOSTER].
                Medice, teipsum;
Protector, see to't well, protect yourself.

KING HENRY
The winds grow high; so do your stomachs, lords.
How irksome is this music to my heart!
When such strings jar, what hope of harmony?
I pray, my lords, let me compound this strife.

Enter a TOWNSMAN *of Saint Alban's,*
crying, A miracle!

GLOSTER
What means this noise?
Fellow, what dost thou proclaim?

TOWNSMAN
A miracle! a miracle!

SUFFOLK
Come to the king, and tell him what miracle.

TOWNSMAN
Forsooth, a blind man at Saint Alban's shrine,
Within this half-hour, hath received his sight;
A man that ne'er saw in his life before.

KING HENRY
Now, God be prais'd, that to believing souls
Gives light in darkness, comfort in despair!

Enter the MAYOR *of Saint Alban's and his brethren,*
bearing SAUNDER SIMPCOX, *between two in a chair,*
his WIFE *and a multitude following.*

CARDINAL BEAUFORT
Here comes the townsmen on procession,
To present your highness with the man.

KING HENRY
Great is his comfort in this earthly vale,
Although by his sight his sin be multiplied.

GLOSTER
Stand by, my masters: — bring him near the king;
His highness' pleasure is to talk with him.

KING HENRY
Good fellow, tell us here the circumstance,
That we for thee may glorify the Lord.
What, hast thou been long blind, and now restored?

SIMPCOX
Born blind, an't please your Grace.

WIFE
                Ay, indeed was he.

SUFFOLK
What woman is this?

WIFE
                His wife, an't like your worship.

GLOSTER
Hadst thou been his mother, thou couldst have better
    told.

KING HENRY
Where wert thou born?

SIMPCOX
At Berwick in the north, an't like your Grace.

KING HENRY
Poor soul, God's goodness hath been great to thee:
Let never day nor night unhallow'd pass,
But still remember what the Lord hath done.

QUEEN MARGARET
Tell me, good fellow, camest thou here by chance,
Or of devotion, to this holy shrine?

SIMPCOX
God knows, of pure devotion; being call'd
A hundred times and oftener, in my sleep,
By good Saint Alban; who said, 'Simpcox, come, —
Come, offer at my shrine, and I will help thee.'

WIFE
Most true, forsooth; and many time and oft
Myself have heard a voice to call him so.

CARDINAL BEAUFORT
What, art thou lame?

SIMPCOX
                Ay, God Almighty help me!

SUFFOLK
How camest thou so?

SIMPCOX
                A fall off of a tree.

WIFE
A plum-tree, master.

GLOSTER
                How long hast thou been blind?

SIMPCOX
O, born so, master.

GLOSTER
                What, and wouldst climb a tree?

TOWNSMAN A miracle!

SIMPCOX
But that in all my life, when I was a youth.

WIFE
Too true; and bought his climbing very dear.

GLOSTER
Mass, thou lovedst plums well, that wouldst venture so.

SIMPCOX
Alas, good master, my wife desired some damsons,
And made me climb, with danger of my life.

GLOSTER
A subtle knave! but yet it shall not serve. —
Let me see thine eyes: wink now; now open them: —
In my opinion yet thou see'st not well.

SIMPCOX
Yes, master, clear as day, I thank God and Saint Alban.

GLOSTER
Say'st thou me so? What colour is this cloak of?

SIMPCOX
Red, master; red as blood.

GLOSTER
Why, that's well said. What colour is my gown of?

SIMPCOX
Black, forsooth; coal-black as jet.

KING HENRY
Why, then, thou know'st what colour jet is of?

SUFFOLK
And yet, I think, jet did he never see.

GLOSTER
But cloaks and gowns, before this day, a many.

WIFE
Never, before this day, in all his life.

GLOSTER
Tell me, sirrah, what's my name?

SIMPCOX
Alas, master, I know not.

GLOSTER
What's his name?

SIMPCOX
I know not.

GLOSTER
Nor his?

SIMPCOX
No, indeed, master.

GLOSTER
What's thine own name?

SIMPCOX
Saunder Simpcox, an if it please you, master.

GLOSTER
Then, Saunder, sit there, the lyingest knave in
Christendom. If thou hadst been born blind, thou
mightst as well have known all our names as thus to
name the several colours we do wear. Sight may
distinguish of colours; but suddenly to nominate them
all, it is impossible. — My lords, Saint Alban here hath
done a miracle; and would ye not think his cunning to
be great that could restore this cripple to his legs again?

SIMPCOX
O master, that you could!

GLOSTER
My masters of Saint Alban's, have you not beadles in
your town, and things call'd whips?

MAYOR OF SAINT ALBAN'S
Yes, my lord, if it please your Grace.

GLOSTER
Then send for one presently.

MAYOR OF SAINT ALBAN'S
Sirrah, go fetch the beadle hither straight.
[*Exit an* ATTENDANT.

GLOSTER
Now fetch me a stool hither by and by. [*A stool brought
out.*] Now, sirrah, if you mean to save yourself from
whipping, leap me over this stool and run away.

SIMPCOX
Alas, master, I am not able to stand alone:
You go about to torture me in vain.

Enter a BEADLE *with whips.*

GLOSTER
Well, sir, we must have you find your legs. — Sirrah
beadle, whip him till he leap over that same stool.

BEADLE
I will, my lord. — Come on, sirrah; off with your
doublet quickly.

SIMPCOX
Alas, master, what shall I do? I am not able to stand.
[*After the* BEADLE *hath hit him once, he leaps over the
stool and runs away; and they follow and cry,* A miracle!

KING HENRY
O God, seest Thou this, and bearest so long?

QUEEN MARGARET
It made me laugh to see the villain run.

GLOSTER
Follow the knave; and take this drab away.

WIFE
Alas, sir, we did it for pure need.

GLOSTER
Let them be whipp'd through every market-town till
they come to Berwick, from whence they came.
[*Exeunt* MAYOR, BEADLE, WIFE, *etc.*

CARDINAL BEAUFORT
Duke Humphrey has done a miracle to-day.

SUFFOLK
True; made the lame to leap and fly away.

GLOSTER
But you have done more miracles than I;
You made in a day, my lord, whole towns to fly.

Enter BUCKINGHAM.

KING HENRY
What tidings with our cousin Buckingham?

BUCKINGHAM
Such as my heart doth tremble to unfold.
A sort of naughty persons, lewdly bent, —
Under the countenance and confederacy
Of Lady Eleanor, the Protector's wife,
The ringleader and head of all this rout, —
Have practis'd dangerously against your state,
Dealing with witches and with conjurers:
Whom we have apprehended in the fact;
Raising up wicked spirits from under ground,
Demanding of King Henry's life and death,
And other of your highness' privy-council,
As more at large your Grace shall understand.

CARDINAL BEAUFORT
And so, my lord Protector, by this means
Your lady is forthcoming yet at London.
[*Aside to* GLOSTER.] This news, I think, hath turn'd
    your weapon's edge;
'Tis like, my lord, you will not keep your hour.

GLOSTER
Ambitious churchman, leave to afflict my heart:
Sorrow and grief have vanquish'd all my powers;
And, vanquish'd as I am, I yield to thee,
Or to the meanest groom.

KING HENRY
O God, what mischiefs work the wicked ones,
Heaping confusion on their own heads thereby!

QUEEN MARGARET
Glóster, see here the tainture of thy nest;
And look thyself be faultless, thou wert best.

GLOSTER
Madam, for thyself, to heaven I do appeal,
How I have lov'd my king and commonweal:
And, for my wife, I know not how it stands;
Sorry I am to hear what I have heard:
Noble she is; but if she have forgot
Honour and virtue, and convers'd with such
As, like to pitch, defile nobility,
I banish her my bed and company,
And give her, as a prey, to law and shame,
That hath dishonour'd Gloster's honest name.

KING HENRY
Well, for this night we will repose us here:
To-morrow toward London back again,
To look into this business thoroughly,
And call these foul offenders to their answers;
And poise the cause in justice' equal scales,
Whose beam stands sure, whose rightful cause
    prevails. [*Flourish. Exeunt.*

SCENE II

London. The DUKE OF YORK'S *garden.*

Enter YORK, SALISBURY, *and* WARWICK.

YORK
Now, my good Lords of Salisbury and Warwick,
Our simple supper ended, give me leave,
In this close walk, to satisfy myself,
In craving your opinion of my title,
Which is infallible, to England's crown.

SALISBURY
My lord, I long to hear it at full.

WARWICK
Sweet York, begin: and if thy claim be good,
The Nevils are thy subjects to command.

YORK
Then thus: —

Edward the Third, my lords, had seven sons:
The first, Edward the Black Prince, Prince of Wales;
The second, William of Hatfield; and the third,
Lionel Duke of Clarence; next to whom
Was John of Gaunt, the Duke of Lancaster;
The fifth was Edmund Langley, Duke of York;
The sixth was Thomas of Woodstock, Duke of Gloster;
William of Windsor was the seventh and last.
Edward the Black Prince died before his father;
And left behind him Richard, his only son,
Who, after Edward the Third's death, reign'd as king;
Till Henry Bolingbroke, Duke of Lancaster,
The eldest son and heir of John of Gaunt,
Crown'd by the name of Henry the Fourth,
Seiz'd on the realm, depos'd the rightful king,
Sent his poor queen to France, from whence she came,
And him to Pomfret, — where, as all you know,
Harmless Richard was murder'd traitorously.

WARWICK
Father, the duke hath told the truth;
Thus got the house of Lancaster the crown.

YORK
Which now they hold by force, and not by right;
For Richard, the first son's heir, being dead,
The issue of the next son should have reign'd.

SALISBURY
But William of Hatfield died without an heir.

YORK
The third son, Duke of Clarence, — from whose line
I claim the crown, — had issue, Philippe, a daughter,
Who married Edmund Mortimer, Earl of March:
Edmund had issue, Roger Earl of March;
Roger had issue, Edmund, Anne, and Eleanor.

SALISBURY
This Edmund, in the reign of Bolingbroke,
As I have read, laid claim unto the crown;
And, but for Owen Glendower, had been king,
Who kept him in captivity till he died.
But, to the rest.

YORK
                His eldest sister, Anne,
My mother, being heir unto the crown,
Married Richard Earl of Cambridge; who was son
To Edmund Langley, Edward the Third's fifth son.
By her I claim the kingdom: she was heir
To Roger Earl of March; who was the son
Of Edmund Mortimer; who married Philippe,
Sole daughter unto Lionel Duke of Clarence:
So, if the issue of the elder son
Succeed before the younger, I am king.

WARWICK
What plain proceeding is more plain than this?
Henry doth claim the crown from John of Gaunt,
The fourth son; York doth claim it from the third.
Till Lionel's issue fails, his should not reign:
It fails not yet, but flourishes in thee,
And in thy sons, fair slips of such a stock. —
Then, father Salisbury, kneel we together;
And, in this private plot, be we the first
That shall salute our rightful sovereign
With honour of his birthright to the crown.

BOTH
Long live our sovereign Richard, England's king!

YORK
We thank you, lords. But I am not your king
Till I be crown'd, and that my sword be stain'd
With heart-blood of the house of Lancaster;
And that's not suddenly to be perform'd,
But with advice and silent secrecy.
Do you as I do in these dangerous days:
Wink at the Duke of Suffolk's insolence,
At Beaufort's pride, at Somerset's ambition,
At Buckingham, and all the crew of them,
Till they have snared the shepherd of the flock,
That virtuous prince, the good Duke Humphrey:
'Tis that they seek; and they, in seeking that,
Shall find their deaths, if York can prophesy.

SALISBURY
My lord, break we off; we know your mind at full.

WARWICK
My heart assures me that the Earl of Warwick
Shall one day make the Duke of York a king.

YORK
And, Nevil, this I do assure myself, —
Richard shall live to make the Earl of Warwick
The greatest man in England but the king. [*Exeunt.*

SCENE III

A hall of justice.

Sound trumpets. Enter the KING, *the* QUEEN, GLOSTER, YORK, SUFFOLK, *and* SALISBURY; *the* DUCHESS OF GLOSTER, MARGERY JOURDAIN, SOUTHWELL, HUME, *and* BOLINGBROKE, *under guard*

KING HENRY
Stand forth, Dame Eleanor Cobham, Gloster's wife:
In sight of God and us, your guilt is great:
Receive the sentence of the law, for sins
Such as by God's book are adjudg'd to death. —
[*To* JOURDAIN, *etc.*] You four, from hence to prison
back again;
From thence unto the place of execution:
The witch in Smithfield shall be burnt to ashes,
And you three shall be strangled on the gallows. —
You, madam, for you are more nobly born,
Despoiled of your honour in your life,
Shall, after three days' open penance done,
Live in your country here, in banishment,
With Sir John Stanley, in the Isle of Man.

DUCHESS OF GLOSTER
Welcome is banishment; welcome were my death.

GLOSTER
Eleanor, the law, thou seest, hath judged thee:
I cannot justify whom the law condemns. —
[*Exeunt the* DUCHESS *and the other prisoners, guarded.*
Mine eyes are full of tears, my heart of grief.
Ah, Humphrey, this dishonour in thine age
Will bring thy head with sorrow to the ground! —
I beseech your majesty, give me leave to go;
Sorrow would solace, and mine age would ease.

KING HENRY
Stay, Humphrey Duke of Gloster: ere thou go,
Give up thy staff: Henry will to himself
Protector be; and God shall be my hope,
My stay, my guide, and lantern to my feet:
And go in peace, Humphrey, — no less beloved
Than when thou wert Protector to thy king.

QUEEN MARGARET
I see no reason why a king of years
Should be to be protected like a child. —
God and King Henry govern England's helm! —
Give up your staff, sir, and the king his realm.

GLOSTER
My staff! here, noble Henry, is my staff:
As willingly do I the same resign
As e'er thy father Henry made it mine;
And even as willingly at thy feet I leave it
As others would ambitiously receive it.
Farewell, good king: when I am dead and gone,
May honourable peace attend thy throne! [*Exit.*

QUEEN MARGARET
Why, now is Henry king, and Margaret queen;
And Humphrey Duke of Gloster scarce himself,
That bears so shrewd a maim; two pulls at once, —
His lady banish'd, and a limb lopp'd off:
This staff of honour raught, there let it stand
Where it best fits to be, — in Henry's hand.

SUFFOLK
Thus droops this lofty pine, and hangs his sprays;
Thus Eleanor's pride dies in her youngest days.

YORK
Lords, let him go. — Please it your majesty,
This is the day appointed for the combat;
And ready are the appellant and defendant,
The armourer and his man, to enter the lists,
So please your highness to behold the fight.

QUEEN MARGARET
Ay, good my lord; for purposely therefore
Left I the court, to see this quarrel tried.

KING HENRY
O' God's name, see the lists and all things fit:
Here let them end it; and God defend the right!

YORK
I never saw a fellow worse bested,
Or more afraid to fight, than is the appellant,
The servant of this armourer, my lords.

Enter, at one door, HORNER, *the Armourer, and his* NEIGHBOURS, *drinking to him so much that he is drunk: and he enters with a drum before him and his staff with a sandbag fasten'd to it; and at the other door* PETER, *his man, with a drum and sandbag, and* PRENTICES *drinking to him.*

FIRST NEIGHBOUR
Here, neighbour Horner, I drink to you in a cup of sack;
and fear not, neighbour, you shall do well enough.

SECOND NEIGHBOUR
And here, neighbour, here's a cup of charneco.

THIRD NEIGHBOUR
And here's a pot of good double-beer, neighbour:
drink, and fear not your man.

HORNER
Let it come, i'faith, and I'll pledge you all; and a fig for
Peter!

FIRST PRENTICE
Here, Peter, I drink to thee: and be not afraid.

SECOND PRENTICE
Be merry, Peter, and fear not thy master: fight for credit
of the prentices.

PETER
I thank you all: drink, and pray for me, I pray you; for I
think I have taken my last draught in this world. —
Here, Robin, an if I die, I give thee my apron: — and,
Will, thou shalt have my hammer: — and here, Tom,
take all the money that I have. — O Lord bless me, I
pray God! for I am never able to deal with my master,
he hath learnt so much fence already.

SALISBURY
Come, leave your drinking, and fall to blows. —
Sirrah, what's thy name?

PETER
Peter, forsooth.

SALISBURY
Peter! what more?

PETER
Thump.

SALISBURY
Thump! then see thou thump thy master well.

HORNER
Masters, I am come hither, as it were, upon my man's
instigation, to prove him a knave, and myself an honest
man: and touching the Duke of York, I will take my
death, I never meant him any ill, nor the king, nor the
queen: and therefore, Peter, have at thee with a
downright blow!

YORK
Dispatch: — this knave's tongue begins to double. —
Sound, trumpets, alarum to the combatants!
[*Alarum. They fight, and* PETER *strikes him down.*

HORNER
Hold, Peter, hold! I confess, I confess treason. [*Dies.*

YORK
Take away his weapon. — Fellow, thank God, and the
good wine in thy master's way.

PETER
O God, have I overcome mine enemy in this presence?
O Peter, thou hast prevail'd in right!

KING HENRY
Go, take hence that traitor from our sight;
For by his death we do perceive his guilt:
And God in justice hath reveal'd to us
The truth and innocence of this poor fellow,
Which he had thought to have murder'd wrongfully. —
Come, fellow, follow us for thy reward.
[*Sound a flourish. Exeunt.*

SCENE IV

A street.

Enter GLOSTER *and his* MEN, *in mourning cloaks.*

GLOSTER
Thus sometimes hath the brightest day a cloud;
And after summer evermore succeeds
Barren winter, with his wrathful nipping cold:
So cares and joys abound, as seasons fleet. —
Sirs, what's o'clock?

SERVING-MAN
'Tis almost ten, my lord.

GLOSTER
Ten is the hour that was appointed me
To watch the coming of my punish'd duchess:
Uneath may she endure the flinty streets,
To tread them with her tender-feeling feet.
Sweet Nell, ill can thy noble mind abrook
The abject people gazing on thy face
With envious looks, still laughing at thy shame,
That erst did follow thy proud chariot-wheels
When thou didst ride in triumph through the streets.
But, soft! I think she comes; and I'll prepare
My tear-stain'd eyes to see her miseries.

Enter the DUCHESS *of* GLOSTER *barefoot, in a white sheet, with verses pinn'd on her back, and a taper burning in her hand; with* SIR JOHN STANLEY, *the* SHERIFF, *and* OFFICERS.

SERVING-MAN
So please your Grace, we'll take her from the sheriff.

GLOSTER
No, stir not, for your lives; let her pass by.

DUCHESS OF GLOSTER
Come you, my lord, to see my open shame?
Now thou dost penance too. Look how they gaze!
See how the giddy multitude do point,
And nod their heads, and throw their eyes on thee!
Ah, Gloster, hide thee from their hateful looks,
And, in thy closet pent up, rue my shame,
And ban thine enemies, both mine and thine!

GLOSTER
Be patient, gentle Nell; forget this grief.

DUCHESS OF GLOSTER
Ah, Gloster, teach me to forget myself!
For whilst I think I am thy married wife,
And thou a prince, Protector of this land,
Methinks I should not thus be led along,
Mail'd up in shame, with papers on my back,
And follow'd with a rabble, that rejoice
To see my tears and hear my deep-fet groans.
The ruthless flint doth cut my tender feet;
And when I start, the envious people laugh,
And bid me be advised how I tread.
Ah, Humphrey, can I bear this shameful yoke?
Trow'st thou that e'er I'll look upon the world,
Or count them happy that enjoy the sun?
No; dark shall be my light, and night my day;
To think upon my pomp shall be my hell.
Sometime I'll say, I am Duke Humphrey's wife;
And he a prince, and ruler of the land:
Yet so he ruled, and such a prince he was,
As he stood by, whilst I, his forlorn duchess,
Was made a wonder and a pointing-stock
To every idle rascal follower.
But be thou mild, and blush not at my shame;
Nor stir at nothing, till the axe of death
Hang over thee, as, sure, it shortly will;
For Suffolk, — he that can do all in all
With her that hateth thee and hates us all, —
And York, and impious Beaufort, that false priest,
Have all limed bushes to betray thy wings,
And, fly thou how thou canst, they'll tangle thee:
But fear not thou, until thy foot be snared,
Nor never seek prevention of thy foes.

GLOSTER
Ah, Nell, forbear! thou aimest all awry;
I must offend before I be attainted:
And had I twenty times so many foes,
And each of them had twenty times their power,
All these could not procure me any scathe,
So long as I am loyal, true, and crimeless.
Wouldst have me rescue thee from this reproach?
Why, yet thy scandal were not wip'd away,
But I in danger for the breach of law.
Thy greatest help is quiet, gentle Nell:
I pray thee, sort thy heart to patience;
These few days' wonder will be quickly worn.

Enter a HERALD.

HERALD
I summon your Grace to his majesty's parliament,
Holden at Bury the first of this next month.

GLOSTER
And my consent ne'er ask'd herein before!
This is close dealing. — Well, I will be there.
[*Exit* HERALD.
My Nell, I take my leave: — and, master sheriff,
Let not her penance exceed the king's commission.

SHERIFF
An't please your Grace, here my commission stays;
And Sir John Stanley is appointed now
To take her with him to the Isle of Man.

GLOSTER
Must you, Sir John, protect my lady here?

STANLEY
So am I given in charge, may't please your Grace.

GLOSTER
Entreat her not the worse, in that I pray
You use her well: the world may laugh again;
And I may live to do you kindness, if
You do it her: and so, Sir John, farewell.

DUCHESS OF GLOSTER
What, gone, my lord, and bid me not farewell!

DUCHESS OF GLOSTER Come you, my lord, to see my open shame?

GLOSTER
Witness my tears, I cannot stay to speak.
[*Exeunt* GLOSTER *and his* MEN.

DUCHESS OF GLOSTER
Art thou gone too? all comfort go with thee!
For none abides with me: my joy is death, —
Death, at whose name I oft have been afeard,
Because I wish'd this world's eternity. —
Stanley, I prithee, go, and take me hence;
I care not whither, for I beg no favour,
Only convey me where thou art commanded.

STANLEY
Why, madam, that is to the Isle of Man;
There to be used according to your state.

DUCHESS OF GLOSTER
That's bad enough, for I am but reproach, —
And shall I, then, be used reproachfully?

STANLEY
Like to a duchess, and Duke Humphrey's lady;
According to that state you shall be used.

DUCHESS OF GLOSTER
Sheriff, farewell, and better than I fare, —
Although thou hast been conduct of my shame.

SHERIFF
It is my office; and, madam, pardon me.

DUCHESS OF GLOSTER
Ay, ay, farewell; thy office is discharged. —
Come, Stanley, shall we go?

STANLEY
Madam, your penance done, throw off this sheet,
And go we to attire you for our journey.

DUCHESS OF GLOSTER
My shame will not be shifted with my sheet:
No, it will hang upon my richest robes,
And show itself, attire me how I can.
Go, lead the way; I long to see my prison. [*Exeunt.*

ACT III

SCENE I

The Abbey at Bury St. Edmund's.

Sound a sennet. Enter KING, QUEEN, CARDINAL
BEAUFORT, SUFFOLK, YORK, BUCKINGHAM,
SALISBURY, *and* WARWICK *to the Parliament.*

KING HENRY
I muse my Lord of Gloster is not come:
'Tis not his wont to be the hindmost man,
Whate'er occasion keeps him from us now.

QUEEN MARGARET
Can you not see? or will ye not observe
The strangeness of his alter'd countenance?
With what a majesty he bears himself;
How insolent of late he is become,
How proud, how peremptory, and unlike himself?
We know the time since he was mild and affable;
And, if we did but glance a far-off look,
Immediately he was upon his knee,
That all the court admired him for submission:
But meet him now, and, be it in the morn,
When every one will give the time of day,
He knits his brow, and shows an angry eye,
And passeth by with stiff unbowed knee,
Disdaining duty that to us belongs.
Small curs are not regarded when they grin;
But great men tremble when the lion roars, —
And Humphrey is no little man in England.
First note, that he is near you in descent;
And, should you fall, he is the next will mount.
Me seemeth, then, it is no policy, —
Respecting what a rancorous mind he bears,
And his advantage following your decease, —
That he should come about your royal person,
Or be admitted to your highness' council.
By flattery hath he won the commons' hearts;
And when he please to make commotion,
'Tis to be fear'd they all will follow him.
Now 'tis the spring, and weeds are shallow-rooted;
Suffer them now, and they'll o'ergrow the garden
And choke the herbs for want of husbandry.
The reverent care I bear unto my lord
Made me collect these dangers in the duke.
If it be fond, call it a woman's fear;
Which fear if better reasons can supplant,
I will subscribe, and say I wrong'd the duke.
My Lord of Suffolk, Buckingham, and York,
Reprove my allegation, if you can;
Or else conclude my words effectual.

SUFFOLK
Well hath your highness seen into this duke;
And, had I first been put to speak my mind,
I think I should have told your Grace's tale.
The duchess, by his subornation,
Upon my life, began her devilish practices:
Or, if he were not privy to those faults,
Yet, by reputing of his high descent, —
As, next the king, he was successive heir, —
And such high vaunts of his nobility, —
Did instigate the bedlam brain-sick duchess
By wicked means to frame our sovereign's fall.
Smooth runs the water where the brook is deep;

And in his simple show he harbours treason.
The fox barks not when he would steal the lamb.
No, no, my sovereign; Gloster is a man
Unsounded yet, and full of deep deceit.

CARDINAL BEAUFORT
Did he not, contrary to form of law,
Devise strange deaths for small offences done?

YORK
And did he not, in his Protectorship,
Levy great sums of money through the realm
For soldiers' pay in France, and never sent it?
By means whereof the towns each day revolted.

BUCKINGHAM
Tut, these are petty faults to faults unknown,
Which time will bring to light in smooth Duke
Humphrey.

KING HENRY
My lords, at once: — the care you have of us,
To mow down thorns that would annoy our foot,
Is worthy praise: but — shall I speak my conscience? —
Our kinsman Gloster is as innocent
From meaning treason to our royal person
As is the sucking lamb or harmless dove:
The duke is virtuous, mild, and too well given
To dream on evil, or to work my downfall.

QUEEN MARGARET
Ah, what's more dangerous than this fond affiance!
Seems he a dove? his feathers are but borrow'd,
For he's disposed as the hateful raven:
Is he a lamb! his skin is surely lent him,
For he's inclin'd as is the ravenous wolf.
Who cannot steal a shape that means deceit?
Take heed, my lord; the welfare of us all
Hangs on the cutting short that fraudful man.
Enter SOMERSET.

SOMERSET
All health unto my gracious sovereign!

KING HENRY
Welcome, Lord Somerset. What news from France?

SOMERSET
That all your interest in those territories
Is utterly bereft you; all is lost.

KING HENRY
Cold news, Lord Somerset: but God's will be done!

YORK [*aside*].
Cold news for me; for I had hope of France
As firmly as I hope for fertile England.
Thus are my blossoms blasted in the bud,
And caterpillars eat my leaves away:
But I will remedy this gear ere long,
Or sell my title for a glorious grave.
Enter GLOSTER.

GLOSTER
All happiness unto my lord the king!
Pardon, my liege, that I have stay'd so long.

SUFFOLK
Nay, Gloster, know that thou art come too soon,
Unless thou wert more loyal than thou art:
I do arrest thee of high treason here.

GLOSTER
Well, Suffolk, well, thou shalt not see me blush
Nor change my countenance for this arrest:
A heart unspotted is not easily daunted.
The purest spring is not so free from mud
As I am clear from treason to my sovereign:
Who can accuse me? wherein am I guilty?

YORK
'Tis thought, my lord, that you took bribes of France,
And, being Protector, stay'd the soldiers' pay;
By means whereof his highness hath lost France.

GLOSTER
Is it but thought so? what are they that think it?
I never robb'd the soldiers of their pay,
Nor ever had one penny bribe from France.
So help me God, as I have watch'd the night, —
Ay, night by night, — in studying good for England!
That doit that e'er I wrested from the king,
Or any groat I hoarded to my use,
Be brought against me at my trial-day!
No; many a pound of mine own proper store,
Because I would not tax the needy commons,
Have I dispursed to the garrisons,
And never ask'd for restitution.

CARDINAL BEAUFORT
It serves you well, my lord, to say so much.

GLOSTER
I say no more than truth, so help me God!

YORK
In your Protectorship you did devise
Strange tortures for offenders, never heard of,
That England was defam'd by tyranny.

GLOSTER
Why, 'tis well known that, whiles I was Protector,
Pity was all the fault that was in me;
For I should melt at an offender's tears,
And lowly words were ransom for their fault.
Unless it were a bloody murderer,
Or foul felonious thief that fleec'd poor passengers,
I never gave them condign punishment:
Murder, indeed, that bloody sin, I tortured
Above the felon or what trespass else.

SUFFOLK
My lord, these faults are easy, quickly answer'd:
But mightier crimes are laid unto your charge,
Whereof you cannot easily purge yourself.
I do arrest you in his highness' name;
And here commit you to my lord cardinal
To keep, until your further time of trial.

KING HENRY
My Lord of Gloster, 'tis my special hope
That you will clear yourself from all suspect:
My conscience tells me you are innocent.

GLOSTER
Ah, gracious lord, these days are dangerous!
Virtue is chok'd with foul ambition,
And charity chas'd hence by rancour's hand;
Foul subornation is predominant,
And equity exiled your highness' land.
I know their complot is to have my life;
And, if my death might make this island happy,
And prove the period of their tyranny,
I would expend it with all willingness:
But mine is made the prologue to their play;
For thousands more, that yet suspect no peril,
Will not conclude their plotted tragedy.
Beaufort's red sparkling eyes blab his heart's malice,
And Suffolk's cloudy brow his stormy hate;
Sharp Buckingham unburdens with his tongue
The envious load that lies upon his heart;
And dogged York, that reaches at the moon,
Whose overweening arm I have pluck'd back,
By false accuse doth level at my life: —
And you, my sovereign lady, with the rest,
Causeless have laid disgraces on my head,
And with your best endeavour have stirr'd up
My liefest liege to be mine enemy: —
Ay, all of you have laid your heads together —
Myself had notice of your conventicles —
And all to make away my guiltless life.
I shall not want false witness to condemn me,
Nor store of treasons to augment my guilt;
The ancient proverb will be well effected, —
A staff is quickly found to beat a dog.

CARDINAL BEAUFORT
My liege, his railing is intolerable:
If those that care to keep your royal person
From treason's secret knife and traitors' rage
Be thus upbraided, chid, and rated at,
And the offender granted scope of speech,
'Twill make them cool in zeal unto your Grace.

SUFFOLK
Hath he not twit our sovereign lady here
With ignominious words, though clerkly couch'd,
As if she had suborned some to swear
False allegations to o'erthrow his state?

QUEEN MARGARET
But I can give the loser leave to chide.

GLOSTER
Far truer spoke than meant: I lose, indeed; —
Beshrew the winners, for they play'd me false!
And well such losers may have leave to speak.

BUCKINGHAM
He'll wrest the sense, and hold us here all day: —
Lord cardinal, he is your prisoner.

CARDINAL BEAUFORT
Sirs, take away the duke, and guard him sure.

GLOSTER
Ah, thus King Henry throws away his crutch,
Before his legs be firm to bear his body!
Thus is the shepherd beaten from thy side,
And wolves are gnarling who shall gnaw thee first.
Ah, that my fear were false! ah, that it were!
For, good King Henry, thy decay I fear.
[Exit GLOSTER, *guarded.*

KING HENRY
My lords, what to your wisdoms seemeth best
Do or undo, as if ourself were here.

QUEEN MARGARET
What, will your highness leave the parliament?

KING HENRY
Ay, Margaret; my heart is drown'd with grief,
Whose flood begins to flow within mine eyes;
My body round engirt with misery, —
For what's more miserable than discontent? —
Ah, uncle Humphrey, in thy face I see
The map of honour, truth, and loyalty!
And yet, good Humphrey, is the hour to come
That e'er I proved thee false, or fear'd thy faith.
What louring star now envies thy estate,
That these great lords, and Margaret our queen,
Do seek subversion of thy harmless life?
Thou never didst them wrong, nor no man wrong:
And as the butcher takes away the calf,
And binds the wretch, and beats it when it strays,
Bearing it to the bloody slaughter-house;
Even so, remorseless, have they borne him hence:
And as the dam runs lowing up and down,
Looking the way her harmless young one went,
And can do naught but wail her darling's loss;
Even so myself bewails good Gloster's case
With sad unhelpful tears; and with dimm'd eyes
Look after him, and cannot do him good, —
So mighty are his vowed enemies.
His fortunes I will weep; and, 'twixt each groan,
Say, 'Who's a traitor, Gloster he is none.'   *[Exit.*

QUEEN MARGARET
Fair lords, cold snow melts with the sun's hot beams.
Henry my lord is cold in great affairs,
Too full of foolish pity: and Gloster's show
Beguiles him, as the mournful crocodile
With sorrow snares relenting passengers;
Or as the snake, roll'd in a flowering bank,
With shining checker'd slough, doth sting a child,
That for the beauty thinks it excellent.
Believe me, lords, were none more wise than I, —
And yet herein I judge mine own wit good, —
This Gloster should be quickly rid the world,
To rid us from the fear we have of him.

CARDINAL BEAUFORT
That he should die is worthy policy;
But yet we want a colour for his death:
'Tis meet he be condemn'd by course of law.

SUFFOLK
But, in my mind, that were no policy:
The king will labour still to save his life;
The commons haply rise to save his life;
And yet we have but trivial argument,
More than mistrust, that shows him worthy death.

YORK
So that, by this, you would not have him die.

SUFFOLK
Ah, York, no man alive so fain as I!

YORK *[aside]*.
'Tis York that hath more reason for his death. —
But, my lord cardinal, and you, my Lord of Suffolk, —
Say as you think, and speak it from your souls, —
Were't not all one, an empty eagle were set
To guard the chicken from a hungry kite,
As place Duke Humphrey for the king's Protector?

QUEEN MARGARET
So the poor chicken should be sure of death.

SUFFOLK
Madam, 'tis true; and were't not madness, then,
To make the fox surveyor of the fold?
Who being accus'd a crafty murderer,
His guilt should be but idly posted over,
Because his purpose is not executed.
No; let him die, in that he is a fox,
By nature proved an enemy to the flock,
Before his chaps be stain'd with crimson blood,
As Humphrey, proved by reasons, to my liege.
And do not stand on quillets how to slay him:
Be it by gins, by snares, by subtlety,
Sleeping or waking, 'tis no matter how,
So he be dead; for that is good deceit
Which mates him first that first intends deceit.

QUEEN MARGARET
Thrice-noble Suffolk, 'tis resolutely spoke.

SUFFOLK
Not resolute, except so much were done;
For things are often spoke, and seldom meant:
But, that my heart accordeth with my tongue, —
Seeing the deed is meritorious,
And to preserve my sovereign from his foe, —
Say but the word, and I will be his priest.

CARDINAL BEAUFORT
But I would have him dead, my Lord of Suffolk,
Ere you can take due orders for a priest:
Say you consent, and censure well the deed,
And I'll provide his executioner, —
I tender so the safety of my liege.

SUFFOLK
Here is my hand, the deed is worthy doing.

QUEEN MARGARET
And so say I.

YORK
And I: and now we three have spoke it,
It skills not greatly who impugns our doom.
Enter a POST.

POST
Great lords, from Ireland am I come amain,
To signify that rebels there are up,
And put the Englishmen unto the sword:
Send succours, lords, and stop the rage betime,
Before the wound do grow uncurable;
For, being green, there is great hope of help.

CARDINAL BEAUFORT
A breach that craves a quick expedient stop!
What counsel give you in this weighty cause?

YORK
That Somerset be sent as regent thither:
'Tis meet that lucky ruler be employ'd;
Witness the fortune he hath had in France.

SOMERSET
If York, with all his far-fet policy,
Had been the regent there instead of me,
He never would have stay'd in France so long.

YORK
No, not to lose it all, as thou hast done:
I rather would have lost my life betimes
Than bring a burden of dishonour home
By staying there so long till all were lost.
Show me one scar character'd on thy skin:
Men's flesh preserv'd so whole do seldom win.

QUEEN MARGARET
Nay, then, this spark will prove a raging fire,
If wind and fuel be brought to feed it with: —
No more, good York; — sweet Somerset, be still: —
Thy fortune, York, hadst thou been regent there,
Might happily have proved far worse than his.

YORK
What, worse than naught? nay, then, a shame take all!

SOMERSET
And, in the number, thee that wishest shame!

CARDINAL BEAUFORT
My Lord of York, try what your fortune is.
Th'uncivil kerns of Ireland are in arms,
And temper clay with blood of Englishmen:
To Ireland will you lead a band of men,
Collected choicely, from each county some,
And try your hap against the Irishmen?

YORK
I will, my lord, so please his majesty.

SUFFOLK
Why, our authority is his consent;
And what we do establish he confirms:
Then, noble York, take thou this task in hand.

YORK
I am content: provide me soldiers, lords,
Whiles I take order for mine own affairs.

SUFFOLK
A charge, Lord York, that I will see perform'd.
But now return we to the false Duke Humphrey.

CARDINAL BEAUFORT
No more of him; for I will deal with him,
That henceforth he shall trouble us no more.
And so break off; the day is almost spent:
Lord Suffolk, you and I must talk of that event.

YORK
My Lord of Suffolk, within fourteen days
At Bristol I expect my soldiers;
For there I'll ship them all for Ireland.

SUFFOLK
I'll see it truly done, my Lord of York.
[Exeunt all except YORK.

YORK
Now, York, or never, steel thy fearful thoughts,
And change misdoubt to resolution:
Be that thou hopest to be; or what thou art
Resign to death, — it is not worth th'enjoying:
Let pale-fac'd fear keep with the mean-born man,
And find no harbour in a royal heart.
Faster than spring-time showers comes thought on
    thought;
And not a thought but thinks on dignity.
My brain, more busy than the labouring spider,

WARWICK Come hither, gracious sovereign, view this body.

Weaves tedious snares to trap mine enemies.
Well, nobles, well, 'tis politicly done,
To send me packing with an host of men:
I fear me you but warm the starved snake,
Who, cherish'd in your breasts, will sting your hearts.
'Twas men I lack'd, and you will give them me:
I take it kindly; yet be well assured
You put sharp weapons in a madman's hands.
Whiles I in Ireland nourish a mighty band,
I will stir up in England some black storm,
Shall blow ten thousand souls to heaven or hell;
And this fell tempest shall not cease to rage
Until the golden circuit on my head,
Like to the glorious sun's transparent beams,
Do calm the fury of this mad-bred flaw.
And for a minister of my intent
I have seduced a headstrong Kentishman,
John Cade of Ashford,
To make commotion, as full well he can,
Under the title of John Mortimer.
In Ireland have I seen this stubborn Cade
Oppose himself against a troop of kerns,
And fought so long, till that his thighs with darts
Were almost like a sharp-quill'd porpentine;
And, in the end being rescued, I have seen
Him caper upright like a wild Morisco,
Shaking the bloody darts as he his bells.
Full often, like a shag-hair'd crafty kern,
Hath he conversed with the enemy,
And, undiscover'd, come to me again,
And given me notice of their villainies.
This devil here shall be my substitute;
For that John Mortimer, which now is dead.
In face, in gait, in speech, he doth resemble:
By this I shall perceive the commons' mind,
How they affect the house and claim of York.

Say he be taken, rack'd, and tortured,
I know no pain they can inflict upon him
Will make him say I moved him to those arms.
Say that he thrive, — as 'tis great like he will, —
Why, then from Ireland come I with my strength,
And reap the harvest which that rascal sow'd;
For, Humphrey being dead, as he shall be,
And Henry put apart, the next for me. [*Exit.*

SCENE II

Bury St. Edmund's. A room of state.

Enter two or three running over the stage, from the murder of DUKE HUMPHREY.

FIRST MURDERER
Run to my Lord of Suffolk; let him know
We have dispatch'd the duke, as he commanded.
SECOND MURDERER
O, that it were to do! — What have we done?
Didst ever hear a man so penitent?
FIRST MURDERER
Here comes my lord.

Enter SUFFOLK.

SUFFOLK
Now, sirs, have you dispatch'd this thing?
FIRST MURDERER
Ay, my good lord, he's dead.
SUFFOLK
Why, that's well said. Go, get you to my house;
I will reward you for this venturous deed.
The king and all the peers are here at hand: —
Have you laid fair the bed? is all things well,
According as I gave directions?

FIRST MURDERER
'Tis, my good lord.
SUFFOLK
Away! be gone. [*Exeunt* MURDERERS.
Sound trumpets. Enter the KING, *the* QUEEN,
CARDINAL BEAUFORT, SOMERSET,
LORDS, *and others.*

KING HENRY
Go, call our uncle to our presence straight;
Say we intend to try his Grace to-day,
If he be guilty, as 'tis published.
SUFFOLK
I'll call him presently, my noble lord. [*Exit.*
KING HENRY
Lords, take your places; and, I pray you all,
Proceed no straiter 'gainst our uncle Gloster
Than from true evidence of good esteem
He be approved in practice culpable.
QUEEN MARGARET
God forbid any malice should prevail,
That faultless may condemn a nobleman!
Pray God he may acquit him of suspicion!
KING HENRY
I thank thee, Meg; these words content me much.
Enter SUFFOLK.
How now! why look'st thou pale? why tremblest thou?
Where is our uncle? what's the matter, Suffolk?
SUFFOLK
Dead in his bed, my lord; Gloster is dead.
QUEEN MARGARET
Marry, God forfend!
CARDINAL BEAUFORT
God's secret judgement: — I did dream to-night
The duke was dumb, and could not speak a word.
[*The* KING *swoons.*
QUEEN MARGARET
How fares my lord? — Help, lords! the king is dead.
SOMERSET
Rear up his body; wring him by the nose.
QUEEN MARGARET
Run, go, help, help! — O Henry, ope thine eyes!
SUFFOLK
He doth revive again: — madam, be patient.
KING HENRY
O heavenly God!
QUEEN MARGARET
                    How fares my gracious lord?
SUFFOLK
Comfort, my sovereign! gracious Henry, comfort!
KING HENRY
What, doth my Lord of Suffolk comfort me?
Came he right now to sing a raven's note,
Whose dismal tune bereft my vital powers;
And thinks he that the chirping of a wren,
By crying comfort from a hollow breast,
Can chase away the first-conceived sound?
Hide not thy poison with such sugar'd words;
Lay not thy hands on me; forbear, I say;
Their touch affrights me as a serpent's sting.
Thou baleful messenger, out of my sight!
Upon thy eyeballs murderous tyranny
Sits in grim majesty, to fright the world.
Look not upon me, for thine eyes are wounding: —
Yet do not go away: — come, basilisk,
And kill the innocent gazer with thy sight;
For in the shade of death I shall find joy, —
In life but double death, now Gloster's dead.
QUEEN MARGARET
Why do you rate my Lord of Suffolk thus?
Although the duke was enemy to him,
Yet he, most Christian-like, laments his death:
And for myself, — foe as he was to me, —
Might liquid tears, or heart-offending groans,
Or blood-consuming sighs recall his life,
I would be blind with weeping, sick with groans,
Look pale as primrose with blood-drinking sighs,
And all to have the noble duke alive.
What know I how the world may deem of me?
For it is known we were but hollow friends:
It may be judg'd I made the duke away;
So shall my name with slander's tongue be wounded,
And princes' courts be fill'd with my reproach.
This get I by his death: ay me, unhappy!
To be a queen, and crown'd with infamy!
KING HENRY
Ah, woe is me for Gloster, wretched man!
QUEEN MARGARET
Be woe for me, more wretched than he is.
What, dost thou turn away, and hide thy face?

I am no loathsome leper? — look on me.
What, art thou, like the adder, waxen deaf?
Be poisonous too, and kill thy forlorn queen.
Is all thy comfort shut in Gloster's tomb?
Why, then, Dame Margaret was ne'er thy joy:
Erect his statua, and worship it,
And make my image but an alehouse sign.
Was I for this nigh wrack'd upon the sea,
And twice by awkward winds from England's bank
Drove back again unto my native clime?
What boded this but well-forewarning winds
Did seem to say, — 'Seek not a scorpion's nest,
Nor set no footing on this unkind shore'?
What did I then but curs'd the gentle gusts,
And he that loos'd them forth their brazen caves;
And bid them blow towards England's blessed shore,
Or turn our stern upon a dreadful rock?
Yet Æolus would not be a murderer,
But left that hateful office unto thee:
The pretty-vaulting sea refus'd to drown me,
Knowing that thou wouldst have me drown'd on shore,
With tears as salt as sea, through thy unkindness:
The splitting rocks cower'd in the sinking sands,
And would not dash me with their ragged sides;
Because thy flinty heart, more hard than they,
Might in thy palace perish Margaret.
As far as I could ken the chalky cliffs,
When from thy shore the tempest beat us back,
I stood upon the hatches in the storm;
And when the dusky sky began to rob
My earnest-gaping sight of thy land's view,
I took a costly jewel from my neck, —
A heart it was, bound in with diamonds, —
And threw it towards thy land: — the sea receiv'd it;
And so I wish'd thy body might my heart:
And even with this I lost fair England's view,
And bid mine eyes be packing with my heart,
And call'd them blind and dusky spectacles,
For losing ken of Albion's wished coast.
How often have I tempted Suffolk's tongue —
The agent of thy foul inconstancy —
To sit and witch me, as Ascanius did
When he to madding Dido would unfold
His father's acts commenc'd in burning Troy!
Am I not witch'd like her? or thou not false like him?
Ay me, I can no more! die, Margaret!
For Henry weeps that thou dost live so long.

Noise within. Enter WARWICK,
SALISBURY, *and many* COMMONS.

WARWICK
It is reported, mighty sovereign,
That good Duke Humphrey traitorously is murder'd
By Suffolk and the Cardinal Beaufort's means.
The commons, like an angry hive of bees
That want their leader, scatter up and down,
And care not who they sting in his revenge.
Myself have calm'd their spleenful mutiny,
Until they hear the order of his death.

KING HENRY
That he is dead, good Warwick, 'tis too true;
But how he died God knows, not Henry:
Enter his chamber, view his breathless corpse,
And comment then upon his sudden death.

WARWICK
That shall I do, my liege. — Stay, Salisbury,
With the rude multitude till I return. [*Exit.*

KING HENRY
O Thou that judgest all things, stay my thoughts, —
My thoughts, that labour to persuade my soul
Some violent hands were laid on Humphrey's life!
If my suspect be false, forgive me, God;
For judgement only doth belong to Thee.
Fain would I go to chafe his paly lips
With twenty thousand kisses, and to rain
Upon his face an ocean of salt tears,
To tell my love unto his dumb deaf trunk,
And with my fingers feel his hand unfeeling:
But all in vain are these mean obsequies;
And to survey his dead and earthy image
What were it but to make my sorrow greater?

[WARWICK *draws the curtains and shows* DUKE
HUMPHREY *in his bed.*

WARWICK
Come hither, gracious sovereign, view this body.

KING HENRY
That is to see how deep my grave is made;
For with his soul fled all my worldly solace,
And seeing him, I see my life in death.

WARWICK
As surely as my soul intends to live

With that dread King that took our state upon Him
To free us from His Father's wrathful curse,
I do believe that violent hands were laid
Upon the life of this thrice-famed duke.

SUFFOLK
A dreadful oath, sworn with a solemn tongue!
What instance gives Lord Warwick for his vow?

WARWICK
See how the blood is settled in his face!
Oft have I seen a timely-parted ghost,
Of ashy semblance, meagre, pale, and bloodless,
Being all descended to the labouring heart;
Who, in the conflict that it holds with death,
Attracts the same for aidance 'gainst the enemy;
Which with the heart there cools, and ne'er returneth
To blush and beautify the cheek again.
But see, his face is black and full of blood;
His eyeballs further out than when he lived,
Staring full ghastly like a strangled man;
His hair uprear'd, his nostrils stretch'd with
    struggling;
His hands abroad display'd, as one that grasp'd
And tugg'd for life, and was by strength subdued:
Look, on the sheets his hair, you see, is sticking;
His well-proportion'd beard made rough and rugged,
Like to the summer's corn by tempest lodg'd.
It cannot be but he was murder'd here;
The least of all these signs were probable.

SUFFOLK
Why, Warwick, who should do the duke to death?
Myself and Beaufort had him in protection;
And we, I hope, sir, are no murderers.

WARWICK
But both of you were vow'd Duke Humphrey's foes;
And you, forsooth, had the good duke to keep:
'Tis like you would not feast him like a friend;
And 'tis well seen he found an enemy.

QUEEN MARGARET
Then you, belike, suspect these noblemen
As guilty of Duke Humphrey's timeless death.

WARWICK
Who finds the heifer dead and bleeding fresh,
And sees fast by a butcher with an axe,
But will suspect 'twas he that made the slaughter?
Who finds the partridge in the puttock's nest,
But may imagine how the bird was dead,
Although the kite soar with unbloodied beak?
Even so suspicious is this tragedy.

QUEEN MARGARET
Are you the butcher, Suffolk? — where's your knife?
Is Beaufort term'd a kite? — where are his talons?

SUFFOLK
I wear no knife to slaughter sleeping men;
But here's a vengeful sword, rusted with ease,
That shall be scoured in his rancorous heart
That slanders me with murder's crimson badge: —
Say, if thou darest, proud Lord of Warwickshire,
That I am faulty in Duke Humphrey's death.

[*Exeunt* CARDINAL, SOMERSET, *and others.*

WARWICK
What dares not Warwick, if false Suffolk dare him?

QUEEN MARGARET
He dares not calm his contumelious spirit,
Nor cease to be an arrogant controller,
Though Suffolk dare him twenty thousand times.

WARWICK
Madam, be still, — with reverence may I say;
For every word you speak in his behalf
Is slander to your royal dignity.

SUFFOLK
Blunt-witted lord, ignoble in demeanour!
If ever lady wrong'd her lord so much,
Thy mother took into her blameful bed
Some stern untutor'd churl, and noble stock
Was graft with crab-tree slip; whose fruit thou art,
And never of the Nevils' noble race.

WARWICK
But that the guilt of murder bucklers thee,
And I should rob the deathsman of his fee,
Quitting thee thereby of ten thousand shames,
And that my sovereign's presence makes me mild,
I would, false murderous coward, on thy knee
Make thee beg pardon for thy passed speech,
And say it was thy mother that thou meant'st, —
That thou thyself was born in bastardy;
And, after all this fearful homage done,
Give thee thy hire, and send thy soul to hell,
Pernicious blood-sucker of sleeping men!

SUFFOLK
Thou shalt be waking while I shed thy blood,

If from this presence thou darest go with me.

WARWICK
Away even now, or I will drag thee hence:
Unworthy though thou art, I'll cope with thee,
And do some service to Duke Humphrey's ghost.
[*Exeunt* SUFFOLK *and* WARWICK.

KING HENRY
What stronger breastplate than a heart untainted!
Thrice is he arm'd that hath his quarrel just;
And he but naked, though lock'd up in steel,
Whose conscience with injustice is corrupted.
[*A noise within.*

QUEEN MARGARET
What noise is this?

Enter SUFFOLK *and* WARWICK, *with their weapons
drawn.*

KING HENRY
Why, how now, lords! your wrathful weapons drawn
Here in our presence! dare you be so bold? —
Why, what tumultuous clamour have we here?

SUFFOLK
The traitorous Warwick, with the men of Bury,
Set all upon me, mighty sovereign.

SALISBURY [*to the* COMMONS *at the door*].
Sirs, stand apart; the king shall know your mind. —
Dread lord, the commons send you word by me,
Unless false Suffolk straight be done to death
Or banished fair England's territories,
They will by violence tear him from your palace,
And torture him with grievous lingering death.
They say, by him the good Duke Humphrey died;
They say, in him they fear your highness' death;
And mere instinct of love and loyalty —
Free from a stubborn opposite intent,
As being thought to contradict your liking —
Makes them thus forward in his banishment.
They say, in care of your most royal person,
That if your highness should intend to sleep,
And charge that no man should disturb your rest,
In pain of your dislike, or pain of death;
Yet, notwithstanding such a strait edict,
Were there a serpent seen, with forked tongue,
That slily glided towards your majesty,
It were but necessary you were waked;
Lest, being suffer'd in that harmful slumber,
The mortal worm might make the sleep eternal:
And therefore do they cry, though you forbid,
That they will guard you, whe'r you will or no,
From such fell serpents as false Suffolk is;
With whose envenomed and fatal sting,
Your loving uncle, twenty times his worth,
They say, is shamefully bereft of life.

COMMONS [*within*].
An answer from the king, my Lord of Salisbury!

SUFFOLK
'Tis like the commons, rude unpolish'd hinds,
Could send such message to their sovereign:
But you, my lord, were glad to be employ'd,
To show how quaint an orator you are:
But all the honour Salisbury hath won
Is, that he was the lord ambassador
Sent from a sort of tinkers to the king.

COMMONS [*within*].
An answer from the king, or we will all break in!

KING HENRY
Go, Salisbury, and tell them all from me,
I thank them for their tender loving care;
And had I not been cited so by them,
Yet did I purpose as they do entreat;
For, sure, my thoughts do hourly prophesy
Mischance unto my state by Suffolk's means:
And therefore, — by His majesty I swear,
Whose far unworthy deputy I am, —
He shall not breathe infection in this air
But three days longer, on the pain of death.
[*Exit* SALISBURY.

QUEEN MARGARET
O, Henry, let me plead for gentle Suffolk!

KING HENRY
Ungentle queen, to call him gentle Suffolk!
No more, I say: if thou dost plead for him,
Thou wilt but add increase unto my wrath.
Had I but said, I would have kept my word;
But when I swear, it is irrevocable. —
If after three days' space thou here be'st found
On any ground that I am ruler of,
The world shall not be ransom for thy life. —
Come, Warwick, come, good Warwick, go with me;
I have great matters to impart to thee.
[*Exeunt all except* QUEEN *and* SUFFOLK.

QUEEN MARGARET
Mischance and sorrow go along with you!
Heart's discontent and sour affliction
Be playfellows to keep you company!
There's two of you; the devil make a third!
And threefold vengeance tend upon your steps!

SUFFOLK
Cease, gentle queen, these execrations,
And let thy Suffolk take his heavy leave.

QUEEN MARGARET
Fie, coward woman, and soft-hearted wretch!
Hast thou not spirit to curse thine enemies?

SUFFOLK
A plague upon them! wherefore should I curse them?
Would curses kill, as doth the mandrake's groan,
I would invent as bitter-searching terms,
As curst, as harsh, and horrible to hear,
Deliver'd strongly through my fixed teeth,
With full as many signs of deadly hate,
As lean-faced Envy in her loathsome cave:
My tongue should stumble in mine earnest words;
Mine eyes should sparkle like the beaten flint;
Mine hair be fix'd on end, as one distract;
Ay, every joint should seem to curse and ban:
And even now my burden'd heart would break,
Should I not curse them. Poison be their drink!
Gall, worse than gall, the dainties that they taste!
Their sweetest shade a grove of cypress-trees!
Their chiefest prospect murdering basilisks!
Their softest touch as smart as lizards' stings!
Their music frightful as the serpent's hiss,
And boding screech-owls make the consort full!
All the foul terrors in dark-seated hell —

QUEEN MARGARET
Enough, sweet Suffolk; thou torment'st thyself;
And these dread curses — like the sun 'gainst glass,
Or like an overcharged gun — recoil,
And turn the force of them upon thyself.

SUFFOLK
You bade me ban, and will you bid me leave?
Now, by the ground that I am banish'd from,
Well could I curse away a winter's night,
Though standing naked on a mountain-top,
Where biting cold would never let grass grow,
And think it but a minute spent in sport.

QUEEN MARGARET
O, let me entreat thee, cease! Give me thy hand,
That I may dew it with my mournful tears;
Nor let the rain of heaven wet this place,
To wash away my woeful monuments.
O, could this kiss be printed in thy hand,
                              [Kisses his hand.
That thou mightst think upon these by the seal,
Through whom a thousand sighs are breath'd for thee!
So, get thee gone, that I may know my grief;
'Tis but surmis'd whiles thou art standing by,
As one that surfeits thinking on a want.
I will repeal thee, or, be well assured,
Adventure to be banished myself:
And banished I am, if but from thee.
Go; speak not to me; even now be gone. —
O, go not yet! — Even thus two friends condemn'd
Embrace, and kiss, and take ten thousand leaves,
Lother a hundred times to part than die.
Yet now farewell; and farewell life with thee!

SUFFOLK
Thus is poor Suffolk ten times banished, —
Once by the king, and three times thrice by thee.
'Tis not the land I care for, wert thou thence;
A wilderness is populous enough,
So Suffolk had thy heavenly company:
For where thou art, there is the world itself,
With every several pleasure in the world;
And where thou art not, desolation.
I can no more: — live thou to joy thy life;
Myself no joy in naught but that thou livest.

Enter VAUX.

QUEEN MARGARET
Whither goes Vaux so fast? what news, I prithee?

VAUX
To signify unto his majesty
That Cardinal Beaufort is at point of death;
For suddenly a grievous sickness took him,
That makes him gasp, and stare, and catch the air,
Blaspheming God, and cursing men on earth.
Sometime he talks as if Duke Humphrey's ghost
Were by his side; sometime he calls the king,
And whispers to his pillow, as to him,
The secrets of his overcharged soul:
And I am sent to tell his majesty

That even now he cries aloud for him.

QUEEN MARGARET
Go tell this heavy message to the king.   [*Exit* VAUX.
Ay me! what is this world! what news are these!
But wherefore grieve I at an hour's poor loss,
Omitting Suffolk's exile, my soul's treasure?
Why only, Suffolk, mourn I not for thee,
And with the southern clouds contend in tears, —
Theirs for the earth's increase, mine for my sorrows?
Now get thee hence: the king, thou know'st, is coming; —
If thou be found by me, thou art but dead.

SUFFOLK
If I depart from thee, I cannot live;
And in thy sight to die, what were it else
But like a pleasant slumber in thy lap?
Here could I breathe my soul into the air,
As mild and gentle as the cradle-babe
Dying with mother's dug between its lips:
Where, from thy sight, I should be raging mad,
And cry out for thee to close up mine eyes,
To have thee with thy lips to stop my mouth;
So shouldst thou either turn my flying soul,
Or I should breathe it so into thy body,
And then it liv'd in sweet Elysium.
To die by thee were but to die in jest;
From thee to die were torture more than death:
O, let me stay, befall what may befall!

QUEEN MARGARET
Away! though parting be a fretful corrosive,
It is applied to a deathful wound.
To France, sweet Suffolk: let me hear from thee;
For wheresoe'er thou art in this world's globe,
I'll have an Iris that shall find thee out.

SUFFOLK
I go.

QUEEN MARGARET
And take my heart with thee.

SUFFOLK
A jewel, lock'd into the woefull'st cask
That ever did contain a thing of worth.
Even as a splitted bark, so sunder we:
This way fall I to death.

QUEEN MARGARET
                    This way for me.
                              [*Exeunt severally.*

SCENE III

The CARDINAL'S bedchamber.

*Enter the KING, SALISBURY, and WARWICK to the
CARDINAL in bed.*

KING HENRY
How fares my lord? speak, Beaufort, to thy
sovereign.

CARDINAL BEAUFORT
If thou be'st Death, I'll give thee England's treasure,
Enough to purchase such another island,
So thou wilt let me live, and feel no pain.

KING HENRY
Ah, what a sign it is of evil life,
Where death's approach is seen so terrible!

WARWICK
Beaufort, it is thy sovereign speaks to thee.

CARDINAL BEAUFORT
Bring me unto my trial when you will.
Died he not in his bed? where should he die?
Can I make men live, whe'r they will or no?
O, torture me no more! I will confess. —
Alive again? then show me where he is:
I'll give a thousand pound to look upon him. —
He hath no eyes, the dust hath blinded them. —
Comb down his hair; look, look! it stands upright,
Like lime-twigs set to catch my winged soul! —
Give me some drink; and bid the apothecary
Bring the strong poison that I bought of him.

KING HENRY
O thou eternal Mover of the heavens,
Look with a gentle eye upon this wretch!
O, beat away the busy-meddling fiend
That lays strong siege unto this wretch's soul,
And from his bosom purge this black despair!

WARWICK
See how the pangs of death do make him grin!

SALISBURY
Disturb him not, let him pass peaceably.

KING HENRY
Peace to his soul, if God's good pleasure be! —
Lord cardinal, if thou think'st on heaven's bliss,
Hold up thy hand, make signal of thy hope. —
He dies, and makes no sign: — O God, forgive him!

WARWICK
So bad a death argues a monstrous life.

KING HENRY
Forbear to judge, for we are sinners all. —
Close up his eyes, and draw the curtain close;
And let us all to meditation.   [*Exeunt.*

ACT IV

SCENE I

The coast of Kent.

*Alarum. Fight at sea. Ordnance goes off. Enter a
CAPTAIN, a MASTER, a MASTER'S-MATE,
WALTER WHITMORE, and others; with them
SUFFOLK and others, prisoners.*

CAPTAIN
The gaudy, blabbing, and remorseful day
Is crept into the bosom of the sea;
And now loud-howling wolves arouse the jades
That drag the tragic melancholy night;
Who, with their drowsy, slow, and flagging wings,
Clip dead men's graves, and from their misty jaws
Breathe foul contagious darkness in the air.
Therefore bring forth the soldiers of our prize;
For, whilst our pinnace anchors in the Downs,
Here shall they make their ransom on the sand,
Or with their blood stain this discolour'd shore. —
Master, this prisoner freely give I thee; —
And thou that art his mate, make boot of this; —
The other [*pointing* to SUFFOLK], Walter Whitmore, is
   thy share.

FIRST GENTLEMAN
What is my ransom, master? let me know.

MASTER
A thousand crowns, or else lay down your head.

MASTER'S-MATE
And so much shall you give, or off goes yours.

CAPTAIN
What, think you much to pay two thousand crowns,
And bear the name and port of gentlemen? —
Cut both the villains' throats; — for die you shall: —
The lives of those which we have lost in fight
Be counterpois'd with such a petty sum!

FIRST GENTLEMAN
I'll give it, sir; and therefore spare my life.

SECOND GENTLEMAN
And so will I, and write home for it straight.

WHITMORE
I lost mine eye in laying the prize aboard,
[*to* SUFFOLK] And therefore, to revenge it, shalt thou
   die;
And so should these, if I might have my will.

CAPTAIN
Be not so rash; take ransom, let him live.

SUFFOLK
Look on my George, — I am a gentleman:
Rate me at what thou wilt, thou shalt be paid.

WHITMORE
And so am I; my name is Walter Whitmore.
How now! why start'st thou? what, doth death affright?

SUFFOLK
Thy name affrights me, in whose sound is death.
A cunning man did calculate my birth,
And told me that by *water* I should die:
Yet let this not make thee be bloody-minded;
Thy name is *Gualtier*, being rightly sounded.

WHITMORE
Gualtier or *Walter*, which it is, I care not:
Never yet did base dishonour blur our name,
But with our sword we wip'd away the blot;
Therefore, when merchant-like I sell revenge,
Broke be my sword, my arms torn and defaced,
And I proclaim'd a coward through the world!
                              [*Lays hold on* SUFFOLK.

SUFFOLK
Stay, Whitmore; for thy prisoner is a prince,
The Duke of Suffolk, William de la Pole.

WHITMORE
The Duke of Suffolk muffled up in rags!

SUFFOLK
Ay, but these rags are no part of the duke:
Jove sometime went disguis'd, and why not I?

CAPTAIN
But Jove was never slain, as thou shalt be.

SUFFOLK
Obscure and lowly swain, King Henry's blood,
The honourable blood of Lancaster,

Must not be shed by such a jaded groom.
Hast thou not kiss'd thy hand, and held my stirrup?
Bare-headed plodded by my foot-cloth mule,
And thought thee happy when I shook my head?
How often hast thou waited at my cup,
Fed from my trencher, kneel'd down at the board,
When I have feasted with Queen Margaret?
Remember it, and let it make thee crest-fall'n,
Ay, and allay this thy abortive pride:
How in our voiding-lobby hast thou stood,
And duly waited for my coming forth?
This hand of mine hath writ in thy behalf,
And therefore shall it charm thy riotous tongue.

WHITMORE
Speak, captain, shall I stab the forlorn swain?

CAPTAIN
First let my words stab him, as he hath me.

SUFFOLK
Base slave, thy words are blunt, and so art thou.

CAPTAIN
Convey him hence, and on our long-boat's side
Strike off his head.

SUFFOLK
       Thou darest not, for thy own.

CAPTAIN
Yes, Pole.

SUFFOLK
    Pole!

CAPTAIN
        Pole! Sir Pole! lord!
Ay, kennel, puddle, sink; whose filth and dirt
Troubles the silver spring where England drinks.
Now will I dam up this thy yawning mouth
For swallowing the treasure of the realm:
Thy lips, that kiss'd the queen, shall sweep the ground;
And thou, that smil'dst at good Duke Humphrey's
   death,
Against the senseless winds shalt grin in vain,
Who, in contempt, shall hiss at thee again:
And wedded be thou to the hags of hell,
For daring to affy a mighty lord
Unto the daughter of a worthless king,
Having neither subject, wealth, nor diadem.
By devilish policy art thou grown great,
And, like ambitious Sylla, overgorged
With gobbets of thy mother's bleeding heart.
By thee Anjou and Maine were sold to France;
The false revolting Normans thorough thee
Disdain to call us lord; and Picardy
Hath slain their governors, surpris'd our forts,
And sent the ragged soldiers wounded home.
The princely Warwick, and the Nevils all, —
Whose dreadful swords were never drawn in vain, —
As hating thee, are rising up in arms:
And now the house of York — thrust from the crown
By shameful murder of a guiltless king
And lofty proud-encroaching tyranny —
Burns with revenging fire; whose hopeful colours
Advance our half-fac'd sun, striving to shine,
Under the which is writ *Invitis nubibus.*
The commons here in Kent are up in arms:
And, to conclude, reproach and beggary
Is crept into the palace of our king,
And all by thee. — Away! convey him hence.

SUFFOLK
O, that I were a god, to shoot forth thunder
Upon these paltry, servile, abject drudges!
Small things make base men proud: this villain here,
Being captain of a pinnace, threatens more
Than Bargulus, the strong Illyrian pirate.
Drones suck not eagles' blood, but rob bee-hives:
It is impossible that I should die
By such a lowly vassal as thyself.
Thy words move rage and not remorse in me:
I go of message from the queen to France;
I charge thee waft me safely cross the Channel.

CAPTAIN
Walter, —

WHITMORE
Come, Suffolk, I must waft thee to thy death.

SUFFOLK
Gelidus timor occupat artus: — it is thee I fear.

WHITMORE
Thou shalt have cause to fear before I leave thee.
What, are ye daunted now? now will ye stoop?

FIRST GENTLEMAN
My gracious lord, entreat him, speak him fair.

SUFFOLK
Suffolk's imperial tongue is stern and rough,
Us'd to command, untaught to plead for favour.

Far be it we should honour such as these
With humble suit: no, rather let my head
Stoop to the block than these knees bow to any,
Save to the God of heaven and to my king;
And sooner dance upon a bloody pole
Than stand uncover'd to the vulgar groom.
True nobility is exempt from fear: —
More can I bear than you dare execute.

CAPTAIN
Hale him away, and let him talk no more.

SUFFOLK
Come, soldiers, show what cruelty ye can,
That this my death may never be forgot! —
Great men oft die by vile besonians:
A Roman sworder and banditto slave
Murder'd sweet Tully; Brutus' bastard hand
Stabb'd Julius Cæsar; savage islanders
Pompey the Great; and Suffolk dies by pirates.
      [*Exeunt* WHITMORE *and others with* SUFFOLK.

CAPTAIN
And as for these whose ransom we have set,
It is our pleasure one of them depart: —
Therefore come you with us, and let him go.
      [*Exeunt all except the* FIRST GENTLEMAN.
    Enter WHITMORE *with* SUFFOLK'S *body.*

WHITMORE
There let his head and lifeless body lie,
Until the queen his mistress bury it.   [*Exit.*

FIRST GENTLEMAN
O barbarous and bloody spectacle!
His body will I bear unto the king:
If he revenge it not, yet will his friends;
So will the queen, that living held him dear.
      [*Exit with the body.*

SCENE II
Blackheath.

Enter GEORGE BEVIS *and* JOHN HOLLAND.

BEVIS
Come, and get thee a sword, though made of a lath:
   they have been up these two days.

HOLLAND
They have the more need to sleep now, then.

BEVIS
I tell thee, Jack Cade the clothier means to dress the
commonwealth, and turn it, and set a new nap upon it.

HOLLAND
So he had need, for 'tis threadbare. Well, I say it was
never merry world in England since gentlemen came
up.

BEVIS
O miserable age! virtue is not regarded in
handicrafts-men.

HOLLAND
The nobility think scorn to go in leather aprons.

BEVIS
Nay, more, the king's council are no good workmen.

HOLLAND
True; and yet it is said, — labour in thy vocation; which
is as much to say as, — let the magistrates be labouring
men; and therefore should we be magistrates.

BEVIS
Thou hast hit it; for there's no better sign of a brave
   mind than a hard hand.

HOLLAND
I see them! I see them! There's Best's son, the tanner of
   Wingham, —

BEVIS
He shall have the skins of our enemies, to make
   dog's-leather of.

HOLLAND
And Dick the butcher, —

BEVIS
Then is sin struck down like an ox, and iniquity's throat
   cut like a calf.

HOLLAND
And Smith the weaver, —

BEVIS
Argo, their thread of life is spun.

HOLLAND
Come, come, let's fall in with them.
   Drum. Enter JACK CADE, DICK *the butcher,* SMITH
   the weaver, and a SAWYER, *with infinite numbers.*

JACK CADE
We John Cade, so term'd of our supposed father, —

DICK [*aside*].
Or rather, of stealing a cade of herrings.

JACK CADE
For our enemies shall fall before us, — inspired with
the spirit of putting down kings and princes, —
Command silence.

DICK
Silence!

JACK CADE
My father was a Mortimer, —

DICK [*aside*].
He was an honest man, and a good bricklayer.

JACK CADE
My mother a Plantagenet, —

DICK [*aside*].
I knew her well; she was a midwife.

JACK CADE
My wife descended of the Lacies, —

DICK [*aside*].
She was, indeed, a pedlar's daughter, and sold many
   laces.

SMITH [*aside*].
But now of late, not able to travel with her furr'd pack,
   she washes bucks here at home.

JACK CADE
Therefore am I of an honourable house.

DICK [*aside*]
Ay, by my faith, the field is honourable; and there was
   he born, under a hedge, — for his father had never a
   house but the cage.

JACK CADE
Valiant I am.

SMITH [*aside*].
'A must needs; for beggary is valiant.

JACK CADE
I am able to endure much.

DICK [*aside*].
No question of that; for I have seen him whipp'd three
   market-days together.

JACK CADE
I fear neither sword nor fire.

SMITH [*aside*].
He need not fear the sword; for his coat is of proof.

DICK [*aside*].
But methinks he should stand in fear of fire, being
   burnt i'th'hand for stealing of sheep.

JACK CADE
Be brave, then; for your captain is brave, and vows
reformation. There shall be in England seven
half-penny loaves sold for a penny: the three-hoop'd
pot shall have ten hoops; and I will make it felony to
drink small beer: all the realm shall be in common; and
in Cheapside shall my palfrey go to grass: and when I
am king, — as king I will be, —

ALL
God save your majesty!

JACK CADE
I thank you, good people: — there shall be no money;
all shall eat and drink on my score; and I will apparel
them all in one livery, that they may agree like brothers,
and worship me their lord.

DICK
The first thing we do, let's kill all the lawyers.

JACK CADE
Nay, that I mean to do. Is not this a lamentable thing,
that of the skin of an innocent lamb should be made
parchment? that parchment, being scribbled o'er,
should undo a man? Some say the bee stings: but I say,
'tis the bee's wax; for I did but seal once to a thing,
and I was never mine own man since. — How now!
who's there?
   Enter some, bringing in the CLERK OF CHATHAM.

SMITH
The clerk of Chatham: he can write and read and cast
   accompt.

JACK CADE
O monstrous!

SMITH
We took him setting of boys' copies.

JACK CADE
Here's a villain!

SMITH
'Has a book in his pocket with red letters in't.

JACK CADE
Nay, then, he is a conjurer.

DICK
Nay, he can make obligations, and write court-hand.

JACK CADE
I am sorry for't: the man is a proper man, of mine
honour; unless I find him guilty, he shall not die. —

Come hither, sirrah, I must examine thee: what is thy
name?

CLERK OF CHATHAM
Emmanuel.

DICK
They use to write it on the top of letters: — 'twill go
hard with you.

JACK CADE
Let me alone. — Dost thou use to write thy name? or
hast thou a mark to thyself, like an honest
plain-dealing man?

CLERK OF CHATHAM
Sir, I thank God, I have been so well brought up that I
can write my name.

ALL
He hath confess'd: away with him! he's a villain and a
traitor.

JACK CADE
Away with him, I say! hang him with his pen and
inkhorn about his neck.   [Exit one with the CLERK.

Enter MICHAEL.

MICHAEL
Where's our general?

JACK CADE
Here I am, thou particular fellow.

MICHAEL
Fly, fly, fly! Sir Humphrey Stafford and his brother are
hard by, with the king's forces.

JACK CADE
Stand, villain, stand, or I'll fell thee down. He shall be
encounter'd with a man as good as himself: he is but
a knight, is 'a?

MICHAEL
No.

JACK CADE
To equal him, I will make myself a knight presently.
[*Kneels.*] Rise up Sir John Mortimer. [*Rises.*] Now
have at him!

Enter SIR HUMPHREY STAFFORD *and his*
BROTHER, *with drum and* SOLDIERS.

STAFFORD
Rebellious hinds, the filth and scum of Kent,
Mark'd for the gallows, lay your weapons down;
Home to your cottages, forsake this groom: —
The king is merciful, if you revolt.

BROTHER
But angry, wrathful, and inclined to blood,
If you go forward; therefore yield, or die.

JACK CADE
As for these silken-coated slaves, I pass not:
It is to you, good people, that I speak,
Over whom, in time to come, I hope to reign;
For I am rightful heir unto the crown.

STAFFORD
Villain, thy father was a plasterer;
And thou thyself a shearman, — art thou not?

JACK CADE
And Adam was a gardener.

BROTHER
And what of that?

JACK CADE
Marry, thus: — Edmund Mortimer, Earl of March,
Married the Duke of Clarence' daughter, — did he not?

STAFFORD
Ay, sir.

JACK CADE
By her he had two children at one birth.

BROTHER
That's false.

JACK CADE
Ay, there's the question; but I say 'tis true:
The elder of them, being put to nurse,,
Was by a beggar-woman stol'n away;
And, ignorant of his birth and parentage,
Became a bricklayer when he came to age:
His son am I; deny it, if you can.

DICK
Nay, 'tis too true; therefore he shall be king.

SMITH
Sir, he made a chimney in my father's house, and the
bricks are alive at this day to testify it; therefore deny
it not.

STAFFORD
And will you credit this base drudge's words,
That speaks he knows not what?

ALL
Ay, marry, will we; therefore get ye gone.

BROTHER
Jack Cade, the Duke of York hath taught you this.

JACK CADE [*aside*].
He lies, for I invented it myself.
Go to, sirrah, tell the king from me, that, for his father's
sake, Henry the Fifth, in whose time boys went to
span-counter for French crowns, I am content he shall
reign; but I'll be Protector over him.

DICK
And furthermore, we'll have the Lord Say's head for
selling the dukedom of Maine.

JACK CADE
And good reason; for thereby is England main'd, and
fain to go with a staff, but that my puissance holds it
up. Fellow kings, I tell you that that Lord Say hath
gelded the commonwealth, and made it an eunuch:
and more than that, he can speak French; and therefore
he is a traitor.

STAFFORD
O gross and miserable ignorance!

JACK CADE
Nay, answer, if you can: — the Frenchmen are our
enemies; go to, then, I ask but this, — can he that
speaks with the tongue of an enemy be a good
counsellor, or no?

ALL
No, no; and therefore we'll have his head.

BROTHER
Well, seeing gentle words will not prevail,
Assail them with the army of the king.

STAFFORD
Herald, away; and throughout every town
Proclaim them traitors that are up with Cade;
That those which fly before the battle ends
May, even in their wives' and children's sight,
Be hang'd up for example at their doors: —
And you that be the king's friends, follow me.
                    [*Exeunt the two* STAFFORDS *and* SOLDIERS.

JACK CADE
And you that love the commons, follow me.
Now show yourselves men; 'tis for liberty.
We will not leave one lord, one gentleman:
Spare none but such as go in clouted shoon;
For they are thrifty honest men, and such
As would — but that they dare not — take our parts.

DICK
They are all in order, and march toward us.

JACK CADE
But then are we in order when we are most out of order.
Come, march forward!   [*Exeunt.

SCENE III

Another part of Blackheath.

Alarums to the fight, wherein both the STAFFORDS *are
slain. Enter* CADE *and the rest.*

JACK CADE
Where's Dick, the butcher of Ashford?

DICK
Here, sir.

JACK CADE
They fell before thee like sheep and oxen, and thou
behavedst thyself as if thou hadst been in thine own
slaughter-house: therefore thus will I reward thee, —
the Lent shall be as long again as it is; and thou shalt
have a licence to kill for a hundred lacking one a week.

DICK
I desire no more.

JACK CADE
And, to speak truth, thou deservest no less. This
monument of the victory will I bear [*putting on* SIR
HUMPHREY'S *brigandine*]; and the bodies shall be
dragg'd at my horse heels till I do come to London,
where we will have the mayor's sword borne before us.

DICK
If we mean to thrive and do good, break open the gaols,
and let out the prisoners.

JACK CADE
Fear not that, I warrant thee. — Come, let's march
towards London.   [*Exeunt.

SCENE IV

London. The palace.

Enter the KING *with a supplication, and the* QUEEN
with SUFFOLK'S *head; the* DUKE OF
BUCKINGHAM *and the* LORD SAY.

QUEEN MARGARET
Oft have I heard that grief softens the mind,

And makes it fearful and degenerate;
Think therefore on revenge, and cease to weep.
But who can cease to weep, and look on this?
Here may his head lie on my throbbing breast:
But where's the body that I should embrace?

BUCKINGHAM
What answer makes your Grace to the rebels'
supplication?

KING HENRY
I'll send some holy bishop to entreat;
For God forbid so many simple souls
Should perish by the sword! And I myself,
Rather than bloody war shall cut them short,
Will parley with Jack Cade their general: —
But stay, I'll read it over once again.

QUEEN MARGARET
Ah, barbarous villains! hath this lovely face
Rul'd, like a wandering planet, over me,
And could it not enforce them to relent,
That were unworthy to behold the same?

KING HENRY
Lord Say, Jack Cade hath sworn to have thy head.

LORD SAY
Ay, but I hope your highness shall have his.

KING HENRY
How now, madam!
Still lamenting, and mourning for Suffolk's death?
I fear me, love, if that I had been dead,
Thou wouldest not have mourn'd so much for me.

QUEEN MARGARET
No, my love, I should not mourn, but die for thee.

Enter a MESSENGER.

KING HENRY
How now! what news? why comest thou in such haste?

MESSENGER
The rebels are in Southwark; fly, my lord!
Jack Cade proclaims himself Lord Mortimer,
Descended from the Duke of Clarence' house;
And calls your Grace usurper openly,
And vows to crown himself in Westminster.
His army is a ragged multitude
Of hinds and peasants, rude and merciless:
Sir Humphrey Stafford and his brother's death
Hath given them heart and courage to proceed:
All scholars, lawyers, courtiers, gentlemen,
They call false caterpillars, and intend their death.

KING HENRY
O graceless men! they know not what they do.

BUCKINGHAM
My gracious lord, retire to Killingworth,
Until a power be rais'd to put them down.

QUEEN MARGARET
Ah, were the Duke of Suffolk now alive,
These Kentish rebels would be soon appeased!

KING HENRY
Lord Say, the traitor hateth thee;
Therefore away with us to Killingworth.

LORD SAY
So might your Grace's person be in danger;
The sight of me is odious in their eyes:
And therefore in this city will I stay,
And live alone as secret as I may.

Enter a second MESSENGER.

SECOND MESSENGER
Jack Cade hath gotten London-bridge;
The citizens fly and forsake their houses:
The rascal people, thirsting after prey,
Join with the traitor; and they jointly swear
To spoil the city and your royal court.

BUCKINGHAM
Then linger not, my lord; away, take horse.

KING HENRY
Come, Margaret; God, our hope, will succour us.

QUEEN MARGARET
My hope is gone, now Suffolk is deceased.

KING HENRY [*to* LORD SAY].
Farewell, my lord: trust not the Kentish rebels.

BUCKINGHAM
Trust nobody, for fear you be betray'd.

LORD SAY
The trust I have is in mine innocence,
And therefore am I bold and resolute.   [*Exeunt.

SCENE V

The same. The Tower.

Enter LORD SCALES *upon the Tower, walking. Then enter two or three* CITIZENS *below.*

SCALES
How now! is Jack Cade slain?

FIRST CITIZEN
No, my lord, nor likely to be slain; for they have won the bridge, killing all those that withstand them: the Lord Mayor craves aid of your honour from the Tower, to defend the city from the rebels.

SCALES
Such aid as I can spare, you shall command;
But I am troubled here with them myself, —
The rebels have assay'd to win the Tower.
But get you to Smithfield, and gather head,
And thither I will send you Matthew Gough:
Fight for your king, your country, and your lives;
And so, farewell, for I must hence again.   [*Exeunt.*

SCENE VI

The same. Cannon-street.

Enter JACK CADE *and the rest, and strikes his staff on London-stone.*

JACK CADE
Now is Mortimer lord of this city. And here, sitting upon London-stone, I charge and command, that, of the city's cost, the pissing-conduit run nothing but claret wine this first year of our reign. And now henceforward it shall be treason for any that calls me other than Lord Mortimer.

Enter a SOLDIER, *running.*

SOLDIER
Jack Cade! Jack Cade!

JACK CADE
Knock him down there.   [*They kill him.*

SMITH
If this fellow be wise, he'll never call ye Jack Cade more: I think he hath a very fair warning.

DICK
My lord, there's an army gather'd together in Smithfield.

JACK CADE
Come, then, let's go fight with them: but first, go and set London-bridge on fire; and, if you can, burn down the Tower too. Come, let's away.   [*Exeunt.*

SCENE VII

The same. Smithfield.

Alarums. MATTHEW GOUGH *is slain, and all the rest. Then enter* JACK CADE, *with his company.*

JACK CADE
So, sirs: — now go some and pull down the Savoy; others to the inns of court; down with them all.

DICK
I have a suit unto your lordship.

JACK CADE
Be it a lordship, thou shalt have it for that word.

DICK
Only, that the laws of England may come out of your mouth.

JOHN HOLLAND [*aside*].
Mass, 'twill be sore law, then; for he was thrust in the mouth with a spear, and 'tis not whole yet.

SMITH [*aside*].
Nay, John, it will be stinking law; for his breath stinks with eating toasted cheese.

JACK CADE
I have thought upon it, it shall be so. Away, burn all the records of the realm: my mouth shall be the parliament of England.

JOHN HOLLAND [*aside*].
Then we are like to have biting statutes, unless his teeth be pull'd out.

JACK CADE
And henceforward all things shall be in common.

Enter a MESSENGER.

MESSENGER
My lord, a prize, a prize! here's the Lord Say, which sold the towns in France; he that made us pay one-and-twenty fifteens, and one shilling to the pound, the last subsidy.

Enter GEORGE BEVIS, *with the* LORD SAY.

JACK CADE
Well, he shall be beheaded for it ten times. — Ah, thou say, thou serge, nay, thou buckram lord! now art thou within point-blank of our jurisdiction regal. What canst thou answer to my majesty for giving up of Normandy unto Monsieur Basimecu, the Dauphin of France? Be it known unto thee by these presence, even the presence of Lord Mortimer, that I am the besom that must sweep the court clean of such filth as thou art. Thou hast most traitorously corrupted the youth of the realm in erecting a grammar-school: and whereas, before, our forefathers had no other books but the score and the tally, thou hast caused printing to be used; and, contrary to the king, his crown, and dignity, thou hast built a paper-mill. It will be proved to thy face that thou hast men about thee that usually talk of a noun and a verb, and such abhominable words as no Christian ear can endure to hear. Thou hast appointed justices of peace, to call poor men before them about matters they were not able to answer. Moreover, thou hast put them in prison; and because they could not read, thou hast hang'd them; when, indeed, only for that cause they have been most worthy to live. Thou dost ride in a foot-cloth, dost thou not?

LORD SAY
What of that?

JACK CADE
Marry, thou ought'st not to let thy horse wear a cloak, when honester men than thou go in their hose and doublets.

DICK
And work in their shirt too; as myself, for example, that am a butcher.

LORD SAY
You men of Kent, —

DICK
What say you of Kent?

LORD SAY
Nothing but this, — 'tis *bona terra, mala gens.*

JACK CADE
Away with him, away with him! he speaks Latin.

LORD SAY
Hear me but speak, and bear me where you will.
Kent, in the Commentaries Cæsar writ,
Is term'd the civill'st place of all this isle:
Sweet is the country, beauteous, full of riches;
The people liberal, valiant, active, wealthy;
Which makes me hope you are not void of pity.
I sold not Maine, I lost not Normandy;
Yet, to recover them, would lose my life.
Justice with favour have I always done;
Prayers and tears have moved me, gifts could never.
When have I aught exacted at your hands,
But to maintain the king, the realm, and you?
Large gifts have I bestow'd on learned clerks,
Because my book preferr'd me to the king:
And, seeing ignorance is the curse of God,
Knowledge the wing wherewith we fly to heaven,
Unless you be possess'd with devilish spirits,
You cannot but forbear to murder me:
This tongue hath parley'd unto foreign kings
For your behoof, —

JACK CADE
Tut, when struck'st thou one blow in the field?

LORD SAY
Great men have reaching hands: oft have I struck
Those that I never saw, and struck them dead.

BEVIS
O monstrous coward! what, to come behind folks?

LORD SAY
These cheeks are pale for watching for your good.

JACK CADE
Give him a box o'th'ear, and that will make 'em red again.

LORD SAY
Long sitting to determine poor men's causes
Hath made me full of sickness and diseases.

JACK CADE
Ye shall have a hempen caudle, then, and the help of hatchet.

DICK
Why dost thou quiver, man?

LORD SAY
It is the palsy, and not fear, provokes me.

JACK CADE
Nay, he nods at us, as who should say, I'll be even with you: I'll see if his head will stand steadier on a pole, or no. Take him away, and behead him.

LORD SAY
Tell me wherein have I offended most?
Have I affected wealth or honour? speak.
Are my chests fill'd up with extorted gold?
Is my apparel sumptuous to behold?
Whom have I injured, that ye seek my death?
These hands are free from guiltless blood-shedding,
This breast from harbouring foul deceitful thoughts.
O, let me live!

JACK CADE [*aside*].
I feel remorse in myself with his words; but I'll bridle it: he shall die, an it be but for pleading so well for his life. — Away with him! he has a familiar under his tongue; he speaks not o' God's name. Go, take him away, I say, and strike off his head presently; and then break into his son-in-law's house, Sir James Cromer, and strike off his head, and bring them both upon two poles hither.

ALL
It shall be done.

LORD SAY
Ah, countrymen! if when you make your prayers,
God should be so obdurate as yourselves,
How would it fare with your departed souls?
And therefore yet relent, and save my life.

JACK CADE
Away with him! and do as I command ye.
          [*Exeunt some with* LORD SAY.
The proudest peer in the realm shall not wear a head on his shoulders, unless he pay me tribute; there shall not a maid be married, but she shall pay to me her maidenhead ere they have it: men shall hold of me *in capite*; and we charge and command that their wives be as free as heart can wish or tongue can tell.

DICK
My lord, when shall we go to Cheapside, and take up commodities upon our bills?

JACK CADE
Marry, presently.

ALL
O, brave!

Enter one with the heads.

JACK CADE
But is not this braver? — Let them kiss one another, for they loved well when they were alive. Now part them again, lest they consult about the giving-up of some more towns in France. Soldiers, defer the spoil of the city until night: for with these borne before us, instead of maces, will we ride through the streets; and at every corner have them kiss. — Away!   [*Exeunt.*

SCENE VIII

Southwark.

Alarum and retreat. Enter again CADE *and all his rabblement.*

JACK CADE
Up Fish-street! down Saint Magnus'-corner! kill and knock down! throw them into Thames! — [*Sound a parley.*] What noise is this I hear? Dare any be so bold to sound retreat or parley, when I command them kill?

Enter BUCKINGHAM *and* OLD CLIFFORD.

BUCKINGHAM
Ay, here they be that dare and will disturb thee:
Know, Cade, we come ambassadors from the king
Unto the commons whom thou hast misled;
And here pronounce free pardon to them all
That will forsake thee and go home in peace.

OLD CLIFFORD
What say ye, countrymen? will ye relent,
And yield to mercy whilst 'tis offer'd you;
Or let a rebel lead you to your deaths?
Who loves the king, and will embrace his pardon,
Fling up his cap, and say, 'God save his majesty!'
Who hateth him, and honours not his father,
Henry the Fifth, that made all France to quake,
Shake he his weapon at us, and pass by.

ALL
God save the king! God save the king!

JACK CADE
What, Buckingham and Clifford, are ye so brave? —
And you, base peasants, do ye believe him? will you needs be hang'd with your pardons about your necks? Hath my sword therefore broke through London gates, that you should leave me at the White Hart in Southwark? I thought ye would never have given out these arms till you had recover'd your ancient freedom: but you are all recreants and dastards, and delight to live in slavery to the nobility. Let them break your backs

with burthens, take your houses over your heads,
ravish your wives and daughters before your faces: for
me, I will make shift for one; and so, God's curse light
upon you all!

ALL
We'll follow Cade! we'll follow Cade!

OLD CLIFFORD
Is Cade the son of Henry the Fifth,
That thus you do exclaim you'll go with him?
Will he conduct you through the heart of France,
And make the meanest of you earls and dukes?
Alas, he hath no home, no place to fly to;
Nor knows he how to live but by the spoil,
Unless by robbing of your friends and us.
Were't not a shame, that whilst you live at jar,
The fearful French, whom you late vanquished,
Should make a start o'er seas, and vanquish you?
Methinks already in this civil broil
I see them lording it in London streets,
Crying 'Viliago!' unto all they meet.
Better ten thousand base-born Cades miscarry
Than you should stoop unto a Frenchman's mercy.
To France, to France, and get what you have lost;
Spare England, for it is your native coast:
Henry hath money, you are strong and manly;
God on our side, doubt not of victory.

ALL
A Clifford! a Clifford! we'll follow the king and Clifford.

JACK CADE [*aside*].
Was ever feather so lightly blown to and fro as this
multitude? the name of Henry the Fifth hales them to
an hundred mischiefs, and makes them leave me
desolate. I see them lay their heads together to surprise
me: my sword make way for me, for here is no staying.
[*Exit.*
— In despite of the devils and hell, have through the
very middest of you! and heavens and honour be
witness, that no want of resolution in me, but only my
followers' base and ignominious treasons, makes me
betake me to my heels.

BUCKINGHAM
What, is he fled? Go some, and follow him;
And he that brings his head unto the king
Shall have a thousand crowns for his reward. —
[*Exeunt some of them.*
Follow me, soldiers: we'll devise a mean
To reconcile you all unto the king. [*Exeunt.*

SCENE IX

Killingworth Castle.

Sound trumpets. Enter KING, QUEEN, *and*
SOMERSET, *on the terrace.*

KING HENRY
Was ever king that joy'd an earthly throne.
And could command no more content than I?
No sooner was I crept out of my cradle
But I was made a king, at nine months old:
Was never subject long'd to be a king
As I do long and wish to be a subject.

Enter BUCKINGHAM *and* OLD CLIFFORD.

BUCKINGHAM
Health and glad tidings to your majesty!

KING HENRY
Why, Buckingham, is the traitor Cade surprised?
Or is he but retired to make him strong?

Enter, below, multitudes, with halters about their necks.

OLD CLIFFORD
He is fled, my lord, and all his powers do yield;
And humbly thus, with halters on their necks,
Expect your highness' doom, of life or death.

KING HENRY
Then, heaven, set ope thy everlasting gates,
To entertain my vows of thanks and praise! —
Soldiers, this day have you redeem'd your lives,
And show'd how well you love your prince and country:
Continue still in this so good a mind,
And Henry, though he be infortunate,
Assure yourselves, will never be unkind:
And so, with thanks and pardon to you all,
I do dismiss you to your several countries.

ALL
God save the king! God save the king!

Enter a MESSENGER.

MESSENGER
Please it your Grace to be advertised
The Duke of York is newly come from Ireland;
And with a puissant and a mighty power

Of gallowglasses and stout kerns
Is marching hitherward in proud array;
And still proclaimeth, as he comes along,
His arms are only to remove from thee
The Duke of Somerset, whom he terms a traitor.

KING HENRY
Thus stands my state, 'twixt Cade and York distress'd;
Like to a ship that, having scaped a tempest,
Is straightway calm'd, and boarded with a pirate:
But now is Cade driven back, his men dispersed;
And now is York in arms to second him. —
I pray thee, Buckingham, go and meet him;
And ask him what's the reason of these arms.
Tell him I'll send Duke Edmund to the Tower; —
And, Somerset, we will commit thee thither,
Until his army be dismiss'd from him.

SOMERSET
My lord,
I'll yield myself to prison willingly,
Or unto death, to do my country good.

KING HENRY
In any case, be not too rough in terms;
For he is fierce, and cannot brook hard language.

BUCKINGHAM
I will, my lord; and doubt not so to deal
As all things shall redound unto your good.

KING HENRY
Come, wife, let's in, and learn to govern better;
For yet may England curse my wretched reign.
[*Flourish. Exeunt.*

SCENE X

Kent. IDEN'S *garden.*

Enter CADE.

JACK CADE
Fie on ambition! fie on myself, that have a sword, and yet
am ready to famish! These five days have I hid me in
these woods; and durst not peep out, for all the country is
laid for me; but now am I so hungry, that if I might have
a lease of my life for a thousand years, I could stay no
longer. Wherefore, on a brick-wall have I climb'd into
this garden, to see if I can eat grass, or pick a sallet
another while, which is not amiss to cool a man's
stomach this hot weather. And I think this word
'sallet'was born to do me good: for many a time, but for a
sallet, my brain-pan had been cleft with a brown bill; and
many a time, when I have been dry, and bravely marching,
it hath served me instead of a quart-pot to drink in; and
now the word 'sallet'must serve me to feed on.

Enter IDEN, *and his* MEN *behind.*

IDEN
Lord, who would live turmoiled in the court,
And may enjoy such quiet walks as these?
This small inheritance my father left me
Contenteth me, and worth a monarchy.
I seek not to wax great by others' waning;
Or gather wealth, I care not with what envy:
Sufficeth that I have maintains my state,
And sends the poor well pleased from my gate.

JACK CADE [*aside*].
Here's the lord of the soil come to seize me for a stray,
for entering his fee-simple without leave. — Ah,
villain, thou wilt betray me, and get a thousand crowns
of the king by carrying my head to him! but I'll make
thee eat iron like an ostrich, and swallow my sword like
a great pin, ere thou and I part.

IDEN
Why, rude companion, whatsoe'er thou be,
I know thee not; why, then, should I betray thee?
Is't not enough to break into my garden,
And, like a thief, to come to rob my grounds,
Climbing my walls in spite of me the owner,
But thou wilt brave me with these saucy terms?

JACK CADE
Brave thee! ay, by the best blood that ever was broach'd,
and beard thee too. Look on me well: I have eat no meat
these five days: yet, come thou and thy five men, and if
I do not leave you all as dead as a door-nail, I pray God I
may never eat grass more.

IDEN
Nay, it shall ne'er be said, while England stands,
That Alexander Iden, an esquire of Kent,
Took odds to combat a poor famish'd man.
Oppose thy steadfast-gazing eyes to mine,
See if thou canst outface me with thy looks:
Set limb to limb, and thou art far the lesser;
Thy hand is but a finger to my fist;
Thy leg a stick compared with this truncheon;
My foot shall fight with all the strength thou hast;

And if mine arm be heaved in the air,
Thy grave is digg'd already in the earth.
As for words, — whose greatness answers words,
Let this my sword report what speech forbears.

JACK CADE
By my valour, the most complete champion that ever I
heard! — Steel, if thou turn the edge, or cut not out the
burly-boned clown in chines of beef ere thou sleep in
thy sheath, I beseech God, on my knees, thou mayst be
turn'd to hobnails. [*Here they fight.* CADE *falls.*] O, I am
slain! famine and no other hath slain me: let ten
thousand devils come against me, and give me but the
ten meals I have lost, and I'ld defy them all. Wither,
garden; and be henceforth a burying-place to all that do
dwell in this house, because the unconquer'd soul of
Cade is fled.

IDEN
Is't Cade that I have slain, that monstrous traitor?
Sword, I will hallow thee for this thy deed,
And hang thee o'er my tomb when I am dead:
Ne'er shall this blood be wiped from thy point;
But thou shalt wear it as a herald's coat,
To emblaze the honour that thy master got.

JACK CADE
Iden, farewell; and be proud of thy victory.
Tell Kent from me, she hath lost her best man; and
exhort all the world to be cowards, — for I, that never
fear'd any, am vanquish'd by famine, not by valour.
[*Dies.*

IDEN
How much thou wrong'st me, heaven be my judge.
Die, damned wretch, the curse of her that bare thee!
And as I thrust thy body in with my sword,
So wish I, I might thrust thy soul to hell.
Hence will I drag thee headlong by the heels
Unto a dunghill, which shall be thy grave,
And there cut off thy most ungracious head;
Which I will bear in triumph to the king,
Leaving thy trunk for crows to feed upon.
[*Exeunt* IDEN, *dragging out the body, and* SERVANTS.

ACT V

SCENE I

Fields between Dartford and Blackheath.

Enter YORK *and his army of Irish,
with drum and colours.*

YORK
From Ireland thus comes York to claim his right,
And pluck the crown from feeble Henry's head:
Ring, bells, aloud; burn, bonfires, clear and bright;
To entertain great England's lawful king.
Ah, *sancta majestas!* who would not buy thee dear?
Let them obey that know not how to rule;
This hand was made to handle naught but gold.
I cannot give due action to my words,
Except a sword or sceptre balance it:
A sceptre shall it have, — have I a soul, —
On which I'll toss the flower-de-luce of France.
Enter BUCKINGHAM [*aside*].
Whom have we here? Buckingham, to disturb me?
The king hath sent him, sure: I must dissemble.

BUCKINGHAM
York, if thou meanest well, I greet thee well.

YORK
Humphrey of Buckingham, I accept thy greeting.
Art thou a messenger, or come of pleasure?

BUCKINGHAM
A messenger from Henry, our dread liege,
To know the reason of these arms in peace;
Or why thou, being a subject as I am,
Against thy oath and true allegiance sworn,
Should raise so great a power without his leave,
Or dare to bring thy force so near the court.

YORK [*aside*].
Scarce can I speak, my choler is so great:
O, I could hew up rocks, and fight with flint,
I am so angry at these abject terms;
And now, like Ajax Telamonius,
On sheep or oxen could I spend my fury!
I am far better born than is the king,
More like a king, more kingly in my thoughts:
But I must make fair weather yet awhile,
Till Henry be more weak, and I more strong. —
Buckingham, I prithee, pardon me,
That I have given no answer all this while;
My mind was troubled with deep melancholy.
The cause why I have brought this army hither

Is, to remove proud Somerset from the king,
Seditious to his Grace and to the state.

BUCKINGHAM
That is too much presumption on thy part:
But if thy arms be to no other end,
The king hath yielded unto thy demand;
The Duke of Somerset is in the Tower.

YORK
Upon thine honour, is he prisoner?

BUCKINGHAM
Upon mine honour, he is prisoner.

YORK
Then, Buckingham, I do dismiss my powers. —
Soldiers, I thank you all; disperse yourselves;
Meet me to-morrow in Saint George's field,
You shall have pay and every thing you wish. —
And let my sovereign, virtuous Henry,
Command my eldest son, nay, all my sons,
As pledges of my fealty and love;
I'll send them all as willing as I live:
Lands, goods, horse, armour, any thing I have,
Is his to use, so Somerset may die.

BUCKINGHAM
York, I commend this kind submission:
We twain will go into his highness' tent.

Enter KING HENRY *and* ATTENDANTS.

KING HENRY
Buckingham, doth York intend no harm to us,
That thus he marcheth with thee arm in arm?

YORK
In all submission and humility
York doth present himself unto your highness.

KING HENRY
Then what intends these forces thou dost bring?

YORK
To heave the traitor Somerset from hence;
And fight against that monstrous rebel Cade,
Who since I heard to be discomfited.

Enter IDEN, *with* CADE'S *head*.

IDEN
If one so rude and of so mean condition
May pass into the presence of a king,
Lo, I present your Grace a traitor's head,
The head of Cade, whom I in combat slew.

KING HENRY
The head of Cade! — Great God, how just art Thou! —
O, let me view his visage, being dead,
That living wrought me such exceeding trouble. —
Tell me, my friend, art thou the man that slew him?

IDEN
I was, an't like your majesty.

KING HENRY
How art thou call'd? and what is thy degree?

IDEN
Alexander Iden, that's my name;
A poor esquire of Kent, that loves his king.

BUCKINGHAM
So please it you, my lord, 'twere not amiss
He were created knight for his good service.

KING HENRY
Iden, kneel down. [*He kneels.*] Rise up a knight.
We give thee for reward a thousand marks;
And will that thou henceforth attend on us.

IDEN
May Iden live to merit such a bounty,
And never live but true unto his liege!

KING HENRY
See, Buckingham! Somerset comes with the queen;
Go, bid her hide him quickly from the duke.

Enter QUEEN MARGARET *and* SOMERSET.

QUEEN MARGARET
For thousand Yorks he shall not hide his head,
But boldly stand, and front him to his face.

YORK
How now! is Somerset at liberty?
Then, York, unloose thy long-imprison'd thoughts,
And let thy tongue be equal with thy heart.
Shall I endure the sight of Somerset? —
False king! why hast thou broken faith with me,
Knowing how hardly I can brook abuse?
King did I call thee? no, thou art not king;
Not fit to govern and rule multitudes,
Which darest not, no, nor canst not rule a traitor.
That head of thine doth not become a crown;
Thy hand is made to grasp a palmer's staff,
And not to grace an awful princely sceptre.
That gold must round engirt these brows of mine;
Whose smile and frown, like to Achilles' spear,

Is able with the change to kill and cure.
Here is a hand to hold a sceptre up,
And with the same to act controlling laws.
Give place: by heaven, thou shalt rule no more
O'er him whom heaven created for thy ruler.

SOMERSET
O monstrous traitor! — I arrest thee, York,
Of capital treason 'gainst the king and crown:
Obey, audacious traitor; kneel for grace.

YORK
Wouldst have me kneel? first let me ask of these,
If they can brook I bow a knee to man. —
Sirrah, call in my sons to be my bail:
                              [*Exit an* ATTENDANT.
I know, ere they will have me go to ward,
They'll pawn their swords for my enfranchisement.

QUEEN MARGARET
Call hither Clifford; bid him come amain,
To say if that the bastard boys of York
Shall be the surety for their traitor father.
                              [*Exit* BUCKINGHAM.

YORK
O blood-bespotted Neapolitan,
Outcast of Naples, England's bloody scourge!
The sons of York, thy betters in their birth,
Shall be their father's bail; and bane to those
That for my surety will refuse the boys!
See where they come: I'll warrant they'll make it good.

Enter EDWARD *and* RICHARD.

QUEEN MARGARET
And here comes Clifford to deny their bail.

Enter OLD CLIFFORD *and his* SON.

OLD CLIFFORD
Health and all happiness to my lord the king!   [*Kneels.*

YORK
I thank thee, Clifford: say, what news with thee?
Nay, do not fright us with an angry look:
We are thy sovereign; Clifford, kneel again;
For thy mistaking so, we pardon thee.

OLD CLIFFORD
This is my king, York; I do not mistake;
But thou mistakest me much to think I do: —
To Bedlam with him! is the man grown mad?

KING HENRY
Ay, Clifford; a bedlam and ambitious humour
Makes him oppose himself against his king.

OLD CLIFFORD
He is a traitor; let him to the Tower,
And chop away that factious pate of his.

QUEEN MARGARET
He is arrested, but will not obey;
His sons, he says, shall give their words for him.

YORK
Will you not, sons?

EDWARD
Ay, noble father, if our words will serve.

RICHARD
And if words will not, then our weapons shall.

OLD CLIFFORD
Why, what a brood of traitors have we here!

YORK
Look in a glass, and call thy image so:
I am thy king, and thou a false-heart traitor. —
Call hither to the stake my two brave bears,
That with the very shaking of their chains
They may astonish these fell-lurking curs:
Bid Salisbury and Warwick come to me.

Enter the EARLS OF WARWICK *and* SALISBURY.

OLD CLIFFORD
Are these thy bears? we'll bait thy bears to death,
And manacle the bear-ward in their chains,
If thou darest bring them to the baiting-place.

RICHARD
Oft have I seen a hot o'erweening cur
Run back and bite, because he was withheld;
Who, being suffer'd with the bear's fell paw,
Hath clapp'd his tail between his legs and cried:
And such a piece of service will you do,
If you oppose yourselves to match Lord Warwick.

OLD CLIFFORD
Hence, heap of wrath, foul indigested lump,
As crooked in thy manners as thy shape!

YORK
Nay, we shall heat you thoroughly anon.

OLD CLIFFORD
Take heed, lest by your heat you burn yourselves.

KING HENRY
Why, Warwick, hath thy knee forgot to bow? —
Old Salisbury, — shame to thy silver hair,
Thou mad misleader of thy brain-sick son! —
What, wilt thou on thy death-bed play the ruffian,
And seek for sorrow with thy spectacles? —
O, where is faith? O, where is loyalty?
If it be banish'd from the frosty head,
Where shall it find a harbour in the earth? —
Wilt thou go dig a grave to find out war,
And shame thine honourable age with blood?
Why art thou old, and want'st experience?
Or wherefore dost abuse it, if thou hast it?
For shame! in duty bend thy knee to me,
That bows unto the grave with mickle age.

SALISBURY
My lord, I have consider'd with myself
The title of this most renowned duke;
And in my conscience do repute his Grace
The rightful heir to England's royal seat.

KING HENRY
Hast thou not sworn allegiance unto me?

SALISBURY
I have.

KING HENRY
Canst thou dispense with heaven for such an oath?

SALISBURY
It is great sin to swear unto a sin;
But greater sin to keep a sinful oath.
Who can be bound by any solemn vow
To do a murderous deed, to rob a man,
To force a spotless virgin's chastity,
To reave the orphan of his patrimony,
To wring the widow from her custom'd right;
And have no other reason for this wrong,
But that he was bound by a solemn oath?

QUEEN MARGARET
A subtle traitor needs no sophister.

KING HENRY
Call Buckingham, and bid him arm himself.

YORK
Call Buckingham, and all the friends thou hast,
I am resolved for death or dignity.

OLD CLIFFORD
The first I warrant thee, if dreams prove true.

WARWICK
You were best to go to bed and dream again,
To keep thee from the tempest of the field.

OLD CLIFFORD
I am resolved to bear a greater storm
Than any thou canst conjure up to-day;
And that I'll write upon thy burgonet,
Might I but know thee by thy household badge.

WARWICK
Now, by my father's badge, old Nevil's crest,
The rampant bear chain'd to the ragged staff,
This day I'll wear aloft my burgonet, —
As on a mountain-top the cedar shows,
That keeps his leaves in spite of any storm, —
Even to affright thee with the view thereof.

OLD CLIFFORD
And from thy burgonet I'll rend thy bear,
And tread it under foot with all contempt,
Despite the bear-ward that protects the bear.

YOUNG CLIFFORD
And so to arms, victorious father,
To quell the rebels and their complices.

RICHARD
Fie! charity, for shame! speak not in spite,
For you shall sup with Jesu Christ to-night.

YOUNG CLIFFORD
Foul stigmatic, that's more than thou canst tell.

RICHARD
If not in heaven, you'll surely sup in hell.
                              [*Exeunt severally.*

SCENE II
Saint Alban's.

Alarums to the battle. Enter WARWICK.

WARWICK
Clifford of Cumberland, 'tis Warwick calls!
And if thou dost not hide thee from the bear,
Now, — when the angry trumpet sounds alarum,
And dead men's cries do fill the empty air, —
Clifford, I say, come forth and fight with me!
Proud northern lord, Clifford of Cumberland,
Warwick is hoarse with calling thee to arms.
                              Enter YORK.
How now, my noble lord! what, all a-foot?

YORK
The deadly-handed Clifford slew my steed;
But match to match I have encounter'd him,
And made a prey for carrion kites and crows
Even of the bonny beast he loved so well.

Enter OLD CLIFFORD.

WARWICK
Of one or both of us the time is come.

YORK
Hold, Warwick, seek thee out some other chase,
For I myself must hunt this deer to death.

WARWICK
Then, nobly, York; 'tis for a crown thou fight'st. —
As I intend, Clifford, to thrive to-day,
It grieves my soul to leave thee unassail'd.   [*Exit.*

OLD CLIFFORD
What seest thou in me, York? why dost thou pause?

YORK
With thy brave bearing should I be in love,
But that thou art so fast mine enemy.

OLD CLIFFORD
Nor should thy prowess want praise and esteem,
But that 'tis shown ignobly and in treason.

YORK
So let it help me now against thy sword,
As I in justice and true right express it!

OLD CLIFFORD
My soul and body on the action both!

YORK
A dreadful lay! — address thee instantly.
                [*They fight.* OLD CLIFFORD *falls.*

OLD CLIFFORD
La fin couronne les œuvres.   [*Dies.*

YORK
Thus war hath given thee peace, for thou art still.
Peace with his soul, heaven, if it be thy will!   [*Exit.*

Enter YOUNG CLIFFORD.

YOUNG CLIFFORD
Shame and confusion! all is on the rout;
Fear frames disorder, and disorder wounds
Where it should guard. O war, thou son of hell,
Whom angry heavens do make their minister,
Throw in the frozen bosoms of our part
Hot coals of vengeance! — Let no soldier fly:
He that is truly dedicate to war
Hath no self-love; nor he that loves himself
Hath not essentially, but by circumstance,
The name of valour. — O, let the vile world end,
                [*Seeing his father's body.*
And the premised flames of the last day
Knit earth and heaven together!
Now let the general trumpet blow his blast,

Particularities and petty sounds
To cease! — Wast thou ordain'd, dear father,
To lose thy youth in peace, and to achieve
The silvery livery of advised age,
And, in thy reverence and thy chair-days, thus
To die in ruffian battle? — Even at this sight
My heart is turn'd to stone: and while 'tis mine,
It shall be stony. York not our old men spares;
No more will I their babes: tears virginal
Shall be to me even as the dew to fire;
And beauty, that the tyrant oft reclaims,
Shall to my flaming wrath be oil and flax.
Henceforth I will not have to do with pity:
Meet I an infant of the house of York,
Into as many gobbets will I cut it,
As wild Medea young Absyrtus did:
In cruelty will I seek out my fame. —
Come, thou new ruin of old Clifford's house.
                [*Taking up the body.*
As did Æneas old Anchises bear,
So bear I thee upon my manly shoulders;
But then Æneas bare a living load,
Nothing so heavy as these woes of mine.   [*Exit.*

Enter RICHARD *and* SOMERSET *to fight.*
SOMERSET *is kill'd.*

RICHARD
So, lie thou there; —
For underneath an alehouse' paltry sign,
The Castle in Saint Alban's, Somerset
Hath made the wizard famous in his death. —
Sword, hold thy temper; heart, be wrathful still:
Priests pray for enemies, but princes kill.   [*Exit.*

Fight. Excursions. Enter KING, QUEEN, *and others.*

QUEEN MARGARET
Away, my lord! you are slow; for shame, away!

KING HENRY
Can we outrun the heavens? good Margaret, stay.

QUEEN MARGARET
What are you made of? you'll nor fight nor fly:
Now is it manhood, wisdom, and defence,
To give the enemy way; and to secure us
By what we can, which can no more but fly.
                [*Alarum afar off.*
If you be ta'en, we then should see the bottom
Of all our fortunes: but if we haply scape, —
As well we may, if not through your neglect, —
We shall to London get: where you are loved;
And where this breach, now in our fortunes made,
May readily be stopp'd.

Enter YOUNG CLIFFORD.

YOUNG CLIFFORD
But that my heart's on future mischief set,

I would speak blasphemy ere bid you fly:
But fly you must; uncurable discomfit
Reigns in the hearts of all our present part.
Away, for your relief! and we will live
To see their day, and them our fortune give:
Away, my lord, away!   [*Exeunt.*

SCENE III

Fields near Saint Alban's.

Alarum. Retreat. Enter YORK, RICHARD,
WARWICK, *and* SOLDIERS, *with drum and colours.*

YORK
Old Salisbury, who can report of him, —
That winter lion, who in rage forgets
Aged contusions and all brush of time,
And, like a gallant in the brow of youth,
Repairs him with occasion? This happy day
Is not itself, nor have we won one foot,
If Salisbury be lost.

RICHARD
                My noble father,
Three times to-day I holp him to his horse,
Three times bestrid him, thrice I led him off,
Persuaded him from any further act:
But still, where danger was, still there I met him;
And like rich hangings in a homely house,
So was his will in his old feeble body.
But, noble as he is, look where he comes.

Enter SALISBURY.

SALISBURY
Now, by my sword, well hast thou fought to-day;
By th'mass, so did we all. — I thank you, Richard:
God knows how long it is I have to live;
And it hath pleas'd him that three times to-day
You have defended me from imminent death. —
Well, lords, we have not got that which we have:
'Tis not enough our foes are this time fled,
Being opposites of such repairing nature.

YORK
I know our safety is to follow them;
For, as I hear, the king is fled to London,
To call a present court of parliament.
Let us pursue him, ere the writs go forth: —
What says Lord Warwick? shall we after them?

WARWICK
After them! nay, before them, if we can.
Now, by my faith, lords, 'twas a glorious day:
Saint Alban's battle, won by famous York,
Shall be eternis'd in all age to come. —
Sound drums and trumpets; and to London all:
And more such days as these to us befall!   [*Exeunt.*

THE THIRD PART OF KING HENRY THE SIXTH

DRAMATIS PERSONAE

KING HENRY THE SIXTH.
EDWARD, *Prince of Wales, his son.*
LOUIS XI, *King of France.*
DUKE OF SOMERSET.
DUKE OF EXETER.
EARL OF OXFORD.
EARL OF NORTHUMBERLAND.
EARL OF WESTMORELAND.
LORD CLIFFORD.
RICHARD PLANTAGENET, *Duke of York.*
EDWARD, *Earl of March,*
　afterwards King Edward IV,
EDMUND, *Earl of Rutland,* } *his sons.*
GEORGE, *afterwards Duke of Clarence,*
RICHARD, *afterwards Duke of Gloster,*

DUKE OF NORFOLK.
MARQUESS OF MONTAGUE.
EARL OF WARWICK.
EARL OF PEMBROKE.
LORD HASTINGS.
LORD STAFFORD.
SIR JOHN MORTIMER, } *uncles to the Duke of York.*
SIR HUGH MORTIMER,
HENRY, *Earl of Richmond, a youth.*
LORD RIVERS, *brother to Lady Grey.*
SIR WILLIAM STANLEY.
SIR JOHN MONTGOMERY.
SIR JOHN SOMERVILLE.
TUTOR TO RUTLAND. MAYOR OF YORK.

LIEUTENANT OF THE TOWER. A NOBLEMAN.
TWO KEEPERS. A HUNTSMAN.
A SON THAT HAS KILL'D HIS FATHER.
A FATHER THAT HAS KILL'D HIS SON.

QUEEN MARGARET.
LADY GREY, *afterwards Queen to Edward IV*
BONA, *sister to the French Queen.*

SOLDIERS, ATTENDANTS, MESSENGERS.
　WATCHMEN, *etc.*

SCENE — *During part of the third Act in France; during the rest of the Play in England.*

ACT I

SCENE I

London. The Parliament-house.

Alarum. Enter the DUKE OF YORK, EDWARD, RICHARD, NORFOLK, MONTAGUE, WARWICK, *and* SOLDIERS.

WARWICK
I wonder how the king escap'd our hands.
YORK
While we pursued the horsemen of the north,
He slily stole away, and left his men:
Whereat the great Lord of Northumberland,
Whose warlike ears could never brook retreat,
Cheer'd up the drooping army; and himself,
Lord Clifford, and Lord Stafford, all a-breast,
Charg'd our main battle's front, and, breaking in,
Were by the swords of common soldiers slain.
EDWARD
Lord Stafford's father, Duke of Buckingham,
Is either slain or wounded dangerous;
I cleft his beaver with a downright blow:
That this is true, father, behold his blood.
　　　　　　　　　[Showing his bloody sword.
MONTAGUE [*to* YORK, *showing his*].
And, brother, here's the Earl of Wiltshire's blood,
Whom I encounter'd as the battles join'd.
RICHARD
Speak thou for me, and tell them what I did.
　　　[Throwing down DUKE OF SOMERSET'S *head.*
YORK
Richard hath best deserv'd of all my sons. —
But is your Grace dead, my Lord of Somerset?
NORFOLK
Such hap have all the line of John of Gaunt!
RICHARD
Thus do I hope to shake King Henry's head.
WARWICK
And so do I. — Victorious Prince of York,
Before I see thee seated in that throne
Which now the house of Lancaster usurps,
I vow by heaven these eyes shall never close.
This is the palace of the fearful king,
And this the regal seat: possess it, York;
For this is thine, and not King Henry's heirs'.
YORK
Assist me, then, sweet Warwick, and I will;
For hither we have broken in by force.
NORFOLK
We'll all assist you; he that flies shall die.
YORK
Thanks, gentle Norfolk: — stay by me, my lords; —
And, soldiers, stay, and lodge by me this night.
WARWICK
And when the king comes, offer him no violence,
Unless he seek to thrust you out perforce. [*They go up.*
YORK
The queen, this day, here holds her parliament,
But little thinks we shall be of her council:
By words or blows here let us win our right.
RICHARD
Arm'd as we are, let's stay within this house.
WARWICK
The bloody parliament shall this be call'd,
Unless Plantagenet, Duke of York, be king,

And bashful Henry depos'd, whose cowardice
Hath made us by-words to our enemies.
YORK
Then leave me not, my lords; be resolute;
I mean to take possession of my right.
WARWICK
Neither the king, nor he that loves him best,
The proudest he that holds up Lancaster,
Dares stir a wing, if Warwick shake his bells.
I'll plant Plantagenet, root him up who dares: —
Resolve thee, Richard; claim the English crown.

Flourish. Enter KING HENRY, CLIFFORD, NORTHUMBERLAND, WESTMORELAND, EXETER, *and the rest.*

KING HENRY
My lords, look where the sturdy rebel sits,
Even in the chair of state! belike he means —
Back'd by the power of Warwick, that false peer —
To aspire unto the crown, and reign as king. —
Earl of Northumberland, he slew thy father;
And thine, Lord Clifford; and you both have vow'd
　revenge
On him, his sons, his favourites, and his friends.
NORTHUMBERLAND
If I be not, heavens be reveng'd on me!
CLIFFORD
The hope thereof makes Clifford mourn in steel.
WESTMORELAND
What, shall we suffer this? let's pluck him down:
My heart for anger burns: I cannot brook it.
KING HENRY
Be patient, gentle Earl of Westmoreland.
CLIFFORD
Patience is for poltroons, such as he:
He durst not sit there, had your father liv'd.
My gracious lord, here in the parliament
Let us assail the family of York.
NORTHUMBERLAND
Well hast thou spoken, cousin: be it so.
KING HENRY
Ah, know you not the city favours them,
And they have troops of soldiers at their beck?
EXETER
But when the duke is slain, they'll quickly fly.
KING HENRY
Far be the thought of this from Henry's heart,
To make a shambles of the parliament-house!
Cousin of Exeter, frowns, words, and threats
Shall be the war that Henry means to use.
Thou factious Duke of York, descend my throne,
And kneel for grace and mercy at my feet;
I am thy sovereign.

RICHARD Speak thou for me, and tell them what I did.

YORK

               Thou'rt deceiv'd; I'm thine.

EXETER

For shame, come down: he made thee Duke of York.

YORK

'Twas my inheritance, as the earldom was.

EXETER

Thy father was a traitor to the crown.

WARWICK

Exeter, thou art a traitor to the crown

In following this usurping Henry.

CLIFFORD

Whom should he follow but his natural king?

WARWICK

True, Clifford; and that's Richard Duke of York.

KING HENRY

And shall I stand, and thou sit in my throne?

YORK

It must and shall be so: content thyself.

WARWICK

Be Duke of Lancaster; let him be king.

WESTMORELAND

He is both king and Duke of Lancaster;

And that the Lord of Westmoreland shall maintain.

WARWICK

And Warwick shall disprove it. You forget

That we are those which chas'd you from the field,

And slew your fathers, and with colours spread

March'd through the city to the palace-gates.

NORTHUMBERLAND

No, Warwick, I remember it to my grief;

And, by his soul, thou and thy house shall rue it.

WESTMORELAND

Plantagenet, of thee, and these thy sons,

Thy kinsman and thy friends, I'll have more lives

Than drops of blood were in my father's veins.

CLIFFORD

Urge it no more; lest that, instead of words,

I send thee, Warwick, such a messenger

As shall revenge his death before I stir.

WARWICK

Poor Clifford! how I scorn his worthless threats!

YORK

Will you we show our title to the crown?

If not, our swords shall plead it in the field.

KING HENRY

What title hast thou, traitor, to the crown?

Thy father was, as thou art, Duke of York;

Thy grandfather, Roger Mortimer, Earl of March:

I am the son of Henry the Fifth,

Who made the Dauphin and the French to stoop

And seiz'd upon their towns and provinces.

WARWICK

Talk not of France, sith thou hast lost it all.

KING HENRY

The lord Protector lost it, and not I:

When I was crown'd, I was but nine months old.

RICHARD

You are old enough now, and yet, methinks, you lose. —

Father, tear the crown from the usurper's head.

EDWARD

Sweet father, do so; set it on your head.

MONTAGUE [to YORK].

Good brother, as thou lov'st and honourest arms,

Let's fight it out, and not stand cavilling thus.

RICHARD

Sound drums and trumpets, and the king will fly.

YORK

Sons, peace!

KING HENRY

Peace thou! and give King Henry leave to speak.

WARWICK

Plantagenet shall speak first: hear him, lords;

And be you silent and attentive too,

For he that interrupts him shall not live.

KING HENRY

Think'st thou that I will leave my kingly throne,

Wherein my grandsire and my father sat?

No; first shall war unpeople this my realm;

Ay, and their colours — often borne in France,

And now in England to our heart's great sorrow —

Shall be my winding-sheet. — Why faint you, lords?

My title's good, and better far than his.

WARWICK

Prove it, Henry, and thou shalt be king.

KING HENRY

Henry the Fourth by conquest got the crown.

YORK

'Twas by rebellion against his king.

KING HENRY [aside].

I know not what to say; my title's weak. —

Tell me, may not a king adopt an heir?

YORK

What then?

KING HENRY

An if he may, then am I lawful king;

For Richard, in the view of many lords,

Resign'd the crown to Henry the Fourth,

Whose heir my father was, and I am his.

YORK

He rose against him, being his sovereign,

And made him to resign his crown perforce.

WARWICK

Suppose, my lords, he did it unconstrain'd,

Think you 'twere prejudicial to his crown?

EXETER

No; for he could not so resign his crown

But that the next heir should succeed and reign.

KING HENRY

Art thou against us, Duke of Exeter?

EXETER

His is the right, and therefore pardon me.

YORK

Why whisper you, my lords, and answer not?

EXETER

My conscience tells me he is lawful king.

KING HENRY [aside].

All will revolt from me, and turn to him.

NORTHUMBERLAND

Plantagenet, for all the claim thou lay'st,

Think not that Henry shall be so deposed.

WARWICK

Deposed he shall be, in despite of all.

NORTHUMBERLAND

Thou art deceiv'd: 'tis not thy southern power.

Of Essex, Norfolk, Suffolk, nor of Kent —

Which makes thee thus presumptuous and proud —

Can set the duke up, in despite of me.

CLIFFORD

King Henry, be thy title right or wrong,

Lord Clifford vows to fight in thy defence:

May that ground gape, and swallow me alive,

Where I shall kneel to him that slew my father!

KING HENRY

O Clifford, how thy words revive my heart!

YORK

Henry of Lancaster, resign thy crown. —

What mutter you, or what conspire you, lords?

WARWICK

Do right unto this princely Duke of York;

Or I will fill the house with armed men,

And over the chair of state, where now he sits,

Write up his title with usurping blood.

[He stamps with his foot, and the SOLDIERS show

themselves.

KING HENRY

My Lord of Warwick, hear me but one word: —

Let me for this my life-time reign as king.

YORK

Confirm the crown to me and to mine heirs,

And thou shalt reign in quiet while thou livest.

KING HENRY

I am content: Richard Plantagenet,

Enjoy the kingdom after my decease.

CLIFFORD

What wrong is this unto the prince your son!

WARWICK

What good is this to England and himself!

WESTMORELAND

Base, fearful, and despairing Henry!

CLIFFORD

How hast thou injur'd both thyself and us!

WESTMORELAND

I cannot stay to hear these articles.

NORTHUMBERLAND

Nor I.

CLIFFORD

Come, cousin, let us tell the queen these news.

WESTMORELAND

Farewell, faint-hearted and degenerate king,

In whose cold blood no spark of honour bides.

NORTHUMBERLAND

Be thou a prey unto the house of York,

And die in bands, for this unmanly deed!

CLIFFORD

In dreadful war mayst thou be overcome,

Or live in peace, abandon'd and despis'd!

[Exeunt NORTHUMBERLAND, CLIFFORD, and

WESTMORELAND.

WARWICK

Turn this way, Henry, and regard them not.

EXETER

They seek revenge, and therefore will not yield.

KING HENRY

Ah, Exeter!

WARWICK

            Why should you sigh, my lord?

KING HENRY

Not for myself, Lord Warwick, but my son,

Whom I unnaturally shall disinherit.

But, be it as it may: — I here entail

The crown to thee, and to thine heirs for ever;

Conditionally, that here thou take an oath

To cease this civil war, and, whilst I live,

To honour me as thy king and sovereign,

And neither by treason nor hostility

To seek to put me down, and reign thyself.

YORK

This oath I willingly take, and will perform.

WARWICK

Long live King Henry! — Plantagenet, embrace him.

KING HENRY

And long live thou, and these thy forward sons!

YORK

Now York and Lancaster are reconciled.

EXETER

Accurst be he that seeks to make them foes!

[Sennet. Here they come down.

YORK

Farewell, my gracious lord; I'll to my castle.

WARWICK

And I'll keep London with my soldiers.

NORFOLK

And I to Norfolk with my followers.

MONTAGUE

And I unto the sea, from whence I came.

[Exeunt YORK and his SONS, WARWICK, NORFOLK,

MONTAGUE, SOLDIERS, and ATTENDANTS.

KING HENRY

And I, with grief and sorrow, to the court.

EXETER

Here comes the queen, whose looks bewray her anger:

I'll steal away. [Going.

KING HENRY

Exeter, so will I. [Going.

Enter QUEEN MARGARET *and the* PRINCE OF

WALES.

QUEEN MARGARET

Nay, go not from me; I will follow thee.

KING HENRY

Be patient, gentle queen, and I will stay.

QUEEN MARGARET

Who can be patient in such extremes?

Ah, wretched man! would I had died a maid,

And never seen thee, never borne thee son,

Seeing thou hast prov'd so unnatural a father!

Hath he deserv'd to lose his birthright thus?

Hadst thou but lov'd him half so well as I,

Or felt that pain which I did for him once,

Or nourish'd him as I did with my blood,

Thou wouldst have left thy dearest heart-blood there,

Rather than have made that savage duke thine heir,

And disinherited thine only son.

PRINCE OF WALES

Father, you cannot disinherit me:

If you be king, why should not I succeed?

KING HENRY

Pardon me, Margaret; — pardon me, sweet son: —

The Earl of Warwick and the duke enforc'd me.

QUEEN MARGARET

Enforc'd thee! art thou king, and wilt be forc'd?

I shame to hear thee speak. Ah, timorous wretch!

Thou hast undone thyself, thy son, and me;

And given unto the house of York such head,

As thou shalt reign but by their sufferance.

To entail him and his heirs unto the crown,

What is it, but to make thy sepulchre,

And creep into it far before thy time?

Warwick is chancellor, and the lord of Calais;

Stern Falconbridge commands the narrow seas;

The duke is made Protector of the realm;

And yet shalt thou be safe? such safety finds

The trembling lamb environed with wolves.
Had I been there, which am a silly woman,
The soldiers should have toss'd me on their pikes
Before I would have granted to that act.
But thou preferr'st thy life before thine honour:
And seeing thou dost, I here divorce myself
Both from thy table, Henry, and thy bed,
Until that act of Parliament be repeal'd,
Whereby my son is disinherited.
The northern lords that have forsworn thy colours
Will follow mine, if once they see them spread;
And spread they shall be, — to thy foul disgrace,
And utter ruin of the house of York.
Thus do I leave thee. — Come, son, let's away;
Our army is ready; come, we'll after them.

KING HENRY
Stay, gentle Margaret, and hear me speak.

QUEEN MARGARET
Thou hast spoke too much already; get thee gone.

KING HENRY
Gentle son Edward, thou wilt stay with me?

QUEEN MARGARET
Ay, to be murder'd by his enemies.

PRINCE OF WALES
When I return with victory from the field,
I'll see your Grace: till then I'll follow her.

QUEEN MARGARET
Come, son, away; we may not linger thus.
          [*Exeunt* QUEEN MARGARET *and the* PRINCE.

KING HENRY
Poor queen! how love to me and to her son
Hath made her break out into terms of rage!
Reveng'd may she be on that hateful duke,
Whose haughty spirit, winged with desire,
Will cost my crown, and like an empty eagle
Tire on the flesh of me and of my son!
The loss of those three lords torments my heart:
I'll write unto them, and entreat them fair: —
Come, cousin, you shall be the messenger.

EXETER
And I, I hope, shall reconcile them all.   [*Exeunt.*

SCENE II

Sandal Castle, near Wakefield.

Enter RICHARD, EDWARD, *and* MONTAGUE.

RICHARD
Brother, though I be youngest, give me leave.

EDWARD
No, I can better play the orator.

MONTAGUE
But I have reasons strong and forcible.
          Enter the DUKE OF YORK.

YORK
Why, how now, sons and brother! at a strife?
What is your quarrel? how began it first?

EDWARD
No quarrel, but a slight contention.

YORK
About what?

RICHARD
About that which concerns your Grace and us, —
The crown of England, father, which is yours.

YORK
Mine, boy? not till King Henry be dead.

RICHARD
Your right depends not on his life or death.

EDWARD
Now you are heir, therefore enjoy it now:
By giving the house of Lancaster leave to breathe,
It will outrun you, father, in the end.

YORK
I took an oath that he should quietly reign.

EDWARD
But, for a kingdom, any oath may be broken:
I would break a thousand oaths to reign one year.

RICHARD
No; God forbid your Grace should be forsworn.

YORK
I shall be, if I claim by open war.

RICHARD
I'll prove the contrary, if you'll hear me speak.

YORK
Thou canst not, son; it is impossible.

RICHARD
An oath is of no moment, being not took
Before a true and lawful magistrate,
That hath authority over him that swears:

Henry had none, but did usurp the place;
Then, seeing 'twas he that made you to depose,
Your oath, my lord, is vain and frivolous.
Therefore, to arms! And, father, do but think
How sweet a thing it is to wear a crown;
Within whose circuit is Elysium,
And all that poets feign of bliss and joy.
Why do we finger thus? I cannot rest
Until the white rose that I wear be dyed
Even in the lukewarm blood of Henry's heart.

YORK
Richard, enough; I will be king, or die.—
Brother, thou shalt to London presently,
And whet-on Warwick to this enterprise. —
Thou, Richard, shalt to the Duke of Norfolk,
And tell him privily of our intent. —
You, Edward, shall unto my Lord Cobham,
With whom the Kentishmen will willingly rise:
In them I trust; for they are soldiers,
Witty, courteous, liberal, full of spirit. —
While you are thus employ'd, what resteth more,
But that I seek occasion how to rise,
And yet the king not privy to my drift,
Nor any of the house of Lancaster?
          Enter a MESSENGER.
But, stay: what news? — Why comest thou in such
     post?

MESSENGER
The queen with all the northern earls and lords
Intend here to besiege you in your castle:
She is hard by with twenty thousand men;
And therefore fortify your hold, my lord.

YORK
Ay, with my sword. What! think'st thou that we fear
     them? —
Edward and Richard, you shall stay with me; —
My brother Montague shall post to London:
Let noble Warwick, Cobham, and the rest,
Whom we have left protectors of the king,
With powerful policy strengthen themselves,
And trust not simple Henry nor his oaths.

MONTAGUE
Brother, I go; I'll win them, fear it not:
And thus most humbly I do take my leave.   [*Exit.*
          Enter SIR JOHN *and* SIR HUGH MORTIMER.

YORK
Sir John and Sir Hugh Mortimer, mine uncles!
You are come to Sandal in a happy hour;
The army of the queen mean to besiege us.

SIR JOHN MORTIMER
She shall not need; we'll meet her in the field.

YORK
What, with five thousand men?

RICHARD
Ay, with five hundred, father, for a need:
A woman's general; what should we fear?
          [*A march afar off.*

EDWARD
I hear their drums: let's set our men in order,
And issue forth, and bid them battle straight.

YORK
Five men to twenty! — though the odds be great,
I doubt not, uncle, of our victory.
Many a battle have I won in France,
Whenas the enemy hath been ten to one:
Why should I not now have the like success?
          [*Alarum. Exeunt.*

SCENE III

Field of battle near Sandal Castle.

Alarums. Enter RUTLAND *and his* TUTOR.

RUTLAND
Ah, whither shall I fly to scape their hands?
Ah, tutor, look where bloody Clifford comes!
          Enter CLIFFORD *and* SOLDIERS.

CLIFFORD
Chaplain, away! thy priesthood saves thy life.
As for the brat of this accursed duke,
Whose father slew my father, — he shall die.

TUTOR
And I, my lord, will bear him company.

CLIFFORD
Soldiers, away with him!

TUTOR
Ah, Clifford, murder not this innocent child,
Lest thou be hated both of God and man!
          [*Exit, forced off by* SOLDIERS.

CLIFFORD
How now! is he dead already? or is it fear
That makes him close his eyes? — I'll open them.

RUTLAND
So looks the pent-up lion o'er the wretch
That trembles under his devouring paws;
And so he walks, insulting o'er his prey,
And so he comes, to rend his limbs asunder. —
Ah, gentle Clifford, kill me with thy sword,
And not with such a cruel threatening look!
Sweet Clifford, hear me speak before I die! —
I am too mean a subject for thy wrath:
Be thou reveng'd on men, and let me live.

CLIFFORD
In vain thou speak'st, poor boy; my father's blood
Hath stopp'd the passage where thy words should enter.

RUTLAND
Then let my father's blood open it again:
He is a man, and, Clifford, cope with him.

CLIFFORD
Had I thy brethren here, their lives and thine
Were not revenge sufficient for me;
No, if I digg'd up thy forefathers' graves,
And hung their rotten coffins up in chains,
It could not slake mine ire nor ease my heart.
The sight of any of the house of York
Is as a fury to torment my soul;
And till I root out their accursed line,
And leave not one alive, I live in hell.
Therefore —   [*Lifting his hand.*

RUTLAND
O, let me pray before I take my death! —
To thee I pray; sweet Clifford, pity me!

CLIFFORD
Such pity as my rapier's point affords.

RUTLAND
I never did thee harm: why wilt thou slay me?

CLIFFORD
Thy father hath.

RUTLAND
          But 'twas ere I was born.
Thou hast one son, — for his sake pity me;
Lest in revenge thereof, — sith God is just, —
He be as miserably slain as I.
Ah, let me live in prison all my days;
And when I give occasion of offence,
Then let me die, for now thou hast no cause!

CLIFFORD
No cause!
Thy father slew my father; therefore, die.   [*Stabs him.*

RUTLAND
Di faciant, laudis summa sit ista tuæ!   [*Dies.*

CLIFFORD
Plantagenet! I come, Plantagenet!
And this thy son's blood cleaving to my blade
Shall rust upon my weapon, till thy blood,
Congeal'd with this, do make me wipe off both.   [*Exit.*

SCENE IV

Another part of the field.

Alarums. Enter RICHARD, DUKE OF YORK.

YORK
The army of the queen hath got the field:
My uncles both are slain in rescuing me;
And all my followers to the eager foe
Turn back, and fly, like ships before the wind,
Or lambs pursued by hunger-starved wolves.
My sons, — God knows what hath bechanced them:
But this I know, they have demean'd themselves
Like men born to renown by life or death.
Three times did Richard make a lane to me,
And thrice cried, 'Courage, father! fight it out!'
And full as oft came Edward to my side,
With purple falchion, painted to the hilt
In blood of those that had encounter'd him:
And when the hardiest warriors did retire,
Richard cried, 'Charge! and give no foot of ground!'
And cried, 'A crown, or else a glorious tomb!
A sceptre, or an earthly sepulchre!'
With this, we charg'd again: but, out, alas!
We bodg'd again: as I have seen a swan
With bootless labour swim against the tide,
And spend her strength with over-matching waves.
          [*A short alarum within.*
Ah, hark! the fatal followers do pursue;
And I am faint, and cannot fly their fury:
And were I strong, I would not shun their fury:
The sands are number'd that make up my life;
Here must I stay, and here my life must end.

QUEEN MARGARET Ay, marry, sir, now looks he like a king!

Enter the QUEEN, CLIFFORD,
NORTHUMBERLAND, *and* SOLDIERS.
Come, bloody Clifford, — rough Northumberland, —
I dare your quenchless fury to more rage:
I am your butt, and I abide your shot.

NORTHUMBERLAND
Yield to our mercy, proud Plantagenet.

CLIFFORD
Ay, to such mercy as his ruthless arm,
With downright payment, show'd unto my father.
Now Phaethon hath tumbled from his car,
And made an evening at the noontide prick.

YORK
My ashes, as the phœnix, may bring forth
A bird that will revenge upon you all;
And in that hope I throw mine eyes to heaven,
Scorning whate'er you can afflict me with.
Why come you not? what! multitudes, and fear?

CLIFFORD
So cowards fight when they can fly no further;
So doves do peck the falcon's piercing talons;
So desperate thieves, all hopeless of their lives,
Breathe out invectives 'gainst the officers.

YORK
O Clifford, but bethink thee once again,
And in thy thought o'er-run my former time;
And, if though canst for blushing, view this face,
And bite thy tongue, that slanders him with cowardice
Whose frown hath made thee faint and fly ere this!

CLIFFORD
I will not bandy with thee word for word,
But buckle with thee blows, twice two for one.   [*Draws.*

QUEEN MARGARET
Hold, valiant Clifford! for a thousand causes
I would prolong awhile the traitor's life. —
Wrath makes him deaf: — speak thou,
   Northumberland.

NORTHUMBERLAND
Hold, Clifford! do not honour him so much
To prick thy finger, though to wound his heart:
What valour were it, when a cur doth grin,
For one to thrust his hand between his teeth,
When he might spurn him with his foot away?
It is war's prize to take all vantages;
And ten to one is no impeach of valour.
      [*They lay hands on* YORK, *who struggles.*

CLIFFORD
Ay, ay, so strives the woodcock with the gin.

NORTHUMBERLAND
So doth the cony struggle in the net.

YORK
So triumph thieves upon their conquer'd booty;
So true men yield, with robbers so o'ermatch'd.

NORTHUMBERLAND
What would your Grace have done unto him now?

QUEEN MARGARET
Brave warriors, Clifford and Northumberland,
Come, make him stand upon this molehill here,
That raught at mountains with outstretched arms,
Yet parted but the shadow with his hand. —
What! was it you that would be England's king?
Was't you that revell'd in our parliament,
And made a preachment of your high descent?
Where are your mess of sons to back you now?
The wanton Edward, and the lusty George?
And where's that valiant crook-back prodigy,
Dicky your boy, that with his grumbling voice
Was wont to cheer his dad in mutinies?

Or, with the rest, where is your darling Rutland?
Look, York: I stain'd this napkin with the blood
That valiant Clifford, with his rapier's point,
Made issue from the bosom of the boy;
And if thine eyes can water for his death,
I give thee this to dry thy cheeks withal.
Alas, poor York! but that I hate thee deadly,
I should lament thy miserable state.
I prithee, grieve, to make me merry, York;
Stamp, rave, and fret, that I may sing and dance.
What! hath thy fiery heart so parch'd thine entrails
That not a tear can fall for Rutland's death?
Why art thou patient, man? thou shouldst be mad;
And I, to make thee mad, do mock thee thus.
Thou wouldst be fee'd, I see, to make me sport:
York cannot speak, unless he wear a crown. —
A crown for York! — and, lords, bow low to him: —
Hold you his hands, whilst I do set it on. —
            [*Putting a paper crown on his head.*
Ay, marry, sir, now looks he like a king!
Ay, this is he that took King Henry's chair;
And this is he was his adopted heir. —
But how is it that great Plantagenet
Is crown'd so soon, and broke his solemn oath?
As I bethink me, you should not be king
Till our King Henry had shook hands with death.
And will you pale your head in Henry's glory,
And rob his temples of the diadem,
Now in his life, against your holy oath?
O, 'tis a fault too-too unpardonable! —
Off with the crown, and, with the crown, his head;
And, whilst we breathe, take time to do him dead.

CLIFFORD
That is my office, for my father's sake.

QUEEN MARGARET
Nay, stay; let's hear the orisons he makes.

YORK
She-wolf of France, but worse than wolves of France,
Whose tongue more poisons than the adder's tooth!
How ill-beseeming is it in thy sex
To triumph, like an Amazonian trull,
Upon their woes whom fortune captivates!
But that thy face is, vizard-like, unchanging,
Made impudent with use of evil deeds,
I would assay, proud queen, to make thee blush:
To tell thee whence thou camest, of whom deriv'd,
Were shame enough to shame thee, wert thou not
   shameless.
Thy father bears the type of King of Naples,
Of both the Sicils and Jerusalem;
Yet not so wealthy as an English yeoman.
Hath that poor monarch taught thee to insult?
It needs not, nor it boots thee not, proud queen;
Unless the adage must be verified,
That beggars mounted run their horse to death.
'Tis beauty that doth oft make women proud;
But, God he knows, thy share thereof is small:
'Tis virtue that doth make them most admired;
The contrary doth make thee wonder'd at:
'Tis government that makes them seem divine;
The want thereof makes thee abominable:
Thou art as opposite to every good
As the Antipodes are unto us,
Or as the south to the septentrion.
O tiger's heart wrapp'd in a woman's hide!
How couldst thou drain the life-blood of the child,
To bid the father wipe his eyes withal,
And yet be seen to bear a woman's face?
Women are soft, mild, pitiful and flexible;
Thou stern, obdurate, flinty, rough, remorseless.
Bidd'st thou me rage? why, now thou hast thy wish:
Wouldst have me weep? why, now thou hast thy will:
For raging wind blows up incessant showers,
And when the rage allays, the rain begins.
These tears are my sweet Rutland's obsequies;
And every drop cries vengeance for his death,
'Gainst thee, fell Clifford, and thee, false
   French-woman.

NORTHUMBERLAND
Beshrew me, but his passion moves me so
That hardly can I check my eyes from tears.

YORK
That face of his the hungry cannibals
Would not have touch'd, would not have stain'd with
   blood:
But you are more inhuman, more inexorable, —
O, ten times more, — than tigers of Hyrcania.
See, ruthless queen, a hapless father's tears:
This cloth thou dipp'dst in blood of my sweet boy,
And I with tears do wash the blood away.
Keep thou the napkin, and go boast of this:

And, if thou tell'st the heavy story right,
Upon my soul, the hearers will shed tears;
Yea, even my foes will shed fast-falling tears,
And say 'Alas, it was a piteous deed!' —
There, take the crown, and, with the crown, my curse;
                                    [*Giving back the paper crown.*
And in thy need such comfort come to thee
As now I reap at thy too cruel hand! —
Hard-hearted Clifford, take me from the world:
My soul to heaven, my blood upon your heads!

NORTHUMBERLAND
Had he been slaughter-man to all my kin,
I should not for my life but weep with him,
To see how inly sorrow gripes his soul.

QUEEN MARGARET
What, weeping-ripe, my Lord Northumberland?
Think but upon the wrong he did us all,
And that will quickly dry thy melting tears.

CLIFFORD
Here's for my oath, here's for my father's death.
                                    [*Stabbing him.*

QUEEN MARGARET
And here's to right our gentle-hearted king.
                                    [*Stabbing him.*

YORK
Open Thy gate of mercy, gracious God!
My soul flies through these wounds to seek out Thee.
                                    [*Dies.*

QUEEN MARGARET
Off with his head, and set it on York gates;
So York may overlook the town of York.
                                    [*Flourish. Exeunt.*

ACT II

SCENE I

A plain near Mortimer's Cross in Herefordshire.

A march. Enter EDWARD, RICHARD,
and their POWER.

EDWARD
I wonder how our princely father scap'd,
Or whether he be scap'd away or no
From Clifford's and Northumberland's pursuit:
Had he been ta'en, we should have heard the news;
Had he been slain, we should have heard the news;
Or had he scap'd, methinks we should have heard
The happy tidings of his good escape. —
How fares my brother? why is he so sad?

RICHARD
I cannot joy, until I be resolved
Where our right valiant father is become.
I saw him in the battle range about;
And watch'd him how he singled Clifford forth.
Methought he bore him in the thickest troop
As doth a lion in a herd of neat;
Or as a bear, encompass'd round with dogs, —
Who having pinch'd a few, and made them cry,
The rest stand all aloof, and bark at him,
So far'd our father with his enemies;
So fled his enemies my warlike father:
Methinks, 'tis prize enough to be his son.
See how the morning opes her golden gates,
And takes her farewell of the glorious sun!
How well resembles it the prime of youth,
Trimm'd like a younker prancing to his love!

EDWARD
Dazzle mine eyes, or do I see three suns?

RICHARD
Three glorious suns, each one a perfect sun;
Not separated with the racking clouds,
But sever'd in a pale clear-shining sky.
See, see! they join, embrace, and seem to kiss,
As if they vow'd some league inviolable:
Now are they but one lamp, one light, one sun.
In this the heaven figures some event.

EDWARD
'Tis wondrous strange, the like yet never heard of.
I think it cites us, brother, to the field, —
That we, the sons of brave Plantagenet,
Each one already blazing by our meeds,
Should, notwithstanding, join our lights together,
And over-shine the earth, as this the world.
Whate'er it bodes, henceforward will I bear
Upon my target three fair-shining suns.

RICHARD
Nay, bear three daughters: — by your leave I speak it,
You love the breeder better than the male.

Enter one blowing.

But what art thou, whose heavy looks foretell
Some dreadful story hanging on thy tongue?

MESSENGER
Ah, one that was a woeful looker-on
Whenas the noble Duke of York was slain,
Your princely father and my loving lord!

EDWARD
O, speak no more! for I have heard too much.

RICHARD
Say how he died, for I will hear it all.

MESSENGER
Environed he was with many foes;
And stood against them as the hope of Troy
Against the Greeks that would have enter'd Troy.
But Hercules himself must yield to odds;
And many strokes, though with a little axe,
Hew down and fell the hardest-timber'd oak.
By many hands your father was subdued;
But only slaughter'd by the ireful arm
Of unrelenting Clifford and the queen,
Who crown'd the gracious duke in high despite;
Laugh'd in his face; and when with grief he wept,
The ruthless queen gave him to dry his cheeks
A napkin steeped in the harmless blood
Of sweet young Rutland, by rough Clifford slain:
And after many scorns, many foul taunts,
They took his head, and on the gates of York
They set the same; and there it doth remain,
The saddest spectacle that e'er I view'd.

EDWARD
Sweet Duke of York, our prop to lean upon,
Now thou art gone, we have no staff, no stay! —
O Clifford, boisterous Clifford, thou hast slain
The flower of Europe for his chivalry;
And treacherously hast thou vanquish'd him,
For hand to hand he would have vanquish'd thee! —
Now my soul's palace is become a prison:
Ah, would she break from hence, that this my body
Might in the ground be closed up in rest!
For never henceforth shall I joy again,
Never, O never, shall I see more joy!

RICHARD
I cannot weep; for all my body's moisture
Scarce serves to quench my furnace-burning heart:
Nor can my tongue unload my heart's great burthen;
For selfsame wind that I should speak withal
Is kindling coals that fires all my breast,
And burns me up with flames that tears would quench.
To weep is to make less the depth of grief:
Tears, then, for babes; blows and revenge for me! —
Richard, I bear thy name; I'll venge thy death,
Or die renowned by attempting it.

EDWARD
His name that valiant duke hath left with thee;
His dukedom and his chair with me is left.

RICHARD
Nay, if thou be that princely eagle's bird,
Show thy descent by gazing 'gainst the sun:
For chair and dukedom, throne and kingdom say;
Either that is thine, or else thou wert not his.

March. Enter WARWICK, MONTAGUE,
and their ARMY.

WARWICK
How now, fair lords! What fare? what news abroad?

RICHARD
Great Lord of Warwick, if we should recount
Our baleful news, and at each word's deliverance
Stab poniards in our flesh till all were told,
The words would add more anguish than the wounds.
O valiant lord, the Duke of York is slain!

EDWARD
O Warwick, Warwick! that Plantagenet,
Which held thee dearly as his soul's redemption,
Is by the stern Lord Clifford done to death.

WARWICK
Ten days ago I drown'd these news in tears;
And now, to add more measure to your woes,
I come to tell you things sith then befall'n.
After the bloody fray at Wakefield fought,
Where your brave father breath'd his latest gasp,
Tidings, as swiftly as the posts could run,
Were brought me of your loss and his depart.
I, then in London, keeper of the king,
Muster'd my soldiers, gather'd flocks of friends,
And very well appointed, as I thought,
March'd toward Saint Alban's to intercept the queen,
Bearing the king in my behalf along;
For by my scouts I was advertised
That she was coming with a full intent

To dash our late decree in parliament
Touching King Henry's oath and your succession.
Short tale to make, — we at Saint Alban's met,
Our battles join'd, and both sides fiercely fought:
But whether 'twas the coldness of the king,
Who look'd full gently on his warlike queen,
That robb'd my soldiers of their heated spleen;
Or whether 'twas report of her success;
Or more than common fear of Clifford's rigour,
Who thunders to his captives blood and death,
I cannot judge: but, to conclude with truth,
Their weapons like to lightning came and went;
Our soldiers — like the night-owl's lazy flight,
Or like an idle thrasher with a flail —
Fell gently down, as if they struck their friends.
I cheer'd them up with justice of our cause,
With promise of high pay and great rewards:
But all in vain; they had no heart to fight,
And we, in them, no hope to win the day;
So that we fled; the king unto the queen,
Lord George your brother, Norfolk, and myself,
In haste, post-haste, are come to join with you;
For in the marches here we heard you were
Making another head to fight again.

EDWARD
Where is the Duke of Norfolk, gentle Warwick?
And when came George from Burgundy to England?

WARWICK
Some six miles off the duke is with his power;
And for your brother, he was lately sent
From your kind aunt, Duchess of Burgundy,
With aid of soldiers to this needful war.

RICHARD
'Twas odds, belike, when valiant Warwick fled:
Oft have I heard his praises in pursuit,
But ne'er till now his scandal of retire.

WARWICK
Nor now my scandal, Richard, dost thou hear;
For thou shalt know this strong right hand of mine
Can pluck the diadem from faint Henry's head,
And wring the awful sceptre from his fist,
Were he as famous and as bold in war
As he is fam'd for mildness, peace, and prayer.

RICHARD
I know it well, Lord Warwick; blame me not:
'Tis love I bear thy glories makes me speak.
But in this troublous time what's to be done?
Shall we go throw away our coats of steel,
And wrap our bodies in black mourning-gowns,
Numbering our Ave-Maries with our beads?
Or shall we on the helmets of our foes
Tell our devotion with revengeful arms?
If for the last, say 'Ay,' and to it, lords.

WARWICK
Why, therefore Warwick came to seek you out;
And therefore comes my brother Montague.
Attend me, lords. The proud insulting queen,
With Clifford and the haught Northumberland,
And of their feather many moe proud birds,
Have wrought the easy-melting king like wax.
He swore consent to your succession,
His oath enrolled in the parliament;
And now to London all the crew are gone,
To frustrate both his oath, and what beside
May make against the house of Lancaster.
Their power, I think, is thirty thousand strong:
Now, if the help of Norfolk and myself,
With all the friends that thou, brave Earl of March,
Amongst the loving Welshmen canst procure,
Will but amount to five-and-twenty thousand,
Why, *Via!* to London will we march amain;
And once again bestride our foaming steeds,
And once again cry, 'Charge! upon our foes!'
But never once again turn back and fly.

RICHARD
Ay, now methinks I hear great Warwick speak:
Ne'er may he live to see a sunshine day,
That cries, 'Retire,' if Warwick bid him stay.

EDWARD
Lord Warwick, on thy shoulder will I lean;
And when thou faint'st, — as God forbid the hour! —
Must Edward fall, which peril heaven forfend!

WARWICK
No longer Earl of March, but Duke of York:
The next degree is England's royal throne;
For King of England shalt thou be proclaim'd
In every borough as we pass along;
And he that throws not up his cap for joy,
Shall for the fault make forfeit of his head.
King Edward, — valiant Richard, — Montague, —
Stay we no longer, dreaming of renown,

QUEEN MARGARET Yonder's the head of that arch-enemy.

But sound the trumpets, and about our task.
RICHARD
Then, Clifford, were thy heart as hard as steel, —
As thou hast shown it flinty by thy deeds, —
I come to pierce it, or to give thee mine.
EDWARD
Then strike up drums: — God and Saint George for us!

Enter a MESSENGER.

WARWICK
How now! what news?
MESSENGER
The Duke of Norfolk sends you word by me
The queen is coming with a puissant host,
And craves your company for speedy counsel.
WARWICK
Why, then it sorts, brave warriors: let's away. [*Exeunt.*

SCENE II
Before York.

Flourish. Enter the KING, QUEEN, *the* PRINCE OF
WALES, CLIFFORD, *and* NORTHUMBERLAND,
with drum and trumpets.

QUEEN MARGARET
Welcome, my lord, to this brave town of York.
Yonder's the head of that arch-enemy
That sought to be encompass'd with your crown:
Doth not the object cheer your heart, my lord?
KING HENRY
Ay, as the rocks cheer them that fear their wrack: —
To see this sight, it irks my very soul. —
Withhold revenge, dear God! 'tis not my fault,
Nor wittingly have I infring'd my vow.

CLIFFORD
My gracious liege, this too much lenity
And harmful pity must be laid aside.
To whom do lions cast their gentle looks?
Not to the beast that would usurp their den.
Whose hand is that the forest bear doth lick?
Not his that spoils her young before her face.
Who scapes the lurking serpent's mortal sting?
Not he that sets his foot upon her back.
The smallest worm will turn being trodden on,
And doves will peck in safeguard of their brood.
Ambitious York did level at thy crown,
Thou smiling while he knit his angry brows:
He, but a duke, would have his son a king,
And raise his issue, like a loving sire;
Thou, being a king, blest with a goodly son,
Didst yield consent to disinherit him,
Which argued thee a most unloving father.
Unreasonable creatures feed their young;
And though man's face be fearful to their eyes,
Yet, in protection of their tender ones,
Who hath not seen them, even with those wings
Which sometime they have us'd in fearful flight,
Make war with him that climb'd unto their nest,
Offering their own lives in their young's defence?
For shame, my liege, make them your precedent!
Were it not pity that this goodly boy
Should lose his birthright by his father's fault,
And long hereafter say unto his child,
'What my great-grandfather and his grandsire got
My careless father fondly gave away'?
Ah, what a shame were this! Look on the boy;
And let his manly face, which promiseth
Successful fortune, steel thy melting heart

To hold thine own, and leave thine own with him.
KING HENRY
Full well hath Clifford play'd the orator,
Inferring arguments of mighty force.
But, Clifford, tell me, didst thou never hear
That things ill-got had ever bad success?
And happy always was it for that son
Whose father for his hoarding went to hell?
I'll leave my son my virtuous deeds behind;
And would my father had left me no more!
For all the rest is held at such a rate
As brings a thousand-fold more care to keep
Than in possession and jot of pleasure. —
Ah, cousin York! would thy best friends did know
How it doth grieve me that thy head is here!
QUEEN MARGARET
My lord, cheer up your spirits: our foes are nigh,
And this soft courage makes your followers faint.
You promis'd knighthood to our forward son:
Unsheathe your sword, and dub him presently. —
Edward, kneel down.
KING HENRY
Edward Plantagenet, arise a knight;
And learn this lesson, — draw thy sword in right.
PRINCE OF WALES
My gracious father, by your kingly leave,
I'll draw it as apparent to the crown,
And in that quarrel use it to the death.
CLIFFORD
Why, that is spoken like a toward prince.

Enter a MESSENGER.

MESSENGER
Royal commanders, be in readiness:
For with a band of thirty thousand men
Comes Warwick, backing of the Duke of York;
And in the towns, as they do march along;
Proclaims him king, and many fly to him:
Darraign your battle, for they are at hand.
CLIFFORD
I would your highness would depart the field:
The queen hath best success when you are absent.
QUEEN MARGARET
Ay, good my lord, and leave us to our fortune.
KING HENRY
Why, that's my fortune too; therefore I'll stay.
NORTHUMBERLAND
Be it with resolution, then, to fight.
PRINCE OF WALES
My royal father, cheer these noble lords,
And hearten those that fight in your defence:
Unsheathe your sword, good father; cry, 'Saint
    George!'

March. Enter EDWARD, GEORGE, RICHARD,
    WARWICK, NORFOLK, MONTAGUE, *and*
        SOLDIERS.

EDWARD
Now, perjur'd Henry! wilt thou kneel for grace,
And set thy diadem upon my head;
Or bide the mortal fortune of the field?
QUEEN MARGARET
Go, rate thy minions, proud insulting boy!
Becomes it thee to be thus bold in terms
Before thy sovereign and thy lawful king?
EDWARD
I am his king, and he should bow his knee;
I was adopted heir by his consent:
Since when, his oath is broke; for, as I hear,
You, that are king, though he do wear the crown,
Have caus'd him, by new act of Parliament,
To blot out me, and put his own son in.
CLIFFORD
And reason too:
Who should succeed the father but the son?
RICHARD
Are you there, butcher? — O, I cannot speak!
CLIFFORD
Ay, crook-back, here I stand to answer thee,
Or any he the proudest of thy sort.
RICHARD
'Twas you that kill'd young Rutland, was it not?
CLIFFORD
Ay, and old York, and yet not satisfied.
RICHARD
For God's sake, lords, give signal to the fight.
WARWICK
What say'st thou, Henry, wilt thou yield the crown?
QUEEN MARGARET
Why, how now, long-tongu'd Warwick!

dare you speak?
When you and I met at Saint Alban's last,
Your legs did better service than your hands.

WARWICK
Then 'twas my turn to fly, and now 'tis thine.

CLIFFORD
You said so much before, and yet you fled.

WARWICK
'Twas not your valour, Clifford, drove me thence.

NORTHUMBERLAND
No, nor your manhood that durst make you stay.

RICHARD
Northumberland, I hold thee reverently. —
Break off the parle; for scarce I can refrain
The execution of my big-swoll'n heart
Upon that Clifford there, that cruel child-killer.

CLIFFORD
I slew thy father, — call'st thou him a child?

RICHARD
Ay, like a dastard and a treacherous coward,
As thou didst kill our tender brother Rutland;
But ere sun set I'll make thee curse the deed.

KING HENRY
Have done with words, my lords, and hear me speak.

QUEEN MARGARET
Defy them, then, or else hold close thy lips.

KING HENRY
I prithee, give no limits to my tongue:
I am a king, and privileg'd to speak.

CLIFFORD
My liege, the wound that bred this meeting here
Cannot be cured by words; therefore be still.

RICHARD
Then, executioner, unsheathe thy sword:
By Him that made us all, I am resolv'd
That Clifford's manhood lies upon his tongue.

EDWARD
Say, Henry, shall I have my right, or no?
A thousand men have broke their fasts to-day
That ne'er shall dine unless thou yield the crown.

WARWICK
If thou deny, their blood upon thy head;
For York in justice puts his armour on.

PRINCE OF WALES
If that be right which Warwick says is right,
There is no wrong, but every thing is right.

RICHARD
Whoever got thee, there thy mother stands;
For, well I wot, thou hast thy mother's tongue.

QUEEN MARGARET
But thou art neither like thy sire nor dam;
But like a foul mis-shapen stigmatic,
Mark'd by the Destinies to be avoided,
As venom toads, or lizards' dreadful stings.

RICHARD
Iron of Naples hid with English gilt,
Whose father bears the title of a king, —
As if a channel should be call'd the sea, —
Shamest thou not, knowing whence thou art extraught,
To let thy tongue detect thy base-born heart?

EDWARD
A wisp of straw were worth a thousand crowns,
To make this shameless callet know herself. —
Helen of Greece was fairer far than thou,
Although thy husband may be Menelaus;
And ne'er was Agamemnon's brother wrong'd
By that false woman as this king by thee.
His father revell'd in the heart of France,
And tam'd the king, and made the Dauphin stoop;
And had he match'd according to his state,
He might have kept that glory to this day;
But when he took a beggar to his bed,
And grac'd thy poor sire with his bridal-day,
Even then that sunshine brew'd a shower for him,
That wash'd his father's fortunes forth of France,
And heap'd sedition on his crown at home.
For what hath broach'd this tumult but thy pride?
Hadst thou been meek, our title still had slept;
And we, in pity of the gentle king,
Had slipp'd our claim until another age.

GEORGE
But when we saw our sunshine made thy spring,
And that thy summer bred us no increase,
We set the axe to thy usurping root;
And though the edge hath something hit ourselves,
Yet, know thou, since we have begun to strike,
We'll never leave till we have hewn thee down,
Or bath'd thy growing with our heated bloods.

EDWARD
And, in this resolution, I defy thee;
Not willing any longer conference,
Since thou deniest the gentle king to speak. —
Sound trumpets! — let our bloody colours wave! —
And either victory, or else a grave.

QUEEN MARGARET
Stay, Edward.

EDWARD
No, wrangling woman, we'll no longer stay;
These words will cost ten thousand lives this day.
        [*Exeunt.*

SCENE III

A field of battle between Towton and Saxton, in Yorkshire.

Alarum. Excursions. Enter WARWICK.

WARWICK
Forspent with toil, as runners with a race,
I lay me down a little while to breathe;
For strokes receiv'd, and many blows repaid,
Have robb'd my strong-knit sinews of their strength,
And, spite of spite, needs must I rest awhile.

Enter EDWARD, *running.*

EDWARD
Smile, gentle heaven! or strike, ungentle death!
For this world frowns, and Edward's sun is clouded.

WARWICK
How now, my lord! what hap? what hope of good?

Enter GEORGE.

GEORGE
Our hap is loss, our hope but sad despair;
Our ranks are broke, and ruin follows us:
What counsel give you? whither shall we fly?

EDWARD
Bootless is flight, — they follow us with wings;
And weak are we, and cannot shun pursuit.

Enter RICHARD.

RICHARD
Ah, Warwick, why hast thou withdrawn thyself?
Thy brother's blood the thirsty earth hath drunk,
Broach'd with the steely point of Clifford's lance;
And, in the very pangs of death he cried,
Like to a dismal clangor heard from far,
'Warwick, revenge! brother, revenge my death!'
So, underneath the belly of their steeds,
That stain'd their fetlocks in his smoking blood,
The noble gentleman gave up the ghost.

WARWICK
Then let the earth be drunken with our blood:
I'll kill my horse, because I will not fly.
Why stand we like soft-hearted women here,
Wailing our losses, whiles the foe doth rage;
And look upon, as if the tragedy
Were play'd in jest by counterfeiting actors?
Here on my knee I vow to God above,
I'll never pause again, never stand still,
Till either death hath clos'd these eyes of mine,
Or fortune given me measure of revenge.

EDWARD
O Warwick, I do bend my knee with thine;
And in this vow do chain my soul to thine!
And, ere my knee rise from the earth's cold face,
I throw my hands, mine eyes, my heart to Thee,
Thou setter-up and plucker-down of kings, —
Beseeching Thee, if with Thy will it stands
That to my foes this body must be prey,
Yet that Thy brazen gates of heaven may ope,
And give sweet passage to my sinful soul! —
Now, lords, take leave until we meet again,
Where'er it be, in heaven or in earth.

RICHARD
Brother, give me thy hand; — and, gentle Warwick,
Let me embrace thee in my weary arms:
I, that did never weep, now melt with woe
That winter should cut off our spring-time so.

WARWICK
Away, away! Once more, sweet lords, farewell.

GEORGE
Yet let us all together to our troops,
And give them leave to fly that will not stay;
And call them pillars that will stand to us;
And, if we thrive, promise them such rewards
As victors wear at the Olympian games:
This may plant courage in their quailing breasts;
For yet is hope of life and victory. —
Forslow no longer, make we hence amain.   [*Exeunt.*

SCENE IV

Another part of the field.

Excursions. Enter RICHARD *and* CLIFFORD.

RICHARD
Now, Clifford, I have singled thee alone:
Suppose this arm is for the Duke of York,
And this for Rutland; both bound to revenge,
Wert thou environ'd with a brazen wall.

CLIFFORD
Now, Richard, I am with thee here alone:
This is the hand that stabb'd thy father York;
And this the hand that slew thy brother Rutland;
And here's the heart that triumphs in their death,
And cheers these hands that slew thy sire and brother,
To execute the like upon thyself;
And so, have at thee!
    [*They fight.* WARWICK *comes;* CLIFFORD *flies.*

RICHARD
Nay, Warwick, single out some other chase;
For I myself will hunt this wolf to death.   [*Exeunt.*

SCENE V

Another part of the field.

Alarum. Enter KING HENRY *alone.*

KING HENRY
This battle fares like to the morning's war,
When dying clouds contend with growing light,
What time the shepherd, blowing of his nails,
Can neither call it perfect day nor night.
Now sways it this way, like a mighty sea
Forc'd by the tide to combat with the wind;
Now sways it that way, like the selfsame sea
Forc'd to retire by fury of the wind:
Sometime the flood prevails, and then the wind;
Now one the better, then another best;
Both tugging to be victors, breast to breast,
Yet neither conqueror nor conquered:
So is the equal poise of this fell war.
Here on this molehill will I sit me down.
To whom God will, there be the victory!
For Margaret my queen, and Clifford too,
Have chid me from the battle; swearing both
They prosper best of all when I am thence.
Would I were dead! if God's good will were so;
For what is in this world but grief and woe?
O God! methinks it were a happy life,
To be no better than a homely swain;
To sit upon a hill, as I do now,
To carve out dials quaintly, point by point,
Thereby to see the minutes how they run, —
How many makes the hour full complete;
How many hours bring about the day;
How many days will finish up the year;
How many years a mortal man may live.
When this is known, then to divide the times: —
So many hours must I tend my flock;
So many hours must I take my rest;
So many hours must I contemplate;
So many hours must I sport myself;
So many days my ewes have been with young;
So many weeks ere the poor fools will ean;
So many months ere I shall shear the fleece:
So minutes, hours, days, months, and years,
Pass'd over to the end they were created,
Would bring white hairs unto a quiet grave.
Ah, what a life were this! how sweet! how lovely!
Gives not the hawthorn-bush a sweeter shade
To shepherds looking on their silly sheep,
Than doth a rich-embroider'd canopy
To kings that fear their subjects' treachery?
O, yes, it doth; a thousand-fold it doth.
And to conclude, — the shepherd's homely curds,
His cold thin drink out of his leather bottle,
His wonted sleep under a fresh tree's shade,
All which secure and sweetly he enjoys,
Is far beyond a prince's delicates,
His viands sparkling in a golden cup,
His body couched in a curious bed,
When care, mistrust, and treason waits on him.

Alarum. Enter a SON *that hath kill'd his father, bringing in the dead body.*

SON
Ill blows the wind that profits nobody.
This man, whom hand to hand I slew in fight,
May be possessed with some store of crowns;
And I, that haply take them from him now,
May yet ere night yield both my life and them
To some man else, as this dead man doth me. —

Who's this? — O God! it is my father's face,
Whom in this conflict I unwares have kill'd.
O heavy times, begetting such events!
From London by the king was I press'd forth;
My father, being the Earl of Warwick's man,
Came on the part of York, press'd by his master;
And I, who at his hands receiv'd my life,
Have by my hands of life bereaved him. —
Pardon me, God, I knew not what I did! —
And pardon, father, for I knew not thee! —
My tears shall wipe away these bloody marks;
And no more words till they have flow'd their fill.

KING HENRY
O piteous spectacle! O bloody times!
Whiles lions war and battle for their dens,
Poor harmless lambs abide their enmity. —
Weep, wretched man, I'll aid thee tear for tear;
And let our hearts and eyes, like civil war,
Be blind with tears, and break o'ercharg'd with grief.

Enter a FATHER, bearing of his son.

FATHER
Thou that so stoutly hast resisted me,
Give me thy gold, if thou hast any gold;
For I have bought it with an hundred blows. —
But let me see: is this our foeman's face?
Ah, no, no, no, it is mine only son!
Ah, boy, if any life be left in thee,
Throw up thine eye! see, see what showers arise,
Blown with the windy tempest of my heart,
Upon thy wounds, that kills mine eye and heart! —
O, pity, pity, this miserable age! —
What stratagems, how fell, how butcherly,
Erroneous, mutinous, and unnatural,
This deadly quarrel daily doth beget! —
O boy, thy father gave thee life too soon,
And hath bereft thee of thy life too late!

KING HENRY
Woe above woe! grief more than common grief!
O, that my death would stay these ruthful deeds!
O pity, pity, gentle heaven, pity! —
The red rose and the white are on his face,
The fatal colours of our striving houses:
The one his purple blood right well resembles;
The other his pale cheeks, methinks, presenteth:
Wither one rose, and let the other flourish;
If you contend, a thousand lives must wither.

SON
How will my mother for a father's death
Take on with me, and ne'er be satisfied!

FATHER
How will my wife for slaughter of my son
Shed seas of tears, and ne'er be satisfied!

KING HENRY
How will the country for these woeful chances
Misthink the king, and not be satisfied!

SON
Was ever son so rued a father's death?

FATHER
Was ever father so bemoan'd his son?

KING HENRY
Was ever king so grieved for subjects' woe?
Much is your sorrow; mine ten times so much.

SON
I'll bear thee hence, where I may weep my fill.
[*Exit with the body.*

FATHER
These arms of mine shall be thy winding-sheet;
My heart, sweet boy, shall be thy sepulchre,
For from my heart thine image ne'er shall go;
My sighing breast shall be thy funeral bell;
And so obsequious will thy father be,
E'en for the loss of thee, having no more,
As Priam was for all his valiant sons.
I'll bear thee hence; and let them fight that will,
For I have murder'd where I should not kill.
[*Exit with the body.*

KING HENRY
Sad-hearted men, much overgone with care,
Here sits a king more woeful than you are.

Alarums. Excursions. Enter the QUEEN, the PRINCE, and EXETER.

PRINCE OF WALES
Fly, father, fly! for all your friends are fled,
And Warwick rages like a chafed bull:
Away! for death doth hold us in pursuit.

QUEEN MARGARET
Mount you, my lord; towards Berwick post amain:
Edward and Richard, like a brace of greyhounds
Having the fearful flying hare in sight,

With fiery eyes sparkling for very wrath,
And bloody steel grasp'd in their ireful hands,
Are at our backs; and therefore hence amain.

EXETER
Away! for vengeance comes along with them:
Nay, stay not to expostulate, — make speed;
Or else come after: I'll away before.

KING HENRY
Nay, take me with thee, good sweet Exeter:
Not that I fear to stay, but love to go
Whither the queen intends. Forward; away! [*Exeunt.*

SCENE VI

Another part of the field.

A loud alarum. Enter CLIFFORD, wounded.

CLIFFORD
Here burns my candle out; — ay, here it dies,
Which, whiles it lasted, gave King Henry light.
O Lancaster, I fear thy overthrow
More than my body's parting with my soul!
My love and fear glued many friends to thee;
And, now I fall, that tough commixture melts.
Impairing Henry, strengthening misproud York,
The common people swarm like summer flies;
And whither fly the gnats but to the sun?
And who shines now but Henry's enemies?
O Phœbus, hadst thou never given consent
That Phæthon should check thy fiery steeds,
Thy burning car never had scorch'd the earth!
And, Henry, hadst thou sway'd as kings should do,
Or as thy father and his father did,
Giving no ground unto the house of York,
I and ten thousand in this luckless realm
Had left no mourning widows for our death;
And thou this day hadst kept thy chair in peace.
For what doth cherish weeds but gentle air?
And what makes robbers bold but too much lenity? —
Bootless are plaints, and cureless are my wounds;
No way to fly, nor strength to hold out flight:
The foe is merciless, and will not pity;
For at their hands I have deserv'd no pity.
The air hath got into my deadly wounds,
And much effuse of blood doth make me faint. —
Come, York and Richard, Warwick and the rest;
I stabb'd your fathers' bosoms, — split my breast.
[*Faints.*

Alarum and retreat. Enter EDWARD, GEORGE, RICHARD, MONTAGUE, WARWICK, and SOLDIERS.

EDWARD
Now breathe we, lords: good fortune bids us pause,
And smooth the frowns of war with peaceful looks. —
Some troops pursue the bloody-minded queen,
That led calm Henry, though he were a king,
As doth a sail, fill'd with a fretting gust,
Command an argosy to stem the waves.
But think you, lords, that Clifford fled with them?

WARWICK
No, 'tis impossible he should escape;
For, though before his face I speak the words,
Your brother Richard mark'd him for the grave:
And wheresoe'er he is, he's surely dead.
[*CLIFFORD groans, and dies.*

EDWARD
Whose soul is that which takes her heavy leave?

RICHARD
A deadly groan, like life and death's departing.

EDWARD
See who it is: and, now the battle's ended,
If friend or foe, let him be gently used.

RICHARD
Revoke that doom of mercy, for 'tis Clifford;
Who not contented that he lopp'd the branch
In hewing Rutland when his leaves put forth,
But set his murdering knife unto the root
From whence that tender spray did sweetly spring, —
I mean our princely father, Duke of York.

WARWICK
From off the gates of York fetch down the head,
Your father's head, which Clifford placed there;
Instead whereof let this supply the room:
Measure for measure must be answered.

EDWARD
Bring forth that fatal screech-owl to our house,
That nothing sung but death to us and ours:
Now death shall stop his dismal-threatening sound,
And his ill-boding tongue no more shall speak.
[*SOLDIERS bring the body forward.*

WARWICK
I think his understanding is bereft. —
Speak, Clifford; dost thou know who speaks to thee? —
Dark cloudy death o'ershades his beams of life,
And he nor sees nor hears us what we say.

RICHARD
O, would he did! and so, perhaps, he doth:
'Tis but his policy to counterfeit,
Because he would avoid such bitter taunts
Which in the time of death he gave our father.

GEORGE
If so thou think'st, vex him with eager words.

RICHARD
Clifford, ask mercy, and obtain no grace.

EDWARD
Clifford, repent in bootless penitence.

WARWICK
Clifford, devise excuses for thy faults.

GEORGE
While we devise fell tortures for thy faults.

RICHARD
Thou didst love York, and I am son to York.

EDWARD
Thou pitied'st Rutland; I will pity thee.

GEORGE
Where's Captain Margaret, to fence you now?

WARWICK
They mock thee, Clifford: swear as thou wast wont.

RICHARD
What, not an oath? nay, then the world goes hard
When Clifford cannot spare his friends an oath. —
I know by that he's dead; and, by my soul,
If this right hand would buy two hours' life,
That I in all despite might rail at him,
This hand should chop it off; and with the issuing
     blood
Stifle the villain whose unstanched thirst
York and young Rutland could not satisfy.

WARWICK
Ay, but he's dead: off with the traitor's head,
And rear it in the place your father stands. —
And now to London with triumphant march,
There to be crowned England's royal king.
From whence shall Warwick cut the sea to France,
And ask the Lady Bona for thy queen:
So shalt thou sinew both these lands together;
And, having France thy friend, thou shalt not dread
The scatter'd foe that hopes to rise again;
For though they cannot greatly sting to hurt,
Yet look to have them buzz to offend thine ears.
First will I see the coronation;
And then to Brittany I'll cross the sea,
To effect this marriage, so it please my lord.

EDWARD
Even as thou wilt, sweet Warwick, let it be;
For in thy shoulder do I build my seat,
And never will I undertake the thing
Wherein thy counsel and consent is wanting. —
Richard, I will create thee Duke of Gloster; —
And George, of Clarence: — Warwick, as ourself,
Shall do and undo as him pleaseth best.

RICHARD
Let me be Duke of Clarence, George of Gloster;
For Gloster's dukedom is too ominous.

WARWICK
Tut, that's a foolish observation:
Richard, be Duke of Gloster. Now to London,
To see these honours in possession. [*Exeunt.*

ACT III

SCENE I

A chase in the north of England.

Enter two KEEPERS, with cross-bows in their hands.

FIRST KEEPER
Under this thick-grown brake we'll shroud ourselves;
For through this laund anon the deer will come;
And in this covert will we make our stand,
Culling the principal of all the deer.

SECOND KEEPER
I'll stay above the hill, so both may shoot.

FIRST KEEPER
That cannot be; the noise of thy cross-bow
Will scare the herd, and so my shoot is lost.
Here stand we both, and aim we at the best:
And, for the time shall not seem tedious,
I'll tell thee what befell me on a day

In this self-place where now we mean to stand.

SECOND KEEPER
Here comes a man; let's stay till he be past.
Enter the KING, *with a prayer-book.*

KING HENRY
From Scotland am I stol'n, even of pure love,
To greet mine own land with my wishful sight.
No, Harry, Harry, 'tis no land of thine;
Thy place is fill'd, thy sceptre wrung from thee,
Thy balm wash'd off wherewith thou wast anointed:
No bending knee will call thee Cæsar now,
No humble suitors press to speak for right,
No, not a man comes for redress of thee;
For how can I help them, and not myself?

FIRST KEEPER
Ay, here's a deer whose skin's a keeper's fee:
This is the *quondam* king; let's seize upon him.

KING HENRY
Let me embrace thee, sour adversity;
For wise men say it is the wisest course.

SECOND KEEPER
Why linger we? let us lay hands upon him.

FIRST KEEPER
Forbear awhile; we'll hear a little more.

KING HENRY
My queen and son are gone to France for aid;
And, as I hear, the great-commanding Warwick
Is thither gone, to crave the French king's sister
To wife for Edward: if this news be true,
Poor queen and son, your labour is but lost;
For Warwick is a subtle orator,
And Louis a prince soon won with moving words.
By this account, then, Margaret may win him;
For she's a woman to be pitied much:
Her sighs will make a battery in his breast;
Her tears will pierce into a marble heart;
The tiger will be mild whiles she doth mourn;
And Nero will be tainted with remorse,
To hear and see her plaints, her brinish tears.
Ay, but she's come to beg; Warwick, to give:
She, on his left side, craving aid for Henry;
He, on his right, asking a wife for Edward.
She weeps, and says her Henry is deposed;
He smiles, and says his Edward is install'd;
That she, poor wretch, for grief can speak no more;
Whiles Warwick tells his title, smooths the wrong,
Inferreth arguments of mighty strength,
And in conclusion wins the king from her,
With promise of his sister, and what else,
To strengthen and support King Edward's place.
O Margaret, thus 'twill be; and thou, poor soul,
Art then forsaken, as thou went'st forlorn!

SECOND KEEPER
Say, what art thou that talk'st of kings and queens?

KING HENRY
More than I seem, and less than I was born to:
A man at least, for less I should not be;
And men may talk of kings, and why not I?

SECOND KEEPER
Ay, but thou talk'st as if thou wert a king.

KING HENRY
Why, so I am — in mind; and that's enough.

SECOND KEEPER
But, if thou be a king, where is thy crown?

KING HENRY
My crown is in my heart, not on my head;
Not deck'd with diamonds and Indian stones,
Nor to be seen: my crown is call'd content —
A crown it is that seldom kings enjoy.

SECOND KEEPER
Well, if you be a king crown'd with content,
Your crown content and you must be contented
To go along with us; for, as we think,
You are the king King Edward hath deposed;
And we his subjects, sworn in all allegiance,
Will apprehend you as his enemy.

KING HENRY
But did you never swear, and break an oath?

SECOND KEEPER
No, never such an oath; nor will not now.

KING HENRY
Where did you dwell when I was king of England?

SECOND KEEPER
Here in this country, where we now remain.

KING HENRY
I was anointed king at nine months old;
My father and my grandfather were kings;
And you were sworn true subjects unto me:
And tell me, then, have you not broke your oaths?

FIRST KEEPER
No;
For we were subjects but while you were king.

KING HENRY
Why, am I dead? do I not breathe a man?
Ah, simple men, you know not what you swear!
Look, as I blow this feather from my face,
And as the air blows it to me again,
Obeying with my wind when I do blow,
And yielding to another when it blows,
Commanded always by the greater gust;
Such is the lightness of you common men.
But do not break your oaths; for of that sin
My mild entreaty shall not make you guilty.
Go where you will, the king shall be commanded;
And be you kings; command, and I'll obey.

FIRST KEEPER
We are true subjects to the king, King Edward.

KING HENRY
So would you be again to Henry,
If he were seated as King Edward is.

FIRST KEEPER
We charge you, in God's name, and the king's,
To go with us unto the officers.

KING HENRY
In God's name, lead; your king's name be obey'd:
And what God will, that let your king perform;
And what he will, I humbly yield unto. [*Exeunt.*

SCENE II

London. A room in the palace.

Enter KING EDWARD, GLOSTER, CLARENCE, *and*
LADY GREY.

KING EDWARD
Brother of Gloster, at Saint Alban's field
This lady's husband, Sir Richard Grey, was slain,
His lands then seiz'd on by the conqueror:
Her suit is now to repossess those lands;
Which we in justice cannot well deny,
Because in quarrel of the house of York
The worthy gentleman did lose his life.

GLOSTER
Your highness shall do well to grant her suit;
It were dishonour to deny it her.

KING EDWARD
It were no less; but yet I'll make a pause.

GLOSTER [*aside to* CLARENCE].
Yea, is it so?
I see the lady hath a thing to grant,
Before the king will grant her humble suit.

CLARENCE [*aside to* GLOSTER].
He knows the game: how true he keeps the wind!

GLOSTER [*aside to* CLARENCE].
Silence!

KING EDWARD
Widow, we will consider of your suit;
And come some other time to know our mind.

LADY GREY
Right gracious lord, I cannot brook delay:
May't please your highness to resolve me now;
And what your pleasure is shall satisfy me.

GLOSTER [*aside*].
Ay, widow? then I'll warrant you all your lands,
An if what pleases him shall pleasure you.
Fight closer, or, good faith, you'll catch a blow.

CLARENCE [*aside to* GLOSTER].
I fear her not, unless she chance to fall.

GLOSTER [*aside to* CLARENCE].
God forbid that! for he'll take vantages.

KING EDWARD
How many children hast thou, widow? tell me.

CLARENCE [*aside to* GLOSTER].
I think he means to beg a child of her.

GLOSTER [*aside to* CLARENCE].
Nay, whip me, then; he'll rather give her two.

LADY GREY
Three, my most gracious lord.

GLOSTER [*aside*].
You shall have four, if you'll be rul'd by him.

KING EDWARD
'Twere pity they should lose their father's lands.

LADY GREY
Be pitiful, dread lord, and grant it, then.

KING EDWARD
Lords, give us leave: I'll try this widow's wit.

GLOSTER [*aside*].
Ay, good leave have you; for you will have leave,
Till youth take leave, and leave you to the crutch.

[*Retires with* CLARENCE.

KING EDWARD
Now tell me, madam, do you love your children?

LADY GREY
Ay, full as dearly as I love myself.

KING EDWARD
And would you not do much to do them good?

LADY GREY
To do them good, I would sustain some harm.

KING EDWARD
Then get your husband's lands, to do them good.

LADY GREY
Therefor I came unto your majesty.

KING EDWARD
I'll tell you how these lands are to be got.

LADY GREY
So shall you bind me to your highness' service.

KING EDWARD
What service wilt thou do me, if I give them?

LADY GREY
What you command, that rests in me to do.

KING EDWARD
But you will take exceptions to my boon.

LADY GREY
No, gracious lord, except I cannot do it.

KING EDWARD
Ay, but thou canst do what I mean to ask.

LADY GREY
Why, then I will do what your Grace commands.

GLOSTER [*aside to* CLARENCE].
He plies her hard; and much rain wears the marble.

CLARENCE [*aside to* GLOSTER].
As red as fire! nay, then her wax must melt.

LADY GREY
Why stops my lord? shall I not hear my task?

KING EDWARD
An easy task; 'tis but to love a king.

LADY GREY
That's soon perform'd, because I am a subject.

KING EDWARD
Why, then, thy husband's lands I freely give thee.

LADY GREY
I take my leave with many thousand thanks.

GLOSTER [*aside to* CLARENCE].
The match is made; she seals it with a curt'sy.

KING EDWARD
But stay thee, — 'tis the fruits of love I mean.

LADY GREY
The fruits of love I mean, my loving liege.

KING EDWARD
Ay, but, I fear me, in another sense.
What love, think'st thou, I sue so much to get?

LADY GREY
My love till death, my humble thanks, my prayers;
That love which virtue begs, and virtue grants.

KING EDWARD
No, by my troth, I did not mean such love.

LADY GREY
Why, then you mean not as I thought you did.

KING EDWARD
But now you partly may perceive my mind.

LADY GREY
My mind will never grant what I perceive
Your highness aims at, if I aim aright.

KING EDWARD
To tell thee plain, I aim to lie with thee.

LADY GREY
To tell you plain, I had rather lie in prison.

KING EDWARD
Why, then thou shalt not have thy husband's lands.

LADY GREY
Why, then mine honesty shall be my dower;
For by that loss I will not purchase them.

KING EDWARD
Therein thou wrong'st thy children mightily.

LADY GREY
Herein your highness wrongs both them and me.
But, mighty lord, this merry inclination
Accords not with the sadness of my suit:
Please you dismiss me, either with 'ay' or 'no.'

KING EDWARD
Ay, if thou wilt say 'ay' to my request;
No, if thou dost say 'no' to my demand.

LADY GREY
Then, no, my lord. My suit is at an end.

GLOSTER [*aside to* CLARENCE].
The widow likes him not, she knits her brows.

CLARENCE [*aside to* GLOSTER].
He is the bluntest wooer in Christendom.

KING EDWARD [*aside*].
Her looks do argue her replete with modesty;
Her words do show her wit incomparable;
All her perfections challenge sovereignty:
One way or other, she is for a king;
And she shall be my love, or else my queen. —
Say that King Edward take thee for his queen?

LADY GREY
'Tis better said than done, my gracious lord:
I am a subject fit to jest withal,
But far unfit to be a sovereign.

KING EDWARD
Sweet widow, by my state I swear to thee
I speak no more than what my soul intends;
And that is, to enjoy thee for my love.

LADY GREY
And that is more than I will yield unto:
I know I am too mean to be your queen,
And yet too good to be your concubine.

KING EDWARD
You cavil, widow: I did mean, my queen.

LADY GREY
'Twill grieve your Grace my sons should call you father.

KING EDWARD
No more than when my daughters call thee mother.
Thou art a widow, and thou hast some children;
And, by God's mother, I, being but a bachelor,
Have other some: why, 'tis a happy thing
To be the father unto many sons.
Answer no more, for thou shalt be my queen.

GLOSTER [*aside to* CLARENCE].
The ghostly father now hath done his shrift.

CLARENCE [*aside to* GLOSTER].
When he was made a shriver, 'twas for shift.

KING EDWARD
Brothers, you muse what chat we two have had.

GLOSTER
The widow likes it not, for she looks sad.

KING EDWARD
You'ld think it strange if I should marry her.

CLARENCE
To whom, my lord?

KING EDWARD
　　　　　　Why, Clarence, to myself.

GLOSTER
That would be ten days' wonder at the least.

CLARENCE
That's a day longer than a wonder lasts.

GLOSTER
By so much is the wonder in extremes.

KING EDWARD
Well, jest on, brothers: I can tell you both
Her suit is granted for her husband's lands.

Enter a NOBLEMAN.

NOBLEMAN
My gracious lord, Henry your foe is taken,
And brought as prisoner to your palace-gate.

KING EDWARD
See that he be convey'd unto the Tower: —
And go we, brothers, to the man that took him,
To question of his apprehension. —
Widow, go you along: — lords, use her honourably.
　　　　　　　　　[*Exeunt all except* GLOSTER.

GLOSTER
Ay, Edward will use women honourably. —
Would he were wasted, marrow, bones and all,
That from his loins no hopeful branch may spring,
To cross me from the golden time I look for!
And yet, between my soul's desire and me —
The lustful Edward's title buried —
Is Clarence, Henry, and his son young Edward,
And all the unlook'd-for issue of their bodies,
To take their rooms, ere I can place myself:
A cold premeditation for my purpose!
Why, then, I do but dream on sovereignty
Like one that stands upon a promontory,
And spies a far-off shore where he would tread,
Wishing his foot were equal with his eye;
And chides the sea that sunders him from thence,
Saying, he'll lade it dry to have his way;
So do I wish the crown, being so far off;
And so I chide the means that keeps me from it;
And so I say, I'll cut the causes off,
Flattering me with impossibilities. —
My eye's too quick, my heart o'erweens too much,
Unless my hand and strength could equal them.
Well, say there is no kingdom, then, for Richard;

What other pleasure can the world afford?
I'll make my heaven in a lady's lap,
And deck my body in gay ornaments,
And witch sweet ladies with my words and looks.
O miserable thought! and more unlikely
Than to accomplish twenty golden crowns!
Why, love forswore me in my mother's womb:
And, for I should not deal in her soft laws,
She did corrupt frail nature with some bribe,
To shrink mine arm up like a wither'd shrub;
To make an envious mountain on my back,
Where sits deformity to mock my body;
To shape my legs of an unequal size;
To disproportion me in every part,
Like to a chaos, or an unlick'd bear-whelp
That carries no impression like the dam.
And am I, then, a man to be beloved?
O monstrous fault, to harbour such a thought!
Then, since this earth affords no joy to me,
But to command, to check, to o'erbear such
As are of better person than myself,
I'll make my heaven to dream upon the crown,
And, whiles I live, t'account this world but hell,
Until my mis-shap'd trunk that bears this head,
Be round impaled with a glorious crown.
And yet I know not how to get the crown,
For many lives stand between me and home:
And I — like one lost in a thorny wood,
That rends the thorns and is rent with the thorns,
Seeking a way, and straying from the way;
Not knowing how to find the open air,
But toiling desperately to find it out —
Torment myself to catch the English crown:
And from that torment I will free myself,
Or hew my way out with a bloody axe.
Why, I can smile, and murder whiles I smile;
And cry 'Content' to that which grieves my heart;
And wet my cheeks with artificial tears,
And frame my face to all occasions:
I'll drown more sailors than the mermaid shall;
I'll slay more gazers than the basilisk;
I'll play the orator as well as Nestor;
Deceive more slily than Ulysses could;
And, like a Sinon, take another Troy:
I can add colours to the chameleon;
Change shapes with Proteus for advantages;
And set the murderous Machiavel to school.
Can I do this, and cannot get a crown?
Tut! were it further off, I'll pluck it down. [*Exit.*

SCENE III

France. The KING'S *palace.*

Flourish. Enter LOUIS *the French king, his sister* BONA,
his Admiral call'd BOURBON; PRINCE EDWARD,
QUEEN MARGARET, *and the* EARL OF OXFORD.
LOUIS *sits, and riseth up again.*

KING LOUIS
Fair Queen of England, worthy Margaret,
Sit down with us: it ill befits thy state
And birth, that thou shouldst stand while Louis doth
　sit.

QUEEN MARGARET
No, mighty King of France: now Margaret
Must strike her sail, and learn awhile to serve,
Where kings command. I was, I must confess,
Great Albion's queen in former golden days:
But now mischance hath trod my title down,
And with dishonour laid me on the ground;
Where I must take like seat unto my fortune,
And to my humble seat conform myself.

KING LOUIS
Why, say, fair queen, whence springs this deep
　despair?

QUEEN MARGARET
From such a cause as fills mine eyes with tears,
And stops my tongue, while heart is drown'd in cares.

KING LOUIS
Whate'er it be, be thou still like thyself,
And sit thee by our side: yield not thy neck.
　　　　　　　　　[*Seats her by him.*
To fortune's yoke, but let thy dauntless mind
Still ride in triumph over all mischance.
Be plain, Queen Margaret, and tell thy grief;
It shall be eas'd, if France can yield relief.

QUEEN MARGARET
Those gracious words revive my drooping thoughts,
And give my tongue-tied sorrows leave to speak.
Now, therefore, be it known to noble Louis,
That Henry, sole possessor of my love,
Is, of a king, become a banish'd man,

And forc'd to live in Scotland a forlorn;
While proud ambitious Edward duke of York
Usurps the regal title and the seat
Of England's true-anointed lawful king.
This is the cause that I, poor Margaret, —
With this my son, Prince Edward, Henry's heir, —
Am come to crave thy just and lawful aid;
And if thou fail us, all our hope is done:
Scotland hath will to help, but cannot help;
Our people and our peers are both misled,
Our treasures seiz'd, our soldiers put to flight,
And, as thou seest, ourselves in heavy plight.

KING LOUIS
Renowned queen, with patience calm the storm,
While we bethink a means to break it off.

QUEEN MARGARET
The more we stay, the stronger grows our foe.

KING LOUIS
The more I stay, the more I'll succour thee.

QUEEN MARGARET
O, but impatience waiteth on true sorrow: —
And see where comes the breeder of my sorrow!

Enter WARWICK, *attended.*

KING LOUIS
What's he approacheth boldly to our presence?

QUEEN MARGARET
Our Earl of Warwick, Edward's greatest friend.

KING LOUIS
Welcome, brave Warwick! What brings thee to France?
　　　　　　　　　[*He descends. She ariseth.*

QUEEN MARGARET [*aside*].
Ay, now begins a second storm to rise;
For this is he that moves both wind and tide.

WARWICK
From worthy Edward, king of Albion,
My lord and sovereign, and thy vowed friend,
I come, in kindness and unfeigned love, —
First, to do greetings to thy royal person;
And then to crave a league of amity;
And lastly, to confirm that amity
With nuptial knot, if thou vouchsafe to grant
That virtuous Lady Bona, thy fair sister,
To England's king in lawful marriage.

QUEEN MARGARET [*aside*].
If that go forward, Henry's hope is done.

WARWICK [*to* BONA].
And, gracious madam, in our king's behalf,
I am commanded, with your leave and favour,
Humbly to kiss your hand, and with my tongue
To tell the passion of my sovereign's heart;
Where fame, late entering at his heedful ears,
Hath plac'd thy beauty's image and thy virtue.

QUEEN MARGARET
King Louis, — and Lady Bona, — hear me speak,
Before you answer Warwick. His demand
Springs not from Edward's well-meant honest love,
But from deceit bred by necessity;
For how can tyrants safely govern home,
Unless abroad they purchase great alliance?
To prove him tyrant this reason may suffice, —
That Henry liveth still; but were he dead,
Yet here Prince Edward stands, King Henry's son.
Look therefore, Louis, that by this league and marriage
Thou draw not on thy danger and dishonour;
For though usurpers sway the rule awhile,
Yet heavens are just, and time suppresseth wrongs.

WARWICK
Injurious Margaret!

PRINCE EDWARD
　　　　　　And why not queen?

WARWICK
Because thy father Henry did usurp;
And thou no more are prince than she is queen.

OXFORD
Then Warwick disannuls great John of Gaunt,
Which did subdue the greatest part of Spain;
And, after John of Gaunt, Henry the Fourth,
Whose wisdom was a mirror to the wisest;
And, after that wise prince, Henry the Fifth,
Who by his prowess conquered all France:
From these our Henry lineally descends.

WARWICK
Oxford, how haps it, in this smooth discourse,
You told not how Henry the Sixth hath lost
All that which Henry the Fifth had gotten?
Methinks these peers of France should smile at that.
But for the rest, — you tell a pedigree
Of threescore and two years; a silly time
To make prescription for a kingdom's worth.

OXFORD
Why, Warwick, canst thou speak against thy liege,
Whom thou obeyed'st thirty and six years,
And not bewray thy treason with a blush?

WARWICK
Can Oxford, that did ever fence the right,
Now buckler falsehood with a pedigree?
For shame! leave Henry, and call Edward king.

OXFORD
Call him my king by whose injurious doom
My elder brother, the Lord Aubrey Vere,
Was done to death? and more than so, my father,
Even in the downfall of his mellow'd years,
When nature brought him to the door of death?
No, Warwick, no; while life upholds this arm,
This arm upholds the house of Lancaster.

WARWICK
And I the house of York.

KING LOUIS
Queen Margaret, Prince Edward, and Oxford,
Vouchsafe, at our request, to stand aside,
While I use further conference with Warwick.
[They stand aloof.

QUEEN MARGARET
Heavens grant that Warwick's words bewitch him not!

KING LOUIS
Now, Warwick, tell me, even upon thy conscience,
Is Edward your true king? for I were loth
To link with him that were not lawful chosen.

WARWICK
Thereon I pawn my credit and mine honour.

KING LOUIS
But is he gracious in the people's eye?

WARWICK
The more that Henry was unfortunate.

KING LOUIS
Then further, — all dissembling set aside,
Tell me for truth the measure of his love
Unto our sister Bona.

WARWICK
Such it seems
As may beseem a monarch like himself.
Myself have often heard him say and swear
That this his love was an eternal plant,
Whereof the root was fix'd in virtue's ground,
The leaves and fruit maintain'd with beauty's sun;
Exempt from envy, but not from disdain,
Unless the Lady Bona quit his pain.

KING LOUIS
Now, sister, let us hear your firm resolve.

BONA
Your grant, or your denial, shall be mine: —
[to WARWICK] Yet I confess that often ere this day,
When I have heard your king's desert recounted,
Mine ear hath tempted judgement to desire.

KING LOUIS
Then, Warwick, thus, — Our sister shall be Edward's;
And now forthwith shall articles be drawn
Touching the jointure that your king must make,
Which with her dowry shall be counterpoised.—
Draw near, Queen Margaret, and be a witness
That Bona shall be wife to the English king.

PRINCE EDWARD
To Edward, but not to the English king.

QUEEN MARGARET
Deceitful Warwick! it was thy device
By this alliance to make void my suit:
Before thy coming, Louis was Henry's friend.

KING LOUIS
And still is friend to him and Margaret:
But if your title to the crown be weak,
As may appear by Edward's good success, —
Then 'tis but reason that I be releas'd
From giving aid which late I promised.
Yet shall you have all kindness at my hand
That your estate requires, and mine can yield.

WARWICK
Henry now lives in Scotland at his ease,
Where having nothing, nothing can he lose.
And as for you yourself, our *quondam* queen,
You have a father able to maintain you;
And better 'twere you troubled him than France.

QUEEN MARGARET
Peace, impudent and shameless Warwick! peace,
Proud setter-up and puller down of kings!
I will not hence till, with my talk and tears,
Both full of truth, I make King Louis behold
Thy sly conveyance and thy lord's false love;
For both of you are birds of selfsame feather.
[POST *blowing a horn within.*

KING LOUIS
Warwick, this is some post to us or thee.
Enter the POST.

POST [*to* WARWICK].
My lord ambassador, these letters are for you,
Sent from your brother, Marquess Montague: —
[to louis] These from our king unto your majesty: —
[to MARGARET] And, madam, these for you; from
whom I know not.
[They all read their letters.

OXFORD
I like it well that our fair queen and mistress
Smiles at her news, while Warwick frowns at his.

PRINCE EDWARD
Nay, mark how Louis stamps, as he were nettled:
I hope all's for the best.

KING LOUIS
Warwick, what are thy news? — and yours, fair queen?

QUEEN MARGARET
Mine such as fill my heart with unhop'd joys.

WARWICK
Mine full of sorrow and heart's discontent.

KING LOUIS
What! has your king married the Lady Grey?
And now, to soothe your forgery and his,
Sends me a paper to persuade me patience?
Is this th'alliance that he seeks with France?
Dare he presume to scorn us in this manner?

QUEEN MARGARET
I told your majesty as much before:
This proveth Edward's love and Warwick's honesty.

WARWICK
King Louis, I here protest, in sight of heaven,
And by the hope I have of heavenly bliss,
That I am clear from this misdeed of Edward's, —
No more my king, for he dishonours me,
But most himself, if he could see his shame.
Did I forget that by the house of York
My father came untimely to his death?
Did I let pass th'abuse done to my niece?
Did I impale him with the regal crown?
Did I put Henry from his native right?
And am I guerdon'd at the last with shame?
Shame on himself! for my desert is honour:
And, to repair my honour lost for him,
I here renounce him, and return to Henry. —
My noble queen, let former grudges pass,
And henceforth I am thy true servitor:
I will revenge his wrong to Lady Bona,
And replant Henry in his former state.

QUEEN MARGARET
Warwick, these words have turn'd my hate to love;
And I forgive and quite forget old faults,
And joy that thou becomest King Henry's friend.

WARWICK
So much his friend, ay, his unfeigned friend,
That, if King Louis vouchsafe to furnish us
With some few bands of chosen soldiers,
I'll undertake to land them on our coast,
And force the tyrant from his seat by war.
'Tis not his new-made bride shall succour him:
And as for Clarence, — as my letters tell me,
He's very likely now to fall from him,
For matching more for wanton lust than honour,
Or than for strength and safety of our country.

BONA
Dear brother, how shall Bona be reveng'd
But by thy help to this distressed queen?

QUEEN MARGARET
Renowned prince, how shall poor Henry live,
Unless thou rescue him from foul despair?

BONA
My quarrel and this English queen's are one.

WARWICK
And mine, fair Lady Bona, joins with yours.

KING LOUIS
And mine with hers and thine and Margaret's:
Therefore, at last, I firmly am resolved
You shall have aid.

QUEEN MARGARET
Let me give humble thanks for all at once.

KING LOUIS
Then, England's messenger, return in post,
And tell false Edward, thy supposed king,
That Louis of France is sending over maskers
To revel it with him and his new bride:
Thou seest what's pass'd, — go fear thy king withal.

BONA
Tell him, in hope he'll prove a widower shortly,
I'll wear the willow-garland for his sake.

QUEEN MARGARET
Tell him, my mourning-weeds are laid aside,
And I am ready to put armour on.

WARWICK
Tell him from me, that he hath done me wrong;
And therefore I'll uncrown him ere't be long.
There's thy reward: be gone. [*Exit* POST.

KING LOUIS
But, Warwick,
Thou and Oxford, with five thousand men,
Shall cross the seas, and bid false Edward battle;
And, as occasion serves, this noble queen
And prince shall follow with a fresh supply.
Yet, ere thou go, but answer me one doubt, —
What pledge have we of thy firm loyalty?

WARWICK
This shall assure my constant loyalty, —
That if our queen and this young prince agree,
I'll join mine eldest daughter and my joy
To him forthwith in holy wedlock-bands.

QUEEN MARGARET
Yes, I agree, and thank you for your motion. —
Son Edward, she is fair and virtuous;
Therefore delay not, give thy hand to Warwick;
And, with thy hand, thy faith irrevocable,
That only Warwick's daughter shall be thine.

PRINCE OF WALES
Yes, I accept her, for she well deserves it;
And here, to pledge my vow, I give my hand.
[*He gives his hand to* WARWICK.

KING LOUIS
Why stay we now? These soldiers shall be levied;
And thou, Lord Bourbon, our high-admiral,
Shall waft them over with our royal fleet. —
I long till Edward fall by war's mischance,
For mocking marriage with a dame of France.
[*Exeunt all except* WARWICK.

WARWICK
I came from Edward as ambassador,
But I return his sworn and mortal foe:
Matter of marriage was the charge he gave me,
But dreadful war shall answer his demand.
Had he none else to make a stale but me?
Then none but I shall turn his jest to sorrow.
I was the chief that rais'd him to the crown,
And I'll be chief to bring him down again:
Not that I pity Henry's misery,
But seek revenge on Edward's mockery. [*Exit.

ACT IV

SCENE I

London. The palace.

Enter GLOSTER, CLARENCE, SOMERSET,
and MONTAGUE.

GLOSTER
Now tell me, brother Clarence, what think you
Of this new marriage with the Lady Grey?
Hath not our brother made a worthy choice?

CLARENCE
Alas, you know 'tis far from hence to France;
How could he stay till Warwick made return?

SOMERSET
My lords, forbear this talk; here comes the king.

GLOSTER
And his well-chosen bride.

CLARENCE
I mind to tell him plainly what I think.

Flourish. Enter KING EDWARD, LADY GREY, *as*
Queen; PEMBROKE, STAFFORD, HASTINGS: *four*
stand on one side and four on the other.

KING EDWARD
Now, brother of Clarence, how like you our choice,
That you stand pensive, as half malcontent?

CLARENCE
As well as Louis of France or the Earl of Warwick;
Which are so weak of courage and in judgement,
That they'll take no offence at our abuse.

KING EDWARD
Suppose they take offence without a cause,
They are but Louis and Warwick: I am Edward,
Your king and Warwick's, and must have my will.

GLOSTER
Ay, and shall have your will, because our king:
Yet hasty marriage seldom proveth well.

WARWICK But Henry now shall wear the English crown.

KING EDWARD
Yea, brother Richard, are you offended too?

GLOSTER
Not I:
No, God forbid that I should wish them sever'd
Whom God hath join'd together; ay, and 'twere pity
To sunder them that yoke so well together.

KING EDWARD
Setting your scorns and your mislike aside,
Tell me some reason why the Lady Grey
Should not become my wife and England's queen: —
And you too, Somerset and Montague,
Speak freely what you think.

CLARENCE
Then this is mine opinion, — that King Louis
Becomes your enemy, for mocking him
About the marriage of the Lady Bona.

GLOSTER
And Warwick, doing what you gave in charge,
Is now dishonoured by this new marriage.

KING EDWARD
What if both Louis and Warwick be appeas'd
By such invention as I can devise?

MONTAGUE
Yet, to have join'd with France in such alliance
Would more have strengthen'd this our
    commonwealth
'Gainst foreign storms than any home-bred marriage.

HASTINGS
Why, knows not Montague that of itself
England is safe, if true within itself?

MONTAGUE
Yes; but the safer when 'tis back'd with France.

HASTINGS
'Tis better using France than trusting France:
Let us be back'd with God, and with the seas
Which He hath given for fence impregnable,
And with their helps only defend ourselves;
In them and in ourselves our safety lies.

CLARENCE
For this one speech Lord Hastings well deserves
To have the heir of the Lord Hungerford.

KING EDWARD
Ay, what of that? it was my will and grant;
And for this once my will shall stand for law.

GLOSTER
And yet methinks your Grace hath not done well,
To give the heir and daughter of Lord Scales
Unto the brother of your loving bride;
She better would have fitted me or Clarence:
But in your bride you bury brotherhood.

CLARENCE
Or else you would not have bestow'd the heir
Of the Lord Bonville on your new wife's son,
And leave your brothers to go speed elsewhere.

KING EDWARD
Alas, poor Clarence! is it for a wife

That thou art malcontent? I will provide thee.

CLARENCE
In choosing for yourself, you show'd your judgement,
Which being shallow, you shall give me leave
To play the broker in mine own behalf;
And to that end I shortly mind to leave you.

KING EDWARD
Leave me, or tarry, Edward will be king,
And not be tied unto his brother's will.

QUEEN ELIZABETH
My lords, before it pleas'd his majesty
To raise my state to title of a queen,
Do me but right, and you must all confess
That I was not ignoble of descent;
And meaner than myself have had like fortune.
But as this title honours me and mine,
So your dislike, to whom I would be pleasing,
Doth cloud my joys with danger and with sorrow.

KING EDWARD
My love, forbear to fawn upon their frowns:
What danger or what sorrow can befall thee,
So long as Edward is thy constant friend,
And their true sovereign, whom they must obey?
Nay, whom they shall obey, and love thee too,
Unless they seek for hatred at my hands;
Which if they do, yet will I keep thee safe,
And they shall feel the vengeance of my wrath.

GLOSTER [*aside*].
I hear, yet say not much, but think the more.

Enter a POST.

KING EDWARD
Now, messenger, what letters or what news
From France?

POST
My sovereign liege, no letters; and few words,
But such as I, without your special pardon,
Dare not relate.

KING EDWARD
Go to, we pardon thee: therefore, in brief,
Tell me their words as near as thou canst guess them.
What answer makes King Louis unto our letters?

POST
At my depart, these were his very words:
'Go tell false Edward, thy supposed king,
That Louis of France is sending over maskers
To revel it with him and his new bride.'

KING EDWARD
Is Louis so brave? belike he thinks me Henry.
But what said Lady Bona to my marriage?

POST
These were her words, utter'd with mild disdain:
'Tell him, in hope he'll prove a widower shortly,
I'll wear the willow-garland for his sake.'

KING EDWARD
I blame not her, she could say little less;
She had the wrong. But what said Henry's queen?
For I have heard that she was there in place.

POST
'Tell him,' quoth she, 'my mourning-weeds are done,
And I am ready to put armour on.'

KING EDWARD
Belike she minds to play the Amazon.
But what said Warwick to these injuries?

POST
He, more incens'd against your majesty
Than all the rest, discharg'd me with these words:
'Tell him from me, that he hath done me wrong,
And therefore I'll uncrown him ere't be long.'

KING EDWARD
Ha! durst the traitor breathe out so proud words?
Well, I will arm me, being thus forewarn'd:
They shall have wars, and pay for their presumption.
But say, is Warwick friends with Margaret?

POST
Ay, gracious sovereign; they are so link'd in
friendship,
That young Prince Edward marries Warwick's
    daughter.

CLARENCE
Belike the elder; Clarence will have the younger.
Now, brother king, farewell, and sit you fast,
For I will hence to Warwick's other daughter;
That, though I want a kingdom, yet in marriage
I may not prove inferior to yourself. —
You that love me and Warwick, follow me.
    [*Exit* CLARENCE, *and* SOMERSET *follows.*]

GLOSTER [*aside*].
Not I:
My thoughts aim at a further matter; I

Stay not for the love of Edward, but the crown.

KING EDWARD
Clarence and Somerset both gone to Warwick!
Yet am I arm'd against the worst can happen;
And haste is needful in this desperate case. —
Pembroke and Stafford, you in our behalf
Go levy men, and make prepare for war;
They are already, or quickly will be landed:
Myself in person will straight follow you.
[*Exeunt* PEMBROKE *and* STAFFORD.
But, ere I go, Hastings and Montague,
Resolve my doubt. You twain, of all the rest,
Are near to Warwick by blood and by alliance:
Tell me if you love Warwick more than me?
If it be so, then both depart to him;
I rather wish you foes than hollow friends:
But if you mind to hold your true obedience,
Give me assurance with some friendly vow,
That I may never have you in suspect.

MONTAGUE
So God help Montague as he proves true!

HASTINGS
And Hastings as he favours Edward's cause!

KING EDWARD
Now, brother Richard, will you stand by us?

GLOSTER
Ay, in despite of all that shall withstand you.

KING EDWARD
Why, so! then am I sure of victory.
Now therefore let us hence; and lose no hour,
Till we meet Warwick with his foreign power. [*Exeunt.*

SCENE II

A plain in Warwickshire.

Enter WARWICK *and* OXFORD,
with French SOLDIERS.

WARWICK
Trust me, my lord, all hitherto goes well;
The common people by numbers swarm to us.
But see where Somerset and Clarence comes!
Enter CLARENCE *and* SOMERSET.
Speak suddenly, my lords, — are we all friends?

CLARENCE
Fear not that, my lord.

WARWICK
Then, gentle Clarence, welcome unto Warwick; —
And welcome, Somerset: — I hold it cowardice
To rest mistrustful where a noble heart
Hath pawn'd an open hand in sign of love;
Else might I think that Clarence, Edward's brother,
Were but a feigned friend to our proceedings:
But welcome, sweet Clarence; my daughter shall be
thine.
And now what rests but, in night's coverture,
Thy brother being carelessly encamp'd,
His soldiers lurking in the towns about,
And but attended by a simple guard,
We may surprise and take him at our pleasure?
Our scouts have found the adventure very easy:
That as Ulysses and stout Diomede
With sleight and manhood stole to Rhesus' tents,
And brought from thence the Thracian fatal steeds;
So we, well cover'd with the night's black mantle,
At unawares may beat down Edward's guard,
And seize himself; I say not, slaughter him,
For I intend but only to surprise him. —
You that will follow me in this attempt
Applaud the name of Henry with your leader.
[*They all cry, 'Henry!'*
Why, then, let's on our way in silent sort:
For Warwick and his friends, God and Saint George!
[*Exeunt.*

SCENE III

EDWARD'S *camp, near Warwick.*

Enter three WATCHMEN, *to guard the* KING'S *tent.*

FIRST WATCHMAN
Come on, my masters, each man take his stand:
The king, by this, is set him down to sleep.

SECOND WATCHMAN
What, will he not to bed?

FIRST WATCHMAN
Why, no; for he hath made a solemn vow
Never to lie and take his natural rest
Till Warwick or himself be quite suppress'd.

SECOND WATCHMAN
To-morrow, then, belike shall be the day,
If Warwick be so near as men report.

THIRD WATCHMAN
But say, I pray, what nobleman is that
That with the king here resteth in his tent?

FIRST WATCHMAN
'Tis the Lord Hastings, the king's chiefest friend.

THIRD WATCHMAN
O, is it so? But why commands the king
That his chief followers lodge in towns about him,
While he himself keeps in the cold field?

SECOND WATCHMAN
'Tis the more honour, because more dangerous.

THIRD WATCHMAN
Ay, but give me worship and quietness;
I like it better than a dangerous honour.
If Warwick knew in what estate he stands,
'Tis to be doubted he would waken him.

FIRST WATCHMAN
Unless our halberds did shut up his passage.

SECOND WATCHMAN
Ay, wherefore else guard we his royal tent,
But to defend his person from night-foes?

Enter WARWICK, CLARENCE, OXFORD,
SOMERSET, *and French* SOLDIERS, *silent all.*

WARWICK
This is his tent; and see where stand his guard.
Courage, my masters! honour now or never!
But follow me, and Edward shall be ours.

FIRST WATCHMAN
Who goes there?

SECOND WATCHMAN
Stay, or thou diest!
[WARWICK *and the rest cry all,* 'Warwick! Warwick!'
and set upon the GUARD, *who fly, crying,* 'Arm! arm!'
WARWICK *and the rest following them.*
The drum playing and trumpet sounding, enter
WARWICK, SOMERSET, *and the rest, bringing*
the KING *out in his gown, sitting in a chair.*
RICHARD *and* HASTINGS *fly over the stage.*

SOMERSET
What are they that fly there?

WARWICK
Richard and Hastings: let them go; here is the duke.

KING EDWARD
The duke! Why, Warwick, when we parted last,
Thou call'dst me king.

WARWICK
                    Ay, but the case is alter'd:
When you disgrac'd me in my embassade,
Then I degraded you from being king,
And come now to create you Duke of York.
Alas, how should you govern any kingdom,
That know not how to use ambassadors;
Nor how to be contented with one wife;
Nor how to use your brothers brotherly;
Nor how to study for the people's welfare;
Nor how to shroud yourself from enemies?

KING EDWARD
Yea, brother of Clarence, are thou here too?
Nay, then I see that Edward needs must down. —
Yet, Warwick, in despite of all mischance,
Of thee thyself and all thy complices,
Edward will always bear himself as king:
Though fortune's malice overthrow my state,
My mind exceeds the compass of her wheel.

WARWICK
Then, for his mind, be Edward England's king:
[*Takes off his crown.*
But Henry now shall wear the English crown,
And be true king indeed; thou but the shadow. —
My Lord of Somerset, at my request,
See that forthwith Duke Edward be convey'd
Unto my brother, Archbishop of York.
When I have fought with Pembroke and his fellows,
I'll follow you, and tell duke what answer
Louis and the Lady Bona send to him. —
Now, for a while farewell, good Duke of York.

KING EDWARD
What fates impose, that men must needs abide;
It boots not to resist both wind and tide.
[*They lead him out forcibly.*

OXFORD
What now remains, my lords, for us to do,
But march to London with our soldiers?

WARWICK
Ay, that's the first thing that we have to do;
To free King Henry from imprisonment,
And see him seated in the regal throne. [*Exeunt.*

SCENE IV

London. The palace.

Enter QUEEN ELIZABETH *and* RIVERS.

RIVERS
Madam, what makes you in this sudden change?

QUEEN ELIZABETH
Why, brother Rivers, are you yet to learn
What late misfortune is befall'n King Edward?

RIVERS
What, loss of some pitch'd battle against Warwick?

QUEEN ELIZABETH
No, but the loss of his own royal person.

RIVERS
Then, is my sovereign slain?

QUEEN ELIZABETH
Ay, almost slain, for he is taken prisoner;
Either betray'd by falsehood of his guard,
Or by his foe surpris'd at unawares:
And, as I further have to understand,
Is new committed to the Bishop of York,
Fell Warwick's brother, and by that our foe.

RIVERS
These news, I must confess, are full of grief;
Yet, gracious madam, bear it as you may:
Warwick may lose, that now hath won the day.

QUEEN ELIZABETH
Till then, fair hope must hinder life's decay.
And I the rather wean me from despair,
For love of Edward's offspring in my womb:
This is it that makes me bridle passion,
And bear with mildness my misfortune's cross;
Ay, ay, for this I draw-in many a tear,
And stop the rising of blood-sucking sighs,
Lest with my sighs or tears I blast or drown
King Edward's fruit, true heir to th'English crown.

RIVERS
But, madam, where is Warwick, then, become?

QUEEN ELIZABETH
I am inform'd that he comes towards London,
To set the crown once more on Henry's head:
Guess thou the rest; King Edward's friends must
    down.
But, to prevent the tyrant's violence, —
For trust not him that hath once broken faith, —
I'll hence forthwith unto the sanctuary,
To save at least the heir of Edward's right:
There shall I rest secure from force and fraud.
Come, therefore, let us fly while we may fly:
If Warwick take us, we are sure to die. [*Exeunt.*

SCENE V

A park near Middleham Castle In Yorkshire.

Enter GLOSTER, HASTINGS, SIR WILLIAM
STANLEY, *and others.*

GLOSTER
Now, my Lord Hastings and Sir William Stanley,
Leave off to wonder why I drew you hither,
Into this chiefest thicket of the park.
Thus stands the case: you know our king, my brother,
Is prisoner to the bishop here, at whose hands
He hath good usage and great liberty;
And, often but attended with weak guard,
Comes hunting this way to disport himself.
I have advertis'd him by secret means,
That if about this hour he make this way,
Under the colour of his usual game,
He shall here find his friends, with horse and men,
To set him free from his captivity.

Enter KING EDWARD *and a* HUNTSMAN.

HUNTSMAN
This way, my lord; for this way lies the game.

KING EDWARD
Nay, this way, man: see where the huntsmen stand. —
Now, brother of Gloster, Lord Hastings, and the rest,
Stand you thus close, to steal the bishop's deer?

GLOSTER
Brother, the time and case requireth haste:
Your horse stands ready at the park-corner.

KING EDWARD
But whither shall we then?

HASTINGS
To Lynn, my lord; and ship from thence to Flanders.

GLOSTER
Well guess'd, believe me; for that was my meaning.

KING EDWARD
Stanley, I will requite thy forwardness.

GLOSTER
But wherefore stay we? 'tis no time to talk.

KING EDWARD
Huntsman, what say'st thou? wilt thou go along?

HUNTSMAN
Better do so than tarry and be hang'd.

GLOSTER
Come then, away; let's ha' no more ado.

KING EDWARD
Bishop, farewell: shield thee from Warwick's frown;
And pray that I may repossess the crown.   [*Exeunt.*

SCENE VI

London. The Tower.

Enter KING HENRY, CLARENCE, WARWICK,
SOMERSET, *young* RICHMOND, OXFORD,
MONTAGUE, *and* LIEUTENANT OF THE TOWER.

KING HENRY
Master lieutenant, now that God and friends
Have shaken Edward from the regal seat,
And turn'd my captive state to liberty,
My fear to hope, my sorrows unto joys, —
At our enlargement what are thy due fees?

LIEUTENANT
Subjects may challenge nothing of their sovereigns;
But if an humble prayer may prevail,
I then crave pardon of your majesty.

KING HENRY
For what, lieutenant? for well-using me?
Nay, be thou sure I'll well requite thy kindness,
For that it made my imprisonment a pleasure;
Ay, such a pleasure as incaged birds
Conceive, when, after many moody thoughts,
At last, by notes of household harmony,
They quite forget their loss of liberty. —
But, Warwick, after God, thou sett'st me free,
And chiefly therefore I thank God and thee;
He was the author, thou the instrument.
Therefore, that I may conquer fortune's spite,
By living low, where fortune cannot hurt me,
And that the people of this blessed land
May not be punish'd with my thwarting stars, —
Warwick, although my head still wear the crown,
I here resign my government to thee,
For thou art fortunate in all thy deeds.

WARWICK
Your Grace hath still been fam'd for virtuous;
And now may seem as wise as virtuous,
By spying and avoiding fortune's malice,
For few men rightly temper with the stars:
Yet in this one thing let me blame your Grace,
For choosing me when Clarence is in place.

CLARENCE
No, Warwick, thou art worthy of the sway,
To whom the heavens, in thy nativity,
Adjudg'd an olive-branch and laurel-crown,
As likely to be blest in peace and war;
And therefore I yield thee my free consent.

WARWICK
And I choose Clarence only for Protector.

KING HENRY
Warwick and Clarence, give me both your hands:
Now join your hands, and with your hands your hearts,
That no dissension hinder government:
I make you both Protectors of this land;
While I myself will lead a private life,
And in devotion spend my latter days,
To sin's rebuke and my Creator's praise.

WARWICK
What answers Clarence to his sovereign's will?

CLARENCE
That he consents, if Warwick yield consent;
For on thy fortune I repose myself.

WARWICK
Why, then, though loth, yet must I be content:
We'll yoke together, like a double shadow
To Henry's body, and supply his place;
I mean, in bearing weight of government,
While he enjoys the honour and his ease.
And, Clarence, now then it is more than needful
Forthwith that Edward be pronounc'd a traitor,
And all his lands and goods be confiscate.

CLARENCE
What else? and that succession be determin'd.

WARWICK
Ay, there'n Clarence shall not want his part.

KING HENRY
But, with the first of all your chief affairs,
Let me entreat — for I command no more —

That Margaret your queen, and my son Edward,
Be sent for, to return from France with speed;
For, till I see them here, by doubtful fear
My joy of liberty is half eclipsed.

CLARENCE
It shall be done, my sovereign, with all speed.

KING HENRY
My Lord of Somerset, what youth is that,
Of whom you seem to have so tender care?

SOMERSET
My liege, it is young Henry, Earl of Richmond.

KING HENRY
Come hither, England's hope. — If secret powers
[*Lays his hand on his head.*
Suggest but truth to my divining thoughts,
This pretty lad will prove our country's bliss.
His looks are full of peaceful majesty;
His head by nature fram'd to wear a crown,
His hand to wield a sceptre; and himself
Likely in time to bless a regal throne.
Make much of him, my lords, for this is he
Must help you more than you are hurt by me.

Enter a POST.

WARWICK
What news, my friend?

POST
That Edward is escaped from your brother,
And fled, as he hears since, to Burgundy.

WARWICK
Unsavoury news! but how made he escape?

POST
He was convey'd by Richard Duke of Gloster,
And the Lord Hastings, who attended him
In secret ambush on the forest-side,
And from the bishop's huntsmen rescued him;
For hunting was his daily exercise.

WARWICK
My brother was too careless of his charge. —
But let us hence, my sovereign, to provide
A salve for any sore that may betide.
[*Exeunt all but* SOMERSET, RICHMOND, *and*
OXFORD.

SOMERSET
My lord, I like not of this flight of Edward's;
For doubtless Burgundy will yield him help,
And we shall have more wars before 'tbe long.
As Henry's late presaging prophecy
Did glad my heart with hope of this young Richmond,
So doth my heart misgive me, in these conflicts
What may befall him, to his harm and ours:
Therefore, Lord Oxford, to prevent the worst,
Forthwith we'll send him hence to Brittany,
Till storms be past of civil enmity.

OXFORD
Ay, for if Edward repossess the crown,
'Tis like that Richmond with the rest shall down.

SOMERSET
It shall be so; he shall to Brittany.
Come, therefore, let's about it speedily.   [*Exeunt.*

SCENE VII

Before York.

Flourish. Enter KING EDWARD, GLOSTER,
HASTINGS, *and* SOLDIERS.

KING EDWARD
Now, brother Richard, Lord Hastings, and the rest,
Yet thus far fortune maketh us amends,
And says, that once more I shall interchange
My waned state for Henry's regal crown.
Well have we pass'd and now repass'd the seas,
And brought desired help from Burgundy:
What, then, remains, we being thus arriv'd
From Ravenspur haven before the gates of York,
But that we enter, as into our dukedom?

GLOSTER
The gates made fast! — Brother, I like not this;
For many men that stumble at the threshold
Are well foretold that danger lurks within.

KING EDWARD
Tush, man, abodements must not now affright us:
By fair or foul means we must enter in,
For hither will our friends repair to us.

HASTINGS
My liege, I'll knock once more to summon them.

Enter, on the walls, the MAYOR OF YORK
and his BRETHREN.

MAYOR OF YORK
My lords, we were forewarned of your coming,
And shut the gates for safety of ourselves;
For now we owe allegiance unto Henry.

KING EDWARD
But, master mayor, if Henry be your king,
Yet Edward at the least is Duke of York.

MAYOR OF YORK
True, my good lord; I know you for no less.

KING EDWARD
Why, and I challenge nothing but my dukedom,
As being well content with that alone.

GLOSTER [*aside*].
But when the fox hath once got in his nose,
He'll soon find means to make the body follow.

HASTINGS
Why, master mayor, why stand you in a doubt?
Open the gates; we are King Henry's friends.

MAYOR OF YORK
Ay, say you so? the gates shall then be open'd.
[*They descend.*

GLOSTER
A wise stout captain, and soon persuaded!

HASTINGS
The good old man would fain that all were well,
So 'twere not long of him; but being enter'd,
I doubt not, I, but we shall soon persuade
Both him and all his brothers unto reason.

Enter the MAYOR *and two* ALDERMEN.

KING EDWARD
So, master mayor: these gates must not be shut
But in the night or in the time of war.
What! fear not, man, but yield me up the keys;
[*Takes his keys.*
For Edward will defend the town and thee,
And all those friends that deign to follow me.

March. Enter MONTGOMERY *with drum and*
SOLDIERS.

GLOSTER
Brother, this is Sir John Montgomery,
Our trusty friend, unless I be deceived.

KING EDWARD
Welcome, Sir John! But why come you in arms?

MONTGOMERY
To help King Edward in his time of storm,
As every loyal subject ought to do.

KING EDWARD
Thanks, good Montgomery: but we now forget
Our title to the crown, and only claim
Our dukedom till God please to send the rest.

MONTGOMERY
Then fare you well, for I will hence again:
I came to serve a king, and not a duke.
Drummer, strike up, and let us march away.
[*The drum begins to march.*

KING EDWARD
Nay, stay, Sir John, awhile; and we'll debate
By what safe means the crown may be recover'd.

MONTGOMERY
What talk you of debating? in few words, —
If you'll not here proclaim yourself our king,
I'll leave you to your fortune, and be gone
To keep them back that come to succour you:
Why shall we fight, if you pretend no title?

GLOSTER
Why, brother, wherefore stand you on nice points?

KING EDWARD
When we grow stronger, then we'll make our claim:
Till then, 'tis wisdom to conceal our meaning.

HASTINGS
Away with scrupulous wit! now arms must rule.

GLOSTER
And fearless minds climb soonest unto crowns.
Brother, we will proclaim you out of hand;
The bruit thereof will bring you many friends.

KING EDWARD
Then be it as you will: for 'tis my right,
And Henry but usurps the diadem.

MONTGOMERY
Ay, now my sovereign speaketh like himself;
And now will I be Edward's champion.

HASTINGS
Sound trumpet; Edward shall be here proclaim'd: —
Come, fellow-soldier, make thou proclamation.
[*Flourish.*

SOLDIER
Edward the Fourth, by the grace of God, king of
England and France, and lord of Ireland, etc.
MONTGOMERY
And whosoe'er gainsays King Edward's right,
By this I challenge him to single fight.
[*Throws down his gauntlet.*
ALL
Long live Edward the Fourth!
KING EDWARD
Thanks, brave Montgomery; — and thanks unto you
all:
If fortune serve me, I'll requite this kindness.
Now, for this night, let's harbour here in York;
And when the morning sun shall raise his car
Above the border of this horizon,
We'll forward towards Warwick and his mates;
For well I wot that Henry is no soldier. —
Ah, forward Clarence! how evil it beseems thee
To flatter Henry, and forsake thy brother!
Yet, as we may, we'll meet both thee and Warwick. —
Come on, brave soldiers: doubt not of the day;
And that once gotten, doubt not of large pay. [*Exeunt.*

SCENE VIII

London. The palace.

Flourish. Enter KING HENRY, WARWICK,
MONTAGUE, CLARENCE, EXETER, *and* OXFORD.

WARWICK
What counsel, lords? Edward from Belgia,
With hasty Germans and blunt Hollanders,
Hath pass'd in safety through the narrow seas,
And with his troops doth march amain to London;
And many giddy people flock to him.
OXFORD
Let's levy men, and beat him back again.
CLARENCE
A little fire is quickly trodden out;
Which, being suffer'd, rivers cannot quench.
WARWICK
In Warwickshire I have true-hearted friends,
Not mutinous in peace, yet bold in war;
Those will I muster up; and thou, son Clarence,
Shalt stir in Suffolk, Norfolk, and in Kent,
The knights and gentlemen to come with thee:
Thou, brother Montague, in Buckingham,
Northampton, and in Leicestershire, shalt find
Men well inclin'd to hear what thou command'st:
And thou, brave Oxford, wondrous well beloved,
In Oxfordshire shalt muster up thy friends.
My sovereign, with the loving citizens, —
Like to his island girt in with the ocean,
Or modest Dian circled with her nymphs, —
Shall rest in London till we come to him.
Fair lords, take leave, and stand not to reply.
Farewell, my sovereign.
KING HENRY
Farewell, my Hector, and my Troy's true hope.
CLARENCE
In sign of truth, I kiss your highness' hand.
KING HENRY
Well-minded Clarence, be thou fortunate!
MONTAGUE
Comfort, my lord; and so I take my leave.
OXFORD [*kissing* HENRY'S *hand*].
And thus I seal my truth, and bid adieu.
KING HENRY
Sweet Oxford, and my loving Montague,
And all at once, once more a happy farewell.
WARWICK
Farewell, sweet lords: let's meet at Coventry.
[*Exeunt all but* KING HENRY *and* EXETER.
KING HENRY
Here at the palace will I rest awhile.
Cousin of Exeter, what thinks your lordship?
Methinks the power that Edward hath in field
Should not be able to encounter mine.
EXETER
The doubt is that he will seduce the rest.
KING HENRY
That's not my fear; my meed hath got me fame:
I have not stopp'd mine ears to their demands,
Nor posted off their suits with slow delays;
My pity hath been balm to heal their wounds,
My mildness hath allay'd their swelling griefs,
My mercy dried their water-flowing tears;
I have not been desirous of their wealth,
Nor much oppress'd them with great subsidies,
Nor forward of revenge, though they much err'd:

Then why should they love Edward more than me?
No, Exeter, these graces challenge grace:
And, when the lion fawns upon the lamb,
The lamb will never cease to follow him.
[*Shout within. 'A York! A York!'*
EXETER
Hark, hark, my lord! what shouts are these?
Enter KING EDWARD, GLOSTER, *and* SOLDIERS.
KING EDWARD
Seize on the shame-fac'd Henry, bear him hence;
And once again proclaim us king of England. —
You are the fount that makes small brooks to flow:
Now stops thy spring; my sea shall suck them dry,
And swell so much the higher by their ebb. —
Hence with him to the Tower; let him not speak.
[*Exeunt some with* KING HENRY.
And, lords, towards Coventry bend we our course,
Where peremptory Warwick now remains:
The sun shines hot; and, if we use delay,
Cold-biting winter mars our hop'd-for hay.
GLOSTER
Away betimes, before his forces join,
And take the great-grown traitor unawares:
Brave warriors, march amain towards Coventry.
[*Exeunt.*

ACT V

SCENE I

Coventry.

Enter WARWICK, *the* MAYOR OF COVENTRY, *two*
MESSENGERS, *and others upon the walls.*

WARWICK
Where is the post that came from valiant Oxford? —
How far hence is thy lord, mine honest fellow?
FIRST MESSENGER
By this at Dunsmore, marching hitherward.
WARWICK
How far off is our brother Montague? —
Where is the post that came from Montague?
SECOND MESSENGER
By this at Daintry, with a puissant troop.
Enter SIR JOHN SOMERVILLE.
WARWICK
Say, Somerville, what says my loving son?
And, by thy guess, how nigh is Clarence now?
SOMERVILLE
At Southam I did leave him with his forces,
And do expect him here some two hours hence.
[*Drum heard.*
WARWICK
Then Clarence is at hand; I hear his drum.
SOMERVILLE
It is not his, my lord; here Southam lies:
The drum your honour hears marcheth from Warwick.
WARWICK
Who should that be? belike, unlook'd-for friends.
SOMERVILLE
They are at hand, and you shall quickly know.
[*Enters the city.*
March. Flourish. Enter KING EDWARD, GLOSTER,
and SOLDIERS.
KING EDWARD
Go, trumpet, to the walls, and sound a parle.
GLOSTER
See how the surly Warwick mans the wall!
WARWICK
O unbid spite! is sportful Edward come?
Where slept our scouts, or how are they seduced,
That we could hear no news of his repair?
KING EDWARD
Now, Warwick, wilt thou ope the city-gates,
Speak gentle words, and humbly bend thy knee,
Call Edward king, and at his hands beg mercy?
And he shall pardon thee these outrages.
WARWICK
Nay, rather, wilt thou draw thy forces hence,
Confess who set thee up and pluck'd thee down,
Call Warwick patron, and be penitent?
And thou shalt still remain the Duke of York.
GLOSTER
I thought at least he would have said the king;
Or did he make the jest against his will?
WARWICK
Is not a dukedom, sir, a goodly gift?

GLOSTER
Ay, by my faith, for a poor earl to give:
I'll do thee service for so good a gift.
WARWICK
'Twas I that gave the kingdom to thy brother.
KING EDWARD
Why, then, 'tis mine, if but by Warwick's gift.
WARWICK
Thou art no Atlas for so great a weight:
And, weakling, Warwick takes his gift again;
And Henry is my king, Warwick his subject.
KING EDWARD
But Warwick's king is Edward's prisoner:
And, gallant Warwick, do but answer this, —
What is the body when the head is off?
GLOSTER
Alas, that Warwick had no more forecast,
But, whiles he thought to steal the single ten,
The king was slily finger'd from the deck!
You left poor Henry at the bishop's palace,
And, ten to one, you'll meet him in the Tower.
KING EDWARD
'Tis even so; yet you are Warwick still.
GLOSTER
Come, Warwick, take the time; kneel down, kneel
down:
Nay, when? strike now, or else the iron cools.
WARWICK
I had rather chop this hand off at a blow,
And with the other fling it at thy face,
Than bear so low a sail, to strike to thee.
KING EDWARD
Sail how thou canst, have wind and tide thy friend,
This hand, fast wound about thy coal-black hair,
Shall, whiles thy head is warm and new cut off,
Write in the dust this sentence with thy blood, —
'Wind-changing Warwick now can change no more.'
Enter OXFORD, *with drum and colours.*
WARWICK
O cheerful colours! see where Oxford comes!
OXFORD
Oxford, Oxford, for Lancaster!
[*He and his* FORCES *enter the city.*
GLOSTER
The gates are open, let us enter too.
KING EDWARD
So other foes may set upon our backs.
Stand we in good array; for they no doubt
Will issue out again and bid us battle:
If not, the city being but of small defence,
We'll quickly rouse the traitors in the same.
WARWICK
O, welcome, Oxford! for we want thy help.
Enter MONTAGUE, *with drum and colours.*
MONTAGUE
Montague, Montague, for Lancaster!
[*He and his* FORCES *enter the city.*
GLOSTER
Thou and thy brother both shall buy this treason
Even with the dearest blood your bodies bear.
KING EDWARD
The harder match'd, the greater victory:
My mind presageth happy gain and conquest.
Enter SOMERSET, *with drum and colours.*
SOMERSET
Somerset, Somerset, for Lancaster!
[*He and his* FORCES *enter the city.*
GLOSTER
Two of thy name, both Dukes of Somerset,
Have sold their lives unto the house of York;
And thou shalt be the third, if this sword hold.
Enter CLARENCE, *with drum and colours.*
WARWICK
And lo, where George of Clarence sweeps along,
Of force enough to bid his brother battle;
With whom an upright zeal to right prevails
More than the nature of a brother's love! —
Come, Clarence, come; thou wilt, if Warwick call.
[*Sound a parley; and* RICHARD *and* CLARENCE
whisper together, and then CLARENCE *takes his red rose
out of his hat and throws it at* WARWICK.
CLARENCE
Father of Warwick, know you what this means?
Look here, I throw my infamy at thee:
I will not ruinate my father's house,
Who gave his blood to lime the stones together,
And set up Lancaster. Why, trow'st thou, Warwick,

That Clarence is so harsh, so blunt, unnatural,
To bend the fatal instruments of war
Against his brother and his lawful king?
Perhaps thou wilt object my holy oath:
To keep that oath were more impiety
Than Jephtha's, when he sacrific'd his daughter.
I am so sorry for my trespass made,
That, to deserve well at my brother's hands,
I here proclaim myself thy mortal foe;
With resolution, wheresoe'er I meet thee, —
As I will meet thee, if thou stir abroad, —
To plague thee for thy foul misleading me.
And so, proud-hearted Warwick, I defy thee,
And to my brother turn my blushing cheeks. —
Pardon me, Edward, I will make amends;
And, Richard, do not frown upon my faults,
For I will henceforth be no more unconstant.

KING EDWARD
Now welcome more and ten times more beloved
Than if thou never hadst deserv'd our hate.

GLOSTER
Welcome, good Clarence; this is brother-like.

WARWICK
O passing traitor, perjured and unjust!

KING EDWARD
What, Warwick, wilt thou leave the town, and fight?
Or shall we beat the stones about thine ears?

WARWICK
Alas, I am not coop'd here for defence!
I will away towards Barnet presently,
And bid thee battle, Edward, if thou darest.

KING EDWARD
Yes, Warwick, Edward dares, and leads the way. —
Lords, to the field; Saint George and victory!

[*Exeunt* KING EDWARD *and his* COMPANY. *March.*
WARWICK *and his* COMPANY *follow.*

SCENE II

A field of battle near Barnet.

Alarum and excursions. Enter KING EDWARD,
bringing forth WARWICK, *wounded.*

KING EDWARD
So, lie thou there: die thou, and die our fear;
For Warwick was a bug that fear'd us all. —
Now, Montague, sit fast; I seek for thee,
That Warwick's bones may keep thine company. [*Exit.*

WARWICK
Ah, who is nigh? come to me, friend or foe,
And tell me who is victor, York or Warwick?
Why ask I that? my mangled body shows,
My blood, my want of strength, my sick heart shows,
That I must yield my body to the earth,
And, by my fall, the conquest to my foe.
Thus yields the cedar to the axe's edge,
Whose arms gave shelter to the princely eagle,
Under whose shade the ramping lion slept,
Whose top-branch overpeer'd Jove's spreading tree,
And kept low shrubs from winter's powerful wind.
These eyes, that now are dimm'd with death's black
  veil,
Have been as piercing as the mid-day sun,
To search the secret treasons of the world:
The wrinkles in my brows, now fill'd with blood,
Were liken'd oft to kingly sepulchres;
For who liv'd king, but I could dig his grave?
And who durst smile when Warwick bent his brow?
Lo, now my glory smear'd in dust and blood!
My parks, my walks, my manors that I had,
Even now forsake me; and of all my lands
Is nothing left me but my body's length!
Why, what is pomp, rule, reign, but earth and dust?
And, live we how we can, yet die we must.

Enter OXFORD *and* SOMERSET.

SOMERSET
Ah, Warwick, Warwick! wert thou as we are,
We might recover all our loss again:
The queen from France hath brought a puissant
  power;
Even now we heard the news: ah, couldst thou fly!

WARWICK
Why, then, I would not fly.— Ah, Montague,
If thou be there, sweet brother, take my hand,
And with thy lips keep in my soul awhile!
Thou lov'st me not; for, brother, if thou didst,
Thy tears would wash this cold congealed blood,
That glues my lips and will not let me speak.
Come quickly, Montague, or I am dead.

SOMERSET
Ah, Warwick! Montague hath breath'd his last;

And to the latest gasp cried out for Warwick,
And said, 'Commend me to my valiant brother.'
And more he would have said; and more he spoke,
Which sounded like a clamour in a vault,
That mought not be distinguish'd; but at last
I well might hear, deliver'd with a groan,
'O, farewell, Warwick!'

WARWICK
Sweet rest his soul! — Fly, lords, and save yourselves.
For Warwick bids you all farewell, to meet in heaven.
[*Dies.*

OXFORD
Away, away, to meet the queen's great power!
[*Here they bear away his body. Exeunt.*

SCENE III

Another part of the field.

Flourish. Enter KING EDWARD *in triumph; with*
GLOSTER, CLARENCE, *and the rest.*

KING EDWARD
Thus far our fortune keeps an upward course,
And we are grac'd with wreaths of victory.
But, in the midst of this bright-shining day,
I spy a black, suspicious, threatening cloud,
That will encounter with our glorious sun
Ere he attain his easeful western bed:
I mean, my lords, those powers that the queen
Hath rais'd in Gallia have arriv'd our coast,
And, as we hear, march on to fight with us.

CLARENCE
A little gale will soon disperse that cloud,
And blow it to the source from whence it came:
The very beams will dry those vapours up;
For every cloud engenders not a storm.

GLOSTER
The queen is valued thirty thousand strong,
And Somerset, with Oxford, fled to her:
If she have time to breathe, be well assured
Her faction will be full as strong as ours.

KING EDWARD
We are advertis'd by our loving friends
That they do hold their course toward Tewksbury:
We, having now the best at Barnet field,
Will thither straight, for willingness rids way;
And, as we march, our strength will be augmented
In every county as we go along. —
Strike up the drum; cry, 'Courage!' and away. [*Exeunt.*

SCENE IV

Plains near Tewksbury.

Flourish. March. Enter QUEEN MARGARET, PRINCE
EDWARD, SOMERSET, OXFORD, *and* SOLDIERS.

QUEEN MARGARET
Great lords, wise men ne'er sit and wail their loss,
But cheerly seek how to redress their harms.
What though the mast be now blown overboard,
The cable broke, the holding-anchor lost,
And half our sailors swallow'd in the flood?
Yet lives our pilot still: is't meet that he
Should leave the helm and, like a fearful lad,
With tearful eyes add water to the sea,
And give more strength to that which hath too much;
Whiles, in his moan, the ship splits on the rock,
Which industry and courage might have saved?
Ah, what a shame! ah, what a fault were this!
Say Warwick was our anchor; what of that?
And Montague our topmost; what of him?
Our slaughter'd friends the tackles; what of these?
Why, is not Oxford here another anchor?
And Somerset another goodly mast?
The friends of France our shrouds and tacklings?
And, though unskilful, why not Ned and I
For once allow'd the skilful pilot's charge?
We will not from the helm to sit and weep;
But keep our course, though the rough wind say no,
From shelves and rocks that threaten us with wrack.
As good to chide the waves as speak them fair.
And what is Edward but a ruthless sea?
What Clarence but a quicksand of deceit?
And Richard but a ragged fatal rock?
All these the enemies to our poor bark.
Say you can swim, — alas, 'tis but awhile!
Tread on the sand, — why, there you quickly sink;
Bestride the rock, — the tide will wash you off,
Or else you famish; that's a threefold death.
This speak I, lords, to let you understand,
If case some one of you would fly from us,
That there's no hop'd-for mercy with the brothers,
More than with ruthless waves, with sands, and rocks.

Why, courage, then! what cannot be avoided
'Twere childish weakness to lament or fear.

PRINCE EDWARD
Methinks a woman of this valiant spirit
Should, if a coward heard her speak these words,
Infuse his breast with magnanimity,
And make him naked foil a man-at-arms.
I speak not this as doubting any here;
For did I but suspect a fearful man,
He should have leave to go away betimes;
Lest in our need he might infect another,
And make him of like spirit to himself.
If any such be here, — as God forbid! —
Let him depart before we need his help.

OXFORD
Women and children of so high a courage,
And warriors faint! why, 'twere perpetual shame. —
O brave young prince! thy famous grandfather
Doth live again in thee: long mayst thou live
To bear his image and renew his glories!

SOMERSET
And he that will not fight for such a hope,
Go home to bed, and, like the owl by day,
If he arise, be mock'd and wonder'd at.

QUEEN MARGARET
Thanks, gentle Somerset; — sweet Oxford, thanks.

PRINCE EDWARD
And take his thanks that yet hath nothing else.

Enter a MESSENGER.

MESSENGER
Prepare you, lords; for Edward is at hand,
Ready to fight; therefore be resolute.

OXFORD
I thought no less: it is his policy
To haste thus fast, to find us unprovided.

SOMERSET
But he's deceiv'd; we are in readiness.

QUEEN MARGARET
This cheers my heart, to see your forwardness.

OXFORD
Here pitch our battle; hence we will not budge.

Flourish and march. Enter KING EDWARD,
GLOSTER, CLARENCE, *and* FORCES.

KING EDWARD
Brave followers, yonder stands the thorny wood,
Which, by the heavens' assistance and your strength,
Must by the roots be hewn up yet ere night.
I need not add more fuel to your fire,
For well I wot ye blaze to burn them out:
Give signal to the fight, and to it, lords.

QUEEN MARGARET
Lords, knights, and gentlemen, what I should say
My tears gainsay; for every word I speak,
Ye see, I drink the water of mine eyes.
Therefore, no more but this: — Henry, your sovereign,
Is prisoner to the foe; his state usurp'd,
His realm a slaughter-house, his subjects slain,
His statutes cancell'd, and his treasure spent;
And yonder is the wolf that makes this spoil.
You fight in justice: then, in God's name, lords,
Be valiant, and give signal to the fight.
[*Alarum. Retreat. Excursions. Exeunt.*

SCENE V

Another part of the field.

Flourish. Enter KING EDWARD, GLOSTER,
CLARENCE, *and* SOLDIERS; *with* QUEEN
MARGARET, OXFORD, *and* SOMERSET, *prisoners.*

KING EDWARD
Lo, here a period of tumultuous broils.
Away with Oxford to Hames Castle straight:
For Somerset, off with his guilty head.
Go, bear them hence; I will not hear them speak.

OXFORD
For my part, I'll not trouble thee with words.

SOMERSET
Nor I, but stoop with patience to my fortune.
[*Exeunt* OXFORD *and* SOMERSET, *guarded.*

QUEEN MARGARET
So part we sadly in this troublous world,
To meet with joy in sweet Jerusalem.

KING EDWARD
Is proclamation made, that who finds Edward
Shall have a high reward, and he his life?

GLOSTER
It is: and lo, where youthful Edward comes!

Enter SOLDIERS, *with* PRINCE EDWARD.

KING EDWARD
Bring forth the gallant, let us hear him speak.
What! can so young a thorn begin to prick? —
Edward, what satisfaction canst thou make
For bearing arms, for stirring up my subjects,
And all the trouble thou hast turn'd me to?

PRINCE EDWARD
Speak like a subject, proud ambitious York!
Suppose that I am now my father's mouth;
Resign thy chair, and where I stand kneel thou,
Whilst I propose the selfsame words to thee,
Which, traitor, thou wouldst have me answer to.

QUEEN MARGARET
Ah, that thy father had been so resolv'd!

GLOSTER
That you might still have worn the petticoat,
And ne'er have stol'n the breech from Lancaster.

PRINCE EDWARD
Let Aesop fable in a winter's night;
His currish riddles sort not with this place.

GLOSTER
By heaven, brat, I'll plague ye for that word.

QUEEN MARGARET
Ay, thou wast born to be a plague to men.

GLOSTER
For God's sake, take away this captive scold.

PRINCE EDWARD
Nay, take away this scolding crook-back rather.

KING EDWARD
Peace, wilful boy, or I will charm your tongue.

CLARENCE
Untutor'd lad, thou art too malapert.

PRINCE EDWARD
I know my duty; you are all undutiful:
Lascivious Edward, — and thou, perjur'd George, —
And thou, mis-shapen Dick, — I tell ye all
I am your better, traitors as ye are; —
And thou usurp'st my father's right and mine.

KING EDWARD
Take that, thou likeness of this railer here. [*Stabs him.*

GLOSTER
Sprawl'st thou? take that, to end thy agony. [*Stabs him.*

CLARENCE
And there's for twitting me with perjury. [*Stabs him.*

QUEEN MARGARET
O, kill me too!

GLOSTER
Marry, and shall. [*Offers to kill her.*

KING EDWARD
Hold, Richard, hold; for we have done too much.

GLOSTER
Why should she live, to fill the world with words?

KING EDWARD
What, doth she swoon? use means for her recovery.

GLOSTER
Clarence, excuse me to the king my brother;
I'll hence to London on a serious matter:
Ere ye come there, be sure to hear some news.

CLARENCE
What? what?

GLOSTER
The Tower, man, the Tower! — I'll root 'em out. [*Exit.*

QUEEN MARGARET
O Ned, sweet Ned! speak to thy mother, boy!
Canst thou not speak? O traitors! murderers!
They that stabb'd Cæsar shed no blood at all,
Did not offend, nor were not worthy blame,
If this foul deed were by to equal it:
He was a man; this, in respect, a child, —
And men ne'er spend their fury on a child.
What's worse than murderer, that I may name it?
No, no, my heart will burst, and if I speak:
And I will speak, that so my heart may burst.
Butchers and villains! bloody cannibals!
How sweet a plant have you untimely cropp'd!
You have no children, butchers! if you had,
The thought of them would have stirr'd up remorse:
But if you ever chance to have a child,
Look in his youth to have him so cut off
As, deathsmen, you have rid this sweet young prince!

KING EDWARD
Away with her; go, bear her hence perforce.

QUEEN MARGARET
Nay, never bear me hence, dispatch me here;
Here sheathe thy sword, I'll pardon thee my death:
What, wilt thou not? — then, Clarence, do it thou.

CLARENCE
By heaven, I will not do thee so much ease.

QUEEN MARGARET
Good Clarence, do; sweet Clarence, do thou do it.

CLARENCE
Didst thou not hear me swear I would not do it?

QUEEN MARGARET
Ay, but thou usest to forswear thyself:
'Twas sin before, but now 'tis charity.
What, wilt thou not? — Where is that devil's butcher,
Hard-favour'd Richard? — Richard, where art thou?
Thou art not here: murder is thy alms deed;
Petitioners for blood thou ne'er put'st back.

KING EDWARD
Away, I say; I charge ye, bear her hence.

QUEEN MARGARET
So come to you and yours, as to this prince!
[*Exit, led out forcibly.*

KING EDWARD
Where's Richard gone?

CLARENCE
To London, all in post; and, as I guess,
To make a bloody supper in the Tower.

KING EDWARD
He's sudden, if a thing comes in his head.
Now march we hence: discharge the common sort
With pay and thanks, and let's away to London,
And see our gentle queen how well she fares, —
By this, I hope, she hath a son for me. [*Exeunt.*

SCENE VI

London. The Tower.

Enter KING HENRY *and* GLOSTER, *with the*
LIEUTENANT, *on the walls.*

GLOSTER
Good day, my lord. What, at your book so hard?

KING HENRY
Ay, my good lord: — my lord, I should say rather;
'Tis sin to flatter; 'good' was little better:
'Good Gloster' and 'good devil' were alike,
And both preposterous; therefore, not 'good lord.'

GLOSTER
Sirrah, leave us to ourselves: we must confer.
[*Exit* LIEUTENANT.

KING HENRY
So flies the reckless shepherd from the wolf;
So first the harmless sheep doth yield his fleece,
And next his throat unto the butcher's knife. —
What scene of death hath Roscius now to act?

GLOSTER
Suspicion always haunts the guilty mind;
The thief doth fear each bush an officer.

KING HENRY
The bird that hath been limed in a bush,
With trembling wings misdoubteth every bush;
And I, the hapless male to one sweet bird,
Have now the fatal object in my eye
Where my poor young was lim'd, was caught, and
  kill'd.

GLOSTER
Why, what a peevish fool was that of Crete,
That taught his son the office of a fowl!
And yet, for all his wings the fool was drown'd.

KING HENRY
I, Dædalus; my poor boy, Icarus;
Thy father, Minos, that denied our course;
The sun, that sear'd the wings of my sweet boy,
Thy brother Edward; and thyself, the sea,
Whose envious gulf did swallow up his life.
Ah, kill me with thy weapon, not with words!
My breast can better brook thy dagger's point
Than can my ears that tragic history.
But wherefore dost thou come? is't for my life?

GLOSTER
Think'st thou I am an executioner?

KING HENRY
A persecutor, I am sure, thou art:
If murdering innocents be executing,
Why, then thou art an executioner.

GLOSTER
Thy son I kill'd for his presumption.

KING HENRY
Hadst thou been kill'd when first thou didst presume,
Thou hadst not lived to kill a son of mine.
And thus I prophesy, — that many a thousand,
Which now mistrust no parcel of my fear,
And many an old man's sigh and many a widow's,
And many an orphan's water-standing eye. —

Men for their sons', wives for their husbands' fate,
And orphans for their parents' timeless death, —
Shall rue the hour that ever thou wast born.
The owl shriek'd at thy birth, — an evil sign;
The night-crow cried, aboding luckless time;
Dogs howl'd, and hideous tempest shook down trees;
The raven rook'd her on the chimney's top,
And chattering pies in dismal discords sung.
Thy mother felt more than a mother's pain,
And yet brought forth less than a mother's hope, —
An indigested and deformed lump,
Not like the fruit of such a goodly tree.
Teeth hadst thou in thy head when thou wast born,
To signify thou cam'st to bite the world:
And, if the rest be true which I have heard,
Thou cam'st —

GLOSTER
I'll hear no more: die, prophet in thy speech:
[*Stabs him.*
For this, amongst the rest, was I ordain'd.

KING HENRY
Ay, and for much more slaughter after this.
O, God forgive my sins, and pardon thee! [*Dies.*

GLOSTER
What, will the aspiring blood of Lancaster
Sink in the ground? I thought it would have mounted.
See how my sword weeps for the poor king's death!
O, may such purple tears be alway shed
From those that wish the downfall of our house!
If any spark of life be yet remaining,
Down, down to hell; and say I sent thee thither,
[*Stabs him again.*
I, that have neither pity, love, nor fear.
Indeed, 'tis true that Henry told me of;
For I have often heard my mother say
I came into the world with my legs forward:
Had I not reason, think ye, to make haste,
And seek their ruin that usurp'd our right?
The midwife wonder'd; and the women cried,
'O, Jesus bless us, he is born with teeth!'
And so I was; which plainly signified
That I should snarl, and bite, and play the dog.
Then, since the heavens have shap'd my body so,
Let hell make crook'd my mind to answer it.
I have no brother, I am like no brother;
And this word 'love,' which greybeards call divine,
Be resident in men like one another,
And not in me: I am myself alone. —
Clarence, beware; thou keep'st me from the light:
But I will sort a pitchy day for thee;
For I will buzz abroad such prophecies,
That Edward shall be fearful of his life;
And then, to purge his fear, I'll be thy death.
King Henry and the prince his son are gone:
Clarence, thy turn is next, and then the rest;
Counting myself but bad till I be best. —
I'll throw thy body in another room,
And triumph, Henry, in thy day of doom.
[*Exit with the body.*

SCENE VII

London. The palace.

Flourish. Enter KING EDWARD, QUEEN
ELIZABETH, GLOSTER, CLARENCE, HASTINGS, *a*
NURSE *with the young* PRINCE, *and* ATTENDANTS.

KING EDWARD
Once more we sit in England's royal throne,
Re-purchas'd with the blood of enemies.
What valiant foemen, like to autumn's corn,
Have we mow'd down in tops of all their pride!
Three Dukes of Somerset, threefold renown'd
For hardy and undoubted champions;
Two Cliffords, as the father and the son;
And two Northumberlands, — two braver men
Ne'er spurr'd their coursers at the trumpet's sound;
With them, the two brave bears, Warwick and
  Montague,
That in their chains fetter'd the kingly lion,
And made the forest tremble when they roar'd.
Thus have we swept suspicion from our seat,
And made our footstool of security. —
Come hither, Bess, and let me kiss my boy.
Young Ned, for thee, thine uncles and myself
Have in our armours watch'd the winter's night;
Went all afoot in summer's scalding heat,
That thou mightst repossess the crown in peace:
And of our labours thou shalt reap the gain.

GLOSTER [*aside*].
I'll blast his harvest, if your head were laid;
For yet I am not look'd on in the world.

This shoulder was ordain'd so thick to heave;
And heave it shall some weight, or break my back: —
Work thou the way, — and thou shalt execute.

KING EDWARD
Clarence and Gloster, love my lovely queen;
And kiss your princely nephew, brothers both.

CLARENCE
The duty that I owe unto your majesty
I seal upon the lips of this sweet babe.

QUEEN ELIZABETH
Thanks, noble Clarence; worthy brother, thanks.

GLOSTER
And, that I love the tree from whence thou sprang'st,
Witness the loving kiss I give the fruit. —
[aside] To say the truth, so Judas kiss'd his Master,
And cried, 'All hail!' whenas he meant all harm.

KING EDWARD
Now am I seated as my soul delights,
Having my country's peace and brothers' loves.

CLARENCE
What will your Grace have done with Margaret?
Reignier, her father, to the king of France

Hath pawn'd the Sicils and Jerusalem,
And hither have they sent it for her ransom.

KING EDWARD
Away with her, and waft her hence to France.
And now what rests, but that we spend the time
With stately triumphs, mirthful comic shows,
Such as befits the pleasure of the court?
Sound drums and trumpets! farewell sour annoy!
For here, I hope, begins our lasting joy.   [*Exeunt.*

KING RICHARD THE THIRD

DRAMATIS PERSONAE

KING EDWARD THE FOURTH.
EDWARD, *Prince of Wales,*
  afterwards King Edward V, } *sons to the King.*
RICHARD, *Duke of York,*
GEORGE, *Duke of Clarence,*
RICHARD, *Duke of Gloster,* } *brothers to the King.*
  afterwards King Richard III,
A YOUNG SON OF CLARENCE.
HENRY, *Earl of Richmond, afterwards King Henry VII.*
CARDINAL BOURCHIER, *Archbishop of Canterbury.*
THOMAS ROTHERHAM, *Archbishop of York.*
JOHN MORTON, *Bishop of Ely.*
DUKE OF BUCKINGHAM.
DUKE OF NORFOLK.
EARL OF SURREY, *his son.*
EARL RIVERS, *brother to Elizabeth.*

MARQUESS OF DORSET *and* LORD GREY, *sons to Elizabeth.*
EARL OF OXFORD.
LORD HASTINGS.
LORD STANLEY, *call'd also Earl of Derby.*
LORD LOVEL.
SIR THOMAS VAUGHAN.
SIR RICHARD RATCLIFF.
SIR WILLIAM CATESBY.
SIR JAMES TYRREL.
SIR JAMES BLOUNT.
SIR WALTER HERBERT.
SIR ROBERT BRAKENBURY, *lieutenant of the Tower.*
CHRISTOPHER URSWICK, *a priest.* ANOTHER PRIEST.
LORD MAYOR OF LONDON. SHERIFF OF WILTSHIRE.

TRESSEL *and* BERKLEY, *attending on Lady Anne.*

ELIZABETH, *queen to King Edward IV.*
MARGARET, *widow of King Henry VI.*
DUCHESS OF YORK, *mother to King Edward IV, Clarence, and Gloster.*
LADY ANNE, *widow of Edward, Prince of Wales, son to King Henry VI; afterwards married to Richard, Duke of Gloster.*
A YOUNG DAUGHTER OF CLARENCE (MARGARET PLANTAGENET).

LORDS *and other* ATTENDANTS; *a* PURSUIVANT, SCRIVENER, CITIZENS, MURDERERS, MESSENGERS, SOLDIERS, etc.

SCENE — *England.*

ACT I

SCENE I

London. A street.

Enter RICHARD, DUKE OF GLOSTER, *solus.*

GLOSTER
Now is the winter of our discontent
Made glorious summer by this sun of York;
And all the clouds that lour'd upon our house
In the deep bosom of the ocean buried.
Now are our brows bound with victorious wreaths;
Our bruised arms hung up for monuments;
Our stern alarums chang'd to merry meetings,
Our dreadful marches to delightful measures.
Grim-visag'd war hath smooth'd his wrinkled front;
And now — instead of mounting barbed steeds
To fright the souls of fearful adversaries —
He capers nimbly in a lady's chamber
To the lascivious pleasing of a lute.
But I, that am not shap'd for sportive tricks,
Nor made to court an amorous looking-glass;
I, that am rudely stamp'd, and want love's majesty
To strut before a wanton ambling nymph;
I, that am curtail'd of this fair proportion,
Cheated of feature by dissembling nature,
Deform'd, unfinish'd, sent before my time
Into this breathing world, scarce half made up,
And that so lamely and unfashionable
That dogs bark at me as I halt by them; —
Why, I, in this weak piping time of peace,
Have no delight to pass away the time,
Unless to spy my shadow in the sun,
And descant on mine own deformity:
And therefore, since I cannot prove a lover,
To entertain these fair well-spoken days,
I am determined to prove a villain,
And hate the idle pleasures of these days.
Plots have I laid, inductions dangerous,
By drunken prophecies, libels, and dreams,
To set my brother Clarence and the king
In deadly hate the one against the other:
And, if King Edward be as true and just
As I am subtle, false, and treacherous,
This day should Clarence closely be mew'd up,
About a prophecy, which says that G
Of Edward's heirs the murderer shall be.
Dive, thoughts, down to my soul: — here Clarence comes.

Enter CLARENCE, *guarded, and* BRAKENBURY.
Brother, good day: what means this armed guard
That waits upon your Grace?

CLARENCE
              His majesty,
Tendering my person's safety, hath appointed
This conduct to convey me to the Tower.

GLOSTER
Upon what cause?

CLARENCE
              Because my name is George.

GLOSTER
Alack, my lord, that fault is none of yours;
He should, for that, commit your godfathers: —
O, belike his majesty hath some intent
That you shall be new-christen'd in the Tower.

But what's the matter, Clarence? may I know?

CLARENCE
Yea, Richard, when I know; for I protest
As yet I do not: but, as I can learn,
He hearkens after prophecies and dreams;
And from the cross-row plucks the letter G,
And says a wizard told him that by G
His issue disinherited should be;
And, for my name of George begins with G,
It follows in his thought that I am he.
These, as I learn, and such-like toys as these,
Have mov'd his highness to commit me now.

GLOSTER
Why, this it is, when men are rul'd by women: —
'Tis not the king that sends you to the Tower;
My Lady Grey his wife, Clarence, 'tis she
That tempers him to this extremity.
Was it not she, and that good man of worship,
Anthony Woodville, her brother there,
That made him send Lord Hastings to the Tower,
From whence this present day he is deliver'd?
We are not safe, Clarence; we are not safe.

CLARENCE
By heaven, I think there's no man is secure
But the queen's kindred, and night-walking heralds
That trudge betwixt the king and Mistress Shore.
Heard ye not what an humble suppliant
Lord Hastings was to her for his delivery?

GLOSTER
Humbly complaining to her deity
Got my lord chamberlain his liberty.
I'll tell you what, — I think it is our way,
If we will keep in favour with the king,
To be her men, and wear her livery:
The jealous o'erworn widow and herself,
Since that our brother dubb'd them gentlewomen,
Are mighty gossips in this monarchy.

BRAKENBURY
I beseech your Graces both to pardon me;
His majesty hath straitly given in charge
That no man shall have private conference,
Of what degree soever, with his brother.

GLOSTER
Even so; an please your worship, Brakenbury,
You may partake of any thing we say:
We speak no treason, man; — we say the king
Is wise and virtuous; and his noble queen
Well struck in years, fair, and not jealous; —
We say that Shore's wife hath a pretty foot,
A cherry lip, a bonny eye, a passing pleasing tongue;
And that the queen's kindred are made

gentle-folks:
How say you, sir? can you deny all this?

BRAKENBURY
With this, my lord, myself have naught to do.

GLOSTER
Naught to do with Mistress Shore! I tell thee, fellow,
He that doth naught with her, excepting one,
Were best to do it secretly, alone.

BRAKENBURY
What one, my lord?

GLOSTER
Her husband, knave: — wouldst thou betray me?

BRAKENBURY
I beseech your Grace to pardon me; and, withal,
Forbear your conference with the noble duke.

CLARENCE
We know thy charge, Brakenbury, and will obey.

GLOSTER
We are the queen's abjects, and must obey. —
Brother, farewell: I will unto the king;
And whatsoe'er you will employ me in, —
Were it to call King Edward's widow sister, —

GLOSTER Now is the winter of our discontent made glorious summer by this sun of York.

I will perform it to enfranchise you.
Meantime, this deep disgrace in brotherhood
Touches me deeper than you can imagine.

CLARENCE
I know it pleaseth neither of us well.

GLOSTER
Well, your imprisonment shall not be long;
I will deliver you, or else lie for you:
Meantime, have patience.

CLARENCE
               I must perforce: farewell.
   [*Exeunt* CLARENCE, BRAKENBURY, *and* GUARD.

GLOSTER
Go, tread the path that thou shalt ne'er return,
Simple, plain Clarence! — I do love thee so,
That I will shortly send thy soul to heaven,
If heaven will take the present at our hands. —
But who comes here? the new-deliver'd Hastings?

             Enter HASTINGS.

HASTINGS
Good time of day unto my gracious lord!

GLOSTER
As much unto my good lord chamberlain!
Well are you welcome to the open air.
How hath your lordship brook'd imprisonment?

HASTINGS
With patience, noble lord, as prisoners must:
But I shall live, my lord, to give them thanks
That were the cause of my imprisonment.

GLOSTER
No doubt, no doubt; and so shall Clarence too;
For they that were your enemies are his,
And have prevail'd as much on him as you.

HASTINGS
More pity that the eagle should be mew'd,
While kites and buzzards prey at liberty.

GLOSTER
What news abroad?

HASTINGS
No news so bad abroad as this at home, —
The king is sickly, weak, and melancholy,
And his physicians fear him mightily.

GLOSTER
Now, by Saint Paul, this news is bad indeed.
O, he hath kept an evil diet long,
And overmuch consum'd his royal person:
'Tis very grievous to be thought upon.
What, is he in his bed?

HASTINGS
He is.

GLOSTER
Go you before, and I will follow you. [*Exit* HASTINGS.
He cannot live, I hope; and must not die
Till George be pack'd with post-horse up to heaven.
I'll in, to urge his hatred more to Clarence,
With lies well steel'd with weighty arguments;
And, if I fail not in my deep intent,
Clarence hath not another day to live:
Which done, God take King Edward to His mercy,
And leave the world for me to bustle in!
For then I'll marry Warwick's youngest daughter:
What though I kill'd her husband and her father?
The readiest way to make the wench amends,
Is to become her husband and her father:
The which will I; not all so much for love
As for another secret close intent,
By marrying her which I must reach unto.
But yet I run before my horse to market:
Clarence still breathes; Edward still lives and reigns:
When they are gone, then must I count my gains. [*Exit.*

SCENE II

The same. Another street.

Enter the corse of HENRY THE SIXTH, *with halberds to
guard it;* LADY ANNE *being the mourner;* TRESSEL
and BERKLEY.

LADY ANNE
Set down, set down your honourable load, —
If honour may be shrouded in a hearse, —
Whilst I awhile obsequiously lament
Th'untimely fall of virtuous Lancaster.
Poor key-cold figure of a holy king!
Pale ashes of the house of Lancaster!
Thou bloodless remnant of that royal blood!
Be it lawful that I invocate thy ghost,
To hear the lamentations of poor Anne,
Wife to thy Edward, to thy slaughter'd son,
Stabb'd by the selfsame hand that made these wounds!

Lo, in these windows that let forth thy life,
I pour the helpless balm of my poor eyes: —
O, cursed be the hand that made these holes!
Cursed the heart that had the heart to do it!
Cursed the blood that let this blood from hence!
More direful hap betide that hated wretch,
That makes us wretched by the death of thee,
Than I can wish to adders, spiders, toads,
Or any creeping venom'd thing that lives!
If ever he have child, abortive be it,
Prodigious, and untimely brought to light,
Whose ugly and unnatural aspect
May fright the hopeful mother at the view;
And that be heir to his unhappiness!
If ever he have wife, let her be made
More miserable by the death of him
Than I am made by my young lord and thee! —
Come now towards Chertsey with your holy load,
Taken from Paul's to be interred there;
And still, as you are weary of the weight,
Rest you, whiles I lament King Henry's corse.

            Enter GLOSTER.

GLOSTER
Stay, you that bear the corse, and set it down.

LADY ANNE
What black magician conjures up this fiend,
To stop devoted charitable deeds?

GLOSTER
Villains, set down the corse; or, by Saint Paul,
I'll make a corse of him that disobeys!

FIRST GENTLEMAN
My lord, stand back, and let the coffin pass.

GLOSTER
Unmanner'd dog! stand thou, when I command:
Advance thy halberd higher than my breast,
Or, by Saint Paul, I'll strike thee to my foot,
And spurn upon thee, beggar, for thy boldness.

LADY ANNE
What, do you tremble? are you all afraid?
Alas, I blame you not; for you are mortal,
And mortal eyes cannot endure the devil. —
Avaunt, thou dreadful minister of hell!
Thou hadst but power over his mortal body,
His soul thou canst not have; therefore, be gone.

GLOSTER
Sweet saint, for charity, be not so curst.

LADY ANNE
Foul devil, for God's sake, hence, and trouble us not;
For thou hast made the happy earth thy hell,
Fill'd it with cursing cries and deep exclaims.
If thou delight to view thy heinous deeds,
Behold this pattern of thy butcheries.
O, gentlemen, see, see! dead Henry's wounds
Open their congeal'd mouths and bleed afresh!
Blush, blush, thou lump of foul deformity;
For 'tis thy presence that exhales this blood
From cold and empty veins, where no blood dwells;
Thy deed, inhuman and unnatural,
Provokes this deluge most unnatural. —
O God, which this blood mad'st, revenge his death!
O earth, which this blood drink'st, revenge his death!
Either heaven with lightning strike the murderer dead;
Or, earth, gape open wide, and eat him quick,
As thou dost swallow up this good king's blood,
Which his hell-govern'd arm hath butchered!

GLOSTER
Lady, you know no rules of charity,
Which renders good for bad, blessings for curses.

LADY ANNE
Villain, thou know'st no law of God nor man:
No beast so fierce but knows some touch of pity.

GLOSTER
But I know none, and therefore am no beast.

LADY ANNE
O wonderful, when devils tell the truth!

GLOSTER
More wonderful, when angels are so angry. —
Vouchsafe, divine perfection of a woman,
Of these supposed evils, to give me leave,
By circumstance, but to acquit myself.

LADY ANNE
Vouchsafe, defus'd infection of a man,
For these known evils, but to give me leave,
By circumstance, to curse thy cursed self.

GLOSTER
Fairer than tongue can name thee, let me have
Some patient leisure to excuse myself.

LADY ANNE
Fouler than heart can think thee, thou canst make

No excuse current, but to hang thyself.

GLOSTER
By such despair, I should accuse myself.

LADY ANNE
And, by despairing, shouldst thou stand excused
For doing worthy vengeance on thyself,
That didst unworthy slaughter upon others.

GLOSTER
Say that I slew them not?

LADY ANNE
             Why, then, they are not dead:
But dead they are, and devilish slave, by thee.

GLOSTER
I did not kill your husband.

LADY ANNE
             Why, then, he is alive.

GLOSTER
Nay, he is dead; and slain by Edward's hand.

LADY ANNE
In thy foul throat thou liest: Queen Margaret saw
Thy murderous falchion smoking in his blood;
The which thou once didst bend against her breast,
But that thy brothers beat aside the point.

GLOSTER
I was provoked by her slanderous tongue,
That laid their guilt upon my guiltless shoulders.

LADY ANNE
Thou wast provoked by thy bloody mind,
That never dreamt on aught but butcheries:
Didst thou not kill this king?

GLOSTER
             I grant ye.

LADY ANNE
Dost grant me, hedgehog? then, God grant me too
Thou mayst be damned for that wicked deed!
O, he was gentle, mild, and virtuous!

GLOSTER
The fitter for the King of heaven, that hath him.

LADY ANNE
He is in heaven, where thou shalt never come.

GLOSTER
Let him thank me, that holp to send him thither;
For he was fitter for that place than earth.

LADY ANNE
And thou unfit for any place but hell.

GLOSTER
Yes, one place else, if you will hear me name it.

LADY ANNE
Some dungeon.

GLOSTER
             Your bed-chamber.

LADY ANNE
Ill rest betide the chamber where thou liest!

GLOSTER
So will it, madam, till I lie with you.

LADY ANNE
I hope so.

GLOSTER
             I know so. But, gentle Lady Anne, —
To leave this keen encounter of our wits,
And fall somewhat into a slower method, —
Is not the causer of the timeless deaths
Of these Plantagenets, Henry and Edward,
As blameful as the executioner?

LADY ANNE
Thou wast the cause and most accurs'd effect.

GLOSTER
Your beauty was the cause of that effect;
Your beauty, that did haunt me in my sleep
To undertake the death of all the world,
So I might live one hour in your sweet bosom.

LADY ANNE
If I thought that, I tell thee, homicide,
These nails should rend that beauty from my cheeks.

GLOSTER
These eyes could not endure that beauty's wrack;
You should not blemish it, if I stood by:
As all the world is cheered by the sun,
So I by that; it is my day, my life.

LADY ANNE
Black night o'ershade thy day, and death thy life!

GLOSTER
Curse not thyself, fair creature; thou art both.

LADY ANNE
I would I were, to be reveng'd on thee.

GLOSTER
It is a quarrel most unnatural,
To be reveng'd on him that loveth thee.

LADY ANNE
It is a quarrel just and reasonable,
To be reveng'd on him that kill'd my husband.
GLOSTER
He that bereft thee, lady, of thy husband,
Did it to help thee to a better husband.
LADY ANNE
His better doth not breathe upon the earth.
GLOSTER
He lives that loves thee better than he could.
LADY ANNE
Name him.
GLOSTER
      Plantagenet.
LADY ANNE
            Why, that was he.
GLOSTER
The selfsame name, but one of better nature.
LADY ANNE
Where is he?
GLOSTER
    Here. [*She spits at him.*] Why dost thou spit at me?
LADY ANNE
Would it were mortal poison, for thy sake!
GLOSTER
Never came poison from so sweet a place.
LADY ANNE
Never hung poison on a fouler toad.
Out of my sight! thou dost infect mine eyes.
GLOSTER
Thine eyes, sweet lady, have infected mine.
LADY ANNE
Would they were basilisks, to strike thee dead!
GLOSTER
I would they were, that I might die at once;
For now they kill me with a living death.
Those eyes of thine from mine have drawn salt tears,
Sham'd their aspects with store of childish drops:
These eyes, which never shed remorseful tear,
No, when my father York and Edward wept
To hear the piteous moan that Rutland made
When black-fac'd Clifford shook his sword at him;
Nor when thy warlike father, like a child,
Told the sad story of my father's death,
And twenty times made pause to sob and weep,
That all the standers-by had wet their cheeks,
Like trees bedash'd with rain; in that sad time
My manly eyes did scorn an humble tear;
And what these sorrows could not thence exhale,
Thy beauty hath, and made them blind with weeping.
I never sued to friend nor enemy;
My tongue could never learn sweet smoothing words;
But, now thy beauty is propos'd my fee,
My proud heart sues, and prompts my tongue to speak.
            [*She looks scornfully at him.*
Teach not thy lips such scorn; for they were made
For kissing, lady, not for such contempt.
If thy revengeful heart cannot forgive,
Lo, here I lend thee this sharp-pointed sword;
Which if thou please to hide in this true breast,
And let the soul forth that adoreth thee,
I lay it naked to the deadly stroke,
And humbly beg the death upon my knee.
      [*He lays his breast open; she offers at it with his sword.*
Nay, do not pause; for I did kill King Henry,
But 'twas thy beauty that provoked me.
Nay, now dispatch; 'twas I that stabb'd young Edward,
But 'twas thy heavenly face that set me on.
            [*She falls the sword.*
Take up the sword again, or take up me.
LADY ANNE
Arise, dissembler: though I wish thy death,
I will not be thy executioner.
GLOSTER
Then bid me kill myself, and I will do it.
LADY ANNE
I have already.
GLOSTER
        That was in thy rage:
Speak it again, and, even with the word,
That hand, which for thy love did kill thy love,
Shall for thy love kill a far truer love;
To both their deaths shalt thou be accessary.
LADY ANNE
I would I knew thy heart.
GLOSTER
'Tis figur'd in my tongue.
LADY ANNE
I fear me both are false.

GLOSTER Nay, do not pause; for I did kill King Henry.

GLOSTER
Then never man was true.
LADY ANNE
Well, well, put up your sword.
GLOSTER
Say, then, my peace is made.
LADY ANNE
That shall thou know hereafter.
GLOSTER
But shall I live in hope?
LADY ANNE
All men, I hope, live so.
GLOSTER
Vouchsafe to wear this ring.
LADY ANNE
To take, is not to give.
GLOSTER
Look, how this ring encompasseth thy finger,
Even so thy breast encloseth my poor heart;
Wear both of them, for both of them are thine.
And if thy poor devoted servant may
But beg one favour at thy gracious hand,
Thou dost confirm his happiness for ever.
LADY ANNE
What is it?
GLOSTER
That it may please you leave these sad designs
To him that hath more cause to be a mourner,
And presently repair to Crosby-place;
Where — after I have solemnly interr'd
At Chertsey monastery this noble king,
And wet his grave with my repentant tears —
I will with all expedient duty see you:
For divers unknown reasons, I beseech you,
Grant me this boon.
LADY ANNE
With all my heart; and much it joys me too
To see you are become so penitent. —
Tressel and Berkley, go along with me.
GLOSTER
Bid me farewell.
LADY ANNE
         'Tis more than you deserve;
But since you teach me how to flatter you,
Imagine I have said farewell already.

      [*Exeunt* LADY ANNE, TRESSEL, *and* BERKLEY.
GLOSTER
Sirs, take up the corse.
GENTLEMEN
         Towards Chertsey, noble lord?
GLOSTER
No, to White-Friars; there attend my coming.
      [*Exeunt all, except* GLOSTER.
Was ever woman in this humour woo'd?
Was ever woman in this humour won?
I'll have her; — but I will not keep her long.
What! I, that kill'd her husband and his father,
To take her in her heart's extremest hate;
With curses in her mouth, tears in her eyes,
The bleeding witness of her hatred by;
Having God, her conscience, and these bars against
    me,
And I no friends to back my suit withal
But the plain devil and dissembling looks,
And yet to win her, — all the world to nothing!
Ha!
Hath she forgot already that brave prince,
Edward, her lord, whom I, some three months since,
Stabb'd in my angry mood at Tewksbury?
A sweeter and a lovelier gentleman —
Fram'd in the prodigality of nature,
Young, valiant, wise, and, no doubt, right royal —
The spacious world cannot again afford:
And will she yet abase her eyes on me,
That cropp'd the golden prime of this sweet prince,
And made her widow to a woeful bed?
On me, whose all not equals Edward's moiety?
On me, that halt and am mis-shapen thus?
My dukedom to a beggarly denier,
I do mistake my person all this while:
Upon my life, she finds, although I cannot,
Myself to be a marvellous proper man.
I'll be at charges for a looking-glass;
And entertain a score or two of tailors
To study fashions to adorn my body:
Since I am crept in favour with myself,
I will maintain it with some little cost.
But first I'll turn yon fellow in his grave;
And then return lamenting to my love. —
Shine out, fair sun, till I have bought a glass,
That I may see my shadow as I pass.   [*Exit.*

SCENE III

The palace.

Enter QUEEN ELIZABETH, RIVERS, *and* GREY.

RIVERS
Have patience, madam: there's no doubt his majesty
Will soon recover his accustom'd health.

GREY
In that you brook it ill, it makes him worse:
Therefore, for God's sake, entertain good comfort,
And cheer his Grace with quick and merry words.

QUEEN ELIZABETH
If he were dead, what would betide of me?

RIVERS
No other harm but loss of such a lord.

QUEEN ELIZABETH
The loss of such a lord includes all harms.

GREY
The heavens have blest you with a goodly son,
To be your comforter when he is gone.

QUEEN ELIZABETH
Ah, he is young; and his minority
Is put unto the trust of Richard Gloster,
A man that loves not me nor none of you.

RIVERS
Is it concluded he shall be Protector?

QUEEN ELIZABETH
It is determin'd, not concluded yet:
But so it must be, if the king miscarry.

Enter BUCKINGHAM *and* DERBY.

GREY
Here come the lords of Buckingham and Derby.

BUCKINGHAM
Good time of day unto your royal Grace!

DERBY
God make your majesty joyful as you have been!

QUEEN ELIZABETH
The Countess Richmond, good my Lord of Derby,
To your good prayer will scarcely say amen.
Yet, Derby, notwithstanding she's your wife,
And loves not me, be you, good lord, assured
I hate not you for her proud arrogance.

DERBY
I do beseech you, either not believe
The envious slanders of her false accusers;
Or, if she be accus'd on true report,
Bear with her weakness, which, I think, proceeds
From wayward sickness, and no grounded malice.

RIVERS
Saw you the king to-day, my Lord of Derby?

DERBY
But now the Duke of Buckingham and I
Are come from visiting his majesty.

QUEEN ELIZABETH
What likelihood of his amendment, lords?

BUCKINGHAM
Madam, good hope; his Grace speaks cheerfully.

QUEEN ELIZABETH
God grant him health! Did you confer with him?

BUCKINGHAM
Ay, madam: he desires to make atonement
Between the Duke of Gloster and your brothers,
And betwixt them and my lord chamberlain;
And sent to warn them to his royal presence.

QUEEN ELIZABETH
Would all were well! — but that will never be:
I fear our happiness is at the height.

Enter GLOSTER, HASTINGS, *and* DORSET.

GLOSTER
They do me wrong, and I will not endure it: —
Who are they that complain unto the king
That I, forsooth, am stern, and love them not?
By holy Paul, they love his Grace but lightly
That fill his ears with such dissentious rumours.
Because I cannot flatter and speak fair,
Smile in men's faces, smooth, deceive, and cog,
Duck with French nods and apish courtesy,
I must be held a rancorous enemy.
Cannot a plain man live and think no harm,
But thus his simple truth must be abused
By silken, sly, insinuating Jacks?

RIVERS
To whom in all this presence speaks your Grace?

GLOSTER
To thee, that hast nor honesty nor grace.
When have I injur'd thee? when done thee wrong? —
Or thee? — or thee? — or any of your faction?

A plague upon you all! His royal Grace —
Whom God preserve better than you would wish! —
Cannot be quiet scarce a breathing-while,
But you must trouble him with lewd complaints.

QUEEN ELIZABETH
Brother of Gloster, you mistake the matter.
The king, of his own royal disposition,
And not provok'd by any suitor else;
Aiming, belike, at your interior hatred,
That in your outward action shows itself
Against my children, brothers, and myself,
Makes him to send, that thereby he may gather
The ground of your ill-will, and so remove it.

GLOSTER
I cannot tell: the world is grown so bad,
That wrens may prey where eagles dare not perch:
Since every Jack became a gentleman,
There's many a gentle person made a Jack.

QUEEN ELIZABETH
Come, come, we know your meaning, brother Gloster;
You envy my advancement and my friends':
God grant we never may have need of you!

GLOSTER
Meantime, God grants that we have need of you:
Our brother is imprison'd by your means,
Myself disgrac'd, and the nobility
Held in contempt; while great promotions
Are daily given to ennoble those
That scarce, some two days since, were worth a noble.

QUEEN ELIZABETH
By Him that rais'd me to this careful height
From that contented hap which I enjoy'd,
I never did incense his majesty
Against the Duke of Clarence, but have been
An earnest advocate to plead for him.
My lord, you do me shameful injury,
Falsely to draw me in these vile suspects.

GLOSTER
You may deny that you were not the cause
Of my Lord Hastings' late imprisonment.

RIVERS
She may, my lord; for —

GLOSTER
She may, Lord Rivers! — why, who knows not so?
She may do more, sir, than denying that:
She may help you to many fair preferments;
And then deny her aiding hand therein,
And lay those honours on your high desert.
What may she not? She may, — ay, marry, may she, —

RIVERS
What, marry, may she?

GLOSTER
What, marry, may she! marry with a king,
A bachelor, a handsome stripling too:
I wis your grandam had a worser match.

QUEEN ELIZABETH
My Lord of Gloster, I have too long borne
Your blunt upbraidings and your bitter scoffs:
By heaven, I will acquaint his majesty
With those gross taunts I often have endured.
I had rather be a country servant-maid
Than a great queen, with this condition, —
To be so baited, scorn'd, and stormed at:
Enter QUEEN MARGARET, *behind.*
Small joy have I in being England's queen.

QUEEN MARGARET [*aside*].
And lessen'd be that small, God, I beseech Him!
Thy honour, state, and seat is due to me.

GLOSTER
What! threat you me with telling of the king?
Tell him, and spare not: look, what I have said
I will avouch in presence of the king:
I dare adventure to be sent to th'Tower.
'Tis time to speak, — my pains are quite forgot.

QUEEN MARGARET [*aside*].
Out, devil! I remember them too well:
Thou kill'dst my husband Henry in the Tower,
And Edward, my poor son, at Tewksbury.

GLOSTER
Ere you were queen, ay, or your husband king,
I was a pack-horse in his great affairs;
A weeder-out of his proud adversaries,
A liberal rewarder of his friends:
To royalise his blood I spilt mine own.

QUEEN MARGARET [*aside*].
Ay, and much better blood than his or thine.

GLOSTER
In all which time you and your husband Grey
Were factious for the house of Lancaster; —
And, Rivers, so were you: — was not your husband

In Margaret's battle at Saint Alban's slain?
Let me put in your minds, if you forget,
What you have been ere now, and what you are;
Withal, what I have been, and what I am.

QUEEN MARGARET [*aside*].
A murderous villain, and so still thou art.

GLOSTER
Poor Clarence did forsake his father, Warwick;
Ay, and forswore himself, — which Jesu pardon! —

QUEEN MARGARET [*aside*].
Which God revenge! —

GLOSTER
To fight on Edward's party, for the crown;
And for his meed, poor lord, he is mew'd up.
I would to God my heart were flint, like Edward's;
Or Edward's soft and pitiful, like mine:
I am too childish-foolish for this world.

QUEEN MARGARET [*aside*].
Hie thee to hell for shame, and leave this world,
Thou cacodemon! there thy kingdom is.

RIVERS
My Lord of Gloster, in those busy days
Which here you urge to prove us enemies,
We follow'd then our lord, our lawful king:
So should we you, if you should be our king.

GLOSTER
If I should be! — I had rather be a pedlar:
Far be it from my heart, the thought of it!

QUEEN ELIZABETH
As little joy, my lord, as you suppose
You should enjoy, were you this country's king, —
As little joy may you suppose in me,
That I enjoy, being the queen thereof.

QUEEN MARGARET [*aside*].
A little joy enjoys the queen thereof;
For I am she, and altogether joyless.
I can no longer hold me patient. —   [*Advancing.*
Hear me, you wrangling pirates, that fall out
In sharing that which you have pill'd from me!
Which of you trembles not that looks on me?
If not, that, I being queen, you bow like subjects,
Yet that, by you depos'd, you quake like rebels? —
Ay, gentle villain, do not turn away!

GLOSTER
Foul wrinkled witch, what mak'st thou in my sight?

QUEEN MARGARET
But repetition of what thou hast marr'd;
That will I make before I let thee go.

GLOSTER
Wert thou not banished on pain of death?

QUEEN MARGARET
I was;
But I do find more pain in banishment
Than death can yield me here by my abode.
A husband and a son thou owest to me, —
And thou a kingdom, — all of you allegiance:
The sorrow that I have, by right is yours;
And all the pleasures you usurp are mine.

GLOSTER
The curse my noble father laid on thee,
When thou didst crown his warlike brows with paper,
And with thy scorns drew'st rivers from his eyes:
And then, to dry them, gav'st the duke a clout
Steep'd in the faultless blood of pretty Rutland; —
His curses, then from bitterness of soul
Denounc'd against thee, are all fall'n upon thee;
And God, not we, hath plagu'd thy bloody deed.

QUEEN ELIZABETH
So just is God, to right the innocent.

HASTINGS
O, 'twas the foulest deed to slay that babe,
And the most merciless that e'er was heard of!

RIVERS
Tyrants themselves wept when it was reported.

DORSET
No man but prophesied revenge for it.

BUCKINGHAM
Northumberland, then present, wept to see it.

QUEEN MARGARET
What! were you snarling all before I came,
Ready to catch each other by the throat,
And turn you all your hatred now on me?
Did York's dread curse prevail so much with heaven,
That Henry's death, my lovely Edward's death,
Their kingdom's loss, my woeful banishment,
Could all but answer for that peevish brat?
Can curses pierce the clouds and enter heaven? —
Why, then, give way, dull clouds, to my quick curses! —
Though not by war, by surfeit die your king,

As ours by murder, to make him a king!
Edward thy son, that now is Prince of Wales,
For Edward my son, that was Prince of Wales,
Die in his youth by like untimely violence!
Thyself a queen, for me that was a queen,
Outlive thy glory, like my wretched self!
Long mayst thou live to wail thy children's loss;
And see another, as I see thee now,
Deck'd in thy rights, as thou art stall'd in mine!
Long die thy happy days before thy death;
And, after many lengthen'd hours of grief,
Die neither mother, wife, nor England's queen! —
Rivers and Dorset, you were standers by, —
And so wast thou, Lord Hastings, — when my son
Was stabb'd with bloody daggers: God, I pray Him,
That none of you may live his natural age,
But by some unlook'd accident cut off!

GLOSTER
Have done thy charm, thou hateful wither'd hag!

QUEEN MARGARET
And leave out thee? stay, dog, for thou shalt hear me.
If heaven have any grievous plague in store
Exceeding those that I can wish upon thee,
O, let them keep it till thy sins be ripe,
And then hurl down their indignation
On thee, the troubler of the poor world's peace!
The worm of conscience still begnaw thy soul!
Thy friends suspect for traitors while thou livest,
And take deep traitors for thy dearest friends!
No sleep close up that deadly eye of thine,
Unless it be while some tormenting dream
Affrights thee with a hell of ugly devils!
Thou elvish-mark'd, abortive, rooting hog!
Thou that wast seal'd in thy nativity
The slave of nature and the son of hell!
Thou slander of thy mother's heavy womb!
Thou loathed issue of thy father's loins!
Thou rag of honour! thou detested —

GLOSTER
Margaret.

QUEEN MARGARET
Richard!

GLOSTER
Ha!

QUEEN MARGARET
I call thee not.

GLOSTER
I cry thee mercy, then; for I did think
That thou hadst call'd me all these bitter names.

QUEEN MARGARET
Why, so I did; but look'd for no reply.
O, let me make the period to my curse!

GLOSTER
'Tis done by me, and ends in — Margaret.

QUEEN ELIZABETH
Thus have you breath'd your curse against yourself.

QUEEN MARGARET
Poor painted queen, vain flourish of my fortune!
Why strew'st thou sugar on that bottled spider,
Whose deadly web ensnareth thee about?
Fool, fool! thou whett'st a knife to kill thyself.
The day will come that thou shalt wish for me
To help thee curse that poisonous bunch-back'd toad.

HASTINGS
False-boding woman, end thy frantic curse,
Lest to thy harm thou move our patience.

QUEEN MARGARET
Foul shame upon you! you have all moved mine.

RIVERS
Were you well serv'd, you would be taught your duty.

QUEEN MARGARET
To serve me well, you all should do me duty,
Teach me to be your queen, and you my subjects:
O, serve me well, and teach yourselves that duty!

DORSET
Dispute not with her, — she is lunatic.

QUEEN MARGARET
Peace, master marquess, you are malapert:
Your fire-new stamp of honour is scarce current:
O, that your young nobility could judge
What 'twere to lose it, and be miserable!
They that stand high have many blasts to shake them;
And if they fall, they dash themselves to pieces.

GLOSTER
Good counsel, marry: — learn it, learn it, marquess.

DORSET
It touches you, my lord, as much as me.

GLOSTER
Ay, and much more: but I was born so high,

Our aery buildeth in the cedar's top,
And dallies with the wind, and scorns the sun.

QUEEN MARGARET
And turns the sun to shade; — alas! alas! —
Witness my son, now in the shade of death;
Whose bright out-shining beams thy cloudy wrath
Hath in eternal darkness folded up.
Your aery buildeth in our aery's nest: —
O God, that seest it, do not suffer it;
As it was won with blood, lost be it so!

BUCKINGHAM
Peace, peace, for shame, if not for charity.

QUEEN MARGARET
Urge neither charity nor shame to me:
Uncharitably with me have you dealt,
And shamefully by you my hopes are butcher'd.
My charity is outrage, life my shame, —
And in that shame still live my sorrow's rage!

BUCKINGHAM
Have done, have done.

QUEEN MARGARET
O princely Buckingham, I'll kiss thy hand,
In sign of league and amity with thee:
Now fair befall thee and thy noble house!
Thy garments are not spotted with our blood,
Nor thou within the compass of my curse.

BUCKINGHAM
Nor no one here; for curses never pass
The lips of those that breathe them in the air.

QUEEN MARGARET
I'll not believe but they ascend the sky,
And there awake God's gentle-sleeping peace.
O Buckingham, take heed of yonder dog!
Look, when he fawns he bites; and when he bites,
His venom tooth will rankle to the death:
Have not to do with him, beware of him;
Sin, death, and hell have set their marks on him,
And all their ministers attend on him.

GLOSTER
What doth she say, my Lord of Buckingham?

BUCKINGHAM
Nothing that I respect, my gracious lord.

QUEEN MARGARET
What, dost thou scorn me for my gentle counsel?
And soothe the devil that I warn thee from?
O, but remember this another day,
When he shall split thy very heart with sorrow,
And say, poor Margaret was a prophetess! —
Live each of you the subjects to his hate,
And he to yours, and all of you to God's.   [Exit.

HASTINGS
My hair doth stand on end to hear her curses.

RIVERS
And so doth mine: I muse why she's at liberty.

GLOSTER
I cannot blame her: by God's holy mother,
She hath had too much wrong; and I repent
My part thereof that I have done to her.

QUEEN ELIZABETH
I never did her any, to my knowledge.

GLOSTER
Yet you have all the vantage of her wrong.
I was too hot to do somebody good
That is too cold in thinking of it now.
Marry, as for Clarence, he is well repaid;
He is frank'd up to fatting for his pains; —
God pardon them that are the cause of it!

RIVERS
A virtuous and a Christian-like conclusion,
To pray for them that have done scathe to us.

GLOSTER [aside].
So do I ever, being well advised;
For had I curs'd now, I had curs'd myself.

Enter CATESBY.

CATESBY
Madam, his majesty doth call for you, —
And for your Grace, — and you, my noble lords.

QUEEN ELIZABETH
Catesby, I come. — Lords, will you go with me?

RIVERS
We wait upon your Grace.
                        [Exeunt all except GLOSTER.

GLOSTER
I do the wrong, and first begin to brawl.
The secret mischiefs that I set abroach
I lay unto the grievous charge of others.
Clarence, — whom I, indeed, have laid in darkness,
I do beweep to many simple gulls;
Namely, to Hastings, Derby, Buckingham;

And say it is the queen and her allies
That stir the king against the duke my brother.
Now, they believe it; and withal whet me
To be reveng'd on Rivers, Vaughan, Grey:
But then I sigh; and, with a piece of Scripture,
Tell them that God bids us do good for evil:
And thus I clothe my naked villainy
With old odd ends stol'n out of holy writ;
And seem a saint, when most I play the devil. —
But, soft! here come my executioners.

Enter two MURDERERS.

How now, my hardy, stout-resolved mates!
Are you now going to dispatch this thing?

FIRST MURDERER
We are, my lord; and come to have the warrant,
That we may be admitted where he is.

GLOSTER
Well thought upon; — I have it here about me:
                        [Gives the warrant.
When you have done, repair to Crosby-place.
But, sirs, be sudden in the execution;
Withal obdurate, do not hear him plead;
For Clarence is well-spoken, and perhaps
May move your hearts to pity, if you mark him.

FIRST MURDERER
Tut, tut, my lord, we will not stand to prate;
Talkers are no good doers: be assured
We go to use our hands, and not our tongues.

GLOSTER
Your eyes drop millstones, when fools' eyes drop tears:
I like you, lads; — about your business straight;
Go, go, dispatch.

FIRST MURDERER
We will, my noble lord.   [Exeunt.

SCENE IV

The Tower.

Enter CLARENCE *and* BRAKENBURY.

BRAKENBURY
Why looks your Grace so heavily to-day?

CLARENCE
O, I have pass'd a miserable night,
So full of fearful dreams, of ugly sights,
That, as I am a Christian faithful man,
I would not spend another such a night,
Though 'twere to buy a world of happy days, —
So full of dismal terror was the time!

BRAKENBURY
What was your dream, my lord? I pray you, tell me.

CLARENCE
Methought that I had broken from the Tower,
And was embark'd to cross to Burgundy;
And, in my company, my brother Gloster;
Who from my cabin tempted me to walk
Upon the hatches: thence we look'd toward England,
And cited up a thousand heavy times,
During the wars of York and Lancaster,
That had befal'n us. As we pac'd along
Upon the giddy footing of the hatches,
Methought that Gloster stumbled; and, in falling,
Struck me, that thought to stay him, overboard
Into the tumbling billows of the main.
Lord, Lord! methought, what pain it was to drown!
What dreadful noise of waters in mine ears!
What ugly sights of death within mine eyes!
Methought I saw a thousand fearful wracks;
Ten thousand men that fishes gnaw'd upon;
Wedges of gold, great anchors, heaps of pearl,
Inestimable stones, unvalued jewels,
All scatt'red in the bottom of the sea:
Some lay in dead men's skulls; and, in those holes
Where eyes did once inhabit, there were crept,
As 'twere in scorn of eyes, reflecting gems,
That woo'd the slimy bottom of the deep,
And mock'd the dead bones that lay scatt'red by.

BRAKENBURY
Had you such leisure in the time of death
To gaze upon the secrets of the deep?

CLARENCE
Methought I had; and often did I strive
To yield the ghost: but still the envious flood
Kept in my soul, and would not let it forth
To seek the empty, vast, and wandering air;
But smother'd it within my panting bulk,
Which almost burst to belch it in the sea.

BRAKENBURY
Awak'd you not with this sore agony?

CLARENCE
No, no, my dream was lengthen'd after life;

O, then began the tempest to my soul!
I pass'd, methought, the melancholy flood,
With that grim ferryman which poets write of,
Unto the kingdom of perpetual night.
The first that there did greet my stranger soul,
Was my great father-in-law, renowned Warwick;
Who cried aloud, 'What scourge for perjury
Can this dark monarchy afford false Clarence?'
And so he vanish'd: then came wandering by
A shadow like an angel, with bright hair
Dabbled in blood; and he shriek'd out aloud,
'Clarence is come; false, fleeting, perjur'd Clarence,
That stabb'd me in the field by Tewksbury:
Seize on him, Furies, take him to your torments!'
With that, methought, a legion of foul fiends
Environ'd me, and howled in mine ears
Such hideous cries, that, with the very noise,
I trembling wak'd, and, for a season after,
Could not believe but that I was in hell, —
Such terrible impression made my dream.

BRAKENBURY
No marvel, lord, though it affrighted you:
I am afraid, methinks, to hear you tell it.

CLARENCE
O Brakenbury, I have done those things,
That now give evidence against my soul,
For Edward's sake; and see how he requites me!
O God! if my deep prayers cannot appease Thee,
But Thou wilt be aveng'd on my misdeeds,
Yet execute Thy wrath in me alone;
O, spare my guiltless wife and my poor children! —
I pray thee, gentle keeper, stay by me;
My soul is heavy, and I fain would sleep.

BRAKENBURY
I will, my lord: God give your Grace good rest! —
                    [CLARENCE *sleeps.*
Sorrow breaks seasons and reposing hours,
Makes the night morning, and the noontide night.
Princes have but their titles for their glories,
An outward honour for an inward toil;
And, for unfelt imaginations,
They often feel a world of restless cares:
So that, betwixt their titles and low names,
There's nothing differs but the outward fame.
                    Enter the two MURDERERS.

FIRST MURDERER
Ho! who's here?

BRAKENBURY
What wouldst thou, fellow? and how camest thou hither?

FIRST MURDERER
I would speak with Clarence, and I came hither on my
legs.

BRAKENBURY
What, so brief?

SECOND MURDERER
'Tis better, sir, than to be tedious. — Let him see our
commission; and talk no more.
                    [BRAKENBURY *reads it.*

BRAKENBURY
I am, in this, commanded to deliver
The noble Duke of Clarence to your hands: —
I will not reason what is meant hereby,
Because I will be guiltless of the meaning.
Here are the keys; — there sits the duke asleep:
I'll to the king; and signify to him
That thus I have resign'd to you my charge.

FIRST MURDERER
You may, sir; 'tis a point of wisdom: fare you well.
                    [*Exit* BRAKENBURY.

SECOND MURDERER
What, shall we stab him as he sleeps?

FIRST MURDERER
No; he'll say 'twas done cowardly, when he wakes.

SECOND MURDERER
When he wakes! why, fool, he shall never wake till the
judgement-day.

FIRST MURDERER
Why, then he'll say we stabb'd him sleeping.

SECOND MURDERER
The urging of that word 'judgement' hath bred a kind of
remorse in me.

FIRST MURDERER
What, art thou afraid?

SECOND MURDERER
Not to kill him, having a warrant for it; but to be
damn'd for killing him, from the which no warrant can
defend me.

FIRST MURDERER
I thought thou hadst been resolute.

SECOND MURDERER
So I am, to let him live.

FIRST MURDERER
I'll back to the Duke of Gloster, and tell him so.

SECOND MURDERER
I pray thee, stay a while: I hope my holy humour will
change; 'twas wont to hold me but while one tells
twenty.

FIRST MURDERER
How dost thou feel thyself now?

SECOND MURDERER
Faith, some certain dregs of conscience are yet within
me.

FIRST MURDERER
Remember our reward, when the deed is done.

SECOND MURDERER
Zounds, he dies: I had forgot the reward.

FIRST MURDERER
Where is thy conscience now?

SECOND MURDERER
In the Duke of Gloster's purse.

FIRST MURDERER
So, when he opens his purse to give us our reward, thy
conscience flies out.

SECOND MURDERER
Let it go; there's few or none will entertain it.

FIRST MURDERER
How if it come to thee again?

SECOND MURDERER
I'll not meddle with it: it is a dangerous thing: it makes
a man a coward: a man cannot steal, but it accuseth
him; he cannot swear, but it checks him; he cannot lie
with his neighbour's wife, but it detects him: it is a
blushing shame-faced spirit that mutinies in a man's
bosom; it fills one full of obstacles: it made me once
restore a purse of gold, that by chance I found; it
beggars any man that keeps it: it is turn'd out of all
towns and cities for a dangerous thing; and every man
that means to live well endeavours to trust to himself
and to live without it.

FIRST MURDERER
Zounds, it is even now at my elbow, persuading me not
to kill the duke.

SECOND MURDERER
Take the devil in thy mind, and believe him not: he
would insinuate with thee but to make thee sigh.

FIRST MURDERER
Tut, I am strong-fram'd, he cannot prevail with me, I
warrant thee.

SECOND MURDERER
Spoke like a tall fellow that respects his reputation.
Come, shall we to this gear?

FIRST MURDERER
Take him over the costard with the hilts of thy sword,
and then we will chop him in the malmsey-butt in the
next room.

SECOND MURDERER
O excellent device! make a sop of him.

FIRST MURDERER
Hark! he stirs: shall I strike?

SECOND MURDERER
No, first let's reason with him.

CLARENCE [*waking*].
Where art thou, keeper? give me a cup of wine.

FIRST MURDERER
You shall have wine enough, my lord, anon.

CLARENCE
In God's name, what art thou?

FIRST MURDERER
A man, as you are.

CLARENCE
But not, as I am, royal.

FIRST MURDERER
Nor you, as we are, loyal.

CLARENCE
Thy voice is thunder, but thy looks are humble.

FIRST MURDERER
My voice is now the king's, my looks mine own.

CLARENCE
How darkly and how deadly dost thou speak!
Your eyes do menace me: why look you pale?
Who sent you hither? Wherefore do you come?

BOTH MURDERERS
To, to, to —

CLARENCE
To murder me?

BOTH MURDERERS
Ay, ay.

CLARENCE
You scarcely have the hearts to tell me so,
And therefore cannot have the hearts to do it.
Wherein, my friends, have I offended you?

FIRST MURDERER
Offended us you have not, but the king.

CLARENCE
I shall be reconcil'd to him again.

SECOND MURDERER
Never, my lord; therefore prepare to die.

CLARENCE
Are you call'd forth from out a world of men
To slay the innocent? What is my offence?
Where are the evidence that do accuse me?
What lawful quest have given their verdict up
Unto the frowning judge? or who pronounc'd
The bitter sentence of poor Clarence' death?
Before I be convict by course of law,
To threaten me with death is most unlawful.
I charge you, as you hope to have redemption
By Christ's dear blood shed for our grievous sins,
That you depart, and lay no hands on me:
The deed you undertake is damnable.

FIRST MURDERER
What we will do, we do upon command.

SECOND MURDERER
And he that hath commanded is the king.

CLARENCE
Erroneous vassal! the great King of kings
Hath in the tables of His law commanded
That thou shalt do no murder: will you, then,
Spurn at His edict, and fulfil a man's?
Take heed; for He holds vengeance in His hand,
To hurl upon their heads that break His law.

SECOND MURDERER
And that same vengeance doth he Hurl on thee,
For false forswearing, and for murder too:
Thou didst receive the sacrament to fight
In quarrel of the house of Lancaster.

FIRST MURDERER
And, like a traitor to the name of God,
Didst break that vow; and with thy treacherous blade
Unripp'dst the bowels of thy sovereign's son.

SECOND MURDERER
Whom thou wert sworn to cherish and defend.

FIRST MURDERER
How canst thou urge God's dreadful law to us,
When thou hast broke it in so dear degree?

CLARENCE
Alas! for whose sake did I that ill deed?
For Edward, for my brother, for his sake:
Why, sirs,
He sends ye not to murder me for this;
For in this sin he is as deep as I.
If God will be revenged for this deed,
O, know you yet, He doth it publicly:
Take not the quarrel from His powerful arm;
He needs no indirect nor lawless course
To cut off those that have offended Him.

FIRST MURDERER
Who made thee, then, a bloody minister,
When gallant-springing brave Plantagenet,
That princely novice, was struck dead by thee?

CLARENCE
My brother's love, the devil, and my rage.

FIRST MURDERER
Thy brother's love, our duty, and thy fault,
Provoke us hither now to slaughter thee.

CLARENCE
O, if you do love my brother, hate not me;
I am his brother, and I love him well.
If you be hired for meed, go back again,
And I will send you to my brother Gloster,
Who shall reward you better for my life
Than Edward will for tidings of my death.

SECOND MURDERER
You are deceiv'd, your brother Gloster hates you.

CLARENCE
O, no, he loves me, and he holds me dear:
Go you to him from me.

BOTH MURDERERS
                    Ay, so we will.

CLARENCE
Tell him, when that our princely father York
Blest his three sons with his victorious arm,
And charg'd us from his soul to love each other,
He little thought of this divided friendship:
Bid Gloster think of this, and he will weep.

FIRST MURDERER
Ay, millstones; as he lesson'd us to weep.
CLARENCE
O, do not slander him, for he is kind.
FIRST MURDERER
Right.
As snow in harvest. — Thou deceiv'st thyself:
'Tis he that sent us hither now to slaughter thee.
CLARENCE
It cannot be; for when I parted with him,
He hugg'd me in his arms, and swore, with sobs,
That he would labour my delivery.
FIRST MURDERER
Why, so he doth, now he delivers thee
From this earth's thraldom to the joys of heaven.
SECOND MURDERER
Make peace with God, for you must die, my lord.
CLARENCE
Hast thou that holy feeling in thy soul,
To counsel me to make my peace with God,
And art thou yet to thy own soul so blind,
That thou wilt war with God by murdering me? —
Ah, sirs, consider, he that set you on
To do this deed will hate you for the deed.
SECOND MURDERER
What shall we do?
CLARENCE
　　　　　Relent, and save your souls.
Which of you, if you were a prince's son,
Being pent from liberty, as I am now,
If two such murderers as yourselves came to you,
Would not entreat for life? As you would beg,
Were you in my distress —
FIRST MURDERER
Relent! 'tis cowardly and womanish.
CLARENCE
Not to relent is beastly, savage, devilish.
My friend, I spy some pity in thy looks;
O, if thine eye be not a flatterer,
Come thou on my side, and entreat for me:
A begging prince what beggar pities not?
SECOND MURDERER
Look behind you, my lord.
FIRST MURDERER
Take that, and that [*stabs him*]: if all this will not do,
I'll drown you in the malmsey-butt within.
　　　　　　　　　　　　　　　[*Exit, with the body.*
SECOND MURDERER
A bloody deed, and desperately dispatch'd!
How fain, like Pilate, would I wash my hands
Of this most grievous guilty murder done!

　　　　　　　Enter FIRST MURDERER.

FIRST MURDERER
How now! what mean'st thou, that thou help'st me
　　not?
By heaven, the duke shall know how slack thou art!
SECOND MURDERER
I would he knew that I had sav'd his brother!
Take thou the fee, and tell him what I say;
For I repent me that the duke is slain. 　　[*Exit.*
FIRST MURDERER
So do not I: go, coward as thou art. —
Well, I'll go hide the body in some hole,
Till that the duke give order for his burial:
And when I have my meed, I will away;
For this will out, and then I must not stay. 　[*Exit.*

ACT II

SCENE I

London. The palace.

Enter the KING, *sick, the* QUEEN, DORSET, RIVERS,
HASTINGS, BUCKINGHAM, GREY, *and others.*

KING EDWARD
Why, so: now have I done a good day's work:
You peers, continue this united league:
I every day expect an embassage
From my Redeemer to redeem me hence;
And now in peace my soul shall part to heaven,
Since I have made my friends at peace on earth.
Rivers and Hastings, take each other's hand;
Dissemble not your hatred, swear your love.
RIVERS
By heaven, my soul is purg'd from grudging hate;
And with my hand I seal my true heart's love.

GLOSTER I every day expect an embassage from my Redeemer to redeem me hence.

HASTINGS
So thrive I, as I truly swear the like!
KING EDWARD
Take heed you dally not before your king;
Lest He that is the supreme King of kings,
Confound your hidden falsehood, and award
Either of you to be the other's end.
HASTINGS
So prosper I, as I swear perfect love!
RIVERS
And I, as I love Hastings with my heart!
KING EDWARD
Madam, yourself are not exempt in this, —
Nor you, son Dorset, — Buckingham, nor you; —
You have been factious one against the other.
Wife, love Lord Hastings, let him kiss your hand;
And what you do, do it unfeignedly.
QUEEN ELIZABETH
There, Hastings; I will never more remember
Our former hatred, so thrive I and mine!
KING EDWARD
Dorset, embrace him; — Hastings, love lord marquess.
DORSET
This interchange of love, I here protest,
Upon my part shall be unviolable.
HASTINGS
And so swear I. 　　　　　　　[*They embrace.*
KING EDWARD
Now, princely Buckingham, seal thou this league
With thy embracements to my wife's allies,
And make me happy in your unity.
BUCKINGHAM 　　[*to the* QUEEN.]
Whenever Buckingham doth turn his hate
Upon your Grace, but with all duteous love
Doth cherish you and yours, God punish me
With hate in those where I expect most love!
When I have most need to employ a friend,
And most assured that he is a friend,
Deep, hollow, treacherous, and full of guile,
Be he unto me! — this do I beg of God,
When I am cold in zeal to you or yours. 　[*They embrace.*
KING EDWARD
A pleasing cordial, princely Buckingham,
Is this thy vow unto my sickly heart.
There wanteth now our brother Gloster here,
To make the perfect period of this peace.
BUCKINGHAM
And, in good time, here comes the noble duke.

　　　　　　　Enter GLOSTER.

GLOSTER
Good morrow to my sovereign king and queen;
And, princely peers, a happy time of day!

KING EDWARD
Happy, indeed, as we have spent the day.
Brother, we have done deeds of charity;
Made peace of enmity, fair love of hate,
Between these swelling wrong-incensed peers.
GLOSTER
A blessed labour, my most sovereign liege.
Among this princely heap, if any here,
By false intelligence or wrong surmise,
Hold me a foe;
If I unwittingly, or in my rage,
Have aught committed that is hardly borne
By any in this presence, I desire
To reconcile me to his friendly peace:
'Tis death to me to be at enmity;
I hate it, and desire all good men's love.
First, madam, I entreat true peace of you,
Which I will purchase with my duteous service;
Of you, my noble cousin Buckingham,
If ever any grudge were lodg'd between us;
Of you, Lord Rivers, and, Lord Grey, of you,
That all without desert have frown'd on me; —
Dukes, earls, lords, gentlemen; — indeed, of all.
I do not know that Englishman alive
With whom my soul is any jot at odds
More than the infant that is born to-night:
I thank my God for my humility.
QUEEN ELIZABETH
A holiday shall this be kept hereafter:
I would to God all strifes were well compounded.
My sovereign lord, I do beseech your highness
To take our brother Clarence to your Grace.
GLOSTER
Why, madam, have I offer'd love for this,
To be so flouted in this royal presence?
Who knows not that the gentle duke is dead?
　　　　　　　　　　　　　[*They all start.*
You do him injury to scorn his corse.
RIVERS
Who knows not he is dead! who knows he is?
QUEEN ELIZABETH
All-seeing heaven, what a world is this!
BUCKINGHAM
Look I so pale, Lord Dorset, as the rest?
DORSET
Ay, my good lord; and no one in this presence
But his red colour hath forsook his cheeks.
KING EDWARD
Is Clarence dead? the order was reversed.
GLOSTER
But he, poor soul, by your order first died,
And that a winged Mercury did bear;
Some tardy cripple bore the countermand,

That came too lag to see him buried.
God grant that some, less noble and less loyal,
Nearer in bloody thoughts, but not in blood,
Deserve not worse than wretched Clarence did,
And yet go current from suspicion!

Enter DERBY.

DERBY
A boon, my sovereign, for my service done!

KING EDWARD
I prithee, peace: my soul is full of sorrow.

DERBY
I will not rise, unless your highness hear me.

KING EDWARD
Then say at once what is it thou request'st.

DERBY
The forfeit, sovereign, of my servant's life;
Who slew to-day a riotous gentleman
Lately attendant on the Duke of Norfolk.

KING EDWARD
Have I a tongue to doom my brother's death,
And shall that tongue give pardon to a slave?
My brother kill'd no man, — his fault was thought,
And yet his punishment was bitter death.
Who sued to me for him? who, in my rage,
Kneel'd at my feet, and bade me be advised?
Who spoke of brotherhood? who spoke of love?
Who told me how the poor soul did forsake
The mighty Warwick, and did fight for me?
Who told me, in the field at Tewksbury,
When Oxford had me down, he rescued me,
And said, 'Dear brother, live, and be a king'?
Who told me, when we both lay in the field
Frozen almost to death, how he did lap me
Even in his garments, and did give himself,
All thin and naked, to the numb-cold night?
All this from my remembrance brutish wrath
Sinfully pluck'd, and not a man of you
Had so much grace to put it in my mind.
But when your carters or your waiting-vassals
Have done a drunken slaughter, and defac'd
The precious image of our dear Redeemer,
You straight are on your knees for pardon, pardon;
And I, unjustly too, must grant it you:
But for my brother not a man would speak,
Nor I, ungracious, speak unto myself
For him, poor soul. The proudest of you all
Have been beholding to him in his life;
Yet none of you would once plead for his life. —
O God, I fear Thy justice will take hold
On me, and you, and mine, and yours for this! —
Come, Hastings, help me to my closet. — Ah,
Poor Clarence!   [*Exeunt some with* KING *and* QUEEN.

GLOSTER
This is the fruit of rashness! — Mark'd you not
How that the guilty kindred of the queen
Look'd pale when they did hear of Clarence' death?
O, they did urge it still unto the king!
God will revenge it. — Come, lords, will you go
To comfort Edward with our company?

BUCKINGHAM
We wait upon your Grace.   [*Exeunt.*

SCENE II

The palace.

Enter the old DUCHESS OF YORK, *with the two*
CHILDREN *of* CLARENCE.

SON
Good grandam, tell us, is our father dead?

DUCHESS OF YORK
No, boy.

DAUGHTER
Why do you weep so oft, and beat your breast,
And cry, 'O Clarence, my unhappy son!'

SON
Why do you look on us, and shake your head,
And call us orphans, wretches, castaways,
If that our noble father be alive?

DUCHESS OF YORK
My pretty cousins, you mistake me both;
I do lament the sickness of the king,
As loth to lose him, not your father's death;
It were lost sorrow to wail one that's lost.

SON
Then, grandam, you conclude that he is dead.
The king my uncle is to blame for this:
God will revenge it; whom I will importune
With daily prayers all to that effect.

DAUGHTER
And so will I.

DUCHESS OF YORK
Peace, children, peace! the king doth love you well:
Incapable and shallow innocents,
You cannot guess who caus'd your father's death.

SON
Grandam, we can; for my good uncle Gloster
Told me, the king, provoked by the queen,
Devis'd impeachments to imprison him:
And when my uncle told me so, he wept,
And pitied me, and kindly kiss'd my cheek;
Bade me rely on him as on my father,
And he would love me dearly as his child.

DUCHESS OF YORK
Ah, that deceit should steal such gentle shapes,
And with a virtuous vizor hide deep vice!
He is my son; ay, and therein my shame;
Yet from my dugs he drew not this deceit.

SON
Think you my uncle did dissemble, grandam?

DUCHESS OF YORK
Ay, boy.

SON
I cannot think it. — Hark! what noise is this?

Enter the QUEEN, *with her hair about her ears;*
RIVERS *and* DORSET *after her.*

QUEEN ELIZABETH
O, who shall hinder me to wail and weep,
To chide my fortune, and torment myself?
I'll join with black despair against my soul,
And to myself become an enemy.

DUCHESS OF YORK
What means this scene of rude impatience?

QUEEN ELIZABETH
To make an act of tragic violence: —
Edward, my lord, thy son, our king, is dead!
Why grow the branches when the root is gone?
Why wither not the leaves that want their sap?
If you will live, lament; if die, be brief,
That our swift-winged souls may catch the king's,
Or, like obedient subjects, follow him
To his new kingdom of ne'er-changing night.

DUCHESS OF YORK
Ah, so much interest have I in thy sorrow
As I had title in thy noble husband!
I have bewept a worthy husband's death,
And liv'd by looking on his images:
But now two mirrors of his princely semblance
Are crack'd in pieces by malignant death,
And I for comfort have but one false glass,
That grieves me when I see my shame in him.
Thou art a widow; yet thou art a mother,
And hast the comfort of thy children left thee:
But death hath snatch'd my husband from mine arms,
And pluck'd two crutches from my feeble hands, —
Clarence and Edward. O, what cause have I —
Thine being but a moiety of my grief —
To over-go thy plaints and drown thy cries!

SON
Ah, aunt, you wept not for our father's death!
How can we aid you with our kindred tears?

DAUGHTER
Our fatherless distress was left unmoan'd;
Your widow-dolour likewise be unwept!

QUEEN ELIZABETH
Give me no help in lamentation;
I am not barren to bring forth complaints:
All springs reduce their currents to mine eyes,
That I, being govern'd by the watery moon,
May send forth plenteous tears to drown the world!
Ah for my husband, for my dear Lord Edward!

CHILDREN
Ah for our father, for our dear Lord Clarence!

DUCHESS OF YORK
Alas for both, both mine, Edward and Clarence!

QUEEN ELIZABETH
What stay had I but Edward? and he's gone.

CHILDREN
What stay had we but Clarence? and he's gone.

DUCHESS OF YORK
What stays had I but they; and they are gone.

QUEEN ELIZABETH
Was never widow had so dear a loss!

CHILDREN
Were never orphans had so dear a loss!

DUCHESS OF YORK
Was never mother had so dear a loss!
Alas, I am the mother of these griefs!
Their woes are parcell'd, mine are general.
She for an Edward weeps, and so do I;

I for a Clarence weep, so doth not she:
These babes for Clarence weep, and so do I;
I for an Edward weep, so do not they: —
Alas, you three, on me, threefold distress'd,
Pour all your tears! I am your sorrow's nurse,
And I will pamper it with lamentations.

DORSET
Comfort, dear mother: God is much displeased
That you take with unthankfulness His doing:
In common worldly things 'tis call'd ungrateful
With dull unwillingness to repay a debt
Which with a bounteous hand was kindly lent;
Much more to be thus opposite with heaven,
For it requires the royal debt it lent you.

RIVERS
Madam, bethink you, like a careful mother,
Of the young prince your son: send straight for him;
Let him be crown'd; in him your comfort lives:
Drown desperate sorrow in dead Edward's grave,
And plant your joys in living Edward's throne.

Enter GLOSTER, BUCKINGHAM, DERBY,
HASTINGS, RATCLIFF, *and others.*

GLOSTER
Sister, have comfort: all of us have cause
To wail the dimming of our shining star;
But none can cure their harms by wailing them. —
Madam, my mother, I do cry you mercy;
I did not see your Grace: — humbly on my knee
I crave your blessing.

DUCHESS OF YORK
God bless thee; and put meekness in thy breast,
Love, charity, obedience, and true duty!

GLOSTER
Amen; — [*aside*] and make me die a good old man!
That is the butt-end of a mother's blessing:
I marvel that her Grace did leave it out.

BUCKINGHAM
You cloudy princes and heart-sorrowing peers,
That bear this mutual heavy load of moan,
Now cheer each other in each other's love:
Though we have spent our harvest of this king,
We are to reap the harvest of his son.
The broken rancour of your high-swoll'n hearts,
But lately splinter'd, knit and join'd together,
Must gently be preserv'd, cherish'd, and kept:
Me seemeth good, that, with some little train,
Forthwith from Ludlow the young prince be fet
Hither to London, to be crown'd our king.

RIVERS
Why with some little train, my Lord of Buckingham?

BUCKINGHAM
Marry, my lord, lest, by a multitude,
The new-heal'd wound of malice should break out;
Which would be so much the more dangerous,
By how much the estate is green and yet ungovern'd:
Where every horse bears his commanding rein,
And may direct his course as please himself,
As well the fear of harm as harm apparent,
In my opinion, ought to be prevented.

GLOSTER
I hope the king made peace with all of us;
And the compact is firm and true in me.

RIVERS
And so in me; and so, I think, in all:
Yet, since it is but green, it should be put
To no apparent likelihood of breach,
Which haply by much company might be urged:
Therefore I say with noble Buckingham,
That it is meet so few should fetch the prince.

HASTINGS
And so say I.

GLOSTER
Then be it so; and go we to determine
Who they shall be that straight shall post to Ludlow.
Madam, — and you, my mother, — will you go
To give your censures in this business?

QUEEN ELIZABETH and **DUCHESS OF YORK**
With all our hearts.
        [*Exeunt all except* BUCKINGHAM *and* GLOSTER.

BUCKINGHAM
My lord, whoever journeys to the prince,
For God's sake, let not us two stay at home;
For, by the way, I'll sort occasion,
As index to the story we late talk'd of,
To part the queen's proud kindred from the prince.

GLOSTER
My other self, my counsel's consistory,
My oracle, my prophet! — my dear cousin,
I, as a child, will go by thy direction.
Towards Ludlow then, for we'll not stay behind.   [*Exeunt.*

SCENE III

London. A street.

Enter two CITIZENS, *meeting.*

FIRST CITIZEN
Good morrow, neighbour: whither away so fast?
SECOND CITIZEN
I promise you I scarcely know myself:
Hear you the news abroad?
FIRST CITIZEN
                    Ay, — that the king is dead.
SECOND CITIZEN
Ill news, by'r lady; seldom comes the better:
I fear, I fear 'twill prove a giddy world.

Enter another CITIZEN.

THIRD CITIZEN
Neighbours, God speed!
FIRST CITIZEN
                    Give you good morrow, sir.
THIRD CITIZEN
Doth the news hold of good King Edward's death?
SECOND CITIZEN
Ay, sir, it is too true; God help, the while!
THIRD CITIZEN
Then, masters, look to see a troublous world.
FIRST CITIZEN
No, no; by God's good grace his son shall reign.
THIRD CITIZEN
Woe to that land that's govern'd by a child!
SECOND CITIZEN
In him there is a hope of government,
That, in his nonage, council under him,
And, in his full and ripen'd years, himself,
No doubt, shall then, and till then, govern well.
FIRST CITIZEN
So stood the state when Henry the Sixth
Was crown'd in Paris but at nine months old.
THIRD CITIZEN
Stood the state so? No, no, good friends, God wot;
For then this land was famously enrich'd
With politic grave counsel; then the king
Had virtuous uncles to protect his Grace.
FIRST CITIZEN
Why, so hath this, both by his father and mother.
THIRD CITIZEN
Better it were they all came by his father,
Or by his father there were none at all;
For emulation now, who shall be nearest,
Will touch us all too near, if God prevent not.
O, full of danger is the Duke of Gloster,
And the queen's sons and brothers haught and proud:
And were they to be rul'd, and not to rule,
This sickly land might solace as before.
FIRST CITIZEN
Come, come, we fear the worst; all will be well.
THIRD CITIZEN
When clouds are seen, wise men put on their cloaks;
When great leaves fall, then winter is at hand;
When the sun sets, who doth not look for night?
Untimely storms make men expect a dearth.
All may be well; but, if God sort it so,
'Tis more than we deserve, or I expect.
SECOND CITIZEN
Truly, the hearts of men are full of fear:
You cannot reason almost with a man
That looks not heavily and full of dread.
THIRD CITIZEN
Before the days of change, still is it so:
By a divine instinct men's minds mistrust
Ensuing danger; as, by proof, we see
The waters swell before a boisterous storm.
But leave it all to God. — Whither away?
SECOND CITIZEN
Marry, we were sent for to the justices.
THIRD CITIZEN
And so was I: I'll bear you company.   [*Exeunt.*

SCENE IV

London. The palace.

Enter the ARCHBISHOP OF YORK, *the young*
DUKE OF YORK, *the* QUEEN, *and the*
DUCHESS OF YORK.

ARCHBISHOP OF YORK
Last night, I hear, they lay at Northampton;
At Stony-Stratford will they be to-night;
To-morrow, or next day, they will be here.

DUCHESS OF YORK
I long with all my heart to see the prince:
I hope he is much grown since last I saw him.
QUEEN ELIZABETH
But I hear, no; they say my son of York
Has almost overta'en him in his growth.
YORK
Ay, mother; but I would not have it so.
DUCHESS OF YORK
Why, my young cousin, it is good to grow.
YORK
Grandam, one night, as we did sit at supper,
My uncle Rivers talk'd how I did grow
More than my brother: 'Ay,' quoth my uncle Gloster,
'Small herbs have grace, great weeds do grow apace':
And since, methinks, I would not grow so fast,
Because sweet flowers are slow, and weeds make haste.
DUCHESS OF YORK
Good faith, good faith, the saying did not hold
In him that did object the same to thee:
He was the wretched'st thing when he was young,
So long a-growing and so leisurely,
That, if his rule were true, he should be gracious.
ARCHBISHOP OF YORK
And so, no doubt, he is, my gracious madam.
DUCHESS OF YORK
I hope he is; but yet let mothers doubt.
YORK
Now, by my troth, if I had been remember'd,
I could have given my uncle's Grace a flout,
To touch his growth nearer than he touch'd mine.
DUCHESS OF YORK
How, my young York? I prithee, let me hear it.
YORK
Marry, they say my uncle grew so fast
That he could gnaw a crust at two hours old:
'Twas full two years ere I could get a tooth.
Grandam, this would have been a biting jest.
DUCHESS OF YORK
I prithee, pretty York, who told thee this?
YORK
Grandam, his nurse.
DUCHESS OF YORK
His nurse! why, she was dead ere thou wast born.
YORK
If 'twere not she, I cannot tell who told me.
QUEEN ELIZABETH
A parlous boy: — go to, you are too shrewd.
ARCHBISHOP OF YORK
Good madam, be not angry with the child.
QUEEN ELIZABETH
Pitchers have ears.
ARCHBISHOP OF YORK
                    Here comes a messenger.

Enter a MESSENGER.

What news?
MESSENGER
Such news, my lord, as grieves me to report.
QUEEN ELIZABETH
How doth the prince?
MESSENGER
                    Well, madam, and in health.
DUCHESS OF YORK
What is thy news, then?
MESSENGER
Lord Rivers and Lord Grey are sent to Pomfret,
With them Sir Thomas Vaughan, prisoners.
DUCHESS OF YORK
Who hath committed them?
MESSENGER
                    The mighty dukes
Gloster and Buckingham.
QUEEN ELIZABETH
                    For what offence?
MESSENGER
The sum of all I can I have disclosed;
Why or for what these nobles were committed
Is all unknown to me, my gracious lady.
QUEEN ELIZABETH
Ay me, I see the downfall of our house!
The tiger now hath seiz'd the gentle hind;
Insulting tyranny begins to jet
Upon the innocent and aweless throne:
Welcome, destruction, blood, and massacre!
I see, as in a map, the end of all.
DUCHESS OF YORK
Accursed and unquiet wrangling days,
How many of you have mine eyes beheld!

My husband lost his life to get the crown;
And often up and down my sons were toss'd,
For me to joy and weep their gain and loss:
And being seated, and domestic broils
Clean over-blown, themselves, the conquerors,
Make war upon themselves; brother to brother,
Blood to blood, self against self: — O, preposterous
And frantic outrage, end thy damned spleen;
Or let me die, to look on death no more!
QUEEN ELIZABETH
Come, come, my boy; we will to sanctuary. —
Madam, farewell.
DUCHESS OF YORK
                    Stay, I will go with you.
QUEEN ELIZABETH
You have no cause.
ARCHBISHOP OF YORK   [*to the* QUEEN.]
                    My gracious lady, go;
And thither bear your treasure and your goods.
For my part, I'll resign unto your Grace
The seal I keep: and so betide to me
As well I tender you and all of yours!
Come, I'll conduct you to the sanctuary.   [*Exeunt.*

ACT III

SCENE I

London. A street.

The trumpets sound. Enter the young PRINCE,
GLOSTER, BUCKINGHAM, CARDINAL
BOURCHIER, CATESBY, *and others.*

BUCKINGHAM
Welcome, sweet prince, to London, to your chamber.
GLOSTER
Welcome, dear cousin, my thoughts' sovereign:
The weary way hath made you melancholy.
PRINCE
No, uncle; but our crosses on the way
Have made it tedious, wearisome, and heavy:
I want more uncles here to welcome me.
GLOSTER
Sweet prince, the untainted virtue of your years
Hath not yet div'd into the world's deceit;
Nor more can you distinguish of a man
Than of his outward show; which, God He knows,
Seldom or never jumpeth with the heart.
Those uncles which you want were dangerous;
Your Grace attended to their sugar'd words,
But look'd not on the poison of their hearts:
God keep you from them, and from such false friends!
PRINCE
God keep me from false friends! but they were none.
GLOSTER
My lord, the mayor of London comes to greet you.

Enter the LORD MAYOR *and his* TRAIN.

MAYOR
God bless your Grace with health and happy days!
PRINCE
I thank you, good my lord; — and thank you all.
                    [MAYOR *and his* TRAIN *retire.*
I thought my mother, and my brother York,
Would long ere this have met us on the way:
Fie, what a slug is Hastings, that he comes not
To tell us whether they will come or no!
BUCKINGHAM
And, in good time, here comes the sweating lord.

Enter HASTINGS.

PRINCE
Welcome, my lord: what, will our mother come?
HASTINGS
On what occasion, God He knows, not I,
The queen your mother, and your brother York,
Have taken sanctuary: the tender prince
Would fain have come with me to meet your Grace,
But by his mother was perforce withheld.
BUCKINGHAM
Fie, what an indirect and peevish course
Is this of hers! — Lord Cardinal, will your Grace
Persuade the queen to send the Duke of York
Unto his princely brother presently?
If she deny, Lord Hastings, go with him,
And from her jealous arms pluck him perforce.
CARDINAL BOURCHIER
My Lord of Buckingham, if my weak oratory
Can from his mother win the Duke of York,
Anon expect him here; but if she be obdurate

GLOSTER Welcome, dear cousin, my thoughts' sovereign.

To mild entreaties, God in heaven forbid
We should infringe the holy privilege
Of blessed sanctuary! not for all this land
Would I be guilty of so great a sin.

BUCKINGHAM
You are too senseless-obstinate, my lord,
Too ceremonious and traditional:
Weigh it but with the grossness of this age,
You break not sanctuary in seizing him.
The benefit thereof is always granted
To those whose dealings have deserv'd the place,
And those who have the wit to claim the place:
This prince hath neither claim'd it nor deserv'd it;
And therefore, in mine opinion, cannot have it:
Then, taking him from thence that is not there,
You break no privilege nor charter there.
Oft have I heard of sanctuary-men;
But sanctuary-children ne'er till now.

CARDINAL BOURCHIER
My lord, you shall o'er-rule my mind for once. —
Come on, Lord Hastings, will you go with me?

HASTINGS
I go, my lord.

PRINCE
Good lords, make all the speedy haste you may.
          [*Exeunt* CARDINAL *and* HASTINGS.
Say, uncle Gloster, if our brother come,
Where shall we sojourn till our coronation?

GLOSTER
Where it seems best unto your royal self.
If I may counsel you, some day or two
Your highness shall repose you at the Tower;
Then where you please, and shall be thought most fit
For your best health and recreation.

PRINCE
I do not like the Tower, of any place. —
Did Julius Cæsar build that place, my lord?

BUCKINGHAM
He did, my gracious lord, begin that place;
Which, since, succeeding ages have re-edified.

PRINCE
Is it upon record, or else reported
Successively from age to age, he built it?

BUCKINGHAM
Upon record, my gracious lord.

PRINCE
But say, my lord, it were not register'd,
Methinks the truth should live from age to age,
As 'twere retail'd to all posterity,
Even to the general all-ending day.

GLOSTER [*aside*].
So wise so young, they say, do never live long.

PRINCE
What say you, uncle?

GLOSTER
I say, without characters, fame lives long. —
[*aside*] Thus, like the formal Vice, Iniquity,
I moralise two meanings in one word.

PRINCE
That Julius Cæsar was a famous man;
With what his valour did enrich his wit,
His wit set down to make his valour live:
Death makes no conquest of this conqueror;
For now he lives in fame, though not in life.
I'll tell you what, my cousin Buckingham, —

BUCKINGHAM
What, my gracious lord?

PRINCE
An if I live until I be a man,
I'll win our ancient right in France again,
Or die a soldier, as I liv'd a king.

GLOSTER [*aside*].
Short summers lightly have a forward spring.

BUCKINGHAM
Now, in good time, here comes the Duke of York.
Enter young YORK, HASTINGS, *and the* CARDINAL.

PRINCE
Richard of York! how fares our loving brother?

YORK
Well, my dread lord; so must I call you now.

PRINCE
Ay, brother, — to our grief, as it is yours:
Too late he died that might have kept that title,
Which by his death hath lost much majesty.

GLOSTER
How fares our cousin, noble Lord of York?

YORK
I thank you, gentle uncle. O, my lord,
You said that idle weeds are fast in growth:
The prince my brother hath outgrown me far.

GLOSTER
He hath, my lord.

YORK
                    And therefore is he idle?

GLOSTER
O, my fair cousin, I must not say so.

YORK
Then he is more beholding to you than I.

GLOSTER
He may command me as my sovereign;
But you have power in me as in a kinsman.

YORK
I pray you, uncle, give me this dagger.

GLOSTER
My dagger, little cousin? with all my heart.

PRINCE
A beggar, brother?

YORK
Of my kind uncle, that I know will give;
And being but a toy, which is no grief to give.

GLOSTER
A greater gift than that I'll give my cousin.

YORK
A greater gift! O, that's the sword to it.

GLOSTER
Ay, gentle cousin, were it light enough.

YORK
O, then, I see you will part but with light gifts;
In weightier things you'll say a beggar nay.

GLOSTER
It is too heavy for your Grace to wear.

YORK
I weigh it lightly, were it heavier.

GLOSTER
What, would you have my weapon, little lord?

YORK
I would, that I might thank you as you call me.

GLOSTER
How?

YORK
Little.

PRINCE
My Lord of York will still be cross in talk: —
Uncle, your Grace knows how to bear with him.

YORK
You mean, to bear me, not to bear with me: —
Uncle, my brother mocks both you and me;
Because that I am little, like an ape,
He thinks that you should bear me on your shoulders.

BUCKINGHAM [*aside to* HASTINGS].
With what a sharp-provided wit he reasons!
To mitigate the scorn he gives his uncle,
He prettily and aptly taunts himself:
So cunning and so young is wonderful.

GLOSTER
My lord, will't please you pass along?
Myself and my good cousin Buckingham
Will to your mother, to entreat of her
To meet you at the Tower and welcome you.

YORK
What, will you go unto the Tower, my lord?

PRINCE
My lord Protector needs will have it so.

YORK
I shall not sleep in quiet at the Tower.

GLOSTER
Why, what should you fear?

YORK
Marry, my uncle Clarence' angry ghost:
My grandam told me he was murder'd there.

PRINCE
I fear no uncles dead.
GLOSTER
Nor none that live, I hope.
PRINCE
An if they live, I hope I need not fear.
But come, my lord; and with a heavy heart,
Thinking on them, go I unto the Tower.
　　[*A sennet. Exeunt all but* GLOSTER, BUCKINGHAM,
　　　　　　　　　　　　　　and CATESBY.

BUCKINGHAM
Think you, my lord, this little prating York
Was not incensed by his subtle mother
To taunt and scorn you thus opprobriously?
GLOSTER
No doubt, no doubt: O, 'tis a parlous boy,
Bold, quick, ingenious, forward, capable:
He is all the mother's, from the top to toe.
BUCKINGHAM
Well, let them rest. — Come hither, Catesby.
Thou art sworn as deeply to effect what we intend
As closely to conceal what we impart:
Thou know'st our reasons urg'd upon the way; —
What think'st thou? is it not an easy matter
To make William Lord Hastings of our mind,
For the instalment of this noble duke
In the seat royal of this famous isle?
CATESBY
He for his father's sake so loves the prince,
That he will not be won to aught against him.
BUCKINGHAM
What think'st thou, then, of Stanley? will not he?
CATESBY
He will do all in all as Hastings doth.
BUCKINGHAM
Well, then, no more but this: go, gentle Catesby,
And, as it were far off, sound thou Lord Hastings,
How he doth stand affected to our purpose;
And summon him to-morrow to the Tower,
To sit about the coronation.
If thou dost find him tractable to us,
Encourage him, and show him all our reasons:
If he be leaden, icy-cold, unwilling,
Be thou so too; and so break off your talk,
And give us notice of his inclination:
For we to-morrow hold divided councils,
Wherein thyself shalt highly be employ'd.
GLOSTER
Commend me to Lord William: tell him, Catesby,
His ancient knot of dangerous adversaries
To-morrow are let blood at Pomfret-castle;
And bid my friend, for joy of this good news,
Give Mistress Shore one gentle kiss the more.
BUCKINGHAM
Good Catesby, go, effect this business soundly.
CATESBY
My good lords both, with all the heed I can.
GLOSTER
Shall we hear from you, Catesby, ere we sleep?
CATESBY
You shall, my lord.
GLOSTER
At Crosby-place, there shall you find us both.
　　　　　　　　　　　　　[*Exit* CATESBY.
BUCKINGHAM
Now, my lord, what shall we do, if we perceive
Lord Hastings will not yield to our complots?
GLOSTER
Chop off his head, man; — somewhat we will do: —
And, look, when I am king, claim thou of me
The earldom of Hereford, and the moveables
Whereof the king my brother stood possess'd.
BUCKINGHAM
I'll claim that promise at your Grace's hand.
GLOSTER
And look to have it yielded with all kindness.
Come, let us sup betimes, that afterwards
We may digest our complots in some form.　　[*Exeunt.*

SCENE II

Before LORD HASTINGS' *house.*

Enter a MESSENGER *to the door of* HASTINGS.

MESSENGER
My lord! my lord! —　　　　　　　　　[*Knocking.*
HASTINGS [*within*].
Who knocks?
MESSENGER
One from the Lord Stanley.

HASTINGS [*within*].
What is't o'clock?
MESSENGER
Upon the stroke of four.
　　　　　　　　Enter HASTINGS.

HASTINGS
Cannot thy master sleep these tedious nights?
MESSENGER
So it appears by that I have to say.
First, he commends him to your noble self.
HASTINGS
What then?
MESSENGER
Then certifies your lordship, that this night
He dreamt the boar had razed off his helm:
Besides, he says there are two councils held;
And that may be determin'd at the one
Which may make you and him to rue at th'other.
Therefore he sends to know your lordship's pleasure, —
If presently you will take horse with him,
And with all speed post with him toward the north,
To shun the danger that his soul divines.
HASTINGS
Go, fellow, go, return unto thy lord;
Bid him not fear the separated councils:
His honour and myself are at the one,
And at the other is my good friend Catesby;
Where nothing can proceed that toucheth us
Whereof I shall not have intelligence.
Tell him his fears are shallow, wanting instance:
And for his dreams, I wonder he's so simple
To trust the mockery of unquiet slumbers:
To fly the boar before the boar pursues,
Were to incense the boar to follow us,
And make pursuit where he did mean no chase.
Go, bid thy master rise and come to me;
And we will both together to the Tower,
Where he shall see the boar will use us kindly.
MESSENGER
I'll go, my lord, and tell him what you say.　　[*Exit.*
　　　　　　　　Enter CATESBY.

CATESBY
Many good morrows to my noble lord!
HASTINGS
Good morrow, Catesby; you are early stirring:
What news, what news, in this our tottering state?
CATESBY
It is a reeling world, indeed, my lord;
And I believe will never stand upright
Till Richard wear the garland of the realm.
HASTINGS
How! wear the garland! dost thou mean the crown?
CATESBY
Ay, my good lord.
HASTINGS
I'll have this crown of mine cut from my shoulders
Before I'll see the crown so foul misplaced.
But canst thou guess that he doth aim at it?
CATESBY
Ay, on my life; and hopes to find forward
Upon his party for the gain thereof:
And thereupon he sends you this good news, —
That this same very day your enemies,
The kindred of the queen, must die at Pomfret.
HASTINGS
Indeed, I am no mourner for that news,
Because they have been still my adversaries:
But, that I'll give my voice on Richard's side,
To bar my master's heirs in true descent,
God knows I will not do it to the death.
CATESBY
God keep your lordship in that gracious mind!
HASTINGS
But I shall laugh at this a twelve-month hence, —
That they who brought me in my master's hate,
I live to look upon their tragedy.
Well, Catesby, ere a fortnight make me older,
I'll send some packing that yet think not on't.
CATESBY
'Tis a vile thing to die, my gracious lord,
When men are unprepared and look not for it.
HASTINGS
O monstrous, monstrous! and so falls it out
With Rivers, Vaughan, Grey: and so 'twill do
With some men else, who think themselves as safe
As thou and I; who, as thou know'st, are dear
To princely Richard and to Buckingham.

CATESBY
The princes both make high account of you, —
[*aside*] For they account his head upon the bridge.
HASTINGS
I know they do; and I have well deserv'd it.
　　　　　　　　Enter STANLEY.
Come on, come on; where is your boar-spear, man?
Fear you the boar, and go so unprovided?
STANLEY
My lord, good morrow; — good morrow, Catesby: —
You may jest on, but, by the holy rood,
I do not like these several councils, I.
HASTINGS
My lord,
I hold my life as dear as you do yours;
And never in my days, I do protest,
Was it more precious to me than 'tis now:
Think you, but that I know our state secure,
I would be so triumphant as I am?
STANLEY
The lords at Pomfret, when they rode from London,
Were jocund, and suppos'd their states were sure, —
And they, indeed, had no cause to mistrust;
But yet, you see, how soon the day o'ercast.
This sudden stab of rancour I misdoubt:
Pray God, I say, I prove a needless coward!
What, shall we toward the Tower? the day is spent.
HASTINGS
Come, come, have with you. — Wot you what, my lord?
To-day the lords you talk of are beheaded.
STANLEY
They, for their truth, might better wear their heads
Than some that have accus'd them wear their hats. —
But come, my lord, let us away.
　　　　　　　　Enter a PURSUIVANT.
HASTINGS
Go on before; I'll talk with this good fellow.
　　　　　　[*Exeunt* STANLEY *and* CATESBY.
How now, sirrah! how goes the world with thee?
PURSUIVANT
The better that your lordship please to ask.
HASTINGS
I tell thee, man, 'tis better with me now
Than when thou mett'st me last where now we meet:
Then was I going prisoner to the Tower,
By the suggestion of the queen's allies;
But now, I tell thee — keep it to thyself —
This day those enemies are put to death,
And I in better state than e'er I was.
PURSUIVANT
God hold it, to your honour's good content!
HASTINGS
Gramercy, fellow: there, drink that for me.
　　　　　　　　　[*Throwing him his purse.*
PURSUIVANT
God save your lordship!　　　　　　　[*Exit.*
　　　　　　　　Enter a PRIEST.
PRIEST
Well met, my lord; I am glad to see your honour.
HASTINGS
I thank thee, good Sir John, with all my heart.
I am in your debt for your last exercise;
Come the next Sabbath, and I will content you.
　　　　　　　　[*He whispers in his ear.*
　　　　　　　　Enter BUCKINGHAM.
BUCKINGHAM
What, talking with a priest, lord chamberlain!
Your friends at Pomfret, they do need the priest;
Your honour hath no shriving-work in hand.
HASTINGS
Good faith, and when I met this holy man,
The men you talk of came into my mind. —
What, go you toward the Tower?
BUCKINGHAM
I do, my lord; but long I cannot stay there:
I shall return before your lordship thence.
HASTINGS
Nay, like enough, for I stay dinner there.
BUCKINGHAM [*aside*].
And supper too, although thou know'st it not. —
Come, will you go?
HASTINGS
I'll wait upon your lordship.　　　　　[*Exeunt.*

SCENE III

Pomfret Castle.

Enter SIR RICHARD RATCLIFF, *with halberds, carrying* RIVERS, GREY, *and* VAUGHAN *to death.*

RATCLIFF
Come, bring forth the prisoners.
RIVERS
Sir Richard Ratcliff, let me tell thee this, —
To-day shalt thou behold a subject die
For truth, for duty, and for loyalty.
GREY
God keep the prince from all the pack of you!
A knot you are of damned blood-suckers.
VAUGHAN
You live that shall cry woe for this hereafter.
RATCLIFF
Dispatch; the limit of your lives is out.
RIVERS
O Pomfret, Pomfret! O thou bloody prison,
Fatal and ominous to noble peers!
Within the guilty closure of thy walls
Richard the Second here was hack'd to death;
And, for more slander to thy dismal seat,
We give thee up our guiltless blood to drink.
GREY
Now Margaret's curse is fall'n upon our heads,
When she exclaim'd on Hastings, you, and I,
For standing by when Richard stabb'd her son.
RIVERS
Then curs'd she Richard, then curs'd she Buckingham,
Then curs'd she Hastings: — O, remember, God,
To hear her prayers for them, as now for us!
And for my sister and her princely sons,
Be satisfied, dear God, with our true blood,
Which, as Thou know'st, unjustly must be spilt.
RATCLIFF
Make haste; the hour of death is expiate.
RIVERS
Come, Grey, — come, Vaughan, — let us here
 embrace:
Farewell, until we meet again in heaven.   [*Exeunt.*

SCENE IV

London. The Tower.

Enter BUCKINGHAM, DERBY, HASTINGS, *the* BISHOP OF ELY, RATCLIFF, LOVEL, *with others, at a table.*

HASTINGS
Now, noble peers, the cause why we are met
Is, to determine of the coronation.
In God's name, speak: — when is the royal day?
BUCKINGHAM
Are all things ready for that royal time?
DERBY
It is; and wants but nomination.
BISHOP OF ELY
To-morrow, then, I judge a happy day.
BUCKINGHAM
Who knows the lord Protector's mind herein?
Who is most inward with the noble duke?
BISHOP OF ELY
Your Grace, we think, should soonest know his mind.
BUCKINGHAM
Who? I, my lord? We know each other's faces,
But for our hearts, he knows no more of mine
Than I of yours; nor I no more of his
Than you of mine.
Lord Hastings, you and he are near in love.
HASTINGS
I thank his Grace, I know he loves me well;
But, for his purpose in the coronation,
I have not sounded him, nor he deliver'd
His gracious pleasure any way therein:
But you, my noble lords, may name the time;
And in the duke's behalf I'll give my voice,
Which, I presume, he'll take in gentle part.
BISHOP OF ELY
In happy time, here comes the duke himself.

Enter GLOSTER.

GLOSTER
My noble lords and cousins all, good morrow.
I have been long a sleeper: but, I trust,
My absence doth neglect no great design,
Which by my presence might have been concluded.
BUCKINGHAM
Had you not come upon your cue, my lord,

William Lord Hastings had pronounc'd your part, —
I mean, your voice, — for crowning of the king.
GLOSTER
Than my Lord Hastings no man might be bolder;
His lordship knows me well, and loves me well. —
My Lord of Ely, when I was last in Holborn,
I saw good strawberries in your garden there:
I do beseech you send for some of them.
BISHOP OF ELY
Marry, and will, my lord, with all my heart.   [*Exit.*
GLOSTER
Cousin of Buckingham, a word with you.
                              [*Takes him aside.*
Catesby hath sounded Hastings in our business,
And finds the testy gentleman so hot,
That he will lose his head ere give consent
His master's child, as worshipfully he terms it,
Shall lose the royalty of England's throne.
BUCKINGHAM
Withdraw you hence, my lord; I'll follow you.
       [*Exit* GLOSTER, *follow'd by* BUCKINGHAM.
DERBY
We have not yet set down this day of triumph.
To-morrow, in my judgement, is too sudden;
For I myself am not so well provided
As else I would be, were the day prolong'd.

Enter BISHOP OF ELY.

BISHOP OF ELY
Where is my lord the Duke of Gloster?
I have sent for these strawberries.
His Grace looks cheerfully and smooth to-day;
There's some conceit or other likes him well,
When he doth bid good-morrow with such a spirit.
I think there's never a man in Christendom
That can less hide his love or hate than he;
For by his face straight shall you know his heart.
DERBY
What of his heart perceive you in his face
By any likelihood he show'd to-day?
HASTINGS
Marry, that with no man here he is offended;
For, were he, he had shown it in his looks.
DERBY
I pray God he be not, I say.

Enter GLOSTER *and* BUCKINGHAM.

GLOSTER
I pray you all, tell me what they deserve
That do conspire my death with devilish plots
Of damned witchcraft, and that have prevail'd
Upon my body with their hellish charms?
HASTINGS
The tender love I bear your Grace, my lord,
Makes me most forward in this noble presence
To doom th'offenders: whosoe'er they be,
I say, my lord, they have deserved death.
GLOSTER
Then be your eyes the witness of their evil:
Look how I am bewitch'd; behold mine arm
Is, like a blasted sapling, wither'd up:
And this is Edward's wife, that monstrous witch,
Consorted with that harlot-strumpet Shore,
That by their witchcraft thus have marked me.
HASTINGS
If they have done this thing, my gracious lord, —
GLOSTER
If! thou protector of this damned strumpet,
Talk'st thou to me of 'ifs'? Thou art a traitor: —
Off with his head! — now, by Saint Paul, I swear
I will not dine until I see the same. —
Lovel and Ratcliff, look that it be done: —
The rest, that love me, rise and follow me.
                    [*Exeunt all, except* HASTINGS,
                         LOVEL, *and* RATCLIFF.
HASTINGS
Woe, woe for England! not a whit for me;
For I, too fond, might have prevented this.
Stanley did dream the boar did raze his helm;
But I disdain'd it, and did scorn to fly:
Three times to-day my foot-cloth horse did stumble
And started when he look'd upon the Tower,
As loth to bear me to the slaughter-house.
O, now I need the priest that spake to me:
I now repent I told the pursuivant,
As too triumphing, how mine enemies
To-day at Pomfret bloodily were butcher'd,
And I myself secure in grace and favour.
O Margaret, Margaret, now thy heavy curse
Is lighted on poor Hastings' wretched head!

RATCLIFF
Dispatch, my lord; the duke would be at dinner:
Make a short shrift; he longs to see your head.
HASTINGS
O momentary grace of mortal men,
Which we more hunt for than the grace of God!
Who builds his hope in air of your fair looks,
Lives like a drunken sailor on a mast,
Ready, with every nod, to tumble down
Into the fatal bowels of the deep.
LOVEL
Come, come, dispatch; 'tis bootless to exclaim.
HASTINGS
O bloody Richard! — miserable England!
I prophesy the fearfull'st time to thee
That ever wretched age hath look'd upon. —
Come, lead me to the block; bear him my head:
They smile at me who shortly shall be dead.   [*Exeunt.*

SCENE V

The Tower-walls.

Enter GLOSTER *and* BUCKINGHAM, *in rotten armour, marvellous ill-favour'd.*

GLOSTER
Come, cousin, canst thou quake, and change thy
 colour,
Murder thy breath in the middle of a word,
And then begin again, and stop again,
As if thou wert distraught and mad with terror?
BUCKINGHAM
Tut, I can counterfeit the deep tragedian;
Speak and look back, and pry on every side,
Tremble and start at wagging of a straw,
Intending deep suspicion: ghastly looks
Are at my service, like enforced smiles;
And both are ready in their offices,
At any time, to grace my stratagems.
But what, is Catesby gone?
GLOSTER
He is; and, see, he brings the mayor along.
BUCKINGHAM
Let me alone to entertain him.
            Enter the MAYOR *and* CATESBY.
                         Lord mayor, —
GLOSTER
Look to the drawbridge there!
BUCKINGHAM
                         Hark! a drum.
GLOSTER
Catesby, o'erlook the walls.
BUCKINGHAM
Lord mayor, the reason we have sent, —
GLOSTER
Look back, defend thee, — here are enemies.
BUCKINGHAM
God and our innocency defend and guard us!
GLOSTER
Be patient, they are friends, — Ratcliff and Lovel.

Enter LOVEL *and* RATCLIFF, *with* HASTINGS' head.

LOVEL
Here is the head of that ignoble traitor,
The dangerous and unsuspected Hastings.
GLOSTER
So dear I lov'd the man, that I must weep.
I took him for the plainest harmless creature
That breath'd upon the earth a Christian;
Made him my book, wherein my soul recorded
The history of all her secret thoughts,
So smooth he daub'd his vice with show of virtue,
That, his apparent open guilt omitted, —
I mean, his conversation with Shore's wife, —
He liv'd from all attainder of suspect.
BUCKINGHAM
Well, well, he was the covert'st shelter'd traitor
That ever liv'd.
Would you imagine, or almost believe, —
Were't not that, by great preservation,
We live to tell it you, — the subtle traitor
This day had plotted, in the council-house,
To murder me and my good Lord of Gloster?
MAYOR OF LONDON
What, had he so?
GLOSTER
What, think you we are Turks or infidels?
Or that we would, against the form of law,
Proceed thus rashly to the villain's death,
But that the extreme peril of the case,
The peace of England and our persons' safety,

Enforc'd us to this execution?

MAYOR OF LONDON
Now, fair befall you! he deserv'd his death;
And your good Graces both have well proceeded,
To warn false traitors from the like attempts.
I never look'd for better at his hands,
After he once fell in with Mistress Shore.

BUCKINGHAM
Yet had we not determin'd he should die,
Until your lordship came to see his end;
Which now the loving haste of these our friends,
Somewhat against our meaning, have prevented;
Because, my lord, we would have had you heard
The traitor speak, and timorously confess
The manner and the purpose of his treason;
That you might well have signified the same
Unto the citizens, who haply may
Misconster us in him, and wail his death.

MAYOR OF LONDON
But, my good lord, your Grace's word shall serve,
As well as I had seen, and heard him speak;
And do not doubt, right noble princes both,
But I'll acquaint our duteous citizens
With all your just proceedings in this case.

GLOSTER
And to that end we wish'd your lordship here,
T'avoid the censures of the carping world.

BUCKINGHAM
But since you come too late of our intent,
Yet witness what you hear we did intend:
And so, my good lord mayor, we bid farewell.
                                        [*Exit* MAYOR.

GLOSTER
Go, after, after, cousin Buckingham.
The mayor towards Guildhall hies him in all post: —
There, at your meetest vantage of the time,
Infer the bastardy of Edward's children:
Tell them how Edward put to death a citizen,
Only for saying he would make his son
Heir to the crown; meaning, indeed, his house,
Which, by the sign thereof, was termed so.
Moreover, urge his hateful luxury,
And bestial appetite in change of lust;
Which stretch'd unto their servants, daughters, wives,
Even where his raging eye or savage heart,
Without control, listed to make a prey.
Nay, for a need, thus far come near my person: —
Tell them, when that my mother went with child
Of that unsatiate Edward, noble York,
My princely father, then had wars in France;
And, by just computation of the time,
Found that the issue was not his begot;
Which well appeared in his lineaments,
Being nothing like the noble duke my father:
Yet touch this sparingly, as 'twere far off;
Because, my lord, you know my mother lives.

BUCKINGHAM
Doubt not, my lord, I'll play the orator
As if the golden fee for which I plead
Were for myself: and so, my lord, adieu.

GLOSTER
If you thrive well, bring them to Baynard's Castle;
Where you shall find me well accompanied
With reverend fathers and well-learned bishops.

BUCKINGHAM
I go; and towards three or four o'clock
Look for the news that the Guildhall affords.   [*Exit*.

GLOSTER
Go, Lovel, with all speed to Doctor Shaw, —
[*to* CATESBY] Go thou to Friar Penker; — bid them
    both
Meet me within this hour at Baynard's Castle.
                    [*Exeunt* LOVEL, CATESBY, *and* RATCLIFF.
Now will I in, to take some privy order,
To draw the brats of Clarence out of sight;
And to give notice that no manner person
Have any time recourse unto the princes.   [*Exit*.

SCENE VI

The same. A street.

Enter a SCRIVENER, *with a paper in his hand.*

SCRIVENER
Here is th'indictment of the good Lord Hastings;
Which in a set hand fairly is engross'd,
That it may be to-day read o'er in Paul's.
And mark how well the sequel hangs together:
Eleven hours I have spent to write it over,
For yesternight by Catesby was it sent me;
The precedent was full as long a-doing:

And yet within these five hours Hastings liv'd,
Untainted, unexamin'd, free, at liberty.
Here's a good world the while! Why, who's so gross
That cannot see this palpable device?
Yet who so bold but says he sees it not?
Bad is the world; and all will come to naught
When such ill dealing must be seen in thought.   [*Exit*.

SCENE VII

Baynard's Castle.

Enter GLOSTER *and* BUCKINGHAM, *meeting.*

GLOSTER
How now, how now! what say the citizens?

BUCKINGHAM
Now, by the holy mother of our Lord,
The citizens are mum, say not a word.

GLOSTER
Touch'd you the bastardy of Edward's children?

BUCKINGHAM
I did; with his contract with Lady Lucy,
And his contract by deputy in France;
Th'insatiate greediness of his desires,
And his enforcement of the city wives;
His tyranny for trifles, his own bastardy, —
As being got, your father then in France,
And his resemblance, being not like the duke:
Withal I did infer your lineaments, —
Being the right idea of your father,
Both in your form and nobleness of mind;
Laid open all your victories in Scotland,
Your discipline in war, wisdom in peace,
Your bounty, virtue, fair humility;
Indeed, left nothing fitting for the purpose
Untouch'd, or slightly handled, in discourse:
And when my oratory drew toward end,
I bade them that did love their country's good
Cry, 'God save Richard, England's royal king!'

GLOSTER
And did they so?

BUCKINGHAM
No, so God help me, they spake not a word;
But, like dumb statuas or breathing stones,
Stared each on other, and look'd deadly pale.
Which when I saw, I reprehended them;
And ask'd the mayor what meant this wilful silence:
His answer was, — the people were not used
To be spoke to but by the recorder.
Then he was urg'd to tell my tale again, —
'Thus saith the duke, thus hath the duke inferr'd';
But nothing spake in warrant from himself.
When he had done, some followers of mine
    own,
At lower end of the hall, hurl'd up their caps,
And some ten voices cried, 'God save King
    Richard!'
And thus I took the vantage of those few, —
'Thanks, gentle citizens and friends,' quoth
    I;
'This general applause and cheerful shout
Argues your wisdom and your love to
    Richard':
And even here brake off, and came away.

GLOSTER
What tongueless blocks were they! would
    they not speak?

BUCKINGHAM
No, by my troth, my lord.

GLOSTER
Will not the mayor, then, and his brethren,
    come?

BUCKINGHAM
The mayor is here at hand. Intend some
    fear;
Be not you spoke with but by mighty suit:
And look you get a prayer-book in your
    hand,
And stand between two churchmen, good
    my lord;
For on that ground I'll make a holy descant:
And be not easily won to our request;
Play the maid's part, — still answer nay, and
    take it.

GLOSTER
I go; and if you plead as well for them
As I can say nay to thee for myself,
No doubt we'll bring it to a happy issue.

BUCKINGHAM
Go, go, up to the leads; the lord mayor
    knocks.

[*Exit* GLOSTER.
Enter the MAYOR, ALDERMEN, *and* CITIZENS.
Welcome, my lord: I dance attendance here;
I think the duke will not be spoke withal.
                    Enter CATESBY.
Now, Catesby, what says your lord to my request?

CATESBY
He doth entreat your Grace, my noble lord,
To visit him to-morrow or next day:
He is within, with two right-reverend fathers,
Divinely bent to meditation:
And in no worldly suit would he be moved,
To draw him from his holy exercise.

BUCKINGHAM
Return, good Catesby, to the gracious duke;
Tell him, myself, the mayor and aldermen,
In deep designs and matters of great moment,
No less importing than our general good,
Are come to have some conference with his Grace.

CATESBY
I'll signify so much unto him straight.   [*Exit*.

BUCKINGHAM
Ah, ha, my lord, this prince is not an Edward!
He is not lolling on a lewd day-bed,
But on his knees at meditation;
Not dallying with a brace of courtezans,
But meditating with two deep divines;
Not sleeping, to engross his idle body,
But praying, to enrich his watchful soul:
Happy were England, would this virtuous prince
Take on himself the sovereignty thereof;
But sure I fear we shall not win him to it.

MAYOR OF LONDON
Marry, God defend his Grace should say us nay!

BUCKINGHAM
I fear he will. Here Catesby comes again.
                    Enter CATESBY.
Now, Catesby, what says his Grace?

CATESBY
He wonders to what end you have assembled
Such troops of citizens to come to him,
His Grace not being warn'd thereof before:
He fears, my lord, you mean no good to him.

BUCKINGHAM
Sorry I am my noble cousin should
Suspect me, that I mean no good to him:
By heaven, we come to him in perfect love;
And so once more return and tell his Grace.
                                        [*Exit* CATESBY.

MAYOR OF LONDON See, where his Grace stands 'tween
two clergymen!

When holy and devout religious men
Are at their beads, 'tis much to draw them thence, —
So sweet is zealous contemplation.

Enter GLOSTER *aloft, between two* BISHOPS.
CATESBY *returns.*

MAYOR OF LONDON
See, where his Grace stands 'tween two clergymen!

BUCKINGHAM
Two props of virtue for a Christian prince,
To stay him from the fall of vanity:
And, see, a book of prayer in his hand, —
True ornaments to know a holy man. —
Famous Plantagenet, most gracious prince,
Lend favourable ear to our request;
And pardon us the interruption
Of thy devotion and right Christian zeal.

GLOSTER
My lord, there needs no such apology:
I rather do beseech you pardon me,
Who, earnest in the service of my God,
Neglect the visitation of my friends.
But, leaving this, what is your Grace's pleasure?

BUCKINGHAM
Even that, I hope, which pleaseth God above,
And all good men of this ungovern'd isle.

GLOSTER
I do suspect I have done some offence
That seems disgracious in the city's eyes;
And that you come to reprehend my ignorance.

BUCKINGHAM
You have, my lord: would it might please your Grace,
On our entreaties, to amend your fault!

GLOSTER
Else wherefore breathe I in a Christian land?

BUCKINGHAM
Know, then, it is your fault that you resign
The supreme seat, the throne majestical,
The sceptred office of your ancestors,
Your state of fortune and your due of birth,
The lineal glory of your royal house,
To the corruption of a blemish'd stock:
Whilst, in the mildness of your sleepy thoughts —
Which here we waken to our country's good —
This noble isle doth want her proper limbs;
Her face defac'd with scars of infamy,
Her royal stock graft with ignoble plants,
And almost shoulder'd in the swallowing gulf
Of dark forgetfulness and deep oblivion.
Which to recure, we heartily solicit
Your gracious self to take on you the charge
And kingly government of this your land; —
Not as protector, steward, substitute,
Or lowly factor for another's gain;
But as successively, from blood to blood,
Your right of birth, your empery, your own.
For this, consorted with the citizens,
Your very worshipful and loving friends,
And by their vehement instigation,
In this just suit come I to move your Grace.

GLOSTER
I cannot tell, if to depart in silence,
Or bitterly to speak in your reproof,
Best fitteth my degree or your condition:
If not to answer, you might haply think
Tongue-tied ambition, not replying, yielded
To bear the golden yoke of sovereignty,
Which fondly you would here impose on me:
If to reprove you for this suit of yours,
So season'd with your faithful love to me,
Then, on the other side, I check'd my friends.
Therefore, — to speak, and to avoid the first,
And then, in speaking not to incur the last, —
Definitively thus I answer you:
Your love deserves my thanks; but my desert
Unmeritable shuns your high request.
First, if all obstacles were cut away,
And that my path were even to the crown,
As the ripe revenue and due of birth;
Yet so much is my poverty of spirit,
So mighty and so many my defects,
That I would rather hide me from my greatness —
Being a bark to brook no mighty sea —
Than in my greatness covet to be hid,
And in the vapour of my glory smother'd.
But, God be thank'd, there is no need of me; —
And much I need to help you, were there need; —
The royal tree hath left us royal fruit,
Which, mellow'd by the stealing hours of time,
Will well become the seat of majesty,
And make, no doubt, us happy by his reign.

On him I lay what you would lay on me,
The right and fortune of his happy stars;
Which God defend that I should wring from him!

BUCKINGHAM
My lord, this argues conscience in your Grace;
But the respects thereof are nice and trivial,
All circumstances well considered.
You say that Edward is your brother's son:
So say we too, but not by Edward's wife;
For first he was contract to Lady Lucy, —
Your mother lives a witness to his vow, —
And afterward by substitute betroth'd
To Bona, sister to the King of France.
These both put by, a poor petitioner,
A care-craz'd mother of a many children,
A beauty-waning and distressed widow,
Even in the afternoon of her best days,
Made prize and purchase of his wanton eye,
Seduc'd the pitch and height of his degree
To base declension and loath'd bigamy:
By her, in his unlawful bed, he got
This Edward, whom our manners call the prince.
More bitterly could I expostulate,
Save that, for reverence to some alive,
I give a sparing limit to my tongue.
Then, good my lord, take to your royal self
This proffer'd benefit of dignity;
If not to bless us and the land withal,
Yet to draw forth your noble ancestry
From the corruption of abusing time
Unto a lineal true-derived course.

MAYOR OF LONDON
Do, good my lord; your citizens entreat you.

BUCKINGHAM
Refuse not, mighty lord, this proffer'd love.

CATESBY
O, make them joyful, grant their lawful suit!

GLOSTER
Alas, why would you heap these cares on me?
I am unfit for state and majesty: —
I do beseech you, take it not amiss;
I cannot nor I will not yield to you.

BUCKINGHAM
If you refuse it, — as, in love and zeal,
Loth to depose the child, your brother's son;
As well we know your tenderness of heart,
And gentle, kind, effeminate remorse,
Which we have noted in you to your kindred,
And egally indeed to all estates, —
Yet whether you accept our suit or no,
Your brother's son shall never reign our king;
But we will plant some other in the throne,
To the disgrace and downfall of your house:
And in this resolution here we leave you. —
Come, citizens: zounds, I'll entreat no more.

GLOSTER
O, do not swear, my lord of Buckingham.
                    [*Exit* BUCKINGHAM *with the* CITIZENS.

CATESBY
Call him again, sweet prince, accept their suit:
If you deny them, all the land will rue it.

GLOSTER
Will you enforce me to a world of cares?
Well, call them again. I am not made of stones,
But penetrable to your kind entreats,
Albeit against my conscience and my soul.
            Enter BUCKINGHAM *and the others.*
Cousin of Buckingham, and you sage, grave men,
Since you will buckle fortune on my back,
To bear her burden, whe'r I will or no,
I must have patience to endure the load:
But if black scandal or foul-fac'd reproach
Attend the sequel of your imposition,
Your mere enforcement shall acquittance me
From all the impure blots and stains thereof;
For God He knows, and you may partly see,
How far I am from the desire of this.

MAYOR OF LONDON
God bless your Grace! we see it, and will say it.

GLOSTER
In saying so, you shall but say the truth.

BUCKINGHAM
Then I salute you with this royal title, —
Long live King Richard, England's worthy king!

ALL
Amen.

BUCKINGHAM
To-morrow may it please you to be crown'd?

GLOSTER
Even when you please, since you will have it so.

BUCKINGHAM
To-morrow, then, we will attend your Grace:
And so, most joyfully, we take our leave.

GLOSTER [*to the* BISHOPS].
Come, let us to our holy work again. —
Farewell, good cousin; farewell, gentle friends.
                                    [*Exeunt.*

ACT IV

SCENE I

London. Before the Tower.

Enter, on one side, QUEEN ELIZABETH, DUCHESS
OF YORK, *and* DORSET; *on the other,* LADY ANNE,
DUCHESS OF GLOSTER, *leading* LADY
MARGARET PLANTAGENET, CLARENCE'S *young
daughter.*

DUCHESS OF YORK
Who meets us here? my niece Plantagenet,
Led in the hand of her kind aunt of Gloster?
Now, for my life, she's wandering to the Tower,
On pure heart's love, to greet the tender princes. —
Daughter, well met.

LADY ANNE
                    God give your Graces both
A happy and a joyful time of day!

QUEEN ELIZABETH
As much to you, good sister! Whither away?

LADY ANNE
No further than the Tower; and, as I guess,
Upon the like devotion as yourselves,
To gratulate the gentle princes there.

QUEEN ELIZABETH
Kind sister, thanks: we'll enter all together: —
And, in good time, here the lieutenant comes.
                    Enter BRAKENBURY.
Master lieutenant, pray you, by your leave,
How doth the prince, and my young son of York?

BRAKENBURY
Right well, dear madam. By your patience,
I may not suffer you to visit them;
The king hath straitly charg'd the contrary.

QUEEN ELIZABETH
The king! who's that?

BRAKENBURY
                    I mean the lord Protector.

QUEEN ELIZABETH
The Lord protect him from that kingly title!
Hath he set bounds between their love and me?
I am their mother; who should bar me from them?

DUCHESS OF YORK
I am their father's mother; I will see them.

LADY ANNE
Their aunt I am in law, in love their mother:
Then bring me to their sights; I'll bear thy blame,
And take thy office from thee, on my peril.

BRAKENBURY
No, madam, no, — I may not leave it so:
I'm bound by oath, and therefore pardon me.   [*Exit.*
                    Enter STANLEY.

STANLEY
Let me but meet you, ladies, one hour hence,
And I'll salute your Grace of York as mother,
And reverend looker-on, of two fair queens. —
[*to the* DUCHESS OF GLOSTER] Come, madam, you
    must straight to Westminster,
There to be crowned Richard's royal queen.

QUEEN ELIZABETH
Ah, cut my lace asunder,
That my pent heart may have some scope to beat,
Or else I swoon with this dead-killing news!

LADY ANNE
Despiteful tidings! O unpleasing news!

DORSET
Be of good cheer: — mother, how fares your Grace?

QUEEN ELIZABETH
O Dorset, speak not to me, get thee hence!
Death and destruction dog thee at the heels;
Thy mother's name is ominous to children.
If thou wilt outstrip death, go cross the seas,
And live with Richmond, from the reach of hell:
Go, hie thee, hie thee from this slaughter-house,
Lest thou increase the number of the dead;
And make me die the thrall of Margaret's curse, —
Nor mother, wife, nor England's counted queen.

STANLEY
Full of wise care is this your counsel, madam. —
Take all the swift advantage of the hours;
You shall have letters from me to my son
In your behalf, to meet you on the way:
Be not ta'en tardy by unwise delay.

DUCHESS OF YORK
O ill-dispersing wind of misery! —
O my accursed womb, the bed of death!
A cockatrice hast thou hatch'd to the world,
Whose unavoided eye is murderous.

STANLEY
Come, madam, come; I in all haste was sent.

LADY ANNE
And I in all unwillingness will go. —
O, would to God that the inclusive verge
Of golden metal that must round my brow
Were red-hot steel, to sear me to the brain!
Anointed let me be with deadly venom;
And die, ere men can say, 'God save the queen!'

QUEEN ELIZABETH
Go, go, poor soul, I envy not thy glory;
To feed my humour, wish thyself no harm.

LADY ANNE
No! why? — When he that is my husband now
Came to me, as I follow'd Henry's corse;
When scarce the blood was well wash'd from his hands
Which issued from my other angel husband,
And that dead saint which then I weeping follow'd;
O, when, I say, I look'd on Richard's face,
This was my wish, — 'Be thou,' quoth I, 'accurst,
For making me, so young, so old a widow!
And, when thou wedd'st, let sorrow haunt thy bed;
And be thy wife — if any be so mad —
More miserable by the life of thee
Than thou hast made me by my dear lord's death!'
Lo, ere I can repeat this curse again,
Even in so short a space, my woman's heart
Grossly grew captive to his honey words,
And prov'd the subject of mine own soul's curse, —
Which ever since hath kept mine eyes from rest;
For never yet one hour in his bed
Have I enjoy'd the golden dew of sleep,
But have been waked by his timorous dreams.
Besides, he hates me for my father Warwick;
And will, no doubt, shortly be rid of me.

QUEEN ELIZABETH
Poor heart, adieu! I pity thy complaining.

LADY ANNE
No more than from my soul I mourn for yours.

QUEEN ELIZABETH
Farewell, thou woeful welcomer of glory!

LADY ANNE
Adieu, poor soul, that takest thy leave of it!

DUCHESS OF YORK [to DORSET].
Go thou to Richmond, and good fortune guide thee! —
[to ANNE] Go thou to Richard, and good angels tend
    thee! —
[to QUEEN ELIZABETH] Go thou to sanctuary, and
    good thoughts possess thee! —
I to my grave, where peace and rest lie with me!
Eighty odd years of sorrow have I seen,
And each hour's joy wrack'd with a week of teen.

QUEEN ELIZABETH
Stay yet, look back with me unto the Tower.
Pity, you ancient stones, those tender babes,
Whom envy hath immur'd within your walls!
Rough cradle for such little pretty ones!
Rude ragged nurse, old sullen playfellow
For tender princes, use my babies well!
So foolish sorrow bids your stones farewell.   [*Exeunt.*

SCENE II

London. The palace.

Sound a sennet. Enter RICHARD, *in pomp, crown'd;*
BUCKINGHAM, CATESBY, *a* PAGE, *and others.*

KING RICHARD
Stand all apart. — Cousin of Buckingham, —

BUCKINGHAM
My gracious sovereign?

KING RICHARD
Give me thy hand. [*Here he ascendeth the throne.*]
        Thus high, by thy advice
And thy assistance, is King Richard seated: —
But shall we wear these honours for a day?
Or shall they last, and we rejoice in them?

BUCKINGHAM
Still live they, and for ever let them last!

DUCHESS OF YORK Who meets us here? my niece Plantagenet.

KING RICHARD
Ah, Buckingham, now do I play the touch,
To try if thou be current gold indeed: —
Young Edward lives; — think now what I would speak.

BUCKINGHAM
Say on, my loving lord.

KING RICHARD
Why, Buckingham, I say, I would be king.

BUCKINGHAM
Why, so you are, my thrice-renowned liege.

KING RICHARD
Ha! am I king? 'tis so: — but Edward lives.

BUCKINGHAM
True, noble prince.

KING RICHARD
                O bitter consequence,
That Edward still should live! 'True, noble prince!'
Cousin, thou wert not wont to be so dull:
Shall I be plain? — I wish the bastards dead;
And I would have it suddenly perform'd.
What say'st thou now? speak suddenly; be brief.

BUCKINGHAM
Your Grace may do your pleasure.

KING RICHARD
Tut, tut, thou art all ice, thy kindness freezes:
Say, have I thy consent that they shall die?

BUCKINGHAM
Give me some breath, some little pause, my lord,
Before I positively speak herein:
I will resolve your Grace immediately.   [*Exit.*

CATESBY [*aside to another.*]
The king is angry; see, he gnaws his lip.

KING RICHARD
I will converse with iron-witted fools
And unrespective boys: none are for me
That look into me with considerate eyes:
High-reaching Buckingham grows circumspect.
Boy! —

PAGE
My lord!

KING RICHARD
Know'st thou not any whom corrupting gold
Would tempt unto a close exploit of death?

PAGE
I know a discontented gentleman,
Whose humble means match not his haughty mind:
Gold were as good as twenty orators,
And will, no doubt, tempt him to any thing.

KING RICHARD
What is his name?

PAGE
                His name, my lord, is Tyrrel.

KING RICHARD
I partly know the man: go call him hither.   [*Exit* PAGE.
The deep-revolving witty Buckingham
No more shall be the neighbour to my counsels:
Hath he so long held out with me untired,
And stops he now for breath? — well, be it so.
                Enter STANLEY.
How now! what news with you?

STANLEY
My lord, I hear the Marquess Dorset's fled
To Richmond, in those parts beyond the seas
Where he abides.

KING RICHARD
Come hither, Catesby: — rumour it abroad
That Anne, my wife, is very grievous sick;
I will take order for her keeping close.
Inquire me out some mean-born gentleman,
Whom I will marry straight to Clarence' daughter; —
The boy is foolish, and I fear not him. —
Look, how thou dream'st! — I say again, give out
That Anne my queen is sick, and like to die:
About it; for it stands me much upon,
To stop all hopes whose growth may damage me.
                [*Exit* CATESBY.
I must be married to my brother's daughter,
Or else my kingdom stands on brittle glass: —
Murder her brothers, and then marry her!
Uncertain way of gain! But I am in
So far in blood, that sin will pluck on sin:
Tear-falling pity dwells not in this eye.
            Enter PAGE, *with* TYRREL.
Is thy name Tyrrel?

TYRREL
James Tyrrel, and your most obedient subject.

KING RICHARD
Art thou, indeed?
TYRREL
　　　　　　Prove me, my gracious sovereign.
KING RICHARD
Darest thou resolve to kill a friend of mine?
TYRREL
Ay, my lord;
But I had rather kill two enemies.
KING RICHARD
Why, then thou hast it: two deep enemies,
Foes to my rest and my sweet sleep's disturbers,
Are they that I would have thee deal upon: —
Tyrrel, I mean those bastards in the Tower.
TYRREL
Let me have open means to come to them,
And soon I'll rid you from the fear of them.
KING RICHARD
Thou sing'st sweet music. Hark, come hither, Tyrrel:
Go, by this token: — rise, and lend thine ear:　[*Whispers.*
There is no more but so: — say it is done,
And I will love thee, and prefer thee for it.
TYRREL
I will dispatch it straight.　　　　　　[*Exit.*

Enter BUCKINGHAM.

BUCKINGHAM
My lord, I have consider'd in my mind
The late demand that you did sound me in.
KING RICHARD
Well, let that rest. Dorset is fled to Richmond.
BUCKINGHAM
I hear the news, my lord.
KING RICHARD
Stanley, he is your wife's son: — well, look to it.
BUCKINGHAM
My lord, I claim the gift, my due by promise,
For which your honour and your faith is pawn'd;
Th'earldom of Hereford, and the movables,
The which you promised I should possess.
KING RICHARD
Stanley, look to your wife: if she convey
Letters to Richmond, you shall answer it.
BUCKINGHAM
What says your highness to my just request?
KING RICHARD
I do remember me, — Henry the Sixth
Did prophesy that Richmond should be king,
When Richmond was a little peevish boy.
A king! perhaps, perhaps —
BUCKINGHAM
My lord, —
KING RICHARD
How chance the prophet could not at that time
Have told me, I being by, that I should kill him?
BUCKINGHAM
My lord, your promise for the earldom, —
KING RICHARD
Richmond! — When last I was at Exeter,
The mayor in courtesy show'd me the castle,
And call'd it Rougemont: at which name I started,
Because a bard of Ireland told me once,
I should not live long after I saw Richmond.
BUCKINGHAM
My lord, —
KING RICHARD
Ay, what's o'clock?
BUCKINGHAM
I am thus bold to put your Grace in mind
Of what you promis'd me.
KING RICHARD
　　　　　　　Well, but what's o'clock?
BUCKINGHAM
Upon the stroke of ten.
KING RICHARD
　　　　　　　Well, let it strike.
BUCKINGHAM
Why let it strike?
KING RICHARD
Because that, like a Jack, thou keep'st the stroke
Betwixt thy begging and my meditation.
I am not in the giving vein to-day.
BUCKINGHAM
Why, then resolve me whether you will or no.
KING RICHARD
Tut, tut,
Thou troublest me; I am not in the vein.
　　　　　　[*Exeunt all except* BUCKINGHAM.

BUCKINGHAM
Is it even so? rewards he my true service
With such contempt? made I him king for this?
O, let me think on Hastings, and be gone
To Brecknock, while my fearful head is on!　[*Exit.*

SCENE III

The same.

Enter TYRREL.

TYRREL
The tyrannous and bloody act is done, —
The most arch deed of piteous massacre
That ever yet this land was guilty of.
Dighton and Forrest, whom I did suborn
To do this ruthless piece of butchery,
Albeit they were flesh'd villains, bloody dogs,
Melting with tenderness and mild compassion,
Wept like two children in their death's sad story.
'Lo, thus,' quoth Dighton, 'lay the gentle babes,' —
'Thus, thus,' quoth Forrest, 'girdling one another
Within their innocent alabaster arms:
Their lips were four red roses on a stalk,
Which in their summer beauty kiss'd each other.
A book of prayers on their pillow lay;
Which once,' quoth Forrest, 'almost chang'd my mind;
But, O, the devil' — there the villain stopp'd;
When Dighton thus told on, — 'We smothered
The most replenished sweet work of nature,
That from the prime creation e'er she fram'd.'
Hence both are gone with conscience and remorse;
They could not speak; and so I left them both,
To bear this tidings to the bloody king: —
And here he comes.

Enter KING RICHARD.
　　　　　All health, my sovereign lord!
KING RICHARD
Kind Tyrrel, am I happy in thy news?
TYRREL
If to have done the thing you gave in charge
Beget your happiness, be happy then,
For it is done.
KING RICHARD
But didst thou see them dead?
TYRREL
I did, my lord.
KING RICHARD
　　　　　And buried, gentle Tyrrel?
TYRREL
The chaplain of the Tower hath buried them;
But where, to say truth, I do not know.
KING RICHARD
Come to me, Tyrrel, soon at after supper,
When thou shalt tell the process of their death.
Meantime, but think how I may do thee good,
And be inheritor of thy desire.
Farewell till then.
TYRREL
　　　　　I humbly take my leave.　[*Exit.*
KING RICHARD
The son of Clarence have I pent up close;
His daughter meanly have I match'd in marriage;
The sons of Edward sleep in Abraham's bosom,
And Anne my wife hath bid the world good night.
Now, for I know the Breton Richmond aims
At young Elizabeth, my brother's daughter,
And, by that knot, looks proudly on the crown,
To her go I, a jolly thriving wooer.

Enter CATESBY.

CATESBY
My lord, —
KING RICHARD
Good news or bad, that thou com'st in so bluntly?
CATESBY
Bad news, my lord: Ely is fled to Richmond;
And Buckingham, back'd with the hardy Welshmen,
Is in the field, and still his power increaseth.
KING RICHARD
Ely with Richmond troubles me more near
Than Buckingham and his rash-levied strength.
Come, — I have learn'd that fearful commenting
Is leaden servitor to dull delay;
Delay leads impotent and snail-pac'd beggary:
Then fiery expedition be my wing,
Jove's Mercury, and herald for a king!
Go, muster men: my counsel is my shield;
We must be brief, when traitors brave the field.
　　　　　　　　　　　[*Exeunt.*

SCENE IV

Before the palace.

Enter QUEEN MARGARET.

QUEEN MARGARET
So, now prosperity begins to mellow,
And drop into the rotten mouth of death.
Here in these confines slily have I lurk'd,
To watch the waning of mine enemies.
A dire induction am I witness to,
And will to France; hoping the consequence
Will prove as bitter, black, and tragical. —
Withdraw thee, wretched Margaret: who comes here?
　　　　　　　　　　　[*Retires.*

Enter QUEEN ELIZABETH *and the* DUCHESS OF
YORK.

QUEEN ELIZABETH
Ah, my poor princes! ah, my tender babes!
My unblown flowers, new-appearing sweets!
If yet your gentle souls fly in the air,
And be not fix'd in doom perpetual,
Hover about me with your airy wings,
And hear your mother's lamentation!
QUEEN MARGARET [*aside*].
Hover about her; say, that right for right
Hath dimm'd your infant morn to aged night.
DUCHESS OF YORK
So many miseries have craz'd my voice,
That my woe-wearied tongue is still and mute. —
Edward Plantagenet, why art thou dead?
QUEEN MARGARET [*aside*].
Plantagenet doth quit Plantagenet,
Edward for Edward pays a dying debt.
QUEEN ELIZABETH
Wilt Thou, O God, fly from such gentle lambs,
And throw them in the entrails of the wolf?
When didst thou sleep, when such a deed was done?
QUEEN MARGARET [*aside*].
When holy Harry died, and my sweet son.
DUCHESS OF YORK
Dead life, blind sight, poor mortal living ghost,
Woe's scene, world's shame, grave's due by life
　　usurp'd,
Brief abstract and record of tedious days,
Rest thy unrest on England's lawful earth,
　　　　　　　　　　　[*Sitting down.*
Unlawfully made drunk with innocents' blood!
QUEEN ELIZABETH
Ah, that thou wouldst as soon afford a grave
As thou canst yield a melancholy seat!
Then would I hide my bones, not rest them here.
Ah, who hath any cause to mourn but I?
　　　　　　　　　　　[*Sitting down by her.*
QUEEN MARGARET [*coming forward.*]
If ancient sorrow be most reverend,
Give mine the benefit of seniory,
And let my griefs frown on the upper hand.
If sorrow can admit society,
　　　　　　　　　　　[*Sitting down with them.*
Tell o'er your woes again by viewing mine: —
I had an Edward, till a Richard kill'd him;
I had a Harry, till a Richard kill'd him:
Thou hadst an Edward, till a Richard kill'd him;
Thou hadst a Richard, till a Richard kill'd him.
DUCHESS OF YORK
I had a Richard too, and thou didst kill him;
I had a Rutland too, thou holp'st to kill him.
QUEEN MARGARET
Thou hadst a Clarence too, and Richard kill'd him.
From forth the kennel of thy womb hath crept
A hell-hound that doth hunt us all to death:
That dog, that had his teeth before his eyes,
To worry lambs, and lap their gentle blood;
That foul defacer of God's handiwork;
That excellent grand tyrant of the earth,
That reigns in galled eyes of weeping souls, —
Thy womb let loose, to chase us to our graves. —
O upright, just, and true-disposing God,
How do I thank thee, that this carnal cur
Preys on the issue of his mother's body,
And makes her pew-fellow with others' moan!
DUCHESS OF YORK
O Harry's wife, triumph not in my woes!
God witness with me, I have wept for thine.
QUEEN MARGARET
Bear with me; I am hungry for revenge,
And now I cloy me with beholding it.
Thy Edward he is dead, that kill'd my Edward:
Thy other Edward dead, to quit my Edward;

DUCHESS OF YORK Thou toad, thou toad, where is thy brother Clarence?

Young York he is but boot, because both they
Match not the high perfection of my loss:
Thy Clarence he is dead that stabb'd my Edward;
And the beholders of this tragic play,
Th'adulterate Hastings, Rivers, Vaughan, Grey,
Untimely smother'd in their dusky graves.
Richard yet lives, hell's black intelligencer;
Only reserv'd their factor, to buy souls,
And send them thither: — but at hand, at hand,
Ensues his piteous and unpitied end:
Earth gapes, hell burns, fiends roar, saints pray,
To have him suddenly convey'd from hence. —
Cancel his bond of life, dear God, I pray,
That I may live to say, 'The dog is dead!'

QUEEN ELIZABETH
O, thou didst prophesy the time would come
That I should wish for thee to help me curse
That bottled spider, that foul bunch-back'd toad!

QUEEN MARGARET
I call'd thee then vain flourish of my fortune;
I call'd thee then poor shadow, painted queen;
The presentation of but what I was;
The flattering index of a direful pageant;
One heav'd a-high, to be hurl'd down below;
A mother only mock'd with two sweet babes;
A dream of what thou wast; a breath, a bubble;
A sign of dignity, a garish flag
To be the aim of every dangerous shot;
A queen in jest, only to fill the scene.
Where is thy husband now? where be thy brothers?
Where be thy two sons? wherein dost thou joy?
Who sues to thee, and cries, 'God save the queen'?
Where be the bending peers that flatter'd thee?
Where be the thronging troops that follow'd thee?
Decline all this, and see what now thou art:
For happy wife, a most distressed widow;
For joyful mother, one that wails the name;
For one being sued-to, one that humbly sues;
For queen, a very caitiff crown'd with care;

For one that scorn'd at me, now scorn'd of me;
For one being fear'd of all, now fearing one;
For one commanding all, obey'd of none;
Thus hath the course of justice wheel'd about,
And left thee but a very prey to time;
Having no more but thought of what thou wast,
To torture thee the more, being what thou art.
Thou didst usurp my place, and dost thou not
Usurp the just proportion of my sorrow?
Now thy proud neck bears half my burden'd yoke;
From which even here I slip my wearied head,
And leave the burden of it all on thee.
Farewell, York's wife; and queen of sad mischance:
These English woes will make me smile in France.

QUEEN ELIZABETH
O thou well skill'd in curses, stay awhile,
And teach me how to curse mine enemies!

QUEEN MARGARET
Forbear to sleep the night, and fast the day;
Compare dead happiness with living woe;
Think that thy babes were fairer than they were,
And he that slew them fouler than he is:
Bettering thy loss makes the bad causer worse:
Revolving this will teach thee how to curse.

QUEEN ELIZABETH
My words are dull; O, quicken them with thine!

QUEEN MARGARET
Thy woes will make them sharp, and pierce like mine.
[Exit.

DUCHESS OF YORK
Why should calamity be full of words?

QUEEN ELIZABETH
Windy attorneys to their client woes,
Airy succeeders of intestate joys,
Poor breathing orators of miseries!
Let them have scope: though what they do impart
Help nothing else, yet do they ease the heart.

DUCHESS OF YORK
If so, then be not tongue-tied: go with me,
And in the breath of bitter words let's smother
My damned son, that thy two sweet sons smother'd.
[Drum within.
I hear his drum: — be copious in exclaims.
Enter KING RICHARD, and his TRAIN, marching,
with drums and trumpets.

KING RICHARD
Who intercepts me in my expedition?

DUCHESS OF YORK
O, she that might have intercepted thee,
By strangling thee in her accursed womb,
From all the slaughters, wretch, that thou hast done!

QUEEN ELIZABETH
Hidest thou that forehead with a golden crown,
Where should be branded, if that right were right,
The slaughter of the prince that owed that crown,
And the dire death of my poor sons and brothers?
Tell me, thou villain-slave, where are my children?

DUCHESS OF YORK
Thou toad, thou toad, where is thy brother Clarence?
And little Ned Plantagenet, his son?

QUEEN ELIZABETH
Where is the gentle Rivers, Vaughan, Grey?

DUCHESS OF YORK
Where is kind Hastings?

KING RICHARD
A flourish, trumpets! strike alarum, drums!
Let not the heavens hear these tell-tale women
Rail on the Lord's anointed: strike, I say!
[Flourish. Alarums.
Either be patient, and entreat me fair,
Or with the clamorous report of war
Thus will I drown your exclamations.

DUCHESS OF YORK
Art thou my son?

KING RICHARD
Ay, I thank God, my father, and yourself.

DUCHESS OF YORK
Then patiently hear my impatience.

KING RICHARD
Madam, I have a touch of your condition,
That cannot brook the accent of reproof.

DUCHESS OF YORK
O, let me speak!

KING RICHARD
Do, then; but I'll not hear.

DUCHESS OF YORK
I will be mild and gentle in my words.

KING RICHARD
And brief, good mother; for I am in haste.

DUCHESS OF YORK
Art thou so hasty? I have stay'd for thee,
God knows, in torment and in agony.

KING RICHARD
And came I not at last to comfort you?

DUCHESS OF YORK
No, by the holy rood, thou know'st it well,
Thou cam'st on earth to make the earth my hell.
A grievous burden was thy birth to me;
Tetchy and wayward was thy infancy;
Thy school-days frightful, desperate, wild, and furious;
Thy prime of manhood daring, bold, and venturous;
Thy age confirm'd, proud, subtle, bloody, treacherous,
More mild, but yet more harmful-kind in hatred:
What comfortable hour canst thou name,
That ever grac'd me in thy company?

KING RICHARD
Faith, none, but Humphrey Hour, that call'd your
 Grace
To breakfast once forth of my company.
If I be so disgracious in your eye,
Let me march on, and not offend you, madam. —
Strike up the drum.

DUCHESS OF YORK
I prithee, hear me speak.

KING RICHARD
You speak too bitterly.

DUCHESS OF YORK
Hear me a word;
For I shall never speak to thee again.

KING RICHARD
So.

DUCHESS OF YORK
Either thou wilt die, by God's just ordinance,
Ere from this war thou turn a conqueror;
Or I with grief and extreme age shall perish,

And never look upon thy face again.
Therefore take with thee my most heavy curse;
Which, in the day of battle, tire thee more
Than all the complete armour that thou wear'st!
My prayers on the adverse party fight;
And there the little souls of Edward's children
Whisper the spirits of thine enemies,
And promise them success and victory.
Bloody thou art, bloody will be thy end;
Shame serves thy life, and doth thy death attend.   [*Exit.*

QUEEN ELIZABETH
Though far more cause, yet much less spirit to curse
Abides in me; I say amen to her.   [*Going.*

KING RICHARD
Stay, madam; I must speak a word with you.

QUEEN ELIZABETH
I have no more sons of the royal blood
For thee to murder: for my daughters, Richard, —
They shall be praying nuns, not weeping queens;
And therefore level not to hit their lives.

KING RICHARD
You have a daughter call'd Elizabeth,
Virtuous and fair, royal and gracious.

QUEEN ELIZABETH
And must she die for this? O, let her live,
And I'll corrupt her manners, stain her beauty;
Slander myself as false to Edward's bed;
Throw over her the veil of infamy:
So she may live unscarr'd of bleeding slaughter,
I will confess she was not Edward's daughter.

KING RICHARD
Wrong not her birth, she is a royal princess.

QUEEN ELIZABETH
To save her life, I'll say she is not so.

KING RICHARD
Her life is safest only in her birth.

QUEEN ELIZABETH
And only in that safety died her brothers.

KING RICHARD
Lo, at their births good stars were opposite.

QUEEN ELIZABETH
No, to their lives ill friends were contrary.

KING RICHARD
All unavoided is the doom of destiny.

QUEEN ELIZABETH
True, when avoided grace makes destiny:
My babes were destin'd to a fairer death,
If grace had blest thee with a fairer life.

KING RICHARD
You speak as if that I had slain my cousins.

QUEEN ELIZABETH
Cousins, indeed; and by their uncle cozen'd
Of comfort, kingdom, kindred, freedom, life.
Whose hand soever lanc'd their tender hearts,
Thy head, all indirectly, gave direction:
No doubt the murderous knife was dull and blunt
Till it was whetted on thy stone-hard heart,
To revel in the entrails of my lambs.
But that still use of grief makes wild grief tame,
My tongue should to thy ears not name my boys
Till that my nails were anchor'd in thine eyes;
And I, in such a desperate bay of death,
Like a poor bark, of sails and tackling reft,
Rush all to pieces on thy rocky bosom.

KING RICHARD
Madam, so thrive I in my enterprise
And dangerous success of bloody wars,
As I intend more good to you and yours
Than ever you and yours by me were harm'd!

QUEEN ELIZABETH
What good is cover'd with the face of heaven,
To be discover'd, that can do me good?

KING RICHARD
Th'advancement of your children, gentle lady.

QUEEN ELIZABETH
Up to some scaffold, there to lose their heads?

KING RICHARD
No, to the dignity and height of honour,
The high imperial type of this earth's glory.

QUEEN ELIZABETH
Flatter my sorrows with report of it;
Tell me what state, what dignity, what honour,
Canst thou demise to any child of mine?

KING RICHARD
Even all I have; ay, and myself and all,
Will I withal endow a child of thine;
So in the Lethe of thy angry soul
Thou drown the sad remembrance of those wrongs
Which thou supposest I have done to thee.

QUEEN ELIZABETH
Be brief, lest that the process of thy kindness
Last longer telling than thy kindness' date.

KING RICHARD
Then know, that from my soul I love thy daughter.

QUEEN ELIZABETH
My daughter's mother thinks it with her soul.

KING RICHARD
What do you think?

QUEEN ELIZABETH
That thou dost love my daughter from thy soul:
So, from thy soul's love, didst thou love her brothers;
And, from my heart's love, I do thank thee for it.

KING RICHARD
Be not so hasty to confound my meaning:
I mean, that with my soul I love thy daughter,
And do intend to make her Queen of England.

QUEEN ELIZABETH
Well, then, who dost thou mean shall be her king?

KING RICHARD
Even he that makes her queen: who else should be?

QUEEN ELIZABETH
What, thou?

KING RICHARD
I, even I: what think you of it, madam?

QUEEN ELIZABETH
How canst thou woo her?

KING RICHARD
                    That would I learn of you,
As one being best acquainted with her humour.

QUEEN ELIZABETH
And wilt thou learn of me?

KING RICHARD
                    Madam, with all my heart.

QUEEN ELIZABETH
Send to her, by the man that slew her brothers,
A pair of bleeding hearts; thereon engrave
'Edward and York'; then haply she will weep:
Therefore present to her — as sometime Margaret
Did to thy father, steep'd in Rutland's blood —
A handkerchief; which, say to her, did drain
The purple sap from her sweet brother's body,
And bid her dry her weeping eyes withal.
If this inducement move her not to love,
Send her a letter of thy noble deeds;
Tell her thou mad'st away her uncle Clarence,
Her uncle Rivers; ay, and, for her sake,
Mad'st quick conveyance with her good aunt Anne.

KING RICHARD
You mock me, madam; this is not the way
To win your daughter.

QUEEN ELIZABETH
                    There is no other way;
Unless thou couldst put on some other shape,
And not be Richard that hath done all this.

KING RICHARD
Say that I did all this for love of her?

QUEEN ELIZABETH
Nay, then indeed she cannot choose but hate thee,
Having bought love with such a bloody spoil.

KING RICHARD
Look, what is done cannot be now amended:
Men shall deal unadvisedly sometimes,
Which after-hours gives leisure to repent.
If I did take the kingdom from your sons,
To make amends, I'll give it to your daughter.
If I have kill'd the issue of your womb,
To quicken your increase, I will beget
Mine issue of your blood upon your daughter:
A grandam's name is little less in love
Than is the doting title of a mother;
They are as children but one step below,
Even of your mettle, of your very blood;
Of all one pain, — save for a night of groans
Endured of her, for whom you bid like sorrow.
Your children were vexation to your youth;
But mine shall be a comfort to your age.
The loss you have is but a son being king,
And by that loss your daughter is made queen.
I cannot make you what amends I would,
Therefore accept such kindness as I can.
Dorset your son, that with a fearful soul
Leads discontented steps in foreign soil,
This fair alliance quickly shall call home
To high promotions and great dignity:
The king, that calls your beauteous daughter wife,
Familiarly shall call thy Dorset brother;
Again shall you be mother to a king,
And all the ruins of distressful times
Repair'd with double riches of content.

What! we have many goodly days to see:
The liquid drops of tears that you have shed
Shall come again, transform'd to orient pearl,
Advantaging their loan with interest
Of ten-times-double gain of happiness.
Go, then, my mother, to thy daughter go;
Make bold her bashful years with your experience;
Prepare her ears to hear a wooer's tale;
Put in her tender heart th'aspiring flame
Of golden sovereignty; acquaint the princess
With the sweet silent hours of marriage joys:
And when this arm of mine hath chastised
The petty rebel, dull-brain'd Buckingham,
Bound with triumphant garlands will I come,
And lead thy daughter to a conqueror's bed;
To whom I will retail my conquest won,
And she shall be sole victress, Cæsar's Cæsar.

QUEEN ELIZABETH
What were I best to say? her father's brother
Would be her lord? or shall I say, her uncle?
Or, he that slew her brothers and her uncles?
Under what title shall I woo for thee,
That God, the law, my honour, and her love,
Can make seem pleasing to her tender years?

KING RICHARD
Infer fair England's peace by this alliance.

QUEEN ELIZABETH
Which she shall purchase with still-lasting war.

KING RICHARD
Tell her, the king, that may command, entreats.

QUEEN ELIZABETH
That at her hands which the king's King forbids.

KING RICHARD
Say, she shall be a high and mighty queen.

QUEEN ELIZABETH
To wail the title, as her mother doth.

KING RICHARD
Say, I will love her everlastingly.

QUEEN ELIZABETH
But how long shall that title 'ever' last?

KING RICHARD
Sweetly in force unto her fair life's end.

QUEEN ELIZABETH
But how long fairly shall her sweet life last?

KING RICHARD
As long as heaven and nature lengthens it.

QUEEN ELIZABETH
As long as hell and Richard likes of it.

KING RICHARD
Say, I, her sovereign, am her subject love.

QUEEN ELIZABETH
But she, your subject, loathes such sovereignty.

KING RICHARD
Be eloquent in my behalf to her.

QUEEN ELIZABETH
An honest tale speeds best being plainly told.

KING RICHARD
Then, plainly to her tell my loving tale.

QUEEN ELIZABETH
Plain and not honest is too harsh a style.

KING RICHARD
Your reasons are too shallow and too quick.

QUEEN ELIZABETH
O, no, my reasons are too deep and dead; —
Too deep and dead, poor infants, in their graves.

KING RICHARD
Harp not on that string, madam; that is past.

QUEEN ELIZABETH
Harp on it still shall I till heart-strings break.

KING RICHARD
Now, by my George, my garter, and my crown, —

QUEEN ELIZABETH
Profan'd, dishonour'd, and the third usurp'd.

KING RICHARD
I swear —

QUEEN ELIZABETH
                    By nothing; for this is no oath:
The George, profan'd, hath lost his holy honour;
The garter, blemish'd, pawn'd his knightly virtue;
The crown, usurp'd, disgrac'd his kingly glory.
If something thou wouldst swear to be believed,
Swear, then, by something that thou hast not wrong'd.

KING RICHARD
Now, by the world, —

QUEEN ELIZABETH
                    'Tis full of thy foul wrongs.

KING RICHARD
My father's death, —

QUEEN ELIZABETH
          Thy life hath that dishonour'd.
KING RICHARD
Then, by myself, —
QUEEN ELIZABETH
          Thyself is self-misused.
KING RICHARD
Why, then, by God, —
QUEEN ELIZABETH
          God's wrong is most of all.
If thou hadst fear'd to break an oath by Him,
The unity the king thy brother made
Had not been broken, nor my brother slain:
If thou hadst fear'd to break an oath by Him,
Th'imperial metal, circling now thy head,
Had grac'd the tender temples of my child;
And both the princes had been breathing here,
Which now, two tender bedfellows for dust,
Thy broken faith hath made a prey for worms.
What canst thou swear by now?
KING RICHARD
          The time to come.
QUEEN ELIZABETH
That thou hast wronged in the time o'erpast;
For I myself have many tears to wash
Hereafter time, for time past wrong'd by thee.
The children live, whose parents thou hast slaughter'd,
Ungovern'd youth, to wail it in their age;
The parents live, whose children thou hast butcher'd,
Old wither'd plants, to wail it with their age.
Swear not by time to come; for that thou hast
Misus'd ere us'd, by time misus'd o'erpast.
KING RICHARD
As I intend to prosper and repent,
So thrive I in my dangerous attempt
Of hostile arms! myself myself confound!
Heaven and fortune bar me happy hours!
Day, yield me not thy light; nor, night, thy rest!
Be opposite all planets of good luck
To my proceedings! — if, with pure heart's love,
Immaculate devotion, holy thoughts,
I tender not thy beauteous princely daughter!
In her consists my happiness and thine;
Without her, follows to myself and thee,
Herself, the land, and many a Christian soul,
Death, desolation, ruin, and decay:
It cannot be avoided but by this;
It will not be avoided but by this.
Therefore, dear mother, — I must call you so, —
Be the attorney of my love to her:
Plead what I will be, not what I have been;
Not my deserts, but what I will deserve:
Urge the necessity and state of times,
And be not peevish-fond in great designs.
QUEEN ELIZABETH
Shall I be tempted of the devil thus?
KING RICHARD
Ay, if the devil tempt thee to do good.
QUEEN ELIZABETH
Shall I forget myself to be myself?
KING RICHARD
Ay, if your self's remembrance wrong yourself.
QUEEN ELIZABETH
But thou didst kill my children.
KING RICHARD
But in your daughter's womb I'll bury them:
Where, in that nest of spicery, they shall breed
Selves of themselves, to your recomforture.
QUEEN ELIZABETH
Shall I go win my daughter to thy will?
KING RICHARD
And be a happy mother by the deed.
QUEEN ELIZABETH
I go. — Write to me very shortly,
And you shall understand from me her mind.
KING RICHARD
Bear her my true love's kiss; and so, farewell.
          [Exit QUEEN ELIZABETH.
Relenting fool, and shallow, changing woman!
      Enter RATCLIFF; CATESBY *following.*
How now! what news?
RATCLIFF
My gracious sovereign, on the western coast
Rideth a puissant navy; to the shore
Throng many doubtful hollow-hearted friends,
Unarm'd, and unresolv'd to beat them back:
'Tis thought that Richmond is their admiral;
And there they hull, expecting but the aid

Of Buckingham to welcome them ashore.
KING RICHARD
Some light-foot friend post to the Duke of Norfolk: —
Ratcliff, thyself, — or Catesby; where is he?
CATESBY
Here, my good lord.
KING RICHARD
Fly to the duke. — [*to* RATCLIFF] Post thou to
    Salisbury:
When thou com'st thither, — [*to* CATESBY] Dull,
    unmindful villain,
Why stay'st thou here, and go'st not to the duke?
CATESBY
First, mighty liege, tell me your highness' pleasure,
What from your Grace I shall deliver to him.
KING RICHARD
O, true, good Catesby: — bid him levy straight
The greatest strength and power he can make,
And meet me suddenly at Salisbury.
CATESBY
I go.   *[Exit.*
RATCLIFF
What, may it please you, shall I do at Salisbury?
KING RICHARD
Why, what wouldst thou do there before I go?
RATCLIFF
Your highness told me I should post before.
             Enter STANLEY.
KING RICHARD
My mind is chang'd. — Stanley, what news with you?
STANLEY
None good, my liege, to please you with the hearing;
Nor none so bad, but well may be reported.
KING RICHARD
Hoyday, a riddle! neither good nor bad!
What need'st thou run so many miles about,
When thou mayst tell thy tale the nearest way?
Once more, what news?
STANLEY
          Richmond is on the seas.
KING RICHARD
There let him sink, and be the seas on him,
White-liver'd runagate! what doth he there?
STANLEY
I know not, mighty sovereign, but by guess.
KING RICHARD
Well, as you guess?
STANLEY
Stirr'd up by Dorset, Buckingham, and Ely,
He makes for England, here, to claim the crown.
KING RICHARD
Is the chair empty? is the sword unsway'd?
Is the king dead? the empire unpossess'd?
What heir of York is there alive but we?
And who is England's king but great York's heir?
Then, tell me, what makes he upon the seas?
STANLEY
Unless for that, my liege, I cannot guess.
KING RICHARD
Unless for that he comes to be your liege,
You cannot guess wherefore the Welshman comes.
Thou wilt revolt, and fly to him, I fear.
STANLEY
No, mighty liege, therefore mistrust me not.
KING RICHARD
Where is thy power, then, to beat him back?
Where be thy tenants and thy followers?
Are they not now upon the western shore,
Safe-conducting the rebels from their ships?
STANLEY
No, my good lord, my friends are in the north.
KING RICHARD
Cold friends to me: what do they in the north,
When they should serve their sovereign in the west?
STANLEY
They have not been commanded, mighty king:
Pleaseth your majesty to give me leave,
I'll muster up my friends, and meet your Grace
Where and what time your majesty shall please.
KING RICHARD
Ay, ay, thou wouldst be gone to join with Richmond:
I will not trust you, sir.
STANLEY
          Most mighty sovereign,
You have no cause to hold my friendship doubtful:
I never was nor never will be false.
KING RICHARD
Go, then, and muster men. But leave behind

Your son, George Stanley: look your faith be firm,
Or else his head's assurance is but frail.
STANLEY
So deal with him as I prove true to you.   *[Exit.*
          Enter a MESSENGER.
MESSENGER
My gracious sovereign, now in Devonshire,
As I by friends am well advertised,
Sir Edward Courtney, and the haughty prelate
Bishop of Exeter, his elder brother,
With many moe confederates, are in arms.
          Enter a second MESSENGER.
SECOND MESSENGER
In Kent, my liege, the Guildfords are in arms;
And every hour more competitors
Flock to the rebels, and their power grows strong.
          Enter a third MESSENGER.
THIRD MESSENGER
My lord, the army of great Buckingham —
KING RICHARD
Out on ye, owls! nothing but songs of death?
                  [He strikes him.
There, take thou that, till thou bring better news.
THIRD MESSENGER
The news I have to tell your majesty
Is, that by sudden floods and fall of waters,
Buckingham's army is dispers'd and scatter'd;
And he himself wander'd away alone,
No man knows whither.
KING RICHARD
          I cry thee mercy:
There is my purse to cure that blow of thine.
Hath any well-advised friend proclaim'd
Reward to him that brings the traitor in?
THIRD MESSENGER
Such proclamation hath been made, my lord.
          Enter a fourth MESSENGER.
FOURTH MESSENGER
Sir Thomas Lovel and Lord Marquess Dorset,
'Tis said, my liege, in Yorkshire are in arms.
But this good comfort bring I to your highness, —
The Breton navy is dispers'd by tempest:
Richmond, in Dorsetshire, sent out a boat
Unto the shore, to ask those on the banks
If they were his assistants, yea or no;
Who answer'd him, they came from Buckingham
Upon his party: he, mistrusting them,
Hois'd sail, and made his course again for Bretagne.
KING RICHARD
March on, march on, since we are up in arms;
If not to fight with foreign enemies,
Yet to beat down these rebels here at home.
          Enter CATESBY.
CATESBY
My liege, the Duke of Buckingham is taken, —
That is the best news: that the Earl of Richmond
Is with a mighty power landed at Milford,
Is colder tidings, yet they must be told.
KING RICHARD
Away towards Salisbury! while we reason here,
A royal battle might be won and lost: —
Some one take order Buckingham be brought
To Salisbury; the rest march on with me.
          [Flourish. Exeunt.

SCENE V

LORD DERBY'S *house.*

Enter DERBY *and* SIR CHRISTOPHER URSWICK.

DERBY
Sir Christopher, tell Richmond this from me: —
That, in the sty of this most bloody boar,
My son George Stanley is frank'd up in hold:
If I revolt, off goes young George's head;
The fear of that withholds my present aid.
But, tell me, where is princely Richmond now?
URSWICK
At Pembroke, or at Ha'rford-west, in Wales.
DERBY
What men of name resort to him?
URSWICK
Sir Walter Herbert, a renowned soldier;
Sir Gilbert Talbot, Sir William Stanley;
Oxford, redoubted Pembroke, Sir James Blunt,
And Rice ap Thomas, with a valiant crew;
And many more of noble fame and worth:
And towards London they do bend their course,

If by the way they be not fought withal.
DERBY
Return unto thy lord; commend me to him:
Tell him the queen hath heartily consented
He shall espouse Elizabeth her daughter.
These letters will resolve him of my mind.
Farewell.   [*Exeunt.*

ACT V

SCENE I

Salisbury. An open place.

Enter the SHERIFF, *and* BUCKINGHAM, *with
halberds, led to execution.*

BUCKINGHAM
Will not King Richard let me speak with him?
SHERIFF
No, my good lord; therefore be patient.
BUCKINGHAM
Hastings, and Edward's children, Rivers, Grey,
Holy King Henry, and thy fair son Edward,
Vaughan, and all that have miscarried
By underhand corrupted foul injustice, —
If that your moody discontented souls
Do through the clouds behold this present hour,
Even for revenge mock my destruction! —
This is All-Souls' day, fellows, is it not?
SHERIFF
It is, my lord.
BUCKINGHAM
Why, then All-Souls' day is my body's doomsday.
This is the day that, in King Edward's time,
I wish'd might fall on me, when I was found
False to his children or his wife's allies;
This is the day wherein I wish'd to fall
By the false faith of him I trusted most;
This, this All-Souls' day to my fearful soul
Is the determin'd respite of my wrongs:
That high All-Seer that I dallied with
Hath turn'd my feigned prayer on my head,
And given in earnest what I begg'd in jest.
Thus doth He force the swords of wicked men
To turn their own points on their masters' bosoms:
Thus Margaret's curse falls heavy on my neck, —
'When he,' quoth she, 'shall split thy heart with sorrow,
Remember, Margaret was a prophetess.'
Come, sirs, convey me to the block of shame;
Wrong hath but wrong, and blame the due of blame.   [*Exeunt.*

SCENE II

Plain near Tamworth.

Enter RICHMOND, OXFORD, HERBERT, BLUNT,
and others, with drum and colours.

RICHMOND
Fellows in arms, and my most loving friends,
Bruis'd underneath the yoke of tyranny,
Thus far into the bowels of the land
Have we march'd on without impediment;
And here receive we from our father Stanley
Lines of fair comfort and encouragement.
The wretched, bloody, and usurping boar,

That spoil'd your summer fields and fruitful vines,
Swills your warm blood like wash, and makes his
    trough
In your embowell'd bosoms, — this foul swine
Lies now even in the centre of this isle,
Near to the town of Leicester, as we learn:
From Tamworth thither is but one day's march.
In God's name, cheerly on, courageous friends,
To reap the harvest of perpetual peace
By this one bloody trial of sharp war.
OXFORD
Every man's conscience is a thousand swords,
To fight against this guilty homicide.
HERBERT
I doubt not but his friends will turn to us.
BLUNT
He hath no friends but what are friends for fear,
Which in his dearest need will shrink from him.
RICHMOND
All for our vantage. Then, in God's name, march:
True hope is swift, and flies with swallow's wings;
Kings it makes gods, and meaner creatures kings.   [*Exeunt.*

SCENE III

Bosworth field.

Enter KING RICHARD *in arms, with* NORFOLK, *the*
EARL OF SURREY, *and others.*

KING RICHARD
Here pitch our tents, even here in Bosworth field.
My Lord of Surrey, why look you so sad?
SURREY
My heart is ten times lighter than my looks.
KING RICHARD
My Lord of Norfolk, —
NORFOLK
              Here, most gracious liege.
KING RICHARD
Norfolk, we must have knocks; ha! must we not?
NORFOLK
We must both give and take, my loving lord.
KING RICHARD
Up with my tent! here will I lie to-night;
    [SOLDIERS *begin to set up the* KING'S *tent.*
But where to-morrow? Well, all's one for that. —
Who hath descried the number of the traitors?
NORFOLK
Six or seven thousand is their utmost power.
KING RICHARD
Why, our battalia trebles that account:
Besides, the king's name is a tower of strength,
Which they upon the adverse party want. —
Up with the tent! — Come, noble gentlemen,
Let us survey the vantage of the ground; —
Call for some men of sound direction: —
Let's lack no discipline, make no delay;
For, lords, to-morrow is a busy day.   [*Exeunt.*

Enter, on the other side of the field, RICHMOND,
BRANDON, OXFORD, *and others. Some of the*
SOLDIERS *pitch* RICHMOND'S *tent.*

RICHMOND
The weary sun hath made a golden set,
And, by the bright track of his fiery car,

Gives token of a goodly day to-morrow. —
Sir William Brandon, you shall bear my standard. —
Give me some ink and paper in my tent:
I'll draw the form and model of our battle,
Limit each leader to his several charge,
And part in just proportion our small power. —
My Lord of Oxford, — you, Sir William Brandon, —
And you, Sir Walter Herbert, — stay with me. —
The Earl of Pembroke keeps his regiment: —
Good Captain Blunt, bear my good-night to him,
And by the second hour in the morning
Desire the earl to see me in my tent: —
Yet one thing more, good captain, do for me, —
Where is Lord Stanley quarter'd, do you know?
BLUNT
Unless I have mista'en his colours much, —
Which well I am assured I have not done, —
His regiment lies half a mile at least
South from the mighty power of the king.
RICHMOND
If without peril it be possible,
Sweet Blunt, make some good means to speak with
    him,
And give him from me this most needful note.
BLUNT
Upon my life, my lord, I'll undertake it;
And so, God give you quiet rest to-night!
RICHMOND
Good night, good Captain Blunt. [*Exit* BLUNT.] Come,
    gentlemen,
Let us consult upon to-morrow's business:
In to my tent; the air is raw and cold.
    [*They withdraw into the tent.*

Enter, to his tent, KING RICHARD, NORFOLK,
RATCLIFF, CATESBY, *and others.*

KING RICHARD
What is't o'clock?
CATESBY
          It's supper-time, my lord;
It's nine o'clock.
KING RICHARD
         I will not sup to-night. —
Give me some ink and paper. —
What, is my beaver easier than it was?
And all my armour laid into my tent?
CATESBY
It is, my liege; and all things are in readiness.
KING RICHARD
Good Norfolk, hie thee to thy charge;
Use careful watch, choose trusty sentinels.
NORFOLK
I go, my lord.
KING RICHARD
Stir with the lark to-morrow, gentle Norfolk.
NORFOLK
I warrant you, my lord.   [*Exit.*
KING RICHARD
Catesby, —
CATESBY
My lord?
KING RICHARD
       Send out a pursuivant-at-arms
To Stanley's regiment; bid him bring his power
Before sunrising, lest his son George fall
Into the blind cave of eternal night.   [*Exit* CATESBY.
Fill me a bowl of wine. — Give me a watch. —
Saddle white Surrey for the field to-morrow. —
Look that my staves be sound, and not too heavy. —
Ratcliff, —
RATCLIFF
My lord?
KING RICHARD
Saw'st thou the melancholy Lord Northumberland?
RATCLIFF
Thomas the Earl of Surrey, and himself,
Much about cock-shut time, from troop to troop
Went through the army, cheering up the soldiers.
KING RICHARD
So, I am satisfied. — Give me a bowl of wine:
I have not that alacrity of spirit,
Nor cheer of mind, that I was wont to have.
    [*Wine brought.*
Set it down. — Is ink and paper ready?
RATCLIFF
It is, my lord.
KING RICHARD
Bid my guard watch; leave me. — Ratcliff,
About the mid of night come to my tent
And help to arm me. — Leave me, I say.

BUCKINGHAM This is the day wherein I wish'd to fall by the false faith of him I trusted most.

[Exeunt RATCLIFF and others.
Enter DERBY to RICHMOND in his tent; LORDS and
GENTLEMEN.

DERBY
Fortune and victory sit on thy helm!
RICHMOND
All comfort that the dark night can afford
Be to thy person, noble father-in-law!
Tell me, how fares our loving mother?
DERBY
I, by attorney, bless thee from thy mother,
Who prays continually for Richmond's good:
So much for that. The silent hours steal on,
And flaky darkness breaks within the east.
In brief, — for so the season bids us be, —
Prepare thy battle early in the morning,
And put thy fortune to th'arbitrement
Of bloody strokes and mortal-staring war.
I, as I may, — that which I would I cannot, —
With best advantage will deceive the time,
And aid thee in this doubtful shock of arms:
But on thy side I may not be too forward,
Lest, being seen, thy brother, tender George,
Be executed in his father's sight.
Farewell: the leisure and the fearful time
Cuts off the ceremonious vows of love
And ample interchange of sweet discourse,
Which so-long-sunder'd friends should dwell upon:
God give us leisure for these rites of love!
Once more, adieu: be valiant, and speed well!
RICHMOND
Good lords, conduct him to his regiment:
I'll strive, with troubled thoughts, to take a nap,
Lest leaden slumber peise me down to-morrow,
When I should mount with wings of victory:
Once more, good night, kind lords and gentlemen.
[Exeunt all but RICHMOND.
O Thou, whose captain I account myself,
Look on my forces with a gracious eye;
Put in their hands Thy bruising irons of wrath,
That they may crush down with a heavy fall
Th'usurping helmets of our adversaries!
Make us Thy ministers of chastisement,
That we may praise Thee in the victory!
To Thee I do commend my watchful soul,
Ere I let fall the windows of mine eyes:
Sleeping and waking, O, defend me still! *[Sleeps.*
Enter the GHOST of PRINCE EDWARD, son to KING
HENRY THE SIXTH.

GHOST *[to KING RICHARD].*
Let me sit heavy on thy soul to-morrow!
Think, how thou stabb'dst me in my prime of youth
At Tewksbury: despair, therefore, and die!
[to RICHMOND] Be cheerful, Richmond; for the
wronged souls
Of butcher'd princes fight in thy behalf:
King Henry's issue, Richmond, comforts thee.
Enter the GHOST of HENRY THE SIXTH.

GHOST *[to KING RICHARD].*
When I was mortal, my anointed body
By thee was punched full of deadly holes:
Think on the Tower and me: despair, and die,
Harry the Sixth bids thee despair and die!
[to RICHMOND] Virtuous and holy, be thou
conqueror!
Harry, that prophesied thou shouldst be king,
Doth comfort thee in thy sleep: live, and flourish!
Enter the GHOST of CLARENCE.

GHOST *[to KING RICHARD].*
Let me sit heavy on thy soul to-morrow!
I, that was wash'd to death with fulsome wine,
Poor Clarence, by thy guile betray'd to death!
To-morrow in the battle think on me,
And fall thy edgeless sword: despair, and die!
[to RICHMOND] Thou offspring of the house of
Lancaster,
The wronged heirs of York do pray for thee:
Good angels guard thy battle! live, and flourish!
Enter the GHOSTS of RIVERS, GREY, and
VAUGHAN.

GHOST OF RIVERS *[to KING RICHARD].*
Let me sit heavy on thy soul to-morrow,
Rivers, that died at Pomfret! despair, and die!
GHOST OF GREY *[to KING RICHARD].*
Think upon Grey, and let thy soul despair!
GHOST OF VAUGHAN *[to KING RICHARD].*
Think upon Vaughan, and, with guilty fear,
Let fall thy lance: despair, and die!

ALL THREE *[to RICHMOND].*
Awake, and think our wrongs in
Richard's bosom
Will conquer him! — awake, and win
the day!
Enter the GHOST of HASTINGS.

GHOST *[to KING RICHARD].*
Bloody and guilty, guiltily awake,
And in a bloody battle end thy days!
Think on Lord Hastings: despair, and
die.
[to RICHMOND] Quiet untroubled
soul, awake, awake!
Arm, fight, and conquer, for fair
England's sake!
Enter the GHOSTS of the two young
PRINCES.

GHOSTS *[to KING RICHARD].*
Dream on thy cousins smothered in
the Tower:
Let us be lead within thy bosom,
Richard,
And weigh thee down to ruin, shame,
and death!
Thy nephews' souls bid thee despair
and die!
[to RICHMOND] Sleep, Richmond,
sleep in peace, and wake in joy;
Good angels guard thee from the
boar's annoy!
Live, and beget a happy race of kings!
Edward's unhappy sons do bid thee
flourish.
Enter the GHOST of ANNE, his wife.

GHOST *[to KING RICHARD].*
Richard, thy wife, that wretched Anne
thy wife,
That never slept a quiet hour with thee,
Now fills thy sleep with perturbations:
To-morrow in the battle think on me,
And fall thy edgeless sword: despair, and die!
[to RICHMOND] Thou quiet soul, sleep thou a quiet
sleep;
Dream of success and happy victory!
Thy adversary's wife doth pray for thee.
Enter the GHOST of BUCKINGHAM.

GHOST *[to KING RICHARD].*
The first was I that help'd thee to the crown;
The last was I that felt thy tyranny:
O, in the battle think on Buckingham,
And die in terror of thy guiltiness!
Dream on, dream on, of bloody deeds and death:
Fainting, despair; despairing, yield thy breath!
[to RICHMOND] I died for hope ere I could lend thee
aid:
But cheer thy heart, and be thou not dismay'd:
God and good angels fight on Richmond's side;
And Richard falls in height of all his pride.
[The GHOSTS vanish. KING RICHARD starts out of his
dream.

KING RICHARD
Give me another horse, — bind up my wounds, —
Have mercy, Jesu! — Soft! I did but dream.
O coward conscience, how dost thou afflict me!
The lights burn blue. It is now dead midnight.
Cold fearful drops stand on my trembling flesh.
What do I fear? myself? there's none else by:
Richard loves Richard; that is, I am I.
Is there a murderer here? No; — yes, I am:
Then fly. What, from myself? Great reason why:
Lest I revenge. What, myself upon myself?
Alack, I love myself. Wherefore? for any good
That I myself have done unto myself?
O, no! alas, I rather hate myself
For hateful deeds committed by myself!
I am a villain: yet I lie, I am not.
Fool, of thyself speak well: — fool, do not flatter.
My conscience hath a thousand several tongues,
And every tongue brings in a several tale,
And every tale condemns me for a villain.
Perjury, perjury, in the high'st degree;
Murder, stern murder, in the direst degree;
All several sins, all used in each degree,
Throng to the bar, crying all 'Guilty! guilty!'
I shall despair. There is no creature loves me;
And if I die, no soul shall pity me:
Nay, wherefore should they, — since that I myself
Find in myself no pity to myself?

GHOST Dream on, dream on, of bloody deeds and death;
fainting, despair; despairing, yield thy breath!

Enter RATCLIFF.

RATCLIFF
My lord, —
KING RICHARD
Who's there?
RATCLIFF
My lord, 'tis I. The early village-cock
Hath twice done salutation to the morn;
Your friends are up, and buckle on their armour.
KING RICHARD
O Ratcliff, I have dream'd a fearful dream! —
What thinkest thou, — will our friends prove all true?
RATCLIFF
No doubt, my lord.
KING RICHARD
O Ratcliff, I fear, I fear! —
Methought the souls of all that I had murder'd
Came to my tent; and every one did threat
To-morrow's vengeance on the head of Richard.
RATCLIFF
Nay, good my lord, be not afraid of shadows.
KING RICHARD
By the apostle Paul, shadows to-night
Have struck more terror to the soul of Richard
Than can the substance of ten thousand soldiers
Armed in proof and led by shallow Richmond.
It is not yet near day. Come, go with me;
Under our tents I'll play the eaves-dropper,
To hear if any mean to shrink from me.
[Exeunt KING RICHARD and RATCLIFF.
Enter the LORDS to RICHMOND, sitting in his tent.

LORDS
Good morrow, Richmond!
RICHMOND *[waking]*
Cry mercy, lords and watchful gentlemen,
That you have ta'en a tardy sluggard here.
LORDS
How have you slept, my lord?
RICHMOND
The sweetest sleep, and fairest-boding dreams
That ever enter'd in a drowsy head,
Have I since your departure had, my lords.
Methought their souls, whose bodies Richard
murder'd,
Came to my tent, and cried on victory:
I promise you, my heart is very jocund
In the remembrance of so fair a dream.
How far into the morning is it, lords?

LORDS
Upon the stroke of four.
RICHMOND
Why, then 'tis time to arm and give direction.
        His oration to his SOLDIERS.
More than I have said, loving countrymen,
The leisure and enforcement of the time
Forbids to dwell upon: yet remember this, —
God and our good cause fight upon our side;
The prayers of holy saints and wronged souls,
Like high-rear'd bulwarks, stand before our faces;
Richard except, those whom we fight against
Had rather have us win than him they follow:
For what is he they follow? truly, gentlemen,
A bloody tyrant and a homicide;
One rais'd in blood, and one in blood establish'd;
One that made means to come by what he hath,
And slaughter'd those that were the means to help him;
A base foul stone, made precious by the foil
Of England's chair, where he is falsely set;
One that hath ever been God's enemy:
Then, if you fight against God's enemy,
God will, in justice, ward you as his soldiers;
If you do sweat to put a tyrant down,
You sleep in peace, the tyrant being slain;
If you do fight against your country's foes,
Your country's fat shall pay your pains the hire;
If you do fight in safeguard of your wives,
Your wives shall welcome home the conquerors;
If you do free your children from the sword,
Your children's children quit it in your age.
Then, in the name of God and all these rights,
Advance your standards, draw your willing swords.
For me, the ransom of my bold attempt
Shall be this cold corpse on the earth's cold face;
But if I thrive, the gain of my attempt
The least of you shall share his part thereof.
Sound drums and trumpets, boldly and cheerfully;
God and Saint George! Richmond and victory!   *[Exeunt.*
      Enter KING RICHARD, RATCLIFF,
        ATTENDANTS, *and* FORCES.

KING RICHARD
What said Northumberland as touching Richmond?
RATCLIFF
That he was never trained up in arms.
KING RICHARD
He said the truth: and what said Surrey, then?
RATCLIFF
He smil'd, and said, 'The better for our purpose.'
KING RICHARD
He was in the right; and so, indeed, it is.   [*Clock strikes.*
Tell the clock there. — Give me a calendar. —
Who saw the sun to-day?
RATCLIFF
Not I, my lord.
KING RICHARD
Then he disdains to shine; for, by the book,
He should have brav'd the east an hour ago:
A black day will it be to somebody. —
Ratcliff, —
RATCLIFF
My lord?
KING RICHARD
The sun will not be seen to-day;
The sky doth frown and lour upon our army.
I would these dewy tears were from the ground.
Not shine to-day! Why, what is that to me
More than to Richmond? for the selfsame heaven
That frowns on me looks sadly upon him.
          Enter NORFOLK.
NORFOLK
Arm, arm, my lord; the foe vaunts in the field.
KING RICHARD
Come, bustle, bustle; — caparison my horse;
Call up Lord Stanley, bid him bring his power:
I will lead forth my soldiers to the plain,
And thus my battle shall be ordered: —
My foreward shall be drawn out all in length,
Consisting equally of horse and foot;
Our archers shall be placed in the midst:
John Duke of Norfolk, Thomas Earl of Surrey,
Shall have the leading of this foot and horse.
They thus directed, we will follow
In the main battle; whose puissance on either side
Shall be well winged with our chiefest horse.
This, and Saint George to boot! — What think'st thou,
  Norfolk?
NORFOLK
A good direction, warlike sovereign.

This found I on my tent this morning.
            [*He sheweth him a paper.*
KING RICHARD   [*reads.*]
'Jockey of Norfolk, be not too bold,
For Dickon thy master is bought and sold.'
A thing devised by the enemy. —
Go, gentlemen, every man unto his charge:
Let not our babbling dreams affright our souls;
Conscience is but a word that cowards use,
Devis'd at first to keep the strong in awe:
Our strong arms be our conscience, swords our law.
March on, join bravely, let us to't pell-mell;
If not to heaven, then hand in hand to hell. —
       His oration to his ARMY.
What shall I say more than I have inferr'd?
Remember whom you are to cope withal; —
A sort of vagabonds, rascals, and runaways,
A scum of Bretons, and base lackey peasants,
Whom their o'er-cloyed country vomits forth
To desperate ventures and assur'd destruction.
You sleeping safe, they bring to you unrest;
You having lands, and blest with beauteous wives,
They would distrain the one, distain the other.
And who doth lead them but a paltry fellow,
Long kept in Bretagne at our mother's cost?
A milk-sop, one that never in his life
Felt so much cold as over shoes in snow?
Let's whip these stragglers o'er the seas again;
Lash hence these overweening rags of France,
These famish'd beggars, weary of their lives;
Who, but for dreaming on this fond exploit,
For want of means, poor rats, had hang'd themselves:
If we be conquer'd, let men conquer us,
And not these bastard Bretons; whom our fathers
Have in their own land beaten, bobb'd, and thump'd,
And, on record, left them the heirs of shame.
Shall these enjoy our lands? lie with our wives?
Ravish our daughters? [*Drum afar off.*] Hark! I hear
  their drum.
Fight, gentlemen of England! fight, bold yeomen!
Draw, archers, draw your arrows to the head!
Spur your proud horses hard, and ride in blood;
Amaze the welkin with your broken staves!
        Enter a MESSENGER.
What says Lord Stanley? will he bring his power?
MESSENGER
My lord, he doth deny to come.
KING RICHARD
Off with his son George's head!
NORFOLK
My lord, the enemy is past the marsh:
After the battle let George Stanley die.
KING RICHARD
A thousand hearts are great within my bosom:
Advance our standards, set upon our foes;
Our ancient word of courage, fair Saint George,
Inspire us with the spleen of fiery dragons!
Upon them! Victory sits on our helms.   [*Exeunt.*

SCENE IV
Another part of the field.

Alarum: excursions. Enter NORFOLK *and* FORCES;
to him CATESBY.

CATESBY
Rescue, my Lord of Norfolk, rescue, rescue!
The king enacts more wonders than a man,
Daring an opposite to every danger:
His horse is slain, and all on foot he fights,

Seeking for Richmond in the throat of death.
Rescue, fair lord, or else the day is lost!
     Alarums. Enter KING RICHARD.
KING RICHARD
A horse! a horse! my kingdom for a horse!
CATESBY
Withdraw, my lord; I'll help you to a horse.
KING RICHARD
Slave, I have set my life upon a cast,
And I will stand the hazard of the die:
I think there be six Richmonds in the field;
Five have I slain to-day instead of him.
A horse! a horse! my kingdom for a horse!   [*Exeunt.*

SCENE V
Another part of the field.

Alarum. Enter RICHARD *and* RICHMOND; *they fight.*
RICHARD *is slain. Retreat and flourish. Re-enter*
RICHMOND, DERBY *bearing the crown,*
with divers other LORDS.

RICHMOND
God and your arms be prais'd, victorious friends!
The day is ours, the bloody dog is dead.
DERBY
Courageous Richmond, well hast thou acquit thee.
Lo, here, this long-usurped royalty
From the dead temples of this bloody wretch
Have I pluck'd off, to grace thy brows withal:
Wear it, enjoy it, and make much of it.
RICHMOND
Great God of heaven, say Amen to all! —
But, tell me, is young George Stanley living?
DERBY
He is, my lord, and safe in Leicester town;
Whither, if't please you, we may now withdraw us.
RICHMOND
What men of name are slain on either side?
DERBY
John Duke of Norfolk, Walter Lord Ferrers,
Sir Robert Brakenbury, and Sir William Brandon.
RICHMOND
Inter their bodies as becomes their births:
Proclaim a pardon to the soldiers fled
That in submission will return to us:
And then, as we have ta'en the sacrament,
We will unite the white rose and the red.
Smile heaven upon this fair conjunction,
That long have frown'd upon their enmity! —
What traitor hears me, and says not Amen?
England hath long been mad and scarr'd herself;
The brother blindly shed the brother's blood,
The father rashly slaughter'd his own son,
The son, compell'd, been butcher to the sire:
All this divided York and Lancaster,
Divided in their dire division,
O, now let Richmond and Elizabeth,
The true succeeders of each royal house,
By God's fair ordinance conjoin together!
And let their heirs — God, if Thy will be so —
Enrich the time to come with smooth-fac'd peace,
With smiling plenty, and fair prosperous days!
Abate the edge of traitors, gracious Lord,
That would reduce these bloody days again,
And make poor England weep in streams of blood!
Let them not live to taste this land's increase
That would with treason wound this fair land's peace!
Now civil wounds are stopp'd, peace lives agen:
That she may long live here, God say Amen!   [*Exeunt.*

TITUS ANDRONICUS

DRAMATIS PERSONAE

SATURNINUS, *son to the late Emperor of Rome, afterwards emperor.*
BASSIANUS, *brother to Saturninus; in love with Lavinia.*
TITUS ANDRONICUS, *a noble Roman, general against the Goths.*
MARCUS ANDRONICUS, *tribune of the people, and brother to Titus.*
LUCIUS,
QUINTUS,
MARTIUS, } *sons to Titus Andronicus.*
MUTIUS,

YOUNG LUCIUS, *a boy, son to Lucius.*
PUBLIUS, *son to Marcus the tribune.*
SEMPRONIUS,
CAIUS, } *kinsmen to Titus.*
VALENTINE,
AEMILIUS, *a noble Roman.*
ALARBUS,
DEMETRIUS, } *sons to Tamora.*
CHIRON,
AARON, *a Moor, beloved by Tamora.*
A CAPTAIN, TRIBUNE, MESSENGER, *and* CLOWN.

ROMANS *and* GOTHS.

TAMORA, *Queen of the Goths.*
LAVINIA, *daughter to Titus Andronicus.*
A NURSE, *and a black* CHILD.

SENATORS, TRIBUNES, OFFICERS, SOLDIERS, *and* ATTENDANTS.

SCENE — *Rome and the country near it.*

ACT I

SCENE I

Rome. Before the Capitol. The Tomb of the Andronici appearing.

Flourish. Enter the TRIBUNES *and* SENATORS *aloft. And then enter, below,* SATURNINUS *and his* FOLLOWERS *at one door; and* BASSIANUS *and his* FOLLOWERS *at the other, with drums and colours.*

SATURNINUS
Noble patricians, patrons of my right,
Defend the justice of my cause with arms;
And, countrymen, my loving followers,
Plead my successive title with your swords:
I am his first-born son, that was the last
That ware the imperial diadem of Rome;
Then let my father's honours live in me,
Nor wrong mine age with this indignity.

BASSIANUS
Romans, — friends, followers, favourers of my right, —
If ever Bassianus, Cæsar's son,
Were gracious in the eyes of royal Rome,
Keep, then, this passage to the Capitol;
And suffer not dishonour to approach
Th'imperial seat, to virtue consecrate,
To justice, continence, and nobility:
But let desert in pure election shine;
And, Romans, fight for freedom in your choice.

Enter MARCUS ANDRONICUS, *aloft, with the crown.*

MARCUS ANDRONICUS
Princes, — that strive by factions and by friends
Ambitiously for rule and empery, —
Know that the people of Rome, for whom we stand
A special party, have, by common voice,
In election for the Roman empery,
Chosen Andronicus, surnamed Pius
For many good and great deserts to Rome:
A nobler man, a braver warrior,
Lives not this day within the city walls:
He by the senate is accited home
From weary wars against the barbarous Goths;
That, with his sons, a terror to our foes,
Hath yok'd a nation strong, train'd up in arms.
Ten years are spent since first he undertook
This cause of Rome, and chastised with arms
Our enemies' pride: five times he hath return'd
Bleeding to Rome, bearing his valiant sons
In coffins from the field;

LAVINIA And at thy feet I kneel, with tears of joy.

And now at last, laden with honour's spoils,
Returns the good Andronicus to Rome,
Renowned Titus, flourishing in arms.
Let us entreat, — by honour of his name,
Whom worthily you would have now succeed,
And in the Capitol and senate's right,
Whom you pretend to honour and adore, —
That you withdraw you, and abate your strength;
Dismiss your followers, and, as suitors should,
Plead your deserts in peace and humbleness.

SATURNINUS
How fair the tribune speaks to calm my thoughts!

BASSIANUS
Marcus Andronicus, so I do affy
In thy uprightness and integrity,
And so I love and honour thee and thine,
Thy noble brother Titus and his sons,
And her to whom my thoughts are humbled all,
Gracious Lavinia, Rome's rich ornament,
That I will here dismiss my loving friends;
And to my fortunes and the people's favour
Commit my cause in balance to be weigh'd.
   [*Exeunt the* FOLLOWERS *of* BASSIANUS.

SATURNINUS
Friends, that have been thus forward in my right,
I thank you all, and here dismiss you all;
And to the love and favour of my country
Commit myself, my person, and the cause.
   [*Exeunt the* FOLLOWERS *of* SATURNINUS.
Rome, be as just and gracious unto me
As I am confident and kind to thee.—
Open the gates, and let me in.

BASSIANUS
Tribunes, and me, a poor competitor.
   [*Flourish.* SATURNINUS *and* BASSIANUS
   go up into the Capitol.

Enter a CAPTAIN.

CAPTAIN
Romans, make way: the good Andronicus,
Patron of virtue, Rome's best champion,
Successful in the battles that he fights,
With honour and with fortune is return'd
From where he circumscribed with his sword,

And brought to yoke, the enemies of Rome.

Sound drums and trumpets, and then enter MARTIUS
and MUTIUS, *two of* TITUS' *sons; after them, two*
MEN *bearing a coffin cover'd with black; then two other*
sons, LUCIUS *and* QUINTUS; *after them,* TITUS
ANDRONICUS; *and then* TAMORA, *the Queen of*
Goths, and her sons ALARBUS, DEMETRIUS, *and*
CHIRON, *with* AARON *the Moor, and others, as many*
as can be. They set down the coffin and TITUS *speaks.*

TITUS ANDRONICUS
Hail, Rome, victorious in thy mourning weeds!
Lo, as the bark that hath discharg'd her fraught
Returns with precious lading to the bay
From whence at first she weigh'd her anchorage,
Cometh Andronicus, bound with laurel-boughs,
To re-salute his country with his tears,
Tears of true joy for his return to Rome. —
Thou great defender of this Capitol,
Stand gracious to the rites that we intend! —
Romans, of five-and-twenty valiant sons,
Half of the number that King Priam had,
Behold the poor remains, alive and dead!
These that survive let Rome reward with love;
These that I bring unto their latest home,
With burial amongst their ancestors:
Here Goths have given me leave to sheathe my sword.
Titus, unkind, and careless of thine own,
Why suffer'st thou thy sons, unburied yet,
To hover on the dreadful shore of Styx? —
Make way to lay them by their brethren. —
   [*They open the tomb.*
There greet in silence, as the dead are wont,
And sleep in peace, slain in your country's wars!
O sacred receptacle of my joys,
Sweet cell of virtue and nobility,
How many sons of mine hast thou in store,
That thou wilt never render to me more!

YOUNG LUCIUS
Give us the proudest prisoner of the Goths,
That we may hew his limbs, and on a pile
Ad manes fratrum sacrifice his flesh,
Before this earthy prison of their bones;
That so the shadows be not unappeased,
Nor we disturb'd with prodigies on earth.

TITUS ANDRONICUS
I give him you, — the noblest that survives,
The eldest son of this distressed queen.

TAMORA
Stay, Roman brethren! — Gracious conqueror,
Victorious Titus, rue the tears I shed,
A mother's tears in passion for her son:
And if thy sons were ever dear to thee,
O, think my son to be as dear to me!
Sufficeth not, that we are brought to Rome,
To beautify thy triumphs and return,
Captive to thee and to thy Roman yoke;
But must my sons be slaughter'd in the streets,
For valiant doings in their country's cause?
O, if to fight for king and commonweal
Were piety in thine, it is in these.
Andronicus, stain not thy tomb with blood:
Wilt thou draw near the nature of the gods?
Draw near them, then, in being merciful:
Sweet mercy is nobility's true badge:
Thrice-noble Titus, spare my first-born son.

TITUS ANDRONICUS
Patient yourself, madam, and pardon me.
These are their brethren, whom you Goths beheld
Alive and dead; and for their brethren slain
Religiously they ask a sacrifice:
To this your son is mark'd; and die he must,
T'appease their groaning shadows that are gone.

LUCIUS
Away with him! and make a fire straight;
And with our swords, upon a pile of wood,
Let's hew his limbs till they be clean consumed.
   [*Exeunt the* SONS *of* ANDRONICUS *with* ALARBUS.

TAMORA
O cruel, irreligious piety!

CHIRON
Was ever Scythia half so barbarous?

DEMETRIUS
Oppose not Scythia to ambitious Rome.
Alarbus goes to rest; and we survive
To tremble under Titus' threatening looks.
Then, madam, stand resolv'd; but hope withal,
The self-same gods, that arm'd the Queen of Troy
With opportunity of sharp revenge
Upon the Thracian tyrant in her tent,
May favour Tamora, the Queen of Goths, —
When Goths were Goths, and Tamora was queen, —
To quit these bloody wrongs upon her foes.

Enter the SONS *of* ANDRONICUS *again,*
with their swords bloody.

LUCIUS
See, lord and father, how we have perform'd
Our Roman rites: Alarbus' limbs are lopp'd,
And entrails feed the sacrificing fire,
Whose smoke, like incense, doth perfume the sky.
Remaineth naught, but to inter our brethren,
And with loud 'larums welcome them to Rome.

TITUS ANDRONICUS
Let it be so; and let Andronicus
Make this his latest farewell to their souls.
   [*Then sound trumpets and lay the coffin in the tomb.*
In peace and honour rest you here, my sons;
Rome's readiest champions, repose you here,
Secure from worldly chances and mishaps!
Here lurks no treason, here no envy swells,
Here grow no damned grudges; here are no storms,
No noise, but silence and eternal sleep:
   Enter LAVINIA.
In peace and honour rest you here, my sons!

LAVINIA
In peace and honour live Lord Titus long;
My noble lord and father, live in fame!
Lo, at this tomb my tributary tears
I render, for my brethren's obsequies;
And at thy feet I kneel, with tears of joy,
Shed on the earth, for thy return to Rome:
O, bless me here with thy victorious hand,
Whose fortunes Rome's best citizens applaud!

TITUS ANDRONICUS
Kind Rome, that hast thus lovingly reserved
The cordial of mine age to glad my heart! —
Lavinia, live; outlive thy father's days,
And fame's eternal date, for virtue's praise!

Enter, below, MARCUS ANDRONICUS
and TRIBUNES; SATURNINUS
and BASSIANUS, *attended.*

MARCUS ANDRONICUS
Long live Lord Titus, my beloved brother,
Gracious triumpher in the eyes of Rome!

TITUS ANDRONICUS
Thanks, gentle tribune, noble brother Marcus.

MARCUS ANDRONICUS
And welcome, nephews, from successful wars,
You that survive, and you that sleep in fame!
Fair lords, your fortunes are alike in all,
That in your country's service drew your swords:
But safer triumph is this funeral pomp,
That hath aspired to Solon's happiness,
And triumphs over chance in honour's bed. —
Titus Andronicus, the people of Rome,
Whose friend in justice thou hast ever been,
Send thee by me, their tribune and their trust,
This palliament of white and spotless hue;
And name thee in election for the empire,
With these our late-deceased emperor's sons:
Be *candidatus*, then, and put it on,
And help to set a head on headless Rome.

TITUS ANDRONICUS
A better head her glorious body fits
Than his that shakes for age and feebleness:
What, should I don this robe, and trouble you?
Be chosen with proclamations to-day,
To-morrow yield up rule, resign my life,
And set abroach new business for you all?
Rome, I have been thy soldier forty years,
And led my country's strength successfully,
And buried one-and-twenty valiant sons,
Knighted in field, slain manfully in arms,
In right and service of their noble country:
Give me a staff of honour for mine age,
But not a sceptre to control the world:
Upright he held it, lords, that held it last.

MARCUS ANDRONICUS
Titus, thou shalt obtain and ask the empery.

SATURNINUS
Proud and ambitious tribune, canst thou tell?

TITUS ANDRONICUS
Patience, Prince Saturnine.

SATURNINUS
                    Romans, do me right; —
Patricians, draw your swords, and sheathe them not
Till Saturninus be Rome's emperor. —
Andronicus, would thou wert shipp'd to hell,
Rather than rob me of the people's hearts!

LUCIUS
Proud Saturnine, interrupter of the good
That noble-minded Titus means to thee!

TITUS ANDRONICUS
Content thee, prince; I will restore to thee
The people's hearts, and wean them from themselves.

BASSIANUS
Andronicus, I do not flatter thee,
But honour thee, and will do till I die:
My faction if thou strengthen with thy friends,
I will most thankful be; and thanks to men
Of noble minds is honourable meed.

TITUS ANDRONICUS
People of Rome, and people's tribunes here,
I ask your voices and your suffrages:
Will you bestow them friendly on Andronicus?

TRIBUNES
To gratify the good Andronicus,
And gratulate his safe return to Rome,
The people will accept whom he admits.

TITUS ANDRONICUS
Tribunes, I thank you: and this suit I make,
That you create your emperor's eldest son,
Lord Saturnine; whose virtues will, I hope,
Reflect on Rome as Titan's rays on earth,
And ripen justice in this commonweal:
Then, if you will elect by my advice,
Crown him, and say, 'Long live our emperor!'

MARCUS ANDRONICUS
With voices and applause of every sort,
Patricians and plebeians, we create
Lord Saturninus Rome's great emperor,
And say, 'Long live our Emperor Saturnine!'
                    [*A long flourish till they come down.*

SATURNINUS
Titus Andronicus, for thy favours done
To us in our election this day
I give thee thanks in part of thy deserts,
And will with deeds requite thy gentleness:
And, for an onset, Titus, to advance
Thy name and honourable family,
Lavinia will I make my empress,
Rome's royal mistress, mistress of my heart,
And in the sacred Pantheon her espouse:
Tell me, Andronicus, doth this motion please thee?

TITUS ANDRONICUS
It doth, my worthy lord; and in this match
I hold me highly honour'd of your Grace:
And here, in sight of Rome, to Saturnine —
King and commander of our commonweal,
The wide world's emperor — do I consecrate
My sword, my chariot, and my prisoners;
Presents well worthy Rome's imperial lord:
Receive them, then, the tribute that I owe,
Mine honour's ensigns humbled at thy feet.

SATURNINUS
Thanks, noble Titus, father of my life!
How proud I am of thee and of thy gifts
Rome shall record; and when I do forget
The least of these unspeakable deserts,
Romans, forget your fealty to me.

TITUS ANDRONICUS [*to* TAMORA].
Now, madam, are you prisoner to an emperor;
To him that, for your honour and your state,
Will use you nobly and your followers.

SATURNINUS [*aside*].
A goodly lady, trust me; of the hue
That I would choose, were I to choose anew. —
Clear up, fair queen, that cloudy countenance:
Though chance of war hath wrought this change of cheer,
Thou com'st not to be made a scorn in Rome:
Princely shall be thy usage every way.
Rest on my word, and let not discontent
Daunt all your hopes: madam, he comforts you
Can make you greater than the Queen of Goths. —
Lavinia, you are not displeas'd with this?

LAVINIA
Not I, my lord; sith true nobility
Warrants these words in princely courtesy.

SATURNINUS
Thanks, sweet Lavinia. — Romans, let us go:
Ransomless here we set our prisoners free:
Proclaim our honours, lords, with trump and drum.
                    [*Flourish.* SATURNINUS *courts*
                    TAMORA *in dumb-show.*

BASSIANUS
Lord Titus, by your leave, this maid is mine.
                    [*Seizing* LAVINIA.

TITUS ANDRONICUS
How, sir! are you in earnest, then, my lord?

BASSIANUS
Ay, noble Titus; and resolv'd withal
To do myself this reason and this right.

MARCUS ANDRONICUS
Suum cuique is our Roman justice:
This prince in justice seizeth but his own.

LUCIUS
And that he will, and shall, if Lucius live.

TITUS ANDRONICUS
Traitors, avaunt! — Where is the emperor's guard? —
Treason, my lord, — Lavinia is surprised!

SATURNINUS
Surpris'd! by whom?

BASSIANUS
                    By him that justly may
Bear his betroth'd from all the world away.
          [*Exeunt* BASSIANUS *and* MARCUS *with* LAVINIA.

MUTIUS
Brothers, help to convey her hence away,
And with my sword I'll keep this door safe.
          [*Exeunt* LUCIUS, QUINTUS, *and* MARTIUS.

TITUS ANDRONICUS
Follow, my lord, and I'll soon bring her back.
          [*Exeunt* SATURNINUS, TAMORA. *and her* SONS,
                    and AARON *the Moor.*

MUTIUS
My lord, you pass not here.

TITUS ANDRONICUS
                    What, villain boy!
Barr'st me my way in Rome?

MUTIUS
                    Help, Lucius, help!
                    [TITUS *kills* MUTIUS.
                    Enter LUCIUS.

LUCIUS
My lord, you are unjust; and, more than so,
In wrongful quarrel you have slain your son.

TITUS ANDRONICUS
Nor thou, nor he, are any sons of mine;
My sons would never so dishonour me:
Traitor, restore Lavinia to the emperor.

LUCIUS
Dead, if you will; but not to be his wife,

That is another's lawful promis'd love.   [*Exit.*
          Enter aloft the Emperor SATURNINUS *with* TAMORA
                    and her two SONS, *and* AARON *the Moor.*

SATURNINUS
No, Titus, no; the emperor needs her not,
Nor her, nor thee, nor any of thy stock:
I'll trust, by leisure, him that mocks me once;
Thee never, nor thy traitorous haughty sons,
Confederates all thus to dishonour me.
Was there none else in Rome to make a stale,
But Saturnine? Full well, Andronicus,
Agree these deeds with that proud brag of thine,
That saidst, I begg'd the empire at thy hands.

TITUS ANDRONICUS
O monstrous! what reproachful words are these?

SATURNINUS
But go thy ways; go, give that changing piece
To him that flourish'd for her with his sword:
A valiant son-in-law thou shalt enjoy;
One fit to bandy with thy lawless sons,
To ruffle in the commonwealth of Rome.

TITUS ANDRONICUS
These words are razors to my wounded heart.

SATURNINUS
And therefore, lovely Tamora, Queen of Goths, —
That, like the stately Phoebe 'mongst her nymphs,
Dost overshine the gallant'st dames of Rome, —
If thou be pleas'd with this my sudden choice,
Behold, I choose thee, Tamora, for my bride,
And will create thee empress of Rome.
Speak, Queen of Goths, dost thou applaud my choice?
And here I swear by all the Roman gods, —
Sith priest and holy water are so near,
And tapers burn so bright, and every thing
In readiness for Hymenæus stand, —
I will not re-salute the streets of Rome,
Or climb my palace, till from forth this place
I lead espous'd my bride along with me.

TAMORA
And here, in sight of heaven, to Rome I swear,
If Saturnine advance the Queen of Goths,
She will a handmaid be to his desires,
A loving nurse, a mother to his youth.

SATURNINUS
Ascend, fair queen, Pantheon. — Lords, accompany
Your noble emperor and his lovely bride,
Sent by the heavens for Prince Saturnine,
Whose wisdom hath her fortune conquered:
There shall we consummate our spousal rites.
                    [*Exeunt all but* TITUS.

TITUS ANDRONICUS
I am not bid to wait upon this bride: —
Titus, when wert thou wont to walk alone,
Dishonour'd thus, and challenged of wrongs?
          Enter MARCUS, LUCIUS, QUINTUS, *and*
                    MARTIUS.

MARCUS ANDRONICUS
O Titus, see, O, see what thou hast done!
In a bad quarrel slain a virtuous son.

TITUS ANDRONICUS
No, foolish tribune, no; no son of mine, —
Nor thou, nor these, confederates in the deed
That hath dishonour'd all our family;
Unworthy brother, and unworthy sons!

LUCIUS
But let us give him burial, as becomes;
Give Mutius burial with our brethren.

TITUS ANDRONICUS
Traitors, away! he rests not in this tomb: —
This monument five hundred years hath stood,
Which I have sumptuously re-edified:
Here none but soldiers and Rome's servitors
Repose in fame; none basely slain in brawls: —
Bury him where you can, he comes not here.

MARCUS ANDRONICUS
My lord, this is impiety in you:
My nephew Mutius' deeds do plead for him;
He must be buried with his brethren.

QUINTUS AND MARTIUS
And shall, or him we will accompany.

TITUS ANDRONICUS
'And shall!' what villain was it spake that word?

QUINTUS
He that would vouch it in any place but here.

TITUS ANDRONICUS
What, would you bury him in my despite?

MARCUS ANDRONICUS
No, noble Titus; but entreat of thee

To pardon Mutius, and to bury him.

TITUS ANDRONICUS
Marcus, even thou hast struck upon my crest,
And, with these boys, mine honour thou hast
  wounded:
My foes I do repute you every one;
So, trouble me no more, but get you gone.

MARTIUS
He is not with himself; let us withdraw.

QUINTUS
Not I, till Mutius' bones be buried.
          [MARCUS *and the* SONS *of* TITUS *kneel.*

MARCUS ANDRONICUS
Brother, for in that name doth nature plead, —

QUINTUS
Father, and in that name doth nature speak, —

TITUS ANDRONICUS
Speak thou no more, if all the rest will speed.

MARCUS ANDRONICUS
Renowned Titus, more than half my soul, —

LUCIUS
Dear father, soul and substance of us all, —

MARCUS ANDRONICUS
Suffer thy brother Marcus to inter
His noble nephew here in virtue's nest,
That died in honour and Lavinia's cause.
Thou art a Roman, — be not barbarous:
The Greeks upon advice did bury Ajax,
That slew himself; and wise Laertes' son
Did graciously plead for his funerals:
Let not young Mutius, then, that was thy joy,
Be barr'd his entrance here.

TITUS ANDRONICUS
                    Rise, Marcus, rise: —
The dismall'st day is this that e'er I saw,
To be dishonour'd by my sons in Rome! —
Well, bury him, and bury me the next.
          [*They put* MUTIUS *in the tomb.*

LUCIUS
There lie thy bones, sweet Mutius, with thy friends,
Till we with trophies do adorn thy tomb.

ALL [*kneeling*].
No man shed tears for noble Mutius;
He lives in fame that died in virtue's cause.

MARCUS ANDRONICUS
My lord, — to step out of these dreary dumps, —
How comes it that the subtle Queen of Goths
Is of a sudden thus advanc'd in Rome?

TITUS ANDRONICUS
I know not, Marcus; but I know it is, —
Whether by device or no, the heavens can tell:
Is she not, then, beholding to the man
That brought her for this high good turn so far?

MARCUS ANDRONICUS
Yes, and will nobly him remunerate.

Flourish. Enter the Emperor SATURNINUS, TAMORA
and her two SONS, *with the* MOOR *at one door; enter at
the other door,* BASSIANUS *and* LAVINIA, *with others.*

SATURNINUS
So, Bassianus, you have play'd your prize:
God give you joy, sir, of your gallant bride!

BASSIANUS
And you of yours, my lord! I say no more,
Nor wish no less; and so, I take my leave.

SATURNINUS
Traitor, if Rome have law, or we have power,
Thou and thy faction shall repent this rape.

BASSIANUS
Rape, call you it, my lord, to seize my own,
My true-betrothed love, and now my wife?
But let the laws of Rome determine all;
Meanwhile, I am possess'd of that is mine.

SATURNINUS
'Tis good, sir: you are very short with us;
But, if we live, we'll be as sharp with you.

BASSIANUS
My lord, what I have done, as best I may,
Answer I must, and shall do with my life.
Only thus much I give your Grace to know, —
By all the duties that I owe to Rome,
This noble gentleman, Lord Titus here,
Is in opinion and in honour wrong'd;
That, in the rescue of Lavinia,
With his own hand did slay his youngest son,
In zeal to you, and highly moved to wrath
To be controll'd in that he frankly gave:
Receive him, then, to favour, Saturnine,
That hath express'd himself in all his deeds
A father and a friend to thee and Rome.

TITUS ANDRONICUS
Prince Bassianus, leave to plead my deeds:
'Tis thou and those that have dishonour'd me.
Rome and the righteous heavens be my judge,
How I have lov'd and honour'd Saturnine!

TAMORA
My worthy lord, if ever Tamora
Were gracious in those princely eyes of thine,
Then hear me speak indifferently for all;
And at my suit, sweet, pardon what is past.

SATURNINUS
What, madam! be dishonour'd openly,
And basely put it up without revenge?

TAMORA
Not so, my lord; the gods of Rome forfend
I should be author to dishonour you!
But on mine honour dare I undertake
For good Lord Titus' innocence in all;
Whose fury not dissembled speaks his griefs:
Then, at my suit, look graciously on him;
Lose not so noble a friend on vain suppose,
Nor with sour looks afflict his gentle heart. —
[*Aside to* SATURNINUS.] My lord, be rul'd by me, be
  won at last;.
Dissemble all your griefs and discontents:
You are but newly planted in your throne;
Lest, then, the people, and patricians too,
Upon a just survey, take Titus' part,
And so supplant you for ingratitude, —
Which Rome reputes to be a heinous sin, —
Yield at entreats; and then let me alone:
I'll find a day to massacre them all,
And raze their faction and their family,
The cruel father and his traitorous sons,
To whom I sued for my dear son's life;
And make them know what 'tis to let a queen
Kneel in the streets and beg for grace in vain. —
Come, come, sweet emperor, — come, Andronicus, —
Take up this good old man, and cheer the heart
That dies in tempest of thy angry frown.

SATURNINUS
Rise, Titus, rise; my empress hath prevail'd.

TITUS ANDRONICUS
I thank your majesty, and her, my lord:
These words, these looks, infuse new life in me.

TAMORA
Titus, I am incorporate in Rome,
A Roman now adopted happily,
And must advise the emperor for his good.
This day all quarrels die, Andronicus; —
And let it be mine honour, good my lord,
That I have reconcil'd your friends and you. —
For you, Prince Bassianus, I have pass'd
My word and promise to the emperor,
That you will be more mild and tractable. —
And fear not, lords, — and you, Lavinia; —
By my advice, all humbled on your knees,
You shall ask pardon of his majesty.
          [MARCUS, LAVINIA, *and the* SONS *of* TITUS *kneel.*

LUCIUS
We do; and vow to heaven, and to his highness,
That what we did was mildly as we might,
Tend'ring our sister's honour and our own.

MARCUS ANDRONICUS
That, on mine honour, here I do protest.

SATURNINUS
Away, and talk not; trouble us no more.

TAMORA
Nay, nay, sweet emperor, we must all be friends:
The tribune and his nephews kneel for grace;
I will not be denied: sweet heart, look back.

SATURNINUS
Marcus, for thy sake and thy brother's here,
And at my lovely Tamora's entreats,
I do remit these young men's heinous faults.
                              [*Stand up.*
Lavinia, though you left me like a churl,
I found a friend; and sure as death I swore
I would not part a bachelor from the priest.
Come, if the emperor's court can feast two brides,
You are my guest, Lavinia, and your friends. —
This day shall be a love-day, Tamora.

TITUS ANDRONICUS
To-morrow, an it please your majesty
To hunt the panther and the hart with me,
With horn and hound we'll give your Grace *bonjour.*

SATURNINUS
Be it so, Titus, and gramercy too.   [*Flourish. Exeunt.*

ACT II

SCENE I

Rome. Before the palace.

Enter AARON *alone.*

AARON
Now climbeth Tamora Olympus' top,
Safe out of fortune's shot; and sits aloft,
Secure of thunder's crack or lightning-flash;
Advanc'd above pale envy's threat'ning reach.
As when the golden sun salutes the morn,
And, having gilt the ocean with his beams,
Gallops the zodiac in his glistering coach,
And overlooks the highest-peering hills;
So Tamora:
Upon her wit doth earthly honour wait,
And virtue stoops and trembles at her frown.
Then, Aaron, arm thy heart, and fit thy thoughts,
To mount aloft with thy imperial mistress,
And mount her pitch, whom thou in triumph long
Hast prisoner held, fetter'd in amorous chains,
And faster bound to Aaron's charming eyes
Than is Prometheus tied to Caucasus.
Away with slavish weeds and servile thoughts!
I will be bright, and shine in pearl and gold,
To wait upon this new-made empress.
To wait, said I? to wanton with this queen,
This goddess, this Semiramis, this nymph,
This siren, that will charm Rome's Saturnine,
And see his shipwrack and his commonweal's. —
Holla! what storm is this?

Enter DEMETRIUS *and* CHIRON, *braving.*

DEMETRIUS
Chiron, thy years want wit, thy wit wants edge,
And manners, to intrude where I am graced;
And may, for aught thou know'st, affected be.

CHIRON
Demetrius, thou dost over-ween in all;
And so in this, to bear me down with braves.
'Tis not the difference of a year or two
Makes me less gracious, or thee more fortunate:
I am as able and as fit as thou
To serve, and to deserve my mistress' grace;
And that my sword upon thee shall approve,
And plead my passions for Lavinia's love.

AARON [*aside*].
Clubs! clubs! these lovers will not keep the peace.

DEMETRIUS
Why, boy, although our mother, unadvis'd,
Gave you a dancing-rapier by your side,
Are you so desperate grown to threat your friends?
Go to; have your lath glued within your sheath
Till you know better how to handle it.

CHIRON
Meanwhile, sir, with the little skill I have,
Full well shalt thou perceive how much I dare.

DEMETRIUS
Ay, boy, grow ye so brave?   [*They draw.*

AARON [*coming forward*].
                    Why, how now, lords!
So near the emperor's palace dare you draw,
And maintain such a quarrel openly?
Full well I wot the ground of all this grudge:
I would not for a million of gold
The cause were known to them it most concerns;
Nor would your noble mother for much more
Be so dishonour'd in the court of Rome.
For shame, put up.

DEMETRIUS
                    Not I, till I have sheath'd
My rapier in his bosom, and withal
Thrust these reproachful speeches down his throat
That he hath breath'd in my dishonour here.

CHIRON
For that I am prepared and full resolv'd, —
Foul-spoken coward, that thunder'st with thy tongue,
And with thy weapon nothing darest perform.

AARON
Away, I say! —
Now, by the gods that warlike Goths adore,
This pretty brabble will undo us all. —
Why, lords, and think you not how dangerous
It is to jet upon a prince's right?
What, is Lavinia, then, become so loose,
Or Bassianus so degenerate,
That for her love such quarrels may be broach'd
Without controlment, justice, or revenge?
Young lords, beware! an should the empress know

This discord's ground, the music would not please.
CHIRON
I care not, I knew she and all the world:
I love Lavinia more than all the world.
DEMETRIUS
Youngling, learn thou to make some meaner choice;
Lavinia is thine elder brother's hope.
AARON
Why, are ye mad? or know ye not, in Rome
How furious and impatient they be,
And cannot brook competitors in love?
I tell you, lords, you do but plot your deaths
By this device.
CHIRON
        Aaron, a thousand deaths
Would I propose to achieve her whom I love.
AARON
To achieve her! — how?
DEMETRIUS
      Why mak'st thou it so strange?
She is a woman, therefore may be woo'd;
She is a woman, therefore may be won;
She is Lavinia, therefore must be lov'd.
What, man! more water glideth by the mill
Than wots the miller of; and easy it is
Of a cut loaf to steal a shive, we know:
Though Bassianus be the emperor's brother,
Better than he have worn Vulcan's badge.
AARON [aside].
Ay, and as good as Saturninus may.
DEMETRIUS
Then why should he despair that knows to court it
With words, fair looks, and liberality?
What, hast not thou full often struck a doe,
And borne her cleanly by the keeper's nose?
AARON
Why, then, it seems, some certain snatch or so
Would serve your turns.
CHIRON
      Ay, so the turn were serv'd.
DEMETRIUS
Aaron, thou hast hit it.
AARON
      Would you had hit it too!
Then should not we be tired with this ado.
Why, hark ye, hark ye, — and are you such fools
To square for this? would it offend you, then,
That both should speed?
CHIRON
Faith, not me.
DEMETRIUS
      Nor me, so I were one.
AARON
For shame, be friends, and join for that you jar:
'Tis policy and stratagem must do
That you affect; and so must you resolve,
That what you cannot as you would achieve,
You must perforce accomplish as you may.
Take this of me, — Lucrece was not more chaste
Than this Lavinia, Bassianus' love.
A speedier course than lingering languishment
Must we pursue, and I have found the path.
My lords, a solemn hunting is in hand;
There will the lovely Roman ladies troop:
The forest-walks are wide and spacious;
And many unfrequented plots there are
Fitted by kind for rape and villainy:
Single you thither, then, this dainty doe,
And strike her home by force, if not by words:
This way, or not at all, stand you in hope.
Come, come, our empress, with her sacred wit
To villainy and vengeance consecrate,
Will we acquaint with all that we intend;
And she shall file our engines with advice,
That will not suffer you to square yourselves,
But to your wishes' height advance you both.
The emperor's court is like the house of Fame,
The palace full of tongues, of eyes, and ears:
The woods are ruthless, dreadful, deaf, and dull;
There speak, and strike, brave boys, and take your
    turns;
There serve your lust, shadow'd from heaven's eye,
And revel in Lavinia's treasury.
CHIRON
Thy counsel, lad, smells of no cowardice.
DEMETRIUS
Sit fas aut nefas, till I find the stream
To cool this heat, a charm to calm these fits,
Per Styga, per manes vehor.   [*Exeunt.*

SCENE II
A forest near Rome.

Enter TITUS ANDRONICUS *and his three* SONS,
making a noise with hounds and horns; and MARCUS.

TITUS ANDRONICUS
The hunt is up, the morn is bright and grey,
The fields are fragrant, and the woods are green:
Uncouple here, and let us make a bay,
And wake the emperor and his lovely bride,
And rouse the prince, and ring a hunter's peal,
That all the court may echo with the noise.
Sons, let it be your charge, as it is ours,
To attend the emperor's person carefully:
I have been troubled in my sleep this night,
But dawning day new comfort hath inspired.
Here a cry of hounds, and wind horns in a peal.
  Enter SATURNINUS, TAMORA, BASSIANUS,
    LAVINIA, DEMETRIUS, CHIRON, *and their*
           ATTENDANTS.
Many good morrows to your majesty; —
Madam, to you as many and as good: —
I promised your Grace a hunter's peal.
SATURNINUS
And you have rung it lustily, my lords;
Somewhat too early for new-married ladies.
BASSIANUS
Lavinia, how say you?
LAVINIA
        I say, no;
I have been broad awake two hours and more.
SATURNINUS
Come on, then; horse and chariots let us have,
And to our sport. — [*to* TAMORA] Madam, now shall
  ye see.
Our Roman hunting.
MARCUS ANDRONICUS
      I have dogs, my lord,
Will rouse the proudest panther in the chase,
And climb the highest promontory top.
TITUS ANDRONICUS
And I have horse will follow where the game
Makes way, and run like swallows o'er the plain.
DEMETRIUS
Chiron, we hunt not, we, with horse nor hound,
But hope to pluck a dainty doe to ground.   [*Exeunt.*

SCENE III
A lonely part of the forest.

Enter AARON *alone, with a bag of gold.*

AARON
He that had wit would think that I had none,
To bury so much gold under a tree,
And never after to inherit it.
Let him that thinks of me so abjectly
Know that this gold must coin a stratagem,
Which, cunningly effected, will beget
A very excellent piece of villainy:
And so repose, sweet gold, for their unrest
             [*Hides the gold.*
That have their alms out of the empress' chest.
    Enter TAMORA *to the Moor.*

TAMORA
My lovely Aaron, wherefore look'st thou sad,
When every thing doth make a gleeful boast?
The birds chant melody on every bush;
The snake lies rolled in the cheerful sun;
The green leaves quiver with the cooling wind,
And make a chequer'd shadow on the ground:
Under their sweet shade, Aaron, let us sit,
And, whilst the babbling echo mocks the
  hounds,
Replying shrilly to the well-tuned horns,
As if a double hunt were heard at once,
Let us sit down and mark their yelping noise;
And — after conflict such as was supposed
The wandering prince and Dido once enjoy'd,
When with a happy storm they were surprised,
And curtain'd with a counsel-keeping cave —
We may, each wreathed in the other's arms,
Our pastimes done, possess a golden slumber;
Whiles hounds and horns and sweet melodious
  birds
Be unto us as is a nurse's song
Of lullaby to bring her babe asleep.
AARON
Madam, though Venus govern your desires,
Saturn is dominator over mine:

What signifies my deadly-standing eye,
My silence and my cloudy melancholy,
My fleece of woolly hair that now uncurls
Even as an adder when she doth unroll
To do some fatal execution?
No, madam, these are no venereal signs:
Vengeance is in my heart, death in my hand,
Blood and revenge are hammering in my head.
Hark, Tamora, — the empress of my soul,
Which never hopes more heaven than rests in thee, —
This is the day of doom for Bassianus:
His Philomel must lose her tongue to-day;
Thy sons make pillage of her chastity,
And wash their hands in Bassianus' blood.
Seest thou this letter? take it up, I pray thee,
And give the king this fatal-plotted scroll. —
Now question me no more, — we are espied;
Here comes a parcel of our hopeful booty,
Which dreads not yet their lives' destruction.
TAMORA
Ah, my sweet Moor, sweeter to me than life!
AARON
No more, great empress, — Bassianus comes:
Be cross with him; and I'll go fetch thy sons
To back thy quarrels, whatsoe'er they be.   [*Exit.*
    Enter BASSIANUS *and* LAVINIA.

BASSIANUS
Who have we here? Rome's royal empress,
Unfurnish'd of her well-beseeming troop?
Or is it Dian, habited like her,
Who hath abandoned her holy groves
To see the general hunting in this forest?
TAMORA
Saucy controller of our private steps!
Had I the power that some say Dian had,
Thy temples should be planted presently
With horns, as was Actæon's; and the hounds
Should drive upon thy new-transformed limbs,
Unmannerly intruder as thou art!
LAVINIA
Under your patience, gentle empress,
'Tis thought you have a goodly gift in horning;
And to be doubted that your Moor and you
Are singled forth to try experiments:
Jove shield your husband from his hounds to-day!
'Tis pity they should take him for a stag.
BASSIANUS
Believe me, queen, your swarth Cimmerian
Doth make your honour of his body's hue,
Spotted, detested, and abominable.
Why are you sequestered from all your train,

TAMORA We may, each wreathed in the other's arms, our pastimes done, possess a golden slumber.

Dismounted from your snow-white goodly steed,
And wander'd hither to an obscure plot,
Accompanied but with a barbarous Moor,
If foul desire had not conducted you?

LAVINIA
And, being intercepted in your sport,
Great reason that my noble lord be rated
For sauciness. — I pray you, let us hence,
And let her joy her raven-colour'd love;
This valley fits the purpose passing well.

BASSIANUS
The king my brother shall have note of this.

LAVINIA
Ay, for thee slips have made him noted long:
Good king, to be so mightily abused!

TAMORA
Why have I patience to endure all this?

Enter DEMETRIUS *and* CHIRON.

DEMETRIUS
How now, dear sovereign and our gracious mother!
Why doth your highness look so pale and wan?

TAMORA
Have I not reason, think you, to look pale?
These two have 'ticed me hither to this place: —
A barren detested vale you see it is;
The trees, though summer, yet forlorn and lean,
O'ercome with moss and baleful mistletoe:
Here never shines the sun; here nothing breeds,
Unless the nightly owl or fatal raven: —
And when they show'd me this abhorred pit,
They told me, here, at dead time of the night,
A thousand fiends, a thousand hissing snakes,
Ten thousand swelling toads, as many urchins,
Would make such fearful and confused cries,
As any mortal body hearing it
Should straight fall mad, or else die suddenly.
No sooner had they told this hellish tale,
But straight they told me they would bind me here
Unto the body of a dismal yew,
And leave me to this miserable death:
And then they call'd me foul adulteress,
Lascivious Goth, and all the bitterest terms
That ever ear did hear to such effect:
And, had you not by wondrous fortune come,
This vengeance on me had they executed.
Revenge it, as you love your mother's life,
Or be ye not henceforth call'd my children.

DEMETRIUS
This is a witness that I am thy son.
[Stabs BASSIANUS.

CHIRON
And this for me, struck home to show my strength.
[Stabs BASSIANUS, *who dies.*

LAVINIA
Ay, come, Semiramis, — nay, barbarous Tamora,
For no name fits thy nature but thy own!

TAMORA
Give me the poniard; — you shall know, my boys,
Your mother's hand shall right your mother's wrong.

DEMETRIUS
Stay, madam; here is more belongs to her;
First thrash the corn, then after burn the straw:
This minion stood upon her chastity,
Upon her nuptial vow, her loyalty,
And with that painted hope she braves your
    mightiness:
And shall she carry this unto her grave?

CHIRON
An if she do, I would I were an eunuch.
Drag hence her husband to some secret hole,
And make his dead trunk pillow to our lust.

TAMORA
But when ye have the honey ye desire,
Let not this wasp outlive, us both to sting.

CHIRON
I warrant you, madam, we will make that sure. —
Come, mistress, now perforce we will enjoy
That nice-preserved honesty of yours.

LAVINIA
O Tamora! thou bear'st a woman's face, —

TAMORA
I will not hear her speak; away with her!

LAVINIA
Sweet lords, entreat her hear me but a word.

DEMETRIUS
Listen, fair madam: let it be your glory
To see her tears; but be your heart to them
As unrelenting flint to drops of rain.

LAVINIA
When did the tiger's young ones teach the dam?
O, do not learn her wrath, — she taught it thee;
The milk thou suck'dst from her did turn to marble;
Even at thy teat thou hadst thy tyranny. —
Yet every mother breeds not sons alike:
[to CHIRON] Do thou entreat her show a woman pity.

CHIRON
What, wouldst thou have me prove myself a bastard?

LAVINIA
'Tis true, — the raven doth not hatch a lark:
Yet have I heard, — O, could I find it now! —
The lion, mov'd with pity, did endure
To have his princely paws pared all away:
Some say that ravens foster forlorn children,
The whilst their own birds famish in their nests:
O, be to me, though thy hard heart say no,
Nothing so kind, but something pitiful!

TAMORA
I know not what it means. — Away with her!

LAVINIA
O, let me teach thee! for my father's sake,
That gave thee life, when well he might have slain thee,
Be not obdurate, open thy deaf ears.

TAMORA
Hadst thou in person ne'er offended me,
Even for his sake am I pitiless. —
Remember, boys, I pour'd forth tears in vain
To save your brother from the sacrifice;
But fierce Andronicus would not relent:
Therefore, away with her, and use her as you will;
The worse to her, the better lov'd of me.

LAVINIA
O Tamora, be call'd a gentle queen,
And with thine own hands kill me in this place!
For 'tis not life that I have begg'd so long;
Poor I was slain when Bassianus died.

TAMORA
What begg'st thou, then? fond woman, let me go.

LAVINIA
'Tis present death I beg; and one thing more
That womanhood denies my tongue to tell:
O, keep me from their worse than killing lust,
And tumble me into some loathsome pit,
Where never man's eye may behold my body:
Do this, and be a charitable murderer.

TAMORA
So should I rob my sweet sons of their fee:
No, let them satisfy their lust on thee.

DEMETRIUS
Away! for thou hast stay'd us here too long.

LAVINIA
No grace? no womanhood? Ah, beastly creature!
The blot and enemy to our general name!
Confusion fall —

CHIRON
Nay, then, I'll stop your mouth. — Bring thou her
    husband:
This is the hole where Aaron bid us hide him.

*[*DEMETRIUS *throws the body of* BASSIANUS
into the pit; then exeunt DEMETRIUS *and* CHIRON,
dragging off LAVINIA.

TAMORA
Farewell, my sons: see that you make her sure: —
Ne'er let my heart know merry cheer indeed
Till all the Andronici be made away.
Now will I hence to seek my lovely Moor,
And let my spleenful sons this trull deflow'r. *[Exit.*

Enter AARON, *with* QUINTUS *and* MARTIUS.

AARON
Come on, my lords, the better foot before:
Straight will I bring you to the loathsome pit
Where I espied the panther fast asleep.

QUINTUS
My sight is very dull, whate'er it bodes.

MARTIUS
And mine, I promise you; were it not for shame,

QUINTUS Thy hand once more; I will not loose again, till thou art here aloft, or I below.

Well could I leave our sport to sleep awhile.
[Falls into the pit.

QUINTUS
What, art thou fall'n? — What subtle hole is this,
Whose mouth is cover'd with rude-growing briers,
Upon whose leaves are drops of new-shed blood
As fresh as morning dew distill'd on flowers?
A very fatal place it seems to me. —
Speak, brother, hast thou hurt thee with the fall?

MARTIUS
O brother, with the dismall'st object hurt
That ever eye with sight made heart lament!

AARON [*aside*].
Now will I fetch the king to find them here,
That he thereby may have a likely guess
How these were they that made away his brother. [*Exit.*

MARTIUS
Why dost not comfort me, and help me out
From this unhallow'd and blood-stained hole?

QUINTUS
I am surprised with an uncouth fear;
A chilling sweat o'er-runs my trembling joints;
My heart suspects more than mine eye can see.

MARTIUS
To prove thou hast a true-divining heart,
Aaron and thou look down into this den,
And see a fearful sight of blood and death.

QUINTUS
Aaron is gone; and my compassionate heart
Will not permit mine eyes once to behold
The thing whereat it trembles by surmise:
O, tell me how it is; for ne'er till now
Was I a child to fear I know not what.

MARTIUS
Lord Bassianus lies embrewed here,
All on a heap, like to a slaughter'd lamb,
In this detested, dark, blood-drinking pit.

QUINTUS
If it be dark, how dost thou know 'tis he?

MARTIUS
Upon his bloody finger he doth wear
A precious ring, that lightens all the hole,
Which, like a taper in some monument,
Doth shine upon the dead man's earthy cheeks,
And shows the ragged entrails of the pit:
So pale did shine the moon on Pyramus
When he by night lay bathed in maiden blood.
O brother, help me with thy fainting hand —
If fear hath made thee faint, as me it hath —
Out of this fell-devouring receptacle,
As hateful as Cocytus' misty mouth.

QUINTUS
Reach me thy hand, that I may help thee out;
Or, wanting strength to do thee so much good,
I may be pluck'd into the swallowing womb
Of this deep pit, poor Bassianus' grave.
I have no strength to pluck thee to the brink.

MARTIUS
Nor I no strength to climb without thy help.

QUINTUS
Thy hand once more; I will not loose again,
Till thou art here aloft, or I below:
Thou canst not come to me, — I come to thee. [*Falls in.*

Enter SATURNINUS with AARON the Moor.

SATURNINUS
Along with me: I'll see what hole is here,
And what he is that now is leap'd into it. —
Say, who art thou that lately didst descend
Into this gaping hollow of the earth?

MARTIUS
The unhappy son of old Andronicus;
Brought hither in a most unlucky hour,
To find thy brother Bassianus dead.

SATURNINUS
My brother dead! I know thou dost but jest:
He and his lady both are at the lodge
Upon the north side of this pleasant chase;
'Tis not an hour since I left him there.

MARTIUS
We know not where you left him all alive;
But, out, alas! here have we found him dead.

*Enter TAMORA, with ATTENDANTS;
TITUS ANDRONICUS, and LUCIUS.*

TAMORA
Where is my lord the king?

SATURNINUS
Here, Tamora; though griev'd with killing grief.

TAMORA
Where is thy brother Bassianus?

SATURNINUS
Now to the bottom dost thou search my wound:
Poor Bassianus here lies murdered.

TAMORA
Then all too late I bring this fatal writ,
[Giving a letter to SATURNINUS.
The complot of this timeless tragedy;
And wonder greatly that man's face can fold
In pleasing smiles such murderous tyranny.

SATURNINUS [*reads*].
'An if we miss to meet him handsomely, —
Sweet huntsman, Bassianus 'tis we mean, —
Do thou so much as dig the grave for him:
Thou know'st our meaning. Look for thy reward
Among the nettles at the elder-tree
Which overshades the mouth of that same pit
Where we decreed to bury Bassianus.
Do this, and purchase us thy lasting friends.' —
O Tamora! was ever heard the like? —
This is the pit, and this the elder-tree. —
Look, sirs, if you can find the huntsman out
That should have murder'd Bassianus here.

AARON
My gracious lord, here is the bag of gold.
[Showing it.

SATURNINUS [*to TITUS*].
Two of thy whelps, fell curs of bloody kind,
Have here bereft my brother of his life. —
Sirs, drag them from the pit unto the prison:
There let them bide until we have devis'd
Some never-heard-of torturing pain for them.

TAMORA
What, are they in this pit? O wondrous thing!
How easily murder is discovered!

TITUS ANDRONICUS
High emperor, upon my feeble knee
I beg this boon, with tears not lightly shed,
That this fell fault of my accursed sons, —
Accursed, if the fault be prov'd in them, —

SATURNINUS
If it be prov'd! you see it is apparent. —
Who found this letter? Tamora, was it you?

TAMORA
Andronicus himself did take it up.

TITUS ANDRONICUS
I did, my lord: yet let me be their bail;
For, by my father's reverend tomb, I vow
They shall be ready at your highness' will
To answer their suspicion with their lives.

SATURNINUS
Thou shalt not bail them: see thou follow me. —
Some bring the murder'd body, some the murderers:
Let them not speak a word, — the guilt is plain;
For, by my soul, were there worse end than death,
That end upon them should be executed.

TAMORA
Andronicus, I will entreat the king:
Fear not thy sons; they shall do well enough.

TITUS ANDRONICUS
Come, Lucius, come; stay not to talk with them.
[Exeunt.

SCENE IV

Another part of the forest.

*Enter the Empress' SONS, DEMETRIUS and
CHIRON, with LAVINIA, her hands cut off, and her
tongue cut out, and ravish'd.*

DEMETRIUS
So, now go tell, an if thy tongue can speak,
Who 'twas that cut thy tongue and ravish'd thee.

CHIRON
Write down thy mind, bewray thy meaning so,
An if thy stumps will let thee play the scribe.

DEMETRIUS
See, how with signs and tokens she can scrowl.

CHIRON
Go home, call for sweet water, wash thy hands.

DEMETRIUS
She hath no tongue to call, nor hands to wash;
And so let's leave her to her silent walks.

CHIRON
An 'twere my case, I should go hang myself.

DEMETRIUS
If thou hadst hands to help thee knit the cord.
[Exeunt DEMETRIUS and CHIRON.

*Wind horns. Enter MARCUS from hunting to
LAVINIA.*

MARCUS ANDRONICUS
Who is this? my niece, that flies away so fast!
Cousin, a word; where is your husband? —
If I do dream, would all my wealth would wake me!
If I do wake, some planet strike me down,
That I may slumber in eternal sleep! —
Speak, gentle niece, what stern ungentle hands
Have lopp'd and hew'd and made thy body bare
Of her two branches, those sweet ornaments,
Whose circling shadows kings have sought to sleep in,
And might not gain so great a happiness
As have thy love? Why dost not speak to me? —
Alas, a crimson river of warm blood,
Like to a bubbling fountain stirr'd with wind,
Doth rise and fall between thy rosed lips,
Coming and going with thy honey breath.
But, sure, some Tereus hath deflower'd thee,
And, lest thou shouldst detect him, cut thy tongue.
Ah, now thou turn'st away thy face for shame! —
And, notwithstanding all this loss of blood, —
As from a conduit with three issuing spouts, —
Yet do thy cheeks look red as Titan's face
Blushing to be encounter'd with a cloud.
Shall I speak for thee? shall I say 'tis so?
O, that I knew thy heart! and knew the beast,
That I might rail at him, to ease my mind!
Sorrow concealed, like an oven stopp'd,
Doth burn the heart to cinders where it is.
Fair Philomela, she but lost her tongue,
And in a tedious sampler sew'd her mind:
But, lovely niece, that mean is cut from thee;
A craftier Tereus, cousin, hast thou met,
And he hath cut those pretty fingers off,
That could have better sew'd than Philomel.
O, had the monster seen those lily hands
Tremble, like aspen-leaves, upon a lute,
And make the silken strings delight to kiss them,
He would not, then, have touch'd them for his life!
Or, had he heard the heavenly harmony
Which that sweet tongue hath made,
He would have dropp'd his knife, and fell asleep
As Cerberus at the Thracian poet's feet.
Come, let us go, and make thy father blind;
For such a sight will blind a father's eye:
One hour's storm will drown the fragrant meads;
What will whole months of tears thy father's eyes?
Do not draw back, for we will mourn with thee:
O, could our mourning ease thy misery! *[Exeunt.*

ACT III

SCENE I

Rome. A street.

*Enter JUDGES, SENATORS, and TRIBUNES, with
TITUS' two SONS, MARTIUS and QUINTUS, bound,
passing on the stage to the place of execution; TITUS
going before, pleading.*

TITUS ANDRONICUS
Hear me, grave fathers! noble tribunes, stay!
For pity of mine age, whose youth was spent
In dangerous wars, whilst you securely slept;
For all my blood in Rome's great quarrel shed;
For all the frosty nights that I have watch'd;
And for these bitter tears, which now you see
Filling the aged wrinkles in my cheeks,
Be pitiful to my condemned sons,
Whose souls are not corrupted as 'tis thought.
For two-and-twenty sons I never wept,
Because they died in honour's lofty bed.
For these, these, tribunes, in the dust I write
[Lieth down, and the JUDGES pass by him, and exeunt.
My heart's deep languor and my soul's sad tears:
Let my tears stanch the earth's dry appetite;
My sons' sweet blood will make it shame and blush.
[Exeunt SENATORS, etc., with the PRISONERS.
O earth, I will befriend thee more with rain,
That shall distil from these two ancient urns,
Than youthful April shall with all his showers:
In summer's drought I'll drop upon thee still;
In winter with warm tears I'll melt the snow,
And keep eternal spring-time on thy face,
So thou refuse to drink my dear sons' blood.

Enter LUCIUS, with his weapon drawn.

O reverend tribunes! O gentle, aged men!
Unbind my sons, reverse the doom of death;
And let me say, that never wept before,

TITUS ANDRONICUS Hear me, grave fathers! noble tribunes, stay!

My tears are now prevailing orators.

LUCIUS
O noble father, you lament in vain:
The tribunes hear you not; no man is by;
And you recount your sorrows to a stone.

TITUS ANDRONICUS
Ah, Lucius, for thy brothers let me plead. —
Grave tribunes, once more I entreat of you, —

LUCIUS
My gracious lord, no tribune hears you speak.

TITUS ANDRONICUS
Why, 'tis no matter, man: if they did hear,
They would not mark me; or if they did mark,
They would not pity me. Yet plead I must:
And bootless unto them ....
Therefore I tell my sorrows to the stones;
Who, though they cannot answer my distress,
Yet in some sort they are better than the tribunes,
For that they will not intercept my tale:
When I do weep, they humbly at my feet
Receive my tears, and seem to weep with me;
And, were they but attired in grave weeds,
Rome could afford no tribune like to these.
A stone is soft as wax, tribunes more hard than
  stones;
A stone is silent, and offendeth not,
And tribunes with their tongues doom men to death. —
                                                    [*Rises.*
But wherefore stand'st thou with thy weapon drawn?

LUCIUS
To rescue my two brothers from their death:
For which attempt the judges have pronounced
My everlasting doom of banishment.

TITUS ANDRONICUS
O happy man! they have befriended thee.
Why, foolish Lucius, dost thou not perceive
That Rome is but a wilderness of tigers?
Tigers must prey; and Rome affords no prey
But me and mine: how happy art thou, then,
From these devourers to be banished! —
But who comes with our brother Marcus here?

                Enter MARCUS *and* LAVINIA.

MARCUS ANDRONICUS
Titus, prepare thy aged eyes to weep;
Or, if not so, thy noble heart to break:
I bring consuming sorrow to thine age.

TITUS ANDRONICUS
Will it consume me? let me see it, then.

MARCUS ANDRONICUS
This was thy daughter.

TITUS ANDRONICUS
                Why, Marcus, so she is.

LUCIUS
Ay me, this object kills me!

TITUS ANDRONICUS
Faint-hearted boy, arise, and look upon her. —
Speak, Lavinia, what accursed hand
Hath made thee handless in thy father's sight?
What fool hath added water to the sea,
Or brought a faggot to bright-burning Troy?
My grief was at the height before thou camest;
And now, like Nilus, it disdaineth bounds. —
Give me a sword, I'll chop off my hands too;
For they have fought for Rome, and all in vain;
And they have nurs'd this woe, in feeding life;
In bootless prayer have they been held up,
And they have serv'd me to effectless use:
Now all the service I require of them
Is, that the one will help to cut the other. —
'Tis well, Lavinia, that thou hast no hands;
For hands, to do Rome service, is but vain.

LUCIUS
Speak, gentle sister, who hath martyr'd thee?

MARCUS ANDRONICUS
O, that delightful engine of her thoughts,
That blabb'd them with such pleasing eloquence,
Is torn from forth that pretty hollow cage,
Where, like a sweet melodious bird, it sung
Sweet varied notes, enchanting every ear!

LUCIUS
O, say thou for her, who hath done this deed?

MARCUS ANDRONICUS
O, thus I found her, straying in the park,
Seeking to hide herself, as doth the deer
That hath receiv'd some unrecuring wound.

TITUS ANDRONICUS
It was my deer; and he that wounded her
Hath hurt me more than had he kill'd me dead:
For now I stand as one upon a rock,
Environ'd with a wilderness of sea;
Who marks the waxing tide grow wave by wave,
Expecting ever when some envious surge
Will in his brinish bowels swallow him.
This way to death my wretched sons are gone;
Here stands my other son, a banish'd man;
And here my brother, weeping at my woes:
But that which gives my soul the greatest spurn,
Is dear Lavinia, dearer than my soul. —
Had I but seen thy picture in this plight,
It would have madded me: what shall I do
Now I behold thy lively body so?
Thou hast no hands to wipe away thy tears;
Nor tongue to tell me who hath martyr'd thee:
Thy husband he is dead; and for his death
Thy brothers are condemn'd, and dead by this. —
Look, Marcus! ah, son Lucius, look on her!
When I did name her brothers, then fresh tears
Stood on her cheeks, as doth the honey-dew
Upon a gather'd lily almost wither'd.

MARCUS ANDRONICUS
Perchance she weeps because they kill'd her husband;
Perchance because she knows them innocent.

TITUS ANDRONICUS
If they did kill thy husband, then be joyful,
Because the law hath ta'en revenge on them. —
No, no, they would not do so foul a deed; —
Witness the sorrow that their sister makes. —
Gentle Lavinia, let me kiss thy lips;
Or make some sign how I may do thee ease:
Shall thy good uncle, and thy brother Lucius,
And thou, and I, sit round about some fountain,
Looking all downwards, to behold our cheeks
How they are stain'd, like meadows, yet not dry,
With miry slime left on them by a flood?
And in the fountain shall we gaze so long
Till the fresh taste be taken from that clearness,
And made a brine-pit with our bitter tears?
Or shall we cut away our hands, like thine?
Or shall we bite our tongues, and in dumb-shows
Pass the remainder of our hateful days?
What shall we do? let us, that have our tongues,
Plot some device of further misery,
To make us wonder'd at in time to come.

LUCIUS
Sweet father, cease your tears; for, at your grief,
See how my wretched sister sobs and weeps.

MARCUS ANDRONICUS
Patience, dear niece. — Good Titus, dry thine eyes.

TITUS ANDRONICUS
Ah, Marcus, Marcus! brother, well I wot
Thy napkin cannot drink a tear of mine,
For thou, poor man, hast drown'd it with thine own.

LUCIUS
Ah, my Lavinia, I will wipe thy cheeks.

TITUS ANDRONICUS
Mark, Marcus, mark! I understand her signs:
Had she a tongue to speak, now would she say
That to her brother which I said to thee:
His napkin, with his true tears all bewet,
Can do no service on her sorrowful cheeks.
O, what a sympathy of woe is this, —
As far from help as Limbo is from bliss!

                Enter AARON *the Moor alone.*

AARON
Titus Andronicus, my lord the emperor
Sends thee this word, — that, if thou love thy sons,
Let Marcus, Lucius, or thyself, old Titus,
Or any one of you, chop off your hand,
And send it to the king: he for the same
Will send thee hither both thy sons alive;
And that shall be the ransom for their fault.

TITUS ANDRONICUS
O gracious emperor! O gentle Aaron!
Did ever raven sing so like a lark,
That gives sweet tidings of the sun's uprise?
With all my heart, I'll send the emperor
My hand:
Good Aaron, wilt thou help to chop it off?

LUCIUS
Stay, father! for that noble hand of thine,
That hath thrown down so many enemies,
Shall not be sent: my hand will serve the turn:
My youth can better spare my blood than you:
And therefore mine shall save my brothers' lives.

MARCUS ANDRONICUS
Which of your hands hath not defended Rome,
And rear'd aloft the bloody battle-axe,
Writing destruction on the enemy's castle?
O, none of both but are of high desert:
My hand hath been but idle; let it serve
To ransom my two nephews from their death;
Then have I kept it to a worthy end.

AARON
Nay, come, agree whose hand shall go along,
For fear they die before their pardon come.

MARCUS ANDRONICUS
My hand shall go.

LUCIUS
                By heaven, it shall not go!

TITUS ANDRONICUS
Sirs, strive no more: such wither'd herbs as these
Are meet for plucking up, and therefore mine.

LUCIUS
Sweet father, if I shall be thought thy son,
Let me redeem my brothers both from death.

MARCUS ANDRONICUS
And, for our father's sake and mother's care,

Now let me show a brother's love to thee.
TITUS ANDRONICUS
Agree between you; I will spare my hand.
LUCIUS
Then I'll go fetch an axe.
MARCUS ANDRONICUS
But I will use the axe.
[*Exeunt* LUCIUS *and* MARCUS.
TITUS ANDRONICUS
Come hither, Aaron; I'll deceive them both:
Lend me thy hand, and I will give thee mine.
AARON [*aside*].
If that be call'd deceit, I TITUS ANDRONICUS
Hear me, grave fathers! noble tribunes, stay!will be
    honest,
And never, whilst I live, deceive men so:
But I'll deceive you in another sort,
And that you'll say, ere half an hour pass.
[*Cuts off* TITUS' hand.
Enter LUCIUS *and* MARCUS *again.*
TITUS ANDRONICUS
Now stay your strife: what shall be is dispatch'd.
Good Aaron, give his majesty my hand:
Tell him it was a hand that warded him
From thousand dangers; bid him bury it;
More hath it merited, — that let it have.
As for my sons, say I account of them
As jewels purchas'd at an easy price;
And yet dear too, because I bought mine own.
AARON
I go, Andronicus: and for thy hand
Look by and by to have thy sons with thee: —
[*aside*] Their heads, I mean. O, how this villainy
Doth fat me with the very thoughts of it!
Let fools do good, and fair men call for grace,
Aaron will have his soul black like his face. [*Exit.*
TITUS ANDRONICUS
O, here I lift this one hand up to heaven,
And bow this feeble ruin to the earth:
If any power pities wretched tears,
To that I call! — [*to* LAVINIA] What, wouldst thou
    kneel with me?
Do, then, dear heart; for heaven shall hear our prayers;
Or with our sighs we'll breathe the welkin dim,
And stain the sun with fog, as sometime clouds
When they do hug him in their melting bosoms.
MARCUS ANDRONICUS
O brother, speak with possibility,
And do not break into these deep extremes.
TITUS ANDRONICUS
Is not my sorrow deep, having no bottom?
Then be my passions bottomless with them.
MARCUS ANDRONICUS
But yet let reason govern thy lament.
TITUS ANDRONICUS
If there were reason for these miseries,
Then into limits could I bind my woes:
When heaven doth weep, doth not the earth o'er-flow?
If the winds rage, doth not the sea wax mad,
Threat'ning the welkin with his big-swoll'n face?
And wilt thou have a reason for this coil?
I am the sea; hark, how her sighs do blow!
She is the weeping welkin, I the earth:
Then must my sea be moved with her sighs;
Then must my earth with her continual tears
Become a deluge, overflow'd and drown'd:
For why my bowels cannot hide her woes,
But like a drunkard must I vomit them.
Then give me leave; for losers will have leave
To ease their stomachs with their bitter tongues.
Enter a MESSENGER, *with two heads and a hand.*
MESSENGER
Worthy Andronicus, ill art thou repaid
For that good hand thou sent'st the emperor.
Here are the heads of thy two noble sons;
And here's thy hand, in scorn to thee sent back, —
Thy griefs their sport, thy resolution mock'd;
That woe is me to think upon thy woes
More than remembrance of my father's death. [*Exit.*
MARCUS ANDRONICUS
Now let hot Aetna cool in Sicily,
And be my heart an ever-burning hell!
These miseries are more than may be borne.
To weep with them that weep doth ease some deal;
But sorrow flouted-at is double death.
LUCIUS
Ah, that this sight should make so deep a wound,
And yet detested life not shrink thereat!
That ever death should let life bear his name,

TITUS ANDRONICUS O, here I lift this one hand up to heaven.

Where life hath no more interest but to breathe!
[LAVINIA *kisses* TITUS.
MARCUS ANDRONICUS
Alas, poor heart, that kiss is comfortless
As frozen water to a starved snake.
TITUS ANDRONICUS
When will this fearful slumber have an end?
MARCUS ANDRONICUS
Now, farewell, flattery: die, Andronicus;
Thou dost not slumber: see, thy two sons' heads,
Thy warlike hand, thy mangled daughter here;
Thy other banish'd son, with this dear sight
Struck pale and bloodless; and thy brother, I,
Even like a stony image, cold and numb.
Ah, now no more will I control thy griefs:
Rent off thy silver hair, thy other hand
Gnawing with thy teeth; and be this dismal sight
The closing up of our most wretched eyes:
Now is a time to storm; why art thou still?
TITUS ANDRONICUS
Ha, ha, ha!
MARCUS ANDRONICUS
Why dost thou laugh? it fits not with this hour.
TITUS ANDRONICUS
Why, I have not another tear to shed:
Besides, this sorrow is an enemy,
And would usurp upon my watery eyes,
And make them blind with tributary tears:
Then which way shall I find Revenge's cave?
For these two heads do seem to speak to me,
And threat me I shall never come to bliss
Till all these mischiefs be return'd again
Even in their throats that have committed them.
Come, let me see what task I have to do. —
You heavy people, circle me about,
That I may turn me to each one of you,
And swear unto my soul to right your wrongs. —
The vow is made. — Come, brother, take a head;
And in this hand the other will I bear. —
Lavinia, thou shalt be employ'd in these things;
Bear thou my hand, sweet wench, between thy teeth. —
As for thee, boy, go get thee from my sight;
Thou art an exile, and thou must not stay:
Hie to the Goths, and raise an army there:
And, if you love me, as I think you do,
Let's kiss and part, for we have much to do.
[*Exeunt* TITUS, MARCUS, *and* LAVINIA.
LUCIUS
Farewell, Andronicus, my noble father, —
The woefull'st man that ever liv'd in Rome:
Farewell, proud Rome; till Lucius come again,
He leaves his pledges dearer than his life:

Farewell, Lavinia, my noble sister;
O, would thou wert as thou tofore hast been!
But now nor Lucius nor Lavinia lives
But in oblivion and hateful griefs.
If Lucius live, he will requite your wrongs;
And make proud Saturnine and his empress
Beg at the gates, like Tarquin and his queen.
Now will I to the Goths, and raise a power,
To be reveng'd on Rome and Saturnine. [*Exit.*

SCENE II

A room in TITUS' *house. A banquet set out.*

Enter TITUS, MARCUS, LAVINIA, *and* YOUNG
LUCIUS, *a boy.*

TITUS ANDRONICUS
So, so; now sit: and look you eat no more
Than will preserve just so much strength in us
As will revenge these bitter woes of ours.
Marcus, unknit that sorrow-wreathen knot:
Thy niece and I, poor creatures, want our hands,
And cannot passionate our tenfold grief
With folded arms. This poor right hand of mine
Is left to tyrannise upon my breast;
Who, when my heart, all mad with misery,
Beats in this hollow prison of my flesh,
Then thus I thump it down. —
[*to* LAVINIA] Thou map of woe, that thus dost talk in
    signs!.
When thy poor heart beats with outrageous beating,
Thou canst not strike it thus to make it still.
Wound it with sighing, girl, kill it with groans;
Or get some little knife between thy teeth,
And just against thy heart make thou a hole;
That all the tears that thy poor eyes let fall
May run into that sink, and, soaking in,
Drown the lamenting fool in sea-salt tears.
MARCUS ANDRONICUS
Fie, brother, fie! teach her not thus to lay
Such violent hands upon her tender life.
TITUS ANDRONICUS
How now! has sorrow made thee dote already?
Why, Marcus, no man should be mad but I.
What violent hands can she lay on her life? —
Ah, wherefore dost thou urge the name of hands; —
To bid Aeneas tell the tale twice o'er,
How Troy was burnt, and he made miserable?
O, handle not the theme, to talk of hands,
Lest we remember still that we have none. —
Fie, fie, how franticly I square my talk, —
As if we should forget we had no hands,
If Marcus did not name the word of hands! —

Come, let's fall to; and, gentle girl, eat this: —
Here is no drink! — Hark, Marcus, what she says; —
I can interpret all her martyr'd signs; —
She says she drinks no other drink but tears,
Brew'd with her sorrow, mash'd upon her cheeks: —
Speechless complainer, I will learn thy thought;
In thy dumb action will I be as perfect
As begging hermits in their holy prayers:
Thou shalt not sigh, nor hold thy stumps to heaven,
Nor wink, nor nod, nor kneel, nor make a sign,
But I of these will wrest an alphabet,
And by still practice learn to know thy meaning.

YOUNG LUCIUS
Good grandsire, leave these bitter deep laments:
Make my aunt merry with some pleasing tale.

MARCUS ANDRONICUS
Alas, the tender boy, in passion moved,

Doth weep to see his grandsire's heaviness.

TITUS ANDRONICUS
Peace, tender sapling; thou art made of tears,
And tears will quickly melt thy life away. —
        [MARCUS *strikes the dish with a knife.*
What dost thou strike at, Marcus, with thy knife?

MARCUS ANDRONICUS
At that that I have kill'd, my lord, — a fly.

TITUS ANDRONICUS
Out on thee, murderer! thou kill'st my heart;
Mine eyes are cloy'd with view of tyranny:
A deed of death done on the innocent
Becomes not Titus' brother: get thee gone;
I see thou art not for my company.

MARCUS ANDRONICUS
Alas, my lord, I have but kill'd a fly.

TITUS ANDRONICUS
But how, if that fly had a father and mother?
How would he hang his slender gilded wings,
And buzz lamenting doings in the air!
Poor harmless fly,
That, with his pretty buzzing melody,
Came here to make us merry! and thou hast kill'd him.

MARCUS ANDRONICUS
Pardon me, sir; it was a black ill-favour'd fly,
Like to the empress' Moor; therefore I kill'd him.

TITUS ANDRONICUS
O, O, O,
Then pardon me for reprehending thee,
For thou hast done a charitable deed.
Give me thy knife, I will insult on him;

Flattering myself, as if it were the Moor
Come hither purposely to poison me. —
There's for thyself, and that's for Tamora. —
Ah, sirrah!
As yet, I think, we are not brought so low
But that between us we can kill a fly
That comes in likeness of a coal-black Moor.

MARCUS ANDRONICUS
Alas, poor man! grief has so wrought on him,
He takes false shadows for true substances.

TITUS ANDRONICUS
Come, take away. — Lavinia, go with me:
I'll to thy closet; and go read with thee
Sad stories chanced in the times of old. —
Come, boy, and go with me: thy sight is young,
And thou shalt read when mine begin to dazzle.
                                    [*Exeunt.*

ACT IV

SCENE I

Rome. The garden of TITUS' *house.*

Enter YOUNG LUCIUS, *and* LAVINIA *running after
him, and the* BOY *flies from her, with his books under his
arm. Then enter* TITUS *and* MARCUS.

YOUNG LUCIUS
Help, grandsire, help! my aunt Lavinia
Follows me every where, I know not why: —
Good uncle Marcus, see how swift she comes. —
Alas, sweet aunt, I know not what you mean.

MARCUS ANDRONICUS
Stand by me, Lucius; do not fear thine aunt.

TITUS ANDRONICUS
She loves thee, boy, too well to do thee harm.

YOUNG LUCIUS
Ay, when my father was in Rome she did.

MARCUS ANDRONICUS
What means my niece Lavinia by these signs?

TITUS ANDRONICUS
Fear her not, Lucius: — somewhat doth she mean: —
See, Lucius, see how much she makes of thee:
Somewhither would she have thee go with her.
Ah, boy, Cornelia never with more care
Read to her sons than she hath read to thee
Sweet poetry and Tully's Orator.

MARCUS ANDRONICUS
Canst thou not guess wherefore she plies thee thus?

YOUNG LUCIUS
My lord, I know not, I, nor can I guess,
Unless some fit or frenzy do possess her:
For I have heard my grandsire say full oft,
Extremity of griefs would make men mad;
And I have read that Hecuba of Troy
Ran mad through sorrow: that made me to fear;
Although, my lord, I know my noble aunt
Loves me as dear as e'er my mother did,
And would not, but in fury, fright my youth:
Which made me down to throw my books, and fly, —
Causeless, perhaps. — But pardon me, sweet aunt:
And, madam, if my uncle Marcus go,
I will most willingly attend your ladyship.

MARCUS ANDRONICUS
Lucius, I will.

                [LAVINIA *turns over with her stumps
                the books which* LUCIUS *has let fall.*

TITUS ANDRONICUS
How now, Lavinia! Marcus, what means this?
Some book there is that she desires to see.
Which is it, girl, of these? Open them, boy.
But thou art deeper read, and better skill'd:
Come, and take choice of all my library,
And so beguile thy sorrow, till the heavens
Reveal the damn'd contriver of this deed. —
Why lifts she up her arms in sequence thus?

MARCUS ANDRONICUS
I think she means that there was more than one
Confederate in the fact; ay, more there was;
Or else to heaven she heaves them for revenge.

TITUS ANDRONICUS
Lucius, what book is that she tosseth so?

YOUNG LUCIUS
Grandsire, 'tis Ovid's Metamorphoses;
My mother gave it me.

MARCUS ANDRONICUS
                For love of her that's gone,
Perhaps she cull'd it from among the rest.

TITUS ANDRONICUS
Soft! so busily she turns the leaves!
Help her:
What would she find? — Lavinia, shall I read?
This is the tragic tale of Philomel,
And treats of Tereus' treason and his rape;
And rape, I fear, was root of thine annoy.

MARCUS ANDRONICUS
See, brother, see; note how she quotes the leaves.

TITUS ANDRONICUS
Lavinia, wert thou thus surpris'd, sweet girl,
Ravish'd and wrong'd, as Philomela was,
Forc'd in the ruthless, vast, and gloomy woods? —
See, see: —
Ay, such a place there is, where we did hunt —
O, had we never, never hunted there! —
Pattern'd by that the poet here describes,
By nature made for murders and for rapes.

MARCUS ANDRONICUS
O, why should nature build so foul a den,
Unless the gods delight in tragedies?

TITUS ANDRONICUS
Give signs, sweet girl, — for here are none but friends, —
What Roman lord it was durst do the deed:
Or slunk not Saturnine, as Tarquin erst,
That left the camp to sin in Lucrece' bed?

MARCUS ANDRONICUS
Sit down, sweet niece: — brother, sit down by me. —
Apollo, Pallas, Jove, or Mercury,
Inspire me, that I may this treason find! —
My lord, look here! — look here, Lavinia:
This sandy plot is plain; guide, if thou canst,
This after me, when I have writ my name
Without the help of any hand at all.
                [He *writes his name with his staff,
                and guides it with feet and mouth.*
Curst be that heart that forc'd us to this shift! —
Write thou, good niece; and here display, at last,
What God will have discover'd for revenge:
Heaven guide thy pen to print thy sorrows plain,
That we may know the traitors and the truth!
                [*She takes the staff in her mouth, and guides it
                with her stumps, and writes.*

TITUS ANDRONICUS
O, do ye read, my lord, what she hath writ? —
'*Stuprum, Chiron, Demetrius.*'

MARCUS ANDRONICUS
What, what! the lustful sons of Tamora
Performers of this heinous, bloody deed?

TITUS ANDRONICUS
Magni dominator poli,
Tam lentus audis scelera? tam lentus vides?
MARCUS ANDRONICUS
O, calm thee, gentle lord; although I know
There is enough written upon this earth
To stir a mutiny in the mildest thoughts,
And arm the minds of infants to exclaims.
My lord, kneel down with me; Lavinia, kneel;
And kneel, sweet boy, the Roman Hector's hope;
And swear with me, — as, with the woeful fere
And father of that chaste dishonour'd dame,
Lord Junius Brutus sware for Lucrece' rape, —
That we will prosecute, by good advice,
Mortal revenge upon these traitorous Goths,
And see their blood, or die with this reproach.
TITUS ANDRONICUS
'Tis sure enough, an you knew how.
But if you hunt these bear-whelps, then beware:
The dam will wake; and, if she wind you once,
She's with the lion deeply still in league,
And lulls him whilst she playeth on her back,
And when he sleeps will she do what she list.
You are a young huntsman, Marcus; let alone;
And, come, I will go get a leaf of brass,
And with a gad of steel will write these words,
And lay it by: the angry northern wind
Will blow these sands, like Sibyl's leaves, abroad,
And where's your lesson, then? — Boy, what say you?
YOUNG LUCIUS
I say, my lord, that if I were a man,
Their mother's bed-chamber should not be safe
For these bad bondmen to the yoke of Rome.
MARCUS ANDRONICUS
Ay, that's my boy! thy father hath full oft
For his ungrateful country done the like.
YOUNG LUCIUS
And, uncle, so will I, an if I live.
TITUS ANDRONICUS
Come, go with me into mine armoury;
Lucius, I'll fit thee; and withal, my boy
Shall carry from me to the empress' sons
Presents that I intend to send them both:
Come, come; thou'lt do thy message, wilt thou not?
YOUNG LUCIUS
Ay, with my dagger in their bosoms, grandsire.
TITUS ANDRONICUS
No, boy, not so; I'll teach thee another course. —
Lavinia, come. — Marcus, look to my house:
Lucius and I'll go brave it at the court;
Ay, marry, will we, sir; and we'll be waited on.
[*Exeunt* TITUS, LAVINIA, *and* YOUNG LUCIUS.
MARCUS ANDRONICUS
O heavens, can you hear a good man groan,
And not relent, or not compassion him? —
Marcus, attend him in his ecstasy,
That hath more scars of sorrow in his heart
Than foemen's marks upon his batter'd shield;
But yet so just that he will not revenge: —
Revenge, ye heavens, for old Andronicus! [*Exit.*

SCENE II

The same. A room in the palace.

Enter AARON, DEMETRIUS, *and* CHIRON, *at one door; at another door* YOUNG LUCIUS, *and* ANOTHER, *with a bundle of weapons, and verses writ upon them.*

CHIRON
Demetrius, here's the son of Lucius;
He hath some message to deliver us.
AARON
Ay, some mad message from his mad grandfather.
YOUNG LUCIUS
My lords, with all the humbleness I may,
I greet your honours from Andronicus, —
[*aside*] And pray the Roman gods confound you both!
DEMETRIUS
Gramercy, lovely Lucius: what's the news?
YOUNG LUCIUS [*aside*].
That you are both decipher'd, that's the news,
For villains mark'd with rape. — May it please you,
My grandsire, well advis'd, hath sent by me
The goodliest weapons of his armoury
To gratify your honourable youth,
The hope of Rome; for so he bid me say;
And so I do, and with his gifts present
Your lordships, that, whenever you have need,
You may be armed and appointed well:
And so I leave you both, — [*aside*] like bloody villains.

[*Exeunt* YOUNG LUCIUS *and* ATTENDANT.
DEMETRIUS
What's here? A scroll; and written round about?
Let's see: —
[*Reads*] *Integer vitæ, scelerisque purus,*
Non eget Mauri jaculis, nec arcu.
CHIRON
O, 'tis a verse in Horace; I know it well:
I read it in the grammar long ago.
AARON
Ay, just, — a verse in Horace; — right, you have it. —
[*aside*] Now, what a thing it is to be an ass!
Here's no sound jest! the old man hath found their
   guilt;
And sends them weapons wrapp'd about with lines
That wound, beyond their feeling, to the quick.
But were our witty empress well a-foot,
She would applaud Andronicus' conceit:
But let her rest in her unrest awhile. —
And now, young lords, was't not a happy star
Led us to Rome, strangers, and more than so,
Captives, to be advanced to this height?
It did me good, before the palace-gate
To brave the tribune in his brother's hearing.
DEMETRIUS
But me more good, to see so great a lord
Basely insinuate and send us gifts.
AARON
Had he not reason, Lord Demetrius?
Did you not use his daughter very friendly?
DEMETRIUS
I would we had a thousand Roman dames
At such a bay, by turn to serve our lust.
CHIRON
A charitable wish and full of love.
AARON
Here lacks but your mother for to say amen.
CHIRON
And that would she for twenty thousand more.
DEMETRIUS
Come, let us go; and pray to all the gods
For our beloved mother in her pains.
AARON
Pray to the devils; the gods have given us over.
[*Flourish within.*
DEMETRIUS
Why do the emperor's trumpets flourish thus?
CHIRON
Belike for joy the emperor hath a son.
DEMETRIUS
Soft! who comes here?

Enter a NURSE, *with a blackamoor* CHILD.

NURSE
                  Good morrow, lords:
O, tell me, did you see Aaron the Moor?
AARON
Well, more or less, or ne'er a whit at all,
Here Aaron is; and what with Aaron now?
NURSE
O gentle Aaron, we are all undone!
Now help, or woe betide thee evermore!
AARON
Why, what a caterwauling dost thou keep!
What dost thou wrap and fumble in thine arms?
NURSE
O, that which I would hide from heaven's eye,
Our empress' shame, and stately Rome's disgrace! —
She is deliver'd, lords, — she is deliver'd.
AARON
To whom?
NURSE
         I mean, she is brought a-bed.
AARON
Well, God give her good rest. What hath he sent her?
NURSE
A devil.
AARON
         Why, then she is the devil's dam;
A joyful issue.
NURSE
A joyless, dismal, black, and sorrowful issue:
Here is the babe, as loathsome as a toad
Amongst the fairest breeders of our clime:
The empress sends it thee, thy stamp, thy seal,
And bids thee christen it with thy dagger's point.
AARON
'Zounds, ye whore! is black so base a hue? —
Sweet blowse, you are a beauteous blossom, sure.

DEMETRIUS
Villain, what hast thou done?
AARON
That which thou canst not undo.
CHIRON
Thou hast undone our mother.
AARON
Villain, I have done thy mother.
DEMETRIUS
And therein, hellish dog, thou hast undone her.
Woe to her chance, and damn'd her loathed choice!
Accurst the offspring of so foul a fiend!
CHIRON
It shall not live.
AARON
It shall not die.
NURSE
Aaron, it must; the mother wills it so.
AARON
What, must it, nurse? then let no man but I
Do execution on my flesh and blood.
DEMETRIUS
I'll broach the tadpole on my rapier's point: —
Nurse, give it me; my sword shall soon dispatch it.
AARON
Sooner this sword shall plough thy bowels up.
   [*Takes the* CHILD *from the* NURSE, *and draws.*
Stay, murderous villains! will you kill your brother?
Now, by the burning tapers of the sky,
That shone so brightly when this boy was got,
He dies upon my scimitar's sharp point
That touches this my first-born son and heir!
I tell you, younglings, not Enceladus,
With all his threat'ning band of Typhon's brood,
Nor great Alcides, nor the god of war,
Shall seize this prey out of his father's hands.
What, what, ye sanguine, shallow-hearted boys!
Ye white-limed walls! ye alehouse painted signs!
Coal-black is better than another hue,
In that it scorns to bear another hue;
For all the water in the ocean
Can never turn the swan's black legs to white,
Although she lave them hourly in the flood.
Tell the empress from me, I am of age
To keep mine own, — excuse it how she can.
DEMETRIUS
Wilt thou betray thy noble mistress thus?
AARON
My mistress is my mistress; this, myself, —
The vigour and the picture of my youth:
This before all the world do I prefer;
This maugre all the world will I keep safe,
Or some of you shall smoke for it in Rome.
DEMETRIUS
By this our mother is for ever shamed.
CHIRON
Rome will despise her for this foul escape.
NURSE
The emperor, in his rage, will doom her death.
CHIRON
I blush to think upon this ignomy.
AARON
Why, there's the privilege your beauty bears:
Fie, treacherous hue, that will betray with blushing
The close enacts and counsels of the heart!
Here's a young lad fram'd of another leer:
Look, how the black slave smiles upon the father,
As who should say, 'Old lad, I am thine own.'
He is your brother, lords; sensibly fed
Of that self-blood that first gave life to you;
And from that womb where you imprison'd were
He is enfranchised and come to light:
Nay, he is your brother by the surer side,
Although my seal be stamped in his face.
NURSE
Aaron, what shall I say unto the empress?
DEMETRIUS
Advise thee, Aaron, what is to be done,
And we will all subscribe to thy advice:
Save thou the child, so we may all be safe.
AARON
Then sit we down, and let us all consult.
My son and I will have the wind of you:
Keep there: now talk at pleasure of your safety.
[*They sit.*
DEMETRIUS
How many women saw this child of his?
AARON
Why, so, brave lords! when we join in league,

I am a lamb: but if you brave the Moor,
The chafed boar, the mountain lioness,
The ocean swells not so as Aaron storms. —
But say, again, how many saw the child?

NURSE
Cornelia the midwife and myself;
And no one else but the deliver'd empress.

AARON
The empress, the midwife, and yourself: —
Two may keep counsel when the third's away: —
Go to the empress, tell her this I said: —   [*He kills her.*
Weke, weke! — so cries a pig prepar'd to th'spit.

DEMETRIUS
What mean'st thou, Aaron? wherefore didst thou this?

AARON
O Lord, sir, 'tis a deed of policy:
Shall she live to betray this guilt of ours, —
A long-tongued babbling gossip? no, lords, no:
And now be it known to you my full intent.
Not far one Muliteus, my countryman,
His wife but yesternight was brought to bed;
His child is like to her, fair as you are:
Go pack with him, and give the mother gold,
And tell them both the circumstance of all;
And how by this their child shall be advanced,
And be received for the emperor's heir,
And substituted in the place of mine,
To calm this tempest whirling in the court;
And let the emperor dandle him for his own.
Hark ye, lords; you see I have given her physic,
                      [*Pointing to the* NURSE.
And you must needs bestow her funeral;
The fields are near, and you are gallant grooms:
This done, see that you take no longer days,
But send the midwife presently to me.
The midwife and the nurse well made away,
Then let the ladies tattle what they please.

CHIRON
Aaron, I see thou wilt not trust the air
With secrets.

DEMETRIUS
For this care of Tamora,
Herself and hers are highly bound to thee.
   [*Exeunt* DEMETRIUS *and* CHIRON, *bearing off the*
                      dead NURSE.

AARON
Now to the Goths, as swift as swallow flies;
There to dispose this treasure in mine arms,
And secretly to greet the empress' friends. —
Come on, you thick-lipp'd slave, I'll bear you hence;
For it is you that puts us to our shifts:
I'll make you feed on berries and on roots,
And feed on curds and whey, and suck the goat,
And cabin in a cave; and bring you up
To be a warrior and command a camp.   [*Exit.*

SCENE III

The same. A public place.

Enter TITUS, MARCUS, YOUNG LUCIUS, *and other*
GENTLEMEN (PUBLIUS, SEMPRONIUS, CAIUS),
with bows; and TITUS *bears the arrows with*
letters at the end of them.

TITUS ANDRONICUS
Come, Marcus, come: — kinsmen, this is the way. —
Sir boy, now let me see your archery;
Look ye draw home enough, and 'tis there straight. —
Terras Astræa reliquit: —
Be you remember'd, Marcus, she's gone, she's fled. —
Sirs, take you to your tools. You, cousins, shall
Go sound the ocean, and cast your nets;
Happily you may catch her in the sea;
Yet there's as little justice as at land: —
No; Publius and Sempronius, you must do it;
'Tis you must dig with mattock and with spade,
And pierce the inmost centre of the earth:
Then, when you come to Pluto's region,
I pray you, deliver him this petition;
Tell him, it is for justice and for aid,
And that it comes from old Andronicus,
Shaken with sorrows in ungrateful Rome. —
Ah, Rome! Well, well; I made thee miserable
What time I threw the people's suffrages
On him that thus doth tyrannise o'er me. —
Go, get you gone; and pray be careful all,
And leave you not a man-of-war unsearch'd:
This wicked emperor may have shipp'd her hence;
And, kinsmen, then we may go pipe for justice.

MARCUS ANDRONICUS
O Publius, is not this a heavy case,
To see thy noble uncle thus distract?

PUBLIUS
Therefore, my lord, it highly us concerns
By day and night t'attend him carefully,
And feed his humour kindly as we may,
Till time beget some careful remedy.

MARCUS ANDRONICUS
Kinsmen, his sorrows are past remedy.
Join with the Goths; and with revengeful
   war
Take wreak on Rome for this ingratitude,
And vengeance on the traitor Saturnine.

TITUS ANDRONICUS
Publius, how now! how now, my masters!
   What,
Have you met with her?

PUBLIUS
No, my good lord; but Pluto sends you
   word,
If you will have Revenge from hell, you
   shall:
Marry, for Justice, she is so employ'd,
He thinks, with Jove in heaven, or
   somewhere else,
So that perforce you must needs stay a time.

TITUS ANDRONICUS
He doth me wrong to feed me with delays.
I'll dive into the burning lake below,
And pull her out of Acheron by the heels. —
Marcus, we are but shrubs, no cedars we,
No big-boned men fram'd of the Cyclops' size;
But metal, Marcus, steel to the very back,
Yet wrung with wrongs more than our backs can bear:
And, sith there's no justice in earth nor hell,
We will solicit heaven, and move the gods
To send down Justice for to wreak our wrongs. —
Come, to this gear. — You are a good archer, Marcus;
              [*He gives them the arrows.*
Ad Jovem, that's for you: — here, *Ad Apollinem:* —
Ad Martem, that's for myself: —
Here, boy, *To Pallas:* — here, *To Mercury:* —
To Saturn, Caius, not to Saturnine;
You were as good to shoot against the wind. —
To it, boy — Marcus, loose when I bid. —
Of my word, I have written to effect;
There's not a god left unsolicited.

MARCUS ANDRONICUS
Kinsmen, shoot all your shafts into the court:
We will afflict the emperor in his pride.

TITUS ANDRONICUS
Now, masters, draw. [*They shoot.*] — O, well said,
   Lucius! —
Good boy, in Virgo's lap; give it Pallas.

MARCUS ANDRONICUS
My lord, I aim a mile beyond the moon;
Your letter is with Jupiter by this.

TITUS ANDRONICUS
Ha, ha!
Publius, Publius, what hast thou done?
See, see, thou hast shot off one of Taurus' horns.

MARCUS ANDRONICUS
This was the sport, my lord: when Publius shot,
The Bull, being gall'd, gave Aries such a knock
That down fell both the Ram's horns in the court;
And who should find them but the empress' villain?
She laugh'd, and told the Moor he should not choose
But give them to his master for a present.

TITUS ANDRONICUS
Why, there it goes: God give his lordship joy!
   Enter a CLOWN, *with a basket, and two pigeons in it.*
News, news from heaven! Marcus, the post is come. —
Sirrah, what tidings? have you any letters?
Shall I have justice? what says Jupiter?

CLOWN
Ho, the gibbet-maker! he says that he hath taken them
down again, for the man must not be hang'd till the
next week.

TITUS ANDRONICUS
But what says Jupiter, I ask thee?

CLOWN
Alas, sir, I know not Jupiter; I never drank with him in
   all my life.

TITUS ANDRONICUS
Why, villain, art not thou the carrier?

CLOWN
Ay, of my pigeons, sir; nothing else.

TITUS ANDRONICUS
Why, didst thou not come from heaven?

CLOWN
From heaven! alas, sir, I never came there: God forbid I
should be so bold to press to heaven in my young days.

TITUS ANDRONICUS Of my word, I have written to effect;
   there's not a god left unsolicited.

Why, I am going with my pigeons to the tribunal plebs,
to take up a matter of brawl betwixt my uncle and one
of the emperial's men.

MARCUS ANDRONICUS
Why, sir, that is as fit as can be to serve for your oration;
and let him deliver the pigeons to the emperor from
you.

TITUS ANDRONICUS
Tell me, can you deliver an oration to the emperor with
a grace?

CLOWN
Nay, truly, sir, I could never say grace in all my life.

TITUS ANDRONICUS
Sirrah, come hither: make no more ado,
But give your pigeons to the emperor:
By me thou shalt have justice at his hands.
Hold, hold; meanwhile here's money for thy charges. —
Give me pen and ink. —
Sirrah, can you with a grace deliver a supplication?

CLOWN
Ay, sir.

TITUS ANDRONICUS
Then here is a supplication for you. And when you
come to him, at the first approach you must kneel; then
kiss his foot; then deliver up your pigeons; and then
look for your reward. I'll be at hand, sir; see you do it
bravely.

CLOWN
I warrant you, sir, let me alone.

TITUS ANDRONICUS
Sirrah, hast thou a knife? come, let me see it. —
Here, Marcus, fold it in the oration;
For thou hast made it like an humble suppliant: —
And when thou hast given it to the emperor,
Knock at my door, and tell me what he says.

CLOWN
God be with you, sir; I will.   [*Exit.*

TITUS ANDRONICUS
Come, Marcus, let us go. — Publius, follow me.
                      [*Exeunt.*

SCENE IV

The same. Before the palace.

Enter SATURNINUS, TAMORA, DEMETRIUS,
CHIRON, LORDS, *and others; the* EMPEROR *brings*
the arrows in his hand that TITUS *shot at him.*

SATURNINUS
Why, lords, what wrongs are these! was ever seen
An emperor in Rome thus overborne,
Troubled, confronted thus; and, for the extent
Of egal justice, used in such contempt?
My lords, you know, as do the mightful gods,
However these disturbers of our peace
Buzz in the people's ears, there naught hath pass'd,
But even with law, against the wilful sons
Of old Andronicus. And what an if
His sorrows have so overwhelm'd his wits, —
Shall we be thus afflicted in his wreaks,
His fits, his frenzy, and his bitterness?
And now he writes to heaven for his redress:
See, here's *To Jove,* and this *To Mercury;*
This *To Apollo;* this *To the god of war;* —

Sweet scrolls to fly about the streets of Rome!
What's this but libelling against the senate,
And blazoning our injustice every where?
A goodly humour, is it not, my lords?
As who would say, in Rome no justice were.
But if I live, his feigned ecstasies
Shall be no shelter to these outrages:
But he and his shall know that justice lives
In Saturninus' health; whom, if she sleep,
He'll so awake, as she in fury shall
Cut off the proud'st conspirator that lives.

TAMORA
My gracious lord, my lovely Saturnine,
Lord of my life, commander of my thoughts,
Calm thee, and bear the faults of Titus' age,
Th'effects of sorrow for his valiant sons,
Whose loss hath pierc'd him deep and scarr'd his
    heart;
And rather comfort his distressed plight
Than prosecute the meanest or the best
For these contempts. — [aside] Why, thus it shall
    become
High-witted Tamora to gloze with all:
But, Titus, I have touch'd thee to the quick,
Thy life-blood out: if Aaron now be wise,
Then is all safe, the anchor's in the port. —
                    Enter CLOWN.
How now, good fellow! wouldst thou speak with us?

CLOWN
Yea, forsooth, an your mister-ship be emperial.

TAMORA
Empress I am, but yonder sits the emperor.

CLOWN
'Tis he. — God and Saint Stephen give you godden: I
    have brought you a letter and a couple of pigeons
    here.
                    [SATURNINUS reads the letter.

SATURNINUS
Go, take him away, and hang him presently.

CLOWN
How much money must I have?

TAMORA
Come, sirrah, you must be hang'd.

CLOWN
Hang'd! by'r lady, then I have brought up a neck to a
    fair end.
                    [Exit, guarded.

SATURNINUS
Despiteful and intolerable wrongs!
Shall I endure this monstrous villainy?
I know from whence this same device proceeds:
May this be borne, — as if his traitorous sons,
That died by law for murder of our brother,
Have by my means been butcher'd wrongfully? —
Go, drag the villain hither by the hair;
Nor age nor honour shall shape privilege:
For this proud mock I'll be thy slaughter-man;
Sly frantic wretch, that holp'st to make me great,
In hope thyself should govern Rome and me.
                    Enter AEMILIUS.
What news with thee, Aemilius?

AEMILIUS
Arm, my lords, — Rome never had more cause!
The Goths have gather'd head; and with a power
Of high-resolved men, bent to the spoil,
They hither march amain, under conduct
Of Lucius, son to old Andronicus;
Who threats, in course of this revenge, to do
As much as ever Coriolanus did.

SATURNINUS
Is warlike Lucius general of the Goths?
These tidings nip me; and I hang the head
As flowers with frost, or grass beat down with storms:
Ay, now begins our sorrows to approach:
'Tis he the common people love so much;
Myself hath often heard them say —
When I have walked like a private man —
That Lucius' banishment was wrongfully,
And they have wish'd that Lucius were their emperor.

TAMORA
Why should you fear? is not your city strong?

SATURNINUS
Ay, but the citizens favour Lucius,
And will revolt from me to succour him.

TAMORA
King, be thy thoughts imperious, like thy name.
Is the sun dimm'd, that gnats do fly in it?
The eagle suffers little birds to sing,
And is not careful what they mean thereby,
Knowing that with the shadow of his wings

He can at pleasure stint their melody:
Even so mayst thou the giddy men of Rome.
Then cheer thy spirit: for know, thou emperor,
I will enchant the old Andronicus
With words more sweet, and yet more dangerous,
Than baits to fish, or honey-stalks to sheep;
Whenas the one is wounded with the bait,
The other rotted with delicious feed.

SATURNINUS
But he will not entreat his son for us.

TAMORA
If Tamora entreat him, then he will:
For I can smooth, and fill his aged ear
With golden promises; that, were his heart
Almost impregnable, his old ears deaf,
Yet should both ear and heart obey my tongue. —
[to AEMILIUS] Go thou before, be our ambassador:
Say that the emperor requests a parley
Of warlike Lucius, and appoint the meeting
Even at his father's house, the old Andronicus.

SATURNINUS
Aemilius, do this message honourably;
And if he stand on hostage for his safety,
Bid him demand what pledge will please him best.

AEMILIUS
Your bidding shall I do effectually.   [Exit.

TAMORA
Now will I to that old Andronicus,
And temper him, with all the art I have,
To pluck proud Lucius from the warlike Goths.
And now, sweet emperor, be blithe again,
And bury all thy fear in my devices.

SATURNINUS
Then go successantly, and plead to him.   [Exeunt.

Imperious, and impatient of your wrongs;
And wherein Rome hath done you any scathe,
Let him make treble satisfaction.

FIRST GOTH
Brave slip, sprung from the great Andronicus,
Whose name was once our terror, now our comfort;
Whose high exploits and honourable deeds
Ingrateful Rome requites with foul contempt,
Be bold in us: we'll follow where thou lead'st, —
Like stinging bees in hottest summer's day,
Led by their master to the flowered fields, —
And be aveng'd on cursed Tamora.

GOTHS
And as he saith, so say we all with him.

LUCIUS
I humbly thank him, and I thank you all. —
But who comes here, led by a lusty Goth?

        Enter a GOTH, leading of AARON with his CHILD in
                            his arms.

SECOND GOTH
Renowned Lucius, from our troops I stray'd
To gaze upon a ruinous monastery;
And, as I earnestly did fix mine eye
Upon the wasted building, suddenly
I heard a child cry underneath a wall.
I made unto the noise; when soon I heard
The crying babe controll'd with this discourse:
'Peace, tawny slave, half me and half thy dam!
Did not thy hue bewray whose brat thou art,
Had nature lent thee but thy mother's look,
Villain, thou mightst have been an emperor:
But where the bull and cow are both milk-white,
They never do beget a coal-black calf.
Peace, villain, peace!' — even thus he rates the babe,
'For I must bear thee to a trusty Goth;
Who, when he knows thou art the empress' babe,

ACT V
SCENE I
Plains near Rome.

Flourish. Enter LUCIUS, *with an army of* GOTHS, *with
            drum and colours.*

LUCIUS
Approved warriors, and my faithful friends,
I have received letters from great Rome,
Which signify what hate they bear their emperor,
And how desirous of our sight they are.
Therefore, great lords, be, as your titles witness,

Will hold thee dearly for thy mother's sake.'
With this, my weapon drawn, I rush'd upon him,
Surpris'd him suddenly; and brought him hither,
To use as you think needful of the man.

LUCIUS
O worthy Goth, this is the incarnate devil
That robb'd Andronicus of his good hand;
This is the pearl that pleas'd your empress' eye;
And here's the base fruit of his burning lust. —
Say, wall-eyed slave, whither wouldst thou convey
This growing image of thy fiend-like face?
Why dost not speak? what, deaf? not a word? —
A halter, soldiers! hang him on this tree.
And by his side his fruit of bastardy.

AARON
Touch not the boy, — he is of royal
  blood.
LUCIUS
Too like the sire for ever being good. —
First hang the child, that he may see it
  sprawl, —
A sight to vex the father's soul withal. —
Get me a ladder.
  [*A ladder brought, which* AARON *is made
                                 to ascend.*

AARON
                    Lucius, save the child,
And bear it from me to the empress.
If thou do this, I'll show thee wondrous
  things,
That highly may advantage thee to hear:
If thou wilt not, befall what may befall,
I'll speak no more but — vengeance rot
  you all!
LUCIUS
Say on: an if it please me which thou
  speak'st,
Thy child shall live, and I will see it
  nourish'd.
AARON
An if it please thee! why, assure thee,
  Lucius,
'Twill vex thy soul to hear what I shall
  speak;
For I must talk of murders, rapes, and
  massacres,
Acts of black night, abominable deeds,
Complots of mischief, treason, villainies
Ruthful to hear, yet piteously perform'd:
And this shall all be buried in my death,
Unless thou swear to me my child shall live.
LUCIUS
Tell on thy mind; I say thy child shall live.
AARON
Swear that he shall, and then I will begin.
LUCIUS
Who should I swear by? thou believ'st no god:
That granted, how canst thou believe an oath?
AARON
What if I do not? as, indeed, I do not;
Yet, for I know thou art religious,
And hast a thing within thee called conscience,
With twenty popish tricks and ceremonies,
Which I have seen thee careful to observe,
Therefore I urge thy oath; for that I know
An idiot holds his bauble for a god,
And keeps the oath which by that god he swears,
To that I'll urge him: — therefore thou shalt vow
By that same god, what god so'er it be,
That thou adorest and hast in reverence, —
To save my boy, to nourish and bring him up;
Or else I will discover naught to thee.
LUCIUS
Even by my god I swear to thee I will.
AARON
First know thou, I begot him on the empress.
LUCIUS
O most insatiate and luxurious woman!
AARON
Tut, Lucius, this was but a deed of charity
To that which thou shalt hear of me anon.
'Twas her two sons that murder'd Bassianus;
They cut thy sister's tongue, and ravish'd her,
And cut her hands, and trimm'd her as thou sawest.
LUCIUS
O detestable villain! call'st thou that trimming?
AARON
Why, she was wash'd, and cut, and trimm'd; and 'twas
Trim sport for them that had the doing of it.
LUCIUS
O barbarous, beastly villains, like thyself!
AARON
Indeed, I was their tutor to instruct them:
That codding spirit had they from their mother,
As sure a card as ever won the set;
That bloody mind, I think, they learn'd of me,
As true a dog as ever fought at head. —
Well, let my deeds be witness of my worth.
I train'd thy brethren to that guileful hole,
Where the dead corpse of Bassianus lay:
I wrote the letter that thy father found,
And hid the gold within the letter mention'd,
Confederate with the queen and her two sons:
And what not done, that thou hast cause to rue,

SECOND GOTH Peace, tawny slave, half me and half thy dam!

Wherein I had no stroke of mischief in it?
I play'd the cheater for thy father's hand;
And, when I had it, drew myself apart,
And almost broke my heart with extreme laughter:
I pried me through the crevice of a wall
When, for his hand, he had his two sons' heads;
Beheld his tears, and laugh'd so heartily,
That both mine eyes were rainy like to his:
And when I told the empress of this sport,
She swounded almost at my pleasing tale,
And for my tidings gave me twenty kisses.
FIRST GOTH
What, canst thou say all this, and never blush?
AARON
Ay, like a black dog, as the saying is.
LUCIUS
Art thou not sorry for these heinous deeds?
AARON
Ay, that I had not done a thousand more.
Even now I curse the day — and yet, I think,
Few come within the compass of my curse —
Wherein I did not some notorious ill:
As, kill a man, or else devise his death;
Ravish a maid, or plot the way to do it;
Accuse some innocent, and forswear myself;
Set deadly enmity between two friends;
Make poor men's cattle break their necks;
Set fire on barns and hay-stacks in the night,
And bid the owners quench them with their tears.
Oft have I digg'd up dead men from their graves,
And set them upright at their dear friends' doors,
Even when their sorrows almost was forgot;
And on their skins, as on the bark of trees,
Have with my knife carved in Roman letters,
'Let not your sorrow die, though I am dead.'
Tut, I have done a thousand dreadful things
As willingly as one would kill a fly;
And nothing grieves me heartily indeed,
But that I cannot do ten thousand more.
LUCIUS
Bring down the devil; for he must not die
So sweet a death as hanging presently.
  [AARON *is brought down from the ladder.*
AARON
If there be devils, would I were a devil,
To live and burn in everlasting fire,
So I might have your company in hell,
But to torment you with my bitter tongue!
LUCIUS
Sirs, stop his mouth, and let him speak no more.
          Enter a GOTH.
THIRD GOTH
My lord, there is a messenger from Rome
Desires to be admitted to your presence.
LUCIUS
Let him come near.
          Enter AEMILIUS.
Welcome, Aemilius: what's the news from Rome?

AEMILIUS
Lord Lucius, and you princes of the Goths,
The Roman emperor greets you all by me;
And, for he understands you are in arms,
He craves a parley at your father's house,
Willing you to demand your hostages,
And they shall be immediately deliver'd.
FIRST GOTH
What says our general?
LUCIUS
Aemilius, let the emperor give his pledges
Unto my father and my uncle Marcus,
And we will come. — March, away! [*Flourish. Exeunt.*

SCENE II

Rome. Before TITUS' *house.*

Enter TAMORA *and her two* SONS, DEMETRIUS *and*
          CHIRON, *disguised.*

TAMORA
Thus, in this strange and sad habiliment,
I will encounter with Andronicus,
And say I am Revenge, sent from below
To join with him and right his heinous wrongs.
Knock at his study, where, they say, he keeps,
To ruminate strange plots of dire revenge;
Tell him Revenge is come to join with him,
And work confusion on his enemies.
          [*They knock and* TITUS *opens his study door.*
TITUS ANDRONICUS
Who doth molest my contemplation?
Is it your trick to make me ope the door,
That so my sad decrees may fly away,
And all my study be to no effect?
You are deceiv'd: for what I mean to do,
See here in bloody lines I have set down;
And what is written shall be executed.
TAMORA
Titus, I am come to talk with thee.
TITUS ANDRONICUS
No, not a word: how can I grace my talk,
Wanting a hand to give it action?
Thou hast the odds of me; therefore no more.
TAMORA
If thou didst know me, thou wouldst talk with me.
TITUS ANDRONICUS
I am not mad; I know thee well enough:
Witness this wretched stump, witness these crimson
  lines;
Witness these trenches made by grief and care;
Witness the tiring day and heavy night;
Witness all sorrow, that I know thee well
For our proud empress, mighty Tamora:
Is not thy coming for my other hand?
TAMORA
Know, thou sad man, I am not Tamora;
She is thy enemy, and I thy friend:
I am Revenge; sent from th'infernal kingdom,
To ease the gnawing vulture of thy mind,
By working wreakful vengeance on thy foes.
Come down, and welcome me to this world's light;
Confer with me of murder and of death:
There's not a hollow cave or lurking-place,
No vast obscurity or misty vale,
Where bloody murder or detested rape
Can couch for fear, but I will find them out;
And in their ears tell them my dreadful name, —
Revenge, — which makes the foul offenders quake.
TITUS ANDRONICUS
Art thou Revenge? and art thou sent to me,
To be a torment to mine enemies?
TAMORA
I am; therefore come down, and welcome me.
TITUS ANDRONICUS
Do me some service, ere I come to thee.
Lo, by thy side where Rape and Murder stand;
Now give me some surance that thou art Revenge, —
Stab them, or tear them on thy chariot-wheels;
And then I'll come and be thy wagoner,
And whirl along with thee about the globe.
Provide thee two proper palfreys, black as jet,
To hale thy vengeful wagon swift away,
And find our murderers in their guilty caves:
And when thy car is loaden with their heads,
I will dismount, and by the wagon-wheel
Trot, like a servile footman, all day long,
Even from Hyperion's rising in the east
Until his very downfall in the sea:
And day by day I'll do this heavy task,
So thou destroy Rapine and Murder there.

TAMORA
These are my ministers, and come with me.
TITUS ANDRONICUS
Are these thy ministers? what are they call'd?
TAMORA
Rapine and Murder; therefore called so,
'Cause they take vengeance of such kind of men.
TITUS ANDRONICUS
Good Lord, how like the empress' sons they are!
And you, the empress! but we worldly men
Have miserable, mad, mistaking eyes.
O sweet Revenge, now do I come to thee;
And, if one arm's embracement will content thee,
I will embrace thee in it by and by.   [*Exit above.*
TAMORA
This closing with him fits his lunacy:
Whate'er I forge to feed his brain-sick fits,
Do you uphold and maintain in your speeches,
For now he firmly takes me for Revenge;
And, being credulous in this mad thought,
I'll make him send for Lucius his son;
And, whilst I at a banquet hold him sure,
I'll find some cunning practice out of hand,
To scatter and disperse the giddy Goths,
Or, at the least, make them his enemies. —
See, here he comes, and I must ply my theme.

    Enter TITUS, *below.*

TITUS ANDRONICUS
Long have I been forlorn, and all for thee:
Welcome, dread Fury, to my woeful house: —
Rapine and Murder, you are welcome too: —
How like the empress and her sons you are!
Well are you fitted, had you but a Moor: —
Could not all hell afford you such a devil? —
For well I wot the empress never wags
But in her company there is a Moor;
And, would you represent our queen aright,
It were convenient you had such a devil:
But welcome, as you are. What shall we do?
TAMORA
What wouldst thou have us do, Andronicus?
DEMETRIUS
Show me a murderer, I'll deal with him.
CHIRON
Show me a villain that hath done a rape,
And I am sent to be reveng'd on him.
TAMORA
Show me a thousand that have done thee wrong,
And I will be revenged on them all.
TITUS ANDRONICUS
Look round about the wicked streets of Rome;
And when thou find'st a man that's like thyself,
Good Murder, stab him; he's a murderer. —
Go thou with him; and when it is thy hap
To find another that is like to thee,
Good Rapine, stab him; he's a ravisher. —
Go thou with them; and in the emperor's court
There is a queen, attended by a Moor;
Well mayst thou know her by thy own proportion,
For up and down she doth resemble thee:
I pray thee, do on them some violent death;
They have been violent to me and mine.
TAMORA
Well hast thou lesson'd us; this shall we do.
But would it please thee, good Andronicus,
To send for Lucius, thy thrice-valiant son,
Who leads towards Rome a band of warlike Goths,
And bid him come and banquet at thy house;
When he is here, even at thy solemn feast,
I will bring in the empress and her sons,
The emperor himself, and all thy foes;
And at thy mercy shall they stoop and kneel,
And on them shalt thou ease thy angry heart.
What says Andronicus to this device?
TITUS ANDRONICUS
Marcus, my brother! 'tis sad Titus calls.
    Enter MARCUS.
Go, gentle Marcus, to thy nephew Lucius;
Thou shalt inquire him out among the Goths:
Bid him repair to me, and bring with him
Some of the chiefest princes of the Goths;
Bid him encamp his soldiers where they are:
Tell him the emperor and the empress too
Feast at my house, and he shall feast with them.
This do thou for my love; and so let him,
As he regards his aged father's life.
MARCUS ANDRONICUS
This will I do, and soon return again.   [*Exit.*
TAMORA
Now will I hence about thy business,

TITUS ANDRONICUS This one hand yet is left to cut your throats.

And take my ministers along with me.
TITUS ANDRONICUS
Nay, nay, let Rape and Murder stay with me;
Or else I'll call my brother back again,
And cleave to no revenge but Lucius.
TAMORA [*aside to* DEMETRIUS *and* CHIRON].
What say you, boys? will you abide with him,
Whiles I go tell my lord the emperor
How I have govern'd our determin'd jest?
Yield to his humour, smooth and speak him fair,
And tarry with him till I turn again.
TITUS ANDRONICUS [*aside*].
I know them all, though they suppose me mad,
And will o'er-reach them in their own devices, —
A pair of cursed hell-hounds and their dam.
DEMETRIUS [*aside to* TAMORA].
Madam, depart at pleasure; leave us here.
TAMORA
Farewell, Andronicus: Revenge now goes
To lay a complot to betray thy foes.
TITUS ANDRONICUS
I know thou dost; and, sweet Revenge, farewell.
                                    [*Exit* TAMORA.
CHIRON
Tell us, old man, how shall we be employ'd?
TITUS ANDRONICUS
Tut, I have work enough for you to do. —
Publius, come hither, Caius, and Valentine!

    Enter PUBLIUS, CAIUS, *and* VALENTINE.

PUBLIUS
What is your will?
TITUS ANDRONICUS
Know you these two?
PUBLIUS
The empress' sons,
I take them, Chiron and Demetrius.
TITUS ANDRONICUS
Fie, Publius, fie! thou art too much deceiv'd. —
The one is Murder, Rape is the other's name;
And therefore bind them, gentle Publius: —
Caius and Valentine, lay hands on them: —
Oft have you heard me wish for such an hour,
And now I find it; therefore bind them sure;
And stop their mouths, if they begin to cry.   [*Exit.*
    [PUBLIUS, *etc., lay hold on* CHIRON *and*
                                    DEMETRIUS.
CHIRON
Villains, forbear! we are the empress' sons.
PUBLIUS
And therefore do we what we are commanded. —
Stop close their mouths, let them not speak a word.
Is he sure bound? look that you bind them fast.
    Enter TITUS, *with a knife, and* LAVINIA, *with a basin.*
TITUS ANDRONICUS
Come, come, Lavinia; look, thy foes are bound. —
Sirs, stop their mouths, let them not speak to me;

But let them hear what fearful words I utter. —
O villains, Chiron and Demetrius!
Here stands the spring whom you have stain'd with
    mud;
This goodly summer with your winter mix'd.
You kill'd her husband; and, for that vile fault,
Two of her brothers were condemn'd to death,
My hand cut off, and made a merry jest;
Both her sweet hands, her tongue, and that more dear
Than hands or tongue, her spotless chastity,
Inhuman traitors, you constrain'd and forc'd.
What would you say, if I should let you speak?
Villains, for shame you could not beg for grace.
Hark, wretches! how I mean to martyr you.
This one hand yet is left to cut your throats,
Whilst that Lavinia 'tween her stumps doth hold
The basin that receives your guilty blood.
You know your mother means to feast with me,
And calls herself Revenge, and thinks me mad: —
Hark, villains! I will grind your bones to dust,
And with your blood and it I'll make a paste;
And of the paste a coffin I will rear,
And make two pasties of your shameful heads;
And bid that strumpet, your unhallow'd dam,
Like to the earth, swallow her own increase.
This is the feast that I have bid her to,
And this the banquet she shall surfeit on;
For worse than Philomel you used my daughter,
And worse than Progne I will be revenged:
And now prepare your throats. — Lavinia, come.
                              [*He cuts their throats.*
Receive the blood: and when that they are dead,
Let me go grind their bones to powder small,
And with this hateful liquor temper it;
And in that paste let their vile heads be bak'd.
Come, come, be every one officious
To make this banquet; which I wish may prove
More stern and bloody than the Centaurs' feast.
So: — now bring them in, for I'll play the cook,
And see them ready 'gainst their mother comes.
                    [*Exeunt, bearing the dead bodies.*

SCENE III

Court of TITUS' *house: tables set out.*

Enter LUCIUS, MARCUS, *and* GOTHS, *with* AARON
                    prisoner.

LUCIUS
Uncle Marcus, since it is my father's mind
That I repair to Rome, I am content.
FIRST GOTH
And ours with thine, befall what fortune will.
LUCIUS
Good uncle, take you in this barbarous Moor,
This ravenous tiger, this accursed devil;
Let him receive no sustenance, fetter him,
Till he be brought unto the empress' face,
For testimony of her foul proceedings:

And see the ambush of our friends be strong;
I fear the emperor means no good to us.

AARON
Some devil whisper curses in my ear,
And prompt me that my tongue may utter forth
The venomous malice of my swelling heart!

LUCIUS
Away, inhuman dog! unhallow'd slave! —
Sirs, help our uncle to convey him in.
[*Exeunt some* GOTHS *with* AARON. *Flourish within.*
The trumpets show the emperor is at hand.

Enter SATURNINUS *and* TAMORA, *with* AEMILIUS,
TRIBUNES, SENATORS, *and others.*

SATURNINUS
What, hath the firmament more suns than one?

LUCIUS
What boots it thee to call thyself a sun?

MARCUS ANDRONICUS
Rome's emperor, and nephew, break the parle;
These quarrels must be quietly debated.
The feast is ready, which the careful Titus
Hath ordain'd to an honourable end,
For peace, for love, for league, and good to Rome:
Please you, therefore, draw nigh, and take your places.

SATURNINUS
Marcus, we will.   [*Hautboys. A table brought in.*

Enter TITUS, *like a cook, placing the meat on the table,*
and LAVINIA *with a veil over her face,* YOUNG
LUCIUS, *and others.*

TITUS ANDRONICUS
Welcome, my gracious lord: welcome, dread queen;
Welcome, ye warlike Goths; welcome, Lucius;
And welcome, all: although the cheer be poor,
'Twill fill your stomachs; please you eat of it.

SATURNINUS
Why art thou thus attired, Andronicus?

TITUS ANDRONICUS
Because I would be sure to have all well,
To entertain your highness and your empress.

TAMORA
We are beholding to you, good Andronicus.

TITUS ANDRONICUS
An if your highness knew my heart, you were. —
My lord the emperor, resolve me this:
Was it well done of rash Virginius
To slay his daughter with his own right hand,
Because she was enforc'd, stain'd, and deflower'd?

SATURNINUS
It was, Andronicus.

TITUS ANDRONICUS
Your reason, mighty lord?

SATURNINUS
Because the girl should not survive her shame,
And by her presence still renew his sorrows.

TITUS ANDRONICUS
A reason mighty, strong, and effectual;
A pattern, precedent, and lively warrant,
For me, most wretched, to perform the like: —
Die, die, Lavinia, and thy shame with thee;
[*He kills her.*
And with thy shame thy father's sorrow die!

SATURNINUS
What hast thou done, unnatural and unkind?

TITUS ANDRONICUS
Kill'd her, for whom my tears have made me blind.
I am as woeful as Virginius was,
And have a thousand times more cause than he
To do this outrage; — and it now is done.

SATURNINUS
What, was she ravish'd? tell who did the deed.

TITUS ANDRONICUS
Will't please you eat? will't please your highness feed?

TAMORA
Why hast thou slain thine only daughter thus?

TITUS ANDRONICUS
Not I; 'twas Chiron and Demetrius:
They ravish'd her, and cut away her tongue;
And they, 'twas they, that did her all this wrong.

SATURNINUS
Go fetch them hither to us presently.

TITUS ANDRONICUS
Why, there they are both, baked in that pie;
Whereof their mother daintily hath fed,
Eating the flesh that she herself hath bred.
'Tis true, 'tis true; witness my knife's sharp point.
[*He stabs the* EMPRESS.

SATURNINUS
Die, frantic wretch, for this accursed deed!

[*Kills* TITUS.

LUCIUS
Can the son's eye behold his father bleed?
There's meed for meed, death for a deadly deed!
[*Kills* SATURNINUS. *A great tumult.* LUCIUS,
MARCUS, *and others go up into a gallery.*

MARCUS ANDRONICUS
You sad-fac'd men, people and sons of Rome,
By uproar sever'd, like a flight of fowl
Scatter'd by winds and high tempestuous gusts,
O, let me teach you how to knit again
This scatter'd corn into one mutual sheaf,
These broken limbs again into one body;
Lest Rome herself be bane unto herself,
And she whom mighty kingdoms court'sy to,
Like a forlorn and desperate castaway,
Do shameful execution on herself.
But if my frosty signs and chaps of age,
Grave witnesses of true experience,
Cannot induce you to attend my words, —
[*to* LUCIUS] Speak, Rome's dear friend: as erst our
          ancestor,
When with his solemn tongue he did discourse
To love-sick Dido's sad-attending ear
The story of that baleful-burning night
When subtle Greeks surpris'd King Priam's Troy, —
Tell us what Sinon hath bewitch'd our ears,
Or who hath brought the fatal engine in
That gives our Troy, our Rome, the civil wound. —
My heart is not compact of flint nor steel;
Nor can I utter all our bitter grief,
But floods of tears will drown my oratory,
And break my utterance, even in the time
When it should move you to attend me most,
And force you to commiseration.
Here's Rome's young captain; let him tell the tale,
While I stand by and weep to hear him speak.

LUCIUS
Then, gracious auditory, be it known to you
That Chiron and the damn'd Demetrius
Were they that murdered our emperor's brother;
And they it were that ravished our sister:
For their fell faults our brothers were beheaded,
Our father's tears despis'd, and basely cozen'd
Of that true hand that fought Rome's quarrel out,
And sent her enemies unto the grave.
Lastly, myself unkindly banished,
The gates shut on me, and turn'd weeping out,
To beg relief among Rome's enemies;
Who drown'd their enmity in my true tears,
And oped their arms to embrace me as a friend:
I am the turn'd forth, be it known to you,
That have preserv'd her welfare in my blood;
And from her bosom took the enemy's point,
Sheathing the steel in my adventurous body.
Alas, you know I am no vaunter, I;
My scars can witness, dumb although they are,
That my report is just and full of truth.
But, soft! methinks I do digress too much,
Citing my worthless praise: O, pardon me;
For when no friends are by, men praise themselves.

MARCUS ANDRONICUS
Now is my turn to speak. Behold this child, —
[*Pointing to the* CHILD *in the arms of an* ATTENDANT.
Of this was Tamora delivered;
The issue of an irreligious Moor,
Chief architect and plotter of these woes:
The villain is alive in Titus' house,
Damn'd as he is, to witness this is true.
Now judge what cause had Titus to revenge
These wrongs, unspeakable, past patience,
Or more than any living man could bear.
Now you have heard the truth, what say you, Romans?
Have we done aught amiss, — show us wherein,
And, from the place where you behold us pleading,
The poor remainder of Andronici
Will, hand in hand, all headlong hurl ourselves,
And on the ragged stones beat forth our brains,
And make a mutual closure of our house.
Speak, Romans, speak; and if you say we shall,
Lo, hand in hand, Lucius and I will fall.

AEMILIUS
Come, come, thou reverend man of Rome,
And bring our emperor gently in thy hand,
Lucius our emperor; for well I know
The common voice do cry it shall be so.

ROMANS
Lucius, all hail, Rome's royal emperor!

MARCUS ANDRONICUS [*to* ATTENDANTS].
Go, go into old Titus' sorrowful house,
And hither hale that misbelieving Moor,
To be adjudg'd some direful-slaughtering death,
As punishment for his most wicked life.
[*Exeunt some* ATTENDANTS.
LUCIUS, MARCUS, *etc., descend*

ROMANS
Lucius, all hail, Rome's gracious governor!

LUCIUS
Thanks, gentle Romans: may I govern so,
To heal Rome's harms, and wipe away her woe!
But, gentle people, give me aim awhile, —
For nature puts me to a heavy task: —
Stand all aloof; — but, uncle, draw you near,
To shed obsequious tears upon this trunk. —
O, take this warm kiss on thy pale cold lips,
[*Kissing* TITUS.
These sorrowful drops upon thy blood-stain'd face,
The last true duties of thy noble son!

MARCUS ANDRONICUS
Tear for tear, and loving kiss for kiss,
Thy brother Marcus tenders on thy lips:
O, were the sum of these that I should pay
Countless and infinite, yet would I pay them!

LUCIUS
Come hither, boy: come, come, and learn of us
To melt in showers: thy grandsire lov'd thee well:
Many a time he danc'd thee on his knee,
Sung thee asleep, his loving breast thy pillow;
Many a story hath he told to thee,
Meet and agreeing with thine infancy;
In that respect, then, like a loving child,
Shed yet some small drops from thy tender spring,
Because kind nature doth require it so:
Friends should associate friends in grief and woe:
Bid him farewell; commit him to the grave;
Do him that kindness, and take leave of him.

YOUNG LUCIUS
O grandsire, grandsire! even with all my heart
Would I were dead, so you did live again! —
O Lord, I cannot speak to him for weeping;
My tears will choke me, if I ope my mouth.

Enter ATTENDANTS *with* AARON.

AEMILIUS
You sad Andronici, have done with woes:
Give sentence on this execrable wretch,
That hath been breeder of these dire events.

LUCIUS
Set him breast-deep in earth, and famish him;
There let him stand, and rave, and cry for food:
If any one relieves or pities him,
For the offence he dies. This is our doom:
Some stay to see him fasten'd in the earth.

AARON
O, why should wrath be mute, and fury dumb?
I am no baby, I, that with base prayers
I should repent the evils I have done:
Ten thousand worse than ever yet I did
Would I perform, if I might have my will:
If one good deed in all my life I did,
I do repent it from my very soul.

LUCIUS
Some loving friends convey the emperor hence,
And give him burial in his father's grave:
My father and Lavinia shall forthwith
Be closed in our household monument.
As for that ravenous tiger, Tamora,
No funeral rite, nor man in mourning weeds,
No mournful bell shall ring her burial;
But throw her forth to beasts and birds of prey:
Her life was beast-like, and devoid of pity;
And, being so, shall have like want of pity.
See justice done on Aaron, that damn'd Moor,
By whom our heavy haps had their beginning:
Then, afterwards, to order well the state,
That like events may ne'er it ruinate.   [*Exeunt.*

THE COMEDY OF ERRORS

DRAMATIS PERSONAE

SOLINUS, *Duke of Ephesus.*
AEGEON, *a merchant of Syracuse.*

ANTIPHOLUS OF EPHESUS, } *twin brothers and*
ANTIPHOLUS OF SYRACUSE, } *sons to Aegeon and*
} *Aemilia.*
DROMIO OF EPHESUS, } *twin brothers, and*
DROMIO OF SYRACUSE, } *attendants on the two*
} *Antipholuses.*

BALTHAZAR, *a merchant.*
ANGELO, *a goldsmith.*
FIRST MERCHANT, *friend to Antipholus of Syracuse.*
SECOND MERCHANT, *to whom Angelo is a debtor.*
PINCH, *a schoolmaster.*

AEMILIA, wife to Aegeon, an abbess at Ephesus.
ADRIANA, wife to Antipholus of Ephesus.

LUCIANA, *her sister.*
LUCE, *servant to Adriana.*
A COURTEZAN.

GAOLER, OFFICERS, *and other* ATTENDANTS.

SCENE — *Ephesus.*

ACT I
SCENE I

A hall in the DUKE'S *palace.*

Enter DUKE, AEGEON, GAOLER, OFFICERS, *and other* ATTENDANTS.

AEGEON
Proceed, Solinus, to procure my fall,
And by the doom of death end woes and all.
DUKE OF EPHESUS
Merchant of Syracusa, plead no more;
I am not partial to infringe our laws:
The enmity and discord which of late
Sprung from the rancorous outrage of your duke
To merchants, our well-dealing countrymen, —
Who, wanting guilders to redeem their lives,
Have seal'd his rigorous statutes with their bloods,

Excludes all pity from our threat'ning looks.
For, since the mortal and intestine jars
'Twixt thy seditious countrymen and us,
It hath in solemn synods been decreed,
Both by the Syracusians and ourselves,
To admit no traffic to our adverse towns:
Nay, more, if any born at Ephesus
Be seen at Syracusian marts and fairs;
Again, if any Syracusian born
Come to the bay of Ephesus, he dies,
His goods confiscate to the duke's dispose,
Unless a thousand marks be levied,
To quit the penalty and to ransom him.
Thy substance, valued at the highest rate,
Cannot amount unto a hundred marks;
Therefore by law thou art condemn'd to die.
AEGEON
Yet this my comfort, — when your words are done,

My woes end likewise with the evening sun.
DUKE OF EPHESUS
Well, Syracusian, say, in brief, the cause
Why thou departed'st from thy native home,
And for what cause thou camest to Ephesus.
AEGEON
A heavier task could not have been imposed
Than I to speak my griefs unspeakable:
Yet, that the world may witness that my end
Was wrought by nature, not by vile offence,
I'll utter what my sorrow gives me leave.
In Syracusa was I born; and wed
Unto a woman, happy but for me,
And by me too, had not our hap been bad.
With her I liv'd in joy; our wealth increased
By prosperous voyages I often made
To Epidamnum; till my factor's death,
And the great care of goods at random left,

Drew me from kind embracements of my spouse:
From whom my absence was not six months old,
Before herself — almost at fainting under
The pleasing punishment that women bear —
Had made provision for her following me,
And soon and safe arrived where I was.
There had she not been long but she became
A joyful mother of two goodly sons;
And, which was strange, the one so like the
    other
As could not be distinguish'd but by names.
That very hour, and in the self-same
    inn,
A meaner woman was delivered
Of such a burden, male twins, both
    alike:
Those, for their parents were
    exceeding poor,
I bought, and brought up to attend
    my sons.
My wife, not meanly proud of two such
    boys,
Made daily motions for our home return:
Unwilling I agreed. Alas, too soon
We came aboard!
A league from Epidamnum had we sail'd,
Before the always-wind-obeying deep
Gave any tragic instance of our harm:

DUKE OF EPHESUS
Nay, forward, old man; do not break off so;
For we may pity, though not pardon thee.
AEGEON
O, had the gods done so, I had not now
    Worthily term'd them merciless to us!
    For, ere the ships could meet by twice five
      leagues,
We were encounter'd by a mighty rock;
Which being violently borne upon,
Our helpful ship was splitted in the midst;
So that, in this unjust divorce of us,
Fortune had left to both of us alike
What to delight in, what to sorrow for.
Her part, poor soul! seeming as burdened
With lesser weight, but not with lesser woe,
Was carried with more speed before the wind;
And in our sight they three were taken up
By fishermen of Corinth, as we thought.
At length, another ship had seiz'd on us;
And, knowing whom it was their hap to save,
Gave healthful welcome to their shipwrack'd
    guests;
And would have reft the fishers of their prey,
Had not their bark been very slow of sail,
And therefore homeward did they bend their
    course. —
Thus have you heard me sever'd from my
    bliss;
That by misfortunes was my life prolong'd,
To tell sad stories of my own mishaps.
    DUKE OF EPHESUS
And, for the sake of them thou sorrowest for,
Do me the favour to dilate at full
What have befall'n of them and thee till now.
    AEGEON
My youngest boy, and yet my eldest care,
At eighteen years became inquisitive
After his brother; and importun'd me
That his attendant — so his case was like,
Reft of his brother, but retain'd his name —
Might bear him company in the quest of him:
Whom whilst I labour'd of a love to see,

DUKE OF EPHESUS For we may pity, though not
pardon thee.

But longer did we not retain much hope;
For what obscured light the heavens did grant
Did but convey unto our fearful minds
A doubtful warrant of immediate death;
Which though myself would gladly have embrac'd,
Yet the incessant weepings of my wife,
Weeping before for what she saw must come,
And piteous plainings of the pretty babes,
That mourn'd for fashion, ignorant what to fear,
Forc'd me to seek delays for them and me.
And this it was, — for other means was none: —
The sailors sought for safety by our boat,
And left the ship, then sinking-ripe, to us:
My wife, more careful for the latter-born,
Had fasten'd him unto a small spare mast,
Such as seafaring men provide for storms;
To him one of the other twins was bound,
Whilst I had been like heedful of the other:
The children thus dispos'd, my wife and I,
Fixing our eyes on whom our care was fix'd,
Fasten'd ourselves at either end the mast;
And floating straight, obedient to the stream,
Was carried towards Corinth, as we thought.
At length the sun, gazing upon the earth,
Dispers'd those vapours that offended us;
And, by the benefit of his wished light,
The seas wax'd calm, and we discovered
Two ships from far making amain to us,
Of Corinth that, of Epidaurus this:
But ere they came, — O, let me say no more!
Gather the sequel by that went before.

I hazarded the loss of whom I lov'd.
Five summers have I spent in furthest Greece,
Roaming clean through the bounds of Asia,
And, coasting homeward, came to Ephesus;
Hopeless to find, yet loth to leave unsought
Or that, or any place that harbours men.
But here must end the story of my life;
And happy were I in my timely death,
Could all my travels warrant me they live.
DUKE OF EPHESUS
Hapless Aegeon, whom the fates have mark'd
To bear the extremity of dire mishap!
Now, trust me, were it not against our laws,
Against my crown, my oath, my dignity, —
Which princes, would they, may not disannul, —
My soul should sue as advocate for thee.
But, though thou art adjudged to the death,
And passed sentence may not be recall'd
But to our honour's great disparagement,
Yet will I favour thee in what I can.
Therefore, merchant, I'll limit thee this day
To seek thy life by beneficial help:
Try all the friends thou hast in Ephesus;
Beg thou, or borrow, to make up the sum,
And live; if no, then thou art doom'd to die. —
Gaoler, take him to thy custody.
GAOLER
I will, my lord.
AEGEON
Hopeless and helpless doth Aegeon wend,
But to procrastinate his lifeless end.   *[Exeunt.*

SCENE II

The Mart.

Enter ANTIPHOLUS OF SYRACUSE, DROMIO OF
SYRACUSE, *and* FIRST MERCHANT.

FIRST MERCHANT
Therefore give out you are of Epidamnum,
Lest that your goods too soon be confiscate.
This very day a Syracusian merchant
Is apprehended for arrival here;
And, not being able to buy out his life,
According to the statute of the town,
Dies ere the weary sun set in the west.
There is your money that I had to keep.
ANTIPHOLUS OF SYRACUSE
Go bear it to the Centaur, where we host,
And stay there, Dromio, till I come to thee.
Within this hour it will be dinner-time:
Till that, I'll view the manners of the town,
Peruse the traders, gaze upon the buildings,
And then return, and sleep within mine inn;
For with long travel I am stiff and weary.
Get thee away.
DROMIO OF SYRACUSE
Many a man would take you at your word,
And go indeed, having so good a mean.   *[Exit.*
ANTIPHOLUS OF SYRACUSE
A trusty villain, sir; that very oft,
When I am dull with care and melancholy,
Lightens my humour with his merry jests.
What, will you walk with me about the town,
And then go to my inn, and dine with me?
FIRST MERCHANT
I am invited, sir, to certain merchants,

ANTIPHOLUS OF SYRACUSE Go bear it to the Centaur.

DROMIO OF EPHESUS O, — sixpence, that I had o' Wednesday last.

Of whom I hope to make much benefit;
I crave your pardon. Soon at five o'clock,
Please you, I'll meet with you upon the mart,
And afterwards consort you till bed-time:
My present business calls me from you now.

ANTIPHOLUS OF SYRACUSE
Farewell till then: I will go lose myself,
And wander up and down to view the city.

FIRST MERCHANT
Sir, I commend you to your own content.   [*Exit.*

ANTIPHOLUS OF SYRACUSE
He that commends me to mine own content
Commends me to the thing I cannot get.
I to the world am like a drop of water,
That in the ocean seeks another drop;
Who, falling there to find his fellow forth,
Unseen, inquisitive, confounds himself:
So I, to find a mother and a brother,
In quest of them, unhappy, lose myself. —
Here comes the almanac of my true date.
        Enter DROMIO OF EPHESUS.
What now? how chance thou art return'd so soon?

DROMIO OF EPHESUS
Return'd so soon! rather approach'd too late:
The capon burns, the pig falls from the spit;
The clock hath strucken twelve upon the bell, —
My mistress made it one upon my cheek:
She is so hot, because the meat is cold;
The meat is cold, because you come not home;
You come not home, because you have no stomach;
You have no stomach, having broke your fast;
But we, that know what 'tis to fast and pray,
Are penitent for your default to-day.

ANTIPHOLUS OF SYRACUSE
Stop in your wind, sir: tell me this, I pray, —
Where have you left the money that I gave you?

DROMIO OF EPHESUS
O, — sixpence, that I had o' Wednesday last
To pay the saddler for my mistress' crupper: —
The saddler had it, sir; I kept it not.

ANTIPHOLUS OF SYRACUSE
I am not in a sportive humour now:
Tell me, and dally not, where is the money?
We being strangers here, how darest thou trust
So great a charge from thine own custody?

DROMIO OF EPHESUS
I pray you, jest, sir, as you sit at dinner:
I from my mistress come to you in post;
If I return, I shall be post indeed,
For she will score your fault upon my pate.
Methinks your maw, like mine, should be your clock,
And strike you home without a messenger.

ANTIPHOLUS OF SYRACUSE
Come, Dromio, come, these jests are out of season;
Reserve them till a merrier hour than this.
Where is the gold I gave in charge to thee?

DROMIO OF EPHESUS
To me, sir! why, you gave no gold to me.

ANTIPHOLUS OF SYRACUSE
Come on, sir knave, have done your foolishness,
And tell me how thou hast dispos'd thy charge.

DROMIO OF EPHESUS
My charge was but to fetch you from the mart
Home to your house, the Phœnix, sir, to dinner:
My mistress and her sister stay for you.

ANTIPHOLUS OF SYRACUSE
Now, as I am a Christian, answer
  me,
In what safe place you have
  bestow'd my money;
Or I shall break that merry sconce
  of yours,
That stands on tricks when I am
  undispos'd:
Where is the thousand marks thou
  hadst of me?

DROMIO OF EPHESUS
I have some marks of yours upon
  my pate,
Some of my mistress' marks upon
  my shoulders;
But not a thousand marks
  between you both.
If I should pay your worship those
  again,
Perchance you will not bear them
  patiently.

ANTIPHOLUS OF SYRACUSE
Thy mistress' marks! what
  mistress, slave, hast thou?

DROMIO OF EPHESUS
Your worship's wife, my mistress at the Phoenix;
She that doth fast till you come home to dinner,
And prays that you will hie you home to dinner.

ANTIPHOLUS OF SYRACUSE
What, wilt thou flout me thus unto my face,
Being forbid? There, take you that, sir knave.
                                    [*Beating him.*

DROMIO OF EPHESUS
What mean you, sir? for God's sake, hold your hands!
Nay, an you will not, sir, I'll take my heels.   [*Exit.*

ANTIPHOLUS OF SYRACUSE
Upon my life, by some device or other
The villain is o'er-raught of all my money.
They say this town is full of cozenage;
As, nimble jugglers that deceive the eye,
Dark-working sorcerers that change the mind,
Soul-killing witches that deform the body,
Disguised cheaters, prating mountebanks,
And many such-like liberties of sin:
If it prove so, I will be gone the sooner.
I'll to the Centaur, to go seek this slave:
I greatly fear my money is not safe.   [*Exit.*

ACT II

SCENE I

Before the house of ANTIPHOLUS OF EPHESUS.

Enter ADRIANA *and* LUCIANA.

ADRIANA
Neither my husband nor the slave return'd,
That in such haste I sent to seek his master!
Sure, Luciana, it is two o'clock.

LUCIANA
Perhaps some merchant hath invited
  him,
And from the mart he's somewhere
  gone to dinner.
Good sister, let us dine, and never
  fret:
A man is master of his liberty:
Time is their master; and, when they
  see time,
They'll go or come: if so, be patient,
  sister.

ADRIANA
Why should their liberty than ours be
  more?

LUCIANA
Because their business still lies out o'
  door.

ADRIANA
Look, when I serve him so, he takes it
  ill.

LUCIANA
O, know he is the bridle of your will.

ADRIANA
There's none but asses will be
  bridled so.

LUCIANA
Why, headstrong liberty is lash'd
  with woe.

There's nothing situate under heaven's eye
But hath his bound, in earth, in sea, in sky:
The beasts, the fishes, and the winged fowls,
Are their males' subjects and at their controls:
Men, more divine, the masters of all these,
Lords of the wide world and wild wat'ry seas,
Indued with intellectual sense and souls,
Of more pre-eminence than fish and fowls,
Are masters to their females and their lords:
Then let your will attend on their accords.

ADRIANA
This servitude makes you to keep unwed.

LUCIANA
Not this, but troubles of the marriage-bed.

ADRIANA
But, were you wedded, you would bear some sway.

LUCIANA
Ere I learn love, I'll practise to obey.

ADRIANA
How if your husband start some other where?

LUCIANA
Till he come home again, I would forbear.

ADRIANA
Patience unmov'd! no marvel though she pause;
They can be meek that have no other cause.
A wretched soul, bruis'd with adversity,
We bid be quiet when we hear it cry;
But were we burden'd with like weight of pain,
As much, or more, we should ourselves complain:
So thou, that hast no unkind mate to grieve thee,
With urging helpless patience would relieve me;
But, if thou live to see like right bereft,
This fool-begg'd patience in thee will be left.

LUCIANA
Well, I will marry one day, but to try. —
Here comes your man; now is your husband nigh.

        Enter DROMIO OF EPHESUS.

ADRIANA
Say, is your tardy master now at hand?

DROMIO OF EPHESUS
Nay, he's at two hands with me, and that my two ears
  can witness.

ADRIANA
Say, didst thou speak with him? know'st thou his
  mind?

DROMIO OF EPHESUS
Ay, ay, he told his mind upon mine ear:
Beshrew his hand, I scarce could understand it.

LUCIANA
Spake he so doubtfully, thou couldst not feel his
  meaning?

DROMIO OF EPHESUS
Nay, he struck so plainly, I could too well feel his blows;
  and withal so doubtfully, that I could scarce
  understand them.

ADRIANA
But say, I prithee, is he coming home?
It seems he hath great care to please his wife.

DROMIO OF EPHESUS
Why, mistress, sure my master is horn-mad.

ANTIPHOLUS OF SYRACUSE There, take you that, sir knave.

ADRIANA
Horn-mad, thou villain!
DROMIO OF EPHESUS
            I mean not cuckold-mad;
But, sure, he is stark mad.
When I desired him to come home to dinner,
He ask'd me for a thousand marks in gold:
''Tis dinner-time,' quoth I; 'My gold,' quoth he:
'Your meat doth burn,' quoth I; 'My gold,' quoth he:
'Will you come home?' quoth I; 'My gold,' quoth he;
'Where is the thousand marks I gave thee, villain?'
'The pig,' quoth I, 'is burnt'; 'My gold,' quoth he:
'My mistress, sir,' quoth I; 'Hang up thy mistress!
I know not thy mistress; out on thy mistress!'
LUCIANA
Quoth who?
DROMIO OF EPHESUS
Quoth my master:
'I know,' quoth he, 'no house, no wife, no mistress.'
So that my arrant, due unto my tongue,
I thank him, I bear home upon my shoulders;
For, in conclusion, he did beat me there.
ADRIANA
Go back again, thou slave, and fetch him home.
DROMIO OF EPHESUS
Go back again, and be new beaten home!
For God's sake, send some other messenger.
ADRIANA
Back, slave, or I will break thy pate across.
DROMIO OF EPHESUS
And he will bless that cross with other beating:
Between you I shall have a holy head.
ADRIANA
Hence, prating peasant! fetch thy master home.
DROMIO OF EPHESUS
Am I so round with you as you with me,
That like a football you do spurn me thus?
You spurn me hence, and he will spurn me hither:
If I last in this service, you must case me in leather.
                        [Exit.
LUCIANA
Fie, how impatience low'reth in your face!
ADRIANA
His company must do his minions grace,
Whilst I at home starve for a merry look.
Hath homely age th'alluring beauty took
From my poor cheek? then he hath wasted it:
Are my discourses dull? barren my wit?
If voluble and sharp discourse be marr'd,
Unkindness blunts it more than marble hard:
Do their gay vestments his affections bait?
That's not my fault, — he's master of my state:
What ruins are in me that can be found
By him not ruin'd? then is he the ground
Of my defeatures. My decayed fair
A sunny look of his would soon repair:
But, too unruly deer, he breaks the pale,
And feeds from home; poor I am but his stale.
LUCIANA
Self-harming jealousy, — fie, beat it hence!
ADRIANA
Unfeeling fools can with such wrongs dispense.
I know his eye doth homage otherwhere;
Or else what lets it but he would be here?
Sister, you know he promis'd me a chain; —
Would that alone alone he would detain,
So he would keep fair quarter with his bed!
I see the jewel best enamelled
Will lose his beauty; and though gold bides still
That tester's touch, yet often-touching will
Wear gold: and so no man that hath a name,
But falsehood and corruption doth it shame.
Since that my beauty cannot please his eye,
I'll weep what's left away, and weeping die.
LUCIANA
How many fond fools serve mad jealousy!   *[Exeunt.*

SCENE II

The Mart.

Enter ANTIPHOLUS OF SYRACUSE.

ANTIPHOLUS OF SYRACUSE
The gold I gave to Dromio is laid up
Safe at the Centaur; and the heedful slave
Is wander'd forth, in care to seek me out.
By computation and mine host's report,
I could not speak with Dromio since at first
I sent him from the mart. — See, here he comes.
        Enter DROMIO OF SYRACUSE.
How now, sir! is your merry humour alter'd?

As you love strokes, so jest with me again.
You know no Centaur? you receiv'd no gold?
Your mistress sent to have me home to dinner?
My house was at the Phoenix? Wast thou mad,
That thus so madly thou didst answer me?
DROMIO OF SYRACUSE
What answer, sir? when spake I such a word?
ANTIPHOLUS OF SYRACUSE
Even now, even here, not half an hour since.
DROMIO OF SYRACUSE
I did not see you since you sent me hence,
Home to the Centaur, with the gold you gave me.
ANTIPHOLUS OF SYRACUSE
Villain, thou didst deny the gold's receipt,
And told'st me of a mistress and a dinner;
For which, I hope, thou felt'st I was displeased.
DROMIO OF SYRACUSE
I am glad to see you in this merry vein:
What means this jest? I pray you, master, tell me.
ANTIPHOLUS OF SYRACUSE
Yea, dost thou jeer and flout me in the teeth?
Think'st thou I jest? Hold, take thou that, and that.
                        [Beats DROMIO.
DROMIO OF SYRACUSE
Hold, sir, for God's sake! now your jest is earnest:
Upon what bargain do you give it me?
ANTIPHOLUS OF SYRACUSE
Because that I familiarly sometimes
Do use you for my fool, and chat with you,
Your sauciness will jest upon my love,
And make a common of my serious hours.
When the sun shines let foolish gnats make sport,
But creep in crannies when he hides his beams.
If you will jest with me, know my aspect,
And fashion your demeanour to my looks,
Or I will beat this method in your sconce.
DROMIO OF SYRACUSE
Sconce call you it? so you would leave battering, I had
rather have it a head: an you use these blows long, I
must get a sconce for my head, and ensconce it too; or
else I shall seek my wit in my shoulders. But, I pray, sir,
why am I beaten?
ANTIPHOLUS OF SYRACUSE
Dost thou not know?
DROMIO OF SYRACUSE
Nothing, sir, but that I am beaten.
ANTIPHOLUS OF SYRACUSE
Shall I tell you why?
DROMIO OF SYRACUSE
Ay, sir, and wherefore; for they say every why hath
a wherefore.
ANTIPHOLUS OF SYRACUSE
Why, first, — for flouting me; and then, wherefore, —
For urging it the second time to me.
DROMIO OF SYRACUSE
Was there ever any man thus beaten out of season,

When in the why and the wherefore is neither rime
nor reason?
Well, sir, I thank you.
ANTIPHOLUS OF SYRACUSE
Thank me, sir! for what?
DROMIO OF SYRACUSE
Marry, sir, for this something that you gave me for
nothing.
ANTIPHOLUS OF SYRACUSE
I'll make you amends next, to give you nothing for
something. But say, sir, is it dinner-time?
DROMIO OF SYRACUSE
No, sir: I think the meat wants that I have.
ANTIPHOLUS OF SYRACUSE
In good time, sir; what's that?
DROMIO OF SYRACUSE
Basting.
ANTIPHOLUS OF SYRACUSE
Well, sir, then 'twill be dry.
DROMIO OF SYRACUSE
If it be, sir, I pray you, eat none of it.
ANTIPHOLUS OF SYRACUSE
Your reason?
DROMIO OF SYRACUSE
Lest it make you choleric, and purchase me another dry
basting.
ANTIPHOLUS OF SYRACUSE
Well, sir, learn to jest in good time: there's a time for all
things.
DROMIO OF SYRACUSE
I durst have denied that, before you were so choleric.
ANTIPHOLUS OF SYRACUSE
By what rule, sir?
DROMIO OF SYRACUSE
Marry, sir, by a rule as plain as the plain bald pate of
father Time himself.
ANTIPHOLUS OF SYRACUSE
Let's hear it.
DROMIO OF SYRACUSE
There's no time for a man to recover his hair that grows
bald by nature.
ANTIPHOLUS OF SYRACUSE
May he not do it by fine and recovery?
DROMIO OF SYRACUSE
Yes, to pay a fine for a periwig, and recover the lost hair
of another man.
ANTIPHOLUS OF SYRACUSE
Why is Time such a niggard of hair, being, as it is, so
plentiful an excrement?
DROMIO OF SYRACUSE
Because it is a blessing that he bestows on beasts: and
what he hath scanted men in hair, he hath given
them in wit.
ANTIPHOLUS OF SYRACUSE
Why, but there's many a man hath more hair than wit.

DROMIO OF EPHESUS Why, mistress, sure my master is horn-mad.

DROMIO OF SYRACUSE
Not a man of those but he hath the wit to lose his hair.

ANTIPHOLUS OF SYRACUSE
Why, thou didst conclude hairy men plain-dealers
    without wit.

DROMIO OF SYRACUSE
The plainer dealer, the sooner lost: yet he loseth it in a
    kind of jollity.

ANTIPHOLUS OF SYRACUSE
For what reason?

DROMIO OF SYRACUSE
For two; and sound ones too.

ANTIPHOLUS OF SYRACUSE
Nay, not sound, I pray you.

DROMIO OF SYRACUSE
Sure ones, then.

ANTIPHOLUS OF SYRACUSE
Nay, not sure, in a thing falsing.

DROMIO OF SYRACUSE
Certain ones, then.

ANTIPHOLUS OF SYRACUSE
Name them.

DROMIO OF SYRACUSE
The one, to save the money that he spends in tiring; the
    other, that at dinner they should not drop in his
    porridge.

ANTIPHOLUS OF SYRACUSE
You would all this time have proved there is no time for
    all things.

DROMIO OF SYRACUSE
Marry, and did, sir; namely, no time to recover hair lost
    by nature.

ANTIPHOLUS OF SYRACUSE
But your reason was not substantial, why there is no
    time to recover.

DROMIO OF SYRACUSE
Thus I mend it: Time himself is bald, and therefore to
    the world's end will have bald followers.

ANTIPHOLUS OF SYRACUSE
I knew 'twould be a bald conclusion:
But, soft! who wafts us yonder?

Enter ADRIANA *and* LUCIANA.

ADRIANA
Ay, ay, Antipholus, look strange and frown:
Some other mistress hath thy sweet aspects;
I am not Adriana nor thy wife.
The time was once when thou unurg'd wouldst vow
That never words were music to thine ear,
That never object pleasing in thine eye,
That never touch well-welcome to thy hand,
That never meat sweet-savour'd in thy taste,
Unless I spake, or look'd, or touch'd, or carv'd to thee.
How comes it now, my husband, O, how comes it,
That thou art then estranged from thyself?
Thyself I call it, being strange to me,
That, undividable, incorporate,
Am better than thy dear self's better part.
Ah, do not tear away thyself from me!
For know, my love, as easy mayst thou fall
A drop of water in the breaking gulf,
And take unmingled thence that drop again,
Without addition or diminishing,
As take from me thyself, and not me too.
How dearly would it touch thee to the quick,
Shouldst thou but hear I were licentious,
And that this body, consecrate to thee,
By ruffian lust should be contaminate!
Wouldst thou not spit at me and spurn at me,
And hurl the name of husband in my face,
And tear the stain'd skin off my harlot-brow,
And from my false hand cut the wedding-ring,
And break it with a deep-divorcing vow?
I know thou canst; and therefore see thou do it.
I am possess'd with an adulterate blot;
My blood is mingled with the grime of lust:
For if we two be one, and thou play false,
I do digest the poison of thy flesh,
Being strumpeted by thy contagion.
Keep, then, fair league and truce with thy true bed;
I live unstain'd, thou undishonoured.

ANTIPHOLUS OF SYRACUSE
Plead you to me, fair dame? I know you not:
In Ephesus I am but two hours old,
As strange unto your town as to your talk;
Who, every word by all my wit being scann'd,
Want wit in all one word to understand.

LUCIANA
Fie, brother! how the world is chang'd with you!
When were you wont to use my sister thus?

She sent for you by Dromio home to dinner.

ANTIPHOLUS OF SYRACUSE
By Dromio?

DROMIO OF SYRACUSE
By me!

ADRIANA
By thee; and this thou didst return from him, —
That he did buffet thee, and, in his blows,
Denied my house for his, me for his wife.

ANTIPHOLUS OF SYRACUSE
Did you converse, sir, with this gentlewoman?
What is the course and drift of your compact?

DROMIO OF SYRACUSE
I, sir! I never saw her till this time.

ANTIPHOLUS OF SYRACUSE
Villain, thou liest; for even her very words
Didst thou deliver to me on the mart.

DROMIO OF SYRACUSE
I never spake with her in all my life.

ANTIPHOLUS OF SYRACUSE
How can she thus, then, call us by our names,
Unless it be by inspiration?

ADRIANA
How ill agrees it with your gravity
To counterfeit thus grossly with your slave,
Abetting him to thwart me in my mood!
Be it my wrong you are from me exempt,
But wrong not that wrong with a more contempt.
Come, I will fasten on this sleeve of thine:
Thou art an elm, my husband, — I a vine,
Whose weakness, married to thy stronger state,
Makes me with thy strength to communicate:
If aught possess thee from me, it is dross,
Usurping ivy, brier, or idle moss;
Who, all for want of pruning, with intrusion
Infect thy sap, and live on thy confusion.

ANTIPHOLUS OF SYRACUSE [*aside*].
To me she speaks; she moves me for her theme:
What, was I married to her in my dream?
Or sleep I now, and think I hear all this?
What error drives our eyes and ears amiss?
Until I know this sure uncertainty,
I'll entertain the offer'd fallacy.

LUCIANA
Dromio, go bid the servants spread for dinner.

DROMIO OF SYRACUSE
O, for my beads! I cross me for a sinner.
This is the fairy land; — O spite of spites! —
We talk with goblins, owls, and elvish sprites:
If we obey them not, this will ensue, —
They'll suck our breath, or pinch us black and blue.

LUCIANA
Why pratest thou to thyself, and answer'st not?
Dromio, thou drone, thou snail, thou slug, thou
    sot!

DROMIO OF SYRACUSE
I am transformed, master, am not I?

ANTIPHOLUS OF SYRACUSE
I think thou art in mind, and so am I.

DROMIO OF SYRACUSE
Nay, master, both in mind and in my shape.

ANTIPHOLUS OF SYRACUSE
Thou hast thine own form.

DROMIO OF SYRACUSE
               No, I am an ape.

LUCIANA
If thou art chang'd to aught, 'tis to an ass.

DROMIO OF SYRACUSE
'Tis true; she rides me, and I long for grass.
'Tis so, I am an ass; else it could never be
But I should know her as well as she knows me.

ADRIANA
Come, come, no longer will I be a fool,
To put the finger in the eye and weep,
Whilst man and master laugh my woes to
    scorn. —
Come, sir, to dinner. — Dromio, keep the gate.
—
Husband, I'll dine above with you to-day,
And shrive you of a thousand idle pranks. —
Sirrah, if any ask you for your master,
Say he dines forth, and let no creature enter. —
Come, sister. — Dromio, play the porter well.

ANTIPHOLUS OF SYRACUSE [*aside*].
Am I in earth, in heaven, or in hell?
Sleeping or waking? mad or well-advised?
Known unto these, and to myself disguised!
I'll say as they say, and persever so,
And in this mist at all adventures go.

DROMIO OF SYRACUSE
Master, shall I be porter at the gate?

ADRIANA
Ay; and let none enter, lest I break your pate.

LUCIANA
Come, come, Antipholus, we dine too late.   [*Exeunt.*

ACT III

SCENE I

Before the house of ANTIPHOLUS OF EPHESUS.

Enter ANTIPHOLUS OF EPHESUS, DROMIO OF
EPHESUS, ANGELO, *and* BALTHAZAR.

ANTIPHOLUS OF EPHESUS
Good Signior Angelo, you must excuse us all;
My wife is shrewish when I keep not hours:
Say that I linger'd with you at your shop
To see the making of her carcanet,
And that to-morrow you will bring it home.
But here's a villain that would face me down
He met me on the mart, and that I beat him,
And charg'd him with a thousand marks in gold,
And that I did deny my wife and house. —
Thou drunkard, thou, what didst thou mean by this?

DROMIO OF EPHESUS
Say what you will, sir, but I know what I know;
That you beat me at the mart, I have your hand to show:
If the skin were parchment, and the blows you gave
    were ink,
Your own handwriting would tell you what I think.

ANTIPHOLUS OF EPHESUS
I think thou art an ass.

DROMIO OF EPHESUS
             Marry, so it doth appear
By the wrongs I suffer and the blows I bear.
I should kick, being kick'd; and, being at that pass,
You would keep from my heels, and beware of an ass.

ANTIPHOLUS OF EPHESUS
You're sad, Signior Balthazar: pray God our cheer
May answer my good will and your good welcome here!

BALTHAZAR
I hold your dainties cheap, sir, and your welcome dear.

ANTIPHOLUS OF EPHESUS
O, Signior Balthazar, either at flesh or fish,
A table full of welcome makes scarce one dainty dish.

BALTHAZAR
Good meat, sir, is common; that every churl affords.

ANTIPHOLUS OF EPHESUS
And welcome more common; for that's nothing but
    words.

ADRIANA Thou art an elm, my husband, — I a vine.

ANTIPHOLUS OF SYRACUSE Villain, thou liest.

BALTHAZAR
Small cheer and great welcome makes a merry feast.
ANTIPHOLUS OF EPHESUS
Ay, to a niggardly host and more sparing guest:
But though my cates be mean, take them in good part:
Better cheer may you have, but not with better heart.
But, soft! my door is lock'd. — Go bid them let us in.
DROMIO OF EPHESUS
Maud, Bridget, Marian, Cicely, Gillian, Ginn!
DROMIO OF SYRACUSE [within].
Mome, malt-horse, capon, coxcomb, idiot, patch!
Either get thee from the door, or sit down at the hatch.
Dost thou conjure for wenches, that thou call'st for
     such store,
When one is one too many? Go get thee from the door.
DROMIO OF EPHESUS
What patch is made our porter? — My master stays in
the street.
DROMIO OF SYRACUSE [within].
Let him walk from whence he came, lest he
     catch cold on's feet.
ANTIPHOLUS OF EPHESUS
Who talks within there? ho, open the door!
DROMIO OF SYRACUSE [within].
Right, sir; I'll tell you when, an you'll tell me wherefore.
ANTIPHOLUS OF EPHESUS
Wherefore? for my dinner: I have not din'd to-day.
DROMIO OF SYRACUSE [within].
Nor to-day here you must not; come again
when you may.
ANTIPHOLUS OF EPHESUS
What art thou that keep'st me out from the house I
     owe?
DROMIO OF SYRACUSE [within].
The porter for this time, sir, and my name
is Dromio.
DROMIO OF EPHESUS
O villain, thou hast stol'n both mine office and my
     name!
The one ne'er got me credit, the other mickle blame.
If thou hadst been Dromio to-day in my place,
Thou wouldst have chang'd thy face for a name, or thy
     name for an ass.
LUCE [within].
What a coil is there, Dromio! who are those
at the gate?
DROMIO OF EPHESUS
Let my master in, Luce.
LUCE [within].
                    Faith, no; he comes too late;
And so tell your master.
DROMIO OF EPHESUS
               O Lord, I must laugh! —
Have at you with a proverb; — Shall I set in my staff?
LUCE [within].
Have at you with another; that's, — When? can you
tell?
DROMIO OF SYRACUSE [within].
If thy name be call'd Luce, — Luce, thou hast answer'd
     him well.

ANTIPHOLUS OF EPHESUS
Do you hear, you minion? you'll let us in, I hope?
LUCE [within].
I thought to have ask'd you.
DROMIO OF SYRACUSE [within].
                    And you said no.
DROMIO OF EPHESUS
So, come, help: — well struck! there was blow for blow.
ANTIPHOLUS OF EPHESUS
Thou baggage, let me in.
LUCE [within].
                    Can you tell for whose sake?
DROMIO OF EPHESUS
Master, knock the door hard.
LUCE [within].
                    Let him knock till it ache.
ANTIPHOLUS OF EPHESUS
You'll cry for this, minion, if I beat the door down.
LUCE [within].
What needs all that, and a pair of stocks in the town?
ADRIANA [within].
Who is that at the door that keeps all this noise?
DROMIO OF SYRACUSE [within].
By my troth, your town is troubled with unruly boys.

ANTIPHOLUS OF EPHESUS
Are you there, wife? you might have come before.
ADRIANA [within].
Your wife, sir knave! go get you from the door.
DROMIO OF EPHESUS
If you went in pain, master, this knave would go sore.
ANGELO
Here is neither cheer, sir, nor welcome: we would fain
     have either.
BALTHAZAR
In debating which was best, we shall part with neither.
DROMIO OF EPHESUS
They stand at the door, master; bid them welcome
     hither.
ANTIPHOLUS OF EPHESUS
There is something in the wind, that we cannot get in.
DROMIO OF EPHESUS
You would say so, master, if your garments were thin.
Your cake there is warm within; you stand here in the
     cold:
It would make a man mad as a buck, to be so bought
     and sold.
ANTIPHOLUS OF EPHESUS
Go fetch me something: I'll break ope the gate.
DROMIO OF SYRACUSE [within].
Break any breaking here, and I'll break your knave's
     pate.
DROMIO OF EPHESUS
A man may break a word with you, sir, and words are
     but wind;
Ay, and break it in your face, so he break it not behind.
DROMIO OF SYRACUSE [within].
It seems thou want'st breaking: out upon thee, hind!
DROMIO OF EPHESUS
Here's too much 'out upon thee!' I pray thee, let me in.
DROMIO OF SYRACUSE [within].
Ay, when fowls have no feathers, and fish have no fin.
ANTIPHOLUS OF EPHESUS
Well, I'll break in: — go borrow me a crow.
DROMIO OF EPHESUS
A crow without feather, — master, mean you so?
For a fish without a fin, there's a fowl without a feather:
If a crow help us in, sirrah, we'll pluck a crow together.
ANTIPHOLUS OF EPHESUS
Go get thee gone; fetch me an iron crow.
BALTHAZAR
Have patience, sir; O, let it not be so!
Herein you war against your reputation,
And draw within the compass of suspect
Th'unviolated honour of your wife.
Once this, — your long experience of her wisdom,
Her sober virtue, years, and modesty,
Plead on her part some cause to you unknown;
And doubt not, sir, but she will well excuse
Why at this time the doors are made against you.
Be rul'd by me: depart in patience,
And let us to the Tiger all to dinner;
And about evening come yourself alone
To know the reason of this strange restraint.
If by strong hand you offer to break in
Now in the stirring passage of the day,
A vulgar comment will be made of it,
And that supposed by the common rout
Against your yet ungalled estimation,
That may with foul intrusion enter in,
And dwell upon your grave when you are dead;
For slander lives upon succession,
For ever housed where it gets possession.
ANTIPHOLUS OF EPHESUS
You have prevail'd: I will depart in quiet,
And, in despite of mirth, mean to be merry.
I know a wench of excellent discourse,
Pretty and witty; wild, and yet, too, gentle:
There will we dine. This woman that I mean,
My wife — but, I protest, without desert —
Hath oftentimes upbraided me withal:
To her will we to dinner. — Get you home,
And fetch the chain; by this I know 'tis made:
Bring it, I pray you, to the Porpentine;
For there's the house: that chain will I bestow —
Be it for nothing but to spite my wife —
Upon mine hostess there: good sir, make haste.
Since mine own doors refuse to entertain me,
I'll knock elsewhere, to see if they'll disdain me.
ANGELO
I'll meet you at that place some hour hence.
ANTIPHOLUS OF EPHESUS
Do so. This jest shall cost me some expense.   [Exeunt.

SCENE II

The same.

Enter LUCIANA and ANTIPHOLUS OF SYRACUSE.

LUCIANA
And may it be that you have quite forgot
  A husband's office? shall, Antipholus,
Even in the spring of love, thy love-springs rot?
  Shall love, in building, grow so ruinous?
If you did wed my sister for her wealth,
  Then for her wealth's sake use her with more
    kindness:
Or if you like elsewhere, do it by stealth;
  Muffle your false love with some show of blindness:
Let not my sister read it in your eye;
  Be not thy tongue thy own shame's orator;
Look sweet, speak fair, become disloyalty;
  Apparel vice like virtue's harbinger;
Bear a fair presence, though your heart be tainted;
  Teach sin the carriage of a holy saint;
Be secret-false: what need she be acquainted?
  What simple thief brags of his own attaint?
'Tis double wrong, to truant with your bed,
  And let her read it in thy looks at board:
Shame hath a bastard fame, well managed;
  Ill deeds is doubled with an evil word.
Alas, poor women! make us but believe,
  Being compact of credit, that you love us;
Though others have the arm, show us the sleeve;
  We in your motion turn, and you may move us.
Then, gentle brother, get you in again;
  Comfort my sister, cheer her, call her wife:
'Tis holy sport, to be a little vain,
  When the sweet breath of flattery conquers strife.

ANTIPHOLUS OF SYRACUSE
Sweet mistress, — what your name is else, I know not,
  Nor by what wonder you do hit of mine, —
Less in your knowledge and your Grace you show not
  Than our earth's wonder; more than earth divine.
Teach me, dear creature, how to think and speak;
  Lay open to my earthy-gross conceit,
Smother'd in errors, feeble, shallow, weak,
  The folded meaning of your words' deceit.
Against my soul's pure truth why labour you
  To make it wander in an unknown field?
Are you a god? would you create me new?
  Transform me, then, and to your power I'll yield.
But if that I am I, then well I know
  Your weeping sister is no wife of mine,
Nor to her bed no homage do I owe:
  Far more, far more to you do I decline.
O, train me not, sweet mermaid, with thy note,
  To drown me in thy sister's flood of tears:
Sing, siren, for thyself and I will dote:
  Spread o'er the silver waves thy golden hairs,
And as a bed I'll take them, and there lie;
  And, in that glorious supposition, think
He gains by death that hath such means to die:
  Let Love, being light, be drowned if she sink!

LUCIANA
What, are you mad, that you do reason so?

ANTIPHOLUS OF SYRACUSE
Not mad, but mated; how, I do not know.

LUCIANA
It is a fault that springeth from your eye.

ANTIPHOLUS OF SYRACUSE
For gazing on your beams, fair sun, being by.

LUCIANA
Gaze where you should, and that will clear your sight.

ANTIPHOLUS OF SYRACUSE
As good to wink, sweet love, as look on night.

LUCIANA
Why call you me love? call my sister so.

ANTIPHOLUS OF SYRACUSE
Thy sister's sister.

LUCIANA
      That's my sister.

ANTIPHOLUS OF SYRACUSE
           No;
It is thyself, mine own self's better part,
Mine eye's clear eye, my dear heart's dearer heart,
My food, my fortune, and my sweet hope's aim,
My sole earth's heaven, and my heaven's claim.

LUCIANA
All this my sister is, or else should be.

ANTIPHOLUS OF SYRACUSE
Call thyself sister, sweet, for I aim thee.
Thee will I love, and with thee lead my life:
Thou hast no husband yet, nor I no wife.
Give me thy hand.

LUCIANA
      O, soft, sir! hold
      you still:
I'll fetch my sister, to get her   [*Exit.*
good-will.

Enter DROMIO of Syracuse.

ANTIPHOLUS OF SYRACUSE
Why, how now, Dromio! where
  runn'st thou so fast?

DROMIO OF SYRACUSE
Do you know me, sir? am I Dromio?
  am I your man? am I myself?

ANTIPHOLUS OF SYRACUSE
Thou art Dromio, thou art my man,
  thou art thyself.

DROMIO OF SYRACUSE
I am an ass, I am a woman's man,
  and besides myself.

ANTIPHOLUS OF SYRACUSE
What woman's man? and how
  besides thyself?

DROMIO OF SYRACUSE
Marry, sir, besides myself, I am due
  to a woman; one
that claims me, one that haunts me,
  one that will have me.

ANTIPHOLUS OF SYRACUSE
What claim lays she to thee?

DROMIO OF SYRACUSE
Marry, sir, such claim as you would
lay to your horse; and she would
have me as a beast: not that, I being
a beast, she would have me; but that
she, being a very beastly creature,
lays claim to me.

ANTIPHOLUS OF SYRACUSE
What is she?

DROMIO OF SYRACUSE
A very reverend body; ay, such a one as a man may not
speak of, without he say 'sir-reverence'. I have but lean
luck in the match, and yet is she a wondrous fat
marriage.

ANTIPHOLUS OF SYRACUSE
How dost thou mean, — a fat marriage?

DROMIO OF SYRACUSE
Marry, sir, she's the kitchen-wench, and all grease; and
I know not what use to put her to, but to make a lamp of
her, and run from her by her own light. I warrant, her
rags, and the tallow in them, will burn a Poland winter:
if she lives till doomsday, she'll burn a week longer
than the whole world.

ANTIPHOLUS OF SYRACUSE
What complexion is she of?

DROMIO OF SYRACUSE
Swart, like my shoe, but her face nothing like so clean
kept: for why? she sweats; a man may go over shoes in
the grime of it.

ANTIPHOLUS OF SYRACUSE
That's a fault that water will mend.

DROMIO OF SYRACUSE
No, sir, 'tis in grain; Noah's flood could not do it.

ANTIPHOLUS OF SYRACUSE
What's her name?

DROMIO OF SYRACUSE
Nell, sir; but her name and three quarters, that's an ell
and three quarters, will not measure her from hip to
hip.

ANTIPHOLUS OF SYRACUSE
Then she bears some breadth?

DROMIO OF SYRACUSE
No longer from head to foot than from hip to hip: she
is spherical, like a globe; I could find out countries in
her.

ANTIPHOLUS OF SYRACUSE
In what part of her body stands Ireland?

DROMIO OF SYRACUSE
Marry, sir, in her buttocks: I found it out by the bogs.

ANTIPHOLUS OF SYRACUSE
Where Scotland?

DROMIO OF SYRACUSE
I found it by the barrenness; hard in the palm of the
  hand.

ANTIPHOLUS OF SYRACUSE
Where France?

DROMIO OF SYRACUSE
In her forehead; arm'd and reverted, making war
against her heir.

ANTIPHOLUS OF EPHESUS Who talks within there? ho, open the door!

ANTIPHOLUS OF SYRACUSE
Where England?

DROMIO OF SYRACUSE
I look'd for the chalky cliffs, but I could find no
whiteness in them; but I guess it stood in her chin, by
the salt rheum that ran between France and it.

ANTIPHOLUS OF SYRACUSE
Where Spain?

DROMIO OF SYRACUSE
Faith, I saw it not; but I felt it hot in her breath.

ANTIPHOLUS OF SYRACUSE
Where America, the Indies?

DROMIO OF SYRACUSE
O, sir, upon her nose, all o'er embellish'd with rubies,
carbuncles, sapphires, declining their rich aspect to the
hot breath of Spain; who sent whole armadoes of
caracks to be ballast at her nose.

ANTIPHOLUS OF SYRACUSE
Where stood Belgia, the Netherlands?

DROMIO OF SYRACUSE
O, sir, I did not look so low. To conclude, this drudge,
or diviner, laid claim to me; call'd me Dromio; swore I
was assured to her; told me what privy marks I had
about me, as, the mark of my shoulder, the mole in my
neck, the great wart on my left arm, that I, amazed, ran
from her as a witch:
And, I think, if my breast had not been made of faith,
  and my heart of steel,
She had transform'd me to a curtal dog, and made me
  turn i'th'wheel.

ANTIPHOLUS OF SYRACUSE
Go hie thee presently post to the road: —
An if the wind blow any way from shore,
I will not harbour in this town to-night: —
If any bark put forth, come to the mart,
Where I will walk till thou return to me.
If every one knows us, and we know none,
'Tis time, I think, to trudge, pack, and be gone.

DROMIO OF SYRACUSE
As from a bear a man would run for life,
So fly I from her that would be my wife.   [*Exit.*

ANTIPHOLUS OF SYRACUSE
There's none but witches do inhabit here;
And therefore 'tis high time that I were hence.
She that doth call me husband, even my soul
Doth for a wife abhor. But her fair sister,
Possess'd with such a gentle sovereign grace,
Of such enchanting presence and discourse,
Hath almost made me traitor to myself:
But, lest myself be guilty to self-wrong,
I'll stop mine ears against the mermaid's song.

DROMIO OF SYRACUSE I, amazed, ran from her as a witch.

Enter ANGELO *with the chain.*

ANGELO
Master Antipholus, —
ANTIPHOLUS OF SYRACUSE
                    Ay, that's my name.
ANGELO
I know it well, sir: — lo, here's the chain.
I thought to have ta'en you at the Porpentine:
The chain unfinish'd made me stay thus long.
ANTIPHOLUS OF SYRACUSE
What is your will that I shall do with this?
ANGELO
What please yourself, sir: I have made it for you.
ANTIPHOLUS OF SYRACUSE
Made it for me, sir! I bespoke it not.
ANGELO
Not once, nor twice, but twenty times you have.
Go home with it, and please your wife withal;
And soon at supper-time I'll visit you,
And then receive my money for the chain.
ANTIPHOLUS OF SYRACUSE
I pray you, sir, receive the money now,
For fear you ne'er see chain nor money more.
ANGELO
You are a merry man, sir: fare you well.   [*Exit.*
ANTIPHOLUS OF SYRACUSE
What I should think of this, I cannot tell:
But this I think, there's no man is so vain
That would refuse so fair an offer'd chain.
I see a man here needs not live by shifts,
When in the streets he meets such golden gifts.
I'll to the mart, and there for Dromio stay:
If any ship put out, then straight away.   [*Exit.*

ACT IV

SCENE I

A public place.

Enter SECOND MERCHANT, ANGELO, *and an*
OFFICER.

SECOND MERCHANT
You know since Pentecost the sum is due,
And since I have not much importun'd you;
Nor now I had not, but that I am bound
To Persia, and want guilders for my voyage:
Therefore make present satisfaction,
Or I'll attach you by this officer.
ANGELO
Even just the sum that I do owe to you
Is growing to me by Antipholus;
And in the instant that I met with you
He had of me a chain: at five o'clock
I shall receive the money for the same.
Pleaseth you walk with me down to his house,
I will discharge my bond, and thank you too.
OFFICER
That labour may you save: see where he comes.

Enter ANTIPHOLUS OF EPHESUS *and* DROMIO
OF EPHESUS *from the* COURTEZAN'S.

ANTIPHOLUS OF EPHESUS
While I go to the goldsmith's house, go thou
And buy a rope's-end: that will I bestow
Among my wife and her confederates
For locking me out of my doors by day. —
But, soft! I see the goldsmith. — Get thee gone;
Buy thou a rope, and bring it home to me.
DROMIO OF EPHESUS
I buy a thousand pound a year! I buy a rope!   [*Exit.*
ANTIPHOLUS OF EPHESUS
A man is well holp up that trusts to you:
You promised your presence and the chain;
But neither chain nor goldsmith came to me.
Belike you thought our love would last too long,
If it were chain'd together, and therefore came not.
ANGELO
Saving your merry humour, here's the note
How much your chain weighs to the utmost carat,
The fineness of the gold, and chargeful fashion,
Which doth amount to three odd ducats more
Than I stand debted to this gentleman:
I pray you, see him presently discharg'd,
For he is bound to sea and stays but for it.
ANTIPHOLUS OF EPHESUS
I am not furnish'd with the present money;
Besides, I have some business in the town.
Good signior, take the stranger to my house,
And with you take the chain, and bid my wife
Disburse the sum on the receipt thereof:
Perchance I will be there as soon as you.
ANGELO
Then you will bring the chain to her yourself?
ANTIPHOLUS OF EPHESUS
No; bear it with you, lest I come not time enough.
ANGELO
Well, sir, I will. Have you the chain about you?
ANTIPHOLUS OF EPHESUS
An if I have not, sir, I hope you have;
Or else you may return without your money.
ANGELO
Nay, come, I pray you, sir, give me the chain:
Both wind and tide stays for this gentleman,
And I, to blame, have held him here too long.
ANTIPHOLUS OF EPHESUS
Good Lord, you use this dalliance to excuse
Your breach of promise to the Porpentine.
I should have chid you for not bringing it,
But, like a shrew, you first begin to brawl.
SECOND MERCHANT
The hour steals on; I pray you, sir, dispatch.
ANGELO
You hear how he importunes me; — the chain! —
ANTIPHOLUS OF EPHESUS
Why, give it to my wife, and fetch your money.
ANGELO
Come, come, you know I gave it you even now.
Either send the chain, or send me by some token.

ANTIPHOLUS OF EPHESUS
Fie, now you run this humour out of breath.
Come, where's the chain? I pray you, let me see it.
SECOND MERCHANT
My business cannot brook this dalliance.
Good sir, say whe'r you'll answer me or no:
If not, I'll leave him to the officer.
ANTIPHOLUS OF EPHESUS
I answer you! what should I answer you?
ANGELO
The money that you owe me for the chain.
ANTIPHOLUS OF EPHESUS
I owe you none till I receive the chain.
ANGELO
You know I gave it you half an hour since.
ANTIPHOLUS OF EPHESUS
You gave me none: you wrong me much to say so.
ANGELO
You wrong me more, sir, in denying it:
Consider how it stands upon my credit.
SECOND MERCHANT
Well, officer, arrest him at my suit.
OFFICER
I do; —
And charge you in the duke's name to obey me.
ANGELO
This touches me in reputation. —
Either consent to pay this sum for me,
Or I attach you by this officer.
ANTIPHOLUS OF EPHESUS
Consent to pay thee that I never had!
Arrest me, foolish fellow, if thou darest.
ANGELO
Here is thy fee; arrest him, officer. —
I would not spare my brother in this case,
If he should scorn me so apparently.
OFFICER
I do arrest you, sir: you hear the suit.
ANTIPHOLUS OF EPHESUS
I do obey thee till I give thee bail. —
But, sirrah, you shall buy this sport as dear
As all the metal in your shop will answer.
ANGELO
Sir, sir, I shall have law in Ephesus,
To your notorious shame; I doubt it not.

Enter DROMIO OF SYRACUSE *from the Bay.*

DROMIO OF SYRACUSE
Master, there's a bark of Epidamnum
That stays but till her owner comes aboard,
And then she bears away. Our fraughtage, sir,
I have convey'd aboard; and I have bought
The oil, the balsamum, and aqua-vitæ.
The ship is in her trim; the merry wind
Blows fair from land: they stay for naught at all
But for their owner, master, and yourself.
ANTIPHOLUS OF EPHESUS
How now! a madman! Why, thou peevish sheep,

OFFICER I do arrest you, sir: you hear the suit.

What ship of Epidamnum stays for me?
DROMIO OF SYRACUSE
A ship you sent me to, to hire waftage.
ANTIPHOLUS OF EPHESUS
Thou drunken slave, I sent thee for a rope,
And told thee to what purpose and what end.
DROMIO OF SYRACUSE
You sent me for a rope's-end as soon:
You sent me to the bay, sir, for a bark.
ANTIPHOLUS OF EPHESUS
I will debate this matter at more leisure,
And teach your ears to list me with more heed.
To Adriana, villain, hie thee straight:
Give her this key, and tell her, in the desk
That's cover'd o'er with Turkish tapestry
There is a purse of ducats; let her send it:
Tell her I am arrested in the street,
And that shall bail me: hie thee, slave, be gone. —
On, officer, to prison till it come.
[*Exeunt* SECOND MERCHANT, ANGELO, OFFICER,
and ANTIPHOLUS OF EPHESUS.
DROMIO OF SYRACUSE
To Adriana! that is where we dined,
Where Dowsabel did claim me for her husband:
She is too big, I hope, for me to compass.
Thither I must, although against my will,
For servants must their masters' minds fulfil.   [*Exit.*

SCENE II

The house of ANTIPHOLUS OF EPHESUS.

Enter ADRIANA *and* LUCIANA.

ADRIANA
Ah, Luciana, did he tempt thee so?
  Mightst thou perceive austerely in his eye
That he did plead in earnest, yea or no?
  Look'd he or red or pale, or sad or merrily?
What observation madest thou, in this case,
Of his heart's meteors tilting in his face?
LUCIANA
First he denied you had in him no right.
ADRIANA
He meant he did me none; the more my spite.
LUCIANA
Then swore he that he was a stranger here.
ADRIANA
And true he swore, though yet forsworn he were.
LUCIANA
Then pleaded I for you.
ADRIANA
                          And what said he?
LUCIANA
That love I begg'd for you he begg'd of me.
ADRIANA
With what persuasion did he tempt thy love?
LUCIANA
With words that in an honest suit might move.
First he did praise my beauty, then my speech.
ADRIANA
Didst speak him fair?
LUCIANA
                  Have patience, I beseech.
ADRIANA
I cannot, nor I will not, hold me still;

My tongue, though not my heart, shall have his will.
He is deformed, crooked, old, and sere,
Ill-fac'd, worse-bodied, shapeless everywhere;
Vicious, ungentle, foolish, blunt, unkind;
Stigmatical in making, worse in mind.
LUCIANA
Who would be jealous, then, of such a one?
No evil lost is wail'd when it is gone.
ADRIANA
Ah, but I think him better than I say,
  And yet would herein others' eyes were worse.
Far from her nest the lapwing cries away:
  My heart prays for him, though my tongue do curse.

Enter DROMIO OF SYRACUSE.

DROMIO OF SYRACUSE
Here, go; the desk, the purse! sweet, now, make haste.
LUCIANA
How hast thou lost thy breath?
DROMIO OF SYRACUSE
                          By running fast.
ADRIANA
Where is thy master, Dromio? is he well?
DROMIO OF SYRACUSE
No, he's in Tartar limbo, worse than hell.
A devil in an everlasting garment hath him;
One whose hard heart is button'd up with steel;
A fiend, a fairy, pitiless and rough;
A wolf, nay, worse, — a fellow all in buff;
A back-friend, a shoulder-clapper, one that
  countermands
The passages of alleys, creeks, and narrow lands;
A hound that runs counter, and yet draws dry-foot well;
One that, before the judgement, carries poor souls to
  hell.
ADRIANA
Why, man, what is the matter?
DROMIO OF SYRACUSE
I do not know the matter: he is 'rested on the case.
ADRIANA
What, is he arrested? tell me at whose suit.
DROMIO OF SYRACUSE
I know not at whose suit he is arrested well;
But is in a suit of buff which 'rested him, that can I tell.
Will you send him, mistress, redemption, the money
  in his desk?
ADRIANA
Go fetch it, sister. — This I wonder at,
                          [*Exit* LUCIANA.
That he, unknown to me, should be in debt. —
Tell me, was he arrested on a band?
DROMIO OF SYRACUSE
Not on a band, but on a stronger thing, —
A chain, a chain: — do you not hear it ring?
ADRIANA
What, the chain?
DROMIO OF SYRACUSE
No, no, the bell: — 'tis time that I were gone:
It was two ere I left him, and now the clock strikes one.
ADRIANA
The hours come back! that did I never hear.
DROMIO OF SYRACUSE
O, yes; if any hour meet a sergeant, 'a turns back for
  very fear.
ADRIANA
As if Time were in debt! how fondly dost thou reason!
DROMIO OF SYRACUSE
Time is a very bankrout, and owes more than he's
  worth to season.
Nay, he's a thief too: have you not heard men say,
That Time comes stealing on by night and day?
If Time be in debt and theft, and a sergeant in the way,
Hath he not reason to turn back an hour in a day?

Enter LUCIANA *with the purse.*

ADRIANA
Go, Dromio; there's the money, bear it straight;
  And bring thy master home immediately. —
Come, sister: I am press'd down with conceit, —
  Conceit, my comfort and my injury.   [*Exeunt.*

SCENE III

A public place.

Enter ANTIPHOLUS OF SYRACUSE.

ANTIPHOLUS OF SYRACUSE
There's not a man I meet but doth salute me
As if I were their well-acquainted friend;
And every one doth call me by my name.
Some tender money to me; some invite me;

Some other give me thanks for kindnesses;
Some offer me commodities to buy; —
Even now a tailor call'd me in his shop,
And show'd me silks that he had bought for me,
And therewithal took measure of my body.
Sure, these are but imaginary wiles,
And Lapland sorcerers inhabit here.

Enter DROMIO OF SYRACUSE.

DROMIO OF SYRACUSE
Master, here's the gold you sent me for. — What, have
  you got the picture of old Adam new-apparell'd?
ANTIPHOLUS OF SYRACUSE
What gold is this? what Adam dost thou mean?
DROMIO OF SYRACUSE
Not that Adam that kept the Paradise, but that Adam
that keeps the prison: he that goes in the calf's skin that
was kill'd for the Prodigal; he that came behind you,
sir, like an evil angel, and bid you forsake your liberty.
ANTIPHOLUS OF SYRACUSE
I understand thee not.
DROMIO OF SYRACUSE
No? why, 'tis a plain case: he that went, like a base-viol,
in a case of leather; the man, sir, that, when gentlemen
are tired, gives them a sob, and 'rests them; he, sir, that
takes pity on decay'd men, and gives them suits of
durance; he that sets up his rest to do more exploits
with his mace than a morris-pike.
ANTIPHOLUS OF SYRACUSE
What, thou mean'st an officer?
DROMIO OF SYRACUSE
Ay, sir, the sergeant of the band; he that brings any
man to answer it that breaks his band; one that thinks a
man always going to bed, and says, 'God give you good
rest!'
ANTIPHOLUS OF SYRACUSE
Well, sir, there rest in your foolery. Is there any ship
puts forth to-night? may we be gone?
DROMIO OF SYRACUSE
Why, sir, I brought you word an hour since, that the
bark Expedition put forth to-night; and then were you
hinder'd by the sergeant, to tarry for the hoy Delay.
Here are the angels that you sent for to deliver you.
ANTIPHOLUS OF SYRACUSE
The fellow is distract, and so am I;
And here we wander in illusions:
Some blessed power deliver us from hence!

Enter a COURTEZAN.

COURTEZAN
Well met, well met, Master Antipholus.
I see, sir, you have found the goldsmith now:
Is that the chain you promis'd me to-day?
ANTIPHOLUS OF SYRACUSE
Satan, avoid! I charge thee, tempt me not.
DROMIO OF SYRACUSE
Master, is this Mistress Satan?
ANTIPHOLUS OF SYRACUSE
It is the devil.
DROMIO OF SYRACUSE
Nay, she is worse, she is the devil's dam; and here she
comes in the habit of a light wench: and thereof comes
that the wenches say, 'God damn me;' that's as much to
say, 'God make me a light wench.' It is written, they
appear to men like angels of light: light is an effect of
fire, and fire will burn; *ergo*, light wenches will burn.
Come not near her.
COURTEZAN
Your man and you are marvellous merry, sir.
Will you go with me? We'll mend our dinner here.
DROMIO OF SYRACUSE
Master, if you do, expect spoon-meat; so bespeak a long
  spoon.
ANTIPHOLUS OF SYRACUSE
Why, Dromio?
DROMIO OF SYRACUSE
Marry, he must have a long spoon that must eat with
  the devil.
ANTIPHOLUS OF SYRACUSE
Avoid, thou fiend! what tell'st thou me of supping?
Thou art, as you are all, a sorceress:
I conjure thee to leave me and be gone.
COURTEZAN
Give me the ring of mine you had at dinner,
Or, for my diamond, the chain you promised;
And I'll be gone, sir, and not trouble you.
DROMIO OF SYRACUSE
Some devils ask but the parings of one's nail,
A rush, a hair, a drop of blood, a pin,
A nut, a cherry-stone;

But she, more covetous, would have a chain.
Master, be wise: an if you give it her,
The devil will shake her chain, and fright us with it.

COURTEZAN
I pray you, sir, my ring, or else the chain:
I hope you do not mean to cheat me so.

ANTIPHOLUS OF SYRACUSE
Avaunt, thou witch! — Come, Dromio, let us go.

DROMIO OF SYRACUSE
'Fly pride,' says the peacock: mistress, that you
    know.

        [*Exeunt* ANTIPHOLUS OF SYRACUSE
                and DROMIO OF SYRACUSE.

COURTEZAN
Now, out of doubt Antipholus is mad,
Else would he never so demean himself.
A ring he hath of mine worth forty ducats,
And for the same he promised me a chain:
Both one and other he denies me now.
The reason that I gather he is mad, —
Besides this present instance of his rage, —
Is a mad tale he told to-day at dinner,
Of his own doors being shut against his entrance.
Belike his wife, acquainted with his fits,
On purpose shut the doors against his way.
My way is now to hie home to his house,
And tell his wife that, being lunatic,
He rush'd into my house, and took perforce
My ring away. This course I fittest choose;
For forty ducats is too much to lose.

                [*Exit.*

SCENE IV

A street.

Enter ANTIPHOLUS OF EPHESUS
and the OFFICER.

ANTIPHOLUS OF EPHESUS
Fear me not, man; I will not break away:
I'll give thee, ere I leave thee, so much money,
To warrant thee, as I am 'rested for.
My wife is in a wayward mood to-day,
And will not lightly trust the messenger:
That I should be attach'd in Ephesus,
I tell you, 'twill sound harshly in her ears. —
Here comes my man; I think he brings the money.

Enter DROMIO OF EPHESUS *with a rope's-end.*
How now, sir! have you that I sent you for?

DROMIO OF EPHESUS
Here's that, I warrant you, will pay them all.

ANTIPHOLUS OF EPHESUS
But where's the money?

DROMIO OF EPHESUS
Why, sir, I gave the money for the rope.

ANTIPHOLUS OF EPHESUS
Five hundred ducats, villain, for a rope?

DROMIO OF EPHESUS
I'll serve you, sir, five hundred at the rate.

ANTIPHOLUS OF EPHESUS
To what end did I bid thee hie thee home?

DROMIO OF EPHESUS
To a rope's-end, sir; and to that end am I return'd.

ANTIPHOLUS OF EPHESUS
And to that end, sir, I will welcome you.   [*Beating him.*

OFFICER
Good sir, be patient.

DROMIO OF EPHESUS
Nay, 'tis for me to be patient; I am in adversity.

OFFICER
Good, now, hold thy tongue.

DROMIO OF EPHESUS
Nay, rather persuade him to hold his hands.

ANTIPHOLUS OF EPHESUS
Thou whoreson, senseless villain!

DROMIO OF EPHESUS
I would I were senseless, sir, that I might not feel your
    blows.

ANTIPHOLUS OF EPHESUS
Thou art sensible in nothing but blows, and so is an
    ass.

DROMIO OF EPHESUS
I am an ass, indeed; you may prove it by my long ears. —
I have served him from the hour of my nativity to this
instant, and have nothing at his hands for my service but
blows. When I am cold, he heats me with beating; when
I am warm, he cools me with beating; I am waked with it
when I sleep; raised with it when I sit; driven out of
doors with it when I go from home; welcomed home
with it when I return: nay, I bear it on my shoulders, as a
beggar wont her brat; and, I think, when he hath lamed

me, I shall beg with it from door to door.

ANTIPHOLUS OF EPHESUS
Come, go along; my wife is coming yonder.

Enter ADRIANA, LUCIANA, *the* COURTEZAN, *and a*
schoolmaster call'd PINCH.

DROMIO OF EPHESUS
Mistress, *respice finem*, respect your end; — or rather,
    the prophecy like the parrot, 'Beware the rope's-end.'

ANTIPHOLUS OF EPHESUS
Wilt thou still talk?   [*Beating him.*

COURTEZAN
How say you now? is not your husband mad?

ADRIANA
His incivility confirms no less. —
Good Doctor Pinch, you are a conjurer;
Establish him in his true sense again,
And I will please you what you will demand.

LUCIANA
Alas, how fiery and how sharp he looks!

COURTEZAN
Mark how he trembles in his ecstasy!

PINCH
Give me your hand, and let me feel your pulse.

ANTIPHOLUS OF EPHESUS
There is my hand, and let it feel your ear.   [*Striking him.*

PINCH
I charge thee, Satan, hous'd within this man,
To yield possession to my holy prayers,
And to thy state of darkness hie thee straight;
I conjure thee by all the saints in heaven!

ANTIPHOLUS OF EPHESUS
Peace, doting wizard, peace! I am not mad.

ADRIANA
O, that thou wert not, poor distressed soul!

ANTIPHOLUS OF EPHESUS
You minion, you, are these your customers?
Did this companion with the saffron face
Revel and feast it at my house to-day,
Whilst upon me the guilty doors were shut,
And I denied to enter in my house?

ADRIANA
O husband, God doth know you din'd at home;
Where would you had remain'd until this time,
Free from these slanders and this open shame!

ANTIPHOLUS OF EPHESUS
Dined at home! — Thou villain, what sayest thou?

DROMIO OF EPHESUS
Sir, sooth to say, you did not dine at home.

ANTIPHOLUS OF EPHESUS
Were not my doors lock'd up, and I shut out?

DROMIO OF EPHESUS
Perdy, your doors were lock'd, and you shut out.

ANTIPHOLUS OF EPHESUS
And did not she herself revile me there?

DROMIO OF EPHESUS
Sans fable, she herself revil'd you there.

ANTIPHOLUS OF EPHESUS
Did not her kitchen-maid rail, taunt, and scorn me?

DROMIO OF EPHESUS
Certes, she did; the kitchen-vestal scorn'd ye.

ANTIPHOLUS OF EPHESUS
And did not I in rage depart from thence?

DROMIO OF EPHESUS
In verity you did; — my bones bear witness,
That since have felt the vigour of his rage.

ADRIANA
Is't good to soothe him in these contraries?

PINCH
It is no shame: the fellow finds his vein,
And, yielding to him, humours well his frenzy.

ANTIPHOLUS OF EPHESUS
Thou hast suborn'd the goldsmith to arrest me.

ADRIANA
Alas, I sent you money to redeem you,
By Dromio here, who came in haste for it.

DROMIO OF EPHESUS
Money by me! heart and good-will you might;
But surely, master, not a rag of money.

ANTIPHOLUS OF EPHESUS
Went'st not thou to her for a purse of ducats?

ADRIANA
He came to me, and I deliver'd it.

LUCIANA
And I am witness with her that she did.

DROMIO OF EPHESUS
God and the rope-maker bear me witness
That I was sent for nothing but a rope!

PINCH [*aside to* ADRIANA].
Mistress, both man and master is possess'd;
I know it by their pale and deadly looks:
They must be bound, and laid in some dark room.

ANTIPHOLUS OF EPHESUS
Say, wherefore didst thou lock me forth to-day —
And why dost thou deny the bag of gold?

ADRIANA
I did not, gentle husband, lock thee forth.

DROMIO OF EPHESUS
And, gentle master, I receiv'd no gold;
But I confess, sir, that we were lock'd out.

ADRIANA
Dissembling villain, thou speak'st false in both.

ANTIPHOLUS OF EPHESUS
Dissembling harlot, thou art false in all;
And art confederate with a damned pack
To make a loathsome abject scorn of me:
But with these nails I'll pluck out those false eyes,
That would behold in me this shameful sport.

ADRIANA
O, bind him, bind him! let him not come near me.

PINCH
More company! — The fiend is strong within him.

LUCIANA
Ay me, poor man, how pale and wan he looks!

Enter three or four, and offer to bind him; he strives.

ANTIPHOLUS OF EPHESUS
What, will you murder me? — Thou gaoler, thou,
I am thy prisoner: wilt thou suffer them
To make a rescue?

OFFICER
            Masters, let him go:
He is my prisoner, and you shall not have him.

PINCH
Go bind this man, for he is frantic too.
            [*They bind* DROMIO OF EPHESUS.

ADRIANA
What wilt thou do, thou peevish officer?
Hast thou delight to see a wretched man
Do outrage and displeasure to himself?

OFFICER
He is my prisoner: if I let him go,
The debt he owes will be required of me.

ADRIANA
I will discharge thee ere I go from thee:
Bear me forthwith unto his creditor,
And, knowing how the debt grows, I will pay it. —
Good master doctor, see him safe convey'd
Home to my house. — O most unhappy day!

ANTIPHOLUS OF EPHESUS
O most unhappy strumpet!

DROMIO OF EPHESUS
Master, I am here enter'd in bond for you.

ANTIPHOLUS OF EPHESUS
Out on thee, villain! wherefore dost thou mad me?

DROMIO OF EPHESUS
Will you be bound for nothing? be mad, good master;
    cry, 'The devil!'

LUCIANA
God help, poor souls, how idly do they talk!

ADRIANA
Go bear him hence. — Sister, go you with me.
            [*Exeunt* PINCH *and* ASSISTANTS,
                with ANTIPHOLUS OF EPHESUS
                and DROMIO OF EPHESUS.
Say now whose suit is he arrested at?

OFFICER
One Angelo, a goldsmith: do you know him?

ADRIANA
I know the man. What is the sum he owes?

OFFICER
Two hundred ducats.

ADRIANA
            Say, how grows it due?

OFFICER
Due for a chain your husband had of him.

ADRIANA
He did bespeak a chain for me, but had it not.

COURTEZAN
Whenas your husband, all in rage, to-day
Came to my house, and took away my ring, —
The ring I saw upon his finger now, —
Straight after did I meet him with a chain.

ADRIANA
It may be so, but I did never see it. —
Come, gaoler, bring me where the goldsmith is:
I long to know the truth hereof at large.

DROMIO OF EPHESUS Here's that, I warrant you, will pay them all.

Enter ANTIPHOLUS OF SYRACUSE *with his rapier drawn, and* DROMIO OF SYRACUSE.

LUCIANA
God, for thy mercy! they are loose again.
ADRIANA
And come with naked swords. Let's call more help,
To have them bound again.
OFFICER
　　　　　　　Away! they'll kill us.

[*Exeunt* ADRIANA, *etc.,*　as fast as may be, frighted.

ANTIPHOLUS OF SYRACUSE
I see these witches are afraid of swords.
DROMIO OF SYRACUSE
She that would be your wife now ran from you.
ANTIPHOLUS OF SYRACUSE
Come to the Centaur; fetch our stuff from thence:
I long that we were safe and sound aboard.
DROMIO OF SYRACUSE
Faith, stay here this night; they will surely do us no
harm: you saw they speak us fair, give us gold:
methinks they are such a gentle nation, that, but for the
mountain of mad flesh that claims marriage of me, I
could find in my heart to stay here still, and turn witch.
ANTIPHOLUS OF SYRACUSE
I will not stay to-night for all the town;
Therefore away, to get our stuff aboard.　　[*Exeunt.*

ACT V

SCENE I

Before an abbey.

Enter SECOND MERCHANT *and* ANGELO.

ANGELO
I am sorry, sir, that I have hinder'd you;
But, I protest, he had the chain of me,
Though most dishonestly he doth deny it.
SECOND MERCHANT
How is the man esteem'd here in the city?
ANGELO
Of very reverend reputation, sir,
Of credit infinite, highly beloved,
Second to none that lives here in the city:
His word might bear my wealth at any time.
SECOND MERCHANT
Speak softly: yonder, as I think, he walks.

Enter ANTIPHOLUS OF SYRACUSE *and* DROMIO
OF SYRACUSE.

ANGELO
'Tis so; and that self chain about his neck,
Which he forswore most monstrously to have.
Good sir, draw near to me, I'll speak to him. —

Signior Antipholus, I wonder much
That you would put me to this shame and trouble;
And, not without some scandal to yourself,
With circumstance and oaths so to deny
This chain, which now you wear so openly:
Beside the charge, the shame, imprisonment,
You have done wrong to this my honest friend;
Who, but for staying on our controversy,
Had hoisted sail and put to sea to-day:
This chain you had of me; can you deny it?
ANTIPHOLUS OF SYRACUSE
I think I had; I never did deny it.
SECOND MERCHANT
Yes, that you did, sir, and forswore it too.
ANTIPHOLUS OF SYRACUSE
Who heard me to deny it or forswear it?
SECOND MERCHANT
These ears of mine, thou know'st, did hear thee:
Fie on thee, wretch! 'tis pity that thou livest
To walk where any honest men resort.

ANTIPHOLUS OF SYRACUSE
Thou art a villain to impeach me thus:
I'll prove mine honour and mine honesty
Against thee presently, if thou dar'st stand.
SECOND MERCHANT
I dare, and do defy thee for a villain.　　[*They draw.*

Enter ADRIANA, LUCIANA,
the COURTEZAN, *and others.*

ADRIANA
Hold, hurt him not, for God's sake! he is mad. —
Some get within him, take his sword away:
Bind Dromio too, and bear them to my house.
DROMIO OF SYRACUSE
Run, master, run; for God's sake, take a house!
This is some priory: — in, or we are spoil'd.

[*Exeunt* ANTIPHOLUS OF SYRACUSE
and DROMIO OF SYRACUSE *to the abbey.*

Enter LADY ABBESS.

ABBESS
Be quiet, people. Wherefore throng you hither?
ADRIANA
To fetch my poor distracted husband hence.
Let us come in, that we may bind him fast,
And bear him home for his recovery.
ANGELO
I knew he was not in his perfect wits.
SECOND MERCHANT
I am sorry now that I did draw on him.
ABBESS
How long hath this possession held the man?
ADRIANA
This week he hath been heavy, sour, sad,
And much different from the man he was;
But till this afternoon his passion
Ne'er brake into extremity of rage.
ABBESS
Hath he not lost much wealth by wrack of sea?
Buried some dear friend? Hath not else his eye
Stray'd his affection in unlawful love, —
A sin prevailing much in youthful men,
Who give their eyes the liberty of gazing?
Which of these sorrows is he subject to?
ADRIANA
To none of these, except it be the last;
Namely, some love that drew him oft from home.
ABBESS
You should for that have reprehended him.
ADRIANA
Why, so I did.
ABBESS
　　　　　Ay, but not rough enough.
ADRIANA
As roughly as my modesty would let me.

PINCH Go bind this man, for he is frantic too.

ABBESS
Haply, in private.
ADRIANA
          And in assemblies too.
ABBESS
Ay, but not enough.
ADRIANA
It was the copy of our conference:
In bed, he slept not for my urging it;
At board, he fed not for my urging it;
Alone, it was the subject of my theme;
In company I often glanced it;
Still did I tell him it was vile and bad.
ABBESS
And thereof came it that the man was mad:
The venom-clamours of a jealous woman
Poisons more deadly than a mad-dog's tooth.
It seems his sleeps were hinder'd by thy railing:
And thereof comes it that his head is light.
Thou say'st his meat was sauc'd with thy upbraidings:
Unquiet meals make ill digestions, —
Thereof the raging fire of fever bred;
And what's a fever but a fit of madness?
Thou say'st his sports were hinder'd by thy brawls:
Sweet recreation barr'd, what doth ensue
But moody and dull melancholy,
Kinsman to grim and comfortless despair;
And at her heels a huge infectious troop
Of pale distemperatures and foes to life?
In food, in sport, and life-preserving rest
To be disturb'd, would mad or man or beast:
The consequence is, then, thy jealous fits
Have scared thy husband from the use of wits.
LUCIANA
She never reprehended him but mildly,
When he demean'd himself rough-rude and wildly. —
Why bear you these rebukes, and answer not?
ADRIANA
She did betray me to my own reproof. —
Good people, enter, and lay hold on him.
ABBESS
No, not a creature enters in my house.
ADRIANA
Then let your servants bring my husband forth.
ABBESS
Neither: he took this place for sanctuary,
And it shall privilege him from your hands
Till I have brought him to his wits again,
Or lose my labour in assaying it.
ADRIANA
I will attend my husband, be his nurse,
Diet his sickness, for it is my office,
And will have no attorney but myself;
And therefore let me have him home with me.
ABBESS
Be patient; for I will not let him stir
Till I have us'd the approved means I have,
With wholesome syrups, drugs, and holy prayers,
To make of him a formal man again:
It is a branch and parcel of mine oath,
A charitable duty of my order.
Therefore depart, and leave him here with me.
ADRIANA
I will not hence, and leave my husband here:
And ill it doth beseem your holiness
To separate the husband and the wife.
ABBESS
Be quiet, and depart: thou shalt not have him.   [*Exit.*
LUCIANA
Complain unto the duke of this indignity.
ADRIANA
Come, go: I will fall prostrate at his feet,
And never rise until my tears and prayers
Have won his grace to come in person hither,
And take perforce my husband from the abbess.
SECOND MERCHANT
By this, I think, the dial points at five:
Anon, I'm sure, the duke himself in person
Comes this way to the melancholy vale,
The place of death and sorry execution,
Behind the ditches of the abbey here.
ANGELO
Upon what cause?
SECOND MERCHANT
To see a reverend Syracusian merchant,
Who put unluckily into this bay
Against the laws and statutes of this town,
Beheaded publicly for his offence.
ANGELO
See where they come: we will behold his death.

SECOND MERCHANT Speak softly: yonder, as I think, he walks.

LUCIANA
Kneel to the duke before he pass the abbey.
   Enter DUKE, *attended*; AEGEON *bareheaded*; *with the*
      HEADSMAN *and other* OFFICERS.
DUKE OF EPHESUS
Yet once again proclaim it publicly,
If any friend will pay the sum for him,
He shall not die, so much we tender him.
ADRIANA
Justice, most sacred duke, against the abbess!
DUKE OF EPHESUS
She is a virtuous and a reverend lady:
It cannot be that she hath done thee wrong.
ADRIANA
May it please your Grace, Antipholus my husband, —
Who I made lord of me and all I had,
At your important letters, — this ill day
A most outrageous fit of madness took him;
That desp'rately he hurried through the street, —
With him his bondman, all as mad as he, —
Doing displeasure to the citizens
By rushing in their houses, bearing thence
Rings, jewels, any thing his rage did like.
Once did I get him bound, and sent him home,
Whilst to take order for the wrongs I went,
That here and there his fury had committed.
Anon, I wot not by what strong escape
He broke from those that had the guard of him;
And both his mad attendant and himself,
Each one with ireful passion, with drawn swords,
Met us again, and, madly bent on us,
Chas'd us away; till, raising of more aid,
We came again to bind them. Then they fled
Into this abbey, whither we pursued them;
And here the abbess shuts the gates on us,
And will not suffer us to fetch him out,
Nor send him forth, that we may bear him hence.
Therefore, most gracious duke, with thy command
Let him be brought forth, and borne hence for help.
DUKE OF EPHESUS
Long since thy husband serv'd me in my wars;
And I to thee engag'd a prince's word,
When thou didst make him master of thy bed,
To do him all the grace and good I could. —
Go, some of you, knock at the abbey-gate,
And bid the lady abbess come to me. —
I will determine this before I stir.
       Enter a SERVANT.
SERVANT
O mistress, mistress, shift and save yourself!

My master and his man are both broke loose,
Beaten the maids a-row, and bound the doctor,
Whose beard they have sing'd off with brands of fire;
And ever, as it blaz'd, they threw on him
Great pails of puddled mire to quench the hair:
My master preaches patience to him, and the while
His man with scissors nicks him like a fool;
And sure, unless you send some present help,
Between them they will kill the conjurer.
ADRIANA
Peace, fool! thy master and his man are here;
And that is false thou dost report to us.
SERVANT
Mistress, upon my life, I tell you true;
I have not breath'd almost since I did see it.
He cries for you, and vows, if he can take you,
To scorch your face, and to disfigure you.   [*Cry within.*
Hark, hark! I hear him, mistress: fly, be gone!
DUKE OF EPHESUS
Come, stand by me; fear nothing. — Guard with
   halberds!
ADRIANA
Ay me, it is my husband! Witness you,
That he is borne about invisible:
Even now we hous'd him in the abbey here;
And now he's there, past thought of human reason.
     Enter ANTIPHOLUS OF EPHESUS
       and DROMIO OF EPHESUS.
ANTIPHOLUS OF EPHESUS
Justice, most gracious duke, O, grant me justice!
Even for the service that long since I did thee,
When I bestrid thee in the wars, and took
Deep scars to save thy life; even for the blood
That then I lost for thee, now grant me justice.
AEGEON
Unless the fear of death doth make me dote,
I see my son Antipholus, and Dromio.
ANTIPHOLUS OF EPHESUS
Justice, sweet prince, against that woman there!
She whom thou gav'st to me to be my wife,
That hath abused and dishonour'd me
Even in the strength and height of injury:
Beyond imagination is the wrong
That she this day hath shameless thrown on me.
DUKE OF EPHESUS
Discover how, and thou shalt find me just.
ANTIPHOLUS OF EPHESUS
This day, great duke, she shut the doors upon me,
While she with harlots feasted in my house.
DUKE OF EPHESUS
A grievous fault. — Say, woman, didst thou so?

DROMIO OF SYRACUSE This is some priory: — in, or we are spoil'd.

ADRIANA
No, my good lord: myself, he, and my sister,
To-day did dine together. So befall my soul
As this is false he burdens me withal!

LUCIANA
Ne'er may I look on day, nor sleep on night,
But she tells to your highness simple truth!

ANGELO
O perjur'd woman! — They are both forsworn:
In this the madman justly chargeth them.

ANTIPHOLUS OF EPHESUS
My liege, I am advised what I say;
Neither disturb'd with the effect of wine,
Nor heady-rash, provok'd with raging ire,
Albeit my wrongs might make one wiser mad.
This woman lock'd me out this day from dinner:
That goldsmith there, were he not pack'd with her,
Could witness it, for he was with me then;
Who parted with me to go fetch a chain,
Promising to bring it to the Porpentine,
Where Balthazar and I did dine together.
Our dinner done, and he not coming thither,
I went to seek him: in the street I met him,
And in his company that gentleman.
There did this perjur'd goldsmith swear me down
That I this day of him receiv'd the chain,
Which, God he knows, I saw not: for the which
He did arrest me with an officer.
I did obey; and sent my peasant home
For certain ducats: he with none return'd.
Then fairly I bespoke the officer
To go in person with me to my house.
By th'way we met
My wife, her sister, and a rabble more
Of vile confederates. Along with them
They brought one Pinch, a hungry lean-fac'd villain,
A mere anatomy, a mountebank,
A threadbare juggler, and a fortune-teller,
A needy, hollow-eyed, sharp-looking wretch,
A living-dead man: this pernicious slave,
Forsooth, took on him as a conjurer;
And, gazing in mine eyes, feeling my pulse,
And with no face, as'twere, outfacing me,
Cries out, I was possess'd. Then all together
They fell upon me, bound me, bore me thence,
And in a dark and dankish vault at home
There left me and my man, both bound together;
Till, gnawing with my teeth my bonds in sunder,
I gain'd my freedom, and immediately
Ran hither to your Grace; whom I beseech
To give me ample satisfaction
For these deep shames and great indignities.

ANGELO
My lord, in truth, thus far I witness with him,
That he din'd not at home, but was lock'd out.

DUKE OF EPHESUS
But had he such a chain of thee or no?

ANGELO
He had, my lord: and when he ran in here,
These people saw the chain about his neck.

SECOND MERCHANT
Besides, I will be sworn these ears of mine
Heard you confess you had the chain of him,
After you first forswore it on the mart:
And thereupon I drew my sword on you;
And then you fled into this abbey here,
From whence, I think, you are come by miracle.

ANTIPHOLUS OF EPHESUS
I never came within these abbey-walls;
Nor ever didst thou draw thy sword on me:
I never saw the chain, so help me heaven!
And this is false you burden me withal!

DUKE OF EPHESUS
Why, what an intricate impeach is this!

I think you all have drunk of Circe's cup.
If here you hous'd him, here he would have been;
If he were mad, he would not plead so coldly: —
You say he din'd at home; the goldsmith here
Denies that saying. — Sirrah, what say you?

DROMIO OF EPHESUS
Sir, he din'd with her there, at the Porpentine.

COURTEZAN
He did; and from my finger snatch'd that ring.

ANTIPHOLUS OF EPHESUS
'Tis true, my liege; this ring I had of her.

DUKE OF EPHESUS
Saw'st thou him enter at the abbey here?

COURTEZAN
As sure, my liege, as I do see your Grace.

DUKE OF EPHESUS
Why, this is strange. — Go call the abbess hither. —
[*Exit one to the* ABBESS.
I think you are all mated or stark mad.

AEGEON
Most mighty duke, vouchsafe me speak a word:
Haply I see a friend will save my life,
And pay the sum that may deliver me.

DUKE OF EPHESUS
Speak freely, Syracusian, what thou wilt.

AEGEON
Is not your name, sir, call'd Antipholus?
And is not that your bondman Dromio?

DROMIO OF EPHESUS
Within this hour I was his bondman, sir,
But he, I thank him, gnaw'd in two my cords:
Now am I Dromio, and his man unbound.

AEGEON
I am sure you both of you remember me.

DROMIO OF EPHESUS
Ourselves we do remember, sir, by you;
For lately we were bound, as you are now.
You are not Pinch's patient, are you, sir?

AEGEON
Why look you strange on me? you know me well.

ANTIPHOLUS OF EPHESUS
I never saw you in my life till now.

AEGEON
O, grief hath chang'd me since you saw me last,
And careful hours with Time's deformed hand
Have written strange defeatures in my face:
But tell me yet, dost thou not know my voice?

ANTIPHOLUS OF EPHESUS
Neither.

AEGEON
Dromio, nor thou?

DROMIO OF EPHESUS
No, trust me, sir, nor I.

ADRIANA Justice, most sacred duke, against the abbess!

AEGEON
I am sure thou dost.

DROMIO OF EPHESUS
Ay, sir, but I am sure I do not; and whatsoever a man
    denies, you are now bound to believe him.

AEGEON
Not know my voice! O time's extremity,
Hast thou so crack'd and splitted my poor tongue
In seven short years, that here my only son
Knows not my feeble key of untuned cares?
Though now this grained face of mine be hid
In sap-consuming winter's drizzled snow,
And all the conduits of my blood froze up,
Yet hath my night of life some memory,
My wasting lamps some fading glimmer left,
My dull deaf ears a little use to hear:
All these old witnesses — I cannot err —
Tell me thou art my son Antipholus.

ANTIPHOLUS OF EPHESUS
I never saw my father in my life.

AEGEON
But seven years since, in Syracusa, boy,
Thou know'st we parted: but perhaps, my son,
Thou sham'st to acknowledge me in misery.

ANTIPHOLUS OF EPHESUS
The duke, and all that know me in the city,
Can witness with me that it is not so:
I ne'er saw Syracusa in my life.

DUKE OF EPHESUS
I tell thee, Syracusian, twenty years
Have I been patron to Antipholus,
During which time he ne'er saw Syracusa:
I see thy age and dangers make thee dote.

Enter ABBESS, *with* ANTIPHOLUS OF SYRACUSE
and DROMIO OF SYRACUSE.

ABBESS
Most mighty duke, behold a man much wrong'd.
               [*All gather to see them.*

ADRIANA
I see two husbands, or mine eyes deceive me.

DUKE OF EPHESUS
One of these men is Genius to the other;
And so of these. Which is the natural man,
And which the spirit? who deciphers them?

DROMIO OF SYRACUSE
I, sir, am Dromio: command him away.

DROMIO OF EPHESUS
I, sir, am Dromio: pray, let me stay.

ANTIPHOLUS OF SYRACUSE
Aegeon art thou not? or else his ghost?

DROMIO OF SYRACUSE
O, my old master! who hath bound him here?

ABBESS
Whoever bound him, I will loose his bonds,
And gain a husband by his liberty. —
Speak, old Aegeon, if thou be'st the man
That hadst a wife once call'd Aemilia,
That bore thee at a burden two fair sons:
O, if thou be'st the same Aegeon, speak,
And speak unto the same Aemilia!

AEGEON
If I dream not, thou art Aemilia:

If thou art she, tell me where is that son
That floated with thee on the fatal raft?

ABBESS
By men of Epidamnum he and I
And the twin Dromio all were taken up;
But by and by rude fishermen of Corinth
By force took Dromio and my son from them,
And me they left with those of Epidamnum.
What then became of them I cannot tell;
I to this fortune that you see me in.

DUKE OF EPHESUS
Why, here begins his morning story right:
These two Antipholus', these two so like,
And these two Dromios, one in semblance, —
Besides her urging of her wrack at sea, —
These are the parents to these children,
Which accidentally are met together. —
Antipholus, thou cam'st from Corinth first?

ANTIPHOLUS OF SYRACUSE
No, sir, not I; I came from Syracuse.

DUKE OF EPHESUS
Stay, stand apart; I know not which is which.

ANTIPHOLUS OF EPHESUS
I came from Corinth, my most gracious lord, —

DROMIO OF EPHESUS
And I with him.

ANTIPHOLUS OF EPHESUS
Brought to this town by that most famous warrior,
Duke Menaphon, your most renowned uncle.

ADRIANA
Which of you two did dine with me to-day?

ANTIPHOLUS OF SYRACUSE
I, gentle mistress.

ADRIANA
           And are not you my husband?

ANTIPHOLUS OF EPHESUS
No; I say nay to that.

ANTIPHOLUS OF SYRACUSE
And so do I; yet did she call me so:
And this fair gentlewoman, her sister here,
Did call me brother. — [*to* LUCIANA] What I told you
    then,
I hope I shall have leisure to make good,
If this be not a dream I see and hear.

ANGELO
That is the chain, sir, which you had of me.

ANTIPHOLUS OF SYRACUSE
I think it be, sir; I deny it not.

ANTIPHOLUS OF EPHESUS
And you, sir, for this chain arrested me.

ANGELO
I think I did, sir; I deny it not.

ADRIANA
I sent you money, sir, to be your bail,
By Dromio; but I think he brought it not.

DROMIO OF EPHESUS
No, none by me.

ANTIPHOLUS OF SYRACUSE
This purse of ducats I receiv'd from you,
And Dromio my man did bring them me.
I see we still did meet each other's man;
And I was ta'en for him, and he for me;

And thereupon these errors are arose.

ANTIPHOLUS OF EPHESUS
These ducats pawn I for my father here.

DUKE OF EPHESUS
It shall not need; thy father hath his life.

COURTEZAN
Sir, I must have that diamond from you.

ANTIPHOLUS OF EPHESUS
There, take it; and much thanks for my good cheer.

ABBESS
Renowned duke, vouchsafe to take the pains
To go with us into the abbey here,
And hear at large discoursed all our fortunes; —
And all that are assembled in this place,
That by this sympathised one day's error
Have suffer'd wrong, go keep us company,
And we shall make full satisfaction. —
Thirty-three years have I but gone in travail
Of you, my sons; and, till this present hour,
My heavy burden ne'er delivered. —
The duke, my husband, and my children both,
And you the calendars of their nativity,
Go to a gossip's feast, and joy with me;
After so long grief, such felicity!

DUKE OF EPHESUS
With all my heart, I'll gossip at this feast.
      [*Exeunt* DUKE, ABBESS, AEGEON,
      COURTEZAN, SECOND MERCHANT,
      ANGELO, *and* ATTENDANTS.

DROMIO OF SYRACUSE
Master, shall I fetch your stuff from shipboard?

ANTIPHOLUS OF EPHESUS
Dromio, what stuff of mine hast thou embark'd?

DROMIO OF SYRACUSE
Your goods that lay at host, sir, in the Centaur.

ANTIPHOLUS OF SYRACUSE
He speaks to me. — I am your master, Dromio:
Come, go with us; we'll look to that anon:
Embrace thy brother there; rejoice with him.
     [*Exeunt* ANTIPHOLUS OF SYRACUSE
     and ANTIPHOLUS OF EPHESUS,
     ADRIANA *and* LUCIANA.

DROMIO OF SYRACUSE
There is a fat friend at your master's house,
That kitchen'd me for you to-day at dinner:
She now shall be my sister, not my wife.

DROMIO OF EPHESUS
Methinks you are my glass, and not my brother:
I see by you I am a sweet-fac'd youth.
Will you walk in to see their gossiping?

DROMIO OF SYRACUSE
Not I, sir; you are my elder.

DROMIO OF EPHESUS
That's a question: how shall we try it?

DROMIO OF SYRACUSE
We'll draw cuts for the senior: till then lead thou first.

DROMIO OF EPHESUS
Nay, then, thus: —
We came into the world like brother and brother;
And now let's go hand in hand, not one before another.
                    [*Exeunt.*

THE TWO GENTLEMEN OF VERONA

DRAMATIS PERSONAE

DUKE OF MILAN, *father to Silvia.*
VALENTINE, } *the two Gentlemen.*
PROTEUS,
ANTONIO, *father to Proteus.*
THURIO, *a foolish rival to Valentine.*
EGLAMOUR, *agent for Silvia in her escape.*
SPEED, *a clownish servant to Valentine.*

LAUNCE, *the like to Proteus.*
PANTHINO, *servant to Antonio.*
HOST, *where Julia lodges.*
OUTLAWS, *with Valentine.*

JULIA, *beloved of Proteus.*
SILVIA, *beloved of Valentine.*

LUCETTA, *waiting-woman to Julia.*

SERVANTS, MUSICIANS.

SCENE — *Verona; Milan; the frontiers of Mantua.*

ACT I

SCENE I

Verona. An open place.

Enter VALENTINE *and* PROTEUS.

VALENTINE
Cease to persuade, my loving Proteus:
Home-keeping youth have ever homely wits.
Were't not affection chains thy tender days
To the sweet glances of thy honour'd love,
I rather would entreat thy company
To see the wonders of the world abroad,
Than, living dully sluggardis'd at home,
Wear out thy youth with shapeless idleness.
But since thou lovest, love still, and thrive therein,
Even as I would, when I to love begin.

PROTEUS
Wilt thou be gone? Sweet Valentine, adieu!
Think on thy Proteus, when thou haply see'st
Some rare note-worthy object in thy travel:
Wish me partaker in thy happiness,
When thou dost meet good hap; and in thy danger,
If ever danger do environ thee,
Commend thy grievance to my holy prayers,
For I will be thy beadsman, Valentine.

VALENTINE
And on a love-book pray for my success?

PROTEUS
Upon some book I love I'll pray for thee.

VALENTINE
That's on some shallow story of deep love;
How young Leander cross'd the Hellespont.

PROTEUS
That's a deep story of a deeper love;
For he was more than over shoes in love.

VALENTINE
'Tis true; for you are over boots in love,
And yet you never swum the Hellespont.

PROTEUS
Over the boots! nay, give me not the boots.

VALENTINE
No, I will not, for it boots thee not.

PROTEUS
                                        What?

VALENTINE
To be in love, where scorn is bought with groans;
Coy looks with heart-sore sighs; one fading moment's mirth
With twenty watchful, weary, tedious nights:

PROTEUS Wilt thou be gone? Sweet Valentine, adieu!

If haply won, perhaps a hapless gain;
If lost, why then a grievous labour won;
However, but a folly bought with wit,
Or else a wit by folly vanquished.

PROTEUS
So, by your circumstance, you call me fool.

VALENTINE
So, by your circumstance, I fear you'll prove.

PROTEUS
'Tis love you cavil at: I am not Love.

VALENTINE
Love is your master, for he masters you:
And he that is so yoked by a fool,
Methinks, should not be chronicled for wise.

PROTEUS
Yet writers say, as in the sweetest bud
The eating canker dwells, so eating love
Inhabits in the finest wits of all.

VALENTINE
And writers say, as the most forward bud
Is eaten by the canker ere it blow,
Even so by love the young and tender wit
Is turn'd to folly; blasting in the bud,
Losing his verdure even in the prime,
And all the fair effects of future hopes.
But wherefore waste I time to counsel thee,
That art a votary to fond desire?
Once more adieu! my father at the road
Expects my coming, there to see me shipp'd.

PROTEUS
And thither will I bring thee, Valentine.

VALENTINE
Sweet Proteus, no; now let us take our leave.
To Milan let me hear from thee by letters
Of thy success in love, and what news else
Betideth here in absence of thy friend;
And likewise will visit thee with mine.

PROTEUS
All happiness bechance to thee in Milan!

VALENTINE
As much to you at home! and so, farewell.   [*Exit.*

PROTEUS
He after honour hunts, I after love:
He leaves his friends to dignify them more;
I leave myself, my friends, and all, for love.
Thou, Julia, thou hast metamorphos'd me, —
Made me neglect my studies, lose my time,
War with good counsel, set the world at naught;
Made wit with musing weak, heart sick with thought.

Enter SPEED.

SPEED
Sir Proteus, save you! Saw you my master?

PROTEUS
But now he parted hence, to embark for Milan.

SPEED
Twenty to one, then, he is shipp'd already,
And I have play'd the sheep in losing him.

PROTEUS
Indeed, a sheep doth very often stray,
An if the shepherd be awhile away.

SPEED
You conclude that my master is a shepherd then, and I a sheep?

PROTEUS
I do.

SPEED
Why, then, my horns are his horns, whether I wake or sleep.

PROTEUS
A silly answer, and fitting well a sheep.

SPEED
This proves me still a sheep.

PROTEUS
True; and thy master a shepherd.

SPEED
Nay, that I can deny by a circumstance.

PROTEUS
It shall go hard but I'll prove it by another.

SPEED
The shepherd seeks the sheep, and not the sheep the shepherd; but I seek my master, and my master seeks not me: therefore I am no sheep.

PROTEUS
The sheep for fodder follow the shepherd, the shepherd for food follows not the sheep; thou for wages followest thy master, thy master for wages follows not thee: therefore thou art a sheep.

SPEED
Such another proof will make me cry 'baa'.

PROTEUS
But, dost thou hear? gavest thou my letter to Julia?

SPEED
Ay, sir: I, a lost mutton, gave your letter to her, a laced mutton; and she, a laced mutton, gave me, a lost mutton, nothing for my labour.

PROTEUS
Here's too small a pasture for such store of muttons.

SPEED
If the ground be overcharged, you were best stick her.

PROTEUS
Nay, in that you are a stray, 'twere best pound you.

SPEED
Nay, sir, less than a pound shall serve me for carrying your letter.

PROTEUS
You mistake; I mean the pound, — a pinfold.

SPEED
From a pound to a pin? fold it over and over,
'Tis threefold too little for carrying a letter to your lover.

PROTEUS
But what said she?

SPEED [*nodding*].
Ay.

PROTEUS
Nod, Ay? — why, that's noddy.

SPEED
You mistook, sir; I say, she did nod: and you ask me if she did nod; and I say, Ay.

PROTEUS
And that set together is — noddy.

SPEED
Now you have taken the pains to set it together, take it for your pains.

PROTEUS
No, no; you shall have it for bearing the letter.

SPEED
Well, I perceive I must be fain to bear with you.

PROTEUS
Why, sir, how do you bear with me?

SPEED
Marry, sir, the letter very orderly; having nothing but the word 'noddy' for my pains.

PROTEUS
Beshrew me, but you have a quick wit.

SPEED
And yet it cannot overtake your slow purse.

PROTEUS
Come, come, open the matter in brief; what said she?

SPEED
Open your purse, that the money and the matter may be both at once deliver'd.

PROTEUS
Well, sir, here is for your pains. [*Giving him money.*] What said she?

SPEED
Truly, sir, I think you'll hardly win her.

PROTEUS
Why, couldst thou perceive so much from her?

SPEED
Sir, I could perceive nothing at all from her; no, not so much as a ducat for delivering your letter: and being so hard to me that brought your mind, I fear she'll prove as hard to you in telling your mind. Give her no token but stones; for she's as hard as steel.

PROTEUS
What? said she nothing?

SPEED
No, not so much as 'Take this for thy pains.' To testify your bounty, I thank you, you have testern'd me; in requital whereof, henceforth carry your letters yourself: and so, sir, I'll commend you to my master.

PROTEUS
Go, go, be gone, to save your ship from wrack,
Which cannot perish having thee aboard,
Being destin'd to a drier death on shore.   [*Exit* SPEED.
I must go send some better messenger:
I fear my Julia would not deign my lines,
Receiving them from such a worthless post.   [*Exit.*

SCENE II

The same. JULIA'S *garden.*

Enter JULIA *and* LUCETTA.

JULIA
But say, Lucetta, now we are alone,
Wouldst thou, then, counsel me to fall in love?

LUCETTA
Ay, madam; so you stumble not unheedfully.

JULIA
Of all the fair resort of gentlemen
That every day with parle encounter me,
In thy opinion which is worthiest love?

LUCETTA
Please you repeat their names, I'll show my mind
According to my shallow simple skill.

JULIA
What think'st thou of the fair Sir Eglamour?

LUCETTA
As of a knight well-spoken, neat, and fine;
But, were I you, he never should be mine.

JULIA
What think'st thou of the rich Mercatio?

LUCETTA
Well of his wealth; but of himself, so-so.

JULIA
What think'st thou of the gentle Proteus?

LUCETTA
Lord, Lord! to see what folly reigns in us!

JULIA
How now! what means this passion at his name?

LUCETTA
Pardon, dear madam: 'tis a passing shame
That I, unworthy body as I am,
Should censure thus on lovely gentlemen.

JULIA
Why not on Proteus, as of all the rest?

LUCETTA
Then thus, — of many good I think him best.

JULIA
Your reason?

LUCETTA
I have no other but a woman's reason;
I think him so, because I think him so.

JULIA
And wouldst thou have me cast my love on him?

LUCETTA
Ay, if you thought your love not cast away.

JULIA
Why, he, of all the rest, hath never mov'd me.

LUCETTA
Yet he, of all the rest, I think, best loves ye.

JULIA
His little speaking shows his love but small.

LUCETTA
Fire that's closest kept burns most of all.
JULIA
They do not love that do not show their love.
LUCETTA
O, they love least that let men know their love.
JULIA
I would I knew his mind.
LUCETTA
Peruse this paper, madam.
JULIA [*reads*].
To Julia. — Say, from whom?
LUCETTA
That the contents will show.
JULIA
Say, say, who gave it thee?
LUCETTA
Sir Valentine's page; and sent, I think, from Proteus.
He would have given it you; but I, being in the way,
Did in your name receive it: pardon the fault, I pray.
JULIA
Now, by my modesty, a goodly broker!
Dare you presume to harbour wanton lines?
To whisper and conspire against my youth?
Now, trust me, 'tis an office of great worth,
And you an officer fit for the place.
There, take the paper: see it be return'd;
Or else return no more into my sight.
LUCETTA
To plead for love deserves more fee than hate.
JULIA
Will ye be gone?
LUCETTA
That you may ruminate.   [*Exit.*
JULIA
And yet I would I had o'erlook'd the letter:
It were a shame to call her back again,
And pray her to a fault for which I chid her.
What fool is she, that knows I am a maid,
And would not force the letter to my view, —
Since maids, in modesty, say 'No' to that
Which they would have the profferer construe 'Ay'!
Fie, fie, how wayward is this foolish love,
That, like a testy babe, will scratch the nurse,
And presently, all humbled, kiss the rod!
How churlishly I chid Lucetta hence,
When willingly I would have had her here!
How angerly I taught my brow to frown,
When inward joy enforc'd my heart to smile!
My penance is, to call Lucetta back,
And ask remission for my folly past. —
What, ho! Lucetta!

Enter LUCETTA.

LUCETTA
                    What would your ladyship?
JULIA
Is't near dinner-time?
LUCETTA
                    I would it were,
That you might kill your stomach on your meat,
And not upon your maid.
JULIA
What is't that you took up so gingerly?
LUCETTA
Nothing.
JULIA
Why didst thou stoop, then?
LUCETTA
To take a paper up that I let fall.
JULIA
And is that paper nothing?
LUCETTA
Nothing concerning me.
JULIA
Then let it lie for those that it concerns.
LUCETTA
Madam, it will not lie where it concerns,
Unless it have a false interpreter.
JULIA
Some love of yours hath writ to you in rhyme.
LUCETTA
That I might sing it, madam, to a tune.
Give me a note: your ladyship can set.
JULIA
As little by such toys as may be possible.
Best sing it to the tune of *Light o' love.*
LUCETTA
It is too heavy for so light a tune.

JULIA
Heavy! belike it hath some burden, then?
LUCETTA
Ay; and melodious were it, would you sing it.
JULIA
And why not you?
LUCETTA
                    I cannot reach so high.
JULIA
Let's see your song. [*Taking the letter.*] How now, minion!
LUCETTA
Keep tune there still, so you will sing it out:
And yet methinks I do not like this tune.
JULIA
You do not?
LUCETTA
                    No, madam; 'tis too sharp.
JULIA
You, minion, are too saucy.
LUCETTA
Nay, now you are too flat,
And mar the concord with too harsh a descant:
There wanteth but a mean to fill your song.
JULIA
The mean is drown'd with your unruly base.
LUCETTA
Indeed, I bid the base for Proteus.
JULIA
This babble shall not henceforth trouble me: —
Here is a coil with protestation! —   [*Tears the letter.*
Go get you gone, and let the papers lie:
You would be fingering them, to anger me.
LUCETTA
She makes it strange; but she would be best pleased
To be so anger'd with another letter.   [*Exit.*
JULIA
Nay, would I were so anger'd with the same!
O hateful hands, to tear such loving words!
Injurious wasps, to feed on such sweet honey,
And kill the bees, that yield it, with your stings!
I'll kiss each several paper for amends.
Look, here is writ — 'kind Julia': — unkind Julia!
As in revenge of thy ingratitude,
I throw thy name against the bruising stones,
Trampling contemptuously on thy disdain.
And here is writ — 'love-wounded Proteus': —
Poor wounded name! my bosom, as a bed,
Shall lodge thee, till thy wound be thoroughly heal'd;
And thus I search it with a sovereign kiss.
But twice or thrice was 'Proteus' written down: —
Be calm, good wind, blow not a word away,
Till I have found each letter in the letter,
Except mine own name: that some whirlwind bear
Unto a ragged, fearful-hanging rock,
And throw it thence into the raging sea! —
Lo, here in one line is his name twice writ, —
'Poor forlorn Proteus, passionate Proteus,
To the sweet Julia:' — that I'll tear away; —
And yet I will not, sith so prettily
He couples it to his complaining names.
Thus will I fold them one upon another:
Now kiss, embrace, contend, do what you will.

Enter LUCETTA.

LUCETTA
Madam,
Dinner is ready, and your father stays.
JULIA
Well, let us go.
LUCETTA
What, shall these papers lie like tell-tales here?
JULIA
If you respect them, best to take them up.
LUCETTA
Nay, I was taken up for laying them down:
Yet here they shall not lie, for catching cold.
JULIA
I see you have a month's mind to them.
LUCETTA
Ay, madam, you may say what sights you see;
I see things too, although you judge I wink.
JULIA
Come, come; will't please you go? [*Exeunt.*

SCENE III

The same. ANTONIO'S *house.*

Enter ANTONIO *and* PANTHINO.

ANTONIO
Tell me, Panthino, what sad talk was that
Wherewith my brother held you in the cloister?
PANTHINO
'Twas of his nephew Proteus, your son.
ANTONIO
Why, what of him?
PANTHINO
                    He wonder'd that your lordship
Would suffer him to spend his youth at home,
While other men, of slender reputation,
Put forth their sons to seek preferment out:
Some to the wars, to try their fortune there;
Some to discover islands far away;
Some to the studious universities.
For any or for all these exercises,
He said that Proteus your son was meet;
And did request me to importune you
To let him spend his time no more at home,
Which would be great impeachment to his age,
In having known no travel in his youth.
ANTONIO
Nor need'st thou much importune me to that
Whereon this month I have been hammering.
I have consider'd well his loss of time,
And how he cannot be a perfect man,
Not being tried and tutor'd in the world:
Experience is by industry achieved,
And perfected by the swift course of time.
Then, tell me, whither were I best to send him?
PANTHINO
I think your lordship is not ignorant
How his companion, youthful Valentine,
Attends the emperor in his royal court.
ANTONIO
I know it well.
PANTHINO
'Twere good, I think, your lordship sent him thither:
There shall he practise tilts and tournaments,
Hear sweet discourse, converse with noblemen,
And be in eye of every exercise
Worthy his youth and nobleness of birth.
ANTONIO
I like thy counsel; well hast thou advised:
And that thou mayst perceive how well I like it,
The execution of it shall make known.
Even with the speediest expedition
I will dispatch him to the emperor's court.
PANTHINO
To-morrow, may it please you, Don Alphonso,
With other gentlemen of good esteem,
Are journeying to salute the emperor,
And to commend their service to his will.
ANTONIO
Good company; with them shall Proteus go:
And, — in good time: — now will we break with him.

Enter PROTEUS.

PROTEUS
Sweet love! sweet lines! sweet life!
Here is her hand, the agent of her heart;
Here is her oath for love, her honour's pawn.

LUCETTA Peruse this paper, madam.

O, that our fathers would applaud our loves,
To seal our happiness with their consents!
O heavenly Julia!

ANTONIO
How now! what letter are you reading there?

PROTEUS
May't please your lordship, 'tis a word or two
Of commendations sent from Valentine,
Deliver'd by a friend that came from him.

ANTONIO
Lend me the letter; let me see what news.

PROTEUS
There is no news, my lord, but that he writes
How happily he lives, how well beloved,
And daily graced by the emperor;
Wishing me with him, partner of his fortune.

ANTONIO
And how stand you affected to his wish?

PROTEUS
As one relying on your lordship's will,
And not depending on his friendly wish.

ANTONIO
My will is something sorted with his wish.
Muse not that I thus suddenly proceed;
For what I will, I will, and there an end.
I am resolv'd that thou shalt spend some time
With Valentinus in the emperor's court:
What maintenance he from his friends receives,
Like exhibition thou shalt have from me.
To-morrow be in readiness to go:
Excuse it not, for I am peremptory.

PROTEUS
My lord, I cannot be so soon provided:
Please you, deliberate a day or two.

ANTONIO
Look, what thou want'st shall be sent after thee:
No more of stay; to-morrow thou must go. —
Come on, Panthino: you shall be employ'd
To hasten on his expedition.
                    [*Exeunt* ANTONIO *and* PANTHINO.

PROTEUS
Thus have I shunn'd the fire for fear of burning,
And drench'd me in the sea, where I am drown'd.
I fear'd to show my father Julia's letter,
Lest he should take exceptions to my love;
And with the vantage of mine own excuse
Hath he excepted most against my love.
O, how this spring of love resembleth
   The uncertain glory of an April day,
Which now shows all the beauty of the sun,
   And by and by a cloud takes all away!

                    Enter PANTHINO.

PANTHINO
Sir Proteus, your father calls for you:
   He is in haste; therefore, I pray you, go.

PROTEUS
Why, this it is, — my heart accords thereto,
   And yet a thousand times it answers, No.   [*Exeunt.*

ACT II

SCENE I

Milan. The DUKE'S *palace.*

Enter VALENTINE *and* SPEED.

SPEED
Sir, your glove.

VALENTINE
                    Not mine; my gloves are on.

SPEED
Why, then, this may be yours, for this is but
   one.

VALENTINE
Ha, let me see: ay, give it me, it's mine: —
Sweet ornament that decks a thing divine!
Ah, Silvia, Silvia!

SPEED
Madam Silvia, Madam Silvia!

VALENTINE
How now, sirrah!

SPEED
She is not within hearing, sir.

VALENTINE
Why, sir, who bade you call her?

SPEED
Your worship, sir; or else I mistook.

VALENTINE
Well, you'll still be too forward.

SPEED
And yet I was last chidden for being too slow.

VALENTINE
Go to, sir: tell me, do you know Madam Silvia?

SPEED
She that your worship loves?

VALENTINE
Why, how know you that I am in love?

SPEED
Marry, by these special marks: first, you have learn'd,
like Sir Proteus, to wreathe your arms, like a
malecontent; to relish a love-song, like a robin-redbreast;
to walk alone, like one that had the pestilence; to sigh,
like a school-boy that had lost his A B C; to weep, like a
young wench that had buried her grandam; to fast, like
one that takes diet; to watch, like one that fears robbing;
to speak puling, like a beggar at Hallowmas. You were
wont, when you laugh'd, to crow like a cock; when you
walk'd, to walk like one of the lions; when you fasted, it
was presently after dinner; when you look'd sadly, it was
for want of money: and now you are metamorphosed
with a mistress, that, when I look on you, I can hardly
think you my master.

VALENTINE
Are all these things perceiv'd in me?

SPEED
They are all perceiv'd without ye.

VALENTINE
Without me? they cannot.

SPEED
Without you! nay, that's certain, for, without you were
so simple, none else would: but you are so without
these follies, that these follies are within you, and shine
through you like the water in an urinal, that not an eye
that sees you but is a physician to comment on your
malady.

VALENTINE
But tell me, dost thou know my lady Silvia?

SPEED
She that you gaze on so as she sits at supper?

VALENTINE
Hast thou observed that? even she I mean.

SPEED
Why, sir, I know her not.

VALENTINE
Dost thou know her by my gazing on her, and yet
   know'st her not?

SPEED
Is she not hard-favour'd, sir?

VALENTINE
Not so fair, boy, as well-favour'd.

SPEED
Sir, I know that well enough.

VALENTINE
What dost thou know?

SPEED
That she is not so fair as, of you, well-favour'd.

VALENTINE Sweet ornament that decks a thing
                divine!

VALENTINE
I mean, that her beauty is exquisite, but her favour
infinite.

SPEED
That's because the one is painted, and the other out of
all count.

VALENTINE
How painted? and how out of count?

SPEED
Marry, sir, so painted, to make her fair, that no man
counts of her beauty.

VALENTINE
How esteem'st thou me? I account of her beauty.

SPEED
You never saw her since she was deform'd.

VALENTINE
How long hath she been deform'd?

SPEED
Ever since you loved her.

VALENTINE
I have loved her ever since I saw her; and still I see her
   beautiful.

SPEED
If you love her, you cannot see her.

VALENTINE
Why?

SPEED
Because Love is blind. O, that you had mine eyes; or
your own eyes had the lights they were wont to have
when you chid at Sir Proteus for going ungarter'd!

VALENTINE
What should I see then?

SPEED
Your own present folly, and her passing deformity: for
he, being in love, could not see to garter his hose; and
you, being in love, cannot see to put on your hose.

VALENTINE
Belike, boy, then, you are in love; for last morning you
could not see to wipe my shoes.

SPEED
True, sir; I was in love with my bed: I thank you, you
swinged me for my love, which makes me the bolder to
chide you for yours.

VALENTINE
In conclusion, I stand affected to her.

SPEED
I would you were set, so your affection would cease.

VALENTINE
Last night she enjoin'd me to write some lines to one
   she loves.

SPEED
And have you?

VALENTINE
I have.

SPEED
Are they not lamely writ?

VALENTINE
No, boy, but as well as I can do them. — Peace!
here she comes.

SPEED [*aside*].
O excellent motion! O exceeding puppet! Now will he interpret to her.

Enter SILVIA.

VALENTINE
Madam and mistress, a thousand good-morrows!

SPEED [*aside*].
O, give ye good even! here's a million of manners.

SILVIA
Sir Valentine and servant, to you two thousand.

SPEED [*aside*].
He should give her interest, and she gives it him.

VALENTINE
As you enjoin'd me, I have writ your letter
Unto the secret nameless friend of yours;
Which I was much unwilling to proceed in
But for my duty to your ladyship.

SILVIA
I thank you, gentle servant: 'tis very clerkly done.

VALENTINE
Now trust me, madam, it came hardly off;
For, being ignorant to whom it goes,
I writ at random, very doubtfully.

SILVIA
Perchance you think too much of so much pains?

VALENTINE
No, madam; so it stead you, I will write,
Please you command, a thousand times as much:
And yet, —

SILVIA
A pretty period! Well, I guess the sequel;
And yet I will not name it; — and yet I care not; —
And yet take this again; — and yet I thank you;
Meaning henceforth to trouble you no more.

SPEED [*aside*].
And yet you will; and yet another 'yet.'

VALENTINE
What means your ladyship? do you not like it?

SILVIA
Yes, yes; the lines are very quaintly writ;
But since unwillingly, take them again;
Nay, take them.

VALENTINE
                        Madam, they are for you.

SILVIA
Ay, ay, you writ them, sir, at my request;
But I will none of them; they are for you:
I would have had them writ more movingly.

VALENTINE
Please you, I'll write your ladyship another.

SILVIA
And when it's writ, for my sake read it over:
And if it please you, so; if not, why, so.

VALENTINE
If it please me, madam! what then?

SILVIA
Why, if it please you, take it for your labour:
And so, good morrow, servant.   [*Exit.*

SPEED
O jest unseen, inscrutable, invisible,
As a nose on a man's face, or a weathercock on a steeple!
My master sues to her; and she hath taught her suitor,
He being her pupil, to become her tutor.
O excellent device! was there ever heard a better,
That my master, being scribe, to himself should write the letter?

VALENTINE
How now, sir? what are you reasoning with yourself?

SPEED
Nay, I was rhyming: 'tis you that have the reason.

VALENTINE
To do what?

SPEED
To be a spokesman for Madam Silvia.

VALENTINE
To whom?

SPEED
To yourself: why, she woos you by a figure.

VALENTINE
What figure?

SPEED
By a letter, I should say.

VALENTINE
Why, she hath not writ to me?

SPEED
What need she, when she hath made you write to yourself? Why, do you not perceive the jest?

VALENTINE
No, believe me.

SPEED
No believing you, indeed, sir. But did you perceive her earnest?

VALENTINE
She gave me none, except an angry word.

SPEED
Why, she hath given you a letter.

VALENTINE
That's the letter I writ to her friend.

SPEED
And that letter hath she deliver'd, and there an end.

VALENTINE
I would it were no worse.

SPEED
I'll warrant you, 'tis as well:
For often have you writ to her; and she, in modesty,
Or else for want of idle time, could not again reply;
Or fearing else some messenger that might her mind discover,
Herself hath taught her love himself to write unto her lover.
All this I speak in print, for in print I found it.
Why muse you, sir? 'tis dinner-time.

VALENTINE
I have dined.

SPEED
Ay, but hearken, sir; though the chameleon Love can feed on the air, I am one that am nourish'd by my victuals, and would fain have meat. O, be not like your mistress; be moved, be moved.   [*Exeunt.*

SCENE II

Verona. JULIA'S *garden.*

Enter PROTEUS *and* JULIA.

PROTEUS
Have patience, gentle Julia.

JULIA
I must, where is no remedy.

PROTEUS
When possibly I can, I will return.

JULIA
If you turn not, you will return the sooner.
Keep this remembrance for thy Julia's sake.
                        [*Gives him a ring.*

PROTEUS
Why, then, we'll make exchange; here, take you this.
                        [*Gives her another.*

JULIA
And seal the bargain with a holy kiss.

PROTEUS
Here is my hand for my true constancy;
And when that hour o'erslips me in the day
Wherein I sigh not, Julia, for thy sake,
The next ensuing hour some foul mischance
Torment me for my love's forgetfulness!
My father stays my coming; answer not;
The tide is now: — nay, not thy tide of tears;
That tide will stay me longer than I should:
Julia, farewell!   [*Exit* JULIA.
                What, gone without a word?
Ay, so true love should do: it cannot speak;
For truth hath better deeds than words to grace it.

Enter PANTHINO.

PANTHINO
Sir Proteus, you are stay'd for.

PROTEUS
Go; I come, I come: —
Alas, this parting strikes poor lovers dumb!   [*Exeunt.*

SCENE III

The same. A street.

Enter LAUNCE, *leading his dog.*

LAUNCE
Nay, 'twill be this hour ere I have done weeping; all the kind of the Launces have this very fault. I have received my proportion, like the prodigious son, and am going with Sir Proteus to the imperial's court. I think Crab my dog be the sourest-natured dog that lives: my mother weeping, my father wailing, my sister crying, our maid howling, our cat wringing her hands, and all our house in a great perplexity, yet did not this cruel-hearted cur shed one tear: he is a stone, a very pebble-stone, and has no more pity in him than a dog: a Jew would have wept to have seen our parting; why, my grandam, having no eyes, look you, wept herself blind at my parting. Nay, I'll show you the manner of it. This shoe is my father; — no, this left shoe is my father; — no, no, this left shoe is my mother; — nay, that cannot be so neither; — yes, it is so, it is so, — it hath the worser sole. This shoe, with the hole in it, is my mother, and this my father; a vengeance on't! there 'tis: now, sir, this staff is my sister; for, look you, she is as white as a lily, and as small as a wand: this hat is Nan, our maid: I am the dog; — no, the dog is himself, and I am the dog, — O, the dog is me, and I am myself; ay, so, so. Now come I to my father; 'Father, your blessing!' now should not the shoe speak a word for weeping: now should I kiss my father; well, he weeps on. Now come I to my mother; — O, that she could speak now like a wood woman! — Well, I kiss her; — why, there 'tis; here's my mother's breath up and down. Now come I to my sister: mark the moan she makes. Now the dog all this while sheds not a tear, nor speaks a word: but see how I lay the dust with my tears.

Enter PANTHINO.

PANTHINO
Launce, away, away, aboard! thy master is shipp'd, and thou art to post after with oars. What's the matter? why weep'st thou, man? Away, ass! you'll lose the tide, if you tarry any longer.

LAUNCE
It is no matter if the tied were lost; for it is the unkindest tied that ever any man tied.

PANTHINO
What's the unkindest tide?

LAUNCE
Why, he that's tied here, — Crab, my dog.

PANTHINO
Tut, man, I mean thou'lt lose the flood, and, in losing the flood, lose thy voyage; and, in losing thy voyage, lose thy master; and, in losing thy master, lose thy service; and, in losing thy service, — Why dost thou stop my mouth?

LAUNCE
For fear thou shouldst lose thy tongue.

PANTHINO
Where should I lose my tongue?

LAUNCE
In thy tale.

PANTHINO
In thy tail!

LAUNCE
Lose the tide, and the voyage, and the master, and the service, and the tied! Why, man, if the river were dry, I am able to fill it with my tears; if the wind were down, I could drive the boat with my sighs.

PANTHINO
Come, come away, man; I was sent to call thee.

LAUNCE
Sir, call me what thou darest.

PANTHINO
Wilt thou go?

LAUNCE
Well, I will go.   [*Exeunt.*

SCENE IV

Milan. The DUKE'S *palace.*

Enter SILVIA, VALENTINE, THURIO, *and* SPEED.

SILVIA
Servant, —

VALENTINE
Mistress?

SPEED
Master, Sir Thurio frowns on you.

VALENTINE
Ay, boy, it's for love.

SPEED
Not of you.

VALENTINE
Of my mistress, then.

SPEED
'Twere good you knock'd him.

SILVIA
Servant, you are sad.

VALENTINE
Indeed, madam, I seem so.

THURIO
Seem you that you are not?

VALENTINE
Haply I do.

THURIO
So do counterfeits.

VALENTINE
So do you.

THURIO
What seem I that I am not?

VALENTINE
Wise.

THURIO
What instance of the contrary?

VALENTINE
Your folly.

THURIO
And how quote you my folly?

VALENTINE
I quote it in your jerkin.

THURIO
My jerkin is a doublet.

VALENTINE
Well, then, I'll double your folly.

THURIO
How!

SILVIA
What, angry, Sir Thurio! do you change colour?

VALENTINE
Give him leave, madam; he is a kind of chameleon.

THURIO
That hath more mind to feed on your blood than live in
  your air.

VALENTINE
You have said, sir.

THURIO
Ay, sir, and done too, for this time.

VALENTINE
I know it well, sir; you always end ere you begin.

SILVIA
A fine volley of words, gentlemen, and quickly shot off.

VALENTINE
'Tis indeed, madam; we thank the giver.

SILVIA
Who is that, servant?

VALENTINE
Yourself, sweet lady; for you gave the fire. Sir Thurio
  borrows his wit from your ladyship's looks, and
  spends what he borrows kindly in your company.

THURIO
Sir, if you spend word for word with me, I shall make
  your wit bankrupt.

VALENTINE
I know it well, sir; you have an exchequer of words, and,
  I think, no other treasure to give your followers, —
  for it appears, by their bare liveries, that they live by
  your bare words.

SILVIA
No more, gentlemen, no more: — here comes my father.

Enter DUKE.

DUKE OF MILAN
Now, daughter Silvia, you are hard beset. —
Sir Valentine, your father's in good health:
What say you to a letter from your friends
Of much good news?

VALENTINE
                    My lord, I will be thankful
To any happy messenger from thence.

DUKE OF MILAN
Know ye Don Antonio, your countryman?

VALENTINE
Ay, my good lord, I know the gentleman
To be of worth and worthy estimation,
And not without desert so well reputed.

DUKE OF MILAN
Hath he not a son?

VALENTINE
Ay, my good lord; a son that well deserves
The honour and regard of such a father.

DUKE OF MILAN
You know him well?

VALENTINE
I know him as myself; for from our infancy
We have convers'd and spent our hours together:
And though myself have been an idle truant,
Omitting the sweet benefit of time
To clothe mine age with angel-like perfection,
Yet hath Sir Proteus, for that's his name,
Made use and fair advantage of his days;
His years but young, but his experience old;
His head unmellow'd, but his judgement ripe;
And, in a word, — for far behind his worth
Comes all the praises that I now bestow, —
He is complete in feature and in mind,

With all good grace to grace a gentleman.

DUKE OF MILAN
Beshrew me, sir, but if he make this good,
He is as worthy for an empress' love
As meet to be an emperor's counsellor.
Well, sir; this gentleman is come to me,
With commendation from great potentates;
And here he means to spend his time awhile:
I think 'tis no unwelcome news to you.

VALENTINE
Should I have wish'd a thing, it had been he.

DUKE OF MILAN
Welcome him, then, according to his worth;
Silvia, I speak to you; and you, Sir Thurio: —
For Valentine, I need not cite him to it:
I will send him hither to you presently.   [*Exit.*

VALENTINE
This is the gentleman I told your ladyship
Had come along with me, but that his mistress
Did hold his eyes lock'd in her crystal looks.

SILVIA
Belike that now she hath enfranchis'd them,
Upon some other pawn for fealty.

VALENTINE
Nay, sure, I think she holds them prisoners still.

SILVIA
Nay, then, he should be blind; and, being blind,
How could he see his way to seek out you?

VALENTINE
Why, lady, Love hath twenty pair of eyes.

THURIO
They say that Love hath not an eye at all.

VALENTINE
To see such lovers, Thurio, as yourself:
Upon a homely object Love can wink.

SILVIA
Have done, have done; here comes the gentleman.

Enter PROTEUS.

VALENTINE
Welcome, dear Proteus! — Mistress, I beseech you,
Confirm his welcome with some special favour.

SILVIA
His worth is warrant for his welcome hither,
If this be he you oft have wish'd to hear from.

VALENTINE
Mistress, it is: sweet lady, entertain him
To be my fellow-servant to your ladyship.

SILVIA
Too low a mistress for so high a servant.

PROTEUS
Not so, sweet lady; but too mean a servant
To have a look of such a worthy mistress.

VALENTINE
Leave off discourse of disability: —
Sweet lady, entertain him for your servant.

PROTEUS
My duty will I boast of, nothing else.

SILVIA
And duty never yet did want his meed:
Servant, you are welcome to a worthless mistress.

PROTEUS
I'll die on him that says so, but yourself.

SILVIA
That you are welcome?

PROTEUS
              That you are worthless.

Enter a SERVANT.

SERVANT
Madam, my lord your father would speak with you.

SILVIA
I wait upon his pleasure.   [*Exit* SERVANT.
              Come, Sir Thurio,
Go with me. — Once more, new servant, welcome:
I'll leave you to confer of home affairs;
When you have done, we look to hear from you.

PROTEUS
We 'll both attend upon your ladyship.
                  [*Exeunt* SILVIA *and* THURIO.

VALENTINE
Now, tell me, how do all from whence you came?

PROTEUS
Your friends are well, and have them much
  commended.

VALENTINE
And how do yours?

PROTEUS
              I left them all in health.

VALENTINE
How does your lady? and how thrives your love?

PROTEUS
My tales of love were wont to weary you;
I know you joy not in a love-discourse.

VALENTINE
Ay, Proteus, but that life is alter'd now.
I have done penance for contemning Love,
Whose high imperious thoughts have punish'd me
With bitter fasts, with penitential groans,
With nightly tears, and daily heart-sore sighs;
For, in revenge of my contempt of love,
Love hath chased sleep from my enthralled eyes,
And made them watchers of mine own heart's sorrow.
O gentle Proteus, Love's a mighty lord,
And hath so humbled me, as, I confess,
There is no woe to his correction,
Nor to his service no such joy on earth!
Now, no discourse, except it be of love;
Now can I break my fast, dine, sup, and sleep,
Upon the very naked name of love.

PROTEUS
Enough; I read your fortune in your eye.
Was this the idol that you worship so?

VALENTINE
Even she; and is she not a heavenly saint?

PROTEUS
No; but she is an earthly paragon.

VALENTINE
Call her divine.

PROTEUS
              I will not flatter her.

VALENTINE
O, flatter me; for love delights in praises.

PROTEUS
When I was sick, you gave me bitter pills;
And I must minister the like to you.

VALENTINE
Then speak the truth by her: if not divine,
Yet let her be a principality,
Sovereign to all the creatures on the earth.

PROTEUS
Except my mistress.

VALENTINE
              Sweet, except not any;
Except thou wilt except against my love.

PROTEUS
Have I not reason to prefer mine own?

VALENTINE
And I will help thee to prefer her too:
She shall be dignified with this high honour, —
To bear my lady's train, lest the base earth
Should from her vesture chance to steal a kiss,
And, of so great a favour growing proud,
Disdain to root the summer-swelling flower,
And make rough winter everlastingly.

PROTEUS
Why, Valentine, what braggardism is this?

VALENTINE
Parden me, Proteus: all I can is nothing
To her, whose worth makes other worthies nothing;
She is alone.

PROTEUS
              Then let her alone.

VALENTINE
Nor for the world: why, man, she is mine own;
And I as rich in having such a jewel
As twenty seas, if all their sand were pearl,
The water nectar, and the rocks pure gold.
Forgive me, that I do not dream on thee,
Because thou see'st me dote upon my love.
My foolish rival, that her father likes
Only for his possessions are so huge,
Is gone with her along; and I must after,
For love, thou know'st, is full of jealousy.

PROTEUS
But she loves you?

VALENTINE
Ay, and we are betroth'd: nay, more, our
  marriage-hour,
With all the cunning manner of our flight,
Determin'd of; how I must climb her window,
The ladder made of cords; and all the means
Plotted and 'greed on for my happiness.
Good Proteus, go with me to my chamber,
In these affairs to aid me with thy counsel.

PROTEUS
Go on before; I shall inquire you forth:
I must unto the road, to disembark

Some necessaries that I needs must use;
And then I'll presently attend you.

VALENTINE
Will you make haste?

PROTEUS
I will.   [*Exeunt* VALENTINE *and* SPEED.
Even as one heat another heat expels,
Or as one nail by strength drives out another,
So the remembrance of my former love
Is by a newer object quite forgotten.
Is it mine eye, or Valentinus' praise,
Her true perfection, or my false transgression,
That makes me, reasonless, to reason thus?
She's fair; and so is Julia, that I love, —
That I did love, for now my love is thaw'd;
Which, like a waxen image 'gainst a fire,
Bears no impression of the thing it was.
Methinks my zeal to Valentine is cold,
And that I love him not as I was wont:
O, but I love his lady too-too much;
And that's the reason I love him so little.
How shall I dote on her with more advice,
That thus without advice begin to love her!
'Tis but her picture I have yet beheld,
And that hath dazzled my reason's light;
But when I look on her perfections,
There is no reason but I shall be blind.
If I can check my erring love, I will;
If not, to compass her I'll use my skill.   [*Exit.*

SCENE V
The same. A street.

Enter SPEED *and* LAUNCE *severally.*

SPEED
Launce! by mine honesty, welcome to Padua!

LAUNCE
Forswear not thyself, sweet youth; for I am not
welcome. I reckon this always — that a man is never
undone till he be hang'd; nor never welcome to a place
till some certain shot be paid, and the hostess say,
'Welcome.'

SPEED
Come on, you madcap, I'll to the alehouse with you
presently; where, for one shot of five pence, thou shalt
have five thousand welcomes. But, sirrah, how did thy
master part with Madam Julia?

LAUNCE
Marry, after they closed in earnest, they parted very
   fairly in jest.

SPEED
But shall she marry him?

LAUNCE
No.

SPEED
How, then? shall he marry her?

LAUNCE
No, neither.

SPEED
What, are they broken?

LAUNCE
No, they are both as whole as a fish.

SPEED
Why, then, how stands the matter with them?

LAUNCE
Marry, thus: when it stands well with him, it stands
well with her.

SPEED
What an ass art thou! I understand thee not.

LAUNCE
What a block art thou, that thou canst not! My staff
understands me.

SPEED
What thou say'st?

LAUNCE
Ay, and what I do too: look thee, I'll but lean, and my
staff understands me.

SPEED
It stands under thee, indeed.

LAUNCE
Why, stand-under and under-stand is all one.

SPEED
But tell me true, will't be a match?

LAUNCE
Ask my dog: if he say ay, it will; if he say no, it will; if he
shake his tail and say nothing, it will.

SPEED
The conclusion is, then, that it will.

LAUNCE
Thou shalt never get such a secret from me but by a parable.

SPEED
'Tis well that I get it so. But, Launce, how say'st thou,
that my master is become a notable lover?

LAUNCE
I never knew him otherwise.

SPEED
Than how?

LAUNCE
A notable lubber, as thou reportest him to be.

SPEED
Why, thou whoreson ass, thou mistakest me.

LAUNCE
Why, fool, I meant not thee; I meant thy master.

SPEED
I tell thee, my master is become a hot lover.

LAUNCE
Why, I tell thee, I care not though he burn himself in
love. If thou wilt, go with me to the alehouse; if not,
thou art an Hebrew, a Jew, and not worth the name of a
Christian.

SPEED
Why?

LAUNCE
Because thou hast not so much charity in thee as to go
to the ale with a Christian. Wilt thou go?

SPEED
At thy service.   [*Exeunt.*

SCENE VI
The same. The DUKE'S *palace.*

Enter PROTEUS.

PROTEUS
To leave my Julia, shall I be forsworn;
To love fair Silvia, shall I be forsworn;
To wrong my friend, I shall be much forsworn;
And even that power, which gave me first my oath,
Provokes me to this threefold perjury:
Love bade me swear, and Love
   bids me forswear:
O sweet-suggesting Love, if
   thou hast sinn'd,
Teach me, thy tempted subject,
   to excuse it!
At first I did adore a twinkling
   star,
But now I worship a celestial
   sun:
Unheedful vows may heedfully
   be broken;
And he wants wit that wants
   resolved will
To learn his wit t'exchange the
   bad for better.
Fie, fie, unreverend tongue! to
   call her bad,
Whose sovereignty so oft thou
   hast preferr'd
With twenty thousand
   soul-confirming oaths.
I cannot leave to love, and yet I
   do;
But there I leave to love where I

should love.
Julia I lose, and Valentine I lose:
If I keep them, I needs must lose myself;
If I lose them, thus find I by their loss, —
For Valentine, myself; for Julia, Silvia.
I to myself am dearer than a friend,
For love is still most precious in itself;
And Silvia — witness Heaven, that made her fair! —
Shows Julia but a swarthy Ethiop.
I will forget that Julia is alive,
Rememb'ring that my love to her is dead;
And Valentine I'll hold an enemy,
Aiming at Silvia as a sweeter friend.
I cannot now prove constant to myself,
Without some treachery used to Valentine.
This night he meaneth with a corded ladder
To climb celestial Silvia's chamber-window,
Myself in counsel his competitor:
Now presently I'll give her father notice
Of their disguising and pretended flight;
Who, all enrag'd, will banish Valentine,
For Thurio, he intends, shall wed his daughter:
But, Valentine being gone, I'll quickly cross,
By some sly trick, blunt Thurio's dull proceeding.
Love, lend me wings to make my purpose swift,
As thou hast lent me wit to plot this drift!   [*Exit.*

SCENE VII
Verona. JULIA'S *house.*

Enter JULIA *and* LUCETTA.

JULIA
Counsel, Lucetta; gentle girl, assist me;
And, even in kind love, I do conjure thee, —
Who art the table wherein all my thoughts
Are visibly character'd and engraved, —
To lesson me; and tell me some good mean,
How, with my honour, I may undertake
A journey to my loving Proteus.

LUCETTA
Alas, the way is wearisome and long!

JULIA
A true-devoted pilgrim is not weary
To measure kingdoms with his feeble steps;
Much less shall she that hath Love's wings to fly,
And when the flight is made to one so dear,
Of such divine perfection, as Sir Proteus.

LUCETTA
Better forbear till Proteus make return.

JULIA
O, know'st thou not, his looks are my soul's food?
Pity the dearth that I have pined in,
By longing for that food so long a time.
Didst thou but know the inly touch of love,
Thou wouldst as soon go kindle fire with snow
As seek to quench the fire of love with words.

LUCETTA
I do not seek to quench your love's hot fire,
But qualify the fire's extreme rage,
Lest it should burn above the bounds of reason.

JULIA
The more thou damm'st it up, the more it burns:
The current that with gentle murmur glides,
Thou know'st, being stopp'd, impatiently doth rage;
But when his fair course is not hindered,
He makes sweet music with th'enamell'd stones,
Giving a gentle kiss to every sedge
He overtaketh in his pilgrimage;
And so by many winding nooks he strays,
With willing sport, to the wide ocean.
Then let me go, and hinder not my course:
I'll be as patient as a gentle stream,
And make a pastime of each weary step,
Till the last step have brought me to my love;
And there I'll rest, as, after much turmoil,
A blessed soul doth in Elysium.

LUCETTA
But in what habit will you go along?

JULIA
Not like a woman; for I would prevent
The loose encounters of lascivious men;
Gentle Lucetta, fit me with such weeds
As may beseem some well-reputed page.

LUCETTA
Why, then, your ladyship must cut your hair.

JULIA
No, girl; I'll knit it up in silken strings,
With twenty odd-conceited true-love knots:
To be fantastic may become a youth
Of greater time than I shall show to be.

SPEED Launce! by mine honesty, welcome to Padua!

JULIA *Counsel, Lucetta; gentle girl, assist me.*

LUCETTA
What fashion, madam, shall I make your breeches?
JULIA
That fits as well as — 'Tell me, good my lord,
What compass will you wear your farthingale?'
Why, even what fashion thou best lik'st, Lucetta.
LUCETTA
You must needs have them with a codpiece, madam.
JULIA
Out, out, Lucetta! that would be ill-favour'd.
LUCETTA
A round hose, madam, now's not worth a pin,
Unless you have a codpiece to stick pins on.
JULIA
Lucetta, as thou lovest me, let me have
What thou think'st meet, and is most mannerly.
But tell me, wench, how will the world repute me
For undertaking so unstaid a journey?
I fear me, it will make me scandalised.
LUCETTA
If you think so, then stay at home, and go not.
JULIA
Nay, that I will not.
LUCETTA
Then never dream on infamy, but go.
If Proteus like your journey when you come,
No matter who's displeas'd when you are gone:
I fear me, he will scarce be pleas'd withal.
JULIA
That is the least, Lucetta, of my fear:
A thousand oaths, an ocean of his tears,
And instances of infinite of love,
Warrant me welcome to my Proteus.
LUCETTA
All these are servants to deceitful men.
JULIA
Base men, that use them to so base effect!
But truer stars did govern Proteus' birth:
His words are bonds, his oaths are oracles;
His love sincere, his thoughts immaculate;
His tears pure messengers sent from his heart;
His heart as far from fraud as heaven from earth.
LUCETTA
Pray heaven he prove so, when you come to him!
JULIA
Now, as thou lov'st me, do him not that wrong,
To bear a hard opinion of his truth:
Only deserve my love by loving him;
And presently go with me to my chamber,
To take a note of what I stand in need of,
To furnish me upon my longing journey.
All that is mine I leave at thy dispose,
My goods, my lands, my reputation;
Only, in lieu thereof, dispatch me hence.
Come, answer not, but to it presently;
I am impatient of my tarriance. [*Exeunt.*

ACT III

SCENE I

Milan. An ante-room in the DUKE'S palace.
Enter DUKE, THURIO, and PROTEUS.

DUKE OF MILAN
Sir Thurio, give us leave, I pray, awhile;
We have some secrets to confer about. [*Exit* THURIO.
Now, tell me, Proteus, what's your will with me?
PROTEUS
My gracious lord, that which I would discover
The law of friendship bids me to conceal;
But when I call to mind your gracious favours
Done to me, undeserving as I am,
My duty pricks me on to utter that
Which else no worldly good should draw from me.
Know, worthy prince, Sir Valentine, my friend,
This night intends to steal away your daughter;
Myself am one made privy to the plot.
I know you have determin'd to bestow her
On Thurio, whom your gentle daughter hates;
And should she thus be stol'n away from you,
It would be much vexation to your age.
Thus, for my duty's sake, I rather chose
To cross my friend in his intended drift
Than, by concealing it, heap on your head
A pack of sorrows, which would press you down,
Being unprevented, to your timeless grave.
DUKE OF MILAN
Proteus, I thank thee for thine honest care;
Which to requite, command me while I live.
This love of theirs myself have often seen,
Haply when they have judg'd me fast asleep;
And oftentimes have purpos'd to forbid
Sir Valentine her company and my court:
But, fearing lest my jealous aim might err,
And so, unworthily, disgrace the man, —
A rashness that I ever yet have shunn'd, —
I gave him gentle looks; thereby to find
That which thyself hast now disclos'd to me.
And, that thou mayst perceive my fear of this,
Knowing that tender youth is soon suggested,
I nightly lodge her in an upper tower,
The key whereof myself have ever kept;
And thence she cannot be convey'd away.
PROTEUS
Know, noble lord, they have devis'd a mean
How he her chamber-window will ascend,
And with a corded ladder fetch her down;
For which the youthful lover now is gone,
And this way comes he with it presently;
Where, if it please you, you may intercept him.
But, good my Lord, do it so cunningly
That my discovery be not aimed at;
For love of you, not hate unto my friend,
Hath made me publisher of this pretence.
DUKE OF MILAN
Upon mine honour, he shall never know
That I had any light from thee of this.
PROTEUS
Adieu, my lord; Sir Valentine is coming. [*Exit.*
Enter VALENTINE.

DUKE OF MILAN
Sir Valentine, whither away so fast?
VALENTINE
Please it your Grace, there is a messenger
That stays to bear my letters to my friends,
And I am going to deliver them.
DUKE OF MILAN
Be they of much import?
VALENTINE
The tenour of them doth but signify
My health, and happy being at your court.
DUKE OF MILAN
Nay, then, no matter; stay with me awhile;
I am to break with thee of some affairs
That touch me near, wherein thou must be secret.
'Tis not unknown to thee that I have sought
To match my friend Sir Thurio to my daughter.
VALENTINE
I know it well, my lord; and, sure, the match
Were rich and honourable; besides, the gentleman
Is full of virtue, bounty, worth, and qualities
Beseeming such a wife as your fair daughter:
Cannot your Grace win her to fancy him?
DUKE OF MILAN
No, trust me; she is peevish, sullen, froward,
Proud, disobedient, stubborn, lacking duty;
Neither regarding that she is my child,
Nor fearing me as if I were her father:
And, may I say to thee, this pride of hers,
Upon advice, hath drawn my love from her;
And, where I thought the remnant of mine age
Should have been cherish'd by her child-like duty,
I now am full resolv'd to take a wife,
And turn her out to who will take her in:
Then let her beauty be her wedding-dower;
For me and my possessions she esteems not.
VALENTINE
What would your Grace have me to do in this?
DUKE OF MILAN
There is a lady of Verona here
Whom I affect; but she is nice and coy,
And naught esteems my aged eloquence:
Now, therefore, would I have thee to my tutor, —
For long agone I have forgot to court;
Besides, the fashion of the time is changed, —
How, and which way, I may bestow myself,
To be regarded in her sun-bright eye.

VALENTINE
Win her with gifts, if she respect not words:
Dumb jewels often, in their silent kind,
More than quick words, do move a woman's mind.
DUKE OF MILAN
But she did scorn a present that I sent her.
VALENTINE
A woman sometimes scorns what best contents her:
Send her another; never give her o'er;
For scorn at first makes after-love the more.
If she do frown, 'tis not in hate of you,
But rather to beget more love in you:
If she do chide, 'tis not to have thee gone;
For why the fools are mad, if left alone.

Take no repulse, whatever she doth say;
For 'get you gone,' she doth not mean 'away!'
Flatter and praise, commend, extol their graces;
Though ne'er so black, say they have angels' faces.
That man that hath a tongue, I say, is no man,
If with his tongue he cannot win a woman.

DUKE OF MILAN
But she I mean is promis'd by her friends
Unto a youthful gentleman of worth;
And kept severely from resort of men,
That no man hath access by day to her.

VALENTINE
Why, then, I would resort to her by night.

DUKE OF MILAN
Ay, but the doors be lock'd, and keys kept safe,
That no man hath recourse to her by night.

VALENTINE
What lets but one may enter at her window?

DUKE OF MILAN
Her chamber is aloft, far from the ground,
And built so shelving, that one cannot climb it
Without apparent hazard of his life.

VALENTINE
Why, then, a ladder, quaintly made of cords,
To cast up, with a pair of anchoring hooks,
Would serve to scale another Hero's tower,
So bold Leander would adventure it.

DUKE OF MILAN
Now, as thou art a gentleman of blood,
Advise me where I may have such a ladder.

VALENTINE
When would you use it? pray, sir, tell me that.

DUKE OF MILAN
This very night; for Love is like a child,
That longs for every thing that he can come by.

VALENTINE
By seven o'clock I'll get you such a ladder.

DUKE OF MILAN
But, hark thee; I will go to her alone:
How shall I best convey the ladder thither?

VALENTINE
It will be light, my lord, that you may bear it
Under a cloak that is of any length.

DUKE OF MILAN
A cloak as long as thine will serve the turn?

VALENTINE
Ay, my good lord.

DUKE OF MILAN
    Then let me see thy cloak:
I'll get me one of such another length.

VALENTINE
Why, any cloak will serve the turn, my lord.

DUKE OF MILAN
How shall I fashion me to wear a cloak? —
I pray thee, let me feel thy cloak upon me. —
What letter is this same? What's here? — *'To Silvia'!*
And here an engine fit for my proceeding!
I'll be so bold to break the seal for once. [*Reads.*
 'My thoughts do harbour with my Silvia nightly;
  And slaves they are to me, that send them flying:
 O, could their master come and go as lightly,
  Himself would lodge where senseless they are
   lying!
 My herald thoughts in thy pure bosom rest them;
  While I, their king, that hither them importune,
 Do curse the grace that with such grace hath blest
  them,
  Because myself do want my servants' fortune:
 I curse myself, for they are sent by me,
 That they should harbour where their lord would
  be.'
What's here?
 'Silvia, this night I will enfranchise thee.'
'Tis so; and here's the ladder for the purpose.
Why, Phaethon, — for thou art Merops' son, —
Wilt thou aspire to guide the heavenly car,
And with thy daring folly burn the world?
Wilt thou reach stars, because they shine on thee?
Go, base intruder! overweening slave!
Bestow thy fawning smiles on equal mates;
And think my patience, more than thy desert,
Is privilege for thy departure hence:
Thank me for this, more than for all the favours
Which, all too much, I have bestow'd on thee.
But if thou linger in my territories
Longer than swiftest expedition
Will give thee time to leave our royal court,
By heaven, my wrath shall far exceed the love
I ever bore my daughter or thyself.
Be gone! I will not hear thy vain excuse;

DUKE OF MILAN A cloak as long as thine will serve the turn?

But, as thou lov'st thy life, make speed from hence.
        [*Exit* DUKE.

VALENTINE
And why not death, rather than living torment?
To die, is to be banish'd from myself;
And Silvia is myself: banish'd from her,
Is self from self, — a deadly banishment!
What light is light, if Silvia be not seen?
What joy is joy, if Silvia be not by?
Unless it be to think that she is by,
And feed upon the shadow of perfection.
Except I be by Silvia in the night,
There is no music in the nightingale;
Unless I look on Silvia in the day,
There is no day for me to look upon:
She is my essence; and I leave to be,
If I be not by her fair influence
Foster'd, illumin'd, cherish'd, kept alive.
I fly not death, to fly his deadly doom:
Tarry I here, I but attend on death;
But, fly I hence, I fly away from life.

   Enter PROTEUS *and* LAUNCE.

PROTEUS
Run, boy, run, run, and seek him out.

LAUNCE
So-ho, so-ho!

PROTEUS
What see'st thou?

LAUNCE
Him we go to find: there's not a hair on's head but 'tis a
 Valentine.

PROTEUS
Valentine!

VALENTINE
No.

PROTEUS
Who then? his spirit?

VALENTINE
Neither.

PROTEUS
What then?

VALENTINE
Nothing.

LAUNCE
Can nothing speak? Master, shall I strike?

PROTEUS
Who wouldst thou strike?

LAUNCE
Nothing.

PROTEUS
Villain, forbear.

LAUNCE
Why, sir, I'll strike nothing: I pray you, —

PROTEUS
Sirrah, I say, forbear. — Friend Valentine, a word.

VALENTINE
My ears are stopp'd and cannot hear good news,
So much of bad already hath possess'd them.

PROTEUS
Then in dumb silence will I bury mine,
For they are harsh, untuneable, and bad.

VALENTINE
Is Silvia dead?

PROTEUS
No, Valentine.

VALENTINE
No Valentine, indeed, for sacred Silvia! —
Hath she forsworn me?

PROTEUS
No, Valentine.

VALENTINE
No Valentine, if Silvia have forsworn me! —
What is your news?

LAUNCE
Sir, there is a proclamation that you are vanish'd.

PROTEUS
That thou art banished — O, that's the news! —
From hence, from Silvia, and from me thy friend,

VALENTINE
O, I have fed upon this woe already,
And now excess of it will make me surfeit.
Doth Silvia know that I am banished?

PROTEUS
Ay, ay; and she hath offer'd to the doom —
Which, unrevers'd, stands in effectual force —
A sea of melting pearl, which some call tears;
Those at her father's churlish feet she tender'd;
With them, upon her knees, her humble self;
Wringing her hands, whose whiteness so became
 them
As if but now they waxed pale for woe:
But neither bended knees, pure hands held up,
Sad sighs, deep groans, nor silver-shedding tears,
Could penetrate her uncompassionate sire;
But Valentine, if he be ta'en, must die.
Besides, her intercession chafed him so,
When she for thy repeal was suppliant,
That to close prison he commanded her,
With many bitter threats of biding there.

VALENTINE
No more; unless the next word that thou speak'st
Have some malignant power upon my life:
If so, I pray thee, breathe it in mine ear,
As ending anthem of my endless dolour.

PROTEUS
Cease to lament for that thou canst not help,
And study help for that which thou lamentest.
Time is the nurse and breeder of all good.
Here if thou stay, thou canst not see thy love;
Besides, thy staying will abridge thy life.
Hope is a lover's staff; walk hence with that,

And manage it against despairing thoughts.
Thy letters may be here, though thou art hence;
Which, being writ to me, shall be deliver'd
Even in the milk-white bosom of thy love.
The time now serves not to expostulate:
Come, I'll convey thee through the city-gate;
And, ere I part with thee, confer at large
Of all that may concern thy love-affairs.
As thou lovest Silvia, though not for thyself,
Regard thy danger, and along with me.

VALENTINE
I pray thee, Launce, an if thou see'st my boy,
Bid him make haste, and meet me at the north-gate.

PROTEUS
Go, sirrah, find him out. — Come, Valentine.

VALENTINE
O my dear Silvia! — Hapless Valentine!

[*Exeunt* VALENTINE *and* PROTEUS.

LAUNCE
I am but a fool, look you; and yet I have the wit to think
my master is a kind of a knave; but that's all one, if he
be but one knave. He lives not now that knows me to be
in love; yet I am in love; but a team of horse shall not
pluck that from me; nor who 'tis I love; and yet 'tis a
woman; but what woman, I will not tell myself; and yet
'tis a milkmaid; yet 'tis not a maid, for she hath had
gossips; yet 'tis a maid, for she is her master's maid,
and serves for wages. She hath more qualities than a
water-spaniel, — which is much in a bare Christian.
[*Pulling out a paper.*] Here is the cate-log of her
condition. [*Reads.*] 'Imprimis, She can fetch and carry.'
Why, a horse can do no more: nay, a horse cannot fetch,
but only carry; therefore she is better than a jade. 'Item,
She can milk'; look you, a sweet virtue in a maid with
clean hands.

Enter SPEED.

SPEED
How now, Signior Launce! what news with your
    mastership?

LAUNCE
With my master's ship? why, it is at sea.

SPEED
Well, your old vice still; mistake the word. What news,
then, in your paper?

LAUNCE
The black'st news that ever thou heard'st.

SPEED
Why, man, how black?

LAUNCE
Why, as black as ink.

SPEED
Let me read them.

LAUNCE
Fie on thee, jolt-head! thou canst not read.

SPEED
Thou liest; I can.

LAUNCE
I will try thee. Tell me this: who begot thee?

SPEED
Marry, the son of my grandfather.

LAUNCE
O illiterate loiterer! it was the son of thy grandmother:
this proves that thou canst not read.

SPEED
Come, fool, come; try me in thy paper.

LAUNCE
There; and Saint Nicholas be thy speed!

SPEED [*reads*].
'Imprimis, She can milk.'

LAUNCE
Ay, that she can.

SPEED
'Item, She brews good ale.'

LAUNCE
And thereof comes the proverb, — Blessing of your
heart, you brew good ale.

SPEED
'Item: She can sew.'

LAUNCE
That's as much as to say, Can she so?

SPEED
'Item, She can knit.'

LAUNCE
What need a man care for a stock with a wench, when
she can knit him a stock?

SPEED
'Item, She can wash and scour.'

SPEED Come, fool, come; try me in thy paper.

LAUNCE
A special virtue; for then she need not be wash'd and
scour'd.

SPEED
'Item, She can spin.'

LAUNCE
Then may I set the world on wheels, when she can spin
for her living.

SPEED
'Item, She hath many nameless virtues.'

LAUNCE
That's as much as to say, bastard virtues; that, indeed,
know not their fathers, and therefore have no names.

SPEED
'Here follow her vices.'

LAUNCE
Close at the heels of her virtues.

SPEED
'Item, She is not to be kiss'd fasting, in respect of her
    breath.'

LAUNCE
Well, that fault may be mended with a breakfast. Read
    on.

SPEED
'Item, She hath a sweet mouth.'

LAUNCE
That makes amends for her sour breath.

SPEED
'Item, She doth talk in her sleep.'

LAUNCE
It's no matter for that, so she sleep not in her talk.

SPEED
'Item, She is slow in words.'

LAUNCE
O villain, that set this down among her vices! To be
slow in words is a woman's only virtue: I pray thee, out
with't, and place it for her chief virtue.

SPEED
'Item, She is proud.'

LAUNCE
Out with that too; it was Eve's legacy, and cannot be
ta'en from her.

SPEED
'Item, She hath no teeth.'

LAUNCE
I care not for that neither, because I love crusts.

SPEED
'Item, She is curst.'

LAUNCE
Well, the best is, she hath no teeth to bite.

SPEED
'Item, She will often praise her liquor.'

LAUNCE
If her liquor be good, she shall: if she will not, I will; for
good things should be praised.

SPEED
'Item, She is too liberal.'

LAUNCE
Of her tongue she cannot, for that's writ down she is
slow of; of her purse she shall not, for that I'll keep
shut: now, of another thing she may, and that cannot I
help. Well, proceed.

SPEED
'Item, She hath more hair than wit, and more faults
    than hairs, and more wealth than faults.'

LAUNCE
Stop there; I'll have her: she was mine, and not mine,
twice or thrice in that last article. Rehearse that once
more.

SPEED
'Item, She hath more hair than wit,' —

LAUNCE
More hair than wit, — it may be: I'll prove it. The cover
of the salt hides the salt, and therefore it is more than
the salt; the hair that covers the wit is more than the
wit, for the greater hides the less. What's next?

SPEED
'And more faults than hairs,' —

LAUNCE
That's monstrous: O, that that were out!

SPEED
'And more wealth than faults.'

LAUNCE
Why, that word makes the faults gracious. Well, I'll have
her: and if it be a match, as nothing is impossible, —

SPEED
What then?

LAUNCE
Why, then will I tell thee — that thy master stays for
thee at the north-gate.

SPEED
For me!

LAUNCE
For thee! ay; who art thou? he hath stay'd for a better
man than thee.

SPEED
And must I go to him?

LAUNCE
Thou must run to him, for thou hast stay'd so long, that
going will scarce serve the turn.

SPEED
Why didst not tell me sooner? pox of your love-letters!
[*Exit.*

LAUNCE
Now will he be swinged for reading my letter, — an
unmannerly slave, that will thrust himself into secrets!
I'll after, to rejoice in the boy's correction.
[*Exit.*

SCENE II

The same. The DUKE'S *palace.*

Enter DUKE *and* THURIO.

DUKE OF MILAN
Sir Thurio, fear not but that she will love you,
Now Valentine is banish'd from her sight.

THURIO
Since his exile she hath despis'd me most,
Forsworn my company, and rail'd at me,
That I am desperate of obtaining her.

DUKE OF MILAN
This weak impress of love is as a figure
Trenched in ice, which with an hour's heat
Dissolves to water, and doth lose his form.
A little time will melt her frozen thoughts,
And worthless Valentine shall be forgot.
                    Enter PROTEUS.
How now, Sir Proteus! Is your countryman,
According to our proclamation, gone?

PROTEUS
Gone, my good lord.

DUKE OF MILAN
My daughter takes his going grievously.

PROTEUS
A little time, my lord, will kill that grief.

DUKE OF MILAN
So I believe; but Thurio thinks not so.
Proteus, the good conceit I hold of thee —
For thou hast shown some sign of good desert —
Makes me the better to confer with thee.

PROTEUS
Longer than I prove loyal to your Grace
Let me not live to look upon your Grace.

DUKE OF MILAN
Thou know'st how willingly I would effect
The match between Sir Thurio and my daughter?

PROTEUS
I do, my lord.

DUKE OF MILAN
And also, I think, thou art not ignorant
How she opposes her against my will.

PROTEUS
She did, my lord, when Valentine was here.

DUKE OF MILAN
Ay, and perversely she persevers so.
What might we do to make the girl forget
The love of Valentine, and love Sir Thurio?

PROTEUS
The best way is to slander Valentine
With falsehood, cowardice, and poor descent, —
Three things that women highly hold in hate.

DUKE OF MILAN
Ay, but she'll think that it is spoke in hate.

PROTEUS
Ay, if his enemy deliver it:
Therefore it must with circumstance be spoken
By one whom she esteemeth as his friend.

DUKE OF MILAN
Then you must undertake to slander him.

PROTEUS
And that, my lord, I shall be loath to do:
'Tis an ill office for a gentleman,
Especially against his very friend.

DUKE OF MILAN
Where your good word cannot advantage him,
Your slander never can endamage him;
Therefore the office is indifferent,
Being entreated to it by your friend.

PROTEUS
You have prevail'd, my lord: if I can do it
By aught that I can speak in his dispraise,
She shall not long continue love to him.
But say this weed her love from Valentine,
It follows not that she will love Sir Thurio.

THURIO
Therefore, as you unwind her love from him,
Lest it should ravel and be good to none,
You must provide to bottom it on me;
Which must be done by praising me as much
As you in worth dispraise Sir Valentine.

DUKE OF MILAN
And, Proteus, we dare trust you in this kind,
Because we know, on Valentine's report,
You are already Love's firm votary,
And cannot soon revolt and change your mind.
Upon this warrant shall you have access
Where you with Silvia may confer at large;
For she is lumpish, heavy, melancholy,

And, for your friend's sake, will be glad of you;
Where you may temper her, by your persuasion,
To hate young Valentine, and love my friend.

PROTEUS
As much as I can do, I will effect: —
But you, Sir Thurio, are not sharp enough;
You must lay lime to tangle her desires
By wailful sonnets, whose composed rhymes
Should be full-fraught with serviceable vows.

DUKE OF MILAN
Ay,
Much is the force of heaven-bred poesy.

PROTEUS
Say, that upon the altar of her beauty
You sacrifice your tears, your sighs, your heart:
Write till your ink be dry, and with your tears
Moist it again, and frame some feeling line
That may discover such integrity:
For Orpheus' lute was strung with poets' sinews;
Whose golden touch could soften steel and stones,
Make tigers tame, and huge leviathans
Forsake unsounded deeps to dance on sands.
After your dire-lamenting elegies,
Visit by night your lady's chamber-window
With some sweet consort; to their instruments
Tune a deploring dump: the night's dead silence
Will well become such sweet-complaining grievance.
This, or else nothing, will inherit her.

DUKE OF MILAN
This discipline shows thou hast been in love.

THURIO
And thy advice this night I'll put in practice.
Therefore, sweet Proteus, my direction-giver,
Let us into the city presently
To sort some gentlemen well skill'd in music:
I have a sonnet that will serve the turn
To give the onset to thy good advice.

DUKE OF MILAN
About it, gentlemen.

PROTEUS
We'll wait upon your Grace till after supper,
And afterward determine our proceedings.

DUKE OF MILAN
Even now about it; I will pardon you.   [*Exeunt.*

ACT IV

SCENE I

A forest.

Enter certain OUTLAWS.

FIRST OUTLAW
Fellows, stand fast; I see a passenger.

SECOND OUTLAW
If there be ten, shrink not, but down with 'em.

Enter VALENTINE *and* SPEED.

THIRD OUTLAW
Stand, sir, and throw us that you have about ye:
If not, we'll make you sit, and rifle you.

SPEED
Sir, we are undone! these are the villains
That all the travellers do fear so much.

VALENTINE
My friends, —

FIRST OUTLAW
That's not so, sir, — we are your enemies.

SECOND OUTLAW
Peace! we'll hear him.

THIRD OUTLAW
Ay, by my beard, will we; for he is a proper man.

VALENTINE
Then know that I have little wealth to lose;
A man I am cross'd with adversity:
My riches are these poor habiliments,
Of which if you should here disfurnish me,
You take the sum and substance that I have.

SECOND OUTLAW
Whither travel you?

VALENTINE
To Verona.

FIRST OUTLAW
Whence came you?

VALENTINE
From Milan.

THIRD OUTLAW
Have you long sojourn'd there?

VALENTINE
Some sixteen months; and longer might have stay'd,
If crooked fortune had not thwarted me.

FIRST OUTLAW
What, were you banish'd thence?

VALENTINE
I was.

SECOND OUTLAW
For what offence?

VALENTINE
For that which now torments me to rehearse:
I kill'd a man, whose death I much repent;
But yet I slew him manfully in fight,
Without false vantage or base treachery.

FIRST OUTLAW
Why, ne'er repent it, if it were done so.
But were you banish'd for so small a fault?

VALENTINE
I was, and held me glad of such a doom.

SECOND OUTLAW
Have you the tongues?

VALENTINE
My youthful travel therein made me happy,
Or else I often had been miserable.

THIRD OUTLAW
By the bare scalp of Robin Hood's fat friar

PROTEUS We'll wait upon your Grace till after supper.

This fellow were a king for our wild faction!

FIRST OUTLAW
We'll have him: — sirs, a word.

SPEED
Master, be one of them; it's an honourable kind of
thievery.

VALENTINE
Peace, villain!

SECOND OUTLAW
Tell us this: have you any thing to take to?

VALENTINE
Nothing but my fortune.

THIRD OUTLAW
Know, then, that some of us are gentlemen,
Such as the fury of ungovern'd youth
Thrust from the company of awful men:
Myself was from Verona banished
For practising to steal away a lady,
An heir, and near allied unto the duke.

SECOND OUTLAW
And I from Mantua, for a gentleman,
Who, in my mood, I stabb'd unto the heart.

FIRST OUTLAW
And I for such-like petty crimes as these.
But to the purpose, — for we cite our faults,
That they may hold excus'd our lawless lives;
And partly, seeing you are beautified
With goodly shape, and by your own report
A linguist, and a man of such perfection
As we do in our quality much want, —

SECOND OUTLAW
Indeed, because you are a banish'd man,
Therefore, above the rest, we parley to you:
Are you content to be our general?
To make a virtue of necessity,
And live, as we do, in this wilderness?

THIRD OUTLAW
What say'st thou? wilt thou be of our consort?
Say ay, and be the captain of us all:
We'll do thee homage and be rul'd by thee,
Love thee as our commander and our king.

FIRST OUTLAW
But if thou scorn our courtesy, thou diest.

SECOND OUTLAW
Thou shalt not live to brag what we have offer'd.

VALENTINE
I take your offer, and will live with you,
Provided that you do no outrages
On silly women or poor passengers.

THIRD OUTLAW
No, we detest such vile base practices.
Come, go with us, we'll bring thee to our crews,
And show thee all the treasure we have got;
Which, with ourselves, all rest at thy dispose.   [*Exeunt.*

SCENE II

Milan. The court of the DUKE'S *palace.*

Enter PROTEUS.

PROTEUS
Already have I been false to Valentine,
And now I must be as unjust to Thurio.
Under the colour of commending him,
I have access my own love to prefer:
But Silvia is too fair, too true, too holy,
To be corrupted with my worthless gifts.
When I protest true loyalty to her,
She twits me with my falsehood to my friend;
When to her beauty I commend my vows,
She bids me think how I have been forsworn
In breaking faith with Julia whom I lov'd:
And notwithstanding all her sudden quips,
The least whereof would quell a lover's hope,
Yet, spaniel-like, the more she spurns my love,
The more it grows, and fawneth on her still.
But here comes Thurio: now must we to her window,
And give some evening music to her ear.

Enter THURIO *and* MUSICIANS.

THURIO
How now, Sir Proteus! are you crept before us?

PROTEUS
Ay, gentle Thurio; for you know that love
Will creep in service where it cannot go.

THURIO
Ay, but I hope, sir, that you love not here.

PROTEUS
Sir, but I do; or else I would be hence.

THURIO
Who? Silvia?

PROTEUS
Ay, Silvia, — for
your sake.

THURIO
I thank you for your own. —
Now, gentlemen,
Let's tune, and to it lustily
awhile.

Enter, at a distance, HOST, *and*
JULIA *in boy's clothes.*

HOST
Now, my young guest, —
methinks you're allicholly: I pray
you, why is it?

JULIA
Marry, mine host, because I
cannot be merry.

HOST
Come, we'll have you merry: I'll
bring you where you shall hear
music, and see the gentleman
that you ask'd for.

JULIA
But shall I hear him speak?

HOST
Ay, that you shall.

JULIA
That will be music.   [*Music plays.*

HOST
Hark, hark!

JULIA
Is he among these?

HOST
Ay: but, peace! let's hear 'em.
Song.

Who is Silvia? what is she,
    That all our swains commend her?
Holy, fair, and wise is she;
    The heaven such grace did lend her,
That she might admired be.

Is she kind as she is fair, —
    For beauty lives with kindness?
Love doth to her eyes repair,
    To help him of his blindness;
And, being help'd, inhabits there.

Then to Silvia let us sing,
    That Silvia is excelling;
She excels each mortal thing
    Upon the dull earth dwelling:
To her let us garlands bring.

HOST
How now! are you sadder than you were before?
How do you, man? the music likes you not.

JULIA
You mistake; the musician likes me not.

HOST
Why, my pretty youth?

JULIA
He plays false, father.

HOST
How? out of tune on the strings?

JULIA
Not so; but yet so false that he grieves my very
    heart-strings.

HOST
You have a quick ear.

JULIA
Ay, I would I were deaf; it makes me have a slow heart.

HOST
I perceive you delight not in music.

JULIA
Not a whit, when it jars so.

HOST
Hark, what fine change is in the music!

JULIA
Ay, that change is the spite.

HOST
You would have them always play but one thing?

JULIA
I would always have one play but one thing.
But, host, doth this Sir Proteus that we talk on
Often resort unto this gentlewoman?

HOST
I tell you what Launce, his man, told me, — he loved
    her out of all nick.

THIRD OUTLAW Stand, sir, and throw us that you have about ye.

JULIA
Where is Launce?

HOST
Gone to seek his dog; which to-morrow, by his master's
    command, he must carry for a present to his lady.

JULIA
Peace! stand aside: the company parts.

PROTEUS
Sir Thurio, fear not you: I will so plead,
That you shall say my cunning drift excels.

THURIO
Where meet we?

PROTEUS
                    At Saint Gregory's well.

THURIO
                            Farewell.
        [*Exeunt* THURIO *and* MUSICIANS.
    SILVIA *appears above, at her window.*

PROTEUS
Madam, good even to your ladyship.

SILVIA
I thank you for your music, gentlemen.
Who is that that spake?

PROTEUS
One, lady, if you knew his pure heart's truth,
You would quickly learn to know him by his voice.

SILVIA
Sir Proteus, as I take it.

PROTEUS
Sir Proteus, gentle lady, and your servant.

SILVIA
What is your will?

PROTEUS
                    That I may compass yours.

SILVIA
You have your wish; my will is even this, —
That presently you hie you home to bed.
Thou subtle, perjured, false, disloyal man!
Think'st thou I am so shallow, so conceitless,
To be seduced by thy flattery,
That hast deceiv'd so many with thy vows?
Return, return, and make thy love amends.
For me, — by this pale queen of night I swear,
I am so far from granting thy request,
That I despise thee for thy wrongful suit;
And by and by intend to chide myself
Even for this time I spend in talking to thee.

PROTEUS
I grant, sweet love, that I did love a lady;
But she is dead.

JULIA [*aside*].
                'Twere false, if I should speak it;
For I am sure she is not buried.

SILVIA
Say that she be; yet Valentine thy friend
Survives; to whom, thyself art witness,
I am betroth'd: and art thou not asham'd

To wrong him with thy importunacy?
PROTEUS
I likewise hear that Valentine is dead.
SILVIA
And so suppose am I; for in his grave
Assure thyself my love is buried.
PROTEUS
Sweet lady, let me rake it from the earth.
SILVIA
Go to thy lady's grave, and call hers thence;
Or, at the least, in hers sepulchre thine.
JULIA [aside].
He heard not that.
PROTEUS
Madam, if your heart be so obdurate,
Vouchsafe me yet your picture for my love,
The picture that is hanging in your chamber;
To that I'll speak, to that I'll sigh and weep:
For since the substance of your perfect self
Is else devoted, I am but a shadow;
And to your shadow will I make true love.
JULIA [aside].
If 'twere a substance, you would, sure, deceive it,
And make it but a shadow, as I am.
SILVIA
I am very loath to be your idol, sir;
But since your falsehood shall become you well
To worship shadows and adore false shapes,
Send to me in the morning, and I'll send it:
And so good rest.
PROTEUS
   As wretches have o'ernight
That wait for execution in the morn.
   [Exeunt PROTEUS, and SILVIA above.
JULIA
Host, will you go?
HOST
By my halidom, I was fast asleep.
JULIA
Pray you, where lies Sir Proteus?
HOST
Marry, at my house. Trust me, I think 'tis almost day.
JULIA
Not so; but it hath been the longest night
That e'er I watch'd, and the most heaviest. [Exeunt.

SCENE III
The same.

Enter EGLAMOUR.

EGLAMOUR
This is the hour that Madam Silvia
Entreated me to call and know her mind:
There's some great matter she'ld employ me in. —
Madam, madam!

  SILVIA *above, at her window.*

SILVIA
   Who calls?
EGLAMOUR
   Your servant and your friend;
One that attends your ladyship's command.
SILVIA
Sir Eglamour, a thousand times good morrow.
EGLAMOUR
As many, worthy lady, to yourself.
According to your ladyship's impose,
I am thus early come to know what service
It is your pleasure to command me in.
SILVIA
O Eglamour, thou art a gentleman,
(Think not I flatter, for I swear I do not)
Valiant, wise, remorseful, well accomplish'd:
Thou art not ignorant what dear good will
I bear unto the banish'd Valentine;
Nor how my father would enforce me marry
Vain Thurio, whom my very soul abhors.
Thyself hast lov'd; and I have heard thee say
No grief did ever come so near thy heart
As when thy lady and thy true love died,
Upon whose grave thou vow'dst pure chastity.
Sir Eglamour, I would to Valentine,
To Mantua, where I hear he makes abode;
And, for the ways are dangerous to pass,
I do desire thy worthy company,
Upon whose faith and honour I repose.
Urge not my father's anger, Eglamour,
But think upon my grief, — a lady's grief, —
And on the justice of my flying hence,
To keep me from a most unholy match,
Which heaven and fortune still
 rewards with plagues.
I do desire thee, even from a heart
As full of sorrows as the sea of
 sands,
To bear me company, and go with
 me:
If not, to hide what I have said to
 thee,
That I may venture to depart
 alone.
EGLAMOUR
Madam, I pity much your
 grievances;
Which since I know they
 virtuously are plac'd,
I give consent to go along with
 you;
Recking as little what betideth me
As much I wish all good befortune
 you.
When will you go?
SILVIA
   This evening coming.
EGLAMOUR
Where shall I meet you?
SILVIA
   At Friar Patrick's cell,
Where I intend holy confession.
EGLAMOUR
I will not fail your ladyship. Good morrow,
Gentle lady.
SILVIA
  Good morrow, kind Sir Eglamour.

  [Exeunt EGLAMOUR, and SILVIA above.

SCENE IV
The same.

Enter LAUNCE, *with his dog.*

LAUNCE
When a man's servant shall play the cur with him, look
you, it goes hard: one that I brought up of a puppy; one
that I saved from drowning, when three or four of his
blind brothers and sisters went to it! I have taught him,
even as one would say precisely, 'Thus I would teach a
dog.' I was sent to deliver him as a present to Mistress
Silvia from my master; and I came no sooner into the
dining-chamber, but he steps me to her trencher, and
steals her capon's leg: O, 'tis a foul thing when a cur
cannot keep himself in all companies! I would have, as
one should say, one that takes upon him to be a dog
indeed, to be, as it were, a dog at all things. If I had not
had more wit than he, to take a fault upon me that he
did, I think verily he had been hang'd for't; sure as I
live, he had suffer'd for't: you shall judge. He thrusts
me himself into the company of three or four
gentlemanlike dogs, under the duke's table: he had not
been there (bless the mark!) a pissing while, but all the
chamber smelt him. 'Out with the dog,' says one;
'What cur is that?' says another; 'Whip him out,' says
the third; 'Hang him up,' says the duke. I, having been
acquainted with the smell before, knew it was Crab;
and goes me to the fellow that whips the
dogs: 'Friend,' quoth I, 'you mean to whip
the dog?' 'Ay, marry, do I,' quoth he. 'You
do him the more wrong,' quoth I; ''twas I
did the thing you wot of.' He makes me no
more ado, but whips me out of the
chamber. How many masters would do
this for his servant? Nay, I'll be sworn, I
have sat in the stocks for puddings he hath
stolen, otherwise he had been executed; I
have stood on the pillory for geese he hath
kill'd, otherwise he had suffer'd for't. —
Thou think'st not of this now! Nay, I
remember the trick you served me when I
took my leave of Madam Silvia; did not I
bid thee still mark me, and do as I do?
when didst thou see me heave up my leg,
and make water against a gentlewoman's
farthingale? didst thou ever see me do such
a trick?

 Enter PROTEUS, *and* JULIA *in boy's
 clothes.*

PROTEUS
Sebastian is thy name? I like thee well,
And will employ thee in some service
 presently.

SECOND OUTLAW And live, as we do, in this wilderness?

JULIA
In what you please: I will do what I can.
PROTEUS
I hope thou wilt. — How now, you whoreson peasant!
Where have you been these two days loitering?
LAUNCE
Marry, sir, I carried Mistress Silvia the dog you bade
me.
PROTEUS
And what says she to my little jewel?
LAUNCE
Marry, she says your dog was a cur, and tells you
currish thanks is good enough for such a present.
PROTEUS
But she received my dog?
LAUNCE
No, indeed, did she not: here have I brought him back
again.
PROTEUS
What, didst thou offer her this from me?
LAUNCE
Ay, sir; the other squirrel was stolen from me by the
hangman boys in the market-place: and then I offer'd
her mine own, — who is a dog as big as ten of yours,
and therefore the gift the greater.
PROTEUS
Go get thee hence, and find my dog again,
Or ne'er return again into my sight.
Away, I say! stay'st thou to vex me here?
A slave, that still an end turns me to shame!
   [Exit LAUNCE.
Sebastian, I have entertained thee,
Partly that I have need of such a youth,
That can with some discretion do my business,
For 'tis no trusting to yond foolish lout;
But chiefly for thy face and thy behaviour,
Which — if my augury deceive me not —
Witness good bringing up, fortune, and truth:
Therefore know thou, for this I entertain thee.

HOST I perceive you delight not in music.

LAUNCE 'What cur is that?' says another.

Go presently, and take this ring with thee;
Deliver it to Madam Silvia:
She lov'd me well deliver'd it to me.
JULIA
It seems you lov'd not her, to leave her token.
She is dead, belike?
PROTEUS
          Not so; I think she lives.
JULIA
Alas!
PROTEUS
Why dost thou cry, 'Alas'?
JULIA
              I cannot choose
But pity her.
PROTEUS
          Wherefore shouldst thou pity her?
JULIA
Because methinks that she lov'd you as well
As you do love your lady Silvia:
She dreams on him that has forgot her love;
You dote on her that cares not for your love.
'Tis pity love should be so contrary;
And thinking on it makes me cry, 'Alas!'
PROTEUS
Well: give her that ring, and therewithal
This letter: — that's her chamber: — tell my lady
I claim the promise for her heavenly picture.
Your message done, hie home unto my chamber,
Where thou shalt find me, sad and solitary.   *[Exit.*
JULIA
How many women would do such a message?
Alas, poor Proteus! thou hast entertain'd
A fox to be the shepherd of thy lambs: —
Alas, poor fool! why do I pity him,
That with his very heart despiseth me?
Because he loves her, he despiseth me;
Because I love him, I must pity him.
This ring I gave him when he parted from me,
To bind him to remember my good will:
And now am I — unhappy messenger —
To plead for that which I would not obtain;
To carry that which I would have refused;
To praise his faith which I would have dispraised.
I am my master's true-confirmed love;
But cannot be true servant to my master,
Unless I prove false traitor to myself.
Yet will I woo for him; but yet so coldly
As, heaven it knows, I would not have him speed.
        Enter SILVIA, *attended.*
Gentlewoman, good day! I pray you, be my mean
To bring me where to speak with Madam Silvia.
SILVIA
What would you with her, if that I be she?
JULIA
If you be she, I do entreat your patience
To hear me speak the message I am sent on.
SILVIA
From whom?

JULIA
From my master, Sir Proteus, madam.
SILVIA
O, — he sends you for a picture?
JULIA
Ay, madam.
SILVIA
Ursula, bring my picture there. —
Go give your master this: tell him, from me,
One Julia, that his changing thoughts forget,
Would better fit his chamber than this shadow.
JULIA
Madam, please you peruse this letter. —
Pardon me, madam; I have unadvised
Deliver'd you a paper that I should not:
This is the letter to your ladyship.
SILVIA
I pray thee, let me look on that again.
JULIA
It may not be; good madam, pardon me.
SILVIA
There, hold: —
I will not look upon your master's lines:
I know they are stuff'd with protestations,
And full of new-found oaths; which he will break
As easily as I do tear his paper.
JULIA
Madam, he sends your ladyship this ring.
SILVIA
The more shame for him that he sends it me;
For I have heard him say a thousand times
His Julia gave it him at his departure.
Though his false finger have profan'd the ring,
Mine shall not do his Julia so much wrong.
JULIA
She thanks you.
SILVIA
What say'st thou?
JULIA
I thank you, madam, that you tender her.
Poor gentlewoman! my master wrongs her much.
SILVIA
Dost thou know her?
JULIA
Almost as well as I do know myself:
To think upon her woes I do protest
That I have wept a hundred several times.
SILVIA
Belike she thinks that Proteus hath forsook her.
JULIA
I think she doth; and that's her cause of sorrow.
SILVIA
Is she not passing fair?
JULIA
She hath been fairer, madam, than she is:
When she did think my master lov'd her well,
She, in my judgement, was as fair as you;
But since she did neglect her looking-glass,
And threw her sun-expelling mask away,
The air hath starv'd the roses in her cheeks,
And pinch'd the lily-tincture of her face,
That now she is become as black as I.
SILVIA
How tall was she?
JULIA
About my stature: for, at Pentecost,
When all our pageants of delight were play'd,
Our youth got me to play the woman's part,
And I was trimm'd in Madam Julia's gown;
Which served me as fit, by all men's judgements,
As if the garment had been made for me:
Therefore I know she is about my height.
And at that time I made her weep a-good,
For I did play a lamentable part;
Madam, 'twas Ariadne, passioning
For Theseus' perjury and unjust flight;
Which I so lively acted with my tears,
That my poor mistress, moved therewithal,
Wept bitterly; and, would I might be dead,
If I in thought felt not her very sorrow!
SILVIA
She is beholding to thee, gentle youth.
Alas, poor lady, desolate and left!
I weep myself to think upon thy words.
Here, youth, there is my purse: I give thee this
For thy sweet mistress' sake, because thou lov'st her.
Farewell.
JULIA
And she shall thank you for't, if e'er you know her.
        [Exit SILVIA, *attended.*
A virtuous gentlewoman, mild and beautiful!
I hope my master's suit will be but cold,
Since she respects my mistress' love so much.
Alas! how love can trifle with itself!
Here is her picture: let me see; I think,
If I had such a the, this face of mine
Were full as lovely as is this of hers:
And yet the painter flatter'd her a little,
Unless I flatter with myself too much.
Her hair is auburn, mine is perfect yellow:
If that be all thje difference in his love,
I'll get me such a colour'd periwig.
Her eyes are grey as glass; and so are mine:
Ay, but her forehead's low, and mine's as high.
What should it be that he respective in her,
But I can make respective in myself,
If this fond Love were not a blinded god?
Come, shadow, come, and take this shadow up,
For 'tis thy rival. O thou senseless form,
Thou shalt be worshipp'd, kiss'd, lov'd and adored!
And, were there sense in his idolatry,
My substance should be statue in thy stead.
I'll use thee kindly for thy mistress' sake,
That used me so; or else, by Jove I vow,
I should have scratch'd out your unseeing eyes,
To make my master out of love with thee!   *[Exit.*

ACT V

SCENE I

Milan. An abbey.

Enter EGLAMOUR.

EGLAMOUR
The sun begins to gild the western sky;
And now it is about the very hour
That Silvia, at Friar Patrick's cell, should meet me.
She will not fail; for lovers break not hours,
Unless it be to come before their time;
So much they spur their expedition.
See where she comes.
        Enter SILVIA.
          Lady, a happy evening!
SILVIA
Amen, amen! Go on, good Eglamour,
Out at the postern by the abbey-wall:
I fear I am attended by some spies.
EGLAMOUR
Fear not: the forest is not three leagues off;
If we recover that, we are sure enough.   *[Exeunt.*

SCENE II

The same. The DUKE'S *palace.*

Enter THURIO, PROTEUS, *and* JULIA *in boy's clothes.*

THURIO
Sir Proteus, what says Silvia to my suit?
PROTEUS
O, sir, I find her milder than she was;
And yet she takes exceptions at your person.
THURIO
What, that my leg is too long?
PROTEUS
No; that it is too little.
THURIO
I'll wear a boot, to make it somewhat rounder.
JULIA [*aside*].
But love will not be spurr'd to what it loathes.
THURIO
What says she to my face?
PROTEUS
She says it is a fair one.
THURIO
Nay, then, the wanton lies; my face is black.
PROTEUS
But pearls are fair; and the old saying is,
Black men are pearls in beauteous ladies' eyes.
JULIA [*aside*].
'Tis true, such pearls as put out ladies' eyes:
For I had rather wink than look on them.
THURIO
How likes she my discourse?
PROTEUS
Ill, when you talk of war.
THURIO
But well, when I discourse of love and peace.

JULIA [*aside*].
But better, indeed, when you hold your peace.

THURIO
What says she to my birth?

PROTEUS
O, sir, she makes no doubt of that.

JULIA [*aside*].
She needs not, when she knows it cowardice.

THURIO
What says she to my valour?

PROTEUS
That you are well derived.

JULIA [*aside*].
True; from a gentleman to a fool.

THURIO
Considers she my possessions?

PROTEUS
O, ay; and pities them.

THURIO
Wherefore?

JULIA [*aside*].
That such an ass should owe them.

PROTEUS
That they are out by lease.

JULIA
Here comes the duke.

Enter DUKE OF MILAN.

DUKE OF MILAN
How now, Sir Proteus! how now, Thurio!
Which of you saw Sir Eglamour of late?

THURIO
Not I.

PROTEUS
            Nor I.

DUKE OF MILAN
            Saw you my daughter?

PROTEUS
                        Neither.

DUKE OF MILAN
Why, then,
She's fled unto that peasant Valentine;
And Eglamour is in her company.
'Tis true; for Friar Laurence met them both,
As he in penance wander'd through the forest:
Him he knew well; and guess'd that it was she,
But, being mask'd, he was not sure of it:
Besides, she did intend confession
At Patrick's cell this even; and there she was not:
These likelihoods confirm her flight from hence.
Therefore, I pray you, stand not to discourse,
But mount you presently; and meet with me
Upon the rising of the mountain-foot
That leads toward Mantua, whither they are fled:
Dispatch, sweet gentlemen, and follow me.   [*Exit.*

THURIO
Why, this it is to be a peevish girl,
That flies her fortune when it follows her.
I'll after, more to be reveng'd on Eglamour
Than for the love of reckless Silvia.   [*Exit.*

PROTEUS
And I will follow, more for Silvia's love
Than hate of Eglamour, that goes with her.   [*Exit.*

JULIA
And I will follow, more to cross that love
Than hate for Silvia, that is gone for love.   [*Exit.*

SCENE III

The forest.

Enter OUTLAWS *with* SILVIA.

FIRST OUTLAW
Come, come;
Be patient; we must bring you to our captain.

SILVIA
A thousand more mischances than this one
Have learn'd me how to brook this patiently.

SECOND OUTLAW
Come, bring her away.

FIRST OUTLAW
Where is the gentleman that was with her?

THIRD OUTLAW
Being nimble-footed, he hath outrun us,
But Moyses and Valerius follow him.
Go thou with her to the west end of the wood;
There is our captain: we'll follow him that's fled;
The thicket is beset, he cannot scape.

FIRST OUTLAW
Come, I must bring you to our captain's cave:

Fear not; he bears an honourable mind,
And will not use a woman lawlessly.

SILVIA
O Valentine, this I endure for thee!
                        [*Exeunt.*

SCENE IV

Another part of the forest.

Enter VALENTINE.

VALENTINE
How use doth breed a habit in a man!
This shadowy desert, unfrequented woods,
I better brook than flourishing peopled towns:
Here can I sit alone, unseen of any,
And to the nightingale's complaining notes
Tune my distresses and record my woes.
O thou that dost inhabit in my breast,
Leave not the mansion so long tenantless,
Lest, growing ruinous, the building fall,
And leave no memory of what it was!
Repair me with thy presence, Silvia!
Thou gentle nymph, cherish thy forlorn swain!
                        [*Noise within.*
What halloing and what stir is this to-day?
These are my mates, that make their wills their law,
Have some unhappy passenger in chase:
They love me well; yet I have much to do
To keep them from uncivil outrages. —
Withdraw thee, Valentine: who's this comes here?
                        [*Retires.*

Enter PROTEUS, SILVIA, *and* JULIA *in boy's clothes.*

PROTEUS
Madam, this service I have done for you, —
Though you respect not aught your servant doth, —
To hazard life, and rescue you from him
That would have forc'd your honour and your love:
Vouchsafe me, for my meed, but one fair look;
A smaller boon than this I cannot beg,
And less than this, I am sure, you cannot give.

VALENTINE [*aside*].
How like a dream is this I see and hear!
Love, lend me patience to forbear awhile.

SILVIA
O miserable, unhappy that I am!

PROTEUS
Unhappy were you, madam, ere I came;
But by my coming I have made you happy.

SILVIA
By thy approach thou makest me most unhappy.

JULIA [*aside*].
And me, when he approacheth to your presence.

SILVIA
Had I been seized by a hungry lion,
I would have been a breakfast to the beast,
Rather than have false Proteus rescue me.
O, Heaven be judge how I love Valentine,
Whose life's as tender to me as my soul;
And full as much — for more there cannot be —
I do detest false perjur'd Proteus!
Therefore be gone, solicit me no more.

PROTEUS
What dangerous action, stood it next to death,
Would I not undergo for one calm look!.
O, 'tis the curse in love, and still approved,
When women cannot love where they're beloved!

SILVIA
When Proteus cannot love where he's beloved.
Read over Julia's heart, thy first best love,

SILVIA What would you with her, if that I be she?

For whose dear sake thou didst then rend thy faith
Into a thousand oaths; and all those oaths
Descended into perjury, to love me.
Thou hast no faith left now, unless thou'dst two,
And that's far worse than none; better have none
Than plural faith, which is too much by one:
Thou counterfeit to thy true friend!

PROTEUS
                        In love
Who respects friend?

SILVIA
                        All men but Proteus.

PROTEUS
Nay, if the gentle spirit of moving words
Can no way change you to a milder form,
I'll woo you like a soldier, at arms' end,
And love you 'gainst the nature of love, — force ye.

SILVIA
O heaven!

PROTEUS
                        I'll force thee yield to my desire.

VALENTINE [*coming forward*].
Ruffian, let go that rude uncivil touch, —
Thou friend of an ill fashion!

PROTEUS
                        Valentine!

VALENTINE
Thou common friend, that's without faith or love,
For such is a friend now; treacherous man!
Thou hast beguil'd my hopes; naught but mine eye
Could have persuaded me: now I dare not say
I have one friend alive; thou wouldst disprove me.
Who should be trusted now, when one's right hand
Is perjur'd to the bosom? Proteus,

SILVIA I fear I am attended by some spies.

VALENTINE Ruffian, let go that rude uncivil touch.

I am sorry I must never trust thee more,
But count the world a stranger for thy sake.
The private wound is deepest: O time most accurst!
'Mongst all foes that a friend should be the worst!

PROTEUS
My shame and guilt confounds me.
Forgive me, Valentine: if hearty sorrow
Be a sufficient ransom for offence,
I tender't here; I do as truly suffer
As e'er I did commit.

VALENTINE
       Then I am paid;
And once again I do receive thee honest.
Who by repentance is not satisfied
Is nor of heaven nor earth; for these are pleas'd;
By penitence th'Eternal wrath's appeas'd:
And, that my love may appear plain and free,
All that was mine in Silvia I give thee.

JULIA
O me unhappy!   [*Faints.*

PROTEUS
Look to the boy.

VALENTINE
Why, boy! why, wag! how now! what's the matter?
Look up; speak.

JULIA
       O good sir, my master charg'd me
To deliver a ring to Madam Silvia;
Which, out of my neglect, was never done.

PROTEUS
Where is that ring, boy?

JULIA
        Here 'tis; this is it.
         [*Gives a ring.*

PROTEUS
How! let me see: —
Why, this is the ring I gave to Julia.

JULIA
O, cry you mercy, sir, I have mistook:
This is the ring you sent to Silvia.
         [*Shows another ring.*

PROTEUS
But how cam'st thou by this ring? At
   my depart I gave this unto Julia.

JULIA
And Julia herself did give it me;
And Julia herself hath brought it hither.

PROTEUS
How! Julia!

JULIA
Behold her that gave aim to all thy oaths,
And entertain'd 'em deeply in her
   heart:
How oft hast thou with perjury cleft
   the root!
O Proteus, let this habit make thee
   blush!
Be thou asham'd that I have took
   upon me
Such an immodest raiment, — if
   shame live
In a disguise of love:
   It is the lesser blot, modesty finds,
Women to change their shapes than men their minds.

PROTEUS
Than men their minds! 'tis true. O heaven, were man
But constant, he were perfect! that one error
Fills him with faults; makes him run through all
   th'sins:
Inconstancy falls off ere it begins.
What is in Silvia's face, but I may spy
More fresh in Julia's with a constant eye?

VALENTINE
Come, come, a hand from either:
Let me be blest to make this happy close;
'Twere pity two such friends should be long foes.

PROTEUS
Bear witness, Heaven, I have my wish for ever.

JULIA
And I mine.

    Enter OUTLAWS, *with* DUKE *and* THURIO.

OUTLAWS
A prize, a prize, a prize!

VALENTINE
Forbear, forbear, I say! it is my lord the duke. —
Your grace is welcome to a man disgrac'd,
Banished Valentine.

DUKE OF MILAN
        Sir Valentine!

THURIO
Yonder is Silvia; and Silvia's mine.

VALENTINE
Thurio, give back, or else embrace thy death;
Come not within the measure of my wrath:
Do not name Silvia thine; if once again,
Verona shall not hold thee. Here she stands:
Take but possession of her with a touch; —
I dare thee but to breathe upon my love.

THURIO
Sir Valentine, I care not for her, I;
I hold him but a fool that will endanger
His body for a girl that loves him not:
I claim her not, and therefore she is thine.

DUKE OF MILAN
The more degenerate and base art thou,
To make such means for her as thou hast done,
And leave her on such slight conditions. —
Now, by the honour of my ancestry,
I do applaud thy spirit, Valentine,
And think thee worthy of an empress' love:
Know, then, I here forget all former griefs,
Cancel all grudge, repeal thee home again,
Plead a new state in thy unrivall'd merit,
To which I thus subscribe, — Sir Valentine,
Thou art a gentleman, and well deriv'd;
Take thou thy Silvia, for thou hast deserv'd her.

VALENTINE
I thank your Grace; the gift hath made me happy.
I now beseech you, for your daughter's sake,
To grant one boon that I shall ask of you.

DUKE OF MILAN
I grant it, for thine own, whate'er it be.

VALENTINE
These banish'd men, that I have kept withal,
Are men endued with worthy qualities:
Forgive them what they have committed here,
And let them be recall'd from their exile:
They are reformed, civil, full of good,
And fit for great employment, worthy lord.

DUKE OF MILAN
Thou hast prevail'd; I pardon them and thee:
Dispose of them as thou know'st their deserts. —
Come, let us go: we will include all jars
With triumphs, mirth, and rare solemnity.

VALENTINE
And, as we walk along, I dare be bold
With our discourse to make your Grace to smile.
What think you of this page, my lord?

DUKE OF MILAN
I think the boy hath grace in him; he blushes.

VALENTINE
I warrant you, my lord, more grace than boy.

DUKE OF MILAN
What mean you by that saying?

VALENTINE
Please you, I'll tell you as we pass along,
That you will wonder what hath fortuned.
Come, Proteus; 'tis your penance but to hear
The story of your loves discovered:
That done, our day of marriage shall be yours;
One feast, one house, one mutual happiness. [*Exeunt.*

LOVE'S LABOUR'S LOST

DRAMATIS PERSONAE

FERDINAND, *King of Navarre.*
BEROWNE,
LONGAVILLE, } *lords attending on the King.*
DUMAINE,
BOYET,
MERCADÉ, } *lords attending on the Princess of France.*
DON ADRIANO DE ARMADO, *a fantastical
Spaniard.*

SIR NATHANIEL, *a curate.*
HOLOFERNES, *a schoolmaster.*
DULL, *a constable.*
COSTARD, *a clown.*
MOTH, *page to Armado.*
A FORESTER.

PRINCESS OF FRANCE.

ROSALINE,
MARIA, } *ladies attending on the Princess.*
KATHARINE,
JAQUENETTA, *a country wench.*

LORDS, ATTENDANTS, etc.

SCENE — *Navarre.*

ACT I

SCENE I

Navarre. A park with a palace in it.

Enter the KING, BEROWNE, LONGAVILLE, *and*
DUMAINE.

KING
Let fame, that all hunt after in their lives,
Live register'd upon our brazen tombs,
And then grace us in the disgrace of death;
When, spite of cormorant devouring Time,
Th'endeavour of this present breath may buy
That honour which shall bate his scythe's keen edge,
And make us heirs of all eternity.
Therefore, brave conquerors, — for so you are,
That war against your own affections,
And the huge army of the world's desires, —
Our late edict shall strongly stand in force:
Navarre shall be the wonder of the world;
Our court shall be a little Academe,
Still and contemplative in living art.
You three, Berowne, Dumaine, and Longaville,
Have sworn for three years' term to live with me
My fellow-scholars, and to keep those statutes
That are recorded in this schedule here:
Your oaths are pass'd; and now subscribe your names,
That his own hand may strike his honour down
That violates the smallest branch herein:
If you are arm'd to do as sworn to do,
Subscribe to your deep oaths, and keep it too.

LONGAVILLE
I am resolv'd; 'tis but a three years' fast:
The mind shall banquet, though the body pine:
Fat paunches have lean pates; and dainty bits
Make rich the ribs, but bankrout quite the wits.

DUMAINE
My loving lord, Dumaine is mortify'd:
The grosser manner of these world's delights
He throws upon the gross world's baser slaves:
To love, to wealth, to pomp, I pine and die;
With all these living in philosophy.

BEROWNE
I can but say their protestation over;
So much, dear liege, I have already sworn,
That is, to live and study here three years.
But there are other strict observances:
As, not to see a woman in that term, —
Which I hope well is not enrolled there;
And one day in a week to touch no food,
And but one meal on every day beside, —
The which I hope is not enrolled there;
And then, to sleep but three hours in the night,
And not be seen to wink of all the day
(When I was wont to think no harm all night,
And make a dark night too of half the day), —
Which I hope well is not enrolled there:
O, these are barren tasks, too hard to keep, —
Not to see ladies, study, fast, not sleep!

KING
Your oath is pass'd to pass away from these.

BEROWNE
Let me say no, my liege, an if you please:
I only swore to study with your Grace,
And stay here in your court for three years' space.

LONGAVILLE
You swore to that, Berowne, and to the rest.

BEROWNE
By yea and nay, sir, then I swore in jest. —
What is the end of study? let me know.

KING
Why, that to know, which else we should not know.

BEROWNE
Things hid and barr'd, you mean, from common
sense?

KING
Ay, that is study's god-like recompense.

BEROWNE
Come on, then; I will swear to study so,
To know the thing I am forbid to know:
As thus, — to study where I well may dine,
When I to feast expressly am forbid;
Or study where to meet some mistress fine,
When mistresses from common sense are hid;
Or, having sworn too hard-a-keeping oath
Study to break it, and not break my troth.
If study's gain be thus, and this be so,
Study knows that which yet it doth not know:
Swear me to this, and I will ne'er say no.

KING
These be the stops that hinder study quite,
And train our intellects to vain delight.

BEROWNE
Why, all delights are vain: but that most vain,
Which, with pain purchas'd, doth inherit pain:
As, painfully to pore upon a book
To seek the light of truth: while truth the while
Doth falsely blind the eyesight of his look:
Light, seeking light, doth light of light beguile:
So, ere you find where light in darkness lies,
Your light grows dark by losing of your eyes.
Study me how to please the eye indeed,
By fixing it upon a fairer eye;
Who dazzling so, that eye shall be his heed,
And give him light that it was blinded by.
Study is like the heaven's glorious sun,
That will not be deep-search'd with saucy looks:
Small have continual plodders ever won,
Save base authority from others' books.
These earthly godfathers of heaven's lights,
That give a name to every fixed star,
Have no more profit of their shining nights
Than those that walk and wot not
what they are.
Too much to know, is to know naught
but fame;
And every godfather can give a name.

KING
How well he's read, to reason against
reading!

DUMAINE
Proceeded well, to stop all good
proceeding!

LONGAVILLE
He weeds the corn, and still lets grow
the weeding.

BEROWNE
The spring is near, when green geese
are a-breeding.

DUMAINE
How follows that?

BEROWNE
Fit in his place and time.

DUMAINE
In reason nothing.

BEROWNE
Something, then, in rime.

KING
Berowne is like an envious-sneaping
frost,
That bites the first-born infants of the
spring.

BEROWNE
Well, say I am; why should proud summer boast,
Before the birds have any cause to sing?
Why should I joy in any abortive birth?
At Christmas I no more desire a rose
Than wish a snow in May's new-fangled earth;
But like of each thing that in season grows.
So you — to study now it is too late —
Climb o'er the house to unlock the little gate.

KING
Well, sit you out: go home, Berowne: adieu.

BEROWNE
No, my good lord; I have sworn to stay with you:
And though I have for barbarism spoke more
Than for that angel knowledge you can say,
Yet confident I'll keep what I have swore,
And bide the penance of each three years' day.
Give me the paper, — let me read the same;
And to the strict'st decrees I'll write my name.

KING
How well this yielding rescues thee from shame!

BEROWNE [*reads*].
'Item, That no woman shall come within a mile
of my court,' — Hath this been proclaim'd?

LONGAVILLE
Four days ago.

BEROWNE
Let's see the penalty. — [*Reads.*] 'On pain of losing her
tongue.' — Who devised this penalty?

LONGAVILLE
Marry, that did I.

BEROWNE
Sweet lord, and why?

LONGAVILLE
To fright them hence with that dread penalty.

BEROWNE
A dangerous law against gentility!
[*Reads.*] 'Item, If any man be seen to talk with a
woman within the term of three years, he shall endure
such public shame as the rest of the court can possibly
devise.'

BEROWNE Let's see the penalty.

This article, my liege, yourself must break;
  For well you know here comes in embassy
The French king's daughter with yourself to speak, —
  A maid of grace and complete majesty, —
About surrender-up of Aquitaine
  To her decrepit, sick, and bed-rid father:
Therefore this article is made in vain,
  Or vainly comes th'admired princess hither.

KING
What say you, lords? why, this was quite forgot.

BEROWNE
So study evermore is overshot:
While it doth study to have what it would,
It doth forget to do the thing it should;
And when it hath the thing it hunteth most,
'Tis won as towns with fire, — so won, so lost.

KING
We must of force dispense with this decree;
She must lie here on mere necessity.

BEROWNE
Necessity will make us all forsworn
  Three thousand times within this three years' space;
For every man with his affects is born,
  Not by might master'd, but by special grace:
If I break faith, this word shall speak for me,
I am forsworn on mere necessity. —
So to the laws at large I write my name: [*Subscribes.*
  And he that breaks them in the least degree
Stands in attainder of eternal shame:
  Suggestions are to other as to me;
But I believe, although I seem so loth,
I am the last that will last keep his oath.
But is there no quick recreation granted?

KING
Ay, that there is. Our court, you know, is haunted
With a refined traveller of Spain;
A man in all the world's new fashion planted,
That hath a mint of phrases in his brain;
One whom the music of his own vain tongue
Doth ravish like enchanting harmony;
A man of complements, whom right and wrong
Have chose as umpire of their mutiny:
This child of fancy, that Armado hight,
For interim to our studies, shall relate,
In high-born words, the worth of many a knight
From tawny Spain, lost in the world's debate.
How you delight, my lords, I know not, I;
But, I protest, I love to hear him lie,
And I will use him for my minstrelsy.

BEROWNE
Armado is a most illustrious wight,
A man of fire-new words, fashion's own knight.

LONGAVILLE
Costard the swain and he shall be our sport;
And, so to study, three years is but short.

Enter DULL *with a letter, and* COSTARD.

DULL
Which is the duke's own person?

BEROWNE
This, fellow: what wouldst?

DULL
I myself reprehend his own person, for I am his
Grace's tharborough: but I would see his own person
in flesh and blood.

BEROWNE
This is he.

DULL
Signior Arme — Arme — commends you. There's
villainy abroad: this letter will tell you more.

COSTARD
Sir, the contempts thereof are as touching me.

KING
A letter from the magnificent Armado.

BEROWNE
How low soever the matter, I hope in God for high
  words.

LONGAVILLE
A high hope for a low having: God grant us patience!

BEROWNE
To hear? or forbear laughing?

LONGAVILLE
To hear meekly, sir, and to laugh moderately; or to
forbear both.

BEROWNE
Well, sir, be it as the style shall give us cause to climb in
  the merriness.

COSTARD
The matter is to me, sir, as concerning Jaquenetta. The
  manner of it is, I was taken with the manner.

BEROWNE
In what manner?

COSTARD
In manner and form following, sir; all those three: I
was seen with her in the manor-house, sitting with her
upon the form, and taken following her into the park;
which, put together, is in manner and form following.
Now, sir, for the manner, — it is the manner of a man
to speak to a woman: for the form, — in some form.

BEROWNE
For the following, sir?

COSTARD
As it shall follow in my correction: and God defend the
  right!

KING
Will you hear this letter with attention?

BEROWNE
As we would hear an oracle.

COSTARD
Such is the simplicity of man to hearken after the flesh.

KING [*reads*].
Great deputy, the welkin's vicegerent, and sole
dominator of Navarre, my soul's earth's god and body's
fostering patron, —

COSTARD
Not a word of Costard yet.

KING [*reads*].
So it is, —

COSTARD
It may be so: but if he says it is so, he is, in telling true,
  but so —

KING
Peace!

COSTARD
Be to me, and every man that dares not fight!

KING
No words!

COSTARD
Of other men's secrets, I beseech you.

KING [*reads*].
So it is, besieged with sable-colour'd melancholy, I did
commend the black-oppressing humour to the most
wholesome physic of thy health-giving air; and, as I am
a gentleman, betook myself to walk. The time when?
About the sixth hour; when beasts most graze, birds
best peck, and men sit down to that nourishment
which is call'd supper; so much for the time when.
Now for the ground which; which, I mean, I walk'd
upon: it is ycleped thy park. Then for the place where;
where, I mean, I did encounter that obscene and most
preposterous event, that draweth from my snow-white
pen the ebon-colour'd ink, which here thou viewest,
beholdest, surveyest, or seest: but to the place where, — it
standeth north-north-east and by east from the west
corner of thy curious-knotted garden: there did I see that
low-spirited swain, that base minnow of thy mirth, —

COSTARD
Me?

KING [*reads*].
that unletter'd small-knowing soul, —

COSTARD
Me?

KING [*reads*].
that shallow vassal, —

COSTARD
Still me?

KING [*reads*].
which, as I remember, hight Costard, —

COSTARD
O, me!

KING [*reads*].
sorted and consorted, contrary to thy establish'd
proclaim'd edict and continent canon, with — with, —
O, with — but with this I passion to say wherewith, —

COSTARD
With a wench.

KING [*reads*].
with a child of our grandmother Eve, a female; or, for
thy more sweet understanding, a woman. Him I — as
my ever-esteem'd duty pricks me on — have sent to
thee, to receive the meed of punishment, by thy sweet
Grace's officer, Anthony Dull; a man of good repute,
carriage, bearing, and estimation.

DULL
Me, an't shall please you; I am Antony Dull.

KING [*reads*].
For Jaquenetta, — so is the weaker vessel call'd which I
apprehended with the aforesaid swain, — I keep her as

a vessel of thy law's fury; and shall, at the least of thy
sweet notice, bring her to trial. Thine, in all
compliements of devoted and heart-burning heat of
duty.
            DON ADRIANO DE ARMADO.

BEROWNE
This is not so well as I look'd for, but the best that ever I
  heard.

KING
Ay, the best for the worst. — But, sirrah, what say you
  to this?

COSTARD
Sir, I confess the wench.

KING
Did you hear the proclamation?

COSTARD
I do confess much of the hearing it, but little of the
  marking of it.

KING
It was proclaim'd a year's imprisonment, to be taken
  with a wench.

COSTARD
I was taken with none, sir: I was taken with a damsel.

KING
Well, it was proclaim'd damsel.

COSTARD
This was no damsel neither, sir; she was a virgin.

KING
It is so varied too; for it was proclaim'd virgin.

COSTARD
If it were, I deny her virginity: I was taken with a maid.

KING
This maid will not serve your turn, sir.

COSTARD
This maid will serve my turn, sir.

KING
Sir, I will pronounce your sentence: you shall fast
a week with bran and water.

COSTARD
I had rather pray a month with mutton and porridge.

KING
And Don Armado shall be your keeper. —
My Lord Berowne, see him deliver'd o'er: —
And go we, lords, to put in practise that
  Which each to other hath so strongly sworn.
    [*Exeunt* KING, LONGAVILLE, *and* DUMAINE.

BEROWNE
I'll lay my head to any good man's hat,
These oaths and laws will prove an idle scorn. —
Sirrah, come on.

COSTARD
I suffer for the truth, sir; for true it is, I was taken with
Jaquenetta, and Jaquenetta is a true girl; and therefore,
Welcome the sour cup of prosperity! Affliction may
one day smile again; and till then, sit thee down,
sorrow!
                    [*Exeunt.*

SCENE II

The same.

Enter ARMADO *and* MOTH, *his page.*

ARMADO
Boy, what sign is it when a man of great spirit grows
  melancholy?

MOTH
A great sign, sir, that he will look sad.

ARMADO
Why, sadness is one and the selfsame thing, dear imp.

MOTH
No, no; O lord, sir, no.

ARMADO
How canst thou part sadness and melancholy, my
  tender juvenal?

MOTH
By a familiar demonstration of the working, my tough
  signior.

ARMADO
Why tough signior? why tough signior?

MOTH
Why tender juvenal? why tender juvenal?

ARMADO
I spoke it, tender juvenal, as a congruent epitheton
appertaining to thy young days, which we may
nominate tender.

MOTH
And I, tough signior, as an appertinent title to your old
time, which we may name tough.

ARMADO
Pretty and apt.
MOTH
How mean you, sir? I pretty, and my saying apt? or I apt, and my saying pretty?
ARMADO
Thou pretty, because little.
MOTH
Little pretty, because little. Wherefore apt?
ARMADO
And therefore apt, because quick.
MOTH
Speak you this in my praise, master?
ARMADO
In thy condign praise.
MOTH
I will praise an eel with the same praise.
ARMADO
What, that an eel is ingenious?
MOTH
That an eel is quick.
ARMADO
I do say thou art quick in answers: thou heat'st my blood.
MOTH
I am answered, sir.
ARMADO
I love not to be cross'd.
MOTH [aside].
He speaks the mere contrary, — crosses love not him.
ARMADO
I have promised to study three years with the duke.
MOTH
You may do it in an hour, sir.
ARMADO
Impossible.
MOTH
How many is one thrice told?
ARMADO
I am ill at reck'ning, — it fitteth the spirit of a tapster.
MOTH
You are a gentleman and a gamester, sir.
ARMADO
I confess both: they are both the varnish of a complete man.
MOTH
Then, I am sure, you know how much the gross sum of deuce-ace amounts to.
ARMADO
It doth amount to one more than two.
MOTH
Which the base vulgar do call three.
ARMADO
True.
MOTH
Why, sir, is this such a piece of study? Now here's three studied, ere you'll thrice wink: and how easy it is to put years to the word three, and study three years in two words, the dancing horse will tell you.
ARMADO
A most fine figure!
MOTH [aside].
To prove you a cipher.
ARMADO
I will hereupon confess I am in love: and as it is base for a soldier to love, so am I in love with a base wench. If drawing my sword against the humour of affection would deliver me from the reprobate thought of it, I would take Desire prisoner, and ransom him to any French courtier for a new-devised courtesy. I think scorn to sigh: methinks I should outswear Cupid. Comfort me, boy: what great men have been in love?
MOTH
Hercules, master.
ARMADO
Most sweet Hercules! — More authority, dear boy, name more; and, sweet my child, let them be men of good repute and carriage.
MOTH
Samson, master: he was a man of good carriage, great carriage, — for he carried the town-gates on his back like a porter: and he was in love.
ARMADO
O well-knit Samson! strong-jointed Samson! I do excel thee in my rapier as much as thou didst me in carrying gates. I am in love too: — who was Samson's love, my dear Moth?

MOTH
A woman, master.
ARMADO
Of what complexion?
MOTH
Of all the four, or the three, or the two; or one of the four.
ARMADO
Tell me precisely of what complexion.
MOTH
Of the sea-water green, sir.
ARMADO
Is that one of the four complexions?
MOTH
As I have read, sir; and the best of them too.
ARMADO
Green, indeed, is the colour of lovers; but to have a love of that colour, methinks Samson had small reason for it. He surely affected her for her wit.
MOTH
It was so, sir; for she had a green wit.
ARMADO
My love is most immaculate white and red.
MOTH
Most maculate thoughts, master, are mask'd under such colours.
ARMADO
Define, define, well-educated infant.
MOTH
My father's wit and my mother's tongue assist me!
ARMADO
Sweet invocation of a child; most pretty and pathetical!
MOTH
　　If she be made of white and red,
　　　Her faults will ne'er be known;
　　For blushing cheeks by faults are bred,
　　　And fears by pale white shown:
　　Then if she fear, or be to blame,
　　　By this you shall not know;
　　For still her cheeks possess the same,
　　　Which native she doth owe.
A dangerous rime, master, against the reason of white and red.
ARMADO
Is there not a ballad, boy, of the King and the Beggar?
MOTH
The world was very guilty of such a ballad some three ages since: but, I think, now 'tis not to be found; or, if it were, it would neither serve for the writing nor the tune.
ARMADO
I will have that subject newly writ o'er, that I may example my digression by some mighty precedent. Boy, I do love that country girl that I took in the park with the rational hind Costard: she deserves well.
MOTH [aside].
To be whipp'd; and yet a better love than my master.
ARMADO
Sing, boy; my spirit grows heavy in love.
MOTH
And that's great marvel, loving a light wench.
ARMADO
I say, sing.
MOTH
Forbear till this company be past.
　　Enter DULL, COSTARD, *and*
　　　JAQUENETTA.
DULL
Sir, the duke's pleasure is, that you keep Costard safe: and you must let him take no delight nor no penance; but a' must fast three days a week. For this damsel, I must keep her at the park: she is allowed for the day-woman. Fare you well.
ARMADO
I do betray myself with blushing. — Maid, —
JAQUENETTA
Man.
ARMADO
I will visit thee at the lodge.
JAQUENETTA
That's hereby.

ARMADO
I know where it is situate.
JAQUENETTA
Lord, how wise you are!
ARMADO
I will tell thee wonders.
JAQUENETTA
With that face?
ARMADO
I love thee.
JAQUENETTA
So I heard you say.
ARMADO
And so, farewell.
JAQUENETTA
Fair weather after you!
DULL
Come, Jaquenetta, away!
　　　[*Exeunt* DULL *and* JAQUENETTA.
ARMADO
Villain, thou shalt fast for thy offences ere thou be pardoned.
COSTARD
Well, sir, I hope, when I do it, I shall do it on a full stomach.
ARMADO
Thou shalt be heavily punished.
COSTARD
I am more bound to you than your fellows, for they are but lightly rewarded.
ARMADO
Take away this villain; shut him up.
MOTH
Come, you transgressing slave; away!
COSTARD
Let me not be pent up, sir: I will fast, being loose.
MOTH
No, sir; that were fast and loose: thou shalt to prison.
COSTARD
Well, if ever I do see the merry days of desolation that I have seen, some shall see —
MOTH
What shall some see?
COSTARD
Nay, nothing, Master Moth, but what they look upon. It is not for prisoners to be too silent in their words; and therefore I will say nothing: I thank God I have as little patience as another man; and therefore I can be quiet.
　　　[*Exeunt* MOTH *and* COSTARD.
ARMADO
I do affect the very ground, which is base, where her shoe, which is baser, guided by her foot, which is basest, doth tread. I shall be forsworn, — which is a great argument of falsehood, — if I love. And how can that be true love which is falsely attempted? Love is a familiar; Love is a devil: there is no evil angel but love.

ARMADO I do betray myself with blushing.

BOYET Proud of employment, willingly I go.

Yet was Samson so tempted, — and he had an excellent strength; yet was Solomon so seduced, — and he had a very good wit. Cupid's buttshaft is too hard for Hercules' club; and therefore too much odds for a Spaniard's rapier. The first and second cause will not serve my turn; the passado he respects not, the duello he regards not: his disgrace is to be called boy; but his glory is to subdue men. Adieu, valour! rust, rapier! be still, drum! for your manager is in love; yea, he loveth. Assist me some extemporal god of rime, for I am sure I shall turn sonnet. Devise, wit, — write, pen; for I am for whole volumes in folio.

ACT II

SCENE I

The same.

Enter the PRINCESS OF FRANCE, ROSALINE, MARIA, KATHARINE, BOYET, LORDS, *and other* ATTENDANTS.

BOYET
Now, madam, summon up your dearest spirits:
Consider who the king your father sends;
To whom he sends; and what's his embassy:
Yourself, held precious in the world's esteem,
To parley with the sole inheritor
Of all perfections that a man may owe,
Matchless Navarre; the plea of no less weight
Than Aquitaine, — a dowry for a queen.
Be now as prodigal of all dear grace,
As Nature was in making graces dear,
When she did starve the general world beside,
And prodigally gave them all to you.

PRINCESS
Good Lord Boyet, my beauty, though but mean,
Needs not the painted flourish of your praise:
Beauty is bought by judgement of the eye,
Not utter'd by base sale of chapmen's tongues:
I am less proud to hear you tell my worth
Than you much willing to be counted wise
In spending your wit in the praise of mine.
But now to task the tasker: — good Boyet,
You are not ignorant, all-telling fame
Doth noise abroad, Navarre hath made a vow,
Till painful study shall outwear three years,
No woman may approach his silent court:
Therefore to's seemeth it a needful course,
Before we enter his forbidden gates,
To know his pleasure; and in that behalf,
Bold of your worthiness, we single you
As our best-moving fair solicitor.
Tell him, the daughter of the King of France,
On serious business, craving quick dispatch,
Importunes personal conference with his Grace:
Haste, signify so much; while we attend,
Like humble-visag'd suitors, his high will.

BOYET
Proud of employment, willingly I go.

PRINCESS
All pride is willing pride, and yours is so.
[*Exit* BOYET.
Who are the votaries, my loving lords,
That are vow-fellows with this virtuous duke?

FIRST LORD
Lord Longaville is one.

PRINCESS
Know you the man?

MARIA
I know him, madam: at a marriage-feast,
Between Lord Perigort and the beauteous heir
Of Jaques Falconbridge, solemnised
In Normandy, saw I this Longaville:
A man of sovereign parts he is esteem'd;
Well-fitted in arts, glorious in arms:
Nothing becomes him ill that he would well.
The only soil of his fair virtue's gloss —
If virtue's gloss will stain with any soil —
Is a sharp wit match'd with too blunt a will;
Whose edge hath power to cut, whose will still wills
It should none spare that come within his power.

PRINCESS
Some merry mocking lord, belike; is't so?

MARIA
They say so most that most his humours know.

PRINCESS
Such short-liv'd wits do wither as they grow.
Who are the rest?

KATHARINE
The young Dumaine, a well-accomplish'd youth,
Of all that virtue love for virtue lov'd:
Most power to do most harm, least knowing ill;
For he hath wit to make an ill shape good,
And shape to win grace, though he had no wit.
I saw him at the Duke Alençon's once;
And much too little of that good I saw
Is my report to his great worthiness.

ROSALINE
Another of these students at that time
Was there with him: if I have heard a truth,

Berowne they call him; but a merrier man,
Within the limit of becoming mirth,
I never spent an hour's talk withal:
His eye begets occasion for his wit;
For every object that the one doth catch,
The other turns to a mirth-moving jest,
Which his fair tongue — conceit's expositor —
Delivers in such apt and gracious words,
That aged ears play truant at his tales,
And younger hearings are quite ravished;
So sweet and voluble is his discourse.

PRINCESS
God bless my ladies! are they all in love,
That every one her own hath garnished
With such bedecking ornaments of praise?

FIRST LORD
Here comes Boyet.

Enter BOYET.

PRINCESS
Now, what admittance, lord?

BOYET
Navarre had notice of your fair approach;
And he and his competitors in oath
Were all address'd to meet you, gentle lady,
Before I came. Marry, thus much I have learnt, —
He rather means to lodge you in the field,
Like one that comes here to besiege his court,
Than seek a dispensation for his oath,
To let you enter his unpeopled house.
Here comes Navarre. [*The ladies mask.*

Enter KING, LONGAVILLE, DUMAINE, BEROWNE,
and ATTENDANTS.

KING
Fair princess, welcome to the court of Navarre.

PRINCESS
'Fair' I give you back again; and 'welcome' I have not
yet: the roof of this court is too high to be yours; and
welcome to the wide fields too base to be mine.

KING
You shall be welcome, madam, to my court.

PRINCESS
I will be welcome, then: conduct me thither.

KING
Hear me, dear lady, — I have sworn an oath.

PRINCESS
Our Lady help my lord! he'll be forsworn.

KING
Not for the world, fair madam, by my will.

PRINCESS
Why, will shall break it; will and nothing else.

KING
Your ladyship is ignorant what it is.

PRINCESS
Were my lord so, his ignorance were wise,
Where now his knowledge must prove ignorance.
I hear your Grace hath sworn-out house-keeping:
'Tis deadly sin to keep that oath, my lord,
And sin to break it.
But pardon me, I am too sudden-bold:
To teach a teacher ill beseemeth me.
Vouchsafe to read the purpose of my coming,
And suddenly resolve me in my suit. [*Gives a paper.*

KING
Madam, I will, if suddenly I may.

PRINCESS
You will the sooner, that I were away;
For you'll prove perjur'd, if you make me stay.

BEROWNE
Did not I dance with you in Brabant once?

ROSALINE
Did not I dance with you in Brabant once?

BEROWNE
I know you did.

ROSALINE
How needless was it, then, to ask the question!

BEROWNE
You must not be so quick.

ROSALINE
'Tis 'long of you that spur me with such questions.

BEROWNE
Your wit's too hot, it speeds too fast, 'twill tire.

ROSALINE
Not till it leave the rider in the mire.

BEROWNE
What time o' day?

ROSALINE
The hour that fools should ask.

BEROWNE
Now fair befall your mask!
ROSALINE
Fair fall the face it covers!
BEROWNE
And send you many lovers!
ROSALINE
Amen, so you be none.
BEROWNE
Nay, then will I be gone.
KING
Madam, your father here doth intimate
The payment of a hundred thousand
 crowns;
Being but th'one-half of an entire sum
Disbursed by my father in his wars.
But say that he or we — as neither have —
Receiv'd that sum, yet there remains
 unpaid
A hundred thousand more; in surety of
 the which,
One part of Aquitaine is bound to us,
Although not valu'd to the money's
 worth.
If, then, the king your father will restore
But that one-half which is unsatisfied,
We will give up our right in Aquitaine,
And hold fair friendship with his
 majesty.
But that, it seems, he little purposeth,
For here he doth demand to have repaid
A hundred thousand crowns; and not
 demands,
On payment of a hundred thousand
 crowns,
To have his title live in Aquitaine,
Which we much rather had depart
 withal,
And have the money by our father lent,
Than Aquitaine so gelded as it is.
Dear Princess, were not his requests so far
From reason's yielding, your fair self should make
A yielding, 'gainst some reason, in my breast,
And go well satisfied to France again.
PRINCESS
You do the king my father too much wrong,
And wrong the reputation of your name,
In so unseeming to confess receipt
Of that which hath so faithfully been paid.
KING
I do protest I never heard of it;
And if you prove it, I'll repay it back,
Or yield up Aquitaine.
PRINCESS
                    We arrest your word. —
Boyet, you can produce acquittances
For such a sum from special officers
Of Charles his father.
KING
                    Satisfy me so.
BOYET
So please your Grace, the packet is not come,
Where that and other specialties are bound:
To-morrow you shall have a sight of them.
KING
It shall suffice me: at which interview
All liberal reason I will yield unto.
Meantime receive such welcome at my hand
As honour, without breach of honour, may
Make tender of to thy true worthiness:
You may not come, fair princess, in my gates;
But here without you shall be so receiv'd
As you shall deem yourself lodg'd in my heart,
Though so denied fair harbour in my house.
Your own good thoughts excuse me, and farewell:
To-morrow shall we visit you again.
PRINCESS
Sweet health and fair desires consort your Grace!
KING
Thy own wish wish I thee in every place!
                    [*Exit* KING *attended.*
BEROWNE
Lady, I will commend you to mine own heart.
ROSALINE
Pray you, do my commendations; I would be glad
to see it.
BEROWNE
I would you heard it groan.
ROSALINE
Is the fool sick?

BEROWNE Did not I dance with you in Brabant once?

BEROWNE
Sick at the heart.
ROSALINE
Alack, let it blood.
BEROWNE
Would that do it good?
ROSALINE
My physic says ay.
BEROWNE
Will you prick't with your eye?
ROSALINE
No point, with my knife.
BEROWNE
Now, God save thy life!
ROSALINE
And yours from long living!
BEROWNE
I cannot stay thanksgiving.   [*Retiring.*
DUMAINE
Sir, I pray you, a word: what lady is that same?
BOYET
The heir of Alençon, Katharine her name.
DUMAINE
A gallant lady. Monsieur, fare you well.   [*Exit.*
LONGAVILLE
I beseech you, a word: what is she in the white?
BOYET
A woman sometimes, an you saw her in the light.
LONGAVILLE
Perchance light in the light. I desire her name.
BOYET
She hath but one for herself; to desire that were a
shame.
LONGAVILLE
Pray you, sir, whose daughter?
BOYET
Her mother's, I have heard.
LONGAVILLE
God's blessing on your beard!
BOYET
Good sir, be not offended.
She is an heir of Falconbridge.
LONGAVILLE
Nay, my choler is ended.
She is a most sweet lady.
BOYET
Not unlike, sir, that may be.   [*Exit* LONGAVILLE.
BEROWNE
What's her name in the cap?

BOYET
Rosaline, by good hap.
BEROWNE
Is she wedded or no?
BOYET
To her will, sir, or so.
BEROWNE
You are welcome, sir: adieu.
BOYET
Farewell to me, sir, and welcome to you.
                [*Exit* BEROWNE. *Ladies unmask.*
MARIA
That last is Berowne, the merry madcap lord:
Not a word with him but a jest.
BOYET
                    And every jest but a word.
PRINCESS
It was well done of you to take him at his word.
BOYET
I was as willing to grapple as he was to board.
MARIA
Two hot sheeps, marry.
BOYET
                    And wherefore not ships?
No sheep, sweet lamb, unless we feed on your lips.
MARIA
You sheep, and I pasture: shall that finish the jest?
BOYET
So you grant pasture for me.   [*Offering to kiss her.*
MARIA
                    Not so, gentle beast:
My lips are no common, though several they be.
BOYET
Belonging to whom?
MARIA
                    To my fortunes and me.
PRINCESS
Good wits will be jangling; but, gentles, agree:
This civil war of wits were much better used
On Navarre and his book-men; for here 'tis abused.
BOYET
If my observation, — which very seldom lies, —
By the heart's still rhetoric disclos'd with eyes,
Deceive me not now, Navarre is infected.
PRINCESS
With what?
BOYET
With that which we lovers entitle affected.
PRINCESS
Your reason?
BOYET
Why, all his behaviours did make their retire
To the court of his eye, peeping thorough desire:
His heart, like an agate, with your print impress'd,
Proud with his form, in his eye pride express'd:
His tongue, all impatient to speak and not see,
Did stumble with haste in his eyesight to be;
All senses to that sense did make their repair,
To feel only looking on fairest of fair:
Methought all his senses were lock'd in his eye,
As jewels in crystal for some prince to buy;
Who, tend'ring their own worth from where they were
 glass'd,
Did point you to buy them, along as you pass'd:
His face's own margent did cote such amazes,
That all eyes saw his eyes enchanted with gazes.
I'll give you Aquitaine, and all that is his,
An you give him for my sake but one loving kiss.
PRINCESS
Come to our pavilion: Boyet is disposed.
BOYET
But to speak that in words which his eye hath
 disclosed:
I only have made a mouth of his eye,
By adding a tongue which I know will not lie.
ROSALINE
Thou art an old love-monger, and speakest skilfully.
MARIA
He is Cupid's grandfather, and learns news of him.
ROSALINE
Then was Venus like her mother: for her father is but
 grim.
BOYET
Do you hear, my mad wenches?
MARIA
                    No.

ARMADO Warble, child; make passionate my sense o' hearing.

BOYET
What then? do you see?
ROSALINE
Ay, our way to be gone.
BOYET
You are too hard for me.
[*Exeunt.*

ACT III

SCENE I

The same.

Enter ARMADO *and* MOTH.

ARMADO
Warble, child; make passionate my sense o' hearing.
MOTH
Concolinel — [*Singing.*
ARMADO
Sweet air! — Go, tenderness of years; take this key, give
enlargement to the swain, bring him festinately hither:
I must employ him in a letter to my love.
MOTH
Master, will you win your love with a French brawl?
ARMADO
How meanest thou? brawling in French?
MOTH
No, my complete master: but to jig off a tune at the
tongue's end, canary to it with your feet, humour it
with turning up your eyelids; sigh a note and sing a
note, — sometime through the throat, as if you
swallow'd love with singing love, — sometime through
the nose, as if you snuff'd up love by smelling love; with
your hat penthouse-like, o'er the shop of your eyes;
with your arms crossed on your thin-belly doublet, like
a rabbit on a spit; or your hands in your pocket, like a
man after the old painting; and keep not too long in one
tune, but a snip and away. These are complements,
these are humours; these betray nice wenches, — that
would be betray'd without these; and make them men
of note — do you note me? — that most are affected to
these.
ARMADO
How hast thou purchas'd this experience?
MOTH
By my penny of observation.
ARMADO
But O, — but O, —
MOTH
'The hobby-horse is forgot.'
ARMADO
Call'st thou my love hobby-horse?
MOTH
No, master; the hobby-horse is but a colt, and your
love perhaps a hackney. But have you forgot your love?
ARMADO
Almost I had.

MOTH
Negligent student! learn her by heart.
ARMADO
By heart and in heart, boy.
MOTH
And out of heart, master: all those three I will prove.
ARMADO
What wilt thou prove?
MOTH
A man, if I live; — and this, by, in, and without, upon
the instant: by heart you love her, because your heart
cannot come by her; in heart you love her, because your
heart is in love with her; and out of heart you love her,
being out of heart that you cannot enjoy her.
ARMADO
I am all these three.
MOTH
And three times as much more, — and yet nothing at
all.
ARMADO
Fetch hither the swain: he must carry me a letter.
MOTH
A message well sympathised; a horse to be ambassador
for an ass.
ARMADO
Ha, ha! what sayest thou?
MOTH
Marry, sir, you must send the ass upon the horse, for
he is very slow-gaited. But I go.
ARMADO
The way is but short: away!
MOTH
As swift as lead, sir.
ARMADO
The meaning, pretty ingenious?
Is not lead a metal heavy, dull, and slow?
MOTH
Minime, honest master; or rather, master, no.
ARMADO
I say lead is slow.
MOTH
You are too swift, sir, to say so:
Is that lead slow which is fired from a gun?
ARMADO
Sweet smoke of rhetoric!
He reputes me a cannon; and the bullet, that's he: —
I shoot thee at the swain.
MOTH
Thump, then, and I flee. [*Exit.*
ARMADO
A most acute juvenal; voluble and free of grace! —
By thy favour, sweet welkin, I must sigh in thy face: —
Most rude melancholy, valour gives thee place. —
My herald is return'd.

Enter MOTH *with* COSTARD.

MOTH
A wonder, master! here's a Costard broken in a shin.

ARMADO
Some enigma, some riddle: come, — thy *l'envoy*; —
begin.
COSTARD
No egma, no riddle, no *l'envoy*; no salve in the mail, sir:
O, sir, plantain, a plain plantain! no *l'envoy*, no *l'envoy*;
no salve, sir, but a plantain!
ARMADO
By virtue, thou enforcest laughter; thy silly thought, my
spleen: the heaving of my lungs provokes me to
ridiculous smiling, — O, pardon me, my stars! Doth
the inconsiderate take salve for *l'envoy*, and the word
l'envoy for a salve?
MOTH
Do the wise think them other? is not *l'envoy* a salve?
ARMADO
No, page: it is an epilogue or discourse, to make plain
Some obscure precedence that hath tofore been sain.
I will example it:
The fox, the ape, and the humble-bee,
Were still at odds, being but three.
There's the moral. Now the *l'envoy*.
MOTH
I will add the *l'envoy*. Say the moral again.
ARMADO
The fox, the ape, and the humble-bee,
Were still at odds, being but three.
MOTH
Until the goose came out of door,
And stay'd the odds by adding four.
Now will I begin your moral, and do you follow with my
l'envoy.
The fox, the ape, and the humble-bee,
Were still at odds, being but three.
ARMADO
Until the goose came out of door,
Staying the odds by adding four.
MOTH
A good *l'envoy*, ending in the goose: would you desire
more?
COSTARD
The boy hath sold him a bargain, a goose, that's flat. —
Sir, your pennyworth is good, an your goose be fat. —
To sell a bargain well is as cunning as fast and loose:
Let me see — a fat *l'envoy*; ay, that's a fat goose.
ARMADO
Come hither, come hither. How did this argument
begin?
MOTH
By saying that a Costard was broken in a shin.
Then call'd you for the *l'envoy*.
COSTARD
True, and I for a plantain: thus came your argument in;
Then the boy's fat *l'envoy*, the goose that you bought;
And he ended the market.
ARMADO
But tell me; how was there a Costard broken in a shin?
MOTH
I will tell you sensibly.
COSTARD
Thou hast no feeling of it, Moth: I will speak that
l'envoy:
I, Costard, running out, that was safely within,
Fell over the threshold, and broke my shin.
ARMADO
We will talk no more of this matter.
COSTARD
Till there be more matter in the shin.
ARMADO
Sirrah Costard, I will enfranchise thee.
COSTARD
O, marry me to one Frances: — I smell some *l'envoy*,
some goose, in this.
ARMADO
By my sweet soul, I mean setting thee at liberty,
enfreedoming thy person: thou wert immured,
restrain'd, captivated, bound.
COSTARD
True, true; and now you will be my purgation, and let
me loose.
ARMADO
I give thee thy liberty, set thee from durance; and, in
lieu thereof, impose on thee nothing but this: — bear
this significant [*giving a letter*] to the country maid
Jaquenetta: there is remuneration [*giving money*]; for
the best ward of mine honour is rewarding my
dependents. — Moth, follow. [*Exit.*
MOTH
Like the sequel, I. — Signior Costard, adieu.

COSTARD
My sweet ounce of man's flesh! my incony Jew! —
[*Exit* MOTH.
Now will I look to his remuneration. Remuneration! O,
that's the Latin word for three farthings: three
farthings — remuneration. — 'What's the price of this
inkle?' — 'A penny.' — 'No, I'll give you a
remuneration': why, it carries it. — Remuneration! —
why, it is a fairer name than French crown. I will never
buy and sell out of this word.

Enter BEROWNE.

BEROWNE
O, my good knave Costard! exceedingly well met.
COSTARD
Pray you, sir, how much carnation ribbon may a man
  buy for a remuneration?
BEROWNE
What is a remuneration?
COSTARD
Marry, sir, halfpenny farthing.
BEROWNE
O, why, then, three-farthing-worth of silk.
COSTARD
I thank your worship: God be wi' you!
BEROWNE
O, stay, slave; I must employ thee:
As thou wilt win my favour, good my knave,
Do one thing for me that I shall entreat.
COSTARD
When would you have it done, sir?
BEROWNE
O, this afternoon.
COSTARD
Well, I will do it, sir: fare you well.
BEROWNE
O, thou knowest not what it is.
COSTARD
I shall know, sir, when I have done it.
BEROWNE
Why, villain, thou must know first.
COSTARD
I will come to your worship to-morrow morning.
BEROWNE
It must be done this afternoon. Hark, slave, it is but
  this: —
The princess comes to hunt here in the park,
And in her train there is a gentle lady;
When tongues speak sweetly, then they name her
  name,
And Rosaline they call her: ask for her;
And to her white hand see thou do commend
This seal'd-up counsel. There's thy guerdon; go.
[*Giving money.*
COSTARD
Gardon, — O sweet gardon! better than remuneration;
eleven-pence farthing better: most sweet gardon! — I
will do it, sir, in print. — Gardon — remuneration!
[*Exit.*
BEROWNE
O, — and I, forsooth, in love! I, that have been love's
  whip;
A very beadle to a humorous sigh;
A critic, nay, a night-watch constable;
A domineering pedant o'er the boy,
Than whom no mortal so magnificent!
This wimpled, whining, purblind, wayward boy;
This signior-junior, giant-dwarf, Dan Cupid;
Regent of love-rimes, lord of folded arms,
Th' anointed sovereign of sighs and groans,
Liege of all loiterers and malecontents,
Dread prince of plackets, king of codpieces,
Sole imperator and great general
Of trotting paritors: — O my little heart! —
And I to be a corporal of his field,
And wear his colours like a tumbler's hoop!
What! I love! I sue! I seek a wife!
A woman, that is like a German clock,
Still a-repairing; ever out of frame;
And never going aright, being a watch,
But being watch'd that it may still go right!
Nay, to be perjur'd, which is worst of all;
And, among three, to love the worst of all;
A whitely wanton with a velvet brow,
With two pitch-balls stuck in her face for eyes;
Ay, and, by heaven, one that will do the deed,
Though Argus were her eunuch and her guard:
And I to sigh for her! to watch for her!
To pray for her! Go to; it is a plague
That Cupid will impose for my neglect

BEROWNE O, — and I, forsooth, in love!

Of his almighty dreadful little might.
Well, I will love, write, sigh, pray, sue, and groan:
Some men must love my lady, and some Joan. [*Exit.*

ACT IV

SCENE I

The same.

Enter the PRINCESS, ROSALINE, MARIA,
KATHARINE, BOYET, LORDS, ATTENDANTS, *and*
a FORESTER.

PRINCESS
Was that the king, that spurr'd his horse so hard
Against the steep uprising of the hill?
BOYET
I know not; but I think it was not he.
PRINCESS
Whoe'er a' was, a' show'd a mounting mind.
Well, lords, to-day we shall have our dispatch:
On Saturday we will return to France. —
Then, forester, my friend, where is the bush
That we must stand and play the murderer in?
FORESTER
Hereby, upon the edge of yonder coppice;
A stand where you may make the fairest shoot.
PRINCESS
I thank my beauty, I am fair that shoot,
And thereupon thou speak'st the fairest shoot.
FORESTER
Pardon me, madam, for I meant not so.
PRINCESS
What, what? first praise me, and again say no?
O short-lived pride! Not fair? alack for woe!
FORESTER
Yes, madam, fair.
PRINCESS
      Nay, never paint me now:
Where fair is not, praise cannot mend the brow.
Here, good my glass, take this for telling true:
[*Giving him money.*
Fair payment for foul words is more than due.
FORESTER
Nothing but fair is that which you inherit.
PRINCESS
See, see, my beauty will be sav'd by merit!
O heresy in fair, fit for these days!
A giving hand, though foul, shall have fair praise. —
But come, the bow: — now mercy goes to kill,
And shooting well is then accounted ill.
Thus will I save my credit in the shoot:
Not wounding, pity would not let me do't;
If wounding, then it was to show my skill,
That more for praise than purpose meant to kill.
And, out of question, so it is sometimes, —
Glory grows guilty of detested crimes,
When, for fame's sake, for praise, an outward part,
We bend to that the working of the heart;
As I for praise alone now seek to spill

The poor deer's blood, that my heart means no ill.
BOYET
Do not curst wives hold that self-sovereignty
Only for praise' sake, when they strive to be
Lords o'er their lords?
PRINCESS
Only for praise: and praise we may afford
To any lady that subdues a lord.
BOYET
Here comes a member of the commonwealth.

Enter COSTARD.

COSTARD
God dig-you-den all! Pray you, which is the head lady?
PRINCESS
Thou shalt know her, fellow, by the rest that have no
  heads.
COSTARD
Which is the greatest lady, the highest?
PRINCESS
The thickest and the tallest.
COSTARD
The thickest and the tallest! it is so; truth is truth.
An your waist, mistress, were as slender as my wit,
One o' these maids' girdles for your waist should be fit.
Are not you the chief woman? you are the thickest here.
PRINCESS
What's your will, sir? what's your will?
COSTARD
I have a letter from Monsieur Berowne to one
  Lady Rosaline.
PRINCESS
O, thy letter, thy letter! he's a good friend of mine:
Stand aside, good bearer. — Boyet, you can carve;
Break up this capon.
BOYET
      I am bound to serve. —
This letter is mistook, it importeth none here;
It is writ to Jaquenetta.
PRINCESS
      We will read it, I swear.
Break the neck of the wax, and every one give ear.
BOYET [*reads*].
By heaven, that thou art fair, is most infallible; true,
that thou art beauteous; truth itself, that thou art lovely.
More fairer than fair, beautiful than beauteous, truer
than truth itself, have commiseration on thy heroical
vassal! The magnanimous and most illustrate King
Cophetua set eye upon the pernicious and indubitate
beggar Zenelophon; and he it was that might rightly say,
Veni, vidi, vici; which to annothanise in the vulgar, — O
base and obscure vulgar! — *videlicet*, he came, saw and
overcame: he came, one; saw, two; overcame, three.
Who came? the king: why did he come? to see: why did
he see? to overcome: to whom came he? to the beggar:
what saw he? the beggar: who overcame he? the beggar.
The conclusion is victory: on whose side? the king's.
The captive is enrich'd: on whose side? the beggar's.
The catastrophe is a nuptial: on whose side? the king's,
— no, on both in one, or one in both. I am the king; for
so stands the comparison: thou the beggar; for so

SIR NATHANIEL Truly, Master Holofernes, the
epithets are sweetly varied.

witnesseth thy lowliness. Shall I command thy love? I
may: shall I enforce thy love? I could: shall I entreat thy
love? I will. What shalt thou exchange for rags? robes;
for tittles? titles; for thyself? me. Thus, expecting thy
reply, I profane my lips on thy foot, my eyes on thy
picture, and my heart on thy every part. — Thine, in the
dearest design of industry,
       DON ADRIANO DE ARMADO.
Thus dost thou hear the Nemean lion roar
 'Gainst thee, thou lamb, that standest as his prey.
Submissive fall his princely feet before,
 And he from forage will incline to play:
But if thou strive, poor soul, what art thou then?
Food for his rage, repasture for his den.

PRINCESS
What plume of feathers is he that indited this letter?
What vane? what weathercock? did you ever hear
 better?

BOYET
I am much deceived but I remember the style.

PRINCESS
Else your memory is bad, going o'er it erewhile.

BOYET
This Armado is a Spaniard, that keeps here in court;
A phantasm, a Monarcho, and one that makes sport
To the prince and his book-mates.

PRINCESS
         Thou fellow, a word:
Who gave thee this letter?

COSTARD
        I told you; my lord.

PRINCESS
To whom shouldst thou give it?

COSTARD
       From my lord to my lady.

PRINCESS
From which lord to which lady?

COSTARD
From my Lord Berowne, a good master of mine,
To a lady of France that he call'd Rosaline.

PRINCESS
Thou hast mistaken his letter. — Come, lords, away. —
Here, sweet, put up this: 'twill be thine another day.
       [*Exit* PRINCESS *attended.*

BOYET
Who is the suitor? who is the suitor?

ROSALINE
       Shall I teach you to know?

BOYET
Ay, my continent of beauty.

ROSALINE
       Why, she that bears the bow.
Finely put off!

BOYET
My lady goes to kill horns; but, if thou marry,
Hang me by the neck, if horns that year miscarry.
Finely put on!

ROSALINE
Well, then, I am the shooter.

BOYET
       And who is your deer?

ROSALINE
If we choose by the horns, yourself: come not near.
Finely put on, indeed!

MARIA
You still wrangle with her, Boyet, and she strikes at the
brow.

BOYET
But she herself is hit lower: have I hit her now?

ROSALINE
Shall I come upon thee with an old saying, that was a
man when King Pepin of France was a little boy, as
touching the hit it?

BOYET
So I may answer thee with one as old, that was a
woman when Queen Guinever of Britain was a little
wench, as touching the hit it.

ROSALINE
   Thou canst not hit it, hit it, hit it,
   Thou canst not hit it, my good man.

BOYET
   An I cannot, cannot, cannot,
   An I cannot, another can.
     [*Exeunt* ROSALINE *and* KATHARINE.

COSTARD
By my troth, most pleasant: how both did fit it!

MARIA
A mark marvellous well shot, for they both did hit it.

BOYET
A mark! O, mark but that mark! A mark, says my lady!
Let the mark have a prick in't, to mete at, if it may be.

MARIA
Wide o'th'bow-hand! i'faith, your hand is out.

COSTARD
Indeed, a' must shoot nearer, or he'll ne'er hit the
clout.

BOYET
An if my hand be out, then belike your hand is in.

COSTARD
Then will she get the upshoot by cleaving the pin.

MARIA
Come, come, you talk greasily; your lips grow foul.

COSTARD
She's too hard for you at pricks, sir challenge her to
bowl.

BOYET
I fear too much rubbing. Good night, my good owl.
      [*Exeunt* BOYET *and* MARIA.

COSTARD
By my soul, a swain! a most simple clown!
Lord, Lord, how the ladies and I have put him down!
O' my troth, most sweet jests! most incony vulgar wit!
When it comes so smoothly off, so obscenely, as it
 were, so fit.
Armado o'th'one side; — O, a most dainty man!
To see him walk before a lady and to bear her fan!
To see him kiss his hand! and how most sweetly a' will
 swear! —
And his page o' t'other side, that handful of wit!
Ah, heavens, it is a most pathetical nit!
Sola, sola!

    [*Shout within. Exit* COSTARD, *running.*

SCENE II

The same.

Enter HOLOFERNES, SIR NATHANIEL, *and* DULL.

SIR NATHANIEL
Very reverend sport, truly; and done in the testimony of
a good conscience.

HOLOFERNES
The deer was, as you know, *sanguis*, — in blood; ripe as
a pomewater, who now hangeth like a jewel in the ear
of *cœlo*, — the sky, the welkin, the heaven; and anon
falleth like a crab on the face of *terra*, — the soil, the
land, the earth.

SIR NATHANIEL
Truly, Master Holofernes, the epithets are sweetly
varied, like a scholar at the least: but, sir, I assure ye, it
was a buck of the first head.

HOLOFERNES
Sir Nathaniel, *haud credo.*

DULL
'Twas not a *haud credo*; 'twas a pricket.

HOLOFERNES
Most barbarous intimation! yet a kind of insinuation,
as it were, *in via*, in way, of explication; *facere*, as it were,
replication, or, rather, *ostentare*, to show, as it were, his
inclination, — after his undress'd, unpolish'd,
uneducated, unpruned, untrain'd, or, rather,
unletter'd, or, ratherest, unconfirm'd fashion, — to
insert again my *haud credo* for a deer.

DULL
I said the deer was not a *haud credo*; 'twas a pricket.

HOLOFERNES
Twice-sod simplicity, *bis coctus!*
O thou monster Ignorance, how deform'd dost thou
look!

SIR NATHANIEL
Sir, he hath never fed of the dainties that are bred in a
book;
he hath not eat paper, as it were; he hath not drunk ink:
his intellect is not replenish'd; he is only an animal,
only sensible in the duller parts:
And such barren plants are set before us, that we
thankful should be —
Which we of taste and feeling are — for those parts that
do fructify in us more than he.
For as it would ill become me to be vain, indiscreet, or a
fool,
So, were there a patch set on learning, to see him in a
school:
But, *omne bene*, say I; being of an old father's mind, —
'Many can brook the weather that love not the wind.'

DULL
You two are book-men: can you tell me by your wit
What was a month old at Cain's birth, that's not five
weeks old as yet?

HOLOFERNES
Dictynna, goodman Dull; Dictynna, goodman Dull.

DULL
What is Dictynna?

SIR NATHANIEL
A title to Phœbe, to Luna, to the moon.

HOLOFERNES
The moon was a month old when Adam was no more,
And raught not to five weeks when he came to
five-score.
Th'allusion holds in the exchange.

DULL
'Tis true indeed; the collusion holds in the exchange.

HOLOFERNES
God comfort thy capacity! I say, th'allusion holds in the
exchange.

DULL
And I say, the pollusion holds in the exchange; for the
moon is never but a month old: and I say beside, that
'twas a pricket that the princess kill'd.

HOLOFERNES
Sir Nathaniel, will you hear an extemporal epitaph on
the death of the deer? and, to humour the ignorant, I
have call'd the deer the princess kill'd a pricket.

SIR NATHANIEL
Perge, good Master Holofernes, *perge*; so it shall please
you to abrogate scurrility.

HOLOFERNES
I will something affect the letter, for it argues facility.
   The preyful princess pierc'd and prick'd
    a pretty pleasing pricket;
   Some say a sore; but not a sore,
    till now made sore with shooting.
   The dogs did yell: put *l* to sore,
    then sorel jumps from thicket;
   Or pricket, sore, or else sorel;
    the people fall a-hooting.
   If sore be sore, then *l* to sore
    makes fifty sores: O sore *l*!
   Of one sore I an hundred make
    by adding but one more *l*.

SIR NATHANIEL
A rare talent!

DULL [*aside*].
If a talent be a claw, look how he claws him with a
talent.

HOLOFERNES
This is a gift that I have, simple, simple; a foolish
extravagant spirit, full of forms, figures, shapes,
objects, ideas, apprehensions, motions, revolutions:
these are begot in the ventricle of memory, nourish'd
in the womb of *pia mater,* and deliver'd upon the
mellowing of occasion. But the gift is good in those in
whom it is acute, and I am thankful for it.

SIR NATHANIEL
Sir, I praise the Lord for you: and so may my
parishioners; for their sons are well tutor'd by you, and
their daughters profit very greatly under you: you are a
good member of the commonwealth.

HOLOFERNES
Mehercle, if their sons be ingenious, they shall want no
instruction; if their daughters be capable, I will put it to

COSTARD Have with thee, my girl.

them: but, *vir sapit qui pauca loquitur.* A soul feminine saluteth us.

Enter JAQUENETTA *and* COSTARD.

JAQUENETTA
God give you good morrow, master person.
HOLOFERNES
Master person, — *quasi* pers-on. An if one should be pierced, which is the one?
COSTARD
Marry, master schoolmaster, he that is likest to a hogshead.
HOLOFERNES
O piercing a hogshead! a good lustre of conceit in a turf of earth; fire enough for a flint, pearl enough for a swine: 'tis pretty; it is well.
JAQUENETTA
Good master person, be so good as read me this letter: it was given me by Costard, and sent me from Don Armado: I beseech you, read it.
HOLOFERNES
Fauste, precor, gelidâ quando pecus omne sub umbrâ Ruminat, — and so forth. Ah, good old Mantuan! I may speak of thee as the traveller doth of Venice;
—— *Venetia, Venetia,*
Chi non te vede, non ti pretia.
Old Mantuan, old Mantuan! who understandeth not, loves thee not. — *Ut, re, sol, la, mi, fa.* — Under pardon, sir, what are the contents? or rather, as Horace says in his — What, my soul, verses?
SIR NATHANIEL
Ay, sir, and very learned.
HOLOFERNES
Let me hear a staff, a stanze, a verse; *lege, domine.*
SIR NATHANIEL [*reads*].
If love make me forsworn, how shall I swear to love?
  Ah, never faith could hold, if not to beauty vow'd!
Though to myself forsworn, to thee I'll faithful prove;
  Those thoughts to me were oaks, to thee like osiers bow'd.
Study his bias leaves, and makes his book thine eyes,
  Where all those pleasures live that art would comprehend:
If knowledge be the mark, to know thee shall suffice;
  Well learned is that tongue that well can thee commend;
All ignorant that soul that sees thee without wonder, —
  Which is to me some praise that I thy parts admire:
Thy eye Jove's lightning bears, thy voice his dreadful thunder,
  Which, not to anger bent, is music and sweet fire.
Celestial as thou art, O, pardon, love, this wrong,

That sings heaven's praise with such an earthly tongue.
HOLOFERNES
You find not the apostrophes, and so miss the accent: let me supervise the canzonet. Here are only numbers ratified; but, for the elegancy, facility, and golden cadence of poesy, *caret.* Ovidius Naso was the man: and why, indeed, Naso, but for smelling out the odoriferous flowers of fancy, the jerks of invention? *Imitari* is nothing: so doth the hound his master, the ape his keeper, the tired horse his rider. — But, damosella virgin, was this directed to you?
JAQUENETTA
Ay, sir, from one Monsieur Berowne, one of the strange queen's lords.
HOLOFERNES
I will overglance the superscript: 'To the snow-white hand of the most beauteous Lady Rosaline.' I will look again on the intellect of the letter, for the nomination of the party writing to the person written unto: 'Your ladyship's in all desired employment, Berowne.' — Sir Nathaniel, this Berowne is one of the votaries with the king; and here he hath framed a letter to a sequent of the stranger queen's, which accidentally, or by the way of progression, hath miscarried. — Trip and go, my sweet; deliver this paper into the royal hand of the king: it may concern much. Stay not thy compliment; I forgive thy duty: adieu.
JAQUENETTA
Good Costard, go with me. — Sir, God save your life!
COSTARD
Have with thee, my girl.
[*Exeunt* COSTARD *and* JAQUENETTA.
SIR NATHANIEL
Sir, you have done this in the fear of God, very religiously; and, as a certain father saith —
HOLOFERNES
Sir, tell not me of the father; I do fear colourable colours. But to return to the verses: did they please you, Sir Nathaniel?
SIR NATHANIEL
Marvellous well for the pen.
HOLOFERNES
I do dine to-day at the father's of a certain pupil of mine; where, if, before repast, it shall please you to gratify the table with a grace, I will, on my privilege I have with the parents of the foresaid child or pupil, undertake your *ben venuto;* where I will prove those verses to be very unlearned, neither savouring of poetry, wit, nor invention: I beseech your society.
SIR NATHANIEL
And thank you too; for society, saith the text, is the happiness of life.
HOLOFERNES
And, certes, the text most infallibly concludes it. — [to DULL] Sir, I do invite you too; you shall not say me nay: *pauca verba.* Away! the gentles are at their game, and we will to our recreation. [*Exeunt.*

SCENE III
The same.

Enter BEROWNE, *with a paper in his hand, alone.*

BEROWNE
The king he is hunting the deer; I am coursing myself: they have pitch'd a toil; I am toiling in a pitch, — pitch that defiles: defile! a foul word. Well, set thee down, sorrow! for so they say the fool said, and so say I, and I the fool: well proved, wit! By the Lord, this love is as mad as Ajax: it kills sheep; it kills me, I a sheep: well proved again o' my side! I will not love: if I do, hang me; i'faith, I will not. O, but her eye, — by this light, but for her eye, I would not love her; yes, for her two eyes. Well, I do nothing in the world but lie, and lie in my throat. By heaven, I do love: and it hath taught me to rime, and to be mallicholy; and here is part of my rime, and here my mallicholy. Well, she hath one o' my sonnets already: the clown bore it, the fool sent it, and the lady hath it: sweet clown, sweeter fool, sweetest lady! By the world, I would not care a pin, if the other three were in. — Here comes one with a paper: God give him grace to groan!
[*He stands aside.*

The KING *ent'reth.*

KING
Ay me!
BEROWNE [*aside*].
Shot, by heaven! — proceed, sweet Cupid: thou hast thump'd him with thy bird-bolt under the left pap. — In faith, secrets!

KING [*reads*].
'So sweet a kiss the golden sun gives not
  To those fresh morning drops upon the rose,
As thy eye-beams, when their fresh rays have smot
  The night of dew that on my cheeks down flows:
Nor shines the silver moon one half so bright
  Through the transparent bosom of the deep,
As doth thy face through tears of mine give light;
  Thou shin'st in every tear that I do weep:
No drop but as a coach doth carry thee;
  So ridest thou triumphing in my woe.
Do but behold the tears that swell in me,
  And they thy glory through my grief will show:
But do not love thyself; then thou wilt keep
My tears for glasses, and still make me weep.
O queen of queens! how far dost thou excel,
No thought can think, nor tongue of mortal tell.' —
How shall she know my griefs? I'll drop the paper: —
Sweet leaves, shade folly. — Who is he comes here?
[*Steps aside.*
What, Longaville! and reading! listen, ear.
BEROWNE [*aside*].
Now, in thy likeness, one more fool appear!

Enter LONGAVILLE.

LONGAVILLE
Ay me, I am forsworn!
BEROWNE [*aside*].
Why, he comes in like a perjure, wearing papers.
KING [*aside*].
In love, I hope: sweet fellowship in shame!
BEROWNE [*aside*].
One drunkard loves another of the name.
LONGAVILLE
Am I the first that have been perjured so?
BEROWNE [*aside*].
I could put thee in comfort, — not by two that I know:
Thou makest the triumviry, the corner-cap of society,
The shape of Love's Tyburn that hangs up simplicity.
LONGAVILLE
I fear these stubborn lines lack power to move: —
O sweet Maria, empress of my love! —
These numbers will I tear, and write in prose.
BEROWNE [*aside*].
O, rimes are guards on wanton Cupid's hose:
Disfigure not his shop.
LONGAVILLE
                     This same shall go. —   [*Reads.*
Did not the heavenly rhetoric of thine eye,
  'Gainst whom the world cannot hold argument,
Persuade my heart to this false perjury?
  Vows for thee broke deserve not punishment.
A woman I forswore; but I will prove,
  Thou being a goddess, I forswore not thee:
My vow was earthly, thou a heavenly love;
  Thy grace being gain'd cures all disgrace in me.
Vows are but breath, and breath a vapour is:
  Then thou, fair sun, which on my earth dost shine,
Exhalest this vapour-vow; in thee it is:
  If broken then, it is no fault of mine:
If by me broke, what fool is not so wise
To lose an oath to win a paradise?
BEROWNE [*aside*].
This is the liver-vein, which makes flesh a deity,
A green goose a goddess: pure, pure idolatry,
God amend us, God amend! we are much out o'th'way.
LONGAVILLE
By whom shall I send this? — Company! stay.
[*Steps aside.*
BEROWNE [*aside*].
All hid, all hid, an old infant play.
Like a demigod here sit I in the sky,
And wretched fools' secrets heedfully o'er-eye.
More sacks to the mill! O heavens, I have my wish!

Enter DUMAINE.

Dumaine transform'd! four woodcocks in a dish!
DUMAINE
O most divine Kate!
BEROWNE [*aside*].
O most profane coxcomb!
DUMAINE
By heaven, the wonder in a mortal eye!
BEROWNE [*aside*].
By earth she is not, corporal: there you lie.
DUMAINE
Her amber hairs for foul hath amber quoted.
BEROWNE [*aside*].
An amber-colour'd raven was well noted.

DUMAINE
As upright as the cedar.
BEROWNE [*aside*].
        Stoop, I say;
Her shoulder is with child.
DUMAINE
          As fair as day.
BEROWNE [*aside*].
Ay, as some days; but then no sun must shine.
DUMAINE
O, that I had my wish!
LONGAVILLE [*aside*].
        And I had mine!
KING [*aside*].
And I mine too, good Lord!
BEROWNE [*aside*].
Amen, so I had mine: is not that a good word?
DUMAINE
I would forget her; but a fever she
Reigns in my blood and will remember'd be.
BEROWNE [*aside*].
A fever in your blood! why, then incision
Would let her out in saucers: sweet misprision!
DUMAINE
Once more I'll read the ode that I have writ.
BEROWNE [*aside*].
Once more I'll mark how love can vary wit.
DUMAINE [*reads*].
    'On a day — alack the day! —
    Love, whose month is ever May,
    Spied a blossom passing fair
    Playing in the wanton air:
    Through the velvet leaves the wind,
    All unseen, can passage find;
    That the lover, sick to death,
    Wish'd himself the heaven's breath.
    Air, quoth he, thy cheeks may blow;
    Air, would I might triumph so!
    But, alack, my hand is sworn
    Ne'er to pluck thee from thy thorn; —
    Vow, alack, for youth unmeet,
    Youth so apt to pluck a sweet!
    Do not call it sin in me,
    That I am forsworn for thee;
    Thou for whom Jove would swear
    Juno but an Ethiope were;
    And deny himself for Jove,
    Turning mortal for thy love.'
This will I send, and something else more plain,
That shall express my true love's fasting pain.
O, would the king, Berowne, and Longaville,
Were lovers too! Ill, to example ill,
Would from my forehead wipe a perjured note;
For none offend where all alike do dote.
LONGAVILLE [*advancing*].
Dumaine, thy love is far from charity,
That in love's grief desir'st society:
You may look pale, but I should blush, I know,
To be o'erheard and taken napping so.
KING [*advancing*].
Come, sir, you blush: as his your case is such;
You chide at him, offending twice as much:
You do not love Maria? Longaville
Did never sonnet for her sake compile,
Nor never lay his wreathed arms athwart
His loving bosom, to keep down his heart!
I have been closely shrouded in this bush,
And mark'd you both, and for you both did blush:
I heard your guilty rimes, observ'd your fashion,
Saw sighs reek from you, noted well your passion:
Ay me! says one: O Jove! the other cries;
One her hairs were gold, crystal the other's eyes:
You would for paradise break faith and troth;
                  [*To* LONGAVILLE.
And Jove, for your love, would infringe an oath.
                  [*To* DUMAINE.
What will Berowne say when that he shall hear
A faith infringed, which such zeal did swear?
How will he scorn! how will he spend his wit!
How will he triumph, leap, and laugh at it!
For all the wealth that ever I did see,
I would not have him know so much by me.
BEROWNE
Now step I forth to whip hypocrisy.   [*Advancing*.
Ah, good my liege, I pray thee, pardon me!
Good heart, what grace hast thou, thus to reprove
These worms for loving, that art most in love?
Your eyes do make no coaches; in your tears
There is no certain princess that appears;
You'll not be perjured, 'tis a hateful thing;

Tush, none but minstrels like of sonneting!
But are you not asham'd? nay, are you not,
All three of you, to be thus much o'ershot?
You found his mote; the king your mote did see;
But I a beam do find in each of three.
O, what a scene of foolery have I seen,
Of sighs, of groans, of sorrow, and of teen!
O me, with what strict patience have I sat,
To see a king transformed to a gnat!
To see great Hercules whipping a gig,
And profound Solomon to tune a jig,
And Nestor play at push-pin with the boys,
And critic Timon laugh at idle toys!
Where lies thy grief, O tell me, good
    Dumaine?
And, gentle Longaville, where lies thy pain?
And where my liege's? all about the breast: —
A caudle, ho!
KING
         Too bitter is thy jest.
Are we betray'd thus to thy over-view?
BEROWNE
Not you to me, but I betray'd by you:
I, that am honest; I, that hold it sin
To break the vow I am engaged in;
I am betray'd, by keeping company
With men like you, men of inconstancy.
When shall you see me write a thing in rime?
Or groan for Joan? or spend a minute's time
In pruning me? When shall you hear that I
Will praise a hand, a foot, a face, an eye,
A gait, a state, a brow, a breast, a waist,
A leg, a limb? —
KING
        Soft! whither away so fast?
A true man or a thief that gallops so?
BEROWNE
I post from love: good lover, let me go.

    Enter JAQUENETTA *and* COSTARD.

JAQUENETTA
God bless the king!
KING
        What present hast thou there?
COSTARD
Some certain treason.
KING
        What makes treason here?
COSTARD
Nay, it makes nothing, sir.
KING
        If it mar nothing neither,
The treason and you go in peace away together.
JAQUENETTA
I beseech your Grace, let this letter be read:
Our person misdoubts it; 'twas treason, he said.
KING
Berowne, read it over.   [*Giving him the letter*.
Where hadst thou it?
JAQUENETTA
Of Costard.
KING
Where hadst thou it?
COSTARD
Of Dun Adramadio, Dun Adramadio.
              [BEROWNE *tears the letter*.
KING
How now! what is in you? why dost thou tear it?
BEROWNE
A toy, my liege, a toy: your Grace needs not fear it.
LONGAVILLE
It did move him to passion, and therefore let's hear it.
DUMAINE
It is Berowne's writing, and here is his name.
           [*Picking up the pieces*.
BEROWNE [*to* COSTARD].
Ah, you whoreson loggerhead! you were born to do me
   shame. —
Guilty, my lord, guilty! I confess, I confess.
KING
What?
BEROWNE
       That you three fools lack'd me fool to make up
the mess:
He, he, and you, and you, my liege, and I,
Are pick-purses in love, and we deserve to die.
O, dismiss this audience, and I shall tell you more.
DUMAINE
Now the number is even.

DUMAINE Once more I'll read the ode that I
    have writ.

BEROWNE
          True, true; we are four.
Will these turtles be gone?
KING
          Hence, sirs; away!
COSTARD
Walk aside the true folk, and let the traitors stay.
        [*Exeunt* COSTARD *and* JAQUENETTA.
BEROWNE
Sweet lords, sweet lovers, O, let us embrace!
   As true we are as flesh and blood can be:
The sea will ebb and flow, heaven show his face;
   Young blood doth not obey an old decree:
We cannot cross the cause why we were born;
Therefore of all hands must we be forsworn.
KING
What, did these rent lines show some love of thine?
BEROWNE
Did they, quoth you? Who sees the heavenly Rosaline,
That, like a rude and savage man of Inde,
   At the first opening of the gorgeous east,
Bows not his vassal head and strucken blind
   Kisses the base ground with obedient breast?
What peremptory eagle-sighted eye
   Dares look upon the heaven of her brow,
That is not blinded by her majesty?
KING
What zeal, what fury hath inspired thee now?
My love, her mistress, is a gracious moon;
   She an attending star, scarce seen a light.
BEROWNE
My eyes are then no eyes, nor I Berowne:
   O, but for my love, day would turn to night!
Of all complexions the cull'd sovereignty
   Do meet, as at a fair, in her fair cheek,
Where several worthies make one dignity,
   Where nothing wants that want itself doth seek.
Lend me the flourish of all gentle tongues, —
   Fie, painted rhetoric! O, she needs it not:
To things of sale a seller's praise belongs,
   She passes praise; then praise too short doth blot.
A wither'd hermit, five-score winters worn,
   Might shake off fifty, looking in her eye:
Beauty doth varnish age, as if new-born,
   And gives the crutch the cradle's infancy:
O, 'tis the sun that maketh all things shine.
KING
By heaven, thy love is black as ebony.

BEROWNE
Is ebony like her? O wood divine!
  A wife of such wood were felicity.
O, who can give an oath? where is a book?
  That I may swear beauty doth beauty lack,
If that she learn not of her eye to look:
  No face is fair that is not full so black.

KING
O paradox! Black is the badge of hell,
  The hue of dungeons and the suit of night;
And beauty's crest becomes the heavens well.

BEROWNE
  Devils soonest tempt, resembling spirits of light.
O, if in black my lady's brows be deck'd,
  It mourns that painting and usurping hair
Should ravish doters with a false aspect;
  And therefore is she born to make black fair.
Her favour turns the fashion of the days,
  For native blood is counted painting now;
And therefore red, that would avoid dispraise,
  Paints itself black, to imitate her brow.

DUMAINE
To look like her are chimney-sweepers black.

LONGAVILLE
And since her time are colliers counted bright.

KING
And Ethiopes of their sweet complexion crack.

DUMAINE
Dark needs no candles now, for dark is light.

BEROWNE
Your mistresses dare never come in rain,
For fear their colours should be wash'd away.

KING
'Twere good, yours did; for, sir, to tell you plain,
I'll find a fairer face not wash'd to-day.

BEROWNE
I'll prove her fair, or talk till doomsday here.

KING
No devil will fright thee then so much as she.

DUMAINE
I never knew man hold vile stuff so dear.

LONGAVILLE
Look, here's thy love: my foot and her face see.

BEROWNE
O, if the streets were paved with thine eyes,
Her feet were much too dainty for such tread!

DUMAINE
O, vile! then, as she goes, what upward lies
The street should see as she walk'd overhead.

KING
But what of this? are we not all in love?

BEROWNE
Nothing so sure; and thereby all forsworn.

KING
Then leave this chat; and, good Berowne, now prove
Our loving lawful, and our faith not torn.

DUMAINE
Ay, marry, there; some flattery for this evil.

LONGAVILLE
O, some authority how to proceed;
Some tricks, some quillets, how to cheat the devil.

DUMAINE
Some salve for perjury.

BEROWNE
            'Tis more than need.
Have at you, then, affection's men-at-arms.
Consider what you first did swear unto,
To fast, to study, and to see no woman;
Flat treason 'gainst the kingly state of youth.
Say, can you fast? your stomachs are too young;
And abstinence engenders maladies.
And where that you have vow'd to study, lords,
In that each of you have forsworn his book,
Can you still dream and pore and thereon look?
For when would you, my lord, or you, or you,
Have found the ground of study's excellence
Without the beauty of a woman's face?
[From women's eyes this doctrine I derive;
They are the ground, the books, the academes
From whence doth spring the true Promethean fire.]
Why, universal plodding poisons up
The nimble spirits in the arteries,
As motion and long-during action tires
The sinewy vigour of the traveller.
Now, for not looking on a woman's face,
You have in that forsworn the use of eyes,
And study too, the causer of your vow;
For where is any author in the world
Teaches such beauty as a woman's eye?

Learning is but an adjunct to ourself
And where we are our learning likewise is:
Then when ourselves we see in ladies' eyes,
Do we not likewise see our learning there?
O, we have made a vow to study, lords,
And in that vow we have forsworn our books.
For when would you, my liege, or you, or you,
In leaden contemplation have found out
Such fiery numbers as the prompting eyes
Of beauty's tutors have enrich'd you with?
Other slow arts entirely keep the brain;
And therefore, finding barren practisers,
Scarce show a harvest of their heavy toil:
But love, first learned in a lady's eyes,
Lives not alone immured in the brain;
But, with the motion of all elements,
Courses as swift as thought in every power,
And gives to every power a double power,
Above their functions and their offices.
It adds a precious seeing to the eye;
A lover's eyes will gaze an eagle blind;
A lover's ear will hear the lowest sound,
When the suspicious head of theft is stopp'd:
Love's feeling is more soft and sensible
Than are the tender horns of cockled snails;
Love's tongue proves dainty Bacchus gross in taste:
For valour, is not Love a Hercules,
Still climbing trees in the Hesperides?
Subtle as Sphinx; as sweet and musical
As bright Apollo's lute, strung with his hair:
And when Love speaks, the voice of all the gods
Make heaven drowsy with the harmony.
Never durst poet touch a pen to write
Until his ink were temper'd with Love's sighs;
O, then his lines would ravish savage ears
And plant in tyrants mild humility.
From women's eyes this doctrine I derive:
They sparkle still the right Promethean fire;
They are the books, the arts, the academes,
That show, contain and nourish all the world:
Else none at all in aught proves excellent.
Then fools you were these women to forswear,
Or keeping what is sworn, you will prove fools.
For wisdom's sake, a word that all men love,
Or for love's sake, a word that loves all men,
Or for men's sake, the authors of these women,
Or women's sake, by whom we men are men,
Let us once lose our oaths to find ourselves,
Or else we lose ourselves to keep our oaths.
It is religion to be thus forsworn,
For charity itself fulfils the law,
And who can sever love from charity?

KING
Saint Cupid, then! and, soldiers, to the field!

BEROWNE
Advance your standards, and upon them, lords;
Pell-mell, down with them! but be first advis'd,
In conflict that you get the sun of them.

LONGAVILLE
Now to plain-dealing; lay these glozes by:
Shall we resolve to woo these girls of France?

KING
And win them too: therefore let us devise
Some entertainment for them in their tents.

BEROWNE
First, from the park let us conduct them thither;
Then homeward every man attach the hand
Of his fair mistress: in the afternoon
We will with some strange pastime solace them,
Such as the shortness of the time can shape;
For revels, dances, masks and merry hours
Forerun fair Love, strewing her way with flowers.

KING
Away, away! no time shall be omitted
That will betime, and may by us be fitted.

BEROWNE
Allons! allons! Sow'd cockle reap'd no corn;
  And justice always whirls in equal measure:
Light wenches may prove plagues to men forsworn;
  If so, our copper buys no better treasure.   [*Exeunt.*

ACT V

SCENE I

The same.

Enter HOLOFERNES, SIR NATHANIEL, *and* DULL.

HOLOFERNES
Satis quod sufficit.

SIR NATHANIEL
I praise God for you, sir: your reasons at dinner have
been sharp and sententious; pleasant without
scurrility, witty without affection, audacious without
impudency, learned without opinion, and strange
without heresy. I did converse this quondam day with a
companion of the king's, who is intituled, nominated,
or call'd, Don Adriano de Armado.

HOLOFERNES
Novi hominem tanquam te: his humour is lofty, his
discourse peremptory, his tongue filed, his eye
ambitious, his gait majestical, and his general behaviour
vain, ridiculous, and thrasonical. He is too pick'd, too
spruce, too affected, too odd, as it were, too peregrinate,
as I may call it.

SIR NATHANIEL
A most singular and choice epithet.
          [*Draws out his table-book.*

HOLOFERNES
He draweth out the thread of his verbosity finer than
the staple of his argument. I abhor such fanatical
phantasms, such insociable and point-device
companions; such rackers of orthography, as to speak
dout, fine, when he should say doubt; det, when he
should pronounce debt, — d, e, b, t, not d, e, t: he
clepeth a calf, cauf; half, hauf; neighbour *vocatur*
nebour; neigh abbreviated ne. This is abhominable, —
which he would call abbominable: it insinuateth me of
insanie: *ne intelligis, domine?* to make frantic, lunatic.

ARMADO Men of peace, well encounter'd.

SIR NATHANIEL
Laus Deo, bone intelligo.
HOLOFERNES
Bone? — *bone,* for *bene!* Priscian a little scratch'd,
'twill serve.
SIR NATHANIEL
Videsne quis venit?
HOLOFERNES
Video, et gaudeo.

Enter ARMADO, MOTH, *and* COSTARD.

ARMADO [*to* MOTH].
Chirrah!
HOLOFERNES
Quare chirrah, not sirrah?
ARMADO
Men of peace, well encounter'd.
HOLOFERNES
Most military sir, salutation.
MOTH [*aside to* COSTARD].
They have been at a great feast of languages, and stolen
the scraps.
COSTARD
O, they have lived long on the alms-basket of words. I
marvel thy master hath not eaten thee for a word; for
thou art not so long by the head as
honorificabilitudinitatibus; thou art easier swallow'd
than a flap-dragon.
MOTH
Peace! the peal begins.
ARMADO [*to* HOLOFERNES].
Monsieur, are you not letter'd?
MOTH
Yes, yes; he teaches boys the horn-book. What is a, b,
spelt backward, with the horn on his head?
HOLOFERNES
Ba, *pueritia,* with a horn added.
MOTH
Ba, most silly sheep with a horn. You hear his learning.
HOLOFERNES
Quis, quis, thou consonant?
MOTH
The last of the five vowels, if You repeat them; or
the fifth, if I.
HOLOFERNES
I will repeat them, — a, e, i, —
MOTH
The sheep: the other two concludes it, — o, u.
ARMADO
Now, by the salt wave of the Mediterraneum, a sweet
touch, a quick venue of wit! snip, snap, quick and
home! it rejoiceth my intellect: true wit!
MOTH
Offer'd by a child to an old man; which is wit-old.
HOLOFERNES
What is the figure? what is the figure?
MOTH
Horns.
HOLOFERNES
Thou disputes like an infant: go, whip thy gig.
MOTH
Lend me your horn to make one, and I will whip about
your infamy *circum circa,* — a gig of a cuckold's horn.
COSTARD
An I had but one penny in the world, thou shouldst
have it to buy gingerbread: hold, there is the very
remuneration I had of thy master, thou halfpenny
purse of wit, thou pigeon-egg of discretion. O, an the
heavens were so pleased that thou wert but my bastard,
what a joyful father wouldst thou make me! Go to; thou
hast it *ad dunghill,* at the fingers' ends, as they say.
HOLOFERNES
O, I smell false Latin; dunghill for *unguem.*
ARMADO
Arts-man, *præmbula,* we will be singled from the
barbarous. Do you not educate youth at the
charge-house on the top of the mountain?
HOLOFERNES
Or *mons,* the hill.
ARMADO
At your sweet pleasure, for the mountain.
HOLOFERNES
I do, sans question.
ARMADO
Sir, it is the king's most sweet pleasure and affection to
congratulate the princess at her pavilion in the
posteriors of this day, which the rude multitude call the
afternoon.

HOLOFERNES
The posterior of the day, most generous sir, is liable,
congruent and measurable for the afternoon: the word
is well cull'd, chose, sweet and apt, I do assure you, sir,
I do assure.
ARMADO
Sir, the king is a noble gentleman, and my familiar, I
do assure ye, very good friend: for what is inward
between us, let it pass. I do beseech thee, remember thy
courtesy; I beseech thee, apparel thy head: and among
other importunate and most serious designs, and of
great import indeed, too, but let that pass: for I must
tell thee, it will please his Grace, by the world,
sometime to lean upon my poor shoulder, and with his
royal finger, thus, dally with my excrement, with my
mustachio; but, sweet heart, let that pass. By the world,
I recount no fable: some certain special honours it
pleaseth his greatness to impart to Armado, a soldier, a
man of travel, that hath seen the world; but let that
pass. The very all of all is, — but, sweet heart, I do
implore secrecy, — that the king would have me
present the princess, sweet chuck, with some
delightful ostentation, or show, or pageant, or antick,
or firework. Now, understanding that the curate and
your sweet self are good at such eruptions and sudden
breaking out of mirth, as it were, I have acquainted you
withal, to the end to crave your assistance.
HOLOFERNES
Sir, you shall present before her the Nine Worthies. Sir
Nathaniel, as concerning some entertainment of time,
some show in the posterior of this day, to be render'd
by our assistance, the king's command, and this most
gallant, illustrate, and learned gentleman, before the
princess; I say none so fit as to present the Nine
Worthies.
SIR NATHANIEL
Where will you find men worthy enough to present
them?
HOLOFERNES
Joshua, yourself; myself or this gallant gentleman,
Judas Maccabæus; this swain, because of his great
limb or joint, shall pass Pompey the Great; the
page, Hercules, —
ARMADO
Pardon, sir; error: he is not quantity enough for that
Worthy's thumb: he is not so big as the end of his club.
HOLOFERNES
Shall I have audience? he shall present Hercules in
minority: his enter and exit shall be strangling a snake;
and I will have an apology for that purpose.
MOTH
An excellent device! so, if any of the audience hiss, you
may cry, 'Well done, Hercules! now thou crushest the
snake!' that is the way to make an offence gracious,
though few have the grace to do it.
ARMADO
For the rest of the Worthies? —
HOLOFERNES
I will play three myself.
MOTH
Thrice-worthy gentleman!
ARMADO
Shall I tell you a thing?
HOLOFERNES
We attend.
ARMADO
We will have, if this fadge not, an antick. I beseech you,
follow.
HOLOFERNES
Via, goodman Dull! thou hast spoken no word all this
while.
DULL
Nor understood none neither, sir.
HOLOFERNES
Allons! we will employ thee.
DULL
I'll make one in a dance, or so; or I will play
On the tabor to the Worthies, and let them dance the
hay.
HOLOFERNES
Most dull, honest Dull! To our sport, away!   [*Exeunt.*

SCENE II

The same.   Before the princess's pavilion.

Enter the PRINCESS, KATHARINE, ROSALINE, *and*
MARIA.

PRINCESS
Sweet hearts, we shall be rich ere we depart,

If fairings come thus plentifully in:
A lady wall'd about with diamonds!
Look you what I have from the loving king.
ROSALINE
Madam, came nothing else along with that?
PRINCESS
Nothing but this! yes, as much love in rime
As would be cramm'd up in a sheet of paper,
Writ o' both sides the leaf, margent and all,
That he was fain to seal on Cupid's name.
ROSALINE
That was the way to make his godhead wax,
For he hath been five thousand years a boy.
KATHARINE
Ay, and a shrewd unhappy gallows too.
ROSALINE
You'll ne'er be friends with him; a' kill'd your sister.
KATHARINE
He made her melancholy, sad, and heavy;
And so she died: had she been light, like you,
Of such a merry, nimble, stirring spirit,
She might ha' been a grandam ere she died:
And so may you; for a light heart lives long.
ROSALINE
What's your dark meaning, mouse, of this light word?
KATHARINE
A light condition in a beauty dark.
ROSALINE
We need more light to find your meaning out.
KATHARINE
You'll mar the light by taking it in snuff;
Therefore I'll darkly end the argument.
ROSALINE
Look, what you do, you do it still i'th'dark.
KATHARINE
So do not you, for you are a light wench.
ROSALINE
Indeed I weigh not you, and therefore light.
KATHARINE
You weigh me not? O, that's you care not for me.
ROSALINE
Great reason; for 'past cure is still past care.'
PRINCESS
Well bandied both; a set of wit well play'd.
But, Rosaline, you have a favour too:
Who sent it? and what is it?
ROSALINE
                    I would you knew:
An if my face were but as fair as yours,
My favour were as great; be witness this.
Nay, I have verses too, I thank Berowne:
The numbers true; and, were the numb'ring too,
I were the fairest goddess on the ground:
I am compared to twenty thousand fairs.
O, he hath drawn my picture in his letter!
PRINCESS
Any thing like?
ROSALINE
Much in the letters; nothing in the praise.
PRINCESS
Beauteous as ink; a good conclusion.
KATHARINE
Fair as a text B in a copy-book.
ROSALINE
'Ware pencils, ho! let me not die your debtor,
My red dominical, my golden letter:
O, that your face were not so full of O's!
PRINCESS
A pox of that jest! and I beshrew all shrows.
But, Katharine, what was sent to you from fair
Dumaine?
KATHARINE
Madam, this glove.
PRINCESS
                    Did he not send you twain?
KATHARINE
Yes, madam, and moreover
Some thousand verses of a faithful lover,
A huge translation of hypocrisy,
Vilely compil'd, profound simplicity.
MARIA
This and these pearls to me sent Longaville:
The letter is too long by half a mile.
PRINCESS
I think no less. Dost thou not wish in heart
The chain were longer and the letter short?
MARIA
Ay, or I would these hands might never part.

BOYET O, I am stabb'd with laughter!

PRINCESS
We are wise girls to mock our lovers so.
ROSALINE
They are worse fools to purchase mocking so.
That same Berowne I'll torture ere I go:
O that I knew he were but in by th'week!
How I would make him fawn and beg and seek
And wait the season and observe the times,
And spend his prodigal wits in bootless rimes,
And shape his service wholly to my hests,
And make him proud to make me proud that jests!
So pertaunt-like would I o'ersway his state
That he should be my fool and I his fate.
PRINCESS
None are so surely caught, when they are catch'd,
As wit turn'd fool: folly, in wisdom hatch'd,
Hath wisdom's warrant and the help of school
And wit's own grace to grace a learned fool.
ROSALINE
The blood of youth burns not with such excess
As gravity's revolt to wantonness.
MARIA
Folly in fools bears not so strong a note
As foolery in the wise, when wit doth dote;
Since all the power thereof it doth apply
To prove, by wit, worth in simplicity.
PRINCESS
Here comes Boyet, and mirth is in his face.

Enter BOYET.

BOYET
O, I am stabb'd with laughter! Where's her Grace?
PRINCESS
Thy news, Boyet?
BOYET
                    Prepare, madam, prepare!
Arm, wenches, arm! encounters mounted are
Against your peace: Love doth approach disguised,
Armed in arguments; you'll be surprised:
Muster your wits; stand in your own defence;
Or hide your heads like cowards, and fly hence.
PRINCESS
Saint Denis to Saint Cupid! What are they
That charge their breath against us? say, scout, say.
BOYET
Under the cool shade of a sycamore
I thought to close mine eyes some half an hour;
When, lo! to interrupt my purpos'd rest,
Toward that shade I might behold address'd
The king and his companions: warily
I stole into a neighbour thicket by,
And overheard what you shall overhear;
That, by and by, disguis'd they will be here.
Their herald is a pretty knavish page,
That well by heart hath conn'd his embassage:

Action and accent did they teach him there;
'Thus must thou speak,' and 'thus thy body bear':
And ever and anon they made a doubt
Presence majestical would put him out;
'For,' quoth the king, 'an angel shalt thou see;
Yet fear not thou, but speak audaciously.'
The boy replied, 'An angel is not evil;
I should have fear'd her had she been a devil.'
With that, all laugh'd and clapp'd him on the shoulder,
Making the bold wag by their praises bolder:
One rubb'd his elbow thus, and fleer'd and swore
A better speech was never spoke before;
Another, with his finger and his thumb,
Cried, 'Via! we will do't, come what will come';
The third he caper'd, and cried, 'All goes well';
The fourth turn'd on the toe, and down he fell.
With that, they all did tumble on the ground,
With such a zealous laughter, so profound,
That in this spleen ridiculous appears,
To cheque their folly, passion's solemn tears.
PRINCESS
But what, but what, come they to visit us?
BOYET
They do, they do: and are apparell'd thus,
Like Muscovites or Russians, as I guess.
Their purpose is to parle, to court and dance;
And every one his love-feat will advance
Unto his several mistress, which they'll know
By favours several which they did bestow.
PRINCESS
And will they so? the gallants shall be task'd;
For, ladies, we will every one be mask'd;
And not a man of them shall have the grace,
Despite of suit, to see a lady's face.
Hold, Rosaline, this favour thou shalt wear,
And then the king will court thee for his dear;
Hold, take thou this, my sweet, and give me thine,
So shall Berowne take me for Rosaline.
And change your favours too; so shall your loves
Woo contrary, deceiv'd by these removes.
ROSALINE
Come on, then; wear the favours most in sight.
KATHARINE
But in this changing what is your intent?
PRINCESS
The effect of my intent is to cross theirs:
They do it but in mocking merriment;
And mock for mock is only my intent.
Their several counsels they unbosom shall
To loves mistook, and so be mock'd
    withal
Upon the next occasion that we meet,
With visages display'd, to talk and greet.
ROSALINE
But shall we dance, if they desire to't?
PRINCESS
No, to the death, we will not move a foot;
Nor to their penn'd speech render we no
    grace,
But while 'tis spoke each turn away her
    face.
BOYET
Why, that contempt will kill the
    speaker's heart,
And quite divorce his memory from his
    part.
PRINCESS
Therefore I do it; and I make no doubt
The rest will ne'er come in, if he be out.
There's no such sport as sport by sport
    o'erthrown,
To make theirs ours and ours none but
    our own:
So shall we stay, mocking intended game,
And they, well mock'd, depart away with
    shame.
                    [*Trumpets sound within.*
BOYET
The trumpet sounds: be mask'd; the
    maskers come.
                    [*The ladies mask.*
Enter BLACKAMOORS *with music;*
    MOTH *with a speech; the* KING,
    BEROWNE, LONGAVILLE, *and*
    DUMAINE, *disguised as Russians.*
MOTH
All hail, the richest beauties on the
    earth! —
BOYET
Beauties no richer than rich taffeta.

MOTH
A holy parcel of the fairest dames
                    [*The ladies turn their backs to him.*
That ever turn'd their — backs — to mortal views!
BEROWNE [*aside to* MOTH].
Their eyes, villain, their eyes.
MOTH
That ever turn'd their eyes to mortal views! —
Out —
BOYET
True; out indeed.
MOTH
Out of your favours, heavenly spirits, vouchsafe
Not to behold —
BEROWNE [*aside to* MOTH].
Once to behold, rogue.
MOTH
Once to behold with your sun-beamed eyes,
——with your sun-beamed eyes —
BOYET
They will not answer to that epithet;
You were best call it 'daughter-beamed eyes.'
MOTH
They do not mark me, and that brings me out.
BEROWNE
Is this your perfectness? be gone, you rogue!
                    [*Exit* MOTH.
ROSALINE
What would these strangers? know their minds, Boyet:
If they do speak our language, 'tis our will
That some plain man recount their purposes:
Know what they would
BOYET
                    What would you with the princess?
BEROWNE
Nothing but peace and gentle visitation.
ROSALINE
What would they, say they?
BOYET
Nothing but peace and gentle visitation.
ROSALINE
Why, that they have; and bid them so be gone.
BOYET
She says, you have it, and you may be gone.

MOTH All hail, the richest beauties on the earth!

KING
Say to her, we have measur'd many miles
To tread a measure with her on this grass.
BOYET
They say, that they have measur'd many a mile
To tread a measure with you on this grass.
ROSALINE
It is not so. Ask them how many inches
Is in one mile: if they have measur'd many,
The measure then of one is easily told.
BOYET
If to come hither you have measur'd miles,
And many miles, the princess bids you tell
How many inches doth fill up one mile.
BEROWNE
Tell her, we measure them by weary steps.
BOYET
She hears herself.
ROSALINE
         How many weary steps,
Of many weary miles you have o'ergone,
Are number'd in the travel of one mile?
BEROWNE
We number nothing that we spend for you:
Our duty is so rich, so infinite,
That we may do it still without accompt.
Vouchsafe to show the sunshine of your face,
That we, like savages, may worship it.
ROSALINE
My face is but a moon, and clouded too.
KING
Blessed are clouds, to do as such clouds do!
Vouchsafe, bright moon, and these thy stars, to
   shine,
Those clouds remov'd, upon our watery eyne.
ROSALINE
O vain petitioner! beg a greater matter;
Thou now requests but moonshine in the water.
KING
Then, in our measure do but vouchsafe one change.
Thou bid'st me beg: this begging is not strange.
ROSALINE
Play, music, then! Nay, you must do it soon.
                   [Music plays.
Not yet! no dance! Thus change I like the moon.
KING
Will you not dance? How come you thus estranged?
ROSALINE
You took the moon at full, but now she's changed.
KING
Yet still she is the moon, and I the man.
The music plays; vouchsafe some motion to it.
ROSALINE
Our ears vouchsafe it.
KING
        But your legs should do it.
ROSALINE
Since you are strangers and come here by chance,
We'll not be nice: take hands. We will not dance.
KING
Why take we hands, then?
ROSALINE
          Only to part friends:
Curtsy, sweet hearts; and so the measure ends.
KING
More measure of this measure; be not nice.
ROSALINE
We can afford no more at such a price.
KING
Price you yourselves: what buys your company?
ROSALINE
Your absence only.
KING
        That can never be.
ROSALINE
Then cannot we be bought: and so, adieu;
Twice to your visor, and half once to you.
KING
If you deny to dance, let's hold more chat.
ROSALINE
In private, then.
KING
        I am best pleas'd with that.
                   [They converse apart.
BEROWNE
White-handed mistress, one sweet word with thee.
PRINCESS
Honey, and milk, and sugar; there is three.

BEROWNE
Nay then, two treys, and if you grow so nice,
Metheglin, wort, and malmsey: well run, dice!
There's half-a-dozen sweets.
PRINCESS
             Seventh sweet, adieu:
Since you can cog, I'll play no more with you.
BEROWNE
One word in secret.
PRINCESS
         Let it not be sweet.
BEROWNE
Thou grievest my gall.
PRINCESS
        Gall! bitter.
BEROWNE
             Therefore meet.
                [They converse apart.
DUMAINE
Will you vouchsafe with me to change a word?
MARIA
Name it.
DUMAINE
     Fair lady, —
MARIA
           Say you so? Fair lord, —
Take that for your fair lady.
DUMAINE
            Please it you,
As much in private, and I'll bid adieu.
                [They converse apart.
KATHARINE
What, was your visard made without a tongue?
LONGAVILLE
I know the reason, lady, why you ask.
KATHARINE
O for your reason! quickly, sir; I long.
LONGAVILLE
You have a double tongue within your mask,
And would afford my speechless visard half.
KATHARINE
Veal, quoth the Dutchman. Is not 'veal' a calf?
LONGAVILLE
A calf, fair lady!
KATHARINE
        No, a fair lord calf.
LONGAVILLE
Let's part the word.
KATHARINE
        No, I'll not be your half:
Take all, and wean it; it may prove an ox.
LONGAVILLE
Look, how you butt yourself in these sharp mocks!
Will you give horns, chaste lady? do not so.
KATHARINE
Then die a calf, before your horns do grow.
LONGAVILLE
One word in private with you, ere I die.
KATHARINE
Bleat softly then; the butcher hears you cry.
                [They converse apart.
BOYET
The tongues of mocking wenches are as keen
  As is the razor's edge invisible,
Cutting a smaller hair than may be seen,
  Above the sense of sense; so sensible
Seemeth their conference; their conceits have wings
Fleeter than arrows, bullets, wind, thought, swifter
   things.
ROSALINE
Not one word more, my maids; break off, break off.
BEROWNE
By heaven, all dry-beaten with pure scoff!
KING
Farewell, mad wenches; you have simple wits.
PRINCESS
Twenty adieus, my frozen Muscovits.
      [Exeunt KING, LORDS, and BLACKAMOORS.
Are these the breed of wits so wonder'd at?
BOYET
Tapers they are, with your sweet breaths puff'd out.
ROSALINE
Well-liking wits they have; gross, gross; fat, fat.
PRINCESS
O poverty in wit, kingly-poor flout!
Will they not, think you, hang themselves to-night?
  Or ever, but in visards, show their faces?
This pert Berowne was out of countenance quite.

ROSALINE
O, they were all in lamentable cases!
The king was weeping-ripe for a good word.
PRINCESS
Berowne did swear himself out of all suit.
MARIA
Dumaine was at my service, and his sword:
No point, quoth I; my servant straight was mute.
KATHARINE
Lord Longaville said, I came o'er his heart;
And trow you what he call'd me?
PRINCESS
              Qualm, perhaps.
KATHARINE
Yes, in good faith.
PRINCESS
         Go, sickness as thou art!
ROSALINE
Well, better wits have worn plain statute-caps.
But will you hear? the king is my love sworn.
PRINCESS
And quick Berowne hath plighted faith to me.
KATHARINE
And Longaville was for my service born.
MARIA
Dumaine is mine, as sure as bark on tree.
BOYET
Madam, and pretty mistresses, give ear:
Immediately they will again be here
In their own shapes; for it can never be
They will digest this harsh indignity.
PRINCESS
Will they return?
BOYET
        They will, they will, God knows;
And leap for joy, though they are lame with blows:
Therefore change favours; and, when they repair,
Blow like sweet roses in this summer air.
PRINCESS
How blow? how blow? speak to be understood.
BOYET
Fair ladies mask'd are roses in their bud;
Dismask'd, their damask sweet commixture shown,
Are angels vailing clouds, or roses blown.
PRINCESS
Avaunt, perplexity! What shall we do,
If they return in their own shapes to woo?
ROSALINE
Good madam, if by me you'll be advised,
Let's mock them still, as well known as disguised:
Let us complain to them what fools were here,
Disguis'd like Muscovites, in shapeless gear;
And wonder what they were and to what end
Their shallow shows and prologue vilely penn'd,
And their rough carriage so ridiculous,
Should be presented at our tent to us.
BOYET
Ladies, withdraw: the gallants are at hand.
PRINCESS
Whip to our tents, as roes run o'er land.
           [Exeunt PRINCESS, ROSALINE,
             KATHARINE, and MARIA.

    Enter the KING, BEROWNE, LONGAVILLE, and
        DUMAINE, in their proper habits.

KING
Fair sir, God save you! Where is the princess?
BOYET
Gone to her tent. Please it your majesty
Command me any service to her thither?
KING
That she vouchsafe me audience for one word.
BOYET
I will; and so will she, I know, my lord.   *[Exit.*
BEROWNE
This fellow pecks up wit as pigeons pease,
And utters it again when God doth please:
He is wit's pedlar, and retails his wares
At wakes and wassails, meetings, markets, fairs;
And we that sell by gross, the Lord doth know,
Have not the grace to grace it with such show.
This gallant pins the wenches on his sleeve;
Had he been Adam, he had tempted Eve;
A' can carve too, and lisp: why, this is he
That kiss'd his hand away in courtesy;
This is the ape of form, monsieur the nice,
That, when he plays at tables, chides the dice
In honourable terms: nay, he can sing
A mean most meanly; and in ushering

Mend him who can: the ladies call him sweet;
The stairs, as he treads on them, kiss his feet:
This is the flower that smiles on every one,
To show his teeth as white as whales bone;
And consciences, that will not die in debt,
Pay him the due of honey-tongued Boyet.

KING
A blister on his sweet tongue, with my heart,
That put Armado's page out of his part!

BEROWNE
See where it comes! Behaviour, what wert thou
Till this madman show'd thee? and what art thou now?

Enter the PRINCESS, *usher'd by* BOYET; ROSALINE,
MARIA, *and* KATHARINE.

KING
All hail, sweet madam, and fair time of day!

PRINCESS
'Fair' in 'all hail' is foul, as I conceive.

KING
Construe my speeches better, if you may.

PRINCESS
Then wish me better; I will give you leave.

KING
We came to visit you, and purpose now
To lead you to our court; vouchsafe it then.

PRINCESS
This field shall hold me; and so hold your vow:
Nor God, nor I, delights in perjur'd men.

KING
Rebuke me not for that which you provoke:
The virtue of your eye must break my oath.

PRINCESS
You nickname virtue; vice you should have spoke;
  For virtue's office never breaks men's troth.
Now by my maiden honour, yet as pure
  As the unsullied lily, I protest,
A world of torments though I should endure,
  I would not yield to be your house's guest;
So much I hate a breaking cause to be
Of heavenly oaths, vow'd with integrity.

KING
O, you have liv'd in desolation here,
Unseen, unvisited, much to our shame.

PRINCESS
Not so, my lord; it is not so, I swear;
We have had pastimes here and pleasant game:
A mess of Russians left us but of late.

KING
How, madam! Russians!

PRINCESS
                    Ay, in truth, my lord;
Trim gallants, full of courtship and of state.

ROSALINE
Madam, speak true. It is not so, my lord:
My lady, to the manner of the days,
In courtesy gives undeserving praise.
We four indeed confronted were with four
In Russian habit: here they stay'd an hour,
And talk'd apace; and in that hour, my lord,
They did not bless us with one happy word.
I dare not call them fools; but this I think,
When they are thirsty, fools would fain have drink.

BEROWNE
This jest is dry to me. Fair gentle sweet,
Your wit makes wise things foolish: when we greet,
With eyes best seeing, heaven's fiery eye,
By light we lose light: your capacity
Is of that nature that to your huge store
Wise things seem foolish and rich things but poor.

ROSALINE
This proves you wise and rich, for in my eye, —

BEROWNE
I am a fool, and full of poverty.

ROSALINE
But that you take what doth to you belong,
It were a fault to snatch words from my tongue.

BEROWNE
O, I am yours, and all that I possess!

ROSALINE
All the fool mine?

BEROWNE
                I cannot give you less.

ROSALINE
Which of the visards was it that you wore?

BEROWNE
Where? when? what visard? why demand you this?

ROSALINE
There, then, that visard; that superfluous case

That hid the worse and show'd the better face.

KING
We are descried; they'll mock us now downright.

DUMAINE
Let us confess and turn it to a jest.

PRINCESS
Amaz'd, my lord? why looks your highness sad?

ROSALINE
Help, hold his brows! he'll swound! Why look you pale?
Sea-sick, I think, coming from Muscovy.

BEROWNE
Thus pour the stars down plagues for perjury.
  Can any face of brass hold longer out?
Here stand I, lady: dart thy skill at me;
  Bruise me with scorn, confound me with a flout;
Thrust thy sharp wit quite through my ignorance;
  Cut me to pieces with thy keen conceit;
And I will wish thee never more to dance,
  Nor never more in Russian habit wait.
O, never will I trust to speeches penn'd,
  Nor to the motion of a schoolboy's tongue,
Nor never come in visard to my friend,
  Nor woo in rime, like a blind harper's song!
Taffeta phrases, silken terms precise,
  Three-pil'd hyperboles, spruce affectation,
Figures pedantical; these summer-flies
  Have blown me full of maggot ostentation:
I do forswear them; and I here protest,
  By this white glove, — how white the hand, God
    knows! —
Henceforth my wooing mind shall be express'd
  In russet yeas and honest kersey noes:
And, to begin, wench, — so God help me, la! —
My love to thee is sound, sans crack or flaw.

ROSALINE
Sans sans, I pray you.

BEROWNE
                    Yet I have a trick
Of the old rage: bear with me, I am sick;
I'll leave it by degrees. Soft, let us see:
Write, 'Lord have mercy on us' on those three;
They are infected; in their hearts it lies;
They have the plague, and caught it of your eyes;
These lords are visited; you are not free,
For the Lord's tokens on you do I see.

PRINCESS
No, they are free that gave these tokens to us.

BEROWNE
Our states are forfeit: seek not to undo us.

ROSALINE
It is not so; for how can this be true,
That you stand forfeit, being those that sue?

BEROWNE
Peace! for I will not have to do with you.

ROSALINE
Nor shall not, if I do as I intend.

BEROWNE
Speak for yourselves; my wit is at an end.

KING
Teach us, sweet madam, for our rude transgression
Some fair excuse.

PRINCESS
                The fairest is confession.
Were not you here but even now disguised?

KING
Madam, I was.

PRINCESS
              And were you well advised?

KING
I was, fair madam.

PRINCESS
                  When you then were here,
What did you whisper in your lady's ear?

KING
That more than all the world I did respect her.

PRINCESS
When she shall challenge this, you will reject her.

KING
Upon mine honour, no.

PRINCESS
                    Peace, peace! forbear:
Your oath once broke, you force not to forswear.

KING
Despise me, when I break this oath of mine.

PRINCESS
I will: and therefore keep it. Rosaline,
What did the Russian whisper in your ear?

ROSALINE
Madam, he swore that he did hold me dear

As precious eyesight, and did value me
Above this world; adding thereto, moreover,
That he would wed me, or else die my lover.

PRINCESS
God give thee joy of him! the noble lord
Most honourably doth unhold his word.

KING
What mean you, madam? by my life, my troth,
I never swore this lady such an oath.

ROSALINE
By heaven, you did; and to confirm it plain,
You gave me this: but take it, sir, again.

KING
My faith and this the princess I did give:
I knew her by this jewel on her sleeve.

PRINCESS
Pardon me, sir, this jewel did she wear;
And Lord Berowne, I thank him, is my dear.
What, will you have me, or your pearl again?

BEROWNE
Neither of either; I remit both twain.
I see the trick on't: here was a consent,
Knowing aforehand of our merriment,
To dash it like a Christmas comedy:
Some carry-tale, some please-man, some slight zany,
Some mumble-news, some trencher-knight, some
  Dick,
That smiles his cheek in years and knows the trick
To make my lady laugh when she's disposed,
Told our intents before; which once disclosed,
The ladies did change favours: and then we,
Following the signs, woo'd but the sign of she.
Now, to our perjury to add more terror,
We are again forsworn, in will and error.
Much upon this it is: and might not you [*to* BOYET.
Forestall our sport, to make us thus untrue?
Do not you know my lady's foot by th'squier,
  And laugh upon the apple of her eye?
And stand between her back, sir, and the fire,
  Holding a trencher, jesting merrily?
You put our page out: go, you are allow'd;
Die when you will, a smock shall be your shroud.
You leer upon me, do you? there's an eye
Wounds like a leaden sword.

BOYET
                        Full merrily
Hath this brave manage, this career, been run.

BEROWNE
Lo, he is tilting straight! Peace! I have done.

Enter COSTARD.

Welcome, pure wit! thou partest a fair fray.

COSTARD
O Lord, sir, they would know
Whether the three Worthies shall come in or no.

BEROWNE
What, are there but three?

COSTARD
                        No, sir; but it is vara fine,
For every one pursents three.

BEROWNE
                          And three times thrice is nine.

COSTARD
Not so, sir; under correction, sir; I hope it is not so.
You cannot beg us, sir, I can assure you, sir; we know
  what we know:
I hope, sir, three times thrice, sir, —

BEROWNE
                                — Is not nine.

COSTARD
Under correction, sir, we know whereuntil it doth
  amount.

BEROWNE
By Jove, I always took three threes for nine.

COSTARD
O Lord, sir, it were pity you should get your living
by reck'ning, sir.

BEROWNE
How much is it?

COSTARD
O Lord, sir, the parties themselves, the actors, sir, will
show whereuntil it doth amount: for mine own part, I
am, as they say, but to parfect one man in one poor
man, Pompey the Great, sir.

BEROWNE
Art thou one of the Worthies?

COSTARD
It pleased them to think me worthy of Pompey the
Great: for mine own part, I know not the degree of the
Worthy, but I am to stand for him.

BEROWNE
Go, bid them prepare.

COSTARD
We will turn it finely off, sir; we will take some care. [*Exit.*

KING
Berowne, they will shame us: let them not approach.

BEROWNE
We are shame-proof, my lord: and 'tis some policy
To have one show worse than the king's and his
company.

KING
I say they shall not come.

PRINCESS
Nay, my good lord, let me o'errule you now:
That sport best pleases that doth least know how:
Where zeal strives to content, and the contents
Dies in the zeal of that which it presents:
Their form confounded makes most form in mirth,
When great things labouring perish in their birth.

BEROWNE
A right description of our sport, my lord.

Enter ARMADO.

ARMADO
Anointed, I implore so much expense of thy royal sweet
breath as will utter a brace of words.
[*Converses apart with the* KING, *and delivers him a paper.*

PRINCESS
Doth this man serve God?

BEROWNE
Why ask you?

PRINCESS
A' speaks not like a man of God his making.

ARMADO
That is all one, my fair, sweet, honey monarch; for, I
protest, the schoolmaster is exceeding fantastical; too
too vain, too too vain: but we will put it, as they say, to
fortune de la guerra. I wish you the peace of mind,
most royal couplement! [*Exit.*

KING
Here is like to be a good presence of Worthies. He
presents Hector of Troy; the swain, Pompey the Great;
the parish curate, Alexander; Armado's page, Hercules;
the pedant, Judas Maccabæus: And if these four
Worthies in their first show thrive.
These four will change habits, and present the other
five.

BEROWNE
There is five in the first show.

KING
You are deceived; 'tis not so.

BEROWNE
The pedant, the braggart, the hedge-priest, the fool
and the boy: —
Abate throw at novum, and the whole world again
Cannot pick out five such, take each one in his vein.

KING
The ship is under sail, and here she comes amain.

Enter COSTARD, *for* POMPEY.

COSTARD
I Pompey am, —

BOYET
                    You lie, you are not he.

COSTARD
I Pompey am, —

BOYET
With libbard's head on knee.

BEROWNE
Well said, old mocker: I must needs be friends with
thee.

COSTARD
I Pompey am, Pompey surnam'd the Big, —

DUMAINE
The Great.

COSTARD
It is 'Great,' sir: —
            Pompey surnam'd the Great;
That oft in field, with targe and shield, did make my foe
to sweat:
And travelling along this coast, I here am come by
chance,
And lay my arms before the legs of this sweet lass of
France.
If your ladyship would say, 'Thanks, Pompey,' I had
done.

PRINCESS
Great thanks, great Pompey.

COSTARD
'Tis not so much worth; but I hope I was perfect: I
made a little fault in 'Great.'

BEROWNE
My hat to a halfpenny, Pompey proves the best
Worthy.

Enter SIR NATHANIEL, *for* ALEXANDER.

SIR NATHANIEL
When in the world I liv'd, I was the world's commander;
By east, west, north, and south, I spread my
conquering might:
My scutcheon plain declares that I am Alisander, —

BOYET
Your nose says, no, you are not; for it stands too right.

BEROWNE
Your nose smells 'no' in this, most tender-smelling
knight.

PRINCESS
The conqueror is dismay'd. Proceed, good Alexander.

SIR NATHANIEL
When in the world I liv'd, I was the world's commander.

BOYET
Most true, 'tis right; you were so, Alisander.

BEROWNE
Pompey the Great, —

COSTARD
Your servant, and Costard.

BEROWNE
Take away the conqueror, take away Alisander.

COSTARD [*to* SIR NATHANIEL].
O, sir, you have overthrown Alisander the conqueror!
You will be scraped out of the painted cloth for this:
your lion, that holds his poll-axe sitting on a close-stool,
will be given to Ajax: he will be the ninth Worthy. A
conqueror, and afeard to speak! run away for shame,
Alisander. [SIR NATHANIEL *retires.*] There an't shall
please you; a foolish mild man; an honest man, look
you, and soon dash'd. He is a marvellous good
neighbour, faith, and a very good bowler: but, for
Alisander, — alas, you see how 'tis, — a little
o'erparted. But there are Worthies a-coming will speak
their mind in some other sort.

PRINCESS
Stand aside, good Pompey.

Enter HOLOFERNES, *for* JUDAS;
and MOTH, *for* HERCULES.

HOLOFERNES
Great Hercules is presented by this imp,
    Whose club kill'd Cerberus, that three-headed canis;
And when he was a babe, a child, a shrimp,
    Thus did he strangle serpents in his manus.
Quoniam he seemeth in minority,
Ergo I come with this apology.
— Keep some state in thy exit, and vanish.
                                    [MOTH *retires.*
Judas I am, —

DUMAINE
A Judas!

HOLOFERNES
Not Iscariot, sir.
Judas I am, ycliped Maccabæus.

DUMAINE
Judas Maccabæus clipp'd is plain Judas.

BEROWNE
A kissing traitor. How art thou proved Judas?

HOLOFERNES
Judas I am, —

DUMAINE
The more shame for you, Judas.

HOLOFERNES
What mean you, sir?

BOYET
To make Judas hang himself.

HOLOFERNES
Begin, sir; you are my elder.

BEROWNE
Well follow'd: Judas was hang'd on an elder.

HOLOFERNES
I will not be put out of countenance.

BEROWNE
Because thou hast no face.

HOLOFERNES
What is this?

BOYET
A cittern-head.

DUMAINE
The head of a bodkin.

BEROWNE
A Death's face in a ring.

LONGAVILLE
The face of an old Roman coin, scarce seen.

BOYET
The pommel of Cæsar's falchion.

DUMAINE
The carved-bone face on a flask.

BEROWNE
Saint George's half-cheek in a brooch.

DUMAINE
Ay, and in a brooch of lead.

BEROWNE
Ay, and worn in the cap of a tooth-drawer.
And now forward; for we have put thee in countenance.

HOLOFERNES
You have put me out of countenance.

BEROWNE
False; we have given thee faces.

HOLOFERNES
But you have out-faced them all.

BEROWNE
An thou wert a lion, we would do so.

BOYET
Therefore, as he is an ass, let him go.
And so adieu, sweet Jude! nay, why dost thou stay?

DUMAINE
For the latter end of his name.

BEROWNE
For the ass to the Jude; give it him: — Jud-as, away!

HOLOFERNES
This is not generous, not gentle, not humble.

BOYET
A light for Monsieur Judas! it grows dark, he may
stumble.
                                    [HOLOFERNES *retires.*

PRINCESS
Alas, poor Maccabæus, how hath he been baited!

Enter ARMADO, *for* HECTOR.

BEROWNE
Hide thy head, Achilles: here comes Hector in arms.

DUMAINE
Though my mocks come home by me, I will now be
merry.

KING
Hector was but a Troyan in respect of this.

BOYET
But is this Hector?

KING
I think Hector was not so clean-timber'd.

LONGAVILLE
His leg is too big for Hector's.

DUMAINE
More calf, certain.

BOYET
No; he is best indued in the small.

BEROWNE
This cannot be Hector.

DUMAINE
He's a god or a painter; for he makes faces.

ARMADO
The armipotent Mars, of lances the almighty,
Gave Hector a gift, —

DUMAINE
A gilt nutmeg.

BEROWNE
A lemon.

LONGAVILLE
Stuck with cloves.

DUMAINE
No, cloven.

ARMADO
Peace! —
The armipotent Mars, of lances the almighty,
    Gave Hector a gift, the heir of Ilion;
A man so breath'd, that certain he would fight; yea
    From morn till night, out of his pavilion.
I am that flower, —

DUMAINE
                    That mint.

LONGAVILLE
                              That columbine.

ARMADO
Sweet Lord Longaville, rein thy tongue.

LONGAVILLE
I must rather give it the rein, for it runs against
Hector.

DUMAINE
Ay, and Hector's a greyhound.
ARMADO
The sweet war-man is dead and rotten; sweet chucks, beat not the bones of the buried: when he breathed, he was a man. But I will forward with my device. [*To the* PRINCESS] Sweet royalty, bestow on me the sense of hearing. [BEROWNE *steps forth.*
PRINCESS
Speak, brave Hector: we are much delighted.
ARMADO
I do adore thy sweet Grace's slipper.
BOYET [*aside to* DUMAINE].
Loves her by the foot.
DUMAINE [*aside to* BOYET].
He may not by the yard.
ARMADO
This Hector far surmounted Hannibal, —
COSTARD
The party is gone.
Fellow Hector, she is gone; she is two months on her way.
ARMADO
What meanest thou?
COSTARD
Faith, unless you play the honest Troyan, the poor wench is cast away; she's quick; the child brags in her belly already: 'tis yours.
ARMADO
Dost thou infamonise me among potentates? thou shalt die.
COSTARD
Then shall Hector be whipp'd for Jaquenetta that is quick by him and hang'd for Pompey that is dead by him.
DUMAINE
Most rare Pompey!
BOYET
Renowned Pompey!
BEROWNE
Greater than great, great, great, great Pompey!
Pompey the Huge!
DUMAINE
Hector trembles.
BEROWNE
Pompey is moved. More Ates, more Ates! stir them on! stir them on!
DUMAINE
Hector will challenge him.
BEROWNE
Ay, if a' have no man's blood in's belly than will sup a flea.
ARMADO
By the north pole, I do challenge thee.
COSTARD
I will not fight with a pole, like a northern man: I'll slash; I'll do it by the sword. I bepray you, let me borrow my arms again.
DUMAINE
Room for the incensed Worthies!
COSTARD
I'll do it in my shirt.
DUMAINE
Most resolute Pompey!
MOTH
Master, let me take you a button-hole lower. Do you not see Pompey is uncasing for the combat? What mean you? You will lose your reputation.
ARMADO
Gentlemen and soldiers, pardon me; I will not combat in my shirt.
DUMAINE
You may not deny it: Pompey hath made the challenge.
ARMADO
Sweet bloods, I both may and will.
BEROWNE
What reason have you for't?
ARMADO
The naked truth of it is, I have no shirt; I go woolward for penance.
BOYET
True, and it was enjoin'd him in Rome for want of linen: since when, I'll be sworn, he wore none but a dishclout of Jaquenetta's, and that a' wears next his heart for a favour.

Enter a messenger, MONSIEUR MERCADÉ

MERCADÉ
God save you, madam!
PRINCESS
Welcome, Mercadé;
But that thou interrupt'st our merriment.
MERCADÉ
I am sorry, madam; for the news I bring
Is heavy in my tongue. The king your father —
PRINCESS
Dead, for my life!
MERCADÉ
Even so; my tale is told.
BEROWNE
Worthies, away! the scene begins to cloud.
ARMADO
For mine own part, I breathe free breath. I have seen the day of wrong through the little hole of discretion, and I will right myself like a soldier.
[*Exeunt* WORTHIES.
KING
How fares your majesty?
PRINCESS
Boyet, prepare; I will away to-night.
KING
Madam, not so; I do beseech you, stay.
PRINCESS
Prepare, I say. I thank you, gracious lords,
For all your fair endeavours; and entreat,
Out of a new-sad soul, that you vouchsafe
In your rich wisdom to excuse or hide
The liberal opposition of our spirits,
If over-boldly we have borne ourselves
In the converse of breath: your gentleness
Was guilty of it. Farewell, worthy lord!
A heavy heart bears not a humble tongue:
Excuse me so, coming too short of thanks
For my great suit so easily obtain'd.
KING
The extreme pace of time extremely forms
All causes to the purpose of his speed,
And often at his very loose decides
That which long process could not arbitrate:
And though the mourning brow of progeny
Forbid the smiling courtesy of love
The holy suit which fain it would convince,
Yet, since love's argument was first on foot,
Let not the cloud of sorrow justle it
From what it purpos'd; since, to wail friends lost
Is not by much so wholesome-profitable
As to rejoice at friends but newly found.
PRINCESS
I understand you not: my griefs are double.
BEROWNE
Honest plain words best pierce the ear of grief;
And by these badges understand the king.
For your fair sakes have we neglected time,
Play'd foul play with our oaths: your beauty, ladies,
Hath much deform'd us, fashioning our humours
Even to the opposed end of our intents:
And what in us hath seem'd ridiculous, —
As love is full of unbefitting strains,
All wanton as a child, skipping and vain,
Form'd by the eye and therefore, like the eye,
Full of straying shapes, of habits, and of forms,
Varying in subjects as the eye doth roll
To every varied object in his glance:
Which parti-coated presence of loose love
Put on by us, if, in your heavenly eyes,
Have misbecom'd our oaths and gravities,
Those heavenly eyes, that look into these faults,
Suggested us to make. Therefore, ladies,
Our love being yours, the error that love makes
Is likewise yours: we to ourselves prove false,
By being once false for ever to be true
To those that make us both, — fair ladies, you:
And even that falsehood, in itself a sin,
Thus purifies itself and turns to grace.
PRINCESS
We have receiv'd your letters full of love;
Your favours, the ambassadors of love;
And, in our maiden council, rated them
At courtship, pleasant jest and courtesy,
As bombast and as lining to the time:
But more devout than this in our respects
Have we not been; and therefore met your loves
In their own fashion, like a merriment.
DUMAINE
Our letters, madam, show'd much more than jest.
LONGAVILLE
So did our looks.
ROSALINE
We did not cote them so.

KING
Now, at the latest minute of the hour,
Grant us your loves.
PRINCESS
A time, methinks, too short
To make a world-without-end bargain in.
No, no, my lord, your Grace is perjur'd much,
Full of dear guiltiness; and therefore this: —
If for my love, as there is no such cause,
You will do aught, this shall you do for me:
Your oath I will not trust; but go with speed
To some forlorn and naked hermitage,
Remote from all the pleasures of the world;
There stay until the twelve celestial signs
Have brought about their annual reckoning.
If this austere insociable life
Change not your offer made in heat of blood;
If frosts and fasts, hard lodging and thin weeds
Nip not the gaudy blossoms of your love,
But that it bear this trial and last love;
Then, at the expiration of the year,
Come challenge me, challenge by these deserts,
And, by this virgin palm now kissing thine,
I will be thine; and till that instant shut
My woeful self up in a mourning house,
Raining the tears of lamentation
For the remembrance of my father's death.
If this thou do deny, let our hands part,
Neither intitled in the other's heart.
KING
If this, or more than this, I would deny,
To flatter up these powers of mine with rest,
The sudden hand of death close up mine eye!
Hence hermit then, my heart is in thy breast.
BEROWNE
And what to me, my love? and what to me?
ROSALINE
You must be purged too, your sins are rack'd:
You are attaint with faults and perjury:
Therefore if you my favour mean to get,
A twelvemonth shall you spend, and never rest,
But seek the weary beds of people sick.]
DUMAINE
But what to me, my love? but what to me?
KATHARINE
A wife? — A beard, fair health, and honesty;
With three-fold love I wish you all these three.
DUMAINE
O, shall I say, I thank you, gentle wife?
KATHARINE
Not so, my lord; a twelvemonth and a day
I'll mark no words that smooth-fac'd wooers say:
Come when the king doth to my lady come;
Then, if I have much love, I'll give you some.
DUMAINE
I'll serve thee true and faithfully till then.
KATHARINE
Yet swear not, lest ye be forsworn again.
LONGAVILLE
What says Maria?
MARIA
At the twelvemonth's end
I'll change my black gown for a faithful friend.
LONGAVILLE
I'll stay with patience; but the time is long.
MARIA
The liker you; few taller are so young.
BEROWNE
Studies my lady? mistress, look on me;
Behold the window of my heart, mine eye,
What humble suit attends thy answer there:
Impose some service on me for thy love.
ROSALINE
Oft have I heard of you, my Lord Berowne,
Before I saw you; and the world's large tongue
Proclaims you for a man replete with mocks,
Full of comparisons and wounding flouts,
Which you on all estates will execute
That lie within the mercy of your wit.
To weed this wormwood from your fruitful brain,
And therewithal to win me, if you please,
Without the which I am not to be won,
You shall this twelvemonth term from day to day
Visit the speechless sick and still converse
With groaning wretches; and your task shall be,
With all the fierce endeavour of your wit
To enforce the pained impotent to smile.
BEROWNE
To move wild laughter in the throat of death?
It cannot be; it is impossible:

Mirth cannot move a soul in agony.

ROSALINE
Why, that's the way to choke a gibing spirit,
Whose influence is begot of that loose grace
Which shallow laughing hearers give to fools:
A jest's prosperity lies in the ear
Of him that hears it, never in the tongue
Of him that makes it: then, if sickly ears,
Deaf'd with the clamours of their own dear groans,
Will hear your idle scorns, continue then,
And I will have you and that fault withal;
But if they will not, throw away that spirit,
And I shall find you empty of that fault,
Right joyful of your reformation.

BEROWNE
A twelvemonth! well; befall what will befall,
I'll jest a twelvemonth in an hospital.

PRINCESS [*to the* KING].
Ay, sweet my lord; and so I take my leave.

KING
No, madam; we will bring you on your way.

BEROWNE
Our wooing doth not end like an old play;
Jack hath not Jill: these ladies' courtesy
Might well have made our sport a comedy.

KING
Come, sir, it wants a twelvemonth and a day,
And then 'twill end.

BEROWNE
            That's too long for a play.
            Enter ARMADO.

ARMADO
Sweet majesty, vouchsafe me, —

PRINCESS
Was not that Hector?

DUMAINE
The worthy knight of Troy.

ARMADO
I will kiss thy royal finger, and take leave.
I am a votary; I have vow'd to Jaquenetta to hold the
plough for her sweet love three years. But, most
esteem'd greatness, will you hear the dialogue that the
two learned men have compiled in praise of the owl
and the cuckoo? It should have follow'd in the end of
our show.

KING
Call them forth quickly; we will do so.

ARMADO
Holla! approach.

            Enter HOLOFERNES, SIR NATHANIEL, MOTH,
                COSTARD, *and others.*

This side is Hiems, Winter, this Ver, the Spring; the
one maintain'd by the owl, the other by the cuckoo.
Ver, begin.

The Song

SPRING
When daisies pied and violets blue,
        And lady-smocks all silver-white,
And cuckoo-buds of yellow hue
        Do paint the meadows with delight,
The cuckoo then on every tree
Mocks married men; for thus sings he,
                Cuckoo;
Cuckoo, cuckoo: O word of fear,
Unpleasing to a married ear!

When shepherds pipe on oaten straws,
        And merry larks are ploughmen's clocks
When turtles tread, and rooks, and daws,
        And maidens bleach their summer smocks,
The cuckoo then on every tree,
        Mocks married men; for thus sings he,
                Cuckoo;
Cuckoo, cuckoo: O word of fear,
Unpleasing to a married ear!

WINTER
When icicles hang by the wall,
        And Dick the shepherd blows his nail,
And Tom bears logs into the hall,
        And milk comes frozen home in pail,
When blood is nipp'd and ways be foul,
        Then nightly sings the staring owl,
                Tu-whit;
Tu-who, a merry note,
While greasy Joan doth keel the pot.

When all aloud the wind doth blow,
        And coughing drowns the parson's saw,
And birds sit brooding in the snow,
        And Marian's nose looks red and raw,
When roasted crabs hiss in the bowl,
        Then nightly sings the staring owl,
                Tu-whit;
Tu-who, a merry note,
While greasy Joan doth keel the pot.

ARMADO
The words of Mercury are harsh after the songs of
Apollo. You that way: we this way.   [*Exeunt.*

ROMEO AND JULIET

DRAMATIS PERSONAE

ESCALUS, *prince of Verona.*
PARIS, *a young nobleman, kinsman to the prince.*
MONTAGUE, } *heads of two houses at variance*
CAPULET, } *with each other.*
AN OLD MAN, *of the Capulet family.*
ROMEO, *son to Montague.*
MERCUTIO, *kinsman to the prince, and friend to Romeo.*
BENVOLIO, *nephew to Montague, and friend to Romeo.*
TYBALT, *nephew to Lady Capulet.*
FRIAR LAURENCE, *a Franciscan.*

FRIAR JOHN, *of the same order.*
BALTHASAR, *servant to Romeo.*
SAMPSON, } *servants to Capulet.*
GREGORY, }
PETER, *servant to Juliet's nurse.*
ABRAHAM, *servant to Montague.*
AN APOTHECARY.
THREE MUSICIANS.
PAGE *to Paris; another* PAGE; *an* OFFICER.
LADY MONTAGUE, *wife to Montague.*

LADY CAPULET, *wife to Capulet.*
JULIET, *daughter to Capulet.*
NURSE *to Juliet.*

CITIZENS *of Verona;* KINSFOLK *of both houses;*
MASKERS, GUARDS, WATCHMEN, *and*
ATTENDANTS. CHORUS.

SCENE — *Verona; once, in the fifth act, at Mantua.*

PROLOGUE

Enter CHORUS.

CHORUS
Two households, both alike in dignity,
   In fair Verona, where we lay our scene,
From ancient grudge break to new mutiny,
   Where civil blood makes civil hands unclean.
From forth the fatal loins of these two foes
   A pair of star-cross'd lovers take their life;
Whose misadventur'd piteous overthrows
   Doth with their death bury their parents' strife.
The fearful passage of their death-mark'd love,
   And the continuance of their parents' rage,
Which, but their children's end, naught could remove,
   Is now the two hours' traffic of our stage;
The which if you with patient ears attend,
What here shall miss, our toil shall strive to mend.
                      [*Exit.*

ACT I

SCENE I

Verona. A public place.

Enter SAMPSON *and* GREGORY, *of the house of*
CAPULET, *with swords and bucklers.*

SAMPSON
Gregory, o' my word, we'll not carry coals.
GREGORY
No, for then we should be colliers.
SAMPSON
I mean, an we be in choler, we'll draw.
GREGORY
Ay, while you live, draw your neck out o'th'collar.
SAMPSON
I strike quickly, being moved.
GREGORY
But thou art not quickly moved to strike.
SAMPSON
A dog of the house of Montague moves me.
GREGORY
To move is to stir; and to be valiant is to stand:
therefore, if thou art moved, thou runn'st away.

SAMPSON
A dog of that house shall move me to stand: I will take
the wall of any man or maid of Montague's.
GREGORY
That shows thee a weak slave; for the weakest goes to
the wall.
SAMPSON
'Tis True; and therefore women, being the weaker
vessels, are ever thrust to the wall: — therefore I will
push Montague's men from the wall, and thrust his
maids to the wall.
GREGORY
The quarrel is between our masters and us their men.
SAMPSON
'Tis all one, I will show myself a tyrant: when I have
fought with the men, I will be cruel with the maids, and
cut off their heads.
GREGORY
The heads of the maids?
SAMPSON
Ay, the heads of the maids, or their maidenheads; take
it in what sense thou wilt.
GREGORY
They must take it in sense that feel it.
SAMPSON
Me they shall feel while I am able to stand: and 'tis
known I am a pretty piece of flesh.
GREGORY
'Tis well thou art not fish; if thou hadst, thou hadst
been Poor-John. — Draw thy tool; here comes two of
the house of the Montagues.

Enter ABRAHAM *and* BALTHASAR, *two*
SERVING-MEN *of the* MONTAGUES.

SAMPSON
My naked weapon is out: quarrel; I will back thee.
GREGORY
How! turn thy back and run?
SAMPSON
Fear me not.
GREGORY
No, marry; I fear thee!
SAMPSON
Let us take the law of our sides; let them begin.
GREGORY
I will frown as I pass by; and let them take it as they list.

SAMPSON
Nay, as they dare. I will bite my thumb at them; which
is a disgrace to them, if they bear it.
ABRAHAM
Do you bite your thumb at us, sir?
SAMPSON
I do bite my thumb, sir.
ABRAHAM
Do you bite your thumb at us, sir?
SAMPSON [*aside to* GREGORY].
Is the law of our side, if I say ay?
GREGORY [*aside to* SAMPSON].
No.
SAMPSON
No, sir, I do not bite my thumb at you, sir; but I bite my
thumb, sir.
GREGORY
Do you quarrel, sir?
ABRAHAM
Quarrel sir! no, sir.
SAMPSON
If you do, sir, I am for you; I serve as good a man as you.
ABRAHAM
No better.
SAMPSON
Well, sir.
GREGORY [*aside to* SAMPSON].
Say 'better': here comes one of my master's kinsmen.
SAMPSON
Yes, better, sir.
ABRAHAM
You lie.
SAMPSON
Draw, if you be men. — Gregory, remember thy
swashing blow.   [*They fight.*

Enter BENVOLIO.

BENVOLIO
Part, fools!   [*Beats down their swords.*
Put up your swords; you know not what you do.

Enter TYBALT.

TYBALT
What, art thou drawn among these heartless hinds?
Turn thee, Benvolio, look upon thy death.

ABRAHAM Do you bite your thumb at us, sir?

BENVOLIO
I do but keep the peace: put up thy sword,
Or manage it to part these men with me.

TYBALT
What, drawn, and talk of peace! I hate the word,
As I hate hell, all Montagues, and thee:
Have at thee, coward! [*They fight.*
Enter several of both houses, who join the fray; then enter
three or four CITIZENS *with clubs.*

CITIZENS
Clubs, bills, and partisans! strike! beat them down!
Down with the Capulets! down with the Montagues!
Enter old CAPULET *in his gown, and* LADY CAPULET.

CAPULET
What noise is this? — Give me my long sword, ho!

LADY CAPULET
A crutch, a crutch! — why call you for a sword?

CAPULET
My sword, I say! — Old Montague is come,
And flourishes his blade in spite of me.
Enter old MONTAGUE *and* LADY MONTAGUE.

MONTAGUE
Thou villain Capulet! — Hold me not, let me go.

LADY MONTAGUE
Thou shalt not stir one foot to seek a foe.
Enter PRINCE ESCALUS *with his* TRAIN.

PRINCE ESCALUS
Rebellious subjects, enemies to peace,
Profaners of this neighbour-stained steel, —
Will they not hear? — what, ho! you men, you beasts,
That quench the fire of your pernicious rage
With purple fountains issuing from your veins, —
On pain of torture, from those bloody hands
Throw your mistemper'd weapons to the ground,
And hear the sentence of your moved prince.
Three civil brawls, bred of an airy word,
By thee, old Capulet, and Montague,
Have thrice disturb'd the quiet of our streets;
And made Verona's ancient citizens
Cast-by their grave beseeming ornaments,
To wield old partisans, in hands as old,
Canker'd with peace, to part your canker'd hate:
If ever you disturb our streets again,
Your lives shall pay the forfeit of the peace.
For this time, all the rest depart away: —
You, Capulet, shall go along with me; —
And, Montague, come you this afternoon,
To know our further pleasure in this case,
To old Freetown, our common judgement-place. —
Once more, on pain of death, all men depart.
[*Exeunt all but* MONTAGUE,
LADY MONTAGUE, *and* BENVOLIO.

MONTAGUE
Who set this ancient quarrel new abroach? —
Speak, nephew, were you by when it began?

BENVOLIO
Here were the servants of your adversary,
And yours, close fighting, ere I did approach:
I drew to part them: in the instant came
The fiery Tybalt, with his sword prepared;
Which, as he breath'd defiance to my ears,
He swung about his head, and cut the winds,
Who, nothing hurt withal, hiss'd him in scorn:
While we were interchanging thrusts and blows,
Came more and more, and fought on part and part,
Till the prince came, who parted either part.

LADY MONTAGUE
O, where is Romeo? — saw you him to-day? —
Right glad am I he was not at this fray.

BENVOLIO
Madam, an hour before the worshipp'd sun
Peer'd forth the golden window of the east,
A troubled mind drave me to walk abroad;
Where — underneath the grove of sycamore
That westward rooteth from the city's side —
So early walking did I see your son:
Towards him I made; but he was ware of me,
And stole into the covert of the wood:
I, measuring his affections by my own,
Which then most sought where most might not be found,
Being one too many by my weary self,
Pursued my humour, not pursuing his,
And gladly shunn'd who gladly fled from me.

MONTAGUE
Many a morning hath he there been seen,
With tears augmenting the fresh morning's dew,
Adding to clouds more clouds with his deep sighs:
But all so soon as the all-cheering sun
Should in the farthest east begin to draw
The shady curtains from Aurora's bed,
Away from light steals home my heavy son,
And private in his chamber pens himself;
Shuts up his windows, locks fair daylight out,
And makes himself an artificial night:
Black and portentous must this humour prove,
Unless good counsel may the cause remove.

BENVOLIO
My noble uncle, do you know the cause?

MONTAGUE
I neither know it nor can learn of him.

BENVOLIO
Have you importun'd him by any means?

MONTAGUE
Both by myself and many other friends:
But he, his own affections' counsellor,
Is to himself, — I will not say how true, —

But to himself so secret and so close,
So far from sounding and discovery,
As is the bud bit with an envious worm,
Ere he can spread his sweet leaves to the air,
Or dedicate his beauty to the sun.
Could we but learn from whence his sorrows grow,
We would as willingly give cure as know.
Enter ROMEO

BENVOLIO
See, where he comes: so please you, step aside;
I'll know his grievance, or be much denied.

MONTAGUE
I would thou wert so happy by thy stay
To hear true shrift. — Come, madam, let's away.
[*Exeunt* MONTAGUE *and* LADY.

BENVOLIO
Good morrow, cousin.

ROMEO
                    Is the day so young?

BENVOLIO
But new struck nine.

ROMEO
                    Ay me! sad hours seem long.
Was that my father that went hence so fast?

BENVOLIO
It was. — What sadness lengthens Romeo's hours?

ROMEO
Not having that, which having makes them short.

BENVOLIO
In love?

ROMEO
Out —

BENVOLIO
Of love?

ROMEO
Out of her favour, where I am in love.

BENVOLIO
Alas, that love, so gentle in his view,
Should be so tyrannous and rough in proof!

ROMEO
Alas, that love, whose view is muffled still,
Should, without eyes, see pathways to his will! —
Where shall we dine? — O me! — What fray was here?
Yet tell me not, for I have heard it all.
Here's much to do with hate, but more with love:
Why, then, O brawling love! O loving hate!
O any thing, of nothing first create!
O heavy lightness! serious vanity!
Mis-shapen chaos of well-seeming forms!
Feather of lead, bright smoke, cold fire, sick health!
Still-waking sleep, that is not what it is! —
This love feel I, that feel no love in this.
Dost thou not laugh?

BENVOLIO
                    No, coz, I rather weep.

ROMEO
Good heart, at what?

BENVOLIO
                    At thy good heart's oppression.

ROMEO
Why, such is love's transgression. —
Griefs of mine own lie heavy in my breast;
Which thou wilt propagate, to have it press'd
With more of thine: this love, that thou hast shown,
Doth add more grief to too much of mine own.
Love is a smoke rais'd with the fume of sighs;
Being purg'd, a fire sparkling in lovers' eyes;
Being vex'd a sea nourish'd with lovers' tears:
What is it else? a madness most discreet,
A choking gall, and a preserving sweet. —
Farewell, my coz.

BENVOLIO
                    Soft! I will go along:
An if you leave me so, you do me wrong.

ROMEO
Tut, I have lost myself; I am not here;
This is not Romeo, he's some other where.

BENVOLIO
Tell me in sadness, who is that you love.

ROMEO
What, shall I groan, and tell thee?

BENVOLIO
                    Groan! why, no;
But sadly tell me who.

ROMEO
Bid a sick man in sadness make his will, —
Ah, word ill urg'd to one that is so ill! —
In sadness, cousin, I do love a woman.

BENVOLIO
I aim'd so near, when I suppos'd you lov'd.
ROMEO
A right good mark-man! — And she's fair I
   love.
BENVOLIO
A right fair mark, fair coz, is soonest hit.
ROMEO
Well, in that hit you miss: she'll not be hit
With Cupid's arrow, — she hath Dian's wit;
And, in strong proof of chastity well arm'd,
From love's weak childish bow she lives
   unharm'd.
She will not stay the siege of loving terms,
Nor bide th'encounter of assailing eyes,
Nor ope her lap to saint-seducing gold:
O, she is rich in beauty; only poor,
That, when she dies, with beauty dies her
   store.
BENVOLIO
Then she hath sworn that she will still live
   chaste?
ROMEO
She hath, and in that sparing makes huge
   waste;
For beauty, starv'd with her severity,
Cuts beauty off from all posterity.
She is too fair, too wise; wisely too fair,
To merit bliss by making me despair:
She hath forsworn to love; and in that vow
Do I live dead that live to tell it now.
BENVOLIO
Be rul'd by me, forget to think of her.
ROMEO
O, teach me how I should forget to think.
BENVOLIO
By giving liberty unto thine eyes;
Examine other beauties.
ROMEO
                    'Tis the way
To call hers, exquisite, in question more:
These happy masks that kiss fair ladies' brows,
Being black, put us in mind they hide the fair;
He that is strucken blind cannot forget
The precious treasure of his eyesight lost:
Show me a mistress that is passing fair,
What doth her beauty serve, but as a note
Where I may read who past that passing fair?
Farewell: thou canst not teach me to forget.
BENVOLIO
I'll pay that doctrine, or else die in debt.   [*Exeunt.*

SCENE II

The same. A street.

Enter CAPULET, COUNTY PARIS, *and* SERVANT.

CAPULET
But Montague is bound as well as I,
In penalty alike; and 'tis not hard, I think,
For men so old as we to keep the peace.
PARIS
Of honourable reckoning are you both;
And pity 'tis you liv'd at odds so long.
But now, my lord, what say you to my suit?
CAPULET
But saying o'er what I have said before:
My child is yet a stranger to the world,
She hath not seen the change of fourteen years;
Let two more summers wither in their pride
Ere we may think her ripe to be a bride.
PARIS
Younger than she are happy mothers made.
CAPULET
And too soon marr'd are those so early made.
The earth hath swallow'd all my hopes but she,
She is the hopeful lady of my earth:
But woo her, gentle Paris, get her heart,
My will to her consent is but a part;
An she agree, within her scope of choice
Lies my consent and fair-according voice.
This night I hold an old-accustom'd feast,
Whereto I have invited many a guest,
Such as I love; and you, among the store,
One more, most welcome, makes my number more.
At my poor house look to behold this night
Earth-treading stars that make dark heaven light:
Such comfort as do lusty young men feel
When well-apparell'd April on the heel
Of limping Winter treads, even such delight
Among fresh female buds shall you this night

SERVANT   Can never find what names the writing
person hath here writ.

Inherit at my house; hear all, all see,
And like her most whose merit most shall be:
Which on more view of many, mine, being one,
May stand in number, though in reckoning none.
Come, go with me. — [*To the* SERVANT, *giving him a
   paper.*] Go, sirrah, trudge about
Through fair Verona; find those persons out
Whose names are written there, and to them say,
My house and welcome on their pleasure stay.
                    [*Exeunt* CAPULET *and* PARIS.
SERVANT
Find them out whose names are written here! It is
written that the shoemaker should meddle with his
yard, and the tailor with his last, the fisher with his
pencil, and the painter with his nets; but I am sent to
find those persons whose names are here writ, and can
never find what names the writing person hath here
writ. I must to the learned: — in good time.

Enter BENVOLIO *and* ROMEO.

BENVOLIO
Tut, man, one fire burns out another's burning,
   One pain is lessen'd by another's anguish;
Turn giddy, and be holp by backward turning;
   One desperate grief cures with another's languish:
Take thou some new infection to thy eye,
And the rank poison of the old will die.
ROMEO
Your plaintain-leaf is excellent for that.
BENVOLIO
For what, I pray thee?
ROMEO
                    For your broken shin.
BENVOLIO
Why, Romeo, art thou mad?
ROMEO
Not mad, but bound more than a madman is;
Shut up in prison, kept without my food,
Whipp'd and tormented, and — God-den, good fellow.
SERVANT
God gi' god-den. — I pray, sir, can you read?
ROMEO
Ay, mine own fortune in my misery.
SERVANT
Perhaps you have learn'd it without book; but, I pray,
   can you read any thing you see?
ROMEO
Ay, if I know the letters and the language.
SERVANT
Ye say honestly: rest you merry!
ROMEO
Stay, fellow; I can read.   [*He reads the paper.*
'Signior Martino and his wife and daughters; County
Anselme and his beauteous sisters; the lady widow of
Vitruvio; Signior Placentio and his lovely nieces;
Mercutio and his brother Valentine; mine uncle
Capulet, his wife, and daughters; my fair niece

Rosaline; Livia; Signior Valentio and his cousin Tybalt;
Lucio and the lively Helena.'   [*Giving back the paper.*
A fair assembly: whither should they come?
SERVANT
Up.
ROMEO
Whither?
SERVANT
To supper to our house.
ROMEO
Whose house?
SERVANT
My master's.
ROMEO
Indeed, I should have ask'd you that before.
SERVANT
Now I'll tell you without asking: my master is the great
rich Capulet; and if you be not of the house of
Montagues, I pray, come and crush a cup of wine. Rest
you merry!
                    [*Exit.*
BENVOLIO
At this same ancient feast of Capulet's
Sups the fair Rosaline whom thou so lovest;
With all the admired beauties of Verona:
Go thither; and, with unattainted eye,
Compare her face with some that I shall show,
And I will make thee think thy swan a crow.
ROMEO
When the devout religion of mine eye
   Maintains such falsehood, then turn tears to fires;
And these, — who, often drown'd could never die, —
   Transparent heretics, be burnt for liars!
One fairer than my love! the all-seeing sun
Ne'er saw her match since first the world begun.
BENVOLIO
Tut, you saw her fair, none else being by,
Herself pois'd with herself in either eye:
But in that crystal scales let there be weigh'd
Your lady-love against some other maid
That I will show you shining at this feast,
And she shall scant show well that now shows best.
ROMEO
I'll go along, no such sight to be shown,
But to rejoice in splendour of mine own.   [*Exeunt.*

SCENE III

The same. A room in CAPULET'S *house.*

Enter LADY CAPULET *and* NURSE.

LADY CAPULET
Nurse, where's my daughter? call her forth to me.
NURSE
Now, by my maidenhead, — at twelve year old, —
I bade her come. What, lamb! what, lady-bird!
God forbid! — where's this girl? — What, Juliet!

Enter JULIET.

JULIET
How now! who calls?
NURSE
Your mother.
JULIET
Madam, I am here, what is your will?
LADY CAPULET
This is the matter, — nurse, give leave awhile,
We must talk in secret: — nurse, come back again;
I have remember'd me, thou's hear our counsel.
Thou know'st my daughter's of a pretty age.
NURSE
Faith, I can tell her age unto an hour.
LADY CAPULET
She's not fourteen.
NURSE
I'll lay fourteen of my teeth, — and yet, to my teen be it
spoken, I have but four, — she's not fourteen. How
long is it now to Lammas-tide?
LADY CAPULET
A fortnight and odd days.
NURSE
Even or odd, of all days in the year,
Come Lammas-eve at night shall she be fourteen.
Susan and she — God rest all Christian souls! —
Were of an age: well, Susan is with God;
She was too good for me:— but, as I said,
On Lammas-eve at night shall she be fourteen;
That shall she, marry; I remember it well.
'Tis since the earthquake now eleven years;
And she was wean'd, — I never shall forget it, —

NURSE A man, young lady! lady, such a man, as all the world — why, he's a man of wax.

Of all the days of the year, upon that day:
For I had then laid wormwood to my dug,
Sitting in the sun under the dove-house wall;
My lord and you were then at Mantua: —
Nay, I do bear a brain: — but, as I said,
When it did taste the wormwood on the nipple
Of my dug, and felt it bitter, pretty fool,
To see it tetchy, and fall out with the dug!
Shake, quoth the dove-house: 'twas no need, I trow,
To bid me trudge:
And since that time it is eleven years;
For then she could stand high-lone; nay, by th'rood,
She could have run and waddled all about;
For even the day before, she broke her brow:
And then my husband — God be with his soul!
A' was a merry man — took up the child:
'Yea,' quoth he, 'dost thou fall upon thy face?
Thou wilt fall backward when thou hast more wit;
Wilt thou not, Jule?' and, by my holidame,
The pretty wretch left crying, and said 'Ay.'
To see, now, how a jest shall come about!
I warrant, an I should live a thousand years,
I never should forget it: 'Wilt thou not, Jule?' quoth he;
And, pretty fool, it stinted, and said 'Ay.'

LADY CAPULET
Enough of this; I pray thee, hold thy peace.

NURSE
Yes, madam: — yet I cannot choose but laugh,
To think it should leave crying, and say 'Ay':
And yet, I warrant, it had upon its brow
A bump as big as a young cockerel's stone;
A perilous knock; and it cried bitterly:
'Yea,' quoth my husband, 'fall'st upon thy face?
Thou wilt fall backward when thou comest to age;
Wilt thou not, Jule?' it stinted, and said 'Ay.'

JULIET
And stint thou too, I pray thee, nurse, say I.

NURSE
Peace, I have done. God mark thee to His grace!
Thou wast the prettiest babe that e'er I nurs'd;
An I might live to see thee married once,
I have my wish.

LADY CAPULET
Marry, that 'marry' is the very theme
I came to talk of: — tell me, daughter Juliet,
How stands your disposition to be married?

JULIET
It is an honour that I dream not of.

NURSE
An honour! were not I thine only nurse,
I would say thou hadst suck'd wisdom from thy teat.

LADY CAPULET
Well, think of marriage now; younger than you,
Here in Verona, ladies of esteem,
Are made already mothers: by my count,
I was your mother much upon these years
That you are now a maid. Thus, then, in brief; —
The valiant Paris seeks you for his love.

NURSE
A man, young lady! lady, such a man
As all the world — why, he's a man of wax.

LADY CAPULET
Verona's summer hath not such a flower.

NURSE
Nay, he's a flower; in faith, a very flower.

LADY CAPULET
What say you? can you love the gentleman?
This night you shall behold him at our feast;
Read o'er the volume of young Paris' face,
And find delight writ there with beauty's pen;
Examine every married lineament,
And see how one another lends content;
And what obscured in this fair volume lies
Find written in the margent of his eyes.
This precious book of love, this unbound lover,
To beautify him only lacks a cover:
The fish lives in the sea; and 'tis much pride
For fair without the fair within to hide:
That book in many's eyes doth share the glory,
That in gold clasps locks in the golden story;
So shall you share all that he doth possess,
By having him, making yourself no less.

NURSE
No less! nay, bigger; women grow by men.

LADY CAPULET
Speak briefly, can you like of Paris' love?

JULIET
I'll look to like, if looking liking move:
But no more deep will I endart mine eye
Than your consent gives strength to make it fly.

Enter a SERVANT.

SERVANT
Madam, the guests are come, supper served up, you
call'd, my young lady ask'd for, the nurse curs'd in
the pantry, and every thing in extremity. I must
hence to wait; I beseech you, follow straight.

LADY CAPULET
We follow thee. [*Exit* SERVANT.] — Juliet, the county
stays.

NURSE
Go, girl, seek happy nights to happy days. [*Exeunt.*

SCENE IV

The same. A street.

Enter ROMEO, MERCUTIO, BENVOLIO, *with five or*
six other MASKERS, *and* TORCH-BEARERS.

ROMEO
What, shall this speech be spoke for our excuse?
Or shall we on without apology?

BENVOLIO
The date is out of such prolixity:
We'll have no Cupid hoodwink'd with a scarf,
Bearing a Tartar's painted bow of lath,
Scaring the ladies like a crow-keeper;
Nor no without-book prologue, faintly spoke
After the prompter, for our entrance:
But, let them measure us by what they will,
We'll measure them a measure, and be gone.

ROMEO
Give me a torch, I am not for this ambling;
Being but heavy, I will bear the light.

MERCUTIO
Nay, gentle Romeo, we must have you dance.

ROMEO
Not I, believe me: you have dancing-shoes
With nimble soles: I have a soul of lead,
So stakes me to the ground I cannot move.

MERCUTIO
You are a lover; borrow Cupid's wings,
And soar with them above a common bound.

MERCUTIO Give me a case to put my visage in.

ROMEO
I am too sore enpierced with his shaft,
To soar with his light feathers; and so bound,
I cannot bound a pitch above dull woe:
Under love's heavy burden do I sink.

MERCUTIO
And, to sink in it, should you burden love;
Too great oppression for a tender thing.

ROMEO
Is love a tender thing? it is too rough,
Too rude, too boisterous, and it pricks like thorn.

MERCUTIO
If love be rough with you, be rough with love;
Prick love for pricking, and you beat love down. —
Give me a case to put my visage in: [*Putting on a mask.*
A visor for a visor! — what care I
What curious eye doth quote deformities?
Here are the beetle-brows shall blush for me.

BENVOLIO
Come, knock and enter; and no sooner in,
But every man betake him to his legs.

ROMEO
A torch for me: let wantons, light of heart,
Tickle the senseless rushes with their heels;
For I am proverb'd with a grandsire phrase, —
I'll be a candle-holder, and look on, —
The game was ne'er so fair, and I am done.

MERCUTIO
Tut, dun's the mouse, the constable's own word:
If thou art Dun, we'll draw thee from the mire
Of this sir-reverence love, wherein thou stick'st
Up to the ears. — Come, we burn daylight, ho!

ROMEO
Nay, that's not so.

MERCUTIO
      I mean, sir, in delay
We waste our lights in vain, like lamps by day.
Take our good meaning, for our judgement sits
Five times in that, ere once in our five wits.

ROMEO
And we mean well, in going to this mask;
But 'tis no wit to go.

MERCUTIO
      Why, may one ask?

ROMEO
I dream'd a dream to-night.

MERCUTIO
      And so did I.

ROMEO
Well, what was yours?

MERCUTIO
      That dreamers often lie.

ROMEO
In bed asleep, while they do dream things true.

MERCUTIO
O, then, I see Queen Mab hath been with you.
She is the fairies' midwife; and she comes
In shape no bigger than an agate-stone
On the fore-finger of an alderman,
Drawn with a team of little atomies
Athwart men's noses as they lie asleep:
Her wagon-spokes made of long spinners' legs;
The cover, of the wings of grasshoppers;
The traces, of the smallest spider's web;
The collars, of the moonshine's watery beams;
Her whip, of cricket's bone; the lash, of film;
Her wagoner, a small gray-coated gnat,
Not half so big as a round little worm
Prick'd from the lazy finger of a maid;
Her chariot is an empty hazel-nut,
Made by the joiner squirrel or old grub,
Time out o' mind the fairies' coachmakers.
And in this state she gallops night by night
Through lovers' brains, and then they dream of love;
O'er courtiers' knees, that dream on court'sies straight;
O'er lawyers' fingers, who straight dream on fees;
O'er ladies' lips, who straight on kisses dream, —
Which oft the angry Mab with blisters plagues,
Because their breaths with sweetmeats tainted are:
Sometime she gallops o'er a courtier's nose,
And then dreams he of smelling out a suit;
And sometime comes she with a tithe-pig's tail
Tickling a parson's nose as 'a lies asleep,
Then dreams he of another benefice:
Sometime she driveth o'er a soldier's neck,
And then dreams he of cutting foreign throats,
Of breaches, ambuscadoes, Spanish blades,
Of healths five-fadom deep; and then anon
Drums in his ear, at which he starts, and wakes;
And, being thus frighted, swears a prayer or two,

And sleeps again. This is that very Mab
That plats the manes of horses in the night;
And bakes the elf-locks in foul sluttish hairs,
Which once untangled, much misfortune bodes:
This is the hag, when maids lie on their backs,
That presses them, and learns them first to bear,
Making them women of good carriage:
This is she —

ROMEO
      Peace, peace, Mercutio, peace!
Thou talk'st of nothing.

MERCUTIO
      True, I talk of dreams;
Which are the children of an idle brain,
Begot of nothing but vain fantasy;
Which is as thin of substance as the air;
And more inconstant than the wind, who wooes
Even now the frozen bosom of the north,
And, being anger'd, puffs away from thence,
Turning his face to the dew-dropping south.

BENVOLIO
This wind, you talk of, blows us from ourselves;
Supper is done, and we shall come too late.

ROMEO
I fear, too early: for my mind misgives
Some consequence, yet hanging in the stars,
Shall bitterly begin his fearful date
With this night's revels; and expire the term
Of a despised life, clos'd in my breast,
By some vile forfeit of untimely death:
But He, that hath the steerage of my course,
Direct my sail! — On, lusty gentlemen!

BENVOLIO
Strike, drum.

      [*They march about the stage, and exeunt.*

SCENE V

The same. A hall in CAPULET'S *house.*

MUSICIANS *waiting.* SERVING-MEN
come forth with their napkins.

FIRST SERVING-MAN
Where's Potpan, that he helps not to take away? he shift a trencher! he scrape a trencher!

SECOND SERVING-MAN
When good manners shall lie all in one or two men's hands, and they unwash'd too, 'tis a foul thing.

FIRST SERVING-MAN
Away with the joint-stools, remove the court-cupboard, look to the plate: — good thou, save me a piece of marchpane; and, as thou lovest me, let the porter let in Susan Grindstone and Nell. — Antony and Potpan!

SECOND SERVING-MAN
Ay, boy, ready.

FIRST SERVING-MAN
You are look'd for and call'd for, ask'd for and sought for, in the great chamber.

THIRD SERVING-MAN
We cannot be here and there too. — Cheerly, boys; be brisk awhile, and the longer liver take all.

      [*They retire behind.*

Enter CAPULET, LADY CAPULET, JULIET,
TYBALT, *and others of the house, with the*
GUESTS *and* MASKERS.

CAPULET
Welcome, gentlemen! ladies that have their toes
Unplagued with corns will have a bout with you: —
Ah ha, my mistresses! which of you all
Will now deny to dance? she that makes dainty,
She, I'll swear, hath corns; am I come near ye now? —
Welcome, gentlemen! I have seen the day
That I have worn a visor; and could tell
A whispering tale in a fair lady's ear,
Such as would please: 'tis gone, 'tis gone, 'tis gone:
You are welcome, gentlemen! Come, musicians, play.
A hall, a hall! give room! and foot it, girls. —
      [*Music plays, and they dance.*
More light, you knaves; and turn the tables up,
And quench the fire, the room is grown too hot. —
Ah, sirrah, this unlook'd-for sport comes well.
Nay, sit, nay, sit, good cousin Capulet;
For you and I are past our dancing days:
How long is't now since last yourself and I
Were in a mask?

SECOND CAPULET
      By 'r lady, thirty years.

CAPULET
What, man! 'tis not so much, 'tis not so much:
'Tis since the nuptial of Lucentio,

Come Pentecost as quickly as it will,
Some five-and-twenty years; and then we mask'd.

SECOND CAPULET
'Tis more, 'tis more: his son is elder, sir;
His son is thirty.

CAPULET
      Will you tell me that?
His son was but a ward two years ago.

ROMEO [*to a* SERVANT].
What lady's that, which doth enrich the hand
Of yonder knight?

SERVANT
I know not, sir.

ROMEO
O, she doth teach the torches to burn bright!
Her beauty hangs upon the cheek of night
Like a rich jewel in an Ethiop's ear;
Beauty too rich for use, for earth too dear!
So shows a snowy dove trooping with crows,
As yonder lady o'er her fellows shows.
The measure done, I'll watch her place of stand,
And, touching hers, make blessed my rude hand.
Did my heart love till now? forswear it, sight!
For I ne'er saw true beauty till this night.

TYBALT
This, by his voice, should be a Montague: —
Fetch me my rapier, boy: — what, dares the slave
Come hither, cover'd with an antic face,
To fleer and scorn at our solemnity?
Now, by the stock and honour of my kin,
To strike him dead I hold it not a sin.

CAPULET
Why, how now, kinsman! wherefore storm you so?

TYBALT
Uncle, this is a Montague, our foe;
A villain, that is hither come in spite,
To scorn at our solemnity this night.

CAPULET
Young Romeo is it?

TYBALT
      'Tis he, that villain Romeo.

CAPULET
Content thee, gentle coz, let him alone,
He bears him like a portly gentleman;
And, to say truth, Verona brags of him
To be a virtuous and well-govern'd youth:
I would not for the wealth of all this town
Here in my house do him disparagement:
Therefore be patient, take no note of him, —
It is my will, the which if thou respect,
Show a fair presence, and put off these frowns,
And ill-beseeming semblance for a feast.

TYBALT
It fits, when such a villain is a guest:
I'll not endure him.

CAPULET
      He shall be endured:
What, goodman boy! — I say, he shall; — go to;
Am I the master here, or you? go to.
You'll not endure him! — God shall mend my soul,
You'll make a mutiny among my guests!
You will set cock-a-hoop! you'll be the man!

TYBALT
Why, uncle, 'tis a shame—

CAPULET
      Go to, go to;
You are a saucy boy: — is't so, indeed? —
This trick may chance to scathe you, — I know what:
You must contrary me! marry, 'tis time. —
Well said, my hearts! — You are a princox; go:
Be quiet, or — More light, more light! — For shame!
I'll make you quiet: what! — Cheerly, my hearts!

TYBALT
Patience perforce with wilful choler meeting
Makes my flesh tremble in their different greeting,
I will withdraw: but this intrusion shall,
Now seeming sweet, convert to bitter gall.   [*Exit.*

ROMEO [*to* JULIET].
If I profane with my unworthiest hand
  This holy shrine, the gentle fine is this, —
My lips, two blushing pilgrims, ready stand
  To smooth that rough touch with a tender kiss.

JULIET
Good pilgrim, you do wrong your hand too much,
  Which mannerly devotion shows in this;
For saints have hands that pilgrims' hands do touch,
  And palm to palm is holy palmers' kiss.

ROMEO
Have not saints lips, and holy palmers too?

JULIET Good pilgrim, you do wrong your hand too much.

JULIET
Ay, pilgrim, lips that they must use in prayer.
ROMEO
O, then, dear saint, let lips do what hands do;
They pray; grant thou, lest faith turn to despair.
JULIET
Saints do not move, though grant for prayers' sake.
ROMEO
Then move not, while my prayer's effect I take.
Thus from my lips, by yours, my sin is purged.
　　　　　　　　　　　　　　　　[Kissing her.
JULIET
Then have my lips the sin that they have took.
ROMEO
Sin from my lips? O trespass sweetly urged!
Give me my sin again.　　　*[Kissing her again.*
JULIET
　　　　　　　You kiss by th'book.
NURSE
Madam, your mother craves a word with you.
ROMEO
What is her mother?
NURSE
　　　　　　Marry, bachelor,
Her mother is the lady of the house,
And a good lady, and a wise and virtuous:
I nurs'd her daughter, that you talk'd withal;
I tell you, he that can lay hold of her
Shall have the chinks.
ROMEO
　　　　　　Is she a Capulet?
O dear account! my life is my foe's debt.
BENVOLIO
Away, be gone; the sport is at the best.
ROMEO
Ay, so I fear; the more is my unrest.
CAPULET
Nay, gentlemen, prepare not to be gone;
We have a trifling foolish banquet towards. —
Is it e'en so? why, then, I thank you all;

I thank you, honest gentlemen; good night. —
More torches here! — Come on, then, let's to bed.
[to SECOND CAPULET] Ah, sirrah, by my fay, it waxes late:
I'll to my rest.

　　　　　[Exeunt all but JULIET *and* NURSE.

JULIET
Come hither, nurse. What is yond gentleman?
NURSE
The son and heir of old Tiberio.
JULIET
What's he that now is going out of door?
NURSE
Marry, that, I think, be young Petruchio.
JULIET
What's he that follows there, that would not dance?
NURSE
I know not.
JULIET
Go, ask his name: — if he be married,
My grave is like to be my wedding-bed.
NURSE
His name is Romeo, and a Montague;
The only son of your great enemy.
JULIET
My only love sprung from my only hate!
Too early seen unknown, and known too late!
Prodigious birth of love it is to me,
That I must love a loathed enemy.
NURSE
What's this? what's this?
JULIET
　　　　　　　A rime I learn'd even now
Of one I danc'd withal.
　　　　　　　　　[One calls within, Juliet.
NURSE
　　　　　　Anon, anon!—
Come, let's away; the strangers all are gone.
　　　　　　　　　　　　　　*[Exeunt.

ACT II

PROLOGUE
Enter CHORUS.

CHORUS
Now old desire doth in his death-bed lie,
And young affection gapes to be his heir;
That fair, for which love groan'd for, and would die,
　　With tender Juliet match'd, is now not fair.
Now Romeo is belov'd and loves again,
　　Alike bewitched by the charm of looks;
But to his foe suppos'd he must complain,
　　And she steal love's sweet bait from fearful hooks:
Being held a foe, he may not have access
　　To breathe such vows as lovers use to swear;
And she as much in love, her means much less
　　To meet her new-beloved any where:
But passion lends them power, time means, to meet,
Tempering extremities with extreme sweet.　　*[Exit.*

JULIET What's he that now is going out of door?

SCENE I

Verona. CAPULET'S *orchard.*

Enter ROMEO, *alone.*

ROMEO
Can I go forward when my heart is here?
Turn back, dull earth, and find thy centre out.
        [*He leaps the orchard-wall.*
        Enter BENVOLIO *with* MERCUTIO.

BENVOLIO
Romeo! my cousin Romeo!

MERCUTIO
                        He is wise;
And, on my life, hath stol'n him home to bed.

BENVOLIO
He ran this way, and leap'd this orchard-wall:
Call, good Mercutio.

MERCUTIO
                        Nay, I'll conjure too. —
Romeo! humours! madman! passion! lover!
Appear thou in the likeness of a sigh:
Speak but one rime, and I am satisfied;
Cry but 'Ay me!' pronounce but 'love' and 'dove';
Speak to my gossip Venus one fair word,
One nickname for her purblind son and heir,
Young Adam Cupid, he that shot so trim,
When King Cophetua lov'd the beggar-maid! —
He heareth not, he stirreth not, he moveth not;
The ape is dead, and I must conjure him. —
I conjure thee by Rosaline's bright eyes,
By her high forehead and her scarlet lip,
By her fine foot, straight leg, and quivering thigh,
And the demesnes that there adjacent lie,
That in thy likeness thou appear to us!

BENVOLIO
An if he hear thee, thou wilt anger him.

MERCUTIO
This cannot anger him: 'twould anger him
To raise a spirit in his mistress' circle
Of some strange nature, letting it there stand
Till she had laid it and conjured it down;
That were some spite: my invocation
Is fair and honest, and, in his mistress' name,
I conjure only but to raise up him.

BENVOLIO
Come, he hath hid himself among these trees,
To be consorted with the humorous night:
Blind is his love, and best befits the dark.

MERCUTIO
If love be blind, love cannot hit the mark.
Now will he sit under a medlar-tree,
And wish his mistress were that kind of fruit
As maids call medlars, when they laugh alone. —
O, Romeo, that she were, O, that she were
An open *et-cætera*, thou a poperin pear!
Romeo, good night: — I'll to my truckle-bed;
This field-bed is too cold for me to sleep:
Come, shall we go?

BENVOLIO
                        Go, then; for 'tis in vain
To seek him here that means not to be found.
                        [*Exeunt.*

ROMEO [*coming forward*].
He jests at scars that never felt a wound. —
        [JULIET *appears above at a window.*
But, soft! what light through yonder window breaks?
It is the east, and Juliet is the sun! —
Arise, fair sun, and kill the envious moon,
Who is already sick and pale with grief,
That thou her maid art far more fair than she:
Be not her maid, since she is envious;
Her vestal livery is but sick and green,
And none but fools do wear it; cast it off. —
It is my lady; O, it is my love!
O, that she knew she were! —
She speaks, yet she says nothing: what of that?
Her eye discourses; I will answer it. —
I am too bold; 'tis not to me she speaks:
Two of the fairest stars in all the heaven,
Having some business, do entreat her eyes
To twinkle in their spheres till they return.
What if her eyes were there, they in her head?
The brightness of her cheek would shame those stars,
As daylight doth a lamp; her eyes in heaven
Would through the airy region stream so bright,
That birds would sing, and think it were not night.
See, how she leans her cheek upon her hand!
O, that I were a glove upon that hand,
That I might touch that cheek!

BENVOLIO He ran this way, and leap'd this orchard-wall.

JULIET
                        Ay me!

ROMEO
                        She speaks: —
O, speak again, bright angel! for thou art
As glorious to this night, being o'er my head,
As is a winged messenger of heaven
Unto the white-upturned wondering eyes
Of mortals that fall back to gaze on him
When he bestrides the lazy-pacing clouds
And sails upon the bosom of the air.

JULIET
O Romeo, Romeo! wherefore art thou Romeo?
Deny thy father, and refuse thy name;
Or, if thou wilt not, be but sworn my love,
And I'll no longer be a Capulet.

ROMEO [*aside*].
Shall I hear more, or shall I speak at this?

JULIET
'Tis but thy name that is my enemy; —
Thou art thyself though, not a Montague.
What's Montague? it is nor hand, nor foot,
Nor arm, nor face, nor any other part
Belonging to a man. O, be some other name!
What's in a name! that which we call a rose
By any other name would smell as sweet;
So Romeo would, were he not Romeo call'd,
Retain that dear perfection which he owes
Without that title: — Romeo, doff thy name;
And for that name, which is no part of thee,
Take all myself.

ROMEO
                        I take thee at thy word:
Call me but love, and I'll be new baptised;
Henceforth I never will be Romeo.

JULIET
What man art thou, that, thus bescreen'd in night,
So stumblest on my counsel?

ROMEO
                        By a name
I know not how to tell thee who I am:
My name, dear saint, is hateful to myself,
Because it is an enemy to thee;
Had I it written, I would tear the word.

JULIET
My ears have not yet drunk a hundred words
Of that tongue's utterance, yet I know the sound:
Art thou not Romeo and a Montague?

ROMEO
Neither, fair saint, if either thee dislike.

JULIET
How cam'st thou hither, tell me, and wherefore?
The orchard-walls are high and hard to climb;
And the place death, considering who thou art,
If any of my kinsmen find thee here.

ROMEO
With love's light wings did I o'er-perch these walls;
For stony limits cannot hold love out:
And what love can do, that dares love attempt;
Therefore thy kinsmen are no let to me.

JULIET
If they do see thee, they will murder thee.

ROMEO
Alack, there lies more peril in thine eye
Than twenty of their swords: look thou but sweet,
And I am proof against their enmity.

JULIET
I would not for the world they saw thee here.

ROMEO
I have night's cloak to hide me from their sight;
And but thou love me, let them find me here:
My life were better ended by their hate
Than death prorogued, wanting of thy love.

JULIET
By whose direction found'st thou out this place?

ROMEO
By love, who first did prompt me to inquire;
He lent me counsel, and I lent him eyes.
I am no pilot; yet, wert thou as far
As that vast shore wash'd with the farthest sea,
I would adventure for such merchandise.

JULIET
Thou know'st the mask of night is on my face,
Else would a maiden blush depaint my cheek
For that which thou hast heard me speak to-night.
Fain would I dwell on form, fain, fain deny
What I have spoke: but farewell compliment!
Dost thou love me? I know thou wilt say 'Ay';
And I will take thy word: yet, if thou swear'st,
Thou mayst prove false; at lovers' perjuries,
Then say, Jove laughs. O gentle Romeo,
If thou dost love, pronounce it faithfully:
Or if thou think'st I am too quickly won,
I'll frown, and be perverse, and say thee nay,
So thou wilt woo; but else, not for the world.
In truth, fair Montague, I am too fond;
And therefore thou mayst think my haviour light:
But trust me, gentleman, I'll prove more true
Than those that have more cunning to be strange.
I should have been more strange, I must confess,
But that thou overheard'st, ere I was ware,
My true love's passion: therefore pardon me;
And not impute this yielding to light love,
Which the dark night hath so discovered.

ROMEO
Lady, by yonder blessed moon I swear,
That tips with silver all these fruit-tree tops, —

JULIET
O, swear not by the moon, th'inconstant moon,
That monthly changes in her circled orb,
Lest that thy love prove likewise variable.

ROMEO
What shall I swear by?

JULIET
                        Do not swear at all;
Or, if thou wilt, swear by thy gracious self,
Which is the god of my idolatry,
And I'll believe thee.

ROMEO
                        If my heart's dear love —

JULIET
Well, do not swear: although I joy in thee,
I have no joy of this contract to-night:
It is too rash, too unadvis'd, too sudden;

FRIAR LAURENCE I must up-fill this osier-cage of ours with baleful weeds and precious-juiced flowers.

Too like the lightning, which doth cease to be
Ere one can say 'It lightens.' Sweet, good night!
This bud of love, by summer's ripening breath,
May prove a beauteous flower when next we meet.
Good night, good night! as sweet repose and rest
Come to thy heart as that within my breast!

ROMEO
O, wilt thou leave me so unsatisfied?

JULIET
What satisfaction canst thou have to-night?

ROMEO
Th'exchange of thy love's faithful vow for mine.

JULIET
I gave thee mine before thou didst request it:
And yet I would it were to give again.

ROMEO
Wouldst thou withdraw it? for what purpose, love?

JULIET
But to be frank, and give it thee again.
And yet I wish but for the thing I have:
My bounty is as boundless as the sea,
My love as deep; the more I give to thee,
The more I have, for both are infinite.
I hear some noise within; dear love, adieu! —
                  [NURSE *calls within.*
Anon, good nurse! — Sweet Montague, be true.
Stay but a little, I will come again.   [*Exit above.*

ROMEO
O blessed, blessed night! I am afeard,
Being in night, all this is but a dream,
Too flattering-sweet to be substantial.

Enter JULIET *above.*

JULIET
Three words, dear Romeo, and good night indeed.
If that thy bent of love be honourable,
Thy purpose marriage, send me word to-morrow,
By one that I'll procure to come to thee,
Where and what time thou wilt perform the rite;
And all my fortunes at thy foot I'll lay,
And follow thee my lord throughout the world.

NURSE [*within*].
Madam!

JULIET
I come, anon: — But if thou mean'st not well,
I do beseech thee —

NURSE [*within*].
Madam!

JULIET
        By and by, I come: —
To cease thy suit, and leave me to my grief:
To-morrow will I send.

ROMEO
               So thrive my soul —

JULIET
A thousand times good night!   [*Exit above.*

ROMEO
A thousand times the worse, to want thy light. —
Love goes toward love, as schoolboys from their books;
But love from love, toward school with heavy looks.
                        [*Retiring.*

Enter JULIET *again.*

JULIET
Hist! Romeo, hist! — O, for a falconer's voice,
To lure this tassel-gentle back again!
Bondage is hoarse, and may not speak aloud;
Else would I tear the cave where Echo lies,
And make her airy tongue more hoarse than mine,
With repetition of my Romeo's name.
Romeo!

ROMEO
It is my soul that calls upon my name:
How silver-sweet sound lovers' tongues by night,
Like softest music to attending ears!

JULIET
Romeo!

ROMEO
   My dear?

JULIET
           At what o'clock to-morrow
Shall I send to thee?

ROMEO
            At the hour of nine.

JULIET
I will not fail: 'tis twenty years till then.
I have forgot why I did call thee back.

ROMEO
Let me stand here till thou remember it.

JULIET
I shall forget, to have thee still stand there,
Remembering how I love thy company.

ROMEO
And I'll still stay, to have thee still forget,
Forgetting any other home but this.

JULIET
'Tis almost morning; I would have thee gone, —
And yet no further than a wanton's bird,
Who lets it hop a little from her hand,
Like a poor prisoner in his twisted gyves,
And with a silk thread plucks it back again,
So loving-jealous of his liberty.

ROMEO
I would I were thy bird.

JULIET
                Sweet, so would I:
Yet I should kill thee with much cherishing.
Good night, good night! parting is such sweet sorrow,
That I shall say good night till it be morrow.
                     [*Exit above.*

ROMEO
Sleep dwell upon thine eyes, peace in thy breast! —
Would I were sleep and peace, so sweet to rest!
Hence will I to my ghostly father's cell,
His help to crave, and my dear hap to tell.   [*Exit.*

SCENE II

The same. FRIAR LAURENCE'S *cell.*

Enter FRIAR LAURENCE, *alone, with a basket.*

FRIAR LAURENCE
The grey-eyed morn smiles on the frowning night,
Chequering the eastern clouds with streaks of light;
And flecked darkness like a drunkard reels
From forth day's path and Titan's fiery wheels:
Now, ere the sun advance his burning eye,
The day to cheer, and night's dank dew to dry,
I must up-fill this osier-cage of ours
With baleful weeds and precious-juiced flowers.
The earth, that's nature's mother, is her tomb;
What is her burying grave, that is her womb:
And from her womb children of divers kind
We sucking on her natural bosom find;
Many for many virtues excellent,
None but for some, and yet all different.
O, mickle is the powerful grace that lies
In herbs, plants, stones, and their true qualities:
For naught so vile that on the earth doth live,
But to the earth some special good doth give;
Nor aught so good, but, strain'd from that fair use,
Revolts from true birth, stumbling on abuse:
Virtue itself turns vice, being misapplied;
And vice sometime's by action dignified.
Within the infant rind of this small flower
Poison hath residence, and medicine power:
For this, being smelt, with that part cheers each part;
Being tasted, slays all senses with the heart.
Two such opposed kings encamp them still
In man as well as herbs, — grace and rude will;
And where the worser is predominant,
Full soon the canker death eats up that plant.

Enter ROMEO.

ROMEO
Good morrow, father.

FRIAR LAURENCE
           Benedicite!
What early tongue so sweet saluteth me? —
Young son, it argues a distemper'd head
So soon to bid good morrow to thy bed:
Care keeps his watch in every old man's eye,
And where care lodges sleep will never lie;
But where unbruised youth with unstuff'd brain
Doth couch his limbs, there golden sleep doth reign:
Therefore thy earliness doth me assure
Thou art up-rous'd by some distemperature;
Or if not so, then here I hit it right, —
Our Romeo hath not been in bed to-night.

ROMEO
That last is true; the sweeter rest was mine.

FRIAR LAURENCE
God pardon sin! wast thou with Rosaline?

ROMEO
With Rosaline, my ghostly father? no;
I have forgot that name, and that name's woe.

FRIAR LAURENCE
That's my good son: but where hast thou been, then?

ROMEO
I'll tell thee, ere thou ask it me agen.
I have been feasting with mine enemy;
Where, on a sudden, one hath wounded me,
That's by me wounded: both our remedies
Within thy help and holy physic lies:
I bear no hatred, blessed man; for, lo,
My intercession likewise steads my foe.

FRIAR LAURENCE
Be plain, good son, and homely in thy drift;
Riddling confession finds but riddling shrift.

ROMEO
Then plainly know my heart's dear love is set
On the fair daughter of rich Capulet:
As mine on hers, so hers is set on mine;
And all combin'd, save what thou must combine
By holy marriage: when, and where, and how,
We met, we woo'd, and made exchange of vow,
I'll tell thee as we pass; but this I pray,
That thou consent to marry us to-day.

FRIAR LAURENCE
Holy Saint Francis, what a change is here!
Is Rosaline, whom thou didst love so dear,
So soon forsaken? young men's love, then, lies
Not truly in their hearts, but in their eyes.
Jesu Maria, what a deal of brine
Hath wash'd thy sallow cheeks for Rosaline!
How much salt water thrown away in waste,
To season love, that of it doth not taste!
The sun not yet thy sighs from heaven clears,
Thy old groans ring yet in mine ancient ears;
Lo, here upon thy cheek the stain doth sit
Of an old tear that is not wash'd off yet:
If e'er thou wast thyself, and these woes thine,
Thou and these woes were all for Rosaline:
And art thou chang'd? pronounce this sentence, then, —
Women may fall, when there's no strength in men.

ROMEO
Thou chidd'st me oft for loving Rosaline.

FRIAR LAURENCE
For doting, not for loving, pupil mine.

ROMEO
And bad'st me bury love.

FRIAR LAURENCE
                    Not in a grave,
To lay one in, another out to have.

ROMEO
I pray thee, chide not: she whom I love now
Doth grace for grace and love for love allow;
The other did not so.

FRIAR LAURENCE
                    O, she knew well
Thy love did read by rote, and could not spell.
But come, young waverer, come, go with me,
In one respect I'll thy assistant be;
For this alliance may so happy prove,
To turn your households' rancour to pure love.

ROMEO
O, let us hence; I stand on sudden haste.

FRIAR LAURENCE
Wisely, and slow; they stumble that run fast.   [*Exeunt.*

SCENE III

A street.

Enter BENVOLIO *and* MERCUTIO.

MERCUTIO
Why, where the devil should this Romeo be? —
Came he not home to-night?

BENVOLIO
Not to his father's; I spoke with his man.

MERCUTIO
Ah, that same pale hard-hearted wench, that Rosaline,
Torments him so, that he will sure run mad.

BENVOLIO
Tybalt, the kinsman to old Capulet,
Hath sent a letter to his father's house.

MERCUTIO
A challenge, on my life.

BENVOLIO
Romeo will answer it.

MERCUTIO
Any man that can write may answer a letter.

BENVOLIO
Nay, he will answer the letter's master, how he dares,
     being dared.

MERCUTIO
Alas, poor Romeo, he is already dead! stabb'd with a
white wench's black eye; shot through the ear with a
love-song; the very pin of his heart cleft with the blind
bow-boy's butt-shaft; and is he a man to encounter
Tybalt?

BENVOLIO
Why, what is Tybalt?

MERCUTIO
More than prince of cats, I can tell you. O, he is the
courageous captain of complements. He fights as you
sing prick-song, keeps time, distance, and proportion;
rests me his minim rest, one, two, and the third in your
bosom: the very butcher of a silk button, a duellist, a
duellist; a gentleman of the very first house, — of the
first and second cause: ah, the immortal passado! the
punto reverso! the hay! —

BENVOLIO
The what?

MERCUTIO
The pox of such antic, lisping, affecting fantasticoes;
these new tuners of accents! — 'By Jesu, a very good
blade! — a very tall man! — a very good whore!' —
Why, is not this a lamentable thing, grandsire, that we
should be thus afflicted with these strange flies, these
fashion-mongers, these *pardonnez-mois*, who stand so
much on the new form that they cannot sit at ease on
the old bench? O, their *bons*, their *bons*!

BENVOLIO
Here comes Romeo, here comes Romeo.

MERCUTIO
Without his roe, like a dried herring: — O flesh, flesh,
how art thou fishified! — Now is he for the numbers
that Petrarch flow'd in; Laura, to his lady, was but a
kitchen-wench, — marry, she had a better love to
be-rime her; Dido, a dowdy; Cleopatra, a gipsy; Helen
and Hero, hildings and harlots; Thisbe, a grey eye or so,
but not to the purpose: —

Enter ROMEO.

Signior Romeo, *bon jour!* there's a French salutation to
your French slop. You gave us the counterfeit fairly last
night.

ROMEO
Good morrow to you both. What counterfeit did I give
you?

MERCUTIO
The slip, sir, the slip; can you not conceive?

ROMEO
Pardon, good Mercutio, my business was great; and in
such a case as mine a man may strain courtesy.

MERCUTIO
That's as much as to say, Such a case as yours
constrains a man to bow in the hams.

ROMEO
Meaning, to court'sy.

MERCUTIO
Thou hast most kindly hit it.

ROMEO
A most courteous exposition.

MERCUTIO
Nay, I am the very pink of courtesy.

ROMEO
Pink for flower.

MERCUTIO
Right.

ROMEO
Why, then is my pump well-flower'd.

MERCUTIO
Well said: follow me this jest now, till
thou hast worn out thy pump; that,
when the single sole of it is worn, the
jest may remain, after the wearing,
solely singular.

ROMEO
O single-soled jest, solely singular for
the singleness!

MERCUTIO
Come between us, good Benvolio, for
my wits fail.

ROMEO
Switch and spurs, switch and spurs;
or I'll cry a match.

MERCUTIO
Nay, if thy wits run the wild-goose
chase, I have done; for thou hast more
of the wild-goose in one of thy wits
than, I am sure, I have in my whole
five: was I with you there for the
goose?

ROMEO
Thou wast never with me for any
thing when thou wast not there for the
goose.

MERCUTIO
I will bite thee by the ear for that jest.

ROMEO
Nay, good goose, bite not.

MERCUTIO
Thy wit is a very bitter sweeting; it is a
most sharp sauce.

ROMEO
And is it not well served in to a sweet goose?

MERCUTIO
O, here's a wit of cheveril, that stretches from an inch
narrow to an ell broad!

ROMEO
I stretch it out for that word 'broad'; which, added to the
goose, proves thee far and wide a broad goose.

MERCUTIO
Why, is not this better now than groaning for love? now
art thou sociable, now art thou Romeo; now art thou
what thou art, by art as well as by nature: for this
drivelling love is like a great natural, that runs lolling
up and down to hide his bauble in a hole.

BENVOLIO
Stop there, stop there.

MERCUTIO
Thou desirest me to stop in my tale against the hair.

BENVOLIO
Thou wouldst else have made thy tale large.

MERCUTIO
O, thou art deceived; I would have made it short: for I
was come to the whole depth of my tale; and meant,
indeed, to occupy the argument no longer.

ROMEO
Here's goodly gear!

Enter NURSE *and her man* PETER.

MERCUTIO
A sail, a sail, a sail!

BENVOLIO
Two, two; a shirt and a smock.

NURSE
Peter!

PETER
Anon?

NURSE
My fan, Peter.

MERCUTIO
Good Peter, to hide her face; for her fan's the fairer face.

NURSE
God ye good morrow, gentlemen.

MERCUTIO
God ye good den, fair gentlewoman.

NURSE
Is it good den?

MERCUTIO
'Tis no less, I tell you; for the bawdy hand of the dial is
now upon the prick of noon.

NURSE
Out upon you! what a man are you!

ROMEO
One, gentlewoman, that God hath made, for himself to
mar.

NURSE My fan, Peter.

NURSE *I am a-weary, give me leave awhile.*

NURSE
By my troth, it is well said; — 'for himself to mar,' quoth a'? — Gentlemen, can any of you tell me where I may find the young Romeo?

ROMEO
I can tell you; but young Romeo will be older when you have found him than he was when you sought him: I am the youngest of that name, for fault of a worse.

NURSE
You say well.

MERCUTIO
Yea, is the worst well? very well took, i'faith; wisely, wisely.

NURSE
If you be he, sir, I desire some confidence with you.

BENVOLIO
She will indite him to some supper.

MERCUTIO
A bawd, a bawd, a bawd! So-ho!

ROMEO
What hast thou found?

MERCUTIO
No hare, sir; unless a hare, sir, in a Lenten pie, that is something stale and hoar ere it be spent.
[*He walks by them and sings.*

An old hare hoar,
And an old hare hoar,
Is very good meat in Lent:
But a hare that is hoar
Is too much for a score,
When it hoars ere it be spent. —

Romeo, will you come to your father's? we'll to dinner, thither.

ROMEO
I will follow you.

MERCUTIO
Farewell, ancient lady; farewell, — [*singing*] lady, lady, lady. [*Exeunt* MERCUTIO *and* BENVOLIO.

NURSE
Marry, farewell! — I pray you, sir, what saucy merchant was this, that was so full of his ropery?

ROMEO
A gentleman, nurse, that loves to hear himself talk, and will speak more in a minute than he will stand to in a month.

NURSE
An a' speak any thing against me, I'll take him down, an a' were lustier than he is, and twenty such Jacks; and if I cannot, I'll find those that shall. Scurvy knave! I am

none of his flirt-gills; I am none of his skains-mates. — And thou [*she turns to* PETER *her man*] must stand by too, and suffer every knave to use me at his pleasure?

PETER
I saw no man use you at his pleasure; if I had, my weapon should quickly have been out, I warrant you: I dare draw as soon as another man, if I see occasion in a good quarrel, and the law on my side.

NURSE
Now, afore God, I am so vex'd, that every part about me quivers. Scurvy knave! — Pray you, sir, a word: and, as I told you, my young lady bade me inquire you out; what she bade me say, I will keep to myself: but first let me tell ye, if ye should lead her into a fool's-paradise, as they say, it were a very gross kind of behaviour, as they say: for the gentlewoman is young; and therefore, if you should deal double with her, truly it were an ill thing to be offer'd to any gentlewoman, and very weak dealing.

ROMEO
Nurse, commend me to thy lady and mistress. I protest unto thee —

NURSE
Good heart, and, i'faith, I will tell her as much:
Lord, Lord, she will be a joyful woman.

ROMEO
What wilt thou tell her, nurse? thou dost not mark me.

NURSE
I will tell her, sir, — that you do protest; which, as I take it, is a gentlemanlike offer.

ROMEO
Bid her devise some means to come to shrift
This afternoon;
And there she shall at Friar Laurence' cell
Be shriv'd and married. Here is for thy pains.

NURSE
No, truly, sir; not a penny.

ROMEO
Go to, I say you shall.

NURSE
This afternoon, sir? well, she shall be there.

ROMEO
And stay, good nurse, behind the abbey-wall:
Within this hour my man shall be with thee,
And bring thee cords made like a tackled stair;
Which to the high top-gallant of my joy
Must be my convoy in the secret night.
Farewell; be trusty, and I'll quite thy pains:
Farewell; commend me to thy mistress.

NURSE
Now God in heaven bless thee! — Hark you, sir.

ROMEO
What say'st thou, my dear nurse?

NURSE
Is your man secret? Did you ne'er hear say,
Two may keep counsel, putting one away?

ROMEO
I warrant thee, my man's as true as steel.

NURSE
Well, sir; my mistress is the sweetest lady — Lord, Lord! when 'twas a little prating thing, — O, there is a nobleman in town, one Paris, that would fain lay knife aboard; but she, good soul, had as lief see a toad, a very toad, as see him. I anger her sometimes, and tell her that Paris is the properer man; but, I'll warrant you, when I say so, she looks as pale as any clout in the versal world. Doth not rosemary and Romeo begin both with a letter?

ROMEO
Ay, nurse; what of that? both with an R.

NURSE
Ah, mocker! that's the dog's name; R is for the — No; I know it begins with some other letter: — and she hath the prettiest sententious of it, of you and rosemary, that it would do you good to hear it.

ROMEO
Commend me to thy lady.

NURSE
Ay, a thousand times. [*Exit* ROMEO.] — Peter!

PETER
Anon?

NURSE
Peter, take my fan, and go before. [*Exeunt.*

SCENE IV
The same. CAPULET'S *orchard.*

Enter JULIET.

JULIET
The clock struck nine when I did send the nurse;
In half an hour she promis'd to return.
Perchance she cannot meet him: — that's not so. —
O, she is lame! love's heralds should be thoughts,
Which ten times faster glide than the sun's beams,
Driving back shadows over louring hills:
Therefore do nimble-pinion'd doves draw love,
And therefore hath the wind-swift Cupid wings.
Now is the sun upon the highmost hill
Of this day's journey; and from nine till twelve
Is three long hours, — yet she is not come.
Had she affections and warm youthful blood,
She'ld be as swift in motion as a ball;
My words would bandy her to my sweet love,
And his to me:
But old folks, many feign as they were dead;
Unwieldy, slow, heavy and pale as lead. —
O God, she comes!
Enter NURSE *and her man* PETER.
O honey nurse, what news?
Hast thou met with him? Send thy man away.

NURSE
Peter, stay at the gate. [*Exit* PETER.

JULIET
Now, good sweet nurse, — O Lord, why look'st thou sad?
Though news be sad, yet tell them merrily;
If good, thou sham'st the music of sweet news
By playing it to me with so sour a face.

NURSE
I am a-weary, give me leave awhile: —
Fie, how my bones ache! what a jaunt have I had!

JULIET
I would thou hadst my bones, and I thy news:
Nay, come, I pray thee, speak; — good, good nurse, speak.

NURSE
Jesu, what haste? can you not stay awhile?
Do you not see that I am out of breath?

JULIET
How art thou out of breath, when thou hast breath
To say to me that thou art out of breath?
The excuse that thou dost make in this delay
Is longer than the tale thou dost excuse.
Is thy news good or bad? answer to that;
Say either, and I'll stay the circumstance:
Let me be satisfied, is't good or bad?

NURSE
Well, you have made a simple choice; you know not how to choose a man: Romeo! no, not he; though his face be better than any man's, yet his leg excels all men's; and for a hand, and a foot, and a body, —

though they be not to be talk'd on, yet they are past
compare: he is not the flower of courtesy, but, I'll
warrant him, as gentle as a lamb. — Go thy ways,
wench; serve God. — What, have you dined at home?

JULIET
No, no: but all this did I know before.
What says he of our marriage? what of that?

NURSE
Lord, how my head aches! what a head have I!
It beats as it would fall in twenty pieces.
My back o' t'other side, — ah, my back, my back! —
Beshrew your heart for sending me about,
To catch my death with jaucing up and down!

JULIET
I'faith, I am sorry that thou art not well.
Sweet, sweet, sweet nurse, tell me, what says my love?

NURSE
Your love says, like an honest gentleman, and a
courteous, and a kind, and a handsome, and, I warrant,
a virtuous, — Where is your mother?

JULIET
Where is my mother! — why, she is within;
Where should she be? How oddly thou repliest!
'Your love says, like an honest gentleman, —
Where is your mother?'

NURSE
              O God's lady dear!
Are you so hot? marry, come up, I trow;
Is this the poultice for my aching bones?
Henceforward do your messages yourself.

JULIET
Here's such a coil! — come, what says Romeo?

NURSE
Have you got leave to go to shrift to-day?

JULIET
I have.

NURSE
Then hie you hence to Friar Laurence' cell;
There stays a husband to make you a wife:
Now comes the wanton blood up in your cheeks,
They'll be in scarlet straight at any news.
Hie you to church; I must another way,
To fetch a ladder, by the which your love
Must climb a bird's-nest soon when it is dark:
I am the drudge, and toil in your delight;
But you shall bear the burden soon at night.
Go; I'll to dinner; hie you to the cell.

JULIET
Hie to high fortune! — Honest nurse, farewell.

                              [*Exeunt.*

SCENE V

FRIAR LAURENCE'S *cell.*

Enter FRIAR LAURENCE *and* ROMEO.

FRIAR LAURENCE
So smile the heavens upon this holy act,
That after-hours with sorrow chide us not!

ROMEO
Amen, amen! but come what sorrow can,
It cannot countervail the exchange of joy
That one short minute gives me in her sight.
Do thou but close our hands with holy words,
Then love-devouring death do what he dare, —
It is enough I may but call her mine.

FRIAR LAURENCE
These violent delights have violent ends,
And in their triumph die; like fire and powder,
Which, as they kiss, consume: the sweetest honey
Is loathsome in his own deliciousness,
And in the taste confounds the appetite:
Therefore, love moderately; long love doth so;
Too swift arrives as tardy as too slow. —
Here comes the lady: — O, so light a foot
Will ne'er wear out the everlasting flint:
A lover may bestride the gossamer
That idles in the wanton summer air,
And yet not fall; so light is vanity.

Enter JULIET *somewhat fast, and embraceth* ROMEO.

JULIET
Good even to my ghostly confessor.

FRIAR LAURENCE
Romeo shall thank thee, daughter, for us both.

JULIET
As much to him, else is his thanks too much.

ROMEO
Ah, Juliet, if the measure of thy joy
Be heap'd like mine, and that thy skill be more
To blazon it, then sweeten with thy breath

This neighbour air, and let rich music's tongue
Unfold the imagin'd happiness that both
Receive in either by this dear encounter.

JULIET
Conceit, more rich in matter than in words,
Brags of his substance, not of ornament:
They are but beggars that can count their worth;
But my true love is grown to such excess,
I cannot sum up sum of half my wealth.

FRIAR LAURENCE
Come, come with me, and we will make short work;
For, by your leaves, you shall not stay alone
Till holy church incorporate two in one.   [*Exeunt.*

ACT III

SCENE I

Verona. A public place.

Enter MERCUTIO, BENVOLIO, PAGE, *and*
SERVANTS.

BENVOLIO
I pray thee, good Mercutio, let's retire:
The day is hot, the Capulets abroad,
And if we meet, we shall not scape a brawl;
For now, these hot days, is the mad blood stirring.

MERCUTIO
Thou art like one of those fellows that, when he enters
the confines of a tavern, claps me his sword upon the
table, and says, 'God send me no need of thee!' and, by
the operation of the second cup, draws it on the drawer,
when, indeed, there is no need.

BENVOLIO
Am I like such a fellow?

MERCUTIO
Come, come, thou art as hot a Jack in thy mood as any
in Italy; and as soon moved to be moody, and as soon
moody to be moved.

BENVOLIO
And what to?

MERCUTIO
Nay, an there were two such, we should have none
shortly, for one would kill the other. Thou! why, thou
wilt quarrel with a man that hath a hair more or a hair
less in his beard than thou hast: thou wilt quarrel with
a man for cracking nuts, having no other reason but
because thou hast hazel eyes; — what eye, but such an
eye, would spy out such a quarrel? Thy head is as full of
quarrels as an egg is full of meat; and yet thy head hath
been beaten as addle as an egg for quarrelling: thou
hast quarrell'd with a man for coughing in the street,
because he hath waken'd thy dog that hath lain asleep

in the sun: didst thou not fall out with a tailor for
wearing his new doublet before Easter? with another,
for tying his new shoes with old riband? and yet thou
wilt tutor me from quarrelling!

BENVOLIO
An I were so apt to quarrel as thou art, any man should
buy the fee-simple of my life for an hour and a quarter.

MERCUTIO
The fee-simple! O simple!

            Enter TYBALT *and others.*

BENVOLIO
By my head, here come the Capulets.

MERCUTIO
By my heel, I care not.

TYBALT
Follow me close, for I will speak to them. —
Gentlemen, good den: a word with one of you.

MERCUTIO
And but one word with one of us? couple it with
something; make it a word and a blow.

TYBALT
You shall find me apt enough to that, sir, an you will
give me occasion.

MERCUTIO
Could you not take some occasion without giving?

TYBALT
Mercutio, thou consort'st with Romeo, —

MERCUTIO
Consort! what, dost thou make us minstrels? an thou
make minstrels of us, look to hear nothing but
discords: here's my fiddlestick; here's that shall make
you dance. Zounds, consort!

BENVOLIO
We talk here in the public haunt of men:
Either withdraw unto some private place,
And reason coldly of your grievances,
Or else depart; here all eyes gaze on us.

MERCUTIO
Men's eyes were made to look, and let them gaze;
I will not budge for no man's pleasure, I.

TYBALT
Well, peace be with you, sir:—here comes my man.

              Enter ROMEO.

MERCUTIO
But I'll be hang'd, sir, if he wear your livery:
Marry, go before to field, he'll be your follower;
Your worship in that sense may call him man.

TYBALT
Romeo, the hate I bear thee can afford
No better term than this, — thou art a villain.

ROMEO
Tybalt, the reason that I have to love thee

MERCUTIO I am hurt; — A plague o' both your houses! — I am sped.

Doth much excuse the appertaining rage
To such a greeting: — villain am I none:
Therefore farewell; I see thou know'st me not.

TYBALT
Boy, this shall not excuse the injuries
That thou hast done me; therefore turn, and draw.

ROMEO
I do protest, I never injured thee;
But love thee better than thou canst devise,
Till thou shalt know the reason of my love:
And so, good Capulet, — which name I tender
As dearly as my own, — be satisfied.

MERCUTIO
O calm, dishonourable, vile submission!
Alla stoccata carries it away. —   [*Draws.*
Tybalt, you rat-catcher, will you walk?

TYBALT
What wouldst thou have with me?

MERCUTIO
Good king of cats, nothing but one of your nine lives;
that I mean to make bold withal, and, as you shall use
me hereafter, dry-beat the rest of the eight. Will you
pluck your sword out of his pilcher by the ears? make
haste, lest mine be about your ears ere it be out.

TYBALT
I am for you.   [*Drawing.*

ROMEO
Gentle Mercutio, put thy rapier up.

MERCUTIO
Come, sir, your passado.   [*They fight.*

ROMEO
Draw, Benvolio; beat down their weapons. —
Gentlemen, for shame, forbear this outrage!
Tybalt, — Mercutio, — the prince expressly hath
Forbidden bandying in Verona streets: —
Hold, Tybalt! — good Mercutio, —
                    [TYBALT *under* ROMEO'S *arm thrusts*
                              MERCUTIO, *and flies.*

MERCUTIO
                                        I am hurt; —
A plague o' both your houses! — I am sped: —
Is he gone, and hath nothing?

BENVOLIO
                              What, art thou hurt?

MERCUTIO
Ay, ay, a scratch, a scratch; marry, 'tis enough.
Where is my page? — Go, villain, fetch a surgeon.
                                        [*Exit* PAGE.

ROMEO
Courage, man; the hurt cannot be much.

MERCUTIO
No, 'tis not so deep as a well, nor so wide as a
church-door; but 'tis enough, 'twill serve: ask for me
to-morrow, and you shall find me a grave man. I am
pepper'd, I warrant, for this world: — a plague o' both
your houses! — Zounds, a dog, a rat, a mouse, a cat, to
scratch a man to death! a braggart, a rogue, a villain,
that fights by the book of arithmetic! — Why, the devil,
came you between us? I was hurt under your arm.

ROMEO
I thought all for the best.

MERCUTIO
Help me into some house, Benvolio,
Or I shall faint. — A plague o' both your houses!
They have made worms'-meat of me: I have it,
And soundly too: — your houses!
                    [*Exit, led by* BENVOLIO *and* SERVANTS.

ROMEO
This gentleman, the prince's near ally,
My very friend, hath got his mortal hurt
In my behalf; my reputation stain'd
With Tybalt's slander, — Tybalt, that an hour
Hath been my kinsman: — O sweet Juliet,
Thy beauty hath made me effeminate,
And in my temper soften'd valour's steel!

                    Enter BENVOLIO.

BENVOLIO
O Romeo, Romeo, brave Mercutio's dead!
That gallant spirit hath aspired the clouds,
Which too untimely here did scorn the earth.

ROMEO
This day's black fate on more days doth depend;
This but begins the woe others must end.

                    Enter TYBALT.

BENVOLIO
Here comes the furious Tybalt back again.

ROMEO
Alive, in triumph! and Mercutio slain!

Away to heaven respective lenity,
And fire-eyed fury be my conduct now!
Now, Tybalt, take the 'villain' back again
That late thou gavest me; for Mercutio's soul
Is but a little way above our heads,
Staying for thine to keep him company:
Either thou or I, or both, must go with him.

TYBALT
Thou, wretched boy, that didst consort him here,
Shalt with him hence.

ROMEO
                    This shall determine that.
                    [*They fight;* TYBALT *falls.*

BENVOLIO
Romeo, away, be gone!
The citizens are up, and Tybalt slain: —
Stand not amaz'd: — the prince will doom thee death,
If thou art taken: — hence, be gone, away!

ROMEO
O, I am fortune's fool!

BENVOLIO
                    Why dost thou stay?
                              [*Exit* ROMEO.

          Enter CITIZENS *and* OFFICERS.

FIRST OFFICER
Which way ran he that kill'd Mercutio?
Tybalt, that murderer, which way ran he?

BENVOLIO
There lies that Tybalt.

FIRST OFFICER
                    Up, sir, go with me;
I charge thee in the prince's name, obey.

          Enter PRINCE, *old* MONTAGUE, CAPULET, *their*
                    WIVES *and all.*

PRINCE ESCALUS
Where are the vile beginners of this fray?

BENVOLIO
O noble prince, I can discover all
The unlucky manage of this fatal brawl:
There lies the man, slain by young Romeo,
That slew thy kinsman, brave Mercutio.

LADY CAPULET
Tybalt, my cousin! O my brother's child!
O prince! O cousin! husband! O, the blood is spilt
Of my dear kinsman! Prince, as thou art true,
For blood of ours shed blood of Montague. —
O cousin, cousin!

PRINCE ESCALUS
Benvolio, who began this bloody fray?

BENVOLIO
Tybalt, here slain, whom Romeo's hand did slay;
Romeo, that spoke him fair, bade him bethink
How nice the quarrel was, and urg'd withal
Your high displeasure: — all this — uttered
With gentle breath, calm look, knees humbly bow'd —
Could not take truce with the unruly spleen
Of Tybalt deaf to peace, but that he tilts
With piercing steel at bold Mercutio's breast;
Who, all as hot, turns deadly point to point,
And, with a martial scorn, with one hand beats
Cold death aside, and with the other sends
It back to Tybalt, whose dexterity
Retorts it: Romeo he cries aloud,
'Hold, friends! friends, part!' and, swifter than
          his tongue,
His agile arm beats down their fatal points,
And 'twixt them rushes; underneath whose arm
An envious thrust from Tybalt hit the life
Of stout Mercutio, and then Tybalt fled:
But by and by comes back to Romeo,
Who had but newly entertain'd revenge,
And to't they go like lightning; for, ere I
Could draw to part them, was stout Tybalt slain;
And, as he fell, did Romeo turn and fly: —
This is the truth, or let Benvolio die.

LADY CAPULET
He is a kinsman to the Montague;
Affection makes him false; he speaks not true:
Some twenty of them fought in this black strife,
And all those twenty could but kill one life.
I beg for justice, which thou, prince, must give;
Romeo slew Tybalt, Romeo must not live.

PRINCE ESCALUS
Romeo slew him, he slew Mercutio;
Who now the price of his dear blood doth owe?

MONTAGUE
Not Romeo, prince, he was Mercutio's friend;
His fault concludes but what the law should end,
The life of Tybalt.

PRINCE ESCALUS
                    And for that offence
Immediately we do exile him hence:
I have an interest in your hate's proceeding:
My blood for your rude brawls doth lie a-bleeding,
But I'll amerce you with so strong a fine,
That you shall all repent the loss of mine:
I will be deaf to pleading and excuses;
Nor tears nor prayers shall purchase out abuses,
Therefore use none: let Romeo hence in haste,
Else, when he's found, that hour is his last.
Bear hence this body, and attend our will:
Mercy but murders, pardoning those that kill.
                                        [*Exeunt.*

SCENE II

The same. CAPULET'S *orchard.*

          Enter JULIET.

JULIET
Gallop apace, you fiery-footed steeds,
Towards Phœbus' lodging: such a wagoner
As Phæthon would whip you to the west,
And bring in cloudy night immediately.
Spread thy close curtain, love-performing night,
That runaway's eyes may wink, and Romeo
Leap to these arms untalk'd-of and unseen.
Lovers can see to do their amorous rites
By their own beauties; or, if love be blind,
It best agrees with night. — Come, civil night,
Thou sober-suited matron, all in black,
And learn me how to lose a winning match,
Play'd for a pair of stainless maidenhoods:
Hood my unmann'd blood, bating in my cheeks,
With thy black mantle; till strange love, grown bold,
Think true love acted simple modesty.
Come, night; come, Romeo; come, thou day in night;
For thou wilt lie upon the wings of night
Whiter than new snow on a raven's back. —
Come, gentle night, — come, loving, black-brow'd
          night,
Give me my Romeo; and, when he shall die,
Take him and cut him out in little stars,
And he will make the face of heaven so fine,
That all the world will be in love with night,
And pay no worship to the garish sun. —
O, I have bought the mansion of a love,
But not possess'd it, and, though I am sold,
Not yet enjoy'd: so tedious is this day,
As is the night before some festival
To an impatient child that hath new robes
And may not wear them. — O, here comes my nurse,
And she brings news; and every tongue that speaks
But Romeo's name speaks heavenly eloquence.

          Enter NURSE, *wringing her hands, with the ladder of*
                    cords in her lap.

Now, nurse, what news? What hast thou there? the
          cords
That Romeo bid thee fetch?

NURSE
                    Ay, ay, the cords.
                    [*Throws them down.*

JULIET
Ay me! what news? why dost thou wring thy hands?

NURSE
Ah, well-a-day! he's dead, he's dead, he's dead!
We are undone, lady, we are undone! —
Alack the day! — he's gone, he's kill'd, he's dead!

JULIET
Can heaven be so envious?

NURSE
                    Romeo can,
Though heaven cannot: — O Romeo, Romeo! —
Who ever would have thought it? — Romeo!

JULIET
What devil art thou, that dost torment me thus?
This torture should be roar'd in dismal hell.
Hath Romeo slain himself? say thou but 'I',
And that bare vowel 'I' shall poison more
Than the death-darting eye of cockatrice:
I am not I, if there be such an 'I';
Or those eyes shut, that make thee answer 'I',
If he be slain, say 'I'; or if not, 'no':
Brief sounds determine of my weal or woe.

NURSE
I saw the wound, I saw it with mine eyes, —
God save the mark! — here on his manly breast:
A piteous corse, a bloody piteous corse;
Pale, pale as ashes, all bedaub'd in blood,
All in gore-blood: — I swounded at the sight.

JULIET
O, break, my heart! poor bankrout, break at once!
To prison, eyes, ne'er look on liberty!
Vile earth, to earth resign; end motion here;
And thou and Romeo press one heavy bier!

NURSE
O Tybalt, Tybalt, the best friend I had!
O courteous Tybalt! honest gentleman!
That ever I should live to see thee dead!

JULIET
What storm is this that blows so contrary?
Is Romeo slaughter'd, and is Tybalt dead?
My dear-lov'd cousin, and my dearer lord? —
Then, dreadful trumpet, sound the general doom!
For who is living, if those two are gone?

NURSE
Tybalt is gone, and Romeo banished;
Romeo that kill'd him, he is banished.

JULIET
O God! did Romeo's hand shed Tybalt's blood?

NURSE
It did, it did; alas the day, it did!

JULIET
O serpent heart, hid with a flow'ring face!
Did ever dragon keep so fair a cave?
Beautiful tyrant! fiend angelical!
Dove-feather'd raven! wolvish-ravening lamb!
Despised substance of divinest show!
Just opposite to what thou justly seem'st,
A damned saint, an honourable villain! —
O nature, what hadst thou to do in hell,
When thou didst bower the spirit of a fiend
In mortal paradise of such sweet flesh?
Was ever book containing such vile matter
So fairly bound? O, that deceit should dwell
In such a gorgeous palace!

NURSE
There's no trust,
No faith, no honesty in men; all perjured,
All forsworn, all naught, all dissemblers. —
Ah, where's my man? give me some *aqua vitæ:* —
These griefs, these woes, these sorrows make me old.
Shame come to Romeo!

JULIET
Blister'd be thy tongue
For such a wish! he was not born to shame:
Upon his brow shame is asham'd to sit;
For 'tis a throne where honour may be crown'd
Sole monarch of the universal earth.
O, what a beast was I to chide at him!

NURSE
Will you speak well of him that kill'd your cousin?

JULIET
Shall I speak ill of him that is my husband?
Ah, poor my lord, what tongue shall smooth thy name,
When I, thy three-hours' wife, have mangled it? —
But wherefore, villain, didst thou kill my cousin?
That villain cousin would have kill'd my husband:
Back, foolish tears, back to your native spring;
Your tributary drops belong to woe,
Which you, mistaking, offer up to joy.
My husband lives, that Tybalt would have slain;
And Tybalt's dead, that would have slain my husband:
All this is comfort; wherefore weep I, then?
Some word there was, worser than Tybalt's death,
That murder'd me: I would forget it fain;
But, O, it presses to my memory,
Like damned guilty deeds to sinners' minds:
'Tybalt is dead, and Romeo — banished';
That 'banished,' that one word 'banished,'
Hath slain ten thousand Tybalts. Tybalt's death
Was woe enough, if it had ended there:
Or, — if sour woe delights in fellowship,
And needly will be rank'd with other griefs, —
Why follow'd not, when she said 'Tybalt's dead,'
Thy father, or thy mother, nay, or both,
Which modern lamentation might have moved?
But with a rear-ward following Tybalt's death,
'Romeo is banished,' — to speak that word,
Is father, mother, Tybalt, Romeo, Juliet,
All slain, all dead: — 'Romeo is banished,' —
There is no end, no limit, measure, bound,
In that word's death; no words can that woe sound. —
Where is my father, and my mother, nurse?

NURSE
Weeping and wailing over Tybalt's corse:
Will you go to them? I will bring you thither.

JULIET
Wash they his wounds with tears: mine shall be spent,
When theirs are dry, for Romeo's banishment.

Take up those cords: — poor ropes, you are beguiled,
Both you and I; for Romeo is exiled:
He made you for a highway to my bed;
But I, a maid, die maiden-widowed.
Come, cords; come, nurse; I'll to my wedding-bed;
And death, not Romeo, take my maidenhead!

NURSE
Hie to your chamber: I'll find Romeo
To comfort you: — I wot well where he is.
Hark ye, your Romeo will be here at night:
I'll to him; he is hid at Laurence' cell.

JULIET
O, find him! give this ring to my true knight,
And bid him come to take his last farewell.   [*Exeunt.*

SCENE III
FRIAR LAURENCE'S *cell.*

Enter FRIAR LAURENCE.

FRIAR LAURENCE
Romeo, come forth; come forth, thou fearful man:
Affliction is enamour'd of thy parts,
And thou art wedded to calamity.

Enter ROMEO.

ROMEO
Father, what news? what is the prince's doom?
What sorrow craves acquaintance at my hand,
That I yet know not?

FRIAR LAURENCE
Too familiar
Is my dear son with such sour company:
I bring thee tidings of the prince's doom.

ROMEO
What less than doomsday is the prince's doom?

FRIAR LAURENCE
A gentler judgement — 'banish'd' — from his lips;
Not body's death, but body's banishment.

ROMEO
Ha, banishment! be merciful, say 'death';
For exile hath more terror in his look,
Much more than death: do not say 'banishment.'

FRIAR LAURENCE
Hence from Verona art thou banished:
Be patient, for the world is broad and wide.

ROMEO
There is no world without Verona walls,
But purgatory, torture, hell itself.
Hence-banished is banish'd from the world,
And world's exile is death: — then 'banished'
Is death mis-term'd: calling death 'banished,'
Thou cutt'st my head off with a golden axe,
And smilest upon the stroke that murders me.

FRIAR LAURENCE
O deadly sin! O rude unthankfulness!
Thy fault our law calls death; but the kind prince,

Taking thy part, hath rush'd aside the law,
And turn'd that black word death to banishment:
This is dear mercy, and thou seest it not.

ROMEO
'Tis torture, and not mercy: heaven is here,
Where Juliet lives; and every cat, and dog,
And little mouse, every unworthy thing,
Live here in heaven, and may look on her;
But Romeo may not: — more validity,
More honourable state, more courtship lives
In carrion-flies than Romeo: they may seize
On the white wonder of dear Juliet's hand,
And steal immortal blessing from her lips;
Who, even in pure and vestal modesty,
Still blush, as thinking their own kisses sin;
But Romeo may not, — he is banished:
This may flies do, when I from this must fly: —
And say'st thou yet, that exile is not death?
Hadst thou no poison mix'd, no sharp-ground knife,
No sudden mean of death, though ne'er so mean,
But 'banished' to kill me, — 'banished'?
O friar, the damned use that word in hell;
Howling attends it: how hast thou the heart,
Being a divine, a ghostly confessor,
A sin-absolver, and my friend profess'd,
To mangle me with that word 'banished'?

FRIAR LAURENCE
Thou fond mad man, hear me a little speak.

ROMEO
O, thou wilt speak again of banishment.

FRIAR LAURENCE
I'll give thee armour to keep off that word;
Adversity's sweet milk, philosophy,
To comfort thee, though thou art banished.

ROMEO
Yet 'banished'? — Hang up philosophy!
Unless philosophy can make a Juliet,
Displant a town, reverse a prince's doom,
It helps not, it prevails not: talk no more.

FRIAR LAURENCE
O, then I see that madmen have no ears.

ROMEO
How should they, when that wise men have no eyes?

FRIAR LAURENCE
Let me dispute with thee of thy estate.

ROMEO
Thou canst not speak of that thou dost not feel:
Wert thou as young as I, Juliet thy love,
An hour but married, Tybalt murdered,
Doting like me, and like me banished,
Then mightst thou speak, then mightst thou tear thy
    hair,
And fall upon the ground, as I do now,
Taking the measure of an unmade grave.
                            [NURSE *knocks.*

ROMEO And fall upon the ground, as I do now, taking the measure of an unmade grave.

FRIAR LAURENCE
Arise; one knocks; good Romeo, hide thyself.
ROMEO
Not I; unless the breath of heart-sick groans,
Mist-like, infold me from the search of eyes.
                                              [*She knocks again.*
FRIAR LAURENCE
Hark, how they knock! — Who's there? — Romeo,
    arise;
Thou wilt be taken. — Stay awhile! — Stand up;
                                              [*Knock.*
Run to my study. — By and by! — God's will,
What simpleness is this! — I come, I come!   [*Knock.*
Who knocks so hard? whence come you? what's your
    will?
NURSE [*within*].
Let me come in, and you shall know my errand;
I come from Lady Juliet.
FRIAR LAURENCE
                        Welcome, then.
                    Enter NURSE.

NURSE
O holy friar, O, tell me, holy friar,
Where is my lady's lord, where's Romeo?
FRIAR LAURENCE
There on the ground, with his own tears made drunk.
NURSE
O, he is even in my mistress' case,
Just in her case!
FRIAR LAURENCE
                O woeful sympathy!
Piteous predicament!
NURSE
                    Even so lies she,
Blubbering and weeping, weeping and blubbering. —
Stand up, stand up; stand, an you be a man:
For Juliet's sake, for her sake, rise and stand.
Why should you fall into so deep an O?   [*He rises.*
ROMEO
Nurse! —
NURSE
Ah sir! ah sir! — Well, death's the end of all.
ROMEO
Spakest thou of Juliet? how is it with her?
Doth she not think me an old murderer,
Now I have stain'd the childhood of our joy
With blood remov'd but little from her own?
Where is she? and how doth she? and what says
My conceal'd lady to our cancell'd love?
NURSE
O, she says nothing, sir, but weeps and weeps;
And now falls on her bed; and then starts up,
And Tybalt calls; and then on Romeo cries,
And then falls down again.
ROMEO
                        As if that name,
Shot from the deadly level of a gun,
Did murder her; as that name's cursed hand
Murder'd her kinsman. — O, tell me, friar, tell me,
In what vile part of this anatomy
Doth my name lodge? tell me, that I may sack
The hateful mansion.
    [*He offers to stab himself, and* NURSE *snatches the dagger
                                                    away.*
FRIAR LAURENCE
                    Hold thy desperate hand:
Art thou a man? thy form cries out thou art:
Thy tears are womanish; thy wild acts denote
The unreasonable fury of a beast:
Unseemly woman in a seeming man!
Or ill-beseeming beast in seeming both!
Thou hast amaz'd me: by my holy order,
I thought thy disposition better temper'd.
Hast thou slain Tybalt? wilt thou slay thyself?
And slay thy lady that in thy life lives,
By doing damned hate upon thyself?
Why rail'st thou on thy birth, the heaven, and earth?
Since birth, and heaven, and earth, all three do meet
In thee at once; which thou at once wouldst lose.
Fie, fie, thou shamest thy shape, thy love, thy wit;
Which, like a usurer, abound'st in all,
And usest none in that true use indeed
Which should bedeck thy shape, thy love, thy wit:
Thy noble shape is but a form of wax,
Digressing from the valour of a man;
Thy dear love, sworn, but hollow perjury,
Killing that love which thou hast vow'd to cherish;
Thy wit, that ornament to shape and love,
Mis-shapen in the conduct of them both,

Like powder in a skilless soldier's flask,
Is set a-fire by thine own ignorance,
And thou dismember'd with thine own defence.
What, rouse thee, man! thy Juliet is alive,
For whose dear sake thou wast but lately dead;
There art thou happy: Tybalt would kill thee,
But thou slew'st Tybalt; there art thou happy too:
The law, that threaten'd death, becomes thy friend,
And turns it to exile; there art thou happy:
A pack of blessings lights upon thy back;
Happiness courts thee in her best array;
But, like a misbehav'd and sullen wench,
Thou pout'st upon thy fortune and thy love: —
Take heed, take heed, for such die miserable.
Go, get thee to thy love, as was decreed,
Ascend her chamber, hence and comfort her:
But look thou stay not till the watch be set,
For then thou canst not pass to Mantua;
Where thou shalt live, till we can find a time
To blaze your marriage, reconcile your friends,
Beg pardon of the prince, and call thee back
With twenty hundred thousand times more joy
Than thou went'st forth in lamentation. —
Go before, nurse: commend me to thy lady;
And bid her hasten all the house to bed,
Which heavy sorrow makes them apt unto:
Romeo is coming.
NURSE
O Lord, I could have stay'd here all the night
To hear good counsel: O, what learning is! —
My lord, I'll tell my lady you will come.
ROMEO
Do so, and bid my sweet prepare to chide.
NURSE
Here is a ring, sir, that she bade me give you:
                    [NURSE *offers to go in and turns again.*
Hie you, make haste, for it grows very late.   [*Exit.*

ROMEO
How well my comfort is reviv'd by this!
FRIAR LAURENCE
Go hence; good night; and here stands all your state: —
Either be gone before the watch be set,
Or by the break of day disguis'd from hence:
Sojourn in Mantua; I'll find out your man,
And he shall signify from time to time
Every good hap to you that chances here:
Give me thy hand; 'tis late: farewell; good night.
ROMEO
But that a joy past joy calls out on me,
It were a grief so brief to part with thee:
Farewell.   [*Exeunt.*

SCENE IV

The same. A room in CAPULET'S *house.*

Enter old CAPULET, LADY CAPULET, *and*
COUNTY PARIS.

CAPULET
Things have fall'n out, sir, so unluckily,
That we have had no time to move our daughter:
Look you, she lov'd her kinsman Tybalt dearly,
And so did I: — well, we were born to die.
'Tis very late, she'll not come down to-night:
I promise you, but for your company,
I would have been a-bed an hour ago.
PARIS
These times of woe afford no time to woo. —
Madam, good night: commend me to your daughter.
LADY CAPULET
I will, and know her mind early to-morrow;
To-night she's mew'd up to her heaviness.
        [PARIS *offers to go in and* CAPULET *calls him again.*

ROMEO Farewell, farewell! one kiss, and I'll descend.

CAPULET
Sir Paris, I will make a desperate tender
Of my child's love: I think she will be ruled
In all respects by me; nay, more, I doubt it not. —
Wife, go you to her ere you go to bed;
Acquaint her here of my son Paris' love;
And bid her, mark you me, on Wednesday next —
But, soft! what day is this?

PARIS
                                    Monday, my lord,

CAPULET
Monday! ha, ha! Well, Wednesday is too soon,
O' Thursday let it be: — o' Thursday, tell her,
She shall be married to this noble earl. —
Will you be ready? do you like this haste?
We'll keep no great ado, — a friend or two;
For, hark you, Tybalt being slain so late,
It may be thought we held him carelessly,
Being our kinsman, if we revel much:
Therefore we'll have some half-a-dozen friends,
And there an end. But what say you to Thursday?

PARIS
My lord, I would that Thursday were to-morrow.

CAPULET
Well, get you gone: — o' Thursday be it, then. —
Go you to Juliet ere you go to bed,
Prepare her, wife, against this wedding-day.—
Farewell, my lord. — Light to my chamber, ho! —
Afore me, it is so very late, that we
May call it early by and by: — good night.   [*Exeunt.*

SCENE V

JULIET'S *chamber.*

Enter ROMEO *and* JULIET *at the window.*

JULIET
Wilt thou be gone? it is not yet near day:
It was the nightingale, and not the lark,
That pierc'd the fearful hollow of thine ear;
Nightly she sings on yond pomegranate-tree:
Believe me, love, it was the nightingale.

ROMEO
It was the lark, the herald of the morn,
No nightingale: look, love, what envious streaks
Do lace the severing clouds in yonder east:
Night's candles are burnt out, and jocund day
Stands tiptoe on the misty mountain tops.
I must be gone and live, or stay and die.

JULIET
Yon light is not day-light, I know it, I:
It is some meteor that the sun exhales,
To be to thee this night a torch-bearer,
And light thee on thy way to Mantua:
Therefore stay yet, — thou need'st not to be gone.

ROMEO
Let me be ta'en, let me be put to death;
I am content, so thou wilt have it so.
I'll say yon grey is not the morning's eye,
'Tis but the pale reflex of Cynthia's brow;
Nor that is not the lark, whose notes do beat
The vaulty heaven so high above our heads:
I have more care to stay than will to go: —
Come, death, and welcome! Juliet wills it so. —
How is't, my soul? let's talk, — it is not day.

JULIET
It is, it is, — hie hence, be gone, away!
It is the lark that sings so out of tune,
Straining harsh discords and unpleasing sharps.
Some say the lark makes sweet division;
This doth not so, for she divideth us:
Some say the lark and loathed toad change eyes;
O, now I would they had chang'd voices too!
Since arm from arm that voice doth us affray,
Hunting thee hence with hunt's-up to the day.
O, now be gone; more light and light it grows.

ROMEO
More light and light, — more dark and dark our woes!

Enter NURSE.

NURSE
Madam!

JULIET
Nurse?

NURSE
Your lady mother is coming to your chamber:
The day is broke; be wary, look about.   [*Exit.*

JULIET
Then, window, let day in, and let life out.

ROMEO
Farewell, farewell! one kiss, and I'll descend.

                                    [*He goeth down.*

JULIET
Art thou gone so? my lord, my love, my friend!
I must hear from thee every day in the hour,
For in a minute there are many days:
O, by this count I shall be much in years
Ere I again behold my Romeo!

ROMEO
Farewell!
I will omit no opportunity
That may convey my greetings, love, to thee.

JULIET
O, think'st thou we shall ever meet again?

ROMEO
I doubt it not; and all these woes shall serve
For sweet discourses in our time to come.

JULIET
O God, I have an ill-divining soul!
Methinks I see thee, now thou art below,
As one dead in the bottom of a tomb:
Either my eyesight fails, or thou look'st pale.

ROMEO
And trust me, love, in my eye so do you:
Dry sorrow drinks our blood. Adieu, adieu!

                                    [*Exit below.*

JULIET
O fortune, fortune! all men call thee fickle:
If thou art fickle, what dost thou with him
That is renown'd for faith? Be fickle, fortune;
For then, I hope, thou wilt not keep him long,
But send him back.

LADY CAPULET [*within*].
                    Ho, daughter! are you up?

JULIET
Who is't that calls? is it my lady mother?
Is she not down so late, or up so early?
What unaccustom'd cause procures her hither?

Enter LADY CAPULET.

LADY CAPULET
Why, how now, Juliet!

JULIET
                    Madam, I am not well.

LADY CAPULET
Evermore weeping for your cousin's death?
What, wilt thou wash him from his grave with tears?
An if thou couldst, thou couldst not make him live;
Therefore have done: some grief shows much of love;
But much of grief shows still some want of wit.

JULIET
Yet let me weep for such a feeling loss.

LADY CAPULET
So shall you feel the loss, but not the friend
Which you weep for.

JULIET
                    Feeling so the loss,
I cannot choose but ever weep the friend.

LADY CAPULET
Well, girl, thou weep'st not so much for his death,
As that the villain lives which slaughter'd him.

JULIET
What villain, madam?

LADY CAPULET
                    That same villain, Romeo.

JULIET [*aside*].
Villain and he be many miles asunder. —
God pardon him! I do, with all my heart;
And yet no man like he doth grieve my heart.

LADY CAPULET
That is, because the traitor murderer lives.

JULIET
Ay, madam, from the reach of these my hands: —
Would none but I might venge my cousin's death!

LADY CAPULET
We will have vengeance for it, fear thou not:
Then weep no more. I'll send to one in Mantua, —
Where that same banish'd runagate doth live, —
Shall give him such an unaccustom'd dram,
That he shall soon keep Tybalt company:
And then, I hope, thou wilt be satisfied.

JULIET
Indeed, I never shall be satisfied
With Romeo, till I behold him — dead —
Is my poor heart so for a kinsman vex'd:
Madam, if you could find out but a man
To bear a poison, I would temper it;
That Romeo should, upon receipt thereof,
Soon sleep in quiet. O, how my heart abhors
To hear him nam'd, — and cannot come to him,

To wreak the love I bore my cousin Tybalt
Upon his body that hath slaughter'd him!

LADY CAPULET
Find thou the means, and I'll find such a man.
But now I'll tell thee joyful tidings, girl.

JULIET
And joy comes well in such a needful time:
What are they, I beseech your ladyship?

LADY CAPULET
Well, well, thou hast a careful father, child;
One who, to put thee from thy heaviness,
Hath sorted out a sudden day of joy,
That thou expect'st not, nor I look'd not for.

JULIET
Madam, in happy time, what day is that?

LADY CAPULET
Marry, my child, early next Thursday morn,
The gallant, young, and noble gentleman,
The County Paris, at Saint Peter's Church,
Shall happily make thee there a joyful bride.

JULIET
Now, by Saint Peter's Church, and Peter too,
He shall not make me there a joyful bride.
I wonder at this haste; that I must wed
Ere he, that should be husband, comes to woo.
I pray you, tell my lord and father, madam,
I will not marry yet; and when I do, I swear
It shall be Romeo, whom you know I hate,
Rather than Paris: — these are news indeed!

LADY CAPULET
Here comes your father; tell him so yourself,
And see how he will take it at your hands.

Enter CAPULET *and* NURSE.

CAPULET
When the sun sets, the air doth drizzle dew;
But for the sunset of my brother's son
It rains downright. —
How now! a conduit, girl? what, still in tears?
Evermore showering? In one little body
Thou counterfeit'st a bark, a sea, a wind:
For still thy eyes, which I may call the sea,
Do ebb and flow with tears; the bark thy body is,
Sailing in this salt flood; the winds, thy sighs;
Who, — raging with thy tears, and they with them, —
Without a sudden calm, will overset
Thy tempest-tossed body. — How now, wife!
Have you deliver'd to her our decree?

LADY CAPULET
Ay, sir; but she will none, she gives you thanks.
I would the fool were married to her grave!

CAPULET
Soft! take me with you, take me with you, wife.
How! will she none? doth she not give us thanks?
Is she not proud? doth she not count her blest,
Unworthy as she is, that we have wrought
So worthy a gentleman to be her bridegroom?

JULIET
Not proud, you have; but thankful, that you have:
Proud can I never be of what I hate;
But thankful even for hate, that is meant love.

CAPULET
How now, how now, chop-logic! What is this?
'Proud,' — and 'I thank you,' — and 'I thank you not'; —
And yet 'not proud': — mistress minion, you,
Thank me no thankings, nor proud me no prouds,
But fettle your fine joints 'gainst Thursday next,
To go with Paris to Saint Peter's Church,
Or I will drag thee on a hurdle thither.
Out, you green-sickness carrion! out, you baggage!
You tallow-face!

LADY CAPULET
                    Fie, fie! what, are you mad?

JULIET
Good father, I beseech you on my knees,
                                    [*She kneels down.*
Hear me with patience but to speak a word.

CAPULET
Hang thee, young baggage! disobedient wretch!
I tell thee what, — get thee to church o' Thursday,
Or never after look me in the face:
Speak not, reply not, do not answer me;
My fingers itch. — Wife, we scarce thought us blest
That God had sent us but this only child;
But now I see this one is one too much,
And that we have a curse in having her:
Out on her, hilding!

NURSE
                    God in heaven bless her! —
You are to blame, my lord, to rate her so.

153

JULIET Good father, I beseech you on my knees, hear me with patience but to speak a word.

CAPULET
And why, my lady wisdom? hold your tongue,
Good prudence; smatter with your gossips, go.
NURSE
I speak no treason.
CAPULET
        O, God ye god-den.
NURSE
May not one speak?
CAPULET
        Peace, you mumbling fool!
Utter your gravity o'er a gossip's bowl;
For here we need it not.
LADY CAPULET
        You are too hot.
CAPULET
God's bread! it makes me mad: day, night, late, early,
At home, abroad, alone, in company,
Waking, or sleeping, still my care hath been
To have her match'd: and having now provided
A gentleman of princely parentage,
Of fair demesnes, youthful, and nobly train'd,
Stuff'd, as they say, with honourable parts,
Proportion'd as one's thought would wish a man, —
And then to have a wretched puling fool,
A whining mammet, in her fortune's tender,
To answer — 'I'll not wed, — I cannot love,
I am too young, — I pray you, pardon me'; —
But, an you will not wed, I'll pardon you:
Graze where you will, you shall not house with me:
Look to't, think on't, I do not use to jest.
Thursday is near; lay hand on heart, advise:
An you be mine, I'll give you to my friend;
An you be not, hang, beg, starve, die in the streets,
For, by my soul, I'll ne'er acknowledge thee,
Nor what is mine shall never do thee good:
Trust to't, bethink you; I'll not be forsworn.   [*Exit.*
JULIET
Is there no pity sitting in the clouds,
That sees into the bottom of my grief?
O, sweet my mother, cast me not away!
Delay this marriage for a month, a week;
Or, if you do not, make the bridal bed
In that dim monument where Tybalt lies.
LADY CAPULET
Talk not to me, for I'll not speak a word:
Do as thou wilt, for I have done with thee.   [*Exit.*
JULIET
O God! — O nurse, how shall this be prevented?
My husband is on earth, my faith in heaven;
How shall that faith return again to earth,
Unless that husband send it me from heaven
By leaving earth? — comfort me, counsel me. —
Alack, alack, that heaven should practise stratagems
Upon so soft a subject as myself! —
What say'st thou? hast thou not a word of joy?
Some comfort, nurse.
NURSE
        Faith, here it is. Romeo
Is banished; and all the world to nothing,
That he dares ne'er come back to challenge you;
Or, if he do, it needs must be by stealth.
Then, since the case so stands as now it doth,
I think it best you married with the county.
O, he's a lovely gentleman!
Romeo's a dishclout to him: an eagle, madam,
Hath not so green, so quick, so fair an eye
As Paris hath. Beshrew my very heart,

I think you are happy in this second match,
For it excels your first; or if it did not,
Your first is dead; or 'twere as good he were,
As living here, and you no use of him.
JULIET
Speakest thou from thy heart?
NURSE
And from my soul too; else beshrew them both.
JULIET
Amen!
NURSE
What?
JULIET
Well, thou hast comforted me marvellous much.
Go in; and tell my lady I am gone,
Having displeas'd my father, to Laurence' cell,
To make confession, and to be absolved.
NURSE
Marry, I will; and this is wisely done.   [*Exit.*
JULIET
Ancient damnation! O most cursed fiend!
        [*She looks after* NURSE.
Is it more sin to wish me thus forsworn,
Or to dispraise my lord with that same tongue
Which she hath prais'd him with above compare
So many thousand times? — Go, counsellor;
Thou and my bosom henceforth shall be twain. —
I'll to the friar, to know his remedy:
If all else fail, myself have power to die.   [*Exit.*

ACT IV

SCENE I

Verona. FRIAR LAURENCE'S *cell.*

Enter FRIAR LAURENCE *and* PARIS.

FRIAR LAURENCE
On Thursday, sir? the time is very short.
PARIS
My father Capulet will have it so;
And I am nothing slow to slack his haste.
FRIAR LAURENCE
You say you do not know the lady's mind:
Uneven is the course; I like it not.
PARIS
Immoderately she weeps for Tybalt's death,
And therefore have I little talk'd of love;
For Venus smiles not in a house of tears.
Now, sir, her father counts it dangerous
That she doth give her sorrow so much sway;
And, in his wisdom, hastes our marriage,
To stop the inundation of her tears;
Which, too much minded by herself alone,
May be put from her by society:
Now do you know the reason of this haste.
FRIAR LAURENCE   [*aside*].
I would I knew not why it should be slow'd. —
Look, sir, here comes the lady toward my cell.

        Enter JULIET.

PARIS
Happily met, my lady and my wife!
JULIET
That may be, sir, when I may be a wife.
PARIS
That may be must be, love, on Thursday next.
JULIET
What must be shall be.
FRIAR LAURENCE
        That's a certain text.
PARIS
Come you to make confession to this father?
JULIET
To answer that, were to confess to you.
PARIS
Do not deny to him that you love me.
JULIET
I will confess to you that I love him.
PARIS
So will ye, I am sure, that you love me.
JULIET
If I do so, it will be of more price,
Being spoke behind your back, than to your face.
PARIS
Poor soul, thy face is much abus'd with tears.
JULIET
The tears have got small victory by that;

JULIET I'll to the friar, to know his remedy: if all else fail, myself have power to die.

For it was bad enough before their spite.
PARIS
Thou wrong'st it, more than tears, with that report.
JULIET
That is no slander, sir, which is a truth;
And what I spake, I spake it to my face.
PARIS
Thy face is mine, and thou hast slander'd it.
JULIET
It may be so, for it is not mine own. —
Are you at leisure, holy father, now;
Or shall I come to you at evening mass?
FRIAR LAURENCE
My leisure serves me, pensive daughter, now. —
My lord, we must entreat the time alone.
PARIS
God shield I should disturb devotion! —
Juliet, on Thursday early will I rouse ye:
Till then, adieu; and keep this holy kiss.   [*Exit.*
JULIET
O, shut the door! and when thou hast done so,
Come weep with me; past hope, past cure, past help!
FRIAR LAURENCE
Ah, Juliet, I already know thy grief;
It strains me past the compass of my wits:
I hear thou must, and nothing may prorogue it,
On Thursday next be married to this county.
JULIET
Tell me not, friar, that thou hear'st of this,
Unless thou tell me how I may prevent it:
If, in thy wisdom, thou canst give no help,
Do thou but call my resolution wise,
And with this knife I'll help it presently.
God join'd my heart and Romeo's, thou our hands;
And ere this hand, by thee to Romeo seal'd,
Shall be the label to another deed,
Or my true heart with treacherous revolt
Turn to another, this shall slay them both:
Therefore, out of thy long-experienc'd time,
Give me some present counsel; or, behold,
'Twixt my extremes and me this bloody knife
Shall play the umpire; arbitrating that
Which the commission of thy years and art
Could to no issue of true honour bring.
Be not so long to speak; I long to die,
If what thou speak'st speak not of remedy.
FRIAR LAURENCE
Hold, daughter: I do spy a kind of hope,
Which craves as desperate an execution
As that is desperate which we would prevent.
If, rather than to marry County Paris,
Thou hast the strength of will to slay thyself,
Then is it likely thou wilt undertake
A thing like death to chide away this shame,
That copest with death himself to scape from it;
And, if thou darest, I'll give thee remedy.
JULIET
O, bid me leap, rather than marry Paris,
From off the battlements of yonder tower;
Or walk in thievish ways; or bid me lurk
Where serpents are; chain me with roaring bears;
Or shut me nightly in a charnel-house,
O'er-cover'd quite with dead men's rattling bones,

With reeky shanks, and yellow chapless skulls;
Or bid me go into a new-made grave,
And hide me with a dead man in his shroud;
Things that, to hear them told, have made me tremble;
And I will do it without fear or doubt,
To live an unstain'd wife to my sweet love.
FRIAR LAURENCE
Hold, then; go home, be merry, give consent
To marry Paris: Wednesday is to-morrow;
To-morrow night look that thou lie alone,
Let not thy nurse lie with thee in thy chamber:
Take thou this vial, being then in bed,
And this distilled liquor drink thou off:
When, presently, through all thy veins shall run
A cold and drowsy humour; for no pulse
Shall keep his native progress, but surcease:
No warmth, no breath, shall testify thou livest;
The roses in thy lips and cheeks shall fade
To paly ashes; thy eyes' windows fall,
Like death, when he shuts up the day of life;
Each part, depriv'd of supple government,
Shall, stiff and stark and cold, appear like death:
And in this borrow'd likeness of shrunk death
Thou shalt continue two-and-forty hours,
And then awake as from a pleasant sleep.
Now, when the bridegroom in the morning comes
To rouse thee from thy bed, there art thou dead:
Then, as the manner of our country is,
In thy best robes, uncover'd, on the bier,
Thou shalt be borne to that same ancient vault
Where all the kindred of the Capulets lie.
In the mean time, against thou shalt awake,
Shall Romeo by my letters know our drift;
And hither shall he come: and he and I
Will watch thy waking, and that very night
Shall Romeo bear thee hence to Mantua.
And this shall free thee from this present shame;
If no inconstant toy, nor womanish fear,
Abate thy valour in the acting it.
JULIET
Give me, give me! O, tell not me of fear!
FRIAR LAURENCE
Hold; get you gone, be strong and prosperous
In this resolve: I'll send a friar with speed
To Mantua, with my letters to thy lord.
JULIET
Love give me strength! and strength shall help afford.
Farewell, dear father!   [*Exeunt.*

SCENE II

Hall in CAPULET'S *house.*

Enter CAPULET, LADY CAPULET, NURSE, *and*
SERVING-MEN *two or three.*

CAPULET
So many guests invite as here are writ. —
                [*Exit* FIRST SERVANT.
Sirrah, go hire me twenty cunning cooks.
SECOND SERVING-MAN
You shall have none ill, sir; for I'll try if they can lick
their fingers.
CAPULET
How canst thou try them so?
SECOND SERVING-MAN
Marry, sir, 'tis an ill cook that cannot lick his own
fingers: therefore he that cannot lick his fingers goes
not with me.
CAPULET
Go, be gone.—   [*Exit* SECOND SERVANT.
We shall be much unfurnish'd for this time. —
What, is my daughter gone to Friar Laurence?
NURSE
Ay, forsooth.
CAPULET
Well, he may chance to do some good on her:
A peevish self-will'd harlotry it is.
NURSE
See where she comes from shrift with merry look.

Enter JULIET.

CAPULET
How now, my headstrong! where have you been
        gadding?
JULIET
Where I have learn'd me to repent the sin
Of disobedient opposition
To you and your behests; and am enjoin'd
By holy Laurence to fall prostrate here,
And beg your pardon: — pardon, I beseech you!
Henceforward I am ever rul'd by you.

FRIAR LAURENCE Ah, Juliet, I already know thy grief; it strains me past the compass of my wits.

CAPULET
Send for the county; go tell him of this:
I'll have this knot knit up to-morrow morning.
JULIET
I met the youthful lord at Laurence' cell;
And gave him what becomed love I might,
Not stepping o'er the bounds of modesty.
CAPULET
Why, I am glad on't; this is well, — stand up, —
This is as't should be. — Let me see the county;
Ay, marry, go, I say, and fetch him hither. —
Now, afore God, this reverend holy friar,
All our whole city is much bound to him.
JULIET
Nurse, will you go with me into my closet,
To help me sort such needful ornaments
As you think fit to furnish me to-morrow?
LADY CAPULET
No, not till Thursday; there is time enough.
CAPULET
Go, nurse, go with her: — we'll to church to-morrow.
[*Exeunt* JULIET *and* NURSE.
LADY CAPULET
We shall be short in our provision:
'Tis now near night.
CAPULET
        Tush, I will stir about,
And all things shall be well, I warrant thee, wife:
Go thou to Juliet, help to deck up her;
I'll not to bed to-night; — let me alone;
I'll play the housewife for this once. — What, ho! —
They are all forth: well, I will walk myself
To County Paris, to prepare him up
Against to-morrow: my heart is wondrous light,
Since this same wayward girl is so reclaim'd.
                    [*Exeunt.*

SCENE III

JULIET'S *chamber.*

Enter JULIET *and* NURSE.

JULIET
Ay, those attires are best: — but, gentle nurse,
I pray thee, leave me to myself to-night;
For I have need of many orisons
To move the heavens to smile upon my state,
Which, well thou know'st, is cross and full of sin.

Enter LADY CAPULET.

LADY CAPULET
What, are you busy, ho? need you my help?
JULIET
No, madam; we have cull'd such necessaries
As are behoveful for our state to-morrow:
So please you, let me now be left alone,
And let the nurse this night sit up with you;
For, I am sure, you have your hands full all
In this so sudden business.
LADY CAPULET
           Good night:
Get thee to bed, and rest; for thou hast need.
[*Exeunt* LADY CAPULET *and* NURSE.
JULIET
Farewell! — God knows when we shall meet again.
I have a faint cold fear thrills through my veins,
That almost freezes up the heat of life:
I'll call them back again to comfort me; —
Nurse! — What should she do here?
My dismal scene I needs must act alone. —
Come, vial. —
What if this mixture do not work at all?
Must I of force be married to the county?
No, no; — this shall forbid it: — lie thou there. —
              [*Laying down her dagger.*
What if it be a poison, which the friar
Subtly hath minister'd to have me dead,
Lest in this marriage he should be dishonour'd,
Because he married me before to Romeo?
I fear it is: and yet, methinks, it should not,
For he hath still been tried a holy man. —
I will not entertain so bad a thought. —
How if, when I am laid into the tomb,
I wake before the time that Romeo
Come to redeem me? there's a fearful point!
Shall I not, then, be stifled in the vault,
To whose foul mouth no healthsome air breathes in,
And there die strangled ere my Romeo comes?
Or, if I live, is it not very like,
The horrible conceit of death and night,
Together with the terror of the place, —
As in a vault, an ancient receptacle,

Where, for this many hundred years, the bones
Of all my buried ancestors are pack'd;
Where bloody Tybalt, yet but green in earth,
Lies festering in his shroud; where, as they say,
At some hours in the night spirits resort; —
Alack, alack, is it not like that I,
So early waking, — what with loathsome smells;
And shrieks like mandrakes' torn out of the earth,
That living mortals, hearing them, run mad; —
O, if I wake, shall I not be distraught,
Environed with all these hideous fears?
And madly play with my forefathers' joints?
And pluck the mangled Tybalt from his shroud?
And, in this rage, with some great kinsman's bone,
As with a club, dash out my desperate brains? —
O, look! methinks I see my cousin's ghost
Seeking out Romeo, that did spit his body
Upon a rapier's point: — stay, Tybalt, stay! —
Romeo, I come! this do I drink to thee.
    [*She falls upon her bed within the curtains.*

SCENE IV

Hall in CAPULET'S *house.*

Enter LADY CAPULET *and* NURSE.

LADY CAPULET
Hold, take these keys, and fetch more spices, nurse.
NURSE
They call for dates and quinces in the pastry.

Enter CAPULET.

CAPULET
Come, stir, stir, stir! the second cock hath crow'd,
The curfew-bell hath rung, 'tis three o'clock: —
Look to the bak'd meats, good Angelica:
Spare not for cost.
NURSE
         Go, you cot-quean, go,
Get you to bed; faith, you'll be sick to-morrow
For this night's watching.
CAPULET
No, not a whit: what! I have watch'd ere now
All night for lesser cause, and ne'er been sick.
LADY CAPULET
Ay, you have been a mouse-hunt in your time;
But I will watch you from such watching now.
      [*Exeunt* LADY CAPULET *and* NURSE.
CAPULET
A jealous-hood, a jealous-hood!

Enter three or four SERVING-MEN *with spits, and logs, and baskets.*

               Now, fellow,
What's there?
FIRST SERVING-MAN
Things for the cook, sir; but I know not what.
CAPULET
Make haste, make haste. [*Exit* FIRST SERVING-MAN.]
  — Sirrah, fetch drier logs:
Call Peter, he will show thee where they are.
SECOND SERVING-MAN
I have a head, sir, that will find out logs,
And never trouble Peter for the matter.   [*Exit.*
CAPULET
Mass, and well said; a merry whoreson, ha!
Thou shalt be logger-head. — Good faith, 'tis day:
The county will be here with music straight,
For so he said he would: — I hear him near. —
                   [*Play music.*
Nurse! — wife! — what, ho! — what, nurse, I say!

Enter NURSE.

Go waken Juliet, go and trim her up;
I'll go and chat with Paris: — hie, make haste,
Make haste; the bridegroom he is come already:
Make haste, I say.   [*Exeunt.*

SCENE V

JULIET'S *chamber.*

Enter NURSE.

NURSE
Mistress! — what, mistress! — Juliet! — fast,
I warrant her, she: —
Why, lamb! — why, lady! — fie, you slug-a-bed! —
Why, love, I say! — madam! sweetheart! — why, bride!
What, not a word? — you take your pennyworths now;
Sleep for a week; for the next night, I warrant,
The County Paris hath set up his rest
That you shall rest but little. — God forgive me,
Marry, and amen, how sound is she asleep!

I must needs wake her. — Madam, madam, madam!
Ay, let the county take you in your bed;
He'll fright you up, i'faith. — Will it not be?
What, dress'd! and in your clothes! and down again!
I must needs wake you: — Lady! lady! lady! —
Alas, alas! — Help, help! my lady's dead! —
O, well-a-day, that ever I was born! —
Some *aqua-vitæ*, ho! — My lord! my lady!

Enter LADY CAPULET.

LADY CAPULET
What noise is here?
NURSE
         O lamentable day!
LADY CAPULET
What is the matter?
NURSE
        Look, look! O heavy day!
LADY CAPULET
O me, O me! — My child, my only life,
Revive, look up, or I will die with thee! —
Help, help! — call help.

Enter CAPULET.

CAPULET
For shame, bring Juliet forth; her lord is come.
NURSE
She's dead, deceas'd, she's dead; alack the day!
LADY CAPULET
Alack the day, she's dead, she's dead, she's dead!
CAPULET
Ha! let me see her: — out, alas! she's cold;
Her blood is settled, and her joints are stiff;
Life and these lips have long been separated:
Death lies on her like an untimely frost
Upon the sweetest flower of all the field.
NURSE
O lamentable day!
LADY CAPULET
        O woeful time!
CAPULET
Death, that hath ta'en her hence to make me wail,
Ties up my tongue, and will not let me speak.

Enter FRIAR LAURENCE *and* PARIS, *with* MUSICIANS.

FRIAR LAURENCE
Come, is the bride ready to go to church?
CAPULET
Ready to go, but never to return: —
O son, the night before thy wedding-day
Hath Death lain with thy wife: — see there she lies,
Flower as she was, deflowered by him.
Death is my son-in-law, Death is my heir;
My daughter he hath wedded: I will die,
And leave him all; life, living, all is Death's.
PARIS
Have I thought long to see this morning's face,
And doth it give me such a sight as this?
LADY CAPULET
Accurst, unhappy, wretched, hateful day!
Most miserable hour that e'er time saw
In lasting labour of his pilgrimage!
But one, poor one, one poor and loving child,
But one thing to rejoice and solace in,
And cruel Death hath catch'd it from my sight!
NURSE
O woe! O woeful, woeful, woeful day!
Most lamentable day, most woeful day,
That ever, ever, I did yet behold!
O day! O day! O day! O hateful day!
Never was seen so black a day as this:
O woeful day, O woeful day!
PARIS
Beguil'd, divorced, wronged, spited, slain!
Most detestable Death, by thee beguiled,
By cruel cruel thee quite overthrown! —
O love! O life! — not life, but love in death!
CAPULET
Despis'd, distressed, hated, martyr'd, kill'd! —
Uncomfortable time, why camest thou now
To murder, murder our solemnity? —
O child! O child! — my soul, and not my child! —
Dead art thou! — alack, my child is dead;
And with my child my joys are buried!
FRIAR LAURENCE
Peace, ho, for shame! confusion's cure lives not
In these confusions. Heaven and yourself
Had part in this fair maid; now heaven hath all,
And all the better is it for the maid:
Your part in her you could not keep from death;

But heaven keeps his part in eternal life.
The most you sought was her promotion;
For 'twas your heaven she should be advanced:
And weep ye now, seeing she is advanced
Above the clouds, as high as heaven itself?
O, in this love, you love your child so ill,
That you run mad, seeing that she is well:
She's not well married that lives married long;
But she's best married that dies married young.
Dry up your tears, and stick your rosemary
On this fair corse; and, as the custom is,
In all her best array bear her to church:
For though fond nature bids us all lament,
Yet nature's tears are reason's merriment.

CAPULET
All things that we ordained festival
Turn from their office to black funeral:
Our instruments to melancholy bells;
Our wedding cheer to a sad burial feast;
Our solemn hymns to sullen dirges change;
Our bridal flowers serve for a burial corse;
And all things change them to the contrary.

FRIAR LAURENCE
Sir, go you in, — and, madam, go with him; —
And go, Sir Paris; — every one prepare
To follow this fair corse unto her grave:
The heavens do lour upon you for some ill;
Move them no more by crossing their high will.
        [*They all, but the* NURSE *and* MUSICIANS, *go forth,*
                        casting rosemary on her.

FIRST MUSICIAN
Faith, we may put up our pipes and be gone.

NURSE
Honest good fellows, ah, put up, put up;
For, well you know, this is a pitiful case.   [*Exit.*

FIRST MUSICIAN
Ay, by my troth, the case may be amended.

            Enter PETER.

PETER
Musicians, O, musicians, 'Heart's ease, Heart's ease':
O, an you will have me live, play 'Heart's ease.'

FIRST MUSICIAN
Why 'Heart's ease'?

PETER
O, musicians, because my heart itself plays 'My heart is
full of woe': O, play me some merry dump, to comfort
me.

FIRST MUSICIAN
Not a dump we; 'tis no time to play now.

PETER
You will not, then?

FIRST MUSICIAN
No.

PETER
I will, then, give it you soundly.

FIRST MUSICIAN
What will you give us?

PETER
No money, on my faith; but the gleek, — I will give you
the minstrel.

FIRST MUSICIAN
Then will I give you the serving-creature.

PETER
Then will I lay the serving-creature's dagger on your
pate. I will carry no crotchets: I'll *re* you, I'll *fa* you; do
you note me?

FIRST MUSICIAN
An you *re* us and *fa* us, you note us.

SECOND MUSICIAN
Pray you, put up your dagger, and put out your wit.

PETER
Then have at you with my wit! I will dry-beat you with
an iron wit, and put up my iron dagger. — Answer me
like men:

        When griping grief the heart doth wound,
            And doleful dumps the mind oppress,
        Then music with her silver sound —

why 'silver sound'? why 'music with her silver sound'?
— What say you, Simon Catling?

FIRST MUSICIAN
Marry, sir, because silver hath a sweet sound.

PETER
Pretty! — What say you, Hugh Rebeck?

SECOND MUSICIAN
I say 'silver sound,' because musicians sound for silver.

PETER
Pretty too! — What say you, James Soundpost?

THIRD MUSICIAN
Faith, I know not what to say.

PETER
O, I cry you mercy; you are the singer: I will say for you.
It is 'music with her silver sound,' because such fellows
as you have seldom gold for sounding: —

        Then music with her silver sound
            With speedy help doth lend redress.
                                            [*Exit.*

FIRST MUSICIAN
What a pestilent knave is this same!

SECOND MUSICIAN
Hang him, Jack! — Come, we'll in here; tarry for the
mourners, and stay dinner.   [*Exeunt.*

ACT V

SCENE I

Mantua. A street.

Enter ROMEO.

ROMEO
If I may trust the flattering eye of sleep,
My dreams presage some joyful news at hand:
My bosom's lord sits lightly in his throne;
And all this day an unaccustom'd spirit
Lifts me above the ground with cheerful thoughts.
I dreamt my lady came and found me dead, —
Strange dream, that gives a dead man leave to think! —
And breath'd such life with kisses in my lips,
That I reviv'd, and was an emperor.
Ah me! how sweet is love itself possess'd,
When but love's shadows are so rich in joy!

        Enter BALTHASAR, *his man, booted.*

News from Verona! — How now, Balthasar!
Dost thou not bring me letters from the friar?
How doth my lady? Is my father well?
How fares my Juliet? that I ask again;
For nothing can be ill, if she be well.

BALTHASAR
Then she is well, and nothing can be ill:
Her body sleeps in Capels' monument,
And her immortal part with angels lives.
I saw her laid low in her kindred's vault,
And presently took post to tell it you:
O, pardon me for bringing these ill news,
Since you did leave it for my office, sir.

ROMEO
Is it even so? then I defy you, stars! —
Thou know'st my lodging: get me ink and paper,
And hire post-horses; I will hence to-night.

BALTHASAR
I do beseech you, sir, have patience:
Your looks are pale and wild, and do import
Some misadventure.

ROMEO
                Tush, thou art deceived:
Leave me, and do the thing I bid thee do.
Hast thou no letters to me from the friar?

BALTHASAR
No, my good lord.

ROMEO
                No matter: get thee gone,
And hire those horses; I'll be with thee straight.
                        [*Exit* BALTHASAR.
Well, Juliet, I will lie with thee to-night.
Let's see for means: — O mischief, thou art swift
To enter in the thoughts of desperate men!
I do remember an apothecary, —
And hereabouts he dwells, — which late I noted
In tatter'd weeds, with overwhelming brows,
Culling of simples; meagre were his looks,
Sharp misery had worn him to the bones:
And in his needy shop a tortoise hung,
An alligator stuff'd, and other skins
Of ill-shap'd fishes; and about his shelves

PETER   O, an you will have me live, play 'Heart's ease.'

A beggarly account of empty boxes,
Green earthen pots, bladders, and musty seeds,
Remnants of packthread, and old cakes of roses,
Were thinly scatter'd, to make up a show.
Noting this penury, to myself I said,
'An if a man did need a poison now,
Whose sale is present death in Mantua,
Here lives a caitiff wretch would sell it him.'
O, this same thought did but forerun my need;
And this same needy man must sell it me.
As I remember, this should be the house:
Being holiday, the beggar's shop is shut. —
What, ho! apothecary!

Enter APOTHECARY.

APOTHECARY

        Who calls so loud?

ROMEO

Come hither, man. — I see that thou art poor;
Hold, there is forty ducats: let me have
A dram of poison; such soon-speeding gear
As will disperse itself through all the veins,
That the life-weary taker may fall dead;
And that the trunk may be discharg'd of breath
As violently as hasty powder fired
Doth hurry from the fatal cannon's womb.

APOTHECARY

Such mortal drugs I have; but Mantua's law
Is death to any he that utters them.

ROMEO

Art thou so bare and full of wretchedness,
And fear'st to die? famine is in thy cheeks,
Need and oppression starveth in thine eyes,
Contempt and beggary hangs upon thy back,
The world is not thy friend, nor the world's law:
The world affords no law to make thee rich;
Then be not poor, but break it, and take this.

APOTHECARY

My poverty, but not my will, consents.

ROMEO

I pay thy poverty, and not thy will.

APOTHECARY

Put this in any liquid thing you will,
And drink it off; and, if you had the strength
Of twenty men, it would dispatch you straight.

ROMEO

There is thy gold; worse poison to men's souls,
Doing more murders in this loathsome world,
Than these poor compounds that thou mayst not sell:
I sell thee poison: thou hast sold me none.
Farewell: buy food, and get thyself in flesh. —
Come, cordial, and not poison, go with me
To Juliet's grave; for there must I use thee.   [*Exeunt.*

SCENE II

Verona. FRIAR LAURENCE'S *cell.*

Enter FRIAR JOHN.

FRIAR JOHN

Holy Franciscan friar! brother, ho!

Enter FRIAR LAURENCE.

FRIAR LAURENCE

This same should be the voice of Friar John. —
Welcome from Mantua: what says Romeo?
Or, if his mind be writ, give me his letter.

FRIAR JOHN

Going to find a barefoot brother out,
One of our order, to associate me,
Here in this city visiting the sick,
And finding him, the searchers of the town,
Suspecting that we both were in a house
Where the infectious pestilence did reign,
Seal'd up the doors, and would not let us forth;
So that my speed to Mantua there was stay'd.

FRIAR LAURENCE

Who bare my letter, then, to Romeo?

FRIAR JOHN

I could not send it, — here it is again, —
Nor get a messenger to bring it thee,
So fearful were they of infection.

FRIAR LAURENCE

Unhappy fortune! by my brotherhood,
The letter was not nice, but full of charge
Of dear import; and the neglecting it
May do much danger. Friar John, go hence;
Get me an iron crow, and bring it straight
Unto my cell.

FRIAR JOHN

Brother, I'll go and bring it thee.   [*Exit.*

FRIAR LAURENCE

Now must I to the monument alone;
Within this three hours will fair Juliet wake:
She will beshrew me much that Romeo
Hath had no notice of these accidents;
But I will write again to Mantua,
And keep her at my cell till Romeo come; —
Poor living corse, clos'd in a dead man's tomb!   [*Exit.*

SCENE III

The same. A churchyard; in it a monument belonging to the CAPULETS.

Enter COUNTY PARIS *and his* PAGE, *with flowers and sweet water.*

PARIS

Give me thy torch, boy; hence, and stand aloof: —
Yet put it out, for I would not be seen.
Under yond yew-trees lay thee all along,
Holding thine ear close to the hollow ground;
So shall no foot upon the churchyard tread —
Being loose, unfirm, with digging-up of graves —
But thou shalt hear it: whistle then to me,
As signal that thou hear'st something approach.
Give me those flowers. Do as I bid thee, go.

PAGE [*aside*].

I am almost afraid to stand alone
Here in the churchyard; yet I will adventure.   [*Retires.*

PARIS

Sweet flower, with flowers thy bridal bed I strew:
    [PARIS *strews the tomb with flowers.*
  O woe, thy canopy is dust and stones!
Which with sweet water nightly I will dew;
  Or, wanting that, with tears distill'd by moans:
The obsequies that I for thee will keep,
Nightly shall be to strew thy grave and weep.
    [BOY *whistles.*
The boy gives warning something doth approach.
What cursed foot wanders this way to-night,
To cross my obsequies and true love's rite?
What, with a torch! — muffle me, night, awhile.
    [*Retires.*

Enter ROMEO, *and* BALTHASAR, *with a torch, a mattock, and a crow of iron.*

ROMEO

Give me that mattock and the wrenching-iron.
Hold, take this letter; early in the morning
See thou deliver it to my lord and father.
Give me the light: upon thy life, I charge thee,
Whate'er thou hear'st or seest, stand all aloof,
And do not interrupt me in my course.
Why I descend into this bed of death,
Is partly to behold my lady's face;
But chiefly to take thence from her dead finger
A precious ring, — a ring that I must use
In dear employment: therefore hence, be gone: —
But if thou, jealous, dost return to pry
In what I further shall intend to do,
By heaven, I will tear thee joint by joint,
And strew this hungry churchyard with thy limbs:
The time and my intents are savage-wild;
More fierce and more inexorable far
Than empty tigers or the roaring sea.

BALTHASAR

I will be gone, sir, and not trouble you.

ROMEO

So shalt thou show me friendship. — Take thou that:
Live, and be prosperous: and farewell, good fellow.

BALTHASAR [*aside*].

For all this same, I'll hide me hereabout:
  His looks I fear, and his intents I doubt.   [*Retires.*

ROMEO

Thou detestable maw, thou womb of death,
Gorg'd with the dearest morsel of the earth,
Thus I enforce thy rotten jaws to open,
    [ROMEO *opens the tomb.*
And, in despite, I'll cram thee with more food!

PARIS

This is that banish'd haughty Montague
That murder'd my love's cousin, — with which grief,
It is supposed, the fair creature died, —
And here is come to do some villainous shame
To the dead bodies: I will apprehend him. —
Stop thy unhallow'd toil, vile Montague!
Can vengeance be pursued further than death?
Condemned villain, I do apprehend thee:
Obey, and go with me; for thou must die.

ROMEO

I must indeed; and therefore came I hither. —
Good gentle youth, tempt not a desperate man;

APOTHECARY Put this in any liquid thing you will, and drink it off.

Fly hence, and leave me: — think upon these gone;
Let them affright thee. — I beseech thee, youth,
Put not another sin upon my head,
By urging me to fury: — O, be gone!
By heaven, I love thee better than myself;
For I come hither arm'd against myself:
Stay not, be gone; — live, and hereafter say,
A madman's mercy bid thee run away.

PARIS
I do defy thy conjurations,
And apprehend thee for a felon here.

ROMEO
Wilt thou provoke me? then have at thee, boy!
                                        [*They fight.*

PAGE
O Lord, they fight! I will go call the watch.
                          [*Exit.* — PARIS *falls.*

PARIS
O, I am slain! — If thou be merciful,
Open the tomb, lay me with Juliet.

ROMEO
In faith, I will. — Let me peruse this face: —
Mercutio's kinsman, noble County Paris! —
What said my man, when my betossed soul
Did not attend him as we rode? I think
He told me Paris should have married Juliet:
Said he not so? or did I dream it so?
Or am I mad, hearing him talk of Juliet,
To think it was so? — O, give me thy hand,
One writ with me in sour misfortune's book!
I'll bury thee in a triumphant grave; —
A grave? O, no, a lantern, slaughter'd youth,
For here lies Juliet, and her beauty makes
This vault a feasting presence full of light.
Death, lie thou there, by a dead man interr'd.
                      [*Laying* PARIS *in the tomb.*
How oft when men are at the point of death
Have they been merry! which their keepers call
A lightning before death: O, how may I
Call this a lightning! O my love! my wife!
Death, that hath suck'd the honey of thy breath,
Hath had no power yet upon thy beauty:
Thou art not conquer'd; beauty's ensign yet
Is crimson in thy lips and in thy cheeks,
And death's pale flag is not advanced there.
Tybalt, liest thou there in thy bloody sheet?
O, what more favour can I do to thee,
Than with that hand that cut thy youth in twain
To sunder his that was thine enemy?
Forgive me, cousin! — Ah, dear Juliet,
Why art thou yet so fair? shall I believe
That unsubstantial Death is amorous;
And that the lean abhorred monster keeps
Thee here in dark to be his paramour?
For fear of that, I still will stay with thee;
And never from this palace of dim night
Depart again: here, here will I remain
With worms that are thy chamber-maids; O, here
Will I set up my everlasting rest;
And shake the yoke of inauspicious stars
From this world-wearied flesh. — Eyes, look your last!
Arms, take your last embrace! and, lips, O you
The doors of breath, seal with a righteous kiss
A dateless bargain to engrossing death! —
Come, bitter conduct, come, unsavoury guide!
Thou desperate pilot, now at once run on
The dashing rocks thy sea-sick weary bark!
Here's to my love! [*drinks*] — O true apothecary!
Thy drugs are quick. — Thus with a kiss I die.   [*Dies.*

Enter, at the other end of the churchyard, FRIAR
LAURENCE, *with a lantern, crow, and spade.*

FRIAR LAURENCE
Saint Francis be my speed! how oft to-night
Have my old feet stumbled at graves! — Who's there?

BALTHASAR
Here's one, a friend, and one that knows you well.

FRIAR LAURENCE
Bliss be upon you! Tell me, good my friend,
What torch is yond, that vainly lends his light
To grubs and eyeless skulls? as I discern,
It burneth in the Capels' monument.

BALTHASAR
It doth so, holy sir; and there's my master,
One that you love.

FRIAR LAURENCE
                    Who is it?

BALTHASAR
                              Romeo.

FRIAR LAURENCE
How long hath he been there?

BALTHASAR
                              Full half an hour.

FRIAR LAURENCE
Go with me to the vault.

BALTHASAR
                    I dare not, sir:
My master knows not but I am gone hence;
And fearfully did menace me with death,
If I did stay to look on his intents.

FRIAR LAURENCE
Stay, then; I'll go alone. — Fear comes upon me;
O, much I fear some ill unlucky thing.

BALTHASAR
As I did sleep under this yew-tree here,
I dream'd my master and another fought,
And that my master slew him.

FRIAR LAURENCE
                        Romeo! —
Alack, alack, what blood is this, which stains
              [*Stoops and looks on the blood and weapons.*
The stony entrance of this sepulchre? —
What mean these masterless and gory swords
To lie discolour'd by this place of peace?
                              [*Enters the tomb.*
Romeo! O, pale! — Who else? what, Paris too?
And steep'd in blood? — Ah, what an unkind hour
Is guilty of this lamentable chance! —
The lady stirs.   [JULIET *wakes.*

JULIET
O comfortable friar! where is my lord? —
I do remember well where I should be,
And there I am: where is my Romeo?   [*Noise within.*

FRIAR LAURENCE
I hear some noise. Lady, come from that nest
Of death, contagion, and unnatural sleep:
A greater power than we can contradict
Hath thwarted our intents: come, come away:
Thy husband in thy bosom there lies dead;
And Paris too: come, I'll dispose of thee
Among a sisterhood of holy nuns:
Stay not to question, for the watch is coming;
Come, go, good Juliet; I dare no longer stay.   [*Exit.*

JULIET
Go, get thee hence, for I will not away.
What's here? a cup, clos'd in my true love's hand?
Poison, I see, hath been his timeless end: —
O churl! drunk all, and left no friendly drop
To help me after? — I will kiss thy lips;
Haply some poison yet doth hang on them,
To make me die with a restorative.   [*Kisses him.*
Thy lips are warm!

FIRST WATCH [*within*].
Lead, boy: — which way?

JULIET
Yea, noise? — then I'll be brief. — O happy dagger!
                        [*Snatching* ROMEO'S *dagger.*
This is thy sheath; there rust, and let me die.
                              [*She stabs herself and falls.*

Enter WATCH, *with the* PAGE *of* PARIS.

PAGE
This is the place; there, where the torch doth burn.

FIRST WATCHMAN
The ground is bloody; search about the church-yard:
Go, some of you, whoe'er you find attach.
                        [*Exeunt some of the* WATCH.
Pitiful sight! here lies the county slain; —
And Juliet bleeding; warm, and newly dead,
Who here hath lain these two days buried. —
Go, tell the prince, — run to the Capulets, —
Raise up the Montagues, — some others search: —
We see the ground whereon these woes do lie;
But the true ground of all these piteous woes
We cannot without circumstance descry.

Enter some of the WATCH, *with* BALTHASAR.

SECOND WATCHMAN
Here's Romeo's man; we found him in the churchyard.

FIRST WATCHMAN
Hold him in safety, till the prince come hither.

Enter FRIAR LAURENCE, *and another* WATCHMAN.

THIRD WATCHMAN
Here is a friar, that trembles, sighs, and weeps:
We took this mattock and this spade from him,
As he was coming from this churchyard side.

FIRST WATCHMAN
A great suspicion: stay the friar too.

Enter the PRINCE *and* ATTENDANTS.

PRINCE ESCALUS
What misadventure is so early up,
That calls our person from our morning rest?

Enter old CAPULET, LADY CAPULET, *and others.*

CAPULET
What should it be, that they so shriek abroad?

LADY CAPULET
The people in the street cry 'Romeo',
Some 'Juliet', and some 'Paris'; and all run,
With open outcry, toward our monument.

PRINCE ESCALUS
What fear is this which startles in our ears?

FIRST WATCHMAN
Sovereign, here lies the County Paris slain;
And Romeo dead; and Juliet, dead before,
Warm, and new kill'd.

PRINCE ESCALUS
Search, seek, and know how this foul murder comes.

FIRST WATCHMAN
Here is a friar, and slaughter'd Romeo's man;
With instruments upon them, fit to open
These dead men's tombs.

CAPULET
O heaven! — O wife, look how our daughter bleeds!
This dagger hath mista'en, — for, lo, his house
Is empty on the back of Montague, —
And it mis-sheathed in my daughter's bosom!

LADY CAPULET
O me! this sight of death is as a bell,
That warns my old age to a sepulchre.

Enter old MONTAGUE *and others.*

PRINCE ESCALUS
Come, Montague; for thou art early up,
To see thy son and heir more early down.

MONTAGUE
Alas, my liege, my wife is dead to-night;
Grief of my son's exile hath stopp'd her breath:
What further woe conspires against mine age?

PRINCE ESCALUS
Look, and thou shalt see.

MONTAGUE
O thou untaught! what manners is in this,
To press before thy father to a grave?

PRINCE ESCALUS
Seal up the mouth of outrage for a while,
Till we can clear these ambiguities,
And know their spring, their head, their true descent;
And then will I be general of your woes,
And lead you even to death: meantime forbear,
And let mischance be slave to patience. —
Bring forth the parties of suspicion.

FRIAR LAURENCE
I am the greatest, able to do least,
Yet most suspected, as the time and place
Doth make against me, of this direful murder;
And here I stand, both to impeach and purge
Myself condemned and myself excused.

PRINCE ESCALUS
Then say at once what thou dost know in this.

FRIAR LAURENCE
I will be brief, for my short date of breath
Is not so long as is a tedious tale.
Romeo, there dead, was husband to that Juliet;
And she, there dead, that Romeo's faithful wife:
I married them; and their stol'n marriage-day
Was Tybalt's dooms-day, whose untimely death
Banish'd the new-made bridegroom from this city;
For whom, and not for Tybalt, Juliet pined.
You, to remove that siege of grief from her,
Betroth'd, and would have married she per force,
To County Paris: — then comes she to me;
And, with wild looks, bid me devise some means
To rid her from this second marriage,
Or in my cell there would she kill herself.
Then gave I her, so tutor'd by my art,
A sleeping potion; which so took effect
As I intended, for it wrought on her
The form of death: meantime I writ to Romeo,
That he should hither come as this dire night,
To help to take her from her borrow'd grave,
Being the time the potion's force should cease.
But he which bore my letter, Friar John,
Was stay'd by accident; and yesternight
Return'd my letter back. Then all alone
At the prefixed hour of her waking,
Came I to take her from her kindred's vault;
Meaning to keep her closely at my cell

Till I conveniently could send to Romeo:
But when I came, — some minute ere the time
Of her awaking, — here untimely lay
The noble Paris and true Romeo dead.
She wakes; and I entreated her come forth,
And bear this work of heaven with patience:
But then a noise did scare me from the tomb;
And she, too desperate, would not go with me,
But, as it seems, did violence on herself.
All this I know; and to the marriage
Her nurse is privy: and, if aught in this
Miscarried by my fault, let my old life
Be sacrific'd, some hour before his time,
Unto the rigour of severest law.

PRINCE ESCALUS
We still have known thee for a holy man. —
Where's Romeo's man? what can he say in this?

BALTHASAR
I brought my master news of Juliet's death;
And then in post he came from Mantua
To this same place, to this same monument.
This letter he early bid me give his father;

And threaten'd me with death, going in the vault,
If I departed not, and left him there.

PRINCE ESCALUS
Give me the letter, — I will look on it. —
Where is the county's page, that rais'd the watch? —
Sirrah, what made your master in this place?

PAGE
He came with flowers to strew his lady's grave;
And bid me stand aloof, and so I did:
Anon comes one with light to ope the tomb;
And by and by my master drew on him;
And then I ran away to call the watch.

PRINCE ESCALUS
This letter doth make good the friar's words,
Their course of love, the tidings of her death:
And here he writes that he did buy a poison
Of a poor pothecary, and therewithal
Came to this vault to die, and lie with Juliet.
Where be these enemies? Capulet, Montague,
See, what a scourge is laid upon your hate,
That heaven finds means to kill your joys with love!
And I, for winking at your discords too,
Have lost a brace of kinsmen: all are punish'd.

CAPULET
O brother Montague, give me thy hand:
This is my daughter's jointure, for no more
Can I demand.

MONTAGUE
But I can give thee more:
For I will raise her statue in pure gold;
That while Verona by that name is known,
There shall no figure at such rate be set
As that of true and faithful Juliet.

CAPULET
As rich shall Romeo by his lady lie;
Poor sacrifices of our enmity!

PRINCE ESCALUS
A glooming peace this morning with it brings;
The sun, for sorrow, will not show his head:
Go hence, to have more talk of these sad things;
Some shall be pardon'd, and some punished:
For never was a story of more woe
Than this of Juliet and her Romeo.   [*Exeunt.*

A MIDSUMMER NIGHT'S DREAM

DRAMATIS PERSONAE

THESEUS, *Duke of Athens.*
EGEUS, *father to Hermia.*
LYSANDER, } *in love with Hermia.*
DEMETRIUS, }
PHILOSTRATE, *master of the revels to Theseus.*
QUINCE, *a carpenter.*
SNUG, *a joiner.*
BOTTOM, *a weaver.*
FLUTE, *a bellows-mender.*
SNOUT, *a tinker.*
STARVELING, *a tailor.*

HIPPOLYTA, *queen of the Amazons, betrothed to Theseus.*
HERMIA, *daughter to Egeus, in love with Lysander.*
HELENA, *in love with Demetrius.*
OBERON, *king of the fairies.*
TITANIA, *queen of the fairies.*
PUCK, *or Robin Goodfellow.*
PEAS-BLOSSOM, }
COBWEB, }
MOTH, } *fairies.*
MUSTARD-SEED, }

PYRAMUS, }
THISBE, }
WALL, } *characters in the interlude*
MOONSHINE, } *perform'd by the Clowns.*
LION, }

Other FAIRIES *attending their* KING *and* QUEEN.
ATTENDANTS *on* THESEUS *and* HIPPOLYTA.

SCENE — *Athens, and a wood near it.*

HIPPOLYTA Four nights will quickly dream away the time.

ACT I

SCENE I

Athens. The palace of THESEUS.

Enter THESEUS, HIPPOLYTA, PHILOSTRATE, *and* ATTENDANTS.

THESEUS
Now, fair Hippolyta, our nuptial hour
Draws on apace; four happy days bring in
Another moon: but, O, methinks, how slow
This old moon wanes! she lingers my desires
Like to a step-dame, or a dowager,
Long withering out a young man's revenue.

HIPPOLYTA
Four days will quickly steep themselves in night;
Four nights will quickly dream away the time;
And then the moon, like to a silver bow
New-bent in heaven, shall behold the night
Of our solemnities.

THESEUS
                    Go, Philostrate,

Stir up the Athenian youth to merriments;
Awake the pert and nimble spirit of mirth:
Turn melancholy forth to funerals, —
The pale companion is not for our pomp.
                    [*Exit* PHILOSTRATE.
Hippolyta, I woo'd thee with my sword,
And won thy love, doing thee injuries;
But I will wed thee in another key,
With pomp, with triumph, and with revelling.

Enter EGEUS *and his daughter* HERMIA, LYSANDER, *and* DEMETRIUS.

EGEUS
Happy be Theseus, our renowned duke!

THESEUS
Thanks, good Egeus: what's the news with thee?

EGEUS
Full of vexation come I, with complaint
Against my child, my daughter Hermia.
Stand forth, Demetrius. My noble lord,
This man hath my consent to marry her.
Stand forth, Lysander: and, my gracious duke,
This hath bewitch'd the bosom of my child: —
Thou, thou, Lysander, thou hast given her rimes,

And interchang'd love-tokens with my child:
Thou hast by moonlight at her window sung,
With feigning voice, verses of feigning love;
And stol'n the impression of her fantasy
With bracelets of thy hair, rings, gauds, conceits,
Knacks, trifles, nosegays, sweetmeats, — messengers
Of strong prevailment in unharden'd youth:
With cunning hast thou filch'd my daughter's heart;
Turn'd her obedience, which is due to me,
To stubborn harshness: — and, my gracious duke,
Be it so she will not here before your Grace
Consent to marry with Demetrius,
I beg the ancient privilege of Athens, —
As she is mine, I may dispose of her:
Which shall be either to this gentleman
Or to her death, according to our law
Immediately provided in that case.

THESEUS
What say you, Hermia? be advis'd, fair maid:
To you your father should be as a god;
One that compos'd your beauties; yea, and one
To whom you are but as a form in wax,
By him imprinted, and within his power
To leave the figure, or disfigure it.
Demetrius is a worthy gentleman.

HERMIA
So is Lysander.

THESEUS
                    In himself he is;
But in this kind, wanting your father's voice,
The other must be held the worthier.

HERMIA
I would my father look'd but with my eyes.

THESEUS
Rather your eyes must with his judgement look.

HERMIA
I do entreat your Grace to pardon me.
I know not by what power I am made bold,
Nor how it may concern my modesty,
In such a presence here to plead my thoughts;
But I beseech your Grace that I may know
The worst that may befall me in this case,
If I refuse to wed Demetrius.

THESEUS
Either to die the death, or to abjure
For ever the society of men.
Therefore, fair Hermia, question your desires;
Know of your youth, examine well your blood,
Whether, if you yield not to your father's choice,
You can endure the livery of a nun;
For aye to be in shady cloister mew'd,
To live a barren sister all your life,
Chanting faint hymns to the cold fruitless moon.
Thrice-blessed they that master so their blood,
To undergo such maiden pilgrimage;
But earthlier-happy is the rose distill'd
Than that which, withering on the virgin thorn,
Grows, lives, and dies in single blessedness.

HERMIA
So will I grow, so live, so die, my lord,
Ere I will yield my virgin patent up
Unto his lordship, whose unwished yoke
My soul consents not to give sovereignty.

THESEUS
Take time to pause; and, by the next new moon, —
The sealing-day betwixt my love and me,
For everlasting bond of fellowship, —
Upon that day either prepare to die
For disobedience to your father's will,

Or else to wed Demetrius, as he would;
Or on Diana's altar to protest
For aye austerity and single life.

DEMETRIUS
Relent, sweet Hermia: — and, Lysander, yield
Thy crazed title to my certain right.

LYSANDER
You have her father's love, Demetrius;
Let me have Hermia's: do you marry him.

EGEUS
Scornful Lysander! true, he hath my love, —
And what is mine my love shall render him;
And she is mine, — and all my right of her
I do estate unto Demetrius.

LYSANDER
I am, my lord, as well deriv'd as he,
As well possess'd; my love is more than his;
My fortunes every way as fairly rank'd,
If not with vantage, as Demetrius';
And, which is more than all these boasts can be,
I am belov'd of beauteous Hermia:
Why should not I, then, prosecute my right?
Demetrius, I'll avouch it to his head,
Made love to Nedar's daughter, Helena,
And won her soul; and she, sweet lady, dotes,
Devoutly dotes, dotes in idolatry,
Upon this spotted and inconstant man.

THESEUS
I must confess that I have heard so much,
And with Demetrius thought to have spoke thereof;
But, being over-full of self-affairs,
My mind did lose it. But, Demetrius, come;
And come, Egeus; you shall go with me,
I have some private schooling for you both.
For you, fair Hermia, look you arm yourself
To fit your fancies to your father's will;
Or else the law of Athens yields you up —
Which by no means we may extenuate —
To death, or to a vow of single life.
Come, my Hippolyta: what cheer, my love?
Demetrius, and Egeus, go along:
I must employ you in some business
Against our nuptial; and confer with you
Of something nearly that concerns yourselves.

EGEUS
With duty and desire we follow you.

[*Exeunt* THESEUS, HIPPOLYTA, EGEUS,
DEMETRIUS, *and* TRAIN.

LYSANDER
How now, my love! why is your cheek so pale?
How chance the roses there do fade so fast?

HERMIA
Belike for want of rain, which I could well
Beteem them from the tempest of my eyes.

LYSANDER
Ay me! for aught that I could ever read,
Could ever hear by tale or history,
The course of true love never did run smooth;
But, either it was different in blood, —

HERMIA
O cross! too high to be enthrall'd to low!

LYSANDER
Or else misgraffed in respect of years, —

HERMIA
O spite! too old to be engag'd to young!

LYSANDER
Or else it stood upon the choice of friends, —

HERMIA
O hell! to choose love by another's eyes!

LYSANDER
Or, if there were a sympathy in choice,
War, death, or sickness did lay siege to it,
Making it momentany as a sound,
Swift as a shadow, short as any dream;
Brief as the lightning in the collied night,
That, in a spleen, unfolds both heaven and earth,
And ere a man hath power to say, 'Behold!'
The jaws of darkness do devour it up:
So quick bright things come to confusion.

HERMIA
If, then, true lovers have been ever cross'd,
It stands as an edict in destiny:
Then let us teach our trial patience,
Because it is a customary cross,
As due to love as thoughts, and dreams, and sighs,
Wishes, and tears, poor fancy's followers.

LYSANDER
A good persuasion: therefore, hear me, Hermia.
I have a widow aunt, a dowager
Of great revenue, and she hath no child:

From Athens is her house remote seven leagues;
And she respects me as her only son.
There, gentle Hermia, may I marry thee;
And to that place the sharp Athenian law
Cannot pursue us. If thou lovest me, then,
Steal forth thy father's house to-morrow night;
And in the wood, a league without the town,
Where I did meet thee once with Helena,
To do observance to a morn of May,
There will I stay for thee.

HERMIA
My good Lysander!
I swear to thee, by Cupid's strongest bow,
By his best arrow with the golden head,
By the simplicity of Venus' doves,
By that which knitteth souls and prospers loves,
And by that fire which burnt the Carthage queen,
When the false Troyan under sail was seen;
By all the vows that ever men have broke,
In number more than ever women spoke; —
In that same place thou hast appointed me,
To-morrow truly will I meet with thee.

LYSANDER
Keep promise, love. Look, here comes Helena.

Enter HELENA.

HERMIA
God speed fair Helena! whither away?

HELENA
Call you me fair? that fair again unsay.
Demetrius loves your fair: O happy fair!
Your eyes are lode-stars; and your tongue's sweet air
More tuneable than lark to shepherd's ear,
When wheat is green, when hawthorn buds appear.
Sickness is catching: O, were favour so,
Yours would I catch, fair Hermia! ere I go,
My hair should catch your hair, my eye your eye,
My tongue should catch your tongue's sweet melody.
Were the world mine, Demetrius being bated,
The rest I'd give to be to you translated.
O, teach me how you look; and with what art
You sway the motion of Demetrius' heart!

HERMIA
I frown upon him, yet he loves me still.

HELENA
O, that your frowns would teach my smiles such skill!

HERMIA
I give him curses, yet he gives me love.

HELENA
O, that my prayers could such affection move!

HERMIA
The more I hate, the more he follows me.

HELENA
The more I love, the more he hateth me.

HERMIA
His folly, Helena, is no fault of mine.

HELENA
None, but your beauty: would that fault were mine!

HERMIA
Take comfort: he no more shall see my face;
Lysander and myself will fly this place.
Before the time I did Lysander see,
Seem'd Athens as a paradise to me:
O, then, what graces in my love do dwell,
That he hath turn'd a heaven unto a hell!

LYSANDER
Helen, to you our minds we will unfold:
To-morrow night, when Phœbe doth behold
Her silver visage in the watery glass,
Decking with liquid pearl the bladed grass, —
A time that lovers' flights doth still conceal, —
Through Athens' gates have we devis'd to steal.

HERMIA
And in the wood, where often you and I
Upon faint primrose-beds were wont to lie,
Emptying our bosoms of their counsel sweet,
There my Lysander and myself shall meet;
And thence from Athens turn away our eyes,
To seek new friends and stranger companies.
Farewell, sweet playfellow: pray thou for us;
And good luck grant thee thy Demetrius! —
Keep word, Lysander: we must starve our sight
From lovers' food till morrow deep midnight.

LYSANDER
I will, my Hermia. [*Exit* HERMIA.
Helena, adieu:
As you on him, Demetrius dote on you! [*Exit.*

HELENA
How happy some o'er other-some can be!
Through Athens I am thought as fair as she.

But what of that? Demetrius thinks not so;
He will not know what all but he do know:
And as he errs, doting on Hermia's eyes,
So I, admiring of his qualities.
Things base and vile, holding no quantity,
Love can transpose to form and dignity:
Love looks not with the eyes, but with the mind;
And therefore is wing'd Cupid painted blind:
Nor hath love's mind of any judgement taste;
Wings, and no eyes, figure unheedy haste:
And therefore is Love said to be a child,
Because in choice he is so oft beguil'd.
As waggish boys in game themselves forswear,
So the boy Love is perjur'd every where:
For ere Demetrius look'd on Hermia's eyne,
He hail'd down oaths that he was only mine;
And when this hail some heat from Hermia's felt,
So he dissolv'd, and showers of oaths did melt.
I will go tell him of fair Hermia's flight:
Then to the wood will he to-morrow night
Pursue her; and for this intelligence
If I have thanks, it is a dear expense:
But herein mean I to enrich my pain,
To have his sight thither and back again. [*Exit.*

SCENE II

The same. A room in QUINCE'S *house.*

Enter QUINCE *the carpenter,* SNUG *the joiner,*
BOTTOM *the weaver,* FLUTE *the bellows-mender,*
SNOUT *the tinker, and* STARVELING *the tailor.*

QUINCE
Is all our company here?

BOTTOM
You were best to call them generally, man by man,
according to the scrip.

QUINCE
Here is the scroll of every man's name, which is
thought fit, through all Athens, to play in our interlude
before the duke and the duchess on his wedding-day at
night.

BOTTOM
First, good Peter Quince, say what the play treats on;
then read the names of the actors; and so grow to a
point.

QUINCE
Marry, our play is *The most lamentable comedy and most
cruel death of Pyramus and Thisby.*

BOTTOM
A very good piece of work, I assure you, and a merry. —
Now, good Peter Quince, call forth your actors by the
scroll. — Masters, spread yourselves.

QUINCE
Answer as I call you. — Nick Bottom the weaver.

BOTTOM
Ready. Name what part I am for, and proceed.

QUINCE
You, Nick Bottom, are set down for Pyramus.

BOTTOM
What is Pyramus? a lover, or a tyrant?

QUINCE
A lover, that kills himself most gallant for love.

BOTTOM
That will ask some tears in the true performing of it:
if I do it, let the audience look to their eyes; I will
move storms, I will condole in some measure. To the
rest: yet my chief humour is for a tyrant: I could play
Ercles rarely, or a part to tear a cat in, to make all
split.

> The raging rocks
> And shivering shocks
> Shall break the locks
> Of prison-gates;
> And Phibbus' car
> Shall shine from far,
> And make and mar
> The foolish Fates.

This was lofty! — Now name the rest of the players. —
This is Ercles' vein, a tyrant's vein; — a lover is more
condoling.

QUINCE
Francis Flute the bellows-mender.

FLUTE
Here, Peter Quince.

QUINCE
You must take Thisby on you.

FLUTE
What is Thisby? a wandering knight?

QUINCE Here is the scroll of every man's name.

QUINCE
It is the lady that Pyramus must love.

FLUTE
Nay, faith, let not me play a woman; I have a beard coming.

QUINCE
That's all one: you shall play it in a mask, and you may speak as small as you will.

BOTTOM
An I may hide my face, let me play Thisby too: I'll speak in a monstrous little voice; — 'Thisne, Thisne,' — 'Ah, Pyramus, my lover dear! thy Thisby dear, and lady dear!'

QUINCE
No, no; you must play Pyramus: — and, Flute, you Thisby.

BOTTOM
Well, proceed.

QUINCE
Robin Starveling the tailor.

STARVELING
Here, Peter Quince.

QUINCE
Robin Starveling, you must play Thisby's mother. — Tom Snout the tinker.

SNOUT
Here, Peter Quince.

QUINCE
You, Pyramus' father; myself, Thisby's father; — Snug the joiner, you, the lion's part: — and, I hope, here is a play fitted.

SNUG
Have you the lion's part written? pray you, if it be, give it me, for I am slow of study.

QUINCE
You may do it extempore, for it is nothing but roaring.

BOTTOM
Let me play the lion too: I will roar, that I will do any man's heart good to hear me; I will roar, that I will make the duke say, 'Let him roar again, let him roar again.'

QUINCE
An you should do it too terribly, you would fright the duchess and the ladies, that they would shriek; and that were enough to hang us all.

ALL
That would hang us, every mother's son.

BOTTOM
I grant you, friends, if you should fright the ladies out of their wits, they would have no more discretion but to hang us: but I will aggravate my voice so, that I will roar you as gently as any sucking dove; I will roar you an'twere any nightingale.

QUINCE
You can play no part but Pyramus; for Pyramus is a sweet-faced man; a proper man as one shall see in a summer's day; a most lovely, gentleman-like man: therefore you must needs play Pyramus.

BOTTOM
Well, I will undertake it. What beard were I best to play it in?

QUINCE
Why, what you will.

BOTTOM
I will discharge it in either your straw-colour beard, your orange-tawny beard, your purple-in-grain beard, or your French-crown-colour beard, your perfect yellow.

QUINCE
Some of your French crowns have no hair at all, and then you will play barefaced. — But, masters, here are your parts: and I am to entreat you, request you, and desire you, to con them by to-morrow night; and meet me in the palace-wood, a mile without the town, by moonlight: there will we rehearse, for if we meet in the city, we shall be dogg'd with company, and our devices known. In the mean time I will draw a bill of properties, such as our play wants. I pray you, fail me not.

BOTTOM
We will meet; and there we may rehearse most obscenely and courageously.

QUINCE
Take pains; be perfit: adieu. At the duke's oak we meet.

BOTTOM
Enough; hold, or cut bow-strings.   [*Exeunt.*

ACT II

SCENE I

A wood near Athens.

Enter a FAIRY *at one door and* PUCK *at another.*

PUCK
How now, spirit! whither wander you?

FAIRY
        Over hill, over dale,

PUCK How now, spirit! whither wander you?

FAIRY Are you not he, that frights the maidens of the villagery.

Thorough bush, thorough brier,
Over park, over pale,
   Thorough flood, thorough fire,
I do wander every where,
Swifter than the moon's sphere;
And I serve the fairy queen,
To dew her orbs upon the green.
The cowslips tall her pensioners be:
In their gold coats spots you see;
Those be rubies, fairy favours,
In those freckles live their savours:
I must go seek some dewdrops here,
And hang a pearl in every cowslip's ear.
Farewell, thou lob of spirits; I'll be gone:
Our queen and all her elves come here anon.

PUCK
The king doth keep his revels here to-night:
Take heed the queen come not within his sight;
For Oberon is passing fell and wrath,
Because that she, as her attendant, hath
A lovely boy, stol'n from an Indian king;
She never had so sweet a changeling:
And jealous Oberon would have the child
Knight of his train, to trace the forests wild;
But she perforce withholds the loved boy,
Crowns him with flowers, and makes him all her joy:
And now they never meet in grove or green,
By fountain clear or spangled starlight sheen,
But they do square, that all their elves, for fear,
Creep into acorn-cups, and hide them there.

FAIRY
Either I mistake your shape and making quite,
Or else you are that shrewd and knavish sprite
Call'd Robin Goodfellow: are you not he
That frights the maidens of the villagery;
Skim milk, and sometimes labour in the quern,
And bootless make the breathless housewife churn;
And sometime make the drink to bear no barm;
Mislead night-wanderers, laughing at their harm?
Those that Hobgoblin call you, and sweet Puck,
You do their work, and they shall have good luck:
Are not you he?

PUCK
       Thou speak'st aright;
I am that merry wanderer of the night,
I jest to Oberon, and make him smile,
When I a fat and bean-fed horse beguile,
Neighing in likeness of a filly foal:
And sometime lurk I in a gossip's bowl,
In very likeness of a roasted crab;
And when she drinks, against her lips I bob,
And on her wither'd dewlap pour the ale.
The wisest aunt, telling the saddest tale,
Sometime for three-foot stool mistaketh me;
Then slip I from her bum, down topples she,
And 'tailor' cries, and falls into a cough;
And then the whole quire hold their hips and loff,
And waxen in their mirth, and neeze, and swear
A merrier hour was never wasted there. —
But room, fairy! here comes Oberon.

FAIRY
And here my mistress, — Would that he were gone!
Enter OBERON, *at one door, with his* TRAIN, *and*
TITANIA, *at another, with hers.*

OBERON
Ill met by moonlight, proud Titania.

TITANIA
What, jealous Oberon! — Fairies, skip hence:
I have forsworn his bed and company.

OBERON
Tarry, rash wanton: am not I thy lord?

TITANIA
Then I must be thy lady: but I know
When thou hast stol'n away from fairy-land,
And in the shape of Corin sat all day,
Playing on pipes of corn, and versing love
To amorous Phyllida. Why art thou here,
Come from the furthest steep of India,
But that, forsooth, the bouncing Amazon,
Your buskin'd mistress and your warrior love,
To Theseus must be wedded? and you come
To give their bed joy and prosperity.

OBERON
How canst thou thus, for shame, Titania,
Glance at my credit with Hippolyta,
Knowing I know thy love to Theseus?
Didst thou not lead him through the glimmering night
From Perigenia, whom he ravished?

And make him with fair Aegle break his faith,
With Ariadne and Antiopa?

TITANIA
These are the forgeries of jealousy:
And never, since the middle summer's spring,
Met we on hill, in dale, forest, or mead,
By paved fountain or by rushy brook,
Or in the beached margent of the sea,
To dance our ringlets to the whistling wind,
But with thy brawls thou hast disturb'd our sport.
Therefore the winds, piping to us in vain,
As in revenge, have suck'd up from the sea
Contagious fogs; which falling in the land,
Hath every pelting river made so proud,
That they have overborne their continents:
The ox hath therefore stretch'd his yoke in vain,
The ploughman lost his sweat; and the green corn
Hath rotted ere his youth attain'd a beard:
The fold stands empty in the drowned field,
And crows are fatted with the murrion flock;
The nine-men's-morris is fill'd up with mud;
And the quaint mazes in the wanton green,
For lack of tread, are undistinguishable:
The human mortals want their winter cheer;
No night is now with hymn or carol blest: —
Therefore the moon, the governess of floods,
Pale in her anger, washes all the air,
That rheumatic diseases do abound:
And thorough this distemperature we see
The seasons alter: hoary-headed frosts
Fall in the fresh lap of the crimson rose;
And on old Hiems' chin and icy crown
An odorous chaplet of sweet summer buds
Is, as in mockery, set: the spring, the summer,
The childing autumn, angry winter, change
Their wonted liveries; and the mazed world,
By their increase, now knows not which is which:
And this same progeny of evils comes
From our debate, from our dissension;
We are their parents and original.

OBERON
Do you amend it, then; it lies in you:
Why should Titania cross her Oberon?
I do but beg a little changeling boy,
To be my henchman.

TITANIA
       Set your heart at rest:
The fairy-land buys not the child of me.
His mother was a vot'ress of my order:
And, in the spiced Indian air, by night,
Full often hath she gossip'd by my side;
And sat with me on Neptune's yellow sands,
Marking th'embarked traders on the flood;
When we have laugh'd to see the sails conceive
And grow big-bellied with the wanton wind;
Which she, with pretty and with swimming gait
Following, — her womb then rich with my young
   squire, —
Would imitate, and sail upon the land,
To fetch me trifles, and return again,

FAIRY Mislead night-wanderers.

As from a voyage, rich with merchandise.
But she, being mortal, of that boy did die;
And for her sake do I rear up her boy;
And for her sake I will not part with him.

OBERON
How long within this wood intend you stay?

TITANIA
Perchance till after Theseus' wedding-day.
If you will patiently dance in our round,
And see our moonlight revels, go with us;
If not, shun me, and I will spare your haunts.

OBERON
Give me that boy, and I will go with thee.

TITANIA
Not for thy fairy kingdom. — Fairies, away!
We shall chide downright, if I longer stay.
[*Exit* TITANIA *with her* TRAIN.

OBERON
Well, go thy way: thou shalt not from this grove
Till I torment thee for this injury. —
My gentle Puck, come hither. Thou remember'st
Since once I sat upon a promontory,
And heard a mermaid, on a dolphin's back,
Uttering such dulcet and harmonious breath,
That the rude sea grew civil at her song,
And certain stars shot madly from their spheres,
To hear the sea-maid's music.

PUCK
                                    I remember.

OBERON
That very time I saw — but thou couldst not —
Flying between the cold moon and the earth,
Cupid all arm'd: a certain aim he took
At a fair vestal throned by the west,
And loos'd his love-shaft smartly from his bow,
As it should pierce a hundred-thousand hearts:
But I might see young Cupid's fiery shaft
Quench'd in the chaste beams of the watery moon,
And the imperial vot'ress passed on,
In maiden meditation, fancy-free,
Yet mark'd I where the bolt of Cupid fell:
It fell upon a little western flower,
Before milk-white, now purple with love's wound,
And maidens call it love-in-idleness.
Fetch me that flower; the herb I shew'd thee once:
The juice of it on sleeping eyelids laid
Will make or man or woman madly dote
Upon the next live creature that it sees.
Fetch me this herb; and be thou here again
Ere the leviathan can swim a league.

PUCK
I'll put a girdle round about the earth
In forty minutes.   [*Exit.*

OBERON
                    Having once this juice,
I'll watch Titania when she is asleep,
And drop the liquor of it in her eyes.
The next thing then she waking looks upon, —
Be it on lion, bear, or wolf, or bull,
On meddling monkey or on busy ape, —
She shall pursue it with the soul of love:
And ere I take this charm off from her sight,
As I can take it with another herb,
I'll make her render up her page to me.
But who comes here? I am invisible;
And I will overhear their conference.

Enter DEMETRIUS, HELENA *following him.*

DEMETRIUS
I love thee not, therefore pursue me not.
Where is Lysander and fair Hermia?
The one I'll slay, the other slayeth me.
Thou told'st me they were stol'n unto this wood;
And here am I, and wood within this wood,
Because I cannot meet my Hermia.
Hence, get thee gone, and follow me no more.

HELENA
You draw me, you hard-hearted adamant;
But yet you draw not iron, for my heart
Is true as steel: leave you your power to draw,
And I shall have no power to follow you.

DEMETRIUS
Do I entice you? do I speak you fair?
Or, rather, do I not in plainest truth
Tell you I do not nor I cannot love you?

HELENA
And even for that do I love you the more.
I am your spaniel; and, Demetrius,
The more you beat me, I will fawn on you:
Use me but as your spaniel, spurn me, strike me,
Neglect me, lose me; only give me leave,

Unworthy as I am, to follow you.
What worser place can I beg in your love, —
And yet a place of high respect with me, —
Than to be used as you use your dog?

DEMETRIUS
Tempt not too much the hatred of my spirit;
For I am sick when I do look on thee.

HELENA
And I am sick when I look not on you.

DEMETRIUS
You do impeach your modesty too much,
To leave the city, and commit yourself
Into the hands of one that loves you not;
To trust the opportunity of night,
And the ill counsel of a desert place,
With the rich worth of your virginity.

HELENA
Your virtue is my privilege: for that
It is not night when I do see your face,
Therefore I think I am not in the night;
Nor doth this wood lack worlds of company,
For you in my respect are all the world:
Then how can it be said I am alone,
When all the world is here to look on me?

DEMETRIUS
I'll run from thee and hide me in the brakes,
And leave thee to the mercy of wild-beasts.

HELENA
The wildest hath not such a heart as you.
Run when you will, the story shall be chang'd, —
Apollo flies, and Daphne holds the chase;
The dove pursues the griffin; the mild hind
Makes speed to catch the tiger, — bootless speed,
When cowardice pursues, and valour flies!

DEMETRIUS
I will not stay thy questions; let me go:
Or, if thou follow me, do not believe
But I shall do thee mischief in the wood.

HELENA
Ay, in the temple, in the town, the field,
You do me mischief. Fie, Demetrius!
Your wrongs do set a scandal on my sex:
We cannot fight for love, as men may do;
We should be woo'd, and were not made to woo.
I'll follow thee, and make a heaven of hell,
To die upon the hand I love so well.
[*Exeunt* DEMETRIUS *and* HELENA.

OBERON
Fare thee well, nymph: ere he do leave this grove,
Thou shalt fly him, and he shall seek thy love.
Enter PUCK.
Hast thou the flower there? Welcome, wanderer.

PUCK
Ay, there it is.

OBERON
                    I pray thee, give it me.
I know a bank where the wild thyme blows,
Where oxlips and the nodding violet grows;
Quite over-canopied with lush woodbine,
With sweet musk-roses, and with eglantine:
There sleeps Titania sometime of the night,
Lull'd in these flowers with dances and delight;
And there the snake throws her enamell'd skin,
Weed wide enough to wrap a fairy in:
And with the juice of this I'll streak her eyes,
And make her full of hateful fantasies.
Take thou some of it, and seek through this grove:
A sweet Athenian lady is in love
With a disdainful youth: anoint his eyes;
But do it when the next thing he espies
May be the lady: thou shalt know the man
By the Athenian garments he hath on.
Effect it with some care, that he may prove
More fond on her than she upon her love:
And look thou meet me ere the first cock crow.

PUCK
Fear not, my lord, your servant shall do so. [*Exeunt.*

SCENE II

Another part of the wood.

Enter TITANIA, *with her* TRAIN.

TITANIA
Come, now a roundel and a fairy song;
Then, for the third part of a minute, hence; —
Some, to kill cankers in the musk-rose buds;
Some, war with rere-mice for their leathern wings,
To make my small elves coats; and some, keep back
The clamorous owl, that nightly hoots and wonders
At our quaint spirits. Sing me now asleep;

Then to your offices, and let me rest.
                    Song.
FIRST FAIRY
        You spotted snakes with double tongue,
            Thorny hedgehogs, be not seen;
        Newts and blind-worms, do no wrong,
            Come not near our fairy queen.
                Chorus.
        Philomel, with melody
        Sing in our sweet lullaby;
        Lulla, lulla, lullaby; lulla, lulla, lullaby:
                Never harm,
                Nor spell nor charm,
            Come our lovely lady nigh;
        So, good night, with lullaby.

SECOND FAIRY
        Weaving spiders, come not here;
            Hence, you long-legg'd spinners, hence!
        Beetles black, approach not near;
            Worm nor snail, do no offence.
                Chorus.
        Philomel, with melody, *etc.*
FIRST FAIRY
Hence, away! now all is well:
One aloof stand sentinel.
        [*Exeunt* FAIRIES. TITANIA *sleeps.*

Enter OBERON.

OBERON
What thou see'st when thou dost wake,
        [*Squeezes the flower on* TITANIA'S *eyelids.*
Do it for thy true-love take;
Love and languish for his sake:
Be it ounce, or cat, or bear,
Pard, or boar with bristled hair,
In thy eye that shall appear
When thou wakest, it is thy dear:
Wake when some vile thing is near.   [*Exit.*
Enter LYSANDER *and* HERMIA.

LYSANDER
Fair love, you faint with wandering in the wood;
    And to speak troth, I have forgot our way:
We'll rest us, Hermia, if you think it good,
    And tarry for the comfort of the day.

HERMIA
Be it so, Lysander: find you out a bed;
For I upon this bank will rest my head.

LYSANDER
One turf shall serve as pillow for us both;
One heart, one bed, two bosoms, and one troth.

HERMIA
Nay, good Lysander; for my sake, my dear,
Lie further off yet, do not lie so near.

LYSANDER
O, take the sense, sweet, of my innocence!
Love takes the meaning in love's conference.
I mean, that my heart unto yours is knit,
So that but one heart we can make of it:
Two bosoms interchained with an oath;
So then two bosoms and a single troth.
Then by your side no bed-room me deny;
For lying so, Hermia, I do not lie.

HERMIA
Lysander riddles very prettily: —
Now much beshrew my manners and my pride,
If Hermia meant to say Lysander lied.
But, gentle friend, for love and courtesy
Lie further off; in human modesty,
Such separation as may well be said
Becomes a virtuous bachelor and a maid,
So far be distant; and, good night, sweet friend:
Thy love ne'er alter till thy sweet life end!

LYSANDER
Amen, amen, to that fair prayer, say I;
And then end life when I end loyalty!
Here is my bed: sleep give thee all his rest!

HERMIA
With half that wish the wisher's eyes be press'd!
                                [*They sleep.*

Enter PUCK.

PUCK
        Through the forest have I gone,
        But Athenian found I none,
        On whose eyes I might approve
        This flower's force in stirring love.
        Night and silence! who is here?
        Weeds of Athens he doth wear:

This is he my master said
Despised the Athenian maid;
And here the maiden, sleeping sound,
On the dank and dirty ground: —
Pretty soul! she durst not lie
Near this lack-love, this kill-court'sy.
Churl, upon thy eyes I throw
    [*Squeezes the flower on* LYSANDER'S *eyelids.*
All the power this charm doth owe.
When thou wakest, let love forbid
Sleep his seat on thy eyelid:
So awake when I am gone;
For I must now to Oberon.   [*Exit.*
  Enter DEMETRIUS *and* HELENA, *running.*

HELENA
Stay, though thou kill me, sweet Demetrius.
DEMETRIUS
I charge thee, hence, and do not haunt me thus.
HELENA
O, wilt thou darkling leave me? do not so.
DEMETRIUS
Stay, on thy peril: I alone will go.   [*Exit.*
HELENA
O, I am out of breath in this fond chase!
The more my prayer, the lesser is my grace.
Happy is Hermia, wheresoe'er she lies;
For she hath blessed and attractive eyes.
How came her eyes so bright? Not with salt tears:
If so, my eyes are oftener wash'd than hers.
No, no, I am as ugly as a bear;
For beasts that meet me run away for fear:
Therefore no marvel though Demetrius
Do, as a monster, fly my presence thus.
What wicked and dissembling glass of mine
Made me compare with Hermia's sphery eyne? —
But who is here? — Lysander! on the ground!
Dead? or asleep? — I see no blood, no wound. —
Lysander, if you live, good sir, awake.
LYSANDER [*starting up*].
And run through fire I will for thy sweet sake.
Transparent Helena! Nature shows art,
That through thy bosom makes me see thy heart.
Where is Demetrius? O, how fit a word
Is that vile name to perish on my sword!
HELENA
Do not say so, Lysander; say not so.
What though he love your Hermia? Lord, what though?
Yet Hermia still loves you: then be content.
LYSANDER
Content with Hermia! No; I do repent
The tedious minutes I with her have spent.
Not Hermia, but Helena I love:
Who will not change a raven for a dove?
The will of man is by his reason sway'd;
And reason says you are the worthier maid.
Things growing are not ripe until their season:
So I, being young, till now ripe not to reason;
And touching now the point of human skill,
Reason becomes the marshal to my will,
And leads me to your eyes; where I o'erlook
Love's stories, written in Love's richest book.
HELENA
Wherefore was I to this keen mockery born?
When at your hands did I deserve this scorn?
Is't not enough, is't not enough, young man,
That I did never, no, nor never can,
Deserve a sweet look from Demetrius' eye,
But you must flout my insufficiency?
Good troth, you do me wrong, — good sooth, you do, —
In such disdainful manner me to woo.
But fare you well: perforce I must confess
I thought you lord of more true gentleness.
O, that a lady, of one man refused,
Should of another therefore be abused!   [*Exit.*
LYSANDER
She sees not Hermia. — Hermia, sleep thou there:
And never mayst thou come Lysander near!
For, as a surfeit of the sweetest things
The deepest loathing to the stomach brings;
Or, as the heresies that men do leave
Are hated most of those they did deceive;
So thou, my surfeit and my heresy,
Of all be hated, but the most of me!
And, all my powers, address your love and might
To honour Helen, and to be her knight!   [*Exit.*
HERMIA [*awaking*].
Help me, Lysander, help me! do thy best
To pluck this crawling serpent from my breast!
Ay me, for pity! — what a dream was here!
Lysander, look how I do quake with fear:

Methought a serpent eat my heart away,
And you sat smiling at his cruel prey. —
Lysander! — what, remov'd? — Lysander! lord! —
What, out of hearing? gone? no sound, no word?
Alack, where are you? speak, an if you hear;
Speak, of all loves! I swoon almost with fear.
No? — then I well perceive you are not nigh:
Either death or you I'll find immediately.   [*Exit.*

ACT III

SCENE I

The wood. TITANIA *lying asleep.*

Enter QUINCE, SNUG, BOTTOM, FLUTE, SNOUT, *and* STARVELING.

BOTTOM
Are we all met?
QUINCE
Pat, pat; and here's a marvellous convenient place for
our rehearsal. This green plot shall be our stage, this
hawthorn-brake our tiring-house; and we will do it in
action as we will do it before the duke.
BOTTOM
Peter Quince, —
QUINCE
What say'st thou, bully Bottom?
BOTTOM
There are things in this comedy of *Pyramus and Thisby*
that will never please. First, Pyramus must draw a
sword to kill himself; which the ladies cannot abide.

How answer you that?
SNOUT
By'r lakin, a parlous fear.
STARVELING
I believe we must leave the killing out, when all is done.
BOTTOM
Not a whit: I have a device to make all well. Write me a
prologue; and let the prologue seem to say, we will do
no harm with our swords, and that Pyramus is not
kill'd indeed; and, for the more better assurance, tell
them that I Pyramus am not Pyramus, but Bottom the
weaver: this will put them out of fear.
QUINCE
Well, we will have such a prologue; and it shall be
written in eight and six.
BOTTOM
No, make it two more: let it be written in eight and
eight.
SNOUT
Will not the ladies be afeard of the lion?
STARVELING
I fear it, I promise you.
BOTTOM
Masters, you ought to consider with yourselves: to bring
in, — God shield us! — a lion among ladies is a most
dreadful thing; for there is not a more fearful wild-fowl
than your lion living; and we ought to look to't.
SNOUT
Therefore another prologue must tell he is not a lion.
BOTTOM
Nay, you must name his name, and half his face must
be seen through the lion's neck; and he himself must

BOTTOM Are we all met?

speak through, saying thus, or to the same defect, —
'Ladies,' — or, 'Fair ladies, — I would wish you,' — or,
'I would request you,' — or, 'I would entreat you, — not
to fear, not to tremble: my life for yours. If you think I
come hither as a lion, it were pity of my life: no, I am no
such thing; I am a man as other men are': — and there,
indeed, let him name his name, and tell them plainly
he is Snug the joiner.

QUINCE
Well, it shall be so. But there is two hard things, — that
is, to bring the moonlight into a chamber; for, you
know, Pyramus and Thisby meet by moonlight.

SNUG
Doth the moon shine that night we play our play?

BOTTOM
A calendar, a calendar! look in the almanac; find out
moonshine, find out moonshine.

QUINCE
Yes, it doth shine that night.

BOTTOM
Why, then may you leave a casement of the great
chamber-window, where we play, open, and the moon
may shine in at the casement.

QUINCE
Ay; or else one must come in with a bush of thorns and
a lantern, and say he comes to disfigure, or to present,
the person of moonshine. Then, there is another thing:
we must have a wall in the great chamber; for Pyramus
and Thisby, says the story, did talk through the chink of
a wall.

SNOUT O Bottom, thou art chang'd! what do I see on thee.

SNUG
You can never bring in a wall.—What say you, Bottom?

BOTTOM
Some man or other must present wall: and let him
have some plaster, or some loam, or some rough-cast
about him, to signify wall; and let him hold his fingers
thus, and through that cranny shall Pyramus and
Thisby whisper.

QUINCE
If that may be, then all is well. Come, sit down, every
mother's son, and rehearse your parts. Pyramus, you
begin: when you have spoken your speech, enter into
that brake; — and so every one according to his cue.

Enter PUCK behind.

PUCK
What hempen home-spuns have we swaggering
    here,
So near the cradle of the fairy queen?
What, a play toward! I'll be an auditor;
An actor too perhaps, if I see cause.

QUINCE
Speak, Pyramus. — Thisby, stand forth.

BOTTOM
Thisby, the flowers of odious savours sweet, —

QUINCE
Odours, odours.

BOTTOM
            — odours savours sweet:
    So hath thy breath, my dearest Thisby dear. —
But hark, a voice! stay thou but here awhile,
    And by and by I will to thee appear.   [*Exit.*

PUCK [*aside*].
A stranger Pyramus than e'er play'd here.   [*Exit.*

FLUTE
Must I speak now?

QUINCE
Ay, marry, must you; for you must understand he goes
but to see a noise that he heard, and is to come again.

FLUTE
Most radiant Pyramus, most lily-white of hue,
    Of colour like the red rose on triumphant brier,
Most brisky juvenal, and eke most lovely Jew,
    As true as truest horse, that yet would never tire,
I'll meet thee, Pyramus, at Ninny's tomb.

QUINCE
'Ninus' tomb,' man: — why, you must not speak that
yet; that you answer to Pyramus: you speak all your part
at once, cues and all. — Pyramus enter: your cue is
past; it is, 'never tire.'

FLUTE
O, — As true as truest horse, that yet would never tire.

Enter PUCK, and BOTTOM with an ass-head.

BOTTOM
If I were fair, Thisby, I were only thine: —

QUINCE
O monstrous! O strange! we are haunted. —
Pray, masters! fly, masters! — Help!
[*Exit with* SNUG, FLUTE, SNOUT, *and* STARVELING.

PUCK
I'll follow you, I'll lead you about a round,
    Through bog, through bush, through brake, through
        brier:
Sometime a horse I'll be, sometime a hound,
    A hog, a headless bear, sometime a fire;
And neigh, and bark, and grunt, and roar, and burn,
Like horse, hound, hog, bear, fire, at every turn.   [*Exit.*

BOTTOM
Why do they run away? this is a knavery of them to
make me afeard.

Enter SNOUT.

SNOUT
O Bottom, thou art chang'd! what do I see on
thee?

BOTTOM
What do you see? you see an ass-head of your own,
do you?
                                        [*Exit* SNOUT.

Enter QUINCE.

QUINCE
Bless thee, Bottom! bless thee! thou art translated.
                                        [*Exit.*

BOTTOM
I see their knavery: this is to make an ass of me; to
fright me, if they could. But I will not stir from this
place, do what they can: I will walk up and down here,
and I will sing, that they shall hear I am not afraid.
                                        [*Sings.*

    The ousel-cock so black of hue,
        With orange-tawny bill,
    The throstle with his note so true,
        The wren with little quill: —

TITANIA [*awaking*].
What angel wakes me from my flowery bed?

BOTTOM [*sings*].
    The finch, the sparrow, and the lark,
        The plain-song cuckoo grey,
    Whose note full many a man doth mark,
        And dares not answer nay; —
for, indeed, who would set his wit to so foolish a bird?
who would give a bird the lie, though he cry 'cuckoo'
never so?

TITANIA
I pray thee, gentle mortal, sing again:
Mine ear is much enamour'd of thy note;
So is mine eye enthrallèd to thy shape;
And thy fair virtue's force perforce doth move me,
On the first view, to say, to swear, I love thee.

BOTTOM
Methinks, mistress, you should have little reason for
that: and yet, to say the truth, reason and love keep little
company together now-a-days; — the more the pity
that some honest neighbours will not make them
friends. Nay, I can gleek upon occasion.

TITANIA
Thou art as wise as thou art beautiful.

BOTTOM
Not so, neither: but if I had wit enough to get out of this
wood, I have enough to serve mine own turn.

TITANIA
Out of this wood do not desire to go:
Thou shalt remain here, whether thou wilt or no.
I am a spirit of no common rate, —
The summer still doth tend upon my state;
And I do love thee: therefore, go with me;
I'll give thee fairies to attend on thee;
And they shall fetch thee jewels from the deep,
And sing, while thou on pressed flowers dost sleep:
And I will purge thy mortal grossness so,
That thou shalt like an airy spirit go. —
Peas-blossom! Cobweb! Moth! and Mustard-seed!

Enter four FAIRIES.

FIRST FAIRY
Ready.

SECOND FAIRY
    And I.

THIRD FAIRY
        And I.

FOURTH FAIRY
            And I.

ALL
                Where shall we go?

TITANIA
Be kind and courteous to this gentleman, —
Hop in his walks, and gambol in his eyes;
Feed him with apricocks and dewberries,
With purple grapes, green figs, and mulberries;
The honey-bags steal from the humble-bees,
And for night-tapers crop their waxen thighs,
And light them at the fiery glow-worm's eyes,
To have my love to bed and to arise;
And pluck the wings from painted butterflies
To fan the moonbeams from his sleeping eyes:
Nod to him, elves, and do him courtesies.

FIRST FAIRY
Hail, mortal!

SECOND FAIRY
Hail!

THIRD FAIRY
Hail!

FOURTH FAIRY
Hail!

BOTTOM I cry your worships mercy heartily.

BOTTOM
I cry your worships mercy heartily. — I beseech your
worship's name.

COBWEB
Cobweb.

BOTTOM
I shall desire you of more acquaintance, good Master
Cobweb: if I cut my finger, I shall make bold with you.
— Your name, honest gentleman?

PEAS-BLOSSOM
Peas-blossom.

BOTTOM
I pray you, commend me to Mistress Squash, your
mother, and to Master Peascod, your father. Good
Master Peas-blossom, I shall desire you of more
acquaintance too. — Your name, I beseech you, sir?

MUSTARD-SEED
Mustard-seed.

BOTTOM
Good Master Mustard-seed, I know your patience well:
that same cowardly, giant-like ox-beef hath devour'd
many a gentleman of your house: I promise you your
kindred hath made my eyes water ere now. I desire you
more acquaintance, good Master Mustard-seed.

TITANIA
Come, wait upon him; lead him to my bower.
    The moon methinks looks with a watery eye;
And when she weeps, weeps every little flower,
    Lamenting some enforced chastity.
    Tie up my love's tongue, bring him silently. [*Exeunt.*

SCENE II
Another part of the wood.

Enter OBERON.

OBERON
I wonder if Titania be awak'd;
Then, what it was that next came in her eye,
Which she must dote on in extremity. —
Here comes my messenger.
            Enter PUCK.
                    How now, mad spirit!
What night-rule now about this haunted grove?

PUCK
My mistress with a monster is in love.
Near to her close and consecrated bower,
While she was in her dull and sleeping hour,
A crew of patches, rude mechanicals,
That work for bread upon Athenian stalls,
Were met together to rehearse a play,
Intended for great Theseus' nuptial day.
The shallowest thickskin of that barren sort,
Who Pyramus presented in their sport,

Forsook his scene, and enter'd in a brake:
When I did him at this advantage take,
An ass's nowl I fixed on his head:
Anon his Thisbe must be answered,
And forth my mimic comes. When they him spy,
As wild geese that the creeping fowler eye,
Or russet-pated choughs, many in sort,
Rising and cawing at the gun's report,
Sever themselves, and madly sweep the sky,
So, at his sight, away his fellows fly;
And, at our stamp, here o'er and o'er one falls;
He murder cries, and help from Athens calls.
Their sense thus weak, lost with their fears thus strong,
Made senseless things begin to do them wrong;
For briers and thorns at their apparel snatch;
Some, sleeves, — some, hats; — from yielders all
    things catch.
I led them on in this distracted fear,
And left sweet Pyramus translated there:
When in that moment, — so it came to pass, —
Titania wak'd, and straightway lov'd an ass.

OBERON
This falls out better than I could devise.
But hast thou yet latch'd the Athenian's eyes
With the love-juice, as I did bid thee do?

PUCK
I took him sleeping, — that is finish'd too, —
And the Athenian woman by his side;
That, when he wak'd, of force she must be ey'd.
        Enter HERMIA *and* DEMETRIUS.

OBERON
Stand close: this is the same Athenian.

PUCK
This is the woman, but not this the man.

DEMETRIUS
O, why rebuke you him that loves you so?
Lay breath so bitter on your bitter foe.

HERMIA
Now I but chide; but I should use thee worse,
For thou, I fear, hast given me cause to curse.
If thou hast slain Lysander in his sleep,
Being o'er shoes in blood, plunge in the deep,
And kill me too.
The sun was not so true unto the day
As he to me: would he have stol'n away
From sleeping Hermia? I'll believe as soon
This whole earth may be bor'd; and that the moon
May through the centre creep, and so displease
Her brother's noontide with th'Antipodes.
It cannot be but thou hast murder'd him;
So should a murderer look, — so dead, so grim.

DEMETRIUS
So should the murder'd look; and so should I,
Pierc'd through the heart with your stern cruelty:
Yet you, the murderer, look as bright, as clear,
As yonder Venus in her glimmering sphere.

HERMIA
What's this to my Lysander? where is he?
Ah, good Demetrius, wilt thou give him me?

DEMETRIUS
I had rather give his carcass to my hounds.

HERMIA
Out, dog! out, cur! thou drivest me past the bounds
Of maiden's patience. Hast thou slain him, then?
Henceforth be never number'd among men!
O, once tell true, tell true, even for my sake!
Durst thou have look'd upon him being awake,
And hast thou kill'd him sleeping? O brave touch!
Could not a worm, an adder, do so much?
An adder did it; for with doubler tongue
Than mine, thou serpent, never adder stung.

DEMETRIUS
You spend your passion on a mispris'd mood:
I am not guilty of Lysander's blood;
Nor is he dead, for aught that I can tell.

HERMIA
I pray thee, tell me, then, that he is well.

DEMETRIUS
An if I could, what should I get therefore?

HERMIA
A privilege, never to see me more: —
And from thy hated presence part I so:
See me no more, whether he be dead or no.   [*Exit.*

DEMETRIUS
There is no following her in this fierce vein:

OBERON Here comes my messenger. How now, mad spirit!

168

PUCK An ass's nowl I fixed on his head.

Here therefore for a while I will remain.
So sorrow's heaviness doth heavier grow
For debt that bankrout sleep doth sorrow owe;
Which now in some slight measure it will pay,
If for his tender here I make some stay.

[Lies down and sleeps.

OBERON
What hast thou done? thou hast mistaken quite,
And laid the love-juice on some true-love's sight:
Of thy misprision must perforce ensue
Some true-love turn'd, and not a false turn'd true.

PUCK
Then fate o'er-rules; that, one man holding troth,
A million fail, confounding oath on oath.

OBERON
About the wood go swifter than the wind,
And Helena of Athens look thou find:
All fancy-sick she is, and pale of cheer
With sighs of love, that costs the fresh blood dear:
By some illusion see thou bring her here:
I'll charm his eyes against she do appear.

PUCK
I go, I go; look how I go, —
Swifter than arrow from the Tartar's bow.   *[Exit.*

OBERON
        Flower of this purple dye,
        Hit with Cupid's archery,
[Squeezes the flower on DEMETRIUS'S *eyelids.*
        Sink in apple of his eye!
        When his love he doth espy,
        Let her shine as gloriously
        As the Venus of the sky. —
        When thou wakest, if she be by,
        Beg of her for remedy.
            Enter PUCK.

PUCK
        Captain of our fairy band,
        Helena is here at hand;
        And the youth, mistook by me,
        Pleading for a lover's fee.
        Shall we their fond pageant see?
        Lord, what fools these mortals be!

OBERON
        Stand aside: the noise they make
        Will cause Demetrius to awake.

PUCK
        Then will two at once woo one, —
        That must needs be sport alone;
        And those things do best please me
        That befall preposterously.
            Enter HELENA *and* LYSANDER.

LYSANDER
Why should you think that I should woo in scorn?
    Scorn and derision never come in tears:
Look, when I vow, I weep; and vows so born,
    In their nativity all truth appears.
How can these things in me seem scorn to you,
Bearing the badge of faith, to prove them true?

HELENA
You do advance your cunning more and more.

When truth kills truth, O devilish-holy fray!
These vows are Hermia's: will you give her o'er?
    Weigh oath with oath, and you will nothing weigh:
Your vows to her and me, put in two scales,
Will even weigh; and both as light as tales.

LYSANDER
I had no judgement when to her I swore.

HELENA
Nor none, in my mind, now you give her o'er.

LYSANDER
Demetrius loves her, and he loves not you.

DEMETRIUS *[awaking].*
O Helen, goddess, nymph, perfect, divine!
To what, my love, shall I compare thine eyne?
Crystal is muddy. O, how ripe in show
Thy lips, those kissing cherries, tempting grow!
That pure congealed white, high Taurus' snow,
Fann'd with the eastern wind, turns to a crow
When thou hold'st up thy hand: O, let me kiss
This princess of pure white, this seal of bliss!

HELENA
O spite! O hell! I see you all are bent
To set against me for your merriment:
If you were civil and knew courtesy,
You would not do me thus much injury.
Can you not hate me, as I know you do,
But you must join in souls to mock me too?
If you were men, as men you are in show,
You would not use a gentle lady so;
To vow, and swear, and superpraise my parts,
When I am sure you hate me with your hearts.
You both are rivals, and love Hermia;
And now both rivals, to mock Helena:
A trim exploit, a manly enterprise,
To conjure tears up in a poor maid's eyes
With your derision! none of noble sort
Would so offend a virgin, and extort
A pour soul's patience, all to make you sport.

LYSANDER
You are unkind, Demetrius; be not so;
For you love Hermia; — this you know I know:
And here, with all good will, with all my heart,
In Hermia's love I yield you up my part;
And yours of Helena to me bequeath,
Whom I do love, and will do to my death.

HELENA
Never did mockers waste more idle breath.

DEMETRIUS
Lysander, keep thy Hermia; I will none:
If e'er I lov'd her, all that love is gone.
My heart to her but as guest-wise sojourn'd,
And now to Helen is it home return'd,
There to remain.

LYSANDER
Helen, it is not so.

DEMETRIUS
Disparage not the faith thou dost not know,
Lest, to thy peril, thou aby it dear. —
Look, where thy love comes; yonder is thy dear.
            Enter HERMIA.

HERMIA
Dark night, that from the eye his function takes,

The ear more quick of apprehension makes;
Wherein it doth impair the seeing sense,
It pays the hearing double recompense. —
Thou art not by mine eye, Lysander, found;
Mine ear, I thank it, brought me to thy sound.
But why unkindly didst thou leave me so?

LYSANDER
Why should he stay, whom love doth press to go?

HERMIA
What love could press Lysander from my side?

LYSANDER
Lysander's love, that would not let him bide, —
Fair Helena; who more engilds the night
Than all yon fiery O's and eyes of light.
Why seek'st thou me? could not this make thee know,
The hate I bear thee made me leave thee so?

HERMIA
You speak not as you think: it cannot be.

HELENA
Lo, she is one of this confederacy!
Now I perceive they have conjoin'd all three
To fashion this false sport in spite of me.
Injurious Hermia! most ungrateful maid!
Have you conspir'd, have you with these contriv'd
To bait me with this foul derision?
Is all the counsel that we two have shared,
The sisters' vows, the hours that we have spent,
When we have chid the hasty-footed time
For parting us, — O, and is all forgot?
All school-days' friendship, childhood innocence?
We, Hermia, like two artificial gods,
Have with our neelds created both one flower,
Both on one sampler, sitting on one cushion,
Both warbling of one song, both in one key;
As if our hands, our sides, voices, and minds,
Had been incorporate. So we grew together,
Like to a double cherry, seeming parted,
But yet an union in partition;
Two lovely berries moulded on one stem;
So, with two seeming bodies, but one heart;
Two of the first, like coats in heraldry,
Due but to one, and crowned with one crest.
And will you rent our ancient love asunder,
To join with men in scorning your poor friend?
It is not friendly, 'tis not maidenly:
Our sex, as well as I, may chide you for it,
Though I alone do feel the injury.

HERMIA
I am amazed at your passionate words.
I scorn you not: it seems that you scorn me.

HELENA
Have you not set Lysander, as in scorn,
To follow me, and praise my eyes and face?
And made your other love, Demetrius —
Who even but now did spurn me with his foot —
To call me goddess, nymph, divine, and rare,
Precious, celestial? Wherefore speaks he this
To her he hates? and wherefore doth Lysander
Deny your love, so rich within his soul,
And tender me, forsooth, affection,
But by your setting on, by your consent?
What though I be not so in grace as you,
So hung upon with love, so fortunate;
But miserable most, to love unlov'd?
This you should pity rather than despise.

HERMIA
I understand not what you mean by this.

HELENA
Ay, do, persever, counterfeit sad looks;
Make mouths upon me when I turn my back;
Wink each at other; hold the sweet jest up:
This sport, well carried, shall be chronicled.
If you have any pity, grace, or manners,
You would not make me such an argument.
But, fare ye well: 'tis partly mine own fault;
Which death or absence soon shall remedy.

LYSANDER
Stay, gentle Helena; hear my excuse:
My love, my life, my soul, fair Helena!

HELENA
O excellent!

HERMIA
        Sweet, do not scorn her so.

DEMETRIUS
If she cannot entreat, I can compel.

LYSANDER
Thou canst compel no more than she entreat:
Thy threats have no more strength than her weak
    prayers. —
Helen, I love thee; by my life, I do:

Although I hate her, I'll not harm her so.

HERMIA
What, can you do me greater harm than hate?
Hate me! wherefore? O me! what news, my love?
Am not I Hermia? are not you Lysander?
I am as fair now as I was erewhile.
Since night you lov'd me; yet since night you left me:
Why, then you left me, — O, the gods forbid! —
In earnest, shall I say?

LYSANDER
        Ay, by my life;
And never did desire to see thee more.
Therefore be out of hope, of question, doubt;
Be certain, nothing truer; 'tis no jest
That I do hate thee, and love Helena.

HERMIA
O me! — you juggler! you canker-blossom!
You thief of love! what, have you come by night
And stol'n my love's heart from him?

HELENA
        Fine, i'faith!
Have you no modesty, no maiden shame,
No touch of bashfulness? What, will you tear
Impatient answers from my gentle tongue?
Fie, fie! you counterfeit, you puppet, you!

HERMIA
Puppet! why, so; ay, that way goes the game.
Now I perceive that she hath made compare
Between our statures; she hath urg'd her height;
And with her personage, her tall personage,
Her height, forsooth, she hath prevail'd with him.
And are you grown so high in his esteem,
Because I am so dwarfish and so low?
How low am I, thou painted maypole? speak;
How low am I? I am not yet so low
But that my nails can reach unto thine eyes.

HELENA
I pray you, though you mock me, gentlemen,
Let her not hurt me: I was never curst;
I have no gift at all in shrewishness;
I am a right maid for my cowardice:
Let her not strike me. You perhaps may think,
Because she is something lower than myself,
That I can match her.

HERMIA
        Lower! hark, again.

HELENA
Good Hermia, do not be so bitter with me.
I evermore did love you, Hermia,
Did ever keep your counsels, never wrong'd you;
Save that, in love unto Demetrius,
I told him of your stealth unto this wood,
He follow'd you; for love I follow'd him;
But he hath chid me hence, and threaten'd me
To strike me, spurn me, nay, to kill me too:
And now, so you will let me quiet go,
To Athens will I bear my folly back,
And follow you no further: let me go:
You see how simple and how fond I am.

HERMIA
Why, get you gone: who is't that hinders you?

HELENA
A foolish heart, that I leave here behind.

HERMIA
What, with Lysander?

HELENA
        With Demetrius.

LYSANDER
Be not afraid; she shall not harm thee, Helena.

DEMETRIUS
No, sir, she shall not, though you take her part.

HELENA
O, when she's angry, she is keen and shrewd!
She was a vixen when she went to school;
And though she be but little, she is fierce.

HERMIA
Little again! nothing but low and little! —
Why will you suffer her to flout me thus?
Let me come to her.

LYSANDER
        Get you gone, you dwarf;
You minimus, of hind'ring knot-grass made;
You bead, you acorn.

DEMETRIUS
        You are too officious
In her behalf that scorns your services.
Let her alone: speak not of Helena;
Take not her part; for, if thou dost intend
Never so little show of love to her,
Thou shalt aby it.

I swear by that which I will lose for thee,
To prove him false that says I love thee not.

DEMETRIUS
I say I love thee more than he can do.

LYSANDER
If thou say so, withdraw, and prove it too.

DEMETRIUS
Quick, come!

HERMIA
        Lysander, whereto tends all this?

LYSANDER
Away, you Ethiop!

DEMETRIUS
        No, no, sir;
Seem to break loose, take on as you would follow,
But yet come not: you are a tame man, go!

LYSANDER
Hang off, thou cat, thou burr! vile thing, let loose,
Or I will shake thee from me like a serpent!

HERMIA
Why are you grown so rude? what change is this,
Sweet love?

LYSANDER
        Thy love! out, tawny Tartar, out!
Out, loathed medicine! O hated potion, hence!

HERMIA
Do you not jest?

HELENA
        Yes, sooth; and so do you.

LYSANDER
Demetrius, I will keep my word with thee.

DEMETRIUS
I would I had your bond, for I perceive
A weak bond holds you: I'll not trust your word.

LYSANDER
What, should I hurt her, strike her, kill her dead?

LYSANDER
      Now she holds me not;
Now follow, if thou darest, to try whose right,
Of thine or mine, is most in Helena.

DEMETRIUS
Follow! nay, I'll go with thee, cheek by jole.
    [*Exeunt* LYSANDER *and* DEMETRIUS.

HERMIA
You, mistress, all this coil is 'long of you:
Nay, go not back.

HELENA
     I will not trust you, I,
Nor longer stay in your curst company,
Your hands than mine are quicker for a fray;
My legs are longer though, to run away. [*Exit.*

HERMIA
I am amaz'd, and know not what to say. [*Exit.*

OBERON
This is thy negligence: still thou mistakest,
Or else committ'st thy knaveries wilfully.

PUCK
Believe me, king of shadows, I mistook.
Did not you tell me I should know the man
By the Athenian garment he had on?
And so far blameless proves my enterprise,
That I have 'nointed an Athenian's eyes;
And so far am I glad it so did sort,
As this their jangling I esteem a sport.

OBERON
Thou see'st these lovers seek a place to fight:
Hie therefore, Robin, overcast the night;
The starry welkin cover thou anon
With drooping fog, as black as Acheron;
And lead these testy rivals so astray,
As one come not within another's way.
Like to Lysander sometime frame thy tongue,
Then stir Demetrius up with bitter wrong;
And sometime rail thou like Demetrius;
And from each other look thou lead them thus,
Till o'er their brows death-counterfeiting sleep
With leaden legs and batty wings doth creep:
Then crush this herb into Lysander's eye;
Whose liquor hath this virtuous property,
To take from thence all error with his might,
And make his eyeballs roll with wonted sight.
When they next wake, all this derision
Shall seem a dream and fruitless vision;
And back to Athens shall the lovers wend,
With league whose date till death shall never end.
Whiles I in this affair do thee employ,
I'll to my queen and beg her Indian boy;
And then I will her charmed eye release
From monster's view, and all things shall be peace.

PUCK
My fairy lord, this must be done with haste,
For Night's swift dragons cut the clouds full fast,
And yonder shines Aurora's harbinger;
At whose approach, ghosts, wandering here and there,
Troop home to churchyards: damned spirits all,
That in crossways and floods have burial,
Already to their wormy beds are gone;
For fear lest day should look their shames upon,
They wilfully themselves exile from light,
And must for aye consort with black-brow'd night.

OBERON
But we are spirits of another sort:
I with the Morning's love have oft made sport;
And, like a forester, the groves may tread,
Even till the eastern gate, all fiery-red,
Opening on Neptune, with fair blessed beams
Turns into yellow gold his salt green streams.
But, notwithstanding, haste; make no delay:
We may effect this business yet ere day. [*Exit.*

PUCK
    Up and down, up and down,
    I will lead them up and down:
    I am fear'd in field and town:
    Goblin, lead them up and down.
Here comes one.

     Enter LYSANDER.

LYSANDER
Where art thou, proud Demetrius? speak thou now.

PUCK
Here, villain; drawn and ready. Where art thou?

LYSANDER
I will be with thee straight.

PUCK
      Follow me, then,
To plainer ground.

LYSANDER He goes before me and still dares me on.

[*Exit* LYSANDER, *as following the voice.*
  Enter DEMETRIUS.

DEMETRIUS
     Lysander! speak agen:
Thou runaway, thou coward, art thou fled?
Speak! in some bush? where dost thou hide thy head?

PUCK
Thou coward, art thou bragging to the stars,
Telling the bushes that thou look'st for wars,
And wilt not come? Come, recreant; come, thou child;
I'll whip thee with a rod: he is defil'd
That draws a sword on thee.

DEMETRIUS
     Yea, art thou there?

PUCK
Follow my voice: we'll try no manhood here.
       [*Exeunt.*

    Enter LYSANDER.

LYSANDER
He goes before me and still dares me on:
When I come where he calls, then he is gone.
The villain is much lighter-heel'd than I:
I follow'd fast, but faster he did fly;
That fall'n am I in dark uneven way,
And here will rest me. [*Lies down.*] Come, thou gentle
  day!
For if but once thou show me thy grey light,
I'll find Demetrius, and revenge this spite. [*Sleeps.*

   Enter PUCK *and* DEMETRIUS.

PUCK
Ho, ho, ho! Coward, why comest thou not?

DEMETRIUS
Abide me, if thou darest; for well I wot
Thou runn'st before me, shifting every place,
And darest not stand, nor look me in the face.
Where art thou now?

PUCK
    Come hither: I am here.

DEMETRIUS
Nay, then, thou mock'st me. Thou shalt buy this dear,
If ever I thy face by daylight see:
Now, go thy way. Faintness constraineth me
To measure out my length on this cold bed.

By day's approach look to be visited.
      [*Lies down and sleeps.*

    Enter HELENA.

HELENA
O weary night, O long and tedious night,
 Abate thy hours! Shine comforts from the east,
That I may back to Athens by daylight,
 From these that my poor company detest:
And sleep, that sometime shuts up sorrow's eye,
Steal me awhile from mine own company.
      [*Lies down and sleeps.*

PUCK
    Yet but three? Come one more;
    Two of both kinds make up four.
    Here she comes, curst and sad: —
    Cupid is a knavish lad,
    Thus to make poor females mad.
     Enter HERMIA.

HERMIA
Never so weary, never so in woe;
 Bedabbled with the dew, and torn with briers;
I can no further crawl, no further go;
 My legs can keep no pace with my desires.
Here will I rest me till the break of day.
Heavens shield Lysander, if they mean a fray!
      [*Lies down and sleeps.*

PUCK
    On the ground
    Sleep sound:
    I'll apply
    To your eye,
    Gentle lover, remedy.
[*Squeezing the herb on* LYSANDER'S *eyelids.*
    When thou wakest,
    Thou takest
    True delight
    In the sight
    Of thy former lady's eye:
    And the country proverb known,
    That every man should take his own,
    In your waking shall be shown:
    Jack shall have Jill;
    Nought shall go ill;
The man shall have his mare again, and all shall
 be well.
        [*Exit.*

TITANIA Come, sit thee down upon this flowery bed.

ACT IV

SCENE I

The wood. LYSANDER, DEMETRIUS, HELENA, *and* HERMIA, *lying asleep.*

Enter TITANIA *and* BOTTOM; PEAS-BLOSSOM, COBWEB, MOTH, MUSTARD-SEED, *and other* FAIRIES *attending;* OBERON *behind unseen.*

TITANIA
Come, sit thee down upon this flowery bed,
While I thy amiable cheeks do coy,
And stick musk-roses in thy sleek smooth head,
   And kiss thy fair large ears, my gentle joy.

BOTTOM
Where's Peas-blossom?

PEAS-BLOSSOM
Ready.

BOTTOM
Scratch my head, Peas-blossom. — Where's Monsieur Cobweb?

COBWEB
Ready.

BOTTOM
Monsieur Cobweb, good monsieur, get your weapons in your hand, and kill me a red-hipp'd humble-bee on the top of a thistle; and, good monsieur, bring me the honey-bag. Do not fret yourself too much in the action, monsieur; and, good monsieur, have a care the honey-bag break not; I would be loth to have you overflown with a honey-bag, signior. — Where's Monsieur Mustard-seed?

MUSTARD-SEED
Ready.

BOTTOM
Give me your neif, Monsieur Mustard-seed.
Pray you, leave your courtesy, good monsieur.

MUSTARD-SEED
What's your will?

BOTTOM
Nothing, good monsieur, but to help Cavalery Peas-blossom to scratch. I must to the barber's, monsieur; for methinks I am marvellous hairy about the face; and I am such a tender ass, if my hair do but tickle me, I must scratch.

TITANIA
What, wilt thou hear some music, my sweet love?

BOTTOM
I have a reasonable good ear in music: let's have the tongs and bones.

[Tongs. Rural music.

TITANIA
Or say, sweet love, what thou desirest to eat.

BOTTOM
Truly, a peck of provender: I could munch your good dry oats. Methinks I have a great desire to a bottle of hay: good hay, sweet hay hath no fellow.

TITANIA
I have a venturous fairy that shall seek
The squirrel's hoard, and fetch thee hence new nuts.

BOTTOM
I had rather have a handful or two of dried peas. But, I pray you, let none of your people stir me: I have an exposition of sleep come upon me.

TITANIA
Sleep thou, and I will wind thee in my arms. —
Fairies, be gone, and be all ways away.

[Exeunt FAIRIES.
So doth the woodbine the sweet honeysuckle
Gently entwist; the female ivy so
Enrings the barky fingers of the elm.
O, how I love thee! how I dote on thee!

[They sleep.

Enter PUCK.

OBERON [*advancing*].
Welcome, good Robin. See'st thou this sweet sight?
Her dotage now I do begin to pity:
For, meeting her of late behind the wood,
Seeking sweet favours for this hateful fool,
I did upbraid her, and fall out with her;
For she his hairy temples then had rounded
With coronet of fresh and fragrant flowers;
And that same dew, which sometime on the buds
Was wont to swell, like round and orient pearls,
Stood now within the pretty flowerets' eyes,
Like tears, that did their own disgrace bewail.
When I had at my pleasure taunted her,
And she in mild terms begg'd my patience,
I then did ask of her her changeling child;
Which straight she gave me, and her fairy sent
To bear him to my bower in fairy-land.
And now I have the boy, I will undo
This hateful imperfection of her eyes:
And, gentle Puck, take this transformed scalp
From off the head of this Athenian swain;
That he, awaking when the other do,
May all to Athens back again repair,
And think no more of this night's accidents,
But as the fierce vexation of a dream.
But first I will release the fairy queen.
      Be as thou wast wont to be;
              [Touching her eyes with a herb.
      See as thou wast wont to see:
      Dian's bud o'er Cupid's flower
      Hath such force and blessed power.
Now, my Titania: wake you, my sweet queen.

TITANIA
My Oberon! what visions have I seen!
Methought I was enamour'd of an ass.

OBERON
There lies your love.

TITANIA
           How came these things to pass?
O, how mine eyes do loathe his visage now!

OBERON
Silence awhile. — Robin, take off this head. —
Titania, music call; and strike more dead
Than common sleep of all these five the sense.

TITANIA
Music, ho! music, such as charmeth sleep!

[Music, still.

PUCK
Now, when thou wak'st, with thine own fool's eyes peep.

OBERON
Sound, music! — Come, my queen, take hands with me,
And rock the ground whereon these sleepers be.
Now thou and I are new in amity,
And will to-morrow midnight solemnly
Dance in Duke Theseus' house triumphantly,
And bless it to all fair prosperity:
There shall the pairs of faithful lovers be
Wedded, with Theseus, all in jollity.

PUCK
      Fairy king, attend, and mark:
      I do hear the morning lark.

OBERON

Then, my queen, in silence sad,
Trip we after the night's shade:
We the globe can compass soon,
Swifter than the wandering moon.

TITANIA

Come, my lord; and in our flight,
Tell me how it came this night
That I sleeping here was found
With these mortals on the ground.

[*Exeunt. Wind horns.*

Enter THESEUS, HIPPOLYTA, EGEUS, *and* TRAIN.

THESEUS

Go, one of you, find out the forester;
For now our observation is perform'd;
And since we have the vaward of the day,
My love shall hear the music of my hounds:
Uncouple in the western valley; go: —
Dispatch, I say, and find the forester. —

[*Exit an* ATTENDANT.

We will, fair queen, up to the mountain's top,
And mark the musical confusion
Of hounds and echo in conjunction.

HIPPOLYTA

I was with Hercules and Cadmus once,
When in a wood of Crete they bay'd the bear
With hounds of Sparta: never did I hear
Such gallant chiding; for, besides the groves,
The skies, the fountains, every region near
Seem all one mutual cry: I never heard
So musical a discord, such sweet thunder.

THESEUS

My hounds are bred out of the Spartan kind,
So flew'd, so sanded; and their heads are hung
With ears that sweep away the morning dew;
Crook-knee'd, and dew-lapt like Thessalian bulls;
Slow in pursuit, but match'd in mouth like bells,
Each under each. A cry more tuneable
Was never holla'd to, nor cheer'd with horn,
In Crete, in Sparta, nor in Thessaly:
Judge when you hear. — But, soft! what nymphs are
these?

EGEUS

My lord, this is my daughter here asleep
And this, Lysander; this Demetrius is;
This Helena, old Nedar's Helena:
I wonder of their being here together.

THESEUS

No doubt they rose up early to observe
The rites of May; and, hearing our intent,
Came here in grace of our solemnity. —
But speak, Egeus; is not this the day
That Hermia should give answer of her choice?

EGEUS

It is, my lord.

THESEUS

Go, bid the huntsmen wake them with their horns.
[*Horns, and they wake. Shout within. and they all start up.*
Good morrow, friends. — Saint Valentine is past:
Begin these wood-birds but to couple now?

LYSANDER

Pardon, my lord.

THESEUS

I pray you all, stand up.
I know you two are rival enemies:
How comes this gentle concord in the world,
That hatred is so far from jealousy,
To sleep by hate, and fear no enmity?

LYSANDER

My lord, I shall reply amazedly,
Half sleep, half waking: but as yet, I swear,
I cannot truly say how I came here;
But, as I think, — for truly would I speak,
And now I do bethink me, so it is, —
I came with Hermia hither: our intent
Was to be gone from Athens, where we might,
Without the peril of the Athenian law, —

EGEUS

Enough, enough, my lord; you have enough:
I beg the law, the law, upon his head. —
They would have stol'n away; they would, Demetrius,
Thereby to have defeated you and me,
You of your wife, and me of my consent, —
Of my consent that she should be your wife.

DEMETRIUS

My lord, fair Helen told me of their stealth,
Of this their purpose hither to this wood;
And I in fury hither follow'd them,
Fair Helena in fancy following me.

But, my good lord, I wot not by what power, —
But by some power it is, — my love to Hermia,
Melted as the snow, seems to me now
As the remembrance of an idle gaud,
Which in my childhood I did dote upon;
And all the faith, the virtue of my heart,
The object, and the pleasure of mine eye,
Is only Helena. To her, my lord,
Was I betroth'd ere I saw Hermia:
But, like in sickness, did I loathe this food;
But, as in health, come to my natural taste,
Now do I wish it, love it, long for it,
And will for evermore be true to it.

THESEUS

Fair lovers, you are fortunately met:
Of this discourse we more will hear anon. —
Egeus, I will overbear your will;
For in the temple, by and by, with us
These couples shall eternally be knit:
And, for the morning now is something worn,
Our purpos'd hunting shall be set aside.
Away with us to Athens! three and three,
We'll hold a feast in great solemnity.
Come, Hippolyta.

[*Exeunt* THESEUS, HIPPOLYTA,
EGEUS, *and* TRAIN.

DEMETRIUS

These things seem small and undistinguishable,
Like far-off mountains turned into clouds.

HERMIA

Methinks I see these things with parted eye,
When every thing seems double.

HELENA

So methinks:
And I have found Demetrius like a gemel,
Mine own, and not mine own.

DEMETRIUS

Are you sure
That we are awake? It seems to me
That yet we sleep, we dream. — Do not you think
The duke was here, and bid us follow him?

HERMIA

Yea; and my father.

HELENA

And Hippolyta.

LYSANDER

And he did bid us follow to the temple.

DEMETRIUS

Why, then, we are awake: let's follow him;
And, by the way, let us recount our dreams.

[*Exeunt.*

BOTTOM [*awaking*].

When my cue comes, call me, and I will
answer: — my next is, 'Most fair Pyramus,' —
Heigh-ho! — Peter Quince! Flute the
bellows-mender! Snout the tinker! Starveling!
— God's my life, stol'n hence, and left me
asleep! I have had a most rare vision. I have
had a dream, — past the wit of man to say what
dream it was: man is but an ass, if he go about
to expound this dream. Methought I was —
there is no man can tell what. Methought I
was, and methought I had, — but man is but a
patch'd fool, if he will offer to say what
methought I had. The eye of man hath not
heard, the ear of man hath not seen, man's
hand is not able to taste, his tongue to
conceive, nor his heart to report, what my
dream was. I will get Peter Quince to write a
ballet of this dream: it shall be called Bottom's
Dream, because it hath no bottom; and I will
sing it in the latter end of a play before the
duke: peradventure, to make it the more
gracious, I shall sing it at her death.

[*Exit.*

SCENE II

Athens. A room in QUINCE'S *house.*

Enter QUINCE, FLUTE, SNOUT, *and*
STARVELING.

QUINCE

Have you sent to Bottom's house? is he come
home yet?

STARVELING

He cannot be heard of. Out of doubt he is
transported.

FLUTE

If he come not, then the play is marr'd: it goes not
forward, doth it?

QUINCE

It is not possible: you have not a man in all Athens able
to discharge Pyramus but he.

FLUTE

No, he hath simply the best wit of any handicraft man
in Athens.

QUINCE

Yea, and the best person too; and he is a very paramour
for a sweet voice.

FLUTE

You must say paragon: a paramour is, God bless us, a
thing of naught.

Enter SNUG.

SNUG

Masters, the duke is coming from the temple, and
there is two or three lords and ladies more married: if
our sport had gone forward, we had all been made
men.

FLUTE

O sweet bully Bottom! Thus hath he lost sixpence a day
during his life; he could not have scaped sixpence a
day: an the duke had not given him sixpence a day for
playing Pyramus, I'll be hang'd; he would have
deserved it: sixpence a day in Pyramus, or nothing.

Enter BOTTOM.

BOTTOM

Where are these lads? where are these hearts?

QUINCE

Bottom! — O most courageous day! O most happy
hour!

BOTTOM

Masters, I am to discourse wonders: but ask me not
what; for if I tell you, I am no true Athenian. I will tell
you every thing, right as it fell out.

QUINCE

Let us hear, sweet Bottom.

BOTTOM

Not a word of me. All that I will tell you is, that the duke
hath dined. Get your apparel together, good strings to
your beards, new ribbons to your pumps; meet
presently at the palace; every man look o'er his part; for
the short and the long is, our play is preferr'd. In any
case, let Thisby have clean linen; and let not him that
plays the lion pare his nails, for they shall hang out for
the lion's claws. And, most dear actors, eat no onions
nor garlic, for we are to utter sweet breath; and I do not
doubt but to hear them say it is a sweet comedy. No
more words: away! go; away!

[*Exeunt.*

ACT V

SCENE I

Athens. An apartment in the palace of THESEUS.

Enter THESEUS, HIPPOLYTA, PHILOSTRATE,
LORDS, *and* ATTENDANTS.

HIPPOLYTA
'Tis strange, my Theseus, that these lovers speak of.
THESEUS
More strange than true: I never may believe
These antick fables nor these fairy toys.
Lovers and madmen have such seething brains,
Such shaping fantasies, that apprehend
More than cool reason ever comprehends.
The lunatic, the lover, and the poet
Are of imagination all compact: —
One sees more devils than vast hell can hold, —
That is, the madman: the lover, all as frantic,
Sees Helen's beauty in a brow of Egypt:
The poet's eye, in a fine frenzy rolling,
Doth glance from heaven to earth, from earth to
    heaven;
And, as imagination bodies forth
The forms of things unknown, the poet's pen
Turns them to shapes, and gives to airy nothing
A local habitation and a name.
Such tricks hath strong imagination,
That, if it would but apprehend some joy,
It comprehends some bringer of that joy;
Or in the night, imagining some fear,
How easy is a bush suppos'd a bear!
HIPPOLYTA
But all the story of the night told over,
And all their minds transfigured so together,
More witnesseth than fancy's images,
And grows to something of great constancy;
But, howsoever, strange and admirable.

THESEUS
Here come the lovers, full of joy and mirth.

Enter LYSANDER, DEMETRIUS, HERMIA, *and*
HELENA.

Joy, gentle friends! joy and fresh days of love
Accompany your hearts!
LYSANDER
                    More than to us
Wait in your royal walks, your board, your bed!
THESEUS
Come now; what masks, what dances shall we have,
To wear away this long age of three hours
Between our after-supper and bed-time?
Where is our usual manager of mirth?
What revels are in hand? Is there no play,
To ease the anguish of a torturing hour?
Call Philostrate.
PHILOSTRATE
                    Here, mighty Theseus.
THESEUS
Say, what abridgement have you for this evening?
What mask? what music? How shall we beguile
The lazy time, if not with some delight?
PHILOSTRATE
There is a brief how many sports are ripe:
Make choice of which your highness will see first.
                                    [*Giving a paper.*
THESEUS [*reads*].
'The battle with the Centaurs, to be sung
By an Athenian eunuch to the harp.'
We'll none of that: that have I told my love,
In glory of my kinsman Hercules. —
[*Reads.*] 'The riot of the tipsy Bacchanals,
Tearing the Thracian singer in their rage.'
That is an old device; and it was play'd
When I from Thebes came last a conqueror. —
[*Reads.*] 'The thrice-three Muses mourning for the
    death
Of Learning, late deceas'd in beggary.'

That is some satire, keen and critical,
Not sorting with a nuptial ceremony. —
[*Reads.*] 'A tedious brief scene of young Pyramus
And his love Thisbe; very tragical mirth.'
Merry and tragical! tedious and brief!
That is, hot ice and wondrous strange snow.
How shall we find the concord of this discord?
PHILOSTRATE
A play there is, my lord, some ten words long,
Which is as brief as I have known a play;
But by ten words, my lord, it is too long,
Which makes it tedious; for in all the play
There is not one word apt, one player fitted:
And tragical, my noble lord, it is;
For Pyramus therein doth kill himself.
Which, when I saw rehears'd, I must confess,
Made mine eyes water; but more merry tears
The passion of loud laughter never shed.
THESEUS
What are they that do play it?
PHILOSTRATE
Hard-handed men, that work in Athens here,
Which never labour'd in their minds till now;
And now have toil'd their unbreath'd memories
With this same play, against your nuptial.
THESEUS
And we will hear it.
PHILOSTRATE
                    No, my noble lord;
It is not for you: I have heard it over,
And it is nothing, nothing in the world;
Unless you can find sport in their intents,
Extremely stretch'd and conn'd with cruel pain,
To do you service.
THESEUS
                    I will hear that play;
For never any thing can be amiss,
When simpleness and duty tender it.
Go, bring them in: — and take your places, ladies.
                                [*Exit* PHILOSTRATE.
HIPPOLYTA
I love not to see wretchedness o'ercharged,
And duty in his service perishing.
THESEUS
Why, gentle sweet, you shall see no such thing.
HIPPOLYTA
He says they can do nothing in this kind.
THESEUS
The kinder we, to give them thanks for nothing.
Our sport shall be to take what they mistake:
And what poor duty cannot do,
Noble respect takes it in might, not merit.
Where I have come, great clerks have purposed
To greet me with premeditated welcomes;
Where I have seen them shiver and look pale,
Make periods in the midst of sentences,
Throttle their practis'd accent in their fears,
And, in conclusion, dumbly have broke off,
Not paying me a welcome. Trust me, sweet,
Out of this silence yet I pick'd a welcome;
And in the modesty of fearful duty
I read as much as from the rattling tongue
Of saucy and audacious eloquence.
Love, therefore, and tongue-tied simplicity,
In least speak most, to my capacity.

Enter PHILOSTRATE.

PHILOSTRATE
So please your Grace, the Prologue is address'd.
THESEUS
Let him approach.   [*Flourish of trumpets.*

Enter the PROLOGUE.

PROLOGUE
If we offend, it is with our good will.
    That you should think, we come not to offend,
But with good will. To show our simple skill,
    That is the true beginning of our end.
Consider, then, we come but in despite.
    We do not come as minding to content you,
Our true intent is. All for your delight,
    We are not here. That you should here repent you,
The actors are at hand; and, by their show,
You shall know all that you are like to know.
THESEUS
This fellow doth not stand upon points.
LYSANDER
He hath rid his prologue like a rough colt; he knows
not the stop. A good moral, my lord: it is not enough to
speak, but to speak true.

HIPPOLYTA
Indeed he hath play'd on his prologue like a child on a recorder; a sound, but not in government.
THESEUS
His speech was like a tangled chain; nothing impair'd, but all disorder'd. Who is next?

Enter PYRAMUS *and* THISBE, WALL,
MOONSHINE, *and* LION.

PROLOGUE
Gentles, perchance you wonder at this show;
   But wonder on, till truth make all things plain.
This man is Pyramus, if you would know;
   This beauteous lady, Thisbe is certain.
This man, with lime and rough-cast, doth present
   Wall, that vile Wall which did these lovers sunder;
And through Wall's chink, poor souls, they are content
   To whisper; at the which let no man wonder.
This man, with lantern, dog, and bush of thorn,
   Presenteth Moonshine; for, if you will know
By moonshine did these lovers think no scorn
   To meet at Ninus' tomb, there, there to woo.
This grisly beast, which by name Lion hight,
   The trusty Thisbe, coming first by night,
Did scare away, or rather did affright;
   And, as she fled, her mantle she did fall,
Which Lion vile with bloody mouth did stain.
Anon comes Pyramus, sweet youth and tall,
   And finds his trusty Thisbe's mantle slain:
Whereat, with blade, with bloody blameful blade,
   He bravely broach'd his boiling bloody breast;
And Thisbe, tarrying in mulberry shade,
   His dagger drew, and died. For all the rest,
Let Lion, Moonshine, Wall, and lovers twain,
At large discourse, while here they do remain.

[Exeunt PROLOGUE, PYRAMUS, THISBE, LION,
and MOONSHINE.

THESEUS
I wonder if the lion be to speak.
DEMETRIUS
No wonder, my lord: one lion may, when many asses do.
WALL
In this same interlude it doth befall
That I, one Snout by name, present a wall;
And such a wall, as I would have you think,
That had in it a crannied hole or chink,
Through which the lovers, Pyramus and Thisbe,
Did whisper often very secretly.
This loam, this rough-cast, and this stone, doth show
That I am that same wall; the truth is so:
And this the cranny is, right and sinister,
Through which the fearful lovers are to whisper.
THESEUS
Would you desire lime and hair to speak better?
DEMETRIUS
It is the wittiest partition that ever I heard discourse, my lord.
THESEUS
Pyramus draws near the wall: silence!

Enter PYRAMUS.

PYRAMUS
O grim-look'd night! O night with hue so black!
O night, which ever art when day is not!
O night, O night! alack, alack, alack,
   I fear my Thisbe's promise is forgot! —
And thou, O wall, O sweet, O lovely wall,
   That stand'st between her father's ground and mine!
Thou wall, O wall, O sweet and lovely wall,
   Show me thy chink, to blink through with mine eyne!
     [WALL holds up his fingers.
Thanks, courteous wall: Jove shield thee well for this!
   But what see I? No Thisbe do I see.
O wicked wall, through whom I see no bliss!
   Cursed be thy stones for thus deceiving me!
THESEUS
The wall, methinks, being sensible, should curse again.
BOTTOM
No, in truth, sir, he should not. 'Deceiving me' is Thisbe's cue: she is to enter now, and I am to spy her through the wall. You shall see, it will fall pat as I told you. — Yonder she comes.

Enter THISBE.

THISBE
O wall, full often hast thou heard my moans,
   For parting my fair Pyramus and me!
My cherry lips have often kiss'd thy stones,
   Thy stones with lime and hair knit up in thee.

PYRAMUS
I see a voice: now will I to the chink,
To spy an I can hear my Thisbe's face. —
Thisbe!
THISBE
My love! thou art my love, I think.
PYRAMUS
Think what thou wilt, I am thy lover's grace;
And, like Limander, am I trusty still.
THISBE
And I like Helen, till the Fates me kill.
PYRAMUS
Not Shafalus to Procrus was so true.
THISBE
As Shafalus to Procrus, I to you.
PYRAMUS
O, kiss me through the hole of this vile wall!
THISBE
I kiss the wall's hole, not your lips at all.
PYRAMUS
Wilt thou at Ninny's tomb meet me straightway?
THISBE
'Tide life, 'tide death, I come without delay.
    [Exeunt PYRAMUS *and* THISBE.

WALL
Thus have I, wall, my part discharged so;
And, being done, thus wall away doth go.
    [Exit.
THESEUS
Now is the mural down between the two neighbours.
DEMETRIUS
No remedy, my lord, when walls are so wilful to hear without warning.
HIPPOLYTA
This is the silliest stuff that e'er I heard.
THESEUS
The best in this kind are but shadows; and the worst are no worse, if imagination amend them.
HIPPOLYTA
It must be your imagination then, and not theirs.
THESEUS
If we imagine no worse of them than they of themselves, they may pass for excellent men. — Here come two noble beasts in, a moon and a lion.

Enter LION *and* MOONSHINE.

LION
You, ladies, you, whose gentle hearts do fear,
   The smallest monstrous mouse that creeps on floor,
May now perchance both quake and tremble here,
   When lion rough in wildest rage doth roar.
Then know that I one Snug the joiner am,
No lion fell, nor else no lion's dam;
For, if I should as lion come in strife
Into this place, 'twere pity on my life.
THESEUS
A very gentle beast, and of a good conscience.
DEMETRIUS
The very best at a beast, my lord, that e'er I saw.
LYSANDER
This lion is a very fox for his valour.
THESEUS
True; and a goose for his discretion.
DEMETRIUS
Not so, my lord; for his valour cannot carry his discretion; and the fox carries the goose.
THESEUS
His discretion, I am sure, cannot carry his valour; for the goose carries not the fox. It is well: leave it to his discretion, and let us listen to the moon.
MOONSHINE
This lantern doth the horned moon present; —
DEMETRIUS
He should have worn the horns on his head.
THESEUS
He is no crescent, and his horns are invisible within the circumference.
MOONSHINE
This lantern doth the horned moon present;
Myself the man-i'-th'- moon do seem to be.
THESEUS
This is the greatest error of all the rest: the man should be put into the lantern. How is it else the man-i-th'-moon?
DEMETRIUS
He dares not come there for the candle; for, you see, it is already in snuff.

HIPPOLYTA
I am a-weary of this moon: would he would change!
THESEUS
It appears, by his small light of discretion, that he is in the wane; but yet, in courtesy, in all reason, we must stay the time.
LYSANDER
Proceed, moon.
MOONSHINE
All that I have to say is, to tell you that the lantern is the moon; I, the man-i'-th'-moon; this thorn-bush, my thorn-bush; and this dog, my dog.
DEMETRIUS
Why, all these should be in the lantern; for all these are in the moon. But, silence! here comes Thisbe.

Enter THISBE.

THISBE
This is old Ninny's tomb. Where is my love?
LION
O —   *[The* LION *roars;* THISBE *runs off.*
DEMETRIUS
Well roar'd, lion.
THESEUS
Well run, Thisbe.
HIPPOLYTA
Well shone, moon. — Truly, the moon shines with a good grace.
    [The LION *tears* THISBE'S *mantle, and exit.*
THESEUS
Well mous'd, lion.
DEMETRIUS
And then came Pyramus.
LYSANDER
And so the lion vanish'd.

Enter PYRAMUS.

PYRAMUS
Sweet moon, I thank thee for thy sunny beams;
   I thank thee, moon, for shining now so bright;
For, by thy gracious, golden, glittering streams,
   I trust to taste of truest Thisbe's sight.

       But stay, — O spite! —
       But mark, poor knight,
   What dreadful dole is here!
       Eyes, do you see?
       How can it be?
O dainty duck! O dear!
       Thy mantle good,
   What, stain'd with blood?
Approach, ye Furies fell!
       O Fates, come, come,
       Cut thread and thrum;
Quail, crush, conclude, and quell!
THESEUS
This passion, and the death of a dear friend, would go near to make a man look sad.
HIPPOLYTA
Beshrew my heart, but I pity the man.
PYRAMUS
O, wherefore, Nature, didst thou lions frame?
Since lion vile hath here deflower'd my dear:
Which is — no, no — which was the fairest dame
   That liv'd, that lov'd, that lik'd, that look'd with cheer.

       Come, tears, confound;
       Out, sword, and wound
The pap of Pyramus, —
       Ay, that left pap,
       Where heart doth hop: —
         [Stabs himself.
Thus die I, thus, thus, thus.
       Now am I dead,
       Now am I fled;
My soul is in the sky:
       Tongue, lose thy light;
       Moon, take thy flight: —
         [Exit MOONSHINE.
Now die, die, die, die, die.   *[Dies.*
DEMETRIUS
No die, but an ace, for him; for he is but one.
LYSANDER
Less than an ace, man; for he is dead; he is nothing.
THESEUS
With the help of a surgeon he might yet recover; and prove an ass.
HIPPOLYTA
How chance Moonshine is gone before Thisbe comes back to find her lover?

THESEUS
She will find him by starlight. — Here she comes, and
her passion ends the play.
Enter THISBE.

HIPPOLYTA
Methinks she should not use a long one for such a
Pyramus: I hope she will be brief.

DEMETRIUS
A mote will turn the balance, which Pyramus, which
Thisbe, is the better; he for a man, God warrant us, —
she for a woman, God bless us.

LYSANDER
She hath spied him already with those sweet eyes.

DEMETRIUS
And thus she moans, *videlicet*:

THISBE
   Asleep, my love?
    What, dead, my dove?
   O Pyramus, arise!
     Speak, speak. Quite dumb?
     Dead, dead? A tomb
   Must cover thy sweet eyes.
    These lily lips,
    This cherry nose,
   These yellow cowslip cheeks,
    Are gone, are gone:
   Lovers, make moan:
   His eyes were green as leeks.
    O Sisters Three,
    Come, come to me,
   With hands as pale as milk;
    Lay them in gore,
    Since you have shore
   With shears his thread of silk.
    Tongue, not a word:
    Come, trusty sword;
   Come, blade, my breast imbrue;
          [*Stabs herself.*
    And, farewell, friends, —
    Thus Thisbe ends, —
   Adieu, adieu, adieu.   [*Dies.*

THESEUS
Moonshine and Lion are left to bury the dead.

DEMETRIUS
Ay, and Wall too.

BOTTOM
No, I assure you; the wall is down that parted their
fathers. Will it please you to see the epilogue, or to hear
a Bergomask dance between two of our company?

THESEUS
No epilogue, I pray you; for your play needs no excuse.
Never excuse; for when the players are all dead, there
need none to be blamed. Marry, if he that writ it had
play'd Pyramus and hang'd himself in Thisbe's garter,
it would have been a fine tragedy: and so it is, truly; and
very notably discharg'd. But, come, your Bergomask:
let your epilogue alone.   [*A dance.*
The iron tongue of midnight hath told twelve: —
Lovers, to bed; 'tis almost fairy-time.
I fear we shall out-sleep the coming morn,
As much as we this night have overwatch'd.
This palpable-gross play hath well beguil'd
The heavy gait of night. — Sweet friends, to bed. —
A fortnight hold we this solemnity
In nightly revels and new jollity.   [*Exeunt.*

Enter PUCK.

PUCK
Now the hungry lion roars,
 And the wolf behowls the moon;
Whilst the heavy ploughman snores,
 All with weary task fordone.
Now the wasted brands do glow,
 Whilst the screech-owl, screeching loud,
Puts the wretch that lies in woe
 In remembrance of a shroud.
Now it is the time of night,
 That the graves, all gaping wide,
Every one lets forth his sprite,
 In the church-way paths to glide:
And we fairies, that do run
 By the triple Hecate's team
From the presence of the sun,
 Following darkness like a dream,
Now are frolic: not a mouse
Shall disturb this hallow'd house:
I am sent, with broom, before,
To sweep the dust behind the door.

Enter OBERON *and* TITANIA, *with their* TRAIN.

OBERON
Through the house give glimmering light,
 By the dead and drowsy fire;
Every elf and fairy sprite
 Hop as light as bird from brier;
And this ditty, after me,
Sing, and dance it trippingly.

TITANIA
First, rehearse your song by rote,
To each word a warbling note:
Hand in hand, with fairy grace,
Will we sing, and bless this place. [*Song and dance.*

OBERON
Now, until the break of day,
Through this house each fairy stray.
To the best bride-bed will we,
Which by us shall blessed be;
And the issue there create
Ever shall be fortunate.
So shall all the couples three
Ever true in loving be;
And the blots of Nature's hand
Shall not in their issue stand;
Never mole, hare-lip, nor scar,
Nor mark prodigious, such as are
Despised in nativity,
Shall upon their children be.
With this field-dew consecrate,
Every fairy take his gait;
And each several chamber bless,
Through this palace, with sweet peace:
Ever shall in safety rest,
And the owner of it blest.
   Trip away;
   Make no stay;
Meet me all by break of day.

   [*Exeunt* OBERON, TITANIA, *and* TRAIN.

PUCK
If we shadows have offended,
Think but this, and all is mended, —
That you have but slumber'd here,
While these visions did appear.
And this weak and idle theme,
No more yielding but a dream,
Gentles, do not reprehend:
If you pardon, we will mend.
And, as I am an honest Puck,
If we have unearned luck,
Now to 'scape the serpent's tongue,
We will make amends ere long;
Else the Puck a liar call:
So, good-night unto you all.
Give me your hands, if we be friends,
And Robin shall restore amends. [*Exit.*

KING JOHN

DRAMATIS PERSONAE

KING JOHN.
PRINCE HENRY, *his son; afterwards King Henry III.*
ARTHUR, *Duke of Bretagne, son of Geffrey, late Duke of Bretagne, the elder brother to King John.*
WILLIAM MARESHALL, *Earl of Pembroke.*
GEFFREY FITZ-PETER, *Earl of Essex, chief-justiciary of England.*
WILLIAM LONGSWORD, *Earl of Salisbury.*
ROBERT BIGOT, *Earl of Norfolk.*
HUBERT DE BURGH, *chamberlain to the King.*
ROBERT FAULCONBRIDGE, *son to Sir Robert Faulconbridge.*

PHILIP FAULCONBRIDGE, *his half-brother, bastard son to King Richard the First.*
JAMES GURNEY, *servant to Lady Faulconbridge.*
PETER *of Pomfret, a prophet.*

PHILIP, *King of France.*
LOUIS, *the Dauphin.*
ARCHDUKE OF AUSTRIA.
CARDINAL PANDULPH, *the Pope's legate.*
MELUN, *a French lord.*
CHATILLON, *ambassador from France to King John.*

ELINOR, *widow of King Henry II. and mother to King John.*

CONSTANCE, *mother to Arthur.*
BLANCH, *daughter to Alphonso, King of Castile, and niece to King John.*
LADY FAULCONBRIDGE, *mother to the Bastard and Robert Faulconbridge.*

LORDS, CITIZENS OF ANGIERS, SHERIFF, HERALDS, OFFICERS, SOLDIERS, MESSENGERS, *and other* ATTENDANTS.

SCENE — *Sometimes in England, and sometimes in France.*

KING JOHN So, hence! Be thou the trumpet of our wrath, and sullen presage of your own decay.

ACT I

SCENE I

KING JOHN'S *palace.*

Enter KING JOHN, QUEEN ELINOR, PEMBROKE, ESSEX, SALISBURY, *and others, with* CHATILLON.

KING JOHN
Now, say, Chatillon, what would France with us?
CHATILLON
Thus, after greeting, speaks the King of France,
In my behaviour, to the majesty,
The borrow'd majesty, of England here.
QUEEN ELINOR
A strange beginning: — borrow'd majesty!
KING JOHN
Silence, good mother; hear the embassy.

CHATILLON
Philip of France, in right and true behalf
Of thy deceased brother Geffrey's son,
Arthur Plantagenet, lays most lawful claim
To this fair island and the territories, —
To Ireland, Poictiers, Anjou, Touraine, Maine;
Desiring thee to lay aside the sword
Which sways usurpingly these several titles,
And put the same into young Arthur's hand,
Thy nephew and right royal sovereign.
KING JOHN
What follows, if we disallow of this?
CHATILLON
The proud control of fierce and bloody war,
To enforce these rights so forcibly withheld.
KING JOHN
Here have we war for war, and blood for blood,
Controlment for controlment: so answer France.
CHATILLON
Then take my king's defiance from my mouth,

The furthest limit of my embassy.
KING JOHN
Bear mine to him, and so depart in peace:
Be thou as lightning in the eyes of France;
For ere thou canst report I will be there,
The thunder of my cannon shall be heard:
So, hence! Be thou the trumpet of our wrath,
And sullen presage of your own decay. —
An honourable conduct let him have: —
Pembroke, look to't. — Farewell, Chatillon.
                    [*Exeunt* CHATILLON *and* PEMBROKE.
QUEEN ELINOR
What now, my son! have I not ever said
How that ambitious Constance would not cease
Till she had kindled France and all the world
Upon the right and party of her son?
This might have been prevented and made whole
With very easy arguments of love;
Which now the manage of two kingdoms must
With fearful bloody issue arbitrate.

KING JOHN
Our strong possession and our right for us.

QUEEN ELINOR [*aside to* KING JOHN].
Your strong possession much more than your right,
Or else it must go wrong with you and me:
So much my conscience whispers in your ear,
Which none but heaven and you and I shall hear.

Enter a SHERIFF.

ESSEX
My liege, here is the strangest controversy,
Come from the country to be judg'd by you,
That e'er I heard: shall I produce the men?

KING JOHN
Let them approach. —   [*Exit* SHERIFF.
Our abbeys and our priories shall pay
This expedition's charge.

Enter SHERIFF, *with* ROBERT FAULCONBRIDGE,
and PHILIP, *his bastard brother.*
                    What men are you?

BASTARD
Your faithful subject I, a gentleman
Born in Northamptonshire, and eldest son,
As I suppose, to Robert Faulconbridge,
A soldier, by the honour-giving hand
Of Cœur-de-lion knighted in the field.

KING JOHN
What art thou?

ROBERT FAULCONBRIDGE
The son and heir to that same Faulconbridge.

KING JOHN
Is that the elder, and art thou the heir?
You came not of one mother, then, it seems.

BASTARD
Most certain of one mother, mighty king;
That is well known; and, as I think, one father:
But for the certain knowledge of that truth,
I put you o'er to heaven and to my mother:
Of that I doubt, as all men's children may.

QUEEN ELINOR
Out on thee, rude man! thou dost shame thy mother
And wound her honour with this diffidence.

BASTARD
I, madam? no, I have no reason for it, —
That is my brother's plea, and none of mine;
The which if he can prove, a' pops me out
At least from fair five hundred pound a year:
Heaven guard my mother's honour and my land!

KING JOHN
A good blunt fellow. — Why, being younger born,
Doth he lay claim to thine inheritance?

BASTARD
I know not why, except to get the land.
But once he slander'd me with bastardy:
But whe'r I be as true begot or no,
That still I lay upon my mother's head;
But, that I am as well begot, my liege, —
Fair fall the bones that took the pains for me! —
Compare our faces, and be judge yourself.
If old Sir Robert did beget us both
And were our father and this son like him,
O old Sir Robert, father, on my knee
I give heaven thanks I was not like to thee!

KING JOHN
Why, what a madcap hath heaven lent us here!

QUEEN ELINOR
He hath a trick of Cœur-de-lion's face;
The accent of his tongue affecteth him:
Do you not read some tokens of my son
In the large composition of this man?

KING JOHN
Mine eye hath well examined his parts,
And finds them perfect Richard. — Sirrah, speak,
What doth move you to claim your brother's land?

BASTARD
Because he hath a half-face, like my father,
With that half-face would he have all my land:
A half-fac'd groat five hundred pound a year!

ROBERT FAULCONBRIDGE
My gracious liege, when that my father liv'd,
Your brother did employ my father much, —

BASTARD
Well, sir, by this you cannot get my land:
Your tale must be, how he employ'd my mother.

ROBERT FAULCONBRIDGE
And once dispatch'd him in an embassy
To Germany, there with the emperor
To treat of high affairs touching that time.
Th'advantage of his absence took the king,
And in the meantime sojourn'd at my father's;

Where how he did prevail, I shame to speak,
But truth is truth: large lengths of seas and shores
Between my father and my mother lay, —
As I have heard my father speak himself, —
When this same lusty gentleman was got.
Upon his death-bed he by will bequeath'd
His lands to me; and took it, on his death,
That this, my mother's son, was none of his;
And if he were, he came into the world
Full fourteen weeks before the course of time.
Then, good my liege, let me have what is mine,
My father's land, as was my father's will.

KING JOHN
Sirrah, your brother is legitimate;
Your father's wife did after wedlock bear him;
And if she did play false, the fault was hers;
Which fault lies on the hazards of all husbands
That marry wives. Tell me, how if my brother,
Who, as you say, took pains to get this son,
Had of your father claim'd this son for his?
In sooth, good friend, your father might have kept
This calf, bred from his cow, from all the world;
In sooth, he might: then, if he were my brother's,
My brother might not claim him; nor your father,
Being none of his, refuse him: this concludes, —
My mother's son did get your father's heir;
Your father's heir must have your father's land.

ROBERT FAULCONBRIDGE
Shall, then, my father's will be of no force
To dispossess that child which is not his?

BASTARD
Of no more force to dispossess me, sir,
Than was his will to get me, as I think.

QUEEN ELINOR
Whether hadst thou rather be a Faulconbridge,
And like thy brother, to enjoy thy land,
Or the reputed son of Cœur-de-lion,
Lord of thy presence, and no land beside?

BASTARD
Madam, an if my brother had my shape,
And I had his, Sir Robert's his, like him;
And if my legs were two such riding-rods,
My arms such eel-skins stuff'd; my face so thin,
That in mine ear I durst not stick a rose,
Lest men should say, 'Look, where three-farthings
  goes!'
And, to his shape, were heir to all this land, —
Would I might never stir from off this place,
I'ld give it every foot to have this face;
I would not be Sir Nob in any case.

QUEEN ELINOR
I like thee well: wilt thou forsake thy fortune,
Bequeath thy land to him, and follow me?
I am a soldier, and now bound to France.

BASTARD
Brother, take you my land, I'll take my chance:
Your face hath got five hundred pound a year;
Yet sell your face for five pence, and 'tis dear. —
Madam, I'll follow you unto the death.

QUEEN ELINOR
Nay, I would have you go before me thither.

BASTARD
Our country manners give our betters way.

KING JOHN
What is thy name?

BASTARD
Philip, my liege, — so is my name begun, —
Philip, good old Sir Robert's wife's eldest son.

KING JOHN
From henceforth bear his name whose form thou
  bear'st:
Kneel thou down Philip, but rise more great, —
Arise Sir Richard and Plantagenet.

BASTARD
Brother by the mother's side, give me your hand:
My father gave me honour, yours gave land. —
Now blessed be the hour, by night or day,
When I was got, Sir Robert was away!

QUEEN ELINOR
The very spirit of Plantagenet! —
I am thy grandam, Richard; call me so.

BASTARD
Madam, by chance, but not by truth: what though?
Something about, a little from the right,
  In at the window, or else o'er the hatch;
Who dares not stir by day must walk by night;
  And have is have, however men do catch;
Near or far off, well won is still well shot;
And I am I, howe'er I was begot.

KING JOHN
Go, Faulconbridge: now hast thou thy desire;
A landless knight makes thee a landed squire. —
Come, madam, — and come, Richard; we must speed
For France, for France, for it is more than need.

BASTARD
Brother, adieu: good fortune come to thee!
For thou wast got i'th'way of honesty.
                    [*Exeunt all but* BASTARD.
A foot of honour better than I was;
But many a many foot of land the worse.
Well, now can I make any Joan a lady: —
'Good den, Sir Richard': — 'God-a-mercy, fellow';
And if his name be George, I'll call him Peter;
For new-made honour doth forget men's names, —
'Tis too respective and too sociable
For your conversion. Now your traveller, —
He and his toothpick at my worship's mess;
And when my knightly stomach is sufficed,
Why then I suck my teeth, and catechise
My picked man of countries: — 'My dear sir,'
Thus, leaning on mine elbow, I begin,
'I shall beseech you' — that is question now;
And then comes answer like an Absey-book: —
'O sir,' says answer, 'at your best command;
At your employment; at your service, sir':
'No, sir,' says question, 'I, sweet sir, at yours':
And so, ere answer knows what question would, —
Saving in dialogue of compliment,
And talking of the Alps and Apennines,
The Pyrenean and the river Po, —
It draws toward supper in conclusion so.
But this is worshipful society,
And fits the mounting spirit like myself;
For he is but a bastard to the time,
That doth not smack of observation;
And so am I, whether I smack or no;
And not alone in habit and device,
Exterior form, outward accoutrement,
But from the inward motion to deliver
Sweet, sweet, sweet poison for the age's tooth:
Which, though I will not practise to deceive,
Yet to avoid deceit, I mean to learn;
For it shall strew the footsteps of my rising. —
But who comes in such haste in riding-robes?
What woman-post is this? hath she no husband,
That will take pains to blow a horn before her?

Enter LADY FAULCONBRIDGE *and* JAMES
  GURNEY.

O me! it is my mother. — How now, good lady!
What brings you here to court so hastily?

LADY FAULCONBRIDGE
Where is that slave, thy brother? where is he,
That holds in chase mine honour up and down?

BASTARD
My brother Robert? old Sir Robert's son?
Colbrand the giant, that same mighty man?
Is it Sir Robert's son that you seek so?

LADY FAULCONBRIDGE
Sir Robert's son! Ay, thou unreverend boy,
Sir Robert's son: why scorn'st thou at Sir Robert?
He is Sir Robert's son; and so art thou.

BASTARD
James Gurney, wilt thou give us leave awhile?

JAMES GURNEY
Good leave, good Philip.

BASTARD
                    Philip? — sparrow! — James,
There's toys abroad: anon I'll tell thee more.
                    [*Exit* GURNEY.
Madam, I was not old Sir Robert's son;
Sir Robert might have eat his part in me
Upon Good Friday, and ne'er broke his fast:
Sir Robert could do well: marry to confess,
Could he get me? Sir Robert could not do it, —
We know his handiwork: — therefore, good mother,
To whom am I beholding for these limbs?
Sir Robert never holp to make this leg.

LADY FAULCONBRIDGE
Hast thou conspired with thy brother too,
That for thine own gain shouldst defend mine honour?
What means this scorn, thou most untoward knave?

BASTARD
Knight, knight, good mother, — Basilisco-like:
What! I am dubb'd; I have it on my shoulder.
But, mother, I am not Sir Robert's son;
I have disclaim'd Sir Robert and my land;
Legitimation, name, and all is gone:
Then, good my mother, let me know my father, —
Some proper man, I hope: who was it, mother?

LADY FAULCONBRIDGE
Hast thou denied thyself a Faulconbridge?
BASTARD
As faithfully as I deny the devil.
LADY FAULCONBRIDGE
King Richard Cœur-de-lion was thy father:
By long and vehement suit I was seduced
To make room for him in my husband's bed: —
Heaven lay not my transgression to my charge!
Thou art the issue of my dear offence,
Which was so strongly urg'd, past my defence.
BASTARD
Now, by this light, were I to get again,
Madam, I would not wish a better father.
Some sins do bear their privilege on earth,
And so doth yours; your fault was not your folly:
Needs must you lay your heart at his dispose,
Subjected tribute to commanding love,
Against whose fury and unmatched force
The aweless lion could not wage the fight,
Nor keep his princely heart from Richard's hand:
He that perforce robs lions of their hearts
May easily win a woman's. Ay, my mother,
With all my heart I thank thee for my father!
Who lives and dares but say, thou didst not well
When I was got, I'll send his soul to hell.
Come, lady, I will show thee to my kin;
   And they shall say, when Richard me begot,
If thou hadst said him nay, it had been sin:
   Who says it was, he lies; I say 'twas not.   [*Exeunt.*

ACT II

SCENE I

France. Before the walls of Angiers.

Enter, on one side, PHILIP, *king of France,* louis,
CONSTANCE, ARTHUR, *and* FORCES; *on the other,*
the ARCHDUKE OF AUSTRIA *and* FORCES.

KING PHILIP
Before Angiers well met, brave Austria. —
Arthur, that great forerunner of thy blood,
Richard, that robb'd the lion of his heart,
And fought the holy wars in Palestine,
By this brave duke came early to his grave:
And, for amends to his posterity,
At our importance hither is he come,
To spread his colours, boy, in thy behalf;
And to rebuke the usurpation
Of thy unnatural uncle, English John:
Embrace him, love him, give him welcome hither.
ARTHUR
God shall forgive you Cœur-de-lion's death
The rather that you give his offspring life,
Shadowing their right under your wings of war:
I give you welcome with a powerless hand,
But with a heart full of unstained love:

Welcome before the gates of Angiers, duke.
KING PHILIP
A noble boy! Who would not do thee right?
AUSTRIA
Upon thy cheek lay I this zealous kiss,
As seal to this indenture of my love; —
That to my home I will no more return,
Till Angiers, and the right thou hast in France,
Together with that pale, that white-fac'd shore,
Whose foot spurns back the ocean's roaring tides,
And coops from other lands her islanders, —
Even till that England, hedg'd in with the main,
That water-walled bulwark, still secure
And confident from foreign purposes, —
Even till that utmost corner of the west
Salute thee for her king: till then, fair boy,
Will I not think of home, but follow arms.
CONSTANCE
O, take his mother's thanks, a widow's thanks,
Till your strong hand shall help to give him strength
To make a more requital to your love!
AUSTRIA
The peace of heaven is theirs that lift their swords
In such a just and charitable war.
KING PHILIP
Well, then, to work: our cannon shall be bent
Against the brows of this resisting town. —
Call for our chiefest men of discipline,
To cull the plots of best advantages:
We'll lay before this town our royal bones,
Wade to the market-place in Frenchmen's blood,
But we will make it subject to this boy.
CONSTANCE
Stay for an answer to your embassy,
Lest unadvis'd you stain your swords with blood:
My Lord Chatillon may from England bring
That right in peace, which here we urge in war;
And then we shall repent each drop of blood
That hot rash haste so indirectly shed.
KING PHILIP
A wonder, lady, — lo, upon thy wish,
Our messenger Chatillon is arriv'd!

Enter CHATILLON.

What England says, say briefly, gentle lord;
We coldly pause for thee; Chatillon, speak.
CHATILLON
Then turn your forces from this paltry siege,
And stir them up against a mightier task.
England, impatient of your just demands,
Hath put himself in arms: the adverse winds,
Whose leisure I have stay'd, have given him time
To land his legions all as soon as I;
His marches are expedient to this town,
His forces strong, his soldiers confident.
With him along is come the mother-queen,
An Ate, stirring him to blood and strife;
With her her niece, the Lady Blanch of Spain;
With them a bastard of the king's deceased:

And all th'unsettled humours of the land, —
Rash, inconsiderate, fiery voluntaries,
With ladies' faces and fierce dragons' spleens, —
Have sold their fortunes at their native homes,
Bearing their birthrights proudly on their backs,
To make a hazard of new fortunes here:
In brief, a braver choice of dauntless spirits,
Than now the English bottoms have waft o'er,
Did never float upon the swelling tide,
To do offence and scathe in Christendom.
The interruption of their churlish drums
                                       [*Drum beats.*
Cuts off more circumstance: they are at hand,
To parley or to fight; therefore prepare.
KING PHILIP
How much unlook'd for is this expedition!
AUSTRIA
By how much unexpected, by so much
We must awake endeavour for defence;
For courage mounteth with occasion:
Let them be welcome, then; we are prepared.

Enter KING JOHN, ELINOR, BLANCH, BASTARD,
LORDS, *and* FORCES.

KING JOHN
Peace be to France, if France in peace permit
Our just and lineal entrance to our own!
If not, bleed France, and peace ascend to heaven!
Whiles we, God's wrathful agent, do correct
Their proud contempt that beats His peace to heaven.
KING PHILIP
Peace be to England, if that war return
From France to England, there to live in peace!
England we love; and for that England's sake
With burden of our armour here we sweat.
This toil of ours should be a work of thine;
But thou from loving England art so far,
That thou hast under-wrought his lawful king,
Cut off the sequence of posterity,
Out-faced infant state, and done a rape
Upon the maiden virtue of the crown.
Look here upon thy brother Geffrey's face; —
These eyes, these brows, were moulded out of his:
This little abstract doth contain that large
Which died in Geffrey; and the hand of time
Shall draw this brief into as huge a volume.
That Geffrey was thy elder brother born,
And this his son; England was Geffrey's right,
And this is Geffrey's: in the name of God,
How comes it, then, that thou art call'd a king,
When living blood doth in these temples beat,
Which owe the crown that thou o'ermasterest?
KING JOHN
From whom hast thou this great commission, France,
To draw my answer from thy articles?
KING PHILIP
From that supernal judge, that stirs good thoughts
In any breast of strong authority,
To look into the blots and stains of right.
That judge hath made me guardian to this boy:
Under whose warrant I impeach thy wrong;
And by whose help I mean to chastise it.
KING JOHN
Alack, thou dost usurp authority.
KING PHILIP
Excuse, — it is to beat usurping down.
QUEEN ELINOR
Who is it thou dost call usurper, France?
CONSTANCE
Let me make answer; — thy usurping son.
QUEEN ELINOR
Out, insolent! thy bastard shall be king,
That thou mayst be a queen, and check the world!
CONSTANCE
My bed was ever to thy son as true
As thine was to thy husband; and this boy
Liker in feature to his father Geffrey
Than thou and John in manners, — being as like
As rain to water, or devil to his dam.
My boy a bastard! By my soul, I think
His father never was so true begot:
It cannot be, an if thou wert his mother.
QUEEN ELINOR
There's a good mother, boy, that blots thy father.
CONSTANCE
There's a good grandam, boy, that would blot thee.
AUSTRIA
Peace!
BASTARD
          Hear the crier.

ARTHUR I give you welcome with a powerless hand, but with a heart full of unstained love.

AUSTRIA

What the devil art thou?

BASTARD
One that will play the devil, sir, with you,
An a' may catch your hide and you alone:
You are the hare of whom the proverb goes,
Whose valour plucks dead lions by the beard:
I'll smoke your skin-coat, an I catch you right;
Sirrah, look to't; i'faith, I will, i'faith.

BLANCH
O, well did he become that lion's robe
That did disrobe the lion of that robe!

BASTARD
It lies as sightly on the back of him
As great Alcides' shows upon an ass: —
But, ass, I'll take that burden from your back,
Or lay on that shall make your shoulders crack.

AUSTRIA
What cracker is this same that deafs our ears
With this abundance of superfluous breath? —
King Philip, determine what we shall do straight.

KING PHILIP
Women and fools, break off your conference.
King John, this is the very sum of all, —
England and Ireland, Anjou, Touraine, Maine,
In right of Arthur do I claim of thee:
Wilt thou resign them, and lay down thy arms?

KING JOHN
My life as soon: — I do defy thee, France. —
Arthur of Bretagne, yield thee to my hand;
And, out of my dear love, I'll give thee more
Than e'er the coward hand of France can win:
Submit thee, boy.

QUEEN ELINOR

Come to thy grandam, child.

CONSTANCE
Do, child, go to it grandam, child;
Give grandam kingdom, and it grandam will
Give it a plum, a cherry, and a fig:
There's a good grandam.

ARTHUR

Good my mother, peace!
I would that I were low laid in my grave:
I am not worth this coil that's made for me.

QUEEN ELINOR
His mother shames him so, poor boy, he weeps.

CONSTANCE
Now shame upon you, whe'r she does or no!
His grandam's wrongs, and not his mother's shames,
Draws those heaven-moving pearls from his poor eyes,
Which heaven shall take in nature of a fee;
Ay, with these crystal beads heaven shall be brib'd
To do him justice, and revenge on you.

QUEEN ELINOR
Thou monstrous slanderer of heaven and earth!

CONSTANCE
Thou monstrous injurer of heaven and earth!
Call me not slanderer; thou and thine usurp
The dominations, royalties, and rights
Of this oppressed boy: this is thy eld'st son's son,
Infortunate in nothing but in thee:
Thy sins are visited in this poor child;
The canon of the law is laid on him,
Being but the second generation
Removed from thy sin-conceiving womb.

KING JOHN
Bedlam, have done.

CONSTANCE

I have but this to say, —
That he is not only plagued for her sin,
But God hath made her sin and her the plague
On this removed issue, plagu'd for her,
And with her plague; her sin his injury,
Her injury the beadle to her sin;
All punish'd in the person of this child,
And all for her; a plague upon her!

QUEEN ELINOR
Thou unadvised scold, I can produce
A will that bars the title of thy son.

CONSTANCE
Ay, who doubts that? a will! a wicked will;
A woman's will; a canker'd grandam's will!

KING PHILIP
Peace, lady! pause, or be more temperate:
It ill beseems this presence to cry aim
To these ill-tuned repetitions. —
Some trumpet summon hither to the walls
These men of Angiers: let us hear them speak,
Whose title they admit, Arthur's or John's.

Trumpet sounds. Enter CITIZENS *upon the walls.*

FIRST CITIZEN
Who is it that hath warn'd us to the walls?

KING PHILIP
'Tis France, for England.

KING JOHN

England, for itself: —
You men of Angiers, and my loving subjects, —

KING PHILIP
You loving men of Angiers, Arthur's subjects,
Our trumpet call'd you to this gentle parle, —

KING JOHN
For our advantage; therefore hear us first.
These flags of France, that are advanced here
Before the eye and prospect of your town,
Have hither march'd to your endamagement:
The cannons have their bowels full of wrath,
And ready mounted are they to spit forth
Their iron indignation 'gainst your walls:
All preparation for a bloody siege
And merciless proceeding by these French
Confronts your city's eyes, your winking gates;
And, but for our approach, those sleeping stones,
That as a waist doth girdle you about,
By the compulsion of their ordinance
By this time from their fixed beds of lime
Had been dishabited, and wide havoc made
For bloody power to rush upon your peace.
But, on the sight of us, your lawful king, —
Who painfully, with much expedient march,
Have brought a countercheck before your gates,
To save unscratch'd your city's threaten'd cheeks, —
Behold, the French, amaz'd, vouchsafe a parle;
And now, instead of bullets wrapp'd in fire,
To make a shaking fever in your walls,
They shoot but calm words, folded up in smoke,
To make a faithless error in your ears:
Which trust accordingly, kind citizens,
And let us in, your king; whose labour'd spirits,
Forwearied in this action of swift speed,
Crave harbourage within your city-walls.

KING PHILIP
When I have said, make answer to us both.
Lo, in this right hand, whose protection
Is most divinely vow'd upon the right
Of him it holds, stands young Plantagenet,
Son to the elder brother of this man,
And king o'er him, and all that he enjoys:
For this down-trodden equity, we tread
In warlike march these greens before your town;
Being no further enemy to you
Than the constraint of hospitable zeal
In the relief of this oppressed child
Religiously provokes. Be pleased, then,
To pay that duty which you truly owe
To him that owes it, namely, this young prince:
And then our arms, like to a muzzled bear,
Save in aspect, hath all offence seal'd up:
Our cannons' malice vainly shall be spent
Against th'invulnerable clouds of heaven;
And with a blessed and unvex'd retire,
With unhack'd swords and helmets all unbruised,
We will bear home that lusty blood again,
Which here we came to spout against your town,
And leave your children, wives, and you in peace.
But if you fondly pass our proffer'd offer,
'Tis not the roundure of your old-fac'd walls
Can hide you from our messengers of war,
Though all these English, and their discipline,
Were harbour'd in their rude circumference.
Then, tell us, shall your city call us lord,
In that behalf which we have challenged it?
Or shall we give the signal to our rage,
And stalk in blood to our possession?

FIRST CITIZEN
In brief, we are the king of England's subjects:
For him, and in his right, we hold this town.

KING JOHN
Acknowledge, then, the king, and let me in.

FIRST CITIZEN
That can we not; but he that proves the king,
To him will we prove loyal: till that time
Have we ramm'd up our gates against the world.

KING JOHN
Doth not the crown of England prove the king?
And if not that, I bring you witnesses,
Twice fifteen thousand hearts of England's breed, —

BASTARD
Bastards, and else.

KING JOHN
To verify our title with their lives.

KING PHILIP
As many and as well-born bloods as those, —

BASTARD
Some bastards too.

KING PHILIP
Stand in his face, to contradict his claim.

FIRST CITIZEN
Till you compound whose right is worthiest,
We for the worthiest hold the right from both.

KING JOHN
Then God forgive the sin of all those souls
That to their everlasting residence,
Before the dew of evening fall, shall fleet,
In dreadful trial of our kingdom's king!

KING PHILIP
Amen, amen! — Mount, chevaliers! to arms!

BASTARD
Saint George, that swing'd the dragon, and e'er since
Sits on his horse back at mine hostess' door,
Teach us some fence! — [*to* AUSTRIA] Sirrah, were I at home,
At your den, sirrah, with your lioness,
I'ld set an ox-head to your lion's hide,
And make a monster of you.

AUSTRIA

Peace! no more.

BASTARD
O, tremble, for you hear the lion roar!

KING JOHN
Up higher to the plain; where we'll set forth
In best appointment all our regiments.

FIRST CITIZEN Till you compound whose right is worthiest, we for the worthiest hold the right from both.

BASTARD
Speed, then, to take advantage of the field.

KING PHILIP
It shall be so; — [to LOUIS] and at the other hill
Command the rest to stand. — God and our right!

[Exeunt, severally, the English and French KINGS, etc.
Here, after excursions, enter the HERALD OF FRANCE,
with trumpets, to the gates.

FRENCH HERALD
You men of Angiers, open wide your gates,
And let young Arthur, Duke of Bretagne, in,
Who, by the hand of France, this day hath made
Much work for tears in many an English mother,
Whose sons lie scatter'd on the bleeding ground:
Many a widow's husband grovelling lies,
Coldly embracing the discolour'd earth;
And victory, with little loss, doth play
Upon the dancing banners of the French,
Who are at hand, triumphantly display'd,
To enter conquerors, and to proclaim
Arthur of Bretagne England's king and yours.

Enter ENGLISH HERALD, *with trumpet.*

ENGLISH HERALD
Rejoice, you men of Angiers, ring your bells;
King John, your king and England's, doth approach,
Commander of this hot malicious day:
Their armours, that march'd hence so silver-bright,
Hither return all gilt with Frenchmen's blood;
There stuck no plume in any English crest
That is removed by a staff of France;
Our colours do return in those same hands
That did display them when we first march'd forth;
And, like a jolly troop of huntsmen, come
Our lusty English, all with purpled hands,
Dyed in the dying slaughter of their foes:
Open your gates, and give the victors way.

FIRST CITIZEN
Heralds, from off our towers we might behold,
From first to last, the onset and retire
Of both your armies; whose equality
By our best eyes cannot be censured:
Blood hath bought blood, and blows have answer'd
    blows;
Strength match'd with strength, and power confronted
    power:
Both are alike; and both alike we like.
One must prove greatest: while they weight so even,
We hold our town for neither; yet for both.

Enter the two KINGS, *with their powers, severally.*

KING JOHN
France, hast thou yet more blood to cast away?
Say, shall the current of our right run on?
Whose passage, vex'd with thy impediment,
Shall leave his native channel, and o'erswell
With course disturb'd even thy confining shores,
Unless thou let his silver water keep
A peaceful progress to the ocean.

KING PHILIP
England, thou hast not sav'd one drop of blood,
In this hot trial, more than we of France;
Rather, lost more: and by this hand I swear,
That sways the earth this climate overlooks,
Before we will lay down our just-borne arms,
We'll put thee down, 'gainst whom these arms we bear,
Or add a royal number to the dead,
Gracing the scroll that tells of this war's loss
With slaughter coupled to the name of kings.

BASTARD
Ha, majesty! how high thy glory towers,
When the rich blood of kings is set on fire!
O, now doth Death line his dead chaps with steel;
The swords of soldiers are his teeth, his fangs;
And now he feasts, mousing the flesh of men,
In undetermin'd differences of kings. —
Why stand these royal fronts amazed thus?
Cry 'havoc,' kings! back to the stained field,
You equal-potent, fiery-kindled spirits!
Then let confusion of one part confirm
The other's peace; till then, blows, blood, and death!

KING JOHN
Whose party do the townsmen yet admit?

KING PHILIP
Speak, citizens, for England; who's your king?

FIRST CITIZEN
The king of England, when we know the king.

KING PHILIP
Know him in us, that here hold up his right.

KING JOHN
In us, that are our own great deputy,

And bear possession of our person here;
Lord of our presence, Angiers, and of you.

FIRST CITIZEN
A greater power then we denies all this;
And till it be undoubted, we do lock
Our former scruple in our strong-barr'd gates;
King'd of our fears, until our fears, resolved,
Be by some certain king purged and deposed.

BASTARD
By heaven, these scroyles of Angiers flout you, kings,
And stand securely on their battlements,
As in a theatre, whence they gape and point
At your industrious scenes and acts of death.
Your royal presences be rul'd by me: —
Do like the mutines of Jerusalem,
Be friends awhile, and both conjointly bend
Your sharpest deeds of malice on this town:
By east and west let France and England mount
Their battering cannon, charged to the mouths,
Till their soul-fearing clamours have brawl'd down
The flinty ribs of this contemptuous city:
I'ld play incessantly upon these jades,
Even till unfenced desolation
Leave them as naked as the vulgar air.
That done, dissever your united strengths,
And part your mingled colours once again;
Turn face to face, and bloody point to point;
Then, in a moment, Fortune shall cull forth
One of one side her happy minion,
To whom in favour she shall give the day,
And kiss him with a glorious victory.
How like you this wild counsel, mighty states?
Smacks it not something of the policy?

KING JOHN
Now, by the sky that hangs above our heads,
I like it well. — France, shall we knit our powers,
And lay this Angiers even with the ground;
Then, after, fight who shall be king of it?

BASTARD
An if thou hast the mettle of a king, —
Being wrong'd, as we are, by this peevish town, —
Turn thou the mouth of thy artillery,
As we will ours, against these saucy walls;
And when that we have dash'd them to the ground,
Why, then defy each other, and, pell-mell,
Make work upon ourselves, for heaven or hell.

KING PHILIP
Let it be so. — Say, where will you assault?

KING JOHN
We from the west will send destruction
Into this city's bosom.

AUSTRIA
I from the north.

KING PHILIP
                    Our thunder from the south
Shall rain their drift of bullets on this town.

BASTARD [*aside*].
O prudent discipline! From north to south, —
Austria and France shoot in each other's mouth:
I'll stir them to it. — Come, away, away!

FIRST CITIZEN
Hear us, great kings: vouchsafe awhile to stay,
And I shall show you peace and fair-fac'd league;
Win you this city without stroke or wound;
Rescue those breathing lives to die in beds,
That here come sacrifices for the field:
Persever not, but hear me, mighty kings.

KING JOHN
Speak on, with favour; we are bent to hear.

FIRST CITIZEN
That daughter there of Spain, the Lady Blanch,
Is niece to England: — look upon the years
Of Louis the Dauphin and that lovely maid:
If lusty love should go in quest of beauty,
Where should he find it fairer than in Blanch?
If zealous love should go in search of virtue,
Where should he find it purer than in Blanch?
If love ambitious sought a match of birth,
Whose veins bound richer blood than Lady Blanch?
Such as she is, in beauty, virtue, birth,
Is the young Dauphin every way complete, —
If not complete, O, say he is not she;
And she again wants nothing, to name want,
It want it be not, that she is not he:
He is the half part of a blessed man,
Left to be finished by such as she;
And she a fair divided excellence,
Whose fulness of perfection lies in him.
O, two such silver currents, when they join,
Do glorify the banks that bound them in;

And two such shores to two such streams made one,
Two such controlling bounds shall you be, kings,
To these two princes, if you marry them.
This union shall do more than battery can
To our fast-closed gates; for, at this match,
With swifter spleen than powder can enforce,
The mouth of passage shall we fling wide ope,
And give you entrance: but without this match,
The sea enraged is not half so deaf,
Lions more confident, mountains and rocks
More free from motion; no, not Death himself
In mortal fury half so peremptory,
As we to keep this city.

BASTARD
                    Here's a stay,
That shakes the rotten carcass of old Death
Out of his rags! Here's a large mouth, indeed,
That spits forth death and mountains, rocks and seas;
Talks as familiarly of roaring lions
As maids of thirteen do of puppy-dogs!
What cannoneer begot this lusty blood?
He speaks plain cannon, — fire and smoke and
    bounce;
He gives the bastinado with his tongue:
Our ears are cudgell'd; not a word of his
But buffets better than a fist of France:
Zounds, I was never so bethump'd with words
Since I first call'd my brother's father dad.

QUEEN ELINOR [*aside to* KING JOHN].
Son, list to this conjunction, make this match;
Give with our niece a dowry large enough:
For by this knot thou shalt so surely tie
Thy now-unsured assurance to the crown,
That yon green boy shall have no sun to ripe
The bloom that promiseth a mighty fruit.
I see a yielding in the looks of France;
Mark, how they whisper: urge them while their souls
Are capable of this ambition,
Lest zeal, now melted by the windy breath
Of soft petitions, pity, and remorse,
Cool and congeal again to what it was.

FIRST CITIZEN
Why answer not the double majesties
This friendly treaty of our threat'ned town?

KING PHILIP
Speak England first, that hath been forward first
To speak unto this city: what say you?

KING JOHN
If that the Dauphin there, thy princely son,
Can in this book of beauty read 'I love,'
Her dowry shall weigh equal with a queen:
For Anjou, and fair Touraine, Maine, Poictiers,
And all that we upon this side the sea —
Except this city now by us besieged —
Find liable to our crown and dignity,
Shall gild her bridal bed; and make her rich
In titles, honours, and promotions,
As she in beauty, education, blood,
Holds hand with any princess of the world.

KING PHILIP
What say'st thou, boy? look in the lady's face.

LOUIS
I do, my lord; and in her eye I find
A wonder, or a wondrous miracle,
The shadow of myself form'd in her eye;
Which, being but the shadow of your son,
Becomes a sun, and makes your son a shadow:
I do protest I never lov'd myself,
Till now infixed I beheld myself
Drawn in the flattering table of her eye.
                    [*Whispers with* BLANCH.

BASTARD [*aside*].
Drawn in the flattering table of her eye! —
    Hang'd in the frowning wrinkle of her brow! —
And quarter'd in her heart! — he doth espy
    Himself love's traitor: — this is pity now,
That, hang'd and drawn and quarter'd, there should be
In such a love so vile a lout as he.

BLANCH
My uncle's will in this respect is mine:
If he see aught in you that makes him like,
That any thing he sees, which moves his liking,
I can with ease translate it to my will;
Or if you will, to speak more properly,
I will enforce it easily to my love.
Further I will not flatter you, my lord,
That all I see in you is worthy love,
Than this, — that nothing do I see in you,
Though churlish thoughts themselves should be your
    judge,
That I can find should merit any hate.

KING JOHN
What say these young ones? — What say you, my
  niece?

BLANCH
That she is bound in honour still to do
What you in wisdom still vouchsafe to say.

KING JOHN
Speak then, Prince Dauphin; can you love this lady?

LOUIS
Nay, ask me if I can refrain from love;
For I do love her most unfeignedly.

KING JOHN
Then do I give Volquessen, Touraine, Maine,
Poictiers, and Anjou, these five provinces,
With her to thee; and this addition more,
Full thirty thousand marks of English coin. —
Philip of France, if thou be pleas'd withal,
Command thy son and daughter to join hands.

KING PHILIP
It likes us well. — Young princes, close your hands.

AUSTRIA
And your lips too; for I am well assured
That I did so when I was first assured.

KING PHILIP
Now, citizens of Angiers, ope your gates,
Let in that amity which you have made;
For at Saint Mary's chapel presently
The rites of marriage shall be solemnis'd. —
Is not the Lady Constance in this troop?
I know she is not; for this match made up
Her presence would have interrupted much:
Where is she and her son? tell me, who knows.

LOUIS
She is sad and passionate at your highness' tent.

KING PHILIP
And, by my faith, this league that we have made
Will give her sadness very little cure. —
Brother of England, how may we content
This widow lady? In her right we came;
Which we, God knows, have turn'd another way,
To our own vantage.

KING JOHN
                      We will heal up all;
For we'll create young Arthur Duke of Bretagne
And Earl of Richmond; and this rich fair town
We make him lord of. — Call the Lady Constance;
Some speedy messenger bid her repair
To our solemnity: — I trust we shall,
If not fill up the measure of her will,
Yet in some measure satisfy her so
That we shall stop her exclamation.
Go we, as well as haste will suffer us,
To this unlook'd-for, unprepared pomp.
                  [Exeunt all but BASTARD.

BASTARD
Mad world! mad kings! mad composition!
John, to stop Arthur's title in the whole,
Hath willingly departed with a part;
And France, — whose armour conscience buckled on,
Whom zeal and charity brought to the field
As God's own soldier, — rounded in the ear
With that same purpose-changer, that sly devil;
That broker, that still breaks the pate of faith;
That daily break-vow; he that wins of all,
Of kings, of beggars, old men, young men, maids, —
Who having no external thing to lose
But the word 'maid', cheats the poor maid of that;
That smooth-fac'd gentleman, tickling Commodity, —
Commodity, the bias of the world;
The world, who of itself is peised well,
Made to run even upon even ground,
Till this advantage, this vile-drawing bias,
This sway of motion, this Commodity,
Makes it take head from all indifferency,
From all direction, purpose, course, intent:
And this same bias, this Commodity,
This bawd, this broker, this all-changing word,
Clapp'd on the outward eye of fickle France,
Hath drawn him from his own determin'd aid,
From a resolv'd and honourable war,
To a most base and vile-concluded peace. —
And why rail I on this Commodity?
But for because he hath not woo'd me yet:
Not that I have the power to clutch my hand,
When his fair angels would salute my palm;
But for my hand, as unattempted yet,
Like a poor beggar, raileth on the rich.
Well, whiles I am a beggar, I will rail,
And say, There is no sin but to be rich:
And being rich, my virtue then shall be,
To say, There is no vice but beggary:

Since kings break faith upon commodity,
Gain, be my lord, — for I will worship thee!   [Exit.

ACT III

SCENE I

France. The French KING'S *tent.*

Enter CONSTANCE, ARTHUR, *and* SALISBURY.

CONSTANCE
Gone to be married! gone to swear a peace!
False blood to false blood join'd! gone to be friends!
Shall Louis have Blanch? and Blanch those provinces?
It is not so; thou hast misspoke, misheard;
Be well advis'd, tell o'er thy tale again:
It cannot be; thou dost but say 'tis so:
I trust I may not trust thee; for thy word
Is but the vain breath of a common man:
Believe me, I do not believe thee, man;
I have a king's oath to the contrary.
Thou shalt be punish'd for thus frighting me,
For I am sick, and capable of fears;
Oppress'd with wrongs, and therefore full of fears;
A widow, husbandless, subject to fears;
A woman, naturally born to fears;
And though thou now confess thou didst but jest,
With my vex'd spirits I cannot take a truce,
But they will quake and tremble all this day.
What dost thou mean by shaking of thy head?
Why dost thou look so sadly on my son?
What means that hand upon that breast of thine?
Why holds thine eye that lamentable rheum,
Like a proud river peering o'er his bounds?
Be these sad signs confirmers of thy words?
Then speak again, — not all thy former tale,
But this one word, whether thy tale be true.

SALISBURY
As true as I believe you think them false
That give you cause to prove my saying true.

CONSTANCE
O, if thou teach me to believe this sorrow,
Teach thou this sorrow how to make me die;
And let belief and life encounter so
As doth the fury of two desperate men,
Which in the very meeting fall and die! —
Louis marry Blanch! O, boy, then where art thou?
France friend with England! what becomes of me? —
Fellow, be gone: I cannot brook thy sight;
This news hath made thee a most ugly man.

SALISBURY
What other harm have I, good lady, done,
But spoke the harm that is by others done?

CONSTANCE
Which harm within itself so heinous is,
As it makes harmful all that speak of it.

ARTHUR
I do beseech you, madam, be content.

CONSTANCE
If thou, that bidd'st me be content, wert grim,
Ugly, and slanderous to thy mother's womb,
Full of unpleasing blots and sightless stains,
Lame, foolish, crooked, swart, prodigious,
Patch'd with foul moles and eye-offending marks,
I would not care, I then would be content;
For then I should not love thee; no, nor thou
Become thy great birth, nor deserve a crown.
But thou art fair; and at thy birth, dear boy,
Nature and Fortune join'd to make thee great:
Of Nature's gifts thou mayst with lilies boast
And with the half-blown rose: but Fortune, O!
She is corrupted, chang'd, and won from thee;
Sh'adulterates hourly with thine uncle John;
And with her golden hand hath pluck'd on France
To tread down fair respect of sovereignty,
And made his majesty the bawd to theirs.
France is a bawd to Fortune and King John,
That strumpet Fortune, that usurping John!
Tell me, thou fellow, is not France forsworn?
Envenom him with words: or get thee gone,
And leave those woes alone which I alone
Am bound to under-bear.

SALISBURY
                      Pardon me, madam,
I may not go without you to the kings.

CONSTANCE
Thou mayst, thou shalt; I will not go with thee:
I will instruct my sorrows to be proud;
For grief is proud, and makes his owner stout.
To me, and to the state of my great grief,

Let kings assemble; for my grief's so great,
That no supporter but the huge firm earth
Can hold it up: here I and sorrows sit;
Here is my throne, bid kings come bow to it.
                  [Seats herself on the ground.

Enter KING JOHN, KING PHILIP, LOUIS,
BLANCH, ELINOR, BASTARD, AUSTRIA, *and*
ATTENDANTS.

KING PHILIP
'Tis true, fair daughter; and this blessed day
Ever in France shall be kept festival;
To solemnise this day the glorious sun
Stays in his course, and plays the alchemist,
Turning with splendour of his precious eye
The meagre cloddy earth to glittering gold:
The yearly course that brings this day about
Shall never see it but a holiday.

CONSTANCE
A wicked day, and not a holy day! —   [Rising.
What hath this day deserv'd? what hath it done,
That it in golden letters should be set
Among the high tides in the calendar?
Nay, rather turn this day out of the week,
This day of shame, oppression, perjury:
Or, if it must stand still, let wives with child
Pray that their burdens may not fall this day,
Lest that their hopes prodigiously be cross'd:
But on this day let seamen fear no wrack;
No bargains break that are not this day made:
This day, all things begun come to ill end, —
Yea, faith itself to hollow falsehood change!

KING PHILIP
By heaven, lady, you shall have no cause
To curse the fair proceedings of this day:
Have I not pawn'd to you my majesty?

CONSTANCE
You have beguil'd me with a counterfeit
Resembling majesty; which, being touch'd and tried,
Proves valueless: you are forsworn, forsworn;
You came in arms to spill mine enemies' blood,
But now in arms you strengthen it with yours:
The grappling vigour and rough frown of war
Is cold in amity and painted peace,
And our oppression hath made up this league.
Arm, arm, you heavens, against these perjur'd kings!
A widow cries; be husband to me, heavens!
Let not the hours of this ungodly day
Wear out the day in peace; but, ere sunset,
Set armed discord 'twixt these perjur'd kings!
Hear me, O, hear me!

AUSTRIA
                    Lady Constance, peace!

CONSTANCE
War! war! no peace! peace is to me a war.
O Limoges! O Austria! thou dost shame
That bloody spoil: thou slave, thou wretch, thou
  coward!
Thou little valiant, great in villainy!
Thou ever strong upon the stronger side!
Thou Fortune's champion that dost never fight
But when her humorous ladyship is by
To teach thee safety! thou art perjur'd too,
And sooth'st up greatness. What a fool art thou,
A ramping fool, to brag, and stamp, and swear,
Upon my party! Thou cold-blooded slave,
Hast thou not spoke like thunder on my side?
Been sworn my soldier? bidding me depend
Upon thy stars, thy fortune, and thy strength?
And dost thou now fall over to my foes?
Thou wear a lion's hide! doff it for shame,
And hang a calf's-skin on those recreant limbs.

AUSTRIA
O, that a man should speak those words to me!

BASTARD
And hang a calf's-skin on those recreant limbs.

AUSTRIA
Thou darest not say so, villain, for thy life.

BASTARD
And hang a calf's-skin on those recreant limbs.

KING JOHN
We like not this; thou dost forget thyself.

KING PHILIP
Here comes the holy legate of the Pope.

Enter PANDULPH, *attended.*

PANDULPH
Hail, you anointed deputies of heaven!
To thee, King John, my holy errand is.
I Pandulph, of fair Milan cardinal,
And from Pope Innocent the legate here,

CONSTANCE Arm, arm, you heavens, against these perjur'd kings!

BLANCH
     That's the curse of Rome.
CONSTANCE
O Louis, stand fast! the devil tempts thee here
In likeness of a new untrimmed bride.
BLANCH
The Lady Constance speaks not from her faith,
But from her need.
CONSTANCE
    O, if thou grant my need,
Which only lives but by the death of faith,
That need must needs infer this principle, —
That faith would live again by death of need!
O, then, tread down my need, and faith mounts up;
Keep my need up, and faith is trodden down!
KING JOHN
The king is mov'd, and answers not to this.
CONSTANCE
O, be remov'd from him, and answer well!
AUSTRIA
Do so, King Philip; hang no more in doubt.
BASTARD
Hang nothing but a calf's-skin, most sweet lout.
KING PHILIP
I am perplex'd, and know not what to say.
PANDULPH
What canst thou say but will perplex thee more,
If thou stand excommunicate and curs'd?
KING PHILIP
Good reverend father, make my person yours,
And tell me how you would bestow yourself.
This royal hand and mine are newly knit,
And the conjunction of our inward souls
Married in league, coupled and link'd together
With all religious strength of sacred vows;
The latest breath that gave the sound of words
Was deep-sworn faith, peace, amity, true love
Between our kingdoms and our royal selves;
And even before this truce, but new before, —
No longer than we well could wash our hands,
To clap this royal bargain up of peace, —
Heaven knows, they were besmear'd and over-stain'd
With slaughter's pencil, where revenge did paint
The fearful difference of incensed kings:
And shall these hands, so lately purg'd of blood,
So newly join'd in love, so strong in both,
Unyoke this seizure and this kind regreet?
Play fast and loose with faith? so jest with heaven,
Make such unconstant children of ourselves,
As now again to snatch our palm from palm;
Unswear faith sworn; and on the marriage-bed
Of smiling peace to march a bloody host,
And make a riot on the gentle brow
Of true sincerity? O, holy sir,
My reverend father, let it not be so!
Out of your Grace devise, ordain, impose
Some gentle order; and then we shall be blest
To do your pleasure, and continue friends.
PANDULPH
All form is formless, order orderless,
Save what is opposite to England's love.
Therefore, to arms! be champion of our church!
Or let the church, our mother, breathe her curse, —
A mother's curse, — on her revolting son.
France, thou mayst hold a serpent by the tongue,
A chafed lion by the mortal paw,
A fasting tiger safer by the tooth,
Than keep in peace that hand which thou dost hold.
KING PHILIP
I may disjoin my hand, but not my faith.
PANDULPH
So mak'st thou faith an enemy to faith;
And, like a civil war, sett'st oath to oath,
Thy tongue against thy tongue. O, let thy vow
First made to heaven, first be to heaven perform'd, —
That is, to be the champion of our church!
What since thou sworest is sworn against thyself,
And may not be performed by thyself:
For that which thou hast sworn to do amiss
Is not amiss when it is truly done;
And being not done, where doing tends to ill,
The truth is then most done, not doing it:
The better act of purposes mistook
Is to mistake again; though indirect,
Yet indirection thereby grows direct,
And falsehood falsehood cures; as fire cools fire
Within the scorched veins of one new-burn'd.
It is religion that doth make vows kept;
But thou hast sworn against religion,
By what thou swear'st against the thing thou swear'st,

Do in his name religiously demand,
Why thou against the church, our holy mother,
So wilfully dost spurn, and, force perforce,
Keep Stephen Langton, chosen archbishop
Of Canterbury, from that holy see?
This, in our foresaid holy father's name,
Pope Innocent, I do demand of thee.
KING JOHN
What earthy name to interrogatories
Can task the free breath of a sacred king?
Thou canst not, cardinal, devise a name
So slight, unworthy, and ridiculous,
To charge me to an answer, as the Pope.
Tell him this tale; and from the mouth of England
Add thus much more, — that no Italian priest
Shall tithe or toll in our dominions;
But as we, under heaven, are supreme head,
So, under Him, that great supremacy,
Where we do reign, we will alone uphold,
Without th'assistance of a mortal hand:
So tell the Pope; all reverence set apart
To him and his usurp'd authority.
KING PHILIP
Brother of England, you blaspheme in this.
KING JOHN
Though you, and all the kings of Christendom,
Are led so grossly by this meddling priest,
Dreading the curse that money may buy out;
And by the merit of vile gold, dross, dust,
Purchase corrupted pardon of a man,
Who in that sale sells pardon from himself;
Though you and all the rest, so grossly led,
This juggling witchcraft with revenue cherish;
Yet I, alone, alone do me oppose
Against the Pope, and count his friends my foes.
PANDULPH
Then, by the lawful power that I have,
Thou shalt stand curs'd and excommunicate:
And blessed shall he be that doth revolt
From his allegiance to an heretic;
And meritorious shall that hand be call'd,
Canonised, and worshipp'd as a saint,
That takes away by any secret course
Thy hateful life.

CONSTANCE
    O, lawful let it be
That I have room with Rome to curse awhile!
Good father cardinal, cry thou amen
To my keen curses; for without my wrong
There is no tongue hath power to curse him right.
PANDULPH
There's law and warrant, lady, for my curse.
CONSTANCE
And for mine too: when law can do no right,
Let it be lawful that law bar no wrong:
Law cannot give my child his kingdom here;
For he that holds his kingdom holds the law:
Therefore, since law itself is perfect wrong,
How can the law forbid my tongue to curse?
PANDULPH
Philip of France, on peril of a curse,
Let go the hand of that arch-heretic;
And raise the power of France upon his head,
Unless he do submit himself to Rome.
QUEEN ELINOR
Look'st thou pale, France? do not let go thy hand.
CONSTANCE
Look to that, devil; lest that France repent,
And by disjoining hands, hell lose a soul.
AUSTRIA
King Philip, listen to the cardinal.
BASTARD
And hang a calf's-skin on his recreant limbs.
AUSTRIA
Well, ruffian, I must pocket up these wrongs,
 Because —
BASTARD
    Your breeches best may carry them.
KING JOHN
Philip, what say'st thou to the cardinal?
CONSTANCE
What should he say, but as the cardinal?
LOUIS
Bethink you, father; for the difference
Is, purchase of a heavy curse from Rome,
Or the light loss of England for a friend:
Forgo the easier.

And mak'st an oath the surety for thy truth
Against an oath: the truth thou art unsure
To swear, swears only not to be forsworn;
Else what a mockery should it be to swear!
But thou dost swear only to be forsworn;
And most forsworn, to keep what thou dost swear.
Therefore thy later vows against thy first
Is in thyself rebellion to thyself;
And better conquest never canst thou make
Than arm thy constant and thy nobler parts
Against these giddy loose suggestions:
Upon which better part our prayers come in,
If thou vouchsafe them; but if not, then know
The peril of our curses light on thee,
So heavy as thou shalt not shake them off,
But in despair die under their black weight.

AUSTRIA
Rebellion, flat rebellion!

BASTARD
     Will't not be?
Will not a calf's-skin stop that mouth of thine?

LOUIS
Father, to arms!

BLANCH
    Upon thy wedding day?
Against the blood that thou hast married?
What, shall our feast be kept with slaughter'd men?
Shall braying trumpets and loud churlish drums, —
Clamours of hell, — be measures to our pomp?
O husband, hear me! — ay, alack, how new
Is husband in my mouth! — even for that name,
Which till this time my tongue did ne'er pronounce,
Upon my knee I beg, go not to arms
Against mine uncle.

CONSTANCE
    O, upon my knee,
Made hard with kneeling, I do pray to thee,
Thou virtuous Dauphin, alter not the doom
Forethought by heaven!

BLANCH
Now shall I see thy love: what motive may
Be stronger with thee than the name of wife?

CONSTANCE
That which upholdeth him that thee upholds,
His honour: — O, thine honour, Louis, thine honour!

LOUIS
I muse your majesty doth seem so cold,
When such profound respects do pull you on.

PANDULPH
I will denounce a curse upon his head.

KING PHILIP
Thou shalt not need. — England, I will fall from thee.

CONSTANCE
O fair return of banish'd majesty!

QUEEN ELINOR
O foul revolt of French inconstancy!

KING JOHN
France, thou shalt rue this hour within this hour.

BASTARD
Old Time the clock-setter, that bald sexton Time,
Is it as he will? well, then, France shall rue.

BLANCH
The sun's o'ercast with blood: fair day, adieu!
Which is the side that I must go withal?
I am with both: each army hath a hand;
And in their rage, I having hold of both,
They whirl asunder and dismember me.
Husband, I cannot pray that thou mayst win;
Uncle, I needs must pray that thou mayst lose;
Father, I may not wish the fortune thine;
Grandam, I will not wish thy wishes thrive:
Whoever wins, on that side shall I lose;
Assured loss before the match be play'd.

LOUIS
Lady, with me; with me thy fortune lies.

BLANCH
There where my fortune lives, there my life dies.

KING JOHN
Cousin, go draw our puissance together.

          [*Exit* BASTARD.

France, I am burn't up with inflaming wrath;
A rage whose heat hath this condition,
That nothing can allay, nothing but blood, —
The blood, and dearest-valued blood of France.

KING PHILIP
Thy rage shall burn thee up, and thou shalt turn
To ashes, ere our blood shall quench that fire:
Look to thyself, thou art in jeopardy.

KING JOHN
No more than he that threats. — To arms let's
hie!

          [*Exeunt.*

SCENE II

The same. Plains near Angiers.

Alarums, excursions. Enter BASTARD, *with*
AUSTRIA'S *head.*

BASTARD
Now, by my life, this day grows wondrous hot;
Some airy devil hovers in the sky,
And pours down mischief. — Austria's head
lie there,
While Philip breathes.

Enter KING JOHN, ARTHUR, *and* HUBERT.

KING JOHN
Hubert, keep this boy. — Philip, make up:
My mother is assailed in our tent,
And ta'en, I fear.

BASTARD
    My lord, I rescued her;
Her highness is in safety, fear you not:
But on, my liege; for very little pains
Will bring this labour to an happy end. [*Exeunt.*

SCENE III

The same.

Alarums, excursions, retreat. Enter KING
JOHN, ELINOR, ARTHUR, BASTARD,
HUBERT, *and* LORDS.

KING JOHN [*to* QUEEN ELINOR].
So shall it be; your Grace shall stay behind,
So strongly guarded. — [*to* ARTHUR] Cousin,
 look not sad:
Thy grandam loves thee; and thy uncle will
As dear be to thee as thy father was.

ARTHUR
O, this will make my mother die with grief!

KING JOHN [*to* BASTARD].
Cousin, away for England: haste before:
And ere our coming, see thou shake the bags
Of hoarding abbots; their imprison'd angels
Set thou at liberty: the fat ribs of peace
Must by the hungry now be fed upon:
Use our commission in his utmost force.

BASTARD
Bell, book, and candle shall not drive me back,
When gold and silver becks me to come on.
I leave your highness. — Grandam, I will pray —
If ever I remember to be holy —
For your fair safety; so, I kiss your hand.

QUEEN ELINOR
Farewell, gentle cousin.

KING JOHN
    Coz, farewell.

          [*Exit* BASTARD.

QUEEN ELINOR
Come hither, little kinsman; hark, a word.

        [*Takes* ARTHUR *aside.*

KING JOHN
Come hither, Hubert. O my gentle Hubert,
We owe thee much! within this wall of flesh
There is a soul counts thee her creditor,
And with advantage means to pay thy love:
And, my good friend, thy voluntary oath
Lives in this bosom, dearly cherished.
Give me thy hand. I had a thing to say, —
But I will fit it with some better time.
By heaven, Hubert, I am almost asham'd
To say what good respect I have of thee.

HUBERT
I am much bounden to your majesty.

KING JOHN
Good friend, thou hast no cause to say so yet:
But thou shalt have: and creep time ne'er so slow,
Yet it shall come for me to do thee good.
I had a thing to say, — but let it go:
The sun is in the heaven, and the proud day,
Attended with the pleasures of the world,
Is all too wanton and too full of gauds
To give me audience: — if the midnight bell
Did, with his iron tongue and brazen mouth,
Sound one into the drowsy ear of night;
If this same were a churchyard where we stand,
And thou possessed with a thousand wrongs;
Or if that surly spirit, melancholy,

BASTARD Austria's head lie there, while Philip breathes.

Had bak'd thy blood, and made it heavy-thick,
Which else runs tickling up and down the veins,
Making that idiot, laughter, keep men's eyes,
And strain their cheeks to idle merriment, —
A passion hateful to my purposes;
Or if that thou couldst see me without eyes,
Hear me without thine ears, and make reply
Without a tongue, using conceit alone,
Without eyes, ears, and harmful sound of words;
Then, in despite of brooded watchful day,
I would into thy bosom pour my thoughts:
But, ah, I will not! — yet I love thee well;
And, by my troth, I think thou lov'st me well.

HUBERT
So well, that what you bid me undertake,
Though that my death were adjunct to my act,
By heaven, I would do it.

KING JOHN
    Do not I know thou wouldst?
Good Hubert, Hubert, Hubert, throw thine eye
On yon young boy: I'll tell thee what, my friend,
He is a very serpent in my way;
And wheresoe'er this foot of mine doth tread,
He lies before me: — dost thou understand me?
Thou art his keeper.

HUBERT
    And I'll keep him so,
That he shall not offend your majesty.

KING JOHN
      Death.

HUBERT
My lord?

KING JOHN
  A grave.

HUBERT
    He shall not live.

KING JOHN
      Enough.
I could be merry now. Hubert, I love thee;
Well, I'll not say what I intend for thee:
Remember. — Madam, fare you well:
I'll send those powers o'er to your majesty.

QUEEN ELINOR
My blessing go with thee!

KING JOHN
    For England, cousin, go:
Hubert shall be your man, attend on you
With all true duty. — On toward Calais, ho! [*Exeunt.*

SCENE IV

The same. The French KING'S *tent.*

Enter KING PHILIP, LOUIS, PANDULPH, *and*
ATTENDANTS.

KING PHILIP
So, by a roaring tempest on the flood,
A whole armado of convented sail
Is scatter'd and disjoin'd from fellowship.

PANDULPH
Courage and comfort! all shall yet go well.

KING PHILIP
What can go well, when we have run so ill?
Are we not beaten? Is not Angiers lost?
Arthur ta'en prisoner? divers dear friends slain?
And bloody England into England gone,
O'erbearing interruption, spite of France?

LOUIS
What he hath won, that hath he fortified:
So hot a speed with such advice disposed,
Such temperate order in so fierce a course,
Doth want example: who hath read or heard
Of any kindred action like to this?

KING PHILIP
Well could I bear that England had this praise,
So we could find some pattern of our shame. —
Look, who comes here! a grave unto a soul;
Holding th'eternal spirit, against her will,
In the vile prison of afflicted breath.

Enter CONSTANCE.

I prithee, lady, go away with me.

CONSTANCE
Lo, now! now see the issue of your peace!

KING PHILIP
Patience, good lady! comfort, gentle Constance!

CONSTANCE
No, I defy all counsel, all redress,
But that which ends all counsel, true redress,
Death, death: — O amiable lovely death!
Thou odoriferous stench! sound rottenness!
Arise forth from the couch of lasting night,
Thou hate and terror to prosperity,
And I will kiss thy detestable bones;
And put my eyeballs in thy vaulty brows;
And ring these fingers with thy household worms;
And stop this gap of breath with fulsome dust;
And be a carrion monster like thyself:
Come, grin on me: and I will think thou smilest,
And buss thee as thy wife! Misery's love,
O, come to me!

KING PHILIP
O fair affliction, peace!

CONSTANCE
No, no, I will not, having breath to cry:
O, that my tongue were in the thunder's mouth!
Then with a passion would I shake the world,
And rouse from sleep that fell anatomy
Which cannot hear a lady's feeble voice,
Which scorns a modern invocation.

PANDULPH
Lady, you utter madness, and not sorrow.

CONSTANCE
Thou art not holy to belie me so;
I am not mad: this hair I tear is mine;
My name is Constance; I was Geffrey's wife;
Young Arthur is my son, and he is lost:
I am not mad; — I would to heaven I were!
For then 'tis like I should forget myself:
O, if I could, what grief should I forget! —
Preach some philosophy to make me mad,
And thou shalt be canonis'd, cardinal;
For, being not mad, but sensible of grief,
My reasonable part produces reason
How I may be deliver'd of these woes,
And teaches me to kill or hang myself:
If I were mad, I should forget my son,
Or madly think a babe of clouts were he:
I am not mad; too well, too well I feel
The different plague of each calamity.

KING PHILIP
Bind up those tresses. — O, what love I note
In the fair multitude of those her hairs!
Where but by chance a silver drop hath fall'n,
Even to that drop ten thousand wiry friends
Do glue themselves in sociable grief;
Like true, inseparable, faithful loves,
Sticking together in calamity.

CONSTANCE
To England, if you will.

KING PHILIP
Bind up your hairs.

CONSTANCE
Yes, that I will; and wherefore will I do it?
I tore them from their bonds, and cried aloud,
'O, that these hands could so redeem my son,
As they have given these hairs their liberty!'
But now I envy at their liberty,
And will again commit them to their bonds,
Because my poor child is a prisoner. —
And, father cardinal, I have heard you say
That we shall see and know our friends in heaven:
If that be true, I shall see my boy again;
For since the birth of Cain, the first male child,
To him that did but yesterday suspire,
There was not such a gracious creature born.
But now will canker-sorrow eat my bud,
And chase the native beauty from his cheek,
And he will look as hollow as a ghost,
As dim and meagre as an ague's fit;
And so he'll die; and, rising so again,
When I shall meet him in the court of heaven,
I shall not know him: therefore never, never
Must I behold my pretty Arthur more.

PANDULPH
You hold too heinous a respect of grief.

CONSTANCE
He talks to me that never had a son.

KING PHILIP
You are as fond of grief as of your child.

CONSTANCE
Grief fills the room up of my absent child,
Lies in his bed, walks up and down with me,
Puts on his pretty looks, repeats his words,
Remembers me of all his gracious parts,
Stuffs out his vacant garments with his form;
Then have I reason to be fond of grief.
Fare you well: had you such a loss as I,
I could give better comfort than you do. —
I will not keep this form upon my head,
When there is such disorder in my wit.
O Lord! my boy, my Arthur, my fair son!
My life, my joy, my food, my all the world!
My widow-comfort, and my sorrows' cure! [*Exit.*

KING PHILIP
I fear some outrage, and I'll follow her. [*Exit.*

LOUIS
There's nothing in this world can make me joy:
Life is as tedious as a twice-told tale
Vexing the dull ear of a drowsy man;
And bitter shame hath spoil'd the sweet world's taste,
That it yields naught but shame and bitterness.

PANDULPH
Before the curing of a strong disease,
Even in the instant of repair and health,
The fit is strongest; evils that take leave,
On their departure most of all show evil:
What have you lost by losing of this day?

LOUIS
All days of glory, joy and happiness.

PANDULPH
If you had won it, certainly you had.
No, no; when Fortune means to men most good,
She looks upon them with a threatening eye.
'Tis strange to think how much King John hath lost
In this which he accounts so clearly won:
Are not you griev'd that Arthur is his prisoner?

LOUIS
As heartily as he is glad he hath him.

PANDULPH
Your mind is all as youthful as your blood.
Now hear me speak with a prophetic spirit;
For even the breath of what I mean to speak
Shall blow each dust, each straw, each little rub,
Out of the path which shall directly lead
Thy foot to England's throne; and therefore mark.
John hath seiz'd Arthur; and it cannot be,
That, whiles warm life plays in that infant's veins,
The misplac'd John should entertain an hour,
One minute, nay, one quiet breath of rest:
A sceptre snatch'd with an unruly hand
Must be as boisterously maintain'd as gain'd;
And he that stands upon a slippery place
Makes nice of no vile hold to stay him up:
That John may stand, then Arthur needs must fall;
So be it, for it cannot be but so.

LOUIS
But what shall I gain by young Arthur's fall?

PANDULPH
You, in the right of Lady Blanch your wife,
May then make all the claim that Arthur did.

LOUIS
And lose it, life and all, as Arthur did.

PANDULPH
How green you are, and fresh in this old world!
John lays you plots; the times conspire with you;
For he that steeps his safety in true blood
Shall find but bloody safety and untrue.
This act, so evilly borne, shall cool the hearts
Of all his people, and freeze up their zeal,
That none so small advantage shall step forth
To check his reign, but they will cherish it;
No natural exhalation in the sky,
No scape of nature, no distemper'd day,

CONSTANCE O, that these hands could so redeem my son, as they have given these hairs their liberty!

No common wind, no customed event,
But they will pluck away his natural cause,
And call them meteors, prodigies, and signs,
Abortives, presages, and tongues of heaven,
Plainly denouncing vengeance upon John.

LOUIS
May be he will not touch young Arthur's life,
But hold himself safe in his prisonment.

PANDULPH
O, sir, when he shall hear of your approach,
If that young Arthur be not gone already,
Even at that news he dies; and then the hearts
Of all his people shall revolt from him,
And kiss the lips of unacquainted change;
And pick strong matter of revolt and wrath
Out of the bloody fingers' ends of John.
Methinks I see this hurly all on foot:
And, O, what better matter breeds for you
Than I have nam'd! — The bastard Faulconbridge
Is now in England, ransacking the church,
Offending charity: if but a dozen French
Were there in arms, they would be as a call
To train ten thousand English to their side;
Or as a little snow, tumbled about,
Anon becomes a mountain. O noble Dauphin,
Go with me to the king: — 'tis wonderful
What may be wrought out of their discontent,
Now that their souls are topful of offence:
For England go: — I will whet on the king.

LOUIS
Strong reasons make strong actions: let us go:
If you say ay, the king will not say no. *[Exeunt.*

ACT IV

SCENE I

A room in a castle.

Enter HUBERT *and* EXECUTIONERS.

HUBERT
Heat me these irons hot; and look thou stand
Within the arras: when I strike my foot
Upon the bosom of the ground, rush forth,
And bind the boy which you shall find with me
Fast to the chair: be heedful: hence, and watch.

FIRST EXECUTIONER
I hope your warrant will bear out the deed.

HUBERT
Uncleanly scruples! fear not you: look to't.
                    [Exeunt EXECUTIONERS.
Young lad, come forth; I have to say with you.
                    Enter ARTHUR.

ARTHUR
Good morrow, Hubert.

HUBERT
                    Good morrow, little prince.

ARTHUR
As little prince, having so great a title
To be more prince, as may be. — You are sad.

HUBERT
Indeed, I have been merrier.

ARTHUR
                    Mercy on me!
Methinks no body should be sad but I:
Yet, I remember, when I was in France,
Young gentlemen would be as sad as night,
Only for wantonness. By my Christendom,
So I were out of prison, and kept sheep,
I should be as merry as the day is long;
And so I would be here, but that I doubt
My uncle practises more harm to me:
He is afraid of me, and I of him:
Is it my fault that I was Geffrey's son?
No, indeed, is't not; and I would to heaven
I were your son, so you would love me, Hubert.

HUBERT [*aside*].
If I talk to him, with his innocent prate
He will awake my mercy, which lies dead:
Therefore I will be sudden and dispatch.

ARTHUR
Are you sick, Hubert? you look pale to-day:
In sooth, I would you were a little sick,
That I might sit all night and watch with you:
I warrant I love you more than you do me.

HUBERT [*aside*].
His words do take possession of my bosom. —
Read here, young Arthur.   [*Showing a paper.*
          [*Aside*] How now, foolish rheum!

Turning dispiteous torture out of door!
I must be brief, lest resolution drop
Out at mine eyes in tender womanish tears. —
Can you not read it, is it not fair writ?

ARTHUR
Too fairly, Hubert, for so foul effect:
Must you with hot irons burn out both mine eyes?

HUBERT
Young boy, I must.

ARTHUR
                    And will you?

HUBERT
                    And I will.

ARTHUR
Have you the heart? When your head did but ache,
I knit my handkercher about your brows, —
The best I had, a princess wrought it me, —
And I did never ask it you again;
And with my hand at midnight held your head;
And like the watchful minutes to the hour,
Still and anon cheer'd up the heavy time,
Saying, 'What lack you?' and, 'Where lies your grief?'
Or, 'What good love may I perform for you?'
Many a poor man's son would have lien still,
And ne'er have spoke a loving word to you;
But you at your sick service had a prince.
Nay, you may think my love was crafty love,
And call it cunning: — do, an if you will:
If heaven be pleas'd that you must use me ill,
Why, then you must. — Will you put out mine eyes?
These eyes that never did nor never shall
So much as frown on you.

HUBERT
                    I have sworn to do it;
And with hot irons must I burn them out.

ARTHUR
Ah, none but in this iron age would do it!
The iron of itself, though heat red-hot,
Approaching near these eyes, would drink my tears,
And quench his fiery indignation
Even in the water of mine innocence;
Nay, after that, consume away in rust,
But for containing fire to harm mine eye.
Are you more stubborn-hard than hammer'd iron?
An if an angel should have come to me,
And told me Hubert should put out mine eyes,
I would not have believ'd him, — no tongue but
   Hubert's.

HUBERT
Come forth!   [*Stamps.*
     Enter EXECUTIONERS, *with cord, irons, etc.*
Do as I bid you do.

ARTHUR
O, save me, Hubert, save me! my eyes are out
Even with the fierce looks of these bloody men.

HUBERT
Give me the iron, I say, and bind him here.

ARTHUR
Alas, what need you be so boisterous-rough?
I will not struggle, I will stand stone-still.
For heaven sake, Hubert, let me not be bound!
Nay, hear me, Hubert! — drive these men away,
And I will sit as quiet as a lamb;
I will not stir, nor wince, nor speak a word,
Nor look upon the iron angerly:
Thrust but these men away, and I'll forgive you,
Whatever torment you do put me to.

HUBERT
Go, stand within; let me alone with him.

FIRST EXECUTIONER
I am best pleas'd to be from such a deed.
                    [*Exeunt* EXECUTIONERS.

ARTHUR
Alas, I then have chid away my friend!
He hath a stern look, but a gentle heart: —
Let him come back, that his compassion may
Give life to yours.

HUBERT
                    Come, boy, prepare yourself.

ARTHUR
Is there no remedy?

HUBERT
                    None, but to lose your eyes.

ARTHUR
O heaven! — that there were but a mote in yours,
A grain, a dust, a gnat, a wandering hair,
Any annoyance in that precious sense!
Then, feeling what small things are boisterous there,
Your vile intent must needs seem horrible.

HUBERT
Is this your promise? go to, hold your tongue.

ARTHUR
Hubert, the utterance of a brace of tongues
Must needs want pleading for a pair of eyes:
Let me not hold my tongue, — let me not, Hubert;
Or, Hubert, if you will, cut out my tongue,
So I may keep mine eyes: O, spare mine eyes,
Though to no use but still to look on you! —
Lo, by my troth, the instrument is cold,
And would not harm me.

HUBERT
                    I can heat it, boy.

ARTHUR
No, in good sooth; the fire is dead with grief,
Being create for comfort, to be used
In undeserv'd extremes: see else yourself;
There is no malice in this burning coal;
The breath of heaven hath blown his spirit out,
And strew'd repentant ashes on his head.

HUBERT
But with my breath I can revive it, boy.

ARTHUR
An if you do, you will but make it blush,

HUBERT Heat me these irons hot.

And glow with shame of your proceedings, Hubert:
Nay, it perchance will sparkle in your eyes;
And, like a dog that is compell'd to fight,
Snatch at his master that doth tarre him on.
All things that you should use to do me wrong
Deny their office: only you do lack
That mercy which fierce fire and iron extends,
Creatures of note for mercy-lacking uses.

HUBERT
Well, see to live; I will not touch thine eye
For all the treasure that thine uncle owes:
Yet am I sworn, and I did purpose, boy,
With this same very iron to burn them out.

ARTHUR
O, now you look like Hubert! all this while
You were disguised.

HUBERT
                    Peace; no more. Adieu.
Your uncle must not know but you are dead;
I'll fill these dogged spies with false reports:
And, pretty child, sleep doubtless and secure
That Hubert, for the wealth of all the world,
Will not offend thee.

ARTHUR
                    O heaven! I thank you, Hubert.

HUBERT
Silence; no more: go closely in with me:
Much danger do I undergo for thee.   [*Exeunt.*

SCENE II
KING JOHN'S *palace.*

Enter KING JOHN, PEMBROKE, SALISBURY, *and*
other LORDS.

KING JOHN
Here once again we sit, once again crown'd,
And look'd upon, I hope, with cheerful eyes.

PEMBROKE
This once again, but that your highness pleas'd,
Was once superfluous: you were crown'd before,
And that high royalty was ne'er pluck'd off;
The faiths of men ne'er stained with revolt;
Fresh expectation troubled not the land
With any long'd-for change or better state.

SALISBURY
Therefore, to be possess'd with double pomp,
To guard a title that was rich before,
To gild refined gold, to paint the lily,
To throw a perfume on the violet,
To smooth the ice, or add another hue
Unto the rainbow, or with taper-light
To seek the beauteous eye of heaven to garnish,
Is wasteful and ridiculous excess.

PEMBROKE
But that your royal pleasure must be done,
This act is as an ancient tale new-told,
And in the last repeating troublesome,
Being urged at a time unseasonable.

SALISBURY
In this, the antique and well-noted face
Of plain old form is much disfigured;
And, like a shifted wind unto a sail,
It makes the course of thoughts to fetch about;
Startles and frights consideration;
Makes sound opinion sick, and truth suspected,
For putting on so new a fashion'd robe.

PEMBROKE
When workmen strive to do better than well,
They do confound their skill in covetousness;
And oftentimes excusing of a fault
Doth make the fault the worse by the excuse, —
As patches set upon a little breach
Discredit more in hiding of the fault
Than did the fault before it was so patch'd.

SALISBURY
To this effect, before you were new-crown'd,
We breath'd our counsel: but it pleas'd your highness
To overbear it; and we are all well pleased,
Since all and every part of what we would
Doth make a stand at what your highness will.

KING JOHN
Some reasons of this double coronation
I have possess'd you with, and think them strong;
And more, more strong, than lesser is my fear,
I shall indue you with: meantime but ask
What you would have reform'd that is not well,
And well shall you perceive how willingly
I will both hear and grant you your requests.

PEMBROKE
Then I — as one that am the tongue of these,

To sound the purposes of all their hearts,
Both for myself and them, but, chief of all,
Your safety, for the which myself and them
Bend their best studies — heartily request
Th'enfranchisement of Arthur; whose restraint
Doth move the murmuring lips of discontent
To break into this dangerous argument, —
If what in rest you have in right you hold,
Why, then your fears — which, as they say, attend
The steps of wrong — should move you to mew up
Your tender kinsman, and to choke his days
With barbarous ignorance, and deny his youth
The rich advantage of good exercise.
That the time's enemies may not have this
To grace occasions, let it be our suit,
That you have bid us ask, his liberty;
Which for our goods we do no further ask
Than whereupon our weal, on you depending,
Counts it your weal he have his liberty.

KING JOHN
Let it be so: I do commit his youth
To your direction.
                    Enter HUBERT.
                    Hubert, what news with you?

PEMBROKE
This is the man should do the bloody deed;
He show'd his warrant to a friend of mine:
The image of a wicked heinous fault
Lives in his eye; that close aspect of his
Does show the mood of a much-troubled breast;
And I do fearfully believe 'tis done,
What we so fear'd he had a charge to do.

SALISBURY
The colour of the king doth come and go
Between his purpose and his conscience,
Like heralds 'twixt two dreadful battles set:
His passion is so ripe, it needs must break.

PEMBROKE
And when it breaks, I fear will issue thence
The foul corruption of a sweet child's death.

KING JOHN
We cannot hold mortality's strong hand: —
Good lords, although my will to give is living,
The suit which you demand is gone and dead:
He tells us Arthur is deceas'd to-night.

SALISBURY
Indeed, we fear'd his sickness was past cure.

PEMBROKE
Indeed, we heard how near his death he was
Before the child himself felt he was sick:
This must be answer'd either here or hence.

KING JOHN
Why do you bend such solemn brows on me?
Think you I bear the shears of destiny?
Have I commandment on the pulse of life?

SALISBURY
It is apparent foul-play; and 'tis shame
That greatness should so grossly offer it:
So thrive it in your game! and so, farewell.

PEMBROKE
Stay yet, Lord Salisbury; I'll go with thee,
And find th'inheritance of this poor child,
His little kingdom of a forced grave.
That blood which ow'd the breadth of all this isle,
Three foot of it doth hold: — bad world the while!
This must not be thus borne: this will break out
To all our sorrows, and ere long I doubt.
                    [*Exeunt* LORDS.

KING JOHN
They burn in indignation. I repent:
There is no sure foundation set on blood,
No certain life achiev'd by others' death. —
                    Enter a MESSENGER.
A fearful eye thou hast: where is that blood
That I have seen inhabit in those cheeks?
So foul a sky clears not without a storm:
Pour down thy weather: how goes all in France?

MESSENGER
From France to England. Never such a power
For any foreign preparation
Was levied in the body of a land.
The copy of your speed is learn'd by them;
For when you should be told they do prepare,
The tidings come that they are all arrived.

KING JOHN
O, where hath our intelligence been drunk?
Where hath it slept? Where is my mother's ear,
That such an army could be drawn in France,
And she not hear of it?

MESSENGER
                    My liege, her ear
Is stopp'd with dust; the first of April died
Your noble mother; and, as I hear, my lord,
The Lady Constance in a frenzy died
Three days before; but this from rumour's tongue
I idly heard; if true or false I know not.

KING JOHN
Withhold thy speed, dreadful occasion!
O, make a league with me, till I have pleased
My discontented peers! What! mother dead!
How wildly, then, walks my estate in France! —
Under whose conduct came those powers of France

PEMBROKE Heartily request th'enfranchisement of Arthur.

KING JOHN There is no sure foundation set on blood, no certain life achiev'd by others' death.

That thou for truth givest out are landed here?

MESSENGER
Under the Dauphin.

KING JOHN
          Thou hast made me giddy
With these ill tidings.

Enter BASTARD *and* PETER *of Pomfret.*

          Now, what says the world
To your proceedings? do not seek to stuff
My head with more ill news, for it is full.

BASTARD
But if you be afeard to hear the worst,
Then let the worst, unheard, fall on your bead.

KING JOHN
Bear with me, cousin; for I was amazed
Under the tide: but now I breathe again
Aloft the flood; and can give audience
To any tongue, speak it of what it will.

BASTARD
How I have sped among the clergy-men,
The sums I have collected shall express.
But as I travell'd hither through the land,
I find the people strangely fantasied;
Possess'd with rumours, full of idle dreams,
Not knowing what they fear, but full of fear:
And here's a prophet, that I brought with me
From forth the streets of Pomfret, whom I found
With many hundreds treading on his heels;
To whom he sung, in rude harsh-sounding rimes,
That, ere the next Ascension-day at noon,
Your highness should deliver up your crown.

KING JOHN
Thou idle dreamer, wherefore didst thou so?

PETER
Foreknowing that the truth will fall out so.

KING JOHN
Hubert, away with him; imprison him;
And on that day at noon, whereon he says
I shall yield up my crown, let him be hang'd.
Deliver him to safety; and return,
For I must use thee.   [*Exit* HUBERT *with* PETER.
          O my gentle cousin,
Hear'st thou the news abroad, who are arrived?

BASTARD
The French, my lord: men's mouths are full of it:
Besides, I met Lord Bigot and Lord Salisbury
With eyes as red as new-enkindled fire,
And others more, going to seek the grave
Of Arthur, who, they say, is kill'd to-night
On your suggestion.

KING JOHN
          Gentle kinsman, go,
And thrust thyself into their companies:
I have a way to win their loves again;
Bring them before me.

BASTARD
          I will seek them out.

KING JOHN
Nay, but make haste; the better foot before.
O, let me have no subject enemies,
When adverse foreigners affright my towns
With dreadful pomp of stout invasion!
Be Mercury, set feathers to thy heels,
And fly like thought from them to me again.

BASTARD
The spirit of the time shall teach me speed.

KING JOHN
Spoke like a sprightful noble gentleman.
               [*Exit* BASTARD.
Go after him; for he perhaps shall need
Some messenger betwixt me and the peers;
And be thou he.

MESSENGER
        With all my heart, my liege.   [*Exit.*

KING JOHN
My mother dead!

Enter HUBERT.

HUBERT
My lord, they say five moons were seen to-night;
Four fixed; and the fifth did whirl about
The other four in wondrous motion.

KING JOHN
Five moons!

HUBERT
        Old men and beldams in the streets
Do prophesy upon it dangerously:
Young Arthur's death is common in their mouths:
And when they talk of him, they shake their heads,
And whisper one another in the ear;
And he that speaks doth gripe the hearer's wrist,
Whilst he that hears makes fearful action,
With wrinkled brows, with nods, with rolling eyes.
I saw a smith stand with his hammer, thus,
The whilst his iron did on the anvil cool,
With open mouth swallowing a tailor's news;
Who, with his shears and measure in his hand,
Standing on slippers, which his nimble haste
Had falsely thrust upon contrary feet,
Told of a many thousand warlike French
That were embattailed and rank'd in Kent:
Another lean unwash'd artificer
Cuts off his tale, and talks of Arthur's death.

KING JOHN
Why seek'st thou to possess me with these fears?
Why urgest thou so oft young Arthur's death?
Thy hand hath murder'd him: I had a mighty cause
To wish him dead, but thou hadst none to kill him.

HUBERT
No had, my lord! why, did you not provoke me?

KING JOHN
It is the curse of kings to be attended
By slaves that take their humours for a warrant
To break within the bloody house of life;
And, on the winking of authority,
To understand a law; to know the meaning
Of dangerous majesty, when perchance it frowns
More upon humour than advis'd respect.

HUBERT
Here is your hand and seal for what I did.

KING JOHN
O, when the last account 'twixt heaven and earth
Is to be made, then shall this hand and seal
Witness against us to damnation!
How oft the sight of means to do ill deeds
Make deeds ill done! Hadst not thou been by,
A fellow by the hand of nature mark'd,
Quoted, and sign'd, to do a deed of shame,
This murder had not come into my mind:
But, taking note of thy abhorr'd aspect,

Finding thee fit for bloody villainy,
Apt, liable to be employ'd in danger,
I faintly broke with thee of Arthur's death;
And thou, to be endeared to a king,
Made it no conscience to destroy a prince.

HUBERT
My lord, —

KING JOHN
Hadst thou but shook thy head, or made a pause,
When I spake darkly what I purposed,
Or turn'd an eye of doubt upon my face,
As bid me tell my tale in express words,
Deep shame had struck me dumb, made me break off,
And those thy fears might have wrought fears in me:
But thou didst understand me by my signs,
And didst in signs again parley with sin;
Yea, without stop, didst let thy heart consent,
And consequently thy rude hand to act
The deed, which both our tongues held vile to name. —
Out of my sight, and never see me more!
My nobles leave me; and my state is braved,
Even at my gates, with ranks of foreign powers:
Nay, in the body of this fleshly land,
This kingdom, this confine of blood and breath,
Hostility and civil tumult reigns
Between my conscience and my cousin's death.

HUBERT
Arm you against your other enemies,
I'll make a peace between your soul and you.
Young Arthur is alive: this hand of mine
Is yet a maiden and an innocent hand,
Not painted with the crimson spots of blood.
Within this bosom never enter'd yet
The dreadful motion of a murderous thought;
And you have slander'd nature in my form,
Which, howsoever rude exteriorly,
Is yet the cover of a fairer mind
Than to be butcher of an innocent child.

KING JOHN
Doth Arthur live? O, haste thee to the peers,
Throw this report on their incensed rage,
And make them tame to their obedience!
Forgive the comment that my passion made
Upon thy feature; for my rage was blind,
And foul imaginary eyes of blood
Presented thee more hideous than thou art.
O, answer not; but to my closet bring
The angry lords with all expedient haste!
I conjure thee but slowly; run more fast.   [*Exeunt.*

SCENE III

Before a castle.

Enter ARTHUR *on the walls.*

ARTHUR
The wall is high, and yet will I leap down:
Good ground, be pitiful, and hurt me not!
There's few or none do know me: if they did,
This ship-boy's semblance hath disguis'd me quite.
I am afraid; and yet I'll venture it.
If I get down, and do not break my limbs,
I'll find a thousand shifts to get away:
As good to die and go, as die and stay.
               [*Leaps down.*
O me! my uncle's spirit is in these stones:
Heaven take my soul, and England keep my bones!
                   [*Dies.*

Enter PEMBROKE, SALISBURY, *and* BIGOT.

SALISBURY
Lords, I will meet him at Saint Edmunds-Bury:
It is our safety, and we must embrace
This gentle offer of the perilous time.

PEMBROKE
Who brought that letter from the cardinal?

SALISBURY
The Count Melun, a noble lord of France;
Whose private with me of the Dauphin's love
Is much more general than these lines import.

BIGOT
To-morrow morning let us meet him, then.

SALISBURY
Or rather then set forward; for 'twill be
Two long days' journey, lords, or e're we meet.

Enter BASTARD.

BASTARD
Once more to-day well met, distemper'd lords!
The king by me requests your presence straight.

SALISBURY
The king hath dispossess'd himself of us:

We will not line his thin bestained cloak
With our pure honours, nor attend the foot
That leaves the print of blood where'er it walks.
Return and tell him so: we know the worst.

BASTARD
Whate'er you think, good words, I think, were best.

SALISBURY
Our griefs, and not our manners, reason now.

BASTARD
But there is little reason in your grief;
Therefore 'twere reason you had manners now.

PEMBROKE
Sir, sir, impatience hath his privilege.

BASTARD
'Tis true, — to hurt his master, no man else.

SALISBURY
This is the prison: — what is he lies here?
                                    [*Seeing* ARTHUR.

PEMBROKE
O death, made proud with pure and princely beauty!
The earth had not a hole to hide this deed.

SALISBURY
Murder, as hating what himself hath done,
Doth lay it open to urge on revenge.

BIGOT
Or, when he doom'd this beauty to a grave,
Found it too precious-princely for a grave.

SALISBURY
Sir Richard, what think you? Have you beheld,
Or have you read or heard? or could you think?
Or do you almost think, although you see,
That you do see? could thought, without this object,
Form such another? This is the very top,
The height, the crest, or crest unto the crest,
Of murder's arms: this is the bloodiest shame,
The wildest savagery, the vilest stroke,
That ever wall-eyed wrath or staring rage
Presented to the tears of soft remorse.

PEMBROKE
All murders past do stand excus'd in this:
And this, so sole and so unmatchable,
Shall give a holiness, a purity,
To the yet-unbegotten sin of times;
And prove a deadly bloodshed but a jest,
Exampled by this heinous spectacle.

BASTARD
It is a damned and a bloody work;
The graceless action of a heavy hand, —
If that it be the work of any hand.

SALISBURY
If that it be the work of any hand! —
We had a kind of light what would ensue:
It is the shameful work of Hubert's hand;
The practice and the purpose of the king: —
From whose obedience I forbid my soul,
Kneeling before this ruin of sweet life,
And breathing to his breathless excellence
The incense of a vow, a holy vow,
Never to taste the pleasures of the world,
Never to be infected with delight,
Nor conversant with ease and idleness,
Till I have set a glory to this hand,
By giving it the worship of revenge.

PEMBROKE *and* **BIGOT**
Our souls religiously confirm thy words.
                        Enter HUBERT.

HUBERT
Lords, I am hot with haste in seeking you:
Arthur doth live; the king hath sent for you.

SALISBURY
O, he is bold, and blushes not at death: —
Avaunt, thou hateful villain, get thee gone!

HUBERT
I am no villain.

SALISBURY
                Must I rob the law?
                            [*Drawing his sword.*

BASTARD
Your sword is bright, sir; put it up again.

SALISBURY
Not till I sheathe it in a murderer's skin.

HUBERT
Stand back, Lord Salisbury, — stand back, I say;
By heaven, I think my sword's as sharp as yours:
I would not have you, lord, forget yourself,
Nor tempt the danger of my true defence;
Lest I, by marking of your rage, forget
Your worth, your greatness, and nobility.

HUBERT Young Arthur's death is common in their mouths: and when they talk of him, they shake their heads.

BIGOT
Out, dunghill! darest thou brave a nobleman?

HUBERT
Not for my life: but yet I dare defend
My innocent life against an emperor.

SALISBURY
Thou art a murderer.

HUBERT
                Do not prove me so;
Yet I am none: whose tongue soe'er speaks false,
Not truly speaks; who speaks not truly, lies.

PEMBROKE
Cut him to pieces.

BASTARD
                Keep the peace, I say.

SALISBURY
Stand by, or I shall gall you, Faulconbridge.

BASTARD
Thou wert better gall the devil, Salisbury:
If thou but frown on me, or stir thy foot,
Or teach thy hasty spleen to do me shame,
I'll strike thee dead. Put up thy sword betime;
Or I'll so maul you and your toasting-iron,
That you shall think the devil is come from hell.

BIGOT
What wilt thou do, renowned Faulconbridge?
Second a villain and a murderer?

HUBERT
Lord Bigot, I am none.

BIGOT
                Who kill'd this prince?

HUBERT
'Tis not an hour since I left him well:
I honour'd him, I lov'd him; and will weep
My date of life out for his sweet life's loss.

SALISBURY
Trust not those cunning waters of his eyes,
For villainy is not without such rheum;
And he, long traded in it, makes it seem
Like rivers of remorse and innocency.
Away with me, all you whose souls abhor
Th'uncleanly savours of a slaughter-house;
For I am stifled with this smell of sin.

BIGOT
Away toward Bury, to the Dauphin there!

PEMBROKE
There, tell the king, he may inquire us out.
                            [*Exeunt* LORDS.

BASTARD
Here's a good world! — Knew you of this fair work?
Beyond the infinite and boundless reach
Of mercy, if thou didst this deed of death,
Art thou damn'd, Hubert.

HUBERT
                Do but hear me, sir: —

BASTARD
Ha! I'll tell thee what;
Thou'rt damn'd as black — nay, nothing is so black;
Thou art more deep damn'd than Prince Lucifer:
There is not yet so ugly a fiend of hell
As thou shalt be, if thou didst kill this child.

HUBERT
Upon my soul, —

BASTARD
                If thou didst but consent
To this most cruel act, do but despair;
And if thou want'st a cord, the smallest thread
That ever spider twisted from her womb
Will serve to strangle thee; a rush will be a beam
To hang thee on; or wouldst thou drown thyself,
Put but a little water in a spoon,
And it shall be as all the ocean,
Enough to stifle such a villain up.
I do suspect thee very grievously.

HUBERT
If I in act, consent, or sin of thought,
Be guilty of the stealing that sweet breath
Which was embounded in this beauteous clay,
Let hell want pains enough to torture me!
I left him well.

BASTARD
                Go, bear him in thine arms. —
I am amaz'd, methinks; and lose my way
Among the thorns and dangers of this world. —
How easy dost thou take all England up!
From forth this morsel of dead royalty,
The life, the right, and truth of all this realm
Is fled to heaven; and England now is left
To tug and scamble, and to part by th'teeth
The unowed interest of proud-swelling state.
Now for the bare-pick'd bone of majesty
Doth dogged war bristle his angry crest,
And snarleth in the gentle eyes of peace:
Now powers from home and discontents at home
Meet in one line; and vast confusion waits,
As doth a raven on a sick-fall'n beast,
The imminent decay of wrested pomp.
Now happy he whose cloak and cincture can
Hold out this tempest. — Bear away that child,
And follow me with speed: I'll to the king:
A thousand businesses are brief in hand,
And heaven itself doth frown upon the land.   [*Exeunt.*

ACT V

SCENE I

KING JOHN'S *palace.*

Enter KING JOHN, PANDULPH *with the crown, and*
ATTENDANTS.

KING JOHN
Thus have I yielded up into your hand
The circle of my glory.

PANDULPH
                Take again   [*Giving back the crown.*
From this my hand, as holding of the Pope
Your sovereign greatness and authority.

KING JOHN
Now keep your holy word: go meet the French;
And from his holiness use all your power
To stop their marches 'fore we are inflamed.
Our discontented counties do revolt;
Our people quarrel with obedience;
Swearing allegiance and the love of soul
To stranger blood, to foreign royalty.
This inundation of mistemper'd humour
Rests by you only to be qualified:

Then pause not; for the present time's so sick,
That present medicine must be minister'd,
Or overthrow incurable ensues.

PANDULPH
It was my breath that blew this tempest up,
Upon your stubborn usage of the Pope:
But since you are a gentle convertite,
My tongue shall hush again this storm of war,
And make fair weather in your blustering land.
On this Ascension-day, remember well,
Upon your oath of service to the Pope,
Go I to make the French lay down their arms. [*Exit.*

KING JOHN
Is this Ascension-day? Did not the prophet
Say, that before Ascension-day at noon
My crown I should give off? Even so I have:
I did suppose it should be on constraint;
But, heaven be thank'd, it is but voluntary.

Enter BASTARD.

BASTARD
All Kent hath yielded; nothing there holds out
But Dover Castle: London hath received,
Like a kind host, the Dauphin and his powers:
Your nobles will not hear you, but are gone
To offer service to your enemy;
And wild amazement hurries up and down
The little number of your doubtful friends.

KING JOHN
Would not my lords return to me again,
After they heard young Arthur was alive?

BASTARD
They found him dead, and cast into the streets;
An empty casket, where the jewel of life
By some damn'd hand was robb'd and ta'en away.

KING JOHN
That villain Hubert told me he did live.

BASTARD
So, on my soul, he did, for aught he knew.
But wherefore do you droop? why look you sad?
Be great in act, as you have been in thought;
Let not the world see fear and sad distrust
Govern the motion of a kingly eye:
Be stirring as the time; be fire with fire;
Threaten the threatener, and outface the brow
Of bragging horror: so shall inferior eyes,
That borrow their behaviours from the great,
Grow great by your example, and put on
The dauntless spirit of resolution.
Away, and glister like the god of war,
When he intendeth to become the field:
Show boldness and aspiring confidence.
What, shall they seek the lion in his den,
And fright him there? and make him tremble there?
O, let it not be said! — Forage, and run
To meet displeasure further from the doors,
And grapple with him ere he come so nigh.

KING JOHN
The legate of the Pope hath been with me,
And I have made a happy peace with him;
And he hath promis'd to dismiss the powers
Led by the Dauphin.

BASTARD
          O inglorious league!
Shall we, upon the footing of our land,
Send fair-play orders, and make compromise,
Insinuation, parley, and base truce,
To arms invasive? shall a beardless boy,
A cocker'd silken wanton, brave our fields,
And flesh his spirit in a warlike soil,
Mocking the air with colours idly spread,
And find no check? Let us, my liege, to arms:
Perchance the cardinal cannot make your peace;
Or if he do, let it at least be said
They saw we had a purpose of defence.

KING JOHN
Have thou the ordering of this present time.

BASTARD
Away, then, with good courage! yet, I know,
Our party may well meet a prouder foe. [*Exeunt.*

SCENE II

Near St. Edmunds-Bury. The French camp.
Enter, in arms, LOUIS, SALISBURY, MELUN,
PEMBROKE, BIGOT, *and* SOLDIERS.

LOUIS
My Lord Melun, let this be copied out,
And keep it safe for our remembrance:
Return the precedent to these lords again;
That, having our fair order written down,
Both they and we, perusing o'er these notes,
May know wherefore we took the sacrament,
And keep our faiths firm and inviolable.

SALISBURY
Upon our sides it never shall be broken.
And, noble Dauphin, albeit we swear
A voluntary zeal and unurg'd faith
To your proceedings; yet, believe me, prince,
I am not glad that such a sore of time
Should seek a plaster by contemn'd revolt,
And heal the inveterate canker of one wound
By making many. O, it grieves my soul,
That I must draw this metal from my side
To be a widow-maker! O, and there
Where honourable rescue and defence
Cries out upon the name of Salisbury!
But such is the infection of the time,
That, for the health and physic of our right,
We cannot deal but with the very hand
Of stern injustice and confused wrong.
And is't not pity, O my grieved friends,
That we, the sons and children of this isle,
Were born to see so sad an hour as this;
Wherein we step after a stranger, march
Upon her gentle bosom, and fill up
Her enemies' ranks, — I must withdraw and weep
Upon the spot of this enforced cause, —
To grace the gentry of a land remote,
And follow unacquainted colours here?
What, here? O nation, that thou couldst remove!
That Neptune's arms, who clippeth thee about,
Would bear thee from the knowledge of thyself,
And grapple thee unto a pagan shore;
Where these two Christian armies might combine
The blood of malice in a vein of league,
And not to spend it so unneighbourly!

LOUIS
A noble temper dost thou show in this;
And great affections wrestling in thy bosom
Do make an earthquake of nobility.
O, what a noble combat hast thou fought
Between compulsion and a brave respect!
Let me wipe off this honourable dew
That silverly doth progress on thy cheeks:
My heart hath melted at a lady's tears,
Being an ordinary inundation;
But this effusion of such manly drops,
This shower, blown up by tempest of the soul,
Startles mine eyes, and makes me more amazed
Than had I seen the vaulty top of heaven
Figur'd quite o'er with burning
  meteors.
Lift up thy brow, renowned
  Salisbury,
And with a great heart heave
  away this storm:
Commend these waters to those
  baby eyes
That never saw the giant world
  enraged;
Nor met with fortune other than
  at feasts,
Full of warm blood, of mirth, of
  gossiping.
Come, come; for thou shalt
  thrust thy hand as deep
Into the purse of rich prosperity
As Louis himself: — so, nobles,
  shall you all,
That knit your sinews to the
  strength of mine. —
And even there, methinks, an
  angel spake:
Look, where the holy legate
  comes apace,
To give us warrant from the hand
  of heaven,
And on our actions set the name
  of right
With holy breath.

Enter PANDULPH, *attended.*

PANDULPH
Hail, noble Prince of France!
The next is this, — King John
  hath reconciled
Himself to Rome; his spirit is
  come in,
That so stood out against the holy
  church,
The great metropolis and see of
  Rome:
Therefore thy threatening colours now wind up;
And tame the savage spirit of wild war,
That, like a lion foster'd-up at hand,
It may lie gently at the foot of peace,
And be no further harmful than in show.

LOUIS
Your Grace shall pardon me, I will not back:
I am too high-born to be propertied,
To be a secondary at control,
Or useful serving-man, and instrument,
To any sovereign state throughout the world.
Your breath first kindled the dead coal of wars
Between this chastis'd kingdom and myself,
And brought in matter that should feed this fire;
And now 'tis far too huge to be blown out
With that same weak wind which enkindled it.
You taught me how to know the face of right,
Acquainted me with interest to this land,
Yea, thrust this enterprise into my heart;
And come ye now to tell me John hath made
His peace with Rome? What is that peace to me?
I, by the honour of my marriage-bed,
After young Arthur, claim this land for mine:
And, now it is half-conquer'd, must I back
Because that John hath made his peace with Rome?
Am I Rome's slave? What penny hath Rome borne,
What men provided, what munition sent,
To underprop this action? Is't not I
That undergo this charge? who else but I,
And such as to my claim are liable,
Sweat in this business and maintain this war?
Have I not heard these islanders shout out,
Vive le roi! as I have bank'd their towns?
Have I not here the best cards for the game
To win this easy match play'd for a crown?
And shall I now give o'er the yielded set?
No, no, on my soul, it never shall be said.

PANDULPH
You look but on the outside of this work.

LOUIS
Outside or inside, I will not return
Till my attempt so much be glorified
As to my ample hope was promised
Before I drew this gallant head of war,
And cull'd these fiery spirits from the world,
To outlook conquest, and to win renown
Even in the jaws of danger and of death. —
         [*Trumpet sounds.*
What lusty trumpet thus doth summon us?

KING JOHN Thus have I yielded up into your hand the circle of my glory.

Enter BASTARD, *attended.*

BASTARD
According to the fair-play of the world,
Let me have audience; I am sent to speak: —
My holy lord of Milan, from the king
I come, to learn how you have dealt for him;
And, as you answer, I do know the scope
And warrant limited unto my tongue.

PANDULPH
The Dauphin is too wilful-opposite,
And will not temporise with my entreaties;
He flatly says he'll not lay down his arms.

BASTARD
By all the blood that ever fury breathed,
The youth says well. — Now hear our English king;
For thus his royalty doth speak in me.
He is prepared; and reason too he should:
This apish and unmannerly approach,
This harness'd mask and unadvised revel,
This unhair'd sauciness and boyish troops,
The king doth smile at; and is well prepared
To whip this dwarfish war, these pigmy arms,
From out the circle of his territories.
That hand which had the strength, even at your door,
To cudgel you, and make you take the hatch;
To dive, like buckets, in concealed wells;
To crouch in litter of your stable planks;
To lie, like pawns, lock'd up in chests and trunks;
To hug with swine; to seek sweet safety out
In vaults and prisons; and to thrill and shake
Even at the crying of your nation's crow,
Thinking his voice an armed Englishman; —
Shall that victorious hand be feebled here,
That in your chambers gave you chastisement?
No: know the gallant monarch is in arms;
And, like an eagle o'er his aery, towers,
To souse annoyance that comes near his nest. —
And you degenerate, you ingrate revolts,
You bloody Neroes, ripping up the womb
Of your dear mother England, blush for shame;
For your own ladies and pale-visag'd maids,
Like Amazons, come tripping after drums,
Their thimbles into armed gauntlets change,
Their needles to lances, and their gentle hearts
To fierce and bloody inclination.

LOUIS
There end thy brave, and turn thy face in peace;
We grant thou canst outscold us: fare thee well;
We hold our time too precious to be spent
With such a brabbler.

PANDULPH
                    Give me leave to speak.

BASTARD
No, I will speak.

LOUIS
                 We will attend to neither. —
Strike up the drums; and let the tongue of war
Plead for our interest and our being here.

BASTARD
Indeed, your drums, being beaten, will cry out;
And so shall you, being beaten: do but start
An echo with the clamour of thy drum,
And even at hand a drum is ready braced
That shall reverberate all as loud as thine;
Sound but another, and another shall,
As loud as thine, rattle the welkin's ear,
And mock the deep-mouth'd thunder: for at hand —
Not trusting to this halting legate here,
Whom he hath used rather for sport than need —
Is warlike John; and in his forehead sits
A bare-ribb'd death, whose office is this day
To feast upon whole thousands of the French.

LOUIS
Strike up our drums, to find this danger out.

BASTARD
And thou shalt find it, Dauphin, do not doubt.   [*Exeunt.*

SCENE III
The field of battle.

Alarums. Enter KING JOHN *and* HUBERT.

KING JOHN
How goes the day with us? O, tell me, Hubert.

HUBERT
Badly, I fear. How fares your majesty?

KING JOHN
This fever, that hath troubled me so long,
Lies heavy on me; — O, my heart is sick!

Enter a MESSENGER.

MESSENGER
My lord, your valiant kinsman, Faulconbridge,
Desires your majesty to leave the field,
And send him word by me which way you go.

KING JOHN
Tell him, toward Swinstead, to the abbey there.

MESSENGER
Be of good comfort; for the great supply,
That was expected by the Dauphin here,
Are wrack'd three nights ago on Goodwin Sands.
This news was brought to Richard but even now:
The French fight coldly, and retire themselves.

KING JOHN
Ay me! this tyrant fever burns me up,
And will not let me welcome this good news! —
Set on toward Swinstead: to my litter straight;
Weakness possesseth me, and I am faint.   [*Exeunt.*

SCENE IV
Another part of the field.

Enter SALISBURY, PEMBROKE, *and* BIGOT.

SALISBURY
I did not think the king so stored with friends.

PEMBROKE
Up once again; put spirit in the French:
If they miscarry, we miscarry too.

SALISBURY
That misbegotten devil, Faulconbridge,
In spite of spite, alone upholds the day.

PEMBROKE
They say King John sore-sick hath left the field.

Enter MELUN, *wounded.*

MELUN
Lead me to the revolts of England here.

SALISBURY
When we were happy, we had other names.

PEMBROKE
It is the Count Melun.

SALISBURY
                    Wounded to death.

MELUN
Fly, noble English, you are bought and sold;
Unthread the rude eye of rebellion,
And welcome home again discarded faith.
Seek out King John, and fall before his feet;
For if the French be lords of this loud day,
He means to recompense the pains you take
By cutting off your heads: thus hath he sworn,
And I with him, and many more with me,
Upon the altar at Saint Edmunds-Bury;
Even on that altar where we swore to you
Dear amity and everlasting love.

SALISBURY
May this be possible? may this be true?

MELUN
Have I not hideous death within my view,
Retaining but a quantity of life,
Which bleeds away, even as a form of wax
Resolveth from his figure 'gainst the fire?
What in the world should make me now deceive,
Since I must lose the use of all deceit?
Why should I, then, be false, since it is true
That I must die here, and live hence by truth?
I say again, if Louis do win the day,
He is forsworn, if e'er those eyes of yours
Behold another day break in the east:
But even this night, — whose black contagious breath
Already smokes about the burning crest
Of the old, feeble, and day-wearied sun, —
Even this ill night, your breathing shall expire
Paying the fine of rated treachery
Even with a treacherous fine of all your lives,
If Louis by your assistance win the day.
Commend me to one Hubert, with your king:
The love of him, — and this respect besides,
For that my grandsire was an Englishman, —
Awakes my conscience to confess all this.
In lieu whereof, I pray you, bear me hence
From forth the noise and rumour of the field;
Where I may think the remnant of my thoughts
In peace, and part this body and my soul
With contemplation and devout desires.

SALISBURY
We do believe thee: — and beshrew my soul
But I do love the favour and the form
Of this most fair occasion, by the which
We will untread the steps of damned flight;

And, like a bated and retired flood,
Leaving our rankness and irregular course,
Stoop low within those bounds we have o'erlook'd.
And calmly run on in obedience,
Even to our ocean, to our great King John. —
My arm shall give thee help to bear thee hence;
For I do see the cruel pangs of death
Right in thine eye. — Away, my friends! New flight;
And happy newness, that intends old right.
            [*Exeunt, leading off* MELUN.

SCENE V
The French camp.

Enter LOUIS *and his* TRAIN.

LOUIS
The sun of heaven methought was loth to set,
But stay'd, and made the western welkin blush,
When th'English measure backward their own ground
In faint retire. O, bravely came we off,
When with a volley of our needless shot,
After such bloody toil, we bid good night;
And wound our tottering colours clearly up,
Last in the field, and almost lords of it!

Enter a MESSENGER.

MESSENGER
Where is my prince, the Dauphin?

LOUIS
                    Here: — what news?

MESSENGER
The Count Melun is slain; the English lords,
By his persuasion, are again fall'n off;
And your supply, which you have wish'd so long,
Are cast away and sunk on Goodwin Sands.

LOUIS
Ah, foul shrewd news! — beshrew thy very heart! —
I did not think to be so sad to-night
As this hath made me. — Who was he that said
King John did fly an hour or two before
The stumbling night did part our weary powers?

MESSENGER
Whoever spoke it, it is true, my lord.

LOUIS
Well; keep good quarter and good care to-night:
The day shall not be up so soon as I,
To try the fair adventure of to-morrow.   [*Exeunt.*

SCENE VI
An open place near Swinstead Abbey.

Enter BASTARD *and* HUBERT, *severally.*

HUBERT
Who's there? speak, ho! speak quickly, or I shoot.

BASTARD
A friend. — What art thou?

HUBERT
                    Of the part of England.

BASTARD
Whither dost thou go?

HUBERT
What's that to thee? Why may not I demand
Of thine affairs, as well as thou of mine?

BASTARD
Hubert, I think?

HUBERT
                Thou hast a perfect thought:
I will, upon all hazards, well believe
Thou art my friend, that know'st my tongue so well.
Who art thou?

BASTARD
            Who thou wilt: an if thou please,
Thou mayst befriend me so much as to think
I come one way of the Plantagenets.

HUBERT
Unkind remembrance! thou and eyeless night
Have done me shame: — brave soldier, pardon me,
That any accent breaking from thy tongue
Should scape the true acquaintance of mine ear.

BASTARD
Come, come; sans compliment, what news abroad?

HUBERT
Why, here walk I, in the black brow of night,
To find you out.

BASTARD
                Brief, then; and what's the news?

HUBERT
O, my sweet sir, news fitting to the night, —
Black, fearful, comfortless, and horrible.

BASTARD
Show me the very wound of this ill news:
I am no woman, I'll not swound at it.
HUBERT
The king, I fear, is poison'd by a monk:
I left him almost speechless; and broke out
To acquaint you with this evil, that you might
The better arm you to the sudden time,
Than if you had at leisure known of this.
BASTARD
How did he take it? who did taste to him?
HUBERT
A monk, I tell you; a resolved villain,
Whose bowels suddenly burst out: the king
Yet speaks, and peradventure may recover.
BASTARD
Who didst thou leave to tend his majesty?
HUBERT
Why, know you not the lords are all come back,
And brought Prince Henry in their company?
At whose request the king hath pardon'd them,
And they are all about his majesty.
BASTARD
Withhold thine indignation, mighty heaven,
And tempt us not to bear above our power! —
I'll tell thee, Hubert, half my power this night,
Passing these flats, are taken by the tide, —
These Lincoln Washes have devoured them;
Myself, well-mounted, hardly have escaped.
Away, before! conduct me to the king;
I doubt he will be dead or e're I come. [*Exeunt.*

SCENE VII

The orchard of Swinstead Abbey.

Enter PRINCE HENRY, SALISBURY, *and* BIGOT.

PRINCE HENRY
It is too late: the life of all his blood
Is touch'd corruptibly; and his pure brain —
Which some suppose the soul's frail dwelling-house —
Doth, by the idle comments that it makes,
Foretell the ending of mortality.

Enter PEMBROKE.

PEMBROKE
His highness yet doth speak; and holds belief
That, being brought into the open air,
It would allay the burning quality
Of that fell poison which assaileth him.
PRINCE HENRY
Let him be brought into the orchard here. —
Doth he still rage? [*Exit* BIGOT.
PEMBROKE
                    He is more patient
Than when you left him; even now he sung.
PRINCE HENRY
O vanity of sickness! fierce extremes
In their continuance will not feel themselves.
Death, having prey'd upon the outward parts,
Leaves them invisible; and his siege is now
Against the mind, the which he pricks and wounds
With many legions of strange fantasies,
Which, in their throng and press to that last hold,

Confound themselves. 'Tis strange that death should
sing. —
I am the cygnet to this pale faint swan,
Who chants a doleful hymn to his own death,
And from the organ-pipe of frailty sings
His soul and body to their lasting rest.
SALISBURY
Be of good comfort, prince; for you are born
To set a form upon that indigest
Which he hath left so shapeless and so rude.
                    KING JOHN *brought in.*
KING JOHN
Ay, marry, now my soul hath elbow-room;
It would not out at windows nor at doors.
There is so hot a summer in my bosom,
That all my bowels crumble up to dust:
I am a scribbled form, drawn with a pen
Upon a parchment; and against this fire
Do I shrink up.
PRINCE HENRY
                    How fares your majesty?
KING JOHN
Poison'd, — ill fare; — dead, forsook, cast off:
And none of you will bid the winter come,
To thrust his icy fingers in my maw;
Nor let my kingdom's rivers take their course
Through my burnt bosom; nor entreat the north
To make his bleak winds kiss my parched lips,
And comfort me with cold: — I do not ask you much,
I beg cold comfort; and you are so strait,
And so ingrateful, you deny me that.
PRINCE HENRY
O, that there were some virtue in my tears,
That might relieve you!
KING JOHN
                    The salt in them is hot. —
Within me is a hell; and there the poison
Is, as a fiend, confin'd to tyrannise
On unreprievable condemned blood.
                    Enter BASTARD.
BASTARD
O, I am scalded with my violent motion,
And spleen of speed to see your majesty!
KING JOHN
O cousin, thou art come to set mine eye:
The tackle of my heart is crack'd and burn'd;
And all the shrouds, wherewith my life should sail,
Are turned to one thread, one little hair:
My heart hath one poor string to stay it by,
Which holds but till thy news be uttered;
And then all this thou see'st is but a clod,
And module of confounded royalty.
BASTARD
The Dauphin is preparing hitherward,
Where heaven he knows how we shall answer him;
For in a night the best part of my power,
As I upon advantage did remove,
Were in the Washes all unwarily
Devoured by the unexpected flood.
                    [KING JOHN *dies.*
SALISBURY
You breathe these dead news in as dead an ear. —
My liege! my lord! — but now a king, — now thus.

PRINCE HENRY
Even so must I run on, and even so stop.
What surety of the world, what hope, what stay,
When this was now a king, and now is clay?
BASTARD
Art thou gone so? I do but stay behind
To do the office for thee of revenge,
And then my soul shall wait on thee to heaven,
As it on earth hath been thy servant still. —
Now, now, you stars that move in your right spheres,
Where be your powers? show now your mended faiths;
And instantly return with me again,
To push destruction and perpetual shame
Out of the weak door of our fainting land.
Straight let us seek, or straight we shall be sought;
The Dauphin rages at our very heels.
SALISBURY
It seems you know not, then, so much as we:
The Cardinal Pandulph is within at rest,
Who half an hour since came from the Dauphin,
And brings from him such offers of our peace
As we with honour and respect may take,
With purpose presently to leave this war.
BASTARD
He will the rather do it when he sees
Ourselves well sinewed to our defence.
SALISBURY
Nay, it is in a manner done already;
For many carriages he hath dispatch'd
To the sea-side, and put his cause and quarrel
To the disposing of the cardinal:
With whom yourself, myself, and other lords,
If you think meet, this afternoon will post
To consummate this business happily.
BASTARD
Let it be so: — and you, my noble prince,
With other princes that may best be spared,
Shall wait upon your father's funeral.
PRINCE HENRY
At Worcester must his body be interr'd;
For so he will'd it.
BASTARD
                    Thither shall it, then:
And happily may your sweet self put on
The lineal state and glory of the land!
To whom, with all submission, on my knee,
I do bequeath my faithful services
And true subjection everlastingly.
SALISBURY
And the like tender of our love we make,
To rest without a spot for evermore.
PRINCE HENRY
I have a kind soul that would give you thanks,
And knows not how to do it but with tears.
BASTARD
O, let us pay the time but needful woe,
Since it hath been beforehand with our griefs. —
This England never did, nor never shall,
Lie at the proud foot of a conqueror,
But when it first did help to wound itself.
Now these her princes are come home again,
Come the three corners of the world in arms,
And we shall shock them; naught shall make us rue,
If England to itself do rest but true. [*Exeunt.*

THE TAMING OF THE SHREW

DRAMATIS PERSONAE

A LORD.
CHRISTOPHER SLY, *a tinker.*
HOSTESS, PAGE, PLAYERS,
HUNTSMEN, *and* SERVANTS.
} *persons in the Induction.*

BAPTISTA, *a rich gentleman of Padua.*
VINCENTIO, *an old gentleman of Pisa.*
LUCENTIO, *son to Vincentio, in love with Bianca.*

PETRUCHIO, *a gentleman of Verona, a suitor to Katharina.*
GREMIO,
HORTENSIO, } *suitors to Bianca.*
TRANIO,
BIONDELLO, } *servants to Lucentio.*
GRUMIO,
CURTIS, } *servants to Petruchio.*
PEDANT.

KATHARINA *the shrew,*
BIANCA, } *daughters to Baptista.*
WIDOW.
TAILOR, HABERDASHER, *and* SERVANTS.

SCENE — *Padua, and sometimes in Petruchio's house in the country.*

INDUCTION

SCENE I

Before an alehouse on a heath.

Enter HOSTESS *and* SLY.

SLY
I'll pheeze you, in faith.

HOSTESS
A pair of stocks, you rogue!

SLY
Y'are a baggage: the Slys are no rogues; look in the
Chronicles; we came in with Richard Conqueror.
Therefore, *paucas pallabris;* let the world slide:
sessa!

HOSTESS
You will not pay for the glasses you have burst?

SLY
No, not a denier. Go by, Jeronimy; go to thy cold bed,
and warm thee.

HOSTESS
I know my remedy; I must go fetch the third-borough.
[*Exit.*

SLY
Third, or fourth, or fifth borough, I'll answer him
by law: I'll not budge an inch, boy: let him come,
and kindly.
[*Lies down on the ground and falls asleep.*
Horns winded. Enter a LORD *from hunting, with*
HUNTSMEN *and* SERVANTS.

LORD
Huntsman, I charge thee, tender well my hounds:
Brach Merriman, the poor cur is imboss'd;
And couple Clowder with the deep-mouth'd brach.
Saw'st thou not, boy, how Silver made it good
At the hedge-corner, in the coldest fault?
I would not lose the dog for twenty pound.

FIRST HUNTSMAN
Why, Belman is as good as he, my lord;
He cried upon it at the merest loss,
And twice to-day pick'd out the dullest scent:
Trust me, I take him for the better dog.

LORD
Thou art a fool: if Echo were as fleet,
I would esteem him worth a dozen such.
But sup them well, and look unto them all:
To-morrow I intend to hunt again.

FIRST HUNTSMAN
I will, my lord.

LORD
What's here? one dead, or drunk? See, doth he breathe?

SECOND HUNTSMAN
He breathes, my lord. Were he not warm'd with ale,
This were a bed but cold to sleep so soundly.

LORD
O monstrous beast! how like a swine he lies! —
Grim death, how foul and loathsome is thine image! —
Sirs, I will practise on this drunken man.
What think you, if he were convey'd to bed,
Wrapp'd in sweet clothes, rings put upon his fingers,
A most delicious banquet by his bed,
And brave attendants near him when he wakes, —
Would not the beggar then forget himself?

FIRST HUNTSMAN
Believe me, lord, I think he cannot choose.

SECOND HUNTSMAN
It would seem strange unto him when he waked.

LORD
Even as a flattering dream or worthless fancy.
Then take him up, and manage well the jest: —
Carry him gently to my fairest chamber,
And hang it round with all my wanton pictures:
Balm his foul head in warm distilled waters,
And burn sweet wood to make the lodging sweet:
Procure me music ready, when he wakes,
To make a dulcet and a heavenly sound;
And if he chance to speak, be ready straight
And with a low submissive reverence
Say, 'What is it your honour will command?'
Let one attend him with a silver basin
Full of rose-water, and bestrew'd with flowers;
Another bear the ewer, the third a diaper,
And say, 'Will't please your lordship cool your hands?'
Some one be ready with a costly suit,
And ask him what apparel he will wear;
Another tell him of his hounds and horse,
And that his lady mourns at his disease:
Persuade him that he hath been lunatic;
And when he says he is — say that he dreams,
For he is nothing but a mighty lord.
This do, and do it kindly, gentle sirs:
It will be pastime passing excellent,
If it be husbanded with modesty.

FIRST HUNTSMAN
My lord, I warrant you, we'll play our part,
As he shall think, by our true diligence,
He is no less than what we say he is.

LORD
Take him up gently, and to bed with him;
And each one to his office when he wakes.
[SLY *is borne out. Sound trumpets.*
Sirrah, go see what trumpet 'tis that sounds: —
[*Exit* SERVANT.
Belike, some noble gentleman, that means,
Travelling some journey, to repose him here. —
Enter SERVANT.
How now! who is it?

SERVANT
An it please your honour,
Players that offer service to your lordship.

LORD
Bid them come near.
Enter PLAYERS.
Now, fellows, you are welcome.

PLAYERS
We thank your honour.
LORD
Do you intend to stay with me to-night?
SECOND PLAYER
So please your lordship to accept our duty.
LORD
With all my heart. — This fellow I remember,
Since once he play'd a farmer's eldest son: —
'Twas where you woo'd the gentlewoman so well:
I have forgot your name; but, sure, that part
Was aptly fitted, and naturally perform'd.
FIRST PLAYER
I think 'twas Soto that your honour means.
LORD
'Tis very true: thou didst it excellent. —
Well, you are come to me in a happy time;
The rather for I have some sport in hand,
Wherein your cunning can assist me much.
There is a lord will hear you play to-night:
But I am doubtful of your modesties;
Lest, over-eyeing of his odd behavior, —
For yet his honour never heard a play, —
You break into some merry passion,
And so offend him; for, I tell you, sirs,
If you should smile, he grows impatient.
FIRST PLAYER
Fear not, my lord; we can contain ourselves,
Were he the veriest antic in the world.
LORD
Go, sirrah, take them to the buttery,
And give them friendly welcome every one:
Let them want nothing that my house affords.
  [Exit one with the PLAYERS.
Sirrah, go you to Barthol'mew my page,
  [To another SERVANT.
And see him dress'd in all suits like a lady:
That done, conduct him to the drunkard's chamber;
And call him madam, do him obeisance.
Tell him from me, — as he will win my love, —
He bear himself with honourable action,
Such as he hath observ'd in noble ladies
Unto their lords, by them accomplished:
Such duty to the drunkard let him do,
With soft low tongue and lowly courtesy;
And say, 'What is't your honour will command,
Wherein your lady and your humble wife
May show her duty and make known her love?'
And then, — with kind embracements, tempting
  kisses,
And with declining head into his bosom, —
Bid him shed tears, as being overjoy'd
To see her noble lord restored to health,
Who for twice seven years hath esteemed him
No better than a poor and loathsome beggar:
And if the boy have not a woman's gift
To rain a shower of commanded tears,
An onion will do well for such a shift;
Which in a napkin being close convey'd
Shall in despite enforce a watery eye.
See this dispatch'd with all the haste thou canst:
Anon I'll give thee more instructions. *[Exit* SERVANT.
I know the boy will well usurp the grace,
Voice, gait, and action of a gentlewoman:
I long to hear him call the drunkard husband;
And how my men will stay themselves from laughter
When they do homage to this simple peasant.
I'll in to counsel them: haply my presence
May well abate the over-merry spleen
Which otherwise would grow into extremes. *[Exeunt.*

SCENE II

A bedchamber in the LORD'S *house.*

Enter aloft the drunkard SLY, *with* ATTENDANTS;
*some with apparel, basin, ewer, and other appurtenances;
and* LORD.

SLY
For God's sake, a pot of small ale.
FIRST SERVANT
Will't please your lordship drink a cup of sack?
SECOND SERVANT
Will't please your honour taste of these conserves?
THIRD SERVANT
What raiment will your honour wear to-day?
SLY
I am Christopher Sly; call not me honour nor lordship:
I ne'er drank sack in my life; and if you give me any
conserves, give me conserves of beef: ne'er ask me
what raiment I'll wear; for I have no more doublets

than backs, no more stockings than legs, nor no more
shoes than feet, — nay, sometime more feet than
shoes, or such shoes as my toes look through the
overleather.
LORD
Heaven cease this idle humour in your honour!
O, that a mighty man, of such descent,
Of such possessions, and so high esteem,
Should be infused with so foul a spirit!
SLY
What, would you make me mad? Am not I Christopher
Sly, old Sly's son of Burton-heath; by birth a pedlar, by
education a card-maker, by transmutation a bear-herd,
and now by present profession a tinker? Ask Marian
Hacket, the fat ale-wife of Wincot, if she know me not:
if she say I am not fourteen pence on the score for
sheer ale, score me up for the lying'st knave in
Christendom. What! I am not bestraught: here's —
FIRST SERVANT
O, this it is that makes your lady mourn!
SECOND SERVANT
O, this it is that makes your servants droop!
LORD
Hence comes it that your kindred shuns your house,
As beaten hence by your strange lunacy.
O noble lord, bethink thee of thy birth;
Call home thy ancient thoughts from banishment,
And banish hence these abject lowly dreams.
Look how thy servants do attend on thee,
Each in his office ready at thy beck.
Wilt thou have music? hark! Apollo plays,
  [Music.
And twenty caged nightingales do sing:
Or wilt thou sleep? we'll have thee to a couch
Softer and sweeter than the lustful bed
On purpose trimm'd up for Semiramis.
Say thou wilt walk; we will bestrew the ground:
Or wilt thou ride? thy horses shall be trapp'd,
Their harness studded all with gold and pearl.
Dost thou love hawking? thou hast hawks will soar
Above the morning lark: or wilt thou hunt?
Thy hounds shall make the welkin answer them,
And fetch shrill echoes from the hollow earth.
FIRST SERVANT
Say thou wilt course; thy greyhounds are as swift
As breathed stags, ay, fleeter than the roe.
SECOND SERVANT
Dost thou love pictures? we will fetch thee straight
Adonis painted by a running brook,
And Cytherea all in sedges hid,
Which seem to move and wanton with her breath,
Even as the waving sedges play with wind.
LORD
We'll show thee Io as she was a maid,
And how she was beguiled and surprised,
As lively painted as the deed was done.
THIRD SERVANT
Or Daphne roaming through a thorny wood,
Scratching her legs, that one shall swear she bleeds;
And at that sight shall sad Apollo weep,
So workmanly the blood and tears are drawn.
LORD
Thou art a lord, and nothing but a lord:
Thou hast a lady far more beautiful
Than any woman in this waning age.
FIRST SERVANT
And, till the tears that she hath shed for thee,
Like envious floods, o'er-run her lovely face,
She was the fairest creature in the world;
And yet she is inferior to none.
SLY
Am I a lord? and have I such a lady?
Or do I dream? or have I dream'd till now?
I do not sleep: I see, I hear, I speak;
I smell sweet savours, and I feel soft things: —
Upon my life, I am a lord indeed;
And not a tinker, nor Christophero Sly.
Well, bring our lady hither to our sight;
And once again a pot o'th'smallest ale.
SECOND SERVANT
Will't please your mightiness to wash your hands?
  [SERVANTS present a ewer, basin, and napkin.
O, how we joy to see your wit restored!
O, that once more you knew but what you are!
These fifteen years you have been in a dream;
Or when you wak'd, so wak'd as if you slept.
SLY
These fifteen years! by my fay, a goodly nap.
But did I never speak of all that time?

FIRST SERVANT
O, yes, my lord; but very idle words:
For though you lay here in this goodly chamber,
Yet would you say ye were beaten out of door;
And rail upon the hostess of the house;
And say, you would present her at the leet,
Because she brought stone jugs and no seal'd quarts:
Sometimes you would call out for Cicely Hacket.
SLY
Ay, the woman's maid of the house.
THIRD SERVANT
Why, sir, you know no house, nor no such maid;
Nor no such men as you have reckon'd up, —
As Stephen Sly, and old John Naps of Greece,
And Peter Turf, and Henry Pimpernell;
And twenty more such names and men as these,
Which never were, nor no man ever saw.
SLY
Now, Lord be thanked for my good amends!
ALL
Amen.
SLY
I thank thee: thou shalt not lose by it.
  Enter the PAGE *as a lady, with* ATTENDANTS.
PAGE
How fares my noble lord?
SLY
Marry, I fare well; for here is cheer enough.
Where is my wife?
PAGE
Here, noble lord: what is thy will with her?
SLY
Are you my wife, and will not call me husband?
My men should call me lord: I am your goodman.
PAGE
My husband and my lord, my lord and husband;
I am your wife in all obedience.
SLY
I know it well. — What must I call her?
LORD
Madam.
SLY
Al'ce madam, or Joan madam?
LORD
Madam, and nothing else: so lords call ladies.
SLY
Madam wife, they say that I have dream'd,
And slept above some fifteen year or more.
PAGE
Ay, and the time seems thirty unto me,
Being all this time abandon'd from your bed.
SLY
'Tis much. — Servants, leave me and her alone. —
Madam, undress you, and come now to bed.
PAGE
Thrice-noble lord, let me entreat of you
To pardon me yet for a night or two;
Or, if not so, until the sun be set:
For your physicians have expressly charged,
In peril to incur your former malady,
That I should yet absent me from your bed:
I hope this reason stands for my excuse.
SLY
Ay, it stands so that I may hardly tarry so long. But I
  would be loth to fall into my dreams again: I will
  therefore tarry, in despite of the flesh and the blood.
  Enter a MESSENGER.
SERVANT
Your honour's players, hearing your amendment,
Are come to play a pleasant comedy;
For so your doctors hold it very meet,
Seeing too much sadness hath congeal'd your blood,
And melancholy is the nurse of frenzy:
Therefore they thought it good you hear a play,
And frame your mind to mirth and merriment,
Which bars a thousand harms and lengthens life.
SLY
Marry, I will; let them play it. Is not a commonty a
  Christmas gambol or a tumbling-trick?
PAGE
No, my good lord; it is more pleasing stuff.
SLY
What, household stuff?
PAGE
It is a kind of history.
SLY
Well, we'll see't. — Come, madam wife, sit by my side,
  and let the world slip: we shall ne'er be younger.

SLY Come, madam wife, sit by my side, and let the world slip.

ACT I

SCENE I

Padua. A public place.

Flourish. Enter LUCENTIO *and his man* TRANIO.

LUCENTIO
Tranio, since, for the great desire I had
To see fair Padua, nursery of arts,
I am arriv'd for fruitful Lombardy,
The pleasant garden of great Italy;
And, by my father's love and leave, am arm'd
With his good will, and thy good company,
My trusty servant, well approv'd in all;
Here let us breathe, and haply institute
A course of learning and ingenious studies.
Pisa, renowned for grave citizens,
Gave me my being and my father first,
A merchant of great traffic through the world,
Vincentio, come of the Bentivolii.
Lucentio his son, brought up in Florence,
It shall become, to serve all hopes conceived,
To deck his fortune with his virtuous deeds:
And therefore, Tranio, for the time I study,
Virtue, and that part of philosophy
Will I apply, that treats of happiness
By virtue specially to be achieved.
Tell me thy mind; for I have Pisa left,
And am to Padua come, as he that leaves
A shallow plash, to plunge him in the deep,
And with satiety seeks to quench his thirst.

TRANIO
Mi perdonate, gentle master mine,
I am in all affected as yourself;
Glad that you thus continue your resolve
To suck the sweets of sweet philosophy.
Only, good master, while we do admire
This virtue and this moral discipline,
Let's be no stoics nor no stocks, I pray;
Or so devote to Aristotle's ethics,
As Ovid be an outcast quite abjured:
Balk logic with acquaintance that you have,
And practise rhetoric in your common talk;
Music and poesy use to quicken you;
The mathematics and the metaphysics,
Fall to them, as you find your stomach serves you;
No profit grows, where is no pleasure ta'en:

In brief, sir, study what you most affect.

LUCENTIO
Gramercies, Tranio, well dost thou advise.
If, Biondello, thou wert come ashore,
We could at once put us in readiness,
And take a lodging, fit to entertain
Such friends as time in Padua shall beget.
But stay awhile: what company is this?

TRANIO
Master, some show, to welcome us to town.

Enter BAPTISTA *with his two daughters,* KATHARINA
and BIANCA; GREMIO, *a pantaloon; and*
HORTENSIO, *suitor to* BIANCA. LUCENTIO *and*
TRANIO *stand by.*

BAPTISTA
Gentlemen, importune me no farther,
For how I firmly am resolv'd you know;
That is, not to bestow my youngest daughter
Before I have a husband for the elder:
If either of you both love Katharina,
Because I know you well, and love you well,
Leave shall you have to court her at your pleasure.

GREMIO
To cart her rather: she's too rough for me. —
There, there, Hortensio, will you any wife?

KATHARINA [*to* BAPTISTA].
I pray you, sir, is it your will
To make a stale of me among these mates?

HORTENSIO
Mates, maid! how mean you that? no mates for you,
Unless you were of gentler, milder mould.

KATHARINA
I'faith, sir, you shall never need to fear:
I wis it is not half way to her heart;
But if it were, doubt not her care should be
To comb your noddle with a three-legg'd stool,
And paint your face, and use you like a fool.

HORTENSIO
From all such devils, good Lord, deliver us!

GREMIO
And me too, good Lord!

TRANIO [*aside to* LUCENTIO].
Hush, master! here's some good pastime toward:
That wench is stark mad, or wonderful froward.

LUCENTIO [*aside to* TRANIO].
But in the other's silence do I see
Maid's mild behaviour and sobriety.
Peace, Tranio!

TRANIO [*aside to* LUCENTIO].
Well said, master; mum! and gaze your fill.

BAPTISTA
Gentlemen, that I may soon make good
What I have said, Bianca, get you in:
And let it not displease thee, good Bianca;
For I will love thee ne'er the less, my girl.

KATHARINA
A pretty peat! it is best put finger in the eye, an she
knew why.

BIANCA
Sister, content you in my discontent. —
Sir, to your pleasure humbly I subscribe:
My books and instruments shall be my company,
On them to look, and practise by myself.

LUCENTIO [*aside to* TRANIO].
Hark, Tranio! thou mayst hear Minerva speak.

HORTENSIO
Signior Baptista, will you be so strange?
Sorry am I that our good will effects
Bianca's grief.

GREMIO
                         Why, will you mew her up,
Signior Baptista, for this fiend of hell,
And make her bear the penance of her tongue?

BAPTISTA
Gentlemen, content ye; I am resolved: —
Go in, Bianca: —   [*Exit* BIANCA.
And for I know she taketh most delight
In music, instruments, and poetry,
Schoolmasters will I keep within my house,
Fit to instruct her youth. If you, Hortensio,
Or Signior Gremio, you, know any such,
Prefer them hither; for to cunning men
I will be very kind, and liberal
To mine own children in good bringing-up:
And so, farewell. — Katharina, you may stay;
For I have more to commune with Bianca.   [*Exit.*

KATHARINA
Why, and I trust I may go too, may I not? What, shall I
be appointed hours; as though, belike, I knew not what
to take, and what to leave, ha?
                                                          [*Exit.*

GREMIO
You may go to the devil's dam: your gifts are so good,
here's none will hold you. — Our love is not so great,
Hortensio, but we may blow our nails together, and
fast it fairly out: our cake's dough on both sides.
Farewell: yet, for the love I bear my sweet Bianca, if I
can by any means light on a fit man to teach her that
wherein she delights, I will wish him to her father.

HORTENSIO
So will I, Signior Gremio: but a word, I pray. Though
the nature of our quarrel yet never brook'd parle, know
now, upon advice, it toucheth us both, — that we may
yet again have access to our fair mistress, and be happy
rivals in Bianca's love, — to labour and effect one thing
specially.

GREMIO
What's that, I pray?

HORTENSIO
Marry, sir, to get a husband for her sister.

GREMIO
A husband! a devil.

HORTENSIO
I say, a husband.

GREMIO
I say, a devil. Think'st thou, Hortensio, though her
father be very rich, any man is so very a fool to be
married to hell?

HORTENSIO
Tush, Gremio, though it pass your patience and mine
to endure her loud alarums, why, man, there be good
fellows in the world, an a man could light on them,
would take her with all faults and money enough.

GREMIO
I cannot tell; but I had as lief take her dowry with this
condition, — to be whipp'd at the high-cross every
morning.

HORTENSIO
Faith, as you say, there's small choice in rotten apples.
But, come; since this bar in law makes us friends, it
shall be so far forth friendly maintain'd, till by helping
Baptista's eldest daughter to a husband, we set his
youngest free for a husband, and then have to't afresh. —
Sweet Bianca! — Happy man be his dole! He that runs
fastest gets the ring. How say you, Signior Gremio?

GREMIO
I am agreed: and would I had given him the best horse
in Padua to begin his wooing, that would thoroughly

woo her, wed her, and bed her, and rid the house of her!
Come on.

[*Exeunt* GREMIO *and* HORTENSIO.

TRANIO
I pray, sir, tell me, — is it possible
That love should of a sudden take such hold?

LUCENTIO
O Tranio, till I found it to be true,
I never thought it possible or likely;
But, see! while idly I stood looking on,
I found the effect of love in idleness:
And now in plainness do confess to thee, —
That art to me as secret and as dear
As Anna to the Queen of Carthage was, —
Tranio, I burn, I pine, I perish, Tranio,
If I achieve not this young modest girl.
Counsel me, Tranio, for I know thou canst;
Assist me, Tranio, for I know thou wilt.

TRANIO
Master, it is no time to chide you now;
Affection is not rated from the heart:
If love have touch'd you, naught remains but so, —
Redime te captum quam queas minimo.

LUCENTIO
Gramercies, lad; go forward; this contents:
The rest will comfort, for thy counsel's sound.

TRANIO
Master, you look'd so longly on the maid,
Perhaps you mark'd not what's the pith of all.

LUCENTIO
O, yes, I saw sweet beauty in her face,
Such as the daughter of Agenor had,
That made great Jove to humble him to her hand,
When with his knees he kiss'd the Cretan strand.

TRANIO
Saw you no more? mark'd you not how her sister
Began to scold, and raise up such a storm,
That mortal ears might hardly endure the din?

LUCENTIO
Tranio, I saw her coral lips to move,
And with her breath she did perfume the air:
Sacred and sweet was all I saw in her.

TRANIO
Nay, then, 'tis time to stir him from his trance. —
I pray, awake, sir: if you love the maid,
Bend thoughts and wits to achieve her. Thus it stands:
Her eldest sister is so curst and shrewd,
That, till the father rid his hands of her,
Master, your love must live a maid at home;
And therefore has he closely mew'd her up,
Because she will not be annoy'd with suitors.

LUCENTIO
Ah, Tranio, what a cruel father's he!
But art thou not advis'd, he took some care
To get her cunning schoolmasters to instruct her?

TRANIO
Ay, marry, am I, sir; and now 'tis plotted.

LUCENTIO
I have it, Tranio.

TRANIO
Master, for my hand,
Both our inventions meet and jump in one.

LUCENTIO
Tell me thine first.

TRANIO
You will be schoolmaster,
And undertake the teaching of the maid:
That's your device.

LUCENTIO
It is: may it be done?

TRANIO
Not possible; for who shall bear your part,
And be in Padua here Vincentio's son,
Keep house, and ply his book; welcome his friends;
Visit his countrymen, and banquet them?

LUCENTIO
Basta; content thee; for I have it full.
We have not yet been seen in any house;
Nor can we be distinguish'd by our faces
For man or master: then it follows thus; —
Thou shalt be master, Tranio, in my stead,
Keep house, and port, and servants, as I should:
I will some other be; some Florentine,
Some Neapolitan, or meaner man of Pisa.
'Tis hatch'd, and shall be so: — Tranio, at once
Uncase thee; take my colour'd hat and cloak:
When Biondello comes, he waits on thee;
But I will charm him first to keep his tongue.

TRANIO
So had you need.

[*They exchange habits.*

In brief, sir, sith it your pleasure is,
And I am tied to be obedient, —
For so your father charg'd me at our parting: —
'Be serviceable to my son,' quoth he,
Although I think 'twas in another sense, —
I am content to be Lucentio,
Because so well I love Lucentio.

LUCENTIO
Tranio, be so, because Lucentio loves:
And let me be a slave, t'achieve that maid
Whose sudden sight hath thrall'd my
wounded eye. —
Here comes the rogue.

Enter BIONDELLO.
Sirrah, where have you been?

BIONDELLO
Where have I been! Nay, how now! where are
you? Master, has my fellow Tranio stol'n
your clothes? or you stol'n his? or both? pray,
what's the news?

LUCENTIO
Sirrah, come hither: 'tis no time to jest,
And therefore frame your manners to the
time.
Your fellow Tranio here, to save my life,
Puts my apparel and my countenance on,
And I for my escape have put on his;
For in a quarrel, since I came ashore,
I kill'd a man, and fear I was descried:
Wait you on him, I charge you, as becomes,
While I make way from hence to save my life:
You understand me?

BIONDELLO
I, sir! Ne'er a whit.

LUCENTIO
And not a jot of Tranio in your mouth:
Tranio is chang'd into Lucentio.

BIONDELLO
The better for him: would I were so too!

TRANIO
So could I, faith, boy, to have the next wish
after,
That Lucentio indeed had Baptista's youngest
daughter.
But, sirrah, — not for my sake, but your master's, —
I advise
You use your manners discreetly in all kind of
companies:
When I am alone, why, then I am Tranio;
But in all places else your master Lucentio.

LUCENTIO
Tranio, let's go:
One thing more rests, that thyself execute, —
To make one among these wooers: if thou ask me why, —
Sufficeth, my reasons are both good and weighty.

[*Exeunt.*

The presenters above speak.

FIRST SERVANT
My lord, you nod; you do not mind the play.

SLY
Yes, by Saint Anne, do I. A good matter, surely:
comes there any more of it?

PAGE
My lord, 'tis but begun.

SLY
'Tis a very excellent piece of work, madam lady;
would 'twere done!

[*They sit and mark.*

SCENE II

The same. Before HORTENSIO'S *house.*

Enter PETRUCHIO *and his man* GRUMIO.

PETRUCHIO
Verona, for awhile I take my leave,
To see my friends in Padua, but, of all,
My best beloved and approved friend,
Hortensio; and I trow this is his house. —
Here, sirrah Grumio; knock, I say.

GRUMIO
Knock, sir! whom should I knock? is there any man has
rebused your worship?

PETRUCHIO
Villain, I say, knock me here soundly.

GRUMIO
Knock you here, sir! why, sir, what am I, sir, that I
should knock you here, sir?

PETRUCHIO
Villain, I say, knock me at this gate,
And rap me well, or I'll knock your knave's pate.

PETRUCHIO Faith, sirrah, an you'll not knock, I'll wring it.

GRUMIO
My master is grown quarrelsome. — I should knock
you first,
And then I know after who comes by the worst.

PETRUCHIO
Will it not be?
Faith, sirrah, an you'll not knock, I'll wring it;
I'll try how you can *sol, fa,* and sing it.

[*He wrings him by the ears.*

GRUMIO
Help, masters, help! my master is mad.

PETRUCHIO
Now, knock when I bid you, sirrah villain!

Enter HORTENSIO.

HORTENSIO
How now! what's the matter? — My old friend
Grumio! and my good friend Petruchio! — How do you
all at Verona?

PETRUCHIO
Signior Hortensio, come you to part the fray?
Con tutto il cuore ben trovato, may I say.

HORTENSIO
*Alla nostra casa ben venuto, molto honorato signor mio
Petruchio.*—
Rise, Grumio, rise: we will compound this quarrel.

GRUMIO [*rising*].
Nay, 'tis no matter, sir, what he 'leges in Latin. — If this
be not a lawful cause for me to leave his service, — look
you, sir, — he bid me knock him and rap him soundly,
sir: well, was it fit for a servant to use his master so;
being perhaps, for aught I see, two-and-thirty, — a pip
out?
Whom would to God I had well knock'd at first,
Then had not Grumio come by the worst.

PETRUCHIO
A senseless villain! — Good Hortensio,
I bade the rascal knock upon your gate,
And could not get him for my heart to do it.

GRUMIO
Knock at the gate! — O heavens! Spake you not these
words plain, — 'Sirrah, knock me here, rap me here,
knock me well, and knock me soundly'? And come you
now with — knocking at the gate?

PETRUCHIO
Sirrah, be gone, or talk not, I advise you.

HORTENSIO
Petruchio, patience; I am Grumio's pledge:
Why, this' a heavy chance 'twixt him and you,

Your ancient, trusty, pleasant servant Grumio.
And tell me now, sweet friend, what happy gale
Blows you to Padua here, from old Verona?

PETRUCHIO
Such wind as scatters young men through the world,
To seek their fortunes further than at home,
Where small experience grows. But, in a few,
Signior Hortensio, thus it stands with me: —
Antonio, my father, is deceased;
And I have thrust myself into this maze,
Haply to wive and thrive as best I may:
Crowns in my purse I have, and goods at home,
And so am come abroad to see the world.

HORTENSIO
Petruchio, shall I, then, come roundly to thee,
And wish thee to a shrewd ill-favour'd wife?
Thou'ldst thank me but a little for my counsel:
And yet I'll promise thee she shall be rich,
And very rich: but thou'rt too much my friend,
And I'll not wish thee to her.

PETRUCHIO
Signior Hortensio, 'twixt such friends as we
Few words suffice; and therefore, if thou know
One rich enough to be Petruchio's wife, —
As wealth is burthen of my wooing dance, —
Be she as foul as was Florentius' love,
As old as Sibyl, and as curst and shrewd
As Socrates' Xanthippe, or a worse,
She moves me not, or not removes, at least,
Affection's edge in me, were she as rough
As are the swelling Adriatic seas:
I come to wive it wealthily in Padua;
If wealthily, then happily in Padua.

GRUMIO
Nay, look you, sir, he tells you flatly what his mind is:
Why, give him gold enough and marry him to a puppet
or an aglet-baby; or an old trot with ne'er a tooth in her
head, though she have as many diseases as two and
fifty horses: why, nothing comes amiss, so money
comes withal.

HORTENSIO
Petruchio, since we are stepp'd thus far in,
I will continue that I broach'd in jest.
I can, Petruchio, help thee to a wife
With wealth enough, and young and beauteous;
Brought up as best becomes a gentlewoman:
Her only fault — and that is faults enough —
Is, that she is intolerable curst,
And shrewd, and froward; so beyond all measure,
That, were my state far worser than it is,
I would not wed her for a mine of gold.

PETRUCHIO
Hortensio, peace! thou know'st not gold's effect:
Tell me her father's name, and 'tis enough;
For I will board her, though she chide as loud
As thunder when the clouds in autumn crack.

HORTENSIO
Her father is Baptista Minola,
An affable and courteous gentleman:
Her name is Katharina Minola,
Renown'd in Padua for her scolding tongue.

PETRUCHIO
I know her father, though I know not her:
And he knew my deceased father well.
I will not sleep, Hortensio, till I see her;
And therefore let me be thus bold with you
To give you over at this first encounter,
Unless you will accompany me thither.

GRUMIO
I pray you, sir, let him go while the humour lasts. O'
my word, an she knew him as well as I do, she would
think scolding would do little good upon him: she may,
perhaps, call him half a score knaves, or so: why, that's
nothing; an he begin once, he'll rail in his rope-tricks.
I'll tell you what, sir, — an she stand him but a little, he
will throw a figure in her face, and so disfigure her with
it, that she shall have no more eyes to see withal than a
cat. You know him not, sir.

HORTENSIO
Tarry, Petruchio, I must go with thee;
For in Baptista's keep my treasure is:
He hath the jewel of my life in hold,
His youngest daughter, beautiful Bianca;
And her withholds from me and other more,
Suitors to her and rivals in my love:
Supposing it a thing impossible, —
For those defects I have before rehearsed, —
That ever Katharina will be woo'd;
Therefore this order hath Baptista ta'en,
That none shall have access unto Bianca
Till Katharina the curst have got a husband.

GRUMIO
Katharina the curst!
A title for a maid, of all titles the worst.

HORTENSIO
Now shall my friend Petruchio do me grace;
And offer me, disguis'd in sober robes,
To old Baptista as a schoolmaster
Well seen in music, to instruct Bianca;
That so I may, by this device, at least
Have leave and leisure to make love to her,
And unsuspected court her by herself.

GRUMIO
Here's no knavery! See, to beguile the old folks,
how the young folks lay their heads together!

Enter GREMIO *and* LUCENTIO *disguised.*

Master, master, look about you: who goes there, ha?

HORTENSIO
Peace, Grumio! it is the rival of my love. —
Petruchio, stand by awhile.

GRUMIO
A proper stripling and an amorous!

[*They stand aside.*

GREMIO
O, very well; I have perus'd the note.
Hark you, sir; I'll have them very fairly bound:
All books of love, see that at any hand;
And see you read no other lectures to her:
You understand me: — over and beside
Signior Baptista's liberality,
I'll mend it with a largess: — take your papers too,
And let me have them very well perfumed;
For she is sweeter than perfume itself,
To whom they go to. What will you read to her?

LUCENTIO
Whate'er I read to her, I'll plead for you
As for my patron, — stand you so assured, —
As firmly as yourself were still in place:
Yea, and perhaps with more successful words
Than you, unless you were a scholar, sir.

GREMIO
O this learning! what a thing it is!

GRUMIO
O this woodcock, what an ass it is!

PETRUCHIO
Peace, sirrah!

HORTENSIO
Grumio, mum! — [*coming forward*] God save you,
    Signior Gremio!

GREMIO
And you are well met, Signior Hortensio.
Trow you whither I am going? — To Baptista Minola.
I promis'd to inquire carefully
About a schoolmaster for the fair Bianca:
And, by good fortune, I have lighted well
On this young man; for learning and behaviour
Fit for her turn; well read in poetry,
And other books, — good ones, I warrant ye.

HORTENSIO
'Tis well: and I have met a gentleman
Hath promis'd me to help me to another,
A fine musician to instruct our mistress;
So shall I no whit be behind in duty
To fair Bianca, so belov'd of me.

GREMIO
Belov'd of me, — and that my deeds shall prove.

GRUMIO [*aside*].
And that his bags shall prove.

HORTENSIO
Gremio, 'tis now no time to vent our love:
Listen to me; and if you speak me fair,
I'll tell you news indifferent good for either.
Here is a gentleman, whom by chance I met,
Upon agreement from us to his liking,
Will undertake to woo curst Katharina,
Yea, and to marry her, if her dowry please.

GREMIO
So said, so done, is well: —
Hortensio, have you told him all her faults?

PETRUCHIO
I know she is an irksome brawling scold:
If that be all, masters, I hear no harm.

GREMIO
No, say'st me so, friend? What countryman?

PETRUCHIO
Born in Verona, old Antonio's son:
My father dead, my fortune lives for me;
And I do hope good days and long to see.

GREMIO
O, sir, such a life, with such a wife, were strange!

But if you have a stomach, to't o' God's name:
You shall have me assisting you in all.
But will you woo this wild-cat?

PETRUCHIO
                    Will I live?

GRUMIO
Will he woo her? ay, or I'll hang her.

PETRUCHIO
Why came I hither but to that intent?
Think you a little din can daunt mine ears?
Have I not in my time heard lions roar?
Have I not heard the sea, puff'd up with winds,
Rage like an angry boar chafed with sweat?
Have I not heard great ordnance in the field,
And heaven's artillery thunder in the skies?
Have I not in a pitched battle heard
Loud 'larums, neighing steeds, and trumpets' clang
And do you tell me of a woman's tongue,
That gives not half so great a blow to th'ear
As will a chestnut in a farmer's fire?
Tush, tush! fear boys with bugs.

GRUMIO
                    For he fears none.

GREMIO
Hortensio, hark:
This gentleman is happily arrived,
My mind presumes, for his own good and ours.

HORTENSIO
I promis'd we would be contributors,
And bear his charging of wooing, whatsoe'er.

GREMIO
And so we will, — provided that he win her.

GRUMIO
I would I were as sure of a good dinner.

Enter TRANIO *brave, and* BIONDELLO.

TRANIO
Gentlemen, God save you! If I may be bold,
Tell me, I beseech you, which is the readiest way
To th'house of Signior Baptista Minola?

GREMIO
He that has the two fair daughters, — is't he you mean?

TRANIO
Even he. — Biondello, —

GREMIO
Hark you, sir; you mean not her to —

TRANIO
Perhaps, him and her, sir: what have you to do?

PETRUCHIO
Not her that chides, sir, at any hand, I pray.

TRANIO
I love no chiders, sir. — Biondello, let's away.

LUCENTIO [*aside*].
Well begun, Tranio.

HORTENSIO
                    Sir, a word ere you go; —
Are you a suitor to the maid you talk of, yea or no?

TRANIO
And if I be, sir, is it any offence?

GREMIO
No; if without more words you will get you hence.

TRANIO
Why, sir, I pray, are not the streets as free
For me as for you?

GREMIO
                    But so is not she.

TRANIO
For what reason, I beseech you?

GREMIO
                    For this reason, if you'll know, —
That she's the choice love of Signior Gremio.

HORTENSIO
That she's the chosen of Signior Hortensio.

TRANIO
Softly, my masters! if you be gentlemen,
Do me this right, — hear me with patience.
Baptista is a noble gentleman,
To whom my father is not all unknown;
And, were his daughter fairer than she is,
She may more suitors have, and me for one.
Fair Leda's daughter had a thousand wooers;
Then well one more may fair Bianca have:
And so she shall; Lucentio shall make one,
Though Paris came in hope to speed alone.

GREMIO
What, this gentleman will out-talk us all!

LUCENTIO
Sir, give him head: I know he'll prove a jade.

BAPTISTA Why, how now, dame! whence grows this insolence?

PETRUCHIO
Hortensio, to what end are all these words?
HORTENSIO
Sir, let me be so bold as ask you,
Did you yet ever see Baptista's daughter?
TRANIO
No, sir; but hear I do that he hath two;
The one as famous for a scolding tongue,
As is the other for beauteous modesty.
PETRUCHIO
Sir, sir, the first's for me; let her go by.
GREMIO
Yea, leave that labour to great Hercules;
And let it be more than Alcides' twelve.
PETRUCHIO
Sir, understand you this of me, in sooth:
The youngest daughter, whom you hearken for,
Her father keeps from all access of suitors;
And will not promise her to any man
Until the elder sister first be wed:
The younger then is free, and not before.
TRANIO
If it be so, sir, that you are the man
Must stead us all, and me amongst the rest;
And if you break the ice, and do this feat,
Achieve the elder, set the younger free
For our access, — whose hap shall be to have her
Will not so graceless be to be ingrate.
HORTENSIO
Sir, you say well, and well you do conceive;
And since you do profess to be a suitor,
You must, as we do, gratify this gentleman,
To whom we all rest generally beholding.
TRANIO
Sir, I shall not be slack: in sign whereof,
Please ye we may contrive this afternoon,
And quaff carouses to our mistress' health;
And do as adversaries do in law, —
Strive mightily, but eat and drink as friends.
GRUMIO and **BIONDELLO**
O excellent motion! Fellows, let's be gone.
HORTENSIO
The motion's good indeed, and be it so: —
Petruchio, I shall be your *ben venuto*.   [*Exeunt.*

ACT II

SCENE I

Padua. A room in BAPTISTA'S house.

*Enter KATHARINA, and BIANCA with her hands
bound.*

BIANCA
Good sister, wrong me not, nor wrong yourself,
To make a bondmaid and a slave of me;
That I disdain: but for these other gauds,
Unbind my hands, I'll pull them off myself,
Yea, all my raiment, to my petticoat;
Or, what you will command me, will I do.
So well I know my duty to my elders.
KATHARINA
Of all thy suitors, here I charge thee, tell
Whom thou lov'st best: see thou dissemble not.
BIANCA
Believe me, sister, of all the men alive,
I never yet beheld that special face
Which I could fancy more than any other.
KATHARINA
Minion, thou liest: is't not Hortensio?
BIANCA
If you affect him, sister, here I swear
I'll plead for you myself, but you shall have him.
KATHARINA
O, then, belike, you fancy riches more:
You will have Gremio to keep you fair.
BIANCA
Is it for him you do envy me so?
Nay, then, you jest; and now I well perceive
You have but jested with me all this while:
I prithee, sister Kate, untie my hands.
KATHARINA
If that be jest, then all the rest was so.   [*Strikes her.*

Enter BAPTISTA.

BAPTISTA
Why, how now, dame! whence grows this insolence? —
Bianca, stand aside: — Poor girl! she weeps: —
Go ply thy needle; meddle not with her. —
For shame, thou hilding of a devilish spirit,
Why dost thou wrong her that did ne'er wrong thee?
When did she cross thee with a bitter word?
KATHARINA
Her silence flouts me, and I'll be revenged.
[*Flies after BIANCA.*
BAPTISTA [*holding her back*].
What, in my sight? — Bianca, get thee in.
[*Exit BIANCA.*
KATHARINA
What, will you not suffer me? Nay, now I see
She is your treasure, she must have a husband;
I must dance barefoot on her wedding-day,
And, for your love to her, lead apes in hell.
Talk not to me: I will go sit and weep,
Till I can find occasion of revenge.   [*Exit.*
BAPTISTA
Was ever gentleman thus griev'd as I?
But who comes here?

*Enter GREMIO, with LUCENTIO in the habit of a
mean man; PETRUCHIO, with HORTENSIO as a
musician; and TRANIO, with BIONDELLO bearing a
lute and books.*

GREMIO
Good morrow, neighbour Baptista.
BAPTISTA
Good morrow, neighbour Gremio. — God save you,
gentlemen!

PETRUCHIO
And you, good sir! Pray, have you not a daughter
Call'd Katharina, fair and virtuous?
BAPTISTA
I have a daughter, sir, call'd Katharina.
GREMIO
You are too blunt: go to it orderly.
PETRUCHIO
You wrong me, Signior Gremio: give me leave. —
I am a gentleman of Verona, sir,
That, hearing of her beauty and her wit,
Her affability and bashful modesty,
Her wondrous qualities and mild behaviour,
Am bold to show myself a forward guest
Within your house, to make mine eye the witness
Of that report which I so oft have heard.
And, for an entrance to my entertainment,
I do present you with a man of mine,

[*presenting* HORTENSIO.

Cunning in music and the mathematics,
To instruct her fully in those sciences,
Whereof I know she is not ignorant:
Accept of him, or else you do me wrong:
His name is Licio, born in Mantua.
BAPTISTA
You're welcome, sir; and he, for your good sake.
But for my daughter Katharina, — this I know,
She is not for your turn, the more my grief.
PETRUCHIO
I see you do not mean to part with her;
Or else you like not of my company.
BAPTISTA
Mistake me not; I speak but as I find.
Whence are you, sir? what may I call your name?
PETRUCHIO
Petruchio is my name; Antonio's son,
A man well known throughout all Italy.
BAPTISTA
I know him well: you are welcome for his sake.
GREMIO
Saving your tale, Petruchio, I pray,
Let us, that are poor petitioners, speak too:
Baccare! you are marvellous forward.
PETRUCHIO
O, pardon me, Signior Gremio; I would fain be doing.
GREMIO
I doubt it not, sir; but you will curse your wooing.
Neighbour, this is a gift very grateful, I am sure of it. To
express the like kindness myself, that have been more
kindly beholding to you than any, I freely give unto you
this young scholar [*presenting* LUCENTIO], that hath
been long studying at Rheims; as cunning in Greek,
Latin, and other languages, as the other in music and
mathematics: his name is Cambio: pray, accept his
service.
BAPTISTA
A thousand thanks, Signior Gremio. — Welcome,
good Cambio. — But, gentle sir [*to* TRANIO],
me-thinks you walk like a stranger: may I be so bold to
know the cause of your coming?
TRANIO
Pardon me, sir, the boldness is mine own;
That, being a stranger in this city here,
Do make myself a suitor to your daughter,
Unto Bianca, fair and virtuous.
Nor is your firm resolve unknown to me,
In the preferment of the eldest sister.
This liberty is all that I request, —
That, upon knowledge of my parentage,
I may have welcome 'mongst the rest that woo,
And free access and favour as the rest:
And, toward the education of your daughters,
I here bestow a simple instrument,
And this small packet of Greek and Latin books:
If you accept them, then their worth is great.
Lucentio is my name.
BAPTISTA
                    Of whence, I pray?
TRANIO
Of Pisa, sir; son to Vincentio.
BAPTISTA
A mighty man of Pisa; by report
I know him well: you are very welcome, sir. —
Take you [*to* HORTENSIO] the lute, and you
      [*to* LUCENTIO] the set of books;
You shall go see your pupils presently. —
Holla, within!

Enter a SERVANT.

Sirrah, lead these gentlemen

To my two daughters; and tell them both
These are their tutors: bid them use them well.
[*Exit* SERVANT, *with* HORTENSIO, LUCENTIO, *and*
BIONDELLO.
We will go walk a little in the orchard,
And then to dinner. You are passing welcome,
And so I pray you all to think yourselves.

PETRUCHIO
Signior Baptista, my business asketh haste,
And every day I cannot come to woo.
You knew my father well; and in him, me,
Left solely heir to all his lands and goods,
Which I have better'd rather than decreas'd:
Then tell me, — if I get your daughter's love,
What dowry shall I have with her to wife?

BAPTISTA
After my death, the one half of my lands,
And in possession twenty thousand crowns.

PETRUCHIO
And, for that dowry, I'll assure her of
Her widowhood, be it that she survive me,
In all my lands and leases whatsoever:
Let specialties be therefore drawn between us,
That covenants may be kept on either hand.

BAPTISTA
Ay, when the special thing is well obtain'd,
That is, her love; for that is all in all.

PETRUCHIO
Why, that is nothing; for I tell you, father,
I am as peremptory as she proud-minded;
And where two raging fires meet together,
They do consume the thing that feeds their fury:
Though little fire grows great with little wind,
Yet extreme gusts will blow out fire and all:
So I to her, and so she yields to me;
For I am rough, and woo not like a babe.

BAPTISTA
Well mayst thou woo, and happy be thy speed!
But be thou arm'd for some unhappy words.

PETRUCHIO
Ay, to the proof; as mountains are for winds,
That shake not, though they blow perpetually.
Enter HORTENSIO, *with his head broke.*

BAPTISTA
How now, my friend! why dost thou look so pale?

HORTENSIO
For fear, I promise you, if I look pale.

BAPTISTA
What, will my daughter prove a good musician?

HORTENSIO
I think she'll sooner prove a soldier:
Iron may hold with her, but never lutes.

BAPTISTA
Why, then thou canst not break her to the lute?

HORTENSIO
Why, no; for she hath broke the lute to me.
I did but tell her she mistook her frets,
And bow'd her hand to teach her fingering;
When, with a most impatient devilish spirit,
'Frets call you these?' quoth she; 'I'll fume with them':
And, with that word, she struck me on the head,
And through the instrument my pate made way;
And there I stood amazed for a while,
As on a pillory, looking through the lute;
While she did call me rascal fiddler
And twangling Jack with twenty such vile terms,
As had she studied to misuse me so.

PETRUCHIO
Now, by the world, it is a lusty wench;
I love her ten times more than e'er I did:
O, how I long to have some chat with her!

BAPTISTA
Well, go with me, and be not so discomfited:
Proceed in practise with my younger daughter;
She's apt to learn, and thankful for good turns. —
Signior Petruchio, will you go with us,
Or shall I send my daughter Kate to you?

PETRUCHIO
I pray you do; I will attend her here, —
[*Exeunt* BAPTISTA, GREMIO, TRANIO, *and*
HORTENSIO.
And woo her with some spirit when she comes.
Say that she rail; why, then, I'll tell her plain,
She sings as sweetly as a nightingale:
Say that she frown; I'll say, she looks as clear
As morning roses newly wash'd with dew:
Say she be mute and will not speak a word;
Then I'll commend her volubility,
And say she uttereth piercing eloquence:

If she do bid me pack, I'll give her thanks,
As though she bid me stay by her a week:
If she deny to wed, I'll crave the day
When I shall ask the banns, and when be married. —
But here she comes; and now, Petruchio, speak.

Enter KATHARINA.

Good morrow, Kate; for that's your name, I hear.

KATHARINA
Well have you heard, but something hard of hearing:
They call me Katharina that do talk of me.

PETRUCHIO
You lie, in faith; for you are call'd plain Kate,
And bonny Kate, and sometimes Kate the curst;
But, Kate, the prettiest Kate in Christendom,
Kate of Kate-Hall, my super-dainty Kate,
For dainties are all kates, — and therefore, Kate,
Take this of me, Kate of my consolation; —
Hearing thy mildness prais'd in every town,
Thy virtues spoke of, and thy beauty sounded,
Yet not so deeply as to thee belongs, —
Myself am mov'd to woo thee for my wife.

KATHARINA
Mov'd! in good time: let him that mov'd you hither
Remove you hence: I knew you at the first,
You were a moveable.

PETRUCHIO
Why, what's a moveable?

KATHARINA
A joint-stool.

PETRUCHIO
Thou hast hit it: come, sit on me.

KATHARINA
Asses are made to bear, and so are you.

PETRUCHIO
Women are made to bear, and so are you.

KATHARINA
No such jade as you, if me you mean.

PETRUCHIO
Alas, good Kate! I will not burthen thee!
For, knowing thee to be but young and light —

KATHARINA
Too light for such a swain as you to catch;
And yet as heavy as my weight should be.

PETRUCHIO
Should be! Should — buzz!

KATHARINA
Well ta'en, and like a buzzard.

PETRUCHIO
O slow-wing'd turtle! shall a buzzard take thee?

KATHARINA
Ay, for a turtle, — as he takes a buzzard.

PETRUCHIO
Come, come, you wasp; i'faith, you are too angry.

KATHARINA
If I be waspish, best beware my sting.

PETRUCHIO
My remedy is then, to pluck it out.

KATHARINA
Ay, if the fool could find it where it lies.

PETRUCHIO
Who knows not where a wasp does wear his sting?
In his tail.

KATHARINA
In his tongue.

PETRUCHIO
Whose tongue?

KATHARINA
Yours, if you talk of tails: and so farewell.

PETRUCHIO
What, with my tongue in your tail? nay, come again,
Good Kate; I am a gentleman.

KATHARINA
That I'll try.
[*She strikes him.*

PETRUCHIO
I swear I'll cuff you, if you strike again.

KATHARINA
So may you lose your arms:
If you strike me, you are no gentleman;
And if no gentleman, why, then no arms.

PETRUCHIO
A herald, Kate? O, put me in thy books!

KATHARINA
What is your crest? a coxcomb?

PETRUCHIO
A combless cock, so Kate will be my hen.

KATHARINA
No cock of mine; you crow too like a craven.

PETRUCHIO
Nay, come, Kate, come; you must not look so sour.

KATHARINA
It is my fashion when I see a crab.

PETRUCHIO
Why, here's no crab; and therefore look not sour.

KATHARINA
There is, there is.

PETRUCHIO
Then show it me.

KATHARINA
Had I a glass, I would.

PETRUCHIO
What, you mean my face?

KATHARINA
Well aim'd of such a young one.

PETRUCHIO
Now, by Saint George, I am too young for you.

KATHARINA
Yet you are wither'd.

PETRUCHIO
'Tis with cares.

KATHARINA
I care not.

PETRUCHIO
Nay, hear you, Kate: in sooth, you scape not so.

PETRUCHIO Thou must be married to no man but me.

KATHARINA
I chafe you, if I tarry: let me go.
PETRUCHIO
No, not a whit: I find you passing gentle.
'Twas told me you were rough, and coy, and sullen,
And now I find report a very liar;
For thou are pleasant, gamesome, passing courteous;
But slow in speech, yet sweet as spring-time flowers:
Thou canst not frown, thou canst not look askance,
Nor bite the lip, as angry wenches will;
Nor hast thou pleasure to be cross in talk;
But thou with mildness entertain'st thy wooers,
With gentle conference, soft and affable.
Why does the world report that Kate doth limp?
O slanderous world! Kate, like the hazel-twig,
Is straight and slender; and as brown in hue
As hazel-nuts, and sweeter than the kernels.
O, let me see thee walk: thou dost not halt.
KATHARINA
Go, fool, and whom thou keep'st, command.
PETRUCHIO
Did ever Dian so become a grove,
As Kate this chamber with her princely gait?
O, be thou Dian, and let her be Kate;
And then let Kate be chaste, and Dian sportful!
KATHARINA
Where did you study all this goodly speech?
PETRUCHIO
It is extempore, from my mother-wit.
KATHARINA
A witty mother! witless else her son.
PETRUCHIO
Am I not wise?
KATHARINA
       Yes; keep you warm.
PETRUCHIO
Marry, so I mean, sweet Katharina, in thy bed:
And therefore, setting all this chat aside,
Thus in plain terms: — your father hath consented
That you shall be my wife; your dowry 'greed on;
And, will you, nill you, I will marry you.
Now, Kate, I am a husband for your turn;
For, by this light, whereby I see thy beauty, —
Thy beauty, that doth make me like thee well, —
Thou must be married to no man but me;
For I am he am born to tame you, Kate,
And bring you from a wild Kate to a Kate
Conformable, as other household Kates.
Here comes your father: never make denial;
I must and will have Katharina to my wife.

Enter BAPTISTA, GREMIO, *and* TRANIO.

BAPTISTA
Now, Signior Petruchio, how speed you with
My daughter?
PETRUCHIO
      How but well, sir? how but well?
It were impossible I should speed amiss.
BAPTISTA
Why, how now, daughter Katharina! in your dumps?
KATHARINA
Call you me daughter? now, I promise you,
You have show'd a tender fatherly regard,
To wish me wed to one half lunatic;
A mad-cap ruffian and a swearing Jack,
That thinks with oaths to face the matter out.
PETRUCHIO
Father, 'tis thus: — yourself and all the world,
That talk'd of her, have talk'd amiss of her:
If she be curst, it is for policy,
For she's not froward, but modest as the dove;
She is not hot, but temperate as the morn;
For patience she will prove a second Grissel,
And Roman Lucrece for her chastity:
And to conclude, — we have 'greed so well together,
That upon Sunday is the wedding-day.
KATHARINA
I'll see thee hang'd on Sunday first.
GREMIO
Hark, Petruchio; she says, she'll see thee hang'd first.
TRANIO
Is this your speeding? nay, then, good night our part!
PETRUCHIO
Be patient, gentlemen; I choose her for myself:
If she and I be pleas'd, what's that to you?
'Tis bargain'd 'twixt us twain, being alone,
That she shall still be curst in company.
I tell you, 'tis incredible to believe
How much she loves me: O, the kindest Kate! —
She hung about my neck; and kiss on kiss

She vied so fast, protesting oath on oath,
That in a twink she won me to her love.
O, you are novices! 'tis a world to see,
How tame, when men and women are alone,
A meacock wretch can make the curstest shrew. —
Give me thy hand, Kate: I will unto Venice,
To buy apparel 'gainst the wedding-day. —
Provide the feast, father, and bid the guests;
I will be sure my Katharina shall be fine.
BAPTISTA
I know not what to say: but give me your hands;
God send you joy, Petruchio! 'tis a match.
GREMIO *and* **TRANIO**
Amen, say we: we will be witnesses.
PETRUCHIO
Father, and wife, and gentlemen, adieu;
I will to Venice; Sunday comes apace: —
We will have rings, and things, and fine array;
And kiss me, Kate; we will be married o' Sunday.
      [*Exeunt* PETRUCHIO *and* KATHARINA *severally.*
GREMIO
Was ever match clapp'd up so suddenly?
BAPTISTA
Faith, gentlemen, now I play a merchant's part,
And venture madly on a desperate mart.
TRANIO
'Twas a commodity lay fretting by you:
'Twill bring you gain, or perish on the seas.
BAPTISTA
The gain I seek is, quiet in the match.
GREMIO
No doubt but he hath got a quiet catch.
But now, Baptista, to your younger daughter:
Now is the day we long have looked for:
I am your neighbour, and was suitor first.
TRANIO
And I am one that love Bianca more
Than words can witness, or your thoughts can guess.
GREMIO
Youngling, thou canst not love so dear as I.
TRANIO
Greybeard, thy love doth freeze.
GREMIO
          But thine doth fry.
Skipper, stand back: 'tis age that nourisheth.
TRANIO
But youth in ladies' eyes that flourisheth.
BAPTISTA
Content you, gentlemen: I will compound this strife:
'Tis deeds must win the prize; and he, of both,
That can assure my daughter greatest dower
Shall have Bianca's love. —
Say, Signior Gremio, what can you assure her?
GREMIO
First, as you know, my house within the city
Is richly furnished with plate and gold;
Basins and ewers, to lave her dainty hands;
My hangings all of Tyrian tapestry;
In ivory coffers I have stuff'd my crowns;
In cypress chests my arras-counterpoints,
Costly apparel, tents, and canopies,
Fine linen, Turkey cushions boss'd with pearl,
Valance of Venice gold in needlework;
Pewter and brass, and all things that belong
To house or housekeeping: then, at my farm
I have a hundred milch-kine to the pail,
Six score fat oxen standing in my stalls;
And all things answerable to this portion.
Myself am struck in years, I must confess;
And if I die to-morrow, this is hers,
If whilst I live she will be only mine.
TRANIO
That 'only' came well in. — Sir, list to me:
I am my father's heir and only son:
If I may have your daughter to my wife,
I'll leave her houses three or four as good,
Within rich Pisa walls, as any one
Old Signior Gremio has in Padua;
Besides two thousand ducats by the year
Of fruitful land, all which shall be her jointure. —
What, have I pinch'd you, Signior Gremio?
GREMIO
Two thousand ducats by the year of land!
My land amounts but to so much in all:
That she shall have: besides an argosy
That now is lying in Marseilles' road. —
What, have I chok'd you with an argosy?
TRANIO
Gremio, 'tis known my father hath no less
Than three great argosies; besides two galliasses,

And twelve tight galleys: these I will assure her,
And twice as much, whate'er thou offer'st next.
GREMIO
Nay, I have offer'd all, — I have no more;
And she can have no more than all I have: —
If you like me, she shall have me and mine.
TRANIO
Why, then, the maid is mine from all the world,
By your firm promise: Gremio is out-vied.
BAPTISTA
I must confess your offer is the best;
And, let your father make her the assurance,
She is your own; else, you must pardon me:
If you should die before him, where's her dower?
TRANIO
That's but a cavil: he is old, I young.
GREMIO
And may not young men die, as well as old?
BAPTISTA
Well, gentlemen,
I am thus resolv'd: — on Sunday next you know
My daughter Katharina is to be married:
Now, on the Sunday following, shall Bianca
Be bride to you, if you make this assurance;
If not, Signior Gremio:
And so, I take my leave, and thank you both.
GREMIO
Adieu, good neighbour.   [*Exit* BAPTISTA.
         Now I fear thee not:
Sirrah young gamester, your father were a fool
To give thee all, and in his waning age
Set foot under thy table: tut, a toy!
An old Italian fox is not so kind, my boy.   [*Exit.*
TRANIO
A vengeance on your crafty wither'd hide!
Yet I have fac'd it with a card of ten.
'Tis in my head to do my master good:
I see no reason but suppos'd Lucentio
Must get a father, call'd — suppos'd Vincentio;
And that's a wonder: fathers commonly
Do get their children; but in this case of wooing,
A child shall get a sire, if I fail not of my cunning. [*Exit.*

ACT III

SCENE I

Padua. A room in BAPTISTA'S *house.*

Enter LUCENTIO, HORTENSIO, *and* BIANCA.

LUCENTIO
Fiddler, forbear; you grow too forward, sir:
Have you so soon forgot the entertainment
Her sister Katharina welcom'd you withal?
HORTENSIO
But, wrangling pedant, this' the patroness
Of heavenly harmony:
Then give me leave to have prerogative;
And when in music we have spent an hour,
Your lecture shall have leisure for as much.
LUCENTIO
Preposterous ass, that never read so far
To know the cause why music was ordain'd!
Was it not to refresh the mind of man
After his studies or his usual pain?
Then give me leave to read philosophy,
And while I pause, serve in your harmony.
HORTENSIO
Sirrah, I will not bear these braves of thine.
BIANCA
Why, gentlemen, you do me double wrong,
To strive for that which resteth in my choice:
I am no breeching scholar in the schools;
I'll not be tied to hours nor 'pointed times,
But learn my lessons as I please myself.
And, to cut off all strife, here sit we down: —
Take you your instrument, play you the whiles;
His lecture will be done ere you have tuned.
HORTENSIO
You'll leave his lecture when I am in tune?
      [*To* BIANCA. HORTENSIO *retires.*
LUCENTIO
That will be never: — tune your instrument.
BIANCA
Where left we last?
LUCENTIO
Here, madam: —   [*Reads.*

BIANCA I must believe my master; else, I promise you, I should be arguing still upon that doubt.

Hac ibat Simois; hic est Sigeia tellus;
Hic steterat Priami regia celsa senis.

BIANCA
Conster them.
LUCENTIO
Hac ibat, as I told you before, — *Simois,* I am Lucentio, — *hic est,* son unto Vincentio of Pisa, — *Sigeia tellus,* disguised thus to get your love; — *Hic steterat,* and that Lucentio that comes a-wooing, — *Priami,* is my man Tranio, — *regia,* bearing my port, — *celsa senis,* that we might beguile the old pantaloon.
HORTENSIO [*coming forward*].
Madam, my instrument's in tune.
BIANCA
                    Let's hear. [*HORTENSIO plays.*
O fie! the treble jars.
LUCENTIO
                    Spit in the hole, man,
And tune again.
BIANCA
Now let me see if I can construe it: —
Hac ibat Simois, I know you not, — *hic est Sigeia tellus,* I trust you not; — *Hic steterat Priami,* take heed he hear us not, — *regia,* presume not, — *celsa senis,* despair not.
HORTENSIO
Madam, 'tis now in tune.
LUCENTIO
                    All but the base.
HORTENSIO
The base is right; 'tis the base knave that jars. —
[*aside*] How fiery and forward our pedant is!
Now, for my life, the knave doth court my love:
Pedascule, I'll watch you better yet.
BIANCA
In time I may believe, yet I mistrust.
LUCENTIO
Mistrust it not; for, sure, Aeacides
Was Ajax, — call'd so from his grandfather.
BIANCA
I must believe my master; else, I promise you,
I should be arguing still upon that doubt:
But let it rest. — Now, Licio, to you: —
Good masters, take it not unkindly, pray,
That I have been thus pleasant with you both.

HORTENSIO [*to LUCENTIO*].
You may go walk, and give me leave awhile:
My lessons make no music in three parts.
LUCENTIO
Are you so formal, sir? well, I must wait,
[*aside*] And watch withal; for, but I be deceived,
Our fine musician groweth amorous.
HORTENSIO
Madam, before you touch the instrument,
To learn the order of my fingering,
I must begin with rudiments of art;
To teach you gamut in a briefer sort,
More pleasant, pithy, and effectual,
Than hath been taught by any of my trade:
And there it is in writing, fairly drawn.
BIANCA
Why, I am past my gamut long ago.
HORTENSIO
Yet read the gamut of Hortensio.
BIANCA [*reads*].
        '*Gamut* I am, the ground of all accord,
            A re, to plead Hortensio's passion;
        B mi, Bianca, take him for thy lord,
            C fa ut, that loves with all affection:
        D sol re, one cliff, two notes have I:
        E la mi, show pity, or I die.'
Call you this gamut? tut, I like it not:
Old fashions please me best; I am not so nice,
To change true rules for old inventions.

                    Enter a SERVANT.

SERVANT
Mistress, your father prays you leave your books,
And help to dress your sister's chamber up:
You know to-morrow is the wedding-day.
BIANCA
Farewell, sweet masters, both; I must be gone.
                    [*Exeunt* BIANCA *and* SERVANT.
LUCENTIO
Faith, mistress, then I have no cause to stay. [*Exit.*
HORTENSIO
But I have cause to pry into this pedant:
Methinks he looks as though he were in love: —
Yet if thy thoughts, Bianca, be so humble,
To cast thy wandering eyes on every stale,

Seize thee that list: if once I find thee ranging,
Hortensio will be quit with thee by changing.   [*Exit.*

SCENE II

The same. Before BAPTISTA'S *house.*

Enter BAPTISTA, GREMIO, TRANIO, KATHARINA,
BIANCA, LUCENTIO, *and others, with*
ATTENDANTS.

BAPTISTA [*to* TRANIO].
Signior Lucentio, this is the 'pointed day
That Katharina and Petruchio should be married,
And yet we hear not of our son-in-law.
What will be said? what mockery will it be,
To want the bridegroom when the priest attends
To speak the ceremonial rites of marriage!
What says Lucentio to this shame of ours?
KATHARINA
No shame but mine: I must, forsooth, be forc'd
To give my hand, opposed against my heart,
Unto a mad-brain rudesby, full of spleen;
Who woo'd in haste, and means to wed at leisure.
I told you, I, he was a frantic fool,
Hiding his bitter jests in blunt behaviour:
And, to be noted for a merry man,
He'll woo a thousand, 'point the day of marriage,
Make feasts, invite friends, and proclaim the banns;
Yet never means to wed where he hath woo'd.
Now must the world point at poor Katharina,
And say, 'Lo, there is mad Petruchio's wife,
If it would please him come and marry her!'
TRANIO
Patience, good Katharina, and Baptista too.
Upon my life, Petruchio means but well,
Whatever fortune stays him from his word:
Though he be blunt, I know him passing wise;
Though he be merry, yet withal he's honest.
KATHARINA
Would Katharina had never seen him, though!
                    [*Exit weeping, follow'd by* BIANCA *and others.*
BAPTISTA
Go, girl; I cannot blame thee now to weep;
For such an injury would vex a saint,
Much more a shrew of thy impatient humour.

                    Enter BIONDELLO.

BIONDELLO
Master, master! news, old news, and such news as you
        never heard of!
BAPTISTA
Is it new and old too? how may that be?
BIONDELLO
Why, is it not news, to hear of Petruchio's coming?
BAPTISTA
Is he come?
BIONDELLO
Why, no, sir.
BAPTISTA
What then?
BIONDELLO
He is coming.
BAPTISTA
When will he be here?
BIONDELLO
When he stands where I am, and sees you there.
TRANIO
But, say, what to thine old news?
BIONDELLO
Why, Petruchio is coming, in a new hat and an old
jerkin; a pair of old breeches, thrice turn'd; a pair of
boots that have been candle-cases, one buckled, another
laced; an old rusty sword ta'en out of the town-armoury,
with a broken hilt, and chapeless; with two broken
points: his horse hipp'd with an old mothy saddle, and
stirrups of no kindred; besides, possess'd with the
glanders, and like to mose in the chine; troubled with the
lampass, infected with the fashions, full of windgalls,
sped with spavins, ray'd with yellows, past cure of the
fives, stark spoil'd with the staggers, begnawn with the
bots; sway'd in the back, and shoulder-shotten;
near-legg'd before, and with a half-cheek'd bit, and a
headstall of sheep's leather, which, being restrain'd to
keep him from stumbling, hath been often burst, and
new-repair'd with knots; one girth six times pieced, and
a woman's crupper of velure, which hath two letters for
her name fairly set down in studs, and here and there
pieced with packthread.
BAPTISTA
Who comes with him?

BIONDELLO
O, sir, his lackey, for all the world caparison'd like the
horse; with a linen stock on one leg, and a kersey
boot-hose on the other, garter'd with a red and blue list;
an old hat, and *The Humour of Forty Fancies* prick'd in't
for a feather: a monster, a very monster in apparel; and
not like a Christian footboy or a gentleman's lackey.

TRANIO
'Tis some odd humour pricks him to this fashion;
Yet oftentimes he goes but mean-apparell'd.

BAPTISTA
I am glad he's come, howsoe'er he comes.

BIONDELLO
Why, sir, he comes not.

BAPTISTA
Didst thou not say he comes?

BIONDELLO
Who? that Petruchio came?

BAPTISTA
Ay, that Petruchio came.

BIONDELLO
No, sir; I say his horse comes, with him on his back.

BAPTISTA
Why, that's all one.

BIONDELLO
    Nay, by Saint Jamy,
  I hold you a penny,
     A horse and a man
     Is more than one,
  And yet not many.
     Enter PETRUCHIO *and* GRUMIO.

PETRUCHIO
Come, where be these gallants? who's at home?

BAPTISTA
You're welcome, sir.

PETRUCHIO
       And yet I come not well.

BAPTISTA
And yet you halt not.

TRANIO
       Not so well apparell'd
As I wish you were.

PETRUCHIO
Were it better, I should rush in thus.
But where is Kate? where is my lovely bride? —
How does my father? — Gentles, methinks you frown:
And wherefore gaze this goodly company,
As if they saw some wondrous monument,
Some comet or unusual prodigy?

BAPTISTA
Why, sir, you know this is your wedding-day:
First we were sad, fearing you would not come;
Now sadder, that you come so unprovided.
Fie, doff this habit, shame to your estate,
An eye-sore to our solemn festival!

TRANIO
And tells us, what occasion of import
Hath all so long detain'd you from your wife,
And sent you hither so unlike yourself?

PETRUCHIO
Tedious it were to tell, and harsh to hear:
Sufficeth, I am come to keep my word,
Though in some part enforced to digress;
Which, at more leisure, I will so excuse
As you shall well be satisfied withal.
But where is Kate? I stay too long from her:
The morning wears, 'tis time we were at church.

TRANIO
See not your bride in these unreverent robes:
Go to my chamber; put on clothes of mine.

PETRUCHIO
Not I, believe me: thus I'll visit her.

BAPTISTA
But thus, I trust, you will not marry her.

PETRUCHIO
Good sooth, even thus; therefore ha' done with words:
To me she's married, not unto my clothes:
Could I repair what she will wear in me,
As I can change these poor accoutrements,
'Twere well for Kate, and better for myself.
But what a fool am I to chat with you,
When I should bid good morrow to my bride,
And seal the title with a lovely kiss!
     [*Exeunt* PETRUCHIO *and* GRUMIO.

TRANIO
He hath some meaning in his mad attire:
We will persuade him, be it possible,
To put on better ere he go to church.

BAPTISTA
I'll after him, and see the event of this.
    [*Exeunt* BAPTISTA, GREMIO, *and* ATTENDANTS.

TRANIO
But, sir, to her love concerneth us to add
Her father's liking: which to bring to pass,
As I before imparted to your worship,
I am to get a man, — whate'er he be,
It skills not much, we'll fit him to our turn, —
And he shall be Vincentio of Pisa;
And make assurance here in Padua
Of greater sums than I have promised.
So shall you quietly enjoy your hope,
And marry sweet Bianca with consent.

LUCENTIO
Were it not that my fellow-schoolmaster
Doth watch Bianca's steps so narrowly,
'Twere good, methinks, to steal our marriage;
Which once perform'd, let all the world say no,
I'll keep mine own, despite of all the world.

TRANIO
That by degrees we mean to look into,
And watch our vantage in this business:
We'll over-reach the greybeard, Gremio,
The narrow-prying father, Minola,
The quaint musician, amorous Licio;
All for my master's sake, Lucentio.
     Enter GREMIO.
Signior Gremio, came you from the church?

GREMIO
As willingly as e'er I came from school.

TRANIO
And is the bride and bridegroom coming home?

GREMIO
A bridegroom say you? 'tis a groom indeed,
A grumbling groom, and that the girl shall find.

TRANIO
Curster than she? why, 'tis impossible.

GREMIO
Why, he's a devil, a devil, a very fiend.

TRANIO
Why, she's a devil, a devil, the devil's dam.

GREMIO
Tut, she's a lamb, a dove, a fool to him.
I'll tell you, Sir Lucentio: when the priest
Should ask, if Katharina should be his wife,
'Ay, by gogs-wouns,' quoth he; and swore so loud,
That, all-amaz'd, the priest let fall the book;
And, as he stoop'd again to pick it up,
The mad-brain'd bridegroom took him such a cuff,
That down fell priest and book, and book and priest:
'Now take them up,' quoth he, 'if any list.'

TRANIO
What said the wench when he rose again?

GREMIO
Trembled and shook; for why he stamp'd and swore,
As if the vicar meant to cozen him.
But after many ceremonies done,
He calls for wine: 'A health!' quoth he, as if
He had been aboard, carousing to his mates
After a storm; quaff'd off the muscadel,
And threw the sops all in the sexton's face;
Having no other reason
But that his beard grew thin and hungerly,
And seem'd to ask him sops as he was drinking.
This done, he took the bride about the neck,
And kiss'd her lips with such a clamorous smack,
That, at the parting, all the church did echo:
And I, seeing this, came thence for very shame;
And after me, I know, the rout is coming.
Such a mad marriage never was before: —
Hark, hark! I hear the minstrels play.   [*Music plays.*

    Enter PETRUCHIO, KATHARINA, BIANCA,
    BAPTISTA, GRUMIO; *with* HORTENSIO *and*
         TRAIN.

PETRUCHIO
Gentlemen and friends, I thank you for your pains:
I know you think to dine with me to-day,
And have prepared great store of wedding cheer;
But so it is, my haste doth call me hence,
And therefore here I mean to take my leave.

BAPTISTA
Is't possible you will away to-night?

PETRUCHIO
I must away to-day, before night come:
Make it no wonder; if you knew my business,
You would entreat me rather go than stay.
And, honest company, I thank you all,
That have beheld me give away myself
To this most patient, sweet, and virtuous wife:

PETRUCHIO Grumio, draw forth thy weapon, we are beset with thieves.

Dine with my father, drink a health to me;
For I must hence; and farewell to you all.

TRANIO
Let us entreat you stay till after dinner.

PETRUCHIO
It may not be.

GREMIO
   Let me entreat you.

PETRUCHIO
It cannot be.

KATHARINA
   Let me entreat you.

PETRUCHIO
I am content.

KATHARINA
   Are you content to stay?

PETRUCHIO
I am content you shall entreat me stay;
But yet not stay, entreat me how you can.

KATHARINA
Now, if you love me, stay.

PETRUCHIO
   Grumio, my horse.

GRUMIO
Ay, sir, they be ready: the oats have eaten the horses.

KATHARINA
Nay, then,
Do what thou canst, I will not go to-day;
No, nor to-morrow, not till I please myself.
The door is open, sir; there lies your way;
You may be jogging whiles your boots are green;
For me, I'll not be gone till I please myself:
'Tis like you'll prove a jolly surly groom,
That take it on you at the first so roundly.

PETRUCHIO
O, Kate, content thee; prithee, be not angry.

KATHARINA
I will be angry: what hast thou to do? —
Father, be quiet: he shall stay my leisure.

GREMIO
Ay, marry, sir, now it begins to work.

KATHARINA
Gentlemen, forward to the bridal dinner:
I see a woman may be made a fool,
If she had not a spirit to resist.

PETRUCHIO
They shall go forward, Kate, at thy command. —
Obey the bride, you that attend on her;
Go to the feast, revel and domineer,
Carouse full measure to her maidenhead,
Be mad and merry, — or go hang yourselves:
But for my bonny Kate, she must with me.
Nay, look not big, nor stamp, nor stare, nor fret;
I will be master of what is mine own:
She is my goods, my chattels; she is my house,
My household-stuff, my field, my barn,
My horse, my ox, my ass, my anything;
And here she stands, touch her whoever dare;
I'll bring mine action on the proudest he
That stops my way in Padua. — Grumio,
Draw forth thy weapon, we are beset with thieves;
Rescue thy mistress, if thou be a man. —
Fear not, sweet wench, they shall not touch thee, Kate:
I'll buckler thee against a million.

[*Exeunt* PETRUCHIO, KATHARINA, *and* GRUMIO.

BAPTISTA
Nay, let them go, a couple of quiet ones.

GREMIO
Went they not quickly, I should die with laughing.

TRANIO
Of all mad matches never was the like.

LUCENTIO
Mistress, what's your opinion of your sister?

BIANCA
That, being mad herself, she's madly mated.

GREMIO
I warrant him, Petruchio is Kated.

BAPTISTA
Neighbours and friends, though bride and
bridegroom wants
For to supply the places at the table,
You know there wants no junkets at the feast. —
Lucentio, you shall supply the bridegroom's place;
And let Bianca take her sister's room.

TRANIO
Shall sweet Bianca practise how to bride it?

BAPTISTA
She shall, Lucentio. — Come, gentlemen, let's go.
[*Exeunt.*

ACT IV

SCENE I

PETRUCHIO'S *country house.*

Enter GRUMIO.

GRUMIO
Fie, fie on all tired jades, on all mad
masters, and all foul ways! Was ever
man so beaten? was ever man so ray'd?
was ever man so weary? I am sent
before to make a fire, and they are
coming after to warm them. Now, were
not I a little pot, and soon hot, my very
lips might freeze to my teeth, my
tongue to the roof of my mouth, my
heart in my belly, ere I should come by a
fire to thaw me: — but I, with blowing
the fire, shall warm myself; for,
considering the weather, a taller man
than I will take cold. — Holla, ho! Curtis.

Enter CURTIS.

CURTIS
Who is that calls so coldly?

GRUMIO
A piece of ice: if thou doubt it, thou
mayst slide from my shoulder to my
heel with no greater a run but my head
and my neck. A fire, good Curtis.

CURTIS
Is my master and his wife coming,
Grumio?

GRUMIO
O, ay, Curtis, ay: and therefore fire, fire;
cast on no water.

CURTIS
Is she so hot a shrew as she's reported?

GRUMIO
She was, good Curtis, before this frost: but, thou
know'st, winter tames man, woman and beast; for it
hath tamed my old master, and my new mistress and
myself, fellow Curtis.

CURTIS
Away, you three-inch fool! I am no beast.

GRUMIO
Am I but three inches? why, thy horn is a foot; and so
long am I at the least. But wilt thou make a fire, or shall
I complain on thee to our mistress, whose hand — she
being now at hand — thou shalt soon feel, to thy cold
comfort, for being slow in thy hot office?

CURTIS
I prithee, good Grumio, tell me, how goes the world?

GRUMIO
A cold world, Curtis, in every office but thine; and
therefore fire: do thy duty, and have thy duty; for my
master and mistress are almost frozen to death.

CURTIS
There's fire ready; and therefore, good Grumio, the
news?

GRUMIO
Why, 'Jack, boy! ho, boy!' and as much news as wilt
thou.

CURTIS
Come, you are so full of cony-catching! —

GRUMIO
Why, therefore fire; for I have caught extreme cold.
Where's the cook? is supper ready, the house trimm'd,
rushes strew'd, cobwebs swept, the serving-men in
their new fustian, their white stockings, and every
officer his wedding-garment on? Be the jacks fair
within, the jills fair without, the carpets laid, and every
thing in order?

CURTIS
All ready; and therefore, I pray thee, news?

GRUMIO
First, know, my horse is tired; my master and mistress
fallen out.

CURTIS
How?

GRUMIO
Out of their saddles into the dirt; and thereby hangs a tale.

CURTIS
Let's ha't, good Grumio.

GRUMIO
Lend thine ear.

CURTIS
Here.

GRUMIO Fie, fie on all tired jades, on all mad masters,
and all foul ways!

GRUMIO
There.   [*Striking him.*

CURTIS
This is to feel a tale, not to hear a tale.

GRUMIO
And therefore 'tis call'd a sensible tale: and this cuff
was but to knock at your ear, and beseech listening.
Now I begin: *Imprimis*, we came down a foul hill, my
master riding behind my mistress: —

CURTIS
Both of one horse?

GRUMIO
What's that to thee?

CURTIS
Why, a horse.

GRUMIO
Tell thou the tale: — but hadst thou not cross'd me,
thou shouldst have heard how her horse fell, and she
under her horse; thou shouldst have heard, in how
miry a place; how she was bemoil'd; how he left her
with the horse upon her; how he beat me because her
horse stumbled; how she waded through the dirt to
pluck him off me; how he swore; how she pray'd —
that never pray'd before; how I cried; how the horses
ran away; how her bridle was burst; how I lost my
crupper; — with many things of worthy memory,
which now shall die in oblivion, and thou return
unexperienced to thy grave.

CURTIS
By this reckoning, he is more shrew than she.

GRUMIO
Ay; and that thou and the proudest of you all shall find
when he comes home. But what talk I of this? — Call
forth Nathaniel, Joseph, Nicholas, Philip, Walter,
Sugarsop, and the rest: let their heads be slickly
comb'd, their blue coats brush'd, and their garters of
an indifferent knit: let them curtsy with their left legs;
and not presume to touch a hair of my master's
horse-tail till they kiss their hands. Are they all ready?

CURTIS
They are.

GRUMIO
Call them forth.

CURTIS
Do you hear, ho? you must meet my master, to
countenance my mistress!

GRUMIO
Why, she hath a face of her own.

CURTIS
Who knows not that?

GRUMIO
Thou, it seems, that calls for company to countenance
her.

NATHANIEL All things is ready. How near is our master?

CURTIS
I call them forth to credit her.
GRUMIO
Why, she comes to borrow nothing of them.

Enter four or five SERVING-MEN.

NATHANIEL
Welcome home, Grumio!
PHILIP
How now, Grumio!
JOSEPH
What, Grumio!
NICHOLAS
Fellow Grumio!
NATHANIEL
How now, old lad!
GRUMIO
Welcome, you! — how now, you! — what, you! —
fellow, you! — and thus much for greeting. Now, my
spruce companions, is all ready, and all things neat?
NATHANIEL
All things is ready. How near is our master?
GRUMIO
E'en at hand, alighted by this; and therefore be not —
Cock's passion, silence! — I hear my master.

Enter PETRUCHIO and KATHARINA.

PETRUCHIO
Where be these knaves? What, no man at door
To hold my stirrup nor to take my horse!
Where is Nathaniel, Gregory, Philip? —
ALL SERVANTS
Here, here, sir; here, sir.
PETRUCHIO
Here, sir! here, sir! here, sir! here, sir! —
You logger-headed and unpolish'd grooms!
What, no attendance? no regard? no duty? —
Where is the foolish knave I sent before?
GRUMIO
Here, sir: as foolish as I was before.
PETRUCHIO
You peasant swain! you whoreson malt-horse drudge!
Did I not bid thee meet me in the park,
And bring along these rascal knaves with thee?

GRUMIO
Nathaniel's coat, sir, was not fully made,
And Gabriel's pumps were all unpink'd i'th'heel;
There was no link to colour Peter's hat,
And Walter's dagger was not come from sheathing:
There were none fine but Adam, Rafe, and Gregory;
The rest were ragged, old, and beggarly;
Yet, as they are, here are they come to meet you.
PETRUCHIO
Go, rascals, go, and fetch my supper in. —
[Exeunt SERVANTS.
[*Sings.*] Where is the life that late I led —
Where are those — Sit down, Kate, and welcome. —
Soud, soud, soud, soud!

Enter SERVANTS with supper.

Why, when, I say? — Nay, good sweet Kate, be merry. —
Off with my boots, you rogues! you villains, when?
[*Sings.*] It was the friar of orders grey,
    As he forth walked on his way: —
Out, you rogue! you pluck my foot awry:
Take that, and mend the plucking off the other. —
[Strikes him.
Be merry, Kate. — Some water, here; what, ho!
Where's my spaniel Troilus? — Sirrah, get you hence,
And bid my cousin Ferdinand come hither: —
[Exit SERVANT.
One, Kate, that you must kiss, and be acquainted with. —
Where are my slippers? — Shall I have some water?
Enter one with water.
Come, Kate, and wash, and welcome heartily. —
You whoreson villain! will you let it fall?
[Strikes him.
KATHARINA
Patience, I pray you; 'twas a fault unwilling.
PETRUCHIO
A whoreson, beetle-headed, flap-ear'd knave! —
Come, Kate, sit down; I know you have a stomach.
Will you give thanks, sweet Kate; or else shall I?
What's this? mutton?
FIRST SERVANT
                    Ay.
PETRUCHIO
                            Who brought it?
PETER
                                            I.
PETRUCHIO
'Tis burnt; and so is all the meat.
What dogs are these! — Where is the rascal cook?
How durst you, villains, bring it from the dresser,
And serve it thus to me that love it not?
There, take it to you, trenchers, cups, and all:
[Throws the meat, etc., at them.
You heedless joltheads and unmanner'd slaves!
What, do you grumble? I'll be with you straight.
[Exeunt SERVANTS.
KATHARINA
I pray you, husband, be not so disquiet:
The meat was well, if you were so contented.
PETRUCHIO
I tell thee, Kate, 'twas burnt and dried away;
And I expressly am forbid to touch it,
For it engenders choler, planteth anger;
And better 'twere that both of us did fast, —
Since, of ourselves, ourselves are choleric, —
Than feed it with such over-roasted flesh.
Be patient; to-morrow't shall be mended,
And, for this night, we'll fast for company: —
Come, I will bring thee to thy bridal chamber. [*Exeunt.*

Enter SERVANTS severally.

NATHANIEL
Peter, didst ever see the like?

PETRUCHIO What, no attendance? no regard? no duty?

PETER

                      He kills her
In her own humour.

Enter CURTIS.

GRUMIO

                 Where is he?

CURTIS

                     In her chamber,
Making a sermon of continency to her;
And rails, and swears, and rates, that she, poor soul,
Knows not which way to stand, to look, to speak,
And sits as one new-risen from a dream. —
Away, away! for he is coming hither.   [*Exeunt.*

Enter PETRUCHIO.

PETRUCHIO

Thus have I politicly begun my reign,
And 'tis my hope to end successfully.
My falcon now is sharp, and passing empty;
And, till she stoop, she must not be full-gorged,
For then she never looks upon her lure.
Another way I have to man my haggard,
To make her come, and know her keeper's call,
That is, to watch her, as we watch these kites
That bate, and beat, and will not be obedient.
She eat no meat to-day, nor none shall eat;
Last night she slept not, nor to-night she shall not;
As with the meat, some undeserved fault
I'll find about the making of the bed;
And here I'll fling the pillow, there the bolster,
This way the coverlet, another way the sheets: —
Ay, and amid this hurly, I intend
That all is done in reverent care of her;
And, in conclusion, she shall watch all night:
And, if she chance to nod, I'll rail and brawl,
And with the clamour keep her still awake.
This is a way to kill a wife with kindness;
And thus I'll curb her mad and headstrong humour. —
He that knows better how to tame a shrew,
Now let him speak: 'tis charity to shew.   [*Exit.*

SCENE II

Padua. Before BAPTISTA'S *house.*

Enter TRANIO *and* HORTENSIO.

TRANIO

Is't possible, friend Licio, that Mistress Bianca
Doth fancy any other but Lucentio?
I tell you, sir, she bears me fair in hand.

HORTENSIO

Sir, to satisfy you in what I have said,
Stand by, and mark the manner of his teaching.

                        [*They stand aside.*

Enter BIANCA *and* LUCENTIO.

LUCENTIO

Now, mistress, profit you in what you read?

BIANCA

What, master, read you? first resolve me that.

LUCENTIO

I read that I profess, the Art to Love.

BIANCA

And may you prove, sir, master of your art!

LUCENTIO

While you, sweet dear, prove mistress of my heart!

                        [*They retire.*

HORTENSIO

Quick proceeders, marry! Now, tell me, I pray,
You that durst swear at your mistress Bianca
Lov'd none in the world so well as Lucentio, —

TRANIO

O despiteful love! unconstant womankind! —
I tell thee, Licio, this is wonderful.

HORTENSIO

Mistake no more: I am not Licio,
Nor a musician, as I seem to be;
But one that scorn to live in this disguise,
For such a one as leaves a gentleman,
And makes a god of such a cullion:
Know, sir, that I am call'd Hortensio.

TRANIO

Signior Hortensio, I have often heard
Of your entire affection to Bianca;
And since mine eyes are witness of her lightness,
I will with you, — if you be so contented, —
Forswear Bianca and her love for ever.

HORTENSIO

See, how they kiss and court! — Signior Lucentio,
Here is my hand, and here I firmly vow
Never to woo her more; but do forswear her,

As one unworthy all the former favours
That I have fondly flatter'd her withal.

TRANIO

And here I take the unfeigned oath,
Never to marry with her though she would entreat:
Fie on her! see, how beastly she doth court him!

HORTENSIO

Would all the world but he had quite forsworn!
For me, that I may surely keep mine oath,
I will be married to a wealthy widow,
Ere three days pass, which hath as long lov'd me
As I have lov'd this proud disdainful haggard.
And so farewell, Signior Lucentio. —
Kindness in women, not their beauteous looks,
Shall win my love: — and so, I take my leave,
In resolution as I swore before.

    [*Exit* HORTENSIO; LUCENTIO *and* BIANCA *advance.*

TRANIO

Mistress Bianca, bless you with such grace
As 'longeth to a lover's blessed case!
Nay, I have ta'en you napping, gentle love;
And have forsworn you, with Hortensio.

BIANCA

Tranio, you jest: but have you both forsworn me?

TRANIO

Mistress, we have.

LUCENTIO

                Then we are rid of Licio.

TRANIO

I'faith, he'll have a lusty widow now,
That shall be woo'd and wedded in a day.

BIANCA

God give him joy!

TRANIO

Ay, and he'll tame her.

BIANCA

                He says so, Tranio.

TRANIO

Faith, he is gone unto the taming-school.

BIANCA

The taming-school! what, is there such a place?

TRANIO

Ay, mistress, and Petruchio is the master;
That teacheth tricks eleven and twenty long,
To tame a shrew, and charm her chattering tongue.

Enter BIONDELLO.

BIONDELLO

O master, master, I have watch'd so long
That I am dog-weary! but at last I spied
An ancient angel coming down the hill,
Will serve the turn.

TRANIO

            What is he, Biondello?

BIONDELLO

Master, a mercatante, or a pedant,
I know not what; but format in apparel,
In gait and countenance surely like a father.

LUCENTIO

And what of him, Tranio?

TRANIO

If he be credulous and trust my tale,
I'll make him glad to seem Vincentio;
And give assurance to Baptista Minola,
As if he were the right Vincentio.
Take in your love, and then let me alone.

         [*Exeunt* LUCENTIO *and* BIANCA.

Enter a PEDANT.

PEDANT

God save you, sir!

TRANIO

         And you, sir! you are welcome.
Travel you far on, or are you at the furthest?

PEDANT

Sir, at the furthest for a week or two:
But then up further, and as far as Rome;
And so to Tripoli, if God lend me life.

TRANIO

What countryman, I pray?

PEDANT

               Of Mantua.

TRANIO

Of Mantua, sir? — marry, God forbid!
And come to Padua, careless of your life?

PEDANT

My life, sir! how, I pray? for that goes hard.

TRANIO

'Tis death for any one in Mantua

To come to Padua. Know you not the cause?
Your ships are stay'd at Venice, and the duke —
For private quarrel 'twixt your duke and him —
Hath publish'd and proclaim'd it openly:
'Tis marvel, but that you are but newly come,
You might have heard it else proclaim'd about.

PEDANT

Alas, sir, it is worse for me than so!
For I have bills for money by exchange
From Florence, and must here deliver them.

TRANIO

Well, sir, to do you courtesy,
This will I do, and this I will advise you: —
First, tell me, have you ever been at Pisa?

PEDANT

Ay, sir, in Pisa have I often been;
Pisa renowned for grave citizens.

TRANIO

Among them know you one Vincentio?

PEDANT

I know him not, but I have heard of him;
A merchant of incomparable wealth.

TRANIO

He is my father, sir; and, sooth to say,
In countenance somewhat doth resemble you.

BIONDELLO [*aside*].

As much as an apple doth an oyster, and all one.

TRANIO

To save your life in this extremity,
This favour will I do you for his sake;
And think it not the worst of all your fortunes
That you are like to Sir Vincentio.
His name and credit shall you undertake,
And in my house you shall be friendly lodged: —
Look that you take upon you as you should;
You understand me, sir: — so shall you stay
Till you have done your business in the city:
If this be courtesy, sir, accept of it.

PEDANT

O, sir, I do; and will repute you ever
The patron of my life and liberty.

TRANIO

Then go with me, to make the matter good.
This, by the way, I let you understand; —
My father is here look'd for every day,
To pass assurance of a dower in marriage
'Twixt me and one Baptista's daughter here:
In all these circumstances I'll instruct you:
Go with me, sir, to clothe you as becomes you.

                        [*Exeunt.*

SCENE III

A room in PETRUCHIO'S *house.*

Enter KATHARINA *and* GRUMIO.

GRUMIO

No, no, forsooth; I dare not, for my life.

KATHARINA

The more my wrong, the more his spite appears:
What, did he marry me to famish me?
Beggars, that come unto my father's door,
Upon entreaty have a present alms;
If not, elsewhere they meet with charity:
But I, — who never knew how to entreat,
Nor never needed that I should entreat, —
Am starv'd for meat, giddy for lack of sleep;
With oaths kept waking, and with brawling fed:
And that which spites me more than all these wants,
He does it under name of perfect love;
As who should say, if I should sleep or eat,
'Twere deadly sickness or else present death. —
I prithee go, and get me some repast;
I care not what, so it be wholesome food.

GRUMIO

What say you to a neat's foot?

KATHARINA

'Tis passing good: I prithee let me have it.

GRUMIO

I fear it is too choleric a meat.
How say you to a fat tripe finely broil'd?

KATHARINA

I like it well: good Grumio, fetch it me.

GRUMIO

I cannot tell; I fear 'tis choleric.
What say you to a piece of beef and mustard?

KATHARINA

A dish that I do love to feed upon.

GRUMIO

Ay, but the mustard is too hot a little.

GRUMIO What say you to a piece of beef and mustard?

KATHARINA
Why, then the beef, and let the mustard rest.
GRUMIO
Nay, then I will not: you shall have the mustard,
Or else you get no beef of Grumio.
KATHARINA
Then both, or one, or any thing thou wilt.
GRUMIO
Why, then the mustard without the beef.
KATHARINA
Go, get thee gone, thou false deluding slave,
                                              [*Beats him.*
That feed'st me with the very name of meat:
Sorrow on thee, and all the pack of you,
That triumph thus upon my misery!
Go, get thee gone, I say.
    Enter PETRUCHIO *and* HORTENSIO *with meat.*

PETRUCHIO
How fares my Kate? What, sweeting, all amort?
HORTENSIO
Mistress, what cheer?
KATHARINA
                    Faith, as cold as can be.
PETRUCHIO
Pluck up thy spirits, look cheerfully upon me.
Here, love; thou see'st how diligent I am
To dress thy meat myself, and bring it thee:
I am sure, sweet Kate, this kindness merits thanks.
What, not a word? Nay, then thou lov'st it not;
And all my pains are sorted to no proof. —
Here, take away this dish.
KATHARINA
                    I pray you, let it stand.
PETRUCHIO
The poorest service is repaid with thanks;
And so shall mine, before you touch the meat.
KATHARINA
I thank you, sir.
HORTENSIO
Signior Petruchio, fie! you are to blame. —
Come, Mistress Kate, I'll bear you company.
PETRUCHIO [*aside to* HORTENSIO].
Eat it up all, Hortensio, if thou lov'st me. —
[*To* KATHARINA.] Much good do it unto thy gentle
    heart!

Kate, eat apace: — and now, my honey
    love,
Will we return unto thy father's house,
And revel it as bravely as the best,
With silken coats, and caps, and golden
    rings,
With ruffs, and cuffs, and farthingales,
    and things;
With scarfs, and fans, and double
    change of bravery,
With amber bracelets, beads, and all this
    knavery.
What, hast thou din'd? The tailor stays
    thy leisure,
To deck thy body with his ruffling
    treasure.
            Enter TAILOR.
Come, tailor, let us see these ornaments;
Lay forth the gown.
            Enter HABERDASHER.
    What news with you, sir?
HABERDASHER
Here is the cap your worship did
bespeak.
PETRUCHIO
Why, this was moulded on a porringer;
A velvet dish: — fie, fie! 'tis lewd and
    filthy:
Why, 'tis a cockle or a walnut-shell,
A knack, a toy, a trick, a baby's cap:
Away with it! come, let me have a bigger.
KATHARINA
I'll have no bigger: this doth fit the time,
And gentlewomen wear such caps as
    these.
PETRUCHIO
When you are gentle, you shall have one
    too,
And not till then.
HORTENSIO [*aside*].
    That will not be in haste.
KATHARINA
Why, sir, I trust I may have leave to
    speak;
And speak I will; I am no child, no babe:
Your betters have endured me say my mind;
And if you cannot, best you stop your ears.
My tongue will tell the anger of my heart;
Or else my heart, concealing it, will break:
And rather than it shall, I will be free
Even to the uttermost, as I please, in words.
PETRUCHIO
Why, thou say'st true: it is a paltry cap,
A custard-coffin, a bauble, a silken pie:
I love thee well, in that thou lik'st it not.
KATHARINA
Love me or love me not, I like the cap;
And it I will have, or I will have none.
PETRUCHIO
Thy gown? why, ay: — come, tailor, let us see't.
O, mercy, God! what masking stuff is here?
What's this? a sleeve? 'tis like a demi-cannon:
What, up and down, carv'd like an apple-tart?
Here's snip, and nip, and cut, and slish, and slash,
Like to a censer in a barber's shop: —
Why, what, o' devil's name, tailor, call'st thou this?
HORTENSIO [*aside*].
I see she's like to have neither cap nor gown.
TAILOR
You bid me make it orderly and well,
According to the fashion and the time.
PETRUCHIO
Marry, and did; but if you be remember'd,
I did not bid you mar it to the time.
Go, hop me over every kennel home,
For you shall hop without my custom, sir:
I'll none of it: hence! make your best of it.
KATHARINA
I never saw a better-fashion'd gown,
More quaint, more pleasing, nor more commendable:
Belike you mean to make a puppet of me.
PETRUCHIO
Why, true; he means to make a puppet of thee.
TAILOR
She says your worship means to make a puppet of her.
PETRUCHIO
O monstrous arrogance! Thou liest, thou thread,
Thou thimble,
Thou yard, three-quarters, half-yard, quarter, nail!
Thou flea, thou nit, thou winter-cricket thou! —

Brav'd in mine own house with a skein of thread?
Away, thou rag, thou quantity, thou remnant;
Or I shall so be-mete thee with thy yard,
As thou shalt think on prating whilst thou livest!
I tell thee, I, that thou hast marr'd her gown.
TAILOR
Your worship is deceiv'd; the gown is made
Just as my master had direction:
Grumio gave order how it should be done.
GRUMIO
I gave him no order; I gave him the stuff.
TAILOR
But how did you desire it should be made?
GRUMIO
Marry, sir, with needle and thread.
TAILOR
But did you not request to have it cut?
GRUMIO
Thou hast faced many things; —
TAILOR
I have.
GRUMIO
Face not me: thou hast braved many men; brave not
me: I will neither be faced nor braved. I say unto thee, I
bid thy master cut out the gown; but I did not bid him
cut it to pieces: *ergo*, thou liest.
TAILOR
Why, here is the note of the fashion to testify.
PETRUCHIO
Read it.
GRUMIO
The note lies in's throat, if he say I said so.
TAILOR [*reads*].
Imprimis, a loose-bodied gown: —
GRUMIO
Master, if ever I said loose-bodied gown, sew me in the
skirts of it, and beat me to death with a bottom of
brown thread: I said a gown.
PETRUCHIO
Proceed.
TAILOR [*reads*].
With a small compassed cape: —
GRUMIO
I confess the cape.
TAILOR [*reads*].
With a trunk sleeve: —
GRUMIO
I confess two sleeves.
TAILOR [*reads*].
The sleeves curiously cut.
PETRUCHIO
Ay, there's the villainy.
GRUMIO
Error i'th'bill, sir; error i'th'bill. — I commanded the
sleeves should be cut out, and sew'd up again; and that
I'll prove upon thee, though thy little finger be arm'd in
a thimble.
TAILOR
This is true that I say; an I had thee in place where, thou
shouldst know it.
GRUMIO
I am for thee straight: take thou the bill, give me thy
mete-yard, and spare not me.
HORTENSIO
God-a-mercy, Grumio! then he shall have no odds.
PETRUCHIO
Well, sir, in brief, the gown is not for me.
GRUMIO
You are i'th'right, sir: 'tis for my mistress.
PETRUCHIO
Go take it up unto thy master's use.
GRUMIO
Villain, not for thy life: take up my mistress' gown for
thy master's use!
PETRUCHIO
Why, sir, what's your conceit in that?
GRUMIO
O, sir, the conceit is deeper than you think for:
Take up my mistress' gown to his master's use!
O, fie, fie, fie!
PETRUCHIO [*aside to* HORTENSIO].
Hortensio, say thou wilt see the tailor paid. —
[*To* TAILOR.] Go take it hence; be gone, and say no
    more.
HORTENSIO
Tailor, I'll pay thee for thy gown to-morrow:
Take no unkindness of his hasty words:
Away! I say; commend me to thy master.

[Exeunt TAILOR *and* HABERDASHER.

PETRUCHIO
Well, come, my Kate; we will unto your father's,
Even in these honest mean habiliments:
Our purses shall be proud, our garments poor;
For 'tis the mind that makes the body rich;
And as the sun breaks through the darkest clouds,
So honour peereth in the meanest habit.
What, is the jay more precious than the lark,
Because his feathers are more beautiful?
Or is the adder better than the eel,
Because his painted skin contents the eye?
O, no, good Kate; neither art thou the worse
For this poor furniture and mean array.
If thou account'st it shame, lay it on me;
And therefore frolic: we will hence forthwith,
To feast and sport us at thy father's house. —
Go call my men, and let us straight to him;
And bring our horses unto Long-lane end;
There will we mount, and thither walk on foot. —
Let's see; I think 'tis now some seven o'clock,
And well we may come there by dinner-time.

KATHARINA
I dare assure you, sir, 'tis almost two;
And 'twill be supper-time ere you come there.

PETRUCHIO
It shall be seven ere I go to horse:
Look, what I speak, or do, or think to do,
You are still crossing it. — Sirs, let's alone:
I will not go to-day; and ere I do,
It shall be what o'clock I say it is.

HORTENSIO
Why, so! this gallant will command the sun!   *[Exeunt.*

SCENE IV

Padua. Before BAPTISTA'S *house.*

Enter TRANIO, *and the* PEDANT *dress'd like*
VINCENTIO.

TRANIO
Sir, this is the house: please it you that I call?

PEDANT
Ay, what else? and, but I be deceived,
Signior Baptista may remember me,
Near twenty years ago, in Genoa,
Where we were lodgers at the Pegasus.

TRANIO
'Tis well; and hold your own, in any case,
With such austerity as 'longeth to a father.

PEDANT
I warrant you. But, sir, here comes your boy;
'Twere good he were school'd.

Enter BIONDELLO.

TRANIO
Fear you not him. — Sirrah Biondello,
Now do your duty throughly, I advise you:
Imagine 'twere the right Vincentio.

BIONDELLO
Tut, fear not me.

TRANIO
But hast thou done thy errand to Baptista?

BIONDELLO
I told him that your father was at Venice;
And that you look'd for him this day in Padua.

TRANIO
Thou'rt a tall fellow: hold thee that to drink.
Here comes Baptista: — set your countenance, sir.

Enter BAPTISTA *and* LUCENTIO.

Signior Baptista, you are happily met. —
[To the PEDANT.*]* Sir, this is the gentleman I told you of:
I pray you, stand good father to me now.
Give me Bianca for my patrimony.

PEDANT
Soft, son! —
Sir, by your leave: having come to Padua
To gather in some debts, my son Lucentio
Made me acquainted with a weighty cause
Of love between your daughter and himself:
And, — for the good report I hear of you,
And for the love he beareth to your daughter,
And she to him, — to stay him not too long,
I am content, in a good father's care,
To have him match'd; and, if you please to like
No worse than I, upon some agreement,
Me shall you find ready and willing
With one consent to have her so bestow'd;
For curious I cannot be with you,
Signior Baptista, of whom I hear so well.

BAPTISTA
Sir, pardon me in what I have to say:
Your plainness and your shortness please me well.
Right true it is, your son Lucentio here
Doth love my daughter, and she loveth him,
Or both dissemble deeply their affections:
And therefore, if you say no more than this,
That like a father you will deal with him,
And pass my daughter a sufficient dower,
The match is made, and all is done:
Your son shall have my daughter with consent.

TRANIO
I thank you, sir. Where, then, do you hold best
We be affied, and such assurance ta'en
As shall with either part's agreement stand?

BAPTISTA
Not in my house, Lucentio; for, you know,
Pitchers have ears, and I have many servants:
Besides, old Gremio is hearkening still;
And happily we might be interrupted.

TRANIO
Then at my lodging, an it like you:
There doth my father lie; and there, this night,
We'll pass the business privately and well.
Send for your daughter by your servant here;
My boy shall fetch the scrivener presently.
The worst is this, — that at so slender warning,
You are like to have a thin and slender pittance.

BAPTISTA
It likes me well. Biondello, hie you home,
And bid Bianca make her ready straight;
And, if you will, tell what hath happened —
Lucentio's father is arriv'd in Padua,
And how she's like to be Lucentio's wife.

BIONDELLO
I pray the gods she may with all my heart!

TRANIO
Dally not with the gods, but get thee gone. —
[Exit BIONDELLO.
Signior Baptista, shall I lead the way?
Welcome! one mess is like to be your cheer:
Come, sir; we will better it in Pisa.

BAPTISTA
I follow you.

[Exeunt TRANIO, PEDANT, *and* BAPTISTA.
Enter BIONDELLO.

BIONDELLO
Cambio, —

LUCENTIO
What say'st thou, Biondello?

BIONDELLO
You saw my master wink and laugh upon you?

LUCENTIO
Biondello, what of that?

BIONDELLO
Faith, nothing; but 'has left me here behind, to
expound the meaning or moral of his signs and tokens.

LUCENTIO
I pray thee, moralise them.

BIONDELLO
Then thus. Baptista is safe, talking with the deceiving
father of a deceitful son.

LUCENTIO
And what of him?

BIONDELLO
His daughter is to be brought by you to the supper.

LUCENTIO
And then?

BIONDELLO
The old priest at Saint Luke's church is at your
command at all hours.

LUCENTIO
And what of all this?

BIONDELLO
I cannot tell, except, while they are busied about a
counterfeit assurance, take you assurance of her, *cum
privilegio ad imprimendum solum:* to th'church; — take
the priest, clerk, and some sufficient honest witnesses:
If this be not that you look for, I have no more to say,
But bid Bianca farewell for ever and a day.   *[Going.*

LUCENTIO
Hear'st thou, Biondello?

BIONDELLO
I cannot tarry: I knew a wench married in an afternoon
as she went to the garden for parsley to stuff a rabbit;
and so may you, sir: and so, adieu, sir. My master hath
appointed me to go to Saint Luke's, to bid the priest be
ready to come against you come with your appendix.
[Exit.

LUCENTIO
I may, and will, if she be so contented:
She will be pleased; then wherefore should I doubt?
Hap what hap may, I'll roundly go about her:
It shall go hard if Cambio go without her.   *[Exit.*

SCENE V

A public road.

Enter PETRUCHIO, KATHARINA, *and*
HORTENSIO.

PETRUCHIO
Come on, o' God's name; once more toward our
father's.
Good Lord, how bright and goodly shines the moon!

KATHARINA
The moon! the sun: it is not moonlight now.

PETRUCHIO
I say it is the moon that shines so bright.

KATHARINA
I know it is the sun that shines so bright.

PETRUCHIO
Now, by my mother's son, and that's myself,
It shall be moon, or star, or what I list,
Or e're I journey to your father's house. —
Go one, and fetch our horses back again. —
Evermore cross'd and cross'd; nothing but cross'd!

HORTENSIO *[aside to* KATHARINA*]*.
Say as he says, or we shall never go.

KATHARINA
Forward, I pray, since we have come so far,
And be it moon, or sun, or what you please:
An if you please to call it a rush-candle,
Henceforth I vow it shall be so for me.

PETRUCHIO
I say it is the moon.

KATHARINA
                                I know it is the moon.

PETRUCHIO
Nay, then, you lie: it is the blessed sun.

KATHARINA
Then, God be bless'd, it is the blessed sun: —
But sun it is not, when you say it is not;
And the moon changes, even as your mind.
What you will have it nam'd, even that it is;
And so it shall be still for Katharina.

HORTENSIO *[aside]*.
Petruchio, go thy ways; the field is won.

PETRUCHIO
Well, forward, forward! thus the bowl should run,
And not unluckily against the bias. —
But, soft! what company is coming here?
Enter VINCENTIO.
[To VINCENTIO.*]* Good morrow, gentle mistress:
where away? —
Tell me, sweet Kate, and tell me truly too,
Hast thou beheld a fresher gentlewoman?
Such war of white and red within her cheeks!
What stars do spangle heaven with such beauty,
As those two eyes become that heavenly face? —
Fair lovely maid, once more good day to thee. —
Sweet Kate, embrace her for her beauty's sake.

HORTENSIO *[aside]*.
A' will make the man mad, to make a woman of him.

KATHARINA
Young budding virgin, fair and fresh and sweet,
Whither away; or where is thy abode?
Happy the parents of so fair a child;
Happier the man whom favourable stars
Allot thee for his lovely bedfellow!

PETRUCHIO
Why, how now, Kate! I hope thou art not mad:
This is a man, old, wrinkled, faded, wither'd;
And not a maiden, as thou say'st he is.

KATHARINA
Pardon, old father, my mistaking eyes,
That have been so bedazzled with the sun,
That every thing I look on seemeth green:
Now I perceive thou art a reverend father;
Pardon, I pray thee, for my mad mistaking.

PETRUCHIO
Do, good old grandsire; and withal make known
Which way thou travellest: if along with us,
We shall be joyful of thy company.

VINCENTIO
Fair sir, and you my merry mistress,
That with your strange encounter much amaz'd me,
My name is call'd Vincentio; my dwelling Pisa;
And bound I am to Padua; there to visit

A son of mine, which long I have not seen.

PETRUCHIO
What is his name?

VINCENTIO
Lucentio, gentle sir.

PETRUCHIO
Happily met; the happier for thy son.
And now by law, as well as reverend age,
I may entitle thee my loving father:
The sister to my wife, this gentlewoman,
Thy son by this hath married. Wonder not,
Nor be not griev'd: she is of good esteem,
Her dowry wealthy, and of worthy birth;
Beside, so qualified as may beseem
The spouse of any noble gentleman.
Let me embrace with old Vincentio:
And wander we to see thy honest son,
Who will of thy arrival be full joyous.

VINCENTIO
But is this true? or is it else your pleasure,
Like pleasant travellers, to break a jest
Upon the company you overtake?

HORTENSIO
I do assure thee, father, so it is.

PETRUCHIO
Come, go along, and see the truth hereof;
For our first merriment hath made thee jealous.
[Exeunt PETRUCHIO, KATHARINA, and
VINCENTIO.

HORTENSIO
Well, Petruchio, this has put me in heart.
Have to my widow! and if she be froward,
Then hast thou taught Hortensio to be untoward. [Exit.

ACT V

SCENE I

Padua. Before LUCENTIO'S *house.*

Enter BIONDELLO, LUCENTIO, *and* BIANCA;
GREMIO *is out before.*

BIONDELLO
Softly and swiftly, sir; for the priest is ready.

LUCENTIO
I fly, Biondello: but they may chance to need thee at
home; therefore leave us.

BIONDELLO
Nay, faith, I'll see the church o' your back; and then
come back to my master as soon as I can.
[Exeunt LUCENTIO, BIANCA, and BIONDELLO.

GREMIO
I marvel Cambio comes not all this while.

Enter PETRUCHIO, KATHARINA, VINCENTIO,
GRUMIO, *and* ATTENDANTS.

PETRUCHIO
Sir, here's the door, this is Lucentio's house:
My father's bears more toward the market-place;
Thither must I; and here I leave you, sir.

VINCENTIO
You shall not choose but drink before you go:
I think I shall command your welcome here,
And, by all likelihood, some cheer is toward.
[Knocks.

GREMIO
They're busy within; you were best knock louder.
PEDANT *looks out of the window.*

PEDANT
What's he that knocks as he would beat down the gate?

VINCENTIO
Is Signior Lucentio within, sir?

PEDANT
He's within, sir, but not to be spoken withal.

VINCENTIO
What if a man bring him a hundred pound or two, to
make merry withal?

PEDANT
Keep your hundred pounds to yourself: he shall need
none, so long as I live.

PETRUCHIO
Nay, I told you your son was well beloved in Padua. —
Do you hear, sir? — to leave frivolous circumstances, —
I pray you, tell Signior Lucentio that his father is come
from Pisa, and is here at the door to speak with him.

PEDANT
Thou liest: his father is come from Pisa, and here
looking out at the window.

VINCENTIO
Art thou his father?

PEDANT
Ay, sir; so his mother says, if I may believe her.

PETRUCHIO [*to* VINCENTIO].
Why, how now, gentleman! why, this is flat knavery, to
take upon you another man's name.

PEDANT
Lay hands on the villain: I believe a' means to cozen
somebody in this city under my countenance.

Enter BIONDELLO.

BIONDELLO
I have seen them in the church together: God send 'em
good shipping! — But who is here? mine old master
Vincentio! now we are undone, and brought to
nothing.

VINCENTIO
Come hither, crack-hemp.

BIONDELLO
I hope I may choose, sir.

VINCENTIO
Come hither, you rogue. What, have you forgot me?

BIONDELLO
Forgot you! no, sir: I could not forget you, for I never
saw you before in all my life.

VINCENTIO
What, you notorious villain, didst thou never see thy
master's father, Vincentio?

BIONDELLO
What, my old worshipful old master? yes, marry, sir:
see where he looks out of the window.

VINCENTIO
Is't so, indeed? [*He beats* BIONDELLO.

BIONDELLO
Help, help, help! here's a madman will murder me.
[Exit.

PEDANT
Help, son! help, Signior Baptista!

PETRUCHIO
Prithee, Kate, let's stand aside, and see the end of
this controversy. [They retire.

Enter PEDANT *below;* BAPTISTA, TRANIO *and*
SERVANTS.

TRANIO
Sir, what are you that offer to beat my servant?

VINCENTIO
What am I, sir! nay, what are you, sir? — O immortal
gods! O fine villain! A silken doublet! a velvet hose! a
scarlet cloak! and a copatain hat! — O, I am undone! I
am undone! while I play the good husband at home,
my son and my servant spend all at the university.

TRANIO
How now! what's the matter?

BAPTISTA
What, is the man lunatic?

TRANIO
Sir, you seem a sober ancient gentleman by your habit,
but your words show you a madman. Why, sir, what
'cerns it you if I wear pearl and gold? I thank my good
father, I am able to maintain it.

VINCENTIO
Thy father! O villain! he is a sail-maker in Bergamo.

BAPTISTA
You mistake, sir, you mistake, sir. Pray, what do you
think is his name?

VINCENTIO
His name! as if I knew not his name: I have brought
him up ever since he was three years old, and his name
is Tranio.

PEDANT
Away, away, mad ass! his name is Lucentio; and he is
mine only son, and heir to the lands of me, Signior
Vincentio.

VINCENTIO
Lucentio! O, he hath murder'd his master! — Lay hold
on him, I charge you, in the duke's name. — O, my
son, my son! — Tell me, thou villain, where is my son
Lucentio?

TRANIO
Call forth an officer.

SERVANT *brings in an* **OFFICER**
Carry this mad knave to the gaol. — Father Baptista,
I charge you see that he be forthcoming.

VINCENTIO
Carry me to the gaol!

GREMIO
Stay, officer: he shall not go to prison.

BAPTISTA
Talk not, Signior Gremio: I say he shall go to prison.

GREMIO
Take heed, Signior Baptista, lest you be cony-catch'd in
this business: I dare swear this is the right Vincentio.

PEDANT
Swear, if thou darest.

GREMIO
Nay, I dare not swear it.

TRANIO
Then thou wert best say that I am not Lucentio.

GREMIO
Yes, I know thee to be Signior Lucentio.

BAPTISTA
Away with the dotard! to the gaol with him!

VINCENTIO
Thus strangers may be haled and abused: —
O monstrous villainy!

Enter BIONDELLO, *with* LUCENTIO *and* BIANCA.

BIONDELLO
O, we are spoil'd! and yonder he is: deny him, forswear
him, or else we are all undone.

LUCENTIO
Pardon, sweet father. [Kneeling.

VINCENTIO
Lives my sweet son?
[Exeunt BIONDELLO, TRANIO, and PEDANT, *as fast
as may be.*

BIANCA
Pardon, dear father.   [*Kneeling.*
BAPTISTA
      How hast thou offended? —
Where is Lucentio?
LUCENTIO
      Here's Lucentio,
Right son unto the right Vincentio;
That have by marriage made thy daughter mine,
While counterfeit supposes blear'd thine eyne.
GREMIO
Here's packing, with a witness, to deceive us all!
VINCENTIO
Where is that damned villain Tranio,
That fac'd and brav'd me in this matter so?
BAPTISTA
Why, tell me, is not this my Cambio?
BIANCA
Cambio is chang'd into Lucentio.
LUCENTIO
Love wrought these miracles. Bianca's love
Made me exchange my state with Tranio,
While he did bear my countenance in the town,
And happily I have arriv'd at last
Unto the wished haven of my bliss.
What Tranio did, myself enforc'd him to;
Then pardon him, sweet father, for my sake.
VINCENTIO
I'll slit the villain's nose, that would have sent me to the
      gaol.
BAPTISTA [*to* LUCENTIO].
But do you hear, sir? have you married my daughter
    without asking my good-will?
VINCENTIO
Fear not, Baptista; we will content you, go to: but
I will in, to be revenged for this villainy.   [*Exit.*
BAPTISTA
And I, to sound the depth of this knavery.   [*Exit.*
LUCENTIO
Look not pale, Bianca; thy father will not frown.
          [*Exeunt* LUCENTIO *and* BIANCA.
GREMIO
My cake is dough: but I'll in among the rest;
Out of hope of all, but my share of the feast.   [*Exit.*
    PETRUCHIO *and* KATHARINA *come forward.*
KATHARINA
Husband, let's follow, to see the end of this ado.
PETRUCHIO
First kiss me, Kate, and we will.
KATHARINA
What, in the midst of the street?
PETRUCHIO
What, art thou asham'd of me?
KATHARINA
No, sir, God forbid; but asham'd to kiss.
PETRUCHIO
Why, then, let's home again: come, sirrah, let's away.
KATHARINA
Nay, I will give thee a kiss [*kisses him*]: now, pray thee,
    love, stay.
PETRUCHIO
Is not this well? — Come, my sweet Kate:
Better once than never, for never too late.   [*Exeunt.*

SCENE II

A room in LUCENTIO'S *house.*

Enter BAPTISTA, VINCENTIO, GREMIO, *the*
PEDANT, LUCENTIO, BIANCA, PETRUCHIO,
KATHARINA, HORTENSIO *and* WIDOW, TRANIO,
BIONDELLO *and* GRUMIO; *the* SERVING-MEN *with*
TRANIO *bringing in a banquet.*

LUCENTIO
At last, though long, our jarring notes agree:
And time it is, when raging war is done,
To smile at scapes and perils overblown.
My fair Bianca, bid my father welcome,
While I with selfsame kindness welcome thine.
Brother Petruchio, sister Katharina,
And thou, Hortensio, with thy loving widow, —
Feast with the best, and welcome to my house:
My banquet is to close our stomachs up,
After our great good cheer. Pray you, sit down;
For now we sit to chat, as well as eat.
          [*They sit at table.*
PETRUCHIO
Nothing but sit and sit, and eat and eat!

PETRUCHIO Nay, that you shall not: since you have begun, have at you for a bitter jest or two!

BAPTISTA
Padua affords this kindness, son Petruchio.
PETRUCHIO
Padua affords nothing but what is kind.
HORTENSIO
For both our sakes, I would that word were true.
PETRUCHIO
Now, for my life, Hortensio fears his widow.
WIDOW
Then never trust me, if I be afeard.
PETRUCHIO
You are very sensible, and yet you miss my sense:
I mean, Hortensio is afeard of you.
WIDOW
He that is giddy thinks the world turns round.
PETRUCHIO
Roundly replied.
KATHARINA
      Mistress, how mean you that?
WIDOW
Thus I conceive by him.
PETRUCHIO
Conceives by me! — How likes Hortensio that?
HORTENSIO
My widow says, thus she conceives her tale.
PETRUCHIO
Very well mended. — Kiss him for that, good widow.
KATHARINA
He that is giddy thinks the world turns round: —
I pray you, tell me what you meant by that.
WIDOW
Your husband, being troubled with a shrew,
Measures my husband's sorrow by his woe:
And now you know my meaning.
KATHARINA
A very mean meaning.
WIDOW
       Right, I mean you.
KATHARINA
And I am mean, indeed, respecting you.
PETRUCHIO
To her, Kate!
HORTENSIO
To her, widow!
PETRUCHIO
A hundred marks, my Kate does put her down.
HORTENSIO
That's my office.
PETRUCHIO
Spoke like an officer: — ha' to thee, lad!
         [*Drinks to* HORTENSIO.
BAPTISTA
How likes Gremio these quick-witted folks?
GREMIO
Believe me, sir, they butt together well.

BIANCA
Head and butt! an hasty-witted body
Would say your head and butt were head and horn.
VINCENTIO
Ay, mistress bride, hath that awaken'd you?
BIANCA
Ay, but not frighted me; therefore I'll sleep again.
PETRUCHIO
Nay, that you shall not: since you have begun,
Have at you for a bitter jest or two!
BIANCA
Am I your bird? I mean to shift my bush;
And then pursue me as you draw your bow. —
You are welcome all.
      [*Exeunt* BIANCA, KATHARINA, *and* WIDOW.
PETRUCHIO
She hath prevented me. — Here, Signior Tranio,
This bird you aim'd at, though you hit her not;
Therefore a health to all that shot and miss'd.
TRANIO
O, sir, Lucentio slipp'd me like his greyhound,
Which runs himself, and catches for his master.
PETRUCHIO
A good swift simile, but something currish.
TRANIO
'Tis well, sir, that you hunted for yourself:
'Tis thought your deer does hold you at a bay.
BAPTISTA
O, ho, Petruchio! Tranio hits you now.
LUCENTIO
I thank thee for that gird, good Tranio.
HORTENSIO
Confess, confess, hath he not hit you here?
PETRUCHIO
A' has a little gall'd me, I confess;
And, as the jest did glance away from me,
'Tis ten to one it maim'd you two outright.
BAPTISTA
Now, in good sadness, son Petruchio,
I think thou hast the veriest shrew of all.
PETRUCHIO
Well, I say no: and therefore, for assurance,
Let's each one send unto his wife;
And he whose wife is most obedient
To come at first when he doth send for her,
Shall win the wager which we will propose.
HORTENSIO
Content. What is the wager?
LUCENTIO
         Twenty crowns.
PETRUCHIO
Twenty crowns!
I'll venture so much of my hawk or hound,
But twenty times so much upon my wife.
LUCENTIO
A hundred, then.

HORTENSIO
Content.

PETRUCHIO
A match! 'tis done.

HORTENSIO
Who shall begin?

LUCENTIO
That will I. —
Go, Biondello, bid your mistress come to me.

BIONDELLO
I go.   [*Exit.*

BAPTISTA
Son, I'll be your half, Bianca comes.

LUCENTIO
I'll have no halves; I'll bear it all myself.

Enter BIONDELLO.

How now! what news?

BIONDELLO
Sir, my mistress sends you word
That she is busy, and she cannot come.

PETRUCHIO
How! she is busy, and she cannot come!
Is that an answer?

GREMIO
Ay, and a kind one too:
Pray God, sir, your wife send you not a worse.

PETRUCHIO
I hope, better.

HORTENSIO
Sirrah Biondello, go and entreat my wife
To come to me forthwith.   [*Exit* BIONDELLO.

PETRUCHIO
O, ho! entreat her!
Nay, then she must needs come.

HORTENSIO
I am afraid, sir,
Do what you can, yours will not be entreated.

Enter BIONDELLO.

Now, where's my wife?

BIONDELLO
She says you have some goodly jest in hand:
She will not come; she bids you come to her.

PETRUCHIO
Worse and worse; she will not come! O vile,
Intolerable, not to be endured! —
Sirrah Grumio, go to your mistress;
Say, I command her to come to me.   [*Exit* GRUMIO.

HORTENSIO
I know her answer.

PETRUCHIO
What?

HORTENSIO
She will not come.

PETRUCHIO
The fouler fortune mine, and there an end.

BAPTISTA
Now, by my holidame, here comes Katharina!

Enter KATHARINA.

KATHARINA
What is your will, sir, that you send for me?

PETRUCHIO
Where is your sister, and Hortensio's wife?

KATHARINA
They sit conferring by the parlour fire.

PETRUCHIO
Go fetch them hither: if they deny to come,
Swinge me them soundly forth unto their husbands:
Away, I say, and bring them hither straight.
[*Exit* KATHARINA.

LUCENTIO
Here is a wonder, if you talk of a wonder.

HORTENSIO
And so it is: I wonder what it bodes.

PETRUCHIO
Marry, peace it bodes, and love, and quiet life,
An awful rule, and right supremacy,
And, to be short, what not that's sweet and happy?

BAPTISTA
Now, fair befall thee, good Petruchio!
The wager thou hast won; and I will add
Unto their losses twenty thousand crowns;
Another dowry to another daughter,
For she is chang'd, as she had never been.

PETRUCHIO
Nay, I will win my wager better yet,
And show more sign of her obedience,
Her new-built virtue and obedience.
See, where she comes, and brings your froward wives
As prisoners to her womanly persuasion.
Enter KATHARINA, *with* BIANCA *and* WIDOW.
Katharina, that cap of yours becomes you not:
Off with that bauble, throw it under-foot.   [*She obeys.*

WIDOW
Lord, let me never have a cause to sigh,
Till I be brought to such a silly pass!

BIANCA
Fie, what a foolish duty call you this?

LUCENTIO
I would your duty were as foolish too:
The wisdom of your duty, fair Bianca,
Hath cost me an hundred crowns since supper-time.

BIANCA
The more fool you, for laying on my duty.

PETRUCHIO
Katharina, I charge thee, tell these headstrong women
What duty they do owe their lords and husbands.

WIDOW
Come, come, you're mocking: we will have no telling.

PETRUCHIO
Come on, I say; and first begin with her.

WIDOW
She shall not.

PETRUCHIO
I say she shall: — and first begin with her.

KATHARINA
Fie, fie! unknit that threatening unkind brow:
And dart not scornful glances from those eyes,
To wound thy lord, thy king, thy governor:
It blots thy beauty, as frosts do bite the meads;
Confounds thy fame, as whirlwinds shake fair buds;
And in no sense is meet or amiable.
A woman mov'd is like a fountain troubled,
Muddy, ill-seeming, thick, bereft of beauty;
And while it is so, none so dry or thirsty
Will deign to sip, or touch one drop of it.
Thy husband is thy lord, thy life, thy keeper,
Thy head, thy sovereign; one that cares for thee,
And for thy maintenance commits his body
To painful labour both by sea and land,
To watch the night in storms, the day in cold,
Whilst thou liest warm at home, secure and safe;
And craves no other tribute at thy hands
But love, fair looks, and true obedience, —
Too little payment for so great a debt.
Such duty as the subject owes the prince,
Even such a woman oweth to her husband;
And when she is froward, peevish, sullen, sour,
And not obedient to his honest will,
What is she but a foul contending rebel,
And graceless traitor to her loving lord?
I am asham'd that women are so simple
To offer war, where they should kneel for peace;
Or seek for rule, supremacy, and sway,
When they are bound to serve, love, and obey.
Why are our bodies soft and weak and smooth,
Unapt to toil and trouble in the world,
But that our soft conditions and our hearts
Should well agree with our external parts?
Come, come, you froward and unable worms!
My mind hath been as big as one of yours,
My heart as great; my reason, haply, more,
To bandy word for word and frown for frown:
But now I see our lances are but straws;
Our strength as weak, our weakness past compare, —
That seeming to be most, which we indeed least are.
Then vail your stomachs, for it is no boot,
And place your hands below your husband's foot:
In token of which duty, if he please,
My hand is ready, may it do him ease.

PETRUCHIO
Why, there's a wench! — Come on, and kiss me, Kate.

LUCENTIO
Well, go thy ways, old lad; for thou shalt ha't.

VINCENTIO
'Tis a good hearing when children are toward.

LUCENTIO
But a harsh hearing when women are froward.

PETRUCHIO
Come, Kate, we'll to bed. —
We three are married, but you two are sped.
'Twas I won the wager, though you hit the white;
[*To* LUCENTIO.
And, being a winner, God give you good night!
[*Exeunt* PETRUCHIO *and* KATHARINA.

HORTENSIO
Now, go thy ways; thou hast tam'd a curst shrew.

LUCENTIO
'Tis a wonder, by your leave, she will be tam'd so.
[*Exeunt.*

KING RICHARD THE SECOND

DRAMATIS PERSONAE

KING RICHARD THE SECOND.
JOHN OF GAUNT, *Duke of Lancaster,*
EDMUND OF LANGLEY, *Duke of York,* } *uncles to the King.*
HENRY, surnamed BOLINGBROKE, *Duke of Hereford, son to John of Gaunt; afterwards King Henry IV.*
DUKE OF AUMERLE, *son to the Duke of York.*
THOMAS MOWBRAY, *Duke of Norfolk.*
DUKE OF SURREY.
EARL OF SALISBURY.
LORD BERKLEY.

BUSHY,
BAGOT, } *creatures to King Richard.*
GREEN,
EARL OF NORTHUMBERLAND.
HENRY PERCY, *his son.*
LORD ROSS.
LORD WILLOUGHBY.
LORD FITZWATER.
BISHOP OF CARLISLE.
ABBOT OF WESTMINSTER.
LORD MARSHAL.
SIR STEPHEN SCROOP.
SIR PIERCE OF EXTON.

CAPTAIN OF A BAND OF WELSHMEN.

QUEEN *to King Richard.*
DUCHESS OF YORK.
DUCHESS OF GLOSTER.
LADIES *attending on the Queen.*

LORDS, HERALDS, OFFICERS, SOLDIERS, TWO GARDENERS, KEEPER, MESSENGER, GROOM, *and other* ATTENDANTS.

SCENE — *England and Wales.*

NORFOLK Myself I throw, dread sovereign, at thy foot.

ACT I

SCENE I

London. KING RICHARD'S *palace.*

Enter KING RICHARD, JOHN OF GAUNT, *with other* NOBLES *and* ATTENDANTS.

KING RICHARD
Old John of Gaunt, time-honour'd Lancaster,
Hast thou, according to thy oath and band,
Brought hither Henry Hereford thy bold son,
Here to make good the boisterous late appeal,
Which then our leisure would not let us hear,
Against the Duke of Norfolk, Thomas Mowbray?

JOHN OF GAUNT
I have, my liege.

KING RICHARD
Tell me, moreover, hast thou sounded him,
If he appeal the duke on ancient malice;
Or worthily, as a good subject should,
On some known ground of treachery in him?

JOHN OF GAUNT
As near as I could sift him on that argument, —
On some apparent danger seen in him
Aim'd at your highness, — no inveterate malice.

KING RICHARD
Then call them to our presence: face to face,
And frowning brow to brow, ourselves will hear
Th'accuser and the accused freely speak: —
High-stomach'd are they both, and full of ire,
In rage deaf as the sea, hasty as fire.

Enter BOLINGBROKE *and* NORFOLK.

BOLINGBROKE
Many years of happy days befall
My gracious sovereign, my most loving liege!

NORFOLK
Each day still better other's happiness;
Until the heavens, envying earth's good hap,
Add an immortal title to your crown!

KING RICHARD
We thank you both: yet one but flatters us,
As well appeareth by the cause you come;
Namely, to appeal each other of high treason. —
Cousin of Hereford, what dost thou object
Against the Duke of Norfolk, Thomas Mowbray?

BOLINGBROKE
First, — heaven be the record to my speech! —
In the devotion of a subject's love,
Tendering the precious safety of my prince,
And free from other misbegotten hate,
Come I appellant to this princely presence. —
Now, Thomas Mowbray, do I turn to thee,
And mark my greeting well; for what I speak
My body shall make good upon this earth,
Or my divine soul answer it in heaven.
Thou art a traitor and a miscreant,
Too good to be so, and too bad to live, —
Since the more fair and crystal is the sky,
The uglier seem the clouds that in it fly.
Once more, the more to aggravate the note,
With a foul traitor's name stuff I thy throat.
And wish, — so please my sovereign, — ere I move,
What my tongue speaks, my right-drawn sword may prove.

NORFOLK
Let not my cold words here accuse my zeal:
'Tis not the trial of a woman's war,
The bitter clamour of two eager tongues,
Can arbitrate this cause betwixt us twain;
The blood is hot that must be cool'd for this:
Yet can I not of such tame patience boast
As to be hush'd, and naught at all to say:
First, the fair reverence of your highness curbs me
From giving reins and spurs to my free speech;
Which else would post until it had return'd
These terms of treason doubled down his throat.
Setting aside his high blood's royalty,
And let him be no kinsman to my liege,
I do defy him, and I spit at him;
Call him a slanderous coward and a villain:
Which to maintain, I would allow him odds;
And meet him, were I tied to run a-foot
Even to the frozen ridges of the Alps,
Or any other ground inhabitable,
Wherever Englishman durst set his foot.
Meantime let this defend my loyalty, —
By all my hopes, most falsely doth he lie.

BOLINGBROKE
Pale trembling coward, there I throw my gage,
Disclaiming here the kindred of the king;
And lay aside my high blood's royalty,
Which fear, not reverence, makes thee to except.
If guilty dread have left thee so much strength
As to take up mine honour's pawn, then stoop:
By that and all the rites of knighthood else,
Will I make good against thee, arm to arm,
What I have spoke, or thou canst worse devise.

NORFOLK
I take it up; and by that sword I swear,
Which gently laid my knighthood on my shoulder,
I'll answer thee in any fair degree,
Or chivalrous design of knightly trial:
And when I mount, alive may I not light,
If I be traitor or unjustly fight!

KING RICHARD
What doth our cousin lay to Mowbray's charge?
It must be great that can inherit us
So much as of a thought of ill in him.

BOLINGBROKE
Look, what I speak, my life shall prove it true: —
That Mowbray hath receiv'd eight thousand nobles
In name of lendings for your highness' soldiers,
The which he hath detain'd for lewd employments,
Like a false traitor and injurious villain.
Besides, I say, and will in battle prove, —
Or here, or elsewhere to the furthest verge
That ever was survey'd by English eye, —
That all the treasons for these eighteen years
Complotted and contrived in this land
Fetch from false Mowbray their first head and spring.
Further, I say, — and further will maintain
Upon his bad life to make all this good, —
That he did plot the Duke of Gloster's death,
Suggest his soon-believing adversaries,
And consequently, like a traitor-coward,
Sluic'd out his innocent soul through streams of blood:
Which blood, like sacrificing Abel's, cries,
Even from the tongueless caverns of the earth,
To me for justice and rough chastisement;
And, by the glorious worth of my descent,
This arm shall do it, or this life be spent.

KING RICHARD
How high a pitch his resolution soars! —

Thomas of Norfolk, what say'st thou to this?

NORFOLK
O, let my sovereign turn away his face,
And bid his ears a little while be deaf,
Till I have told this slander of his blood,
How God and good men hate so foul a liar!

KING RICHARD
Mowbray, impartial are our eyes and ears:
Were he my brother, nay, my kingdom's heir, —
As he is but my father's brother's son, —
Now, by my sceptre's awe, I make a vow,
Such neighbour-nearness to our sacred blood
Should nothing privilege him, nor partialise
The unstooping firmness of my upright soul:
He is our subject, Mowbray; so art thou:
Free speech and fearless I to thee allow.

NORFOLK
Then, Bolingbroke, as low as to thy heart,
Through the false passage of thy throat, thou liest!
Three parts of that receipt I had for Calais
Disburs'd I duly to his highness' soldiers;
The other part reserv'd I by consent,
For that my sovereign liege was in my debt
Upon remainder of a dear account,
Since last I went to France to fetch his queen:
Now swallow down that lie. — For Gloster's death —
I slew him not; but, to my own disgrace,
Neglected my sworn duty in that case. —
For you, my noble Lord of Lancaster,
The honourable father to my foe,
Once did I lay an ambush for your life, —
A trespass that doth vex my grieved soul:
But, ere I last receiv'd the sacrament,
I did confess it; and exactly begg'd
Your Grace's pardon, and I hope I had it.
This is my fault: as for the rest appeal'd,
It issues from the rancour of a villain,
A recreant and most degenerate traitor:
Which in myself I boldly will defend;
And interchangeably hurl down my gage
Upon this overweening traitor's foot,
To prove myself a loyal gentleman
Even in the best blood chamber'd in his bosom.
In haste whereof, most heartily I pray
Your highness to assign our trial-day.

KING RICHARD
Wrath-kindled gentlemen, be rul'd by me;
Let's purge this choler without letting blood:
This we prescribe, though no physician;
Deep malice makes too deep incision:
Forget, forgive; conclude and be agreed;
Our doctors say this is no month to bleed. —
Good uncle, let this end where it begun;
We'll calm the Duke of Norfolk, you your son.

JOHN OF GAUNT
To be a make-peace shall become my age: —
Throw down, my son, the Duke of Norfolk's gage.

KING RICHARD
And, Norfolk, throw down his.

JOHN OF GAUNT
                    When, Harry? when?
Obedience bids I should not bid agen.

KING RICHARD
Norfolk, throw down; we bid; there is no boot.

NORFOLK
Myself I throw, dread sovereign, at thy foot.
My life thou shalt command, but not my shame:
The one my duty owes; but my fair name —
Despite of death, that lives upon my grave, —
To dark dishonour's use thou shalt not have.
I am disgrac'd, impeach'd, and baffled here;
Pierc'd to the soul with slander's venom'd spear,
The which no balm can cure but his heart-blood
Which breath'd this poison.

KING RICHARD
                    Rage must be withstood: —
Give me his gage: — lions make leopards tame.

NORFOLK
Yea, but not change his spots: take but my shame,
And I resign my gage. My dear dear lord,
The purest treasure mortal times afford
Is spotless reputation; that away,
Men are but gilded loam or painted clay.
A jewel in a ten-times-barr'd-up chest
Is a bold spirit in a loyal breast.
Mine honour is my life; both grow in one;
Take honour from me, and my life is done:
Then, dear my liege, mine honour let me try;
In that I live, and for that will I die.

KING RICHARD
Cousin, throw down your gage; do you begin.

BOLINGBROKE
O, God defend my soul from such deep sin!
Shall I seem crest-fall'n in my father's sight?
Or with pale beggar-fear impeach my height
Before this outdared dastard? Ere my tongue
Shall wound my honour with such feeble wrong,
Or sound so base a parle, my teeth shall tear
The slavish motive of recanting fear,
And spit it bleeding in his high disgrace,
Where shame doth harbour, even in Mowbray's face.
[*Exit* GAUNT.

KING RICHARD
We were not born to sue, but to command; —
Which since we cannot do to make you friends,
Be ready, as your lives shall answer it,
At Coventry, upon Saint Lambert's day:
There shall your swords and lances arbitrate
The swelling difference of your settled hate:
Since we cannot atone you, we shall see
Justice design the victor's chivalry. —
Lord marshal, command our officers-at-arms
Be ready to direct these home-alarms.   [*Exeunt.*

SCENE II

The same. A room in the DUKE OF
LANCASTER'S *palace.*

Enter GAUNT *and* DUCHESS OF GLOSTER.

GAUNT
Alas, the part I had in Woodstock's blood
Doth more solicit me than your exclaims,
To stir against the butchers of his life!
But since correction lieth in those hands
Which made the fault that we cannot correct,
Put we our quarrel to the will of heaven;
Who, when they see the hours ripe on earth,
Will rain hot vengeance on offenders' heads.

DUCHESS OF GLOSTER
Finds brotherhood in thee no sharper spur?
Hath love in thy old blood no living fire?
Edward's seven sons, whereof thyself art one,
Were as seven vials of his sacred blood,
Or seven fair branches springing from one root:
Some of those seven are dried by nature's course,
Some of those branches by the Destinies cut;
But Thomas, my dear lord, my life, my Gloster,
One vial full of Edward's sacred blood,
One flourishing branch of his most royal root,
Is crack'd, and all the precious liquor spilt,
Is hack'd down, and his summer-leaves all faded,
By envy's hand and murder's bloody axe.
Ah, Gaunt, his blood was thine! that bed, that womb,
That metal, that self-mould, that fashion'd thee,
Made him a man; and though thou liv'st and breathest,
Yet art thou slain in him: thou dost consent
In some large measure to thy father's death,
In that thou seest thy wretched brother die,
Who was the model of thy father's life.
Call it not patience, Gaunt, — it is despair:
In suffering thus thy brother to be slaughter'd,
Thou show'st the naked pathway to thy life,
Teaching stern murder how to butcher thee:
That which in mean men we entitle patience,
Is pale cold cowardice in noble breasts.
What shall I say? to safeguard thine own life,
The best way is to venge my Gloster's death.

GAUNT
God's is the quarrel; for God's
    substitute,
His deputy anointed in His sight,
Hath caus'd his death: the which if
    wrongfully,
Let heaven revenge; for I may never lift
An angry arm against his minister.

DUCHESS OF GLOSTER
Where, then, alas, may I complain
    myself?

GAUNT
To God, the widow's champion and
    defence.

DUCHESS OF GLOSTER
Why, then, I will. Farewell, old Gaunt:
Thou go'st to Coventry, there to behold
Our cousin Hereford and fell Mowbray
    fight:
O, sit my husband's wrongs on
    Bolingbroke,
That it may enter butcher Mowbray's
    breast!

Or, if misfortune miss the first career,
Be Mowbray's sins so heavy in his bosom,
That they may break his foaming courser's back,
And throw the rider headlong in the lists,
A caitiff recreant to my cousin Hereford!
Farewell, old Gaunt: thy sometimes brother's wife
With her companion grief must end her life.

GAUNT
Sister, farewell; I must to Coventry:
As much good stay with thee as go with me!

DUCHESS OF GLOSTER
Yet one word more: — grief boundeth where it falls,
Not with the empty hollowness, but weight:
I take my leave before I have begun:
For sorrow ends not when it seemeth done.
Commend me to thy brother, Edmund York.
Lo, this is all: — nay, yet depart not so;
Though this be all, do not so quickly go;
I shall remember more. Bid him — ah, what? —
With all good speed at Plashy visit me.
Alack, and what shall good old York there see,
But empty lodgings and unfurnish'd walls,
Unpeopled offices, untrodden stones?
And what cheer there for welcome, but my groans?
Therefore commend me; let him not come there,
To seek out sorrow that dwells every where.
Desolate, desolate, will I hence and die:
The last leave of thee takes my weeping eye.   [*Exeunt.*

SCENE III

Gosford Green, near Coventry.

Lists set out, and a throne; with ATTENDANTS.

Enter the LORD MARSHAL *and* AUMERLE.

LORD MARSHAL
My Lord Aumerle, is Harry Hereford arm'd?

AUMERLE
Yea, at all points; and longs to enter in.

LORD MARSHAL
The Duke of Norfolk, sprightfully and bold,
Stays but the summons of the appellant's trumpet.

AUMERLE
Why, then, the champions are prepared, and stay
For nothing but his majesty's approach.

The trumpets sound, and the KING *enters with his
    nobles,* GAUNT, BUSHY, BAGOT, GREEN, *and
    others. When they are set, enter the* DUKE OF
    NORFOLK *in arms, defendant, with a* HERALD.

KING RICHARD
Marshal, demand of yonder champion
The cause of his arrival here in arms:
Ask him his name; and orderly proceed
To swear him in the justice of his cause.

LORD MARSHAL
In God's name and the king's, say who thou art,
And why thou comest thus knightly clad in arms;
Against what man thou comest, and what thy quarrel:
Speak truly, on thy knighthood and thy oath;
As so defend thee heaven and thy valour!

NORFOLK
My name is Thomas Mowbray, Duke of Norfolk;
Who hither come engaged by my oath, —
Which God defend a knight should violate! —
Both to defend my loyalty and truth
To God, my king, and my succeeding issue,
Against the Duke of Hereford that appeals me;

DUCHESS OF GLOSTER To safeguard thine own life, the best way
is to venge my Gloster's death.

And, by the grace of God and this mine arm,
To prove him, in defending of myself,
A traitor to my God, my king, and me:
And as I truly fight, defend me heaven!

*The trumpets sound. Enter BOLINGBROKE, appellant,
in armour, with a HERALD.*

KING RICHARD
Marshal, ask yonder knight in arms,
Both who he is, and why he cometh hither
Thus plated in habiliments of war;
And formally, according to our law,
Depose him in the justice of his cause.
LORD MARSHAL
What is thy name? and wherefore comest thou hither,
Before King Richard in his royal lists?
Against whom comest thou? and what's thy quarrel?
Speak like a true knight, so defend thee heaven!
BOLINGBROKE
Harry of Hereford, Lancaster, and Derby,
Am I; who ready here do stand in arms,
To prove, by God's grace, and my body's valour,
In lists, on Thomas Mowbray, Duke of Norfolk,
That he is a traitor, foul and dangerous,
To God of heaven, King Richard, and to me:
And as I truly fight, defend me heaven!
LORD MARSHAL
On pain of death, no person be so bold
Or daring-hardy as to touch the lists,
Except the marshal and such officers
Appointed to direct these fair designs.
BOLINGBROKE
Lord marshal, let me kiss my sovereign's hand,
And bow my knee before his majesty:
For Mowbray and myself are like two men
That vow a long and weary pilgrimage;
Then let us take a ceremonious leave
And loving farewell of our several friends.
LORD MARSHAL
The appellant in all duty greets your highness,
And craves to kiss your hand and take his leave.
KING RICHARD
We will descend and fold him in our arms. —
Cousin of Hereford, as thy cause is right,
So be thy fortune in this royal fight!
Farewell, my blood; which if to-day thou shed,
Lament we may, but not revenge thee dead.
BOLINGBROKE
O, let no noble eye profane a tear
For me, if I be gored with Mowbray's spear:
As confident as is the falcon's flight
Against a bird, do I with Mowbray fight. —
[*to LORD MARSHAL*] My loving lord, I take my leave of
    you; —
Of you, my noble cousin, Lord Aumerle;
Not sick, although I have to do with death,
But lusty, young, and cheerly drawing breath. —
Lo, as at English feasts, so I regreet
The daintiest last, to make the end most sweet:
[*to GAUNT*] O thou, the earthly author of my blood, —
Whose youthful spirit, in me regenerate,
Doth with a twofold vigour lift me up
To reach at victory above my head, —
Add proof unto mine armour with thy prayers;
And with thy blessings steel my lance's point,
That it may enter Mowbray's waxen coat,
And furbish new the name of John o' Gaunt,
Even in the lusty haviour of his son.
GAUNT
God in thy good cause make thee prosperous!
Be swift like lightning in the execution;
And let thy blows, doubly redoubled,
Fall like amazing thunder on the casque
Of thy adverse pernicious enemy:
Rouse up thy youthful blood, be valiant and live.
BOLINGBROKE
Mine innocency and Saint George to thrive!
NORFOLK
However God or fortune cast my lot,
There lives or dies, true to King Richard's throne,
A loyal, just, and upright gentleman:
Never did captive with a freer heart
Cast off his chains of bondage, and embrace
His golden uncontroll'd enfranchisement,
More than my dancing soul doth celebrate
This feast of battle with mine adversary. —
Most mighty liege, and my companion peers,
Take from my mouth the wish of happy years:
As gentle and as jocund as to jest
Go I to fight: truth hath a quiet breast.

KING RICHARD
Farewell, my lord: securely I espy
Virtue with valour couched in thine eye. —
Order the trial, marshal, and begin.
LORD MARSHAL
Harry of Hereford, Lancaster, and Derby,
Receive thy lance; and God defend the right!
BOLINGBROKE
Strong as a tower in hope, I cry amen.
LORD MARSHAL [*to an* OFFICER].
Go bear this lance to Thomas, Duke of Norfolk.
FIRST HERALD
Harry of Hereford, Lancaster, and Derby,
Stands here for God, his sovereign, and himself,
On pain to be found false and recreant,
To prove the Duke of Norfolk, Thomas Mowbray,
A traitor to his God, his king, and him;
And dares him to set forward to the fight.
SECOND HERALD
Here standeth Thomas Mowbray, Duke of Norfolk,
On pain to be found false and recreant,
Both to defend himself, and to approve
Henry of Hereford, Lancaster, and Derby,
To God, his sovereign, and to him disloyal;
Courageously, and with a free desire,
Attending but the signal to begin.
LORD MARSHAL
Sound, trumpets; and set forward, combatants.
                              [*A charge sounded.*
Stay, the king hath thrown his warder down.
KING RICHARD
Let them lay by their helmets and their spears,
And both return back to their chairs again: —
Withdraw with us: — and let the trumpets sound
While we return these dukes what we decree. —
                              [*A long flourish.*
Draw near,
And list what with our council we have done.
For that our kingdom's earth should not be soil'd
With that dear blood which it hath fostered;
And for our eyes do hate the dire aspect
Of civil wounds plough'd up with neighbours'
    sword;
And for we think the eagle-winged pride
Of sky-aspiring and ambitious thoughts,
With rival-hating envy, set on you
To wake our peace, which in our country's cradle
Draws the sweet infant breath of gentle sleep;
Which so rous'd up with boist'rous untuned drums
With harsh-resounding trumpets'
    dreadful bray,
And grating shock of wrathful iron
    arms,
Might from our quiet confines fright
    fair peace,
And make us wade even in our
    kindred's blood; —
Therefore we banish you our
    territories; —
You, cousin Hereford, upon pain of
    life,
Till twice five summers have
    enrich'd our fields,
Shall not regreet our fair dominions,
But tread the stranger paths of
    banishment.
BOLINGBROKE
Your will be done: this must my
    comfort be, —
That sun that warms you here shall
    shine on me;
And those his golden beams to you
    here lent
Shall point on me and gild my
    banishment.
KING RICHARD
Norfolk, for thee remains a heavier
    doom,
Which I with some unwillingness
    pronounce:
The sly slow hours shall not
    determinate
The dateless limit of thy dear
    exile; —
The hopeless word of 'never to
    return'
Breathe I against thee, upon pain of
    life.
NORFOLK
A heavy sentence, my most
    sovereign liege,

And all unlook'd-for from your highness' mouth:
A dearer merit, not so deep a maim
As to be cast forth in the common air,
Have I deserved at your highness' hands.
The language I have learn'd these forty years,
My native English, now I must forgo:
And now my tongue's use is to me no more
Than an unstringed viol or a harp;
Or like a cunning instrument cased up,
Or, being open, put into his hands
That knows no touch to tune the harmony:
Within my mouth you have engaol'd my tongue,
Doubly portcullis'd with my teeth and lips;
And dull, unfeeling, barren ignorance
Is made my gaoler to attend on me.
I am too old to fawn upon a nurse,
Too far in years to be a pupil now:
What is thy sentence, then, but speechless death,
Which robs my tongue from breathing native
    breath?
KING RICHARD
It boots thee not to be compassionate:
After our sentence plaining comes too late.
NORFOLK
Then thus I turn me from my country's light,
To dwell in solemn shades of endless night.
KING RICHARD
Return again, and take an oath with thee.
Lay on our royal sword your banish'd hands;
Swear by the duty that you owe to God, —
Our part therein we banish with yourselves, —
To keep the oath that we administer: —
You never shall — so help you truth and God! —
Embrace each other's love in banishment;
Nor never look upon each other's face;
Nor never write, regreet, nor reconcile
This louring tempest of your home-bred hate;
Nor never by advised purpose meet
To plot, contrive, or complot any ill
'Gainst us, our state, our subjects, or our land.
BOLINGBROKE
I swear.
NORFOLK
And I, to keep all this.
BOLINGBROKE
Norfolk, so far as to mine enemy; —
By this time, had the king permitted us,
One of our souls had wander'd in the air,
Banish'd this frail sepulchre of our flesh,

LORD MARSHAL Stay, the king hath thrown his warder down.

As now our flesh is banish'd from this land:
Confess thy treasons, ere thou fly the realm;
Since thou hast far to go, bear not along
The clogging burden of a guilty soul.

NORFOLK
No, Bolingbroke: if ever I were traitor,
My name be blotted from the book of life,
And I from heaven banish'd, as from hence!
But what thou art, God, thou, and I do know;
And all too soon, I fear, the king shall rue. —
Farewell, my liege. — Now no way can I stray:
Save back to England, all the world's my way.   [*Exit.*

KING RICHARD
Uncle, even in the glasses of thine eyes
I see thy grieved heart: thy sad aspect
Hath from the number of his banish'd years
Pluck'd four away. — [*to* BOLINGBROKE] Six frozen
    winters spent,
Return with welcome home from banishment.

BOLINGBROKE
How long a time lies in one little word!
Four lagging winters and four wanton springs
End in a word: such is the breath of kings.

GAUNT
I thank my liege, that in regard of me
He shortens four years of my son's exile:
But little vantage shall I reap thereby;
For, ere the six years that he hath to spend
Can change their moons and bring their times about,
My oil-dried lamp and time-bewasted light
Shall be extinct with age and endless night;
My inch of taper will be burnt and done,
And blindfold death not let me see my son.

KING RICHARD
Why, uncle, thou hast many years to live.

GAUNT
But not a minute, king, that thou canst give:
Shorten my days thou canst with sullen sorrow,
And pluck nights from me, but not lend a morrow;
Thou canst help time to furrow me with age,
But stop no wrinkle in his pilgrimage;
Thy word is current with him for my death,
But dead, thy kingdom cannot buy my breath.

KING RICHARD
Thy son is banish'd upon good advice,
Whereto thy tongue a party-verdict gave:
Why at our justice seem'st thou, then, to lour?

GAUNT
Things sweet to taste prove in digestion sour.
You urg'd me as a judge; but I had rather
You would have bid me argue like a father.
O, had it been a stranger, not my child,
To smooth his fault I should have been more mild:
A partial slander sought I to avoid,
And in the sentence my own life destroy'd.
Alas, I look'd when some of you should say,
I was too strict to make mine own away;
But you gave leave to my unwilling tongue
Against my will to do myself this wrong.

KING RICHARD
Cousin, farewell; — and, uncle, bid him so:
Six years we banish him, and he shall go.

            [*Flourish. Exeunt* KING RICHARD *and* TRAIN.

AUMERLE
Cousin, farewell: what presence must not know,
From where you do remain let paper show.

LORD MARSHAL
My lord, no leave take I; for I will ride,
As far as land will let me, by your side.

GAUNT
O, to what purpose dost thou hoard thy words,
That thou return'st no greeting to thy friends?

BOLINGBROKE
I have too few to take my leave of you,
When the tongue's office should be prodigal
To breathe th'abundant dolour of the heart.

GAUNT
Thy grief is but thy absence for a time.

BOLINGBROKE
Joy absent, grief is present for that time.

GAUNT
What is six winters? they are quickly gone.

BOLINGBROKE
To men in joy; but grief makes one hour ten.

GAUNT
Call it a travel that thou tak'st for pleasure.

BOLINGBROKE
My heart will sigh when I miscall it so,
Which finds it an inforced pilgrimage.

GAUNT
The sullen passage of thy weary steps
Esteem as foil, wherein thou art to set
The precious jewel of thy home-return.

BOLINGBROKE
Nay, rather, every tedious stride I make
Will but remember me what deal of world
I wander from the jewels that I love.
Must I not serve a long apprenticehood
To foreign passages; and in the end,
Having my freedom, boast of nothing else
But that I was a journeyman to grief?

GAUNT
All places that the eye of heaven visits
Are to a wise man ports and happy havens.
Teach thy necessity to reason thus;
There is no virtue like necessity.
Think not the king did banish thee,
But thou the king; woe doth the heavier sit,
Where it perceives it is but faintly borne.
Go say, I sent thee forth to purchase honour,
And not, the king exil'd thee; or suppose
Devouring pestilence hangs in our air,
And thou art flying to a fresher clime:
Look, what thy soul holds dear, imagine it
To lie that way thou go'st, not whence thou comest:
Suppose the singing-birds musicians,
The grass whereon thou tread'st, the presence strew'd,
The flowers fair ladies, and thy steps no more
Than a delightful measure or a dance;
For gnarling sorrow hath less power to bite
The man that mocks at it and sets it light.

BOLINGBROKE
O, who can hold a fire in his hand
By thinking on the frosty Caucasus?
Or cloy the hungry edge of appetite
By bare imagination of a feast?
Or wallow naked in December snow
By thinking on fantastic summer's heat?
O, no! the apprehension of the good
Gives but the greater feeling to the worse:
Fell sorrow's tooth doth never rankle more
Than when he bites, but lanceth not the sore.

GAUNT
Come, come, my son, I'll bring thee on thy way:
Had I thy youth and cause, I would not stay.

BOLINGBROKE
Then, England's ground, farewell; sweet soil, adieu;
My mother, and my nurse, that bears me yet!
Where'er I wander, boast of this I can, —
Though banish'd, yet a true-born Englishman.

                    [*Exeunt.*

SCENE IV

The court.

Enter, from one side, KING RICHARD, BAGOT, *and*
GREEN; *from the other,* AUMERLE.

KING RICHARD
We did observe. — Cousin Aumerle,
How far brought you high Hereford on his way?

AUMERLE
I brought high Hereford, if you call him so,
But to the next highway, and there I left him.

KING RICHARD
And say, what store of parting tears were shed?

AUMERLE
Faith, none for me; except the north-east wind,
Which then blew bitterly against our faces,
Awaked the sleeping rheum, and so by chance
Did grace our hollow parting with a tear.

KING RICHARD
What said our cousin when you parted with him?

AUMERLE
'Farewell';
And, for my heart disdained that my tongue
Should so profane the word, that taught me craft
To counterfeit oppression of such grief,
That words seem'd buried in my sorrow's grave.
Marry, would the word 'farewell' have lengthen'd hours,
And added years to his short banishment,
He should have had a volume of 'farewells';
But since it would not, he had none of me.

KING RICHARD
He is our cousin, cousin; but 'tis doubt,
When time shall call him home from banishment,
Whether our kinsman come to see his friends.
Ourself, and Bushy, Bagot here, and Green,
Observ'd his courtship to the common people;
How he did seem to dive into their hearts
With humble and familiar courtesy;
What reverence he did throw away on slaves;
Wooing poor craftsmen with the craft of smiles,
And patient underbearing of his fortune,
As 'twere to banish their affects with him.
Off goes his bonnet to an oyster-wench;
A brace of draymen bid God speed him well,
And had the tribute of his supple knee,
With 'Thanks, my countrymen, my loving friends';
As were our England in reversion his,
And he our subjects' next degree in hope.

GREEN
Well, he is gone; and with him go these thoughts.
Now for the rebels which stand out in Ireland, —
Expedient manage must be made, my liege,
Ere further leisure yield them further means
For their advantage and your highness' loss.

KING RICHARD
We will ourself in person to this war:
And, for our coffers, with too great a court
And liberal largess, are grown somewhat light,
We are inforc'd to farm our royal realm;
The revenue whereof shall furnish us
For our affairs in hand. If that come short,
Our substitutes at home shall have blank charters;
Whereto, when they shall know what men are rich,
They shall subscribe them for large sums of gold,
And send them after to supply our wants;
For we will make for Ireland presently.
                    Enter BUSHY.
Bushy, what news?

BUSHY
Old John of Gaunt is grievous sick, my lord,

KING RICHARD How far brought you high Hereford on his way?

Suddenly taken; and hath sent post-haste
To entreat your majesty to visit him.

KING RICHARD
Where lies he?

BUSHY
At Ely-house.

KING RICHARD
Now put it, God, in the physician's mind
To help him to his grave immediately!
The lining of his coffers shall make coats
To deck our soldiers for these Irish wars. —
Come, gentlemen, let's all go visit him:
Pray God we may make haste, and come too late!

ALL
Amen.   [*Exeunt.*

ACT II

SCENE I

London. A room in Ely-house.

Enter GAUNT sick, with the DUKE OF YORK and others.

GAUNT
Will the king come, that I may breathe my last
In wholesome counsel to his unstaid youth?

YORK
Vex not yourself, nor strive not with your breath;
For all in vain comes counsel to his ear.

GAUNT
O, but they say the tongues of dying men
Enforce attention like deep harmony:
Where words are scarce, they are seldom spent in vain;
For they breathe truth that breathe their words in pain.
He that no more must say is listen'd more
    Than they whom youth and ease have taught to
        gloze;
More are men's ends mark'd than their lives before:
    The setting sun, and music at the close,
As the last taste of sweets, is sweetest last,
Writ in remembrance more than things long past:
Though Richard my life's counsel would not hear,
My death's sad tale may yet undeaf his ear.

YORK
No; it is stopp'd with other flattering sounds,
As, praises of his state: then there are found
Lascivious metres, to whose venom sound
The open ear of youth doth always listen;
Report of fashions in proud Italy,
Whose manners still our tardy apish nation
Limps after in base imitation.
Where doth the world thrust forth a vanity, —
So it be new, there's no respect how vile, —
That is not quickly buzz'd into his ears?
Then all too late comes counsel to be heard,
Where will doth mutiny with wit's regard.
Direct not him, whose way himself will choose:
'Tis breath thou lack'st, and that breath wilt thou lose.

GAUNT
Methinks I am a prophet new-inspired,
And thus, expiring, do foretell of him:
His rash fierce blaze of riot cannot last,
For violent fires soon burn out themselves;
Small showers last long, but sudden storms are short;
He tires betimes that spurs too fast betimes;
With eager feeding food doth choke the feeder:
Light vanity, insatiate cormorant,
Consuming means, soon preys upon itself.
This royal throne of kings, this sceptred isle,
This earth of majesty, this seat of Mars,
This other Eden, demi-Paradise;
This fortress built by Nature for herself
Against infection and the hand of war;
This happy breed of men, this little world;
This precious stone set in the silver sea,
Which serves it in the office of a wall,
Or as a moat defensive to a house,
Against the envy of less happier lands;
This blessed plot, this earth, this realm, this England,
This nurse, this teeming womb of royal kings,
Fear'd by their breed, and famous by their birth,
Renowned for their deeds as far from home, —
For Christian service and true chivalry, —
As is the sepulchre, in stubborn Jewry,
Of the world's ransom, blessed Mary's Son; —
This land of such dear souls, this dear dear land,
Dear for her reputation through the world,
Is now leas'd out — I die pronouncing it —
Like to a tenement or pelting farm:

England, bound in with the triumphant sea,
Whose rocky shore beats back the envious siege
Of watery Neptune, is now bound in with shame,
With inky blots, and rotten parchment bonds:
That England, that was wont to conquer others,
Hath made a shameful conquest of itself.
Ah, would the scandal vanish with my life,
How happy then were my ensuing death!

Enter KING RICHARD and QUEEN,
AUMERLE, BUSHY, GREEN, BAGOT,
ROSS, and WILLOUGHBY.

YORK
The king is come: deal mildly with his youth;
For young hot colts being rag'd do rage the more.

QUEEN
How fares our noble uncle, Lancaster?

KING RICHARD
What comfort, man? how is't with aged Gaunt?

GAUNT
O, how that name befits my composition!
Old Gaunt, indeed; and gaunt in being old:
Within me grief hath kept a tedious fast;
And who abstains from meat, that is not gaunt?
For sleeping England long time have I watch'd;
Watching breeds leanness, leanness is all gaunt:
The pleasure that some fathers feed upon,
Is my strict fast, — I mean, my children's looks;
And therein fasting, hast thou made me gaunt:
Gaunt am I for the grave, gaunt as a grave,
Whose hollow womb inherits naught but bones.

GAUNT Ah, would the scandal vanish with my life, how happy then were my ensuing death!

KING RICHARD
Can sick men play so nicely with their names?

GAUNT
No, misery makes sport to mock itself:
Since thou dost seek to kill my name in me,
I mock my name, great king, to flatter thee.

KING RICHARD
Should dying men flatter with those that live?

GAUNT
No, no, men living flatter those that die.

KING RICHARD
Thou, now a-dying, say'st thou flatter'st me.

GAUNT
O, no! thou diest, though I the sicker be.

KING RICHARD
I am in health, I breathe, and see thee ill.

GAUNT
Now, He that made me knows I see thee ill;
Ill in myself to see, and in thee seeing ill.
Thy death-bed is no lesser than thy land,
Wherein thou liest in reputation sick;
And thou, too careless patient as thou art,
Committ'st thy 'nointed body to the cure
Of those physicians that first wounded thee:
A thousand flatterers sit within thy crown,
Whose compass is no bigger than thy head;
And yet, incaged in so small a verge,
The waste is no whit lesser than thy land.
O, had thy grandsire, with a prophet's eye,
Seen how his son's son should destroy his sons,
From forth thy reach he would have laid thy shame,
Deposing thee before thou wert possess'd,

Which art possess'd now to depose thyself.
Why, cousin, wert thou regent of the world,
It were a shame to let this land by lease;
But for thy world enjoying but this land,
Is it not more than shame to shame it so?
Landlord of England art thou now, not king:
Thy state of law is bond-slave to the law;
And thou —

KING RICHARD
            A lunatic lean-witted fool,
Presuming on an ague's privilege,
Darest with thy frozen admonition
Make pale our cheek, chasing the royal blood
With fury from his native residence.
Now, by my seat's right royal majesty,
Wert thou not brother to great Edward's son,
This tongue that runs so roundly in thy head
Should run thy head from thy unreverent shoulders.

GAUNT
O, spare me not, my brother Edward's son,
For that I was his father Edward's son; —
That blood already, like the pelican,
Hast thou tapp'd out, and drunkenly carousel:
My brother Gloster, plain well-meaning soul, —
Whom fair befall in heaven 'mongst happy souls! —
May be a precedent and witness good
That thou respect'st not spilling Edward's blood:
Join with the present sickness that I have;
And thy unkindness be like crooked age,
To crop at once a too-long wither'd flower.
Live in thy shame, but die not shame with thee! —
These words hereafter thy tormentors be! —
Convey me to my bed, then to my grave:
Love they to live that love and honour have.
            [*Exit, borne out by his* ATTENDANTS.

KING RICHARD
And let them die that age and sullens have;
For both hast thou, and both become the grave.

YORK
I do beseech your majesty, impute his words
To wayward sickliness and age in him:
He loves you, on my life, and holds you dear
As Harry, Duke of Hereford, were he here.

KING RICHARD
Right, you say true: as Hereford's love, so his;
As theirs, so mine; and all be as it is.

Enter NORTHUMBERLAND.

NORTHUMBERLAND
My liege, old Gaunt commends him to your majesty.

KING RICHARD
What says he?

NORTHUMBERLAND
            Nay, nothing; all is said:
His tongue is now a stringless instrument;
Words, life, and all, old Lancaster hath spent.

YORK
Be York the next that must be bankrupt so!
Though death be poor, it ends a mortal woe.

KING RICHARD
The ripest fruit falls first, and so doth he;
His time is spent, our pilgrimage must be:
So much for that. — Now for our Irish wars:
We must supplant these rough rug-headed kerns,
Which live like venom, where no venom else

GAUNT Convey me to my bed, then to my grave.

But only they have privilege to live.
And for these great affairs do ask some charge,
Towards our assistance we do seize to us
The plate, corn, revenues, and movables,
Whereof our uncle Gaunt did stand possess'd.

YORK
How long shall I be patient? ah, how long
Shall tender duty make me suffer wrong?
Not Gloster's death, nor Hereford's banishment,
Not Gaunt's rebukes, nor England's private wrongs,
Nor the prevention of poor Bolingbroke
About his marriage, nor my own disgrace,
Have ever made me sour my patient cheek,
Or bend one wrinkle on my sovereign's face.
I am the last of noble Edward's sons,
Of whom thy father, Prince of Wales, was first:
In war was never lion rag'd more fierce,
In peace was never gentle lamb more mild,
Than was that young and princely gentleman.
His face thou hast, for even so look'd he,
Accomplish'd with the number of thy hours;
But when he frown'd, it was against the French,
And not against his friends: his noble hand
Did win what he did spend, and spent not that
Which his triumphant father's hand had won:
His hands were guilty of no kindred's blood,
But bloody with the enemies of his kin.
O Richard! York is too far gone with grief,
Or else he never would compare between.

KING RICHARD
Why, uncle, what's the matter?

YORK
O my liege,
Pardon me, if you please; if not, I, pleased
Not to be pardon'd, am content withal.
Seek you to seize, and gripe into your hands,
The royalties and rights of banish'd Hereford?
Is not Gaunt dead? and doth not Hereford live?
Was not Gaunt just? and is not Harry true?
Did not the one deserve to have an heir?
Is not his heir a well-deserving son?
Take Hereford's rights away, and take from Time
His charters and his customary rights;
Let not to-morrow, then, ensue to-day;
Be not thyself, — for how art thou a king
But by fair sequence and succession?
Now, afore God, — God forbid I say true! —
If you do wrongfully seize Hereford's rights,
Call in the letters-patents that he hath
By his attorneys-general to sue
His livery, and deny his offer'd homage,
You pluck a thousand dangers on your head,
You lose a thousand well-disposed hearts,
And prick my tender patience to those thoughts
Which honour and allegiance cannot think.

KING RICHARD
Think what you will, we seize into our hands
His plate, his goods, his money, and his lands.

YORK
I'll not be by the while: my liege, farewell:
What will ensue hereof, there's none can tell;
But by bad courses may be understood
That their events can never fall out good. [Exit.

KING RICHARD
Go, Bushy, to the Earl of Wiltshire straight:
Bid him repair to us to Ely-house
To see this business. To-morrow next
We will for Ireland; and 'tis time, I trow:
And we create, in absence of ourself,
Our uncle York lord governor of England;
For he is just, and always lov'd us well. —
Come on, our queen: to-morrow must we part;
Be merry, for our time of stay is short.

[Flourish. Exeunt KING, QUEEN, AUMERLE,
BUSHY, GREEN, and BAGOT.

NORTHUMBERLAND
Well, lords, the Duke of Lancaster is dead.

ROSS
And living too; for now his son is duke.

WILLOUGHBY
Barely in title, not in revenues.

NORTHUMBERLAND
Richly in both, if justice had her right.

ROSS
My heart is great; but it must break with silence,
Ere't be disburden'd with a liberal tongue.

NORTHUMBERLAND
Nay, speak thy mind; and let him ne'er speak more
That speaks thy words again to do thee harm!

WILLOUGHBY
Tends that thou wouldst speak to the Duke of
Hereford?
If it be so, out with it boldly, man;
Quick is mine ear to hear of good towards him.

ROSS
No good at all, that I can do for him;
Unless you call it good to pity him,
Bereft and gelded of his patrimony.

NORTHUMBERLAND
Now, afore God, 'tis shame such wrongs are borne
In him, a royal prince, and many more
Of noble blood in this declining land.
The king is not himself, but basely led
By flatterers; and what they will inform,
Merely in hate, 'gainst any of us all,
That will the king severely prosecute
'Gainst us, our lives, our children, and our heirs.

ROSS
The commons hath he pill'd with grievous taxes,
And quite lost their hearts: the nobles hath he fined
For ancient quarrels, and quite lost their hearts.

WILLOUGHBY
And daily new exactions are devised, —
As blanks, benevolences, and I wot not what:
But what, o' God's name, doth become of this?

NORTHUMBERLAND
Wars have not wasted it, for warr'd he hath not,
But basely yielded upon compromise
That which his ancestors achiev'd with blows:
More hath he spent in peace than they in wars.

ROSS
The Earl of Wiltshire hath the realm in farm.

WILLOUGHBY
The king's grown bankrupt, like a broken man.

NORTHUMBERLAND
Reproach and dissolution hangeth over him.

ROSS
He hath not money for these Irish wars,
His burdenous taxations notwithstanding,
But by the robbing of the banish'd duke.

NORTHUMBERLAND
His noble kinsman: — most degenerate king!
But, lords, we hear this fearful tempest sing,
Yet seek no shelter to avoid the storm;
We see the wind sit sore upon our sails,
And yet we strike not, but securely perish.

ROSS
We see the very wrack that we must suffer;
And unavoided is the danger now,
For suffering so the causes of our wrack.

NORTHUMBERLAND
Not so; even through the hollow eyes of death
I spy life peering; but I dare not say
How near the tidings of our comfort is.

WILLOUGHBY
Nay, let us share thy thoughts, as thou dost ours.

ROSS
Be confident to speak, Northumberland:
We three are but thyself; and, speaking so,
Thy words are but as thoughts; therefore, be bold.

NORTHUMBERLAND
Then thus: — I have from Port le Blanc, a bay
In Brittany, received intelligence
That Harry, Duke of Hereford, Rainold, Lord Cobham,
That late broke from the Duke of Exeter,
His brother, Archbishop late of Canterbury,
Sir Thomas Erpingham, Sir John Ramston,
Sir John Norbery, Sir Robert Waterton, and Francis
Quoint, —
All these well furnish'd by the Duke of Bretagne,
With eight tall ships, three thousand men of war,
Are making hither with all due expedience,
And shortly mean to touch our northern shore:
Perhaps they had ere this, but that they stay
The first departing of the king for Ireland.
If, then, we shall shake off our slavish yoke,
Imp out our drooping country's broken wing,
Redeem from broking pawn the blemish'd crown,
Wipe off the dust that hides our sceptre's gilt,
And make high majesty look like itself,
Away with me in post to Ravenspurg;
But if you faint, as fearing to do so,
Stay, and be secret, and myself will go.

ROSS
To horse! to horse! urge doubts to them that fear.

WILLOUGHBY
Hold out my horse, and I will first be there. [Exeunt.

SCENE II
The Court.

Enter QUEEN, BUSHY, and BAGOT.

BUSHY
Madam, your majesty is too much sad:
You promis'd, when you parted with the king,
To lay aside life-harming heaviness,
And entertain a cheerful disposition.

QUEEN
To please the king, I did; to please myself,
I cannot do it; yet I know no cause
Why I should welcome such a guest as grief,
Save bidding farewell to so sweet a guest
As my sweet Richard: yet, again, methinks
Some unborn sorrow, ripe in fortune's womb,
Is coming towards me; and my inward soul
With nothing trembles: at something it grieves,
More than with parting from my lord the king.

BUSHY
Each substance of a grief hath twenty shadows,
Which shows like grief itself, but is not so;
For sorrow's eye, glazed with blinding tears,
Divides one thing entire to many objects;
Like perspectives, which rightly gazed upon,
Show nothing but confusion, — eyed awry,
Distinguish form: so your sweet majesty,
Looking awry upon your lord's departure,
Find shapes of grief, more than himself, to wail;
Which, look'd on as it is, is naught but shadows
Of what it is not. Then, thrice-gracious queen,
More than your lord's departure weep not, — more's
not seen;
Or if it be, 'tis with false sorrow's eye,
Which for things true weeps things imaginary.

QUEEN

It may be so; but yet my inward soul
Persuades me it is otherwise: howe'er it be,
I cannot but be sad; so heavy sad,
As, though, on thinking, on no thought I think,
Makes me with heavy nothing faint and shrink.

BUSHY

'Tis nothing but conceit, my gracious lady.

QUEEN

'Tis nothing less: conceit is still derived
From some forefather grief; mine is not so,
For nothing hath begot my something grief;
Or something hath the nothing that I grieve:
'Tis in reversion that I do possess;
But what it is, that is not yet known; what
I cannot name; 'tis nameless woe, I wot.

Enter GREEN.

GREEN

God save your majesty! and well met, gentlemen:
I hope the king is not yet shipp'd for Ireland.

QUEEN

Why hopest thou so? 'tis better hope he is;
For his designs crave haste, his haste good hope;
Then wherefore dost thou hope he is not shipp'd?

GREEN

That he, our hope, might have retired his power,
And driven into despair an enemy's hope,
Who strongly hath set footing in this land:
The banish'd Bolingbroke repeals himself,
And with uplifted arms is safe arrived
At Ravenspurg.

QUEEN

Now God in heaven forbid!

GREEN

Ah, madam, 'tis too true: and that is worse,
The Lord Northumberland, his son young Henry
Percy,
The Lords of Ross, Beaumond, and Willoughby,
With all their powerful friends, are fled to him.

BUSHY

Why have you not proclaim'd Northumberland
And all the rest revolted faction traitors?

GREEN

We have: whereupon the Earl of Worcester
Hath broke his staff, resign'd his stewardship,
And all the household servants fled with him
To Bolingbroke.

QUEEN

So, Green, thou art the midwife to my woe,
And Bolingbroke my sorrow's dismal heir:
Now hath my soul brought forth her prodigy;
And I, a gasping new-deliver'd mother,
Have woe to woe, sorrow to sorrow join'd.

BUSHY

Despair not, madam.

QUEEN

Who shall hinder me?
I will despair, and be at enmity
With cozening hope, — he is a flatterer,
A parasite, a keeper-back of death,
Who gently would dissolve the bands of life,
Which false hope lingers in extremity.

GREEN

Here comes the Duke of York.

QUEEN

With signs of war about his aged neck:
O, full of careful business are his looks!

Enter YORK.

Uncle, for God's sake, speak comfortable words.

YORK

Should I do so, I should belie my thoughts:
Comfort's in heaven; and we are on the earth,
Where nothing lives but crosses, cares, and grief.
Your husband, he is gone to save far off,
Whilst others come to make him lose at home:
Here am I left to underprop his land,
Who, weak with age, cannot support myself:
Now comes the sick hour that his surfeit made;
Now shall he try his friends that flatter'd him.

Enter a SERVANT.

SERVANT

My lord, your son was gone before I came.

YORK

He was? — Why, so! — go all which way it will! —
The nobles they are fled, the commons they are cold,
And will, I fear, revolt on Hereford's side. —
Sirrah, get thee to Plashy, to my sister Gloster;
Bid her send me presently a thousand pound: —

BUSHY Madam, your majesty is too much sad.

Hold, take my ring.

SERVANT

My lord, I had forgot to tell your lordship,
To-day, as I came by, I called there; —
But I shall grieve you to report the rest.

YORK

What is it, knave?

SERVANT

An hour before I came, the duchess died.

YORK

God for his mercy! what a tide of woes
Comes rushing on this woeful land at once!
I know not what to do: — I would to God, —
So my untruth had not provok'd him to it, —
The king had cut off my head with my brother's. —
What, are there no posts dispatch'd for Ireland? —
How shall we do for money for these wars? —
Come, sister, — cousin, I would say, — pray, pardon
me. —
Go, fellow, get thee home, provide some carts,
And bring away the armour that is there.

[Exit SERVANT.

Gentlemen, will you go muster men? If I
Know how or which way to order these affairs,
Thus disorderly thrust into my hands,
Never believe me. Both are my kinsmen: —
Th'one is my sovereign, whom both my oath
And duty bids defend; th'other, again,
Is my kinsman, whom the king hath wrong'd,
Whom conscience and my kindred bids to right.
Well, somewhat we must do. — Come, cousin, I'll
dispose of you. —
Gentlemen, go muster up your men,
And meet me presently at Berkley.
I should to Plashy too; —
But time will not permit: — all is uneven,
And every thing is left at six and seven.

[Exeunt YORK and QUEEN.

BUSHY

The wind sits fair for news to go to Ireland,
But none returns. For us to levy power
Proportionable to the enemy
Is all unpossible.

GREEN

Besides, our nearness to the king in love
Is near the hate of those love not the king.

BAGOT

And that's the wavering commons: for their love
Lies in their purses; and whoso empties them,
By so much fills their hearts with deadly hate.

BUSHY

Wherein the king stands generally condemn'd.

BAGOT

If judgement lie in them, then so do we,
Because we ever have been near the king.

GREEN

Well, I will for refuge straight to Bristol-castle:
The Earl of Wiltshire is already there.

BUSHY

Thither will I with you; for little office
The hateful commons will perform for us,
Except like curs to tear us all to pieces. —
Will you go along with us?

BAGOT

No; I will to Ireland to his majesty.
Farewell: if heart's presages be not vain,
We three here part that ne'er shall meet again.

BUSHY

That's as York thrives to beat back Bolingbroke.

GREEN

Alas, poor duke! the task he undertakes
Is numbering sands, and drinking oceans dry:
Where one on his side fights, thousands will fly.
Farewell at once, — for once, for all, and ever.

BUSHY

Well, we may meet again.

BAGOT

I fear me, never. *[Exeunt.*

SCENE III

The wilds in Glostershire.

*Enter BOLINGBROKE and NORTHUMBERLAND,
with FORCES.*

BOLINGBROKE

How far is it, my lord, to Berkley now?

NORTHUMBERLAND

Believe me, noble lord,
I am a stranger here in Glostershire:
These high wild hills and rough uneven ways
Draw out our miles, and make them wearisome;
And yet your fair discourse hath been as sugar,
Making the hard way sweet and delectable.
But I bethink me what a weary way
From Ravenspurg to Cotswold will be found
In Ross and Willoughby, wanting your company,
Which, I protest, hath very much beguil'd
The tediousness and process of my travel:
But theirs is sweeten'd with the hope to have
The present benefit which I possess;
And hope to joy is little less in joy
Than hope enjoy'd: by this the weary lords
Shall make their way seem short; as mine hath done
By sight of what I have, your noble company.

BOLINGBROKE

Of much less value is my company
Than your good words. — But who comes here?

NORTHUMBERLAND

It is my son, young Harry Percy,
Sent from my brother Worcester, whencesoever.

Enter PERCY.

Harry, how fares your uncle?

PERCY
I had thought, my lord, to have learn'd his health of
    you.

NORTHUMBERLAND
Why, is he not with the queen?

PERCY
No, my good lord; he hath forsook the court,
Broken his staff of office, and dispersed
The household of the king.

NORTHUMBERLAND
What was his reason?
He was not so resolv'd when last we spake together.

PERCY
Because your lordship was proclaimed traitor.
But he, my lord, is gone to Ravenspurg,
To offer service to the Duke of Hereford;
And sent me over by Berkley, to discover
What power the Duke of York had levied there;
Then with directions to repair to Ravenspurg.

NORTHUMBERLAND
Have you forgot the Duke of Hereford, boy?

PERCY
No, my good lord; for that is not forgot
Which ne'er I did remember: to my knowledge,
I never in my life did look on him.

NORTHUMBERLAND
Then learn to know him now; this is the duke.

PERCY
My gracious lord, I tender you my service,
Such as it is, being tender, raw, and young;
Which elder days shall ripen, and confirm
To more approved service and desert.

BOLINGBROKE
I thank thee, gentle Percy; and be sure
I count myself in nothing else so happy
As in a soul remembering my good friends;
And, as my fortune ripens with thy love,
It shall be still thy true love's recompense:
My heart this covenant makes, my hand thus seals it.

NORTHUMBERLAND
How far is it to Berkley? and what stir
Keeps good old York there with his men of war?

PERCY
There stands the castle, by yond tuft of trees,
Mann'd with three hundred men, as I have heard;
And in it are the Lords of York, Berkley, and Seymour, —
None else of name and noble estimate.

NORTHUMBERLAND
Here come the Lords of Ross and Willoughby,
Bloody with spurring, fiery-red with haste.

Enter ROSS *and* WILLOUGHBY.

BOLINGBROKE
Welcome, my lords. I wot your love pursues
A banish'd traitor: all my treasury
Is yet but unfelt thanks, which more enrich'd,
Shall be your love and labour's recompense.

ROSS
Your presence makes us rich, most noble lord.

WILLOUGHBY
And far surmounts our labour to attain it.

BOLINGBROKE
Evermore thanks, the exchequer of the poor;
Which, till my infant fortune comes to years,
Stands for my bounty. — But who comes here?

NORTHUMBERLAND
It is my Lord of Berkley, as I guess.

Enter BERKLEY.

BERKLEY
My Lord of Hereford, my message is to you.

BOLINGBROKE
My lord, my answer is — 'to Lancaster';
And I am come to seek that name in England;
And I must find that title in your tongue,
Before I make reply to aught you say.

BERKLEY
Mistake me not, my lord; 'tis not my meaning
To raze one title of your honour out: —
To you, my lord, I come, — what lord you will, —
From the most gracious regent of this land,
The Duke of York, to know what pricks you on
To take advantage of the absent time,
And fright our native peace with self-born arms.

BOLINGBROKE
I shall not need transport my words by you;
Here comes his Grace in person.

Enter YORK *attended.*
                        My noble uncle! [*Kneels.*

YORK
Show me thy humble heart, and not thy knee,
Whose duty is deceivable and false.

BOLINGBROKE
My gracious uncle!

YORK
Tut, tut!
Grace me no grace, nor uncle me no uncle:
I am no traitor's uncle; and that word 'grace'
In an ungracious mouth is but profane.
Why have those banish'd and forbidden legs
Dared once to touch a dust of England's ground?
But, then, more 'why?' — why have they dared to
    march
So many miles upon her peaceful bosom,
Frighting her pale-fac'd villages with war
And ostentation of despised arms?
Comest thou because th'anointed king is hence?
Why, foolish boy, the king is left behind,
And in my loyal bosom lies his power.
Were I but now the lord of such hot youth
As when brave Gaunt thy father, and myself,
Rescued the Black Prince, that young Mars of men,
From forth the ranks of many thousand French,
O, then, how quickly should this arm of mine,
Now prisoner to the palsy, chastise thee,
And minister correction to thy fault!

BOLINGBROKE
My gracious uncle, let me know my fault;
On what condition stands it and wherein?

YORK
Even in condition of the worst degree, —
In gross rebellion and detested treason:
Thou art a banish'd man; and here art come
Before the expiration of thy time,
In braving arms against thy sovereign.

BOLINGBROKE
As I was banish'd, I was banish'd Hereford;
But as I come, I come for Lancaster.
And, noble uncle, I beseech your Grace
Look on my wrongs with an indifferent eye:
You are my father, for methinks in you
I see old Gaunt alive; O, then, my father,
Will you permit that I shall stand condemn'd
A wandering vagabond; my rights and royalties
Pluck'd from my arms perforce, and given away
To upstart unthrifts? Wherefore was I born?
If that my cousin king be King of England,
It must be granted I am Duke of Lancaster.
You have a son, Aumerle, my noble cousin;
Had you first died, and he been thus trod down,
He should have found his uncle Gaunt a father,
To rouse his wrongs, and chase them to the bay.
I am denied to sue my livery here,
And yet my letters-patents give me leave:
My father's goods are all distrain'd and sold;
And these and all are all amiss employ'd.
What would you have me do? I am a subject,
And I challenge law: attorneys are denied me;
And therefore personally I lay my claim
To my inheritance of free descent.

NORTHUMBERLAND
The noble duke hath been too much abused.

ROSS
It stands your Grace upon to do him right.

WILLOUGHBY
Base men by his endowments are made great.

YORK
My lords of England, let me tell you this: —
I have had feeling of my cousin's wrongs,
And labour'd all I could to do him right;
But in this kind to come, in braving arms,
Be his own carver, and cut out his way,
To find out right with wrong, — it may not be;
And you that do abet him in this kind
Cherish rebellion and are rebels all.

NORTHUMBERLAND
The noble duke hath sworn his coming is
But for his own; and for the right of that
We all have strongly sworn to give him aid;
And let him ne'er see joy that breaks that oath!

YORK
Well, well, I see the issue of these arms;
I cannot mend it, I must needs confess,
Because my power is weak and all ill left:
But if I could, by him that gave me life,
I would attach you all, and make you stoop
Unto the sovereign mercy of the king;
But since I cannot, be it known to you
I do remain as neuter. So, fare you well; —
Unless you please to enter in the castle,
And there repose you for this night.

BOLINGBROKE
An offer, uncle, that we will accept:
But we must win your Grace to go with us
To Bristol-castle, which they say is held
By Bushy, Bagot and their complices,
The caterpillars of the commonwealth,
Which I have sworn to weed and pluck away.

YORK
It may be I will go with you: — but yet I'll pause;
For I am loth to break our country's laws.
Nor friends nor foes, to me welcome you are:
Things past redress are now with me past care.
                                        [*Exeunt.*

SCENE IV

A camp in Wales.

Enter SALISBURY *and a* CAPTAIN.

CAPTAIN
My lord of Salisbury, we have stay'd ten days,
And hardly kept our countrymen together,
And yet we hear no tidings from the king;
Therefore we will disperse ourselves: farewell.

SALISBURY
Stay yet another day, thou trusty Welshman:
The king reposeth all his confidence in thee.

CAPTAIN
'Tis thought the king is dead; we will not stay.
The bay-trees in our country are all wither'd,
And meteors fright the fixed stars of heaven;
The pale-fac'd moon looks bloody on the earth,
And lean-look'd prophets whisper fearful change;
Rich men look sad, and ruffians dance and leap, —
The one in fear to lose what they enjoy,
The other to enjoy by rage and war:
These signs forerun the death or fall of kings. —
Farewell: our countrymen are gone and fled,
As well assured Richard their king is dead. [*Exit.*

SALISBURY
Ah, Richard, with the eyes of heavy mind,
I see thy glory, like a shooting star,
Fall to the base earth from the firmament!
Thy sun sets weeping in the lowly west,
Witnessing storms to come, woe, and unrest:
Thy friends are fled, to wait upon thy foes;
And crossly to thy good all fortune goes. [*Exit.*

ACT III

SCENE I

BOLINGBROKE'S *camp at Bristol.*

Enter BOLINGBROKE, YORK,
NORTHUMBERLAND, PERCY, WILLOUGHBY,
with BUSHY *and* GREEN, *prisoners.*

BOLINGBROKE
Bring forth these men.
Bushy and Green, I will not vex your souls —
Since presently your souls must part your bodies —
With too much urging your pernicious lives,
For 'twere no charity; yet, to wash your blood
From off my hands, here, in the view of men,
I will unfold some causes of your deaths.
You have misled a prince, a royal king,
A happy gentleman in blood and lineaments,
By you unhappied and disfigured clean:
You have in manner with your sinful hours
Made a divorce betwixt his queen and him;
Broke the possession of a royal bed,
And stain'd the beauty of a fair queen's cheeks
With tears drawn from her eyes by your foul wrongs.
Myself, — a prince by fortune of my birth,
Near to the king in blood, and near in love
Till you did make him misinterpret me, —
Have stoop'd my neck under your injuries,
And sigh'd my English breath in foreign clouds,
Eating the bitter bread of banishment;
Whilst you have fed upon my signories,
Dispark'd my parks, and fell'd my forest-woods,
From my own windows torn my household coat,
Raz'd out my imprese, leaving me no sign,
Save men's opinions and my living blood,
To show the world I am a gentleman.
This and much more, much more than twice all this,
Condemns you to the death. — See them deliver'd over
To execution and the hand of death.

BUSHY
More welcome is the stroke of death to me

BOLINGBROKE Bring forth these men.

Than Bolingbroke to England. — Lords, farewell.

GREEN
My comfort is, that heaven will take our souls,
And plague injustice with the pains of hell.

BOLINGBROKE
My Lord Northumberland, see them dispatch'd.
　　[*Exeunt* NORTHUMBERLAND *and others, with the*
　　　　　　　　　　　　　　PRISONERS.
Uncle, you say the queen is at your house:
For God's sake, fairly let her be entreated:
Tell her I send to her my kind commends;
Take special care my greetings be deliver'd.

YORK
A gentleman of mine I have dispatch'd
With letters of your love to her at large.

BOLINGBROKE
Thanks, gentle uncle. — Come, lords, away,
To fight with Glendower and his complices:
Awhile to work, and after holiday. 　　　[*Exeunt.*

SCENE II

The coast of Wales. A castle in view.

Drums: flourish and colours. Enter KING RICHARD,
the BISHOP OF CARLISLE,
AUMERLE, *and* SOLDIERS.

KING RICHARD
Barkloughly-castle call they this at hand?

AUMERLE
Yea, my lord. How brooks your Grace the air,
After your late tossing on the breaking seas?

KING RICHARD
Needs must I like it well: I weep for joy
To stand upon my kingdom once again. —
Dear earth, I do salute thee with my hand,
Though rebels wound thee with their horses' hoofs:
As a long-parted mother with her child
Plays fondly with her tears and smiles in meeting,
So, weeping, smiling, greet I thee, my earth,
And do thee favours with my royal hands.
Feed not thy sovereign's foe, my gentle earth,
Nor with thy sweets comfort his ravenous sense;
But let thy spiders, that suck up thy venom,
And heavy-gaited toads, lie in their way,
Doing annoyance to the treacherous feet
Which with usurping steps do trample thee:
Yield stinging nettles to mine enemies;
And when they from thy bosom pluck a flower,
Guard it, I pray thee, with a lurking adder,
Whose double tongue may with a mortal touch
Throw death upon thy sovereign's enemies. —
Mock not my senseless conjuration, lords:
This earth shall have a feeling, and these stones
Prove armed soldiers, ere her native king
Shall falter under foul rebellion's arms.

BISHOP OF CARLISLE
Fear not, my lord: that Power that made you king
Hath power to keep you king in spite of all.
The means that heaven yields must be embraced,
And not neglected; else, if heaven would,
And we will not, heaven's offer we refuse,
The proffer'd means of succour and redress.

AUMERLE
He means, my lord, that we are too remiss;
Whilst Bolingbroke, through our security,
Grows strong and great in substance and in friends.

KING RICHARD
Discomfortable cousin! know'st thou not
That when the searching eye of heaven is hid,
Behind the globe, that lights the lower world,
Then thieves and robbers range abroad unseen,
In murders and in outrage boldly here;
But when, from under this terrestrial ball,
He fires the proud tops of the eastern pines,
And darts his light through every guilty hole,
Then murders, treasons, and detested sins,
The cloak of night being pluck'd from off their backs,
Stand bare and naked, trembling at themselves?
So when this thief, this traitor, Bolingbroke, —
Who all this while hath revell'd in the night,
Whilst we were wandering with the Antipodes, —
Shall see us rising in our throne, the east,
His treasons will sit blushing in his face,
Not able to endure the sight of day,
But self-affrighted tremble at his sin.
Not all the water in the rough rude sea
Can wash the balm from an anointed king;
The breath of worldly men cannot depose
The deputy elected by the Lord:
For every man that Bolingbroke hath press'd
To lift shrewd steel against our golden crown,
God for his Richard hath in heavenly pay
A glorious angel: then, if angels fight,
Weak men must fall; for heaven still guards the right.

Enter SALISBURY.

Welcome, my lord: how far off lies your power?

SALISBURY
Not near nor farther off, my gracious lord,
Than this weak arm: discomfort guides my tongue,
And bids me speak of nothing but despair.
One day too late, I fear me, noble lord,
Hath clouded all thy happy days on earth:
O, call back yesterday, bid time return,
And thou shalt have twelve thousand fighting men!
To-day, to-day, unhappy day, too late,
O'erthrows thy joys, friends, fortune, and thy state;
For all the Welshmen, hearing thou wert dead,
Are gone to Bolingbroke, dispers'd and fled.

AUMERLE
Comfort, my liege: why looks your Grace so pale?

KING RICHARD
But now the blood of twenty thousand men
Did triumph in my face, and they are fled;
And, till so much blood thither come agen,
Have I not reason to look pale and dead?
All souls that will be safe, fly from my side;
For time hath set a blot upon my pride.

AUMERLE
Comfort, my liege; remember who you are.

KING RICHARD
I had forgot myself: am I not king?
Awake, thou coward majesty! thou sleepest.
Is not the king's name twenty thousand names?
Arm, arm, my name! a puny subject strikes
At thy great glory. — Look not to the ground,

Ye favourites of a king: are we not high?
High be our thoughts: I know my uncle York
Hath power enough to serve our turn. —
But who comes here?

Enter SCROOP.

SCROOP
More health and happiness betide my liege
Than can my care-tun'd tongue deliver him!

KING RICHARD
Mine ear is open and my heart prepared:
The worst is worldly loss thou canst unfold.
Say, is my kingdom lost? why, 'twas my care;
And what loss is it to be rid of care?
Strives Bolingbroke to be as great as we?
Greater he shall not be; if he serve God,
We'll serve Him too, and be his fellow so:
Revolt our subjects? that we cannot mend;
They break their faith to God as well as us:
Cry woe, destruction, ruin, loss, decay;
The worst is death, and death will have his day.

SCROOP
Glad am I that your highness is so arm'd
To bear the tidings of calamity.
Like an unseasonable stormy day,
Which makes the silver rivers drown their shores,
As if the world were all dissolv'd to tears;
So high above his limits swells the rage
Of Bolingbroke, covering your fearful land
With hard bright steel, and hearts harder than steel.
White-beards have arm'd their thin and hairless scalps
Against thy majesty; boys with women's voices
Strive to speak big, and clap their female joints
In stiff unwieldy arms against thy crown;
The very beadsmen learn to bend their bows
Of double-fatal yew against thy state;
Yea, distaff-women manage rusty bills
Against thy seat: both young and old rebel,
And all goes worse than I have power to tell.

KING RICHARD
Too well, too well thou tell'st a tale so ill.
Where is the Earl of Wiltshire? where is Bagot?
What is become of Bushy? where is Green?
That they have let the dangerous enemy
Measure our confines with such peaceful steps?
If we prevail, their heads shall pay for it:
I warrant they have made peace with Bolingbroke.

SCROOP
Peace have they made with him, indeed, my lord.

KING RICHARD
O villains, vipers, damn'd without redemption!
Dogs, easily won to fawn on any man!
Snakes, in my heart-blood warm'd, that sting my heart!
Three Judases, each one thrice worse than Judas!
Would they make peace? terrible hell make war
Upon their spotted souls for this offence!

SCROOP
Sweet love, I see, changing his property,
Turns to the sourest and most deadly hate: —
Again uncurse their souls; their peace is made
With heads, and not with hands: those whom you curse
Have felt the worst of death's destroying wound,
And lie full low, grav'd in the hollow ground.

AUMERLE
Is Bushy, Green, and the Earl of Wiltshire dead?

SCROOP
Ay, all of them at Bristol lost their heads.

AUMERLE
Where is the duke my father with his power?

KING RICHARD
No matter where; — of comfort no man speak:
Let's talk of graves, of worms, and epitaphs;
Make dust our paper, and with rainy eyes
Write sorrow on the bosom of the earth.
Let's choose executors, and talk of wills:
And yet not so, — for what can we bequeath,
Save our deposed bodies to the ground?
Our lands, our lives, and all are Bolingbroke's,
And nothing can we call our own but death,
And that small model of the barren earth
Which serves as paste and cover to our bones.
For God's sake, let us sit upon the ground,
And tell sad stories of the death of kings: —
How some have been depos'd; some slain in war;
Some haunted by the ghosts they have depos'd;
Some poison'd by their wives; some sleeping kill'd;
All murder'd: — for within the hollow crown
That rounds the mortal temples of a king
Keeps Death his court; and there the antick sits,
Scoffing his state, and grinning at his pomp;
Allowing him a breath, a little scene,

To monarchise, be fear'd, and kill with looks;
Infusing him with self and vain conceit, —
As if this flesh, which walls about our life,
Were brass impregnable; and humour'd thus,
Comes at the last, and with a little pin
Bores through his castle-wall, and — farewell king!
Cover your heads, and mock not flesh and blood
With solemn reverence; throw away respect,
Tradition, form, and ceremonious duty;
For you have but mistook me all this while:
I live with bread like you, feel want,
Taste grief, need friends: — subjected thus,
How can you say to me, I am a king?

CARLISLE
My lord, wise men ne'er sit and wail their woes,
But presently prevent the ways to wail.
To fear the foe, since fear oppresseth strength,
Gives, in your weakness, strength unto your foe,
And so your follies fight against yourself.
Fear, and be slain; no worse can come to fight:
And fight and die is death destroying death;
Where fearing dying pays death servile breath.

AUMERLE
My father hath a power; inquire of him;
And learn to make a body of a limb.

KING RICHARD
Thou chidest me well: — proud Bolingbroke, I come
To change blows with thee for our day of doom.
This ague-fit of fear is over-blown;
An easy task it is to win our own. —
Say, Scroop, where lies our uncle with his power?
Speak sweetly, man, although thy looks be sour.

SCROOP
Men judge by the complexion of the sky
    The state and inclination of the day;
So may you by my dull and heavy eye,
    My tongue hath but a heavier tale to say.
I play the torturer, by small and small
To lengthen out the worst that must be spoken: —
Your uncle York is join'd with Bolingbroke,
And all your northern castles yielded up,
And all your southern gentlemen in arms
Upon his party.

KING RICHARD
                Thou hast said enough. —
[*to* AUMERLE] Beshrew thee, cousin, which didst lead
    me forth
Of that sweet way I was in to despair!
What say you now? what comfort have we now?
By heaven, I'll hate him everlastingly
That bids me be of comfort any more.
Go to Flint-castle: there I'll pine away;
A king, woe's slave, shall kingly woe obey.
That power I have, discharge; and let them go
To ear the land that hath some hope to grow,
For I have none: — let no man speak again
To alter this, for counsel is but vain.

AUMERLE
My liege, one word.

KING RICHARD
                He does me double wrong
That wounds me with the flatteries of his tongue.
Discharge my followers: let them hence away,
From Richard's night to Bolingbroke's fair day.
[*Exeunt.*

SCENE III

Wales. Before Flint-castle.

Enter, with drums and colours, BOLINGBROKE,
YORK, NORTHUMBERLAND, *and* FORCES.

BOLINGBROKE
So that by this intelligence we learn
The Welshmen are dispers'd; and Salisbury
Is gone to meet the king, who lately landed
With some few private friends upon this coast.

NORTHUMBERLAND
The news is very fair and good, my lord:
Richard not far from hence hath hid his head.

YORK
It would beseem the Lord Northumberland
To say 'King Richard': — alack the heavy day
When such a sacred king should hide his head!

NORTHUMBERLAND
Your Grace mistakes; only to be brief,
Left I his title out.

YORK
                The time hath been,
Would you have been so brief with him, he would
Have been so brief with you, to shorten you,

For taking so the head, your whole head's length.

BOLINGBROKE
Mistake not, uncle, further than you should.

YORK
Take not, good cousin, further than you should,
Lest you mistake: the heavens are over our heads.

BOLINGBROKE
I know it, uncle; and oppose not myself
Against their will. — But who comes here?
                Enter PERCY.
Welcome, Harry: what, will not this castle yield?

PERCY
The castle royally is mann'd, my lord,
Against thy entrance.

BOLINGBROKE
Royally!
Why, it contains no king?

PERCY
                Yes, my good lord,
It doth contain a king; King Richard lies
Within the limits of yon lime and stone:
And with him are the Lord Aumerle, Lord Salisbury,
Sir Stephen Scroop; besides a clergyman
Of holy reverence; who I cannot learn.

NORTHUMBERLAND
O, belike it is the Bishop of Carlisle.

BOLINGBROKE
[*to* NORTHUMBERLAND] Noble lord,
Go to the rude ribs of that ancient castle;
Through brazen trumpet send the breath of parley
Into his ruin'd ears, and thus deliver: —
Henry Bolingbroke
On both his knees doth kiss King Richard's hand,
And sends allegiance and true faith of heart
To his most royal person; hither come
Even at his feet to lay my arms and power,
Provided that my banishment repeal'd
And lands restored again be freely granted:
If not, I'll use th'advantage of my power,
And lay the summer's dust with showers of blood
Rain'd from the wounds of slaughter'd Englishmen:
The which, how far off from the mind of Bolingbroke
It is, such crimson tempest should bedrench
The fresh green lap of fair King Richard's land,
My stooping duty tenderly shall show.
Go, signify as much, while here we march
Upon the grassy carpet of this plain.
Let's march without the noise of threatening drum,
That from this castle's tatter'd battlements
Our fair appointments may be well perused.
Methinks King Richard and myself should meet
With no less terror than the elements
Of fire and water, when their thundering shock
At meeting tears the cloudy cheeks of heaven.
Be he the fire, I'll be the yielding water:
The rage be his, while on the earth I rain
My waters, — on the earth, and not on him.
March on, and mark King Richard how he looks.

*Parle without, and answer within. Then a flourish. Enter,
on the walls,* KING RICHARD, *the* BISHOP OF
CARLISLE, AUMERLE, SCROOP, *and* SALISBURY.

YORK
See, see, King Richard doth himself appear,
As doth the blushing discontented sun
From out the fiery portal of the east,
When he perceives the envious clouds are bent
To dim his glory, and to stain the track
Of his bright passage to the occident.
Yet looks he like a king: behold, his eye,
As bright as is the eagle's, lightens forth
Controlling majesty: — alack, alack, for woe,
That any harm should stain so fair a show!

KING RICHARD [*to* NORTHUMBERLAND].
We are amaz'd; and thus long have we stood
To watch the fearful bending of thy knee,
Because we thought ourself thy lawful king:
And if we be, how dare thy joints forget
To pay their awful duty to our presence?
If we be not, show us the hand of God
That hath dismiss'd us from our stewardship;
For well we know, no hand of blood and bone
Can gripe the sacred handle of our sceptre,
Unless he do profane, steal, or usurp.
And though you think that all, as you have done,
Have torn their souls by turning them from us,
And we are barren and bereft of friends;
Yet know, — my master, God omnipotent,
Is mustering in his clouds, on our behalf,
Armies of pestilence; and they shall strike
Your children yet unborn and unbegot,

That lift your vassal hands against my head,
And threat the glory of my precious crown.
Tell Bolingbroke, — for yond methinks he stands, —
That every stride he makes upon my land
Is dangerous treason: he is come to ope
The purple testament of bleeding war;
But ere the crown he looks for live in peace,
Ten thousand bloody crowns of mothers' sons
Shall ill become the flower of England's face,
Change the complexion of her maid-pale peace
To scarlet indignation, and bedew
Her pastures' grass with faithful English blood.

NORTHUMBERLAND
The king of heaven forbid our lord the king
Should so with civil and uncivil arms
Be rush'd upon! Thy thrice-noble cousin
Harry Bolingbroke doth humbly kiss thy hand;
And by the honourable tomb he swears
That stands upon your royal grandsire's bones,
And by the royalties of both your bloods, —
Currents that spring from one most gracious head, —
And by the buried hand of warlike Gaunt,
And by the worth and honour of himself,
Comprising all that may be sworn or said, —
His coming hither hath no further scope
Than for his lineal royalties, and to beg
Enfranchisement immediate on his knees:
Which on thy royal party granted once,
His glittering arms he will commend to rust,
His barbed steeds to stables, and his heart
To faithful service of your majesty.
This swears he, as he is a prince, is just;
And, as I am a gentleman, I credit him.

KING RICHARD
Northumberland, say thus the king returns: —
His noble cousin is right welcome hither;
And all the number of his fair demands
Shall be accomplish'd without contradiction:
With all the gracious utterance thou hast
Speak to his gentle hearing kind commends. —
[*to* AUMERLE] We do debase ourself, cousin, do we
    not,
To look so poorly, and to speak so fair?
Shall we call back Northumberland, and send
Defiance to the traitor, and so die?

AUMERLE
No, good my lord; let's fight with gentle words
Till time lend friends, and friends their helpful
    swords.

KING RICHARD
O God, O God! that e'er this tongue of mine,
That laid the sentence of dread banishment
On yond proud man, should take it off again
With words of sooth! O, that I were as great
As is my grief, or lesser than my name!
Or that I could forget what I have been!
Or not remember what I must be now!
Swell'st thou, proud heart? I'll give thee scope to beat,
Since foes have scope to beat both thee and me.

AUMERLE
Northumberland comes back from Bolingbroke.

KING RICHARD
What must the king do now? must he submit?
The king shall do it: must he be deposed?
The king shall be contented: must he lose
The name of king? o' God's name, let it go:
I'll give my jewels for a set of beads,
My gorgeous palace for a hermitage,
My gay apparel for an almsman's gown,
My figured goblets for a dish of wood,
My sceptre for a palmer's walking-staff,
My subjects for a pair of carved saints,
And my large kingdom for a little grave,
A little little grave, an obscure grave; —
Or I'll be buried in the king's highway,
Some way of common trade, where subjects' feet
May hourly trample on their sovereign's head;
For on my heart they tread now whilst I live;
And buried once, why not upon my head? —
Aumerle, thou weep'st, — my tender-hearted
    cousin! —
We'll make foul weather with despised tears;
Our sighs and they shall lodge the summer corn,
And make a dearth in this revolting land.
Or shall we play the wantons with our woes,
And make some pretty match with shedding tears?
As thus; — to drop them still upon one place,
Till they have fretted us a pair of graves
Within the earth; and, therein laid, — 'There lies
Two kinsmen digg'd their graves with weeping
    eyes.'

Would not this ill do well? — Well, well, I see
I talk but idly, and you laugh at me. —
Most mighty prince, my Lord Northumberland,
What says King Bolingbroke? will his majesty
Give Richard leave to live till Richard die?
You make a leg, and Bolingbroke says ay.

NORTHUMBERLAND
My lord, in the base court he doth attend
To speak with you; — may it please you to come down.

KING RICHARD
Down, down I come; like glistering Phaëton,
Wanting the manage of unruly jades.
In the base court? Base court, where kings grow base,
To come at traitors' calls, and do them grace.
In the base court? Come down? Down, court! down,
    king!
For night-owls shriek where mounting larks should
    sing.   [Exeunt above.

BOLINGBROKE
What says his majesty?

NORTHUMBERLAND
                    Sorrow and grief of heart
Makes him speak fondly, like a frantic man:
Yet he is come.

        Enter KING RICHARD attended, below.

BOLINGBROKE
Stand all apart,
And show fair duty to his majesty. —
My gracious lord, —   [Kneeling.

KING RICHARD
Fair cousin, you debase your princely knee
To make the base earth proud with kissing it:
Me rather had my heart might feel your love
Than my unpleas'd eye see your courtesy.
Up, cousin, up; — your heart is up, I know.
Thus high at least [touching his own head], although
    your knee be low.

BOLINGBROKE
My gracious lord, I come but for mine own.

KING RICHARD
Your own is yours, and I am yours, and all.

BOLINGBROKE
So far be mine, my most redoubted lord,
As my true service shall deserve your love.

KING RICHARD
Well you deserve: — they well deserve to have,
That know the strong'st and surest way to get. —
Uncle, give me your hands: nay, dry your eyes;
Tears show their love, but want their remedies. —
Cousin, I am too young to be your father,
Though you are old enough to be my heir.
What you will have, I'll give, and willing too;
For do we must what force will have us do. —
Set on towards London: — cousin, is it so?

BOLINGBROKE
Yea, my good lord.

KING RICHARD
                    Then I must not say no.
                        [Flourish. Exeunt.

SCENE IV

Langley. The DUKE OF YORK'S garden.

Enter the QUEEN and two LADIES.

QUEEN
What sport shall we devise here in this garden,
To drive away the heavy thought of care?

FIRST LADY
Madam, we'll play at bowls.

QUEEN
'Twill make me think the world is full of rubs,
And that my fortune runs against the bias.

FIRST LADY
Madam, we'll dance.

QUEEN
My legs can keep no measure in delight,
When my poor heart no measure keeps in grief:
Therefore, no dancing, girl; some other sport.

FIRST LADY
Madam, we'll tell tales.

QUEEN
Of sorrow or of joy?

FIRST LADY
                Of either, madam.

QUEEN
Of neither, girl:
For if of joy, being altogether wanting,
It doth remember me the more of sorrow;
Or if of grief, being altogether had,

It adds more sorrow to my want of joy:
For what I have, I need not to repeat;
And what I want, it boots not to complain.

FIRST LADY
Madam, I'll sing.

QUEEN
                'Tis well that thou hast cause;
But thou shouldst please me better, wouldst thou
    weep.

FIRST LADY
I could weep, madam, would it do you good.

QUEEN
And I could weep, would weeping do me good,
And never borrow any tear of thee. —
But stay, here come the gardeners:
Let's step into the shadow of these trees.
My wretchedness unto a row of pins,
They'll talk of state; for every one doth so
Against a change; woe is forerun with woe.
                [QUEEN and LADIES retire.
        Enter a GARDENER and two SERVANTS.

GARDENER
Go, bind thou up yon dangling apricocks,
Which, like unruly children, make their sire
Stoop with oppression of their prodigal weight:
Give some supportance to the bending twigs. —
Go thou, and, like an executioner,
Cut off the heads of too-fast-growing sprays,
That look too lofty in our commonwealth:
All must be even in our government. —
You thus employ'd, I will go root away
The noisome weeds, that without profit suck
The soil's fertility from wholesome flowers.

FIRST SERVANT
Why should we, in the compass of a pale,
Keep law and form and due proportion,
Showing, as in a model, our firm estate,
When our sea-walled garden, the whole land,
Is full of weeds; her fairest flowers chok'd up,
Her fruit-trees all unprun'd, her hedges ruin'd,
Her knots disorder'd, and her wholesome herbs
Swarming with caterpillars?

GARDENER
                        Hold thy peace: —
He that hath suffer'd this disorder'd spring
Hath now himself met with the fall of leaf:
The weeds which his broad-spreading leaves did
    shelter,
That seem'd in eating him to hold him up,
Are pluck'd up root and all by Bolingbroke, —
I mean the Earl of Wiltshire, Bushy, Green.

FIRST SERVANT
What, are they dead?

GARDENER
                They are; and Bolingbroke
Hath seiz'd the wasteful king. — O, what pity is it
That he had not so trimm'd and dress'd his land
As we this garden! We at time of year
Do wound the bark, the skin of our fruit-trees,
Lest, being over-proud in sap and blood,
With too much riches it confound itself:
Had he done so to great and growing men,
They might have liv'd to bear, and he to taste,
Their fruits of duty. All superfluous branches
We lop away, that bearing boughs may live:
Had he done so, himself had borne the crown,
Which waste of idle hours hath quite thrown down.

FIRST SERVANT
What, think you, then, the king shall be depos'd?

GARDENER
Depress'd he is already; and depos'd
'Tis doubt he will be: letters came last night
To a dear friend of the good Duke of York's,
That tell black tidings.

QUEEN
O, I am press'd to death through want of speaking! —
                [Comes forward with LADIES.
Thou, old Adam's likeness, set to dress this garden,
How dares thy harsh rude tongue sound this
    unpleasing news?
What Eve, what serpent, hath suggested thee
To make a second fall of cursed man?
Why dost thou say King Richard is depos'd?
Darest thou, thou little better thing than earth,
Divine his downfall? Say, where, when, and how,
Camest thou by this ill tidings? speak, thou wretch.

GARDENER
Pardon me, madam: little joy have I
To breathe this news: yet what I say is true.
King Richard, he is in the mighty hold

Of Bolingbroke: their fortunes both are weigh'd:
In your lord's scale is nothing but himself,
And some few vanities that make him light;
But in the balance of great Bolingbroke,
Besides himself, are all the English peers,
And with that odds he weighs King Richard down.
Post you to London, and you will find it so;
I speak no more than every man doth know.

QUEEN
Nimble mischance, that art so light of foot,
Doth not thy embassage belong to me,
And am I last that knows it? O, thou think'st
To serve me last, that I may longest keep
Thy sorrow in my breast. — Come, ladies, go,
To meet at London London's king in woe. —
What, was I born to this, that my sad look
Should grace the triumph of great Bolingbroke?
Gardener, for telling me this news of woe,
Pray God the plants thou graft'st may never grow.
                [Exeunt QUEEN and LADIES.

GARDENER
Poor queen! so that thy state might be no worse,
I would my skill were subject to thy curse. —
Here did she fall a tear; here, in this place,
I'll set a bank of rue, sour herb of grace:
Rue, even for ruth, here shortly shall be seen,
In the remembrance of a weeping queen.   [Exeunt.

ACT IV

SCENE I

Westminster Hall.

Enter as to the Parliament BOLINGBROKE,
AUMERLE, NORTHUMBERLAND, PERCY,
FITZWATER, SURREY, another LORD, the BISHOP
OF CARLISLE, the ABBOT OF WESTMINSTER, and
ATTENDANTS. HERALD, OFFICERS, and BAGOT.

BOLINGBROKE
Call forth Bagot.
Now, Bagot, freely speak thy mind;
What dost thou know of noble Gloster's death;
Who wrought it with the king, and who perform'd
The bloody office of his timeless end.

BAGOT
Then set before my face the Lord Aumerle.

BOLINGBROKE
Cousin, stand forth, and look upon that man.

BAGOT
My Lord Aumerle, I know your daring tongue
Scorns to unsay what once it hath deliver'd.
In that dead time when Gloster's death was plotted,
I heard you say, — 'Is not my arm of length,
That reacheth from the restful English court
As far as Calais, to my uncle's head?'
Amongst much other talk, that very time,
I heard you say that you had rather refuse
The offer of an hundred thousand crowns
Than Bolingbroke's return to England;
Adding withal, how blest this land would be
In this your cousin's death.

AUMERLE
                    Princes, and noble lords,
What answer shall I make to this base man?
Shall I so much dishonour my fair stars,
On equal terms to give him chastisement?
Either I must, or have mine honour soil'd
With the attainder of his slanderous lips. —
There is my gage, the manual seal of death,
That marks thee out for hell! I say, thou liest,
And will maintain what thou hast said is false
In thy heart-blood, though being all too base
To stain the temper of my knightly sword.

BOLINGBROKE
Bagot, forbear; thou shalt not take it up.

AUMERLE
Excepting one, I would he were the best
In all this presence that hath mov'd me so.

FITZWATER
If that thy valour stand on sympathy,
There is my gage, Aumerle, in gage to thine:
By that fair sun which shows me where thou stand'st,
I heard thee say, and vauntingly thou spakest it,
That thou wert cause of noble Gloster's death.
If thou deny'st it twenty times, thou liest;
And I will turn thy falsehood to thy heart,
Where it was forged, with my rapier's point.

AUMERLE
Thou darest not, coward, live to see that day.

KING RICHARD Up, cousin, up; — your heart is up, I know, thus high at least.

FITZWATER
Now, by my soul, I would it were this hour.

AUMERLE
Fitzwater, thou art damn'd to hell for this.

PERCY
Aumerle, thou liest; his honour is as true
In this appeal as thou art all unjust;
And that thou art so, there I throw my gage,
To prove it on thee to th'extremest point
Of mortal breathing: seize it, if thou darest.

AUMERLE
And if I do not, may my hands rot off,
And never brandish more revengeful steel
Over the glittering helmet of my foe!

ANOTHER LORD
I task the earth to the like, forsworn Aumerle;
And spur thee on with full as many lies
As may be holla'd in thy treacherous ear
From sun to sun: there is my honour's pawn;
Engage it to the trial, if thou darest.

AUMERLE
Who sets me else? by heaven, I'll throw at all:
I have a thousand spirits in one breast,
To answer twenty thousand such as you.

SURREY
My Lord Fitzwater, I do remember well
The very time Aumerle and you did talk.

FITZWATER
'Tis very true: you were in presence then;
And you can witness with me this is true.

SURREY
As false, by heaven, as heaven itself is true.

FITZWATER
Surrey, thou liest.

SURREY
                    Dishonourable boy!
That lie shall lie so heavy on my sword,
That it shall render vengeance and revenge
Till thou the lie-giver and that lie do lie
In earth as quiet as thy father's skull:
In proof whereof, there is my honour's pawn;
Engage it to the trial, if thou darest.

FITZWATER
How fondly dost thou spur a forward horse!
If I dare eat, or drink, or breathe, or live,
I dare meet Surrey in a wilderness,
And spit upon him, whilst I say he lies,
And lies, and lies: there is my bond of faith,
To tie thee to my strong correction. —
As I intend to thrive in this new world,
Aumerle is guilty of my true appeal:
Besides, I heard the banish'd Norfolk say
That thou, Aumerle, didst send two of thy men
To execute the noble duke at Calais.

AUMERLE
Some honest Christian trust me with a gage,
That Norfolk lies: here do I throw down this,

If he may be repeal'd, to try his honour.

BOLINGBROKE
These differences shall all rest under gage
Till Norfolk be repeal'd: repeal'd he shall be,
And, though mine enemy, restored again
To all his lands and signories: when he's return'd,
Against Aumerle we will enforce his trial.

BISHOP OF CARLISLE
That honourable day shall ne'er be seen.
Many a time hath banish'd Norfolk fought
For Jesu Christ in glorious Christian field,
Streaming the ensign of the Christian cross
Against black pagans, Turks, and Saracens;
And toil'd with works of war, retired himself
To Italy; and there, at Venice, gave
His body to that pleasant country's earth,
And his pure soul unto his captain Christ,
Under whose colours he had fought so long.

BOLINGBROKE
Why, bishop, is Norfolk dead?

BISHOP OF CARLISLE
As surely as I live, my lord.

BOLINGBROKE
Sweet peace conduct his sweet soul to the bosom
Of good old Abraham! — Lords appellants,
Your differences shall all rest under gage
Till we assign you to your days of trial.

Enter YORK, attended.

YORK
Great Duke of Lancaster, I come to thee
From plume-pluck'd Richard; who with willing soul

Adopts thee heir, and his high sceptre yields
To the possession of thy royal hand:
Ascend his throne, descending now from him, —
And long live Henry, fourth of that name!

BOLINGBROKE
In God's name, I'll ascend the regal throne.

BISHOP OF CARLISLE
Marry. God forbid! —
Worst in this royal presence may I speak,
Yet best beseeming me to speak the truth.
Would God that any in this noble presence
Were enough noble to be upright judge
Of noble Richard! then true noblesse would
Learn him forbearance from so foul a wrong.
What subject can give sentence on his king?
And who sits here that is not Richard's subject?
Thieves are not judg'd but they are by to hear,
Although apparent guilt be seen in them;
And shall the figure of God's majesty,
His captain, steward, deputy elect,
Anointed, crowned, planted many years,
Be judg'd by subject and inferior breath,
And he himself not present? O, forfend it, God,
That in a Christian climate, souls refined
Should show so heinous, black, obscene a deed!
I speak to subjects, and a subject speaks,
Stirr'd up by God, thus boldly for his king.
My Lord of Hereford here, whom you call king,
Is a foul traitor to proud Hereford's king;
And if you crown him, let me prophesy, —
The blood of English shall manure the ground,
And future ages groan for this foul act;
Peace shall go sleep with Turks and infidels,
And in this seat of peace tumultuous wars
Shall kin with kin and kind with kind confound;
Disorder, horror, fear, and mutiny,
Shall here inhabit, and this land be call'd
The field of Golgotha and dead men's skulls.
O, if you raise this house against this house,
It will the woefullest division prove
That ever fell upon this cursed earth.
Prevent, resist it, let it not be so,
Lest child, child's children cry against you 'woe!'

NORTHUMBERLAND
Well have you argued, sir; and, for your pains,
Of capital treason we arrest you here. —
My Lord of Westminster, be it your charge
To keep him safely till his day of trial. —
May it please you, lords, to grant the commons' suit.

BOLINGBROKE
Fetch hither Richard, that in common view
He may surrender; so we shall proceed
Without suspicion.

YORK
                    I will be his conduct.   [*Exit.*

BOLINGBROKE
Lords, you that here are under our arrest,
Procure your sureties for your days of answer. —
Little are we beholding to your love,   [*To* CARLISLE.
And little look'd for at your helping hands.

Enter YORK, with KING RICHARD, *and* OFFICERS
bearing the crown, etc.

KING RICHARD
Alack, why am I sent for to a king,

FIRST SERVANT What, think you, then, the king shall be depos'd?

Before I have shook off the regal thoughts
Wherewith I reign'd? I hardly yet have learn'd
To insinuate, flatter, bow, and bend my knee:
Give sorrow leave awhile to tutor me
To this submission. Yet I well remember
The favours of these men: were they not mine?
Did they not sometime cry, 'All hail!' to me?
So Judas did to Christ: but he, in twelve,
Found truth in all but one; I, in twelve thousand, none.
God save the king! — Will no man say amen?
Am I both priest and clerk? well then, amen.
God save the king! although I be not he;
And yet, amen, if heaven do think him me. —
To do what service am I sent for hither?

YORK
To do that office of thine own good will
Which tired majesty did make thee offer, —
The resignation of thy state and crown
To Henry Bolingbroke.

KING RICHARD
Give me the crown. — Here, cousin, seize the crown;
Here, cousin:
On this side my hand, and on that side yours.
Now is this golden crown like a deep well
That owes two buckets, filling one another;
The emptier ever dancing in the air,
The other down, unseen, and full of water:
That bucket down and full of tears am I,
Drinking my griefs, whilst you mount up on high.

BOLINGBROKE
I thought you had been willing to resign.

KING RICHARD
My crown I am; but still my griefs are mine:
You may my glories and my state depose,
But not my griefs; still am I king of those.

BOLINGBROKE
Part of your cares you give me with your crown.

KING RICHARD
Your cares set up do not pluck my cares down.
My care is, loss of care, by old care done;
Your care is, gain of care, by new care won:
The cares I give, I have, though given away;
They tend the crown, yet still with me they stay.

BOLINGBROKE
Are you contented to resign the crown?

KING RICHARD
Ay, no; — no, ay; for I must nothing be;
Therefore no no, for I resign to thee.
Now mark me, how I will undo myself: —
I give this heavy weight from off my head,
And this unwieldy sceptre from my hand,
The pride of kingly sway from out my heart;
With mine own tears I wash away my balm,
With mine own hands I give away my crown,
With mine own tongue deny my sacred state,
With mine own breath release all duty's rites:
All pomp and majesty I do forswear;
My manors, rents, revenues I forgo;
My acts, decrees, and statutes I deny:
God pardon all oaths that are broke to me!
God keep all vows unbroke that swear to thee!
Make me, that nothing have, with nothing grieved,
And thou with all pleas'd, that hast all achieved!
Long mayst thou live in Richard's seat to sit,
And soon lie Richard in an earthy pit!
God save King Henry, unking'd Richard says,
And send him many years of sunshine days! —
What more remains?

NORTHUMBERLAND
                              No more, but that you read
                              [*Offering a paper.*
These accusations, and these grievous crimes
Committed by your person and your followers
Against the state and profit of this land;
That, by confessing them, the souls of men
May deem that you are worthily depos'd.

KING RICHARD
Must I do so? and must I ravel out
My weav'd-up follies? Gentle Northumberland,
If thy offences were upon record,
Would it not shame thee in so fair a troop
To read a lecture of them? If thou wouldst,
There shouldst thou find one heinous article, —
Containing the deposing of a king,
And cracking the strong warrant of an oath, —
Mark'd with a blot, damn'd in the book of heaven: —
Nay, all of you that stand and look upon,
Whilst that my wretchedness doth bait myself, —
Though some of you, with Pilate, wash your hands,
Showing an outward pity; yet you Pilates
Have here deliver'd me to my sour cross,

BOLINGBROKE Cousin, stand forth, and look upon that man.

And water cannot wash away your sin.

NORTHUMBERLAND
My lord, dispatch; read o'er these articles.

KING RICHARD
Mine eyes are full of tears, I cannot see:
And yet salt water blinds them not so much
But they can see a sort of traitors here.
Nay, if I turn mine eyes upon myself,
I find myself a traitor with the rest;
For I have given here my soul's consent
T'undeck the pompous body of a king;
Made glory base, and sovereignty a slave,
Proud majesty a subject, state a peasant.

NORTHUMBERLAND
My lord, —

KING RICHARD
No lord of thine, thou haught-insulting man,
Nor no man's lord; I have no name, no title, —
No, not that name was given me at the font, —
But 'tis usurp'd: — alack the heavy day,
That I have worn so many winters out,
And know not now what name to call myself!
O, that I were a mockery-king of snow,
Standing before the sun of Bolingbroke,
To melt myself away in water-drops! —
Good king, — great king, — and yet not greatly good, —
An if my word be sterling yet in England,
Let it command a mirror hither straight,
That it may show me what a face I have,
Since it is bankrupt of his majesty.

BOLINGBROKE
Go, some of you, and fetch a looking-glass.
                              [*Exit an* ATTENDANT.

NORTHUMBERLAND
Read o'er this paper while the glass doth come.

KING RICHARD
Fiend, thou torment'st me ere I come to hell!

BOLINGBROKE
Urge it no more, my Lord Northumberland.

NORTHUMBERLAND
The commons will not, then, be satisfied.

KING RICHARD
They shall be satisfied: I'll read enough,
When I do see the very book indeed
Where all my sins are writ, and that's myself.

Enter ATTENDANT *with a glass.*

Give me the glass, and therein will I read. —
No deeper wrinkles yet? hath sorrow struck
So many blows upon this face of mine,
And made no deeper wounds! — O flattering glass,
Like to my followers in prosperity,
Thou dost beguile me! Was this face the face
That every day under his household roof
Did keep ten thousand men? was this the face
That, like the sun, did make beholders wink?
Was this the face that fac'd so many follies,
And was at last out-fac'd by Bolingbroke?
A brittle glory shineth in this face:
As brittle as the glory is the face;
                              [*Dashes the glass against the ground.*
For there it is, crack'd in a hundred shivers. —
Mark, silent king, the moral of this sport, —
How soon my sorrow hath destroy'd my face.

BOLINGBROKE
The shadow of your sorrow hath destroy'd
The shadow or your face.

KING RICHARD
                              Say that again.
The shadow of my sorrow? ha! let's see: —
'Tis very true, my grief lies all within;
And these external manners of lament
Are merely shadows to the unseen grief
That swells with silence in the tortured soul;
There lies the substance: and I thank thee, king,
For thy great bounty, that not only givest
Me cause to wail, but teachest me the way
How to lament the cause. I'll beg one boon,
And then be gone and trouble you no more.
Shall I obtain it?

BOLINGBROKE
                              Name it, fair cousin.

KING RICHARD
Fair cousin! I am greater than a king:
For when I was a king, my flatterers
Were then but subjects; being now a subject,
I have a king here to my flatterer.
Being so great, I have no need to beg.

BOLINGBROKE
Yet ask.

KING RICHARD
And shall I have?

BOLINGBROKE
You shall.

KING RICHARD
Then give me leave to go.

BOLINGBROKE
Whither?

KING RICHARD
Whither you will, so I were from your sights.

BOLINGBROKE
Go, some of you convey him to the Tower.

KING RICHARD
O, good! convey? — conveyers are you all,
That rise thus nimbly by a true king's fall.
                              [*Exeunt* KING RICHARD, *some* LORDS, *and a*
                              GUARD.

BOLINGBROKE
On Wednesday next we solemnly set down
Our coronation: lords, prepare yourselves.
                              [*Exeunt all except the* BISHOP OF CARLISLE, *the*
                              ABBOT OF WESTMINSTER, *and* AUMERLE.

ABBOT OF WESTMINSTER
A woeful pageant have we here beheld.

BISHOP OF CARLISLE
The woe's to come; the children yet unborn
Shall feel this day as sharp to them as thorn.

AUMERLE
You holy clergymen, is there no plot
To rid the realm of this pernicious blot?

ABBOT OF WESTMINSTER
My lord,
Before I freely speak my mind herein,
You shall not only take the sacrament
To bury mine intents, but also to effect
Whatever I shall happen to devise. —
I see your brows are full of discontent,
Your hearts of sorrow, and your eyes of tears:

Come home with me to supper: I will lay
A plot shall show us all a merry day.   [*Exeunt.*

ACT V

SCENE I

London. A street leading to the Tower.

Enter QUEEN *and* LADIES.

QUEEN
This way the king will come; this is the way
To Julius Cæsar's ill-erected tower,
To whose flint bosom my condemned lord
Is doom'd a prisoner by proud Bolingbroke:
Here let us rest, if this rebellious earth
Have any resting for her true king's queen. —
But soft, but see, or rather do not see,
My fair rose wither: yet look up, behold,
That you in pity may dissolve to dew,
And wash him fresh again with true-love tears.

Enter KING RICHARD *and* GUARDS.

Ah, thou, the model where old Troy did stand,
Thou map of honour, thou King Richard's tomb,
And not King Richard; thou most beauteous inn,
Why should hard-favour'd grief be lodg'd in thee,
When triumph is become an alehouse guest?

KING RICHARD
Join not with grief, fair woman, do not so,
To make my end too sudden: learn, good soul,
To think our former state a happy dream;
From which awak'd, the truth of what we are
Shows us but this: I am sworn brother, sweet,
To grim Necessity; and he and I
Will keep a league till death. Hie thee to France,
And cloister thee in some religious house:
Our holy lives must win a new world's crown,
Which our profane hours here have stricken down.

QUEEN
What, is my Richard both in shape and mind
Transform'd and weaken'd? hath Bolingbroke depos'd
Thine intellect? hath he been in thy heart?
The lion dying thrusteth forth his paw,
And wounds the earth, if nothing else, with rage
To be o'erpower'd; and wilt thou, pupil-like,
Take thy correction mildly, kiss the rod,
And fawn on rage with base humility,
Which art a lion and a king of beasts?

KING RICHARD
A king of beasts, indeed; if aught but beasts,
I had been still a happy king of men.
Good sometime queen, prepare thee hence for France:
Think I am dead; and that even here thou takest,
As from my death-bed, thy last living leave.
In winter's tedious nights sit by the fire
With good old folks, and let them tell thee tales
Of woeful ages long ago betid:
And ere thou bid good night, to quit their griefs
Tell thou the lamentable tale of me,
And send the hearers weeping to their beds:
For why the senseless brands will sympathise
The heavy accent of thy moving tongue,
And in compassion weep the fire out;
And some will mourn in ashes, some coal-black,
For the deposing of a rightful king.

Enter NORTHUMBERLAND, *attended.*

NORTHUMBERLAND
My lord, the mind of Bolingbroke is changed;
You must to Pomfret, not unto the Tower. —
And, madam, there is order ta'en for you;
With all swift speed you must away to France.

KING RICHARD
Northumberland, thou ladder wherewithal
The mounting Bolingbroke ascends my throne,
The time shall not be many hours of age
More than it is, ere foul sin gathering head
Shall break into corruption: thou shalt think,
Though he divide the realm, and give thee half,
It is too little, helping him to all;
And he shall think, that thou, which know'st the way
To plant unrightful kings, wilt know again,
Being ne'er so little urged, another way
To pluck him headlong from th'usurped throne.
The love of wicked friends converts to fear;
That fear to hate; and hate turns one or both
To worthy danger and deserved death.

NORTHUMBERLAND
My guilt be on my head, and there an end.
Take leave, and part; for you must part forthwith.

KING RICHARD
Doubly divorc'd! — Bad men, you violate
A twofold marriage, — 'twixt my crown and me,
And then betwixt me and my married wife. —
Let me unkiss the oath 'twixt thee and me;
And yet not so, for with a kiss 'twas made. —
Part us, Northumberland; I towards the north,
Where shivering cold and sickness pines the clime;
My wife to France, — from whence, set forth in pomp,
She came adorned hither like sweet May,
Sent back to Hallowmas or short'st of day.

QUEEN
And must we be divided? must we part?

KING RICHARD
Ay, hand from hand, my love, and heart from heart.

QUEEN
Banish us both, and send the king with me.

NORTHUMBERLAND
That were some love, but little policy.

QUEEN
Then whither he goes, thither let me go.

KING RICHARD
So two, together weeping, make one woe.
Weep thou for me in France, I for thee here;
Better far off than near, be ne'er the near.
Go, count thy way with sighs; I, mine with groans.

QUEEN
So longest way shall have the longest moans.

KING RICHARD
Twice for one step I'll groan, the way being short,
And piece the way out with a heavy heart.
Come, come, in wooing sorrow let's be brief,
Since, wedding it, there is such length in grief:
One kiss shall stop our mouths, and dumbly part;
Thus give I mine, and thus take I thy heart.   [*They kiss.*

QUEEN
Give me mine own again; 'twere no good part
To take on me to keep and kill thy heart.
          [*They kiss again.*
So, now I have mine own again, be gone,
That I may strive to kill it with a groan.

KING RICHARD
We make woe wanton with this fond delay:
Once more, adieu; the rest let sorrow say.   [*Exeunt.*

SCENE II

The DUKE OF YORK'S *palace.*

Enter YORK *and his* DUCHESS.

DUCHESS OF YORK
My lord, you told me you would tell the rest,
When weeping made you break the story off
Of our two cousins coming into London.

YORK
Where did I leave?

DUCHESS OF YORK
          At that sad stop, my lord,
Where rude misgovern'd hands from windows' tops
Threw dust and rubbish on King Richard's head.

YORK
Then, as I said, the duke, great Bolingbroke, —
Mounted upon a hot and fiery steed,
Which his aspiring rider seem'd to know, —
With slow but stately pace kept on his course,
While all tongues cried, 'God save thee, Bolingbroke!'
You would have thought the very windows spake,
So many greedy looks of young and old
Through casements darted their desiring eyes
Upon his visage; and that all the walls
With painted imagery had said at once,
'Jesu preserve thee! welcome, Bolingbroke!'
Whilst he, from the one side to the other turning,
Bareheaded, lower than his proud steed's neck,
Bespake them thus, — 'I thank you, countrymen':
And thus still doing, thus he pass'd along.

DUCHESS OF YORK
Alack, poor Richard! where rode he the whilst?

YORK
As in a theatre, the eyes of men,
After a well-grac'd actor leaves the stage,
Are idly bent on him that enters next,
Thinking his prattle to be tedious;
Even so, or with much more contempt, men's eyes
Did scowl on gentle Richard; no man cried, 'God save
          him!'
No joyful tongue gave him his welcome home:
But dust was thrown upon his sacred head;
Which with such gentle sorrow he shook off, —
His face still combating with tears and smiles,
The badges of his grief and patience, —

That had not God, for some strong purpose, steel'd
The hearts of men, they must perforce have melted,
And barbarism itself have pitied him.
But heaven hath a hand in these events,
To whose high will we bound our calm contents.
To Bolingbroke are we sworn subjects now,
Whose state and honour I for aye allow.

DUCHESS OF YORK
Here comes my son Aumerle.

YORK
          Aumerle that was;
But that is lost for being Richard's friend,
And, madam, you must call him Rutland now:
I am in parliament pledge for his truth
And lasting fealty to the new-made king.

Enter AUMERLE.

DUCHESS OF YORK
Welcome, my son: who are the violets now
That strew the green lap of the new-come spring?

AUMERLE
Madam, I know not, nor I greatly care not:
God knows I had as lief be none as one.

YORK
Well, bear you well in this new spring of time,
Lest you be cropp'd before you come to prime.
What news from Oxford? — hold those justs and
          triumphs?

AUMERLE
For aught I know, my lord, they do.

YORK
You will be there, I know.

AUMERLE
If God prevent not, I do purpose so.

YORK
What seal is that that hangs without thy bosom?
Yea, look'st thou pale? let me see the writing.

AUMERLE
My lord, 'tis nothing.

YORK
          No matter, then, who see it:
I will be satisfied; let me see the writing.

AUMERLE
I do beseech your Grace to pardon me:
It is a matter of small consequence,
Which for some reasons I would not have seen.

YORK
Which for some reasons, sir, I mean to see.
I fear, I fear, —

DUCHESS OF YORK
          What should you fear?
'Tis nothing but some band that he is enter'd into
For gay apparel 'gainst the triumph-day.

YORK
Bound to himself! what doth he with a bond
That he is bound to? Wife, thou art a fool. —
Boy, let me see the writing.

AUMERLE
I do beseech you, pardon me; I may not show it.

YORK
I will be satisfied: let me see't, I say.
          [*He plucks it out of his bosom and reads it.*
Treason! foul treason! — Villain! traitor! slave!

DUCHESS OF YORK
What is the matter, my lord?

YORK
Ho! who is within there? ho!
          Enter a SERVANT.
          Saddle my horse. —
God for his mercy, what treachery is here!

DUCHESS OF YORK
Why, what is it, my lord?

YORK
Give me my boots, I say; saddle my horse. —
          [*Exit* SERVANT.
Now, by mine honour, by my life, by my troth,
I will appeach the villain.

DUCHESS OF YORK
          What is the matter?

YORK
Peace, foolish woman.

DUCHESS OF YORK
I will not peace. — What is the matter, Aumerle?

AUMERLE
Good mother, be content; it is no more
Than my poor life must answer.

DUCHESS OF YORK
          Thy life answer!

YORK
Bring me my boots: — I will unto the king.
His MAN *enters with his boots.*

DUCHESS OF YORK
Strike him, Aumerle. — Poor boy, thou art amazed. —
Hence, villain! never more come in my sight.

YORK
Give me my boots, I say.

DUCHESS OF YORK
Why, York, what wilt thou do?
Wilt thou not hide the trespass of thine own?
Have we more sons? or are we like to have?
Is not my teeming date drunk up with time?
And wilt thou pluck my fair son from mine age,
And rob me of a happy mother's name?
Is he not like thee? is he not thine own?

YORK
Thou fond mad woman,
Wilt thou conceal this dark conspiracy?
A dozen of them here have ta'en the sacrament,
And interchangeably set down their hands,
To kill the king at Oxford.

DUCHESS OF YORK
He shall be none;
We'll keep him here: then what is that to him?

YORK
Away, fond woman! were he twenty times my son,
I would appeach him.

DUCHESS OF YORK
Hadst thou groan'd for him
As I have done, thou wouldst be more pitiful.
But now I know thy mind; thou dost suspect
That I have been disloyal to thy bed,
And that he is a bastard, not thy son:
Sweet York, sweet husband, be not of that mind:
He is as like thee as a man may be,
Not like to me, nor any of my kin,
And yet I love him.

YORK
Make way, unruly woman! [*Exit.*

DUCHESS OF YORK
After, Aumerle, mount thee upon his horse;
Spur post, and get before him to the king,
And beg thy pardon ere he do accuse thee.
I'll not be long behind; though I be old,
I doubt not but to ride as fast as York;
And never will I rise up from the ground
Till Bolingbroke have pardon'd thee. Away, be gone!
[*Exeunt.*

SCENE III
Windsor Castle.

Enter BOLINGBROKE, PERCY, *and other* LORDS.

BOLINGBROKE
Can no man tell me of my unthrifty son?
'Tis full three months since I did see him last: —
If any plague hang over us, 'tis he.
I would to God, my lords, he might be found:
Inquire at London, 'mongst the taverns there,
For there, they say, he daily doth frequent,
With unrestrained loose companions, —
Even such, they say, as stand in narrow lanes,
And beat our watch, and rob our passengers;
Which he, young wanton and effeminate boy,
Takes on the point of honour to support
So dissolute a crew.

PERCY
My lord, some two days since I saw the prince,
And told him of those triumphs held at Oxford.

BOLINGBROKE
And what said the gallant?

PERCY
His answer was, — he would unto the stews,
And from the common'st creature pluck a glove,
And wear it as a favour; and with that
He would unhorse the lustiest challenger.

BOLINGBROKE
As dissolute as desperate; yet through both
I see some sparks of better hope,
Which elder days may happily bring forth. —
But who comes here?

Enter AUMERLE, *hastily.*

AUMERLE
Where is the king?

BOLINGBROKE
What means
Our cousin, that he stares and looks so wildly?

AUMERLE
God save your Grace! I do beseech your majesty,
To have some conference with your Grace alone.

BOLINGBROKE
Withdraw yourselves, and leave us here alone.
[*Exeunt* PERCY *and* LORDS.
What is the matter with our cousin now?

AUMERLE
For ever may my knees grow to the earth, [*Kneels.*
My tongue cleave to my roof within my mouth,
Unless a pardon ere I rise or speak.

BOLINGBROKE
Intended or committed was this fault?
If on the first, how heinous e'er it be,
To win thy after-love I pardon thee.

AUMERLE
Then give me leave that I may turn the key,
That no man enter till my tale be done.

BOLINGBROKE
Have thy desire.

YORK [*within*].
My liege, beware; look to thyself;
Thou hast a traitor in thy presence there.

BOLINGBROKE
Villain, I'll make thee safe. [*Drawing.*

AUMERLE
Stay thy revengeful hand; thou hast no cause to fear.

YORK [*within*].
Open the door, secure, foolhardy king:
Shall I, for love, speak treason to thy face?
Open the door, or I will break it open.

Enter YORK.

BOLINGBROKE
What is the matter, uncle? speak;
Recover breath; tell us how near is danger,
That we may arm us to encounter it.

YORK
Peruse this writing here, and thou shalt know
The treason that my haste forbids me show.

AUMERLE
Remember, as thou read'st, thy promise past:
I do repent me; read not my name there;
My heart is not confederate with my hand.

YORK
It was, villain, ere thy hand did set it down. —
I tore it from the traitor's bosom, king;
Fear, and not love, begets his penitence:
Forget to pity him, lest thy pity prove
A serpent that will sting thee to the heart.

BOLINGBROKE
O heinous, strong, and bold conspiracy! —
O loyal father of a treacherous son!
Thou sheer, immaculate, and silver fountain,
From whence this stream through muddy passages
Hath held his current, and defiled himself!
Thy overflow of good converts to bad;
And thy abundant goodness shall excuse
This deadly blot in thy digressing son.

YORK
So shall my virtue be his vice's bawd;
And he shall spend mine honour with his shame,
As thriftless sons their scraping fathers' gold.
Mine honour lives when his dishonour dies,
Or my sham'd life in his dishonour lies:
Thou kill'st me in his life; giving him breath,
The traitor lives, the true man's put to death.

DUCHESS OF YORK [*within*].
What ho, my liege! for God's sake, let me in.

BOLINGBROKE
What shrill-voic'd suppliant makes this eager cry?

DUCHESS OF YORK [*within*].
A woman, and thy aunt, great king; 'tis I.
Speak with me, pity me, open the door:
A beggar begs that never begg'd before.

BOLINGBROKE
Our scene is alter'd from a serious thing,
And now chang'd to 'The Beggar and the King.' —
My dangerous cousin, let your mother in:
I know she is come to pray for your foul sin.

YORK
If thou do pardon, whosoever pray,
More sins, for this forgiveness, prosper may.
This fester'd joint cut off, the rest rest sound;
This let alone will all the rest confound.

Enter DUCHESS.

DUCHESS OF YORK
O king, believe not this hard-hearted man!
Love, loving not itself, none other can.

YORK
Thou frantic woman, what dost thou make here?
Shall thy old dugs once more a traitor rear?

DUCHESS OF YORK
Sweet York, be patient. — Hear me, gentle liege.
[*Kneels.*

BOLINGBROKE
Rise up, good aunt.

DUCHESS OF YORK
Not yet, I thee beseech:
For ever will I walk upon my knees,
And never see day that the happy sees,
Till thou give joy; until thou bid me joy,
By pardoning Rutland, my transgressing boy.

AUMERLE
Unto my mother's prayers I bend my knee. [*Kneels.*

YORK
Against them both my true joints bended be. [*Kneels.*
Ill mayst thou thrive, if thou grant any grace!

DUCHESS OF YORK
Pleads he in earnest? look upon his face;
His eyes do drop no tears, his prayers are in jest;
His words come from his mouth, ours from our breast:
He prays but faintly, and would be denied;
We pray with heart and soul, and all beside:
His weary joints would gladly rise, I know;
Our knees shall kneel till to the ground they grow:
His prayers are full of false hypocrisy;
Ours of true zeal and deep integrity.
Our prayers do out-pray his; then let them have
That mercy which true prayer ought to have.

BOLINGBROKE
Good aunt, stand up.

DUCHESS OF YORK
Nay, do not say, 'stand up';
But 'pardon' first, and afterwards 'stand up'.
An if I were thy nurse, thy tongue to teach,
'Pardon' should be the first word of thy speech.
I never long'd to hear a word till now;
Say 'pardon' king; let pity teach thee how:
The word is short, but not so short as sweet;
No word like 'pardon' for kings' mouths so meet.

YORK
Speak it in French, king; say, *pardonne moi.*

DUCHESS OF YORK
Dost thou teach pardon pardon to destroy?
Ah, my sour husband, my hard-hearted lord,
That sett'st the word itself against the word! —
Speak 'pardon' as 'tis current in our land;
The chopping French we do not understand.
Thine eye begins to speak, set thy tongue there:
Or in thy piteous heart plant thou thine ear;
That hearing how our plaints and prayers do pierce,
Pity may move thee 'pardon' to rehearse.

BOLINGBROKE
Good aunt, stand up.

DUCHESS OF YORK
I do not sue to stand;
Pardon is all the suit I have in hand.

BOLINGBROKE
I pardon him, as God shall pardon me.

DUCHESS OF YORK
O happy vantage of a kneeling knee!
Yet am I sick for fear: speak it again;
Twice saying 'pardon' doth not pardon twain,
But makes one pardon strong.

BOLINGBROKE
With all my heart
I pardon him.

DUCHESS OF YORK
A god on earth thou art.

BOLINGBROKE
But for our trusty brother-in-law, and the abbot,
With all the rest of that consorted crew,
Destruction straight shall dog them at the heels. —
Good uncle, help to order several powers
To Oxford, or where'er these traitors are:
They shall not live within this world, I swear,
But I will have them, if I once know where.
Uncle, farewell: — and, cousin too, adieu:
Your mother well hath pray'd, and prove you true.

DUCHESS OF YORK
Come, my old son: — I pray God make thee new.
[*Exeunt.*

SCENE IV

The same.

Enter SIR PIERCE OF EXTON *and a* SERVANT.

EXTON
Didst thou not mark the king, what words he spake, —
'Have I no friend will rid me of this living fear?'
Was it not so?

SERVANT
           Those were his very words.

EXTON
'Have I no friend?' quoth he: he spake it twice,
And urg'd it twice together, — did he not?

SERVANT
He did.

EXTON
And speaking it, he wistly look'd on me;
As who should say, — 'I would thou wert the man
That would divorce this terror from my heart,' —
Meaning the king at Pomfret. Come, let's go:
I am the king's friend, and will rid his foe.   [*Exeunt.*

SCENE V

Pomfret Castle.

Enter KING RICHARD.

KING RICHARD
I have been studying how I may compare
This prison where I live unto the world:
And, for because the world is populous,
And here is not a creature but myself,
I cannot do it; — yet I'll hammer it out.
My brain I'll prove the female to my soul,
My soul the father: and these two beget
A generation of still-breeding thoughts,
And these same thoughts people this little world;
In humours like the people of this world,
For no thought is contented. The better sort, —
As thoughts of things divine, — are intermix'd
With scruples, and do set the word itself
Against the word:
As thus, 'Come, little ones'; and then again,
'It is as hard to come as for a camel
To thread the postern of a small needle's eye.'
Thoughts tending to ambition, they do plot
Unlikely wonders; how these vain weak nails
May tear a passage through the flinty ribs
Of this hard world, my ragged prison-walls;
And, for they cannot, die in their own pride.
Thoughts tending to content flatter themselves
That they are not the first of fortune's slaves,
Nor shall not be the last; like silly beggars,
Who, sitting in the stocks, refuge their shame,
That many have and others must sit there;
And in this thought they find a kind of ease,
Bearing their own misfortunes on the back
Of such as have before endured the like.
Thus play I, in one person, many people,
And none contented: sometimes am I king;
Then treason makes me wish myself a beggar,
And so I am: then crushing penury
Persuades me I was better when a king;
Then am I king'd again: and by and by
Think that I am unking'd by Bolingbroke,
And straight am nothing: — but whate'er I be,
Nor I, nor any man that but man is,
With nothing shall be pleas'd, till he be eas'd
With being nothing. — Music do I hear?   [*Music.*
Ha, ha! keep time: — how sour sweet music is,
When time is broke and no proportion kept!
So is it in the music of men's lives.
And here have I the daintiness of ear
To check time broke in a disorder'd string;
But, for the concord of my state and time,
Had not an ear to hear my true time broke.
I wasted time, and now doth time waste me;
For now hath time made me his numbering clock;
My thoughts are minutes; and with sighs they jar
Their watches to mine eyes, the outward watch,
Whereto my finger, like a dial's point,
Is pointing still, in cleansing them from tears:
Now, sir, the sound that tells what hour it is,
Are clamorous groans, which strike upon my heart,
Which is the bell: so sighs and tears and groans
Show minutes, times, and hours: — but my time

Runs posting on in Bolingbroke's proud joy,
While I stand fooling here, his Jack o'th'clock.
This music mads me; let it sound no more;
For though it have holp madmen to their wits,
In me it seems it will make wise men mad.
Yet, blessing on his heart that gives it me!
For 'tis a sign of love; and love to Richard
Is a strange brooch in this all-hating world.

Enter GROOM.

GROOM
Hail, royal prince!

KING RICHARD
           Thanks, noble peer;
The cheapest of us is ten groats too dear.
What art thou? and how comest thou hither,
Where no man never comes, but that sad dog
That brings me food to make misfortune live?

GROOM
I was a poor groom of thy stable, king,
When thou wert king; who, travelling towards York,
With much ado at length have gotten leave
To look upon my sometimes royal master's face.
O, how it yearn'd my heart, when I beheld,
In London streets, that coronation-day,
When Bolingbroke rode on roan Barbary, —
That horse that thou so often hast bestrid,
That horse that I so carefully have dress'd!

KING RICHARD
Rode he on Barbary? Tell me, gentle friend,
How went he under him?

GROOM
So proudly as if he disdain'd the ground.

KING RICHARD
So proud that Bolingbroke was on his back!
That jade hath eat bread from my royal hand;
This hand hath made him proud with clapping him.
Would he not stumble? would he not fall down, —
Since pride must have a fall, — and break the neck
Of that proud man that did usurp his back?
Forgiveness, horse! why do I rail on thee,
Since thou, created to be awed by man,
Wast born to bear? I was not made a horse;
And yet I bear a burden like an ass,
Spur-gall'd and tired by jauncing Bolingbroke.

Enter KEEPER, *with a dish.*

KEEPER [*to the* GROOM].
Fellow, give place; here is no longer stay.

KING RICHARD
If thou love me, 'tis time thou wert away.

GROOM
What my tongue dares not, that my heart shall say.
    [*Exit.*

KEEPER
My lord, will't please you to fall to?

KING RICHARD
Taste of it first, as thou art wont to do.

KEEPER
My lord, I dare not. Sir Pierce of Exton,
Who lately came from th'king, commands the
    contrary.

KING RICHARD
The devil take Henry of Lancaster and thee!
Patience is stale, and I am weary of it.
    [*Beats the* KEEPER.

KEEPER
Help, help, help!

Enter SIR PIERCE OF EXTON *and* SERVANTS,
arm'd.

KING RICHARD
How now! what means death in this rude assault?
Villain, thy own hand yields thy death's instrument.
    [*Snatching a weapon, and killing a* SERVANT.
Go thou, and fill another room in hell.
    [*He kills another* SERVANT. *Then* EXTON *strikes him
down.*
That hand shall burn in never-quenching fire
That staggers thus my person. — Exton, thy fierce
    hand
Hath with the king's blood stain'd the king's own land.
Mount, mount, my soul! thy seat is up on high;
Whilst my gross flesh sinks downward, here to die.
    [*Dies.*

EXTON
As full of valour as of royal blood:
Both have I spilt; — O, would the deed were good!
For now the devil, that told me I did well,
Says that this deed is chronicled in hell.
This dead king to the living king I'll bear: —
Take hence the rest, and give them burial here.
    [*Exeunt.*

SCENE VI

Windsor Castle.

Flourish. Enter BOLINGBROKE, YORK, LORDS, *and*
ATTENDANTS.

BOLINGBROKE
Kind uncle York, the latest news we hear
Is that the rebels have consum'd with fire
Our town of Cicester in Glostershire;
But whether they be ta'en or slain we hear not.

Enter NORTHUMBERLAND.

Welcome, my lord: what is the news?

NORTHUMBERLAND
First, to thy sacred state wish I all happiness.
The next news is, I have to London sent
The heads of Oxford, Salisbury, Blunt, and Kent:
The manner of their taking may appear
At large discoursed in this paper here.

BOLINGBROKE
We thank thee, gentle Percy, for thy pains;
And to thy worth will add right worthy gains.

Enter FITZWATER.

FITZWATER
My lord, I have from Oxford sent to London
The heads of Brocas and Sir Bennet Seely,
Two of the dangerous consorted traitors
That sought at Oxford thy dire overthrow.

BOLINGBROKE
Thy pains, Fitzwater, shall not be forgot;
Right noble is thy merit, well I wot.

Enter PERCY, *with the* BISHOP OF CARLISLE.

PERCY
The grand conspirator, Abbot of Westminster,
With clog of conscience and sour melancholy,
Hath yielded up his body to the grave;
But here is Carlisle living, to abide
Thy kingly doom and sentence of his pride.

BOLINGBROKE
Carlisle, this is your doom: —
Choose out some secret place, some reverend room,
More than thou hast, and with it joy thy life;
So, as thou liv'st in peace, die free from strife:
For though mine enemy thou hast ever been,
High sparks of honour in thee have I seen.

Enter SIR PIERCE OF EXTON, *with a coffin.*

EXTON
Great king, within this coffin I present
Thy buried fear: herein all breathless lies
The mightiest of thy greatest enemies,
Richard of Bordeaux, by me hither brought.

BOLINGBROKE
Exton, I thank thee not; for thou hast wrought
A deed of slander, with thy fatal hand,
Upon my head and all this famous land.

EXTON
From your own mouth, my lord, did I this deed.

BOLINGBROKE
They love not poison that do poison need,
Nor do I thee: though I did wish him dead,
I hate the murderer, love him murdered.
The guilt of conscience take thou for thy labour,
But neither my good word nor princely favour:
With Cain go wander through the shades of night,
And never show thy head by day nor light. —
Lords, I protest, my soul is full of woe
That blood should sprinkle me to make me grow:
Come, mourn with me for that I do lament,
And put on sullen black incontinent:
I'll make a voyage to the Holy Land,
To wash this blood off from my guilty hand: —
March sadly after; grace my mournings here,
In weeping after this untimely bier.   [*Exeunt.*

THE MERCHANT OF VENICE

DRAMATIS PERSONAE

DUKE OF VENICE.
PRINCE OF MOROCCO, } suitors to Portia.
PRINCE OF ARAGON, }
ANTONIO, *a merchant of Venice.*
BASSANIO, *his kinsman and friend.*
SOLANIO,
SALARINO, } *friends to Antonio and Bassanio.*
GRATIANO,
LORENZO, *in love with Jessica.*

SHYLOCK, *a rich Jew.*
TUBAL, *a Jew, his friend.*
LAUNCELOT GOBBO, *a clown, servant to Shylock.*
OLD GOBBO, *father to Launcelot.*
LEONARDO, *servant to Bassanio.*
BALTHAZAR, } *servants to Portia.*
STEPHANO,
PORTIA, *a rich heiress.*
NERISSA, *her waiting-maid.*

JESSICA, *daughter to Shylock.*

MAGNIFICOES OF VENICE, OFFICERS OF THE
 COURT OF JUSTICE, GAOLER, SERVANTS, *and*
 other ATTENDANTS.

SCENE — *Partly at Venice, and partly at Belmont, the
 seat of Portia, on the Continent.*

ACT I

SCENE I

Venice. A street.

Enter ANTONIO, SALARINO, *and* SOLANIO.

ANTONIO
In sooth, I know not why I am so sad:
It wearies me; you say it wearies you;
But how I caught it, found it, or came by it,
What stuff 'tis made of, whereof it is born,
I am to learn;
And such a want-wit sadness makes of me,
That I have much ado to know myself.

SALARINO
Your mind is tossing on the ocean;
There, where your argosies with portly sail, —
Like signiors and rich burghers on the flood,
Or, as it were, the pageants of the sea, —
Do overpeer the petty traffickers,
That curtsey to them, do them reverence,
As they fly by them with their woven wings.

SOLANIO
Believe me, sir, had I such venture forth,
The better part of my affections would
Be with my hopes abroad. I should be still
Plucking the grass, to know where sits the wind;
Peering in maps for ports, and piers, and roads;
And every object that might make me fear
Misfortune to my ventures, out of doubt

Would make me sad.

SALARINO
                    My wind, cooling my broth,
Would blow me to an ague, when I thought
What harm a wind too great might do at sea.
I should not see the sandy hour-glass run,
But I should think of shallows and of flats;
And see my wealthy Andrew dock'd in sand,
Vailing her high-top lower than her ribs,
To kiss her burial. Should I go to church,
And see the holy edifice of stone,
And not bethink me straight of dangerous rocks,
Which touching but my gentle vessel's side,
Would scatter all her spices on the stream;
Enrobe the roaring waters with my silks;
And, in a word, but even now worth this,
And now worth nothing? Shall I have the thought
To think on this; and shall I lack the thought,
That such a thing bechanc'd would make me sad?
But tell not me; I know Antonio
Is sad to think upon his merchandise.

ANTONIO
Believe me, no: I thank my fortune for it,
My ventures are not in one bottom trusted,
Nor to one place; nor is my whole estate
Upon the fortune of this present year:
Therefore my merchandise makes me not sad.

SALARINO
Why, then you are in love.

ANTONIO
                            Fie, fie!

SALARINO
Not in love neither? Then let's say you're sad,
Because you are not merry: and 'twere as easy
For you to laugh, and leap, and say you are merry,
Because you are not sad. Now, by two-headed Janus,
Nature hath fram'd strange fellows in her time:
Some that will evermore peep through their eyes,
And laugh, like parrots, at a bag-piper;
And other of such vinegar aspect,
That they'll not show their teeth in way of smile,
Though Nestor swear the jest be laughable.

SOLANIO
Here comes Bassanio, your most noble kinsman,
Gratiano, and Lorenzo. Fare ye well:
We leave you now with better company.

SALARINO
I would have stay'd till I had made you merry,
If worthier friends had not prevented me.

ANTONIO
Your worth is very dear in my regard.
I take it, your own business calls on you,
And you embrace th'occasion to depart.

Enter BASSANIO, LORENZO, *and* GRATIANO.

SALARINO
Good morrow, my good lords.

BASSANIO
Good signiors both, when shall we laugh? say, when?
You grow exceeding strange: must it be so?

SALARINO
We'll make our leisures to attend on yours.
                    [*Exeunt* SALARINO *and* SOLANIO.

LORENZO
My Lord Bassanio, since you have found Antonio,
We two will leave you: but, at dinner-time,
I pray you, have in mind where we must meet.

BASSANIO
I will not fail you.

GRATIANO
You look not well, Signior Antonio;
You have too much respect upon the world:
They lose it that do buy it with much care:
Believe me, you are marvellously changed.

ANTONIO
I hold the world but as the world, Gratiano;
A stage, where every man must play a part,
And mine a sad one.

GRATIANO
                    Let me play the fool:
With mirth and laughter let old wrinkles come;
And let my liver rather heat with wine
Than my heart cool with mortifying groans.
Why should a man, whose blood is warm within,
Sit like his grandsire cut in alabaster?
Sleep when he wakes? and creep into the jaundice
By being peevish? I tell thee what, Antonio, —
I love thee, and it is my love that speaks, —
There are a sort of men, whose visages
Do cream and mantle like a standing pond;
And do a wilful stillness entertain,
With purpose to be dress'd in an opinion
Of wisdom, gravity, profound conceit;
As who should say, 'I am Sir Oracle,
And when I ope my lips, let no dog bark!'
O my Antonio, I do know of these,
That therefore only are reputed wise
For saying nothing; when, I am very sure,
If they should speak, would almost damn those ears,
Which, hearing them, would call their brothers fools.
I'll tell thee more of this another time:
But fish not, with this melancholy bait,
For this fool-gudgeon, this opinion. —
Come, good Lorenzo. — Fare ye well awhile:

I'll end my exhortation after dinner.

LORENZO
Well, we will leave you, then, till dinner-time:
I must be one of these same dumb wise men,
For Gratiano never lets me speak.

GRATIANO
Well, keep me company but two years more,
Thou shalt not know the sound of thine own tongue.

ANTONIO
Farewell: I'll grow a talker for this gear.

GRATIANO
Thanks, i'faith; for silence is only commendable
In a neat's tongue dried, and a maid not vendible.
[*Exeunt* GRATIANO *and* LORENZO.

ANTONIO
Is that any thing now?

BASSANIO
Gratiano speaks an infinite deal of nothing, more
than any man in all Venice. His reasons are as two
grains of wheat hid in two bushels of chaff: you
shall seek all day ere you find them; and when you
have them, they are not worth the search.

ANTONIO
Well; tell me now, what lady is the same
To whom you swore a secret pilgrimage,
That you to-day promis'd to tell me of?

BASSANIO
'Tis not unknown to you, Antonio,
How much I have disabled mine estate,
By something showing a more swelling port
Than my faint means would grant continuance:
Nor do I now make moan to be abridg'd
From such a noble rate; but my chief care
Is, to come fairly off from the great debts,
Wherein my time, something too prodigal,
Hath left me gaged. To you, Antonio,
I owe the most, in money and in love;
And from your love I have a warranty
To unburden all my plots and purposes
How to get clear of all the debts I owe.

ANTONIO
I pray you, good Bassanio, let me know it;
And if it stand, as you yourself still do,
Within the eye of honour, be assured
My purse, my person, my extremest means,
Lie all unlock'd to your occasions.

BASSANIO
In my school-days, when I had lost one shaft,
I shot his fellow of the selfsame flight
The selfsame way with more advised watch,
To find the other forth; and by advent'ring both,
I oft found both: I urge this childhood proof,
Because what follows is pure innocence.
I owe you much; and, like a wilful youth,
That which I owe is lost: but if you please
To shoot another arrow that self way
Which you did shoot the first, I do not doubt,
As I will watch the aim, or to find both,
Or bring your latter hazard back again,
And thankfully rest debtor for the first.

ANTONIO
You know me well; and herein spend but time
To wind about my love with circumstance;
And out of doubt you do me now more wrong
In making question of my uttermost,
Than if you had made waste of all I have:
Then do but say to me what I should do,
That in your knowledge may by me be done,
And I am prest unto it: therefore, speak.

BASSANIO
In Belmont is a lady richly left;
And she is fair, and, fairer than that word,
Of wondrous virtues: sometimes from her eyes
I did receive fair speechless messages:
Her name is Portia; nothing undervalu'd
To Cato's daughter, Brutus' Portia:
Nor is the wide world ignorant of her worth;
For the four winds blow in from every coast
Renowned suitors: and her sunny locks
Hang on her temples like a golden fleece;
Which makes her seat of Belmont Colchos' strond,
And many Jasons come in quest of her.
O my Antonio, had I but the means
To hold a rival place with one of them,
I have a mind presages me such thrift,
That I should questionless be fortunate!

ANTONIO
Thou know'st that all my fortunes are at sea;
Neither have I money, nor commodity
To raise a present sum: therefore, go forth;
Try what my credit can in Venice do:
That shall be rack'd, even to the uttermost,
To furnish thee to Belmont, to fair Portia.
Go, presently inquire, and so will I,
Where money is; and I no question make,
To have it of my trust, or for my sake.
[*Exeunt.*

SCENE II

Belmont. A room in PORTIA'S *house.*

Enter PORTIA *and* NERISSA.

PORTIA
By my troth, Nerissa, my little body is aweary of this
great world.

NERISSA
You would be, sweet madam, if your miseries were in
the same abundance as your good fortunes are: and yet,
for aught I see, they are as sick that surfeit with too
much, as they that starve with nothing. It is no mean
happiness, therefore, to be seated in the mean:
superfluity comes sooner by white hairs; but
competency lives longer.

PORTIA
Good sentences, and well pronounced.

NERISSA
They would be better, if well followed.

PORTIA
If to do were as easy as to know what were good to do,
chapels had been churches, and poor men's cottages
princes' palaces. It is a good divine that follows his own
instructions: I can easier teach twenty what were good
to be done, than be one of the twenty to follow mine
own teaching. The brain may devise laws for the blood;
but a hot temper leaps o'er a cold decree: such a hare is
madness the youth, to skip o'er the meshes of
good-counsel the cripple. But this reasoning is not in
the fashion to choose me a husband: — O me, the word
'choose'! I may neither choose who I would, nor refuse
who I dislike; so is the will of a living daughter curb'd
by the will of a dead father. — Is it not hard, Nerissa,
that I cannot choose one, nor refuse none?

NERISSA
Your father was ever virtuous; and holy men, at their
death, have good inspirations: therefore, the lottery,
that he hath devised in these three chests of gold, silver,
and lead, — whereof who chooses his meaning
chooses you, — will, no doubt, never be chosen by any
rightly, but one who shall rightly love. But what
warmth is there in your affection towards any of these
princely suitors that are already come?

PORTIA
I pray thee, over-name them; and as thou namest them,
I will describe them; and, according to my description,
level at my affection.

NERISSA
First, there is the Neapolitan prince.

PORTIA
Ay, that's a colt indeed, for he doth nothing but talk of
his horse; and he makes it a great appropriation to his
own good parts, that he can shoe him himself. I am
much afeard my lady his mother play'd false with a
smith.

NERISSA
Then there is the County Palatine.

PORTIA
He doth nothing but frown; as who should say, 'An you
will not have me, choose': he hears merry tales, and
smiles not: I fear he will prove the weeping
philosopher when he grows old, being so full of
unmannerly sadness in his youth. I had rather be
married to a Death's-head with a bone in his mouth
than to either of these: — God defend me from these
two!

NERISSA
How say you by the French lord, Monsieur Le Bon?

PORTIA
God made him, and therefore let him pass for a man.
In truth, I know it is a sin to be a mocker: but, he! —
why, he hath a horse better than the Neapolitan's; a
better bad habit of frowning than the Count Palatine:
he is every man in no man; if a throstle sing, he falls
straight a-capering; he will fence with his own shadow:
if I should marry him, I should marry twenty
husbands. If he would despise me, I would forgive
him; for if he love me to madness, I shall never requite
him.

NERISSA
What say you, then, to Falconbridge, the young baron
of England?

PORTIA
You know I say nothing to him: for he understands me
not, nor I him: he hath neither Latin, French, nor
Italian; and you will come into the court and swear that
I have a poor pennyworth in the English. He is a proper
man's picture; but, alas, who can converse with a
dumb-show? How oddly he is suited! I think he bought
his doublet in Italy, his round hose in France, his
bonnet in Germany, and his behaviour every where.

NERISSA
What think you of the Scottish lord, his neighbour?

PORTIA
That he hath a neighbourly charity in him; for he
borrow'd a box of the ear of the Englishman, and swore
he would pay him again when he was able: I think the
Frenchman became his surety, and seal'd under for
another.

NERISSA
How like you the young German, the Duke of Saxony's
nephew?

PORTIA
Very vilely in the morning, when he is sober; and most
vilely in the afternoon, when he is drunk: when he is
best, he is a little worse than a man; and when he is
worst, he is little better than a beast. An the worst fall
that ever fell, I hope I shall make shift to go without
him.

NERISSA
If he should offer to choose, and choose the right
casket, you should refuse to perform your father's will,
if you should refuse to accept him.

PORTIA
Therefore, for fear of the worst, I pray thee, set a deep
glass of Rhenish wine on the contrary casket; for, if the
devil be within, and that temptation without, I know he
will choose it. I will do any thing, Nerissa, ere I will be
married to a sponge.

NERISSA
You need not fear, lady, the having any of these lords:
they have acquainted me with their determinations;
which is, indeed, to return to their home, and to trouble
you with no more suit, unless you may be won by some
other sort than your father's imposition, depending on
the caskets.

PORTIA
If I live to be as old as Sibylla, I will die as chaste as
Diana, unless I be obtain'd by the manner of my
father's will. I am glad this parcel of wooers are so
reasonable; for there is not one among them but I dote
on his very absence; and I pray God grant them a fair
departure.

NERISSA
Do you not remember, lady, in your father's time, a
Venetian, a scholar and a soldier, that came hither in
company of the Marquis of Montferrat?

PORTIA
Yes, yes, it was Bassanio: as I think, so was he call'd.

NERISSA
True, madam: he, of all the men that ever my foolish
eyes look'd upon, was the best deserving a fair lady.

PORTIA
I remember him well; and I remember him worthy of
thy praise.

Enter a SERVANT.
How now! what news?

SERVANT
The four strangers seek for you, madam, to take their
leave: and there is a forerunner come from a fifth, the
Prince of Morocco; who brings word, the prince his
master will be here to-night.

PORTIA
If I could bid the fifth welcome with so good a heart as I
can bid the other four farewell, I should be glad of his
approach: if he have the condition of a saint and the
complexion of a devil, I had rather he should shrive me
than wive me.
Come, Nerissa. — Sirrah, go before. —
Whiles we shut the gates upon one wooer, another
knocks at the door.
[*Exeunt.*

SCENE III

Venice. A public place.

Enter BASSANIO *with* SHYLOCK *the Jew.*

SHYLOCK
Three thousand ducats, — well.

BASSANIO
Ay, sir, for three months.

SHYLOCK
For three months, — well.
BASSANIO
For the which, as I told you, Antonio shall be bound.
SHYLOCK
Antonio shall become bound, — well.
BASSANIO
May you stead me? will you pleasure me? shall I know
your answer?
SHYLOCK
Three thousand ducats for three months, and Antonio
bound.
BASSANIO
Your answer to that.
SHYLOCK
Antonio is a good man.
BASSANIO
Have you heard any imputation to the contrary?
SHYLOCK
Ho, no, no, no, no; — my meaning, in saying he is a
good man, is to have you understand me that he is
sufficient. Yet his means are in supposition: he hath an
argosy bound to Tripolis, another to the Indies; I
understand, moreover, upon the Rialto, he hath a third
at Mexico, a fourth for England, — and other ventures
he hath, squander'd abroad. But ships are but boards,
sailors but men: there be land-rats and water-rats,
water-thieves and land-thieves, I mean pirates; and
then there is the peril of waters, winds, and rocks. The
man is, notwithstanding, sufficient: — three thousand
ducats: — I think I may take his bond.
BASSANIO
Be assured you may.
SHYLOCK
I will be assured I may; and, that I may be assured, I
will bethink me. May I speak with Antonio?
BASSANIO
If it please you to dine with us.
SHYLOCK
Yes, to smell pork; to eat of the habitation which your
prophet the Nazarite conjured the devil into. I will buy
with you, sell with you, talk with you, walk with you,
and so following; but I will not eat with you, drink with
you, nor pray with you. What news on the Rialto? —
Who is he comes here?

Enter ANTONIO.

BASSANIO
This is Signior Antonio.
SHYLOCK [*aside*].
How like a fawning publican he looks!
I hate him for he is a Christian!
But more, for that, in low simplicity,
He lends out money gratis, and brings down
The rate of usance here with us in Venice.
If I can catch him once upon the hip,
I will feed fat the ancient grudge I bear him.
He hates our sacred nation; and he rails,
Even there where merchants most do congregate,
On me, my bargains, and my well-won thrift,
Which he calls interest. Cursed be my tribe,
If I forgive him!
BASSANIO
Shylock, do you hear?
SHYLOCK
I am debating of my present store;
And, by the near guess of my memory,
I cannot instantly raise up the gross
Of full three thousand ducats. What of that?
Tubal, a wealthy Hebrew of my tribe,
Will furnish me. But soft! how many months
Do you desire? — Rest you fair, good signior;
[*To* ANTONIO.
Your worship was the last man in our mouths.
ANTONIO
Shylock, although I neither lend nor borrow
By taking nor by giving of excess,
Yet, to supply the ripe wants of my friend,
I'll break a custom. — Is he yet possess'd
How much ye would?
SHYLOCK
Ay, ay, three thousand ducats.
ANTONIO
And for three months.
SHYLOCK
I had forgot, — three months, you told me so.
Well, then, your bond; and let me see, — but hear you;
Methought you said you neither lend nor borrow
Upon advantage.

ANTONIO
I do never use it.
SHYLOCK
When Jacob graz'd his uncle Laban's sheep, —
This Jacob from our holy Abram was
(As his wise mother wrought in his behalf)
The third possessor; ay, he was the third, —
ANTONIO
And what of him? did he take interest?
SHYLOCK
No, not take interest; not as you would say,
Directly interest: mark what Jacob did.
When Laban and himself were compromis'd
That all the eanlings which were streaked and pied
Should fall as Jacob's hire, the ewes, being rank,
In th'end of autumn turned to the rams;
And when the work of generation was
Between these woolly breeders in the act,
The skilful shepherd peel'd me certain wands,
And, in the doing of the deed of kind,
He stuck them up before the fulsome ewes,
Who, then conceiving, did in eaning time
Fall parti-colour'd lambs, and those were Jacob's.
This was a way to thrive, and he was blest:
And thrift is blessing, if men steal it not.
ANTONIO
This was a venture, sir, that Jacob serv'd for;
A thing not in his power to bring to pass,
But sway'd and fashion'd by the hand of heaven.
Was this inserted to make interest good?
Or is your gold and silver ewes and rams?
SHYLOCK
I cannot tell: I make it breed as fast: —
But note me, signior.
ANTONIO
Mark you this, Bassanio,
The devil can cite Scripture for his purpose.
An evil soul, producing holy witness,
Is like a villain with a smiling cheek;
A goodly apple rotten at the heart:
O, what a goodly outside falsehood hath!
SHYLOCK
Three thousand ducats, — 'tis a good round sum.
Three months from twelve, — then, let me see, the rate —
ANTONIO
Well, Shylock, shall we be beholden to you?
SHYLOCK
Signior Antonio, many a time and oft,
In the Rialto, you have rated me
About my moneys and my usances:
Still have I borne it with a patient shrug;
For sufferance is the badge of all our tribe:
You call me misbeliever, cut-throat dog,
And spit upon my Jewish gaberdine,
And all for use of that which is mine own.
Well, then, it now appears you need my help:
Go to, then; you come to me, and you say,
'Shylock, we would have moneys': — you say so;
You, that did void your rheum upon my beard,
And foot me as you spurn a stranger cur
Over your threshold: moneys is your suit.
What should I say to you? Should I not say,
'Hath a dog money? is it possible
A cur can lend three thousand ducats?' or
Shall I bend low, and in a bondman's key,
With bated breath and whispering humbleness,
Say this, —
'Fair sir, you spit on me on Wednesday last;
You spurn'd me such a day; another time
You call'd me dog; and for these courtesies
I'll lend you thus much moneys'?
ANTONIO
I am as like to call thee so again,
To spit on thee again, to spurn thee too.
If thou wilt lend this money, lend it not
As to thy friends — for when did friendship take
A breed for barren metal of his friend? —
But lend it rather to thine enemy;
Who if he break, thou mayst with better face
Exact the penalty.
SHYLOCK
Why, look you, how you storm!
I would be friends with you, and have your love,
Forget the shames that you have stain'd me with,
Supply your present wants, and take no doit
Of usance for my moneys,
And you'll not hear me: this is kind I offer.
BASSANIO
This were kindness.

SHYLOCK
This kindness will I show: —
Go with me to a notary, seal me there
Your single bond; and, in a merry sport,
If you repay me not on such a day,
In such a place, such sum or sums as are
Express'd in the condition, let the forfeit
Be nominated for an equal pound
Of your fair flesh, to be cut off and taken
In what part of your body pleaseth me.
ANTONIO
Content, i'faith: I'll seal to such a bond,
And say there is much kindness in the Jew.
BASSANIO
You shall not seal to such a bond for me:
I'll rather dwell in my necessity.
ANTONIO
Why, fear not, man; I will not forfeit it:
Within these two months, that's a month before
This bond expires, I do expect return
Of thrice three times the value of this bond.
SHYLOCK
O father Abram, what these Christians are,
Whose own hard dealings teaches them suspect
The thoughts of others! — Pray you, tell me this:
If he should break his day, what should I gain
By the exaction of the forfeiture?
A pound of man's flesh taken from a man
Is not so estimable, profitable neither,
As flesh of muttons, beefs, or goats. I say,
To buy his favour, I extend this friendship:
If he will take it, so; if not, adieu;
And, for my love, I pray you wrong me not.
ANTONIO
Yes, Shylock, I will seal unto this bond.
SHYLOCK
Then meet me forthwith at the notary's, —
Give him direction for this merry bond;
And I will go and purse the ducats straight;
See to my house, left in the fearful guard
Of an unthrifty knave; and presently
I will be with you.
ANTONIO
Hie thee, gentle Jew.
[*Exit* SHYLOCK.
The Hebrew will turn Christian: he grows kind.
BASSANIO
I like not fair terms and a villain's mind.
ANTONIO
Come on: in this there can be no dismay;
My ships come home a month before the day.
[*Exeunt.*

ACT II

SCENE I

Belmont. A room in PORTIA'S *house.*

Enter the PRINCE OF MOROCCO, *a tawny Moor all
in white, and three or four* FOLLOWERS *accordingly,
with* PORTIA, NERISSA, *and their* TRAIN. *Flourish of
cornets.*

PRINCE OF MOROCCO
Mislike me not for my complexion,
The shadow'd livery of the burnish'd sun,
To whom I am a neighbour and near bred.
Bring me the fairest creature northward born,
Where Phœbus' fire scarce thaws the icicles,
And let us make incision for your love,
To prove whose blood is reddest, his or mine.
I tell thee, lady, this aspect of mine
Hath fear'd the valiant: by my love, I swear
The best-regarded virgins of our clime
Hath lov'd it too: I would not change this hue,
Except to steal your thoughts, my gentle queen.
PORTIA
In terms of choice I am not solely led
By nice direction of a maiden's eyes;
Besides, the lottery of my destiny
Bars me the right of voluntary choosing:
But, if my father had not scanted me,
And hedg'd me by his will, to yield myself
His wife who wins me by that means I told you,
Yourself, renowned prince, then stood as fair
As any comer I have look'd on yet
For my affection.
PRINCE OF MOROCCO
Even for that I thank you:
Therefore, I pray you, lead me to the caskets,

To try my fortune. By this scimitar,
That slew the Sophy and a Persian prince,
That won three fields of Sultan Solyman,
I would outstare the sternest eyes that look,
Outbrave the heart most daring on the earth,
Pluck the young sucking-cubs from the she-bear,
Yea, mock the lion when he roars for prey,
To win thee, lady. But, alas the while!
If Hercules and Lichas play at dice
Which is the better man, the greater throw
May turn by fortune from the weaker hand:
So is Alcides beaten by his page;
And so may I, blind Fortune leading me,
Miss that which one unworthier may attain,
And die with grieving.

PORTIA
               You must take your chance;
And either not attempt to choose at all,
Or swear before you choose, — if you choose wrong,
Never to speak to lady afterward
In way of marriage: therefore be advised.

PRINCE OF MOROCCO
Nor will not. Come, bring me unto my chance.

PORTIA
First, forward to the temple: after dinner
Your hazard shall be made.

PRINCE OF MOROCCO
               Good fortune, then!
To make me blest or cursed'st among men.
               [Cornets, and exeunt.

SCENE II

Venice. A street.

Enter LAUNCELOT *the Clown, alone.*

LAUNCELOT
Certainly my conscience will serve me to run from this
Jew my master. The fiend is at mine elbow, and tempts
me, saying to me, 'Gobbo, Launcelot Gobbo, good
Launcelot,' or 'good Gobbo,' or 'good Launcelot Gobbo,
use your legs, take the start, run away.' My conscience
says, 'No, take heed, honest Launcelot; take heed,
honest Gobbo,' or, as aforesaid, 'honest Launcelot
Gobbo; do not run; scorn running with thy heels.' Well,
the most courageous fiend bids me pack: '*Via!*' says the
fiend, 'away!' says the fiend; 'for the heavens, rouse up
a brave mind,' says the fiend, 'and run.' Well, my
conscience, hanging about the neck of my heart, says
very wisely to me, 'My honest friend Launcelot, being
an honest man's son,' — or rather an honest woman's
son; — for, indeed, my father did something smack,
something grow to, — he had a kind of taste; — well,
my conscience says, 'Launcelot, budge not.' 'Budge,'
says the fiend. 'Budge not,' says my conscience.
'Conscience,' say I, 'you counsel well'; 'fiend,' say I,
'you counsel well': to be ruled by my conscience, I
should stay with the Jew my master, who — God bless

the mark! — is a kind of devil; and, to run away from
the Jew, I should be ruled by the fiend, who, saving
your reverence, is the devil himself. Certainly the Jew is
the very devil incarnal; and, in my conscience, my
conscience is but a kind of hard conscience, to offer to
counsel me to stay with the Jew. The fiend gives the
more friendly counsel: I will run, fiend; my heels are at
your command; I will run.

Enter OLD GOBBO, *with a basket.*

OLD GOBBO
Master young man, you, I pray you, which is the way to
master Jew's?

LAUNCELOT [*aside*].
O heavens, this is my true-begotten father! who, being
more than sand-blind, high-gravel-blind, knows me
not: — I will try confusions with him.

OLD GOBBO
Master young gentleman, I pray you, which is the way
to master Jew's?

LAUNCELOT
Turn up on your right hand at the next turning, but, at
the next turning of all, on your left; marry, at the very
next turning, turn of no hand, but turn down indirectly
to the Jew's house.

OLD GOBBO
By God's sonties, 'twill be a hard way to hit. Can you tell
me whether one Launcelot, that dwells with him, dwell
with him or no?

LAUNCELOT
Talk you of young Master Launcelot? — [*aside*].
Mark me now; now will I raise the waters. — Talk you
of young Master Launcelot?

OLD GOBBO
No master, sir, but a poor man's son: his father, though
I say it, is an honest exceeding poor man, and, God be
thank'd, well to live.

LAUNCELOT
Well, let his father be what a' will, we talk of young
Master Launcelot.

OLD GOBBO
Your worship's friend, and Launcelot, sir.

LAUNCELOT
But, I pray you, *ergo*, old man, *ergo*, I beseech you, talk
you of young Master Launcelot?

OLD GOBBO
Of Launcelot, an't please your mastership.

LAUNCELOT
Ergo, Master Launcelot. Talk not of Master Launcelot,
father; for the young gentleman — according to Fates
and Destinies, and such odd sayings, the Sisters Three,
and such branches of learning — is, indeed, deceased;
or, as you would say in plain terms, gone to heaven.

OLD GOBBO
Marry, God forbid! the boy was the very staff of my age,
my very prop.

LAUNCELOT
Do I look like a cudgel or a hovel-post, a staff, or a
prop? — Do you know me, father? —

OLD GOBBO
Alack the day, I know you not, young gentleman: but, I
pray you, tell me, is my boy — God rest his soul! —
alive or dead?

LAUNCELOT
Do you not know me, father?

OLD GOBBO
Alack, sir, I am sand-blind; I know you not.

LAUNCELOT
Nay, indeed, if you had your eyes, you might fail of the
knowing me: it is a wise father that knows his own
child. Well, old man, I will tell you news of your son:
give me your blessing [*kneels*]: truth will come to light;
murder cannot be hid long, — a man's son may; but, in
the end, truth will out.

OLD GOBBO
Pray you, sir, stand up: I am sure you are not Launcelot,
my boy.

LAUNCELOT
Pray you, let's have no more fooling about it, but give
me your blessing: I am Launcelot, your boy that was,
your son that is, your child that shall be.

OLD GOBBO
I cannot think you are my son.

LAUNCELOT
I know not what I shall think of that: but I am
Launcelot, the Jew's man; and I am sure Margery your
wife is my mother.

OLD GOBBO
Her name is Margery, indeed: I'll be sworn, if thou be
Launcelot, thou art mine own flesh and blood. Lord
worship'd might he be! what a beard hast thou got!
thou hast got more hair on thy chin than Dobbin my
fill-horse has on his tail.

LAUNCELOT [*rising*].
It should seem, then, that Dobbin's tail grows
backward; I am sure he had more hair of his tail than I
have of my face when I last saw him.

OLD GOBBO
Lord, how art thou changed! How dost thou and thy
master agree? I have brought him a present. How 'gree
you now?

LAUNCELOT
Well, well: but, for mine own part, as I have set up my
rest to run away, so I will not rest till I have run some
ground. My master's a very Jew: give him a present!
give him a halter: I am famish'd in his service; you may
tell every finger I have with my ribs. Father, I am glad
you are come: give me your present to one Master
Bassanio, who, indeed, gives rare new liveries: if I serve
not him, I will run as far as God has any ground. — O
rare fortune! here comes the man: — to him, father; for
I am a Jew, if I serve the Jew any longer.

Enter BASSANIO, *with* LEONARDO *and a*
FOLLOWER *or two.*

BASSANIO
You may do so; — but let it be so hasted, that supper be
ready at the furthest by five of the clock. See these
letters deliver'd; put the liveries to making; and desire
Gratiano to come anon to my lodging.
               [Exit a SERVANT.

LAUNCELOT
To him, father.

OLD GOBBO
God bless your worship!

BASSANIO
Gramercy: wouldst thou aught with me?

OLD GOBBO
Here's my son, sir, a poor boy, —

LAUNCELOT
Not a poor boy, sir, but the rich Jew's man; that would,
sir, — as my father shall specify, —

OLD GOBBO
He hath a great infection, sir, as one would say, to
serve, —

LAUNCELOT
Indeed, the short and the long is, I serve the Jew, and
have a desire, — as my father shall specify, —

OLD GOBBO
His master and he — saving your worship's reverence
— are scarce cater-cousins, —

LAUNCELOT
To be brief, the very truth is, that the Jew having done
me wrong, doth cause me, — as my father, being, I
hope, an old man, shall frutify unto you, —

LAUNCELOT Do I look like a cudgel or a hovel-post, a staff, or a prop?

OLD GOBBO
I have here a dish of doves that I would bestow upon
your worship; and my suit is, —
LAUNCELOT
In very brief, the suit is impertinent to myself, as your
worship shall know by this honest old man; and,
though I say it, though old man, yet poor man, my
father.
BASSANIO
One speak for both. — What would you?
LAUNCELOT
Serve you, sir.
OLD GOBBO
That is the very defect of the matter, sir.
BASSANIO
I know thee well; thou hast obtain'd thy suit:
Shylock thy master spoke with me this day,
And hath preferr'd thee, — if it be preferment
To leave a rich Jew's service, to become
The follower of so poor a gentleman.
LAUNCELOT
The old proverb is very well parted between my master
Shylock and you, sir: you have the grace of God, sir, and
he hath enough.
BASSANIO
Thou speak'st it well. — Go, father, with thy son. —
Take leave of thy old master, and inquire
My lodging out. — Give him a livery
More guarded than his fellows': see it done.
LAUNCELOT
Father, in. — I cannot get a service, no; — I have ne'er a
tongue in my head. — Well [*looking on his palm*], if any
man in Italy have a fairer table, which doth offer to
swear upon a book, I shall have good fortune! — Go to,
here's a simple line of life! here's a small trifle of wives!
alas, fifteen wives is nothing! eleven widows and nine
maids is a simple coming-in for one man; and then to
scape drowning thrice, and to be in peril of my life with
the edge of a feather-bed, — here are simple scapes!
Well, if Fortune be a woman, she's a good wench for
this gear. — Father, come; I'll take my leave of the Jew
in the twinkling of an eye.
[*Exeunt LAUNCELOT and OLD GOBBO.*
BASSANIO
I pray thee, good Leonardo, think on this:
These things being bought and orderly bestow'd,
Return in haste, for I do feast to-night
My best-esteem'd acquaintance: hie thee, go.
LEONARDO
My best endeavours shall be done herein.

Enter GRATIANO.

GRATIANO
Where's your master?
LEONARDO
                Yonder, sir, he walks.   [*Exit.*
GRATIANO
Signior Bassanio, —
BASSANIO
Gratiano!
GRATIANO
I have a suit to you.
BASSANIO
                You have obtain'd it.
GRATIANO
You must not deny me: I must go with you to Belmont.
BASSANIO
Why, then you must. But hear thee, Gratiano:
Thou art too wild, too rude, and bold of voice, —
Parts that become thee happily enough,
And in such eyes as ours appear not faults;
But where thou art not known, why, there they show
Something too liberal. Prithee, take pain
To allay with some cold drops of modesty
Thy skipping spirit; lest, through thy wild behaviour,
I be misconstrued in the place I go to,
And lose my hopes.
GRATIANO
                Signior Bassanio, hear me:
If I do not put on a sober habit,
Talk with respect, and swear but now and then,
Wear prayer-books in my pocket, look demurely;
Nay, more, while grace is saying, hood mine eyes
Thus with my hat, and sigh, and say amen;
Use all the observance of civility,
Like one well studied in a sad ostent
To please his grandam, — never trust me more.
BASSANIO
Well, we shall see your bearing.

GRATIANO
Nay, but I bar to-night: you shall not gauge me
By what we do to-night.
BASSANIO
                No, that were pity:
I would entreat you rather to put on
Your boldest suit of mirth, for we have friends
That purpose merriment. But fare ye well:
I have some business.
GRATIANO
And I must to Lorenzo and the rest:
But we will visit you at supper-time.   [*Exeunt.*

SCENE III

The same. A room in SHYLOCK'S house.

Enter JESSICA and LAUNCELOT.

JESSICA
I am sorry thou wilt leave my father so:
Our house is hell: and thou, a merry devil,
Didst rob it of some taste of tediousness.
But fare thee well; there is a ducat for thee:
And, Launcelot, soon at supper shalt thou see
Lorenzo, who is thy new master's guest:
Give him this letter; do it secretly; —
And so farewell: I would not have my father
See me in talk with thee.
LAUNCELOT
Adieu; tears exhibit my tongue. Most beautiful pagan,
most sweet Jew! if a Christian did not play the knave
and get thee, I am much deceived. But, adieu: these
foolish drops do something drown my manly spirit:
adieu.
JESSICA
Farewell, good Launcelot. —   [*Exit LAUNCELOT.*
Alack, what heinous sin is it in me
To be asham'd to be my father's child!
But though I am a daughter to his blood,
I am not to his manners. O Lorenzo,
If thou keep promise, I shall end this strife, —
Become a Christian, and thy loving wife!   [*Exit.*

SCENE IV

The same. A street.

*Enter GRATIANO, LORENZO, SALARINO, and
SOLANIO.*

LORENZO
Nay, we will slink away in supper-time,
Disguise us at my lodging, and return
All in an hour.
GRATIANO
We have not made good preparation.
SALARINO
We have not spoke us yet of torch-bearers.
SOLANIO
'Tis vile, unless it may be quaintly order'd,
And better in my mind not undertook.
LORENZO
'Tis now but four o'clock: we have two hours
To furnish us.
            Enter LAUNCELOT, with a letter.
                Friend Launcelot, what's the news?
LAUNCELOT
An it shall please you to break up this, it shall seem to
   signify.
LORENZO
I know the hand: in faith, 'tis a fair hand;
And whiter than the paper it writ on,
Is the fair hand that writ.
GRATIANO
                Love-news, in faith.
LAUNCELOT
By your leave, sir.
LORENZO
Whither goest thou?
LAUNCELOT
Marry, sir, to bid my old master the Jew to sup to-night
with my new master the Christian.
LORENZO
Hold here, take this [*gives money*]; — tell gentle Jessica
I will not fail her; speak it privately; go. —
                        [*Exit LAUNCELOT.*
Gentlemen, will you prepare you for this mask
   to-night?
I am provided of a torch-bearer.
SALARINO
Ay, marry, I'll be gone about it straight.

SOLANIO
And so will I.
LORENZO
                Meet me and Gratiano
At Gratiano's lodging some hour hence.
SALARINO
'Tis good we do so.
                [*Exeunt SALARINO and SOLANIO.*
GRATIANO
Was not that letter from fair Jessica?
LORENZO
I must needs tell thee all. She hath directed
How I shall take her from her father's house;
What gold and jewels she is furnish'd with;
What page's suit she hath in readiness.
If e'er the Jew her father come to heaven,
It will be for his gentle daughter's sake:
And never dare misfortune cross her foot,
Unless she do it under this excuse, —
That she is issue to a faithless Jew.
Come, go with me: peruse this as thou goest:
Fair Jessica shall be my torch-bearer.   [*Exeunt.*

SCENE V

The same. Before SHYLOCK'S house.

Enter SHYLOCK and LAUNCELOT.

SHYLOCK
Well, thou shalt see, thy eyes shall be thy judge,
The difference of old Shylock and Bassanio: —
What, Jessica! — thou shalt not gormandise,
As thou hast done with me; — What, Jessica! —
And sleep and snore, and rend apparel out; —
Why, Jessica, I say!
LAUNCELOT
                Why, Jessica!
SHYLOCK
Who bids thee call? I do not bid thee call.
LAUNCELOT
Your worship was wont to tell me that I could do
nothing without bidding.

Enter JESSICA.

JESSICA
Call you? what is your will?
SHYLOCK
I am bid forth to supper, Jessica:
There are my keys. — But wherefore should I go?
I am not bid for love; they flatter me:
But yet I'll go in hate, to feed upon
The prodigal Christian. — Jessica, my girl,
Look to my house. — I am right loth to go:
There is some ill a-brewing towards my rest,
For I did dream of money-bags to-night.
LAUNCELOT
I beseech you, sir, go: my young master doth expect
your reproach.
SHYLOCK
So do I his.
LAUNCELOT
And they have conspired together, — I will not say you
shall see a mask; but if you do, then it was not for
nothing that my nose fell a-bleeding on Black-Monday
last at six o'clock i'th'morning, falling out that year on
Ash-Wednesday was four year, in th'afternoon.
SHYLOCK
What, are there masks? — Hear you me, Jessica:
Lock up my doors; and when you hear the drum,
And the vile squealing of the wry-neck'd fife,
Clamber not you up to the casements then,
Nor thrust your head into the public street,
To gaze on Christian fools with varnish'd faces;
But stop my house's ears, I mean my casements:
Let not the sound of shallow foppery enter
My sober house. — By Jacob's staff, I swear
I have no mind of feasting forth to-night:
But I will go. — Go you before me, sirrah;
Say I will come.
LAUNCELOT
                I will go before, sir. —
Mistress, look out at window for all this;
            There will come a Christian by
            Will be worth a Jewess' eye.   [*Exit.*
SHYLOCK
What says that fool of Hagar's offspring, ha?
JESSICA
His words were, 'Farewell, mistress'; nothing else.
SHYLOCK
The patch is kind enough; but a huge feeder,
Snail-slow in profit, and he sleeps by day

More than the wild-cat: drones hive not with me;
Therefore I part with him; and part with him
To one that I would have him help to waste
His borrow'd purse. — Well, Jessica, go in:
Perhaps I will return immediately:
Do as I bid you; shut doors after you:
Fast bind, fast find, —
A proverb never stale in thrifty mind.   *[Exit.*

JESSICA
Farewell; and if my fortune be not cross'd,
I have a father, you a daughter, lost.   *[Exit.*

    Enter the maskers GRATIANO *and* SALARINO.

GRATIANO
This is the pent-house under which Lorenzo
Desired us to make stand.

SALARINO
              His hour is almost past.

GRATIANO
And it is marvel he out-dwells his hour,
For lovers ever run before the clock.

SALARINO
O, ten times faster Venus' pigeons fly
To seal love's bonds new-made than they are wont
To keep obliged faith unforfeited!

GRATIANO
That ever holds: who riseth from a feast
With that keen appetite that he sits down?
Where is the horse that doth untread again
His tedious measures with the unbated fire
That he did pace them first? All things that are,
Are with more spirit chased than enjoy'd.
How like a younker or a prodigal
The scarfed bark puts from her native bay,
Hugg'd and embraced by the strumpet wind!
How like the prodigal doth she return,
With over-weather'd ribs, and ragged sails,
Lean, rent, and beggar'd by the strumpet wind!

SALARINO
Here comes Lorenzo: — more of this hereafter.

    Enter LORENZO.

LORENZO
Sweet friends, your patience for my long abode;
Not I, but my affairs, have made you wait:
When you shall please to play the thieves for wives,
I'll watch as long for you then. — Approach;
Here dwells my father Jew. — Ho! who's within?

    Enter JESSICA, *above, in boy's clothes.*

JESSICA
Who are you? Tell me, for more certainty,
Albeit I'll swear that I do know your tongue.

LORENZO
Lorenzo, and thy love.

JESSICA
Lorenzo, certain; and my love, indeed, —
For who love I so much? And now who knows
But you, Lorenzo, whether I am yours?

LORENZO
Heaven and thy thoughts are witness that thou art.

JESSICA
Here, catch this casket; it is worth the pains.
I am glad 'tis night, you do not look on me,
For I am much asham'd of my exchange:
But love is blind, and lovers cannot see
The pretty follies that themselves commit;
For if they could, Cupid himself would blush
To see me thus transformed to a boy.

LORENZO
Descend, for you must be my torch-bearer.

JESSICA
What, must I hold a candle to my shames?
They in themselves, good sooth, are too-too light.
Why, 'tis an office of discovery, love;
And I should be obscured.

LORENZO
              So are you, sweet,
Even in the lovely garnish of a boy.
But come at once;
For the close night doth play the runaway,
And we are stay'd for at Bassanio's feast.

JESSICA
I will make fast the doors, and gild myself
With some more ducats, and be with you straight.
    [Exit above.

GRATIANO
Now, by my hood, a Gentile, and no Jew.

LORENZO
Beshrew me but I love her heartily;
For she is wise, if I can judge of her;

And fair she is, if that mine eyes be true;
And true she is, as she hath prov'd herself;
And therefore, like herself, wise, fair, and true,
Shall she be placed in my constant soul.

    Enter JESSICA, *below.*

What, art thou come? — On, gentlemen; away!
Our masking mates by this time for us stay.
    [Exit with JESSICA *and* SALARINO.

    Enter ANTONIO.

ANTONIO
Who's there?

GRATIANO
Signior Antonio!

ANTONIO
Fie, fie, Gratiano! where are all the rest?
'Tis nine o'clock; our friends all stay for you.
No mask to-night; the wind is come about;
Bassanio presently will go aboard;
I have sent twenty out to seek for you.

GRATIANO
I am glad on't: I desire no more delight
Than to be under sail and gone to-night.   *[Exeunt.*

SCENE VI

Belmont. A room in PORTIA'S *house.*

Enter PORTIA, *with the* PRINCE OF MOROCCO, *and their* TRAINS. *Flourish cornets.*

PORTIA
Go draw aside the curtains, and discover
The several caskets to this noble prince. —
Now make your choice.

PRINCE OF MOROCCO
The first, of gold, who this inscription bears, —
'Who chooseth me shall gain what many men desire';
The second, silver, which this promise carries, —
'Who chooseth me shall get as much as he deserves';
This third, dull lead, with warning all as blunt, —
'Who chooseth me must give and hazard all he hath.' —
How shall I know if I do choose the right?

PORTIA
The one of them contains my picture, prince:
If you choose that, then I am yours withal.

PRINCE OF MOROCCO
Some god direct my judgement! Let me see;
I will survey the inscriptions back again.
What says this leaden casket?
'Who chooseth me must give and hazard all he hath.'
Must give, — for what? for lead? hazard for lead?
This casket threatens: men that hazard all
Do it in hope of fair advantages:
A golden mind stoops not to shows of dross;
I'll then nor give nor hazard aught for lead.
What says the silver, with her virgin hue?
'Who chooseth me shall get as much as he deserves.'
As much as he deserves! — Pause there, Morocco,
And weigh thy value with an even hand:
If thou be'st rated by thy estimation,
Thou dost deserve enough; and yet enough

May not extend so far as to the lady:
And yet to be afeard of my deserving,
Were but a weak disabling of myself.
As much as I deserve! — Why, that's the lady:
I do in birth deserve her, and in fortunes,
In graces, and in qualities of breeding;
But more than these, in love I do deserve.
What if I stray'd no further, but chose here? —
Let's see once more this saying grav'd in gold:
'Who chooseth me shall gain what many men desire.'
Why, that's the lady; all the world desires her;
From the four corners of the earth they come,
To kiss this shrine, this mortal-breathing saint:
The Hyrcanian deserts and the vasty wilds
Of wide Arabia are as throughfares now
For princes to come view fair Portia:
The watery kingdom, whose ambitious head
Spits in the face of heaven, is no bar
To stop the foreign spirits; but they come,
As o'er a brook, to see fair Portia.
One of these three contains her heavenly picture.
Is't like that lead contains her? 'Twere damnation
To think so base a thought: it were too gross
To rib her cerecloth in the obscure grave.
Or shall I think in silver she's immured,
Being ten times undervalued to tried gold?
O sinful thought! Never so rich a gem
Was set in worse than gold. They have in England
A coin that bears the figure of an angel
Stamped in gold, — but that's insculp'd upon;
But here an angel in a golden bed
Lies all within. — Deliver me the key:
Here do I choose, and thrive as I may!

PORTIA
There, take it, prince; and if my form lie there,
Then I am yours.   *[He opens the golden casket.*

PRINCE OF MOROCCO
          O hell! what have we here?
A carrion Death, within whose empty eye
There is a written scroll! I'll read the writing.

    All that glisters is not gold, —
    Often have you heard that told:
    Many a man his life hath sold
    But my outside to behold:
    Gilded tombs do worms enfold.
    Had you been as wise as bold,
    Young in limbs, in judgement old,
    Your answer had not been inscroll'd:
    Fare you well; your suit is cold.

    Cold, indeed; and labour lost:
    Then, farewell, heat; and welcome, frost! —
Portia, adieu. I have too griev'd a heart
To take a tedious leave: thus losers part.
    [Exit with his TRAIN. *Cornets.*

PORTIA
A gentle riddance. — Draw the curtains, go. —
Let all of his complexion choose me so.   *[Exeunt.*

SOLANIO My daughter! — O my ducats! — O my daughter!

SCENE VII

Venice. A street.

Enter SALARINO *and* SOLANIO.

SALARINO
Why, man, I saw Bassanio under sail:
With him is Gratiano gone along;
And in their ship I am sure Lorenzo is not.

SOLANIO
The villain Jew with outcries rais'd the duke,
Who went with him to search Bassanio's ship.

SALARINO
He came too late, the ship was under sail:
But there the duke was given to understand
That in a gondola were seen together
Lorenzo and his amorous Jessica:
Besides, Antonio certified the duke
They were not with Bassanio in his ship.

SOLANIO
I never heard a passion so confused,
So strange, outrageous, and so variable,
As the dog Jew did utter in the streets:
'My daughter! — O my ducats! — O my daughter!
Fled with a Christian! — O my Christian ducats! —
Justice! the law! my ducats, and my daughter!
A sealed bag, two sealed bags of ducats,
Of double ducats, stol'n from me by my daughter!
And jewels, — two stones, two rich and precious
   stones,
Stol'n by my daughter! — Justice! find the girl!
She hath the stones upon her, and the ducats!'

SALARINO
Why, all the boys in Venice follow him,
Crying, — his stones, his daughter, and his ducats.

SOLANIO
Let good Antonio look he keep his day,
Or he shall pay for this.

SALARINO
                    Marry, well remember'd.
I reason'd with a Frenchman yesterday,
Who told me, — in the narrow seas that part
The French and English, there miscarried
A vessel of our country richly fraught:
I thought upon Antonio when he told me;
And wish'd in silence that it were not his.

SOLANIO
You were best to tell Antonio what you hear;
Yet do not suddenly, for it may grieve him.

SALARINO
A kinder gentleman treads not the earth.
I saw Bassanio and Antonio part:
Bassanio told him he would make some speed
Of his return: he answer'd, 'Do not so;
Slubber not business for my sake, Bassanio,
But stay the very riping of the time;
And for the Jew's bond which he hath of me,
Let it not enter in your mind of love:
Be merry; and employ your chiefest thoughts
To courtship, and such fair ostents of love
As shall conveniently become you there':
And even there, his eye being big with tears,
Turning his face, he put his hand behind him,
And with affection wondrous sensible
He wrung Bassanio's hand; and so they parted.

SOLANIO
I think he only loves the world for him.
I pray thee, let us go and find him out,
And quicken his embraced heaviness
With some delight or other.

SALARINO
                    Do we so.   [*Exeunt.*

SCENE VIII

Belmont. A room in PORTIA'S *house.*

Enter NERISSA *and a* SERVITOR.

NERISSA
Quick, quick, I pray thee; draw the curtain straight:
The Prince of Arragon hath ta'en his oath,
And comes to his election presently.

Enter PRINCE OF ARRAGON, *his* TRAIN, *and*
PORTIA. *Flourish of cornets.*

PORTIA
Behold, there stand the caskets, noble prince:
If you choose that wherein I am contain'd,
Straight shall our nuptial rites be solemnised:
But if you fail, without more speech, my lord,
You must be gone from hence immediately.

PRINCE OF ARRAGON
I am enjoin'd by oath to observe three things: —
First, never to unfold to any one
Which casket 'twas I chose; next, if I fail
Of the right casket, never in my life
To woo a maid in way of marriage; lastly,
If I do fail in fortune of my choice,
Immediately to leave you and be gone.

PORTIA
To these injunctions every one doth swear
That comes to hazard for my worthless self.

PRINCE OF ARRAGON
And so have I address'd me. Fortune now
To my heart's hope! — Gold, silver, and base lead.
'Who chooseth me must give and hazard all he hath.'
You shall look fairer, ere I give or hazard.
What says the golden chest? ha! let me see:
'Who chooseth me shall gain what many men desire.'
What many men desire! — that many may be meant
By the fool multitude, that choose by show,
Not learning more than the fond eye doth teach;
Which pries not to th'interior, but, like the martlet,
Builds in the weather on the outward wall,
Even in the force and road of casualty.
I will not choose what many men desire,
Because I will not jump with common spirits,
And rank me with the barbarous multitudes.
Why, then to thee, thou silver treasure-house;
Tell me once more what title thou dost bear:
'Who chooseth me shall get as much as he deserves':
And well said too; for who shall go about
To cozen fortune, and be honourable
Without the stamp of merit? Let none presume
To wear an undeserved dignity.
O, that estates, degrees, and offices,
Were not deriv'd corruptly! and that clear honour
Were purchas'd by the merit of the wearer!
How many then should cover that stand bare!
How many be commanded that command!
How much low peasantry would then be glean'd
From the true seed of honour! and how much honour
Pick'd from the chaff and ruin of the times,
To be new-varnish'd! Well, but to my choice:
'Who chooseth me shall get as much as he deserves.'
I will assume desert. — Give me a key for this,
And instantly unlock my fortunes here.

                    [*He opens the silver casket.*

PORTIA [*aside*].
Too long a pause for that which you find there.

PRINCE OF ARRAGON
What's here? the portrait of a blinking idiot,
Presenting me a schedule! I will read it.
How much unlike art thou to Portia!
How much unlike my hopes and my deservings!
'Who chooseth me shall have as much as he deserves.'
Did I deserve no more than a fool's head?
Is that my prize? are my deserts no better?

PORTIA
To offend, and judge, are distinct offices,
And of opposed natures.

PRINCE OF ARRAGON
                    What is here?

   The fire seven times tried this:
   Seven times tried that judgement is,
   That did never choose amiss.
   Some there be that shadows kiss;
   Such have but a shadow's bliss.
   There be fools alive, I wis,
   Silver'd o'er; and so was this.
   Take what wife you will to bed,
   I will ever be your head:
   So be gone; you are sped.

Still more fool I shall appear
By the time I linger here:
With one fool's head I came to woo,
But I go away with two. —
Sweet, adieu. I'll keep my oath,
Patiently to bear my wroth.   [*Exit with his* TRAIN.

PORTIA
Thus hath the candle sing'd the moth.
O, these deliberate fools! when they do choose,
They have the wisdom by their wit to lose.

NERISSA
The ancient saying is no heresy, —
Hanging and wiving goes by destiny.

PORTIA
Come, draw the curtain, Nerissa.

Enter a SERVANT.

SERVANT
Where is my lady?

PORTIA
                    Here: what would my lord?

SERVANT
Madam, there is alighted at your gate
A young Venetian, one that comes before
To signify th'approaching of his lord;
From whom he bringeth sensible regreets,
To wit, besides commends and courteous breath,
Gifts of rich value. Yet I have not seen
So likely an ambassador of love:
A day in April never came so sweet,
To show how costly summer was at hand,
As this fore-spurrer comes before his lord.

PORTIA
No more, I pray thee: I am half afeard
Thou wilt say anon he is some kin to thee,
Thou spend'st such high-day wit in praising him. —
Come, come, Nerissa; for I long to see
Quick Cupid's post that comes so mannerly.

NERISSA
Bassanio, lord Love, if thy will it be!   [*Exeunt.*

ACT III

SCENE I

Venice. A street.

Enter SOLANIO *and* SALARINO.

SOLANIO
Now, what news on the Rialto?

SALARINO
Why, yet it lives there uncheck'd, that Antonio hath a
ship of rich lading wrack'd on the narrow seas; the
Goodwins, I think they call the place; a very dangerous
flat and fatal, where the carcasses of many a tall ship lie
buried, as they say, if my gossip Report be an honest
woman of her word.

SOLANIO
I would she were as lying a gossip in that as ever
knapp'd ginger, or made her neighbours believe she
wept for the death of a third husband. But it is true, —
without any slips of prolixity, or crossing the plain
highway of talk, — that the good Antonio, the honest
Antonio, — O, that I had a title good enough to keep his
name company! —

SALARINO
Come, the full stop.

SOLANIO
Ha, — what sayest thou? — Why, the end is, he hath
lost a ship.

SALARINO
I would it might prove the end of his losses.

SOLANIO
Let me say amen betimes, lest the devil cross my
prayer, — for here he comes in the likeness of a Jew.
                    Enter SHYLOCK.
How now, Shylock! what news among the merchants?

SHYLOCK
You knew, none so well, none so well as you, of my
daughter's flight.

SALARINO
That's certain: I, for my part, knew the tailor that made
the wings she flew withal.

SOLANIO
And Shylock, for his own part, knew the bird was
fledged; and then it is the complexion of them all to
leave the dam.

SHYLOCK
She is damn'd for it.

SALARINO
That's certain, if the devil may be her judge.

SHYLOCK
My own flesh and blood to rebel!

SOLANIO
Out upon it, old carrion! rebels it at these years?

SHYLOCK
I say my daughter is my flesh and blood.

SALARINO
There is more difference between thy flesh and hers
than between jet and ivory; more between your bloods
than there is between red wine and rhenish. — But tell
us, do you hear whether Antonio have had any loss at
sea or no?

SHYLOCK The curse never fell upon our nation till now; I never felt it till now.

SHYLOCK
There I have another bad match: a bankrout, a prodigal, who dare scarce show his head on the Rialto; — a beggar, that was used to come so smug upon the mart; — let him look to his bond; he was wont to call me usurer; — let him look to his bond: he was wont to lend money for a Christian courtesy: — let him look to his bond.

SALARINO
Why, I am sure, if he forfeit, thou wilt not take his flesh: what's that good for?

SHYLOCK
To bait fish withal: if it will feed nothing else, it will feed my revenge. He hath disgraced me, and hinder'd me half a million; laugh'd at my losses, mock'd at my gains, scorn'd my nation, thwarted my bargains, cool'd my friends, heated mine enemies; and what's his reason? I am a Jew. Hath not a Jew eyes? hath not a Jew hands, organs, dimensions, senses, affections, passions? fed with the same food, hurt with the same weapons, subject to the same diseases, heal'd by the same means, warm'd and cool'd by the same winter and summer, as a Christian is? If you prick us, do we not bleed? if you tickle us, do we not laugh? if you poison us, do we not die? and if you wrong us, shall we not revenge? If we are like you in the rest, we will resemble you in that. If a Jew wrong a Christian, what is his humility? revenge: if a Christian wrong a Jew, what should his sufferance be by Christian example? why, revenge. The villainy you teach me, I will execute; and it shall go hard but I will better the instruction.

Enter a SERVANT *from* ANTONIO.

SERVANT
Gentlemen, my master Antonio is at his house, and desires to speak with you both.

SALARINO
We have been up and down to seek him.

SOLANIO
Here comes another of the tribe: a third cannot be match'd, unless the devil himself turn Jew.

[*Exeunt* SOLANIO, SALARINO, *and* SERVANT.
Enter TUBAL.

SHYLOCK
How now, Tubal! what news from Genoa? hast thou found my daughter?

TUBAL
I often came where I did hear of her, but cannot find her.

SHYLOCK
Why, there, there, there, there! a diamond gone, cost me two thousand ducats in Frankfort! The curse never fell upon our nation till now; I never felt it till now: — two thousand ducats in that; and other precious, precious jewels. — I would my daughter were dead at my foot, and the jewels in her ear! would she were hearsed at my foot, and the ducats in her coffin! No news of them? — Why, so: — and I know not what's spent in the search: why, thou, loss upon loss! the thief gone with so much, and so much to find the thief; and no satisfaction, no revenge: nor no ill luck stirring but what lights on my shoulders; no sighs but of my breathing; no tears but of my shedding.

TUBAL
Yes, other men have ill luck too: Antonio, as I heard in Genoa, —

SHYLOCK
What, what, what? ill luck, ill luck?

TUBAL
Hath an argosy cast away, coming from Tripolis.

SHYLOCK
I thank God, I thank God! — Is't true, is't true?

TUBAL
I spoke with some of the sailors that escaped the wrack.

SHYLOCK
I thank thee, good Tubal: — good news, good news! ha, ha! — where? in Genoa?

TUBAL
Your daughter spent in Genoa, as I heard, in one night fourscore ducats.

SHYLOCK
Thou stick'st a dagger in me: — I shall never see my gold again: fourscore ducats at a sitting! fourscore ducats!

TUBAL
There came divers of Antonio's creditors in my company to Venice, that swear he cannot choose but break.

SHYLOCK
I am very glad of it: — I'll plague him; I'll torture him: — I am glad on't.

TUBAL
One of them show'd me a ring that he had of your daughter for a monkey.

SHYLOCK
Out upon her! Thou torturest me, Tubal: it was my turquoise; I had it of Leah when I was a bachelor: I would not have given it for a wilderness of monkeys.

TUBAL
But Antonio is certainly undone.

SHYLOCK
Nay, that's true, that's very true. Go, Tubal, fee me an officer; bespeak him a fortnight before. I will have the heart of him, if he forfeit; for, were he out of Venice, I can make what merchandise I will. Go, Tubal, and meet me at our synagogue; go, good Tubal; at our synagogue, Tubal.

[*Exeunt.*

SCENE II

Belmont. A room in PORTIA'S *house.*

Enter BASSANIO, PORTIA, GRATIANO, NERISSA, *and all their* TRAIN.

PORTIA
I pray you, tarry: pause a day or two
Before you hazard; for, in choosing wrong,
I lose your company: therefore, forbear awhile.
There's something tells me — but it is not love —
I would not lose you; and, you know yourself,
Hate counsels not in such a quality.

SHYLOCK You knew, none so well, none so well as you, of my daughter's flight.

But lest you should not understand me well, —
And yet a maiden hath no tongue but thought, —
I would detain you here some month or two
Before you venture for me. I could teach you
How to choose right, but then I am forsworn;
So will I never be: so may you miss me;
But if you do, you'll make me wish a sin,
That I had been forsworn. Beshrew your eyes,
They have o'erlook'd me, and divided me;
One half of me is yours, the other half yours, —
Mine own, I would say; but if mine, then yours,
And so all yours! O, these naughty times
Put bars between the owners and their rights!
And so, though yours, not yours. — Prove it so,
Let fortune go to hell for it, — not I.
I speak too long; but 'tis to peize the time,
To eke it, and to draw it out in length,
To stay you from election.

BASSANIO
               Let me choose;
For, as I am, I live upon the rack.

PORTIA
Upon the rack, Bassanio! then confess
What treason there is mingled with your love.

BASSANIO
None but that ugly treason of mistrust,
Which makes me fear the enjoying of my love:
There may as well be amity and league
'Tween snow and fire, as treason and my love.

PORTIA
Ay, but I fear you speak upon the rack,
Where men enforced do speak anything.

BASSANIO
Promise me life, and I'll confess the truth.

PORTIA
Well then, confess, and live.

BASSANIO
               'Confess', and 'love',
Had been the very sum of my confession:
O happy torment, when my torturer
Doth teach me answers for deliverance!
But let me to my fortune and the caskets.

PORTIA
Away, then! I am lock'd in one of them:
If you do love me, you will find me out. —
Nerissa, and the rest, stand all aloof. —
Let music sound while he doth make his choice;
Then, if he lose, he makes a swan-like end,
Fading in music: that the comparison
May stand more proper, my eye shall be the stream
And watery death-bed for him. He may win;
And what is music then? then music is
Even as the flourish when true subjects bow
To a new-crowned monarch: such it is
As are those dulcet sounds in break of day
That creep into the dreaming bridegroom's ear,
And summon him to marriage. — Now he goes,
With no less presence, but with much more love,
Than young Alcides, when he did redeem
The virgin tribute paid by howling Troy
To the sea-monster: I stand for sacrifice;
The rest aloof are the Dardanian wives,
With bleared visages, come forth to view
The issue of th'exploit. Go, Hercules!
Live thou, I live: — with much much more dismay
I view the fight than thou that mak'st the fray.

Here music. — A song, the whilst BASSANIO *comments
on the caskets to himself.*

Tell me where is fancy bred,
  Or in the heart or in the head?
  How begot, how nourished?
      Reply, reply.
It is engender'd in the eyes,
With gazing fed; and fancy dies
In the cradle where it lies.
   Let us all ring fancy's knell;
   I'll begin it, — Ding, dong, bell.

All. Ding, dong, bell.

BASSANIO
So may the outward shows be least themselves:
The world is still deceiv'd with ornament.
In law, what plea so tainted and corrupt,
But, being season'd with a gracious voice,
Obscures the show of evil? In religion,
What damned error, but some sober brow
Will bless it, and approve it with a text,
Hiding the grossness with fair ornament?
There is no vice so simple, but assumes
Some mark of virtue on his outward parts:

How many cowards, whose hearts are all as false
As stairs of sand, wear yet upon their chins
The beards of Hercules and frowning Mars;
Who, inward search'd, have livers white as milk;
And these assume but valour's excrement
To render them redoubted! Look on beauty,
And you shall see 'tis purchas'd by the weight;
Which therein works a miracle in nature,
Making them lightest that wear most of it:
So are those crisped snaky golden locks,
Which make such wanton gambols with the wind,
Upon supposed fairness, often known
To be the dowry of a second head,
The skull that bred them in the sepulchre.
Thus ornament is but the guiled shore
To a most dangerous sea; the beauteous scarf
Veiling an Indian beauty; in a word,
The seeming truth which cunning times put on
To entrap the wisest. Therefore, thou gaudy gold,
Hard food for Midas, I will none of thee;
Nor none of thee, thou stale and common drudge
'Tween man and man: but thou, thou meagre lead,
Which rather threatenest than dost promise aught,
Thy paleness moves me more than eloquence;
And here choose I: — joy be the consequence!

PORTIA [*aside*].
How all the other passions fleet to air, —
As doubtful thoughts, and rash-embrac'd despair,
And shuddering fear, and green-eyed jealousy!
O love, be moderate: allay thy ecstasy;
In measure rein thy joy; scant this excess!
I feel too much thy blessing: make it less,
For fear I surfeit!

BASSANIO
             What find I here?
          [*Opening the leaden casket.*
Fair Portia's counterfeit! What demi-god
Hath come so near creation? Move these eyes?
Or whether, riding on the balls of mine,
Seem they in motion? Here are sever'd lips,
Parted with sugar breath: so sweet a bar
Should sunder such sweet friends. Here in her hairs
The painter plays the spider; and hath woven
A golden mesh t'entrap the hearts of men,
Faster than gnats in cobwebs: but her eyes, —
How could he see to do them? having made one,
Methinks it should have power to steal both his,
And leave itself unfurnish'd. Yet look, how far
The substance of my praise doth wrong this shadow
In underprizing it, so far this shadow
Doth limp behind the substance. — Here's the scroll,
The continent and summary of my fortune.

    You that choose not by the view,
    Chance as fair, and choose as true!
    Since this fortune falls to you,
    Be content, and seek no new.
    If you be well pleas'd with this,
    And hold your fortune for your bliss,
    Turn you where your lady is,
    And claim her with a loving kiss.

A gentle scroll. — Fair lady, by your leave;   [*Kissing her.*
I come by note, to give and to receive.
Like one of two contending in a prize,
That thinks he hath done well in people's eyes,
Hearing applause and universal shout,
Giddy in spirit, still gazing in a doubt
Whether those peals of praise be his or no;
So, thrice-fair lady, stand I, even so;
As doubtful whether what I see be true,
Until confirm'd, sign'd, ratified by you.

PORTIA
You see me, Lord Bassanio, where I stand,
Such as I am: though for myself alone
I would not be ambitious in my wish,
To wish myself much better; yet for you
I would be trebled twenty times myself;
A thousand times more fair, ten thousand times more
   rich;
That, only to stand high in your account,
I might in virtues, beauties, livings, friends,
Exceed account: but the full sum of me
Is sum of nothing: which, to term in gross,
Is an unlesson'd girl, unschool'd, unpractis'd:
Happy in this, she is not yet so old
But she may learn; happier than this,
She is not bred so dull but she can learn;
Happiest of all is that her gentle spirit
Commits itself to yours to be directed,
As from her lord, her governor, her king.
Myself and what is mine to you and yours

Is now converted: but now I was the lord
Of this fair mansion, master of my servants,
Queen o'er myself; and even now, but now,
This house, these servants, and this same myself,
Are yours, my lord: I give them with this ring;
Which when you part from, lose, or give away,
Let it presage the ruin of your love,
And be my vantage to exclaim on you.

BASSANIO
Madam, you have bereft me of all words,
Only my blood speaks to you in my veins:
And there is such confusion in my powers,
As, after some oration fairly spoke
By a beloved prince, there doth appear
Among the buzzing pleased multitude;
Where every something, being blent together,
Turns to a wild of nothing, save of joy,
Express'd and not express'd. But when this ring
Parts from this finger, then parts life from hence:
O, then be bold to say Bassanio's dead!

NERISSA
My lord and lady, it is now our time,
That have stood by, and seen our wishes prosper,
To cry, good joy: — good joy, my lord and lady!

GRATIANO
My Lord Bassanio and my gentle lady,
I wish you all the joy that you can wish;
For I am sure you can wish none from me:
And, when your honours mean to solemnise
The bargain of your faith, I do beseech you,
Even at that time I may be married too.

BASSANIO
With all my heart, so thou canst get a wife.

GRATIANO
I thank your lordship, you have got me one.
My eyes, my lord, can look as swift as yours:
You saw the mistress, I beheld the maid;
You lov'd, I lov'd; for intermission
No more pertains to me, my lord, than you.
Your fortune stood upon the caskets there;
And so did mine too, as the matter falls;
For wooing here, until I sweat again,
And swearing, till my very roof was dry
With oaths of love, at last, — if promise last, —
I got a promise of this fair one here,
To have her love, provided that your fortune
Achiev'd her mistress.

PORTIA
             Is this true, Nerissa?

NERISSA
Madam, it is, so you stand pleased withal.

BASSANIO
And do you, Gratiano, mean good faith?

GRATIANO
Yes, faith, my lord.

BASSANIO
Our feast shall be much honour'd in your marriage.

GRATIANO
We'll play with them the first boy for a thousand
   ducats.

NERISSA
What, and stake down?

GRATIANO
No; we shall ne'er win at that sport, and stake down. —
But who comes here? Lorenzo and his infidel?
What, and my old Venetian friend Solanio?

Enter LORENZO, JESSICA, *and* SOLANIO.

BASSANIO
Lorenzo and Solanio, welcome hither;
If that the youth of my new interest here
Have power to bid you welcome. — By your leave,
I bid my very friends and countrymen,
Sweet Portia, welcome.

PORTIA
             So do I, my lord;
They are entirely welcome.

LORENZO
I thank your honour. — For my part, my lord,
My purpose was not to have seen you here;
But meeting with Solanio by the way,
He did entreat me, past all saying nay,
To come with him along.

SOLANIO
             I did, my lord;
And I have reason for't. Signior Antonio
Commends him to you.   [*Gives* BASSANIO *a letter.*

BASSANIO
             Ere I ope his letter,
I pray you, tell me how my good friend doth.

SOLANIO
Not sick, my lord, unless it be in mind;
Nor well, unless in mind: his letter there
Will show you his estate.
                       [BASSANIO *reads the letter.*

GRATIANO
Nerissa, cheer yon stranger; bid her welcome. —
Your hand, Solanio: what's the news from Venice?
How doth that royal merchant, good Antonio?
I know he will be glad of our success;
We are the Jasons, we have won the fleece.

SOLANIO
I would you had won the fleece that he hath lost!

PORTIA
There are some shrewd contents in yon same paper,
That steals the colour from Bassanio's cheek:
Some dear friend dead; else nothing in the world
Could turn so much the constitution
Of any constant man. What, worse and worse! —
With leave, Bassanio; I am half yourself,
And I must freely have the half of any thing
That this same paper brings you.

BASSANIO
                   O sweet Portia,
Here are a few of the unpleasant'st words
That ever blotted paper! Gentle lady,
When I did first impart my love to you,
I freely told you, all the wealth I had
Ran in my veins, — I was a gentleman;
And then I told you true: and yet, dear lady,
Rating myself at nothing, you shall see
How much I was a braggart. When I told you
My state was nothing, I should then have told you
That I was worse than nothing; for, indeed,
I have engag'd myself to a dear friend,
Engag'd my friend to his mere enemy,
To feed my means. Here is a letter, lady, —
The paper as the body of my friend,
And every word in it a gaping wound,
Issuing life-blood. — But is it true, Solanio?
Have all his ventures fail'd? What, not one hit?
From Tripolis, from Mexico, and England,
From Lisbon, Barbary, and India?
And not one vessel scape the dreadful touch
Of merchant-marring rocks?

SOLANIO
                   Not one, my lord.
Besides, it should appear, that if he had
The present money to discharge the Jew,
He would not take it. Never did I know
A creature, that did bear the shape of man,
So keen and greedy to confound a man;
He plies the duke at morning and at night;
And doth impeach the freedom of the state,
If they deny him justice: twenty merchants,
The duke himself, and the magnificoes
Of greatest port, have all persuaded with him;
But none can drive him from the envious plea
Of forfeiture, of justice, and his bond.

JESSICA
When I was with him, I have heard him swear,
To Tubal and to Chus, his countrymen,
That he would rather have Antonio's flesh
Than twenty times the value of the sum
That he did owe him: and I know, my lord,
If law, authority, and power deny not,
It will go hard with poor Antonio.

PORTIA
Is it your dear friend that is thus in trouble?

BASSANIO
The dearest friend to me, the kindest man,
The best-condition'd and unwearied spirit
In doing courtesies; and one in whom
The ancient Roman honour more appears
Than any that draws breath in Italy.

PORTIA
What sum owes he the Jew?

BASSANIO
For me three thousand ducats.

PORTIA
                  What, no more?
Pay him six thousand, and deface the bond;
Double six thousand, and then treble that,
Before a friend of this description
Shall lose a hair through Bassanio's fault.
First go with me to church and call me wife,
And then away to Venice to your friend;
For never shall you lie by Portia's side
With an unquiet soul. You shall have gold
To pay the petty debt twenty times over:
When it is paid, bring your true friend along.

SHYLOCK Gaoler, look to him: — tell not me of mercy; — this is the fool that lent out money gratis.

My maid Nerissa and myself meantime
Will live as maids and widows. Come, away!
For you shall hence upon your wedding-day:
Bid your friends welcome, show a merry cheer:
Since you are dear-bought, I will love you dear. —
But let me hear the letter of your friend.

BASSANIO [*reads*].
Sweet Bassanio, my ships have all miscarried, my
creditors grow cruel, my estate is very low, my bond to
the Jew is forfeit; and since in paying it, it is impossible
I should live, all debts are clear'd between you and I, if I
might but see you at my death. Notwithstanding, use
your pleasure: if your love do not persuade you to
come, let not my letter.

PORTIA
O love, dispatch all business, and be gone!

BASSANIO
Since I have your good leave to go away,
  I will make haste: but, till I come again,
No bed shall e'er be guilty of my stay,
  No rest be interposer 'twixt us twain.
                       [*Exeunt.*

SCENE III

Venice. A street.

Enter SHYLOCK, SALARINO, ANTONIO, *and*
GAOLER.

SHYLOCK
Gaoler, look to him: — tell not me of mercy; —
This is the fool that lent out money gratis: —
Gaoler, look to him.

ANTONIO
            Hear me yet, good Shylock.

SHYLOCK
I'll have my bond; speak not against my bond:
I have sworn an oath that I will have my bond.
Thou call'dst me dog before thou hadst a cause;
But, since I am a dog, beware my fangs:
The duke shall grant me justice. — I do wonder,
Thou naughty gaoler, that thou art so fond
To come abroad with him at his request.

ANTONIO
I pray thee, hear me speak.

SHYLOCK
I'll have my bond; I will not hear thee speak:
I'll have my bond; and therefore speak no more.
I'll not be made a soft and dull-eyed fool,
To shake the head, relent, and sigh, and yield
To Christian intercessors. Follow not;
I'll have no speaking: I will have my bond.   [*Exit.*

SALARINO
It is the most impenetrable cur
That ever kept with men.

ANTONIO
              Let him alone:
I'll follow him no more with bootless prayers.
He seeks my life; his reason well I know:
I oft deliver'd from his forfeitures
Many that have at times made moan to me;
Therefore he hates me.

SALARINO
              I am sure the duke
Will never grant this forfeiture to hold.

ANTONIO
The duke cannot deny the course of law;
For the commodity that strangers have
With us in Venice, if it be denied,
Will much impeach the justice of the state;
Since that the trade and profit of the city
Consisteth of all nations. Therefore, go:
These griefs and losses have so bated me,
That I shall hardly spare a pound of flesh
To-morrow to my bloody creditor. —
Well, gaoler, on. — Pray God, Bassanio come
To see me pay his debt, — and then I care not!   [*Exeunt.*

SCENE IV

Belmont. A room in PORTIA'S *house.*

Enter PORTIA, NERISSA, LORENZO, JESSICA, *and*
BALTHAZAR, *a man of* PORTIA'S.

LORENZO
Madam, although I speak it in your presence,
You have a noble and a true conceit
Of god-like amity; which appears most strongly
In bearing thus the absence of your lord.
But if you knew to whom you show this honour,
How true a gentleman you send relief,
How dear a lover of my lord your husband,
I know you would be prouder of the work
Than customary bounty can enforce you.

PORTIA
I never did repent for doing good,
Nor shall not now: for in companions
That do converse and waste the time together,
Whose souls do bear an equal yoke of love,
There must be needs a like proportion
Of lineaments, of manners, and of spirit;
Which makes me think that this Antonio,
Being the bosom lover of my lord,
Must needs be like my lord. If it be so,
How little is the cost I have bestow'd
In purchasing the semblance of my soul
From out the state of hellish cruelty!
This comes too near the praising of myself;
Therefore no more of it: hear other things. —
Lorenzo, I commit into your hands
The husbandry and manage of my house
Until my lord's return: for mine own part,
I have toward heaven breath'd a secret vow
To live in prayer and contemplation,
Only attended by Nerissa here,
Until her husband and my lord's return:
There is a monastery two miles off;
And there will we abide. I do desire you
Not to deny this imposition;
The which my love and some necessity
Now lays upon you.

LORENZO
             Madam, with all my heart;
I shall obey you in all fair commands.

PORTIA
My people do already know my mind,
And will acknowledge you and Jessica
In place of Lord Bassanio and myself.
So fare you well, till we shall meet again.

LORENZO
Fair thoughts and happy hours attend on you!
JESSICA
I wish your ladyship all heart's content.
PORTIA
I thank you for your wish, and am well pleased
To wish it back on you: fare you well, Jessica.
[*Exeunt* JESSICA *and* LORENZO.
Now, Balthazar,
As I have ever found thee honest-true,
So let me find thee still. Take this same letter,
And use thou all the endeavour of a man
In speed to Padua: see thou render this
Into my cousin's hand, Doctor Bellario;
And, look, what notes and garments he doth give thee,
Bring them, I pray thee, with imagin'd speed
Unto the tranect, to the common ferry
Which trades to Venice. Waste no time in words,
But get thee gone: I shall be there before thee.
BALTHAZAR
Madam, I go with all convenient speed.   [*Exit.*
PORTIA
Come on, Nerissa; I have work in hand
That you yet know not of: we'll see our husbands
Before they think of us.
NERISSA
                    Shall they see us?
PORTIA
They shall, Nerissa; but in such a habit,
That they shall think we are accomplished
With that we lack. I'll hold thee any wager,
When we are both accoutred like young men,
I'll prove the prettier fellow of the two,
And wear my dagger with the braver grace;
And speak between the change of man and boy
With a reed voice; and turn two mincing steps
Into a manly stride; and speak of frays,
Like a fine-bragging youth; and tell quaint lies,
How honourable ladies sought my love,
Which I denying, they fell sick and died, —
I could not do withal; — then I'll repent,
And wish, for all that, that I had not kill'd them:
And twenty of these puny lies I'll tell;
That men shall swear I have discontinued school
Above a twelvemonth: — I have within my mind
A thousand raw tricks of these bragging Jacks,
Which I will practise.
NERISSA
                    Why, shall we turn to men?
PORTIA
Fie, what a question's that,
If thou wert near a lewd interpreter!
But come, I'll tell thee all my whole device
When I am in my coach, which stays for us
At the park-gate; and therefore haste away,
For we must measure twenty miles to-day.
[*Exeunt.*

SCENE V

The same. A garden.

Enter LAUNCELOT *and* JESSICA.

LAUNCELOT
Yes, truly; for, look you, the sins of the father are to be
laid upon the children: therefore, I promise ye, I fear
you. I was always plain with you, and so now I speak
my agitation of the matter: therefore be o' good cheer;
for, truly, I think you are damn'd. There is but one hope
in it that can do you any good; and that is but a kind of
bastard hope neither.
JESSICA
And what hope is that, I pray thee?
LAUNCELOT
Marry, you may partly hope that your father got you
not, — that you are not the Jew's daughter.
JESSICA
That were a kind of bastard hope, indeed: so the sins of
my mother should be visited upon me.
LAUNCELOT
Truly, then, I fear you are damn'd both by father and
mother: thus when I shun Scylla, your father, I fall into
Charybdis, your mother: well, you are gone both ways.
JESSICA
I shall be saved by my husband; he hath made me a
Christian.
LAUNCELOT
Truly, the more to blame he: we were Christians enow
before; e'en as many as could well live, one by another.
This making of Christians will raise the price of hogs: if
we grow all to be pork-eaters, we shall not shortly have
a rasher on the coals for money.

JESSICA
I'll tell my husband, Launcelot, what you say: here he
comes.

Enter LORENZO.

LORENZO
I shall grow jealous of you shortly, Launcelot, if you
thus get my wife into corners.
JESSICA
Nay, you need not fear us, Lorenzo: Launcelot and I are
out. He tells me flatly, there's no mercy for me in
heaven, because I am a Jew's daughter: and he says,
you are no good member of the commonwealth; for, in
converting Jews to Christians, you raise the price of
pork.
LORENZO
I shall answer that better to the commonwealth than
you can the getting up of the negro's belly: the Moor's
with child by you, Launcelot.
LAUNCELOT
It is much that the Moor should be more than reason:
but if she be less than an honest woman, she is indeed
more than I took her for.
LORENZO
How every fool can play upon the word! I think the best

grace of wit will shortly turn into silence, and discourse
grow commendable in none only but parrots. — Go in,
sirrah; bid them prepare for dinner.
LAUNCELOT
That's done, sir; they have all stomachs.
LORENZO
Goodly Lord, what a wit-snapper are you! then bid
them prepare dinner.
LAUNCELOT
That is done too, sir; only 'cover' is the word.
LORENZO
Will you cover, then, sir?
LAUNCELOT
Not so, sir, neither; I know my duty.
LORENZO
Yet more quarrelling with occasion! Wilt thou show the
whole wealth of thy wit in an instant? I pray thee,
understand a plain man in his plain meaning: go to thy
fellows, bid them cover the table, serve in the meat, and
we will come in to dinner.
LAUNCELOT
For the table, sir, it shall be serv'd in; for the meat, sir, it
shall be cover'd; for your coming in to dinner, sir, why,
let it be as humours and conceits shall govern.
[*Exit.*
LORENZO
O dear discretion, how his words are suited!
The fool hath planted in his memory
An army of good words; and I do know
A many fools, that stand in better place,
Garnish'd like him, that for a tricksy word
Defy the matter. — How cheer'st thou, Jessica?
And now, good sweet, say thy opinion, —
How dost thou like the Lord Bassanio's wife?
JESSICA
Past all expressing. It is very meet
The Lord Bassanio live an upright life;

For, having such a blessing in his lady,
He finds the joys of heaven here on earth;
And if on earth he do not mean it, then
In reason he should never come to heaven.
Why, if two gods should play some heavenly match,
And on the wager lay two earthly women,
And Portia one, there must be something else
Pawn'd with the other; for the poor rude world
Hath not her fellow.
LORENZO
                    Even such a husband
Hast thou of me as she is for a wife.
JESSICA
Nay, but ask my opinion too of that.
LORENZO
I will anon: first, let us go to dinner.
JESSICA
Nay, let me praise you while I have a stomach.
LORENZO
No, prithee, let it serve for table-talk;
Then, howsoe'er thou speak'st, 'mong other things
I shall digest it.
JESSICA
                    Well, I'll set you forth.   [*Exeunt.*

ACT IV

SCENE I

Venice. A court of justice.

Enter the DUKE, *the* MAGNIFICOES, ANTONIO,
BASSANIO, GRATIANO, SOLANIO, SALARINO,
and others.

DUKE OF VENICE
What, is Antonio here?
ANTONIO
Ready, so please your Grace.
DUKE OF VENICE
I am sorry for thee: thou art come to answer
A stony adversary, an inhuman wretch
Uncapable of pity, void and empty
From any dram of mercy.
ANTONIO
                    I have heard
Your grace hath ta'en great pains to qualify
His rigorous course; but since he stands obdurate,
And that no lawful means can carry me
Out of his envy's reach, I do oppose
My patience to his fury, and am arm'd
To suffer, with a quietness of spirit,
The very tyranny and rage of his.
DUKE OF VENICE
Go one, and call the Jew into the court.
SOLANIO
He's ready at the door: he comes, my lord.

Enter SHYLOCK.

DUKE OF VENICE
Make room, and let him stand before our face. —
Shylock, the world thinks, and I think so too,
That thou but lead'st this fashion of thy malice

To the last hour of act; and then 'tis thought
Thou'lt show thy mercy and remorse more strange
Than is thy strange apparent cruelty;
And where thou now exact'st the penalty, —
Which is a pound of this poor merchant's flesh, —
Thou wilt not only loose the forfeiture,
But, touch'd with human gentleness and love,
Forgive a moiety of the principal;
Glancing an eye of pity on his losses,
That have of late so huddled on his back,
Enow to press a royal merchant down,
And pluck commiseration of his state
From brassy bosoms and rough hearts of flint,
From stubborn Turks and Tartars, never train'd
To offices of tender courtesy.
We all expect a gentle answer, Jew.
SHYLOCK
I have possess'd your Grace of what I purpose;
And by our holy Sabbath have I sworn
To have the due and forfeit of my bond:
If you deny it, let the danger light
Upon your charter and your city's freedom.
You'll ask me, why I rather choose to have
A weight of carrion-flesh than to receive
Three thousand ducats: I'll not answer that;
But say it is my humour: is it answer'd?
What if my house be troubled with a rat,
And I be pleas'd to give ten thousand ducats
To have it ban'd! What, are you answer'd yet?
Some men there are love not a gaping pig;
Some, that are mad if they behold a cat;
And others, when the bag-pipe sings i'th'nose,
Cannot contain their urine: for affection,
Mistress of passion, sways it to the mood
Of what it likes or loathes. Now, for your answer:
As there is no firm reason to be render'd,
Why he cannot abide a gaping pig;
Why he, a harmless necessary cat;
Why he, a woollen bag-pipe — but of force
Must yield to such inevitable shame
As to offend himself, being offended;
So can I give no reason, nor I will not,
More than a lodg'd hate and a certain loathing
I bear Antonio, that I follow thus
A losing suit against him. Are you answer'd?
BASSANIO
This is no answer, thou unfeeling man,
To excuse the current of thy cruelty.
SHYLOCK
I am not bound to please thee with my answer.
BASSANIO
Do all men kill the things they do not love?
SHYLOCK
Hates any man the thing he would not kill?
BASSANIO
Every offence is not a hate at first.
SHYLOCK
What, would'st thou have a serpent sting thee twice?
ANTONIO
I pray you, think you question with the Jew:
You may as well go stand upon the beach,
And bid the main flood bate his usual height;
You may as well use question with the wolf,
Why he hath made the ewe bleat for the lamb;
You may as well forbid the mountain pines
To wag their high tops, and to make no noise,
When they are fretten with the gusts of heaven;
You may as well do anything most hard,
As seek to soften that, — than which what's harder? —
His Jewish heart: — therefore, I do beseech you,
Make no more offers, use no further means,
But, with all brief and plain conveniency,
Let me have judgement, and the Jew his will.
BASSANIO
For thy three thousand ducats here is six.
SHYLOCK
If every ducat in six thousand ducats
Were in six parts, and every part a ducat,
I would not draw them, — I would have my bond.
DUKE OF VENICE
How shalt thou hope for mercy, rendering none?
SHYLOCK
What judgement shall I dread, doing no wrong?
You have among you many a purchas'd slave,
Which, like your asses and your dogs and mules,
You use in abject and in slavish parts
Because you bought them: — shall I say to you,
Let them be free, marry them to your heirs?
Why sweat they under burdens? let their beds
Be made as soft as yours, and let their palates

Be season'd with such viands? You will answer,
The slaves are ours: — so do I answer you:
The pound of flesh, which I demand of him,
Is dearly bought, 'tis mine, and I will have it.
If you deny me, fie upon your law!
There is no force in the decrees of Venice.
I stand for judgement: answer, — shall I have it?
DUKE OF VENICE
Upon my power I may dismiss this court,
Unless Bellario, a learned doctor,
Whom I have sent for to determine this,
Come here to-day.
SOLANIO
        My lord, here stays without
A messenger with letters from the doctor,
New come from Padua.
DUKE OF VENICE
Bring us the letters; call the messenger.
BASSANIO
Good cheer, Antonio! What, man, courage yet!
The Jew shall have my flesh, blood, bones, and all,
Ere thou shalt lose for me one drop of blood.
ANTONIO
I am a tainted wether of the flock,
Meetest for death: the weakest kind of fruit
Drops earliest to the ground; and so let me:
You cannot better be employ'd, Bassanio,
Than to live still, and write mine epitaph.
   Enter NERISSA, dressed like a lawyer's clerk.
DUKE OF VENICE
Came you from Padua, from Bellario?
NERISSA
From both, my lord. Bellario greets your Grace.
             [Presents a letter.
BASSANIO
Why dost thou whet thy knife so earnestly?
SHYLOCK
To cut the forfeiture from that bankrupt there.
GRATIANO
Not on thy sole, but on thy soul, harsh Jew,
Thou mak'st thy knife keen; but no metal can,
No, not the hangman's axe, bear half the keenness
Of thy sharp envy. Can no prayers pierce thee?
SHYLOCK
No, none that thou hast wit enough to make.
GRATIANO
O, be thou damn'd, inexecrable dog!
And for thy life let justice be accused.
Thou almost mak'st me waver in my faith,
To hold opinion with Pythagoras,
That souls of animals infuse themselves
Into the trunks of men: thy currish spirit
Govern'd a wolf, who, hang'd for human slaughter,
Even from the gallows did his fell soul fleet,
And, whilst thou lay'st in thy unhallow'd dam,
Infus'd itself in thee; for thy desires
Are wolfish, bloody, starv'd and ravenous.
SHYLOCK
Till thou canst rail the seal from off my bond,
Thou but offend'st thy lungs to speak so loud:
Repair thy wit, good youth, or it will fall
To cureless ruin. — I stand here for law.
DUKE OF VENICE
This letter from Bellario doth commend
A young and learned doctor to our court. —
Where is he?
NERISSA
        He attendeth here hard by,
To know your answer, whether you'll admit him.
DUKE OF VENICE
With all my heart. — Some three or four of you
Go give him courteous conduct to this place. —
Meantime the court shall hear Bellario's letter.
CLERK [*reads*].
Your Grace shall understand, that at the receipt of your
letter I am very sick: but in the instant that your
messenger came, in loving visitation was with me a
young doctor of Rome; his name is Balthazar. I
acquainted him with the cause in controversy between
the Jew and Antonio the merchant: we turn'd o'er
many books together: he is furnis'd with my opinion;
which, better'd with his own learning, — the greatness
whereof I cannot enough commend, — comes with
him, at my importunity, to fill up your Grace's request
in my stead. I beseech you, let his lack of years be no
impediment to let him lack a reverend estimation; for I
never knew so young a body with so old a head. I leave
him to your gracious acceptance, whose trial shall
better publish his commendation.

DUKE OF VENICE
You hear the learned Bellario, what he writes:
And here, I take it, is the doctor come.
   Enter PORTIA for BALTHAZAR.
Give me your hand. Come you from old Bellario?
PORTIA
I did, my lord.
DUKE OF VENICE
        You are welcome: take your place.
Are you acquainted with the difference
That holds this present question in the court?
PORTIA
I am informed throughly of the cause. —
Which is the merchant here, and which the Jew?
DUKE OF VENICE
Antonio and old Shylock, both stand forth.
PORTIA
Is your name Shylock?
SHYLOCK
        Shylock is my name.
PORTIA
Of a strange nature is the suit you follow;
Yet in such rule, that the Venetian law
Cannot impugn you as you do proceed. —
You stand within his danger, do you not?
ANTONIO
Ay, so he says.
PORTIA
        Do you confess the bond?
ANTONIO
I do.
PORTIA
        Then must the Jew be merciful.
SHYLOCK
On what compulsion must I? tell me that.
PORTIA
The quality of mercy is not strain'd, —
It droppeth as the gentle rain from heaven
Upon the place beneath: it is twice blest, —
It blesseth him that gives, and him that takes:
'Tis mightiest in the mightiest: it becomes
The throned monarch better than his crown;
His sceptre shows the force of temporal power,
The attribute to awe and majesty,
Wherein doth sit the dread and fear of kings;
But mercy is above this sceptred sway, —
It is enthroned in the hearts of kings,
It is an attribute to God himself;
And earthly power doth then show likest God's
When mercy seasons justice. Therefore, Jew,
Though justice be thy plea, consider this, —
That, in the course of justice, none of us
Should see salvation: we do pray for mercy;
And that same prayer doth teach us all to render
The deeds of mercy. I have spoke thus much
To mitigate the justice of thy plea;
Which if thou follow, this strict court of Venice
Must needs give sentence 'gainst the merchant there.
SHYLOCK
My deeds upon my head! I crave the law,
The penalty and forfeit of my bond.
PORTIA
Is he not able to discharge the money?
BASSANIO
Yes, here I tender it for him in the court;
Yea, thrice the sum: if that will not suffice,
I will be bound to pay it ten times o'er,
On forfeit of my hands, my head, my heart:
If this will not suffice, it must appear
That malice bears down truth. And I beseech you,
Wrest once the law to your authority:
To do a great right, do a little wrong;
And curb this cruel devil of his will.
PORTIA
It must not be; there is no power in Venice
Can alter a decree established:
'Twill be recorded for a precedent;
And many an error, by the same example,
Will rush into the state: it cannot be.
SHYLOCK
A Daniel come to judgement! yea, a Daniel! —
O wise young judge, how I do honour thee!
PORTIA
I pray you, let me look upon the bond.
SHYLOCK
Here 'tis, most reverend doctor, here it is.
PORTIA
Shylock, there's thrice thy money offer'd thee.

PORTIA Take then thy bond.

SHYLOCK
An oath, an oath, I have an oath in heaven:
Shall I lay perjury upon my soul?
No, not for Venice.

PORTIA
                    Why, this bond is forfeit;
And lawfully by this the Jew may claim
A pound of flesh, to be by him cut off
Nearest the merchant's heart. — Be merciful:
Take thrice thy money; bid me tear the bond.

SHYLOCK
When it is paid according to the tenour. —
It doth appear you are a worthy judge;
You know the law, your exposition
Hath been most sound: I charge you by the law,
Whereof you are a well-deserving pillar,
Proceed to judgement: by my soul I swear
There is no power in the tongue of man
To alter me: I stay here on my bond.

ANTONIO
Most heartily I do beseech the court
To give the judgement.

PORTIA
                    Why then, thus it is: —
You must prepare your bosom for his knife.

SHYLOCK
O noble judge! O excellent young man!

PORTIA
For the intent and purpose of the law
Hath full relation to the penalty,
Which here appeareth due upon the bond.

SHYLOCK
'Tis very true: O wise and upright judge!
How much more elder art thou than thy looks!

PORTIA
Therefore lay bare your bosom.

SHYLOCK
                    Ay, his breast:
So says the bond: — doth it not, noble judge? —
Nearest his heart: those are the very words.

PORTIA
It is so. Are there balance here to weigh
The flesh?

SHYLOCK
I have them ready.

PORTIA
Have by some surgeon,
  Shylock, on your charge,
  To stop his wounds, lest he do
  bleed to death.

SHYLOCK
Is it so nominated in the bond?

PORTIA
It is not so express'd: but what
  of that?
'Twere good you do so much
  for charity.

SHYLOCK
I cannot find it; 'tis not in the
  bond.

PORTIA
You, merchant, have you any
  thing to say?

ANTONIO
But little: I am arm'd and well
  prepared. —
Give me your hand, Bassanio:
  fare you well!
Grieve not that I am fall'n to
  this for you;
For herein Fortune shows
  herself more kind
Than is her custom: it is still
  her use
To let the wretched man
  outlive his wealth,
To view with hollow eye and
  wrinkled brow
An age of poverty; from which
  lingering penance
Of such misery doth she cut
  me off.
Commend me to your
  honourable wife:
Tell her the process of
  Antonio's end;
Say how I lov'd you, speak me
  fair in death;
And, when the tale is told, bid
  her be judge
Whether Bassanio had not once a love.
Repent but you that you shall lose your friend,
And he repents not that he pays your debt;
For, if the Jew do cut but deep enough,
I'll pay it presently with all my heart.

BASSANIO
Antonio, I am married to a wife
Which is as dear to me as life itself;
But life itself, my wife, and all the world,
Are not with me esteem'd above thy life:
I would lose all, ay, sacrifice them all
Here to this devil, to deliver you.

PORTIA
Your wife would give you little thanks for that,
If she were by, to hear you make the offer.

GRATIANO
I have a wife, whom, I protest, I love:
I would she were in heaven, so she could
Entreat some power to change this currish Jew.

NERISSA
'Tis well you offer it behind her back;
The wish would make else an unquiet house.

SHYLOCK [aside].
These be the Christian husbands! I have a
  daughter;
Would any of the stock of Barabbas
Had been her husband rather than a Christian! —
We trifle time: I pray thee, pursue sentence.

PORTIA
A pound of that same merchant's flesh is thine:
The court awards it, and the law doth give it.

SHYLOCK
Most rightful judge!

PORTIA
And you must cut this flesh from off his breast:
The law allows it, and the court awards it.

SHYLOCK
Most learned judge! — A sentence! Come,
  prepare!

PORTIA
Tarry a little; there is something else.
This bond doth give thee here no jot of blood, —
The words expressly are, 'a pound of flesh':
Take then thy bond, take thou thy pound of flesh;
But, in the cutting it, if thou dost shed

One drop of Christian blood, thy lands and goods
Are, by the laws of Venice, confiscate
Unto the state of Venice.

GRATIANO
O upright judge! — Mark, Jew: — O learned judge!

SHYLOCK
Is that the law?

PORTIA
                    Thyself shalt see the act:
For, as thou urgest justice, be assured
Thou shalt have justice, more than thou desirest.

GRATIANO
O learned judge! — Mark, Jew: — a learned judge!

SHYLOCK
I take this offer, then; — pay the bond thrice,
And let the Christian go.

BASSANIO
                    Here is the money.

PORTIA
                              Soft!
The Jew shall have all justice; — soft! no haste: —
He shall have nothing but the penalty.

GRATIANO
O Jew! an upright judge, a learned judge!

PORTIA
Therefore prepare thee to cut off the flesh.
Shed thou no blood; nor cut thou less nor more
But just a pound of flesh: if thou cutt'st more
Or less than a just pound, — be it but so much
As makes it light or heavy in the substance,
Or the division of the twentieth part
Of one poor scruple, nay, if the scale do turn
But in the estimation of a hair, —
Thou diest, and all thy goods are confiscate.

GRATIANO
A second Daniel, a Daniel, Jew!
Now, infidel, I have you on the hip.

PORTIA
Why doth the Jew pause? take thy forfeiture.

SHYLOCK
Give me my principal, and let me go.

BASSANIO
I have it ready for thee; here it is.

PORTIA
He hath refus'd it in the open court:
He shall have merely justice and his bond.

GRATIANO
A Daniel, still say I, a second Daniel! —
I thank thee, Jew, for teaching me that word.

SHYLOCK
Shall I not have barely my principal?

PORTIA
Thou shalt have nothing but the forfeiture,
To be so taken at thy peril, Jew.

SHYLOCK
Why, then the devil give him good of it!

PORTIA Then must the Jew be merciful.

GRATIANO Beg that thou mayst have leave to hang thyself.

I'll stay no longer question.

PORTIA

     Tarry, Jew:
The law hath yet another hold on you.
It is enacted in the laws of Venice, —
If it be prov'd against an alien
That by direct or indirect attempts
He seek the life of any citizen,
The party 'gainst the which he doth contrive
Shall seize one half his goods; the other half
Comes to the privy coffer of the state;
And the offender's life lies in the mercy
Of the duke only, 'gainst all other voice.
In which predicament, I say, thou stand'st;
For it appears, by manifest proceeding,
That indirectly, and directly too,
Thou hast contriv'd against the very life
Of the defendant; and thou hast incurr'd
The danger formerly by me rehearsed.
Down, therefore, and beg mercy of the duke.

GRATIANO

Beg that thou mayst have leave to hang thyself:
And yet, thy wealth being forfeit to the state,
Thou hast not left the value of a cord;
Therefore thou must be hang'd at the state's charge.

DUKE OF VENICE

That thou shalt see the difference of our spirits,
I pardon thee thy life before thou ask it:
For half thy wealth, it is Antonio's;
The other half comes to the general state,
Which humbleness may drive unto a fine.

PORTIA

Ay, for the state, — not for Antonio.

SHYLOCK

Nay, take my life and all; pardon not that:
You take my house, when you do take the prop
That doth sustain my house; you take my life,
When you do take the means whereby I live.

PORTIA

What mercy can you render him, Antonio?

GRATIANO

A halter gratis; nothing else, for God's sake.

ANTONIO

So please my lord the duke and all the court
To quit the fine for one half of his goods,
I am content; so he will let me have
The other half in use, to render it,
Upon his death, unto the gentleman
That lately stole his daughter:
Two things provided more, — that, for this favour,
He presently become a Christian;
The other, that he do record a gift,
Here in the court, of all he dies possess'd,
Unto his son Lorenzo and his daughter.

DUKE OF VENICE

He shall do this; or else I do recant
The pardon that I late pronounced here.

PORTIA

Art thou contented, Jew? what dost thou say?

SHYLOCK

I am content.

PORTIA

    Clerk, draw a deed of gift.

SHYLOCK

I pray you, give me leave to go
 from hence;
I am not well: send the deed after
 me,
And I will sign it.

DUKE OF VENICE

 Get thee gone, but do it.

GRATIANO

In christening shalt thou have two
 godfathers:
Had I been judge, thou shouldst
 have had ten more,
To bring thee to the gallows, not
 the font.

      [*Exit* SHYLOCK.

DUKE OF VENICE

Sir, I entreat you home with me to
 dinner.

PORTIA

I humbly do desire your Grace of
 pardon:
I must away this night toward
 Padua,
And it is meet I presently set forth.

DUKE OF VENICE

I am sorry that your leisure serves you not. —
Antonio, gratify this gentleman;
For, in my mind, you are much bound to him.

    [*Exeunt* DUKE *and his* TRAIN.

BASSANIO

Most worthy gentleman, I and my friend
Have by your wisdom been this day acquitted
Of grievous penalties; in lieu whereof
Three thousand ducats, due unto the Jew,
We freely cope your courteous pains withal.

ANTONIO

And stand indebted, over and above,
In love and service to you evermore.

PORTIA

He is well paid that is well satisfied;
And I, delivering you, am satisfied,
And therein do account myself well paid:
My mind was never yet more mercenary.
I pray you, know me when we meet again:
I wish you well, and so I take my leave.

BASSANIO

Dear sir, of force I must attempt you further:
Take some remembrance of us, as a tribute,
Not as a fee: grant me two things, I pray you, —
Not to deny me, and to pardon me.

PORTIA

You press me far, and therefore I will yield.
[*to* ANTONIO] Give me your gloves, I'll wear them for
 your sake;
[*to* BASSANIO] And, for your love, I'll take this ring
 from you: —
Do not draw back your hand; I'll take no more;
And you in love shall not deny me this.

BASSANIO

This ring, good sir, — alas, it is a trifle!
I will not shame myself to give you this.

PORTIA

I will have nothing else but only this;
And now methinks I have a mind to it.

BASSANIO

There's more depends on this than on the value.
The dearest ring in Venice will I give you,
And find it out by proclamation:
Only for this, I pray you, pardon me.

PORTIA

I see, sir, you are liberal in offers:
You taught me first to beg; and now methinks
You teach me how a beggar should be answer'd.

BASSANIO

Good sir, this ring was given me by my wife;
And, when she put it on, she made me vow
That I should neither sell nor give nor lose it.

PORTIA

That 'scuse serves many men to save their gifts.
An if your wife be not a mad woman,
And know how well I have deserv'd the ring,
She would not hold out enemy for ever
For giving it to me. Well, peace be with you!

    [*Exeunt* PORTIA *and* NERISSA.

ANTONIO

My Lord Bassanio, let him have the ring:
Let his deservings, and my love withal,
Be valued 'gainst your wife's commandment.

BASSANIO

Go, Gratiano, run and overtake him;
Give him this ring; and bring him, if thou canst,
Unto Antonio's house: — away! make haste.

    [*Exit* GRATIANO.

Come, you and I will thither presently;
And in the morning early will we both
Fly toward Belmont: come, Antonio. [*Exeunt*

SCENE II

The same. A street.

Enter PORTIA *and* NERISSA.

PORTIA

Inquire the Jew's house out, give him this deed,
And let him sign it: we'll away to-night,
And be a day before our husbands home:
This deed will be well welcome to Lorenzo.

Enter GRATIANO.

GRATIANO

Fair sir, you are well o'erta'en:
My Lord Bassanio, upon more advice,
Hath sent you here this ring; and doth entreat
Your company at dinner.

PORTIA

     That cannot be:
His ring I do accept most thankfully;
And so, I pray you, tell him: furthermore,
I pray you, show my youth old Shylock's house.

GRATIANO

That will I do.

NERISSA

    Sir, I would speak with you. —
[*to* PORTIA] I'll see if I can get my husband's ring,
Which I did make him swear to keep for ever.

PORTIA [*to* NERISSA].

Thou mayst, I warrant. We shall have old swearing
That they did give the rings away to men;
But we'll outface them, and outswear them too. —
Away! make haste: thou know'st where I will tarry.

NERISSA

Come, good sir, will you show me to this house?

      [*Exeunt*

ACT V

SCENE I

Belmont. Avenue to PORTIA'S *house.*

Enter LORENZO *and* JESSICA.

LORENZO

The moon shines bright: — in such a night as this,
When the sweet wind did gently kiss the trees,
And they did make no noise, — in such a night
Troilus methinks mounted the Troyan walls,
And sigh'd his soul toward the Grecian tents,
Where Cressid lay that night.

JESSICA

     In such a night

Did Thisbe fearfully o'ertrip the dew,
And saw the lion's shadow ere himself,
And ran dismay'd away.
LORENZO
    In such a night
Stood Dido with a willow in her hand
Upon the wild sea-banks, and waft her love
To come again to Carthage.
JESSICA
    In such a night
Medea gather'd the enchanted herbs
That did renew old Aeson.
LORENZO
    In such a night
Did Jessica steal from the wealthy Jew,
And with an unthrift love did run from Venice
As far as Belmont.
JESSICA
    In such a night
Did young Lorenzo swear he lov'd her well,
Stealing her soul with many vows of faith,
And ne'er a true one.
LORENZO
    In such a night
Did pretty Jessica, like a little shrew,
Slander her love, and he forgave it her.
JESSICA
I would out-night you, did no body come:
But, hark, I hear the footing of a man.
Enter STEPHANO.
LORENZO
Who comes so fast in silence of the night?
STEPHANO
A friend.
LORENZO
A friend! what friend? your name, I pray you, friend?
STEPHANO
Stephano is my name; and I bring word
My mistress will before the break of day
Be here at Belmont: she doth stray about
By holy crosses, where she kneels and prays
For happy wedlock hours.
LORENZO
    Who comes with her?
STEPHANO
None but a holy hermit and her maid.
I pray you, is my master yet return'd?
LORENZO
He is not, nor we have not heard from him. —
But go we in, I pray thee, Jessica,
And ceremoniously let us prepare
Some welcome for the mistress of the house.
Enter LAUNCELOT.
LAUNCELOT
Sola, sola! wo ha, ho! sola, sola!
LORENZO
Who calls?
LAUNCELOT
Sola! — did you see Master Lorenzo? Master
Lorenzo! — sola, sola!
LORENZO
Leave hollaing, man: — here.
LAUNCELOT
Sola! — where? where?
LORENZO
Here.
LAUNCELOT
Tell him there's a post come from my master, with his
horn full of good news: my master will be here ere
morning.
    [Exit.
LORENZO
Sweet soul, let's in, and there expect their coming.
And yet no matter: — why should we go in? —
My friend Stephano, signify, I pray you,
Within the house, your mistress is at hand;
And bring your music forth into the air.
    [Exit STEPHANO.
How sweet the moonlight sleeps upon this bank!
Here will we sit, and let the sounds of music
Creep in our ears: soft stillness and the night
Becomes the touches of sweet harmony.
Sit, Jessica. Look, how the floor of heaven
Is thick inlaid with patines of bright gold:
There's not the smallest orb which thou behold'st
But in his motion like an angel sings,
Still quiring to the young-eyed cherubins, —
Such harmony is in immortal souls;

But whilst this muddy vesture of decay
Doth grossly close it in, we cannot hear it.
Enter MUSICIANS.
Come, ho, and wake Diana with a hymn!
With sweetest touches pierce your mistress' ear,
And draw her home with music.   *[Music plays.*
JESSICA
I am never merry when I hear sweet music.
LORENZO
The reason is, your spirits are attentive:
For do but note a wild and wanton herd,
Or race of youthful and unhandled colts,
Fetching mad bounds, bellowing, and neighing loud,
Which is the hot condition of their blood;
If they but hear perchance a trumpet sound,
Or any air of music touch their ears,
You shall perceive them make a mutual stand,
Their savage eyes turn'd to a modest gaze
By the sweet power of music: therefore the poet
Did feign that Orpheus drew trees, stones, and floods;
Since naught so stockish, hard, and full of rage,
But music for the time doth change his nature.
The man that hath no music in himself,
Nor is not mov'd with concord of sweet sounds,
Is fit for treasons, stratagems, and spoils;
The motions of his spirit are dull as night,
And his affections dark as Erebus:
Let no such man be trusted. — Mark the music.
Enter PORTIA and NERISSA.
PORTIA
That light we see is burning in my hall.
How far that little candle throws his beams!
So shines a good deed in a naughty world.
NERISSA
When the moon shone, we did not see the candle.
PORTIA
So doth the greater glory dim the less:
A substitute shines brightly as a king,
Until the king be by; and then his state
Empties itself, as doth an inland brook
Into the main of waters. — Music! hark!
NERISSA
It is your music, madam, of the house.
PORTIA
Nothing is good, I see, without respect:
Methinks it sounds much sweeter than by day.
NERISSA
Silence bestows that virtue on it, madam.
PORTIA
The crow doth sing as sweetly as the lark,
When neither is attended; and I think
The nightingale, if she should sing by day,
When every goose is cackling, would be thought
No better a musician than the wren.
How many things by season season'd are
To their right praise and true perfection! —
Peace, ho! the moon sleeps with Endymion,
And would not be awak'd.   *[Music ceases.*
LORENZO
    That is the voice,
Or I am much deceiv'd, of Portia.
PORTIA
He knows me, as the blind man knows the cuckoo,

By the bad voice.
LORENZO
    Dear lady, welcome home.
PORTIA
We have been praying for our husbands' health,
Which speed, we hope, the better for our words.
Are they return'd?
LORENZO
    Madam, they are not yet;
But there is come a messenger before,
To signify their coming.
PORTIA
    Go in, Nerissa;
Give orders to my servants that they take
No note at all of our being absent hence; —
Nor you, Lorenzo; — Jessica, nor you. *[A tucket sounds.*
LORENZO
Your husband is at hand; I hear his trumpet:
We are no tell-tales, madam; fear you not.
PORTIA
This night methinks is but the daylight sick;
It looks a little paler: 'tis a day,
Such as the day is when the sun is hid.
Enter BASSANIO, ANTONIO, GRATIANO, and their
    FOLLOWERS.
BASSANIO
We should hold day with the Antipodes,
If you would walk in absence of the sun.
PORTIA
Let me give light, but let me not be light;
For a light wife doth make a heavy husband,
And never be Bassanio so for me:
But God sort all! — You're welcome home, my lord.
BASSANIO
I thank you, madam. Give welcome to my friend:
This is the man, this is Antonio,
To whom I am so infinitely bound.
PORTIA
You should in all sense be much bound to him,
For, as I hear, he was much bound for you.
ANTONIO
No more than I am well acquitted of.
PORTIA
Sir, you are very welcome to our house:
It must appear in other ways than words,
Therefore I scant this breathing courtesy.
GRATIANO *[to NERISSA].*
By yonder moon I swear you do me wrong;
In faith, I gave it to the judge's clerk:
Would he were gelt that had it, for my part,
Since you do take it, love, so much at heart.
PORTIA
A quarrel, ho, already! what's the matter?
GRATIANO
About a hoop of gold, a paltry ring
That she did give me; whose posy was
For all the world like cutler's poetry
Upon a knife, 'Love me, and leave me not.'
NERISSA
What talk you of the posy or the value?
You swore to me, when I did give it you,
That you would wear it till your hour of death;

JESSICA I would out-night you, did no body come.

And that it should lie with you in your grave:
Though not for me, yet for your vehement oaths,
You should have been respective, and have kept it.
Gave it a judge's clerk! no, God's my judge,
The clerk will ne'er wear hair on's face that had it.

GRATIANO
He will, an if he live to be a man.

NERISSA
Ay, if a woman live to be a man.

GRATIANO
Now, by this hand, I gave it to a youth, —
A kind of boy; a little scrubbed boy,
No higher than thyself, the judge's clerk;
A prating boy, that begg'd it as a fee:
I could not for my heart deny it him.

PORTIA
You were to blame, — I must be plain with you, —
To part so slightly with your wife's first gift;
A thing stuck on with oaths upon your finger,
And so riveted with faith unto your flesh.
I gave my love a ring, and made him swear
Never to part with it; and here he stands, —
I dare be sworn for him, he would not leave it,
Nor pluck it from his finger, for the wealth
That the world masters. Now, in faith, Gratiano,
You give your wife too unkind a cause of grief:
An 'twere to me, I should be mad at it.

BASSANIO [aside].
Why, I were best to cut my left hand off,
And swear I lost the ring defending it.

GRATIANO
My Lord Bassanio gave his ring away
Unto the judge that begg'd it, and indeed
Deserv'd it too; and then the boy, his clerk,
That took some pains in writing, he begg'd mine:
And neither man nor master would take aught
But the two rings.

PORTIA
                    What ring gave you, my lord?
Not that, I hope, which you receiv'd of me.

BASSANIO
If I could add a lie unto a fault,
I would deny it; but you see my finger
Hath not the ring upon it, — it is gone.

PORTIA
Even so void is your false heart of truth.
By heaven, I will ne'er come in your bed
Until I see the ring.

NERISSA
                    Nor I in yours
Till I again see mine.

BASSANIO
                    Sweet Portia,
If you did know to whom I gave the ring,
If you did know for whom I gave the ring,
And would conceive for what I gave the ring,
And how unwillingly I left the ring,
When naught would be accepted but the ring,
You would abate the strength of your displeasure.

PORTIA
If you had known the virtue of the ring,
Or half her worthiness that gave the ring,
Or your own honour to contain the ring,
You would not then have parted with the ring.
What man is there so much unreasonable,
If you had pleas'd to have defended it
With any terms of zeal, wanted the modesty
To urge the thing held as a ceremony?
Nerissa teaches me what to believe:

I'll die for't but some woman had the ring.

BASSANIO
No, by my honour, madam, by my soul,
No woman had it, but a civil doctor,
Which did refuse three thousand ducats of me,
And begg'd the ring; the which I did deny him,
And suffer'd him to go displeas'd away;
Even he that did uphold the very life
Of my dear friend. What should I say, sweet lady?
I was enforc'd to send it after him:
I was beset with shame and courtesy;
My honour would not let ingratitude
So much besmear it. Pardon me, good lady;
For, by these blessed candles of the night,
Had you been there, I think, you would have begg'd
The ring of me to give the worthy doctor.

PORTIA
Let not that doctor e'er come near my house:
Since he hath got the jewel that I lov'd,
And that which you did swear to keep for me,
I will become as liberal as you;
I'll not deny him any thing I have,
No, not my body nor my husband's bed:
Know him I shall, I am well sure of it:
Lie not a night from home; watch me like Argus:
If you do not, if I be left alone,
Now, by mine honour, which is yet mine own,
I'll have that doctor for my bedfellow.

NERISSA
And I his clerk; therefore be well advised
How you do leave me to mine own protection.

GRATIANO
Well, do you so: let me not take him, then;
For if I do, I'll mar the young clerk's pen.

ANTONIO
I am the unhappy subject of these quarrels.

PORTIA
Sir, grieve not you; you are welcome notwithstanding.

BASSANIO
Portia, forgive me this enforced wrong;
And, in the hearing of these many friends,
I swear to thee, even by thine own fair eyes,
Wherein I see myself, —

PORTIA
                    Mark you but that!
In both my eyes he doubly sees himself;
In each eye, one: — swear by your double self,
And there's an oath of credit.

BASSANIO
                    Nay, but hear me:
Pardon this fault, and by my soul I swear
I never more will break an oath with thee.

ANTONIO
I once did lend my body for his wealth;
Which, but for him that had your husband's ring,
Had quite miscarried: I dare be bound again,
My soul upon the forfeit, that your lord
Will never more break faith advisedly.

PORTIA
Then you shall be his surety. Give him this;
And bid him keep it better than the other.

ANTONIO
Here, Lord Bassanio; swear to keep this ring.

BASSANIO
By heaven, it is the same I gave the doctor!

PORTIA
I had it of him: pardon me, Bassanio;
For, by this ring, the doctor lay with me.

NERISSA
And pardon me, my gentle Gratiano;
For that same scrubbed boy, the doctor's clerk,
In lieu of this, last night did lie with me.

GRATIANO
Why, this is like the mending of highways
In summer, where the ways are fair enough:
What, are we cuckolds ere we have deserv'd it?

PORTIA
Speak not so grossly. — You are all amaz'd:
Here is a letter; read it at your leisure;
It comes from Padua, from Bellario:
There you shall find that Portia was the doctor;
Nerissa there her clerk: Lorenzo here
Shall witness I set forth as soon as you,
And even but now return'd; I have not yet
Enter'd my house. — Antonio, you are welcome;
And I have better news in store for you
Than you expect: unseal this letter soon;
There you shall find three of your argosies
Are richly come to harbour suddenly:
You shall not know by what strange accident
I chanced on this letter.

ANTONIO
                    I am dumb.

BASSANIO
Were you the doctor, and I knew you not?

GRATIANO
Were you the clerk that is to make me cuckold?

NERISSA
Ay, but the clerk that never means to do it,
Unless he live until he be a man.

BASSANIO
Sweet doctor, you shall be my bedfellow:
When I am absent, then lie with my wife.

ANTONIO
Sweet lady, you have given me life and living;
For here I read for certain that my ships
Are safely come to road.

PORTIA
                    How now, Lorenzo!
My clerk hath some good comforts too for you.

NERISSA
Ay, and I'll give them him without a fee. —
There do I give to you and Jessica,
From the rich Jew, a special deed of gift,
After his death, of all he dies possess'd of.

LORENZO
Fair ladies, you drop manna in the way
Of starved people.

PORTIA
                    It is almost morning,
And yet I am sure you are not satisfied
Of these events at full. Let us go in;
And charge us there upon inter'gatories,
And we will answer all things faithfully.

GRATIANO
Let it be so: the first inter'gatory
That my Nerissa shall be sworn on is,
Whether till the next night she had rather stay,
Or go to bed now, being two hours to day:
But were the day come, I should wish it dark,
That I were couching with the doctor's clerk.
Well, while I live I'll fear no other thing
So sore as keeping safe Nerissa's ring.   [Exeunt.

THE FIRST PART OF KING HENRY THE FOURTH

DRAMATIS PERSONAE

KING HENRY THE FOURTH.
HENRY, *Prince of Wales,*
PRINCE JOHN *of Lancaster,* } *sons to the King.*
EARL OF WESTMORELAND.
SIR WALTER BLUNT.
THOMAS PERCY, *Earl of Worcester.*
HENRY PERCY, *Earl of Northumberland.*
HENRY PERCY, *surnamed* HOTSPUR, *his son.*
EDMUND MORTIMER, *Earl of March.*
SCROOP, *Archbishop of York.*

ARCHIBALD, *Earl of Douglas.*
OWEN GLENDOWER.
SIR RICHARD VERNON.
SIR JOHN FALSTAFF.
SIR MICHAEL, *a friend to the Archbishop of York.*
POINTZ.
GADSHILL.
PETO.
BARDOLPH.

LADY PERCY, *wife to Hotspur, and sister to Mortimer.*
LADY MORTIMER, *daughter to Glendower, and wife to Mortimer.*
MISTRESS QUICKLY, *hostess of a tavern in East-cheap.*

LORDS, OFFICERS, SHERIFF, VINTNER, CHAMBERLAIN, DRAWERS, TWO CARRIERS, TRAVELLERS, *and* ATTENDANTS.

SCENE — *England.*

WESTMORELAND My liege, this haste was hot in question.

ACT I

SCENE I

London. The palace.

Enter KING HENRY, WESTMORELAND, SIR WALTER BLUNT, *and others.*

KING HENRY
So shaken as we are, so wan with care,
Find we a time for frighted peace to pant,
And breathe short-winded accents of new broils
To be commenc'd in stronds afar remote.
No more the thirsty entrance of this soil
Shall daub her lips with her own children's blood;
No more shall trenching war channel her fields,
Nor bruise her flowerets with the armed hoofs
Of hostile paces: those opposed eyes,
Which, like the meteors of a troubled heaven,
All of one nature, of one substance bred,
Did lately meet in the intestine shock
And furious close of civil butchery,
Shall now, in mutual well-beseeming ranks,
March all one way, and be no more opposed
Against acquaintance, kindred, and allies:
The edge of war, like an ill-sheathed knife,
No more shall cut his master. Therefore, friends,
As far as to the sepulchre of Christ, —
Whose soldier now, under whose blessed cross
We are impressed and engag'd to fight, —
Forthwith a power of English shall we levy;
Whose arms were moulded in their mothers' womb
To chase these pagans in those holy fields
Over whose acres walk'd those blessed feet
Which fourteen hundred years ago were nail'd
For our advantage on the bitter cross.
But this our purpose now is twelve month old,
And bootless 'tis to tell you we will go:
Therefore we meet not now. — Then let me hear
Of you, my gentle cousin Westmoreland,
What yesternight our council did decree
In forwarding this dear expedience.

WESTMORELAND
My liege, this haste was hot in question,
And many limits of the charge set down
But yesternight: when, all athwart, there came
A post from Wales loaden with heavy news;
Whose worst was, — that the noble Mortimer,
Leading the men of Herefordshire to fight
Against the irregular and wild Glendower,
Was by the rude hands of that Welshman taken,
A thousand of his people butchered;
Upon whose dead corpse there was such misuse,
Such beastly, shameless transformation,
By those Welshwomen done, as may not be
Without much shame re-told or spoken of.

KING HENRY
It seems, then, that the tidings of this broil
Brake off our business for the Holy Land.

WESTMORELAND
This, match'd with other, did, my gracious lord;
For more uneven and unwelcome news
Came from the north, and thus it did import:
On Holy-rood day, the gallant Hotspur there,
Young Harry Percy, and brave Archibald,
That ever-valiant and approved Scot,
At Holmedon met,
Where they did spend a sad and bloody hour,
As by discharge of their artillery,
And shape of likelihood, the news was told;
For he that brought them, in the very heat
And pride of their contention did take horse,
Uncertain of the issue any way.

KING HENRY
Here is a dear, a true industrious friend,
Sir Walter Blunt, new lighted from his horse,
Stain'd with the variation of each soil
Betwixt that Holmedon and this seat of ours;
And he hath brought us smooth and welcome news.
The Earl of Douglas is discomfited;
Ten thousand bold Scots, two-and-twenty knights,
Balk'd in their own blood, did Sir Walter see
On Holmedon's plains: of prisoners, Hotspur took
Mordake the Earl of Fife, and eldest son
To beaten Douglas; and the Earl of Athol,
Of Murray, Angus, and Menteith:
And is not this an honourable spoil,
A gallant prize? ha, cousin, is it not?

WESTMORELAND
In faith,
It is a conquest for a prince to boast of.

KING HENRY
Yea, there thou mak'st me sad, and mak'st me sin
In envy that my Lord Northumberland
Should be the father to so blest a son, —
A son who is the theme of honour's tongue;
Amongst a grove, the very straightest plant;
Who is sweet Fortune's minion and her pride:
Whilst I, by looking on the praise of him,
See riot and dishonour stain the brow
Of my young Harry. O, that it could be prov'd
That some night-tripping fairy had exchang'd
In cradle-clothes our children where they lay,
And call'd mine Percy, his Plantagenet!
Then would I have his Harry, and he mine:
But let him from my thoughts. — What think you, coz,
Of this young Percy's pride? the prisoners,
Which he in this adventure hath surpris'd,
To his own use he keeps; and sends me word
I shall have none but Mordake Earl of Fife.

WESTMORELAND
This is his uncle's teaching, this is Worcester,
Malevolent to you in all aspects;
Which makes him prune himself, and bristle up
The crest of youth against your dignity.

KING HENRY
But I have sent for him to answer this;
And for this cause awhile we must neglect
Our holy purpose to Jerusalem.
Cousin, on Wednesday next our council we
Will hold at Windsor, — so inform the lords:
But come yourself with speed to us again;
For more is to be said and to be done
Than out of anger can be uttered.

WESTMORELAND
I will, my liege. [*Exeunt.*

PRINCE HENRY What say'st thou to a hare, or the melancholy of Moor-ditch?

SCENE II

London. A tavern.

Enter PRINCE HENRY *and* FALSTAFF.

FALSTAFF
Now, Hal, what time of day is it, lad?

PRINCE HENRY
Thou art so fat-witted, with drinking of old sack, and unbuttoning thee after supper, and sleeping upon benches after noon, that thou hast forgotten to demand that truly which thou wouldst truly know. What a devil hast thou to do with the time of the day? unless hours were cups of sack, and minutes capons, and clocks the tongues of bawds, and dials the signs of leaping-houses, and the blessed sun himself a fair hot wench in flame-colour'd taffeta, — I see no reason why thou shouldst be so superfluous to demand the time of the day.

FALSTAFF
Indeed, you come near me now, Hal; for we that take purses go by the moon and the seven stars, and not by Phœbus, he, 'that wandering knight so fair.' And, I prithee, sweet wag, when thou art king, — as, God save thy Grace, — majesty I should say, for grace thou wilt have none, —

PRINCE HENRY
What, none?

FALSTAFF
No, by my troth, — not so much as will serve to prologue to an egg and butter.

PRINCE HENRY
Well, how then? come, roundly, roundly.

FALSTAFF
Marry, then, sweet wag, when thou art king, let not us that are squires of the night's body be call'd thieves of the day's beauty: let us be Diana's foresters, gentlemen of the shade, minions of the moon; and let men say we be men of good government, being govern'd, as the sea is, by our noble and chaste mistress the moon, under whose countenance we steal.

PRINCE HENRY
Thou say'st well, and it holds well too; for the fortune of us that are the moon's men doth ebb and flow like the sea, being govern'd, as the sea is, by the moon. As, for proof, now: a purse of gold most resolutely snatch'd on Monday night, and most dissolutely spent on Tuesday morning; got with swearing 'lay by', and spent with crying 'bring in'; now in as low an ebb as the foot of the ladder, and by and by in as high a flow as the ridge of the gallows.

FALSTAFF
By the Lord, thou say'st true, lad. And is not my hostess of the tavern a most sweet wench?

PRINCE HENRY
As the honey of Hybla, my old lad of the castle. And is not a buff jerkin a most sweet robe of durance?

FALSTAFF
How now, how now, mad wag! what, in thy quips and thy quiddities? what a plague have I to do with a buff jerkin?

PRINCE HENRY
Why, what a pox have I to do with my hostess of the tavern?

FALSTAFF
Well, thou hast call'd her to a reckoning many a time and oft.

PRINCE HENRY
Did I ever call for thee to pay thy part?

FALSTAFF
No; I'll give thee thy due, thou hast paid all there.

PRINCE HENRY
Yea, and elsewhere, so far as my coin would stretch; and where it would not, I have used my credit.

FALSTAFF
Yea, and so used it, that, were it not here apparent that thou art heir apparent — But, I prithee, sweet wag, shall there be gallows standing in England when thou art king? and resolution thus fobb'd as it is with the rusty curb of old father antic the law? Do not thou, when thou art king, hang a thief.

PRINCE HENRY
No; thou shalt.

FALSTAFF
Shall I? O rare! By the Lord, I'll be a brave judge.

PRINCE HENRY
Thou judgest false already: I mean, thou shalt have the hanging of the thieves, and so become a rare hangman.

FALSTAFF
Well, Hal, well; and in some sort it jumps with my humour as well as waiting in the court, I can tell you.

PRINCE HENRY
For obtaining of suits?

FALSTAFF
Yea, for obtaining of suits, whereof the hangman hath no lean wardrobe. 'Sblood, I am as melancholy as a gib-cat or a lugg'd bear.

PRINCE HENRY
Or an old lion, or a lover's lute.

FALSTAFF
Yea, or the drone of a Lincolnshire bagpipe.

PRINCE HENRY
What say'st thou to a hare, or the melancholy of Moor-ditch?

FALSTAFF
Thou hast the most unsavoury similes, and art, indeed, the most comparative, rascalliest, — sweet young prince. But, Hal, I prithee, trouble me no more with vanity. I would to God thou and I knew where a commodity of good names were to be bought. An old lord of the council rated me the other day in the street about you, sir, — but I mark'd him not; and yet he talk'd very wisely, — but I regarded him not; and yet he talk'd wisely, and in the street too.

PRINCE HENRY
Thou didst well; for wisdom cries out in the streets, and no man regards it.

FALSTAFF
O, thou hast damnable iteration, and art, indeed, able to corrupt a saint. Thou hast done much harm upon me, Hal, — God forgive thee for it! Before I knew thee,

Hal, I knew nothing; and now am I, if a man should speak truly, little better than one of the wicked. I must give over this life, and I will give it over; by the Lord, and I do not, I am a villain: I'll be damn'd for never a king's son in Christendom.

PRINCE HENRY
Where shall we take a purse to-morrow, Jack?

FALSTAFF
Zounds, where thou wilt, lad; I'll make one: an I do not, call me villain, and baffle me.

PRINCE HENRY
I see a good amendment of life in thee, — from praying to purse-taking.

Enter POINTZ.

FALSTAFF
Why, Hal, 'tis my vocation, Hal; 'tis no sin for a man to labour in his vocation. — Pointz! — Now shall we know if Gadshill have set a match. — O, if men were to be saved by merit, what hole in hell were hot enough for him? This is the most omnipotent villain that ever cried 'stand' to a true man.

PRINCE HENRY
Good morrow, Ned.

POINTZ
Good morrow, sweet Hal. — What says Monsieur Remorse? what says Sir John Sack-and-Sugar? Jack, how agrees the devil and thee about thy soul, that thou soldest him on Good-Friday last for a cup of Madeira and a cold capon's leg?

PRINCE HENRY
Sir John stands to his word, — the devil shall have his bargain; for he was never yet a breaker of proverbs, — he will give the devil his due.

POINTZ
Then art thou damn'd for keeping thy word with the devil.

PRINCE HENRY
Else he had been damn'd for cozening the devil.

POINTZ
But, my lads, my lads, to-morrow morning, by four o'clock, early at Gadshill! there are pilgrims going to Canterbury with rich offerings, and traders riding to London with fat purses: I have vizards for you all; you have horses for yourselves: Gadshill lies to-night in Rochester: I have bespoke supper to-morrow night in Eastcheap: we may do it as secure as sleep. If you will go, I will stuff our purses full of crowns; if you will not, tarry at home and be hang'd.

FALSTAFF
Hear ye, Yedward; if I tarry at home and go not, I'll hang you for going.

POINTZ
You will, chops?

FALSTAFF
Hal, wilt thou make one?

PRINCE HENRY
Who, I rob? I a thief? not I, by my faith.

FALSTAFF
There's neither honesty, manhood, nor good fellowship in thee, nor thou camest not of the blood royal, if thou darest not stand for ten shillings.

PRINCE HENRY
Well, then, once in my days I'll be a madcap.

FALSTAFF
Why, that's well said.

PRINCE HENRY
Well, come what will, I'll tarry at home.

FALSTAFF
By the Lord, I'll be a traitor, then, when thou art king.

PRINCE HENRY
I care not.

POINTZ
Sir John, I prithee, leave the prince and me alone: I will lay him down such reasons for this adventure, that he shall go.

FALSTAFF
Well, God give thee the spirit of persuasion, and him the ears of profiting, that what thou speakest may move, and what he hears may be believed, that the true prince may, for recreation sake, prove a false thief; for the poor abuses of the time want countenance. Farewell: you shall find me in Eastcheap.

PRINCE HENRY
Farewell, thou latter spring! farewell, All-hallown summer!

[*Exit* FALSTAFF.

POINTZ
Now, my good sweet honey lord, ride with us to-morrow: I

have a jest to execute that I cannot manage alone. Falstaff,
Bardolph, Peto, and Gadshill, shall rob those men that we
have already waylaid; yourself and I will not be there; and
when they have the booty, if you and I do not rob them, cut
this head from my shoulders.

PRINCE HENRY
But how shall we part with them in setting forth?

POINTZ
Why, we will set forth before or after them, and appoint
them a place of meeting, wherein it is at our pleasure to
fail, and then will they adventure upon the exploit
themselves, which they shall have no sooner achieved,
but we'll set upon them.

PRINCE HENRY
Yea, but 'tis like that they will know us by our horses, by
our habits, and by every other appointment, to be
ourselves.

POINTZ
Tut! our horses they shall not see, — I'll tie them in the
wood; our vizards we will change, after we leave them;
and, sirrah, I have cases of buckram for the nonce, to
immask our noted outward garments.

PRINCE HENRY
Yea, but I doubt they will be too hard for us.

POINTZ
Well, for two of them, I know them to be as true-bred
cowards as ever turn'd back; and for the third, if he
fight longer than he sees reason, I'll forswear arms.
The virtue of this jest will be, the incomprehensible lies
that this same fat rogue will tell us when we meet at
supper: how thirty, at least, he fought with; what wards,
what blows, what extremities he endured; and in the
reproof of this lies the jest.

PRINCE HENRY
Well, I'll go with thee: provide us all things necessary,
and meet me to-night in Eastcheap; there I'll sup.
Farewell.

POINTZ
Farewell, my lord. [*Exit.*

PRINCE HENRY
I know you all, and will awhile uphold
The unyok'd humour of your idleness:
Yet herein will I imitate the sun,
Who doth permit the base contagious clouds
To smother up his beauty from the world,
That, when he please again to be himself,
Being wanted, he may be more wonder'd at,
By breaking through the foul and ugly mists
Of vapours that did seem to strangle him.
If all the year were playing holidays,
To sport would be as tedious as to work;
But when they seldom come, they wish'd for come,
And nothing pleaseth but rare accidents.
So, when this loose behaviour I throw off,
And pay the debt I never promised,
By how much better than my word I am,
By so much shall I falsify men's hopes;
And, like bright metal on a sullen ground,
My reformation, glittering o'er my fault,
Shall show more goodly and attract more eyes
Than that which hath no foil to set it off.
I'll so offend, to make offence a skill;
Redeeming time, when men think least I will. [*Exit.*

SCENE III

London. The palace.

Enter KING HENRY, NORTHUMBERLAND,
WORCESTER, HOTSPUR, SIR WALTER BLUNT,
and others.

KING HENRY
My blood hath been too cold and temperate,
Unapt to stir at these indignities,
And you have found me; for accordingly
You tread upon my patience: but be sure
I will from henceforth rather be myself,
Mighty and to be fear'd, than my condition;
Which hath been smooth as oil, soft as young down,
And therefore lost that title of respect
Which the proud soul ne'er pays but to the proud.

WORCESTER
Our house, my sovereign liege, little deserves
The scourge of greatness to be used on it;
And that same greatness too which our own hands
Have holp to make so portly.

NORTHUMBERLAND
My lord, —

KING HENRY
Worcester, get thee gone; for I do see
Danger and disobedience in thine eye:

KING HENRY Worcester, get thee gone.

O, sir, your presence is too bold and peremptory,
And majesty might never yet endure
The moody frontier of a servant brow.
You have good leave to leave us: when we need
Your use and counsel, we shall send for you.
[*Exit* WORCESTER.
[*to* NORTHUMBERLAND] You were about to speak.

NORTHUMBERLAND
                              Yea, my good lord.
Those prisoners in your highness' name demanded,
Which Harry Percy here at Holmedon took,
Were, as he says, not with such strength denied
As is deliver'd to your majesty:
Either envy, therefore, or misprison
Is guilty of this fault, and not my son.

HOTSPUR
My liege, I did deny no prisoners.
But I remember, when the fight was done,
When I was dry with rage and extreme toil,
Breathless and faint, leaning upon my sword,
Came there a certain lord, neat, and trimly dress'd,
Fresh as a bridegroom; and his chin new reap'd
Show'd like a stubble-land at harvest-home;
He was perfumed like a milliner;
And 'twixt his finger and his thumb he held
A pouncet-box, which ever and anon
He gave his nose, and took't away again; —
Who therewith angry, when it next came there,
Took it in snuff: — and still he smil'd and talk'd;
And as the soldiers bore dead bodies by,
He call'd them untaught knaves, unmannerly,
To bring a slovenly unhandsome corse
Betwixt the wind and his nobility.
With many holiday and lady terms
He question'd me; amongst the rest, demanded
My prisoners in your majesty's behalf.
I then, all smarting with my wounds being cold,
To be so pester'd with a popinjay,
Out of my grief and my impatience,
Answer'd neglectingly, I know not what, —
He should, or he should not; for he made me mad
To see him shine so brisk, and smell so sweet,
And talk so like a waiting-gentlewoman
Of guns and drums and wounds, — God save the
    mark! —
And telling me the sovereign'st thing on earth
Was parmaceti for an inward bruise;
And that it was great pity, so it was,
This villainous salt-petre should be digg'd

Out of the bowels of the harmless earth,
Which many a good tall fellow had destroy'd
So cowardly; and but for these vile guns,
He would himself have been a soldier.
This bald unjointed chat of his, my lord,
I answer'd indirectly, as I said;
And I beseech you, let not his report
Come current for an accusation
Betwixt my love and your high majesty.

SIR WALTER BLUNT
The circumstance consider'd, good my lord,
Whate'er Lord Harry Percy then had said
To such a person, and in such a place,
At such a time, with all the rest re-told,
May reasonably die, and never rise
To do him wrong, or any way impeach
What then he said, so he unsay it now.

KING HENRY
Why, yet he doth deny his prisoners,
But with proviso and exception, —
That we at our own charge shall ransom straight
His brother-in-law, the foolish Mortimer;
Who, on my soul, hath wilfully betray'd
The lives of those that he did lead to fight
Against that great magician, damn'd Glendower,
Whose daughter, as we hear, that Earl of March
Hath lately married. Shall our coffers, then,
Be emptied to redeem a traitor home?
Shall we buy treason? and indent with fears,
When they have lost and forfeited themselves?
No, on the barren mountains let him starve;
For I shall never hold that man my friend
Whose tongue shall ask me for one penny cost
To ransom home revolted Mortimer.

HOTSPUR
Revolted Mortimer!
He never did fall off, my sovereign liege,
But by the chance of war: — to prove that true
Needs no more but one tongue for all those wounds,
Those mouthed wounds, which valiantly he took,
When on the gentle Severn's sedgy bank,
In single opposition, hand to hand,
He did confound the best part of an hour
In changing hardiment with great Glendower:
Three times they breath'd, and three times did they
    drink,
Upon agreement, of swift Severn's flood;
Who then, affrighted with their bloody looks,
Ran fearfully among the trembling reeds,

And hid his crisp head in the hollow bank
Blood-stained with these valiant combatants.
Never did base and rotten policy
Colour her working with such deadly wounds;
Nor never could the noble Mortimer
Receive so many, and all willingly:
Then let him not be slander'd with revolt.

KING HENRY
Thou dost belie him, Percy, thou dost belie him;
He never did encounter with Glendower:
I tell thee,
He durst as well have met the devil alone
As Owen Glendower for an enemy.
Art thou not ashamed? But, sirrah, henceforth
Let me not hear you speak of Mortimer:
Send me your prisoners with the speediest means,
Or you shall hear in such a kind from me
As will displease you. — My Lord Northumberland,
We licence your departure with your son. —
Send us your prisoners, or you will hear of it.
            [Exeunt KING HENRY, BLUNT, and TRAIN.

HOTSPUR
An if the devil come and roar for them,
I will not send them: — I will after straight
And tell him so: for I will ease my heart,
Albeit I make a hazard of my head.

NORTHUMBERLAND
What, drunk with choler? stay, and pause awhile:
Here comes your uncle.

            Enter WORCESTER.

HOTSPUR
                    Speak of Mortimer!
Zounds, I will speak of him; and let my soul
Want mercy, if I do not join with him:
Yea, on his part I'll empty all these veins,
And shed my dear blood drop by drop i'th'dust,
But I will lift the down-trod Mortimer
As high i'th'air as this unthankful king,
As this ingrate and canker'd Bolingbroke.

NORTHUMBERLAND
[to WORCESTER] Brother, the king hath made your
    nephew mad.

WORCESTER
Who struck this heat up after I was gone?

HOTSPUR
He will, forsooth, have all my prisoners;
And when I urg'd the ransom once again
Of my wife's brother, then his cheek look'd pale,
And on my face he turn'd an eye of death,
Trembling even at the name of Mortimer.

WORCESTER
I cannot blame him: was not he proclaim'd
By Richard that dead is the next of blood?

NORTHUMBERLAND
He was; I heard the proclamation:
And then it was when the unhappy king —
Whose wrongs in us God pardon! — did set forth
Upon his Irish expedition;
From whence he intercepted did return
To be depos'd, and shortly murdered.

WORCESTER
And for whose death we in the world's wide mouth
Live scandalis'd and foully spoken of.

HOTSPUR
But, soft, I pray you; did King Richard then
Proclaim my brother Edmund Mortimer
Heir to the crown?

NORTHUMBERLAND
                    He did; myself did hear it.

HOTSPUR
Nay, then I cannot blame his cousin king,
That wish'd him on the barren mountains starve.
But shall it be, that you, that set the crown
Upon the head of this forgetful man,
And for his sake wear the detested blot
Of murderous subornation, — shall it be,
That you a world of curses undergo,
Being the agents, or base second means,
The cords, the ladder, or the hangman rather? —
O, pardon me, that I descend so low,
To show the line and the predicament
Wherein you range under this subtle king; —
Shall it, for shame, be spoken in these days,
Or fill up chronicles in time to come,
That men of your nobility and power
Did gage them both in an unjust behalf, —
As both of you, God pardon it! have done, —
To put down Richard, that sweet lovely rose,
And plant this thorn, this canker, Bolingbroke?
And shall it, in more shame, be further spoken,

That you are fool'd, discarded,
    and shook off
By him for whom these shames
    ye underwent?
No; yet time serves, wherein
    you may redeem
Your banish'd honours, and
    restore yourselves
Into the good thoughts of the
    world again;
Revenge the jeering and
    disdain'd contempt
Of this proud king, who studies
    day and night
To answer all the debt he owes
    to you
Even with the bloody payment
    of your deaths:
Therefore, I say, —

WORCESTER
        Peace, cousin,
                    say no more:
And now I will unclasp a secret
    book,
And to your quick-conceiving discontents
I'll read you matter deep and dangerous;
As full of peril and adventurous spirit
As to o'er-walk a current roaring loud
On the unsteadfast footing of a spear.

HOTSPUR
If he fall in, good night! — or sink or swim: —
Send danger from the east unto the west,
So honour cross it from the north to south,
And let them grapple: — O, the blood more stirs
To rouse a lion than to start a hare!

NORTHUMBERLAND
Imagination of some great exploit
Drives him beyond the bounds of patience.

HOTSPUR
By heaven, methinks it were an easy leap,
To pluck bright honour from the pale-fac'd moon;
Or dive into the bottom of the deep,
Where fadom-line could never touch the ground,
And pluck up drowned honour by the locks;
So he that doth redeem her thence might wear
Without corrival, all her dignities:
But out upon this half-fac'd fellowship!

WORCESTER
He apprehends a world of figures here,
But not the form of what he should attend. —
Good cousin, give me audience for a while.

HOTSPUR
I cry you mercy.

WORCESTER
            Those same noble Scots
That are your prisoners, —

HOTSPUR
                    I'll keep them all;
By God, he shall not have a Scot of them;
No, if a Scot would save his soul, he shall not:
I'll keep them, by this hand.

WORCESTER
            You start away,
And lend no ear unto my purposes. —
Those prisoners you shall keep.

HOTSPUR
                    Nay, I will; that's flat: —
He said he would not ransom Mortimer;
Forbad my tongue to speak of Mortimer;
But I will find him when he lies asleep,
And in his ear I'll holla 'Mortimer!'
Nay, I'll have a starling shall be taught to speak
Nothing but 'Mortimer', and give it him,
To keep his anger still in motion.

WORCESTER
Hear you, cousin; a word.

HOTSPUR
All studies here I solemnly defy,
Save how to gall and pinch this Bolingbroke:
And that same sword-and-buckler Prince of Wales, —
But that I think his father loves him not,
And would be glad he met with some mischance,
I would have him poison'd with a pot of ale.

WORCESTER
Farewell, kinsman: I'll talk to you
When you are better temper'd to attend.

NORTHUMBERLAND
Why, what a wasp-stung and impatient fool
Art thou to break into this woman's mood,
Tying thine ear to no tongue but thine own!

HOTSPUR Came there a certain lord, neat, and trimly dress'd.

HOTSPUR
Why, look you, I am whipp'd and scourg'd with rods,
Nettled, and stung with pismires, when I hear
Of this vile politician, Bolingbroke.
In Richard's time, — what do you call the place? —
A plague upon't — it is in Glostershire; —
'Twas where the madcap duke his uncle kept, —
His uncle York; — where I first bow'd my knee
Unto this king of smiles, this Bolingbroke, —
'Sblood! —
When you and he came back from Ravenspurg.

NORTHUMBERLAND
At Berkley-castle.

HOTSPUR
You say true: —
Why, what a candy deal of courtesy
This fawning greyhound then did proffer me!
Look, 'when his infant fortune came to age',
And, 'gentle Harry Percy', and, 'kind cousin', —
O, the devil take such cozeners! — God forgive me! —
Good uncle, tell your tale; I have done.

WORCESTER
Nay, if you have not, to it again;
We will stay your leisure.

HOTSPUR
                    I have done, i'faith.

WORCESTER
Then once more to your Scottish prisoners.
Deliver them up without their ransom straight,
And make the Douglas' son your only mean
For powers in Scotland; which, for divers reasons
Which I shall send you written, be assured,
Will easily be granted. — [to NORTHUMBERLAND]
    You, my lord,
Your son in Scotland being thus employ'd,
Shall secretly into the bosom creep
Of that same noble prelate, well beloved,
The archbishop.

HOTSPUR
Of York, is it not?

WORCESTER
True; who bears hard
His brother's death at Bristol, the Lord Scroop.
I speak not this in estimation,
As what I think might be, but what I know
Is ruminated, plotted, and set down,
And only stays but to behold the face
Of that occasion that shall bring it on.

HOTSPUR
I smell it: upon my life, it will do well.

NORTHUMBERLAND
Before the game is a-foot, thou still lett'st slip.

HOTSPUR
Why, it cannot choose but be a noble plot: —
And then the power of Scotland and of York,
To join with Mortimer, ha?

WORCESTER
                    And so they shall.

HOTSPUR
In faith, it is exceedingly well aim'd.

WORCESTER
And 'tis no little reason bids us speed,
To save our heads by raising of a head;
For, bear ourselves as even as we can,
The king will always think him in our debt,
And think we think ourselves unsatisfied,

Till he hath found a time to pay us home:
And see already how he doth begin
To make us strangers to his looks of love.

HOTSPUR
He does, he does; we'll be revenged on him.

WORCESTER
Cousin, farewell: — no further go in this
Than I by letters shall direct your course.
When time is ripe, — which will be suddenly, —
I'll steal to Glendower and Lord Mortimer;
Where you and Douglas, and our powers at once,
As I will fashion it, shall happily meet,
To bear our fortunes in our own strong arms,
Which now we hold at much uncertainty.

NORTHUMBERLAND
Farewell, good brother: we shall thrive, I trust.

HOTSPUR
Uncle, adieu: — O, let the hours be short,
Till fields and blows and groans applaud our sport!

[*Exeunt.*

ACT II

SCENE I

Rochester. An inn-yard.

Enter a CARRIER *with a lantern in his hand.*

FIRST CARRIER
Heigh-ho! an't be not four by the day, I'll be hang'd:
Charles' wain is over the new chimney, and yet our
horse not pack'd. — What, ostler!

OSTLER [*within*].
Anon, anon.

FIRST CARRIER
I prithee, Tom, beat Cut's saddle, put a few flocks in
the point; poor jade is wrung in the withers out of
all cess.

Enter another CARRIER.

SECOND CARRIER
Peas and beans are as dank here as a dog, and that is
the next way to give poor jades the bots: this house is
turn'd upside down since Robin ostler died.

FIRST CARRIER
Poor fellow! never joy'd since the price of oats rose; it
was the death of him.

SECOND CARRIER
I think this be the most villainous house in all London
road for fleas: I am stung like a tench.

FIRST CARRIER
Like a tench! by the mass, there is ne'er a king christen
could be better bit than I have been since the first cock.

SECOND CARRIER
Why, they will allow us ne'er a jordan, and then we leak
in your chimney; and your chamber-lie breeds fleas
like a loach.

FIRST CARRIER
What, ostler! come away, and be hang'd! come away.

SECOND CARRIER
I have a gammon of bacon and two razes of ginger, to
be deliver'd as far as Charing-cross.

FIRST CARRIER
God's body, the turkeys in my pannier are quite
starved. — What, ostler! — A plague on thee! hast thou
never an eye in thy head? canst not hear? An'twere not
as good a deed as drink, to break the pate on thee, I am
a very villain. — Come, and be hang'd! — hast no faith
in thee?

Enter GADSHILL.

GADSHILL
Good morrow, carriers. What's o'clock?

FIRST CARRIER
I think it be two o'clock.

GADSHILL
I prithee, lend me thy lantern, to see my gelding in the
stable.

FIRST CARRIER
Nay, by God, soft; I know a trick worth two of that,
i'faith.

GADSHILL
I pray thee, lend me thine.

SECOND CARRIER
Ay, when? canst tell? — Lend me thy lantern, quoth
a? — marry, I'll see thee hang'd first.

GADSHILL
Sirrah carrier, what time do you mean to come to
London?

SECOND CARRIER
Time enough to go to bed with a candle, I warrant
thee. — Come, neighbour Mugs, we'll call up the
gentlemen: they will along with company, for they
have great charge.

[*Exeunt* CARRIERS.

GADSHILL
What, ho! chamberlain!

CHAMBERLAIN [*within*].
At hand, quoth pick-purse.

GADSHILL
That's even as fair as — at hand, quoth the
chamberlain; for thou variest no more from picking of
purses than giving direction doth from labouring; thou
lay'st the plot how.

Enter CHAMBERLAIN.

CHAMBERLAIN
Good morrow, Master Gadshill. It holds current that I
told you yesternight: — there's a franklin in the wild of
Kent hath brought three hundred marks with him in
gold: I heard him tell it to one of his company last night
at supper; a kind of auditor; one that hath abundance of
charge too, God knows what. They are up already, and
call for eggs and butter; they will away presently.

GADSHILL
Sirrah, if they meet not with Saint Nicholas' clerks, I'll
give thee this neck.

CHAMBERLAIN
No, I'll none of it: I prithee, keep that for the hangman;
for I know thou worship'st Saint Nicholas as truly as a
man of falsehood may.

GADSHILL
What talkest thou to me of the hangman? if I hang, I'll
make a fat pair of gallows; for if I hang, old Sir John
hangs with me, and thou know'st he's no starveling! Tut!
there are other Trojans that thou dream'st not of, the
which, for sport sake, are content to do the profession
some grace; that would, if matters should be look'd into,
for their own credit sake, make all whole. I am joined
with no foot land-rakers, no long-staff sixpenny strikers,
none of these mad mustachio purple-hued malt-worms;
but with nobility and tranquillity, burgomasters and
great oneyers, such as can hold in, such as will strike
sooner than speak, and speak sooner than drink, and
drink sooner than pray: and yet, zounds, I lie; for they
pray continually to their saint, the commonwealth; or,
rather, not pray to her, but prey on her, — for they ride
up and down on her, and make her their boots.

CHAMBERLAIN
What, the commonwealth their boots? will she hold out
water in foul way?

GADSHILL
She will, she will; justice hath liquor'd her. We steal as in
a castle, cock-sure; we have the receipt of fern-seed, —
we walk invisible.

CHAMBERLAIN
Nay, by my faith, I think you are more beholding to the
night than to fern-seed for your walking invisible.

FIRST CARRIER What, ostler!

GADSHILL
Give me thy hand: thou shalt have a share in our
purchase, as I am a true man.

CHAMBERLAIN
Nay, rather let me have it, as you are a false thief.

GADSHILL
Go to; *homo* is a common name to all men. Bid the
ostler bring my gelding out of the stable. Farewell, you
muddy knave.

[*Exeunt.*

SCENE II

The road by Gadshill.

Enter PRINCE HENRY *and* POINTZ; BARDOLPH
and PETO *at some distance.*

POINTZ
Come, shelter, shelter: I have removed Falstaff's horse,
and he frets like a gumm'd velvet.

PRINCE HENRY
Stand close.   [*They retire.*

Enter FALSTAFF.

FALSTAFF
Pointz! Pointz, and be hang'd! Pointz!

PRINCE HENRY [*coming forward*].
Peace, ye fat-kidney'd rascal! what a brawling dost thou
keep!

FALSTAFF
Where's Pointz, Hal?

PRINCE HENRY
He is walk'd up to the top of the hill: I'll go seek him.
[*Retires.*

FALSTAFF
I am accurst to rob in that thief's company: the rascal
hath removed my horse, and tied him I know not where.
If I travel but four foot by the squier further a-foot, I shall
break my wind. Well, I doubt not but to die a fair death
for all this, if I scape hanging for killing that rogue. I
have forsworn his company hourly any time this
two-and-twenty year, and yet I am bewitch'd with the
rogue's company. If the rascal hath not given me
medicines to make me love him, I'll be hang'd; it could
not be else; I have drunk medicines. — Pointz! H—al!
— a plague upon you both! — Bardolph! — Peto! — I'll
starve, ere I'll rob a foot further. An'twere not as good a
deed as drink, to turn true man, and to leave these
rogues, I am the veriest varlet that ever chew'd with a
tooth. Eight yards of uneven ground is threescore and
ten miles a-foot with me; and the stony-hearted villains
know it well enough: a plague upon't, when thieves
cannot be true one to another! [*They whistle.*] Whew! — A
plague upon you all! Give me my horse, you rogues; give
me my horse, and be hang'd!

PRINCE HENRY [*coming forward*].
Peace, ye fat-guts! lie down; lay thine ear close to the
ground, and list if thou canst hear the tread of
travellers.

FALSTAFF
Have you any levers to lift me up again, being down?

'Sblood, I'll not bear mine own flesh so far a-foot again
for all the coin in thy father's exchequer. What a plague
mean ye to colt me thus?

PRINCE HENRY
Thou liest; thou art not colted, thou art uncolted.

FALSTAFF
I prithee, good Prince Hal, help me to my horse, good
king's son.

PRINCE HENRY
Out, ye rogue! shall I be your ostler?

FALSTAFF
Go, hang thyself in thine own heir-apparent garters!
If I be ta'en, I'll peach for this. An I have not ballads
made on you all, and sung to filthy tunes, let a cup of
sack be my poison: — when a jest is so forward, and
a-foot too! — I hate it.

Enter GADSHILL.

GADSHILL
Stand!

FALSTAFF
So I do, against my will.

POINTZ
O, 'tis our setter: I know his voice.
　　　　[*Coming forward with* BARDOLPH *and* PETO.

BARDOLPH
What news?

GADSHILL
Case ye, case ye; on with your vizards: there's money of
the king's coming down the hill; 'tis going to the king's
exchequer.

FALSTAFF
You lie, ye rogue; 'tis going to the king's tavern.

GADSHILL
There's enough to make us all.

FALSTAFF
To be hang'd.

PRINCE HENRY
Sirs, you four shall front them in the narrow lane; Ned
Pointz and I will walk lower: if they scape from your
encounter, then they light on us.

PETO
How many be there of them?

GADSHILL
Some eight or ten.

FALSTAFF
Zounds, will they not rob us?

PRINCE HENRY
What, a coward, Sir John Paunch?

FALSTAFF
Indeed, I am not John of Gaunt, your grandfather; but
yet no coward, Hal.

PRINCE HENRY
Well, we leave that to the proof.

POINTZ
Sirrah Jack, thy horse stands behind the hedge: when
thou need'st him, there thou shalt find him. Farewell,
and stand fast.

FALSTAFF
Now cannot I strike him, if I should be hang'd.

PRINCE HENRY [*aside to* POINTZ].
Ned, where are our disguises?

POINTZ [*aside to* PRINCE HENRY].
Here, hard by: stand close.
　　　　[*Exeunt* PRINCE HENRY *and* POINTZ.

FALSTAFF
Now, my masters, happy man be his dole, say I: every
man to his business.

Enter the TRAVELLERS.

FIRST TRAVELLER
Come, neighbour: the boy shall lead our horses down
the hill; we'll walk a-foot awhile, and ease our legs.

THIEVES
Stand!

TRAVELLERS
Jesus bless us!

FALSTAFF
Strike; down with them; cut the villains' throats: — ah,
whoreson caterpillars! bacon-fed knaves! they hate us
youth: — down with them; fleece them.

TRAVELLERS
O, we are undone, both we and ours for ever!

FALSTAFF
Hang ye, gorbellied knaves, are ye undone? No, ye fat
chuffs: I would your store were here! On, bacons, on!
What, ye knaves! young men must live. You are
grand-jurors, are ye? we'll jure ye, i'faith.
　　　　[*Here they rob them and bind them. Exeunt.*

Enter PRINCE HENRY and POINTZ
disguised.

PRINCE HENRY
The thieves hath bound the true men. Now
could thou and I rob the thieves, and go
merrily to London, it would be argument for
a week, laughter for a month, and a good jest
for ever.

POINTZ
Stand close: I hear them coming. [*They retire.*
　　　　Enter THIEVES again.

FALSTAFF
Come, my masters, let us share, and then to
horse before day. An the Prince and Pointz
be not two arrant cowards, there's no equity
stirring: there's no more valour in that
Pointz than in a wild-duck.

PRINCE HENRY
Your money!

POINTZ
Villains!
　　[*As they are sharing, the* PRINCE *and*
POINTZ *set upon them. They all run away,*
and FALSTAFF *after a blow or two runs away*
too, leaving the booty behind them.

PRINCE HENRY
Got with much ease. Now merrily to horse:
The thieves are scatter'd, and possess'd with
　fear
So strongly that they dare not meet each other;
Each takes his fellow for an officer.
Away, good Ned. Falstaff sweats to death,
And lards the lean earth as he walks along:
Were't not for laughing, I should pity him.

POINTZ
How the rogue roar'd!
　　　　　　　　　　　　　　[*Exeunt.*

SCENE III

Warkworth Castle.

Enter HOTSPUR solus, reading a letter.

HOTSPUR
' — But, for mine own part, my lord, I could be well
contented to be there, in respect of the love I bear your
house.' — He could be contented, — why is he not,
then? In respect of the love he bears our house: — he
shows in this, he loves his own barn better than he
loves our house. Let me see some more. 'The purpose
you undertake is dangerous': — why, that's certain: 'tis
dangerous to take a cold, to sleep, to drink; but I tell
you, my lord fool, out of this nettle, danger, we pluck
this flower, safety. 'The purpose you undertake is
dangerous; the friends you have named uncertain; the
time itself unsorted; and your whole plot too light for
the counterpoise of so great an opposition.' — Say you
so, say you so? I say unto you again, you are a shallow,
cowardly hind, and you lie. What a lack-brain is this! By
the Lord, our plot is a good plot as ever was laid; our
friends true and constant: a good plot, good friends,
and full of expectation; an excellent plot, very good
friends. What a frosty-spirited rogue is this! Why, my
Lord of York commends the plot and the general
course of action. Zounds, an I were now by this rascal, I
could brain him with his lady's fan. Is there not my
father, my uncle, and myself? Lord Edmund Mortimer,
my lord of York, and Owen Glendower? is there not,
besides, the Douglas? have I not all their letters to meet
me in arms by the ninth of the next month? and are
they not some of them set forward already? What a
pagan rascal is this! an infidel! Ha! you shall see now,
in very sincerity of fear and cold heart, will he to the
king, and lay open all our proceedings. O, could I
divide myself, and go to buffets, for moving such a dish
of skim milk with so honourable an action! Hang him!
let him tell the king: we are prepared. I will set forward
to-night.

Enter LADY PERCY.

How now, Kate! I must leave you within these two
hours.

LADY PERCY
O, my good lord, why are you thus alone?
For what offence have I this fortnight been
A banish'd woman from my Harry's bed?
Tell me, sweet lord, what is't that takes from thee
Thy stomach, pleasure and thy golden sleep?
Why dost thou bend thine eyes upon the earth,
And start so often when thou sitt'st alone?
Why hast thou lost the fresh blood in thy cheeks;
And given my treasures and my rights of thee
To thick-eyed musing and curst melancholy?

HOTSPUR 'The purpose you undertake is dangerous': —
why, that's certain.

In thy faint slumbers I by thee have watch'd,
And heard thee murmur tales of iron wars;
Speak terms of manage to thy bounding steed;
Cry, 'Courage! to the field!' — and thou hast talk'd
Of sallies and retires, of trenches, tents,
Of palisadoes, frontiers, parapets,
Of basilisks, of cannon, culverin,
Of prisoners' ransom, and of soldiers slain,
And all the currents of a heady fight.
Thy spirit within thee hath been so at war,
And thus hath so bestirr'd thee in thy sleep,
That beads of sweat have stood upon thy brow,
Like bubbles in a late-disturbed stream;
And in thy face strange motions have appear'd,
Such as we see when men restrain their breath
On some great sudden hest. O, what portents are
　these?
Some heavy business hath my lord in hand,
And I must know it, else he loves me not.

HOTSPUR
What, ho!

Enter a SERVANT.

Is Gilliams with the packet gone?

SERVANT
He is, my lord, an hour ago.

HOTSPUR
Hath Butler brought those horses from the sheriff?

SERVANT
One horse, my lord, he brought even now.

HOTSPUR
What horse? a roan, a crop-ear, is it not?

SERVANT
It is, my lord.

HOTSPUR
　　　　That roan shall be my throne.
Well, I will back him straight: O *esperance!* —
Bid Butler lead him forth into the park.
　　　　　　　　　　　　[*Exit SERVANT.*

LADY PERCY
But hear you, my lord.

HOTSPUR
　　　　　　What say'st thou, my lady?

LADY PERCY
What is it carries you away?

HOTSPUR
　　　　　　Why, my horse,
My love, — my horse.

LADY PERCY
　　　　　　Out, you mad-headed ape!
A weasel hath not such a deal of spleen
As you are toss'd with. In faith,
I'll know your business, Harry, — that I will.
I fear my brother Mortimer doth stir
About his title, and hath sent for you
To line his enterprise: but if you go, —

HOTSPUR
So far a-foot, I shall be weary, love.

LADY PERCY
Come, come, you paraquito, answer me
Directly unto this question that I ask:

In faith, I'll break thy little finger, Harry,
An if thou wilt not tell me all things true.

HOTSPUR
Away, away, you trifler! — Love! — I love thee not,
I care not for thee, Kate: this is no world
To play with mammets and to tilt with lips:
We must have bloody noses and crack'd crowns,
And pass them current too. — God's me, my horse! —
What say'st thou, Kate? what wouldst thou have with
    me?

LADY PERCY
Do you not love me? do you not, indeed?
Well, do not, then; for since you love me not,
I will not love myself. Do you not love me?
Nay, tell me if you speak in jest or no.

HOTSPUR
Come, wilt thou see me ride?
And when I am o' horseback, I will swear
I love thee infinitely. But hark you, Kate;
I must not have you henceforth question me
Whither I go, nor reason whereabout:
Whither I must, I must; and, to conclude,
This evening must I leave you, gentle Kate.
I know you wise; but yet no further wise
Than Harry Percy's wife: constant you are;
But yet a woman: and for secrecy,
No lady closer; for I well believe
Thou wilt not utter what thou dost not know, —
And so far will I trust thee, gentle Kate.

LADY PERCY
How! so far?

HOTSPUR
Not an inch further. But hark you, Kate:
Whither I go, thither shall you go too;
To-day will I set forth, to-morrow you. —
Will this content you, Kate?

LADY PERCY
                It must of force. [*Exeunt.*

SCENE IV

Eastcheap. The Boar's-Head Tavern.

Enter PRINCE HENRY.

PRINCE HENRY
Ned, prithee, come out of that fat room, and lend me
thy hand to laugh a little.

Enter POINTZ.

POINTZ
Where hast been, Hal?

PRINCE HENRY
With three or four loggerheads amongst three or four
score hogsheads. I have sounded the very base-string of
humility. Sirrah, I am sworn brother to a leash of
drawers; and can call them all by their christen names,
as, — Tom, Dick, and Francis. They take it already
upon their salvation, that though I be but the prince of
Wales, yet I am the king of courtesy; and tell me flatly I
am no proud Jack, like Falstaff, but a Corinthian, a lad
of mettle, a good boy, by the Lord, so they call me, and
when I am king of England, I shall command all the
good lads in Eastcheap. They call drinking deep, dying
scarlet; and when you breathe in your watering, they
cry 'hem!' and bid you play it off. To conclude, I am so
good a proficient in one quarter of an hour, that I can
drink with any tinker in his own language during my
life. I tell thee, Ned, thou hast lost much honour, that
thou wert not with me in this action. But, sweet Ned, —
to sweeten which name of Ned, I give thee this
pennyworth of sugar, clapp'd even now into my hand
by an under-skinker, one that never spake other
English in his life than 'Eight shillings and sixpence',
and 'You are welcome', with this shrill addition, 'Anon,
anon, sir! Score a pint of bastard in the Half-Moon', or
so: — but, Ned, to drive away the time till Falstaff
come, I prithee, do thou stand in some by-room, while
I question my puny drawer to what end he gave me the
sugar; and do thou never leave calling 'Francis', that his
tale to me may be nothing but 'anon'. Step aside, and
I'll show thee a precedent.

                [*Exit* POINTZ.

POINTZ [*within*].
Francis!

PRINCE HENRY
Thou art perfect.

POINTZ [*within*].
Francis!

Enter FRANCIS.

FRANCIS
Anon, anon, sir. — Look down into the Pomgarnet,

Ralph.

PRINCE HENRY
Come hither, Francis.

FRANCIS
My lord?

PRINCE HENRY
How long hast thou to serve, Francis?

FRANCIS
Forsooth, five years, and as much as to —

POINTZ [*within*].
Francis!

FRANCIS
Anon, anon, sir.

PRINCE HENRY
Five years! by 'r lady, a long lease for the clinking of
pewter. But, Francis, darest thou be so valiant as to play
the coward with thy indenture and show it a fair pair of
heels and run from it?

FRANCIS
O Lord, sir, I'll be sworn upon all the books in
England, I could find in my heart —

POINTZ [*within*].
Francis!

FRANCIS
Anon, anon, sir.

PRINCE HENRY
How old art thou, Francis?

FRANCIS
Let me see, — about Michaelmas next I shall be —

POINTZ [*within*].
Francis!

FRANCIS
Anon, sir. — Pray you, stay a little, my lord.

PRINCE HENRY
Nay, but hark you, Francis: for the sugar thou gavest
me, — 'twas a pennyworth, was't not? —

FRANCIS
O Lord, sir, I would it had been two!

PRINCE HENRY
I will give thee for it a thousand pound: ask me when
thou wilt, and thou shalt have it.

POINTZ [*within*].
Francis!

FRANCIS
Anon, anon.

PRINCE HENRY
Anon, Francis? No, Francis; but to-morrow, Francis;
or, Francis, o' Thursday; or, indeed, Francis, when
thou wilt. But, Francis, —

FRANCIS
My lord?

PRINCE HENRY
Wilt thou rob this leathern-jerkin, crystal-button,
nott-pated, agate-ring, puke-stocking, caddis-garter,
smooth-tongue, Spanish-pouch, —

FRANCIS
O Lord, sir, who do you mean?

PRINCE HENRY
Why, then, your brown bastard is your only drink; for,
look you, Francis, your white canvas doublet will sully:
in Barbary, sir, it cannot come to so much.

FRANCIS
What, sir?

POINTZ [*within*].
Francis!

PRINCE HENRY
Away, you rogue! dost thou not hear them call?
    [*Here they both call him; the* DRAWER *stands amazed,
            not knowing which way to go.*

Enter VINTNER.

VINTNER
What, stand'st thou still, and hear'st such a calling?
Look to the guests within. [*Exit* FRANCIS.] My lord, old
Sir John, with half-a-dozen more, are at the door: shall I
let them in?

PRINCE HENRY
Let them alone awhile, and then open the door. [*Exit*
VINTNER.] Pointz!

Enter POINTZ.

POINTZ
Anon, anon, sir.

PRINCE HENRY
Sirrah, Falstaff and the rest of the thieves are at the
door: shall we be merry?

POINTZ
As merry as crickets, my lad. But hark ye; what cunning
match have you made with this jest of the drawer?

come, what's the issue?

PRINCE HENRY
I am now of all humours that have show'd themselves
humours since the old days of good-man Adam to the
pupil age of this present twelve o'clock at midnight. —
What's o'clock, Francis?

FRANCIS [*within*].
Anon, anon, sir.

PRINCE HENRY
That ever this fellow should have fewer words than a
parrot, and yet the son of a woman! His industry is
up-stairs and down-stairs; his eloquence the parcel of a
reckoning. I am not yet of Percy's mind, the Hotspur of
the north; he that kills me some six or seven dozen of
Scots at a breakfast, washes his hands, and says to his
wife, 'Fie upon this quiet life! I want work.' 'O my sweet
Harry', says she, 'how many hast thou kill'd to-day?'
'Give my roan horse a drench', says he; and answers,
'Some fourteen', an hour after, — 'a trifle, a trifle'. I
prithee, call in Falstaff: I'll play Percy, and that damn'd
brawn shall play Dame Mortimer his wife. 'Rivo,' says
the drunkard. Call in ribs, call in tallow.

    Enter FALSTAFF, GADSHILL, BARDOLPH, *and*
        PETO; *followed by* FRANCIS *with wine.*

POINTZ
Welcome, Jack: where hast thou been?

FALSTAFF
A plague of all cowards, I say, and a vengeance too!
marry, and amen! — Give me a cup of sack, boy. — Ere
I lead this life long, I'll sew netherstocks, and mend
them and foot them too. A plague of all cowards! —
Give me a cup of sack, rogue. — Is there no virtue
extant?
                [*Drinks.*

PRINCE HENRY
Didst thou never see Titan kiss a dish of butter
(pitiful-hearted Titan!) that melted at the sweet tale of
the sun! if thou didst, then behold that compound.

FALSTAFF
You rogue, here's lime in this sack, too: there is
nothing but roguery to be found in villainous man: yet
a coward is worse than a cup of sack with lime in it, — a
villainous coward. — Go thy ways, old Jack; die when
thou wilt, if manhood, good manhood, be not forgot
upon the face of the earth, then am I a shotten herring.
There lives not three good men unhang'd in England;
and one of them is fat, and grows old: God help the
while! a bad world, I say. I would I were a weaver; I
could sing psalms or any thing. A plague of all cowards!
I say still.

PRINCE HENRY
How now, wool-sack! what mutter you?

FALSTAFF
A king's son! If I do not beat thee out of thy kingdom
with a dagger of lath, and drive all thy subjects afore
thee like a flock of wild-geese, I'll never wear hair on
my face more. You Prince of Wales!

PRINCE HENRY
Why, you whoreson round man, what's the matter?

FALSTAFF
Are not you a coward? answer me to that: — and Pointz
there?

POINTZ
Zounds, ye fat paunch, an ye call me coward, by the
Lord, I'll stab thee.

FALSTAFF
I call thee coward! I'll see thee damn'd ere I call thee
coward: but I would give a thousand pound, I could run
as fast as thou canst. You are straight enough in the
shoulders, — you care not who sees your back: call you
that backing of your friends? A plague upon such
backing! give me them that will face me. — Give me a
cup of sack: — I am a rogue, if I drunk to-day.

PRINCE HENRY
O villain! thy lips are scarce wiped since thou drunk'st
last.

FALSTAFF
All's one for that. A plague of all cowards! still say I.
                [*Drinks.*

PRINCE HENRY
What's the matter?

FALSTAFF
What's the matter! there be four of us here have ta'en a
thousand pound this day morning.

PRINCE HENRY
Where is it, Jack? where is it?

FALSTAFF
Where is it? taken from us it is: a hundred upon poor
four of us.

FALSTAFF I am a rogue, if I were not at half-sword with a dozen of them.

PRINCE HENRY
What, a hundred, man?

FALSTAFF
I am a rogue, if I were not at half-sword with a dozen of them two hours together. I have scaped by miracle. I am eight times thrust through the doublet, four through the hose; my buckler cut through and through; my sword hack'd like a hand-saw — *ecce signum!* I never dealt better since I was a man: all would not do. A plague of all cowards! — Let them speak: if they speak more or less than truth, they are villains and the sons of darkness.

PRINCE HENRY
Speak, sirs; how was it?

GADSHILL
We four set upon some dozen, —

FALSTAFF
Sixteen at least, my lord.

GADSHILL
And bound them.

PETO
No, no, they were not bound.

FALSTAFF
You rogue, they were bound, every man of them; or I am a Jew else, an Ebrew Jew.

GADSHILL
As we were sharing, some six or seven fresh men set upon us, —

FALSTAFF
And unbound the rest, and then come in the other.

PRINCE HENRY
What, fought you with them all?

FALSTAFF
All! I know not what you call all; but if I fought not with fifty of them, I am a bunch of radish: if there were not two or three and fifty upon poor old Jack, then am I no two-legg'd creature.

PRINCE HENRY
Pray God you have not murder'd some of them.

FALSTAFF
Nay, that's past praying for: I have pepper'd two of them; two I am sure I have paid, — two rogues in buckram suits. I tell thee what, Hal, — if I tell thee a lie, spit in my face, call me horse. Thou knowest my old ward; — here I lay, and thus I bore my point. Four rogues in buckram let drive at me, —

PRINCE HENRY
What, four? thou saidst but two even now.

FALSTAFF
Four, Hal; I told thee four.

POINTZ
Ay, ay, he said four.

FALSTAFF
These four came all a-front, and mainly thrust at me. I made me no more ado but took all their seven points in my target, thus.

PRINCE HENRY
Seven? why, there were but four even now.

FALSTAFF
In buckram?

POINTZ
Ay, four, in buckram suits.

FALSTAFF
Seven, by these hilts, or I am a villain else.

PRINCE HENRY
Prithee, let him alone; we shall have more anon.

FALSTAFF
Dost thou hear me, Hal?

PRINCE HENRY
Ay, and mark thee too, Jack.

FALSTAFF
Do so, for it is worth the listening to. These nine in buckram that I told thee of, —

PRINCE HENRY
So, two more already.

FALSTAFF
Their points being broken, —

POINTZ
Down fell their hose.

FALSTAFF
Began to give me ground: but I follow'd me close, came in foot and hand; and with a thought seven of the eleven I paid.

PRINCE HENRY
O monstrous! eleven buckram men grown out of two!

FALSTAFF
But, as the devil would have it, three misbegotten knaves in Kendal green came at my back and let drive at me; — for it was so dark, Hal, that thou couldst not see thy hand.

PRINCE HENRY
These lies are like their father that begets them, — gross as a mountain, open, palpable. Why, thou clay-brain'd guts, thou nott-pated fool, thou whoreson, obscene, greasy tallow-keech, —

FALSTAFF
What, art thou mad? art thou mad? is not the truth the truth?

PRINCE HENRY
Why, how couldst thou know these men in Kendal green, when it was so dark thou couldst not see thy hand? come, tell us your reason: what say'st thou to this?

POINTZ
Come, your reason, Jack, your reason.

FALSTAFF
What, upon compulsion? Zounds, an I were at the strappado, or all the racks in the world, I would not tell you on compulsion. Give you a reason on compulsion! if reasons were as plentiful as blackberries, I would give no man a reason upon compulsion, I.

PRINCE HENRY
I'll be no longer guilty of this sin; this sanguine coward, this bed-presser, this horse-back-breaker, this huge hill of flesh, —

FALSTAFF
Away, you starveling, you eel-skin, you dried neat's-tongue, you bull's-pizzle, you stock-fish, — O, for breath to utter what is like thee! — you tailor's-yard, you sheath, you bow-case; you vile standing-tuck, —

PRINCE HENRY
Well, breathe awhile, and then to it again: and when thou hast tired thyself in base comparisons, hear me speak but this.

POINTZ
Mark, Jack.

PRINCE HENRY
We two saw you four set on four and bound them, and were masters of their wealth. — Mark now, how a plain tale shall put you down. — Then did we two set on you four; and, with a word, out-faced you from your prize, and have it; yea, and can show it you here in the house: — and, Falstaff, you carried your guts away as nimbly, with as quick dexterity, and roar'd for mercy, and still ran and roar'd, as ever I heard bull-calf. What a slave art thou, to hack thy sword as thou hast done, and then say it was in fight! What trick, what device, what starting-hole, canst thou now find out to hide thee from this open and apparent shame?

POINTZ
Come, let's hear, Jack; what trick hast thou now?

FALSTAFF
By the Lord, I knew ye as well as he that made ye. Why, hear you, my masters: was it for me to kill the heir-apparent? should I turn upon the true prince? why, thou knowest I am as valiant as Hercules: but beware instinct; the lion will not touch the true prince. Instinct is a great matter; I was a coward on instinct. I shall think the better of myself and thee during my life; I for a valiant lion, and thou for a true prince. But, by

FALSTAFF I made me no more ado but took all their seven points in my target, thus.

the Lord, lads, I am glad you have the money. —
Hostess, clap-to the doors [to HOSTESS within]: —
watch to-night, pray to-morrow. — Gallants, lads, boys,
hearts of gold, all the titles of good fellowship come to
you! What, shall we be merry? shall we have a play
extempore?

PRINCE HENRY
Content; — and the argument shall be thy running
away.

FALSTAFF
Ah, no more of that, Hal, an thou lovest me!

Enter HOSTESS.

HOSTESS
O Jesu, my lord the prince, —

PRINCE HENRY
How now, my lady the hostess! what say'st thou to me?

HOSTESS
Marry, my lord, there is a nobleman of the court at door
would speak with you: he says he comes from your
father.

PRINCE HENRY
Give him as much as will make him a royal man, and
send him back again to my mother.

FALSTAFF
What manner of man is he?

HOSTESS
An old man.

FALSTAFF
What doth gravity out of his bed at midnight? —
Shall I give him his answer?

PRINCE HENRY
Prithee, do, Jack.

FALSTAFF
Faith, and I'll send him packing.   [*Exit.*

PRINCE HENRY
Now, sirs: — by 'r lady, you fought fair; — so did you,
Peto; — so did you, Bardolph: you are lions too, you ran
away upon instinct, you will not touch the true prince;
no, — fie!

BARDOLPH
Faith, I ran when I saw others run.

PRINCE HENRY
Faith, tell me now in earnest, how came Falstaff's
sword so hack'd?

PETO
Why, he hack'd it with his dagger; and said he would
swear truth out of England, but he would make you
believe it was done in fight; and persuaded us to do the
like.

BARDOLPH
Yea, and to tickle our noses with spear-grass to make
them bleed; and then to beslubber our garments with
it, and swear it was the blood of true men. I did that I
did not this seven year before, — I blush'd to hear his
monstrous devices.

PRINCE HENRY
O villain, thou stolest a cup of sack eighteen years ago,
and wert taken with the manner, and ever since thou
hast blush'd extempore. Thou hadst fire and sword on
thy side, and yet thou ran'st away: what instinct hadst
thou for it?

BARDOLPH
My lord, do you see these meteors? do you behold these
exhalations?

PRINCE HENRY
I do.

BARDOLPH
What think you they portend?

PRINCE HENRY
Hot livers and cold purses.

BARDOLPH
Choler, my lord, if rightly taken.

PRINCE HENRY
No, if rightly taken, halter. — Here comes lean Jack,
here comes bare-bone.

Enter FALSTAFF.

How now, my sweet creature of bombast! How long is't
ago, Jack, since thou saw'st thine own knee?

FALSTAFF
My own knee! when I was about thy years, Hal, I was
not an eagle's talon in the waist; I could have crept into
any alderman's thumb-ring: a plague of sighing and
grief! it blows a man up like a bladder. — There's
villainous news abroad: here was Sir John Bracy from
your father; you must to the court in the morning. That
same mad fellow of the north, Percy; and he of Wales,
that gave Amaimon the bastinado, and made Lucifer
cuckold, and swore the devil his true liegeman upon

the cross of a Welsh hook, — what, a plague, call you
him? —

POINTZ
O, Glendower.

FALSTAFF
Owen, Owen, — the same; and his son-in-law
Mortimer, and old Northumberland; and that sprightly
Scot of Scots, Douglas, that runs o' horseback up a hill
perpendicular, —

PRINCE HENRY
He that rides at high speed and with his pistol kills a
sparrow flying.

FALSTAFF
You have hit it.

PRINCE HENRY
So did he never the sparrow.

FALSTAFF
Well, that rascal hath good mettle in him; he will not
run.

PRINCE HENRY
Why, what a rascal art thou, then, to praise him so for
running!

FALSTAFF
O' horseback, ye cuckoo; but a-foot he will not budge a
foot.

PRINCE HENRY
Yes, Jack, upon instinct.

FALSTAFF
I grant ye, upon instinct. — Well, he is there too, and
one Mordake, and a thousand blue-caps more:
Worcester is stolen away to-night; thy father's beard is
turn'd white with the news: you may buy land now as
cheap as stinking mackerel.

PRINCE HENRY
Why, then, it is like, if there come a hot June, and this
civil buffeting hold, we shall buy maidenheads as they
buy hob-nails, by the hundreds.

FALSTAFF
By the mass, lad, thou say'st true; it is like we shall have
good trading that way. — But tell me, Hal, art thou not
horribly afeard? thou being heir-apparent, could the
world pick thee out three such enemies again as that
fiend Douglas, that spirit Percy, and that devil
Glendower? art thou not horribly afraid? doth not thy
blood thrill at it?

PRINCE HENRY
Not a whit, i'faith; I lack some of thy instinct.

FALSTAFF
Well, thou wilt be horribly chid to-morrow when thou
comest to thy father: if thou love me, practise an
answer.

PRINCE HENRY
Do thou stand for my father, and examine me upon the
particulars of my life.

FALSTAFF
Shall I? content: — this chair shall be my state, this
dagger my sceptre, and this cushion my crown.

PRINCE HENRY
Thy state is taken for a joined-stool, thy golden sceptre
for a leaden dagger, and thy precious rich crown for a
pitiful bald crown!

FALSTAFF
Well, an the fire of grace be not quite out of thee, now
shalt thou be moved. — Give me a cup of sack to make
my eyes look red, that it may be thought I have wept; for
I must speak in passion, and I will do it in King
Cambyses' vein.
                                                    [*Drinks.*

PRINCE HENRY
Well, here is my leg.

FALSTAFF
And here is my speech. — Stand aside, nobility.

HOSTESS
O Jesu, this is excellent sport, i'faith!

FALSTAFF
Weep not, sweet queen; for trickling tears are vain.

HOSTESS
O, the father, how he holds his countenance!

FALSTAFF
For God's sake, lords, convey my tristful queen;
For tears do stop the flood-gates of her eyes.

HOSTESS
O Jesu, he doth it as like one of these harlotry
players as ever I see!

FALSTAFF
Peace, good pint-pot; peace, good tickle-brain. —
Harry, I do not only marvel where thou spendest thy
time, but also how thou art accompanied: for though
the camomile, the more it is trodden on, the faster it

grows, yet youth, the more it is wasted, the sooner it
wears. That thou art my son, I have partly thy mother's
word, partly my own opinion; but chiefly a villainous
trick of thine eye, and a foolish hanging of thy nether
lip, that doth warrant me. If, then, thou be son to me,
here lies the point; — why, being son to me, art thou so
pointed at? Shall the blessed sun of heaven prove a
micher, and eat blackberries? a question not to be
ask'd. Shall the son of England prove a thief, and take
purses? a question to be ask'd. There is a thing, Harry,
which thou hast often heard of, and it is known to
many in our land by the name of pitch: this pitch, as
ancient writers do report, doth defile; so doth the
company thou keepest: for, Harry, now I do not speak
to thee in drink, but in tears; not in pleasure, but in
passion; not in words only, but in woes also: — and yet
there is a virtuous man whom I have often noted in thy
company, but I know not his name.

PRINCE HENRY
What manner of man, an it like your majesty?

FALSTAFF
A goodly portly man, i'faith, and a corpulent; of a
cheerful look, a pleasing eye, and a most noble
carriage; and, as I think, his age some fifty, or, by 'r
lady, inclining to three-score; and now I remember me,
his name is Falstaff: if that man should be lewdly
given, he deceiveth me; for, Harry, I see virtue in his
looks. If, then, the tree may be known by the fruit, as
the fruit by the tree, then, peremptorily I speak it, there
is virtue in that Falstaff: him keep with, the rest banish.
And tell me now, thou naughty varlet, tell me where
hast thou been this month?

PRINCE HENRY
Dost thou speak like a king? Do thou stand for me, and
I'll play my father.

FALSTAFF
Depose me? if thou dost it half so gravely, so
majestically, both in word and matter, hang me up by
the heels for a rabbit-sucker or a poulter's hare.

PRINCE HENRY
Well, here I am set.

FALSTAFF
And here I stand: — judge, my masters.

PRINCE HENRY
Now, Harry, whence come you?

FALSTAFF
My noble lord, from Eastcheap.

PRINCE HENRY
The complaints I hear of thee are grievous.

FALSTAFF
'Sblood, my lord, they are false: — nay, I'll tickle ye for
a young prince, i'faith.

PRINCE HENRY
Swearest thou, ungracious boy? henceforth ne'er look
on me. Thou art violently carried away from grace:
there is a devil haunts thee, in the likeness of an old
fat man, — a tun of man is thy companion. Why dost
thou converse with that trunk of humours, that
bolting-hutch of beastliness, that swoll'n parcel of
dropsies, that huge bombard of sack, that stuff'd
cloakbag of guts, that roasted Manningtree ox with
the pudding in his belly, that reverend vice, that grey
iniquity, that father ruffian, that vanity in years?
Wherein is he good, but to taste sack and drink it?
wherein neat and cleanly, but to carve a capon and eat
it? wherein cunning, but in craft? wherein crafty, but
in villainy? wherein villainous, but in all things?
wherein worthy, but in nothing?

FALSTAFF
I would your Grace would take me with you: whom
means your Grace?

PRINCE HENRY
That villainous abominable misleader of youth,
Falstaff, that old white-bearded Satan.

FALSTAFF
My lord, the man I know.

PRINCE HENRY
I know thou dost.

FALSTAFF
But to say I know more harm in him than in myself,
were to say more than I know. That he is old, — the more
the pity, — his white hairs do witness it; but that he is —
saving your reverence — a whoremaster, that I utterly
deny. If sack and sugar be a fault, God help the wicked! if
to be old and merry be a sin, then many an old host that I
know is damn'd: if to be fat be to be hated, then
Pharaoh's lean kine are to be loved. No, my good lord;
banish Peto, banish Bardolph, banish Pointz: but, for
sweet Jack Falstaff, kind Jack Falstaff, true Jack Falstaff,
valiant Jack Falstaff, and therefore more valiant, being,

FALSTAFF This chair shall be my state, this dagger my sceptre, and this cushion my crown.

And, sheriff, I will engage my word to thee,
That I will, by to-morrow dinner-time,
Send him to answer thee, or any man,
For any thing he shall be charg'd withal:
And so, let me entreat you leave the house.

SHERIFF
I will, my lord. There are two gentlemen
Have in this robbery lost three hundred marks.

PRINCE HENRY
It may be so: if he have robb'd these men,
He shall be answerable; and so, farewell.

SHERIFF
Good night, my noble lord.

PRINCE HENRY
I think it is good morrow, is it not?

SHERIFF
Indeed, my lord, I think it be two o'clock.
[*Exeunt* SHERIFF *and* CARRIER.

PRINCE HENRY
This oily rascal is known as well as Paul's.
Go, call him forth.

POINTZ
Falstaff! — fast asleep behind the arras, and snorting
like a horse.

PRINCE HENRY
Hark, how hard he fetches breath. Search his pockets.
[*He searcheth his pockets, and findeth certain papers.*]
What hast thou found?

POINTZ
Nothing but papers, my lord.

PRINCE HENRY
Let's see what they be: read them.

POINTZ [*reads*].

Item, A capon,	.	.	2s. 2d.
Item, Sauce,	.	.	4d.
Item, Sack, two gallons,	.	.	5s. 8d.
Item, Anchovies and sack after supper,			2s. 6d.
Item, Bread,	.	.	ob.

PRINCE HENRY
O monstrous! but one half-pennyworth of bread to this
intolerable deal of sack! — What there is else, keep
close; we'll read it at more advantage: there let him
sleep till day. I'll to the court in the morning. We must
all to the wars, and thy place shall be honourable. I'll
procure this fat rogue a charge of foot; and I know his
death will be a march of twelve-score. The money shall
be paid back again with advantage. Be with me betimes
in the morning; and so, good morrow, Pointz.

POINTZ
Good morrow, good my lord. [*Exeunt.*

as he is, old Jack Falstaff, banish not him thy Harry's
company, banish not him thy Harry's company: —
banish plump Jack, and banish all the world.

PRINCE HENRY
I do, I will. [*A knocking heard.*
[*Exeunt* HOSTESS, FRANCIS, *and* BARDOLPH.
Enter BARDOLPH, *running.*

BARDOLPH
O, my lord, my lord! the sheriff with a most monstrous
watch is at the door.

FALSTAFF
Out, ye rogue! — Play out the play: I have much to say
in the behalf of that Falstaff.
Enter HOSTESS, *hastily.*

HOSTESS
O Jesu, my lord, my lord, —

PRINCE HENRY
Heigh, heigh! the devil rides upon a fiddlestick: what's
the matter?

HOSTESS
The sheriff and all the watch are at the door: they are
come to search the house. Shall I let them in?

FALSTAFF
Dost thou hear, Hal? never call a true piece of gold a
counterfeit: thou art essentially mad, without seeming
so.

PRINCE HENRY
And thou a natural coward, without instinct.

FALSTAFF
I deny your *major*: if you will deny the sheriff, so; if not,
let him enter: if I become not a cart as well as another
man, a plague on my bringing up! I hope I shall as soon
be strangled with a halter as another.

PRINCE HENRY
Go, hide thee behind the arras: —
the rest walk up above. Now, my
masters, for a true face and good
conscience.

FALSTAFF
Both which I have had: but their
date is out, and therefore I'll hide
me.

PRINCE HENRY
Call in the sheriff.
[*Exeunt all except* PRINCE HENRY
and POINTZ.
Enter SHERIFF *and* CARRIER.

Now, master sheriff, what's your
will with me?

SHERIFF
First, pardon me, my lord. A hue
and cry
Hath follow'd certain men unto this
house.

PRINCE HENRY
What men?

SHERIFF
One of them is well known, my
gracious lord,
A gross fat man.

CARRIER
As fat as butter.

PRINCE HENRY
The man, I do assure you, is not
here;
For I myself at this time have
employ'd him.

ACT III

SCENE I

Bangor. The Archdeacon's house.

Enter HOTSPUR, WORCESTER, MORTIMER, *and*
GLENDOWER.

MORTIMER
These promises are fair, the parties sure,
And our induction full of prosperous hope.

HOTSPUR
Lord Mortimer, — and cousin Glendower, —
Will you sit down? —
And uncle Worcester: — a plague upon it!
I have forgot the map.

GLENDOWER
   No, here it is.
Sit, cousin Percy; — sit, good cousin Hotspur,
For by that name as oft as Lancaster
Doth speak of you, his cheek looks pale, and with
A rising sigh he wisheth you in heaven.

HOTSPUR
And you in hell, as oft as he hears Owen Glendower
spoke of.

GLENDOWER
I cannot blame him: at my nativity
The front of heaven was full of fiery shapes,
Of burning cressets; and at my birth
The frame and huge foundation of the earth
Shak'd like a coward.

HOTSPUR
Why, so it would have done at the same season, if your
mother's cat had but kitten'd, though yourself had
never been born.

GLENDOWER
I say the earth did shake when I was born.

HOTSPUR
And I say the earth was not of my mind,
If you suppose as fearing you it shook.

GLENDOWER
The heavens were all on fire, the earth did tremble.

HOTSPUR
O, then the earth shook to see the heavens on fire,
And not in fear of your nativity.
Diseased nature oftentimes breaks forth
In strange eruptions; oft the teeming earth
Is with a kind of colic pinch'd and vex'd
By the imprisoning of unruly wind
Within her womb; which, for enlargement striving,
Shakes the old beldam earth, and topples down
Steeples and moss-grown towers. At your birth
Our grandam earth, having this distemperature,
In passion shook.

GLENDOWER
   Cousin, of many men
I do not bear these crossings. Give me leave
To tell you once again, that at my birth
The front of heaven was full of fiery shapes;
The goats ran from the mountains, and the herds
Were strangely clamorous to the frighted fields.
These signs have mark'd me extraordinary;
And all the courses of my life do show
I am not in the roll of common men.
Where is he living, — clipp'd in with the sea
That chides the banks of England, Scotland, Wales, —
Which calls me pupil, or hath read to me?
And bring him out that is but woman's son
Can trace me in the tedious ways of art,
And hold me pace in deep experiments.

HOTSPUR
I think there is no man speaks better Welsh. —
I'll to dinner.

MORTIMER
Peace, cousin Percy; you will make him mad.

GLENDOWER
I can call spirits from the vasty deep.

HOTSPUR
Why, so can I, or so can any man;
But will they come when you do call for them?

GLENDOWER
Why, I can teach you, cousin, to command
The devil.

HOTSPUR
And I can teach thee, coz, to shame the devil
By telling truth: tell truth, and shame the devil. —
If thou have power to raise him, bring him hither,
And I'll be sworn I have power to shame him hence.
O, while you live, tell truth, and shame the devil!

MORTIMER
Come, come, no more of this unprofitable chat.

GLENDOWER
Three times hath Henry Bolingbroke made head
Against my power; thrice from the banks of Wye
And sandy-bottom'd Severn have I sent him
Bootless home and weather-beaten back.

HOTSPUR
Home without boots, and in foul weather too!
How scapes he agues, in the devil's name?

GLENDOWER
Come, here's the map: shall we divide our right
According to our threefold order ta'en?

MORTIMER
The archdeacon hath divided it
Into three limits very equally: —
England, from Trent and Severn hitherto,
By south and east is to my part assign'd:
All westward, Wales beyond the Severn shore,
And all the fertile land within that bound,
To Owen Glendower: — and, dear coz, to you
The remnant northward, lying off from Trent.
And our indentures tripartite are drawn;
Which being sealed interchangeably, —
A business that this night may execute, —
To-morrow, cousin Percy, you, and I,
And my good Lord of Worcester, will set forth
To meet your father and the Scottish power,
As is appointed us, at Shrewsbury.
My father Glendower is not ready yet,
Not shall we need his help these fourteen days: —
[*to* GLENDOWER] Within that space you may have
   drawn together
Your tenants, friends and neighbouring gentlemen.

GLENDOWER
A shorter time shall send me to you, lords:
And in my conduct shall your ladies come;
From whom you now must steal, and take no leave,
For there will be a world of water shed
Upon the parting of your wives and you.

HOTSPUR
Methinks my moiety, north from Burton here,
In quantity equals not one of yours:
See how this river comes me cranking in,
And cuts me from the best of all my land
A huge half-moon, a monstrous cantle out.
I'll have the current in this place damm'd up;
And here the smug and silver Trent shall run
In a new channel, fair and evenly:
It shall not wind with such a deep indent,
To rob me of so rich a bottom here.

GLENDOWER
Not wind? it shall, it must; you see it doth.

MORTIMER
Yea, but
Mark how he bears his course, and runs me up
With like advantage on the other side;
Gelding the opposed continent as much
As on the other side it takes from you.

WORCESTER
Yea, but a little charge will trench him here,
And on this north side win this cape of land;
And then he runs straight and even.

HOTSPUR
I'll have it so: a little charge will do it.

GLENDOWER
I'll not have it alter'd.

HOTSPUR
   Will not you?

GLENDOWER
No, nor you shall not.

HOTSPUR
   Who shall say me nay?

GLENDOWER
Why, that will I.

HOTSPUR
   Let me not understand you, then;
Speak it in Welsh.

GLENDOWER
I can speak English, lord, as well as you;
For I was train'd up in the English court;
Where, being but young, I framed to the harp
Many an English ditty lovely well,
And gave the tongue a helpful ornament, —
A virtue that was never seen in you.

HOTSPUR
Marry, and I am glad of it with all my heart:
I had rather be a kitten, and cry mew,
Than one of these same metre ballet-mongers;
I had rather hear a brazen canstick turn'd,

Or a dry wheel grate on the axletree;
And that would set my teeth nothing on edge,
Nothing so much as mincing poetry: —
'Tis like the forc'd gait of a shuffling nag.

GLENDOWER
Come, you shall have Trent turn'd.

HOTSPUR
I do not care: I'll give thrice so much land
To any well-deserving friend;
But in the way of bargain, mark ye me,
I'll cavil on the ninth part of a hair.
Are the indentures drawn? shall we be gone?

GLENDOWER
The moon shines fair; you may away by night:
I'll in and haste the writer, and withal
Break with your wives of your departure hence:
I am afraid my daughter will run mad,
So much she doteth on her Mortimer. [*Exit.*

MORTIMER
Fie, cousin Percy! how you cross my father!

HOTSPUR
I cannot choose: sometime he angers me
With telling me of the mouldwarp and the ant,
Of the dreamer Merlin and his prophecies,
And of a dragon and a finless fish,
A clip-wing'd griffin and a moulten raven,
A couching lion and a ramping cat,
And such a deal of skimble-skamble stuff
As puts me from my faith. I tell you what, —
He held me last night at least nine hours
In reckoning up the several devils' names
That were his lackeys: I cried 'hum', and 'well, go to',
But mark'd him not a word. O, he is as tedious
As a tired horse, a railing wife;
Worse than a smoky house: — I had rather live
With cheese and garlic in a windmill, far,
Than feed on cates and have him talk to me
In any summer-house in Christendom.

MORTIMER
In faith, he is a worthy gentleman;
Exceedingly well-read, and profited
In strange concealments; valiant as a lion,
And wondrous affable, and as bountiful
As mines of India. Shall I tell you, cousin?
He holds your temper in a high respect,
And curbs himself even of his natural scope
When you do cross his humour; faith, he does:
I warrant you, that man is not alive
Might so have tempted him as you have done,
Without the taste of danger and reproof:
But do not use it oft, let me entreat you.

WORCESTER
In faith, my lord, you are too wilful-blame;
And since your coming hither have done enough
To put him quite beside his patience.
You must needs learn, lord, to amend this fault:
Though sometimes it show greatness, courage, blood, —
And that's the dearest grace it renders you, —
Yet oftentimes it doth present harsh rage,
Defect of manners, want of government,
Pride, haughtiness, opinion, and disdain:
The least of which haunting a nobleman
Loseth men's hearts, and leaves behind a stain
Upon the beauty of all parts besides,
Beguiling them of commendation.

HOTSPUR
Well, I am school'd: good manners be your speed!
Here come our wives, and let us take our leave.

Enter GLENDOWER, *with the* LADIES.

MORTIMER
This is the deadly spite that angers me, —
My wife can speak no English, I no Welsh.

GLENDOWER
My daughter weeps: she will not part with you;
She'll be a soldier too, she'll to the wars.

MORTIMER
Good father, tell her that she and my aunt Percy
Shall follow in your conduct speedily.
[GLENDOWER *speaks to* LADY MORTIMER *in Welsh,*
and she answers him in the same.

GLENDOWER
She is desperate here; a peevish self-will'd harlotry,
one that no persuasion can do good upon.
   [*The* LADY *speaks in Welsh.*

MORTIMER
I understand thy looks: that pretty Welsh
Which thou pour'st down from these swelling heavens
I am too perfect in; and, but for shame,
In such a parley should I answer thee.
   [*The* LADY *speaks again in Welsh.*

I understand thy kisses, and thou mine,
And that's a feeling disputation:
But I will never be a truant, love,
Till I have learn'd thy language; for thy tongue
Makes Welsh as sweet as ditties highly penn'd,
Sung by a fair queen in a summer's bower,
With ravishing division, to her lute.

GLENDOWER
Nay, if you melt, then will she run quite mad.
[*The* LADY *speaks again in Welsh.*

MORTIMER
O, I am ignorance itself in this!

GLENDOWER
She bids you on the wanton rushes lay you down,
And rest your gentle head upon her lap,
And she will sing the song that pleaseth you,
And on your eyelids crown the god of sleep,
Charming your blood with pleasing heaviness;
Making such difference 'twixt wake and sleep,
As is the difference betwixt day and night,
The hour before the heavenly-harness'd team
Begins his golden progress in the east.

MORTIMER
With all my heart I'll sit and hear her sing:
By that time will our book, I think, be drawn.

GLENDOWER
Do so;
And those musicians that shall play to you
Hang in the air a thousand leagues from hence;
And straight they shall be here: sit, and attend.

HOTSPUR
Come, Kate, thou art perfect in lying down: come,
quick, quick, that I may lay my head in thy lap.

LADY PERCY
Go, ye giddy goose. [*The music plays.*

HOTSPUR
Now I perceive the devil understands Welsh;
And 'tis no marvel he is so humorous.
By 'r lady, he is a good musician.

LADY PERCY
Then should you be nothing but musical; for you are
altogether govern'd by humours. Lie still, ye thief,
and hear the lady sing in Welsh.

HOTSPUR
I had rather hear Lady, my brach, howl in Irish.

LADY PERCY
Wouldst thou have thy head broken?

HOTSPUR
No.

LADY PERCY
Then be still.

HOTSPUR
Neither; 'tis a woman's fault.

LADY PERCY
Now God help thee!

HOTSPUR
To the Welsh lady's bed.

LADY PERCY
What's that?

HOTSPUR
Peace! she sings.
[*Here the* LADY *sings a Welsh song.*
Come, Kate, I'll have your song too.

LADY PERCY
Not mine, in good sooth.

HOTSPUR
Not yours, in good sooth! Heart! you swear like a
comfit-maker's wife. 'Not you, in good sooth'; and 'as
true as I live'; and 'as God shall mend me'; and 'as sure
as day';
And givest such sarcenet surety for thy oaths,
As if thou never walk'st further than Finsbury.
Swear me, Kate, like a lady as thou art,
A good mouth-filling oath; and leave 'in sooth',
And such protest of pepper-gingerbread,
To velvet-guards and Sunday-citizens.
Come, sing.

LADY PERCY
I will not sing.

HOTSPUR
'Tis the next way to turn tailor, or be red-breast teacher.
An the indentures be drawn, I'll away within these two
hours; and so, come in when ye will.
[*Exit.*

GLENDOWER
Come, come, Lord Mortimer; you are as slow
As hot Lord Percy is on fire to go.
By this our book is drawn; we'll but seal, and then
To horse immediately.

MORTIMER
With all my heart.
[*Exeunt.*

SCENE II

London. The palace.

Enter KING HENRY, PRINCE
HENRY, *and* LORDS.

KING HENRY
Lords, give us leave; the Prince of
Wales and I
Must have some private conference:
but be near at hand,
For we shall presently have need of
you.
[*Exeunt* LORDS.
I know not whether God will have it
so,
For some displeasing service I have
done,
That, in his secret doom, out of my
blood
He'll breed revengement and a
scourge for me;
But thou dost, in thy passages of life,
Make me believe that thou art only
mark'd
For the hot vengeance and the rod of
heaven
To punish my mistreadings. Tell me else,
Could such inordinate and low desires,
Such poor, such base, such lewd, such mean attempts,
Such barren pleasures, rude society,
As thou art match'd withal and grafted to,
Accompany the greatness of thy blood,
And hold their level with thy princely heart?

PRINCE HENRY
So please your majesty, I would I could
Quit all offences with as clear excuse
As well as I am doubtless I can purge
Myself of many I am charg'd withal:
Yet such extenuation let me beg,
As, in reproof of many tales devised, —
which oft the ear of greatness needs must hear, —
By smiling pick-thanks and base news-mongers,
I may, for some things true, wherein my youth
Hath faulty wander'd and irregular,
Find pardon on my true submission.

KING HENRY
God pardon thee! — yet let me wonder, Harry,
At thy affections, which do hold a wing
Quite from the flight of all thy ancestors.
Thy place in council thou hast rudely lost,
Which by thy younger brother is supplied;
And art almost an alien to the hearts
Of all the court and princes of my blood:
The hope and expectation of thy time
Is ruin'd; and the soul of every man
Prophetically do forethink thy fall.
Had I so lavish of my presence been,
So common-hackney'd in the eyes of men,
So stale and cheap to vulgar company, —
Opinion, that did help me to the crown,
Had still kept loyal to possession,
And left me in reputeless banishment,
A fellow of no mark nor likelihood.
By being seldom seen, I could not stir
But, like a comet, I was wonder'd at;
That men would tell their children, 'This is he';
Others would say, 'Where, which is Bolingbroke?'
And then I stole all courtesy from heaven,
And dress'd myself in such humility
That I did pluck allegiance from men's hearts,
Loud shouts and salutations from their mouths,
Even in the presence of the crowned king.
Thus did I keep my person fresh and new;
My presence, like a robe pontifical,
Ne'er seen but wonder'd at: and so my state,
Seldom but sumptuous, show'd like a feast,
And won by rareness such solemnity.
The skipping king, he ambled up and down
With shallow jesters and rash bavin wits,
Soon kindled and soon burnt; carded his state;
Mingled his royalty with capering fools;
Had his great name profaned with their scorns;
And gave his countenance, against his name,
To laugh at gibing boys, and stand the push
Of every beardless vain comparative;
Grew a companion to the common streets,
Enfeoff'd himself to popularity;

HOTSPUR I'll have the current in this place damm'd up.

That, being daily swallow'd by men's eyes,
They surfeited with honey, and began
To loathe the taste of sweetness, whereof a little
More than a little is by much too much.
So, when he had occasion to be seen,
He was but as the cuckoo is in June,
Heard, not regarded, — seen, but with such eyes
As, sick and blunted with community,
Afford no extraordinary gaze,
Such as is bent on sun-like majesty
When it shines seldom in admiring eyes;
But rather drowz'd, and hung their eyelids down,
Slept in his face, and render'd such aspect
As cloudy men use to their adversaries,
Being with his presence glutted, gorg'd, and full.
And in that very line, Harry, stand'st thou;
For thou hast lost thy princely privilege
With vile participation: not an eye
But is a-weary of thy common sight,
Save mine, which hath desired to see thee more;
Which now doth that I would not have it do, —
Make blind itself with foolish tenderness.

PRINCE HENRY
I shall hereafter, my thrice-gracious lord,
Be more myself.

KING HENRY
For all the world,
As thou art to this hour, was Richard then
When I from France set foot at Ravenspurg;
And even as I was then is Percy now.
Now, by my sceptre, and my soul to boot,
He hath more worthy interest to the state
Than thou, the shadow of succession;
For, of no right, nor colour like to right,
He doth fill fields with harness in the realm;
Turns head against the lion's armed jaws;
And, being no more in debt to years than thou,
Leads ancient lords and reverend bishops on
To bloody battles and to bruising arms.
What never-dying honour hath he got
Against renowned Douglas! whose high deeds,
Whose hot incursions, and great name in arms,
Holds from all soldiers chief majority
And military title capital
Through all the kingdoms that acknowledge Christ:
Thrice hath this Hotspur, Mars in swathling-clothes,
This infant warrior, in his enterprises
Discomfited great Douglas: ta'en him once,
Enlarged him, and made a friend of him,
To fill the mouth of deep defiance up,
And shake the peace and safety of our throne.
And what say you to this? Percy, Northumberland,
The Archbishop's Grace of York, Douglas, Mortimer,
Capitulate against us, and are up.
But wherefore do I tell these news to thee?
Why, Harry, do I tell thee of my foes,
Which art my near'st and dearest enemy?
Thou that art like enough, — through vassal fear,
Base inclination, and the start of spleen, —
To fight against me under Percy's pay,
To dog his heels, and court'sy at his frowns,
To show how much thou art degenerate.

PRINCE HENRY
Do not think so; you shall not find it so:
And God forgive them that so much have sway'd
Your majesty's good thoughts away from me!
I will redeem all this on Percy's head,
And, in the closing of some glorious day,
Be bold to tell you that I am your son;
When I will wear a garment all of blood,
And stain my favours in a bloody mask,
Which, wash'd away, shall scour my shame with it:
And that shall be the day, whene'er it lights,
That this same child of honour and renown,
This gallant Hotspur, this all-praised knight,
And your unthought-of Harry, chance to meet.
For every honour sitting on his helm,
Would they were multitudes, and on my head
My shames redoubled! for the time will come,
That I shall make this northern youth exchange
His glorious deeds for my indignities.
Percy is but my factor, good my lord,
To engross up glorious deeds on my behalf;
And I will call him to so strict account,
That he shall render every glory up,
Yea, even the slightest worship of his time,
Or I will tear the reckoning from his heart.
This, in the name of God, I promise here:
The which if He be pleas'd I shall perform,
I do beseech your majesty, may salve
The long-grown wounds of my intemperance:
If not, the end of life cancels all bands;
And I will die a hundred thousand deaths
Ere break the smallest parcel of this vow.

KING HENRY
A hundred thousand rebels die in this: —
Thou shalt have charge and sovereign trust herein.

Enter SIR WALTER BLUNT.

How now, good Blunt? thy looks are full of speed.

SIR WALTER BLUNT
So hath the business that I come to speak of.
Lord Mortimer of Scotland hath sent word
That Douglas and the English rebels met
The eleventh of this month at Shrewsbury:
A mighty and a fearful head they are,
If promises be kept on every hand,
As ever offer'd foul play in a state.

KING HENRY
The Earl of Westmoreland set forth to-day;
With him my son, Lord John of Lancaster;
For this advertisement is five days old: —
On Wednesday next, Harry, you shall set forward;
On Thursday we ourselves will march:
Our meeting is Bridgenorth: and, Harry, you
Shall march through Glostershire; by which account,
Our business valued, some twelve days hence
Our general forces at Bridgenorth shall meet.
Our hands are full of business: let's away;
Advantage feeds him fat, while men delay.   [*Exeunt.*

SCENE III

Eastcheap. The Boar's-Head Tavern.

Enter FALSTAFF *and* BARDOLPH.

FALSTAFF
Bardolph, am I not fall'n away vilely since this last action? do I not bate? do I not dwindle? Why, my skin hangs about me like an old lady's loose gown; I am wither'd like an old apple-john. Well, I'll repent, and that suddenly, while I am in some liking; I shall be out of heart shortly, and then I shall have no strength to repent. An I have not forgotten what the inside of a church is made of, I am a peppercorn, a brewer's horse: the inside of a church! Company, villainous company, hath been the spoil of me.

BARDOLPH
Sir John, you are so fretful, you cannot live long.

FALSTAFF
Why, there is it: — come, sing me a bawdy song; make me merry. I was as virtuously given as a gentleman need to be; virtuous enough; swore little; diced not above seven times a week; went to a bawdy-house not above once in a quarter — of an hour; paid money that I borrow'd — three or four times; lived well and in good compass: and now I live out of all order, out of all compass.

BARDOLPH
Why, you are so fat, Sir John, that you must needs be out of all compass, — out of all reasonable compass, Sir John.

FALSTAFF
Do thou amend thy face, and I'll amend my life: thou art our admiral, thou bearest the lantern in the poop, —

but 'tis in the nose of thee; thou art the Knight of the Burning Lamp.

BARDOLPH
Why, Sir John, my face does you no harm.

FALSTAFF
No, I'll be sworn; I make as good use of it as many a man doth of a death's-head or a *memento mori:* I never see thy face but I think upon hell-fire, and Dives that lived in purple; for there he is in his robes, burning, burning. If thou wert any way given to virtue, I would swear by thy face; my oath should be, 'By this fire, that's God's angel': but thou art altogether given over; and wert indeed, but for the light in thy face, the son of utter darkness. When thou ran'st up Gadshill in the night to catch my horse, if I did not think thou hadst been an *ignis fatuus* or a ball of wildfire, there's no purchase in money. O, thou art a perpetual triumph, an everlasting bonfire-light! Thou hast saved me a thousand marks in links and torches, walking with thee in the night betwixt tavern and tavern: but the sack that thou hast drunk me would have bought me lights as good cheap at the dearest chandler's in Europe. I have maintain'd that salamander of yours with fire any time this two-and-thirty years; God reward me for it!

BARDOLPH
'Sblood, I would my face were in your belly!

FALSTAFF
God-a-mercy! so should I be sure to be heart-burn'd.

Enter HOSTESS.

How now, Dame Partlet the hen! have you inquired yet who pick'd my pocket?

HOSTESS
Why, Sir John, what do you think, Sir John? do you think I keep thieves in my house? I have search'd, I have inquired, so has my husband, man by man, boy by boy, servant by servant: the tithe of a hair was never lost in my house before.

FALSTAFF
Ye lie, hostess: Bardolph was shaved, and lost many a hair; and I'll be sworn my pocket was pick'd. Go to, you are a woman, go.

HOSTESS
Who, I? no; I defy thee: God's light, I was never call'd so in mine own house before.

FALSTAFF
Go to, I know you well enough.

HOSTESS
No, Sir John; you do not know me, Sir John. I know you, Sir John: you owe me money, Sir John; and now you pick a quarrel to beguile me of it: I bought you a dozen of shirts to your back.

FALSTAFF
Dowlas, filthy dowlas: I have given them away to bakers' wives, and they have made bolters of them.

HOSTESS
Now, as I am a true woman, holland of eight shillings an ell. You owe money here besides, Sir John, for your diet and by-drinkings, and money lent you, four-and-twenty pound.

FALSTAFF
He had his part of it; let him pay.

HOSTESS
He? alas, he is poor; he hath nothing.

FALSTAFF
How! poor? look uponc his face; what call you rich? let them coin his nose, let them coin his cheeks: I'll not pay a denier. What, will you make a younker of me? shall I not take mine ease in mine inn, but I shall have my pocket pick'd? I have lost a seal-ring of my grandfather's worth forty mark.

HOSTESS
O Jesu, I have heard the prince tell him, I know not how oft, that that ring was copper!

FALSTAFF
How! the prince is a Jack, a sneak-cup:'sblood, an he were here, I would cudgel him like a dog, if he would say so.

Enter the PRINCE *and* POINTZ, *marching, and*
FALSTAFF *meets them, playing on his truncheon like a fife.*
How now, lad! is the wind in that door, i'faith? must we all march?

BARDOLPH
Yea, two and two, Newgate-fashion.

HOSTESS
My lord, I pray you, hear me.

PRINCE HENRY
What say'st thou, Mistress Quickly! How doth thy husband? I love him well; he is an honest man.

BARDOLPH Why, Sir John, my face does you no harm.

HOSTESS
Good my lord, hear me.

FALSTAFF
Prithee, let her alone, and list to me.

PRINCE HENRY
What say'st thou, Jack?

FALSTAFF
The other night I fell asleep here behind the arras, and had my pocket pick'd: this house is turn'd bawdy-house; they pick pockets.

PRINCE HENRY
What didst thou lose, Jack?

FALSTAFF
Wilt thou believe me, Hal? three or four bonds of forty pound a-piece, and a seal-ring of my grandfather's.

PRINCE HENRY
A trifle, some eight-penny matter.

HOSTESS
So I told him, my lord; and I said I heard your Grace say so: and, my lord, he speaks most vilely of you, like a foul-mouth'd man as he is; and said he would cudgel you.

PRINCE HENRY
What! he did not?

HOSTESS
There's neither faith, truth, nor womanhood in me else.

FALSTAFF
There's no more faith in thee than in a stew'd prune; nor no more truth in thee than in a drawn fox; and for womanhood, Maid Marian may be the deputy's wife of the ward to thee. Go, you thing, go.

HOSTESS
Say, what thing? what thing?

FALSTAFF
What thing! why, a thing to thank God on.

HOSTESS
I am no thing to thank God on, I would thou shouldst know it; I am an honest man's wife: and, setting thy knighthood aside, thou art a knave to call me so.

FALSTAFF
Setting thy womanhood aside, thou art a beast to say otherwise.

HOSTESS
Say, what beast, thou knave, thou?

FALSTAFF
What beast! why, an otter.

PRINCE HENRY
An otter, Sir John! why an otter?

FALSTAFF
Why, she's neither fish nor flesh; a man knows not where to have her.

HOSTESS
Thou art an unjust man in saying so: thou or any man knows where to have me, thou knave, thou!

PRINCE HENRY
Thou say'st true, hostess; and he slanders thee most grossly.

HOSTESS
So he doth you, my lord; and said this other day you

FALSTAFF Company, villainous company, hath been the spoil of me.

ought him a thousand pound.

PRINCE HENRY
Sirrah, do I owe you a thousand pound?

FALSTAFF
A thousand pound, Hal! a million: thy love is worth a million; thou owest me thy love.

HOSTESS
Nay, my lord, he call'd you Jack, and said he would cudgel you.

FALSTAFF
Did I, Bardolph?

BARDOLPH
Indeed, Sir John, you said so.

FALSTAFF
Yea, — if he said my ring was copper.

PRINCE HENRY
I say 'tis copper: darest thou be as good as thy word now?

FALSTAFF
Why, Hal, thou know'st, as thou art but man, I dare; but as thou art prince, I fear thee as I fear the roaring of the lion's whelp.

PRINCE HENRY
And why not as the lion?

FALSTAFF
The king himself is to be fear'd as the lion: dost thou think I'll fear thee as I fear thy father? nay, an I do, I pray God my girdle break.

PRINCE HENRY
O, if it should, how would thy guts fall about thy knees! But, sirrah, there's no room for faith, truth, nor honesty in this bosom of thine, — it is all fill'd up with guts and midriff. Charge an honest woman with picking thy pocket! why, thou whoreson, impudent, emboss'd rascal, if there were anything in thy pocket but tavern-reckonings, memorandums of bawdy-houses, and one poor pennyworth of sugar-candy to make thee long-winded, — if thy pocket were enrich'd with any other injuries but these, I am a villain: and yet you will stand to it; you will not pocket-up wrong: art thou not ashamed?

FALSTAFF
Dost thou hear, Hal? thou know'st in the state of innocency Adam fell; and what should poor Jack Falstaff do in the days of villainy? Thou seest I have more flesh than another man; and therefore more frailty. You confess, then, you pick'd my pocket?

PRINCE HENRY
It appears so by the story.

FALSTAFF
Hostess, I forgive thee: go, make ready breakfast; love thy husband, look to thy servants, cherish thy guests: thou shalt find me tractable to any honest reason; thou seest I am pacified still. — Nay, prithee, be gone. [*Exit* HOSTESS.] Now, Hal, to the news at court: for the robbery, lad, — how is that answer'd?

PRINCE HENRY
O, my sweet beef, I must still be good angel to thee: — the money is paid back again.

FALSTAFF
O, I do not like that paying back; 'tis a double labour.

PRINCE HENRY
I am good friends with my father, and may do any thing.

FALSTAFF
Rob me the exchequer the first thing thou dost, and do it with unwash'd hands too.

BARDOLPH
Do, my lord.

PRINCE HENRY
I have procured thee, Jack, a charge of foot.

FALSTAFF
I would it had been of horse. Where shall I find one that can steal well? O, for a fine thief, of the age of two-and-twenty or thereabouts! I am heinously unprovided. Well, God be thank'd for these rebels, — they offend none but the virtuous: I laud them, I praise them.

PRINCE HENRY
Bardolph, —

BARDOLPH
My lord?

PRINCE HENRY
Go bear this letter to Lord John of Lancaster, to my brother John; this to my Lord of Westmoreland. [*Exit* BARDOLPH.] Go, Pointz, to horse, to horse; for thou and I have thirty miles to ride yet ere dinner-time. [*Exit* POINTZ.] Jack, meet me to-morrow in the Temple-hall at two o'clock in the afternoon:
There shalt thou know thy charge; and there receive Money and order for their furniture.
The land is burning; Percy stands on high;
And either we or they must lower lie. [*Exit.*

FALSTAFF
Rare words! brave world! — Hostess, my breakfast; come: —
O, I could wish this tavern were my drum! [*Exit.*

ACT IV

SCENE I

The rebel camp near Shrewsbury.

Enter HOTSPUR, WORCESTER, *and* DOUGLAS.

HOTSPUR
Well said, my noble Scot: if speaking truth
In this fine age were not thought flattery,
Such attribution should the Douglas have,
As not a soldier of this season's stamp
Should go so general current through the world.
By God, I cannot flatter; I defy
The tongues of soothers; but a braver place
In my heart's love hath no man than yourself:
Nay, task me to my word; approve me, lord.

DOUGLAS
Thou art the king of honour:
No man so potent breathes upon the ground
But I will beard him.

HOTSPUR
Do so, and 'tis well. —
Enter a MESSENGER *with letters.*
What letters hast thou there? — I can but thank you.

MESSENGER
These letters come from your father.

HOTSPUR
Letters from him! why comes he not himself?

MESSENGER
He cannot come, my lord; he is grievous sick.

HOTSPUR
Zounds! how has he the leisure to be sick
In such a justling time? Who leads his power?
Under whose government come they along?

MESSENGER
His letters bear his mind, not I, my lord.

WORCESTER
I prithee, tell me, doth he keep his bed?

MESSENGER
He did, my lord, four days ere I set forth;
And at the time of my departure thence
He was much fear'd by his physicians.

WORCESTER
I would the state of time had first been whole
Ere he by sickness had been visited:
His health was never better worth than now.

HOTSPUR
Sick now! droop now! this sickness doth infect
The very life-blood of our enterprise;
'Tis catching hither, even to our camp. —
He writes me here, that inward sickness, —
And that his friends by deputation could not
So soon be drawn; nor did he think it meet
To lay so dangerous and dear a trust
On any soul remov'd, but on his own.
Yet doth he give us bold advertisement,
That with our small conjunction we should on,
To see how fortune is dispos'd to us;
For, as he writes, there is no quailing now,
Because the king is certainly possess'd
Of all our purposes. What say you to it?

WORCESTER
Your father's sickness is a maim to us.

HOTSPUR
A perilous gash, a very limb lopp'd off: —
And yet, in faith, it is not; his present want
Seems more than we shall find it: — were it good
To set the exact wealth of all our states
All at one cast? to set so rich a main
On the nice hazard of one doubtful hour?
It were not good; for therein should we read
The very bottom and the soul of hope,
The very list, the very utmost bound
Of all our fortunes.

FALSTAFF Go, you thing, go.

DOUGLAS
          Faith, and so we should;
Where now remains a sweet reversion,
We may boldly spend upon the hope of what
Is to come in:
A comfort of retirement lives in this.

HOTSPUR
A rendezvous, a home to fly unto,
If that the devil and mischance look big
Upon the maidenhead of our affairs.

WORCESTER
But yet I would your father had been here.
The quality and hair of our attempt
Brooks no division: it will be thought
By some, that know not why he is away,
That wisdom, loyalty, and mere dislike
Of our proceedings, kept the earl from hence:
And think how such an apprehension
May turn the tide of fearful faction,
And breed a kind of question in our cause;
For well you know we of the offering side
Must keep aloof from strict arbitrement,
And stop all sight-holes, every loop from whence
The eye of reason may pry in upon us:
This absence of your father's draws a curtain,
That shows the ignorant a kind of fear
Before not dreamt of.

HOTSPUR
          You strain too far.
I, rather, of his absence make this use: —
It lends a lustre and more great opinion,
A larger dare to our great enterprise,
Than if the earl were here; for men must think,
If we, without his help, can make a head
To push against a kingdom, with his help
We shall o'erturn it topsy-turvy down. —
Yet all goes well, yet all our joints are whole.

DOUGLAS
As heart can think: there is not such a word
Spoke of in Scotland as this term of fear.

Enter SIR RICHARD VERNON.

HOTSPUR
My cousin Vernon! welcome, by my soul.

VERNON
Pray God my news be worth a welcome, lord.
The Earl of Westmoreland, seven thousand strong,
Is marching hitherwards; with him Prince John.

HOTSPUR
No harm: — what more?

VERNON
          And further, I have learn'd,
The king himself in person is set forth,
Or hitherwards intended speedily,
With strong and mighty preparation.

HOTSPUR
He shall be welcome too. Where is his son,
The nimble-footed madcap Prince of Wales,
And his comrades, that daff'd the world aside,
And bid it pass?

VERNON
          All furnish'd, all in arms;
All plum'd like estridges that wing the wind;
Bated like eagles having lately bathed;
Glittering in golden coats, like images;
As full of spirit as the month of May,
And gorgeous as the sun at midsummer;
Wanton as youthful goats, wild as young bulls.
I saw young Harry, — with his beaver on,
His cuisses on his thighs, gallantly arm'd, —
Rise from the ground like feather'd Mercury,
And vaulted with such ease into his seat,
As if an angel dropp'd down from the clouds,
To turn and wind a fiery Pegasus,
And witch the world with noble horsemanship.

HOTSPUR
No more, no more: worse than the sun in March,
This praise doth nourish agues. Let them come;
They come like sacrifices in their trim,
And to the fire-eyed maid of smoky war,
All hot and bleeding, will we offer them:
The mailed Mars shall on his altar sit
Up to the ears in blood. I am on fire
To hear this rich reprisal is so nigh,
And yet not ours. — Come, let me taste my horse,
Who is to bear me, like a thunderbolt,
Against the bosom of the Prince of Wales:
Harry to Harry shall, hot horse to horse,
Meet, and ne'er part till one drop down a corse. —
O, that Glendower were come!

VERNON
          There is more news:
I learn'd in Worcester, as I rode along,
He cannot draw his power this fourteen days.

DOUGLAS
That's the worst tidings that I hear of yet.

WORCESTER
Ay, by my faith, that bears a frosty sound.

HOTSPUR
What may the king's whole battle reach unto?

VERNON
To thirty thousand.

HOTSPUR
          Forty let it be:
My father and Glendower being both away,
The powers of us may serve so great a day.
Come, let us take a muster speedily:
Doomsday is near; die all, die merrily.

DOUGLAS
Talk not of dying: I am out of fear
Of death or death's hand for this one half-year. [*Exeunt.*

SCENE II

A public road near Coventry.

Enter FALSTAFF *and* BARDOLPH.

FALSTAFF
Bardolph, get thee before to Coventry; fill me a bottle of sack: our soldiers shall march through; we'll to Sutton Co'fil' to-night.

BARDOLPH
Will you give me money, captain?

FALSTAFF
Lay out, lay out.

BARDOLPH
This bottle makes an angel.

FALSTAFF
An if it do, take it for thy labour; and if it make twenty, take them all; I'll answer the coinage. Bid my lieutenant Peto meet me at town's end.

BARDOLPH
I will, captain: farewell.   [*Exit.*

FALSTAFF
If I be not ashamed of my soldiers, I am a soused gurnet. I have misused the king's press damnably. I have got, in exchange of a hundred and fifty soldiers, three hundred and odd pounds. I press me none but good householders, yeoman's sons; inquire me out contracted bachelors, such as had been ask'd twice on the banns; such a commodity of warm slaves as had as lieve hear the devil as a drum; such as fear the report of a caliver worse than a struck fowl or a hurt wild-duck. I press'd me none but such toasts-and-butter, with

hearts in their bellies no bigger than pins'-heads, and they have bought out their services; and now my whole charge consists of ancients, corporals, lieutenants, gentlemen of companies, slaves as ragged as Lazarus in the painted cloth, where the glutton's dogs lick'd his sores; and such as, indeed, were never soldiers, but discarded unjust serving-men, younger sons to younger brothers, revolted tapsters, and ostlers trade-fall'n; the cankers of a calm world and a long peace; ten times more dishonourable ragged than an old-faced ancient: and such have I, to fill up the rooms of them that have bought out their services, that you would think that I had a hundred and fifty tatter'd prodigals lately come from swine-keeping, from eating draff and husks. A mad fellow met me on the way, and told me I had unloaded all the gibbets, and press'd the dead bodies. No eye hath seen such scarecrows. I'll not march through Coventry with them, that's flat: — nay, and the villains march wide betwixt the legs, as if they had gyves on; for, indeed, I had the most of them out of prison. There's but a shirt and a half in all my company; and the half-shirt is two napkins tack'd together and thrown over the shoulders like a herald's coat without sleeves; and the shirt, to say the truth, stolen from my host at Saint Alban's, or the red-nose innkeeper of Daventry. But that's all one; they'll find linen enough on every hedge.

Enter the PRINCE *and* WESTMORELAND.

PRINCE HENRY
How now, blown Jack! how now, quilt!

FALSTAFF
What, Hal! how now, mad wag! what a devil dost thou in Warwickshire? — My good Lord of Westmoreland, I cry you mercy: I thought your honour had already been at Shrewsbury.

WESTMORELAND
Faith, Sir John, 'tis more than time that I were there, and you too; but my powers are there already. The king, I can tell you, looks for us all: we must away all night.

FALSTAFF
Tut, never fear me: I am as vigilant as a cat to steal cream.

PRINCE HENRY
I think, to steal cream, indeed; for thy theft hath already made thee butter. But tell me, Jack, whose fellows are these that come after?

FALSTAFF
Mine, Hal, mine.

PRINCE HENRY
I did never see such pitiful rascals.

FALSTAFF
Tut, tut; good enough to toss; food for powder, food for powder; they'll fill a pit as well as better: tush, man,

HOTSPUR As he writes, there is no quailing now.

mortal men, mortal men.

WESTMORELAND
Ay, but, Sir John, methinks they are exceeding poor and bare, — too beggarly.

FALSTAFF
Faith, for their poverty, I know not where they had that; and for their bareness, I am sure they never learn'd that of me.

PRINCE HENRY
No, I'll be sworn; unless you call three fingers on the ribs bare. But, sirrah, make haste: Percy is already in the field.

[*Exit.*

FALSTAFF
What, is the king encamp'd?

WESTMORELAND
He is, Sir John: I fear we shall stay too long.   [*Exit.*

FALSTAFF
Well,
To the latter end of a fray and the beginning of a feast
Fits a dull fighter and a keen guest.   [*Exit.*

SCENE III

The rebel camp near Shrewsbury.

Enter HOTSPUR, WORCESTER,
DOUGLAS, *and* VERNON.

HOTSPUR
We'll fight with him to-night.

WORCESTER
                        It may not be.

DOUGLAS
You give him, then, advantage.

VERNON
                        Not a whit.

HOTSPUR
Why say you so? looks he not for supply?

VERNON
So do we.

HOTSPUR
        His is certain, ours is doubtful.

WORCESTER
Good cousin, be advis'd; stir not to-night.

VERNON
Do not, my lord.

DOUGLAS
            You do not counsel well:
You speak it out of fear and cold heart.

VERNON
Do me no slander, Douglas: by my life, —
And I dare well maintain it with my life, —
If well-respected honour bid me on,
I hold as little counsel with weak fear
As you, my lord, or any Scot that this day lives: —
Let it be seen to-morrow in the battle
Which of us fears.

DOUGLAS
            Yea, or to-night.

VERNON
                        Content.

HOTSPUR
To-night, say I.

VERNON
Come, come it may not be. I wonder much,
Being men of such great leading as you are,
That you foresee not what impediments
Drag back our expedition: certain horse
Of my cousin Vernon's are not yet come up:
Your uncle Worcester's horse came but to-day;
And now their pride and mettle is asleep,
Their courage with hard labour tame and dull,
That not a horse is half the half of himself.

HOTSPUR
So are the horses of the enemy
In general, journey-bated and brought low:
The better part of ours are full of rest.

WORCESTER
The number of the king exceedeth ours:
For God's sake, cousin, stay till all come in.

[*The trumpet sounds a parley.*

Enter SIR WALTER BLUNT.

BLUNT
I come with gracious offers from the king,
If you vouchsafe me hearing and respect.

HOTSPUR
Welcome, Sir Walter Blunt; and would to God
You were of our determination!
Some of us love you well; and even those some

Envy your great deservings
and good name,
Because you are not of our
quality,
But stand against us like an
enemy.

BLUNT
And God defend but still I
should stand so,
So long as out of limit and
true rule
You stand against anointed
majesty!
But, to my charge! — The
king hath sent to know
The nature of your griefs; and
whereupon
You conjure from the breast
of civil peace
Such bold hostility, teaching
his duteous land
Audacious cruelty. If that the
king
Have any way your good
deserts forgot,
Which he confesseth to be
manifold,
He bids you name your griefs;
and with all speed
You shall have your desires
with interest,
And pardon absolute for
yourself and these
Herein misled by your
suggestion.

HOTSPUR
The king is kind; and well we know the king
Knows at what time to promise, when to pay.
My father and my uncle and myself
Did give him that same royalty he wears;
And when he was not six-and-twenty strong,
Sick in the world's regard, wretched and low,
A poor unminded outlaw sneaking home,
My father gave him welcome to the shore;
And when he heard him swear and vow to God,
He came but to be Duke of Lancaster,
To sue his livery and beg his peace,
With tears of innocency and terms of zeal, —
My father, in kind heart and pity moved,
Swore him assistance, and perform'd it too.
Now, when the lords and barons of the realm
Perceiv'd Northumberland did lean to him,
The more and less came in with cap and knee;
Met him in boroughs, cities, villages,
Attended him on bridges, stood in lanes,
Laid gifts before him, proffer'd him their oaths,
Gave him their heirs as pages, follow'd him
Even at the heels in golden multitudes.
He presently, — as greatness knows itself, —
Steps me a little higher than his vow
Made to my father, while his blood was poor,
Upon the naked shore at Ravenspurg;
And now, forsooth, takes on him to reform
Some certain edicts and some strait decrees
That lie too heavy on the commonwealth;
Cries out upon abuses, seems to weep
Over his country's wrongs; and, by this face,
This seeming brow of justice, did he win
The hearts of all that he did angle for:
Proceeded further; cut me off the heads
Of all the favourites, that the absent king
In deputation left behind him here
When he was personal in the Irish war.

BLUNT
Tut, I came not to hear this.

HOTSPUR
                    Then to the point.
In short time after, he depos'd the king;
Soon after that, depriv'd him of his life;
And, in the neck of that, task'd the whole state:
To make that worse, suffer'd his kinsman March, —
Who is, if every owner were well placed,
Indeed his king, — to be engag'd in Wales,
There without ransom to lie forfeited;
Disgrac'd me in my happy victories,
Sought to entrap me by intelligence;
Rated my uncle from the council-board;
In rage dismiss'd my father from the court;
Broke oath on oath, committed wrong on wrong;
And, in conclusion, drove us to seek out
This head of safety; and withal to pry

FALSTAFF If I be not ashamed of my soldiers, I am a soused gurnet.

Into his title, the which we find
Too indirect for long continuance.

BLUNT
Shall I return this answer to the king?

HOTSPUR
Not so, Sir Walter: we'll withdraw awhile.
Go to the king; and let there be impawn'd
Some surety for a safe return again,
And in the morning early shall mine uncle
Bring him our purposes: and so, farewell.

BLUNT
I would you would accept of grace and love.

HOTSPUR
And may be so we shall.

BLUNT
                    Pray God you do.   [*Exeunt.*

SCENE IV

York. The ARCHBISHOP'S *palace.*

Enter the ARCHBISHOP OF YORK
and SIR MICHAEL.

ARCHBISHOP OF YORK
Hie, good Sir Michael; bear this sealed brief
With winged haste to the lord marshal;
This to my cousin Scroop; and all the rest
To whom they are directed. If you knew
How much they do import, you would make haste.

SIR MICHAEL
My good lord,
I guess their tenour.

ARCHBISHOP OF YORK
                Like enough you do.
To-morrow, good Sir Michael, is a day
Wherein the fortune of ten thousand men
Must bide the touch; for, sir, at Shrewsbury,
As I am truly given to understand,
The king, with mighty and quick-raised power,
Meets with Lord Harry: and, I fear, Sir Michael,
What with the sickness of Northumberland,
Whose power was in the first proportion,
And what with Owen Glendower's absence thence,
Who with them was a rated sinew too,
And comes not in, o'er-rul'd by prophecies, —
I fear the power of Percy is too weak
To wage an instant trial with the king.

SIR MICHAEL
Why, my good lord, you need not fear;
There is Douglas and Lord Mortimer.

ARCHBISHOP OF YORK
No, Mortimer is not there.

SIR MICHAEL
But there is Mordake, Vernon, Lord Harry Percy,
And there is my Lord of Worcester; and a head
Of gallant warriors, noble gentlemen.

ARCHBISHOP OF YORK
And so there is: but yet the king hath drawn
The special head of all the land together; —
The Prince of Wales, Lord John of Lancaster,
The noble Westmoreland, and warlike Blunt;
And many more corrivals and dear men
Of estimation and command in arms.

SIR MICHAEL
Doubt not, my lord, they shall be well opposed.

ARCHBISHOP OF YORK
I hope no less, yet needful 'tis to fear;
And, to prevent the worst, Sir Michael, speed:
For if Lord Percy thrive not, ere the king
Dismiss his power, he means to visit us,
For he hath heard of our confederacy, —
And 'tis but wisdom to make strong against him:
Therefore make haste. I must go write again
To other friends; and so, farewell, Sir Michael. [*Exeunt.*

ACT V

SCENE I

The KING'S *camp near Shrewsbury.*

Enter the KING, PRINCE HENRY, PRINCE JOHN
OF LANCASTER, SIR WALTER BLUNT,
and FALSTAFF.

KING HENRY
How bloodily the sun begins to peer
Above yon busky hill! the day looks pale
At his distemperature.

PRINCE HENRY
     The southern wind
Doth play the trumpet to his purposes;
And by his hollow whistling in the leaves
Foretells a tempest and a blustering day.

KING HENRY
Then with the losers let it sympathise,
For nothing can seem foul to those that win.
        [*The trumpet sounds.*
   Enter WORCESTER *and* VERNON.
How now, my Lord of Worcester! 'tis not well
That you and I should meet upon such terms
As now we meet. You have deceiv'd our trust;
And made us doff our easy robes of peace,
To crush our old limbs in ungentle steel:
This is not well, my lord, this is not well.
What say you to it? will you again unknit
This churlish knot of all-abhorred war?
And move in that obedient orb again
Where you did give a fair and natural light;
And be no more an exhaled meteor,
A prodigy of fear, and a portent
Of broached mischief to the unborn times?

WORCESTER
Hear me, my liege:
For mine own part, I could be well content
To entertain the lag-end of my life
With quiet hours; for, I do protest,
I have not sought the day of this dislike.

KING HENRY
You have not sought it! how comes it, then?

FALSTAFF
Rebellion lay in his way, and he found it.

PRINCE HENRY
Peace, chewet, peace!

WORCESTER
It pleas'd your majesty to turn your looks
Of favour from myself and all our house;
And yet I must remember you, my lord,
We were the first and dearest of your friends.
For you my staff of office did I break
In Richard's time; and posted day and night
To meet you on the way, and kiss your hand,
When yet you were in place and in account
Nothing so strong and fortunate as I.
It was myself, my brother, and his son,
That brought you home, and boldly did outdare
The dangers of the time. You swore to us,
And you did swear that oath at Doncaster,
That you did nothing purpose 'gainst the state;
Nor claim no further than your new-fall'n right,
The seat of Gaunt, dukedom of Lancaster:
To this we swore our aid. But in short space
It rain'd down fortune showering on your head;
And such a flood of greatness fell on you, —
What with our help, what with the absent king,
What with the injuries of a wanton time,
The seeming sufferances that you had borne,

And the contrarious winds that held the king
So long in his unlucky Irish wars
That all in England did repute him dead, —
And from this swarm of fair advantages
You took occasion to be quickly woo'd
To gripe the general sway into your hand;
Forget your oath to us at Doncaster;
And, being fed by us, you used us so
As that ungentle gull, the cuckoo's bird,
Useth the sparrow, — did oppress our nest;
Grew by our feeding to so great a bulk,
That even our love durst not come near your sight
For fear of swallowing; but with nimble wing
We were enforc'd, for safety sake, to fly
Out of your sight, and raise this present head:
Whereby we stand opposed by such means
As you yourself have forg'd against yourself,
By unkind usage, dangerous countenance,
And violation of all faith and troth
Sworn to us in your younger enterprise.

KING HENRY
These things, indeed, you have articulate,
Proclaim'd at market-crosses, read in churches,
To face the garment of rebellion
With some fine colour that may please the eye
Of fickle changelings and poor discontents,
Which gape and rub the elbow at the news
Of hurlyburly innovation:
And never yet did insurrection want
Such water-colours to impaint his cause;
Nor moody beggars, starving for a time
Of pellmell havoc and confusion.

PRINCE HENRY
In both your armies there is many a soul
Shall pay full dearly for this encounter,
If once they join in trial. Tell your nephew,
The Prince of Wales doth join with all the world
In praise of Henry Percy: by my hopes,
This present enterprise set off his head,
I do not think a braver gentleman,
More active-valiant or more valiant-young,
More daring or more bold, is now alive
To grace this latter age with noble deeds.
For my part, I may speak it to my shame,
I have a truant been to chivalry;
And so I hear he doth account me too:
Yet this before my father's majesty, —
I am content that he shall take the odds
Of his great name and estimation,
And will, to save the blood on either side,
Try fortune with him in a single fight.

KING HENRY
And, Prince of Wales, so dare we venture thee,
Albeit considerations infinite
Do make against it. — No, good Worcester, no,
We love our people well; even those we love
That are misled upon your cousin's part;
And, will they take the offer of our grace,
Both he, and they, and you, yea, every man
Shall be my friend again, and I'll be his:
So tell your cousin, and bring me word
What he will do: but if he will not yield,
Rebuke and dread correction wait on us,
And they shall do their office. So, be gone;
We will not now be troubled with reply:
We offer fair; take it advisedly.
     [*Exeunt* WORCESTER *and* VERNON.

PRINCE HENRY
It will not be accepted, on my life:
The Douglas and the Hotspur both together
Are confident against the world in arms.

KING HENRY
Hence, therefore, every leader to his charge;
For, on their answer, will we set on them:
And God befriend us, as our cause is just!
    [*Exeunt the* KING, BLUNT, *and* PRINCE JOHN.

FALSTAFF
Hal, if thou see me down in the battle, and bestride me,
so; 'tis a point of friendship.

PRINCE HENRY
Nothing but a colossus can do thee that friendship. Say
thy prayers, and farewell.

FALSTAFF
I would 'twere bedtime, Hal, and all well.

PRINCE HENRY
Why, thou owest God a death.   [*Exit.*

FALSTAFF
'Tis not due yet; I would be loath to pay him before his
day. What need I be so forward with him that calls not
on me? Well, 'tis no matter; honour pricks me on. Yea,
but how if honour prick me off when I come on? how
then? Can honour set to a leg? no: or an arm? no: or
take away the grief of a wound? no. Honour hath no
skill in surgery, then? no. What is honour? a word.
What is that word honour? air. A trim reckoning! —
Who hath it? he that died o' Wednesday. Doth he feel
it? no.Doth he hear it? no. 'Tis insensible, then? yea, to
the dead. But will it not live with the living? no. Why?
detraction will not suffer it. Therefore I'll none of it:
honour is a mere scutcheon: — and so ends my
catechism.
                [*Exit.*

ARCHBISHOP OF YORK Bear this sealed brief with winged haste.

KING HENRY Hence, therefore, every leader to his charge.

SCENE II

The rebel camp.

Enter WORCESTER *and* VERNON.

WORCESTER
O no, my nephew must not know, Sir Richard,
The liberal and kind offer of the king.

VERNON
'Twere best he did.

WORCESTER
       Then are we all undone.
It is not possible, it cannot be,
The king should keep his word in loving us;
He will suspect us still, and find a time
To punish this offence in other faults:
Suspicion all our lives shall be stuck full of eyes;
For treason is but trusted like the fox,
Who, ne'er so tame, so cherish'd, and lock'd up,
Will have a wild trick of his ancestors.
Look how we can, or sad or merrily,
Interpretation will misquote our looks;
And we shall feed like oxen at a stall,
The better cherish'd, still the nearer death.
My nephew's trespass may be well forgot, —
It hath the excuse of youth and heat of blood,
And an adopted name of privilege, —
A hare-brain'd Hotspur, govern'd by a spleen:
All his offences live upon my head
And on his father's: we did train him on;
And, his corruption being ta'en from us,
We, as the spring of all, shall pay for all.
Therefore, good cousin, let not Harry know,
In any case, the offer of the king.

VERNON
Deliver what you will, I'll say 'tis so.
Here comes your cousin.

Enter HOTSPUR *and* DOUGLAS; OFFICERS *and*
SOLDIERS *behind.*

HOTSPUR
My uncle is return'd: —
Deliver up, my Lord of Westmoreland. —
Uncle, what news?

WORCESTER
The king will bid you battle presently.

DOUGLAS
Defy him by the Lord of Westmoreland.

HOTSPUR
Lord Douglas, go you and tell him so.

DOUGLAS
Marry, and shall, and very willingly.   [*Exit.*

WORCESTER
There is no seeming mercy in the king.

HOTSPUR
Did you beg any? God forbid!

WORCESTER
I told him gently of our grievances,
Of his oath-breaking; which he mended thus,
By now forswearing that he is forsworn:
He calls us rebels, traitors; and will scourge
With haughty arms this hateful name in us.

Enter DOUGLAS.

DOUGLAS
Arm, gentlemen; to arms! for I have thrown
A brave defiance in King Henry's teeth,
And Westmoreland, that was engag'd, did bear it;
Which cannot choose but bring him quickly on.

WORCESTER
The Prince of Wales stepp'd forth before the king,
And, nephew, challeng'd you to single fight.

HOTSPUR
O, would the quarrel lay upon our heads;
And that no man might draw short breath to-day
But I and Harry Monmouth! Tell me, tell me,
How show'd his tasking? seem'd it in contempt?

VERNON
No, by my soul; I never in my life
Did hear a challenge urg'd more modestly,
Unless a brother should a brother dare
To gentle exercise and proof of arms.
He gave you all the duties of a man;
Trimm'd up your praises with a princely tongue:
Spoke your deservings like a chronicle;
Making you ever better than his praise,
By still dispraising praise valued with you;
And, which became him like a prince indeed,
He made a blushing cital of himself;
And chid his truant youth with such a grace,
As if he master'd there a double spirit,
Of teaching and of learning instantly.
There did he pause: but let me tell the world, —
If he outlive the envy of this day,
England did never owe so sweet a hope,
So much misconstrued in his wantonness.

HOTSPUR
Cousin, I think thou art enamoured
On his follies: never did I hear
Of any prince so wild a libertine.
But be he as he will, yet once ere night
I will embrace him with a soldier's arm,
That he shall shrink under my courtesy. —
Arm, arm with speed: — and, fellows, soldiers, friends,
Better consider what you have to do

Than I, that have not well the gift of tongue,
Can lift your blood up with persuasion.

Enter a MESSENGER.

MESSENGER
My lord, here are letters for you.

HOTSPUR
I cannot read them now. —
O gentlemen, the time of life is short!
To spend that shortness basely were too long,
If life did ride upon a dial's point,
Still ending at the arrival of an hour.
An if we live, we live to tread on kings;
If die, brave death, when princes die with us!
Now, for our consciences, — the arms are fair,
When the intent of bearing them is just.

Enter another MESSENGER.

MESSENGER
My lord, prepare; the king comes on apace.

HOTSPUR
I thank him, that he cuts me from my tale,
For I profess not talking; only this, —
Let each man do his best: and here draw I
A sword, whose temper I intend to stain
With the best blood that I can meet withal
In the adventure of this perilous day.
Now, — *Esperance!* — Percy! — and set on. —
Sound all the lofty instruments of war,
And by that music let us all embrace;
For, heaven to earth, some of us never shall
A second time do such a courtesy.

    [*The trumpets sound. They embrace, and exeunt.*

SCENE III

Plain between the camps.

The KING *enters with his Power. Alarum to the battle.*
Then enter DOUGLAS *and* SIR WALTER BLUNT.

BLUNT
What is thy name, that in the battle thus
Thou crossest me? what honour dost thou seek
Upon my head?

DOUGLAS
       Know, then, my name is Douglas;
And I do haunt thee in the battle thus
Because some tell me that thou art a king.

BLUNT
They tell thee true.

DOUGLAS
The Lord of Stafford dear to-day hath bought
Thy likeness, for, instead of thee, King Harry,
This sword hath ended him: so shall it thee,
Unless thou yield thee as my prisoner.

BLUNT
I was not born a yielder, thou proud Scot;
And thou shalt find a king that will revenge
Lord Stafford's death.

    [*They fight;* DOUGLAS *kills* BLUNT.
    Enter HOTSPUR.

HOTSPUR
O Douglas, hadst thou fought at Holmedon thus,
I never had triumph'd upon a Scot.

DOUGLAS
All's done, all's won; here breathless lies the king.

HOTSPUR
Where?

DOUGLAS
Here.

HOTSPUR
This, Douglas? no; I know this face full well:
A gallant knight he was, his name was Blunt;
Semblably furnish'd like the king himself.

DOUGLAS
A fool go with thy soul, whither it goes!
A borrow'd title hast thou bought too dear:
Why didst thou tell me that thou wert a king?

HOTSPUR
The king hath many masking in his coats.

DOUGLAS
Now, by my sword, I will kill all his coats;
I'll murder all his wardrobe piece by piece,
Until I meet the king.

HOTSPUR
       Up, and away!
Our soldiers stand full fairly for the day.   [*Exeunt.*
    Alarum. Enter FALSTAFF *solus.*

FALSTAFF
Though I could scape shot-free at London, I fear the

shot here; here's no scoring but upon the pate. —
Soft! who are you? Sir Walter Blunt: — there's
honour for you! here's no vanity! — I am as hot as
molten lead, and as heavy too: God keep lead out of
me! I need no more weight than mine own bowels.
— I have led my ragamuffins where they are
pepper'd: there's but three of my hundred and fifty
left alive; and they are for the town's end, — to beg
during life. — But who comes here?

Enter PRINCE HENRY.

PRINCE HENRY
What, stand'st thou idle here? lend me thy sword:
Many a nobleman lies stark and stiff
Under the hoofs of vaunting enemies,
Whose deaths are yet unrevenged:
I prithee, lend me thy sword.

FALSTAFF
O Hal, I prithee, give me leave to breathe awhile. —
Turk Gregory never did such deeds in arms as I have
done this day. I have paid Percy, I have made him
sure.

PRINCE HENRY
He is, indeed; and living to kill thee. I prithee, lend
me thy sword.

FALSTAFF
Nay, before God, Hal, if Percy be alive, thou gett'st
not my sword; but take my pistol, if thou wilt.

PRINCE HENRY
Give it me: what, is it in the case?

FALSTAFF
Ay, Hal. 'Tis hot, 'tis hot; there's that will sack a city.
[*The* PRINCE *draws it out, and finds it to be
a bottle of sack.*

PRINCE HENRY
What, is it a time to jest and dally now?
[*He throws the bottle at him. Exit.*

FALSTAFF
Well, if Percy be alive, I'll pierce him. If he do come in
my way, so; if he do not, if I come in his willingly, let
him make a carbonado of me. I like not such grinning
honour as Sir Walter hath: give me life; which if I can
save, so; if not, honour come unlook'd for, and there's
an end.
[*Exit.*

SCENE IV

Another part of the field.

Alarum. Excursions. Enter the KING, PRINCE
HENRY, PRINCE JOHN OF LANCASTER, *and*
WESTMORELAND.

KING HENRY
I prithee,
Harry, withdraw thyself; thou bleed'st too much. —
Lord John of Lancaster, go you with him.

LANCASTER
Not I, my lord, unless I did bleed too.

PRINCE HENRY
I beseech your majesty, make up,
Lest your retirement do amaze your friends.

KING HENRY
I will do so. —
My Lord of Westmoreland, lead him to his tent.

WESTMORELAND
Come, my lord, I will lead you to your tent.

PRINCE HENRY
Lead me, my lord? I do not need your help:
And God forbid, a shallow scratch should drive
The Prince of Wales from such a field as this,
Where stain'd nobility lies trodden on,
and rebels' arms triumph in massacres!

PRINCE JOHN
We breathe too long: — come, cousin Westmoreland,
Our duty this way lies; for God's sake, come.
[*Exeunt* PRINCE JOHN *and* WESTMORELAND.

PRINCE HENRY
By God, thou hast deceiv'd me, Lancaster;
I did not think thee lord of such a spirit:
Before, I lov'd thee as a brother, John;
But now, I do respect thee as my soul.

KING HENRY
I saw him hold Lord Percy at the point
With lustier maintenance than I did look for
Of such an ungrown warrior.

PRINCE HENRY
O, this boy
Lends mettle to us all! [*Exit.*

PRINCE HENRY I am the Prince of Wales.

Enter DOUGLAS.

DOUGLAS
Another king! they grow like Hydra's heads:
I am the Douglas, fatal to all those
That wear those colours on them: — what art thou,
That counterfeit'st the person of a king?

KING HENRY
The king himself; who, Douglas, grieves at heart,
So many of his shadows thou hast met,
And not the very king. I have two boys
Seek Percy and thyself about the field:
But, seeing thou fall'st on me so luckily,
I will assay thee: so, defend thyself.

DOUGLAS
I fear thou art another counterfeit;
And yet, in faith, thou bear'st thee like a king:
But mine I am sure thou art, whoe'er thou be,
And thus I win thee.
[*They fight; the* KING *being in danger,
enter* PRINCE HENRY.

PRINCE HENRY
Hold up thy head, vile Scot, or thou art like
Never to hold it up again! the spirits
Of valiant Shirley, Stafford, Blunt, are in my arms:
It is the Prince of Wales that threatens thee;
Who never promiseth but he means to pay.
[*They fight;* DOUGLAS *flies.*
Cheerly, my lord: how fares your Grace? —
Sir Nicholas Gawsey hath for succour sent,
And so hath Clifton: I'll to Clifton straight.

KING HENRY
Stay, and breathe awhile: —
Thou hast redeem'd thy lost opinion;
And show'd thou makest some tender of my life,
In this fair rescue thou hast brought to me.

PRINCE HENRY
O God, they did me too much injury
That ever said I hearken'd for your death!
If it were so, I might have let alone
The insulting hand of Douglas over you,
Which would have been as speedy in your end
As all the poisonous potions in the world,
And saved the treacherous labour of your son.

KING HENRY
Make up to Clifton: I'll to Sir Nicholas Gawsey. [*Exit.*

Enter HOTSPUR.

HOTSPUR
If I mistake not, thou art Harry Monmouth.

PRINCE HENRY
Thou speak'st as if I would deny my name.

HOTSPUR
My name is Harry Percy.

PRINCE HENRY
Why, then I see
A very valiant rebel of the name.
I am the Prince of Wales; and think not, Percy,
To share with me in glory any more:
Two stars keep not their motion in one sphere;
Nor can one England brook a double reign,
Of Harry Percy and the Prince of Wales.

HOTSPUR
Nor shall it, Harry, for the hour is come
To end the one of us; and would to God
Thy name in arms were now as great as mine!

PRINCE HENRY
I'll make it greater ere I part from thee;
And all the budding honours on thy crest
I'll crop, to make a garland for my head.

HOTSPUR
I can no longer brook thy vanities. [*They fight.*

Enter FALSTAFF.

FALSTAFF
Well said, Hal! to it, Hal! — Nay, you shall find no boy's
play here, I can tell you.

Enter DOUGLAS; *he fights with* FALSTAFF, *who falls
down as if he were dead, and exit* DOUGLAS. *The*
PRINCE *killeth* PERCY.

HOTSPUR
O Harry, thou hast robb'd me of my youth!
I better brook the loss of brittle life
Than those proud titles thou hast won of me;
They wound my thoughts worse than sword my
flesh: —
But thought's the slave of life, and life time's fool;
And time, that takes survey of all the world,
Must have a stop. O, I could prophesy,
But that the earthy and cold hand of death
Lies on my tongue: — no, Percy, thou art dust,
And food for — [*Dies.*

PRINCE HENRY
For worms, brave Percy: fare thee well, great heart! —
Ill-weav'd ambition, how much art thou shrunk!
When that this body did contain a spirit,
A kingdom for it was too small a bound;
But now two paces of the vilest earth
Is room enough: — this earth that bears thee dead
Bears not alive so stout a gentleman.
If thou wert sensible of courtesy,
I should not make so dear a show of zeal: —
But let my favours hide thy mangled face;
And, even in thy behalf, I'll thank myself
For doing these fair rites of tenderness.
Adieu, and take thy praise with thee to heaven!
Thy ignomy sleep with thee in the grave,
But not remember'd in thy epitaph! —
                    [*He spieth* FALSTAFF *on the ground.*
What, old acquaintance! could not all this flesh
Keep in a little life? Poor Jack, farewell!
I could have better spared a better man:
O, I should have a heavy miss of thee,
If I were much in love with vanity!
Death hath not struck so fat a deer to-day,
Though many dearer, in this bloody fray.
Embowell'd will I see thee by and by:
Till then in blood by noble Percy lie.   [*Exit.*
                    [FALSTAFF *riseth up.*

FALSTAFF
Embowell'd! if thou embowel me to-day, I'll give you
leave to powder me and eat me too to-morrow.
'Sblood, 'twas time to counterfeit, or that hot
termagant Scot had paid me scot and lot too.
Counterfeit? I lie, I am no counterfeit: to die, is to be
a counterfeit; for he is but the counterfeit of a man
who hath not the life of a man: but to counterfeit
dying, when a man thereby liveth, is to be no
counterfeit, but the true and perfect image of life
indeed. The better part of valour is discretion; in the
which better part I have saved my life. Zounds, I am
afraid of this gunpowder Percy, though he be dead:
how, if he should counterfeit too, and rise? by my
faith, I am afraid he would prove the better
counterfeit. Therefore I'll make him sure; yea, and
I'll swear I kill'd him. Why may not he rise as well as
I? Nothing confutes me but eyes, and nobody sees
me. Therefore, sirrah [*stabbing him*], with a new
wound in your thigh, come you along with me.
                    [*He takes up* HOTSPUR *on his back.*
Enter PRINCE HENRY *and* PRINCE JOHN OF
LANCASTER.

PRINCE HENRY
Come, brother John; full bravely hast thou flesh'd
Thy maiden sword.

PRINCE JOHN
                    But, soft! whom have we here?

Did you not tell me this fat man was dead?

PRINCE HENRY
I did; I saw him dead,
Breathless and bleeding on the ground. —
Art thou alive? or is it fantasy
That plays upon our eyesight? I prithee, speak;
We will not trust our eyes without our ears: —
Thou art not what thou seem'st.

FALSTAFF
No, that's certain; I am not a double man: but if I be not
Jack Falstaff, then am I a Jack. There is Percy [*throwing
the body down*]: if your father will do me any honour, so;
if not, let him kill the next Percy himself. I look to be
either earl or duke, I can assure you.

PRINCE HENRY
Why, Percy I kill'd myself, and saw thee dead.

FALSTAFF
Didst thou? — Lord, Lord, how this world is given to
lying! — I grant you I was down and out of breath; and
so was he: but we rose both at an instant, and fought a
long hour by Shrewsbury clock. If I may be believed, so;
if not, let them that should reward valour bear the sin
upon their own heads. I'll take it upon my death, I gave
him this wound in the thigh: if the man were alive, and
would deny it, zounds, I would make him eat a piece of
my sword.

PRINCE JOHN
This is the strangest tale that e'er I heard.

PRINCE HENRY
This is the strangest fellow, brother John. —
Come, bring your luggage nobly on your back:
For my part, if a lie may do thee grace,
I'll gild it with the happiest terms I have.
                    [*A retreat is sounded.*
The trumpet sounds retreat; the day is ours.
Come, brother, let's to the highest of the field,
To see what friends are living, who are dead.
                    [*Exeunt* PRINCES.

FALSTAFF
I'll follow, as they say, for reward. He that rewards me,
God reward him! If I do grow great, I'll grow less; for
I'll purge, and leave sack, and live cleanly as a
nobleman should do.
                    [*Exit, bearing off the body.*

SCENE V
Another part of the field.

The trumpets sound. Enter the KING, PRINCE HENRY,
PRINCE JOHN OF LANCASTER,
WESTMORELAND, *and others, with* WORCESTER
and VERNON *prisoners.*

KING HENRY
Thus ever did rebellion find rebuke. —

Ill-spirited Worcester! did we not send grace,
Pardon, and terms of love to all of you?
And wouldst thou turn our offers contrary?
Misuse the tenour of thy kinsman's trust?
Three knights upon our party slain to-day,
A noble earl, and many a creature else,
Had been alive this hour,
If, like a Christian, thou hadst truly borne
Betwixt our armies true intelligence.

WORCESTER
What I have done my safety urg'd me to;
And I embrace this fortune patiently,
Since not to be avoided it falls on me.

KING HENRY
Bear Worcester to the death, and Vernon too:
Other offenders we will pause upon. —
                    [*Exeunt* WORCESTER *and* VERNON, *guarded.*
How goes the field?

PRINCE HENRY
The noble Scot, Lord Douglas, when he saw
The fortune of the day quite turn'd from him,
The noble Percy slain, and all his men
Upon the foot of fear, — fled with the rest;
And falling from a hill, he was so bruised
That the pursuers took him. At my tent
The Douglas is; and I beseech your Grace
I may dispose of him.

KING HENRY
                    With all my heart.

PRINCE HENRY
Then, brother John of Lancaster, to you
This honourable bounty shall belong:
Go to the Douglas, and deliver him
Up to his pleasure, ransomless and free;
His valour, shown upon our crests to-day,
Hath taught us how to cherish such high deeds
Even in the bosom of our adversaries.

PRINCE JOHN
I thank your Grace for this high courtesy
Which I shall give away immediately.

KING HENRY
Then this remains, — that we divide our power. —
You, son John, and my cousin Westmoreland,
Towards York shall bend you with your dearest speed,
To meet Northumberland and the prelate Scroop,
Who, as we hear, are busily in arms:
Myself, — and you, son Harry, — will towards Wales,
To fight with Glendower and the Earl of March.
Rebellion in this land shall lose his sway,
Meeting the checkof such another day:
And since this business so fair is done,
Let us not leave till all our own be won.   [*Exeunt.*

THE SECOND PART OF KING HENRY THE FOURTH

DRAMATIS PERSONAE

RUMOUR, *the Presenter.*
KING HENRY THE FOURTH.
PRINCE HENRY, *afterwards crown'd* KING HENRY THE FIFTH.
PRINCE JOHN *of Lancaster,*
HUMPHREY *of Gloster,*
THOMAS *of Clarence,* } *sons to Henry the Fourth and brethren to Henry the Fifth.*
NORTHUMBERLAND,
THE ARCHBISHOP OF YORK,
MOWBRAY,
HASTINGS,
LORD BARDOLPH,
TRAVERS,
MORTON,
COLEVILE, } *opposites to King Henry the Fourth.*

WARWICK,
WESTMORELAND,
SURREY,
GOWER,
HARCOURT,
BLUNT, } *of the King's Priory.*
LORD CHIEF JUSTICE.
POINTZ.
FALSTAFF.
BARDOLPH.
PISTOL.
PETO.
PAGE.
A SERVANT *of the Chief Justice.*
SHALLOW,
SILENCE, } *both Country Justices.*

DAVY, *servant to Shallow.*
FANG *and* SNARE, *two Sergeants.*
MOULDY,
SHADOW,
WART,
FEEBLE,
BULLCALF, } *recruits.*
DRAWERS. BEADLES. GROOMS. PORTER.

NORTHUMBERLAND'S WIFE.
PERCY'S WIDOW.
HOSTESS QUICKLY.
DOLL TEARSHEET.
EPILOGUE.

SCENE — *England.*

INDUCTION

Warkworth. Before the castle.

Enter RUMOUR, *painted full of tongues.*

RUMOUR
Open your ears; for which of you will stop
The vent of hearing when loud Rumour speaks?
I, from the orient to the drooping west,
Making the wind my post-horse, still unfold
The acts commenced on this ball of earth:
Upon my tongues continual slanders ride,
The which in every language I pronounce,
Stuffing the ears of men with false reports.
I speak of peace, while covert enmity,
Under the smile of safety, wounds the world:
And who but Rumour, who but only I,
Make fearful musters and prepared defence,
Whilst the big year, swol'n with some other grief,
Is thought with child by the stern tyrant war,
And no such matter? Rumour is a pipe
Blown by surmises, jealousies, conjectures;
And of so easy and so plain a stop,
That the blunt monster with uncounted heads,
The still-discordant wavering multitude,
Can play upon it. But what need I thus
My well-known body to anatomise
Among my household? Why is Rumour here?
I run before King Harry's victory;
Who, in a bloody field by Shrewsbury,
Hath beaten down young Hotspur and his troops,
Quenching the flame of bold rebellion
Even with the rebel's blood. But what mean I
To speak so true at first? my office is
To noise abroad, that Harry Monmouth fell
Under the wrath of noble Hotspur's sword;
And that the king before the Douglas' rage
Stoop'd his anointed head as low as death.
This have I rumour'd through the peasant towns
Between that royal field of Shrewsbury
And this worm-eaten hold of ragged stone,
Where Hotspur's father, old Northumberland,
Lies crafty-sick: the posts come tiring on,
And not a man of them brings other news
Than they have learn'd of me: from Rumour's tongues
They bring smooth comforts false, worse than true
wrongs.   [*Exit.*

ACT I

SCENE I

The same.

Enter LORD BARDOLPH; *the* PORTER *at the gate.*

LORD BARDOLPH
Who keeps the gate here, ho? Where is the earl?
PORTER
What shall I say you are?
LORD BARDOLPH
                                Tell thou the earl
That the Lord Bardolph doth attend him here.
PORTER
His lordship is walk'd forth into the orchard:
Please it your honour, knock but at the gate,
And he himself will answer.

PORTER   Please it your honour, knock but at the gate, and he himself will answer.

LORD BARDOLPH
                        Here comes the earl.
                                [*Exit* PORTER.

Enter NORTHUMBERLAND.

NORTHUMBERLAND
What news, Lord Bardolph? every minute now
Should be the father of some stratagem:
The times are wild; contention, like a horse
Full of high feeding, madly hath broke loose,
And bears down all before him.
LORD BARDOLPH
                                Noble earl,
I bring you certain news from Shrewsbury.
NORTHUMBERLAND
Good, an God will!
LORD BARDOLPH
                        As good as heart can wish: —
The king is almost wounded to the death;
And, in the fortune of my lord your son,
Prince Harry slain outright; and both the Blunts
Kill'd by the hand of Douglas; young Prince John
And Westmoreland and Stafford fled the field;
And Harry Monmouth's brawn, the hulk Sir John,

Is prisoner to your son: O, such a day,
So fought, so follow'd, and so fairly won,
Came not till now to dignify the times,
Since Cæsar's fortunes!
NORTHUMBERLAND
                        How is this derived?
Saw you the field? came you from Shrewsbury?
LORD BARDOLPH
I spake with one, my lord, that came from thence,
A gentleman well bred and of good name,
That freely render'd me these news for true.
NORTHUMBERLAND
Here comes my servant Travers, whom I sent
On Tuesday last to listen after news.
LORD BARDOLPH
My lord, I over-rode him on the way;
And he is furnish'd with no certainties
More than he haply may retail from me.

Enter TRAVERS.

NORTHUMBERLAND
Now, Travers, what good tidings comes with you?
TRAVERS
My lord, Sir John Umfrevile turn'd me back

With joyful tidings; and, being better hors'd,
Out-rode me. After him came spurring hard
A gentleman, almost forspent with speed,
That stopp'd by me to breathe his bloodied horse.
He ask'd the way to Chester; and of him
I did demand what news from Shrewsbury:
He told me that rebellion had ill luck,
And that young Harry Percy's spur was cold.
With that, he gave his able horse the head,
And, bending forward, struck his armed heels
Against the panting sides of his poor jade
Up to the rowel-head; and starting so,
He seem'd in running to devour the way,
Staying no longer question.

NORTHUMBERLAND
       Ha! — Again:
Said he young Harry Percy's spur was cold?
Of Hotspur, Coldspur? that rebellion
Had met ill luck?

LORD BARDOLPH
      My lord, I'll tell you what;
If my young lord your son have not the day,
Upon mine honour, for a silken point
I'll give my barony: ne'er talk of it.

NORTHUMBERLAND
Why should that gentleman that rode by Travers
Give, then, such instances of loss?

LORD BARDOLPH
         Who, he?
He was some hilding fellow, that had stol'n
The horse he rode on; and, upon my life,
Spoke at a venture. — Look, here comes more news.

Enter MORTON.

NORTHUMBERLAND
Yea, this man's brow, like to a title-leaf,
Foretells the nature of a tragic volume:
So looks the strond whereon the imperious flood
Hath left a witness'd usurpation. —
Say, Morton, didst thou come from Shrewsbury?

MORTON
I ran from Shrewsbury, my noble lord;
Where hateful death put on his ugliest mask
To fright our party.

NORTHUMBERLAND
      How doth my son and brother?
Thou tremblest; and the whiteness in thy cheek
Is apter than thy tongue to tell thy errand.
Even such a man, so faint, so spiritless,
So dull, so dead in look, so woe-begone,
Drew Priam's curtain in the dead of night,
And would have told him half his Troy was burnt;
But Priam found the fire ere he his tongue,
And I my Percy's death ere thou report'st it.
This thou wouldst say, 'Your son did thus and thus;
Your brother thus; so fought the noble Douglas';
Stopping my greedy ear with their bold deeds:
But in the end, to stop my ear indeed,
Thou hast a sigh to blow away this praise,
Ending with 'Brother, son, and all are dead.'

MORTON
Douglas is living, and your brother, yet;
But, for my lord your son, —

NORTHUMBERLAND
        Why, he is dead.
See what a ready tongue suspicion hath!
He that but fears the thing he would not know
Hath by instinct knowledge from others' eyes,
That what he fear'd is chanced. Yet speak, Morton;
Tell thou thy earl his divination lies,
And I will take it as a sweet disgrace,
And make thee rich for doing me such wrong.

MORTON
You are too great to be by me gainsaid:
Your spirit is too true, your fears too certain.

NORTHUMBERLAND
Yet, for all this, say not that Percy's dead.
I see a strange confession in thine eye:
Thou shakest thy head, and hold'st it fear or sin
To speak a truth. If he be slain, say so;
The tongue offends not that reports his death:
And he doth sin that doth belie the dead;
Not he which says the dead is not alive.
Yet the first bringer of unwelcome news
Hath but a losing office; and his tongue
Sounds ever after as a sullen bell,
Remember'd tolling a departing friend.

LORD BARDOLPH
I cannot think, my lord, your son is dead.

MORTON
I am sorry I should force you to believe

That which I would to God I had not seen;
But these mine eyes saw him in bloody state,
Rendering faint quittance, wearied and out-breathed,
To Harry Monmouth; whose swift wrath beat down
The never-daunted Percy to the earth,
From whence with life he never more sprung up.
In few, his death — whose spirit lent a fire
Even to the dullest peasant in his camp —
Being bruited once, took fire and heat away
From the best-temper'd courage in his troops;
For from his metal was his party steel'd;
Which once in him abated, all the rest
Turn'd on themselves, like dull and heavy lead:
And as the thing that's heavy in itself,
Upon enforcement flies with greatest speed,
So did our men, heavy in Hotspur's loss,
Lend to this weight such lightness with their fear,
That arrows fled not swifter toward their aim
Than did our soldiers, aiming at their safety,
Fly from the field. Then was the noble Worcester
Too soon ta'en prisoner; and that furious Scot,
The bloody Douglas, whose well-labouring sword
Had three times slain th'appearance of the king,
Gan vail his stomach, and did grace the shame
Of those that turn'd their backs; and in his flight,
Stumbling in fear, was took. The sum of all
Is, that the king hath won; and hath sent out
A speedy power to encounter you, my lord,
Under the conduct of young Lancaster
And Westmoreland. This is the news at full.

NORTHUMBERLAND
For this I shall have time enough to mourn.
In poison there is physic; and these news,
Having been well, that would have made me sick,
Being sick, have in some measure made me well:
And as the wretch, whose fever-weaken'd joints,
Like strengthless hinges, buckle under life,
Impatient of his fit, breaks like a fire
Out of his keeper's arms; even so my limbs,
Weaken'd with grief, being now enrag'd with grief,
Are thrice themselves. Hence, therefore, thou nice
  crutch!
A scaly gauntlet now, with joints of steel,
Must glove this hand: and hence, thou sickly quoif!
Thou art a guard too wanton for the head
Which princes, flesh'd with conquest, aim to hit.
Now bind my brows with iron; and approach
The ragged'st hour that time and spite dare bring
To frown upon th'enrag'd Northumberland!
Let heaven kiss earth! now let not Nature's hand
Keep the wild flood confin'd! let order die!
And let this world no longer be a stage
To feed contention in a lingering act;
But let one spirit of the first-born Cain
Reign in all bosoms, that, each heart being set
On bloody courses, the rude scene may end,
And darkness be the burier of the dead!

TRAVERS
This strained passion doth you wrong, my lord.

LORD BARDOLPH
Sweet earl, divorce not wisdom from your honour.

MORTON
The lives of all your loving complices
Lean on your health; the which, if you give o'er
To stormy passion, must perforce decay.
You cast th'event of war, my noble lord,
And summ'd the account of chance, before you said,
'Let us make head.' It was your presurmise
That, in the dole of blows, your son might drop;
You knew he walk'd o'er perils on an edge,
More likely to fall in than to get o'er;
You were advis'd his flesh was capable
Of wounds and scars, and that his forward spirit
Would lift him where most trade of danger rang'd:
Yet did you say, 'Go forth'; and none of this,
Though strongly apprehended, could restrain
The stiff-borne action: what hath, then, befall'n,
Or what hath this bold enterprise brought forth,
More than that being which was like to be?

LORD BARDOLPH
We all that are engaged to this loss
Knew that we ventur'd on such dangerous seas,
That if we wrought our life, 'twas ten to one;
And yet we ventur'd, for the gain propos'd
Chok'd the respect of likely peril fear'd;
And since we are o'erset, venture again.
Come, we will all put forth, body and goods.

MORTON
'Tis more than time: and, my most noble lord,
I hear for certain, and do speak the truth,
The gentle Archbishop of York is up

With well-appointed powers: he is a man
Who with a double surety binds his followers.
My lord your son had only but the corpse,
But shadows and the shows of men, to fight;
For that same word, rebellion, did divide
The action of their bodies from their souls;
And they did fight with queasiness, constrain'd,
As men drink potions; that their weapons only
Seem'd on our side, but, for their spirits and souls,
This word, rebellion, it had froze them up,
As fish are in a pond. But now the bishop
Turns insurrection to religion:
Suppos'd sincere and holy in his thoughts,
He's follow'd both with body and with mind;
And doth enlarge his rising with the blood
Of fair King Richard, scrap'd from Pomfret stones;
Derives from heaven his quarrel and his cause;
Tells them he doth bestride a bleeding land,
Gasping for life under great Bolingbroke;
And more and less do flock to follow him.

NORTHUMBERLAND
I knew of this before; but, to speak truth,
This present grief had wip'd it from my mind.
Go in with me; and counsel every man
The aptest way for safety and revenge:
Get posts and letters, and make friends with speed, —
Never so few, and never yet more need. *[Exeunt.*

SCENE II
London. A street.

Enter FALSTAFF, *with his* PAGE *bearing his sword and
buckler.*

FALSTAFF
Sirrah, you giant, what says the doctor to my water?

PAGE
He said, sir, the water itself was a good healthy water;
but, for the party that owed it, he might have more
diseases than he knew for.

FALSTAFF
Men of all sorts take a pride to gird at me: the brain of
this foolish-compounded clay, man, is not able to
invent anything that tends to laughter, more than I
invent or is invented on me: I am not only witty in
myself, but the cause that wit is in other men. I do
here walk before thee like a sow that hath overwhelm'd
all her litter but one. If the prince put thee into my
service for any other reason than to set me off, why
then I have no judgement. Thou whoreson mandrake,
thou art fitter to be worn in my cap than to wait at my
heels. I was never mann'd with an agate till now: but I
will inset you neither in gold nor silver, but in vile
apparel, and send you back again to your master, for a
jewel, — the juvenal, the prince your master, whose
chin is not yet fledged. I will sooner have a beard grow
in the palm of my hand than he shall get one on his
cheek; and yet he will not stick to say his face is a
face-royal: God may finish it when he will, 'tis not a
hair amiss yet: he may keep it still at a face-royal, for a
barber shall never earn sixpence out of it; and yet he'll
be crowing as if he had writ man ever since his father
was a bachelor. He may keep his own grace, but he's
almost out of mine, I can assure him. — What said
Master Dombledon about the satin for my short cloak
and my slops?

PAGE
He said, sir, you should procure him better assurance
than Bardolph: he would not take his bond and yours;
he liked not the security.

FALSTAFF
Let him be damn'd, like the glutton! pray God his tongue
be hotter! — A whoreson Achitophel! a rascally
yea-forsooth knave! to bear a gentleman in hand, and
then stand upon security! — The whoreson
smooth-pates do now wear nothing but high shoes, and
bunches of keys at their girdles; and if a man is through
with them in honest taking-up, then they must stand
upon security. I had as lief they would put ratsbane in
my mouth as offer to stop it with security. I look'd a'
should have sent me two-and-twenty yards of satin, as I
am a true knight, and he sends me security. Well, he
may sleep in security; for he hath the horn of abundance,
and the lightness of his wife shines through it: and yet
cannot he see, though he have his own lantern to light
him. — Where's Bardolph?

PAGE
He's gone into Smithfield to buy your worship a horse.

FALSTAFF
I bought him in Paul's, and he'll buy me a horse in
Smithfield: an I could get me but a wife in the stews, I
were mann'd, horsed, and wived.

PAGE
Sir, here comes the nobleman that committed the prince for striking him about Bardolph.

FALSTAFF
Wait close; I will not see him.

Enter the LORD CHIEF JUSTICE *and* SERVANT.

LORD CHIEF JUSTICE
What's he that goes there?

SERVANT
Falstaff, an't please your lordship.

LORD CHIEF JUSTICE
He that was in question for the robbery?

SERVANT
He, my lord: but he hath since done good service at Shrewsbury; and, as I hear, is now going with some charge to the Lord John of Lancaster.

LORD CHIEF JUSTICE
What, to York? Call him back again.

SERVANT
Sir John Falstaff!

FALSTAFF
Boy, tell him I am deaf.

PAGE
You must speak louder; my master is deaf.

LORD CHIEF JUSTICE
I am sure he is, to the hearing of any thing good. — Go, pluck him by the elbow; I must speak with him.

SERVANT
Sir John, —

FALSTAFF
What! a young knave, and begging! Is there not wars? is there not employment? doth not the king lack subjects? do not the rebels need soldiers? Though it be a shame to be on any side but one, it is worse shame to beg than to be on the worst side, were it worse than the name of rebellion can tell how to make it.

SERVANT
You mistake me, sir.

FALSTAFF
Why, sir, did I say you were an honest man? setting my knighthood and my soldiership aside, I had lied in my throat, if I had said so.

SERVANT
I pray you, sir, then set your knighthood and your soldiership aside; and give me leave to tell you, you lie in your throat, if you say I am any other than an honest man.

FALSTAFF
I give thee leave to tell me so! I lay aside that which grows to me! If thou gett'st any leave of me, hang me; if thou takest leave, thou wert better be hang'd. You hunt-counter: hence! avaunt!

SERVANT
Sir, my lord would speak with you.

LORD CHIEF JUSTICE
Sir John Falstaff, a word with you.

FALSTAFF
My good lord! — God give your lordship good time of day. I am glad to see your lordship abroad: I heard say your lordship was sick: I hope your lordship goes abroad by advice. Your lordship, though not clean past your youth, hath yet some smack of age in you, some relish of the saltness of time; and I most humbly beseech your lordship to have a reverend care of your health.

LORD CHIEF JUSTICE
Sir John, I sent for you before your expedition to Shrewsbury.

FALSTAFF
An't please your lordship, I hear his majesty is return'd with some discomfort from Wales.

LORD CHIEF JUSTICE
I talk not of his majesty: — you would not come when I sent for you.

FALSTAFF
And I hear, moreover, his highness is fall'n into this same whoreson apoplexy.

LORD CHIEF JUSTICE
Well, God mend him! — I pray you, let me speak with you.

FALSTAFF
This apoplexy is, as I take it, a kind of lethargy, an't please your lordship; a kind of sleeping in the blood, a whoreson tingling.

LORD CHIEF JUSTICE
What tell you me of it? be it as it is.

FALSTAFF
It hath its original from much grief, from study, and perturbation of the brain: I have read the cause of his effects in Galen: it is a kind of deafness.

LORD CHIEF JUSTICE
I think you are fall'n into the disease; for you hear not what I say to you.

FALSTAFF
Very well, my lord, very well: rather, an't please you, it is the disease of not listening, the malady of not marking, that I am troubled withal.

LORD CHIEF JUSTICE
To punish you by the heels would amend the attention of your ears; and I care not if I do become your physician.

FALSTAFF
I am as poor as Job, my lord, but not so patient: your lordship may minister the potion of imprisonment to me in respect of poverty; but how I should be your patient to follow your prescriptions, the wise may make some dram of a scruple, or, indeed, a scruple itself.

LORD CHIEF JUSTICE
I sent for you, when there were matters against you for your life, to come speak with me.

FALSTAFF
As I was then advised by my learned counsel in the laws of this land-service, I did not come.

LORD CHIEF JUSTICE
Well, the truth is, Sir John, you live in great infamy.

FALSTAFF
He that buckles him in my belt cannot live in less.

LORD CHIEF JUSTICE
Your means are very slender, and your waste is great.

FALSTAFF
I would it were otherwise; I would my means were greater, and my waist slenderer.

LORD CHIEF JUSTICE
You have misled the youthful prince.

FALSTAFF
The young prince hath misled me: I am the fellow with the great belly, and he my dog.

LORD CHIEF JUSTICE
Well, I am loth to gall a new-heal'd wound: your day's service at Shrewsbury hath a little gilded over your night's exploit on Gadshill: you may thank the unquiet time for your quiet o'er-posting that action.

FALSTAFF
My lord, —

LORD CHIEF JUSTICE
But since all is well, keep it so: wake not a sleeping wolf.

FALSTAFF
To wake a wolf is as bad as to smell a fox.

LORD CHIEF JUSTICE
What! you are as a candle, the better part burnt out.

FALSTAFF
A wassail candle, my lord; all tallow: if I did say of wax, my growth would approve the truth.

LORD CHIEF JUSTICE
There is not a white hair on your face but should have his effect of gravity.

FALSTAFF
His effect of gravy, gravy, gravy.

LORD CHIEF JUSTICE
You follow the young prince up and down, like his ill angel.

FALSTAFF
Not so, my lord; your ill angel is light; but I hope he that looks upon me will take me without weighing: and yet, in some respects, I grant, I cannot go: — I cannot tell. Virtue is of so little regard in these costermonger times, that true valour is turn'd bear-herd: pregnancy is made a tapster, and hath his quick wit wasted in giving reckonings: all the other gifts appertinent to man, as the malice of this age shapes them, are not worth a gooseberry. You that are old consider not the capacities of us that are young; you measure the heat of our livers with the bitterness of your galls: and we that are in the vaward of our youth, I must confess, are wags too.

LORD CHIEF JUSTICE
Do you set down your name in the scroll of youth, that are written down old with all the characters of age? Have you not a moist eye? a dry hand? a yellow cheek? a white beard? a decreasing leg? an increasing belly? is

FALSTAFF Wait close; I will not see him.

not your voice broken? your wind short? your chin double? your wit single? and every part about you blasted with antiquity? and will you yet call yourself young? Fie, fie, fie, Sir John!

FALSTAFF
My lord, I was born about three of the clock in the afternoon, with a white head and something a round belly. For my voice, — I have lost it with hallooing, and singing of anthems. To approve my youth further, I will not: the truth is, I am only old in judgement and understanding; and he that will caper with me for a thousand marks, let him lend me the money, and have at him. For the box of th'ear that the prince gave you, — he gave it like a rude prince, and you took it like a sensible lord. I have check'd him for it; and the young lion repents, — marry, not in ashes and sackcloth, but in new silk and old sack.

LORD CHIEF JUSTICE
Well, God send the prince a better companion!

FALSTAFF
God send the companion a better prince! I cannot rid my hands of him.

LORD CHIEF JUSTICE
Well, the king hath sever'd you and Prince Harry: I hear you are going with Lord John of Lancaster against the Archbishop and the Earl of Northumberland.

FALSTAFF
Yea; I thank your pretty sweet wit for it. But look you pray, all you that kiss my lady Peace at home, that our armies join not in a hot day; for, by the Lord, I take but two shirts out with me, and I mean not to sweat extraordinarily: if it be a hot day, an I brandish any thing but a bottle, I would I might never spit white again. There is not a dangerous action can peep out his head, but I am thrust upon it: well, I cannot last ever: but it was alway yet the trick of our English nation, if they have a good thing, to make it too common. If ye will needs say I am an old man, you should give me rest. I would to God, my name were not so terrible to the enemy as it is: I were better to be eaten to death with a rust than to be scour'd to nothing with perpetual motion.

LORD CHIEF JUSTICE
Well, be honest, be honest; and God bless your expedition!

FALSTAFF
Will your lordship lend me a thousand pound to furnish me forth?

LORD CHIEF JUSTICE
Not a penny, not a penny; you are too impatient to bear crosses. Fare you well: commend me to my cousin Westmoreland.

[Exeunt CHIEF JUSTICE *and* SERVANT.

FALSTAFF
If I do, fillip me with a three-man beetle. — A man can
no more separate age and covetousness than a' can part
young limbs and lechery: but the gout galls the one,
and the pox pinches the other; and so both the degrees
prevent my curses. — Boy!

PAGE
Sir?

FALSTAFF
What money is in my purse?

PAGE
Seven groats and two pence.

FALSTAFF
I can get no remedy against this consumption of the
purse: borrowing only lingers and lingers it out, but the
disease is incurable. — Go bear this letter to my Lord of
Lancaster; this to the prince; this to the Earl of
Westmoreland; and this to old Mistress Ursula, whom
I have weekly sworn to marry since I perceived the first
white hair on my chin. About it: you know where to
find me. [*Exit* PAGE.] A pox of this gout! or, a gout of
this pox! for the one or the other plays the rogue with
my great toe. 'Tis no matter if I do halt; I have the wars
for my colour, and my pension shall seem the more
reasonable. A good wit will make use of any thing: I will
turn diseases to commodity. [*Exit.*

SCENE III

York. The ARCHBISHOP'S *palace.*

Enter the ARCHBISHOP, HASTINGS, MOWBRAY,
and LORD BARDOLPH.

ARCHBISHOP OF YORK
Thus have you heard our cause and know our means;
And, my most noble friends, I pray you all
Speak plainly your opinions of our hopes: —
And first, lord marshal, what say you to it?

MOWBRAY
I well allow the occasion of our arms;
But gladly would be better satisfied
How, in our means, we should advance ourselves
To look with forehead bold and big enough
Upon the power and puissance of the king.

HASTINGS
Our present musters grow upon the file
To five-and-twenty thousand men of choice;
And our supplies live largely in the hope
Of great Northumberland, whose bosom burns
With an incensed fire of injuries.

LORD BARDOLPH
The question, then, Lord Hastings, standeth thus; —
Whether our present five-and-twenty thousand
May hold up head without Northumberland?

HASTINGS
With him, we may.

LORD BARDOLPH
Yea, marry, there's the point:
But if without him we be thought too feeble,
My judgement is, we should not step too far
Till we had his assistance by the hand;
For, in a theme so bloody-fac'd as this,
Conjecture, expectation, and surmise
Of aids incertain should not be admitted.

ARCHBISHOP OF YORK
'Tis very true, Lord Bardolph; for, indeed,
It was young Hotspur's case at Shrewsbury.

LORD BARDOLPH
It was, my lord; who lined himself with hope,
Eating the air on promise of supply,
Flattering himself with project of a power
Much smaller than the smallest of his thoughts:
And so, with great imagination,
Proper to madmen, led his powers to death,
And, winking, leapt into destruction.

HASTINGS
But, by your leave, it never yet did hurt
To lay down likelihoods and forms of hope.

LORD BARDOLPH
Yes, if this present quality of war; —
Indeed, the instant action — a cause on foot —
Lives so in hope, as in an early spring
We see th' appearing buds; which to prove fruit,
Hope gives not so much warrant, as despair
That frosts will bite them. When we mean to build,
We first survey the plot, then draw the model;
And when we see the figure of the house,
Then must we rate the cost of the erection;
Which if we find outweighs ability,
What do we then but draw anew the model
In fewer offices, or at last desist

To build at all? Much more, in this great work —
Which is almost to pluck a kingdom down,
And set another up — should we survey
The plot of situation and the model,
Consent upon a sure foundation,
Question surveyors, know our own estate,
How able such a work to undergo,
To weigh against his opposite; or else
We fortify in paper and in figures,
Using the names of men instead of men:
Like one that draws the model of a house
Beyond his power to build it; who, half through,
Gives o'er, and leaves his part-created cost
A naked subject to the weeping clouds,
And waste for churlish winter's tyranny.

HASTINGS
Grant that our hopes — yet likely of fair birth —
Should be still-born, and that we now possess'd
The utmost man of expectation;
I think we are a body strong enough,
Even as we are, to equal with the king.

LORD BARDOLPH
What, is the king but five-and-twenty thousand?

HASTINGS
To us no more; nay, not so much, Lord Bardolph.
For his divisions, as the times do brawl,
Are in three heads: one power against the French,
And one against Glendower; perforce a third
Must take up us: so is the unfirm king
In three divided; and his coffers sound
With hollow poverty and emptiness.

ARCHBISHOP OF YORK
That he should draw his several strengths together,
And come against us in full puissance,
Need not be dreaded.

HASTINGS
If he should do so,
He leaves his back unarm'd, the French and Welsh
Baying him at the heels: never fear that.

LORD BARDOLPH
Who is it like should lead his forces hither?

HASTINGS
The Duke of Lancaster and Westmoreland;
Against the Welsh, himself and Harry Monmouth:
But who is substituted 'gainst the French,
I have no certain notice.

ARCHBISHOP OF YORK
Let us on,
And publish the occasion of our arms.
The commonwealth is sick of their own choice;
Their over-greedy love hath surfeited:
An habitation giddy and unsure
Hath he that buildeth on the vulgar heart.
O thou fond many! with what loud applause
Didst thou beat heaven with blessing Bolingbroke,
Before he was what thou wouldst have him be!
And being now trimmed in thine own desires,
Thou, beastly feeder, art so full of him,
That thou provokest thyself to cast him up.
So, so, thou common dog, didst thou disgorge
Thy glutton bosom of the royal Richard;
And now thou wouldst eat thy dead vomit up,

And howl'st to find it. What trust is in these times?
They that, when Richard liv'd, would have him die,
Are now become enamour'd on his grave:
Thou, that threw'st dust upon his goodly head
When through proud London he came sighing on
After th' admired heels of Bolingbroke,
Cry'st now, 'O earth, yield us that king again,
And take thou this!' O thoughts of men accurs'd!
Past, and to come, seems best; things present, worst.

MOWBRAY
Shall we go draw our numbers, and set on?

HASTINGS
We are time's subjects, and time bids be gone. [*Exeunt.*

ACT II

SCENE I

London. A street.

Enter HOSTESS, FANG *and his* BOY *with her, and*
SNARE *following.*

HOSTESS
Master Fang, have you enter'd the exion?

FANG
It is enter'd.

HOSTESS
Where's your yeoman? Is't a lusty yeoman? will a'
stand to't?

FANG
Sirrah, where's Snare?

HOSTESS
O Lord, ay! good Master Snare.

SNARE
Here, here.

FANG
Snare, we must arrest Sir John Falstaff.

HOSTESS
Yes, good Master Snare; I have enter'd him and all.

SNARE
It may chance cost some of us our lives, for he will stab.

HOSTESS
Alas the day! take heed of him; he stabb'd me in mine
own house, and that most beastly: in good faith, a'
cares not what mischief he doth, if his weapon be out:
he will foin like any devil; he will spare neither man,
woman, nor child.

FANG
If I can close with him, I care not for his thrust.

HOSTESS
No, nor I neither: I'll be at your elbow.

FANG
An I but fist him once; an a' come but within my vice, —

HOSTESS
I am undone by his going; I warrant you, he's an
infinitive thing upon my score: — good Master Fang,
hold him sure; — good Master Snare, let him not
scape. A' comes continuantly to Pie-corner — saving
your manhoods — to buy a saddle; and he is indited to
dinner to the Lubber's-head in Lumbert-street, to

HOSTESS Good Master Fang, hold him sure; — good Master Snare, let him not scape.

Master Smooth's the silkman: I pray ye, since my exion is enter'd, and my case so openly known to the world, let him be brought in to his answer. A hundred mark is a long one for a poor lone woman to bear: and I have borne, and borne, and borne; and have been fubb'd off, and fubb'd off, and fubb'd off, from this day to that day, that it is a shame to be thought on. There is no honesty in such dealing; unless a woman should be made an ass and a beast, to bear every knave's wrong. — Yonder he comes; and that arrant malmsey-nose knave, Bardolph with him. Do your offices, do your offices, Master Fang and Master Snare; do me, do me, do me your offices.

Enter FALSTAFF, PAGE, *and* BARDOLPH.

FALSTAFF
How now! whose mare's dead? what's the matter?

FANG
Sir John, I arrest you at the suit of Mistress Quickly.

FALSTAFF
Away, varlets! — Draw, Bardolph: cut me off the villain's head; throw the quean in the channel.

HOSTESS
Throw me in the channel! I'll throw thee in the channel. Wilt thou? wilt thou? thou bastardly rogue! — Murder, murder! Ah, thou honey-suckle villain! wilt thou kill God's officers and the king's? Ah, thou honey-seed rogue! thou art a honey-seed, a man-queller, and a woman-queller.

FALSTAFF
Keep them off, Bardolph.

FANG
A rescue! a rescue!

HOSTESS
Good people, bring a rescue or two. — Thou wo't, wo't thou? thou wo't, wo't ta? do, do, thou rogue! do, thou hemp-seed!

FALSTAFF
Away, you scullion! you rampallian! you fustilarian! I'll tickle your catastrophe.

Enter the LORD CHIEF JUSTICE, *and his men.*

LORD CHIEF JUSTICE
What is the matter? keep the peace here, ho!

HOSTESS
Good my lord, be good to me! I beseech you, stand to me!

LORD CHIEF JUSTICE
How now, Sir John! what are you brawling here? Doth this become your place, your time, and business? You should have been well on your way to York. — Stand from him, fellow: wherefore hang'st upon him?

HOSTESS
O my most worshipful lord, an't please your Grace, I am a poor widow of Eastcheap, and he is arrested at my suit.

LORD CHIEF JUSTICE
For what sum?

HOSTESS
It is more than for some, my lord; it is for all, — all I have. He hath eaten me out of house and home; he hath put all my substance into that fat belly of his: — but I will have some of it out again, or I will ride thee o' nights like the mare.

FALSTAFF
I think I am as like to ride the mare, if I have any vantage of ground to get up.

LORD CHIEF JUSTICE
How comes this, Sir John? Fie! what man of good temper would endure this tempest of exclamation? Are you not ashamed to enforce a poor widow to so rough a course to come by her own?

FALSTAFF
What is the gross sum that I owe thee?

HOSTESS
Marry, if thou wert an honest man, thyself and the money too. Thou didst swear to me upon a parcel-gilt goblet, sitting in my Dolphin-chamber, at the round table, by a sea-coal fire, upon Wednesday in Wheeson-week, when the prince broke thy head for liking his father to a singing-man of Windsor, — thou didst swear to me then, as I was washing thy wound, to marry me, and make me my lady thy wife. Canst thou deny it? Did not goodwife Keech, the butcher's wife, come in then, and call me gossip Quickly? coming in to borrow a mess of vinegar; telling us she had a good dish of prawns; whereby thou didst desire to eat some; whereby I told thee they were ill for a green wound? And didst thou not, when she was gone down stairs, desire me to be no more so familiarity with such poor

HOSTESS I put thee now to thy book-oath: deny it, if thou canst.

people; saying that ere long they should call me madam? And didst thou not kiss me, and bid me fetch thee thirty shillings? I put thee now to thy book-oath: deny it, if thou canst.

FALSTAFF
My lord, this is a poor mad soul; and she says, up and down the town, that her eldest son is like you: she hath been in good case, and the truth is, poverty hath distracted her. But for these foolish officers, I beseech you I may have redress against them.

LORD CHIEF JUSTICE
Sir John, Sir John, I am well acquainted with your manner of wrenching the true cause the false way. It is not a confident brow, nor the throng of words that come with such more than impudent sauciness from you, can thrust me from a level consideration: you have, as it appears to me, practised upon the easy-yielding spirit of this woman, and made her serve your uses both in purse and in person.

HOSTESS
Yea, in truth, my lord.

LORD CHIEF JUSTICE
Pray thee, peace. — Pay her the debt you owe her, and unpay the villainy you have done her: the one you may do with sterling money, and the other with current repentance.

FALSTAFF
My lord, I will not undergo this sneap without reply. You call honourable boldness impudent sauciness: if a man will make court'sy, and say nothing, he is virtuous: — no, my lord, my humble duty remember'd, I will not be your suitor. I say to you, I do desire deliverance from these officers, being upon hasty employment in the king's affairs.

LORD CHIEF JUSTICE
You speak as having power to do wrong: but answer in the effect of your reputation, and satisfy this poor woman.

FALSTAFF
Come hither, hostess.   [*Takes her aside.*

Enter GOWER.

LORD CHIEF JUSTICE
Now, Master Gower, what news?

GOWER
The king, my lord, and Harry Prince of Wales
Are near at hand: the rest the paper tells.   [*Gives a letter.*

FALSTAFF
As I am a gentleman, —

HOSTESS
Faith, you said so before.

FALSTAFF
As I am a gentleman: — come, no more words of it.

HOSTESS
By this heavenly ground I tread on, I must be fain to pawn both my plate and the tapestry of my dining-chambers.

FALSTAFF
Glasses, glasses, is the only drinking: and for thy walls, — a pretty slight drollery, or the story of the Prodigal, or the German Hunting in water-work, is worth a thousand of these bed-hangings and these fly-bitten tapestries. Let it be ten pound, if thou canst. Come, an'twere not for thy humours, there's not a better wench in England. Go, wash thy face, and draw the action. Come, thou must not be in this humour with me; dost not know me? come, come, I know thou wast set on to this.

HOSTESS
Pray thee, Sir John, let it be but twenty nobles: i'faith, I am loth to pawn my plate, so God save me, la.

FALSTAFF
Let it alone; I'll make other shift: you'll be a fool still.

HOSTESS
Well, you shall have it, though I pawn my gown. I hope you'll come to supper. You'll pay me all together?

FALSTAFF
Will I live? — [*to* BARDOLPH] Go, with her, with her; hook on, hook on.

HOSTESS
Will you have Doll Tearsheet meet you at supper?

FALSTAFF
No more words; let's have her.
[*Exeunt* HOSTESS, BARDOLPH, OFFICERS, *and* BOY.

LORD CHIEF JUSTICE
I have heard better news.

FALSTAFF
What's the news, my lord?

LORD CHIEF JUSTICE
Where lay the king last night?

GOWER
At Basingstoke, my lord.

FALSTAFF
I hope, my lord, all's well: what is the news, my lord?

LORD CHIEF JUSTICE
Come all his forces back?

GOWER
No; fifteen hundred foot, five hundred horse,
Are march'd up to my Lord of Lancaster,
Against Northumberland and the Archbishop.

FALSTAFF
Comes the king back from Wales, my noble lord?

LORD CHIEF JUSTICE
You shall have letters of me presently:
Come, go along with me, good Master Gower.

FALSTAFF
My lord!

LORD CHIEF JUSTICE
What's the matter?

FALSTAFF
Master Gower, shall I entreat you with me to dinner?

GOWER
I must wait upon my good lord here, — I thank you, good Sir John.

LORD CHIEF JUSTICE
Sir John, you loiter here too long, being you are to take soldiers up in counties as you go.

FALSTAFF
Will you sup with me, Master Gower?

LORD CHIEF JUSTICE
What foolish master taught you these manners, Sir John?

FALSTAFF
Master Gower, if they become me not, he was a fool that taught them me. — This is the right fencing grace, my lord; tap for tap, and so part fair.

LORD CHIEF JUSTICE
Now, the Lord lighten thee! thou art a great fool.

[*Exeunt.*

SCENE II

London. Another street.

Enter PRINCE HENRY *and* POINTZ.

PRINCE HENRY
Before God, I am exceeding weary.

POINTZ
Is't come to that? I had thought weariness durst not have attach'd one of so high blood.

PRINCE HENRY
Faith, it does me; though it discolours the complexion of my greatness to acknowledge it. Doth it not show vilely in me to desire small beer?

POINTZ
Why, a prince should not be so loosely studied as to remember so weak a composition.

PRINCE HENRY
Belike, then, my appetite was not princely got; for, by my troth, I do now remember the poor creature, small beer. But, indeed, these humble considerations make me out of love with my greatness. What a disgrace is it to me to remember thy name! or to know thy face to-morrow! or to take note how many pair of silk stockings thou hast, viz. these, and those that were thy peach-colour'd ones! or to bear the inventory of thy shirts, as, one for superfluity, and one other for use! — but that the tennis-court keeper knows better than I; for it is a low ebb of linen with thee when thou keepest not racket there; as thou hast not done a great while, because the rest of thy low-countries have made a shift to eat up thy holland: and God knows whether those that bawl out the ruins of thy linen shall inherit his kingdom: but the midwives say the children are not in the fault; whereupon the world increases, and kindreds are mightily strengthen'd.

POINTZ
How ill it follows, after you have labour'd so hard, you should talk so idly! Tell me, how many good young princes would do so, their fathers being so sick as yours at this time is?

PRINCE HENRY
Shall I tell thee one thing, Pointz?

POINTZ
Yes, faith; and let it be an excellent good thing.

PRINCE HENRY
It shall serve among wits of no higher breeding than thine.

POINTZ
Go to; I stand the push of your one thing that you will tell.

PRINCE HENRY
Marry, I tell thee, — it is not meet that I should be sad, now my father is sick: albeit I could tell to thee, — as to one it pleases me, for fault of a better, to call my friend, — I could be sad, and sad indeed too.

POINTZ
Very hardly upon such a subject.

PRINCE HENRY
By this hand, thou think'st me as far in the devil's book as thou and Falstaff for obduracy and persistency: let the end try the man. But I tell thee, my heart bleeds inwardly that my father is so sick: and keeping such vile company as thou art hath in reason taken from me all ostentation of sorrow.

POINTZ
The reason?

PRINCE HENRY
What wouldst thou think of me, if I should weep?

POINTZ
I would think thee a most princely hypocrite.

PRINCE HENRY
It would be every man's thought; and thou art a blessed fellow to think as every man thinks: never a man's thought in the world keeps the road-way better than thine: every man would think me an hypocrite indeed. And what accites your most worshipful thought to think so?

POINTZ
Why, because you have been so lewd, and so much engraff'd to Falstaff.

PRINCE HENRY
And to thee.

POINTZ
By this light, I am well spoke on; I can hear it with mine own ears: the worst that they can say of me is, that I am a second brother, and that I am a proper fellow of my hands; and those two things, I confess, I cannot help. — By the mass, here comes Bardolph.

PRINCE HENRY
And the boy that I gave Falstaff: a' had him from me Christian; and look, if the fat villain have not transform'd him ape.

Enter BARDOLPH *and* PAGE.

BARDOLPH
God save your Grace!

PRINCE HENRY
And yours, most noble Bardolph!

BARDOLPH [*to the* PAGE].
Come, you virtuous ass, you bashful fool, must you be blushing? wherefore blush you now? What a maidenly man-at-arms are you become! Is't such a matter to get a pottle-pot's maidenhead?

PAGE
A' calls me e'en now, my lord, through a red lattice, and I could discern no part of his face from the window: at last I spied his eyes; and methought he had made two holes in the alewife's new petticoat, and so peep'd through.

PRINCE HENRY
Hath not the boy profited?

BARDOLPH
Away, you whoreson upright rabbit, away!

PAGE
Away, you rascally Althæa's dream, away!

PRINCE HENRY
Instruct us, boy; what dream, boy?

PAGE
Marry, my lord, Althæa dream'd she was deliver'd of a firebrand; and therefore I call him her dream.

PRINCE HENRY
A crown's worth of good interpretation: — there 'tis, boy.

[*Gives money.*

POINTZ
O, that this good blossom could be kept from cankers! — Well, there is sixpence to preserve thee.

[*Gives money.*

BARDOLPH
An you do not make him hang'd among you, the gallows shall have wrong.

PRINCE HENRY
And how doth thy master, Bardolph?

BARDOLPH
Well, my lord. He heard of your Grace's coming to town; there's a letter for you.

[*Gives a letter.*

POINTZ
Deliver'd with good respect. — And how doth the martlemas, your master?

BARDOLPH
In bodily health, sir.

POINTZ
Marry, the immortal part needs a physician; but that moves not him: though that be sick, it dies not.

PRINCE HENRY
I do allow this wen to be as familiar with me as my dog: and he holds his place; for look you how he writes.

POINTZ [*reads*].
'John Falstaff, knight,' — every man must know that, as oft as he has occasion to name himself: even like those that are kin to the king; for they never prick their finger but they say, 'There's some of the king's blood spilt.' 'How comes that?' says he, that takes upon him not to conceive. The answer is as ready as a borrower's cap, 'I am the king's poor cousin, sir.'

PRINCE HENRY
Nay, they will be kin to us, or they will fetch it from Japhet. But to the letter: —

POINTZ [*reads*].
'Sir John Falstaff, knight, to the son of the king, nearest his father, Harry Prince of Wales, greeting.' — Why, this is a certificate.

PRINCE HENRY
Peace!

POINTZ [*reads*].
'I will imitate the honourable Roman in brevity': — sure means brevity in breath, short-winded. — 'I commend me to thee, I commend thee, and I leave thee. Be not too familiar with Pointz; for he misuses thy favours so much, that he swears thou art to marry his sister Nell. Repent at idle times as thou may'st; and so, farewell.

'Thine, by yea and no (which is as much as to say, as thou usest him), JACK FALSTAFF with my familiars, JOHN with my brothers and sisters, and SIR JOHN with all Europe.'
My lord, I'll steep this letter in sack, and make him eat it.

PRINCE HENRY
That's to make him eat twenty of his words. But do you use me thus, Ned? must I marry your sister?

POINTZ
God send the wench no worse fortune! but I never said so.

PRINCE HENRY
Well, thus we play the fools with the time; and the spirits of the wise sit in the clouds and mock us. — Is your master here in London?

BARDOLPH
Yes, my lord.

PRINCE HENRY
Where sups he? doth the old boar feed in the old frank?

BARDOLPH
At the old place, my lord, — in Eastcheap.

PRINCE HENRY
What company?

PAGE
Ephesians, my lord, — of the old church.

PRINCE HENRY
Sup any women with him?

PAGE
None, my lord, but old Mistress Quickly and Mistress Doll Tearsheet.

PRINCE HENRY
What pagan may that be?

PAGE
A proper gentlewoman, sir, and a kinswoman of my master's.

PRINCE HENRY
Even such kin as the parish heifers are to the town bull. — Shall we steal upon them, Ned, at supper?

POINTZ
I am your shadow, my lord; I'll follow you.

PRINCE HENRY
Sirrah, you boy, — and Bardolph, — no word to your master that I am yet come to town: there's for your silence.

[*Gives money.*

BARDOLPH
I have no tongue, sir.

PAGE
And for mine, sir, — I will govern it.

PRINCE HENRY
Fare you well; go. [*Exeunt* BARDOLPH *and* PAGE.] — This Doll Tearsheet should be some road.

POINTZ
I warrant you, as common as the way between Saint Alban's and London.

PRINCE HENRY
How might we see Falstaff bestow himself to-night in his true colours, and not ourselves be seen?

POINTZ
Put on two leathern jerkins and aprons, and wait upon him at his table as drawers.

PRINCE HENRY
From a god to a bull? a heavy descension! it was Jove's case. From a prince to a prentice? a low transformation! that shall be mine; for in every thing the purpose must weigh with the folly. Follow me, Ned.

[*Exeunt.*

SCENE III

Warkworth. Before the castle.

Enter NORTHUMBERLAND, LADY NORTHUMBERLAND, *and* LADY PERCY.

NORTHUMBERLAND
I pray thee, loving wife, and gentle daughter,
Give even way unto my rough affairs:
Put not you on the visage of the times,

LADY PERCY O, yet, for God's sake, go not to these wars!

And be, like them, to Percy troublesome.
LADY NORTHUMBERLAND
I have given over, I will speak no more:
Do what you will; your wisdom be your guide.
NORTHUMBERLAND
Alas, sweet wife, my honour is at pawn;
And, but my going, nothing can redeem it.
LADY PERCY
O, yet, for God's sake, go not to these wars!
The time is, father, that you broke your word,
When you were more endear'd to it than now;
When your own Percy, when my heart's dear Harry,
Threw many a northward look to see his father
Bring up his powers; but he did long in vain.
Who then persuaded you to stay at home?
There were two honours lost, — yours and your son's.
For yours, — the God of heaven brighten it!
For his, — it stuck upon him, as the sun
In the grey vault of heaven; and by his light
Did all the chivalry of England move
To do brave acts: he was, indeed, the glass
Wherein the noble youth did dress themselves:
He had no legs that practis'd not his gait;
And speaking thick, which nature made his blemish,
Became the accents of the valiant;
For those that could speak low and tardily
Would turn their own perfection to abuse,
To seem like him: so that in speech, in gait,
In diet, in affections of delight,
In military rules, humours of blood,
He was the mark and glass, copy and book,
That fashion'd others. And him, — O wondrous him!
O miracle of men! — him did you leave —
Second to none, unseconded by you —
To look upon the hideous god of war
In disadvantage; to abide a field
Where nothing but the sound of Hotspur's name
Did seem defensible: — so you left him.
Never, O never, do his ghost the wrong
To hold your honour more precise and nice
With others than with him! let them alone:
The marshal and the archbishop are strong:
Had my sweet Harry had but half their numbers,
To-day might I, hanging on Hotspur's neck,
Have talk'd of Monmouth's grave.
NORTHUMBERLAND
                                  Beshrew your heart,
Fair daughter, you do draw my spirits from me
With new lamenting ancient oversights.
But I must go, and meet with danger there;
Or it will seek me in another place,
And find me worse provided.
LADY NORTHUMBERLAND
                                  O, fly to Scotland,
Till that the nobles and the armed commons
Have of their puissance made a little taste.
LADY PERCY
If they get ground and vantage of the king,
Then join you with them, like a rib of steel,

To make strength stronger; but, for all our loves,
First let them try themselves. So did your son;
He was so suffer'd: so came I a widow;
And never shall have length of life enough
To rain upon remembrance with mine eyes,
That it may grow and sprout as high as heaven,
For recordation to my noble husband.
NORTHUMBERLAND
Come, come, go in with me. 'Tis with my mind
As with the tide swell'd up unto his height,
That makes a still-stand, running neither way:
Fain would I go to meet the archbishop,
But many thousand reasons hold me back.
I will resolve for Scotland: there am I,
Till time and vantage crave my company.   [*Exeunt.*

SCENE IV

London. The Boar's-Head Tavern in Eastcheap.

Enter two DRAWERS.

FIRST DRAWER
What the devil hast thou brought there? apple-johns?
thou know'st Sir John cannot endure an apple-john.
SECOND DRAWER
Mass, thou say'st true. The prince once set a dish of
apple-johns before him, and told him there were five
more Sir Johns; and, putting off his hat, said, 'I will
now take my leave of these six dry, round, old, wither'd
knights.' It anger'd him to the heart: but he hath forgot
that.
FIRST DRAWER
Why, then, cover, and set them down: and see if thou
canst find out Sneak's noise; Mistress Tearsheet would
fain hear some music. Dispatch: — the room where
they supp'd is too hot; they'll come in straight.
SECOND DRAWER
Sirrah, here will be the prince and Master Pointz anon;
and they will put on two of our jerkins and aprons; and
Sir John must not know of it: Bardolph hath brought
word.
FIRST DRAWER
By the mass, here will be old utis: it will be an excellent
stratagem.
SECOND DRAWER
I'll see if I can find out Sneak.   [*Exit.*

Enter HOSTESS *and* DOLL TEARSHEET.

HOSTESS
I'faith, sweetheart, methinks now you are in an
excellent good temperality: your pulsidge beats as
extraordinarily as heart would desire; and your colour,
I warrant you, is as red as any rose, in good truth, la:
but, i'faith, you have drunk too much canaries; and
that's a marvellous searching wine, and it perfumes
the blood ere one can say 'What's this?' — How do you
now?
DOLL TEARSHEET
Better than I was: — hem.

HOSTESS
Why, that's well said; a good heart's worth gold. — Lo,
here comes Sir John.

Enter FALSTAFF.

FALSTAFF [*singing*].
'When Arthur first in court'— Empty the jordan. [*Exit*
FIRST DRAWER.]—[*singing*] 'And was a worthy king.'—
How now, Mistress Doll!
HOSTESS
Sick of a calm; yea, good faith.
FALSTAFF
So is all her sect; an they be once in a calm, they are
sick.
DOLL TEARSHEET
You muddy rascal, is that all the comfort you give me?
FALSTAFF
You make fat rascals, Mistress Doll.
DOLL TEARSHEET
I make them! gluttony and diseases make them; I make
them not.
FALSTAFF
If the cook help to make the gluttony, you help to make
the diseases, Doll; we catch of you, Doll, we catch of
you; grant that, my poor virtue, grant that.
DOLL TEARSHEET
Yea, joy, — our chains and our jewels.
FALSTAFF
'Your brooches, pearls, and ouches': — for to serve
bravely is to come halting off, you know: to come off the
breach with his pike bent bravely, and to surgery bravely;
to venture upon the charged chambers bravely, —
DOLL TEARSHEET
Hang yourself, you muddy conger, hang yourself!
HOSTESS
By my troth, this is the old fashion; you two never meet
but you fall to some discord: you are both, i' good truth,
as rheumatic as two dry toasts; you cannot one bear with
another's confirmities. What the good-year! one must
bear, and that must be you [*to* DOLL TEARSHEET]: you
are the weaker vessel, as they say, the emptier vessel.
DOLL TEARSHEET
Can a weak empty vessel bear such a huge full
hogshead? there's a whole merchant's venture of
Bourdeaux stuff in him; you have not seen a hulk better
stuff'd in the hold. — Come, I'll be friends with thee,
Jack: thou art going to the wars; and whether I shall ever
see thee again or no, there is nobody cares.

Enter FIRST DRAWER.

FIRST DRAWER
Sir, Ancient Pistol's below, and would speak with you.
DOLL TEARSHEET
Hang him, swaggering rascal! let him not come hither:
it is the foul-mouth'dst rogue in England.
HOSTESS
If he swagger, let him not come here: no, by my faith; I
must live among my neighbours; I'll no swaggerers: I
am in good name and fame with the very best: — shut
the door; — there comes no swaggerers here: I have not
lived all this while, to have swaggering now: — shut the
door, I pray you.
FALSTAFF
Dost thou hear, hostess? —
HOSTESS
Pray ye, pacify yourself, Sir John: there comes no
swaggerers here.
FALSTAFF
Dost thou hear? it is mine ancient.
HOSTESS
Tilly-fally, Sir John, ne'er tell me: your ancient
swaggerer comes not in my doors. I was before Master
Tisick, the deputy, t'other day; and, as he said to me,
'twas no longer ago than Wednesday last, 'I' good faith,
neighbour Quickly,' says he; — Master Dumbe, our
minister, was by then; — 'neighbour Quickly,' says he,
'receive those that are civil; for,' saith he, 'you are in an
ill name': — now a' said so, I can tell whereupon; 'for,'
says he, 'you are an honest woman, and well thought
on; therefore take heed what guests you receive:
receive,' says he, 'no swaggering companions.' There
comes none here: you would bless you to hear what he
said: no, I'll no swaggerers.
FALSTAFF
He's no swaggerer, hostess; a tame cheater, i'faith; you
may stroke him as gently as a puppy greyhound; he'll
not swagger with a Barbary hen, if her feathers turn
back in any show of resistance. — Call him up, drawer.
          [*Exit* FIRST DRAWER.

HOSTESS
Cheater, call you him? I will bar no honest man my
house, nor no cheater: but I do not love swaggering;
by my troth, I am the worse when one says 'swagger':
feel, masters, how I shake; look you, I warrant you.

DOLL TEARSHEET
So you do, hostess.

HOSTESS
Do I? yea, in very truth, do I, an'twere an aspenleaf: I
cannot abide swaggerers.

Enter PISTOL, BARDOLPH, *and* PAGE.

PISTOL
God save you, Sir John!

FALSTAFF
Welcome, Ancient Pistol. Here, Pistol, I charge you with
a cup of sack: do you discharge upon mine hostess.

PISTOL
I will discharge upon her, Sir John, with two bullets.

FALSTAFF
She is pistol-proof, sir; you shall hardly offend her.

HOSTESS
Come, I'll drink no proofs nor no bullets: I'll drink no
more than will do me good, for no man's pleasure, I.

PISTOL
Then to you, Mistress Dorothy; I will charge you.

DOLL TEARSHEET
Charge me! I scorn you, scurvy companion. What!
you poor, base, rascally, cheating, lack-linen mate!
Away, you mouldy rogue, away! I am meat for your
master.

PISTOL
I know you, Mistress Dorothy.

DOLL TEARSHEET
Away, you cut-purse rascal! you filthy bung, away! by
this wine, I'll thrust my knife in your mouldy chaps, an
you play the saucy cuttle with me. Away, you bottle-ale
rascal! you basket-hilt stale juggler, you! — Since
when, I pray you, sir? — God's light, with two points on
your shoulder? much!

PISTOL
God let me not live, but I will murder your ruff for
this.

FALSTAFF
No more, Pistol; I would not have you go off here:
discharge yourself of our company, Pistol.

HOSTESS
No, Good Captain Pistol; not here, sweet captain.

DOLL TEARSHEET
Captain! thou abominable damn'd cheater, art thou not
ashamed to be call'd captain? An captains were of my
mind, they would truncheon you out, for taking their
names upon you before you have earn'd them. You a
captain! you slave, for what? for tearing a poor whore's
ruff in a bawdy-house! — He a captain! hang him,
rogue! he lives upon mouldy stew'd prunes and dried
cakes. A captain! God's light, these villains will make
the word as odious as the word 'occupy'; which was an
excellent good word before it was ill sorted: therefore
captains had need look to't.

BARDOLPH
Pray thee, go down, good ancient.

FALSTAFF
Hark thee hither, Mistress Doll.

PISTOL
Not I: I tell thee what, Corporal Bardolph, — I could
tear her: I'll be revenged of her.

PAGE
Pray thee, go down.

PISTOL
I'll see her damned first; — to Pluto's damned lake, by
this hand, to the infernal deep, with Erebus and
tortures vile also. Hold hook and line, say I. Down,
down, dogs! down, faitors! Have we not Hiren here?

HOSTESS
Good Captain Peesel, be quiet; 'tis very late, i'faith: I
beseek you now, aggravate your choler.

PISTOL
These be good humours, indeed! Shall pack-horses,
And hollow pamper'd jades of Asia,
Which cannot go but thirty mile a-day,
Compare with Cæsars, and with Cannibals,
And Trojan Greeks? nay, rather damn them with
King Cerberus; and let the welkin roar.
Shall we fall foul for toys?

HOSTESS
By my troth, captain, these are very bitter words.

BARDOLPH
Be gone, good ancient: this will grow to a brawl anon.

PISTOL
Die men like dogs! give crowns like pins! Have we not
Hiren here?

HOSTESS
O' my word, captain, there's none such here. What the
good-year! do you think I would deny her? For God's
sake, be quiet.

PISTOL
Then feed, and be fat, my fair Calipolis.
Come, give's some sack.
Si fortune me tormente, sperato me contento. —
Fear we broadsides? no, let the fiend give fire:
Give me some sack: — and, sweetheart, lie thou there.
[*Laying down his sword.*
Come we to full points here, and are etceteras nothing?

FALSTAFF
Pistol, I would be quiet.

PISTOL
Sweet knight, I kiss thy neif: what! we have seen the
seven stars.

DOLL TEARSHEET
For God's sake, thrust him down stairs: I cannot endure
such a fustian rascal.

PISTOL
Thrust him down stairs! know we not Galloway nags?

FALSTAFF
Quoit him down, Bardolph, like a shove-groat shilling:
nay, an a' do nothing but speak nothing, a' shall be
nothing here.

BARDOLPH
Come, get you down stairs.

PISTOL
What! shall we have incision? shall we imbrue? —
[*Snatching up his sword.*
Then death rock me asleep, abridge my doleful days!
Why, then, let grievous, ghastly, gaping wounds
Untwine the Sisters Three! Come, Atropos, I say!

HOSTESS
Here's goodly stuff toward!

FALSTAFF
Give me my rapier, boy.

DOLL TEARSHEET
I pray thee, Jack, I pray thee, do not draw.

FALSTAFF
Get you down stairs.
[*Drawing, and driving* PISTOL *out.*

HOSTESS
Here's a goodly tumult! I'll forswear keeping house,
afore I'll be in these tirrits and frights. So; murder, I
warrant now. — Alas, alas! put up your naked weapons,
put up your naked weapons.
[*Exeunt* PISTOL *and* BARDOLPH.

DOLL TEARSHEET
I pray thee, Jack, be quiet; the rascal's gone. Ah, you
whoreson little valiant villain, you!

HOSTESS
Are you not hurt i'th'groin?
methought a' made a shrewd thrust
at your belly.
Enter BARDOLPH.

FALSTAFF
Have you turn'd him out o' doors?

BARDOLPH
Yes, sir. The rascal's drunk; you have
hurt him, sir, i'th'shoulder.

FALSTAFF
A rascal! to brave me!

DOLL TEARSHEET
Ah, you sweet little rogue, you! Alas,
poor ape, how thou sweat'st! come, let
me wipe thy face; come on, you
whoreson chops: — ah, rogue! i'faith, I
love thee: thou art as valorous as Hector
of Troy, worth five of Agamemnon, and
ten times better than the Nine
Worthies: ah, villain!

FALSTAFF
A rascally slave! I will toss the rogue
in a blanket.

DOLL TEARSHEET
Do, an thou darest for thy heart: an
thou dost,
I'll canvass thee between a pair of
sheets.
Enter MUSICIANS.

PAGE
The music is come, sir.

FALSTAFF
Let them play: — play, sirs. — Sit on my knee, Doll.
[*Music.*] A rascal bragging slave! the rogue fled from me
like quicksilver.

DOLL TEARSHEET
I'faith, and thou follow'dst him like a church. Thou
whoreson little tidy Bartholomew boar-pig, when wilt
thou leave fighting o' days and foining o' nights, and
begin to patch up thine old body for heaven?
Enter, behind, PRINCE HENRY *and* POINTZ *disguised
as* DRAWERS.

FALSTAFF
Peace, good Doll! do not speak like a death's-head; do
not bid me remember mine end.

DOLL TEARSHEET
Sirrah, what humour's the prince of?

FALSTAFF
A good shallow young fellow: a' would have made a
good pantler, a' would ha' chipp'd bread well.

DOLL TEARSHEET
They say Pointz has a good wit.

FALSTAFF
He a good wit? hang him, baboon! his wit's as thick as
Tewkesbury mustard; there's no more conceit in him
than is in a mallet.

DOLL TEARSHEET
Why does the prince love him so, then?

FALSTAFF
Because their legs are both of a bigness; and a' plays at
quoits well; and eats conger and fennel; and drinks off
candles' ends for flap-dragons; and rides the wild-mare
with the boys; and jumps upon joint-stools; and swears
with a good grace; and wears his boots very smooth,
like unto the sign of the leg; and breeds no bate with
telling of discreet stories; and such other gambol
faculties a' has, that show a weak mind and an able
body, for the which the prince admits him: for the
prince himself is such another; the weight of a hair will
turn the scales between their avoirdupois.

PRINCE HENRY
Would not this nave of a wheel have his ears cut off?

POINTZ
Let's beat him before his whore.

PRINCE HENRY
Look, whether the wither'd elder hath not his poll claw'd
like a parrot.

POINTZ
Is it not strange that desire should so many years
outlive performance?

FALSTAFF
Kiss me, Doll.

PRINCE HENRY
Saturn and Venus this year in conjunction! what says
the almanac to that?

POINTZ
And, look, whether the fiery Trigon, his man, be not

FALSTAFF Kiss me, Doll.

lisping to his master's own tables, his note-book, his counsel-keeper.

FALSTAFF
Thou dost give me flattering busses.

DOLL TEARSHEET
By my troth, I kiss thee with a most constant heart.

FALSTAFF
I am old, I am old.

DOLL TEARSHEET
I love thee better than I love e'er a scurvy young boy of them all.

FALSTAFF
What stuff wilt have a kirtle of? I shall receive money o' Thursday: shalt have a cap to-morrow. A merry song, come: it grows late; we'll to bed. Thou'lt forget me when I am gone.

DOLL TEARSHEET
By my troth, thou'lt set me a-weeping, an thou say'st so: prove that ever I dress myself handsome till thy return: — well, hearken the end.

FALSTAFF
Some sack, Francis.

PRINCE HENRY and POINTZ
Anon, anon, sir.   [*Advancing.*

FALSTAFF
Ha! a bastard son of the king's? — And art not thou Pointz his brother?

PRINCE HENRY
Why, thou globe of sinful continents! what a life dost thou lead!

FALSTAFF
A better than thou: I am a gentleman; thou art a drawer.

PRINCE HENRY
Very true, sir; and I come to draw you out by the ears.

HOSTESS
O, the Lord preserve thy good Grace! by my troth, welcome to London. Now, the Lord bless that sweet face of thine! O Jesu, are you come from Wales?

FALSTAFF
Thou whoreson mad compound of majesty, — by this light flesh and corrupt blood, thou art welcome.

      [*Leaning his hand upon* DOLL TEARSHEET.

DOLL TEARSHEET
How, you fat fool! I scorn you.

POINTZ
My lord, he will drive you out of your revenge, and turn all to a merriment, if you take not the heat.

PRINCE HENRY
You whoreson candle-mine, you, how vilely did you speak of me even now before this honest, virtuous, civil gentlewoman!

HOSTESS
God's blessing of your good heart! and so she is, by my troth.

FALSTAFF
Didst thou hear me?

PRINCE HENRY
Yea; and you knew me, as you did when you ran away by Gadshill: you knew I was at your back, and spoke it on purpose to try my patience.

FALSTAFF
No, no, no; not so; I did not think thou wast within hearing.

PRINCE HENRY
I shall drive you, then, to confess the wilful abuse; and then I know how to handle you.

FALSTAFF
No abuse, Hal, o' mine honour; no abuse.

PRINCE HENRY
Not, — to dispraise me, and call me pantler, and bread-chipper, and I know not what!

FALSTAFF
No abuse, Hal!

POINTZ
No abuse!

FALSTAFF
No abuse, Ned, i'th'world; honest Ned, none. I dispraised him before the wicked, that the wicked might not fall in love with him; — in which doing, I have done the part of a careful friend and a true subject, and thy father is to give me thanks for it. No abuse, Hal; — none, Ned, none; — no, faith, boys, none.

PRINCE HENRY
See now, whether pure fear and entire cowardice doth not make thee wrong this virtuous gentlewoman to close with us. Is she of the wicked! is thine hostess here of the wicked? or is thy boy of the wicked? or honest Bardolph, whose zeal burns in his nose, of the wicked?

POINTZ
Answer, thou dead elm, answer.

FALSTAFF
The fiend hath prick'd down Bardolph irrecoverable; and his face is Lucifer's privy-kitchen, where he doth nothing but roast malt-worms. For the boy, — there is a good angel about him; but the devil outbids him too.

PRINCE HENRY
For the women?

FALSTAFF
For one of them, — she is in hell already, and burns, poor soul! For the other, — I owe her money; and whether she be damn'd for that, I know not.

HOSTESS
No, I warrant you.

FALSTAFF
No, I think thou art not; I think thou art quit for that. Marry, there is another indictment upon thee, for suffering flesh to be eaten in thy house, contrary to the law; for the which I think thou wilt howl.

HOSTESS
All victuallers do so: what's a joint of mutton or two in a whole Lent?

PRINCE HENRY
You, gentlewoman, —

DOLL TEARSHEET
What says your Grace?

FALSTAFF
His Grace says that which his flesh rebels against.

       [*Knocking within.*

HOSTESS
Who knocks so loud at door? — Look to the door there, Francis.

         Enter PETO.

PRINCE HENRY
Peto, how now! what news?

PETO
The king your father is at Westminster;
And there are twenty weak and wearied posts
Come from the north: and, as I came along,
I met and overtook a dozen captains,
Bare-headed, sweating, knocking at the taverns,
And asking every one for Sir John Falstaff.

PRINCE HENRY
By heaven, Pointz, I feel me much to blame,
So idly to profane the precious time;
When tempest of commotion, like the south,
Borne with black vapour, doth begin to melt,
And drop upon our bare unarmed heads.
Give me my sword and cloak. — Falstaff, good-night.

    [*Exeunt* PRINCE HENRY, POINTZ, PETO, *and*
                 BARDOLPH.

FALSTAFF
Now comes in the sweetest morsel of the night, and we must hence, and leave it unpick'd. [*Knocking within.*] More knocking at the door!

         Enter BARDOLPH.
How now! what's the matter?

BARDOLPH
You must away to court, sir, presently;
A dozen captains stay at door for you.

FALSTAFF   [*to the* PAGE.]
Pay the musicians, sirrah. — Farewell, hostess; — farewell, Doll. — You see, my good wenches, how men of merit are sought after: the undeserver may sleep, when the man of action is call'd on. Farewell, good wenches: if I be not sent away post, I will see you again ere I go.

DOLL TEARSHEET
I cannot speak; — if my heart be not ready to burst, — well, sweet Jack, have a care of thyself.

FALSTAFF
Farewell, farewell.

        [*Exeunt* FALSTAFF *and* BARDOLPH.

HOSTESS
Well, fare thee well: I have known thee these twenty-nine years, come peascod-time; but an honester and truer-hearted man, — well, fare thee well.

BARDOLPH   [*within*].
Mistress Tearsheet!

HOSTESS
What's the matter?

BARDOLPH   [*within*].
Bid Mistress Tearsheet come to my master.

HOSTESS
O, run, Doll, run; run, good Doll: come [*she comes blubber'd*]; yea, will you come, Doll?

                      [*Exeunt.*

ACT III

SCENE I

Westminster. A room in the palace.

Enter KING HENRY *in his nightgown, with a* PAGE.

KING HENRY
Go call the Earls of Surrey and of Warwick;
But, ere they come, bid them o'er-read these letters,
And well consider of them: make good speed.

              [*Exit* PAGE.

How many thousand of my poorest subjects
Are at this hour asleep! — O sleep, O gentle sleep,
Nature's soft nurse, how have I frighted thee,
That thou no more wilt weigh my eyelids down,
And steep my senses in forgetfulness?
Why rather, sleep, liest thou in smoky cribs,
Upon uneasy pallets stretching thee,
And hush'd with buzzing night-flies to thy slumber,
Than in the perfum'd chambers of the great,
Under the canopies of costly state,
And lull'd with sound of sweetest melody?
O thou dull god, why liest thou with the vile
In loathsome beds, and leavest the kingly couch
A watch-case or a common 'larum-bell?
Wilt thou upon the high and giddy mast
Seal up the ship-boy's eyes, and rock his brains
In cradle of the rude imperious surge,
And in the visitation of the winds,
Who take the ruffian billows by the top,
Curling their monstrous heads, and hanging them
With deafening clamour in the slippery shrouds,
That, with the hurly, death itself awakes? —
Canst thou, O partial sleep, give thy repose
To the wet sea-boy in an hour so rude;
And in the calmest and most stillest night,
With all appliances and means to boot,
Deny it to a king? Then, happy low, lie down!
Uneasy lies the head that wears a crown.

       Enter WARWICK *and* SURREY.

WARWICK
Many good morrows to your majesty!

KING HENRY
Is it good morrow, lords?

WARWICK
'Tis one o'clock, and past.

KING HENRY
Why, then, good morrow to you all, my lords.
Have you read o'er the letters that I sent you?

WARWICK
We have, my liege.

KING HENRY
Then you perceive the body of our kingdom
How foul it is; what rank diseases grow,
And with what danger, near the heart of it.

WARWICK
It is but as a body yet distemper'd;
Which to his former strength may be restored
With good advice and little medicine:
My Lord Northumberland will soon be cool'd.

KING HENRY
O God! that one might read the book of fate,
And see the revolution of the times
Make mountains level, and the continent,
Weary of solid firmness, melt itself
Into the sea! and, other times, to see
The beachy girdle of the ocean
Too wide for Neptune's hips; how chances mock,
And changes fill the cup of alteration
With divers liquors! O, if this were seen,
The happiest youth, — viewing his progress through,
What perils past, what crosses to ensue, —
Would shut the book, and sit him down and die.
'Tis not ten years gone
Since Richard and Northumberland, great friends,
Did feast together, and in two years after
Were they at wars: it is but eight years since
This Percy was the man nearest my soul;
Who like a brother toil'd in my affairs,
And laid his love and life under my foot;
Yea, for my sake, even to the eyes of Richard
Gave him defiance. But which of you was by —
[*to* WARWICK] You, cousin Nevil, as I may remember,
When Richard, — with his eye brimful of tears,
Then check'd and rated by Northumberland, —
Did speak these words, now prov'd a prophecy?
'Northumberland, thou ladder by the which
My cousin Bolingbroke ascends my throne,' —
Though then, God knows, I had no such intent,

SHALLOW I would have done any thing indeed too, and roundly too.

But that necessity so bow'd the state,
That I and greatness were compell'd to kiss: —
'The time shall come,' thus did he follow it,
'The time will come, that foul sin, gathering head,
Shall break into corruption': — so went on,
Foretelling this same time's condition,
And the division of our amity.

WARWICK
There is a history in all men's lives,
Figuring the nature of the times deceas'd;
The which observ'd, a man may prophesy,
With a near aim, of the main chance of things
As yet not come to life, which in their seeds
And weak beginnings lie intreasured.
Such things become the hatch and brood of time;
And, by the necessary form of this,
King Richard might create a perfect guess,
That great Northumberland, then false to him,
Would of that seed grow to a greater falseness;
Which should not find a ground to root upon,
Unless on you.

KING HENRY
Are these things, then, necessities?
Then let us meet them like necessities; —
And that same word even now cries out on us:
They say the bishop and Northumberland
Are fifty thousand strong.

WARWICK
It cannot be, my lord;
Rumour doth double, like the voice and echo,
The numbers of the fear'd. Please it your Grace
To go to bed. Upon my soul, my lord,
The powers that you already have sent forth
Shall bring this prize in very easily.
To comfort you the more, I have received
A certain instance that Glendower is dead.
Your majesty hath been this fortnight ill;
And these unseason'd hours perforce must add
Unto your sickness.

KING HENRY
I will take your counsel:
And were these inward wars once out of hand,
We would, dear lords, unto the Holy Land. [*Exeunt.*

SCENE II

Glostershire. Court before JUSTICE SHALLOW'S *house.*

Enter SHALLOW *and* SILENCE; MOULDY,
SHADOW, WART, FEEBLE, BULLCALF, *and*
SERVANTS, *behind.*

SHALLOW
Come on, come on, come on, sir; give me your hand,
sir, give me your hand, sir: an early stirrer, by the rood!
And how doth my good cousin Silence?

SILENCE
Good morrow, good cousin Shallow.

SHALLOW
And how doth my good cousin, your bedfellow? and
your fairest daughter and mine, my god-daughter Ellen?

SILENCE
Alas, a black ousel, cousin Shallow!

SHALLOW
By yea and nay, sir, I dare say my cousin William is
become a good scholar: he is at Oxford still, is he not?

SILENCE
Indeed, sir, to my cost.

SHALLOW
A' must, then, to the inns o' court shortly: I was once of
Clement's-inn, where I think they will talk of mad
Shallow yet.

SILENCE
You were call'd 'lusty Shallow' then, cousin.

SHALLOW
By the mass, I was call'd any thing; and I would have
done any thing indeed too, and roundly too. There was I,
and little John Doit of Staffordshire, and black George
Barnes, and Francis Pickbone, and Will Squele a Cotsall
man, — you had not four such swinge-bucklers in all the
inns o' court again: and, I may say to you, we knew
where the bona-robas were, and had the best of them all
at commandment. Then was Jack Falstaff, now Sir John,
a boy, and page to Thomas Mowbray, Duke of Norfolk.

SILENCE
This Sir John, cousin, that comes hither anon about
soldiers?

SHALLOW
The same Sir John, the very same. I see him break
Skogan's head at the court-gate, when a' was a crack
not thus high: and the very same day did I fight with
one Sampson Stockfish, a fruiterer, behind Gray's-inn.
Jesu, Jesu, the mad days that I have spent! and to see
how many of my old acquaintance are dead!

SILENCE
We shall all follow, cousin.

SHADOW
Certain, 'tis certain; very sure, very sure: death, as the
Psalmist says, is certain to all; all shall die. — How a
good yoke of bullocks at Stamford fair?

SILENCE
Truly, cousin, I was not there.

SHALLOW
Death is certain. — Is old Double of your town living
yet?

SILENCE
Dead, sir.

SHALLOW
Jesu, Jesu, dead! — a' drew a good bow; — and dead! —
a' shot a fine shoot: — John o' Gaunt loved him well,
and betted much money on his head. Dead! — a' would
have clapp'd i'th'clout at twelve score; and carried you
a forehand shaft a fourteen and fourteen and a half,
that it would have done a man's heart good to see. —

How a score of ewes now?

SILENCE
Thereafter as they be: a score of good ewes may be
worth ten pounds.

SHALLOW
And is old Double dead?

SILENCE
Here come two of Sir John Falstaff's men, as I think.

Enter BARDOLPH *and one with him.*

BARDOLPH
Good morrow, honest gentlemen: I beseech you,
which is Justice Shallow?

SHALLOW
I am Robert Shallow, sir; a poor esquire of this county,
and one of the king's justices of the peace: what is your
good pleasure with me?

BARDOLPH
My captain, sir, commends him to you; my captain, Sir
John Falstaff, — a tall gentleman, by heaven, and a
most gallant leader.

SHALLOW
He greets me well, sir. I knew him a good backsword
man. How doth the good knight? may I ask how my
lady his wife doth?

BARDOLPH
Sir, pardon; a soldier is better accommodated than
with a wife.

SHALLOW
It is well said, in faith, sir; and it is well said indeed too.
Better accommodated! — it is good; yea, indeed, is it:
good phrases are surely, and ever were, very
commendable. Accommodated! — it comes of
accommodo: very good; a good phrase.

BARDOLPH
Pardon, sir; I have heard the word. Phrase call you it?
by this good day, I know not the phrase; but I will
maintain the word with my sword to be a soldier-like
word, and a word of exceeding good command, by
heaven. Accommodated; that is, when a man is, as they
say, accommodated; or when a man is, being, whereby
a' may be thought to be accommodated; which is an
excellent thing.

SHALLOW
It is very just. — Look, here comes good Sir John.

Enter FALSTAFF.

Give me your good hand, give me your worship's good
hand: by my troth, you like well, and bear your years
very well: welcome, good Sir John.

FALSTAFF
I am glad to see you well, good Master Robert Shallow: —
Master Surecard, as I think?

SHALLOW
No, Sir John; it is my cousin Silence, in commission
with me.

FALSTAFF
Good Master Silence, it well befits you should be of the
peace.

SILENCE
Your good worship is welcome.

FALSTAFF
Fie! this is hot weather, gentlemen. Have you provided
me here half a dozen sufficient men?

SHALLOW
Marry, have we, sir. Will you sit?

FALSTAFF
Let me see them, I beseech you.

SHALLOW
Where's the roll? where's the roll? where's the roll?
Let me see, let me see, let me see. So, so, so, so, so, so,
so: yea, marry, sir: — Ralph Mouldy! — let them
appear as I call; let them do so, let them do so. — Let
me see; where is Mouldy?

MOULDY
Here, an't please you.

SHALLOW
What think you, Sir John? a good-limb'd fellow; young,
strong, and of good friends.

FALSTAFF
Is thy name Mouldy?

MOULDY
Yea, an't please you.

FALSTAFF
'Tis the more time thou wert used.

SHALLOW
Ha, ha, ha! most excellent, i'faith! things that are
mouldy lack use: very singular good! — in faith, well
said, Sir John, very well said.

FALSTAFF [*to* SHALLOW].
Prick him.
MOULDY
I was prick'd well enough before, an you could have let me alone: my old dame will be undone now, for one to do her husbandry and her drudgery: you need not to have prick'd me; there are other men fitter to go out than I.
FALSTAFF
Go to: peace, Mouldy; you shall go. Mouldy, it is time you were spent.
MOULDY
Spent!
SHALLOW
Peace, fellow, peace; stand aside: know you where you are? — For th'other, Sir John: — let me see; — Simon Shadow!
FALSTAFF
Yea, marry, let me have him to sit under: he's like to be a cold soldier.
SHALLOW
Where's Shadow?
SHADOW
Here, sir.
FALSTAFF
Shadow, whose son art thou?
SHADOW
My mother's son, sir.
FALSTAFF
Thy mother's son! like enough; and thy father's shadow: so the son of the female is the shadow of the male: it is often so, indeed; but much of the father's substance!
SHALLOW
Do you like him, Sir John?
FALSTAFF
Shadow will serve for summer, — prick him; for we have a number of shadows to fill up the muster-book.
SHALLOW
Thomas Wart!
FALSTAFF
Where's he?
WART
Here, sir.
FALSTAFF
Is thy name Wart?
WART
Yea, sir.
FALSTAFF
Thou art a very ragged wart.
SHALLOW
Shall I prick him, Sir John?
FALSTAFF
It were superfluous; for his apparel is built upon his back, and the whole frame stands upon pins: prick him no more.
SHALLOW
Ha, ha, ha! — you can do it, sir; you can do it: I commend you well. — Francis Feeble!
FEEBLE
Here, sir.
FALSTAFF
What trade art thou, Feeble?
FEEBLE
A woman's tailor, sir.
SHALLOW
Shall I prick him, sir?
FALSTAFF
You may: but if he had been a man's tailor, he'ld ha' prick'd you. — Wilt thou make as many holes in an enemy's battle as thou hast done in a woman's petticoat?
FEEBLE
I will do my good will, sir; you can have no more.
FALSTAFF
Well said, good woman's tailor! well said, courageous Feeble! thou wilt be as valiant as the wrathful dove or most magnanimous mouse. — Prick the woman's tailor well, Master Shallow; deep, Master Shallow.
FEEBLE
I would Wart might have gone, sir.
FALSTAFF
I would thou wert a man's tailor, that thou mightst mend him, and make him fit to go. I cannot put him to a private soldier, that is the leader of so many thousands: let that suffice, most forcible Feeble.
FEEBLE
It shall suffice, sir.

SHALLOW What think you, Sir John? a good-limb'd fellow; young, strong, and of good friends.

FALSTAFF
I am bound to thee, reverend Feeble. — Who is next?
SHALLOW
Peter Bullcalf o'th'green!
FALSTAFF
Yea, marry, let's see Bullcalf.
BULLCALF
Here, sir.
FALSTAFF
'Fore God, a likely fellow! — Come, prick me Bullcalf till he roar again.
BULLCALF
O Lord! good my lord captain, —
FALSTAFF
What, dost thou roar before thou art prick'd?
BULLCALF
O Lord, sir! I am a diseased man.
FALSTAFF
What disease hast thou?
BULLCALF
A whoreson cold, sir, — a cough, sir, — which I caught with ringing in the king's affairs upon his coronation-day, sir.
FALSTAFF
Come, thou shalt go to the wars in a gown; we will have away thy cold; and I will take such order, that thy friends shall ring for thee. — Is here all?
SHALLOW
Here is two more call'd than your number; you must have but four here, sir: — and so, I pray you, go in with me to dinner.
FALSTAFF
Come, I will go drink with you, but I cannot tarry dinner. I am glad to see you, by my troth, Master Shallow.
SHALLOW
O, Sir John, do you remember since we lay all night in the windmill in Saint George's field?
FALSTAFF
No more of that, good Master Shallow, no more of that.
SHALLOW
Ha! 'twas a merry night. And is Jane Nightwork alive?
FALSTAFF
She lives, Master Shallow.
SHALLOW
She never could away with me.
FALSTAFF
Never, never; she would always say she could not abide Master Shallow.
SHALLOW
By the mass, I could anger her to the heart. She was then a bona-roba. Doth she hold her own well?
FALSTAFF
Old, old, Master Shallow.

SHALLOW
Nay, she must be old; she cannot choose but be old; certain she's old; and had Robin Nightwork by old Nightwork before I came to Clement's-Inn.
SILENCE
That's fifty-five year ago.
SHALLOW
Ha, cousin Silence, that thou hadst seen that that this knight and I have seen! — Ha, Sir John, said I well?
FALSTAFF
We have heard the chimes at midnight, Master Shallow.
SHALLOW
That we have, that we have, that we have; in faith, Sir John, we have: our watch-word was, 'Hem, boys!' — Come, let's to dinner; come, let's to dinner: — Jesus, the days that we have seen! — come, come.
[*Exeunt* FALSTAFF, SHALLOW, *and* SILENCE.
BULLCALF
Good master corporate Bardolph, stand my friend; and here's four Harry ten shillings in French crowns for you. In very truth, sir, I had as lief be hang'd, sir, as go: and yet, for mine own part, sir, I do not care; but rather, because I am unwilling, and, for mine own part, have a desire to stay with my friends; else, sir, I did not care, for mine own part, so much.
BARDOLPH
Go to; stand aside.
MOULDY
And, good master corporal captain, for my old dame's sake, stand my friend: she has nobody to do any thing about her when I am gone; and she is old, and cannot help herself: you shall have forty, sir.
BARDOLPH
Go to; stand aside.
FEEBLE
By my troth, I care not; a man can die but once; — we owe God a death: I'll ne'er bear a base mind: an't be my destiny, so; an't be not, so: no man's too good to serve's prince; and let it go which way it will, he that dies this year is quit for the next.
BARDOLPH
Well said; thou'rt a good fellow.
FEEBLE
Faith, I'll bear no base mind.
Enter FALSTAFF, SHALLOW, *and* SILENCE.
FALSTAFF
Come, sir, which men shall I have?
SHALLOW
Four of which you please.
BARDOLPH
Sir, a word with you: — I have three pound to free Mouldy and Bullcalf.
FALSTAFF
Go to; well.

SHALLOW
Come, Sir John, which four will you have?

FALSTAFF
Do you choose for me.

SHALLOW
Marry, then, — Mouldy, Bullcalf, Feeble, and Shadow.

FALSTAFF
Mouldy and Bullcalf: — for you, Mouldy, stay at home till you are past service: — and for your part, Bullcalf, grow till you come unto it: — I will none of you.

SHALLOW
Sir John, Sir John, do not yourself wrong: they are your likeliest men, and I would have you served with the best.

FALSTAFF
Will you tell me, Master Shallow, how to choose a man? Care I for the limb, the thews, the stature, bulk, and big assemblance of a man! Give me the spirit, Master Shallow. — Here's Wart; — you see what a ragged appearance it is: a' shall charge you, and discharge you, with the motion of a pewterer's hammer; come off, and on, swifter than he that gibbets-on the brewer's bucket. And this same half-faced fellow, Shadow, — give me this man: he presents no mark to the enemy; — the foeman may with as great aim level at the edge of a penknife. And, for a retreat, — how swiftly will this Feeble, the woman's tailor, run off! O, give me the spare men, and spare me the great ones. — Put me a caliver into Wart's hand, Bardolph.

BARDOLPH
Hold, Wart, traverse; thus, thus, thus.

FALSTAFF
Come, manage me your caliver. So: — very well — go to: — very good: — exceeding good: — O, give me always a little, lean, old, chapp'd, bald shot. — Well said, i'faith, Wart: thou'rt a good scab: hold, there's a tester for thee.

SHALLOW
He is not his craft's-master; he doth not do it right. I remember at Mile-end Green, — when I lay at Clement's-Inn, — I was then Sir Dagonet in Arthur's show, — there was a little quiver fellow, and a' would manage you his piece thus; and a' would about and about, and come you in and come you in: 'rah, tah, tah,' would a' say; 'bounce' would a' say; and away again would a' go, and again would a' come: — I shall ne'er see such a fellow.

FALSTAFF
These fellows will do well, Master Shallow. — God keep you, Master Silence: I will not use many words with you. — Fare you well, gentlemen both: I thank you: I must a dozen mile to-night. — Bardolph, give the soldiers coats.

SHALLOW
Sir John, the Lord bless you! God prosper your affairs! God send us peace! At your return, visit our house; let our old acquaintance be renew'd: peradventure I will with ye to the court.

FALSTAFF
'Fore God, I would you would, Master Shallow.

SHALLOW
Go to; I have spoke at a word; God keep you.

FALSTAFF
Fare you well, gentle gentlemen. [*Exeunt* SHALLOW *and* SILENCE.] On, Bardolph; lead the men away. [*Exeunt* BARDOLPH, RECRUITS, *etc.*] As I return, I will fetch off these justices: I do see the bottom of Justice Shallow. Lord, Lord, how subject we old men are to this vice of lying! This same starved justice hath done nothing but prate to me of the wildness of his youth, and the feats he hath done about Turnbull-Street; and every third word a lie, duer paid to the hearer than the Turk's tribute. I do remember him at Clement's-Inn, like a man made after supper of a cheese-paring: when a' was naked, he was, for all the world, like a fork'd radish, with a head fantastically carved upon it with a knife: a' was so forlorn, that his dimensions to any thick sight were invisible: a' was the very genius of famine; yet lecherous as a monkey, and the whores call'd him mandrake: a' came ever in the rearward of the fashion; and sung those tunes to the overscutch'd huswives that he heard the carmen whistle, and swear they were his Fancies or his Good-nights. And now is this Vice's dagger become a squire, and talks as familiarly of John o' Gaunt as if he had been sworn brother to him; and I'll be sworn a' ne'er saw him but once in the Tilt-yard; and then he burst his head for crowding among the marshal's men. I saw it, and told John o' Gaunt he beat his own name; for you might have thrust him and all his apparel into an eel-skin; the case of a treble hautboy was a mansion for

him, a court: — and now has he land and beefs. Well, I'll be acquainted with him, if I return; and it shall go hard but I'll make him a philosopher's two stones to me: if the young dace be a bait for the old pike, I see no reason, in the law of nature, but I may snap at him. Let time shape, and there an end.

[*Exit.*

ACT IV

SCENE I

Yorkshire. Gaultree Forest.

Enter the ARCHBISHOP OF YORK, MOWBRAY, HASTINGS, *and others.*

ARCHBISHOP OF YORK
What is this forest call'd?

HASTINGS
'Tis Gaultree Forest, an't shall please your Grace.

ARCHBISHOP OF YORK
Here stand, my lords; and send discoverers forth
To know the numbers of our enemies.

HASTINGS
We have sent forth already.

ARCHBISHOP OF YORK
⠀⠀⠀⠀⠀⠀⠀⠀⠀⠀'Tis well done.
My friends and brethren in these great affairs,
I must acquaint you that I have received
New-dated letters from Northumberland;
Their cold intent, tenour, and substance, thus: —
Here doth he wish his person, with such powers
As might hold sortance with his quality,
The which he could not levy; whereupon
He is retired, to ripe his growing fortunes,
To Scotland; and concludes in hearty prayers
That your attempts may overlive the hazard
And fearful melting of their opposite.

MOWBRAY
Thus do the hopes we have in him touch ground,
And dash themselves to pieces.

Enter a MESSENGER.

HASTINGS
⠀⠀⠀⠀⠀⠀⠀⠀⠀⠀Now, what news?

MESSENGER
West of this forest, scarcely off a mile,
In goodly form comes on the enemy;
And, by the ground they hide, I judge their number
Upon or near the rate of thirty thousand.

MOWBRAY
The just proportion that we gave them out.
Let us sway on, and face them in the field.

ARCHBISHOP OF YORK
What well-appointed leader fronts us here?

MOWBRAY
I think it is my Lord of Westmoreland.

Enter WESTMORELAND.

WESTMORELAND
Health and fair greeting from our general,
The prince, Lord John and Duke of Lancaster.

ARCHBISHOP OF YORK
Say on, my Lord of Westmoreland, in peace:
What doth concern your coming?

WESTMORELAND
⠀⠀⠀⠀⠀⠀⠀⠀⠀⠀Then, my lord,
Unto your Grace do I in chief address
The substance of my speech. If that rebellion
Came like itself, in base and abject routs,
Led on by heady youth, guarded with rags,
And countenanc'd by boys and beggary, —
I say, if damn'd commotion so appear'd,
In his true, native, and most proper shape,
You, reverend father, and these noble lords,
Had not been here, to dress the ugly form
Of base and bloody insurrection
With your fair honours. You, lord archbishop, —
Whose see is by a civil peace maintain'd;
Whose beard the silver hand of peace hath touch'd;
Whose learning and good letters peace hath tutor'd;
Whose white investments figure innocence,
The dove and very blessed spirit of peace, —
Wherefore do you so ill translate yourself
Out of the speech of peace, that bears such grace,
Into the harsh and boisterous tongue of war;
Turning your books to greaves, your ink to blood,
Your pens to lances, and your tongue divine
To a loud trumpet and a point of war?

ARCHBISHOP OF YORK
Wherefore do I this? — so the question stands.
Briefly to this end: — we are all diseased;
And with our surfeiting and wanton hours
Have brought ourselves into a burning fever,
And we must bleed for it: of which disease
Our late king, Richard, being infected, died.
But, my most noble Lord of Westmoreland,
I take not on me here as a physician;
Nor do I, as an enemy to peace,
Troop in the throngs of military men;
But, rather, show awhile like fearful war,
To diet rank minds sick of happiness,
And purge th'obstructions which begin to stop
Our very veins of life. Hear me more plainly.
I have in equal balance justly weigh'd
What wrongs our arms may do, what wrongs we suffer,
And find our griefs heavier than our offences.
We see which way the stream of time doth run,
And are enforc'd from our most quiet sphere
By the rough torrent of occasion;
And have the summary of all our griefs,
When time shall serve, to show in articles;
Which long ere this we offer'd to the king,
And might by no suit gain our audience:
When we are wrong'd, and would unfold our griefs,
We are denied access unto his person
Even by those men that most have done us wrong.
The dangers of the days but newly gone,
Whose memory is written on the earth
With yet-appearing blood, and the examples
Of every minute's instance, present now,
Have put us in these ill-beseeming arms;
Not to break peace, or any branch of it,
But to establish here a peace indeed,
Concurring both in name and quality.

WESTMORELAND
When ever yet was your appeal denied?
Wherein have you been galled by the king?
What peer hath been suborn'd to grate on you; —
That you should seal this lawless bloody book
Of forg'd rebellion with a seal divine,
And consecrate commotion's bitter edge?

ARCHBISHOP OF YORK
My brother general, the commonwealth,
To brother born an household cruelty,
I make my quarrel in particular.

WESTMORELAND
There is no need of any such redress;
Or if there were, it not belongs to you.

MOWBRAY
Why not to him in part, and to us all
That feel the bruises of the days before,
And suffer the condition of these times
To lay a heavy and unequal hand
Upon our honours?

WESTMORELAND
⠀⠀⠀⠀⠀⠀⠀⠀O, my good Lord Mowbray,
Construe the times to their necessities,
And you shall say indeed, it is the time,
And not the king, that doth you injuries.
Yet, for your part, it not appears to me,
Either from the king, or in the present time,
That you should have an inch of any ground
To build a grief on: were you not restor'd
To all the Duke of Norfolk's signiories,
Your noble and right-well-remember'd father's?

MOWBRAY
What thing, in honour, had my father lost,
That need to be reviv'd and breath'd in me?
The king, that lov'd him, as the state stood then,
Was, force perforce, compell'd to banish him:
And then that Harry Bolingbroke and he —
Being mounted and both roused in their seats,
Their neighing coursers daring of the spur,
Their armed staves in charge, their beavers down,
Their eyes of fire sparking through sights of steel,
And the loud trumpet blowing them together, —
Then, then, when there was nothing could have stay'd
My father from the breast of Bolingbroke,
O, when the king did throw his warder down,
His own life hung upon the staff he threw:
Then threw he down himself, and all their lives
That by indictment and by dint of sword
Have since miscarried under Bolingbroke.

WESTMORELAND
You speak, Lord Mowbray, now you know not what.
The Earl of Hereford was reputed then
In England the most valiant gentleman:
Who knows on whom fortune would then have smil'd?
But if your father had been victor there,

He ne'er had borne it out of Coventry:
For all the country, in a general voice,
Cried hate upon him; and all their prayers and love
Were set on Hereford, whom they doted on,
And bless'd and grac'd indeed, more than the king.
But this is mere digression from my purpose. —
Here come I from our princely general
To know your griefs; to tell you from his Grace
That he will give you audience; and wherein
It shall appear that your demands are just,
You shall enjoy them, — every thing set off
That might so much as think you enemies.

MOWBRAY
But he hath forc'd us to compel this offer;
And it proceeds from policy, not love.

WESTMORELAND
Mowbray, you overween to take it so;
This offer comes from mercy, not from fear:
For, lo! within a ken our army lies;
Upon mine honour, all too confident
To give admittance to a thought of fear.
Our battle is more full of names than yours,
Our men more perfect in the use of arms,
Our armour all as strong, our cause the best;
Then reason will our heart should be as good:
Say you not, then, our offer is compell'd.

MOWBRAY
Well, by my will we shall admit no parley.

WESTMORELAND
That argues but the shame of your offence:
A rotten case abides no handling.

HASTINGS
Hath the Prince John a full commission,
In very ample virtue of his father,
To hear and absolutely to determine
Of what conditions we shall stand upon?

WESTMORELAND
That is intended in the general's name:
I muse you make so slight a question.

ARCHBISHOP OF YORK
Then take, my Lord of Westmoreland, this schedule,
For this contains our general grievances:
Each several article herein redress'd,
All members of our cause, both here and hence,
That are insinew'd to this action,
Acquitted by a true substantial form
And present execution of our wills
To us and to our purposes consign'd, —
We come within our awful banks again,
And knit our powers to the arm of peace.

WESTMORELAND
This will I show the general. Please you, lords,
In sight of both our battles we may meet;
And either end in peace, — which God so frame! —
Or to the place of difference call the swords
Which must decide it.

ARCHBISHOP OF YORK
My lord, we will do so.
[*Exit* WESTMORELAND.

MOWBRAY
There is a thing within my bosom tells me
That no conditions of our peace can stand.

HASTINGS
Fear you not that: if we can make our peace
Upon such large terms and so absolute
As our conditions shall consist upon,
Our peace shall stand as firm as rocky mountains.

MOWBRAY
Yea, but our valuation shall be such,
That every slight and false-derived cause,
Yea, every idle, nice, and wanton reason
Shall to the king taste of this action;
That, were our royal faiths martyrs in love,
We shall be winnow'd with so rough a wind,
That even our corn shall seem as light as chaff,
And good from bad find no partition.

ARCHBISHOP OF YORK
No, no, my lord. Note this, — the king is weary
Of dainty and such picking grievances:
For he hath found, to end one doubt by death
Revives two greater in the heirs of life;
And therefore will he wipe his tables clean,
And keep no tell-tale to his memory,
That may repeat and history his loss
To new remembrance: for full well he knows
He cannot so precisely weed this land
As his misdoubts present occasion:
His foes are so enrooted with his friends,
That, plucking to unfix an enemy,
He doth unfasten so and shake a friend.

ARCHBISHOP OF YORK My lord, we come.

So that this land, like an offensive wife
That hath enrag'd him on to offer strokes,
As he is striking, holds his infant up,
And hangs resolv'd correction in the arm
That was uprear'd to execution.

HASTINGS
Besides, the king hath wasted all his rods
On late offenders, that he now doth lack
The very instruments of chastisement:
So that his power, like to a fangless lion,
May offer, but not hold.

ARCHBISHOP OF YORK
'Tis very true:
And therefore be assur'd, my good lord marshal,
If we do now make our atonement well,
Our peace will, like a broken limb united,
Grow stronger for the breaking.

MOWBRAY
Be it so.
Here is return'd my Lord of Westmoreland.
Enter WESTMORELAND.

WESTMORELAND
The prince is here at hand: pleaseth your lordship
To meet his Grace just distance 'tween our armies.

MOWBRAY
Your Grace of York, in God's name, then, set forward.

ARCHBISHOP OF YORK
Before, and greet his Grace: — my lord, we come.
[*Exeunt.*

SCENE II
Another part of the forest.

Enter, from one side, MOWBRAY, *the* ARCHBISHOP,
HASTINGS, *and others; from the other side,* PRINCE
JOHN OF LANCASTER, WESTMORELAND,
OFFICERS, *and* ATTENDANTS.

PRINCE JOHN
You are well encounter'd here, my cousin Mowbray: —
Good day to you, gentle lord archbishop; —
And so to you, Lord Hastings, — and to all. —

My Lord of York, it better show'd with you,
When that your flock, assembled by the bell,
Encircled you to hear with reverence
Your exposition on the holy text,
Than now to see you here an iron man,
Cheering a rout of rebels with your drum,
Turning the word to sword, and life to death.
That man that sits within a monarch's heart,
And ripens in the sunshine of his favour,
Would he abuse the countenance of the king,
Alack, what mischiefs might he set abroach,
In shadow of such greatness! With you, lord bishop,
It is even so. Who hath not heard it spoken,
How deep you were within the books of God?
To us the speaker in his parliament;
To us th'imagined voice of God himself;
The very opener and intelligencer
Between the grace, the sanctities of heaven
And our dull workings. O, who shall believe,
But you misuse the reverence of your place,
Employ the countenance and grace of heaven,
As a false favourite doth his prince's name,
In deeds dishonourable? You have ta'en up,
Under the counterfeited zeal of God,
The subjects of his substitute, my father,
And both against the peace of heaven and him
Have here up-swarm'd them.

ARCHBISHOP OF YORK
Good my Lord of Lancaster,
I am not here against your father's peace;
But, as I told my Lord of Westmoreland,
The time misorder'd doth, in common sense,
Crowd us and crush us to this monstrous form,
To hold our safety up. I sent your Grace
The parcels and particulars of our grief, —
The which hath been with scorn shov'd from the
court, —
Whereon this Hydra son of war is born;
Whose dangerous eyes may well be charm'd asleep
With grant of our most just and right desires,
And true obedience, of this madness cured,
Stoop tamely to the foot of majesty.

PRINCE JOHN
                    Go, my lord,
And let our army be discharged too.
                    [*Exit* WESTMORELAND.
And, good my lord, so please you, let our trains
March by us, that we may peruse the men
We should have coped withal.

ARCHBISHOP OF YORK
                    Go, good Lord Hastings,
And, ere they be dismiss'd, let them march by.
                    [*Exit* HASTINGS.

PRINCE JOHN
I trust, lords, we shall lie to-night together.
                    Enter WESTMORELAND.
Now, cousin, wherefore stands our army still?

WESTMORELAND
The leaders, having charge from you to stand,
Will not go off until they hear you speak.

PRINCE JOHN
They know their duties.

                    Enter HASTINGS.

HASTINGS
My lord, our army is dispers'd already:
Like youthful steers unyok'd, they take their courses
East, west, north, south; or, like a school broke up,
Each hurries toward his home and sporting-place.

WESTMORELAND
Good tidings, my Lord Hastings; for the which
I do arrest thee, traitor, of high treason: —
And you, lord archbishop, — and you, Lord Mowbray, —
Of capitol treason I attach you both.

MOWBRAY
Is this proceeding just and honourable?

WESTMORELAND
Is your assembly so?

ARCHBISHOP OF YORK
Will you thus break your faith!

PRINCE JOHN
                    I pawn'd thee none:
I promised you redress of these same grievances
Whereof you did complain; which, by mine honour,
I will perform with a most Christian care.
But for you, rebels, — look to taste the due
Meet for rebellion and such acts as yours.
Most shallowly did you these arms commence,
Fondly brought here, and foolishly sent hence. —
Strike up our drums, pursue the scatter'd stray:
God, and not we, hath safely fought to-day. —
Some guard these traitors to the block of death,
Treason's true bed and yielder-up of breath.   [*Exeunt.*

SCENE III

Another part of the forest.

Alarums: excursions. Enter FALSTAFF *and* COLEVILE, *meeting.*

FALSTAFF
What's your name, sir? of what condition are you, and of what place, I pray?

COLEVILE
I am a knight, sir; and my name is Colevile of the dale.

FALSTAFF
Well, then, Colevile is your name, a knight is your degree, and your place the dale: Colevile shall be still your name, a traitor your degree, and the dungeon your place, — a dale deep enough; so shall you be still Colevile of the dale.

COLEVILE
Are not you Sir John Falstaff?

FALSTAFF
As good a man as he, sir, whoe'er I am. Do ye yield, sir? or shall I sweat for you? If I do sweat, they are the drops of thy lovers, and they weep for thy death: therefore rouse up fear and trembling, and do observance to my mercy.

COLEVILE
I think you are Sir John Falstaff; and in that thought yield me.

FALSTAFF
I have a whole school of tongues in this belly of mine; and not a tongue of them all speaks any other word but my name. An I had but a belly of any indifferency, I were simply the most active fellow in Europe: my womb, my womb, my womb, undoes me. — Here comes our general.

Enter PRINCE JOHN OF LANCASTER, WESTMORELAND, BLUNT, *and others.*

PRINCE JOHN The word of peace is render'd: hark, how they shout!

MOWBRAY
If not, we ready are to try our fortunes
To the last man.

HASTINGS
                    And though we here fall down,
We have supplies to second our attempt:
If they miscarry, theirs shall second them;
And so success of mischief shall be born,
And heir from heir shall hold this quarrel up,
Whiles England shall have generation.

PRINCE JOHN
You are too shallow, Hastings, much too shallow,
To sound the bottom of the after-times.

WESTMORELAND
Pleaseth your Grace to answer them directly,
How far-forth you do like their articles.

PRINCE JOHN
I like them all, and do allow them well;
And swear here, by the honour of my blood,
My father's purposes have been mistook;
And some about him have too lavishly
Wrested his meaning and authority. —
My lord, these griefs shall be with speed redress'd;
Upon my soul, they shall. If this may please you,
Discharge your powers unto their several counties,
As we will ours: and here, between the armies,
Let's drink together friendly and embrace,
That all their eyes may bear those tokens home
Of our restored love and amity.

ARCHBISHOP OF YORK
I take your princely word for these redresses.

PRINCE JOHN
I give it you, and will maintain my word:
And thereupon I drink unto your Grace.   [*Drinks.*

HASTINGS [*to an* OFFICER].
Go, captain, and deliver to the army
This news of peace: let them have pay, and part:
I know it will well please them. Hie thee, captain.

[*Exit* OFFICER.

ARCHBISHOP OF YORK
To you, my noble Lord of Westmoreland.   [*Drinks.*

WESTMORELAND
I pledge your Grace [*drinks*]; and, if you knew what pains
I have bestow'd to breed this present peace,
You would drink freely: but my love to ye
Shall show itself more openly hereafter.

ARCHBISHOP OF YORK
I do not doubt you.

WESTMORELAND
                    I am glad of it. —
Health to my lord and gentle cousin, Mowbray.
                    [*Drinks.*

MOWBRAY
You wish me health in very happy season;
For I am, on the sudden, something ill.

ARCHBISHOP OF YORK
Against ill chances men are ever merry;
But heaviness foreruns the good event.

WESTMORELAND
Therefore be merry, coz; since sudden sorrow
Serves to say thus, 'Some good thing comes
    to-morrow.'

ARCHBISHOP OF YORK
Believe me, I am passing light in spirit.

MOWBRAY
So much the worse, if your own rule be true.
                    [*Shouts within.*

PRINCE JOHN
The word of peace is render'd: hark, how they shout!

MOWBRAY
This had been cheerful after victory.

ARCHBISHOP OF YORK
A peace is of the nature of a conquest;
For then both parties nobly are subdued,
And neither party loser.

PRINCE JOHN
The heat is past; follow no further now: —
Call in the powers, good cousin Westmoreland.
     [*Exit* WESTMORELAND.
Now, Falstaff, where have you been all this while?
When every thing is ended, then you come:
These tardy tricks of yours will, on my life,
One time or other break some gallows' back.

FALSTAFF
I would be sorry, my lord, but it should be thus: I never
knew yet but rebuke and check was the reward of valour.
Do you think me a swallow, an arrow, or a bullet? have I,
in my poor and old motion, the expedition of thought? I
have speeded hither with the very extremest inch of
possibility; I have founder'd nine-score and odd posts:
and here, travel-tainted as I am, have, in my pure and
immaculate valour, taken Sir John Colevile of the dale, a
most furious knight and valorous enemy. But what of
that? he saw me, and yielded; that I may justly say with
the hook-nosed fellow of Rome, — I came, saw, and
overcame.

PRINCE JOHN
It was more of his courtesy than your deserving.

FALSTAFF
I know not: — here he is, and here I yield him: and I
beseech your Grace, let it be book'd with the rest of this
day's deeds; or, by the Lord, I will have it in a particular
ballad else, with mine own picture on the top of it,
Colevile kissing my foot: to the which course if I be
enforced, if you do not all show like gilt twopences to
me, and I, in the clear sky of fame o'ershine you as
much as the full moon doth the cinders of the element,
which show like pins' heads to her, believe not the
word of the noble: therefore let me have right, and let
desert mount.

PRINCE JOHN
Thine's too heavy to mount.

FALSTAFF
Let it shine, then.

PRINCE JOHN
Thine's too thick to shine.

FALSTAFF
Let it do something, my good lord, that may do me
good, and call it what you will.

PRINCE JOHN
Is thy name Colevile?

COLEVILE
It is, my lord.

PRINCE JOHN
A famous rebel art thou, Colevile.

FALSTAFF
And a famous true subject took him.

COLEVILE
I am, my lord, but as my betters are,
That led me hither: had they been ruled by me,
You should have won them dearer than you have.

FALSTAFF
I know not how they sold themselves: but thou, like a
kind fellow, gavest thyself away gratis; and I thank thee
for thee.

Enter WESTMORELAND.

PRINCE JOHN
Now, have you left pursuit?

WESTMORELAND
Retreat is made, and execution stay'd.

PRINCE JOHN
Send Colevile, with his confederates,
To York, to present execution: —
Blunt, lead him hence; and see you guard him sure.
    [*Exeunt* BLUNT *and others with* COLEVILE.
And now dispatch we toward the court, my lords:
I hear the king my father is sore sick:
Our news shall go before us to his majesty, —
Which, cousin, you shall bear, — to comfort him;
And we with sober speed will follow you.

FALSTAFF
My lord, I beseech you, give me leave to go
Through Glostershire: and, when you come to court,
Stand my good lord, pray, in your good report.

PRINCE JOHN
Fare you well, Falstaff: I, in my condition,
Shall better speak of you than you deserve.
    [*Exeunt all except* FALSTAFF.

FALSTAFF
I would you had but the wit: 'twere better than your
dukedom. — Good faith, this same young sober-blooded
boy doth not love me; nor a man cannot make him laugh;
— but that's no marvel, he drinks no wine. There's never
none of these demure boys come to any proof; for thin

drink doth so over-cool their blood, and making many
fish-meals, that they fall into a kind of male green-
sickness; and then, when they marry, they get wenches:
they are generally fools and cowards; — which some of us
should be too, but for inflammation. A good sherris-sack
hath a twofold operation in it. It ascends me into the
brain; dries me there all the foolish and dull and curdy
vapours which environ it; makes it apprehensive, quick,
forgetive, full of nimble, fiery, and delectable shapes;
which, deliver'd o'er to the voice, the tongue, which is the
birth, becomes excellent wit. The second property of your
excellent sherris is, the warming of the blood; which,
before cold and settled, left the liver white and pale, which
is the badge of pusillanimity and cowardice; but the
sherris warms it, and makes it course from the inwards to
the parts extreme: it illumineth the face, which, as a
beacon, gives warning to all the rest of this little kingdom,
man, to arm; and then the vital commoners and inland
petty spirits muster me all to their captain, the heart, who,
great and puff'd up with this retinue, doth any deed of
courage: and this valour comes of sherris. So that skill in
the weapon is nothing without sack, for that sets it a-work;
and learning, a mere hoard of gold kept by a devil, till sack
commences it, and sets it in act and use. Hereof comes it,
that Prince Harry is valiant; for the cold blood he did
naturally inherit of his father, he hath, like lean, sterile,
and bare land, manured, husbanded, and till'd, with
excellent endeavour of drinking good and good store of
fertile sherris, that he is become very hot and valiant. If I
had a thousand sons, the first humane principle I would
teach them should be, — to forswear thin potations, and
to addict themselves to sack.

Enter BARDOLPH.
How now, Bardolph!

BARDOLPH
The army is discharged all, and gone.

FALSTAFF
Let them go. I'll through Glostershire; and there will I
visit Master Robert Shallow, esquire: I have him already
tempering between my finger and my thumb, and
shortly will I seal with him. Come away.
     [*Exeunt.*

SCENE IV

Westminster. The Jerusalem Chamber.

Enter the KING, THOMAS DUKE OF CLARENCE,
HUMPHREY OF GLOSTER, WARWICK, *and others.*

KING HENRY
Now, lords, if God doth give successful end
To this debate that bleedeth at our doors,
We will our youth lead on to higher fields,
And draw no swords but what are sanctified.
Our navy is address'd, our power collected,
Our substitutes in absence well invested,

And every thing lies level to our wish:
Only, we want a little personal strength;
And pause us, till these rebels, now afoot,
Come underneath the yoke of government.

WARWICK
Both which we doubt not but your majesty
Shall soon enjoy.

KING HENRY
    Humphrey, my son of Gloster,
Where is the prince your brother?

GLOSTER
I think he's gone to hunt, my lord, at Windsor.

KING HENRY
And how accompanied?

GLOSTER
    I do not know, my lord.

KING HENRY
Is not his brother, Thomas of Clarence, with him?

GLOSTER
No, my good lord; he is in presence here.

CLARENCE
What would my lord and father?

KING HENRY
Nothing but well to thee, Thomas of Clarence.
How chance thou art not with the prince thy brother?
He loves thee, and thou dost neglect him, Thomas;
Thou hast a better place in his affection
Than all thy brothers: cherish it, my boy;
And noble offices thou mayst effect
Of mediation, after I am dead,
Between his greatness and thy other brethren:
Therefore omit him not; blunt not his love,
Nor lose the good advantage of his grace
By seeming cold or careless of his will;
For he is gracious, if he be observed:
He hath a tear for pity, and a hand
Open as day for melting charity:
Yet notwithstanding, being incens'd, he's flint:
As humorous as winter, and as sudden
As flaws congealed in the spring of day.
His temper, therefore, must be well observed:
Chide him for faults, and do it reverently,
When you perceive his blood inclin'd to mirth;
But, being moody, give him line and scope,
Till that his passions, like a whale on ground,
Confound themselves with working. Learn this,
  Thomas,
And thou shalt prove a shelter to thy friends;
A hoop of gold to bind thy brothers in,
That the united vessel of their blood,
Mingled with venom of suggestion —
As, force perforce, the age will pour it in —
Shall never leak, though it do work as strong
As aconitum or rash gunpowder.

KING HENRY My grief stretches itself beyond the hour of death.

CLARENCE
I shall observe him with all care and love.
KING HENRY
Why art thou not at Windsor with him, Thomas?
CLARENCE
He is not there to-day; he dines in London.
KING HENRY
And how accompanied? canst thou tell that?
CLARENCE
With Pointz, and other his continual followers.
KING HENRY
Most subject is the fattest soil to weeds;
And he, the noble image of my youth,
Is overspread with them: therefore my grief
Stretches itself beyond the hour of death:
The blood weeps from my heart, when I do shape,
In forms imaginary, th'unguided days
And rotten times that you shall look upon
When I am sleeping with my ancestors.
For when his headstrong riot hath no curb,
When rage and hot blood are his counsellors,
When means and lavish manners meet together,
O, with what wings shall his affections fly
Towards fronting peril and oppos'd decay!
WARWICK
My gracious lord, you look beyond him quite:
The prince but studies his companions,
Like a strange tongue; wherein, to gain the language,
'Tis needful that the most immodest word
Be look'd upon and learn'd; which once attain'd,
Your highness knows, comes to no further use
But to be known and hated. So, like gross terms,
The prince will, in the perfectness of time,
Cast off his followers; and their memory
Shall as a pattern or a measure live,
By which his Grace must mete the lives of others,
Turning past evils to advantages.
KING HENRY
'Tis seldom when the bee doth leave her comb
In the dead carrion.
Enter WESTMORELAND.
Who's here? Westmoreland?
WESTMORELAND
Health to my sovereign, and new happiness
Added to that that I am to deliver!
Prince John, your son, doth kiss your Grace's hand:
Mowbray, the Bishop Scroop, Hastings, and all,
Are brought to the correction of your law;
There is not now a rebel's sword unsheath'd,
But Peace puts forth her olive every where:
The manner how this action hath been borne,
Here at more leisure may your highness read,
With every course in his particular.
[Giving packet.
KING HENRY
O Westmoreland, thou art a summer bird,
Which ever in the haunch of winter sings
The lifting-up of day. — Look, here's more news.
Enter HARCOURT.
HARCOURT
From enemies heaven keep your majesty;
And, when they stand against you, may they fall
As those that I am come to tell you of!
The Earl Northumberland and the Lord Bardolph,
With a great power of English and of Scots,
Are by the shrieve of Yorkshire overthrown:
The manner and true order of the fight,
This packet, please it you, contains at large.
[Giving packet.
KING HENRY
And wherefore should these good news make me sick?
Will Fortune never come with both hands full,
But write her fair words still in foulest letters?
She either gives a stomach, and no food, —
Such are the poor, in health; or else a feast,
And takes away the stomach — such are the rich,
That have abundance, and enjoy it not.
I should rejoice now at this happy news;
And now my sight fails, and my brain is giddy: —
O me! come near me; now I am much ill. *[Falls back.*
GLOSTER
Comfort, your majesty!
CLARENCE
O my royal father!
WESTMORELAND
My sovereign lord, cheer up yourself, look up.
WARWICK
Be patient, princes; you do know, these fits
Are with his highness very ordinary.

KING HENRY   I pray you, take me up, and bear me hence, into some other chamber.

Stand from him, give him air; he'll straight be well.
CLARENCE
No, no, he cannot long hold out these pangs:
Th'incessant care and labour of his mind
Hath wrought the mure, that should confine it in,
So thin that life looks through and will break out.
GLOSTER
The people fear me; for they do observe
Unfather'd heirs and loathly births of nature:
The seasons change their manners, as the year
Had found some months asleep, and leap'd them over.
CLARENCE
The river hath thrice flow'd, no ebb between;
And the old folk, time's doting chronicles,
Say it did so a little time before
That our great-grandsire, Edward, sick'd and died.
WARWICK
Speak lower, princes, for the king recovers.
GLOSTER
This apoplex will certain be his end.
KING HENRY
I pray you, take me up, and bear me hence
Into some other chamber: softly, pray.
[They lay the KING *on a bed in an inner room.*
Let there be no noise made, my gentle friends;
Unless some dull and favourable hand
Will whisper music to my weary spirit.
WARWICK
Call for the music in the other room.
KING HENRY
Set me the crown upon my pillow here.
CLARENCE
His eye is hollow, and he changes much.
WARWICK
Less noise, less noise!
Enter PRINCE HENRY.
PRINCE HENRY
Who saw the Duke of Clarence?
CLARENCE
I am here, brother, full of heaviness.
PRINCE HENRY
How now! rain within doors, and none abroad!
How doth the king?

GLOSTER
Exceeding ill.
PRINCE HENRY
Heard he
The good news yet? tell it him.
GLOSTER
He alter'd much
Upon the hearing it.
PRINCE HENRY
If he be sick with joy, he'll recover without physic.
WARWICK
Not so much noise, my lords: — sweet prince, speak low;
The king your father is dispos'd to sleep.
CLARENCE
Let us withdraw into the other room.
WARWICK
Will't please your Grace to go along with us?
PRINCE HENRY
No; I will sit and watch here by the king.
[Exeunt all except PRINCE HENRY.
Why doth the crown lie there upon his pillow,
Being so troublesome a bedfellow?
O polish'd perturbation! golden care!
That keep'st the ports of slumber open wide
To many a watchful night! — sleep with it now!
Yet not so sound and half so deeply sweet
As he whose brow with homely biggen bound
Snores out the watch of night. O majesty!
When thou dost pinch thy bearer, thou dost sit
Like a rich armour worn in heat of day,
That scalds with safety. By his gates of breath
There lies a downy feather which stirs not:
Did he suspire, that light and weightless down
Perforce must move. — My gracious lord! my father! –
This sleep is sound indeed; this is a sleep,
That from this golden rigol hath divorced
So many English kings. Thy due from me
Is tears and heavy sorrows of the blood,
Which nature, love, and filial tenderness,
Shall, O dear father, pay thee plenteously:
My due from thee is this imperial crown,
Which, as immediate from thy place and blood,
Derives itself to me. Lo, here it sits, —

[Putting it on his head.

Which God shall guard: and put the world's whole
   strength
Into one giant arm, it shall not force
This lineal honour from me: this from thee
Will I to mine leave, as 'tis left to me.   *[Exit.*

KING HENRY
Warwick! Gloster! Clarence!

Enter WARWICK *and the rest.*

CLARENCE
Doth the king call?

WARWICK
What would your majesty? how fares your Grace?

KING HENRY
Why did you leave me here alone, my lords?

CLARENCE
We left the prince my brother here, my liege,
Who undertook to sit and watch by you.

KING HENRY
The Prince of Wales! Where is he? let me see him:
He is not here.

WARWICK
This door is open; he is gone this way.

GLOSTER
He came not through the chamber where we stay'd.

KING HENRY
Where is the crown? who took it from my pillow?

WARWICK
When we withdrew, my liege, we left it here.

KING HENRY
The prince hath ta'en it hence: — go, seek him out.
Is he so hasty, that he doth suppose
My sleep my death? —
Find him, my Lord of Warwick; chide him hither.
                       [Exit WARWICK.
This part of his conjoins with my disease,
And helps to end me. — See, sons, what things you are!
How quickly nature falls into revolt
When gold becomes her object!
For this the foolish over-careful fathers
Have broke their sleep with thought, their brains with
   care,
Their bones with industry;
For this they have engross'd and piled up
The canker'd heaps of strange-achieved gold;
For this they have been thoughtful to invest
Their sons with arts and martial exercises:
When, like the bee, culling from every flower
The virtuous sweets,
Our thighs pack'd with wax, our mouths with honey,
We bring it to the hive; and, like the bees,
Are murder'd for our pains. This bitter taste
Yield his engrossments to the ending father.
              Enter WARWICK.
Now, where is he that will not stay so long
Till his friend sickness hath determined me?

WARWICK
My lord, I found the prince in the next room,
Washing with kindly tears his gentle cheeks;
With such a deep demeanour in great sorrow,
That tyranny, which never quaff'd but blood,
Would, by beholding him, have wash'd his knife
With gentle eye-drops. He is coming hither.

KING HENRY
But wherefore did he take away the crown?

Enter PRINCE HENRY.

Lo, where he comes. — Come hither to me, Harry. —
Depart the chamber, leave us here alone.
[Exeunt all except KING HENRY *and* PRINCE HENRY.

PRINCE HENRY
I never thought to hear you speak again.

KING HENRY
Thy wish was father, Harry, to that thought:
I stay too long by thee, I weary thee.
Dost thou so hunger for mine empty chair,
That thou wilt needs invest thee with my honours
Before thy hour be ripe? O foolish youth!
Thou seek'st the greatness that will overwhelm thee.
Stay but a little; for my cloud of dignity
Is held from falling with so weak a wind
That it will quickly drop: my day is dim.
Thou hast stol'n that which, after some few hours,
Were thine without offence; and at my death
Thou hast seal'd up my expectation:
Thy life did manifest thou loved'st me not,
And thou wilt have me die assured of it.
Thou hidest a thousand daggers in thy thoughts,
Which thou hast whetted on thy stony heart
To stab at half an hour of my life.

PRINCE HENRY   Lo, here it sits, — which God shall guard.

What! canst thou not forbear me half an hour?
Then, get thee gone, and dig my grave thyself;
And bid the merry bells ring to thine ear,
That thou art crowned, not that I am dead.
Let all the tears that should bedew my hearse
Be drops of balm to sanctify thy head:
Only compound me with forgotten dust;
Give that which gave thee life unto the worms.
Pluck down my officers, break my decrees;
For now a time is come to mock at form: —
Harry the Fifth is crown'd: — up, vanity!
Down, royal state! all you sage counsellors, hence!
And to the English court assemble now,
From every region, apes of idleness!
Now, neighbour confines, purge you of your scum:
Have you a ruffian that will swear, drink, dance,
Revel the night, rob, murder, and commit
The oldest sins the newest kind of ways?
Be happy, he will trouble you no more;
England shall double-gild his treble guilt, —
England shall give him office, honour, might;
For the Fifth Harry from curb'd licence plucks
The muzzle of restraint, and the wild dog
Shall flesh his tooth in every innocent.
O my poor kingdom, sick with civil blows!
When that my care could not withhold thy riots,
What wilt thou do when riot is thy care?
O, thou wilt be a wilderness again,
Peopled with wolves, thy old inhabitants!

PRINCE HENRY
O, pardon me, my liege! but for my tears,   *[Kneeling.*
The moist impediments unto my speech,
I had forestall'd this dear and deep rebuke,
Ere you with grief had spoke, and I had heard
The course of it so far. There is your crown;
And He that wears the crown immortally
Long guard it yours! If I affect it more
Than as your honour and as your renown,
Let me no more from this obedience rise, —
Which my most inward true and duteous spirit
Teacheth, — this prostrate and exterior bending!
God witness with me, when I here came in,   *[Rising.*
And found no course of breath within your majesty,
How cold it struck my heart! If I do feign,
O, let me in my present wildness die,

And never live to show th'incredulous world
The noble change that I have purposed!
Coming to look on you, thinking you dead, —
And dead almost, my liege, to think you were, —
I spake unto this crown as having sense,
And thus upbraided it: 'The care on thee depending
Hath fed upon the body of my father;
Therefore, thou, best of gold, art worst of gold:
Other, less fine in carat, is more precious,
Preserving life in medicine potable;
But thou, most fine, most honour'd, most renown'd,
Hast eat thy bearer up.' Thus, my most royal liege,
Accusing it, I put it on my head,
To try with it — as with an enemy
That had before my face murder'd my father —
The quarrel of a true inheritor.
But if it did infect my blood with joy,
Or swell my thoughts to any strain of pride;
If any rebel or vain spirit of mine
Did with the least affection of a welcome
Give entertainment to the might of it, —
Let God for ever keep it from my head,
And make me as the poorest vassal is,
That doth with awe and terror kneel to it!

KING HENRY
O my son,
God put it in thy mind to take it hence,
That thou mightst win the more thy father's love,
Pleading so wisely in excuse of it!
Come hither, Harry, sit thou by my bed;
And hear, I think, the very latest counsel
That ever I shall breathe. God knows, my son,
By what by-paths and indirect crook'd ways
I met this crown; and I myself know well
How troublesome it sat upon my head:
To thee it shall descend with bitter quiet,
Better opinion, better confirmation;
For all the soil of the achievement goes
With me into the earth. It seem'd in me
But as an honour snatch'd with boisterous hand;
And I had many living to upbraid
My gain of it by their assistances;
Which daily grew to quarrel and to bloodshed,
Wounding supposed peace: all these bold fears
Thou see'st with peril I have answered;

FALSTAFF I'll follow you, good Master Robert Shallow.

For all my reign hath been but as a scene
Acting that argument: and now my death
Changes the mode; for what in me was purchas'd,
Falls upon thee in a more fairer sort;
So thou the garland wear'st successively.
Yet, though thou stand'st more sure than I could do,
Thou art not firm enough, since griefs are green;
And all my foes, which thou must make thy friends,
Have but their stings and teeth newly ta'en out;
By whose fell working I was first advanced,
And by whose power I well might lodge a fear
To be again displaced: which to avoid,
I cut some off, and had a purpose now
To lead out many to the Holy Land,
Lest rest and lying still might make them look
Too near unto my state. Therefore, my Harry,
Be it thy course to busy giddy minds
With foreign quarrels; that action, hence borne out,
May waste the memory of the former days.
More would I, but my lungs are wasted so
That strength of speech is utterly denied me.
How I came by the crown, O God forgive;
And grant it may with thee in true peace live!

PRINCE HENRY
My gracious liege,
You won it, wore it, kept it, gave it me;
Then plain and right must my possession be:
Which I with more than with a common pain
'Gainst all the world will rightfully maintain.

KING HENRY
Look, look, here comes my John of Lancaster.

Enter PRINCE JOHN OF LANCASTER, WARWICK,
LORDS, *and others.*

PRINCE JOHN
Health, peace, and happiness to my royal father!

KING HENRY
Thou bring'st me happiness and peace, son John;
But health, alack, with youthful wings is flown
From this bare wither'd trunk: upon thy sight
My worldly business makes a period. —
Where is my Lord of Warwick?

PRINCE HENRY
My Lord of Warwick!

KING HENRY
Doth any name particular belong
Unto the lodging where I first did swoon?

WARWICK
'Tis call'd Jerusalem, my noble lord.

KING HENRY
Laud be to God! — even there my life must end.
It hath been prophesied to me many years,
I should not die but in Jerusalem;
Which vainly I suppos'd the Holy Land: —
But bear me to that chamber; there I'll lie;
In that Jerusalem shall Harry die.   [*Exeunt.*

ACT V

SCENE I

Glostershire. SHALLOW'S *house.*

Enter SHALLOW, FALSTAFF, BARDOLPH, *and*
PAGE.

SHALLOW
By cock and pie, sir, you shall not away to-night. —
What, Davy, I say!

FALSTAFF
You must excuse me, Master Robert Shallow.

SHALLOW
I will not excuse you; you shall not be excused; excuses
shall not be admitted; there is no excuse shall serve;
you shall not be excused. — Why, Davy!

Enter DAVY.

DAVY
Here, sir.

SHALLOW
Davy, Davy, Davy, Davy, — let me see, Davy; let me see,
Davy; let me see: — yea, marry, William cook, bid him
come hither. — Sir John, you shall not be excused.

DAVY
Marry, sir, thus; those precepts cannot be served: and
again, sir, — shall we sow the headland with wheat?

SHALLOW
With red wheat, Davy. But for William cook: — are
there no young pigeons?

DAVY
Yes, sir. — Here is now the smith's note for shoeing
and plough-irons.

SHALLOW
Let it be cast, and paid. — Sir John, you shall not be
excused.

DAVY
Now, sir, a new link to the bucket must needs be had: —
and, sir, do you mean to stop any of William's wages,
about the sack he lost the other day at Hinckley fair?

SHALLOW
A' shall answer it. — Some pigeons, Davy, a couple of
short-legg'd hens, a joint of mutton, and any pretty
little tiny kickshaws, tell William cook.

DAVY
Doth the man of war stay all night, sir?

SHALLOW
Yea, Davy. I will use him well: a friend i'th'court is
better than a penny in purse. Use his men well, Davy;
for they are arrant knaves, and will backbite.

DAVY
No worse than they are backbitten, sir; for they have
marvellous foul linen.

SHALLOW
Well conceited, Davy: — about thy business, Davy.

DAVY
I beseech you, sir, to countenance William Visor of
Woncot against Clement Perkes o'th'hill.

SHALLOW
There is many complaints, Davy, against that Visor:
that Visor is an arrant knave, on my knowledge.

DAVY
I grant your worship that he is a knave, sir; but yet, God
forbid, sir, but a knave should have some countenance at
his friend's request. An honest man, sir, is able to speak
for himself, when a knave is not. I have served your
worship truly, sir, this eight years; and if I cannot once or
twice in a quarter bear out a knave against an honest
man, I have but a very little credit with your worship.
The knave is mine honest friend, sir; therefore, I
beseech your worship, let him be countenanced.

SHALLOW
Go to; I say he shall have no wrong. Look about, Davy.
[*Exit* DAVY.] Where are you, Sir John? Come, come,
come, off with your boots. — Give me your hand,
Master Bardolph.

BARDOLPH
I am glad to see your worship.

SHALLOW
I thank thee with all my heart, kind Master Bardolph:
[*to the* PAGE] and welcome, my tall fellow. — Come, Sir
John.

FALSTAFF
I'll follow you, good Master Robert Shallow. [*Exit*
SHALLOW.] Bardolph, look to our horses. [*Exeunt*
BARDOLPH *and* PAGE.] If I were saw'd into
quantities, I should make four dozen of such bearded
hermits'-staves as Master Shallow. It is a wonderful
thing to see the semblable coherence of his men's
spirits and his: they, by observing of him, do bear
themselves like foolish justices; he, by conversing
with them, is turn'd into a justice-like serving-man:
their spirits are so married in conjunction with the
participation of society, that they flock together in
consent, like so many wild-geese. If I had a suit to
Master Shallow, I would humour his men with the
imputation of being near their master: if to his men, I
would curry with Master Shallow, that no man could
better command his servants. It is certain that either
wise bearing or ignorant carriage is caught, as men
take diseases, one of another: therefore let men take
heed of their company. I will devise matter enough
out of this Shallow to keep Prince Harry in continual
laughter the wearing-out of six fashions, — which is
four terms, or two actions, — and a' shall laugh
without *intervallums*. O, it is much that a lie with a
slight oath, and a jest with a sad brow, will do with a
fellow that never had the ache in his shoulders! O, you
shall see him laugh till his face be like a wet cloak ill
laid up!

SHALLOW [*within*].
Sir John!

FALSTAFF
I come, Master Shallow; I come, Master Shallow.
                                                      [*Exit.*

SCENE II

Westminster. The palace.

Enter WARWICK *and the* LORD CHIEF JUSTICE,
meeting.

WARWICK
How now, my lord chief justice! whither away?

LORD CHIEF JUSTICE
How doth the king?

WARWICK
Exceeding well; his cares are now all ended.

LORD CHIEF JUSTICE
I hope, not dead.

WARWICK
He's walk'd the way of nature;
And, to our purposes, he lives no more.

LORD CHIEF JUSTICE
I would his majesty had call'd me with him:
The service that I truly did his life
Hath left me open to all injuries.

WARWICK
Indeed I think the young king loves you not.

LORD CHIEF JUSTICE
I know he doth not; and do arm myself
To welcome the condition of the time;
Which cannot look more hideously upon me
Than I have drawn it in my fantasy.

WARWICK
Here come the heavy issue of dead Harry:
O, that the living Harry had the temper
Of him, the worst of these three gentlemen!
How many nobles then should hold their places,
That must strike sail to spirits of vile sort!
LORD CHIEF JUSTICE
O God, I fear all will be overturn'd!

Enter JOHN OF LANCASTER, CLARENCE,
GLOSTER, WESTMORELAND, *and others.*

PRINCE JOHN
Good morrow, cousin Warwick, good morrow.
GLOSTER *and* **CLARENCE**
Good morrow, cousin.
PRINCE JOHN
We meet like men that had forgot to speak.
WARWICK
We do remember; but our argument
Is all too heavy to admit much talk.
PRINCE JOHN
Well, peace be with him that hath made us heavy!
LORD CHIEF JUSTICE
Peace be with us, lest we be heavier!
GLOSTER
O, good my lord, you've lost a friend indeed;
And I dare swear you borrow not that face
Of seeming sorrow, — it is sure your own.
PRINCE JOHN
Though no man be assured what grace to find,
You stand in coldest expectation:
I am the sorrier; would 'twere otherwise.
CLARENCE
Well, you must now speak Sir John Falstaff fair;
Which swims against your stream of quality.
LORD CHIEF JUSTICE
Sweet princes, what I did, I did in honour,
Led by th'impartial conduct of my soul;
And never shall you see that I will beg
A ragged and forestall'd remission.
If truth and upright innocency fail me,
I'll to the king my master that is dead,
And tell him who hath sent me after him.
WARWICK
Here comes the prince.

Enter KING HENRY THE FIFTH, *attended.*

LORD CHIEF JUSTICE
Good morrow; and God save your majesty!
KING HENRY THE FIFTH
This new and gorgeous garment, majesty,
Sits not so easy on me as you think. —
Brothers, you mix your sadness with some fear:
This is the English, not the Turkish court;
Not Amurath an Amurath succeeds,
But Harry Harry. Yet be sad, good brothers,

For, by my faith, it very well becomes you:
Sorrow so royally in you appears,
That I will deeply put the fashion on,
And wear it in my heart: why, then, be sad;
But entertain no more of it, good brothers,
Than a joint burden laid upon us all.
For me, by heaven, I bid you be assured,
I'll be your father and your brother too;
Let me but bear your love, I'll bear your cares:
Yet weep that Harry's dead; and so will I;
But Harry lives, that shall convert those tears,
By number, into hours of happiness.
    CLARENCE, PRINCE JOHN OF LANCASTER, *and*
            GLOSTER.
We hope no other from your majesty.
KING HENRY THE FIFTH
You all look strangely on me: — and you most;
                    [*To the* CHIEF JUSTICE.
You are, I think, assured I love you not.
LORD CHIEF JUSTICE
I am assured, if I be measur'd rightly,
Your majesty hath no just cause to hate me.
KING HENRY THE FIFTH
No!
How might a prince of my great hopes forget
So great indignities you laid upon me?
What! rate, rebuke, and roughly send to prison
Th'immediate heir of England? Was this easy?
May this be wash'd in Lethe and forgotten?
LORD CHIEF JUSTICE
I then did use the person of your father;
The image of his power lay then in me:
And in th'administration of his law,
Whiles I was busy for the commonwealth,
Your highness pleased to forget my place,
The majesty and power of law and justice,
The image of the king whom I presented,
And struck me in my very seat of judgement;
Whereon, as an offender to your father,
I gave bold way to my authority,
And did commit you. If the deed were ill,
Be you contented, wearing now the garland,
To have a son set your decrees at naught,
To pluck down justice from your awful bench,
To trip the course of law, and blunt the sword
That guards the peace and safety of your person;
Nay, more, to spurn at your most royal image,
And mock your workings in a second body.
Question your royal thoughts, make the case yours;
Be now the father, and propose a son;
Hear your own dignity so much profaned,
See your most dreadful laws so loosely slighted,
Behold yourself so by a son disdained;
And then imagine me taking your part,
And, in your power, soft silencing your son:
After this cold consideration, sentence me;

And, as you are a king, speak in your state
What I have done that misbecame my place,
My person, or my liege's sovereignty.
KING HENRY THE FIFTH
You are right, justice, and you weigh this well;
Therefore still bear the balance and the sword:
And I do wish your honours may increase,
Till you do live to see a son of mine
Offend you, and obey you, as I did.
So shall I live to speak my father's words:
'Happy am I, that have a man so bold
That dares do justice on my proper son;
And not less happy, having such a son
That would deliver up his greatness so
Into the hands of justice.' — You did commit me:
For which, I do commit into your hand
Th'unstained sword that you have used to bear;
With this remembrance, — that you use the same
With the like bold, just, and impartial spirit
As you have done 'gainst me. There is my hand.
You shall be as a father to my youth:
My voice shall sound as you do prompt mine ear;
And I will stoop and humble my intents
To your well-practis'd wise directions. —
And, princes all, believe me, I beseech you; —
My father is gone wild into his grave,
For in his tomb lie my affections;
And with his spirit sadly I survive,
To mock the expectation of the world,
To frustrate prophecies, and to raze out
Rotten opinion, who hath writ me down
After my seeming. The tide of blood in me
Hath proudly flow'd in vanity till now:
Now doth it turn, and ebb back to the sea,
Where it shall mingle with the state of floods,
And flow henceforth in formal majesty.
Now call we our high court of parliament:
And let us choose such limbs of noble counsel,
That the great body of our state may go
In equal rank with the best-govern'd nation;
That war, or peace, or both at once, may be
As things acquainted and familiar to us;
In which you, father, shall have foremost hand.
Our coronation done, we will accite,
As I before remember'd, all our state:
And, God consigning to my good intents,
No prince nor peer shall have just cause to say,
God shorten Harry's happy life one day!   [*Exeunt.*

SCENE III

Glostershire. SHALLOW'S *orchard.*

Enter FALSTAFF, SHALLOW, SILENCE,
BARDOLPH, the PAGE, *and* DAVY.

SHALLOW
Nay, you shall see my orchard, where, in an arbour, we
will eat a last year's pippin of my own graffing, with a
dish of caraways, and so forth: — come, cousin Silence: —
and then to bed.
FALSTAFF
'Fore God, you have here a goodly dwelling and a rich.
SHALLOW
Barren, barren, barren; beggars all, beggars all, Sir
John: — marry, good air. — Spread, Davy; spread,
Davy: well said, Davy.
FALSTAFF
This Davy serves you for good uses; he is your
serving-man and your husband.
SHALLOW
A good varlet, a good varlet, a very good varlet, Sir John: —
by the mass, I have drunk too much sack at supper: — a
good varlet. Now sit down, now sit down: — come, cousin.
SILENCE
Ah, sirrah! quoth-a, — we shall   [*Singing.*
    Do nothing but eat, and make good cheer,
    And praise God for the merry year;
    When flesh is cheap and females dear,
    And lusty lads roam here and there
            So merrily,
    And ever among so merrily.
FALSTAFF
There's a merry heart! — Good Master Silence, I'll give
you a health for that anon.
SHALLOW
Give Master Bardolph some wine, Davy.
DAVY
Sweet sir, sit; I'll be with you anon; most sweet sir, sit. —
Master Page, good master page, sit. — Proface! What
you want in meat, we'll have in drink: but you must
bear; — the heart's all.   [*Exit.*

LORD CHIEF JUSTICE Good morrow; and God save your majesty!

PISTOL   Puff in thy teeth, most recreant coward base!

SHALLOW
Be merry, Master Bardolph; — and, my little soldier there, be merry.
SILENCE [*singing*].
    Be merry, be merry, my wife has all;
    For women are shrews, both short and tall:
    'Tis merry in hall when beards wag all,
        And welcome merry Shrove-tide.
    Be merry, be merry.
FALSTAFF
I did not think Master Silence had been a man of this mettle.
SILENCE
Who, I? I have been merry twice and once ere now.

Enter DAVY.

DAVY
There's a dish of leather-coats for you.
            [*Setting them before* BARDOLPH.
SHALLOW
Davy, —
DAVY
Your worship? — [*to* BARDOLPH] I'll be with you straight. — A cup of wine, sir?
SILENCE [*singing*].
        A cup of wine that's brisk and fine,
        And drink unto the leman mine;
            And a merry heart lives long-a.
FALSTAFF
Well said, Master Silence.
SILENCE
An we shall be merry; — now comes in the sweet o'th'night.
FALSTAFF
Health and long life to you, Master Silence!
SILENCE [*singing*].
        Fill the cup, and let it come;
        I'll pledge you a mile to the bottom.
SHALLOW
Honest Bardolph, welcome: if thou want'st any thing, and wilt not call, beshrew thy heart. — [*to the* PAGE] Welcome, my little tiny thief, and welcome indeed too. — I'll drink to Master Bardolph, and to all the cavaleroes about London.
DAVY
I hope to see London once ere I die.
BARDOLPH
An I might see you there, Davy, —
SHALLOW
By the mass, you'll crack a quart together, — ha! will you not, Master Bardolph?

BARDOLPH
Yea, sir, in a pottle-pot.
SHALLOW
By God's liggens, I thank thee: — the knave will stick by thee, I can assure thee that: a' will not out; he is true bred.
BARDOLPH
And I'll stick by him, sir.
SHALLOW
Why, there spoke a king. Lack nothing: be merry. [*Knocking within.*] Look who's at door there, ho! who knocks?   [*Exit* DAVY.
FALSTAFF
Why, now you have done me right.
            [*To* SILENCE, *who has drunk a bumper.*
SILENCE [*singing*].
        Do me right,
        And dub me knight:
            Samingo.
Is't not so?
FALSTAFF
'Tis so.
SILENCE
Is't so? Why, then, say an old man can do somewhat.

Enter DAVY.

DAVY
An't please your worship, there's one Pistol come from the court with news.
FALSTAFF
From the court! let him come in.
                Enter PISTOL.
How now, Pistol!
PISTOL
Sir John, God save you!
FALSTAFF
What wind blew you hither, Pistol?
PISTOL
Not the ill wind which blows no man to good. — Sweet knight, thou art now one of the greatest men in this realm.
SILENCE
By'r lady, I think a' be, but goodman Puff of Barson.
PISTOL
Puff!
Puff in thy teeth, most recreant coward base! —
Sir John, I am thy Pistol and thy friend,
And helter-skelter have I rode to thee;
And tidings do I bring, and lucky joys,
And golden times, and happy news of price.
FALSTAFF
I pray thee, now, deliver them like a man of this world.

PISTOL
A foutre for the world and worldlings base!
I speak of Africa and golden joys.
FALSTAFF
O base Assyrian knight, what is thy news?
Let King Cophetua know the truth thereof.
SILENCE [*singing*].
        And Robin Hood, Scarlet, and John.
PISTOL
Shall dunghill curs confront the Helicons?
And shall good news be baffled?
Then, Pistol, lay thy head in Furies' lap.
SILENCE
Honest gentleman, I know not your breeding.
PISTOL
Why, then, lament therefore.
SHALLOW
Give me pardon, sir: — if, sir, you come with news from the court, I take it there's but two ways, — either to utter them, or to conceal them. I am, sir, under the king, in some authority.
PISTOL
Under which king, Besonian? speak, or die.
SHALLOW
Under King Harry.
PISTOL
                Harry the Fourth? or Fifth?
SHALLOW
Harry the Fourth.
PISTOL
                A foutre for thine office! —
Sir John, thy tender lambkin now is king;
Harry the Fifth's the man. I speak the truth:
When Pistol lies, do this; and fig me, like
The bragging Spaniard.
FALSTAFF
What, is the old king dead?
PISTOL
As nail in door: the things I speak are just.
FALSTAFF
Away, Bardolph! saddle my horse. — Master Robert Shallow, choose what office thou wilt in the land, 'tis thine. — Pistol, I will double-charge thee with dignities.
BARDOLPH
O joyful day! —
I would not take a knighthood for my fortune.
PISTOL
What! I do bring good news?
FALSTAFF
Carry Master Silence to bed. — Master Shallow, my Lord Shallow, be what thou wilt; I am fortune's steward. Get on thy boots: we'll ride all night. — O sweet Pistol! — Away, Bardolph! [*Exit* BARDOLPH.] — Come, Pistol, utter more to me; and, withal, devise something to do thyself good. — Boot, boot, Master Shallow! I know the young king is sick for me. Let us take any man's horses; the laws of England are at my commandment. Blessed are they that have been my friends; and woe to my lord chief justice!
PISTOL
Let vultures vile seize on his lungs also!
'Where is the life that late I led?' say they:
Why, here it is; — welcome this pleasant day!
                                [*Exeunt.

SCENE IV

London. A street.

Enter HOSTESS QUICKLY, DOLL TEARSHEET, *and*
BEADLES.

HOSTESS
No, thou arrant knave: I would to God that I might die, that I might have thee hang'd: thou hast drawn my shoulder out of joint.
FIRST BEADLE
The constables have deliver'd her over to me; and she shall have whipping-cheer enough, I warrant her: there hath been a man or two lately kill'd about her.
DOLL TEARSHEET
Nut-hook, nut-hook, you lie. Come on; I'll tell thee what, thou damn'd tripe-visaged rascal, an the child I go with do miscarry, thou wert better thou hadst struck thy mother, thou paper-faced villain.
HOSTESS
O the Lord, that Sir John were come! he would make this a bloody day to somebody. But I pray God the fruit of her womb miscarry!
FIRST BEADLE
If it do, you shall have a dozen of cushions again; you

have but eleven now. Come, I charge you both go with me; for the man is dead that you and Pistol beat amongst you.

DOLL TEARSHEET
I'll tell thee what, thou thin man in a censer, I will have you as soundly swinged for this, — you blue-bottle rogue, you filthy famish'd correctioner, if you be not swinged, I'll forswear half-kirtles.

FIRST BEADLE
Come, come, you she knight-errant, come.

HOSTESS
O God, that right should thus overcome might! Well, of sufferance comes ease.

DOLL TEARSHEET
Come, you rogue, come; bring me to a justice.

HOSTESS
Ay, come, you starved bloodhound.

DOLL TEARSHEET
Goodman death, goodman bones!

HOSTESS
Thou atomy, thou!

DOLL TEARSHEET
Come, you thin thing; come, you rascal.

FIRST BEADLE
Very well.   [*Exeunt.*

SCENE V

A public place near Westminster Abbey.

Enter two GROOMS, *strewing rushes.*

FIRST GROOM
More rushes, more rushes.

SECOND GROOM
The trumpets have sounded twice.

FIRST GROOM
'Twill be two o'clock ere they come from the coronation: Dispatch, dispatch.   [*Exeunt.*

Enter FALSTAFF, SHALLOW, PISTOL, BARDOLPH, *and* PAGE.

FALSTAFF
Stand here by me, Master Robert Shallow; I will make the king do you grace: I will leer upon him as a' comes by; and do but mark the countenance that he will give me.

PISTOL
God bless thy lungs, good knight.

FALSTAFF
Come here, Pistol; stand behind me! — [*to* SHALLOW] O, if I had had time to have made new liveries, I would have bestow'd the thousand pound I borrow'd of you. But 'tis no matter; this poor show doth better: this doth infer the zeal I had to see him; —

SHALLOW
It doth so.

FALSTAFF
It shows my earnestness of affection, —

SHALLOW
It doth so.

FALSTAFF
My devotion, —

SHALLOW
It doth, it doth, it doth.

FALSTAFF
As it were, to ride day and night; and not to deliberate, not to remember, not to have patience to shift me, —

SHALLOW
It is best, certain.

FALSTAFF
But to stand stain'd with travel, and sweating with desire to see him; thinking of nothing else, putting all affairs else in oblivion, as if there were nothing else to be done but to see him.

PISTOL
'Tis *semper idem*, for *obsque hoc nihil est*: 'tis all in every part.

SHALLOW
'Tis so, indeed.

PISTOL
My knight, I will inflame thy noble liver, And make thee rage. Thy Doll, and Helen of thy noble thoughts, Is in base durance and contagious prison; Haled thither By most mechanical and dirty hand: — Rouse up revenge from ebon den with fell Alecto's snake, For Doll is in. Pistol speaks naught but truth.

FALSTAFF
I will deliver her.
     [*Shouts within, and the trumpets sound.*

PISTOL
There roar'd the sea, and trumpet-clangor sounds.

Enter the KING *and his* TRAIN, *the* LORD CHIEF JUSTICE *among them.*

FALSTAFF
God save thy Grace, King Hal! my royal Hal!

PISTOL
The heavens thee guard and keep, most royal imp of fame!

FALSTAFF
God save thee, my sweet boy!

KING HENRY THE FIFTH
My lord chief justice, speak to that vain man.

LORD CHIEF JUSTICE
Have you your wits? know you what 'tis you speak?

FALSTAFF
My king! my Jove! I speak to thee, my heart!

KING HENRY THE FIFTH
I know thee not, old man: fall to thy prayers; How ill white hairs become a fool and jester! I have long dream'd of such a kind of man, So surfeit-swell'd, so old, and so profane; But, being awak'd, I do despise my dream. Make less thy body hence, and more thy grace; Leave gormandizing; know the grave doth gape For thee thrice wider than for other men. — Reply not to me with a fool-born jest: Presume not that I am the thing I was; For God doth know, so shall the world perceive, That I have turn'd away my former self; So will I those that kept me company. When thou dost hear I am as I have been, Approach me, and thou shalt be as thou wast, The tutor and the feeder of my riots: Till then, I banish thee, on pain of death, — As I have done the rest of my misleaders, — Not to come near our person by ten mile. For competence of life I will allow you, That lack of means enforce you not to evil: And, as we hear you do reform yourselves, We will, according to your strengths and qualities, Give you advancement. — Be it your charge, my lord, To see perform'd the tenour of our word. — Set on.   [*Exeunt* KING *and his* TRAIN.

FALSTAFF
Master Shallow, I owe you a thousand pound.

SHALLOW
Yea, marry, Sir John; which I beseech you to let me have home with me.

FALSTAFF
That can hardly be, Master Shallow. Do not you grieve at this; I shall be sent for in private to him: look you, he

FALSTAFF   God save thy Grace, King Hal! my royal Hal!

must seem thus to the world: fear not your advancements; I will be the man yet that shall make you great.

SHALLOW
I cannot well perceive how, — unless you should give me your doublet, and stuff me out with straw. I beseech you, good Sir John, let me have five hundred of my thousand.

FALSTAFF
Sir, I will be as good as my word: this that you heard was but a colour.

SHALLOW
A colour that I fear you will die in, Sir John.

FALSTAFF
Fear no colours: go with me to dinner: — come, Lieutenant Pistol; — come, Bardolph: — I shall be sent for soon at night.

Enter PRINCE JOHN OF LANCASTER, *the* LORD CHIEF JUSTICE, OFFICERS *etc.*

LORD CHIEF JUSTICE
Go, carry Sir John Falstaff to the Fleet; Take all his company along with him.

FALSTAFF
My lord, my lord, —

LORD CHIEF JUSTICE
I cannot now speak: I will hear you soon. — Take them away.

PISTOL
Si fortuna me tormenta, spero contenta.
     [*Exeunt all but* PRINCE JOHN *and* CHIEF JUSTICE.

PRINCE JOHN
I like this fair proceeding of the king's: He hath intent his wonted followers Shall all be very well provided for; But all are banish'd till their conversations Appear more wise and modest to the world.

LORD CHIEF JUSTICE
And so they are.

PRINCE JOHN
The king hath call'd his parliament, my lord.

LORD CHIEF JUSTICE
He hath.

PRINCE JOHN
I will lay odds that, ere this year expire, We bear our civil swords and native fire As far as France: I heard a bird so sing, Whose music, to my thinking, pleas'd the king. Come, will you hence?   [*Exeunt.*

EPILOGUE

Spoken by a DANCER.

First my fear; then my court'sy; last my speech. My fear is, your displeasure; my court'sy, my duty; and my speech, to beg your pardons. If you look for a good speech now, you undo me: for what I have to say is of

283

mine own making; and what indeed I should say will, I doubt, prove mine own marring. But to the purpose, and so to the venture. — Be it known to you, — as it is very well, — I was lately here in the end of a displeasing play, to pray your patience for it, and to promise you a better. I meant, indeed, to pay you with this; which, if, like an ill venture, it come unluckily home, I break, and you, my gentle creditors, lose. Here I promised you I would be, and here I commit my body to your mercies: bate me some, and I will pay you some, and, as most debtors do, promise you infinitely.

If my tongue cannot entreat you to acquit me, will you command me to use my legs? and yet that were but light payment, — to dance out of your debt. But a good conscience will make any possible satisfaction, and so would I. All the gentlewomen here have forgiven me: if the gentlemen will not, then the gentlemen do not agree with the gentlewomen, which was never seen before in such an assembly.

One word more, I beseech you. If you be not too much cloy'd with fat meat, our humble author will continue the story, with Sir John in it, and make you merry with fair Katharine of France: where, for any thing I know, Falstaff shall die of a sweat, unless already a' be kill'd with your hard opinions; for Oldcastle died a martyr, and this is not the man. My tongue is weary; when my legs are too, I will bid you good night; and so kneel down before you; — but, indeed, to pray for the queen.

KING HENRY THE FIFTH

DRAMATIS PERSONAE

KING HENRY THE FIFTH.
DUKE OF GLOSTER, } *brothers to the King.*
DUKE OF BEDFORD,
DUKE OF EXETER, *uncle to the King.*
DUKE OF YORK, *cousin to the King.*
EARL OF SALISBURY.
EARL OF WESTMORELAND.
EARL OF WARWICK.
ARCHBISHOP OF CANTERBURY.
BISHOP OF ELY.
EARL OF CAMBRIDGE.
LORD SCROOP.
SIR THOMAS GREY.
SIR THOMAS ERPINGHAM, GOWER, FLUELLEN,
   MACMORRIS, JAMY, *officers in King Henry's army.*

JOHN BATES, ALEXANDER COURT, MICHAEL
   WILLIAMS, *soldiers in the same.*
PISTOL.
NYM.
BARDOLPH.
BOY.
A HERALD.
CHARLES THE SIXTH, *King of France.*
LOUIS, *the Dauphin.*
DUKE OF BURGUNDY.
DUKE OF ORLEANS.
DUKE OF BOURBON.
THE CONSTABLE OF FRANCE.
RAMBURES, GRANDPRÉ, *French lords.*
GOVERNOR OF HARFLEUR.

MONTJOY, *a French herald.*
AMBASSADORS *to the King of England.*

ISABEL, *Queen of France.*
KATHARINE, *daughter to Charles and Isabel.*
ALICE, *a lady attending on her.*
HOSTESS *of a tavern in Eastcheap (formerly Mistress
   Quickly, and now married to Pistol).*

LORDS, LADIES, OFFICERS, SOLDIERS, CITIZENS,
   MESSENGERS, *and* ATTENDANTS.

CHORUS.

SCENE — *England; afterwards France.*

PROLOGUE

Enter CHORUS.

CHORUS
O for a Muse of fire, that would ascend
The brightest heaven of invention, —
A kingdom for a stage, princes to act,
And monarchs to behold the swelling scene!
Then should the warlike Harry, like himself,
Assume the port of Mars; and at his heels,
Leash'd-in like hounds, should famine, sword, and
   fire,
Crouch for employment. But pardon, gentles all,
The flat unraised spirits that have dared
On this unworthy scaffold to bring forth
So great an object: can this cockpit hold
The vasty fields of France? or may we cram
Within this wooden O the very casques
That did affright the air at Agincourt?
O, pardon! since a crooked figure may
Attest in little place a million;
And let us, ciphers to this great accompt,
On your imaginary forces work.
Suppose within the girdle of these walls
Are now confin'd two mighty monarchies,
Whose high-upreared and abutting fronts
The perilous narrow ocean parts asunder:
Piece-out our imperfections with your thoughts;
Into a thousand parts divide one man,
And make imaginary puissance;
Think, when we talk of horses, that you see them
Printing their proud hoofs i'th' receiving earth; —
For 'tis your thoughts that now must deck our kings,

Carry them here and there; jumping o'er times,
Turning th'accomplishment of many years
Into an hour-glass: for the which supply,
Admit me Chorus to this history;
Who, prologue-like, your humble patience pray,
Gently to hear, kindly to judge, our play.   [*Exit.*

ACT I

SCENE I

London. An ante-chamber in the KING'S *palace.*

Enter the ARCHBISHOP OF CANTERBURY *and the*
BISHOP OF ELY.

ARCHBISHOP OF CANTERBURY
My lord, I'll tell you, — that self bill is urged,
Which in th'eleventh year of the last king's reign
Was like, and had indeed against us pass'd,
But that the scambling and unquiet time
Did push it out of further question.

BISHOP OF ELY
But how, my lord, shall we resist it now?

ARCHBISHOP OF CANTERBURY
It must be thought on. If it pass against us,
We lose the better half of our possession;
For all the temporal lands, which men devout
By testament have given to the church,
Would they strip from us; being valued thus, —
As much as would maintain, to the king's honour,
Full fifteen earls and fifteen hundred knights,

Six thousand and two hundred good esquires;
And, to relief of lazars and weak age,
Of indigent faint souls past corporal toil,
A hundred almshouses right well supplied;
And to the coffers of the king, beside,
A thousand pounds by th'year: thus runs the bill.

BISHOP OF ELY
This would drink deep.

ARCHBISHOP OF CANTERBURY
                              'Twould drink the cup and all.

BISHOP OF ELY
But what prevention?

ARCHBISHOP OF CANTERBURY
The king is full of grace and fair regard.

BISHOP OF ELY
And a true lover of the holy church.

ARCHBISHOP OF CANTERBURY
The courses of his youth promis'd it not.
The breath no sooner left his father's body,
But that his wildness, mortified in him,
Seem'd to die too; yea, at that very moment,
Consideration, like an angel, came,
And whipp'd th'offending Adam out of him,
Leaving his body as a paradise,
T'envelop and contain celestial spirits.
Never was such a sudden scholar made;
Never came reformation in a flood,
With such a heady current, scouring faults;
Nor never Hydra-headed wilfulness
So soon did lose his seat, and all at once,
As in this king.

BISHOP OF ELY
We are blessed in the change.
ARCHBISHOP OF CANTERBURY
Hear him but reason in divinity,
And, all-admiring, with an inward wish
You would desire the king were made a prelate:
Hear him debate of commonwealth affairs,
You would say it hath been all-in-all his study:
List his discourse of war, and you shall hear
A fearful battle render'd you in music:
Turn him to any cause of policy,
The Gordian knot of it he will unloose,
Familiar as his garter: — that, when he speaks,
The air, a charter'd libertine, is still,
And the mute wonder lurketh in men's ears,
To steal his sweet and honey'd sentences;
So that the art and practic part of life
Must be the mistress to this theoric:
Which is a wonder how his Grace should glean it,
Since his addiction was to courses vain;
His companies unletter'd, rude, and shallow;
His hours fill'd up with riots, banquets, sports;
And never noted in him any study,
Any retirement, any sequestration
From open haunts and popularity.
BISHOP OF ELY
The strawberry grows underneath the nettle,
And wholesome berries thrive and ripen best
Neighbour'd by fruit of baser quality:
And so the prince obscur'd his contemplation
Under the veil of wildness; which, no doubt,
Grew like the summer grass, fastest by night,
Unseen, yet crescive in his faculty.
ARCHBISHOP OF CANTERBURY
It must be so; for miracles are ceas'd;
And therefore we must needs admit the means
How things are perfected.
BISHOP OF ELY
                          But, my good lord,
How now for mitigation of this bill
Urg'd by the commons? Doth his majesty
Incline to it, or no?
ARCHBISHOP OF CANTERBURY
                          He seems indifferent;
Or, rather, swaying more upon our part
Than cherishing th'exhibiters against us:
For I have made an offer to his majesty, —
Upon our spiritual convocation,
And in regard of causes now in hand,
Which I have open'd to his Grace at large,
As touching France, — to give a greater sum
Than ever at one time the clergy yet
Did to his predecessors part withal.
BISHOP OF ELY
How did this offer seem receiv'd, my lord?
ARCHBISHOP OF CANTERBURY
With good acceptance of his majesty;
Save that there was not time enough to hear —
As, I perceiv'd, his Grace would fain have done —
The severals and unhidden passages
Of his true titles to some certain dukedoms,
And, generally, to the crown and seat of France,
Deriv'd from Edward, his great-grandfather.
BISHOP OF ELY
What was th'impediment that broke this off?
ARCHBISHOP OF CANTERBURY
The French ambassador upon that instant
Crav'd audience; — and the hour, I think, is come
To give him hearing: is it four o'clock?
BISHOP OF ELY
It is.
ARCHBISHOP OF CANTERBURY
Then go we in, to know his embassy;
Which I could, with a ready guess, declare,
Before the Frenchman speak a word of it.
BISHOP OF ELY
I'll wait upon you; and I long to hear it.   [*Exeunt.*

SCENE II

The same. The Presence-chamber.

Enter KING HENRY, GLOSTER, BEDFORD,
EXETER, WARWICK, WESTMORELAND, *and*
ATTENDANTS.

KING HENRY
Where is my gracious Lord of Canterbury?
EXETER
Not here in presence.
KING HENRY
                          Send for him, good uncle.

WESTMORELAND
Shall we call in th'ambassador, my liege?
KING HENRY
Not yet, my cousin: we would be resolved,
Before we hear him, of some things of weight,
That task our thoughts, concerning us and France.

Enter the ARCHBISHOP OF CANTERBURY *and the*
BISHOP OF ELY.

ARCHBISHOP OF CANTERBURY
God and his angels guard your sacred throne,
And make you long become it!
KING HENRY
                          Sure, we thank you.
My learned lord, we pray you to proceed,
And justly and religiously unfold
Why the law Salique, that they have in France,
Or should, or should not, bar us in our claim:
And God forbid, my dear and faithful lord,
That you should fashion, wrest, or bow your reading,
Or nicely charge your understanding soul
With opening titles miscreate, whose right
Suits not in native colours with the truth;
For God doth know how many, now in health,
Shall drop their blood in approbation
Of what your reverence shall incite us to.
Therefore take heed how you impawn our person,
How you awake our sleeping sword of war:
We charge you, in the name of God, take heed;
For never two such kingdoms did contend
Without much fall of blood; whose guiltless drops
Are every one a woe, a sore complaint
'Gainst him whose wrongs give edge unto the swords
That make such waste in brief mortality.
Under this conjuration, speak, my lord;
For we will hear, note, and believe in heart
That what you speak is in your conscience wash'd
As pure as sin with baptism.
ARCHBISHOP OF CANTERBURY
Then hear me, gracious sovereign, — and you peers,
That owe yourselves, your lives, and services
To this imperial throne. — There is no bar
To make against your highness' claim to France
But this, which they produce from Pharamond, —
In terram Salicam mulieres ne succedant,
'No woman shall succeed in Salique land':
Which Salique land the French unjustly gloze
To be the realm of France, and Pharamond
The founder of this law and female bar.
Yet their own authors faithfully affirm
That the land Salique is in Germany,
Between the floods of Sala and of Elbe;
Where Charles the Great, having subdued the Saxons,
There left behind and settled certain French;
Who, holding in disdain the German women
For some dishonest manners of their life,
Establish'd then this law, — to wit, no female
Should be inheritrix in Salique land:
Which Salique, as I said, 'twixt Elbe and Sala,
Is at this day in Germany call'd Meisen.
Then doth it well appear, the Salique law
Was not devised for the realm of France:
Nor did the French possess the Salique land
Until four hundred one and twenty years
After defunction of King Pharamond,
Idly suppos'd the founder of this law;
Who died within the year of our redemption
Four hundred twenty-six; and Charles the Great
Subdued the Saxons, and did seat the French
Beyond the river Sala, in the year
Eight hundred five. Besides, their writers say,
King Pepin, which deposed Childeric,
Did, as heir general, being descended
Of Blithild, which was daughter to King Clothair,
Make claim and title to the crown of France.
Hugh Capet also, — who usurp'd the crown
Of Charles the Duke of Lorraine, sole heir male
Of the true line and stock of Charles the Great, —
To find his title with some shows of truth,
Though, in pure truth, it was corrupt and naught,
Convey'd himself as heir to th'Lady Lingare,
Daughter to Charlemain, who was the son
To Louis the emperor, and Louis the son
Of Charles the Great. Also King Louis the Tenth,
Who was sole heir to the usurper Capet,
Could not keep quiet in his conscience,
Wearing the crown of France, till satisfied
That fair Queen Isabel, his grandmother,
Was lineal of the Lady Ermengare,
Daughter to Charles the foresaid Duke of Lorraine:
By the which marriage the line of Charles the Great
Was re-united to the crown of France.

So that, as clear as is the summer's sun,
King Pepin's title, and Hugh Capet's claim,
King Louis his satisfaction, all appear
To hold in right and title of the female:
So do the kings of France unto this day;
Howbeit they would hold up this Salique law
To bar your highness claiming from the female;
And rather choose to hide them in a net
Than amply to imbar their crooked titles,
Usurp'd from you and your progenitors.
KING HENRY
May I with right and conscience make this claim?
ARCHBISHOP OF CANTERBURY
The sin upon my head, dread sovereign!
For in the Book of Numbers is it writ, —
When the man dies, let the inheritance
Descend unto the daughter. Gracious lord,
Stand for your own; unwind your bloody flag;
Look back into your mighty ancestors:
Go, my dread lord, to your great-grandsire's tomb,
From whom you claim; invoke his warlike spirit,
And your great-uncle's, Edward the Black Prince,
Who on the French ground play'd a tragedy,
Making defeat on the full power of France,
Whiles his most mighty father on a hill
Stood smiling to behold his lion's whelp
Forage in blood of French nobility.
O noble English, that could entertain
With half their forces the full pride of France,
And let another half stand laughing by,
All out of work and cold for action!
BISHOP OF ELY
Awake remembrance of these valiant dead,
And with your puissant arm renew their feats:
You are their heir; you sit upon their throne;
The blood and courage that renowned them
Runs in your veins; and my thrice-puissant liege
Is in the very May-morn of his youth,
Ripe for exploits and mighty enterprises.
EXETER
Your brother kings and monarchs of the earth
Do all expect that you should rouse yourself,
As did the former lions of your blood.
WESTMORELAND
They know your Grace hath cause and means and
          might;
So hath your highness; never king of England
Had nobles richer and more loyal subjects,
Whose hearts have left their bodies here in England,
And lie pavilion'd in the fields of France.
ARCHBISHOP OF CANTERBURY
O, let their bodies follow, my dear liege,
With blood and sword and fire to win your right:
In aid whereof we of the spirituality
Will raise your highness such a mighty sum
As never did the clergy at one time
Bring in to any of your ancestors.
KING HENRY
We must not only arm t'invade the French,
But lay down our proportions to defend
Against the Scot, who will make road upon us
With all advantages.
ARCHBISHOP OF CANTERBURY
They of those marches, gracious sovereign,
Shall be a wall sufficient to defend
Our inland from the pilfering borderers.
KING HENRY
We do not mean the coursing snatchers only,
But fear the main intendment of the Scot,
Who hath been still a giddy neighbour to us;
For you shall read that my great-grandfather
Never went with his forces into France,
But that the Scot on his unfurnish'd kingdom
Came pouring, like the tide into a breach,
With ample and brim fulness of his force;
Galling the gleaned land with hot assays,
Girding with grievous siege castles and towns;
That England, being empty of defence,
Hath shook and trembled at th'ill neighbourhood.
ARCHBISHOP OF CANTERBURY
She hath been then more fear'd than harm'd, my liege;
For hear her but exampled by herself: —
When all her chivalry hath been in France,
And she a mourning widow of her nobles,
She hath herself not only well defended,
But taken, and impounded as a stray,
The King of Scots; whom she did send to France,
To fill King Edward's fame with prisoner kings,
And make her chronicle as rich with praise
As is the ooze and bottom of the sea
With sunken wrack and sumless treasuries.

KING HENRY Tell the Dauphin, his jest will savour but of shallow wit, when thousands weep.

WESTMORELAND
But there's a saying, very old and true, —
　　'If that you will France win,
　　Then with Scotland first begin':
For once the eagle England being in prey,
To her unguarded nest the weasel Scot
Comes sneaking, and so sucks her princely eggs;
Playing the mouse in absence of the cat,
To spoil and havoc more than she can eat.

EXETER
It follows, then, the cat must stay at home:
Yet that is but a curs'd necessity,
Since we have locks to safeguard necessaries,
And pretty traps to catch the petty thieves.
While that the armed hand doth fight abroad,
Th'advised head defends itself at home;
For government, though high, and low, and lower,
Put into parts, doth keep in one concent,
Congreeing in a full and natural close,
Like music.

ARCHBISHOP OF CANTERBURY
　　　True: therefore doth heaven divide
The state of man in divers functions,
Setting endeavour in continual motion;
To which is fixed, as an aim or butt,
Obedience: for so work the honey-bees,
Creatures that, by a rule in nature, teach
The art of order to a peopled kingdom.
They have a king, and officers of sorts:
Where some, like magistrates, correct at home;
Others, like merchants, venture trade abroad;
Others, like soldiers, armed in their stings,
Make boot upon the summer's velvet buds;
Which pillage they with merry march bring home
To the tent-royal of their emperor:
Who, busied in his majesty, surveys
The singing masons building roofs of gold;
The civil citizens kneading-up the honey;
The poor mechanic porters crowding in
Their heavy burdens at his narrow gate;
The sad-eyed justice, with his surly hum,
Delivering o'er to executors pale
The lazy yawning drone. I this infer, —

That many things, having full reference
To one concent, may work contrariously:
As many arrows, loosed several ways,
Fly to one mark;
As many several ways meet in one town;
As many fresh streams meet in one self sea;
As many lines close in the dial's centre;
So may a thousand actions, once afoot,
End in one purpose, and be all well borne
Without defeat. Therefore to France, my liege.
Divide your happy England into four;
Whereof take you one quarter into France,
And you withal shall make all Gallia shake.
If we, with thrice such powers left at home,
Cannot defend our own doors from the dog,
Let us be worried, and our nation lose
The name of hardiness and policy.

KING HENRY
Call in the messengers sent from the Dauphin.
　　　　　[*Exeunt some* ATTENDANTS.
Now are we well resolv'd; and, by God's help,
And yours, the noble sinews of our power,
France being ours, we'll bend it to our awe,
Or break it all to pieces: or there we'll sit,
Ruling in large and ample empery
O'er France and all her almost kingly dukedoms,
Or lay these bones in an unworthy urn,
Tombless, with no remembrance over them:
Either our history shall with full mouth
Speak freely of our acts, or else our grave,
Like Turkish mute, shall have a tongueless mouth,
Not worshipp'd with a waxen epitaph.
　　　Enter AMBASSADORS *of France, attended.*
Now are we well prepared to know the pleasure
Of our fair cousin Dauphin; for we hear
Your greeting is from him, not from the king.

FIRST AMBASSADOR
May't please your majesty to give us leave
Freely to render what we have in charge;
Or shall we sparingly show you far off
The Dauphin's meaning and our embassy?

KING HENRY
We are no tyrant, but a Christian king;

Unto whose grace our passion is as subject
As are our wretches fetter'd in our prisons:
Therefore with frank and with uncurbed plainness
Tell us the Dauphin's mind.

FIRST AMBASSADOR
　　　　　Thus, then, in few.
Your highness, lately sending into France,
Did claim some certain dukedoms, in the right
Of your great predecessor, King Edward the Third.
In answer of which claim, the prince our master
Says, that you savour too much of your youth;
And bids you be advis'd, there's naught in France
That can be with a nimble galliard won; —
You cannot revel into dukedoms there.
He therefore sends you, meeter for your spirit,
This tun of treasure; and, in lieu of this,
Desires you let the dukedoms that you claim
Hear no more of you. This the Dauphin speaks.

KING HENRY
What treasure, uncle?

EXETER
　　　　　Tennis-balls, my liege.

KING HENRY
We are glad the Dauphin is so pleasant with us;
His present and your pains we thank you for:
When we have match'd our rackets to these balls,
We will, in France, by God's grace, play a set
Shall strike his father's crown into the hazard.
Tell him he hath made a match with such a wrangler
That all the courts of France will be disturb'd
With chases. And we understand him well,
How he comes o'er us with our wilder days,
Not measuring what use we made of them.
We never valued this poor seat of England;
And therefore, living hence, did give ourself
To barbarous licence; as 'tis ever common
That men are merriest when they are from home.
But tell the Dauphin, I will keep my state,
Be like a king, and show my sail of greatness,
When I do rouse me in my throne of France:
For that I have laid by my majesty,
And plodded like a man for working-days;
But I will rise there with so full a glory,
That I will dazzle all the eyes of France,
Yea, strike the Dauphin blind to look on us.
And tell the pleasant prince, this mock of his
Hath turn'd his balls to gun-stones; and his soul
Shall stand sore charged for the wasteful vengeance
That shall fly with them: for many a thousand widows
Shall this his mock mock out of their dear husbands;
Mock mothers from their sons, mock castles down;
And some are yet ungotten and unborn
That shall have cause to curse the Dauphin's scorn.
But this lies all within the will of God,
To whom I do appeal; and in whose name,
Tell you the Dauphin, I am coming on,
To venge me as I may, and to put forth
My rightful hand in a well-hallow'd cause.
So, get you hence in peace; and tell the Dauphin,
His jest will savour but of shallow wit,
When thousands weep, more than did laugh at it. —
Convey them with safe conduct. — Fare you well.
　　　　　[*Exeunt* AMBASSADORS.

EXETER
This was a merry message.

KING HENRY
We hope to make the sender blush at it.
Therefore, my lords, omit no happy hour
That may give furtherance to our expedition;
For we have now no thought in us but France,
Save those to God, that run before our business.
Therefore let our proportions for these wars
Be soon collected, and all things thought upon
That may with reasonable swiftness add
More feathers to our wings; for, God before,
We'll chide this Dauphin at his father's door.
Therefore let every man now task his thought,
That this fair action may on foot be brought.
　　　　　[*Flourish. Exeunt.*

ACT II

PROLOGUE

Enter CHORUS.

CHORUS
Now all the youth of England are on fire,
And silken dalliance in the wardrobe lies:
Now thrive the armourers, and honour's thought
Reigns solely in the breast of every man:

They sell the pasture now to buy the horse;
Following the mirror of all Christian kings,
With winged heels, as English Mercuries.
For now sits Expectation in the air,
And hides a sword from hilts unto the point
With crowns imperial, crowns, and coronets,
Promis'd to Harry and his followers.
The French, advis'd by good intelligence
Of this most dreadful preparation,
Shake in their fear; and with pale policy
Seek to divert the English purposes.
O England! — model to thy inward greatness,
Like little body with a mighty heart, —
What mightst thou do, that honour would thee do,
Were all thy children kind and natural!
But see thy fault! France hath in thee found out
A nest of hollow bosoms, which he fills
With treacherous crowns; and three corrupted men, —
One, Richard Earl of Cambridge; and the second,
Henry Lord Scroop of Masham; and the third,
Sir Thomas Grey, knight, of Northumberland, —
Have, for the gilt of France — O guilt indeed! —
Confirm'd conspiracy with fearful France;
And by their hands this grace of kings must die,
If hell and treason hold their promises,
Ere he take ship for France, and in Southampton.
Linger your patience on; and we'll digest
Th'abuse of distance; force a play.
The sum is paid; the traitors are agreed;
The king is set from London; and the scene
Is now transported, gentles, to Southampton, —
There is the playhouse now, there must you sit:
And thence to France shall we convey you safe,
And bring you back, charming the narrow seas
To give you gentle pass; for, if we may,
We'll not offend one stomach with our play.
But, till the king come forth, and not till then,
Unto Southampton do we shift our scene.   [*Exit.*

SCENE I

London. Before the Boar's-Head Tavern, Eastcheap.

Enter CORPORAL NYM *and* LIEUTENANT
BARDOLPH.

BARDOLPH
Well met, Corporal Nym.
NYM
Good morrow, Lieutenant Bardolph.
BARDOLPH
What, are Ancient Pistol and you friends yet?
NYM
For my part, I care not: I say little; but when time shall
serve, there shall be smites; — but that shall be as it
may. I dare not fight; but I will wink, and hold out mine
iron: it is a simple one; but what though? it will toast
cheese, and it will endure cold as another man's sword
will: and there's the humour of it.
BARDOLPH
I will bestow a breakfast to make you friends; and we'll
be all three sworn brothers to France: let's it be so, good
Corporal Nym.
NYM
Faith, I will live so long as I may, that's the certain of it;
and when I cannot live any longer, I will do as I may:
that is my rest, that is the rendezvous of it.
BARDOLPH
It is certain, corporal, that he is married to Nell Quickly:
and, certainly, she did you wrong; for you were
troth-plight to her.
NYM
I cannot tell: — things must be as they may: men may
sleep, and they may have their throats about them at
that time; and, some say, knives have edges. It must be
as it may: though patience be a tired mare, yet she will
plod. There must be conclusions. Well, I cannot tell.
BARDOLPH
Here comes Ancient Pistol and his wife: — good
corporal, be patient here.
                    Enter PISTOL *and* HOSTESS.
How now, mine host Pistol!
PISTOL
Base tike, call'st thou me host?
Now, by this hand, I swear, I scorn the term;
Nor shall my Nell keep lodgers.
HOSTESS
No, by my troth, not long; for we cannot lodge and board
a dozen or fourteen gentlewomen that live honestly by
the prick of their needles, but it will be thought we keep a
bawdy-house straight. [NYM *and* PISTOL *draw.*] O

well-a-day, Lady, if he be not drawn now! We shall see
wilful adultery and murder committed.
BARDOLPH
Good lieutenant, — good corporal, — offer nothing
here.
NYM
Pish!
PISTOL
Pish for thee, Iceland dog! thou prick-ear'd cur of Iceland!
HOSTESS
Good Corporal Nym, show thy valour, and put up your
sword.
NYM
Will you shog off? I would have you *solus.*
PISTOL
Solus, egregious dog? O viper vile!
The *solus* in thy most mervailous face;
The *solus* in thy teeth, and in thy throat,
And in thy hateful lungs, yea, in thy maw, perdy,
And, which is worse, within thy nasty mouth!
I do retort the *solus* in thy bowels;
For I can take, and Pistol's cock is up,
And flashing fire will follow.
NYM
I am not Barbason; you cannot conjure me. I have an
humour to knock you indifferently well. If you grow
foul with me, Pistol, I will scour you with my rapier, as
I may, in fair terms: if you would walk off, I would prick
your guts a little, in good terms, as I may: and that's the
humour of it.
PISTOL
O braggart vile, and damned furious wight!
The grave doth gape, and doting death is near;
Therefore exhale.
BARDOLPH
Hear me, hear me what I say: — he that strikes the first
stroke, I'll run him up to the hilts, as I am a soldier.
                    [*Draws.*
PISTOL
An oath of mickle might; and fury shall abate. —
Give me thy fist, thy fore-foot to me give:
Thy spirits are most tall.   [*They sheath their swords.*
NYM
I will cut thy throat, one time or other, in fair terms:
that is the humour of it.
PISTOL
Couple a gorge!
That is the word. I thee defy again.
O hound of Crete, think'st thou my spouse to get?
No; to the spital go,
And from the powdering-tub of infamy
Fetch forth the lazar kite of Cressid's kind,
Doll Tearsheet she by name, and her espouse:
I have, and I will hold, the *quondam* Quickly
For the only she; and — *pauca,* there's enough.
Go to.

                    Enter BOY.

BOY
Mine host Pistol, you must come to my master, — and
you, hostess: — he is very sick, and would to bed. — Good
Bardolph, put thy face between his sheets, and do the
office of a warming-pan. — Faith, he's very ill.
BARDOLPH
Away, you rogue!
HOSTESS
By my troth, he'll yield the crow a pudding one of these
days: the king has kill'd his heart. — Good husband,
come home presently.
                    [*Exeunt* HOSTESS *and* BOY.
BARDOLPH
Come, shall I make you two friends? We must to
France together: why the devil should we keep knives
to cut one another's throats?
PISTOL
Let floods o'erswell, and fiends for food howl on!
NYM
You'll pay me the eight shillings I won of you at
betting?
PISTOL
Base is the slave that pays.
NYM
That now I will have: that's the humour of it.
PISTOL
As manhood shall compound: push home.
                    [*They draw.*
BARDOLPH
By this sword, he that makes the first thrust, I'll kill
him; by this sword, I will.   [*Draws.*

PISTOL
Sword is an oath, and oaths must have their course.
BARDOLPH
Corporal Nym, an thou wilt be friends, be friends: an
thou wilt not, why, then, be enemies with me too.
Prithee, put up.
NYM
I shall have my eight shillings I won of you at betting?
PISTOL
A noble shalt thou have, and present pay;
And liquor likewise will I give to thee,
And friendship shall combine and brotherhood;
I'll live by Nym, and Nym shall live by me; —
Is not this just? — for I shall sutler be
Unto the camp, and profits will accrue.
Give me thy hand.   [*They sheathe their swords.*
NYM
I shall have my noble?
PISTOL
In cash most justly paid.
NYM
Well, then, that's the humour of it.

                    Enter HOSTESS.

HOSTESS
As ever you came of women, come in quickly to Sir
John. Ah, poor heart! he is so shaked of a burning
quotidian tertian, that it is most lamentable to behold.
Sweet men, come to him.
NYM
The king hath run bad humours on the knight, that's
the even of it.
PISTOL
Nym, thou hast spoke the right;
His heart is fracted and corroborate.
NYM
The king is a good king: but it must be as it may; he
passes some humours and careers.
PISTOL
Let us condole the knight; for, lambkins, we will live.
                    [*Exeunt.*

SCENE II

Southampton. A council-chamber.

Enter EXETER, BEDFORD, *and* WESTMORELAND.

BEDFORD
'Fore God, his Grace is bold, to trust these traitors.
EXETER
They shall be apprehended by and by.
WESTMORELAND
How smooth and even they do bear themselves!
As if allegiance in their bosoms sat,
Crowned with faith and constant loyalty.
BEDFORD
The king hath note of all that they intend,
By interception which they dream not of.
EXETER
Nay, but the man that was his bedfellow,
Whom he hath dull'd and cloy'd with gracious favours,
That he should, for a foreign purse, so sell
His sovereign's life to death and treachery!
Trumpets sound. Enter KING HENRY, CAMBRIDGE,
SCROOP, GREY, LORDS, *and* ATTENDANTS.
KING HENRY
Now sits the wind fair, and we will aboard.
My Lord of Cambridge, — and my kind Lord of
Masham, —
And you, my gentle knight, — give me your thoughts:
Think you not that the powers we bear with us
Will cut their passage through the force of France,
Doing the execution and the act
For which we have in head assembled them?
SCROOP
No doubt, my liege, if each man do his best.
KING HENRY
I doubt not that; since we are well persuaded
We carry not a heart with us from hence
That grows not in a fair consent with ours,
Nor leave not one behind that doth not wish
Success and conquest to attend on us.
CAMBRIDGE
Never was monarch better fear'd and lov'd
Than is your majesty: there's not, I think, a subject,
That sits in heart-grief and uneasiness
Under the sweet shade of your government.
GREY
True: those that were your father's enemies
Have steep'd their galls in honey, and do serve you
With hearts create of duty and of zeal.

KING HENRY

We therefore have great cause of thankfulness;
And shall forget the office of our hand,
Sooner than quittance of desert and merit
According to the weight and worthiness.

SCROOP

So service shall with steeled sinews toil,
And labour shall refresh itself with hope,
To do your Grace incessant services.

KING HENRY

We judge no less. — uncle of Exeter,
Enlarge the man committed yesterday,
That rail'd against our person: we consider
It was excess of wine that set him on;
And, on his more advice, we pardon him.

SCROOP

That's mercy, but too much security:
Let him be punish'd, sovereign; lest example
Breed, by his sufferance, more of such a kind.

KING HENRY

O, let us yet be merciful.

CAMBRIDGE

So may your highness, and yet punish too.

GREY

Sir, you show great mercy, if you give him life,
After the taste of much correction.

KING HENRY

Alas, your too much love and care of me
Are heavy orisons 'gainst this poor wretch!
If little faults, proceeding on distemper,
Shall not be wink'd at, how shall we stretch our eye
When capital crimes, chew'd, swallow'd, and digested,
Appear before us? — We'll yet enlarge that man,
Though Cambridge, Scroop, and Grey, in their dear
        care
And tender preservation of our person,
Would have him punish'd. And now to our French
        causes:
Who are the late commissioners?

CAMBRIDGE

I one, my lord:
Your highness bade me ask for it to-day.

SCROOP

So did you me, my liege.

GREY

And me, my royal sovereign.

KING HENRY

Then, Richard Earl of Cambridge, there is yours; —
There yours, Lord Scroop of Masham; — and, sir
        knight,
Grey of Northumberland, this same is yours: —
Read them; and know, I know your worthiness. —
My Lord of Westmoreland, and uncle Exeter,
We will aboard to-night. — Why, how now, gentlemen!
What see you in those papers, that you lose
So much complexion? — Look ye, how they change!
Their cheeks are paper. — Why, what read you there,
That hath so cowarded and chas'd your blood
Out of appearance?

CAMBRIDGE

                I do confess my fault;
And do submit me to your highness' mercy.

GREY and **SCROOP**

To which we all appeal.

KING HENRY

The mercy that was quick in us but late,
By your own counsel is suppress'd and kill'd:
You must not dare, for shame, to talk of mercy;
For your own reasons turn into your bosoms,
As dogs upon their masters, worrying you. —
See you, my princes and my noble peers,
These English monsters! My Lord of Cambridge here, —
You know how apt our love was to accord
To furnish him with all appertinents
Belonging to his honour; and this man
Hath, for a few light crowns, lightly conspired,
And sworn unto the practices of France,
To kill us here in Hampton: to the which
This knight, no less for bounty bound to us
Than Cambridge is, hath likewise sworn. — But, O,
What shall I say to thee, Lord Scroop? thou cruel,
Ingrateful, savage, and inhuman creature!
Thou that didst bear the key of all my counsels,
That knew'st the very bottom of my soul,
That almost mightst have coin'd me into gold,
Wouldst thou have practis'd on me for thy use, —
May it be possible, that foreign hire
Could out of thee extract one spark of evil
That might annoy my finger? 'tis so strange,
That, though the truth of it stands off as gross

As black and white, my eye will scarcely see it.
Treason and murder ever kept together,
As two yoke-devils sworn to either's purpose,
Working so grossly in a natural cause,
That admiration did not whoop at them:
But thou, 'gainst all proportion, didst bring in
Wonder to wait on treason and on murder:
And whatsoever cunning fiend it was
That wrought upon thee so preposterously,
Hath got the voice in hell for excellence:
All other devils, that suggest by treasons,
Do botch and bungle up damnation
With patches, colours, and with forms being fetch'd
From glistering semblances of piety;
But he that temper'd thee bade thee stand up,
Gave thee no instance why thou shouldst do treason,
Unless to dub thee with the name of traitor.
If that same demon that hath gull'd thee thus
Should with his lion-gait walk the whole world,
He might return to vasty Tartar back,
And tell the legions, 'I can never win
A soul so easy as that Englishman's.'
O, how hast thou with jealousy infected
The sweetness of affiance! Show men dutiful?
Why, so didst thou: seem they grave and learned?
Why, so didst thou: come they of noble family?
Why, so didst thou: seem they religious?
Why, so didst thou: or are they spare in diet;
Free from gross passion, or of mirth or anger;
Constant in spirit, not swerving with the blood;
Garnish'd and deck'd in modest complement;
Not working with the eye without the ear,
And but in purged judgement trusting neither?
Such and so finely bolted didst thou seem:
And thus thy fall hath left a kind of blot,
To mark the full-fraught man and best indued
With some suspicion. I will weep for thee;
For this revolt of thine, methinks, is like
Another fall of man. — Their faults are open:
Arrest them to the answer of the law; —
And God acquit them of their practices!

EXETER

I arrest thee of high treason, by the name of Richard
        Earl of Cambridge.
I arrest thee of high treason, by the name of
        Henry Lord Scroop of Masham.
I arrest thee of high treason, by the name of
        Thomas Grey, knight, of Northumberland.

SCROOP

Our purposes God justly hath discover'd;
And I repent my fault more than my death;
Which I beseech your highness to forgive,
Although my body pay the price of it.

CAMBRIDGE

For me, — the gold of France did not seduce;
Although I did admit it as a motive
The sooner to effect what I intended;
But God be thanked for prevention;
Which I in sufferance heartily will rejoice,
Beseeching God and you to pardon me.

GREY

Never did faithful subject more rejoice
At the discovery of most dangerous treason
Than I do at this hour joy o'er myself,
Prevented from a damned enterprise:
My fault, but not my body, pardon, sovereign.

KING HENRY

God quit you in his mercy! Hear your sentence.
You have conspired against our royal person,
Join'd with an enemy proclaim'd, and from his coffers
Receiv'd the golden earnest of our death;
Wherein you would have sold your king to slaughter,
His princes and his peers to servitude,
His subjects to oppression and contempt,
And his whole kingdom into desolation.
Touching our person, seek we no revenge;
But we our kingdom's safety must so tender,
Whose ruin you have sought, that to her laws
We do deliver you. Get you, therefore, hence,
Poor miserable wretches, to your death:
The taste whereof, God of his mercy give
You patience to endure, and true repentance
Of all your dear offences! — Bear them hence.
        [*Exeunt* CAMBRIDGE, SCROOP, *and* GREY, *guarded.*
Now, lords, for France; the enterprise whereof
Shall be to you as us like glorious.
We doubt not of a fair and lucky war,
Since God so graciously hath brought to light
This dangerous treason, lurking in our way
To hinder our beginnings; we doubt not now
But every rub is smoothed on our way.

Then, forth, dear countrymen: let us deliver
Our puissance into the hand of God,
Putting it straight in expedition.
Cheerly to sea; the signs of war advance:
No king of England, if not king of France.   [*Exeunt.*

SCENE III

London. Before the Boar's-Head Tavern, Eastcheap.

Enter PISTOL, HOSTESS, NYM, BARDOLPH, *and*
BOY.

HOSTESS

Prithee, honey-sweet husband, let me bring thee to
Staines.

PISTOL

No; for my manly heart doth yearn. —
Bardolph, be blithe; — Nym, rouse thy vaunting veins; —
Boy, bristle thy courage up; — for Falstaff he is dead,
And we must yearn therefore.

BARDOLPH

Would I were with him, wheresome'er he is, either in
heaven or in hell!

HOSTESS

Nay, sure, he's not in hell: he's in Arthur's bosom, if
ever man went to Arthur's bosom. A' made a finer
end, and went away, an it had been any christom
child; a' parted ev'n just between twelve and one, ev'n
at the turning o'th'tide: for after I saw him fumble
with the sheets, and play with flowers, and smile
upon his fingers' ends, I knew there was but one way;
for his nose was as sharp as a pen, and a' babbled of
green fields. 'How now, sir John!' quoth I: 'what,
man! be o' good cheer.' So a' cried out 'God, God,
God!' three or four times. Now I, to comfort him, bid
him a' should not think of God; I hoped there was no
need to trouble himself with any such thoughts yet.
So a' bade me lay more clothes on his feet: I put my
hand into the bed and felt them, and they were as cold
as any stone; then I felt to his knees, and they were as
cold as any stone, and so upward and upward, and all
was as cold as any stone.

NYM

They say he cried out of sack.

HOSTESS

Ay, that a' did.

BARDOLPH

And of women.

HOSTESS

Nay, that a' did not.

BOY

Yes, that a' did; and said they were devils incarnate.

HOSTESS

A' could never abide carnation; 'twas a colour he
never liked.

BOY

A' said once, the devil would have him about women.

HOSTESS

A' did in some sort, indeed, handle women; but then he
was rheumatic, and talk'd of the whore of Babylon.

BOY

Do you not remember, a' saw a flea stick upon Bardolph's
nose, and a' said it was a black soul burning in
hell-fire?

BARDOLPH

Well, the fuel is gone that maintain'd that fire: that's all
the riches I got in his service.

NYM

Shall we shog? the king will be gone from
Southampton.

PISTOL

Come, let's away. — My love, give me thy lips.
Look to my chattels and my movables:
Let senses rule; the word is 'Pitch and Pay';
Trust none;
For oaths are straws, men's faiths are wafer-cakes,
And hold-fast is the only dog, my duck:
Therefore, *caveto* be thy counsellor.
Go, clear thy crystals. — Yoke-fellows in arms,
Let us to France; like horse-leeches, my boys,
To suck, to suck, the very blood to suck!

BOY

And that's but unwholesome food, they say.

PISTOL

Touch her soft mouth, and march.

BARDOLPH

Farewell, hostess.   [*Kissing her.*

NYM

I cannot kiss, that is the humour of it; but, adieu.

PISTOL
Let housewifery appear: keep close, I thee command.
HOSTESS
Farewell; adieu.   [*Exeunt.*

SCENE IV

France. A room in the French KING'S *palace.*

Flourish. Enter the FRENCH KING, *the* DAUPHIN, *the*
DUKE OF BURGUNDY, *the* CONSTABLE, *and others.*

FRENCH KING
Thus comes the English with full power upon us;
And more than carefully it us concerns
To answer royally in our defences.
Therefore the Dukes of Berri and of Bretagne,
Of Brabant and of Orleans, shall make forth, —
And you, Prince Dauphin, — with all swift dispatch,
To line and new repair our towns of war
With men of courage and with means defendant;
For England his approaches makes as fierce
As waters to the sucking of a gulf.
It fits us, then, to be as provident
As fear may teach us, out of late examples
Left by the fatal and neglected English
Upon our fields.
DAUPHIN
                    My most redoubted father,
It is most meet we arm us 'gainst the foe;
For peace itself should not so dull a kingdom,
Though war nor no known quarrel were in question,
But that defences, musters, preparations,
Should be maintain'd, assembled, and collected,
As were a war in expectation.
Therefore, I say 'tis meet we all go forth
To view the sick and feeble parts of France:
And let us do it with no show of fear;
No, with no more than if we heard that England
Were busied with a Whitsun morris-dance:
For, my good liege, she is so idly king'd,
Her sceptre so fantastically borne
By a vain, giddy, shallow, humorous youth,
That fear attends her not.
CONSTABLE
                    O peace, Prince Dauphin!
You are too much mistaken in this king:
Question your Grace the late ambassadors, —
With what great state he heard their embassy,
How well supplied with noble counsellors,
How modest in exception, and withal
How terrible in constant resolution, —
And you shall find his vanities forespent
Were but the outside of the Roman Brutus,
Covering discretion with a coat of folly;
As gardeners do with ordure hide those roots
That shall first spring and be most delicate.
DAUPHIN
Well, 'tis not so, my lord high-constable;
But though we think it so, it is no matter:
In cases of defence 'tis best to weigh
The enemy more mighty than he seems:
So the proportions of defence are fill'd;
Which, of a weak and niggardly projection,
Doth, like a miser, spoil his coat with scanting
A little cloth.
FRENCH KING
                    Think we King Harry strong;
And princes, look you strongly arm to meet him.
The kindred of him hath been flesh'd upon us;
And he is bred out of that bloody strain
That haunted us in our familiar paths:
Witness our too-much memorable shame
When Cressy battle fatally was struck,
And all our princes captiv'd by the hand
Of that black name, Edward, Black Prince of Wales;
Whiles that his mountain sire, — on mountain
          standing,
Up in the air, crown'd with the golden sun, —
Saw his heroical seed, and smil'd to see him,
Mangle the work of nature, and deface
The patterns that by God and by French fathers
Had twenty years been made. This is a stem
Of that victorious stock; and let us fear
The native mightiness and fate of him.
                    Enter a MESSENGER.
MESSENGER
Ambassadors from Harry king of England
Do crave admittance to your majesty.
FRENCH KING
We'll give them present audience. Go, and bring them.
                    [*Exeunt* MESSENGER *and certain* LORDS.
You see this chase is hotly follow'd, friends.

DAUPHIN
Turn head, and stop pursuit; for coward dogs
Most spend their mouths, when what they seem to
          threaten
Runs far before them. Good my sovereign,
Take up the English short; and let them know
Of what a monarchy you are the head:
Self-love, my liege, is not so vile a sin
As self-neglecting.

          Enter LORDS, *with* EXETER *and* TRAIN.

FRENCH KING
                    From our brother England?
EXETER
From him; and thus he greets your majesty.
He wills you, in the name of God Almighty,
That you divest yourself, and lay apart
The borrow'd glories, that, by gift of heaven,
By law of nature and of nations, 'longs
To him and to his heirs; namely, the crown,
And all wide-stretched honours that pertain,
By custom and the ordinance of times,
Unto the crown of France. That you may know
'Tis no sinister nor no awkward claim,
Pick'd from the worm-holes of long-vanish'd days,
Nor from the dust of old oblivion rak'd,
He sends you this most memorable line,
                                        [*Gives a paper.*
In every branch truly demonstrative;
Willing to overlook this pedigree:
And when you find him evenly derived
From his most fam'd of famous ancestors,
Edward the Third, he bids you then resign
Your crown and kingdom, indirectly held
From him the native and true challenger.
FRENCH KING
Or else what follows?
EXETER
Bloody constraint; for if you hide the crown
Even in your hearts, there will he rake for it:
Therefore in fierce tempest is he coming,
In thunder and in earthquake, like a Jove,
That, if requiring fail, he will compel;
And bids you, in the bowels of the Lord,
Deliver up the crown; and to take mercy
On the poor souls for whom this hungry war
Opens his vasty jaws: and on your head
Turns he the widows' tears, the orphans' cries,
The dead men's blood, the pining maidens' groans,
For husbands, fathers, and betrothed lovers,
That shall be swallow'd in this controversy.
This is his claim, his threatening, and my message;
Unless the Dauphin be in presence here,
To whom expressly I bring greeting too.
FRENCH KING
For us, we will consider of this further:
To-morrow shall you bear our full intent
Back to our brother England.
DAUPHIN
                    For the Dauphin,
I stand here for him: what to him from England?
EXETER
Scorn and defiance; slight regard, contempt,
And any thing that may not misbecome
The mighty sender, doth he prize you at.
Thus says my king: an if your father's highness
Do not, in grant of all demands at large,
Sweeten the bitter mock you sent his majesty,
He'll call you to so hot an answer of it,
That caves and womby vaultages of France
Shall chide your trespass, and return your mock
In second accent of his ordnance.
DAUPHIN
Say, if my father render fair return,
It is against my will; for I desire
Nothing but odds with England: to that end,
As matching to his youth and vanity,
I did present him with the Paris balls.
EXETER
He'll make your Paris Louvre shake for it,
Were it the mistress-court of mighty Europe:
And, be assured, you'll find a difference,
As we, his subjects, have in wonder found,
Between the promise of his greener days
And these he masters now: now he weighs time,
Even to the utmost grain: — that you shall read
In your own losses, if he stay in France.
FRENCH KING
To-morrow shall you know our mind at full.
EXETER
Dispatch us with all speed, lest that our king

Come here himself to question our delay;
For he is footed in this land already.
FRENCH KING
You shall be soon dispatch'd with fair conditions:
A night is but small breath and little pause
To answer matters of this consequence.
                    [*Flourish. Exeunt.*

ACT III

PROLOGUE

Enter CHORUS.

CHORUS
Thus with imagin'd wing our swift scene flies,
In motion of no less celerity
Than that of thought. Suppose that you have seen
The well-appointed king at Hampton pier
Embark his royalty; and his brave fleet
With silken streamers the young Phœbus fanning:
Play with your fancies; and in them behold
Upon the hempen tackle ship-boys climbing;
Hear the shrill whistle which doth order give
To sounds confus'd; behold the threaden sails,
Borne with th'invisible and creeping wind,
Draw the huge bottoms through the furrow'd sea,
Breasting the lofty surge: O, do but think
You stand upon the rivage, and behold
A city on th'inconstant billows dancing;
For so appears this fleet majestical,
Holding due course to Harfleur. Follow, follow!
Grapple your minds to sternage of this navy;
And leave your England, as dead midnight still,
Guarded with grandsires, babies, and old women,
Either past, or not arriv'd to, pith and puissance;
For who is he, whose chin is but enrich'd
With one appearing hair, that will not follow
These cull'd and choice-drawn cavaliers to France?
Work, work your thoughts, and therein see a siege;
Behold the ordnance on their carriages,
With fatal mouths gaping on girded Harfleur.
Suppose th'ambassador from the French comes back;
Tells Harry that the king doth offer him
Katharine his daughter; and with her, to dowry,
Some petty and unprofitable dukedoms.
The offer likes not: and the nimble gunner
With linstock now the devilish cannon touches,
                    [*Alarum, and chambers go off, within.*
And down goes all before them. Still be kind,
And eke out our performance with your mind.   [*Exit.*

SCENE I

France. Before Harfleur.

Alarums. Enter KING HENRY, EXETER, BEDFORD,
GLOSTER, *and* SOLDIERS, *with scaling-ladders.*

KING HENRY
Once more unto the breach, dear friends, once more;
Or close the wall up with our English dead!
In peace there's nothing so becomes a man
As modest stillness and humility:
But when the blast of war blows in our ears,
Then imitate the action of the tiger;
Stiffen the sinews, summon up the blood,
Disguise fair nature with hard-favour'd rage:
Then lend the eye a terrible aspect;
Let it pry through the portage of the head
Like the brass cannon; let the brow o'erwhelm it
As fearfully as doth a galled rock
O'erhang and jutty his confounded base,
Swill'd with the wild and wasteful ocean.
Now set the teeth, and stretch the nostril wide;
Hold hard the breath, and bend up every spirit
To his full height! — On, on, you noble English,
Whose blood is fet from fathers of war-proof! —
Fathers that, like so many Alexanders,
Have in these parts from morn till even fought,
And sheath'd their swords for lack of argument: —
Dishonour not your mothers; now attest
That those whom you call'd fathers did beget you!
Be copy now to men of grosser blood,
And teach them how to war! — And you, good yeoman,
Whose limbs were made in England, show us here
The mettle of your pasture; let us swear
That you are worth your breeding: which I doubt not;
For there is none of you so mean and base,
That hath not noble lustre in your eyes.
I see you stand like greyhounds in the slips,
Straining upon the start. The game's afoot:
Follow your spirit; and, upon this charge,
Cry 'God for Harry, England, and Saint George!'
                    [*Exeunt. Alarum, and chambers go off, within.*

SCENE II.

The same.

Enter NYM, BARDOLPH, PISTOL, *and* BOY.

BARDOLPH
On, on, on, on, on! to the breach, to the breach!

NYM
Pray thee, corporal, stay: the knocks are too hot; and, for
mine own part, I have not a case of lives: the humour of it
is too hot, that is the very plain-song of it.

PISTOL
The plain-song is most just; for humours do abound;
Knocks go and come; God's vassals drop and die;
      And sword and shield,
        In bloody field,
      Doth win immortal fame.

BOY
Would I were in an alehouse in London! I would give
  all my fame for a pot of ale and safety.

PISTOL
And I:
      If wishes would prevail with me,
      My purpose should not fail with me,
        But thither would I hie.

BOY
      As duly, but not as truly,
      As bird doth sing on bough.
         Enter FLUELLEN.

FLUELLEN
God's plood! — Up to the preaches, you rascals! will
you not up to the preaches?
              [Driving them forward.

PISTOL
Be merciful, great duke, to men of mould!
Abate thy rage, abate thy manly rage!
Abate thy rage, great duke!
Good bawcock, bate thy rage! use lenity, sweet chuck!

NYM
These be good humours! — your honour runs bad
humours.
  [Exeunt NYM, BARDOLPH, *and* PISTOL, *driven in by*
                  FLUELLEN.

BOY
As young as I am, I have observed these three
swashers. I am boy to them all three: but all they three,
though they would serve me, could not be man to me;
for, indeed, three such antics do not amount to a man.
For Bardolph, — he is white-liver'd and red-faced; by
the means whereof a' faces it out, but fights not. For
Pistol, — he hath a killing tongue and a quiet sword; by
the means whereof a' break words, and keeps whole
weapons. For Nym, — he hath heard that men of few
words are the best men; and therefore he scorns to say
his prayers, lest a' should be thought a coward: but his
few bad words are match'd with as few good deeds; for
a' never broke any man's head but his own, and that
was against a post when he was drunk. They will steal
any thing, and call it purchase. Bardolph stole a
lute-case, bore it twelve leagues, and sold it for
three-half-pence. Nym and Bardolph are sworn
brothers in filching; and in Calais they stole a
fire-shovel: I knew by that piece of service the men
would carry coals. They would have me as familiar with
men's pockets as their gloves or their handkerchers:
which makes much against my manhood, if I should
take from another's pocket to put into mine; for it is
plain pocketing-up of wrongs. I must leave them, and
seek some better service: their villany goes against my
weak stomach, and therefore I must cast it up.
                        [Exit.

Enter FLUELLEN, GOWER *following.*

GOWER
Captain Fluellen, you must come presently to the
mines; the Duke of Gloster would speak with you.

FLUELLEN
To the mines! tell you the duke, it is not so good to
come to the mines; for, look you, the mines is not
according to the disciplines of the war: the concavities
of it is not sufficient; for, look you, th'athversary — you
may discuss unto the duke, look you — is digg'd
himself four yard under the countermines: by Cheshu,
I think a' will plough up all, if there is not petter
directions.

GOWER
The Duke of Gloster, to whom the order of the siege is
given, is altogether directed by an Irishman, — a very
valiant gentleman, i'faith.

FLUELLEN
It is Captain Macmorris, is it not?

GOWER
I think it be.

FLUELLEN
By Cheshu, he is an ass, as in the 'orld: I will verify as
much in his peard: he has no more directions in the
true disciplines of the wars, look you, of the Roman
disciplines, than is a puppy-dog.

GOWER
Here a' comes; and the Scots captain, Captain Jamy,
with him.

FLUELLEN
Captain Jamy is a marvellous falorous gentleman, that
is certain; and of great expedition and knowledge in
th'auncient wars, upon my particular knowledge of his
directions: by Cheshu, he will maintain his argument
as well as any military man in the 'orld, in the
disciplines of the pristine wars of the Romans.

Enter MACMORRIS *and* JAMY.

JAMY
I say gude-day, Captain Fluellen.

FLUELLEN
Got-den to your worship, goot Captain Jamy.

GOWER
How now, Captain Macmorris! have you quit the
mines? have the pioners given o'er?

MACMORRIS
By Chrish, la, tish ill done; the work ish give over, the
trompet sound the retreat. By my hand, I swear, and
my father's soul, the work ish ill done; it ish give over: I
would have blow'd up the town, so Chrish save me, la,
in an hour: O, tish ill done, tish ill done; by my hand,
tish ill done!

FLUELLEN
Captain Macmorris, I peseech you now, will you
voutsafe me, look you, a few disputations with you, as
partly touching or concerning the disciplines of the
war, the Roman wars, in the way of argument, look
you, and friendly communication; partly to satisfy my
opinion, and partly for the satisfaction, look you, of my
mind, as touching the direction of the military
discipline; that is the point.

JAMY
It sall be vary gude, gude feith, gud captains baith: and
I sall quit you with gude leve, as I may pick occasion;
that sall I, marry.

MACMORRIS
It is no time to discourse, so Chrish save me: the day is
hot, and the weather, and the wars, and the king, and
the dukes: it is no time to discourse. The town is
beseech'd, and the trompet call us to the breach; and
we talk, and, be Chrish, do nothing: 'tis shame for us
all: so God sa' me, 'tis shame to stand still; it is shame,
by my hand: and there is throats to be cut, and works to
be done; and there ish nothing done, so Chrish sa' me,
la.

JAMY
By the mess, ere theise eyes of mine take themselves to
slomber, ay'll de gude service, or ay'll lig i'th'grund for
it; ay, or go to death; and ay'll pay't as valorously as I
may, that sall I suerly do, that is the breff and the long.
Marry, I wad full fain heard some question 'tween you
tway.

FLUELLEN
Captain Macmorris, I think, look you, under your
correction, there is not many of your nation —

MACMORRIS
Of my nation! What ish my nation? Ish a villain, and a
bastard, and a knave, and a rascal. What ish my nation?
Who talks of my nation?

FLUELLEN
Look you, if you take the matter otherwise than is
meant, Captain Macmorris, peradventure I shall think
you do not use me with that affability as in discretion
you ought to use me, look you; being as goot a man as
yourself, both in the disciplines of war, and in the
derivation of my birth, and in other particularities.

MACMORRIS
I do not know you so good a man as myself: so Chrish
save me, I will cut off your head.

GOWER
Gentlemen both, you will mistake each other.

JAMY
A! that's a foul fault.   *[A parley sounded.*

GOWER
The town sounds a parley.

FLUELLEN
Captain Macmorris, when there is more petter
opportunity to be required, look you, I will be so pold as

to tell you I know the disciplines of war; and there is an
end.
                        [Exeunt.

SCENE III

The same.

The GOVERNOR *and some* CITIZENS *on the walls; the
English forces below. Enter* KING HENRY *and his
TRAIN before the gates.*

KING HENRY
How yet resolves the governor of the town?
This is the latest parle we will admit:
Therefore, to our best mercy give yourselves;
Or, like to men proud of destruction,
Defy us to our worst: for, as I am a soldier,
A name that, in my thoughts, becomes me best,
If I begin the battery once again,
I will not leave the half-achiev'd Harfleur
Till in her ashes she lie buried.
The gates of mercy shall be all shut up;
And the flesh'd soldier, — rough and hard of heart, —
In liberty of bloody hand shall range
With conscience wide as hell; mowing like grass
Your fresh-fair virgins and your flowering infants.
What is it then to me, if impious war, —
Array'd in flames, like to the prince of fiends, —
Do, with his smirch'd complexion, all fell feats
Enlink'd to waste and desolation?
What is't to me, when you yourselves are cause,
If your pure maidens fall into the hand
Of hot and forcing violation?
What rein can hold licentious wickedness
When down the hill he holds his fierce career?
We may as bootless spend our vain command
Upon th'enraged soldiers in their spoil,
As send precepts to the leviathan
To come ashore. Therefore, you men of Harfleur,
Take pity of your town and of your people,
Whiles yet my soldiers are in my command;
Whiles yet the cool and temperate wind of grace
O'erblows the filthy and contagious clouds
Of heady murder, spoil, and villainy.
If not, why, in a moment, look to see
The blind and bloody soldier with foul hand
Defile the locks of your shrill-shrieking daughters;
Your fathers taken by the silver beards,
And their most reverend heads dash'd to the walls;
Your naked infants spitted upon pikes,
Whiles the mad mothers with their howls confused
Do break the clouds, as did the wives of Jewry
At Herod's bloody-hunting slaughtermen.
What say you? will you yield, and this avoid?
Or, guilty in defence, be thus destroy'd?

GOVERNOR OF HARFLEUR
Our expectation hath this day an end:
The Dauphin, whom of succour we entreated,
Returns us, that his powers are yet not ready
To raise so great a siege. Therefore, dread king,
We yield our town and lives to thy soft mercy.
Enter our gates; dispose of us and ours;
For we no longer are defensible.

KING HENRY
Open your gates. — Come, uncle Exeter,
Go you and enter Harfleur; there remain,
And fortify it strongly 'gainst the French:
Use mercy to them all. For us, dear uncle, —
The winter coming on, and sickness growing
Upon our soldiers, — we will retire to Calais.
To-night in Harfleur will we be your guest;
To-morrow for the march are we address'd.
        [Flourish, and enter the town.

SCENE IV

The French KING'S *palace.*

Enter KATHARINE *and* ALICE.

KATHARINE
Alice, tu as été en Angleterre, et tu parles bien le langage.

ALICE
Un peu, madame.

KATHARINE
*Je te prie, m'enseignez; il faut que j'apprenne à parler.
Comment appelez-vous la main en Anglois?*

ALICE
La main? elle est appelée de hand.

KATHARINE
De hand. *Et les doigts?*

ALICE

Les doigts? ma foi, j'oublie les doigts; mais je me souviendrai. Les doigts? je pense qu'ils sont appelés de fingres; oui, de fingres.

KATHARINE

La main, de hand; les doigts, de fingres. Je pense que je suis le bon écolier; j'ai gagné deux mots d'Anglois vitement. Comment appelez-vous les ongles?

ALICE

Les ongles? nous les appelons de nails.

KATHARINE

De nails. Écoutez; dites-moi, si je parle bien: de hand, de fingres, et de nails.

ALICE

C'est bien dit, madame; il est fort bon Anglois.

KATHARINE

Dites-moi l'Anglois pour le bras.

ALICE

De arm, madame.

KATHARINE

Et le coude?

ALICE

D'elbow.

KATHARINE

D'elbow. Je m'en fais la répétition de tous les mots que vous m'avez appris dès à présent.

ALICE

Il est trop difficile, madame, comme je pense.

KATHARINE

Excusez-moi, Alice; écoutez: d'hand, de fingres, de nails, *d'arm, de bilbow.*

ALICE

D'elbow, madame.

KATHARINE

O Seigneur Dieu, je m'en oublie! d'elbow. *Comment appelez-vous le col?*

ALICE

De neck, madame.

KATHARINE

De nick. Et le menton?

ALICE

De chin.

KATHARINE

De sin. Le col, de nick; le menton, de sin.

ALICE

Oui. Sauf votre honneur, en vérité, vous prononcez les mots aussi droit que les natifs d'Angleterre.

KATHARINE

Je ne doute point d'apprendre, par la grace de Dieu, et en peu de temps.

ALICE

N'avez-vous pas déjà oublié ce que je vous ai enseigné?

KATHARINE

Non, je réciterai à vous promptement: d'hand, de fingres, de mails, —

ALICE

De nails, madame.

KATHARINE

De nails, de arm, de ilbow.

ALICE

Sauf votre honneur, d'elbow.

KATHARINE

Ainsi dis-je; d'elbow, de nick, *et de sin. Comment appelez-vous le pied et la robe?*

ALICE

De foot, madame; et de coun.

KATHARINE

De foot et de coun! O Seigneur Dieu! ce sont mots de son mauvais, corruptible, gros, et impudique, et non pour les dames d'honneur d'user: je ne voudrais prononcer ces mots devant les seigneurs de France pour tout le monde. Foh! le foot *et le* coun! *Néanmoins, je réciterai une autre fois ma leçon ensemble:* d'hand, de fingres, de nails, d'arm, d'elbow, de nick, de sin, de foot, de coun.

ALICE

Excellent, madame!

KATHARINE

C'est assez pour une fois: allons-nous à diner. [*Exeunt.*

SCENE V

The same.

Enter the KING OF FRANCE, *the* DAUPHIN, BOURBON, *the* CONSTABLE OF FRANCE, *and others.*

FRENCH KING

'Tis certain he hath pass'd the river Somme.

CONSTABLE

And if he be not fought withal, my lord,

Let us not live in France; let us quit all,
And give our vineyards to a barbarous people.

DAUPHIN

O *Dieu vivant!* shall a few sprays of us,
The emptying of our fathers' luxury,
Our scions, put in wild and savage stock,
Spirit up so suddenly into the clouds,
And overlook their grafters?

BOURBON

Normans, but bastard Normans, Norman bastards!
Mort de ma vie! if they march along
Unfought withal, but I will sell my dukedom,
To buy a slobbery and a dirty farm
In that nook-shotten isle of Albion.

CONSTABLE

Dieu de batailles! where have they this mettle?
Is not their climate foggy, raw, and dull;
On whom, as in despite, the sun looks pale,
Killing their fruit with frowns? Can sodden water,
A drench for sur-rein'd jades, their barley-broth,
Decoct their cold blood to such valiant heat?
And shall our quick blood, spirited with wine,
Seem frosty? O, for honour of our land,
Let us not hang like roping icicles
Upon our houses' thatch, whiles a more frosty people
Sweat drops of gallant youth in our rich fields, —
Poor we may call them in their native lords!

DAUPHIN

By faith and honour,
Our madams mock at us, and plainly say
Our mettle is bred out, and they will give
Their bodies to the lust of English youth
To new-store France with bastard warriors.

BOURBON

They bid us to the English dancing-schools,
And teach lavoltas high and swift corantos;
Saying our grace is only in our heels,
And that we are most lofty runaways.

FRENCH KING

Where is Montjoy the herald? speed him hence;
Let him greet England with our sharp defiance. —
Up, princes! and, with spirit of honour edged
More sharper than your swords, hie to the field:
Charles Delabreth, high-Constable of France;
You Dukes of Orleans, Bourbon, and of Berri,
Alençon, Brabant, Bar, and Burgundy;
Jaques Chatillon, Rambures, Vaudemont,
Beaumont, Grandpré, Roussi, and Fauconberg,
Foix, Lestrale, Boucicqualt, and Charolois;
High dukes, great princes, barons, lords, and knights,
For your great seats now quit you of great shames.
Bar Harry England, that sweeps through our land
With pennons painted in the blood of Harfleur:
Rush on his host, as doth the melted snow
Upon the valleys, whose low vassal seat
The Alps doth spit and void his rheum upon:
Go down upon him, — you have power enough, —
And in a captive chariot into Rouen
Bring him our prisoner.

CONSTABLE

                              This becomes the great.
Sorry am I his numbers are so few,
His soldiers sick, and famish'd in their march;
For I am sure, when he shall see our army,
He'll drop his heart into the sink of fear,
And for achievement offer us his ransom.

FRENCH KING

Therefore, lord Constable, haste on Montjoy;
And let him say to England, that we send
To know what willing ransom he will give. —
Prince Dauphin, you shall stay with us in Rouen.

DAUPHIN

Not so, I do beseech your majesty.

FRENCH KING

Be patient; for you shall remain with us.
Now forth, lord Constable, and princes all,
And quickly bring us word of England's fall. [*Exeunt.*

SCENE VI

The English camp in Picardy.

Enter GOWER *and* FLUELLEN, *meeting.*

GOWER

How now, Captain Fluellen! come you from the bridge?

FLUELLEN

I assure you, there is very excellent services committed at the pridge.

GOWER

Is the Duke of Exeter safe?

FLUELLEN

The Duke of Exeter is as magnanimous as Agamemnon; and a man that I love and honour with my soul, and my heart, and my duty, and my life, and my living, and my uttermost power: he is not — Got be praised and plest! — any hurt in the 'orld; but keeps the pridge most valiantly, with excellent discipline. There is an auncient there at the pridge, — I think in my very conscience he is as valiant a man as Mark Antony; and he is a man of no estimation in the 'orld; but I did see him do gallant service.

GOWER

What do you call him?

FLUELLEN

He is called Auncient Pistol.

GOWER

I know him not.

FLUELLEN

Here is the man.

Enter PISTOL.

PISTOL

Captain, I thee beseech to do me favours:
The Duke of Exeter doth love thee well.

FLUELLEN

Ay, I praise Got; and I have merited some love at his hands.

PISTOL

Bardolph, a soldier, firm and sound of heart,
And of buxom valour, hath, by cruel fate,
And giddy Fortune's furious fickle wheel, —
That goddess blind,
That stands upon the rolling restless stone, —

FLUELLEN

By your patience, Auncient Pistol. Fortune is painted plind, with a muffler afore her eyes, to signify to you that Fortune is plind; and she is painted also with a wheel, to signify to you, which is the moral of it, that she is turning, and inconstant, and mutability, and variation: and her foot, look you, is fix'd upon a spherical stone, which rolls, and rolls, and rolls: — in good truth, the poet makes a most excellent description of it: Fortune is an excellent moral.

PISTOL

Fortune is Bardolph's foe, and frowns on him;
For he hath stol'n a pax, and hanged must a' be, —
A damned death!
Let gallows gape for dog; let man go free,
And let not hemp his windpipe suffocate:
But Exeter hath given the doom of death
For pax of little price.
Therefore, go speak, — the duke will hear thy voice;
And let not Bardolph's vital thread be cut
With edge of penny cord and vile reproach:
Speak, captain, for his life, and I will thee requite.

FLUELLEN

Auncient Pistol, I do partly understand your meaning.

PISTOL

Why, then, rejoice therefore.

FLUELLEN

Certainly, auncient, it is not a thing to rejoice at: for if, look you, he were my prother, I would desire the duke to use his goot pleasure, and put him to execution; for discipline ought to be used.

PISTOL

Die and be damn'd! and figo for thy friendship!

FLUELLEN

It is well.

PISTOL

The fig of Spain! [*Exit.*

FLUELLEN

Very goot.

GOWER

Why, this is an arrant counterfeit rascal; I remember him now; a bawd, a cutpurse.

FLUELLEN

I'll assure you, a' utter'd as prave 'ords at the pridge as you shall see in a summer's day. But it is very well; what he has spoke to me, that is well, I warrant you, when time is serve.

GOWER

Why, 'tis a gull, a fool, a rogue, that now and then goes to the wars, to grace himself, at his return into London, under the form of a soldier. And such fellows are perfect in the great commanders' names: and they will learn you by rote where services were done; — at such and such a sconce, at such a breach, at such a convoy; who came off bravely, who was shot, who disgraced, what terms the enemy stood on; and this they con perfectly in the phrase of war, which they trick up with new-turn'd oaths: and what a beard of the general's cut, and a horrid suit of the camp, will do among foaming bottles and ale-wash'd wits, is wonderful to be thought on. But you must learn to know such slanders of the age, or else you may be marvellously mistook.

FLUELLEN
I tell you what, Captain Gower; — I do perceive he is not the man that he would gladly make show to the 'orld he is: if I find a hole in his coat, I will tell him my mind. [*Drum within.*] Hark you, the king is coming; and I must speak with him from the pridge.
Drum and colours. Enter KING HENRY, GLOSTER, *and his poor* SOLDIERS.
Got pless your majesty!

KING HENRY
How now, Fluellen! camest thou from the bridge?

FLUELLEN
Ay, so please your majesty. The Duke of Exeter has very gallantly maintain'd the pridge: the French is gone off, look you; and there is gallant and most prave passages: marry, th'athversary was have possession of the pridge; but he is enforced to retire, and the Duke of Exeter is master of the pridge: I can tell your majesty, the duke is a prave man.

KING HENRY
What men have you lost, Fluellen?

FLUELLEN
The perdition of th'athversary hath been very great, reasonable great: marry, for my part, I think the duke hath lost never a man, but one that is like to be executed for robbing a church, — one Bardolph, if your majesty know the man: his face is all bubukles, and whelks, and knobs, and flames o' fire: and his lips plows at his nose, and it is like a coal of fire, sometimes plue and sometimes red; but his nose is executed, and his fire's out.

KING HENRY
We would have all such offenders so cut off: — and we give express charge that, in our marches through the country, there be nothing compell'd from the villages, nothing taken but paid for, none of the French upbraided or abused in disdainful language; for when lenity and cruelty play for a kingdom, the gentler gamester is the soonest winner.
Tucket. Enter MONTJOY.

MONTJOY
You know me by my habit.

KING HENRY
Well, then, I know thee: what shall I know of thee?

MONTJOY
My master's mind.

KING HENRY
Unfold it.

MONTJOY
Thus says my king: — Say thou to Harry of England: Though we seem'd dead, we did but sleep; advantage is a better soldier than rashness. Tell him, we could have rebuked him at Harfleur, but that we thought not good to bruise an injury till it were full ripe: — now we speak upon our cue, and our voice is imperial: England shall repent his folly, see his weakness, and admire our sufferance. Bid him, therefore, consider of his ransom; which must proportion the losses we have borne, the subjects we have lost, the disgrace we have digested; which, in weight to re-answer, his pettiness would bow under. For our losses, his exchequer is too poor; for th'effusion of our blood, the muster of his kingdom too faint a number, and for our disgrace, his own person, kneeling at our feet, but a weak and worthless satisfaction. To this add defiance: and tell him, for conclusion, he hath betray'd his followers, whose condemnation is pronounced. So far my king and master; so much my office.

KING HENRY
What is thy name? I know thy quality.

MONTJOY
Montjoy.

KING HENRY
Thou dost thy office fairly. Turn thee back,
And tell thy king, — I do not seek him now;
But could be willing to march on to Calais
Without impeachment: for, to say the sooth, —
Though 'tis no wisdom to confess so much
Unto an enemy of craft and vantage, —
My people are with sickness much enfeebled;
My numbers lessen'd; and those few I have,
Almost no better than so many French;
Who when they were in health, I tell thee, herald,
I thought upon one pair of English legs
Did march three Frenchmen. — Yet, forgive me, God,

That I do brag thus! — this your air of France
Hath blown that vice in me; I must repent.
Go, therefore, tell thy master here I am;
My ransom is this frail and worthless trunk;
My army but a weak and sickly guard:
Yet, God before, tell him we will come on,
Though France himself, and such another neighbour,
Stand in our way. There's for thy labour, Montjoy.
[*Gives a purse.*
Go, bid thy master well advise himself:
If we may pass, we will; if we be hinder'd,
We shall your tawny ground with your red blood
Discolour: and so, Montjoy, fare you well.
The sum of all our answer is but this:
We would not seek a battle, as we are;
Nor, as we are, we say, we will not shun it:
So tell your master.

MONTJOY
I shall deliver so. Thanks to your highness. [*Exit.*

GLOSTER
I hope they will not come upon us now.

KING HENRY
We are in God's hand, brother, not in theirs.
March to the bridge; it now draws toward night: —
Beyond the river we'll encamp ourselves;
And on to-morrow bid them march away. [*Exeunt.*

SCENE VII

The French camp near Agincourt.

Enter the CONSTABLE OF FRANCE, *the* LORD RAMBURES, ORLEANS, *the* DAUPHIN, *and others.*

CONSTABLE
Tut! I have the best armour of the world. — Would it were day!

ORLEANS
You have an excellent armour; but let my horse have his due.

CONSTABLE
It is the best horse of Europe.

ORLEANS
Will it never be morning?

DAUPHIN
My Lord of Orleans, and my lord high-Constable, you talk of horse and armour?

ORLEANS
You are as well provided of both as any prince in the world.

DAUPHIN
What a long night is this! — I will not change my horse with any that treads but on four pasterns. *Ça, ha!* he bounds from the earth, as if his entrails were hairs; *le cheval volant*, the Pegasus, *qui a les narines de feu!* When I bestride him, I soar, I am a hawk: he trots the air; the earth sings when he touches it; the basest horn of his hoof is more musical than the pipe of Hermes.

ORLEANS
He's of the colour of the nutmeg.

DAUPHIN
And of the heat of the ginger. It is a beast for Perseus: he is pure air and fire; and the dull elements of earth and water never appear in him, but only in patient stillness while his rider mounts him: he is, indeed, a horse; and all other jades you may call beasts.

CONSTABLE
Indeed, my lord, it is a most absolute and excellent horse.

DAUPHIN
It is the prince of palfreys; his neigh is like the bidding of a monarch, and his countenance enforces homage.

ORLEANS
No more, cousin.

DAUPHIN
Nay, the man hath no wit that cannot, from the rising of the lark to the lodging of the lamb, vary deserved praise on my palfrey: it is a theme as fluent as the sea; turn the sands into eloquent tongues, and my horse is argument for them all: 'tis a subject for a sovereign to reason on, and for a sovereign's sovereign to ride on; and for the world, familiar to us and unknown, to lay apart their particular functions, and wonder at him. I once writ a sonnet in his praise, and began thus: 'Wonder of nature,' —

ORLEANS
I have heard a sonnet begin so to one's mistress.

DAUPHIN
Then did they imitate that which I composed to my courser; for my horse is my mistress.

ORLEANS
Your mistress bears well.

DAUPHIN
Me well; which is the prescript praise and perfection of a good and particular mistress.

CONSTABLE
Ma foi, methought yesterday your mistress shrewdly shook your back.

DAUPHIN
So, perhaps, did yours.

CONSTABLE
Mine was not bridled.

DAUPHIN
O, then, belike she was old and gentle; and you rode, like a kern of Ireland, your French hose off, and in your strait strossers.

CONSTABLE
You have good judgement in horsemanship.

DAUPHIN
Be warn'd by me, then: they that ride so, and ride not warily, fall into foul bogs. I had rather have my horse to my mistress.

CONSTABLE
I had as lief have my mistress a jade.

DAUPHIN
I tell thee, Constable, my mistress wears his own hair.

CONSTABLE
I could make as true a boast as that, if I had a sow to my mistress.

DAUPHIN
Le chien est retourné à son propre vomissement, et la truie lavée au bourbier: thou makest use of any thing.

CONSTABLE
Yet do I not use my horse for my mistress; or any such proverb, so little kin to the purpose.

RAMBURES
My lord Constable, the armour that I saw in your tent to-night, — are those stars or suns upon it?

CONSTABLE
Stars, my lord.

DAUPHIN
Some of them will fall to-morrow, I hope.

CONSTABLE
And yet my sky shall not want.

DAUPHIN
That may be, for you bear a many superfluously, and 'twere more honour some were away.

CONSTABLE
Even as your horse bears your praises; who would trot as well, were some of your brags dismounted.

DAUPHIN
Would I were able to load him with his desert! — Will it never be day? — I will trot to-morrow a mile, and my way shall be paved with English faces.

CONSTABLE
I will not say so, for fear I should be faced out of my way: but I would it were morning; for I would fain be about the ears of the English.

RAMBURES
Who will go to hazard with me for twenty prisoners?

CONSTABLE
You must first go yourself to hazard, ere you have them.

DAUPHIN
'Tis midnight; I'll go arm myself. [*Exit.*

ORLEANS
The Dauphin longs for morning.

RAMBURES
He longs to eat the English.

CONSTABLE
I think he will eat all he kills.

ORLEANS
By the white hand of my lady, he's a gallant prince.

CONSTABLE
Swear by her foot, that she may tread out the oath.

ORLEANS
He is, simply, the most active gentleman of France.

CONSTABLE
Doing is activity; and he will still be doing.

ORLEANS
He never did harm, that I heard of.

CONSTABLE
Nor will do none to-morrow: he will keep that good name still.

ORLEANS
I know him to be valiant.

CONSTABLE
I was told that by one that knows him better than you.

ORLEANS
What's he?

CONSTABLE
Marry, he told me so himself; and he said he cared not who knew it.

ORLEANS
He needs not; it is no hidden virtue in him.

CONSTABLE
By my faith, sir, but it is; never any body saw it but his lackey: 'tis a hooded valour; and when it appears, it will bate.

ORLEANS
Ill-will never said well.

CONSTABLE
I will cap that proverb with — There is flattery in friendship.

ORLEANS
And I will take up that with — Give the devil his due.

CONSTABLE
Well placed: there stands your friend for the devil: have at the very eye of that proverb, with — A pox of the devil.

ORLEANS
You are the better at proverbs, by how much — A fool's bolt is soon shot.

CONSTABLE
You have shot over.

ORLEANS
'Tis not the first time you were overshot.

Enter a MESSENGER.

MESSENGER
My lord high-Constable, the English lie within fifteen hundred paces of your tents.

CONSTABLE
Who hath measured the ground?

MESSENGER
The Lord Grandpré.

CONSTABLE
A valiant and most expert gentleman. — Would it were day! — Alas, poor Harry of England! he longs not for the dawning, as we do.

ORLEANS
What a wretched and peevish fellow is this king of England, to mope with his fat-brain'd followers so far out of his knowledge!

CONSTABLE
If the English had any apprehension, they would run away.

ORLEANS
That they lack; for if their heads had any intellectual armour, they could never wear such heavy head-pieces.

RAMBURES
That island of England breeds very valiant creatures; their mastiffs are of unmatchable courage.

ORLEANS
Foolish curs, that run winking into the mouth of a Russian bear, and have their heads crush'd like rotten apples! You may as well say, that's a valiant flea that dare eat his breakfast on the lip of a lion.

CONSTABLE
Just, just; and the men do sympathise with the mastiffs in robustious and rough coming-on, leaving their wits with their wives: and then give them great meals of beef, and iron and steel, they will eat like wolves, and fight like devils.

ORLEANS
Ay, but these English are shrewdly out of beef.

CONSTABLE
Then shall we find to-morrow they have only stomachs to eat, and none to fight. Now is it time to arm: come, shall we about it?

ORLEANS
It is now two o'clock: but, let me see, — by ten We shall have each a hundred Englishmen. [*Exeunt.*

ACT IV

PROLOGUE

Enter CHORUS.

CHORUS
Now entertain conjecture of a time
When creeping murmur and the poring dark
Fills the wide vessel of the universe.
From camp to camp, through the foul womb of night,
The hum of either army stilly sounds,
That the fix'd sentinels almost receive
The secret whispers of each other's watch:
Fire answers fire; and through their paly flames
Each battle sees the other's umber'd face:

Steed threatens steed, in high and boastful neighs
Piercing the night's dull ear; and from the tents,
The armourers, accomplishing the knights,
With busy hammers closing rivets up,
Give dreadful note of preparation:
The country cocks do crow, the clocks do toll,
And the third hour of drowsy morning name.
Proud of their numbers, and secure in soul,
The confident and over-lusty French
Do the low-rated English play at dice;
And chide the cripple tardy-gaited night,
Who, like a foul and ugly witch, doth limp
So tediously away. The poor condemned English,
Like sacrifices, by their watchful fires
Sit patiently, and inly ruminate
The morning's danger; and their gesture sad
Investing lank-lean cheeks, and war-worn coats,
Presenteth them unto the gazing moon
So many horrid ghosts. O, now, who will behold
The royal captain of this ruin'd band
Walking from watch to watch, from tent to tent,
Let him cry, 'Praise and glory on his head!'
For forth he goes and visits all his host;
Bids them good morrow with a modest smile,
And calls them brothers, friends, and countrymen.
Upon his royal face there is no note
How dread an army hath enrounded him;
Nor doth he dedicate one jot of colour
Unto the weary and all-watched night,
But freshly looks, and over-bears attaint
With cheerful semblance and sweet majesty;
That every wretch, pining and pale before,
Beholding him, plucks comfort from his looks:
A largess universal, like the sun,
His liberal eye doth give to every one,
Thawing cold fear. Then, mean and gentle all,
Behold, as may unworthiness define,
A little touch of Harry in the night:
And so our scene must to the battle fly;
Where — O for pity! — we shall much disgrace
With four or five most vile and ragged foils,
Right ill-dispos'd, in brawl ridiculous,
The name of Agincourt. Yet, sit and see;
Minding true things by what their mockeries be. [*Exit.*

SCENE I

The English camp at Agincourt.

Enter KING HENRY, BEDFORD, *and* GLOSTER.

KING HENRY
Gloster, 'tis true that we are in great danger;
The greater therefore should our courage be. —
Good morrow, brother Bedford. — God Almighty!
There is some soul of goodness in things evil,
Would men observingly distil it out;
For our bad neighbour makes us early stirrers,
Which is both healthful and good husbandry:
Besides, they are our outward consciences,
And preachers to us all; admonishing
That we should dress us fairly for our end.
Thus may we gather honey from the weed,
And make a moral of the devil himself.

Enter ERPINGHAM.

Good morrow, old Sir Thomas Erpingham:
A good soft pillow for that good white head
Were better than a churlish turf of France.

ERPINGHAM
Not so, my liege: this lodging likes me better,
Since I may say, 'Now lie I like a king.'

KING HENRY
'Tis good for men to love their present pains
Upon example; so the spirit is eased:
And when the mind is quicken'd, out of doubt
The organs, though defunct and dead before,
Break up their drowsy grave, and newly move
With casted slough and fresh legerity.
Lend me thy cloak, Sir Thomas. — Brothers both,
Commend me to the princes in our camp;
Do my good morrow to them; and anon
Desire them all to my pavilion.

GLOSTER
We shall, my liege.

ERPINGHAM
Shall I attend your Grace?

KING HENRY
                    No, my good knight;
Go with my brothers to my lords of England:
I and my bosom must debate awhile,
And then I would no other company.

ERPINGHAM
The Lord in heaven bless thee, noble Harry!

[*Exeunt* GLOSTER, BEDFORD, *and* ERPINGHAM.

KING HENRY
God-a-mercy, old heart! thou speak'st cheerfully.

Enter PISTOL.

PISTOL
Qui va là?

KING HENRY
A friend.

PISTOL
Discuss unto me; art thou officer?
Or art thou base, common, and popular?

KING HENRY
I am a gentleman of a company.

PISTOL
Trail'st thou the puissant pike?

KING HENRY
Even so. What are you?

PISTOL
As good a gentleman as the emperor.

KING HENRY
Then you are a better than the king.

PISTOL
The king's a bawcock, and a heart of gold,
A lad of life, an imp of fame;
Of parents good, of fist most valiant:
I kiss his dirty shoe, and from heart-string
I love the lovely bully. — What is thy name?

KING HENRY
Harry *le Roy.*

PISTOL
Le Roy!
A Cornish name: art thou of Cornish crew?

KING HENRY
No, I am a Welshman.

PISTOL
Know'st thou Fluellen?

KING HENRY
Yes.

PISTOL
Tell him, I'll knock his leek about his pate
Upon Saint Davy's day.

KING HENRY
Do not you wear your dagger in your cap that day, lest he knock that about yours.

PISTOL
Art thou his friend?

KING HENRY
And his kinsman too.

PISTOL
The figo for thee, then!

KING HENRY
I thank you: God be with you!

PISTOL
My name is Pistol call'd. [*Exit.*

KING HENRY
It sorts well with your fierceness.

Enter FLUELLEN *and* GOWER, *severally.*

GOWER
Captain Fluellen!

FLUELLEN
So! in the name of Cheshu Christ, speak lower. It is the greatest admiration of the universal 'orld, when the true and auncient prerogatifs and laws of the wars is not kept: if you would take the pains but to examine the wars of Pompey the Great, you shall find, I warrant you, that there is no tiddle-taddle nor pibble-pabble in Pompey's camp; I warrant you, you shall find the ceremonies of the wars, and the cares of it, and the forms of it, and the sobriety of it, and the modesty of it, to be otherwise.

GOWER
Why, the enemy is loud; you heard him all night.

FLUELLEN
If the enemy is an ass, and a fool, and a prating coxcomb, is it meet, think you, that we should also, look you, be an ass, and a fool, and a prating coxcomb, — in your own conscience, now?

GOWER
I will speak lower.

FLUELLEN
I pray you, and peseech you, that you will.

[*Exeunt* GOWER *and* FLUELLEN.

KING HENRY
Though it appear a little out of fashion,
There is much care and valour in this Welshman.

Enter three SOLDIERS, JOHN BATES, ALEXANDER COURT, *and* MICHAEL WILLIAMS.

ALEXANDER COURT
Brother John Bates, is not that the morning which breaks yonder?

JOHN BATES
I think it be: but we have no great cause to desire the approach of day.

MICHAEL WILLIAMS
We see yonder the beginning of the day, but I think we shall never see the end of it. — Who goes there?

KING HENRY
A friend.

MICHAEL WILLIAMS
Under what captain serve you?

KING HENRY
Under Sir Thomas Erpingham.

MICHAEL WILLIAMS
A good old commander and a most kind gentleman: I pray you, what thinks he of our estate?

KING HENRY
Even as men wreck'd upon a sand, that look to be wash'd off the next tide.

JOHN BATES
He hath not told his thought to the king?

KING HENRY
No; nor is it meet he should. For, though I speak it to you, I think the king is but a man, as I am: the violet smells to him as it doth to me; the element shows to him as it doth to me; all his senses have but human conditions: his ceremonies laid by, in his nakedness he appears but a man; and though his affections are higher mounted than ours, yet, when they stoop, they stoop with the like wing. Therefore when he sees reason of fears, as we do, his fears, out of doubt, be of the same relish as ours are: yet, in reason, no man should possess him with any appearance of fear, lest he, by showing it, should dishearten his army.

JOHN BATES
He may show what outward courage he will; but I believe, as cold a night as 'tis, he could wish himself in Thames up to the neck; — and so I would he were, and I by him, at all adventures, so we were quit here.

KING HENRY
By my troth, I will speak my conscience of the king: I think he would not wish himself any where but where he is.

JOHN BATES
Then I would he were here alone; so should he be sure to be ransom'd, and a many poor men's lives saved.

KING HENRY
I dare say you love him not so ill, to wish him here alone, howsoever you speak this, to feel other men's minds: methinks I could not die any where so contented as in the king's company, — his cause being just, and his quarrel honourable.

MICHAEL WILLIAMS
That's more than we know.

JOHN BATES
Ay, or more than we should seek after; for we know enough, if we know we are the king's subjects: if his cause be wrong, our obedience to the king wipes the crime of it out of us.

MICHAEL WILLIAMS
But if the cause be not good, the king himself hath a heavy reckoning to make, when all those legs and arms and heads, chopp'd off in battle, shall join together at the latter day, and cry all, 'We died at such a place'; some swearing; some crying for a surgeon; some, upon their wives left poor behind them; some, upon the debts they owe; some, upon their children rawly left. I am afeard there are few die well that die in battle, for how can they charitably dispose of any thing, when blood is their argument? Now, if these men do not die well, it will be a black matter for the king that led them to it; who to disobey were against all proportion of subjection.

KING HENRY
So, if a son, that is by his father sent about merchandise, do sinfully miscarry upon the sea, the imputation of his wickedness, by your rule, should be imposed upon his father that sent him: or if a servant, under his master's command transporting a sum of money, be assail'd by robbers, and die in many irreconciled iniquities, you may call the business of the master the author of the servant's damnation: — but this is not so: the king is not bound to answer the particular endings of his soldiers, the father of his son, nor the master of his servant; for they purpose not their death, when they purpose their services. Besides, there is no king, be his cause never so spotless, if it come to the arbitrement of swords, can try it out with all unspotted soldiers: some peradventure have on them the guilt of premeditated and contrived murder; some, of beguiling virgins with the broken seals of perjury; some, making the wars their bulwark, that have before gored the gentle bosom of peace with pillage and robbery. Now, if these men have defeated the law and outrun native punishment, though they can outstrip men, they have no wings to fly from God: war is his beadle, war is his vengeance; so that here men are punish'd for before-breach of the king's laws in now the king's quarrel: where they fear'd the death, they have borne life away; and where they would be safe, they perish: then if they die unprovided, no more is the king guilty of their damnation, than he was before guilty of those impieties for the which they are now visited. Every subject's duty is the king's; but every subject's soul is his own. Therefore should every soldier in the wars do as every sick man in his bed, — wash every mote out of his conscience and dying so, death is to him advantage; or not dying, the time was blessedly lost wherein such preparation was gain'd: and in him that escapes, it were not sin to think that, making God so free an offer, He let him outlive that day to see His greatness, and to teach others how they should prepare.

MICHAEL WILLIAMS
'Tis certain, every man that dies ill, the ill upon his own head, — the king is not to answer it.

JOHN BATES
I do not desire he should answer for me; and yet I determine to fight lustily for him.

KING HENRY
I myself heard the king say he would not be ransom'd.

MICHAEL WILLIAMS
Ay, he said so, to make us fight cheerfully: but when our throats are cut, he may be ransom'd, and we ne'er the wiser.

KING HENRY
If I live to see it, I will never trust his word after.

MICHAEL WILLIAMS
'Mass, you'll pay him then! That's a perilous shot out of an elder-gun, that a poor and private displeasure can do against a monarch! you may as well go about to turn the sun to ice with fanning in his face with a peacock's feather. You'll never trust his word after! come, 'tis a foolish saying.

KING HENRY
Your reproof is something too round: I should be angry with you, if the time were convenient.

MICHAEL WILLIAMS
Let it be a quarrel between us, if you live.

KING HENRY
I embrace it.

MICHAEL WILLIAMS
How shall I know thee again?

KING HENRY
Give me any gage of thine, and I will wear it in my bonnet: then, if ever thou darest acknowledge it, I will make it my quarrel.

MICHAEL WILLIAMS
Here's my glove: give me another of thine.

KING HENRY
There.

MICHAEL WILLIAMS
This will I also wear in my cap: if ever thou come to me and say, after to-morrow, 'This is my glove,' by this hand, I will take thee a box on the ear.

KING HENRY
If ever I live to see it, I will challenge it.

MICHAEL WILLIAMS
Thou darest as well be hang'd.

KING HENRY
Well, I will do it, though I take thee in the king's company.

MICHAEL WILLIAMS
Keep thy word: fare thee well.

JOHN BATES
Be friends, you English fools, be friends: we have French quarrels enow, if you could tell how to reckon.

KING HENRY
Indeed, the French may lay twenty French crowns to one, they will beat us; for they bear them on their shoulders: but it is no English treason to cut French crowns; and to-morrow the king himself will be a clipper.   [*Exeunt* SOLDIERS.
Upon the king! — let us our lives, our souls, Our debts, our careful wives, Our children, and our sins, lay on the king! We must bear all. O hard condition, Twin-born with greatness, subject to the breath Of every fool, whose sense no more can feel But his own wringing! What infinite heart's-ease must kings neglect, That private men enjoy! And what have kings, that privates have not too, Save ceremony, — save general ceremony? And what art thou, thou idol ceremony? What kind of god art thou, that suffer'st more Of mortal griefs than do thy worshippers? What are thy rents? what are thy comings-in? O ceremony, show me but thy worth! What is thy soul, O adoration? Art thou aught else but place, degree, and form, Creating awe and fear in other men? Wherein thou art less happy being fear'd Than they in fearing. What drink'st thou oft, instead of homage sweet, But poison'd flattery? O, be sick, great greatness, And bid thy ceremony give thee cure! Think'st thou the fiery fever will go out With titles blown from adulation? Will it give place to flexure and low bending? Canst thou, when thou command'st the beggar's knee, Command the health of it? No, thou proud dream, That play'st so subtly with a king's repose: I am a king that find thee; and I know 'Tis not the balm, the sceptre, and the ball, The sword, the mace, the crown imperial, The intertissued robe of gold and pearl, The farced title running 'fore the king, The throne he sits on, nor the tide of pomp That beats upon the high shore of this world, — No, not all these, thrice-gorgeous ceremony, Not all these, laid in bed majestical, Can sleep so soundly as the wretched slave, Who, with a body fill'd and vacant mind, Gets him to rest, cramm'd with distressful bread; Never sees horrid night, the child of hell; But, like a lackey, from the rise to set, Sweats in the eye of Phœbus and all night Sleeps in Elysium; next day, after dawn, Doth rise, and help Hyperion to his horse; And follows so the ever-running year, With profitable labour, to his grave: And, but for ceremony, such a wretch, Winding up days with toil and nights with sleep, Had the fore-hand and vantage of a king. The slave, a member of the country's peace, Enjoys it; but in gross brain little wots What watch the king keeps to maintain the peace, Whose hours the peasant best advantages.

Enter ERPINGHAM.

ERPINGHAM
My lord, your nobles, jealous of your absence, Seek through your camp to find you.

KING HENRY
                                    Good old knight, Collect them all together at my tent: I'll be before thee.

ERPINGHAM
                    I shall do't, my lord.   [*Exit.*

KING HENRY
O God of battles! steel my soldiers' hearts; Possess them not with fear; take from them now The sense of reckoning, if th'opposed numbers Pluck their hearts from them! — Not to-day, O Lord, O, not to-day, think not upon the fault My father made in compassing the crown! I Richard's body have interred new; And on it have bestow'd more contrite tears Than from it issued forced drops of blood: Five hundred poor I have in yearly pay, Who twice a-day their wither'd hands hold up Toward heaven, to pardon blood; and I have built Two chantries, where the sad and solemn priests Sing still for Richard's soul. More will I do; Though all that I can do is nothing worth, Since that my penitence comes after all, Imploring pardon.

Enter GLOSTER.

GLOSTER
My liege!

KING HENRY
                    My brother Gloster's voice? — Ay; I know thy errand, I will go with thee: — The day, my friends, and all things stay for me.
                                                    [*Exeunt.*

SCENE II

The French camp.

Enter the DAUPHIN, ORLEANS,
RAMBURES, *and others.*

ORLEANS
The sun doth gild our armour; up, my lords!
DAUPHIN
Montez à cheval! — My horse! *varlet, laquais!* ha!
ORLEANS
O brave spirit!
DAUPHIN
Via! — *les eaux et la terre,* —
ORLEANS
Rien puis? l'air et le feu, —
DAUPHIN
Ciel! cousin Orleans.
Enter CONSTABLE.
Now, my lord Constable!
CONSTABLE
Hark, how our steeds for present service neigh!
DAUPHIN
Mount them, and make incision in their hides,
That their hot blood may spin in English eyes,
And dout them with superfluous courage, ha!
RAMBURES
What, will you have them weep our horses' blood?
How shall we, then, behold their natural tears?
Enter a MESSENGER.
MESSENGER
The English are embattled, you French peers.
CONSTABLE
To horse, you gallant princes! straight to horse!
Do but behold yond poor and starved band,
And your fair show shall suck away their souls,
Leaving them but the shales and husks of men.
There is not work enough for all our hands;
Scarce blood enough in all their sickly veins
To give each naked curtle-axe a stain,
That our French gallants shall to-day draw out,
And sheathe for lack of sport: let us but blow on them,
The vapour of our valour will o'erturn them.
'Tis positive 'gainst all exceptions, lords,
That our superfluous lackeys and our peasants, —
Who in unnecessary action swarm
About our squares of battle, — were enow
To purge this field of such a hilding foe;
Though we upon this mountain's basis by
Took stand for idle speculation, —
But that our honours must not. What's to say?
A very little little let us do,
And all is done. Then let the trumpets sound
The tucket-sonance and the note to mount:
For our approach shall so much dare the field,
That England shall couch down in fear, and yield.
Enter GRANDPRÉ.
GRANDPRÉ
Why do you stay so long, my lords of France?
Yond island carrions, desperate of their bones,
Ill-favouredly become the morning field:
Their ragged curtains poorly are let loose,
And our air shakes them passing scornfully:
Big Mars seems bankrout in their beggar'd host,
And faintly through a rusty beaver peeps:
The horsemen sit like fixed candlesticks,
With torch-staves in their hand; and their poor jades
Lob down their heads, dropping the hides and hips,
The gum down-roping from their pale-dead eyes,
And in their pale dull mouths the gimmal-bit
Lies foul with chew'd grass, still and motionless;
And their executors, the knavish crows,
Fly o'er them, all impatient for their hour.
Description cannot suit itself in words
To demonstrate the life of such a battle
In life so lifeless as it shows itself.
CONSTABLE
They have said their prayers, and they stay for death.
DAUPHIN
Shall we go send them dinners and fresh suits,
And give their fasting horses provender,
And after fight with them?
CONSTABLE
I stay but for my guidon: — to the field! —
I will the banner from a trumpet take,
And use it for my haste. Come, come, away!
The sun is high, and we outwear the day. [*Exeunt.*

SCENE III

The English camp.

Enter GLOSTER, BEDFORD, EXETER,
ERPINGHAM, *with all his host;* SALISBURY, *and*
WESTMORELAND.

GLOSTER
Where is the king?
BEDFORD
The king himself is rode to view the battle.
WESTMORELAND
Of fighting-men they have full three-score thousand.
EXETER
There's five to one; besides, they all are fresh.
SALISBURY
God's arm strike with us! 'tis a fearful odds.
God b' wi' you, princes all; I'll to my charge:
If we no more meet till we meet in heaven,
Then, joyfully, — my noble Lord of Bedford, —
My dear Lord Gloster, — and my good Lord Exeter, —
And my kind kinsman, — warriors all, adieu!
BEDFORD
Farewell, good Salisbury; and good luck go with thee!
EXETER
Farewell, kind lord; fight valiantly to-day:
And yet I do thee wrong to mind thee of it,
For thou art fram'd of the firm truth of valour.
[*Exit* SALISBURY.
BEDFORD
He is as full of valour as of kindness;
Princely in both.
Enter KING HENRY.
WESTMORELAND
O, that we now had here
But one ten thousand of those men in England
That do no work to-day!
KING HENRY
What's he that wishes so?
My cousin Westmoreland? — No, my fair cousin:
If we are mark'd to die, we are enow
To do our country loss; and if to live,
The fewer men, the greater share of honour.
God's will! I pray thee, wish not one man more.
By Jove, I am not covetous for gold;
Nor care I who doth feed upon my cost;
It yearns me not if men my garments wear;
Such outward things dwell not in my desires:
But if it be a sin to covet honour,
I am the most offending soul alive.
No, faith, my coz, wish not a man from England:
God's peace! I would not lose so great an honour,
As one man more, methinks, would share from me,
For the best hope I have. O, do not wish one more!
Rather proclaim it, Westmoreland, through my host,
That he which hath no stomach to this fight,
Let him depart; his passport shall be made,
And crowns for convoy put into his purse:
We would not die in that man's company
That fears his fellowship to die with us.
This day is call'd the feast of Crispian:
He that outlives this day, and comes safe home,
Will stand a tip-toe when the day is named,
And rouse him at the name of Crispian.
He that shall live this day, and see old age,
Will yearly on the vigil feast his neighbours,
And say, 'To-morrow is Saint Crispian':
Then will he strip his sleeve and show his scars,
And say, 'These wounds I had on Crispin's day.'
Old men forget: yet all shall be forgot,
But he'll remember with advantages
What feats he did that day: then shall our names,
Familiar in their mouths as household words, —
Harry the king, Bedford and Exeter,
Warwick and Talbot, Salisbury and Gloster, —
Be in their flowing cups freshly remember'd.
This story shall the good man teach his son;
And Crispin Crispian shall ne'er go by,
From this day to the ending of the world,
But we in it shall be remembered, —
We few, we happy few, we band of brothers;
For he to-day that sheds his blood with me
Shall be my brother; be he ne'er so vile,
This day shall gentle his condition:
And gentlemen in England now a-bed
Shall think themselves accurs'd they were not here;
And hold their manhoods cheap whiles any speaks
That fought with us upon Saint Crispin's day.

Enter SALISBURY.

SALISBURY
My sovereign lord, bestow yourself with speed:
The French are bravely in their battles set,
And will with all expedience charge on us.
KING HENRY
All things are ready, if our minds be so.
WESTMORELAND
Perish the man whose mind is backward now!
KING HENRY
Thou dost not wish more help from England, coz?
WESTMORELAND
God's will! my liege, would you and I alone,
Without more help, could fight this royal battle out!
KING HENRY
Why, now thou hast unwish'd five thousand men;
Which likes me better than to wish us one. —
You know your places: God be with you all!

Tucket. Enter MONTJOY.

MONTJOY
Once more I come to know of thee, King Harry,
If for thy ransom thou wilt now compound,
Before thy most assured overthrow:
For certainly thou art so near the gulf,
Thou needs must be englutted. Besides, in mercy,
The Constable desires thee thou wilt mind
Thy followers of repentance; that their souls
May make a peaceful and a sweet retire
From off these fields, where, wretches, their poor
    bodies
Must lie and fester.
KING HENRY
Who hath sent thee now?
MONTJOY
The Constable of France.
KING HENRY
I pray thee, bear my former answer back:
Bid them achieve me, and then sell my bones.
Good God! why should they mock poor fellows thus?
The man that once did sell the lion's skin
While the beast liv'd, was kill'd with hunting him.
A many of our bodies shall no doubt
Find native graves; upon the which, I trust,
Shall witness live in brass of this day's work:
And those that leave their valiant bones in France,
Dying like men, though buried in your dunghills,
They shall be fam'd; for there the sun shall greet them,
And draw their honours reeking up to heaven;
Leaving their earthly parts to choke your clime,
The smell whereof shall breed a plague in France.
Mark, then, abounding valour in our English;
That, being dead, like to the bullet's grazing,
Break out into a second course of mischief,
Killing in relapse of mortality.
Let me speak proudly: — tell the Constable
We are but warriors for the working-day;
Our gayness and our gilt are all besmirch'd
With rainy marching in the painful field;
There's not a piece of feather in our host, —
Good argument, I hope, we will not fly, —
And time hath worn us into slovenry:
But, by the mass, our hearts are in the trim;
And my poor soldiers tell me, yet ere night
They'll be in fresher robes; or they will pluck
The gay new coats o'er the French soldiers' heads,
And turn them out of service. If they do this, —
As, if God please, they shall, — my ransom then
Will soon be levied. Herald, save thou thy labour;
Come thou no more for ransom, gentle herald:
They shall have none, I swear, but these my joints, —
Which if they have as I will leave 'em them,
Shall yield them little, tell the Constable.
MONTJOY
I shall, King Harry. And so, fare thee well:
Thou never shalt hear herald any more. [*Exit.*
KING HENRY
I fear thou'lt once more come again for ransom.

Enter YORK.

YORK
My lord, most humbly on my knee I beg
The leading of the vaward.
KING HENRY
Take it, brave York. — Now, soldiers, march away: —
And how thou pleasest, God, dispose the day! [*Exeunt.*

PISTOL Bid him prepare; for I will cut his throat.

SCENE IV

The field of battle.

Alarum: excursions. Enter PISTOL, *French* SOLDIER, *and* BOY.

PISTOL
Yield, cur!

FRENCH SOLDIER
Je pense que vous êtes le gentilhomme de bonne qualité.

PISTOL
Qualitie calmie custure me! Art thou a gentleman? what
is thy name? discuss.

FRENCH SOLDIER
O Seigneur Dieu!

PISTOL
O, Signieur Dew should be a gentleman: —
Perpend my words, O Signieur Dew, and mark; —
O Signieur Dew, thou diest on point of fox,
Except, O Signieur, thou do give to me
Egregious ransom.

FRENCH SOLDIER
O, prenez miséricorde! ayez pitié de moy!

PISTOL
Moy shall not serve; I will have forty moys;
Or I will fetch thy rim out at thy throat
In drops of crimson blood.

FRENCH SOLDIER
Est-il impossible d'échapper la force de ton bras?

PISTOL
Brass, cur!
Thou damned and luxurious mountain-goat,
Offer'st me brass?

FRENCH SOLDIER
O, pardonnez-moy!

PISTOL
Say'st thou me so? is that a ton of moys? —
Come hither, boy: ask me this slave in French
What is his name.

BOY
Écoutez: comment êtes-vous appelé?

FRENCH SOLDIER
Monsieur le Fer.

BOY
He says his name is Master Fer.

PISTOL
Master Fer! I'll fer him, and firk him, and ferret him: —
Discuss the same in French unto him.

BOY
I do not know the French for fer, and ferret, and firk.

PISTOL
Bid him prepare; for I will cut his throat.

FRENCH SOLDIER
Que dit-il, monsieur?

BOY
*Il me commande de vous dire que vous faites vous prêt; car
ce soldat ici est disposé tout à cette heure de couper votre
gorge.*

PISTOL
Owy, cuppele gorge, permafoy,
Peasant, unless thou give me crowns, brave crowns;

Or mangled shalt thou be by this my sword.

FRENCH SOLDIER
*O, je vous supplie, pour l'amour de Dieu, me pardonner! Je
suis gentilhomme de bonne maison: gardez ma vie, et je
vous donnerai deux cents écus.*

PISTOL
What are his words?

BOY
He prays you to save his life: he is a gentleman of a
good house; and for his ransom he will give you two
hundred crowns.

PISTOL
Tell him my fury shall abate, and I
The crowns will take.

FRENCH SOLDIER
Petit monsieur, que dit-il?

BOY
*Encore qu'il est contre son jurement de pardonner aucun
prisonnier, néanmoins, pour les écus que vous l'avez
promis, il est content de vous donner la liberté, le
franchisement.*

FRENCH SOLDIER
*Sur mes genoux je vous donne mille remercîmes; et je
m'estime heureux que je suis tombé entre les mains d'un
chevalier, je pense, le plus brave, vaillant, et très distingué
seigneur d'Angleterre.*

PISTOL
Expound unto me, boy.

BOY
He gives you, upon his knees, a thousand thanks; and
he esteems himself happy that he hath fall'n into the
hands of one, as he thinks, the most brave, valorous,
and thrice-worthy signieur of England.

PISTOL
As I suck blood, I will some mercy show. — Follow me,
cur. [*Exit.*

BOY
Suivez-vous le grand capitaine. [*Exit* FRENCH SOLDIER.] I
did never know so full a voice issue from so empty a
heart: but the saying is true, — The empty vessel
makes the greatest sound. Bardolph and Nym had ten
times more valour than this roaring devil i'th' old play,
that every one may pare his nails with a wooden
dagger; and they are both hang'd; and so would this be,
if he durst steal any thing adventurously. I must stay
with the lackeys, with the luggage of our camp: the
French might have a good prey of us, if he knew of it;
for there is none to guard it but boys. [*Exit.*

SCENE V

Another part of the field.

Enter CONSTABLE, ORLEANS, BOURBON,
DAUPHIN, RAMBURES, *and others.*

CONSTABLE
O diable!

ORLEANS
O Seigneur! — le jour est perdu, tout est perdu!

DAUPHIN
Mort de ma vie! all is confounded, all!
Reproach and everlasting shame
Sits mocking in our plumes. — *O méchante fortune!* —

Do not run away. [*A short alarum.*

CONSTABLE
Why, all our ranks are broke.

DAUPHIN
O perdurable shame! — let's stab ourselves.
Be these the wretches that we play'd at dice for?

ORLEANS
Is this the king we sent to for his ransom?

BOURBON
Shame, and eternal shame, nothing but shame!
Let's die in honour: once more back again;
And he that will not follow Bourbon now,
Let him go hence, and with his cap in hand,
Like a base pandar, hold the chamber-door
Whilst by a slave, no gentler than my dog,
His fairest daughter is contaminate.

CONSTABLE
Disorder, that hath spoil'd us, friend us now!
Let us on heaps go offer up our lives.

ORLEANS
We are enow, yet living in the field,
To smother up the English in our throngs,
If any order might be thought upon.

BOURBON
The devil take order now! I'll to the throng:
Let life be short; else shame will be too long. [*Exeunt.*

SCENE VI

Another part of the field.

Alarum. Enter KING HENRY *and* FORCES, EXETER,
and others.

KING HENRY
Well have we done, thrice-valiant countrymen:
But all's not done; yet keep the French the field.

EXETER
The Duke of York commends him to your majesty.

KING HENRY
Lives he, good uncle? thrice within this hour
I saw him down; thrice up again, and fighting;
From helmet to the spur all blood he was.

EXETER
In which array, brave soldier, doth he lie,
Larding the plain; and by his bloody side,
Yoke-fellow to his honour-owing wounds,
The noble Earl of Suffolk also lies.
Suffolk first died: and York, all haggled over,
Comes to him, where in gore he lay insteep'd,
And takes him by the beard; kisses the gashes
That bloodily did yawn upon his face;
And cries aloud, 'Tarry, dear cousin Suffolk!
My soul shall thine keep company to heaven;
Tarry, sweet soul, for mine; then fly abreast;
As in this glorious and well-foughten field
We kept together in our chivalry!'
Upon these words I came, and cheer'd him up:
He smil'd me in the face, raught me his hand,
And, with a feeble gripe, says, 'Dear my lord,
Commend my service to my sovereign.'
So did he turn, and over Suffolk's neck
He threw his wounded arm, and kiss'd his lips;
And so, espous'd to death, with blood he seal'd
A testament of noble-ending love.
The pretty and sweet manner of it forc'd
Those waters from me which I would have stopp'd;
But I had not so much of man in me,
And all my mother came into mine eyes,
And gave me up to tears.

KING HENRY
                              I blame you not;
For, hearing this, I must perforce compound
With mistful eyes, or they will issue too. — [*Alarum.*
But, hark! what new alarum is this same? —
The French have reinforc'd their scatter'd men: —
Then every soldier kill his prisoners;
Give the word through. [*Exeunt.*

SCENE VII

Another part of the field.

Enter FLUELLEN *and* GOWER.

FLUELLEN
Kill the poys and the luggage! 'tis expressly against the
law of arms: 'tis as arrant a piece of knavery, mark you
now, as can be offer't; in your conscience, now, is it
not?

GOWER
'Tis certain there's not a boy left alive; and the cowardly
rascals that ran from the battle ha' done this slaughter:
besides, they have burn'd and carried away all that was

in the king's tent; wherefore the king, most worthily, hath caused every soldier to cut his prisoner's throat. O, 'tis a gallant king!

FLUELLEN
Ay, he was porn at Monmouth, Captain Gower. What call you the town's name where Alexander the Pig was porn!

GOWER
Alexander the Great.

FLUELLEN
Why, I pray you, is not pig great? the pig, or the great, or the mighty, or the huge, or the magnanimous, are all one reckonings, save the phrase is a little variations.

GOWER
I think Alexander the Great was born in Macedon: his father was call'd Philip of Macedon, as I take it.

FLUELLEN
I think it is in Macedon where Alexander is porn. I tell you, captain, if you look in the maps of the 'orld, I warrant you sall find, in the comparisons between Macedon and Monmouth, that the situations, look you, is both alike. There is a river in Macedon; and there is also moreover a river at Monmouth: it is called Wye at Monmouth; but it is out of my prains what is the name of the other river; but 'tis all one, 'tis alike as my fingers is to my fingers, and there is salmons in both. If you mark Alexander's life well, Harry of Monmouth's life is come after it indifferent well; for there is figures in all things. Alexander, — Got knows, and you know, — in his rages, and his furies, and his wraths, and his cholers, and his moods, and his displeasures, and his indignations, and also being a little intoxicates in his prains, did, in his ales and his angers, look you, kill his pest friend, Cleitus.

GOWER
Our king is not like him in that: he never kill'd any of his friends.

FLUELLEN
It is not well done, mark you now, take the tales out of my mouth, ere it is made and finish't. I speak but in the figures and comparisons of it: as Alexander kill'd his friend Cleitus, being in his ales and his cups; so also Harry Monmouth, being in his right wits and his goot judgements, turn'd away the fat knight with the great-pelly doublet: he was full of jests, and gipes, and knaveries, and mocks; I have forgot his name.

GOWER
Sir John Falstaff.

FLUELLEN
That is he: — I'll tell you there is goot men porn at Monmouth.

GOWER
Here comes his majesty.

Alarum. Enter KING HENRY, and FORCES; WARWICK, GLOSTER, EXETER, and others.

KING HENRY
I was not angry since I came to France
Until this instant. — Take a trumpet, herald;
Ride thou unto the horsemen on yond hill:
If they will fight with us, bid them come down,
Or void the field; they do offend our sight:
If they'll do neither, we will come to them,
And make them skirr away, as swift as stones
Enforced from the old Assyrian slings:
Besides, we'll cut the throats of those we have;
And not a man of them that we shall take
Shall taste our mercy: — go, and tell them so.

EXETER
Here comes the herald of the French, my liege.

GLOSTER
His eyes are humbler than they us'd to be.

Enter MONTJOY.

KING HENRY
How now! what means this, herald? know'st thou not
That I have fin'd these bones of mine for ransom?
Comest thou again for ransom?

MONTJOY
                              No, great king:
I come to thee for charitable licence
That we may wander o'er this bloody field
To look our dead, and then to bury them;
To sort our nobles from our common men;
For many of our princes — woe the while —
Lie drown'd and soak'd in mercenary blood;
So do our vulgar drench their peasant limbs
In blood of princes; and their wounded steeds
Fret fetlock deep in gore, and with wild rage
Yerk out their armed heels at their dead masters,
Killing them twice. O, give us leave, great king,
To view the field in safety, and dispose
Of their dead bodies!

KING HENRY
                    I tell thee truly, herald,
I know not if the day be ours or no;
For yet a many of your horsemen peer
And gallop o'er the field.

MONTJOY
                         The day is yours.

KING HENRY
Praised be God, and not our strength, for it! —
What is this castle call'd that stands hard by?

MONTJOY
They call it Agincourt.

KING HENRY
Then call we this the field of Agincourt,
Fought on the day of Crispin Crispianus.

FLUELLEN
Your grandfather of famous memory, an't please your majesty, and your great-uncle Edward the Plack Prince of Wales, as I have read in the chronicles, fought a most prave pattle here in France.

KING HENRY
They did, Fluellen.

FLUELLEN
Your majesty says very true: if your majesties is remember'd of it, the Welshmen did goot service in a garden where leeks did grow, wearing leeks in their Monmouth caps; which, your majesty knows, to this hour is an honourable padge of the service; and I do pelieve your majesty takes no scorn to wear the leek upon Saint Tavy's day.

KING HENRY
I wear it for a memorable honour;
For I am Welsh, you know, good countryman.

FLUELLEN
All the water in Wye cannot wash your majesty's Welsh plood out of your pody, I can tell you that: God pless it, and preserve it, as long as it pleases his Grace, and his majesty too!

KING HENRY
Thanks, good my countryman.

FLUELLEN
By Cheshu, I am your majesty's countryman, I care not who know it; I will confess it to all the 'orld: I need not to be ashamed of your majesty, praised be Got, so long as your majesty is an honest man.

KING HENRY
God keep me so! — Our heralds go with him:
Bring me just notice of the numbers dead
On both our parts. — Call yonder fellow hither.

[Points to WILLIAMS.
Exeunt HERALDS with MONTJOY.

EXETER
Soldier, you must come to the king.

KING HENRY
Soldier, why wear'st thou that glove in thy cap?

MICHAEL WILLIAMS
An't please your majesty, 'tis the gage of one that I should fight withal, if he be alive.

KING HENRY
An Englishman?

MICHAEL WILLIAMS
An't please your majesty, a rascal that swagger'd with me last night; who, if alive, and ever dare to challenge this glove, I have sworn to take him a box o'th'ear: or if I can see my glove in his cap, which he swore, as he was a soldier, he would wear if alive, I will strike it out soundly.

KING HENRY
What think you, Captain Fluellen? is it fit this soldier keep his oath?

FLUELLEN
He is a craven and a villain else, an't please your majesty, in my conscience.

KING HENRY
It may be his enemy is a gentleman of great sort, quite from the answer of his degree.

FLUELLEN
Though he be as goot a gentleman as the tevil is, as Lucifer and Belzebub himself, it is necessary, look your Grace, that he keep his vow and his oath: if he be perjured, see you now, his reputation is as arrant a villain and a Jack-sauce, as ever his plack shoe trod upon Got's ground and his earth, in my conscience, la.

KING HENRY
Then keep thy vow, sirrah, when thou meet'st the fellow.

MICHAEL WILLIAMS
So I will, my liege, as I live.

KING HENRY
Who servest thou under?

MICHAEL WILLIAMS
Under Captain Gower, my liege.

FLUELLEN
Gower is a goot captain, and is good knowledge and literatured in the wars.

KING HENRY
Call him hither to me, soldier.

MICHAEL WILLIAMS
I will, my liege.   *[Ex*

KING HENRY
Here, Fluellen; wear thou this favour for me, and stick it in thy cap: when Alençon and myself were down together, I pluck'd this glove from his helm: if any ma challenge this, he is a friend to Alençon, and an enem to our person; if thou encounter any such, apprehend him, an thou dost me love.

FLUELLEN
Your Grace does me as great honours as can be desire in the hearts of his subjects: I would fain see the man, that has but two legs, that shall find himself aggriefed at this glove; that is all; but I would fain see it once, an please Got of his grace that I might see.

KING HENRY
Know'st thou Gower?

FLUELLEN
He is my dear friend, an please you.

KING HENRY
Pray thee, go seek him, and bring him to my tent.

FLUELLEN
I will fetch him.

KING HENRY
My Lord of Warwick, and my brother Gloster,
Follow Fluellen closely at the heels:
The glove which I have given him for a favour
May haply purchase him a box o'th'ear;
It is the soldier's; I, by bargain, should
Wear it myself. Follow, good cousin Warwick:
If that the soldier strike him, — as I judge
By his blunt bearing, he will keep his word, —
Some sudden mischief may arise of it;
For I do know Fluellen valiant,
And, touch'd with choler, hot as gunpowder,
And quickly will return an injury:
Follow, and see there be no harm between them. —
Go you with me, uncle of Exeter.   *[Exeur*

SCENE VIII

Before KING HENRY'S pavilion.

Enter GOWER and WILLIAMS.

MICHAEL WILLIAMS
I warrant it is to knight you, captain.

Enter FLUELLEN.

FLUELLEN
God's will and his pleasure, captain, I peseech you now, come apace to the king: there is more goot towar you peradventure than is in your knowledge to dream of.

MICHAEL WILLIAMS
Sir, know you this glove?

FLUELLEN
Know the glove! I know the glove is a glove.

MICHAEL WILLIAMS
I know this; and thus I challenge it.   *[Strikes hir*

FLUELLEN
'Splood, an arrant traitor as any's in the universal 'orld or in France, or in England!

GOWER
How now, sir! you villain!

MICHAEL WILLIAMS
Do you think I'll be forsworn?

FLUELLEN
Stand away, Captain Gower; I will give treason his payment into plows, I warrant you.

MICHAEL WILLIAMS
I am no traitor.

FLUELLEN
That's a lie in thy throat. — I charge you in his majesty's name, apprehend him: he's a friend of the Duke Alençon's.

Enter WARWICK and GLOSTER.

WARWICK
How now, how now! what's the matter?

FLUELLEN
My Lord of Warwick, here is — praised be Got for it! — most contagious treason come to light, look you, as you shall desire in a summer's day. — Here is his majesty.

Enter KING HENRY *and* EXETER.

KING HENRY
How now! what's the matter?

FLUELLEN
My liege, here is a villain and a traitor, that, look your grace, has struck the glove which your majesty is take out of the helmet of Alençon.

MICHAEL WILLIAMS
My liege, this was my glove; here is the fellow of it; and he that I gave it to in change promised to wear it in his cap: I promised to strike him, if he did: I met this man with my glove in his cap, and I have been as good as my word.

FLUELLEN
Your majesty hear now, saving your majesty's manhood, what an arrant, rascally, beggarly, lousy knave it is: I hope your majesty is pear me testimony, and witness, and will avouchment, that this is the glove of Alençon, that your majesty is give me, in your conscience, now.

KING HENRY
Give me thy glove, soldier: look, here is the fellow of it. 'Twas I, indeed, thou promised'st to strike; and thou hast given me most bitter terms.

FLUELLEN
An please your majesty, let his neck answer for it, if there is any martial law in the 'orld.

KING HENRY
How canst thou make me satisfaction?

MICHAEL WILLIAMS
All offences, my liege, come from the heart: never came any from mine that might offend your majesty.

KING HENRY
It was ourself thou didst abuse.

MICHAEL WILLIAMS
Your majesty came not like yourself: you appear'd to me but as a common man; witness the night, your garments, your lowliness; and what your highness suffer'd under that shape, I beseech you take it for your own fault, and not mine: for had you been as I took you for, I made no offence; therefore, I beseech your highness, pardon me.

KING HENRY
Here, uncle Exeter, fill this glove with crowns, and give it to this fellow. — Keep it, fellow; and wear it for an honour in thy cap till I do challenge it. — Give him the crowns: — and, captain, you must needs be friends with him.

FLUELLEN
By this day and this light, the fellow has mettle enough in his pelly. — Hold, there is twelve pence for you; and I pray you to serve Got, and keep you out of prawls, and prabbles, and quarrels, and dissensions, and, I warrant you, it is the better for you.

MICHAEL WILLIAMS
I will none of your money.

FLUELLEN
It is with a goot will; I can tell you, it will serve you to mend your shoes: come, wherefore should you be so pashful? your shoes is not so goot; 'tis a good silling, I warrant you, or I will change it.

Enter an English HERALD.

KING HENRY
Now, herald, — are the dead number'd?

HERALD
Here is the number of the slaughter'd French.
[*Delivers a paper.*

KING HENRY
What prisoners of good sort are taken, uncle?

EXETER
Charles Duke of Orleans, nephew to the king;
John Duke of Bourbon, and Lord Bouciqualt:
Of other lords and barons, knights and squires,
Full fifteen hundred, besides common men.

KING HENRY
This note doth tell me of ten thousand French
That in the field lie slain: of princes, in this number,
And nobles bearing banners, there lie dead
One hundred twenty-six: added to these,
Of knights, esquires, and gallant gentlemen,
Eight thousand four hundred; of the which,
Five hundred were but yesterday dubb'd knights:
So that, in these ten thousand they have lost,
There are but sixteen hundred mercenaries;

The rest are princes, barons, lords, knights, squires,
And gentlemen of blood and quality.
The names of those their nobles that lie dead, —
Charles Delabreth, high-Constable of France;
Jaques of Chatillon, admiral of France;
The master of the cross-bows, Lord Rambures;
Great-master of France, the brave Sir Guiscard Dauphin;
John Duke of Alençon; Antony Duke of Brabant,
The brother of the Duke of Burgundy;
And Edward Duke of Bar: of lusty earls,
Grandpré and Roussi, Fauconberg and Foix,
Beaumont and Marle, Vaudemont and Lestrale.
Here was a royal fellowship of death! —
Where is the number of our English dead? —
[HERALD *presents another paper.*
Edward the Duke of York, the Earl of Suffolk,
Sir Richard Ketly, Davy Gam, esquire;
None else of name; and of all other men
But five and twenty. — O God, Thy arm was here;
And not to us, but to Thy arm alone,
Ascribe we all! — When, without stratagem,
But in plain shock and even play of battle,
Was ever known so great and little loss
On one part and on th'other? — Take it, God,
For it is only thine!

EXETER
'Tis wonderful!

KING HENRY
Come, go we in procession to the village:
And be it death proclaimed through our host
To boast of this, or take the praise from God
Which is His only.

FLUELLEN
Is it not lawful, an please your majesty, to tell how many is kill'd?

KING HENRY
Yes, captain; but with this acknowledgement,
That God fought for us.

FLUELLEN
Yes, my conscience, He did us great goot.

KING HENRY
Do we all holy rites:
Let there be sung *Non nobis* and *Te Deum.*
The dead with charity enclos'd in clay,
We'll then to Calais; and to England then;
Where ne'er from France arriv'd more happy men.
[*Exeunt.*

ACT V

PROLOGUE
Enter CHORUS.

CHORUS
Vouchsafe to those that have not read the story,
That I may prompt them: and of such as have,
I humbly pray them to admit th'excuse
Of time, of numbers, and due course of things,
Which cannot in their huge and proper life
Be here presented. Now we bear the king
Toward Calais: grant him there; there seen,
Heave him away upon your winged thoughts
Athwart the sea. Behold, the English beach
Pales in the flood with men, with wives, and boys,
Whose shouts and claps out-voice the deep-mouth'd sea,
Which, like a mighty whiffler 'fore the king,
Seems to prepare his way: so let him land;
And solemnly see him set on to London.
So swift a pace hath thought, that even now
You may imagine him upon Blackheath;
Where that his lords desire him to have borne
His bruised helmet and his bended sword
Before him through the city: he forbids it,
Being free from vainness and self-glorious pride;
Giving full trophy, signal, and ostent,
Quite from himself to God. But now behold,
In the quick forge and working-house of thought,
How London doth pour out her citizens!
The mayor, and all his brethren, in best sort, —
Like to the senators of th'antique Rome,
With the plebeians swarming at their heels, —
Go forth, and fetch their conquering Cæsar in:
As, by a lower but loving likelihood,
Were now the general of our gracious empress —
As in good time he may — from Ireland coming,
Bringing rebellion broached on his sword,
How many would the peaceful city quit,
To welcome him! much more, and much more cause,

Did they this Harry. Now in London place him; —
As yet the lamentation of the French
Invites the King of England's stay at home; —
The emperor's coming in behalf of France,
To order peace between them; — and omit
All the occurrences, whatever chanc'd,
Till Harry's back-return again to France:
There must we bring him; and myself have play'd
The interim, by remembering you 'tis past.
Then brook abridgement; and your eyes advance,
After your thoughts, straight back again to France.
[*Exit.*

SCENE I
France. The English camp.

Enter FLUELLEN *and* GOWER.

GOWER
Nay, that's right; but why wear you your leek to-day?
Saint Davy's day is past.

FLUELLEN
There is occasions and causes why and wherefore in all things: I will tell you, asse my friend, Captain Gower: — the rascally, scald, peggarly, lousy, pragging knave, Pistol, — which you and yourself, and all the 'orld, know to be no petter than a fellow, look you now, of no merits, — he is come to me, and prings me 'pread and salt yesterday, look you, and pid me eat my leek: it was in a place where I could not preed no contention with him; but I will be so pold as to wear it in my cap till I see him once again, and then I will tell him a little piece of my desires.

GOWER
Why, here he comes, swelling like a turkeycock.

FLUELLEN
'Tis no matter for his swellings nor his turkeycocks.

Enter PISTOL.

God pless you, Auncient Pistol! you scurvy, lousy knave, God pless you!

PISTOL
Ha! art thou bedlam? dost thou thirst, base Trojan,
To have me fold up Parca's fatal web?
Hence! I am qualmish at the smell of leek.

FLUELLEN
I peseech you heartily, scurvy, lousy knave, at my desires, and my requests, and my petitions, to eat, look you, this leek: because, look you, you do not love it, nor your affections, and your appetites, and your digestions, does not agree with it, I would desire you to eat it.

PISTOL
Not for Cadwallader and all his goats.

FLUELLEN
There is one goat for you. [*Strikes him.*] Will you be so goot, scald knave, as eat it?

PISTOL
Base Trojan, thou shalt die.

FLUELLEN
You say very true, scald knave, — when Got's will is: I will desire you to live in the mean time, and eat your victuals: come, there is sauce for it. [*Strikes him again.*] You call'd me yesterday mountain-squire; but I will make you to-day a squire of low degree. I pray you, fall to: if you can mock a leek, you can eat a leek.

GOWER
Enough, captain: you have astonish'd him.

FLUELLEN
I say, I will make him eat some part of my leek, or I will peat his pate four days. — Pite, I pray you; it is good for your green wound and your ploody coxcomb.

PISTOL
Must I bite?

FLUELLEN
Yes, certainly, and out of doubt, and out of question too, and ambiguities.

PISTOL
By this leek, I will most horribly revenge:
I eat and eat, I swear —

FLUELLEN
Eat, I pray you: will you have some more sauce to your leek? there is not enough leek to swear by.

PISTOL
Quiet thy cudgel; thou dost see I eat.

FLUELLEN
Much goot do you, scald knave, heartily. Nay, pray you, throw none away; the skin is goot for your proken coxcomb. When you take occasions to see leeks hereafter, I pray you, mock at 'em; that is all.

PISTOL
Good.

FLUELLEN I pray you, fall to: if you can mock a leek, you can eat a leek.

FLUELLEN
Ay, leeks is goot: — hold you, there is a groat to heal
your pate.

PISTOL
Me a groat!

FLUELLEN
Yes, verily and in truth, you shall take it; or I have
another leek in my pocket, which you shall eat.

PISTOL
I take thy groat in earnest of revenge.

FLUELLEN
If I owe you any thing, I will pay you in cudgels; you shall
be a woodmonger, and buy nothing of me but cudgels.
Got b' wi' you, and keep you, and heal your pate.   [*Exit.*

PISTOL
All hell shall stir for this.

GOWER
Go, go; you are a counterfeit cowardly knave. Will you
mock at an ancient tradition, — begun upon an
honourable respect, and worn as a memorable trophy
of predeceased valour, — and dare not avouch in your
deeds any of your words? I have seen you gleeking and
galling at this gentleman twice or thrice. You thought,
because he could not speak English in the native garb,
he could not therefore handle an English cudgel: you
find it otherwise; and henceforth let a Welsh correction
teach you a good English condition. Fare ye well.   [*Exit.*

PISTOL
Doth Fortune play the huswife with me now?
News have I, that my Nell is dead i' the spital
Of malady of France;
And there my rendezvous is quite cut off.
Old I do wax; and from my weary limbs
Honour is cudgell'd. Well, bawd will I turn,
And something lean to cutpurse of quick hand.
To England will I steal, and there I'll steal:
And patches will I get unto these scars,
And swear I got them in the Gallia wars.   [*Exit.*

SCENE II

France. The French KING'S *palace.*

Enter, at one door, KING HENRY, BEDFORD,
GLOSTER, EXETER, WARWICK,
WESTMORELAND, *and other* LORDS; *at another, the*
French KING, QUEEN ISABEL, *the* PRINCESS
KATHARINE, ALICE, *other* LADIES, *and* LORDS; *the*
DUKE *of* BURGUNDY, *and his* TRAIN.

KING HENRY
Peace to this meeting, wherefore we are met!
Unto our brother France, and to our sister,
Health and fair time of day; — joy and good wishes
To our most fair and princely cousin Katharine; —
And, as a branch and member of this royalty,

By whom this great assembly is contrived,
We do salute you, Duke of Burgundy; —
And, princes French, and peers, health to you all!

FRENCH KING
Right joyous are we to behold your face,
Most worthy brother England; fairly met: —
So are you, princes English, every one.

QUEEN ISABEL
So happy be the issue, brother England,
Of this good day and of this gracious meeting,
As we are now glad to behold your eyes;
Your eyes, which hitherto have borne in them
Against the French, that met them in their bent,
The fatal balls of murdering basilisks:
The venom of such looks, we fairly hope,
Have lost their quality; and that this day
Shall change all griefs and quarrels into love.

KING HENRY
To cry amen to that, thus we appear.

QUEEN ISABEL
You English princes all, I do salute you.

BURGUNDY
My duty to you both, on equal love,
Great Kings of France and England! That I have
  labour'd,
With all my wits, my pains, and strong endeavours,
To bring your most imperial majesties
Unto this bar and royal interview,
Your mightiness on both parts best can witness.
Since, then, my office hath so far prevail'd,
That, face to face and royal eye to eye,
You have congreeted, let it not disgrace me,
If I demand, before this royal view,
What rub or what impediment there is,
Why that the naked, poor, and mangled Peace,
Dear nurse of arts, plenties, and joyful births,
Should not, in this best garden of the world,
Our fertile France, put up her lovely visage?
Alas, she hath from France too long been chased!
And all her husbandry doth lie on heaps,
Corrupting in its own fertility.
Her vine, the merry cheerer of the heart,
Unpruned dies; her hedges even-pleach'd,
Like prisoners wildly overgrown with hair,
Put forth disorder'd twigs; her fallow leas
The darnel, hemlock, and rank fumitory,
Do root upon, while that the coulter rusts,
That should deracinate such savagery;
The even mead, that erst brought sweetly forth
The freckled cowslip, burnet, and green clover,
Wanting the scythe, all uncorrected, rank,
Conceives by idleness, and nothing teems
But hateful docks, rough thistles, kecksies, burs,
Losing both beauty and utility.
And as our vineyards, fallows, meads, and hedges,
Defective in their natures, grow to wildness,
Even so our houses, and ourselves, and children,

Have lost, or do not learn for want of time,
The sciences that should become our country;
But grow, like savages, — as soldiers will,
That nothing do but meditate on blood, —
To swearing, and stern looks, diffus'd attire,
And every thing that seems unnatural.
Which to reduce into our former favour,
You are assembled: and my speech entreats
That I may know the let, why gentle Peace
Should not expel these inconveniences,
And bless us with her former qualities.

KING HENRY
If, Duke of Burgundy, you would the peace,
Whose want gives growth to th'imperfections
Which you have cited, you must buy that peace
With full accord to all our just demands;
Whose tenours and particular effects
You have, enschedul'd briefly, in your hands.

BURGUNDY
The king hath heard them; to the which as yet
There is no answer made.

KING HENRY
                Well, then, the peace,
Which you before so urg'd, lies in his answer.

FRENCH KING
I have but with a cursorary eye
O'erglanc'd the articles: pleaseth your Grace
To appoint some of your council presently
To sit with us once more, with better heed
To re-survey them, we will suddenly
Pass our accept and peremptory answer.

KING HENRY
Brother, we shall. — Go, uncle Exeter, —
And brother Clarence, — and you, brother Gloster, —
Warwick, — and Huntingdon, — go with the king;
And take with you free power to ratify,
Augment, or alter, as your wisdoms best
Shall see advantageable for our dignity,
Any thing in or out of our demands;
And we'll consign thereto. — Will you, fair sister,
Go with the princes, or stay here with us?

QUEEN ISABEL
Our gracious brother, I will go with them:
Haply a woman's voice may do some good,
When articles too nicely urg'd be stood on.

KING HENRY
Yet leave our cousin Katharine here with us:
She is our capital demand, comprised
Within the fore-rank of our articles.

QUEEN ISABEL
She hath good leave.

           [*Exeunt all except* KING HENRY,
               KATHARINE, *and* ALICE

KING HENRY
           Fair Katharine, and most fair!
Will you vouchsafe to teach a soldier terms
Such as will enter at a lady's ear,
And plead his love-suit to her gentle heart?

KATHARINE
Your majesty shall mock at me; I cannot speak your
England.

KING HENRY
O fair Katharine, if you will love me soundly with your
French heart, I will be glad to hear you confess it
brokenly with your English tongue. Do you like me,
Kate?

KATHARINE
Pardonnez-moi, I cannot tell vat is 'like me'.

KING HENRY
An angel is like you, Kate, and you are like an angel.

KATHARINE
Que dit-il? que je suis semblable à les anges?

ALICE
Oui, vraiment, sauf votre grace, ainsi dit-il.

KING HENRY
I said so, dear Katharine; and I must not blush to affirm
it.

KATHARINE
O bon Dieu! les langues des hommes sont pleines de
tromperies.

KING HENRY
What says she, fair one? that the tongues of men are
full of deceits?

ALICE
Oui, dat de tongues of de mans is be full of deceits —
dat is de princess.

KING HENRY
The princess is the better Englishwoman. I'faith, Kate
my wooing is fit for thy understanding: I am glad thou

FRENCH KING Right joyous are we to behold your face, most worthy brother England.

canst speak no better English; for, if thou couldst, thou wouldst find me such a plain king, that thou wouldst think I had sold my farm to buy my crown. I know no ways to mince it in love, but directly to say 'I love you': then, if you urge me farther than to say, 'Do you in faith?' I wear out my suit. Give me your answer; i'faith, do; and so clap hands and a bargain: how say you, lady?

KATHARINE
Sauf votre honneur, me understand vell.

KING HENRY
Marry, if you would put me to verses or to dance for your sake, Kate, why, you undid me: for the one, I have neither words nor measure; and for the other, I have no strength in measure, yet a reasonable measure in strength. If I could win a lady at leap-frog, or by vaulting into my saddle with my armour on my back, under the correction of bragging be it spoken, I should quickly leap into a wife. Or if I might buffet for my love, or bound my horse for her favours, I could lay on like a butcher, and sit like a jack-an-apes, never off. But, before God, Kate, I cannot look greenly, nor gasp out my eloquence, nor I have no cunning in protestation; only downright oaths, which I never use till urged, nor never break for urging. If thou canst love a fellow of this temper, Kate, whose face is not worth sun-burning, that never looks in his glass for love of any thing he sees there, — let thine eye be thy cook. I speak to thee plain soldier: if thou canst love me for this, take me; if not, to say to thee that I shall die, is true, — but for thy love, by the Lord, no; yet I love thee too. And while thou livest, dear Kate, take a fellow of plain and uncoin'd constancy; for he perforce must do thee right, because he hath not the gift to woo in other places: for these fellows of infinite tongue, that can rime themselves into ladies' favours, they do always reason themselves out again. What! a speaker is but a prater; a rime is but a ballad. A good leg will fall; a straight back will stoop; a black beard will turn white; a curl'd pate will grow bald; a fair face will wither; a full eye will wax hollow: but a good heart, Kate, is the sun and the moon; or, rather, the sun, and not the moon, — for it shines bright, and never changes, but keeps his course truly. If thou would have such a one, take me: and take me, take a soldier; take a soldier, take a king: and what say'st thou, then, to my love? speak, my fair, and fairly, I pray thee.

KATHARINE
Is it possible dat I sould love de enemy of France?

KING HENRY
No; it is not possible you should love the enemy of France, Kate: but, in loving me, you should love the friend of France; for I love France so well, that I will not part with a village of it; I will have it all mine: and, Kate, when France is mine and I am yours, then yours is France and you are mine.

KATHARINE
I cannot tell vat is dat.

KING HENRY
No, Kate? I will tell thee in French; which I am sure will hang upon my tongue like a new-married wife about her husband's neck, hardly to be shook off. *Je quand sur le possession de France, et quand vous avez le possession de moi,* — let me see, what then? Saint Denis be my speed! — *donc votre est France et vous êtes mienne.* It is as easy for me, Kate, to conquer the kingdom, as to speak so much more French: I shall never move thee in French, unless it be to laugh at me.

KATHARINE
Sauf votre honneur, le Français que vous parlez, il est meilleur que l'Anglais lequel je parle.

KING HENRY
No, faith, is't not, Kate: but thy speaking of my tongue, and I thine, most truly-falsely, must needs be granted to be much at one. But, Kate, dost thou understand thus much English, — Canst thou love me?

KATHARINE
I cannot tell.

KING HENRY
Can any of your neighbours tell, Kate? I'll ask them. Come, I know thou lovest me: and at night, when you come into your closet, you'll question this gentlewoman about me; and I know, Kate, you will to her dispraise those parts in me that you love with your heart: but, good Kate, mock me mercifully; the rather, gentle princess, because I love thee cruelly. If ever thou beest mine, Kate, — as I have a saving faith within me tells me thou shalt, — I get thee with scambling, and thou must therefore needs prove a good soldier-breeder: shall not thou and I, between Saint Denis and Saint George, compound a boy, half French, half English, that shall go to Constantinople and take the Turk by the beard? shall we not? what say'st thou, my fair flower-de-luce?

KATHARINE
I do not know dat.

KING HENRY
No; 'tis hereafter to know, but now to promise: do but now promise, Kate, you will endeavour for your French part of such a boy; and for my English moiety take the word of a king and a bachelor. How answer you, *la plus belle Katharine du monde, mon très-chère et devin déesse?*

KATHARINE
Your majestee ave *fausse* French enough to deceive de most *sage demoiselle* dat is *en France.*

KING HENRY
Now, fie upon my false French! By mine honour, in true English, I love thee, Kate: by which honour I dare not swear thou lovest me; yet my blood begins to flatter me that thou dost, notwithstanding the poor and untempering effect of my visage. Now, beshrew my father's ambition! he was thinking of civil wars when he got me: therefore was I created with a stubborn outside, with an aspect of iron, that, when I come to woo ladies, I fright them. But, in faith, Kate, the elder I wax, the better I shall appear: my comfort is, that old age, that ill layer-up of beauty, can do no more spoil upon my face: thou hast me, if thou hast me, at the worst; and thou shalt wear me, if thou wear me, better and better: — and therefore tell me, most fair Katharine, will you have me? Put off your maiden blushes; avouch the thoughts of your heart with the looks of an empress; take me by the hand, and say, 'Henry of England, I am thine': which word thou shalt no sooner bless mine ear withal, but I will tell thee aloud, 'England is thine, Ireland is thine, France is thine, and Henry Plantagenet is thine'; who, though I speak it before his face, if he be not fellow with the best king, thou shalt find the best king of good fellows. Come, your answer in broken music, — for thy voice is music and thy English broken; therefore, queen of all Katharines, break thy mind to me in broken English, — wilt thou have me?

KATHARINE
Dat is as it sall please de *roi mon père.*

KING HENRY
Nay, it will please him well, Kate, — it shall please him, Kate.

KATHARINE
Den it sall also content me.

KING HENRY
Upon that I kiss your hand, and I call you my queen.

KATHARINE
Laissez, mon seigneur, laissez, laissez: ma foi, je ne veux point que vous abaissiez votre grandeur en baisant la main d'une de votre indigne serviteur; excusez-moi, je vous supplie, mon très-puissant seigneur.

KING HENRY
Then I will kiss your lips, Kate.

KATHARINE
Les dames et demoiselles pour être baisées devant leur noces, il n'est pas la coutume de France.

KING HENRY
Madam my interpreter, what says she?

ALICE
Dat it is not be de fashion *pour les* ladies of France, — I cannot tell vat is *baiser en* Anglish.

KING HENRY
To kiss.

ALICE
Your majestee *entendre* bettre *que moi.*

KING HENRY
It is not a fashion for the maids in France to kiss before they are married, would she say?

ALICE
Oui, vraiment.

KING HENRY

O Kate, nice customs court'sy to great kings. Dear Kate, you and I cannot be confined within the weak list of a country's fashion: we are the makers of manners, Kate; and the liberty that follows our places stops the mouth of all find-faults, — as I will do yours for upholding the nice fashion of your country in denying me a kiss: therefore, patiently and yielding. [*Kissing her.*] You have witchcraft in your lips, Kate: there is more eloquence in a sugar touch of them than in the tongues of the French council; and they should sooner persuade Harry of England than a general petition of monarchs. — Here comes your father.

Enter the French KING *and* QUEEN, BURGUNDY, BEDFORD, GLOSTER, EXETER, WESTMORELAND, WARWICK, *etc.*

BURGUNDY

God save your majesty! my royal cousin,
Teach you our princess English?

KING HENRY

I would have her learn, my fair cousin, how perfectly I love her; and that is good English.

BURGUNDY

Is she not apt?

KING HENRY

Our tongue is rough, coz, and my condition is not smooth; so that, having neither the voice nor the heart of flattery about me, I cannot so conjure up the spirit of love in her, that he will appear in his true likeness.

BURGUNDY

Pardon the frankness of my mirth, if I answer you for that. If you would conjure in her, you must make a circle; if conjure up love in her in his true likeness, he must appear naked and blind. Can you blame her, then, being a maid yet rosed-over with the virgin crimson of modesty, if she deny the appearance of a naked blind boy in her naked seeing self? It were, my lord, a hard condition for a maid to consign to.

KING HENRY

Yet they do wink and yield, — as love is blind and enforces.

BURGUNDY

They are then excused, my lord, when they see not what they do.

KING HENRY

Then, good my lord, teach your cousin to consent winking.

BURGUNDY

I will wink on her to consent, my lord, if you will teach her to know my meaning: for maids, well summer'd and warm kept, are like flies at Bartholomew-tide, blind, though they have their eyes; and then they will

endure handling, which before would not abide looking on.

KING HENRY

This moral ties me over to time and a hot summer; and so I shall catch the fly, your cousin, in the latter end, and she must be blind too.

BURGUNDY

As love is, my lord, before it loves.

KING HENRY

It is so: and you may, some of you, thank love for my blindness, who cannot see many a fair French city for one fair French maid that stands in my way.

FRENCH KING

Yes, my lord, you see them perspectively, the cities turn'd into a maid; for they are all girdled with maiden walls that war hath never enter'd.

KING HENRY

Shall Kate be my wife?

FRENCH KING

So please you.

KING HENRY

I am content; so the maiden cities you talk of may wait on her: so the maid that stood in the way for my wish shall show me the way to my will.

FRENCH KING

We have consented to all terms of reason.

KING HENRY

Is't so, my lords of England?

WESTMORELAND

The king hath granted every article: —
His daughter first; and then, in sequel, all,
According to their firm proposed natures.

EXETER

Only, he hath not yet subscribed this:
Where your majesty demands, that the King of France, having any occasion to write for matter of grant, shall name your highness in this form and with this addition, in French, *Notre très-cher fils Henri, roi d'Angleterre, héritier de France*; and thus in Latin, *Præclarissimus filius noster Henricus, rex Angliæ, et hæres Franciæ.*

FRENCH KING

Nor this I have not, brother, so denied,
But your request shall make me let it pass.

KING HENRY

I pray you, then, in love and dear alliance,
Let that one article rank with the rest;
And thereupon give me your daughter.

FRENCH KING

Take her, fair son; and from her blood raise up
Issue to me; that the contending kingdoms
Of France and England, whose very shores look pale

With envy of each other's happiness,
May cease their hatred; and this dear conjunction
Plant neighbourhood and Christian-like accord
In their sweet bosoms, that never war advance
His bleeding sword 'twixt England and fair France.

ALL

Amen!

KING HENRY

Now, welcome, Kate; — and bear me witness all,
That here I kiss her as my sovereign queen. [*Flourish.*

QUEEN ISABEL

God, the best maker of all marriages,
Combine your hearts in one, your realms in one!
As man and wife, being two, are one in love,
So be there 'twixt your kingdoms such a spousal,
That never may ill office, or fell jealousy,
Which troubles oft the bed of blessed marriage,
Thrust in between the paction of these kingdoms,
To make divorce of their incorporate league;
That English may as French, French Englishmen,
Receive each other! — God speak this Amen!

ALL

Amen!

KING HENRY

Prepare we for our marriage: — on which day,
My Lord of Burgundy, we'll take your oath,
And all the peers', for surety of our leagues.
Then shall I swear to Kate, and you to me;
And may our oaths well kept and prosperous be!
[*Sennet. Exeunt.*

EPILOGUE

Enter CHORUS.

CHORUS

Thus far, with rough and all unable pen,
   Our bending author hath pursued the story;
In little room confining mighty men,
   Mangling by starts the full course of their glory.
Small time, but in that small, most greatly liv'd
   This star of England: fortune made his sword;
By which the world's best garden be achiev'd,
   And of it left his son imperial lord.
Henry the Sixth, in infant bands crown'd king
   Of France and England, did this king succeed;
Whose state so many had the managing,
   That they lost France, and made his England bleed:
Which oft our stage hath shown; and for their sake,
In your fair minds let this acceptance take. [*Exit.*

MUCH ADO ABOUT NOTHING

DRAMATIS PERSONAE

DON PEDRO, *prince of Arragon.*
DON JOHN, *his bastard brother.*
CLAUDIO, *a young lord of Florence.*
BENEDICK, *a young lord of Padua.*
LEONATO, *governor of Messina.*
ANTONIO, *his brother.*
BALTHAZAR, *attendant on Don Pedro.*

BORACHIO, } *followers of Don John.*
CONRADE, }
FRIAR FRANCIS.
DOGBERRY, *a constable.*
VERGES, *a headborough.*
A SEXTON.
A BOY.

HERO, *daughter to Leonato.*
BEATRICE, *niece to Leonato.*
MARGARET, } *gentlewomen attending on Hero.*
URSULA, }

MESSENGERS, WATCH, ATTENDANTS, *etc.*

SCENE — *Messina.*

ACT I

SCENE I

Before LEONATO'S *house.*

Enter LEONATO, HERO, *and* BEATRICE, *with a* MESSENGER.

LEONATO
I learn in this letter that Don Pedro of Arragon comes this night to Messina.

MESSENGER
He is very near by this: he was not three leagues off when I left him.

LEONATO
How many gentlemen have you lost in this action?

MESSENGER
But few of any sort, and none of name.

LEONATO
A victory is twice itself when the achiever brings home full numbers. I find here that Don Pedro hath bestow'd much honour on a young Florentine called Claudio.

MESSENGER
Much deserved on his part, and equally remember'd by Don Pedro. He hath borne himself beyond the promise of his age; doing, in the figure of a lamb, the feats of a lion: he hath, indeed, better better'd expectation than you must expect of me to tell you how.

LEONATO
He hath an uncle here in Messina will be very much glad of it.

MESSENGER
I have already deliver'd him letters, and there appears much joy in him; even so much, that joy could not show itself modest enough without a badge of bitterness.

LEONATO
Did he break out into tears?

MESSENGER
In great measure.

LEONATO
A kind overflow of kindness: there are no faces truer than those that are so wash'd. How much better is it to weep at joy than to joy at weeping!

BEATRICE
I pray you, is Signior Mountanto return'd from the wars or no?

MESSENGER
I know none of that name, lady: there was none such in the army of any sort.

LEONATO
What is he that you ask for, niece?

HERO
My cousin means Signior Benedick of Padua.

MESSENGER
O, he's return'd; and as pleasant as ever he was.

BEATRICE
He set up his bills here in Messina, and challenged Cupid at the flight; and my uncle's fool, reading the challenge, subscribed for Cupid, and challenged him at the birdbolt. — I pray you, how many hath he kill'd and

eaten in these wars? But how many hath he kill'd? for, indeed, I promised to eat all of his killing.

LEONATO
Faith, niece, you tax Signior Benedick too much; but he'll be meet with you, I doubt it not.

MESSENGER
He hath done good service, lady, in these wars.

BEATRICE
You had musty victual, and he hath holp to eat it: he's a very valiant trencher-man; he hath an excellent stomach.

MESSENGER
And a good soldier too, lady.

BEATRICE
And a good soldier to a lady: — but what is he to a lord?

MESSENGER
A lord to a lord, a man to a man; stuff'd with all honourable virtues.

BEATRICE
It is so, indeed; he is no less than a stuff'd man: but for the stuffing, — well, we are all mortal.

LEONATO
You must not, sir, mistake my niece. There is a kind of merry war betwixt Signior Benedick and her: they never meet but there's a skirmish of wit between them.

BEATRICE
Alas, he gets nothing by that! In our last conflict four of his five wits went halting off, and now is the whole man govern'd with one: so that if he have wit enough to keep himself warm, let him bear it for a difference between

BENEDICK I would my horse had the speed of your tongue,
and so good a continuer.

himself and his horse; for it is all the wealth that he
hath left, to be known a reasonable creature. — Who is
his companion now? He hath every month a new
sworn brother.

MESSENGER
Is't possible?

BEATRICE
Very easily possible: he wears his faith but as the
fashion of his hat; it ever changes with the next block.

MESSENGER
I see, lady, the gentleman is not in your books.

BEATRICE
No; an he were, I would burn my study. But, I pray you,
who is his companion? Is there no young squarer now
that will make a voyage with him to the devil?

MESSENGER
He is most in the company of the right noble Claudio.

BEATRICE
O Lord, he will hang upon him like a disease: he is
sooner caught than the pestilence, and the taker runs
presently mad. God help the noble Claudio! If he have
caught the Benedick, it will cost him a thousand pound
ere a' be cured.

MESSENGER
I will hold friends with you, lady.

BEATRICE
Do, good friend.

LEONATO
You will never run mad, niece.

BEATRICE
No, not till a hot January.

MESSENGER
Don Pedro is approach'd.

Enter DON PEDRO, DON JOHN, CLAUDIO,
BENEDICK, *and* BALTHAZAR.

DON PEDRO
Good Signior Leonato, you are come to meet your
trouble: the fashion of the world is to avoid cost, and
you encounter it.

LEONATO
Never came trouble to my house in the likeness of your
Grace: for trouble being gone, comfort should remain;
but when you depart from me, sorrow abides, and
happiness takes his leave.

DON PEDRO
You embrace your charge too willingly. — I think this
is your daughter.

LEONATO
Her mother hath many times told me so.

BENEDICK
Were you in doubt, sir, that you ask'd
her?

LEONATO
Signior Benedick, no; for then were you a
child.

DON PEDRO
You have it full, Benedick: we may guess
by this what you are, being a man. —
Truly, the lady fathers herself. — Be
happy, lady; for you are like an
honourable father.

BENEDICK
If Signior Leonato be her father, she
would not have his head on her shoulders
for all Messina, as like him as she is.

BEATRICE
I wonder that you will still be talking,
Signior Benedick: nobody marks you.

BENEDICK
What, my dear Lady Disdain! are you yet
living?

BEATRICE
Is it possible disdain should die while she
hath such meet food to feed it as Signior
Benedick? Courtesy itself must convert to
disdain, if you come in her presence.

BENEDICK
Then is courtesy a turncoat. — But it is
certain I am loved of all ladies, only you
excepted: and I would I could find in my
heart that I had not a hard heart; for,
truly, I love none.

BEATRICE
A dear happiness to women: they would
else have been troubled with a pernicious
suitor. I thank God and my cold blood, I am
of your humour for that: I had rather hear
my dog bark at a crow than a man swear he
loves me.

BENEDICK
God keep your ladyship still in that mind! so some
gentleman or other shall scape a predestinate scratch'd
face.

BEATRICE
Scratching could not make it worse, an'twere such a
face as yours were.

BENEDICK
Well, you are a rare parrot-teacher.

BEATRICE
A bird of my tongue is better than a beast of yours.

BENEDICK
I would my horse had the speed of your tongue, and so
good a continuer. But keep your way, i' God's name; I
have done.

BEATRICE
You always end with a jade's trick: I know you of old.

DON PEDRO
That is the sum of all: Leonato, — Signior Claudio and
Signior Benedick, — my dear friend Leonato hath
invited you all. I tell him we shall stay here at the least a
month; and he heartily prays some occasion may
detain us longer: I dare swear he is no hypocrite, but
prays from his heart.

LEONATO
If you swear, my lord, you shall not be forsworn. — Let
me bid you welcome, my lord: being reconciled to the
prince your brother, I owe you all duty.

DON JOHN
I thank you: I am not of many words, but I thank you.

LEONATO
Please it your Grace lead on?

DON PEDRO
Your hand, Leonato; we will go together.

[*Exeunt all except* BENEDICK *and* CLAUDIO.

CLAUDIO
Benedick, didst thou note the daughter of Signior
Leonato?

BENEDICK
I noted her not; but I look'd on her.

CLAUDIO
Is she not a modest young lady?

BENEDICK
Do you question me, as an honest man should do, for
my simple true judgement, or would you have me
speak after my custom, as being a profess'd tyrant to
their sex?

CLAUDIO
No; I pray thee speak in sober judgement.

BENEDICK
Why, i'faith, methinks she's too low for a high praise,
too brown for a fair praise, and too little for a great
praise: only this commendation I can afford her, —
that were she other than she is, she were unhandsome;
and being no other but as she is, I do not like her.

CLAUDIO
Thou think'st I am in sport: I pray thee tell me truly
how thou likest her.

BENEDICK
Would you buy her, that you inquire after her?

CLAUDIO
Can the world buy such a jewel?

BENEDICK
Yea, and a case to put it into. But speak you this with a
sad brow? or do you play the flouting Jack, to tell us
Cupid is a good hare-finder, and Vulcan a rare
carpenter? Come, in what key shall a man take you, to
go in the song?

CLAUDIO
In mine eye she is the sweetest lady that ever I look'd
on.

BENEDICK
I can see yet without spectacles, and I see no such
matter: there's her cousin, an she were not possess'd
with a fury, exceeds her as much in beauty as the first of
May doth the last of December. But I hope you have no
intent to turn husband, have you?

CLAUDIO
I would scarce trust myself, though I had sworn the
contrary, if Hero would be my wife.

BENEDICK
Is't come to this? In faith, hath not the world one man
but he will wear his cap with suspicion? Shall I never
see a bachelor of threescore again? Go to, i'faith; an
thou wilt needs thrust thy neck into a yoke, wear the
print of it, and sigh away Sundays. Look; Don Pedro is
return'd to seek you.

Enter DON PEDRO.

DON PEDRO
What secret hath held you here, that you follow'd not to
Leonato's?

BENEDICK
I would your Grace would constrain me to tell.

DON PEDRO
I charge thee on thy allegiance.

BENEDICK
You hear, Count Claudio: I can be secret as a dumb man,
I would have you think so; but on my allegiance, — mark
you this, on my allegiance. — He is in love. With who? —
now that is your Grace's part. — Mark how short his
answer is; — With Hero, Leonato's short daughter.

CLAUDIO
If this were so, so were it utter'd.

BENEDICK
Like the old tale, my lord: 'it is not so, nor 'twas not so;
but indeed, God forbid it should be so.'

CLAUDIO
If my passion change not shortly, God forbid it should
be otherwise.

DON PEDRO
Amen, if you love her; for the lady is very well worthy.

CLAUDIO
You speak this to fetch me in, my lord.

DON PEDRO
By my troth, I speak my thought.

CLAUDIO
And, in faith, my lord, I spoke mine.

BENEDICK
And, by my two faiths and troths, my lord, I spoke
mine.

CLAUDIO
That I love her, I feel.

DON PEDRO
That she is worthy, I know.

BENEDICK
That I neither feel how she should be loved, nor know
how she should be worthy, is the opinion that fire
cannot melt out of me: I will die in it at the stake.

DON PEDRO
Thou wast ever an obstinate heretic in the despite of
beauty.

CLAUDIO
And never could maintain his part but in the force of
his will.

BENEDICK
That a woman conceived me, I thank her; that she
brought me up, I likewise give her most humble

thanks: but that I will have a recheat winded in my forehead, or hang my bugle in an invisible baldrick, all women shall pardon me. Because I will not do them the wrong to mistrust any, I will do myself the right to trust none; and the fine is (for the which I may go the finer), I will live a bachelor.

DON PEDRO
I shall see thee, ere I die, look pale with love.

BENEDICK
With anger, with sickness, or with hunger, my lord; not with love: prove that ever I lose more blood with love than I will get again with drinking, pick out mine eyes with a ballet-maker's pen, and hang me up at the door of a brothel-house for the sign of blind Cupid.

DON PEDRO
Well, if ever thou dost fall from this faith, thou wilt prove a notable argument.

BENEDICK
If I do, hang me in a bottle like a cat, and shoot at me; and he that hits me, let him be clapp'd on the shoulder, and called Adam.

DON PEDRO
Well, as time shall try:
'In time the savage bull doth bear the yoke.'

BENEDICK
The savage bull may; but if ever the sensible Benedick bear it, pluck off the bull's horns, and set them in my forehead; and let me be vilely painted; and in such great letters as they write, 'Here is good horse to hire,' let them signify under my sign, 'Here you may see Benedick the married man.'

CLAUDIO
If this should ever happen, thou wouldst be horn-mad.

DON PEDRO
Nay, if Cupid have not spent all his quiver in Venice, thou wilt quake for this shortly.

BENEDICK
I look for an earthquake too, then.

DON PEDRO
Well, you will temporise with the hours. In the meantime, good Signior Benedick, repair to Leonato's: commend me to him, and tell him I will not fail him at supper; for indeed he hath made great preparation.

BENEDICK
I have almost matter enough in me for such an embassage; and so I commit you, —

CLAUDIO
To the tuition of God: From my house (if I had it), —

DON PEDRO
The sixth of July: Your loving friend, Benedick.

BENEDICK
Nay, mock not, mock not. The body of your discourse is sometime guarded with fragments, and the guards are but slightly basted on neither: ere you flout old ends any further, examine your conscience: and so I leave you. *[Exit.*

CLAUDIO
My liege, your highness now may do me good.

DON PEDRO
My love is thine to teach: teach it but how,
And thou shalt see how apt it is to learn
Any hard lesson that may do thee good.

CLAUDIO
Hath Leonato any son, my lord?

DON PEDRO
No child but Hero; she's his only heir.
Dost thou affect her, Claudio?

CLAUDIO
                    O, my lord,
When you went onward on this ended action,
I look'd upon her with a soldier's eye,
That lik'd, but had a rougher task in hand
Than to drive liking to the name of love:
But now I am return'd, and that war-thoughts
Have left their places vacant, in their rooms
Come thronging soft and delicate desires,
All prompting me how fair young Hero is,
Saying, I lik'd her ere I went to wars.

DON PEDRO
Thou wilt be like a lover presently
And tire the hearer with a book of words.
If thou dost love fair Hero, cherish it;
And I will break with her and with her father,
And thou shalt have her. Was't not to this end
That thou began'st to twist so fine a story?

CLAUDIO
How sweetly you do minister to love,
That know love's grief by his complexion!
But lest my liking might too sudden seem,

I would have salv'd it with a longer treatise.

DON PEDRO
What need the bridge much broader than the flood?
The fairest grant is the necessity.
Look, what will serve is fit: 'tis once, thou lovest;
And I will fit thee with the remedy.
I know we shall have revelling to-night:
I will assume thy part in some disguise,
And tell fair Hero I am Claudio;
And in her bosom I'll unclasp my heart,
And take her hearing prisoner with the force
And strong encounter of my amorous tale:
Then after to her father will I break;
And the conclusion is, she shall be thine.
In practice let us put it presently. *[Exeunt.*

SCENE II
A room in LEONATO'S *house.*

Enter, severally, LEONATO *and* ANTONIO.

LEONATO
How now, brother! Where is my cousin, your son? hath he provided this music?

ANTONIO
He is very busy about it. But, brother, I can tell you strange news, that you yet dream'd not of.

LEONATO
Are they good?

ANTONIO
As the event stamps them: but they have a good cover; they show well outward. The prince and Count Claudio, walking in a thick-pleach'd alley in my orchard, were thus much overheard by a man of mine: the prince discover'd to Claudio that he loved my niece your daughter, and meant to acknowledge it this night in a dance; and if he found her accordant, he meant to take the present time by the top, and instantly break with you of it.

LEONATO
Hath the fellow any wit that told you this?

ANTONIO
A good sharp fellow: I will send for him; and question him yourself.

LEONATO
No, no; we will hold it as a dream till it appear itself: but I will acquaint my daughter withal, that she may be the better prepared for an answer, if peradventure this be true. Go you and tell her of it. [*Exit* ANTONIO. — *Several persons cross the stage.*] Cousins, you know what you have to do. — O, I cry you mercy, friend; go you with me, and I will use your skill. — Good cousin, have a care this busy time. *[Exit.*

SCENE III
Another room in LEONATO'S *house.*

Enter DON JOHN *and* CONRADE.

CONRADE
What the good-year, my lord! why are you thus out of measure sad?

DON JOHN
There is no measure in the occasion that breeds it; therefore the sadness is without limit.

CONRADE
You should hear reason.

DON JOHN
And when I have heard it, what blessing bringeth it?

CONRADE
If not a present remedy, yet a patient sufferance.

DON JOHN
I wonder that thou, being (as thou say'st thou art) born under Saturn, goest about to apply a moral medicine to a mortifying mischief. I cannot hide what I am: I must be sad when I have cause, and smile at no man's jests; eat when I have stomach, and wait for no man's leisure; sleep when I am drowsy, and tend on no man's business; laugh when I am merry, and claw no man in his humour.

CONRADE
Yea, but you must not make the full show of this till you may do it without controlment. You have of late stood out against your brother, and he hath ta'en you newly into his grace; where it is impossible you should take true root but by the fair weather that you make yourself: it is needful that you frame the season for your own harvest.

DON JOHN
I had rather be a canker in a hedge than a rose in his

ANTONIO But, brother, I can tell you strange news, that you yet dream'd not of.

grace; and it better fits my blood to be disdain'd of all than to fashion a carriage to rob love from any: in this, though I cannot be said to be a flattering honest man, it must not be denied but I am a plain-dealing villain. I am trusted with a muzzle, and enfranchised with a clog; therefore I have decreed not to sing in my cage. If I had my mouth, I would bite; if I had my liberty, I would do my liking: in the mean time let me be that I am, and seek not to alter me.

CONRADE
Can you make no use of your discontent?

DON JOHN
I make all use of it, for I use it only. — Who comes here?

Enter BORACHIO.

What news, Borachio?

BORACHIO
I came yonder from a great supper: the prince your brother is royally entertain'd by Leonato; and I can give you intelligence of an intended marriage.

DON JOHN
Will it serve for any model to build mischief on? What is he for a fool that betroths himself to unquietness?

BORACHIO
Marry, it is your brother's right hand.

DON JOHN
Who, the most exquisite Claudio?

BORACHIO
Even he.

DON JOHN
A proper squire! And who, and who? which way looks he?

BORACHIO
Marry, on Hero, the daughter and heir of Leonato.

DON JOHN
A very forward March-chick! How came you to this?

BORACHIO
Being entertain'd for a perfumer, as I was smoking a musty room, comes me the prince and Claudio, hand in hand, in sad conference: I whipp'd me behind the arras; and there heard it agreed upon, that the prince should woo Hero for himself, and having obtain'd her, give her to Count Claudio.

DON JOHN
Come, come, let us thither: this may prove food to my displeasure. That young start-up hath all the glory of my overthrow: if I can cross him any way, I bless myself every way. You are both sure, and will assist me?

CONRADE
To the death, my lord.

DON JOHN
Let us to the great supper: their cheer is the greater that I am subdued. Would the cook were of my mind! — Shall we go prove what's to be done?

BORACHIO
We'll wait upon your lordship. *[Exeunt.*

ACT II

SCENE I

A hall in LEONATO'S *house.*

Enter LEONATO, ANTONIO, HERO, BEATRICE, *and others.*

LEONATO
Was not Count John here at supper?

ANTONIO
I saw him not.

BEATRICE
How tartly that gentleman looks! I never can see him but I am heart-burn'd an hour after.

HERO
He is of a very melancholy disposition.

BEATRICE
He were an excellent man that were made just in the midway between him and Benedick: the one is too like an image, and says nothing; and the other too like my lady's eldest son, evermore tattling.

LEONATO
Then half Signior Benedick's tongue in Count John's mouth, and half Count John's melancholy in Signior Benedick's face, —

BEATRICE
With a good leg and a good foot, uncle, and money enough in his purse, such a man would win any woman in the world, — if a' could get her good-will.

LEONATO
By my troth, niece, thou wilt never get thee a husband, if thou be so shrewd of thy tongue.

ANTONIO
In faith, she's too curst.

BEATRICE
Too curst is more than curst: I shall lessen God's sending that way; for it is said, 'God sends a curst cow short horns'; but to a cow too curst he sends none.

LEONATO
So, by being too curst, God will send you no horns.

BEATRICE
Just, if he send me no husband; for the which blessing I am at him upon my knees every morning and evening. Lord, I could not endure a husband with a beard on his face: I had rather lie in the woollen.

LEONATO
You may light on a husband that hath no beard.

BEATRICE
What should I do with him? dress him in my apparel, and make him my waiting-gentlewoman? He that hath a beard is more than a youth; and he that hath no beard is less than a man: and he that is more than a youth is not for me; and he that is less than a man, I am not for him: therefore I will even take sixpence in earnest of the bear-ward, and lead his apes into hell.

LEONATO
Well, then, go you into hell?

BEATRICE
No; but to the gate; and there will the devil meet me, like an old cuckold, with horns on his head, and say, 'Get you to heaven, Beatrice, get you to heaven; here's no place for you maids': so deliver I up my apes, and away to Saint Peter for the heavens; he shows me where the bachelors sit, and there live we as merry as the day is long.

ANTONIO
Well, niece [*to* HERO], I trust you will be ruled by your father.

BEATRICE
Yes, faith; it is my cousin's duty to make curtsey, and say, 'Father, as it please you': — but yet for all that, cousin, let him be a handsome fellow, or else make another curtsey, and say, 'Father, as it please me.'

LEONATO
Well, niece, I hope to see you one day fitted with a husband.

BEATRICE
Not till God make men of some other metal than earth. Would it not grieve a woman to be overmaster'd with a piece of valiant dust? to make an account of her life to a clod of wayward marl? No, uncle, I'll none: Adam's sons are my brethren; and, truly, I hold it a sin to match in my kindred.

LEONATO
Daughter, remember what I told you: if the prince do solicit you in that kind, you know your answer.

BEATRICE
The fault will be in the music, cousin, if you be not woo'd in good time: if the prince be too important, tell him there is measure in every thing, and so dance out the answer. For, hear me, Hero: — wooing, wedding, and repenting, is as a Scotch jig, a measure, and a cinque-pace: the first suit is hot and hasty, like a Scotch jig, and full as fantastical; the wedding, mannerly-modest, as a measure, full of state and ancientry; and then comes repentance, and, with his bad legs, falls into the cinque-pace faster and faster, till he sink into his grave.

LEONATO
Cousin, you apprehend passing shrewdly.

BEATRICE
I have a good eye, uncle; I can see a church by daylight.

LEONATO
The revellers are ent'ring, brother: make good room.

Enter DON PEDRO, CLAUDIO, BENEDICK, BALTHAZAR, DON JOHN, BORACHIO, MARGARET, URSULA, *and others, mask'd; with a drum.*

DON PEDRO
Lady, will you walk about with your friend?

HERO
So you walk softly, and look sweetly, and say nothing, I am yours for the walk; and especially when I walk away.

DON PEDRO
With me in your company?

HERO
I may say so, when I please.

DON PEDRO
And when please you to say so?

HERO
When I like your favour; for God defend the lute should be like the case!

DON PEDRO
My visor is Philemon's roof; within the house is Jove.

HERO
Why, then, your visor should be thatch'd.

DON PEDRO
Speak low, if you speak love.   [*Takes her aside.*

BALTHAZAR
Well, I would you did like me.

MARGARET
So would not I, for your own sake; for I have many ill qualities.

BALTHAZAR
Which is one?

MARGARET
I say my prayers aloud.

BALTHAZAR
I love you the better: the hearers may cry, Amen.

MARGARET
God match me with a good dancer!

BALTHAZAR
Amen.

MARGARET
And God keep him out of my sight when the dance is done! — Answer, clerk.

BALTHAZAR
No more words: the clerk is answer'd.

URSULA
I know you well enough; you are Signior Antonio.

ANTONIO
At a word, I am not.

URSULA
I know you by the waggling of your head.

ANTONIO
To tell you true, I counterfeit him.

URSULA
You could never do him so ill-well, unless you were the very man. Here's his dry hand up and down: you are he, you are he.

ANTONIO
At a word, I am not.

URSULA
Come, come, do you think I do not know you by your excellent wit? can virtue hide itself? Go to, mum, you are he: graces will appear, and there's an end.

BEATRICE
Will you not tell me who told you so?

BENEDICK
No, you shall pardon me.

BEATRICE
Nor will you not tell me who you are?

BENEDICK
Not now.

BEATRICE
That I was disdainful, and that I had my good wit out of the *Hundred Merry Tales*: — well, this was Signior Benedick that said so.

BENEDICK
What's he?

BEATRICE
I am sure you know him well enough.

BENEDICK
Not I, believe me.

BEATRICE
Did he never make you laugh?

BENEDICK
I pray you, what is he?

BEATRICE
Why, he is the prince's jester: a very dull fool; only his gift is in devising impossible slanders: none but libertines delight in him; and the commendation is not in his wit, but in his villainy; for he both pleases men and angers them, and then they laugh at him and beat him. I am sure he is in the fleet: I would he had boarded me.

BENEDICK
When I know the gentleman, I'll tell him what you say.

BEATRICE
Do, do: he'll but break a comparison or two on me; which, peradventure, not mark'd, or not laugh'd at, strikes him into melancholy; and then there's a partridge wing saved, for the fool will eat no supper that night. [*Music within.*] We must follow the leaders.

BENEDICK
In every good thing.

BEATRICE
Nay, if they lead to any ill, I will leave them at the next turning.
          [*Music. Dance. Then exeunt all except* DON JOHN, BORACHIO, *and* CLAUDIO.

DON JOHN
Sure my brother is amorous on Hero, and hath withdrawn her father to break with him about it. The ladies follow her, and but one visor remains.

BORACHIO
And that is Claudio: I know him by his bearing.

DON JOHN
Are not you Signior Benedick?

CLAUDIO
You know me well; I am he.

DON JOHN
Signior, you are very near my brother in his love: he is enamour'd on Hero; I pray you, dissuade him from her: she is no equal for his birth: you may do the part of an honest man in it.

CLAUDIO
How know you he loves her?

DON JOHN
I heard him swear his affection.

BORACHIO
So did I too; and he swore he would marry her to-night.

DON JOHN
Come, let us to the banquet.
          [*Exeunt* DON JOHN *and* BORACHIO.

CLAUDIO
Thus answer I in the name of Benedick,
But hear these ill news with the ears of Claudio.
'Tis certain so; — the prince wooes for himself.
Friendship is constant in all other things
Save in the office and affairs of love:
Therefore all hearts in love use their own tongues;
Let every eye negotiate for itself,
And trust no agent; for beauty is a witch,
Against whose charms faith melteth into blood.
This is an accident of hourly proof,
Which I mistrusted not. Farewell, therefore, Hero!

Enter BENEDICK.

BENEDICK
Count Claudio?

CLAUDIO
Yea, the same.

BENEDICK
Come, will you go with me?

CLAUDIO
Whither?

BENEDICK
Even to the next willow, about your own business, county. What fashion will you wear the garland of? about your neck, like an usurer's chain? or under your arm, like a lieutenant's scarf? You must wear it one way, for the prince hath got your Hero.

CLAUDIO

I wish him joy of her.

BENEDICK

Why, that's spoken like an honest drovier: so they sell bullocks. But did you think the prince would have served you thus?

CLAUDIO

I pray you, leave me.

BENEDICK

Ho! now you strike like the blind man: 'twas the boy that stole your meat, and you'll beat the post.

CLAUDIO

If it will not be, I'll leave you. [*Exit.*

BENEDICK

Alas, poor hurt fowl! now will he creep into sedges. — But, that my Lady Beatrice should know me, and not know me! The prince's fool! — Ha! It may be I go under that title because I am merry. — Yea, but so I am apt to do myself wrong; I am not so reputed: it is the base thought, bitter disposition, of Beatrice that puts the world into her person, and so gives me out. Well, I'll be revenged as I may.

Enter DON PEDRO.

DON PEDRO

Now, signior, where's the count? did you see him?

BENEDICK

Troth, my lord, I have play'd the part of Lady Fame. I found him here as melancholy as a lodge in a warren: I told him, and I think I told him true, that your Grace had got the good-will of this young lady; and I offer'd him my company to a willow-tree, either to make him a garland, as being forsaken, or to bind him up a rod, as being worthy to be whipp'd.

DON PEDRO

To be whipp'd! What's his fault?

BENEDICK

The flat transgression of a school-boy, who, being overjoy'd with finding a bird's-nest, shows it his companion, and he steals it.

DON PEDRO

Wilt thou make a trust a transgression? The transgression is in the stealer.

BENEDICK

Yet it had not been amiss the rod had been made, and the garland too; for the garland he might have worn himself, and the rod he might have bestow'd on you, who, as I take it, have stolen his bird's-nest.

DON PEDRO

I will but teach them to sing, and restore them to the owner.

BENEDICK

If their singing answer your saying, by my faith, you say honestly.

DON PEDRO

The Lady Beatrice hath a quarrel to you: the gentleman that danced with her told her she is much wrong'd by you.

BENEDICK

O, she misused me past the endurance of a block! an oak but with one green leaf on it would have answer'd her; my very visor began to assume life and scold with her. She told me, — not thinking I had been myself, — that I was the prince's jester, and that I was duller than a great thaw; huddling jest upon jest with such impossible conveyance upon me that I stood like a man at a mark, with a whole army shooting at me. She speaks poniards, and every word stabs: if her breath were as terrible as her terminations, there were no living near her; she would infect to the north star. I would not marry her, though she were endow'd with all that Adam had left him before he transgress'd: she would have made Hercules have turn'd spit, yea, and have cleft his club to make the fire too. Come, talk not of her: you shall find her the infernal Ate in good apparel. I would to God some scholar would conjure her; for certainly, while she is here, a man may live as quiet in hell as in a sanctuary; and people sin upon purpose, because they would go thither; so, indeed, all disquiet, horror, and perturbation follow her.

DON PEDRO

Look, here she comes.

Enter CLAUDIO, BEATRICE, HERO, *and* LEONATO.

BENEDICK

Will your Grace command me any service to the world's end? I will go on the slightest errand now to the Antipodes that you can devise to send me on; I will fetch you a toothpicker now from the furthest inch of Asia; bring you the length of Prester John's foot; fetch you a hair off the great Cham's beard; do you any embassage to the Pigmies; — rather than hold three words' conference with this harpy. You have no employment for me?

DON PEDRO

None, but to desire your good company.

BENEDICK

O God, sir, here's a dish I love not: I cannot endure my Lady Tongue. [*Exit.*

DON PEDRO

Come, lady, come; you have lost the heart of Signior Benedick.

BEATRICE

Indeed, my lord, he lent it me awhile; and I gave him use for it, — a double heart for his single one: marry, once before he won it of me with false dice, therefore your Grace may well say I have lost it.

DON PEDRO

You have put him down, lady, you have put him down.

BEATRICE

So I would not he should do me, my lord, lest I should prove the mother of fools. — I have brought Count Claudio, whom you sent me to seek.

DON PEDRO

Why, how now, count! wherefore are you sad?

CLAUDIO

Not sad, my lord.

DON PEDRO

How then? sick?

CLAUDIO

Neither, my lord.

BEATRICE

The count is neither sad, nor sick, nor merry, nor well; but civil, count, — civil as an orange, and something of that jealous complexion.

DON PEDRO

I'faith, lady, I think your blazon to be true; though, I'll be sworn, if he be so, his conceit is false. — Here, Claudio, I have woo'd in thy name, and fair Hero is won: I have broke with her father, and, his good-will obtain'd, name the day of marriage, and God give thee joy!

LEONATO

Count, take of me my daughter, and with her my fortunes: his grace hath made the match, and all grace say Amen to it!

BEATRICE

Speak, count, 'tis your cue.

CLAUDIO

Silence is the perfectest herald of joy: I were but little happy, if I could say how much. — Lady, as you are mine, I am yours: I give away myself for you, and dote upon the exchange.

BEATRICE

Speak, cousin; or, if you cannot, stop his mouth with a kiss, and let not him speak neither.

DON PEDRO

In faith, lady, you have a merry heart.

BEATRICE

Yea, my lord; I thank it, poor fool, it keeps on the windy side of care. — My cousin tells him in his ear that he is in her heart.

CLAUDIO

And so she doth, cousin.

BEATRICE

Good Lord, for alliance! — Thus goes every one to the world but I, and I am sun-burn'd; I may sit in a corner, and cry heigh-ho for a husband!

DON PEDRO

Lady Beatrice, I will get you one.

BEATRICE

I would rather have one of your father's getting. Hath your Grace ne'er a brother like you? Your father got excellent husbands, if a maid could come by them.

DON PEDRO

Will you have me, lady?

BEATRICE

No, my lord, unless I might have another for working-days: your Grace is too costly to wear every day. But, I beseech your Grace, pardon me: I was born to speak all mirth and no matter.

DON PEDRO

Your silence most offends me, and to be merry best becomes you; for, out of question, you were born in a merry hour.

BEATRICE

No, sure, my lord, my mother cried; but then there was a star danced, and under that was I born. — Cousins, God give you joy!

LEONATO

Niece, will you look to those things I told you of?

BEATRICE

I cry you mercy, uncle. — By your Grace's pardon. [*Exit.*

DON PEDRO

By my troth, a pleasant-spirited lady.

LEONATO

There's little of the melancholy element in her, my lord: she is never sad but when she sleeps; and not ever sad then; for I have heard my daughter say, she hath often dream'd of unhappiness, and waked herself with laughing.

DON PEDRO

She cannot endure to hear tell of a husband.

LEONATO

O, by no means: she mocks all her wooers out of suit.

DON PEDRO

She were an excellent wife for Benedick.

LEONATO

O Lord, my lord, if they were but a week married, they would talk themselves mad!

DON PEDRO

County Claudio, when mean you to go to church?

CLAUDIO

To-morrow, my lord: time goes on crutches till love have all his rites.

LEONATO

Not till Monday, my dear son, which is hence a just seven-night; and a time too brief, too, to have all things answer my mind.

DON PEDRO

Come, you shake the head at so long a breathing: but, I warrant thee, Claudio, the time shall not go dully by us. I will, in the interim, undertake one of Hercules' labours; which is, to bring Signior Benedick and the Lady Beatrice into a mountain of affection the one with the other. I would fain have it a match; and I doubt not but to fashion it, if you three will but minister such assistance as I shall give you direction.

LEONATO

My lord, I am for you, though it cost me ten nights' watchings.

CLAUDIO

And I, my lord.

DON PEDRO

And you too, gentle Hero?

HERO

I will do any modest office, my lord, to help my cousin to a good husband.

DON PEDRO

And Benedick is not the unhopefullest husband that I know. Thus far can I praise him; he is of a noble strain, of approved valour, and confirm'd honesty. I will teach you how to humour your cousin, that she shall fall in love with Benedick; — and I, with your two helps, will so practise on Benedick, that, in despite of his quick wit and his queasy stomach, he shall fall in love with Beatrice. If we can do this, Cupid is no longer an archer: his glory shall be ours, for we are the only love-gods. Go in with me, and I will tell you my drift.

[*Exeunt.*

SCENE II

Another room in LEONATO'S *house.*

Enter DON JOHN *and* BORACHIO.

DON JOHN

It is so; the Count Claudio shall marry the daughter of Leonato.

BORACHIO

Yea, my lord; but I can cross it.

DON JOHN

Any bar, any cross, any impediment will be medicinable to me: I am sick in displeasure to him; and whatsoever comes athwart his affection ranges evenly with mine. How canst thou cross this marriage?

BORACHIO

Not honestly, my lord; but so covertly that no dishonesty shall appear in me.

DON JOHN

Show me briefly how.

BORACHIO

I think I told your lordship, a year since, how much I am in the favour of Margaret, the waiting gentlewoman to Hero.

DON JOHN

I remember.

BORACHIO

I can, at any unseasonable instant of the night, appoint her to look out at her lady's chamber window.

DON JOHN

What life is in that, to be the death of this marriage?

BORACHIO

The poison of that lies in you to temper. Go you to the prince your brother; spare not to tell him that he hath wrong'd his honour in marrying the renown'd Claudio (whose estimation do you mightily hold up) to a contaminated stale, such a one as Hero.

DON JOHN

What proof shall I make of that?

BORACHIO

Proof enough to misuse the prince, to vex Claudio, to undo Hero, and kill Leonato. Look you for any other issue?

DON JOHN

Only to despite them, I will endeavour any thing.

BORACHIO

Go, then; find me a meet hour to draw Don Pedro and the Count Claudio alone: tell them that you know that Hero loves me; intend a kind of zeal both to the prince and Claudio, as, — in love of your brother's honour, who hath made this match, and his friend's reputation, who is thus like to be cozen'd with the semblance of a maid, — that you have discover'd thus. They will scarcely believe this without trial: offer them instances; which shall bear no less likelihood than to see me at her chamber-window; hear me call Margaret, Hero; hear Margaret term me Claudio; and bring them to see this the very night before the intended wedding, — for in the mean time I will so fashion the matter that Hero shall be absent, and there shall appear such seeming truth of Hero's disloyalty, that jealousy shall be call'd assurance, and all the preparation overthrown.

DON JOHN

Grow this to what adverse issue it can, I will put it in practice. Be cunning in the working this, and thy fee is a thousand ducats.

BORACHIO

Be you constant in the accusation, and my cunning shall not shame me.

DON JOHN

I will presently go learn their day of marriage.   [*Exeunt.*

SCENE III

LEONATO'S *orchard.*

Enter BENEDICK *alone.*

BENEDICK

Boy, —

Enter BOY.

BOY

Signior?

BENEDICK

In my chamber-window lies a book: bring it hither to me in the orchard.

BOY

I am here already, sir.

BENEDICK

I know that; but I would have thee hence, and here again. [*Exit* BOY.] — I do much wonder that one man, seeing how much another man is a fool when he dedicates his behaviours to love, will, after he hath laugh'd at such shallow follies in others, become the argument of his own scorn by failing in love: and such a man is Claudio. I have known when there was no music with him but the drum and the fife; and now had he rather hear the tabor and the pipe: I have known when he would have walk'd ten mile a-foot to see a good armour; and now will he lie ten nights awake, carving the fashion of a new doublet. He was wont to speak plain and to the purpose, like an honest man and a soldier; and now is he turn'd orthography; his words are a very fantastical banquet, — just so many strange dishes. May I be so converted, and see with these eyes? I cannot tell; I think not: I will not be sworn but love may transform me to an oyster; but I'll take my oath on it, till he have made an oyster of me, he shall never make me such a fool. One woman is fair, — yet I am well; another is wise, — yet I am well; another virtuous, — yet I am well: but till all graces be in one woman, one woman shall not come in my grace. Rich she shall be, that's certain; wise, or I'll none; virtuous, or I'll never cheapen her; fair, or I'll never look on her; mild, or come not near me; noble, or not I for an angel; of good discourse, an excellent musician, and her hair shall be of what colour it please God. — Ha, the prince and Monsieur Love! I will hide me in the arbour.

[*Withdraws into the arbour.*

Enter DON PEDRO, CLAUDIO, LEONATO, BALTHAZAR, *and* MUSICIANS.

DON PEDRO

Come, shall we hear this music?

CLAUDIO

Yea, my good lord. — How still the evening is, As hush'd on purpose to grace harmony!

DON PEDRO

See you where Benedick hath hid himself?

CLAUDIO

O, very well, my lord: the music ended, We'll fit the kid-fox with a pennyworth.

DON PEDRO

Come, Balthazar, we'll hear that song again.

BALTHAZAR

O, good my lord, tax not so bad a voice To slander music any more than once.

DON PEDRO

It is the witness still of excellency To put a strange face on his own perfection: — I pray thee, sing, and let me woo no more.

BALTHAZAR

Because you talk of wooing, I will sing; Since many a wooer doth commence his suit To her he thinks not worthy; yet he wooes, Yet will he swear he loves.

DON PEDRO

Nay, pray thee, come; Or, if thou wilt hold longer argument, Do it in notes.

BALTHAZAR

Note this before my notes, — There's not a note of mine that's worth the noting.

DON PEDRO

Why, these are very crotchets that he speaks; Note notes, forsooth, and nothing!   [*Music.*

BENEDICK [*aside*].

Now, 'Divine air!' now is his soul ravish'd! — Is it not strange that sheeps' guts should hale souls out of men's bodies? — Well, a horn for my money, when all's done.

BALTHAZAR [*sings.*]

Sigh no more, ladies, sigh no more,
     Men were deceivers ever;
One foot in sea, and one on shore;
     To one thing constant never:
          Then sigh not so,
          But let them go,
     And be you blithe and bonny;
Converting all your sounds of woe
     Into Hey nonny, nonny.

Sing no more ditties, sing no more
     Of dumps so dull and heavy;
The fraud of men was ever so,
     Since summer first was leavy.
          Then sigh not so, *etc.*

DON PEDRO

By my troth, a good song.

BALTHAZAR

And an ill singer, my lord.

DON PEDRO

Ha, no, no, faith; thou sing'st well enough for a shift.

BENEDICK [*aside*].

An he had been a dog that should have howl'd thus, they would have hang'd him: and I pray God his bad voice bode no mischief! I had as lief have heard the night-raven, come what plague could have come after it.

DON PEDRO

Yea, marry, dost thou hear, Balthazar? I pray thee, get us some excellent music; for to-morrow night we would have it at the Lady Hero's chamber-window.

BALTHAZAR

The best I can, my lord.

DON PEDRO

Do so: farewell. [*Exeunt* BALTHAZAR *and* MUSICIANS.] — Come hither, Leonato. What was it you told me of to-day, — that your niece Beatrice was in love with Signior Benedick?

CLAUDIO

O, ay: — stalk on, stalk on; the fowl sits.[*aside to* PEDRO]. — I did never think that lady would have loved any man.

LEONATO

No, nor I neither; but most wonderful that she should so dote on Signior Benedick, whom she hath in all outward behaviours seem'd ever to abhor.

BENEDICK [*aside*].

Is't possible? Sits the wind in that corner?

LEONATO

By my troth, my lord, I cannot tell what to think of it: but that she loves him with an enraged affection, — it is past the infinite of thought.

DON PEDRO

May be she doth but counterfeit.

CLAUDIO

Faith, like enough.

LEONATO

O God, counterfeit! There was never counterfeit of passion came so near the life of passion as she discovers it.

DON PEDRO

Why, what effects of passion shows she?

CLAUDIO [*aside*].

Bait the hook well; this fish will bite.

LEONATO

What effects, my lord! — She will sit you, — you heard my daughter tell you how.

CLAUDIO

She did, indeed.

DON PEDRO

How, how, I pray you? You amaze me: I would have thought her spirit had been invincible against all assaults of affection.

LEONATO

I would have sworn it had, my lord; especially against Benedick.

BENEDICK [*aside*].

I should think this a gull, but that the white-bearded fellow speaks it: knavery cannot, sure, hide himself in such reverence.

CLAUDIO [*aside*].

He hath ta'en th'infection: hold it up.

DON PEDRO

Hath she made her affection known to Benedick?

LEONATO

No; and swears she never will: that's her torment.

CLAUDIO

'Tis true, indeed; so your daughter says: 'Shall I,' says she, 'that have so oft encounter'd him with scorn, write to him that I love him?'

LEONATO

This says she now when she is beginning to write to him; for she'll be up twenty times a night; and there will she sit in her smock till she have writ a sheet of paper: — my daughter tells us all.

CLAUDIO

Now you talk of a sheet of paper, I remember a pretty jest your daughter told us of.

LEONATO

O, — when she had writ it, and was reading it over, she found Benedick and Beatrice between the sheet? —

CLAUDIO

That.

LEONATO

O, she tore the letter into a thousand halfpence; rail'd at herself, that she should be so immodest to write to one that she knew would flout her; 'I measure him,' says she, 'by my own spirit; for I should flout him, if he writ to me; yea, though I love him, I should.'

CLAUDIO

Then down upon her knees she falls, weeps, sobs, beats her heart, tears her hair, prays, curses; — 'O sweet Benedick! God give me patience!'

LEONATO

She doth indeed; my daughter says so: and the ecstasy hath so much overborne her, that my daughter is sometime afeard she will do a desperate outrage to herself: it is very true.

DON PEDRO

It were good that Benedick knew of it by some other, if she will not discover it.

CLAUDIO

To what end? He would but make a sport of it, and torment the poor lady worse.

DON PEDRO

An he should, it were an alms to hang him. She's an excellent-sweet lady; and, out of all suspicion, she is virtuous.

CLAUDIO

And she is exceeding wise.

DON PEDRO

In everything but in loving Benedick.

BENEDICK I should think this a gull, but that the white-bearded fellow speaks it.

LEONATO
O, my lord, wisdom and blood combating in so tender a body, we have ten proofs to one that blood hath the victory. I am sorry for her, as I have just cause, being her uncle and her guardian.

DON PEDRO
I would she had bestow'd this dotage on me: I would have daff'd all other respects, and made her half myself. I pray you, tell Benedick of it, and hear what he will say.

LEONATO
Were it good, think you?

CLAUDIO
Hero thinks surely she will die; for she says she will die, if he love her not; and she will die, ere she make her love known; and she will die, if he woo her, rather than she will bate one breath of her accustom'd crossness.

DON PEDRO
She doth well: if she should make tender of her love, 'tis very possible he'll scorn it; for the man, as you know all, hath a contemptible spirit.

CLAUDIO
He is a very proper man.

DON PEDRO
He hath indeed a good outward happiness.

CLAUDIO
Fore God, and in my mind, very wise.

DON PEDRO
He doth indeed show some sparks that are like wit.

LEONATO
And I take him to be valiant.

DON PEDRO
As Hector, I assure you: and in the managing of quarrels you may say he is wise; for either he avoids them with great discretion, or undertakes them with a most Christian-like fear.

LEONATO
If he do fear God, a' must necessarily keep the peace: if he break the peace, he ought to enter into a quarrel with fear and trembling.

DON PEDRO
And so will he do; for the man doth fear God, howsoever it seems not in him by some large jests he will make. Well, I am sorry for your niece. Shall we go seek Benedick, and tell him of her love?

CLAUDIO
Never tell him, my lord: let her wear it out with good counsel.

LEONATO
Nay, that's impossible: she may wear her heart out first.

DON PEDRO
Well, we will hear further of it by your daughter: let it cool the while. I love Benedick well; and I could wish he would modestly examine himself, to see how much he is unworthy so good a lady.

LEONATO
My lord, will you walk? dinner is ready.

CLAUDIO [aside].
If he do not dote on her upon this, I will never trust my expectation.

DON PEDRO [aside].
Let there be the same net spread for her: and that must your daughter and her gentlewomen carry. The sport will be, when they hold one an opinion of another's dotage, and no such matter: that's the scene that I would see, which will be merely a dumb-show. Let us send her to call him in to dinner.

[Exeunt DON PEDRO, CLAUDIO, and LEONATO.

BENEDICK [coming forward].
This can be no trick: the conference was sadly borne. They have the truth of this from Hero. They seem to pity the lady: it seems her affections have their full bent. Love me! why, it must be requited. I hear how I am censured: they say I will bear myself proudly, if I perceive the love come from her; they say too that she will rather die than give any sign of affection. — I did never think to marry. — I must not seem proud: — happy are they that hear their detractions, and can put them to mending. They say the lady is fair, — 'tis a truth, I can bear them witness; and virtuous, — 'tis so, I cannot reprove it; and wise, but for loving me, — by my troth, it is no addition to her wit, nor no great argument of her folly, for I will be horribly in love with her. I may chance have some odd quirks and remnants of wit broken on me, because I have rail'd so long against marriage: but doth not the appetite alter? a man loves the meat in his youth that he cannot endure in his age. Shall quips and sentences, and these paper bullets of the brain, awe a man from the career of his humour? no, the world must be peopled. When I said I would die a bachelor, I did not think I should live till I were married. — Here comes Beatrice. By this day, she's a fair lady: I do spy some marks of love in her.

Enter BEATRICE.

BEATRICE
Against my will I am sent to bid you come in to dinner.

BENEDICK
Fair Beatrice, I thank you for your pains.

BEATRICE
I took no more pains for those thanks than you take pains to thank me: if it had been painful, I would not have come.

BENEDICK
You take pleasure, then, in the message?

BEATRICE
Yea, just so much as you may take upon a knife's point, and choke a daw withal. — You have no stomach, signior: fare you well. [Exit.

BENEDICK
Ha! 'Against my will I am sent to bid you come in to dinner,' — there's a double meaning in that. 'I took no more pains for those thanks than you took pains to thank me,' — that's as much as to say, Any pains that I take for you is as easy as thanks. — If I do not take pity of her, I am a villain; if I do not love her, I am a Jew. I will go get her picture. [Exit.

SCENE I

LEONATO'S *orchard.*

Enter HERO *and two gentlewomen,*
MARGARET *and* URSULA.

HERO
Good Margaret, run thee to the parlour;
There shalt thou find my cousin Beatrice
Proposing with the prince and Claudio:
Whisper her ear, and tell her, I and Ursula
Walk in the orchard, and our whole discourse
Is all of her; say that thou overheard'st us;
And bid her steal into the pleached bower,
Where honeysuckles, ripen'd by the sun,
Forbid the sun to enter; — like favourites,
Made proud by princes, that advance their pride
Against that power that bred it: — there will she hide
   her,
To listen our purpose. This is thy office:
Bear thee well in it, and leave us alone.

MARGARET
I'll make her come, I warrant you, presently.   [Exit.

HERO
Now, Ursula, when Beatrice doth come,
As we do trace this alley up and down,
Our talk must only be of Benedick.
When I do name him, let it be thy part
To praise him more than ever man did merit:
My talk to thee must be, how Benedick
Is sick in love with Beatrice. Of this matter
Is little Cupid's crafty arrow made,
That only wounds by hearsay. Now begin;
      Enter BEATRICE, *behind.*
For look where Beatrice, like a lapwing, runs
Close by the ground, to hear our conference.

URSULA
The pleasant'st angling is to see the fish
Cut with her golden oars the silver stream,
And greedily devour the treacherous bait:
So angle we for Beatrice; who even now
Is couched in the woodbine coverture.
Fear you not my part of the dialogue.

HERO
Then go we near her, that her ear lose nothing
Of the false-sweet bait that we lay for it. —
      [*They advance to the bower.*
No, truly, Ursula, she's too disdainful;
I know her spirits are as coy and wild
As haggards of the rock.

URSULA
            But are you sure
That Benedick loves Beatrice so entirely?

HERO
So says the prince and my new-trothed lord.

URSULA
And did they bid you tell her of it, madam?

HERO
They did entreat me to acquaint her of it;
But I persuaded them, if they lov'd Benedick,
To wish him wrestle with affection,
And never to let Beatrice know of it.

URSULA
Why did you so? Doth not the gentleman
Deserve as full as fortunate a bed
As ever Beatrice shall couch upon?

HERO
O god of love! I know he doth deserve
As much as may be yielded to a man:
But Nature never fram'd a woman's heart
Of prouder stuff than that of Beatrice;
Disdain and scorn ride sparkling in her eyes,
Misprising what they look on; and her wit
Values itself so highly, that to her
All matter else seems weak; she cannot love,
Nor take no shape nor project of affection,
She is so self-endeared.

URSULA
            Sure, I think so;
And therefore certainly it were not good
She knew his love, lest she make sport at it.

HERO
Why, you speak truth. I never yet saw man,
How wise, how noble, young, how rarely-featur'd,
But she would spell him backward: if fair-fac'd,
She'd swear the gentleman should be her sister;
If black, why, Nature, drawing of an antic,
Made a foul blot; if tall, a lance ill-headed;

If low, an agate very vilely cut;
If speaking, why, a vane blown with all winds;
If silent, why, a block moved with none.
So turns she every man the wrong side out;
And never gives to truth and virtue that
Which simpleness and merit purchaseth.

URSULA
Sure, sure, such carping is not commendable.

HERO
No, not to be so odd, and from all fashions,
As Beatrice is, cannot be commendable:
But who dare tell her so? If I should speak,
She would mock me into air; O, she would laugh me
Out of myself, press me to death with wit!
Therefore let Benedick, like cover'd fire,
Consume away in sighs, waste inwardly:
It were a better death than die with mocks,
Which is as bad as die with tickling.

URSULA
Yet tell her of it: hear what she will say.

HERO
No; rather I will go to Benedick,
And counsel him to fight against his passion.
And, truly, I'll devise some honest slanders
To stain my cousin with: one doth not know
How much an ill word may empoison liking.

URSULA
O, do not do your cousin such a wrong!
She cannot be so much without true judgement
(Having so swift and excellent a wit
As she is priz'd to have) as to refuse
So rare a gentleman as Signior Benedick.

HERO
He is the only man of Italy,
Always excepted my dear Claudio.

URSULA
I pray you, be not angry with me, madam,
Speaking my fancy: Signior Benedick,
For shape, for bearing, argument, and valour,
Goes foremost in report through Italy.

HERO
Indeed, he hath an excellent good name.

URSULA
His excellence did earn it, ere he had it. —
When are you married, madam?

HERO
Why, every day, to-morrow. Come, go in:
I'll show thee some attires; and have thy counsel
Which is the best to furnish me to-morrow.

URSULA [aside].
She's lim'd, I warrant you: we have caught her,
madam.

HERO [aside].
If it prove so, then loving goes by haps:
Some Cupid kills with arrows, some with traps.
[Exeunt HERO and URSULA.

BEATRICE [coming forward].
What fire is in mine ears? Can this be true?
   Stand I condemn'd for pride and scorn so much?
Contempt, farewell! and maiden pride, adieu!
   No glory lives behind the back of such.
And, Benedick, love on; I will requite thee,
   Taming my wild heart to thy loving hand:
If thou dost love, my kindness shall incite thee
   To bind our loves up in a holy band;
For others say, thou dost deserve, and I
Believe it better than reportingly.   [Exit.

SCENE II

A room in LEONATO'S house.

Enter DON PEDRO, CLAUDIO, BENEDICK,
and LEONATO.

DON PEDRO
I do but stay till your marriage be consummate, and
   then go I toward Arragon.

CLAUDIO
I'll bring you thither, my lord, if you'll vouchsafe me.

DON PEDRO
Nay, that would be as great a soil in the new gloss of
your marriage, as to show a child his new coat, and
forbid him to wear it. I will only be bold with Benedick
for his company; for, from the crown of his head to the
sole of his foot, he is all mirth: he hath twice or thrice
cut Cupid's bow-string, and the little hangman dare
not shoot at him; he hath a heart as sound as a bell, and
his tongue is the clapper, — for what his heart thinks,
his tongue speaks.

BENEDICK
Gallants, I am not as I have been.

LEONATO
So say I: methinks you are sadder.

CLAUDIO
I hope he be in love.

DON PEDRO
Hang him, truant! there's no true drop of blood in him,
to be truly touch'd with love: if he be sad, he wants
money.

BENEDICK
I have the toothache.

DON PEDRO
Draw it.

BENEDICK
Hang it!

CLAUDIO
You must hang it first, and draw it afterwards.

DON PEDRO
What! sigh for the toothache?

LEONATO
Where is but a humour or a worm?

BENEDICK
Well, every one can master a grief but he that has it.

CLAUDIO
Yet say I he is in love.

DON PEDRO
There is no appearance of fancy in him, unless it be a
fancy that he hath to strange disguises; as, to be a
Dutchman to-day, a Frenchman to-morrow; or in the
shape of two countries at once, as, a German from the
waist downward, all slops, and a Spaniard from the hip
upward, no doublet. Unless he have a fancy to this
foolery, as it appears he hath, he is no fool for fancy, as
you would have it appear he is.

CLAUDIO
If he be not in love with some woman, there is no
believing old signs: a' brushes his hat o' mornings;
what should that bode?

DON PEDRO
Hath any man seen him at the barber's?

CLAUDIO
No, but the barber's man hath been seen with him; and
the old ornament of his cheek hath already stuff'd
tennis-balls.

LEONATO
Indeed, he looks younger than he did, by the loss of a
beard.

DON PEDRO
Nay, a' rubs himself with civet: can you smell him out
by that?

CLAUDIO
That's as much as to say, the sweet youth's in love.

DON PEDRO
The greatest note of it is his melancholy.

CLAUDIO
And when was he wont to wash his face?

DON PEDRO
Yea, or to paint himself? for the which, I hear what they
say of him.

CLAUDIO
Nay, but his jesting spirit; which is now crept into a
lute-string, and new-govern'd by stops.

DON PEDRO
Indeed, that tells a heavy tale for him. Conclude,
conclude he is in love.

CLAUDIO
Nay, but I know who loves him.

DON PEDRO
That would I know too: I warrant, one that knows him
not.

CLAUDIO
Yes, and his ill conditions; and, in despite of all, dies for
him.

DON PEDRO
She shall be buried with her face upwards.

BENEDICK
Yet is this no charm for the toothache. — Old signior,
walk aside with me: I have studied eight or nine wise
words to speak to you, which these hobby-horses must
not hear.   [Exeunt BENEDICK and LEONATO.

DON PEDRO
For my life, to break with him about Beatrice.

CLAUDIO
'Tis even so. Hero and Margaret have by this play'd
their parts with Beatrice; and then the two bears will
not bite one another when they meet.

Enter DON JOHN.

DON JOHN
My lord and brother, God save you!

DON PEDRO
Good den, brother.

DON JOHN
If your leisure served, I would speak with you.

DON PEDRO
In private?

DON JOHN
If it please you: yet Count Claudio may hear: for what I
would speak of concerns him.

DON PEDRO
What's the matter?

DON JOHN [to CLAUDIO].
Means your lordship to be married to-morrow?

DON PEDRO
You know he does.

DON JOHN
I know not that, when he knows what I know.

CLAUDIO
If there be any impediment, I pray you discover it.

DON JOHN
You may think I love you not: let that appear hereafter,
and aim better at me by that I now will manifest. For
my brother, I think he holds you well; and in dearness
of heart hath help to effect your ensuing marriage, —
surely suit ill spent and labour ill bestow'd.

DON PEDRO
Why, what's the matter?

DON JOHN
I came hither to tell you; and, circumstances shorten'd
(for she hath been too long a talking of), the lady is
disloyal.

CLAUDIO
Who, Hero?

DON JOHN
Even she; Leonato's Hero, your Hero, every man's
Hero.

CLAUDIO
Disloyal!

DON JOHN
The word is too good to paint out her wickedness; I
could say she were worse: think you of a worse title, and
I will fit her to it. Wonder not till further warrant: go
but with me to-night, you shall see her
chamber-window enter'd, even the night before her
wedding-day: if you love her then, to-morrow wed her;
but it would better fit your honour to change your
mind.

CLAUDIO
May this be so?

DON PEDRO
I will not think it.

DON JOHN
If you dare not trust that you see, confess not that you
know: if you will follow me, I will show you enough;
and when you have seen more, and heard more,
proceed accordingly.

CLAUDIO
If I see any thing to-night why I should not marry her
to-morrow, in the congregation, where I should wed
her, there will I shame her.

DON PEDRO
And, as I woo'd for thee to obtain her, I will join with
thee to disgrace her.

DON JOHN
I will disparage her no further till you are my
witnesses: bear it coldly but till midnight, and let the
issue show itself.

DON PEDRO
O day untowardly turn'd!

CLAUDIO
O mischief strangely thwarting!

DON JOHN
O plague right well prevented! so will you say when you
have seen the sequel.   [Exeunt.

SCENE III

A street.

Enter DOGBERRY and his compartner VERGES,
with the WATCH.

DOGBERRY
Are you good men and true?

VERGES
Yea, or else it were pity but they should suffer salvation
body and soul.

DOGBERRY
Nay, that were a punishment too good for them, if they should have any allegiance in them, being chosen for the prince's watch.

VERGES
Well, give them their charge, neighbour Dogberry.

DOGBERRY
First, who think you the most desartless man to be constable?

FIRST WATCHMAN
Hugh Oatcake, sir, or George Seacoal; for they can write and read.

DOGBERRY
Come hither, neighbour Seacoal. God hath blest you with a good name; to be a well-favour'd man is the gift of fortune; but to write and read comes by nature.

SECOND WATCHMAN
Both which, master constable, —

DOGBERRY
You have: I knew it would be your answer. Well, for your favour, sir, why, give God thanks, and make no boast of it; and for your writing and reading, let that appear when there is no need of such vanity. You are thought here to be the most senseless and fit man for the constable of the watch; therefore bear you the lantern. This is your charge: — you shall comprehend all vagrom men; you are to bid any man stand, in the prince's name.

SECOND WATCHMAN
How if a' will not stand?

DOGBERRY
Why, then, take no note of him, but let him go; and presently call the rest of the watch together, and thank God you are rid of a knave.

VERGES
If he will not stand when he is bidden, he is none of the prince's subjects.

DOGBERRY
True, and they are to meddle with none but the prince's subjects. — You shall also make no noise in the streets; for for the watch to babble and talk is most tolerable and not to be endured.

SECOND WATCHMAN
We will rather sleep than talk: we know what belongs to a watch.

DOGBERRY
Why, you speak like an ancient and most quiet watchman; for I cannot see how sleeping should offend: only, have a care that your bills be not stolen. — Well, you are to call at all the ale-houses, and bid those that are drunk get them to bed.

SECOND WATCHMAN
How if they will not?

DOGBERRY
Why, then, let them alone till they are sober: if they make you not then the better answer, you may say they are not the men you took them for.

SECOND WATCHMAN
Well, sir.

DOGBERRY
If you meet a thief, you may suspect him, by virtue of your office, to be no true man; and, for such kind of men, the less you meddle or make with them, why, the more is for your honesty.

SECOND WATCHMAN
If we know him to be a thief, shall we not lay hands on him?

DOGBERRY
Truly, by your office, you may; but I think they that touch pitch will be defiled: the most peaceable way for you, if you do take a thief, is to let him show himself what he is, and steal out of your company.

VERGES
You have been always call'd a merciful man, partner.

DOGBERRY
Truly, I would not hang a dog by my will, much more a man who hath any honesty in him.

VERGES
If you hear a child cry in the night, you must call to the nurse and bid her still it.

SECOND WATCHMAN
How if the nurse be asleep and will not hear us?

DOGBERRY
Why, then, depart in peace, and let the child wake her with crying; for the ewe that will not hear her lamb when it baes will never answer a calf when he bleats.

VERGES
'Tis very true.

DOGBERRY
This is the end of the charge: — you, constable, are to present the prince's own person: if you meet the prince in the night, you may stay him.

VERGES
Nay, by'r lady, that I think a' cannot.

DOGBERRY
Five shillings to one on't, with any man that knows the statutes, he may stay him: marry, not without the prince be willing; for, indeed, the watch ought to offend no man; and it is an offence to stay a man against his will.

VERGES
By'r lady, I think it be so.

DOGBERRY
Ha, ah-ha! Well, masters, good night: an there be any matter of weight chances, call up me: keep your fellows' counsels and your own; and good night. — Come, neighbour.

FIRST WATCHMAN
Well, masters, we hear our charge: let us go sit here upon the church-bench till two, and then all to bed.

DOGBERRY
One word more, honest neighbours. I pray you, watch about Signior Leonato's door; for the wedding being there to-morrow, there is a great coil to-night. Adieu: be vigilant, I beseech you.
                    [*Exeunt* DOGBERRY *and* VERGES.
            Enter BORACHIO *and* CONRADE.

BORACHIO
What, Conrade! —

FIRST WATCHMAN   [*aside*].
Peace! stir not.

BORACHIO
Conrade, I say! —

CONRADE
Here, man; I am at thy elbow.

BORACHIO
Mass, and my elbow itch'd; I thought there would a scab follow.

CONRADE
I will owe thee an answer for that: and now forward with thy tale.

BORACHIO
Stand thee close, then, under this pent-house, for it drizzles rain; and I will, like a true drunkard, utter all to thee.

FIRST WATCHMAN   [*aside*].
Some treason, masters; yet stand close.

BORACHIO
Therefore know I have earn'd of Don John a thousand ducats.

CONRADE
Is it possible that any villainy should be so dear?

BORACHIO
Thou shouldst rather ask, if it were possible any villainy should be so rich; for when rich villains have need of poor ones, poor ones may make what price they will.

CONRADE
I wonder at it.

BORACHIO
That shows thou art unconfirm'd. Thou knowest that the fashion of a doublet, or a hat, or a cloak, is nothing to a man.

CONRADE
Yes, it is apparel.

BORACHIO
I mean, the fashion.

CONRADE
Yes, the fashion is the fashion.

BORACHIO
Tush! I may as well say the fool's the fool. But seest thou not what a deform'd thief this fashion is?

FIRST WATCHMAN   [*aside*].
I know that Deform'd; a' has been a vile thief this seven year; a' goes up and down like a gentleman: I remember his name.

BORACHIO
Didst thou not hear somebody?

CONRADE
No; 'twas the vane on the house.

BORACHIO
Seest thou not, I say, what a deform'd thief this fashion is? how giddily 'a turns about all the hot bloods between fourteen and five-and-thirty? sometimes fashioning them like Pharaoh's soldiers in the reechy painting, sometime like god Bel's priests in the old

church-window, sometime like the shaven Hercules in the smirch'd worm-eaten tapestry, where his codpiece seems as massy as his club?

CONRADE
All this I see; and I see that the fashion wears out more apparel than the man. But art not thou thyself giddy with the fashion too, that thou hast shifted out of thy tale into telling me of the fashion?

BORACHIO
Not so, neither: but know that I have to-night woo'd Margaret, the Lady Hero's gentlewoman, by the name of Hero: she leans me out at her mistress' chamber-window, bids me a thousand times good night, — I tell this tale vilely: — I should first tell thee how the prince, Claudio, and my master, planted and placed and possess'd by my master Don John, saw afar off in the orchard this amiable encounter.

CONRADE
And thought they Margaret was Hero?

BORACHIO
Two of them did, the prince and Claudio; but the devil my master knew she was Margaret; and partly by his oaths, which first possess'd them, partly by the dark night, which did deceive them, but chiefly by my villainy, which did confirm any slander that Don John had made, away went Claudio enrag'd; swore he would meet her, as he was appointed, next morning at the temple, and there, before the whole congregation, shame her with what he saw o'ernight, and send her home again without a husband.

FIRST WATCHMAN
We charge you, in the prince's name, stand!

SECOND WATCHMAN
Call up the right master constable. We have here recover'd the most dangerous piece of lechery that ever was known in the commonwealth.

FIRST WATCHMAN
And one Deform'd is one of them: I know him; a' wears a lock.

CONRADE
Masters, masters, —

SECOND WATCHMAN
You'll be made bring Deform'd forth, I warrant you.

CONRADE
Masters, —

FIRST WATCHMAN
Never speak: we charge you let us obey you to go with us.

BORACHIO
We are like to prove a goodly commodity, being taken up of these men's bills.

CONRADE
A commodity in question, I warrant you. — Come, we'll obey you.   [*Exeunt.*

SCENE IV

A room in LEONATO'S *house.*

Enter HERO, MARGARET, *and* URSULA.

HERO
Good Ursula, wake my cousin Beatrice, and desire her to rise.

URSULA
I will, lady.

HERO
And bid her come hither.

URSULA
Well.   [*Exit.*

MARGARET
Troth, I think your other rabato were better.

HERO
No, pray thee, good Meg, I'll wear this.

MARGARET
By my troth, 's not so good; and I warrant your cousin will say so.

HERO
My cousin's a fool, and thou art another: I'll wear none but this.

MARGARET
I like the new tire within excellently, if the hair were a thought browner; and your gown's a most rare fashion, i' faith. I saw the Duchess of Milan's gown that they praise so.

HERO
O, that exceeds, they say.

MARGARET
By my troth, 's but a night-gown in respect of yours, — cloth-o'-gold, and cuts, and laced with silver, set with pearls, down sleeves, side sleeves, and skirts round

VERGES If you hear a child cry in the night, you must call to the nurse and bid her still it.

underborne with a bluish tinsel: but for a fine, quaint, graceful, and excellent fashion, yours is worth ten on't.

HERO
God give me joy to wear it! for my heart is exceeding heavy.

MARGARET
'Twill be heavier soon by the weight of a man.

HERO
Fie upon thee! art not ashamed?

MARGARET
Of what, lady? of speaking honourably? Is not marriage honourable in a beggar? Is not your lord honourable without marriage? I think you would have me say, 'saving your reverence, a husband'; an bad thinking do not wrest true speaking, I'll offend nobody: is there any harm in 'the heavier for a husband'? None, I think, an it be the right husband and the right wife; otherwise 'tis light, and not heavy: ask my Lady Beatrice else; here she comes.

Enter BEATRICE.

HERO
Good morrow, coz.

BEATRICE
Good morrow, sweet Hero.

HERO
Why, how now! do you speak in the sick tune?

BEATRICE
I am out of all other tune, methinks.

MARGARET
Clap's into *Light o' love*; that goes without a burden: do you sing it, and I'll dance it.

BEATRICE
Ye light o' love, with your heels! — then, if your husband have stables enough, you'll see he shall lack no barns.

MARGARET
O illegitimate construction! I scorn that with my heels.

BEATRICE
'Tis almost five o'clock, cousin; 'tis time you were ready. — By my troth, I am exceeding ill: — heigh-ho!

MARGARET
For a hawk, a horse, or a husband?

BEATRICE
For the letter that begins them all, H.

MARGARET
Well, and you be not turn'd Turk, there's no more sailing by the star.

BEATRICE
What means the fool, trow?

MARGARET
Nothing I; but God send every one their heart's desire!

HERO
These gloves the Count sent me; they are an excellent perfume.

BEATRICE
I am stuff'd, cousin; I cannot smell.

MARGARET
A maid, and stuff'd! there's goodly catching of cold.

BEATRICE
O, God help me! God help me! how long have you profess'd apprehension?

MARGARET
Ever since you left it. Doth not my wit become me rarely?

BEATRICE
It is not seen enough; you should wear it in your cap. — By my troth, I am sick.

MARGARET
Get you some of this distill'd Carduus Benedictus, and lay it to your heart: it is the only thing for a qualm.

HERO
There thou prick'st her with a thistle.

BEATRICE
Benedictus! why Benedictus? you have some moral in this Benedictus.

MARGARET
Moral! no, by my troth, I have no moral meaning; I meant, plain holy-thistle. You may think perchance that I think you are in love: nay, by'r lady, I am not such a fool to think what I list; nor I list not to think what I can; nor, indeed, I cannot think, if I would think my heart out of thinking, that you are in love, or that you will be in love, or that you can be in love. Yet Benedick was such another, and now is he become a man: he swore he would never marry; and yet now, in despite of his heart, he eats his meat without grudging: and how you may be converted, I know not; but methinks you look with your eyes as other women do.

BEATRICE
What pace is this that thy tongue keeps?

MARGARET
Not a false gallop.

Enter URSULA.

URSULA
Madam, withdraw: the prince, the count, Signior Benedick, Don John, and all the gallants of the town, are come to fetch you to church.

HERO
Help to dress me, good coz, good Meg, good Ursula.

[*Exeunt.*

SCENE V

Another room in LEONATO'S *house.*

Enter LEONATO, *with the* CONSTABLE DOGBERRY *and the* HEADBOROUGH VERGES.

LEONATO
What would you with me, honest neighbour?

DOGBERRY
Marry, sir, I would have some confidence with you that decerns you nearly.

LEONATO
Brief, I pray you; for you see it is a busy time with me.

DOGBERRY
Marry, this it is, sir, —

VERGES
Yes, in truth it is, sir.

LEONATO
What is it, my good friends?

DOGBERRY
Goodman Verges, sir, speaks a little off the matter: an old man, sir, and his wits are not so blunt as, God help, I would desire they were; but, in faith, honest as the skin between his brows.

VERGES
Yes, I thank God I am as honest as any man living that is an old man and no honester than I.

FIRST WATCHMAN Some treason, masters; yet stand close.

DOGBERRY
Comparisons are odorous: *palabras*, neighbour Verges.

LEONATO
Neighbours, you are tedious.

DOGBERRY
It pleases your worship to say so, but we are the poor duke's officers; but truly, for mine own part, if I were as tedious as a king, I could find it in my heart to bestow it all of your worship.

LEONATO
All thy tediousness on me, ha!

DOGBERRY
Yea, an'twere a thousand pound more than 'tis, for I hear as good exclamation on your worship as of any man in the city; and though I be but a poor man, I am glad to hear it.

VERGES
And so am I.

LEONATO
I would fain know what you have to say.

VERGES
Marry, sir, our watch to-night, excepting your worship's presence, ha' ta'en a couple of as arrant knaves as any in Messina.

DOGBERRY
A good old man, sir; he will be talking: as they say, When the age is in, the wit is out: God help us! it is a world to see! — Well said, i'faith, neighbour Verges: — well, God's a good man; an two men ride of a horse, one must ride behind. — An honest soul, i'faith, sir; by my troth, he is, as ever broke bread: but God is to be worshipp'd, all men are not alike, — alas, good neighbour!

LEONATO
Indeed, neighbour, he comes too short of you.

DOGBERRY
Gifts that God gives.

LEONATO
I must leave you.

DOGBERRY
One word, sir: our watch, sir, have indeed comprehended two aspicious persons, and we would have them this morning examined before your worship.

LEONATO
Take their examination yourself, and bring it me: I am now in great haste, as it may appear unto you.

DOGBERRY
It shall be suffigance.

LEONATO
Drink some wine ere you go: fare you well.

Enter a MESSENGER.

MESSENGER
My lord, they stay for you to give your daughter to her husband.

LEONATO
I'll wait upon them: I am ready.

[*Exeunt* LEONATO *and* MESSENGER.

DOGBERRY
Go, good partner, go, get you to Francis Seacoal; bid him bring his pen and inkhorn to the gaol: we are now to examination these men.

VERGES
And we must do it wisely.

DOGBERRY
We will spare for no wit, I warrant you: here's that shall drive some of them to a non-come; only get the learned writer to set down our excommunication, and meet me at the gaol. [*Exeunt.*

ACT IV

SCENE I

A church.

Enter DON PEDRO, DON JOHN, LEONATO, FRIAR FRANCIS, CLAUDIO, BENEDICK, HERO, BEATRICE, *and* ATTENDANTS.

LEONATO
Come, Friar Francis, be brief; only to the plain form of marriage, and you shall recount their particular duties afterwards.

FRIAR FRANCIS
You come hither, my lord, to marry this lady?

CLAUDIO
No.

LEONATO
To be married to her: — friar, you come to marry her.

FRIAR FRANCIS
Lady, you come hither to be married to this count?

HERO
I do.

FRIAR FRANCIS
If either of you know any inward impediment why you should not be conjoin'd, I charge you, on your souls, to utter it.

CLAUDIO
Know you any, Hero?

HERO
None, my lord.

FRIAR FRANCIS
Know you any, count?

LEONATO
I dare make his answer, — none.

CLAUDIO
O, what men dare do! what men may do! what men daily do, not knowing what they do!

BENEDICK
How now! interjections? Why, then, some be of laughing, as, Ah, ha, he!

CLAUDIO
Stand thee by, friar. — Father, by your leave:
Will you with free and unconstrained soul
Give me this maid, your daughter?

LEONATO
As freely, son, as God did give her me.

CLAUDIO
And what have I to give you back, whose worth
May counterpoise this rich and precious gift?

DON PEDRO
Nothing, unless you render her again.

CLAUDIO
Sweet prince, you learn me noble thankfulness. —
There, Leonato, take her back again:
Give not this rotten orange to your friend;
She's but the sign and semblance of her honour. —
Behold how like a maid she blushes here!
O, what authority and show of truth
Can cunning sin cover itself withal!
Comes not that blood as modest evidence
To witness simple virtue? Would you not swear,
All you that see her, that she were a maid,
By these exterior shows? But she is none:
She knows the heat of a luxurious bed;
Her blush is guiltiness, not modesty.

LEONATO
What do you mean, my lord?

CLAUDIO
Not to be married, not to knit my soul
To an approved wanton.

LEONATO
Dear my lord, if you, in your own proof,
Have vanquish'd the resistance of her youth,
And made defeat of her virginity, —

CLAUDIO
I know what you would say: if I have known her,
You will say she did embrace me as a husband,
And so extenuate the 'forehand sin:
No, Leonato,
I never tempted her with word too large;
But, as a brother to his sister, show'd
Bashful sincerity and comely love.

HERO
And seem'd I ever otherwise to you?

CLAUDIO
Out on thee, seeming! I will write against it:
You seem to me as Dian in her orb,
As chaste as is the bud ere it be blown;
But you are more intemperate in your blood
Than Venus, or those pamper'd animals
That rage in savage sensuality.

HERO
Is my lord well, that he doth speak so wide?

CLAUDIO
Sweet prince, why speak not you?

DON PEDRO
        What should I speak?
I stand dishonour'd, that have gone about
To link my dear friend to a common stale.

LEONATO
Are these things spoken? or do I but dream?

DON JOHN
Sir, they are spoken, and these things are true.

BENEDICK
This looks not like a nuptial.

HERO
        True! — O God!

CLAUDIO
Leonato, stand I here?
Is this the prince? is this the prince's brother?
Is this face Hero's? are our eyes our own?

LEONATO
All this is so: but what of this, my lord?

CLAUDIO
Let me but move one question to your daughter;
And, by that fatherly and kindly power
That you have in her, bid her answer truly.

LEONATO
I charge thee do so, as thou art my child.

HERO
O, God defend me! how am I beset! —
What kind of catechising call you this?

CLAUDIO
To make you answer truly to your name.

HERO
Is it not Hero? Who can blot that name
With any just reproach?

CLAUDIO
        Marry, that can Hero;
Hero itself can blot out Hero's virtue.
What man was he talk'd with you yesternight
Out at your window betwixt twelve and one?
Now, if you are a maid, answer to this.

HERO
I talk'd with no man at that hour, my lord.
DON PEDRO
Why, then are you no maiden. — Leonato,
I am sorry you must hear: upon mine honour,
Myself, my brother, and this grieved count
Did see her, hear her, at that hour last night
Talk with a ruffian at her chamber-window;
Who hath indeed, most like a liberal villain,
Confess'd the vile encounters they have had
A thousand times in secret.
DON JOHN
Fie, fie! they are not to be nam'd, my lord,
Not to be spoke of;
There is not chastity enough in language,
Without offence to utter them. — Thus, pretty lady,
I am sorry for thy much misgovernment.
CLAUDIO
O Hero, what a Hero hadst thou been,
If half thy outward graces had been plac'd
About thy thoughts and counsels of thy heart!
But fare thee well, most foul, most fair! farewell,
Thou pure impiety and impious purity!
For thee I'll lock up all the gates of love,
And on my eyelids shall conjecture hang,
To turn all beauty into thoughts of harm,
And never shall it more be gracious.
LEONATO
Hath no man's dagger here a point for me?

[HERO *swoons*.

BEATRICE
Why, how now, cousin! wherefore sink you down?
DON JOHN
Come, let us go. These things, come thus to light,
Smother her spirits up.

[*Exeunt* DON PEDRO, DON JOHN,
CLAUDIO, *and* ATTENDANTS.

BENEDICK
How doth the lady?
BEATRICE
Dead, I think: — help, uncle: —
Hero! why, Hero! — uncle! — Signior Benedick! —
friar!
LEONATO
O Fate, take not away thy heavy hand!
Death is the fairest cover for her shame
That may be wish'd for.
BEATRICE
How now, cousin Hero!
FRIAR FRANCIS
Have comfort, lady.
LEONATO
Dost thou look up?
FRIAR FRANCIS
Yea, wherefore should she not?
LEONATO
Wherefore! Why, doth not every earthly thing
Cry shame upon her? Could she here deny
The story that is printed in her blood? —
Do not live, Hero; do not ope thine eyes:
For, did I think thou wouldst not quickly die,
Thought I thy spirits were stronger than thy shames,
Myself would, on the rearward of reproaches,
Strike at thy life. Griev'd I, I had but one?
Chid I for that at frugal nature's frame?
O, one too much by thee! Why had I one?
Why ever wast thou lovely in my eyes?
Why had I not with charitable hand
Took up a beggar's issue at my gates,
Who smirched thus and mired with infamy,
I might have said, 'No part of it is mine,
This shame derives itself from unknown loins'?
But mine, and mine I lov'd, and mine I prais'd,
And mine that I was proud on; mine so much
That I myself was to myself not mine,
Valuing of her; why, she — O, she is fall'n
Into a pit of ink, that the wide sea
Hath drops too few to wash her clean again,
And salt too little which may season give
To her foul-tainted flesh!
BENEDICK
Sir, sir, be patient.
For my part, I am so attir'd in wonder,
I know not what to say.
BEATRICE
O, on my soul, my cousin is belied!
BENEDICK
Lady, were you her bedfellow last night?

BEATRICE
No, truly, not; although, until last night,
I have this twelvemonth been her bedfellow.
LEONATO
Confirm'd, confirm'd! O, that is stronger made
Which was before barr'd up with ribs of iron!
Would the two princes lie? and Claudio lie,
Who lov'd her so, that, speaking of her foulness,
Wash'd it with tears? Hence from her! let her die.
FRIAR FRANCIS
Hear me a little;
For I have only been silent so long,
And given way unto this course of fortune,
By noting of the lady: I have mark'd
A thousand blushing apparitions
To start into her face; a thousand innocent shames
In angel whiteness beat away those blushes;
And in her eye there hath appear'd a fire,
To burn the errors that these princes hold
Against her maiden truth. Call me a fool;
Trust not my reading nor my observations,
Which with experimental seal doth warrant
The tenour of my book; trust not my age,
My reverence, calling, nor divinity,
If this sweet lady lie not guiltless here
Under some biting error.
LEONATO
Friar, it cannot be.
Thou see'st that all the grace that she hath left
Is that she will not add to her damnation
A sin of perjury; she not denies it:
Why seek'st thou, then, to cover with excuse
That which appears in proper nakedness?
FRIAR FRANCIS
Lady, what man is he you are accus'd of?
HERO
They know that do accuse me; I know none:
If I know more of any man alive
Than that which maiden modesty doth warrant,
Let all my sins lack mercy! — O my father,
Prove you that any man with me convers'd
At hours unmeet, or that I yesternight
Maintain'd the change of words with any creature,
Refuse me, hate me, torture me to death!
FRIAR FRANCIS
There is some strange misprision in the princes.
BENEDICK
Two of them have the very bent of honour;
And if their wisdoms be misled in this,
The practice of it lives in John the bastard,
Whose spirits toil in frame of villainies.
LEONATO
I know not. If they speak but truth of her,
These hands shall tear her; if they wrong her honour,
The proudest of them shall well hear of it.
Time hath not yet so dried this blood of mine,
Nor age so eat up my invention,
Nor fortune made such havoc of my means,
Nor my bad life reft me so much of friends,
But they shall find, awak'd in such a kind,
Both strength of limb and policy of mind,
Ability in means and choice of friends,
To quit me of them thoroughly.
FRIAR FRANCIS
Pause awhile,
And let my counsel sway you in this case.
Your daughter here the princes left for dead,
Let her awhile be secretly kept in,
And publish it that she is dead indeed;
Maintain a mourning ostentation,
And on your family's old monument
Hang mournful epitaphs, and do all rites
That appertain unto a burial.
LEONATO
What shall become of this? what will this do?
FRIAR FRANCIS
Marry, this, well carried, shall on her behalf
Change slander to remorse; — that is some good:
But not for that dream I on this strange course,
But on this travail look for greater birth.
She dying, as it must be so maintain'd,
Upon the instant that she was accused,
Shall be lamented, pitied, and excused
Of every hearer: for it so falls out,
That what we have we prize not to the worth
Whiles we enjoy it; but being lack'd and lost,
Why, then we rack the value, then we find
The virtue that possession would not show us
Whiles it was ours. So will it fare with Claudio:
When he shall hear she died upon his words,

Th'idea of her life shall sweetly creep
Into his study of imagination;
And every lovely organ of her life
Shall come apparell'd in more precious habit,
More moving-delicate and full of life,
Into the eye and prospect of his soul,
Than when she liv'd indeed; then shall he mourn
(If ever love had interest in his liver),
And wish he had not so accused her, —
No, though he thought his accusation true.
Let this be so, and doubt not but success
Will fashion the event in better shape
Than I can lay it down in likelihood.
But if all aim but this be levell'd false,
The supposition of the lady's death
Will quench the wonder of her infamy:
And if it sort not well, you may conceal her
(As best befits her wounded reputation)
In some reclusive and religious life,
Out of all eyes, tongues, minds, and injuries.
BENEDICK
Signior Leonato, let the friar advise you:
And though you know my inwardness and love
Is very much unto the prince and Claudio,
Yet, by mine honour, I will deal in this
As secretly and justly as your soul
Should with your body.
LEONATO
Being that I flow in grief,
The smallest twine may lead me.
FRIAR FRANCIS
'Tis well consented: presently away;
For to strange sores strangely they strain the cure. —
Come, lady, die to live: this wedding-day
Perhaps is but prolong'd: have patience and endure.

[*Exeunt* FRIAR FRANCIS, HERO, *and* LEONATO.

BENEDICK
Lady Beatrice, have you wept all this while?
BEATRICE
Yea, and I will weep a while longer.
BENEDICK
I will not desire that.
BEATRICE
You have no reason; I do it freely.
BENEDICK
Surely I do believe your fair cousin is wrong'd.
BEATRICE
Ah, how much might the man deserve of me that
would right her!
BENEDICK
Is there any way to show such friendship?
BEATRICE
A very even way, but no such friend.
BENEDICK
May a man do it?
BEATRICE
It is a man's office, but not yours.
BENEDICK
I do love nothing in the world so well as you: is not that
strange?
BEATRICE
As strange as the thing I know not. It were as possible
for me to say I loved nothing so well as you: but believe
me not; and yet I lie not; I confess nothing, nor I deny
nothing. — I am sorry for my cousin.
BENEDICK
By my sword, Beatrice, thou lovest me.
BEATRICE
Do not swear by it, and eat it.
BENEDICK
I will swear by it that you love me; and I will make him
eat it that says I love not you.
BEATRICE
Will you not eat your word?
BENEDICK
With no sauce that can be devised to it. I protest I love
thee.
BEATRICE
Why, then, God forgive me!
BENEDICK
What offence, sweet Beatrice?
BEATRICE
You have stay'd me in a happy hour: I was about to
protest I loved you.
BENEDICK
And do it with all thy heart.
BEATRICE
I love you with so much of my heart, that none is left to
protest.

BENEDICK
Come, bid me do any thing for thee.
BEATRICE
Kill Claudio.
BENEDICK
Ha! not for the wide world.
BEATRICE
You kill me to deny it. Farewell.
BENEDICK
Tarry, sweet Beatrice.
BEATRICE
I am gone, though I am here: — there is no love in you: — nay, I pray you, let me go.
BENEDICK
Beatrice, —
BEATRICE
In faith, I will go.
BENEDICK
We'll be friends first.
BEATRICE
You dare easier be friends with me than fight with mine enemy.
BENEDICK
Is Claudio thine enemy?
BEATRICE
Is he not approved in the height a villain, that hath slander'd, scorn'd, dishonour'd my kinswoman? — O that I were a man! — What, bear her in hand until they come to take hands; and then, with public accusation, uncover'd slander, unmitigated rancour, — O God, that I were a man! I would eat his heart in the market-place.
BENEDICK
Hear me, Beatrice, —
BEATRICE
Talk with a man out at a window! — a proper saying!
BENEDICK
Nay, but, Beatrice, —
BEATRICE
Sweet Hero! — she is wrong'd, she is slander'd, she is undone.
BENEDICK
Beat —
BEATRICE
Princes and counties! Surely, a princely testimony, a goodly count, Count Comfect; a sweet gallant, surely! O that I were a man for his sake! or that I had any friend would be a man for my sake! But manhood is melted into curtsies, valour into compliment, and men are only turn'd into tongue, and trim ones too: he is now as valiant as Hercules that only tells a lie, and swears it. — I cannot be a man with wishing, therefore I will die a woman with grieving.
BENEDICK
Tarry, good Beatrice. By this hand, I love thee.
BEATRICE
Use it for my love some other way than swearing by it.
BENEDICK
Think you in your soul the Count Claudio hath wrong'd Hero?
BEATRICE
Yea, as sure as I have a thought or a soul.
BENEDICK
Enough, I am engaged; I will challenge him. I will kiss your hand, and so I leave you. By this hand, Claudio shall render me a dear account. As you hear of me, so think of me. Go, comfort your cousin: I must say she is dead: and so, farewell. [Exeunt.

SCENE II
A prison.

Enter DOGBERRY *and* VERGES, *and* SEXTON, *in gowns; and the* WATCH, *with* CONRADE *and* BORACHIO.

DOGBERRY
Is our whole dissembly appear'd?
VERGES
O, a stool and a cushion for the sexton.
SEXTON
Which be the malefactors?
DOGBERRY
Marry, that am I and my partner.
VERGES
Nay, that's certain; we have the exhibition to examine.
SEXTON
But which are the offenders that are to be examined? let them come before master constable.

DOGBERRY
Yea, marry, let them come before me. — What is your name friend?
BORACHIO
Borachio.
DOGBERRY
Pray, write down — Borachio. — Yours, sirrah?
CONRADE
I am a gentleman, sir, and my name is Conrade.
DOGBERRY
Write down — master gentleman Conrade. — Masters, do you serve God?
CONRADE *and* **BORACHIO.**
Yea, sir, we hope.
DOGBERRY
Write down — that they hope they serve God: — and write God first; for God defend but God should go before such villains! — Masters, it is proved already that you are little better than false knaves; and it will go near to be thought so shortly. How answer you for yourselves?
CONRADE
Marry, sir, we say we are none.
DOGBERRY
A marvellous witty fellow, I assure you; but I will go about with him. — Come you hither, sirrah: a word in your ear, sir; I say to you, it is thought you are false knaves.
BORACHIO
Sir, I say to you we are none.
DOGBERRY
Well, stand aside. — 'Fore God, they are both in a tale. Have you writ down — that they are none?
SEXTON
Master constable, you go not the way to examine: you must call forth the watch that are their accusers.
DOGBERRY
Yea, marry, that's the eftest way. — Let the watch come forth. — Masters, I charge you, in the prince's name, accuse these men.
FIRST WATCHMAN
This man said, sir, that Don John, the prince's brother, was a villain.
DOGBERRY
Write down — Prince John a villain. — Why, this is flat perjury, to call a prince's brother villain.
BORACHIO
Master constable, —
DOGBERRY
Pray thee, fellow, peace: I do not like thy look, I promise thee.
SEXTON
What heard you him say else?

SECOND WATCHMAN
Marry, that he had received a thousand ducats of Don John for accusing the Lady Hero wrongfully.
DOGBERRY
Flat burglary as ever was committed.
VERGES
Yea, by th'mass, that it is.
SEXTON
What else, fellow?
FIRST WATCHMAN
And that Count Claudio did mean, upon his words, to disgrace Hero before the whole assembly, and not marry her.
DOGBERRY
O villain! thou wilt be condemn'd into everlasting redemption for this.
SEXTON
What else?
SECOND WATCHMAN
This is all.
SEXTON
And this is more, masters, than you can deny. Prince John is this morning secretly stolen away; Hero was in this manner accused, in this very manner refused, and upon the grief of this suddenly died. — Master constable, let these men be bound, and brought to Leonato's: I will go before and show him their examination. [Exit.
DOGBERRY
Come, let them be opinion'd.
VERGES
Let them be in the hands —
CONRADE
Off, coxcomb!
DOGBERRY
God's my life, where's the sexton? let him write down — the prince's officer, coxcomb. — Come, bind them. — Thou naughty varlet!
CONRADE
Away! you are an ass, you are an ass.
DOGBERRY
Dost thou not suspect my place? dost thou not suspect my years? — O that he were here to write me down an ass! — but, masters, remember that I am an ass; though it be not written down, yet forget not that I am an ass. — No, thou villain, thou art full of piety, as shall be proved upon thee by good witness. I am a wise fellow; and, which is more, an officer; and, which is more, a householder; and, which is more, as pretty a piece of flesh as any in Messina; and one that knows the law, go to; and a rich fellow enough, go to; find a fellow that hath had losses; and one that hath two gowns, and every thing handsome about him. — Bring him away. — O that I had been writ down an ass! [Exeunt.

BENEDICK Tarry, sweet Beatrice.

DOGBERRY Is our whole dissembly appear'd?

ACT V

SCENE I

Before LEONATO'S *house.*

Enter LEONATO *and his brother* ANTONIO.

ANTONIO
If you go on thus, you will kill yourself;
And 'tis not wisdom thus to second grief
Against yourself.

LEONATO
        I pray thee, cease thy counsel,
Which falls into mine ears as profitless
As water in a sieve: give not me counsel;
Nor let no comforter delight mine ear
But such a one whose wrongs do suit with mine.
Bring me a father that so lov'd his child,
Whose joy of her is overwhelm'd like mine,
And bid him speak of patience;
Measure his woe the length and breadth of mine,
And let it answer every strain for strain,
As thus for thus, and such a grief for such,
In every lineament, branch, shape, and form:
If such a one will smile, and stroke his beard,
Bid sorrow wag, cry 'hem' when he should groan,
Patch grief with proverbs, make misfortune drunk
With candle-wasters, — bring him yet to me,
And I of him will gather patience.
But there is no such man: for, brother, men
Can counsel and speak comfort to that grief
Which they themselves not feel; but, tasting it,
Their counsel turns to passion, which before
Would give preceptial medicine to rage,
Fetter strong madness in a silken thread,
Charm ache with air, and agony with words:
No, no, 'tis all men's office to speak patience
To those that wring under the load of sorrow,
But no man's virtue nor sufficiency
To be so moral when he shall endure
The like himself. Therefore give me no counsel:
My griefs cry louder than advertisement.

ANTONIO
Therein do men from children nothing differ.

LEONATO
I pray thee, peace, — I will be flesh and blood;
For there was never yet philosopher
That could endure the toothache patiently,
However they have writ the style of gods,
And made a push at chance and sufferance.

ANTONIO
Yet bend not all the harm upon yourself;
Make those that do offend you suffer too.

LEONATO
There thou speak'st reason: nay, I will do so.
My soul doth tell me Hero is belied;
And that shall Claudio know; so shall the prince,
And all of them that thus dishonour her.

ANTONIO
Here comes the prince and Claudio hastily.

Enter DON PEDRO *and* CLAUDIO.

DON PEDRO
Good den, good den.

CLAUDIO
        Good day to both of you.

LEONATO
Hear you, my lords, —

DON PEDRO
        We have some haste, Leonato.

LEONATO
Some haste, my lord! — well, fare you well, my lord: —
Are you so hasty now? — well, all is one.

DON PEDRO
Nay, do not quarrel with us, good old man.

ANTONIO
If he could right himself with quarrelling,
Some of us would lie low.

CLAUDIO
        Who wrongs him?

LEONATO
Marry, thou dost wrong me; thou dissembler, thou: —
Nay, never lay thy hand upon thy sword;
I fear thee not.

CLAUDIO
        Marry, beshrew my hand,
If it should give your age such cause of fear:
In faith, my hand meant nothing to my sword.

LEONATO
Tush, tush, man; never fleer and jest at me:
I speak not like a dotard nor a fool,
As, under privilege of age, to brag
What I have done, being young, or what would do,
Were I not old. Know, Claudio, to thy head,
Thou hast so wrong'd mine innocent child and me,
That I am forc'd to lay my reverence by,
And, with grey hairs and bruise of many days,
Do challenge thee to trial of a man.
I say thou hast belied mine innocent child;
Thy slander hath gone through and through her heart,
And she lies buried with her ancestors, —
O, in a tomb where never scandal slept,
Save this of hers, fram'd by thy villainy!

CLAUDIO
My villainy?

LEONATO
        Thine, Claudio; thine, I say.

DON PEDRO
You say not right, old man.

LEONATO
        My lord, my lord,
I'll prove it on his body, if he dare,
Despite his nice fence and his active practice,
His May of youth and bloom of lustihood.

CLAUDIO
Away! I will not have to do with you.

LEONATO
Canst thou so daff me? Thou hast kill'd my child:
If thou kill'st me, boy, thou shalt kill a man.

ANTONIO
He shall kill two of us, and men indeed:
But that's no matter; let him kill one first; —
Win me and wear me, — let him answer me. —
Come, follow me, boy; come, sir boy, come, follow me:
Sir boy, I'll whip you from your foining fence;
Nay, as I am a gentleman, I will.

LEONATO
Brother, —

ANTONIO
Content yourself. God knows I lov'd my niece;
And she is dead, slander'd to death by villains,
That dare as well answer a man indeed
As I dare take a serpent by the tongue;

Boys, apes, braggarts, Jacks, milksops!

LEONATO
                              Brother Antony, —

ANTONIO
Hold you content. What, man! I know them, yea,
And what they weigh, even to the utmost scruple, —
Scrambling, out-facing, fashion-mong'ring boys,
That lie, and cog, and flout, deprave, and slander,
Go antickly, show outward hideousness,
And speak off half a dozen dangerous words,
How they might hurt their enemies, if they durst;
And this is all.

LEONATO
But, brother Antony, —

ANTONIO
                              Come, 'tis no matter:
Do not you meddle; let me deal in this.

DON PEDRO
Gentlemen both, we will not wake your patience.
My heart is sorry for your daughter's death:
But, on my honour, she was charg'd with nothing
But what was true, and very full of proof.

LEONATO
My lord, my lord, —

DON PEDRO
                              I will not hear you.

LEONATO
                                             No? —
Come, brother, away. — I will be heard.

ANTONIO
                                   And shall,
Or some of us will smart for't.
                    [*Exeunt* LEONATO *and* ANTONIO.

DON PEDRO
See, see; here comes the man we went to seek.

                    Enter BENEDICK.

CLAUDIO
Now, signior, what news?

BENEDICK
Good day, my lord.

DON PEDRO
Welcome, signior: you are almost come to part almost a fray.

CLAUDIO
We had like to have had our two noses snapp'd off with two old men without teeth.

DON PEDRO
Leonato and his brother. What think'st thou? Had we fought, I doubt we should have been too young for them.

BENEDICK
In a false quarrel there is no true valour. I came to seek you both.

CLAUDIO
We have been up and down to seek thee; for we are high-proof melancholy, and would fain have it beaten away. Wilt thou use thy wit?

BENEDICK
It is in my scabbard: shall I draw it?

DON PEDRO
Dost thou wear thy wit by thy side?

CLAUDIO
Never any did so, though very many have been beside their wit. — I will bid thee draw, as we do the minstrels; draw, to pleasure us.

DON PEDRO
As I am an honest man, he looks pale. — Art thou sick, or angry?

CLAUDIO
What, courage, man! What though care kill'd a cat, thou hast mettle enough in thee to kill care.

BENEDICK
Sir, I shall meet your wit in the career, an you charge it against me. I pray you choose another subject.

CLAUDIO
Nay, then, give him another staff: this last was broke cross.

DON PEDRO
By this light, he changes more and more: I think he be angry indeed.

CLAUDIO
If he be, he knows how to turn his girdle.

BENEDICK
Shall I speak a word in your ear?

CLAUDIO
God bless me from a challenge!

BENEDICK
You are a villain; — I jest not: — I will make it good

how you dare, with what you dare, and when you dare. — Do me right, or I will protest your cowardice. You have kill'd a sweet lady, and her death shall fall heavy on you. Let me hear from you.

CLAUDIO
Well, I will meet you, so I may have good cheer.

DON PEDRO
What, a feast? a feast?

CLAUDIO
I'faith, I thank him; he hath bid me to a calf's-head and a capon; the which if I do not carve most curiously, say my knife's naught. — Shall I not find a woodcock too?

BENEDICK
Sir, your wit ambles well; it goes easily.

DON PEDRO
I'll tell thee how Beatrice praised thy wit the other day. I said, thou hadst a fine wit: 'True', says she, 'a fine little one'. 'No', said I, 'a great wit': 'Right', says she, 'a great gross one'. 'Nay', said I, 'a good wit': 'Just', said she, 'it hurts nobody'. 'Nay', said I, 'the gentleman is wise': 'Certain', said she, 'a wise gentleman'. 'Nay', said I, 'he hath the tongues': 'That I believe', said she, 'for he swore a thing to me on Monday night, which he forswore on Tuesday morning; there's a double tongue; there's two tongues'. Thus did she, an hour together, trans-shape thy particular virtues: yet at last she concluded with a sigh, thou wast the properest man in Italy.

CLAUDIO
For the which she wept heartily, and said she cared not.

DON PEDRO
Yea, that she did; but yet, for all that, an if she did not hate him deadly, she would love him dearly: — the old man's daughter told us all.

CLAUDIO
All, all; and, moreover, God saw him when he was hid in the garden.

DON PEDRO
But when shall we set the savage bull's horns on the sensible Benedick's head?

CLAUDIO
Yea, and text underneath, 'Here dwells Benedick, the married man'?

BENEDICK
Fare you well, boy: you know my mind. I will leave you now to your gossip-like humour: you break jests as braggarts do their blades, which, God be thank'd, hurt not. — My lord, for your many courtesies I thank you: I must discontinue your company: your brother the bastard is fled from Messina: you have among you kill'd a sweet and innocent lady. For my Lord Lackbeard there, he and I shall meet: and till then peace be with him.   [*Exit.*

DON PEDRO
He is in earnest.

CLAUDIO
In most profound earnest; and, I'll warrant you, for the love of Beatrice.

DON PEDRO
And hath challenged thee.

CLAUDIO
Most sincerely.

DON PEDRO
What a pretty thing man is when he goes in his doublet and hose, and leaves off his wit!

CLAUDIO
He is then a giant to an ape: but then is an ape a doctor to such a man.

DON PEDRO
But, soft you, let me be: pluck up, my heart, and be sad!
    Did he not say, my brother was fled?

            Enter DOGBERRY *and* VERGES, *and the* WATCH,
                    with CONRADE *and* BORACHIO.

DOGBERRY
Come, you, sir: if justice cannot tame you, she shall ne'er weigh more reasons in her balance: nay, an you be a cursing hypocrite once, you must be look'd to.

DON PEDRO
How now! two of my brother's men bound! Borachio one!

CLAUDIO
Hearken after their offence, my lord.

DON PEDRO
Officers, what offence have these men done?

DOGBERRY
Marry, sir, they have committed false report; moreover, they have spoken untruths; secondarily, they are slanders; sixth and lastly, they have belied a lady;

thirdly, they have verified unjust things; and, to conclude, they are lying knaves.

DON PEDRO
First, I ask thee what they have done; thirdly, I ask thee what's their offence; sixth and lastly, why they are committed; and, to conclude, what you lay to their charge.

CLAUDIO
Rightly reason'd, and in his own division; and, by my troth, there's one meaning well suited.

DON PEDRO
Who have you offended, masters, that you are thus bound to your answer? this learned constable is too cunning to be understood: what's your offence?

BORACHIO
Sweet prince, let me go no further to mine answer: do you hear me, and let this count kill me. I have deceived even your very eyes: what your wisdoms could not discover, these shallow fools have brought to light; who, in the night, overheard me confessing to this man, how Don John your brother incensed me to slander the Lady Hero; how you were brought into the orchard, and saw me court Margaret in Hero's garments; how you disgraced her, when you should marry her: my villainy they have upon record; which I had rather seal with my death than repeat over to my shame. The lady is dead upon mine and my master's false accusation; and, briefly, I desire nothing but the reward of a villain.

DON PEDRO
Runs not this speech like iron through your blood?

CLAUDIO
I have drunk poison whiles he utter'd it.

DON PEDRO
But did my brother set thee on to this?

BORACHIO
Yea, and paid me richly for the practice of it.

DON PEDRO
He is compos'd and fram'd of treachery:
And fled he is upon this villainy.

CLAUDIO
Sweet Hero! now thy image doth appear
In the rare semblance that I lov'd it first.

DOGBERRY
Come, bring away the plaintiffs: by this time our sexton hath reform'd Signior Leonato of the matter: and, masters, do not forget to specify, when time and place shall serve, that I am an ass.

VERGES
Here, here comes master Signior Leonato, and the Sexton too.

        Enter LEONATO *and* ANTONIO, *with the* SEXTON.

LEONATO
Which is the villain? let me see his eyes,
That, when I note another man like him,
I may avoid him: which of these is he?

BORACHIO
If you would know your wronger, look on me.

LEONATO
Art thou the slave that with thy breath hast kill'd
Mine innocent child?

BORACHIO
                              Yea, even I alone.

LEONATO
No, not so, villain; thou beliest thyself:
Here stand a pair of honourable men,
A third is fled, that had a hand in it. —
I thank you, princes, for my daughter's death:
Record it with your high and worthy deeds;
'Twas bravely done, if you bethink you of it.

CLAUDIO
I know not how to pray your patience;
Yet I must speak. Choose your revenge yourself;
Impose me to what penance your invention
Can lay upon my sin: yet sinn'd I not
But in mistaking.

DON PEDRO
                              By my soul, nor I:
And yet, to satisfy this good old man,
I would bend under any heavy weight
That he'll enjoin me to.

LEONATO
I cannot bid you bid my daughter live, —
That were impossible: but, I pray you both,
Possess the people in Messina here
How innocent she died; and if your love
Can labour aught in sad invention,
Hang her an epitaph upon her tomb,
And sing it to her bones, — sing it to-night: —

DON PEDRO See, see; here comes the man we went to seek.

To-morrow morning come you to my house;
And since you could not be my son-in-law,
Be yet my nephew: my brother hath a daughter,
Almost the copy of my child that's dead,
And she alone is heir to both of us:
Give her the right you should have given her cousin,
And so dies my revenge.

CLAUDIO
        O noble sir,
Your over-kindness doth wring tears from me!
I do embrace your offer; and dispose
For henceforth of poor Claudio.

LEONATO
To-morrow, then, I will expect your coming;
To-night I take my leave. — This naughty man
Shall face to face be brought to Margaret,
Who I believe was pack'd in all this wrong,
Hired to it by your brother.

BORACHIO
        No, by my soul, she was not;
Nor knew not what she did when she spoke to me;
But always hath been just and virtuous
In any thing that I do know by her.

DOGBERRY
Moreover, sir (which indeed is not under white and
black), this plaintiff here, the offender, did call me ass:
I beseech you, let it be remember'd in his punishment.
And also, the watch heard them talk of one Deform'd:
they say he wears a key in his ear, and a lock hanging by
it: and borrows money in God's name, — the which he
hath used so long and never paid, that now men grow
hard-hearted, and will lend nothing for God's sake:
pray you, examine him upon that point.

LEONATO
I thank thee for thy care and honest pains.

DOGBERRY
Your worship speaks like a most thankful and reverend
youth; and I praise God for you.

LEONATO
There's for thy pains.

DOGBERRY
God save the foundation!

LEONATO
Go, I discharge thee of thy prisoner, and I thank thee.

DOGBERRY
I leave an arrant knave with your worship; which I
beseech your worship to correct yourself, for the
example of others. God keep your worship! I wish your
worship well; God restore you to health! I humbly give
you leave to depart; and if a merry meeting may be
wish'd, God prohibit it! — Come, neighbour.
        [*Exeunt* DOGBERRY *and* VERGES.

LEONATO
Until to-morrow morning, lords, farewell.

ANTONIO
Farewell, my lords: we look for you to-morrow.
DON PEDRO
We will not fail.
CLAUDIO
        To-night I'll mourn with Hero.
        [*Exeunt* DON PEDRO *and* CLAUDIO.
LEONATO [*to the* WATCH].
Bring you these fellows on. We'll talk with Margaret
How her acquaintance grew with this lewd fellow.
        [*Exeunt severally.*

SCENE II
LEONATO'S *garden*.

Enter, severally, BENEDICK *and* MARGARET.

BENEDICK
Pray thee, sweet Mistress Margaret, deserve well at my
hands by helping me to the speech of Beatrice.

MARGARET
Will you, then, write me a sonnet in praise of my
beauty?
BENEDICK
In so high a style, Margaret, that no man living shall
come over it; for, in most comely truth, thou deservest
it.
MARGARET
To have no man come over me! why, shall I always keep
below stairs?
BENEDICK
Thy wit is as quick as the greyhound's mouth, — it
catches.
MARGARET
And yours as blunt as the fencer's foils, which hit, but
hurt not.
BENEDICK
A most manly wit, Margaret; it will not hurt a woman:
and so, I pray thee, call Beatrice: I give thee the
bucklers.
MARGARET
Give us the swords; we have bucklers of our own.
BENEDICK
If you use them, Margaret, you must put in the pikes
with a vice; and they are dangerous weapons for maids.
MARGARET
Well, I will call Beatrice to you, who I think hath legs.
BENEDICK
And therefore will come.   [*Exit* MARGARET.
        [*He sings.*
        The god of love,
        That sits above,
    And knows me, and knows me,
        How pitiful I deserve, —
I mean in singing; but in loving, — Leander the good
swimmer, Troilus the first employer of pandars, and a
whole book full of these quondam carpet-mongers,
whose names yet run smoothly in the even road of a
blank verse, — why, they were never so truly turn'd
over and over as my poor self in love. Marry, I cannot
show it in rime; I have tried: I can find out no rime to
'lady' but 'baby,' — an innocent rime; for 'scorn',
'horn,' — a hard rime; for 'school,' 'fool,' — a babbling
rime; very ominous endings: no, I was not born under
a riming planet, nor I cannot woo in festival terms.
        Enter BEATRICE.
Sweet Beatrice, wouldst thou come when I call'd thee?
BEATRICE
Yea, signior, and depart when you bid me.
BENEDICK
O, stay but till then!
BEATRICE
'Then' is spoken; fare you well now: — and yet, ere I go,
let me go with that I came; which is, with knowing
what hath pass'd between you and Claudio.

BENEDICK Thy wit is as quick as the greyhound's mouth, — it catches.

BENEDICK
Only foul words; and thereupon I will kiss thee.

BEATRICE
Foul words is but foul wind, and foul wind is but foul breath, and foul breath is noisome; therefore I will depart unkiss'd.

BENEDICK
Thou hast frighted the word out of his right sense, so forcible is thy wit. But I must tell thee plainly, Claudio undergoes my challenge; and either I must shortly hear from him, or I will subscribe him a coward. And, I pray thee now, tell me for which of my bad parts didst thou first fall in love with me?

BEATRICE
For them all together; which maintain'd so politic a state of evil, that they will not admit any good part to intermingle with them. But for which of my good parts did you first suffer love for me?

BENEDICK
Suffer love, — a good epithet! I do suffer love indeed, for I love thee against my will.

BEATRICE
In spite of your heart, I think; alas, poor heart! If you spite it for my sake, I will spite it for yours; for I will never love that which my friend hates.

BENEDICK
Thou and I are too wise to woo peaceably.

BEATRICE
It appears not in this confession: there's not one wise man among twenty that will praise himself.

BENEDICK
An old, an old instance, Beatrice, that lived in the time of good neighbours. If a man do not erect in this age his own tomb ere he dies, he shall live no longer in monument than the bell rings and the widow weeps.

BEATRICE
And how long is that, think you?

BENEDICK
Question: — why, an hour in clamour, and a quarter in rheum: therefore is it most expedient for the wise, if Don Worm, his conscience, find no impediment to the contrary, to be the trumpet of his own virtues, as I am to myself. So much for praising myself, who, I myself will bear witness, is praiseworthy: and now tell me, how doth your cousin?

BEATRICE
Very ill.

BENEDICK
And how do you?

BEATRICE
Very ill too.

BENEDICK
Serve God, love me, and mend. There will I leave you too, for here comes one in haste.

Enter URSULA.

URSULA
Madam, you must come to your uncle. Yonder's old coil at home: it is proved my Lady Hero hath been falsely accused, the prince and Claudio mightily abused; and Don John is the author of all, who is fled and gone. Will you come presently?

BEATRICE
Will you go hear this news, signior?

BENEDICK
I will live in thy heart, die in thy lap, and be buried in thy eyes; and moreover I will go with thee to thy uncle's.   [*Exeunt.*

SCENE III

A church.

Enter DON PEDRO, CLAUDIO,
and three or four with tapers.

CLAUDIO
Is this the monument of Leonato?

ATTENDANT
It is, my lord.

CLAUDIO [*reads from a scroll*].

Done to death by slanderous tongues
    Was the Hero that here lies;
Death, in guerdon of her wrongs,
    Gives her fame which never dies.
So the life that died with shame
Lives in death with glorious fame.
Hang thou there upon the tomb,
Praising her when I am dumb. —

Now, music, sound, and sing your solemn hymn.

Song.
Pardon, goddess of the night,
Those that slew thy virgin knight;
For the which, with songs of woe,
Round about her tomb they go.
Midnight, assist our moan;
Help us to sigh and groan,
        Heavily, heavily;
Graves, yawn, and yield your dead,
Till death be uttered,
        Heavily, heavily.

CLAUDIO
Now, unto thy bones good night! —
Yearly will I do this rite.

DON PEDRO
Good morrow, masters; put your torches out:
    The wolves have prey'db; and look, the gentle day,
Before the wheels of Phœus, round about
    Dapples the drowsy east with spots of grey.
Thanks to you all, and leave us: fare you well.

CLAUDIO
Good morrow, masters: each his several way.

DON PEDRO
Come, let us hence, and put on other weeds;
    And then to Leonato's we will go.

CLAUDIO
And Hymen now with luckier issue speed's
    Than this for whom we render'd up this woe!
                                                      [*Exeunt.*

SCENE IV

A room in LEONATO'S *house.*

Enter LEONATO, ANTONIO, BENEDICK,
BEATRICE, MARGARET, URSULA, FRIAR
FRANCIS, *and* HERO.

FRIAR FRANCIS
Did I not tell you she was innocent?

LEONATO
So are the prince and Claudio, who accus'd her
Upon the error that you heard debated:
But Margaret was in some fault for this,
Although against her will, as it appears
In the true course of all the question.

ANTONIO
Well, I am glad that all things sort so well.

BENEDICK
And so am I, being else by faith enforced
To call young Claudio to a reckoning for it.

LEONATO
Well, daughter, and you gentlewomen all,
Withdraw into a chamber by yourselves,
And when I send for you, come hither mask'd:
The prince and Claudio promis'd by this hour
To visit me. — You know your office, brother:
                                            [*Exeunt* LADIES.
You must be father to your brother's daughter,
And give her to young Claudio.

ANTONIO
Which I will do with confirm'd countenance.

BENEDICK
Friar, I must entreat your pains, I think.

FRIAR FRANCIS
To do what, signior?

BENEDICK
To bind me, or undo me; one of them. —
Signior Leonato, truth it is, good signior,
Your niece regards me with an eye of favour.

LEONATO
That eye my daughter lent her: 'tis most true.

BENEDICK
And I do with an eye of love requite her.

LEONATO
The sight whereof I think you had from me,
From Claudio, and the prince: but what's your will?

BENEDICK
Your answer, sir, is enigmatical:
But, for my will, my will is, your good-will
May stand with ours, this day to be conjoin'd
In the state of honourable marriage: —
In which, good friar, I shall desire your help.

LEONATO
My heart is with your liking.

FRIAR FRANCIS
                            And my help. —
Here comes the prince and Claudio.

Enter DON PEDRO *and* CLAUDIO, *with*
ATTENDANTS.

DON PEDRO
Good morrow to this fair assembly.

LEONATO
Good morrow, prince; good morrow, Claudio:
We here attend you. Are you yet determin'd
To-day to marry with my brother's daughter?

CLAUDIO
I'll hold my mind, were she an Ethiop.

LEONATO
Call her forth, brother; here's the friar ready.
                                            [*Exit* ANTONIO.

DON PEDRO
Good morrow, Benedick. Why, what's the matter,
That you have such a February face,
So full of frost, of storm, and cloudiness?

CLAUDIO
I think he thinks upon the savage bull. —
Tush, fear not, man; we'll tip thy horns with gold,
And all Europa shall rejoice at thee;
As once Europa did at lusty Jove,
When he would play the noble beast in love.

BENEDICK
Bull Jove, sir, had an amiable low;
And some such strange bull leapt your father's cow,
And got a calf in that same noble feat
Much like to you, for you have just his bleat.

CLAUDIO
For this I owe you: here come other reck'nings.
        Enter ANTONIO, *with the* LADIES *mask'd.*
Which is the lady I must seize upon?

ANTONIO
This same is she, and I do give you her.

CLAUDIO
Why, then she's mine. — Sweet, let me see your face.

LEONATO
No, that you shall not, till you take her hand
Before this friar, and swear to marry her.

CLAUDIO
Give me your hand before this holy friar:
I am your husband, if you like of me.

HERO
And when I liv'd, I was your other wife: [*Unmasking.*
And when you lov'd, you were my other husband.

CLAUDIO
Another Hero!

HERO
                    Nothing certainer:
One Hero died defil'd; but I do live,
And surely as I live, I am a maid.

DON PEDRO
The former Hero! Hero that is dead!

LEONATO
She died, my lord, but whiles her slander liv'd.

FRIAR FRANCIS
All this amazement can I qualify;
When after that the holy rites are ended,
I'll tell you largely of fair Hero's death:
Meantime let wonder seem familiar,
And to the chapel let us presently.

BENEDICK
Soft and fair, friar. — Which is Beatrice?

BEATRICE [*Unmasking*].
I answer to that name. What is your will?

BENEDICK
Do not you love me?

BEATRICE
                            Why, no; no more than reason.

BENEDICK
Why, then your uncle, and the prince, and Claudio
Have been deceiv'd; for they swore you did.

BEATRICE
Do not you love me?

BENEDICK
                            Troth, no; no more than reason.

BEATRICE
Why, then my cousin, Margaret, and Ursula
Are much deceiv'd; for they did swear you did.

BENEDICK
They swore that you were almost sick for me.

BEATRICE
They swore that you were well-nigh dead for me.

BENEDICK
'Tis no such matter. — Then you do not love me?

BEATRICE
No, truly, but in friendly recompense.

LEONATO
Come, cousin, I am sure you love the gentleman.
CLAUDIO
And I'll be sworn upon't that he loves her;
For here's a paper, written in his hand,
A halting sonnet of his own pure brain
Fashion'd to Beatrice.
HERO
           And here's another,
Writ in my cousin's hand, stol'n from her pocket,
Containing her affection unto Benedick.
BENEDICK
A miracle! here's our own hands against our hearts. —
Come, I will have thee; but, by this light, I take thee for
pity.
BEATRICE
I would not deny you; — but, by this good day, I yield
upon great persuasion; and partly to save your life, for I
was told you were in a consumption.
BENEDICK
Peace! I will stop your mouth.   [*Kissing her.*

DON PEDRO
How dost thou, Benedick, the married man?
BENEDICK
I'll tell thee what, prince; a college of wit-crackers
cannot flout me out of my humour. Dost thou think I
care for a satire or an epigram? No: if a man will be
beaten with brains, a' shall wear nothing handsome
about him. In brief, since I do purpose to marry, I will
think nothing to any purpose that the world can say
against it; and therefore never flout at me for what I
have said against it; for man is a giddy thing, and this is
my conclusion. — For thy part, Claudio, I did think to
have beaten thee; but in that thou art like to be my
kinsman, live unbruised, and love my cousin.
CLAUDIO
I had well hoped thou wouldst have denied Beatrice,
that I might have cudgell'd thee out of thy single life, to
make thee a double-dealer; which, out of question,
thou wilt be, if my cousin do not look exceeding
narrowly to thee.

BENEDICK
Come, come, we are friends. — Let's have a dance ere
we are married, that we may lighten our own hearts
and our wives' heels.
LEONATO
We'll have dancing afterward.
BENEDICK
First, of my word; therefore play, music! — Prince,
thou art sad; get thee a wife, get thee a wife: there is no
staff more reverend than one tipp'd with horn.
       Enter a MESSENGER.
MESSENGER
My lord, your brother John is ta'en in flight,
And brought with arm'd men back to Messina.
BENEDICK
Think not on him till to-morrow: I'll devise thee brave
punishments for him. — Strike up, pipers!
       [*Dance. Exeunt.*

THE MERRY WIVES OF WINDSOR

DRAMATIS PERSONAE

SIR JOHN FALSTAFF.
FENTON, *a gentleman.*
SHALLOW, *a country justice.*
SLENDER, *cousin to Shallow.*
FORD, } *two gentlemen dwelling at Windsor.*
PAGE, }
WILLIAM PAGE, *a boy, son to Page.*
SIR HUGH EVANS, *a Welsh parson.*

DOCTOR CAIUS, *a French physician.*
HOST OF THE GARTER INN.
BARDOLPH, }
PISTOL, } *followers of Falstaff.*
NYM, }
ROBIN, *page to Falstaff.*
SIMPLE, *servant to Slender.*
RUGBY, *servant to Doctor Caius.*

MISTRESS FORD.
MISTRESS PAGE.
ANNE PAGE, *her daughter.*
MISTRESS QUICKLY, *servant to Doctor Caius.*

SERVANTS *to Page, Ford, etc.*

SCENE — *Windsor, and the neighbourhood.*

SHALLOW Sir Hugh, persuade me not; I will make a Star-Chamber matter of it.

ACT I

SCENE I

Windsor. Before PAGE'S *house.*

Enter JUSTICE SHALLOW, SLENDER, *and* SIR HUGH EVANS.

SHALLOW
Sir Hugh, persuade me not; I will make a Star-Chamber matter of it: if he were twenty Sir John Falstaffs, he shall not abuse Robert Shallow, esquire.
SLENDER
In the county of Gloster, justice of peace and *coram.*
SHALLOW
Ay, cousin Slender, and *cust-alorum.*
SLENDER
Ay, and *rato-lorum* too; and a gentleman born, master parson; who writes himself *armigero,* — in any bill, warrant, quittance, or obligation, *armigero.*
SHALLOW
Ay, that I do; and have done any time these three hundred years.
SLENDER
All his successors gone before him hath done't; and all his ancestors that come after him may: they may give the dozen white luces in their coat.
SHALLOW
It is an old coat.
EVANS
The dozen white louses do become an old coat well; it agrees well, passant; it is a familiar beast to man, and signifies — love.
SHALLOW
The luce is the fresh fish; the salt fish is an old coat.
SLENDER
I may quarter, coz?

SHALLOW
You may, by marrying.
EVANS
It is marring indeed, if he quarter it.
SHALLOW
Not a whit.
EVANS
Yes, py'r lady; if he has a quarter of your coat, there is but three skirts for yourself, in my simple conjectures: but that is all one. If Sir John Falstaff have committed disparagements unto you, I am of the church, and will be glad to do my benevolence to make atonements and compremises between you.
SHALLOW
The Council shall hear it; it is a riot.
EVANS
It is not meet the Council hear a riot; there is no fear of Got in a riot: the Council, look you, shall desire to hear the fear of Got, and not to hear a riot; take your vizaments in that.
SHALLOW
Ha! o' my life, if I were young again, the sword should end it.
EVANS
It is petter that friends is the sword, and end it: and there is also another device in my prain, which peradventure prings goot discretions with it: — there is Anne Page, which is daughter to Master George Page, which is pretty virginity.
SLENDER
Mistress Anne Page! She has brown hair, and speaks small like a woman.
EVANS
It is that fery person for all the 'orld, as just as you will desire; and seven hundred pounds of moneys, and gold, and silver, is her grandsire upon his death's-bed (Got deliver to a joyful resurrections!) give, when she is able to overtake seventeen years old. It were a goot

motion if we leave our pribbles and prabbles, and desire a marriage between Master Abraham and Mistress Anne Page.
SHALLOW
Did her grandsire leave her seven hundred pound?
EVANS
Ay, and her father is make her a petter penny.
SHALLOW
I know the young gentlewoman; she has good gifts.
EVANS
Seven hundred pounds and possibilities is goot gifts.
SHALLOW
Well, let us see honest Master Page. Is Falstaff there?
EVANS
Shall I tell you a lie? I do despise a liar as I do despise one that is false, or as I despise one that is not true. The knight, Sir John, is there; and, I beseech you, be ruled by your well-willers. I will peat the door for Master Page. [*Knocks.*] What, ho! Got pless your house here!
PAGE [*within*].
Who's there?
EVANS
Here is Got's plessing, and your friend, and Justice Shallow; and here young Master Slender, that peradventures shall tell you another tale, if matters grow to your likings.

Enter PAGE.

PAGE
I am glad to see your worships well. I thank you for my venison, Master Shallow.
SHALLOW
Master Page, I am glad to see you: much good do it your good heart! I wish'd your venison better; it was ill kill'd. — How doth good Mistress Page? — and I thank you always with my heart, la; with my heart.
PAGE
Sir, I thank you.
SHALLOW
Sir, I thank you; by yea and no, I do.
PAGE
I am glad to see you, good Master Slender.
SLENDER
How does your fallow greyhound, sir? I heard say he was outrun on Cotsall.
PAGE
It could not be judged, sir.
SLENDER
You'll not confess, you'll not confess.
SHALLOW
That he will not. — 'Tis your fault, 'tis your fault: — 'tis a good dog.
PAGE
A cur, sir.
SHALLOW
Sir, he's a good dog, and a fair dog: can there be more said? he is good and fair. — Is Sir John Falstaff here?
PAGE
Sir, he is within; and I would I could do a good office between you.
EVANS
It is spoke as a Christians ought to speak.
SHALLOW
He hath wrong'd me, Master Page.
PAGE
Sir, he doth in some sort confess it.
SHALLOW
If it be confess'd, it is not redress'd: is not that so, Master Page? He hath wrong'd me; indeed he hath; — at a word, he hath; — believe me; Robert Shallow, esquire, saith he is wrong'd.

SLENDER By these gloves, then, 'twas he.

PAGE
Here comes Sir John.

Enter SIR JOHN FALSTAFF, BARDOLPH, NYM, *and*
PISTOL.

FALSTAFF
Now, Master Shallow, — you'll complain of me to the
king?

SHALLOW
Knight, you have beaten my men, killed my deer, and
broke open my lodge.

FALSTAFF
But not kiss'd your keeper's daughter?

SHALLOW
Tut, a pin! this shall be answer'd.

FALSTAFF
I will answer it straight; I have done all this: — that is
now answer'd.

SHALLOW
The Council shall know this.

FALSTAFF
'Twere better for you if it were known in counsel: you'll
be laugh'd at.

EVANS
Pauca verba, Sir John, goot worts.

FALSTAFF
Good worts! good cabbage. — Slender, I broke your
head: what matter have you against me?

SLENDER
Marry, sir, I have matter in my head against you, and
against your cony-catching rascals, Bardolph, Nym,
and Pistol; they carried me to the tavern and made me
drunk, and afterwards pick'd my pocket.

BARDOLPH
You Banbury cheese!

SLENDER
Ay, it is no matter.

PISTOL
How now, Mephostophilus!

SLENDER
Ay, it is no matter.

NYM
Slice, I say! *pauca, pauca;* slice! that's my humour.

SLENDER
Where's Simple, my man? — can you tell, cousin?

EVANS
Peace, I pray you. — Now let us understand. There is
three umpires in this matter, as I understand; that is,
Master Page, *fidelicet* Master Page; and there is myself,
fidelicet myself; and the three party is, lastly and finally,
mine host of the Garter.

PAGE
We three, to hear it and end it between them.

EVANS
Fery goot: I will make a prief of it in my note-book; and
we will afterwards ork upon the cause with as great
discreetly as we can.

FALSTAFF
Pistol, —

PISTOL
He hears with ears.

EVANS
The tevil and his tam! what phrase is this, 'He hears
with ear'? why, it is affectations.

FALSTAFF
Pistol, did you pick Master Slender's purse?

SLENDER
Ay, by these gloves, did he — or I would I might never
come in mine own great chamber again else — of
seven groats in mill-sixpences, and two Edward
shovel-boards, that cost me two shilling and two pence
a-piece of Yead Miller, by these gloves.

FALSTAFF
Is this true, Pistol?

EVANS
No; it is false, if it is a pick-purse.

PISTOL
Ha, thou mountain-foreigner! — Sir John and
   master mine,
I combat challenge of this latten bilbo. —
Word of denial in thy labras here;
Word of denial: — froth and scum, thou liest!

SLENDER
By these gloves, then, 'twas he.

NYM
Be avised, sir, and pass good humours: I will say 'marry
trap' with you, if you run the nuthook's humour on me;
that is the very note of it.

SLENDER
By this hat, then, he in the red face had it; for though I
cannot remember what I did when you made me
drunk, yet I am not altogether an ass.

FALSTAFF
What say you, Scarlet and John?

BARDOLPH
Why, sir, for my part, I say the gentleman had drunk
himself out of his five sentences, —

EVANS
It is his five senses: fie, what the ignorance is!

BARDOLPH
And being fap, sir, was, as they say, cashiered; and so
conclusions passed the careires.

SLENDER
Ay, you spake in Latin then too; but 'tis no matter: I'll
ne'er be drunk whilst I live again, but in honest, civil,
godly company, for this trick: if I be drunk, I'll be drunk
with those that have the fear of God, and not with
drunken knaves.

EVANS
So Got udge me, that is a virtuous mind.

FALSTAFF
You hear all these matters denied, gentlemen; you hear it.

Enter ANNE PAGE, *with wine;* MISTRESS FORD
and MISTRESS PAGE.

PAGE
Nay, daughter, carry the wine in; we'll drink within.

[*Exit* ANNE PAGE.

SLENDER
O heaven! this is Mistress Anne Page.

PAGE
How now, Mistress Ford!

FALSTAFF
Mistress Ford, by my troth, you are very well met: by
your leave, good mistress.   [*Kisses her.*

PAGE
Wife, bid these gentlemen welcome. — Come, we have
a hot venison-pasty to dinner: come, gentlemen, I hope
we shall drink down all unkindness.

[*Exeunt all except* SHALLOW, SLENDER, *and* EVANS.

SLENDER
I had rather than forty shillings I had my Book of Songs
and Sonnets here.

Enter SIMPLE.

How now, Simple! where have you been? I must wait
on myself, must I? You have not the Book of Riddles
about you, have you?

SIMPLE
Book of Riddles! why, did you not lend it to Alice
Shortcake upon All-hallowmas last, a fortnight afore
Michaelmas?

SHALLOW
Come, coz; come, coz; we stay for you. A word with you,
coz; marry, this, coz; — there is, as'twere, a tender, a
kind of tender, made afar off by Sir Hugh here. Do you
understand me?

SLENDER
Ay, sir, you shall find me reasonable; if it be so, I shall
do that that is reason.

SHALLOW
Nay, but understand me.

SLENDER
So I do, sir.

EVANS
Give ear to his motions, Master Slender: I will
description the matter to you, if you be capacity of it.

SLENDER
Nay, I will do as my cousin Shallow says: I pray you,
pardon me; he's a justice of peace in his country,
simple though I stand here.

EVANS
But that is not the question: the question is concerning
your marriage.

SHALLOW
Ay, there's the point, sir.

EVANS
Marry, is it; the very point of it; to Mistress Anne Page.

SLENDER
Why, if it be so, I will marry her upon any reasonable
demands.

EVANS
But can you affection the oman? Let us command to
know that of your mouth or of your lips; for divers
philosophers hold that the lips is parcel of the mouth.
Therefore, precisely, can you carry your good will to the
maid?

SHALLOW
Cousin Abraham Slender, can you love her?

SLENDER
I hope, sir, I will do as it shall become one that would
do reason.

EVANS
Nay, Got's lords and his ladies, you must speak
positable, if you can carry her your desires towards her.

SHALLOW
That you must. Will you, upon good dowry, marry her?

SLENDER
I will do a greater thing than that, upon your request,
cousin, in any reason.

SHALLOW
Nay, conceive me, conceive me, sweet coz: what I do is
to pleasure you, coz. Can you love the maid?

SLENDER
I will marry her, sir, at your request: but if there be no
great love in the beginning, yet heaven may decrease it
upon better acquaintance, when we are married and
have more occasion to know one another; I hope, upon
familiarity will grow more content: but if you say,
'marry her', I will marry her; that I am freely dissolved,
and dissolutely.

EVANS
It is a fery discretion answer; save the faul is in the ort
'dissolutely': the ort is, according to our meaning,
'resolutely', — his meaning is goot.

SHALLOW
Ay, I think my cousin meant well.

SLENDER
Ay, or else I would I might be hang'd, la.

SHALLOW
Here comes fair Mistress Anne.

Enter ANNE PAGE.

Would I were young for your sake, Mistress Anne!

ANNE PAGE
The dinner is on the table; my father desires your worships' company.

SHALLOW
I will wait on him, fair Mistress Anne.

EVANS
Od's plessed will! I will not be absence at the grace.

[Exeunt SHALLOW *and* EVANS.

ANNE PAGE
Will't please your worship to come in, sir?

SLENDER
No, I thank you, forsooth, heartily; I am very well.

ANNE PAGE
The dinner attends you, sir.

SLENDER
I am not a-hungry, I thank you, forsooth. — Go, sirrah, for all you are my man, go wait upon my cousin Shallow. [*Exit* SIMPLE.] A justice of peace sometime may be beholding to his friend for a man. — I keep but three men and a boy yet, till my mother be dead: but what though? yet I live like a poor gentleman born.

ANNE PAGE
I may not go in without your worship: they will not sit till you come.

SLENDER
I'faith, I'll eat nothing; I thank you as much as though I did.

ANNE PAGE
I pray you, sir, walk in.

SLENDER
I had rather walk here, I thank you. I bruised my shin th'other day with playing at sword and dagger with a master of fence, — three veneys for a dish of stew'd prunes; and, by my troth, I cannot abide the smell of hot meat since. — Why do your dogs bark so? be there bears i'th'town?

ANNE PAGE
I think there are, sir; I heard them talk'd of.

SLENDER
I love the sport well; but I shall as soon quarrel at it as any man in England. You are afraid, if you see the bear loose, are you not?

ANNE PAGE
Ay, indeed, sir.

SLENDER
That's meat and drink to me, now. I have seen Sackerson loose twenty times, and have taken him by the chain; but, I warrant you, the women have so cried and shriek'd at it, that it pass'd: — but women, indeed, cannot abide 'em; they are very ill-favour'd rough things.

Enter PAGE.

PAGE
Come, gentle Master Slender, come; we stay for you.

SLENDER
I'll eat nothing, I thank you, sir.

PAGE
By cock and pie, you shall not choose, sir: come, come.

SLENDER
Nay, pray you, lead the way.

PAGE
Come on, sir.

SLENDER
Mistress Anne, yourself shall go first.

ANNE PAGE
Not I, sir; pray you, keep on.

SLENDER
Truly, I will not go first; truly, la; I will not do you that wrong.

ANNE PAGE
I pray you, sir.

SLENDER
I'll rather be unmannerly than troublesome.
You do yourself wrong, indeed, la. *[Exeunt.*

SCENE II

The same.

Enter SIR HUGH EVANS *and* SIMPLE.

EVANS
Go your ways, and ask of Doctor Caius' house which is the way: and there dwells one Mistress Quickly, which is in the manner of his nurse, or his try nurse, or his cook, or his laundry, his washer, and his wringer.

SIMPLE
Well, sir.

EVANS
Nay, it is petter yet. — Give her this letter; for it is a oman that altogether's acquaintance with Mistress Anne Page: and the letter is, to desire and require her to solicit your master's desires to Mistress Anne Page. I pray you, be gone: I will make an end of my dinner; there's pippins and seese to come. *[Exeunt.*

SCENE III

A room in the Garter Inn.

Enter FALSTAFF, HOST, BARDOLPH, NYM,
PISTOL, *and* ROBIN.

FALSTAFF
Mine host of the Garter, —

HOST
What says my bully-rook? speak scholarly and wisely.

FALSTAFF
Truly, mine host, I must turn away some of my followers.

HOST
Discard, bully Hercules; cashier: let them wag; trot, trot.

FALSTAFF
I sit at ten pounds a-week.

HOST
Thou'rt an emperor, Cæsar, Keisar, and Pheezar. I will entertain Bardolph; he shall draw, he shall tap: said I well, bully Hector?

FALSTAFF
Do so, good mine host.

HOST
I have spoke; let him follow. — Let me see thee froth and lime: I am at a word; follow.

[Exit.

FALSTAFF
Bardolph, follow him. A tapster is a good trade: an old cloak makes a new jerkin; a wither'd serving-man a fresh tapster. Go; adieu.

BARDOLPH
It is a life that I have desired: I will thrive.

PISTOL
O base Hungarian wight! wilt thou the spigot wield?

[Exit BARDOLPH.

NYM
He was gotten in drink: is not the humour conceited? His mind is not heroic, and there's the humour of it.

FALSTAFF
I am glad I am so acquit of this tinder-box: his thefts were too open; his filching was like an unskilful singer, — he kept not time.

NYM
The good humour is to steal at a minim's rest.

PISTOL
'Convey' the wise it call. 'Steal'! foh! a fico for the phrase!

FALSTAFF
Well, sirs, I am almost out at heels.

PISTOL
Why, then, let kibes ensue.

FALSTAFF
There is no remedy; I must cony-catch; I must shift.

PISTOL
Young ravens must have food.

FALSTAFF
Which of you know Ford of this town?

PISTOL
I ken the wight: he is of substance good.

FALSTAFF
My honest lads, I will tell you what I am about.

PISTOL
Two yards, and more.

FALSTAFF
No quips now, Pistol: — indeed, I am in the waist two yards about; but I am now about no waste; I am about thrift. Briefly, I do mean to make love to Ford's wife: I spy entertainment in her; she discourses, she carves, she gives the leer of invitation: I can construe the action of her familiar style; and the hardest voice of her behaviour, to be English'd rightly, is, 'I am Sir John Falstaff's.'

PISTOL
He hath studied her well, and translated her well, — out of honesty into English.

NYM
The anchor is deep: will that humour pass?

FALSTAFF
Now, the report goes she has all the rule of her husband's purse: — he hath a legion of angels.

PISTOL
As many devils entertain; and, 'To her, boy,' say I.

NYM
The humour rises; it is good: humour me the angels.

FALSTAFF
I have writ me here a letter to her: and here another to Page's wife, who even now gave me good eyes too, examined my parts with most judicious œillades; sometimes the beam of her view gilded my foot, sometimes my portly belly.

PISTOL
Then did the sun on dunghill shine.

NYM
I thank thee for that humour.

FALSTAFF
O, she did so course o'er my exteriors with such a greedy intention, that the appetite of her eye did seem

FALSTAFF I have writ me here a letter to her.

CAIUS *O diable, diable!* vat is in my closet?

to scorch me up like a burning-glass! Here's another letter to her: she bears the purse too; she is a region in Guiana, all gold and bounty. I will be cheaters to them both, and they shall be exchequers to me; they shall be my East and West Indies, and I will trade to them both. Go bear thou this letter to Mistress Page; and thou this to Mistress Ford: we will thrive, lads, we will thrive.

PISTOL
Shall I Sir Pandarus of Troy become,
And by my side wear steel? then, Lucifer take all!

NYM
I will run no base humour: here, take the humour-letter:
I will keep the haviour of reputation.

FALSTAFF [*to* ROBIN].
Hold, sirrah, bear you these letters tightly;
Sail like my pinnace to these golden shores. —
Rogues, hence, avaunt! vanish like hailstones, go;
Trudge, plod away o'th'hoof; seek shelter, pack!
Falstaff will learn the humour of the age,
French thrift, you rogues; myself and skirted page.
　　　　　　　　　　　[*Exeunt* FALSTAFF *and* ROBIN.

PISTOL
Let vultures gripe thy guts! for gourd and fullam holds,
And high and low beguiles the rich and poor:
Tester I'll have in pouch when thou shalt lack,
Base Phrygian Turk!

NYM
I have operations in my head, which be humours of revenge.

PISTOL
Wilt thou revenge?

NYM
By welkin and her star!

PISTOL
With wit or steel?

NYM
With both the humours, I:
I will discuss the humour of this love to Page.

PISTOL
　　　And I to Ford shall eke unfold
　　　　　How Falstaff, varlet vile,
　　　His dove will prove, his gold will hold,
　　　　　And his soft couch defile.

NYM
My humour shall not cool: I will incense Page to deal with poison; I will possess him with yellowness, for the revolt of mien is dangerous: that is my true humour.

PISTOL
Thou art the Mars of malecontents: I second thee;
troop on.　　　　　　　　　　　　　　[*Exeunt.*

SCENE IV

A room in DOCTOR CAIUS'S *house.*

Enter MISTRESS QUICKLY *and* SIMPLE.

MISTRESS QUICKLY
What, John Rugby!
　　　　　　　Enter RUGBY.
I pray thee, go to the casement, and see if you can see my master, Master Doctor Caius, coming. If he do,

i'faith, and find any body in the house, here will be an old abusing of God's patience and the king's English.

RUGBY
I'll go watch.

MISTRESS QUICKLY
Go; and we'll have a posset for't soon at night, in faith, at the latter end of a sea-coal fire. [*Exit* RUGBY.] An honest, willing, kind fellow, as ever servant shall come in house withal; and, I warrant you, no tell-tale nor no breed-bate: his worst fault is, that he is given to prayer; he is something peevish that way: but nobody but has his fault; — but let that pass. — Peter Simple you say your name is?

SIMPLE
Ay, for fault of a better.

MISTRESS QUICKLY
And Master Slender's your master?

SIMPLE
Ay, forsooth.

MISTRESS QUICKLY
Does he not wear a great round beard, like a glover's paring-knife?

SIMPLE
No, forsooth: he hath but a little wee face, with a little yellow beard, — a Cain-colour'd beard.

MISTRESS QUICKLY
A softly-sprighted man, is he not?

SIMPLE
Ay, forsooth: but he is as tall a man of his hands as any is between this and his head; he hath fought with a warrener.

MISTRESS QUICKLY
How say you? — O, I should remember him: does he not hold up his head, as it were, and strut in his gait?

SIMPLE
Yes, indeed, does he.

MISTRESS QUICKLY
Well, heaven send Anne Page no worse fortune! Tell Master Parson Evans I will do what I can for your master: Anne is a good girl, and I wish —

　　　　　　　Enter RUGBY.

RUGBY
Out, alas! here comes my master.

MISTRESS QUICKLY
We shall all be shent. [*Exit* RUGBY.] — Run in here, good young man; go into this closet: — he will not stay long. [*Shuts* SIMPLE *in the closet.*] — What, John Rugby! John! what, John, I say! Go, John, go inquire for my master; I doubt he be not well, that he comes not home. 　　　　　　　　　　　　　　[*Sings.*
　　And down, down, adown-a, *etc.*

　　　　　　　Enter DOCTOR CAIUS.

CAIUS
Vat is you sing? I do not like dese toys. Pray you, go and vetch me in my closet *un boitier vert,* — a box, a green-a box: do intend vat I speak? a green-a box.

MISTRESS QUICKLY
Ay, forsooth; I'll fetch it you. — [*aside*] I am glad he

went not in himself: if he had found the young man, he would have been horn-mad.

CAIUS
Fe, fe, fe, fe! ma foi, il fait fort chaud. Je m'en vais à la cour, — la grande affaire.

MISTRESS QUICKLY
Is it this, sir?

CAIUS
Oui; mette le au mon pocket: *dépêche,* quickly. — Vere is dat knave Rugby?

MISTRESS QUICKLY
What, John Rugby! John!

　　　　　　　Enter RUGBY.

RUGBY
Here, sir!

CAIUS
You are John Rugby, and you are Jack Rugby. Come, take-a your rapier, and come after my heel to de court.

RUGBY
'Tis ready, sir, here in the porch.

CAIUS
By my trot, I tarry too long. — Od's me! *Qu'ai-j'oublié!* dere is some simples in my closet, dat I vill not for de varld I shall leave behind.

MISTRESS QUICKLY
Ay me, he'll find the young man there, and be mad!

CAIUS
O diable, diable! vat is in my closet? Villain! *larron!* [*Pulling* SIMPLE *out.*] — Rugby, my rapier!

MISTRESS QUICKLY
Good master, be content.

CAIUS
Verefore shall I be content-a?

MISTRESS QUICKLY
The young man is an honest man.

CAIUS
Vat shall de honest man do in my closet? dere is no honest man dat shall come in my closet.

MISTRESS QUICKLY
I beseech you, be not so phlegmatic. Hear the truth of it: he came of an errand to me from Parson Hugh.

CAIUS
Vell.

SIMPLE
Ay, forsooth; to desire her to —

MISTRESS QUICKLY
Peace, I pray you.

CAIUS
Peace-a your tongue. — Speak-a your tale.

SIMPLE
To desire this honest gentlewoman, your maid, to speak a good word to Mistress Anne Page for my master in the way of marriage.

MISTRESS QUICKLY
This is all, indeed, la; but I'll ne'er put my finger in the fire, and need not.

CAIUS
Sir Hugh send-a you? — Rugby, *baille* me some paper. — Tarry you a little-a while. 　　　　　　　　[*Writes.*

MISTRESS QUICKLY
I am glad he is so quiet: if he had been throughly moved, you should have heard him so loud and so melancholy. — But notwithstanding, man, I'll do you your master what good I can: and the very yea and the no is, the French doctor, my master, — I may call him my master, look you, for I keep his house; and I wash, wring, brew, bake, scour, dress meat and drink, make the beds, and do all myself, —

SIMPLE
'Tis a great charge to come under one body's hand.

MISTRESS QUICKLY
Are you avised o' that? you shall find it a great charge: and to be up early and down late; — but notwithstanding, to tell you in your ear, — I would have no words of it, — my master himself is in love with Mistress Anne Page: but notwithstanding that, I know Anne's mind, — that's neither here nor there.

CAIUS
You jack'nape, — give-a dis letter to Sir Hugh; by gar, it is a challenge: I vill cut his troat in de park; and I vill teach a scurvy jack-a-nape priest to meddle or make: — you may be gone; it is not good you tarry here: — by gar, I vill cut all his two stones; by gar, he shall not have a stone to trow at his dog. 　　　　　　[*Exit* SIMPLE.

MISTRESS QUICKLY
Alas, he speaks but for his friend.

CAIUS
It is no matter-a ver dat: — do not you tell-a me dat I

shall have Anne Page for myself? — by gar, I vill kill de
Jack priest; and I have appointed mine host of de
Garter to measure our weapon: — by gar, I vill myself
have Anne Page.

MISTRESS QUICKLY
Sir, the maid loves you, and all shall be well. We must
give folks leave to prate: what, the good-jer!

CAIUS
Rugby, come to de court vit me. — By gar, if I have not
Anne Page, I shall turn your head out of my door. —
Follow my heels, Rugby.

[*Exeunt* CAIUS *and* RUGBY.

MISTRESS QUICKLY
You shall have An fool's-head of your own. No, I know
Anne's mind for that: never a woman in Windsor
knows more of Anne's mind than I do; nor can do more
than I do with her, I thank heaven.

FENTON [*within*].
Who's within there? ho!

MISTRESS QUICKLY
Who's there, I trow? Come near the house, I pray you.

Enter FENTON.

FENTON
How now, good woman! how dost thou?

MISTRESS QUICKLY
The better that it pleases your good worship to ask.

FENTON
What news? how does pretty Mistress Anne?

MISTRESS QUICKLY
In truth, sir, and she is pretty, and honest, and gentle;
and one that is your friend, I can tell you that by the
way; I praise heaven for it.

FENTON
Shall I do any good, think'st thou? shall I not lose my
suit?

MISTRESS QUICKLY
Troth, sir, all is in his hands above: but
notwithstanding, Master Fenton, I'll be sworn on a
book, she loves you. — Have not your worship a wart
above your eye?

FENTON
Yes, marry, have I; what of that?

MISTRESS QUICKLY
Well, thereby hangs a tale: — good faith, it is such
another Nan; — but, I detest, an honest maid as ever
broke bread: — we had an hour's talk of that wart: — I
shall never laugh but in that maid's company! — But,
indeed, she is given too much to allicholy and musing:
but for you — well, go to.

FENTON
Well, I shall see her to-day. Hold, there's money for
thee; let me have thy voice in my behalf: if thou see'st
her before me, commend me.

MISTRESS QUICKLY
Will I? i'faith, that we will; and I will tell your worship
more of the wart the next time we have confidence; and
of other wooers.

FENTON
Well, farewell; I am in great haste now.

MISTRESS QUICKLY
Farewell to your worship. [*Exit* FENTON.] Truly, an
honest gentleman: but Anne loves him not; for I know
Anne's mind as well as another does. — Out upon't!
what have I forgot?

[*Exit.*

ACT II

SCENE I

Before PAGE'S *house.*

Enter MISTRESS PAGE, *with a letter.*

MISTRESS PAGE
What, have I scaped love-letters in the holiday-time of
my beauty, and am I now a subject for them? Let me
see.

[*Reads.*

Ask me no reason why I love you; for though Love use
Reason for his physician, he admits him not for his
counsellor. You are not young, no more am I; go to,
then, there's sympathy: you are merry, so am I; ha, ha!
then there's more sympathy: you love sack, and so do I;
would you desire better sympathy? Let it suffice thee,
Mistress Page, — at the least, if the love of soldier can
suffice, — that I love thee. I will not say, pity me, — 'tis
not a soldier-like phrase; but I say, love me. By me,

    Thine own true knight,
      By day or night,
      Or any kind of light,

MISTRESS PAGE Letter for letter, but that the name of Page and Ford differs!

    With all his might
    For thee to fight,   JOHN FALSTAFF.
What a Herod of Jewry is this! — O wicked, wicked
world! — one that is well-nigh worn to pieces with age
to show himself a young gallant! What an unweigh'd
behaviour hath this Flemish drunkard pick'd — with
the devil's name — out of my conversation, that he
dares in this manner assay me? Why, he hath not been
thrice in my company! — What should I say to him? — I
was then frugal of my mirth: — Heaven forgive me! —
Why, I'll exhibit a bill in the parliament for the
putting-down of fat men. How shall I be revenged on
him? for revenged I will be, as sure as his guts are made
of puddings.

Enter MISTRESS FORD.

MISTRESS FORD
Mistress Page! trust me, I was going to your house.

MISTRESS PAGE
And, trust me, I was coming to you. You look very ill.

MISTRESS FORD
Nay, I'll ne'er believe that; I have to show to the contrary.

MISTRESS PAGE
Faith, but you do, in my mind.

MISTRESS FORD
Well, I do, then; yet, I say, I could show you to the
contrary. O Mistress Page, give me some counsel!

MISTRESS PAGE
What's the matter, woman?

MISTRESS FORD
O woman, if it were not for one trifling respect, I could
come to such honour!

MISTRESS PAGE
Hang the trifle, woman! take the honour. What is it? —
dispense with trifles; — what is it?

MISTRESS FORD
If I would but go to hell for an eternal moment or so, I
could be knighted.

MISTRESS PAGE
What? thou liest! — Sir Alice Ford! These knights will
hack; and so thou shouldst not alter the article of thy
gentry.

MISTRESS FORD
We burn daylight: — here, read, read; perceive how I
might be knighted. — I shall think the worse of fat
men, as long as I have an eye to make difference of
men's liking: and yet he would not swear; praised
women's modesty; and gave such orderly and
well-behaved reproof to all uncomeliness, that I would

have sworn his disposition would have gone to the
truth of his words; but they do no more adhere and
keep place together than the Hundredth Psalm to the
tune of *Green Sleeves*. What tempest, I trow, threw this
whale, with so many tuns of oil in his belly, ashore at
Windsor? How shall I be revenged on him? I think the
best way were to entertain him with hope, till the
wicked fire of lust have melted him in his own grease.
— Did you ever hear the like?

MISTRESS PAGE
Letter for letter, but that the name of Page and Ford
differs! — To thy great comfort in this mystery of ill
opinions, here's the twin-brother of thy letter: but let
thine inherit first; for, I protest, mine never shall. I
warrant he hath a thousand of these letters, writ with
blank space for different names, — sure, more, — and
these are of the second edition: he will print them, out
of doubt; for he cares not what he puts into the press,
when he would put us two. I had rather be a giantess,
and lie under Mount Pelion. Well, I will find you
twenty lascivious turtles, ere one chaste man.

MISTRESS FORD
Why, this is the very same; the very hand, the very
words. What doth he think of us?

MISTRESS PAGE
Nay, I know not: it makes me almost ready to wrangle
with mine own honesty. I'll entertain myself like one
that I am not acquainted withal; for, sure, unless he
know some strain in me, that I know not myself, he
would never have boarded me in this fury.

MISTRESS FORD
Boarding, call you it? I'll be sure to keep him above
deck.

MISTRESS PAGE
So will I: if he come under my hatches, I'll never to sea
again. Let's be revenged on him: let's appoint him a
meeting; give him a show of comfort in his suit; and
lead him on with a fine-baited delay, till he hath pawn'd
his horses to mine host of the Garter.

MISTRESS FORD
Nay, I will consent to act any villainy against him, that
may not sully the chariness of our honesty. O, that my
husband saw this letter! it would give eternal food to
his jealousy.

MISTRESS PAGE
Why, look where he comes; — and my good man, too:
he's as far from jealousy as I am from giving him
cause; and that, I hope, is an unmeasurable distance.

MISTRESS FORD
You are the happier woman.

MISTRESS PAGE
Let's consult together against this greasy knight.
Come hither. [*They retire.*

Enter FORD, PISTOL, PAGE, *and* NYM.

FORD
Well, I hope it be not so.

PISTOL
Hope is a curtal dog in some affairs:
Sir John affects thy wife.

FORD
Why, sir, my wife is not young.

PISTOL
He woos both high and low, both rich and poor,
Both young and old, one with another, Ford;
He loves the gallimaufry: Ford, perpend.

FORD
Love my wife!

PISTOL
With liver burning hot. Prevent, or go thou,
Like Sir Actæon he, with Ringwood at thy heels: —
O, odious is the name!

FORD
What name, sir?

PISTOL
The horn, I say. Farewell.
Take heed; have open eye; for thieves do foot by night:
Take heed, ere summer comes, or cuckoo-birds do
    sing. —
Away, Sir Corporal Nym! —
Believe it, Page; he speaks sense. [*Exit.*

FORD
I will be patient; I will find out this.

NYM [*to* PAGE].
And this is true; I like not the humour of lying. He hath
wrong'd me in some humours: I should have borne the
humour'd letter to her; but I have a sword, and it shall
bite upon my necessity. He loves your wife; there's the
short and the long. My name is Corporal Nym; I speak,
and I avouch 'tis true: my name is Nym, and Falstaff
loves your wife. — Adieu. I love not the humour of
bread and cheese; and there's the humour of it. Adieu.
[*Exit.*

PAGE
'The humour of it,' quoth a'! here's a fellow frights
humour out of his wits.

FORD
I will seek out Falstaff.

PAGE
I never heard such a drawling, affecting rogue.

FORD
If I do find it: — well.

PAGE
I will not believe such a Cataian, though the priest
o'th'town commended him for a true man.

FORD
'Twas a good sensible fellow: — well.
[MISTRESS PAGE *and*
MISTRESS FORD *come forward.*

PAGE
How now, Meg!

MISTRESS PAGE
Whither go you, George? — Hark you.

MISTRESS FORD
How now, sweet Frank! why art thou melancholy?

FORD
I melancholy! I am not melancholy. —Get you home,
go.

MISTRESS FORD
Faith, thou hast some crotchets in thy head now,. —
Will you go, Mistress Page?

MISTRESS PAGE
Have with you. — You'll come to dinner, George? —
[*Aside to* MISTRESS FORD.] Look who comes yonder:
she shall be our messenger to this paltry knight.

MISTRESS FORD [*aside to* MISTRESS PAGE].
Trust me, I thought on her: she'll fit it.

Enter MISTRESS QUICKLY.

MISTRESS PAGE
You are come to see my daughter Anne?

MISTRESS QUICKLY
Ay, forsooth; and, I pray, how does good Mistress
Anne?

MISTRESS PAGE
Go in with us and see: we have an hour's talk with you.

[*Exeunt* MISTRESS PAGE, MISTRESS FORD,
and MISTRESS QUICKLY.

PAGE
How now, Master Ford!

FORD
You heard what this knave told me, did you not?

PAGE
Yes: and you heard what the other told me?

FORD
Do you think there is truth in them?

PAGE
Hang 'em, slaves! I do not think the knight would offer
it: but these that accuse him in his intent towards our
wives are a yoke of his discarded men; very rogues, now
they be out of service.

FORD
Were they his men?

PAGE
Marry, were they.

FORD
I like it never the better for that. — Does he lie at the
Garter?

PAGE
Ay, marry, does he. If he should intend this voyage
toward my wife, I would turn her loose to him; and
what he gets more of her than sharp words, let it lie on
my head.

FORD
I do not misdoubt my wife; but I would be loth to turn
them together. A man may be too confident: I would
have nothing lie on my head: I cannot be thus satisfied.

PAGE
Look where my ranting host of the Garter comes: there
is either liquor in his pate, or money in his purse, when
he looks so merrily.

Enter HOST.

How now, mine host!

HOST
How now, bully-rook! thou'rt a gentleman. —
Cavalero-justice, I say!

Enter SHALLOW.

SHALLOW
I follow, mine host, I follow. — Good even and twenty,
good Master Page! Master Page, will you go with us? we
have sport in hand.

HOST
Tell him, cavalero-justice; tell him, bully-rook.

SHALLOW
Sir, there is a fray to be fought between Sir High the
Welsh priest and Caius the French doctor.

FORD
Good mine host o'th'Garter, a word with you.

HOST
What say'st thou, my bully-rook? [*They go aside.*

SHALLOW [*to* PAGE].
Will you go with us to behold it? My merry host hath
had the measuring of their weapons; and, I think, hath
appointed them contrary places; for, believe me, I hear
the parson is no jester. Hark, I will tell you what our
sport shall be. [*They go aside.*

HOST
Hast thou no suit against my knight, my guest-cavalier?

FORD
None, I protest: but I'll give you a pottle of burnt sack to
give me recourse to him, and tell him my name is
Brook, only for a jest.

HOST
My hand, bully; thou shalt have egress and regress; —
said I well? — and thy name shall be Brook. It is a
merry knight. — Will you go, myn-heers?

SHALLOW
Have with you, mine host.

PAGE
I have heard the Frenchman hath good skill in his
rapier.

SHALLOW
Tut, sir, I could have told you more. In these times you
stand on distance, your passes, stoccadoes, and I know
not what: 'tis the heart, Master Page; 'tis here, 'tis here.
I have seen the time, with my long sword I would have
made you four tall fellows skip like rats.

HOST
Here, boys, here, here! shall we wag?

PAGE
Have with you. — I had rather hear them scold than
fight. [*Exeunt* HOST, SHALLOW, *and* PAGE.

FORD
Though Page be a secure fool, and stands so firmly on
his wife's frailty, yet I cannot put off my opinion so
easily: she was in his company at Page's house; and
what they made there, I know not. Well, I will look
further into't: and I have a disguise to sound Falstaff. If
I find her honest, I lose not my labour, if she be
otherwise, 'tis labour well bestow'd. [*Exit.*

SCENE II

A room in the Garter Inn.

Enter FALSTAFF *and* PISTOL.

FALSTAFF
I will not lend thee a penny.

PISTOL
Why, then the world's mine oyster,
Which I with sword will open. —
I will retort the sum in equipage.

FALSTAFF
Not a penny. I have been content, sir, you should lay my
countenance to pawn. I have grated upon my good
friends for three reprieves for you and your coach-fellow
Nym; or else you had look'd through the grate, like a
geminy of baboons. I am damn'd in hell for swearing to
gentlemen my friends you were good soldiers and tall
fellows; and when Mistress Bridget lost the handle of
her fan, I took't upon mine honour thou hadst it not.

PISTOL
Didst not thou share? hadst thou not fifteen pence?

FALSTAFF
Reason, you rogue, reason: think'st thou I'll endanger
my soul gratis? At a word, hang no more about me, I am
no gibbet for you: — go: — a short knife and a throng; —
to your manor of Pickt-hatch, go. — You'll not bear a

FALSTAFF Reason, you rogue, reason.

etter for me, you rogue! — you stand upon your honour! — Why, thou unconfinable baseness, it is as much as I can do to keep the terms of my honour precise; I, I, I myself sometimes, leaving the fear of God on the left hand, and hiding mine honour in my necessity, am fain to shuffle, to hedge, and to lurch; and yet you, rogue, will ensconce your rags, your cat-a-mountain looks, your red-lattice phrases, and your bold-beating oaths, under the shelter of your honour! You will not do it, you!

PISTOL
I do relent: — what would thou more of man?

FALSTAFF
Well, go to, away, no more!

Enter ROBIN.

ROBIN
Sir, here's a woman would speak with you.

FALSTAFF
Let her approach.

Enter MISTRESS QUICKLY.

MISTRESS QUICKLY
Give your worship good morrow.

FALSTAFF
Good morrow, good wife.

MISTRESS QUICKLY
Not so, an't please your worship.

FALSTAFF
Good maid, then.

MISTRESS QUICKLY
I'll be sworn;
As my mother was, the first hour I was born.

FALSTAFF
I do believe the swearer. What with me?

MISTRESS QUICKLY
Shall I vouchsafe your worship a word or two?

FALSTAFF
Two thousand, fair woman: and I'll vouchsafe thee the hearing.

MISTRESS QUICKLY
There is one Mistress Ford, sir: — I pray, come a little nearer this ways: — I myself dwell with Master Doctor Caius, —

FALSTAFF
Well, on: Mistress Ford, you say, —

MISTRESS QUICKLY
Your worship says very true: — I pray your worship, come a little nearer this ways.

FALSTAFF
I warrant thee, nobody hears; — mine own people, mine own people.

MISTRESS QUICKLY
Are they so? God bless them, and make them his servants!

FALSTAFF
Well, Mistress Ford; — what of her?

MISTRESS QUICKLY
Why, sir, she's a good creature. — Lord, Lord! your worship's a wanton! Well, heaven forgive you, and all of us, I pray! —

FALSTAFF
Mistress Ford; — come, Mistress Ford, —

MISTRESS QUICKLY
Marry, this is the short and the long of it; you have brought her into such a canaries as 'tis wonderful. The best courtier of them all, when the court lay at Windsor, could never have brought her to such a canary. Yet there has been knights, and lords, and gentlemen, with their coaches; I warrant you, coach after coach, letter after letter, gift after gift; smelling so sweetly — all musk — and so rushling, I warrant you, in silk and gold; and in such alligant terms; and in such wine and sugar of the best and the fairest, that would have won any woman's heart; and, I warrant you, they could never get an eye-wink of her: — I had myself twenty angels given me this morning; but I defy all angels — in any such sort, as they say — but in the way of honesty: — and, I warrant you, they could never get her so much as sip on a cup with the proudest of them all: and yet there has been earls, nay, which is more, pensioners; but, I warrant you, all is one with her.

FALSTAFF
But what says she to me? be brief, my good she-Mercury.

MISTRESS QUICKLY
Marry, she hath received your letter; for the which she thanks you a thousand times: and she gives you to notify, that her husband will be absence from his house between ten and eleven.

FALSTAFF
Ten and eleven?

MISTRESS QUICKLY
Ay, forsooth; and then you may come and see the picture, she says, that you wot of; — Master Ford, her husband, will be from home. Alas! the sweet woman leads an ill life with him! he's a very jealousy man: she leads a very frampold life with him, good heart.

FALSTAFF
Ten and eleven: — woman, commend me to her; I will not fail her.

MISTRESS QUICKLY
Why, you say well. But I have another messenger to your worship. Mistress Page hath her hearty commendations to you, too: — and let me tell you in your ear, she's as fartuous a civil modest wife, and one, I tell you, that will not miss you morning nor evening prayer, as any is in Windsor, whoe'er be the other: — and she bade me tell your worship that her husband is seldom from home; but, she hopes, there will come a time. I never knew a woman so dote upon a man: surely, I think you have charms, la; yes, in truth.

FALSTAFF
Not I, I assure thee: setting the attraction of my good parts aside, I have no other charms.

MISTRESS QUICKLY
Blessing on your heart for't!

FALSTAFF
But, I pray thee, tell me this, — has Ford's wife and Page's wife acquainted each other how they love me?

MISTRESS QUICKLY
That were a jest indeed! — they have not so little grace, I hope: — that were a trick indeed! — But Mistress Page would desire you to send her your little page, of all loves: her husband has a marvellous infection to the little page; and, truly, Master Page is an honest man. Never a wife in Windsor leads a better life than she does: do what she will, say what she will, take all, pay all, go to bed when she list, rise when she list, all is as she will: and, truly, she deserves it; for if there be a kind woman in Windsor, she is one. You must send her your page; no remedy.

FALSTAFF
Why, I will.

MISTRESS QUICKLY
Nay, but do so, then: and, look you, he may come and go between you both; and, in any case, have a nay-word, that you may know one another's mind, and the boy never need to understand any thing; for 'tis not good that children should know any wickedness: old folks, you know, have discretion, as they say, and know the world.

FALSTAFF
Fare thee well: commend me to them both: there's my purse; I am yet thy debtor. — Boy, go along with this woman. [*Exeunt* MISTRESS QUICKLY *and* ROBIN.] — This news distracts me!.

PISTOL
This punk is one of Cupid's carriers: —
Clap on more sails; pursue; up with your fights;
Give fire; she is my prize, or ocean whelm them all!
[*Exit.*

FALSTAFF
Say'st thou so, old Jack? go thy ways: I'll make more of thy old body than I have done. Will they yet look after thee? Wilt thou, after the expense of so much money, be now a gainer? Good body, I thank thee. Let them say 'tis grossly done; so it be fairly done, no matter.

Enter BARDOLPH, with a cup of sack.

BARDOLPH
Sir John, there's one Master Brook below would fain speak with you, and be acquainted with you; and hath sent your worship a morning's draught of sack.

FALSTAFF
Brook is his name?

BARDOLPH
Ay, sir.

FALSTAFF
Call him in. [*Exit* BARDOLPH.] Such Brooks are welcome to me, that o'erflow such liquor. — Ah, ha! Mistress Ford and Mistress Page, have I encompass'd you? go to; *via!*

Enter BARDOLPH, with FORD disguised.

FORD
Bless you, sir!

FALSTAFF
And you, sir! Would you speak with me?

FORD
I make bold to press with so little preparation upon you.

FALSTAFF
You're welcome. What's your will? — Give us leave, drawer. [*Exit* BARDOLPH.

FORD
Sir, I am a gentleman that have spent much; my name is Brook.

FALSTAFF
Good Master Brook, I desire more acquaintance of you.

FORD
Good Sir John, I sue for yours: not to charge you; for I must let you understand I think myself in better plight for a lender than you are: the which hath something embolden'd me to this unseason'd intrusion; for they say, if money go before, all ways do lie open.

FALSTAFF
Money is a good soldier, sir, and will on.

FORD
Troth, and I have a bag of money here troubles me: if you will help to bear it, Sir John, take all, or half, for easing me of the carriage.

FALSTAFF
Sir, I know not how I may deserve to be your porter.

FORD
I will tell you, sir, if you will give me the hearing.

FALSTAFF
Speak, good Master Brook: I shall be glad to be your servant.

FORD
Sir, I hear you are a scholar, — I will be brief with you; — and you have been a man long known to me, though I had never so good means, as desire, to make myself acquainted with you. I shall discover a thing to you, wherein I must very much lay open mine own imperfection: but, good Sir John, as you have one eye upon my follies, as you hear them unfolded, turn another into the register of your own; that I may pass with a reproof the easier, sith you yourself know how easy it is to be such an offender.

FALSTAFF
Very well, sir; proceed.

FORD
There is a gentlewoman in this town, her husband's name is Ford.

FALSTAFF
Well, sir.

FORD
I have long loved her, and, I protest to you, bestow'd much on her: follow'd her with a doting observance; engross'd opportunities to meet her; fee'd every slight occasion that could but niggardly give me sight of her; not only bought many presents to give her, but have given largely to many to know what she would have given; briefly, I have pursued her as love hath pursued me; which hath been on the wing of all occasions. But whatsoever I have merited, either in my mind or in my means, meed, I am sure, I have received none; unless experience be a jewel: that I have purchased at an infinite rate; and that hath taught me to say this:
Love like a shadow flies when substance love pursues;
Pursuing that that flies, and flying what pursues.

FALSTAFF
Have you received no promise of satisfaction at her hands?

FORD
Never.

FALSTAFF
Have you importuned her to such a purpose?

FORD
Never.

FALSTAFF
Of what quality was your love, then?

FORD
Like a fair house built on another man's ground; so that I have lost my edifice by mistaking the place where I erected it.

FALSTAFF
To what purpose have you unfolded this to me?

FORD
When I have told you that, I have told you all. Some say, that though she appear honest to me, yet in other places she enlargeth her mirth so far that there is shrewd construction made of her. Now, Sir John, here is the heart of my purpose: you are a gentleman of excellent breeding, admirable discourse, of great admittance, authentic in your place and person, generally allow'd for your many war-like, court-like, and learned preparations, —

FORD O, understand my drift. She dwells so securely on the excellency of her honour.

FALSTAFF
O, sir!

FORD
Believe it, for you know it. — There is money; spend it, spend it; spend more; spend all I have; only give me so much of your time in exchange of it, as to lay an amiable siege to the honesty of this Ford's wife: use your art of wooing; win her to consent to you: if any man may, you may as soon as any.

FALSTAFF
Would it apply well to the vehemency of your affection, that I should win what you would enjoy? Methinks you prescribe to yourself very preposterously.

FORD
O, understand my drift. She dwells so securely on the excellency of her honour, that the folly of my soul dares not present itself: she is too bright to be look'd against. Now, could I come to her with any detection in my hand, my desires had instance and argument to commend themselves: I could drive her then from the ward of her purity, her reputation, her marriage-vow, and a thousand other her defences, which now are too-too strongly embattled against me. What say you to't, Sir John?

FALSTAFF
Master Brook, I will first make bold with your money; next, give me your hand; and last, as I am a gentleman, you shall, if you will, enjoy Ford's wife.

FORD
O, good sir!

FALSTAFF
Master Brook, I say you shall.

FORD
Want no money, Sir John; you shall want none.

FALSTAFF
Want no Mistress Ford, Master Brook; you shall want none. I shall be with her — I may tell you — by her own appointment; even as you came in to me, her assistant, or go-between, parted from me: I say I shall be with her between ten and eleven; for at that time the jealous rascally knave her husband will be forth. Come you to me at night; you shall know how I speed.

FORD
I am blest in your acquaintance. Do you know Ford, sir?

FALSTAFF
Hang him, poor cuckoldly knave! I know him not: — yet I wrong him to call him poor; they say the jealous wittolly knave hath masses of money; for the which his wife seems to me well-favour'd. I will use her as the key of the cuckoldly rogue's coffer; and there's my harvest-home.

FORD
I would you knew Ford, sir, that you might avoid him, if you saw him.

FALSTAFF
Hang him, mechanical salt-butter rogue! I will stare him out of his wits; I will awe him with my cudgel, — it shall hang like a meteor o'er the cuckold's horns. Master Brook, thou shalt know I will predominate over the peasant, and thou shalt lie with his wife. — Come to me soon at night: — Ford's a knave, and I will aggravate his style; thou, Master Brook, shalt know him for knave and cuckold: — come to me soon at night.

[Exit.

FORD
What a damn'd Epicurean rascal is this! — My heart is ready to crack with impatience. — Who says this is improvident jealousy? my wife hath sent to him, the hour is fix'd, the match is made. Would any man have thought this? — See the hell of having a false woman! My bed shall be abused, my coffers ransack'd, my reputation gnawn at; and I shall not only receive this villainous wrong, but stand under the adoption of abominable terms, and by him that does me this wrong. Terms! names! — Amaimon sounds well; Lucifer, well; Barbason, well; yet they are devils' additions, the names of fiends: but cuckold! wittol! — Cuckold! the devil himself hath not such a name. Page is an ass, a secure ass: he will trust his wife; he will not be jealous. I will rather trust a Fleming with my butter, Parson Hugh the Welshman with my cheese, an Irishman with my aqua-vitæ bottle, or a thief to walk my ambling gelding, than my wife with herself: then she plots, then she ruminates, then she devises; and what they think in their hearts they may effect, they will break their hearts but they will effect. Heaven be praised for my jealousy! — Eleven o'clock the hour: — I will prevent this, detect my wife, be revenged on Falstaff, and laugh at Page. I will about it; better three hours too soon than a minute too late. Fie, fie, fie! cuckold! cuckold! cuckold! [Exit.

SCENE III

A field near Windsor.

Enter CAIUS and RUGBY.

CAIUS
Jack Rugby, —

RUGBY
Sir?

CAIUS
Vat is de clock, Jack?

RUGBY
'Tis past the hour, sir, that Sir Hugh promised to meet.

CAIUS
By gar, he has save his soul, dat he is no come; he has pray his Pible vell, dat he is no come: by gar, Jack Rugby, he is dead already, if he be come.

RUGBY
He is wise, sir; he knew your worship would kill him, if he came.

CAIUS
By gar, de herring is no dead so as I vill kill him. Take your rapier, Jack; I vill tell you how I vill kill him.

RUGBY
Alas, sir, I cannot fence.

CAIUS
Villainy, take your rapier.

RUGBY
Forbear; here's company.

Enter HOST, SHALLOW, SLENDER, and PAGE.

HOST
'Bless thee, bully doctor!

SHALLOW
'Save you, Master Doctor Caius!

PAGE
Now, good master doctor!

SLENDER
'Give you good morrow, sir.

CAIUS
Vat be all you, one, two, tree, four, come for?

HOST
To see thee fight, to see thee foin, to see thee traverse; to see thee here, to see thee there; to see thee pass thy punto, thy stock, thy reverse, thy distance, thy montant. Is he dead, my Ethiopian? is he dead, my Francisco? ha, bully! What says my Aesculapius? my Galen? my heart of elder? ha! is he dead, bully-stale? is he dead?

CAIUS
By gar, he is de coward Jack priest of de vorld; he is not show his face.

HOST
Thou art a Castilian, King Urinal! Hector of Greece, my boy!

CAIUS
I pray you, bear vitness that me have stay six or seven, two, tree hours for him, and he is no come.

SHALLOW
He is the wiser man, master doctor: he is a curer of souls, and you a curer of bodies; if you should fight, you go against the hair of your professions. — Is it not true, Master Page?

PAGE
Master Shallow, you have yourself been a great fighter, though now a man of peace.

SHALLOW
Bodikins, Master Page, though I now be old, and of the peace, if I see a sword out, my finger itches to make one. Though we are justices, and doctors, and churchmen, Master Page, we have some salt of our youth in us; we are the sons of women, Master Page.

PAGE
'Tis true, Master Shallow.

SHALLOW
It will be found so, Master Page. — Master Doctor Caius, I am come to fetch you home. I am sworn of the peace: you have show'd yourself a wise physician, and Sir Hugh hath shown himself a wise and patient churchman. You must go with me, master doctor.

HOST
Pardon, guest-justice. — A word, Monsieur Mock-water.

CAIUS
Mock-vater! vat is dat?

HOST
Mock-water, in our English tongue, is valour, bully.

CAIUS
By gar, den, I have as mush mock-water as de Englishman. — Scurvy jack-dog priest! by gar, me vill cut his ears.

HOST
He will clapper-claw thee tightly, bully.

CAIUS
Clapper-de-claw! vat is dat?

HOST
That is, he will make thee amends.

CAIUS
By gar, me do look he shall clapper-de-claw me; for, by gar, me vill have it.

HOST
And I will provoke him to't, or let him wag.

CAIUS
Me tank you for dat.

HOST
And, moreover, bully, — But first, master guest, and Master Page, and eke Cavalero Slender, go you through the town to Frogmore. [*Aside to them*

PAGE
Sir Hugh is there, is he?

HOST
He is there: see what humour he is in; and I will bring the doctor about by the fields. Will it do well?

SHALLOW
We will do it.

PAGE, SHALLOW, *and* **SLENDER**
Adieu, good master doctor.
[*Exeunt* PAGE, SHALLOW, *and* SLENDER

CAIUS
By gar, me vill kill de priest; for he speak for a
Jack-an-ape to Anne Page.

HOST
Let him die; sheathe thy impatience, throw cold water
on thy choler: go about the fields with me through
Frogmore: I will bring thee where Mistress Anne Page
is, at a farm-house a-feasting; and thou shalt woo her.
Cried I aim? said I well?

CAIUS
By gar, me dank you vor dat: by gar, I love you; and I
shall procure-a you de good guest, de earl, de knight, de
lords, de gentlemen, my patients.

HOST
For the which I will be thy adversary toward Anne
Page. Said I well?

CAIUS
By gar, 'tis good; vell said.

HOST
Let us wag, then.

CAIUS
Come at my heels, Jack Rugby.   [*Exeunt.*

ACT III

SCENE I

A field near Frogmore.

Enter SIR HUGH EVANS *and* SIMPLE.

EVANS
I pray you now, good master Slender's serving-man,
and friend Simple by your name, which way have you
look'd for Master Caius, that calls himself doctor of
physics?

SIMPLE
Marry, sir, the pittie-ward, the park-ward, every way;
Old Windsor way, and every way but the town way.

EVANS
I most fehemently desire you you will also look that
way.

SIMPLE
I will, sir.   [*Retires.*

EVANS
Pless my soul, how full of cholers I am, and trembling
of mind! — I shall be glad if he have deceived me: —
how melancholies I am! — I will knog his urinals about
his knave's costard when I have goot opportunities for
the ork: — Pless my soul!   [*Sings.*
    To shallow rivers, to whose falls
    Melodious birds sings madrigals;
    There will we make our peds of roses,
    And a thousand fragrant posies.
    To shallow —
Mercy on me! I have a great dispositions to cry. —
      [*Sings.*

    Melodious birds sing madrigals; —
    Whenas I sat in Pabylon, —
    And a thousand vagram posies.
    To shallow, *etc.*

SIMPLE [*coming forward*].
Yonder he is coming, this way, Sir Hugh.

EVANS
He's welcome. —   [*Sings.*
    To shallow rivers, to whose falls —
Heaven prosper the right! — What weapons is he?

SIMPLE
No weapons, sir. There comes my master, Master
Shallow, and another gentleman, from Frogmore, over
the stile, this way.

EVANS
Pray you, give me my gown; or else keep it in your arms.
    Enter PAGE, SHALLOW, *and* SLENDER.

SHALLOW
How now, master parson! Good morrow, good Sir
Hugh. Keep a gamester from the dice, and a good
student from his book, and it is wonderful.

SLENDER [*aside*].
Ah, sweet Anne Page!

PAGE
'Save you, good Sir Hugh!

EVANS
'Pless you from his mercy sake,
all of you!

SHALLOW
What, the sword and the word!
do you study them both, master
parson?

PAGE
And youthful still, in your
doublet and hose this raw
rheumatic day?

EVANS
There is reasons and causes
for it.

PAGE
We are come to you to do a good
office, master parson.

EVANS
Fery well: what is it?

PAGE
Yonder is a most reverend
gentleman, who, belike having
received wrong by some person,
is at most odds with his own
gravity and patience that ever
you saw.

SHALLOW
I have lived fourscore years and
upward; I never heard a man of
his place, gravity, and learning,
so wide of his own respect.

EVANS
What is he?

PAGE
I think you know him; Master Doctor Caius, the
renown'd French physician.

EVANS
Got's will, and his passion of my heart! I had as lief you
would tell me of a mess of porridge.

PAGE
Why?

EVANS
He has no more knowledge in Hibbocrates and Galen, —
and he is a knave besides; a cowardly knave as you would
desires to be acquainted withal.

PAGE
I warrant you, he's the man should fight with him.

SLENDER [*aside*].
O sweet Anne Page!

SHALLOW
It appears so, by his weapons. — Keep them asunder: —
here comes Doctor Caius.

    Enter HOST, CAIUS, *and* RUGBY.

PAGE
Nay, good master parson, keep in your weapon.

SHALLOW
So do you, good master doctor.

HOST
Disarm them, and let them question; let them keep
their limbs whole, and hack our English.

CAIUS
I pray you, let-a me speak a word vit your ear.

Vherefore vill you not meet-a me?

EVANS [*aside to* CAIUS].
Pray you, use your patience: in good time. .

CAIUS
By gar, you are de coward, de Jack dog, John ape.

EVANS [*aside to* CAIUS].
Pray you, let us not be laughing-stogs to other men's
humours; I desire you in friendship, and I will one way
or other make you amends. — [*aloud*] I will knog your
urinals about your knave's cogs-comb for missing your
meetings and appointments.

CAIUS
Diable! — Jack Rugby, — mine host de Jarteer, — have
I not stay for him to kill him? have I not, at de place I
did appoint?

EVANS
As I am a Christians soul, now, look you, this is the
place appointed: I'll be judgement by mine host of the
Garter.

HOST
Peace, I say, Gallia and Guallia, French and Welsh,
soul-curer and body-curer!

CAIUS
Ay, dat is very good; excellent.

HOST
Peace, I say! hear mine host of the Garter. Am I politic?
am I subtle? am I a Machivell? Shall I lose my doctor?
no; he gives me the potions and the motions. Shall I
lose my parson, my priest, my Sir Hugh? no; he gives
me the proverbs and the noverbs. — Give me thy hand,
terrestrial; so. — Give me thy hand, celestial; so. —
Boys of art, I have deceived you both; I have directed
you to wrong places: your hearts are mighty, your skins
are whole, and let burnt sack be the issue. — Come, lay
their swords to pawn. — Follow me, lads of peace;
follow, follow, follow.

SHALLOW
Trust me, a mad host. — Follow, gentlemen, follow.

SLENDER [*aside*].
O sweet Anne Page!
    [*Exeunt* SHALLOW, SLENDER, PAGE, *and* HOST.

CAIUS
Ha, do I perceive dat? have you make-a de sot of us, ha,
ha?

EVANS
This is well; he has made us his vlouting-stog. — I
desire you that we may be friends; and let us knog our
prains together to be revenge on this same scall, scurvy,
cogging companion, the host of the Garter.

CAIUS
By gar, vit all my heart. He promise to bring me vere is
Anne Page; by gar, he deceive me too.

EVANS
Well, I will smite his noddles. Pray you, follow.
      [*Exeunt.*

SCENE II

The street, in Windsor.

Enter MISTRESS PAGE *and* ROBIN.

MISTRESS PAGE
Nay, keep your way, little gallant; you were wont to be a
follower, but now you are a leader. Whether had you
rather lead mine eyes, or eye your master's heels?

ROBIN
I had rather, forsooth, go before you like a man than
follow him like a dwarf.

MISTRESS PAGE
O, you are a flattering boy: now I see you'll be a
courtier.

    Enter FORD.

FORD
Well met, Mistress Page. Whither go you?

MISTRESS PAGE
Truly, sir, to see your wife. Is she at home?

FORD
Ay, and as idle as she may hang together, for want of
company. I think, if your husbands were dead, you two
would marry.

MISTRESS PAGE
Be sure of that, — two other husbands.

FORD
Where had you this pretty weathercock?

MISTRESS PAGE
I cannot tell what the dickens his name is my husband
had him of. — What do you call your knight's name,
sirrah?

FALSTAFF Have I caught thee, my heavenly jewel?

ROBIN
Sir John Falstaff.
FORD
Sir John Falstaff!
MISTRESS PAGE
He, he; I can never hit on's name. — There is such a league between my good man and he! — Is your wife at home indeed?
FORD
Indeed she is.
MISTRESS PAGE
By your leave, sir: I am sick till I see her.
[*Exeunt* MISTRESS PAGE *and* ROBIN.
FORD
Has Page any brains? hath he any eyes? hath he any thinking? Sure, they sleep; he hath no use of them. Why, this boy will carry a letter twenty mile as easy as a cannon will shoot point-blank twelve score. He pieces out his wife's inclination; he gives her folly motion and advantage: and now she's going to my wife, and Falstaff's boy with her: — a man may hear this shower sing in the wind: — and Falstaff's boy with her! — Good plots, — they are laid; and our revolted wives share damnation together. Well; I will take him, then torture my wife, pluck the borrow'd veil of modesty from the so seeming Mistress Page, divulge Page himself for a secure and wilful Actæon; and to these violent proceedings all my neighbours shall cry aim. [*Clock strikes.*] The clock gives me my cue, and my assurance bids me search: there I shall find Falstaff: I shall be rather praised for this than mock'd; for it is as positive as the earth is firm that Falstaff is there: I will go.

Enter PAGE, SHALLOW, SLENDER, HOST,
SIR HUGH EVANS, CAIUS, *and* RUGBY.

SHALLOW, PAGE, *etc*
Well met, Master Ford.
FORD
Trust me, a good knot: I have good cheer at home; and I pray you all, go with me.
SHALLOW
I must excuse myself, Master Ford.
SLENDER
And so must I, sir: we have appointed to dine with Mistress Anne, and I would not break with her for more money than I'll speak of.
SHALLOW
We have linger'd about a match between Anne Page and my cousin Slender, and this day we shall have our answer.
SLENDER
I hope I have your good will, father Page.
PAGE
You have, Master Slender; I stand wholly for you: — but my wife, master doctor, is for you altogether.

CAIUS
Ay, by gar; and de maid is love-a me; my nursh-a Quickly tell me so mush.
HOST
What say you to young Master Fenton? he capers, he dances, he has eyes of youth, he writes verses, he speaks holiday, he smells April and May: he will carry't, he will carry't; 'tis in his buttons; he will carry't.
PAGE
Not by my consent, I promise you. The gentleman is of no having: he kept company with the wild prince and Pointz; he is of too high a region; he knows too much. No, he shall not knit a knot in his fortunes with the finger of my substance: if he take her, let him take her simply; the wealth I have waits on my consent, and my consent goes not that way.
FORD
I beseech you heartily, some of you go home with me to dinner: besides your cheer, you shall have sport; I will show you a monster. — Master doctor, you shall go; — so shall you, Master Page; — and you, Sir Hugh.
SHALLOW
Well, fare you well: we shall have the freer wooing at Master Page's.
[*Exeunt* SHALLOW *and* SLENDER.
CAIUS
Go home, John Rugby; I come anon. [*Exit* RUGBY.
HOST
Farewell, my hearts: I will to my honest knight Falstaff, and drink canary with him. [*Exit.*
FORD [*aside*].
I think I shall drink in pipe-wine first with him; I'll make him dance. — Will you go, gentles?
ALL
Have with you to see this monster. [*Exeunt.*

SCENE III

A room in FORD'S *house.*

Enter MISTRESS FORD *and* MISTRESS PAGE.

MISTRESS FORD
What, John! What, Robert!
MISTRESS PAGE
Quickly, quickly: — is the buck-basket —
MISTRESS FORD
I warrant. — What, Robin, I say!
Enter SERVANTS *with a basket.*
MISTRESS PAGE
Come, come, come.
MISTRESS FORD
Here, set it down.
MISTRESS PAGE
Give your men the charge: we must be brief.
MISTRESS FORD
Marry, as I told you before, John and Robert, be ready here hard by in the brew-house; and when I suddenly call you, come forth, and, without any pause or staggering, take this basket on your shoulders: that done, trudge with it in all haste, and carry it among the whitsters in Datchet-mead, and there empty it in the muddy ditch close by the Thames side.
MISTRESS PAGE
You will do it?
MISTRESS FORD
I ha' told them over and over; they lack no direction. — Be gone, and come when you are called.
[*Exeunt* SERVANTS.
MISTRESS PAGE
Here comes little Robin.
Enter ROBIN.
MISTRESS FORD
How now, my eyas-musket! what news with you?
ROBIN
My master, Sir John, is come in at your back-door, Mistress Ford, and requests your company.

MISTRESS PAGE
You little Jack-a-Lent, have you been true to us?
ROBIN
Ay, I'll be sworn. My master knows not of your being here, and hath threaten'd to put me into everlasting liberty, if I tell you of it; for he swears he'll turn me away.
MISTRESS PAGE
Thou'rt a good boy: this secrecy of thine shall be a tailor to thee, and shall make thee a new doublet and hose. — I'll go hide me.
MISTRESS FORD
Do so. — Go tell thy master I am alone. — Mistress Page, remember you your cue. [*Exit* ROBIN.
MISTRESS PAGE
I warrant thee; if I do not act it, hiss me. [*Exit.*
MISTRESS FORD
Go to, then: we'll use this unwholesome humidity, this gross watery pumpion; we'll teach him to know turtles from jays.

Enter FALSTAFF.

FALSTAFF
Have I caught thee, my heavenly jewel? Why, now let me die, for I have lived long enough; this is the period of my ambition: O this blessed hour!
MISTRESS FORD
O sweet Sir John!
FALSTAFF
Mistress Ford, I cannot cog, I cannot prate, Mistress Ford. Now shall I sin in my wish, — I would thy husband were dead; I'll speak it before the best lord, — I would make thee my lady.
MISTRESS FORD
I your lady, Sir John! alas, I should be a pitiful lady!
FALSTAFF
Let the court of France show me such another. I see how thine eye would emulate the diamond: thou hast the right arch'd beauty of the brow that becomes the ship-tire, the tire-valiant, or any tire of Venetian admittance.
MISTRESS FORD
A plain kerchief, Sir John: my brows become nothing else; nor that well neither.
FALSTAFF
By the Lord, thou art a traitor to say so: thou wouldst make an absolute courtier; and the firm fixture of thy foot would give an excellent motion to thy gait in a semi-circled farthingale. I see what thou wert, if Fortune thy foe were not, Nature thy friend. Come, thou canst not hide it.
MISTRESS FORD
Believe me, there's no such thing in me.
FALSTAFF
What made me love thee? let that persuade thee there's something extraordinary in thee. Come, I cannot cog, and say thou art this and that, like a many of these lisping hawthorn-buds, that come like women in men's apparel, and smell like Bucklersbury in simple-time; I cannot: but I love thee; none but thee; and thou deservest it.
MISTRESS FORD
Do not betray me, sir. I fear you love Mistress Page.
FALSTAFF
Thou mightst as well say I love to walk by the Counter-gate, which is as hateful to me as the reek of a lime-kiln.
MISTRESS FORD
Well, heaven knows how I love you; and you shall one day find it.
FALSTAFF
Keep in that mind; I'll deserve it.
MISTRESS FORD
Nay, I must tell you, so you do; or else I could not be in that mind.
ROBIN [*within*].
Mistress Ford, Mistress Ford! here's Mistress Page at the door, sweating, and blowing, and looking wildly, and would needs speak with you presently.
FALSTAFF
She shall not see me: I will ensconce me behind the arras.
MISTRESS FORD
Pray you, do so: she's a very tattling woman.
[FALSTAFF *hides himself behind the arras.*
Enter MISTRESS PAGE *and* ROBIN.
What's the matter? how now!
MISTRESS PAGE
O Mistress Ford, what have you done? You're shamed, you're overthrown, you're undone for ever!

MISTRESS FORD
What's the matter, good Mistress Page?

MISTRESS PAGE
O well-a-day, Mistress Ford! having an honest man to your husband, to give him such cause of suspicion!

MISTRESS FORD
What cause of suspicion?

MISTRESS PAGE
What cause of suspicion! Out upon you! how am I mistook in you!

MISTRESS FORD
Why, alas, what's the matter?

MISTRESS PAGE
Your husband's coming hither, woman, with all the officers in Windsor, to search for a gentleman that he says is here now in the house, by your consent, to take an ill advantage of his absence: you are undone.

MISTRESS FORD
'Tis not so, I hope.

MISTRESS PAGE
Pray heaven it be not so, that you have such a man here! but 'tis most certain your husband's coming, with half Windsor at his heels, to search for such a one. I come before to tell you. If you know yourself clear, why, I am glad of it; but if you have a friend here, convey, convey him out. Be not amazed; call all your senses to you; defend your reputation, or bid farewell to your good life for ever.

MISTRESS FORD
What shall I do? — There is a gentleman my dear friend; and I fear not mine own shame so much as his peril! I had rather than a thousand pound he were out of the house.

MISTRESS PAGE
For shame! never stand 'you had rather' and 'you had rather': your husband's here at hand; bethink you of some conveyance: in the house you cannot hide him. — O, how have you deceiv'd me! — Look, here is a basket: if he be of any reasonable stature, he may creep in here; and throw foul linen upon him, as if it were going to bucking: or, — it is whiting-time, — send him by your two men to Datchet-mead.

MISTRESS FORD
He's too big to go in there. What shall I do?

Enter FALSTAFF.

FALSTAFF
Let me see't, let me see't, O, let me see't! — I'll in, I'll in: — follow your friend's counsel: — I'll in.

MISTRESS PAGE
What, Sir John Falstaff! Are these your letters, knight?

FALSTAFF [*aside to* MISTRESS PAGE].
I love thee, and none but thee: — [*aloud*] help me away: let me creep in here. I'll never —
[*Goes into the basket; they cover him with foul linen.*

MISTRESS PAGE
Help to cover your master, boy. — Call your men, Mistress Ford. — You dissembling knight!
[*Exit* ROBIN.

MISTRESS FORD
What, John! Robert! John!
Enter SERVANTS.
Go take up these clothes here quickly: — where's the cowl-staff? look, how you drumble! — carry them to the laundress in Datchet-mead; quickly, come.
Enter FORD, PAGE, CAIUS, *and* SIR HUGH EVANS.

FORD
Pray you, come near: if I suspect without cause, why then make sport at me; then let me be your jest; I deserve it. — How now! whither bear you this?

SERVANTS
To the laundress, forsooth.

MISTRESS FORD
Why, what have you to do whither they bear it? You were best meddle with buck-washing.

FORD
Buck! — I would I could wash myself of the buck! — Buck, buck, buck! Ay, buck; I warrant you, buck; and of the season too, it shall appear. [*Exeunt* SERVANTS *with the basket.*] — Gentlemen, I have dream'd to-night; I'll tell you my dream. Here, here, here be my keys; ascend my chambers; search, seek, find out: I'll warrant we'll unkennel the fox. — Let me stop this way first [*Locks the door.*] — So, now uncape.

PAGE
Good Master Ford, be contented: you wrong yourself too much.

FORD
True, Master Page. — Up, gentlemen; you shall see

MISTRESS FORD Carry them to the laundress in Datchet-mead.

sport anon: follow me, gentlemen.
[*Exit.*

EVANS
This is fery fantastical humours and jealousies.

CAIUS
By gar, 'tis no de fashion of France; it is not jealous in France.

PAGE
Nay, follow him, gentlemen; see the issue of his search.
[*Exeunt* PAGE, CAIUS, *and* EVANS.

MISTRESS PAGE
Is there not a double excellency in this?

MISTRESS FORD
I know not which pleases me better, that my husband is deceived, or Sir John.

MISTRESS PAGE
What a taking was he in when your husband ask'd what was in the basket!

MISTRESS FORD
I am half afraid he will have need of washing; so throwing him into the water will do him a benefit.

MISTRESS PAGE
Hang him, dishonest rascal! I would all of the same strain were in the same distress.

MISTRESS FORD
I think my husband hath some special suspicion of Falstaff's being here; for I never saw him so gross in his jealousy till now.

MISTRESS PAGE
I will lay a plot to try that; and we will yet have more tricks with Falstaff: his dissolute disease will scarce obey this medicine.

MISTRESS FORD
Shall we send that foolish carrion Mistress Quickly to him, and excuse his throwing into the water; and give him another hope, to betray him to another punishment?

MISTRESS PAGE
We will do it: let him be sent for to-morrow eight o'clock, to have amends.
Enter FORD, PAGE, CAIUS, *and* SIR HUGH EVANS.

FORD
I cannot find him: may be the knave bragg'd of that he could not compass.

MISTRESS PAGE [*aside to* MISTRESS FORD].
Heard you that?

MISTRESS FORD [*aside to* MISTRESS PAGE].
Ay, ay, peace. — You use me well, Master Ford, do you?

FORD
Ay, I do so.

MISTRESS FORD
Heaven make you better than your thoughts!

FORD
Amen!

MISTRESS PAGE
You do yourself mighty wrong, Master Ford.

FORD
Ay, ay; I must bear it.

EVANS
If there be any pody in the house, and in the chambers, and in the coffers, and in the presses, heaven forgive my sins at the day of judgement!

CAIUS
By gar, nor I too: dere is no bodies.

PAGE
Fie, fie, Master Ford! are you not ashamed? What spirit, what devil suggests this imagination? I would not ha' your distemper in this kind for the wealth of Windsor Castle.

FORD
'Tis my fault, Master Page: I suffer for it.

EVANS
You suffer for a pad conscience: your wife is as honest a omans as I will desires among five thousand, and five hundred too.

CAIUS
By gar, I see 'tis an honest woman.

FORD
Well; — I promised you a dinner: — come, come, walk in the Park: I pray you, pardon me; I will hereafter make known to you why I have done this. — Come, wife; — come, Mistress Page. — I pray you, pardon me; pray heartily, pardon me.

PAGE
Let's go in, gentlemen; but, trust me, we'll mock him. I do invite you to-morrow morning to my house to breakfast; after, we'll a-birding together; I have a fine hawk for the bush. Shall it be so?

FORD
Any thing.

EVANS
If there is one, I shall make two in the company.

CAIUS
If dere be one or two, I shall make-a de turd.

EVANS
In your teeth: for shame!

FORD
Pray you, go, Master Page.

EVANS
I pray you now, remembrance to-morrow on the lousy knave, mine host.

CAIUS
Dat is good; by gar, vit all my heart!

EVANS
A lousy knave, to have his gibes and his mockeries!
[*Exeunt.*

SCENE IV

A room in PAGE'S *house.*

Enter FENTON *and* ANNE PAGE.

FENTON
I see I cannot get thy father's love;
Therefore no more turn me to him, sweet Nan.

ANNE PAGE
Alas, how then?

FENTON
Why, thou must be thyself.
He doth object I am too great of birth;
And that, my state being gall'd with my expense,
I seek to heal it only by his wealth:
Besides these, other bars he lays before me, —
My riots past, my wild societies;
And tells me 'tis a thing impossible
I should love thee but as a property.

ANNE PAGE
May be he tells you true.

FENTON
No, heaven so speed me in my time to come!
Albeit, I will confess, thy father's wealth
Was the first motive that I woo'd thee, Anne;
Yet, wooing thee, I found thee of more value
Than stamps in gold or sums in sealed bags;
And 'tis the very riches of thyself
That now I aim at.

ANNE PAGE
Gentle Master Fenton,
Yet seek my father's love; still seek it, sir:
If opportunity and humblest suit
Cannot attain it, why, then, — Hark you hither!
[*They converse apart.*

Enter SHALLOW, SLENDER,
and MISTRESS QUICKLY.

SHALLOW
Break their talk, Mistress Quickly: my kinsman shall
speak for himself.

SLENDER
I'll make a shaft or a bolt on't: 'slid, 'tis but venturing.

SHALLOW
Be not dismay'd.

SLENDER
No, she shall not dismay me: I care not for that, — but
that I am afeard.

MISTRESS QUICKLY
Hark ye: Master Slender would speak a word with you.

ANNE PAGE
I come to him. — [*aside*] This is my father's choice.
O, what a world of vile ill-favour'd faults
Looks handsome in three hundred pounds a-year!

MISTRESS QUICKLY
And how does good Master Fenton? Pray you, a word
with you.

SHALLOW
She's coming; to her, coz. O boy, thou hadst a father!

SLENDER
I had a father, Mistress Anne; — my uncle can tell you
good jests of him. — Pray you, uncle, tell Mistress
Anne the jest, how my father stole two geese out of a
pen, good uncle.

SHALLOW
Mistress Anne, my cousin loves you.

SLENDER
Ay, that I do; as well as I love any woman in
Glostershire.

SHALLOW
He will maintain you like a gentlewoman.

SLENDER
Ay, that I will, come cut and long-tail, under the degree
of a squire.

SHALLOW
He will make you a hundred and fifty pounds jointure.

ANNE PAGE
Good Master Shallow, let him woo for himself.

SHALLOW
Marry, I thank you for it; I thank you for that good
comfort. — She calls you, coz: I'll leave you.

ANNE PAGE
Now, Master Slender, —

SLENDER
Now, good Mistress Anne, —

ANNE PAGE
What is your will?

SLENDER
My will! od's heartlings, that's a pretty jest indeed! I
ne'er made my will yet, I thank heaven; I am not such a
sickly creature, I give heaven praise.

ANNE PAGE
I mean, Master Slender, what would you with me?

SLENDER
Truly, for mine own part, I would little or nothing with
you. Your father and my uncle hath made motions: if it
be my luck, so; if not, happy man be his dole! They can
tell you how things go better than I can: you may ask
your father; here he comes.

Enter PAGE *and* MISTRESS PAGE.

PAGE
Now, Master Slender: — love him, daughter Anne. —
Why, how now! what does Master Fenton here?
You wrong me, sir, thus still to haunt my house:
I told you, sir, my daughter is dispos'd of.

FENTON
Nay, Master Page, be not impatient.

MISTRESS PAGE
Good Master Fenton, come not to my child.

PAGE
She is no match for you.

FENTON
Sir, will you hear me?

PAGE
No, good Master Fenton.—
Come, Master Shallow; come, son Slender; in. —
Knowing my mind, you wrong me, Master Fenton.
[*Exeunt* PAGE, SHALLOW, *and* SLENDER.

MISTRESS QUICKLY
Speak to Mistress Page.

FENTON
Good Mistress Page, for that I love your daughter
In such a righteous fashion as I do,
Perforce, against all checks, rebukes, and manners,
I must advance the colours of my love,
And not retire: let me have your good will.

ANNE PAGE
Good mother, do not marry me to yond fool.

MISTRESS PAGE
I mean it not; I seek you a better husband.

MISTRESS QUICKLY
That's my master, master doctor.

ANNE PAGE
Alas, I had rather be set quick i'th'earth,
And bowl'd to death with turnips!

MISTRESS PAGE
Come, trouble not yourself. — Good Master Fenton,
I will not be your friend nor enemy:
My daughter will I question how she loves you,
And as I find her, so am I affected.
Till then farewell, sir: she must needs go in;
Her father will be angry.

FENTON
Farewell, gentle mistress. — Farewell, Nan.
[*Exeunt* MISTRESS PAGE *and* ANNE PAGE.

MISTRESS QUICKLY
This is my doing now: — 'Nay,' said I, 'will you cast
away your child on a fool and a physician? Look on
Master Fenton': — this is my doing.

FENTON
I thank thee; and I pray thee, once to-night
Give my sweet Nan this ring: there's for thy pains.

MISTRESS QUICKLY
Now heaven send thee good fortune! [*Exit* FENTON.] A
kind heart he hath: a woman would run through fire
and water for such a kind heart. But yet I would my
master had Mistress Anne; or I would Master Slender
had her; or, in sooth, I would Master Fenton had her: I
will do what I can for them all three; for so I have
promised, and I'll be as good as my word; but
speciously for Master Fenton. Well, I must of another
errand to Sir John Falstaff from my two mistresses:
what a beast am I to slack it! [*Exit.*

SCENE V

A room in the Garter Inn.

Enter FALSTAFF *and* BARDOLPH.

FALSTAFF
Bardolph, I say, —

BARDOLPH
Here, sir.

FALSTAFF
Go fetch me a quart of sack; put a toast in't. [*Exit*
BARDOLPH.] Have I lived to be carried in a basket, like
a barrow of butcher's offal, and to be thrown in the
Thames? Well, if I be served such another trick, I'll
have my brains ta'en out, and butter'd, and give them
to a dog for a new-year's gift. The rogues slighted me
into the river with as little remorse as they would have
drown'd a bitch's blind puppies, fifteen i'th'litter: and
you may know by my size that I have a kind of alacrity
in sinking; if the bottom were as deep as hell, I should
down. I had been drown'd, but that the shore was
shelvy and shallow, — a death that I abhor; for the
water swells a man; and what a thing should I have
been when I had been swell'd! I should have been a
mountain of mummy.

Enter BARDOLPH *with sack.*

BARDOLPH
Here's Mistress Quickly, sir, to speak with you.

FALSTAFF
Come, let me pour in some sack to the Thames water;
for my belly's as cold as if I had swallow'd snowballs for
pills to cool the reins. Call her in.

BARDOLPH
Come in, woman!

Enter MISTRESS QUICKLY.

MISTRESS QUICKLY
By your leave; I cry you mercy: — give your worship
good morrow.

FALSTAFF
Take away these chalices. Go brew me a pottle of sack
finely.

BARDOLPH
With eggs, sir?

FALSTAFF
Simple of itself; I'll no pullet-sperm in my brewage.
[*Exit* BARDOLPH.] How now!

MISTRESS QUICKLY
Marry, sir, I come to your worship from Mistress Ford.

FALSTAFF
Mistress Ford! I have had ford enough; I was thrown
into the ford; I have my belly full of ford.

MISTRESS QUICKLY
Alas the day! good heart, that was not her fault: she
does so take on with her men; they mistook their
erection.

FALSTAFF
So did I mine, to build upon a foolish woman's promise.

MISTRESS QUICKLY
Well, she laments, sir, for it, that it would yearn your
heart to see it. Her husband goes this morning
a-birding; she desires you once more to come to her
between eight and nine: I must carry her word quickly:
she'll make you amends, I warrant you.

FALSTAFF
Well, I will visit her: tell her so; and bid her think what
a man is: let her consider his frailty, and then judge of
my merit.

MISTRESS QUICKLY
I will tell her.

FALSTAFF
Do so. Between nine and ten, say'st thou?

MISTRESS QUICKLY
Eight and nine, sir.

FALSTAFF
Well, be gone: I will not miss her.

MISTRESS QUICKLY
Peace be with you, sir. [*Exit.*

FALSTAFF
I marvel I hear not of Master Brook; he sent me word to
stay within: I like his money well. — O, here he comes.

Enter FORD *disguised.*

FORD
Bless you, sir!

FALSTAFF
Now, Master Brook, — you come to know what hath
pass'd between me and Ford's wife?

FORD
That, indeed, Sir John, is my business.

FALSTAFF
Master Brook, I will not lie to you: I was at her house
the hour she appointed me.

FORD
And how sped you, sir?

FALSTAFF
Very ill-favour'dly, Master Brook.

FORD
How so, sir? Did she change her determination?

FALSTAFF
No, Master Brook; but the peaking cornuto her
husband, Master Brook, dwelling in a continual 'larum
of jealousy, comes me in the instant of our encounter,
after we had embraced, kiss'd, protested, and, as it
were, spoke the prologue of our comedy; and at his
heels a rabble of his companions, thither provoked and
instigated by his distemper, and, forsooth, to search his
house for his wife's love.

FORD
What, while you were there?

FALSTAFF
While I was there.

FORD
And did he search for you, and could not find you?

FALSTAFF
You shall hear. As good luck would have it, comes in one Mistress Page; gives intelligence of Ford's approach; and, in her invention and Ford's wife's distraction, they convey'd me into a buck-basket.

FORD
A buck-basket!

FALSTAFF
By the Lord, a buck-basket! — ramm'd me in with foul shirts and smocks, socks, foul stockings, greasy napkins; that, Master Brook, there was the rankest compound of villainous smell that ever offended nostril.

FORD
And how long lay you there?

FALSTAFF
Nay, you shall hear, Master Brook, what I have suffer'd to bring this woman to evil for your good. Being thus cramm'd in the basket, a couple of Ford's knaves, his hinds, were call'd forth by their mistress to carry me in the name of foul clothes to Datchet-lane: they took me on their shoulders; met the jealous knave their master in the door, who ask'd them once or twice what they had in their basket: I quaked for fear, lest the lunatic knave would have search'd it; but fate, ordaining he should be a cuckold, held his hand. Well: on went he for a search, and away went I for foul clothes. But mark the sequel, Master Brook: I suffer'd the pangs of three several deaths; first, an intolerable fright, to be detected with a jealous rotten bell-wether; next, to be compass'd, like a good bilbo, in the circumference of a peck, hilt to point, heel to head; and then, to be stopp'd in, like a strong distillation, with stinking clothes that fretted in their own grease: think of that, — a man of my kidney, — think of that, — that am as subject to heat as butter; a man of continual dissolution and thaw; — it was a miracle to scape suffocation. And in the height of this bath, when I was more than half stew'd in grease, like a Dutch dish, to be thrown into the Thames, and cool'd, glowing hot, in that surge, like a horse-shoe; think of that, — hissing hot, — think of that, Master Brook.

FORD
In good sadness, sir, I am sorry that for my sake you have suffer'd all this. My suit, then, is desperate; you'll undertake her no more?

FALSTAFF
Master Brook, I will be thrown into Etna, as I have been into Thames, ere I will leave her thus. Her husband is this morning gone a-birding: I have received from her another embassy of meeting; 'twixt eight and nine is the hour, Master Brook.

FORD
'Tis past eight already, sir.

FALSTAFF
Is it? I will then address me to my appointment. Come to me at your convenient leisure, and you shall know how I speed; and the conclusion shall be crown'd with your enjoying her. Adieu. You shall have her, Master Brook; Master Brook, you shall cuckold Ford.   [*Exit.*

FORD
Hum, — ha! is this a vision? is this a dream? do I sleep? Master Ford, awake! awake, Master Ford! there's a hole made in your best coat, Master Ford. This 'tis to be married! this 'tis to have linen and buck-baskets! — Well, I will proclaim myself what I am: I will now take the lecher; he is at my house; he cannot scape me; 'tis impossible he should; he cannot creep into a halfpenny purse, nor into a pepper-box: but, lest the devil that guides him should aid him, I will search impossible places. Though what I am I cannot avoid, yet to be what I would not shall not make me tame: if I have horns to make one mad, let the proverb go with me, — I'll be horn-mad.   [*Exit.*

ACT IV

SCENE I

The street.

Enter MISTRESS PAGE,
MISTRESS QUICKLY, *and* WILLIAM.

MISTRESS PAGE
Is he at Master Ford's already, think'st thou?

MISTRESS QUICKLY
Sure he is by this, or will be presently: but, truly, he is very courageous mad about his throwing into the water. Mistress Ford desires you to come suddenly.

MISTRESS PAGE
I'll be with her by and by; I'll but bring my young man here to school. Look, where his master comes: 'tis a playing-day, I see.

Enter EVANS.
How now, Sir Hugh! no school to-day?

EVANS
No; Master Slender is let the boys leave to play.

MISTRESS QUICKLY
Blessing of his heart!

MISTRESS PAGE
Sir Hugh, my husband says my son profits nothing in the world at his book. I pray you, ask him some questions in his accidence.

EVANS
Come hither, William; hold up your head; come.

MISTRESS PAGE
Come on, sirrah; hold up your head; answer your master, be not afraid.

EVANS
William, how many numbers is in nouns?

WILLIAM PAGE
Two.

MISTRESS QUICKLY
Truly, I thought there had been one number more, because they say, Od's-nouns.

EVANS
Peace your tattlings. — What is *fair*, William?

WILLIAM PAGE
Pulcher.

MISTRESS QUICKLY
Polecats! there are fairer things than polecats, sure.

EVANS
You are a very simplicity oman: I pray you, peace. — What is *lapis*, William?

WILLIAM PAGE
A stone.

EVANS
And what is a stone, William?

WILLIAM PAGE
A pebble.

EVANS
No, it is *lapis:* I pray you, remember in your prain.

WILLIAM PAGE
Lapis.

EVANS
That is a good William. What is he, William, that does lend articles?

WILLIAM PAGE
Articles are borrowed of the pronoun, and be thus declined, *Singulariter, nominativo, hic, hæc, hoc.*

EVANS
Nominativo, hig, hag, hog; — pray you, mark: *genitivo, hujus.* Well, what is your accusative case?

WILLIAM PAGE
Accusativo, hinc.

EVANS
I pray you, have your remembrance, child; *accusativo, hung, hang, hog.*

MISTRESS QUICKLY
Hang-hog is Latin for bacon, I warrant you.

EVANS
Leave your prabbles, oman. — What is the focative case, William?

WILLIAM PAGE
O, — vocativo, O.

EVANS
Remember, William; focative is *caret.*

MISTRESS QUICKLY
And that's a good root.

EVANS
Oman, forbear.

MISTRESS PAGE
Peace!

EVANS
What is your genitive case plural, William?

WILLIAM PAGE
Genitive case!

EVANS
Ay.

WILLIAM PAGE
Genitivo, — horum, harum, horum.

MISTRESS QUICKLY
Vengeance of Jenny's case! fie on her! — never name her, child, if she be a whore.

EVANS
For shame, oman.

MISTRESS QUICKLY
You do ill to teach the child such words: — he teaches him to hick and to hack, which they'll do fast enough of themselves, and to call whorum: — fie upon you!

EVANS
Oman, art thou lunatics? hast thou no understandings for thy cases, and the numbers of the genders? Thou art as foolish Christian creatures as I would desires.

MISTRESS PAGE
Prithee, hold thy peace.

EVANS
Show me now, William, some declensions of your pronouns.

WILLIAM PAGE
Forsooth, I have forgot.

EVANS
It is *qui, quæ, quod:* if you forget your *quies*, your *quæs*, and your *quods*, you must be preeches. Go your ways, and play; go.

MISTRESS PAGE
He is a better scholar than I thought he was.

EVANS
He is a good sprag memory. Farewell, Mistress Page.

MISTRESS PAGE
Adieu, good Sir Hugh. [*Exit* EVANS.] — Get you home, boy. — Come, we stay too long.   [*Exeunt.*

EVANS Come hither, William; hold up your head; come.

SCENE II

A room in FORD'S *house.*

Enter FALSTAFF *and* MISTRESS FORD.

FALSTAFF
Mistress Ford, your sorrow hath eaten up my sufferance. I see you are obsequious in your love, and I profess requital to a hair's breadth; not only, Mistress Ford, in the simple office of love, but in all the accoutrement, complement, and ceremony of it. But are you sure of your husband now?

MISTRESS FORD
He's a-birding, sweet Sir John.

MISTRESS PAGE [*within*].
What, ho, gossip Ford! what, ho!

MISTRESS FORD
Step into the chamber, Sir John.   [*Exit* FALSTAFF.

Enter MISTRESS PAGE.

MISTRESS PAGE
How now, sweetheart! who's at home besides yourself?

MISTRESS FORD
Why, none but mine own people.

MISTRESS PAGE
Indeed!

MISTRESS FORD
No, certainly. [*Aside to her.*] Speak louder.

MISTRESS PAGE
Truly, I am so glad you have nobody here.

MISTRESS FORD
Why?

MISTRESS PAGE
Why, woman, your husband is in his old lunes again: he so takes on yonder with my husband; so rails against all married mankind; so curses all Eve's daughters, of what complexion soever; and so buffets himself on the forehead, crying, 'Peer out, peer out!' that any madness I ever yet beheld seem'd but tameness, civility, and patience, to this his distemper he is in now: I am glad the fat knight is not here.

MISTRESS FORD
Why, does he talk of him?

MISTRESS PAGE
Of none but him; and swears he was carried out, the last time he search'd for him, in a basket; protests to my husband he is now here; and hath drawn him and the rest of their company from their sport, to make another experiment of his suspicion: but I am glad the knight is not here; now he shall see his own foolery.

MISTRESS FORD
How near is he, Mistress Page?

MISTRESS PAGE
Hard by; at street end; he will be here anon.

MISTRESS FORD
I am undone! — the knight is here.

MISTRESS PAGE
Why, then, you are utterly shamed, and he's but a dead man. What a woman are you! — Away with him, away with him! better shame than murder.

MISTRESS FORD
Which way should he go? how should I bestow him? Shall I put him into the basket again?

Enter FALSTAFF.

FALSTAFF
No, I'll come no more i'th'basket. May I not go out ere he come?

MISTRESS PAGE
Alas, three of Master Ford's brothers watch the door with pistols, that none shall issue out; otherwise you might slip away ere he came. But what make you here?

FALSTAFF
What shall I do? — I'll creep up into the chimney.

MISTRESS FORD
There they always use to discharge their birding-pieces.

MISTRESS PAGE
Creep into the kiln-hole.

FALSTAFF
Where is it?

MISTRESS FORD
He will seek there, on my word. Neither press, coffer, chest, trunk, well, vault, but he hath an abstract for the remembrance of such places, and goes to them by his note: there is no hiding you in the house.

FALSTAFF
I'll go out, then.

MISTRESS PAGE
If you go out in your own semblance, you die, Sir John. Unless you go out disguised, —

MISTRESS FORD
How might we disguise him?

MISTRESS PAGE
Alas the day, I know not! There is no woman's gown big enough for him; otherwise he might put on a hat, a muffler, and a kerchief, and so escape.

FALSTAFF
Good hearts, devise something: any extremity rather than a mischief.

MISTRESS FORD
My maid's aunt, the fat woman of Brainford, has a gown above.

MISTRESS PAGE
On my word, it will serve him; she's as big as he is: and there's her thrumm'd hat, and her muffler too. — Run up, Sir John.

MISTRESS FORD
Go, go, sweet Sir John: Mistress Page and I will look some linen for your head.

MISTRESS PAGE
Quick, quick! we'll come dress you straight: put on the gown the while.   [*Exit* FALSTAFF.

MISTRESS FORD
I would my husband would meet him in this shape: he cannot abide the old woman of Brainford; he swears she's a witch; forbade her my house, and hath threaten'd to beat her.

MISTRESS PAGE
Heaven guide him to thy husband's cudgel, and the devil guide his cudgel afterwards!

MISTRESS FORD
But is my husband coming?

MISTRESS PAGE
Ay, in good sadness, is he; and talks of the basket too, howsoever he hath had intelligence.

MISTRESS FORD
We'll try that; for I'll appoint my men to carry the basket again, to meet him at the door with it, as they did last time.

MISTRESS PAGE
Nay, but he'll be here presently: let's go dress him like the witch of Brainford.

MISTRESS FORD
I'll first direct my men what they shall do with the basket. Go up; I'll bring linen for him straight.
        [*Exit.*

MISTRESS PAGE
Hang him, dishonest varlet! we cannot misuse him enough.
We'll leave a proof, by that which we will do,
Wives may be merry, and yet honest too:
We do not act that often jest and laugh;
'Tis old, but true, — Still swine eats all the draff.   [*Exit.*

Enter MISTRESS FORD *with two* SERVANTS.

MISTRESS FORD
Go, sirs, take the basket again on your shoulders: your master is hard at door; if he bid you set it down, obey him: quickly, dispatch.   [*Exit.*

FIRST SERVANT
Come, come, take it up.

SECOND SERVANT
Pray heaven it be not full of knight again.

FIRST SERVANT
I hope not; I had as lief bear so much lead.

Enter FORD, PAGE, SHALLOW, CAIUS, *and*
SIR HUGH EVANS.

FORD
Ay, but if it prove true, Master Page, have you any way then to unfool me again? — Set down the basket, villain! — Somebody call my wife. — You, youth in a basket, come out here! — O you panderly rascals! there's a knot, a ging, a pack, a conspiracy against me: now shall the devil be shamed. — What, wife, I say! come, come forth! behold what honest clothes you send forth to bleaching!

MISTRESS PAGE
Why, this passes! Master Ford, you are not to go loose any longer; you must be pinion'd.

EVANS
Why, this is lunatics! this is mad as a mad dog!

SHALLOW
Indeed, Master Ford, this is not well; indeed.

FORD
So say I too, sir.

Enter MISTRESS FORD.

Come hither, Mistress Ford; Mistress Ford, the honest woman, the modest wife, the virtuous creature, that hath the jealous fool to her husband! — I suspect

without cause, mistress, do I?

MISTRESS FORD
Heaven be my witness you do, if you suspect me in any dishonesty.

FORD
Well said, brazen-face! hold it out. — Come forth, sirrah!   [*Pulling the clothes out of the basket.*

PAGE
This passes!

MISTRESS FORD
Are you not ashamed? let the clothes alone.

FORD
I shall find you anon.

EVANS
'Tis unreasonable! Will you take up your wife's clothes? Come away.

FORD
Empty the basket, I say!

MISTRESS FORD
Why, man, why, —

FORD
Master Page, as I am a man, there was one convey'd out of my house yesterday in this basket: why may not he be there again? In my house I am sure he is: my intelligence is true; my jealousy is reasonable. — Pluck me out all the linen.

MISTRESS FORD
If you find a man there, he shall die a flea's death.

PAGE
Here's no man.

SHALLOW
By my fidelity, this is not well, Master Ford; this wrongs you.

EVANS
Master Ford, you must pray, and not follow the imaginations of your own heart: this is jealousies.

FORD
Well, he's not here I seek for.

PAGE
No, nor nowhere else but in your brain.

FORD
Help to search my house this one time. If I find not what I seek, show no colour for my extremity; let me for ever be your table-sport; let them say of me, 'As jealous as Ford, that search'd a hollow walnut for his wife's leman.' Satisfy me once more; once more search with me.

MISTRESS FORD
What, ho, Mistress Page! come you and the old woman down; my husband will come into the chamber.

FORD
Old woman! what old woman's that?

MISTRESS FORD
Why, it is my maid's aunt of Brainford.

FORD
A witch, a quean, an old cozening quean! Have I not forbid her my house? She comes of errands, does she? We are simple men; we do not know what's brought to pass under the profession of fortune-telling. She works by charms, by spells, by th'figure; and such daubery as this is beyond our element; we know nothing. — Come down, you witch, you hag, you; come down, I say!

MISTRESS FORD
Nay, good, sweet husband, — Good gentlemen, let him not strike the old woman.

Enter FALSTAFF *in woman's clothes, led by*
MISTRESS PAGE.

MISTRESS PAGE
Come, Mother Prat; come, give me your hand.

FORD
I'll prat her. — [*Beating him.*] Out of my door, you witch, you rag, you baggage, you polecat, you ronyon! out, out! I'll conjure you, I'll fortune-tell you.
        [*Exit* FALSTAFF.

MISTRESS PAGE
Are you not ashamed? I think you have kill'd the poor woman.

MISTRESS FORD
Nay, he will do it. — 'Tis a goodly credit for you.

FORD
Hang her, witch!

EVANS
By yea and no, I think the oman is a witch indeed: I like not when a oman has a great peard; I spy a great peard under her muffler.

FORD
Will you follow, gentlemen? I beseech you, follow; see but the issue of my jealousy: if I cry out thus upon no

trail, never trust me when I open again.

PAGE
Let's obey his humour a little further: come, gentlemen.
[*Exeunt* FORD, PAGE, SHALLOW, CAIUS, *and* EVANS.

MISTRESS PAGE
Trust me, he beat him most pitifully.

MISTRESS FORD
Nay, by th'mass, that he did not; he beat him most unpitifully methought.

MISTRESS PAGE
I'll have the cudgel hallow'd, and hung o'er the altar; it hath done meritorious service.

MISTRESS FORD
What think you? may we, with the warrant of womanhood and the witness of a good conscience, pursue him with any further revenge?

MISTRESS PAGE
The spirit of wantonness is, sure, scared out of him: if the devil have him not in fee-simple, with fine and recovery, he will never, I think, in the way of waste, attempt us again.

MISTRESS FORD
Shall we tell our husbands how we have served him?

MISTRESS PAGE
Yes, by all means; if it be but to scrape the figures out of your husband's brains. If they can find in their hearts the poor unvirtuous fat knight shall be any further afflicted, we two will still be the ministers.

MISTRESS FORD
I'll warrant they'll have him publicly shamed: and methinks there would be no period to the jest, should he not be publicly shamed.

MISTRESS PAGE
Come, to the forge with it, then; shape it: I would not have things cool. [*Exeunt.*

SCENE III

A room in the Garter Inn.

Enter HOST *and* BARDOLPH.

BARDOLPH
Sir, the Germans desire to have three of your horses: the duke himself will be to-morrow at court, and they are going to meet him.

HOST
What duke should that be comes so secretly? I hear not of him in the court. Let me speak with the gentlemen: they speak English?

BARDOLPH
Ay, sir; I'll call them to you.

HOST
They shall have my horses; but I'll make them pay; I'll sauce them: they have had my house a week at command; I have turn'd away my other guests: they must come off; I'll sauce them. Come. [*Exeunt.*

SCENE IV

A room in FORD'S *house.*

Enter PAGE, FORD, MISTRESS PAGE, MISTRESS FORD, *and* SIR HUGH EVANS.

EVANS
'Tis one of the best discretions of a oman as ever I did look upon.

PAGE
And did he send you both these letters at an instant?

MISTRESS PAGE
Within a quarter of an hour.

FORD
Pardon me, wife. Henceforth do what thou wilt;
I rather will suspect the sun with cold
Than thee with wantonness: now doth thy honour stand,
In him that was of late an heretic,
As firm as faith.

PAGE
                'Tis well, 'tis well; no more:
Be not as extreme in submission
As in offence.
But let our plot go forward: let our wives
Yet once again, to make us public sport,
Appoint a meeting with this old fat fellow,
Where we may take him, and disgrace him for it.

FORD
There is no better way than that they spoke of.

PAGE
How! to send him word they'll meet him in the Park at midnight? Fie, fie! he'll never come.

EVANS
You say he has been thrown in the rivers; and has been grievously peaten, as an old oman: methinks there should be terrors in him that he should not come; methinks his flesh is punish'd, he shall have no desires.

PAGE
So think I too.

MISTRESS FORD
Devise but how you'll use him when he comes,
And let us two devise to bring him thither.

MISTRESS PAGE
There is an old tale goes that Herne the Hunter,
Sometime a keeper here in Windsor forest,
Doth all the winter-time, at still midnight,
Walk round about an oak, with great ragg'd horns;
And there he blasts the tree, and takes the cattle,
And makes milch-kine yield blood, and shakes a chain
In a most hideous and dreadful manner:
You have heard of such a spirit; and well you know
The superstitious idle-headed eld
Received, and did deliver to our age,
This tale of Herne the hunter for a truth.

PAGE
Why, yet there want not many that do fear
In deep of night to walk by this Herne's oak:
But what of this?

MISTRESS FORD
                Marry, this is our device:
That Falstaff at that oak shall meet with us,
Disguis'd like Herne, with huge horns on his head.

PAGE
Well, let it not be doubted but he'll come:
And in this shape when you have brought him thither,
What shall be done with him? what is your plot?

MISTRESS PAGE
That likewise have we thought upon, and thus:
Nan Page my daughter, and my little son,
And three or four more of their growth, we'll dress
Like urchins, ouphs, and fairies, green and white,
With rounds of waxen tapers on their heads,
And rattles in their hands: upon a sudden,
As Falstaff, she, and I, are newly met,
Let them from forth a sawpit rush at once
With some diffused song: upon their sight,
We two in great amazedness will fly:
Then let them all encircle him about,
And, fairy-like, to-pinch the unclean knight;
And ask him why, that hour of fairy revel
In their so sacred paths he dares to tread
In shape profane.

MISTRESS FORD
                And till he tell the truth,
Let the supposed fairies pinch him sound,
And burn him with their tapers.

MISTRESS PAGE
                The truth being known,
We'll all present ourselves, dis-horn the spirit,
And mock him home to Windsor.

FORD
                The children must
Be practis'd well to this, or they'll ne'er do't.

EVANS
I will teach the children their behaviours; and I will be like a jack-an-apes also, to burn the knight with my taber.

FORD
That will be excellent. I'll go buy them vizards.

MISTRESS PAGE
My Nan shall be the queen of all the fairies,
Finely attired in a robe of white.

PAGE
That silk will I go buy: — [*aside*] and in that time
Shall Master Slender steal my Nan away,
And marry her at Eton. — Go send to Falstaff straight.

FORD
Nay, I'll to him again in name of Brook;
He'll tell me all his purpose: sure, he'll come.

MISTRESS PAGE
Fear not you that. Go get us properties
And tricking for our fairies.

EVANS
Let us about it: it is admirable pleasures and fery honest knaveries. [*Exeunt* PAGE, FORD, *and* EVANS.

MISTRESS PAGE
Go, Mistress Ford,
Send quickly to Sir John, to know his mind.
[*Exit* MISTRESS FORD.
I'll to the doctor: he hath my good will,

And none but he, to marry with Nan Page.
That Slender, though well landed, is an idiot;
And he my husband best of all affects.
The doctor is well money'd, and his friends
Potent at court: he, none but he, shall have her,
Though twenty thousand worthier come to crave her.
[*Exit.*

SCENE V

A room in the Garter Inn.

Enter HOST *and* SIMPLE.

HOST
What wouldst thou have, boor? what, thick-skin? speak, breathe, discuss; brief, short, quick, snap.

SIMPLE
Marry, sir, I come to speak with Sir John Falstaff from Master Slender.

HOST
There's his chamber, his house, his castle, his standing-bed, and truckle-bed; 'tis painted about with the story of the Prodigal, fresh and new. Go knock and call; he'll speak like an Anthropophaginian unto thee: knock, I say.

SIMPLE
There's an old woman, a fat woman, gone up into his chamber: I'll be so bold as stay, sir, till she come down; I come to speak with her, indeed.

HOST
Ha! a fat woman! the knight may be robb'd: I'll call. — Bully knight! bully Sir John! speak from thy lungs military: art thou there? it is thine host, thine Ephesian, calls.

FALSTAFF [*above*].
How now, mine host!

HOST
Here's a Bohemian-Tartar tarries the coming down of thy fat woman. Let her descend, bully, let her descend; my chambers are honourable: fie! privacy? fie!

Enter FALSTAFF.

FALSTAFF
There was, mine host, an old fat woman even now with me; but she's gone.

SIMPLE
Pray you, sir, was't not the wise-woman of Brainford?

FALSTAFF
Ay, marry, was it, mussel-shell: what would you with her?

SIMPLE
My master, sir, Master Slender, sent to her, seeing her go through the streets, to know, sir, whether one Nym, sir, that beguiled him of a chain, had the chain or no.

FALSTAFF
I spake with the old woman about it.

SIMPLE
And what says she, I pray, sir?

FALSTAFF
Marry, she says that the very same man that beguiled Master Slender of his chain cozen'd him of it.

SIMPLE
I would I could have spoken with the woman herself; I had other things to have spoken with her too from him.

FALSTAFF
What are they? let us know.

HOST
Ay, come; quick.

SIMPLE
I may not conceal them, sir.

HOST
Conceal them, or thou diest.

SIMPLE
Why, sir, they were nothing but about Mistress Anne Page; to know if it were my master's fortune to have her or no.

FALSTAFF
'Tis, 'tis his fortune.

SIMPLE
What, sir?

FALSTAFF
To have her, — or no. Go; say the woman told me so.

SIMPLE
May I be bold to say so, sir?

FALSTAFF
Ay, sir Tike! — who more bold?

SIMPLE
I thank your worship: I shall make my master glad with these tidings. [*Exit.*

HOST
Thou art clerkly, thou art clerkly, Sir John. Was there a wise woman with thee?

FALSTAFF
Ay, that there was, mine host; one that hath taught me more wit than ever I learn'd before in my life; and I paid nothing for it neither, but was paid for my learning.

Enter BARDOLPH.

BARDOLPH
Out, alas, sir! cozenage, mere cozenage!

HOST
Where be my horses? speak well of them, varletto.

BARDOLPH
Run away with the cozeners: for so soon as I came beyond Eton, they threw me off, from behind one of them, in a slough of mire; and set spurs and away, like three German devils, three Dr. Faustuses.

HOST
They are gone but to meet the duke, villain: do not say they be fled; Germans are honest men.

Enter SIR HUGH EVANS.

EVANS
Where is mine host?

HOST
What is the matter, sir?

EVANS
Have a care of your entertainments: there is a friend of mine come to town, tells me there is three cozen-germans that has cozen'd all the hosts of Readins, of Maidenhead, of Colebrook, of horses and money. I tell you for good will, look you: you are wise, and full of gibes and vlouting-stogs, and 'tis not convenient you should be cozen'd. Fare you well. [*Exit.*

Enter DOCTOR CAIUS.

CAIUS
Vere is mine host de Jarteer?

HOST
Here, master doctor, in perplexity and doubtful dilemma.

CAIUS
I cannot tell vat is dat: but it is tell-a me dat you make grand preparation for a duke de Jamany: by my trot, dere is no duke dat de court is know to come. I tell you for good vill: adieu. [*Exit.*

HOST
Hue and cry, villain, go! — Assist me, knight. — I am undone! — Fly, run, hue and cry, villain! — I am undone! [*Exeunt* HOST *and* BARDOLPH.

FALSTAFF
I would all the world might be cozen'd; for I have been cozen'd and beaten too. If it should come to the ear of the court, how I have been transform'd, and how my transformation hath been wash'd and cudgell'd, they would melt me out of my fat drop by drop, and liquor fishermen's boots with me: I warrant they would whip me with their fine wits till I were as crest-fallen as a dried pear. I never prosper'd since I forswore myself at primero. Well, if my wind were but long enough to say my prayers, I would repent.

Enter MISTRESS QUICKLY.

Now, whence come you?

MISTRESS QUICKLY
From the two parties, forsooth.

FALSTAFF
The devil take one party. and his dam the other! and so they shall be both bestow'd. I have suffer'd more for their sakes, more than the villainous inconstancy of man's disposition is able to bear.

MISTRESS QUICKLY
And have not they suffer'd? Yes, I warrant; speciously one of them; Mistress Ford, good heart, is beaten black and blue, that you cannot see a white spot about her.

FALSTAFF
What tell'st thou me of black and blue? I was beaten myself into all the colours of the rainbow; and I was like to be apprehended for the witch of Brainford: but that my admirable dexterity of wit, my counterfeiting the action of an old woman, deliver'd me, the knave constable had set me i'th'stocks, i'th'common stocks, for a witch.

MISTRESS QUICKLY
Sir, let me speak with you in your chamber: you shall hear how things go; and, I warrant, to your content. Here is a letter will say somewhat. Good hearts, what ado here is to bring you together! Sure, one of you does not serve heaven well, that you are so cross'd.

FALSTAFF
Come up into my chamber. [*Exeunt.*

SCENE VI

Another room in the Garter Inn.

Enter FENTON *and* HOST.

HOST
Master Fenton, talk not to me; my mind is heavy: I will give over all.

FENTON
Yet hear me speak. Assist me in my purpose,
And, as I am a gentleman, I'll give thee
A hundred pound in gold more than your loss.

HOST
I will hear you, Master Fenton; and I will at the least keep your counsel.

FENTON
From time to time I have acquainted you
With the dear love I bear to fair Anne Page;
Who mutually hath answer'd my affection,
So far forth as herself might be her chooser,
Even to my wish: I have a letter from her
Of such contents as you will wonder at;
The mirth whereof so larded with my matter,
That neither singly can be manifested
Without the show of both; — wherein fat Falstaff
Hath a great scene: the image of the jest
I'll show you here at large. Hark, good mine host.
To-night at Herne's oak, just 'twixt twelve and one,
Must my sweet Nan present the Fairy Queen;
The purpose why, is here: in which disguise,
While other jests are something rank on foot,
Her father hath commanded her to slip
Away with Slender, and with him at Eton
Immediately to marry: she hath consented:
Now, sir,
Her mother, even strong against that match,
And firm for Doctor Caius, hath appointed
That he shall likewise shuffle her away,
While other sports are tasking of their minds,
And at the deanery, where a priest attends,
Straight marry her: to this her mother's plot
She, seemingly obedient, likewise hath
Made promise to the doctor. — Now, thus it rests:
Her father means she shall be all in white;
And in that habit, when Slender sees his time
To take her by the hand, and bid her go,
She shall go with him: her mother hath intended,
The better to denote her to the doctor, —
For they must all be mask'd and vizarded, —
That quaint in green she shall be loose enrobed,
With ribands pendent, flaring 'bout her head;
And when the doctor spies his vantage ripe,
To pinch her by the hand, and, on that token,
The maid hath given consent to go with him.

HOST
Which means she to deceive, father or mother?

FENTON
Both, my good host, to go along with me:
And here it rests, — that you'll procure the vicar
To stay for me at church 'twixt twelve and one,
And, in the lawful name of marrying,
To give our hearts united ceremony.

HOST
Well, husband your device; I'll to the vicar:
Bring you the maid, you shall not lack a priest.

FENTON
So shall I evermore be bound to thee;
Besides, I'll make a present recompense. [*Exeunt.*

ACT V

SCENE I

A room in the Garter Inn.

Enter FALSTAFF *and* MISTRESS QUICKLY.

FALSTAFF
Prithee, no more prattling; go: — I'll hold. This is the third time; I hope good luck lies in odd numbers. Away! go. They say there is divinity in odd numbers, either in nativity, chance, or death. Away!

MISTRESS QUICKLY
I'll provide you a chain; and I'll do what I can to get you a pair of horns.

FALSTAFF
Away, I say; time wears: hold up your head, and mince. [*Exit* MISTRESS QUICKLY.

Enter FORD *disguised.*

How now, Master Brook! Master Brook, the matter will be known to-night, or never. Be you in the Park about midnight, at Herne's oak, and you shall see wonders.

FORD
Went you not to her yesterday, sir, as you told me you had appointed?

FALSTAFF
I went to her, Master Brook, as you see, like a poor old man: but I came from her, Master Brook, like a poor old woman. That same knave Ford, her husband, hath the finest mad devil of jealousy in him, Master Brook, that ever govern'd frenzy: — I will tell you: — he beat me grievously, in the shape of a woman; for in the shape of man, Master Brook, I fear not Goliath with a weaver's beam; because I know also life is a shuttle. I am in haste; go along with me: I'll tell you all, Master Brook. Since I pluck'd geese, play'd truant, and whipp'd top, I knew not what 'twas to be beaten till lately. Follow me: I'll tell you strange things of this knave Ford; on whom to-night I will be revenged, and I will deliver his wife into your hand. Follow: — strange things in hand, Master Brook: — follow. [*Exeunt.*

SCENE II

Windsor Park.

Enter PAGE, SHALLOW, *and* SLENDER.

PAGE
Come, come; we'll couch i'th'castle-ditch till we see the light of our fairies. — Remember, son Slender, my daughter.

SLENDER
Ay, forsooth; I have spoke with her, and we have a nay-word how to know one another: I come to her in white, and cry 'mum'; she cries 'budget'; and by that we know one another.

SHALLOW
That's good too; but what needs either your 'mum' or her 'budget'? the white will decipher her well enough. — It hath struck ten o'clock.

PAGE
The night is dark; light and spirits will become it well. Heaven prosper our sport! No man means evil but the devil, and we shall know him by his horns. Let's away; follow me. [*Exeunt.*

SCENE III

A street leading to the Park.

Enter MISTRESS PAGE, MISTRESS FORD, *and* DOCTOR CAIUS.

MISTRESS PAGE
Master doctor, my daughter is in green: when you see your time, take her by the hand, away with her to the deanery, and dispatch it quickly. Go before into the Park: we two must go together.

CAIUS
I know vat I have to do. Adieu.

MISTRESS PAGE
Fare you well, sir. [*Exit* CAIUS.] — My husband will not rejoice so much at the abuse of Falstaff as he will chafe at the doctor's marrying my daughter: but 'tis no matter; better a little chiding than a great deal of heart-break.

MISTRESS FORD
Where is Nan now and her troop of fairies, and the Welsh devil Hugh?

MISTRESS PAGE
They are all couch'd in a pit hard by Herne's oak, with obscured lights; which, at the very instant of Falstaff's and our meeting, they will at once display to the night.

MISTRESS FORD
That cannot choose but amaze him.

MISTRESS PAGE
If he be not amazed, he will be mock'd; if he be amazed, he will every way be mock'd.

MISTRESS FORD
We'll betray him finely.

MISTRESS PAGE
Against such lewdsters and their lechery
Those that betray them do no treachery.

MISTRESS FORD
The hour draws on. To the oak, to the oak! [*Exeunt.*

SCENE IV

Windsor Park.

Enter SIR HUGH EVANS *disguised as a Satyr, with* ANNE PAGE *and others as fairies.*

EVANS
Trib, trib, fairies; come; and remember your parts: be pold, I pray you; follow me into the pit; and when I give the watch-ords, do as I pid you: come, come; trib, trib. [*Exeunt.*

SCENE V

Another part of the Park.

Enter FALSTAFF, *with a buck's head upon him.*

FALSTAFF
The Windsor bell hath struck twelve; the minute draws on. Now, the hot-blooded gods assist me! — Remember, Jove, thou wast a bull for thy Europa; love set on thy horns: — O powerful love! that, in some respects, makes a beast a man; in some other, a man a beast. — You were also, Jupiter, a swan for the love of Leda: — O omnipotent love! how near the god drew to the complexion of a goose! — A fault done first in the form of a beast; — O Jove, a beastly fault! and then another fault in the semblance of a fowl; — think on't, Jove; a foul fault! When gods have hot backs, what shall poor men do? For me, I am here a Windsor stag; and the fattest, I think, i'th'forest. — Send me a cool rut-time, Jove, or who can blame me to piss my tallow? — Who comes here? my doe?

Enter MISTRESS FORD *and* MISTRESS PAGE.

MISTRESS FORD
Sir John! art thou there, my deer? my male deer?

FALSTAFF
My doe with the black scut! — Let the sky rain potatoes; let it thunder to the tune of *Green Sleeves*, hail kissing-comfits, and snow eryngoes; let there come a tempest of provocation, I will shelter me here.
[Embracing her.

MISTRESS FORD
Mistress Page is come with me, sweetheart.

FALSTAFF
Divide me like a brib'd-buck, each a haunch: I will keep my sides to myself, my shoulders for the fellow of this walk, and my horns I bequeath your husbands. Am I a woodman, ha? Speak I like Herne the hunter? — Why, now is Cupid a child of conscience; he makes restitution. As I am a true spirit, welcome!
[Noise of horns within.

MISTRESS PAGE
Alas, what noise?

MISTRESS FORD
Heaven forgive our sins!

FALSTAFF
What should this be?

MISTRESS FORD *and* **MISTRESS PAGE**
Away, away! *[They run off.*

FALSTAFF
I think the devil will not have me damn'd, lest the oil that's in me should set hell on fire; he would never else cross me thus.

Enter SIR HUGH EVANS *as a Satyr,* PISTOL *as Hobgoblin,* ANNE PAGE *as Fairy Queen, and others as fairies.*

ANNE PAGE
Fairies, black, grey, green, and white,
You moonshine revellers, and shades of night,
You orphan heirs of fixed destiny,
Attend your office and your quality. —
Crier Hobgoblin, make the fairy oyes.

PISTOL
Elves, list your names; silence, you airy toys.
Cricket, to Windsor chimneys shalt thou leap:
Where fires thou find'st unrak'd and hearths unswept,
There pinch the maids as blue as bilberry:
Our radiant queen hates sluts and sluttery.

FALSTAFF
They are fairies; he that speaks to them shall die:
I'll wink and couch: no man their works must eye.
[Lies down upon his face.

EVANS
Where's Pead? — Go you, and where you find a maid
That, ere she sleep, has thrice her prayers said,
Raise up the organs of her fantasy,
Sleep she as sound as careless infancy:
But those as sleep and think not on their sins,
Pinch them, arms, legs, backs, shoulders, sides, and shins.

ANNE PAGE
About, about;
Search Windsor Castle, elves, within and out:
Strew good luck, ouphs, on every sacred room;
That it may stand till the perpetual doom,
In site as wholesome as in state 'tis fit,
Worthy the owner, and the owner it.
The several chairs of order look you scour
With juice of balm and every precious flower:
Each fair instalment, coat, and several crest,

ANNE PAGE With trial-fire touch me his finger-end.

With loyal blazon, evermore be blest!
And nightly, meadow-fairies, look you sing,
Like to the Garter's compass, in a ring:
Th'expressure that it bears, green let it be,
More fertile-fresh than all the field to see;
And *Honi soit qui maly pense* write
In emerald tufts, flowers purple, blue, and white;
Like sapphire, pearl, and rich embroidery,
Buckled below fair knighthood's bending knee: —
Fairies use flowers for their charactery.
Away; disperse: but till 'tis one o'clock,
Our dance of custom round about the oak
Of Herne the hunter let us not forget.

EVANS
Pray you, lock hand in hand; yourselves in order set;
And twenty glow-worms shall our lanterns be,
To guide our measure round about the tree. —
But stay; I smell a man of middle-earth.

FALSTAFF
Heavens defend me from that Welsh fairy, lest he transform me to a piece of cheese!

PISTOL
Vile worm, thou wast o'erlook'd even in thy birth.

ANNE PAGE
With trial-fire touch me his finger-end:
If he be chaste, the flame will back descend,
And turn him to no pain; but if he start,
It is the flesh of a corrupted heart.

PISTOL
A trial, come.

EVANS
Come, will this wood take fire?
[They put the tapers to his fingers and he starts.

FALSTAFF
O, O, O!

ANNE PAGE
Corrupt, corrupt, and tainted in desire! —
About him, fairies; sing a scornful rhyme;
And, as you trip, still pinch him to your time.

EVANS
It is right; indeed he is full of lecheries and iniquity.

Song.
Fie on sinful fantasy!
Fie on lust and luxury!
Lust is but a bloody fire,
Kindled with unchaste desire,
Fed in heart; whose flames aspire,
As thoughts do blow them, higher and higher.
Pinch him, fairies, mutually;
Pinch him for his villainy;
Pinch him, and burn him, and turn him about,
Till candles and starlight and moonshine be out.

Here they pinch him and sing about him, and the DOCTOR *comes one way, and steals away a Boy in green;* SLENDER *another way, and takes off a Boy in white; and* FENTON *steals* ANNE PAGE. *A noise of hunting is made within. All the fairies run away.* FALSTAFF *pulls off his buck's head, and rises.*

Enter PAGE, FORD, MISTRESS PAGE, *and* MISTRESS FORD.

PAGE
Nay, do not fly; I think we have watch'd you now:
Will none but Herne the hunter serve your turn?

MISTRESS PAGE
I pray you, come, hold up the jest no higher. —
Now, good Sir John, how like you Windsor wives? —
See you these, husband? do not these fair yokes
Become the forest better than the town?

FORD
Now, sir, who's a cuckold now? — Master Brook, Falstaff's a knave, a cuckoldly knave; here are his horns, Master Brook: and, Master Brook, he hath enjoy'd nothing of Ford's but his buck-basket, his cudgel, and twenty pounds of money, which must be paid to Master Brook; his horses are arrested for it, Master Brook.

MISTRESS FORD
Sir John, we have had ill luck; we could never meet. I will never take you for my love again; but I will always count you my deer.

FALSTAFF
I do begin to perceive that I am made an ass.

FORD
Ay, and an ox too: both the proofs are extant.

FALSTAFF
And these are not fairies? I was three or four times in the thought they were not fairies: and yet the guiltiness of my mind, the sudden surprise of my powers, drove the grossness of the foppery into a received belief, in despite of the teeth of all rhyme and reason, that they were fairies. See now how wit may be made a Jack-a-Lent, when 'tis upon ill employment!

EVANS
Sir John Falstaff, serve Got, and leave your desires, and fairies will not pinse you.

FORD
Well said, fairy Hugh.

EVANS
And leave you your jealousies too, I pray you.

FORD
I will never mistrust my wife again, till thou art able to woo her in good English.

FALSTAFF
Have I laid my brain in the sun, and dried it, that it wants matter to prevent so gross o'er-reaching as this? Am I ridden with a Welsh goat too? shall I have a coxcomb of frize? 'Tis time I were choked with a piece of toasted cheese.

EVANS
Seese is not to give putter; your belly is all putter.

FALSTAFF
'Seese' and 'putter'! have I lived to stand at the taunt of one that makes fritters of English? This is enough to be the decay of lust and late-walking through the realm.

MISTRESS PAGE
Why, Sir John, do you think, though we would have thrust virtue out of our hearts by the head and shoulders, and have given ourselves without scruple to hell, that ever the devil could have made you our delight?

FORD
What, a hodge-pudding? a bag of flax?

MISTRESS PAGE
A puff'd man?

PAGE
Old, cold, wither'd, and of intolerable entrails?

FORD
And one that is as slanderous as Satan?

PAGE
And as poor as Job?

FORD
And as wicked as his wife?

EVANS
And given to fornications, and to taverns, and sack, and wine, and metheglins, and to drinkings, and swearings and starings, pribbles and prabbles?

FALSTAFF
Well, I am your theme: you have the start of me; I am dejected; I am not able to answer the Welsh flannel; ignorance itself is a plummet o'er me: use me as you will.

FORD
Marry, sir, we'll bring you to Windsor, to one Master Brook, that you have cozen'd of money, to whom you should have been a pandar: over and above that you have suffer'd, I think to repay that money will be a biting affliction.

MISTRESS FORD
Nay, husband, let that go to make amends; Forgive that sum, and so we'll all be friends.

FORD
Well, here is my hand; all's forgiven at last.

PAGE
Yet be cheerful, knight: thou shalt eat a posset to-night at my house; where I will desire thee to laugh at my wife, that now laughs at thee: tell her Master Slender hath married her daughter.

MISTRESS PAGE [aside].
Doctors doubt that: if Anne Page be my daughter, she is, by this, Doctor Caius' wife.

Enter SLENDER.

SLENDER
Whoa, ho! ho, father Page!

PAGE
Son, how now! how now, son! have you dispatch'd?

SLENDER
Dispatch'd! — I'll make the best in Glostershire know on't; would I were hang'd, la, else!

PAGE
Of what, son?

SLENDER
I came yonder at Eton to marry Mistress Anne Page, and she's a great lubberly boy. If it had not been i'th'church, I would have swinged him, or he should have swinged me. If I did not think it had been Anne Page, would I might never stir! — and 'tis a postmaster's boy.

PAGE
Upon my life, then, you took the wrong.

SLENDER
What need you tell me that? I think so, when I took a boy for a girl. If I had been married to him, for all he was in woman's apparel, I would not have had him.

PAGE
Why, this is your own folly. Did not I tell you how you should know my daughter by her garments?

SLENDER
I went to her in white, and cried 'mum,' and she cried 'budget,' as Anne and I had appointed; and yet it was not Anne, but a postmaster's boy.

EVANS
Jeshu, Master Slender! cannot you see but marry boys?

PAGE
O, I am vex'd at heart! what shall I do?

MISTRESS PAGE
Good George, be not angry: I knew of your purpose; turn'd my daughter into green; and, indeed, she is now with the doctor at the deanery, and there married.

Enter CAIUS.

CAIUS
Vere is Mistress Page? By gar, I am cozen'd: I ha' married *un garçon*, a boy; *un paysan*, by gar, a boy; it is not Anne Page: by gar, I am cozen'd.

MISTRESS PAGE
Why, did you take her in green?

CAIUS
Ay, by gar, and 'tis a boy: by gar, I'll raise all Windsor.
[*Exit.*

FORD
This is strange. Who hath got the right Anne?

PAGE
My heart misgives me: — here comes Master Fenton.

Enter FENTON *and* ANNE PAGE.
How now, Master Fenton!

ANNE PAGE
Pardon, good father! — good my mother, pardon!

PAGE
Now, mistress, — how chance you went not with Master Slender?

MISTRESS PAGE
Why went you not with master doctor, maid?

FENTON
You do amaze her: hear the truth of it.
You would have married her most shamefully,
Where there was no proportion held in love.
The truth is, she and I, long since contracted,
Are now so sure that nothing can dissolve us.
Th'offence is holy that she hath committed,
And this deceit loses the name of craft,
Of disobedience, or unduteous title,
Since therein she doth evitate and shun
A thousand irreligious cursed hours,
Which forced marriage would have brought upon her.

FORD
Stand not amaz'd: here is no remedy:
In love the heavens themselves do guide the state;
Money buys lands, and wives are sold by fate.

FALSTAFF
I am glad, though you have ta'en a special stand to strike at me, that your arrow hath glanced.

PAGE
Well, what remedy? — Fenton, heaven give thee joy!
What cannot be eschew'd must be embrac'd.

FALSTAFF
When night-dogs run, all sorts of deer are chas'd.

EVANS
I will also dance and eat plums at your weddings.

MISTRESS PAGE
Well, I will muse no further. — Master Fenton,
Heaven give you many, many merry days! —
Good husband, let us every one go home,
And laugh this sport o'er by a country fire;
Sir John and all.

FORD
Let it be so. — Sir John,
To Master Brook you yet shall hold your word;
For he to-night shall lie with Mistress Ford. [*Exeunt.*

JULIUS CAESAR

DRAMATIS PERSONAE

JULIUS CAESAR.
OCTAVIUS CAESAR, } *triumvirs after the death*
MARCUS ANTONIUS, } *of Julius Cæsar.*
M. AEMILIUS LEPIDUS, }
CICERO, }
PUBLIUS, } *senators.*
POPILIUS LENA, }
MARCUS BRUTUS, }
CASSIUS, }
CASCA, } *conspirators against*
TREBONIUS, } *Julius Cæsar.*
LIGARIUS, }
DECIUS BRUTUS, }
METELLUS CIMBER, }

CINNA, *conspirator against Julius Cæsar.*
FLAVIUS *and* MARULLUS, *tribunes.*
ARTEMIDORUS, *a sophist of Cnidos.*
A SOOTHSAYER.
CINNA, *a poet.*
ANOTHER POET.
LUCILIUS, }
TITINIUS, }
MESSALA, } *friends to Brutus and Cassius.*
YOUNG CATO, }
VOLUMNIUS, }
VARRO, }
CLITUS, } *servants to Brutus.*
CLAUDIUS, }

STRATO, }
LUCIUS, } *servants to Brutus.*
DARDANIUS, }
PINDARUS, *servant to Cassius.*

CALPHURNIA, *wife to Cæsar.*
PORTIA, *wife to* BRUTUS.

SENATORS, CITIZENS, GUARDS, ATTENDANTS, *etc.*

SCENE — *During a great part of the play at Rome;*
afterwards near Sardis, and near Philippi.

ACT I

SCENE I

Rome. A street.

Enter FLAVIUS, MARULLUS, *and certain*
COMMONERS *over the stage.*

FLAVIUS
Hence! home, you idle creatures, get you home:
Is this a holiday? what! know you not,
Being mechanical, you ought not walk
Upon a labouring day without the sign
Of your profession? — Speak, what trade art thou?

FIRST CITIZEN
Why, sir, a carpenter.

MARULLUS
Where is thy leather apron and thy rule?
What dost thou with thy best apparel on? —
You, sir, what trade are you?

SECOND CITIZEN
Truly, sir, in respect of a fine workman, I am but, as
you would say, a cobbler.

MARULLUS
But what trade art thou? answer me directly.

SECOND CITIZEN
A trade, sir, that I hope I may use with a safe conscience;
which is, indeed, sir, a mender of bad soles.

MARULLUS
What trade, thou knave? thou naughty knave, what
trade?

SECOND CITIZEN
Nay, I beseech you, sir, be not out with me: yet if you be
out, sir, I can mend you.

MARULLUS
What meanest thou by that? mend me, thou saucy
fellow!

SECOND CITIZEN
Why, sir, cobble you.

FLAVIUS
Thou art a cobbler, art thou?

SECOND CITIZEN
Truly, sir, all that I live by is with the awl: I meddle with
no tradesman's matters, nor women's matters, but
with awl. I am, indeed, sir, a surgeon to old shoes;
when they are in great danger, I recover them. As
proper men as ever trod upon neats-leather have gone
upon my handiwork.

FLAVIUS
But wherefore art not in thy shop to-day?
Why dost thou lead these men about the streets?

SECOND CITIZEN
Truly, sir, to wear out their shoes, to get myself into
more work. But, indeed, sir, we make holiday, to see
Cæsar, and to rejoice in his triumph.

MARULLUS
Wherefore rejoice? What conquest brings he home?
What tributaries follow him to Rome,
To grace in captive bonds his chariot-wheels?
You blocks, you stones, you worse than senseless
    things!
O you hard hearts, you cruel men of Rome,
Knew you not Pompey? Many a time and oft
Have you climb'd up to walls and battlements,
To towers and windows, yea, to chimney-tops,
Your infants in your arms, and there have sat
The live-long day, with patient expectation,
To see great Pompey pass the streets of Rome:
And when you saw his chariot but appear,
Have you not made an universal shout,
That Tiber trembled underneath her banks,
To hear the replication of your sounds
Made in her concave shores?
And do you now put on your best attire?
And do you now cull out a holiday?
And do you now strew flowers in his way
That comes in triumph over Pompey's blood?
Be gone!

Run to your houses, fall upon your knees,
Pray to the gods to intermit the plague
That needs must light on this ingratitude.
FLAVIUS
Go, go, good countrymen, and, for this fault,
Assemble all the poor men of your sort;
Draw them to Tiber banks, and weep your tears
Into the channel, till the lowest stream
Do kiss the most exalted shores of all.
                    [*Exeunt all the* COMMONERS.
See, whe'r their basest metal be not mov'd!
They vanish tongue-tied in their guiltiness.
Go you down that way towards the Capitol;
This way will I: disrobe the images,
If you do find them deck'd with ceremonies.
MARULLUS
May we do so?
You know it is the feast of Lupercal.
FLAVIUS
It is no matter; let no images
Be hung with Cæsar's trophies. I'll about,
And drive away the vulgar from the streets:
So do you too, where you perceive them thick.
These growing feathers pluck'd from Cæsar's wing
Will make him fly an ordinary pitch;
Who else would soar above the view of men,
And keep us all in servile fearfulness.   [*Exeunt.*

SCENE II

The same. A public place.

Enter CAESAR; ANTONY, *for the course;*
CALPHURNIA, PORTIA, DECIUS, CICERO,
BRUTUS, CASSIUS, *and* ASCA; *a great crowd*
following, among them a SOOTHSAYER.

CAESAR
Calphurnia, —
CASCA
Peace, ho! Cæsar speaks.   [*Music ceases.*
CAESAR
                    Calphurnia, —
CALPHURNIA
Here, my lord.
CAESAR
Stand you directly in Antonius' way,
When he doth run his course. — Antonius, —
ANTONY
Cæsar, my lord?
CAESAR
Forget not, in your speed, Antonius,
To touch Calphurnia; for our elders say,
The barren, touched in this holy chase,
Shake off their sterile curse.
ANTONY
                    I shall remember:
When Cæsar says 'Do this,' it is perform'd.
CAESAR
Set on; and leave no ceremony out.   [*Music.*
SOOTHSAYER
Cæsar!
CAESAR
Ha! who calls?
CASCA
Bid every noise be still: — peace yet again!
                    [*Music ceases.*
CAESAR
Who is it in the press that calls on me?
I hear a tongue, shriller than all the music,
Cry 'Cæsar.' Speak; Cæsar is turn'd to hear.
SOOTHSAYER
Beware the ides of March.
CAESAR
                    What man is that?
BRUTUS
A soothsayer bids you beware the ides of March.
CAESAR
Set him before me; let me see his face.
CASSIUS
Fellow, come from the throng; look upon Cæsar.
CAESAR
What say'st thou to me now? speak once again.
SOOTHSAYER
Beware the ides of March.
CAESAR
He is a dreamer; let us leave him: — pass.
          [*Sennet. Exeunt all but* BRUTUS *and* CASSIUS.
CASSIUS
Will you go see the order of the course?

BRUTUS
Not I.
CASSIUS
I pray you, do.
BRUTUS
I am not gamesome: I do lack some part
Of that quick spirit that is in Antony.
Let me not hinder, Cassius, your desires;
I'll leave you.
CASSIUS
Brutus, I do observe you now of late:
I have not from your eyes that gentleness
And show of love as I was wont to have:
You bear too stubborn and too strange a hand
Over your friend that loves you.
BRUTUS
                    Cassius,
Be not deceived: if I have veil'd my look,
I turn the trouble of my countenance
Merely upon myself. Vexed I am,
Of late, with passions of some difference,
Conceptions only proper to myself,
Which give some soil, perhaps, to my behaviours;
But let not therefore my good friends be griev'd, —
Among which number, Cassius, be you one, —
Nor construe any further my neglect,
Than that poor Brutus, with himself at war,
Forgets the shows of love to other men.
CASSIUS
Then, Brutus, I have much mistook your passion;
By means whereof this breast of mine hath buried
Thoughts of great value, worthy cogitations.
Tell me, good Brutus, can you see your face?
BRUTUS
No, Cassius; for the eye sees not itself
But by reflection from some other thing.
CASSIUS
'Tis just:
And it is very much lamented, Brutus,
That you have no such mirrors as will turn
Your hidden worthiness into your eye,
That you might see your shadow. I have heard,
Where many of the best respect in Rome, —
Except immortal Cæsar, — speaking of Brutus,
And groaning underneath this age's yoke,
Have wish'd that noble Brutus had his eyes.
BRUTUS
Into what dangers would you lead me, Cassius,
That you would have me seek into myself
For that which is not in me?
CASSIUS
Therefore, good Brutus, be prepared to hear:
And, since you know you cannot see yourself
So well as by reflection, I, your glass,
Will modestly discover to yourself
That of yourself which you yet know not of.
And be not jealous on me, gentle Brutus:
Were I a common laughter, or did use
To stale with ordinary oaths my love
To every new protester; if you know
That I do fawn on men, and hug them hard,
And after scandal them; or if you know
That I profess myself in banqueting
To all the rout, then hold me dangerous.
                    [*Flourish and shout.*
BRUTUS
What means this shouting? I do fear, the people
Choose Cæsar for their king.
CASSIUS
                    Ay, do you fear it?
Then must I think you would not have it so.
BRUTUS
I would not, Cassius; yet I love him well. —
But wherefore do you hold me here so long?
What is it that you would impart to me?
If it be aught toward the general good,
Set honour in one eye, and death i'th'other,
And I will look on both indifferently;
For, let the gods so speed me as I love
The name of honour more than I fear death.
CASSIUS
I know that virtue to be in you, Brutus,
As well as I do know your outward favour.
Well, honour is the subject of my story. —
I cannot tell what you and other men
Think of this life; but, for my single self,
I had as lief not be as live to be
In awe of such a thing as I myself.
I was born free as Cæsar; so were you:
We both have fed as well; and we can both

Endure the winter's cold as well as he:
For once, upon a raw and gusty day,
The troubled Tiber chafing with her shores,
Cæsar said to me, 'Darest thou, Cassius, now
Leap in with me into this angry flood,
And swim to yonder point?' Upon the word,
Accoutred as I was, I plunged in,
And bade him follow: so, indeed, he did.
The torrent roar'd; and we did buffet it
With lusty sinews, throwing it aside
And stemming it with hearts of controversy:
But ere we could arrive the point proposed,
Cæsar cried, 'Help me, Cassius, or I sink!'
I, as Aeneas, our great ancestor,
Did from the flames of Troy upon his shoulder
The old Anchises bear, so from the waves of Tiber
Did I the tired Cæsar: and this man
Is now become a god; and Cassius is
A wretched creature, and must bend his body,
If Cæsar carelessly but nod on him.
He had a fever when he was in Spain,
And, when the fit was on him, I did mark
How he did shake: 'tis true, this god did shake:
His coward lips did from their colour fly;
And that same eye, whose bend doth awe the world,
Did lose his lustre: I did hear him groan:
Ay, and that tongue of his, that bade the Romans
Mark him, and write his speeches in their books,
Alas, it cried, 'Give me some drink, Titinius,'
As a sick girl. Ye gods, it doth amaze me,
A man of such a feeble temper should
So get the start of the majestic world,
And bear the palm alone.   [*Flourish and shout.*
BRUTUS
Another general shout!
I do believe that these applauses are
For some new honours that are heap'd on Cæsar.
CASSIUS
Why, man, he doth bestride the narrow world
Like a Colossus; and we petty men
Walk under his huge legs, and peep about
To find ourselves dishonourable graves.
Men at some time are masters of their fates:
The fault, dear Brutus, is not in our stars,
But in ourselves, that we are underlings.
Brutus, and Cæsar: what should be in that Cæsar?
Why should that name be sounded more than yours?
Write them together, yours is as fair a name;
Sound them, it doth become the mouth as well;
Weigh them, it is as heavy; conjure with 'em,
Brutus will start a spirit as soon as Cæsar.
Now, in the names of all the gods at once,
Upon what meat doth this our Cæsar feed,
That he is grown so great? Age, thou art shamed!
Rome, thou hast lost the breed of noble bloods!
When went there by an age, since the great flood,
But it was fam'd with more than with one man?
When could they say, till now, that talk'd of Rome,
That her wide walls encompass'd but one man?
Now is it Rome indeed, and room enough,
When there is in it but one only man.
O, you and I have heard our fathers say,
There was a Brutus once that would have brook'd
Th'eternal devil to keep his state in Rome
As easily as a king.
BRUTUS
That you do love me, I am nothing jealous;
What you would work me to, I have some aim:
How I have thought of this, and of these times,
I shall recount hereafter; for this present,
I would not, so with love I might entreat you,
Be any further mov'd. What you have said,
I will consider; what you have to say,
I will with patience hear; and find a time
Both meet to hear and answer such high things.
Till then, my noble friend, chew upon this;
Brutus had rather be a villager
Than to repute himself a son of Rome
Under these hard conditions as this time
Is like to lay upon us.
CASSIUS
                    I am glad
That my weak words have struck but this much show
Of fire from Brutus.
BRUTUS
The games are done, and Cæsar is returning.
CASSIUS
As they pass by, pluck Casca by the sleeve;
And he will, after his sour fashion, tell you
What hath proceeded worthy note to-day.

Enter CAESAR *and his* TRAIN.

BRUTUS
I will do so: — but, look you, Cassius,
The angry spot doth glow on Cæsar's brow,
And all the rest look like a chidden train:
Calphurnia's cheek is pale; and Cicero
Looks with such ferret and such fiery eyes
As we have seen him in the Capitol,
Being cross'd in conference by some senator.

CASSIUS
Casca will tell us what the matter is.

CAESAR
Antonius, —

ANTONY
Cæsar?

CAESAR
Let me have men about me that are fat;
Sleek-headed men, and such as sleep o' nights:
Yond Cassius has a lean and hungry look;
He thinks too much: such men are dangerous.

ANTONY
Fear him not, Cæsar; he's not dangerous;
He is a noble Roman, and well given.

CAESAR
Would he were fatter! — but I fear him not;
Yet if my name were liable to fear,
I do not know the man I should avoid
So soon as that spare Cassius. He reads much;
He is a great observer, and he looks
Quite through the deeds of men: he loves no plays,
As thou dost, Antony; he hears no music;
Seldom he smiles; and smiles in such a sort
As if he mock'd himself, and scorn'd his spirit
That could be mov'd to smile at any thing.
Such men as he be never at heart's ease
Whiles they behold a greater than themselves;
And therefore are they very dangerous.
I rather tell thee what is to be fear'd
Than what I fear, — for always I am Cæsar.
Come on my right hand, for this ear is deaf,
And tell me truly what thou think'st of him.
[*Exeunt* CAESAR *and all his* TRAIN *but* CASCA.

CASCA
You pull'd me by the cloak; would you speak with me?

BRUTUS
Ay, Casca; tell us what hath chanc'd to-day,
That Cæsar looks so sad.

CASCA
Why, you were with him, were you not?

BRUTUS
I should not, then, ask Casca what had chanc'd.

CASCA
Why, there was a crown offer'd him; and being offer'd
him, he put it by with the back of his hand, thus; and
then the people fell a-shouting.

BRUTUS
What was the second noise for?

CASCA
Why, for that too.

CASSIUS
They shouted thrice: what was the last cry for?

CASCA
Why, for that too.

BRUTUS
Was the crown offer'd him thrice?

CASCA
Ay, marry, was't, and he put it by thrice, every time
gentler than other; and at every putting-by mine honest
neighbours shouted.

CASSIUS
Who offer'd him the crown?

CASCA
Why, Antony.

BRUTUS
Tell us the manner of it, gentle Casca.

CASCA
I can as well be hang'd as tell the manner of it: it was
mere foolery; I did not mark it. I saw Mark Antony offer
him a crown; — yet 'twas not a crown neither, 'twas one
of these coronets; — and, as I told you, he put it by
once: but, for all that, to my thinking, he would fain
have had it. Then he offer'd it to him again; then he put
it by again: but, to my thinking, he was very loth to lay
his fingers off it. And then he offer'd it the third time;
he put it the third time by; and still as he refused it, the
rabblement shouted, and clapp'd their chopp'd hands,
and threw up their sweaty nightcaps, and utter'd such a
deal of stinking breath because Cæsar refused the
crown, that it had almost choked Cæsar; for he

CASCA You pull'd me by the cloak; would you speak with me?

swounded, and fell down at it: and for my own part, I
durst not laugh, for fear of opening my lips and
receiving the bad air.

CASSIUS
But, soft, I pray you: what, did Cæsar swound?

CASCA
He fell down in the market-place, and foam'd at mouth,
and was speechless.

BRUTUS
'Tis very like he hath the falling-sickness.

CASSIUS
No, Cæsar hath it not: but you, and I,
And honest Casca, we have the falling-sickness.

CASCA
I know not what you mean by that; but, I am sure,
Cæsar fell down. If the tag-rag people did not clap him
and hiss him, according as he pleased and displeased
them, as they use to do the players in the theatre, I am
no true man.

BRUTUS
What said he when he came unto himself?

CASCA
Marry, before he fell down, when he perceived the
common herd was glad he refused the crown, he
pluck'd me ope his doublet, and offer'd them his throat
to cut: — an I had been a man of any occupation, if I
would not have taken him at a word, I would I might go
to hell among the rogues: — and so he fell. When he
came to himself again, he said, if he had done or said
any thing amiss, he desired their worships to think it
was his infirmity. Three or four wenches, where I
stood, cried, 'Alas, good soul!' and forgave him with all
their hearts: but there's no heed to be taken of them; if
Cæsar had stabb'd their mothers, they would have
done no less.

BRUTUS
And after that, he came, thus sad, away?

CASCA
Ay.

CASSIUS
Did Cicero say any thing?

CASCA
Ay, he spoke Greek.

CASSIUS
To what effect?

CASCA
Nay, an I tell you that, I'll ne'er look you i'th'face again:
but those that understood him smiled at one another,
and shook their heads; but, for mine own part, it was
Greek to me. I could tell you more news too: Marullus
and Flavius, for pulling scarfs off Cæsar's images, are
put to silence. Fare you well. There was more foolery
yet, if I could remember it.

CASSIUS
Will you sup with me to-night, Casca?

CASCA
No, I am promised forth.

CASSIUS
Will you dine with me to-morrow?

CASCA
Ay, if I be alive, and your mind hold, and your dinner
worth the eating.

CASSIUS
Good; I will expect you.

CASCA
Do so: farewell, both. [*Exit.*

BRUTUS
What a blunt fellow is this grown to be!
He was quick mettle when he went to school.

CASSIUS
So is he now, in execution
Of any bold or noble enterprise,
However he puts on this tardy form.
This rudeness is a sauce to his good wit,
Which gives men stomach to digest his words
With better appetite.

BRUTUS
And so it is. For this time I will leave you:
To-morrow, if you please to speak with me,
I will come home to you; or, if you will,
Come home to me, and I will wait for you.

CASSIUS
I will do so: — till then, think of the world.
[*Exit* BRUTUS.

Well, Brutus, thou art noble; yet, I see,
Thy honourable mettle may be wrought
From that it is dispos'd: therefore 'tis meet
That noble minds keep ever with their likes;
For who so firm that cannot be seduced?
Cæsar doth bear me hard; but he loves Brutus:
If I were Brutus now, and he were Cassius,
He should not humour me. I will this night,
In several hands, in at his windows throw,
As if they came from several citizens,
Writings, all tending to the great opinion
That Rome holds of his name; wherein obscurely
Cæsar's ambition shall be glanced at:
And, after this, let Cæsar seat him sure;
For we will shake him, or worse days endure. [*Exit.*

SCENE III

The same. A street.

Thunder and lightning. Enter, from opposite sides,
CASCA, *with his sword drawn, and* CICERO.

CICERO
Good even, Casca: brought you Cæsar home?
Why are you breathless? and why stare you so?

CASCA
Are not you mov'd, when all the sway of earth
Shakes like a thing unfirm? O Cicero,
I have seen tempests, when the scolding winds
Have riv'd the knotty oaks; and I have seen
Th'ambitious ocean swell and rage and foam,
To be exalted with the threat'ning clouds:
But never till to-night, never till now,
Did I go through a tempest dropping fire.
Either there is a civil strife in heaven,
Or else the world, too saucy with the gods,
Incenses them to send destruction.

CICERO
Why, saw you any thing more wonderful?
CASCA
A common slave — you know him well by sight —
Held up his left hand, which did flame and burn
Like twenty torches join'd; and yet his hand,
Not sensible of fire, remain'd unscorch'd.
Besides, — I ha' not since put up my sword, —
Against the Capitol I met a lion,
Who glared upon me, and went surly by,
Without annoying me: and there were drawn
Upon a heap a hundred ghastly women,
Transformed with their fear; who swore they saw
Men, all in fire, walk up and down the streets.
And yesterday the bird of night did sit
Even at noonday upon the market-place,
Hooting and shrieking. When these prodigies
Do so conjointly meet, let not men say,
'These are their reasons, — they are natural';
For, I believe, they are portentous things
Unto the climate that they point upon.
CICERO
Indeed, it is a strange-disposed time:
But men may construe things after their fashion,
Clean from the purpose of the things themselves.
Comes Cæsar to the Capitol to-morrow?
CASCA
He doth: for he did bid Antonius
Send word to you he would be there to-morrow.
CICERO
Good night, then, Casca: this disturbed sky
Is not to walk in.
CASCA
　　　　　Farewell, Cicero.　　[Exit CICERO.
　　　　　Enter CASSIUS.

CASSIUS
Who's there?
CASCA
　　　　　A Roman.
CASSIUS
　　　　　　　Casca, by your voice.
CASCA
Your ear is good. Cassius, what night is this!
CASSIUS
A very pleasing night to honest men.
CASCA
Who ever knew the heavens menace so?
CASSIUS
Those that have known the earth so full of faults.
For my part, I have walk'd about the streets,
Submitting me unto the perilous night;
And, thus unbraced, Casca, as you see,
Have bared my bosom to the thunder-stone:
And when the cross blue lightning seem'd to open
The breast of heaven, I did present myself
Even in the aim and very flash of it.
CASCA
But wherefore did you so much tempt the heavens?
It is the part of men to fear and tremble,
When the most mighty gods by tokens send
Such dreadful heralds to astonish us.
CASSIUS
You are dull, Casca; and those sparks of life
That should be in a Roman you do want,
Or else you use not. You look pale, and gaze,
And put on fear, and cast yourself in wonder,
To see the strange impatience of the heavens:
But if you would consider the true cause
Why all these fires, why all these gliding ghosts,
Why birds and beasts from quality and kind —
Why old men, fools, and children calculate;
Why all these things change from their ordinance,
Their natures, and pre-formed faculties,
To monstrous quality; — why, you shall find
That heaven hath infus'd them with these spirits,
To make them instruments of fear and warning
Unto some monstrous state.
Now could I, Casca, name to thee a man
Most like this dreadful night,
That thunders, lightens, opens graves, and roars
As doth the lion in the Capitol, —
A man no mightier than thyself or me
In personal action; yet prodigious grown,
And fearful, as these strange eruptions are.
CASCA
'Tis Cæsar that you mean; is it not, Cassius?
CASSIUS
Let it be who it is; for Romans now
Have thews and limbs like to their ancestors;

But, woe the while! our fathers' minds are dead,
And we are govern'd with our mothers' spirits;
Our yoke and sufferance show us womanish.
CASCA
Indeed, they say the senators to-morrow
Mean to establish Cæsar as a king;
And he shall wear his crown by sea and land,
In every place, save here in Italy.
CASSIUS
I know where I will wear this dagger, then;
Cassius from bondage will deliver Cassius:
Therein, ye gods, you make the weak most strong;
Therein, ye gods, you tyrants do defeat:
Nor stony tower, nor walls of beaten brass,
Nor airless dungeon, nor strong links of iron,
Can be retentive to the strength of spirit;
But life, being weary of these worldly bars,
Never lacks power to dismiss itself.
If I know this, know all the world besides,
That part of tyranny that I do bear
I can shake off at pleasure.　　　[Thunder still.
CASCA
　　　　　　　So can I:
So every bondman in his own hand bears
The power to cancel his captivity.
CASSIUS
And why should Cæsar be a tyrant, then?
Poor man! I know he would not be a wolf,
But that he sees the Romans are but sheep:
He were no lion, were not Romans hinds.
Those that with haste will make a mighty fire
Begin it with weak straws: what trash is Rome,
What rubbish, and what offal, when it serves
For the base matter to illuminate
So vile a thing as Cæsar! But, O grief,
Where hast thou led me? I perhaps speak this
Before a willing bondman: then I know
My answer must be made; but I am arm'd,
And dangers are to me indifferent.
CASCA
You speak to Casca; and to such a man
That is no fleering tell-tale. Hold, my hand:
Be factious for redress of all these griefs;
And I will set this foot of mine as far
As who goes farthest.
CASSIUS
　　　　　There's a bargain made.
Now know you, Casca, I have mov'd already
Some certain of the noblest-minded Romans
To undergo with me an enterprise
Of honourable-dangerous consequence;
And I do know, by this, they stay for me
In Pompey's porch: for now, this fearful night,
There is no stir or walking in the streets;
And the complexion of the element
In's favour's like the work we have in hand,
Most bloody, fiery and most terrible.
CASCA
Stand close awhile, for here comes one in haste.
CASSIUS
'Tis Cinna, — I do know him by his gait;
He is a friend.
　　　　　Enter CINNA.
　　　　Cinna, where haste you so?
CINNA
To find out you. Who's that? Metellus Cimber?
CASSIUS
No, it is Casca; one incorporate
To our attempts. Am I not stay'd for, Cinna?
CINNA
I am glad on't. What a fearful night is this!
There's two or three of us have seen strange sights.
CASSIUS
Am I not stay'd for? tell me.
CINNA
　　　　　Yes, you are. —
O Cassius, if you could
But win the noble Brutus to our party —
CASSIUS
Be you content: good Cinna, take this paper,
And look you lay it in the prætor's chair,
Where Brutus may but find it; and throw this
In at his window; set this up with wax
Upon old Brutus' statue: all this done,
Repair to Pompey's porch, where you shall find us.
Is Decius Brutus and Trebonius there?
CINNA
All but Metellus Cimber; and he's gone
To seek you at your house. Well, I will hie,
And so bestow these papers as you bade me.

CASSIUS
That done, repair to Pompey's theatre.　[Exit CINNA.
Come, Casca, you and I will yet, ere day,
See Brutus at his house: three parts of him
Is ours already; and the man entire,
Upon the next encounter, yields him ours.
CASCA
O, he sits high in all the people's hearts:
And that which would appear offence in us,
His countenance, like richest alchemy,
Will change to virtue and to worthiness.
CASSIUS
Him, and his worth, and our great need of him,
You have right well conceited. Let us go,
For it is after midnight; and, ere day,
We will awake him, and be sure of him.　　[Exeunt

ACT II

SCENE I

Rome. BRUTUS' orchard.

Enter BRUTUS.

BRUTUS
What, Lucius, ho! —
I cannot, by the progress of the stars,
Give guess how near to day. — Lucius, I say! —
I would it were my fault to sleep so soundly. —
When, Lucius, when? awake, I say! what, Lucius!
　　　　　Enter LUCIUS.
LUCIUS
Call'd you, my lord?
BRUTUS
Get me a taper in my study, Lucius:
When it is lighted, come and call me here.
LUCIUS
I will, my lord.　　　　　　　　　[Exit.
BRUTUS
It must be by his death: and, for my part,
I know no personal cause to spurn at him,
But for the general. He would be crown'd: —
How that might change his nature, there's the
　　question:
It is the bright day that brings forth the adder;
And that craves wary walking. Crown him? — that; —
And then, I grant, we put a sting in him,
That at his will he may do danger with.
Th'abuse of greatness is, when it disjoins
Remorse from power: and, to speak truth of Cæsar,
I have not known when his affections sway'd
More than his reason. But 'tis a common proof,
That lowliness is young ambition's ladder,
Whereto the climber-upward turns his face;
But when he once attains the upmost round,
He then unto the ladder turns his back,

Looks in the clouds, scorning the base degrees
By which he did ascend: so Cæsar may;
Then, lest he may, prevent. And, since the quarrel
Will bear no colour for the thing he is,
Fashion it thus: that what he is, augmented,
Would run to these and these extremities:
And therefore think him as a serpent's egg,
Which, hatch'd, would, as his kind, grow mischievous;
And kill him in the shell.

Enter LUCIUS.

LUCIUS
The taper burneth in your closet, sir.
Searching the window for a flint, I found
        [Gives him the letter.
This paper, thus seal'd up; and, I am sure,
It did not lie there when I went to bed.

BRUTUS
Get you to bed again; it is not day.
Is not to-morrow, boy, the ides of March?

LUCIUS
I know not, sir.

BRUTUS
Look in the calendar, and bring me word.

LUCIUS
I will, sir.   *[Exit.*

BRUTUS
The exhalations, whizzing in the air,
Give so much light, that I may read by them.
      [Opens the letter and reads.
'Brutus, thou sleep'st; awake, and see thyself.
Shall Rome, etc. Speak, strike, redress!' —
'Brutus, thou sleep'st: awake!' —
Such instigations have been often dropp'd
Where I have took them up.
'Shall Rome, etc.' Thus must I piece it out;
Shall Rome stand under one man's awe? What, Rome?
My ancestors did from the streets of Rome
The Tarquin drive, when he was call'd a king.
'Speak, strike, redress!' — Am I entreated
To speak and strike? O Rome, I make thee promise,
If the redress will follow, thou receivest
Thy full petition at the hand of Brutus!

Enter LUCIUS.

LUCIUS
Sir, March is wasted fifteen days.   *[Knock within.*

BRUTUS
'Tis good. Go to the gate; somebody knocks,
      [Exit LUCIUS.
Since Cassius first did whet me against Cæsar,
I have not slept.
Between the acting of a dreadful thing
And the first motion, all the interim is
Like a phantasma or a hideous dream:
The Genius and the mortal instruments
Are then in council; and the state of man,
Like to a little kingdom, suffers then
The nature of an insurrection.

Enter LUCIUS.

LUCIUS
Sir, 'tis your brother Cassius at the door,
Who doth desire to see you.

BRUTUS
        Is he alone?

LUCIUS
No, sir, there are more with him.

BRUTUS
        Do you know them?

LUCIUS
No, sir; their hats are pluck'd about their ears,
And half their faces buried in their cloaks,
That by no means I may discover them
By any mark of favour.

BRUTUS
        Let 'em enter.
      [Exit LUCIUS.
They are the faction. O conspiracy,
Shamest thou to show thy dangerous brow by night,
When evils are most free? O, then, by day
Where wilt thou find a cavern dark enough
To mask thy monstrous visage? Seek none, conspiracy;
Hide it in smiles and affability:
For if thou put thy native semblance on,
Not Erebus itself were dim enough
To hide thee from prevention.

Enter the Conspirators, CASSIUS, CASCA, DECIUS,
   CINNA, METELLUS CIMBER, *and* TREBONIUS.

CASSIUS
I think we are too bold upon your rest:

Good morrow, Brutus; do we
  trouble you?

BRUTUS
I have been up this hour; awake all
  night.
Know I these men that come along
  with you?

CASSIUS
Yes, every man of them; and no
  man here
But honours you; and every one
  doth wish
You had but that opinion of yourself
Which every noble Roman bears of
  you. —
This is Trebonius.

BRUTUS
      He is welcome hither.

CASSIUS
This, Decius Brutus.

BRUTUS
      He is welcome too.

CASSIUS
This, Casca; this, Cinna; and this,
  Metellus Cimber.

BRUTUS
They are all welcome. —
What watchful cares do interpose
  themselves
Betwixt your eyes and night?

CASSIUS
Shall I entreat a word? *[They whisper.*

DECIUS
Here lies the east: doth not the day
  break here?

CASCA
No.

CINNA
O, pardon, sir, it doth; and yon grey
  lines
That fret the clouds are messengers
  of day.

CASCA
You shall confess that you are both
  deceived.
Here, as I point my sword, the sun
  arises;
Which is a great way growing on the
  south,
Weighing the youthful season of the year.
Some two months hence, up higher toward the north
He first presents his fire; and the high east
Stands, as the Capitol, directly here.

BRUTUS
Give me your hands all over, one by one.

CASSIUS
And let us swear our resolution.

BRUTUS
No, not an oath: if not the face of men,
The sufferance of our souls, the time's abuse, —
If these be motives weak, break off betimes,
And every man hence to his idle bed;
So let high-sighted tyranny range on,
Till each man drop by lottery. But if these,
As I am sure they do, bear fire enough
To kindle cowards, and to steel with valour
The melting spirits of women; then, countrymen,
What need we any spur, but our own cause,
To prick us to redress? what other bond
Than secret Romans, that have spoke the word,
And will not palter? and what other oath
Than honesty to honesty engaged,
That this shall be, or we will fall for it?
Swear priests, and cowards, and men cautelous,
Old feeble carrions, and such suffering souls
That welcome wrongs; unto bad causes swear
Such creatures as men doubt: but do not stain
The even virtue of our enterprise,
Nor th'insuppressive mettle of our spirits,
To think that or our cause or our performance
Did need an oath; when every drop of blood
That every Roman bears, and nobly bears,
Is guilty of a several bastardy,
If he do break the smallest particle
Of any promise that hath pass'd from him.

CASSIUS
But what of Cicero? shall we sound him?
I think he will stand very strong with us.

CASCA
Let us not leave him out.

CINNA
      No, by no means.

METELLUS
O, let us have him; for his silver hairs
Will purchase us a good opinion,
And buy men's voices to commend our deeds:
It shall be said, his judgement rul'd our hands;
Our youths and wildness shall no whit appear,
But all be buried in his gravity.

BRUTUS
O, name him not: let us not break with him;
For he will never follow any thing
That other men begin.

CASSIUS
      Then leave him out.

CASCA
Indeed he is not fit.

DECIUS
Shall no man else be touch'd but only Cæsar?

CASSIUS
Decius, well urg'd: — I think it is not meet,
Mark Antony, so well belov'd of Cæsar,
Should outlive Cæsar: we shall find of him
A shrewd contriver; and, you know, his means,
If he improve them, may well stretch so far
As to annoy us all: which to prevent,
Let Antony and Cæsar fall together.

BRUTUS
Our course will seem too bloody, Caius Cassius,
To cut the head off, and then hack the limbs, —
Like wrath in death, and envy afterwards;
For Antony is but a limb of Cæsar:
Let's be sacrificers, but not butchers, Caius.
We all stand up against the spirit of Cæsar;
And in the spirit of men there is no blood:
O, that we, then, could come by Cæsar's spirit,
And not dismember Cæsar! But, alas,
Cæsar must bleed for it! And, gentle friends,
Let's kill him boldly, but not wrathfully;
Let's carve him as a dish fit for the gods,
Not hew him as a carcass fit for hounds:
And let our hearts, as subtle masters do,

PORTIA Tell me your counsels; I will not disclose 'em.

Stir up their servants to an act of rage,
And after seem to chide 'em. This shall make
Our purpose necessary, and not envious:
Which so appearing to the common eyes,
We shall be call'd purgers, not murderers.
And for Mark Antony, think not of him;
For he can do no more than Cæsar's arm
When Cæsar's head is off.

CASSIUS
                    Yet I fear him;
For in the ingrafted love he bears to Cæsar —

BRUTUS
Alas, good Cassius, do not think of him:
If he love Cæsar, all that he can do
Is to himself, — take thought, and die for Cæsar:
And that were much he should; for he is given
To sports, to wildness, and much company.

TREBONIUS
There is no fear in him; let him not die;
For he will live, and laugh at this hereafter.
                                        [*Clock strikes.*

BRUTUS
Peace! count the clock.

CASSIUS
                    The clock hath stricken three.

TREBONIUS
'Tis time to part.

CASSIUS
                    But it is doubtful yet,
Whether Cæsar will come forth to-day or no;
For he is superstitious grown of late;
Quite from the main opinion he held once
Of fantasy, of dreams, and ceremonies:
It may be, these apparent prodigies,
The unaccustom'd terror of this night,
And the persuasion of his augurers,
May hold him from the Capitol to-day.

DECIUS
Never fear that: if he be so resolved,
I can o'ersway him; for he loves to hear
That unicorns may be betray'd with trees,
And bears with glasses, elephants with holes,
Lions with toils, and men with flatterers:
But when I tell him he hates flatterers,
He says he does, — being then most flattered.
Let me work;
For I can give his humour the true bent,
And I will bring him to the Capitol.

CASSIUS
Nay, we will all of us be there to fetch him.

BRUTUS
By the eighth hour: is that the uttermost?

CINNA
Be that the uttermost, and fail not then.

METELLUS
Caius Ligarius doth bear Cæsar hard,
Who rated him for speaking well of Pompey:
I wonder none of you have thought of him.

BRUTUS
Now, good Metellus, go along by him:
He loves me well, and I have given him reasons;
Send him but hither, and I'll fashion him.

CASSIUS
The morning comes upon's: we'll leave you, Brutus: —
And, friends, disperse yourselves; but all remember
What you have said, and show yourselves true Romans

BRUTUS
Good gentlemen, look fresh and merrily;
Let not our looks put on our purposes;
But bear it as our Roman actors do,
With untired spirits and formal constancy:
And so, good morrow to you every one.
                    [*Exeunt all but* BRUTUS
Boy! Lucius! — Fast asleep? It is no matter;
Enjoy the honey-heavy dew of slumber:
Thou hast no figures nor no fantasies,
Which busy care draws in the brains of men;
Therefore thou sleep'st so sound.

                    Enter PORTIA.

PORTIA
                              Brutus, my lord!

BRUTUS
Portia, what mean you? wherefore rise you now?
It is not for your health thus to commit
Your weak condition to the raw-cold morning.

PORTIA
Nor for yours neither. Y' have ungently, Brutus,
Stole from my bed: and yesternight, at supper,
You suddenly arose, and walk'd about,
Musing and sighing, with your arms across;
And when I ask'd you what the matter was,
You stared upon me with ungentle looks:
I urg'd you further; then you scratch'd your head,
And too impatiently stamp'd with your foot:
Yet I insisted, yet you answer'd not;
But, with an angry wafture of your hand,
Gave sign for me to leave you: so I did;
Fearing to strengthen that impatience
Which seem'd too much enkindled; and withal
Hoping it was but an effect of humour,
Which sometime hath his hour with every man.
It will not let you eat, nor talk, nor sleep;
And, could it work so much upon your shape,
As it hath much prevail'd on your condition,
I should not know you, Brutus. Dear my lord,
Make me acquainted with your cause of grief.

BRUTUS
I am not well in health, and that is all.

PORTIA
Brutus is wise, and, were he not in health,
He would embrace the means to come by it.

BRUTUS
Why, so I do. — Good Portia, go to bed.

PORTIA
Is Brutus sick, — and is it physical
To walk unbraced, and suck up the humours
Of the dank morning? What, is Brutus sick, —
And will he steal out of his wholesome bed,
To dare the vile contagion of the night,
And tempt the rheumy and unpurged air
To add unto his sickness? No, my Brutus;
You have some sick offence within your mind,
Which, by the right and virtue of my place,
I ought to know of: and, upon my knees,
I charm you, by my once-commended beauty,
By all your vows of love, and that great vow
Which did incorporate and make us one,
That you unfold to me, yourself, your half,
Why you are heavy; and what men to-night
Have had resort to you, — for here have been
Some six or seven, who did hide their faces
Even from darkness.

BRUTUS
                    Kneel not, gentle Portia.

PORTIA
I should not need, if you were gentle Brutus.
Within the bond of marriage, tell me, Brutus,
Is it excepted I should know no secrets
That appertain to you? Am I yourself
But, as it were, in sort or limitation, —
To keep with you at meals, comfort your bed,
And talk to you sometimes? Dwell I but in the suburbs
Of your good pleasure? If it be no more,
Portia is Brutus' harlot, not his wife.

BRUTUS
You are my true and honourable wife;
As dear to me as are the ruddy drops
That visit my sad heart.

PORTIA
If this were true, then should I know this secret.
I grant I am a woman; but withal
A woman that Lord Brutus took to wife:
I grant I am a woman; but withal
A woman well-reputed, — Cato's daughter.
Think you I am no stronger than my sex,
Being so father'd and so husbanded?
Tell me your counsels; I will not disclose 'em:
I have made strong proof of my constancy,
Giving myself a voluntary wound
Here, in the thigh: can I bear that with patience,
And not my husband's secrets?

BRUTUS
              O ye gods,
Render me worthy of this noble wife!   [*Knock.*
Hark, hark! one knocks: Portia, go in awhile;
And by and by thy bosom shall partake
The secrets of my heart:
All my engagements I will construe to thee,
All the charactery of my sad brows: —
Leave me with haste. [*Exit* PORTIA.] — Lucius, who's
    that knocks?

Enter LUCIUS *with* LIGARIUS.

LUCIUS
Here is a sick man that would speak with you.

BRUTUS
Caius Ligarius, that Metellus spake of. —
Boy, stand aside. — Caius Ligarius, — how!

LIGARIUS
Vouchsafe good-morrow from a feeble tongue.

BRUTUS
O, what a time have you chose out, brave Caius,
To wear a kerchief! Would you were not sick!

LIGARIUS
I am not sick, if Brutus have in hand
Any exploit worthy the name of honour.

BRUTUS
Such an exploit have I in hand, Ligarius,
Had you a healthful ear to hear of it.

LIGARIUS
By all the gods that Romans bow before,
I here discard my sickness! Soul of Rome!
Brave son, deriv'd from honourable loins!
Thou, like an exorcist, hast conjur'd up
My mortified spirit. Now bid me run,
And I will strive with things impossible;
Yea, get the better of them. What's to do?

BRUTUS
A piece of work that will make sick men whole.

LIGARIUS
But are not some whole that we must make sick?

BRUTUS
That must we also. What it is, my Caius,
I shall unfold to thee, as we are going
To whom it must be done.

LIGARIUS
            Set on your foot;
And, with a heart new-fired, I follow you,
To do I know not what: but it sufficeth
That Brutus leads me on.

BRUTUS
        Follow me, then.   [*Exeunt.*

SCENE II

The same. A hall in CAESAR'S *palace.*

Thunder and lightning. Enter JULIUS CAESAR, *in his
nightgown.*

CAESAR
Nor heaven nor earth have been at peace to-night:
Thrice hath Calphurnia in her sleep cried out,
'Help, ho! they murder Cæsar!' — Who's within?

Enter a SERVANT.

SERVANT
My lord?

CAESAR
Go bid the priests do present sacrifice,
And bring me their opinions of success.

SERVANT
I will, my lord.   [*Exit.*

Enter CALPHURNIA.

CALPHURNIA
What mean you, Cæsar? think you to walk forth?

You shall not stir out of your house to-day.

CAESAR
Cæsar shall forth: the things that threaten'd me
Ne'er look'd but on my back; when they shall see
The face of Cæsar, they are vanished.

CALPHURNIA
Cæsar, I never stood on ceremonies,
Yet now they fright me. There is one within,
Besides the things that we have heard and seen,
Recounts most horrid sights seen by the watch.
A lioness hath whelped in the streets;
And graves have yawn'd, and yielded up their dead;
Fierce fiery warriors fight upon the clouds,
In ranks and squadrons and right form of war,
Which drizzled blood upon the Capitol;
The noise of battle hurtled in the air;
Horses did neigh, and dying men did groan;
And ghosts did shriek and squeal about the streets.
O Cæsar, these things are beyond all use,
And I do fear them!

CAESAR
          What can be avoided
Whose end is purpos'd by the mighty gods?
Yet Cæsar shall go forth; for these predictions
Are to the world in general as to Cæsar.

CALPHURNIA
When beggars die, there are no comets seen;
The heavens themselves blaze forth the death of
    princes.

CAESAR
Cowards die many times before their deaths;
The valiant never taste of death but once.
Of all the wonders that I yet have heard,
It seems to me most strange that men should fear;
Seeing that death, a necessary end,
Will come when it will come.

Enter SERVANT.
          What say the augurers?

SERVANT
They would not have you to stir forth to-day.
Plucking the entrails of an offering forth,
They could not find a heart within the beast.

CAESAR
The gods do this in shame of cowardice:
Cæsar should be a beast without a heart,
If he should stay at home to-day for fear.
No, Cæsar shall not: danger knows full well
That Cæsar is more dangerous than he:
We are two lions litter'd in one day,
And I the elder and more terrible: —
And Cæsar shall go forth.

CALPHURNIA
          Alas, my lord,
Your wisdom is consum'd in confidence.
Do not go forth to-day: call it my fear
That keeps you in the house, and not your own.
We'll send Mark Antony to the senate-house;
And he shall say you are not well to-day:
Let me, upon my knee, prevail in this.

CAESAR
Mark Antony shall say I am not well;
And, for thy humour, I will stay at home.

Enter DECIUS.
Here's Decius Brutus, he shall tell them so.

DECIUS
Cæsar, all hail! good morrow, worthy Cæsar:
I come to fetch you to the senate-house.

CAESAR
And you are come in very happy time,
To bear my greeting to the senators,
And tell them that I will not come to-day;
Cannot, is false; and that I dare not, falser:
I will not come to-day, — tell them so, Decius.

CALPHURNIA
Say he is sick.

CAESAR
          Shall Cæsar send a lie?
Have I in conquest stretch'd mine arm so far
To be afeard to tell greybeards the truth?
Decius, go tell them Cæsar will not come.

DECIUS
Most mighty Cæsar, let me know some cause,
Lest I be laugh'd at when I tell them so.

CAESAR
The cause is in my will, — I will not come;
That is enough to satisfy the senate.
But, for your private satisfaction,
Because I love you, I will let you know, —
Calphurnia here, my wife, stays me at home:
She dream'd to-night she saw my statua,
Which, like a fountain with an hundred spouts,
Did run pure blood; and many lusty Romans
Came smiling, and did bathe their hands in it:
And these does she apply for warnings and portents
And evils imminent; and on her knee
Hath begg'd that I will stay at home to-day.

DECIUS
This dream is all amiss interpreted;
It was a vision fair and fortunate:
Your statue spouting blood in many pipes,
In which so many smiling Romans bath'd,
Signifies that from you great Rome shall suck

PORTIA How hard it is for women to keep counsel!

Reviving blood; and that great men shall press
For tinctures, stains, relics, and recognisance.
This by Calphurnia's dream is signified.

CAESAR
And this way have you well expounded it.

DECIUS
I have, when you have heard what I can say:
And know it now, — the senate have concluded
To give, this day, a crown to mighty Cæsar.
If you shall send them word you will not come,
Their minds may change. Besides, it were a mock
Apt to be render'd, for some one to say,
'Break up the senate till another time,
When Cæsar's wife shall meet with better dreams.'
If Cæsar hide himself, shall they not whisper,
'Lo, Cæsar is afraid'?
Pardon me, Cæsar; for my dear dear love
To your proceeding bids me tell you this;
And reason to my love is liable.

CAESAR
How foolish do your fears seem now, Calphurnia!
I am ashamed I did yield to them. —
Give me my robe, for I will go: —

Enter PUBLIUS, BRUTUS, LIGARIUS, METELLUS,
CASCA, TREBONIUS, *and* CINNA.

And look where Publius is come to fetch me.

PUBLIUS
Good morrow, Cæsar.

CAESAR
Welcome, Publius. —
What, Brutus, are you stirr'd so early too? —
Good morrow, Casca. — Caius Ligarius,
Cæsar was ne'er so much your enemy
As that same ague which hath made you lean. —
What is't o'clock?

DECIUS
Cæsar, 'tis strucken eight.

CAESAR
I thank you for your pains and courtesy.
Enter ANTONY.
See! Antony, that revels long o' nights,
Is notwithstanding up. — Good morrow, Antony.

ANTONY
So to most noble Cæsar.

CAESAR
Bid them prepare within: —
I am to blame to be thus waited for. —
Now, Cinna: — now, Metellus: — what, Trebonius!
I have an hour's talk in store for you;
Remember that you call on me to-day:
Be near me, that I may remember you.

TREBONIUS
Cæsar, I will: — [*aside*] and so near will I be,
That your best friends shall wish I had been further.

CAESAR
Good friends, go in, and taste some wine with me;
And we, like friends, will straightway go together.

DECIUS [*aside*].
That every like is not the same, O Cæsar,
The heart of Brutus yearns to think upon! [*Exeunt.*

SCENE III

The same. A street near the Capitol.

Enter ARTEMIDORUS, *reading a paper.*

ARTEMIDORUS
Cæsar, beware of Brutus; take heed of Cassius; come
not near Casca; have an eye to Cinna; trust not
Trebonius; mark well Metellus Cimber; Decius Brutus
loves thee not: thou hast wrong'd Caius Ligarius. There
is but one mind in all these men, and it is bent against
Cæsar. If thou beest not immortal, look about you:
security gives way to conspiracy. The mighty gods
defend thee! Thy lover,
ARTEMIDORUS
Here will I stand till Cæsar pass along,
And as a suitor will I give him this.
My heart laments that virtue cannot live
Out of the teeth of emulation.
If thou read this, O Cæsar, thou mayst live;
If not, the Fates with traitors do contrive. [*Exit.*

SCENE IV

*The same. Another part of the same street, before the
house of* BRUTUS.

Enter PORTIA *and* LUCIUS.

PORTIA
I prithee, boy, run to the senate-house;
Stay not to answer me, but get thee gone:

Why dost thou stay?

LUCIUS
To know my errand, madam.

PORTIA
I would have had thee there, and here again,
Ere I can tell thee what thou shouldst do there. —
[*aside*] O constancy, be strong upon my side;
Set a huge mountain 'tween my heart and tongue!
I have a man's mind, but a woman's might.
How hard it is for women to keep counsel! —
Art thou here yet?

LUCIUS
Madam, what should I do?
Run to the Capitol, and nothing else?
And so return to you, and nothing else?

PORTIA
Yes, bring me word, boy, if thy lord look well,
For he went sickly forth: and take good note
What Cæsar doth, what suitors press to him.
Hark, boy! what noise is that?

LUCIUS
I hear none, madam.

PORTIA
Prithee, listen well:
I heard a bustling rumour, like a fray,
And the wind brings it from the Capitol.

LUCIUS
Sooth, madam, I hear nothing.

Enter the SOOTHSAYER.

PORTIA
Come hither, fellow: which way hast thou been?

SOOTHSAYER
At mine own house, good lady.

PORTIA
What is't o'clock?

SOOTHSAYER
About the ninth hour, lady.

PORTIA
Is Cæsar yet gone to the Capitol?

SOOTHSAYER
Madam, not yet: I go to take my stand,
To see him pass on to the Capitol.

PORTIA
Thou hast some suit to Cæsar, hast thou not?

SOOTHSAYER
That I have, lady: if it will please Cæsar
To be so good to Cæsar as to hear me,
I shall beseech him to befriend himself.

PORTIA
Why, know'st thou any harm's intended towards
him?

SOOTHSAYER
None that I know will be, much that I fear may chance.

Good morrow to you. — Here the street is narrow:
The throng that follows Cæsar at the heels,
Of senators, of prætors, common suitors,
Will crowd a feeble man almost to death:
I'll get me to a place more void, and there
Speak to great Cæsar as he comes along. [*Exit.*

PORTIA
I must go in. — [*aside*] Ay me, how weak a thing
The heart of woman is! O Brutus,
The heavens speed thee in thine enterprise! —
Sure, the boy heard me. — Brutus hath a suit
That Cæsar will not grant. — O, I grow faint. —
Run, Lucius, and commend me to my lord;
Say I am merry: come to me again,
And bring me word what he doth say to thee.
[*Exeunt severally.*

ACT III

SCENE I

Rome. Before the Capitol; the SENATE *sitting.*

A crowd of people; among them ARTEMIDORUS *and
the* SOOTHSAYER. *Flourish. Enter* CAESAR,
BRUTUS, CASSIUS, CASCA, DECIUS, METELLUS,
TREBONIUS, CINNA, ANTONY, LEPIDUS,
POPILIUS, PUBLIUS, *and others.*

CAESAR
The ides of March are come.

SOOTHSAYER
Ay, Cæsar; but not gone.

ARTEMIDORUS
Hail, Cæsar! read this schedule.

DECIUS
Trebonius doth desire you to o'er-read,
At your best leisure, this his humble suit.

ARTEMIDORUS
O Cæsar, read mine first; for mine's a suit
That touches Cæsar nearer; read it, great Cæsar.

CAESAR
What touches us ourself, shall be last serv'd.

ARTEMIDORUS
Delay not, Cæsar; read it instantly.

CAESAR
What, is the fellow mad?

PUBLIUS
Sirrah, give place.

CASSIUS
What, urge you your petitions in the street?
Come to the Capitol.

*CAESAR enters the Capitol, the rest following.
All the SENATORS rise.*

POPILIUS
I wish your enterprise to-day may thrive.
CASSIUS
What enterprise, Popilius?
POPILIUS
         Fare you well.   [*Advances to* CAESAR.
BRUTUS
What said Popilius Lena?
CASSIUS
He wish'd to-day our enterprise might thrive.
I fear our purpose is discovered.
BRUTUS
Look, how he makes to Cæsar: mark him.
CASSIUS
                     Casca,
Be sudden, for we fear prevention. —
Brutus, what shall be done? If this be known,
Cassius or Cæsar never shall turn back,
For I will slay myself.
BRUTUS
          Cassius, be constant:
Popilius Lena speaks not of our purpose;
For, look, he smiles, and Cæsar doth not change.
CASSIUS
Trebonius knows his time; for, look you, Brutus,
He draws Mark Antony out of the way.

     [*Exeunt* ANTONY *and* TREBONIUS.
     CAESAR *and the* SENATORS *take their seats.*

DECIUS
Where is Metellus Cimber? Let him go,
And presently prefer his suit to Cæsar.
BRUTUS
He is address'd: press near and second him.
CINNA
Casca, you are the first that rears your hand.
CAESAR
Are we all ready? What is now amiss
That Cæsar and his senate must redress?
METELLUS
Most high, most mighty, and most puissant Cæsar,
Metellus Cimber throws before thy seat
An humble heart, —   [*Kneeling.*
CAESAR
         I must prevent thee, Cimber.
These couchings and these lowly courtesies
Might fire the blood of ordinary men,
And turn pre-ordinance and first decree
Into the law of children. Be not fond,
To think that Cæsar bears such rebel blood
That will be thaw'd from the true quality
With that which melteth fools; I mean, sweet words,
Low-crooked curt'sies, and base spaniel-fawning.
Thy brother by decree is banished:
If thou dost bend, and pray, and fawn for him,
I spurn thee like a cur out of my way.
Know, Cæsar doth not wrong; nor without cause
Will he be satisfied.
METELLUS
Is there no voice more worthy than my own,
To sound more sweetly in great Cæsar's ear
For the repealing of my banish'd brother?
BRUTUS
I kiss thy hand, but not in flattery, Cæsar;
Desiring thee that Publius Cimber may
Have an immediate freedom of repeal.
CAESAR
What, Brutus!
CASSIUS
      Pardon, Cæsar; Cæsar, pardon:
As low as to thy foot doth Cassius fall,
To beg enfranchisement for Publius Cimber.
CAESAR
I could be well mov'd, if I were as you;
If I could pray to move, prayers would move me:
But I am constant as the northern star,
Of whose true-fix'd and resting quality
There is no fellow in the firmament.
The skies are painted with unnumber'd sparks;
They are all fire, and every one doth shine;
But there's but one in all doth hold his place:
So in the world; — 'tis furnish'd well with men,
And men are flesh and blood, and apprehensive;
Yet in the number I do know but one
That unassailable holds on his rank,
Unshak'd of motion: and that I am he,
Let me a little show it, even in this, —
That I was constant Cimber should be banish'd,
And constant do remain to keep him so.

CINNA
O Cæsar, —
CAESAR
        Hence! wilt thou lift up Olympus?
DECIUS
Great Cæsar, —
CAESAR
         Doth not Brutus bootless kneel?
CASCA
Speak, hands, for me!   [*They stab* CAESAR.
CAESAR
Et tu, Brute? — Then fall, Cæsar!   [*Dies.*
CINNA
Liberty! Freedom! Tyranny is dead! —
Run hence, proclaim, cry it about the streets.
CASSIUS
Some to the common pulpits, and cry out,
'Liberty, freedom, and enfranchisement!'
BRUTUS
People, and senators, be not affrighted;
Fly not; stand still: — ambition's debt is paid.
CASCA
Go to the pulpit, Brutus.
DECIUS
           And Cassius too.
BRUTUS
Where's Publius?
CINNA
Here, quite confounded with this mutiny.
METELLUS
Stand fast together, lest some friend of Cæsar's
Should chance —
BRUTUS
Talk not of standing. — Publius, good cheer;
There is no harm intended to your person,
Nor to no Roman else: so tell them, Publius.
CASSIUS
And leave us, Publius; lest that the people,
Rushing on us, should do your age some mischief.
BRUTUS
Do so: — and let no man abide this deed,
But we the doers.

     Enter TREBONIUS.

CASSIUS
Where is Antony?
TREBONIUS
           Fled to his house amazed:
Men, wives, and children stare, cry out, and run
As it were doomsday.
BRUTUS
       Fates, we will know your pleasures: —
That we shall die, we know; 'tis but the time,
And drawing days out, that men stand upon.
CASSIUS
Why, he that cuts off twenty years of life
Cuts off so many years of fearing death.
BRUTUS
Grant that, and then is death a benefit:
So are we Cæsar's friends, that have abridg'd
His time of fearing death. — Stoop, Romans, stoop,
And let us bathe our hands in Cæsar's blood
Up to the elbows, and besmear our swords:
Then walk we forth, even to the market-place,
And, waving our red weapons o'er our heads,
Let's all cry 'Peace, freedom, and liberty!'
CASSIUS
Stoop, then, and wash. — How many ages hence
Shall this our lofty scene be acted over
In states unborn and accents yet unknown!
BRUTUS
How many times shall Cæsar bleed in sport,
That now on Pompey's basis lies along
No worthier than the dust!
CASSIUS
          So oft as that shall be,
So often shall the knot of us be call'd
The men that gave their country liberty.
DECIUS
What, shall we forth?
CASSIUS
         Ay, every man away:
Brutus shall lead; and we will grace his heels
With the most boldest and best hearts of Rome.
BRUTUS
Soft! who comes here?

     Enter a SERVANT.
     A friend of Antony's.

SERVANT
Thus, Brutus, did my master bid me kneel;
Thus did Mark Antony bid me fall down;
And, being prostrate, thus he bade me say: —
Brutus is noble, wise, valiant, and honest;
Cæsar was mighty, bold, royal, and loving:
Say I love Brutus, and I honour him;
Say I fear'd Cæsar, honour'd him, and lov'd him.
If Brutus will vouchsafe that Antony
May safely come to him, and be resolv'd
How Cæsar hath deserv'd to lie in death,
Mark Antony shall not love Cæsar dead
So well as Brutus living; but will follow
The fortunes and affairs of noble Brutus
Through the hazards of this untrod state
With all true faith. So says my master Antony.
BRUTUS
Thy master is a wise and valiant Roman;
I never thought him worse.
Tell him, so please him come unto this place,
He shall be satisfied; and, by my honour,
Depart untouch'd.
SERVANT
       I'll fetch him presently.   [*Exit.*
BRUTUS
I know that we shall have him well to friend.
CASSIUS
I wish we may: but yet have I a mind
That fears him much; and my misgiving still
Falls shrewdly to the purpose.
BRUTUS
But here comes Antony.
        Enter ANTONY.
          Welcome, Mark Antony.
ANTONY
O mighty Cæsar! dost thou lie so low?
Are all thy conquests, glories, triumphs, spoils,
Shrunk to this little measure? Fare thee well. —
I know not, gentlemen, what you intend,
Who else must be let blood, who else is rank:
If I myself, there is no hour so fit
As Cæsar's death's hour: nor no instrument
Of half that worth as those your swords, made rich
With the most noble blood of all this world.
I do beseech ye, if you bear me hard,
Now, whilst your purpled hands do reek and smoke,
Fulfil your pleasure. Live a thousand years,
I shall not find myself so apt to die:
No place will please me so, no mean of death
As here by Cæsar, and by you cut off,
The choice and master spirits of this age.
BRUTUS
O Antony, beg not your death of us.
Though now we must appear bloody and cruel,
As, by our hands and this our present act,
You see we do; yet see you but our hands,
And this the bleeding business they have done:
Our hearts you see not, — they are pitiful;
And pity to the general wrong of Rome —
As fire drives out fire, so pity pity —
Hath done this deed on Cæsar. For your part,
To you our swords have leaden points, Mark Antony,
Our arms no strength of malice; and our hearts,
Of brothers' temper, do receive you in
With all kind love, good thoughts, and reverence.
CASSIUS
Your voice shall be as strong as any man's
In the disposing of new dignities.
BRUTUS
Only be patient till we have appeased
The multitude, beside themselves with fear,
And then we will deliver you the cause,
Why I, that did love Cæsar when I struck him,
Have thus proceeded.
ANTONY
       I doubt not of your wisdom.
Let each man render me his bloody hand:
First, Marcus Brutus, will I shake with you: —
Next, Caius Cassius, do I take your hand; —
Now, Decius Brutus, yours; — now yours, Metellus; —
Yours, Cinna; — and, my valiant Casca, yours; —
Though last, not least in love, yours, good Trebonius.
Gentlemen all, — alas, what shall I say?
My credit now stands on such slippery ground,
That one of two bad ways you must conceit me,
Either a coward or a flatterer. —
That I did love thee, Cæsar, O, 'tis true:
If, then, thy spirit look upon us now,
Shall it not grieve thee dearer than thy death,
To see thy Antony making his peace,
Shaking the bloody fingers of thy foes,

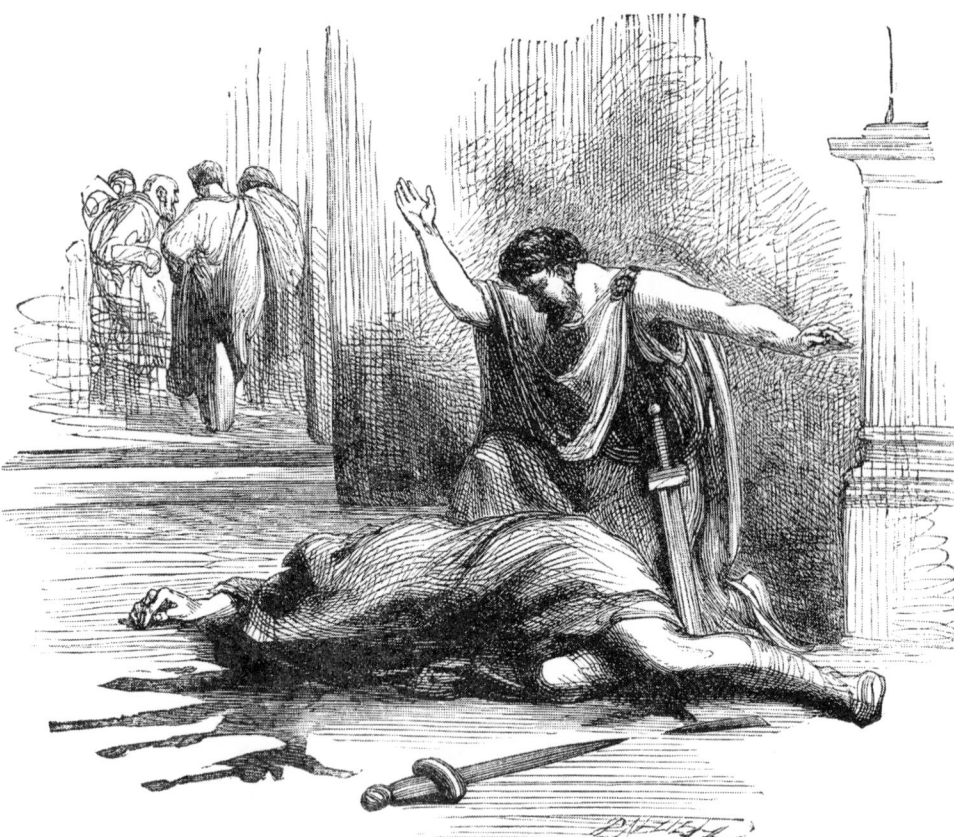

ANTONY How like a deer, strucken by many princes, dost thou here lie!

Most noble! in the presence of thy corse?
Had I as many eyes as thou hast wounds,
Weeping as fast as they stream forth thy blood,
It would become me better than to close
In terms of friendship with thine enemies.
Pardon me, Julius! — Here wast thou bay'd, brave hart;
Here didst thou fall; and here thy hunters stand,
Sign'd in thy spoil, and crimson'd in thy lethe. —
O world, thou wast the forest to this hart;
And this, indeed, O world, the heart of thee. —
How like a deer, strucken by many princes,
Dost thou here lie!
CASSIUS
Mark Antony, —
ANTONY
        Pardon me, Caius Cassius:
The enemies of Cæsar shall say this;
Then, in a friend, it is cold modesty.
CASSIUS
I blame you not for praising Cæsar so;
But what compact mean you to have with us?
Will you be prick'd in number of our friends;
Or shall we on, and not depend on you?
ANTONY
Therefore I took your hands; but was, indeed,
Sway'd from the point, by looking down on Cæsar.
Friends am I with you all, and love you all;
Upon this hope, that you shall give me reasons
Why and wherein Cæsar was dangerous.
BRUTUS
Or else were this a savage spectacle:
Our reasons are so full of good regard,
That were you, Antony, the son of Cæsar,
You should be satisfied.
ANTONY
        That's all I seek:
And am moreover suitor that I may
Produce his body to the market-place;
And in the pulpit, as becomes a friend,
Speak in the order of his funeral.
BRUTUS
You shall, Mark Antony.
CASSIUS
        Brutus, a word with you.
[aside to BRUTUS] You know not what you do: do not
   consent
That Antony speak in his funeral:
Know you how much the people may be mov'd
By that which he will utter?

BRUTUS [aside to CASSIUS].
        By your pardon; —
I will myself into the pulpit first,
And show the reason of our Cæsar's death:
What Antony shall speak, I will protest
He speaks by leave and by permission;
And that we are contented Cæsar shall
Have all true rites and lawful ceremonies.
It shall advantage more than do us wrong.
CASSIUS [aside to BRUTUS].
I know not what may fall; I like it not.
BRUTUS
Mark Antony, here, take you Cæsar's body.
You shall not in your funeral speech blame us,
But speak all good you can devise of Cæsar;
And say you do't by our permission;
Else shall you not have any hand at all
About his funeral: and you shall speak
In the same pulpit whereto I am going,
After my speech is ended.
ANTONY
        Be it so;
I do desire no more.
BRUTUS
Prepare the body, then, and follow us.
        [Exeunt all but ANTONY.
ANTONY
O, pardon me, thou bleeding piece of earth,
That I am meek and gentle with these butchers!
Thou art the ruins of the noblest man
That ever lived in the tide of times.
Woe to the hand that shed this costly blood!
Over thy wounds now do I prophesy, —
Which, like dumb mouths, do ope their ruby lips,
To beg the voice and utterance of my tongue, —
A curse shall light upon the limbs of men;
Domestic fury and fierce civil strife
Shall cumber all the parts of Italy;
Blood and destruction shall be so in use,
And dreadful objects so familiar,
That mothers shall but smile when they behold
Their infants quarter'd with the hands of war;
All pity chok'd with custom of fell deeds:
And Cæsar's spirit, ranging for revenge,
With Ate by his side come hot from hell,
Shall in these confines with a monarch's voice
Cry 'Havoc,' and let slip the dogs of war;
That this foul deed shall smell above the earth
With carriovn men, groaning for burial.

Enter OCTAVIUS' SERVANT.
You serve Octavius Cæsar, do you not?
SERVANT
I do, Mark Antony.
ANTONY
Cæsar did write for him to come to Rome.
SERVANT
He did receive his letters, and is coming;
And bid me say to you by word of mouth —
O Cæsar! —   [Seeing the body.
ANTONY
Thy heart is big, get thee apart and weep.
Passion, I see, is catching; for mine eyes,
Seeing those beads of sorrow stand in thine,
Begin to water. Is thy master coming?
SERVANT
He lies to-night within seven leagues of Rome.
ANTONY
Post back with speed, and tell him what hath chanc'd:
Here is a mourning Rome, a dangerous Rome,
No Rome of safety for Octavius yet;
Hie hence, and tell him so. Yet, stay awhile;
Thou shalt not back till I have borne this corse
Into the market-place: there shall I try,
In my oration, how the people take
The cruel issue of these bloody men;
According to the which, thou shalt discourse
To young Octavius of the state of things.
Lend me your hand.   [Exeunt with CAESAR'S body.

SCENE II
The same. The Forum.

Enter BRUTUS *and* CASSIUS, *and a throng of*
CITIZENS.

CITIZENS
We will be satisfied; let us be satisfied
BRUTUS
Then follow me, and give me audience, friends.
Cassius, go you into the other street,
And part the numbers.
Those that will hear me speak, let 'em stay here;
Those that will follow Cassius, go with him;
And public reasons shall be rendered
Of Cæsar's death.
FIRST CITIZEN
        I will hear Brutus speak.
SECOND CITIZEN
I will hear Cassius; and compare their reasons,
When severally we hear them rendered.
   [Exit CASSIUS, with some of the CITIZENS. BRUTUS
                            goes into the pulpit.
THIRD CITIZEN
The noble Brutus is ascended: silence!
BRUTUS
Be patient till the last.
Romans, countrymen, and lovers! hear me for my
cause; and be silent, that you may hear: believe me for
mine honour; and have respect to mine honour, that
you may believe: censure me in your wisdom; and
awake your senses, that you may the better judge. If
there be any in this assembly, any dear friend of
Cæsar's, to him I say, that Brutus' love to Cæsar was no
less than his. If, then, that friend demand why Brutus
rose against Cæsar, this is my answer, — Not that I
loved Cæsar less, but that I loved Rome more. Had you
rather Cæsar were living, and die all slaves, than that
Cæsar were dead, to live all free men? As Cæsar loved
me, I weep for him; as he was fortunate, I rejoice at it;
as he was valiant, I honour him: but, as he was
ambitious, I slew him. There is tears for his love; joy for
his fortune; honour for his valour; and death for his
ambition. Who is here so base that would be a
bondman? If any, speak; for him have I offended. Who
is here so rude that would not be a Roman? If any,
speak; for him have I offended. Who is here so vile that
will not love his country? If any, speak; for him have I
offended. I pause for a reply.
CITIZENS
None, Brutus, none.
BRUTUS
Then none have I offended. I have done no more to
Cæsar than you shall do to Brutus. The question of his
death is enroll'd in the Capitol; his glory not
extenuated, wherein he was worthy; nor his offences
enforced, for which he suffer'd death. Here comes his
body, mourn'd by Mark Antony:
     Enter ANTONY *with* CAESAR'S *body.*
who, though he had no hand in his death, shall receive
the benefit of his dying, a place in the commonwealth;

BRUTUS Romans, countrymen, and lovers! hear me for my cause.

as which of you shall not? With this I depart, — that, as
I slew my best lover for the good of Rome, I have the
same dagger for myself, when it shall please my
country to need my death.

CITIZENS
Live, Brutus! live, live!

FIRST CITIZEN
Bring him with triumph home unto his house.

SECOND CITIZEN
Give him a statue with his ancestors.

THIRD CITIZEN
Let him be Cæsar.

FOURTH CITIZEN
          Cæsar's better parts
Shall be crown'd in Brutus.

FIRST CITIZEN
We'll bring him to his house with shouts and
   clamours.

BRUTUS
My countrymen, —

SECOND CITIZEN
         Peace, silence! Brutus speaks.

FIRST CITIZEN
Peace, ho!

BRUTUS
Good countrymen, let me depart alone,
And, for my sake, stay here with Antony:
Do grace to Cæsar's corpse, and grace his speech
Tending to Cæsar's glories; which Mark Antony,
By our permission, is allow'd to make.
I do entreat you, not a man depart,
Save I alone, till Antony have spoke.   [*Exit.*

FIRST CITIZEN
Stay, ho! and let us hear Mark Antony.

THIRD CITIZEN
Let him go up into the public chair;

We'll hear him. — Noble Antony, go up.

ANTONY
For Brutus' sake, I am beholding to you.   [*Goes up.*

FOURTH CITIZEN
What does he say of Brutus?

THIRD CITIZEN
             He says, for Brutus' sake,
He finds himself beholding to us all.

FOURTH CITIZEN
'Twere best he speak no harm of Brutus here.

FIRST CITIZEN
This Cæsar was a tyrant.

THIRD CITIZEN
          Nay, that's certain:
We are blest that Rome is rid of him.

SECOND CITIZEN
Peace! let us hear what Antony can say.

ANTONY
You gentle Romans, —

CITIZENS
         Peace, ho! let us hear him.

ANTONY
Friends, Romans, countrymen, lend me your ears;
I come to bury Cæsar, not to praise him.
The evil that men do lives after them;
The good is oft interred with their bones:
So let it be with Cæsar. The noble Brutus
Hath told you Cæsar was ambitious:
If it were so, it was a grievous fault;
And grievously hath Cæsar answer'd it.
Here, under leave of Brutus and the rest, —
For Brutus is an honourable man;
So are they all, all honourable men, —
Come I to speak in Cæsar's funeral.
He was my friend, faithful and just to me:
But Brutus says he was ambitious;

And Brutus is an honourable man.
He hath brought many captives home to Rome,
Whose ransoms did the general coffers fill:
Did this in Cæsar seem ambitious?
When that the poor have cried, Cæsar hath wept:
Ambition should be made of sterner stuff:
Yet Brutus says he was ambitious;
And Brutus is an honourable man.
You all did see that on the Lupercal
I thrice presented him a kingly crown,
Which he did thrice refuse: was this ambition?
Yet Brutus says he was ambitious;
And, sure, he is an honourable man.
I speak not to disprove what Brutus spoke,
But here I am to speak what I do know.
You all did love him once, — not without cause:
What cause withholds you, then, to mourn for him?
O judgement, thou art fled to brutish beasts,
And men have lost their reason! — Bear with me;
My heart is in the coffin there with Cæsar,
And I must pause till it come back to me.

FIRST CITIZEN
Methinks there is much reason in his sayings.

SECOND CITIZEN
If thou consider rightly of the matter,
Cæsar has had great wrong.

THIRD CITIZEN
             Has he, masters?
I fear there will a worse come in his place.

FOURTH CITIZEN
Mark'd ye his words? He would not take the crown;
Therefore 'tis certain he was not ambitious.

FIRST CITIZEN
If it be found so, some will dear abide it.

SECOND CITIZEN
Poor soul! his eyes are red as fire with weeping.

THIRD CITIZEN
There's not a nobler man in Rome than Antony.

FOURTH CITIZEN
Now mark him, he begins again to speak.

ANTONY
But yesterday the word of Cæsar might
Have stood against the world: now lies he there,
And none so poor to do him reverence.
O masters, if I were dispos'd to stir
Your hearts and minds to mutiny and rage,
I should do Brutus wrong, and Cassius wrong,
Who, you all know, are honourable men:
I will not do them wrong; I rather choose
To wrong the dead, to wrong myself, and you,
Than I will wrong such honourable men.
But here's a parchment with the seal of Cæsar, —
I found it in his closet, — 'tis his will:
Let but the commons hear this testament, —
Which, pardon me, I do not mean to read, —
And they would go and kiss dead Cæsar's wounds,
And dip their napkins in his sacred blood;
Yea, beg a hair of him for memory,
And, dying, mention it within their wills,
Bequeathing it, as a rich legacy,
Unto their issue.

FOURTH CITIZEN
We'll hear the will: read it, Mark Antony.

CITIZENS
The will, the will! we will hear Cæsar's will.

ANTONY
Have patience, gentle friends, I must not read it;
It is not meet you know how Cæsar lov'd you.
You are not wood, you are not stones, but men;
And, being men, hearing the will of Cæsar,
It will inflame you, it will make you mad:
'Tis good you know not that you are his heirs;
For, if you should, O, what would come of it!

FOURTH CITIZEN
Read the will: we'll hear it, Antony;
You shall read us the will, — Cæsar's will.

ANTONY
Will you be patient? will you stay awhile?
I have o'ershot myself to tell you of it:
I fear I wrong the honourable men
Whose daggers have stabb'd Cæsar; I do fear it.

FOURTH CITIZEN
They were traitors: honourable men!

CITIZENS
The will! the testament!

SECOND CITIZEN
They were villains, murderers: the will! read the will.

ANTONY
You will compel me, then, to read the will?
Then make a ring about the corpse of Cæsar,

And let me show you him that made the will.
Shall I descend? and will you give me leave?

CITIZENS
Come down.

SECOND CITIZEN
Descend.

THIRD CITIZEN
You shall have leave.   [ANTONY *comes down.*

FOURTH CITIZEN
A ring; stand round.

FIRST CITIZEN
Stand from the hearse, stand from the body.

SECOND CITIZEN
Room for Antony, — most noble Antony.

ANTONY
Nay, press not so upon me; stand far off.

CITIZENS
Stand back; room; bear back.

ANTONY
If you have tears, prepare to shed them now.
You all do know this mantle: I remember
The first time ever Cæsar put it on;
'Twas on a summer's evening, in his tent,
That day he overcame the Nervii: —
Look, in this place ran Cassius' dagger through:
See what a rent the envious Casca made:
Through this the well-beloved Brutus stabb'd;
And, as he pluck'd his cursed steel away,
Mark how the blood of Cæsar follow'd it,
As rushing out of doors, to be resolved
If Brutus so unkindly knock'd, or no;
For Brutus, as you know, was Cæsar's angel:
Judge, O you gods, how dearly Cæsar lov'd him!
This was the most unkindest cut of all;
For when the noble Cæsar saw him stab,
Ingratitude, more strong than traitors' arms,
Quite vanquish'd him: then burst his mighty heart;
And, in his mantle muffling up his face,
Even at the base of Pompey's statua,
Which all the while ran blood, great Cæsar fell.
O, what a fall was there, my countrymen!
Then I, and you, and all of us fell down,
Whilst bloody treason flourish'd over us.
O, now you weep; and, I perceive, you feel
The dint of pity: these are gracious drops.
Kind souls, what, weep you when you but behold
Our Cæsar's vesture wounded? Look you here,
Here is himself, marr'd, as you see, with traitors.

FIRST CITIZEN
O piteous spectacle!

SECOND CITIZEN
O noble Cæsar!

THIRD CITIZEN
O woeful day!

FOURTH CITIZEN
O traitors, villains!

FIRST CITIZEN
O most bloody sight!

SECOND CITIZEN
We will be revenged.

CITIZENS
Revenge, — about, — seek, — burn, — fire, — kill, —
slay, — let not a traitor live!

ANTONY
Stay, countrymen.

FIRST CITIZEN
Peace there! hear the noble Antony.

SECOND CITIZEN
We'll hear him, we'll follow him, we'll die with him.

ANTONY
Good friends, sweet friends, let me not stir you up
To such a sudden flood of mutiny.
They that have done this deed are honourable; —
What private griefs they have, alas, I know not,
That made them do it; — they are wise and honourable,
And will, no doubt, with reasons answer you.
I come not, friends, to steal away your hearts:
I am no orator, as Brutus is;
But, as you know me all, a plain blunt man,
That love my friend; and that they know full well
That gave me public leave to speak of him:
For I have neither wit, nor words, nor worth,
Action, nor utterance, nor the power of speech,
To stir men's blood: I only speak right on;
I tell you that which you yourselves do know;
Show you sweet Cæsar's wounds, poor poor dumb
    mouths,
And bid them speak for me: but were I Brutus,
And Brutus Antony, there were an Antony

Would ruffle up your spirits, and put a tongue
In every wound of Cæsar, that should move
The stones of Rome to rise and mutiny.

CITIZENS
We'll mutiny.

FIRST CITIZEN
We'll burn the house of Brutus.

THIRD CITIZEN
Away, then! come, seek the conspirators.

ANTONY
Yet hear me, countrymen; yet hear me speak.

CITIZENS
Peace, ho! hear Antony, — most noble Antony.

ANTONY
Why, friends, you go to do you know not what:
Wherein hath Cæsar thus deserv'd your loves?
Alas, you know not, — I must tell you, then: —
You have forgot the will I told you of.

CITIZENS
Most true; the will: — let's stay and hear the will.

ANTONY
Here is the will, and under Cæsar's seal: —
To every Roman citizen he gives,
To every several man, seventy-five drachmas.

SECOND CITIZEN
Most noble Cæsar! — we'll revenge his death.

THIRD CITIZEN
O royal Cæsar!

ANTONY
Hear me with patience.

CITIZENS
Peace, ho!

ANTONY
Moreover, he hath left you all his walks,
His private arbours, and new-planted orchards,
On this side Tiber; he hath left them you,
And to your heirs for ever, — common pleasures,
To walk abroad, and recreate yourselves.
Here was a Cæsar! when comes such another?

FIRST CITIZEN
Never, never. — Come, away, away!
We'll burn his body in the holy place,
And with the brands fire the traitors' houses.
Take up the body.

SECOND CITIZEN
Go fetch fire.

THIRD CITIZEN
Pluck down benches.

FOURTH CITIZEN
Pluck down forms, windows, any thing.
                    [*Exeunt* CITIZENS *with the body.*

ANTONY
Now let it work: — mischief, thou art afoot,
Take thou what course thou wilt!
                    Enter SERVANT.
                                How now, fellow!

SERVANT
Sir, Octavius is already come to Rome.

ANTONY
Where is he?

SERVANT
He and Lepidus are at Cæsar's house.

ANTONY
And thither will I straight to visit him:
He comes upon a wish. Fortune is
    merry,
And in this mood will give us any thing.

SERVANT
I heard him say, Brutus and Cassius
Are rid like madmen through the gates
    of Rome.

ANTONY
Belike they had some notice of the
    people
How I had mov'd them. Bring me to
Octavius.   [*Exeunt.*

SCENE III
The same. A street.

Enter CINNA *the poet, and after him the* CITIZENS.

CINNA
I dreamt to-night that I did feast with Cæsar,
And things unlucky charge my fantasy:
I have no will to wander forth of doors,
Yet something leads me forth.

FIRST CITIZEN
What is your name?

SECOND CITIZEN
Whither are you going?

THIRD CITIZEN
Where do you dwell?

FOURTH CITIZEN
Are you a married man or a bachelor?

SECOND CITIZEN
Answer every man directly.

FIRST CITIZEN
Ay, and briefly.

FOURTH CITIZEN
Ay, and wisely.

THIRD CITIZEN
Ay, and truly, you were best.

CINNA
What is my name? Whither am I going? Where do I
dwell? Am I a married man or a bachelor? Then, to
answer every man directly and briefly, wisely and truly: —
wisely I say, I am a bachelor.

SECOND CITIZEN
That's as much as to say, they are fools that marry: —
you'll bear me a bang for that, I fear. Proceed; directly.

CINNA
Directly, I am going to Cæsar's funeral.

FIRST CITIZEN
As a friend or an enemy?

CINNA
As a friend.

SECOND CITIZEN
That matter is answer'd directly.

FOURTH CITIZEN
For your dwelling, — briefly.

CINNA
Briefly, I dwell by the Capitol.

THIRD CITIZEN
Your name, sir, truly.

CINNA
Truly, my name is Cinna.

FIRST CITIZEN
Tear him to pieces; he's a conspirator.

CINNA
I am Cinna the poet, I am Cinna the poet.

FOURTH CITIZEN
Tear him for his bad verses, tear him for his bad verses.

CINNA
I am not Cinna the conspirator.

FOURTH CITIZEN
It is no matter, his name's Cinna; pluck but his name
out of his heart, and turn him going.

THIRD CITIZEN
Tear him, tear him! Come, brands, ho! fire-brands: to
Brutus', to Cassius'; burn all: some to Decius' house,
and some to Casca's; some to Ligarius': away, go!
                                        [*Exeunt*

ACT IV

SCENE I
Rome. A room in ANTONY'S *house.*

ANTONY, OCTAVIUS, *and* LEPIDUS,
seated at a table.

ANTONY
These many, then, shall die; their names are prick'd.

OCTAVIUS
Your brother too must die; consent you, Lepidus?

LEPIDUS
I do consent, —
OCTAVIUS
          Prick him down, Antony.
LEPIDUS
Upon condition Publius shall not live,
Who is your sister's son, Mark Antony.
ANTONY
He shall not live; look, with a spot I damn him.
But, Lepidus, go you to Cæsar's house;
Fetch the will hither, and we shall determine
How to cut off some charge in legacies.
LEPIDUS
What, shall I find you here?
OCTAVIUS
          Or here, or at
The Capitol.   [*Exit* LEPIDUS.
ANTONY
This is a slight unmeritable man,
Meet to be sent on errands: is it fit,
The threefold world divided, he should stand
One of the three to share it?
OCTAVIUS
          So you thought him;
And took his voice who should be prick'd to die,
In our black sentence and proscription.
ANTONY
Octavius, I have seen more days than you:
And though we lay these honours on this man,
To ease ourselves of divers slanderous loads,
He shall but bear them as the ass bears gold,
To groan and sweat under the business,
Either led or driven, as we point the way;
And having brought our treasure where we will,
Then take we down his load, and turn him off,
Like to the empty ass, to shake his ears,
And graze in commons.
OCTAVIUS
          You may do your will:
But he's a tried and valiant soldier.
ANTONY
So is my horse, Octavius; and for that
I do appoint him store of provender:
It is a creature that I teach to fight,
To wind, to stop, to run directly on, —
His corporal motion govern'd by my spirit.
And, in some taste, is Lepidus but so;
He must be taught, and train'd, and bid go forth: —
A barren-spirited fellow; one that feeds
On objects, arts, and imitations,
Which, out of use and stal'd by other men,
Begin his fashion: do not talk of him
But as a property. And now, Octavius,
Listen great things: — Brutus and Cassius
Are levying powers: we must straight make head:
Therefore let our alliance be combined,
Our best friends made, and our best means stretch'd out;
And let us presently go sit in council,
How covert matters may be best disclosed,
And open perils surest answered.
OCTAVIUS
Let us do so: for we are at the stake,
And bay'd about with many enemies;
And some that smile have in their hearts, I fear,
Millions of mischiefs.   [*Exeunt.*

SCENE II

Before BRUTUS' tent, in the camp near Sardis.

Drum. Enter BRUTUS, LUCILIUS, LUCIUS, and the
ARMY; TITINIUS *and* PINDARUS *meet them.*

BRUTUS
Stand, ho!
LUCILIUS
Give the word, ho! and stand.
BRUTUS
What now, Lucilius! is Cassius near?
LUCILIUS
He is at hand; and Pindarus is come
To do you salutation from his master.
BRUTUS
He greets me well. — Your master, Pindarus,
In his own change, or by ill officers,
Hath given me some worthy cause to wish
Things done, undone: but, if he be at hand
I shall be satisfied.
PINDARUS
          I do not doubt
But that my noble master will appear
Such as he is, full of regard and honour.

BRUTUS
He is not doubted. — A word, Lucilius;
How he receiv'd you, let me be resolv'd.
LUCILIUS
With courtesy and with respect enough;
But not with such familiar instances,
Nor with such free and friendly conference,
As he hath used of old.
BRUTUS
          Thou hast described
A hot friend cooling: ever note, Lucilius,
When love begins to sicken and decay,
It useth an enforced ceremony.
There are no tricks in plain and simple faith:
But hollow men, like horses hot at hand,
Make gallant show and promise of their mettle;
But when they should endure the bloody spur,
They fall their crests, and, like deceitful jades,
Sink in the trial. Comes his army on?
LUCILIUS
They mean this night in Sardis to be quarter'd;
The greater part, the horse in general,
Are come with Cassius.   [*Low march within.*
BRUTUS
          Hark! he is arriv'd: —
March gently on to meet him.
      Enter CASSIUS *and his* POWERS.
CASSIUS
Stand, ho!
BRUTUS
Stand, ho! Speak the word along.
FIRST SOLDIER
Stand!
SECOND SOLDIER
Stand!
THIRD SOLDIER
Stand!
CASSIUS
Most noble brother, you have done me wrong.
BRUTUS
Judge me, you gods! wrong I mine enemies?
And if not so, how should I wrong a brother?
CASSIUS
Brutus, this sober form of yours hides wrongs;
And when you do them —
BRUTUS
          Cassius, be content;
Speak your griefs softly, — I do know you well: —
Before the eyes of both our armies here,
Which should perceive nothing but love from us,
Let us not wrangle: bid them move away;
Then in my tent, Cassius, enlarge your griefs,
And I will give you audience.
CASSIUS
          Pindarus,
Bid our commanders lead their charges off
A little from this ground.
BRUTUS
Lucilius, do you the like; and let no man
Come to our tent till we have done our conference.
Let Lucius and Titinius guard our door.   [*Exeunt.*

SCENE III

Within the tent of BRUTUS.

Enter BRUTUS and CASSIUS.

CASSIUS
That you have wrong'd me doth appear in this:
You have condemn'd and noted Lucius Pella
For taking bribes here of the Sardians;
Wherein my letters, praying on his side,
Because I knew the man, were slighted off.
BRUTUS
You wrong'd yourself to write in such a case.
CASSIUS
In such a time as this it is not meet
That every nice offence should bear his comment.
BRUTUS
Let me tell you, Cassius, you yourself
Are much condemn'd to have an itching palm;
To sell and mart your offices for gold
To undeservers.
CASSIUS
          I an itching palm!
You know that you are Brutus that speak this,
Or, by the gods, this speech were else your last.
BRUTUS
The name of Cassius honours this corruption,
And chastisement doth therefore hide his head.

CASSIUS
Chastisement!
BRUTUS
Remember March, the ides of March remember:
Did not great Julius bleed for justice' sake?
What villain touch'd his body, that did stab,
And not for justice? What, shall one of us,
That struck the foremost man of all this world
But for supporting robbers, shall we now
Contaminate our fingers with base bribes,
And sell the mighty space of our large honours
For so much trash as may be grasped thus? —
I had rather be a dog, and bay the moon,
Than such a Roman.
CASSIUS
          Brutus, bay not me, —
I'll not endure it: you forget yourself,
To hedge me in; I am a soldier, I,
Older in practice, abler than yourself
To make conditions.
BRUTUS
          Go to; you are not, Cassius.
CASSIUS
I am.
BRUTUS
I say you are not.
CASSIUS
Urge me no more, I shall forget myself;
Have mind upon your health, tempt me no further.
BRUTUS
Away, slight man!
CASSIUS
Is't possible?
BRUTUS
          Hear me, for I will speak.
Must I give way and room to your rash choler?
Shall I be frighted when a madman stares?
CASSIUS
O ye gods, ye gods! must I endure all this?
BRUTUS
All this! ay, more: fret till your proud heart break;
Go show your slaves how choleric you are,
And make your bondmen tremble. Must I budge?
Must I observe you? must I stand and crouch
Under your testy humour? By the gods,
You shall digest the venom of your spleen,
Though it do split you; for, from this day forth,
I'll use you for my mirth, yea, for my laughter,
When you are waspish.
CASSIUS
          Is it come to this?
BRUTUS
You say you are a better soldier:
Let it appear so; make your vaunting true,
And it shall please me well: for mine own part,
I shall be glad to learn of noble men.
CASSIUS
You wrong me every way; you wrong me, Brutus;
I said, an elder soldier, not a better:
Did I say 'better'?
BRUTUS
          If you did, I care not.
CASSIUS
When Cæsar liv'd, he durst not thus have mov'd me.
BRUTUS
Peace, peace! you durst not so have tempted him.
CASSIUS
I durst not!
BRUTUS
No.
CASSIUS
What, durst not tempt him!
BRUTUS
          For your life you durst not.
CASSIUS
Do not presume too much upon my love;
I may do that I shall be sorry for.
BRUTUS
You have done that you should be sorry for.
There is no terror, Cassius, in your threats;
For I am arm'd so strong in honesty,
That they pass by me as the idle wind,
Which I respect not. I did send to you
For certain sums of gold, which you denied me;
For I can raise no money by vile means:
By heaven, I had rather coin my heart,
And drop my blood for drachmas, than to wring
From the hard hands of peasants their vile trash
By any indirection; — I did send

To you for gold to pay my legions,
Which you denied me: was that done like Cassius?
Should I have answer'd Caius Cassius so?
When Marcus Brutus grows so covetous,
To lock such rascal counters from his friends,
Be ready, gods, with all your thunderbolts;
Dash him to pieces!
CASSIUS
     I denied you not.
BRUTUS
You did.
CASSIUS
I did not: — he was but a fool that brought
My answer back. — Brutus hath riv'd my heart:
A friend should bear his friend's infirmities,
But Brutus makes mine greater than they are.
BRUTUS
I do not, till you practise them on me.
CASSIUS
You love me not.
BRUTUS
    I do not like your faults.
CASSIUS
A friendly eye could never see such faults.
BRUTUS
A flatterer's would not, though they do appear
As huge as high Olympus.
CASSIUS
Come, Antony, and young Octavius, come,
Revenge yourselves alone on Cassius,
For Cassius is a-weary of the world;
Hated by one he loves; brav'd by his brother;
Check'd like a bondman; all his faults observed,
Set in a note-book, learn'd, and conn'd by rote,
To cast into my teeth. O, I could weep
My spirit from mine eyes! — There is my dagger,
And here my naked breast; within, a heart
Dearer than Pluto's mine, richer than gold:
If that thou be'st a Roman, take it forth;
I, that denied thee gold, will give my heart:
Strike, as thou didst at Cæsar; for, I know,
When thou didst hate him worst, thou lovedst him
  better
Than ever thou lovedst Cassius.
BRUTUS
     Sheathe your dagger:
Be angry when you will, it shall have scope;
Do what you will, dishonour shall be humour.
O Cassius, you are yoked with a lamb
That carries anger as the flint bears fire;
Who, much enforced, shows a hasty spark,
And straight is cold again.
CASSIUS
    Hath Cassius liv'd
To be but mirth and laughter to his Brutus,
When grief, and blood ill-temper'd, vexeth him?
BRUTUS
When I spoke that, I was ill-temper'd too.
CASSIUS
Do you confess so much? Give me your hand.
BRUTUS
And my heart too.
CASSIUS
   O Brutus, —
BRUTUS
     What's the matter?
CASSIUS
Have not you love enough to bear with me,
When that rash humour which my mother gave me
Makes me forgetful?
BRUTUS
   Yes, Cassius; and, from henceforth,
When you are over-earnest with your Brutus,
He'll think your mother chides, and leave you so.
POET [within]
Let me go in to see the generals;
There is some grudge between 'em, 'tis not meet
They be alone.
LUCILIUS [within].
You shall not come to them.
POET [within].
Nothing but death shall stay me.

  Enter POET, follow'd by LUCILIUS,
   TITINIUS, and LUCIUS.

CASSIUS
How now! what's the matter?
POET
For shame, you generals! what do you mean?

Love, and be friends, as two such men should be;
For I have seen more years, I'm sure, than ye.
CASSIUS
Ha, ha! how vilely doth this cynic rime!
BRUTUS
Get you hence, sirrah; saucy fellow, hence!
CASSIUS
Bear with him, Brutus; 'tis his fashion.
BRUTUS
I'll know his humour, when he knows his time:
What should the wars do with these jigging fools? —
Companion, hence!
CASSIUS
   Away, away, be gone!
       [*Exit* POET.
BRUTUS
Lucilius and Titinius, bid the commanders
Prepare to lodge their companies to-night.
CASSIUS
And come yourselves, and bring Messala with you
Immediately to us.
  [*Exeunt* LUCILIUS *and* TITINIUS.
BRUTUS
   Lucius, a bowl of wine!
CASSIUS
I did not think you could have been so angry.
BRUTUS
O Cassius, I am sick of many griefs.
CASSIUS
Of your philosophy you make no use,
If you give place to accidental evils.
BRUTUS
No man bears sorrow better: — Portia is dead.
CASSIUS
Ha! Portia!
BRUTUS
She is dead.
CASSIUS
How scap'd I killing when I cross'd you so? —
O insupportable and touching loss! —
Upon what sickness?
BRUTUS
   Impatient of my absence,
And grief that young Octavius with Mark Antony
Have made themselves so strong; — for with her
  death
That tidings came; — with this she fell distract,
And, her attendants absent, swallow'd fire.
CASSIUS
And died so?
BRUTUS
   Even so.
CASSIUS
   O ye immortal gods!
 Enter LUCIUS, *with wine and taper.*
BRUTUS
Speak no more of her. — Give me a bowl of wine. —
In this I bury all unkindness, Cassius. [*Drinks.*
CASSIUS
My heart is thirsty for that noble pledge. —
Fill, Lucius, till the wine o'erswell the cup;
I cannot drink too much of Brutus' love. [*Drinks.*
BRUTUS
Come in, Titinius!   [*Exit* LUCIUS.
 Enter TITINIUS, *with* MESSALA.
  Welcome, good Messala. —
Now sit we close about this taper here,
And call in question our necessities.
CASSIUS
Portia, art thou gone?
BRUTUS
   No more, I pray you. —
Messala, I have here received letters,
That young Octavius and Mark Antony
Come down upon us with a mighty power,
Bending their expedition toward Philippi.
MESSALA
Myself have letters of the selfsame tenour.
BRUTUS
With what addition?
MESSALA
That by proscription and bills of outlawry,
Octavius, Antony, and Lepidus
Have put to death an hundred senators.
BRUTUS
Therein our letters do not well agree;
Mine speak of seventy senators that died
By their proscriptions, Cicero being one.

CASSIUS
Cicero one!
MESSALA
   Cicero is dead,
And by that order of proscription. —
Had you your letters from your wife, my lord?
BRUTUS
No, Messala.
MESSALA
Nor nothing in your letters writ of her?
BRUTUS
Nothing, Messala.
MESSALA
   That, methinks, is strange.
BRUTUS
Why ask you? hear you aught of her in yours?
MESSALA
No, my lord.
BRUTUS
Now, as you are a Roman, tell me true.
MESSALA
Then like a Roman bear the truth I tell:
For certain she is dead, and by strange manner.
BRUTUS
Why, farewell, Portia. — We must die, Messala:
With meditating that she must die once,
I have the patience to endure it now.
MESSALA
Even so great men great losses should endure.
CASSIUS
I have as much of this in art as you,
But yet my nature could not bear it so.
BRUTUS
Well, to our work alive. What do you think
Of marching to Philippi presently?
CASSIUS
I do not think it good.
BRUTUS
   Your reason?
CASSIUS
    This it is: —
'Tis better that the enemy seek us:
So shall he waste his means, weary his soldiers,
Doing himself offence; whilst we, lying still,
Are full of rest, defence, and nimbleness.
BRUTUS
Good reasons must, of force, give place to better.
The people 'twixt Philippi and this ground
Do stand but in a forc'd affection;
For they have grudg'd us contribution:
The enemy, marching along by them,
By them shall make a fuller number up,
Come on refresh'd, new-added, and encourag'd;
From which advantage shall we cut him off,
If at Philippi we do face him there,
These people at our back.
CASSIUS
   Hear me, good brother.
BRUTUS
Under your pardon. — You must note beside,
That we have tried the utmost of our friends,
Our legions are brim-full, our cause is ripe:
The enemy increaseth every day;
We, at the height, are ready to decline.
There is a tide in the affairs of men,
Which, taken at the flood, leads on to fortune;
Omitted, all the voyage of their life
Is bound in shallows and in miseries.
On such a full sea are we now afloat;
And we must take the current when it serves,
Or lose our ventures.
CASSIUS
   Then, with your will, go on;
We'll along ourselves, and meet them at Philippi.
BRUTUS
The deep of night is crept upon our talk,
And nature must obey necessity;
Which we will niggard with a little rest.
There is no more to say?
CASSIUS
   No more. Good night:
Early to-morrow will we rise, and hence.
BRUTUS
Lucius, my gown! — Farewell, good Messala: —
Good night, Titinius: — noble, noble Cassius,
Good night, and good repose.
CASSIUS
   O my dear brother!
This was an ill beginning of the night:

Never come such division 'tween our souls!
Let it not, Brutus.

BRUTUS
Every thing is well.

CASSIUS
Good night, my lord.

BRUTUS
Good night, good brother.

TITINIUS and MESSALA
Good night, Lord Brutus.

BRUTUS
Farewell, every one.

[*Exeunt* CASSIUS, TITINIUS, *and* MESSALA.
Enter LUCIUS, *with the gown.*

Give me the gown. Where is thy instrument?

LUCIUS
Here in the tent.

BRUTUS
What, thou speak'st drowsily?
Poor knave, I blame thee not; thou art o'er-watch'd.
Call Claudius and some other of my men;
I'll have them sleep on cushions in my tent.

LUCIUS
Varro and Claudius!

Enter VARRO *and* CLAUDIUS.

VARRO
Calls my lord?

BRUTUS
I pray you, sirs, lie in my tent and sleep;
It may be I shall raise you by and by
On business to my brother Cassius.

VARRO
So please you, we will stand and watch your pleasure.

BRUTUS
I will not have it so: lie down, good sirs;
It may be I shall otherwise bethink me. —
Look, Lucius, here's the book I sought for so;
I put it in the pocket of my gown.

[VARRO *and* CLAUDIUS *lie down.*

LUCIUS
I was sure your lordship did not give it me.

BRUTUS
Bear with me, good boy, I am much forgetful.
Canst thou hold up thy heavy eyes awhile,
And touch thy instrument a strain or two?

LUCIUS
Ay, my lord, an't please you.

BRUTUS
It does, my boy:
I trouble thee too much, but thou art willing.

LUCIUS
It is my duty, sir.

BRUTUS
I should not urge thy duty past thy might;
I know young bloods look for a time of rest.

LUCIUS
I have slept, my lord, already.

BRUTUS
It was well done; and thou shalt sleep again;
I will not hold thee long: if I do live,
I will be good to thee.   [*Music, and a song.*
This is a sleepy tune: — O murderous slumber,
Lay'st thou thy leaden mace upon my boy,
That plays thee music? — Gentle knave, good night:
I will not do thee so much wrong to wake thee:
If thou dost nod, thou break'st thy instrument;
I'll take it from thee; and, good boy, good night. —
Let me see, let me see; — is not the leaf turn'd down
Where I left reading? Here it is, I think.

Enter the GHOST OF CAESAR.

How ill this taper burns! — Ha! who comes here?
I think it is the weakness of mine eyes
That shapes this monstrous apparition.
It comes upon me. — Art thou any thing?
Art thou some god, some angel, or some devil,
That makest my blood cold, and my hair to stare?
Speak to me what thou art.

GHOST OF CAESAR
Thy evil spirit, Brutus.

BRUTUS
Why comest thou?

GHOST OF CAESAR
To tell thee thou shalt see me at Philippi.

BRUTUS
Well; then I shall see thee again?

GHOST OF CAESAR
Ay, at Philippi.

BRUTUS
Why, I will see thee at Philippi, then.
[GHOST *vanishes.*
Now I have taken heart thou vanishest:
Ill spirit, I would hold more talk with thee. —
Boy, Lucius! — Varro! Claudius! — Sirs, awake! —
Claudius!

LUCIUS
The strings, my lord, are false.

BRUTUS
He thinks he still is at his instrument. —
Lucius, awake!

LUCIUS
My lord?

BRUTUS
Didst thou dream, Lucius, that thou so criedst out?

LUCIUS
My lord, I do not know that I did cry.

BRUTUS
Yes, that thou didst: didst thou see any thing?

LUCIUS
Nothing, my lord.

BRUTUS
Sleep again, Lucius. — Sirrah, Claudius! —
[*to* VARRO] Fellow thou, awake!

VARRO
My lord?

CLAUDIUS
My lord?

BRUTUS
Why did you so cry out, sirs, in your sleep?

VARRO and CLAUDIUS
Did we, my lord?

BRUTUS
Ay: saw you any thing?

VARRO
No, my lord, I saw nothing.

CLAUDIUS
Nor I, my lord.

BRUTUS
Go and commend me to my brother Cassius;
Bid him set on his powers betimes before,
And we will follow.

VARRO and CLAUDIUS
It shall be done, my lord.   [*Exeunt.*

ACT V

SCENE I

The plains of Philippi.

Enter OCTAVIUS, ANTONY, *and their* ARMY.

OCTAVIUS
Now, Antony, our hopes are answered:
You said the enemy would not come down,
But keep the hills and upper regions:
It proves not so; their battles are at hand;
They mean to warn us at Philippi here,
Answering before we do demand of them.

ANTONY
Tut, I am in their bosoms, and I know
Wherefore they do it: they could be content
To visit other places; and come down

With fearful bravery, thinking by this face
To fasten in our thoughts that they have courage;
But 'tis not so.

Enter a MESSENGER.

MESSENGER
Prepare you, generals:
The enemy comes on in gallant show;
Their bloody sign of battle is hung out,
And something to be done immediately.

ANTONY
Octavius, lead your battle softly on,
Upon the left hand of the even field.

OCTAVIUS
Upon the right hand I; keep thou the left.

ANTONY
Why do you cross me in this exigent?

OCTAVIUS
I do not cross you; but I will do so.   [*March.*
Drum. Enter BRUTUS, CASSIUS, *and their* ARMY;
LUCILIUS, TITINIUS, MESSALA, *and others.*

BRUTUS
They stand, and would have parley.

CASSIUS
Stand fast, Titinius: we must out and talk.

OCTAVIUS
Mark Antony, shall we give sign of battle?

ANTONY
No, Cæsar, we will answer on their charge.
Make forth; the generals would have some words.

OCTAVIUS
Stir not until the signal.

BRUTUS
Words before blows: — is it so, countrymen?

OCTAVIUS
Not that we love words better, as you do.

BRUTUS
Good words are better than bad strokes, Octavius.

ANTONY
In your bad strokes, Brutus, you give good words;
Witness the hole you made in Cæsar's heart,
Crying, 'Long live! hail, Cæsar!'

CASSIUS
Antony,
The posture of your blows are yet unknown;
But for your words, they rob the Hybla bees,
And leave them honeyless.

ANTONY
Not stingless too.

BRUTUS
O, yes, and soundless, too;
For you have stol'n their buzzing, Antony,
And very wisely threat before you sting.

ANTONY
Villains, you did not so, when your vile daggers
Hack'd one another in the sides of Cæsar:
You show'd your teeth like apes, and fawn'd like
          hounds,
And bow'd like bondmen, kissing Cæsar's feet;
Whilst damned Casca, like a cur, behind
Struck Cæsar on the neck. O you flatterers!

CASSIUS
Flatterers! — Now, Brutus, thank yourself:
This tongue had not offended so to-day,
If Cassius might have rul'd.

OCTAVIUS
Come, come, the cause: if arguing make us sweat,
The proof of it will turn to redder drops.
Look, —
I draw a sword against conspirators;
When think you that the sword goes up again? —
Never, till Cæsar's three-and-thirty wounds
Be well avenged; or till another Cæsar
Have added slaughter to the words of traitors.

BRUTUS
Cæsar, thou canst not die by traitors' hands,
Unless thou bring'st them with thee.

OCTAVIUS
      So I hope;
I was not born to die on Brutus' sword.

BRUTUS
O, if thou wert the noblest of thy strain,
Young man, thou couldst not die more honourable.

CASSIUS
A peevish schoolboy, worthless of such honour,
Join'd with a masker and a reveller!

ANTONY
Old Cassius still!

OCTAVIUS
    Come, Antony; away! —
Defiance, traitors, hurl we in your teeth:
If you dare fight to-day, come to the field;
If not, when you have stomachs.

  [*Exeunt* OCTAVIUS, ANTONY, *and their* ARMY.

CASSIUS
Why, now, blow wind, swell billow, and swim bark!
The storm is up, and all is on the hazard.

BRUTUS
Ho,
Lucilius! hark; a word with you.

LUCILIUS
    My lord?
  [BRUTUS *and* LUCILIUS *converse apart.*

CASSIUS
Messala, —

MESSALA
   What says my general?

CASSIUS
     Messala,
This is my birth-day; as this very day
Was Cassius born. Give me thy hand, Messala:
Be thou my witness that, against my will,
As Pompey was, am I compell'd to set
Upon one battle all our liberties.
You know that I held Epicurus strong,
And his opinion: now I change my mind,
And partly credit things that do presage.
Coming from Sardis, on our former ensign
Two mighty eagles fell; and there they perch'd,
Gorging and feeding from our soldiers' hands;
Who to Philippi here consorted us:
This morning are they fled away and gone;
And in their steads do ravens, crows, and kites,
Fly o'er our heads, and downward look on us,
As we were sickly prey: their shadows seem
A canopy most fatal, under which
Our army lies, ready to give up the ghost.

MESSALA
Believe not so.

CASSIUS
   I but believe it partly;
For I am fresh of spirit, and resolved
To meet all perils very constantly.

BRUTUS
Even so, Lucilius.

CASSIUS
    Now, most noble Brutus,
The gods to-day stand friendly, that we may,
Lovers in peace, lead on our days to age!
But, since the affairs of men rest still incertain,
Let's reason with the worst that may befall.
If we do lose this battle, then is this
The very last time we shall speak together:
What are you, then, determined to do?

BRUTUS
Even by the rule of that philosophy
By which I did blame Cato for the death
Which he did give himself: — I know not how,
But I do find it cowardly and vile,
For fear of what might fall, so to prevent
The time of life: — arming myself with patience
To stay the providence of some high powers
That govern us below.

CASSIUS
    Then, if we lose this battle,

You are contented to be led in triumph
Through the streets of Rome?

BRUTUS
No, Cassius, no: think not, thou noble Roman,
That ever Brutus will go bound to Rome;
He bears too great a mind. But this same day
Must end that work the ides of March begun;
And whether we shall meet again I know not.
Therefore our everlasting farewell take: —
For ever, and for ever, farewell, Cassius!
If we do meet again, why, we shall smile;
If not, why, then, this parting was well made.

CASSIUS
For ever, and for ever, farewell, Brutus!
If we do meet again, we'll smile indeed;
If not, 'tis true this parting was well made.

BRUTUS
Why, then, lead on. — O, that a man might know
The end of this day's business ere it come!
But it sufficeth that the day will end,
And then the end is known. — Come, ho! away!

  [*Exeunt.*

SCENE II

The same. The field of battle.

Alarums. Enter BRUTUS *and* MESSALA.

BRUTUS
Ride, ride, Messala, ride, and give these bills
Unto the legions on the other side:

Let them set on at once; for I perceive
But cold demeanour in Octavius' wing,
And sudden push gives them the overthrow.
Ride, ride, Messala: let them all come down. [*Exeunt.*

SCENE III

The same. Another part of the field.

Alarums. Enter CASSIUS *and* TITINIUS.

CASSIUS
O look, Titinius, look, the villains fly!
Myself have to mine own turn'd enemy:
This ensign here of mine was turning back;
I slew the coward, and did take it from him.

TITINIUS
O Cassius, Brutus gave the word too early;
Who, having some advantage on Octavius,
Took it too eagerly: his soldiers fell to spoil,
Whilst we by Antony are all enclosed.

Enter PINDARUS.

PINDARUS
Fly further off, my lord, fly further off;
Mark Antony is in your tents, my lord:
Fly, therefore, noble Cassius, fly far off.

CASSIUS
This hill is far enough. — Look, look, Titinius;
Are those my tents where I perceive the fire?

TITINIUS
They are, my lord.

CASSIUS Come down, behold no more.

CASSIUS
Titinius, if thou lov'st me,
Mount thou my horse, and hide thy spurs in him,
Till he have brought thee up to yonder troops,
And here again; that I may rest assured
Whether yond troops are friend or enemy.

TITINIUS
I will be here again, even with a thought.   [*Exit.*

CASSIUS
Go, Pindarus, get higher on that hill;
My sight was ever thick; regard Titinius,
And tell me what thou notest about the field. —
               [*PINDARUS goes up.*
This day I breathed first: time is come round,
And where I did begin, there shall I end;
My life is run his compass. — Sirrah, what news?

PINDARUS [*above*].
O my lord!

CASSIUS
What news?

PINDARUS [*above*].
Titinius is enclosed round about
With horsemen, that make to him on the spur; —
Yet he spurs on. — Now they are almost on him; —
Now, Titinius! —
Now some light: O, he lights too: he's ta'en; [*shout*] and,
   hark!
They shout for joy.

CASSIUS
        Come down, behold no more. —
O, coward that I am, to live so long,
To see my best friend ta'en before my face!

    PINDARUS descends.

Come hither, sirrah:
In Parthia did I take thee prisoner;
And then I swore thee, saving of thy life,
That whatsoever I did bid thee do,
Thou shouldst attempt it. Come now, keep thine oath;
Now be a freeman; and, with this good sword,
That ran through Cæsar's bowels, search this bosom.
Stand not to answer: here, take thou the hilts;
And, when my face is cover'd, as 'tis now,
Guide thou the sword. — Cæsar, thou art revenged,
Even with the sword that kill'd thee.   [*Dies.*

PINDARUS
So, I am free; yet would not so have been,
Durst I have done my will. O Cassius!
Far from this country Pindarus shall run,
Where never Roman shall take note of him.   [*Exit.*

    Enter TITINIUS with MESSALA.

MESSALA
It is but change, Titinius; for Octavius
Is overthrown by noble Brutus' power,
As Cassius' legions are by Antony.

TITINIUS
These tidings will well comfort Cassius.

MESSALA
Where did you leave him?

TITINIUS
           All disconsolate,
With Pindarus his bondman, on this hill.

MESSALA
Is not that he that lies upon the ground?

TITINIUS
He lies not like the living. O my heart!

MESSALA
Is not that he?

TITINIUS
       No, this was he, Messala,
But Cassius is no more. — O setting sun,
As in thy red rays thou dost sink to night,
So in his red blood Cassius' day is set, —
The sun of Rome is set! Our day is gone;
Clouds, dews, and dangers come; our deeds are done!
Mistrust of my success hath done this deed.

MESSALA
Mistrust of good success hath done this deed.
O hateful Error, Melancholy's child,
Why dost thou show to the apt thoughts of men
The things that are not? O Error, soon conceived,
Thou never comest unto a happy birth,
But kill'st the mother that engender'd thee!

TITINIUS
What, Pindarus! where art thou, Pindarus?

MESSALA
Seek him, Titinius, whilst I go to meet
The noble Brutus, thrusting this report
Into his ears: I may say, thrusting it;

For piercing steel, and darts envenomed,
Shall be as welcome to the ears of Brutus
As tidings of this sight.

TITINIUS
        Hie you, Messala,
And I will seek for Pindarus the while.
                  [*Exit* MESSALA.
Why didst thou send me forth, brave Cassius?
Did I not meet thy friends? and did not they
Put on my brows this wreath of victory,
And bid me give it thee? Didst thou not hear their
   shouts?
Alas, thou hast misconstrued every thing!
But, hold thee, take this garland on thy brow;
Thy Brutus bid me give it thee, and I
Will do his bidding. — Brutus, come apace,
And see how I regarded Caius Cassius. —
By your leave, gods: — this is a Roman's part:
Come, Cassius' sword, and find Titinius' heart.
                       [*Dies.*

*Alarums. Enter MESSALA, with BRUTUS, young
CATO, STRATO, VOLUMNIUS, and LUCILIUS.*

BRUTUS
Where, where, Messala, doth his body lie?

MESSALA
Lo, yonder; and Titinius mourning it.

BRUTUS
Titinius' face is upward.

YOUNG CATO
          He is slain.

BRUTUS
O Julius Cæsar, thou art mighty yet!
Thy spirit walks abroad, and turns our swords
In our own proper entrails.   [*Low alarums.*

YOUNG CATO
          Brave Titinius!
Look, whe'r he have not crown'd dead Cassius!

BRUTUS
Are yet two Romans living such as these? —
The last of all the Romans, fare thee well!
It is impossible that ever Rome
Should breed thy fellow. — Friends, I owe more tears
To this dead man than you shall see me pay. —
I shall find time, Cassius, I shall find time. —
Come, therefore, and to Thasos send his body:
His funerals shall not be in our camp,
Lest it discomfort us. — Lucilius, come; —
And come, young Cato; — let us to the field. —
Labeo and Flavius, set our battles on: —
'Tis three o'clock; and, Romans, yet ere night
We shall try fortune in a second fight.   [*Exeunt.*

SCENE IV

The same. Another part of the field.

*Alarum. Enter, fighting, SOLDIERS of both armies; then
BRUTUS, YOUNG CATO, LUCILIUS, and others.*

BRUTUS
Yet, countrymen, O, yet hold up your heads!

YOUNG CATO
What bastard doth not? Who will go with me?
I will proclaim my name about the field: —
I am the son of Marcus Cato, ho!
A foe to tyrants, and my country's friend;
I am the son of Marcus Cato, ho!

BRUTUS
And I am Brutus, Marcus Brutus, I;
Brutus, my country's friend; know me for Brutus!
                       [*Exit.*

LUCILIUS
O young and noble Cato, art thou down?
Why, now thou diest as bravely as Titinius;
And mayst be honour'd, being Cato's son.

FIRST SOLDIER
Yield, or thou diest.

LUCILIUS
        Only I yield to die:
There is so much that thou wilt kill me straight;
                 [*Offering money.*
Kill Brutus, and be honour'd in his death.

FIRST SOLDIER
We must not. — A noble prisoner!

SECOND SOLDIER
Room, ho! Tell Antony, Brutus is ta'en.

FIRST SOLDIER
I'll tell the news: — here comes the general.
        Enter ANTONY.
Brutus is ta'en, Brutus is ta'en, my lord.

ANTONY
Where is he?

LUCILIUS
Safe, Antony; Brutus is safe enough:
I dare assure thee that no enemy
Shall ever take alive the noble Brutus:
The gods defend him from so great a shame!
When you do find him, or alive or dead,
He will be found like Brutus, like himself.

ANTONY
This is not Brutus, friend; but, I assure you,
A prize no less in worth: keep this man safe,
Give him all kindness: I had rather have
Such men my friends than enemies. Go on,
And see whe'r Brutus be alive or dead:
And bring us word unto Octavius' tent
How every thing is chanced.   [*Exeunt.*

SCENE V

The same. Another part of the field.

*Enter BRUTUS, DARDANIUS, CLITUS, STRATO,
and VOLUMNIUS.*

BRUTUS
Come, poor remains of friends, rest on this rock.

CLITUS
Statilius show'd the torch-light; but, my lord,
He came not back: he is or ta'en or slain.

BRUTUS
Sit thee down, Clitus: slaying is the word;
It is a deed in fashion. Hark thee, Clitus.
                  [*Whispers him.*

CLITUS
What, I, my lord? No, not for all the world.

BRUTUS
Peace, then, no words.

CLITUS
        I'll rather kill myself.

BRUTUS
Hark thee, Dardanius.   [*Whispers him.*

DARDANIUS
        Shall I do such a deed?

CLITUS
O Dardanius!

DARDANIUS
O Clitus!

CLITUS
What ill request did Brutus make to thee?

DARDANIUS
To kill him, Clitus. Look, he meditates.

CLITUS
Now is that noble vessel full of grief,
That it runs over even at his eyes.

BRUTUS
Come hither, good Volumnius; list a word.

VOLUMNIUS
What says my lord?

BRUTUS
        Why, this, Volumnius:
The ghost of Cæsar hath appear'd to me
Two several times by night, — at Sardis once,
And, this last night, here in Philippi fields:
I know my hour is come.

VOLUMNIUS
        Not so, my lord.

BRUTUS
Nay, I am sure it is, Volumnius.
Thou seest the world, Volumnius, how it goes;
Our enemies have beat us to the pit: [*Low alarums.*
It is more worthy to leap in ourselves,
Than tarry till they push us. Good Volumnius,
Thou know'st that we two went to school together;
Even for that our love of old, I prithee,
Hold thou my sword-hilts, whilst I run on it.

VOLUMNIUS
That's not an office for a friend, my lord.
                  [*Alarum still.*

CLITUS
Fly, fly, my lord; there is no tarrying here.

BRUTUS
Farewell to you; — and you; — and you, Volumnius. —
Strato, thou hast been all this while asleep;
Farewell to thee too, Strato. — Countrymen,
My heart doth joy, that yet, in all my life,
I found no man but he was true to me.
I shall have glory by this losing day,
More than Octavius and Mark Antony
By this vile conquest shall attain unto.
So, fare you well at once; for Brutus' tongue

Hath almost ended his life's history:
Night hangs upon mine eyes; my bones would rest,
That have but labour'd to attain this hour.
                              [*Alarums. Cry within, 'Fly, fly, fly!'*

CLITUS
Fly, my lord, fly.

BRUTUS
                              Hence! I will follow.
              [*Exeunt* CLITUS, DARDANIUS, *and* VOLUMNIUS.
I prithee, Strato, stay thou by thy lord:
Thou art a fellow of a good respect;
Thy life hath had some smatch of honour in it:
Hold, then, my sword, and turn away thy face,
While I do run upon it. Wilt thou, Strato?

STRATO
Give me your hand first: fare you well, my lord.

BRUTUS
Farewell, good Strato. — Cæsar, now be still:
I kill'd not thee with half so good a will.
                              [*He runs on his sword, and dies.*
      Alarums. Retreat. Enter OCTAVIUS, ANTONY,
          MESSALA, LUCILIUS, *and the* ARMY.

OCTAVIUS
What man is that?

MESSALA
My master's man. — Strato, where is thy master?

STRATO
Free from the bondage you are in, Messala:
The conquerors can but make a fire of him;
For Brutus only overcame himself,
And no man else hath honour by his death.

LUCILIUS
So Brutus should be found. — I thank thee, Brutus,
That thou hast prov'd Lucilius' saying true.

OCTAVIUS
All that serv'd Brutus, I will entertain them. —
Fellow, wilt thou bestow thy time with me?

STRATO
Ay, if Messala will prefer me to you.

OCTAVIUS
Do so, good Messala.

MESSALA
How died my master, Strato?

STRATO
I held the sword, and he did run on it.

MESSALA
Octavius, then take him to follow thee,
That did the latest service to my master.

ANTONY
This was the noblest Roman of them all:
All the conspirators, save only he,
Did that they did in envy of great Cæsar;
He only, in a general honest thought,
And common good to all, made one of them.
His life was gentle; and the elements
So mix'd in him, that Nature might stand up
And say to all the world, 'This was a man!'

OCTAVIUS
According to his virtue let us use him,
With all respect and rites of bur ial.
Within my tent his bones to-night shall lie,
Most like a soldier, order'd honourably. —
So, call the field to rest: and let's away,
To part the glories of this happy day.   [*Exeunt.*

AS YOU LIKE IT

DRAMATIS PERSONAE

DUKE, *living in banishment.*
FREDERICK, *his brother, and usurper of his dominions.*
AMIENS, } *lords attending on the banish'd Duke.*
JAQUES, }
LE BEAU, *a courtier attending on Frederick.*
CHARLES, *wrestler to Frederick.*
OLIVER, }
JAQUES, } *sons of Sir Rowland de Boys.*
ORLANDO, }

ADAM, } *servants to Oliver.*
DENIS, }
TOUCHSTONE, *a clown.*
SIR OLIVER MARTEXT, *a vicar.*
CORIN, } *shepherds.*
SILVIUS, }
WILLIA M, *a country fellow, in love with Audrey.*
A person representing HYMEN.

ROSALIND, *daughter to the banish'd Duke.*

CELIA, *daughter to Frederick.*
PHEBE, *a shepherdess.*
AUDREY, *a country wench.*

LORDS, PAGES, *and* ATTENDANTS, *etc.*

SCENE — *Oliver's house; Duke Frederick's court; and the Forest of Arden.*

OLIVER Wilt thou lay hands on me, villain?

ACT I

SCENE I

Orchard of OLIVER'S *house.*

Enter ORLANDO *and* ADAM.

ORLANDO
As I remember, Adam, it was upon this fashion: a' bequeath'd me by will but poor a thousand crowns, and, as thou say'st, charged my brother, on his blessing, to breed me well: and there begins my sadness. My brother Jaques he keeps at school, and report speaks goldenly of his profit; for my part, he keeps me rustically at home, or, to speak more properly, stays me here at home unkept; for call you that keeping for a gentleman of my birth, that differs not from the stalling of an ox? His horses are bred better; for, besides that they are fair with their feeding, they are taught their manage, and to that end riders dearly hired: but I, his brother, gain nothing under him but growth; for the which his animals on his dunghills are as much bound to him as I. Besides this nothing that he so plentifully gives me, the something that nature gave me his countenance seems to take from me: he lets me feed with his hinds, bars me the place of a brother, and, as much as in him lies, mines my gentility with my education. This is it, Adam, that grieves me; and the spirit of my father, which I think is within me, begins to mutiny against this servitude: I will no longer endure it, though yet I know no wise remedy how to avoid it.

ADAM
Yonder comes my master, your brother.

ORLANDO
Go apart, Adam, and thou shalt hear how he will shake me up.

Enter OLIVER.

OLIVER
Now, sir! what make you here?

ORLANDO
Nothing: I am not taught to make anything.

OLIVER
What mar you then, sir?

ORLANDO
Marry, sir, I am helping you to mar that which God made, a poor unworthy brother of yours, with idleness.

OLIVER
Marry, sir, be better employ'd, and be naught awhile.

ORLANDO
Shall I keep your hogs, and eat husks with them? What prodigal's portion have I spent that I should come to such penury?

OLIVER
Know you where you are, sir?

ORLANDO
O, sir, very well: here in your orchard.

OLIVER
Know you before whom, sir?

ORLANDO
Ay, better than him I am before knows me. I know you are my eldest brother; and, in the gentle condition of blood, you should so know me. The courtesy of nations allows you my better, in that you are the first-born; but the same tradition takes not away my blood, were there twenty brothers betwixt us: I have as much of my father in me as you; albeit, I confess, your coming before me is nearer to his reverence.

OLIVER
What, boy!

ORLANDO
Come, come, elder brother, you are too young in this.

OLIVER
Wilt thou lay hands on me, villain?

ORLANDO
I am no villain; I am the youngest son of Sir Rowland de Boys; he was my father, and he is thrice a villain that says such a father begot villains. Wert thou not my brother, I would not take this hand from thy throat till this other had pull'd out thy tongue for saying so; thou hast rail'd on thyself.

ADAM
Sweet masters, be patient: for your father's remembrance, be at accord.

OLIVER
Let me go, I say.

ORLANDO
I will not, till I please: you shall hear me. My father charged you in his will to give me good education: you have train'd me like a peasant, obscuring and hiding from me all gentleman-like qualities. The spirit of my father grows strong in me, and I will no longer endure it: therefore allow me such exercises as may become a gentleman, or give me the poor allottery my father left me by testament; with that I will go buy my fortunes.

OLIVER
And what wilt thou do? beg, when that is spent? Well, sir, get you in: I will not long be troubled with you; you shall have some part of your will: I pray you, leave me.

ORLANDO
I will no further offend you than becomes me for my good.

OLIVER
Get you with him, you old dog.

ADAM
Is 'old dog' my reward? Most true, I have lost my teeth in your service. — God be with my old master! he would not have spoke such a word.

[*Exeunt* ORLANDO *and* ADAM.

OLIVER
Is it even so? begin you to grow upon me? I will physic your rankness, and yet give no thousand crowns neither. — Holla, Denis!

Enter DENIS.

DENIS
Calls your worship?

OLIVER
Was not Charles, the duke's wrestler, here to speak with me?

DENIS
So please you, he is here at the door, and importunes access to you.

OLIVER
Call him in. [*Exit* DENIS.] 'Twill be a good way; and to-morrow the wrestling is.

Enter CHARLES.

CHARLES
Good morrow to your worship.

OLIVER
Good morrow, Monsieur Charles. — What's the new news at the new court?

CHARLES
There's no news at the court, sir, but the old news: that is, the old duke is banish'd by his younger brother the new duke; and three or four loving lords have put themselves into voluntary exile with him, whose lands and revenues enrich the new duke; therefore he gives them good leave to wander.

OLIVER
Can you tell if Rosalind, the duke's daughter, be banish'd with her father?

CHARLES
O, no; for the duke's daughter, her cousin, so loves her, being ever from their cradles bred together, that she would have follow'd her exile, or have died to stay behind her. She is at the court, and no less beloved of her uncle than his own daughter; and never two ladies loved as they do.

OLIVER
Where will the old duke live?

CHARLES
They say he is already in the forest of Arden, and a many merry men with him; and there they live like the old Robin Hood of England: they say many young gentlemen flock to him every day, and fleet the time carelessly, as they did in the golden world.

OLIVER
What, you wrestle to-morrow before the new duke?

CHARLES
Marry, do I, sir; and I came to acquaint you with a matter. I am given, sir, secretly to understand that your younger brother Orlando hath a disposition to come in disguised against me to try a fall. To-morrow, sir, I wrestle for my credit; and he that escapes me without some broken limb shall acquit him well. Your brother is but young and tender; and, for your love, I would be loath to foil him, as I must, for my own honour, if he come in: therefore, out of my love to you, I came hither to acquaint you withal, that either you might stay him from his intendment or brook such disgrace well as he shall run into, in that it is a thing of his own search and altogether against my will.

OLIVER
Charles, I thank thee for thy love to me, which thou shalt find I will most kindly requite. I had myself notice of my brother's purpose herein, and have by underhand means labour'd to dissuade him from it; but he is resolute. I'll tell thee, Charles: it is the stubbornest young fellow of France; full of ambition, an envious emulator of every man's good parts, a secret and villainous contriver against me his natural brother; therefore use thy discretion; I had as lief thou didst break his neck as his finger. And thou wert best look to't; for if thou dost him any slight disgrace, or if he do not mightily grace himself on thee, he will practise against thee by poison, entrap thee by some treacherous device, and never leave thee till he hath ta'en thy life by some indirect means or other; for, I assure thee, and almost with tears I speak it, there is not one so young and so villainous this day living. I speak but brotherly of him; but should I anatomise him to thee as he is, I must blush and weep, and thou must look pale and wonder.

CHARLES
I am heartily glad I came hither to you. If he come to-morrow, I'll give him his payment: if ever he go alone again, I'll never wrestle for prize more: and so, God keep your worship!

OLIVER
Farewell, good Charles. [*Exit* CHARLES.] Now will I stir this gamester: I hope I shall see an end of him; for my soul, yet I know not why, hates nothing more than he. Yet he's gentle; never school'd, and yet learned; full of noble device; of all sorts enchantingly beloved; and, indeed, so much in the heart of the world, and especially of my own people, who best know him, that I am altogether misprised: but it shall not be so long; this wrestler shall clear all: nothing remains but that I kindle the boy thither; which now I'll go about.   [*Exit.*

SCENE II

Lawn before the DUKE'S *palace.*

Enter ROSALIND *and* CELIA.

CELIA
I pray thee, Rosalind, sweet my coz, be merry.

ROSALIND
Dear Celia, I show more mirth than I am mistress of; and would you yet I were merrier? Unless you could teach me to forget a banish'd father, you must not learn me how to remember any extraordinary pleasure.

CELIA
Herein I see thou lovest me not with the full weight that I love thee. If my uncle, thy banish'd father, had banish'd thy uncle, the duke my father, so thou hadst been still with me, I could have taught my love to take thy father for mine: so wouldst thou, if the truth of thy love to me were so righteously temper'd as mine is to thee.

ROSALIND
Well, I will forget the condition of my estate, to rejoice in yours.

CELIA
You know my father hath no child but I, nor none is like to have: and, truly, when he dies, thou shalt be his heir; for what he hath taken away from thy father perforce, I will render thee again in affection; by mine honour, I will; and when I break that oath, let me turn monster: therefore, my sweet Rose, my dear Rose, be merry.

ROSALIND
From henceforth I will, coz, and devise sports. Let me see: what think you of falling in love?

CELIA
Marry, I prithee, do, to make sport withal: but love no man in good earnest; nor no further in sport neither than with safety of a pure blush thou mayst in honour come off again.

ROSALIND
What shall be our sport, then?

CELIA
Let us sit and mock the good housewife Fortune from her wheel, that her gifts may henceforth be bestow'd equally.

ROSALIND
I would we could do so; for her benefits are mightily misplaced; and the bountiful blind woman doth most mistake in her gifts to women.

CELIA
'Tis true; for those that she makes fair, she scarce makes honest; and those that she makes honest, she makes very ill-favour'dly.

ROSALIND
Nay, now thou goest from Fortune's office to Nature's: Fortune reigns in gifts of the world, not in the lineaments of Nature.

Enter TOUCHSTONE.

CELIA
No? when Nature hath made a fair creature, may she not by Fortune fall into the fire? Though Nature hath given us wit to flout at Fortune, hath not Fortune sent in this fool to cut off the argument?

ROSALIND
Indeed, there is Fortune too hard for Nature, when Fortune makes Nature's natural the cutter-off of Nature's wit.

CELIA
Peradventure this is not Fortune's work neither, but Nature's; who perceiveth our natural wits too dull to reason of such goddesses and hath sent this natural for our whetstone; for always the dullness of the fool is the whetstone of the wits. — How now, wit! whither wander you?

TOUCHSTONE
Mistress, you must come away to your father.

CELIA
Were you made the messenger?

TOUCHSTONE
No, by mine honour; but I was bid to come for you.

ROSALIND
Where learn'd you that oath, fool?

TOUCHSTONE
Of a certain knight that swore by his honour they were good pancakes, and swore by his honour the mustard was naught: now I'll stand to it, the pancakes were naught, and the mustard was good; and yet was not the knight forsworn.

CELIA
How prove you that, in the great heap of your knowledge?

ROSALIND
Ay, marry, now unmuzzle your wisdom.

TOUCHSTONE
Stand you both forth now: stroke your chins, and swear by your beards that I am a knave.

CELIA
By our beards, if we had them, thou art.

TOUCHSTONE
By my knavery, if I had it, then I were; but if you swear by that that is not, you are not forsworn: no more was

ROSALIND What think you of falling in love?

this knight, swearing by his honour, for he never had any; or if he had, he had sworn it away before ever he saw those pancakes or that mustard.

CELIA
Prithee, who is't that thou mean'st?

TOUCHSTONE
One that old Frederick, your father, loves.

CELIA
My father's love is enough to honour him enough: speak no more of him; you'll be whipp'd for taxation one of these days.

TOUCHSTONE
The more pity, that fools may not speak wisely what wise men do foolishly.

CELIA
By my troth, thou sayest true; for since the little wit that fools have was silenced, the little foolery that wise men have makes a great show. — Here comes Monsieur Le Beau.

ROSALIND
With his mouth full of news.

CELIA
Which he will put on us, as pigeons feed their young.

ROSALIND
Then shall we be news-cramm'd.

CELIA
All the better; we shall be the more marketable.
Enter LE BEAU.
Bon jour, Monsieur Le Beau: what's the news?

LE BEAU
Fair princess, you have lost much good sport.

CELIA
Sport! of what colour?

LE BEAU
What colour, madam! how shall I answer you?

ROSALIND
As wit and fortune will.

TOUCHSTONE
Or as the Destinies decrees.

CELIA
Well said: that was laid on with a trowel.

TOUCHSTONE
Nay, if I keep not my rank, —

ROSALIND
Thou losest thy old smell.

LE BEAU
You amaze me, ladies: I would have told you of good wrestling, which you have lost the sight of.

ROSALIND
Yet tell us the manner of the wrestling.

LE BEAU
I will tell you the beginning; and, if it please your ladyships, you may see the end; for the best is yet to do; and here, where you are, they are coming to perform it.

CELIA
Well, — the beginning, that is dead and buried.

LE BEAU
There comes an old man and his three sons, —

CELIA
I could match this beginning with an old tale.

LE BEAU
Three proper young men, of excellent growth and presence.

ROSALIND
With bills on their necks, 'Be it known unto all men by these presents.'

LE BEAU
The eldest of the three wrestled with Charles, the duke's wrestler; which Charles in a moment threw him, and broke three of his ribs, that there is little hope of life in him: so he served the second, and so the third. Yonder they lie; the poor old man, their father, making such pitiful dole over them, that all the beholders take his part with weeping.

ROSALIND
Alas!

TOUCHSTONE
But what is the sport, monsieur, that the ladies have lost?

LE BEAU
Why, this that I speak of.

TOUCHSTONE
Thus men may grow wiser every day! it is the first time that ever I heard breaking of ribs was sport for ladies.

CELIA
Or I, I promise thee.

ROSALIND
But is there any else longs to see this broken music in his sides? is there yet another dotes upon rib-breaking? — Shall we see this wrestling, cousin?

LE BEAU
You must, if you stay here; for here is the place appointed for the wrestling, and they are ready to perform it.

CELIA
Yonder, sure, they are coming: let us now stay and see it.

Flourish. Enter DUKE FREDERICK, LORDS, ORLANDO, CHARLES, *and* ATTENDANTS.

DUKE FREDERICK
Come on: since the youth will not be entreated, his own peril on his forwardness.

ROSALIND
Is yonder the man?

LE BEAU
Even he, madam.

CELIA
Alas, he is too young! yet he looks successfully.

DUKE FREDERICK
How now, daughter, and cousin! are you crept hither to see the wrestling?

ROSALIND
Ay, my liege, so please you give us leave.

DUKE FREDERICK
You will take little delight in it, I can tell you, there is such odds in the men. In pity of the challenger's youth, I would fain dissuade him, but he will not be entreated. Speak to him, ladies; see if you can move him.

CELIA
Call him hither, good Monsieur Le Beau.

DUKE FREDERICK
Do so: I'll not be by.

LE BEAU
Monsieur the challenger, the princess call for you.

ORLANDO
I attend them with all respect and duty.

ROSALIND
Young man, have you challenged Charles the wrestler?

ORLANDO
No, fair princess; he is the general challenger: I come but in, as others do, to try with him the strength of my youth.

CELIA
Young gentleman, your spirits are too bold for your years. You have seen cruel proof of this man's strength: if you saw yourself with your eyes, or knew yourself with your judgement, the fear of your adventure would counsel you to a more equal enterprise. We pray you, for your own sake, to embrace your own safety, and

give over this attempt.

ROSALIND
Do, young sir; your reputation shall not therefore be misprised: we will make it our suit to the duke that the wrestling might not go forward.

ORLANDO
I beseech you, punish me not with your hard thoughts: wherein I confess me much guilty, to deny so fair and excellent ladies any thing. But let your fair eyes and gentle wishes go with me to my trial; wherein if I be foil'd, there is but one shamed that was never gracious; if kill'd, but one dead that is willing to be so: I shall do my friends no wrong, for I have none to lament me; the world no injury, for in it I have nothing; only in the world I fill up a place, which may be better supplied when I have made it empty.

ROSALIND
The little strength that I have, I would it were with you.

CELIA
And mine, to eke out hers.

ROSALIND
Fare you well: pray heaven I be deceiv'd in you!

CELIA
Your heart's desires be with you!

CHARLES
Come, where is this young gallant that is so desirous to lie with his mother earth?

ORLANDO
Ready, sir; but his will hath in it a more modest working.

DUKE FREDERICK
You shall try but one fall.

CHARLES
No, I warrant your Grace, you shall not entreat him to a second, that have so mightily persuaded him from a first.

ORLANDO
An you mean to mock me after, you should not have mock'd me before: but come your ways.

ROSALIND
Now Hercules be thy speed, young man!

CELIA
I would I were invisible, to catch the strong fellow by the leg.   [*Wrestle.*

ROSALIND
O excellent young man!

CELIA
If I had a thunderbolt in mine eye, I can tell who should down.   [*Shout.* CHARLES *is thrown.*

DUKE FREDERICK
No more, no more.

ORLANDO
Yes, I beseech your Grace: I am not yet well breath'd.

DUKE FREDERICK
How dost thou, Charles?

LE BEAU
He cannot speak, my lord.

DUKE FREDERICK
Bear him away. What is thy name, young man?

ORLANDO
Orlando, my liege; the youngest son of Sir Rowland de Boys.

DUKE FREDERICK
I would thou hadst been son to some man else:

LE BEAU He cannot speak, my lord.

The world esteem'd thy father honourable,
But I did find him still mine enemy:
Thou shouldst have better pleas'd me with this deed,
Hadst thou descended from another house.
But fare thee well; thou art a gallant youth:
I would thou hadst told me of another father.

[*Exeunt* DUKE FREDERICK, TRAIN, *and* LE BEAU.

CELIA
Were I my father, coz, would I do this?

ORLANDO
I am more proud to be Sir Rowland's son,
His youngest son; — and would not change that
   calling,
To be adopted heir to Frederick.

ROSALIND
My father lov'd Sir Rowland as his soul,
And all the world was of my father's mind:
Had I before known this young man his son,
I should have given him tears unto entreaties,
Ere he should thus have ventur'd.

CELIA
                              Gentle cousin,
Let us go thank him and encourage him:
My father's rough and envious disposition
Sticks me at heart. — Sir, you have well deserv'd:
If you do keep your promises in love
But justly, as you have exceeded all promise,
Your mistress shall be happy.

ROSALIND
                              Gentleman,
[*Giving him a chain from her neck.*
Wear this for me, one out of suits with fortune,
That would give more, but that her hand lacks means.
— Shall we go, coz?

CELIA
              Ay. — Fare you well, fair gentleman.

ORLANDO
Can I not say, I thank you? My better parts
Are all thrown down, and that which here stands up
Is but a quintain, a mere lifeless block.

ROSALIND
He calls us back: my pride fell with my fortunes;
I'll ask him what he would. — Did you call, sir? —
Sir, you have wrestled well, and overthrown
More than your enemies.

CELIA
                    Will you go, coz?

ROSALIND
Have with you. — Fare you well.
              [*Exeunt* ROSALIND *and* CELIA.

ORLANDO
What passion hangs these weights upon my tongue?
I cannot speak to her, yet she urg'd conference.
O poor Orlando, thou art overthrown!
Or Charles or something weaker masters thee.

Enter LE BEAU.

LE BEAU
Good sir, I do in friendship counsel you
To leave this place. Albeit you have deserv'd
High commendation, true applause and love,
Yet such is now the duke's condition
That he misconstrues all that you have done.
The duke is humorous: what he is, indeed,
More suits you to conceive than I to speak of.

ORLANDO
I thank you, sir: and, pray you, tell me this, —
Which of the two was daughter of the duke,
That here was at the wrestling?

LE BEAU
Neither his daughter, if we judge by manners;
But yet, indeed, the smaller is his daughter:
The other is daughter to the banish'd duke,
And here detain'd by her usurping uncle,
To keep his daughter company: whose loves
Are dearer than the natural bond of sisters.
But I can tell you that of late this duke
Hath ta'en displeasure 'gainst his gentle niece,
Grounded upon no other argument
But that the people praise her for her virtues
And pity her for her good father's sake;
And, on my life, his malice 'gainst the lady
Will suddenly break forth. — Sir, fare you well:
Hereafter, in a better world than this,
I shall desire more love and knowledge of you.

ORLANDO
I rest much bounden to you: fare you well.
              [*Exit* LE BEAU.
Thus must I from the smoke into the smother;

From tyrant duke unto a tyrant brother: —
But heavenly Rosalind!   [*Exit.*

SCENE III

A room in the palace.

Enter CELIA *and* ROSALIND.

Why, cousin; why, Rosalind; — Cupid have mercy! —
not a word?

ROSALIND
Not one to throw at a dog.

CELIA
No, thy words are too precious to be cast away upon curs;
throw some of them at me; come, lame me with reasons.

ROSALIND
Then there were two cousins laid up, when the one
should be lamed with reasons, and the other mad
without any.

CELIA
But is all this for your father?

ROSALIND
No, some of it is for my father's child. O, how full of
briers is this working-day world!

CELIA
They are but burs, cousin, thrown upon thee in holiday
foolery: if we walk not in the trodden paths, our very
petticoats will catch them.

ROSALIND
I could shake them off my coat: these burs are in my
heart.

CELIA
Hem them away.

ROSALIND
I would try, if I could cry 'hem', and have him.

CELIA
Come, come, wrestle with thy affections.

ROSALIND
O, they take the part of a better wrestler than myself!

CELIA
O, a good wish upon you! you will try in time, in despite
of a fall. — But, turning these jests out of service, let us
talk in good earnest: is it possible, on such a sudden,
you should fall into so strong a liking with old Sir
Rowland's youngest son?

ROSALIND
The duke my father lov'd his father dearly.

CELIA
Doth it therefore ensue that you should love his son
dearly? By this kind of chase, I should hate him, for my
father hated his father dearly; yet I hate not Orlando.

ROSALIND
No, faith, hate him not, for my sake.

CELIA
Why should I? doth he not deserve well?

ROSALIND
Let me love him for that; and do you love him because I
do. — Look, here comes the duke.

CELIA
With his eyes full of anger.

Enter DUKE FREDERICK, *with* LORDS.

DUKE FREDERICK
Mistress, dispatch you with your safest haste,
And get you from our court.

ROSALIND
                    Me, uncle?

DUKE FREDERICK
                              You, cousin:
Within these ten days if that thou be'st found
So near our public court as twenty miles,
Thou diest for it.

ROSALIND
              I do beseech your Grace,
Let me the knowledge of my fault bear with me:
If with myself I hold intelligence,
Or have acquaintance with mine own desires;
If that I do not dream, or be not frantic,
As I do trust I am not, — then, dear uncle,
Never so much as in a thought unborn
Did I offend your highness.

DUKE FREDERICK
                    Thus do all traitors:
If their purgation did consist in words,
They are as innocent as grace itself:
Let it suffice thee that I trust thee not.

ROSALIND
Yet your mistrust cannot make me a traitor:
Tell me whereon the likelihood depends.

DUKE FREDERICK
Thou art thy father's daughter; there's enough.

ROSALIND
So was I when your highness took his dukedom;
So was I when your highness banish'd him:
Treason is not inherited, my lord;
Or, if we did derive it from our friends,
What's that to me? my father was no traitor:
Then, good my liege, mistake me not so much
To think my poverty is treacherous.

CELIA
Dear sovereign, hear me speak.

DUKE FREDERICK
Ay, Celia; we stay'd her for your sake,
Else had she with her father rang'd along.

CELIA
I did not then entreat to have her stay;
It was your pleasure and your own remorse:
I was too young that time to value her;
But now I know her: if she be a traitor,
Why, so am I; we still have slept together,
Rose at an instant, learn'd, play'd, eat together;
And wheresoe'er we went, like Juno's swans,
Still we went coupled and inseparable.

DUKE FREDERICK
She is too subtle for thee; and her smoothness,
Her very silence and her patience
Speak to the people, and they pity her.
Thou art a fool: she robs thee of thy name;
And thou wilt show more bright and seem more
   virtuous
When she is gone. Then open not thy lips:
Firm and irrevocable is my doom
Which I have pass'd upon her; — she is banish'd.

CELIA
Pronounce that sentence then on me, my liege:
I cannot live out of her company.

DUKE FREDERICK
You are a fool. — You, niece, provide yourself:
If you outstay the time, upon mine honour,
And in the greatness of my word, you die.
              [*Exeunt* DUKE FREDERICK *and* LORDS

CELIA
O my poor Rosalind! whither wilt thou go?
Wilt thou change fathers? I will give thee mine.
I charge thee, be not thou more griev'd than I am.

ROSALIND
I have more cause.

CELIA
Thou hast not, cousin;
Prithee, be cheerful: know'st thou not, the duke
Hath banish'd me, his daughter?

ROSALIND
                              That he hath not.

CELIA
No, hath not? Rosalind lacks then the love
Which teacheth me that thou and I am one:
Shall we be sunder'd? shall we part, sweet girl?
No: let my father seek another heir.
Therefore devise with me how we may fly,
Whither to go and what to bear with us:
And do not seek to take the charge upon you,
To bear your griefs yourself and leave me out:
For, by this heaven, now at our sorrows pale,
Say what thou canst, I'll go along with thee.

ROSALIND
Why, whither shall we go?

CELIA
To seek my uncle in the forest of Arden.

ROSALIND
Alas, what danger will it be to us,
Maids as we are, to travel forth so far!
Beauty provoketh thieves sooner than gold.

CELIA
I'll put myself in poor and mean attire,
And with a kind of umber smirch my face;
The like do you: so shall we pass along
And never stir assailants.

ROSALIND
                    Were it not better,
Because that I am more than common tall,
That I did suit me all points like a man?
A gallant curtle-axe upon my thigh,
A boar-spear in my hand; and — in my heart
Lie there what hidden woman's fear there will —
We'll have a swashing and a martial outside;
As many other mannish cowards have
That do outface it with their semblances.

CELIA
What shall I call thee when thou art a man?

ROSALIND
I'll have no worse a name than Jove's own page;
And therefore look you call me Ganymede.
But what will you be call'd?
CELIA
Something that hath a reference to my state;
No longer Celia, but Aliena.
ROSALIND
But, cousin, what if we assay'd to steal
The clownish fool out of your father's court?
Would he not be a comfort to our travel?
CELIA
He'll go along o'er the wide world with me;
Leave me alone to woo him. Let's away,
And get our jewels and our wealth together;
Devise the fittest time and safest way
To hide us from pursuit that will be made
After my flight. Now go we in content,
To liberty and not to banishment. [*Exeunt.*

ACT II

SCENE I

The Forest of Arden.

Enter DUKE SENIOR, AMIENS, *and two or three*
LORDS, *like foresters.*

DUKE SENIOR
Now, my co-mates and brothers in exile,
Hath not old custom made this life more sweet
Than that of painted pomp? Are not these woods
More free from peril than the envious court?
Here feel we but the penalty of Adam,
The seasons' difference; as the icy fang
And churlish chiding of the winter's wind,
Which, when it bites and blows upon my body,
Even till I shrink with cold, I smile, and say:
'This is no flattery; these are counsellors
That feelingly persuade me what I am.'
Sweet are the uses of adversity;
Which, like the toad, ugly and venomous,
Wears yet a precious jewel in his head;
And this our life, exempt from public haunt,
Finds tongues in trees, books in the running brooks,
Sermons in stones, and good in every thing:
I would not change it.
AMIENS
                              Happy is your Grace,
That can translate the stubbornness of fortune
Into so quiet and so sweet a style.
DUKE SENIOR
Come, shall we go and kill us venison?
And yet it irks me the poor dappled fools,
Being native burghers of this desert city,
Should in their own confines with forked heads
Have their round haunches gored.
FIRST LORD
                              Indeed, my lord,
The melancholy Jaques grieves at that;
And, in that kind, swears you do more usurp
Than doth your brother that hath banish'd you.
To-day my Lord of Amiens and myself
Did steal behind him, as he lay along
Under an oak, whose antique root peeps out
Upon the brook that brawls along this wood:
To the which place a poor sequester'd stag,
That from the hunter's aim had ta'en a hurt,
Did come to languish; and, indeed, my lord,
The wretched animal heav'd forth such groans,
That their discharge did stretch his leathern coat
Almost to bursting; and the big round tears
Cours'd one another down his innocent nose
In piteous chase: and thus the hairy fool,
Much marked of the melancholy Jaques,
Stood on th'extremest verge of the swift brook,
Augmenting it with tears.
DUKE SENIOR
But what said Jaques?
Did he not moralise this spectacle?
FIRST LORD
O, yes, into a thousand similes.
First, for his weeping into the needless stream:
'Poor deer,' quoth he, 'thou makest a testament
As worldlings do, giving thy sum of more
To that which had too much': then, being there alone,
Left and abandon'd of his velvet friends,
''Tis right,' quoth he; 'thus misery doth part
The flux of company': anon, a careless herd,
Full of the pasture, jumps along by him,

And never stays to greet him: 'Ay,' quoth Jaques,
'Sweep on, you fat and greasy citizens;
'Tis just the fashion: wherefore do you look
Upon that poor and broken bankrupt there?'
Thus most invectively he pierceth through
The body of the country, city, court,
Yea, and of this our life: swearing that we
Are mere usurpers, tyrants, and what's worse,
To fright the animals, and to kill them up,
In their assign'd and native dwelling-place.
DUKE SENIOR
And did you leave him in this contemplation?
SECOND LORD
We did, my lord, weeping and commenting
Upon the sobbing deer.
DUKE SENIOR
                              Show me the place:
I love to cope him in these sullen fits,
For then he's full of matter.
FIRST LORD
I'll bring you to him straight. [*Exeunt.*

SCENE II

A room in the palace.

Enter DUKE FREDERICK, *with* LORDS.

DUKE FREDERICK
Can it be possible that no man saw them?
It cannot be: some villains of my court
Are of consent and sufferance in this.
FIRST LORD
I cannot hear of any that did see her.
The ladies, her attendants of her chamber,
Saw her a-bed; and, in the morning early,
They found the bed untreasur'd of their mistress.
SECOND LORD
My lord, the roynish clown, at whom so oft
Your Grace was wont to laugh, is also missing.
Hesperia, the princess' gentlewoman,
Confesses that she secretly o'erheard
Your daughter and her cousin much commend
The parts and graces of the wrestler
That did but lately foil the sinewy Charles;
And she believes, wherever they are gone,
That youth is surely in their company.
DUKE FREDERICK
Send to his brother's; fetch that gallant hither:
If he be absent, bring his brother to me;
I'll make him find him: do this suddenly;
And let not search and inquisition quail
To bring again these foolish runaways. [*Exeunt.*

SCENE III

Before OLIVER'S *house.*

Enter ORLANDO *and* ADAM, *meeting.*

ORLANDO
Who's there?
ADAM
What, my young master? O my gentle master!
O my sweet master! O you memory
Of old Sir Rowland! why, what make you here?
Why are you virtuous? why do people love you?
And wherefore are you gentle, strong and valiant?
Why would you be so fond to overcome
The bony priser of the humorous duke?
Your praise is come too swiftly home before you.
Know you not, master, to some kind of men
Their graces serve them but as enemies?
No more do yours: your virtues, gentle master,
Are sanctified and holy traitors to you.
O, what a world is this, when what is comely
Envenoms him that bears it!
ORLANDO
Why, what's the matter?
ADAM
                              O, unhappy youth!
Come not within these doors; within this roof
The enemy of all your Graces lives:
Your brother — no, no brother; yet the son —
Yet not the son, I will not call him son
Of him I was about to call his father —
Hath heard your praises, and this night he means
To burn the lodging where you use to lie,
And you within it: if he fail of that,
He will have other means to cut you off:
I overheard him and his practices.
This is no place; this house is but a butchery:
Abhor it, fear it, do not enter it.

ORLANDO
Why, whither, Adam, wouldst thou have me go?
ADAM
No matter whither, so you come not here.
ORLANDO
What, wouldst thou have me go and beg my food?
Or with a base and boisterous sword enforce
A thievish living on the common road?
This I must do, or know not what to do:
Yet this I will not do, do how I can;
I rather will subject me to the malice
Of a diverted blood and bloody brother.
ADAM
But do not so. I have five hundred crowns,
The thrifty hire I sav'd under your father,
Which I did store to be my foster-nurse
When service should in my old limbs lie lame
And unregarded age in corners thrown:
Take that; and he that doth the ravens feed,
Yea, providently caters for the sparrow,
Be comfort to my age! Here is the gold;
All this I give you. Let me be your servant:
Though I look old, yet I am strong and lusty:
For in my youth I never did apply
Hot and rebellious liquors in my blood,
Nor did not with unbashful forehead woo
The means of weakness and debility;
Therefore my age is as a lusty winter,
Frosty, but kindly: let me go with you;
I'll do the service of a younger man
In all your business and necessities.
ORLANDO
O good old man, how well in thee appears
The constant service of the antique world,
When service sweat for duty, not for meed!
Thou art not for the fashion of these times,
Where none will sweat but for promotion,
And having that, do choke their service up
Even with the having: it is not so with thee.
But, poor old man, thou prunest a rotten tree,
That cannot so much as a blossom yield
In lieu of all thy pains and husbandry.
But come thy ways: we'll go along together;
And ere we have thy youthful wages spent,
We'll light upon some settled low content.
ADAM
Master, go on, and I will follow thee,
To the last gasp, with truth and loyalty.
From seventeen years till now almost fourscore
Here lived I, but now live here no more.
At seventeen years many their fortunes seek;
But at fourscore it is too late a week:
Yet fortune cannot recompense me better
Than to die well and not my master's debtor.
                              [*Exeunt.*

SCENE IV

The Forest of Arden.

Enter ROSALIND *for* GANYMEDE, CELIA *for*
ALIENA, *and* TOUCHSTONE.

ROSALIND
O Jupiter, how weary are my spirits!
TOUCHSTONE
I care not for my spirits, if my legs were not weary.
ROSALIND
I could find in my heart to disgrace my man's apparel
and to cry like a woman; but I must comfort the weaker
vessel, as doublet and hose ought to show itself
courageous to petticoat: therefore courage, good
Aliena!
CELIA
I pray you, bear with me; I cannot go no further.
TOUCHSTONE
For my part, I had rather bear with you than bear you;
yet I should bear no cross, if I did bear you, for I think
you have no money in your purse.
ROSALIND
Well, this is the forest of Arden.
TOUCHSTONE
Ay, now am I in Arden; the more fool I; when I was at
home, I was in a better place: but travellers must be
content.
ROSALIND
Ay, be so, good Touchstone.
                    Enter CORIN *and* SILVIUS.
Look you, who comes here; a young man and an old in
solemn talk.
CORIN
That is the way to make her scorn you still.

ROSALIND Well, this is the Forest of Arden.

SILVIUS
O Corin, that thou knew'st how I do love her!
CORIN
I partly guess; for I have lov'd ere now.
SILVIUS
No, Corin, being old, thou canst not guess;
Though in thy youth thou wast as true a lover
As ever sigh'd upon a midnight pillow:
But if thy love were ever like to mine, —
As sure I think did never man love so, —
How many actions most ridiculous
Hast thou been drawn to by thy fantasy?
CORIN
Into a thousand that I have forgotten.
SILVIUS
O, thou didst then never love so heartily!
If thou remember'st not the slightest folly
That ever love did make thee run into,
Thou hast not loved:
Or if thou hast not sat as I do now,
Wearing thy hearer in thy mistress' praise,
Thou hast not loved:
Or if thou hast not broke from company
Abruptly, as my passion now makes me,
Thou hast not loved.
O Phebe, Phebe, Phebe!   [*Exit.*

ROSALIND
Alas, poor shepherd! searching of thy wound, I have by
hard adventure found mine own.
TOUCHSTONE
And I mine. I remember, when I was in love I broke my
sword upon a stone, and bid him take that for coming
a-night to Jane Smile: and I remember the kissing of
her batlet, and the cow's dugs that her pretty chopp'd
hands had milk'd: and I remember the wooing of a
peascod instead of her; from whom I took two cods,
and, giving her them again, said with weeping tears,
'Wear these for my sake.' We that are true lovers run
into strange capers; but as all is mortal in nature, so is
all nature in love mortal in folly.
ROSALIND
Thou speak'st wiser than thou art ware of.
TOUCHSTONE
Nay, I shall ne'er be ware of mine own wit till I break
my shins against it.
ROSALIND
    Jove, Jove! this shepherd's passion
    Is much upon my fashion.
TOUCHSTONE
And mine; but it grows something stale with me.

CELIA
I pray you, one of you question yond man,
If he for gold will give us any food:
I faint almost to death.
TOUCHSTONE
                    Holla, you clown!
ROSALIND
Peace, fool: he's not thy kinsman.
CORIN
                    Who calls?
TOUCHSTONE
Your betters, sir.
CORIN
Else are they very wretched.
ROSALIND
Peace, I say. — Good even to you, friend.
CORIN
And to you, gentle sir, and to you all.
ROSALIND
I prithee, shepherd, if that love or gold
Can in this desert place buy entertainment,
Bring us where we may rest ourselves and feed:
Here's a young maid with travel much oppress'd,
And faints for succour.
CORIN
                    Fair sir, I pity her,
And wish, for her sake more than for mine own,
My fortunes were more able to relieve her;
But I am shepherd to another man
And do not shear the fleeces that I graze:
My master is of churlish disposition,
And little recks to find the way to heaven
By doing deeds of hospitality:
Besides, his cote, his flocks, and bounds of feed,
Are now on sale; and at our sheepcote now,
By reason of his absence, there is nothing
That you will feed on; but what is, come see,
And in my voice most welcome shall you be.
ROSALIND
What is he that shall buy his flock and pasture?
CORIN
That young swain that you saw here but erewhile,
That little cares for buying any thing.
ROSALIND
I pray thee, if it stand with honesty,
Buy thou the cottage, pasture, and the flock,
And thou shalt have to pay for it of us.
CELIA
And we will mend thy wages. I like this place,
And willingly could waste my time in it.
CORIN
Assuredly the thing is to be sold:
Go with me: if you like, upon report,
The soil, the profit, and this kind of life,
I will your very faithful feeder be,
And buy it with your gold right suddenly.   [*Exeunt.*

SCENE V

The forest.

Enter AMIENS, JAQUES, *and others.*

AMIENS [*sings*].
        Under the greenwood tree
            Who loves to lie with me,
        And turn his merry note
        Unto the sweet bird's throat,
Come hither, come hither, come hither:
            Here shall he see
            No enemy
But winter and rough weather.
JAQUES
More, more, I prithee, more.
AMIENS
It will make you melancholy, Monsieur Jaques.
JAQUES
I thank it. More, I prithee, more. I can suck melancholy
out of a song, as a weasel sucks eggs. More, I prithee,
more.
AMIENS
My voice is ragged: I know I cannot please you.
JAQUES
I do not desire you to please me; I do desire you to sing.
Come, more; another stanzo: call you 'em stanzos?
AMIENS
What you will, Monsieur Jaques.
JAQUES
Nay, I care not for their names; they owe me nothing.
Will you sing?

AMIENS

More at your request than to please myself.

JAQUES

Well, then, if ever I thank any man, I'll thank you: but that they call compliment is like th'encounter of two dog-apes; and when a man thanks me heartily, methinks I have given him a penny and he renders me the beggarly thanks. Come, sing; and you that will not, hold your tongues.

AMIENS

Well, I'll end the song. — Sirs, cover the while; the duke will drink under this tree. — He hath been all this day to look you.

JAQUES

And I have been all this day to avoid him. He is too disputable for my company: I think of as many matters as he; but I give heaven thanks, and make no boast of them. Come, warble, come.

Song.

Who doth ambition shun   *[All together here.*
   And loves to live i'th'sun,
Seeking the food he eats
And pleased with what he gets,
Come hither, come hither, come hither:
   Here shall he see
   No enemy
But winter and rough weather.

JAQUES

I'll give you a verse to this note, that I made yesterday in despite of my invention.

AMIENS

And I'll sing it.

JAQUES

Thus it goes: —
   If it do come to pass
   That any man turn ass,
   Leaving his wealth and ease,
   A stubborn will to please,
Ducdame, ducdame, ducdame:
   Here shall he see
   Gross fools as he,
An if he will come to me.

AMIENS

What's that 'ducdame'?

JAQUES

'Tis a Greek invocation, to call fools into a circle. I'll go sleep, if I can; if I cannot, I'll rail against all the first-born of Egypt.

AMIENS

And I'll go seek the duke: his banquet is prepared.

        [Exeunt severally.

SCENE VI

The forest.

Enter ORLANDO and ADAM.

ADAM

Dear master, I can go no further: O, I die for food! Here lie I down, and measure out my grave. Farewell, kind master.

ORLANDO

Why, how now, Adam! no greater heart in thee? Live a little; comfort a little; cheer thyself a little. If this uncouth forest yield any thing savage, I will either be food for it or bring it for food to thee. Thy conceit is nearer death than thy powers. For my sake be comfortable; hold death awhile at the arm's end: I will here be with thee presently; and if I bring thee not something to eat, I will give thee leave to die: but if thou diest before I come, thou art a mocker of my labour. Well said! thou look'st cheerly; and I'll be with thee quickly. Yet thou liest in the bleak air: come, I will bear thee to some shelter; and thou shalt not die for lack of a dinner, if there live any thing in this desert. Cheerly, good Adam!   *[Exeunt.*

SCENE VII

The forest. A table set out.

Enter DUKE SENIOR, AMIENS, and LORDS like OUTLAWS.

DUKE SENIOR

I think he be transform'd into a beast;
For I can no where find him like a man.

FIRST LORD

My lord, he is but even now gone hence:
Here was he merry, hearing of a song.

DUKE SENIOR

If he, compact of jars, grow musical,
We shall have shortly discord in the spheres.
Go, seek him: tell him I would speak with him.

      Enter JAQUES.

FIRST LORD

He saves my labour by his own approach.

DUKE SENIOR

Why, how now, monsieur! what a life is this,
That your poor friends must woo your company!
What, you look merrily!

JAQUES

A fool, a fool! I met a fool i'th'forest,
A motley fool; a miserable world!
As I do live by food, I met a fool;
Who laid him down and bask'd him in the sun,
And rail'd on Lady Fortune in good terms,
In good set terms, and yet a motley fool.
'Good morrow, fool,' quoth I. 'No, sir,' quoth he,
'Call me not fool till heaven hath sent me fortune':
And then he drew a dial from his poke,
And, looking on it with lack-lustre eye,
Says very wisely, 'It is ten o'clock:
Thus we may see,' quoth he, 'how the world wags:
'Tis but an hour ago since it was nine,
And after one hour more 'twill be eleven;
And so, from hour to hour, we ripe and ripe,
And then, from hour to hour, we rot and rot;
And thereby hangs a tale.' When I did hear
The motley fool thus moral on the time,
My lungs began to crow like chanticleer,
That fools should be so deep-contemplative;
And I did laugh sans intermission
An hour by his dial. O noble fool!
A worthy fool! Motley's the only wear.

DUKE SENIOR

What fool is this?

JAQUES

O worthy fool! One that hath been a courtier;
And says, if ladies be but young and fair,
They have the gift to know it: and in his brain, —
Which is as dry as the remainder biscuit
After a voyage, — he hath strange places cramm'd
With observation, the which he vents
In mangled forms. — O, that I were a fool!
I am ambitious for a motley coat.

DUKE SENIOR

Thou shalt have one.

JAQUES

      It is my only suit;
Provided that you weed your better judgements
Of all opinion that grows rank in them
That I am wise. I must have liberty
Withal, as large a charter as the wind,
To blow on whom I please; for so fools have:
And they that are most galled with my folly,
They most must laugh. And why, sir, must they so?
The 'why' is plain as way to parish church:
He that a fool doth very wisely hit
Doth very foolishly, although he smart,
Not to seem senseless of the bob: if not,
The wise man's folly is anatomis'd
Even by the squandering glances of the fool.
Invest me in my motley; give me leave
To speak my mind, and I will through and through
Cleanse the foul body of th'infected world,
If they will patiently receive my medicine.

DUKE SENIOR

Fie on thee! I can tell what thou wouldst do.

JAQUES

What, for a counter, would I do but good?

DUKE SENIOR

Most mischievous foul sin, in chiding sin:
For thou thyself hast been a libertine,
As sensual as the brutish sting itself;
And all th'imbossed sores and headed evils,
That thou with licence of free foot hast caught,
Wouldst thou disgorge into the general world.

JAQUES

Why, who cries out on pride,
That can therein tax any private party?
Doth it not flow as hugely as the sea,
Till that the weary very means do ebb?
What woman in the city do I name,
When that I say the city-woman bears
The cost of princes on unworthy shoulders?
Who can come in and say that I mean her,
When such a one as she such is her neighbour?
Or what is he of basest function,
That says his bravery is not on my cost,

Thinking that I mean him, but therein suits
His folly to the mettle of my speech?
There then; how then? what then? Let me see wherein
My tongue hath wrong'd him: if it do him right,
Then he hath wrong'd himself; if he be free,
Why, then my taxing like a wild-goose flies,
Unclaim'd of any man. — But who comes here?

   Enter ORLANDO, with his sword drawn.

ORLANDO

Forbear, and eat no more!

JAQUES

      Why, I have eat none yet.

ORLANDO

Nor shalt not, till necessity be served.

JAQUES

Of what kind should this cock come of?

DUKE SENIOR

Art thou thus bolden'd, man, by thy distress,
Or else a rude despiser of good manners,
That in civility thou seem'st so empty?

ORLANDO

You touch'd my vein at first: the thorny point
Of bare distress hath ta'en from me the show
Of smooth civility: yet am I inland bred,
And know some nurture. But forbear, I say:
He dies that touches any of this fruit
Till I and my affairs are answered.

JAQUES

An you will not be answer'd with reason, I must die.

DUKE SENIOR

What would you have? Your gentleness shall force
More than your force move us to gentleness.

ORLANDO

I almost die for food; and let me have it.

DUKE SENIOR

Sit down and feed, and welcome to our table.

ORLANDO

Speak you so gently? Pardon me, I pray you:
I thought that all things had been savage here;
And therefore put I on the countenance
Of stern commandment. But whate'er you are,
That in this desert inaccessible,
Under the shade of melancholy boughs,
Lose and neglect the creeping hours of time;
If ever you have look'd on better days,
If ever been where bells have knoll'd to church,
If ever sat at any good man's feast,
If ever from your eyelids wip'd a tear,
And know what 'tis to pity and be pitied, —
Let gentleness my strong enforcement be:
In the which hope I blush, and hide my sword.

DUKE SENIOR

True is it that we have seen better days,
And have with holy bell been knoll'd to church,
And sat at good men's feasts, and wip'd our eyes
Of drops that sacred pity hath engender'd:
And therefore sit you down in gentleness,
And take upon command what help we have,
That to your wanting may be minister'd.

ORLANDO

Then but forbear your food a little while,
Whiles, like a doe, I go to find my fawn,
And give it food. There is an old poor man,
Who after me hath many a weary step
Limp'd in pure love: till he be first sufficed, —
Oppress'd with two weak evils, age and hunger, —
I will not touch a bit.

DUKE SENIOR

      Go find him out,
And we will nothing waste till you return.

ORLANDO

I thank ye; and be blest for your good comfort!   *[Exit.*

DUKE SENIOR

Thou seest we are not all alone unhappy:
This wide and universal theatre
Presents more woeful pageants than the scene
Wherein we play in.

JAQUES

      All the world's a stage,
And all the men and women merely players:
They have their exits and their entrances;
And one man in his time plays many parts,
His acts being seven ages. As, first the infant,
Mewling and puking in the nurse's arms.
And then the whining schoolboy, with his satchel
And shining morning face, creeping like snail
Unwillingly to school. And then the lover,
Sighing like furnace, with a woeful ballad
Made to his mistress' eyebrow. Then the soldier,

Full of strange oaths, and bearded like the pard,
Jealous in honour, sudden and quick in quarrel,
Seeking the bubble reputation
Even in the cannon's mouth. And then the justice,
In fair round belly with good capon lined,
With eyes severe and beard of formal cut,
Full of wise saws and modern instances;
And so he plays his part. The sixth age shifts
Into the lean and slipper'd pantaloon,
With spectacles on nose and pouch on side;
His youthful hose, well sav'd, a world too wide
For his shrunk shank; and his big manly voice,
Turning again toward childish treble, pipes
And whistles in his sound. Last scene of all,
That ends this strange eventful history,
Is second childishness and mere oblivion,
Sans teeth, sans eyes, sans taste, sans everything.

Enter ORLANDO, *with* ADAM.

DUKE SENIOR
Welcome. Set down your venerable burthen,
And let him feed.
ORLANDO
I thank you most for him.
ADAM
         So had you need: —
I scarce can speak to thank you for myself.
DUKE SENIOR
Welcome; fall to: I will not trouble you
As yet, to question you about your fortunes. —
Give us some music; and, good cousin, sing.
AMIENS
    Blow, blow, thou winter wind,
    Thou art not so unkind
       As man's ingratitude;
    Thy tooth is not so keen,
    Because thou art not seen,
       Although thy breath be rude.
Heigh-ho! sing, heigh-ho! unto the green holly:
Most friendship is feigning, most loving mere folly:
    Then, heigh-ho, the holly!
       This life is most jolly.

    Freeze, freeze, thou bitter sky,
    That dost not bite so nigh
       As benefits forgot:
    Though thou the waters warp,
    Thy sting is not so sharp
       As friend remember'd not.
Heigh-ho! Sing, heigh-ho! *etc.*
DUKE SENIOR
If that you were the good Sir Rowland's son,

As you have whisper'd faithfully you were,
And as mine eye doth his effigies witness
Most truly limn'd and living in your face, —
Be truly welcome hither: I am the duke,
That lov'd your father: the residue of your fortune,
Go to my cave and tell me. — Good old man,
Thou art right welcome as thy master is. —
Support him by the arm. — Give me your hand,
And let me all your fortunes understand.   [*Exeunt.*

ACT III

SCENE I

A room in the palace.

Enter DUKE FREDERICK, LORDS, *and* OLIVER.

DUKE FREDERICK
Not see him since? Sir, sir, that cannot be:
But were I not the better part made mercy,
I should not seek an absent argument
Of my revenge, thou present. But look to it:
Find out thy brother, wheresoe'er he is;
Seek him with candle; bring him dead or living
Within this twelvemonth, or turn thou no more
To seek a living in our territory.
Thy lands, and all things that thou dost call thine
Worth seizure, do we seize into our hands,
Till thou canst quit thee by thy brother's mouth
Of what we think against thee.
OLIVER
O, that your highness knew my heart in this!
I never lov'd my brother in my life.
DUKE FREDERICK
More villain thou. — Well, push him out of doors;
And let my officers of such a nature
Make an extent upon his house and lands:
Do this expediently, and turn him going.   [*Exeunt.*

SCENE II

The forest.

Enter ORLANDO, *with a paper.*

ORLANDO
Hang there, my verse, in witness of my love:
And thou, thrice-crowned queen of night, survey
With thy chaste eye, from thy pale sphere above,
   Thy huntress' name, that my full life doth sway.
O Rosalind! these trees shall be my books,
   And in their barks my thoughts I'll character;
That every eye, which in this forest looks,

Shall see thy virtue witness'd every where.
Run, run, Orlando; carve on every tree
The fair, the chaste, and unexpressive she.   [*Exit.*

Enter CORIN *and* TOUCHSTONE.

CORIN
And how like you this shepherd's life, Master
Touchstone?
TOUCHSTONE
Truly, shepherd, in respect of itself, it is a good life; but
in respect that it is a shepherd's life, it is naught. In
respect that it is solitary, I like it very well; but in
respect that it is private, it is a very vile life. Now, in
respect it is in the fields, it pleaseth me well; but in
respect it is not in the court, it is tedious. As it is a spare
life, look you, it fits my humour well; but as there is no
more plenty in it, it goes much against my stomach.
Hast any philosophy in thee, shepherd?
CORIN
No more but that I know the more one sickens the
worse at ease he is; and that he that wants money,
means, and content, is without three good friends; that
the property of rain is to wet, and fire to burn; that good
pasture makes fat sheep; and that a great cause of the
night is lack of the sun; that he that hath learn'd no wit
by nature nor art may complain of good breeding, or
comes of a very dull kindred.
TOUCHSTONE
Such a one is a natural philosopher. Wast ever in court,
shepherd?
CORIN
No, truly.
TOUCHSTONE
Then thou art damn'd.
CORIN
Nay, I hope, —
TOUCHSTONE
Truly, thou art damn'd; like an ill-roasted egg, all on
one side.
CORIN
For not being at court? Your reason?
TOUCHSTONE
Why, if thou never wast at court, thou never saw'st
good manners; if thou never saw'st good manners,
then thy manners must be wicked; and wickedness is
sin, and sin is damnation. Thou art in a parlous state,
shepherd.
CORIN
Not a whit, Touchstone: those that are good manners at
the court, are as ridiculous in the country as the
behaviour of the country is most mockable at the court.
You told me you salute not at the court, but you kiss

DUKE FREDERICK Find out thy brother, wheresoe'er he is.

your hands: that courtesy would be uncleanly, if
courtiers were shepherds.

TOUCHSTONE
Instance, briefly; come, instance.

CORIN
Why, we are still handling our ewes; and their fells, you
know, are greasy.

TOUCHSTONE
Why, do not your courtier's hands sweat? and is not the
grease of a mutton as wholesome as the sweat of a
man? Shallow, shallow. A better instance, I say; come.

CORIN
Besides, our hands are hard.

TOUCHSTONE
Your lips will feel them the sooner. Shallow again. A
more sounder instance, come.

CORIN
And they are often tarr'd over with the surgery of our
sheep; and would you have us kiss tar? The courtier's
hands are perfumed with civet.

TOUCHSTONE
Most shallow man! thou worms-meat, in respect of a
good piece of flesh, indeed! — Learn of the wise, and
perpend: civet is of a baser birth than tar, — the very
uncleanly flux of a cat. Mend the instance, shepherd.

CORIN
You have too courtly a wit for me: I'll rest.

TOUCHSTONE
Wilt thou rest damn'd? God help thee, shallow man!
God make incision in thee! thou art raw.

CORIN
Sir, I am a true labourer: I earn that I eat, get that I
wear; owe no man hate, envy no man's happiness; glad
of other men's good, content with my harm; and the
greatest of my pride is, to see my ewes graze and my
lambs suck.

TOUCHSTONE
That is another simple sin in you; to bring the ewes
and the rams together, and to offer to get your living by
the copulation of cattle; to be bawd to a bell-wether; and
to betray a she-lamb of a twelvemonth to a crooked-
pated, old, cuckoldly ram, out of all reasonable match.
If thou be'st not damn'd for this, the devil himself will
have no shepherds; I cannot see else how thou shouldst
scape.

CORIN
Here comes young Master Ganymede, my new
mistress's brother.

Enter ROSALIND, *with a paper, reading.*

ROSALIND
    From the east to western Ind,
    No jewel is like Rosalind.
    Her worth, being mounted on the wind,
    Through all the world bears Rosalind.
    All the pictures fairest lin'd
    Are but black to Rosalind.
    Let no face be kept in mind
    But the fair of Rosalind.

TOUCHSTONE
I'll rime you so eight years together, dinners and
suppers and sleeping-hours excepted: it is the right
butter-women's rank to market.

ROSALIND
Out, fool!

TOUCHSTONE
For a taste:
    If a hart do lack a hind,
    Let him seek out Rosalind.
    If the cat will after kind,
    So be sure will Rosalind.
    Winter garments must be lin'd,
    So must slender Rosalind.
    They that reap must sheaf and bind;
    Then to cart with Rosalind.
    Sweetest nut hath sourest rind,
    Such a nut is Rosalind.
    He that sweetest rose will find,
    Must find love's prick and Rosalind.
This is the very false gallop of verses: why do you
infect yourself with them?

ROSALIND
Peace, you dull fool! I found them on a tree.

TOUCHSTONE
Truly, the tree yields bad fruit.

ROSALIND
I'll graff it with you, and then I shall graff it with a
meddler: then it will be the earliest fruit i'th'country;
for you'll be rotten ere you be half ripe, and that's the
right virtue of the medlar.

ORLANDO Hang there, my verse, in witness of my love.

TOUCHSTONE
You have said; but whether wisely or no, let the forest
judge.

Enter CELIA, *with a writing.*

ROSALIND
Peace!
Here comes my sister, reading: stand aside.

CELIA [*reads*].
    Why should this a desert be?
      For it is unpeopled? No;
    Tongues I'll hang on every tree,
      That shall civil sayings show:
    Some, how brief the life of man
      Runs his erring pilgrimage,
    That the stretching of a span
      Buckles in his sum of age;
    Some, of violated vows
      'Twixt the souls of friend and friend:
    But upon the fairest boughs,
      Or at every sentence end,
    Will I Rosalinda write;
      Teaching all that read to know
    The quintessence of every sprite
      Heaven would in little show.
    Therefore Heaven Nature charged
      That one body should be fill'd
    With all graces wide-enlarged:
      Nature presently distill'd
    Helen's cheek, but not her heart;
      Cleopatra's majesty;
    Atalanta's better part;
      Sad Lucretia's modesty.
    Thus Rosalind of many parts
      By heavenly synod was devised;
    Of many faces, eyes, and hearts,
      To have the touches dearest prized.
Heaven would that she these gifts should have,
And I to live and die her slave.

ROSALIND
O most gentle pulpiter! — what tedious homily of love
have you wearied your parishioners withal, and never
cried, 'Have patience, good people!'

CELIA
How now! back, friends: — shepherd, go off a little: —
go with him, sirrah.

TOUCHSTONE
Come, shepherd, let us make an honourable retreat;
though not with bag and baggage, yet with scrip and
scrippage.

[*Exeunt* CORIN *and* TOUCHSTONE.

CELIA
Didst thou hear these verses?

ROSALIND
O, yes, I heard them all, and more too; for some of
them had in them more feet than the verses would
bear.

CELIA
That's no matter: the feet might bear the verses.

ROSALIND
Ay, but the feet were lame, and could not bear
themselves without the verse, and therefore stood
lamely in the verse.

CELIA
But didst thou hear without wondering how thy name
should be hang'd and carved upon these trees?

ROSALIND
I was seven of the nine days out of the wonder before
you came; for look here what I found on a palm-tree: —
I was never so berimed since Pythagoras' time, that I
was an Irish rat, which I can hardly remember.

CELIA
Trow you who hath done this?

ROSALIND
Is it a man?

TOUCHSTONE Hang there, my verse, in witness of my love.

CELIA
And a chain, that you once wore, about his neck.
Change you colour?

ROSALIND
I prithee, who?

CELIA
O Lord, Lord! it is a hard matter for friends to meet; but mountains may be removed with earthquakes and so encounter.

ROSALIND
Nay, but who is it?

CELIA
Is it possible?

ROSALIND
Nay, I prithee now with most petitionary vehemence, tell me who it is.

CELIA
O wonderful, wonderful, and most wonderful wonderful! and yet again wonderful, and after that, out of all whooping!

ROSALIND
Good my complexion! dost thou think, though I am caparison'd like a man, I have a doublet and hose in my disposition? One inch of delay more is a South-sea of discovery; I prithee, tell me who is it quickly, and speak apace. I would thou couldst stammer, that thou mightest pour this conceal'd man out of thy mouth, as wine comes out of a narrow-mouth'd bottle, — either too much at once, or none at all. I prithee, take the cork out of thy mouth, that I may drink thy tidings.

CELIA
So you may put a man in your belly.

ROSALIND
Is he of God's making? What manner of man? Is his head worth a hat, or his chin worth a beard?

CELIA
Nay, he hath but a little beard.

ROSALIND
Why, God will send more, if the man will be thankful: let me stay the growth of his beard, if thou delay me not the knowledge of his chin.

CELIA
It is young Orlando, that tripp'd up the wrestler's heels and your heart both in an instant.

ROSALIND
Nay, but the devil take mocking: speak, sad brow and true maid.

CELIA
I'faith, coz, 'tis he.

ROSALIND
Orlando?

CELIA
Orlando.

ROSALIND
Alas the day! what shall I do with my doublet and hose? — What did he when thou saw'st him? What said he? How look'd he? Wherein went he? What makes he here? Did he ask for me? Where remains he? How parted he with thee? and when shalt thou see him again? Answer me in one word.

CELIA
You must borrow me Gargantua's mouth first: 'tis a word too great for any mouth of this age's size. To say ay and no to these particulars is more than to answer in a catechism.

ROSALIND
But doth he know that I am in this forest, and in man's apparel? Looks he as freshly as he did the day he wrestled?

CELIA
It is as easy to count atomies as to resolve the propositions of a lover: — but take a taste of my finding him, and relish it with good observance. I found him under a tree, like a dropp'd acorn.

ROSALIND
It may well be call'd Jove's tree, when it drops forth such fruit.

CELIA
Give me audience, good madam.

ROSALIND
Proceed.

CELIA
There lay he, stretch'd along, like a wounded knight.

ROSALIND
Though it be pity to see such a sight, it well becomes the ground.

CELIA
Cry, holla! to thy tongue, I prithee; it curvets unseasonably. He was furnish'd like a hunter.

ROSALIND
O, ominous, he comes to kill my heart.

CELIA
I would sing my song without a burden: thou bring'st me out of tune.

ROSALIND
Do you not know I am a woman? when I think, I must speak. Sweet, say on.

CELIA
You bring me out. — Soft! comes he not here?

ROSALIND
'Tis he: slink by, and note him.

[CELIA *and* ROSALIND *retire.*

Enter ORLANDO *and* JAQUES.

JAQUES
I thank you for your company; but, good faith, I had as lief have been myself alone.

ORLANDO
And so had I; but yet, for fashion sake,
I thank you too for your society.

JAQUES
God b' wi' you! let's meet as little as we can.

ORLANDO
I do desire we may be better strangers.

JAQUES
I pray you, mar no more trees with writing love-songs in their barks.

ORLANDO
I pray you, mar no more of my verses with reading them ill-favour'dly.

JAQUES
Rosalind is your love's name?

ORLANDO
Yes, just.

JAQUES
I do not like her name.

ORLANDO
There was no thought of pleasing you when she was christen'd.

JAQUES
What stature is she of?

ORLANDO
Just as high as my heart.

JAQUES
You are full of pretty answers. Have you not been acquainted with goldsmiths' wives, and conn'd them out of rings?

ORLANDO
Not so; but I answer you right painted cloth, from whence you have studied your questions.

JAQUES
You have a nimble wit: I think 'twas made of Atalanta's heels. Will you sit down with me? and we two will rail against our mistress the world and all our misery.

ORLANDO
I will chide no breather in the world but myself, against whom I know most faults.

JAQUES
The worst fault you have is to be in love.

ORLANDO
'Tis a fault I will not change for your best virtue.
I am weary of you.

JAQUES
By my troth, I was seeking for a fool when I found you.

ORLANDO
He is drown'd in the brook: look but in, and you shall see him.

JAQUES
There I shall see mine own figure.

ORLANDO
Which I take to be either a fool or a cipher.

JAQUES
I'll tarry no longer with you: farewell, good Signior Love.

ORLANDO
I am glad of your departure: adieu, good Monsieur Melancholy.

[*Exit* JAQUES, CELIA *and* ROSALIND *come forward.*

ROSALIND [*aside to* CELIA].
I will speak to him like a saucy lackey, and under that habit play the knave with him. — Do you hear, forester?

ORLANDO
Very well: what would you?

ROSALIND
I pray you, what is't o'clock?

ORLANDO
You should ask me, what time o'day: there's no clock in the forest.

ROSALIND
Then there is no true lover in the forest; else sighing every minute, and groaning every hour, would detect the lazy foot of Time as well as a clock.

ORLANDO
And why not the swift foot of Time? had not that been as proper?

ROSALIND
By no means, sir. Time travels in divers paces with divers persons: I'll tell you who Time ambles withal, who Time trots withal, who Time gallops withal, and who he stands still withal.

ORLANDO
I prithee, who doth he trot withal?

ROSALIND
Marry, he trots hard with a young maid between the contract of her marriage and the day it is solemnised: if the interim be but a se'nnight, Time's pace is so hard that it seems the length of seven year.

ORLANDO
Who ambles Time withal?

ROSALIND
With a priest that lacks Latin, and a rich man that hath not the gout; for the one sleeps easily, because he cannot study; and the other lives merrily, because he feels no pain: the one lacking the burden of lean and wasteful learning; the other knowing no burthen of heavy tedious penury: these Time ambles withal.

ORLANDO
Who doth he gallop withal?

ROSALIND
With a thief to the gallows; for though he go as softly as foot can fall, he thinks himself too soon there.

ORLANDO
Who stays it still withal?

ROSALIND
With lawyers in the vacation; for they sleep between term and term, and then they perceive not how Time moves.

ORLANDO
Where dwell you, pretty youth?

ROSALIND
With this shepherdess, my sister; here in the skirts of the forest, like fringe upon a petticoat.

ORLANDO
Are you native of this place?

ROSALIND
As the cony, that you see dwell where she is kindled.

ORLANDO
Your accent is something finer than you could purchase in so removed a dwelling.

ROSALIND
I have been told so of many: but indeed an old religious uncle of mine taught me to speak, who was in his youth an inland man; one that knew courtship too well, for there he fell in love. I have heard him read many lectures against it; and I thank God I am not a woman, to be touch'd with so many giddy offences as he hath generally taxed their whole sex withal.

ORLANDO
Can you remember any of the principal evils that he laid to the charge of women?

ROSALIND
There were none principal: they were all like one another as half-pence are; every one fault seeming monstrous till his fellow-fault came to match it.

ORLANDO
I prithee, recount some of them.

ROSALIND
No, I will not cast away my physic but on those that are sick. There is a man haunts the forest, that abuses our young plants with carving Rosalind on their barks; hangs odes upon hawthorns, and elegies on brambles; all, forsooth, deifying the name of Rosalind: if I could meet that fancy-monger, I would give him some good counsel, for he seems to have the quotidian of love upon him.

ORLANDO
I am he that is so love-shaked: I pray you, tell me your remedy.

TOUCHSTONE I would fain see this meeting.

ROSALIND
There is none of my uncle's marks upon you: he taught me how to know a man in love; in which cage of rushes I am sure you are not prisoner.

ORLANDO
What were his marks?

ROSALIND
A lean cheek, — which you have not; a blue eye and sunken, — which you have not; an unquestionable spirit, — which you have not; a beard neglected, — which you have not; — but I pardon you for that; for simply your having in beard is a younger brother's revenue: — then your hose should be ungarter'd, your bonnet unbanded, your sleeve unbutton'd, your shoe untied, and every thing about you demonstrating a careless desolation; — but you are no such man, — you are rather point-device in your accoutrements, as loving yourself than seeming the lover of any other.

ORLANDO
Fair youth, I would I could make thee believe I love.

ROSALIND
Me believe it! you may as soon make her that you love believe it; which, I warrant, she is apter to do than to confess she does: that is one of the points in which women still give the lie to their consciences. But, in good sooth, are you he that hangs the verses on the trees, wherein Rosalind is so admired?

ORLANDO
I swear to thee, youth, by the white hand of Rosalind, I am that he, that unfortunate he.

ROSALIND
But are you so much in love as your rimes speak?

ORLANDO
Neither rime nor reason can express how much.

ROSALIND
Love is merely a madness; and, I tell you, deserves as well a dark house and a whip as madmen do: and the reason why they are not so punish'd and cured is, that the lunacy is so ordinary, that the whippers are in love too. Yet I profess curing it by counsel.

ORLANDO
Did you ever cure any so?

ROSALIND
Yes, one; and in this manner. He was to imagine me his love, his mistress; and I set him every day to woo me: at which time would I, being but a moonish youth, grieve, be effeminate, changeable, longing, and liking; proud, fantastical, apish, shallow, inconstant, full of tears, full of smiles; for every passion something, and for no passion truly any thing, as boys and women are for the most part cattle of this colour: would now like him, now loathe him; then entertain him, then forswear him; now weep for him, then spit at him; that I drave my suitor from his mad humour of love to a living humour of madness; which was, to forswear the full stream of the world, and to live in a nook merely monastic. And thus I cured him; and this way will I take upon me to wash your liver as clean as a sound sheep's heart, that there shall not be one spot of love in't.

ORLANDO
I would not be cured, youth.

ROSALIND
I would cure you, if you would but call me Rosalind, and come every day to my cote and woo me.

ORLANDO
Now, by the faith of my love, I will: tell me where it is.

ROSALIND
Go with me to it, and I'll show it you: and, by the way, you shall tell me where in the forest you live. Will you go?

ORLANDO
With all my heart, good youth.

ROSALIND
Nay, you must call me Rosalind. — Come, sister, will you go? [*Exeunt.*

SCENE III

The forest.

Enter TOUCHSTONE *and* AUDREY; JAQUES *behind.*

TOUCHSTONE
Come apace, good Audrey: I will fetch up your goats,
Audrey. And how, Audrey? am I the man yet? doth my
simple feature content you?

AUDREY
Your features! Lord warrant us! what features?

TOUCHSTONE
I am here with thee and thy goats, as the most
capricious poet, honest Ovid, was among the Goths.

JAQUES [*aside*].
O knowledge ill-inhabited, — worse than Jove in a
thatch'd house!

TOUCHSTONE
When a man's verses cannot be understood, nor a man's
good wit seconded with the forward child
Understanding, it strikes a man more dead than a great
reckoning in a little room. — Truly, I would the gods had
made thee poetical.

AUDREY
I do not know what 'poetical' is: is it honest in deed and
word? is it a true thing?

TOUCHSTONE
No, truly; for the truest poetry is the most feigning; and
lovers are given to poetry; and what they swear in
poetry may be said as lovers they do feign.

AUDREY
Do you wish, then, that the gods had made me
poetical?

TOUCHSTONE
I do, truly; for thou swear'st to me thou art honest: now,
if thou wert a poet, I might have some hope thou didst
feign.

AUDREY
Would you not have me honest?

TOUCHSTONE
No, truly, unless thou wert hard-favour'd; for honesty
coupled to beauty is to have honey a sauce to sugar.

JAQUES [*aside*].
A material fool!

AUDREY
Well, I am not fair; and therefore I pray the gods make
me honest.

TOUCHSTONE
Truly, and to cast away honesty upon a foul slut, were
to put good meat into an unclean dish.

AUDREY
I am not a slut, though I thank the gods I am foul.

TOUCHSTONE
Well, praised be the gods for thy foulness! sluttishness
may come hereafter. But be it as it may be, I will marry
thee: and to that end I have been with Sir Oliver
Martext, the vicar of the next village; who hath
promised to meet me in this place of the forest, and to
couple us.

JAQUES [*aside*].
I would fain see this meeting.

AUDREY
Well, the gods give us joy!

TOUCHSTONE
Amen. A man may, if he were of a fearful heart, stagger
in this attempt; for here we have no temple but the
wood, no assembly but horn-beasts. But what though?
Courage! As horns are odious, they are necessary. It is
said, 'Many a man knows no end of his goods': right;
many a man has good horns, and knows no end of
them. Well, that is the dowry of his wife; 'tis none of his
own getting. Horns? even so; poor men alone? No, no;
the noblest deer hath them as huge as the rascal. Is the
single man therefore blessed? No: as a wall'd town is
more worthier than a village, so is the forehead of a
married man more honourable than the bare brow of a
bachelor; and by how much defence is better than no
skill, by so much is a horn more precious than to want.
— Here comes Sir Oliver.

Enter SIR OLIVER MARTEXT.

Sir Oliver Martext, you are well met: will you dispatch
us here under this tree, or shall we go with you to your
chapel?

MARTEXT
Is there none here to give the woman?

TOUCHSTONE
I will not take her on gift of any man.

MARTEXT
Truly, she must be given, or the marriage is not lawful.

JAQUES [*coming forward*].
Proceed, proceed: I'll give her.

TOUCHSTONE
Good even, good Master What-ye-call't: how do you,
sir? You are very well met: God ild you for your last
company: I am very glad to see you: — even a toy in
hand here, sir: — nay, pray be cover'd.

JAQUES
Will you be married, motley?

TOUCHSTONE
As the ox hath his bow, sir, the horse his curb, and the
falcon her bells, so man hath his desires; and as
pigeons bill, so wedlock would be nibbling.

JAQUES
And will you, being a man of your breeding, be married
under a bush like a beggar? Get you to church and have
a good priest that can tell you what marriage is: this
fellow will but join you together as they join wainscot;
then one of you will prove a shrunk panel, and like
green timber, warp, warp.

TOUCHSTONE [*aside*].
I am not in the mind but I were better to be married of
him than of another: for he is not like to marry me well;
and not being well married, it will be a good excuse for
me hereafter to leave my wife.

JAQUES
Go thou with me, and let me counsel thee.

TOUCHSTONE
Come, sweet Audrey:
We must be married, or we must live in bawdry. —
Farewell, good Master Oliver: — not,
     O sweet Oliver,
     O brave Oliver,
    Leave me not behind thee; —
but,

     Wind away,
     Be gone, I say,
  I will not to wedding with thee.
[*Exeunt* JAQUES, TOUCHSTONE, *and* AUDREY.

MARTEXT
'Tis no matter: ne'er a fantastical knave of them all
shall flout me out of my calling.   [*Exit.*

SCENE IV

The forest.

Enter ROSALIND *and* CELIA.

ROSALIND
Never talk to me; I will weep.

CELIA
Do, I prithee; but yet have the grace to consider that
tears do not become a man.

ROSALIND
But have I not cause to weep?

CELIA
As good cause as one would desire: therefore weep.

ROSALIND
His very hair is of the dissembling colour.

CELIA
Something browner than Judas's: marry, his kisses are
Judas's own children.

ROSALIND
I'faith, his hair is of a good colour.

CELIA
An excellent colour: your chestnut was ever the only
colour.

ROSALIND
And his kissing is as full of sanctity as the touch of holy
bread.

CELIA
He hath bought a pair of cast lips of Diana: a nun of
winter's sisterhood kisses not more religiously; the
very ice of chastity is in them.

ROSALIND
But why did he swear he would come this morning,
and comes not?

CELIA
Nay, certainly, there is no truth in him.

ROSALIND
Do you think so?

CELIA
Yes; I think he is not a pick-purse nor a horse-stealer;
but for his verity in love, I do think him as concave as a
cover'd goblet or a worm-eaten nut.

ROSALIND
Not true in love?

CELIA
Yes, when he is in; but I think he is not in.

ROSALIND
You have heard him swear downright he was.

CELIA
'Was' is not 'is': besides, the oath of a lover is no
stronger than the word of a tapster; they are both the
confirmers of false reckonings. He attends here in the
forest on the duke your father.

ROSALIND
I met the duke yesterday, and had much question with
him: he ask'd me, of what parentage I was; I told him,
of as good as he; so he laugh'd, and let me go. But what
talk we of fathers, when there is such a man as
Orlando?

CELIA
O, that's a brave man! he writes brave verses, speaks
brave words, swears brave oaths, and breaks them
bravely, quite traverse, athwart the heart of his lover; as
a puisny tilter, that spurs his horse but on one side,
breaks his staff like a noble goose: but all's brave that
youth mounts and folly guides. — Who comes here?

Enter CORIN.

CORIN
Mistress and master, you have oft inquired
After the shepherd that complain'd of love,
Who you saw sitting by me on the turf,
Praising the proud disdainful shepherdess
That was his mistress.

CELIA
          Well, and what of him?

CORIN
If you will see a pageant truly play'd,
Between the pale complexion of true love
And the red glow of scorn and proud disdain,
Go hence a little, and I shall conduct you,
If you will mark it.

ROSALIND
        O, come, let us remove:
The sight of lovers feedeth those in love. —
Bring us to this sight, and you shall say
I'll prove a busy actor in their play.   [*Exeunt.*

SCENE V

The forest.

Enter SILVIUS *and* PHEBE.

SILVIUS
Sweet Phebe, do not scorn me; do not, Phebe:
Say that you love me not; but say not so
In bitterness. The common executioner,
Whose heart th'accustom'd sight of death makes hard,
Falls not the axe upon the humbled neck
But first begs pardon: will you sterner be
Than he that dies and lives by bloody drops?

Enter ROSALIND *and* CELIA; CORIN *behind.*

PHEBE
I would not be thy executioner:
I fly thee, for I would not injure thee.
Thou tell'st me there is murder in mine eye:
'Tis pretty, sure, and very probable,
That eyes — that are the frail'st and softest things,
Who shut their coward gates on atomies —
Should be call'd tyrants, butchers, murderers!
Now I do frown on thee with all my heart;
And, if mine eyes can wound, now let them kill thee:
Now counterfeit to swoon; why, now fall down;
Or, if thou canst not, O, for shame, for shame,
Lie not, to say mine eyes are murderers!
Now show the wound mine eye hath made in thee:
Scratch thee but with a pin, and there remains
Some scar of it; lean but upon a rush,
The cicatrice and capable impressure
Thy palm some moment keeps: but now mine eyes,
Which I have darted at thee, hurt thee not;
Nor, I am sure, there is no force in eyes
That can do hurt.

SILVIUS
         O dear Phebe,
If ever — as that ever may be near —
You meet in some fresh cheek the power of fancy,
Then shall you know the wounds invisible
That love's keen arrows make.

PHEBE
          But, till that time,
Come not thou near me: and, when that time comes,
Afflict me with thy mocks, pity me not;
As, till that time, I shall not pity thee.

ROSALIND [*coming forward*].
And why, I pray you? Who might be your mother,
That you insult, exult, and all at once,

Over the wretched? What though you have no beauty,—
As, by my faith, I see no more in you
Than without candle may go dark to bed,—
Must you be therefore proud and pitiless?
Why, what means this? Why do you look on me?
I see no more in you than in the ordinary
Of nature's sale-work:—'Od's my little life,
I think she means to tangle my eyes too!—
No, faith, proud mistress, hope not after it:
'Tis not your inky brows, your black-silk hair,
Your bugle eyeballs, nor your cheek of cream,
That can entame my spirits to your worship.—
You foolish shepherd, wherefore do you follow her,
Like foggy south, puffing with wind and rain?
You are a thousand times a properer man
Than she a woman: 'tis such fools as you
That makes the world full of ill-favour'd children:
'Tis not her glass, but you, that flatters her;
And out of you she sees herself more proper
Than any of her lineaments can show her.—
But, mistress, know yourself: down on your knees,
And thank heaven, fasting, for a good man's love:
For I must tell you friendly in your ear,—
Sell when you can: you are not for all markets:
Cry the man mercy; love him; take his offer:
Foul is most foul, being foul to be a scoffer.—
So, take her to thee, shepherd:—fare you well.

PHEBE
Sweet youth, I pray you, chide a year together:
I had rather hear you chide than this man woo.

ROSALIND
He's fall'n in love with her foulness, and she'll fall in
love with my anger:—If it be so, as fast as she answers
thee with frowning looks, I'll sauce her with bitter
words.—Why look you so upon me?

PHEBE
For no ill will I bear you.

ROSALIND
I pray you, do not fall in love with me,
For I am falser than vows made in wine:
Besides, I like you not.—If you will know my house,
'Tis at the tuft of olives here hard by.—
Will you go, sister?—Shepherd, ply her hard.—
Come, sister.—Shepherdess, look on him better,
And be not proud: though all the world could see,
None could be so abus'd in sight as he.—
Come, to our flock.

[*Exeunt* ROSALIND, CELIA, *and* CORIN.

PHEBE
Dead shepherd, now I find thy saw of might,—
'Who ever lov'd that lov'd not at first sight?'

SILVIUS
Sweet Phebe,—

PHEBE
Ha, what say'st thou, Silvius?

SILVIUS
Sweet Phebe, pity me.

PHEBE
Why, I am sorry for thee, gentle Silvius.

SILVIUS
Wherever sorrow is, relief would be:
If you do sorrow at my grief in love,
By giving love, your sorrow and my grief
Were both extermined.

PHEBE
Thou hast my love: is not that neighbourly?

SILVIUS
I would have you.

PHEBE
Why, that were covetousness.
Silvius, the time was, that I hated thee;
And yet it is not that I bear thee love:
But since that thou canst talk of love so well,
Thy company, which erst was irksome to me,
I will endure; and I'll employ thee too:
But do not look for further recompense
Than thine own gladness that thou art employ'd.

SILVIUS
So holy and so perfect is my love,
And I in such a poverty of grace,
That I shall think it a most plenteous crop
To glean the broken ears after the man
That the main harvest reaps: loose now and then
A scatter'd smile, and that I'll live upon.

PHEBE
Know'st thou the youth that spoke to me erewhile?

SILVIUS
Not very well, but I have met him oft;
And he hath bought the cottage and the bounds
That the old carlot once was master of.

PHEBE
Think not I love him, though I ask for him;
'Tis but a peevish boy:—yet he talks well;—
But what care I for words? yet words do well,
When he that speaks them pleases those that hear.
It is a pretty youth:—not very pretty:—
But, sure, he's proud; and yet his pride becomes him:
He'll make a proper man: the best thing in him
Is his complexion; and faster than his tongue
Did make offence, his eye did heal it up.
He is not very tall; yet for his years he's tall:
His leg is but so-so; and yet 'tis well:
There was a pretty redness in his lip,
A little riper and more lusty red
Than that mix'd in his cheek; 'twas just the difference
Betwixt the constant red and mingled damask.
There be some women, Silvius, had they mark'd him
In parcels as I did, would have gone near
To fall in love with him: but, for my part,
I love him not, nor hate him not; and yet
I have more cause to hate him than to love him:
For what had he to do to chide at me?
He said mine eyes were black, and my hair black;
And, now I am remember'd, scorn'd at me:
I marvel why I answer'd not again:
But that's all one; omittance is no quittance.
I'll write to him a very taunting letter,
And thou shalt bear it; wilt thou, Silvius?

SILVIUS
Phebe, with all my heart.

PHEBE
⠀⠀⠀⠀⠀⠀⠀⠀⠀⠀I'll write it straight;
The matter's in my head and in my heart:
I will be bitter with him and passing short.
Go with me, Silvius.⠀⠀⠀⠀⠀⠀⠀⠀⠀⠀[*Exeunt.*

ACT IV

SCENE I

The forest.

Enter ROSALIND, CELIA, *and* JAQUES.

JAQUES
I prithee, pretty youth, let me be better acquainted with
thee.

ROSALIND
They say you are a melancholy fellow.

JAQUES
I am so; I do love it better than laughing.

ROSALIND
Those that are in extremity of either are abominable
fellows, and betray themselves to every modern
censure worse than drunkards.

JAQUES
Why, 'tis good to be sad and say nothing.

ROSALIND
Why, then 'tis good to be a post.

JAQUES
I have neither the scholar's melancholy, which is
emulation; nor the musician's, which is fantastical; nor
the courtier's, which is proud; nor the soldier's, which
is ambitious; nor the lawyer's, which is politic; nor the
lady's, which is nice; nor the lover's, which is all these;
—but it is a melancholy of mine own, compounded of
many simples, extracted from many objects, and,
indeed, the sundry contemplation of my travels, which,
by often rumination, wraps me in a most humorous
sadness.

ROSALIND
A traveller! By my faith, you have great reason to be sad:
I fear you have sold your own lands, to see other men's;
then, to have seen much, and to have nothing, is to
have rich eyes and poor hands.

JAQUES
Yes, I have gain'd my experience.

ROSALIND
And your experience makes you sad: I had rather have a
fool to make me merry than experience to make me
sad; and to travel for it too!

Enter ORLANDO.

ORLANDO
Good day and happiness, dear Rosalind!

JAQUES
Nay, then, God b'wi'you, an you talk in blank verse!
⠀⠀⠀⠀⠀⠀⠀⠀⠀⠀[*Exit.*

ROSALIND
Farewell, Monsieur Traveller: look you lisp, and wear
strange suits; disable all the benefits of your own

country; be out of love with your nativity, and almost
chide God for making you that countenance you are; or
I will scarce think you have swam in a gondola. Why,
how now, Orlando! where have you been all this while?
You a lover!—An you serve me such another trick,
never come in my sight more.

ORLANDO
My fair Rosalind, I come within an hour of my
promise.

ROSALIND
Break an hour's promise in love! He that will divide a
minute into a thousand parts, and break but a part of
the thousandth part of a minute in the affairs of love, it
may be said of him, that Cupid hath clapp'd him
o'th'shoulder, but I'll warrant him heart-whole.

ORLANDO
Pardon me, dear Rosalind.

ROSALIND
Nay, an you be so tardy, come no more in my sight: had
as lief be woo'd of a snail.

ORLANDO
Of a snail!

ROSALIND
Ay, of a snail; for though he comes slowly, he carries his
house on his head,—a better jointure, I think, than you
make a woman: besides, he brings his destiny with him.

ORLANDO
What's that?

ROSALIND
Why, horns; which such as you are fain to be beholding
to your wives for: but he comes arm'd in his fortune,
and prevents the slander of his wife.

ORLANDO
Virtue is no horn-maker; and my Rosalind is virtuous.

ROSALIND
And I am your Rosalind.

CELIA
It pleases him to call you so; but he hath a Rosalind of a
better leer than you.

ROSALIND
Come, woo me, woo me; for now I am in a holiday
humour, and like enough to consent.—What would
you say to me now, an I were your very very Rosalind?

ORLANDO
I would kiss before I spoke.

ROSALIND
Nay, you were better speak first; and when you were
gravell'd for lack of matter, you might take occasion to
kiss. Very good orators, when they are out, they will
spit; and for lovers, lacking (God warn us!) matter, the
cleanliest shift is to kiss.

ORLANDO
How if the kiss be denied?

ROSALIND
Then she puts you to entreaty, and there begins new
matter.

ORLANDO
Who could be out, being before his beloved mistress?

ROSALIND
Marry, that should you, if I were your mistress; or I
should think my honesty ranker than my wit.

ORLANDO
What, of my suit?

ROSALIND
Not out of your apparel, and yet out of your suit.
Am not I your Rosalind?

ORLANDO
I take some joy to say you are, because I would be
talking of her.

ROSALIND
Well, in her person, I say,—I will not have you.

ORLANDO
Then, in mine own person, I die.

ROSALIND
No, faith, die by attorney. The poor world is almost six
thousand years old, and in all this time there was not
any man died in his own person, *videlicet*, in a
love-cause. Troilus had his brains dash'd out with a
Grecian club; yet he did what he could to die before;
and he is one of the patterns of love. Leander, he would
have lived many a fair year, though Hero had turn'd
nun, if it had not been for a hot midsummer night; for,
good youth, he went but forth to wash him in the
Hellespont, and, being taken with the cramp, was
drown'd: and the foolish chroniclers of that age found
it was—Hero of Sestos. But these are all lies: men
have died from time to time, and worms have eaten

ORLANDO I take thee, Rosalind, for wife.

them, but not for love.

ORLANDO
I would not have my right Rosalind of this mind; for, I protest, her frown might kill me.

ROSALIND
By this hand, it will not kill a fly. But come, now I will be your Rosalind in a more coming-on disposition; and ask me what you will, I will grant it.

ORLANDO
Then love me, Rosalind.

ROSALIND
Yes, faith, will I, Fridays and Saturdays and all.

ORLANDO
And wilt thou have me?

ROSALIND
Ay, and twenty such.

ORLANDO
What sayest thou?

ROSALIND
Are you not good?

ORLANDO
I hope so.

ROSALIND
Why, then, can one desire too much of a good thing? — Come, sister, you shall be the priest, and marry us. — Give me your hand, Orlando. — What do you say, sister?

ORLANDO
Pray thee, marry us.

CELIA
I cannot say the words.

ROSALIND
You must begin, — 'Will you, Orlando,' —

CELIA
Go to. — Will you, Orlando, have to wife this Rosalind?

ORLANDO
I will.

ROSALIND
Ay, but when?

ORLANDO
Why now; as fast as she can marry us.

ROSALIND
Then you must say, — 'I take thee, Rosalind, for wife.'

ORLANDO
I take thee, Rosalind, for wife.

ROSALIND
I might ask you for your commission; but, — I do take thee, Orlando, for my husband: — there's a girl goes before the priest; and, certainly, a woman's thought runs before her actions.

ORLANDO
So do all thoughts, — they are wing'd.

ROSALIND
Now tell me how long you would have her, after you have possess'd her.

ORLANDO
For ever and a day.

ROSALIND
Say a day, without the ever. No, no, Orlando; men are April when they woo, December when they wed: maids are May when they are maids, but the sky changes when they are wives. I will be more jealous of thee than a Barbary cock-pigeon over his hen; more clamorous than a parrot against rain; more new-fangled than an ape; more giddy in my desires than a monkey: I will weep for nothing, like Diana in the fountain, and I will do that when you are disposed to be merry; I will laugh like a hyen, and that when thou art inclined to weep.

ORLANDO
But will my Rosalind do so?

ROSALIND
By my life, she will do as I do.

ORLANDO
O, but she is wise.

ROSALIND
Or else she could not have the wit to do this: the wiser, the waywarder: make the doors upon a woman's wit, and it will out at the casement; shut that, and 'twill out at the key-hole; stop that, 'twill fly with the smoke out at the chimney.

ORLANDO
A man that had a wife with such a wit, he might say, — 'Wit, whither wilt?'

ROSALIND
Nay, you might keep that check for it till you met your wife's wit going to your neighbour's bed.

ORLANDO
And what wit could wit have to excuse that?

ROSALIND
Marry, to say, — she came to seek you there. You shall never take her without her answer, unless you take her without her tongue. O, that woman that cannot make her fault her husband's occasion, let her never nurse her child herself, for she will breed it like a fool!

ORLANDO
For these two hours, Rosalind, I will leave thee.

ROSALIND
Alas! dear love, I cannot lack thee two hours!

ORLANDO
I must attend the duke at dinner: by two o'clock I will be with thee again.

ROSALIND
Ay, go your ways, go your ways; — I knew what you would prove: my friends told me as much, and I thought no less: — that flattering tongue of yours won me: — 'tis but one cast away, and so, — come, death! — Two o'clock is your hour?

ORLANDO
Ay, sweet Rosalind.

ROSALIND
By my troth, and in good earnest, and so God mend me, and by all pretty oaths that are not dangerous, if you break one jot of your promise, or come one minute behind your hour, I will think you the most pathetical break-promise, and the most hollow lover, and the most unworthy of her you call Rosalind, that may be chosen out of the gross band of the unfaithful: therefore beware my censure, and keep your promise.

ORLANDO
With no less religion than if thou wert indeed my Rosalind: so, adieu.

ROSALIND
Well, Time is the old justice that examines all such offenders, and let Time try: adieu.   [*Exit* ORLANDO.

CELIA
You have simply misused our sex in your love-prate: we must have your doublet and hose pluck'd over your head, and show the world what the bird hath done to her own nest.

ROSALIND
O coz, coz, coz, my pretty little coz, that thou didst know how many fathom deep I am in love! But it cannot be sounded: my affection hath an unknown bottom, like the bay of Portugal.

CELIA
Or rather, bottomless; that as fast as you pour affection in, it runs out.

ROSALIND
No, that same wicked bastard of Venus, that was begot of thought, conceived of spleen, and born of madness; that blind rascally boy, that abuses every one's eyes, because his own are out, let him be judge how deep I am in love: — I'll tell thee, Aliena, I cannot be out of the sight of Orlando; I'll go find a shadow, and sigh till he come.

CELIA
And I'll sleep.   [*Exeunt*

SCENE II

The forest.

Enter JAQUES, LORDS, *and* FORESTERS.

JAQUES
Which is he that kill'd the deer?

A LORD
Sir, it was I.

JAQUES
Let's present him to the duke, like a Roman conqueror; and it would do well to set the deer's horns upon his head, for a branch of victory. — Have you no song, forester, for this purpose?

FORESTER
Yes, sir.

JAQUES
Sing it: 'tis no matter how it be in tune, so it make noise enough.

> *Song.*
> What shall he have that kill'd the deer?
> His leather skin and horns to wear.
>   Then sing him home!
>   [*The rest shall bear this burthen*
> Take thou no scorn to wear the horn;

It was a crest ere thou wast born;
  Thy father's father wore it,
  And thy father bore it:
The horn, the horn, the lusty horn
Is not a thing to laugh to scorn. [*Exeunt.*

SCENE III

The forest.

Enter ROSALIND *and* CELIA.

ROSALIND
How say you now? Is it not past two o'clock? and here
much Orlando!

CELIA
I warrant you, with pure love and troubled brain, he
hath ta'en his bow and arrows, and is gone forth — to
sleep. Look, who comes here.

Enter SILVIUS.

SILVIUS
My errand is to you, fair youth; —
My gentle Phebe bid me give you this:
    [*Gives a letter.*
I know not the contents; but, as I guess
By the stern brow and waspish action
Which she did use as she was writing of it,
It bears an angry tenor: pardon me,
I am but as a guiltless messenger.

ROSALIND
Patience herself would startle at this letter,
And play the swaggerer; bear this, bear all:
She says I am not fair; that I lack manners;
She calls me proud; and that she could not love me,
Were man as rare as phœnix. 'Od's my will!
Her love is not the hare that I do hunt:
Why writes she so to me? — Well, shepherd, well,
This is a letter of your own device.

SILVIUS
No, I protest, I know not the contents:
Phebe did write it.

ROSALIND
    Come, come, you are a fool,
And turn'd into the extremity of love.
I saw her hand: she has a leathern hand,
A freestone-colour'd hand; I verily did think
That her old gloves were on, but 'twas her hands:
She has a housewife's hand; but that's no matter:
I say, she never did invent this letter;
This is a man's invention, and his hand.

SILVIUS
Sure, it is hers.

ROSALIND
Why, 'tis a boisterous and a cruel style,
A style for challengers: why, she defies me,
Like Turk to Christian: women's gentle brain
Could not drop forth such giant-rude invention,
Such Ethiop words, blacker in their effect
Than in their countenance. — Will you hear me letter?

SILVIUS
So please you, for I never heard it yet;
Yet heard too much of Phebe's cruelty.

ROSALIND
She Phebes me: mark how the tyrant writes.
[*Reads*] Art thou god to shepherd turn'd,
  That a maiden's heart hath burn'd? —
Can a woman rail thus?

SILVIUS
Call you this railing?

ROSALIND [*reads*].
  Why, thy godhead laid apart,
  Warr'st thou with a woman's heart? —
Did you ever hear such railing? —
  Whiles the eye of man did woo me,
  That could do no vengeance to me. —
Meaning me a beast. —
  If the scorn of your bright eyne
  Have power to raise such love in mine,
  Alack, in me what strange effect
  Would they work in mild aspect!
  Whiles you chid me, I did love;
  How, then, might your prayers move!
  He that brings this love to thee
  Little knows this love in me:
  And by him seal up thy mind;
  Whether that thy youth and kind
  Will the faithful offer take
  Of me, and all that I can make;
  Or else by him my love deny,
  And then I'll study how to die.

SILVIUS
Call you this chiding?

CELIA
Alas, poor shepherd!

ROSALIND
Do you pity him? no, he deserves no pity. Wilt thou love
such a woman? What, to make thee an instrument, and
play false strains upon thee! not to be endured! Well, go
your way to her, for I see love hath made thee a tame
snake, and say this to her: — that if she love me, I
charge her to love thee; if she will not, I will never have
her, unless thou entreat for her. — If you be a true
lover, hence, and not a word; for here comes more
company. [*Exit* SILVIUS.

Enter OLIVER.

OLIVER
Good morrow, fair ones: pray you, if you know,
Where in the purlieus of this forest stands
A sheep-cote fenc'd about with olive-trees?

CELIA
West of this place, down in the neighbour bottom:
The rank of osiers, by the murmuring stream,
Left on your right hand, brings you to the place.
But at this hour the house doth keep itself;
There's none within.

OLIVER
If that an eye may profit by a tongue,
Then should I know you by description;
Such garments and such years: — 'The boy is fair,
Of female favour, and bestows himself
Like a ripe sister: the woman low,
And browner than her brother.' Are not you
The owners of the house I did inquire for?

CELIA
It is no boast, being ask'd, to say we are.

OLIVER
Orlando doth commend him to you both;
And to that youth he calls his Rosalind
He sends this bloody napkin; — are you he?

ROSALIND
I am: what must we understand by this?

OLIVER
Some of my shame; if you will know of me
What man I am, and how, and why, and where
This handkercher was stain'd.

CELIA
    I pray you, tell it.

OLIVER
When last the young Orlando parted from you,
He left a promise to return again
Within an hour; and, pacing through the forest,
Chewing the food of sweet and bitter fancy,
Lo, what befell! he threw his eye aside,
And, mark, what object did present itself:
Under an oak, whose boughs were moss'd with age,
And high top bald with dry antiquity,
A wretched ragged man, o'ergrown with hair,
Lay sleeping on his back: about his neck
A green and gilded snake had wreath'd itself,
Who with her head, nimble in threats, approach'd
The opening of his mouth; but suddenly,
Seeing Orlando, it unlink'd itself,
And with indented glides did slip away
Into a bush: under which bush's shade
A lioness, with udders all drawn dry,
Lay couching, head on ground, with catlike watch,
When that the sleeping man should stir; for 'tis
The royal disposition of that beast
To prey on nothing that doth seem as dead:
This seen, Orlando did approach the man,
And found it was his brother, his elder brother.

CELIA
O, I have heard him speak of that same brother;
And he did render him the most unnatural
That liv'd 'mongst men.

OLIVER
   And well he might so do,
For well I know he was unnatural.

ROSALIND
But, to Orlando: — did he leave him there,
Food to the suck'd and hungry lioness?

OLIVER
Twice did he turn his back, and purpos'd so;
But kindness, nobler ever than revenge,
And nature, stronger than his just occasion,
Made him give battle to the lioness,
Who quickly fell before him: in which hurtling
From miserable slumber I awak'd.

CELIA
Are you his brother?

ROSALIND
    Was't you he rescued?

CELIA
Was't you that did so oft contrive to kill him?

OLIVER
'Twas I: but 'tis not I: I do not shame
To tell you what I was, since my conversion
So sweetly tastes, being the thing I am.

ROSALIND
But, for the bloody napkin?

OLIVER
    By and by.
When from the first to last, betwixt us two,
Tears our recountments had most kindly bathed,
As how I came into that desert place; —
In brief, he led me to the gentle duke,
Who gave me fresh array and entertainment,
Committing me unto my brother's love;
Who led me instantly unto his cave,
There stripp'd himself, and here upon his arm
The lioness had torn some flesh away,
Which all this while had bled; and now he fainted
And cried, in fainting, upon Rosalind.
Brief, I recover'd him, bound up his wound;
And, after some small space, being strong at heart,
He sent me hither, stranger as I am,
To tell this story, that you might excuse
His broken promise, and to give this napkin,
Dyed in his blood, unto the shepherd youth
That he in sport doth call his Rosalind.

CELIA
Why, how now, Ganymede! sweet Ganymede!
    [ROSALIND *faints.*

OLIVER
Many will swoon when they do look on blood.

CELIA
There is more in it. — Cousin Ganymede!

OLIVER
Look, he recovers.

ROSALIND
I would I were at home.

CELIA
    We'll lead you thither. —
I pray you, will you take him by the arm?

OLIVER
Be of good cheer, youth: — you a man? you lack a
man's heart.

ROSALIND
I do so, I confess it! Ah, sirrah, a body would think this
was well counterfeited! I pray you, tell your brother
how well I counterfeited. — Heigh-ho!

OLIVER
This was not counterfeit: there is too great testimony in
your complexion, that it was a passion of earnest.

ROSALIND
Counterfeit, I assure you.

OLIVER
Well, then, take a good heart, and counterfeit to be a
man.

ROSALIND
So I do: but, i'faith, I should have been a woman by
right.

CELIA
Come, you look paler and paler: pray you, draw
homewards. — Good sir, go with us.

OLIVER
That will I, for I must bear answer back
How you excuse my brother, Rosalind.

ROSALIND
I shall devise something: but, I pray you, commend my
counterfeiting to him: — Will you go? [*Exeunt.*

ACT V

SCENE I

The forest.

Enter TOUCHSTONE *and* AUDREY.

TOUCHSTONE
We shall find a time, Audrey; patience, gentle Audrey.

AUDREY
Faith, the priest was good enough, for all the old
gentleman's saying.

TOUCHSTONE
A most wicked Sir Oliver, Audrey, a most vile Martext.

TOUCHSTONE Therefore, you clown, abandon.

But, Audrey, there is a youth here in the forest lays claim to you.

AUDREY
Ay, I know who 'tis; he hath no interest in me in the world: here comes the man you mean.

TOUCHSTONE
It is meat and drink to me to see a clown: by my troth, we that have good wits have much to answer for; we shall be flouting; we cannot hold.

Enter WILLIAM.

WILLIAM
Good even, Audrey.

AUDREY
God ye good even, William.

WILLIAM
And good even to you, sir.

TOUCHSTONE
Good even, gentle friend. Cover thy head, cover thy head: nay, prithee, be cover'd. How old are you, friend?

WILLIAM
Five and twenty, sir.

TOUCHSTONE
A ripe age. Is thy name William?

WILLIAM
William, sir.

TOUCHSTONE
A fair name. Wast born i'th'forest here?

WILLIAM
Ay, sir, I thank God.

TOUCHSTONE
Thank God; — a good answer. Art rich?

WILLIAM
Faith, sir, so-so.

TOUCHSTONE
So-so is good, very good, very excellent good: — and yet it is not; it is but so-so. Art thou wise?

WILLIAM
Ay, sir, I have a pretty wit.

TOUCHSTONE
Why, thou say'st well. I do now remember a saying, 'The fool doth think he is wise; but the wise man knows himself to be a fool.' The heathen philosopher, when he had a desire to eat a grape, would open his lips when he put it into his mouth; meaning thereby, that grapes were made to eat, and lips to open. You do love this maid?

WILLIAM
I do, sir.

TOUCHSTONE
Give me your hand. Art thou learned?

WILLIAM
No, sir.

TOUCHSTONE
Then learn this of me: — to have, is to have; for it is a figure in rhetoric, that drink, being pour'd out of a cup into a glass, by filling the one doth empty the other; for all your writers do consent that *ipse* is he: now, you are not *ipse*, for I am he.

WILLIAM
Which he, sir?

TOUCHSTONE
He, sir, that must marry this woman. Therefore, you clown, abandon, — which is in the vulgar leave, — the society, — which in the boorish is company, — of this female, — which in the common is woman; which together is, abandon the society of this female, or, clown, thou perishest; or, to thy better understanding, diest; or (to wit) I kill thee, make thee away, translate thy life into death, thy liberty into bondage: I will deal in poison with thee, or in bastinado, or in steel; I will bandy with thee in faction; I will o'er-run thee with policy; I will kill thee a hundred and fifty ways: therefore tremble, and depart.

AUDREY
Do, good William.

WILLIAM
God rest you merry, sir.   [*Exit.*

Enter CORIN.

CORIN
Our master and mistress seek you; come, away, away!

TOUCHSTONE
Trip, Audrey, trip, Audrey. — I attend, I attend.
                                         [*Exeunt.*

The forest.

Enter ORLANDO *and* OLIVER.

ORLANDO
Is't possible that, on so little acquaintance, you should like her? that, but seeing, you should love her? and, loving, woo? and, wooing, she should grant? and will you persever to enjoy her?

OLIVER
Neither call the giddiness of it in question, the poverty of her, the small acquaintance, my sudden wooing, no her sudden consenting; but say with me, I love Aliena; say with her, that she loves me; consent with both, that we may enjoy each other: it shall be to your good; for my father's house, and all the revenue that was old Sir Rowland's, will I estate upon you, and here live and die a shepherd.

ORLANDO
You have my consent. Let your wedding be to-morrow thither will I invite the duke, and all's contented followers. Go you and prepare Aliena; for, look you, here comes my Rosalind.

Enter ROSALIND.

ROSALIND
God save you, brother.

OLIVER
And you, fair sister.   [*Exi*

ROSALIND
O, my dear Orlando, how it grieves me to see thee wear thy heart in a scarf!

ORLANDO
It is my arm.

ROSALIND
I thought thy heart had been wounded with the claws of a lion.

ORLANDO
Wounded it is, but with the eyes of a lady.

ROSALIND
Did your brother tell you how I counterfeited to swoon when he show'd me your handkercher?

ORLANDO
Ay, and greater wonders than that.

ROSALIND
O, I know where you are: — nay, 'tis true: there was never any thing so sudden, but the fight of two rams, and Cæsar's thrasonical brag of — 'I came, saw, and overcame': for your brother and my sister no sooner met, but they look'd; no sooner look'd, but they loved; no sooner loved, but they sigh'd; no sooner sigh'd, but they ask'd one another the reason; no sooner knew the reason, but they sought the remedy: and in these degrees have they made a pair of stairs to marriage, which they will climb incontinent, or else be incontinent before marriage: they are in the very wrath of love, and they will together; clubs cannot part them.

ORLANDO
They shall be married to-morrow; and I will bid the duke to the nuptial. But, O, how bitter a thing it is to look into happiness through another man's eyes! By so much the more shall I to-morrow be at the height of heart-heaviness, by how much I shall think my brother happy in having what he wishes for.

ROSALIND
Why, then, to-morrow I cannot serve your turn for Rosalind?

ORLANDO
I can live no longer by thinking.

ROSALIND
I will weary you, then, no longer with idle talking. Know of me, then — for now I speak to some purpose, — that I know you are a gentleman of good conceit: I speak not this, that you should bear a good opinion of my knowledge, insomuch I say I know you are; neither do I labour for a greater esteem than may in some little measure draw a belief from you, to do yourself good, and not to grace me. Believe, then, if you please, that I can do strange things: I have, since I was three year old conversed with a magician, most profound in his art, and yet not damnable. If you do love Rosalind so near the heart as your gesture cries it out, when your brother marries Aliena, shall you marry her: I know into what straits of fortune she is driven; and it is not impossible to me, if it appear not inconvenient to you, to set her before your eyes to-morrow human as she is, and without any danger.

ORLANDO
Speak'st thou in sober meanings?

ROSALIND
By my life I do; which I tender dearly, though I say I am
a magician. Therefore, put you in your best array, bid
your friends; for if you will be married to-morrow, you
shall; and to Rosalind, if you will. — Look, here comes
a lover of mine, and a lover of hers.

Enter SILVIUS *and* PHEBE.

PHEBE
Youth, you have done me much ungentleness,
To show the letter that I writ to you.

ROSALIND
I care not, if I have: it is my study
To seem despiteful and ungentle to you:
You are there follow'd by a faithful shepherd;
Look upon him, love him; he worships you.

PHEBE
Good shepherd, tell this youth what 'tis to love.

SILVIUS
It is to be all made of sighs and tears; —
And so am I for Phebe.

PHEBE
And I for Ganymede.

ORLANDO
And I for Rosalind.

ROSALIND
And I for no woman.

SILVIUS
It is to be all made of faith and service; —
And so am I for Phebe.

PHEBE
And I for Ganymede.

ORLANDO
And I for Rosalind.

ROSALIND
And I for no woman.

SILVIUS
It is to be all made of fantasy,
All made of passion, and all made of wishes;
All adoration, duty, and observance,
All humbleness, all patience, and impatience,
All purity, all trial, all deservings; —
And so am I for Phebe.

PHEBE
And so am I for Ganymede.

ORLANDO
And so am I for Rosalind.

ROSALIND
And so am I for no woman.

PHEBE [*to* ROSALIND].
If this be so, why blame you me to love you?

SILVIUS [*to* PHEBE].
If this be so, why blame you me to love you?

ORLANDO
If this be so, why blame you me to love you?

ROSALIND
Who do you speak to, — 'Why blame you me to love
you?'

ORLANDO
To her that is not here, nor doth not hear.

ROSALIND
Pray you, no more of this; 'tis like the howling of Irish
wolves against the moon. — I will help you [*to*
SILVIUS], if I can: — I would love you [*to* PHEBE], if I
could. — To-morrow meet me all together. — I will
marry you [*to* PHEBE], if ever I marry woman, and I'll
be married to-morrow: — I will satisfy you [*to*
ORLANDO], if ever I satisfy man, and you shall be
married to-morrow: — I will content you [*to* SILVIUS],
if what pleases you contents you, and you shall be
married to-morrow. — As you [*to* ORLANDO] love
Rosalind, meet: — as you [*to* SILVIUS] love Phebe,
meet: and as I love no woman, I'll meet. — So, fare you
well: I have left you commands.

SILVIUS
I'll not fail, if I live.

PHEBE
Nor I.

ORLANDO
Nor I. [*Exeunt.*

SCENE III

The forest.

Enter TOUCHSTONE *and* AUDREY.

TOUCHSTONE
To-morrow is the joyful day, Audrey; to-morrow will we
be married.

AUDREY
I do desire it with all my heart; and I hope it is no
dishonest desire, to desire to be a woman of the world.
Here come two of the banish'd duke's pages.

Enter two PAGES.

FIRST PAGE
Well met, honest gentleman.

TOUCHSTONE
By my troth, well met. Come, sit, sit, and a song.

SECOND PAGE
We are for you: sit i'th'middle.

FIRST PAGE
Shall we clap into't roundly, without hawking, or
spitting, or saying we are hoarse, which are the only
prologues to a bad voice?

SECOND PAGE
I'faith, i'faith; and both in a tune, like two gipsies on a
horse.

Song.
It was a lover and his lass,
    With a hey, and a ho, and a hey nonino,
That o'er the green corn-field did pass
    In spring-time, the only pretty ring-time,
When birds do sing, hey ding a ding, ding:
Sweet lovers love the spring.

Between the acres of the rye,
    With a hey, and a ho, and a hey nonino,
These pretty country-folks would lie
    In spring-time, *etc.*

This carol they began that hour,
    With a hey, and a ho, and a hey nonino,
How that a life was but a flower
    In spring-time, *etc.*

And therefore take the present time,
    With a hey, and a ho, and a hey nonino;
For love is crowned with the prime
    In spring time, *etc.*

TOUCHSTONE
Truly, young gentlemen, though there was no great
matter in the ditty, yet the note was very untuneable.

FIRST PAGE
You are deceived, sir: we kept time, we lost not our
time.

TOUCHSTONE
By my troth, yes; I count it but time lost to hear such a
foolish song. God b' wi' you; and God mend your
voices! — Come, Audrey. [*Exeunt.*

SCENE IV

The forest.

Enter DUKE SENIOR, AMIENS, JAQUES,
ORLANDO, OLIVER, *and* CELIA.

DUKE SENIOR
Dost thou believe, Orlando, that the boy
Can do all this that he hath promised?

ORLANDO
I sometimes do believe, and sometimes do not;
As those that fear, — they hope, and know they fear.

Enter ROSALIND, SILVIUS, *and* PHEBE.

ROSALIND
Patience once more, whiles our compact is urged; —
You say, if I bring in your Rosalind, [*To the* DUKE.
You will bestow her on Orlando here?

DUKE SENIOR
That would I, had I kingdoms to give with her.

ROSALIND [*to* ORLANDO].
And you say, you will have her, when I bring her?

ORLANDO
That would I, were I of all kingdoms king.

ROSALIND [*to* PHEBE].
You say, you'll marry me, if I be willing?

PHEBE
That will I, should I die the hour after.

ROSALIND
But if you do refuse to marry me,
You'll give yourself to this most faithful shepherd?

PHEBE
So is the bargain.

ROSALIND [*to* SILVIUS].
You say, that you'll have Phebe, if she will?

SILVIUS
Though to have her and death were both one thing.

ROSALIND
I have promised to make all this matter even.
Keep you your word, O duke, to give your daughter; —

You yours, Orlando, to receive his daughter: —
Keep your word, Phebe, that you'll marry me,
Or else, refusing me, to wed this shepherd: —
Keep your word, Silvius, that you'll marry her,
If she refuse me: — and from hence I go,
To make these doubts all even.
[*Exeunt* ROSALIND *and* CELIA.

DUKE SENIOR
I do remember in this shepherd boy
Some lively touches of my daughter's favour.

ORLANDO
My lord, the first time that I ever saw him
Methought he was a brother to your daughter:
But, my good lord, this boy is forest-born,
And hath been tutor'd in the rudiments
Of many desperate studies by his uncle,
Whom he reports to be a great magician,
Obscured in the circle of this forest.

JAQUES
There is, sure, another flood toward, and these couples
are coming to the ark. Here comes a pair of very
strange beasts, which in all tongues are call'd fools.

Enter TOUCHSTONE *and* AUDREY.

TOUCHSTONE
Salutation and greeting to you all!

JAQUES
Good my lord, bid him welcome: this is the
motley-minded gentleman that I have so often met in
the forest: he hath been a courtier, he swears.

TOUCHSTONE
If any man doubt that, let him put me to my purgation.
I have trod a measure; I have flatter'd a lady; I have
been politic with my friend, smooth with mine enemy;
I have undone three tailors; I have had four quarrels,
and like to have fought one.

JAQUES
And how was that ta'en up?

TOUCHSTONE
Faith, we met, and found the quarrel was upon the
seventh cause.

JAQUES
How seventh cause? — Good my lord, like this fellow.

DUKE SENIOR
I like him very well.

TOUCHSTONE
God ild you, sir; I desire you of the like. I press in here,
sir, amongst the rest of the country copulatives, to
swear and to forswear; according as marriage binds
and blood breaks: — a poor virgin, sir, an ill-favour'd
thing, sir, but mine own; a poor humour of mine, sir, to
take that that no man else will: rich honesty dwells like
a miser, sir, in a poor house; as your pearl in your foul
oyster.

DUKE SENIOR
By my faith, he is very swift and sententious.

TOUCHSTONE
According to the fool's bolt, sir, and such dulcet
diseases.

JAQUES
But, for the seventh cause; how did you find the quarrel
on the seventh cause?

TOUCHSTONE
Upon a lie seven times removed: — bear your body
more seeming, Audrey: — as thus, sir: I did dislike the
cut of a certain courtier's beard: he sent me word, if I
said his beard was not cut well, he was in the mind it
was: this is call'd the Retort Courteous. If I sent him
word again it was not well cut, he would send me word
he cut it to please himself: this is call'd the Quip
Modest. If again it was not well cut, he disabled my
judgement: this is call'd the Reply Churlish. If again it
was not well cut, he would answer I spake not true: this
is call'd the Reproof Valiant. If again it was not well cut,
he would say I lie: this is call'd the Counter-check
Quarrelsome: and so to the Lie Circumstantial and the
Lie Direct.

JAQUES
And how oft did you say his beard was not well cut?

TOUCHSTONE
I durst go no further than the Lie Circumstantial, nor
he durst not give me the Lie Direct; and so we
measured swords, and parted.

JAQUES
Can you nominate in order now the degrees of the lie?

TOUCHSTONE
O sir, we quarrel in print, by the book; as you have
books for good manners: I will name you the degrees.
The first, the Retort Courteous; the second, the Quip

Modest; the third, the Reply Churlish; the fourth, the Reproof Valiant; the fifth, the Countercheck Quarrelsome; the sixth, the Lie with Circumstance; the seventh, the Lie Direct. All these you may avoid, but the Lie Direct; and you may avoid that too with an 'if'. I knew when seven justices could not take up a quarrel; but when the parties were met themselves, one of them thought but of an 'if', as, 'If you said so, then I said so'; and they shook hands, and swore brothers. Your 'if' is the only peacemaker; much virtue in 'if'.

JAQUES

Is not this a rare fellow, my lord? he's as good at any thing, and yet a fool.

DUKE SENIOR

He uses his folly like a stalking-horse, and under the presentation of that he shoots his wit.

Enter HYMEN leading ROSALIND in woman's clothes, and CELIA.

Still music.

HYMEN

Then is there mirth in heaven,
When earthly things made even
    Atone together.
Good duke, receive thy daughter:
Hymen from heaven brought her,
    Yea, brought her hither,
That thou mightst join her hand with his
Whose heart within his bosom is.

ROSALIND   [*to* DUKE SENIOR].

To you I give myself, for I am yours. —
[*to* ORLANDO] To you I give myself, for I am yours.

DUKE SENIOR

If there be truth in sight, you are my daughter.

ORLANDO

If there be truth in sight, you are my Rosalind.

PHEBE

If sight and shape be true,
Why, then, — my love adieu!

ROSALIND   [*to* DUKE SENIOR].

I'll have no father, if you be not he: —
[*to* ORLANDO] I'll have no husband, if you be not he: —
[*to* PHEBE] Nor ne'er wed woman, if you be not she.

HYMEN

Peace, ho! I bar confusion:
'Tis I must make conclusion
Of these most strange events:
Here's eight that must take hands
To join in Hymen's bands,
    If truth holds true contents.
You and you no cross shall part: —
         [*To* ORLANDO *and* ROSALIND.
You and you are heart in heart: —
         [*To* OLIVER *and* CELIA.
You to his love must accord,   [*To* PHEBE.

Or have a woman to your lord: —
You and you are sure together,

         [*To* TOUCHSTONE *and* AUDREY.

As the winter to foul weather.
Whiles a wedlock-hymn we sing,
Feed yourselves with questioning;
That reason wonder may diminish,
How thus we met, and these things finish.
         Song.
Wedding is great Juno's crown:
    O blessed bond of board and bed!
'Tis Hymen peoples every town;
    High wedlock, then, be honoured:
Honour, high honour, and renown,
To Hymen, god of every town!

DUKE SENIOR

O my dear niece, welcome thou art to me,
Even daughter-welcome, in no less degree.

PHEBE   [*to* SILVIUS].

I will not eat my word, now thou art mine;
Thy faith my fancy to thee doth combine.

        Enter JAQUES DE BOYS.

JAQUES DE BOYS

Let me have audience for a word or two:
I am the second son of old Sir Rowland,
That bring these tidings to this fair assembly. —
Duke Frederick, hearing how that every day
Men of great worth resorted to this forest,
Address'd a mighty power; which were on foot,
In his own conduct, purposely to take
His brother here, and put him to the sword:
And to the skirts of this wild wood he came;
Where meeting with an old religious man,
After some question with him, was converted
Both from his enterprise and from the world;
His crown bequeathing to his banish'd brother,
And all their lands restored to them again
That were with him exil'd. This to be true,
I do engage my life.

DUKE SENIOR

          Welcome, young man;
Thou offer'st fairly to thy brothers' wedding:
To one, his lands withheld; and to the other,
A land itself at large, a potent dukedom.
First, in this forest, let us do those ends
That here were well begun and well begot:
And after, every of this happy number,
That have endured shrewd days and nights with us,
Shall share the good of our returned fortune,
According to the measure of their states.
Meantime forget this new-fall'n dignity,
And fall into our rustic revelry. —
Play, music! — and you, brides and bridegrooms all,
With measure heap'd in joy, to th'measures fall.

JAQUES

Sir, by your patience. — If I heard you rightly,
The duke hath put on a religious life,
And thrown into neglect the pompous court?

JAQUES DE BOYS

He hath.

JAQUES

To him will I: out of these convertites
There is much matter to be heard and learn'd. —
You [*to* DUKE SENIOR] to your former honour I
    bequeath;
Your patience and your virtue well deserves it: —
You [*to* ORLANDO] to a love that your true faith doth
    merit: —
You [*to* OLIVER] to your land, and love, and great allies: —
You [*to* SILVIUS] to a long and well-deserved bed: —
And you [*to* TOUCHSTONE] to wrangling; for thy
    loving voyage
Is but for two months victuall'd. — So, to your
    pleasures:
I am for other than for dancing measures.

DUKE SENIOR

Stay, Jaques, stay.

JAQUES

To see no pastime I: — what you would have
I'll stay to know at your abandon'd cave.   [*Exit*

DUKE SENIOR

Proceed, proceed: we will begin these rites,
As we do trust they'll end, in true delights.   [*A dance*

EPILOGUE

ROSALIND

It is not the fashion to see the lady the epilogue; but it is no more unhandsome than to see the lord the prologue. If it be true that good wine needs no bush, 'tis true that a good play needs no epilogue: yet to good wine they do use good bushes; and good plays prove the better by the help of good epilogues. What a case am I in, then, that am neither a good epilogue, nor cannot insinuate with you in the behalf of a good play! I am not furnish'd like a beggar, therefore to beg will not become me: my way is, to conjure you; and I'll begin with the women. I charge you, O women, for the love you bear to men, to like as much of this play as please you: and I charge you, O men, for the love you bear to women (as I perceive by your simpering, none of you hates them), that between you and the women the play may please. If I were a woman, I would kiss as many of you as had beards that pleased me, complexions that liked me, and breaths that I defied not: and, I am sure, as many as have good beards, or good faces, or sweet breaths, will, for my kind offer, when I make curtsy, bid me farewell.   [*Exeunt*

TWELFTH NIGHT; OR, WHAT YOU WILL

DRAMATIS PERSONAE

ORSINO, *Duke of Illyria.*
SEBASTIAN, *a young gentleman.*
ANTONIO, *a sea captain, friend to Sebastian.*
A SEA CAPTAIN, *friend to Viola.*
VALENTINE, } *gentlemen attending on the Duke.*
CURIO,
SIR TOBY BELCH, *uncle to Olivia.*

SIR ANDREW AGUECHEEK.
MALVOLIO, *steward to Olivia.*
FABIAN, } *servants to Olivia.*
CLOWN,

OLIVIA.
VIOLA, *sister to Sebastian.*

MARIA, *Olivia's woman.*

LORDS, *a* PRIEST, SAILORS, OFFICERS,
MUSICIANS, *and* ATTENDANTS.

SCENE — *A city in Illyria, and the sea-coast near it.*

ACT I

SCENE I

The DUKE'S *palace.*

Enter DUKE, LORDS, *and* CURIO;
MUSICIANS *attending.*

DUKE
If music be the food of love, play on;
Give me excess of it, that, surfeiting,
The appetite may sicken, and so die. —
That strain again! — it had a dying fall:
O, it came o'er my ear like the sweet sound,
That breathes upon a bank of violets,
Stealing and giving odour! — Enough; no more;
'Tis not so sweet now as it was before.
O spirit of love, how quick and fresh art thou!
That, notwithstanding thy capacity
Receiveth as the sea, naught enters there,
Of what validity and pitch soe'er,
But falls into abatement and low price,
Even in a minute! so full of shapes is fancy,
That it alone is high-fantastical.

CURIO
Will you go hunt, my lord?

DUKE
What, Curio?

CURIO
The hart.

DUKE
Why, so I do, the noblest that I have:
O, when mine eyes did see Olivia first,
Methought she purg'd the air of pestilence!
That instant was I turn'd into a hart;
And my desires, like fell and cruel hounds,
E'er since pursue me.

Enter VALENTINE.
How now! what news from her?

VALENTINE
So please my lord, I might not be admitted;
But from her handmaid do return this answer:
The element itself, till seven years hence,
Shall not behold her face at ample view;
But, like a cloistress, she will veiled walk,
And water once a day her chamber round
With eye-offending brine: all this to season
A brother's dead love, which she would keep fresh
And lasting in her sad remembrance.

DUKE
O, she that hath a heart of that fine frame
To pay this debt of love but to a brother,

How will she love, when the rich golden shaft
Hath kill'd the flock of all affections else
That live in her; when liver, brain, and heart,
These sovereign thrones, are all supplied, and fill'd
Her sweet perfections with one self king! —
Away before me to sweet beds of flowers:
Love-thoughts lie rich when canopied with bowers.
[*Exeunt.*

SCENE II

The sea-coast.

Enter VIOLA, CAPTAIN, *and* SAILORS.

VIOLA
What country, friends, is this?

CAPTAIN
This is Illyria, lady.

VIOLA
And what should I do in Illyria?
My brother he is in Elysium.
Perchance he is not drown'd: — what think you,
    sailors?

CAPTAIN
It is perchance that you yourself were saved.

VIOLA
O my poor brother! and so perchance may he be.

CAPTAIN
True, madam; and, to comfort you with chance,
Assure yourself, after our ship did split,
When you, and those poor number sav'd with you,
Hung on our driving boat, I saw your brother,
Most provident in peril, bind himself —
Courage and hope both teaching him the practice —
To a strong mast that liv'd upon the sea;
Where, like Arion on the dolphin's back,
I saw him hold acquaintance with the waves
So long as I could see.

VIOLA
For saying so, there's gold:
Mine own escape unfoldeth to my hope,
Whereto thy speech serves for authority,
The like of him. Know'st thou this country?

CAPTAIN
Ay, madam, well; for I was bred and born
Not three hours' travel from this very place.

VIOLA
Who governs here?

CAPTAIN
A noble duke, in nature as in name.

VIOLA
What is his name?

CAPTAIN
Orsino.

VIOLA
Orsino! I have heard my father name him:
He was a bachelor then.

CAPTAIN
And so is now, or was so very late;
For but a month ago I went from hence,
And then 'twas fresh in murmur, — as, you know,
What great ones do, the less will prattle of, —
That he did seek the love of fair Olivia.

VIOLA
What's she?

CAPTAIN
A virtuous maid, the daughter of a count
That died some twelvemonth since; then leaving her
In the protection of his son, her brother,
Who shortly also died: for whose dear loss,
They say, she hath abjur'd the company
And sight of men.

VIOLA
O, that I serv'd that lady,
And might not be deliver'd to the world,
Till I had made mine own occasion mellow,
What my estate is!

CAPTAIN
That were hard to compass;
Because she will admit no kind of suit,
No, not the duke's.

VIOLA
There is a fair behaviour in thee, captain;
And though that nature with a beauteous wall
Doth oft close in pollution, yet of thee
I will believe thou hast a mind that suits
With this thy fair and outward character.
I prithee, — and I'll pay thee bounteously, —
Conceal me what I am; and be my aid
For such disguise as haply shall become
The form of my intent. I'll serve this duke:
Thou shalt present me as an eunuch to him:
It may be worth thy pains; for I can sing,
And speak to him in many sorts of music,
That will allow me very worth his service.
What else may hap, to time I will commit;
Only shape thou thy silence to my wit.

CAPTAIN
Be you his eunuch, and your mute I'll be:
When my tongue blabs, then let mine eyes not see.

VIOLA
I thank thee: lead me on.   [*Exeunt.*

SCENE III

Olivia's house.

Enter SIR TOBY BELCH *and* MARIA.

SIR TOBY
What a plague means my niece, to take the death of her
brother thus? I am sure care's an enemy to life.

MARIA
By my troth, Sir Toby, you must come in earlier o'nights:
your cousin, my lady, takes great exceptions to your ill
hours.

SIR TOBY
Why, let her except before excepted.

MARIA
Ay, but you must confine yourself within the modest
limits of order.

SIR TOBY
Confine! I'll confine myself no finer than I am: these
clothes are good enough to drink in; and so be these
boots too, — an they be not, let them hang themselves
in their own straps.

MARIA
That quaffing and drinking will undo you: I heard my
lady talk of it yesterday; and of a foolish knight that you
brought in one night here to be her wooer.

SIR TOBY
Who, Sir Andrew Aguecheek?

MARIA
Ay, he.

SIR TOBY
He's as tall a man as any's in Illyria.

MARIA
What's that to th'purpose?

SIR TOBY
Why, he has three thousand ducats a year.

MARIA
Ay, but he'll have but a year in all these ducats: he's a
very fool and a prodigal.

SIR TOBY
Fie, that you'll say so! he plays o'th'viol-de-gamboys,
and speaks three or four languages word for word
without book, and hath all the good gifts of nature.

MARIA
He hath, indeed, almost natural: for, besides that he's a
fool, he's a great quarreller; and, but that he hath the
gift of a coward to allay the gust he hath in quarrelling,
'tis thought among the prudent he would quickly have
the gift of a grave.

SIR TOBY
By this hand, they are scoundrels and substractors that
say so of him. Who are they?

MARIA
They that add, moreover, he's drunk nightly in your
company.

SIR TOBY
With drinking healths to my niece: I'll drink to her as
long as there is a passage in my throat and drink in
Illyria: he's a coward and a coistrel that will not drink to
my niece till his brains turn o'th'toe like a parish-top.
What, wench! *Castiliano volto*; for here comes Sir
Andrew Agueface.

Enter SIR ANDREW AGUECHEEK.

SIR ANDREW
Sir Toby Belch, — how now, Sir Toby Belch!

SIR TOBY
Sweet Sir Andrew!

SIR ANDREW
Bless you, fair shrew.

MARIA
And you too, sir.

SIR TOBY
Accost, Sir Andrew, accost.

SIR ANDREW
What's that?

SIR TOBY
My niece's chambermaid.

SIR ANDREW
Good Mistress Accost, I desire better acquaintance.

MARIA
My name is Mary, sir.

SIR ANDREW
Good Mistress Mary Accost, —

SIR TOBY
You mistake, knight: 'accost' is front her, board her,
woo her, assail her.

SIR ANDREW
By my troth, I would not undertake her in this company.
Is that the meaning of 'accost'?

MARIA
Fare you well, gentlemen.

SIR TOBY
An thou let part so, Sir Andrew, would thou mightst
never draw sword again.

SIR ANDREW
An you part so, mistress, I would I might never draw
sword again. Fair lady, do you think you have fools in
hand?

MARIA
Sir, I have not you by th'hand.

SIR ANDREW
Marry, but you shall have; and here's my hand.

SIR TOBY I am sure care's an enemy to life.

MARIA
Now, sir, thought is free: I pray you, bring your hand to th'buttery-bar, and let it drink.

SIR ANDREW
Wherefore, sweet-heart? what's your metaphor?

MARIA
It's dry, sir.

SIR ANDREW
Why, I think so: I am not such an ass but I can keep my hand dry. But what's your jest?

MARIA
A dry jest, sir.

SIR ANDREW
Are you full of them?

MARIA
Ay, sir, I have them at my fingers' ends: marry, now I let go your hand, I am barren.   [*Exit.*

SIR TOBY
O knight, thou lack'st a cup of canary: when did I see thee so put down?

SIR ANDREW
Never in your life, I think; unless you see canary put me down. Methinks sometimes I have no more wit than a Christian or an ordinary man has: but I am a great eater of beef, and I believe that does harm to my wit.

SIR TOBY
No question.

SIR ANDREW
An I thought that, I'ld forswear it. I'll ride home to-morrow, Sir Toby.

SIR TOBY
Pourquoi, my dear knight?

SIR ANDREW
What is *pourquoi?* do or not do? I would I had bestow'd that time in the tongues that I have in fencing, dancing, and bear-baiting: O, had I but follow'd the arts!

SIR TOBY
Then hadst thou had an excellent head of hair.

SIR ANDREW
Why, would that have mended my hair?

SIR TOBY
Past question; for thou seest it will not curl by nature.

SIR ANDREW
But it becomes me well enough, does't not?

SIR TOBY
Excellent; it hangs like flax on a distaff; and I hope to see a housewife take thee between her legs and spin it off.

SIR ANDREW
Faith, I'll home to-morrow, Sir Toby: your niece will not be seen; or if she be, it's four to one she'll none of me: the count himself here hard by woos her.

SIR TOBY
She'll none o'th'count: she'll not match above her degree, neither in estate, years, nor wit; I have heard her swear't. Tut, there's life in't, man.

SIR ANDREW
I'll stay a month longer. I am a fellow o'th'strangest mind i'th'world; I delight in masks and revels sometimes altogether.

SIR TOBY
Art thou good at these kickshawses, knight?

SIR ANDREW
As any man in Illyria, whatsoever he be, under the degree of my betters; and yet I will not compare with an obleman.

SIR TOBY
What is thy excellence in a galliard, knight?

SIR ANDREW
Faith, I can cut a caper.

SIR TOBY
And I can cut the mutton to't.

SIR ANDREW
And I think I have the back-trick simply as strong as any man in Illyria.

SIR TOBY
Wherefore are these things hid? wherefore have these gifts a curtain before 'em? are they like to take dust, like Mistress Mall's picture? why dost thou not go to church in a galliard, and come home in a coranto? My very walk should be a jig; I would not so much as make water but in a sink-a-pace. What dost thou mean? is it a world to hide virtues in? I did think, by the excellent constitution of thy leg, it was form'd under the star of a galliard.

SIR ANDREW
Ay, 'tis strong, and it does indifferent well in a flame-colour'd stock. Shall we set about some revels?

SIR TOBY
What shall we do else? were we not born under Taurus?

SIR ANDREW Fair lady, do you think you have fools in hand?

SIR ANDREW
Taurus! that's sides and heart.

SIR TOBY
No, sir; it is legs and thighs. Let me see thee caper [SIR ANDREW *dances*]: ha! higher: ha, ha! excellent!
            [*Exeunt.*

SCENE IV

The Duke's palace.

Enter VALENTINE, *and* VIOLA *in man's attire.*

VALENTINE
If the duke continue these favours towards you, Cesario, you are like to be much advanced: he hath known you but three days, and already you are no stranger.

VIOLA
You either fear his humour or my negligence, that you call in question the continuance of his love: is he inconstant, sir, in his favours?

VALENTINE
No, believe me.

VIOLA
I thank you. Here comes the count.

Enter DUKE, CURIO, *and* ATTENDANTS.

DUKE
Who saw Cesario, ho?

VIOLA
On your attendance, my lord; here.

DUKE
Stand you awhile aloof. — Cesario,
Thou know'st no less but all; I have unclasp'd
To thee the book even of my secret soul:
Therefore, good youth, address thy gait unto her,
Be not denied access, stand at her doors,
And tell them, there thy fixed foot shall grow
Till thou have audience.

VIOLA
                    Sure, my noble lord,
If she be so abandon'd to her sorrow
As it is spoke, she never will admit me.

DUKE
Be clamorous, and leap all civil bounds,
Rather than make unprofited return.

VIOLA
Say I do speak with her, my lord, what then?

DUKE
O, then unfold the passion of my love,
Surprise her with discourse of my dear faith!
It shall become thee well to act my woes;
She will attend it better in thy youth
Than in a nuncio of more grave aspect.

VIOLA
I think not so, my lord.

DUKE
                    Dear lad, believe it;
For they shall yet belie thy happy years,
That say thou art a man: Diana's lip
Is not more smooth and rubious; thy small pipe

Is as the maiden's organ, shrill and sound;
And all is semblative a woman's part.
I know thy constellation is right apt
For this affair: — some four or five attend him;
All, if you will; for I myself am best
When least in company: — prosper well in this,
And thou shalt live as freely as thy lord,
To call his fortunes thine.

VIOLA
                    I'll do my best
To woo your lady: — [*aside*] yet, a barful strife!
Whoe'er I woo, myself would be his wife.   [*Exeunt.*

SCENE V

OLIVIA'S *house.*

Enter MARIA *and* CLOWN.

MARIA
Nay, either tell me where thou hast been, or I will not open my lips so wide as a bristle may enter in way of thy excuse: my lady will hang thee for thy absence.

CLOWN
Let her hang me: he that is well hang'd in this world needs to fear no colours.

MARIA
Make that good.

CLOWN
He shall see none to fear.

MARIA
A good lenten answer: I can tell thee where that saying was born, of, — I fear no colours.

CLOWN
Where, good Mistress Mary?

MARIA
In the wars; and that may you be bold to say in your foolery.

CLOWN
Well, God give them wisdom that have it; and those that are fools, let them use their talents.

MARIA
Yet you will be hang'd for being so long absent; or, to be turn'd away, — is not that as good as a hanging to you?

CLOWN
Many a good hanging prevents a bad marriage; and, for turning away, let summer bear it out.

MARIA
You are resolute, then?

CLOWN
Not so, neither; but I am resolved on two points.

MARIA
That if one break, the other will hold; or, if both break, your gaskins fall.

CLOWN
Apt, in good faith; very apt. Well, go thy way; if Sir Toby would leave drinking, thou wert as witty a piece of Eve's flesh as any in Illyria.

MARIA
Peace, you rogue, no more o' that. Here comes my lady: make your excuse wisely, you were best.   [*Exit.*

CLOWN
Wit, an't be thy will, put me into good fooling! Those wits, that think they have thee, do very oft prove fools; and I, that am sure I lack thee, may pass for a wise man: for what says Quinapalus? 'Better a witty fool than a foolish wit.'

Enter LADY OLIVIA *with* MALVOLIO.
God bless thee, lady!

OLIVIA
Take the fool away.

CLOWN
Do you not hear, fellows? Take away the lady.

OLIVIA
Go to, y'are a dry fool: I'll no more of you: besides, you grow dishonest.

CLOWN
Two faults, madonna, that drink and good counsel will amend: for give the dry fool drink, then is the fool not dry: bid the dishonest man mend himself; if he mend, he is no longer dishonest: if he cannot, let the botcher mend him: any thing that's mended is but patch'd: virtue that transgresses is but patch'd with sin; and sin that amends is but patch'd with virtue: if that this simple syllogism will serve, so; if it will not, what remedy? As there is no true cuckold but calamity, so beauty's a flower. — The lady bade take away the fool; therefore, I say again, take her away.

OLIVIA
Sir, I bade them take away you.

CLOWN
Misprision in the highest degree! — Lady, *cucullus non facit monachum*; that's as much to say as, I wear not motley in my brain. Good madonna, give me leave to prove you a fool.

OLIVIA
Can you do it?

CLOWN
Dexteriously, good madonna.

OLIVIA
Make your proof.

CLOWN
I must catechise you for it, madonna: good my mouse of virtue, answer me.

OLIVIA
Well, sir, for want of other idleness, I'll bide your proof.

CLOWN
Good madonna, why mourn'st thou?

OLIVIA
Good fool, for my brother's death.

CLOWN
I think his soul is in hell, madonna.

OLIVIA
I know his soul is in heaven, fool.

CLOWN
The more fool, madonna, to mourn for your brother's soul being in heaven. — Take away the fool, gentlemen.

OLIVIA
What think you of this fool, Malvolio? doth he not mend?

MALVOLIO
Yes, and shall do till the pangs of death shake him: infirmity, that decays the wise, doth ever make the better fool.

CLOWN
God send you, sir, a speedy infirmity, for the better increasing your folly! Sir Toby will be sworn that I am no fox; but he will not pass his word for twopence that you are no fool.

OLIVIA
How say you to that, Malvolio?

MALVOLIO
I marvel your ladyship takes delight in such a barren rascal: I saw him put down the other day with an ordinary fool, that has no more brain than a stone. Look you now, he's out of his guard already; unless you laugh and minister occasion to him, he is gagg'd. I protest, I take these wise men, that crow so at these set kind of fools, no better than the fools' zanies.

OLIVIA
O, you are sick of self-love, Malvolio, and taste with a distemper'd appetite. To be generous, guiltless, and of free disposition, is to take those things for bird-bolts that you deem cannon-bullets: there is no slander in an allow'd fool, though he do nothing but rail; nor no railing in a known discreet man, though he do nothing but reprove.

CLOWN
Now Mercury endue thee with leasing, for thou speak'st well of fools!

Enter MARIA.

MARIA
Madam, there is at the gate a young gentleman much desires to speak with you.

OLIVIA
From the Count Orsino, is it?

MARIA
I know not, madam: 'tis a fair young man, and well attended.

OLIVIA
Who of my people hold him in delay?

MARIA
Sir Toby, madam, your kinsman.

OLIVIA
Fetch him off, I pray you; he speaks nothing but madman: fie on him! [*Exit* MARIA.] Go you, Malvolio: if it be a suit from the count, I am sick, or not at home; what you will, to dismiss it. [*Exit* MALVOLIO.] Now you see, sir, how your fooling grows old, and people dislike it.

CLOWN
Thou hast spoke for us, madonna, as if thy eldest son should be a fool; whose skull Jove cram with brains! for — here he comes — one of thy kin has a most weak *pia mater*.

Enter SIR TOBY.

OLIVIA
By mine honour, half drunk. — What is he at the gate, cousin?

SIR TOBY
A gentleman.

OLIVIA
A gentleman! what gentleman?

SIR TOBY
'Tis a gentleman here — a plague o' these pickle-herring! — How now, sot!

CLOWN
Good Sir Toby! —

OLIVIA
Cousin, cousin, how have you come so early by this lethargy?

SIR TOBY
Lechery! I defy lechery. There's one at the gate.

OLIVIA
Ay, marry, what is he?

SIR TOBY
Let him be the devil, an he will, I care not: give me faith, say I. Well, it's all one. [*Exit*.

OLIVIA
What's a drunken man like, fool?

CLOWN
Like a drown'd man, a fool, and a madman: one draught above heat makes him a fool; the second mads him; and a third drowns him.

OLIVIA
Go thou and seek the crowner, and let him sit o' my coz; for he's in the third degree of drink, — he's drown'd: go, look after him.

CLOWN
He is but mad yet, madonna; and the fool shall look to the madman. [*Exit*.

Enter MALVOLIO.

MALVOLIO
Madam, yond young fellow swears he will speak with you. I told him you were sick; he takes on him to understand so much, and therefore comes to speak with you: I told him you were asleep; he seems to have a foreknowledge of that too, and therefore comes to speak with you. What is to be said to him, lady? he's fortified against any denial.

OLIVIA
Tell him he shall not speak with me.

MALVOLIO
Has been told so; and he says, he'll stand at your door like a sheriff's post, and be the supporter to a bench, but he'll speak with you.

OLIVIA
What kind o' man is he?

MALVOLIO
Why, of mankind.

OLIVIA
What manner of man?

MALVOLIO
Of very ill manner; he'll speak with you, will you or no.

OLIVIA
Of what personage and years is he?

MALVOLIO
Not yet old enough for a man, nor young enough for a boy; as a squash is before 'tis a peascod, or a codling when 'tis almost an apple: 'tis with him e'en standing water, between boy and man. He is very well-favour'd, and he speaks very shrewishly; one would think his mother's milk were scarce out of him.

OLIVIA
Let him approach: call in my gentlewoman.

MALVOLIO
Gentlewoman, my lady calls. [*Exit*

Enter MARIA.

OLIVIA
Give me my veil: come, throw it o'er my face. We'll once more hear Orsino's embassy.

Enter VIOLA.

VIOLA
The honourable lady of the house, which is she?

OLIVIA
Speak to me; I shall answer for her. Your will?

VIOLA
Most radiant, exquisite, and unmatchable beauty, — I pray you, tell me if this be the lady of the house, for I never saw her: I would be loth to cast away my speech; for, besides that it is excellently well penn'd, I have taken great pains to con it. Good beauties, let me sustain no scorn; I am very comptible, even to the least sinister usage.

OLIVIA
Whence came you, sir?

VIOLA
I can say little more than I have studied, and that question's out of my part. Good gentle one, give me modest assurance if you be the lady of the house, that I may proceed in my speech.

OLIVIA
Are you a comedian?

VIOLA
No, my profound heart: and yet, by the very fangs of malice I swear I am not that I play. Are you the lady of the house?

OLIVIA
If I do not usurp myself, I am.

VIOLA
Most certain, if you are she, you do usurp yourself; for, what is yours to bestow is not yours to reserve. But this is from my commission: I will on with my speech in your praise, and then show you the heart of my message.

OLIVIA
Come to what is important in't: I forgive you the praise.

VIOLA
Alas, I took great pains to study it, and 'tis poetical.

OLIVIA
It is the more like to be feign'd: I pray you, keep it in. I heard you were saucy at my gates; and allow'd your approach rather to wonder at you than to hear you. If you be mad, be gone; if you have reason, be brief: 'tis not that time of moon with me to make one in so skipping a dialogue.

MARIA
Will you hoist sail, sir? here lies your way.

VIOLA
No, good swabber; I am to hull here a little longer. Some mollification for your giant, sweet lady. Tell me your mind: I am a messenger.

OLIVIA
Sure, you have some hideous matter to deliver, when the courtesy of it is so fearful. Speak your office.

VIOLA
It alone concerns your ear. I bring no overture of war, no taxation of homage: I hold the olive in my hand; my words are as full of peace as matter.

OLIVIA
Yet you began rudely. What are you? what would you?

VIOLA
The rudeness that hath appear'd in me have I learn'd from my entertainment. What I am, and what I would, are as secret as maidenhead: to your ears, divinity; to any other's, profanation.

OLIVIA
Give us the place alone: we will hear this divinity. [*Exit* MARIA.] Now, sir, what is your text?

VIOLA
Most sweet lady, —

OLIVIA
A comfortable doctrine, and much may be said of it. Where lies your text?

VIOLA
In Orsino's bosom.
OLIVIA
In his bosom! In what chapter of his bosom?
VIOLA
To answer by the method, in the first of his heart.
OLIVIA
O, I have read it: it is heresy. Have you no more to say?
VIOLA
Good madam, let me see your face.
OLIVIA
Have you any commission from your lord to negotiate
with my face? You are now out of your text: but we will
draw the curtain, and show you the picture. Look you,
sir, such a one I was, this presents: is't not well done?
[*Unveiling.*
VIOLA
Excellently done, if God did all.
OLIVIA
'Tis in grain, sir; 'twill endure wind and weather.
VIOLA
'Tis beauty truly blent, whose red and white
Nature's own sweet and cunning hand laid on:
Lady, you are the cruell'st she alive,
If you will lead these graces to the grave,
And leave the world no copy.
OLIVIA
O, sir, I will not be so hard-hearted; I will give out
divers schedules of my beauty: it shall be inventoried,
and every particle and utensil labell'd to my will: — as,
item, two lips, indifferent red; item, two grey eyes, with
lids to them; item, one neck, one chin, and so forth.
Were you sent hither to 'praise me?
VIOLA
I see you what you are, — you are too proud;
But, if you were the devil, you are fair.
My lord and master loves you: O, such love
Could be but recompens'd, though you were crown'd
The nonpareil of beauty!
OLIVIA
How does he love me?
VIOLA
With adorations, with fertile tears,
With groans that thunder love, with sighs of fire.
OLIVIA
Your lord does know my mind; I cannot love him:
Yet I suppose him virtuous, know him noble,
Of great estate, of fresh and stainless youth;
In voices well divulg'd, free, learn'd, and valiant;
And, in dimension and the shape of nature,
A gracious person: but yet I cannot love him;
He might have took his answer long ago.
VIOLA
If I did love you in my master's flame,
With such a suffering, such a deadly life,
In your denial I would find no sense;
I would not understand it.
OLIVIA
Why, what would you?
VIOLA
Make me a willow cabin at your gate,
And call upon my soul within the house;
Write loyal cantons of contemned love,
And sing them loud even in the dead of night;
Holla your name to the reverberate hills,
And make the babbling gossip of the air
Cry out, 'Olivia!' O, you should not rest
Between the elements of air and earth,
But you should pity me!
OLIVIA
You might do much. What is your parentage?
VIOLA
Above my fortunes, yet my state is well:
I am a gentleman.
OLIVIA
Get you to your lord;
I cannot love him: let him send no more;
Unless, perchance, you come to me again,
To tell me how he takes it. Fare you well:
I thank you for your pains: spend this for me.
VIOLA
I am no fee'd post, lady; keep your purse:
My master, not myself, lacks recompense.
Love make his heart of flint, that you shall love;
And let your fervour, like my master's, be
Plac'd in contempt! Farewell, fair cruelty. [*Exit.*
OLIVIA
'What is your parentage?'
'Above my fortunes, yet my state is well:

SEBASTIAN I am bound to the Count Orsino's court: farewell.

I am a gentleman.' I'll be sworn thou art;
Thy tongue, thy face, thy limbs, actions, and spirit,
Do give thee fivefold blazon: — not too fast; —
Soft, soft! —
Unless the master were the man. — How now!
Even so quickly may one catch the plague?
Methinks I feel this youth's perfections
With an invisible and subtle stealth
To creep in at mine eyes. Well, let it be. —
What, ho, Malvolio!

Enter MALVOLIO.

MALVOLIO
Here, madam, at your service.
OLIVIA
Run after that same peevish messenger,
The county's man: he left this ring behind him,
Would I or not: tell him I'll none of it.
Desire him not to flatter with his lord,
Nor hold him up with hopes; I am not for him:
If that the youth will come this way to-morrow,
I'll give him reasons for't. Hie thee, Malvolio.
MALVOLIO
Madam, I will. [*Exit.*
OLIVIA
I do I know not what; and fear to find
Mine eye too great a flatterer for my mind.
Fate, show thy force: ourselves we do not owe;
What is decreed must be, — and be this so! [*Exit.*

ACT II

SCENE I

The sea-coast.

Enter ANTONIO *and* SEBASTIAN.

ANTONIO
Will you stay no longer? nor will you not that I go with
you?
SEBASTIAN
By your patience, no. My stars shine darkly over me:
the malignancy of my fate might perhaps distemper
yours; therefore I shall crave of you your leave that I
may bear my evils alone: it were a bad recompense for
your love, to lay any of them on you.
ANTONIO
Let me yet know of you whither you are bound.
SEBASTIAN
No, sooth, sir: my determinate voyage is mere
extravagancy. But I perceive in you so excellent a touch
of modesty, that you will not extort from me what I am
willing to keep in; therefore it charges me in manners
the rather to express myself. You must know of me,
then, Antonio, my name is Sebastian, which I call'd
Roderigo. My father was that Sebastian of Messaline,
whom I know you have heard of. He left behind him
myself and a sister, both born in an hour: if the heavens
had been pleased, would we had so ended! but you, sir,

altered that; for some hour before you took me from
the breach of the sea was my sister drown'd.
ANTONIO
Alas the day!
SEBASTIAN
A lady, sir, though it was said she much resembled me,
was yet of many accounted beautiful: but, though I
could not, with such estimable wonder, overfar believe
that, yet thus far I will boldly publish her, — she bore a
mind that envy could not but call fair. She is drown'd
already, sir, with salt water, though I seem to drown
her remembrance again with more.
ANTONIO
Pardon me, sir, your bad entertainment.
SEBASTIAN
O good Antonio, forgive me your trouble!
ANTONIO
If you will not murder me for my love, let me be your
servant.
SEBASTIAN
If you will not undo what you have done, that is, kill
him whom you have recover'd, desire it not. Fare ye
well at once: my bosom is full of kindness; and I am yet
so near the manners of my mother, that, upon the least
occasion more, mine eyes will tell tales of me. I am
bound to the Count Orsino's court: farewell. [*Exit.*
ANTONIO
The gentleness of all the gods go with thee!
I have many enemies in Orsino's court,
Else would I very shortly see thee there:
But, come what may, I do adore thee so,
That danger shall seem sport, and I will go. [*Exit.*

SCENE II

A street.

Enter VIOLA, MALVOLIO *following.*

MALVOLIO
Were not you even now with the Countess Olivia?
VIOLA
Even now, sir; on a moderate pace I have since arrived
but hither.
MALVOLIO
She returns this ring to you, sir: you might have saved me
my pains, to have taken it away yourself. She adds,
moreover, that you should put your lord into a desperate
assurance she will none of him: and one thing more, that
you be never so hardy to come again in his affairs, unless
it be to report your lord's taking of this. Receive it so.
VIOLA
She took no ring of me; — I'll none of it.
MALVOLIO
Come, sir, you peevishly threw it to her; and her will is,
it should be so return'd: if it be worth stooping for,
there it lies in your eye; if not, be it his that finds it.
[*Exit.*

MALVOLIO Is there no respect of place, persons, nor time, in you?

VIOLA
I left no ring with her: what means this lady?
Fortune forbid, my outside have not charm'd her!
She made good view of me; indeed, so much,
That, sure, methought, her eyes had lost her tongue,
For she did speak in starts distractedly.
She loves me, sure; the cunning of her passion
Invites me in this churlish messenger.
None of my lord's ring! why, he sent her none.
I am the man: if it be so, as 'tis,
Poor lady, she were better love a dream.
Disguise, I see, thou art a wickedness,
Wherein the pregnant enemy does much.
How easy is it for the proper-false
In women's waxen hearts to set their forms!
Alas, our frailty is the cause, not we!
For such as we are made of, such we be.
How will this fadge? my master loves her dearly;
And I, poor monster, fond as much on him;
And she, mistaken, seems to dote on me.
What will become of this? As I am man,
My state is desperate for my master's love;
As I am woman, — now, alas the day! —
What thriftless sighs shall poor Olivia breathe!
O Time, thou must untangle this, not I;
It is too hard a knot for me t'untie!   [*Exit.*

SCENE III
Olivia's house.

Enter SIR TOBY *and* SIR ANDREW.

SIR TOBY
Approach, Sir Andrew: not to be a-bed after midnight is
to be up betimes; and *diluculo surgere*, thou know'st, —
SIR ANDREW
Nay, by my troth, I know not: but I know, to be up late is
to be up late.
SIR TOBY
A false conclusion: I hate it as an unfill'd can. To be up

after midnight, and to go to bed then, is early: so that to
go to bed after midnight is to go to bed betimes. Does
not our life consist of the four elements?
SIR ANDREW
Faith, so they say; but, I think, it rather consists of
eating and drinking.
SIR TOBY
Th'art a scholar: let us therefore eat and drink. —
Marian, I say! a stoup of wine!
SIR ANDREW
Here comes the fool, i'faith.

Enter CLOWN.

CLOWN
How now, my hearts! did you never see the picture of
We Three?
SIR TOBY
Welcome, ass. Now let's have a catch.
SIR ANDREW
By my troth, the fool has an excellent breast. I had
rather than forty shillings I had such a leg, and so sweet
a breath to sing, as the fool has. In sooth, thou wast in
very gracious fooling last night, when thou spokest of
Pigrogromitus, of the Vapians passing the equinoctial
of Queubus: 'twas very good, i'faith. I sent thee
sixpence for thy leman: hadst it?
CLOWN
I did impeticos thy gratillity; for Malvolio's nose is no
whipstock; my lady has a white hand, and the
Myrmidons are no bottle-ale houses.
SIR ANDREW
Excellent! why, this is the best fooling, when all is done.
Now, a song.
SIR TOBY
Come on; there is sixpence for you: let's have a song.
SIR ANDREW
There's a testril of me too; if one knight give a —
CLOWN
Would you have a love-song, or a song of good life?

SIR TOBY
A love-song, a love-song.
SIR ANDREW
Ay, ay: I care not for good life.
CLOWN [*sings*].
    O mistress mine, where are you roaming?
    O, stay and hear; your true-love's coming,
        That can sing both high and low:
    Trip no further, pretty sweeting;
    Journeys end in lovers' meeting,
        Every wise man's son doth know.
SIR ANDREW
Excellent good, i'faith.
SIR TOBY
Good, good.
CLOWN
    What is love? 'tis not hereafter;
    Present mirth hath present laughter;
        What's to come is still unsure:
    In delay there lies no plenty;
    Then come kiss me, sweet-and-twenty,
        Youth's a stuff will not endure.
SIR ANDREW
A mellifluous voice, as I am true knight.
SIR TOBY
A contagious breath.
SIR ANDREW
Very sweet and contagious, i'faith.
SIR TOBY
To hear by the nose, it is dulcet in contagion. But shall
we make the welkin dance indeed? shall we rouse the
night-owl in a catch that will draw three souls out of
one weaver? shall we do that?
SIR ANDREW
An you love me, let's do't: I am dog at a catch.
CLOWN
By'r lady, sir, and some dogs will catch well.
SIR ANDREW
Most certain. Let our catch be, 'Thou knave.'
CLOWN
'Hold thy peace, thou knave,' knight? I shall be
constrain'd in't to call thee knave, knight.
SIR ANDREW
'Tis not the first time I have constrain'd one to call me
knave. Begin, fool: it begins, 'Hold thy peace.'
CLOWN
I shall never begin, if I hold my peace.
SIR ANDREW
Good, i'faith. Come, begin.   [*Catch sung.*

Enter MARIA.

MARIA
What a caterwauling do you keep here! If my lady have
not call'd up her steward Malvolio, and bid him turn
you out of doors, never trust me.
SIR TOBY
My lady's a Cataian, we are politicians, Malvolio's a
Peg-a-Ramsey, and 'Three merry men be we.' Am not I
consanguineous? am I not of her blood? Tilly-vally,
lady! [*Sings*] 'There dwelt a man in Babylon, lady, lady!'
CLOWN
Beshrew me, the knight's in admirable fooling.
SIR ANDREW
Ay, he does well enough if he be disposed, and so do I
too: he does it with a better grace, but I do it more
natural.
SIR TOBY
'O, the twelfth day of December, —'
MARIA
For the love o' God, peace!

Enter MALVOLIO.

MALVOLIO
My masters, are you mad? or what are you? Have you
no wit, manners, nor honesty, but to gabble like tinkers
at this time of night? Do ye make an ale-house of my
lady's house, that ye squeak out your cosiers' catches
without any mitigation or remorse of voice? Is there no
respect of place, persons, nor time, in you?
SIR TOBY
We did keep time, sir, in our catches. Sneck-up!
MALVOLIO
Sir Toby, I must be round with you. My lady bade me
tell you, that, though she harbours you as her kinsman,
she's nothing allied to your disorders. If you can
separate yourself and your misdemeanours, you are
welcome to the house; if not, an it would please you to
take leave of her, she is very willing to bid you farewell.

SIR TOBY
'Farewell, dear heart, since I must needs be gone.'

MARIA
Nay, good Sir Toby.

CLOWN
'His eyes do show his days are almost done.'

MALVOLIO
Is't even so?

SIR TOBY
'But I will never die.'

CLOWN
Sir Toby, there you lie.

MALVOLIO
This is much credit to you.

SIR TOBY
'Shall I bid him go?'

CLOWN
'What an if you do?'

SIR TOBY
'Shall I bid him go, and spare not?'

CLOWN
'O, no, no, no, no, you dare not.'

SIR TOBY
Out o' time, sir? ye lie. — Art any more than a steward?
Dost thou think, because thou art virtuous, there shall
be no more cakes and ale?

CLOWN
Yes, by Saint Anne; and ginger shall be hot i'th'mouth
too.

SIR TOBY
Th'art i'th'right. — Go, sir, rub your chain with
crumbs. — A stoup of wine, Maria!

MALVOLIO
Mistress Mary, if you prized my lady's favour at any
thing more than contempt, you would not give means
for this uncivil rule: she shall know of it, by this hand.
[*Exit.*

MARIA
Go shake your ears.

SIR ANDREW
'Twere as good a deed as to drink when a man's
a-hungry, to challenge him the field, and then to break
promise with him, and make a fool of him.

SIR TOBY
Do't, knight: I'll write thee a challenge; or I'll deliver
thy indignation to him by word of mouth.

MARIA
Sweet Sir Toby, be patient for to-night; since the youth
of the count's was to-day with my lady, she is much out
of quiet. For Monsieur Malvolio, let me alone with
him: if I do not gull him into a nayword, and make him
a common recreation, do not think I have wit enough
to lie straight in my bed: I know I can do it.

SIR TOBY
Possess us, possess us; tell us something of him.

MARIA
Marry, sir, sometimes he is a kind of puritan.

SIR ANDREW
O, if I thought that I'ld beat him like a dog!

SIR TOBY
What, for being a puritan? thy exquisite reason, dear
knight?

SIR ANDREW
I have no exquisite reason for't, but I have reason good
enough.

MARIA
The devil a puritan that he is, or any thing constantly,
but a time-pleaser; an affection'd ass, that cons state
without book, and utters it by great swarths: the best
persuaded of himself, so cramm'd, as he thinks, with
excellencies, that it is his grounds of faith that all that
look on him love him; and on that vice in him will my
revenge find notable cause to work.

SIR TOBY
What wilt thou do?

MARIA
I will drop in his way some obscure epistles of love;
wherein, by the colour of his beard, the shape of his leg,
the manner of his gait, the expressure of his eye,
forehead, and complexion, he shall find himself most
feelingly personated. I can write very like my lady, your
niece; on a forgotten matter we can hardly make
distinction of our hands.

SIR TOBY
Excellent! I smell a device.

SIR ANDREW
I have't in my nose too.

SIR TOBY
He shall think, by the letters that thou wilt drop, that
they come from my niece, and that she's in love with him.

MARIA
My purpose is, indeed, a horse of that colour.

SIR TOBY
And your horse now would make him an ass.

MARIA
Ass, I doubt not.

SIR ANDREW
O, 'twill be admirable!

MARIA
Sport royal, I warrant you: I know my physic will work
with him. I will plant you two, and let the fool make a
third, where he shall find the letter: observe his
construction of it. For this night, to bed, and dream on
the event. Farewell.

SIR TOBY
Good night, Penthesilea. [*Exit* MARIA.

SIR ANDREW
Before me, she's a good wench.

SIR TOBY
She's a beagle, true-bred, and one that adores me: what
o' that?

SIR ANDREW
I was adored once too.

SIR TOBY
Let's to bed, knight. — Thou hadst need send for more
money.

SIR ANDREW
If I cannot recover your niece, I am a foul way out.

SIR TOBY
Send for money, knight: if thou hast her not i'th'end,
call me cut.

SIR ANDREW
If I do not, never trust me, take it how you will.

SIR TOBY
Come, come; I'll go burn some sack; 'tis too late to go to
bed now: come, knight; come, knight. [*Exeunt.*

SCENE IV

The DUKE'S *palace.*

Enter DUKE, VIOLA, CURIO, *and others.*

DUKE
Give me some music: — now, good morrow, friends: —
Now, good Cesario, but that piece of song,
That old and antique song we heard last night:
Methought it did relieve my passion much,
More than light airs and recollected terms
Of these most brisk and giddy-paced times: —
Come, but one verse.

CURIO
He is not here, so please your lordship, that should
sing it.

DUKE
Who was it?

CURIO
Feste, the jester, my lord; a fool that the Lady Olivia's
father took much delight in: he is about the house.

DUKE
Seek him out: and play the tune the while.
[*Exit* CURIO. *Music plays.*
Come hither, boy: if ever thou shalt love,
In the sweet pangs of it remember me;
For such as I am all true lovers are,
Unstaid and skittish in all motions else,
Save in the constant image of the creature
That is beloved. — How dost thou like this tune?

VIOLA
It gives a very echo to the seat
Where Love is thron'd.

DUKE
Thou dost speak masterly:
My life upon't, young though thou art, thine eye
Hath stay'd upon some favour that it loves; —
Hath it not, boy?

VIOLA
A little, by your favour.

DUKE
What kind of woman is't?

VIOLA
Of your complexion.

DUKE
She is not worth thee, then. What years, i'faith?

VIOLA
About your years, my lord.

DUKE
Too old, by heaven: let still the woman take
An elder than herself; so wears she to him,
So sways she level in her husband's heart:
For, boy, however we do praise ourselves,
Our fancies are more giddy and unfirm,
More longing, wavering, sooner lost and worn,
Than women's are.

VIOLA
I think it well, my lord.

DUKE
Then let thy love be younger than thyself,
Or thy affection cannot hold the bent;
For women are as roses, whose fair flower
Being once display'd, doth fall that very hour.

VIOLA
And so they are: alas, that they are so, —
To die, even when they to perfection grow!

Enter CURIO *and* CLOWN.

DUKE
O, fellow, come, the song we had last night. —
Mark it, Cesario; it is old and plain:
The spinsters and the knitters in the sun,
And the free maids that weave their thread with bones,
Do use to chant it: it is silly sooth,
And dallies with the innocence of love,
Like the old age.

CLOWN
Are you ready, sir?

DUKE
Ay; prithee, sing. [*Music.*

CLOWN
Come away, come away, death,
And in sad cypress let me be laid;
Fly away, fly away, breath;
I am slain by a fair cruel maid.
My shroud of white, stuck all with yew,
O, prepare it!
My part of death, no one so true
Did share it.

Not a flower, not a flower sweet,
On my black coffin let there be strown;
Not a friend, not a friend greet
My poor corpse, where my bones shall be
thrown:
A thousand thousand sighs to save,
Lay me, O, where
Sad true lover never find my grave,
To weep there!

DUKE
There's for thy pains.

CLOWN
No pains, sir; I take pleasure in singing, sir.

DUKE
I'll pay thy pleasure, then.

CLOWN
Truly, sir, and pleasure will be paid, one time or
another.

DUKE
Give me now leave to leave thee.

CLOWN
Now, the melancholy god protect thee; and the tailor
make thy doublet of changeable taffeta, for thy mind is
a very opal! I would have men of such constancy put to
sea, that their business might be every thing, and their
intent every where; for that's it that always makes a
good voyage of nothing. Farewell. [*Exit.*

DUKE
Let all the rest give place.

[*Exeunt* CURIO *and* ATTENDANTS.
Once more, Cesario,
Get thee to yond same sovereign cruelty:
Tell her, my love, more noble than the world,
Prizes not quantity of dirty lands;
The parts that Fortune hath bestow'd upon her,
Tell her, I hold as giddily as Fortune;
But 'tis that miracle and queen of gems,
That nature pranks her in, attracts my soul.

VIOLA
But if she cannot love you, sir?

DUKE
I cannot be so answer'd.

VIOLA
Sooth, but you must.
Say that some lady — as, perhaps, there is —
Hath for your love as great a pang of heart
As you have for Olivia: you cannot love her;
You tell her so; must she not, then, be answer'd?

MARIA Get ye all three into the box-tree: Malvolio's coming down this walk.

DUKE
There is no woman's sides
Can bide the beating of so strong a passion
As love doth give my heart; no woman's heart
So big, to hold so much; they lack retention.
Alas, their love may be call'd appetite, —
No motion of the liver, but the palate, —
That suffer surfeit, cloyment, and revolt;
But mine is all as hungry as the sea,
And can digest as much: make no compare
Between that love a woman can bear me
And that I owe Olivia.

VIOLA
Ay, but I know, —

DUKE
What dost thou know?

VIOLA
Too well what love women to men may owe:
In faith, they are as true of heart as we.
My father had a daughter lov'd a man,
As it might be, perhaps, were I a woman,
I should your lordship.

DUKE
And what's her history?

VIOLA
A blank, my lord. She never told her love,
But let concealment, like a worm i'th'bud,
Feed on her damask cheek: she pin'd in thought;
And, with a green and yellow melancholy,
She sat like Patience on a monument,
Smiling at grief. Was not this love indeed?
We men may say more, swear more: but, indeed,
Our shows are more than will; for still we prove
Much in our vows, but little in our love.

DUKE
But died thy sister of her love, my boy?

VIOLA
I am all the daughters of my father's house,
And all the brothers too; — and yet I know not. —
Sir, shall I to this lady?

DUKE
Ay, that's the theme.
To her in haste; give her this jewel; say,
My love can give no place, bide no denay.
[*Exeunt.*

SCENE V

OLIVIA'S *garden.*

Enter SIR TOBY, SIR ANDREW, *and* FABIAN.

SIR TOBY
Come thy ways, Signior Fabian.

FABIAN
Nay, I'll come: if I lose a scruple of this sport, let me be
boil'd to death with melancholy.

SIR TOBY
Wouldst thou not be glad to have the niggardly rascally
sheep-biter come by some notable shame?

FABIAN
I would exult, man: you know he brought me out o'
favour with my lady about a bear-baiting here.

SIR TOBY
To anger him, we'll have the bear again; and we will
fool him black and blue: — shall we not, Sir Andrew?

SIR ANDREW
An we do not, it is pity of our lives.

SIR TOBY
Here comes the little villain.

Enter MARIA.

How now, my metal of India!

MARIA
Get ye all three into the box-tree: Malvolio's coming
down this walk: he has been yonder i' the sun
practising behaviour to his own shadow this half-hour:
observe him, for the love of mockery; for I know this
letter will make a contemplative idiot of him. Close, in
the name of jesting! Lie thou there [*throws down a letter*];
for here comes the trout that must be caught with
tickling. [*Exit.*

Enter MALVOLIO.

MALVOLIO
'Tis but fortune; all is fortune. Maria once told me she
did affect me: and I have heard herself come thus near,
that, should she fancy, it should be one of my
complexion. Besides, she uses me with a more exalted
respect than any one else that follows her. What should
I think on't?

SIR TOBY
Here's an overweening rogue!

FABIAN
O, peace! Contemplation makes a rare turkey-cock of
him: how he jets under his advanced plumes!

SIR ANDREW
'Slight, I could so beat the rogue!

SIR TOBY
Peace, I say.

MALVOLIO
To be Count Malvolio, —

SIR TOBY
Ah, rogue!

SIR ANDREW
Pistol him, pistol him.

SIR TOBY
Peace, peace!

MALVOLIO
There is example for't; the lady of the Strachy married
the yeoman of the wardrobe.

SIR ANDREW
Fie on him, Jezebel!

FABIAN
O, peace! now he's deeply in: look how imagination
blows him.

MALVOLIO
Having been three months married to her, sitting in
my state, —

SIR TOBY
O, for a stone-bow, to hit him in the eye!

MALVOLIO
Calling my officers about me, in my branch'd velvet
gown; having come from a day-bed, where I have left
Olivia sleeping, —

SIR TOBY
Fire and brimstone!

FABIAN
O, peace, peace!

MALVOLIO
And then to have the humour of state; and after a
demure travel of regard, — telling them I know my
place, as I would they should do theirs, — to ask for my
kinsman Toby, —

SIR TOBY
Bolts and shackles!

FABIAN
O, peace, peace, peace! now, now.

MALVOLIO
Seven of my people, with an obedient start, make out
for him: I frown the while; and perchance wind up my
watch, or play with some rich jewel. Toby approaches;
court'sies there to me, —

SIR TOBY
Shall this fellow live?

FABIAN
Though our silence be drawn from us with cars, yet
peace.

MALVOLIO
I extend my hand to him thus, quenching my familiar
smile with an austere regard of control,—

SIR TOBY
And does not Toby take you a blow o' the lips then?

MALVOLIO
Saying, 'Cousin Toby, my fortunes having cast me on
your niece, give me this prerogative of speech,' —

SIR TOBY
What, what?

MALVOLIO
'You must amend your drunkenness.'

SIR TOBY
Out, scab!

FABIAN
Nay, patience, or we break the sinews of our plot.

MALVOLIO
'Besides, you waste the treasure of your time with a
foolish knight,' —

SIR ANDREW
That's me, I warrant you.

MALVOLIO
'One Sir Andrew,' —

SIR ANDREW
I knew 'twas I; for many do call me fool.

MALVOLIO
What employment have we here? [*Taking up the letter.*

FABIAN
Now is the woodcock near the gin.

SIR TOBY
O peace! and the spirit of humours intimate reading
aloud to him!

MALVOLIO
By my life, this is my lady's hand: these be her very C's,
her U's, and her T's; and thus makes she her great P's.
It is, in contempt of question, her hand.

SIR ANDREW
Her C's, her U's, and her T's: why that?

MALVOLIO [*reads*].
To the unknown beloved, this, and my good wishes:
her very phrases! — By your leave, wax. — Soft! — and
the impressure her Lucrece, with which she uses to
seal: 'tis my lady. To whom should this be?

FABIAN
This wins him, liver and all.

MALVOLIO I will smile; I will do every thing that thou wilt have me.

MALVOLIO [reads].
Jove knows I love:
　　But who?
Lips, do not move;
　　No man must know.
'No man must know.' — What follows? the numbers alter'd! — 'No man must know': — if this should be thee, Malvolio?

SIR TOBY
Marry, hang thee, brock!

MALVOLIO [reads].
I may command where I adore;
　　But silence, like a Lucrece knife,
With bloodless stroke my heart doth gore:
　　M, O, A, I, doth sway my life.

FABIAN
A fustian riddle!

SIR TOBY
Excellent wench, say I.

MALVOLIO
'M, O, A, I, doth sway my life.' — Nay, but first, let me see, — let me see, — let me see.

FABIAN
What dish o' poison has she dress'd him!

SIR TOBY
And with what wing the staniel checks at it!

MALVOLIO
'I may command where I adore.' Why, she may command me: I serve her; she is my lady. Why, this is evident to any formal capacity; there is no obstruction in this: — and the end, — what should that alphabetical position portend? if I could make that resemble something in me, — Softly! — M, O, A, I, —

SIR TOBY
O, ay, make up that: — he is now at a cold scent.

FABIAN
Sowter will cry upon't, for all this, though it be as rank as a fox.

MALVOLIO
M, — Malvolio; — M, — why, that begins my name.

FABIAN
Did not I say he would work it out? the cur is excellent at faults.

MALVOLIO
M, — but then there is no consonancy in the sequel; that suffers under probation: A should follow, but O does.

FABIAN
And O shall end, I hope.

SIR TOBY
Ay, or I'll cudgel him, and make him cry O!

MALVOLIO
And then I comes behind.

FABIAN
Ay, an you had any eye behind you, you might see more detraction at your heels than fortunes before you.

MALVOLIO
M, O, A, I; — this simulation is not as the former: — and yet, to crush this a little, it would bow to me, for every one of these letters are in my name. Soft! here follows prose. — [reads] 'If this fall into thy hand, revolve. In my stars I am above thee; but be not afraid of greatness: some are born great, some achieve greatness, and some have greatness thrust upon 'em. Thy Fates open their hands; let thy blood and spirit embrace them: and, to inure thyself to what thou art like to be, cast thy humble slough, and appear fresh. Be opposite with a kinsman, surly with servants; let thy tongue tang arguments of state; put thyself into the trick of singularity: she thus advises thee that sighs for thee. Remember who commended thy yellow stockings, and wish'd to see thee ever cross-garter'd: I say, remember. Go to, thou art made, if thou desirest to be so; if not, let me see thee a steward still, the fellow of servants, and not worthy to touch Fortune's fingers. Farewell. She that would alter services with thee,

THE FORTUNATE-UNHAPPY.'

Daylight and champain discovers not more: this is open. I will be proud, I will read politic authors, I will baffle Sir Toby, I will wash off gross acquaintance, I will be point-devise the very man. I do not now fool myself, to let imagination jade me; for every reason excites to this, that my lady loves me. She did commend my yellow stockings of late, she did praise my leg being

cross-garter'd; and in this she manifests herself to my love, and, with a kind of injunction, drives me to these habits of her liking. I thank my stars, I am happy. I will be strange, stout, in yellow stockings, and cross-garter'd, even with the swiftness of putting on. Jove and my stars be praised! — Here is yet a postscript. [reads] 'Thou canst not choose but know who I am. If thou entertain'st my love, let it appear in thy smiling: thy smiles become thee well; therefore in my presence still smile, dear my sweet, I prithee.' Jove, I thank thee: — I will smile; I will do every thing that thou wilt have me. [Exit.

FABIAN
I will not give my part of this sport for a pension of thousands to be paid from the Sophy.

SIR TOBY
I could marry this wench for this device, —

SIR ANDREW
So could I too.

SIR TOBY
And ask no other dowry with her but such another jest.

SIR ANDREW
Nor I neither.

FABIAN
Here comes my noble gull-catcher.

Enter MARIA.

SIR TOBY
Wilt thou set thy foot o'my neck?

SIR ANDREW
Or o' mine either?

SIR TOBY
Shall I play my freedom at tray-trip, and become thy bond-slave?

SIR ANDREW
I'faith, or I either?

SIR TOBY
Why, thou hast put him in such a dream, that, when the image of it leaves him, he must run mad.

MARIA
Nay, but say true; does it work upon him?

SIR TOBY
Like aqua-vitæ with a midwife.

MARIA
If you will then see the fruits of the sport, mark his first approach before my lady: he will come to her in yellow stockings, and 'tis a colour she abhors, and cross-garter'd, a fashion she detests; and he will smile upon her, which will now be so unsuitable to her disposition, being addicted to a melancholy as she is, that it cannot but turn him into a notable contempt. If you will see it, follow me.

SIR TOBY
To the gates of Tartar, thou most excellent devil of wit!

SIR ANDREW
I'll make one too.
[Exeunt.

ACT III

SCENE I

OLIVIA'S *garden.*

Enter VIOLA, *and* CLOWN *with a tabor.*

VIOLA
Save thee, friend, and thy music! dost thou live by thy tabor?

CLOWN
No, sir, I live by the church.

VIOLA
Art thou a churchman?

CLOWN
No such matter, sir: I do live by the church; for I do live at my house, and my house doth stand by the church.

VIOLA
So thou mayst say, the king lies by a beggar, if a beggar dwell near him; or, the church stands by thy tabor, if thy tabor stand by the church.

CLOWN
You have said, sir. — To see this age! A sentence is but a cheveril glove to a good wit: how quickly the wrong side may be turn'd outward!

VIOLA
Nay, that's certain; they that dally nicely with words may quickly make them wanton.

CLOWN
I would, therefore, my sister had had no name, sir.

VIOLA
Why, man?

CLOWN
Why, sir, her name's a word; and to dally with that word might make my sister wanton. But, indeed, words are very rascals, since bonds disgraced them.

VIOLA
Thy reason, man?

CLOWN
Troth, sir, I can yield you none without words; and words are grown so false, I am loth to prove reason with them.

VIOLA
I warrant thou art a merry fellow, and carest for nothing.

CLOWN
Not so, sir; I do care for something; but in my conscience, sir, I do not care for you: if that be to care for nothing, sir, I would it would make you invisible.

VIOLA
Art not thou the Lady Olivia's fool?

CLOWN
No, indeed, sir; the Lady Olivia has no folly: she will keep no fool, sir, till she be married; and fools are as like husbands as pilchers are to herrings, — the husband's the bigger: I am, indeed, not her fool, but her corrupter of words.

VIOLA
I saw thee late at the Count Orsino's.

CLOWN
Foolery, sir, does walk about the orb like the sun, it shines every where. I would be sorry, sir, but the fool should be as oft with your master as with my mistress: I think I saw your wisdom there.

VIOLA
Nay, an thou pass upon me, I'll no more with thee. Hold, there's expenses for thee.

CLOWN
Now Jove, in his next commodity of hair, send thee a beard!

VIOLA
By my troth, I'll tell thee, I am almost sick for one: though I would not have it grow on my chin. Is thy lady within?

CLOWN
Would not a pair of these have bred, sir?

VIOLA
Yes, being kept together and put to use.

CLOWN
I would play Lord Pandarus of Phrygia, sir, to bring a Cressida to this Troilus.

VIOLA
I understand you, sir; 'tis well begg'd.

CLOWN
The matter, I hope, is not great, sir, begging but a beggar: Cressida was a beggar. My lady is within, sir. I will conster to them whence you come; who you are, and what you would, are out of my welkin, — I might say element, but the word is over-worn. *[Exit.*

VIOLA
This fellow is wise enough to play the fool;
And to do that well craves a kind of wit:
He must observe their mood on whom he jests,
The quality of persons, and the time;
Not, like the haggard, check at every feather
That comes before his eye. This is a practice
As full of labour as a wise man's art:
For folly, that he wisely shows, is fit;
But wise men, folly-fall'n, quite taint their wit.

Enter SIR TOBY *and* SIR ANDREW.

SIR TOBY
Save you, gentleman!

VIOLA
And you, sir.

SIR ANDREW
Dieu vous garde, monsieur.

VIOLA
Et vous aussi; votre serviteur.

SIR ANDREW
I hope, sir, you are; and I am yours.

SIR TOBY
Will you encounter the house? my niece is desirous you should enter, if your trade be to her.

VIOLA
I am bound to your niece, sir; I mean, she is the list of my voyage.

SIR TOBY
Taste your legs, sir; put them to motion.

VIOLA
My legs do better understand me, sir, than I understand what you mean by bidding me taste my legs.

SIR TOBY
I mean, to go, sir, to enter.

VIOLA
I will answer you with gait and entrance: — but we are prevented.

Enter OLIVIA *and* MARIA.

Most excellent accomplish'd lady, the heavens rain odours on you!

SIR ANDREW [*aside*].
That youth's a rare courtier: 'Rain odours': — well.

VIOLA
My matter hath no voice, lady, but to your own most pregnant and vouchsafed ear.

SIR ANDREW [*aside*].
'Odours,' 'pregnant,' and 'vouchsafed': — I'll get 'em all three all ready.

OLIVIA
Let the garden-door be shut, and leave me to my hearing. [*Exeunt* SIR TOBY, SIR ANDREW, *and* MARIA.] Give me your hand, sir.

VIOLA
My duty, madam, and most humble service.

OLIVIA
What is your name?

VIOLA
Cesario is your servant's name, fair princess.

OLIVIA
My servant, sir! 'Twas never merry world
Since lowly feigning was call'd compliment:
Y'are servant to the Count Orsino, youth.

VIOLA
And he is yours, and his must needs be yours:
Your servant's servant is your servant, madam.

OLIVIA
For him, I think not on him: for his thoughts,
Would they were blanks, rather than fill'd with me!

VIOLA
Madam, I come to whet your gentle thoughts
On his behalf: —

OLIVIA
                    O, by your leave, I pray you, —
I bade you never speak again of him:
But, would you undertake another suit,
I had rather hear you to solicit that
Than music from the spheres.

VIOLA
                            Dear lady, —

OLIVIA
Give me leave, beseech you. I did send,
After the last enchantment you did here,
A ring in chase of you: so did I abuse
Myself, my servant, and, I fear me, you:
Under your hard construction must I sit,
To force that on you, in a shameful cunning,
Which you knew none of yours: what might you think?
Have you not set mine honour at the stake,
And baited it with all th'unmuzzled thoughts
That tyrannous heart can think? To one of your receiving
Enough is shown: a cypress, not a bosom,
Hides my poor heart. So, let me hear you speak.

VIOLA
I pity you.

OLIVIA
            That's a degree to love.

VIOLA
No, not a grise; for 'tis a vulgar proof,
That very oft we pity enemies.

OLIVIA
Why, then, methinks 'tis time to smile again.
O world, how apt the poor are to be proud!
If one should be a prey, how much the better
To fall before the lion than the wolf! *[Clock strikes.*
The clock upbraids me with the waste of time. —
Be not afraid, good youth, I will not have you:

And yet, when wit and youth is come to harvest,
Your wife is like to reap a proper man:
There lies your way, due west.

VIOLA
                            Then westward-ho! —
Grace and good disposition attend your ladyship!
You'll nothing, madam, to my lord by me?

OLIVIA
Stay:
I prithee, tell me what thou think'st of me.

VIOLA
That you do think you are not what you are.

OLIVIA
If I think so, I think the same of you.

VIOLA
Then think you right: I am not what I am.

OLIVIA
I would you were as I would have you be!

VIOLA
Would it be better, madam, than I am,
I wish it might; for now I am your fool.

OLIVIA
O, what a deal of scorn looks beautiful
In the contempt and anger of his lip!
A murderous guilt shows not itself more soon
Than love that would seem hid: love's night is noon.
Cesario, by the roses of the spring,
By maidhood, honour, truth, and every thing,
I love thee so, that, maugre all thy pride,
Nor wit nor reason can my passion hide.
Do not extort thy reasons from this clause,
For that I woo, thou therefore hast no cause;
But, rather, reason thus with reason fetter, —
Love sought is good, but given unsought is better.

VIOLA
By innocence I swear, and by my youth,
I have one heart, one bosom, and one truth, —
And that no woman has; nor never none
Shall mistress be of it, save I alone.
And so adieu, good madam: never more
Will I my master's tears to you deplore.

OLIVIA
Yet come again; for thou perhaps mayst move
That heart, which now abhors, to like his love. *[Exeunt.*

SCENE II

OLIVIA'S *house.*

Enter SIR TOBY, SIR ANDREW, *and* FABIAN.

SIR ANDREW
No, faith, I'll not stay a jot longer.

SIR TOBY
Thy reason, dear venom; give thy reason.

FABIAN
You must needs yield your reason, Sir Andrew.

SIR ANDREW
Marry, I saw your niece do more favours to the count's serving-man than ever she bestow'd upon me; I saw't i'th'orchard.

SIR TOBY
Did she see thee the while, old boy? tell me that.

SIR ANDREW
As plain as I see you now.

FABIAN
This was a great argument of love in her toward you.

SIR ANDREW
'Slight, will you make an ass o'me?

FABIAN
I will prove it legitimate, sir, upon the oaths of judgement and reason.

SIR TOBY
And they have been grand-jurymen since before Noah was a sailor.

FABIAN
She did show favour to the youth in your sight only to exasperate you, to awake your dormouse valour, to put fire in your heart, and brimstone in your liver. You should then have accosted her; and with some excellent jests, fire-new from the mint, you should have bang'd the youth into dumbness. This was look'd for at your hand, and this was balk'd: the double gilt of this opportunity you let time wash off, and you are now sail'd into the north of my lady's opinion; where you will hang like an icicle on a Dutchman's beard, unless you do redeem it by some laudable attempt either of valour or policy.

SIR ANDREW
An't be any way, it must be with valour; for policy I hate: I had as lief be a Brownist as a politician.

SIR TOBY

Why, then, build me thy fortunes upon the basis of valour. Challenge me the count's youth to fight with him; hurt him in eleven places: my niece shall take note of it; and assure thyself, there is no love-broker in the world can more prevail in man's commendation with woman than report of valour.

FABIAN

There is no way but this, Sir Andrew.

SIR ANDREW

Will either of you bear me a challenge to him?

SIR TOBY

Go, write it in a martial hand; be curst and brief; it is no matter how witty, so it be eloquent and full of invention: taunt him with the licence of ink: if thou 'thou'st'him some thrice, it shall not be amiss; and as many lies as will lie in thy sheet of paper, although the sheet were big enough for the bed of Ware in England, set 'em down: go, about it. Let there be gall enough in thy ink, though thou write with a goose-pen, no matter: about it.

SIR ANDREW

Where shall I find you?

SIR TOBY

We'll call thee at the *cubiculo*: go. [*Exit* SIR ANDREW.

FABIAN

This is a dear manakin to you, Sir Toby.

SIR TOBY

I have been dear to him, lad, — some two thousand strong, or so.

FABIAN

We shall have a rare letter from him: but you'll not deliver't?

SIR TOBY

Never trust me, then; and by all means stir on the youth to an answer. I think oxen and wainropes cannot hale them together. For Andrew, if he were open'd, and you find so much blood in his liver as will clog the foot of a flea, I'll eat the rest of th'anatomy.

FABIAN

And his opposite, the youth, bears in his visage no great presage of cruelty.

SIR TOBY

Look, where the youngest wren of nine comes.

Enter MARIA.

MARIA

If you desire the spleen, and will laugh yourselves into stitches, follow me. Yond gull Malvolio is turn'd heathen, a very renegado; for there is no Christian, that means to be saved by believing rightly, can ever believe such impossible passages of grossness. He's in yellow stockings.

SIR TOBY

And cross-garter'd?

MARIA

Most villainously; like a pedant that keeps a school i'th'church. — I have dogg'd him, like his murderer. He does obey every point of the letter that I dropp'd to betray him: he does smile his face into more lines than is in the new map, with the augmentation of the Indies: you have not seen such a thing as 'tis; I can hardly forbear hurling things at him. I know my lady will strike him: if she do, he'll smile, and take't for a great favour.

SIR TOBY

Come, bring us, bring us where he is. [*Exeunt.*

SCENE III

A street.

Enter SEBASTIAN *and* ANTONIO.

SEBASTIAN

I would not, by my will, have troubled you;
But, since you make your pleasure of your pains,
I will no further chide you.

ANTONIO

I could not stay behind you: my desire,
More sharp than filed steel, did spur me forth;
And not all love to see you, — though so much
As might have drawn me to a longer voyage, —
But jealousy what might befall your travel,
Being skilless in these parts; which to a stranger,
Unguided and unfriended, often prove
Rough and unhospitable: my willing love,
The rather by these arguments of fear,
Set forth in your pursuit.

SEBASTIAN

My kind Antonio,
I can no other answer make, but thanks,
And thanks, and ever; oft good turns

Are shuffled off with such uncurrent pay:
But, were my worth, as is my conscience, firm,
You should find better dealing. What's to do?
Shall we go see the reliques of this town?

ANTONIO

To-morrow, sir; best first go see your lodging.

SEBASTIAN

I am not weary, and 'tis long to night:
I pray you, let us satisfy our eyes
With the memorials and the things of fame
That do renown this city.

ANTONIO

Would you'ld pardon me;
I do not without danger walk these streets:
Once, in a sea-fight, 'gainst the count his galleys
I did some service; of such note, indeed,
That, were I ta'en here, it would scarce be answer'd.

SEBASTIAN

Belike you slew great number of his people?

ANTONIO

Th'offence is not of such a bloody nature;
Albeit the quality of the time and quarrel
Might well have given us bloody argument.
It might have since been answer'd in repaying
What we took from them; which, for traffic's sake,
Most of our city did: only myself stood out;
For which, if I be lapsed in this place,
I shall pay dear.

SEBASTIAN

Do not, then, walk too open.

ANTONIO

It doth not fit me. Hold, sir, here's my purse.
In the south suburbs, at the Elephant,
Is best to lodge: I will bespeak our diet,
Whiles you beguile the time and feed your knowledge
With viewing of the town: there shall you have me.

SEBASTIAN

Why I your purse?

ANTONIO

Haply your eye shall light upon some toy
You have desire to purchase; and your store,
I think, is not for idle markets, sir.

SEBASTIAN

I'll be your purse-bearer, and leave you for
An hour.

ANTONIO

To th'Elephant.

SEBASTIAN

I do remember. [*Exeunt.*

SCENE IV

OLIVIA'S *garden.*

Enter OLIVIA *and* MARIA.

OLIVIA

I have sent after him: he says he'll come; —
How shall I feast him? what bestow of him?
For youth is bought more oft than begg'd or borrow'd.
I speak too loud. —
Where is Malvolio? — he is sad and civil,
And suits well for a servant with my fortunes: —
Where is Malvolio?

MARIA

He's coming, madam; but in very strange manner. He is, sure, possess'd, madam.

OLIVIA

Why, what's the matter? does he rave?

MARIA

No, madam, he does nothing but smile: your ladyship were best to have some guard about you, if he come; for, sure, the man is tainted in's wits.

OLIVIA

Go call him hither. [*Exit* MARIA.] I am as mad as he,
If sad and merry madness equal be.

Enter MARIA, *with* MALVOLIO.

How now, Malvolio!

MALVOLIO

Sweet lady, ho, ho. [*Smiles fantastically.*

OLIVIA

Smilest thou?
I sent for thee upon a sad occasion.

MALVOLIO

Sad, lady! I could be sad: this does make some obstruction in the blood, this cross-gartering; but what of that? if it please the eye of one, it is with me as the very true sonnet is, 'Please one, and please all.'

OLIVIA

Why, how dost thou, man? what is the matter with thee?

MALVOLIO

Not black in my mind, though yellow in my legs. It did come to his hands, and commands shall be executed: I think we do know the sweet Roman hand.

OLIVIA

Wilt thou go to bed, Malvolio?

MALVOLIO

To bed! ay, sweet-heart; and I'll come to thee.

OLIVIA

God comfort thee! Why dost thou smile so, and kiss thy hand so oft?

MARIA

How do you, Malvolio?

MALVOLIO

At your request! yes; nightingales answer daws.

MARIA

Why appear you with this ridiculous boldness before my lady?

MALVOLIO

'Be not afraid of greatness': — 'twas well writ.

OLIVIA

What mean'st thou by that, Malvolio?

MALVOLIO

'Some are born great,' —

OLIVIA

Ha!

MALVOLIO

'Some achieve greatness,' —

OLIVIA

What say'st thou?

MALVOLIO

'And some have greatness thrust upon them.'

OLIVIA

Heaven restore thee!

MALVOLIO

'Remember who commended thy yellow stockings,' —

OLIVIA

Thy yellow stockings!

MALVOLIO

'And wish'd to see thee cross-garter'd.'

OLIVIA

Cross-garter'd!

MALVOLIO

'Go to, thou art made, if thou desirest to be so'; —

OLIVIA

Am I made?

MALVOLIO

'If not, let me see thee a servant still.'

OLIVIA

Why, this is very midsummer madness.

Enter a SERVANT.

SERVANT

Madam, the young gentleman of the Count Orsino's is return'd: I could hardly entreat him back: he attends your ladyship's pleasure.

OLIVIA

I'll come to him. [*Exit* SERVANT.] Good Maria, let this fellow be look'd to. Where's my cousin Toby? Let some of my people have a special care of him: I would not have him miscarry for the half of my dowry.

[*Exeunt* OLIVIA *and* MARIA.

MALVOLIO

O, ho! do you come near me now? no worse man than Sir Toby to look to me? This concurs directly with the letter: she sends him on purpose, that I may appear stubborn to him; for she incites me to that in the letter. 'Cast thy humble slough,' says she; 'be opposite with a kinsman, surly with servants; let thy tongue tang with arguments of state; put thyself into the trick of singularity'; — and, consequently, sets down the manner how; as, a sad face, a reverend carriage, a slow tongue, in the habit of some sir of note, and so forth. I have limed her; but it is Jove's doing, and Jove make me thankful! And, when she went away now, 'Let this fellow be look'd to': fellow! not Malvolio, nor after my degree, but fellow. Why, every thing adheres together, that no dram of a scruple, no scruple of a scruple, no obstacle, no incredulous or unsafe circumstance — What can be said? Nothing, that can be, can come between me and the full prospect of my hopes. Well, Jove, not I, is the doer of this, and he is to be thank'd.

Enter MARIA *with* SIR TOBY *and* FABIAN.

SIR TOBY

Which way is he, in the name of sanctity? If all the devils of hell be drawn in little, and Legion himself possess'd him, yet I'll speak to him.

MALVOLIO Go off; I discard you: let me enjoy my private: go off.

FABIAN
Here he is, here he is. — How is't with you, sir? how is't with you, man?
MALVOLIO
Go off; I discard you: let me enjoy my private: go off.
MARIA
Lo, how hollow the fiend speaks within him; did not I tell you? — Sir Toby, my lady prays you to have a care of him.
MALVOLIO
Ah, ha! does she so?
SIR TOBY
Go to, go to; peace, peace; we must deal gently with him: let me alone. — How do you, Malvolio? how is't with you? What, man! defy the devil: consider, he's an enemy to mankind.
MALVOLIO
Do you know what you say?
MARIA
La you, an you speak ill of the devil, how he takes it at heart! Pray God, he be not bewitch'd!
FABIAN
Carry his water to th'wise woman.
MARIA
Marry, and it shall be done to-morrow morning, if I live. My lady would not lose him for more than I'll say.
MALVOLIO
How now, mistress!
MARIA
O Lord!
SIR TOBY
Prithee, hold thy peace; this is not the way: do you not see you move him? let me alone with him.
FABIAN
No way but gentleness; gently, gently: the fiend is

rough, and will not be roughly used.
SIR TOBY
Why, how now, my bawcock! how dost thou, chuck?
MALVOLIO
Sir!
SIR TOBY
Ay, Biddy, come with me. What, man! 'tis not for gravity to play at cherry-pit with Satan: hang him, foul collier!
MARIA
Get him to say his prayers; good Sir Toby; get him to pray.
MALVOLIO
My prayers, minx!
MARIA
No, I warrant you, he will not hear of godliness.
MALVOLIO
Go, hang yourselves all! you are idle shallow things: I am not of your element: you shall know more hereafter.   [Exit.
SIR TOBY
Is't possible?
FABIAN
If this were play'd upon a stage now, I could condemn it as an improbable fiction.
SIR TOBY
His very genius hath taken the infection of the device, man.
MARIA
Nay, pursue him now, lest the device take air, and taint.
FABIAN
Why, we shall make him mad indeed.
MARIA
The house will be the quieter.
SIR TOBY
Come, we'll have him in a dark room and bound.

My niece is already in the belief that he's mad; we may carry it thus, for our pleasure and his penance, till our very pastime, tired out of breath, prompt us to have mercy on him: at which time we will bring the device to the bar, and crown thee for a finder of madmen. — But see, but see.
FABIAN
More matter for a May morning.
                    Enter SIR ANDREW.
SIR ANDREW
Here's the challenge, read it: warrant there's vinegar and pepper in't.
FABIAN
Is't so saucy?
SIR ANDREW
Ay, is't, I warrant him: do but read.
SIR TOBY
Give me. [reads] Youth, whatsoever thou art, thou art but a scurvy fellow.
FABIAN
Good, and valiant.
SIR TOBY [reads].
Wonder not, nor admire not in thy mind, why I do call thee so, for I will show thee no reason for't.
FABIAN
A good note: that keeps you from the blow of the law.
SIR TOBY [reads].
Thou comest to the Lady Olivia, and in my sight she uses thee kindly: but thou liest in thy throat; that is not the matter I challenge thee for.
FABIAN
Very brief, and to exceeding good sense — less.
SIR TOBY [reads].
I will waylay thee going home; where if it be thy chance to kill me, —
FABIAN
Good.
SIR TOBY [reads].
Thou kill'st me like a rogue and a villain.
FABIAN
Still you keep o'th'windy side of the law: good.
SIR TOBY [reads].
Fare thee well; and God have mercy upon one of our souls! He may have mercy upon mine; but my hope is better, and so look to thyself. Thy friend, as thou usest him, and thy sworn enemy,
                    ANDREW AGUECHEEK.
If this letter move him not, his legs cannot: I'll give't him.
MARIA
You may have very fit occasion for't: he is now in some commerce with my lady, and will by and by depart.
SIR TOBY
Go, Sir Andrew; scout me for him at the corner of the orchard, like a bum-baily: so soon as ever thou seest him, draw; and, as thou draw'st, swear horrible; for it comes to pass oft, that a terrible oath, with a swaggering accent sharply twang'd off, gives manhood more approbation than ever proof itself would have earn'd him. Away!
SIR ANDREW
Nay, let me alone for swearing.   [Exit.
SIR TOBY
Now will not I deliver his letter: for the behaviour of the young gentleman gives him out to be of good capacity and breeding: his employment between his lord and my niece confirms no less: therefore this letter, being so excellently ignorant, will breed no terror in the youth: he will find it comes from a clodpole. But, sir, I will deliver his challenge by word of mouth; set upon Aguecheek a notable report of valour; and drive the gentleman — as I know his youth will aptly receive it — into a most hideous opinion of his rage, skill, fury, and impetuosity. This will so fright them both, that they will kill one another by the look, like cockatrices.
FABIAN
Here he comes with your niece: give them way till he take leave, and presently after him.
SIR TOBY
I will meditate the while upon some horrid message for a challenge.
                    [Exeunt SIR TOBY, FABIAN, and MARIA.
                    Enter OLIVIA, with VIOLA.
OLIVIA
I have said too much unto a heart of stone,
And laid mine honour too unchary out:
There's something in me that reproves my fault;
But such a headstrong potent fault it is,

That it but mocks reproof.

VIOLA
With the same 'haviour that your passion bears,
Goes on my master's griefs.

OLIVIA
Here, wear this jewel for me, 'tis my picture:
Refuse it not: it hath no tongue to vex you:
And, I beseech you, come again to-morrow.
What shall you ask of me that I'll deny,
That honour sav'd may upon asking give?

VIOLA
Nothing but this, — your true love for my master.

OLIVIA
How with mine honour may I give him that
Which I have given to you?

VIOLA
                    I will acquit you.

OLIVIA
Well, come again to-morrow; fare thee well:
A fiend like thee might bear my soul to hell. [*Exit.*

Enter SIR TOBY *and* FABIAN.

SIR TOBY
Gentleman, God save thee!

VIOLA
And you, sir.

SIR TOBY
That defence thou hast, betake thee to't: of what nature
the wrongs are thou hast done him, I know not: but thy
intercepter, full of despite, bloody as the hunter,
attends thee at the orchard-end: dismount thy tuck, be
yare in thy preparation; for thy assailant is quick,
skilful, and deadly.

VIOLA
You mistake, sir; I am sure no man hath any quarrel to
me: my remembrance is very free and clear from any
image of offence done to any man.

SIR TOBY
You'll find it otherwise, I assure you: therefore, if you
hold your life at any price, betake you to your guard; for
your opposite hath in him what youth, strength, skill,
and wrath can furnish man withal.

VIOLA
I pray you, sir, what is he?

SIR TOBY
He is knight, dubb'd with unhatch'd rapier and on
carpet consideration; but he is a devil in private brawl:
souls and bodies hath he divorced three; and his
incensement at this moment is so implacable, that
satisfaction can be none but by pangs of death and
sepulchre: hob-nob is his word; give't or take't.

VIOLA
I will return again into the house, and desire some
conduct of the lady. I am no fighter. I have heard of
some kind of men that put quarrels purposely on
others, to taste their valour; belike this is a man of that
quirk.

SIR TOBY
Sir, no; his indignation derives itself out of a very
competent injury: therefore, get you on, and give him
his desire. Back you shall not to the house, unless you
undertake that with me which with as much safety you
might answer him: therefore, on, or strip your sword
stark naked; for meddle you must, that's certain, or
forswear to wear iron about you.

VIOLA
This is as uncivil as strange. I beseech you, do me this
courteous office, as to know of the knight what my
offence to him is: it is something of my negligence,
nothing of my purpose.

SIR TOBY
I will do so. — Signior Fabian, stay you by this
gentleman till my return. [*Exit.*

VIOLA
Pray you, sir, do you know of this matter?

FABIAN
I know the knight is incensed against you, even to a
mortal arbitrement; but nothing of the circumstance
more.

VIOLA
I beseech you, what manner of man is he?

FABIAN
Nothing of that wonderful promise, to read him by his
form, as you are like to find him in the proof of his
valour. He is, indeed, sir, the most skilful, bloody, and
fatal opposite that you could possibly have found in any
part of Illyria. Will you walk towards him? I will make
your peace with him, if I can.

VIOLA
I shall be much bound to you for't: I am one that had

rather go with sir priest than sir knight: I care not who
knows so much of my mettle. [*Exeunt.*

Enter SIR TOBY *and* SIR ANDREW.

SIR TOBY
Why, man, he's a very devil; I have not seen such a
firago. I had a pass with him, rapier, scabbard, and all,
and he gives me the stuck-in with such a mortal
motion, that it is inevitable; and on the answer, he pays
you as surely as your feet hit the ground they step on:
they say he has been fencer to the Sophy.

SIR ANDREW
Pox on't, I'll not meddle with him.

SIR TOBY
Ay, but he will not now be pacified: Fabian can scarce
hold him yonder.

SIR ANDREW
Plague on't, an I thought he had been valiant and so
cunning in fence, I'ld have seen him damn'd ere I'ld
have challenged him. Let him let the matter slip, and
I'll give him my horse, grey Capulet.

SIR TOBY
I'll make the motion: stand here, make a good show
on't: this shall end without the perdition of souls. —
[*aside*] Marry, I'll ride your horse as well as I ride you.

Enter FABIAN *and* VIOLA.

[*to* FABIAN] I have his horse to take up the quarrel: I
have persuaded him the youth's a devil.

FABIAN
He is as horribly conceited of him; and pants and looks
pale, as if a bear were at his heels.

SIR TOBY [*to* VIOLA].
There's no remedy, sir; he will fight with you for's
oath-sake: marry, he hath better bethought him of his
quarrel, and he finds that now scarce to be worth
talking of: therefore draw, for the supportance of his
vow; he protests he will not hurt you.

VIOLA [*aside*].
Pray God defend me! A little thing would make me tell
them how much I lack of a man.

FABIAN
Give ground, if you see him furious.

SIR TOBY
Come, Sir Andrew, there's no remedy; the gentleman
will, for his honour's sake, have one bout with you; he
cannot by the duello avoid it: but he has promised me,
as he is a gentleman and a soldier, he will not hurt you.
Come on, to't.

SIR ANDREW
Pray God, he keep his oath! [*Draws.*

VIOLA
I do assure you, 'tis against my will. [*Draws.*

Enter ANTONIO.

ANTONIO
Put up your sword. If this young gentleman
Have done offence, I take the fault on me:
If you offend him, I for him defy you.

SIR TOBY
You, sir! why, what are you?

ANTONIO [*drawing*].
One, sir, that for his love dares yet do more
Than you have heard him brag to you he will.

SIR TOBY
Nay, if you be an undertaker, I am for you. [*Draws.*

FABIAN
O good Sir Toby, hold! here come the officers.

SIR TOBY [*to* ANTONIO].
I'll be with you anon.

VIOLA [*to* ANTONIO].
Pray, sir, put your sword up, if you please.

SIR ANDREW
Marry, will I, sir; and, for that I promised you,
I'll be as good as my word: he will bear you easily, and
reins well.

Enter OFFICERS.

FIRST OFFICER
This is the man; do thy office.

SECOND OFFICER
Antonio, I arrest thee at the suit of Count Orsino.

ANTONIO
You do mistake me, sir.

FIRST OFFICER
No, sir, no jot; I know your favour well,
Though now you have no sea-cap on your head. —
Take him away: he knows I know him well.

ANTONIO
I must obey. [*to* VIOLA] This comes with seeking you:
But there's no remedy; I shall answer it.

What will you do, now my necessity
Makes me to ask you for my purse? It grieves me
Much more for what I cannot do for you
Than what befalls myself. You stand amazed;
But be of comfort.

SECOND OFFICER
                    Come, sir, away.

ANTONIO
I must entreat of you some of that money.

VIOLA
What money, sir?
For the fair kindness you have show'd me here,
And, part, being prompted by your present trouble,
Out of my lean and low ability
I'll lend you something: my having is not much;
I'll make division of my present with you:
Hold, there's half my coffer.

ANTONIO
                    Will you deny me now?
Is't possible that my deserts to you
Can lack persuasion? Do not tempt my misery,
Lest that it makes me so unsound a man
As to upbraid you with those kindnesses
That I have done for you.

VIOLA
                    I know of none;
Nor know I you by voice or any feature:
I hate ingratitude more in a man
Than lying, vainness, babbling, drunkenness,
Or any taint of vice whose strong corruption
Inhabits our frail blood.

ANTONIO
                    O heavens themselves!

SECOND OFFICER
Come, sir, I pray you, go.

ANTONIO
Let me speak a little. This youth that you see here
I snatch'd one half out of the jaws of death,
Reliev'd him with such sanctity of love,
And to his image, which methought did promise
Most venerable worth, did I devotion.

FIRST OFFICER
What's that to us? The time goes by: away!

ANTONIO
But, O, how vile an idol proves this god!
Thou hast, Sebastian, done good feature shame.
In nature there's no blemish but the mind;
None can be call'd deform'd but the unkind:
Virtue is beauty, but the beauteous evil
Are empty trunks, o'erflourish'd by the devil.

FIRST OFFICER
The man grows mad: away with him! — come, come,
sir.

ANTONIO
Lead me on. [*Exit with* OFFICERS.

VIOLA
Methinks his words do from such passion fly,
That he believes himself: so do not I.
Prove true, imagination, O, prove true,
That I, dear brother, be now ta'en for you!

SIR TOBY
Come hither, knight; come hither, Fabian: we'll
whisper o'er a couplet or two of most sage saws.

VIOLA
He nam'd Sebastian: I my brother know
Yet living in my glass; even such, and so,
In favour was my brother; and he went
Still in this fashion, colour, ornament, —
For him I imitate: O, if it prove,
Tempests are kind, and salt waves fresh in love! [*Exit.*

SIR TOBY
A very dishonest paltry boy, and more a coward than a
hare: his dishonesty appears in leaving his friend here
in necessity, and denying him; and for his cowardship,
ask Fabian.

FABIAN
A coward, a most devout coward, religious in it.

SIR ANDREW
'Slid, I'll after him again, and beat him.

SIR TOBY
Do; cuff him soundly, but never draw thy sword.

SIR ANDREW
An I do not, — [*Exit.*

FABIAN
Come, let's see the event.

SIR TOBY
I dare lay any money 'twill be nothing yet. [*Exeunt.*

Against thy peace. Go with me to my house;
And hear thou there how many fruitless pranks
This ruffian hath botch'd up, that thou thereby
Mayst smile at this: thou shalt not choose but go:
Do not deny. Beshrew his soul for me,
He started one poor heart of mine in thee.

SEBASTIAN
What relish is in this? how runs the stream?
Or I am mad, or else this is a dream:
Let fancy still my sense in Lethe steep;
If it be thus to dream, still let me sleep!

OLIVIA
Nay, come, I prithee: would thou'ldst be rul'd by me!

SEBASTIAN
Madam, I will.

OLIVIA
　　　　O, say so, and so be! 　　[*Exeunt*

SCENE II

OLIVIA'S *house.*

Enter MARIA *and* CLOWN.

MARIA
Nay, I prithee, put on this gown and this beard; make
him believe thou art Sir Topas the curate: do it quickly;
I'll call Sir Toby the whilst. 　　[*Exit*

CLOWN
Well, I'll put it on, and I will dissemble myself in't; and
I would I were the first that ever dissembled in such a
gown. I am not tall enough to become the function
well; nor lean enough to be thought a good student: but
to be said an honest man and a good housekeeper, goes
as fairly as to say a careful man and a great scholar. The
competitors enter.

Enter SIR TOBY *and* MARIA.

SIR TOBY
Jove bless thee, master parson.

CLOWN
Bonos dies, Sir Toby: for, as the old hermit of Prague,
that never saw pen and ink, very wittily said to a niece

ACT IV

SCENE I

Before OLIVIA'S *house.*
Enter SEBASTIAN *and* CLOWN.

CLOWN
Will you make me believe that I am not sent for you?

SEBASTIAN
Go to, go to, thou art a foolish fellow:
Let me be clear of thee.

CLOWN
Well held out, i'faith! No, I do not know you; nor I am
not sent to you by my lady, to bid you come speak with
her; nor your name is not Master Cesario; nor this is
not my nose neither. Nothing that is so is so.

SEBASTIAN
I prithee, vent thy folly somewhere else;
Thou know'st not me.

CLOWN
Vent my folly! he has heard that word of some great
man, and now applies it to a fool: vent my folly! I am
afraid this great lubber, the world, will prove a cockney.
— I prithee, now, ungird thy strangeness, and tell me
what I shall vent to my lady: shall I vent to her that thou
art coming?

SEBASTIAN
I prithee, foolish Greek, depart from me:
There's money for thee: if you tarry longer,
I shall give worse payment.

CLOWN
By my troth, thou hast an open hand. — These wise
men, that give fools money, get themselves a good
report after fourteen years' purchase.

Enter SIR ANDREW.

SIR ANDREW
Now, sir, have I met you again? there's for you.
　　　　　　　　[*Striking* SEBASTIAN.

SEBASTIAN
Why, there's for thee, and there, and there!
　　　　　　　　[*Beating* SIR ANDREW.
Are all the people mad?

Enter SIR TOBY *and* FABIAN.

SIR TOBY
Hold, sir, or I'll throw your dagger o'er the house.

CLOWN
This will I tell my lady straight: I would not be in some
of your coats for twopence. 　　[*Exit.*

SIR TOBY
Come on, sir; hold.

SIR ANDREW
Nay, let him alone: I'll go another way to work with
him: I'll have an action of battery against him, if there
be any law in Illyria: though I struck him first, yet it's
no matter for that.

SEBASTIAN
Let go thy hand.

SIR TOBY
Come, sir, I will not let you go. Come, my young
soldier, put up your iron: you are well flesh'd; come on.

SEBASTIAN
I will be free from thee. What wouldst thou now?
If thou darest tempt me further, draw thy sword.
　　　　　　　　[*Draws.*

SIR TOBY
What, what? Nay, then I must have an ounce or two of
this malapert blood from you. 　　[*Draws.*

Enter OLIVIA.

OLIVIA
Hold, Toby; on thy life, I charge thee, hold!

SIR TOBY
Madam!

OLIVIA
Will it be ever thus? Ungracious wretch,
Fit for the mountains and the barbarous caves,
Where manners ne'er were preach'd! out of my sight! —
Be not offended, dear Cesario. —
Rudesby, be gone!
　　　[*Exeunt* SIR TOBY, SIR ANDREW, *and* FABIAN.
　　　I prithee, gentle friend,
Let thy fair wisdom, not thy passion, sway
In this uncivil and unjust extent

SEBASTIAN Why, there's for thee, and there, and there! Are all the people mad?

of King Gorboduc, 'That that is is'; so I, being master parson, am master parson; for, what is that but that, and is but is?

SIR TOBY
To him, Sir Topas.

CLOWN
What, ho, I say, — peace in this prison!

SIR TOBY
The knave counterfeits well; a good knave.

MALVOLIO [within].
Who calls there?

CLOWN
Sir Topas the curate, who comes to visit Malvolio the lunatic.

MALVOLIO
Sir Topas, Sir Topas, good Sir Topas, go to my lady.

CLOWN
Out, hyperbolical fiend! how vexest thou this man! talkest thou nothing but of ladies?

SIR TOBY
Well said, master parson.

MALVOLIO
Sir Topas, never was man thus wrong'd: good Sir Topas, do not think I am mad: they have laid me here in hideous darkness.

CLOWN
Fie, thou dishonest Satan! I call thee by the most modest terms; for I am one of those gentle ones that will use the devil himself with courtesy: say'st thou that house is dark?

MALVOLIO
As hell, Sir Topas.

CLOWN
Why, it hath bay windows transparent as barricadoes, and the clearstories toward the south-north are as lustrous as ebony; and yet complainest thou of obstruction?

MALVOLIO
I am not mad, Sir Topas: I say to you, this house is dark.

CLOWN
Madman, thou errest: I say, there is no darkness but ignorance; in which thou art more puzzled than the Egyptians in their fog.

MALVOLIO
I say, this house is as dark as ignorance, though ignorance were as dark as hell; and I say, there was never man thus abused. I am no more mad than you are: make the trial of it in any constant question.

CLOWN
What is the opinion of Pythagoras concerning wildfowl?

MALVOLIO
That the soul of our grandam might haply inhabit a bird.

CLOWN
What think'st thou of his opinion?

MALVOLIO
I think nobly of the soul, and no way approve his opinion.

CLOWN
Fare thee well. Remain thou still in darkness: thou shalt hold the opinion of Pythagoras ere I will allow of thy wits; and fear to kill a woodcock, lest thou dispossess the soul of thy grandam. Fare thee well.

MALVOLIO
Sir Topas, Sir Topas, —

SIR TOBY
My most exquisite Sir Topas!

CLOWN
Nay, I am for all waters.

MARIA
Thou mightst have done this without thy beard and gown: he sees thee not.

SIR TOBY
To him in thine own voice, and bring me word how thou find'st him: I would we were well rid of this knavery. If he may be conveniently deliver'd, I would he were; for I am now so far in offence with my niece, that I cannot pursue with any safety this sport to the upshot. Come by and by to my chamber. [Exeunt SIR TOBY and MARIA.

CLOWN [singing].
    Hey, Robin, jolly Robin,
        Tell me how thy lady does.

MALVOLIO
Fool, —

CLOWN
'My lady is unkind, perdy.'

MALVOLIO
Fool, —

CLOWN
'Alas, why is she so?'

MALVOLIO
Fool, I say, —

CLOWN
'She loves another' — Who calls, ha?

MALVOLIO
Good fool, as ever thou wilt deserve well at my hand, help me to a candle, and pen, ink and paper: as I am a gentleman, I will live to be thankful to thee for't.

CLOWN
Master Malvolio!

MALVOLIO
Ay, good fool.

CLOWN
Alas, sir, how fell you besides your five wits?

MALVOLIO
Fool, there was never a man so notoriously abused: I am as well in my wits, fool, as thou art.

CLOWN
But as well? then you are mad indeed, if you be no better in your wits than a fool.

MALVOLIO
They have here propertied me; keep me in darkness, send ministers to me, asses, and do all they can to face me out of my wits.

CLOWN
Advise you what you say; the minister is here. — Malvolio, Malvolio, thy wits the heavens restore! endeavour thyself to sleep, and leave thy vain bibble-babble.

MALVOLIO
Sir Topas, —

CLOWN
Maintain no words with him, good fellow. — Who, I, sir? not I, sir. God b'wi' you, good Sir Topas! — Marry, amen. — I will, sir, I will.

MALVOLIO
Fool, fool, fool, I say, —

CLOWN
Alas, sir, be patient. What say you sir? I am shent for speaking to you.

MALVOLIO
Good fool, help me to some light and some paper: I tell thee, I am as well in my wits as any man in Illyria.

CLOWN
Well-a-day, that you were, sir!

MALVOLIO
By this hand, I am. Good fool, some ink, paper, and light; and convey what I will set down to my lady: it shall advantage thee more than ever the bearing of letter did.

CLOWN
I will help you to't. But tell me true, are you not mad indeed? or do you but counterfeit?

MALVOLIO
Believe me, I am not; I tell thee true.

CLOWN
Nay, I'll ne'er believe a madman till I see his brains. I will fetch you light, and paper, and ink.

MALVOLIO
Fool, I'll requite it in the highest degree: I prithee, be gone.

CLOWN [singing].
    I am gone, sir;
        And anon, sir,
    I'll be with you again,
        In a trice,
        Like to the old Vice,
    Your need to sustain;
    Who, with dagger of lath,
    In his rage and his wrath,
        Cries, ah, ha! to the devil:
    Like a mad lad,
    Pare thy nails, dad;
        Adieu, goodman devil.   [Exit.

SCENE III

OLIVIA'S *garden*.

Enter SEBASTIAN.

SEBASTIAN
This is the air; that is the glorious sun;
This pearl she gave me, I do feel't and see't:
And though 'tis wonder that enwraps me thus,
Yet 'tis not madness. Where's Antonio, then?
I could not find him at the Elephant:
Yet there he was; and there I found this credit,
That he did range the town to seek me out.
His counsel now might do me golden service;
For though my soul disputes well with my sense,
That this may be some error, but no madness,
Yet doth this accident and flood of fortune
So far exceed all instance, all discourse,
That I am ready to distrust mine eyes,
And wrangle with my reason, that persuades me
To any other trust but that I am mad
Or else the lady's mad; yet, if 'twere so,
She could not sway her house, command her followers,
Take and give back affairs, and their dispatch,
With such a smooth, discreet, and stable bearing,
As I perceive she does: there's something in't
That is deceivable. But here the lady comes.

Enter OLIVIA *and a* PRIEST.

OLIVIA
Blame not this haste of mine. If you mean well,
Now go with me and with this holy man
Into the chantry by: there, before him,
And underneath that consecrated roof,
Plight me the full assurance of your faith;
That my most jealous and too doubtful soul
May live at peace: he shall conceal it,
Whiles you are willing it shall come to note,
What time we will our celebration keep
According to my birth. — What do you say?

SEBASTIAN
I'll follow this good man, and go with you;
And, having sworn truth, ever will be true.

OLIVIA
Then lead the way, good father; and heavens so shine,
That they may fairly note this act of mine!   [Exeunt.

ACT V

SCENE I

Before OLIVIA'S *house.*

Enter CLOWN *and* FABIAN.

FABIAN
Now, as thou lovest me, let me see his letter.
CLOWN
Good Master Fabian, grant me another request.
FABIAN
Any thing.
CLOWN
Do not desire to see this letter.
FABIAN
This is, to give a dog, and in recompense desire my dog
again.

Enter DUKE, VIOLA, CURIO, *and* ATTENDANTS.

DUKE
Belong you to the Lady Olivia, friends?
CLOWN
Ay, sir; we are some of her trappings.
DUKE
I know thee well: how dost thou, my good fellow?
CLOWN
Truly, sir, the better for my foes, and the worse for my
friends.
DUKE
Just the contrary; the better for thy friends.
CLOWN
No, sir, the worse.
DUKE
How can that be?
CLOWN
Marry, sir, they praise me, and make an ass of me; now
my foes tell me plainly I am an ass: so that by my foes,
sir, I profit in the knowledge of myself; and by my
friends I am abused: so that, conclusions to be as
kisses, if your four negatives make your two
affirmatives, why, then, the worse for my friends, and
the better for my foes.
DUKE
Why, this is excellent.
CLOWN
By my troth, sir, no; though it please you to be one of
my friends.
DUKE
Thou shalt not be the worse for me: there's gold.
[*Gives money.*
CLOWN
But that it would be double-dealing, sir, I would you
could make it another.
DUKE
O, you give me ill counsel.
CLOWN
Put your Grace in your pocket, sir, for this once, and let
your flesh and blood obey it.
DUKE
Well, I will be so much a sinner to be a double-dealer:
there's another. [*Gives money.*
CLOWN
Primo, secundo, tertio, is a good play; and the old saying
is, the third pays for all: the *triplex,* sir, is a good
tripping measure; or the bells of Saint Bennet, sir, may
put you in mind, — one, two, three.
DUKE
You can fool no more money out of me at this throw: if
you will let your lady know I am here to speak with her,
and bring her along with you, it may awake my bounty
further.
CLOWN
Marry, sir, lullaby to your bounty till I come again. I go,
sir; but I would not have you to think that my desire of
having is the sin of covetousness: but, as you say, sir, let
your bounty take a nap, I will awake it anon. [*Exit.*
VIOLA
Here comes the man, sir, that did rescue me.

Enter OFFICERS, *with* ANTONIO.

DUKE
That face of his I do remember well;
Yet, when I saw it last, it was besmear'd
As black as Vulcan in the smoke of war:
A bawbling vessel was he captain of,
For shallow draught and bulk unprizable;
With which such scatheful grapple did he make
With the most noble bottom of our fleet,
That very envy and the tongue of loss
Cried fame and honour on him. — What's the matter?
FIRST OFFICER
Orsino, this is that Antonio
That took the Phœnix and her fraught from Candy;
And this is he that did the Tiger board,
When your young nephew Titus lost his leg:
Here in the streets, desperate of shame and state,
In private brabble did we apprehend him.
VIOLA
He did me kindness, sir; drew on my side;
But, in conclusion, put strange speech upon me, —
I know not what 'twas but distraction.
DUKE
Notable pirate! thou salt-water thief!
What foolish boldness brought thee to their mercies,
Whom thou, in terms so bloody and so dear,
Hast made thine enemies?
ANTONIO
                          Orsino, noble sir,
Be pleas'd that I shake off these names you give me:
Antonio never yet was thief or pirate,
Though, I confess, on base and ground enough,
Orsino's enemy. A witchcraft drew me hither:
That most ingrateful boy there by your side,
From the rude sea's enrag'd and foamy mouth
Did I redeem; a wreck past hope he was:
His life I gave him, and did thereto add
My love, without retention or restraint,
All his in dedication; for his sake
Did I expose myself, pure for his love,
Into the danger of this adverse town;
Drew to defend him when he was beset:
Where being apprehended, his false cunning,
Not meaning to partake with me in danger,
Taught him to face me out of his acquaintance,
And grew a twenty-years-removed thing
While one would wink; denied me mine own purse,
Which I had recommended to his use
Not half an hour before.
VIOLA
                          How can this be?
DUKE
When came he to this town?
ANTONIO
To-day, my lord: and for three months before —
No interim, not a minute's vacancy —
Both day and night did we keep company.
DUKE
Here comes the countess: now heaven walks on earth. —
But for thee, fellow; fellow, thy words are madness:
Three months this youth hath tended upon me;
But more of that anon. Take him aside.

Enter OLIVIA *and* ATTENDANTS.

OLIVIA
What would my lord, but that he may not have,
Wherein Olivia may seem serviceable? —
Cesario, you do not keep promise with me.
VIOLA
Madam!
DUKE
Gracious Olivia, —
OLIVIA
What do you say, Cesario? Good my lord, —
VIOLA
My lord would speak; my duty hushes me.
OLIVIA
If it be aught to the old tune, my lord,
It is as fat and fulsome to mine ear
As howling after music.
DUKE
                          Still so cruel?
OLIVIA
Still so constant, lord.
DUKE
What, to perverseness? you uncivil lady,
To whose ingrate and unauspicious altars
My soul the faithfull'st offerings hath breath'd out
That e'er devotion tender'd! What shall I do?
OLIVIA
Even what it please my lord, that shall become him.
DUKE
Why should I not, had I the heart to do it,
Like to th'Egyptian thief at point of death,
Kill what I love? a savage jealousy
That sometimes savours nobly. — But hear me this:
Since you to non-regardance cast my faith,
And that I partly know the instrument
That screws me from my true place in your favour,
Live you, the marble-breasted tyrant, still;
But this your minion, whom I know you love,
And whom, by heaven I swear, I tender dearly,
Him will I tear out of that cruel eye,
Where he sits crowned in his master's spite. —
Come, boy, with me; my thoughts are ripe in mischief:
I'll sacrifice the lamb that I do love,
To spite a raven's heart within a dove.
VIOLA
And I, most jocund, apt, and willingly,
To do you rest, a thousand deaths would die.
OLIVIA
Where goes Cesario?
VIOLA
                          After him I love
More than I love these eyes, more than my life,
More, by all mores, than e'er I shall love wife.
If I do feign, you witnesses above
Punish my life for tainting of my love!
OLIVIA
Ay me, detested! how am I beguiled!
VIOLA
Who does beguile you? who does do you wrong?
OLIVIA
Hast thou forgot thyself? is it so long?
Call forth the holy father. [*Exit an* ATTENDANT
DUKE
                          Come, away! [*To* VIOLA
OLIVIA
Whither, my lord? — Cesario, husband, stay.
DUKE
Husband!
OLIVIA
                          Ay, husband: can he that deny?
DUKE
Her husband, sirrah!
VIOLA
                          No, my lord, not I.
OLIVIA
Alas, it is the baseness of thy fear
That makes thee strangle thy propriety:
Fear not, Cesario; take thy fortunes up;
Be that thou know'st thou art, and then thou art
As great as that thou fear'st.

Enter ATTENDANT, *with* PRIEST.

                          O, welcome, father!
Father, I charge thee, by thy reverence,
Here to unfold — though lately we intended
To keep in darkness what occasion now
Reveals before 'tis ripe — what thou dost know
Hath newly pass'd between this youth and me.
PRIEST
A contract of eternal bond of love,
Confirm'd by mutual joinder of your hands,
Attested by the holy close of lips,
Strengthen'd by interchangement of your rings;
And all the ceremony of this compact
Seal'd in my function, by my testimony:
Since when, my watch hath told me, toward my grave
I have travell'd but two hours.
DUKE
O thou dissembling cub! what wilt thou be
When time hath sow'd a grizzle on thy case?
Or will not else thy craft so quickly grow,
That thine own trip shall be thine overthrow?
Farewell, and take her; but direct thy feet
Where thou and I henceforth may never meet.
VIOLA
My lord, I do protest, —
OLIVIA
                          O, do not swear!
Hold little faith, though thou hast too much fear.

Enter SIR ANDREW.

SIR ANDREW
For the love of God, a surgeon! send one presently to
Sir Toby.
OLIVIA
What's the matter?
SIR ANDREW
'Has broke my head across, and has given Sir Toby a
bloody coxcomb too: for the love of God, your help! I
had rather than forty pound I were at home.
OLIVIA
Who has done this, Sir Andrew?
SIR ANDREW
The count's gentleman, one Cesario: we took him for a
coward, but he's the very devil incardinate.

DUKE
My gentleman Cesario?

SIR ANDREW
'Od's lifelings, here he is! — You broke my head for nothing; and that that I did, I was set on to do't by Sir Toby.

VIOLA
Why do you speak to me? I never hurt you:
You drew your sword upon me without cause;
But I bespake you fair, and hurt you not.

SIR ANDREW
If a bloody coxcomb be a hurt, you have hurt me: I think you set nothing by a bloody coxcomb. — Here comes Sir Toby halting; you shall hear more: but if he had not been in drink, he would have tickled you othergates than he did.

Enter SIR TOBY *and* CLOWN.

DUKE
How now, gentleman! how is't with you?

SIR TOBY
That's all one: 'has hurt me, and there's the end on't. — Sot, didst see Dick surgeon, sot?

CLOWN
O, he's drunk, Sir Toby, an hour agone; his eyes were set at eight i'th' morning.

SIR TOBY
Then he's a rogue and a passy-measures pavin: I hate a drunken rogue.

OLIVIA
Away with him! Who hath made this havoc with them?

SIR ANDREW
I'll help you, Sir Toby, because we'll be dress'd together.

SIR TOBY
Will you help? an ass-head and a coxcomb and a knave, a thin-faced knave, a gull?

OLIVIA
Get him to bed, and let his hurt be look'd to.

[*Exeunt* CLOWN, FABIAN, SIR TOBY, *and* SIR ANDREW.

Enter SEBASTIAN.

SEBASTIAN
I am sorry, madam, I have hurt your kinsman;
But, had it been the brother of my blood,
I must have done no less with wit and safety.
You throw a strange regard upon me, and by that
I do perceive it hath offended you:
Pardon me, sweet one, even for the vows
We made each other but so late ago.

DUKE
One face, one voice, one habit, and two persons, —
A natural perspective, that is and is not!

SEBASTIAN
Antonio, O my dear Antonio!
How have the hours rack'd and tortured me,
Since I have lost thee!

ANTONIO
Sebastian are you?

SEBASTIAN
Fear'st thou that, Antonio?

ANTONIO
How have you made division of yourself?
An apple, cleft in two, is not more twin
Than these two creatures. Which is Sebastian?

OLIVIA
Most wonderful!

SEBASTIAN
Do I stand there? I never had a brother;
Nor can there be that deity in my nature,
Of here and every where. I had a sister,
Whom the blind waves and surges have devour'd. —
Of charity, what kin are you to me?   [*To* VIOLA.
What countryman? what name? what parentage?

VIOLA
Of Messaline: Sebastian was my father;
Such a Sebastian was my brother too,
So went he suited to his watery tomb,
If spirits can assume both form and suit,
You come to fright us.

SEBASTIAN
A spirit I am indeed;
But am in that dimension grossly clad,
Which from the womb I did participate.
Were you a woman, as the rest goes even,
I should my tears let fall upon your cheek,
And say, 'Thrice-welcome, drowned Viola!'

VIOLA
My father had a mole upon his brow, —

SEBASTIAN
And so had mine.

VIOLA
And died that day when Viola from her birth
Had number'd thirteen years.

SEBASTIAN
O, that record is lively in my soul!
He finished, indeed, his mortal act
That day that made my sister thirteen years.

VIOLA
If nothing lets to make us happy both
But this my masculine usurp'd attire,
Do not embrace me till each circumstance
Of place, time, fortune, do cohere and jump,
That I am Viola: which to confirm,
I'll bring you to a captain in this town,
Where lie my maiden weeds; by whose gentle help
I was preserv'd to serve this noble count.
All the occurrence of my fortune since
Hath been between this lady and this lord.

SEBASTIAN [*to* OLIVIA].
So comes it, lady, you have been mistook:
But nature to her bias drew in that.
You would have been contracted to a maid;
Nor are you therein, by my life, deceived, —
You are betrothed both to a maid and man.

DUKE
Be not amaz'd; right noble is his blood. —
If this be so, as yet the glass seems true,
I shall have share in this most happy wrack. —
[*to* VIOLA] Boy, thou hast said to me a thousand times
Thou never shouldst love woman like to me.

VIOLA
And all those sayings will I over-swear;
And all those swearings keep as true in soul
As doth that orbed continent the fire
That severs day from night.

DUKE
Give me thy hand;
And let me see thee in thy woman's weeds.

VIOLA
The captain that did bring me first on shore
Hath my maid's garments: he, upon some action,
Is now in durance, at Malvolio's suit,
A gentleman and follower of my lady's.

OLIVIA
He shall enlarge him: — fetch Malvolio hither: —
And yet, alas, now I remember me,
They say, poor gentleman, he's much distract.

Enter CLOWN *with a letter, and* FABIAN.

A most extracting frenzy of mine own
From my remembrance clearly banish'd his. —
How does he, sirrah?

CLOWN
Truly, madam, he holds Beelzebub at the stave's end as well as a man in his case may do: has here writ a letter to you; I should have given't you to-day morning, but as a madman's epistles are no gospels, so it skills not much when they are deliver'd.

OLIVIA
Open't, and read it.

CLOWN
Look, then, to be well edified when the fool delivers the madman. [*reads*] By the Lord, madam, —

OLIVIA
How now! art thou mad?

CLOWN
No, madam, I do but read madness: an your ladyship will have it as it ought to be, you must allow *vox*.

OLIVIA
Prithee, read i' thy right wits.

CLOWN
So I do, madonna; but to read his right wits is to read thus: therefore perpend, my princess, and give ear.

OLIVIA
Read it you, sirrah.   [*to* FABIAN.

FABIAN [*reads*].
By the Lord, madam, you wrong me, and the world shall know it: though you have put me into darkness, and given your drunken cousin rule over me, yet have I the benefit of my senses as well as your ladyship. I have your own letter that induced me to the semblance I put on; with the which I doubt not but to do myself much right, or you much shame. Think of me as you please. I leave my duty a little unthought of, and speak out of my injury.

THE MADLY-USED MALVOLIO.

OLIVIA
Did he write this?

CLOWN
Ay, madam.

DUKE
This savours not much of distraction.

OLIVIA
See him deliver'd, Fabian; bring him hither.

[*Exit* FABIAN.

My lord, so please you, these things further thought on,
To think me as well a sister as a wife,
One day shall crown th'alliance on't, so please you,
Here at my house, and at my proper cost.

DUKE
Madam, I am most apt t'embrace your offer. —
[*to* VIOLA] Your master quits you; and, for your service done him,
So much against the mettle of your sex,
So far beneath your soft and tender breeding,
And since you call'd me master for so long,
Here is my hand: you shall from this time be
Your master's mistress.

OLIVIA
A sister! — you are she.

Enter FABIAN, *with* MALVOLIO.

DUKE
Is this the madman?

OLIVIA
Ay, my lord, this same. —
How now, Malvolio!

MALVOLIO
Madam, you have done me wrong,
Notorious wrong.

OLIVIA
Have I, Malvolio? no.

MALVOLIO
Lady, you have. Pray you, peruse that letter:
You must not now deny it is your hand, —
Write from it, if you can, in hand or phrase;
Or say 'tis not your seal, nor your invention:
You can say none of this: well, grant it then,
And tell me, in the modesty of honour,
Why you have given me such clear lights of favour,
Bade me come smiling and cross-garter'd to you,
To put on yellow stockings, and to frown
Upon Sir Toby and the lighter people;
And, acting this in an obedient hope,
Why have you suffer'd me to be imprison'd,
Kept in a dark house, visited by the priest,
And made the most notorious geck and gull
That e'er invention play'd on? tell me why.

OLIVIA
Alas, Malvolio, this is not my writing,
Though, I confess, much like the character:
But, out of question, 'tis Maria's hand.
And now I do bethink me, it was she
First told me thou wast mad: thou camest in smiling,
And in such forms which here were presupposed
Upon thee in the letter. Prithee, be content:
This practice hath most shrewdly pass'd upon thee;
But, when we know the grounds and authors of it,
Thou shalt be both the plaintiff and the judge
Of thine own cause.

FABIAN
Good madam, hear me speak:
And let no quarrel nor no brawl to come
Taint the condition of this present hour,
Which I have wonder'd at. In hope it shall not,
Most freely I confess, myself and Toby
Set this device against Malvolio here,
Upon some stubborn and uncourteous parts
We had conceiv'd in him: Maria writ
The letter at Sir Toby's great importance;
In recompense whereof he hath married her.
How with a sportful malice it was follow'd,
May rather pluck on laughter than revenge;
If that the injuries be justly weigh'd
That have on both sides passed.

OLIVIA
Alas, poor fool, how have they baffled thee!

CLOWN
Why, 'some are born great, some achieve greatness, and some have greatness thrown upon them.' I was one, sir, in this interlude, — one Sir Topas, sir; but that's all one. — 'By the Lord, fool, I am not mad'; — but do you remember? 'Madam, why laugh you at such a barren rascal? an you smile not, he's gagg'd': and thus the whirligig of time brings in his revenges.

MALVOLIO
I'll be revenged on the whole pack of you.   [*Exit*.

OLIVIA
He hath been most notoriously abused.
DUKE
Pursue him, and entreat him to a peace: —
He hath not told us of the captain yet:
When that is known, and golden time convents,
A solemn combination shall be made
Of our dear souls. Meantime, sweet sister,
We will not part from hence. — Cesario, come;
For so you shall be, while you are a man;
But when in other habits you are seen,
Orsino's mistress and his fancy's queen.
[Exeunt all, except CLOWN.

CLOWN [*sings*].
When that I was and a little tiny boy,
  With hey, ho, the wind and the rain,
A foolish thing was but a toy,
  For the rain it raineth every day.

But when I came to man's estate,
  With hey, ho, the wind and the rain,
'Gainst knaves and thieves men shut their gate,
  For the rain it raineth every day.

But when I came, alas! to wive,
  With hey, ho, the wind and the rain,
By swaggering could I never thrive,
  For the rain it raineth every day.

But when I came unto my beds,
  With hey, ho, the wind and the rain,
With toss-pots still had drunken heads,
  For the rain it raineth every day.

A great while ago the world begun,
  With hey, ho, the wind and the rain: —
But that's all one, our play is done,
  And we'll strive to please you every day.
[Exit.

HAMLET, PRINCE OF DENMARK

DRAMATIS PERSONAE

CLAUDIUS, *King of Denmark.*
HAMLET, *son to the late, and nephew to the present king.*
POLONIUS, *lord chamberlain.*
HORATIO, *friend to Hamlet.*
LAERTES, *son to Polonius.*
VOLTIMAND,
CORNELIUS,
ROSENCRANTZ, } *courtiers.*
GUILDENSTERN,
OSRIC,
A GENTLEMAN,

A PRIEST.
MARCELLUS, }
BERNARDO, } *officers.*
FRANCISCO, *a soldier.*
REYNALDO, *servant to Polonius.*
PLAYERS.
TWO CLOWNS, *grave-diggers.*
FORTINBRAS, *Prince of Norway.*
A CAPTAIN.
ENGLISH AMBASSADORS.

GERTRUDE, *Queen of Denmark, and mother to Hamlet.*
OPHELIA, *daughter to Polonius.*

LORDS, LADIES, OFFICERS, SOLDIERS, SAILORS,
MESSENGERS, *and other* ATTENDANTS.

GHOST *of Hamlet's father.*

SCENE — *Denmark.*

BERNARDO   Looks it not like the king? mark it, Horatio.

ACT I

SCENE I

Elsinore. A platform before the castle.

FRANCISCO *at his post. Enter to him* BERNARDO.

BERNARDO
Who's there?
FRANCISCO
Nay, answer me: stand, and unfold yourself.
BERNARDO
Long live the king!
FRANCISCO
Bernardo?
BERNARDO
He.
FRANCISCO
You come most carefully upon your hour.
BERNARDO
'Tis now struck twelve; get thee to bed, Francisco.
FRANCISCO
For this relief much thanks: 'tis bitter cold,
And I am sick at heart.

BERNARDO
Have you had quiet guard?
FRANCISCO
Not a mouse stirring.
BERNARDO
Well, good night.
If you do meet Horatio and Marcellus,
The rivals of my watch, bid them make haste.
FRANCISCO
I think I hear them. — Stand, ho! Who's there?
Enter HORATIO *and* MARCELLUS.
HORATIO
Friends to this ground.
MARCELLUS
And liegemen to the Dane.
FRANCISCO
Give you good night.
MARCELLUS
O, farewell, honest soldier:
Who hath reliev'd you?
FRANCISCO
Bernardo has my place.
Give you good night.   [*Exit.*
MARCELLUS
Holla! Bernardo!

BERNARDO
Say, —
What, is Horatio there?
HORATIO
A piece of him.
BERNARDO
Welcome, Horatio: — welcome, good Marcellus.
MARCELLUS
What, has this thing appear'd again to-night?
BERNARDO
I have seen nothing.
MARCELLUS
Horatio says 'tis but our fantasy,
And will not let belief take hold of him
Touching this dreaded sight, twice seen of us:
Therefore I have entreated him along
With us to watch the minutes of this night;
That, if again this apparition come,
He may approve our eyes, and speak to it.
HORATIO
Tush, tush, 'twill not appear.
BERNARDO
Sit down awhile;
And let us once again assail your ears,
That are so fortified against our story,
What we two nights have seen.
HORATIO
Well, sit we down,
And let us hear Bernardo speak of this.
BERNARDO
Last night of all,
When yond samestar that's westward from the pole
Had made his course t'illume that part of heaven
Where now it burns, Marcellus and myself,
The bell then beating one, —
MARCELLUS
Peace, break thee off; look, where it comes again!
Enter GHOST.
BERNARDO
In the same figure, like the king that's dead.
MARCELLUS
Thou art a scholar; speak to it, Horatio.
BERNARDO
Looks it not like the king? mark it, Horatio.
HORATIO
Most like: — it harrows me with fear and wonder.
BERNARDO
It would be spoke to.
MARCELLUS
Question it, Horatio.
HORATIO
What art thou, that usurp'st this time of night,
Together with that fair and warlike form
In which the majesty of buried Denmark
Did sometimes march? by heaven I charge thee, speak!
MARCELLUS
It is offended.
BERNARDO
See, it stalks away!
HORATIO
Stay! speak, speak! I charge thee, speak!   [*Exit* GHOST.
MARCELLUS
'Tis gone, and will not answer.
BERNARDO
How now, Horatio! you tremble, and look pale:
Is not this something more than fantasy?
What think you on't?
HORATIO
Before my God, I might not this believe

Without the sensible and true avouch
Of mine own eyes.

MARCELLUS
      Is it not like the king?

HORATIO
As thou art to thyself:
Such was the very armour he had on
When he th'ambitious Norway combated;
So frown'd he once, when, in an angry parle,
He smote the sledded Polacks on the ice.
'Tis strange.

MARCELLUS
Thus twice before, and jump at this dead hour,
With martial stalk hath he gone by our watch.

HORATIO
In what particular thought to work I know not;
But, in the gross and scope of my opinion,
This bodes some strange eruption to our state.

MARCELLUS
Good now, sit down, and tell me, he that knows,
Why this same strict and most observant watch
So nightly toils the subject of the land;
And why such daily cast of brazen cannon,
And foreign mart for implements of war;
Why such impress of shipwrights, whose sore task
Does not divide the Sunday from the week;
What might be toward, that this sweaty haste
Doth make the night joint-labourer with the day:
Who is't that can inform me?

HORATIO
      That can I;
At least, the whisper goes so. Our last king,
Whose image even but now appear'd to us,
Was, as you know, by Fortinbras of Norway,
Thereto prick'd on by a most emulate pride,
Dar'd to the combat; in which our valiant Hamlet —
For so this side of our known world esteem'd him —
Did slay this Fortinbras; who, by a seal'd compact,
Well ratified by law and heraldry,
Did forfeit, with his life, all those his lands
Which he stood seiz'd of to the conqueror:
Against the which, a moiety competent
Was gaged by our king; which had return'd
To the inheritance of Fortinbras,
Had he been vanquisher; as, by the same cov'nant
And carriage of the article design'd,
His fell to Hamlet. Now, sir, young Fortinbras,
Of unimproved mettle hot and full,
Hath in the skirts of Norway, here and there,
Shark'd up a list of lawless resolutes,
For food and diet, to some enterprise
That hath a stomach in't: which is no other —
As it doth well appear unto our state —
But to recover of us, by strong hand
And terms compulsative, those foresaid lands
So by his father lost: and this, I take it,
Is the main motive of our preparations,
The source of this our watch, and the chief head
Of this post-haste and romage in the land.

BERNARDO
I think it be no other but e'en so:
Well may it sort, that this portentous figure
Comes armed through our watch; so like the king
That was and is the question of these wars.

HORATIO
A mote it is to trouble the mind's eye.
In the most high and palmy state of Rome,
A little ere the mightiest Julius fell,
The graves stood tenantless, and the sheeted dead
Did squeak and gibber in the Roman streets:
As, stars with trains of fire, and dews of blood,
Disasters in the sun; and the moist star,
Upon whose influence Neptune's empire stands,
Was sick almost to doomsday with eclipse:
And even the like precurse of fierce events —
As harbingers preceding still the fates,
And prologue to the omen coming on —
Have heaven and earth together demonstrated
Unto our climatures and countrymen. —
But, soft, behold! lo, where it comes again!

Enter GHOST *again.*

I'll cross it, though it blast me. — Stay, illusion!
If thou hast any sound, or use of voice,
Speak to me:
If there be any good thing to be done,
That may to thee do ease, and grace to me,
Speak to me:
If thou art privy to thy country's fate,
Which happily foreknowing may avoid,
O, speak!
Or if thou hast uphoarded in thy life

Extorted treasure in the womb of earth,
For which, they say, you spirits oft walk in death,
          [*Cock crows.*
Speak of it: — stay, and speak! — Stop it, Marcellus.

MARCELLUS
Shall I strike at it with my partisan?

HORATIO
Do, if it will not stand.

BERNARDO
      'Tis here!

HORATIO
        'Tis here!

MARCELLUS
'Tis gone!   [*Exit* GHOST.
We do it wrong, being so majestical,
To offer it the show of violence;
For it is, as the air, invulnerable,
And our vain blows malicious mockery.

BERNARDO
It was about to speak when the cock crew.

HORATIO
And then it started like a guilty thing
Upon a fearful summons. I have heard,
The cock, that is the trumpet to the morn,
Doth with his lofty and shrill-sounding throat
Awake the god of day; and at his warning,
Whether in sea or fire, in earth or air,
Th'extravagant and erring spirit hies
To his confine: and of the truth herein
This present object made probation.

MARCELLUS
It faded on the crowing of the cock.
Some say, that ever 'gainst that season comes
Wherein our Saviour's birth is celebrated,
The bird of dawning singeth all night long:
And then, they say, no spirit dare stir abroad;
The nights are wholesome; then no planets strike,
No fairy takes, nor witch hath power to charm;
So hallow'd and so gracious is the time.

HORATIO
So have I heard, and do in part believe it.
But, look, the morn, in russet mantle clad,
Walks o'er the dew of yon high eastern hill:
Break we our watch up: and, by my advice,
Let us impart what we have seen to-night
Unto young Hamlet; for, upon my life,
This spirit, dumb to us, will speak to him:
Do you consent we shall acquaint him with it,
As needful in our loves, fitting our duty?

MARCELLUS
Let's do't, I pray; and I this morning know
Where we shall find him most convenient. [*Exeunt.*

SCENE II

A room of state in the castle.

Enter the KING, QUEEN, HAMLET, POLONIUS,
LAERTES, VOLTIMAND, CORNELIUS,
LORDS, *and* ATTENDANTS.

KING
Though yet of Hamlet our dear brother's death
The memory be green; and that it us befitted
To bear our hearts in grief, and our whole kingdom
To be contracted in one brow of woe;
Yet so far hath discretion fought with nature,
That we with wisest sorrow think on him,
Together with remembrance of ourselves.
Therefore our sometime sister, now our queen,
Th'imperial jointress of this warlike state,
Have we, as 'twere with a defeated joy, —
With one auspicious, and one dropping eye,
With mirth in funeral, and with dirge in marriage,
In equal scale weighing delight and dole, —
Taken to wife: nor have we herein barr'd
Your better wisdoms, which have freely gone
With this affair along: — for all, our thanks.
Now follows, that you know, young Fortinbras,
Holding a weak supposal of our worth,
Or thinking by our late dear brother's death
Our state to be disjoint and out of frame,
Colleagued with the dream of his advantage, —
He hath not fail'd to pester us with message,
Importing the surrender of those lands
Lost by his father, with all bands of law,
To our most valiant brother. So much for him. —
Now for ourself, and for this time of meeting:
Thus much the business is: — we have here writ
To Norway, uncle of young Fortinbras, —
Who, impotent and bed-rid, scarcely hears
Of this his nephew's purpose, — to suppress

His further gait herein; in that the levies,
The lists, and full proportions, are all made
Out of his subject: — and we here dispatch
You, good Cornelius, and you, Voltimand,
For bearers of this greeting to old Norway;
Giving to you no further personal power
To business with the king, more than the scope
Of these delated articles allow.
Farewell; and let your haste commend your duty.

CORNELIUS *and* **VOLTIMAND**
In that and all things will we show our duty.

KING
We doubt it nothing: heartily farewell.
    [*Exeunt* VOLTIMAND *and* CORNELIUS.
And now, Laertes, what's the news with you?
You told us of some suit; what is't, Laertes?
You cannot speak of reason to the Dane,
And lose your voice: what would'st thou beg, Laertes,
That shall not be my offer, not thy asking?
The head is not more native to the heart,
The hand more instrumental to the mouth,
Than is the throne of Denmark to thy father.
What wouldst thou have, Laertes?

LAERTES
        Dread my lord,
Your leave and favour to return to France;
From whence though willingly I came to Denmark,
To show my duty in your coronation,
Yet now, I must confess, that duty done,
My thoughts and wishes bend again toward France,
And bow them to your gracious leave and pardon.

KING
Have you your father's leave? What says Polonius?

POLONIUS
He hath, my lord, wrung from me my slow leave
By laboursome petition; and, at last,
Upon his will I seal'd my hard consent:
I do beseech you, give him leave to go.

KING
Take thy fair hour, Laertes; time be thine,
And thy best graces spend it at thy will! —
But now, my cousin Hamlet, and my son, —

HAMLET [*aside*].
A little more than kin, and less than kind.

KING
How is it that the clouds still hang on you?

HAMLET
Not so, my lord; I am too much i'th'sun.

QUEEN
Good Hamlet, cast thy nighted colour off,
And let thine eye look like a friend on Denmark.
Do not for ever with thy vailed lids
Seek for thy noble father in the dust:
Thou know'st 'tis common, — all that live must die,
Passing through nature to eternity.

HAMLET
Ay, madam, it is common.

QUEEN
      If it be,
Why seems it so particular with thee?

HAMLET
Seems, madam! nay, it is; I know not 'seems'.
'Tis not alone my inky cloak, good mother,
Nor customary suits of solemn black,
Nor windy suspiration of forc'd breath,
No, nor the fruitful river in the eye,
Nor the dejected haviour of the visage,
Together with all forms, moods, shows of grief,
That can denote me truly: these, indeed, seem,
For they are actions that a man might play:
But I have that within which passeth show;
These but the trappings and the suits of woe.

KING
'Tis sweet and commendable in your nature, Hamlet,
To give these mourning duties to your father:
But, you must know, your father lost a father;
That father lost, lost his; and the survivor bound,
In filial obligation, for some term
To do obsequious sorrow: but to persever
In obstinate condolement, is a course
Of impious stubbornness; 'tis unmanly grief:
It shows a will most incorrect to heaven;
A heart unfortified, a mind impatient;
An understanding simple and unschool'd:
For what we know must be, and is as common
As any the most vulgar thing to sense,
Why should we, in our peevish opposition,
Take it to heart? Fie! 'tis a fault to heaven,
A fault against the dead, a fault to nature,
To reason most absurd; whose common theme

s death of fathers, and who still hath cried,
'rom the first corse till he that died to-day,
This must be so.' We pray you, throw to earth
This unprevailing woe; and think of us
As of a father: for let the world take note,
'ou are the most immediate to our throne;
And with no less nobility of love
'han that which dearest father bears his son,
Do I impart toward you. For your intent
In going back to school in Wittenberg,
't is most retrograde to our desire:
And we beseech you, bend you to remain
Here, in the cheer and comfort of our eye,
Our chiefest courtier, cousin, and our son.

QUEEN
Let not thy mother lose her prayers, Hamlet:
I pray thee, stay with us; go not to Wittenberg.

HAMLET
I shall in all my best obey you, madam.

KING
Why, 'tis a loving and a fair reply:
Be as ourself in Denmark. — Madam, come;
This gentle and unforc'd accord of Hamlet
Sits smiling to my heart: in grace whereof,
No jocund health that Denmark drinks to-day,
But the great cannon to the clouds shall tell;
And the king's rouse the heaven shall bruit again,
Re-speaking earthly thunder. Come away.
                    [*Exeunt all but* HAMLET.

HAMLET
O, that this too too solid flesh would melt,
Thaw, and resolve itself into a dew!
Or that the Everlasting had not fix'd
His canon 'gainst self-slaughter! O God! God!
How weary, stale, flat, and unprofitable
Seem to me all the uses of this world!
Fie on't! O, fie! 'tis an unweeded garden,
That grows to seed; things rank and gross in nature
Possess it merely. That it should come to this!
But two months dead! — nay, not so much, not two:
So excellent a king; that was, to this,
Hyperion to a satyr: so loving to my mother,
That he might not beteem the winds of heaven
Visit her face too roughly. Heaven and earth!
Must I remember? why, she would hang on him,
As if increase of appetite had grown
By what it fed on: and yet, within a month, —
Let me not think on't, — Frailty, thy name is
    woman! —
A little month; or e'er those shoes were old
With which she follow'd my poor father's body,
Like Niobe, all tears; — why she, even she —
O God! a beast, that wants discourse of reason,
Would have mourn'd longer — married with my uncle,
My father's brother; but no more like my father
Than I to Hercules: within a month;
Ere yet the salt of most unrighteous tears
Had left the flushing in her galled eyes,
She married: — O, most wicked speed, to post
With such dexterity to incestuous sheets!
It is not nor it cannot come to good:
But break, my heart, — for I must hold my tongue!

Enter HORATIO, MARCELLUS, *and* BERNARDO.

HORATIO
Hail to your lordship!

HAMLET
                I am glad to see you well:
Horatio, — or I do forget my self.

HORATIO
The same, my lord, and your poor servant ever.

HAMLET
Sir, my good friend; I'll change that name with you:
And what make you from Wittenberg, Horatio? —
    Marcellus?

MARCELLUS
My good lord, —

HAMLET
I am very glad to see you. Good even, sir. —
But what, in faith, make you from Wittenberg?

HORATIO
A truant disposition, good my lord.

HAMLET
I would not hear your enemy say so;
Nor shall you do mine ear that violence
To make it truster of your own report
Against yourself: I know you are no truant.
But what is your affair in Elsinore?
We'll teach you to drink deep ere you depart.

HORATIO
My lord, I came to see your father's funeral.

QUEEN I pray thee, stay with us; go not to Wittenberg.

HAMLET
I pray thee, do not mock me, fellow-student;
I think it was to see my mother's wedding.

HORATIO
Indeed, my lord, it follow'd hard upon.

HAMLET
Thrift, thrift, Horatio! the funeral baked meats
Did coldly furnish forth the marriage tables.
Would I had met my dearest foe in heaven
Or ever I had seen that day, Horatio! —
My father, — methinks I see my father.

HORATIO
O, where, my lord?

HAMLET
                In my mind's eye, Horatio.

HORATIO
I saw him once; he was a goodly king.

HAMLET
He was a man, take him for all in all,
I shall not look upon his like again.

HORATIO
My lord, I think I saw him yesternight.

HAMLET
Saw? who?

HORATIO
My lord, the king your father.

HAMLET
                The king my father!

HORATIO
Season your admiration for a while
With an attent ear; till I may deliver,
Upon the witness of these gentlemen,
This marvel to you.

HAMLET
                For God's love, let me hear.

HORATIO
Two nights together had these gentlemen,
Marcellus and Bernardo, on their watch,
In the dead vast and middle of the night,
Been thus encounter'd. A figure like your father,
Armed at point exactly, cap-a-pe,
Appears before them, and with solemn march
Goes slow and stately by them: thrice he walk'd
By their oppress'd and fear-surprised eyes,
Within his truncheon's length; whilst they, distill'd
Almost to jelly with the act of fear,
Stand dumb, and speak not to him. This to me
In dreadful secrecy impart they did;
And I with them the third night kept the watch:
Where, as they had deliver'd, both in time,
Form of the thing, each word made true and good,
The apparition comes: I knew your father;
These hands are not more like.

HAMLET
                But where was this?

MARCELLUS
My lord, upon the platform where we watch'd.

HAMLET
Did you not speak to it?

HORATIO
                My lord, I did;
But answer made it none: yet once methought
It lifted up its head, and did address
Itself to motion, like as it would speak:
But even then the morning cock crew loud;
And at the sound it shrunk in haste away,
And vanish'd from our sight.

HAMLET
                'Tis very strange.

HORATIO
As I do live, my honour'd lord, 'tis true;
And we did think it writ down in our duty
To let you know of it.

HAMLET
Indeed, indeed, sirs, but this troubles me.
Hold you the watch to-night?

MARCELLUS and BERNARDO
                We do, my lord.

HAMLET
Arm'd, say you?

MARCELLUS and BERNARDO
Arm'd, my lord.

HAMLET
From top to toe?

MARCELLUS and BERNARDO
                My lord, from head to foot.

HAMLET
Then saw you not his face?

HORATIO
O, yes, my lord; he wore his beaver up.

HAMLET
What, look'd he frowningly?

HORATIO
A countenance more in sorrow than in anger.

HAMLET
Pale or red?

HORATIO
Nay, very pale.

HAMLET
                And fix'd his eyes upon you?

HORATIO
Most constantly.

HAMLET
                I would I had been there.

HORATIO
It would have much amaz'd you.

HAMLET
Very like, very like. Stay'd it long?

HORATIO
While one with moderate haste might tell a hundred.

MARCELLUS and BERNARDO
Longer, longer.

HORATIO
Not when I saw't.

HAMLET Did you not speak to it?

HAMLET
        His beard was grizzled, — no?

HORATIO
It was, as I have seen it in his life,
A sable silver'd.

HAMLET
        I will watch to-night;
Perchance 'twill walk again.

HORATIO
        I warrant it will.

HAMLET
If it assume my noble father's person,
I'll speak to it, though hell itself should gape,
And bid me hold my peace. I pray you all,
If you have hitherto conceal'd this sight,
Let it be tenable in your silence still;
And whatsoever else shall hap to-night,
Give it an understanding, but no tongue:
I will requite your loves. So, fare you well:
Upon the platform, 'twixt eleven and twelve,
I'll visit you.

ALL
        Our duty to your honour.

HAMLET
Your loves, as mine to you: farewell.
        [Exeunt all but HAMLET.
My father's spirit in arms! all is not well!
I doubt some foul play: would the night were come!
Till then sit still, my soul: foul deeds will rise,
Though all the earth o'erwhelm them, to men's eyes.
        [Exit.

SCENE III

A room in POLONIUS' *house.*

Enter LAERTES *and* OPHELIA.

LAERTES
My necessaries are embark'd: farewell:
And, sister, as the winds give benefit,
And convoy is assistant, do not sleep,
But let me hear from you.

OPHELIA
        Do you doubt that?

LAERTES
For Hamlet, and the trifling of his favour,
Hold it a fashion, and a toy in blood;
A violet in the youth of primy nature,
Forward, not permanent, sweet, not lasting,
The perfume and suppliance of a minute;
No more.

OPHELIA
        No more but so?

LAERTES
        Think it no more:
For nature, crescent, does not grow alone
In thews and bulk; but, as this temple waxes,
The inward service of the mind and soul
Grows wide withal. Perhaps he loves you now;
And now no soil nor cautel doth besmirch
The virtue of his will: but you must fear,
His greatness weigh'd, his will is not his own;
For he himself is subject to his birth:
He may not, as unvalued persons do,
Carve for himself; for on his choice depends
The safety and health of this whole state;
And therefore must his choice be circumscribed
Unto the voice and yielding of that body,
Whereof he is the head. Then if he says he loves you,
It fits your wisdom so far to believe it,
As he in his particular act and place
May give his saying deed; which is no further
Than the main voice of Denmark goes withal.
Then weigh what loss your honour may sustain,
If with too credent ear you list his songs;
Or lose your heart; or your chaste treasure open
To his unmaster'd importunity.
Fear it, Ophelia, fear it, my dear sister;
And keep you in the rear of your affection,
Out of the shot and danger of desire.
The chariest maid is prodigal enough,
If she unmask her beauty to the moon:
Virtue itself scapes not calumnious strokes:
The canker galls the infants of the spring,
Too oft before their buttons be disclosed;
And in the morn and liquid dew of youth
Contagious blastments are most imminent.
Be wary, then; best safety lies in fear:
Youth to itself rebels, though none else near.

OPHELIA
I shall th'effect of this good lesson keep,
As watchman to my heart. But, good my brother,
Do not, as some ungracious pastors do,
Show me the steep and thorny way to heaven;
Whilst, like a puff'd and reckless libertine,
Himself the primrose path of dalliance treads,
And recks not his own rede.

LAERTES
        O, fear me not.
I stay too long: — but here my father comes.
        Enter POLONIUS.
A double blessing is a double grace;
Occasion smiles upon a second leave.

POLONIUS
Yet here, Laertes! aboard, aboard, for shame!
The wind sits in the shoulder of your sail,
And you are stay'd for. There, — my blessing with thee!
        [Laying his hand on LAERTES' *head.*
And these few precepts in thy memory
See thou character. Give thy thoughts no tongue,
Nor any unproportion'd thought his act.
Be thou familiar, but by no means vulgar.
The friends thou hast, and their adoption tried,
Grapple them to thy soul with hoops of steel;
But do not dull thy palm with entertainment
Of each new-hatch'd, unfledg'd comrade. Beware
Of entrance to a quarrel; but being in,
Bear't, that th'opposed may beware of thee.
Give every man thine ear, but few thy voice:
Take each man's censure, but reserve thy judgement.
Costly thy habit as thy purse can buy,
But not express'd in fancy; rich, not gaudy:
For the apparel oft proclaims the man;
And they in France of the best rank and station
Are most select and generous, chief in that.
Neither a borrower nor a lender be:
For loan oft loses both itself and friend;
And borrowing dulls the edge of husbandry.
This above all, — to thine own self be true;
And it must follow, as the night the day,
Thou canst not then be false to any man.
Farewell: my blessing season this in thee!

LAERTES
Most humbly do I take my leave, my lord.

POLONIUS
The time invites you; go, your servants tend.

LAERTES
Farewell, Ophelia; and remember well
What I have said to you.

OPHELIA
        'Tis in my memory lock'd,
And you yourself shall keep the key of it.

LAERTES
Farewell.   *[Exit*

POLONIUS
What is't, Ophelia, he hath said to you?

OPHELIA
So please you, something touching the Lord Hamlet.

POLONIUS
Marry, well bethought:
'Tis told me, he hath very oft of late
Given private time to you; and you yourself
Have of your audience been most free and bounteous:
If it be so, — as so 'tis put on me,
And that in way of caution, — I must tell you,
You do not understand yourself so clearly
As it behoves my daughter and your honour.
What is between you? give me up the truth.

OPHELIA
He hath, my lord, of late made many tenders
Of his affection to me.

POLONIUS
Affection! pooh! you speak like a green girl,
Unsifted in such perilous circumstance.
Do you believe his tenders, as you call them?

OPHELIA
I do not know, my lord, what I should think.

POLONIUS
Marry, I'll teach you: think yourself a baby;
That you have ta'en these tenders for true pay,
Which are not sterling. Tender yourself more dearly;
Or — not to crack the wind of the poor phrase,
Running it thus — you'll tender me a fool.

OPHELIA
My lord, he hath importun'd me with love
In honourable fashion.

POLONIUS
Ay, fashion you may call't; go to, go to.

OPHELIA
And hath given countenance to his speech, my lord,
With almost all the holy vows of heaven.

POLONIUS
Ay, springes to catch woodcocks. I do know,
When the blood burns, how prodigal the soul
Lends the tongue vows: these blazes, daughter,
Giving more light than heat, — extinct in both,
Even in their promise, as it is a-making, —
You must not take for fire. From this time
Be somewhat scanter of your maiden presence;
Set your entreatments at a higher rate
Than a command to parley. For Lord Hamlet,
Believe so much in him, that he is young;
And with a larger tether may he walk
Than may be given you: in few, Ophelia,
Do not believe his vows; for they are brokers, —
Not of that dye which their investments show,
But mere implorators of unholy suits,
Breathing like sanctified and pious bawds,
The better to beguile. This is for all, —
I would not, in plain terms, from this time forth,
Have you so slander any moment leisure
As to give words or talk with the Lord Hamlet.
Look to't, I charge you: come your ways.

OPHELIA
I shall obey, my lord.   *[Exeunt*

SCENE IV

The platform before the castle.

Enter HAMLET, HORATIO, *and* MARCELLUS.

HAMLET
The air bites shrewdly; it is very cold.

HORATIO
It is a nipping and an eager air.

HAMLET
What hour now?

HORATIO
                    I think it lacks of twelve.

MARCELLUS
No, it is struck.

HORATIO
Indeed? I heard it not: then it draws near the season
Wherein the spirit held his wont to walk.
        [*A flourish of trumpets, and ordnance shot off, within.*
What does this mean, my lord?

HAMLET
The king doth wake to-night, and takes his rouse,
Keeps wassail, and the swaggering upspring reels;
And, as he drains his draughts of Rhenish down,
The kettle-drum and trumpet thus bray out
The triumph of his pledge.

HORATIO
                    Is it a custom?

HAMLET
Ay, marry, is't:
But to my mind, — though I am native here,
And to the manner born, — it is a custom
More honour'd in the breach than the observance.
This heavy-headed revel east and west
Makes us traduc'd and tax'd of other nations:
They clepe us drunkards, and with swinish phrase
Soil our addition; and, indeed, it takes
From our achievements, though perform'd at height,
The pith and marrow of our attribute.
So, oft it chances in particular men,
That, for some vicious mole of nature in them,
As, in their birth, — wherein they are not guilty,
Since nature cannot choose his origin, —
By the o'ergrowth of some complexion,
Oft breaking down the pales and forts of reason;
Or by some habit, that too much o'er-leavens
The form of plaus
ive manners; — that these men, —
Carrying, I say, the stamp of one defect,
Being nature's livery, or fortune's star, —
His virtues else — be they as pure as grace,
As infinite as man may undergo —
Shall in the general censure take corruption
From that particular fault: the dram of eale
Doth all the noble substance of adoubt
To his own scandal.

HORATIO
                    Look, my lord, it comes!
                    Enter GHOST.

HAMLET
Angels and ministers of grace defend us! —
Be thou a spirit of health or goblin damn'd,
Bring with thee airs from heaven or blasts from hell,
Be thy intents wicked or charitable,
Thou comest in such a questionable shape,
That I will speak to thee: I'll call thee Hamlet,
King, father, royal Dane: O, answer me!
Let me not burst in ignorance; but tell
Why thy canoniz'd bones, hearsed in death,
Have burst their cerements; why the sepulchre,
Wherein we saw thee quietly inurn'd,
Hath oped his ponderous and marble jaws
To cast thee up again! What may this mean,
That thou, dead corse, again, in complete steel,
Revisits thus the glimpses of the moon,
Making night hideous; and we fools of nature
So horridly to shake our disposition
With thoughts beyond the reaches of our souls?
Say, why is this? wherefore? what should we do?
                [GHOST *beckons* HAMLET.

HORATIO
It beckons you to go away with it,
As if it some impartment did desire
To you alone.

MARCELLUS
            Look, with what courteous action
It waves you to a more removed ground:
But do not go with it.

HORATIO
                    No, by no means.

HORATIO Then it draws near the season wherein the spirit held his wont to walk.

HAMLET
It will not speak; then I will follow it.

HORATIO
Do not, my lord.

HAMLET
                    Why, what should be the fear?
I do not set my life at a pin's fee;
And for my soul, what can it do to that,
Being a thing immortal as itself?
It waves me forth again; — I'll follow it.

HORATIO
What if it tempt you toward the flood, my lord,
Or to the dreadful summit of the cliff
That beetles o'er his base into the sea,
And there assume some other horrible form,
Which might deprive your sovereignty of reason,
And draw you into madness? think of it:
The very place puts toys of desperation,
Without more motive, into every brain,
That looks so many fathoms to the sea,
And hears it roar beneath.

HAMLET
                    It waves me still. —
Go on; I'll follow thee.

MARCELLUS
You shall not go, my lord.

HAMLET
                    Hold off your hands.

HORATIO
Be rul'd; you shall not go.

HAMLET
                    My fate cries out,
And makes each petty artery in this body
As hardy as the Nemean lion's nerve. —
Still am I call'd: — unhand me, gentlemen; —
By heaven, I'll make a ghost of him that lets me: —
I say, away! — Go on; I'll follow thee.
                [*Exeunt* GHOST *and* HAMLET.

HORATIO
He waxes desperate with imagination.

MARCELLUS
Let's follow; 'tis not fit thus to obey him.

HORATIO
Have after. — To what issue will this come?

MARCELLUS
Something is rotten in the state of Denmark.

HORATIO
Heaven will direct it.

MARCELLUS
                    Nay, let's follow him.   [*Exeunt.*

SCENE V

Another part of the platform.

Enter GHOST *and* HAMLET.

HAMLET
Where wilt thou lead me? speak; I'll go no further.

GHOST
Mark me.

HAMLET
        I will.

GHOST
                    My hour is almost come,

When I to sulphurous and tormenting flames
Must render up myself.

HAMLET
                    Alas, poor ghost!

GHOST
Pity me not, but lend thy serious hearing
To what I shall unfold.

HAMLET
                    Speak; I am bound to hear.

GHOST
So art thou to revenge, when thou shalt hear.

HAMLET
What?

GHOST
I am thy father's spirit;
Doom'd for a certain term to walk the night,
And for the day confin'd to fast in fires,
Till the foul crimes done in my days of nature
Are burnt and purg'd away. But that I am forbid
To tell the secrets of my prison-house,
I could a tale unfold, whose lightest word
Would harrow up thy soul; freeze thy young blood;
Make thy two eyes, like stars, start from their spheres;
Thy knotted and combined locks to part,
And each particular hair to stand on end,
Like quills upon the fretful porpentine:
But this eternal blazon must not be
To ears of flesh and blood. — List, list, O, list! —
If thou didst ever thy dear father love, —

HAMLET
O God!

GHOST
Revenge his foul and most unnatural murder.

HAMLET
Murder!

GHOST
Murder most foul, as in the best it is;
But this most foul, strange, and unnatural.

HAMLET
Haste me to know't, that I, with wings as swift
As meditation or the thoughts of love,
May sweep to my revenge.

GHOST
                    I find thee apt;
And duller shouldst thou be than the fat weed
That roots itself in ease on Lethe wharf,
Wouldst thou not stir in this. Now, Hamlet, hear:
'Tis given out that, sleeping in my orchard,
A serpent stung me; so the whole ear of Denmark
Is by a forged process of my death
Rankly abus'd: but know, thou noble youth,
The serpent that did sting thy father's life
Now wears his crown.

HAMLET
                    O my prophetic soul!
My uncle!

GHOST
Ay, that incestuous, that adulterate beast,
With witchcraft of his wit, with traitorous gifts, —
O wicked wit and gifts, that have the power
So to seduce! — won to his shameful lust
The will of my most seeming-virtuous queen:
O, Hamlet, what a falling-off was there!

From me, whose love was of that dignity,
That it went hand in hand even with the vow
I made to her in marriage; and to decline
Upon a wretch, whose natural gifts were poor
To those of mine!
But virtue, as it never will be moved,
Though lewdness court it in a shape of heaven;
So lust, though to a radiant angel link'd,
Will sate itself in a celestial bed,
And prey on garbage.
But, soft! methinks I scent the morning air;
Brief let me be. — Sleeping within my orchard,
My custom always in the afternoon,
Upon my secure hour thy uncle stole,
With juice of cursed hebenon in a vial,
And in the porches of mine ears did pour
The leperous distilment; whose effect
Holds such an enmity with blood of man,
That, swift as quicksilver, it courses through
The natural gates and alleys of the body;
And, with a sudden vigour, it doth posset
And curd, like eager droppings into milk,
The thin and wholesome blood: so did it mine;
And a most instant tetter bark'd about,
Most lazar-like, with vile and loathsome crust
All my smooth body.
Thus was I, sleeping, by a brother's hand
Of life, of crown, of queen, at once dispatch'd:
Cut off even in the blossoms of my sin,
Unhousell'd, disappointed, unaneled;
No reckoning made, but sent to my account
With all my imperfections on my head:
O, horrible! O, horrible! most horrible!
If thou hast nature in thee, bear it not;
Let not the royal bed of Denmark be
A couch for luxury and damn'd incest.
But, howsoever thou pursuest this act,
Taint not thy mind, nor let thy soul contrive
Against thy mother aught: leave her to heaven,
And to those thorns that in her bosom lodge
To prick and sting her. Fare thee well at once!
The glow-worm shows the matin to be near,
And 'gins to pale his uneffectual fire:
Adieu, adieu, adieu! remember me.   [Exit.

HAMLET
O all you host of heaven! O earth! what else?
And shall I couple hell? — O, fie! — Hold, hold, my
    heart;
And you, my sinews, grow not instant old,
But bear me stiffly up. — Remember thee!
Ay, thou poor ghost, while memory holds a seat
In this distracted globe. Remember thee!
Yea, from the table of my memory
I'll wipe away all trivial fond records,
All saws of books, all forms, all pressures past,
That youth and observation copied there;
And thy commandment all alone shall live
Within the book and volume of my brain,
Unmix'd with baser matter: yes, by heaven! —
O most pernicious woman!
O villain, villain, smiling, damned villain!
My tables, — meet it is I set it down,
That one may smile, and smile, and be a villain;
At least I'm sure it may be so in Denmark: [Writing.
So, uncle, there you are. Now to my word;
It is, 'Adieu, adieu! remember me':
I have sworn't.

HORATIO [within].
My lord, my lord, —
MARCELLUS [within].
                    Lord Hamlet, —
HORATIO [within].
                              Heaven secure him!
HAMLET
So be it!
HORATIO [within].
Illo, ho, ho, my lord!
HAMLET
Hillo, ho, ho, boy! come, bird, come.

Enter HORATIO *and* MARCELLUS.

MARCELLUS
How is't, my noble lord?
HORATIO
                    What news, my lord?
HAMLET
O, wonderful!
HORATIO
Good my lord, tell it.
HAMLET
                    No; you will reveal it.

HORATIO
Not I, my lord, by heaven.
MARCELLUS
                    Nor I, my lord.
HAMLET
How say you, then; would heart of man once think it?
But you'll be secret?
HORATIO and MARCELLUS
                    Ay, by heaven, my lord.
HAMLET
There's ne'er a villain dwelling in all Denmark
But he's an arrant knave.
HORATIO
There needs no ghost, my lord, come from the grave
To tell us this.
HAMLET
                    Why, right; you are i'th'right;
And so, without more circumstance at all,
I hold it fit that we shake hands and part:
You, as your business and desire shall point you, —
For every man hath business and desire,
Such as it is; — and for mine own poor part,
Look you, I'll go pray.
HORATIO
These are but wild and whirling words, my lord.
HAMLET
I'm sorry they offend you, heartily;
Yes, faith, heartily.
HORATIO
                    There's no offence, my lord.
HAMLET
Yes, by Saint Patrick, but there is, Horatio,
And much offence too. Touching this vision here, —
It is an honest ghost, that let me tell you:
For your desire to know what is between us,
O'ermaster't as you may. And now, good friends,
As you are friends, scholars, and soldiers,
Give me one poor request.
HORATIO
What is't, my lord? we will.
HAMLET
Never make known what you have seen to-night.
HORATIO and MARCELLUS
My lord, we will not.
HAMLET
                    Nay, but swear't.
HORATIO
                              In faith,
My lord, not I.
MARCELLUS
                    Nor I, my lord, in faith.
HAMLET
Upon my sword.
MARCELLUS
                    We have sworn, my lord, already.
HAMLET
Indeed, upon my sword, indeed.
GHOST [cries under the stage].
Swear.
HAMLET
Ah, ha, boy! say'st thou so? art thou there, truepenny?
Come on, — you hear this fellow in the cellarage, —
Consent to swear.
HORATIO
                    Propose the oath, my lord.
HAMLET
Never to speak of this that you have seen,
Swear by my sword.
GHOST [beneath].
Swear.
HAMLET
Hic et ubique? then we'll shift our ground. —
Come hither, gentlemen,
And lay your hands again upon my sword:
Never to speak of this that you have heard,
Swear by my sword.
GHOST [beneath].
Swear.
HAMLET
Well said, old mole! canst work i'th'earth so fast?
A worthy pioneer! — Once more remove, good friends.
HORATIO
O day and night, but this is wondrous strange!
HAMLET
And therefore as a stranger give it welcome.
There are more things in heaven and earth, Horatio,
Than are dreamt of in your philosophy.
But come; —

Here, as before, never, so help you mercy, —
How strange or odd soe'er I bear myself, —
As I, perchance, hereafter shall think meet
To put an antic disposition on, —
That you, at such times seeing me, never shall,
With arms encumber'd thus, or this head-shake,
Or by pronouncing of some doubtful phrase,
As 'Well, well, we know,' or 'We could, an if we would,'
Or 'If we list to speak,' or 'There be, an if they might,'
Or such ambiguous giving out, to note
That you know aught of me: — this not to do,
So grace and mercy at your most need help you,
Swear.
GHOST [beneath].
Swear.
HAMLET
Rest, rest, perturbed spirit! — So, gentlemen,
With all my love I do commend me to you:
And what so poor a man as Hamlet is
May do t'express his love and friending to you,
God willing, shall not lack. Let us go in together;
And still your fingers on your lips, I pray.
The time is out of joint: — O cursed spite,
That ever I was born to set it right! —
Nay, come, let's go together.   [Exeunt.

ACT II

SCENE I

Elsinore. A room in POLONIUS' *house.*

Enter POLONIUS *and* REYNALDO.

POLONIUS
Give him this money and these notes, Reynaldo.
REYNALDO
I will, my lord.
POLONIUS
You shall do marvellous wisely, good Reynaldo,
Before you visit him, to make inquiry
Of his behaviour.
REYNALDO
                    My lord, I did intend it.
POLONIUS
Marry, well said; very well said. Look you, sir,
Inquire me first what Danskers are in Paris;
And how, and who, what means, and where they keep,
What company, at what expense; and finding,
By this encompassment and drift of question,
That they do know my son, come you more nearer
Than your particular demands will touch it:
Take you, as 'twere, some distant knowledge of him;
As thus, 'I know his father and his friends,
And in part him'; — do you mark this, Reynaldo?
REYNALDO
Ay, very well, my lord.
POLONIUS
'And in part him; — but,' you may say, 'not well:
But, if't be he I mean, he's very wild;
Addicted so and so'; — and there put on him
What forgeries you please; marry, none so rank
As may dishonour him; take heed of that;
But, sir, such wanton, wild, and usual slips
As are companions noted and most known
To youth and liberty.
REYNALDO
                    As gaming, my lord.
POLONIUS
Ay, or drinking, fencing, swearing,
Quarrelling, drabbing: — you may go so far.
REYNALDO
My lord, that would dishonour him.
POLONIUS
Faith, no; as you may season it in the charge.
You must not put another scandal on him,
That he is open to incontinency;
That's not my meaning: but breathe his faults so
    quaintly,
That they may seem the taints of liberty;
The flash and outbreak of a fiery mind;
A savageness in unreclaimed blood,
Of general assault.
REYNALDO
                    But, my good lord, —
POLONIUS
Wherefore should you do this?
REYNALDO
                              Ay, my lord,
I would know that.

POLONIUS

       Marry, sir, here's my drift;
And, I believe, it is a fetch of warrant:
You laying these slight sullies on my son,
As 'twere a thing a little soil'd i'th'working,
Mark you,
Your party in converse, him you would sound,
Having ever seen in the prenominate crimes
The youth you breathe of guilty, be assured
He closes with you in this consequence;
'Good sir,' or so; or 'friend,' or 'gentleman,' —
According to the phrase, or the addition,
Of man and country.

REYNALDO

       Very good, my lord.

POLONIUS

And then, sir, does he this, — he does — What was I
about to say? — By the mass, I was about to say
something: — where did I leave?

REYNALDO

At 'closes in the consequence,' at 'friend or so,' and
'gentleman.'

POLONIUS

At 'closes in the consequence,' — ay, marry;
He closes with you thus: 'I know the gentleman;
I saw him yesterday, or t'other day,
Or then, or then; with such, or such; and, as you say,
There was a' gaming; there o'ertook in's rouse;
There falling out at tennis': or perchance,
I saw him enter such a house of sale,' —
Videlicet, a brothel, — or so forth. —
See you now;
Your bait of falsehood takes this carp of truth:
And thus do we of wisdom and of reach,
With windlasses and with assays of bias,
By indirections find directions out:
So, by my former lecture and advice,
Shall you my son. You have me, have you not?

REYNALDO

My lord, I have.

POLONIUS

       God be wi' ye! fare ye well.

REYNALDO

Good my lord!

POLONIUS

Observe his inclination in yourself.

REYNALDO

I shall, my lord.

POLONIUS

And let him ply his music.

REYNALDO

       Well, my lord.

POLONIUS

Farewell!

           [*Exit* REYNALDO.
      Enter OPHELIA.

      How now, Ophelia! what's the matter?

OPHELIA

O, my lord, my lord, I have been so affrighted!

POLONIUS

With what, i'th'name of God?

OPHELIA

My lord, as I was sewing in my chamber,
Lord Hamlet, — with his doublet all unbraced;
No hat upon his head; his stockings foul'd,
Ungarter'd, and down-gyved to his ancle;
Pale as his shirt; his knees knocking each other;
And with a look so piteous in purport
As if he had been loosed out of hell
To speak of horrors, — he comes before me.

POLONIUS

Mad for thy love?

OPHELIA

      My lord, I do not know;
But, truly, I do fear it.

POLONIUS

       What said he?

OPHELIA

He took me by the wrist, and held me hard;
Then goes he to the length of all his arm;
And, with his other hand thus o'er his brow,
He falls to such perusal of my face
As he would draw it. Long stayed he so;
At last, — a little shaking of mine arm,
And thrice his head thus waving up and down, —
He rais'd a sigh so piteous and profound,
That it did seem to shatter all his bulk,
And end his being: that done, he lets me go:
And, with his head over his shoulder turn'd,
He seem'd to find his way without his eyes;

For out o' doors he went without their help,
And, to the last, bended their light on me.

POLONIUS

Come, go with me: I will go seek the king.
This is the very ecstasy of love;
Whose violent property fordoes itself,
And leads the will to desperate undertakings,
As oft as any passion under heaven
That does afflict our natures. I am sorry, —
What, have you given him any hard words of late?

OPHELIA

No, my good lord; but, as you did command,
I did repel his letters, and denied
His access to me.

POLONIUS

       That hath made him mad. —
I am sorry that with better heed and judgement
I had not quoted him: I fear'd he did but trifle,
And meant to wrack thee; but, beshrew my jealousy!
It seems is as proper to our age
To cast beyond ourselves in our opinions,
As it is common for the younger sort
To lack discretion. Come, go we to the king:
This must be known; which, being kept close, might
    move
More grief to hide than hate to utter love.
Come.
                [*Exeunt.*

SCENE II

A room in the castle.

Enter KING, QUEEN, ROSENCRANTZ,
GUILDENSTERN, *and* ATTENDANTS.

KING

Welcome, dear Rosencrantz and Guildenstern!
Moreover that we much did long to see you,
The need we have to use you did provoke
Our hasty sending. Something have you heard
Of Hamlet's transformation; so call it,
Since nor th'exterior nor the inward man
Resembles that it was. What it should be,
More than his father's death, that thus hath put him
So much from th'understanding of himself,
I cannot dream of: I entreat you both,
That, being of so young days brought up with him,
And sith so neighbour'd to his youth and haviour,
That you vouchsafe your rest here in our court
Some little time: so by your companies
To draw him on to pleasures, and to gather,
So much as from occasion you may glean,
Whether aught, to us unknown, afflicts him thus,
That, open'd, lies within our remedy.

QUEEN

Good gentlemen, he hath much talk'd of you;
And sure I am two men there are not living
To whom he more adheres. If it will please you
To show us so much gentry and good will
As to expend your time with us awhile,
For the supply and profit of our hope,
Your visitation shall receive such thanks
As fits a king's remembrance.

ROSENCRANTZ

          Both your majesties
Might, by the sovereign power you have of us,
Put your dread pleasures more into command
Than to entreaty.

GUILDENSTERN

       But we both obey,
And here give up ourselves, in the full bent,
To lay our service freely at your feet,
To be commanded.

KING

Thanks, Rosencrantz and gentle Guildenstern.

QUEEN

Thanks, Guildenstern and gentle Rosencrantz:
And I beseech you instantly to visit
My too-much-changed son. — Go, some of you,
And bring these gentlemen where Hamlet is.

GUILDENSTERN

Heavens make our presence and our practices
Pleasant and helpful to him!

QUEEN

       Ay, amen!
[*Exeunt* ROSENCRANTZ, GUILDENSTERN, *and some*
                ATTENDANTS.

Enter POLONIUS.

POLONIUS

Th'ambassadors from Norway, my good lord,
Are joyfully return'd.

KING

Thou still hast been the father of good news.

POLONIUS

Have I, my lord? Assure you, my good liege,
I hold my duty, as I hold my soul,
Both to my God and to my gracious king:
And I do think — or else this brain of mine
Hunts not the trail of policy so sure
As it hath us'd to do — that I have found
The very cause of Hamlet's lunacy.

KING

O, speak of that; that do I long to hear.

POLONIUS

Give first admittance to th'ambassadors;
My news shall be the fruit to that great feast.

KING

Thyself do grace to them, and bring them in.
             [*Exit* POLONIUS.
He tells me, my dear Gertrude, he hath found
The head and source of all your son's distemper.

QUEEN

I doubt it is no other but the main, —
His father's death, and our o'erhasty marriage.

KING

Well, we shall sift him.

     Enter POLONIUS, *with* VOLTIMAND
         and CORNELIUS.

       Welcome, my good friends!
Say, Voltimand, what from our brother Norway?

VOLTIMAND

Most fair return of greetings and desires.
Upon our first, he sent out to suppress
His nephew's levies; which to him appear'd
To be a preparation 'gainst the Polack;
But, better look'd into, he truly found
It was against your highness: whereat grieved, —
That so his sickness, age, and impotence,
Was falsely borne in hand, — sends out arrests
On Fortinbras; which he, in brief, obeys;
Receives rebuke from Norway; and, in fine,
Makes vow before his uncle never more
To give th'assay of arms against your majesty.
Whereon old Norway, overcome with joy,
Gives him three thousand crowns in annual fee;
And his commission to employ these soldiers,
So levied as before, against the Polack:
With an entreaty, herein further shown, [*Gives a paper.*
That it might please you to give quiet pass
Through your dominions for this enterprise,
On such regards of safety and allowance
As therein are set down.

KING

       It likes us well;
And at our more consider'd time we'll read,
Answer, and think upon this business.
Meantime we thank you for your well-took labour:
Go to your rest; at night we'll feast together:
Most welcome home!
      [*Exeunt* VOLTIMAND *and* CORNELIUS.

POLONIUS

      This business is well ended. —
My liege, and madam, — to expostulate
What majesty should be, what duty is,
Why day is day, night night, and time is time,
Were nothing but to waste night, day, and time.
Therefore, since brevity is the soul of wit,
And tediousness the limbs and outward flourishes,
I will be brief: — your noble son is mad:
Mad call I it; for, to define true madness,
What is't but to be nothing else but mad?
But let that go.

QUEEN

      More matter, with less art.

POLONIUS

Madam, I swear I use no art at all.
That he is mad, 'tis true: 'tis true, 'tis pity,
And pity 'tis 'tis true: a foolish figure;
But farewell it, for I will use no art.
Mad let us grant him, then: and now remains
That we find out the cause of this effect, —
Or rather say, the cause of this defect,
For this effect defective comes by cause:
Thus it remains, and the remainder thus.
Perpend.
I have a daughter, — have whilst she is mine, —
Who, in her duty and obedience, mark,
Hath given me this: now gather, and surmise. [*Reads.*
'To the celestial and my soul's idol, the most beautified
  Ophelia,' —
That's an ill phrase, a vile phrase, — 'beautified' is

a vile phrase: but you shall hear. Thus: [*Reads.*
'In her excellent white bosom,' these, etc. —

QUEEN
Came this from Hamlet to her?

POLONIUS
Good madam, stay awhile; I will be faithful.   [*Reads.*
    Doubt thou the stars are fire;
      Doubt that the sun doth move;
      Doubt truth to be a liar;
      But never doubt I love.
  O dear Ophelia, I am ill at these numbers; I have not
art to reckon my groans: but that I love thee best, O
most best, believe it. Adieu.
    Thine evermore, most dear lady, whilst
      this machine is to him,   HAMLET.
This, in obedience, hath my daughter shown me:
And more above, hath his solicitings,
As they fell out by time, by means, and place,
All given to mine ear.

KING
              But how hath she
Receiv'd his love?

POLONIUS
              What do you think of me?

KING
As of a man faithful and honourable.

POLONIUS
I would fain prove so. But what might you think,
When I had seen this hot love on the wing, —
As I perceiv'd it, I must tell you that, —
Before my daughter told me, — what might you,
Or my dear majesty your queen here, think,
If I had play'd the desk or table-book;
Or given my heart a winking, mute and dumb;
Or look'd upon this love with idle sight; —
What might you think? No, I went round to work,
And my young mistress thus I did bespeak:
'Lord Hamlet is a prince, out of thy star;
This must not be': and then I prescripts gave her,
That she should lock herself from his resort,
Admit no messengers, receive no tokens.
Which done, she took the fruits of my advice;
And he, repulsed, — a short tale to make, —
Fell into a sadness; then into a fast;
Thence to a watch; thence into a weakness;
Thence to a lightness; and, by this declension,
Into the madness wherein now he raves,
And all we mourn for.

KING
              Do you think 'tis this?

QUEEN
It may be, very like.

POLONIUS
Hath there been such a time — I'ld fain know that —
That I have positively said ''Tis so,'
When it prov'd otherwise?

KING
              Not that I know.

POLONIUS [*pointing to his head and shoulder*].
Take this from this, if this be otherwise:
If circumstances lead me, I will find
Where truth is hid, though it were hid indeed
Within the centre.

KING
              How may we try it further?

POLONIUS
You know, sometimes he walks four hours together
Here in the lobby.

QUEEN
              So he does indeed.

POLONIUS
At such a time I'll loose my daughter to him:
Be you and I behind an arras then;
Mark the encounter: if he love her not,
And be not from his reason fall'n thereon,
Let me be no assistant for a state,
But keep a farm and carters.

KING
              We will try it.

QUEEN
But, look, where sadly the poor wretch comes reading.

POLONIUS
Away, I do beseech you, both away:
I'll board him presently: — O, give me leave.

      [*Exeunt* KING, QUEEN, *and* ATTENDANTS.
      Enter HAMLET, *reading on a book.*

How does my good Lord Hamlet?

HAMLET
Well, God-a-mercy.

POLONIUS
Do you know me, my lord?

HAMLET
Excellent well; you are a fishmonger.

POLONIUS
Not I, my lord.

HAMLET
Then I would you were so honest a man.

POLONIUS
Honest, my lord!

HAMLET
Ay, sir; to be honest, as this world goes, is to
be one man pick'd out of ten thousand.

POLONIUS
That's very true, my lord.

HAMLET
For if the sun breed maggots in a dead dog,
being a god kissing carrion, — Have you a
daughter?

POLONIUS
I have, my lord.

HAMLET
Let her not walk i'th'sun: conception is a
blessing; but not as your daughter may
conceive: — friend, look to't.

POLONIUS [*aside*].
How say you by that? Still harping on my
daughter: — yet he knew me not at first; he
said I was a fishmonger: he is far gone, far
gone: and truly in my youth I suffer'd
much extremity for love; very near this. I'll
speak to him again. — What do you read,
my lord?

HAMLET
Words, words, words.

POLONIUS
What is the matter, my lord?

HAMLET
Between who?

POLONIUS
I mean, the matter that you read, my lord.

HAMLET
Slanders, sir: for the satirical rogue says here, that old
men have grey beards; that their faces are wrinkled;
their eyes purging thick amber and plum-tree gum;
and that they have a plentiful lack of wit, together with
most weak hams: all which, sir, though I most
powerfully and potently believe, yet I hold it not
honesty to have it thus set down; for yourself, sir, shall
grow old as I am, if, like a crab, you could go backward.

POLONIUS [*aside*].
Though this be madness, yet there is method in't. —
Will you walk out of the air, my lord?

HAMLET
Into my grave?

POLONIUS
Indeed, that is out o'th'air. — [*aside*] How pregnant
sometimes his replies are! a happiness that often
madness hits on, which reason and sanity could not so
prosperously be deliver'd of. I will leave him, and
suddenly contrive the means of meeting between him
and my daughter. — My honourable lord, I will most
humbly take my leave of you.

HAMLET
You cannot, sir, take from me any thing that I will more
willingly part withal, — except my life, except my life,
except my life.

POLONIUS
Fare you well, my lord.

HAMLET
These tedious old fools!

      Enter ROSENCRANTZ *and* GUILDENSTERN.

POLONIUS
You go to seek the Lord Hamlet; there he is.

ROSENCRANTZ [*to* POLONIUS].
God save you, sir!   [*Exit* POLONIUS.

GUILDENSTERN
My honour'd lord!

ROSENCRANTZ
My most dear lord!

HAMLET
My excellent good friends! How dost thou, Guildenstern?
Ah, Rosencrantz! Good lads, how do ye both?

ROSENCRANTZ
As the indifferent children of the earth.

GUILDENSTERN
Happy, in that we are not overhappy;
On Fortune's cap we are not the very button.

HAMLET For if the sun breed maggots in
     a dead dog.

HAMLET
Nor the soles of her shoe?

ROSENCRANTZ
Neither, my lord.

HAMLET
Then you live about her waist, or in the middle of her
favours?

GUILDENSTERN
Faith, her privates we.

HAMLET
In the secret parts of Fortune? O, most true; she is a
strumpet. What's the news?

ROSENCRANTZ
None, my lord, but that the world's grown honest.

HAMLET
Then is doomsday near: but your news is not true. Let
me question more in particular: what have you, my
good friends, deserved at the hands of Fortune, that
she sends you to prison hither?

GUILDENSTERN
Prison, my lord!

HAMLET
Denmark's a prison.

ROSENCRANTZ
Then is the world one.

HAMLET
A goodly one; in which there are many confines, wards,
and dungeons, Denmark being one o'th'worst.

ROSENCRANTZ
We think not so, my lord.

HAMLET
Why, then, 'tis none to you: for there is nothing either
good or bad, but thinking makes it so: to me it is a
prison.

ROSENCRANTZ
Why, then, your ambition makes it one; 'tis too narrow
for your mind.

HAMLET
O God, I could be bounded in a nut-shell, and count
myself a king of infinite space, were it not that I have
bad dreams.

GUILDENSTERN
Which dreams indeed, are ambition; for the very
substance of the ambitious is merely the shadow of a
dream.

HAMLET
A dream itself is but a shadow.

ROSENCRANTZ
Truly, and I hold ambition of so airy and light a quality that it is but a shadow's shadow.

HAMLET
Then are our beggars bodies, and our monarchs and outstretch'd heroes the beggars' shadows. Shall we to th'court? for, by my fay, I cannot reason.

ROSENCRANTZ *and* **GUILDENSTERN**
We'll wait upon you.

HAMLET
No such matter: I will not sort you with the rest of my servants; for, to speak to you like an honest man, I am most dreadfully attended. But, in the beaten way of friendship, what make you at Elsinore?

ROSENCRANTZ
To visit you, my lord; no other occasion.

HAMLET
Beggar that I am, I am even poor in thanks; but I thank you: and sure, dear friends, my thanks are too dear a halfpenny. Were you not sent for? Is it your own inclining? Is it a free visitation? Come, deal justly with me: come, come; nay, speak.

GUILDENSTERN
What should we say, my lord?

HAMLET
Why, any thing — but to the purpose. You were sent for; and there is a kind of confession in your looks which your modesties have not craft enough to colour: I know the good king and queen have sent for you.

ROSENCRANTZ
To what end, my lord?

HAMLET
That you must teach me. But let me conjure you, by the rights of our fellowship, by the consonancy of our youth, by the obligation of our ever-preserved love, and by what more dear a better proposer could charge you withal, be even and direct with me, whether you were sent for, or no.

ROSENCRANTZ [*aside to* GUILDENSTERN].
What say you?

HAMLET [*aside*].
Nay, then, I have an eye of you. — If you love me, hold not off.

GUILDENSTERN
My lord, we were sent for.

HAMLET
I will tell you why; so shall my anticipation prevent your discovery, and your secrecy to the king and queen moult no feather. I have of late — but wherefore I know not — lost all my mirth, forgone all custom of exercises; and, indeed, it goes so heavily with my disposition that this goodly frame, the earth, seems to me a sterile promontory; this most excellent canopy, the air, look you, this brave o'erhanging firmament, this majestical roof fretted with golden fire, — why, it appears no other thing to me than a foul and pestilent congregation of vapours. What a piece of work is a man! how noble in reason! how infinite in faculty! in form and moving how express and admirable! in action how like an angel! in apprehension how like a god! the beauty of the world! the paragon of animals! And yet, to me, what is this quintessence of dust? man delights not me: no, nor woman neither, though by your smiling you seem to say so.

ROSENCRANTZ
My lord, there was no such stuff in my thoughts.

HAMLET
Why did you laugh, then, when I said 'man delights not me'?

ROSENCRANTZ
To think, my lord, if you delight not in man, what lenten entertainment the players shall receive from you: we coted them on the way; and hither are they coming, to offer you service.

HAMLET
He that plays the king shall be welcome, — his majesty shall have tribute of me; the adventurous knight shall use his foil and target; the lover shall not sigh gratis; the humorous man shall end his part in peace; the clown shall make those laugh whose lungs are tickled o'th'sere; and the lady shall say her mind freely, or the blank verse shall halt for't. — What players are they?

ROSENCRANTZ
Even those you were wont to take delight in, the tragedians of the city.

HAMLET
How chances it they travel? their residence, both in reputation and profit, was better both ways.

ROSENCRANTZ
I think their inhibition comes by the means of the late innovation.

HAMLET
Do they hold the same estimation they did when I was in the city? are they so follow'd?

ROSENCRANTZ
No, indeed, they are not.

HAMLET
How comes it? do they grow rusty?

ROSENCRANTZ
Nay, their endeavour keeps in the wonted pace: but there is, sir, an aery of children, little eyases, that cry out on the top of question, and are most tyrannically clapp'd for't: these are now the fashion, and so berattle the common stages, — so they call them, — that many wearing rapiers are afraid of goose-quills, and dare scarce come thither.

HAMLET
What, are they children? who maintains 'em? how are they escoted? Will they pursue the quality no longer than they can sing? will they not say afterwards, if they should grow themselves to common players, — as it is most like, if their means are no better, — their writers do them wrong, to make them exclaim against their own succession?

ROSENCRANTZ
Faith, there has been much to do on both sides; and the nation holds it no sin to tarre them to controversy; there was, for a while, no money bid for argument, unless the poet and the player went to cuffs in the question.

HAMLET
Is't possible?

GUILDENSTERN
O, there has been much throwing about of brains.

HAMLET
Do the boys carry it away?

ROSENCRANTZ
Ay, that they do, my lord; Hercules and his load too.

HAMLET
It is not very strange; for my uncle is king of Denmark, and those that would make mows at him while my father lived, give twenty, forty, fifty, an hundred ducats a-piece for his picture in little. 'Sblood, there is something in this more than natural, if philosophy could find it out. [*Flourish of trumpets within.*]

GUILDENSTERN
There are the players.

HAMLET
Gentlemen, you are welcome to Elsinore. Your hands, come: the appurtenance of welcome is fashion and ceremony: let me comply with you in this garb; lest my extent to the players, which, I tell you, must show fairly outward, should more appear like entertainment than yours. You are welcome: but my uncle-father and aunt-mother are deceived.

GUILDENSTERN
In what, my dear lord?

HAMLET
I am but mad north-nort-west: when the wind is southerly I know a hawk from a handsaw.

Enter POLONIUS.

POLONIUS
Well be with you, gentlemen!

HAMLET
Hark you, Guildenstern; — and you too; — at each ear a hearer: that great baby you see there is not yet out of his swaddling-clouts.

ROSENCRANTZ
Happily he's the second time come to them; for they say an old man is twice a child.

HAMLET
I will prophesy he comes to tell me of the players; mark it. — You say right, sir: o' Monday morning; 'twas then, indeed.

POLONIUS
My lord, I have news to tell you.

HAMLET
My lord, I have news to tell you. When Roscius was an actor in Rome, —

HAMLET There is a kind of confession in your looks: I know the good king and queen have sent for you.

POLONIUS
The actors are come hither, my lord.

HAMLET
Buz, buz!

POLONIUS
Upon mine honour, —

HAMLET
Then came each actor on his ass, —

POLONIUS
The best actors in the world, either for tragedy, comedy, history, pastoral, pastoral-comical, historical-pastoral, tragical-historical, tragical-comical-historical-pastoral, scene individable, or poem unlimited: Seneca cannot be too heavy, nor Plautus too light. For the law of writ and the liberty, these are the only men.

HAMLET
O Jephthah, judge of Israel, what a treasure hadst thou!

POLONIUS
What a treasure had he, my lord?

HAMLET
Why,
　　'One fair daughter, and no more,
　　　　The which he loved passing well.'

POLONIUS [*aside*].
Still on my daughter.

HAMLET
Am I not i'th'right, old Jephthah?

POLONIUS
If you call me Jephthah, my lord, I have a daughter that I love passing well.

HAMLET
Nay, that follows not.

POLONIUS
What follows, then, my lord?

HAMLET
Why,
　　'As by lot, God wot,'
and then, you know,
　　'It came to pass, as most like it was,' —
the first row of the pious chanson will show you more; for look, where my abridgement comes.
　　Enter four or five PLAYERS.
You are welcome, masters; welcome, all; I am glad to see thee well; welcome, good friends. — O, my old friend! Why, thy face is valenced since I saw thee last; comest thou to beard me in Denmark? — What, my young lady and mistress! By'r lady, your ladyship is nearer to heaven than when I saw you last by the altitude of a chopine. Pray God, your voice, like a piece of uncurrent gold, be not crack'd within the ring. — Masters, you are all welcome. We'll e'en to't like French falconers, fly at any thing we see: we'll have a speech straight: come, give us a taste of your quality; come: a passionate speech.

FIRST PLAYER
What speech, my good lord?

HAMLET
I heard thee speak me a speech once, — but it was never acted; or, if it was, not above once; for the play, I remember, pleased not the million; 'twas caviare to the general: but it was — as I received it, and others, whose judgements in such matters cried in the top of mine —

an excellent play, well digested in the scenes, set down with as much modesty as cunning. I remember, one said there were no sallets in the lines to make the matter savoury, nor no matter in the phrase that might indict the author of affection: but call'd it an honest method, as wholesome as sweet, and by very much more handsome than fine. One speech in it I chiefly loved: 'twas Aeneas' tale to Dido; and thereabout of it especially, where he speaks of Priam's slaughter: if it live in your memory, begin at this line; — let me see, let me see;

'The rugged Pyrrhus, like th'Hyrcanian beast,' — 'tis not so: — it begins with Pyrrhus;

'The rugged Pyrrhus, — he whose sable arms,
Black as his purpose, did the night resemble
When he lay couched in the ominous horse, —
Hath now this dread and black complexion smear'd
With heraldry more dismal; head to foot
Now is he total gules; horridly trick'd
With blood of fathers, mothers, daughters, sons,
Bak'd and impasted with the parching streets,
That lend a tyrannous and damned light
To their vile murder: roasted in wrath and fire,
And thus o'er-sized with coagulate gore,
With eyes like carbuncles, the hellish Pyrrhus
Old grandsire Priam seeks.' —

So, proceed you.

POLONIUS
'Fore God, my lord, well spoken, with good accent and good discretion.

FIRST PLAYER
                         'Anon he finds him
Striking too short at Greeks; his antique sword,
Rebellious to his arm, lies where it falls,
Repugnant to command: unequal match'd,
Pyrrhus at Priam drives; in rage strikes wide;
But with the whiff and wind of his fell sword
Th'unnerved father falls. Then senseless Ilium,
Seeming to feel this blow, with flaming top
Stoops to his base; and with a hideous crash
Takes prisoner Pyrrhus' ear: for, lo! his sword,
Which was declining on the milky head
Of reverend Priam, seem'd i'th'air to stick:
So, as a painted tyrant, Pyrrhus stood;
And, like a neutral to his will and matter,
Did nothing.
But, as we often see, against some storm,
A silence in the heavens, the rack stand still,
The bold winds speechless, and the orb below
As hush as death, anon the dreadful thunder
Doth rend the region; so, after Pyrrhus' pause,
Aroused vengeance sets him new a-work;
And never did the Cyclops' hammers fall
On Mars his armour, forg'd for proof eterne,
With less remorse than Pyrrhus' bleeding sword
Now falls on Priam. —
Out, out, thou strumpet, Fortune! All you gods,
In general synod, take away her power;
Break all the spokes and fellies from her wheel,
And bowl the round nave down the hill of heaven,
As low as to the fiends!'

POLONIUS
This is too long.

HAMLET
It shall to th'barber's, with your beard. — Prithee, say on: — he's for a jig or a tale of bawdry, or he sleeps: — say on: come to Hecuba.

FIRST PLAYER
       'But who, O, who had seen the mobled queen — '

HAMLET
'The mobled queen?'

POLONIUS
That's good, 'mobled queen' is good.

FIRST PLAYER
       'Run barefoot up and down, threat'ning the flames
With bisson rheum; a clout upon that head
Where late the diadem stood; and for a robe,
About her lank and all o'er-teemed loins,
A blanket, in th'alarm of fear caught up; —
Who this had seen, with tongue in venom steep'd,
'Gainst Fortune's state would treason have pronounced:
But if the gods themselves did see her then,
When she saw Pyrrhus make malicious sport
In mincing with his sword her husband's limbs,
The instant burst of clamour that she made —
Unless things mortal move them not at all —
Would have made milch the burning

eyes of heaven,
       And passion in the gods.'

POLONIUS
Look, whe'r he has not turn'd his colour, and has tears in's eyes. — Pray you, no more.

HAMLET
'Tis well; I'll have thee speak out the rest soon. — Good my lord, will you see the players well bestow'd? Do you hear, let them be well used; for they are the abstract and brief chronicles of the time: after your death you were better have a bad epitaph than their ill report while you live.

POLONIUS
My lord, I will use them according to their desert.

HAMLET
God's bodykins, man, better: use every man after his desert, and who should scape whipping? Use them after your own honour and dignity: the less they deserve, the more merit is in your bounty. Take them in.

POLONIUS
Come, sirs.

HAMLET
Follow him, friends: we'll hear a play to-morrow. [*Exit* POLONIUS *with all the* PLAYERS *but the First.*] Dost thou hear me, old friend; can you play the Murder of Gonzago?

FIRST PLAYER
Ay, my lord.

HAMLET
We'll ha't to-morrow night. You could, for a need, study a speech of some dozen or sixteen lines, which I would set down and insert in't, could you not?

FIRST PLAYER
Ay, my lord.

HAMLET
Very well. — Follow that lord; and look you mock him not. [*Exit* FIRST PLAYER.] My good friends, I'll leave you till night: you are welcome to Elsinore.

ROSENCRANTZ
Good my lord!

HAMLET
Ay, so, God be wi' ye! [*Exeunt* ROSENCRANTZ *and* GUILDENSTERN.] Now I am alone.
O, what a rogue and peasant slave am I!
Is it not monstrous, that this player here,
But in a fiction, in a dream of passion,
Could force his soul so to his own conceit,
That, from her working, all his visage wann'd;
Tears in his eyes, distraction in's aspect,
A broken voice, and his whole function suiting
With forms to his conceit? and all for nothing!
For Hecuba!
What's Hecuba to him, or he to Hecuba,
That he should weep for her? What would he do,
Had he the motive and the cue for passion
That I have? He would drown the stage with tears,
And cleave the general ear with horrid speech;
Make mad the guilty, and appal the free,
Confound the ignorant, and amaze, indeed,
The very faculties of eyes and ears.
Yet I,
A dull and muddy-mettled rascal, peak,
Like John-a-dreams, unpregnant of my cause,
And can say nothing; no, not for a king,
Upon whose property and most dear life
A damn'd defeat was made. Am I a coward?
Who calls me villain? breaks my pate across?
Plucks off my beard, and blows it in my face?
Tweaks me by th'nose? gives me the lie i'th'throat,
As deep as to the lungs? who does me this, ha?
'Swounds, I should take it: for it cannot be
But I am pigeon-liver'd, and lack gall
To make oppression bitter; or, ere this,
I should have fatted all the region kites
With this slave's offal: — bloody, bawdy villain!
Remorseless, treacherous, lecherous, kindless villain!
O, vengeance!
Why, what an ass am I! This is most brave,
That I, the son of a dear father murder'd,
Prompted to my revenge by heaven and hell,
Must, like a whore, unpack my heart with words,
And fall a-cursing, like a very drab,
A scullion!
Fie upon't! foh! — About, my brain! I have heard
That guilty creatures sitting at a play
Have by the very cunning of the scene
Been struck so to the soul, that presently
They have proclaim'd their malefactions;
For murder, though it have no tongue, will speak
With most miraculous organ. I'll have these players

Play something like the murder of my father
Before mine uncle: I'll observe his looks;
I'll tent him to the quick: if he but blench,
I know my course. The spirit that I have seen
May be the devil: and the devil hath power
T'assume a pleasing shape; yea, and perhaps
Out of my weakness and my melancholy,
As he is very potent with such spirits,
Abuses me to damn me: I'll have grounds
More relative than this: — the play's the thing
Wherein I'll catch the conscience of the king. [*Exit.*

ACT III

SCENE I

Elsinore. A room in the castle.

Enter KING, QUEEN, POLONIUS, OPHELIA, ROSENCRANTZ, *and* GUILDENSTERN.

KING
And can you, by no drift of circumstance,
Get from him why he puts on this confusion,
Grating so harshly all his days of quiet
With turbulent and dangerous lunacy?

ROSENCRANTZ
He does confess he feels himself distracted;
But from what cause he will by no means speak.

GUILDENSTERN
Nor do we find him forward to be sounded;
But, with a crafty madness, keeps aloof,
When we would bring him on to some confession
Of his true state.

QUEEN
                    Did he receive you well?

ROSENCRANTZ
Most like a gentleman.

GUILDENSTERN
But with much forcing of his disposition.

ROSENCRANTZ
Niggard of question; but, of our demands,
Most free in his reply.

QUEEN
                    Did you assay him
To any pastime?

ROSENCRANTZ
Madam, it so fell out, that certain players
We o'er-raught on the way: of these we told him;
And there did seem in him a kind of joy
To hear of it: they are about the court;
And, as I think, they have already order
This night to play before him.

POLONIUS
                    'Tis most true:
And he beseech'd me to entreat your majesties
To hear and see the matter.

KING
With all my heart; and it doth much content me
To hear him so inclined. —
Good gentlemen, give him a further edge,
And drive his purpose on to these delights.

ROSENCRANTZ
We shall, my lord.
       [*Exeunt* ROSENCRANTZ *and* GUILDENSTERN.

KING
                    Sweet Gertrude, leave us too;
For we have closely sent for Hamlet hither,
That he, as 'twere by accident, may here
Affront Ophelia;
Her father and myself — lawful espials —
Will so bestow ourselves that, seeing, unseen,
We may of their encounter frankly judge;
And gather by him, as he is behaved,
If 't be th'affliction of his love or no
That thus he suffers for.

QUEEN
                    I shall obey you: —
And for your part, Ophelia, I do wish
That your good beauties be the happy cause
Of Hamlet's wildness: so shall I hope your virtues
Will bring him to his wonted way again,
To both your honours.

OPHELIA
                    Madam, I wish it may.
       [*Exit* QUEEN.

POLONIUS
Ophelia, walk you here. — Gracious, so please you,
We will bestow ourselves. — [*to* OPHELIA] Read on this book;

That show of such an exercise may colour
Your loneliness. — We are oft to blame in this, —
'Tis too much prov'd, — that with devotion's visage
And pious action we do sugar o'er
The devil himself.

KING [aside].

O, 'tis too true!
How smart a lash that speech doth give my conscience!
The harlot's cheek, beautied with plastering art,
Is not more ugly to the thing that helps it
Than is my deed to my most painted word:
O heavy burden!

POLONIUS
I hear him coming: let's withdraw, my lord.

[Exeunt KING and POLONIUS.

Enter HAMLET.

HAMLET
To be, or not to be, — that is the question: —
Whether 'tis nobler in the mind to suffer
The slings and arrows of outrageous fortune,
Or to take arms against a sea of troubles,
And by opposing end them? — To die — to sleep, —
No more; and by a sleep to say we end
The heart-ache, and the thousand natural shocks
That flesh is heir to, 'tis a consummation
Devoutly to be wish'd. To die — to sleep; —
To sleep! perchance to dream: ay, there's the rub;
For in that sleep of death what dreams may come,
When we have shuffled off this mortal coil,
Must give us pause: there's the respect
That makes calamity of so long life;
For who would bear the whips and scorns of time,
The oppressor's wrong, the proud man's contumely,
The pangs of despised love, the law's delay,
The insolence of office, and the spurns
That patient merit of the unworthy takes,
When he himself might his quietus make
With a bare bodkin? who would fardels bear,
To grunt and sweat under a weary life,
But that the dread of something after death, —
The undiscover'd country, from whose bourn
No traveller returns, — puzzles the will,
And makes us rather bear those ills we have
Than fly to others that we know not of?
Thus conscience does make cowards of us all;
And thus the native hue of resolution
Is sicklied o'er with the pale cast of thought;
And enterprises of great pith and moment,
With this regard, their currents turn awry,
And lose the name of action. — Soft you now!
The fair Ophelia! — Nymph, in thy orisons
Be all my sins remember'd.

OPHELIA

Good my lord,

How does your honour for this many a day?

HAMLET
I humbly thank you; well, well, well.

OPHELIA
My lord, I have remembrances of yours,
That I have longed long to re-deliver;
I pray you, now receive them.

HAMLET

No, not I;

I never gave you aught.

OPHELIA
My honour'd lord, you know right well you did;
And, with them, words of so sweet breath composed
As made the things more rich: their perfume lost,
Take these again; for to the noble mind
Rich gifts wax poor when givers prove unkind.
There, my lord.

HAMLET
Ha, ha! are you honest?

OPHELIA
My lord?

HAMLET
Are you fair?

OPHELIA
What means your lordship?

HAMLET
That if you be honest and fair, your honesty should
admit no discourse to your beauty.

OPHELIA
Could beauty, my lord, have better commerce than
with honesty?

HAMLET
Ay, truly; for the power of beauty will sooner transform
honesty from what it is to a bawd than the force of
honesty can translate beauty into his likeness: this was

sometime a paradox, but now
the time gives it proof. I did
love you once.

OPHELIA
Indeed, my lord, you made
me believe so.

HAMLET
You should not have believed
me; for virtue cannot so
inoculate our old stock, but
we shall relish of it: I loved
you not.

OPHELIA
I was the more deceived.

HAMLET
Get thee to a nunnery: why
wouldst thou be a breeder of
sinners? I am myself
indifferent honest: but yet I
could accuse me of such
things, that it were better my
mother had not borne me: I
am very proud, revengeful, ambitious; with more
offences at my beck than I have thoughts to put them
in, imagination to give them shape, or time to act them
in. What should such fellows as I do crawling between
earth and heaven? We are arrant knaves, all; believe
none of us. Go thy ways to a nunnery. Where's your
father?

OPHELIA
At home, my lord.

HAMLET
Let the doors be shut upon him, that he may play the
fool no where but in's own house. Farewell.

OPHELIA
O, help him, you sweet heavens!

HAMLET
If thou dost marry, I'll give thee this plague for thy
dowry, — be thou as chaste as ice, as pure as snow,
thou shalt not escape calumny. Get thee to a nunnery,
go: farewell. Or, if thou wilt needs marry, marry a fool;
for wise men know well enough what monsters you
make of them. To a nunnery, go; and quickly too.
Farewell.

OPHELIA
O heavenly powers, restore him!

HAMLET
I have heard of your paintings too, well enough; God
has given you one face, and you make yourselves
another: you jig, you amble, and you lisp, and
nickname God's creatures, and make your wantonness
your ignorance. Go to, I'll no more on't; it hath made
me mad. I say, we will have no more marriages: those
that are married already, all but one, shall live; the rest
shall keep as they are. To a nunnery, go. [Exit.

OPHELIA
O, what a noble mind is here o'erthrown!
The courtier's, soldier's, scholar's eye, tongue, sword;
Th'expectancy and rose of the fair state,
The glass of fashion and the mould of form,
Th'observ'd of all observers, — quite, quite down!
And I, of ladies most deject and wretched,
That suck'd the honey of his music vows,
Now see that noble and most sovereign reason,
Like sweet bells jangled, out of tune and harsh;
That unmatch'd form and feature of blown youth
Blasted with ecstasy: O, woe is me
T'have seen what I have seen, see what I see!

Enter KING and POLONIUS.

KING
Love! his affections do not that way tend;
Nor what he spake, though it lack'd form a little,
Was not like madness. There's something in his soul
O'er which his melancholy sits on brood;
And I do doubt the hatch and the disclose
Will be some danger: which for to prevent,
I have in quick determination
Thus set it down: — he shall with speed to England,
For the demand of our neglected tribute:
Haply, the seas, and countries different,
With variable objects, shall expel
This something-settled matter in his heart;
Whereon his brains still beating puts him thus
From fashion of himself. What think you on't?

POLONIUS
It shall do well: but yet do I believe
The origin and commencement of his grief
Sprung from neglected love. — How now, Ophelia!
You need not tell us what Lord Hamlet said;
We heard it all. — My lord, do as you please;

QUEEN Did you assay him to any pastime?

But, if you hold it fit, after the play,
Let his queen mother all alone entreat him
To show his grief: let her be round with him;
And I'll be plac'd, so please you, in the ear
Of all their conference. If she find him not,
To England send him; or confine him where
Your wisdom best shall think.

KING

It shall be so:

Madness in great ones must not unwatch'd go. [Exeunt.

SCENE II
A hall in the castle.

Enter HAMLET and two or three of the PLAYERS.

HAMLET
Speak the speech, I pray you, as I pronounced it to you,
trippingly on the tongue: but if you mouth it, as many
of your players do, I had as lief the town-crier spoke my
lines. Nor do not saw the air too much with your hand,
thus; but use all gently: for in the very torrent, tempest,
and, as I may say, the whirlwind of passion, you must
acquire and beget a temperance that may give it
smoothness. O, it offends me to the soul to hear a
robustious periwig-pated fellow tear a passion to
tatters, to very rags, to split the ears of the groundlings,
who, for the most part, are capable of nothing but
inexplicable dumb-shows and noise: I would have such
a fellow whipped for o'erdoing Termagant; it
out-herods Herod: pray you, avoid it.

FIRST PLAYER
I warrant your honour.

HAMLET
Be not too tame neither, but let your own discretion be
your tutor: suit the action to the word, the word to the
action; with this special observance, that you o'erstep
not the modesty of nature: for anything so overdone is
from the purpose of playing, whose end, both at the
first and now, was and is, to hold, as 'twere, the mirror
up to nature; to show virtue her own feature, scorn her
own image, and the very age and body of the time his
form and pressure. Now, this overdone, or come tardy
off, though it make the unskilful laugh, cannot but
make the judicious grieve; the censure of the which
one must, in your allowance, o'erweigh a whole theatre
of others. O, there be players that I have seen play, —
and heard others praise, and that highly, — not to
speak it profanely, that, neither having the accent of
Christians, nor the gait of Christian, pagan, nor man,
have so strutted and bellow'd, that I have thought some
of nature's journeymen had made them, and not made
them well, they imitated humanity so abominably.

FIRST PLAYER
I hope we have reform'd that indifferently with us, sir.

HAMLET
O, reform it altogether. And let those that play your
clowns speak no more than is set down for them: for
there be of them that will themselves laugh, to set on
some quantity of barren spectators to laugh too;
though, in the mean time, some necessary question of
the play be then to be consider'd; that's villainous, and
shows a most pitiful ambition in the fool that uses it.
Go, make you ready. [Exeunt PLAYERS.

Enter POLONIUS, ROSENCRANTZ, and
GUILDENSTERN.

How now, my lord! I will the king hear this piece of
work?

POLONIUS
And the queen too, and that presently.

HAMLET To a nunnery, go; and quickly too.

HAMLET
Bid the players make haste.   [*Exit* POLONIUS.
Will you two help to hasten them?
ROSENCRANTZ and GUILDENSTERN.
We will, my lord.
    [*Exeunt* ROSENCRANTZ *and* GUILDENSTERN.
HAMLET
What, ho, Horatio!

    Enter HORATIO.

HORATIO
Here, sweet lord, at your service.
HAMLET
Horatio, thou art e'en as just a man
As e'er my conversation coped withal.
HORATIO
O, my dear lord, —
HAMLET
        Nay, do not think I flatter;
For what advancement may I hope from thee,
That no revenue hast, but thy good spirits,
To feed and clothe thee? Why should the poor be
    flatter'd?
No, let the candied tongue lick absurd pomp;
And crook the pregnant hinges of the knee
Where thrift may follow fawning. Dost thou hear?
Since my dear soul was mistress of her choice,
And could of men distinguish, her election
Hath seal'd thee for herself: for thou hast been
As one, in suffering all, that suffers nothing;
A man that fortune's buffets and rewards
Hast ta'en with equal thanks: and blest are those
Whose blood and judgement are so well commingled,
That they are not a pipe for fortune's finger
To sound what stop she please. Give me that man
That is not passion's slave, and I will wear him
In my heart's core, ay, in my heart of heart,
As I do thee. — Something too much of this. —
There is a play to-night before the king;
One scene of it comes near the circumstance
Which I have told thee of my father's death:
I prithee, when thou seest that act a-foot,
Even with the very comment of thy soul
Observe my uncle: if his occulted guilt
Do not itself unkennel in one speech,
It is a damned ghost that we have seen;
And my imaginations are as foul
As Vulcan's stithy. Give him heedful note:

For I mine eyes will rivet to his face;
And, after, we will both our judgements join
In censure of his seeming.
HORATIO
          Well, my lord:
If he steal aught the whilst this play is playing,
And scape detecting, I will pay the theft.
HAMLET
They're coming to the play; I must be idle:
Get you a place.
    Danish march. A flourish. Enter KING, QUEEN,
    POLONIUS, OPHELIA, ROSENCRANTZ,
    GUILDENSTERN, *and other* LORDS *attendant*,
    with the GUARD *carrying torches.*
KING
How fares our cousin Hamlet?
HAMLET
Excellent, i'faith; of the chameleon's dish: I eat the air,
promise-cramm'd: you cannot feed capons so.
KING
I have nothing with this answer, Hamlet; these words
are not mine.
HAMLET
No, nor mine now. — [*to* POLONIUS] My lord, you
play'd once i'th'university, you say?
POLONIUS
That did I, my lord; and was accounted a good actor.
HAMLET
And what did you enact?
POLONIUS
I did enact Julius Cæsar: I was killed i'th'Capitol;
Brutus kill'd me.
HAMLET
It was a brute part of him to kill so capital a calf there.
— Be the players ready?
ROSENCRANTZ
Ay, my lord; they stay upon your patience.
QUEEN
Come hither, my dear Hamlet, sit by me.
HAMLET
No, good mother; here's metal more attractive.
POLONIUS [*to the* KING].
O, ho! do you mark that?
HAMLET
Lady, shall I lie in your lap?
    [*Lying down at* OPHELIA'S *feet.*

OPHELIA
No, my lord.
HAMLET
I mean, my head upon your lap?
OPHELIA
Ay, my lord.
HAMLET
Do you think I meant country matters?
OPHELIA
I think nothing, my lord.
HAMLET
That's a fair thought to lie between maids' legs.
OPHELIA
What is, my lord?
HAMLET
Nothing.
OPHELIA
You are merry, my lord,
HAMLET
Who, I?
OPHELIA
Ay, my lord.
HAMLET
O God, your only jig-maker. What should a man do but
be merry? for, look you, how cheerfully my mother
looks, and my father died within's two hours.
OPHELIA
Nay, 'tis twice two months, my lord.
HAMLET
So long? Nay, then, let the devil wear black, for I'll have
a suit of sables. O heavens! die two months ago, and
not forgotten yet? Then there's hope a great man's
memory may outlive his life half a year: but, by'r lady,
he must build churches, then; or else shall he suffer
not thinking on, with the hobby-horse, whose epitaph
is, 'For, O, for, O, the hobby-horse is forgot.'
    Hautboys play. The dumb-show enters.
    Enter a KING *and a* QUEEN *very lovingly; the* QUEEN
    embracing him, and he her. She kneels, and makes show of
    protestation unto him. He takes her up, and declines his
    head upon her neck; lays him down upon a bank of flowers:
    she, seeing him asleep, leaves him. Anon comes in a fellow,
    takes off his crown, kisses it, and pours poison in the
    KING'S *ears, and exit. The* QUEEN *returns; finds the*
    KING *dead, and makes passionate action. The*
    POISONER, *with some two or three* MUTES, *comes in*
    again, seeming to lament with her. The dead body is
    carried away. The POISONER *wooes the* QUEEN *with*
    gifts: she seems loth and unwilling awhile, but
    in the end accepts his love.   [*Exeunt.*
OPHELIA
What means this, my lord?
HAMLET
Marry, this is miching mallecho; it means mischief.
OPHELIA
Belike this show imports the argument of the play.
    Enter PROLOGUE.
HAMLET
We shall know by this fellow: the players cannot keep
counsel; they'll tell all.
OPHELIA
Will he tell us what this show meant?
HAMLET
Ay, or any show that you'll show him: be not you
ashamed to show, he'll not shame to tell you what it
means.
OPHELIA
You are naught, you are naught: I'll mark the play.
PROLOGUE
    For us, and for our tragedy,
    Here stooping to your clemency,
    We beg your hearing patiently.   [*Exit.*
HAMLET
Is this a prologue, or the posy of a ring?
OPHELIA
'Tis brief, my lord.
HAMLET
As woman's love.
    Enter two PLAYERS, KING *and* QUEEN.
PLAYER KING
Full thirty times hath Phœbus' cart gone round
Neptune's salt wash and Tellus' orbed ground,
And thirty dozen moons with borrow'd sheen
About the world have times twelve thirties been,
Since love our hearts, and Hymen did our hands
Unite commutual in most sacred bands.

PLAYER QUEEN
So many journeys may the sun and moon
Make us again count o'er ere love be done!
But, woe is me, you are so sick of late,
So far from cheer and from your former state,
That I distrust you. Yet, though I distrust,
Discomfort you, my lord, it nothing must:
For women's fear and love holds quantity;
In neither aught, or in extremity.
Now, what my love is, proof hath made you know;
And as my love is siz'd, my fear is so:
Where love is great, the littlest doubts are fear;
Where little fears grow great, great love grows there.

PLAYER KING
Faith, I must leave thee, love, and shortly too;
My operant powers their functions leave to do:
And thou shalt live in this fair world behind,
Honour'd, belov'd; and haply one as kind
For husband shalt thou —

PLAYER QUEEN
⠀⠀⠀⠀⠀⠀⠀⠀⠀⠀O, confound the rest!
Such love must needs be treason in my breast:
In second husband let me be accurst!
None wed the second but who kill'd the first.

HAMLET [aside].
Wormwood, wormwood.

PLAYER QUEEN
The instances that second marriage move
Are base respects of thrift, but none of love:
A second time I kill my husband dead
When second husband kisses me in bed.

PLAYER KING
I do believe you think what now you speak;
But what we do determine oft we break.
Purpose is but the slave to memory;
Of violent birth, but poor validity;
Which now, like fruit unripe, sticks on the tree;
But fall, unshaken, when they mellow be.
Most necessary 'tis that we forget
To pay ourselves what to ourselves is debt:
What to ourselves in passion we propose,
The passion ending, doth the purpose lose.
The violence of either grief or joy
Their own enactures with themselves destroy:
Where joy most revels, grief doth most lament;
Grief joys, joy grieves, on slender accident.
This world is not for aye; nor 'tis not strange
That even our loves should with our fortunes change;
For 'tis a question left us yet to prove,
Whether love lead fortune, or else fortune love.
The great man down, you mark his favourite flies;
The poor advanc'd makes friends of enemies.
And hitherto doth love on fortune tend:
For who not needs shall never lack a friend;
And who in want a hollow friend doth try,
Directly seasons him his enemy.
But, orderly to end where I begun, —
Our wills and fates do so contrary run,
That our devices still are overthrown;
Our thoughts are ours, their ends none of our own:
So think thou wilt no second husband wed;
But die thy thoughts when thy first lord is dead.

PLAYER QUEEN
Nor earth to me give food, nor heaven light!
Sport and repose lock from me day and night!
To desperation turn my trust and hope!
An anchor's cheer in prison be my scope!
Each opposite that blanks the face of joy
Meet what I would have well, and it destroy!
Both here and hence pursue me lasting strife,
If, once a widow, ever I be wife!

HAMLET
If she should break it now!

PLAYER KING
'Tis deeply sworn. Sweet, leave me here awhile;
My spirits grow dull, and fain I would beguile
The tedious day with sleep. ⠀⠀⠀⠀⠀⠀[Sleeps.

PLAYER QUEEN
⠀⠀⠀⠀⠀⠀Sleep rock thy brain;
And never come mischance between us twain! ⠀[Exit.

HAMLET
Madam, how like you this play?

QUEEN
The lady doth protests too much, methinks.

HAMLET
O, but she'll keep her word.

KING
Have you heard the argument? Is there no offence in't?

HAMLET
No, no, they do but jest, poison in jest; no offence

i'th'world.

KING
What do you call the play?

HAMLET
The Mouse-trap. Marry, how? Tropically. This play is
the image of a murder done in Vienna: Gonzago is the
duke's name; his wife, Baptista: you shall see anon; 'tis
a knavish piece of work: but what o' that? your majesty,
and we that have free souls, it touches us not: let the
gall'd jade wince, our withers are unwrung.

Enter PLAYER, as LUCIANUS.

This is one Lucianus, nephew to the king.

OPHELIA
You are as good as a chorus, my lord.

HAMLET
I could interpret between you and your love, if I could
see the puppets dallying.

OPHELIA
You are keen, my lord, you are keen.

HAMLET
It would cost you a groaning to take off my edge.

OPHELIA
Still better, and worse.

HAMLET
So you mistake your husbands. — Begin, murderer;
pox, leave thy damnable faces, and begin. Come: — the
croaking raven doth bellow for revenge.

LUCIANUS
Thoughts black, hands apt, drugs fit, and time
agreeing;
Confederate season, else no creature seeing;
Thou mixture rank, of midnight weeds collected,
With Hecate's ban thrice blasted, thrice infected,
Thy natural magic and dire property,
On wholesome life usurp immediately.
⠀⠀⠀⠀⠀⠀[Pours the poison in his ears.

HAMLET
He poisons him i'th'garden for's estate. His name's
Gonzago: the story is extant, and writ in choice Italian:
you shall see anon how the murderer gets the love of
Gonzago's wife.

OPHELIA
The king rises.

HAMLET
What, frighted with false fire!

QUEEN
How fares my lord?

POLONIUS
Give o'er the play.

KING
Give me some light: — away!

ALL
Lights, lights, lights.
⠀⠀⠀⠀[Exeunt all but HAMLET and HORATIO.

HAMLET
⠀⠀⠀Why, let the stricken deer go weep,
⠀⠀⠀⠀⠀The hart ungalled play;
⠀⠀⠀For some must watch, while some must sleep;
⠀⠀⠀⠀⠀So runs the world away. —
Would not this, sir, and a forest of feathers, — if the
rest of my fortunes turn Turk with me, — with two
Provincial roses on my razed shoes, get me a
fellowship in a cry of players, sir?

HORATIO
Half a share.

HAMLET
A whole one, I.
⠀⠀⠀For thou dost know, O Damon dear,
⠀⠀⠀⠀⠀This realm dismantled was
⠀⠀⠀Of Jove himself; and now reigns here
⠀⠀⠀⠀⠀A very, very — pajcock.

HORATIO
You might have rimed.

HAMLET
O good Horatio, I'll take the ghost's word for a
thousand pound. Didst perceive?

HORATIO
Very well, my lord.

HAMLET
Upon the talk of the poisoning, —

HORATIO
I did very well note him.

HAMLET
Ah, ha! — Come, some music! come, the recorders! —
For if the king like not the comedy,
Why, then, belike, — he likes it not, perdy. —
Come, some music!

Enter ROSENCRANTZ and GUILDENSTERN.

GUILDENSTERN
Good my lord, vouchsafe me a word with you.

HAMLET
Sir, a whole history.

GUILDENSTERN
The king, sir, —

HAMLET
Ay, sir, what of him?

GUILDENSTERN
Is, in his retirement, marvellous distemper'd.

HAMLET
With drink, sir?

GUILDENSTERN
No, my lord, with choler.

HAMLET
Your wisdom should show itself more richer to signify
this to his doctor; for, for me to put him to his
purgation would perhaps plunge him into far more
choler.

GUILDENSTERN
Good my lord, put your discourse into some frame, and
start not so wildly from my affair.

HAMLET
I am tame, sir: — pronounce.

GUILDENSTERN
The queen, your mother, in most great affliction of
spirit, hath sent me to you.

HAMLET
You are welcome.

GUILDENSTERN
Nay, good my lord, this courtesy is not of the right
breed. If it shall please you to make me a wholesome
answer, I will do your mother's commandment: if not,
your pardon and my return shall be the end of the
business.

HAMLET
Sir, I cannot.

GUILDENSTERN
What, my lord?

HAMLET
Make you a wholesome answer; my wit's diseased: but,
sir, such answer as I can make, you shall command; or,
rather, as you say, my mother: therefore no more, but
to the matter: my mother, you say, —

ROSENCRANTZ
Then thus she says: your behavior hath struck her into
amazement and admiration.

HAMLET
O wonderful son, that can so astonish a mother! — But
is there no sequel at the heels of this mother's
admiration? Impart.

ROSENCRANTZ
She desires to speak with you in her closet, ere you go to
bed.

HAMLET
We shall obey, were she ten times our mother.
Have you any further trade with us?

ROSENCRANTZ
My lord, you once did love me.

HAMLET
And do still, by these pickers and stealers.

ROSENCRANTZ
Good my lord, what is your cause of distemper? you do,
surely, bar the door upon your own liberty, if you deny
your griefs to your friend.

HAMLET
Sir, I lack advancement.

ROSENCRANTZ
How can that be, when you have the voice of the king
himself for your succession in Denmark?

HAMLET
Ay, sir, but 'While the grass grows,' — the proverb is
something musty.
⠀⠀⠀⠀*Enter PLAYERS with recorders.*
O, the recorders: — let me see one. — To withdraw
with you: — why do you go about to recover the wind of
me, as if you would drive me into a toil?

GUILDENSTERN
O, my lord, if my duty be too bold, my love is too
unmannerly.

HAMLET
I do not well understand that. Will you play upon this
pipe?

GUILDENSTERN
My lord, I cannot.

HAMLET
I pray you.

GUILDENSTERN
Believe me, I cannot.
HAMLET
I do beseech you.
GUILDENSTERN
I know no touch of it, my lord.
HAMLET
'Tis as easy as lying: govern these ventages with your
finger and thumb, give it breath with your mouth, and
it will discourse most eloquent music. Look you, these
are the stops.
GUILDENSTERN
But these cannot I command to any utterance of
harmony; I have not the skill.
HAMLET
Why, look you now, how unworthy a thing you make of
me! You would play upon me; you would seem to know
my stops; you would pluck out the heart of my mystery;
you would sound me from my lowest note to the top of
my compass: and there is much music, excellent voice,
in this little organ; yet cannot you make it speak.
'Sblood, do you think I am easier to be play'd on than a
pipe? Call me what instrument you will, though you
can fret me, you cannot play upon me.

Enter POLONIUS.

God bless you, sir!
POLONIUS
My lord, the queen would speak with you, and presently.
HAMLET
Do you see yonder cloud that's almost in shape of a
camel?
POLONIUS
By th'mass, and 'tis like a camel, indeed.
HAMLET
Methinks it is like a weasel.
POLONIUS
It is back'd like a weasel.

HAMLET
Or like a whale?
POLONIUS
Very like a whale.
HAMLET
Then will I come to my mother by and by. — They fool
me to the top of my bent. — I will come by and by.
POLONIUS
I will say so.
HAMLET
By and by is easily said. [*Exit* POLONIUS.] —
Leave me, friends.
 [*Exeunt* ROSENCRANTZ, GUILDENSTERN,
 HORATIO, *and* PLAYERS.
'Tis now the very witching time of night,
When churchyards yawn, and hell itself breathes out
Contagion to this world: now could I drink hot blood,
And do such bitter business as the day
Would quake to look on. Soft! now to my mother. —
O heart, lose not thy nature; let not ever
The soul of Nero enter this firm bosom:
Let me be cruel, not unnatural:
I will speak daggers to her, but use none;
My tongue and soul in this be hypocrites, —
How in my words soever she be shent,
To give them seals never, my soul, consent!   [*Exit.*

SCENE III

A room in the castle.

Enter KING, ROSENCRANTZ,
and GUILDENSTERN.

KING
I like him not, nor stands it safe with us
To let his madness range. Therefore prepare you;
I your commission will forthwith dispatch,
And he to England shall along with you:
The terms of our estate may not endure
Hazard so dangerous as doth hourly grow

Out of his lunacies.
GUILDENSTERN
 We will ourselves provide:
Most holy and religious fear it is
To keep those many many bodies safe
That live and feed upon your majesty.
ROSENCRANTZ
The single and peculiar life is bound,
With all the strength and armour of the mind,
To keep itself from noyance; but much more
That spirit upon whose weal depends and rests
The lives of many. The cease of majesty
Dies not alone; but, like a gulf, doth draw
What's near it with it: 'tis a massy wheel,
Fix'd on the summit of the highest mount,
To whose huge spokes ten thousand lesser things
Are mortis'd and adjoin'd; which, when it falls,
Each small annexment, petty consequence,
Attends the boisterous ruin. Ne'er alone
Did the king sigh, but with a general groan.
KING
Arm you, I pray you, to this speedy voyage;
For we will fetters put upon this fear,
Which now goes too free-footed.
ROSENCRANTZ and GUILDENSTERN
 We will haste us.
 [*Exeunt* ROSENCRANTZ *and* GUILDENSTERN.
 Enter POLONIUS.

POLONIUS
My lord, he's going to his mother's closet:
Behind the arras I'll convey myself,
To hear the process; I'll warrant she'll tax him home:
And, as you said, and wisely was it said,
'Tis meet that some more audience than a mother,
Since nature makes them partial, should o'erhear
The speech, of vantage. Fare you well, my liege:
I'll call upon you ere you go to bed,
And tell you what I know.
KING
 Thanks, dear my lord.
 [*Exit* POLONIUS
O, my offence is rank, it smells to heaven;
It hath the primal eldest curse upon't, —
A brother's murder! — Pray can I not,
Though inclination be as sharp as will:
My stronger guilt defeats my strong intent;
And, like a man to double business bound,
I stand in pause where I shall first begin,
And both neglect. What if this cursed hand
Were thicker than itself with brother's blood,
Is there not rain enough in the sweet heavens
To wash it white as snow? Whereto serves mercy
But to confront the visage of offence?
And what's in prayer but this twofold force, —
To be forestalled ere we come to fall,
Or pardon'd being down? Then I'll look up;
My fault is past. But, O, what form of prayer
Can serve my turn? 'Forgive me my foul murder'?
That cannot be; since I am still possess'd
Of those effects for which I did the murder, —
My crown, mine own ambition, and my queen.
May one be pardon'd, and retain th'offence?
In the corrupted currents of this world
Offence's gilded hand may shove by justice;
And oft 'tis seen the wicked prize itself
Buys out the law: but 'tis not so above;
There is no shuffling, — there the action lies
In his true nature; and we ourselves compell'd,
Even to the teeth and forehead of our faults,
To give in evidence. What then? what rests?
Try what repentance can: what can it not?
Yet what can it when one can not repent?
O wretched state! O bosom black as death!
O limed soul, that, struggling to be free,
Art more engag'd! Help, angels! Make assay:
Bow, stubborn knees; and, heart with strings of steel,
Be soft as sinews of the new-born babe!
All may be well. [*Retires and kneels*

Enter HAMLET.

HAMLET
Now might I do it pat, now he is praying;
And now I'll do't: — and so he goes to heaven;
And so am I reveng'd: — that would be scann'd:
A villain kills my father; and, for that,
I, his sole son, do this same villain send
To heaven.
O, this is hire and salary, not revenge.
He took my father grossly, full of bread;
With all his crimes broad blown, as flush as May;
And how his audit stands who knows save heaven?

HAMLET He poisons him i'th'garden for's estate.

But, in our circumstance and course of thought,
'Tis heavy with him: and am I, then, revenged,
To take him in the purging of his soul,
When he is fit and season'd for his passage?
No.
Up, sword; and know thou a more horrid hent:
When he is drunk asleep, or in his rage;
Or in th'incestuous pleasure of his bed;
At gaming, swearing; or about some act
That has no relish of salvation in't; —
Then trip him, that his heels may kick at heaven;
And that his soul may be as damn'd and black
As hell, whereto it goes. My mother stays:
This physic but prolongs thy sickly days.   [*Exit.*
KING [*rising*].
My words fly up, my thoughts remain below:
Words without thoughts never to heaven go.   [*Exit.*

SCENE IV

The Queen's closet.

Enter QUEEN *and* POLONIUS.

POLONIUS
He will come straight. Look you lay home to him:
Tell him his pranks have been too broad to bear with,
And that your Grace hath screen'd and stood between
Much heat and him. I'll sconce me even here.
Pray you, be round with him.
HAMLET [*within*].
Mother, mother, mother!
QUEEN
I'll warrant you; fear me not: — withdraw,
I hear him coming.   [POLONIUS *goes behind the arras.*
Enter HAMLET.

HAMLET
Now, mother, what's the matter?
QUEEN
Hamlet, thou hast thy father much offended.
HAMLET
Mother, you have my father much offended.
QUEEN
Come, come, you answer with an idle tongue.
HAMLET
Go, go, you question with a wicked tongue.
QUEEN
Why, how now, Hamlet!
HAMLET
                    What's the matter now?
QUEEN
Have you forgot me?
HAMLET
                    No, by the rood, not so:
You are the queen, your husband's brother's wife;
And — would it were not so! — you are my mother.
QUEEN
Nay, then, I'll set those to you that can speak.
HAMLET
Come, come, and sit you down; you shall not budge;
You go not till I set you up a glass
Where you may see the inmost part of you.
QUEEN
What wilt thou do? thou wilt not murder me? —
Help, help, ho!
POLONIUS [*behind*].
What, ho! help, help, help!
HAMLET [*drawing*].
How now! a rat? Dead for a ducat, dead!
                    [*Makes a pass through the arras.*
POLONIUS [*behind*].
O, I am slain!   [*Falls and dies.*
QUEEN
          O me, what hast thou done?
HAMLET
Nay, I know not: is it the king?
QUEEN
O, what a rash and bloody deed is this!
HAMLET
A bloody deed! — almost as bad, good mother,
As kill a king, and marry with his brother.
QUEEN
As kill a king!
HAMLET
          Ay, lady, 'twas my word. —
          [*Lifts up the arras, and sees* POLONIUS.
Thou wretched, rash, intruding fool, farewell!
I took thee for thy better: take thy fortune;
Thou find'st to be too busy is some danger. —
Leave wringing of your hands: peace; sit you down,

KING Give me some light: — away!

And let me wring your heart: for so I shall,
If it be made of penetrable stuff;
If damned custom have not braz'd it so,
That it is proof and bulwark against sense.
QUEEN
What have I done, that thou dar'st wag thy tongue
In noise so rude against me?
HAMLET
                    Such an act
That blurs the grace and blush of modesty;
Calls virtue hypocrite; takes off the rose
From the fair forehead of an innocent love,
And sets a blister there; makes marriage-vows
As false as dicers' oaths: O, such a deed
As from the body of contraction plucks
The very soul; and sweet religion makes
A rhapsody of words: heaven's face doth glow;
Yea, this solidity and compound mass,
With tristful visage, as against the doom,
Is thought-sick at the act.
QUEEN
                    Ay me, what act,
That roars so loud, and thunders in the index?
HAMLET
Look here, upon this picture, and on this,
The counterfeit presentment of two brothers.
See, what a grace was seated on this brow;
Hyperion's curls; the front of Jove himself;
An eye like Mars, to threaten and command;
A station like the herald Mercury
New-lighted on a heaven-kissing hill;
A combination and a form indeed,
Where every god did seem to set his seal,
To give the world assurance of a man:
This was your husband. — Look you now, what
     follows:
Here is your husband; like a mildew'd ear,
Blasting his wholesome brother. Have you eyes?
Could you on this fair mountain leave to feed,

And batten on this moor? Ha! have you eyes?
You cannot call it love; for at your age
The hey-day in the blood is tame, it's humble,
And waits upon the judgement; and what judgement
Would step from this to this? Sense, sure, you have,
Else could you not have motion: but, sure, that sense
Is apoplex'd; for madness would not err;
Nor sense to ecstasy was ne'er so thrall'd
But it reserv'd some quantity of choice,
To serve in such a difference. What devil was't
That thus hath cozen'd you at hoodman-blind?
Eyes without feeling, feeling without sight,
Ears without hands or eyes, smelling sans all,
Or but a sickly part of one true sense
Could not so mope.
O shame! where is thy blush? Rebellious hell,
If thou canst mutine in a matron's bones,
To flaming youth let virtue be as wax,
And melt in her own fire: proclaim no shame
When the compulsive ardour gives the charge,
Since frost itself as actively doth burn,
And reason panders will.
QUEEN
                    O Hamlet, speak no more:
Thou turn'st mine eyes into my very soul;
And there I see such black and grained spots
As will not leave their tinct.
HAMLET
                    Nay, but to live
In the rank sweat of an enseamed bed,
Stew'd in corruption, honeying and making love
Over the nasty sty, —
QUEEN
                    O, speak to me no more;
These words, like daggers, enter in mine ears;
No more, sweet Hamlet!
HAMLET
                    A murderer and a villain;
A slave that is not twentieth part the tithe

HAMLET Now he is praying; and now I'll do't: — and so he goes to heaven.

Of your precedent lord; a vice of kings;
A cutpurse of the empire and the rule,
That from a shelf the precious diadem stole,
And put it in his pocket!

QUEEN
      No more!

HAMLET
A king of shreds and patches, —

Enter GHOST.

Save me, and hover o'er me with your wings,
You heavenly guards! — What would your gracious
    figure?

QUEEN
Alas, he's mad!

HAMLET
Do you not come your tardy son to chide,
That, laps'd in time and passion, lets go by
Th'important acting of your dread command?
O, say!

GHOST
Do not forget: this visitation
Is but to whet thy almost blunted purpose.
But, look, amazement on thy mother sits:
O, step between her and her fighting soul, —
Conceit in weakest bodies strongest works, —
Speak to her, Hamlet.

HAMLET
    How is it with you, lady?

QUEEN
Alas, how is't with you,
That you do bend your eye on vacancy,
And with th'incorporal air do hold discourse?
Forth at your eyes your spirits wildly peep;
And, as the sleeping soldiers in th'alarm,
Your bedded hair, like life in excrements,
Start up, and stand an end. O gentle son,
Upon the heat and flame of thy distemper
Sprinkle cool patience. Whereon do you look?

HAMLET
On him, on him! Look you, how pale he glares!
His form and cause conjoin'd, preaching to stones,
Would make them capable. — Do not look upon me,
Lest with this piteous action you convert
My stern effects: then what I have to do
Will want true colour; tears perchance for blood.

QUEEN
To whom do you speak this?

HAMLET
    Do you see nothing there?

QUEEN
Nothing at all; yet all that is I see.

HAMLET
Nor did you nothing hear?

QUEEN
    No, nothing but ourselves.

HAMLET
Why, look you there! look, how it steals away!
My father, in his habit as he liv'd!
Look, where he goes, even now, out at the portal!
        [*Exit* GHOST.

QUEEN
This the very coinage of your brain:
This bodiless creation ecstasy
Is very cunning in.

HAMLET
    Ecstasy!
My pulse, as yours, doth temperately keep time,
And makes as healthful music: it is not madness
That I have utter'd: bring me to the test,
And I the matter will re-word; which madness
Would gambol from. Mother, for love of grace,
Lay not that flattering unction to your soul,
That not your trespass, but my madness speaks:
It will but skin and film the ulcerous place,
Whilst rank corruption, mining all within,
Infects unseen. Confess yourself to heaven;
Repent what's past; avoid what is to come;
And do not spread the compost on the weeds,
To make them ranker. Forgive me this my virtue;
For in the fatness of these pursy times
Virtue itself of vice must pardon beg,
Yea, curb and woo for leave to do him good.

QUEEN
O Hamlet, thou hast cleft my heart in twain.

HAMLET
O, throw away the worser part of it,
And live the purer with the other half.
Good night: but go not to my uncle's bed;
Assume a virtue, if you have it not.
That monster, custom, who all sense doth eat,
Of habits devil, is angel yet in this,
That to the use of actions fair and good
He likewise gives a frock or livery,
That aptly is put on. Refrain to-night;
And that shall lend a kind of easiness
To the next abstinence: the next more easy;
For use almost can change the stamp of nature,
And either master the devil, or throw him out
With wondrous potency. Once more, good night:
And when you are desirous to be blest,
I'll blessing beg of you. — For this same lord,
        [*Pointing to* POLONIUS.
I do repent: but heaven hath pleas'd it so,
To punish me with this, and this with me,

That I must be their scourge and minister.
I will bestow him, and will answer well
The death I gave him. So, again, good night. —
I must be cruel, only to be kind:
Thus bad begins, and worse remains behind. —
One word more, good lady.

QUEEN
    What shall I do?

HAMLET
Not this, by no means, that I bid you do:
Let the bloat king tempt you again to bed;
Pinch wanton on your cheek; call you his mouse;
And let him, for a pair of reechy kisses,
Or paddling in your neck with his damn'd fingers,
Make you to ravel all this matter out,
That I essentially am not in madness,
But mad in craft. 'Twere good you let him know;
For who, that's but a queen, fair, sober, wise,
Would from a paddock, from a bat, a gib,
Such dear concernings hide? who would do so?
No, in despite of sense and secrecy,
Unpeg the basket on the house's top,
Let the birds fly, and, like the famous ape,
To try conclusions, in the basket creep,
And break your own neck down.

QUEEN
Be thou assured, if words be made of breath
And breath of life, I have no life to breathe
What thou hast said to me.

HAMLET
I must to England; you know that?

QUEEN
    Alack,
I had forgot: 'tis so concluded on.

HAMLET
There's letters seal'd: and my two schoolfellows, —
Whom I will trust as I will adders fang'd, —
They bear the mandate; they must sweep my way,
And marshal me to knavery. Let it work;
For 'tis the sport to have the enginer
Hoist with his own petar: and't shall go hard
But I will delve one yard below their mines,
And blow them at the moon: O, 'tis most sweet
When in one line two crafts directly meet. —
This man shall set me packing:
I'll lug the guts into the neighbour room. —
Mother, good night. — Indeed, this counsellor
Is now most still, most secret, and most grave,
Who was in life a foolish prating knave.
Come, sir, to draw toward an end with you. —
Good night, mother.
    [*Exeunt severally;* HAMLET *tugging in* POLONIUS.

ACT IV

SCENE I

A room in the castle.

Enter KING, QUEEN, ROSENCRANTZ,
and GUILDENSTERN.

KING
There's matter in these sighs, these profound heaves:
You must translate: 'tis fit we understand them.
Where is your son?

QUEEN
Bestow this place on us a little while.
    [*Exeunt* ROSENCRANTZ *and* GUILDENSTERN.
Ah, my good lord, what have I seen to-night!

KING
What, Gertrude? How does Hamlet?

QUEEN
Mad as the sea and wind, when both contend
Which is the mightier: in his lawless fit,
Behind the arras hearing something stir,
Whips out his rapier, cries, 'A rat, a rat!'
And, in this brainish apprehension, kills
The unseen good old man.

KING
    O heavy deed!
It had been so with us, had we been there:
His liberty is full of threats to all;
To you yourself, to us, to every one.
Alas, how shall this bloody deed be answer'd?
It will be laid to us, whose providence
Should have kept short, restrain'd, and out of haunt
This mad young man: but so much was our love,
We would not understand what was most fit;
But, like the owner of a foul disease,
To keep it from divulging, let it feed

Even on the pith of life. Where is he gone?
QUEEN
To draw apart the body he hath kill'd:
O'er whom his very madness, like some ore
Among a mineral of metals base,
Shows itself pure; he weeps for what is done.
KING
O Gertrude, come away!
The sun no sooner shall the mountains touch,
But we will ship him hence: and this vile deed
We must, with all our majesty and skill,
Both countenance and excuse. — Ho, Guildenstern!
Enter ROSENCRANTZ *and* GUILDENSTERN.
Friends both, go join you with some further aid:
Hamlet in madness hath Polonius slain,
And from his mother's closet hath he dragg'd him:
Go seek him out; speak fair, and bring the body
Into the chapel. I pray you, haste in this.
[*Exeunt* ROSENCRANTZ *and* GUILDENSTERN.
Come, Gertrude, we'll call up our wisest friends;
And let them know, both what we mean to do,
And what's untimely done: so, haply, slander —
Whose whisper o'er the world's diameter,
As level as the cannon to his blank,
Transports his poison'd shot — may miss our name,
And hit the woundless air. — O, come away!
My soul is full of discord and dismay. [*Exeunt.*

SCENE II
Another room in the castle.
Enter HAMLET.

HAMLET
Safely stow'd.
ROSENCRANTZ and GUILDENSTERN [*within*].
Hamlet! Lord Hamlet!
HAMLET
What noise? who calls on Hamlet? O, here they come.
Enter ROSENCRANTZ *and* GUILDENSTERN.

ROSENCRANTZ
What have you done, my lord, with the dead body?
HAMLET
Compounded it with dust, whereto 'tis kin.
ROSENCRANTZ
Tell us where 'tis; that we may take it thence,
And bear it to the chapel.
HAMLET
Do not believe it.
ROSENCRANTZ
Believe what?
HAMLET
That I can keep your counsel, and not mine own.
Besides, to be demanded of a sponge! — what
replication should be made by the son of a king?
ROSENCRANTZ
Take you me for a sponge, my lord?
HAMLET
Ay, sir; that soaks up the king's countenance, his
rewards, his authorities. But such officers do the king
best service in the end: he keeps them, like an ape, in
the corner of his jaw; first mouth'd, to be last
swallow'd: when he needs what you have glean'd, it is
but squeezing you, and, sponge, you shall be dry again.
ROSENCRANTZ
I understand you not, my lord.
HAMLET
I am glad of it: a knavish speech sleeps in a foolish ear.
ROSENCRANTZ
My lord, you must tell us where the body is, and go with
us to the king.
HAMLET
The body is with the king, but the king is not with the
body. The king is a thing —
GUILDENSTERN
A thing, my lord?
HAMLET
Of nothing: bring me to him. Hide fox, and all after.
[*Exeunt.*

SCENE III
Another room in the castle.
Enter KING, *attended.*

KING
I have sent to seek him, and to find the body.
How dangerous is it that this man goes loose!
Yet must not we put the strong law on him:
He's lov'd of the distracted multitude,
Who like not in their judgement, but their eyes;

HAMLET Look you, how pale he glares!

And where 'tis so, th'offender's scourge is weigh'd,
But never the offence. To bear all smooth and even,
This sudden sending him away must seem
Deliberate pause: diseases desperate grown
By desperate appliance are relieved,
Or not at all.
Enter ROSENCRANTZ.
How now! what hath befall'n?
ROSENCRANTZ
Where the dead body is bestow'd, my lord,
We cannot get from him.
KING
But where is he?
ROSENCRANTZ
Without, my lord; guarded, to know your pleasure.
KING
Bring him before us.
ROSENCRANTZ
Ho, Guildenstern! bring in my lord.
Enter HAMLET *and* GUILDENSTERN.

KING
Now, Hamlet, where's Polonius?
HAMLET
At supper.
KING
At supper! where?
HAMLET
Not where he eats, but where he is eaten: a certain
convocation of politic worms are e'en at him. Your
worm is your only emperor for diet: we fat all creatures
else to fat us, and we fat ourselves for maggots: your fat
king and your lean beggar is but variable service, —
two dishes, but to one table: that's the end.
KING
Alas, alas!
HAMLET
A man may fish with the worm that hath eat of a king,

and eat of the fish that hath fed of that worm.
KING
What dost thou mean by this?
HAMLET
Nothing but to show you how a king may go a progress
through the guts of a beggar.
KING
Where is Polonius?
HAMLET
In heaven; send thither to see: if your messenger find
him not there, seek him i'th'other place yourself. But,
indeed, if you find him not within this month, you
shall nose him as you go up the stairs into the lobby.
KING
Go seek him there. [*To some* ATTENDANTS.
HAMLET
He will stay till ye come. [*Exeunt* ATTENDANTS.
KING
Hamlet, this deed, for thine especial safety, —
Which we do tender, as we dearly grieve
For that which thou hast done, — must send thee
hence
With fiery quickness: therefore prepare thyself;
The bark is ready, and the wind at help,
Th'associates tend, and every thing is bent
For England.
HAMLET
For England!
KING
Ay, Hamlet.
HAMLET
Good.
KING
So is it, if thou knew'st our purposes.
HAMLET
I see a cherub that sees them. — But, come; for
England! — Farewell, dear mother.

ROSENCRANTZ What have you done, my lord, with the dead body?

KING
Thy loving father, Hamlet.

HAMLET
My mother: father and mother is man and wife; man
and wife is one flesh; and so, my mother. — Come, for
England!   [*Exit.*

KING
Follow him at foot; tempt him with speed aboard;
Delay it not; I'll have him hence to-night:
Away! for every thing is seal'd and done
That else leans on th'affair: pray you, make haste.

    [*Exeunt* ROSENCRANTZ *and* GUILDENSTERN.

And, England, if my love thou hold'st at aught, —
As my great power thereof may give thee sense,
Since yet thy cicatrice looks raw and red
After the Danish sword, and thy free awe
Pays homage to us, — thou mayst not coldly set
Our sovereign process; which imports at full,
By letters congruing to that effect,
The present death of Hamlet. Do it, England;
For like the hectic in my blood he rages,
And thou must cure me: till I know 'tis done,
Howe'er my haps, my joys were ne'er begun.   [*Exit.*

SCENE IV
A plain in Denmark.

Enter FORTINBRAS *with his* ARMY *over the stage.*

FORTINBRAS
Go, captain, from me greet the Danish king;
Tell him that, by his licence, Fortinbras
Claims the conveyance of a promis'd march
Over his kingdom. You know the rendezvous.
If that his majesty would aught with us,
We shall express our duty in his eye;
And let him know so.

CAPTAIN
                    I will do't, my lord.

FORTINBRAS
Go softly on.   [*Exeunt all but* CAPTAIN.

Enter HAMLET, ROSENCRANTZ, GUILDENSTERN,
and others.

HAMLET
Good sir, whose powers are these?

CAPTAIN
They are of Norway, sir.

HAMLET
How purposed, sir, I pray you?

CAPTAIN
Against some part of Poland.

HAMLET
Who commands them, sir?

CAPTAIN
The nephew to old Norway, Fortinbras.

HAMLET
Goes it against the main of Poland, sir,

Or for some frontier?

CAPTAIN
Truly to speak, sir, and with no addition,
We go to gain a little patch of ground
That hath in it no profit but the name.
To pay five ducats, five, I would not farm it;
Nor will it yield to Norway or the Pole
A ranker rate, should it be sold in fee.

HAMLET
Why, then, the Polack never will defend it.

CAPTAIN
Yes, it is already garrison'd.

HAMLET
Two thousand souls and twenty thousand ducats
Will not debate the question of this straw:
This is th'imposthume of much wealth and peace,
That inward breaks, and shows no cause without
Why the man dies. — I humbly thank you, sir.

CAPTAIN
God be wi' you, sir.   [*Exit.*

ROSENCRANTZ
                Will't please you go, my lord?

HAMLET
I'll be with you straight. Go a little before.

                        [*Exeunt all but* HAMLET.

How all occasions do inform against me,
And spur my dull revenge! What is a man
If his chief good and market of his time
Be but to sleep and feed? a beast, no more.
Sure, he that made us with such large discourse,
Looking before and after, gave us not
That capability and godlike reason
To fust in us unus'd. Now, whether it be
Bestial oblivion, or some craven scruple
Of thinking too precisely on the event, —
A thought which, quarter'd, hath but one part wisdom
And ever three parts coward, — I do not know
Why yet I live to say 'This thing's to do';
Sith I have cause, and will, and strength, and means
To do't. Examples, gross as earth, exhort me:
Witness this army, of such mass and charge,
Led by a delicate and tender prince,
Whose spirit, with divine ambition puff'd,
Makes mouths at the invisible event;
Exposing what is mortal and unsure
To all that fortune, death, and danger dare,
Even for an egg-shell. Rightly to be great
Is not to stir without great argument,
But greatly to find quarrel in a straw
When honour's at the stake. How stand I, then,
That have a father kill'd, a mother stain'd,
Excitements of my reason and my blood,
And let all sleep? while, to my shame, I see
The imminent death of twenty thousand men,
That for a fantasy and trick of fame
Go to their graves like beds; fight for a plot
Whereon the numbers cannot try the cause,

Which is not tomb enough and continent
To hide the slain? — O, from this time forth,
My thoughts be bloody, or be nothing worth!   [*Exit.*

SCENE V
Elsinore. A room in the castle.

Enter QUEEN *and* HORATIO.

QUEEN
I will not speak with her.

HORATIO
She is importunate, indeed distract;
Her mood will needs be pitied.

QUEEN
                    What would she have?

HORATIO
She speaks much of her father; says she hears
There's tricks i'th'world; and hems, and beats her
    heart;
Spurns enviously at straws; speaks things in doubt,
That carry but half sense: her speech is nothing,
Yet the unshaped use of it doth move
The hearers to collection; they aim at it,
And botch the words up fit to their own thoughts;
Which, as her winks and nods and gestures yield them,
Indeed would make one think there might be thought,
Though nothing sure, yet much unhappily.
'Twere good she were spoken with; for she may strew
Dangerous conjectures in ill-breeding minds.

QUEEN
Let her come in.   [*Exit* HORATIO.
To my sick soul, as sin's true nature is,
Each toy seems prologue to some great amiss:
So full of artless jealousy is guilt,
It spills itself in fearing to be spilt.

    Enter HORATIO, *with* OPHELIA *distracted.*

OPHELIA
Where is the beauteous majesty of Denmark?

QUEEN
How now, Ophelia!

OPHELIA [*sings*].
        How should I your true-love know
                From another one?
        By his cockle hat and staff,
                And his sandal shoon.

QUEEN
Alas, sweet lady, what imports this song?

OPHELIA
Say you? nay, pray you, mark.   [*Sings.*
        He is dead and gone, lady,
                He is dead and gone;
        At his head a grass-green turf,
                At his heels a stone.

QUEEN
Nay, but, Ophelia, —

OPHELIA
Pray you, mark.   [*Sings.*
        White his shroud as the mountain snow, —
                Enter KING.

QUEEN
Alas, look here, my lord.

OPHELIA [*sings*].
        Larded with sweet flowers;
        Which bewept to the grave did go
                With true-love showers.

KING
How do you, pretty lady?

OPHELIA
Well, God 'ild you! They say the owl was a baker's
daughter. Lord, we know what we are, but know not
what we may be. God be at your table!

KING
Conceit upon her father.

OPHELIA
Pray you, let's have no words of this; but when they ask
you what it means, say you this: [*Sings.*
        To-morrow is Saint Valentine's day,
                All in the morning betime,
        And I a maid at your window,
                To be your Valentine.
        Then up he rose, and donn'd his clothes,
                And dup'd the chamber-door;
        Let in the maid, that out a maid
                Never departed more.

KING
Pretty Ophelia!

OPHELIA
Indeed, la, without an oath, I'll make an end on't:

[*Sings.*

> By Gis and by Saint Charity,
>> Alack, and fie for shame!
> Young men will do't, if they come to't
>> By cock, they are to blame.
> Quoth she, before you tumbled me,
>> You promised me to wed.

He answers:

> So would I ha' done, by yonder sun,
>> An thou hadst not come to my bed.

KING
How long hath she been thus?

OPHELIA
I hope all will be well. We must be patient: but I cannot choose but weep, to think they should lay him i'th'cold ground. My brother shall know of it: and so I thank you for your good counsel. — Come, my coach! — Good night, ladies; good night, sweet ladies; good night, good night. [*Exit.*

KING
Follow her close; give her good watch, I pray you.
[*Exit* HORATIO.
O, this is the poison of deep grief; it springs
All from her father's death. O Gertrude, Gertrude,
When sorrows come, they come not single spies,
But in battalions! First, her father slain:
Next, your son gone; and he most violent author
Of his own just remove: the people muddied,
Thick and unwholesome in their thoughts and
     whispers,
For good Polonius' death; and we have done but
     greenly,
In hugger-mugger to inter him: poor Ophelia
Divided from herself and her fair judgement,
Without the which we are pictures, or mere beasts:
Last, and as much containing as all these,
Her brother is in secret come from France;
Feeds on his wonder, keeps himself in clouds,
And wants not buzzers to infect his ear
With pestilent speeches of his father's death;
Wherein necessity, of matter beggar'd,
Will nothing stick our person to arraign
In ear and ear. O my dear Gertrude, this,
Like to a murdering-piece, in many places
Gives me superfluous death. [*A noise within.*

QUEEN
                    Alack, what noise is this?

KING
Where are my Switzers? Let them guard the door.
Enter a GENTLEMAN.
What is the matter?

GENTLEMAN
               Save yourself, my lord:
The ocean, overpeering of his list,
Eats not the flats with more impetuous haste
Than young Laertes, in a riotous head,
O'erbears your officers. The rabble call him lord;
And, as the world were now but to begin,
Antiquity forgot, custom not known,
The ratifiers and props of every word,
They cry 'Choose we; Laertes shall be king!'
Caps, hands, and tongues applaud it to the clouds:
'Laertes shall be king, Laertes king!'

QUEEN
How cheerfully on the false trail they cry!
O, this is counter, you false Danish dogs!

KING
The doors are broke. [*Noise within.*
Enter LAERTES, *arm'd;* DANES *following.*

LAERTES
Where is this king? — Sirs, stand you all without.

DANES
No, let's come in.

LAERTES
             I pray you, give me leave.

DANES
We will, we will. [*They retire without the door.*

LAERTES
I thank you: — keep the door. — O thou vile king,
Give me my father!

QUEEN
             Calmly, good Laertes.

LAERTES
That drop of blood that's calm proclaims me bastard;
Cries cuckold to my father; brands the harlot
Even here, between the chaste unsmirched brow
Of my true mother.

KING
             What is the cause, Laertes,

That thy rebellion looks so giant-like? —
Let him go, Gertrude; do not fear our person:
There's such divinity doth hedge a king,
That treason can but peep to what it would,
Acts little of his will. — Tell me, Laertes,
Why thou art thus incens'd: — let him go, Gertrude: —
Speak, man.

LAERTES
Where is my father?

KING
                    Dead.

QUEEN
                    But not by him.

KING
Let him demand his fill.

LAERTES
How came he dead? I'll not be juggled with:
To hell, allegiance! vows, to the blackest devil!
Conscience and grace, to the profoundest pit!
I dare damnation: — to this point I stand, —
That both the worlds I give to negligence,
Let come what comes; only I'll be revenged
Most thoroughly for my father.

KING
                    Who shall stay you?

LAERTES
My will, not all the world:
And for my means, I'll husband them so well,
They shall go far with little.

KING
                    Good Laertes,
If you desire to know the certainty
Of your dear father's death, is't writ in your revenge,
That, swoopstake, you will draw both friend and foe,
Winner and loser?

LAERTES
None but his enemies.

KING
                    Will you know them then?

LAERTES
To his good friends thus wide I'll ope my arms,
And, like the kind life-rendering pelican,
Repast them with my blood.

KING
                    Why, now you speak
Like a good child and a true gentleman.
That I am guiltless of your father's death,
And am most sensible in grief for it,
It shall as level to your judgement 'pear
As day does to your eye.

DANES [*within*].
                    Let her come in.

LAERTES
How now! what noise is that?
Enter OPHELIA.
O heat, dry up my brains! tears seven-times salt,
Burn out the sense and virtue of mine eye! —
By heaven, thy madness shall be paid by weight,
Till our scale turn the beam. O rose of May!
Dear maid, kind sister, sweet Ophelia! —
O heavens! is't possible a young maid's wits
Should be as mortal as an old man's life?
Nature is fine in love; and where 'tis fine,
It sends some precious instance of itself
After the thing it loves.

OPHELIA [*sings*].
> They bore him barefac'd on the bier;
> Hey non nonny, nonny, hey nonny;
> And in his grave rain'd many a tear, —

Fare you well, my dove!

LAERTES
Hadst thou thy wits, and didst persuade revenge,
It could not move thus.

OPHELIA
You must sing, 'Down a-down, an you call him a-down-a.' O, how the wheel becomes it! It is the false steward, that stole his master's daughter.

LAERTES
This nothing's more than matter.

OPHELIA
There's rosemary, that's for remembrance; pray you, love, remember: and there is pansies, that's for thoughts.

LAERTES
A document in madness, — thoughts and remembrance fitted.

OPHELIA
There's fennel for you, and columbines: — there's rue for you; and here's some for me: — we may call it

herb-grace o' Sundays: — O, you must wear your rue with a difference. — There's a daisy: — I would give you some violets, but they wither'd all when my father died: — they say he made a good end, — [*Sings.*
> For bonny sweet Robin is all my joy, —

LAERTES
Thought and affliction, passion, hell itself,
She turns to favour and to prettiness.

OPHELIA [*sings*].
> And will a' not come again?
> And will a' not come again?
>> No, no, he is dead:
>> Go to thy death-bed:
> He never will come again.
>
> His beard was as white as snow,
> All flaxen was his poll:
>> He is gone, he is gone,
>> And we cast away moan:
> God ha' mercy on his soul!

And of all Christian souls, I pray God. — God be wi' you. [*Exit.*

LAERTES
Do you see this, O God?

KING
Laertes, I must commune with your grief,
Or you deny me right. Go but apart,
Make choice of whom your wisest friends you will,
And they shall hear and judge 'twixt you and me:
If by direct or by collateral hand
They find us touch'd, we will our kingdom give,
Our crown, our life, and all that we call ours,
To you in satisfaction; but if not,
Be you content to lend your patience to us,
And we shall jointly labour with your soul
To give it due content.

LAERTES
                    Let this be so;
His means of death, his obscure burial, —
No trophy, sword, nor hatchment o'er his bones,
No noble rite nor formal ostentation, —
Cry to be heard, as 'twere from heaven to earth,
That I must call't in question.

KING
                    So you shall;
And where th'offence is let the great axe fall.
I pray you, go with me. [*Exeunt.*

SCENE VI

Another room in the castle.

Enter HORATIO *and a* SERVANT.

HORATIO
What are they that would speak with me?

SERVANT
Seafaring men, sir: they say they have letters for you.

HORATIO
Let them come in. — [*Exit* SERVANT.
I do not know from what part of the world
I should be greeted, if not from Lord Hamlet.
Enter SAILORS.

FIRST SAILOR
God bless you, sir.

HORATIO
Let him bless thee too.

FIRST SAILOR
He shall, sir, an't please Him. There's a letter for you, sir, — it comes from the ambassador that was bound for England, — if your name be Horatio, as I am let to know it is.

HORATIO [*reads*].
Horatio, when thou shalt have overlook'd this, give these fellows some means to the king: they have letters for him. Ere we were two days old at sea, a pirate of very warlike appointment gave us chase. Finding ourselves too slow of sail, we put on a compell'd valour; and in the grapple I boarded them: on the instant they got clear of our ship; so I alone became their prisoner. They have dealt with me like thieves of mercy: but they knew what they did; I am to do a good turn for them. Let the king have the letters I have sent; and repair thou to me with as much speed as thou wouldst fly death. I have words to speak in thine ear will make thee dumb; yet are they much too light for the bore of the matter. These good fellows will bring thee where I am. Rosencrantz and Guildenstern hold their course for England: of them I have much to tell thee. Farewell.
     He that thou knowest thine, HAMLET.
Come, I will make you way for these your letters;
And do't the speedier, that you may direct me
To him from whom you brought them. [*Exeunt.*

OPHELIA There's rosemary, that's for remembrance.

SCENE VII

Another room in the castle.

Enter KING *and* LAERTES.

KING
Now must your conscience my acquittance seal,
And you must put me in your heart for friend,
Sith you have heard, and with a knowing ear,
That he which hath your noble father slain
Pursued my life.

LAERTES
                    It well appears: — but tell me
Why you proceeded not against these feats,
So crimeful and so capital in nature,
As by your safety, wisdom, all things else,
You mainly were stirr'd up.

KING
                    O, for two special reasons;
Which may to you, perhaps, seem much unsinew'd,
But yet to me th'are strong. The queen his mother
Lives almost by his looks; and for myself, —
My virtue or my plague, be it either which, —
She's so conjunctive to my life and soul,
That, as the star moves not but in his sphere,
I could not but by her. The other motive,
Why to a public count I might not go,
Is the great love the general gender bear him;
Who, dipping all his faults in their affection,
Would, like the spring that turneth wood to stone,
Convert his gyves to graces; so that my arrows,
Too slightly timber'd for so loud a wind,
Would have reverted to my bow again,
And not where I had aim'd them.

LAERTES
And so have I a noble father lost;
A sister driven into desperate terms, —
Whose worth, if praises may go back again,
Stood challenger on mount of all the age
For her perfections: — but my revenge will come.

KING
Break not your sleeps for that: you must not think
That we are made of stuff so flat and dull,
That we can let our beard be shook with danger,
And think it pastime. You shortly shall hear more:
I lov'd your father, and we love ourself;
And that, I hope, will teach you to imagine —

Enter a MESSENGER.

How now! what news?

MESSENGER
                    Letters, my lord, from Hamlet:
This to your majesty; this to the queen.

KING
From Hamlet! who brought them?

MESSENGER
Sailors, my lord, they say; I saw them not:
They were given me by Claudio, — he receiv'd them
Of him that brought them.

KING
                    Laertes, you shall hear them. —
Leave us.   [*Exit* MESSENGER.
[*Reads*] 'High and mighty, — You shall know I am set
naked on your kingdom. To-morrow shall I beg leave to
see your kingly eyes: when I shall, first asking your
pardon thereunto, recount the occasion of my sudden
and more strange return.
                                        HAMLET.'
What should this mean? Are all the rest come back?
Or is it some abuse, and no such thing?

LAERTES
Know you the hand?

KING
                    'Tis Hamlet's character: — 'Naked'. —
And in a postscript here, he says 'alone'.

Can you advise me?

LAERTES
I'm lost in it, my lord. But let him come;
It warms the very sickness in my heart,
That I shall live and tell him to his teeth,
'Thus didest thou.'

KING
                    If it be so, Laertes, —
As how should it be so? how otherwise? —
Will you be ruled by me?

LAERTES
                    Ay, my lord;
So you will not o'errule me to a peace.

KING
To thine own peace. If he be now return'd, —
As checking at his voyage, and that he means
No more to undertake it, — I will work him
To an exploit, now ripe in my device,
Under the which he shall not choose but fall:
And for his death no wind of blame shall breathe;
But even his mother shall uncharge the practice,
And call it accident.

LAERTES
                    My lord, I will be ruled;
The rather, if you could devise it so,
That I might be the organ.

KING
                    It falls right.
You have been talk'd of since your travel much,
And that in Hamlet's hearing, for a quality
Wherein, they say, you shine: your sum of parts
Did not together pluck such envy from him,
As did that one; and that, in my regard,
Of the unworthiest siege.

LAERTES
                    What part is that, my lord?

KING
A very riband in the cap of youth,
Yet needful too; for youth no less becomes
The light and careless livery that it wears
Than settled age his sables and his weeds,
Importing health and graveness. — Two months since,
Here was a gentleman of Normandy, —
I've seen myself, and serv'd against, the French,
And they can well on horseback: but this gallant
Had witchcraft in't; he grew unto his seat;
And to such wondrous doing brought his horse,
As he had been incorps'd and demi-natured
With the brave beast: so far he topp'd my thought,
That I, in forgery of shapes and tricks,
Come short of what he did.

LAERTES
                    A Norman was't?

KING
A Norman.

LAERTES
Upon my life, Lamond.

KING
                    The very same.

LAERTES
I know him well: he is the brooch, indeed,
And gem of all the nation.

KING
He made confession of you;
And gave you such a masterly report,
For art and exercise in your defence,
And for your rapier most especially,
That he cried out, 'twould be a sight indeed,
If one could match you: th'scrimers of their nation,
He swore, had neither motion, guard, nor eye,
If you oppos'd them. Sir, this report of his
Did Hamlet so envenom with his envy,
That he could nothing do but wish and beg
Your sudden coming o'er, to play with him.
Now, out of this, —

LAERTES
                    What out of this, my lord?

KING
Laertes, was your father dear to you?
Or are you like the painting of a sorrow,
A face without a heart?

LAERTES
                    Why ask you this?

KING
Not that I think you did not love your father;
But that I know love is begun by time;
And that I see, in passages of proof,
Time qualifies the spark and fire of it.
There lives within the very flame of love
A kind of wick or snuff that will abate it;

FIRST SAILOR There's a letter for you, sir.

And nothing is at a like goodness still;
For goodness, growing to a plurisy,
Dies in his own too-much: that we would do,
We should do when we would; for this 'would'
    changes,
And hath abatements and delays as many
As there are tongues, are hands, are accidents;
And then this 'should' is like a spendthrift sigh,
That hurts by easing. But, to th'quick o' th'ulcer: —
Hamlet comes back: what would you undertake,
To show yourself your father's son in deed
More than in words?

LAERTES
                To cut his throat i'th'church.

KING
No place, indeed, should murder sanctuarise;
Revenge should have no bounds. But, good Laertes,
Will you do this, keep close within your chamber.
Hamlet return'd shall know you are come home:
We'll put on those shall praise your excellence,
And set a double varnish on the fame
The Frenchman gave you; bring you, in fine, together,
And wager on your heads: he, being remiss,
Most generous, and free from all contriving,
Will not peruse the foils; so that, with ease,
Or with a little shuffling, you may choose
A sword unbated, and, in a pass of practice,
Requite him for your father.

LAERTES
                I will do't:
And for that purpose, I'll anoint my sword.
I bought an unction of a mountebank,
So mortal, that but dip a knife in it,
Where it draws blood no cataplasm so rare,
Collected from all simples that have virtue
Under the moon, can save the thing from death
That is but scratch'd withal: I'll touch my point
With this contagion, that, if I gall him slightly,
It may be death.

KING
              Let's further think of this;
Weigh what convenience both of time and means
May fit us to our shape: if this should fail,
And that our drift look through our bad performance,
'Twere better not assay'd: therefore this project
Should have a back or second, that might hold,
If this should blast in proof. Soft! — let me see: —
We'll make a solemn wager on your cunnings, —
I ha't:
When in your motion you are hot and dry, —
As make your bouts more violent to that end, —
And that he calls for drink, I'll have prepared him
A chalice for the nonce; whereon but sipping,
If he by chance escape your venom'd stuck,
Our purpose may hold there. But stay! what noise? —
        Enter QUEEN.
How now, sweet queen!

QUEEN
One woe doth tread upon another's heel,
So fast they follow: — your sister's drown'd, Laertes.

LAERTES
Drown'd! O, where?

QUEEN
There is a willow grows aslant a brook,
That shows his hoar leaves in the glassy stream;
There with fantastic garlands did she come
Of crow-flowers, nettles, daisies, and long purples
That liberal shepherds give a grosser name,
But our cold maids do dead men's fingers call them:
There, on the pendent boughs her coronet weeds
Clambering to hang, an envious sliver broke;
When down her weedy trophies and herself
Fell in the weeping brook. Her clothes spread wide,
And, mermaid-like, awhile they bore her up;
Which time she chanted snatches of old tunes,
As one incapable of her own distress,
Or like a creature native and indued
Unto that element: but long it could not be
Till that her garments, heavy with their drink,
Pull'd the poor wretch from her melodious lay
To muddy death.

LAERTES
              Alas, then, she is drown'd?

QUEEN
Drown'd, drown'd.

LAERTES
Too much of water hast thou, poor Ophelia,
And therefore I forbid my tears: but yet
It is our trick; nature her custom holds,
Let shame say what it will: when these are gone,
The woman will be out. — Adieu, my lord:
I have a speech of fire, that fain would blaze,
But that this folly douts it.   [*Exit.*

KING
              Let's follow, Gertrude:
How much I had to do to calm his rage!
Now fear I this will give it start again;
Therefore let's follow.   [*Exeunt.*

ACT V

SCENE I

Elsinore. A churchyard.

Enter two CLOWNS, *with spades, etc.*

FIRST CLOWN
Is she to be buried in Christian burial that wilfully
seeks her own salvation?

SECOND CLOWN
I tell thee she is; and therefore make her grave straight:
the crowner hath sat on her, and finds it Christian
burial.

FIRST CLOWN
How can that be, unless she drown'd herself in her
own defence?

SECOND CLOWN
Why, 'tis found so.

FIRST CLOWN
It must be *se offendendo*; it cannot be else. For here lies
the point: if I drown myself wittingly, it argues an act:
and an act hath three branches; it is, to act, to do, to
perform: argal, she drown'd herself wittingly.

SECOND CLOWN
Nay, but hear you, goodman delver, —

FIRST CLOWN
Give me leave. Here lies the water; good: here stands
the man; good: if the man go to this water and drown
himself, it is, will he, nill he, he goes, — mark you that;
but if the water come to him and drown him, he
drowns not himself: argal, he that is not guilty of his
own death shortens not his own life.

SECOND CLOWN
But is this law?

FIRST CLOWN
Ay, marry, is't; crowner's quest-law.

SECOND CLOWN
Will you ha' the truth on't? If this had not been a
gentlewoman, she should have been buried out o'
Christian burial.

FIRST CLOWN
Why, there thou sayst: and the more pity that great folk
should have countenance in this world to drown or
hang themselves, more than their even Christian. —
Come, my spade. There is no ancient gentleman but
gardeners, ditchers, and grave-makers: they hold up
Adam's profession.

SECOND CLOWN
Was he a gentleman?

FIRST CLOWN
A' was the first that ever bore arms.

SECOND CLOWN
Why, he had none.

FIRST CLOWN
What, art a heathen? How dost thou understand the
Scripture? The Scripture says, Adam digg'd: could he
dig without arms? I'll put another question to thee: if
thou answerest me not to the purpose, confess
thyself —

SECOND CLOWN
Go to.

FIRST CLOWN
What is he that builds stronger than either the mason,
the shipwright, or the carpenter?

SECOND CLOWN
The gallows-maker; for that frame outlives a thousand
tenants.

FIRST CLOWN
I like thy wit well, in good faith: the gallows does well;
but how does it well? it does well to those that do ill:
now, thou dost ill to say the gallows is built stronger
than the church: argal, the gallows may do well to thee.
To't again, come.

SECOND CLOWN
'Who builds stronger than a mason, a shipwright, or a
carpenter?'

FIRST CLOWN
Ay, tell me that, and unyoke.

SECOND CLOWN
Marry, now I can tell.

FIRST CLOWN
To't.

SECOND CLOWN
Mass, I cannot tell.

      Enter HAMLET *and* HORATIO, *afar off.*

FIRST CLOWN
Cudgel thy brains no more about it, for your dull ass will
not mend his pace with beating; and when you are ask'd
this question next, say 'a grave-maker': the houses that he
makes last till doomsday. Go, get thee to Yaughan; fetch
me a stoop of liquor.   [*Exit* SECOND CLOWN.
                   [*He digs, and sings.*
    In youth, when I did love, did love,
      Methought it was very sweet,
    To contract, O, the time, for, ah, my behove,
      O, methought there was nothing meet.

HAMLET
Has this fellow no feeling of his business, that he sings
at grave-making?

HORATIO
Custom hath made it in him a property of easiness.

HAMLET
'Tis e'en so: the hand of little employment hath the daintier sense.

FIRST CLOWN [sings].
But age, with his stealing steps,
    Hath claw'd me in his clutch,
And hath shipp'd me intil the land,
    As if I had never been such.
                                    [Throws up a skull.

HAMLET
That skull had a tongue in it, and could sing once: how the knave jowls it to the ground, as if it were Cain's jaw-bone, that did the first murder! It might be the pate of a politician, which this ass now o'er-reaches; one that would circumvent God, might it not?

HORATIO
It might, my lord.

HAMLET
Or of a courtier; which could say 'Good morrow, sweet lord! How dost thou, good lord?' This might be my lord such-a-one, that praised my lord such-a-one's horse, when he meant to beg it, — might it not?

HORATIO
Ay, my lord.

HAMLET
Why, e'en so: and now my Lady Worm's; chapless, and knock'd about the mazard with a sexton's spade: here's fine revolution, an we had the trick to see't. Did these bones cost no more the breeding, but to play at loggats with 'em? mine ache to think on't.

FIRST CLOWN [sings].
A pickaxe, and a spade, a spade,
    For and a shrouding sheet:
O, a pit of clay for to be made
    For such a guest is meet.
                                    [Throws up another skull.

HAMLET
There's another: why may not that be the skull of a lawyer? Where be his quiddits now, his quillets, his cases, his tenures, and his tricks? why does he suffer this rude knave now to knock him about the sconce with a dirty shovel, and will not tell him of his action of battery? Hum! This fellow might be in's time a great buyer of land, with his statutes, his recognisances, his fines, his double vouchers, his recoveries: is this the fine of his fines, and the recovery of his recoveries, to have his fine pate full of fine dirt? will his vouchers vouch him no more of his purchases, and double ones too, than the length and breadth of a pair of indentures? The very conveyances of his lands will hardly lie in this box; and must the inheritor himself have no more, ha?

HORATIO
Not a jot more, my lord.

HAMLET
Is not parchment made of sheep-skins?

HORATIO
Ay, my lord, and of calf-skins too.

HAMLET
They are sheep and calves which seek out assurance in

that. I will speak to this fellow. — Whose grave's this, sirrah?

FIRST CLOWN
Mine, sir. —   [Sings.
    O, a pit of clay for to be made
        For such a guest is meet.

HAMLET
I think it be thine, indeed; for thou liest in't.

FIRST CLOWN
You lie out on't, sir, and therefore it is not yours: for my part, I do not lie in't, and yet it is mine.

HAMLET
Thou dost lie in't, to be in't, and say it is thine: 'tis for the dead, not for the quick; therefore thou liest.

FIRST CLOWN
'Tis a quick lie, sir; 'twill away again, from me to you.

HAMLET
What man dost thou dig it for?

FIRST CLOWN
For no man, sir.

HAMLET
What woman, then?

FIRST CLOWN
For none, neither.

HAMLET
Who is to be buried in't?

FIRST CLOWN
One that was a woman, sir; but, rest her soul, she's dead.

HAMLET
How absolute the knave is! we must speak by the card, or equivocation will undo us. By the Lord, Horatio, this three years I have taken note of it; the age is grown so pick'd, that the toe of the peasant comes so near the heel of the courtier, he galls his kibe. — How long hast thou been a grave-maker?

FIRST CLOWN
Of all the days i'th'year, I came to't that day that our last king Hamlet o'ercame Fortinbras.

HAMLET
How long is that since?

FIRST CLOWN
Cannot you tell that? every fool can tell that: it was that very day that young Hamlet was born, — he that is mad, and sent into England.

HAMLET
Ay, marry, why was he sent into England?

FIRST CLOWN
Why, because a' was mad: a' shall recover his wits there; or, if a' do not, 'tis no great matter there.

HAMLET
Why?

FIRST CLOWN
'Twill not be seen in him there; there the men are as mad as he.

HAMLET
How came he mad?

FIRST CLOWN
Very strangely, they say.

HAMLET
How strangely?

FIRST CLOWN
Faith, e'en with losing his wits.

HAMLET
Upon what ground?

FIRST CLOWN
Why, here in Denmark: I have been sexton here, man and boy, thirty years.

HAMLET
How long will a man lie i'th'earth ere he rot?

FIRST CLOWN
I'faith, if a' be not rotten before a' die, — as we have many pocky corses now-a-days that will scarce hold the laying in, — a' will last you some eight year or nine year: a tanner will last you nine year.

HAMLET
Why he more than another?

FIRST CLOWN
Why, sir, his hide is so tann'd with his trade that a' will keep out water a great while; and your water is a sore decayer of your whoreson dead body. Here's a skull now hath lain you i'th'earth three-and-twenty years.

HAMLET
Whose was it?

FIRST CLOWN
A whoreson mad fellow's it was: whose do you think it was?

HAMLET
Nay, I know not.

FIRST CLOWN
A pestilence on him for a mad rogue! a' pour'd a flagon of Rhenish on my head once. This same skull, sir, was Yorick's skull, the king's jester.

HAMLET
This?

FIRST CLOWN
E'en that.

HAMLET
Let me see. [Takes the skull.] — Alas, poor Yorick! — I knew him, Horatio: a fellow of infinite jest, of most excellent fancy: he hath borne me on his back a thousand times; and now, how abhorr'd in my imagination it is! my gorge rises at it. Here hung those lips that I have kiss'd I know not how oft. Where be your gibes now? your gambols? your songs? your flashes of merriment, that were wont to set the table on a roar? Not one now, to mock your own grinning? quite chop-fall'n? Now get you to my lady's chamber, and tell her, let her paint an inch thick, to this favour she must come; make her laugh at that. — Prithee, Horatio, tell me one thing.

HORATIO
What's that, my lord?

HAMLET
Dost thou think Alexander look'd o' this fashion i'th'earth?

HORATIO
E'en so.

HAMLET
And smelt so? pah!   [Puts down the skull.

HORATIO
E'en so, my lord.

HAMLET
To what base uses we may return, Horatio! Why may not imagination trace the noble dust of Alexander till he find it stopping a bung-hole?

HORATIO
'Twere to consider too curiously, to consider so.

HAMLET
No, faith, not a jot; but to follow him thither with modesty enough, and likelihood to lead it: as thus; Alexander died, Alexander was buried, Alexander returneth into dust; the dust is earth: of earth we make loam; and why of that loam whereto he was converted might they not stop a beer-barrel?
    Imperious Cæsar, dead and turn'd to clay,
        Might stop a hole to keep the wind away:
    O, that that earth which kept the world in awe
        Should patch a wall t'expel the winter flaw! —
But soft! but soft! aside: — here comes the king.

    Enter KING, QUEEN, LAERTES and the Corse;
        PRIESTS, and LORDS attendant.

The queen, the courtiers: who is this they follow?
And with such maimed rites? This doth betoken
The corse they follow did with desperate hand
Fordo its own life: 'twas of some estate.
Couch we awhile, and mark. [Retiring with HORATIO.

FIRST CLOWN Ay, marry, is't; crowner's quest-law.

LAERTES
What ceremony else?

HAMLET
         That is Laertes,
A very noble youth: mark.

LAERTES
What ceremony else?

FIRST PRIEST
Her obsequies have been as far enlarg'd
As we have warrantise: her death was doubtful;
And, but that great command o'ersways the order,
She should in ground unsanctified have lodg'd
Till the last trumpet; for charitable prayers,
Shards, flints, and pebbles should be thrown on her:
Yet here she is allow'd her virgin crants,
Her maiden strewments, and the bringing home
Of bell and burial.

LAERTES
Must there no more be done?

FIRST PRIEST
         No more be done:
We should profane the service of the dead
To sing a requiem, and such rest to her
As to peace-parted souls.

LAERTES
         Lay her i'th'earth; —
And from her fair and unpolluted flesh
May violets spring! — I tell thee, churlish priest,
A minist'ring angel shall my sister be,
When thou liest howling.

HAMLET
         What, the fair Ophelia!

QUEEN
Sweets to the sweet: farewell!   *[Scattering flowers.*
I hop'd thou shouldst have been my Hamlet's wife;
I thought thy bride-bed to have deck'd, sweet maid,
And not have strew'd thy grave.

LAERTES
         O, treble woe
Fall ten times treble on that cursed head
Whose wicked deed thy most ingenious sense
Depriv'd thee of! — Hold off the earth awhile,
Till I have caught her once more in mine arms:
         [Leaps into the grave.
Now pile your dust upon the quick and dead,
Till of this flat a mountain you have made
To o'ertop old Pelion or the skyish head
Of blue Olympus.

HAMLET *[advancing].*
         What is he whose grief
Bears such an emphasis! whose phrase of sorrow
Conjures the wandering stars, and makes them stand
Like wonder-wounded hearers? This is I,
Hamlet the Dane.   *[Leaps into the grave.*

LAERTES
         The devil take thy soul!
         [Grappling with him.

HAMLET
Thou pray'st not well.
I prithee, take thy fingers from my throat;
For, though I am not splenitive and rash,
Yet have I something in me dangerous,
Which let thy wisdom fear: hold off thy hand!

KING
Pluck them asunder.

QUEEN
         Hamlet, Hamlet!

ALL
         Gentlemen, —

HORATIO
Good my lord, be quiet.
[The ATTENDANTS *part them, and they come out of the grave.*

HAMLET
Why, I will fight with him upon this theme
Until my eyelids will no longer wag.

QUEEN
O my son, what theme?

HAMLET
I lov'd Ophelia: forty thousand brothers
Could not, with all their quantity of love,
Make up my sum. — What wilt thou do for her?

KING
O, he is mad, Laertes.

QUEEN
For love of God, forbear him.

HAMLET
'Swounds, show me what thou'lt do:
Woo't weep? woo't fight? woo't fast? woo't tear thyself?

Woo't drink up eisel? eat a crocodile?
I'll do't. — Dost thou come here to whine?
To outface me with leaping in her grave?
Be buried quick with her, and so will I:
And if thou prate of mountains, let them throw
Millions of acres on us, till our ground,
Singeing his pate against the burning zone,
Make Ossa like a wart! Nay, an thou'lt mouth,
I'll rant as well as thou.

QUEEN
         This is mere madness:
And thus awhile the fit will work on him;
Anon, as patient as the female dove
When that her golden couplets are disclosed,
His silence will sit drooping.

HAMLET
         Hear you, sir;
What is the reason that you use me thus?
I lov'd you ever: but it is no matter;
Let Hercules himself do what he may,
The cat will mew, and dog will have his day.   *[Exit.*

KING
I pray you, good Horatio, wait upon him. —
         [Exit HORATIO.
[to LAERTES] Strengthen your patience in our last
  night's speech;
We'll put the matter to the present push. —
Good Gertrude, set some watch over your son. —
This grave shall have a living monument:
An hour of quiet shortly shall we see;
Till then, in patience our proceeding be.   *[Exeunt.*

HAMLET Alas, poor Yorick! — I knew him, Horatio.

SCENE II

A hall in the castle.

Enter HAMLET *and* HORATIO.

HAMLET
So much for this, sir: now shall you see the other; —
You do remember all the circumstance?

HORATIO
Remember it, my lord!

HAMLET
Sir, in my heart there was a kind of fighting,
That would not let me sleep: methought I lay
Worse than the mutines in the bilboes. Rashly,
And prais'd be rashness for it, let us know,
Our indiscretion sometime serves us well,
When our deep plots do pall: and that should learn us
There's a divinity that shapes our ends,
Rough-hew them how we will, —

HORATIO
         That is most certain.

HAMLET
Up from my cabin,
My sea-gown scarf'd about me, in the dark
Grop'd I to find out them: had my desire;
Finger'd their packet; and, in fine, withdrew
To mine own room again: making so bold,
My fears forgetting manners, to unseal
Their grand commission; where I found, Horatio, —
O royal knavery! — an exact command, —
Larded with many several sorts of reasons,
Importing Denmark's health, and England's too,
With, ho! such bugs and goblins in my life, —

That, on the supervise, no leisure bated,
No, not to stay the grinding of the axe,
My head should be struck off.

HORATIO
                              Is't possible?

HAMLET
Here's the commission: read it at more leisure.
But wilt thou hear me how I did proceed?

HORATIO
I beseech you.

HAMLET
Being thus be-netted round with villainies, —
Ere I could make a prologue to my brains,
They had begun the play, — I sat me down;
Devis'd a new commission; wrote it fair: —
I once did hold it, as our statists do,
A baseness to write fair, and labour'd much
How to forget that learning; but, sir, now
It did me yeoman's service: — wilt thou know
The effect of what I wrote?

HORATIO
                              Ay, good my lord.

HAMLET
An earnest conjuration from the king, —
As England was his faithful tributary;
As love between them like the palm might flourish;
As peace should still her wheaten garland wear,
And stand a comma 'tween their amities;
And many such-like As-es of great charge, —
That, on the view and knowing of these contents,
Without debatement further, more or less,
He should the bearers put to sudden death,
Not shriving-time allow'd.

HORATIO
                              How was this seal'd?

HAMLET
Why, even in that was heaven ordinant.
I had my father's signet in my purse,
Which was the model of that Danish seal;
Folded the writ up in form of th'other;
Subscrib'd it; gave't th'impression; plac'd it safely,
The changeling never known. Now, the next day
Was our sea-fight; and what to this was sequent
Thou know'st already.

HORATIO
So Guildenstern and Rosencrantz go to't.

HAMLET
Why, man, they did make love to this employment;
They are not near my conscience; their defeat
Does by their own insinuation grow:
'Tis dangerous when the baser nature comes
Between the pass and fell incensed points
Of mighty opposites.

HORATIO
                              Why, what a king is this!

HAMLET
Does it not, think'st thee, stand me now upon, —
He that hath kill'd my king, and whored my mother;
Popp'd in between th'election and my hopes;
Thrown out his angle for my proper life,
And with such cozenage, — is't not perfect conscience
To quit him with this arm? and is't not to be damn'd,
To let this canker of our nature come
In further evil?

HORATIO
It must be shortly known to him from England
What is the issue of the business there.

HAMLET
It will be short: the interim is mine;
And a man's life's no more than to say 'one'.
But I am very sorry, good Horatio,
That to Laertes I forgot myself;
For, by the image of my cause, I see
The portraiture of his: I'll court his favours:
But, sure, the bravery of his grief did put me
Into a towering passion.

HORATIO
                              Peace! who comes here?

Enter OSRIC.

OSRIC
Your lordship is right welcome back to Denmark.

HAMLET
I humbly thank you, sir. — [*aside to* HORATIO]
Dost know this water-fly?

HORATIO [*aside to* HAMLET].
No, my good lord.

HAMLET [*aside to* HORATIO].
Thy state is the more gracious; for 'tis a vice to know
him. He hath much land, and fertile: let a beast be lord

of beasts, and his crib shall stand at the king's mess: 'tis
a chough; but, as I say, spacious in the possession of
dirt.

OSRIC
Sweet lord, if your lordship were at leisure, I should
impart a thing to you from his majesty.

HAMLET
I will receive it, sir, with all diligence of spirit. Put your
bonnet to his right use; 'tis for the head.

OSRIC
I thank your lordship, it is very hot.

HAMLET
No, believe me, 'tis very cold; the wind is northerly.

OSRIC
It is indifferent cold, my lord, indeed.

HAMLET
But yet methinks it is very sultry and hot for my
complexion.

OSRIC
Exceedingly, my lord; it is very sultry, — as 'twere, — I
cannot tell how. — But, my lord, his majesty bade me
signify to you, that he has laid a great wager on your
head: sir, this is the matter, —

HAMLET
I beseech you, remember —

                    [HAMLET *moves him to put on his hat.*

OSRIC
Nay, good my lord: for mine ease, in good faith. Sir,
here is newly come to court Laertes; believe me, an
absolute gentleman, full of most excellent differences,
of very soft society and great showing: indeed, to speak
feelingly of him, he is the card or calendar of gentry, for
you shall find in him the continent of what part a
gentleman would see.

HAMLET
Sir, his definement suffers no perdition in you; —
though, I know, to divide him inventorially would
dizzy the arithmetic of memory, and yet but yaw
neither, in respect of his quick sail. But, in the verity of
extolment, I take him to be a soul of great article; and
his infusion of such dearth and rareness, as, to make
true diction of him, his semblable is his mirror; and
who else would trace him, his umbrage, nothing more.

OSRIC
Your lordship speaks most infallibly of him.

HAMLET
The concernancy, sir? why do we wrap the gentleman
in our more rawer breath?

OSRIC
Sir?

HORATIO
Is't not possible to understand in another tongue? You
will do't, sir, really.

HAMLET
What imports the nomination of this gentleman?

OSRIC
Of Laertes?

HORATIO [*aside to* HAMLET].
His purse is empty already: all's golden words are
spent.

HAMLET
Of him, sir.

OSRIC
I know you are not ignorant —

HAMLET
I would you did, sir; yet, in faith, if you did, it would not
much approve me: — well, sir.

OSRIC
You are not ignorant of what excellence Laertes is —

HAMLET
I dare not confess that, lest I should compare with him
in excellence; but, to know a man well, were to know
himself.

OSRIC
I mean, sir, for his weapon; but in the imputation laid
on him by them, in his meed he's unfellow'd.

HAMLET
What's his weapon?

OSRIC
Rapier and dagger.

HAMLET
That's two of his weapons: but, well.

OSRIC
The king, sir, hath wager'd with him six Barbary
horses: against the which he has imponed, as I take it,
six French rapiers and poniards, with their assigns, as
girdle, hangers, and so: three of the carriages, in faith,
are very dear to fancy, very responsive to the hilts, most

delicate carriages, and of very liberal conceit.

HAMLET
What call you the carriages?

HORATIO [*aside to* HAMLET].
I knew you must be edified by the margent ere you had
done.

OSRIC
The carriages, sir, are the hangers.

HAMLET
The phrase would be more german to the matter, if
we could carry cannon by our sides: I would it might
be hangers till then. But, on: six Barbary horses
against six French swords, their assigns, and three
liberal-conceited carriages; that's the French bet against
the Danish. Why is this 'imponed'. as you call it?

OSRIC
The king, sir, hath laid, that in a dozen passes between
yourself and him, he shall not exceed you three hits: he
hath laid on twelve for nine; and it would come to
immediate trial, if your lordship would vouchsafe the
answer.

HAMLET
How if I answer no?

OSRIC
I mean, my lord, the opposition of your person in trial.

HAMLET
Sir, I will walk here in the hall: if it please his majesty,
'tis the breathing time of day with me; let the foils be
brought, the gentleman willing, and the king hold his
purpose, I will win for him an I can; if not, I will gain
nothing but my shame and the odd hits.

OSRIC
Shall I re-deliver you e'en so?

HAMLET
To this effect, sir; after what flourish your nature will.

OSRIC
I commend my duty to your lordship.

HAMLET
Yours, yours. [*Exit* OSRIC.] — He does well to
commend it himself; there are no tongues else for's
turn.

HORATIO
This lapwing runs away with the shell on his head.

HAMLET
He did comply with his dug, before he suck'd it. Thus
has he — and many more of the same bevy, that I know
the drossy age dotes on — only got the tune of the time,
and outward habit of encounter; a kind of yesty
collection, which carries them through and through
the most fann'd and winnow'd opinions; and do but
blow them to their trial, the bubbles are out.

Enter a LORD.

LORD
My lord, his majesty commended him to you by young
Osric, who brings back to him, that you attend him in
the hall: he sends to know if your pleasure hold to play
with Laertes, or that you will take longer time.

HAMLET
I am constant to my purpose; they follow the king's
pleasure: if his fitness speaks, mine is ready; now or
whensoever, provided I be so able as now.

LORD
The king and queen and all are coming down.

HAMLET
In happy time.

LORD
The queen desires you to use some gentle
entertainment to Laertes before you fall to play.

HAMLET
She well instructs me.   [*Exit* LORD

HORATIO
You will lose this wager, my lord.

HAMLET
I do not think so; since he went into France, I have been
in continual practice; I shall win at the odds. But thou
wouldst not think how ill all's here about my heart: but
it is no matter.

HORATIO
Nay, good my lord, —

HAMLET
It is but foolery; but it is such a kind of gain-giving as
would perhaps trouble a woman.

HORATIO
If your mind dislike any thing, obey it: I will forestall
their repair hither, and say you are not fit.

HAMLET
Not a whit, we defy augury: there's a special providence
in the fall of a sparrow. If it be now, 'tis not to come; if

be not to come, it will be now; if it be not now, yet it will
come: the readiness is all: since no man knows aught of
what he leaves, what is't to leave betimes? Let be.

Enter KING, QUEEN, LAERTES, LORDS, OSRIC,
and ATTENDANTS *with foils and gauntlets:*
a table and flagons of wine on it.

KING
Come, Hamlet, come, and take this hand from me.

[*The* KING *puts* LAERTES' *hand into* HAMLET'S.

HAMLET
Give me your pardon, sir: I've done you wrong;
But pardon't, as you are a gentleman.
This presence knows,
And you must needs have heard, how I am punish'd
With sore distraction. What I have done,
That might your nature, honour, and exception
Roughly awake, I here proclaim was madness.
Was't Hamlet wrong'd Laertes? Never Hamlet:
If Hamlet from himself be ta'en away,
And when he's not himself does wrong Laertes,
Then Hamlet does it not, Hamlet denies it.
Who does it, then? His madness: if't be so,
Hamlet is of the faction that is wrong'd;
His madness is poor Hamlet's enemy.
Sir, in this audience,
Let my disclaiming from a purpos'd evil
Free me so far in your most generous thoughts,
That I have shot mine arrow o'er the house,
And hurt my brother.

LAERTES
    I am satisfied in nature,
Whose motive, in this case, should stir me most
To my revenge: but in my terms of honour
I stand aloof; and will no reconcilement
Till by some elder masters, of known honour,
I have a voice and precedent of peace,
To keep my name ungored. But till that time
I do receive your offer'd love like love,
And will not wrong it.

HAMLET
    I embrace it freely;
And will this brother's wager frankly play. —
Give us the foils. — Come on.

LAERTES
    Come, one for me.

HAMLET
I'll be your foil, Laertes: in mine ignorance
Your skill shall, like a star i'th'darkest night,
Stick fiery off indeed.

LAERTES
    You mock me, sir.

HAMLET
No, by this hand.

KING
Give them the foils, young Osric. — Cousin Hamlet,
You know the wager?

HAMLET
    Very well, my lord;
Your Grace hath laid the odds o'th'weaker side.

KING
I do not fear it; I have seen you both:
But since he is better'd, we have therefore odds.

LAERTES
This is too heavy, let me see another.

HAMLET
This likes me well. These foils have all a length?
             [*They prepare to play.*

OSRIC
Ay, my good lord.

KING
Set me the stoops of wine upon that table. —
If Hamlet give the first or second hit,
Or quit in answer of the third exchange,
Let all the battlements their ordnance fire;
The king shall drink to Hamlet's better breath;
And in the cup an union shall he throw,
Richer than that which four successive kings
In Denmark's crown have worn. Give me the cups;
And let the kettle to the trumpet speak,
The trumpet to the cannoneer without,
The cannons to the heavens, the heaven to earth,
'Now the king drinks to Hamlet.' — Come, begin;
And you, the judges, bear a wary eye.

HAMLET
Come on, sir.

LAERTES
    Come, my lord.   [*They play.*

HAMLET
        One.

LAERTES
          No.

HAMLET
            Judgement.

OSRIC
A hit, a very palpable hit.

LAERTES
        Well; — again.

KING
Stay; give me drink. — Hamlet, this pearl is thine;
Here's to thy health. [*Trumpets sound, and shot goes off.*
        Give him the cup.

HAMLET
I'll play this bout first; set it by awhile. —
Come. — [*They play.*] Another hit; what say you?

LAERTES
A touch, a touch, I do confess.

KING
Our son shall win.

QUEEN
    He's fat, and scant of breath.
Here, Hamlet, take my napkin, rub thy brows:
The queen carouses to thy fortune, Hamlet.

HAMLET
Good madam!

KING
    Gertrude, do not drink.

QUEEN
I will, my lord; I pray you, pardon me.   [*Drinks.*

KING [*aside*].
It is the poison'd cup; it is too late.

HAMLET
I dare not drink yet, madam; by and by.

QUEEN
Come, let me wipe thy face.

LAERTES
My lord, I'll hit him now.

KING
    I do not think't.

LAERTES [*aside*].
And yet 'tis almost 'gainst my conscience.

HAMLET
Come, for the third, Laertes: you but dally;
I pray you, pass with your best violence;
I am afear'd you make a wanton of me.

LAERTES
Say you so? come on.   [*They play.*

OSRIC
Nothing, neither way.

LAERTES
Have at you now!
    [LAERTES *wounds* HAMLET; *then, in scuffling, they*
      change rapiers, and HAMLET *wounds* LAERTES.

KING
    Part them; they are incensed.

HAMLET
Nay, come, again.   [*The* QUEEN *falls.*

OSRIC
    Look to the queen there, ho!

HORATIO
They bleed on both sides. — How is it, my lord?

OSRIC
How is't, Laertes?

LAERTES
Why, as a woodcock to mine own springe, Osric;
I am justly kill'd with mine own treachery.

HAMLET
How does the queen?

FORTINBRAS This quarry cries on havoc.

KING
            She swounds to see them bleed.

QUEEN
No, no, the drink, the drink, — O my dear Hamlet, —
The drink, the drink! — I am poison'd.   [*Dies.*

HAMLET
O villainy! — Ho! let the door be lock'd:
Treachery! seek it out.   [LAERTES *falls.*

LAERTES
It is here, Hamlet: Hamlet, thou art slain;
No medicine in the world can do thee good,
In thee there is not half an hour of life;
The treacherous instrument is in thy hand,
Unbated and envenom'd: the foul practice
Hath turn'd itself on me; lo, here I lie,
Never to rise again: thy mother's poison'd: —
I can no more: — the king, the king's to blame.

HAMLET
The point envenom'd too! —
Then, venom, to thy work.   [*Stabs the* KING.

ALL
Treason! treason!

KING
O, yet defend me, friends; I am but hurt.

HAMLET
Here, thou incestuous, murderous, damned Dane,
Drink off this potion: — is thy union here?
Follow my mother.   [KING *dies.*

LAERTES
          He is justly served;
It is a poison temper'd by himself. —
Exchange forgiveness with me, noble Hamlet:
Mine and my father's death come not upon thee,
Nor thine on me!   [*Dies.*

HAMLET
Heaven make thee free of it! I follow thee. —
I am dead, Horatio. — Wretched queen, adieu! —
You that look pale and tremble at this chance,
That are but mutes or audience to this act,
Had I but time, — as this fell sergeant, death,
Is strict in his arrest, — O, I could tell you, —
But let it be. — Horatio, I am dead;
Thou liv'st; report me and my cause aright
To the unsatisfied.

HORATIO
          Never believe it:
I am more an antique Roman than a Dane:
Here's yet some liquor left.

HAMLET
          As th'art a man,
Give me the cup: let go; by heaven, I'll have't.
O good Horatio, what a wounded name,
Things standing thus unknown, shall live behind me!
If thou didst ever hold me in thy heart,
Absent thee from felicity awhile,
And in this harsh world draw thy breath in pain,
To tell my story.   [*March afar off, and shot within.*
     What warlike noise is this?

OSRIC
Young Fortinbras, with conquest come from Poland,
To the ambassadors of England gives
This warlike volley.

HAMLET
          O, I die, Horatio;
The potent poison quite o'er-crows my spirit:
I cannot live to hear the news from England;
But I do prophesy th'election lights
On Fortinbras: he has my dying voice;
So tell him, with the occurrents, more and less,
Which have solicited — the rest is silence.   [*Dies.*

HORATIO
Now cracks a noble heart. — Good night, sweet prince;
And flights of angels sing thee to thy rest! —
Why does the drum come hither?   [*March within.*

    Enter FORTINBRAS *and the English*
    AMBASSADORS, *with drum, colours,*
    and ATTENDANTS.

FORTINBRAS
Where is this sight?

HORATIO
          What is it ye would see?
If aught of woe or wonder, cease your search.

FORTINBRAS
This quarry cries on havoc. — O proud Death,
What feast is toward in thine eternal cell,
That thou so many princes at a shot
So bloodily hast struck?

FIRST AMBASSADOR
          The sight is dismal;

And our affairs from England come too late:
The ears are senseless that should give us hearing,
To tell him his commandment is fulfill'd,
That Rosencrantz and Guildenstern are dead:
Where should we have our thanks?

HORATIO
          Not from his mouth,
Had it th'ability of life to thank you:
He never gave commandment for their death.
But since, so jump upon this bloody question,
You from the Polack wars, and you from England,
Are here arriv'd, give order that these bodies
High on a stage be placed to the view;
And let me speak to th'yet unknowing world
How these things came about: so shall you hear
Of carnal, bloody, and unnatural acts;
Of accidental judgements, casual slaughters;
Of deaths put on by cunning and forced cause;
And, in this upshot, purposes mistook
Fall'n on the inventors' heads: all this can I
Truly deliver.

FORTINBRAS
          Let us haste to hear it,
And call the noblest to the audience.
For me, with sorrow I embrace my fortune:
I have some rights of memory in this kingdom,
Which now to claim my vantage doth invite me.

HORATIO
Of that I shall have also cause to speak,
And from his mouth whose voice will draw on more:
But let this same be presently perform'd,
Even while men's minds are wild; lest more
   mischance,
On plots and errors, happen.

FORTINBRAS
          Let four captains
Bear Hamlet, like a soldier, to the stage;
For he was likely, had he been put on,
To have prov'd most royally: and, for his passage,
The soldiers' music and the rites of war
Speak loudly for him. —
Take up the bodies: — such a sight as this
Becomes the field, but here shows much amiss. —
Go, bid the soldiers shoot.
    [*A dead march. Exeunt, bearing off the dead bodies*
    after which a peal of ordnance is shot off.

TROILUS AND CRESSIDA

DRAMATIS PERSONAE

RIAM, *King of Troy.*
HECTOR,
TROILUS,
ARIS,
DEIPHOBUS,
HELENUS, } *his sons.*
MARGARELON, *a bastard son of Priam.*
ENEAS,
NTENOR, } *Trojan commanders.*
CALCHAS, *a Trojan priest, taking part with the Greeks.*
ANDARUS, *uncle to Cressida.*
GAMEMNON, *the Grecian general.*

MENELAUS, *his brother.*
ACHILLES,
AJAX,
ULYSSES,
NESTOR, } *Grecian commanders.*
DIOMEDES,
PATROCLUS,
THERSITES, *a deform'd and scurrilous Grecian.*
ALEXANDER, *servant to Cressida.*
SERVANT *to Troilus.*
SERVANT *to Paris.*
SERVANT *to Diomedes.*

HELEN, *wife to Menelaus.*
ANDROMACHE, *wife to Hector.*
CASSANDRA, *daughter of Priam; a prophetess.*
CRESSIDA, *daughter of Calchas.*

TROJAN and GREEK SOLDIERS, *and* ATTENDANTS.

SCENE — *Troy, and the Grecian camp before it.*

PANDARUS For my part, I'll meddle nor make no more i'th'matter.

PROLOGUE

Troy, there lies the scene. From isles of Greece
he princes orgulous, their high blood chafed,
ave to the port of Athens sent their ships,
raught with the ministers and instruments
f cruel war: sixty and nine, that wore
heir crownets regal, from th'Athenian bay
ut forth toward Phrygia: and their vow is made
o ransack Troy; within whose strong immures
he ravish'd Helen, Menelaus' queen,
Vith wanton Paris sleeps; and that's the quarrel.
o Tenedos they come;
nd the deep-drawing barks do there disgorge
heir warlike fraughtage: now on Dardan plains
he fresh and yet unbruised Greeks do pitch
heir brave pavilions: Priam's six-gated city,
ardan, and Tymbria, Helias, Chetas, Troien,
nd Antenorides, with massy staples,
nd corresponsive and fulfilling bolts,
perr up the sons of Troy.
ow expectation, tickling skittish spirits,
n one and other side, Trojan and Greek,
ets all on hazard: and hither am I come

A prologue arm'd, — but not in confidence
Of author's pen or actor's voice; but suited
In like conditions as our argument, —
To tell you, fair beholders, that our play
Leaps o'er the vaunt and firstlings of those broils,
Beginning in the middle; starting thence away
To what may be digested in a play.
Like, or find fault; do as your pleasures are;
Now good or bad, 'tis but the chance of war.

ACT I

SCENE I

Troy. Before PRIAM'S *palace.*

Enter PANDARUS *and* TROILUS.

TROILUS
Call here my varlet; I'll unarm again:
Why should I war without the walls of Troy,
That find such cruel battle here within?
Each Trojan that is master of his heart,
Let him to field; Troilus, alas, hath none!

PANDARUS
Will this gear ne'er be mended?

TROILUS
The Greeks are strong, and skilful to their strength,
Fierce to their skill, and to their fierceness valiant;
But I am weaker than a woman's tear,
Tamer than sleep, fonder than ignorance,
Less valiant than the virgin in the night,
And skilless as unpractis'd infancy.

PANDARUS
Well, I have told you enough of this: for my part, I'll not meddle nor make no further. He that will have a cake out of the wheat must needs tarry the grinding.

TROILUS
Have I not tarried?

PANDARUS
Ay, the grinding; but you must tarry the bolting.

TROILUS
Have I not tarried?

PANDARUS
Ay, the bolting; but you must tarry the leavening.

TROILUS
Still have I tarried.

PANDARUS
Ay, to the leavening; but here's yet in the word 'hereafter' the kneading, the making of the cake, the heating of the oven, and the baking; nay, you must stay the cooling too, or you may chance to burn your lips.

TROILUS
Patience herself, what goddess e'er she be,
Doth lesser blench at sufferance than I do.
At Priam's royal table do I sit;
And when fair Cressid comes into my thoughts, —
So, traitor! — 'When she comes'! — When is she thence?

PANDARUS
Well, she look'd yesternight fairer than ever I saw her look, or any woman else.

TROILUS
I was about to tell thee, — when my heart,
As wedged with a sigh, would rive in twain;
Lest Hector or my father should perceive me, —
I have — as when the sun doth light a storm —
Buried this sigh in wrinkle of a smile:
But sorrow, that is couch'd in seeming gladness,
Is like that mirth fate turns to sudden sadness.

PANDARUS
An her hair were not somewhat darker than Helen's, — well, go to, — there were no more comparison between the women, — but, for my part, she is my kinswoman; I would not, as they term it, praise her, — but I would somebody had heard her talk yesterday, as I did. I will not dispraise your sister Cassandra's wit; but —

TROILUS
O Pandarus! I tell thee, Pandarus, —
When I do tell thee, there my hopes lie drown'd,
Reply not in how many fadoms deep
They lie indrench'd. I tell thee, I am mad
In Cressid's love: thou answer'st, 'She is fair';
Pour'st in the open ulcer of my heart
Her eyes, her hair, her cheek, her gait, her voice;
Handlest in thy discourse, O, that her hand,
In whose comparison all whites are ink,
Writing their own reproach; to whose soft seizure
The cygnet's down is harsh, and spirit of sense
Hard as the palm of ploughman! — this thou tell'st me,
As true thou tell'st me, when I say I love her;
But, saying thus, instead of oil and balm,
Thou lay'st in every gash that love hath given me
The knife that made it.

CRESSIDA Who were those went by?

PANDARUS
I speak no more than truth.

TROILUS
Thou dost not speak so much.

PANDARUS
Faith, I'll not meddle in't. Let her be as she is: if she be fair, 'tis the better for her: an she be not, she has the mends in her own hands.

TROILUS
Good Pandarus, — how now, Pandarus!

PANDARUS
I have had my labour for my travail; ill-thought on of her, and ill-thought on of you: gone between and between, but small thanks for my labour.

TROILUS
What, art thou angry, Pandarus? what, with me?

PANDARUS
Because she's kin to me, therefore she's not so fair as Helen: an she were not kin to me, she would be as fair on Friday as Helen is on Sunday. But what care I? I care not an she were a black-a-moor; 'tis all one to me.

TROILUS
Say I she is not fair?

PANDARUS
I do not care whether you do or no. She's a fool to stay behind her father; let her to the Greeks; and so I'll tell her the next time I see her: for my part, I'll meddle nor make no more i'th'matter.

TROILUS
Pandarus, —

PANDARUS
Not I.

TROILUS
Sweet Pandarus, —

PANDARUS
Pray you, speak no more to me: I will leave all as I found it, and there an end.
[*Exit* PANDARUS. *Sound alarum.*

TROILUS
Peace, you ungracious clamours! peace, rude sounds!
Fools on both sides! Helen must needs be fair,
When with your blood you daily paint her thus.
I cannot fight upon this argument;
It is too starv'd a subject for my sword.
But Pandarus, — O gods, how do you plague me!
I cannot come to Cressid but by Pandar;
And he's as tetchy to be woo'd to woo,
As she is stubborn-chaste against all suit.
Tell me, Apollo, for thy Daphne's love,
What Cressid is, what Pandar, and what we?
Her bed is India; there she lies, a pearl:

Between our Ilium and where she resides,
Let it be call'd the wild and wandering flood,
Ourself the merchant; and this sailing Pandar,
Our doubtful hope, our convoy, and our bark.
Alarum. Enter AENEAS.

AENEAS
How now, Prince Troilus! wherefore not a-field?

TROILUS
Because not there: this woman's answer sorts,
For womanish it is to be from thence.
What news, Aeneas, from the field to-day?

AENEAS
That Paris is returned home, and hurt.

TROILUS
By whom, Aeneas?

AENEAS
Troilus, by Menelaus.

TROILUS
Let Paris bleed; 'tis but a scar to scorn;
Paris is gor'd with Menelaus' horn. [*Alarum.*

AENEAS
Hark, what good sport is out of town to-day!

TROILUS
Better at home, if 'would I might' were 'may'. —
But to the sport abroad: — are you bound thither?

AENEAS
In all swift haste.

TROILUS
Come, go we, then, together.
[*Exeunt.*

SCENE II
The same. A street.

Enter CRESSIDA *and* ALEXANDER *her* MAN.

CRESSIDA
Who were those went by?

ALEXANDER
Queen Hecuba and Helen.

CRESSIDA
And whither go they?

ALEXANDER
Up to the eastern tower,
Whose height commands as subject all the vale,
To see the battle. Hector, whose patience
Is, as a virtue, fix'd, to-day was moved:
He chid Andromache, and struck his armourer;
And, like as there were husbandry in war,
Before the sun rose, he was harness'd light,
And to the field goes he; where every flower
Did, as a prophet, weep what it foresaw
In Hector's wrath.

CRESSIDA
What was his cause of anger?

ALEXANDER
The noise goes, this: there is among the Greeks
A lord of Trojan blood, nephew to Hector;
They call him Ajax.

CRESSIDA
Good; and what of him?

ALEXANDER
They say he is a very man *per se*,
And stands alone.

CRESSIDA
So do all men, — unless they are drunk, sick, or have no legs.

ALEXANDER
This man, lady, hath robb'd many beasts of their particular additions; he is as valiant as the lion, churlish as the bear, slow as the elephant: a man into whom nature hath so crowded humours, that his valour is crush'd into folly, his folly sauced with discretion: there is no man hath a virtue that he hath not a glimpse of; nor any man an attaint but he carries some stain of it: he is melancholy without cause, and merry against the hair: he hath the joints of every thing; but every thing so out of joint, that he is a gouty Briareus, many hands and no use; or purblind Argus, all eyes and no sight.

CRESSIDA
But how should this man, that makes me smile, make Hector angry?

ALEXANDER
They say he yesterday coped Hector in the battle, and struck him down; the disdain and shame whereof hath

ever since kept Hector fasting and waking.

CRESSIDA
Who comes here?

ALEXANDER
Madam, your uncle Pandarus.

Enter PANDARUS.

CRESSIDA
Hector's a gallant man.

ALEXANDER
As may be in the world, lady.

PANDARUS
What's that? what's that?

CRESSIDA
Good morrow, uncle Pandarus.

PANDARUS
Good morrow, cousin Cressid: what do you talk of? — Good morrow, Alexander. — How do you, cousin? When were you at Ilium?

CRESSIDA
This morning, uncle.

PANDARUS
What were you talking of when I came? Was Hector arm'd and gone, ere ye came to Ilium? Helen was not up, was she?

CRESSIDA
Hector was gone; but Helen was not up.

PANDARUS
E'en so: Hector was stirring early.

CRESSIDA
That were we talking of, and of his anger.

PANDARUS
Was he angry?

CRESSIDA
So he says here.

PANDARUS
True, he was so; I know the cause too; he'll lay about him to-day, I can tell them that: and there's Troilus will not come far behind him; let them take heed of Troilus, I can tell them that too.

CRESSIDA
What, is he angry too?

PANDARUS
Who, Troilus? Troilus is the better man of the two.

CRESSIDA
O Jupiter! there's no comparison.

PANDARUS
What, not between Troilus and Hector? Do you know a man if you see him?

CRESSIDA
Ay, if I ever saw him before, and knew him.

PANDARUS
Well, I say Troilus is Troilus.

CRESSIDA
Then you say as I say; for, I am sure, he is not Hector.

PANDARUS
No, nor Hector is not Troilus in some degrees.

CRESSIDA
'Tis just to each of them; he is himself.

PANDARUS
Himself! Alas, poor Troilus! I would he were, —

CRESSIDA
So he is.

PANDARUS
Condition, I had gone barefoot to India.

CRESSIDA
He is not Hector.

PANDARUS
Himself! no, he's not himself: — would a' were himself! Well, the gods are above; time must friend or end: well, Troilus, well, — I would my heart were in her body! — No, Hector is not a better man than Troilus.

CRESSIDA
Excuse me.

PANDARUS
He is elder.

CRESSIDA
Pardon me, pardon me.

PANDARUS
Th'other's not come to't; you shall tell me another tale, when th'other's come to't. Hector shall not have his wit this year. —

CRESSIDA
He shall not need it, if he have his own.

PANDARUS
Nor his qualities, —

CRESSIDA
No matter.

PANDARUS
Nor his beauty.

CRESSIDA
'Twould not become him, — his own's better.

PANDARUS
You have no judgement, niece: Helen herself swore th'other day, that Troilus, for a brown favour — for so 'tis, I must confess, — not brown neither,—

CRESSIDA
No, but brown.

PANDARUS
Faith, to say truth, brown and not brown.

CRESSIDA
To say the truth, true and not true.

PANDARUS
She praised his complexion above Paris.

CRESSIDA
Why, Paris hath colour enough.

PANDARUS
So he has.

CRESSIDA
Then Troilus should have too much: if she praised him above, his complexion is higher than his; he having colour enough, and the other higher, is too flaming a praise for a good complexion. I had as lief Helen's golden tongue had commended Troilus for a copper nose.

PANDARUS
I swear to you, I think Helen loves him better than Paris.

CRESSIDA
Then she's a merry Greek indeed.

PANDARUS
Nay, I am sure she does. She came to him th'other day into the compass'd window, — and, you know, he has not past three or four hairs on his chin —

CRESSIDA
Indeed, a tapster's arithmetic may soon bring his particulars therein to a total.

PANDARUS
Why, he is very young: and yet will he, within three pound, lift as much as his brother Hector.

CRESSIDA
Is he so young a man, and so old a lifter?

PANDARUS
But, to prove to you that Helen loves him, — she came,and puts me her white hand to his cloven chin —

CRESSIDA
Juno have mercy! how came it cloven?

PANDARUS
Why, you know, 'tis dimpled: I think his smiling becomes him better than any man in all Phrygia.

CRESSIDA
O, he smiles valiantly.

PANDARUS
Does he not?

CRESSIDA
O yes, an 'twere a cloud in autumn.

PANDARUS
Why, go to, then: — but to prove to you that Helen loves Troilus, —

CRESSIDA
Troilus will stand to the proof, if you'll prove it so.

PANDARUS
Troilus! why, he esteems her no more than I esteem an addle egg.

CRESSIDA
If you love an addle egg as well as you love an idle head, you would eat chickens i'th'shell.

PANDARUS
I cannot choose but laugh, to think how she tickled his chin; — indeed, she has a marvellous white hand, I must needs confess, —

CRESSIDA
Without the rack.

PANDARUS
And she takes upon her to spy a white hair on his chin.

CRESSIDA
Alas, poor chin! many a wart is richer.

PANDARUS
But there was such laughing! — Queen Hecuba laugh'd, that her eyes ran o'er, —

CRESSIDA
With mill-stones.

PANDARUS
And Cassandra laugh'd, —

CRESSIDA
But there was more temperate fire under the pot of her eyes: — did her eyes run o'er too?

PANDARUS
And Hector laugh'd.

CRESSIDA
At what was all this laughing?

PANDARUS
Marry, at the white hair that Helen spied on Troilus' chin.

CRESSIDA
An't had been a green hair, I should have laugh'd too.

PANDARUS
They laugh'd not so much at the hair as at his pretty answer.

CRESSIDA
What was his answer?

PANDARUS
Quoth she, 'Here's but two and fifty hairs on your chin, and one of them is white.'

CRESSIDA
This is her question.

PANDARUS
That's true; make no question of that. 'One and fifty hairs,' quoth he, 'and one white: that white hair is my father, and all the rest are his sons.' 'Jupiter!' quoth she, 'which of these hairs is Paris my husband?' 'The fork'd one,' quoth he; 'pluck't out, and give it him.' But there was such laughing! and Helen so blush'd, and Paris so chafed, and all the rest so laugh'd, that it pass'd.

CRESSIDA
So let it now; for it has been a great while going by.

PANDARUS
Well, cousin, I told you a thing yesterday; think on't.

CRESSIDA
So I do.

PANDARUS
I'll be sworn 'tis true; he will weep you, an 'twere-a man born in April.

CRESSIDA
And I'll spring up in his tears, an 'twere a nettle against May. [*A retreat sounded.*

PANDARUS
Hark! they are coming from the field: shall we stand up here, and see them as they pass toward Ilium? good niece, do, — sweet niece Cressida.

CRESSIDA
At your pleasure.

PANDARUS
Here, here, here's an excellent place; here we may see most bravely: I'll tell you them all by their names as they pass by; but mark Troilus above the rest.

CRESSIDA
Speak not so loud.

AENEAS *passes.*

PANDARUS
That's Aeneas: is not that a brave man? he's one of the flowers of Troy, I can tell you: but mark Troilus; you shall see anon.

ANTENOR *passes.*

CRESSIDA
Who's that?

PANDARUS
That's Antenor: he has a shrewd wit, I can tell you; and he's a man good enough: he's one o'th'soundest judgements in Troy, whosoever, and a proper man of person. — When comes Troilus? — I'll show you Troilus anon: if he see me, you shall see him nod at me.

CRESSIDA
Will he give you the nod?

PANDARUS
You shall see.

CRESSIDA
If he do, the rich shall have more.

HECTOR *passes.*

PANDARUS
That's Hector, that, that, look you, that; there's a fellow! — Go thy way, Hector! —There's a brave man, niece. — O brave Hector! — Look how he looks! there's a countenance! is't not a brave man?

CRESSIDA
O, a brave man!

PANDARUS
Is a' not? it does a man's heart good: — look you what hacks are on his helmet! look you yonder, do you see? look you there: there's no jesting; there's laying on, take't off who will, as they say: there be hacks!

CRESSIDA
Be those with swords?

PANDARUS
Swords! any thing, he cares not; an the devil come to him, it's all one: by God's lid, it does one's heart good. — Yonder comes Paris, yonder comes Paris:
PARIS *passes.*
look ye yonder, niece; is't not a gallant man too, is't not? — Why, this is brave now. — Who said he came hurt home to-day? he's not hurt: why, this will do Helen's heart good now, ha! — Would I could see Troilus now! — You shall see Troilus anon.
HELENUS *passes.*

CRESSIDA
Who's that?

PANDARUS
That's Helenus: — I marvel where Troilus is: — that's Helenus: — I think he went not forth to-day: — that's Helenus.

CRESSIDA
Can Helenus fight, uncle?

PANDARUS
Helenus! no; yes, he'll fight indifferent well. — I marvel where Troilus is. — Hark! do you not hear the people cry 'Troilus'? — Helenus is a priest.

CRESSIDA
What sneaking fellow comes yonder?
TROILUS *passes.*

PANDARUS
Where? yonder? that's Deiphobus: 'tis Troilus! there's a man, niece! Hem! Brave Troilus! the prince of chivalry!

CRESSIDA
Peace, for shame, peace!

PANDARUS
Mark him; note him: O brave Troilus! — look well upon him, niece: look you how his sword is bloodied, and his helm more hack'd than Hector's; and how he looks, and how he goes! — O admirable youth! he ne'er saw three-and-twenty. — Go thy way, Troilus, go thy way! — Had I a sister were a grace, or a daughter a goddess, he should take his choice. O admirable man! Paris? — Paris is dirt to him; and, I warrant, Helen, to change, would give an eye to boot.

CRESSIDA
Here come more.
COMMON SOLDIERS *pass.*

PANDARUS
Asses, fools, dolts! chaff and bran, chaff and bran! porridge after meat! — I could live and die i'th'eyes of Troilus. — Ne'er look, ne'er look; the eagles are gone: crows and daws, crows and daws! — I had rather be such a man as Troilus than Agamemnon and all Greece.

CRESSIDA
There is among the Greeks Achilles, — a better man than Troilus.

PANDARUS
Achilles! a drayman, a porter, a very camel.

CRESSIDA
Well, well.

PANDARUS
Well, well! — Why, have you any discretion? have you any eyes? do you know what a man is? Is not birth, beauty, good shape, discourse, manhood, learning, gentleness, virtue, youth, liberality, and such like, the spice and salt that season a man?

CRESSIDA
Ay, a minced man: and then to be baked with no date in the pie, — for then the man's date's out.

PANDARUS
You are such a woman! one knows not at what ward you lie.

CRESSIDA
Upon my back, to defend my belly; upon my wit, to defend my wiles; upon my secrecy, to defend mine honesty; my mask, to defend my beauty; and you, to defend all these: and at all these wards I lie, at a thousand watches.

PANDARUS
Say one of your watches.

CRESSIDA
Nay, I'll watch you for that; and that's one of the chiefest of them too: if I cannot ward what I would not have hit, I can watch you for telling how I took the blow; unless it swell past hiding, and then it's past watching.

PANDARUS
You are such another!
Enter TROILUS' BOY.

BOY
Sir, my lord would instantly speak with you.

PANDARUS
Where?
BOY
At your own house; there he unarms him.
PANDARUS
Good boy, tell him I come. [*Exit* BOY.] I doubt he be
hurt. — Fare ye well, good niece.
CRESSIDA
Adieu, uncle.
PANDARUS
I'll be with you, niece, by and by.
CRESSIDA
To bring, uncle?
PANDARUS
Ay, a token from Troilus.
CRESSIDA
By the same token — you are a bawd.
[*Exit* PANDARUS.
Words, vows, gifts, tears, and love's full sacrifice,
He offers in another's enterprise:
But more in Troilus thousand-fold I see
Than in the glass of Pandar's praise may be;
Yet hold I off. Women are angels, wooing:
Things won are done: joy's soul lies in the doing:
That she belov'd knows naught that knows not this, —
Men prize the thing ungain'd more than it is:
That she was never yet that ever knew
Love got so sweet as when desire did sue:
Therefore this maxim out of love, I teach, —
Achievement is command; ungain'd, beseech:
Then, though my heart's content firm love doth bear,
Nothing of that shall from mine eyes appear. [*Exeunt.*

SCENE III

The Grecian camp. Before AGAMEMNON'S *tent.*

Sennet. Enter AGAMEMNON, NESTOR, ULYSSES,
MENELAUS, *with others.*

AGAMEMNON
Princes,
What grief hath set the jaundice on your cheeks?
The ample proposition that hope makes
In all designs begun on earth below
Fails in the promis'd largeness: checks and disasters
Grow in the veins of actions highest rear'd;
As knots, by the conflux of meeting sap,
Infect the sound pine, and divert his grain
Tortive and errant from his course of growth.
Nor, princes, is it matter new to us,
That we come short of our suppose so far,
That, after seven years' siege, yet Troy walls stand;
Sith every action that hath gone before,
Whereof we have record, trial did draw
Bias and thwart, not answering the aim,
And that unbodied figure of the thought
That gave't surmised shape. Why, then, you princes,
Do you with cheeks abash'd behold our works,
And call them shames, which are, indeed, naught else
But the protractive trials of great Jove
To find persistive constancy in men?
The fineness of which metal is not found
In fortune's love; for then the bold and coward,
The wise and fool, the artist and unread,
The hard and soft, seem all affin'd and kin:
But, in the wind and tempest of her frown,
Distinction, with a broad and powerful fan,
Puffing at all, winnows the light away;
And what hath mass or matter, by itself
Lies rich in virtue and unmingled.
NESTOR
With due observance of thy godlike seat,
Great Agamemnon, Nestor shall apply
Thy latest words. In the reproof of chance
Lies the true proof of men: the sea being smooth,
How many shallow bauble boats dare sail
Upon her patient breast, making their way
With those of nobler bulk!
But let the ruffian Boreas once enrage
The gentle Thetis, and anon, behold
The strong-ribb'd bark through liquid mountains cut,
Bounding between the two moist elements,
Like Perseus' horse: where's then the saucy boat,
Whose weak untimber'd sides but even now
Co-rivall'd greatness? either to harbour fled,
Or made a toast for Neptune. Even so
Doth valour's show and valour's worth divide
In storms of fortune: for in her ray and brightness
The herd hath more annoyance by the breese
Than by the tiger; but when the splitting wind
Makes flexible the knees of knotted oaks,

And flies fled under shade, why, then the thing of
courage,
As rous'd with rage, with rage doth sympathise,
And with an accent tun'd in selfsame key
Returns to chiding fortune.
ULYSSES
Agamemnon, —
Thou great commander, nerve and bone of Greece,
Heart of our numbers, soul and only spirit,
In whom the tempers and the minds of all
Should be shut up, — hear what Ulysses speaks.
Besides th'applause and approbation
The which — [*to* AGAMEMNON] most mighty for thy
place and sway, —
[*to* NESTOR] And thou most reverend for thy
stretch'd-out life —
I give to both your speeches, — which were such
As Agamemnon and the hand of Greece
Should hold up high in brass; and such again
As venerable Nestor, hatch'd in silver,
Should with a bond of air — strong as the axletree
On which heaven rides — knit all the Greekish ears
To his experienc'd tongue, — yet let it please both,
Though great and wise, to hear Ulysses speak.
AGAMEMNON
Speak, Prince of Ithaca; and be't of less expect
That matter needless, of importless burden,
Divide thy lips, than we are confident,
When rank Thersites opes his mastic jaws,
We shall hear music, wit, and oracle.
ULYSSES
Troy, yet upon his basis, had been down,
And the great Hector's sword had lack'd a master,
But for these instances.
The specialty of rule hath been neglected:
And, look, how many Grecian tents do stand
Hollow upon this plain, so many hollow factions.
When that the general is not like the hive,
To whom the foragers shall all repair,
What honey is expected? Degree being vizarded,
Th'unworthiest shows as fairly in the mask.
The heavens themselves, the planets, and this centre,
Observe degree, priority, and place,
Insisture, course, proportion, season, form,
Office, and custom, in all line of order:
And therefore is the glorious planet Sol
In noble eminence enthron'd and sphered
Amidst the other; whose med'cinable eye
Corrects the ill aspects of planets evil,
And posts, like the commandment of a king,
Sans check, to good and bad: but when the planets,
In evil mixture, to disorder wander,
What plagues, and what portents, what mutiny,
What raging of the sea, shaking of earth,
Commotion in the winds, frights, changes, horrors,
Divert and crack, rend and deracinate
The unity and married calm of states
Quite from their fixure! O, when degree is shaked,
Which is the ladder to all high designs,
Then enterprise is sick! How could communities,
Degrees in schools, and brotherhoods in cities,
Peaceful commerce from dividable shores,
The primogenity and due of birth,
Prerogative of age, crowns, sceptres, laurels,
But by degree, stand in authentic place?
Take but degree away, untune that string,
And, hark, what discord follows! each thing meets
In mere oppugnancy: the bounded waters
Should lift their bosoms higher than the shores,
And make a sop of all this solid globe:
Strength should be lord of imbecility,
And the rude son should strike his father dead:
Force should be right; or, rather, right and wrong —
Between whose endless jar justice resides —
Should lose their names, and so should justice too.
Then every thing includes itself in power,
Power into will, will into appetite;
And appetite, an universal wolf,
So doubly seconded with will and power,
Must make perforce an universal prey,
And last eat up himself. Great Agamemnon,
This chaos, when degree is suffocate,
Follows the choking.
And this neglection of degree it is
That by a pace goes backward, with a purpose
It hath to climb. The general's disdain'd
By him one step below; he, by the next;
That next, by him beneath: so every step,
Exampled by the first pace that is sick
Of his superior, grows to an envious fever
Of pale and bloodless emulation:
And 'tis this fever that keeps Troy on foot,

Not her own sinews. To end a tale of length,
Troy in our weakness stands, not in her strength.
NESTOR
Most wisely hath Ulysses here discover'd
The fever whereof all our power is sick.
AGAMEMNON
The nature of the sickness found, Ulysses,
What is the remedy?
ULYSSES
The great Achilles, — whom opinion crowns
The sinew and the forehand of our host, —
Having his ear full of his airy fame,
Grows dainty of his worth, and in his tent
Lies mocking our designs: with him, Patroclus,
Upon a lazy bed, the livelong day
Breaks scurril jests;
And with ridiculous and awkward action —
Which, slanderer, he imitation calls —
He pageants us. Sometime, great Agamemnon,
Thy topless deputation he puts on;
And, like a strutting player, — whose conceit
Lies in his hamstring, and doth think it rich
To hear the wooden dialogue and sound
'Twixt his stretch'd footing and the scaffoldage, —
Such to-be-pitied and o'er-wrested seeming
He acts thy greatness in: and when he speaks,
'Tis like a chime a-mending; with terms unsquared,
Which, from the tongue of roaring Typhon dropp'd,
Would seem hyperboles. At this fusty stuff
The large Achilles, on his press'd bed lolling,
From his deep chest laughs out a loud applause;
Cries, 'Excellent! 'tis Agamemnon just.
Now play me Nestor; hem, and stroke thy beard,
As he being dress'd to some oration.'
That's done; — as near as the extremest ends
Of parallels; as like as Vulcan and his wife:
Yet god Achilles still cries, 'Excellent!
'Tis Nestor right. Now play him me, Patroclus,
Arming to answer in a night-alarm.'
And then, forsooth, the faint defects of age
Must be the scene of mirth; to cough and spit,
And, with a palsy fumbling on his gorget,
Shake in and out the rivet: — and at this sport
Sir Valour dies; cries, 'O, enough, Patroclus;
Or give me ribs of steel! I shall split all
In pleasure of my spleen.' And in this fashion,
All our abilities, gifts, natures, shapes,
Severals and generals of grace exact,
Achievements, plots, orders, preventions,
Excitements to the field, or speech for truce,
Success or loss, what is or is not, serves
As stuff for these two to make paradoxes.
NESTOR
And in the imitation of these twain —
Who, as Ulysses says, opinion crowns
With an imperial voice — many are infect.
Ajax is grown self-will'd; and bears his head
In such a rein, in full as proud a pace
As broad Achilles; keeps his tent like him;
Makes factious feasts; rails on our state of war,
Bold as an oracle; and sets Thersites —
A slave whose gall coins slanders like a mint —
To match us in comparisons with dirt,
To weaken and discredit our exposure,
How rank soever rounded in with danger.
ULYSSES
They tax our policy, and call it cowardice;
Count wisdom as no member of the war;
Forestall prescience, and esteem no act
But that of hand: the still and mental parts,
That do contrive how many hands shall strike,
When fitness calls them on; and know, by measure
Of their observant toil, the enemies' weight, —
Why, this hath not a finger's dignity:
They call this bed-work, mappery, closet-war;
So that the ram that batters down the wall,
For the great swing and rudeness of his poise,
They place before his hand that made the engine,
Or those that with the fineness of their souls
By reason guide his execution.
NESTOR
Let this be granted, and Achilles' horse
Makes many Thetis' sons. [*Tucket*
AGAMEMNON
What trumpet? look, Menelaus.
MENELAUS
From Troy.

Enter AENEAS.

AGAMEMNON
What would you 'fore our tent?

AENEAS
Is this great Agamemnon's tent, I pray you?

AGAMEMNON
Even this.

AENEAS
May one, that is a herald and a prince,
Do a fair message to his kingly ears?

AGAMEMNON
With surety stronger than Achilles' arm
Fore all the Greekish heads, which with one voice
Call Agamemnon head and general.

AENEAS
Fair leave and large security. How may
A stranger to those most imperial looks
Know them from eyes of other mortals?

AGAMEMNON
                              How?

AENEAS
Ay;
I ask, that I might waken reverence,
And bid the cheek be ready with a blush
Modest as morning when she coldly eyes
The youthful Phœbus:
Which is that god in office, guiding men?
Which is the high and mighty Agamemnon?

AGAMEMNON
This Trojan scorns us; or the men of Troy
Are ceremonious courtiers.

AENEAS
Courtiers as free, as debonair, unarm'd,
As bending angels; that's their fame in peace:
But when they would seem soldiers, they have galls,
Good arms, strong joints, true swords; and, Jove's
            accord,
Nothing so full of heart. But peace, Aeneas,
Peace, Trojan; lay thy finger on thy lips!
The worthiness of praise distains his worth,
If that the prais'd himself bring the praise forth:
But what the repining enemy commends,
That breath fame blows; that praise, sole sure,
            transcends.

AGAMEMNON
Sir, you of Troy, call you yourself Aeneas?

AENEAS
Ay, Greek, that is my name.

AGAMEMNON
What's your affair, I pray you?

AENEAS
Sir, pardon; 'tis for Agamemnon's ears.

AGAMEMNON
He hears naught privately that comes from Troy.

AENEAS
Nor I from Troy come not to whisper him:
I bring a trumpet to awake his ear;
To set his sense on the attentive bent,
And then to speak.

AGAMEMNON
              Speak frankly as the wind;
It is not Agamemnon's sleeping hour:
That thou shalt know, Trojan, he is awake,
He tells thee so himself.

AENEAS
              Trumpet, blow loud,
Send thy brass voice through all these lazy tents;
And every Greek of mettle, let him know,
What Troy means fairly shall be spoke aloud.
            [Trumpet sounds.
We have, great Agamemnon, here in Troy
A prince call'd Hector, — Priam is his father, —
Who in this dull and long-continued truce
Is rusty grown: he bade me take a trumpet,
And to this purpose speak. Kings, princes, lords!
If there be one among the fair'st of Greece
That holds his honour higher than his ease;
That seeks his praise more than he fears his peril;
That knows his valour, and knows not his fear;
That loves his mistress more than in confession
With truant vows to her own lips he loves,
And dare avow her beauty and her worth
In other arms than hers, — to him this challenge.
Hector, in view of Trojans and of Greeks,
Shall make it good, or do his best to do it,
He hath a lady, wiser, fairer, truer,
Than ever Greek did compass in his arms;
And will to-morrow with his trumpet call
Midway between your tents and walls of Troy,
To rouse a Grecian that is true in love:
If any come, Hector shall honour him;
If none, he'll say in Troy when he retires,
The Grecian dames are sunburnt, and not worth

The splinter of a lance. Even so much.

AGAMEMNON
This shall be told our lovers, Lord Aeneas;
If none of them have soul in such a kind,
We left them all at home: but we are soldiers;
And may that soldier a mere recreant prove,
That means not, hath not, or is not in love!
If then one is, or hath, or means to be,
That one meets Hector; if none else, I am he.

NESTOR
Tell him of Nestor, one that was a man
When Hector's grandsire suck'd: he is old now;
But if there be not in our Grecian host
One noble man that hath one spark of fire,
To answer for his love, tell him from me, —
I'll hide my silver beard in a gold beaver,
And in my vantbrace put this wither'd brawn;
And, meeting him, will tell him that my lady
Was fairer than his grandam, and as chaste
As may be in the world; his youth in flood,
I'll prove this truth with my three drops of blood.

AENEAS
Now heavens forbid such scarcity of youth!

ULYSSES
Amen.

AGAMEMNON
Fair Lord Aeneas, let me touch your hand;
To our pavilion shall I lead you, sir.
Achilles shall have word of this intent;
So shall each lord of Greece, from tent to tent:
Yourself shall feast with us before you go,
And find the welcome of a noble foe.
            [Exeunt all but ULYSSES and NESTOR.

ULYSSES
Nestor, —

NESTOR
What says Ulysses?

ULYSSES
I have a young conception in my brain;
Be you my time to bring it to some shape.

NESTOR
What is't?

ULYSSES
This 'tis: —
Blunt wedges rive hard knots: the seeded pride
That hath to this maturity blown up
In rank Achilles must or now be cropp'd,
Or, shedding, breed a nursery of like evil,
To overbulk us all.

NESTOR
              Well, and how?

ULYSSES
This challenge that the gallant Hector sends,
However it is spread in general name,
Relates in purpose only to Achilles.

NESTOR
The purpose is perspicuous even as substance
Whose grossness little characters sum up:
And, in the publication, make no strain,
But that Achilles, were his brain as barren
As banks of Libya, — though, Apollo knows,
'Tis dry enough, — will, with great speed of
            judgement,
Ay, with celerity, find Hector's purpose
Pointing on him.

ULYSSES
And wake him to the answer, think you?

NESTOR
                              Yes,
It is most meet: who may you else oppose,
That can from Hector bring his honour off,
If not Achilles? Though't be a sportful combat,
Yet in the trial much opinion dwells;
For here the Trojans taste our dear'st repute
With their finest palate: and trust to me, Ulysses,
Our imputation shall be oddly poised
In this wild action; for the success,
Although particular, shall give a scantling
Of good or bad unto the general;
And in such indexes, although small pricks
To their subsequent volumes, there is seen
The baby figure of the giant mass
Of things to come at large. It is supposed,
He that meets Hector issues from our choice:
And choice, being mutual act of all our souls,
Makes merit her election; and doth boil,
As 'twere from forth us all, a man distill'd
Out of our virtues; who miscarrying,
What heart receives from hence the conquering part,
To steel a strong opinion to themselves?

Which entertain'd, limbs are his instruments,
In no less working than are swords and bows
Directive by the limbs.

ULYSSES
Give pardon to my speech; —
Therefore 'tis meet Achilles meet not Hector.
Let us, like merchants, show our foulest wares,
And think, perchance, they'll sell; if not,
The lustre of the better yet to show,
Shall show the better. Do not, then, consent
That ever Hector and Achilles meet;
For both our honour and our shame in this
Are dogg'd with two strange followers.

NESTOR
I see them not with my old eyes: what are they?

ULYSSES
What glory our Achilles shares from Hector,
Were he not proud, we all should share with him:
But he already is too insolent;
And we were better parch in Afric sun
Than in the pride and salt scorn of his eyes,
Should he scape Hector fair: if he were foil'd,
Why, then we did our main opinion crush
In taint of our best man. No, make a lottery;
And, by device, let blockish Ajax draw
The sort of fight with Hector: among ourselves
Give him allowance as the worthier man;
For that will physic the great Myrmidon
Who broils in loud applause, and make him fall
His crest that prouder than blue Iris bends.
If the dull brainless Ajax come safe off,
We'll dress him up in voices: if he fail,
Yet go we under our opinion still
That we have better men. But, hit or miss,
Our project's life this shape of sense assumes, —
Ajax employ'd plucks down Achilles' plumes.

NESTOR
Ulysses,
Now I begin to relish thy advice;
And I will give a taste of it forthwith
To Agamemnon: go we to him straight.
Two curs shall tame each other: pride alone
Must tarre the mastiffs on, as 'twere their bone.   [Exeunt.

ACT II

SCENE I

A part of the Grecian camp.

Enter AJAX *and* THERSITES.

AJAX
Thersites,

THERSITES
Agamemnon, — how if he had boils, — full, all over,
generally? —

AJAX
Thersites! —

THERSITES
And those boils did run? — Say so, — did not the
general run then? were not that a botchy core? —

AJAX
Dog, —

THERSITES
Then would come some matter from him; I see none
now.

AJAX
Thou bitch-wolf's son, canst thou not hear? Feel, then.
            [Strikes him.

THERSITES
The plague of Greece upon thee, thou mongrel
beef-witted lord!

AJAX
Speak, then, thou vinewedst leaven, speak: I will beat
thee into handsomeness.

THERSITES
I shall sooner rail thee into wit and holiness: but, I
think, thy horse will sooner con an oration than thou
learn a prayer without book. Thou canst strike, canst
thou? a red murrain o' thy jade's tricks!

AJAX
Toadstool, learn me the proclamation.

THERSITES
Dost thou think I have no sense, thou strikest me thus?

AJAX
The proclamation!

THERSITES
Thou art proclaim'd a fool, I think.

THERSITES What modicums of wit he utters! his evasions have ears thus long.

AJAX
Do not, porpentine, do not: my fingers itch.
THERSITES
I would thou didst itch from head to foot, and I had the scratching of thee; I would make thee the loathsom'st scab in Greece. When thou art forth in the incursions, thou strikest as slow as another.
AJAX
I say, the proclamation!
THERSITES
Thou grumblest and railest every hour on Achilles; and thou art as full of envy at his greatness as Cerberus is at Proserpina's beauty, ay, that thou bark'st at him.
AJAX
Mistress Thersites!
THERSITES
Thou shouldst strike him.
AJAX
Cobloaf!
THERSITES
He would pun thee into shivers with his fist, as a sailor breaks a biscuit.
AJAX
You whoreson cur!   *[Beating him.*
THERSITES
Do, do.
AJAX
Thou stool for a witch!
THERSITES
Ay, do, do; thou sodden-witted lord! thou hast no more brain than I have in mine elbows; an assinego may tutor thee: thou scurvy-valiant ass! thou art here but to thrash Trojans; and thou art bought and sold among those of any wit, like a barbarian slave. If thou use to beat me, I will begin at thy heel, and tell what thou art by inches, thou thing of no bowels, thou!
AJAX
You dog!
THERSITES
You scurvy lord!
AJAX
You cur!   *[Beating him.*
THERSITES
Mars his idiot! do, rudeness, do, camel; do, do.
    Enter ACHILLES *and* PATROCLUS.

ACHILLES
Why, how now, Ajax! wherefore do you thus? —
How now, Thersites! what's the matter, man?
THERSITES
You see him there, do you?
ACHILLES
Ay, what's the matter?
THERSITES
Nay, look upon him.
ACHILLES
So I do: what's the matter?
THERSITES
Nay, but regard him well.

ACHILLES
Well! Why, so I do.
THERSITES
But yet you look not well upon him; for, whosoever you take him to be, he is Ajax.
ACHILLES
I know that, fool.
THERSITES
Ay, but that fool knows not himself.
AJAX
Therefore I beat thee.
THERSITES
Lo, lo, lo, lo, what modicums of wit he utters! his evasions have ears thus long. I have bobb'd his brain more than he has beat my bones: I will buy nine sparrows for a penny, and his *pia mater* is not worth the ninth part of a sparrow. This lord, Achilles, Ajax, — who wears his wit in his belly, and his guts in his head, — I'll tell you what I say of him.
ACHILLES
What?
THERSITES
I say, this Ajax —
    [AJAX *offers to beat him,* ACHILLES *interposes.*
ACHILLES
Nay, good Ajax.
THERSITES
Has not so much wit —
ACHILLES
Nay, I must hold you.
THERSITES
As will stop the eye of Helen's needle, for whom he comes to fight.
ACHILLES
Peace, fool!
THERSITES
I would have peace and quietness, but the fool will not: he there; that he; look you there.
AJAX
O thou damn'd cur! I shall —
ACHILLES
Will you set your wit to a fool's?
THERSITES
No, I warrant you; for a fool's will shame it.
PATROCLUS
Good words, Thersites.
ACHILLES
What's the quarrel?
AJAX
I bade the vile owl go learn me the tenour of the proclamation, and he rails upon me.
THERSITES
I serve thee not.
AJAX
Well, go to, go to.
THERSITES
I serve here voluntary.

ACHILLES
Your last service was sufferance, 'twas not voluntary, — no man is beaten voluntary: Ajax was here the voluntary, and you as under an impress.
THERSITES
E'en so; a great deal of your wit, too, lies in your sinews, or else there be liars. Hector shall have a great catch, if he knock out either of your brains: a' were as good crack a fusty nut with no kernel.
ACHILLES
What, with me too, Thersites?
THERSITES
There's Ulysses and old Nestor — whose wit was mouldy ere your grandsires had nails on their toes — yoke you like draught-oxen, and make you plough up the wars.
ACHILLES
What, what?
THERSITES
Yes, good sooth: to, Achilles! to, Ajax! to!
AJAX
I shall cut out your tongue.
THERSITES
'Tis no matter; I shall speak as much as thou afterwards.
PATROCLUS
No more words, Thersites; peace!
THERSITES
I will hold my peace when Achilles' brach bids me, shall I?
ACHILLES
There's for you, Patroclus.
THERSITES
I will see you hang'd, like clotpoles, ere I come any more to your tents: I will keep where there is wit stirring, and leave the faction of fools.   *[Exit.*
PATROCLUS
A good riddance.
ACHILLES
Marry, this, sir, is proclaim'd through all our host: —
That Hector, by the fifth hour of the sun,
Will, with a trumpet, 'twixt our tents and Troy,
To-morrow morning call some knight to arms
That hath a stomach; and such a one that dare
Maintain — I know not what; 'tis trash. Farewell.
AJAX
Farewell. Who shall answer him?
ACHILLES
I know not, — 'tis put to lottery; otherwise
He knew his man.
           [Exeunt ACHILLES *and* PATROCLUS.
AJAX
O, meaning you. — I will go learn more of it.   *[Exit.*

SCENE II

Troy. PRIAM'S *palace.*

Enter PRIAM, HECTOR, TROILUS,
PARIS, *and* HELENUS.

PRIAM
After so many hours, lives, speeches spent,
Thus once again says Nestor from the Greeks: —
'Deliver Helen, and all damage else —
As honour, loss of time, travail, expense,
Wounds, friends, and what else dear that is consumed
In hot digestion of this cormorant war —
Shall be struck off': — Hector, what say you to't?
HECTOR
Though no man lesser fears the Greeks than I
As far as toucheth my particular,
Yet, dread Priam,
There is no lady of more softer bowels,
More spongy to suck in the sense of fear,
More ready to cry out, 'Who knows what follows?'
Than Hector is: the wound of peace is surety,
Surety secure; but modest doubt is call'd
The beacon of the wise, the tent that searches
To th'bottom of the worst. Let Helen go:
Since the first sword was drawn about this question,
Every tithe soul, 'mongst many thousand dismes,
Hath been as dear as Helen, — I mean, of ours:
If we have lost so many tenths of ours,
To guard a thing not ours nor worth to us,
Had it our name, the value of one ten, —
What merit's in that reason which denies
The yielding of her up?
TROILUS
                   Fie, fie, my brother!
Weigh you the worth and honour of a king,

o great as our dread father, in a scale
Of common ounces? will you with counters sum
The past-proportion of his infinite?
And buckle in a waist most fathomless
With spans and inches so diminutive
As fears and reasons? fie, for godly shame!

HELENUS
No marvel, though you bite so sharp at reasons,
You are so empty of them. Should not our father
Bear the great sway of his affairs with reasons,
Because your speech hath none that tells him so?

TROILUS
You are for dreams and slumbers, brother priest;
You fur your gloves with reason. Here are your
  reasons:
You know an enemy intends you harm;
You know a sword employ'd is perilous,
And reason flies the object of all harm:
Who marvels, then, when Helenus beholds
A Grecian and his sword, if he do set
The very wings of reason to his heels,
And fly like chidden Mercury from Jove,
Or like a star disorb'd? Nay, if we talk of reason,
Let's shut our gates, and sleep: manhood and honour
Should have hare-hearts, would they but fat their
  thoughts
With this cramm'd reason: reason and respect
Make livers pale, and lustihood deject.

HECTOR
Brother, she is not worth what she doth cost
The holding.

TROILUS
                   What is aught, but as 'tis valued?

HECTOR
But value dwells not in particular will;
It holds his estimate and dignity
As well therein 'tis precious of itself
As in the prizer: 'tis mad idolatry
To make the service greater than the god;
And the will dotes, that is attributive
To what infectiously itself affects,
Without some image of th'affected merit.

TROILUS
I take to-day a wife, and my election
Is led on in the conduct of my will;
My will enkindled by mine eyes and ears,
Two traded pilots 'twixt the dangerous shores
Of will and judgement: how may I avoid,
Although my will distaste what it elected,
The wife I chose? there can be no evasion
To blench from this, and to stand firm by honour:
We turn not back the silks upon the merchant
When we have soil'd them; nor the remainder viands
We do not throw in unrespective sieve
Because we now are full. It was thought meet
Paris should do some vengeance on the Greeks:
Your breath of full consent bellied his sails;
The seas and winds, old wranglers, took a truce,
And did him service: he touch'd the ports desired,
And, for an old aunt whom the Greeks held captive,
He brought a Grecian queen, whose youth and
  freshness
Wrinkles Apollo's, and makes stale the morning.
Why keep we her? the Grecians keep our aunt:
Is she worth keeping? why, she is a pearl,
Whose price hath launch'd above a thousand ships,
And turn'd crown'd kings to merchants.
If you'll avouch 'twas wisdom Paris went, —
As you must needs, for you all cried, 'Go, go';
If you'll confess he brought home noble prize, —
As you must needs, for you all clapp'd your hands,
And cried, 'Inestimable!' — why do you now
The issue of your proper wisdoms rate,
And do a deed that fortune never did, —
Beggar the estimation which you priz'd
Richer than sea and land? O, theft most base,
That we have stol'n what we do fear to keep!
But, thieves, unworthy of a thing so stol'n,
That in their country did them that disgrace
We fear to warrant in our native place!

CASSANDRA [within].
Cry, Trojans, cry!

PRIAM
                   What noise? what shriek is this?

TROILUS
'Tis our mad sister, I do know her voice.

CASSANDRA [within].
Cry, Trojans!

HECTOR
It is Cassandra.

Enter CASSANDRA, *raving,*
with her hair about her ears.

CASSANDRA
Cry, Trojans, cry! lend me ten thousand eyes,
And I will fill them with prophetic tears.

HECTOR
Peace, sister, peace!

CASSANDRA
Virgins and boys, mid-age and wrinkled eld,
Soft infancy, that nothing canst but cry,
Add to my clamours! let us pay betimes
A moiety of that mass of moan to come.
Cry, Trojans, cry! practise your eyes with tears!
Troy must not be, nor goodly Ilion stand;
Our firebrand brother, Paris, burns us all.
Cry, Trojans, cry! a Helen and a woe!
Cry, cry! Troy burns, or else let Helen go.   [*Exit.*

HECTOR
Now, youthful Troilus, do not these high strains
Of divination in our sister work
Some touches of remorse? or is your blood
So madly hot, that no discourse of reason,
Nor fear of bad success in a bad cause,
Can qualify the same?

TROILUS
                   Why, brother Hector,
We may not think the justness of each act
Such and no other than event doth form it;
Nor once deject the courage of our minds,
Because Cassandra's mad: her brain-sick raptures
Cannot distaste the goodness of a quarrel
Which hath our several honours all engaged
To make it gracious. For my private part,
I am no more touch'd than all Priam's sons:
And Jove forbid there should be done amongst us
Such things as might offend the weakest spleen
To fight for and maintain!

PARIS
Else might the world convince of levity
As well my undertakings as your counsels:
But I attest the gods, your full consent
Gave wings to my propension, and cut off
All fears attending on so dire a project.
For what, alas, can these my single arms?
What propugnation is in one man's valour,
To stand the push and enmity of those
This quarrel would excite? Yet, I protest,
Were I alone to pass the difficulties,
And had as ample power as I have will,
Paris should ne'er retract what he hath done,
Nor faint in the pursuit.

PRIAM
                   Paris, you speak
Like one besotted on your sweet delights:
You have the honey still, but these the gall;
So to be valiant is no praise at all.

PARIS
Sir, I propose not merely to myself
The pleasures such a beauty brings with it;
But I would have the soil of her fair rape
Wip'd off, in honourable keeping her.
What treason were it to the ransack'd queen,
Disgrace to your great worths, and shame to me,
Now to deliver her possession up
On terms of base compulsion! Can it be
That so degenerate a strain as this
Should once set footing in your generous bosoms?
There's not the meanest spirit on our party
Without a heart to dare, or sword to draw,
When Helen is defended; nor none so noble
Whose life were ill bestow'd, or death unfamed,
Where Helen is the subject: then, I say,
Well may we fight for her, whom, we know well,
The world's large spaces cannot parallel.

HECTOR
Paris and Troilus, you have both said well;
And on the cause and question now in hand
Have gloz'd, but superficially; not much
Unlike young men, whom Aristotle thought
Unfit to hear moral philosophy:
The reasons you allege do more conduce
To the hot passion of distemper'd blood
Than to make up a free determination
'Twixt right and wrong; for pleasure and revenge
Have ears more deaf than adders to the voice
Of any true decision. Nature craves
All dues be render'd to their owners: now,
What nearer debt in all humanity
Than wife is to the husband? If this law
Of nature be corrupted through affection,

And that great minds, of partial indulgence
To their benumbed wills, resist the same,
There is a law in each well-order'd nation
To curb those raging appetites that are
Most disobedient and refractory.
If Helen, then, be wife to Sparta's king, —
As it is known she is, — these moral laws
Of nature and of nations speak aloud
To have her back return'd: thus to persist
In doing wrong extenuates not wrong,
But makes it much more heavy. Hector's opinion
Is this, in way of truth: yet, ne'ertheless,
My spritely brethren, I propend to you
In resolution to keep Helen still;
For 'tis a cause that hath no mean dependance
Upon our joint and several dignities.

TROILUS
Why, there you touch'd the life of our design:
Were it not glory that we more affected
Than the performance of our heaving spleens,
I would not wish a drop of Trojan blood
Spent more in her defence. But, worthy Hector,
She is a theme of honour and renown;
A spur to valiant and magnanimous deeds;
Whose present courage may beat down our foes,
And fame in time to come canonise us:
For, I presume, brave Hector would not lose
So rich advantage of a promis'd glory,
As smiles upon the forehead of this action,
For the wide world's revenue.

HECTOR
                   I am yours,
You valiant offspring of great Priamus. —
I have a roisting challenge sent amongst
The dull and factious nobles of the Greeks
Will strike amazement to their drowsy spirits:
I was advertis'd their great general slept,
Whilst emulation in the army crept:
This, I presume, will wake him.   [*Exeunt.*

SCENE III

The Grecian camp. Before ACHILLES' *tent.*

Enter THERSITES.

THERSITES
How now, Thersites! what, lost in the labyrinth of thy
fury! Shall the elephant Ajax carry it thus? he beats me,
and I rail at him: O, worthy satisfaction! would it were
otherwise; that I could beat him, whilst he rail'd at
me:'sfoot, I'll learn to conjure and raise devils, but I'll
see some issue of my spiteful execrations. Then there's
Achilles, — a rare enginer. If Troy be not taken till
these two undermine it, the walls will stand till they fall
of themselves. O thou great thunder-darter of

THERSITES How now, Thersites! what, lost in the
labyrinth of thy fury!

Olympus, forget that thou art Jove, the king of gods; and, Mercury, lose all the serpente craft of thy caduceus; if ye take not that little little less-than-little wit from them that they have! which short-arm'd ignorance itself knows is so abundant scarce, it will not in circumvention deliver a fly from a spider, without drawing their massy irons and cutting the web. After this, the vengeance on the whole camp! or, rather, the Neapolitan bone-ache! for that, methinks, is the curse dependent on those that war for a placket. I have said my prayers; and devil Envy say Amen. — What, ho! my Lord Achilles!

Enter PATROCLUS.

PATROCLUS
Who's there? Thersites! Good Thersites, come in and rail.

THERSITES
If I could ha' remember'd a gilt counterfeit, thou wouldst not have slipp'd out of my contemplation: but it is no matter; thyself upon thyself! The common curse of mankind, folly and ignorance, be thine in great revenue! heaven bless thee from a tutor, and discipline come not near thee! Let thy blood be thy direction till thy death! then if she that lays thee out says thou art a fair corse, I'll be sworn and sworn upon't she never shrouded any but lazars. Amen. — Where's Achilles?

PATROCLUS
What, art thou devout? wast thou in prayer?

THERSITES
Ay; the heavens hear me!

Enter ACHILLES.

ACHILLES
Who's there?

PATROCLUS
Thersites, my lord.

ACHILLES
Where, where? — Art thou come? why, my cheese, my digestion, why hast thou not served thyself in to my table so many meals? Come, — what's Agamemnon?

THERSITES
Thy commander, Achilles. — Then tell me, Patroclus, what's Achilles?

PATROCLUS
Thy lord, Thersites: then tell me, I pray thee, what's thyself?

THERSITES
Thy knower, Patroclus: then tell me, Patroclus, what art thou?

PATROCLUS
Thou mayst tell that know'st.

ACHILLES
O, tell, tell.

THERSITES
I'll decline the whole question. Agamemnon commands Achilles; Achilles is my lord; I am Patroclus' knower; and Patroclus is a fool.

PATROCLUS
You rascal!

THERSITES
Peace, fool! I have not done.

ACHILLES
He is a privileged man. — Proceed, Thersites.

THERSITES
Agamemnon is a fool; Achilles is a fool; Thersites is a fool; and, as aforesaid, Patroclus is a fool.

ACHILLES
Derive this; come.

THERSITES
Agamemnon is a fool to offer to command Achilles; Achilles is a fool to be commanded of Agamemnon; Thersites is a fool to serve such a fool; and Patroclus is a fool positive.

PATROCLUS
Why am I a fool?

THERSITES
Make that demand to the Creator. It suffices me thou art. — Look you, who comes here?

ACHILLES
Patroclus, I'll speak with nobody. — Come in with me, Thersites. [*Exit.*

THERSITES
Here is such patchery, such juggling, and such knavery! all the argument is a cuckold and a whore; a good quarrel to draw emulous factions and bleed to death upon. Now, the dry serpigo on the subject! and war and lechery confound all! [*Exit.*

Enter AGAMEMNON, ULYSSES, NESTOR, DIOMEDES, *and* AJAX.

AGAMEMNON
Where is Achilles?

PATROCLUS
Within his tent: but ill-dispos'd, my lord.

AGAMEMNON
Let it be known to him that we are here.
He shent our messengers; and we lay by
Our appertainments, visiting of him:
Let him be told so; lest perchance he think
We dare not move the question of our place,
Or know not what we are.

PATROCLUS
                    I shall say so to him. [*Exit.*

ULYSSES
We saw him at the opening of his tent:
He is not sick.

AJAX
Yes, lion-sick, sick of proud heart: you may call it melancholy, if you will favour the man; but, by my head, 'tis pride: but why, why? let him show us the cause. — A word, my lord.

[*Takes* AGAMEMNON *aside.*

NESTOR
What moves Ajax thus to bay at him?

ULYSSES
Achilles hath inveigled his fool from him.

NESTOR
Who? Thersites?

ULYSSES
He.

NESTOR
Then will Ajax lack matter, if he have lost his argument.

ULYSSES
No, you see, he is his argument that has his argument, — Achilles.

NESTOR
All the better; their fraction is more our wish than their faction: but it was a strong composure a fool could disunite.

ULYSSES
The amity that wisdom knits not, folly may easily untie. — Here comes Patroclus.

NESTOR
No Achilles with him.

ULYSSES
The elephant hath joints, but none for courtesy: his legs are legs for necessity, not for flexure.

Enter PATROCLUS.

PATROCLUS
Achilles bids me say, he is much sorry,
If any thing more than your sport and pleasure
Did move your greatness and this noble state
To call upon him; he hopes it is no other
But for your health and your digestion sake, —
And after-dinner's breath.

AGAMEMNON
                    Hear you, Patroclus: —
We are too well acquainted with these answers:
But his evasion, wing'd thus swift with scorn,
Cannot outfly our apprehensions.
Much attribute he hath; and much the reason
Why we ascribe it to him; yet all his virtues,
Not virtuously on his own part beheld,
Do in our eyes begin to lose their gloss;
Yea, like fair fruit in an unwholesome dish,
Are like to rot untasted. Go and tell him,
We come to speak with him; and you shall not sin,
If you do say we think him over-proud
And under-honest; in self-assumption greater
Than in the note of judgement; and worthier
        than himself
Here tend the savage strangeness he puts on,
Disguise the holy strength of their command,
And underwrite in an observing kind
His humorous predominance; yea, watch
His pettish lunes, his ebbs, his flows, as if
The passage and whole carriage of this action
Rode on his tide. Go tell him this; and add,
That if he overhold his price so much,
We'll none of him; but let him, like an engine
Not portable, lie under this report, —
'Bring action hither, this cannot go to war:
A stirring dwarf we do allowance give
Before a sleeping giant': — tell him so.

PATROCLUS
I shall; and bring his answer presently. [*Exit.*

AGAMEMNON
In second voice we'll not be satisfied;
We come to speak with him. — Ulysses, enter you.
                                [*Exit* ULYSSES

AJAX
What is he more than another?

AGAMEMNON
No more than what he thinks he is.

AJAX
Is he so much? Do you not think he thinks himself a better man than I am?

AGAMEMNON
No question.

AJAX
Will you subscribe his thought, and say he is?

AGAMEMNON
No, noble Ajax; you are as strong, as valiant, as wise, no less noble, much more gentle, and altogether more tractable.

AJAX
Why should a man be proud? How doth pride grow? I know not what pride is.

AGAMEMNON
Your mind is the clearer, Ajax, and your virtues the fairer. He that is proud eats up himself; pride is his own glass, his own trumpet, his own chronicle; and whatever praises itself but in the deed, devours the deed in the praise.

AJAX
I do hate a proud man, as I hate the engendering of toads.

NESTOR [*aside*].
Yet he loves himself: is't not strange?

Enter ULYSSES.

ULYSSES
Achilles will not to the field to-morrow.

AGAMEMNON
What's his excuse?

ULYSSES
                    He doth rely on none;
But carries on the stream of his dispose,
Without observance or respect of any,
In will peculiar and in self-admission.

AGAMEMNON
Why will he not, upon our fair request,
Untent his person, and share the air with us?

ULYSSES
Things small as nothing, for request's sake only,
He makes important: possess'd he is with greatness;
And speaks not to himself, but with a pride
That quarrels at self-breath: imagin'd worth
Holds in his blood such swol'n and hot discourse,
That 'twixt his mental and his active parts
Kingdom'd Achilles in commotion rages,
And batters down himself: what should I say?
He is so plaguy proud, that the death-tokens of it
Cry 'No recovery.'

AGAMEMNON
                    Let Ajax go to him. —
Dear lord, go you and greet him in his tent:
'Tis said he holds you well; and will be led,
At your request, a little from himself.

ULYSSES
O Agamemnon, let it not be so!
We'll consecrate the steps that Ajax makes
When they go from Achilles: shall the proud lord,
That bastes his arrogance with his own seam,
And never suffers matter of the world
Enter his thoughts, save such as doth revolve
And ruminate himself, — shall he be worshipp'd
Of that we hold an idol more than he?
No, this thrice-worthy and right-valiant lord
Must not so stale his palm, nobly acquired;
Nor, by my will, assubjugate his merit,
As amply titled as Achilles is,
By going to Achilles:
That were to enlard his fat-already pride,
And add more coals to Cancer when he burns
With entertaining great Hyperion.
This lord go to him! Jupiter forbid;
And say in thunder, 'Achilles, go to him.'

NESTOR [*aside*].
O, this is well; he rubs the vein of him.

DIOMEDES [*aside*].
And how his silence drinks up this applause!

AJAX
If I go to him, with my armed fist
I'll pash him o'er the face.

AGAMEMNON
O, no, you shall not go.

AJAX
An a' be proud with me, I'll pheeze his pride:
Let me go to him.

ULYSSES
Not for the worth that hangs upon our quarrel.

AJAX
A paltry, insolent fellow!

NESTOR [aside].
How he describes himself!

AJAX
Can he not be sociable?

ULYSSES [aside].
The raven chides blackness.

AJAX
I'll let his humours blood.

AGAMEMNON [aside].
He will be the physician that should be the patient.

AJAX
An all men were o' my mind, —

ULYSSES [aside].
Wit would be out of fashion.

AJAX
A' should not bear it so, a' should eat swords first:
Shall pride carry it?

NESTOR [aside].
An 'twould, you'ld carry half.

ULYSSES [aside].
A' would have ten shares.

AJAX
I will knead him; I'll make him supple.

NESTOR [aside].
He's not yet through warm: force him with praises:
Pour in, pour in; his ambition is dry.

ULYSSES [to AGAMEMNON].
My lord, you feed too much on this dislike.

NESTOR
Our noble general, do not do so.

DIOMEDES
You must prepare to fight without Achilles.

ULYSSES
Why, 'tis this naming of him does him harm.
Here is a man — but 'tis before his face;
I will be silent.

NESTOR
  Wherefore should you so?
He is not emulous, as Achilles is.

ULYSSES
Know the whole world, he is as valiant.

AJAX
A whoreson dog, that shall palter thus with us!
Would he were a Trojan!

NESTOR
What a vice were it in Ajax now, —

ULYSSES
If he were proud, —

DIOMEDES
Or covetous of praise, —

ULYSSES
Ay, or surly borne, —

DIOMEDES
Or strange, or self-affected!

ULYSSES
Thank the heavens, lord, thou art of sweet composure;
Praise him that got thee, she that gave thee suck:
Fam'd be thy tutor, and thy parts of nature
Thrice-fam'd, beyond all erudition:
But he that disciplin'd thy arms to fight,
Let Mars divide eternity in twain,
And give him half: and, for thy vigour,
Bull-bearing Milo his addition yield
To sinewy Ajax. I will not praise thy wisdom,
Which, like a bourn, a pale, a shore, confines
Thy spacious and dilated parts: here's Nestor, —
Instructed by the antiquary times,
He must, he is, he cannot but be wise: —
But pardon, father Nestor, were your days
As green as Ajax', and your brain so temper'd,
You should not have the eminence of him,
But be as Ajax.

AJAX
  Shall I call you father?

NESTOR
Ay, my good son.

DIOMEDES
  Be rul'd by him, Lord Ajax.

ULYSSES
There is no tarrying here; the hart Achilles
Keeps thicket. Please it our great general

To call together all his state of war;
Fresh kings are come to Troy: to-morrow
We must with all our main of power stand fast:
And here's a lord, — come knights from east to west,
And cull their flower, Ajax shall cope the best.

AGAMEMNON
Go we to council. Let Achilles sleep:
Light boats sail swift, though greater hulks draw deep.
  [Exeunt.

ACT III

SCENE I

Troy. PRIAM'S *palace.*

Enter PANDARUS *and a* SERVANT.

PANDARUS
Friend, you, — pray you, a word: do not you follow
the young Lord Paris?

SERVANT
Ay, sir, when he goes before me.

PANDARUS
You depend upon him, I mean?

SERVANT
Sir, I do depend upon the Lord.

PANDARUS
You depend upon a noble gentleman; I must needs
praise him.

SERVANT
The Lord be praised!

PANDARUS
You know me, do you not?

SERVANT
Faith, sir, superficially.

PANDARUS
Friend, know me better; I am the Lord Pandarus.

SERVANT
I hope I shall know your honour better.

PANDARUS
I do desire it.

SERVANT
You are in the state of grace.

PANDARUS
Grace! not so, friend; honour and lordship are my
titles. [*Music sounds within.*] — What music is this?

SERVANT
I do but partly know, sir: it is music in parts.

PANDARUS
Know you the musicians?

SERVANT
Wholly, sir.

PANDARUS
Who play they to?

SERVANT
To the hearers, sir.

PANDARUS
At whose pleasure, friend?

SERVANT
At mine, sir, and theirs that love music.

PANDARUS
Command, I mean, friend.

SERVANT
Who shall I command, sir?

PANDARUS
Friend, we understand not one another: I am too
courtly and thou art too cunning. At whose request do
these men play?

SERVANT
That's to't, indeed, sir: marry, sir, at the request of Paris
my lord, who's there in person; with him, the mortal
Venus, the heart-blood of beauty, love's invisible soul, —

PANDARUS
Who, my cousin Cressida?

SERVANT
No, sir, Helen: could you not find out that by her
attributes?

PANDARUS
It should seem, fellow, that thou hast not seen the Lady
Cressida. I come to speak with Paris from the Prince
Troilus: I will make a complimental assault upon him,
for my business seethes.

SERVANT
Sodden business! there's a stew'd phrase indeed!

Enter PARIS *and* HELEN, *attended.*

PANDARUS
Fair be to you, my lord, and to all this fair company! fair

desires, in all fair measure, fairly guide them! —
especially to you, fair queen! fair thoughts be your fair
pillow!

HELEN
Dear lord, you are full of fair words.

PANDARUS
You speak your fair pleasure, sweet queen. — Fair
prince, here is good broken music.

PARIS
You have broke it, cousin: and, by my life, you shall
make it whole again; you shall piece it out with a piece
of your performance. — Nell, he is full of harmony.

PANDARUS
Truly, lady, no.

HELEN
O, sir, —

PANDARUS
Rude, in sooth; in good sooth, very rude.

PARIS
Well said, my lord! well, you say so in fits.

PANDARUS
I have business to my lord, dear queen. — My lord, will
you vouchsafe me a word?

HELEN
Nay, this shall not hedge us out: we'll hear you sing,
certainly.

PANDARUS
Well, sweet queen, you are pleasant with me. — But,
marry, thus, my lord, — My dear lord, and most
esteem'd friend, your brother Troilus, —

HELEN
My Lord Pandarus; honey-sweet lord, —

PANDARUS
Go to, sweet queen, to go: — commends himself most
affectionately to you, —

HELEN
You shall not bob us out of our melody: if you do, our
melancholy upon your head!

PANDARUS
Sweet queen, sweet queen; that's a sweet queen, i'faith, —

HELEN
And to make a sweet lady sad is a sour offence. Nay,
that shall not serve your turn; that shall it not, in truth,
la. Nay, I care not for such words; no, no.

PANDARUS
And, my lord, he desires you, that if the king call for
him at supper, you will make his excuse.

HELEN
My Lord Pandarus, —

PANDARUS
What says my sweet queen, — my very very sweet
queen?

PARIS
What exploit's in hand? where sups he to-night?

HELEN
Nay, but, my lord, —

PANDARUS
What says my sweet queen? — My cousin will fall out
with you. You must not know where he sups.

PARIS
I'll lay my life, with my disposer Cressida.

PANDARUS
No, no, no such matter; you are wide: come, your
disposer is sick.

PARIS
Well, I'll make excuse.

PANDARUS
Ay, good my lord. Why should you say Cressida? no,
your poor disposer's sick.

PARIS
I spy.

PANDARUS
You spy! what do you spy? — Come, give me an
instrument. — Now, sweet queen.

HELEN
Why, this is kindly done.

PANDARUS
My niece is horribly in love with a thing you have, sweet
queen.

HELEN
She shall have it, my lord, if it be not my lord Paris.

PANDARUS
He! no, she'll none of him; they two are twain.

HELEN
Falling in, after falling out, may make them three.

PANDARUS
Come, come, I'll hear no more of this; I'll sing you a
song now.

HELEN
Ay, ay, prithee now. By my troth, sweet lord, thou hast a fine forehead.
PANDARUS
Ay, you may, you may.
HELEN
Let thy song be love: this love will undo us all. O Cupid, Cupid, Cupid!
PANDARUS
Love! ay, that it shall, i'faith.
PARIS
Ay, good now, love, love, nothing but love.
PANDARUS
In good troth, it begins so. [*Sings.*
        Love, love, nothing but love, still more!
                For, O, love's bow
                Shoots buck and doe:
                The shaft confounds,
                Not that it wounds,
        But tickles still the sore.
        These lovers cry — Oh! oh! they die!
                Yet that which seems the wound to kill
        Doth turn oh! oh! to ha! ha! he!
                So dying love lives still:
        Oh! oh! a while, but ha! ha! ha!
        Oh! oh! groans out for ha! ha! ha!
        Heigh-ho!
HELEN
In love, i'faith, to the very tip of the nose.
PARIS
He eats nothing but doves, love; and that breeds hot blood, and hot blood begets hot thoughts, and hot thoughts beget hot deeds, and hot deeds is love.
PANDARUS
Is this the generation of love? hot blood, hot thoughts, and hot deeds? Why, they are vipers: is love a generation of vipers? — Sweet lord, who's a-field to-day?
PARIS
Hector, Deiphobus, Helenus, Antenor, and all the gallantry of Troy: I would fain have arm'd to-day, but my Nell would not have it so. How chance my brother Troilus went not?
HELEN
He hangs the lip at something: — you know all, Lord Pandarus.
PANDARUS
Not I, honey-sweet queen. — I long to hear how they sped to-day. — You'll remember your brother's excuse?
PARIS
To a hair.
PANDARUS
Farewell, sweet queen.
HELEN
Commend me to your niece.
PANDARUS
I will, sweet queen. [*Exit.*
[*Sound a retreat.*
PARIS
They're come from field: let us to Priam's hall,
To greet the warriors. Sweet Helen, I must woo you
To help unarm our Hector: his stubborn buckles,
With these your white enchanting fingers touch'd,
Shall more obey than to the edge of steel
Or force of Greekish sinews; you shall do more
Than all the island kings, — disarm great Hector.
HELEN
'Twill make us proud to be his servant, Paris;
Yea, what he shall receive of us in duty
Gives us more palm in beauty than we have,
Yea, overshines ourself.
PARIS
Sweet, above thought I love thee. [*Exeunt.*

SCENE II
PANDARUS' *orchard.*

Enter PANDARUS *and* TROILUS' BOY, *meeting.*

PANDARUS
How now! where's thy master? at my cousin Cressida's?
BOY
No, sir; he stays for you to conduct him thither.
PANDARUS
O, here he comes.

Enter TROILUS.

How now, how now!

TROILUS
Sirrah, walk off. [*Exit* BOY.
PANDARUS
Have you seen my cousin?
TROILUS
No, Pandarus: I stalk about her door,
Like a strange soul upon the Stygian banks
Staying for waftage. O, be thou my Charon,
And give me swift transportance to those fields
Where I may wallow in the lily-beds
Propos'd for the deserver! O gentle Pandarus,
From Cupid's shoulder pluck his painted wings,
And fly with me to Cressid!
PANDARUS
Walk here i'th'orchard; I'll bring her straight. [*Exit.*
TROILUS
I am giddy; expectation whirls me round.
Th'imaginary relish is so sweet
That it enchants my sense: what will it be,
When that the watery palate tastes indeed
Love's thrice-repured nectar? death, I fear me;
Swooning destruction; or some joy too fine,
Too subtle-potent, tun'd too sharp in sweetness,
For the capacity of my ruder powers:
I fear it much; and I do fear besides,
That I shall lose distinction in my joys;
As doth a battle, when they charge on heaps
The enemy flying.

Enter PANDARUS.

PANDARUS
She's making her ready, she'll come straight: you must be witty now. She does so blush, and fetches her wind so short, as if she were fray'd with a sprite: I'll fetch her. It is the prettiest villain: she fetches her breath as short as a new-ta'en sparrow. [*Exit.*
TROILUS
Even such a passion doth embrace my bosom:
My heart beats thicker than a feverous pulse;
And all my powers do their bestowing lose,
Like vassalage at unawares encountering
The eye of majesty.

Enter PANDARUS *with* CRESSIDA.

PANDARUS
Come, come, what need you blush? shame's a baby. — Here she is now: swear the oaths now to her that you have sworn to me. — What, are you gone again? you must be watch'd ere you be made tame, must you? Come your ways, come your ways: an you draw backward, we'll put you i'th'fills. Why do you not speak to her? Come, draw this curtain, and let's see your picture. Alas the day, how loth you are to offend daylight! an 'twere dark, you'ld close sooner. So, so; rub on, and kiss the mistress. How now! a kiss in fee-farm! build there, carpenter; the air is sweet. Nay, you shall fight your hearts out ere I part you. The falcon as the tercel, for all the ducks i'th'river: go to, go to.
TROILUS
You have bereft me of all words, lady.
PANDARUS
Words pay no debts, give her deeds: but she'll bereave you o'th'deeds too, if she call your activity in question. What, billing again? Here's — 'In witness whereof the parties interchangeably' — Come in, come in: I'll go get a fire. [*Exit.*
CRESSIDA
Will you walk in, my lord?
TROILUS
O Cressida, how often have I wish'd me thus!
CRESSIDA
Wish'd, my lord! — The gods grant — O my lord!
TROILUS
What should they grant? what makes this pretty abruption? What too curious dreg espies my sweet lady in the fountain of our love?
CRESSIDA
More dregs than water, if my fears have eyes.
TROILUS
Fears make devils of cherubins; they never see truly.

PANDARUS Come, come, what need you blush? shame's a baby.

CRESSIDA
Blind fear, that seeing reason leads, finds safer footing than blind reason stumbling without fear: to fear the worst oft cures the worst.
TROILUS
O, let my lady apprehend no fear: in all Cupid's pageant there is presented no monster.
CRESSIDA
Nor nothing monstrous neither?
TROILUS
Nothing, but our undertakings; when we vow to weep seas, live in fire, eat rocks, tame tigers; thinking it harder for our mistress to devise imposition enough than for us to undergo any difficulty imposed. This is the monstruosity in love, lady, — that the will is infinite, and the execution confined; that the desire is boundless, and the act a slave to limit.
CRESSIDA
They say, all lovers swear more performance than they are able, and yet reserve an ability that they never perform; vowing more than the perfection of ten, and discharging less than the tenth part of one. They that have the voice of lions and the act of hares, are they not monsters?
TROILUS
Are there such? such are not we: praise us as we are tasted, allow us as we prove; our head shall go bare till merit crown it: no perfection in reversion shall have a praise in present: we will not name desert before his birth; and, being born, his addition shall be humble. Few words to fair faith: Troilus shall be such to Cressid as what envy can say worst shall be a mock for his truth, and what truth can speak truest not truer than Troilus.
CRESSIDA
Will you walk in, my lord?

Enter PANDARUS.

PANDARUS
What, blushing still? have you not done talking yet?
CRESSIDA
Well, uncle, what folly I commit, I dedicate to you.
PANDARUS
I thank you for that: if my lord get a boy of you, you'll give him me. Be true to my lord: if he flinch, chide me for it.
TROILUS
You know now your hostages; your uncle's word and my firm faith.
PANDARUS
Nay, I'll give my word for her too: our kindred, though they be long ere they are woo'd, they are constant being won: they are burs, I can tell you; they'll stick where they are thrown.
CRESSIDA
Boldness comes to me now, and brings me heart: —
Prince Troilus, I have lov'd you night and day
For many weary months.
TROILUS
Why was my Cressid, then, so hard to win?

CRESSIDA

Hard to seem won: but I was won, my lord,
With the first glance that ever — pardon me —
If I confess much, you will play the tyrant.
I love you now; but not, till now, so much
But I might master it: — in faith, I lie;
My thoughts were like unbridled children, grown
Too headstrong for their mother: — see, we fools!
Why have I blabb'd? who shall be true to us
When we are so unsecret to ourselves? —
But, though I lov'd you well, I woo'd you not;
And yet, good faith, I wish'd myself a man,
Or that we women had men's privilege
Of speaking first. Sweet, bid me hold my tongue;
For, in this rapture, I shall surely speak
The thing I shall repent. See, see, your silence,
Cunning in dumbness, from my weakness draws
My very soul of counsel! — stop my mouth.

TROILUS

And shall, albeit sweet music issues thence.

[*Kisses her.*

PANDARUS

Pretty, i'faith.

CRESSIDA

My lord, I do beseech you, pardon me;
'Twas not my purpose thus to beg a kiss:
I am asham'd; — O heavens! what have I done?
For this time will I take my leave, my lord.

TROILUS

Your leave, sweet Cressid!

PANDARUS

Leave! an you take leave till to-morrow morning, —

CRESSIDA

Pray you, content you.

TROILUS

What offends you, lady?

CRESSIDA

Sir, mine own company.

TROILUS

You cannot shun
Yourself.

CRESSIDA

Let me go and try:
I have a kind of self resides with you;
But an unkind self, that itself will leave,
To be another's fool. I would be gone: —
Where is my wit? I know not what I speak.

TROILUS

Well know they what they speak that speak so wisely.

CRESSIDA

Perchance, my lord, I show'd more craft than love;
And fell so roundly to a large confession,
To angle for your thoughts: but you are wise;
Or else you love not; for to be wise and love
Exceeds man's might; that dwells with gods above.

TROILUS

O, that I thought it could be in a woman —
As, if it can, I will presume in you —
To feed for aye her lamp and flames of love;
To keep her constancy in plight and youth,
Outliving beauty's outward, with a mind
That doth renew swifter than blood decays!
Or, that persuasion could but thus convince me, —
That my integrity and truth to you
Might be affronted with the match and weight
Of such a winnow'd purity in love;
How were I then uplifted! but, alas!
I am as true as truth's simplicity,
And simpler than the infancy of truth.

CRESSIDA

In that I'll war with you.

TROILUS

O virtuous fight,
When right with right wars who shall be most right!
True swains in love shall, in the world to come,
Approve their truths by Troilus: when their rimes,
Full of protest, of oath, and big compare,
Want similes, truth tired with iteration, —
As true as steel, as plantage to the moon,
As sun to day, as turtle to her mate,
As iron to adamant, as earth to th'centre, —
Yet, after all comparisons of truth,
'As true as Troilus' shall crown up the verse,
And sanctify the numbers.

CRESSIDA

Prophet may you be!
If I be false, or swerve a hair from truth,
When time is old and hath forgot itself,
When waterdrops have worn the stones of Troy,
And blind oblivion swallow'd cities up,
And mighty states characterless are grated
To dusty nothing; yet let memory,
From false to false, among false maids in love,
Upbraid my falsehood! when they've said 'as false
As air, as water, wind, or sandy earth,
As fox to lamb, as wolf to heifer's calf,
Pard to the hind, or stepdame to her son,' —
'Yea,' let them say, to stick the heart of falsehood
'As false as Cressid.'

PANDARUS

Go to, a bargain made: seal it, seal it; I'll be the witness.
Here I hold your hand; here my cousin's. If ever you
prove false one to another, since I have taken such
pains to bring you together, let all pitiful goers-between
be call'd to the world's end after my name; call them all
Pandars; let all inconstant men be Troiluses, all false
women Cressids, and all brokers-between Pandars!
say, amen.

TROILUS

Amen.

CRESSIDA

Amen.

PANDARUS

Amen. Whereupon I will show you a chamber with a
bed; which bed, because it shall not speak of your pretty
encounters, press it to death: away! And Cupid grant all
tongue-tied maidens here
Bed, chamber, Pandar to provide this gear! [*Exeunt.*

SCENE III

The Grecian camp.

Flourish. Enter AGAMEMNON,
ULYSSES, DIOMEDES, NESTOR, AJAX,
MENELAUS, *and* CALCHAS.

CALCHAS

Now, princes, for the service I have done you,
Th'advantage of the time prompts me aloud
To call for recompense. Appear it to your mind
That, through the sight I bear in things to love,
I have abandon'd Troy, left my possession,
Incurr'd a traitor's name; expos'd myself,
From certain and possess'd conveniences,
To doubtful fortunes; sequest'ring from me all
That time, acquaintance, custom, and condition,
Made tame and most familiar to my nature;
And here, to do you service, am become
As new into the world, strange, unacquainted:
I do beseech you, as in way of taste,
To give me now a little benefit,
Out of those many register'd in promise,
Which, you say, live to come in my behalf.

AGAMEMNON

What wouldst thou of us, Trojan? make demand.

CALCHAS

You have a Trojan prisoner, call'd Antenor,
Yesterday took: Troy holds him very dear.

ACHILLES What, comes the general to speak with me?

Oft have you — often have you thanks therefore —
Desired my Cressid in right great exchange,
Whom Troy hath still denied: but this Antenor,
I know, is such a wrest in their affairs,
That their negotiations all must slack,
Wanting his manage; and they will almost
Give us a prince of blood, a son of Priam,
In change of him: let him be sent, great princes,
And he shall buy my daughter; and her presence
Shall quite strike off all service I have done,
In most accepted pain.

AGAMEMNON

Let Diomedes bear him,
And bring us Cressid hither: Calchas shall have
What he requests of us. — Good Diomed,
Furnish you fairly for this interchange:
Withal, bring word if Hector will to-morrow
Be answer'd in his challenge: Ajax is ready.

DIOMEDES

This shall I undertake; and 'tis a burden
Which I am proud to bear.

[*Exeunt* DIOMEDES *and* CALCHAS.

Enter ACHILLES *and* PATROCLUS, *before their tent.*

ULYSSES

Achilles stands i'th'entrance of his tent: —
Please it our general to pass strangely by him,
As if he were forgot; and, princes all,
Lay negligent and loose regard upon him:
I will come last. 'Tis like he'll question me
Why such unplausive eyes are bent on him:
If so, I have derision medicinable,
To use between your strangeness and his pride,
Which his own will shall have desire to drink:
It may do good: pride hath no other glass
To show itself but pride; for supple knees
Feed arrogance, and are the proud man's fees.

AGAMEMNON

We'll execute your purpose, and put on
A form of strangeness as we pass along: —
So do each lord; and either greet him not,
Or else disdainfully, which shall shake him more
Than if not look'd on. I will lead the way.

ACHILLES

What, comes the general to speak with me?
You know my mind, I'll fight no more 'gainst Troy.

AGAMEMNON

What says Achilles? would he aught with us?

NESTOR

Would you, my lord, aught with the general?

ACHILLES

No.

NESTOR

Nothing, my lord.

AGAMEMNON

The better. [*Exeunt* AGAMEMNON *and* NESTOR.

ACHILLES

Good day, good day.

MENELAUS
How do you? how do you? [*Exit.*

ACHILLES
What, does the cuckold scorn me?

AJAX
How now, Patroclus!

ACHILLES
Good morrow, Ajax.

AJAX
Ha!

ACHILLES
Good morrow.

AJAX
Ay, and good next day too. [*Exit.*

ACHILLES
What mean these fellows? Know they not Achilles?

PATROCLUS
They pass by strangely: they were used to bend,
To send their smiles before them to Achilles;
To come as humbly as they use to creep
To holy altars.

ACHILLES
What, am I poor of late?
'Tis certain, greatness, once fall'n out with fortune,
Must fall out with men too: what the declin'd is,
He shall as soon read in the eyes of others
As feel in his own fall; for men, like butterflies,
Show not their mealy wings but to the summer;
And not a man, for being simply man,
Hath any honour, but honour for those honours
That are without him, as place, riches, favour,
Prizes of accident as oft as merit:
Which when they fall, as being slippery standers,
The love that lean'd on them as slippery too,
Do one pluck down another, and together
Die in the fall. But 'tis not so with me:
Fortune and I are friends: I do enjoy
At ample point all that I did possess,
Save these men's looks; who do, methinks, find out
Something not worth in me such rich beholding
As they have often given. Here is Ulysses:
I'll interrupt his reading. —
How now, Ulysses!

ULYSSES
Now, great Thetis' son!

ACHILLES
What are you reading?

ULYSSES
A strange fellow here
Writes me, 'That man — how dearly ever parted,
How much in having, or without or in —
Cannot make boast to have that which he hath,
Nor feels not what he owes, but by reflection;
As when his virtues shining upon others
Heat them, and they retort that heat again
To the first giver.'

ACHILLES
This is not strange, Ulysses.
The beauty that is borne here in the face
The bearer knows not, but commends itself
To others' eyes: nor doth the eye itself,
That most pure spirit of sense, behold itself,
Not going from itself; but eye to eye opposed
Salutes each other with each other's form:
For speculation turns not to itself,
Till it hath travell'd, and is mirror'd there
Where it may see itself. This is not strange at all.

ULYSSES
I do not strain at the position, —
It is familiar, — but at the author's drift;
Who, in his circumstance, expressly proves
That no man is the lord of any thing,
Though in and of him there be much consisting,
Till he communicate his parts to others;
Nor doth he of himself know them for aught
Till he behold them formed in th'applause
Where they're extended; who, like an arch, reverb'rates
The voice again; or, like a gate of steel
Fronting the sun, receives and renders back
His figure and his heat. I was much rapt in this;
And apprehended here immediately
The unknown Ajax.
Heavens, what a man is there! a very horse;
That has he knows not what. Nature, what things there
are,
Most abject in regard, and dear in use!
What things again most dear in the esteem,
And poor in worth! Now shall we see to-morrow —
An act that very chance doth throw upon him —
Ajax renown'd. O heavens, what some men do,

While some men leave to do!
How some men creep in skittish Fortune's hall,
Whiles others play the idiots in her eyes!
How one man eats into another's pride,
While pride is fasting in his wantonness!
To see these Grecian lords! — why, even already
They clap the lubber Ajax on the shoulder,
As if his foot were on brave Hector's breast,
And great Troy shrieking.

ACHILLES
I do believe it; for they pass'd by me
As misers do by beggars, — neither gave to me
Good word nor look: what, are my deeds forgot?

ULYSSES
Time hath, my lord, a wallet at his back,
Wherein he puts alms for oblivion,
A great-siz'd monster of ingratitudes:
Those scraps are good deeds past; which are devour'd
As fast as they are made, forgot as soon
As done: perseverance, dear my lord,
Keeps honour bright: to have done, is to hang
Quite out of fashion, like a rusty mail
In monumental mockery. Take the instant way;
For honour travels in a strait so narrow,
Where one but goes abreast: keep, then, the path;
For emulation hath a thousand sons,
That one by one pursue: if you give way,
Or hedge aside from the direct forthright,
Like to an enter'd tide, they all rush by,
And leave you hindmost;
Or, like a gallant horse fall'n in first rank,
Lie there for pavement to the abject rear,
O'er-run and trampled on: then what they do in
present,
Though less than yours in past, must o'ertop yours;
For time is like a fashionable host,
That slightly shakes his parting guest by th'hand,
And with his arms outstretch'd, as he would fly,
Grasps-in the comer: welcome ever smiles,
And farewell goes out sighing. O, let not virtue seek
Remuneration for the thing it was;
For beauty, wit,
High birth, vigour of bone, desert in service,
Love, friendship, charity, are subjects all
To envious and calumniating time.
One touch of nature makes the whole world kin, —
That all, with one consent, praise new-born gawds,
Though they are made and moulded of things past,
And give to dust, that is a little gilt,
More laud than gilt o'er-dusted.
The present eye praises the present object:
Then marvel not, thou great and complete man,
That all the Greeks begin to worship Ajax;
Since things in motion sooner catch the eye
Than what not stirs. The cry went once on thee,
And still it might, and yet it may again,
If thou wouldst not entomb thyself alive,
And case thy reputation in thy tent;
Whose glorious deeds, but in these fields of late,
Made emulous missions 'mongst the gods themselves,
And drave great Mars to faction.

ACHILLES
Of this my privacy
I have strong reasons.

ULYSSES
But 'gainst your privacy
The reasons are more potent and heroical:
'Tis known, Achilles, that you are in love
With one of Priam's daughters.

ACHILLES
Ha! known!

ULYSSES
Is that a wonder?
The providence that's in a watchful state
Knows almost every grain of Pluto's gold;
Finds bottom in th'uncomprehensive deeps;
Keeps place with thought, and almost, like the gods,
Does thoughts unveil in their dumb cradles.
There is a mystery — with whom relation
Durst never meddle — in the soul of state;
Which hath an operation more divine
Than breath or pen can give expressure to:
All the commerce that you have had with Troy
As perfectly is ours as yours, my lord;
And better would it fit Achilles much
To throw down Hector than Polyxena:
But it must grieve young Pyrrhus now at home,
When fame shall in our islands sound her trump,
And all the Greekish girls shall tripping sing,
'Great Hector's sister did Achilles win;
But our great Ajax bravely beat down him.'

Farewell, my lord: I as your lover speak;
The fool slides o'er the ice that you should break.
[*Exit.*

PATROCLUS
To this effect, Achilles, have I mov'd you:
A woman impudent and mannish grown
Is not more loath'd than an effeminate man
In time of action. I stand condemn'd for this;
They think, my little stomach to the war,
And your great love to me, restrains you thus:
Sweet, rouse yourself; and the weak wanton Cupid
Shall from your neck unloose his amorous fold,
And, like a dew-drop from the lion's mane,
Be shook to air.

ACHILLES
Shall Ajax fight with Hector?

PATROCLUS
Ay, and perhaps receive much honour by him.

ACHILLES
I see my reputation is at stake;
My fame is shrewdly gored.

PATROCLUS
O, then, beware;
Those wounds heal ill that men do give themselves:
Omission to do what is necessary
Seals a commission to a blank of danger;
And danger, like an ague, subtly taints
Even then when we sit idly in the sun.

ACHILLES
Go call Thersites hither, sweet Patroclus:
I'll send the fool to Ajax, and desire him
T'invite the Trojan lords after the combat
To see us here unarm'd: I have a woman's longing,
An appetite that I am sick withal,
To see great Hector in his weeds of peace;
To talk with him, and to behold his visage,
Even to my full of view. — A labour saved!

Enter THERSITES.

THERSITES
A wonder!

ACHILLES
What?

THERSITES
Ajax goes up and down the field, asking for himself.

ACHILLES
How so?

THERSITES
He must fight singly to-morrow with Hector; and is so
prophetically proud of an heroical cudgelling that he
raves in saying nothing.

ACHILLES
How can that be?

THERSITES
Why, he stalks up and down like a peacock, — a stride
and a stand: ruminates like an hostess that hath no
arithmetic but her brain to set down her reckoning:
bites his lip with a politic regard, as who should say,
'There were wit in this head, an 'twould out'; and so
there is; but it lies as coldly in him as fire in a flint,
which will not show without knocking. The man's
undone for ever; for if Hector break not his neck
i'th'combat, he'll break't himself in vainglory. He
knows not me: I said, 'Good morrow, Ajax'; and he
replies, 'Thanks, Agamemnon.' What think you of this
man, that takes me for the general? He's grown a very
land-fish, languageless, a monster. A plague of
opinion! a man may wear it on both sides, like a leather
jerkin.

ACHILLES
Thou must be my ambassador to him, Thersites.

THERSITES
Who, I? why, he'll answer nobody; he professes not
answering: speaking is for beggars; he wears his
tongue in's arms. I will put on his presence: let
Patroclus make demands to me, you shall see the
pageant of Ajax.

ACHILLES
To him, Patroclus; tell him, — I humbly desire the
valiant Ajax to invite the most valorous Hector to come
unarm'd to my tent; and to procure safe-conduct for his
person of the magnanimous and most illustrious
six-or-seven-times-honour'd captain-general of the
Grecian army, Agamemnon, et cetera. Do this.

PATROCLUS
Jove bless great Ajax!

THERSITES
Hum!

PATROCLUS
I come from the worthy Achilles, —

THERSITES
Ha!
PATROCLUS
Who most humbly desires you to invite Hector to his tent, —
THERSITES
Hum!
PATROCLUS
And to procure safe-conduct from Agamemnon.
THERSITES
Agamemnon!
PATROCLUS
Ay, my lord.
THERSITES
Ha!
PATROCLUS
What say you to't?
THERSITES
God b'wi' you, with all my heart.
PATROCLUS
Your answer, sir.
THERSITES
If to-morrow be a fair day, by eleven o'clock it will go one way or other: howsoever, he shall pay for me ere he has me.
PATROCLUS
Your answer, sir.
THERSITES
Fare you well, with all my heart.
ACHILLES
Why, but he is not in this tune, is he?
THERSITES
No, but he's out o' tune thus. What music will be in him when Hector has knock'd out his brains, I know not; but, I am sure, none, — unless the fiddler Apollo get his sinews to make catlings on.
ACHILLES
Come, thou shalt bear a letter to him straight.
THERSITES
Let me bear another to his horse; for that's the more capable creature.
ACHILLES
My mind is troubled, like a fountain stirr'd;
And I myself see not the bottom of it.
[*Exeunt* ACHILLES *and* PATROCLUS.
THERSITES
Would the fountain of your mind were clear again, that I might water an ass at it! I had rather be a tick in a sheep than such a valiant ignorance. [*Exit.*

ACT IV

SCENE I

Troy. A street.

Enter, at one door, AENEAS, *and* SERVANT *with a torch; at another,* PARIS, DEIPHOBUS, ANTENOR, DIOMEDES *the Grecian, and others, with torches.*

PARIS
See, ho! who is that there?
DEIPHOBUS
It is the Lord Aeneas.
AENEAS
Is the prince there in person? —
Had I so good occasion to lie long
As you, Prince Paris, nothing but heavenly business
Should rob my bed-mate of my company.
DIOMEDES
That's my mind too. — Good morrow, Lord Aeneas.
PARIS
A valiant Greek, Aeneas, — take his hand, —
Witness the process of your speech, wherein
You told how Diomed, a whole week by days,
Did haunt you in the field.
AENEAS
                        Health to you, valiant sir,
During all question of the gentle truce;
But when I meet you arm'd, as black defiance
As heart can think or courage execute.
DIOMEDES
The one and other Diomed embraces.
Our bloods are now in calm; and, so long, health;
But when contention and occasion meet,
By Jove, I'll play the hunter for thy life
With all my force, pursuit, and policy.
AENEAS
And thou shalt hunt a lion, that will fly

With his face backward. — In humane gentleness,
Welcome to Troy! now, by Anchises' life,
Welcome, indeed! By Venus' hand I swear
No man alive can love in such a sort
The thing he means to kill more excellently.
DIOMEDES
We sympathise: — Jove, let Aeneas live,
If to my sword his fate be not the glory,
A thousand complete courses of the sun!
But, in mine emulous honour, let him die,
With every joint a wound, and that to-morrow!
AENEAS
We know each other well.
DIOMEDES
We do; and long to know each other worse.
PARIS
This is the most despiteful gentle greeting,
The noblest hateful love, that e'er I heard of. —
What business, lord, so early?
AENEAS
I was sent for to the king; but why, I know not.
PARIS
His purpose meets you: 'twas to bring this Greek
To Calchas' house; and there to render him,
For the enfreed Antenor, the fair Cressid:
Let's have your company; or, if you please,
Haste there before us: I constantly do think —
Or, rather, call my thought a certain knowledge —
My brother Troilus lodges there to-night:
Rouse him, and give him note of our approach,
With the whole quality wherefore: I fear
We shall be much unwelcome.
AENEAS
                        That I assure you:
Troilus had rather Troy were borne to Greece
Than Cressid borne from Troy.
PARIS
                        There is no help;
The bitter disposition of the time
Will have it so. On, lord; we'll follow you.
AENEAS
Good morrow, all. [*Exit with* SERVANT.
PARIS
And tell me, noble Diomed, — faith, tell me true,
Even in the soul of sound good-fellowship, —
Who, in your thoughts, merits fair Helen best,
Myself or Menelaus?
DIOMEDES
                        Both alike:
He merits well to have her, that doth seek her,
Not making any scruple of her soilure,
With such a hell of pain and world of charge;
And you as well to keep her, that defend her,
Not palating the taste of her dishonour,
With such a costly loss of wealth and friends:
He, like a puling cuckold, would drink up
The lees and dregs of a flat tamed piece;
You, like a lecher, out of whorish loins
Are pleas'd to breed out your inheritors:
Both merits pois'd, each weighs nor less nor more;
But he as he, the heavier for a whore.
PARIS
You are too bitter to your countrywoman.
DIOMEDES
She's bitter to her country: hear me, Paris: —
For every false drop in her bawdy veins
A Grecian's life hath sunk; for every scruple
Of her contaminated carrion weight
A Trojan hath been slain; since she could speak,
She hath not given so many good words breath
As for her Greeks and Trojans suffer'd death.
PARIS
Fair Diomed, you do as chapmen do,
Dispraise the thing that you desire to buy:
But we in silence hold this virtue well, —
We'll not commend what we intend not sell.
Here lies our way. [*Exeunt.*

SCENE II

Court of PANDARUS' *house.*

Enter TROILUS *and* CRESSIDA.

TROILUS
Dear, trouble not yourself: the morn is cold.
CRESSIDA
Then, sweet my lord, I'll call mine uncle down;
He shall unbolt the gates.
TROILUS
                        Trouble him not;
To bed, to bed: sleep kill those pretty eyes,
And give as soft attachment to thy senses
As infants' empty of all thought!
CRESSIDA
                        Good morrow, then.
TROILUS
I prithee now, to bed.
CRESSIDA
                        Are you a-weary of me?
TROILUS
O Cressida! but that the busy day,
Wak'd by the lark, hath rous'd the ribald crows,
And dreaming night will hide our joys no longer,
I would not from thee.
CRESSIDA
                        Night hath been too brief.
TROILUS
Beshrew the witch! with venomous wights she stays
As tediously as hell; but flies the grasps of love
With wings more momentary-swift than thought.
— You will catch cold, and curse me.
CRESSIDA
                        Prithee, tarry; —
You men will never tarry. —
O foolish Cressid! — I might have still held off,
And then you would have tarried. — Hark! there's one up.
PANDARUS [*within*].
What,'s all the doors open here?
TROILUS
It is your uncle.
CRESSIDA
A pestilence on him! now will he be mocking:
I shall have such a life!
                        Enter PANDARUS.
PANDARUS
How now, how now! how go maidenheads? —
Here, you maid! where's my cousin Cressid?

CRESSIDA Good morrow, then.

CRESSIDA
Go hang yourself, you naughty mocking uncle!
You bring me to do — and then you flout me too.
PANDARUS
To do what? to do what? — let her say what: — what
have I brought you to do?
CRESSIDA
Come, come, beshrew your heart! you'll ne'er be good,
Nor suffer others.
PANDARUS
Ha, ha! Alas, poor wretch! ah, poor capocchia! hast not
slept to-night? would he not — a naughty man — let it
sleep? a bugbear take him!
CRESSIDA
Did not I tell you? — would he were knock'd i'th'head! —
                                        [*One knocks.*
Who's that at door? good uncle, go and see. —
My lord, come you again into my chamber:
You smile and mock me, as if I meant naughtily.
TROILUS
Ha, ha!
CRESSIDA
Come, you are deceiv'd: I think of no such thing. —
                                        [*Knock.*
How earnestly they knock! — Pray you, come in:
I would not for half Troy have you seen here.
            [*Exeunt* TROILUS *and* CRESSIDA.
PANDARUS
Who's there? what's the matter? will you beat down the
door? How now! what's the matter?

            Enter AENEAS.

AENEAS
Good morrow, lord, good morrow.
PANDARUS
Who's there? my Lord Aeneas! By my troth,
I knew you not: what news with you so early?
AENEAS
Is not Prince Troilus here?
PANDARUS
Here! what should he do here?
AENEAS
Come, he is here, my lord; do not deny him:
It doth import him much to speak with me.
PANDARUS
Is he here, say you? 'tis more than I know, I'll
be sworn: — for my own part, I came in late. What
should he do here?
AENEAS
Who! — nay, then: — come, come, you'll do him
wrong ere you're ware: you'll be so true to him to be
false to him: do not you know of him, but yet go fetch
him hither; go.

            Enter TROILUS.

TROILUS
How now! what's the matter?
AENEAS
My lord, I scarce have leisure to salute you,
My matter is so rash: there is at hand
Paris your brother, and Deiphobus,
The Grecian Diomed, and our Antenor
Deliver'd to us; and for him forthwith,
Ere the first sacrifice, within this hour,
We must give up to Diomedes' hand
The Lady Cressida.
TROILUS
            Is it so concluded?
AENEAS
By Priam and the general state of Troy:
They are at hand, and ready to effect it.
TROILUS
How my achievements mock me! —
I will go meet them: and, my Lord Aeneas,
We met by chance; you did not find me here.
AENEAS
Good, good, my lord; the secrets of nature
Have not more gift in taciturnity.
            [*Exeunt* TROILUS *and* AENEAS.
PANDARUS
Is't possible? no sooner got but lost? The devil take
Antenor! the young prince will go mad: a plague upon
Antenor! I would they had broke's neck!

            Enter CRESSIDA.

CRESSIDA
How now! what's the matter? who was here?
PANDARUS
Ah, ah!

CRESSIDA
Why sigh you so profoundly? where's my lord? gone?
Tell me, sweet uncle, what's the matter?
PANDARUS
Would I were as deep under the earth as I am above!
CRESSIDA
O the gods! — what's the matter?
PANDARUS
Prithee, get thee in: would thou hadst ne'er been born!
I knew thou wouldst be his death: — O, poor
gentleman! — A plague upon Antenor!
CRESSIDA
Good uncle, I beseech you, on my knees I beseech you,
what's the matter?
PANDARUS
Thou must be gone, wench, thou must be gone; thou
art changed for Antenor: thou must to thy father, and
be gone from Troilus: 'twill be his death; 'twill be his
bane; he cannot bear it.
CRESSIDA
O you immortal gods! — I will not go.
PANDARUS
Thou must.
CRESSIDA
I will not, uncle: I have forgot my father;
I know no touch of consanguinity;
No kin, no love, no blood, no soul so near me
As the sweet Troilus. — O you gods divine,
Make Cressid's name the very crown of falsehood,
If ever she leave Troilus! Time, force, and death,
Do to this body what extremes you can;
But the strong base and building of my love
Is as the very centre of the earth,
Drawing all things to it. — I'll go in and weep, —
PANDARUS
Do, do.
CRESSIDA
Tear my bright hair, and scratch my praised cheeks;
Crack my clear voice with sobs, and break my heart
With sounding 'Troilus'. I will not go from Troy.
                                        [*Exeunt.*

SCENE III
Before PANDARUS' *house.*

Enter PARIS, TROILUS, AENEAS, DEIPHOBUS,
ANTENOR, *and* DIOMEDES.

PARIS
It is great morning; and the hour prefix'd
Of her delivery to this valiant Greek
Comes fast upon: — good my brother Troilus,
Tell you the lady what she is to do,
And haste her to the purpose.
TROILUS
                        Walk into her house;
I'll bring her to the Grecian presently:
And to his hand when I deliver her,
Think it an altar, and thy brother Troilus
A priest, there offering to it his own heart.   [*Exit.*
PARIS
I know what 'tis to love;
And would, as I shall pity, I could help! —
Please you walk in, my lords.   [*Exeunt.*

SCENE IV
A room in PANDARUS' *house.*

Enter PANDARUS *and* CRESSIDA.

PANDARUS
Be moderate, be moderate.
CRESSIDA
Why tell you me of moderation?
The grief is fine, full, perfect, that I taste,
And violenteth in a sense as strong
As that which causeth it: how can I moderate it?
If I could temporise with my affection,
Or brew it to a weak and colder palate,
The like allayment could I give my grief:
My love admits no qualifying dross;
No more my grief, in such a precious loss.
PANDARUS
Here, here, here he comes.
            Enter TROILUS.
Ah, sweet ducks!
CRESSIDA
O Troilus! Troilus!   [*Embracing him.*
PANDARUS
What a pair of spectacles is here! Let me embrace too.
  'O heart,' as the goodly saying is,

'—— O heart, O heavy heart,
    Why sigh'st thou without breaking?'
where he answers again,
    'Because thou canst not ease thy smart
        By friendship nor by speaking.'
There was never a truer rime. Let us cast away nothing,
  for we may live to have need of such a verse: we see it,
  we see it. — How now, lambs!
TROILUS
Cressid, I love thee in so strain'd a purity,
That the blest gods, as angry with my fancy,
More bright in zeal than the devotion which
Cold lips blow to their deities, take thee from me.
CRESSIDA
Have the gods envy?
PANDARUS
Ay, ay, ay, ay; 'tis too plain a case.
CRESSIDA
And is it true that I must go from Troy?
TROILUS
A hateful truth.
CRESSIDA
            What, and from Troilus too?
TROILUS
From Troy and Troilus.
CRESSIDA
            Is it possible?
TROILUS
And suddenly; where injury of chance
Puts back leave-taking, justles roughly by
All time of pause, rudely beguiles our lips
Of all rejoindure, forcibly prevents
Our lock'd embrasures, strangles our dear vows
Even in the birth of our own labouring breath:
We two, that with so many thousand sighs
Did buy each other, must poorly sell ourselves
With the rude brevity and discharge of one.
Injurious time now, with a robber's haste,
Crams his rich thievery up, he knows not how:
As many farewells as be stars in heaven,
With distinct breath and consign'd kisses to them,
He fumbles up into a loose adieu;
And scants us with a single famish'd kiss,
Distasted with the salt of broken tears.
AENEAS [*within*].
My lord, is the lady ready?
TROILUS
Hark! you are call'd: some say the Genius so
Cries 'Come!' to him that instantly must die. —
Bid them have patience; she shall come anon.
PANDARUS
Where are my tears? rain, to lay this wind, or
my heart will be blown up by the root.   [*Exit.*
CRESSIDA
I must, then, to the Grecians?
TROILUS
                        No remedy.
CRESSIDA
A woeful Cressid 'mongst the merry Greeks!
When shall we see again?
TROILUS
Hear me, my love: be thou but true of heart, —
CRESSIDA
I true! how now! what wicked deem is this?
TROILUS
Nay, we must use expostulation kindly,
For it is parting from us:
I speak not 'be thou true,' as fearing thee;
For I will throw my glove to Death himself,
That there's no maculation in thy heart:
But 'be thou true,' say I, to fashion in
My sequent protestation; be thou true,
And I will see thee.
CRESSIDA
O, you shall be expos'd, my lord, to dangers
As infinite as imminent! but I'll be true.
TROILUS
And I'll grow friend with danger. Wear this sleeve.
CRESSIDA
And you this glove. When shall I see you?
TROILUS
I will corrupt the Grecian sentinels,
To give thee nightly visitation.
But yet, be true.
CRESSIDA
            O heavens! — 'be true' again!
TROILUS
Hear why I speak it, love:
The Grecian youths are full of quality;

AGAMEMNON Give with thy trumpet a loud note to Troy.

They're loving, well compos'd with gifts of nature,
And swelling o'er with arts and exercise:
How novelty may move, and parts with person,
Alas, a kind of godly jealousy —
Which, I beseech you, call a virtuous sin —
Makes me afeard.

CRESSIDA

O heavens! you love me not.

TROILUS

Die I a villain, then!
In this I do not call your faith in question
So mainly as my merit: I cannot sing,
Nor heel the high lavolt, nor sweeten talk,
Nor play at subtle games; fair virtues all,
To which the Grecians are most prompt and pregnant:
But I can tell, that in each grace of these
There lurks a still and dumb-discoursive devil
That tempts most cunningly: but be not tempted.

CRESSIDA

Do you think I will?

TROILUS

No.
But something may be done that we will not:
And sometimes we are devils to ourselves,
When we will tempt the frailty of our powers,
Presuming on their changeful potency.

AENEAS [within].

Nay, good my lord, —

TROILUS

Come, kiss; and let us part.

PARIS [within].

Brother Troilus!

TROILUS

Good brother, come you hither;
And bring Aeneas and the Grecian with you.

CRESSIDA

My lord, will you be true?

TROILUS

Who, I? alas, it is my vice, my fault:
Whiles others fish with craft for great opinion,
I with great truth catch mere simplicity;
Whilst some with cunning gild their copper crowns,
With truth and plainness I do wear mine bare.

Fear not my truth: the moral of my wit
Is 'plain and true'; there's all the reach of it.

Enter AENEAS, PARIS, ANTENOR,
DEIPHOBUS, *and* DIOMEDES.

Welcome, Sir Diomed! here is the lady
Which for Antenor we deliver you:
At the port, lord, I'll give her to thy hand;
And by the way possess thee what she is.
Entreat her fair; and, by my soul, fair Greek,
If e'er thou stand at mercy of my sword,
Name Cressid, and thy life shall be as safe
As Priam is in Ilion.

DIOMEDES

Fair Lady Cressid,
So please you, save the thanks this prince expects:
The lustre in your eye, heaven in your cheek,
Pleads your fair usage; and to Diomed
You shall be mistress, and command him wholly.

TROILUS

Grecian, thou dost not use me courteously,
To shame the zeal of my petition to thee
In praising her: I tell thee, lord of Greece,
She is as far high-soaring o'er thy praises
As thou unworthy to be call'd her servant.
I charge thee use her well, even for my charge;
For, by the dreadful Pluto, if thou dost not,
Though the great bulk Achilles be thy guard,
I'll cut thy throat.

DIOMEDES

O, be not mov'd, Prince Troilus:
Let me be privileg'd by my place and message
To be a speaker free; when I am hence,
I'll answer to my lust: and know you, lord,
I'll nothing do on charge: to her own worth
She shall be priz'd; but that you say, 'Be't so,'
I'll speak it in my spirit and honour, 'No.'

TROILUS

Come, to the port. — I'll tell thee, Diomed,
This brave shall oft make thee to hide thy head. —
Lady, give me your hand; and, as we walk,
To our own selves bend we our needful talk.

[*Exeunt* TROILUS, CRESSIDA, *and* DIOMEDES.
Sound trumpet.

PARIS

Hark! Hector's trumpet.

AENEAS

How have we spent this morning!
The prince must think me tardy and remiss,
That swore to ride before him to the field.

PARIS

'Tis Troilus' fault: come, come, to field with him.

DEIPHOBUS

Let us make ready straight.

AENEAS

Yea, with a bridegroom's fresh alacrity,
Let us address to tend on Hector's heels:
The glory of our Troy doth this day lie
On his fair worth and single chivalry. [*Exeunt.*

SCENE V

The Grecian camp. Lists set out.

Enter AJAX, *arm'd;* AGAMEMNON, ACHILLES,
PATROCLUS, MENELAUS, ULYSSES, NESTOR,
and others.

AGAMEMNON

Here art thou in appointment fresh and fair,
Anticipating time with starting courage.
Give with thy trumpet a loud note to Troy,
Thou dreadful Ajax; that the appalled air
May pierce the head of the great combatant,
And hale him hither.

AJAX

Thou, trumpet, there's my purse.
Now crack thy lungs, and split thy brazen pipe:
Blow, villain, till thy sphered bias cheek
Outswell the colic of puff'd Aquilon:
Come, stretch thy chest, and let thy eyes spout blood;
Thou blow'st for Hector. [*Trumpet sounds.*

ULYSSES

No trumpet answers.

ACHILLES

'Tis but early days.

AGAMEMNON

Is not yond Diomed, with Calchas' daughter?

ULYSSES

'Tis he, I ken the manner of his gait;
He rises on the toe: that spirit of his
In aspiration lifts him from the earth.

Enter DIOMEDES *with* CRESSIDA.

AGAMEMNON

Is this the Lady Cressid?

DIOMEDES

Even she.

AGAMEMNON

Most dearly welcome to the Greeks, sweet lady.
[*Kisses her.*

NESTOR

Our general doth salute you with a kiss.

ULYSSES

Yet is the kindness but particular;
'Twere better she were kiss'd in general.

NESTOR

And very courtly counsel: I'll begin. — [*Kisses her.*
So much for Nestor.

ACHILLES

I'll take that winter from your lips, fair lady: [*Kisses her.*
Achilles bids you welcome.

MENELAUS

I had good argument for kissing once.

PATROCLUS

But that's no argument for kissing now;
For this popp'd Paris in his hardiment,
And parted thus you and your argument. [*Kisses her.*

ULYSSES

O deadly gall, and theme of all our scorns!
For which we lose our heads to gild his horns.

PATROCLUS

The first was Menelaus' kiss; — this, mine:
[*Kisses her again.*
Patroclus kisses you.

MENELAUS

O, this is trim!

PATROCLUS

Paris and I kiss evermore for him.

MENELAUS

I'll have my kiss, sir. — Lady, by your leave.

CRESSIDA

In kissing, do you render or receive?

MENELAUS

Both take and give.

CRESSIDA
           I'll make my match to live,
The kiss you take is better than you give;
Therefore no kiss.
MENELAUS
I'll give you boot, I'll give you three for one.
CRESSIDA
You're an odd man; give even, or give none.
MENELAUS
An odd man, lady! every man is odd.
CRESSIDA
No, Paris is not; for you know 'tis true
That you are odd, and he is even with you.
MENELAUS
You fillip me o'th'head.
CRESSIDA
           No, I'll be sworn.
ULYSSES
It were no match, your nail against his horn. —
May I, sweet lady, beg a kiss of you?
CRESSIDA
You may.
ULYSSES
           I do desire it.
CRESSIDA
           Why, beg, then.
ULYSSES
Why, then, for Venus' sake, give me a kiss,
When Helen is a maid again, and his.
CRESSIDA
I am your debtor, claim it when 'tis due.
ULYSSES
Never's my day, and then a kiss of you.
DIOMEDES
Lady, a word: — I'll bring you to your father.
                [Exit with CRESSIDA.
NESTOR
A woman of quick sense.
ULYSSES
           Fie, fie upon her!
There's language in her eye, her cheek, her lip,
Nay, her foot speaks; her wanton spirits look out
At every joint and motive of her body.
O, these encounterers, so glib of tongue,
That give a coasting welcome ere it comes,
And wide unclasp the tables of their thoughts
To every ticklish reader! set them down
For sluttish spoils of opportunity
And daughters of the game.   *[Trumpet within.*
ALL
The Trojans' trumpet.
AGAMEMNON
           Yonder comes the troop.
Flourish. Enter all of Troy; HECTOR, AENEAS,
    TROILUS, *and* ATTENDANTS.
AENEAS
Hail, all you state of Greece! what shall be done
To him that victory commands? or do you purpose
A victor shall be known? will you the knights
Shall to the edge of all extremity
Pursue each other; or shall be divided
By any voice or order of the field?
Hector bade ask.
AGAMEMNON
           Which way would Hector have it?
AENEAS
He cares not; he'll obey conditions.
ACHILLES
'Tis done like Hector; but securely done,
A little proudly, and great deal misprizing
The knight oppos'd.
AENEAS
           If not Achilles, sir,
What is your name?
ACHILLES
           If not Achilles, nothing.
AENEAS
Therefore Achilles: but whate'er, know this: —
In the extremity of great and little,
Valour and pride excel themselves in Hector;
The one almost as infinite as all,
The other blank as nothing. Weigh him well,
And that which looks like pride is courtesy.
This Ajax is half made of Hector's blood:
In love whereof half Hector stays at home;
Half heart, half hand, half Hector comes to seek
This blended knight, half Trojan and half Greek.

ACHILLES
A maiden battle, then? — O, I perceive you.
           Enter DIOMEDES.
AGAMEMNON
Here is Sir Diomed. — Go, gentle knight,
Stand by our Ajax: as you and Lord Aeneas
Consent upon the order of their fight,
So be it; either to the uttermost,
Or else a breath: the combatants being kin
Half stints their strife before their strokes begin.
        *[*AJAX *and* HECTOR *enter the lists.*
ULYSSES
They are oppos'd already.
AGAMEMNON
What Trojan is that same that looks so heavy?
ULYSSES
The youngest son of Priam, a true knight;
Not yet mature, yet matchless: firm of word;
Speaking in deeds, and deedless in his tongue;
Not soon provok'd, nor being provok'd soon calm'd:
His heart and hand both open and both free;
For what he has he gives, what thinks he shows;
Yet gives he not till judgement guide his bounty
Nor dignifies an impair thought with breath:
Manly as Hector, but more dangerous;
For Hector, in his blaze of wrath, subscribes
To tender objects; but he, in heat of action,
Is more vindicative than jealous love:
They call him Troilus; and on him erect
A second hope, as fairly built as Hector.
Thus says Aeneas; one that knows the youth
Even to his inches, and with private soul
Did in great Ilion thus translate him to me.
        [Alarum. HECTOR *and* AJAX *fight.*
AGAMEMNON
They are in action.
NESTOR
Now, Ajax, hold thine own!
TROILUS
           Hector, thou sleep'st;
Awake thee!
AGAMEMNON
His blows are well disposed: — there, Ajax!
DIOMEDES
You must no more.   *[Trumpets cease.*
AENEAS
        Princes, enough, so please you.
AJAX
I am not warm yet; let us fight again.
DIOMEDES
As Hector pleases.
HECTOR
           Why, then will I no more: —
Thou art, great lord, my father's sister's son,
A cousin-german to great Priam's seed;
The obligation of our blood forbids
A gory emulation 'twixt us twain:
Were thy commixtion Greek and Trojan so
That thou couldst say, 'This hand is Grecian all,
And this is Trojan; the sinews of this leg
All Greek, and this all Troy; my mother's blood
Runs on the dexter cheek, and this sinister
Bounds in my father's'; by Jove multipotent,
Thou shouldst not bear from me a Greekish member
Wherein my sword had not impressure made
Of our rank feud: but the just gods gainsay
That any drop thou borrow'dst from thy mother,
My sacred aunt, should by my mortal sword
Be drained! Let me embrace thee, Ajax;
By him that thunders, thou hast lusty arms;
Hector would have them fall upon him thus:
Cousin, all honour to thee!
AJAX
           I thank thee, Hector:
Thou art too gentle and too free a man:
I came to kill thee, cousin, and bear hence
A great addition earned in thy death.
HECTOR
Not Neoptolemus so mirable —
On whose bright crest Fame with her loud'st oyes
Cries 'This is he' — could promise to himself
A thought of added honour torn from Hector.
AENEAS
There is expectance here from both the sides,
What further you will do.
HECTOR
           We'll answer it;
The issue is embracement: — Ajax, farewell.

AJAX
If I might in entreaties find success —
As seld I have the chance — I would desire
My famous cousin to our Grecian tents.
DIOMEDES
'Tis Agamemnon's wish; and great Achilles
Doth long to see unarm'd the valiant Hector.
HECTOR
Aeneas, call my brother Troilus to me:
And signify this loving interview
To the expecters of our Trojan part;
Desire them home. — Give me thy hand, my cousin;
I will go eat with thee, and see your knights.
     AGAMEMNON *and the rest come forward.*

AJAX
Great Agamemnon comes to meet us here.
HECTOR
The worthiest of them tell me name by name;
But for Achilles, mine own searching eyes
Shall find him by his large and portly size.
AGAMEMNON
Worthy of arms! as welcome as to one
That would be rid of such an enemy;
But that's no welcome: understand more clear,
What's past and what's to come is strew'd with husks
And formless ruin of oblivion;
But in this extant moment, faith and troth,
Strain'd purely from all hollow bias-drawing,
Bids thee, with most divine integrity,
From heart of very heart, great Hector, welcome.
HECTOR
I thank thee, most imperious Agamemnon.
AGAMEMNON *[to* TROILUS*]*.
My well-fam'd lord of Troy, no less to you.
MENELAUS
Let me confirm my princely brother's greeting; —
You brace of warlike brothers, welcome hither.
HECTOR
Who must we answer?
AENEAS
           The noble Menelaus.
HECTOR
O, you, my lord? by Mars his gauntlet, thanks!
Mock not, that I affect th'untraded oath;
Your *quondam* wife swears still by Venus' glove:
She's well, but bade me not commend her to you.
MENELAUS
Name her not now, sir; she's a deadly theme.
HECTOR
O, pardon; I offend.
NESTOR
I have, thou gallant Trojan, seen thee oft,
Labouring for destiny, make cruel way
Through ranks of Greekish youth; and I have seen
    thee,
As hot as Perseus, spur thy Phrygian steed,
Despising many forfeits and subduements,
When thou hast hung thy advanc'd sword i'th'air,
Not letting it decline on the declined;
That I have said to some my standers-by,
'Lo, Jupiter is yonder, dealing life!'
And I have seen thee pause and take thy breath,
When that a ring of Greeks have hemm'd thee in,
Like an Olympian wrestling: this have I seen;
But this thy countenance, still lock'd in steel,
I never saw till now. I knew thy grandsire,
And once fought with him: he was a soldier good;
But, by great Mars, the captain of us all,
Never like thee. Let an old man embrace thee;
And, worthy warrior, welcome to our tents.
AENEAS
'Tis the old Nestor.
HECTOR
Let me embrace thee, good old chronicle,
That hast so long walk'd hand in hand with time: —
Most reverend Nestor, I am glad to clasp thee.
NESTOR
I would my arms could match thee in contention,
As they contend with thee in courtesy.
HECTOR
I would they could.
NESTOR
Ha!
By this white beard, I'ld fight with thee to-morrow: —
Well, welcome, welcome! — I have seen the time —
ULYSSES
I wonder now how yonder city stands
When we have here her base and pillar by us.

THERSITES Here's a letter for thee.

HECTOR
I know your favour, Lord Ulysses, well.
Ah, sir, there's many a Greek and Trojan dead,
Since first I saw yourself and Diomed
In Ilion, on your Greekish embassy.
ULYSSES
Sir, I foretold you then what would ensue:
My prophecy is but half his journey yet;
For yonder walls, that pertly front your town,
Yond towers, whose wanton tops do buss the clouds,
Must kiss their own feet.
HECTOR
                    I must not believe you:
There they stand yet; and modestly I think,
The fall of every Phrygian stone will cost
A drop of Grecian blood: the end crowns all;
And that old common arbitrator, Time,
Will one day end it.
ULYSSES
                    So to him we leave it.
Most gentle and most valiant Hector, welcome:
After the general, I beseech you next
To feast with me, and see me at my tent.
ACHILLES
I shall forestall thee, Lord Ulysses, thou! —
Now, Hector, I have fed mine eyes on thee;
I have with exact view perus'd thee, Hector,
And quoted joint by joint.
HECTOR
                    Is this Achilles?
ACHILLES
I am Achilles.
HECTOR
Stand fair, I pray thee: let me look on thee.
ACHILLES
Behold thy fill.
HECTOR
                    Nay, I have done already.
ACHILLES
Thou art too brief: I will the second time,
As I would buy thee, view thee limb by limb.
HECTOR
O, like a book of sport thou'lt read me o'er;
But there's more in me than thou understand'st.
Why dost thou so oppress me with thine eye?
ACHILLES
Tell me, you heavens, in which part of his body
Shall I destroy him? whether there, or there, or there?
That I may give the local wound a name,
And make distinct the very breach whereout
Hector's great spirit flew: answer me, heavens!
HECTOR
It would discredit the blest gods, proud man,
To answer such a question: stand again:
Think'st thou to catch my life so pleasantly
As to prenominate in nice conjecture
Where thou wilt hit me dead?
ACHILLES
                    I tell thee, yea.

HECTOR
Wert thou the oracle to tell me so,
I'ld not believe thee. Henceforth guard thee well;
For I'll not kill thee there, nor there, nor there;
But, by the forge that stithied Mars his helm,
I'll kill thee every where, yea, o'er and o'er. —
You wisest Grecians, pardon me this brag,
His insolence draws folly from my lips;
But I'll endeavour deeds to match these words,
Or may I never —
AJAX
                    Do not chafe thee, cousin: —
And you, Achilles, let these threats alone,
Till accident or purpose bring you to't:
You may have every day enough of Hector,
If you have stomach; the general state, I fear,
Can scarce entreat you to be odd with him.
HECTOR
I pray you, let us see you in the field:
We have had pelting wars, since you refused
The Grecians' cause.
ACHILLES
                    Dost thou entreat me, Hector?
To-morrow do I meet thee, fell as death;
To-night all friends.
HECTOR
                    Thy hand upon that match.
AGAMEMNON
First, all you peers of Greece, go to my tent;
There in the full convive we: afterwards,
As Hector's leisure and your bounties shall
Concur together, severally entreat him. —
Beat loud the tabourines, let the trumpets blow,
That this great soldier may his welcome know.
                    [Exeunt all but TROILUS and ULYSSES.

TROILUS
My Lord Ulysses, tell me, I beseech you,
In what place of the field doth Calchas keep?
ULYSSES
At Menelaus' tent, most princely Troilus:
There Diomed doth feast with him to-night;
Who neither looks upon the heaven nor earth,
But gives all gaze and bent of amorous view
On the fair Cressid.
TROILUS
Shall I, sweet lord, be bound to you so much,
After we part from Agamemnon's tent,
To bring me thither?
ULYSSES
                    You shall command me, sir.
As gentle tell me, of what honour was
This Cressida in Troy? Had she no lover there
That wails her absence?
TROILUS
O, sir, to such as boasting show their scars
A mock is due. Will you walk on, my lord?
She was belov'd, she lov'd; she is, and doth:
But still sweet love is food for fortune's tooth. [Exeunt.

ACT V

SCENE I

The Grecian camp. Before ACHILLES' *tent.*

Enter ACHILLES *and* PATROCLUS.

ACHILLES
I'll heat his blood with Greekish wine to-night,
Which with my scimitar I'll cool to-morrow. —
Patroclus, let us feast him to the height.
PATROCLUS
Here comes Thersites.
                    Enter THERSITES.
ACHILLES
                    How now, thou core of envy!
Thou crusty batch of nature, what's the news?
THERSITES
Why, thou picture of what thou seem'st, and idol of
idiot-worshippers, here's a letter for thee.
ACHILLES
From whence, fragment?
THERSITES
Why, thou full dish of fool, from Troy.
PATROCLUS
Who keeps the tent now?
THERSITES
The surgeon's box, or the patient's wound.
PATROCLUS
Well said, adversity! and what need these tricks?
THERSITES
Prithee, be silent, boy; I profit not by thy talk: thou art
thought to be Achilles' male varlet.
PATROCLUS
Male varlet, you rogue! what's that?
THERSITES
Why, his masculine whore. Now, the rotten diseases of
the south, the guts-griping, ruptures, catarrhs, loads o'
gravel i'th'back, lethargies, cold palsies, raw eyes,
dirt-rotten livers, wheezing lungs, bladders full of
imposthume, sciaticas, limekilns i'th'palm, incurable
bone-ache, and the rivell'd fee-simple of the tetter, take
and take again such preposterous discoveries!
PATROCLUS
Why, thou damnable box of envy, thou, what mean'st
thou to curse thus?
THERSITES
Do I curse thee?
PATROCLUS
Why, no, you ruinous butt; you whoreson
indistinguishable cur, no.
THERSITES
No! why art thou, then, exasperate, thou idle
immaterial skein of sleave-silk, thou green sarcenet
flap for a sore eye, thou tassel of a prodigal's purse,
thou? Ah, how the poor world is pester'd with such
waterflies, — diminutives of nature!
PATROCLUS
Out, gall!
THERSITES
Finch-egg!
ACHILLES
My sweet Patroclus, I am thwarted quite
From my great purpose in to-morrow's battle.
Here is a letter from Queen Hecuba;
A token from her daughter, my fair love;
Both taxing me and gaging me to keep
An oath that I have sworn. I will not break it:
Fall Greeks; fail fame; honour or go or stay;
My major vow lies here, this I'll obey. —
Come, come, Thersites, help to trim my tent;
This night in banqueting must all be spent. —
Away, Patroclus!
                    [Exeunt ACHILLES and PATROCLUS.
THERSITES
With too much blood and too little brain, these two may
run mad; but, if with too much brain and too little
blood they do, I'll be a curer of madmen. Here's
Agamemnon, — an honest fellow enough, and one
that loves quails: but he has not so much brain as
ear-wax: and the goodly transformation of Jupiter
there, his brother, the bull, — the primitive statue, and
oblique memorial of cuckolds; a thrifty shoeing-horn
in a chain, hanging at his brother's leg, — to what
form, but that he is, should wit larded with malice, and
malice forced with wit, turn him to? To an ass, were
nothing; he is both ass and ox: to an ox, were nothing;
he is both ox and ass. To be a dog, a mule, a cat, a

fitchew, a toad, a lizard, an owl, a puttock, or a herring without a roe, I would not care; but to be Menelaus! — I would conspire against destiny. Ask me not what I would be, if I were not Thersites; for I care not to be the louse of a lazar, so I were not Menelaus. — Hoyday! spirits and fires!

Enter HECTOR, TROILUS, AJAX, AGAMEMNON, ULYSSES, NESTOR, MENELAUS, DIOMEDES, *with lights.*

AGAMEMNON
We go wrong, we go wrong.

AJAX
No, yonder 'tis;
There, where we see the lights.

HECTOR
I trouble you.

AJAX
No, not a whit.

ULYSSES
Here comes himself to guide you.
Enter ACHILLES.

ACHILLES
Welcome, brave Hector; welcome, princes all.

AGAMEMNON
So now, fair prince of Troy, I bid good night.
Ajax commands the guard to tend on you.

HECTOR
Thanks and good night to the Greeks' general.

MENELAUS
Good night, my lord.

HECTOR
Good night, sweet Lord Menelaus.

THERSITES
Sweet draught: sweet, quoth a'! sweet sink, sweet
  sewer.

ACHILLES
Good night and welcome, both at once, to those
That go or tarry.

AGAMEMNON
Good night. [*Exeunt* AGAMEMNON *and* MENELAUS.

ACHILLES
Old Nestor tarries; and you too, Diomed,
Keep Hector company an hour or two.

DIOMEDES
I cannot, lord; I have important business,
The tide whereof is now. — Good night, great Hector.

HECTOR
Give me your hand.

ULYSSES [*aside to* TROILUS].
Follow his torch; he goes to Calchas' tent:
I'll keep you company.

TROILUS [*aside to* ULYSSES].
Sweet sir, you honour me.

HECTOR
And so, good night.
  [*Exit* DIOMEDES; ULYSSES *and* TROILUS *following.*

ACHILLES
Come, come, enter my tent.
  [*Exeunt* ACHILLES, HECTOR, AJAX, *and* NESTOR.

THERSITES
That same Diomed's a false-hearted rogue, a most unjust knave; I will no more trust him when he leers than I will a serpent when he hisses: he will spend his mouth, and promise, like Brabbler the hound; but when he performs, astronomers foretell it; it is prodigious, there will come some change; the sun borrows of the moon, when Diomed keeps his word. I will rather leave to see Hector than not to dog him: they say he keeps a Trojan drab, and uses the traitor Calchas' tent: I'll after. — Nothing but lechery! all incontinent varlets! [*Exit.*

SCENE II

The same. Before CALCHAS' *tent.*
Enter DIOMEDES.

DIOMEDES
What, are you up here, ho? speak.

CALCHAS [*within*].
Who calls?

DIOMEDES
Diomed. — Calchas, I think. Where's your daughter?

CALCHAS [*within*].
She comes to you.

Enter TROILUS *and* ULYSSES, *at a distance; after them* THERSITES.

ULYSSES
Stand where the torch may not discover us.
Enter CRESSIDA.

TROILUS
Cressid comes forth to him.

DIOMEDES
How now, my charge!

CRESSIDA
Now, my sweet guardian! — Hark, a word with you.
  [*Whispers.*

TROILUS
Yea, so familiar!

ULYSSES
She will sing any man at first sight.

THERSITES
And any man may sing her, if he can take her cliff: she's noted.

DIOMEDES
Will you remember?

CRESSIDA
Remember! yes.

DIOMEDES
Nay, but do, then;
And let your mind be coupled with your words.

TROILUS
What should she remember?

ULYSSES
List.

CRESSIDA
Sweet honey Greek, tempt me no more to folly.

THERSITES
Roguery!

DIOMEDES
Nay, then, —

CRESSIDA
I'll tell you what, —

DIOMEDES
Foh, foh! come, tell a pin: you are forsworn.

CRESSIDA
In faith, I cannot: what would you have me do?

THERSITES
A juggling trick, — to be secretly open.

DIOMEDES
What did you swear you would bestow on me?

CRESSIDA
I prithee, do not hold me to mine oath;
Bid me do any thing but that, sweet Greek.

DIOMEDES
Good night.

TROILUS
Hold, patience!

ULYSSES
How now, Trojan!

CRESSIDA
Diomed, —

DIOMEDES
No, no, good night: I'll be your fool no more.

TROILUS
Thy better must.

CRESSIDA
Hark, one word in your ear.

TROILUS
O plague and madness!

ULYSSES
You are moved, prince; let us depart, I pray you,
Lest your displeasure should enlarge itself
To wrathful terms: this place is dangerous;
The time right deadly; I beseech you, go.

TROILUS
Behold, I pray you!

ULYSSES
Nay, good my lord, go off:
You flow to great distraction; come, my lord.

TROILUS
I pray thee, stay.

ULYSSES
You have not patience; come.

TROILUS
I pray you, stay; by hell and all hell's torments,
I will not speak a word!

DIOMEDES
And so, good night.

CRESSIDA
Nay, but you part in anger.

TROILUS
Doth that grieve thee?
O wither'd truth!

ULYSSES
Why, how now, lord!

TROILUS
By Jove,
I will be patient.

CRESSIDA
Guardian! — why, Greek!

DIOMEDES
Foh, foh! adieu; you palter.

CRESSIDA
In faith, I do not: come hither once again.

ULYSSES
You shake, my lord, at something: will you go?
You will break out.

TROILUS
She strokes his cheek!

ULYSSES
Come, come.

TROILUS
Nay, stay; by Jove, I will not speak a word:
There is between my will and all offences
A guard of patience: — stay a little while.

THERSITES
How the devil luxury, with his fat rump and potato-finger, tickles these together! Fry, lechery, fry!

DIOMEDES
But will you, then?

CRESSIDA
In faith, I will, la; never trust me else.

DIOMEDES
Give me some token for the surety of it.

CRESSIDA
I'll fetch you one. [*Exit.*

ULYSSES
You have sworn patience.

TROILUS
Fear me not, sweet lord;
I will not be myself, nor have cognition
Of what I feel: I am all patience.
Enter CRESSIDA.

THERSITES
Now the pledge; now, now, now!

CRESSIDA
Here, Diomed, keep this sleeve.

TROILUS
O beauty! where is thy faith?

ULYSSES
My lord, —

TROILUS
I will be patient; outwardly I will.

CRESSIDA
You look upon that sleeve; behold it well. —
He lov'd me — O false wench! — Give't me again.

DIOMEDES
Whose was't?

CRESSIDA
It is no matter, now I have't again.
I will not meet with you to-morrow night:
I prithee, Diomed, visit me no more.

THERSITES
Now she sharpens: — well said, whetstone!

DIOMEDES
I shall have it.

CRESSIDA
What, this?

DIOMEDES
Ay, that.

CRESSIDA
O, all you gods! — O pretty, pretty pledge!
Thy master now lies thinking in his bed
Of thee and me: and sighs, and takes my glove,
And gives memorial dainty kisses to it,
As I kiss thee. — Nay, do not snatch it from me;
He that takes that doth take my heart withal.

DIOMEDES
I had your heart before, this follows it.

TROILUS
I did swear patience.

CRESSIDA
You shall not have it, Diomed; faith, you shall not;
I'll give you something else.

DIOMEDES
I will have this: whose was it?

CRESSIDA
It is no matter.

DIOMEDES
Come, tell me whose it was.

CRESSIDA
'Twas one's that lov'd me better than you will.
But, now you have it, take it.

DIOMEDES
              Whose was it?

CRESSIDA
By all Diana's waiting-women yond,
And by herself, I will not tell you whose.

DIOMEDES
To-morrow will I wear it on my helm;
And grieve his spirit that dares not challenge it.

TROILUS
Wert thou the devil, and worest it on thy horn,
It should be challeng'd.

CRESSIDA
Well, well, 'tis done, 'tis past; — and yet it is not;
I will not keep my word.

DIOMEDES
           Why, then, farewell;
Thou never shalt mock Diomed again.

CRESSIDA
You shall not go: — one cannot speak a word,
But it straight starts you.

DIOMEDES
             I do not like this fooling.

THERSITES
Nor I, by Pluto: but that that likes not you pleases me
best.

DIOMEDES
What, shall I come? the hour?

CRESSIDA
Ay, come: — O Jove! — do come: — I shall be plagued.

DIOMEDES
Farewell till then.

CRESSIDA
        Good night: I prithee, come.
              [*Exit* DIOMEDES.
Troilus, farewell! one eye yet looks on thee;
But with my heart the other eye doth see.
Ah, poor our sex! this fault in us I find,
The error of our eye directs our mind:
What error leads must err; O, then conclude
Minds sway'd by eyes are full of turpitude.   [*Exit*.

THERSITES
A proof of strength she could not publish more,
Unless she said, 'My mind is now turn'd whore.'

ULYSSES
All's done, my lord.

TROILUS
        It is.

ULYSSES
           Why stay we, then?

TROILUS
To make a recordation to my soul
Of every syllable that here was spoke.
But if I tell how these two did co-act,
Shall I not lie in publishing a truth?
Sith yet there is a credence in my heart,
An esperance so obstinately strong,
That doth invert th'attest of eyes and ears;
As if those organs had deceptious functions,
Created only to calumniate.
Was Cressid here?

ULYSSES
        I cannot conjure, Trojan.

TROILUS
She was not, sure.

ULYSSES
        Most sure she was.

TROILUS
Why, my negation hath no taste of madness.

ULYSSES
Nor mine, my lord: Cressid was here but now.

TROILUS
Let it not be believ'd for womanhood!
Think, we had mothers; do not give advantage
To stubborn critics, — apt, without a theme,
For depravation, — to square the general sex
By Cressid's rule: rather think this not Cressid.

ULYSSES
What hath she done, prince, that can soil our mothers?

TROILUS
Nothing at all, unless that this were she.

THERSITES
Will he swagger himself out on's own eyes?

TROILUS
This she? no, this is Diomed's Cressida:
If beauty have a soul, this is not she;

If souls guide vows, if vows be sanctimonies,
If sanctimony be the gods' delight,
If there be rule in unity itself,
This is not she. O madness of discourse,
That cause sets up with and against itself!
Bi-fold authority! where reason can revolt
Without perdition, and loss assume all reason
Without revolt: this is, and is not, Cressid!
Within my soul there doth conduce a fight
Of this strange nature, that a thing inseparate
Divides more wider than the sky and earth;
And yet the spacious breadth of this division
Admits no orifex for a point, as subtle
As Ariachne's broken woof, to enter.
Instance, O instance! strong as Pluto's gates;
Cressid is mine, tied with the bonds of heaven:
Instance, O instance! strong as heaven itself;
The bonds of heaven are slipp'd, dissolv'd, and loos'd;
And with another knot, five-finger-tied,
The fractions of her faith, orts of her love,
The fragments, scraps, the bits, and greasy relics
Of her o'er-eaten faith, are bound to Diomed.

ULYSSES
May worthy Troilus be half attach'd
With that which here his passion doth express?

TROILUS
Ay, Greek, and that shall be divulged well
In characters as red as Mars his heart
Inflam'd with Venus; never did young man fancy
With so eternal and so fix'd a soul.
Hark, Greek: — as much as I do Cressid love,
So much by weight hate I her Diomed:
That sleeve is mine that he'll bear on his helm;
Were it a casque compos'd by Vulcan's skill,
My sword should bite it: not the dreadful spout,
Which shipmen do the hurricano call,
Constring'd in mass by the almighty sun,
Shall dizzy with more clamour Neptune's ear
In his descent than shall my prompted sword
Falling on Diomed.

THERSITES
He'll tickle it for his concupy.

TROILUS
O Cressid! O false Cressid! false, false, false!
Let all untruths stand by thy stained name,
And they'll seem glorious.

ULYSSES
             O, contain yourself;
Your passion draws ears hither.
            Enter AENEAS.

AENEAS
I have been seeking you this hour, my lord:
Hector, by this, is arming him in Troy;
Ajax, your guard, stays to conduct you home.

TROILUS
Have with you, prince. — My courteous lord, adieu. —
Farewell, revolted fair! — and, Diomed,
Stand fast, and wear a castle on thy head!

ULYSSES
I'll bring you to the gates.

TROILUS
Accept distracted thanks.
      [*Exeunt* TROILUS, AENEAS, *and* ULYSSES.

THERSITES
Would I could meet that rogue Diomed! I would croak
like a raven; I would bode, I would bode. Patroclus will
give me any thing for the intelligence of this whore: the
parrot will not do more for an almond than he for a
commodious drab. Lechery, lechery; still, wars and
lechery; nothing else holds fashion: a burning devil
take them!   [*Exit*.

SCENE III

Troy. Before PRIAM'S *palace.*

Enter HECTOR *and* ANDROMACHE.

ANDROMACHE
When was my lord so much ungently temper'd,
To stop his ears against admonishment?
Unarm, unarm, and do not fight to-day.

HECTOR
You train me to offend you; get you in:
By all the everlasting gods, I'll go!

HECTOR Be gone, I say: the gods have heard me swear.

ANDROMACHE
My dreams will, sure, prove ominous to the day.
HECTOR
No more, I say.

Enter CASSANDRA.

CASSANDRA
      Where is my brother Hector?
ANDROMACHE
Here, sister; arm'd, and bloody in intent.
Consort with me in loud and dear petition,
Pursue we him on knees; for I have dream'd
Of bloody turbulence, and this whole night
Hath nothing been but shapes and forms of slaughter.
CASSANDRA
O, 'tis true.
HECTOR
      Ho! bid my trumpet sound!
CASSANDRA
No notes of sally, for the heavens, sweet brother.
HECTOR
Be gone, I say: the gods have heard me swear.
CASSANDRA
The gods are deaf to hot and peevish vows:
They are polluted offerings, more abhorr'd
Than spotted livers in the sacrifice.
ANDROMACHE
O, be persuaded! do not count it holy
To hurt by being just: it is as lawful,
For we would give much, to use violent thefts,
And rob in the behalf of charity.
CASSANDRA
It is the purpose that makes strong the vow;
But vows to every purpose must not hold:
Unarm, sweet Hector.
HECTOR
      Hold you still, I say;
Mine honour keeps the weather of my fate:
Life every man holds dear; but the brave man
Holds honour far more precious-dear than life.

Enter TROILUS.

How now, young man! mean'st thou to fight to-day?
ANDROMACHE
Cassandra, call my father to persuade.

[Exit CASSANDRA.

HECTOR
No, faith, young Troilus; doff thy harness, youth;
I am to-day i'th'vein of chivalry:
Let grow thy sinews till their knots be strong,
And tempt not yet the brushes of the war.
Unarm thee, go; and doubt thou not, brave boy,
I'll stand to-day for thee, and me, and Troy.
TROILUS
Brother, you have a vice of mercy in you,
Which better fits a lion than a man.
HECTOR
What vice is that, good Troilus? chide me for it.
TROILUS
When many times the captive Grecian falls,
Even in the fan and wind of your fair sword,
You bid them rise, and live.
HECTOR
O, 'tis fair play.
TROILUS
      Fool's play, by heaven, Hector.
HECTOR
How now! how now!
TROILUS
      For th'love of all the gods,
Let's leave the hermit pity with our mothers;
And when we have our armours buckled on,
The venom'd vengeance ride upon our swords,
Spur them to ruthful work, rein them from ruth.
HECTOR
Fie, savage, fie!
TROILUS
      Hector, then 'tis wars.
HECTOR
Troilus, I would not have you fight to-day.
TROILUS
Who should withhold me?
Not fate, obedience, nor the hand of Mars
Beckoning with fiery truncheon my retire;
Not Priamus and Hecuba on knees,
Their eyes o'ergalled with recourse of tears;
Not you, my brother, with your true sword drawn,
Oppos'd to hinder me, should stop my way,
But by my ruin.

Enter CASSANDRA with PRIAM.

CASSANDRA
Lay hold upon him, Priam, hold him fast:
He is thy crutch; now if thou lose thy stay,
Thou on him leaning, and all Troy on thee,
Fall all together.
PRIAM
      Come, Hector, come, go back:
Thy wife hath dream'd; thy mother hath had visions;
Cassandra doth foresee; and I myself
Am like a prophet suddenly enrapt,
To tell thee that this day is ominous:
Therefore, come back.
HECTOR
      Aeneas is a-field;
And I do stand engag'd to many Greeks,
Even in the faith of valour, to appear
This morning to them.
PRIAM
      Ay, but thou shalt not go.
HECTOR
I must not break my faith.
You know me dutiful; therefore, dear sir,
Let me not shame respect; but give me leave
To take that course by your consent and voice,
Which you do here forbid me, royal Priam.
CASSANDRA
O Priam, yield not to him!
ANDROMACHE
      Do not, dear father.
HECTOR
Andromache, I am offended with you:
Upon the love you bear me, get you in.

[Exit ANDROMACHE.

TROILUS
This foolish, dreaming, superstitious girl
Makes all these bodements.
CASSANDRA
      O, farewell, dear Hector!
Look, how thou diest! look, how thy eye turns pale!
Look, how thy wounds do bleed at many vents!
Hark, how Troy roars! how Hecuba cries out!
How poor Andromache shrills her dolours forth!
Behold distraction, frenzy, and amazement,
Like witless anticks, one another meet,
And all cry 'Hector! Hector's dead!' O Hector!
TROILUS
Away! away!
CASSANDRA
Farewell: — yet, soft! — Hector, I take my leave:
Thou dost thyself and all our Troy deceive.
                          [Exit.
HECTOR
You are amaz'd, my liege, at her exclaim:
Go in, and cheer the town: we'll forth, and fight;
Do deeds worth praise, and tell you them at night.
PRIAM
Farewell: the gods with safety stand about thee!

[Exeunt severally PRIAM and HECTOR. Alarum.

TROILUS
They are at it, hark! — Proud Diomed, believe,
I come to lose my arm, or win my sleeve.

Enter PANDARUS.

PANDARUS
Do you hear, my lord? do you hear?
TROILUS
What now?
PANDARUS
Here's a letter come from yond poor girl.
TROILUS
Let me read.
PANDARUS
A whoreson tisick, a whoreson rascally tisick so
troubles me, and the foolish fortune of this girl; and
what one thing, what another, that I shall leave you one
o'th's days: and I have a rheum in mine eyes too; and
such an ache in my bones, that, unless a man were
cursed, I cannot tell what to think on't. — What says
she there?
TROILUS
Words, words, mere words, no matter from the heart;
Th'effect doth operate another way. —
                      [Tearing the letter.
Go, wind, to wind, there turn and change together. —
My love with words and errors still she feeds;
But edifies another with her deeds.   *[Exeunt severally.*

SCENE IV

Plains between Troy and the Grecian camp.

Alarums: excursions. Enter THERSITES.

THERSITES
Now they are clapper-clawing one another; I'll go look
on. That dissembling abominable varlet, Diomed, has
got that same scurvy doting foolish young knave's
sleeve of Troy there in his helm: I would fain see them
meet; that that same young Trojan ass, that loves the
whore there, might send that Greekish whore-masterly
villain, with the sleeve, back to the dissembling
luxurious drab of a sleeveless errand. O'th't'other side,
the policy of those crafty swearing rascals — that stale
old mouse-eaten dry cheese, Nestor, and that same
dog-fox, Ulysses — is not proved worth a blackberry: —
they set me up, in policy, that mongrel cur, Ajax,
against that dog of as bad a kind, Achilles: and now is
the cur Ajax prouder than the cur Achilles, and will not
arm to-day; whereupon the Grecians begin to proclaim
barbarism, and policy grows into an ill opinion. —
Soft! here comes sleeve, and t'other.

Enter DIOMEDES and TROILUS.

TROILUS
Fly not: for shouldst thou take the river Styx,
I would swim after.
DIOMEDES
      Thou dost miscall retire:
I do not fly; but advantageous care
Withdrew me from the odds of multitude:
Have at thee!
THERSITES
Hold thy whore, Grecian! now for thy whore,
Trojan! — now the sleeve! now the sleeve!

[Exeunt TROILUS and DIOMEDES, fighting.

Enter HECTOR.

HECTOR
What art thou, Greek? art thou for Hector's match?
Art thou of blood and honour?
THERSITES
No, no, — I am a rascal; a scurvy railing knave; a very
filthy rogue.
HECTOR
I do believe thee; — live.   *[Exit.*
THERSITES
God-a-mercy, that thou wilt believe me; but a plague
break thy neck for frighting me! — What's become of
the wenching rogues? I think they have swallow'd one
another: I would laugh at that Miracle: — yet, in a sort,
lechery eats itself. I'll seek them.   *[Exit.*

SCENE V

Another part of the plains.

Enter DIOMEDES and SERVANT.

DIOMEDES
Go, go, my servant, take thou Troilus' horse;
Present the fair steed to my lady Cressid:
Fellow, commend my service to her beauty;
Tell her I have chastis'd the amorous Trojan,
And am her knight by proof.
SERVANT
      I go, my lord.   *[Exit.*

Enter AGAMEMNON.

AGAMEMNON
Renew, renew! The fierce Polydamas
Hath beat down Menon: bastard Margarelon
Hath Doreus prisoner,
And stands colossus-wise, waving his beam,
Upon the pashed corses of the kings
Epistrophus and Cedius: Polyxenes is slain;
Amphimachus and Thoas deadly hurt;
Patroclus ta'en or slain; and Palamedes
Sore hurt and bruis'd: the dreadful Sagittary
Appals our numbers: — haste we, Diomed,
To reinforcement, or we perish all.

Enter NESTOR.

NESTOR
Go, bear Patroclus' body to Achilles;
And bid the snail-pac'd Ajax arm for shame. —
There is a thousand Hectors in the field:
Now here he fights on Galathe his horse,
And there lacks work; anon he's there afoot,
And there they fly or die, like scaled sculls
Before the belching whale; then is he yonder,
And there the strawy Greeks, ripe for his edge,
Fall down before him, like the mower's swath:

Here, there, and every where, he leaves and takes;
Dexterity so obeying appetite,
That what he will he does; and does so much,
That proof is call'd impossibility.

Enter ULYSSES.

ULYSSES
O, courage, courage, princes! great Achilles
Is arming, weeping, cursing, vowing vengeance:
Patroclus' wounds have rous'd his drowsy blood,
Together with his mangled Myrmidons,
That noseless, handless, hack'd and chipp'd, come to
  him,
Crying on Hector. Ajax hath lost a friend,
And foams at mouth, and he is arm'd and at it,
Roaring for Troilus; who hath done to-day
Mad and fantastic execution;
Engaging and redeeming of himself,
With such a careless force and forceless care,
As if that luck, in very spite of cunning,
Bade him win all.

Enter AJAX.

AJAX
Troilus! thou coward Troilus!   [*Exit.*

DIOMEDES
                    Ay, there, there.

NESTOR
So, so, we draw together.

Enter ACHILLES.

ACHILLES
                    Where is this Hector? —
Come, come, thou boy-queller, show thy face;
Know what it is to meet Achilles angry: —
Hector? where's Hector? I will none but Hector.
                                        [*Exeunt.*

SCENE VI

Another part of the plains.

Enter AJAX.

AJAX
Troilus, thou coward Troilus, show thy head!

ACHILLES Achilles hath the mighty Hector slain.

Enter DIOMEDES.

DIOMEDES
Troilus, I say! where's Troilus?

AJAX
                    What wouldst thou?

DIOMEDES
I would correct him.

AJAX
Were I the general, thou shouldst have my office
Ere that correction. — Troilus, I say! what, Troilus!

Enter TROILUS.

TROILUS
O traitor Diomed! — turn thy false face, thou traitor,
And pay thy life thou owest me for my horse!

DIOMEDES
Ha, art thou there?

AJAX
I'll fight with him alone: stand, Diomed.

DIOMEDES
He is my prize; I will not look upon.

TROILUS
Come, both you cogging Greeks; have at you both!
                            [*Exeunt, fighting.*

Enter HECTOR.

HECTOR
Yea, Troilus? O, well fought, my youngest brother!

Enter ACHILLES.

ACHILLES
Now do I see thee, ha! — have at thee, Hector!

HECTOR
Pause, if thou wilt.

ACHILLES
I do disdain thy courtesy, proud Trojan:
Be happy that my arms are out of use:
My rest and negligence befriends thee now,
But thou anon shalt hear of me again;
Till when, go seek thy fortune.   [*Exit.*

HECTOR
                    Fare thee well: —
I would have been much more a fresher man,
Had I expected thee.

Enter TROILUS.
                    How now, my brother!

TROILUS
Ajax hath ta'en Aeneas: shall it be?
No, by the flame of yonder glorious heaven,
He shall not carry him; I'll be ta'en too,
Or bring him off: — fate, hear me what I say!
I reck not though I end my life to-day.   [*Exit.*

Enter one in sumptuous armour.

HECTOR
Stand, stand, thou Greek; thou art a goodly mark: —
No? wilt thou not? — I like thy armour well;
I'll frush it, and unlock the rivets all,
But I'll be master of it: — wilt thou not, beast, abide?
Why then, fly on, I'll hunt thee for thy hide.   [*Exeunt.*

SCENE VII

Another part of the plains.

Enter ACHILLES with MYRMIDONS.

ACHILLES
Come here about me, you my Myrmidons;
Mark what I say. Attend me where I wheel:
Strike not a stroke, but keep yourselves in breath:
And when I have the bloody Hector found,
Empale him with your weapons round about;
In fellest manner execute your arms.
Follow me, sirs, and my proceedings eye: —
It is decreed Hector the great must die.   [*Exeunt.*

*Enter MENELAUS and PARIS, fighting;
then THERSITES.*

THERSITES
The cuckold and the cuckold-maker are at it. — Now,
bull! now, dog! 'Loo, Paris, 'loo! now my double-henn'd
sparrow! 'loo, Paris, 'loo! — The bull has the game: —
ware horns, ho!   [*Exeunt PARIS and MENELAUS.*

Enter MARGARELON.

MARGARELON
Turn, slave, and fight.

THERSITES
What art thou?

MARGARELON
A bastard son of Priam's.

THERSITES
I am a bastard too; I love bastards: I am a bastard begot,
bastard instructed, bastard in mind, bastard in valour,
in every thing illegitimate. One bear will not bite
another, and wherefore should one bastard? Take
heed, the quarrel's most ominous to us: if the son of a
whore fight for a whore, he tempts judgement:
farewell, bastard.   [*Exit.*

MARGARELON
The devil take thee, coward!   [*Exit.*

SCENE VIII

Another part of the plains.

Enter HECTOR.

HECTOR
Most putrefied core, so fair without,
Thy goodly armour thus hath cost thy life.
Now is my day's work done; I'll take good breath:
Rest, sword; thou hast thy fill of blood and death.
    [*Puts off his helmet, and hangs his shield behind him.*

Enter ACHILLES and MYRMIDONS.

ACHILLES
Look, Hector, how the sun begins to set;
How ugly night comes breathing at his heels:
Even with the vail and darkening of the sun,
To close the day up, Hector's life is done.

HECTOR
I am unarm'd; forgo this vantage, Greek.

ACHILLES
Strike, fellows, strike; this is the man I seek.
                                [*HECTOR falls.*
So, Ilion, fall thou next! now, Troy, sink down!
Here lies thy heart, thy sinews, and thy bone. —
On, Myrmidons; and cry you all amain,
'Achilles hath the mighty Hector slain.' —
                            [*A retreat sounded.*
Hark! a retire upon our Grecian part.

MYRMIDONS
The Trojan trumpets sound the like, my lord.

ACHILLES
The dragon wing of night o'erspreads the earth,
And, stickler-like, the armies separates.
My half-supp'd sword, that frankly would have fed,

Pleas'd with this dainty bait, thus goes to bed.
[*Sheathes his sword.*
Come, tie his body to my horse's tail;
Along the field I will the Trojan trail.   [*Exeunt.*

SCENE IX

Another part of the plains.

Enter AGAMEMNON, AJAX, MENELAUS, NESTOR,
DIOMEDES, *and the rest, marching. Shouts within.*

AGAMEMNON
Hark! hark! what shout is that?
NESTOR
Peace, drums!
[*within*] Achilles! Achilles! Hector's slain! Achilles!
DIOMEDES
The bruit is, Hector's slain, and by Achilles.
AJAX
If it be so, yet bragless let it be;
Great Hector was a man as good as he.
AGAMEMNON
March patiently along: — let one be sent
To pray Achilles see us at our tent. —
If in his death the gods have us befriended,
Great Troy is ours, and our sharp wars are ended.
[*Exeunt, marching.*

SCENE X

Another part of the plains.

Enter AENEAS, PARIS,
ANTENOR, *and* DEIPHOBUS.

AENEAS
Stand, ho! yet are we masters of the field:
Never go home; here starve we out the night.

Enter TROILUS.

TROILUS
Hector is slain.
ALL
Hector! — the gods forbid!
TROILUS
He's dead; and at the murderer's horse's tail,
In beastly sort, dragg'd through the shameful field. —
Frown on, you heavens, effect your rage with speed!
Sit, gods, upon your thrones, and smile at Troy!
I say, at once let your brief plagues be mercy,
And linger not our sure destructions on!
AENEAS
My lord, you do discomfort all the host.
TROILUS
You understand me not that tell me so:
I do not speak of flight, of fear, of death;
But dare all imminence that gods and men
Address their dangers in. Hector is gone:
Who shall tell Priam so, or Hecuba?
Let him that will a screech-owl aye be call'd,
Go in to Troy, and say there, 'Hector's dead':
There is a word will Priam turn to stone;
Make wells and Niobes of the maids and wives,
Cold statues of the youth; and, in a word,
Scare Troy out of itself. But, march away:
Hector is dead; there is no more to say.
Stay yet. — You vile abominable tents,
Thus proudly pight upon our Phrygian plains,
Let Titan rise as early as he dare,
I'll through and through you! — and, thou great-siz'd
coward,
No space of earth shall sunder our two hates:
I'll haunt thee like a wicked conscience still,
That mouldeth goblins swift as frenzy's thoughts. —

Strike a free march to Troy! — with comfort go:
Hope of revenge shall hide our inward woe.
[*Exeunt* AENEAS *and* TROJANS.

As TROILUS *is going out, enter,
from the other side,* PANDARUS.

PANDARUS
But hear you, hear you!
TROILUS
Hence, broker-lackey! ignomy and shame
Pursue thy life, and live aye with thy name!   [*Exit*
PANDARUS
A goodly medicine for my aching bones! — O world!
world! world! thus is the poor agent despised! O traders
and bawds, how earnestly are you set a-work, and how
ill requited! why should our endeavour be so loved, and
the performance so loathed? what verse for it? what
instance for it? — Let me see: —
    Full merrily the humble-bee doth sing,
    Till he hath lost his honey and his sting;
    And being once subdued in armed tail,
    Sweet honey and sweet notes together fail. —
Good traders in the flesh, set this in your painted
    cloths.
As many as be here of pander's hall,
Your eyes, half out, weep out at Pandar's fall;
Or if you cannot weep, yet give some groans,
Though not for me, yet for your aching bones.
Brethren and sisters of the hold-door trade,
Some two months hence my will shall here be made:
It should be now, but that my fear is this, —
Some galled goose of Winchester would hiss:
Till then I'll sweat, and seek about for eases;
And at that time bequeath you my diseases.   [*Exit*

ALL'S WELL THAT ENDS WELL

DRAMATIS PERSONAE

KING OF FRANCE.
DUKE OF FLORENCE.
BERTRAM, *Count of Rousillon.*
LAFEU, *an old lord.*
PAROLLES, *a follower of Bertram.*
Several young French LORDS, *who serve with Bertram in the Florentine war.*

STEWARD,
LAVACHE, *a clown,* } *servants to the Countess of Rousillon.*
A PAGE.
COUNTESS OF ROUSILLON, *mother to Bertram.*
HELENA, *a gentlewoman protected by the Countess.*
A WIDOW *of Florence.*
DIANA, *her daughter.*

VIOLENTA, } *neighbours and friends*
MARIANA, } *to the widow.*

LORDS ATTENDING ON THE KING; OFFICERS,
SOLDIERS, *etc.,* FRENCH AND FLORENTINE.

SCENE — *Rousillon; Paris; Florence; Marseilles.*

COUNTESS In delivering my son from me, I bury a second husband.

ACT I

SCENE I

Rousillon. A hall in the house of the COUNTESS.

Enter BERTRAM, *the* COUNTESS *of* ROUSILLON, HELENA, *and* LAFEU, *all in black.*

COUNTESS
In delivering my son from me, I bury a second husband.

BERTRAM
And I, in going, madam, weep o'er my father's death anew; but I must attend his majesty's command, to whom I am now in ward, evermore in subjection.

LAFEU
You shall find of the king a husband, madam; — you, sir, a father: he that so generally is at all times good, must of necessity hold his virtue to you; whose worthiness would stir it up where it wanted, rather than lack it where there is such abundance.

COUNTESS
What hope is there of his majesty's amendment?

LAFEU
He hath abandon'd his physicians, madam; under whose practices he hath persecuted time with hope; and finds no other advantage in the process but only the losing of hope by time.

COUNTESS
This young gentlewoman had a father, — O, that 'had'! how sad a passage 'tis! — whose skill was almost as great as his honesty; had it stretch'd so far, would have made nature immortal, and death should have play for lack of work. Would, for the king's sake, he were living! I think it would be the death of the king's disease.

LAFEU
How call'd you the man you speak of, madam?

COUNTESS
He was famous, sir, in his profession, and it was his great right to be so, — Gerard de Narbon.

LAFEU
He was excellent indeed, madam: the king very lately spoke of him admiringly and mourningly: he was skilful enough to have lived still, if knowledge could be set up against mortality.

BERTRAM
What is it, my good lord, the king languishes of?

LAFEU
A fistula, my lord.

BERTRAM
I heard not of it before.

LAFEU
I would it were not notorious. —Was this gentlewoman the daughter of Gerard de Narbon?

COUNTESS
His sole child, my lord; and bequeath'd to my overlooking. I have those hopes of her good that her education promises: her dispositions she inherits, which makes fair gifts fairer, for where an unclean mind carries virtuous qualities, there commendations go with pity, — they are virtues and traitors too: in her they are the better for their simpleness; she derives her honesty, and achieves her goodness.

LAFEU
Your commendations, madam, get from her tears.

COUNTESS
'Tis the best brine a maiden can season her praise in. The remembrance of her father never approaches her heart but the tyranny of her sorrows takes all livelihood from her cheek. — No more of this, Helena, — go to, no more; lest it be rather thought you affect a sorrow than to have —

HELENA
I do affect a sorrow, indeed; but I have it too.

LAFEU
Moderate lamentation is the right of the dead; excessive grief the enemy of the living.

COUNTESS
If the living be enemy to the grief, the excess makes it soon mortal.

LAFEU
How understand we that?

BERTRAM
Madam, I desire your holy wishes.

COUNTESS
Be thou blest, Bertram! and succeed thy father
In manners, as in shape! thy blood and virtue
Contend for empire in thee, and thy goodness
Share with thy birthright! Love all, trust a few,
Do wrong to none; be able for thine enemy
Rather in power than use, and keep thy friend
Under thy own life's key: be check'd for silence,
But never tax'd for speech. What heaven more will,
That thee may furnish, and my prayers pluck down,
Fall on thy head! — Farewell, my lord:
'Tis an unseason'd courtier; good my lord,
Advise him.

LAFEU
        He cannot want the best
That shall attend his love.

COUNTESS
Heaven bless him! — Farewell, Bertram.   [*Exit.*

BERTRAM [*to* HELENA].
The best wishes that can be forged in your thoughts be servants to you! Be comfortable to my mother, your mistress, and make much of her.

LAFEU
Farewell, pretty lady: you must hold the credit of your father.   [*Exeunt* BERTRAM *and* LAFEU.

HELENA
O, were that all! I think not on my father;
And these great tears grace his remembrance more
Than those I shed for him. What was he like?
I have forgot him: my imagination
Carries no favour in't but Bertram's.
I am undone: there is no living, none,
If Bertram be away. 'Twere all one
That I should love a bright particular star
And think to wed it, he is so above me:
In his bright radiance and collateral light
Must I be comforted, not in his sphere.
The ambition in my love thus plagues itself:
The hind that would be mated by the lion
Must die for love. 'Twas pretty, though a plague,
To see him every hour; to sit and draw
His arched brows, his hawking eye, his curls,
In our heart's table, — heart too capable
Of every line and trick of his sweet favour:

But now he's gone, and my idolatrous fancy
Must sanctify his reliques. — Who comes here?
One that goes with him: I love him for his sake;
And yet I know him a notorious liar,
Think him a great way fool, solely a coward;
Yet these fix'd evils sit so fit in him,
That they take place, when virtue's steely bones
Look bleak i'th'cold wind: withal, full oft we see
Cold wisdom waiting on superfluous folly.

Enter PAROLLES.

PAROLLES
Save you, fair queen!

HELENA
And you, monarch!

PAROLLES
No.

HELENA
And no.

PAROLLES
Are you meditating on virginity?

HELENA
Ay. You have some stain of soldier in you: let me ask
you a question. Man is enemy to virginity; how may we
barricado it against him?

PAROLLES
Keep him out.

HELENA
But he assails; and our virginity, though valiant in the
defence, yet is weak: unfold to us some warlike
resistance.

PAROLLES
There is none: man, sitting down before you, will
undermine you, and blow you up.

HELENA
Bless our poor virginity from underminers and
blowers-up! — Is there no military policy, how virgins
might blow up men?

PAROLLES
Virginity being blown down, man will quicklier be
blown up: marry, in blowing him down again, with the
breach yourselves made, you lose your city. It is not
politic in the commonwealth of nature to preserve
virginity. Loss of virginity is rational increase; and
there was never virgin got till virginity was first lost.
That you were made of, is metal to make virgins.
Virginity, by being once lost, may be ten times found;
by being ever kept, it is ever lost; 'tis too cold a
companion; away with't!

HELENA
I will stand for't a little, though therefore I die a virgin.

PAROLLES
There's little can be said in't; 'tis against the rule of
nature. To speak on the part of virginity, is to accuse
your mothers; which is most infallible disobedience.
He that hangs himself is a virgin: virginity murders
itself; and should be buried in highways, out of all
sanctified limit, as a desperate offendress against
nature. Virginity breeds mites, much like a cheese;
consumes itself to the very paring, and so dies with
feeding his own stomach. Besides, virginity is peevish,
proud, idle, made of self-love, which is the most
inhibited sin in the canon. Keep it not; you cannot
choose but lose by't: out with't! within ten year it will
make itself ten, which is a goodly increase; and the
principal itself not much the worse: away with't!

HELENA
How might one do, sir, to lose it to her own liking?

PAROLLES
Let me see: marry, ill, to like him that ne'er it likes. 'Tis a
commodity will lose the gloss with lying; the longer kept,
the less worth: off with't while 'tis vendible; answer the
time of request. Virginity, like an old courtier, wears her
cap out of fashion; richly suited, but unsuitable: just like
the brooch and the toothpick, which wear not now. Your
date is better in your pie and your porridge than in your
cheek: and your virginity, your old virginity, is like one of
our French wither'd pears — it looks ill, it eats dryly;
marry, 'tis a wither'd pear; it was formerly better; marry,
yet, 'tis a wither'd pear: will you anything with it?

HELENA
Not my virginity yet …
There shall your master have a thousand loves,
A mother, and a mistress, and a friend,
A phœnix, captain, and an enemy,
A guide, a goddess, and a sovereign,
A counsellor, a traitress, and a dear;
His humble ambition, proud humility,
His jarring concord, and his discord dulcet,
His faith, his sweet disaster; with a world

Of pretty, fond, adoptious Christendoms,
That blinking Cupid gossips. Now shall he —
I know not what he shall: — God send him well! —
The court's a learning-place; — and he is one —

PAROLLES
What one, i'faith?

HELENA
That I wish well. — 'Tis pity —

PAROLLES
What's pity?

HELENA
That wishing well had not a body in't,
Which might be felt; that we, the poorer born,
Whose baser stars do shut us up in wishes,
Might with effects of them follow our friends,
And show what we alone must think; which never
Returns us thanks.

Enter a PAGE.

PAGE
Monsieur Parolles, my lord calls for you.   [*Exit.*

PAROLLES
Little Helen, farewell: if I can remember thee, I will
think of thee at court.

HELENA
Monsieur Parolles, you were born under a charitable
star.

PAROLLES
Under Mars, I.

HELENA
I especially think, under Mars.

PAROLLES
Why under Mars?

HELENA
The wars have so kept you under, that you must needs
be born under Mars.

PAROLLES
When he was predominant.

HELENA
When he was retrograde, I think, rather.

PAROLLES
Why think you so?

HELENA
You go so much backward when you fight.

PAROLLES
That's for advantage.

HELENA
So is running away, when fear proposes the safety: but
the composition, that your valour and fear makes in
you, is a virtue of a good wing, and I like the wear well.

PAROLLES
I am so full of businesses, I cannot answer thee acutely.
I will return perfect courtier; in the which, my
instruction shall serve to naturalise thee, so thou wilt
be capable of a courtier's counsel, and understand what
advice shall thrust upon thee; else thou diest in thine
unthankfulness, and thine ignorance makes thee
away: farewell. When thou hast leisure, say thy prayers;
when thou hast none, remember thy friends: get thee a
good husband, and use him as he uses thee: so,
farewell.   [*Exit.*

HELENA
Our remedies oft in ourselves do lie,
Which we ascribe to heaven: the fated sky
Gives us free scope; only doth backward pull
Our slow designs when we ourselves are dull.
What power is it which mounts my love so high;
That makes me see, and cannot feed mine eye?
The mightiest space in fortune nature brings
To join like likes and kiss like native things.
Impossible be strange attempts to those
That weigh their pains in sense; and do suppose
What hath not been can't be: who ever strove
To show her merit, that did miss her love?
The king's disease, — my project may deceive me,
But my intents are fix'd, and will not leave me.   [*Exit.*

SCENE II

Paris. A room in the KING'S *palace.*

Flourish of cornets. Enter the KING OF FRANCE *with
letters, and divers* ATTENDANTS.

KING
The Florentines and Senoys are by th'ears;
Have fought with equal fortune, and continue
A braving war.

FIRST LORD
So 'tis reported, sir.

KING
Nay, 'tis most credible; we here receive it
A certainty, vouch'd from our cousin Austria,
With caution, that the Florentine will move us
For speedy aid; wherein our dearest friend
Prejudicates the business, and would seem
To have us make denial.

FIRST LORD
                              His love and wisdom,
Approved so to your majesty, may plead
For amplest credence.

KING
                    He hath arm'd our answer,
And Florence is denied before he comes:
Yet, for our gentlemen that mean to see
The Tuscan service, freely have they leave
To stand on either part.

SECOND LORD
                         It well may serve
A nursery to our gentry, who are sick
For breathing and exploit.

KING
                            What's he comes here?

Enter BERTRAM, LAFEU, *and* PAROLLES.

FIRST LORD
It is the Count Rousillon, my good lord,
Young Bertram.

KING
                  Youth, thou bear'st thy father's face;
Frank nature, rather curious than in haste,
Hath well compos'd thee. Thy father's moral parts
Mayst thou inherit too! Welcome to Paris.

BERTRAM
My thanks and duty are your majesty's.

KING
I would I had that corporal soundness now
As when thy father and myself in friendship
First tried our soldiership! He did look far
Into the service of the time, and was
Discipled of the bravest: he lasted long;
But on us both did haggish age steal on,
And wore us out of act. It much repairs me
To talk of your good father. In his youth
He had the wit, which I can well observe
To-day in our young lords; but they may jest,
Till their own scorn return to them unnoted,
Ere they can hide their levity in honour
So like a courtier: contempt nor bitterness
Were in his pride, or sharpness; if they were,
His equal had awak'd them; and his honour,
Clock to itself, knew the true minute when
Exception bid him speak, and at this time
His tongue obey'd his hand: who were below him
He us'd as creatures of another place;
And bow'd his eminent top to their low ranks,
Making them proud of his humility,
In their poor praise he humbled. Such a man
Might be a copy to these younger times;
Which, follow'd well, would demonstrate them now
But goers backward.

BERTRAM
                        His good remembrance, sir,
Lies richer in your thoughts than on his tomb;
So in approof lives not his epitaph
As in your royal speech.

KING
Would I were with him! He would always say, —
Methinks I hear him now; his plausive words
He scatter'd not in ears, but grafted them,
To grow there, and to bear, — 'Let me not live,' —
Thus his good melancholy oft began,
On the catastrophe and heel of pastime,
When it was out, — 'Let me not live,' quoth he,
'After my flame lacks oil, to be the snuff
Of younger spirits, whose apprehensive senses
All but new things disdain; whose judgements are
Mere fathers of their garments; whose constancies
Expire before their fashions': — this he wish'd:
I, after him, do after him wish too,
Since I nor wax nor honey can bring home,
I quickly were dissolved from my hive,
To give some labourer room.

SECOND LORD
                              You are lov'd, sir;
They that least lend it you shall lack you first.

KING
I fill a place, I know't. — How long is't, count,
Since the physician at your father's died?
He was much famed.

RTRAM

    Some six months since, my lord.

NG

e were living, I would try him yet; —
nd me an arm; — the rest have worn me out
th several applications: — nature and sickness
bate it at their leisure. Welcome, count;
son's no dearer.

RTRAM

    Thank your majesty.

        [Exeunt. Flourish.

SCENE III

Rousillon. A room in the house of the COUNTESS.

Enter COUNTESS, STEWARD, *and* CLOWN.

OUNTESS

ill now hear: what say you of this gentlewoman?

EWARD

adam, the care I have had to even your content, I
sh might be found in the calendar of my past
deavours; for then we wound our modesty, and
ake foul the clearness of our deservings, when of
rselves we publish them.

OUNTESS

hat does this knave here? Get you gone, sirrah: the
mplaints I have heard of you I do not all believe: 'tis
y slowness that I do not; for I know you lack not folly
commit them, and have ability enough to make such
averies yours.

LOWN

is not unknown to you, madam, I am a poor fellow.

OUNTESS

ell, sir.

LOWN

o, madam, 'tis not so well that I am poor; though
any of the rich are damn'd: but, if I may have your
dyship's good-will to go to the world, Isbel your
oman and I will do as we may.

OUNTESS

ilt thou needs be a beggar?

LOWN

do beg your good-will in this case.

OUNTESS

what case?

LOWN

Isbel's case and mine own. Service is no heritage:
nd I think I shall never have the blessing of God till I
ave issue o' my body; for they say barns are blessings.

OUNTESS

ell me thy reason why thou wilt marry.

LOWN

ly poor body, madam, requires it: I am driven on by
e flesh; and he must needs go that the devil drives.

OUNTESS

s this all your worship's reason?

LOWN

aith, madam, I have other holy reasons, such as they
re.

OUNTESS

lay the world know them?

LOWN

have been, madam, a wicked creature, as you and all
lesh and blood are; and, indeed, I do marry that I may
epent.

COUNTESS

hy marriage, — sooner than thy wickedness.

LOWN

am out o' friends, madam; and I hope to have friends
for my wife's sake.

COUNTESS

uch friends are thine enemies, knave.

LOWN

'are shallow, madam; e'en great friends; for the
naves come to do that for me, which I am a-weary of.
He that ears my land spares my team, and gives me
eave to in the crop; if I be his cuckold, he's my drudge:
e that comforts my wife is the cherisher of my flesh
nd blood; he that cherishes my flesh and blood loves
my flesh and blood; he that loves my flesh and blood is
my friend: *ergo*, he that kisses my wife is my friend. If
men could be contented to be what they are, there were
no fear in marriage; for young Charbon the puritan and
old Poysam the papist, howsome'er their hearts are
sever'd in religion, their heads are both one, — they
may jowl horns together, like any deer i'th'herd.

COUNTESS

Wilt thou ever be a foul-mouth'd and calumnious knave?

COUNTESS What does this knave here? Get you gone, sirrah.

CLOWN

A prophet I, madam; and I speak the truth the next
way:

    For I the ballad will repeat,
      Which men full true shall find;
    Your marriage comes by destiny,
      Your cuckoo sings by kind.

COUNTESS

Get you gone, sir; I'll talk with you more anon.

STEWARD

May it please you, madam, that he bid Helen come to
you: of her I am to speak.

COUNTESS

Sirrah, tell my gentlewoman I would speak with her;
    Helen, I mean.

CLOWN

    Was this fair face the cause, quoth she,
      Why the Grecians sacked Troy?
    Fond done, done fond,
      Was this King Priam's joy?
    With that she sighed as she stood,
    With that she sighed as she stood,
      And gave this sentence then;
    Among nine bad if one be good,
    Among nine bad if one be good,
      There's yet one good in ten.

COUNTESS

What, one good in ten? you corrupt the song, sirrah.

CLOWN

One good woman in ten, madam; which is a purifying
o'th'song: would God would serve the world so all the
year! we'ld find no fault with the tithe-woman, if I were
the parson: one in ten, quoth a'! an we might have a
good woman born but 'fore every blazing star, or at an
earthquake, 'twould mend the lottery well: a man may
draw his heart out, ere a' pluck one.

COUNTESS

You'll begone, sir knave, and do as I command you?

CLOWN

That man should be at woman's command, and yet no
hurt done! — Though honesty be no puritan, yet it will
do no hurt; it will wear the surplice of humility over the
black gown of a big heart. — I am going, forsooth: the
business is for Helen to come hither.   *[Exit.*

COUNTESS

Well, now.

STEWARD

I know, madam, you love your gentlewoman entirely.

COUNTESS

Faith, I do: her father bequeath'd her to me; and she
herself, without other advantage, may lawfully make

title to as much love as she finds: there is more owing
her than is paid; and more shall be paid her than she'll
demand.

STEWARD

Madam, I was very late more near her than I think she
wish'd me: alone she was, and did communicate to
herself her own words to her own ears; she thought, I
dare vow for her, they touch'd not any stranger sense.
Her matter was, she loved your son: Fortune, she said,
was no goddess, that had put such difference betwixt
their two estates; Love no god, that would not extend
his might, only where qualities were level; Dian no
queen of virgins, that would suffer her poor knight
surprised, without rescue in the first assault, or
ransom afterward. This she deliver'd in the most bitter
touch of sorrow that e'er I heard virgin exclaim in:
which I held my duty speedily to acquaint you withal;
sithence, in the loss that may happen, it concerns you
something to know it.

COUNTESS

You have discharg'd this honestly; keep it to yourself:
many likelihoods inform'd me of this before, which
hung so tottering in the balance, that I could neither
believe nor misdoubt. Pray you, leave me: stall this in
your bosom, and I thank you for your honest care: I will
speak with you further anon.   *[Exit* STEWARD.
Even so it was with me when I was young:
    If we are nature's, these are ours; this thorn
Doth to our rose of youth rightly belong;
    Our blood to us, this to our blood is born;
It is the show and seal of nature's truth,
Where love's strong passion is impress'd in youth:
By our remembrances of days foregone,
Such were our faults; nor then we thought them none.
      Enter HELENA.
Her eye is sick on't: I observe her now.

HELENA

What is your pleasure, madam?

COUNTESS

        You know, Helen,
I am a mother to you.

HELENA

Mine honourable mistress.

COUNTESS

        Nay, a mother:
Why not a mother? When I said a mother,
Methought you saw a serpent: what's in 'mother,'
That you start at it? I say, I am your mother;
And put you in the catalogue of those
That were enwombed mine: 'tis often seen
Adoption strives with nature; and choice breeds
A native slip to us from foreign seeds:

You ne'er oppress'd me with a mother's groan,
Yet I express to you a mother's care: —
God's mercy, maiden! does it curd thy blood,
To say, I am thy mother? What's the matter,
That this distemper'd messenger of wet,
The many-colour'd Iris, rounds thine eye?
Why, — that you are my daughter?

HELENA

                              That I am not.

COUNTESS
I say, I am your mother.

HELENA

                         Pardon, madam:
The Count Rousillon cannot be my brother:
I am from humble, he from honour'd name;
No note upon my parents, his all noble:
My master, my dear lord he is; and I
His servant live, and will his vassal die:
He must not be my brother.

COUNTESS

                    Nor I your mother?

HELENA
You are my mother, madam; would you were —
So that my lord your son were not my brother —
Indeed my mother! — or were you both our mothers,
I care no more for than I do for heaven,
So I were not his sister. Can't no other,
But I your daughter, he must be my brother?

COUNTESS
Yes, Helen, you might be my daughter-in-law:
God shield, you mean it not! 'daughter' and 'mother'
So strive upon your pulse. What, pale again?
My fear hath catch'd your fondness: now I see
The mystery of your loneliness, and find
Your salt tears' head: now to all sense 'tis gross
You love my son; invention is ashamed,
Against the proclamation of thy passion,
To say thou dost not: therefore tell me true;
But tell me then, 'tis so; — for, look, thy cheeks
Confess it, th'one to th'other; and thine eyes
See it so grossly shown in thy behaviours,
That in their kind they speak it: only sin
And hellish obstinacy tie thy tongue,
That truth should be suspected. Speak, is't so?
If it be so, you have wound a goodly clew;
If it be not, forswear't: howe'er, I charge thee,
As heaven shall work in me for thine avail,
To tell me truly.

HELENA

              Good madam, pardon me!

COUNTESS
Do you love my son?

HELENA

                  Your pardon, noble mistress!

COUNTESS
Love you my son?

HELENA

                Do not you love him, madam?

COUNTESS
Go not about; my love hath in't a bond,
Whereof the world takes note: come, come, disclose
The state of your affection; for your passions
Have to the full appeach'd.

HELENA

                        Then, I confess,
Here on my knee, before high heaven and you,
That before you, and next unto high heaven,
I love your son: —
My friends were poor, but honest; so's my love:
Be not offended; for it hurts not him,
That he is lov'd of me: I follow him not
By any token of presumptuous suit;
Nor would I have him till I do deserve him;
Yet never know how that desert should be.
I know I love in vain, strive against hope;
Yet in this captious and intenible sieve
I still pour in the waters of my love,
And lack not to lose still: thus, Indian-like,
Religious in mine error, I adore
The sun, that looks upon his worshipper,
But knows of him no more. My dearest madam,
Let not your hate encounter with my love,
For loving where you do: but, if yourself,
Whose aged honour cites a virtuous youth,
Did ever, in so true a flame of liking,
Wish chastely, and love dearly, that your Dian
Was both herself and Love; O, then, give pity
To her, whose state is such, that cannot choose
But lend and give, where she is sure to lose;
That seeks not to find that her search implies,

But, riddle-like, lives sweetly where she dies!

COUNTESS
Had you not lately an intent, — speak truly, —
To go to Paris?

HELENA

              Madam, I had.

COUNTESS

                          Wherefore?
Tell true.

HELENA
I will tell truth; by grace itself, I swear.
You know my father left me some prescriptions
Of rare and prov'd effects, such as his reading
And manifest experience had collected
For general sovereignty; and that he will'd me
In heedfull'st reservation to bestow them,
As notes, whose faculties inclusive were,
More than they were in note: amongst the rest,
There is a remedy, approv'd, set down,
To cure the desperate languishings whereof
The king is render'd lost.

COUNTESS

                     This was your motive
For Paris, was it? speak.

HELENA
My lord your son made me to think of this;
Else Paris, and the medicine, and the king,
Had from the conversation of my thoughts
Haply been absent then.

COUNTESS

                      But think you, Helen,
If you should tender your supposed aid,
He would receive it? he and his physicians
Are of a mind; he, that they cannot help him;
They, that they cannot help: how shall they credit
A poor unlearned virgin, when the schools,
Embowell'd of their doctrine, have left off
The danger to itself?

HELENA

                   There's something hints,
More than my father's skill, which was the greatest
Of his profession, that his good receipt
Shall, for my legacy, be sanctified
By th'luckiest stars in heaven: and, would your honour
But give me leave to try success, I'ld venture
The well-lost life of mine on his Grace's cure
By such a day and hour.

COUNTESS

                      Dost thou believe't?

HELENA
Ay, madam, knowingly.

COUNTESS
Why, Helen, thou shalt have my leave, and love,
Means, and attendants, and my loving greetings
To those of mine in court: I'll stay at home,
And pray God's blessing into thy attempt:
Be gone to-morrow; and be sure of this,
What I can help thee to, thou shalt not miss. [*Exeunt.*

ACT II

SCENE I

Paris. A room in the KING'S *palace.*

Enter the KING, *with divers young* LORDS, *taking leave
for the Florentine war;* BERTRAM, PAROLLES, *and*
ATTENDANTS. *Flourish of cornets.*

KING
Farewell, young lords; these warlike principles
Do not throw from you: and you, my lords, farewell:
Share the advice betwixt you; if both gain, all
The gift doth stretch itself as 'tis received,
And is enough for both.

FIRST LORD

                     'Tis our hope, sir,
After well-enter'd soldiers, to return
And find your Grace in health.

KING
No, no, it cannot be; and yet my heart
Will not confess he owes the malady
That doth my life besiege. Farewell, young lords;
Whether I live or die, be you the sons
Of worthy Frenchmen: let higher Italy —
Those bated that inherit but the fall
Of the last monarchy — see that you come
Not to woo honour, but to wed it; when
The bravest questant shrinks, find what you seek,
That fame may cry you loud: I say, farewell.

SECOND LORD
Health, at your bidding, serve your majesty!

KING
Those girls of Italy, take heed of them:
They say, our French lack language to deny,
If they demand: beware of being captives,
Before you serve.

BOTH LORDS

              Our hearts receive your warnings.

KING
Farewell. — Come hither to me.   [*Exit, attende*

FIRST LORD
O my sweet lord, that you will stay behind us!

PAROLLES
'Tis not his fault, the spark.

SECOND LORD

                          O, 'tis brave wars!

PAROLLES
Most admirable: I have seen those wars.

BERTRAM
I am commanded here, and kept a coil with
'Too young,' and 'the next year,' and ''tis too early.'

PAROLLES
An thy mind stand to't, boy, steal away bravely.

BERTRAM
I shall stay here the forehorse to a smock,
Creaking my shoes on the plain masonry,
Till honour be bought up, and no sword worn
But one to dance with! By heaven, I'll steal away.

FIRST LORD
There's honour in the theft.

PAROLLES

                         Commit it, count.

SECOND LORD
I am your accessary; and so, farewell.

BERTRAM
I grow to you, and our parting is a tortur'd body.

FIRST LORD
Farewell, captain.

SECOND LORD
Sweet Monsieur Parolles!

PAROLLES
Noble heroes, my sword and yours are kin. Good
sparks and lustrous, a word, good metals: — you shall
find in the regiment of the Spinii one Captain Spurio,
with his cicatrice, an emblem of war, here on his
sinister cheek; it was this very sword entrench'd it: say
to him, I live; and observe his reports for me.

FIRST LORD
We shall, noble captain.

PAROLLES
Mars dote on you for his novices!   [*Exeunt* LORDS

What will ye do?

BERTRAM
Stay; the king!

        Enter KING; BERTRAM *and* PAROLLES *retire.*

PAROLLES
Use a more spacious ceremony to the noble lords; you
have restrain'd yourself within the list of too cold an
adieu: be more expressive to them: for they wear
themselves in the cap of the time, there do muster true
gait, eat, speak, and move under the influence of the
most received star; and though the devil lead the
measure, such are to be follow'd: after them, and take a
more dilated farewell.

BERTRAM
And I will do so.

PAROLLES
Worthy fellows; and like to prove most sinewy sword-men.
              [*Exeunt* BERTRAM *and* PAROLLES.

              Enter LAFEU.

LAFEU [*kneeling*].
Pardon, my lord, for me and for my tidings.

KING
I'll fee thee to stand up.

LAFEU [*rising*].
Then here's a man stands that has brought his pardon.
I would you had kneel'd, my lord, to ask me mercy;
And that, at my bidding, you could so stand up.

KING
I would I had; so I had broke thy pate,
And ask'd thee mercy for't.

LAFEU
Good faith, across: but, my good lord, 'tis thus;
Will you be cured of your infirmity?

KING
No.

LAFEU
O, will you eat no grapes, my royal fox?
Yes, but you will my noble grapes, an if
My royal fox could reach them: I have seen a medicine
That's able to breathe life into a stone,
Quicken a rock, and make you dance canary
With sprightly fire and motion; whose simple touch
Is powerful to araise King Pepin, nay,
To give great Charlemain a pen in's hand,
And write to her a love-line.

KING
What 'her' is this?

LAFEU
Why, doctor she: my lord, there's one arrived,
If you will see her: — now, by my faith and honour,
If seriously I may convey my thoughts
In this my light deliverance, I have spoke
With one that, in her sex, her years, profession,
Wisdom, and constancy, hath amaz'd me more
Than I dare blame my weakness: will you see her, —
For that is her demand, — and know her business?
That done, laugh well at me.

KING
Now, good Lafeu,
Bring in the admiration; that we with thee
May spend our wonder too, or take off thine
By wondering how thou took'st it.

LAFEU
Nay, I'll fit you,
And not be all day neither. [Exit.

KING
Thus he his special nothing ever prologues.
Enter LAFEU, with HELENA.

LAFEU
Nay, come your ways.

KING
This haste hath wings indeed.

LAFEU
Nay, come your ways;
This is his majesty, say your mind to him:
A traitor you do look like; but such traitors
His majesty seldom fears: I am Cressid's uncle,
That dare leave two together; fare you well. [Exit.

KING
Now, fair one, does your business follow us?

HELENA
Ay, my good lord.
Gerard de Narbon was my father; one,
In what he did profess, well found.

KING
I knew him.

HELENA
The rather will I spare my praises towards him;
Knowing him is enough. On's bed of death
Many receipts he gave me; chiefly one,
Which, as the dearest issue of his practice,
And of his old experience th'only darling,
He bade me store up, as a triple eye,
Safer than mine own two, more dear: I have so:
And, hearing your high majesty is touch'd
With that malignant cause, wherein the honour
Of my dear father's gift stands chief in power,
I come to tender it, and my appliance,
With all bound humbleness.

KING
We thank you, maiden;
But may not be so credulous of cure,
When our most learned doctors leave us, and
The congregated college have concluded
That labouring art can never ransom nature
From her inaidable state, — I say we must not
So stain our judgement, or corrupt our hope,
To prostitute our past-cure malady
To empirics; or to dissever so
Our great self and our credit, to esteem
A senseless help, when help past sense we deem.

HELENA
My duty, then, shall pay me for my pains:
I will no more enforce mine office on you;
Humbly entreating from your royal thoughts
A modest one, to bear me back again.

KING
I cannot give thee less, to be call'd grateful:
Thou thought'st to help me; and such thanks I give
As one near death to those that wish him live:
But, what at full I know, thou know'st no part;
I knowing all my peril, thou no art.

HELENA Not helping, death's my fee; but, if I help, what do you promise me?

HELENA
What I can do can do no hurt to try,
Since you set up your rest 'gainst remedy.
He that of greatest works is finisher,
Oft does them by the weakest minister:
So holy writ in babes hath judgement shown,
When judges have been babes; great floods have flown
From simple sources; and great seas have dried,
When miracles have by the greatest been denied.
Oft expectation fails, and most oft there
Where most it promises; and oft it hits
Where hope is coldest, and despair most fits.

KING
I must not hear thee; fare thee well, kind maid;
Thy pains, not us'd, must by thyself be paid:
Proffers not took reap thanks for their reward.

HELENA
Inspired merit so by breath is barr'd:
It is not so with him that all things knows,
As 'tis with us that square our guess by shows;
But most it is presumption in us when
The help of heaven we count the act of men.
Dear sir, to my endeavours give consent;
Of heaven, not me, make an experiment.
I am not an impostor, that proclaim
Myself against the level of mine aim;
But know I think, and think I know most sure,
My art is not past power, nor you past cure.

KING
Are thou so confident? within what space
Hopest thou my cure?

HELENA
The great'st grace lending grace,
Ere twice the horses of the sun shall bring
Their fiery torcher his diurnal ring;
Ere twice in murk and occidental damp
Moist Hesperus hath quench'd his sleepy lamp;
Or four and twenty times the pilot's glass
Hath told the thievish minutes how they pass;
What is infirm from your sound parts shall fly,
Health shall live free, and sickness freely die.

KING
Upon thy certainty and confidence
What darest thou venture?

HELENA
Tax of impudence, —
A strumpet's boldness, a divulged shame, —
Traduc'd by odious ballads; my maiden's name
Sear'd otherwise; nay, worse, if worse, extended
With vilest torture let my life be ended.

KING
Methinks in thee some blessed spirit doth speak,
His powerful sound within an organ weak:
And what impossibility would slay
In common sense, sense saves another way.

Thy life is dear; for all, that life can rate
Worth name of life, in thee hath estimate, —
Youth, beauty, wisdom, courage, all
That happiness and prime can happy call:
Thou this to hazard, needs must intimate
Skill infinite or monstrous desperate.
Sweet practiser, thy physic I will try,
That ministers thine own death, if I die.

HELENA
If I break time, or flinch in property
Of what I spoke, unpitied let me die,
And well deserv'd: not helping, death's my fee;
But, if I help, what do you promise me?

KING
Make thy demand.

HELENA
But will you make it even?

KING
Ay, by my sceptre and my hopes of heaven.

HELENA
Then shalt thou give me with thy kingly hand
What husband in thy power I will command:
Exempted be from me the arrogance
To choose from forth the royal blood of France,
My low and humble name to propagate
With any branch or image of thy state;
But such a one, thy vassal, whom I know
Is free for me to ask, thee to bestow.

KING
Here is my hand; the premises observed,
Thy will by my performance shall be served:
So make the choice of thy own time; for I,
Thy resolved patient, on thee still rely.
More should I question thee, and more I must, —
Though more to know could not be more to trust, —
From whence thou camest, how tended on: but rest
Unquestion'd welcome, and undoubted blest. —
Give me some help here, ho! — If thou proceed
As high as word, my deed shall match thy deed.
[Flourish. Exeunt.

SCENE II
Rousillon. A room in the house of the COUNTESS.

Enter COUNTESS and CLOWN.

COUNTESS
Come on, sir; I shall now put you to the height of your breeding.

CLOWN
I will show myself highly fed and lowly taught: I know my business is but to the court.

COUNTESS
To the court! why, what place make you special, when you put off that with such contempt? But to the court!

CLOWN
Truly, madam, if God have lent a man any manners,
he may easily put it off at court: he that cannot make a
leg, put off's cap, kiss his hand, and say nothing, has
neither leg, hands, lip, nor cap; and, indeed, such a
fellow, to say precisely, were not for the court: but for
me, I have an answer will serve all men.

COUNTESS
Marry, that's a bountiful answer that fits all questions.

CLOWN
It is like a barber's chair, that fits all buttocks, — the
pin-buttock, the quatch-buttock, the brawn-buttock, or
any buttock.

COUNTESS
Will your answer serve fit to all questions?

CLOWN
As fit as ten groats is for the hand of an attorney, as
your French crown for your taffeta punk, as Tib's rush
for Tom's forefinger, as a pancake for Shrove-Tuesday,
a morris for May-day, as the nail to his hole, the
cuckold to his horn, as a scolding queen to a wrangling
knave, as the nun's lip to the friar's mouth, nay, as the
pudding to his skin.

COUNTESS
Have you, I say, an answer of such fitness for all
questions?

CLOWN
From below your duke to beneath your constable, it
will fit any question.

COUNTESS
It must be an answer of most monstrous size that must
fit all demands.

CLOWN
But a trifle neither, in good faith, if the learned should
speak truth of it: here it is, and all that belongs to't. Ask
me if I am a courtier: it shall do you no harm to learn.

COUNTESS
To be young again, if we could: — I will be a fool in
question, hoping to be the wiser by your answer. I pray
you, sir, are you a courtier?

CLOWN
'O Lord, sir!' — there's a simple putting off. —
More, more, a hundred of them.

COUNTESS
Sir, I am a poor friend of yours that loves you.

CLOWN
'O Lord, sir!' — Thick, thick, spare not me.

COUNTESS
I think, sir, you can eat none of this homely meat.

CLOWN
'O Lord, sir!' — Nay, put me to't, I warrant you.

COUNTESS
You were lately whipp'd, sir, as I think.

CLOWN
'O Lord, sir!' — Spare not me.

COUNTESS
Do you cry, 'O Lord, sir!' at your whipping, and 'Spare
not me?' Indeed, your 'O Lord, sir!' is very sequent to
your whipping: you would answer very well to a
whipping, if you were but bound to't.

CLOWN
I ne'er had worse luck in my life in my 'O Lord, sir!' I
see things may serve long, but not serve ever.

COUNTESS
I play the noble housewife with the time,
To entertain it so merrily with a fool.

CLOWN
'O Lord, sir! — why, there't serves well again.

COUNTESS
An end, sir: to your business. Give Helen this,
And urge her to a present answer back:
Commend me to my kinsmen and my son:
This is not much.

CLOWN
Not much commendation to them.

COUNTESS
Not much employment for you: you understand me?

CLOWN
Most fruitfully: I am there before my legs.

COUNTESS
Haste you again.   [*Exeunt severally.*

SCENE III

Paris. A room in the KING'S *palace.*

Enter LAFEU *and* PAROLLES.

LAFEU
They say miracles are past; and we have our
philosophical persons, to make modern and familiar,
things supernatural and causeless. Hence is it that we
make trifles of terrors; ensconcing ourselves into
seeming knowledge, when we should submit ourselves
to an unknown fear. Why, 'tis the rarest argument of
wonder that hath shot out in our latter times.

PAROLLES
And so 'tis.

LAFEU
To be relinquish'd of the artists, —

PAROLLES
So I say.

LAFEU
Both of Galen and Paracelsus, of all the learned and
authentic fellows, —

PAROLLES
Right; so I say.

LAFEU
That gave him out incurable, —

PAROLLES
Why, there 'tis; so say I too.

LAFEU
Not to be help'd, —

PAROLLES
Right; as 'twere, a man assured of a —

LAFEU
Uncertain life, and sure death.

PAROLLES
Just, you say well: so would I have said.

LAFEU
I may truly say, it is a novelty to the world.

PAROLLES
It is, indeed: if you will have it in showing, you
shall read it in — What do ye call there? —

LAFEU
A showing of a heavenly effect in an earthly actor.

PAROLLES
That's it I would have said, the very same.

LAFEU
Why, your dolphin is not lustier: 'fore me, I speak in
respect —

PAROLLES
Nay, 'tis strange, 'tis very strange, that is the brief and
the tedious of it; and he's of a most facinerious spirit
that will not acknowledge it to be the —

LAFEU
Very hand of heaven —

PAROLLES
Ay, so I say.

LAFEU
In a most weak and debile minister great power, great
transcendence: which should, indeed, give us a further
use to be made than alone the recovery of the king.

PAROLLES.
As to be —

LAFEU
Generally thankful.

PAROLLES
I would have said it; you say well. — Here comes the
king.

Enter KING, HELENA, *and* ATTENDANTS.

LAFEU
Lustig, as the Dutchman says: I'll like a maid the better,
whilst I have a tooth in my head: why, he's able to lead
her a coranto.

PAROLLES
Mort du vinaigre! is not this Helen?

LAFEU
'Fore God, I think so.

KING
Go, call before me all the lords in court. —
                    [*Exit an* ATTENDANT.
Sit, my preserver, by thy patient's side;
And with this healthful hand, whose banish'd sense
Thou hast repeal'd, a second time receive
The confirmation of my promis'd gift,
Which but attends thy naming.
            Enter three or four LORDS *and* BERTRAM.
Fair maid, send forth thine eye: this youthful parcel
Of noble bachelors stand at my bestowing,
O'er whom both sovereign power and father's voice
I have to use: thy frank election make;
Thou hast power to choose, and they none to forsake.

HELENA
To each of you one fair and virtuous mistress
Fall, when Love please! — marry, to each, but one!

HELENA I take you; but I give me and my service, ever whilst I live.

LAFEU
I'ld give bay curtal and his furniture,
My mouth no more were broken than these boys',
And writ as little beard.

KING
                    Peruse them well:
Not one of these but had a noble father.

HELENA
Gentlemen,
Heaven hath, through me, restor'd the king to health.

ALL
We understand it, and thank heaven for you.

HELENA
I am a simple maid; and therein wealthiest,
That I protest I simply am a maid. —
Please it your majesty, I have done already:
The blushes in my cheeks thus whisper me,
'We blush that thou shouldst choose; but, be refus'd,
Let the white death sit on thy cheek for ever;
We'll ne'er come there again.'

KING
                    Make choice; and, see,
Who shuns thy love shuns all his love in me.

HELENA
Now, Dian, from thy altar do I fly;
And to imperial Love, that god most high,
Do my sighs stream. — [to FIRST LORD] Sir, will you
          hear my suit?

FIRST LORD
And grant it.

HELENA
                    Thanks, sir; all the rest is mute.

LAFEU
I had rather be in this choice than throw ames-ace for
my life.

HELENA [to SECOND LORD].
The honour, sir, that flames in your fair eyes,
Before I speak, too threateningly replies:
Love make your fortunes twenty times above
Her that so wishes and her humble love!

SECOND LORD
No better, if you please.

HELENA
                    My wish receive,
Which great Love grant! and so, I take my leave.

LAFEU
Do all they deny her? An they were sons of mine,
I'ld have them whipp'd; or I would send them to the
Turk, to make eunuchs of.

HELENA [to THIRD LORD].
Be not afraid that I your hand should take;
I'll never do you wrong for your own sake:
Blessing upon your vows! and in your bed
Find fairer fortune, if you ever wed!

LAFEU
These boys are boys of ice, they'll none have her: sure,
they are bastards to the English; the French ne'er got
'em.

HELENA [to FOURTH LORD].
You are too young, too happy, and too good,
To make yourself a son out of my blood.

FOURTH LORD
Fair one, I think not so.

LAFEU
There's one grape yet, — I am sure thy father drunk
wine: — but if thou be'st not an ass, I am a youth of
fourteen; I have known thee already.

HELENA [to BERTRAM].
I dare not say I take you; but I give
Me and my service, ever whilst I live,
Into your guiding power. — This is the man.

KING
Why, then, young Bertram, take her; she's thy wife.

BERTRAM
My wife, my liege! I shall beseech your highness,
In such a business give me leave to use
The help of mine own eyes.

KING
                    Know'st thou not, Bertram,
What she has done for me?

BERTRAM
                    Yes, my good lord;
But never hope to know why I should marry her.

KING
Thou know'st she has rais'd me from my sickly bed.

BERTRAM
But follows it, my lord, to bring me down
Must answer for your raising? I know her well:
She had her breeding at my father's charge.

A poor physician's daughter my wife! — Disdain
Rather corrupt me ever!

KING
'Tis only title thou disdain'st in her, the which
I can build up. Strange is it that our bloods,
Of colour, weight, and heat, pour'd all together,
Would quite confound distinction, yet stand off
In differences so mighty. If she be
All that is virtuous, — save what thou dislikest,
A poor physician's daughter, — thou dislikest
Of virtue for the name: but do not so:
From lowest place when virtuous things proceed,
The place is dignified by th'doer's deed:
Where great additions swell's, and virtue none,
It is a dropsied honour: good alone
Is good without a name; vileness is so:
The property by what it is should go,
Not by the title. She is young, wise, fair;
In these to nature she's immediate heir;
And these breed honour: that is honour's scorn,
Which challenges itself as honour's born,
And is not like the sire: honours thrive,
When rather from our acts we them derive
Than our foregoers: the mere word's a slave,
Debosh'd on every tomb, on every grave
A lying trophy; and as oft is dumb
Where dust and damn'd oblivion is the tomb
Of honour'd bones indeed. What should be said?
If thou canst like this creature as a maid,
I can create the rest; virtue and she
Is her own dower; honour and wealth from me.

BERTRAM
I cannot love her, nor will strive to do't.

KING
Thou wrong'st thyself, if thou shouldst strive to
choose.

HELENA
That you are well restor'd, my lord, I'm glad:
Let the rest go.

KING
My honour's at the stake; which to defeat,
I must produce my power. Here, take her hand,
Proud scornful boy, unworthy this good gift;
That dost in vile misprision shackle up
My love and her desert; that canst not dream,
We, poising us in her defective scale,
Shall weigh thee to the beam; that wilt not know,
It is in us to plant thine honour where
We please to have it grow. Check thy contempt:
Obey our will, which travails in thy good:
Believe not thy disdain, but presently
Do thine own fortunes that obedient right
Which both thy duty owes and our power claims;
Or I will throw thee from my care for ever
Into the staggers and the careless lapse
Of youth and ignorance; both my revenge and hate
Loosing upon thee, in the name of justice,
Without all terms of pity. Speak; thine answer.

BERTRAM
Pardon, my gracious lord; for I submit
My fancy to your eyes: when I consider
What great creation and what dole of honour
Flies where you bid it, I find that she, which late
Was in my nobler thoughts most base, is now
The praised of the king; who, so ennobled,
Is, as 'twere born so.

KING
                    Take her by the hand,
And tell her she is thine: to whom I promise
A counterpoise; if not to thy estate,
A balance more replete.

BERTRAM
                    I take her hand.

KING
Good fortune and the favour of the king
Smile upon this contract; whose ceremony
Shall seem expedient on the now-born brief,
And be perform'd to-night: the solemn feast
Shall more attend upon the coming space,
Expecting absent friends. As thou lovest her,
Thy love's to me religious; else, does err.

[*Exeunt all but* LAFEU *and* PAROLLES.

LAFEU
Do you hear, monsieur? a word with you.

PAROLLES
Your pleasure, sir?

LAFEU
Your lord and master did well to make his recantation.

PAROLLES
Recantation! — My lord! my master!

LAFEU
Ay; is it not a language I speak?

PAROLLES
A most harsh one, and not to be understood without
bloody succeeding. My master!

LAFEU
Are you companion to the Count Rousillon?

PAROLLES
To any count, — to all counts, — to what is man.

LAFEU
To what is count's man: count's master is of another
style.

PAROLLES
You are too old, sir; let it satisfy you, you are too old.

LAFEU
I must tell thee, sirrah, I write man; to which title age
cannot bring thee.

PAROLLES
What I dare too well do, I dare not do.

LAFEU
I did think thee, for two ordinaries, to be a pretty wise
fellow; thou didst make tolerable vent of thy travel; it
might pass: yet the scarfs and the bannerets about thee
did manifoldly dissuade me from believing thee a
vessel of too great a burthen. I have now found thee;
when I lose thee again, I care not: yet art thou good for
nothing but taking up; and that thou'rt scarce worth.

PAROLLES
Hadst thou not the privilege of antiquity upon thee, —

LAFEU
Do not plunge thyself too far in anger, lest thou hasten
thy trial; which if — Lord have mercy on thee for a hen!
So, my good window of lattice, fare thee well: thy
casement I need not open, for I look through thee. Give
me thy hand.

PAROLLES
My lord, you give me most egregious indignity.

LAFEU
Ay, with all my heart; and thou art worthy of it.

PAROLLES
I have not, my lord, deserved it.

LAFEU
Yes, good faith, every dram of it; and I will not bate thee
a scruple.

PAROLLES
Well, I shall be wiser —

LAFEU
Ev'n as soon as thou can'st, for thou hast to pull at a
smack o'th'contrary. If ever thou be'st bound in thy
scarf and beaten, thou shalt find what it is to be proud
of thy bondage. I have a desire to hold my acquaintance
with thee, or rather my knowledge, that I may say, in
the default, he is a man I know.

PAROLLES
My lord, you do me most insupportable vexation.

LAFEU
I would it were hell-pains for thy sake, and my poor
doing eternal: for doing I am past; as I will by thee, in
what motion age will give me leave.   [*Exit.*

PAROLLES
Well, thou hast a son shall take this disgrace off me;
scurvy, old, filthy, scurvy lord! — Well, I must be
patient; there is no fettering of authority. I'll beat him,
by my life, if I can meet him with any convenience, an
he were double and double a lord. I'll have no more pity
of his age than I would have of — I'll beat him, an if I
could but meet him again.

                    Enter LAFEU.

LAFEU
Sirrah, your lord and master's married; there's news
for you: you have a new mistress.

PAROLLES
I most unfeignedly beseech your lordship to make
some reservation of your wrongs: he is my good lord;
whom I serve above is my master.

LAFEU
Who? God?

PAROLLES
Ay, sir.

LAFEU
The devil it is that's thy master. Why dost thou garter
up thy arms o' this fashion? dost make hose of thy
sleeves? do other servants so? Thou wert best set thy
lower part where thy nose stands. By mine honour, if I
were but two hours younger, I'ld beat thee: methinks,
thou art a general offence, and every man should beat

PAROLLES A young man married is a man that's marr'd.

thee: I think thou wast created for men to breathe themselves upon thee.

PAROLLES
This is hard and undeserved measure, my lord.

LAFEU
Go to, sir; you were beaten in Italy for picking a kernel out of a pomegranate; you are a vagabond, and no true traveller: you are more saucy with lords and honourable personages than the heraldry of your birth and virtue gives you commission. You are not worth another word, else I'ld call you knave. I leave you.

[*Exit.*

PAROLLES
Good, very good; it is so then: — good, very good; let it be conceal'd awhile.

Enter BERTRAM.

BERTRAM
Undone, and forfeited to cares for ever!

PAROLLES
What's the matter, sweet-heart?

BERTRAM
Although before the solemn priest I have sworn,
I will not bed her.

PAROLLES
What, what, sweet-heart?

BERTRAM
O, my Parolles, they have married me! —
I'll to the Tuscan wars, and never bed her.

PAROLLES
France is a dog-hole, and it no more merits
The tread of a man's foot: to th'wars!

BERTRAM
There's letters from my mother: what th'import is, I know not yet.

PAROLLES
Ay, that would be known. To th'wars, my boy, to
    th'wars!
He wears his honour in a box unseen,
That hugs his kicky-wicky here at home,
Spending his manly marrow in her arms,
Which should sustain the bound and high curvet
Of Mars's fiery steed. To other regions!
France is a stable; we that dwell in't jades;
Therefore, to th'wars!

BERTRAM
It shall be so: I'll send her to my house,
Acquaint my mother with my hate to her,
And wherefore I am fled; write to the king
That which I durst not speak: his present gift
Shall furnish me to those Italian fields,
Where noble fellows strike: war is no strife
To the dark house and the detested wife.

PAROLLES
Will this capriccio hold in thee, art sure?

BERTRAM
Go with me to my chamber, and advise me.
I'll send her straight away: to-morrow

I'll to the wars, she to her single sorrow.

PAROLLES
Why, these balls bound; there's noise in it. — 'Tis hard:
A young man married is a man that's marr'd:
Therefore, away, and leave her; bravely go:
The king has done you wrong; but, hush, 'tis so.

[*Exeunt.*

SCENE IV
Paris. The KING'S *palace.*

Enter HELENA *and* CLOWN.

HELENA
My mother greets me kindly: is she well?

CLOWN
She is not well; but yet she has her health: she's very merry; but yet she is not well: but thanks be given, she's very well, and wants nothing i'th'world; but yet she is not well.

HELENA
If she be very well, what does she ail, that she's not very well?

CLOWN
Truly, she's very well indeed, but for two things.

HELENA
What two things?

CLOWN
One, that she's not in heaven, whither God send her quickly! the other, that she's in earth, from whence God send her quickly!

Enter PAROLLES.

PAROLLES
Bless you, my fortunate lady!

HELENA
I hope, sir, I have your good will to have mine own good fortunes.

PAROLLES
You had my prayers to lead them on; and to keep them on, have them still. — O, my knave, — how does my old lady?

CLOWN
So that you had her wrinkles, and I her money, I would she did as you say.

PAROLLES
Why, I say nothing.

CLOWN Truly, she's very well indeed, but for two things.

CLOWN
Marry, you are the wiser man; for many a man's tongue
shakes out his master's undoing: to say nothing, to do
nothing, to know nothing, and to have nothing, is to be
a great part of your title; which is within a very little of
nothing.
PAROLLES
Away! th'art a knave.
CLOWN
You should have said, sir, before a knave th'art a knave;
that's, before me th'art a knave: this had been truth, sir.
PAROLLES
Go to, thou art a witty fool; I have found thee.
CLOWN
Did you find me in yourself, sir? or were you taught to
find me? The search, sir, was profitable; and much fool
may you find in you, even to the world's pleasure and
the increase of laughter.
PAROLLES
A good knave, i'faith, and well fed. —
Madam, my lord will go away to-night;
A very serious business calls on him.
The great prerogative and rite of love,
Which, as your due, time claims, he does acknowledge;
But puts it off by a compell'd restraint;
Whose want, and whose delay, is strew'd with sweets,
Which they distil now in the curbed time,
To make the coming hour o'erflow with joy,
And pleasure drown the brim.
HELENA
What's his will else?
PAROLLES
That you will take your instant leave o'th'king,
And make this haste as your own good proceeding,
Strengthen'd with what apology you think
May make it probable need.
HELENA
What more commands he?
PAROLLES
That, having this obtain'd, you presently
Attend his further pleasure.
HELENA
In every thing I wait upon his will.
PAROLLES
I shall report it so.
HELENA
I pray you.   [*Exit* PAROLLES.
Come, sirrah.   [*Exeunt.*

SCENE V
Paris. The KING'S *palace.*

Enter LAFEU *and* BERTRAM.

LAFEU
But I hope your lordship thinks not him a soldier.
BERTRAM
Yes, my lord, and of very valiant approof.
LAFEU
You have it from his own deliverance.
BERTRAM
And by other warranted testimony.
LAFEU
Then my dial goes not true: I took this lark for a
bunting.
BERTRAM
I do assure you, my lord, he is very great in knowledge,
and accordingly valiant.
LAFEU
I have, then, sinn'd against his experience, and
transgress'd against his valour; and my state that way is
dangerous, since I cannot yet find in my heart to
repent. Here he comes: I pray you, make us friends; I
will pursue the amity.

Enter PAROLLES.

PAROLLES [*to* BERTRAM].
These things shall be done, sir.
LAFEU
Pray you, sir, who's his tailor?
PAROLLES
Sir?
LAFEU
O, I know him well, I, sir; he, sir,'s a good workman, a
very good tailor.
BERTRAM [*aside to* PAROLLES].
Is she gone to the king?
PAROLLES [*aside to* BERTRAM].
She is.

BERTRAM [*aside to* PAROLLES].
Will she away to-night?
PAROLLES [*aside to* BERTRAM].
As you'll have her.
BERTRAM [*aside to* PAROLLES].
I've writ my letters, casketed my treasure,
Given order for our horses; and to-night,
When I should take possession of the bride,
End ere I do begin.
LAFEU
A good traveller is something at the latter end of a
dinner; but one that lies three-thirds, and uses a known
truth to pass a thousand nothings with, should be once
heard, and thrice beaten. — God save you, captain.
BERTRAM
Is there any unkindness between my lord and you,
monsieur?
PAROLLES
I know not how I have deserved to run into my lord's
displeasure.
LAFEU
You have made shift to run into't, boots and spurs and
all, like him that leaped into the custard; and out of it
you'll run again, rather than suffer question for your
residence.
BERTRAM
It may be you have mistaken him, my lord.
LAFEU
And shall do so ever, though I took him at's prayers.
Fare you well, my lord; and believe this of me, there can
be no kernel in this light nut; the soul of this man is his
clothes: trust him not in matter of heavy consequence;
I have kept of them tame, and know their natures. —
Farewell, monsieur: I have spoken better of you than
you have worth or wit to deserve at my hand; but we
must do good against evil.   [*Exit.*
PAROLLES
An idle lord, I swear.
BERTRAM
I think so.
PAROLLES
Why, do you not know him?
BERTRAM
Yes, I do know him well; and common speech
Gives him a worthy pass. — Here comes my clog.

Enter HELENA.

HELENA
I have, sir, as I was commanded from you,
Spoke with the king, and have procur'd his leave
For present parting; only, he desires
Some private speech with you.
BERTRAM
I shall obey his will.
You must not marvel, Helen, at my course,
Which holds not colour with the time, nor does
The ministration and required office
On my particular. Prepared I was not
For such a business; therefore am I found
So much unsettled: this drives me to entreat you,
That presently you take your way for home,
And rather muse than ask why I entreat you;
For my respects are better than they seem,
And my appointments have in them a need
Greater than shows itself, at the first view,
To you that know them not. This to my mother:
     [*Giving a letter.*
'Twill be two days ere I shall see you; so,
I leave you to your wisdom.
HELENA
Sir, I can nothing say,
But that I am your most obedient servant.
BERTRAM
Come, come, no more of that.
HELENA
And ever shall
With true observance seek to eke out that
Wherein toward me my homely stars have fail'd
To equal my great fortune.
BERTRAM
Let that go:
My haste is very great: farewell, hie home.
HELENA
Pray, sir, your pardon.
BERTRAM
Well, what would you say?
HELENA
I am not worthy of the wealth I owe;
Nor dare I say 'tis mine, — and yet it is;
But, like a timorous thief, most fain would steal

What law does vouch mine own.
BERTRAM
What would you have?
HELENA
Something; and scarce so much: — nothing, indeed. —
I would not tell you what I would, my lord: —
Faith, yes; —
Strangers and foes do sunder, and not kiss.
BERTRAM
I pray you, stay not, but in haste to horse.
HELENA
I shall not break your bidding, good my lord.
BERTRAM
Where are my other men, monsieur? — Farewell.
     [*Exit* HELENA.
Go thou toward home; where I will never come,
Whilst I can shake my sword, or hear the drum. —
Away, and for our flight.
PAROLLES
Bravely, coragio!   [*Exeunt.*

ACT III

SCENE I
Florence. A room in the DUKE'S *palace.*

Flourish. Enter the DUKE OF FLORENCE, *two French*
LORDS *and a troop of* SOLDIERS.

DUKE
So that, from point to point, now have you heard
The fundamental reasons of this war;
Whose great decision hath much blood let forth,
And more thirsts after.
FIRST LORD
Holy seems the quarrel
Upon your Grace's part; black and fearful
On the opposer.
DUKE
Therefore we marvel much our cousin France
Would, in so just a business, shut his bosom
Against our borrowing prayers.
SECOND LORD
Good my lord,
The reasons of our state I cannot yield,
But like a common and an outward man,
That the great figure of a council frames
By self-unable motion: therefore dare not
Say what I think of it, since I have found
Myself in my incertain grounds to fail
As often as I guess'd.
DUKE
Be it his pleasure.
SECOND LORD
But I am sure the younger of our nation,
That surfeit on their ease, will day by day
Come here for physic.
DUKE
Welcome shall they be;
And all the honours that can fly from us
Shall on them settle. You know your places well;
When better fall, for your avails they fell:
To-morrow to the field.   [*Flourish. Exeunt.*

SCENE II
Rousillon. A room in the house of the COUNTESS.

Enter COUNTESS *and* CLOWN.

COUNTESS
It hath happen'd all as I would have had it, save that he
comes not along with her.
CLOWN
By my troth, I take my young lord to be a very
melancholy man.
COUNTESS
By what observance, I pray you?
CLOWN
Why, he will look upon his boot, and sing; mend the
ruff, and sing; ask questions, and sing; pick his teeth,
and sing. I know a man that had this trick of
melancholy sold a goodly manor for a song.
COUNTESS
Let me see what he writes, and when he means to come.
     [*Opening a letter.*
CLOWN
I have no mind to Isbel, since I was at court: our old
ling and our Isbels o'th'country are nothing like your
old ling and your Isbels o'th'court: the brains of my

Cupid's knock'd out; and I begin to love, as an old man
loves money, with no stomach.

COUNTESS
What have we here?

CLOWN
E'en that you have there.   [*Exit.*

COUNTESS [*reads*].
I have sent you a daughter-in-law: she hath recover'd
the king, and undone me. I have wedded her, not
bedded her; and sworn to make the 'not' eternal. You
shall hear I am run away: know it before the report
come. If there be breadth enough in the world, I will
hold a long distance. My duty to you. Your unfortunate
son,

                             BERTRAM.

This is not well, rash and unbridled boy,
To fly the favours of so good a king;
To pluck his indignation on thy head
By the misprising of a maid too virtuous
For the contempt of empire.
             Enter CLOWN.

CLOWN
O madam, yonder is heavy news within between two
soldiers and my young lady!

COUNTESS
What is the matter?

CLOWN
Nay, there is some comfort in the news, some comfort;
your son will not be kill'd so soon as I thought he
would.

COUNTESS
Why should he be kill'd?

CLOWN
So say I, madam, if he run away, as I hear he does: the
danger is in standing to't; that's the loss of men,
though it be the getting of children. Here they come
will tell you more: for my part, I only hear your son was
run away.   [*Exit.*
   Enter HELENA *and two* GENTLEMEN.

FIRST GENTLEMAN
Save you, good madam.

HELENA
Madam, my lord is gone, for ever gone.

SECOND GENTLEMAN
Do not say so.

COUNTESS
Think upon patience. — Pray you, gentlemen, —
I have felt so many quirks of joy and grief,
That the first face of neither, on the start,
Can woman me unto't: — where is my son, I pray you?

SECOND GENTLEMAN
Madam, he's gone to serve the Duke of Florence:
We met him thitherward; for thence we came,
And, after some dispatch in hand at court,
Thither we bend again.

HELENA
Look on his letter, madam; here's my passport. [*Reads*]
When thou canst get the ring upon my finger which
never shall come off, and show me a child begotten of
thy body that I am father to, then call me husband: but
in such a 'then' I write a 'never.'
This is a dreadful sentence.

COUNTESS
Brought you this letter, gentlemen?

FIRST GENTLEMAN
                    Ay, madam;
And, for the contents' sake, are sorry for our pains.

COUNTESS
I prithee, lady, have a better cheer;
If thou engrossest all the griefs are thine,
Thou robb'st me of a moiety: he was my son;
But I do wash his name out of my blood,
And thou art all my child. — Towards Florence is he?

SECOND GENTLEMAN
Ay, madam.

COUNTESS
              And to be a soldier?

SECOND GENTLEMAN
Such is his noble purpose: and, believe't,
The duke will lay upon him all the honour
That good convenience claims.

COUNTESS
               Return you thither?

FIRST GENTLEMAN
Ay, madam, with the swiftest wing of speed.

HELENA [*reads*].
'Till I have no wife, I have nothing in France.'
'Tis bitter.

COUNTESS
Find you that there?

HELENA
               Ay, madam.

FIRST GENTLEMAN
'Tis but the boldness of his hand, haply, which his
heart was not consenting to.

COUNTESS
Nothing in France, until he have no wife!
There's nothing here that is too good for him,
But only she; and she deserves a lord,
That twenty such rude boys might tend upon,
And call her hourly mistress. — Who was with him?

FIRST GENTLEMAN
A servant only, and a gentleman
Which I have sometime known.

COUNTESS
              Parolles, was't not?

FIRST GENTLEMAN
Ay, my good lady, he.

COUNTESS
A very tainted fellow, and full of wickedness.
My son corrupts a well-derived nature
With his inducement.

FIRST GENTLEMAN
             Indeed, good lady,
The fellow has a deal of that too much,
Which holds him much to have.

COUNTESS
Y' are welcome, gentlemen.
I will entreat you, when you see my son,
To tell him that his sword can never win
The honour that he loses: more I'll entreat you
Written to bear along.

SECOND GENTLEMAN
             We serve you, madam,
In that and all your worthiest affairs.

COUNTESS
Not so, but as we change our courtesies.
Will you draw near?
        [*Exeunt* COUNTESS *and* GENTLEMEN.

HELENA
'Till I have no wife, I have nothing in France.'
Nothing in France, until he has no wife!
Thou shalt have none, Rousillon, none in France;
Then hast thou all again. Poor lord! is't I
That chase thee from thy country, and expose
Those tender limbs of thine to the event
Of the none-sparing war? and is it I
That drive thee from the sportive court, where thou
Wast shot at with fair eyes, to be the mark
Of smoky muskets? O you leaden messengers,
That ride upon the violent speed of fire,
Fly with false aim; move the still-piecing air,
That sings with piercing; do not touch my lord!
Whoever shoots at him, I set him there;
Whoever charges on his forward breast,
I am the caitiff that do hold him to't;
And, though I kill him not, I am the cause
His death was so effected: better 'twere
I met the ravin lion when he roar'd
With sharp constraint of hunger; better 'twere
That all the miseries which nature owes
Were mine at once. No, come thou home, Rousillon,
Whence honour but of danger wins a scar,
As oft it loses all: I will be gone;
My being here it is that holds thee hence:
Shall I stay here to do't? no, no, although
The air of paradise did fan the house,
The angels offic'd all: I will be gone,
That pitiful rumour may report my flight,
To consolate thine ear. Come, night; end, day!
For with the dark, poor thief, I'll steal away.   [*Exit.*

SCENE III

Florence. Before the DUKE'S *palace.*

Flourish. Enter the DUKE OF FLORENCE,
BERTRAM, PAROLLES, SOLDIERS,
drum, and trumpets.

DUKE
The general of our horse thou art; and we,
Great in our hope, lay our best love and credence
Upon thy promising fortune.

BERTRAM
              Sir, it is
A charge too heavy for my strength; but yet
We'll strive to bear it, for your worthy sake,
To th'extreme edge of hazard.

DUKE
              Then go thou forth;
And Fortune play upon thy prosperous helm,
As thy auspicious mistress!

BERTRAM
             This very day,
Great Mars, I put myself into thy file:
Make me but like my thoughts, and I shall prove
A lover of thy drum, hater of love.   [*Exeunt.*

SCENE IV

Rousillon. A room in the house of the COUNTESS.

Enter COUNTESS *and* STEWARD.

COUNTESS
Alas! and would you take the letter of her?
Might you not know she would do as she has done,
By sending me a letter? Read it again.

STEWARD [*reads*].
I am Saint Jaques' pilgrim, thither gone:
   Ambitious love hath so in me offended,
That barefoot plod I the cold ground upon,
   With sainted vow my faults to have amended.
Write, write, that from the bloody course of war
   My dearest master, your dear son, may hie:
Bless him at home in peace, whilst I from far
   His name with zealous fervour sanctify:
His taken labours bid him me forgive;
   I, his despiteful Juno, sent him forth
From courtly friends, with camping foes to live,
   Where death and danger dogs the heels of worth:
He is too good and fair for death and me;
Whom I myself embrace, to set him free.

COUNTESS
Ah, what sharp stings are in her mildest words! —
Rinaldo, you did never lack advice so much,
As letting her pass so: had I spoke with her,
I could have well diverted her intents,
Which thus she hath prevented.

STEWARD
             Pardon me, madam:
If I had given you this at over-night,
She might have been o'erta'en; and yet she writes,
Pursuit would be but vain.

COUNTESS
           What angel shall
Bless this unworthy husband? he cannot thrive,
Unless her prayers, whom heaven delights to hear,
And loves to grant, reprieve him from the wrath
Of greatest justice. — Write, write, Rinaldo,
To this unworthy husband of his wife;
Let every word weigh heavy of her worth,
That he does weigh too light: my greatest grief,
Though little he do feel it, set down sharply.
Dispatch the most convenient messenger: —
When haply he shall hear that she is gone,
He will return; and hope I may that she,
Hearing so much, will speed her foot again,
Led hither by pure love: which of them both
Is dearest to me, I have no skill in sense
To make distinction: — provide this messenger: —
My heart is heavy and mine age is weak;
Grief would have tears, and sorrow bids me speak.
                          [*Exeunt.*

SCENE V

Without the walls of Florence. A tucket afar off.

Enter an old WIDOW *of Florence,* DIANA, VIOLENTA,
MARIANA, *with other* CITIZENS.

WIDOW
Nay, come; for if they do approach the city, we shall lose
all the sight.

DIANA
They say the French count has done most honourable
service.

WIDOW
It is reported that he has taken their greatest
commander; and that with his own hand he slew the
duke's brother. [*Tucket.*] We have lost our labour; they
are gone a contrary way: hark! you may know by their
trumpets.

MARIANA
Come, let's return again, and suffice ourselves with the
report of it. Well, Diana, take heed of this French earl:
the honour of a maid is her name; and no legacy is so
rich as honesty.

WIDOW
I have told my neighbour how you have been solicited
by a gentleman his companion.

MARIANA

I know that knave; hang him! one Parolles: a filthy officer he is in those suggestions for the young earl. — Beware of them, Diana; their promises, enticements, oaths, tokens, and all these engines of lust, are not the things they go under: many a maid hath been seduced by them; and the misery is, example, that so terrible shows in the wrack of maidenhood, cannot for all that dissuade succession, but that they are limed with the twigs that threaten them. I hope I need not to advise you further; but I hope your own grace will keep you where you are, though there were no further danger known but the modesty which is so lost.

DIANA

You shall not need to fear me.

WIDOW

I hope so. — Look, here comes a pilgrim: I know she will lie at my house; thither they send one another: I'll question her.

Enter HELENA, *in the dress of a pilgrim.*

God save you, pilgrim! whither are you bound?

HELENA

To Saint Jaques le Grand.
Where do the palmers lodge, I do beseech you?

WIDOW

At the Saint Francis here, beside the port.

HELENA

Is this the way?

WIDOW

Ay, marry, is't. — Hark you! they come this way. —
                                        [*A march afar off.*
If you will tarry, holy pilgrim,
But till the troops come by,
I will conduct you where you shall be lodg'd;
The rather, for I think I know your hostess
As ample as myself.

HELENA

                        Is it yourself?

WIDOW

If you shall please so, pilgrim.

HELENA

I thank you, and will stay upon your leisure.

WIDOW

You came, I think, from France?

HELENA

                        I did so.

WIDOW

Here you shall see a countryman of yours
That has done worthy service.

HELENA

                        His name, I pray you.

DIANA

The Count Rousillon: know you such a one?

HELENA

But by the ear, that hears most nobly of him:
His face I know not.

DIANA

                        Whatsome'er he is,
He's bravely taken here. He stole from France
As 'tis reported, for the king had married him
Against his liking: think you it is so?

HELENA

Ay, surely, mere the truth: I know his lady.

DIANA

There is a gentleman that serves the count
Reports but coarsely of her.

HELENA

                        What's his name?

DIANA

Monsieur Parolles.

HELENA

                        O, I believe with him,
In argument of praise, or to the worth
Of the great count himself, she is too mean
To have her name repeated: all her deserving
Is a reserved honesty, and that
I have not heard examin'd.

DIANA

                        Alas, poor lady!
'Tis a hard bondage to become the wife
Of a detesting lord.

WIDOW

I write good creature; wheresoe'er she is,
Her heart weighs sadly: this young maid might do her
A shrewd turn, if she pleas'd.

HELENA

                        How do you mean?
May be the amorous count solicits her
In the unlawful purpose.

WIDOW

He does indeed;
And brokes with all that can in such a suit
Corrupt the tender honour of a maid:
But she is arm'd for him, and keeps her guard
In honestest defence.

MARIANA

                        The gods forbid else!

WIDOW

So, now they come: —

Drum and colours.

Enter BERTRAM, PAROLLES, *and the whole army.*

That is Antonio, the duke's eldest son;
That, Escalus.

HELENA

                        Which is the Frenchman?

DIANA

                        He;
That with the plume: 'tis a most gallant fellow.
I would he lov'd his wife: if he were honester
He were much goodlier: is't not a handsome
        gentleman?

HELENA

I like him well.

DIANA

'Tis pity he is not honest: yond's that same knave
That leads him to these passes: were I his lady,
I would poison that vile rascal.

HELENA

                        Which is he?

DIANA

That jack-an-apes with scarfs: why is he melancholy?

HELENA

Perchance he's hurt i' the battle.

PAROLLES

Lose our drum! well.

MARIANA

He's shrewdly vex'd at something: look, he has spied us.

WIDOW

Marry, hang you!

MARIANA

And your courtesy, for a ring-carrier!
                        [*Exeunt* BERTRAM, PAROLLES, *etc.*

WIDOW

The troop is pass'd. Come, pilgrim, I will bring you
Where you shall host: of enjoin'd penitents
There's four or five, to Great Saint Jaques bound,
Already at my house.

HELENA

                        I humbly thank you:
Please it this matron and this gentle maid
To eat with us to-night, the charge and thanking
Shall be for me; and, to requite you further,
I will bestow some precepts of this virgin
Worthy the note.

BOTH

                We'll take your offer kindly.   [*Exeunt.*

SCENE VI

Camp before Florence.

Enter BERTRAM *and the two French* LORDS.

FIRST LORD

Nay, good my lord, put him to't; let him have his way.

SECOND LORD

If your lordship find him not a hilding, hold me no more in your respect.

FIRST LORD

On my life, my lord, a bubble.

BERTRAM

Do you think I am so far deceived in him?

FIRST LORD

Believe it, my lord, in mine own direct knowledge, without any malice, but to speak of him as my kinsman, he's a most notable coward, an infinite and endless liar, an hourly promise-breaker, the owner of no one good quality worthy your lordship's entertainment.

SECOND LORD

It were fit you knew him; lest, reposing too far in his virtue, which he hath not, he might at some great and trusty business, in a main danger fail you.

BERTRAM

I would I knew in what particular action to try him.

SECOND LORD

None better than to let him fetch off his drum, which you hear him so confidently undertake to do.

FIRST LORD

I, with a troop of Florentines, will suddenly surprise him; such I will have, whom, I am sure, he knows not from the enemy: we will bind and hoodwink him so, that he shall suppose no other but that he is carried into the leaguer of the adversaries, when we bring him to our own tents. Be but your lordship present at his examination: if he do not, for the promise of his life, and in the highest compulsion of base fear, offer to betray you, and deliver all the intelligence in his power against you, and that with the divine forfeit of his soul upon oath, never trust my judgement in any thing.

SECOND LORD

O, for the love of laughter, let him fetch off his drum; he says he has a stratagem for't: when your lordship sees the bottom of his success in't, and to what metal this counterfeit lump of ore will be melted, if you give him not John Drum's entertainment, your inclining cannot be removed. — Here he comes.

FIRST LORD

O, for the love of laughter, hinder not the homour of his design: let him fetch off his drum in any hand.

Enter PAROLLES.

BERTRAM

How now, monsieur! this drum sticks sorely in your disposition.

SECOND LORD

A pox on't, let it go; 'tis but a drum.

PAROLLES

But a drum! is't but a drum? A drum so lost! — There was excellent command, — to charge in with our horse upon our own wings, and to rend our own soldiers!

SECOND LORD

That was not to be blamed in the command of the service: it was a disaster of war that Cæsar himself could not have prevented, if he had been there to command.

BERTRAM

Well, we cannot greatly condemn our success: some dishonour we had in the loss of that drum; but it is not to be recover'd.

PAROLLES

It might have been recover'd.

BERTRAM

It might; but it is not now.

PAROLLES

It is to be recover'd: but that the merit of service is seldom attributed to the true and exact performer, I would have that drum or another, or *hic jacet.*

BERTRAM

Why, if you have a stomach, to't, monsieur, if you think your mystery in stratagem can bring this instrument of honour again into his native quarter, be magnanimous in the enterprise, and go on; I will grace the attempt for a worthy exploit: if you speed well in it, the duke shall both speak of it, and extend to you what further becomes his greatness, even to the utmost syllable of your worthiness.

PAROLLES

By the hand of a soldier, I will undertake it.

BERTRAM

But you must not now slumber in it.

PAROLLES

I'll about it this evening: and I will presently pen down my dilemmas, encourage myself in my certainty, put myself into my mortal preparation; and, by midnight, look to hear further from me.

BERTRAM

May I be bold to acquaint his Grace you are gone about it?

PAROLLES

I know not what the success will be, my lord; but the attempt I vow.

BERTRAM

I know th'art valiant; and, to the possibility of thy soldiership, will subscribe for thee. Farewell.

PAROLLES

I love not many words.   [*Exit.*

FIRST LORD

No more than a fish loves water. — Is not this a strange fellow, my lord, that so confidently seems to undertake this business, which he knows is not to be done; damns himself to do, and dares better be damn'd than to do't?

SECOND LORD

You do not know him, my lord, as we do: certain it is, that he will steal himself into a man's favour, and for a week escape a great deal of discoveries; but when you find him out, you have him ever after.

BERTRAM
Why, do you think he will make no deed at all of this, that so seriously he does address himself unto?

FIRST LORD
None in the world; but return with an invention, and clap upon you two or three probable lies: but we have almost emboss'd him, — you shall see his fall to-night; for indeed he is not for your lordship's respect.

SECOND LORD
We'll make you some sport with the fox, ere we case him. He was first smoked by the old Lord Lafeu: when his disguise and he is parted, tell me what a sprat you shall find him: which you shall see this very night.

FIRST LORD
I must go look my twigs: he shall be caught.

BERTRAM
Your brother, he shall go along with me.

FIRST LORD
As't please your lordship: I'll leave you.   [*Exit.*

BERTRAM
Now will I lead you to the house, and show you The lass I spoke of.

SECOND LORD
But you say she's honest.

BERTRAM
That's all the fault: I spoke with her but once, And found her wondrous cold; but I sent to her, By this same coxcomb that we have i' the wind, Tokens and letters which she did re-send; And this is all I have done. She's a fair creature: Will you go see her?

SECOND LORD
                    With all my heart, my lord. [*Exeunt.*

SCENE VII

Florence. A room in the WIDOW'S *house.*

Enter HELENA *and* WIDOW.

HELENA
If you misdoubt me that I am not she, I know not how I shall assure you further, But I shall lose the grounds I work upon.

WIDOW
Though my estate be fall'n, I was well born, Nothing acquainted with these businesses; And would not put my reputation now In any staining act.

HELENA
                    Nor would I wish you. First, give me trust, the count he is my husband, And what to your sworn counsel I have spoken Is so from word to word; and then you cannot, By the good aid that I of you shall borrow, Err in bestowing it.

WIDOW
                    I should believe you; For you have show'd me that which well approves Y'are great in fortune.

HELENA
                    Take this purse of gold, And let me buy your friendly help thus far, Which I will over-pay and pay again, When I have found it. The count he woos your daughter, Lays down his wanton siege before her beauty, Resolv'd to carry her: let her, in fine, consent, As we'll direct her how 'tis best to bear it; Now his impatient blood will naught deny That she'll demand: a ring the county wears, That downward hath succeeded in his house From son to son, some four or five descents Since the first father wore it: this ring he holds In most rich choice; yet in his idle fire, To buy his will, it would not seem too dear, Howe'er repented after.

WIDOW
                    Now I see The bottom of your purpose.

HELENA
You see it lawful, then: it is no more, But that your daughter, ere she seems as won, Desires this ring; appoints him an encounter; In fine, delivers me to fill the time, Herself most chastely absent: after this, To marry her, I'll add three thousand crowns To what is pass'd already.

WIDOW
                    I have yielded: Instruct my daughter how she shall persever,

That time and place with this deceit so lawful May prove coherent. Every night he comes With music of all sorts, and songs compos'd To her unworthiness: it nothing steads us To chide him from our eaves; for he persists, As if his life lay on't.

HELENA
                    Why, then, to-night Let us assay our plot; which, if it speed, Is wicked meaning in a lawful deed, And lawful meaning in unlawful act; Where both not sin, and yet a sinful fact: But let's about it.   [*Exeunt.*

ACT IV

SCENE I

Without the Florentine camp.

Enter first French LORD, *with five or six other* SOLDIERS, *in ambush.*

FIRST LORD
He can come no other way but by this hedge-corner. When you sally upon him, speak what terrible language you will, — though you understand it not yourselves, no matter; for we must not seem to understand him, unless some one among us, whom we must produce for an interpreter.

FIRST SOLDIER
Good captain, let me be th'interpreter.

FIRST LORD
Art not acquainted with him? knows he not thy voice?

FIRST SOLDIER
No, sir, I warrant you.

FIRST LORD
But what linsey-woolsey hast thou to speak to us again?

FIRST SOLDIER
E'en such as you speak to me.

FIRST LORD
He must think us some band of strangers i' the adversary's entertainment. Now, he hath a smack of all neighbouring languages; therefore we must every one be a man of his own fancy, not to know what we speak one to another; so we seem to know, is to know straight our purpose: choughs' language, gabble enough, and good enough. As for you, interpreter, you must seem very politic. — But couch, ho! here he comes, — to beguile two hours in a sleep, and then to return and swear the lies he forges.

Enter PAROLLES.

PAROLLES
Ten o'clock: within these three hours 'twill be time enough to go home. What shall I say I have done? It must be a very plausive invention that carries it: they begin to smoke me; and disgraces have of late knock'd too often at my door. I find my tongue is too foolhardy; but my heart hath the fear of Mars before it and of his creatures, not daring the reports of my tongue.

FIRST LORD [*aside*].
This is the first truth that e'er thine own tongue was guilty of.

PAROLLES
What the devil should move me to undertake the recovery of this drum, being not ignorant of the impossibility, and knowing I had no such purpose? I must give myself some hurts, and say I got them in exploit: yet slight ones will not carry it; they will say, 'Came you off with so little?' and great ones I dare not give. Wherefore, what's the instance? Tongue, I must put you into a butter-woman's mouth, and buy myself another of Bajazet's mule, if you prattle me into these perils.

FIRST LORD [*aside*].
Is it possible he should know what he is, and be that he is?

PAROLLES
I would the cutting of my garments would serve the turn, or the breaking of my Spanish sword.

FIRST LORD [*aside*].
We cannot afford you so.

PAROLLES
Or the baring of my beard; and to say it was in stratagem.

FIRST LORD [*aside*].
'Twould not do.

PAROLLES
Or to drown my clothes, and say I was stripp'd—

FIRST LORD [*aside*].
Hardly serve.

PAROLLES
Though I swore I leapt from the window of the citadel —

FIRST LORD [*aside*].
How deep?

PAROLLES
Thirty fadom.

FIRST LORD [*aside*].
Three great oaths would scarce make that be believed.

PAROLLES
I would I had any drum of the enemy's: I would swear I recover'd it.

FIRST LORD [*aside*].
You shall hear one anon.   [*Alarum within.*

PAROLLES
A drum now of the enemy's!

FIRST LORD
Throca movousus, cargo, cargo, cargo.

ALL
Cargo, cargo, cargo, villianda par corbo, cargo.

PAROLLES
O, ransom, ransom! — do not hide mine eyes.
          [*They seize and blindfold him.*

FIRST SOLDIER
Boskos thromuldo boskos.

PAROLLES
I know you are the Muskos' regiment; And I shall lose my life for want of language: If there be here German, or Dane, low Dutch, Italian, or French, let him speak to me; I'll discover that which shall undo the Florentine.

FIRST SOLDIER
Boskos vauvado: — I understand thee, and can speak thy tongue: — *Kerelybonto:* — sir, Betake thee to thy faith, for seventeen poniards Are at thy bosom.

PAROLLES
                    O!

FIRST SOLDIER
                    O, pray, pray, pray! — *Manka revania dulche.*

FIRST LORD
Oscorbidulchos volivorco.

FIRST LORD
The general is content to spare thee yet; And, hoodwink'd as thou art, will lead thee on To gather from thee: haply thou mayst inform Something to save thy life.

PAROLLES
                    O, let me live! And all the secrets of our camp I'll show, Their force, their purposes; nay, I'll speak that Which you will wonder at.

FIRST SOLDIER
                    But wilt thou faithfully?

PAROLLES
If I do not, damn me.

FIRST SOLDIER
                    Acordo linta: — Come on; thou art granted space.
          [*Exit, with* PAROLLES *guarded. A short alarum within.*

FIRST LORD
Go, tell the Count Rousillon, and my brother, We have caught the woodcock, and will keep him muffled Till we do hear from them.

SECOND SOLDIER
                    Captain, I will.

FIRST LORD
A' will betray us all unto ourselves: — Inform 'em that.

SECOND SOLDIER
                    So I will, sir.

FIRST LORD
Till then I'll keep him dark and safely lock'd.   [*Exeunt.*

SCENE II

Florence. A room in the WIDOW'S *house.*

Enter BERTRAM *and* DIANA.

BERTRAM
They told me that your name was Fontibell.

DIANA
No, my good lord, Diana.

BERTRAM
                    Titled goddess;

And worth it, with addition! But, fair soul,
In your fine frame hath love no quality?
If the quick fire of youth light not your mind,
You are no maiden, but a monument:
When you are dead, you should be such a one
As you are now, for you are cold and stern;
And now you should be as your mother was
When your sweet self was got.

DIANA
She then was honest.

BERTRAM
          So should you be.

DIANA
                  No:
My mother did but duty; such, my lord,
As you owe to your wife.

BERTRAM
          No more o' that, —
I prithee, do not strive against my vows:
I was compell'd to her; but I love thee
By love's own sweet constraint, and will for ever
Do thee all rights of service.

DIANA
          Ay, so you serve us
Till we serve you; but when you have our roses,
You barely leave our thorns to prick ourselves,
And mock us with our bareness.

BERTRAM
          How have I sworn!

DIANA
'Tis not the many oaths that makes the truth,
But the plain single vow that is vow'd true.
What is not holy, that we swear not by,
But take the High'st to witness: then, pray you, tell me,
If I should swear by Jove's great attributes,
I lov'd you dearly, would you believe my oaths,
When I did love you ill? this has no holding,
To swear by him whom I protest to love,
That I will work against him. Therefore your oaths
Are words and poor conditions; but unseal'd;
At least in my opinion.

BERTRAM
          Change it, change it;
Be not so holy-cruel: love is holy;
And my integrity ne'er knew the crafts
That you do charge men with. Stand no more off,
But give thyself unto my sick desires,
Who then recover: say thou art mine, and ever
My love as it begins shall so persever.

DIANA
I see that men make ropes in such a scarr,
That we'll forsake ourselves. Give me that ring.

BERTRAM
I'll lend it thee, my dear; but have no power
To give it from me.

DIANA
          Will you not, my lord?

BERTRAM
It is an honour 'longing to our house,
Bequeathed down from many ancestors;
Which were the greatest obloquy i' the world
In me to lose.

DIANA
          Mine honour's such a ring:
My chastity's the jewel of our house,
Bequeathed down from many ancestors;
Which were the greatest obloquy i' the world
In me to lose: thus your own proper wisdom
Brings in the champion honour on my part,
Against your vain assault.

BERTRAM
          Here, take my ring:
My house, mine honour, yea, my life, be thine,
And I'll be bid by thee.

DIANA
When midnight comes, knock at my chamber-window:
I'll order take my mother shall not hear.
Now will I charge you in the band of truth,
When you have conquer'd my yet maiden bed,
Remain there but an hour, nor speak to me:
My reasons are most strong; and you shall know them
When back again this ring shall be deliver'd:
And on your finger, in the night, I'll put
Another ring, that what in time proceeds
May token to the future our past deeds.
Adieu, till then; then fail not. You have won
A wife of me, though there my hope be done.

BERTRAM
A heaven on earth I have won by wooing thee.   [*Exit.*

DIANA
For which live long to thank both heaven and me!
You may so in the end. —
My mother told me just how he would woo,
As if she sat in's heart; she says all men
Have the like oaths: he had sworn to marry me
When his wife's dead; therefore I'll lie with him
When I am buried. Since Frenchmen are so braid,
Marry that will, I live and die a maid:
Only, in this disguise, I think't no sin
To cozen him that would unjustly win.   [*Exit.*

SCENE III

The Florentine camp.

Enter the two French LORDS *and some
two or three* SOLDIERS.

FIRST LORD
You have not given him his mother's letter?

SECOND LORD
I have deliver'd it an hour since: there is something in't
that stings his nature; for, on the reading it, he changed
almost into another man.

FIRST LORD
He has much worthy blame laid upon him for shaking
off so good a wife and so sweet a lady.

SECOND LORD
Especially he hath incurr'd the everlasting displeasure
of the king, who had even tuned his bounty to sing
happiness to him. I will tell you a thing, but you shall
let it dwell darkly with you.

FIRST LORD
When you have spoken it, 'tis dead, and I am the grave
of it.

SECOND LORD
He hath perverted a young gentlewoman here in
Florence, of a most chaste renown; and this night he
fleshes his will in the spoil of her honour: he hath given
her his monumental ring, and thinks himself made in
the unchaste composition.

FIRST LORD
Now, God delay our rebellion! as we are ourselves,
what things are we!

SECOND LORD
Merely our own traitors. And as in the common course
of all treasons, we still see them reveal themselves, till
they attain to their abhorr'd ends, so he that in this
action contrives against his own nobility, in his proper
stream o'erflows himself.

FIRST LORD
Is it not meant damnable in us, to be trumpeters of our
unlawful intents? We shall not, then, have his company
to-night?

SECOND LORD
Not till after midnight; for he is dieted to his hour.

FIRST LORD
That approaches apace: I would gladly have him see his
company anatomised, that he might take a measure of
his own judgements, wherein so curiously he had set
this counterfeit.

SECOND LORD
We will not meddle with him till he come; for his
presence must be the whip of the other.

FIRST LORD
In the mean time, what hear you of these wars?

SECOND LORD
I hear there is an overture of peace.

FIRST LORD
Nay, I assure you, a peace concluded.

SECOND LORD
What will Count Rousillon do then? will he travel higher,
or return again into France?

FIRST LORD
I perceive, by this demand, you are not altogether of his
council.

SECOND LORD
Let it be forbid, sir! so should I be a great deal of his act.

FIRST LORD
Sir, his wife, some two months since, fled from his
house; her pretence is a pilgrimage to Saint Jaques le
Grand; which holy undertaking, with most austere
sanctimony, she accomplish'd, and, there residing, the
tenderness of her nature became as a prey to her grief;
in fine, made a groan of her last breath; and now she
sings in heaven.

SECOND LORD
How is this justified?

FIRST LORD
The stronger part of it by her own letters, which make

her story true, even to the point of her death: her death
itself, which could not be her office to say is come, was
faithfully confirm'd by the rector of the place.

SECOND LORD
Hath the count all this intelligence?

FIRST LORD
Ay, and the particular confirmations, point from point,
to the full arming of the verity.

SECOND LORD
I am heartily sorry that he'll be glad of this.

FIRST LORD
How mightily sometimes we make us comforts of our
losses!

SECOND LORD
And how mightily some other times we drown our gain
in tears! The great dignity that his valour hath here
acquired for him shall at home be encounter'd with a
shame as ample.

FIRST LORD
The web of our life is of a mingled yarn, good and ill
together: our virtues would be proud, if our faults
whipp'd them not: and our crimes would despair, if
they were not cherish'd by our virtues.

Enter a MESSENGER.

How now! where's your master?

MESSENGER
He met the duke in the street, sir, of whom he hath
taken a solemn leave: his lordship will next morning
for France. The duke hath offer'd him letters of
commendations to the king.   [*Exit.*

SECOND LORD
They shall be no more than needful there, if they were
more than they can commend.

FIRST LORD
They cannot be too sweet for the king's tartness.
Here's his lordship now.

Enter BERTRAM.

How now, my lord! is't not after midnight?

BERTRAM
I have to-night dispatch'd sixteen businesses, a
month's length a-piece, by an abstract of success: I
have congied with the duke, done my adieu with his
nearest; buried a wife, mourn'd for her; writ to my lady
mother I am returning; entertain'd my convoy; and
between these main parcels of dispatch, effected many
nicer needs: the last was the greatest, but that I have not
ended yet.

SECOND LORD
If the business be of any difficulty, and this morning
your departure hence, it requires haste of your
lordship.

BERTRAM
I mean, the business is not ended, as fearing to hear of it
hereafter. But we shall have this dialogue between the
fool and the soldier? — Come, bring forth this
counterfeit module, has deceiv'd me, like a
double-meaning prophesier.

SECOND LORD
Bring him forth [*exeunt* SOLDIERS]: — has sat i' the
stocks all night, poor gallant knave.

BERTRAM
No matter: his heels have deserved it, in usurping his
spurs so long. How does he carry himself?

SECOND LORD
I have told your lordship already, — the stocks carry
him. But, to answer you as you would be understood;
he weeps like a wench that had shed her milk: he hath
confess'd himself to Morgan, whom he supposes to be
a friar, from the time of his remembrance to this very
instant disaster of his setting i' the stocks: and what
think you he hath confess'd?

BERTRAM
Nothing of me, has a'?

SECOND LORD
His confession is taken, and it shall be read to his face:
if your lordship be in't, as I believe you are, you must
have the patience to hear it.

Enter SOLDIERS *with* PAROLLES *muffled.*

BERTRAM
A plague upon him! muffled! he can say nothing of me.

FIRST LORD
Hush, hush! Hoodman comes. — *Portotartarossa.*

FIRST SOLDIER
He calls for the tortures: what will you say without 'em?

PAROLLES
I will confess what I know without constraint: if ye
pinch me like a pasty, I can say no more.

FIRST SOLDIER
Bosko chimurcho.

FIRST SOLDIER So, look about you: know you any here?

FIRST LORD
Boblibindo chicurmurco.

FIRST SOLDIER
You are a merciful general. — Our general bids you answer to what I shall ask you out of a note.

PAROLLES
And truly, as I hope to live.

FIRST SOLDIER [*reads*].
'First demand of him how many horse the duke is strong.' What say you to that?

PAROLLES
Five or six thousand; but very weak and unserviceable: the troops are all scatter'd, and the commanders very poor rogues, upon my reputation and credit, and as I hope to live.

FIRST SOLDIER
Shall I set down your answer so?

PAROLLES
Do: I'll take the sacrament on't, how and which way you will.

BERTRAM
All's one to him. What a past-saving slave is this!

FIRST LORD
Y'are deceiv'd, my lord: this is Monsieur Parolles, the gallant militarist, — that was his own phrase, — that had the whole theoric of war in the knot of his scarf, and the practice in the chape of his dagger.

SECOND LORD
I will never trust a man again for keeping his sword clean; nor believe he can have every thing in him by wearing his apparel neatly.

FIRST SOLDIER
Well, that's set down.

PAROLLES
Five or six thousand horse, I said, — I will say true, — or thereabouts, set down, — for I'll speak truth.

FIRST LORD
He's very near the truth in this.

BERTRAM
But I con him no thanks for't, in the nature he delivers it.

PAROLLES
Poor rogues, I pray you, say.

FIRST SOLDIER
Well, that's set down.

PAROLLES
I humbly thank you, sir. A truth's a truth, — the rogues are marvellous poor.

FIRST SOLDIER [*reads*].
'Demand of him, of what strength they are a-foot.' What say you to that?

PAROLLES
By my troth, sir, if I were to live this present hour, I will tell true. Let me see: Spurio, a hundred and fifty; Sebastian, so many; Corambus, so many; Jaques, so many; Guiltian, Cosmo, Lodowick, and Gratii, two hundred fifty each; mine own company, Chitopher, Vaumond, Bentii, two hundred fifty each: so that the muster-file, rotten and sound, upon my life, amounts not to fifteen thousand poll; half of the which dare not shake snow from off their cassocks, lest they shake themselves to pieces.

BERTRAM
What shall be done to him?

FIRST LORD
Nothing, but let him have thanks. — Demand of him my condition, and what credit I have with the duke.

FIRST SOLDIER
Well, that's set down. [*Reads*] 'You shall demand of him, whether one Captain Dumain be i' the camp, a Frenchman; what his reputation is with the duke; what his valour, honesty, and expertness in wars; or whether he thinks it were not possible, with well-weighing sums of gold, to corrupt him to revolt.' What say you to this? what do you know of it?

PAROLLES
I beseech you, let me answer to the particular of the inter'gatories: demand them singly.

FIRST SOLDIER
Do you know this Captain Dumain?

PAROLLES
I know him: a' was a botcher's 'prentice in Paris, from whence he was whipp'd for getting the shrieve's fool with child, — a dumb innocent, that could not say him nay. [FIRST LORD *lifts up his hand in anger.*

BERTRAM
Nay, by your leave, hold your hands; though I know his brains are forfeit to the next tile that falls.

FIRST SOLDIER
Well, is this captain in the Duke of Florence's camp?

PAROLLES
Upon my knowledge, he is, and lousy.

FIRST LORD
Nay, look not so upon me; we shall hear of your lordship anon.

FIRST SOLDIER
What is his reputation with the duke?

PAROLLES
The duke knows him for no other but a poor officer of mine; and writ to me this other day to turn him out o' the band: I think I have his letter in my pocket.

FIRST SOLDIER
Marry, we'll search.

PAROLLES
In good sadness, I do not know; either it is there, or it is upon a file, with the duke's other letters, in my tent.

FIRST SOLDIER
Here 'tis; here's a paper: shall I read it to you?

PAROLLES
I do not know if it be it or no.

BERTRAM
Our interpreter does it well.

FIRST LORD
Excellently.

FIRST SOLDIER [*reads*].
Dian, the count's a fool, and full of gold, —

PAROLLES
That is not the duke's letter, sir; that is an advertisement to a proper maid in Florence, one Diana, to take heed of the allurement of one Count Rousillon, a foolish idle boy, but, for all that, very ruttish: I pray you, sir, put it up again.

FIRST SOLDIER
Nay, I'll read it first, by your favour.

PAROLLES
My meaning in't, I protest, was very honest in the behalf of the maid; for I knew the young count to be a dangerous and lascivious boy, who is a whale to virginity, and devours up all the fry it finds.

BERTRAM
Damnable both-sides rogue!

FIRST SOLDIER [*reads*].
When he swears oaths, bid him drop gold, and take it;
   After he scores, he never pays the score:
Half won is match well made; match, and well make it;
   He ne'er pays after-debts, take it before;
And say a soldier, Dian, told thee this,
Men are to mell with, boys are but to kiss:
For count of this, the count's a fool, I know it,
Who pays before, but not when he does owe it.
   Thine, as he vow'd to thee in thine ear,
                        PAROLLES.

BERTRAM
He shall be whipp'd through the army, with this rime in's forehead.

SECOND LORD
This is your devoted friend, sir, the manifold linguist and the armipotent soldier.

BERTRAM
I could endure any thing before but a cat, and now he's a cat to me.

FIRST SOLDIER
I perceive, sir, by the general's looks, we shall be fain to hang you.

PAROLLES
My life, sir, in any case: not that I am afraid to die; but that, my offences being many, I would repent out the remainder of nature: let me live, sir, in a dungeon, i' the stocks, or any where, so I may live.

FIRST SOLDIER
We'll see what may be done, so you confess freely; therefore, once more to this Captain Dumain: you have answer'd to his reputation with the duke, and to his valour: what is his honesty?

PAROLLES
He will steal, sir, an egg out of a cloister: for rapes and

ravishments he parallels Nessus: he professes not keeping of oaths; in breaking 'em he is stronger than Hercules: he will lie, sir, with such volubility, that you would think truth were a fool: drunkenness is his best virtue, for he will be swine-drunk; and in his sleep he does little harm, save to his bed-clothes about him; but they know his conditions, and lay him in straw. I have but little more to say, sir, of his honesty: he has every thing that an honest man should not have; what an honest man should have, he has nothing.

FIRST LORD
I begin to love him for this.

BERTRAM
For this description of thine honesty? A pox upon him for me, he's more and more a cat.

FIRST SOLDIER
What say you to his expertness in war?

PAROLLES
Faith, sir, has led the drum before the English tragedians, — to belie him, I will not, — and more of his soldiership I know not; except, in that country he had the honour to be the officer at a place there called Mile-end, to instruct for the doubling of files: I would do the man what honour I can, but of this I am not certain.

FIRST LORD
He hath out-villain'd villainy so far, that the rarity redeems him.

BERTRAM
A pox on him, he's a cat still.

FIRST SOLDIER
His qualities being at this poor price, I need not to ask you if gold will corrupt him to revolt.

PAROLLES
Sir, for a cardecu he will sell the fee-simple of his salvation, the inheritance of it; and cut th'entail from all remainders, and a perpetual succession for it perpetually.

FIRST SOLDIER
What's his brother, the other Captain Dumain?

SECOND LORD
Why does he ask him of me?

FIRST SOLDIER
What's he?

PAROLLES
E'en a crow o' the same nest; not altogether so great as the first in goodness, but greater a great deal in evil: he excels his brother for a coward, yet his brother is reputed one of the best that is: in a retreat he outruns any lackey; marry, in coming on he has the cramp.

FIRST SOLDIER
If your life be saved, will you undertake to betray the Florentine?

PAROLLES
Ay, and the captain of his horse, Count Rousillon.

FIRST SOLDIER
I'll whisper with the general, and know his pleasure.

PAROLLES [aside].
I'll no more drumming; a plague of all drums! Only to seem to deserve well, and to beguile the supposition of that lascivious young boy the count, have I run into this danger: yet who would have suspected an ambush where I was taken?

FIRST SOLDIER
There is no remedy, sir, but you must die: the general says, you that have so traitorously discover'd the secrets of your army, and made such pestiferous reports of men very nobly held, can serve the world for no honest use; therefore you must die. — Come, headsman, off with his head.

PAROLLES
O Lord, sir, let me live, or let me see my death!

FIRST SOLDIER
That shall you, and take your leave of all your friends.
[Unmuffling him.
So, look about you: know you any here?

BERTRAM
Good morrow, noble captain.

SECOND LORD
God bless you, Captain Parolles.

FIRST LORD
God save you, noble captain.

SECOND LORD
Captain, what greeting will you to my Lord Lafeu? I am for France.

FIRST LORD
Good captain, will you give me a copy of the sonnet you writ to Diana in behalf of the Count Rousillon? an I were not a very coward, I'ld compel it of you; but fare you well.
[Exeunt BERTRAM and LORDS.

FIRST SOLDIER
You are undone, captain; all but your scarf, that has a knot on't yet.

PAROLLES
Who cannot be crush'd with a plot?

FIRST SOLDIER
If you could find out a country where but women were that had received so much shame, you might begin an impudent nation. Fare ye well, sir; I am for France too: we shall speak of you there. [Exit with SOLDIERS.

PAROLLES
Yet am I thankful: if my heart were great,
'Twould burst at this. Captain I'll be no more;
But I will eat and drink, and sleep as soft
As captain shall: simply the thing I am
Shall make me live. Who knows himself a braggart,
Let him fear this; for it will come to pass,
That every braggart shall be found an ass.
Rust, sword! cool, blushes! and, Parolles, live
Safest in shame! being fool'd, by foolery thrive!
There's place and means for every man alive.
I'll after them. [Exit.

SCENE IV

Florence. A room in the WIDOW'S house.

Enter HELENA, WIDOW, and DIANA.

HELENA
That you may well perceive I have not wrong'd you,
One of the greatest in the Christian world
Shall be my surety; 'fore whose throne 'tis needful,
Ere I can perfect mine intents, to kneel:
Time was, I did him a desired office,
Dear almost as his life; which gratitude
Through flinty Tartar's bosom would peep forth,
And answer, thanks: I duly am inform'd
His Grace is at Marseilles; to which place
We have convenient convoy. You must know,
I am supposed dead: the army breaking,
My husband hies him home; where, heaven aiding,
And by the leave of my good lord the king,
We'll be before our welcome.

WIDOW
                    Gentle madam,
You never had a servant to whose trust
Your business was more welcome.

HELENA
                    Nor you, mistress,
Ever a friend whose thoughts more truly labour
To recompense your love: doubt not but heaven
Hath brought me up to be your daughter's dower,
As it hath fated her to be my motive
And helper to a husband. But, O strange men!
That can such sweet use make of what they hate,
When saucy trusting of the cozen'd thoughts
Defiles the pitchy night! so lust doth play
With what it loathes, for that which is away:
But more of this hereafter. — You, Diana,
Under my poor instructions yet must suffer
Something in my behalf.

DIANA
                    Let death and honesty
Go with your impositions, I am yours
Upon your will to suffer.

HELENA
                    Yet, I pray you:
But, with the word, the time will bring on summer,
When briers shall have leaves as well as thorns,
And be as sweet as sharp. We must away;
Our wagon is prepared, and time revives us:
All's Well that Ends Well: still the fine's the crown;
Whate'er the course, the end is the renown. [Exeunt.

SCENE V

Rousillon. A room in the house of the COUNTESS.

Enter COUNTESS, LAFEU, and CLOWN.

LAFEU
No, no, no, your son was misled with a snipt-taffeta fellow there, whose villainous saffron would have made all the unbaked and doughy youth of a nation in his colour: your daughter-in-law had been alive at this hour, and your son here at home, more advanced by the king than by that red-tail'd humble-bee I speak of.

COUNTESS
I would he had not known him! it was the death of the most virtuous gentlewoman that ever nature had praise for creating: if she had partaken of my flesh, and cost me the dearest groans of a mother, I could not have owed her a more rooted love.

LAFEU
'Twas a good lady, 'twas a good lady: we may pick a thousand sallets ere we light on such another herb.

CLOWN
Indeed, sir, she was the sweet marjoram of the sallet, or rather, the herb of grace.

LAFEU
They are not sallet-herbs, you knave; they are nose-herbs.

CLOWN
I am no great Nebuchadnezzar, sir; I have not much skill in grass.

LAFEU
Whether dost thou profess thyself, — a knave or a fool?

CLOWN
A fool, sir, at a woman's service, and a knave at a man's.

LAFEU
Your distinction?

CLOWN
I would cozen the man of his wife, and do his service.

LAFEU
So you were a knave at his service, indeed.

CLOWN
And I would give his wife my bauble, sir, to do her service.

LAFEU
I will subscribe for thee, thou art both knave and fool.

CLOWN
At your service.

LAFEU
No, no, no.

CLOWN
Why, sir, if I cannot serve you, I can serve as great a prince as you are.

LAFEU
Who's that? a Frenchman?

CLOWN
Faith, sir, a' has an English name; but his phisnomy is more hotter in France than there.

LAFEU
What prince is that?

CLOWN
The black prince, sir; *alias*, the prince of darkness; *alias*, the devil.

LAFEU
Hold thee, there's my purse: I give thee not this to suggest thee from thy master thou talk'st of; serve him still.

CLOWN
I am a woodland fellow, sir, that always loved a great fire; and the master I speak of ever keeps a good fire. But, sure, he is the prince of the world; let his nobility remain in's court. I am for the house with the narrow gate, which I take to be too little for pomp to enter: some that humble themselves may; but the many will be too chill and tender, and they'll be for the flowery way that leads to the broad gate and the great fire.

LAFEU
Go thy ways, I begin to be a-weary of thee; and I tell thee so before, because I would not fall out with thee. Go thy ways: let my horses be well look'd to, without any tricks.

CLOWN
If I put any tricks upon 'em, sir, they shall be jades' tricks; which are their own right by the law of nature.
[Exit.

LAFEU
A shrewd knave and an unhappy.

COUNTESS
So he is. My lord that's gone made himself much sport out of him: by his authority he remains here, which he thinks is a patent for his sauciness; and, indeed, he has no pace, but runs where he will.

LAFEU
I like him well; 'tis not amiss. And I was about to tell you, since I heard of the good lady's death, and that my lord your son was upon his return home, I moved the king my master to speak in the behalf of my daughter; which, in the minority of them both, his majesty, out of a self-gracious remembrance, did first propose; his highness hath promised me to do it: and, to stop up the displeasure he hath conceived against your son, there is no fitter matter. How does your ladyship like it?

COUNTESS
With very much content, my lord; and I wish it happily effected.

LAFEU
His highness comes post from Marseilles, of as able body as when he number'd thirty: he will be here to-morrow, or I am deceived by him that in such

intelligence hath seldom fail'd.

COUNTESS
It rejoices me, that I hope I shall see him ere I die. I have letters that my son will be here to-night: I shall beseech your lordship to remain with me till they meet together.

LAFEU
Madam, I was thinking with what manners I might safely be admitted.

COUNTESS
You need but plead your honourable privilege.

LAFEU
Lady, of that I have made a bold charter; but, I thank my God, it holds yet.

Enter CLOWN.

CLOWN
O madam, yonder's my lord your son with a patch of velvet on's face: whether there be a scar under't or no, the velvet knows: but 'tis a goodly patch of velvet: his left cheek is a cheek of two pile and a half, but his right cheek is worn bare.

LAFEU
A scar nobly got, or a noble scar, is a good livery of honour; so belike is that.

CLOWN
But it is your carbonadoed face.

LAFEU
Let us go see your son, I pray you: I long to talk with the young noble soldier.

CLOWN
Faith, there's a dozen of 'em, with delicate fine hats, and most courteous feathers, which bow the head and nod at every man.   [*Exeunt.*

ACT V

SCENE I

Marseilles. A street.

*Enter HELENA, WIDOW, and DIANA,
with two ATTENDANTS.*

HELENA
But this exceeding posting day and night
Must wear your spirits low; we cannot help it:
But, since you have made the days and nights as one,
To wear your gentle limbs in my affairs,
Be bold you do so grow in my requital
As nothing can unroot you. — In happy time; —
Enter a GENTLE ASTRINGER.
This man may help me to his majesty's ear,
If he would spend his power. — God save you, sir.

GENTLE ASTRINGER
And you.

HELENA
Sir, I have seen you in the court of France.

GENTLE ASTRINGER
I have been sometimes there.

HELENA
I do presume, sir, that you are not fall'n
From the report that goes upon your goodness;
An therefore, goaded with most sharp occasions,
Which lay nice manners by, I put you to
The use of your own virtues, for the which
I shall continue thankful.

GENTLE ASTRINGER
                    What's your will?

HELENA
That it will please you
To give this poor petition to the king;
And aid me with that store of power you have
To come into his presence.

GENTLE ASTRINGER
The king's not here.

HELENA
                    Not here, sir!

GENTLE ASTRINGER
                    Not, indeed:
He hence remov'd last night, and with more haste
Than is his use.

WIDOW
                    Lord, how we lose our pains!

HELENA
All's Well that Ends Well yet,
Though time seem so adverse and means unfit. —
I do beseech you, whither is he gone?

GENTLE ASTRINGER
Marry, as I take it, to Rousillon;

Whither I am going.

HELENA
                    I do beseech you, sir,
Since you are like to see the king before me,
Commend the paper to his gracious hand;
Which, I presume, shall render you no blame,
But rather make you thank your pains for it.
I will come after you with what good speed
Our means will make us means.

GENTLE ASTRINGER
                    This I'll do for you.

HELENA
And you shall find yourself to be well thank'd,
Whate'er falls more. — We must to horse again: —
Go, go, provide.   [*Exeunt.*

SCENE II

Rousillon. Before the house of the COUNTESS.

Enter CLOWN and PAROLLES.

PAROLLES
Good Monsieur Lavache, give my Lord Lafeu this letter: I have ere now, sir, been better known to you, when I have held familiarity with fresher clothes; but I am now, sir, muddied in Fortune's mood, and smell somewhat strong of her strong displeasure.

CLOWN
Truly, Fortune's displeasure is but sluttish, if it smell so strongly as thou speak'st of: I will henceforth eat no fish of Fortune's buttering. Prithee, allow the wind.

PAROLLES
Nay, you need not to stop your nose, sir; I spake but by a metaphor.

CLOWN
Indeed, sir, if your metaphor stink, I will stop my nose; or against any man's metaphor. Prithee, get thee further.

PAROLLES
Pray you, sir, deliver me this paper.

CLOWN
Foh, prithee, stand away: a paper from Fortune's close-stool to give to a nobleman! Look, here he comes himself.
Enter LAFEU.
Here is a pur of Fortune's, sir, or of Fortune's cat, — but not a musk-cat, — that has fall'n into the unclean fishpond of her displeasure, and, as he says, is muddied withal: pray you, sir, use the carp as you may: for he looks like a poor, decay'd, ingenious, foolish, rascally knave. I do pity his distress in my similes of comfort, and leave him to your lordship.   [*Exit.*

PAROLLES
My lord, I am a man whom Fortune hath cruelly scratch'd.

LAFEU
And what would you have me to do? 'tis too late to pare her nails now. Wherein have you play'd the knave with Fortune, that she should scratch you, who of herself is a good lady, and would not have knaves thrive long under her? There's a cardecu for you: let the justices make you and Fortune friends; I am for other business.

PAROLLES
I beseech your honour to hear me one single word.

LAFEU
You beg a single penny more: come, you shall ha't; save your word.

PAROLLES
My name, my good lord, is Parolles.

LAFEU
You beg more than 'word', then. — Cox my passion! give me your hand: — how does your drum?

PAROLLES
O my good lord, you were the first that found me!

LAFEU
Was I, in sooth? and I was the first that lost thee.

PAROLLES
It lies in you, my lord, to bring me in some grace, for you did bring me out.

LAFEU
Out upon thee, knave! dost thou put upon me at once both the office of God and the devil? one brings thee in grace, and the other brings thee out. [*Trumpets sound.*] The king's coming; I know by his trumpets. — Sirrah, inquire further after me; I had talk of you last night: though you are a fool and a knave, you shall eat; go to, follow.

PAROLLES
I praise God for you.   [*Exeunt.*

SCENE III

*The same. A room in the house of the COUNTESS.
Flourish. Enter KING, COUNTESS, LAFEU, the two
French LORDS, GENTLEMEN, GUARDS, etc.*

KING
We lost a jewel of her; and our esteem
Was made much poorer by it: but your son,
As mad in folly, lack'd the sense to know
Her estimation home.

COUNTESS
                    'Tis past, my liege;
And I beseech your majesty to make it
Natural rebellion, done i' the blaze of youth;
When oil and fire, too strong for reason's force,
O'erbears it, and burns on.

KING
                    My honour'd lady,
I have forgiven and forgotten all;
Though my revenges were high-bent upon him,
And watch'd the time to shoot.

LAFEU
                    This I must say, —
But first I beg my pardon, — the young lord
Did to his majesty, his mother, and his lady,
Offence of mighty note: but to himself
The greatest wrong of all: he lost a wife,
Whose beauty did astonish the survey
Of richest eyes; whose words all ears took captive;
Whose dear perfection hearts that scorn'd to serve
Humbly call'd mistress.

KING
                    Praising what is lost
Makes the remembrance dear. Well, call him hither;
We are reconciled, and the first view shall kill
All repetition: — let him not ask our pardon;
The nature of his great offence is dead,
And deeper than oblivion we do bury
Th'incensing reliques of it: let him approach,
A stranger, no offender; and inform him
So 'tis our will he should.

FIRST GENTLEMAN
                    I shall, my liege.   [*Exit.*

KING
What says he to your daughter? have you spoke?

LAFEU
All that he is hath reference to your highness.

KING
Then shall we have a match. I have letters sent me
That sets him high in fame.

Enter BERTRAM, with FIRST GENTLEMAN.

LAFEU
                    He looks well on't.

KING
I am not a day of season,
For thou mayst see a sunshine and a hail
In me at once: but to the brightest beams
Distracted clouds give way; so stand thou forth,
The time is fair again.

BERTRAM
                    My high-repented blames,
Dear sovereign, pardon to me.

KING
                    All is whole;
Not one word more of the consumed time.
Let's take the instant by the forward top;
For we are old, and on our quick'st decrees
Th'inaudible and noiseless foot of Time
Steals ere we can effect them. You remember
The daughter of this lord?

BERTRAM
Admiringly, my liege: at first
I stuck my choice upon her, ere my heart
Durst make too bold a herald of my tongue:
Where the impression of mine eye infixing,
Contempt his scornful perspective did lend me,
Which warp'd the line of every other favour;
Scorn'd a fair colour, or express'd it stol'n;
Extended or contracted all proportions
To a most hideous object: thence it came
That she whom all men prais'd, and whom myself,
Since I have lost, have lov'd, was in mine eye
The dust that did offend it.

KING
                    Well excused:
That thou didst love her, strikes some scores away
From the great compt: but love that comes too late,
Like a remorseful pardon slowly carried,
To the great sender turns a sour offence,

Crying, 'That's good that's gone.' Our rasher faults
Make trivial price of serious things we have,
Not knowing them until we know their grave:
Oft our displeasures, to ourselves unjust,
Destroy our friends, and after weep their dust:
Our old love waking cries to see what's done,
While shameful hate sleeps out the afternoon.
Be this sweet Helen's knell, and now forget her.
Send forth your amorous token for fair Maudlin:
The main consents are had; and here we'll stay
To see our widower's second marriage-day.

COUNTESS
Which better than the first, O dear heaven, bless!
Or, ere they meet, in me, O nature, cesse!

LAFEU
Come on, my son, in whom my house's name
Must be digested, give a favour from you,
To sparkle in the spirits of my daughter,
That she may quickly come. —
                    [BERTRAM *gives a ring to* LAFEU.
                    By my old beard,
And every hair that's on't, Helen, that's dead,
Was a sweet creature: such a ring as this,
The last that e'er I took her leave at court,
I saw upon her finger.

BERTRAM
                    Hers it was not.

KING
Now, pray you, let me see it; for mine eye,
While I was speaking, oft was fasten'd to't. —
This ring was mine, and when I gave it Helen,
I bade her, if her fortunes ever stood
Necessitied to help, that by this token
I would relieve her. Had you that craft, to reave her
Of what should stead her most?

BERTRAM
                    My gracious sovereign,
Howe'er it pleases you to take it so,
The ring was never hers.

COUNTESS
                    Son, on my life,
I have seen her wear it; and she reckon'd it
At her life's rate.

LAFEU
                    I am sure I saw her wear it.

BERTRAM
You are deceiv'd, my lord; she never saw it:
In Florence was it from a casement thrown me,
Wrapp'd in a paper, which contain'd the name
Of her that threw it: noble she was, and thought
I stood engag'd: but when I had subscrib'd
To mine own fortune, and inform'd her fully
I could not answer in that course of honour
As she had made the overture, she ceas'd
In heavy satisfaction, and would never
Receive the ring again.

KING
                    Plutus himself,
That knows the tinct and multiplying medicine,
Hath not in nature's mystery more science
Than I have in this ring: 'twas mine, 'twas Helen's,
Whoever gave it you. Then, if you know
That you are well acquainted with yourself,
Confess 'twas hers, and by what rough enforcement
You got it from her: she call'd the saints to surety
That she would never put it from her finger,
Unless she gave it to yourself in bed, —
Where you have never come, — or sent it us
Upon her great disaster.

BERTRAM
                    She never saw it.

KiNG
Thou speak'st it falsely, as I love mine honour;
And makest conjectural fears to come into me,
Which I would fain shut out. If it should prove
That thou art so inhuman, — 'twill not prove so; —
And yet I know not: — thou didst hate her deadly,
And she is dead, which nothing, but to close
Her eyes myself, could win me to believe,
More than to see this ring. — Take him away. —
                    [*Guards seize* BERTRAM.
My fore-past proofs, howe'er the matter fall,
Shall tax my fears of little vanity,
Having vainly fear'd too little. — Away with him! —
We'll sift this matter further.

BERTRAM
                    If you shall prove
This ring was ever hers, you shall as easy
Prove that I husbanded her bed in Florence,
Where yet she never was.   [*Exit, guarded.*

KING
I am wrapp'd in dismal thinkings.

                    Enter a GENTLE ASTRINGER.

GENTLE ASTRINGER
                    Gracious sovereign,
Whether I have been to blame or no, I know not:
Here's a petition from a Florentine,
Who hath for four or five removes come short
To tender it herself. I undertook it,
Vanquish'd thereto by the fair grace and speech
Of the poor suppliant, who by this, I know,
Is here attending: her business looks in her
With an importing visage; and she told me,
In a sweet verbal brief, it did concern
Your highness with herself.

KING [*reads*].
Upon his many protestations to marry me when his
wife was dead, I blush to say it, he won me. Now is the
Count Rousillon a widower: his vows are forfeited to
me, and my honour's paid to him. He stole from
Florence, taking no leave, and I follow him to his
country for justice: grant it me, O king! in you it best
lies; otherwise a seducer flourishes, and a poor maid is
undone.
                    DIANA CAPULET.

LAFEU
I will buy me a son-in-law in a fair, and toll: for this, I'll
none of him.

KING
The heavens have thought well on thee, Lafeu,
To bring forth this discov'ry. — Seek these suitors. —
Go speedily and bring again the count.
            [*Exeunt* GENTLEMAN *and some* ATTENDANTS.
I am afear'd the life of Helen, lady,
Was foully snatch'd.

COUNTESS
                    Now, justice on the doers!

                    Enter BERTRAM, *guarded.*

KING
I wonder, sir, sith wives are monsters to you,
And that you fly them as you swear them lordship,
Yet you desire to marry.

            Enter GENTLEMAN, *with* WIDOW *and* DIANA.
                    What woman's that?

DIANA
I am, my lord, a wretched Florentine,
Derived from the ancient Capulet:
My suit, as I do understand, you know,
And therefore know how far I may be pitied.

WIDOW
I am her mother, sir, whose age and honour
Both suffer under this complaint we bring;
And both shall cease, without your remedy.

KING
Come hither, count: do you know these women?

BERTRAM
My lord, I neither can nor will deny
But that I know them: do they charge me further?

DIANA
Why do you look so strange upon your wife?

BERTRAM
She's none of mine, my lord.

DIANA
                    If you shall marry,
You give away this hand, and that is mine;
You give away heaven's vows, and those are mine;
You give away myself, which is known mine;
For I by vow am so embodied yours,
That she which marries you must marry me, —
Either both or none.

LAFEU [*to* BERTRAM].
Your reputation comes too short for my daughter; you
are no husband for her.

BERTRAM
My lord, this is a fond and desperate creature,
Whom sometime I have laugh'd with: let your
  highness
Lay a more noble thought upon mine honour
Than for to think that I would sink it here.

KING
Sir, for my thoughts, you have them ill to friend
Till your deeds gain them: fairer prove your honour
Than in my thought it lies!

DIANA
                    Good my lord,
Ask him upon his oath, if he does think
He had not my virginity.

KING
What say'st thou to her?

BERTRAM
                    She's impudent, my lord,
And was a common gamester to the camp.

DIANA
He does me wrong, my lord; if I were so,
He might have bought me at a common price:
Do not believe him: O, behold this ring,
Whose high respect and rich validity
Did lack a parallel; yet, for all that,
He gave it to a commoner o' the camp,
If I be one.

COUNTESS
                    He blushes, and 'tis his:
Of six preceding ancestors, that gem,
Conferr'd by testament to the sequent issue,
Hath it been ow'd and worn. This is his wife;
That ring's a thousand proofs.

KING
                    Methought you said
You saw one here in court could witness it.

DIANA
I did, my lord, but loth am to produce
So bad an instrument: his name's Parolles.

LAFEU
I saw the man to-day, if man he be.

KING
Find him, and bring him hither.
                    [*Exit an* ATTENDANT.

BERTRAM
                    What of him?
He's quoted for a most perfidious slave,
With all the spots o' the world tax'd and debosh'd;
Whose nature sickens but to speak a truth,
Am I or that or this for what he'll utter,
That will speak any thing?

KING
                    She hath that ring of yours.

BERTRAM
I think she has: certain it is I lik'd her,
And boarded her i' the wanton way of youth:
She knew her distance, and did angle for me,
Madding my eagerness with her restraint,
As all impediments in fancy's course
Are motives of more fancy; and, in fine,
Her infinite cunning, with her modern grace,
Subdued me to her rate: she got the ring;
And I had that which any inferior might
At market-price have bought.

DIANA
                    I must be patient:
You, that turn'd off a first so noble wife,
May justly diet me. I pray you yet, —
Since you lack virtue, I will lose a husband, —
Send for your ring, I will return it home,
And give me mine again.

BERTRAM
                    I have it not.

KING
What ring was yours, I pray you?

DIANA
                    Sir, much like
The same upon your finger.

KING
Know you this ring? this ring was his of late.

DIANA
And this was it I gave him, being a-bed.

KING
The story, then, goes false, you threw it him
Out of a casement.

DIANA
                    I have spoke the truth.

BERTRAM
My lord, I do confess the ring was hers.

KING
You boggle shrewdly, every feather starts you. —
            Enter PAROLLES, *with* ATTENDANT.
Is this the man you speak of?

DIANA
                    Ay, my lord.

KING
Tell me, sirrah, — but tell me true, I charge you,
Not fearing the displeasure of your master,
Which, on your just proceeding, I'll keep off, —
By him and by this woman here what know you?

PAROLLES
So please your majesty, my master hath been an
honourable gentleman: tricks he hath had in him,

which gentlemen have.

KING
Come, come, to the purpose: did he love this woman?

PAROLLES
Faith, sir, he did love her; but how?

KING
How, I pray you?

PAROLLES
He did love her, sir, as a gentleman loves a woman.

KING
How is that?

PAROLLES
He loved her, sir, and loved her not.

KING
As thou art a knave, and no knave. — What an
    equivocal companion is this!

PAROLLES
I am a poor man, and at your majesty's command.

LAFEU
He's a good drum, my lord, but a naughty orator.

DIANA
Do you know he promised me marriage?

PAROLLES
Faith, I know more than I'll speak.

KING
But wilt thou not speak all thou know'st?

PAROLLES
Yes, so please your majesty. I did go between them, as I
said; but more than that, he loved her, — for, indeed,
he was mad for her, and talk'd of Satan, and of Limbo,
and of Furies, and I know not what: yet I was in that
credit with them at that time, that I knew of their going
to bed; and of other motions, as promising her
marriage, and things which would derive me ill will to
speak of; therefore I will not speak what I know.

KING
Thou hast spoken all already, unless thou canst say
they are married; but thou art too fine in thy evidence;
therefore stand aside. —
This ring, you say, was yours?

DIANA
              Ay, my good lord.

KING
Where did you buy it? or who gave it you?

DIANA
It was not given me, nor I did not buy it.

KING
Who lent it you?

DIANA
          It was not lent me neither.

KING
Where did you find it, then?

DIANA
             I found it not.

KING
If it were yours by none of all these ways,
How could you give it him?

DIANA
           I never gave it him.

LAFEU
This woman's an easy glove, my lord; she goes off and
on at pleasure.

KING
This ring was mine; I gave it his first wife.

DIANA
It might be yours or hers, for aught I know.

KING
Take her away; I do not like her now;
To prison with her: and away with him. —
Unless thou tell'st me where thou hadst this ring,
Thou diest within this hour.

DIANA
           I'll never tell you.

KING
Take her away.

DIANA
        I'll put in bail, my liege.

KING
I think thee now some common customer.

DIANA
By Jove, if ever I knew man, 'twas you.

KING
Wherefore hast thou accus'd him all this while?

DIANA
Because he's guilty, and he is not guilty:
He knows I am no maid, and he'll swear to't;
I'll swear I am a maid, and he knows not.
Great king, I am no strumpet, by my life;
I'm either maid, or else this old man's wife.
                     [*Pointing to* LAFEU.

KING
She does abuse our ears: to prison with her.

DIANA
Good mother, fetch my bail. — Stay, royal sir:
                      [*Exit* WIDOW.
The jeweller that owes the ring is sent for,
And he shall surety me. But for this lord,
Who hath abus'd me, as he knows himself,
Though yet he never harm'd me, here I quit him:
He knows himself my bed he hath defiled;
And at that time he got his wife with child:
Dead though she be, she feels her young one kick:
So there's my riddle, — One that's dead is quick:
And now behold the meaning.

                Enter WIDOW, *with* HELENA.

KING
               Is there no exorcist
Beguiles the truer office of mine eyes?
Is't real that I see?

HELENA
            No, my good lord;
'Tis but the shadow of a wife you see,
The name, and not the thing.

BERTRAM
            Both, both: — O, pardon!

HELENA
O my good lord, when I was like this maid,
I found you wondrous kind. There is your ring;
And, look you, here's your letter; this it says:
'When from my finger you can get this ring,
And are by me with child, etc.' This is done:
Will you be mine, now you are doubly won?

BERTRAM
If she, my liege, can make me know this clearly,
I'll love her dearly, ever, ever dearly.

HELENA
If it appear not plain, and prove untrue,
Deadly divorce step between me and you! —
O my dear mother, do I see you living?

LAFEU
Mine eyes smell onions; I shall weep anon: —
[*to* PAROLLES] Good Tom Drum, lend me a
handkercher: so, I thank thee: wait on me home, I'll
make sport with thee: let thy courtesies alone, they are
scurvy ones.

KING
Let us from point to point this story know,
To make the even truth in pleasure flow. —
[*to* DIANA] If thou be'st yet a fresh uncropped flower,
Choose thou thy husband, and I'll pay thy dower;
For I can guess that, by thy honest aid,
Thou kept'st a wife herself, thyself a maid. —
Of that, and all the progress, more and less,
Resolvedly more leisure shall express:
All yet seems well; and if it end so meet,
The bitter past, more welcome is the sweet.   [*Flourish*

EPILOGUE
Spoken by the KING.

The king's a beggar, now the play is done:
All is well ended, if this suit be won,
That you express content; which we will pay,
With strife to please you, day exceeding day:
Ours be your patience then, and yours our parts;
Your gentle hands lend us, and take our hearts.
                            [*Exeunt*

MEASURE FOR MEASURE

DRAMATIS PERSONAE

VINCENTIO, *the Duke.*
ANGELO, *the Deputy.*
ESCALUS, *an ancient Lord.*
CLAUDIO, *a young Gentleman.*
LUCIO, *a Fantastic.*
TWO OTHER LIKE GENTLEMEN.
PROVOST.
THOMAS, } *two Friars.*
PETER,

A JUSTICE.
VARRIUS.
ELBOW, *a simple Constable.*
FROTH, *a foolish Gentleman.*
POMPEY, *servant to Mistress Overdone.*
ABHORSON, *an Executioner.*
BARNARDINE, *a dissolute Prisoner.*

ISABELLA, *sister to Claudio.*

MARIANA, *betrothed to Angelo.*
JULIET, *beloved of Claudio.*
FRANCISCA, *a Nun.*
MISTRESS OVERDONE, *a Bawd.*

LORDS, OFFICERS, CITIZENS, BOY, *and*
ATTENDANTS.

SCENE — *Vienna.*

ACT I

SCENE I

An apartment in the DUKE'S *palace.*

Enter DUKE, ESCALUS, LORDS,
and ATTENDANTS.

DUKE
Escalus, —
ESCALUS
My lord?
DUKE
Of government the properties to unfold,
Would seem in me t'affect speech and discourse;
Since I am put to know that your own science
Exceeds, in that, the lists of all advice
My strength can give you: then no more remains
But that to your sufficiency
             as your worth is able,
And let them work. The nature of our people,
Our city's institutions, and the terms
For common justice, you're as pregnant in
As art and practice hath enriched any
That we remember. There is our commission,
From which we would not have you warp. — Call
    hither,
I say, bid come before us Angelo.
                [*Exit an* ATTENDANT.
What figure of us think you he will bear?
For, you must know, we have with special soul
Elected him our absence to supply;
Lent him our terror, dress'd him with our love,
And given his deputation all the organs
Of our own power: what think you of it?
ESCALUS
If any in Vienna be of worth
To undergo such ample grace and honour,
It is Lord Angelo.

DUKE
         Look where he comes.

    Enter ANGELO.

ANGELO
Always obedient to your Grace's will,
I come to know your pleasure.
DUKE
              Angelo,
There is a kind of character in thy life,
That to th'observer doth thy history
Fully unfold. Thyself and thy belongings
Are not thine own so proper, as to waste
Thyself upon thy virtues, they on thee.
Heaven doth with us as we with torches do,
Not light them for themselves; for if our virtues
Did not go forth of us, 'twere all alike
As if we had them not. Spirits are not finely touch'd
But to fine issues; nor Nature never lends
The smallest scruple of her excellence
But, like a thrifty goddess, she determines
Herself the glory of a creditor,
Both thanks and use. But I do bend my speech
To one that can my part in him advertise;
Hold, therefore, Angelo: —
In our remove be thou at full ourself;
Mortality and mercy in Vienna
Live in thy tongue and heart: old Escalus,
Though first in question, is thy secondary: —
Take thy commission.
ANGELO
          Now, good my lord,
Let there be some more test made of my metal,
Before so noble and so great a figure
Be stamp'd upon it.
DUKE
        No more evasion:
We have with a leaven'd and prepared choice
Proceeded to you; therefore take your honours.

Our haste from hence is of so quick condition,
That it prefers itself and leaves unquestion'd
Matters of needful value. We shall write to you,
As time and our concernings shall importune,
How it goes with us; and do look to know
What doth befall you here. So, fare you well:
To th'hopeful execution do I leave you
Of your commissions.
ANGELO
         Yet, give leave, my lord,
That we may bring you something on the way.
DUKE
My haste may not admit it;
Nor need you, on mine honour, have to do
With any scruple: your scope is as mine own,
So to enforce or qualify the laws
As to your soul seems good. Give me your hand:
I'll privily away. I love the people,
But do not like to stage me to their eyes:
Though it do well, I do not relish well
Their loud applause and Aves vehement;
Nor do I think the man of safe discretion
That does affect it. Once more, fare you well.
ANGELO
The heavens give safety to your purposes! —
ESCALUS
Lead forth and bring you back in happiness!
DUKE
I thank you. Fare you well.   [*Exit.*
ESCALUS
I shall desire you, sir, to give me leave
To have free speech with you; and it concerns me
To look into the bottom of my place:
A power I have, but of what strength and nature
I am not yet instructed.
ANGELO
'Tis so with me. Let us withdraw together,
And we may soon our satisfaction have
Touching that point.

ESCALUS
I'll wait upon your honour.
[*Exeunt.*

SCENE II

A street.

Enter LUCIO *and two other* GENTLEMEN.

LUCIO
If the duke, with the other dukes, come not to composition with the King of Hungary, why, then, all the dukes fall upon the king.

FIRST GENTLEMAN
Heaven grant us its peace, but not the King of Hungary's!

SECOND GENTLEMAN
Amen.

LUCIO
Thou concludest like the sanctimonious pirate, that went to sea with the Ten Commandments, but scraped one out of the table.

SECOND GENTLEMAN
'Thou shalt not steal'?

LUCIO
Ay, that he razed.

FIRST GENTLEMAN
Why, 'twas a commandment to command the captain and all the rest from their functions: they put forth to steal. There's not a soldier of us all, that, in the thanksgiving before meat, do relish the petition well that prays for peace.

SECOND GENTLEMAN
I never heard any soldier dislike it.

LUCIO
I believe thee; for I think thou never wast where grace was said.

SECOND GENTLEMAN
No? a dozen times at least.

FIRST GENTLEMAN
What, in metre?

LUCIO
In any proportion or in any language.

FIRST GENTLEMAN
I think, or in any religion.

LUCIO
Ay, why not? Grace is grace, despite of all controversy: as, for example, — thou thyself art a wicked villain, despite of all grace.

FIRST GENTLEMAN
Well, there went but a pair of shears between us.

LUCIO
I grant; as there may between the lists and the velvet. Thou art the list.

FIRST GENTLEMAN
And thou the velvet: thou art good velvet; thou'rt a three-piled piece, I warrant thee: I had as lief be a list of an English kersey, as be piled, as thou art piled, for a French velvet. Do I speak feelingly now?

LUCIO
I think thou dost; and, indeed, with most painful feeling of thy speech, I will, out of thine own confession, learn to begin thy health; but, whilst I live, forget to drink after thee.

FIRST GENTLEMAN
I think I have done myself wrong, have I not?

SECOND GENTLEMAN
Yes, that thou hast, whether thou art tainted or free.

LUCIO
Behold, behold, where Madam Mitigation comes!

FIRST GENTLEMAN
I have purchased as many diseases under her roof as come to —

SECOND GENTLEMAN
To what, I pray?

FIRST GENTLEMAN
Judge.

SECOND GENTLEMAN
To three thousand dolours a year.

FIRST GENTLEMAN
Ay, and more.

LUCIO
A French crown more.

FIRST GENTLEMAN
Thou art always figuring diseases in me; but thou art full of error, — I am sound.

LUCIO
Nay, not as one would say, healthy; but so sound as things that are hollow: thy bones are hollow; impiety has made a feast of thee.

Enter MISTRESS OVERDONE.

FIRST GENTLEMAN
How now! which of your hips has the most profound sciatica?

MISTRESS OVERDONE
Well, well; there's one yonder arrested and carried to prison was worth five thousand of you all.

SECOND GENTLEMAN
Who's that, I pray thee?

MISTRESS OVERDONE
Marry, sir, that's Claudio, Signior Claudio.

FIRST GENTLEMAN
Claudio to prison! 'tis not so.

MISTRESS OVERDONE
Nay, but I know 'tis so: I saw him arrested, saw him carried away; and, which is more, within these three days his head to be chopp'd off.

LUCIO
But, after all this fooling, I would not have it so.
Art thou sure of this?

MISTRESS OVERDONE
I am too sure of it: and it is for getting Madam Julietta with child.

LUCIO
Believe me, this may be: he promised to meet me two hours since, and he was ever precise in promise-keeping.

SECOND GENTLEMAN
Besides, you know, it draws something near to the speech we had to such a purpose.

FIRST GENTLEMAN
But, most of all, agreeing with the proclamation.

LUCIO
Away! let's go learn the truth of it.

[*Exeunt* LUCIO *and* GENTLEMEN.

MISTRESS OVERDONE
Thus, what with the war, what with the sweat, what with the gallows, and what with poverty, I am custom-shrunk.

Enter POMPEY.

How now! What's the news with you!

POMPEY
Yonder man is carried to prison.

MISTRESS OVERDONE
Well: what has he done?

POMPEY
A woman.

MISTRESS OVERDONE
But what's his offence?

POMPEY
Groping for trouts in a peculiar river.

MISTRESS OVERDONE
What, is there a maid with child by him?

POMPEY
No, but there's a woman with maid by him. You have not heard of the proclamation, have you?

MISTRESS OVERDONE
What proclamation, man?

POMPEY
All houses in the suburbs of Vienna must be pluck'd down.

MISTRESS OVERDONE
And what shall become of those in the city?

POMPEY
They shall stand for seed: they had gone down too, but that a wise burgher put in for them.

MISTRESS OVERDONE
But shall all our houses of resort in the suburbs be pull'd down?

POMPEY
To the ground, mistress.

MISTRESS OVERDONE
Why, here's a change indeed in the commonwealth! What shall become of me?

POMPEY
Come; fear you not: good counsellors lack no clients: though you change your place, you need not change your trade; I'll be your tapster still. Courage! there will be pity taken on you: you that have worn your eyes almost out in the service, you will be consider'd.

MISTRESS OVERDONE
What's to do here, Thomas Tapster? let's withdraw.

POMPEY
Here comes Signior Claudio, led by the provost to prison; and there's Madam Juliet.   [*Exeunt.*

Enter PROVOST, CLAUDIO, JULIET,
and OFFICERS.

CLAUDIO
Fellow, why dost thou show me thus to th'world?
Bear me to prison, where I am committed.

PROVOST
I do it not in evil disposition,
But from Lord Angelo by special charge.

CLAUDIO
Thus can the demigod Authority
Make us pay down for our offence by weight. —
The words of heaven; — on whom it will, it will;
On whom it will not, so; yet still 'tis just.

Enter LUCIO *and two* GENTLEMEN.

LUCIO
Why, how now, Claudio! whence comes this restraint?

CLAUDIO
From too much liberty, my Lucio, liberty:
As surfeit is the father of much fast,
So every scope by the immoderate use
Turns to restraint. Our natures do pursue,
Like rats that ravin down their proper bane,
A thirsty evil; and when we drink we die.

LUCIO
If I could speak so wisely under an arrest, I would send for certain of my creditors: and yet, to say the truth, I had as lief have the foppery of freedom as the morality of imprisonment. — What's thy offence, Claudio?

CLAUDIO
What but to speak of would offend again.

LUCIO
What, is't murder?

CLAUDIO
No.

LUCIO
Lechery?

LUCIO I believe thee; for I think thou never wast where grace was said.

CLAUDIO
Call it so.

PROVOST
Away, sir! you must go.

CLAUDIO
One word, good friend. — Lucio, a word with you.
[*Takes him aside.*

LUCIO
A hundred, if they'll do you any good. —
Is lechery so look'd after?

CLAUDIO
Thus stands it with me: — upon a true contract
I got possession of Julietta's bed:
You know the lady; she is fast my wife,
Save that we do the denunciation lack
Of outward order: this we came not to,
Only for propagation of a dower
Remaining in the coffer of her friends;
From whom we thought it meet to hide our love
Till time had made them for us. But it chances
The stealth of our most mutual entertainment
With character too gross is writ on Juliet.

LUCIO
With child, perhaps?

CLAUDIO
Unhappily, even so.
And the new deputy now for the duke, —
Whether it be the fault and glimpse of newness,
Or whether that the body public be
A horse whereon the governor doth ride,
Who, newly in the seat, that it may know
He can command, lets it straight feel the spur;
Whether the tyranny be in his place,
Or in his eminence that fills it up,
I stagger in: — but this new governor
Awakes me all the enrolled penalties
Which have, like unscour'd armour, hung by the wall
So long, that nineteen zodiacs have gone round,
And none of them been worn; and, for a name,
Now puts the drowsy and neglected act
Freshly on me: — 'tis surely for a name.

LUCIO
I warrant it is: and thy head stands so tickle on thy
shoulders, that a milkmaid, if she be in love, may sigh
it off. Send after the duke, and appeal to him.

CLAUDIO
I have done so, but he's not to be found.
I prithee, Lucio, do me this kind service: —
This day my sister should the cloister enter,
And there receive her approbation:
Acquaint her with the danger of my state;
Implore her, in my voice, that she make friends
To the strict deputy; bid herself assay him:
I have great hope in that; for in her youth
There is a prone and speechless dialect,
Such as move men; beside, she hath prosperous art
When she will play with reason and discourse,
And well she can persuade.

LUCIO
I pray she may; as well for the encouragement of the
like, which else would stand under grievous
imposition, as for the enjoying of thy life, who I would
be sorry should be thus foolishly lost at a game of
tick-tack. I'll to her.

CLAUDIO
I thank you, good friend Lucio.

LUCIO
Within two hours.

CLAUDIO
Come, officer, away! [*Exeunt.*

SCENE III
A monastery.

Enter DUKE *and* FRIAR THOMAS.

DUKE
No, holy father; throw away that thought;
Believe not that the dribbling dart of love
Can pierce a complete bosom. Why I desire thee
To give me secret harbour, hath a purpose
More grave and wrinkled than the aims and ends
Of burning youth.

FRIAR THOMAS
May your Grace speak of it?

DUKE
My holy sir, none better knows than you
How I have ever lov'd the life remov'd;
And held in idle price to haunt assemblies,
Where youth, and cost, and witless bravery keeps.

I have deliver'd to Lord Angelo —
A man of stricture and firm abstinence —
My absolute power and place here in Vienna,
And he supposes me travell'd to Poland;
For so I have strew'd it in the common ear,
And so it is receiv'd. Now, pious sir,
You will demand of me why I do this?

FRIAR THOMAS
Gladly, my lord.

DUKE
We have strict statutes and most biting laws, —
The needful bits and curbs to headstrong wills, —
Which for this fourteen years we have let slip;
Even like an o'ergrown lion in a cave,
That goes not out to prey. Now, as fond fathers,
Having bound up the threat'ning twigs of birch,
Only to stick it in their children's sight
For terror, not to use, in time the rod
Becomes more mock'd than fear'd; so our decrees,
Dead to infliction, to themselves are dead;
And liberty plucks justice by the nose;
The baby beats the nurse, and quite athwart
Goes all decorum.

FRIAR THOMAS
It rested in your Grace
To unloose this tied-up justice when you pleas'd:
And it in you more dreadful would have seem'd
Than in Lord Angelo.

DUKE
I do fear, too dreadful:
Sith 'twas my fault to give the people scope,
'Twould be my tyranny to strike and gall them
For what I bid them do: for we bid this be done,
When evil deeds have their permissive pass,
And not the punishment. Therefore, indeed, my
father,
I have on Angelo impos'd the office,
Who may, in th'ambush of my name, strike home;
And yet my nature never in the fight
To do it slander. And to behold his sway,
I will, as 'twere a brother of your order,
Visit both prince and people: therefore, I prithee,
Supply me with the habit, and instruct me
How I may formally in person bear me
Like a true friar. More reasons for this action
At our more leisure shall I render you;
Only, this one: — Lord Angelo is precise;
Stands at a guard with envy; scarce confesses
That his blood flows, or that his appetite
Is more to bread than stone: hence shall we see,
If power change purpose, what our seemers be.
[*Exeunt.*

DUKE I will, as 'twere a brother of your order, visit both prince and people.

SCENE IV
A nunnery.

Enter ISABELLA *and* FRANCISCA, *a* NUN.

ISABELLA
And have you nuns no further privileges?

FRANCISCA
Are not these large enough?

ISABELLA
Yes, truly: I speak not as desiring more;
But rather wishing a more strict restraint
Upon the sisterhood, the votarists of Saint Clare.

LUCIO [*within*].
Ho! Peace be in this place!

ISABELLA
Who's that which calls?

FRANCISCA
It is a man's voice. Gentle Isabella,
Turn you the key, and know his business of him;
You may, I may not; you are yet unsworn.
When you have vow'd, you must not speak with men
But in the presence of the prioress:
Then, if you speak, you must not show your face;
Or, if you show your face, you must not speak.
He calls again; I pray you, answer him. [*Exit.*

ISABELLA
Peace and prosperity! Who is't that calls?

Enter LUCIO.

LUCIO
Hail, virgin, if you be, as those cheek-roses
Proclaim you are no less! Can you so stead me
As bring me to the sight of Isabella,
A novice of this place, and the fair sister
To her unhappy brother Claudio?

ISABELLA
Why 'her unhappy brother'? let me ask;
The rather, for I now must make you know
I am that Isabella and his sister.

LUCIO
Gentle and fair, your brother kindly greets you:
Not to be weary with you, he's in prison.

ISABELLA
Woe me! for what?

LUCIO
For that which, if myself might be his judge,
He should receive his punishment in thanks:
He hath got his friend with child.

ISABELLA
Sir, make me not your story.

LUCIO
'Tis true.
I would not — though 'tis my familiar sin
With maids to seem the lapwing, and to jest,
Tongue far from heart — play with all virgins so:
I hold you as a thing ensky'd and sainted;
By your renouncement, an immortal spirit;
And to be talk'd with in sincerity,
As with a saint.

ISABELLA
You do blaspheme the good in mocking me.

LUCIO
Do not believe it. Fewness and truth, 'tis thus: —
Your brother and his lover have embraced:
As those that feed grow full; as blossoming-time,
That from the seedness the bare fallow brings
To teeming foison; even so her plenteous womb
Expresseth his full tilth and husbandry.

ISABELLA
Some one with child by him? — My cousin Juliet?

LUCIO
Is she your cousin?

ISABELLA
Adoptedly; as school-maids change their names
By vain, though apt, affection.

LUCIO
She it is.

ISABELLA
O, let him marry her.

LUCIO
This is the point.
The duke is very strangely gone from hence;
Bore many gentlemen, myself being one,
In hand, and hope of action: but we do learn
By those that know the very nerves of state,
His givings-out were of an infinite distance
From his true-meant design. Upon his place,
And with full line of his authority,
Governs Lord Angelo; a man whose blood
Is very snow-broth; one who never feels
The wanton stings and motions of the sense,
But doth rebate and blunt his natural edge
With profits of the mind, study and fast.
He — to give fear to use and liberty,
Which have for long run by the hideous law,
As mice by lions — hath pick'd out an act,
Under whose heavy sense your brother's life
Falls into forfeit: he arrests him on it;
And follows close the rigour of the statute,
To make him an example. All hope is gone,
Unless you have the grace by your fair prayer
To soften Angelo: and that's my pith
Of business 'twixt you and your poor brother.

ISABELLA
Doth he so seek his life?

LUCIO
Has censur'd him
Already; and, as I hear, the provost hath
A warrant for his execution.

ISABELLA
Alas! what poor ability's in me
To do him good!

LUCIO
Assay the power you have.

ISABELLA
My power! Alas, I doubt, —

LUCIO
Our doubts are traitors,
And make us lose the good we oft might win
By fearing to attempt. Go to Lord Angelo,
And let him learn to know, when maidens sue,
Men give like gods; but when they weep and kneel,
All their petitions are as freely theirs
As they themselves would owe them.

ISABELLA
I'll see what I can do.

LUCIO
But speedily.

ISABELLA
I will about it straight;
No longer staying but to give the mother
Notice of my affair. I humbly thank you:
Commend me to my brother: soon at night
I'll send him certain word of my success.

LUCIO
I take my leave of you.

ISABELLA
Good sir, adieu. [Exeunt.

ISABELLA And have you nuns no further privileges?

ACT II

SCENE I

A hall in ANGELO'S *house.*

Enter ANGELO, ESCALUS, a JUSTICE, PROVOST, OFFICERS, and other ATTENDANTS.

ANGELO
We must not make a scarecrow of the law,
Setting it up to fear the birds of prey,
And let it keep one shape, till custom make it
Their perch and not their terror.

ESCALUS
Ay, but yet
Let us be keen, and rather cut a little,
Than fall, and bruise to death. Alas, this gentleman,
Whom I would save, had a most noble father!
Let but your honour know, —
Whom I believe to be most strait in virtue, —
That, in the working of your own affections,
Had time cohered with place, or place with wishing,
Or that the resolute acting of your blood
Could have attain'd th'effect of your own purpose,
Whether you had not sometime in your life
Err'd in this point which now you censure him,
And pull'd the law upon you.

ANGELO
'Tis one thing to be tempted, Escalus,
Another thing to fall. I not deny,
The jury, passing on the prisoner's life,
May in the sworn twelve have a thief or two
Guiltier than him they try. What's open made to justice,
That justice seizes: what know the laws
That thieves do pass on thieves? 'Tis very pregnant,
The jewel that we find, we stoop and take't,
Because we see it; but what we do not see
We tread upon, and never think of it.
You may not so extenuate his offence,
For I have had such faults; but rather tell me,
When I, that censure him, do so offend,
Let mine own judgement pattern out my death,
And nothing come in partial. Sir, he must die.

ESCALUS
Be it as your wisdom will.

ANGELO
Where is the provost?

PROVOST
Here, if it like your honour.

ANGELO
See that Claudio
Be executed by nine to-morrow morning:
Bring him his confessor, let him be prepared;
For that's the utmost of his pilgrimage.
[Exit PROVOST.

ESCALUS [*aside*].
Well, heaven forgive him! and forgive us all!
Some rise by sin, and some by virtue fall;
Some run from brakes of vice, and answer none;
And some condemned for a fault alone.

Enter ELBOW, and OFFICERS with FROTH and
POMPEY.

ELBOW
Come, bring them away: if these be good people in a commonweal that do nothing but use their abuses in common houses, I know no law: bring them away.

ANGELO
How now, sir! What's your name? and what's the matter?

ELBOW
If it please your honour, I am the poor duke's constable, and my name is Elbow: I do lean upon justice, sir, and do bring in here before your good honour two notorious benefactors.

ANGELO
Benefactors? Well; what benefactors are they? are they not malefactors?

ELBOW
If it please your honour, I know not well what they are: but precise villains they are, that I am sure of; and void of all profanation in the world that good Christians ought to have.

ESCALUS
This comes off well; here's a wise officer.

ANGELO
Go to: — what quality are they of? Elbow is your name? why dost thou not speak, Elbow?

POMPEY
He cannot, sir; he's out at elbow.

ANGELO
What are you, sir?

ELBOW
He, sir! a tapster, sir; parcel-bawd; one that serves a bad woman; whose house, sir, was, as they say, pluck'd down in the suburbs; and now she professes a hot-house, which, I think, is a very ill house too.

ESCALUS
How know you that?

ELBOW
My wife, sir, whom I detest before heaven and your honour, —

ESCALUS
How! thy wife!

ELBOW
Ay, sir; — whom, I thank heaven, is an honest woman, —

ESCALUS
Dost thou detest her therefore?

ELBOW
I say, sir, I will detest myself also, as well as she, that this house, if it be not a bawd's house, it is pity of her life, for it is a naughty house.

POMPEY I beseech you, sir, look in this gentleman's face.

ESCALUS
How dost thou know that, constable?

ELBOW
Marry, sir, by my wife; who, if she had been a woman cardinally given, might have been accused in fornication, adultery, and all uncleanliness there.

ESCALUS
By the woman's means?

ELBOW
Ay, sir, by Mistress Overdone's means: but as she spit in his face, so she defied him.

POMPEY
Sir, if it please your honour, this is not so.

ELBOW
Prove it before these varlets here, thou honourable man; prove it.

ESCALUS [to ANGELO].
Do you hear how he misplaces?

POMPEY
Sir, she came in great with child; and longing — saving your honour's reverence — for stew'd prunes. Sir, we had but two in the house, which at that very distant time stood, as it were, in a fruit-dish, a dish of some three-pence; — your honours have seen such dishes; they are not China dishes, but very good dishes, —

ESCALUS
Go to, go to: no matter for the dish, sir.

POMPEY
No, indeed, sir, not of a pin; you are therein in the right: — but to the point. As I say, this Mistress Elbow, being, as I say, with child, and being great-bellied, and longing, as I said, for prunes; and having but two in the dish, as I said, Master Froth here, this very man, having eaten the rest, as I said, and, as I say, paying for them very honestly; — for, as you know, Master Froth, I could not give you three-pence again, —

FROTH
No, indeed.

POMPEY
Very well; — you being then, if you be remember'd,

cracking the stones of the aforesaid prunes, —

FROTH
Ay, so I did indeed.

POMPEY
Why, very well; — I telling you then, if you be remember'd, that such a one and such a one were past cure of the thing you wot of, unless they kept very good diet, as I told you, —

FROTH
All this is true.

POMPEY
Why, very well, then, —

ESCALUS
Come, you are a tedious fool: to the purpose. What was done to Elbow's wife, that he hath cause to complain of? Come me to what was done to her.

POMPEY
Sir, your honour cannot come to that yet.

ESCALUS
No, sir, nor I mean it not.

POMPEY
Sir, but you shall come to it, by your honour's leave. And, I beseech you, look into Master Froth here, sir; a man of fourscore pound a year; whose father died at Hallowmas: — was't not at Hallowmas, Master Froth? —

FROTH
All-hallond eve.

POMPEY
Why, very well; I hope here be truths. He, sir, sitting, as I say, in a lower chair, sir; — 'twas in the Bunch of Grapes, where, indeed, you have a delight to sit, have you not? —

FROTH
I have so; because it is an open room, and good for winter.

POMPEY
Why, very well, then; I hope here be truths.

ANGELO
This will last out a night in Russia,
When nights are longest there: I'll take my leave,

And leave you to the hearing of the cause;
Hoping you'll find good cause to whip them all.

ESCALUS
I think no less. Good morrow to your lordship.

[*Exit* ANGELO.

Now, sir, come on: what was done to Elbow's wife, once more?

POMPEY
Once, sir! there was nothing done to her once.

ELBOW
I beseech you, sir, ask him what this man did to my wife.

POMPEY
I beseech your honour, ask me.

ESCALUS
Well, sir; what did this gentleman to her?

POMPEY
I beseech you, sir, look in this gentleman's face. — Good Master Froth, look upon his honour; 'tis for a good purpose. — Doth your honour mark his face?

ESCALUS
Ay, sir, very well.

POMPEY
Nay, I beseech you, mark it well.

ESCALUS
Well, I do so.

POMPEY
Doth your honour see any harm in his face?

ESCALUS
Why, no.

POMPEY
I'll be supposed upon a book, his face is the worst thing about him. Good, then; if his face be the worst thing about him, how could Master Froth do the constable's wife any harm? I would know that of your honour.

ESCALUS
He's in the right. — Constable, what say you to it?

ELBOW
First, an it like you, the house is a respected house; next, this is a respected fellow; and his mistress is a respected woman.

POMPEY
By this hand, sir, his wife is a more respected person than any of us all.

ELBOW
Varlet, thou liest; thou liest, wicked varlet! the time is yet to come, that she was ever respected with man, woman, or child.

POMPEY
Sir, she was respected with him before he married with her.

ESCALUS
Which is the wiser here? Justice or Iniquity? — Is this true?

ELBOW
O thou caitiff! O thou varlet! O thou wicked Hannibal! I respected with her before I was married to her! — If ever I was respected with her, or she with me, let not your worship think me the poor duke's officer. — Prove this, thou wicked Hannibal, or I'll have mine action of battery on thee.

ESCALUS
If he took you a box o' th' ear, you might have your action of slander too.

ELBOW
Marry, I thank your good worship for it. — What is't your worship's pleasure I shall do with this wicked caitiff?

ESCALUS
Truly, officer, because he hath some offences in him that thou wouldst discover if thou couldst, let him continue in his courses till thou know'st what they are.

ELBOW
Marry, I thank your worship for it. — Thou seest, thou wicked varlet, now, what's come upon thee: thou art to continue now, thou varlet; thou art to continue.

ESCALUS [to FROTH].
Where were you born, friend?

FROTH
Here in Vienna, sir.

ESCALUS
Are you of fourscore pounds a year?

FROTH
Yes, an't please you, sir.

ESCALUS
So. — [to POMPEY] What trade are you of, sir?

POMPEY
A tapster; a poor widow's tapster.

ESCALUS
Your mistress' name?

POMPEY
Mistress Overdone.

ESCALUS
Hath she had any more than one husband?

POMPEY
Nine, sir; Overdone by the last.

ESCALUS
Nine! — Come hither to me, Master Froth. Master
Froth, I would not have you acquainted with tapsters:
they will draw you, Master Froth, and you will hang
them. Get you gone, and let me hear no more of you.

FROTH
I thank your worship. For mine own part, I never come
into any room in a taphouse, but I am drawn in.

ESCALUS
Well, no more of it, Master Froth: farewell. [*Exit*
FROTH.] Come you hither to me, master tapster.
What's your name, master tapster?

POMPEY
Pompey.

ESCALUS
What else?

POMPEY
Bum, sir.

ESCALUS
Troth, and your bum is the greatest thing about you; so
that, in the beastliest sense, you are Pompey the Great.
Pompey, you are partly a bawd, Pompey, howsoever
you colour it in being a tapster. Are you not? come, tell
me true: it shall be the better for you.

POMPEY
Truly, sir, I am a poor fellow that would live.

ESCALUS
How would you live, Pompey? by being a bawd? What
do you think of the trade, Pompey? is it a lawful trade?

POMPEY
If the law would allow it, sir.

ESCALUS
But the law will not allow it, Pompey; nor it shall not be
allow'd in Vienna.

POMPEY
Does your worship mean to geld and splay all the youth
of the city?

ESCALUS
No, Pompey.

POMPEY
Truly, sir, in my poor opinion, they will to't then. If
your worship will take order for the drabs and the
knaves, you need not to fear the bawds.

ESCALUS
There is pretty orders beginning, I can tell you: it is but
heading and hanging.

POMPEY
If you head and hang all that offend that way but for ten
year together, you'll be glad to give out a commission
for more heads: if this law hold in Vienna ten year, I'll
rent the fairest house in it after three-pence a bay: if you
live to see this come to pass, say Pompey told you so.

ESCALUS
Thank you, good Pompey; and, in requital of your
prophecy, hark you: — I advise you, let me not find you
before me again upon any complaint whatsoever; no,
not for dwelling where you do: if I do, Pompey, I shall
beat you to your tent, and prove a shrewd Cæsar to you;
in plain dealing, Pompey, I shall have you whipp'd: so,
for this time, Pompey, fare you well.

POMPEY
I thank your worship for your good counsel. — [*aside*]
But I shall follow it as the flesh and fortune shall better
determine.
Whip me! No, no; let carman whip his jade:
The valiant's heart's not whipp'd out of his trade. [*Exit.*

ESCALUS
Come hither to me, Master Elbow; come hither, master
constable. How long have you been in this place of
constable?

ELBOW
Seven year and a half, sir.

ESCALUS
I thought, by your readiness in the office, you had
continued in it some time. You say, seven years
together?

ELBOW
And a half, sir.

ESCALUS
Alas, it hath been great pains to you! They do you
wrong to put you so oft upon't: are there not men in
your ward sufficient to serve it?

ELBOW
Faith, sir, few of any wit in such matters: as they are
chosen, they are glad to choose me for them; I do it for
some piece of money, and go through with all.

ESCALUS
Look you bring me in the names of some six or seven,
the most sufficient of your parish.

ELBOW
To your worship's house, sir?

ESCALUS
To my house. Fare you well. [*Exit* ELBOW.
What's o'clock, think you?

JUSTICE
Eleven, sir.

ESCALUS
I pray you home to dinner with me.

JUSTICE
I humbly thank you.

ESCALUS
It grieves me for the death of Claudio;
But there's no remedy.

JUSTICE
Lord Angelo is severe.

ESCALUS
                    It is but needful:
Mercy is not itself, that oft looks so;
Pardon is still the nurse of second woe:
But yet, — poor Claudio! — There is no remedy. —
Come, sir.   [*Exeunt.*

SCENE II

Another room in the same.

Enter PROVOST *and a* SERVANT.

SERVANT
He's hearing of a cause; he will come straight: I'll tell
him of you.

PROVOST
                Pray you, do. [*Exit* SERVANT.] I'll know
His pleasure; may be he will relent. Alas,
He hath but as offended in a dream!
All sects, all ages smack of this vice; and he
To die for't!

Enter ANGELO.

ANGELO
                Now, what's the matter, provost?

PROVOST
Is it your will Claudio shall die to-morrow?

ANGELO
Did not I tell thee yea? hadst thou not
    order?
Why dost thou ask again?

PROVOST
                Lest I might be too rash:
Under your good correction, I have seen,
When, after execution, judgement hath
Repented o'er his doom.

ANGELO
                Go to; let that be mine:
Do you your office, or give up your place,
And you shall well be spar'd.

PROVOST
            I crave your honour's pardon. —
What shall be done, sir, with the groaning
    Juliet?
She's very near her hour.

ANGELO
                Dispose of her
To some more fitter place; and that with
    speed.

Enter SERVANT.

SERVANT
Here is the sister of the man condemn'd
Desires access to you.

ANGELO
                Hath he a sister?

PROVOST
Ay, my good lord; a very virtuous maid,
And to be shortly of a sisterhood,
If not already.

ANGELO
            Well, let her be admitted.
                    [*Exit* SERVANT.
See you the fornicatress be removed:
Let her have needful, but not lavish,
    means;

There shall be order for't.

Enter ISABELLA *and* LUCIO.

PROVOST
                'Save your honour!

ANGELO
Stay a little while. — [*to* ISABELLA] You're welcome:
what's your will?

ISABELLA
I am a woeful suitor to your honour,
Please but your honour hear me.

ANGELO
                Well; what's your suit?

ISABELLA
There is a vice that most I do abhor,
And most desire should meet the blow of justice;
For which I would not plead, but that I must;
For which I must not plead, but that I am
At war 'twixt *will* and *will not*.

ANGELO
                Well; the matter?

ISABELLA
I have a brother is condemn'd to die:
I do beseech you, let it be his fault,
And not my brother.

PROVOST [*aside*].
                Heaven give thee moving graces!

ANGELO
Condemn the fault, and not the actor of it?
Why, every fault's condemn'd ere it be done:
Mine were the very cipher of a function,
To fine the faults whose fine stands in record,
And let go by the actor.

ISABELLA
                O just but severe law!
I had a brother, then. — Heaven keep your honour!

LUCIO [*aside to* ISABELLA].
Give't not o'er so: to him again, entreat him;
Kneel down before him, hang upon his gown:
You are too cold; if you should need a pin,
You could not with more tame a tongue desire it:
To him, I say.

ISABELLA
Must he needs die?

ANGELO
                Maiden, no remedy.

ISABELLA
Yes; I do think that you might pardon him,
And neither heaven nor man grieve at the mercy.

ANGELO
I will not do't.

ANGELO Pray you, be gone.

ISABELLA
But can you, if you would?

ANGELO
Look, what I will not, that I cannot do.

ISABELLA
But might you do't, and do the world no wrong,
If so your heart were touch'd with that remorse
As mine is to him.

ANGELO
He's sentenc'd; 'tis too late.

LUCIO [aside to ISABELLA].
You are too cold.

ISABELLA
Too late?!why, no; I, that do speak a word,
May call it back again. Well, believe this,
No ceremony that to great ones 'longs,
Not the king's crown nor the deputed sword,
The marshal's truncheon nor the judge's robe,
Become them with one half so good a grace
As mercy does.
If he had been as you, and you as he,
You would have slipp'd like him; but he, like you,
Would not have been so stern.

ANGELO
Pray you, be gone.

ISABELLA
I would to heaven I had your potency,
And you were Isabel! should it then be thus?
No; I would tell what 'twere to be a judge,
And what a prisoner.

LUCIO [aside to ISABELLA].
Ay, touch him; there's the vein.

ANGELO
Your brother is a forfeit of the law,
And you but waste your words.

ISABELLA
Alas, alas!
Why, all the souls that were were forfeit once;
And he that might the vantage best have took
Found out the remedy. How would you be,
If he, which is the top of judgement, should
But judge you as you are? O, think on that;
And mercy then will breathe within your lips,
Like man new-made.

ANGELO
Be you content, fair maid;
It is the law, not I, condemn your brother:
Were he my kinsman, brother, or my son,
It should be thus with him: — he must die to-morrow.

ISABELLA
To-morrow! O, that's sudden! Spare him, spare him! —
He's not prepared for death. Even for our kitchens
We kill the fowl of season: shall we serve heaven
With less respect than we do minister
To our gross selves? Good, good my lord, bethink you;
Who is it that hath died for this offence?
There's many have committed it.

LUCIO [aside to ISABELLA].
Ay, well said.

ANGELO
The law hath not been dead, though it hath slept:
Those many had not dared to do that evil,
If the first that did th'edict infringe
Had answer'd for his deed: now 'tis awake,
Takes note of what is done; and, like a prophet,
Looks in a glass, that shows what future evils, —
Either new, or by remissness new-conceived,
And so in progress to be hatch'd and born, —
Are now to have no successive degrees,
But, ere they live, to end.

ISABELLA
Yet show some pity.

ANGELO
I show it most of all when I show justice;
For then I pity those I do not know,
Which a dismiss'd offence would after gall;
And do him right that, answering one foul wrong,
Lives not to act another. Be satisfied;
Your brother dies to-morrow; be content.

ISABELLA
So you must be the first that gives this sentence,
And he that suffers. O, it is excellent
To have a giant's strength; but it is tyrannous
To use it like a giant.

LUCIO [aside to ISABELLA].
That's well said.

ISABELLA
Could great men thunder
As Jove himself does, Jove would ne'er be quiet,
For every pelting, petty officer
Would use his heaven for thunder. Nothing but
thunder!
Merciful Heaven,
Thou rather with thy sharp and sulphurous bolt
Splitt'st the unwedgeable and gnarled oak
Than the soft myrtle: but man, proud man,
Dress'd in a little brief authority, —
Most ignorant of what he's most assured,
His glassy essence, — like an angry ape,
Plays such fantastic tricks before high heaven
As make the angels weep; who, with our spleens,
Would all themselves laugh mortal.

LUCIO [aside to ISABELLA].
O, to him, to him, wench! he will relent;
He's coming; I perceive't.

PROVOST [aside].
Pray heaven she win him!

ISABELLA
We cannot weigh our brother with ourself:
Great men may jest with saints; 'tis wit in them,
But in the less foul profanation.

LUCIO [aside to ISABELLA].
Thou'rt i' the right, girl; more o' that.

ISABELLA
That in the captain's but a choleric word,
Which in the soldier is flat blasphemy.

LUCIO [aside to ISABELLA].
Art avised o' that? more on't.

ANGELO
Why do you put these sayings upon me?

ISABELLA
Because authority, though it err like others,
Hath yet a kind of medicine in itself,
That skins the vice o' the top. Go to your bosom;
Knock there, and ask your heart what it doth know
That's like my brother's fault: if it confess
A natural guiltiness such as is his,
Let it not sound a thought upon your tongue
Against my brother's life.

ANGELO [aside].
She speaks, and 'tis
Such sense, that my sense breeds with't. — Fare you
well.

ISABELLA
Gentle my lord, turn back.

ANGELO
I will bethink me: come again to-morrow.

ISABELLA
Hark how I'll bribe you: good my lord, turn back.

ANGELO
How! bribe me!

ISABELLA
Ay, with such gifts that heaven shall share with you.

LUCIO [aside to ISABELLA].
You had marr'd all else.

ISABELLA
Not with fond shekels of the tested gold,
Or stones, whose rates are either rich or poor
As fancy values them; but with true prayers,
That shall be up at heaven and enter there
Ere sun-rise, — prayers from preserved souls,
From fasting maids, whose minds are dedicate
To nothing temporal.

ANGELO
Well; come to me to-morrow.

LUCIO [aside to ISABELLA].
Go to; 'tis well; away!

ISABELLA
Heaven keep your honour safe!

ANGELO [aside].
Amen; for I
Am that way going to temptation,
Where prayers cross.

ISABELLA
At what hour to-morrow
Shall I attend your lordship?

ANGELO
At any time 'fore noon.

ISABELLA
Save your honour!

[Exeunt ISABELLA, LUCIO, and PROVOST.

ANGELO
From thee, — even from thy virtue! —
What's this, what's this? Is this her fault or mine?
The tempter or the tempted, who sins most, ha?
Not she: nor doth she tempt: but it is I
That, lying by the violet in the sun,
Do as the carrion does, not as the flower,
Corrupt with virtuous season. Can it be
That modesty may more betray our sense
Than woman's lightness? Having waste ground
enough,
Shall we desire to raze the sanctuary,
And pitch our evils there? O, fie, fie, fie!
What dost thou, or what art thou, Angelo?
Dost thou desire her foully for those things
That make her good? O, let her brother live:
Thieves for their robbery have authority
When judges steal themselves. What, do I love her,
That I desire to hear her speak again,
And feast upon her eyes? What is't I dream on?
O cunning enemy, that, to catch a saint,
With saints dost bait thy hook! Most dangerous
Is that temptation that doth goad us on
To sin in loving virtue: never could the strumpet,
With all her double vigour, art and nature,
Once stir my temper; but this virtuous maid
Subdues me quite: — ever till now,
When men were fond, I smil'd and wonder'd how.
[Exit.

SCENE III
A prison.

Enter, severally, DUKE disguised as a friar,
and PROVOST.

DUKE
Hail to you, provost! — so I think you are.

PROVOST
I am the provost. What's your will, good friar?

DUKE
Bound by my charity and my blest order,
I come to visit the afflicted spirits
Here in the prison. Do me the common right
To let me see them, and to make me know
The nature of their crimes, that I may minister
To them accordingly.

PROVOST
I would do more than that, if more were needful.
Look, here comes one, — a gentlewoman of mine,
Who, falling in the flaws of her own youth,
Hath blister'd her report: she is with child;
And he that got it, sentenc'd, — a young man
More fit to do another such offence
Than die for this.

Enter JULIET.

DUKE
When must he die?

PROVOST
As I do think, to-morrow. —
[to JULIET] I have provided for you: stay awhile,
And you shall be conducted.

DUKE
Repent you, fair one, of the sin you carry?

JULIET
I do; and bear the shame most patiently.

DUKE
I'll teach you how you shall arraign your conscience,
And try your penitence, if it be sound,
Or hollowly put on.

JULIET
I'll gladly learn.

DUKE
Love you the man that wrong'd you?

JULIET
Yes, as I love the woman that wrong'd him.

DUKE
So, then, it seems your most offenceful act
Was mutually committed?

JULIET
Mutually.

DUKE
Then was your sin of heavier kind than his.

JULIET
I do confess it, and repent it, father.

DUKE
'Tis meet so, daughter: but lest you do repent,
As that the sin hath brought you to this shame, —
Which sorrow is always toward ourselves, not heaven,
Showing we would not spare heaven as we love it,
But as we stand in fear, —

JULIET
I do repent me, as it is an evil,
And take the shame with joy.

DUKE
There rest.
Your partner, as I hear, must die to-morrow,
And I am going with instruction to him.

DUKE Hail to you, Provost! — so I think you are.

Grace go with you, *Benedicite!*   [*Exit.*

JULIET
Must die to-morrow! O injurious law,
That respites me a life, whose very comfort
Is still a dying horror!

PROVOST
        'Tis pity of him.   [*Exeunt.*

SCENE IV

ANGELO'S *house.*

Enter ANGELO.

ANGELO
When I would pray and think, I think and pray
To several subjects. Heaven hath my empty words;
Whilst my invention, hearing not my tongue,
Anchors on Isabel: Heaven in my mouth,
As if I did but only chew his name;
And in my heart the strong and swelling evil
Of my conception. The state, whereon I studied,
Is like a good thing, being often read,
Grown sear'd and tedious; yea, my gravity,
Wherein — let no man hear me — I take pride,
Could I with boot change for an idle plume,
Which the air beats for vain. O place, O form,
How often dost thou with thy case, thy habit,
Wrench awe from fools, and tie the wiser souls
To thy false seeming! Blood, thou art blood:
Let's write good angel on the devil's horn,
'Tis not the devil's crest.
        Enter SERVANT.
How now! who's there?

SERVANT
        One Isabel, a sister,
Desires access to you.

ANGELO
        Teach her the way.
        [*Exit* SERVANT.
O heavens!
Why does my blood thus muster to my heart,
Making both it unable for itself,
And dispossessing all my other parts
Of necessary fitness?
So play the foolish throngs with one that swoons;
Come all to help him, and so stop the air
By which he should revive: and even so
The general, subject to a well-wish'd king,
Quit their own part, and in obsequious fondness
Crowd to his presence, where their untaught love
Must needs appear offence.
        Enter ISABELLA.
How now, fair maid ı

ISABELLA
        I am come to know your pleasure.

ANGELO
That you might know it, would much better please me
Than to demand what 'tis. Your brother cannot live.

ISABELLA
Even so. — Heaven keep your honour!   [*Retiring.*

ANGELO
Yet may he live awhile; and, it may be,
As long as you or I: yet he must die.

ISABELLA
Under your sentence?

ANGELO
Yea.

ISABELLA
When, I beseech you? that in his reprieve,
Longer or shorter, he may be so fitted
That his soul sicken not.

ANGELO
Ha! fie, these filthy vices! It were as good
To pardon him that hath from nature stol'n
A man already made, as to remit
Their saucy sweetness that do coin heaven's image
In stamps that are forbid: 'tis all as easy
Falsely to take away a life true made,
As to put metal in restrained means
To make a false one.

ISABELLA
'Tis set down so in heaven, but not in earth.

ANGELO
Say you so? then I shall pose you quickly.
Which had you rather, — that the most just law
Now took your brother's life; or, to redeem him,
Give up your body to such sweet uncleanness
As she that he hath stain'd?

ISABELLA
        Sir, believe this,
I had rather give my body than my soul.

ANGELO
I talk not of your soul: our compell'd sins
Stand more for number than for accompt.

ISABELLA
        How say you?

ANGELO
Nay, I'll not warrant that; for I can speak
Against the thing I say. Answer to this: —
I, now the voice of the recorded law,
Pronounce a sentence on your brother's life:
Might there not be a charity in sin
To save this brother's life?

ISABELLA
        Please you to do't,
I'll take it as a peril to my soul,
It is no sin at all, but charity.

ANGELO
Pleas'd you to do't at peril of your soul,
Were equal poise of sin and charity.

ISABELLA
That I do beg his life, if it be sin,
Heaven let me bear it! you granting of my suit,
If that be sin, I'll make it my morn-prayer

To have it added to the faults of mine,
And nothing of your answer.

ANGELO
        Nay, but hear me.
Your sense pursues not mine: either you are ignorant,
Or seem so, craftily; and that's not good.

ISABELLA
Let me be ignorant, and in nothing good,
But graciously to know I am no better.

ANGELO
Thus wisdom wishes to appear most bright
When it doth tax itself; as these black masks
Proclaim an enshield beauty ten times louder
Than beauty could, display'd. — But mark me;
To be received plain, I'll speak more gross:
Your brother is to die.

ISABELLA
So.

ANGELO
And his offence is so, as it appears,
Accountant to the law upon that pain.

ISABELLA
True.

ANGELO
Admit no other way to save his life, —
As I subscribe not that, nor any other,
But in the loss of question, — that you, his sister,
Finding yourself desired of such a person,
Whose credit with the judge, or own great place,
Could fetch your brother from the manacles
Of the all-building law; and that there were
No earthly mean to save him, but that either
You must lay down the treasures of your body
To this suppos'd, or else to let him suffer;
What would you do?

ISABELLA
As much for my poor brother as myself:
That is, were I under the terms of death,
Th'impression of keen whips I'ld wear as rubies
And strip myself to death, as to a bed
That longing have been sick for, ere I'ld yield
My body up to shame.

ANGELO
        Then must
Your brother die.

ISABELLA
        And 'twere the cheaper way:
Better it were a brother died at once,
Than that a sister, by redeeming him,
Should die for ever.

ANGELO
Were not you, then, as cruel as the sentence
That you have slander'd so?

ISABELLA
Ignomy in ransom, and free pardon,
Are of two houses: lawful mercy
Is nothing kin to foul redemption.

ANGELO
You seem'd of late to make the law a tyrant;
And rather prov'd the sliding of your brother
A merriment than a vice.

ISABELLA
O, pardon me, my lord; it oft falls out,
To have what we would have, we speak not what we
    mean:
I something do excuse the thing I hate,
For his advantage that I dearly love.

ANGELO
We are all frail.

ISABELLA
        Else let my brother die,
If not a feodary, but only he,
Owe and succeed this weakness.

ANGELO
        Nay, women are frail too.

ISABELLA
Ay, as the glasses where they view themselves;
Which are as easy broke as they make forms.
Women! — Help heaven! men their creation mar
In profiting by them. Nay, call us ten times frail;
For we are soft as our complexions are,
And credulous to false prints.

ANGELO
        I think it well:
And from this testimony of your own sex, —
Since, I suppose, we are made to be no stronger
Than faults may shake our frames, — let me be bold; —
I do arrest your words. Be that you are,
That is, a woman; if you be more, you're none;
If you be one, — as you are well express'd

By all external warrants, — show it now,
By putting on the destin'd livery.

ISABELLA
I have no tongue but one: gentle my lord,
Let me entreat you speak the former language.

ANGELO
Plainly conceive, I love you.

ISABELLA
My brother did love Juliet; and you tell me
That he shall die for't.

ANGELO
He shall not, Isabel, if you give me love.

ISABELLA
I know your virtue hath a licence in't,
Which seems a little fouler than it is,
To pluck on others.

ANGELO
        Believe me, on mine honour,
My words express my purpose.

ISABELLA
Ha! little honour to be much believed,
And most pernicious purpose! — Seeming, seeming! —
I will proclaim thee, Angelo; look for't:
Sign me a present pardon for my brother,
Or with an outstretch'd throat I'll tell the world
Aloud what man thou art.

ANGELO
        Who will believe thee, Isabel?
My unsoil'd name, th'austereness of my life,
My vouch against you, and my place i' the state,
Will so your accusation overweigh,
That you shall stifle in your own report,
And smell of calumny. I have begun;
And now I give my sensual race the rein:
Fit thy consent to my sharp appetite;
Lay by all nicety and prolixious blushes,
That banish what they sue for; redeem thy brother
By yielding up thy body to my will;
Or else he must not only die the death,
But thy unkindness shall his death draw out
To lingering sufferance. Answer me to-morrow,
Or, by the affection that now guides me most,
I'll prove a tyrant to him. As for you,
Say what you can, my false o'erweighs your true. [*Exit.*

ISABELLA
To whom should I complain? Did I tell this,
Who would believe me? O perilous mouths,
That bear in them one and the self-same tongue,
Either of condemnation or approof;
Bidding the law make court'sy to their will;
Hooking both right and wrong to the appetite,
To follow as it draws! I'll to my brother:
Though he hath fall'n by prompture of the blood,
Yet hath he in him such a mind of honour,
That, had he twenty heads to tender down
On twenty bloody blocks, he'ld yield them up,
Before his sister should her body stoop
To such abhorr'd pollution.
Then, Isabel, live chaste, and, brother, die:
More than our brother is our chastity.
I'll tell him yet of Angelo's request,
And fit his mind to death, for his soul's rest. [*Exit.*

ACT III

SCENE I

The prison.

Enter DUKE *disguised as before,*
CLAUDIO, *and* PROVOST.

DUKE
So, then, you hope of pardon from Lord Angelo?

CLAUDIO
The miserable have no other medicine
But only hope:
I have hope to live, and am prepar'd to die.

DUKE
Be absolute for death; either death or life
Shall thereby be the sweeter. Reason thus with life: —
If I do lose thee, I do lose a thing
That none but fools would keep: a breath thou art,
Servile to all the skyey influences
That do this habitation, where thou keep'st,
Hourly afflict: merely, thou art death's fool;
For him thou labour'st by thy flight to shun,
And yet runn'st toward him still. Thou art not noble;
For all th'accommodations that thou bear'st
Are nurs'd by baseness. Thou'rt by no means valiant;
For thou dost fear the soft and tender fork

Of a poor worm. Thy best of rest is sleep,
And that thou oft provokest; yet grossly fear'st
Thy death, which is no more. Thou art not thyself;
For thou exists on many a thousand grains
That issue out of dust. Happy thou art not;
For what thou hast not, still thou strivest to get,
And what thou hast, forgett'st. Thou art not certain;
For thy complexion shifts to strange effects,
After the moon. If thou art rich, thou'rt poor;
For, like an ass whose back with ingots bows,
Thou bear'st thy heavy riches but a journey,
And death unloads thee. Friend hast thou none;
For thine own bowels, which do call thee sire,
The mere effusions of thy proper loins,
Do curse the gout, serpigo, and the rheum,
For ending thee no sooner. Thou hast nor youth nor
    age,
But, as it were, an after-dinner's sleep,
Dreaming on both; for all thy blessed youth
Becomes as aged, and doth beg the alms
Of palsied eld; and when thou art old and rich,
Thou hast neither heat, affection, limb, nor beauty,
To make thy riches pleasant. What's yet in this
That bears the name of life? Yet in this life
Lie hid more thousand deaths: yet death we fear,
That makes these odds all even.

CLAUDIO
        I humbly thank you.
To sue to live, I find I seek to die;
And, seeking death, find life: let it come on.

ISABELLA [*within*].
What, ho! Peace here; grace and good company!

PROVOST
Who's there? come in: the wish deserves a welcome.

DUKE
Dear sir, ere long I'll visit you again.

CLAUDIO
Most holy sir, I thank you.

Enter ISABELLA.

ISABELLA
My business is a word or two with Claudio.

PROVOST
And very welcome. — Look, signior, here's your sister.

DUKE
Provost, a word with you.

PROVOST
        As many as you please.

DUKE
Bring me to hear them speak, where I may be conceal'd.
        [*Exeunt* DUKE *and* PROVOST.

CLAUDIO
Now, sister, what's the comfort?

ISABELLA
        Why,
As all comforts are; most good, most good indeed.
Lord Angelo, having affairs to heaven,

Intends you for his swift ambassador,
Where you shall be an everlasting leiger:
Therefore your best appointment make with speed;
To-morrow you set on.

CLAUDIO
        Is there no remedy?

ISABELLA
None, but such remedy as, to save a head,
To cleave a heart in twain.

CLAUDIO
        But is there any?

ISABELLA
Yes, brother, you may live:
There is a devilish mercy in the judge,
If you'll implore it, that will free your life,
But fetter you till death.

CLAUDIO
        Perpetual durance?

ISABELLA
Ay, just; perpetual durance, — a restraint,
Though all the world's vastidity you had,
To a determin'd scope.

CLAUDIO
        But in what nature?

ISABELLA
In such a one as, you consenting to't,
Would bark your honour from that trunk you bear,
And leave you naked.

CLAUDIO
        Let me know the point.

ISABELLA
O, I do fear thee, Claudio; and I quake,
Lest thou a feverous life shouldst entertain,
And six or seven winters more respect
Than a perpetual honour. Darest thou die?
The sense of death is most in apprehension;
And the poor beetle that we tread upon,
In corporal sufferance finds a pang as great
As when a giant dies.

CLAUDIO
        Why give you me this shame?
Think you I can a resolution fetch
From flowery tenderness? If I must die,
I will encounter darkness as a bride,
And hug it in mine arms.

ISABELLA
There spake my brother; there my father's grave
Did utter forth a voice! Yes, thou must die:
Thou art too noble to conserve a life
In base appliances. This outward-sainted deputy —
Whose settled visage and deliberate word
Nips youth i' the head, and follies doth emmew
As falcon doth the fowl — is yet a devil;
His filth within being cast, he would appear
A pond as deep as hell.

CLAUDIO
        The priestly Angelo?

DUKE So, then, you hope of pardon from Lord Angelo?

ISABELLA

O, 'tis the cunning livery of hell,
The damned'st body to invest and cover
In priestly guards! Dost thou think, Claudio? —
If I would yield him my virginity,
Thou mightst be freed.

CLAUDIO

O heavens! it cannot be.

ISABELLA

Yes, he would give't thee, from this rank offence,
So to offend him still. This night's the time
That I should do what I abhor to name,
Or else thou diest to-morrow.

CLAUDIO

Thou shalt not do't.

ISABELLA

O, were it but my life,
I'd throw it down for your deliverance
As frankly as a pin.

CLAUDIO

Thanks, dear Isabel.

ISABELLA

Be ready, Claudio, for your death to-morrow.

CLAUDIO

Yes. — Has he affections in him,
That thus can make him bite the law by the nose,
When he would force it? Sure, it is no sin,
Or of the deadly seven it is the least.

ISABELLA

Which is the least?

CLAUDIO

If it were damnable, he being so wise,
Why would he for the momentary trick
Be perdurably fined? — O Isabel!

ISABELLA

What says my brother?

CLAUDIO

Death is a fearful thing.

ISABELLA

And shamed life a hateful.

CLAUDIO

Ay, but to die, and go we know not where;
To lie in cold obstruction, and to rot;
This sensible warm motion to become
A kneaded clod; and the delighted spirit
To bathe in fiery floods, or to reside
In thrilling region of thick-ribbed ice;
To be imprison'd in the viewless winds,
And blown with restless violence round about
The pendent world; or to be worse than worst
Of those that lawless and incertain thought
Imagine howling! — 'tis too horrible!
The weariest and most loathed worldly life
That age, ache, penury, and imprisonment
Can lay on nature, is a paradise
To what we fear of death.

ISABELLA

Alas, alas!

CLAUDIO

Sweet sister, let me live:
What sin you do to save a brother's life,
Nature dispenses with the deed so far
That it becomes a virtue.

ISABELLA

O you beast!
O faithless coward! O dishonest wretch!
Wilt thou be made a man out of my vice?
Is't not a kind of incest, to take life
From thine own sister's shame? What should I think?
Heaven shield my mother play'd my father fair!
For such a warped slip of wilderness
Ne'er issued from his blood. Take my defiance;
Die, perish! might but my bending down
Reprieve thee from thy fate, it should proceed:
I'll pray a thousand prayers for thy death, —
No word to save thee.

CLAUDIO

Nay, hear me, Isabel.

ISABELLA

O, fie, fie, fie!
Thy sin's not accidental, but a trade.
Mercy to thee would prove itself a bawd:
'Tis best thou diest quickly.   [Going.

CLAUDIO

O, hear me, Isabella!

Enter DUKE.

DUKE

Vouchsafe a word, young sister, but one word.

ISABELLA

What is your will?

DUKE

Might you dispense with your leisure, I would by and
by have some speech with you: the satisfaction I would
require is likewise your own benefit.

ISABELLA

I have no superfluous leisure; my stay must be stolen
out of other affairs; but I will attend you awhile.

DUKE

Son, I have overheard what hath pass'd between you
and your sister. Angelo had never the purpose to
corrupt her; only he hath made an assay of her virtue to
practise his judgement with the disposition of natures:
she, having the truth of honour in her, hath made him
that gracious denial which he is most glad to receive. I
am confessor to Angelo, and I know this to be true;
therefore prepare yourself to death: do not satisfy your
resolution with hopes that are fallible: to-morrow you
must die; go to your knees and make ready.

CLAUDIO

Let me ask my sister pardon. I am so out of love with
life, that I will sue to be rid of it.

DUKE

Hold you there: farewell. [*Exit CLAUDIO.*] Provost, a
word with you!

Enter PROVOST.

PROVOST

What's your will, father?

DUKE

That now you are come, you will be gone. Leave me
awhile with the maid: my mind promises with my
habit no loss shall touch her by my company.

PROVOST

In good time.   [*Exit.*

DUKE

The hand that hath made you fair hath made you good:
the goodness that is cheap in beauty makes beauty
brief in goodness; but grace, being the soul of your
complexion, shall keep the body of it ever fair. The
assault that Angelo hath made to you, fortune hath
convey'd to my understanding; and, but that frailty
hath examples for his falling, I should wonder at
Angelo. How will you do to content this substitute, and
to save your brother?

ISABELLA

I am now going to resolve him, I had rather my brother
die by the law than my son should be unlawfully born.
But, O, how much is the good duke deceived in Angelo!
If ever he return, and I can speak to him, I will open my
lips in vain, or discover his government.

DUKE

That shall not be much amiss: yet, as the matter now
stands, he will avoid your accusation, — he made trial
of you only. Therefore fasten your ear on my advisings:
to the love I have in doing good a remedy presents
itself. I do make myself believe that you may most
uprightously do a poor wrong'd lady a merited
benefit; redeem your brother from the angry law; do no
stain to your own gracious person; and much please
the absent duke, if peradventure he shall ever return to
have hearing of this business.

ISABELLA

Let me hear you speak further. I have spirit to do any
thing that appears not foul in the truth of my spirit.

DUKE

Virtue is bold, and goodness never fearful. Have you
not heard speak of Mariana, the sister of Frederick the
great soldier who miscarried at sea?

ISABELLA

I have heard of the lady, and good words went with her
name.

DUKE

She should this Angelo have married; was affianced to
her by oath, and the nuptial appointed: between which
time of the contract and limit of the solemnity, her
brother Frederick was wrack'd at sea, having in that
perish'd vessel the dowry of his sister. But mark how
heavily this befell to the poor gentlewoman: there she
lost a noble and renown'd brother, in his love toward
her ever most kind and natural; with him, the portion
and sinew of her fortune, her marriage-dowry; with
both, her combinate husband, this well-seeming
Angelo.

ISABELLA

Can this be so? did Angelo so leave her?

DUKE

Left her in her tears, and dried not one of them with his
comfort; swallow'd his vows whole, pretending in her

discoveries of dishonour: in few, bestow'd her on her
own lamentation, which she yet wears for his sake; and
he, a marble to her tears, is wash'd with them, but
relents not.

ISABELLA

What a merit were it in death to take this poor maid
from the world! What corruption in this life, that it will
let this man live! — But how out of this can she avail?

DUKE

It is a rupture that you may easily heal: and the cure of
it not only saves your brother, but keeps you from
dishonour in doing it.

ISABELLA

Show me how, good father.

DUKE

This forenam'd maid hath yet in her the continuance of
her first affection: his unjust unkindness, that in all
reason should have quench'd her love, hath, like an
impediment in the current, made it more violent and
unruly. Go you to Angelo; answer his requiring with a
plausible obedience; agree with his demands to the
point; only refer yourself to this advantage, — first, that
your stay with him may not be long; that the time may
have all shadow and silence in it; and the place answer
to convenience. This being granted in course — and
now follows all — we shall advise this wrong'd maid to
stead up your appointment, go in your place; if the
encounter acknowledge itself hereafter, it may compel
him to her recompense: and here, by this, is your
brother saved, your honour untainted, the poor
Mariana advantaged, and the corrupt deputy scaled.
The maid will I frame and make fit for his attempt. If
you think well to carry this as you may, the doubleness
of the benefit defends the deceit from reproof. What
think you of it?

ISABELLA

The image of it gives me content already; and I trust it
will grow to a most prosperous perfection.

DUKE

It lies much in your holding up. Haste you speedily to
Angelo: if for this night he entreat you to his bed, give
him promise of satisfaction. I will presently to Saint
Luke's: there, at the moated grange, resides this
dejected Mariana. At that place call upon me; and
dispatch with Angelo, that it may be quickly.

ISABELLA

I thank you for this comfort. Fare you well, good father.

[*Exeunt.*

SCENE II

The street before the prison.

*Enter DUKE disguised as before; to him, ELBOW and
OFFICERS with POMPEY.*

ELBOW

Nay, if there be no remedy for it, but that you will needs
buy and sell men and women like beasts, we shall have
all the world drink brown and white bastard.

DUKE

O heavens! what stuff is here?

POMPEY

'Twas never merry world since, of two usuries, the
merriest was put down, and the worser allow'd by order
of law a furr'd gown to keep him warm; and furr'd with
fox and lamb-skins too, to signify, that craft, being
richer than innocency, stands for the facing.

ELBOW

Come your way, sir. — 'Bless you, good father friar.

DUKE

And you, good brother father. What offence hath this
man made you, sir?

ELBOW

Marry, sir, he hath offended the law: and, sir, we take
him to be a thief too, sir; for we have found upon him,
sir, a strange picklock, which we have sent to the
deputy.

DUKE

Fie, sirrah! a bawd, a wicked bawd!
The evil that thou causest to be done,
That is thy means to live. Do thou but think
What 'tis to cram a maw or clothe a back
From such a filthy vice: say to thyself, —
From their abominable and beastly touches
I drink, I eat, array myself, and live.
Canst thou believe thy living is a life,
So stinkingly depending? Go mend, go mend.

POMPEY

Indeed, it does stink in some sort, sir; but yet, sir, I
would prove —

ELBOW Marry, sir, he hath offended the law.

DUKE
Nay, if the devil have given thee proofs for sin,
Thou wilt prove his. — Take him to prison, officer:
Correction and instruction must both work
Ere this rude beast will profit.

ELBOW
He must before the deputy, sir; he has given him
warning: the deputy cannot abide a whoremaster: if he
be a whoremonger, and comes before him, he were as
good go a mile on his errand.

DUKE
That we were all, as some would seem to be,
From our faults, or faults from seeming, free!

ELBOW
His neck will come to your waist, — a cord, sir.

POMPEY
I spy comfort; I cry, bail! Here's a gentleman and a
friend of mine.

Enter LUCIO.

LUCIO
How now, noble Pompey! What, at the wheels of
Cæsar! art thou led in triumph? What, is there none of
Pygmalion's images, newly-made woman, to be had
now, for putting the hand in the pocket and extracting
it clutch'd? What reply, ha? What say'st thou to this
tune, matter, and method? Is't not drown'd i' the last
rain, ha? What say'st thou, Trot? Is the world as it was,
man? Which is the way? Is it sad, and few words? or
how? The trick of it?

DUKE
Still thus, and thus; still worse!

LUCIO
How doth my dear morsel, thy mistress? Procures she
still, ha?

POMPEY
Troth, sir, she hath eaten up all her beef, and she is
herself in the tub.

LUCIO
Why, 'tis good; it is the right of it; it must be so: ever
your fresh whore and your powder'd bawd: an
unshunn'd consequence; it must be so. Art going to
prison, Pompey?

POMPEY
Yes, faith, sir.

LUCIO
Why, 'tis not amiss, Pompey. Farewell: go, say I sent
thee thither. For debt, Pompey? or how?

ELBOW
For being a bawd, for being a bawd.

LUCIO
Well, then, imprison him: if imprisonment be the due
of a bawd, why, 'tis his right: bawd is he doubtless, and
of antiquity too; bawd-born. — Farewell, good Pompey.
Commend me to the prison, Pompey: you will turn
good husband now, Pompey; you will keep the house.

POMPEY
I hope, sir, your good worship will be my bail.

LUCIO
No, indeed, will I not, Pompey; it is not the wear. I will
pray, Pompey, to increase your bondage: If you take it

not patiently, why, your mettle is the more. Adieu,
trusty Pompey. — Bless you, friar.

DUKE
And you.

LUCIO
Does Bridget paint still, Pompey, ha?

ELBOW
Come your ways, sir; come.

POMPEY
You will not bail me, then, sir?

LUCIO
Then, Pompey, nor now. — What news abroad, friar,
what news?

ELBOW
Come your ways, sir; come.

LUCIO
Go, — to kennel, Pompey; go. [*Exeunt* ELBOW *and*
OFFICERS *with* POMPEY.] What news, friar, of the
duke?

DUKE
I know none. Can you tell me of any?

LUCIO
Some say he is with the Emperor of Russia; other
some, he is in Rome: but where is he, think you?

DUKE
I know not where; but wheresoever, I wish him well.

LUCIO
It was a mad fantastical trick of him to steal from the
state, and usurp the beggary he was never born to. Lord
Angelo dukes it well in his absence; he puts
transgression to't.

DUKE
He does well in't.

LUCIO
A little more lenity to lechery would do no harm in him:
something too crabb'd that way, friar.

DUKE
It is too general a vice, and severity must cure it.

LUCIO
Yes, in good sooth, the vice is of a great kindred; it is
well allied; but it is impossible to extirp it quite, friar,
till eating and drinking be put down. They say this
Angelo was not made by man and woman, after the
downright way of creation: is it true, think you?

DUKE
How should he be made, then?

LUCIO
Some report a sea-maid spawn'd him; some, that he
was begot between two stock-fishes. But it is certain
that, when he makes water, his urine is congeal'd ice;
that I know to be true: and he is a motion ungenerative;
that's infallible.

DUKE
You are pleasant, sir, and speak apace.

LUCIO
Why, what a ruthless thing is this in him, for the
rebellion of a codpiece to take away the life of a man!
Would the duke that is absent have done this? Ere he
would have hang'd a man for the getting a hundred
bastards, he would have paid for the nursing a

thousand: he had some feeling of the sport; he knew
the service, and that instructed him to mercy.

DUKE
I never heard the absent duke much detected for
women; he was not inclined that way.

LUCIO
O, sir, you are deceived.

DUKE
'Tis not possible.

LUCIO
Who, not the duke? yes, your beggar of fifty; and his
use was to put a ducat in her clack-dish: the duke had
crotchets in him. He would be drunk too; that let me
inform you.

DUKE
You do him wrong, surely.

LUCIO
Sir, I was an inward of his. A sly fellow was the
duke: and I believe I know the cause of his
withdrawing.

DUKE
What, I prithee, might be the cause?

LUCIO
No, — pardon; 'tis a secret must be lock'd within the
teeth and the lips: but this I can let you understand, —
the greater file of the subject held the duke to be wise.

DUKE
Wise! why, no question but he was.

LUCIO
A very superficial, ignorant, unweighing fellow.

DUKE
Either this is the envy in you, folly, or mistaking: the
very stream of his life and the business he hath helm'd
must, upon a warranted need, give him a better
proclamation. Let him be but testimonied in his own
bringings-forth, and he shall appear to the envious a
scholar, a statesman, and a soldier. Therefore you
speak unskilfully; or if your knowledge be more, it is
much darken'd in your malice.

LUCIO
Sir, I know him, and I love him.

DUKE
Love talks with better knowledge, and knowledge with
dearer love.

LUCIO
Come, sir, I know what I know.

DUKE
I can hardly believe that, since you know not what you
speak. But, if ever the duke return, — as our prayers are
he may, — let me desire you to make your answer
before him. If it be honest you have spoke, you have
courage to maintain it: I am bound to call upon you;
and, I pray you, your name?

LUCIO
Sir, my name is Lucio; well known to the duke.

DUKE
He shall know you better, sir, if I may live to report you.

LUCIO
I fear you not.

DUKE
O, you hope the duke will return no more; or you
imagine me too unhurtful an opposite. But, indeed, I
can do you little harm; you'll forswear this again.

LUCIO
I'll be hang'd first: thou art deceived in me, friar. But
no more of this. Canst thou tell if Claudio die
to-morrow or no?

DUKE
Why should he die, sir?

LUCIO
Why, for filling a bottle with a tun-dish. I would the
duke we talk of were return'd again: this ungenitured
agent will unpeople the province with continency;
sparrows must not build in his house-eaves, because
they are lecherous. The duke yet would have dark deeds
darkly answer'd; he would never bring them to light:
would he were return'd! Marry, this Claudio is
condemn'd for untrussing. Farewell, good friar: I
prithee, pray for me. The duke, I say to thee again,
would eat mutton on Fridays. He's now past it; yet, and
I say to thee, he would mouth with a beggar, though
she smelt brown bread and garlick: say that I said so.
Farewell. [*Exit*.

DUKE
No might nor greatness in mortality
Can censure scape; back-wounding calumny
The whitest virtue strikes. What king so strong
Can tie the gall up in the slanderous tongue? —
But who comes here?

Enter ESCALUS, PROVOST, *and* OFFICERS *with* MISTRESS OVERDONE.

ESCALUS
Go; away with her to prison!
MISTRESS OVERDONE
Good my lord, be good to me; your honour is accounted a merciful man; good my lord.
ESCALUS
Double and treble admonition, and still forfeit in the same kind? This would make mercy swear and play the tyrant.
PROVOST
A bawd of eleven years' continuance, may it please your honour.
MISTRESS OVERDONE
My lord, this is one Lucio's information against me. Mistress Kate Keep-down was with child by him in the duke's time; he promised her marriage: his child is a year and a quarter old, come Philip and Jacob: I have kept it myself; and see how he goes about to abuse me!
ESCALUS
That fellow is a fellow of much licence: — let him be call'd before us. — Away with her to prison! — Go to; no more words. [*Exeunt* OFFICERS *with* MISTRESS OVERDONE.] Provost, my brother Angelo will not be alter'd; Claudio must die to-morrow: let him be furnish'd with divines, and have all charitable preparation. If my brother wrought by my pity, it should not be so with him.
PROVOST
So please you, this friar hath been with him, and advised him for the entertainment of death.
ESCALUS
Good even, good father.
DUKE
Bliss and goodness on you!
ESCALUS
Of whence are you?
DUKE
Not of this country, though my chance is now
To use it for my time: I am a brother
Of gracious order, late come from the See
In special business from his holiness.
ESCALUS
What news abroad i' the world?
DUKE
None, but that there is so great a fever on goodness, that the dissolution of it must cure it: novelty is only in request; and it is as dangerous to be aged in any kind of course, as it is virtuous to be constant in any undertaking: there is scarce truth enough alive to make societies secure; but security enough to make fellowships accurs'd: — much upon this riddle runs the wisdom of the world. This news is old enough, yet it is every day's news. I pray you, sir, of what disposition was the duke?
ESCALUS
One that, above all other strifes, contended especially to know himself.
DUKE
What pleasure was he given to?
ESCALUS
Rather rejoicing to see another merry, than merry at any thing which profess'd to make him rejoice: a gentleman of all temperance. But leave we him to his events, with a prayer they may prove prosperous; and let me desire to know how you find Claudio prepared. I am made to understand that you have lent him visitation.
DUKE
He professes to have received no sinister measure from his judge, but most willingly humbles himself to the determination of justice: yet had he framed to himself, by the instruction of his frailty, many deceiving promises of life; which I, by my good leisure, have discredited to him, and now is he resolved to die.
ESCALUS
You have paid the heavens your function, and the prisoner the very debt of your calling. I have labour'd for the poor gentleman to the extremest shore of my modesty: but my brother justice have I found so severe, that he hath forced me to tell him he is indeed Justice.
DUKE
If his own life answer the straitness of his proceeding, it shall become him well; wherein if he chance to fail, he hath sentenced himself.
ESCALUS
I am going to visit the prisoner. Fare you well.
DUKE
Peace be with you!
                [*Exeunt* ESCALUS *and* PROVOST.
He who the sword of heaven will bear
Should be as holy as severe;
Pattern in himself to know,
Grace to stand, and virtue go;
More nor less to others paying
Than by self-offences weighing.
Shame to him whose cruel striking
Kills for faults of his own liking!
Twice treble shame on Angelo,
To weed my vice, and let his grow!
O, what may man within him hide,
Though angel on the outward side!
How may likeness wade in crimes,
Making practice on the times,
To draw with idle spiders' strings
Most ponderous and substantial things
Craft against vice I must apply:
With Angelo to-night shall lie
His old betrothed but despis'd;
So disguise shall, by the disguis'd,
Pay with falsehood false exacting,
And perform an old contracting.   [*Exit.

ACT IV

SCENE I

The Moated Grange.

Enter MARIANA; *a* BOY *singing.*

Song.
Take, O take those lips away,
  That so sweetly were forsworn;
And those eyes, the break of day,
  Lights that do mislead the morn:
But my kisses bring again, bring again;
  Seals of love, but seal'd in vain, seal'd in vain.

MARIANA
Break off thy song, and haste thee quick away:
Here comes a man of comfort, whose advice
Hath often still'd my brawling discontent.   [*Exit* BOY.
      Enter DUKE *disguised as before.*
I cry you mercy, sir; and well could wish
You had not found me here so musical:
Let me excuse me, and believe me so, —
My mirth it much displeas'd, but pleas'd my woe.
DUKE
'Tis good; though music oft hath such a charm
To make bad good, and good provoke to harm. —
I pray you, tell me, hath any body inquired for me here
to-day? much upon this time have I promised here to
meet.
MARIANA
You have not been inquired after: I have sat here all day.
DUKE
I do constantly believe you. — The time is come even now. I shall crave your forbearance a little: may be I will call upon you anon, for some advantage to yourself.
MARIANA
I am always bound to you.   [*Exit.

             Enter ISABELLA.

DUKE
Very well met, and welcome.
What is the news from this good deputy?
ISABELLA
He hath a garden circummured with brick,
Whose western side is with a vineyard back'd;
And to that vineyard is a planched gate,
That makes his opening with this bigger key:
This other doth command a little door
Which from the vineyard to the garden leads;
There have I made my promise
Upon the heavy middle of the night
To call upon him.
DUKE
But shall you on your knowledge find this way?
ISABELLA
I have ta'en a due and wary note upon't:
With whispering and most guilty diligence,
In action all of precept, he did show me
The way twice o'er.
DUKE
          Are there no other tokens
Between you 'greed concerning her observance?
ISABELLA
No, none, but only a repair i' the dark;
And that I have possess'd him my most stay
Can be but brief; for I have made him know
I have a servant comes with me along,
That stays upon me; whose persuasion is
I come about my brother.
DUKE
          'Tis well borne up.
I have not yet made known to Mariana
A word of this. — What, ho! within! come forth!
        Enter MARIANA.
I pray you, be acquainted with this maid;
She comes to do you good.
ISABELLA
          I do desire the like.
DUKE
Do you persuade yourself that I respect you?
MARIANA
Good friar, I know you do, and have found it.
DUKE
Take, then, this your companion by the hand,
Who hath a story ready for your ear.
I shall attend your leisure: but make haste;
The vaporous night approaches.
MARIANA
          Will't please you walk aside?
      [*Exeunt* MARIANA *and* ISABELLA.
DUKE
O place and greatness, millions of false eyes
Are stuck upon thee! volumes of report
Run with these false and most contrarious quests
Upon thy doings! thousand escapes of wit
Make thee the father of their idle dream,
And rack thee in their fancies!
      Enter MARIANA *and* ISABELLA.
          Welcome! How agreed?
ISABELLA
She'll take the enterprise upon her, father,
If you advise it.
DUKE
          It is not my consent,
But my entreaty too.
ISABELLA
          Little have you to say
When you depart from him, but, soft and low,
'Remember now my brother.'
MARIANA
          Fear me not.
DUKE
Nor, gentle daughter, fear you not at all.
He is your husband on a pre-contract:
To bring you thus together, 'tis no sin,
Sith that the justice of your title to him
Doth flourish the deceit. Come, let us go:
Our corn's to reap, for yet our tilth's to sow.   [*Exeunt.

SCENE II

The prison.

Enter PROVOST *and* POMPEY.

PROVOST
Come hither, sirrah. Can you cut off a man's head?
POMPEY
If the man be a bachelor, sir, I can; but if he be a

MARIANA Break off thy song, and haste thee quick away.

married man, he's his wife's head, and I can never cut off a woman's head.
PROVOST
Come, sir, leave me your snatches, and yield me a direct answer. To-morrow morning are to die Claudio and Barnardine. Here is in our prison a common executioner, who in his office lacks a helper: if you will take it on you to assist him, it shall redeem you from your gyves; if not, you shall have your full time of imprisonment, and your deliverance with an unpitied whipping, for you have been a notorious bawd.
POMPEY
Sir, I have been an unlawful bawd time out of mind; but yet I will be content to be a lawful hangman. I would be glad to receive some instruction from my fellow partner.
PROVOST
What, ho, Abhorson! Where's Abhorson, there?

Enter ABHORSON.

ABHORSON
Do you call, sir?
PROVOST
Sirrah, here's a fellow will help you to-morrow in your execution. If you think it meet, compound with him by the year, and let him abide here with you; if not, use him for the present, and dismiss him. He cannot plead his estimation with you; he hath been a bawd.
ABHORSON
A bawd, sir! fie upon him! he will discredit our mystery.
PROVOST
Go to, sir; you weigh equally; a feather will turn the scale. [*Exit.*
POMPEY
Pray, sir, by your good favour, — for surely, sir, a good favour you have, but that you have a hanging look, — do you call, sir, your occupation a mystery?
ABHORSON
Ay, sir; a mystery
POMPEY
Painting, sir, I have heard say, is a mystery; and your whores, sir, being members of my occupation, using painting, do prove my occupation a mystery: but what mystery there should be in hanging, if I should be hang'd, I cannot imagine.
ABHORSON
Sir, it is a mystery.
POMPEY
Proof?
ABHORSON
Every true man's apparel fits your thief: if it be too little for your thief, your true man thinks it big enough; if it be too big for your thief, your thief thinks it little enough: so every true man's apparel fits your thief.

Enter PROVOST.

PROVOST
Are you agreed?
POMPEY
Sir, I will serve him; for I do find your hangman is a more penitent trade than your bawd, — he doth oftener ask forgiveness.
PROVOST
You, sirrah, provide your block and your axe to-morrow four o'clock.
ABHORSON
Come on, bawd; I will instruct thee in my trade, follow.
POMPEY
I do desire to learn, sir: and I hope, if you have occasion to use me for your own turn, you shall find me yare; for, truly, sir, for your kindness I owe you a good turn.
PROVOST
Call hither Barnardine and Claudio:

[*Exeunt* POMPEY *and* ABHORSON.

Th'one has my pity; not a jot the other,
Being a murderer, though he were my brother.

Enter CLAUDIO.

Look, here's the warrant, Claudio, for thy death:
'Tis now dead midnight, and by eight to-morrow
Thou must be made immortal. Where's Barnardine?
CLAUDIO
As fast lock'd up in sleep as guiltless labour,
When it lies starkly in the traveller's bones:
He will not wake.
PROVOST
                    Who can do good on him?
Well, go, prepare thyself. [*Knocking within.*] But, hark, what noise? —
Heaven give your spirits comfort! [*Exit* CLAUDIO.] By and by! —
I hope it is some pardon or reprieve
For the most gentle Claudio.

Enter DUKE *disguised as before.*
                    Welcome, father.

DUKE
The best and wholesom'st spirts of the night
Envelop you, good provost! Who call'd here of late?
PROVOST
None, since the curfew rung.
DUKE
Not Isabel?
PROVOST
                    No.
DUKE
                    They will, then, ere't be long.
PROVOST
What comfort is for Claudio?

DUKE
There's some in hope.
PROVOST
                    It is a bitter deputy.
DUKE
Not so, not so; his life is parallel'd
Even with the stroke and line of his great justice:
He doth with holy abstinence subdue
That in himself which he spurs on his power
To qualify in others: were he meal'd with that
Which he corrects, then were he tyrannous;
But this being so, he's just.   [*Knocking within.*
                    Now are they come.
                              [*Exit* PROVOST.
This is a gentle provost: seldom, when
The steeled gaoler is the friend of men.
                              [*Knocking within.*
How now! what noise? That spirit's possess'd with haste
That wounds th'unsisting postern with these strokes.

Enter PROVOST.

PROVOST
There he must stay until the officer
Arise to let him in: he is call'd up.
DUKE
Have you no countermand for Claudio yet,
But he must die to-morrow?
PROVOST
                    None, sir, none.
DUKE
As near the dawning, provost, as it is,
You shall hear more ere morning.
PROVOST
                    Happily
You something know; yet I believe there comes
No countermand; no such example have we:
Besides, upon the very siege of justice
Lord Angelo hath to the public ear
Profess'd the contrary.

Enter a MESSENGER.
                    This is his lordship's man.
DUKE
And here comes Claudio's pardon.
MESSENGER [*giving a paper*].
My lord hath sent you this note; and by me this further charge, — that you swerve not from the smallest article of it, neither in time, matter, or other circumstance. Good morrow; for, as I take it, it is almost day.
PROVOST
I shall obey him.   [*Exit* MESSENGER.
DUKE [*aside*].
This is his pardon, purchas'd by such sin
For which the pardoner himself is in.
Hence hath offence his quick celerity,
When it is born in high authority:
When vice makes mercy, mercy's so extended,
That for the fault's love is th'offender friended. —
Now, sir, what news?
PROVOST
I told you: Lord Angelo, belike thinking me remiss in mine office, awakens me with this unwonted putting-on; methinks strangely, for he hath not used it before.
DUKE
Pray you, let's hear.
PROVOST [*reads*].
Whatsoever you may hear to the contrary, let Claudio be executed by four of the clock; and in the afternoon Barnardine: for my better satisfaction, let me have Claudio's head sent me by five. Let this be duly perform'd; with a thought that more depends on it than we must yet deliver. Thus fail not to do your office, as you will answer it at your peril.
What say you to this, sir?
DUKE
What is that Barnardine who is to be executed in th'afternoon?
PROVOST
A Bohemian born, but here nursed up and bred; one that is a prisoner nine years old.
DUKE
How came it that the absent duke had not either deliver'd him to his liberty or executed him? I have heard it was ever his manner to do so.
PROVOST
His friends still wrought reprieves for him: and, indeed, his fact, till now in the government of Lord Angelo, came not to an undoubtful proof.

DUKE
It is now apparent?
PROVOST
Most manifest, and not denied by himself.
DUKE
Hath he born himself penitently in prison? How seems
he to be touch'd?
PROVOST
A man that apprehends death no more dreadfully but
as a drunken sleep; careless, reckless, and fearless of
what's past, present, or to come; insensible of
mortality, and desperately mortal.
DUKE
He wants advice.
PROVOST
He will hear none: he hath evermore had the liberty of
the prison; give him leave to escape hence, he would
not: drunk many times a day, if not many days entirely
drunk. We have very oft awaked him, as if to carry him
to execution, and show'd him a seeming warrant for it:
it hath not moved him at all.
DUKE
More of him anon. There is written in your brow,
provost, honesty and constancy: if I read it not truly, my
ancient skill beguiles me; but, in the boldness of my
cunning, I will lay myself in hazard. Claudio, whom
here you have warrant to execute, is no greater forfeit to
the law than Angelo, who hath sentenced him. To
make you understand this in a manifested effect, I
crave but four days' respite; for the which you are to do
me both a present and a dangerous courtesy.
PROVOST
Pray, sir, in what?
DUKE
In the delaying death.
PROVOST
Alack, how may I do it, — having the hour limited, and
an express command, under penalty, to deliver his
head in the view of Angelo? I may make my case as
Claudio's, to cross this in the smallest.
DUKE
By the vow of mine order I warrant you, if my
instructions may be your guide. Let this Barnardine be
this morning executed, and his head borne to Angelo.
PROVOST
Angelo hath seen them both, and will discover the
favour.
DUKE
O, death's a great disguiser; and you may add to it.
Shave the head, and tie the beard; and say it was the
desire of the penitent to be so bared before his death:
you know the course is common. If any thing fall to you
upon this, more than thanks and good fortune, by the
saint whom I profess, I will plead against it with my
life.
PROVOST
Pardon me, good father; it is against my oath.
DUKE
Were you sworn to the duke, or to the deputy?
PROVOST
To him, and to his substitutes.
DUKE
You will think you have made no offence, if the duke
avouch the justice of your dealing?
PROVOST
But what likelihood is in that?
DUKE
Not a resemblance, but a certainty. Yet since I see you
fearful that neither my coat, integrity, nor persuasion
can with ease attempt you, I will go further than I
meant, to pluck all fears out of you. Look you, sir, here
is the hand and seal of the duke: you know the
character, I doubt not; and the signet is not strange to
you.
PROVOST
I know them both.
DUKE
The contents of this is the return of the duke; you shall
anon over-read it at your pleasure; where you shall find,
within these two days he will be here. This is a thing
that Angelo knows not; for he this very day receives
letters of strange tenor; perchance of the duke's death;
perchance entering into some monastery; but, by
chance, nothing of what is writ. Look, th'unfolding star
calls up the shepherd. Put not yourself into
amazement how these things should be: all difficulties
are but easy when they are known. Call your
executioner, and off with Barnardine's head: I will give
him a present shrift, and advise him for a better place.

Yet you are amazed; but this shall absolutely resolve
you. Come away; it is almost clear dawn.   [*Exeunt.*

SCENE III

Another room in the same.

Enter POMPEY.

POMPEY
I am as well acquainted here as I was in our house of
profession: one would think it were Mistress
Overdone's own house, for here be many of her old
customers. First, here's young Master Rash; he's in for
a commodity of brown paper and old ginger,
nine-score and seventeen pounds; of which he made
five marks, ready money; marry, then ginger was not
much in request, for the old women were all dead.
Then is there here one Master Caper, at the suit of
Master Three-pile the mercer, for some four suits of
peach-colour'd satin, which now peaches him a beggar.
Then have we here young Dizzy, and young Master
Deep-vow, and Master Copper-spur, and Master
Starve-lackey, the rapier-and-dagger-man, and young
Drop-heir that kill'd lusty Pudding, and Master
Forthright the tilter, and brave Master Shoe-tie the
great traveller, and wild Half-can that stabb'd Pots,
and, I think, forty more, all great doers in our trade, and
are now 'for the Lord's sake.'

Enter ABHORSON.

ABHORSON
Sirrah, bring Barnardine hither.
POMPEY
Master Barnardine! you must rise and be hang'd,
Master Barnardine!
ABHORSON
What, ho, Barnardine!
BARNARDINE [*within*].
A pox o' your throats! Who makes that noise there?
Who are you?
POMPEY
Your friends, sir; the hangman. You must be so good,
sir, to rise and be put to death.
BARNARDINE [*within*].
Away, you rogue, away! I am sleepy.
ABHORSON
Tell him he must awake, and that quickly too.
POMPEY
Pray, Master Barnardine, awake till you are executed,
and sleep afterwards.
ABHORSON
Go in to him, and fetch him out.
POMPEY
He is coming, sir, he is coming; I hear his straw rustle.
ABHORSON
Is the axe upon the block, sirrah?
POMPEY
Very ready, sir.

Enter BARNARDINE.

BARNARDINE
How now, Abhorson! what's the news with you?
ABHORSON
Truly, sir, I would desire you to clap into your prayers;
for, look you, the warrant's come.
BARNARDINE
You rogue, I have been drinking all night; I am not
fitted for't.
POMPEY
O, the better, sir; for he that drinks all night, and is
hang'd betimes in the morning, may sleep the sounder
all the next day.
ABHORSON
Look you, sir; here comes your ghostly father: do we
jest now, think you?

Enter DUKE *disguised as before.*

DUKE
Sir, induced by my charity, and hearing how hastily
you are to depart, I am come to advise you, comfort you,
and pray with you.
BARNARDINE
Friar, not I: I have been drinking hard all night, and I
will have more time to prepare me, or they shall beat
out my brains with billets: I will not consent to die this
day, that's certain.
DUKE
O, sir, you must: and therefore I beseech you
Look forward on the journey you shall go.

BARNARDINE
I swear I will not die to-day for any man's persuasion.
DUKE
But hear you, —
BARNARDINE
Not a word: if you have anything to say to me, come to
my ward; from thence will not I to-day.   [*Exit.*
DUKE
Unfit to live or die: O gravel heart! —
After him, fellows; bring him to the block.
        [*Exeunt* ABHORSON *and* POMPEY.

Enter PROVOST.

PROVOST
Now, sir, how do you find the prisoner?
DUKE
A creature unprepar'd, unmeet for death;
And to transport him in the mind he is
Were damnable.
PROVOST
                Here in the prison, father,
There died this morning of a cruel fever
One Ragozine, a most notorious pirate,
A man of Claudio's years; his beard and head
Just of his colour. What if we do omit
This reprobate till he were well inclin'd;
And satisfy the deputy with the visage
Of Ragozine, more like to Claudio?
DUKE
O, 'tis an accident that heaven provides!
Dispatch it presently; the hour draws on
Prefix'd by Angelo: see this be done,
And sent according to command; whiles I
Persuade this rude wretch willingly to die.
PROVOST
This shall be done, good father, presently.
But Barnardine must die this afternoon:
And how shall we continue Claudio,
To save me from the danger that might come
If he were known alive?
DUKE
Let this be done, — put them in secret holds,
Both Barnardine and Claudio:
Ere twice the sun hath made his journal greeting
To th'under generation, you shall find
Your safety manifested.
PROVOST
I am your free dependant.
DUKE
                Quick, dispatch,
And send the head to Angelo.   [*Exit* PROVOST.
Now will I write letters to Angelo, —
The provost, he shall bear them, — whose contents
Shall witness to him I am near at home,
And that, by great injunctions, I am bound
To enter publicly: him I'll desire
To meet me at the consecrated fount,
A league below the city; and from thence,
By cold gradation and well-balanc'd form,
We shall proceed with Angelo.

Enter PROVOST *with* RAGOZINE'S *head.*

PROVOST
Here is the head; I'll carry it myself.
DUKE
Convenient is it. Make a swift return;
For I would commune with you of such things
That want no ear but yours.
PROVOST
                I'll make all speed.   [*Exit.*
ISABELLA [*within*].
Peace, ho, be here!
DUKE
The tongue of Isabel. She's come to know
If yet her brother's pardon be come hither:
But I will keep her ignorant of her good,
To make her heavenly comforts of despair,
When it is least expected.

Enter ISABELLA.

ISABELLA
                Ho, by your leave!
DUKE
Good morning to you, fair and gracious daughter.
ISABELLA
The better, given by so holy a man.
Hath yet the deputy sent my brother's pardon?
DUKE
He hath releas'd him, Isabel, from the world:
His head is off, and sent to Angelo.

ISABELLA
Nay, but it is not so.
DUKE
It is no other: show your wisdom, daughter,
In your close patience.
ISABELLA
O, I will to him and pluck out his eyes!
DUKE
You shall not be admitted to his sight.
ISABELLA
Unhappy Claudio! wretched Isabel!
Injurious world! most damned Angelo!
DUKE
This nor hurts him nor profits you a jot;
Forbear it therefore; give your cause to heaven.
Mark what I say, which you shall find
By every syllable a faithful verity:
The duke comes home to-morrow; — nay, dry your
eyes;
One of our convent, and his confessor,
Gives me this instance: already he hath carried
Notice to Escalus and Angelo;
Who do prepare to meet him at the gates,
There to give up their power. If you can, pace your
wisdom
In that good path that I would wish it go;
And you shall have your bosom on this wretch,
Grace of the duke, revenges to your heart,
And general honour.
ISABELLA
        I am directed by you.
DUKE
This letter, then, to Friar Peter give;
'Tis that he sent me of the duke's return:
Say, by this token, I desire his company
At Mariana's house to-night. Her cause and yours
I'll perfect him withal, and he shall bring you
Before the duke; and to the head of Angelo
Accuse him home and home. For my poor self,
I am combined by a sacred vow,
And shall be absent. Wend you with this letter:
Command these fretting waters from your eyes
With a light heart; trust not my holy order,
If I pervert your course. — Who's here?

Enter LUCIO.

LUCIO
Good even. friar: where's the provost?
DUKE
Not within, sir.
LUCIO
O pretty Isabella, I am pale at mine heart to see thine
eyes so red: thou must be patient. I am fain to dine and
sup with water and bran; I dare not for my head fill my
belly; one fruitful meal would set me to't. But they say
the duke will be here to-morrow. By my troth, Isabel, I
loved thy brother: if the old fantastical duke of dark
corners had been at home, he had lived. [*Exit* ISABELLA.
DUKE
Sir, the duke is marvellous little beholding to your
reports; but the best is, he lives not in them.
LUCIO
Friar, thou know'st not the duke so well as I do: he's a
better woodman than thou takest him for.
DUKE
Well, you'll answer this one day. Fare ye well.
LUCIO
Nay, tarry; I'll go along with thee: I can tell thee pretty
tales of the duke.
DUKE
You have told me too many of him already, sir, if they
be true; if not true, none were enough.
LUCIO
I was once before him for getting a wench with child.
DUKE
Did you such a thing?
LUCIO
Yes, marry, did I: but I was fain to forswear it; they
would else have married me to the rotten medlar.
DUKE
Sir, your company is fairer than honest. Rest you well.
LUCIO
By my troth, I'll go with thee to the lane's end: if bawdy
talk offend you, we'll have very little of it. Nay, friar, I
am a kind of burr; I shall stick. [*Exeunt.*

SCENE IV

ANGELO'S *house.*

Enter ANGELO *and* ESCALUS.

ESCALUS
Every letter he hath writ hath disvouch'd other.
ANGELO
In most uneven and distracted manner. His actions
show much like to madness: pray heaven his wisdom
be not tainted! And why meet him at the gates, and
redeliver our authorities there?
ESCALUS
I guess not.
ANGELO
And why should we proclaim it in an hour before his
entering, that if any crave redress of injustice, they
should exhibit their petitions in the street?
ESCALUS
He shows his reason for that; — to have a dispatch of
complaints, and to deliver us from devices hereafter,
which shall then have no power to stand against us.
ANGELO
Well, I beseech you, let it be proclaim'd:
Betimes i' the morn; I'll call you at your house:
Give notice to such men of sort and suit
As are to meet him.
ESCALUS
        I shall, sir. Fare you well.
ANGELO
Good night. [*Exit* ESCALUS.
This deed unshapes me quite, makes me unpregnant,
And dull to all proceedings. A deflower'd maid!
And by an eminent body that enforc'd
The law against it! But that her tender shame
Will not proclaim against her maiden loss,
How might she tongue me! Yet reason dares her no;
For my authority bears of a credent bulk,
That no particular scandal once can touch
But it confounds the breather. He should have liv'd,
Save that riotous youth, with dangerous sense,
Might in the times to come have ta'en revenge,
By so receiving a dishonour'd life
With ransom of such shame. Would yet he had liv'd!
Alack, when once our grace we have forgot,
Nothing goes right, — we would, and we would not!
[*Exit.*

SCENE V

Fields without the town.

Enter DUKE *in his own habit, and* FRIAR PETER.

DUKE
These letters at fit time deliver me: [*Giving letters.*
The provost knows our purpose and our plot.
The matter being afoot, keep your instruction,
And hold you ever to our special drift;
Though sometimes you do blench from this to that,
As cause doth minister. Go call at Flavius' house,
And tell him where I stay: give the like notice
To Valentinus, Rowland, and to Crassus,
And bid them bring the trumpets to the gate;
But send me Flavius first.
FRIAR PETER
        It shall be speeded well. [*Exit.*

Enter VARRIUS.

DUKE
I thank thee, Varrius; thou hast made good haste:
Come, we will walk. There's other of our friends
Will greet us here anon, my gentle Varrius. [*Exeunt.*

SCENE VI

Street near the city-gate.

Enter ISABELLA *and* MARIANA.

ISABELLA
To speak so indirectly I am loth:
I would say the truth; but to accuse him so,
That is your part: yet I am advis'd to do it;
He says, to vailful purpose.
MARIANA
        Be rul'd by him.
ISABELLA
Besides, he tells me that, if peradventure
He speak against me on the adverse side,
I should not think it strange; for 'tis a physic
That's bitter to sweet end.
MARIANA
I would Friar Peter, —

ISABELLA
        O, peace! the friar is come.

Enter FRIAR PETER.

FRIAR PETER
Come, I have found you out a stand most fit,
Where you may have such vantage on the duke,
He shall not pass you. Twice have the trumpets
sounded;
The generous and gravest citizens
Have hent the gates, and very near upon
The duke is ent'ring: therefore, hence, away! [*Exeunt.*

ACT V

SCENE I

A public place near the city-gate.

MARIANA *veiled,* ISABELLA, *and* FRIAR PETER *at
their stand. Enter at opposite doors,* DUKE *in his own
habit,* VARRIUS, LORDS; ANGELO, ESCALUS,
LUCIO, PROVOST, OFFICERS, *and* CITIZENS.

DUKE
My very worthy cousin, fairly met: —
Our old and faithful friend, we are glad to see you.
ANGELO and ESCALUS
Happy return be to your royal grace!
DUKE
Many and hearty thankings to you both.
We have made inquiry of you; and we hear
Such goodness of your justice, that our soul
Cannot but yield you forth to public thanks,
Forerunning more requital.
ANGELO
        You make my bonds still greater.
DUKE
O, your desert speaks loud; and I should wrong it,
To lock it in the wards of covert bosom,
When it deserves, with characters of brass,
A forted residence 'gainst the tooth of time
And razure of oblivion. Give me your hand,
And let the subject see, to make them know
That outward courtesies would fain proclaim
Favours that keep within. — Come, Escalus;
You must walk by us on our other hand: —
And good supporters are you.
        FRIAR PETER *and* ISABELLA *come forward.*
FRIAR PETER
Now is your time: speak loud, and kneel before him.
ISABELLA
Justice, O royal duke! Vail your regard
Upon a wrong'd, I would fain have said, a maid!
O worthy prince, dishonour not your eye
By throwing it on any other object
Till you have heard me in my true complaint,
And given me justice, justice, justice, justice!
DUKE
Relate your wrongs; in what? by whom? be brief.
Here is Lord Angelo shall give you justice.
Reveal yourself to him.
ISABELLA
        O worthy duke,
You bid me seek redemption of the devil:
Hear me yourself; for that which I must speak
Must either punish me, not being believ'd,
Or wring redress from you: hear me, O, hear me, here!
ANGELO
My lord, her wits, I fear me, are not firm:
She hath been a suitor to me for her brother
Cut off by course of justice, —
ISABELLA
        By course of justice!
ANGELO
And she will speak most bitterly and strange.
ISABELLA
Most strange, but yet most truly, will I speak:
That Angelo's forsworn; is it not strange?
That Angelo's a murderer; is't not strange?
That Angelo is an adulterous thief,
An hypocrite, a virgin-violator,
Is it not strange and strange?
DUKE
        Nay, it is ten times strange.
ISABELLA
It is not truer he is Angelo
Than this is all as true as it is strange:
Nay, it is ten times true; for truth is truth
To th'end of reck'ning.

DUKE

       Away with her! — Poor soul,
She speaks this in th'infirmity of sense.

ISABELLA

O prince, I conjure thee, as thou believest
There is another comfort than this world,
That thou neglect me not, with that opinion
That I am touch'd with madness! Make not impossible
That which but seems unlike: 'tis not impossible
But one, the wicked'st caitiff on the ground,
May seem as shy, as grave, as just, as absolute
As Angelo; even so may Angelo,
In all his dressings, characts, titles, forms,
Be an arch-villain; believe it, royal prince:
If he be less, he's nothing; but he's more,
Had I more name for badness.

DUKE

       By mine honesty,
If she be mad, — as I believe no other, —
Her madness hath the oddest frame of sense,
Such a dependency of thing on thing,
As e'er I heard in madness.

ISABELLA

       O gracious duke,
Harp not on that; nor do not banish reason
For inequality; but let your reason serve
To make the truth appear where it seems hid,
And hide the false seems true.

DUKE

       Many that are not mad
Have, sure, more lack of reason. — What would you say?

ISABELLA

I am the sister of one Claudio,
Condemn'd upon the act of fornication
To lose his head; condemn'd by Angelo:
I, in probation of a sisterhood,
Was sent to by my brother; one Lucio
As then the messenger, —

LUCIO

      That's I, an't like your Grace:
I came to her from Claudio, and desired her
To try her gracious fortune with Lord Angelo
For her poor brother's pardon.

ISABELLA

       That's he indeed.

DUKE

You were not bid to speak.

LUCIO

      No, my good lord;
Nor wish'd to hold my peace.

DUKE

      I wish you now, then;
Pray you, take note of it: and when you have
A business for yourself, pray heaven you then
Be perfect.

LUCIO

I warrant your honour.

DUKE

The warrant's for yourself; take heed to't.

ISABELLA

This gentleman told somewhat of my tale, —

LUCIO

Right.

DUKE

It may be right; but you are i' the wrong
To speak before your time. — Proceed.

ISABELLA

       I went
To this pernicious caitiff deputy, —

DUKE

That's somewhat madly spoken.

ISABELLA

      Pardon it;
The phrase is to the matter.

DUKE

Mended again. The matter; — proceed.

ISABELLA

In brief, — to set the needless process by,
How I persuaded, how I pray'd, and kneel'd,
How he refell'd me, and how I replied, —
For this was of much length, — the vile conclusion
I now begin with grief and shame to utter;
He would not, but by gift of my chaste body
To his concupiscible intemperate lust,
Release my brother; and, after much debatement,
My sisterly remorse confutes mine honour,
And I did yield to him; but the next morn betimes,
His purpose surfeiting, he sends a warrant
For my poor brother's head.

DUKE

       This is most likely!

ISABELLA

O, that it were as like as it is true!

DUKE

By heaven, fond wretch, thou know'st not what thou
  speak'st.
Or else thou art suborn'd against his honour
In hateful practice. First, his integrity
Stands without blemish. Next, it imports no reason
That with such vehemency he should pursue
Faults proper to himself: if he had so offended,
He would have weigh'd thy brother by himself,
And not have cut him off. Some one hath set you on:
Confess the truth, and say by whose advice
Thou camest here to complain.

ISABELLA

      And is this all?
Then, O you blessed ministers above,
Keep me in patience, and with ripen'd time
Unfold the evil which is here wrapp'd up
In countenance! — Heaven shield your Grace from
  woe,
As I, thus wrong'd, hence unbelieved go!

DUKE

I know you'ld fain be gone. — An officer!
To prison with her! — Shall we thus permit
A blasting and a scandalous breath to fall
On him so near us? This needs must be a practice. —
Who knew of your intent and coming hither?

ISABELLA

One that I would were here, Friar Lodowick.

DUKE

A ghostly father, belike. — Who knows that Lodowick?

LUCIO

My lord, I know him; 'tis a meddling friar;
I do not like the man: had he been lay, my lord,
For certain words he spake against your Grace
In your retirement, I had swing'd him soundly.

DUKE

Words against me! this' a good friar, belike!
And to set on this wretched woman here
Against our substitute! — Let this friar be found.

LUCIO

But yesternight, my lord, she and that friar,
I saw them at the prison: a saucy friar,
A very scurvy fellow.

FRIAR PETER

      Bless'd be your royal grace!
I have stood by, my lord, and I have heard
Your royal ear abus'd. First, hath this woman
Most wrongfully accus'd your substitute,
Who is as free from touch or soil with her
As she from one ungot.

DUKE

      We did believe no less.
Know you that Friar Lodowick that she speaks of?

FRIAR PETER

I know him for a man divine and holy;
Not scurvy, nor a temporary meddler,
As he's reported by this gentleman;
And, on my trust, a man that never yet
Did, as he vouches, misreport your Grace.

LUCIO

My lord, most villainously; believe it.

FRIAR PETER

Well, he in time may come to clear himself;
But at this instant he is sick, my lord,
Of a strange fever. Upon his mere request, —
Being come to knowledge that there was complaint
Intended 'gainst Lord Angelo, — came I hither,
To speak, as from his mouth, what he doth know
Is true and false; and what he, with his oath
And all probation, will make up full clear,
Whensoever he's convented. First, for this woman, —
To justify this worthy nobleman,
So vulgarly and personally accused, —
Her shall you hear disproved to her eyes,
Till she herself confess it.

DUKE

      Good friar, let's hear it.

    [ISABELLA *is carried off guarded;*
     and MARIANA *comes forward.*

Do you not smile at this, Lord Angelo? —
O heaven, the vanity of wretched fools! —
Give us some seats. — Come, cousin Angelo;
In this I'll be impartial; be you judge
Of your own cause. — Is this the witness, friar?
First, let her show her face, and after speak.

MARIANA

Pardon, my lord; I will not show my face
Until my husband bid me.

DUKE

What, are you married?

MARIANA

No, my lord.

DUKE

Are you a maid?

MARIANA

No, my lord.

DUKE

A widow, then?

MARIANA

Neither, my lord.

DUKE

Why, you are nothing, then: — neither maid, widow,
  nor wife?

LUCIO

My lord, she may be a punk; for many of them are
  neither maid, widow, nor wife.

DUKE

Silence that fellow: I would he had some cause
To prattle for himself.

LUCIO

Well, my lord.

MARIANA

My lord, I do confess I ne'er was married;
And I confess, besides, I am no maid:
I've known my husband; yet my husband knows not
That ever he knew me.

LUCIO

He was drunk, then, my lord: it can be no better.

DUKE

For the benefit of silence, would thou wert so too!

LUCIO

Well, my lord.

DUKE

This is no witness for Lord Angelo.

MARIANA

Now I come to't, my lord:
She that accuses him of fornication,
In self-same manner doth accuse my husband;
And charges him, my lord, with such a time
When I'll depose I had him in mine arms
With all th'effect of love.

ANGELO

Charges she more than me?

MARIANA

      Not that I know.

DUKE

No? you say your husband.

MARIANA

Why, just, my lord, and that is Angelo,
Who thinks he knows that he ne'er knew my body,
But knows he thinks that he knows Isabel's.

ANGELO

This is a strange abuse. — Let's see thy face.

MARIANA

My husband bids me; now I will unmask.
This is that face, thou cruel Angelo,   [*Unveiling.*
Which once thou sworest was worth the looking on;
This is the hand which, with a vow'd contract,
Was fast belock'd in thine; this is the body
That took away the match from Isabel,
And did supply thee at thy garden-house
In her imagin'd person.

DUKE

      Know you this woman?

LUCIO

Carnally, she says.

DUKE

      Sirrah, no more!

LUCIO

Enough, my lord.

ANGELO

My lord, I must confess I know this woman:
And five years since there was some speech of
  marriage
Betwixt myself and her; which was broke off,
Partly for that her promised proportions
Came short of composition; but in chief
For that her reputation was disvalued
In levity: since which time of five years
I never spake with her, saw her, nor heard from her,
Upon my faith and honour.

MARIANA

      Noble prince,

As there comes light from heaven and words from
    breath,
As there is sense in truth and truth in virtue,
I am affianc'd this man's wife as strongly
As words could make up vows: and, my good lord,
But Tuesday night last gone, in's garden-house,
He knew me as a wife. As this is true,
Let me in safety raise me from my knees;
Or else for ever be confixed here,
A marble monument!

ANGELO
                I did but smile till now;
Now, good my lord, give me the scope of justice;
My patience here is touch'd. I do perceive
These poor informal women are no more
But instruments of some more mightier member
That sets them on: let me have way, my lord,
To find this practice out.

DUKE
                Ay, with my heart;
And punish them to your height of pleasure. —
Thou foolish friar; and thou pernicious woman,
Compact with her that's gone, think'st thou thy oaths,
Though they would swear down each particular saint,
Were testimonies against his worth and credit,
That's seal'd in approbation? — You, Lord Escalus,
Sit with my cousin; lend him your kind pains
To find out this abuse, whence 'tis derived. —
There is another friar that set them on;
Let him be sent for.

FRIAR PETER
Would he were here, my lord! for he, indeed,
Hath set the women on to this complaint:
Your provost knows the place where he abides,
And he may fetch him.

DUKE
                Go do it instantly.   [*Exit* PROVOST.
And you, my noble and well-warranted cousin,
Whom it concerns to hear this matter forth,
Do with your injuries as seems you best,
In any chastisement: I for a while will leave you;
But stir not till you have well determined
Upon these slanderers.

ESCALUS
My lord, we'll do it throughly.   [*Exit* DUKE.
Signior Lucio, did not you say you knew that
Friar Lodowick to be a dishonest person?

LUCIO
Cucullus non facit monachum: honest in nothing but in
his clothes; and one that hath spoken most villanous
speeches of the duke.

ESCALUS
We shall entreat you to abide here till he come, and
enforce them against him: we shall find this friar a
notable fellow.

LUCIO
As any in Vienna, on my word.

ESCALUS
Call that same Isabel here once again: I would speak
with her. [*Exit an* ATTENDANT.] — Pray you, my lord,
give me leave to question; you shall see how I'll handle
her.

LUCIO
Not better than he, by her own report.

ESCALUS
Say you?

LUCIO
Marry, sir, I think, if you handled her privately, she
would sooner confess: perchance, publicly, she'll be
ashamed.

ESCALUS
I will go darkly to work with her.

LUCIO
That's the way; for women are light at midnight.

Enter OFFICERS *with* ISABELLA.

ESCALUS [*to* ISABELLA].
Come on, mistress: here's a gentlewoman denies all
that you have said.

LUCIO
My lord, here comes the rascal I spoke of; here with the
provost.

ESCALUS
In very good time: — speak not you to him till we call
upon you.

LUCIO
Mum.

Enter DUKE *disguised as a friar, and* PROVOST.

ESCALUS
Come, sir: did you set these women on to slander
Lord Angelo? they have confess'd you did.

DUKE
'Tis false.

ESCALUS
How! know you where you are?

DUKE
Respect to your great place! and let the devil
Be sometime honour'd for his burning throne! —
Where is the duke? 'tis he should hear me speak.

ESCALUS
The duke's in us; and we will hear you speak:
Look you speak justly.

DUKE
Boldly, at least. — But, O, poor souls,
Come you to seek the lamb here of the fox?
Good night to your redress! Is the duke gone?
Then is your cause gone too. The duke's unjust,
Thus to retort your manifest appeal,
And put your trial in the villain's mouth
Which here you come to accuse.

LUCIO
This is the rascal; this is he I spoke of.

ESCALUS
Why, thou unreverend and unhallow'd friar,
Is't not enough thou hast suborn'd these women
To accuse this worthy man, but, in foul mouth,
And in the witness of his proper ear,
To call him villain? and then to glance from him
To th'duke himself, to tax him with injustice? —
Take him hence; to th'rack with him! — We'll touse
    you
Joint by joint, but we will know his purpose. —
What ,'unjust'?

DUKE
                Be not so hot; the duke
Dare no more stretch this finger of mine than he
Dare rack his own: his subject am I not,
Nor here provincial. My business in this state
Made me a looker-on here in Vienna,
Where I have seen corruption boil and bubble
Till it o'er-run the stew; laws for all faults,
But faults so countenanc'd, that the strong statutes
Stand like the forfeits in a barber's shop,
As much in mock as mark.

ESCALUS
Slander to th'state! — Away with him to prison!

ANGELO
What can you vouch against him, Signior Lucio?
Is this the man that you did tell us of?

LUCIO
'Tis he, my lord. — Come hither, goodman baldpate:
do you know me?

DUKE
I remember you, sir, by the sound of your voice: I met
you at the prison, in the absence of the duke.

LUCIO
O, did you so? And do you remember what you said of
the duke?

DUKE
Most notedly, sir.

LUCIO
Do you so, sir? And was the duke a fleshmonger, a fool,
and a coward, as you then reported him to be?

DUKE
You must, sir, change persons with me, ere you make
that my report; you, indeed, spoke so of him; and much
more, much worse.

LUCIO
O thou damnable fellow! Did not I pluck thee by the
nose for thy speeches?

DUKE
I protest I love the duke as I love myself.

ANGELO
Hark, how the villain would close now, after his
treasonable abuses!

ESCALUS
Such a fellow is not to be talk'd withal. — Away with
him to prison! — Where is the provost? — Away with
him to prison! lay bolts enough upon him: let him
speak no more. — Away with those giglots too, and
with the other confederate companion!

DUKE [*to* PROVOST].
Stay, sir; stay awhile.

ANGELO
What, resists he? — Help him, Lucio.

LUCIO
Come, sir; come, sir; come, sir; foh, sir! Why, you

bald-pated, lying rascal, you must be hooded, must
you? Show your knave's visage, with a pox to you! show
your sheep-biting face, and be hang'd an hour! Will't
not off?

[*Pulls off the* FRIAR's *hood, and discovers the* DUKE.

DUKE
Thou art the first knave that e'er madest a duke. —
First, provost, let me bail these gentle three. —
[*to* LUCIO] Sneak not away, sir; for the friar and you
Must have a word anon. — Lay hold on him.

LUCIO
This may prove worse than hanging.

DUKE [*to* ESCALUS].
What you have spoke I pardon: sit you down:
We'll borrow place of him. — [*to* ANGELO] Sir, by your
    leave.
Hast thou or word, or wit, or impudence,
That yet can do thee office? If thou hast,
Rely upon it till my tale be heard,
And hold no longer out.

ANGELO
                O my dread lord,
I should be guiltier than my guiltiness,
To think I can be undiscernible,
When I perceive your Grace, like power divine,
Hath look'd upon my passes. Then, good prince
No longer session hold upon my shame,
But let my trial be mine own confession:
Immediate sentence then, and sequent death,
Is all the grace I beg.

DUKE
                Come hither, Mariana. —
Say, wast thou e'er contracted to this woman?

ANGELO
I was, my lord.

DUKE
Go take her hence, and marry her instantly. —
Do you the office, friar; which consummate,
Return him here again. — Go with him, provost.
[*Exeunt* ANGELO, MARIANA, FRIAR PETER, *and*
                       PROVOST.

ESCALUS
My lord, I am more amaz'd at his dishonour
Than at the strangeness of it.

DUKE
                Come hither, Isabel.
Your friar is now your prince: as I was then
Advertising and holy to your business,
Not changing heart with habit, I am still
Attorney'd at your service.

ISABELLA
                O, give me pardon,
That I, your vassal, have employ'd and pain'd
Your unknown sovereignty!

DUKE
                You are pardon'd, Isabel:
And now, dear maid, be you as free to us.
Your brother's death, I know, sits at your heart;
And you may marvel why I obscured myself,
Labouring to save his life, and would not rather
Make rash remonstrance of my hidden power
Than let him so be lost. O most kind maid,
It was the swift celerity of his death,
Which I did think with slower foot came on,
That brain'd my purpose — but peace be with him!
That life is better life, past fearing death,
Than that which lives to fear: make it your comfort,
So happy is your brother.

ISABELLA
                I do, my lord.

Enter ANGELO, MARIANA, FRIAR PETER,
and PROVOST.

DUKE
For this new-married man, approaching here,
Whose salt imagination yet hath wrong'd
Your well-defended honour, you must pardon
For Mariana's sake: but as he adjudg'd your brother, —
Being criminal, in double violation
Of sacred chastity, and of promise-breach
Thereon dependent, for your brother's life, —
The very mercy of the law cries out
Most audible, even from his proper tongue,
'An Angelo for Claudio, death for death!'
Haste still pays haste, and leisure answers leisure;
Like doth quit like, and *Measure* still *for measure*.
Then, Angelo, thy fault thus manifested, —
Which, though thou wouldst deny, denies thee
    vantage, —

We do condemn thee to the very block
Where Claudio stoop'd to death, and with like haste. —
Away with him!

MARIANA
        O my most gracious lord,
I hope you will not mock me with a husband.

DUKE
It is your husband mock'd you with a husband.
Consenting to the safeguard of your honour,
I thought your marriage fit; else imputation,
For that he knew you, might reproach your life,
And choke your good to come; for his possessions,
Although by confiscation they are ours,
We do instate and widow you withal,
To buy you a better husband.

MARIANA
        O my dear lord,
I crave no other, nor no better man.

DUKE
Never crave him; we are definitive.

MARIANA
Gentle my liege, —   [Kneeling.

DUKE
        You do but lose your labour. —
Away with him to death! — [to LUCIO] Now, sir, to
    you.

MARIANA
O my good lord! — Sweet Isabel, take my part;
Lend me your knees, and all my life to come
I'll lend you all my life to do you service.

DUKE
Against all sense you do importune her:
Should she kneel down in mercy of this fact,
Her brother's ghost his paved bed would break,
And take her hence in horror.

MARIANA
        Isabel,
Sweet Isabel, do yet but kneel by me;
Hold up your hands, say nothing, — I'll speak all.
They say, best men are moulded out of faults;
And, for the most, become much more the better
For being a little bad: so may my husband.
O Isabel, will you not lend a knee?

DUKE
He dies for Claudio's death.

ISABELLA
        Most bounteous sir,
        [Kneeling.
Look, if it please you, on this man condemn'd,
As if my brother liv'd: I partly think
A due sincerity govern'd his deeds,
Till he did look on me: since it is so,
Let him not die. My brother had but justice,
In that he did the thing for which he died:
For Angelo,
His act did not o'ertake his bad intent;
And must be buried but as an intent
That perish'd by the way: thoughts are no subjects,
Intents but merely thoughts.

MARIANA
        Merely, my lord.

DUKE
Your suit's unprofitable; stand up, I say. —
I have bethought me of another fault. —
Provost, how came it Claudio was beheaded
At an unusual hour?

PROVOST
        It was commanded so.

DUKE
Had you a special warrant for the deed?

PROVOST
No, my good lord; it was by private message.

DUKE
For which I do discharge you of your office:
Give up your keys.

PROVOST
        Pardon me, noble lord:
I thought it was a fault, but knew it not;
Yet did repent me, after more advice:
For testimony whereof, one in the prison,
That should by private order else have died,
I have reserv'd alive.

DUKE
        What's he?

PROVOST
        His name is Barnardine.

DUKE
I would thou hadst done so by Claudio. —
Go fetch him hither; let me look upon him.
        [Exit PROVOST.

ESCALUS
I am sorry, one so learned and so wise
As you, Lord Angelo, have still appear'd,
Should slip so grossly, both in the heat of blood,
And lack of temper'd judgement afterward.

ANGELO
I am sorry that such sorrow I procure:
And so deep sticks it in my penitent heart,
That I crave death more willingly than mercy;
'Tis my deserving, and I do entreat it.

    Enter PROVOST, with BARNARDINE, CLAUDIO
        muffled, and JULIET.

DUKE
Which is that Barnardine?

PROVOST
        This, my lord.

DUKE
There was a friar told me of this man. —
Sirrah, thou art said to have a stubborn soul,
That apprehends no further than this world,
And squarest thy life according. Thou'rt condemn'd:
But, for those earthly faults, I quit them all;
And pray thee take this mercy to provide
For better times to come. — Friar, advise him;
I leave him to your hand. — What muffled fellow's
    that?

PROVOST
This is another prisoner that I saved,
Who should have died when Claudio lost his head;
As like almost to Claudio as himself.
        [Unmuffles CLAUDIO.

DUKE [to ISABELLA].
If he be like your brother, for his sake
Is he pardon'd; and, for your lovely sake,
Give me your hand, and say you will be mine,
He is my brother too: but fitter time for that.
By this Lord Angelo perceives he's safe;
Methinks I see a quick'ning in his eye. —
Well, Angelo, your evil quits you well:
Look that you love your wife; her worth worth yours. —
I find an apt remission in myself;
And yet here's one in place I cannot pardon. —
[to LUCIO] You, sirrah, that knew me for a fool, a
    coward,
One all of luxury, an ass, a madman;
Wherein have I so deserved of you,
That you extol me thus?

LUCIO
Faith, my lord, I spoke it but according to the trick. If
you will hang me for it, you may; but I had rather it
would please you I might be whipp'd.

DUKE
Whipp'd first, sir, and hang'd after. —
Proclaim it, provost, round about the city,
Is any woman wrong'd by this lewd fellow, —
As I have heard him swear himself there's one
Whom he begot with child, — let her appear,
And he shall marry her: the nuptial finish'd,
Let him be whipp'd and hang'd.

LUCIO
I beseech your highness, do not marry me to a whore!
Your highness said even now, I made you a duke: good
my lord, do not recompense me in making me a
cuckold.

DUKE
Upon mine honour, thou shalt marry her.
Thy slanders I forgive; and therewithal
Remit thy other forfeits. — Take him to prison;
And see our pleasure herein executed.

LUCIO
Marrying a punk, my lord, is pressing to death,
whipping, and hanging.

DUKE
Slandering a prince deserves it. —
        [Exeunt OFFICERS with LUCIO.
She, Claudio, that you wrong'd, look you restore. —
Joy to you, Mariana! — Love her, Angelo:
I have confess'd her, and I know her virtue. —
Thanks, good friend Escalus, for thy much goodness:
There's more behind that is more gratulate. —
Thanks, provost, for thy care and secrecy:
We shall employ thee in a worthier place. —
Forgive him, Angelo, that brought you home
The head of Ragozine for Claudio's:
Th'offence pardons itself. — Dear Isabel,
I have a motion much imports your good;
Whereto if you'll a willing ear incline,
What's mine is yours, and what is yours is mine. —
So, bring us to our palace; where we'll show
What's yet behind, that's meet you all should know.
        [Exeunt.

OTHELLO, THE MOOR OF VENICE

DRAMATIS PERSONAE

DUKE OF VENICE.
BRABANTIO, *a senator.*
OTHER SENATORS.
GRATIANO, *brother to a Brabantio.*
LODOVICO, *kinsman to Brabantio.*
OTHELLO, *a noble Moor in the service of the Venetian state.*
CASSIO, *his lieutenant.*

IAGO, *his ancient.*
RODERIGO, *a Venetian gentleman.*
MONTANO, *Othello's predecessor in the government of Cyprus.*
CLOWN, *servant to Othello.*

DESDEMONA, *daughter to Brabantio and wife to Othello*
EMILIA, *wife to Iago.*

BIANCA, *mistress to Cassio.*

SAILOR, MESSENGER, HERALD, OFFICERS, GENTLEMEN, MUSICIANS, *and* ATTENDANTS.

SCENE— *Venice: a seaport in Cyprus.*

ACT I

SCENE I

Venice. A street.

Enter RODERIGO *and* IAGO.

RODERIGO
Tush, never tell me; I take it much unkindly
That thou, Iago, who hast had my purse
As if the strings were thine, shouldst know of this,—

IAGO
'Sblood, but you will not hear me:—
If ever I did dream of such a matter,
Abhor me.

RODERIGO
Thou told'st me thou didst hold him in thy hate.

IAGO
Despise me, if I do not. Three great ones of the city,
In personal suit to make me his lieutenant,
Off-capp'd to him:—and, by the faith of man,
I know my price, I am worth no worse a place:—
But he, as loving his own pride and purposes,
Evades them, with a bombast circumstance
Horribly stuff'd with epithets of war;
And, in conclusion,
Nonsuits my mediators; for, 'Certes,' says he,
'I have already chose my officer.'
And what was he?
Forsooth, a great arithmetician,
One Michael Cassio, a Florentine,
A fellow almost damn'd in a fair wife;
That never set a squadron in the field,
Nor the division of a battle knows
More than a spinster; unless the bookish theoric,
Wherein the toged consuls can propose
As masterly as he: mere prattle, without practice,
Is all his soldiership. But he, sir, had th'election:
And I—of whom his eyes had seen the proof
At Rhodes, at Cyprus, and on other grounds
Christian and heathen—must be be-lee'd and calm'd
By debitor and creditor; this counter-caster,
He, in good time, must his lieutenant be,
And I—God bless the mark!—his Moorship's ancient.

RODERIGO
By heaven, I rather would have been his hangman.

IAGO
Why, there's no remedy; 'tis the curse of service,
Preferment goes by letter and affection,
And not by old gradation, where each second
Stood heir to th'first. Now, sir, be judge yourself,
Whether I in any just term am affined
To love the Moor.

RODERIGO
I would not follow him, then.

IAGO
O, sir, content you;
I follow him to serve my turn upon him:
We cannot all be masters, nor all masters
Cannot be truly follow'd. You shall mark
Many a duteous and knee-crooking knave,
That, doting on his own obsequious bondage,
Wears out his time, much like his master's ass,
For naught but provender; and, when he's old, cashier'd:
Whip me such honest knaves. Others there are,
Who, trimm'd in forms and visages of duty,
Keep yet their hearts attending on themselves;
And, throwing but shows of service on their lords,
Do well thrive by them, and, when they have lin'd their coats,
Do themselves homage: these fellows have some soul;
And such a one do I profess myself.
For, sir,

BRABANTIO What is the reason of this terrible summons?

It is as sure as you are Roderigo,
Were I the Moor, I would not be Iago:
In following him, I follow but myself;
Heaven is my judge, not I for love and duty,
But seeming so, for my peculiar end:
For when my outward action doth demonstrate
The native act and figure of my heart
In compliment extern, 'tis not long after
But I will wear my heart upon my sleeve
For daws to peck at: I am not what I am.

RODERIGO
What a full fortune does the thick-lips owe,
If he can carry't thus!

IAGO
Call up her father,
Rouse him:—make after him, poison his delight,
Proclaim him in the streets; incense her kinsmen:
And though he in a fertile climate dwell,
Plague him with flies; though that his joy be joy,
Yet throw such changes of vexation on't,
As it may lose some colour.

RODERIGO
Here is her father's house; I'll call aloud.

IAGO
Do; with like timorous accent and dire yell
As when, by night and negligence, the fire
Is spied in populous cities.

RODERIGO
What, ho, Brabantio! Signior Brabantio, ho!

IAGO
Awake! what, ho, Brabantio! thieves! thieves! thieves!
Look to your house, your daughter, and your bags!
Thieves! thieves!

BRABANTIO *appears above, at a window.*

BRABANTIO
What is the reason of this terrible summons?
What is the matter there?

RODERIGO
Signior, is all your family within?

IAGO
Are your doors lock'd?

BRABANTIO
Why, wherefore ask you this?

IAGO
Zounds, sir, y' are robb'd; for shame, put on your gown;
Your heart is burst, you have lost half your soul;
Even now, now, very now, an old black ram
Is tupping your white ewe. Arise, arise;
Awake the snorting citizens with the bell,
Or else the devil will make a grandsire of you:
Arise, I say.

BRABANTIO
What, have you lost your wits?

RODERIGO
Most reverend signior, do you know my voice?

BRABANTIO
Not I: what are you?

RODERIGO
My name is Roderigo.

BRABANTIO
The worser welcome:
I have charg'd thee not to haunt about my doors:
In honest plainness thou hast heard me say
My daughter is not for thee; and now, in madness,
Being full of supper and distempering draughts,
Upon malicious bravery, dost thou come
To start my quiet;—

RODERIGO
Sir, sir, sir, —

BRABANTIO
But thou must needs be sure
My spirit and my place have in them power
To make this bitter to thee.

RODERIGO
Patience, good sir.

BRABANTIO
What tell'st thou me of robbing? this is Venice;
My house is not a grange.

RODERIGO
Most grave Brabantio,
In simple and pure soul I come to you.

IAGO
Zounds, sir, you are one of those that will not serve
God, if the devil bid you. Because we come to do you
service, and you think we are ruffians, you'll have your
daughter cover'd with a Barbary horse; you'll have your
nephews neigh to you; you'll have coursers for cousins,
and gennets for germans.

BRABANTIO
What profane wretch art thou?

IAGO
I am one, sir, that comes to tell you your daughter and
the Moor are now making the beast with two backs.

BRABANTIO
Thou art a villain.

IAGO
You are — a senator.

BRABANTIO
This thou shalt answer: I know thee, Roderigo.

RODERIGO
Sir, I will answer any thing. But, I beseech you,
If't be your pleasure and most wise consent,
As partly I find it is, that your fair daughter,
At this odd-even and dull watch o'the night,
Transported, with no worse nor better guard
But with a knave of common hire, a gondolier,
To the gross clasps of a lascivious Moor, —
If this be known to you, and your allowance,
We then have done you bold and saucy wrongs;
But, if you know not this, my manners tell me
We have your wrong rebuke. Do not believe
That, from the sense of all civility,

I thus would play and trifle with your reverence:
Your daughter, — if you have not given her leave, —
I say again, hath made a gross revolt;
Tying her duty, beauty, wit, and fortunes,
In an extravagant and wheeling stranger
Of here and every where. Straight satisfy yourself:
If she be in her chamber or your house,
Let loose on me the justice of the state
For thus deluding you.

BRABANTIO
                    Strike on the tinder, ho!
Give me a taper! — call up all my people! —
This accident is not unlike my dream:
Belief of it oppresses me already. —
Light, I say! light!   [*Exit above.*

IAGO
                    Farewell; for I must leave you:
It seems not meet, nor wholesome to my place,
To be produc'd — as, if I stay, I shall —
Against the Moor: for, I do know, the state,
However this may gall him with some check,
Cannot with safety cast him; for he's embark'd
With such loud reason to the Cyprus wars,
Which even now stand in act, that, for their souls,
Another of his fadom they have none
To lead their business: in which regard,
Though I do hate him as I do hell-pains,
Yet, for necessity of present life,
I must show out a flag and sign of love,
Which is indeed but sign. That you shall surely find
    him,
Lead to the Sagittary the raised search;
And there will I be with him. So, farewell.   [*Exit.*

*Enter, below, BRABANTIO, with SERVANTS and
torches.*

BRABANTIO
It is too true an evil: gone she is;
And what's to come of my despised time
Is naught but bitterness. — Now, Roderigo,
Where didst thou see her? — O unhappy girl! —
With the Moor, say'st thou? — Who would be a father! —
How didst thou know 'twas she? — O, she deceives me
Past thought! — What said she to you? — Get more
    tapers;
Raise all my kindred. — Are they married, think you?

RODERIGO
Truly, I think they are.

BRABANTIO
O heaven! — How got she out? — O treason of the
    blood! —
Fathers, from hence trust not your daughters' minds
By what you see them act. — Is there not charms
By which the property of youth and maidhood
May be abused? Have you not read, Roderigo,
Of some such thing?

RODERIGO
                    Yes, sir, I have indeed.

BRABANTIO
Call up my brother. — O, would you had had her! —
Some one way, some another. — Do you know
Where we may apprehend her and the Moor?

RODERIGO
I think I can discover him, if you please
To get good guard, and go along with me.

BRABANTIO
Pray you, lead on. At every house I'll call;
I may command at most. — Get weapons, ho!
And raise some special officers of night. —
On, good Roderigo; — I'll deserve your pains.   [*Exeunt.*

SCENE II

Another street.

*Enter OTHELLO, IAGO, and ATTENDANTS
with torches.*

IAGO
Though in the trade of war I have slain men,
Yet do I hold it very stuff o'the conscience
To do no contriv'd murder: I lack iniquity
Sometimes to do me service: nine or ten times
I had thought t'have yerk'd him here under the ribs.

OTHELLO
'Tis better as it is.

IAGO
                    Nay, but he prated,
And spoke such scurvy and provoking terms
Against your honour,
That, with the little godliness I have,
I did full hard forbear him. But, I pray you, sir,
Are you fast married? Be assured of this,

That the magnifico is much beloved;
And hath, in his effect, a voice potential
As double as the duke's: he will divorce you;
Or put upon you what restraint and grievance
The law — with all his might t'enforce it on —
Will give him cable.

OTHELLO
                    Let him do his spite:
My services which I have done the signiory
Shall out-tongue his complaints. 'Tis yet to know, —
Which, when I know that boasting is an honour,
I shall promulgate, — I fetch my life and being
From men of royal siege; and my demerits
May speak, unbonneted, to as proud a fortune
As this that I have reach'd: for know, Iago,
But that I love the gentle Desdemona,
I would not my unhoused free condition
Put into circumscription and confine
For the sea's worth. But, look! what lights come yond?

IAGO
Those are the raised father and his friends:
You were best go in.

OTHELLO
                    Not I; I must be found:
My parts, my title, and my perfect soul
Shall manifest me rightly. Is it they?

IAGO
By Janus, I think no.

Enter CASSIO, and certain OFFICERS with torches.

OTHELLO
The servants of the duke, and my lieutenant. —
The goodness of the night upon you, friends!
What is the news?

CASSIO
                    The duke does greet you, general;
And he requires your haste-post-haste appearance
Even on the instant.

OTHELLO
                    What is the matter, think you?

CASSIO
Something from Cyprus, as I may divine:
It is a business of some heat: the galleys
Have sent a dozen sequent messengers
This very night at one another's heels;
And many of the consuls, rais'd and met,
Are at the duke's already: you have been hotly call'd for;
When, being not at your lodging to be found,
The senate hath sent about three several quests
To search you out.

OTHELLO
                    'Tis well I am found by you.
I will but spend a word here in the house,
And go with you.   [*Exit.*

CASSIO
                    Ancient, what makes he here?

IAGO
Faith, he to-night hath boarded a land carack:
If it prove lawful prize, he's made for ever.

CASSIO
I do not understand.

IAGO
                    He's married.

CASSIO
                                        To who?

Enter OTHELLO.

IAGO
Marry, to — Come, captain, will you go?

OTHELLO
                                        Have with you.

CASSIO
Here comes another troop to seek for you.

IAGO
It is Brabantio: — general, be advised;
He comes to bad intent.

*Enter BRABANTIO, RODERIGO, and OFFICERS
with torches and weapons.*

OTHELLO
                    Holla! stand there!

RODERIGO
Signior, it is the Moor.

BRABANTIO
                    Down with him, thief!
                    [*They draw on both sides.*

IAGO
You, Roderigo! come, sir, I am for you.

OTHELLO
Keep up your bright swords, for the dew will rust them. —

Good signior, you shall more command with years
Than with your weapons.

BRABANTIO
O thou foul thief, where hast thou stow'd my daughter?
Damn'd as thou art, thou hast enchanted her;
For I'll refer me to all things of sense,
If she in chains of magic were not bound,
Whether a maid so tender, fair, and happy,
So opposite to marriage that she shunn'd
The wealthy curled darlings of our nation,
Would ever have, t'incur a general mock,
Run from her guardage to the sooty bosom
Of such a thing as thou, — to fear, not to delight.
Judge me the world, if 'tis not gross in sense
That thou hast practis'd on her with foul charms;
Abus'd her delicate youth with drugs or minerals
That weaken motion: — I'll have't disputed on;
'Tis probable, and palpable to thinking.
I therefore apprehend and do attach thee
For an abuser of the world, a practiser
Of arts inhibited and out of warrant. —
Lay hold upon him: if he do resist,
Subdue him at his peril.

OTHELLO
                    Hold your hands,
Both you of my inclining, and the rest:
Were it my cue to fight, I should have known it
Without a prompter. — Where will you that I go
To answer this your charge?

BRABANTIO
                    To prison; till fit time
Of law, and course of direct session,
Call thee to answer.

OTHELLO
                    What if I do obey?
How may the duke be therewith satisfied,
Whose messengers are here about my side,
Upon some present business of the state
To bring me to him?

FIRST OFFICER
                    'Tis true, most worthy signior;
The duke's in council, and your noble self,
I am sure, is sent for.

BRABANTIO
                    How! the duke in council!
In this time of the night! — Bring him away;
Mine's not an idle cause: the duke himself,
Or any of my brothers of the state,
Cannot but feel this wrong as 'twere their own;
For if such actions may have passage free,
Bond-slaves and pagans shall our statesmen be.
                                        [*Exeunt.*

SCENE III

A council-chamber.

*The DUKE and SENATORS sitting at a table;
OFFICERS attending.*

DUKE
There is no composition in these news
That gives them credit.

FIRST SENATOR
                    Indeed, they are disproportion'd;
My letters say a hundred and seven galleys.

DUKE
And mine, a hundred and forty.

SECOND SENATOR
                    And mine, two hundred:
But though they jump not on a just account, —
As in these cases, where the aim reports,
'Tis oft with difference, — yet do they all confirm
A Turkish fleet, and bearing up to Cyprus.

DUKE
Nay, it is possible enough to judgement:
I do not so secure me in the error,
But the main article I do approve
In fearful sense.

SAILOR [*within*].
What, ho! what, ho! what, ho!

FIRST OFFICER
A messenger from the galleys.

Enter a SAILOR.

DUKE
                    Now, what's the business?

SAILOR
The Turkish preparation makes for Rhodes;
So was I bid report here to the state
By Signior Angelo.

DUKE
How say you by this change?
FIRST SENATOR
          This cannot be,
By no assay of reason: 'tis a pageant,
To keep us in false gaze. When we consider
Th'importancy of Cyprus to the Turk;
And let ourselves again but understand,
That as it more concerns the Turk than Rhodes,
So may he with more facile question bear it,
For that it stands not in such warlike brace,
But altogether lacks th'abilities
That Rhodes is dress'd in: — if we make thought of
    this,
We must not think the Turk is so unskilful
To leave that latest which concerns him first,
Neglecting an attempt of ease and gain,
To wake and wage a danger profitless.
DUKE
Nay, in all confidence, he's not for Rhodes.
FIRST OFFICER
Here is more news.

        Enter a MESSENGER.

MESSENGER
The Ottomites, reverend and gracious,
Steering with due course towards the isle of Rhodes,
Have there injointed them with an after fleet.
FIRST SENATOR
Ay, so I thought. How many, as you guess?
MESSENGER
Of thirty sail: and now they do re-stem
Their backward course, bearing with frank appearance
Their purposes toward Cyprus. — Signior Montano,
Your trusty and most valiant servitor,
With his free duty recommends you thus,
And prays you to believe him.
DUKE
'Tis certain, then, for Cyprus. —
Marcus Luccicos, is not he in town?
FIRST SENATOR
He's now in Florence.
DUKE
Write from us to him; post-post-haste dispatch.
FIRST SENATOR
Here comes Brabantio and the valiant Moor.

  Enter BRABANTIO, OTHELLO, IAGO, RODERIGO,
      and OFFICERS.

DUKE
Valiant Othello, we must straight employ you
Against the general enemy Ottoman. —
[*to* BRABANTIO] I did not see you; welcome, gentle
    signior;
We lack'd your counsel and your help to-night.
BRABANTIO
So did I yours. Good your Grace, pardon me;
Neither my place, nor aught I heard of business,
Hath rais'd me from my bed; nor doth the general care
Take hold on me; for my particular grief
Is of so flood-gate and o'erbearing nature
That it engluts and swallows other sorrows,
And it is still itself.
DUKE
         Why, what's the matter?
BRABANTIO
My daughter! O, my daughter!
DUKE *and* **SENATOR**
             Dead?
BRABANTIO
Ay, to me;
She is abus'd, stol'n from me, and corrupted
By spells and medicines bought of mountebanks;
For nature so preposterously to err,
Being not deficient, blind, or lame of sense,
Sans witchcraft could not.
DUKE
Whoe'er he be that, in this foul proceeding,
Hath thus beguil'd your daughter of herself,
And you of her, the bloody book of law
You shall yourself read in the bitter letter
After your own sense; yea, though our proper son
Stood in your action.
BRABANTIO
        Humbly I thank your Grace.
Here is the man, this Moor; whom now, it seems,
Your special mandate, for the state-affairs,
Hath hither brought.
DUKE *and* **SENATOR**
          We are very sorry for't.

DUKE [*to* OTHELLO].
What, in your own part, can you say to this?
BRABANTIO
Nothing, but this is so.
OTHELLO
Most potent, grave, and reverend signiors,
My very noble and approv'd good masters,
That I have ta'en away this old man's daughter,
It is most true; true, I have married her:
The very head and front of my offending
Hath this extent, no more. Rude am I in my speech,
And little blest with the soft phrase of peace;
For since these arms of mine had seven years' pith,
Till now some nine moons wasted, they have us'd
Their dearest action in the tented field;
And little of this great world can I speak,
More than pertains to feats of broil and battle;
And therefore little shall I grace my cause
In speaking for myself. Yet, by your gracious patience,
I will a round unvarnish'd tale deliver
Of my whole course of love; what drugs, what charms,
What conjuration, and what mighty magic, —
For such proceeding I am charg'd withal, —
I won his daughter.
BRABANTIO
         A maiden never bold;
Of spirit so still and quiet, that her motion
Blush'd at herself; and she — in spite of nature,
Of years, of country, credit, every thing —
To fall in love with what she fear'd to look on!
It is a judgement maim'd and most imperfect,
That will confess perfection so could err
Against all rules of nature; and must be driven
To find out practices of cunning hell,
Why this should be. I therefore vouch again,
That with some mixtures powerful o'er the blood,
Or with some dram conjured to this effect,
He wrought upon her.
DUKE
        To vouch this, is no proof,
Without more wider and more overt test
Than these thin habits and poor likelihoods
Of modern seeming do prefer against him.
FIRST SENATOR
But, Othello, speak:
Did you by indirect and forced courses
Subdue and poison this young maid's affections?
Or came it by request, and such fair question
As soul to soul affordeth?
OTHELLO
          I do beseech you,
Send for the lady to the Sagittary,
And let her speak of me before her father:
If you do find me foul in her report,
The trust, the office, I do hold of you,
Not only take away, but let your sentence
Even fall upon my life.
DUKE
        Fetch Desdemona hither.
OTHELLO
Ancient, conduct them, you best know the place. —
        [*Exeunt* IAGO *and* ATTENDANTS.
And, till she come, as truly as to heaven
I do confess the vices of my blood,
So justly to your grave ears I'll present
How I did thrive in this fair lady's love,

    OTHELLO She lov'd me for the dangers I had pass'd.

And she in mine.
DUKE
Say it, Othello.
OTHELLO
Her father lov'd me; oft invited me;
Still question'd me the story of my life,
From year to year, — the battles, sieges, fortunes,
That I have pass'd.
I ran it through, even from my boyish days
To the very moment that he bade me tell it:
Wherein I spake of most disastrous chances,
Of moving accidents by flood and field;
Of hair-breadth scapes i'th'imminent deadly breach;
Of being taken by the insolent foe,
And sold to slavery; of my redemption thence,
And portance in my travel's history:
Wherein of antres vast and deserts idle,
Rough quarries, rocks, and hills whose heads touch
    heaven,
It was my hint to speak, — such was the process;
And of the Cannibals that each other eat,
The Anthropophagi, and men whose heads
Do grow beneath their shoulders. This to hear
Would Desdemona seriously incline:
But still the house-affairs would draw her thence;
Which ever as she could with haste dispatch,
She'ld come again, and with a greedy ear
Devour up my discourse: — which I observing,
Took once a pliant hour; and found good means
To draw from her a prayer of earnest heart
That I would all my pilgrimage dilate,
Whereof by parcels she had something heard,
But not intentively: I did consent;
And often did beguile her of her tears,
When I did speak of some distressful stroke
That my youth suffer'd. My story being done,
She gave me for my pains a world of sighs:
She swore, — in faith,'twas strange, 'twas passing
    strange;
'Twas pitiful, 'twas wondrous pitiful:
She wish'd she had not heard it: yet she wish'd
That heaven had made her such a man: she thank'd
    me;
And bade me, if I had a friend that lov'd her,
I should but teach him how to tell my story,
And that would woo her. Upon this hint I spake:
She lov'd me for the dangers I had pass'd;
And I lov'd her that she did pity them.
This only is the witchcraft I have used: —
Here comes the lady; let her witness it.

  Enter DESDEMONA, *with* IAGO *and* ATTENDANTS.

DUKE
I think this tale would win my daughter too. —
Good Brabantio,
Take up this mangled matter at the best:
Men do their broken weapons rather use
Than their bare hands.
BRABANTIO
         I pray you, hear her speak:
If she confess that she was half the wooer,
Destruction on my head, if my bad blame
Light on the man!— Come hither, gentle mistress:
Do you perceive in all this noble company
Where most you owe obedience?
DESDEMONA
           My noble father,

BRABANTIO I here do give thee that which I would keep from thee.

I do perceive here a divided duty:
To you I am bound for life and education;
My life and education both do learn me
How to respect you; you are the lord of duty, —
I am hitherto your daughter: but here's my husband;
And so much duty as my mother show'd
To you, preferring you before her father,
So much I challenge that I may profess
Due to the Moor my lord.

BRABANTIO
God be wi' you! I have done.
Please it your Grace, on to the state-affairs:
I had rather to adopt a child than get it. —
Come hither, Moor:
I here do give thee that with all my heart
Which, but thou hast already, with all my heart
I would keep from thee. — For your sake, jewel,
I am glad at soul I have no other child;
For thy escape would teach me tyranny,
To hang clogs on them. — I have done, my lord.

DUKE
Let me speak like yourself; and lay a sentence,
Which, as a grise or step, may help these lovers
Into your favour.
When remedies are past, the griefs are ended
By seeing the worst, which late on hopes depended.
To mourn a mischief that is past and gone
Is the next way to draw new mischief on.
What cannot be preserv'd when fortune takes,
Patience her injury a mockery makes.
The robb'd that smiles steals something from the thief;
He robs himself that spends a bootless grief.

BRABANTIO
So let the Turk of Cyprus us beguile;
We lose it not, so long as we can smile.
He bears the sentence well that nothing bears
But the free comfort which from thence he hears;
But he bears both the sentence and the sorrow
That to pay grief must of poor patience borrow.
These sentences, to sugar, or to gall,
Being strong on both sides, are equivocal:
But words are words; I never yet did hear
That the bruis'd heart was pierced through the ear. —
I humbly beseech you, proceed to th'affairs of state.

DUKE
The Turk with a most mighty preparation makes for
Cyprus: — Othello, the fortitude of the place is best
known to you; and though we have there a substitute of
most allow'd sufficiency, yet opinion, a sovereign
mistress of effects, throws a more safer voice on you:
you must therefore be content to slubber the gloss of
your new fortunes with this more stubborn and
boisterous expedition.

OTHELLO
The tyrant custom, most grave senators,
Hath made the flinty and steel couch of war
My thrice-driven bed of down: I do agnize
A natural and prompt alacrity
I find in hardness; and do undertake
This present war against the Ottomites.
Most humbly, therefore, bending to your state,
I crave fit disposition for my wife;
Due reference of place and exhibition;
With such accommodation and besort
As levels with her breeding.

DUKE
If you please,
Be't at her father's.

BRABANTIO
I'll not have it so.

OTHELLO
Nor I.

DESDEMONA
Nor I; I would not there reside,
To put my father in impatient thoughts
By being in his eye. Most gracious duke,
To my unfolding lend your prosperous ear;
And let me find a charter in your voice,
T'assist my simpleness.

DUKE
What would you, Desdemona?

DESDEMONA
That I did love the Moor to live with him,
My downright violence and storm of fortunes
May trumpet to the world: my heart's subdued
Even to the very quality of my lord:
I saw Othello's visage in his mind;
And to his honours and his valiant parts
Did I my soul and fortunes consecrate.
So that, dear lords, if I be left behind,
A moth of peace, and he go to the war,
The rites for which I love him are bereft me,
And I a heavy interim shall support
By his dear absence. Let me go with him.

OTHELLO
Your voices, lords: beseech you, let her will

Have a free way.
Vouch with me, heaven, I therefore beg it not,
To please the palate of my appetite;
Nor to comply with heat — the young affects
In me defunct — and proper satisfaction;
But to be free and bounteous to her mind:
And heaven defend your good souls, that you think
I will your serious and great business scant
For she is with me: no, when light-wing'd toys
Of feather'd Cupid seel with wanton dullness
My speculative and offic'd instruments,
That my disports corrupt and taint my business,
Let housewives make a skillet of my helm,
And all indign and base adversities
Make head against my estimation!

DUKE
Be it as you shall privately determine,
Either for her stay or going: th'affair cries haste,
And speed must answer it.

FIRST SENATOR
You must away to-night.

OTHELLO
With all my heart.

DUKE
At nine i' the morning here we'll meet again. —
Othello, leave some officer behind,
And he shall our commission bring to you;
With such things else of quality and respect
As doth import you.

OTHELLO
So please your Grace, my ancient;
A man he is of honest and trust:
To his conveyance I assign my wife,
With what else needful your good Grace shall think
To be sent after me.

DUKE
Let it be so. —
Good night to every one. — [*to* BRABANTIO] And,
    noble signior,
If virtue no delighted beauty lack,
Your son-in-law is far more fair than black.

FIRST SENATOR
Adieu, brave Moor: use Desdemona well.

BRABANTIO
Look to her, Moor, if thou hast eyes to see:
She has deceiv'd her father, and may thee.
[*Exeunt* DUKE, SENATORS, OFFICERS, *etc.*

OTHELLO
My life upon her faith! — Honest Iago,
My Desdemona must I leave to thee:
I prithee, let thy wife attend on her;
And bring them after in the best advantage. —
Come, Desdemona; I have but an hour
Of love, of worldly matters and direction,
To spend with thee: we must obey the time.
[*Exeunt* OTHELLO *and* DESDEMONA.

RODERIGO
Iago, —

IAGO
What say'st thou, noble heart?

RODERIGO
What will I do, think'st thou?

IAGO
Why, go to bed, and sleep.

RODERIGO
I will incontinently drown myself.

IAGO
If thou dost, I shall never love thee after. Why, thou
silly gentleman!

RODERIGO
It is silliness to live when to live is torment; and then
have we a prescription to die when death is our
physician.

IAGO
O villainous! I have look'd upon the world for four
times seven years; and since I could distinguish
betwixt a benefit and an injury, I never found man that
knew how to love himself. Ere I would say, I would
drown myself for the love of a guinea-hen, I would
change my humanity with a baboon.

RODERIGO
What should I do? I confess it is my shame to be so
fond; but it is not in my virtue to amend it.

IAGO
Virtue! a fig! 'tis in ourselves that we are thus or thus.
Our bodies are gardens; to the which our wills are
gardeners: so that if we will plant nettles, or sow
lettuce; set hyssop, and weed-up thyme; supply it with
one gender of herbs, or distract it with many; either to
have it sterile with idleness, or manured with industry;

why, the power and corrigible authority of this lies in our wills. If the balance of our lives had not one scale of reason to poise another of sensuality, the blood and baseness of our natures would conduct us to most preposterous conclusions: but we have reason to cool our raging motions, our carnal stings, our unbitted lusts; whereof I take this that you call love to be a sect or scion.

RODERIGO
It cannot be.

IAGO
It is merely a lust of the blood and a permission of the will. Come, be a man: drown thyself! drown cats and blind puppies. I have profess'd me thy friend, and I confess me knit to thy deserving with cables of perdurable toughness; I could never better stead thee than now. Put money in thy purse; follow thou the wars; defeat thy favour with an usurp'd beard; I say, put money in thy purse. It cannot be that Desdemona should long continue her love to the Moor, — put money in thy purse, — nor he his to her: it was a violent commencement, and thou shalt see an answerable sequestration; — put but money in thy purse. — These Moors are changeable in their wills: — fill thy purse with money: — the food that to him now is as luscious as locusts shall be to him shortly as bitter as coloquintida. She must change for youth; when she is sated with his body, she will find the error of her choice: she must have change, she must: therefore put money in thy purse. — If thou wilt needs damn thyself, do it a more delicate way than drowning. Make all the money thou canst: if sanctimony and a frail vow betwixt an erring barbarian and a supersubtle Venetian be not too hard for my wits and all the tribe of hell, thou shalt enjoy her; therefore make money. A pox of drowning thyself! it is clean out of the way: seek thou rather to be hang'd in compassing thy joy than to be drown'd and go without her.

RODERIGO
Wilt thou be fast to my hopes, if I depend on the issue?

IAGO
Thou art sure of me: — go, make money: — I have told thee often, and I re-tell thee again and again, I hate the Moor: my cause is hearted; thine hath no less reason. Let us be conjunctive in our revenge against him: if thou canst cuckold him, thou dost thyself a pleasure, me a sport. There are many events in the womb of time, which will be deliver'd. Traverse; go; provide thy money. We will have more of this to-morrow. Adieu.

RODERIGO
Where shall we meet i' the morning?

IAGO
At my lodging.

RODERIGO
I'll be with thee betimes.

IAGO
Go to; farewell. Do you hear, Roderigo?

RODERIGO
What say you?

IAGO
No more of drowning, do you hear?

RODERIGO
I am changed: I'll go sell all my land.

IAGO
Go to; farewell! put money in your purse.

[Exit RODERIGO.

Thus do I ever make my fool my purse;
For I mine own gain'd knowledge should profane,
If I would time expend with such a snipe,
But for my sport and profit. I hate the Moor;
And it is thought abroad, that 'twixt my sheets
'Has done my office: I know not if't be true;
But I, for mere suspicion in that kind,
Will do as if for surety. He holds me well;
The better shall my purpose work on him.
Cassio's a proper man: let me see now;
To get his place, and to plume up my will
In double knavery — How, how? — Let's see: —
After some time, to abuse Othello's ear
That he is too familiar with his wife: —
He hath a person, and a smooth dispose,
To be suspected; fram'd to make women false.
The Moor is of a free and open nature,
That thinks men honest that but seem to be so;
And will as tenderly be led by th'nose
As asses are.
I have't; — It is engender'd: — hell and night
Must bring this monstrous birth to the world's light.
[Exit.

ACT II

SCENE I

A Seaport town in Cyprus. An open place near the Quay.

Enter MONTANO and two GENTLEMEN.

MONTANO
What from the cape can you discern at sea?

FIRST GENTLEMAN
Nothing at all: it is a high-wrought flood;
I cannot 'twixt the heaven and the main
Descry a sail.

MONTANO
Methinks the wind hath spoke aloud at land;
A fuller blast ne'er shook our battlements:
If it hath ruffian'd so upon the sea,
What ribs of oak, when mountains melt on them,
Can hold the mortise? What shall we hear of this?

SECOND GENTLEMAN
A segregation of the Turkish fleet:
For do but stand upon the foaming shore,
The chidden billow seems to pelt the clouds;
The wind-shak'd surge, with high and monstrous mane,
Seems to cast water on the burning bear,
And quench the guards of th'ever-fixed pole:
I never did like molestation view
On the enchafed flood.

MONTANO
If that the Turkish fleet
Be not enshelter'd and embay'd, they are drown'd;
It is impossible they bear it out.

Enter a third GENTLEMAN.

THIRD GENTLEMAN
News, lads! our wars are done.
The desperate tempest hath so bang'd the Turks,
That their designment halts: a noble ship of Venice
Hath seen a grievous wrack and sufferance
On most part of their fleet.

MONTANO
How! is this true?

THIRD GENTLEMAN
The ship is here put in,
A Veronesa; Michael Cassio,
Lieutenant to the warlike Moor Othello,
Is come on shore: the Moor himself's at sea,
And is in full commission here for Cyprus.

MONTANO
I am glad on't; 'tis a worthy governor.

THIRD GENTLEMAN
But this same Cassio, though he speak of comfort
Touching the Turkish loss, yet he looks sadly,
And prays the Moor be safe; for they were parted
With foul and violent tempest.

MONTANO
Pray heavens he be;
For I have serv'd him, and the man commands
Like a full soldier. Let's to the seaside, ho!
As well to see the vessel that's come in
As to throw out our eyes for brave Othello,
Even till we make the main and th'aerial blue
An indistinct regard.

THIRD GENTLEMAN
Come, let's do so;
For every minute is expectancy
Of more arrivance.

Enter CASSIO.

CASSIO
Thanks, you the valiant of this warlike isle,
That so approve the Moor! O, let the heavens
Give him defence against the elements,
For I have lost him on a dangerous sea!

MONTANO
Is he well shipp'd?

CASSIO
His bark is stoutly timber'd, and his pilot
Of very expert and approv'd allowance;
Therefore my hopes, not surfeited to death,
Stand in bold cure.
[Within] A sail, a sail, a sail!

Enter a fourth GENTLEMAN.

CASSIO
What noise?

FOURTH GENTLEMAN
The town is empty; on the brow o'the sea
Stand ranks of people, and they cry, 'A sail!'

CASSIO
My hopes do shape him for the governor. *[Guns within.*

SECOND GENTLEMAN
They do discharge their shot of courtesy:
Our friends at least.

CASSIO
I pray you, sir, go forth,
And give us truth who 'tis that is arrived.

SECOND GENTLEMAN
I shall. *[Exit.*

MONTANO
But, good lieutenant, is your general wiv'd?

CASSIO
Most fortunately: he hath achiev'd a maid
That paragons description and wild fame;
One that excels the quirks of blazoning pens,
And in th'essential vesture of creation
Does tire the ingener.

Enter second GENTLEMAN.

How now! who has put in?

SECOND GENTLEMAN
'Tis one Iago, ancient to the general.

CASSIO
'Has had most favourable and happy speed:
Tempests themselves, high seas, and howling winds,
The gutter'd rocks, and congregated sands, —
Traitors ensteep'd to clog the guiltless keel, —
As having sense of beauty, do omit
Their mortal natures, letting go safely by
The divine Desdemona.

MONTANO
What is she?

CASSIO
She that I spake of, our great captain's captain,
Left in the conduct of the bold Iago;
Whose footing here anticipates our thoughts
A se'nnight's speed. — Great Jove, Othello guard,
And swell his sail with thine own powerful breath,
That he may bless this bay with his tall ship,
Make love's quick pants in Desdemona's arms,
Give renew'd fire to our extincted spirits,
And bring all Cyprus comfort! — O, behold,
*Enter DESDEMONA, EMILIA, IAGO,
RODERIGO, and ATTENDANTS.*
The riches of the ship is come on shore!
Ye men of Cyprus, let her have your knees. —
Hail to thee, lady! and the grace of heaven
Before, behind thee, and on every hand,
Enwheel thee round!

DESDEMONA
I thank you, valiant Cassio.
What tidings can you tell me of my lord?

CASSIO
He is not yet arriv'd: nor know I aught
But that he's well, and will be shortly here.

DESDEMONA
O, but I fear — How lost you company?

CASSIO
The great contention of the sea and skies
Parted our fellowship: — but, hark! a sail.
[Within] A sail, a sail! *[Guns within.*

SECOND GENTLEMAN
They give their greeting to the citadel:
This likewise is a friend.

CASSIO
See for the news. —
[Exit GENTLEMAN.
Good ancient, you are welcome: — *[to EMILIA]*
welcome, mistress: —
Let it not gall your patience, good Iago,
That I extend my manners; 'tis my breeding
That gives me this bold show of courtesy. *[Kissing her.*

IAGO
Sir, would she give you so much of her lips
As of her tongue she oft bestows on me,
You'ld have enough.

DESDEMONA
Alas, she has no speech.

IAGO
In faith, too much;
I find it still, when I have list to sleep:
Marry, before your ladyship, I grant,
She puts her tongue a little in her heart,
And chides with thinking.

EMILIA
You have little cause to say so.

IAGO
Come on, come on; you are pictures out of doors,
Bells in your parlours, wild-cats in your kitchens,

Saints in your injuries, devils being offended,
Players in your housewifery, and housewives in your
    beds.

DESDEMONA
O, fie upon thee, slanderer!

IAGO
Nay, it is true, or else I am a Turk:
You rise to play, and go to bed to work.

EMILIA
You shall not write my praise.

IAGO
                                No, let me not.

DESDEMONA
What wouldst thou write of me, if thou shouldst praise
    me?

IAGO
O gentle lady, do not put me to't;
For I am nothing, if not critical.

DESDEMONA
Come on, assay. — There's one gone to the harbour?

IAGO
Ay, madam.

DESDEMONA
I am not merry; but I do beguile
The thing I am, by seeming otherwise. —
Come, how wouldst thou praise me?

IAGO
I am about it; but, indeed, my invention
Comes from my pate as birdlime does from frize, —
It plucks out brains and all: but my Muse labours,
And thus she is deliver'd.
If she be fair and wise, — fairness and wit,
The one's for use, the other useth it.

DESDEMONA
Well praised! How if she be black and witty?

IAGO
If she be black, and thereto have a wit,
She'll find a white that shall her blackness hit.

DESDEMONA
Worse and worse.

EMILIA
How if fair and foolish?

IAGO
She never yet was foolish that was fair;
For even her folly help'd her to an heir.

DESDEMONA
These are old fond paradoxes to make fools laugh
i'th'alehouse. What miserable praise hast thou for her
that's foul and foolish?

IAGO
There's none so foul, and foolish thereunto,
But does foul pranks which fair and wise ones do.

DESDEMONA
O heavy ignorance! — thou praisest the worst best. But
what praise couldst thou bestow on a deserving woman
indeed, — one that, in the authority of her merit, did
justly put on the vouch of very malice itself?

IAGO
She that was ever fair, and never proud;
Had tongue at will, and yet was never loud;
Never lack'd gold, and yet went never gay;
Fled from her wish, and yet said, 'Now I may';
She that, being anger'd, her revenge being nigh,
Bade her wrong stay, and her displeasure fly;
She that in wisdom never was so frail
To change the cod's head for the salmon's tail;
She that could think, and ne'er disclose her mind;
See suitors following, and not look behind;
She was a wight, if ever such wight were, —

DESDEMONA
To do what?

IAGO
To suckle fools and chronicle small beer.

DESDEMONA
O most lame and impotent conclusion! — Do not learn
of him, Emilia, though he be thy husband. — How say
you, Cassio? is he not a most profane and liberal
counsellor?

CASSIO
He speaks home, madam: you may relish him more in
the soldier than in the scholar.

IAGO [aside].
He takes her by the palm: ay, well said, whisper: with as
little a web as this will I ensnare as great a fly as Cassio.
Ay, smile upon her, do; I will gyve thee in thine own
courtship. You say true; 'tis so, indeed; if such tricks as
these strip you out of your lieutenantry, it had been
better you had not kiss'd your three fingers so oft,
which now again you are most apt to play the sir in.

Very good; well kiss'd! an excellent courtesy! 'tis so,
indeed. Yet again your fingers to your lips? would they
were clyster-pipes for your sake! [Trumpet within.] —
The Moor! I know his trumpet.

CASSIO
'Tis truly so.

DESDEMONA
Let's meet him, and receive him.

CASSIO
Lo, where he comes!

            Enter OTHELLO and ATTENDANTS.

OTHELLO
O my fair warrior!

DESDEMONA
            My dear Othello!

OTHELLO
It gives me wonder great as my content
To see you here before me. O my soul's joy!
If after every tempest come such calms,
May the winds blow till they have waken'd death!
And let the labouring bark climb hills of seas
Olympus-high, and duck again as low
As hell's from heaven! If it were now to die,
'Twere now to be most happy; for, I fear,
My soul hath her content so absolute,
That not another comfort like to this
Succeeds in unknown fate.

DESDEMONA
                        The heavens forbid
But that our loves and comforts should increase,
Even as our days do grow!

OTHELLO
                        Amen to that, sweet powers!
I cannot speak enough of this content;
It stops me here; it is too much of joy:
And this, and this, the greatest discords be [Kissing her.
That e'er our hearts shall make!

IAGO [aside].
                        O, you are well tun'd now!
But I'll set down the pegs that make this music,
As honest as I am.

OTHELLO
                    Come, let us to the castle. —
News, friends; our wars are done, the Turks are
    drown'd.
How does my old acquaintance of this isle? —
Honey, you shall be well desired in Cyprus;
I have found great love amongst them. O my sweet,
I prattle out of fashion, and I dote
In mine own comforts. — I prithee, good Iago,
Go to the bay and disembark my coffers:
Bring thou the master to the citadel;
He is a good one, and his worthiness
Does challenge much respect. — Come, Desdemona,
Once more well met at Cyprus.
            [Exeunt OTHELLO, DESDEMONA, and
                                ATTENDANTS.

IAGO
Do thou meet me presently at the harbour. Come
hither. If thou be'st valiant, — as, they say, base men
being in love have then a nobility in their natures more
than is native to them, — list me. The lieutenant
to-night watches on the court-of-guard: — first, I must
tell thee this — Desdemona is directly in love with him.

RODERIGO
With him! why, 'tis not possible.

IAGO
Lay thy finger thus, and let thy soul be instructed. Mark
me with what violence she first loved the Moor, but for
bragging, and telling her fantastical lies: and will she
love him still for prating? let not thy discreet heart
think it. Her eye must be fed; and what delight shall
she have to look on the devil? When the blood is made
dull with the act of sport, there should be — again to
inflame it, and to give satiety a fresh appetite —
loveliness in favour, sympathy in years, manners, and
beauties; all which the Moor is defective in: now, for
want of these required conveniences, her delicate
tenderness will find itself abused, begin to heave the
gorge, disrelish and abhor the Moor; very nature will
instruct her in it, and compel her to some second
choice. Now, sir, this granted, — as it is a most
pregnant and unforced position, — who stands so
eminent in the degree of this fortune as Cassio does? a
knave very voluble; no further conscionable than in
putting on the mere form of civil and humane
seeming, for the better compassing of his salt and most
hidden loose affection? Why, none; why, none: a
slipper and subtle knave; a finder of occasions; that has
an eye can stamp and counterfeit advantages, though

true advantage never present itself: a devilish knave!
Besides, the knave is handsome, young, and hath all
those requisites in him that folly and green minds look
after: a pestilent complete knave; and the woman hath
found him already.

RODERIGO
I cannot believe that in her; she's full of most blest
condition.

IAGO
Blest fig's-end! the wine she drinks is made of grapes:
if she had been blest, she would never have loved the
Moor: blest pudding! Didst thou not see her paddle
with the palm of his hand? didst not mark that?

RODERIGO
Yes, that I did; but that was but courtesy.

IAGO
Lechery, by this hand; an index and obscure prologue
to the history of lust and foul thoughts. They met so
near with their lips, that their breaths embraced
together. Villainous thoughts, Roderigo! when these
mutualities so marshal the way, hard at hand comes
the master and main exercise, the incorporate
conclusion: pish! — But, sir, be you ruled by me: I have
brought you from Venice. Watch you to-night; for the
command, I'll lay't upon you: Cassio knows you not: —
I'll not be far from you: do you find some occasion to
anger Cassio, either by speaking too loud, or tainting
his discipline; or from what other course you please,
which the time shall more favourably minister.

RODERIGO
Well.

IAGO
Sir, he is rash, and very sudden in choler, and haply
may strike at you: provoke him, that he may; for even
out of that will I cause these of Cyprus to mutiny;
whose qualification shall come into no true taste again
but by the displanting of Cassio. So shall you have a
shorter journey to your desires, by the means I shall
then have to prefer them; and the impediment most
profitably removed, without the which there were no
expectation of our prosperity.

RODERIGO
I will do this, if I can bring it to any opportunity.

IAGO
I warrant thee. Meet me by and by at the citadel:
I must fetch his necessaries ashore. Farewell.

RODERIGO
Adieu.   [Exit.

IAGO
That Cassio loves her, I do well believe it;
That she loves him, 'tis apt, and of great credit:
The Moor — howbeit that I endure him not —
Is of a constant, loving, noble nature;
And I dare think he'll prove to Desdemona
A most dear husband. Now, I do love her too;
Not out of absolute lust, — though peradventure
I stand accountant for as great a sin, —
But partly led to diet my revenge,
For that I do suspect the lusty Moor
Hath leapt into my seat: the thought whereof
Doth, like a poisonous mineral, gnaw my inwards;
And nothing can or shall content my soul
Till I am even'd with him, wife for wife;
Or failing so, yet that I put the Moor
At least into a jealousy so strong
That judgement cannot cure. Which thing to do,
If this poor trash of Venice, whom I trash
For his quick hunting, stand the putting on,
I'll have our Michael Cassio on the hip;
Abuse him to the Moor in the rank garb, —
For I fear Cassio with my night-cap too;
Make the Moor thank me, love me, and reward me,
For making him egregiously an ass,
And practising upon his peace and quiet
Even to madness. 'Tis here, but yet confused:
Knavery's plain face is never seen till used.   [Exit.

SCENE II

A street.

Enter OTHELLO'S HERALD with a proclamation;
PEOPLE following.

HERALD
It is Othello's pleasure, our noble and valiant general,
that, upon certain tidings now arrived, importing the
mere perdition of the Turkish fleet, every man put
himself into triumph; some to dance, some to make
bonfires, each man to what sport and revels his
addiction leads him: for, besides these beneficial news,
it is the celebration of his nuptial: — so much was his

CASSIO To the health of our general!

pleasure should be proclaim'd. All offices are open; and there is full liberty of feasting from this present hour of five till the bell have told eleven. Heaven bless the isle of Cyprus and our noble general Othello!

[*Exeunt.*

SCENE III

A hall in the castle.

Enter OTHELLO, DESDEMONA, CASSIO, *and* ATTENDANTS.

OTHELLO
Good Michael, look you to the guard to-night:
Let's teach ourselves that honourable stop,
Not to outsport discretion.

CASSIO
Iago hath direction what to do;
But, notwithstanding, with my personal eye
Will I look to't.

OTHELLO
   Iago is most honest.
Michael, good night: to-morrow with your earliest
Let me have speech with you. — [*to* DESDEMONA]
 Come, my dear love, —
The purchase made, the fruits are to ensue;
That profit's yet to come 'twixt me and you. —
Good night.

   [*Exeunt* OTHELLO, DESDEMONA,
    and ATTENDANTS.

   Enter IAGO.

CASSIO
Welcome, Iago; we must to the watch.

IAGO
Not this hour, lieutenant; 'tis not yet ten o'the clock. Our general cast us thus early for the love of his Desdemona; who let us not therefore blame; he hath not yet made wanton the night with her; and she is sport for Jove.

CASSIO
She's a most exquisite lady.

IAGO
And, I'll warrant her, full of game.

CASSIO
Indeed, she's a most fresh and delicate creature.

IAGO
What an eye she has! methinks it sounds a parley to provocation.

CASSIO
An inviting eye; and yet methinks right modest.

IAGO
And when she speaks, is it not an alarum to love?

CASSIO
She is, indeed, perfection.

IAGO
Well, happiness to their sheets! Come, lieutenant, I have a stoop of wine; and here without are a brace of Cyprus gallants that would fain have a measure to the health of black Othello.

CASSIO
Not to-night, good Iago: I have very poor and unhappy brains for drinking: I could well wish courtesy would invent some other custom of entertainment.

IAGO
O, they are our friends; but one cup: I'll drink for you.

CASSIO
I have drunk but one cup to-night, and that was craftily qualified too, and, behold, what innovation it makes here: I am unfortunate in the infirmity, and dare not task my weakness with any more.

IAGO
What, man! 'tis a night of revels: the gallants desire it.

CASSIO
Where are they?

IAGO
Here at the door; I pray you, call them in.

CASSIO
I'll do't; but it dislikes me.   [*Exit.*

IAGO
If I can fasten but one cup upon him,
With that which he hath drunk to-night already,
He'll be as full of quarrel and offence
As my young mistress' dog. Now, my sick fool
 Roderigo,
Whom love hath turn'd almost the wrong side out,
To Desdemona hath to-night caroused
Potations pottle-deep; and he's to watch:
Three lads of Cyprus — noble swelling spirits,
That hold their honours in a wary distance,
The very elements of this warlike isle —
Have I to-night fluster'd with flowing cups,
And they watch too. Now, 'mongst this flock of
 drunkards
Am I to put our Cassio in some action
That may offend the isle: — but here they come:
If consequence do but approve my dream,
My boat sails freely, both with wind and stream.

Enter CASSIO, MONTANO *and* GENTLEMEN;
SERVANTS *following with wine.*

CASSIO
'Fore God, they have given me a rouse already.

MONTANO
Good faith, a little one; not past a pint, as I am a soldier.

IAGO
Some wine, ho!   [*Sings.*

 And let me the canakin clink, clink;
 And let me the canakin clink;
  A soldier's a man;
  A life's but a span;
 Why, then, let a soldier drink.

Some wine, boys!

CASSIO
'Fore God, an excellent song.

IAGO
I learn'd it in England, where, indeed, they are most potent in potting: your Dane, your German, and your swag-bellied Hollander, — Drink, ho! — are nothing to your English.

CASSIO
Is your Englishman so expert in his drinking?

IAGO
Why, he drinks you, with facility, your Dane dead drunk; he sweats not to overthrow your Almain; he gives your Hollander a vomit, ere the next pottle can be fill'd.

CASSIO
To the health of our general!

MONTANO
I am for it, lieutenant; and I'll do you justice.

IAGO
O sweet England!   [*Sings.*
 King Stephen was a worthy peer,
  His breeches cost him but a crown;
 He held them sixpence all too dear,
  With that he call'd the tailor lown.

 He was a wight of high renown,
  And thou art but of low degree:
 'Tis pride that pulls the country down;
  Then take thine auld cloak about thee.
Some wine, ho!

CASSIO
Why, this is a more exquisite song than the other.

IAGO
Will you hear't again?

CASSIO
No; for I hold him to be unworthy of his place that does those things. — Well, — God's above all; and there be souls must be saved, and there be souls must not be saved.

IAGO
It's true, good lieutenant.

CASSIO
For mine own part, — no offence to the general, nor any man of quality, — I hope to be saved.

IAGO
And so do I too, lieutenant.

CASSIO
Ay, but, by your leave, not before me; the lieutenant is to be saved before the ancient. Let's have no more of this; let's to our affairs. — God forgive us our sins! — Gentlemen, let's look to our business. Do not think, gentlemen, I am drunk: this is my ancient; — This is my right hand, and this is my left: — I am not drunk now; I can stand well enough, and speak well enough.

ALL
Excellent well.

CASSIO
Why, very well, then; you must not think, then, that I am drunk.   [*Exit.*

MONTANO
To the platform, masters; come, let's set the watch.

IAGO
You see this fellow that is gone before; —
He is a soldier fit to stand by Cæsar
And give direction: and do but see his vice;
'Tis to his virtue a just equinox,
The one as long as th'other: 'tis pity of him.
I fear the trust Othello puts him in,
On some odd time of his infirmity,
Will shake this island.

MONTANO
    But is he often thus?

IAGO
'Tis evermore the prologue to his sleep:
He'll watch the horologe a double set,
If drink rock not his cradle.

MONTANO
    It were well
The general were put in mind of it.
Perhaps he sees it not; or his good nature
Prizes the virtue that appears in Cassio,
And looks not on his evils: is not this true?

Enter RODERIGO.

IAGO [*aside to* RODERIGO].
How now, Roderigo!
I pray you, after the lieutenant; go. [*Exit* RODERIGO.

MONTANO
And 'tis great pity that the noble Moor
Should hazard such a place as his own second
With one of an ingraft infirmity:
It were an honest action to say
So to the Moor.

IAGO
   Not I, for this fair island:
I do love Cassio well; and would do much
To cure him of this evil — But, hark! what noise?

[Cry within, — 'Help! help!'
Enter CASSIO, *driving in* RODERIGO.

CASSIO
Zounds, you rogue! you rascal!

MONTANO
What's the matter, lieutenant?

CASSIO
A knave teach me my duty! but I'll beat the knave into a
twiggen bottle.

RODERIGO
Beat me!

CASSIO
Dost thou prate, rogue?　　　　　*[Striking* RODERIGO.

MONTANO
Nay, good lieutenant; I pray you, sir, hold your hand.

CASSIO
Let me go, sir, or I'll knock you o'er the mazard.

MONTANO
Come, come, you're drunk.

CASSIO
Drunk!　　　　　　　　　　　*[They fight.*

IAGO [*aside to* RODERIGO].
Away, I say, go out; and cry a mutiny!

[Exit RODERIGO.

Nay, good lieutenant, — God's will, gentlemen; —
Help, ho! — Lieutenant, — sir, — Montano, — sir; —
Help, masters! — Here's a goodly watch indeed!

[Bell rings.

Who's that which rings the bell? — Diablo, ho!
The town will rise: God's will, lieutenant, hold;
You will be sham'd for ever.

Enter OTHELLO *and* ATTENDANTS.

OTHELLO
　　　　　　　　What is the matter here?

MONTANO
Zounds, I bleed still; I am hurt to the death.　　*[Faints.*

OTHELLO
Hold, for your lives!

IAGO
Hold, ho! Lieutenant, — sir, — Montano, —
　gentlemen, —
Have you forgot all sense of place and duty?
Hold! the general speaks to you; hold, hold, for shame!

OTHELLO
Why, how now, ho! from whence ariseth this?
Are we turn'd Turks, and to ourselves do that
Which heaven hath forbid the Ottomites?
For Christian shame, put by this barbarous brawl:
He that stirs next to carve for his own rage,
Holds his soul light; he dies upon his motion. —
Silence that dreadful bell! it frights the isle
From her propriety. — What is the matter, masters? —
Honest Iago, that look'st dead with grieving,
Speak, who began this? on thy love, I charge thee.

IAGO
I do not know: — friends all but now, even now,
In quarter, and in terms like bride and groom
Devesting them for bed; and then, but now —
As if some planet had unwitted men —
Swords out, and tilting one at other's breast,
In opposition bloody. I cannot speak
Any beginning to this peevish odds;
And would in action glorious I had lost
Those legs that brought me to a part of it!

OTHELLO
How comes it, Michael, you are thus forgot?

CASSIO
I pray you, pardon me; I cannot speak.

OTHELLO
Worthy Montano, you were wont be civil;
The gravity and stillness of your youth
The world hath noted, and your name is great
In mouths of wisest censure: what's the matter,
That you unlace your reputation thus,
And spend your rich opinion for the name
Of a night-brawler? give me answer to it.

MONTANO
Worthy Othello, I am hurt to danger:
Your officer, Iago, can inform you —
While I spare speech, which something now offends
　me —
Of all that I do know: nor know I aught
By me that's said or done amiss this night;
Unless self-charity be sometimes a vice,
And to defend ourselves it be a sin
When violence assails us.

OTHELLO
　　　　　　　　Now by heaven,

My blood begins my safer guides to rule;
And passion, having my best judgement collied,
Assays to lead the way: — if I once stir,
Or do but lift this arm, the best of you
Shall sink in my rebuke. Give me to know
How this foul rout began, who set it on;
And he that is approv'd in this offence,
Though he had twinn'd with me, both at a birth,
Shall lose me. — What! in a town of war,
Yet wild, the people's hearts brimful of fear,
To manage private and domestic quarrel,
In night, and on the court and guard of safety!
'Tis monstrous — Iago, who began't?

MONTANO
If partially affin'd, or leagued in office,
Thou dost deliver more or less than truth,
Thou art no soldier.

IAGO
　　　　　　　　Touch me not so near:
I had rather have this tongue cut from my mouth
Than it should do offence to Michael Cassio;
Yet, I persuade myself, to speak the truth
Shall nothing wrong him. — Thus it is, general.
Montano and myself being in speech,
There comes a fellow crying out for help;
And Cassio following him with determin'd sword
To execute upon him. Sir, this gentleman
Steps in to Cassio, and entreats his pause:
Myself the crying fellow did pursue,
Lest by his clamour — as it so fell out —
The town might fall in fright: he, swift of foot,
Outran my purpose; and I return'd the rather
For that I heard the clink and fall of swords,
And Cassio high in oath; which till to-night
I ne'er might say before. When I came back, —
For this was brief, — I found them close together,
At blow and thrust; even as again they were
When you yourself did part them.
More of this matter cannot I report: —
But men are men; the best sometimes forget: —
Though Cassio did some little wrong to him, —
As men in rage strike those that wish them best, —
Yet, surely, Cassio, I believe, received
From him that fled some strange indignity,
Which patience could not pass.

OTHELLO
　　　　　　　　I know, Iago,
Thy honesty and love doth mince this matter,
Making it light to Cassio. — Cassio, I love thee;
But never more be officer of mine.

Enter DESDEMONA, *attended.*

Look, if my gentle love be not rais'd up! —
I'll make thee an example.

DESDEMONA
　　　　　　　　What's the matter?

OTHELLO
All's well now, sweeting; come away to bed. —
Sir, for your hurts, myself will be your surgeon:
Lead him off.　　　　　*[Exeunt some with* MONTANO.
Iago, look with care about the town,
And silence those whom this vile brawl distracted. —
Come, Desdemona: 'tis the soldiers' life
To have their balmy slumbers wak'd with strife.

[Exeunt all but IAGO *and* CASSIO.

IAGO
What, are you hurt, lieutenant?

CASSIO
Ay, past all surgery.

IAGO
Marry, heaven forbid!

CASSIO
Reputation, reputation, reputation! O, I have lost my
reputation! I have lost the immortal part of myself, and
what remains is bestial. — My reputation, Iago, my
reputation!

IAGO
As I am an honest man, I thought you had received
some bodily wound; there is more sense in that than in
reputation. Reputation is an idle and most false
imposition; oft got without merit, and lost without
deserving: you have lost no reputation at all, unless you
repute yourself such a loser. What, man! there are ways
to recover the general again: you are but now cast in his
mood, a punishment more in policy than in malice,
even so as one would beat his offenceless dog to
affright an imperious lion: sue to him again, and he's
yours.

CASSIO
I will rather sue to be despised than to deceive so good a
commander with so slight, so drunken, and so
indiscreet an officer. Drunk? and speak parrot? and
squabble? swagger? swear? and discourse fustian with
one's own shadow? — O thou invisible spirit of wine, if
thou hast no name to be known by, let us call thee devil!

IAGO
What was he that you follow'd with your sword?
What had he done to you?

CASSIO
I know not.

IAGO
Is't possible?

CASSIO
I remember a mass of things, but nothing distinctly; a
quarrel, but nothing wherefore. — O God, that men
should put an enemy in their mouths to steal away
their brains! that we should, with joy, pleasance, revel,
and applause, transform ourselves into beasts!

IAGO
Why, but you are now well enough: how came you thus
recover'd?

IAGO What, are you hurt, lieutenant?

CASSIO

It hath pleased the devil drunkenness to give place to the devil wrath: one unperfectness shows me another, to make me frankly despise myself.

IAGO

Come, you are too severe a moraler: as the time, the place, and the condition of this country stands, I could heartily wish this had not befall'n; but, since it is as it is, mend it for your own good.

CASSIO

I will ask him for my place again, — he shall tell me I am a drunkard! Had I as many mouths as Hydra, such an answer would stop them all. To be now a sensible man, by and by a fool, and presently a beast! O strange! — Every inordinate cup is unblest, and the ingredient is a devil.

IAGO

Come, come, good wine is a good familiar creature, if it be well used: exclaim no more against it. And, good lieutenant, I think you think I love you.

CASSIO

I have well approved it, sir. — I drunk!

IAGO

You or any man living may be drunk at a time, man. I'll tell you what you shall do. Our general's wife is now the general; — I may say so in this respect, for that he hath devoted and given up himself to the contemplation, mark, and denotement of her parts and graces: confess yourself freely to her; importune her help to put you in your place again: she is of so free, so kind, so apt, so blessed a disposition, she holds it a vice in her goodness not to do more than she is requested: this broken joint between you and her husband entreat her to splinter; and, my fortunes against any lay worth naming, this crack of your love shall grow stronger than it was before.

CASSIO

You advise me well.

IAGO

I protest, in the sincerity of love and honest kindness.

CASSIO

I think it freely; and betimes in the morning I will beseech the virtuous Desdemona to undertake for me: I am desperate of my fortunes if they check me here.

IAGO

You are in the right. Good night, lieutenant; I must to the watch.

CASSIO

Good night, honest Iago.   [*Exit.*

IAGO

And what's he, then, that says I play the villain?
When this advice is free I give and honest,
Probal to thinking, and, indeed, the course
To win the Moor again? For 'tis most easy
Th'inclining Desdemona to subdue
In any honest suit: she's fram'd as fruitful
As the free elements. And then for her
To win the Moor, — were't to renounce his baptism,
All seals and symbols of redeemed sin,
His soul is so enfetter'd to her love,
That she may make, unmake, do what she list,
Even as her appetite shall play the god
With his weak function. How am I, then, a villain
To counsel Cassio to this parallel course,
Directly to his good? Divinity of hell!
When devils will the blackest sins put on,
They do suggest at first with heavenly shows,
As I do now: for whiles this honest fool
Plies Desdemona to repair his fortunes,
And she for him pleads strongly to the Moor,
I'll pour this pestilence into his ear, —
That she repeals him for her body's lust;
And by how much she strives to do him good,
She shall undo her credit with the Moor.
So will I turn her virtue into pitch;
And out of her own goodness make the net
That shall enmesh them all.

Enter RODERIGO.

                    How now, Roderigo!

RODERIGO

I do follow here in the chase, not like a hound that hunts, but one that fills up the cry. My money is almost spent; I have been to-night exceedingly well cudgell'd; and I think the issue will be — I shall have so much experience for my pains; and so, with no money at all, and a little more wit, return again to Venice.

IAGO

How poor are they that have not patience!
What wound did ever heal but by degrees?
Thou know'st we work by wit, and not by witchcraft;
And wit depends on dilatory time.
Does't not go well? Cassio hath beaten thee,
And thou, by that small hurt, hast cashier'd Cassio:
Though other things grow fair against the sun,
Yet fruits that blossom first will first be ripe:
Content thyself awhile. — By th'mass, 'tis morning;
Pleasure and action make the hours seem short. —
Retire thee; go where thou art billeted:
Away, I say; thou shalt know more hereafter:
Nay, get thee gone. [*Exit* RODERIGO.] Two things are to be done, —
My wife must move for Cassio to her mistress;
I'll set her on;
Myself the while to draw the Moor apart,
And bring him jump when he may Cassio find
Soliciting his wife: — ay, that's the way;
Dull not device by coldness and delay.   [*Exit.*

ACT III

SCENE I

Cyprus. Before the castle.

Enter CASSIO *and some* MUSICIANS.

CASSIO

Masters, play here, — I will content your pains, —
Something that's brief; and bid 'Good morrow,
  general.'   [*Music.*

Enter CLOWN.

CLOWN

Why, masters, have your instruments been in Naples, that they speak i'th'nose thus?

FIRST MUSICIAN

How, sir, how!

CLOWN

Are these, I pray you, wind-instruments?

FIRST MUSICIAN

Ay, marry, are they, sir.

CLOWN

O, thereby hangs a tail.

FIRST MUSICIAN

Whereby hangs a tale, sir?

CLOWN

Marry, sir, by many a wind-instrument that I know. But, masters, here's money for you: and the general so likes your music, that he desires you, of all loves, to make no more noise with it.

FIRST MUSICIAN

Well, sir, we will not.

CLOWN

If you have any music that may not be heard, to't again: but, as they say, to hear music the general does not greatly care.

FIRST MUSICIAN

We have none such, sir.

CLOWN

Then put up your pipes in your bag, for I'll away: go; vanish into air; away!   [*Exeunt* MUSICIANS.

CASSIO

Dost thou hear, my honest friend?

CLOWN

No, I hear not your honest friend; I hear you.

CASSIO

Prithee, keep up thy quillets. There's a poor piece of gold for thee: if the gentlewoman that attends the general's wife be stirring, tell her there's one Cassio entreats her a little favour of speech: wilt thou do this?

CLOWN

She is stirring, sir: if she will stir hither, I shall seem to notify unto her.

CASSIO

Do, good my friend.   [*Exit* CLOWN.

Enter IAGO.

                    In happy time, Iago.

IAGO

You have not been a-bed, then?

CASSIO

Why, no; the day had broke
Before we parted. I have made bold, Iago,
To send in to your wife: my suit to her
Is, that she will to virtuous Desdemona
Procure me some access.

IAGO

                    I'll send her to you presently;
And I'll devise a mean to draw the Moor
Out of the way, that your converse and business
May be more free.

CASSIO

I humbly thank you for't. [*Exit* IAGO.] I never knew
A Florentine more kind and honest.

Enter EMILIA.

EMILIA

Good morrow, good Lieutenant: I am sorry
For your displeasure; but all will sure be well.
The general and his wife are talking of it;
And she speaks for you stoutly: the Moor replies,
That he you hurt is of great fame in Cyprus
And great affinity, and that in wholesome wisdom
He might not but refuse you; but he protests he loves
  you,
And needs no other suitor but his likings
To take the safest occasion by the front
To bring you in again.

CASSIO

                    Yet, I beseech you, —
If you think fit, or that it may be done, —
Give me advantage of some brief discourse
With Desdemona alone.

EMILIA

                    Pray you, come in:
I will bestow you where you shall have time
To speak your bosom freely.

CASSIO

                    I am much bound to you.   [*Exeunt.*

SCENE II

A room in the castle.

Enter OTHELLO, IAGO, *and* GENTLEMEN.

OTHELLO

These letters give, Iago, to the pilot;
And, by him, do my duties to the senate:
That done, I will be walking on the works;
Repair there to me.

IAGO

                    Well, my good lord, I'll do't.

OTHELLO

This fortification, gentlemen, — shall we see't?

GENTLEMAN

We'll wait upon your lordship.   [*Exeunt.*

SCENE III

The garden of the castle.

Enter DESDEMONA, CASSIO, *and* EMILIA.

DESDEMONA

Be thou assured, good Cassio, I will do
All my abilities in thy behalf.

EMILIA

Good madam, do: I warrant it grieves my husband,
As if the case were his.

DESDEMONA

O, that's an honest fellow. — Do not doubt, Cassio,
But I will have my lord and you again
As friendly as you were.

CASSIO

                    Bounteous madam,
Whatever shall become of Michael Cassio,
He's never anything but your true servant.

DESDEMONA

I know't, — I thank you. You do love my lord:
You have known him long; and be you well assured
He shall in strangeness stand no further off
Than in a polite distance.

CASSIO

                    Ay, but, lady,
That policy may either last so long,
Or feed upon such nice and waterish diet,
Or breed itself so out of circumstance,
That, I being absent, and my place supplied,
My general will forget my love and service.

DESDEMONA

Do not doubt that; before Emilia here
I give thee warrant of thy place: assure thee,
If I do vow a friendship, I'll perform it
To the last article: my lord shall never rest;
I'll watch him tame, and talk him out of patience;
His bed shall seem a school, his board a shrift;
I'll intermingle every thing he does
With Cassio's suit: therefore be merry, Cassio;
For thy solicitor shall rather die
Than give thy cause away.

EMILIA

Madam, here comes my lord.

CASSIO

Madam, I'll take my leave.

CASSIO Madam, I'll take my leave.

DESDEMONA
Why, stay, and hear me speak.
CASSIO
Madam, not now: I am very ill at ease,
Unfit for mine own purposes.
DESDEMONA
Well, do your discretion.   [*Exit* CASSIO.

Enter OTHELLO *and* IAGO.

IAGO
Ha! I like not that.
OTHELLO
                    What dost thou say?
IAGO
Nothing, my lord: or if — I know not what.
OTHELLO
Was not that Cassio parted from my wife?
IAGO
Cassio, my lord! No, sure, I cannot think it,
That he would steal away so guilty-like,
Seeing you coming.
OTHELLO
                    I do believe 'twas he.
DESDEMONA
How now, my lord!
I have been talking with a suitor here,
A man that languishes in your displeasure.
OTHELLO
Who is't you mean?
DESDEMONA
Why, your lieutenant, Cassio. Good my lord,
If I have any grace or power to move you,
His present reconciliation take;
For if he be not one that truly loves you,
That errs in ignorance, and not in cunning,
I have no judgement in an honest face:
I prithee, call him back.
OTHELLO
                    Went he hence now?
DESDEMONA
Ay, sooth; so humbled,
That he hath left part of his grief with me,
To suffer with him. Good love, call him back.
OTHELLO
Not now, sweet Desdemona; some other time.
DESDEMONA
But shall't be shortly?
OTHELLO
                    The sooner, sweet, for you.
DESDEMONA
Shall't be to-night at supper?
OTHELLO
                    No, not to-night.

DESDEMONA
To-morrow dinner, then?
OTHELLO
                    I shall not dine at home;
I meet the captains at the citadel.
DESDEMONA
Why, then, to-morrow night; or Tuesday morn;
On Tuesday morn, or night; on Wednesday morn: —
I prithee, name the time; but let it not
Exceed three days: in faith, he's penitent;
And yet his trespass, in our common reason, —
Save that, they say, the wars must make examples
Out of their best, — is not almost a fault
T'incur a private check. When shall he come?
Tell me, Othello: I wonder in my soul,
What you would ask me, that I should deny,
Or stand so mammering on. What! Michael Cassio,
That came a-wooing with you; and so many a time,
When I have spoke of you dispraisingly,
Hath ta'en your part; to have so much to do
To bring him in! Trust me, I could do much —
OTHELLO
Prithee, no more: let him come when he will;
I will deny thee nothing.
DESDEMONA
                    Why, this is not a boon;
'Tis as I should entreat you wear your gloves,
Or feed on nourishing dishes, or keep you warm,
Or sue to you to do a peculiar profit
To your own person: nay, when I have a suit
Wherein I mean to touch your love indeed,
It shall be full of poise and difficult weight,
And fearful to be granted.
OTHELLO
                    I will deny thee nothing:
Whereon, I do beseech thee, grant me this,
To leave me but a little to myself.
DESDEMONA
Shall I deny you? no: farewell, my lord.
OTHELLO
Farewell, my Desdemona: I'll come to thee straight.
DESDEMONA
Emilia, come. — Be as your fancies teach you;
Whate'er you be, I am obedient.   [*Exit, with* EMILIA.
OTHELLO
Excellent wretch! Perdition catch my soul,
But I do love thee! and when I love thee not,
Chaos is come again.
IAGO
My noble lord, —
OTHELLO
                    What does thou say, Iago?
IAGO
Did Michael Cassio, when you woo'd my lady,

Know of your love?
OTHELLO
He did, from first to last: why dost thou ask?
IAGO
But for a satisfaction of my thought;
No further harm.
OTHELLO
                    Why of thy thought, Iago?
IAGO
I did not think he had been acquainted with her.
OTHELLO
O, yes; and went between us very oft.
IAGO
Indeed!
OTHELLO
Indeed! ay, indeed: — discern'st thou aught in that?
Is he not honest?
IAGO
                    Honest, my lord!
OTHELLO
                    Honest! ay, honest.
IAGO
My lord, for aught I know.
OTHELLO
What dost thou think?
IAGO
                    Think, my lord!
OTHELLO
                    Think, my lord!
By heaven, he echoes me,
As if there were some monster in his thought
Too hideous to be shown. — Thou dost mean
    something:
I heard thee say even now, thou likedst not that,
When Cassio left my wife: what didst not like?
And when I told thee he was of my counsel
In my whole course of wooing, thou criedst 'Indeed!'
And didst contract and purse thy brow together,
As if thou then hadst shut up in thy brain
Some horrible conceit: if thou dost love me,
Show me thy thought.
IAGO
My lord, you know I love you.
OTHELLO
                    I think thou dost;
And, for I know thou'rt full of love and honesty,
And weigh'st thy words before thou givest them
    breath,
Therefore these stops of thine fright me the more:
For such things in a false disloyal knave
Are tricks of custom; but in a man that's just
They're close delations, working from the heart,
That passion cannot rule.
IAGO
                    For Michael Cassio,
I dare be sworn I think that he is honest.
OTHELLO
I think so too.
IAGO
                    Men should be what they seem;
Or those that be not, would they might seem none!
OTHELLO
Certain, men should be what they seem.
IAGO
Why, then, I think Cassio's an honest man.
OTHELLO
Nay, yet there's more in this:
I prithee, speak to me as to thy thinkings,
As thou dost ruminate; and give thy worst of thoughts
The worst of words.
IAGO
                    Good my lord, pardon me:
Though I am bound to every act of duty,
I am not bound to that all slaves are free to.
Utter my thoughts? Why, say they are vile and false, —
As where's that palace whereinto foul things
Sometimes intrude not? who has a breast so pure,
But some uncleanly apprehensions
Keep leets and law-days and in session sit
With meditations lawful?
OTHELLO
Thou dost conspire against thy friend, Iago,
If thou but think'st him wrong'd, and makest his ear
A stranger to thy thoughts.
IAGO
                    I do beseech you —
Though I perchance am vicious in my guess,
As, I confess, it is my nature's plague
To spy into abuses, and oft my jealousy

486

Shapes faults that are not — that your wisdom yet,
From one that so imperfectly conceits,
Would take no notice; nor build yourself a trouble
Out of his scattering and unsure observance: —
It were not for your quiet nor your good,
Nor for my manhood, honesty, or wisdom,
To let you know my thoughts.

OTHELLO
                    What dost thou mean?

IAGO
Good name in man and woman, dear my lord,
Is the immediate jewel of their souls:
Who steals my purse steals trash; 'tis something,
    nothing;
'Twas mine, 'tis his, and has been slave to thousands;
But he that filches from me my good name
Robs me of that which not enriches him,
And makes me poor indeed.

OTHELLO
By heaven, I'll know thy thoughts!

IAGO
You cannot, if my heart were in your hand;
Nor shall not, whilst 'tis in my custody.

OTHELLO
Ha!

IAGO
    O, beware, my lord, of jealousy;
It is the green-eyed monster, which doth mock
The meat it feeds on: that cuckold lives in bliss
Who, certain of his fate, loves not his wronger;
But, O, what damned minutes tells he o'er
Who dotes, yet doubts, suspects, yet strongly loves!

OTHELLO
O misery!

IAGO
Poor and content is rich, and rich enough;
But riches fineless is as poor as winter
To him that ever fears he shall be poor: —
Good heaven, the souls of all my tribe defend
From jealousy!

OTHELLO
                    Why, why is this?
Think'st thou I'ld make a life of jealousy,
To follow still the changes of the moon
With fresh suspicions? No; to be once in doubt
Is once to be resolv'd: exchange me for a goat,
When I shall turn the business of my soul
To such exsufflicate and blown surmises,
Matching thy inference. 'Tis not to make me jealous
To say my wife is fair, feeds well, loves company,
Is free of speech, sings, plays, and dances well;
Where virtue is, these are more virtuous:
Nor from mine own weak merits will I draw
The smallest fear or doubt of her revolt;
For she had eyes, and chose me. No, Iago;
I'll see before I doubt; when I doubt, prove;
And, on the proof, there is no more but this, —
Away at once with love or jealousy!

IAGO
I am glad of it; for now I shall have reason
To show the love and duty that I bear you
With franker spirit: therefore, as I am bound,
Receive it from me: — I speak not yet of proof.
Look to your wife; observe her well with Cassio;
Wear your eye thus, not jealous nor secure:
I would not have your free and noble nature,
Out of self-bounty, be abus'd; look to't:
I know our country disposition well;
In Venice they do let heaven see the pranks
They dare not show their husbands; their best
    conscience
Is — not to leave undone, but keep unknown.

OTHELLO
Dost thou say so?

IAGO
She did deceive her father, marrying you;
And when she seem'd to shake and fear your looks,
She lov'd them most.

OTHELLO
                    And so she did.

IAGO
                    Why, go to, then;
She that, so young, could give out such a seeming,
To seel her father's eyes up close as oak —
He thought 'twas witchcraft: — but I am much to blame;
I humbly do beseech you of your pardon
For too much loving you.

OTHELLO
                    I am bound to thee for ever.

IAGO
I see this hath a little dash'd your spirits.

OTHELLO
Not a jot, not a jot.

IAGO
                    I' faith, I fear it has.
I hope you will consider what is spoke
Comes from my love; — but I do see y' are moved: —
I am to pray you not to strain my speech
To grosser issues nor to larger reach
Than to suspicion.

OTHELLO
I will not.

IAGO
                    Should you do so, my lord,
My speech should fall into such vile success
As my thoughts aim not at. Cassio's my worthy friend: —
My lord, I see y' are mov'd.

OTHELLO
                    No, not much mov'd: —
I do not think but Desdemona's honest.

IAGO
Long live she so! and long live you to think so!

OTHELLO
And yet, how nature erring from itself, —

IAGO
Ay, there's the point: — as — to be bold with you —
Not to affect many proposed matches
Of her own clime, complexion, and degree,
Whereto we see in all things nature tends, —
Foh! one may smell in such, a will most rank,
Foul disproportion thoughts unnatural: —
But pardon me: I do not in position
Distinctly speak of her; though I may fear
Her will, recoiling to her better judgement,
May fall to match you with her country forms,
And happily repent.

OTHELLO
                    Farewell, farewell:
If more thou dost perceive, let me know more;
Set on thy wife to observe: leave me, Iago.

IAGO
My lord, I take my leave.   [*Going.*

OTHELLO
Why did I marry? — This honest creature doubtless
Sees and knows more, much more, than he unfolds.

IAGO
My lord, I would I might entreat your honour
                                    [*Returning.*
To scan this thing no further; leave it to time:
Although 'tis fit that Cassio have his place, —
For, sure, he fills it up with great ability, —
Yet, if you please to hold him off awhile,
You shall by that perceive him and his means:
Note if your lady strain his entertainment
With any strong or vehement importunity;
Much will be seen in that. In the mean time
Let me be thought too busy in my fears, —
As worthy cause I have to fear I am, —
And hold her free, I do beseech your honour.

OTHELLO
Fear not my government.

IAGO
I once more take my leave.   [*Exit.*

OTHELLO
This fellow's of exceeding honesty,
And knows all qualities, with a learned spirit,
Of human dealings. If I do prove her haggard,
Though that her jesses were my dear heartstrings,
I'ld whistle her off, and let her down the wind,
To prey at fortune. Haply, for I am black,
And have not those soft parts of conversation
That chamberers have; or, for I am declined
Into the vale of years, — yet that's not much; —
She's gone; I am abus'd; and my relief
Must be to loathe her. O curse of marriage,
That we can call these delicate creatures ours,
And not their appetites! I had rather be a toad,
And live upon the vapour of a dungeon,
Than keep a corner in the thing I love
For others' uses. Yet, 'tis the plague of great ones;
Prerogativ'd are they less than the base;
'Tis destiny unshunnable, like death:
Even then this forked plague is fated to us
When we do quicken. — Desdemona comes:
If she be false, O, then heaven mocks itself! —
I'll not believe't.

Enter DESDEMONA *and* EMILIA.

DESDEMONA
                    How now, my dear Othello!
Your dinner, and the generous islanders
By you invited, do attend your presence.

OTHELLO
I am to blame.

DESDEMONA
                    Why do you speak so faintly?
Are you not well?

OTHELLO
I have a pain upon my forehead here.

DESDEMONA
Faith, that's with watching; 'twill away again:
Let me but bind it hard, within this hour
It will be well.

OTHELLO
                    Your napkin is too little;
            [*He puts the handkerchief from him; and she drops it.*
Let it alone. Come, I'll go in with you.

DESDEMONA
I am very sorry that you are not well.
                [*Exeunt* OTHELLO *and* DESDEMONA.

EMILIA
I am glad I have found this napkin:
This was her first remembrance from the Moor:
My wayward husband hath a hundred times
Woo'd me to steal it; but she so loves the token, —
For he conjured her she should ever keep it, —
That she reserves it evermore about her
To kiss and talk to. I'll have the work ta'en out,
And give't Iago:
What he will do with it heaven knows, not I;
I nothing but to please his fantasy.

Enter IAGO.

IAGO
How now! what do you here alone?

EMILIA
Do not you chide; I have a thing for you.

IAGO
A thing for me! — it is a common thing —

EMILIA
Ha!

IAGO
To have a foolish wife.

EMILIA
O, is that all? What will you give me now
For that same handkerchief?

IAGO
                    What handkerchief?

EMILIA
What handkerchief!
Why, that the Moor first gave to Desdemona;
That which so often you did bid me steal.

IAGO
Hast stol'n it from her?

EMILIA
No, faith; she let it drop by negligence,
And, to th'advantage, I, being here, took't up.
Look, here it is.

IAGO
                    A good wench; give it me.

EMILIA
What will you do with't, that you have been so earnest
To have me filch it?

IAGO
                    Why, what's that to you?
                                    [*Snatching it.*

EMILIA
If't be not for some purpose of import,
Give't me again: poor lady, she'll run mad
When she shall lack it.

IAGO
Be not acknown on't; I have use for it.
Go, leave me.   [*Exit* EMILIA.
I will in Cassio's lodging lose this napkin,
And let him find it. Trifles light as air
Are to the jealous confirmations strong
As proofs of holy writ: this may do something.
The Moor already changes with my poison: —
Dangerous conceits are, in their natures, poisons,
Which at the first are scarce found to distaste,
But, with a little, act upon the blood,
Burn like the mines of sulphur. — I did say so: —
Look, where he comes! Not poppy, nor mandragora,
Nor all the drowsy syrups of the world,
Shall ever medicine thee to that sweet sleep
Which thou owedst yesterday.

Enter OTHELLO.

OTHELLO

Ha! ha! false to me?

IAGO

Why, how now, general! no more of that.

OTHELLO

Avaunt! be gone! thou hast set me on the rack: —
I swear 'tis better to be much abused
Than but to know 't a little.

IAGO

How now, my lord!

OTHELLO

What sense had I of her stol'n hours of lust?
I saw 't not, thought it not, it harm'd not me:
I slept the next night well, was free and merry;
I found not Cassio's kisses on her lips:
He that is robb'd, not wanting what is stol'n,
Let him not know 't, and he's not robb'd at all.

IAGO

I am sorry to hear this.

OTHELLO

I had been happy, if the general camp,
Pioners and all, had tasted her sweet body,
So I had nothing known. O, now, for ever
Farewell the tranquil mind! farewell content!
Farewell the plumed troop, and the big wars,
That make ambition virtue! O, farewell!
Farewell the neighing steed, and the shrill trump,
The spirit-stirring drum, th'ear-piercing fife,
The royal banner, and all quality,
Pride, pomp and circumstance of glorious war!
And, O you mortal engines, whose rude throats
Th'immortal Jove's dread clamours counterfeit,
Farewell! Othello's occupation's gone!

IAGO

Is 't possible, my lord?

OTHELLO

Villain, be sure thou prove my love a whore, —
Be sure of it; give me the ocular proof;
Or, by the worth of man's eternal soul,
Thou hadst been better have been born a dog
Than answer my wak'd wrath!

IAGO

Is 't come to this?

OTHELLO

Make me to see 't; or, at the least, so prove it,
That the probation bear no hinge nor loop
To hang a doubt on; or woe upon thy life!

IAGO

My noble lord, —

OTHELLO

If thou dost slander her, and torture me,
Never pray more; abandon all remorse;
On horror's head horrors accumulate;
Do deeds to make heaven weep, all earth amazed;
For nothing canst thou to damnation add
Greater than that.

IAGO

O grace! O heaven forgive me!
Are you a man? have you a soul or sense? —
God be wi' you! take mine office. — O wretched fool,
That livest to make thine honesty a vice! —
O monstrous world! Take note, take note, O world,
To be direct and honest is not safe. —
I thank you for this profit; and from hence
I'll love no friend, sith love breeds such offence.

OTHELLO

Nay, stay: — thou shouldst be honest.

IAGO

I should be wise; for honesty's a fool,
And loses that it works for.

OTHELLO

By the world,
I think my wife be honest, and think she is not;
I think that thou art just, and think thou art not;
I'll have some proof: her name, that was as fresh
As Dian's visage, is now begrim'd and black
As mine own face. — If there be cords or knives,
Poison, or fire, or suffocating streams,
I'll not endure it. — Would I were satisfied!

IAGO

I see, sir, you are eaten up with passion:
I do repent me that I put it to you.
You would be satisfied?

OTHELLO

Would! nay, I will.

IAGO

And may: but, how? how satisfied, my lord?
Would you, the supervisor, grossly gape on, —

Behold her topp'd?

OTHELLO

Death and damnation! O!

IAGO

It were a tedious difficulty, I think,
To bring them to that prospect: damn them, then,
If ever mortal eyes do see them bolster
More than their own! What then? how then?
What shall I say? Where's satisfaction?
It is impossible you should see this,
Were they as prime as goats, as hot as monkeys,
As salt as wolves in pride, and fools as gross
As ignorance made drunk. But yet, I say,
If imputation and strong circumstances —
Which lead directly to the door of truth —
Will give you satisfaction, you may have 't.

OTHELLO

Give me a living reason she's disloyal.

IAGO

I do not like the office:
But, sith I am enter'd in this cause so far, —
Prick'd to 't by foolish honesty and love, —
I will go on. I lay with Cassio lately;
And, being troubled with a raging tooth,
I could not sleep.
There are a kind of men so loose of soul
That in their sleeps will mutter their affairs;
One of this kind is Cassio:
In sleep I heard him say, 'Sweet Desdemona,
Let us be wary, let us hide our loves';
And then, sir, would he gripe and wring my hand,
Cry 'O sweet creature!' and then kiss me hard,
As if he pluck'd up kisses by the roots
That grew upon my lips: then laid his leg
Over my thigh, and sigh'd, and kiss'd; and then
Cried, 'Cursed fate that gave thee to the Moor!'

OTHELLO

O monstrous! monstrous!

IAGO

Nay, this was but his dream.

OTHELLO

But this denoted a foregone conclusion:
'Tis a shrewd doubt, though it be but a dream.

IAGO

And this may help to thicken other proofs
That do demonstrate thinly.

OTHELLO

I'll tear her all to pieces.

IAGO

Nay, but be wise: yet we see nothing done;
She may be honest yet. Tell me but this, —
Have you not sometimes seen a handkerchief
Spotted with strawberries in your wife's hand?

OTHELLO

I gave her such a one; 'twas my first gift.

IAGO

I know not that: but such a handkerchief —
I am sure it was your wife's — did I to-day
See Cassio wipe his beard with.

OTHELLO

If it be that, —

IAGO

If it be that, or any that was hers,
It speaks against her with the other proofs.

OTHELLO

O, that the slave had forty thousand lives, —
One is too poor, too weak for my revenge!
Now do I see 'tis true. — Look here, Iago;
All my fond love thus do I blow to heaven:
'Tis gone. —
Arise, black vengeance, from thy hollow hell!
Yield up, O love, thy crown and hearted throne
To tyrannous hate! Swell, bosom, with thy fraught,
For 'tis of aspics' tongues!

IAGO

Yet be content.

OTHELLO Now, by yond marble heaven, in the due reverence of a sacred vow I here engage my words.

OTHELLO
O, blood, blood, blood!

IAGO
Patience, I say; your mind perhaps may change.

OTHELLO
Never, Iago. Like to the Pontic sea,
Whose icy current and compulsive course
Ne'er feels retiring ebb, but keeps due on
To the Propontic and the Hellespont;
Even so my bloody thoughts, with violent pace,
Shall ne'er look back, ne'er ebb to humble love,
Till that a capable and wide revenge
Swallow them up. — Now, by yond marble heaven,
In the due reverence of a sacred vow   [*Kneels.*
I here engage my words.

IAGO
                      Do not rise yet. —   [*Kneels.*
Witness, you ever-burning lights above,
You elements that clip us round about, —
Witness that here Iago doth give up
The execution of his wit, hands, heart,
To wrong'd Othello's service! Let him command,
And to obey shall be in me remorse,
What bloody business ever.   [*They rise.*

OTHELLO
                      I greet thy love,
Not with vain thanks, but with acceptance bounteous,
And will upon the instant put thee to't:
Within these three days let me hear thee say
That Cassio's not alive.

IAGO
My friend is dead; 'tis done at your request:
But let her live.

OTHELLO
          Damn her, lewd minx! O, damn her!
Come, go with me apart; I will withdraw,
To furnish me with some swift means of death
For the fair devil. Now art thou my lieutenant.

IAGO
I am your own for ever.   [*Exeunt.*

SCENE IV
Before the castle.

Enter DESDEMONA, EMILIA, *and* CLOWN.

DESDEMONA
Do you know, sirrah, where Lieutenant Cassio lies?

CLOWN
I dare not say he lies any where.

DESDEMONA
Why, man?

CLOWN
He's a soldier; and for one to say a soldier lies, is
stabbing.

DESDEMONA
Go to: where lodges he?

CLOWN
To tell you where he lodges, is to tell you where I lie.

DESDEMONA
Can any thing be made of this?

CLOWN
I know not where he lodges; and for me to devise a
lodging, and say he lies here or he lies there, were to lie
in mine own throat.

DESDEMONA
Can you inquire him out, and be edified by report?

CLOWN
I will catechise the world for him; that is, make
questions, and by them answer.

DESDEMONA
Seek him, bid him come hither: tell him I have moved
my lord on his behalf, and hope all will be well.

CLOWN
To do this is within the compass of man's wit; and
therefore I will attempt the doing it.   [*Exit.*

DESDEMONA
Where should I lose that handkerchief, Emilia?

EMILIA
I know not, madam.

DESDEMONA
Believe me, I had rather have lost my purse
Full of crusadoes: and, but my noble Moor
Is true of mind, and made of no such baseness
As jealous creatures are, it were enough
To put him to ill thinking.

EMILIA
                      Is he not jealous?

DESDEMONA
Who, he? I think the sun where he was born
Drew all such humours from him.

EMILIA
                      Look, where he comes.

DESDEMONA
I will not leave him now till Cassio
Be call'd to him.

Enter OTHELLO.
How is't with you, my lord?

OTHELLO
Well, my good lady. — [*aside*] O, hardness to
dissemble! —
How do you, Desdemona?

DESDEMONA
                      Well, my good lord.

OTHELLO
Give me your hand: this hand is moist, my lady.

DESDEMONA
It yet hath felt no age nor known no sorrow.

OTHELLO
This argues fruitfulness and liberal heart: —
Hot, hot, and moist: this hand of yours requires
A sequester from liberty, fasting and prayer,
Much castigation, exercise devout;
For here's a young and sweating devil here,
That commonly rebels. 'Tis a good hand,
A frank one.

DESDEMONA
                      You may, indeed, say so;
For 'twas that hand that gave away my heart.

OTHELLO
A liberal hand: the hearts of old gave hands;
But our new heraldry is hands, not hearts.

DESDEMONA
I cannot speak of this. Come now, your promise.

OTHELLO
What promise, chuck?

DESDEMONA
I have sent to bid Cassio come speak with you.

OTHELLO
I have a salt and sorry rheum offends me;
Lend me thy handkerchief.

DESDEMONA
                      Here, my lord.

OTHELLO
That which I gave you.

DESDEMONA
                      I have it not about me.

OTHELLO
Not?

DESDEMONA
          No, indeed, my lord.

OTHELLO
                      That is a fault.
That handkerchief
Did an Egyptian to my mother give;
She was a charmer, and could almost read
The thoughts of people: she told her, while she kept it,
'Twould make her amiable, and subdue my father
Entirely to her love; but if she lost it,
Or made gift of it, my father's eye
Should hold her loathed, and his spirits should hunt
After new fancies: she, dying, gave it me;
And bid me, when my fate would have me wive,
To give it her. I did so: and take heed on't;
Make it a darling like your precious eye;
To lose't or give't away were such perdition
As nothing else could match.

DESDEMONA
                      Is't possible?

OTHELLO
'Tis true: there's magic in the web of it:
A sibyl, that had number'd in the world
The sun to course two hundred compasses,
In her prophetic fury sew'd the work;
The worms were hallow'd that did breed the silk;
And it was dyed in mummy which the skilful
Conserv'd of maidens' hearts.

DESDEMONA
                      Indeed! is't true?

OTHELLO
Most veritable; therefore look to't well.

DESDEMONA
Then would to God that I had never seen't!

OTHELLO
Ha! wherefore?

DESDEMONA
Why do you speak so startingly and rash?

OTHELLO
Is't lost? Is't gone? speak; is't out o'the way?

DESDEMONA
Heaven bless us!

OTHELLO
Say you?

DESDEMONA
It is not lost; but what an if it were?

OTHELLO
How!

DESDEMONA
I say, it is not lost.

OTHELLO
                      Fetch't, let me see't.

DESDEMONA
Why, so I can, sir, but I will not now.
This is a trick to put me from my suit:
Pray you, let Cassio be receiv'd again.

OTHELLO
Fetch me the handkerchief: my mind misgives.

DESDEMONA
Come, come;
You'll never meet a more sufficient man.

OTHELLO
The handkerchief!

DESDEMONA
                      I pray, talk me of Cassio.

OTHELLO
The handkerchief!

DESDEMONA
                      A man that all his time
Hath founded his good fortunes on your love,
Shared dangers with you, —

OTHELLO
The handkerchief!

DESDEMONA
In sooth, you are to blame.

OTHELLO
Away!   [*Exit.*

EMILIA
Is not this man jealous?

DESDEMONA
I ne'er saw this before.
Sure, there's some wonder in this handkerchief:
I am most unhappy in the loss of it.

EMILIA
'Tis not a year or two shows us a man:
They are all but stomachs, and we all but food;
They eat us hungerly, and when they are full,
They belch us. — Look you, — Cassio and my
husband.

Enter CASSIO *and* IAGO.

IAGO
There is no other way; 'tis she must do't:
And, lo, the happiness! go, and importune her.

DESDEMONA
How now, good Cassio! what's the news with you?

CASSIO
Madam, my former suit: I do beseech you
That by your virtuous means I may again
Exist, and be a member of his love
Whom I with all the office of my heart
Entirely honour: I would not be delay'd.
If my offence be of such mortal kind
That nor my service past, nor present sorrows,
Nor purpos'd merit in futurity,
Can ransom me into his love again,
But to know so must be my benefit;
So shall I clothe me in a forc'd content,
And shut myself up in some other course,
To fortune's alms.

DESDEMONA
                      Alas, thrice-gentle Cassio!
My advocation is not now in tune;
My lord is not my lord; nor should I know him,
Were he in favour as in humour alter'd.
So help me every spirit sanctified,
As I have spoken for you all my best,
And stood within the blank of his displeasure
For my free speech! you must awhile be patient:
What I can do I will; and more I will
Than for myself I dare: let that suffice you.

IAGO
Is my lord angry?

EMILIA
                      He went hence but now,
And certainly in strange unquietness.

IAGO
Can he be angry? I have seen the cannon,
When it hath blown his ranks into the air,

And, like the devil, from his very arm
Puff'd his own brother; — and can he be angry?
Something of moment, then: I will go meet him:
There's matter in't indeed, if he be angry.

DESDEMONA
I prithee, do so.   [*Exit* IAGO.
                    Something, sure, of state, —
Either from Venice, or some unhatch'd practice
Made demonstrable here in Cyprus to him, —
Hath puddled his clear spirit; and in such cases
Men's natures wrangle with inferior things,
Though great ones are their object. 'Tis even so;
For let our finger ache, and it indues
Our other healthful members even to that sense
Of pain: nay, we must think men are not gods,
Nor of them look for such observancy
As fits the bridal. — Beshrew me much, Emilia,
I was — unhandsome warrior as I am —
Arraigning his unkindness with my soul;
But now I find I had suborn'd the witness,
And he's indicted falsely.

EMILIA
Pray heaven it be state-matters, as you think,
And no conception nor no jealous toy
Concerning you.

DESDEMONA
Alas the day, I never gave him cause!

EMILIA
But jealous souls will not be answer'd so;
They are not ever jealous for the cause,
But jealous for they're jealous: it is a monster
Begot upon itself, born on itself.

DESDEMONA
Heaven keep that monster from Othello's mind!

EMILIA
Lady, amen.

DESDEMONA
I will go seek him. — Cassio, walk hereabout:
If I do find him fit, I'll move your suit,
And seek to effect it to my uttermost.

CASSIO
I humbly thank your ladyship.
                [*Exeunt* DESDEMONA *and* EMILIA.
                    Enter BIANCA.

BIANCA
Save you, friend Cassio!

CASSIO
                    What make you from home?
How is it with you, my most fair Bianca?
I'faith, sweet love, I was coming to your house.

BIANCA
And I was going to your lodging, Cassio.
What, keep a week away? seven days and nights?
Eight score eight hours? and lovers' absent hours
More tedious than the dial eight score times?
O weary reckoning!

CASSIO
                    Pardon me, Bianca:
I have this while with leaden thoughts been press'd;
But I shall, in a more continuate time,
Strike off this score of absence. Sweet Bianca,
        [*Giving her* DESDEMONA'S *handkerchief.*
Take me this work out.

BIANCA
                    O Cassio, whence came this?
This is some token from a newer friend:
To the felt absence now I feel a cause:
Is't come to this? Well, well.

CASSIO
                    Go to, woman!
Throw your vile guesses in the devil's teeth,
From whence you have them. You are jealous now
That this is from some mistress, some remembrance:
No, in good troth, Bianca.

BIANCA
                    Why, whose is it?

CASSIO
I know not neither: I found it in my chamber.
I like the work well: ere it be demanded, —
As like enough it will, — I'd have it copied:
Take it, and do't; and leave me for this time.

BIANCA
Leave you! wherefore?

CASSIO
I do attend here on the general;
And think it no addition, nor my wish,
To have him see me woman'd.

BIANCA
                    Why, I pray you?

CASSIO
Not that I love you not.

BIANCA
                    But that you do not love me.
I pray you, bring me on the way a little;
And say if I shall see you soon at night.

CASSIO
'Tis but a little way that I can bring you;
For I attend here: but I'll see you soon.

BIANCA
'Tis very good; I must be circumstanc'd.   [*Exeunt.*

ACT IV

SCENE I

Cyprus. Before the castle.

Enter OTHELLO *and* IAGO.

IAGO
Will you think so?

OTHELLO
                    Think so, Iago!

IAGO
                            What,
To kiss in private?

OTHELLO
                    An unauthoris'd kiss.

IAGO
Or to be naked with her friend in bed
An hour or more, not meaning any harm?

OTHELLO
Naked in bed, Iago, and not mean harm!
It is hypocrisy against the devil:
They that mean virtuously and yet do so,
The devil their virtue tempts, and they tempt heaven.

IAGO
So they do nothing, 'tis a venial slip:
But if I give my wife a handkerchief, —

OTHELLO
What then?

IAGO
Why, then, 'tis hers, my lord; and, being hers,
She may, I think, bestow't on any man.

OTHELLO
She is protectress of her honour too:
May she give that?

IAGO
Her honour is an essence that's not seen;
They have it very oft that have it not:
But, for the handkerchief, —

OTHELLO
By heaven, I would most gladly have forgot it: —
Thou said'st, — O, it comes o'er my memory,
As doth the raven o'er the infected house,
Boding to all, — he had my handkerchief.

IAGO
Ay, what of that?

OTHELLO
                    That's not so good now.

IAGO
                            What,
If I had said I had seen him do you wrong?
Or heard him say, — as knaves be such abroad,
Who having, by their own importunate suit,
Or voluntary dotage of some mistress,
Convinced or supplied them, cannot choose
But they must blab —

OTHELLO
                    Hath he said any thing?

IAGO
He hath, my lord; but be you well assured,
No more than he'll unswear.

OTHELLO
                    What hath he said?

IAGO
Faith, that he did — I know not what he did.

OTHELLO
What? what?

IAGO
Lie —

OTHELLO
                    With her?

IAGO
                            With her, on her; what you will.

OTHELLO
Lie with her! lie on her! — We say lie on her, when
they belie her. — Lie with her! that's fulsome. —

Handkerchief — confessions — handkerchief! — To
confess, and be hang'd for his labour; — first, to be
hang'd, and then to confess. — I tremble at it. Nature
would not invest herself in such shadowing passion
without some instruction. It is not words that shake me
thus: — pish! — noses, ears, and lips. — Is't possible?
— Confess — handkerchief! — O devil! —
                    [*Falls in a trance.*

IAGO
Work on,
My medicine, work! Thus credulous fools are caught;
And many worthy and chaste dames even thus,
All guiltless, meet reproach. — What, ho! my lord!
My lord, I say! Othello!
                    Enter CASSIO.
                    How now, Cassio!

CASSIO
What's the matter?

IAGO
My lord is fall'n into an epilepsy:
This is his second fit; he had one yesterday.

CASSIO
Rub him about the temples.

IAGO
                    No, forbear;
The lethargy must have his quiet course:
If not, he foams at mouth, and by and by
Breaks out to savage madness. Look, he stirs:
Do you withdraw yourself a little while,
He will recover straight: when he is gone,
I would on great occasion speak with you.
                    [*Exit* CASSIO.
How is it, general? have you not hurt your head?

OTHELLO
Dost thou mock me?

IAGO
                    I mock you! no, by heaven.
Would you would bear your fortune like a man!

OTHELLO
A horned man's a monster and a beast.

IAGO
There's many a beast, then, in a populous city,
And many a civil monster.

OTHELLO
Did he confess it?

IAGO Work on, my medicine, work!

IAGO
Good sir, be a man;
Think every bearded fellow that's but yok'd
May draw with you: there's millions now alive
That nightly lie in those unproper beds
Which they dare swear peculiar: your case is better.
O, 'tis the spite of hell, the fiend's arch-mock,
To lip a wanton in a secure couch,
And to suppose her chaste! No, let me know;
And knowing what I am, I know what she shall be.

OTHELLO
O, thou art wise; 'tis certain.

IAGO
Stand you awhile apart;
Confine yourself but in a patient list.
Whilst you were here o'erwhelmed with your grief, —
A passion most unfitting such a man, —
Cassio came hither: I shifted him away,
And laid good 'scuse upon your ecstasy;
Bade him anon return, and here speak with me;
The which he promis'd. Do but encave yourself,
And mark the fleers, the gibes, and notable scorns,
That dwell in every region of his face;
For I will make him tell the tale anew, —
Where, how, how oft, how long ago, and when
He hath, and is again to cope your wife:
I say, but mark his gesture. Marry, patience;
Or I shall say y'are all in all in spleen,
And nothing of a man.

OTHELLO
Dost thou hear, Iago?
I will be found most cunning in my patience;
But — dost thou hear? — most bloody.

IAGO
That's not amiss;
But yet keep time in all. Will you withdraw?
[OTHELLO retires.
Now will I question Cassio of Bianca,
A housewife that, by selling her desires,
Buys herself bread and clothes: it is a creature
That dotes on Cassio, — as 'tis the strumpet's plague
To beguile many and be beguil'd by one: —
He, when he hears of her, cannot refrain
From the excess of laughter: — here he comes: —
As he shall smile, Othello shall go mad;
And his unbookish jealousy must construe
Poor Cassio's smiles, gestures, and light behaviour,
Quite in the wrong.
Enter CASSIO.
How do you now, lieutenant?

CASSIO
The worser that you give me the addition
Whose want even kills me.

IAGO
Ply Desdemona well, and you are sure on't.
Now, if this suit lay in Bianca's power, [Speaking lower.
How quickly should you speed!

CASSIO
Alas, poor caitiff!

OTHELLO [aside].
Look, how he laughs already!

IAGO
I never knew woman love man so.

CASSIO
Alas, poor rogue! I think, i'faith, she loves me.

OTHELLO [aside].
Now he denies it faintly, and laughs it out.

IAGO
Do you hear, Cassio?

OTHELLO [aside].
Now he importunes him
To tell it o'er: — go to; well said, well said.

IAGO
She gives it out that you shall marry her:
Do you intend it?

CASSIO
Ha, ha, ha!

OTHELLO [aside].
Do you triumph, Roman? do you triumph?

CASSIO
I marry her! — what, a customer! Prithee, bear some
charity to my wit; do not think it so unwholesome: —
ha, ha, ha!

OTHELLO [aside].
So, so, so, so: — they laugh that win.

IAGO
Faith, the cry goes that you shall marry her.

CASSIO
Prithee, say true.

IAGO
I am a very villain else.

OTHELLO [aside].
Have you scored me? Well.

CASSIO
This is the monkey's own giving out: she is persuaded I
will marry her, out of her own love and flattery, not out
of my promise.

OTHELLO [aside].
Iago beckons me; now he begins the story.

CASSIO
She was here even now; she haunts me in every place. I
was, the other day, talking on the sea-bank with certain
Venetians; and thither comes the bauble, and by this
hand she falls me thus about my neck, —

OTHELLO [aside].
Crying 'O dear Cassio!' as it were: his gesture imports
it.

CASSIO
So hangs, and lolls, and weeps upon me; so hales and
pulls me: — ha, ha, ha!

OTHELLO [aside].
Now he tells how she pluck'd him to my chamber. O, I
see that nose of yours, but not that dog I shall throw it
to.

CASSIO
Well, I must leave her company.

IAGO
Before me! look, where she comes.

CASSIO
'Tis such another fitchew! marry, a perfum'd one.
Enter BIANCA.
What do you mean by this haunting of me?

BIANCA
Let the devil and his dam haunt you! What did you
mean by that same handkerchief you gave me even
now? I was a fine fool to take it. I must take out the
work? — A likely piece of work, that you should find it
in your chamber, and not know who left it there! This is
some minx's token, and I must take out the work?
There, — give it your hobby-horse: wheresoever you
had it, I'll take out no work on't.

CASSIO
How now, my sweet Bianca! how now! how now!

OTHELLO [aside].
By heaven, that should be my handkerchief!

BIANCA
An you'll come to supper to-night, you may; an you will
not, come when you are next prepared for. [Exit.

IAGO
After her, after her.

CASSIO
Faith, I must; she'll rail i' the street else.

IAGO
Will you sup there?

CASSIO
Faith, I intend so.

IAGO
Well, I may chance to see you; for I would very fain
speak with you.

CASSIO
Prithee, come; will you?

IAGO
Go to; say no more. [Exit CASSIO.

OTHELLO [coming forward].
How shall I murder him, Iago?

IAGO
Did you perceive how he laugh'd at his vice?

OTHELLO
O Iago!

IAGO
And did you see the handkerchief?

OTHELLO
Was that mine?

IAGO
Yours, by this hand: and to see how he prizes the
foolish woman your wife! she gave it him, and he hath
given it his whore.

OTHELLO
I would have him nine years a-killing. — A fine
woman! a fair woman! a sweet woman!

IAGO
Nay, you must forget that.

OTHELLO
Ay, let her rot, and perish, and be damn'd to-night; for
she shall not live: no, my heart is turn'd to stone; I
strike it, and it hurts my hand. — O, the world hath not
a sweeter creature: she might lie by an emperor's side,

and command him tasks.

IAGO
Nay, that's not your way.

OTHELLO
Hang her! I do but say what she is: — so delicate with
her needle! — an admirable musician! O, she will sing
the savageness out of a bear! — of so high and
plenteous wit and invention! —

IAGO
She's the worse for all this.

OTHELLO
O, a thousand thousand times: — and then, of so
gentle a condition!

IAGO
Ay, too gentle.

OTHELLO
Nay, that's certain: — but yet the pity of it, Iago!
O Iago, the pity of it, Iago!

IAGO
If you are so fond over her iniquity, give her patent to
offend; for, if it touch not you, it comes near nobody.

OTHELLO
I will chop her into messes: — cuckold me!

IAGO
O, 'tis foul in her.

OTHELLO
With mine officer!

IAGO
That's fouler.

OTHELLO
Get me some poison, Iago; this night: — I'll not
expostulate with her, lest her body and beauty
unprovide my mind again: — this night, Iago.

IAGO
Do it not with poison, strangle her in her bed, even the
bed she hath contaminated.

OTHELLO
Good, good: the justice of it pleases: very good.

IAGO
And for Cassio, — let me be his undertaker: you shall
hear more by midnight.

OTHELLO
Excellent good. [A trumpet within.] What trumpet is that
same?

IAGO
Something from Venice, sure. 'Tis Lodovico
Come from the duke: and, see, your wife is with him.
Enter LODOVICO, DESDEMONA, and
ATTENDANTS.

LODOVICO
Save you, worthy general!

OTHELLO
With all my heart, sir.

LODOVICO
The duke and senators of Venice greet you.
[Gives him a packet.

OTHELLO
I kiss the instrument of their pleasures.
[Opens the packet, and reads.

DESDEMONA
And what's the news, good cousin Lodovico?

IAGO
I am very glad to see you, signior;
Welcome to Cyprus.

LODOVICO
I thank you. How does Lieutenant Cassio?

IAGO
Lives, sir.

DESDEMONA
Cousin, there's fall'n between him and my lord
An unkind breach: but you shall make all well.

OTHELLO
Are you sure of that?

DESDEMONA
My lord?

OTHELLO [reads].
This fail you not to do, as you will —

LODOVICO
He did not call; he's busy in the paper.
Is there division 'twixt my lord and Cassio?

DESDEMONA
A most unhappy one: I would do much
T'atone them, for the love I bear to Cassio.

OTHELLO
Fire and brimstone!

DESDEMONA
My lord?

OTHELLO
                    Are you wise?
DESDEMONA
What, is he angry?
LODOVICO
                    May be the letter mov'd him;
For, as I think, they do command him home,
Deputing Cassio in his government.
DESDEMONA
Trust me, I am glad on't.
OTHELLO
                    Indeed!
DESDEMONA
                    My lord?
OTHELLO
I am glad to see you mad.
DESDEMONA
                    Why, sweet Othello, —
OTHELLO
Devil!   [*Striking her.*
DESDEMONA
I have not deserv'd this.
LODOVICO
My lord, this would not be believed in Venice,
Though I should swear I saw't: 'tis very much:
Make her amends; she weeps.
OTHELLO
                    O devil, devil!
If that the earth could teem with woman's tears,
Each drop she falls would prove a crocodile. —
Out of my sight!
DESDEMONA
                    I will not stay to offend you.   [*Going.*
LODOVICO
Truly, an obedient lady: —
I do beseech your lordship, call her back.
OTHELLO
Mistress!
DESDEMONA
                    My lord?
OTHELLO
                    What would you with her, sir?
LODOVICO
Who, I, my lord?
OTHELLO
Ay; you did wish that I would make her turn:
Sir, she can turn, and turn, and yet go on,
And turn again; and she can weep, sir, weep;
And she's obedient, as you say, — obedient, —
Very obedient. — Proceed you in your tears. —
Concerning this, sir, — O well-painted passion! —
I am commanded home. — Get you away;
I'll send for you anon. — Sir, I obey the mandate,
And will return to Venice. — Hence, avaunt!
                    [*Exit* DESDEMONA.
Cassio shall have my place. And, sir, to-night
I do entreat that we may sup together:
You are welcome, sir, to Cyprus. — Goats and
    monkeys!   [*Exit.*
LODOVICO
Is this the noble Moor whom our full senate
Call all-in-all sufficient? — Is this the nature
Whom passion could not shake? whose solid virtue
The shot of accident, nor dart of chance,
Could neither graze nor pierce?
IAGO
                    He is much changed.
LODOVICO
Are his wits safe? is he not light of brain?
IAGO
He's that he is: I may not breathe my censure.
What he might be, — if, what he might, he is not, —
I would to heaven he were!
LODOVICO
                    What, strike his wife!
IAGO
Faith, that was not so well; yet would I knew
That stroke would prove the worst!
LODOVICO
                    Is it his use?
Or did the letters work upon his blood,
And new-create this fault?
IAGO
                    Alas, alas!
It is not honesty in me to speak
What I have seen and known. You shall observe him;
And his own courses will denote him so,
That I may save my speech: do but go after,
And mark how he continues.

DESDEMONA Upon my knees, what doth your speech import?

LODOVICO
I am sorry that I am deceiv'd in him.   [*Exeunt.*

SCENE II
A room in the castle.
Enter OTHELLO *and* EMILIA.

OTHELLO
You have seen nothing, then?
EMILIA
Nor ever heard, nor ever did suspect.
OTHELLO
Yes, you have seen Cassio and she together.
EMILIA
But then I saw no harm, and then I heard
Each syllable that breath made up between them.
OTHELLO
What, did they never whisper?
EMILIA
                    Never, my lord.
OTHELLO
Nor send you out o'th'way?
EMILIA
Never.
OTHELLO
To fetch her fan, her gloves, her mask, nor nothing?
EMILIA
Never, my lord.
OTHELLO
That's strange.
EMILIA
I durst, my lord, to wager she is honest,
Lay down my soul at stake: if you think other,
Remove your thought, — it doth abuse your bosom.
If any wretch have put this in your head,
Let heaven requite it with the serpent's curse!
For, if she be not honest, chaste, and true,
There's no man happy; the purest of their wives
Is foul as slander.
OTHELLO
                    Bid her come hither: — go.
                    [*Exit* EMILIA.
She says enough; — yet she's a simple bawd
That cannot say as much. This is a subtle whore,
A closet-lock-and-key of villainous secrets:
And yet she'll kneel and pray; I have seen her do't.
Enter DESDEMONA *with* EMILIA.

DESDEMONA
My lord, what is your will?
OTHELLO
                    Pray, chuck, come hither.
DESDEMONA
What is your pleasure?

OTHELLO
                    Let me see your eyes;
Look in my face.
DESDEMONA
                    What horrible fancy's this?
OTHELLO [*to* EMILIA].
Some of your function, mistress;
Leave procreants alone, and shut the door;
Cough, or cry 'hem', if anybody come:
Your mystery, your mystery; — nay, dispatch.
                    [*Exit* EMILIA.
DESDEMONA
Upon my knees, what doth your speech import?
I understand a fury in your words,
But not the words.
OTHELLO
Why, what art thou?
DESDEMONA
                    Your wife, my lord; your true
And loyal wife.
OTHELLO
                    Come, swear it, damn thyself;
Lest, being like one of heaven, the devils themselves
Should fear to seize thee: therefore be double damn'd, —
Swear thou art honest.
DESDEMONA
                    Heaven doth truly know it.
OTHELLO
Heaven truly knows that thou art false as hell.
DESDEMONA
To whom, my lord? with whom? how am I false?
OTHELLO
Ah, Desdemona! — away! away! away!
DESDEMONA
Alas the heavy day! — Why do you weep?
Am I the motive of these tears, my lord?
If haply you my father do suspect
An instrument of this your calling back,
Lay not your blame on me: if you have lost him,
Why, I have lost him too.
OTHELLO
                    Had it pleas'd heaven
To try me with affliction; had they rain'd
All kinds of sores and shames on my bare head;
Steep'd me in poverty to the very lips;
Given to captivity me and my utmost hopes;
I should have found in some place of my soul
A drop of patience: but, alas, to make me
A fixed figure for the time of scorn
To point his slow unmoving finger at! —
Yet could I bear that too; well, very well:
But there, where I have garner'd up my heart,
Where either I must live, or bear no life, —
The fountain from the which my current runs,

Or else dries up; to be discarded thence!
Or keep it as a cistern for foul toads
To knot and gender in! — turn thy complexion there,
Patience, thou young and rose-lipp'd cherubin, —
Ay, there, look grim as hell!

DESDEMONA
I hope my noble lord esteems me honest.

OTHELLO
O, ay; as summer flies are in the shambles,
That quicken even with blowing. O thou weed,
Who art so lovely fair, and smell'st so sweet,
That the sense aches at thee, — would thou hadst ne'er
    been born!

DESDEMONA
Alas, what ignorant sin have I committed?

OTHELLO
Was this fair paper, this most goodly book,
Made to write 'whore' upon? What committed!
Committed! — O thou public commoner!
I should make very forges of my cheeks,
That would to cinders burn up modesty,
Did I but speak thy deeds. — What committed!
Heaven stops the nose at it, and the moon winks;
The bawdy wind, that kisses all it meets,
Is hush'd within the hollow mine of earth,
And will not hear it. — What committed! —
Impudent strumpet!

DESDEMONA
    By heaven, you do me wrong.

OTHELLO
Are you not a strumpet?

DESDEMONA
    No, as I am a Christian:
If to preserve this vessel for my lord
From any other foul unlawful touch,
Be not to be a strumpet, I am none.

OTHELLO
What, not a whore?

DESDEMONA
    No, as I shall be saved.

OTHELLO
Is't possible?

DESDEMONA
O, heaven forgive us!

OTHELLO
    I cry you mercy, then:
I took you for that cunning whore of Venice
That married with Othello. — You, mistress,
That have the office opposite to Saint Peter,
And keep the gate of hell!

Enter EMILIA.

    You, you, ay, you!
We have done our course; there's money for your
    pains:
I pray you, turn the key, and keep our counsel.   [*Exit.*

EMILIA
Alas, what does this gentleman conceive? —
How do you, madam? how do you, my good lady?

DESDEMONA
Faith, half asleep.

EMILIA
Good madam, what's the matter with my lord?

DESDEMONA
With who?

EMILIA
Why, with my lord, madam.

DESDEMONA
Who is thy lord?

EMILIA
    He that is yours, sweet lady.

DESDEMONA
I have none: do not talk to me, Emilia;
I cannot weep; nor answer have I none,
But what should go by water. Prithee, to-night
Lay on my bed my wedding-sheets, — remember; —
And call thy husband hither.

EMILIA
    Here's a change indeed!   [*Exit.*

DESDEMONA
'Tis meet I should be us'd so, very meet.
How have I been behav'd, that he might stick
The small'st opinion on my least misuse?

Enter EMILIA *with* IAGO.

IAGO
What is your pleasure, madam? How is't with you?

DESDEMONA
I cannot tell. Those that do teach young babes
Do it with gentle means and easy tasks:

He might have chid me so; for, in good faith,
I am a child to chiding.

IAGO
    What's the matter, lady?

EMILIA
Alas, Iago, my lord hath so bewhored her,
Thrown such despite and heavy terms upon her,
As true hearts cannot bear.

DESDEMONA
Am I that name, Iago?

IAGO
    What name, fair lady?

DESDEMONA
Such as she says my lord did say I was.

EMILIA
He call'd her whore: a beggar in his drink
Could not have laid such terms upon his callet.

IAGO
Why did he so?

DESDEMONA
I do not know; I am sure I am none such.

IAGO
Do not weep, do not weep: — alas the day!

EMILIA
Hath she forsook so many noble matches,
Her father, and her country, and her friends,
To be call'd whore? would it not make one weep?

DESDEMONA
It is my wretched fortune.

IAGO
    Beshrew him for't!
How comes this trick upon him?

DESDEMONA
    Nay, heaven doth know.

EMILIA
I will be hang'd, if some eternal villain,
Some busy and insinuating rogue,
Some cogging, cozening slave, to get some office,
Have not devis'd this slander; I'll be hang'd else.

IAGO
Fie, there is no such man; it is impossible.

DESDEMONA
If any such there be, heaven pardon him!

EMILIA
A halter pardon him! and hell gnaw his bones!
Why should he call her whore? who keeps her
    company?
What place? what time? what form? what likelihood?
The Moor's abus'd by some most villainous knave,
Some base notorious knave, some scurvy fellow: —
O heaven, that such companions thou'ldst unfold,
And put in every honest hand a whip
To lash the rascals naked through the world
Even from the east to th'west!

IAGO
    Speak within door.

EMILIA
O, fie upon them! Some such squire he was
That turn'd your wit the seamy side without,
And made you to suspect me with the Moor.

IAGO
You are a fool; go to.

DESDEMONA
    O good Iago,
What shall I do to win my lord again?
Good friend, go to him; for, by this light of heaven,
I know not how I lost him. Here I kneel: —
If e'er my will did trespass 'gainst his love,
Either in discourse of thought or actual deed;
Or that mine eyes, mine ears, or any sense,
Delighted them in any other form;
Or that I do not yet, and ever did,
And ever will — though he do shake me off
To beggarly divorcement — love him dearly,
Comfort forswear me! Unkindness may do much;
And his unkindness may defeat my life,
But never taint my love. I cannot say 'whore', —
It does abhor me now I speak the word;
To do the act that might the addition earn
Not the world's mass of vanity could make me.

IAGO
I pray you, be content; 'tis but his humour:
The business of the state does him offence,
And he does chide with you.

DESDEMONA
If 'twere no other, —

IAGO
    'Tis but so, I warrant.   [*Trumpets within.*
Hark, how these instruments summon to supper!
The messengers of Venice stay the meat:
Go in, and weep not; all things shall be well.
    [*Exeunt* DESDEMONA *and* EMILIA.
    Enter RODERIGO.
How now, Roderigo!

RODERIGO
I do not find that thou deal'st justly with me.

IAGO
What in the contrary?

RODERIGO
Every day thou daff'st me with some device, Iago; and
rather, as it seems to me now, keep'st from me all
conveniency than suppliest me with the least
advantage of hope. I will, indeed, no longer endure it;
nor am I yet persuaded to put up in peace what already
I have foolishly suffer'd.

IAGO
Will you hear me, Roderigo?

RODERIGO
Faith, I have heard too much; for your words and
performances are no kin together.

IAGO   Go in, and weep not; all things shall be well.

IAGO
You charge me most unjustly.

RODERIGO
With naught but truth. I have wasted myself out of my means. The jewels you have had from me to deliver to Desdemona would half have corrupted a votarist: you have told me she hath received them, and return'd me expectations and comforts of sudden respect and acquaintance; but I find none.

IAGO
Well; go to; very well.

RODERIGO
Very well! go to! I cannot go to, man; nor 'tis not very well: nay, I think it is scurvy, and begin to find myself fopp'd in it.

IAGO
Very well.

RODERIGO
I tell you 'tis not very well. I will make myself known to Desdemona: if she will return me my jewels, I will give over my suit, and repent my unlawful solicitation; if not, assure yourself I will seek satisfaction of you.

IAGO
You have said now.

RODERIGO
Ay, and said nothing but what I protest intendment of doing.

IAGO
Why, now I see there's mettle in thee; and even from this instant to build on thee a better opinion than ever before. Give me thy hand, Roderigo: thou hast taken against me a most just exception; but yet, I protest, I have dealt most directly in thy affair.

RODERIGO
It hath not appear'd.

IAGO
I grant, indeed, it hath not appear'd; and your suspicion is not without wit and judgement. But, Roderigo, if thou hast that in thee indeed, which I have greater reason to believe now than ever, — I mean purpose, courage, and valour, — this night show it: if thou the next night following enjoy not Desdemona, take me from this world with treachery, and devise engines for my life.

RODERIGO
Well, what is it? is it within reason and compass?

IAGO
Sir, there is especial commission come from Venice to depute Cassio in Othello's place.

RODERIGO
Is that true? why, then Othello and Desdemona return again to Venice.

IAGO
O, no; he goes into Mauritania, and takes away with him the fair Desdemona, unless his abode be linger'd here by some accident: wherein none can be so determinate as the removing of Cassio.

RODERIGO
How do you mean, removing of him?

IAGO
Why, by making him uncapable of Othello's place, — knocking out his brains.

RODERIGO
And that you would have me to do?

IAGO
Ay, if you dare do yourself a profit and a right. He sups to-night with a harlotry, and thither will I go to him: — he knows not yet of his honourable fortune. If you will watch his going thence, — which I will fashion to fall out between twelve and one, — you may take him at your pleasure: I will be near to second your attempt, and he shall fall between us. Come, stand not amazed at it, but go along with me; I will show you such a necessity in his death, that you shall think yourself bound to put it on him. It is now high suppertime, and the night grows to waste: about it.

RODERIGO
I will hear further reason for this.

IAGO
And you shall be satisfied.   [*Exeunt.*

SCENE III

Another room in the castle.

Enter OTHELLO, LODOVICO, DESDEMONA,
EMILIA, *and* ATTENDANTS.

LODOVICO
I do beseech you, sir, trouble yourself no further.

OTHELLO
O, pardon me; 'twill do me good to walk.

LODOVICO
Madam, good night; I humbly thank your ladyship.

DESDEMONA
Your honour is most welcome.

OTHELLO
                                   Will you walk, sir?
O, — Desdemona, —

DESDEMONA
My lord?

OTHELLO
Get you to bed on th'instant: I will be return'd forthwith: dismiss your attendant there: look't be done.

DESDEMONA
I will, my lord.
    [*Exeunt* OTHELLO, LODOVICO, *and* ATTENDANTS.

EMILIA
How goes it now? he looks gentler than he did.

DESDEMONA
He says he will return incontinent:
He hath commanded me to go to bed,
And bade me to dismiss you.

EMILIA
                                   Dismiss me!

DESDEMONA
It was his bidding; therefore, good Emilia,
Give me my nightly wearing, and adieu:
We must not now displease him.

EMILIA
I would you had never seen him!

DESDEMONA
So would not I: my love doth so approve him,
That even his stubbornness, his checks, his frowns, —
Prithee, unpin me, — have grace and favour in them.

EMILIA
I have laid those sheets you bade me on the bed.

DESDEMONA
All's one. — Good faith, how foolish are our minds! —
If I do die before thee, prithee, shroud me
In one of those same sheets.

EMILIA
                                   Come, come, you talk.

DESDEMONA
My mother had a maid call'd Barbara:
She was in love; and he she lov'd prov'd mad,
And did forsake her: she had a song of 'willow';
An old thing 'twas, but it express'd her fortune,
And she died singing it: that song to-night
Will not go from my mind; I have much to do,
But to go hang my head all at one side,
And sing it like poor Barbara. — Prithee, dispatch.

EMILIA
Shall I go fetch your night-gown?

DESDEMONA
                                   No, unpin me here. —
This Lodovico is a proper man.

EMILIA
A very handsome man.

DESDEMONA
He speaks well.

EMILIA
I know a lady in Venice would have walk'd barefoot to
Palestine for a touch of his nether lip.

DESDEMONA [*singing*].
        The poor soul sat sighing by a sycamore tree,
            Sing all a green willow;
        Her hand on her bosom, her head on her knee,
            Sing willow, willow, willow:
        The fresh streams ran by her, and murmur'd
        her moans;
            Sing willow, willow, willow;
        Her salt tears fell from her, and soften'd the
        stones; —
Lay by these: —
            Sing willow, willow, willow;
Prithee, hie thee; he'll come anon: —
        Sing all a green willow must be my garland.
        Let nobody blame him; his scorn I approve, —
Nay, that's not next. — Hark! who is't that knocks?

EMILIA
It is the wind.

DESDEMONA
        I call'd my love false love; but what said he then?
            Sing willow, willow, willow;
        If I court moe women, you'll couch with moe
        men: —
So, get thee gone; good night. Mine eyes do itch;
Doth that bode weeping?

EMILIA
                                   'Tis neither here nor there.

DESDEMONA
I have heard it said so. — O, these men, these men! —
Dost thou in conscience think, — tell me, Emilia, —
That there be women do abuse their husbands
In such gross kind?

EMILIA
                                   There be some such, no question.

DESDEMONA
Wouldst thou do such a deed for all the world?

EMILIA
Why, would not you?

DESDEMONA
                                   No, by this heavenly light!

EMILIA
Nor I neither by this heavenly light; I might do't as well
i'th'dark.

DESDEMONA
Wouldst thou do such a deed for all the world?

EMILIA
The world is a huge thing: it is a great price for a small
vice.

DESDEMONA
In troth, I think thou wouldst not.

EMILIA
In troth, I think I should; and undo't when I had done.
Marry, I would not do such a thing for a joint-ring, nor
for measures of lawn, nor for gowns, petticoats, nor
caps, nor any petty exhibition; but, for the whole world,
— why, who would not make her husband a cuckold to
make him a monarch? I should venture purgatory for't.

DESDEMONA
Beshrew me, if I would do such a wrong
For the whole world.

EMILIA
Why, the wrong is but a wrong i'th'world; and having
the world for your labour, 'tis a wrong in your own
world, and you might quickly make it right.

DESDEMONA
I do not think there is any such woman.

EMILIA
Yes, a dozen; and as many to th'vantage as would store
    the world they play'd for.
But I do think it is their husbands' faults
If wives do fall: say that they slack their duties,
And pour our treasures into foreign laps;
Or else break out in peevish jealousies,
Throwing restraint upon us; or say they strike us,
Or scant our former having in despite;
Why, we have galls; and though we have some grace,
Yet have we some revenge. Let husbands know
Their wives have sense like them: they see, and smell,
And have their palates both for sweet and sour,
As husbands have. What is it that they do
When they change us for others? Is it sport?
I think it is: and doth affection breed it?
I think it doth: is't frailty that thus errs?
It is so too: — and have not we affections,
Desires for sport, and frailty, as men have?
Then let them use us well: else let them know,
The ills we do, their ills instruct us so.

DESDEMONA
Good night, good night: heaven me such usage send,
Not to pick bad from bad, but by bad mend!   [*Exeunt.*

ACT V

SCENE I

Cyprus. A street.

Enter IAGO *and* RODERIGO.

IAGO
Here, stand behind this bulk; straight will he come:
Wear thy good rapier bare, and put it home:
Quick, quick; fear nothing; I'll be at thy elbow:
It makes us, or it mars us; think on that,
And fix most firm thy resolution.

RODERIGO
Be near at hand; I may miscarry in't.

IAGO
Here, at thy hand: be bold, and take thy stand.
                        [*Retires to a little distance.*

RODERIGO
I have no great devotion to the deed;
And yet he hath given me satisfying reasons: —
'Tis but a man gone: — forth, my sword; he dies.
                        [*Goes to his stand.*

IAGO Here, stand behind this bulk; straight will he come.

IAGO
I have rubb'd this young quat almost to the sense,
And he grows angry. Now, whether he kill Cassio,
Or Cassio him, or each do kill the other,
Every way makes my gain: live Roderigo,
He calls me to a restitution large
Of gold and jewels that I bobb'd from him,
As gifts to Desdemona;
It must not be: if Cassio do remain,
He hath a daily beauty in his life
That makes me ugly; and, besides, the Moor
May unfold me to him; there stand I in much peril:
No, he must die. But so: I hear him coming.

Enter CASSIO.

RODERIGO
I know his gait, 'tis he. — Villain, thou diest!
        [Makes a pass at CASSIO.

CASSIO
That thrust had been mine enemy indeed,
But that my coat is better than thou know'st:
I will make proof of thine.
    [Draws, and wounds RODERIGO.

RODERIGO
        O, I am slain!
  *[IAGO *cuts* CASSIO *behind in the leg, and exit.*

CASSIO
I am maim'd for ever. — Help, ho! murder! murder!
        [Falls.

Enter OTHELLO, *at some distance.*

OTHELLO
The voice of Cassio: — Iago keeps his word.

RODERIGO
O, villain that I am!

OTHELLO
      It is even so.

CASSIO
O, help, ho! light! a surgeon!

OTHELLO
'Tis he: — O brave Iago, honest and just,
That hast such noble sense of thy friend's wrong!
Thou teachest me: — Minion, your dear lies dead,
And your unblest fate hies: strumpet, I come!
Forth of my heart those charms, thine eyes, are blotted;
Thy bed lust-stain'd shall with lust's blood be spotted.
        [Exit.

Enter LODOVICO *and* GRATIANO.

CASSIO
What, ho! no watch? no passage? murder! murder!

GRATIANO
'Tis some mischance; the cry is very direful.

CASSIO
O, help!

LODOVICO
Hark!

RODERIGO
O wretched villain!

LODOVICO
Two or three groan: — it is a heavy night:
These may be counterfeits: let's think't unsafe
To come in to the cry without more help.

RODERIGO
Nobody come? then shall I bleed to death.

LODOVICO
Hark!

GRATIANO
Here's one comes in his shirt, with light and weapons.

Enter IAGO, *with a light.*

IAGO
Who's there? whose noise is this that cries on murder?

LODOVICO
We do not know.

IAGO
      Did not you hear a cry?

CASSIO
Here, here! for heaven's sake, help me!

IAGO
        What's the matter?

GRATIANO
This is Othello's ancient, as I take it.

LODOVICO
The same indeed; a very valiant fellow.

IAGO
What are you here that cry so grievously?

CASSIO
Iago? O, I am spoil'd, undone by villains!
Give me some help.

IAGO
O me, lieutenant! what villains have done this?

CASSIO
I think that one of them is hereabout,
And cannot make away.

IAGO
        O treacherous villains! —
What are you there? come in, and give some help.
      [To LODOVICO *and* GRATIANO.

RODERIGO
O, help me here!

CASSIO
That's one of them.

IAGO
       O murderous slave! O villain!
        [Stabs RODERIGO.

RODERIGO
O damn'd Iago! O inhuman dog!

IAGO
Kill men i'th'dark! — Where be these bloody thieves? —
How silent is this town! — Ho! murder! murder! —
What may you be? are you of good or evil?

LODOVICO
As you shall prove us, praise us.

IAGO
Signior Lodovico?

LODOVICO
He, sir.

IAGO
I cry you mercy. Here's Cassio hurt by villains.

GRATIANO
Cassio!

IAGO
How is't, brother?

CASSIO
My leg is cut in two.

IAGO
       Marry, heaven forbid! —
Light, gentlemen: — I'll bind it with my shirt.

Enter BIANCA.

BIANCA
What is the matter, ho? who is't that cried?

IAGO
Who is't that cried!

BIANCA
O my dear Cassio! my sweet Cassio!
O Cassio, Cassio, Cassio!

IAGO
O notable strumpet! — Cassio, may you suspect
Who they should be that have thus mangled you?

CASSIO
No.

GRATIANO
I am sorry to find you thus: I have been to seek you.

IAGO
Lend me a garter: — so. — O, for a chair,
To bear him easily hence!

BIANCA
Alas, he faints! — O Cassio, Cassio, Cassio!

IAGO
Gentlemen all, I do suspect this trash
To be a party in this injury. —
Patience awhile, good Cassio. — Come, come;
Lend me a light. — Know we this face or no?
Alas, my friend and my dear countryman
Roderigo? no: — yes, sure; O heaven! Roderigo.

GRATIANO
What, of Venice?

IAGO
Even he, sir: did you know him?

GRATIANO
        Know him! ay.

IAGO
Signior Gratiano? I cry you gentle pardon;
These bloody accidents must excuse my manners
That so neglected you.

GRATIANO
      I am glad to see you.

BIANCA O my dear Cassio! my sweet Cassio!

IAGO
How do you, Cassio? — O, a chair, a chair!
GRATIANO
Roderigo!
IAGO
He, he, 'tis he. — [*A chair brought in.*] O, that's well
  said; — the chair: —
Some good man bear him carefully from hence;
I'll fetch the general's surgeon. — [*to* BIANCA] For
  you, mistress,
Save you your labour. — He that lies slain here, Cassio,
Was my dear friend: what malice was between you?
CASSIO
None in the world; nor do I know the man.
IAGO [*to* BIANCA].
What, look you pale? — O, bear him out o'th'air. —
        [CASSIO *and* RODERIGO *are borne off.*
Stay you, good gentlemen. — Look you pale, mistress? —
Do you perceive the gastness of her eye? —
Nay, if you stare, we shall hear more anon. —
Behold her well; I pray you, look upon her:
Do you see, gentlemen? nay, guiltiness will speak,
Though tongues were out of use.
        Enter EMILIA.
EMILIA
'Las, what's the matter? what's the matter, husband?
IAGO
Cassio hath here been set on in the dark
By Roderigo, and fellows that are scap'd:
He's almost slain, and Roderigo dead.
EMILIA
Alas, good gentleman! alas, good Cassio!
IAGO
This is the fruit of whoring. — Prithee, Emilia,
Go know of Cassio where he supp'd to-night. —
[*to* BIANCA] What, do you shake at that?
BIANCA
He supp'd at my house; but I therefore shake not.
IAGO
O, did he so? I charge you, go with me.
EMILIA
Fie, fie upon thee, strumpet!
BIANCA
I am no strumpet; but of life as honest
As you that thus abuse me.
EMILIA
        As I! foh! fie upon thee!
IAGO
Kind gentlemen, let's go see poor Cassio dress'd. —
[*to* BIANCA] Come, mistress, you must tell's another
  tale. —
Emilia, run you to the citadel,
And tell my lord and lady what hath happ'd. —
Will you go on afore? — [*aside*] This is the night
That either makes me or fordoes me quite.   [*Exeunt.*

SCENE II

A bedchamber in the castle: DESDEMONA
in bed asleep; a light burning.

Enter OTHELLO.

OTHELLO
It is the cause, it is the cause, my soul, —

Let me not name it to you, you chaste stars!
It is the cause. — Yet I'll not shed her blood;
Nor scar that whiter skin of hers than snow,
And smooth as monumental alabaster.
Yet she must die, else she'll betray more men. —
Put out the light, and then put out the light:
If I quench thee, thou flaming minister,
I can again thy former light restore,
Should I repent me: — but once put out thy light,
Thou cunning'st pattern of excelling nature,
I know not where is that Promethean heat
That can thy light relume. When I have pluck'd the
  rose,
I cannot give it vital growth again,
It needs must wither: — I'll smell it on the tree. —
        [*Kissing her.*
O balmy breath, that dost almost persuade
Justice to break her sword! — One more, one more: —
Be thus when thou art dead, and I will kill thee,
And love thee after: — one more, and this the last:
So sweet was ne'er so fatal. I must weep,
But they are cruel tears: this sorrow's heavenly;
It strikes where it doth love. — She wakes.
DESDEMONA
Who's there? Othello?
OTHELLO
        Ay, Desdemona.
DESDEMONA
Will you come to bed, my lord?
OTHELLO
Have you pray'd to-night, Desdemona?
DESDEMONA
        Ay, my lord.
OTHELLO
If you bethink yourself of any crime
Unreconcil'd as yet to heaven and grace,
Solicit for it straight.
DESDEMONA
Alack, my lord, what may you mean by that?
OTHELLO
Well, do it, and be brief; I will walk by:
I would not kill thy unprepared spirit;
No, — heaven forfend! — I would not kill thy soul.
DESDEMONA
Talk you of killing?
OTHELLO
Ay, I do.
DESDEMONA
Then heaven have mercy on me!
OTHELLO
Amen, with all my heart!
DESDEMONA
If you say so, I hope you will not kill me.
OTHELLO
Hum!
DESDEMONA
And yet I fear you; for you are fatal then
When your eyes roll so: why I should fear I know not,
Since guiltiness I know not; but yet I feel I fear.
OTHELLO
Think on thy sins.
DESDEMONA
        They are loves I bear to you.

OTHELLO
Ay, and for that thou diest.
DESDEMONA
That death's unnatural that kills for loving. —
Alas, why gnaw you so your nether lip?
Some bloody passion shakes your very frame:
These are portents; but yet I hope, I hope,
They do not point on me.
OTHELLO
        Peace, and be still.
DESDEMONA
I will so. What's the matter?
OTHELLO
That handkerchief which I so lov'd and gave thee
Thou gavest to Cassio.
DESDEMONA
        No, by my life and soul!
Send for the man, and ask him.
OTHELLO
        Sweet soul, take heed,
Take heed of perjury; thou art on thy death-bed.
DESDEMONA
Ay, but not yet to die.
OTHELLO
        Yes, presently:
Therefore confess thee freely of thy sin;
For to deny each article with oath
Cannot remove nor choke the strong conception
That I do groan withal. Thou art to die.
DESDEMONA
Then Lord have mercy on me!
OTHELLO
        I say, amen.
DESDEMONA
And have you mercy too! — I never did
Offend you in my life; never lov'd Cassio
But with such general warranty of heaven
As I might love; I never gave him token.
OTHELLO
By heaven, I saw my handkerchief in's hand.
O perjured woman! thou dost stone my heart.
And mak'st me call what I intend to do
A murder, which I thought a sacrifice:
I saw the handkerchief.
DESDEMONA
        He found it, then;
I never gave it him: — send for him hither;
Let him confess a truth.
OTHELLO
        He hath confess'd.

OTHELLO Put out the light, and then put out the light

DESDEMONA
What, my lord?
OTHELLO
That he hath us'd thee.
DESDEMONA
           How? unlawfully?
OTHELLO
                      Ay.
DESDEMONA
He will not say so.
OTHELLO
           No, his mouth is stopp'd;
Honest Iago hath ta'en order for't.
DESDEMONA
O, my fear interprets: — what, is he dead?
OTHELLO
Had all his hairs been lives, my great revenge
Had stomach for them all.
DESDEMONA
Alas, he is betray'd, and I undone!
OTHELLO
Out, strumpet! weep'st thou for him to my face?
DESDEMONA
O, banish me, my lord, but kill me not!
OTHELLO
Down, strumpet!
DESDEMONA
Kill me to-morrow; let me live to-night!
OTHELLO
Nay, if you strive, —
DESDEMONA
But half an hour!
OTHELLO
       Being done, there is no pause.
DESDEMONA
But while I say one prayer!
OTHELLO
             It is too late.   [*Smothers her.*
EMILIA [*at the door*].
My lord, my lord! what, ho! my lord, my lord!
OTHELLO
What noise is this? — Not dead? not yet quite dead?
I that am cruel am yet merciful;
I would not have thee linger in thy pain: —
So, so.
EMILIA [*within*].
What, ho! my lord, my lord!
OTHELLO
              Who's there?
EMILIA [*within*].
O, good my lord, I would speak a word with you!
OTHELLO
Yes: 'tis Emilia: — by and by. — She's dead. —
'Tis like she comes to speak of Cassio's death; —
The noise was high. — Ha! no more moving?
Still as the grave. — Shall she come in? were't good? —
I think she stirs again: — no. — What's best to do?
If she come in, she'll sure speak to my wife:
My wife! my wife! what wife? I have no wife.
O, insupportable! O heavy hour!
Methinks it should be now a huge eclipse
Of sun and moon, and that th'affrighted globe
Should yawn at alteration.
EMILIA [*within*].
              I do beseech you
That I may speak with you, O, good my lord!
OTHELLO
I had forgot thee: O, come in, Emilia: —
Soft, — by and by: — let me the curtains draw. —
Where art thou?   [*Opens the door.*

Enter EMILIA.

      What's the matter with thee now?
EMILIA
O, my good lord, yonder's foul murders done!
OTHELLO
What, now?
EMILIA
But now, my lord.
OTHELLO
It is the very error of the moon;
She comes more near the earth than she was wont,
And makes men mad.
EMILIA
Cassio, my lord, hath kill'd a young Venetian
Call'd Roderigo.
OTHELLO
         Roderigo kill'd!

And Cassio kill'd!
EMILIA
         No, Cassio is not kill'd.
OTHELLO
Not Cassio kill'd! then murder's out of tune,
And sweet revenge grows harsh.
DESDEMONA
O falsely, falsely murder'd!
EMILIA
           Alas, what cry is that?
OTHELLO
That! what?
EMILIA
Out, and alas! that was my lady's voice. —
Help! help, ho! help! — O lady, speak again!
Sweet Desdemona! O sweet mistress, speak!
DESDEMONA
A guiltless death I die.
EMILIA
         O, who hath done
This deed?
DESDEMONA
      Nobody, — I myself. Farewell:
Commend me to my kind lord: O, farewell!   [*Dies.*
OTHELLO
Why, how should she be murder'd?
EMILIA
             Alas, who knows?
OTHELLO
You heard her say herself, it was not I.
EMILIA
She said so: I must needs report the truth.
OTHELLO
She's, like a liar, gone to burning hell:
'Twas I that kill'd her.
EMILIA
        O, the more angel she,
And you the blacker devil!
OTHELLO
She turn'd to folly, and she was a whore.
EMILIA
Thou dost belie her, and thou art a devil.
OTHELLO
She was false as water.
EMILIA
        Thou art rash as fire, to say
That she was false: O, she was heavenly true!
OTHELLO
Cassio did top her; ask thy husband else.
O, I were damn'd beneath all depth in hell,
But that I did proceed upon just grounds
To this extremity. Thy husband knew it all.
EMILIA
My husband!
OTHELLO
Thy husband.
EMILIA
That she was false to wedlock?
OTHELLO
Ay, with Cassio. Nay, had she been true,
If heaven would make me such another world
Of one entire and perfect chrysolite,
I'ld not have sold her for it.
EMILIA
My husband!
OTHELLO
      Ay, 'twas he that told me first:
An honest man he is, and hates the slime
That sticks on filthy deeds.
EMILIA
          My husband!
OTHELLO
What needs this iterance, woman? I say thy husband.
EMILIA
O mistress, villainy hath made mocks with love! —
My husband say that she was false!
OTHELLO
             He, woman:
I say thy husband: dost understand the word?
My friend, thy husband, honest, honest Iago.
EMILIA
If he say so, may his pernicious soul
Rot half a grain a day! he lies to th'heart:
She was too fond of her most filthy bargain.
OTHELLO
Ha!
EMILIA
Do thy worst:

This deed of thine is no more worthy heaven
Than thou wast worthy her.
OTHELLO
          Peace, you were best.
EMILIA
Thou hast not half that power to do me harm
As I have to be hurt. O gull! O dolt!
As ignorant as dirt! thou hast done a deed —
I care not for thy sword; I'll make thee known,
Though I lost twenty lives. — Help! help, ho! help!
The Moor hath kill'd my mistress! Murder! murder!

Enter MONTANO, GRATIANO, *and* IAGO.

MONTANO
What is the matter? — How now, general!
EMILIA
O, are you come, Iago? you have done well,
That men must lay their murders on your neck.
GRATIANO
What is the matter?
EMILIA
Disprove this villain, if thou be'st a man:
He says thou told'st him that his wife was false:
I know thou didst not, thou'rt not such a villain:
Speak, for my heart is full.
IAGO
I told him what I thought; and told no more
Than what he found himself was apt and true.
EMILIA
But did you ever tell him she was false?
IAGO
I did.
EMILIA
You told a lie; an odious, damned lie;
Upon my soul, a lie; a wicked lie: —
She false with Cassio! — did you say with Cassio?
IAGO
With Cassio, mistress. Go to, charm your tongue.
EMILIA
I will not charm my tongue; I am bound to speak:
My mistress here lies murder'd in her bed, —
ALL
O heavens forfend!
EMILIA
And your reports have set the murder on.
OTHELLO
Nay, stare not, masters: it is true, indeed.
GRATIANO
'Tis a strange truth.
MONTANO
O monstrous act!
EMILIA
        Villainy, villainy, villainy!
I think upon't, — I think, — I smell't; — O villainy! —
I thought so then; — I'll kill myself for grief: —
O villainy, villainy!
IAGO
What, are you mad? I charge you, get you home.
EMILIA
Good gentlemen, let me have leave to speak:
'Tis proper I obey him, but not now. —
Perchance, Iago, I will ne'er go home.
OTHELLO
O! O! O!   [*Falling on the bed.*
EMILIA
      Nay, lay thee down and roar;
For thou hast kill'd the sweetest innocent
That e'er did lift up eye.
OTHELLO
        O, she was foul! —   [*Rising.*
I scarce did know you, uncle: there lies your niece,
Whose breath, indeed, these hands have newly stopp'd:
I know this act shows horrible and grim.
GRATIANO
Poor Desdemona! I am glad thy father's dead:
Thy match was mortal to him, and pure grief
Shore his old thread in twain: did he live now,
This sight would make him do a desperate turn,
Yea, curse his better angel from his side,
And fall to reprobance.
OTHELLO
'Tis pitiful; but yet Iago knows
That she with Cassio hath the act of shame
A thousand times committed; Cassio confess'd it:
And she did gratify his amorous works
With that recognisance and pledge of love
Which I first gave her; I saw it in his hand:
It was a handkerchief, an antique token
My father gave my mother.

EMILIA
O heaven! O heavenly powers!

IAGO
Come, hold your peace.

EMILIA
    'Twill out, 'twill out: — I peace!
No, I will speak as liberal as the north:
Let heaven and men and devils, let them all,
All, all, cry shame against me, yet I'll speak.

IAGO
Be wise, and get you home.

EMILIA
     I will not.
[IAGO *offers to stab* EMILIA.

GRATIANO
     Fie!
Your sword upon a woman?

EMILIA
O thou dull Moor! that handkerchief thou speak'st of
I found by fortune, and did give my husband;
For often, with a solemn earnestness —
More than, indeed, belong'd to such a trifle —
He begg'd of me to steal it.

IAGO
     Villainous whore!

EMILIA
She give it Cassio! no, alas, I found it,
And I did give't my husband.

IAGO
     Filth, thou liest!

EMILIA
By heaven, I do not, I do not, gentlemen. —
O murderous coxcomb! what should such a fool
Do with so good a wife!

OTHELLO
    Are there no stones in heaven
But what serve for the thunder? — Precious villain!
[*He runs at* IAGO: IAGO *stabs* EMILIA, *and exit.*

GRATIANO
The woman falls; sure, he hath kill'd his wife.

EMILIA
Ay, ay: — O, lay me by my mistress' side.

GRATIANO
He's gone, but his wife's kill'd.

MONTANO
'Tis a notorious villain. Take you this weapon,
Which I have here recover'd from the Moor:
Come, guard the door without; let him not pass,
But kill him rather. I'll after that same villain,
For 'tis a damned slave.
[*Exeunt* MONTANO *and* GRATIANO.

OTHELLO
    I am not valiant neither,
But every puny whipster gets my sword: —
But why should honour outlive honesty?
Let it go all.

EMILIA
    What did thy song bode, lady?
Hark, canst thou hear me? I will play the swan,
And die in music: — 'Willow, willow, willow. — '
[*Singing.*
Moor, she was chaste; she lov'd thee, cruel Moor;
So come my soul to bliss as I speak true;
So speaking as I think, I die, — I die.
[*Dies.*

OTHELLO
I have another weapon in this chamber;
It is a sword of Spain, the ice-brook's temper: —
O, here it is. — uncle, I must come forth.

GRATIANO [*within*].
If thou attempt it, it will cost thee dear:
Thou hast no weapon, and perforce must suffer.

OTHELLO
Look in upon me, then, and speak with me,
Or, naked as I am, I will assault thee.

Enter GRATIANO.

GRATIANO
What is the matter?

OTHELLO
    Behold, I have a weapon;
A better never did itself sustain
Upon a soldier's thigh: I have seen the day
That, with this little arm and this good sword,
I have made my way through more impediments
Than twenty times your stop: — but, O vain boast!
Who can control his fate? 'tis not so now. —
Be not afraid, though you do see me weapon'd;
Here is my journey's end, here is my butt,
And very sea-mark of my utmost sail.
Do you go back dismay'd? 'tis a lost fear;
Man but a rush against Othello's breast,
And he retires: — where should Othello go? —
Now, how dost thou look now? O ill-starr'd wench!
Pale as thy smock! when we shall meet at compt,
This look of thine will hurl my soul from heaven,
And fiends will snatch at it. Cold, cold, my girl!
Even like thy chastity. —
O cursed, cursed slave! — whip me, ye devils,
From the possession of this heavenly sight!
Blow me about in winds! roast me in sulphur! —
Wash me in steep-down gulfs of liquid fire! —
O Desdemona! Desdemona! dead!
O! O! O!

Enter LODOVICO, MONTANO, CASSIO *carried in a*
chair, and OFFICERS *with* IAGO, *prisoner.*

LODOVICO
Where is this rash and most unfortunate man?

OTHELLO
That's he that was Othello; — here I am.

LODOVICO
Where is that viper? bring the villain forth.

OTHELLO
I look down towards his feet, — but that's a fable.
If that thou be'st a devil, I cannot kill thee.
[*Wounds* IAGO.

LODOVICO
Wrench his sword from him. [OTHELLO *is disarm'd.*

IAGO
    I bleed, sir; but not kill'd.

OTHELLO
I am not sorry neither: I'ld have thee live;
For, in my sense, 'tis happiness to die.

LODOVICO
O thou Othello, that wert once so good,
Fall'n in the practice of a damned slave,
What shall be said to thee?

OTHELLO
    Why, any thing:
An honourable murderer, if you will;
For naught I did in hate, but all in honour.

LODOVICO
This wretch hath part confess'd his villainy:
Did you and he consent in Cassio's death?

OTHELLO
Ay.

CASSIO
Dear general, I never gave you cause.

OTHELLO
I do believe it, and I ask your pardon.
Will you, I pray, demand that demi-devil
Why he hath thus ensnared my soul and body?

IAGO
Demand me nothing: what you know, you know:
From this time forth I never will speak word.

LODOVICO
What, not to pray?

GRATIANO
    Torments will ope your lips.

OTHELLO
Well, thou dost best.

LODOVICO
Sir, you shall understand what hath befall'n,
Which, as I think, you know not. Here is a letter
Found in the pocket of the slain Roderigo;
And here another: the one of them imports
The death of Cassio to be undertook
By Roderigo.

OTHELLO
O villain!

CASSIO
    Most heathenish and most gross!

LODOVICO
Now here's another discontented paper,
Found in his pocket too; and this, it seems,
Roderigo meant t'have sent this damned villain;
But that, belike, Iago in the interim
Came in and satisfied him.

OTHELLO
    O the pernicious caitiff! —
How came you, Cassio, by that handkerchief
That was my wife's?

CASSIO
    I found it in my chamber:
And he himself confess'd but even now
That there he dropp'd it for a special purpose
Which wrought to his desire.

OTHELLO
    O fool! fool! fool!

CASSIO
There is besides in Roderigo's letter, —
How he upbraids Iago, that he made him
Brave me upon the watch; whereon it came
That I was cast: and even but now he spake,
After long seeming dead, — Iago hurt him,
Iago set him on.

LODOVICO
You must forsake this room, and go with us:
Your power and your command is taken off,
And Cassio rules in Cyprus. For this slave,
If there be any cunning cruelty
That can torment him much and hold him long,
It shall be his. You shall close prisoner rest,
Till that the nature of your fault be known
To the Venetian state. — Come, bring him away.

OTHELLO
Soft you; a word or two before you go.
I have done the state some service, and they know't; —
No more of that. — I pray you, in your letters,
When you shall these unlucky deeds relate,
Speak of me as I am; nothing extenuate,
Nor set down aught in malice: then must you speak
Of one that lov'd not wisely, but too well;
Of one not easily jealous, but, being wrought,
Perplex'd in the extreme; of one whose hand,
Like the base Indian, threw a pearl away
Richer than all his tribe; of one whose subdued eyes,
Albeit unused to the melting mood,
Drop tears as fast as the Arabian trees
Their medicinable gum. Set you down this;
And say besides, that in Aleppo once,
Where a malignant and a turban'd Turk
Beat a Venetian and traduc'd the state,
I took by th'throat the circumcised dog,
And smote him — thus. [*He stabs himself.*

LODOVICO
O bloody period!

GRATIANO
    All that's spoke is marr'd.

OTHELLO
I kiss'd thee ere I kill'd thee: no way but this,
[*Falling upon* DESDEMONA.
Killing myself, to die upon a kiss.   [*Dies.*

CASSIO
This did I fear, but thought he had no weapon;
For he was great of heart.

LODOVICO [*to* IAGO].
    O Spartan dog,
More fell than anguish, hunger, or the sea!
Look on the tragic loading of this bed;
This is thy work: the object poisons sight;
Let it be hid. Gratiano, keep the house,
And seize upon the fortunes of the Moor,
For they succeed on you. To you, lord governor,
Remains the censure of this hellish villain;
The time, the place, the torture. O, enforce it!
Myself will straight aboard, and to the state
This heavy act with heavy heart relate. [*Exeunt.*

MACBETH

DRAMATIS PERSONAE

DUNCAN, *King of Scotland.*
MALCOLM, }
DONALBAIN, } *his sons.*
MACBETH, }
BANQUO, } *generals of the King's army.*
MACDUFF, }
LENNOX, }
ROSS, }
MENTEITH, } *noblemen of Scotland.*
ANGUS, }
CAITHNESS, }
FLEANCE, *son of Banquo.*

SIWARD, *Earl of Northumberland, general of the English forces.*
YOUNG SIWARD, *his son.*
SEYTON, *an officer attending on Macbeth.*
BOY, *son to Macduff.*
AN ENGLISH DOCTOR.

A SCOTCH DOCTOR.
A SERGEANT.
A PORTER.
AN OLD MAN.

LADY MACBETH.
LADY MACDUFF.

GENTLEWOMAN *attending on Lady Macbeth.*

HECATE.
THREE WITCHES.
APPARITIONS.

LORDS, GENTLEMEN, OFFICERS, SOLDIERS,
  MURDERERS, ATTENDANTS, *and*
  MESSENGERS.

SCENE — *in the end of the fourth Act in England;
  through the rest of the play in Scotland.*

ACT I

SCENE I

An open place.

Thunder and lightning. Enter three WITCHES.

FIRST WITCH
When shall we three meet again
In thunder, lightning, or in rain?
SECOND WITCH
When the hurlyburly's done,
When the battle's lost and won.
THIRD WITCH
That will be ere the set of sun.
FIRST WITCH
Where the place?
SECOND WITCH
                    Upon the heath.
THIRD WITCH
There to meet with Macbeth.
FIRST WITCH
I come, Graymalkin!
SECOND WITCH
Paddock calls: — anon!
ALL
Fair is foul, and foul is fair;
Hover through the fog and filthy air.   [*Exeunt.*

SCENE II

A camp near Forres.

Alarum within. Enter DUNCAN, MALCOLM,
DONALBAIN, LENNOX, *with* ATTENDANTS,
meeting a bleeding SERGEANT.

DUNCAN
What bloody man is that? He can report,
As seemeth by his plight, of the revolt
The newest state.
MALCOLM
                    This is the sergeant,
Who, like a good and hardy soldier, fought
'Gainst my captivity. — Hail, brave friend!
Say to the king thy knowledge of the broil
As thou didst leave it.
SERGEANT
                    Doubtful it stood;
As two spent swimmers, that do cling together
And choke their art. The merciless Macdonwald —
Worthy to be a rebel, for, to that,
The multiplying villainies of nature
Do swarm upon him — from the western isles
Of kerns and gallowglasses is supplied;
And fortune, on his damned quarrel smiling,
Show'd like a rebel's whore: but all's too weak:
For brave Macbeth, — well he deserves that name, —
Disdaining fortune, with his brandish'd steel,
Which smok'd with bloody execution,
Like valour's minion,
Carv'd out his passage till he fac'd the slave;
Which ne'er shook hands, nor bade farewell to him,
Till he unseam'd him from the nave to th'chops,
And fix'd his head upon our battlements.
DUNCAN
O valiant cousin! worthy gentleman!
SERGEANT
As whence the sun 'gins his reflection

Shipwracking storms and direful thunders break;
So from that spring, whence comfort seem'd to come,
Discomfort swells. Mark, King of Scotland, mark:
No sooner justice had, with valour arm'd,
Compell'd these skipping kerns to trust their heels,
But the Norweyan lord, surveying vantage,
With furbish'd arms and new supplies of men,
Began a fresh assault.
DUNCAN
                    Dismay'd not this
Our captains, Macbeth and Banquo?
SERGEANT
                                    Yes;
As sparrows eagles, or the hare the lion.
If I say sooth, I must report they were
As cannons overcharg'd with double cracks;
So they
Doubly redoubled strokes upon the foe:
Except they meant to bathe in reeking wounds,
Or memorise another Golgotha,
I cannot tell: —
But I am faint, my gashes cry for help.
DUNCAN
So well thy words become thee as thy wounds;
They smack of honour both. — Go get him surgeons.
                              [*Exit* SERGEANT, *attended.*
Who comes here?

            Enter ROSS.

MALCOLM
                    The worthy thane of Ross.
LENNOX
What haste looks through his eyes! So should he look
That seems to speak things strange.
ROSS
                              God save the king!
DUNCAN
Whence camest thou, worthy thane?

ROSS
                              From Fife, great king;
Where the Norweyan banners flout the sky
And fan our people cold. Norway himself,
With terrible numbers,
Assisted by that most disloyal traitor
The thane of Cawdor, began a dismal conflict;
Till that Bellona's bridegroom, lapp'd in proof,
Confronted him with self-comparisons,
Point against point rebellious, arm 'gainst arm,
Curbing his lavish spirit: and, to conclude,
The victory fell on us.
DUNCAN
                    Great happiness!
ROSS
That now
Sweno, the Norways' king, craves composition;
Nor would we deign him burial of his men
Till he disbursed, at Saint Colme's-inch,
Ten thousand dollars to our general use.
DUNCAN
No more that thane of Cawdor shall deceive
Our bosom interest: — go pronounce his present
  death,
And with his former title greet Macbeth.
ROSS
I'll see it done.
DUNCAN
What he hath lost noble Macbeth hath won.   [*Exeunt.*

SCENE III

A heath.

Thunder. Enter the three WITCHES.

FIRST WITCH
Where hast thou been, sister?
SECOND WITCH
Killing swine.
THIRD WITCH
Sister, where thou?
FIRST WITCH
A sailor's wife had chestnuts in her lap,
And munch'd, and munch'd, and munch'd: — 'Give
  me,' quoth I:
'Aroint thee, witch!' the rump-fed ronyon cries.
Her husband's to Aleppo gone, master o'th'Tiger:
But in a sieve I'll thither sail,
And, like a rat without a tail,
I'll do, I'll do, and I'll do.
SECOND WITCH
I'll give thee a wind.
FIRST WITCH
Th'art kind.
THIRD WITCH
And I another.
FIRST WITCH
I myself have all the other;
And the very ports they blow,
All the quarters that they know
I'th'shipman's card.
I will drain him dry as hay:
Sleep shall neither night nor day
Hang upon his pent-house lid;
He shall live a man forbid:
Weary se'nnights nine times nine
Shall he dwindle, peak, and pine:
Though his bark cannot be lost,

ALL The weird sisters, hand in hand.

Yet it shall be tempest-toss'd. —
Look what I have.
SECOND WITCH
Show me, show me.
FIRST WITCH
Here I have a pilot's thumb,
Wrack'd as homeward he did come.   [*Drum within.*
THIRD WITCH
A drum, a drum!
Macbeth doth come.
ALL
The weird sisters, hand in hand,
Posters of the sea and land,
Thus do go about, about:
Thrice to thine, and thrice to mine,
And thrice again, to make up nine: —
Peace! — the charm's wound up.
    Enter MACBETH *and* BANQUO; SOLDIERS *at some*
                    distance.

MACBETH
So foul and fair a day I have not seen.
BANQUO
How far is't call'd to Forres? — What are these
So wither'd, and so wild in their attire,
That look not like th'inhabitants o'th'earth,
And yet are on't? — Live you? or are you aught
That man may question? You seem to understand me,
By each at once her choppy finger laying
Upon her skinny lips: — you should be women,
And yet your beards forbid me to interpret
That you are so.
MACBETH
            Speak, if you can; — what are you?
FIRST WITCH
All hail, Macbeth! hail to thee, thane of Glamis!
SECOND WITCH
All hail, Macbeth! hail to thee, thane of Cawdor!
THIRD WITCH
All hail, Macbeth, that shalt be king hereafter!
BANQUO
Good sir, why do you start; and seem to fear
Things that do sound so fair? — I' th'name of truth,
Are ye fantastical, or that indeed
Which outwardly ye show? My noble partner
You greet with present grace, and great prediction
Of noble having and of royal hope,
That he seems rapt withal: — to me you speak not:
If you can look into the seeds of time,

And say which grain will grow, and which will not,
Speak, then, to me, who neither beg nor fear
Your favours nor your hate.
FIRST WITCH
Hail!
SECOND WITCH
Hail!
THIRD WITCH
Hail!
FIRST WITCH
Lesser than Macbeth, and greater.
SECOND WITCH
Not so happy, yet much happier.
THIRD WITCH
Thou shalt get kings, though thou be none:
So, all hail, Macbeth and Banquo!
FIRST WITCH
Banquo and Macbeth, all hail!
MACBETH
Stay, you imperfect speakers, tell me more:
By Sinel's death I know I am thane of Glamis;
But how of Cawdor? the thane of Cawdor lives,
A prosperous gentleman; and to be king
Stands not within the prospect of belief,
No more than to be Cawdor. Say from whence
You owe this strange intelligence? or why
Upon this blasted heath you stop our way
With such prophetic greeting? Speak, I charge you.
                                [WITCHES *vanish.*
BANQUO
The earth hath bubbles, as the water has,
And these are of them: — whither are they vanish'd?
MACBETH
Into the air; and what seem'd corporal melted
As breath into the wind. — Would they had stay'd!
BANQUO
Were such things here as we do speak about?
Or have we eaten on the insane root
That takes the reason prisoner?
MACBETH
Your children shall be kings.
BANQUO
                        You shall be king.
MACBETH
And thane of Cawdor too, — went it not so?
BANQUO
To th'selfsame tune and words. — Who's here?
                Enter ROSS *and* ANGUS.

ROSS
The king hath happily received, Macbeth,
The news of thy success: and when he reads
Thy personal venture in the rebels' fight,
His wonders and his praises do contend
Which should be thine or his: silenc'd with that,
In viewing o'er the rest o'th'selfsame day,
He finds thee in the stout Norweyan ranks,
Nothing afeard of what thyself didst make,
Strange images of death. As thick as hail
Came post with post; and every one did bear
Thy praises in his kingdom's great defence,
And pour'd them down before him.
ANGUS
                        We are sent
To give thee, from our royal master, thanks;
Only to herald thee into his sight, not pay thee.
ROSS
And, for an earnest of a greater honour,
He bade me, from him, call thee thane of Cawdor:
In which addition, hail, most worthy thane!
For it is thine.
BANQUO [*aside*].
What, can the devil speak true?
MACBETH
The thane of Cawdor lives: why do you dress me

In borrow'd robes?
ANGUS
                Who was the thane; lives yet:
But under heavy judgement bears that life
Which he deserves to lose. Whether he was combin'd
With those of Norway, or did line the rebel
With hidden help and vantage, or that with both
He labour'd in his country's wrack, I know not;
But treasons capital, confess'd and proved,
Have overthrown him.
MACBETH [*aside*].
                Glamis, and thane of Cawdor!
The greatest is behind. — [*to* ROSS *and* ANGUS]
    Thanks for your pains. —
[*aside to* BANQUO] Do you not hope your children
    shall be kings,
When those that gave the thane of Cawdor to me
Promis'd no less to them?
BANQUO [*aside to* MACBETH].
                    That, trusted home,
Might yet enkindle you unto the crown,
Besides the thane of Cawdor. But 'tis strange:
And oftentimes, to win us to our harm,
The instruments of darkness tell us truths,
Win us with honest trifles, to betray's
In deepest consequence. —
Cousins, a word, I pray you.
MACBETH [*aside*].
                    Two truths are told,
As happy prologues to the swelling act
Of the imperial theme. — I thank you, gentlemen. —
[*aside*] This supernatural soliciting
Cannot be ill, cannot be good: — if ill,
Why hath it given me earnest of success,
Commencing in a truth? I am thane of Cawdor:
If good, why do I yield to that suggestion
Whose horrid image doth unfix my hair,
And make my seated heart knock at my ribs,
Against the use of nature? Present fears
Are less than horrible imaginings:
My thought, whose murder yet is but fantastical,
Shakes so my single state of man, that function
Is smother'd in surmise; and nothing is
But what is not.
BANQUO
                Look, how our partner's rapt.
MACBETH [*aside*].
If chance will have me king, why, chance may crown me,
Without my stir.
BANQUO
                New honours come upon him,
Like our strange garments, cleave not to their mould
But with the aid of use.
MACBETH [*aside*].
                Come what come may,
Time and the hour runs through the roughest day.
BANQUO
Worthy Macbeth, we stay upon your leisure.
MACBETH
Give me your favour: — my dull brain was wrought
With things forgotten. Kind gentlemen, your pains
Are register'd where every day I turn
The leaf to read them. — Let us toward the king. —
[*aside to* BANQUO] Think upon what hath chanc'd;
    and, at more time,
The interim having weigh'd it, let us speak
Our free hearts each to other.
BANQUO [*aside to* MACBETH].
                        Very gladly.
MACBETH [*aside to* BANQUO].
    Till then, enough. — Come, friends.   [*Exeunt.*

SCENE IV
Forres. A room in the palace.

Flourish. Enter DUNCAN, MALCOLM, DONALBAIN,
    LENNOX, *and* ATTENDANTS.

DUNCAN
Is execution done on Cawdor? Are not
Those in commission yet return'd?
MALCOLM
                        My liege,
They are not yet come back. But I have spoke
With one that saw him die: who did report,
That very frankly he confess'd his treasons;
Implor'd your highness' pardon; and set forth
A deep repentance: nothing in his life
Became him like the leaving it; he died
As one that had been studied in his death
To throw away the dearest thing he owed,

As 'twere a careless trifle.

DUNCAN
There's no art
To find the mind's construction in the face:
He was a gentleman on whom I built
An absolute trust.

Enter MACBETH, BANQUO, ROSS, *and* ANGUS.
O worthiest cousin!
The sin of my ingratitude even now
Was heavy on me: thou art so far before,
That swiftest wing of recompense is slow
To overtake thee. Would thou hadst less deserv'd,
That the proportion both of thanks and payment
Might have been mine! only I have left to say,
More is thy due than more than all can pay.

MACBETH
The service and the loyalty I owe,
In doing it, pays itself. Your highness' part
Is to receive our duties; and our duties
Are to your throne and state children and servants;
Which do but what they should by doing every thing
Safe toward your love and honour.

DUNCAN
Welcome hither:
I have begun to plant thee, and will labour
To make thee full of growing. — Noble Banquo,
That hast no less deserv'd, nor must be known
No less to have done so; let me enfold thee
And hold thee to my heart.

BANQUO
There if I grow,
The harvest is your own.

DUNCAN
My plenteous joys,
Wanton in fulness, seek to hide themselves
In drops of sorrow. — Sons, kinsmen, thanes,
And you whose places are the nearest, know,
We will establish our estate upon
Our eldest, Malcolm; whom we name hereafter
The Prince of Cumberland: which honour must
Not unaccompanied invest him only,
But signs of nobleness, like stars, shall shine
On all deservers. — From hence to Inverness,
And bind us further to you.

MACBETH
The rest is labour, which is not us'd for you:
I'll be myself the harbinger, and make joyful
The hearing of my wife with your approach:
So, humbly take my leave.

DUNCAN
My worthy Cawdor!

MACBETH [*aside*].
The Prince of Cumberland! that is a step
On which I must fall down, or else I o'erleap,
For in my way it lies. Stars, hide your fires;
Let not light see my black and deep desires:
The eye wink at the hand; yet let that be,
Which the eye fears, when it is done, to see. [*Exit.*

DUNCAN
True, worthy Banquo, — he is full so valiant;
And in his commendations I am fed, —
It is a banquet to me. Let's after him,
Whose care is gone before to bid us welcome:
It is a peerless kinsman. [*Flourish. Exeunt.*

SCENE V

Inverness. A room in MACBETH'S *castle.*

Enter LADY MACBETH *alone, with a letter.*

LADY MACBETH
'They met me in the day of success; and I have learn'd
by the perfect'st report, they have more in them than
mortal knowledge. When I burnt in desire to question
them further, they made themselves air, into which
they vanish'd. Whiles I stood rapt in the wonder of it,
came missives from the king, who all-hail'd me "Thane
of Cawdor"; by which title, before, these weird sisters
saluted me, and referr'd me to the coming on of time,
with "Hail, king that shalt be!" This have I thought
good to deliver thee, my dearest partner of greatness,
that thou mightst not lose the dues of rejoicing, by
being ignorant of what greatness is promised thee. Lay
it to thy heart, and farewell.'
Glamis thou art, and Cawdor, and shalt be
What thou art promis'd: yet do I fear thy nature;
It is too full o'th' milk of human kindness
To catch the nearest way: thou wouldst be great;
Art not without ambition; but without
The illness should attend it: what thou wouldst highly,
That wouldst thou holily; wouldst not play false,
And yet wouldst wrongly win: thou'ldst have,

great Glamis,
That which cries 'Thus thou must do, if thou
have it;
And that which rather thou dost fear to do
Than wishest should be undone.' Hie thee
hither,
That I may pour my spirits in thine ear;
And chastise with the valour of my tongue
All that impedes thee from the golden round,
Which fate and metaphysical aid doth seem
To have thee crown'd withal.

Enter a MESSENGER.
What is your tidings?

MESSENGER
The king comes here to-night.

LADY MACBETH
Thou'rt mad to say it:
Is not thy master with him? who, were't so,
Would have inform'd for preparation.

MESSENGER
So please you, it is true: — our thane is coming:
One of my fellows had the speed of him;
Who, almost dead for breath, had scarcely more
Than would make up his message.

LADY MACBETH
Give him tending;
He brings great news. [*Exit* MESSENGER.
The raven himself is hoarse
That croaks the fatal entrance of Duncan
Under my battlements. Come, you spirits
That tend on mortal thoughts, unsex me here;
And fill me, from the crown to the toe, top-full
Of direst cruelty! make thick my blood,
Stop up th'access and passage to remorse,
That no compunctious visitings of nature
Shake my fell purpose, nor keep peace between
Th'effect and it! Come to my woman's breasts,
And take my milk for gall, you murd'ring
ministers,
Wherever in your sightless substances
You wait on nature's mischief! Come, thick night,
And pall thee in the dunnest smoke of hell,
That my keen knife see not the wound it makes,
Nor heaven peep through the blanket of the dark,
To cry 'Hold, hold!'

Enter MACBETH.
Great Glamis! worthy Cawdor!
Greater than both, by the all-hail hereafter!
Thy letters have transported me beyond
This ignorant present, and I feel now
The future in the instant.

MACBETH
My dearest love.
Duncan comes here to-night.

LADY MACBETH
And when goes hence?

MACBETH
To-morrow, as he purposes.

LADY MACBETH
O, never
Shall sun that morrow see!
Your face, my thane, is as a book where men
May read strange matters: — to beguile the time,
Look like the time; bear welcome in your eye,
Your hand, your tongue: look like the innocent flower,
But be the serpent under't. He that's coming
Must be provided for: and you shall put
This night's great business into my dispatch;
Which shall to all our nights and days to come
Give solely sovereign sway and masterdom.

MACBETH
We will speak further.

LADY MACBETH
Only look up clear;
To alter favour ever is to fear:
Leave all the rest to me. [*Exeunt.*

SCENE VI

The same. Before MACBETH'S *castle.*

Hautboys and torches. Enter DUNCAN, MALCOLM,
DONALBAIN, BANQUO, LENNOX, MACDUFF,
ROSS, ANGUS, *and* ATTENDANTS.

DUNCAN
This castle hath a pleasant seat; the air
Nimbly and sweetly recommends itself
Unto our gentle senses.

BANQUO
This guest of summer,
The temple-haunting martlet, does approve,

MACBETH By Sinel's death I know I am
Thane of Glamis.

By his lov'd mansionry, that the heavens' breath
Smells wooingly here: no jutty, frieze,
Buttress, nor coign of vantage, but this bird
Hath made his pendent bed and procreant cradle:
Where they most breed and haunt, I have observ'd
The air is delicate.

Enter LADY MACBETH.

DUNCAN
See, see, our honour'd hostess! —
The love that follows us sometime is our trouble,
Which still we thank as love. Herein I teach you
Now you shall bid God 'ild us for your pains,
And thank us for your trouble.

LADY MACBETH
All our service
In every point twice done, and then done double,
Were poor and single business to contend
Against those honours deep and broad wherewith
Your majesty loads our house: for those of old,
And the late dignities heap'd up to them,
We rest your hermits.

DUNCAN
Where's the thane of Cawdor?
We cours'd him at the heels, and had a purpose
To be his purveyor: but he rides well;
And his great love, sharp as his spur, hath holp him
To his home before us. Fair and noble hostess,
We are your guest to-night.

LADY MACBETH
Your servants ever
Have theirs, themselves, and what is theirs, in compt,
To make their audit at your highness' pleasure,
Still to return your own.

DUNCAN
Give me your hand;
Conduct me to mine host: we love him highly,
And shall continue our graces towards him.
By your leave, hostess. [*Exeunt.*

SCENE VII

The same. A lobby in MACBETH'S *castle.*

Hautboys and torches. Enter a SEWER, *and divers*
SERVANTS *with dishes and service, over the stage.*
Then enter MACBETH.

MACBETH
If it were done — when 'tis done — then 'twere well
It were done quickly: if th'assassination
Could trammel up the consequence, and catch,
With his surcease, success; that but this blow
Might be the be-all and the end-all here,
But here, upon this bank and shoal of time,

LADY MACBETH That my keen knife see not the
wound it makes.

We'ld jump the life to come. But in these cases
We still have judgement here; that we but teach
Bloody instructions, which, being taught, return
To plague th'inventor: this even-handed justice
Commends th'ingredients of our poison'd chaice
To our own lips. He's here in double trust:
First, as I am his kinsman and his subject,
Strong both against the deed; then, as his host,
Who should against his murderer shut the door,
Not bear the knife myself. Besides, this Duncan
Hath borne his faculties so meek, hath been
So clear in his great office, that his virtues
Will plead like angels, trumpet-tongued, against
The deep damnation of his taking-off;
And pity, like a naked new-born babe,
Striding the blast, or heaven's cherubin, hors'd
Upon the sightless couriers of the air,
Shall blow the horrid deed in every eye,
That tears shall drown the wind, — I have no spur
To prick the sides of my intent, but only
Vaulting ambition, which o'erleaps'tself,
And falls on th'other.

     Enter LADY MACBETH.
       How now! what news?

LADY MACBETH
He has almost supp'd: why have you left the chamber?
MACBETH
Hath he ask'd for me?
LADY MACBETH
       Know you not he has?
MACBETH
We will proceed no further in this business:
He hath honour'd me of late; and I have bought
Golden opinions from all sorts of people,
Which would be worn now in their newest gloss,
Not cast aside so soon.
LADY MACBETH
       Was the hope drunk
Wherein you dress'd yourself? hath it slept since?
And wakes it now, to look so green and pale
At what it did so freely? From this time
Such I account thy love. Art thou afeard
To be the same in thine own act and valour
As thou art in desire? Wouldst thou have that
Which thou esteem'st the ornament of life,
And live a coward in thine own esteem,
Letting 'I dare not' wait upon 'I would',
Like the poor cat i'th'adage?
MACBETH
       Prithee, peace:
I dare do all that may become a man;
Who dares do more is none.
LADY MACBETH
       What beast was't, then,
That made you break this enterprise to me?

When you durst do it, then you were a man;
And, to be more than what you were, you would
Be so much more the man. Nor time nor place
Did then adhere, and yet you would make both:
They have made themselves, and that their fitness now
Does unmake you. I have given suck, and know
How tender 'tis to love the babe that milks me:
I would, while it was smiling in my face,
Have pluck'd my nipple from his boneless gums,
And dash'd the brains out, had I so sworn as you
Have done to this.
MACBETH
       If we should fail?
LADY MACBETH
       We fail:
But screw your courage to the sticking-place,
And we'll not fail. When Duncan is asleep, —
Whereto the rather shall his day's hard journey
Soundly invite him, — his two chamberlains
Will I with wine and wassail so convince,
That memory, the warder of the brain,
Shall be a fume, and the receipt of reason
A limbeck only: when in swinish sleep
Their drenched natures lie as in a death,
What cannot you and I perform upon
Th'unguarded Duncan? what not put upon
His spongy officers, who shall bear the guilt
Of our great quell?
MACBETH
       Bring forth men-children only;
For thy undaunted mettle should compose
Nothing but males. Will it not be receiv'd,
When we have mark'd with blood those sleepy two
Of his own chamber, and us'd their very daggers,
That they have done't?
LADY MACBETH
       Who dares receive it other,
As we shall make our griefs and clamour roar.
Upon his death?
MACBETH
       I am settled, and bend up
Each corporal agent to this terrible feat.
Away, and mock the time with fairest show:
False face must hide what the false heart doth know.
                 [*Exeunt.*

ACT II

SCENE I

Inverness. Court of MACBETH'S *castle.*

Enter BANQUO, *and* FLEANCE *with a
torch before him.*

BANQUO
How goes the night, boy?
FLEANCE
The moon is down; I have not heard the clock.
BANQUO
And she goes down at twelve.
FLEANCE
       I take't, 'tis later, sir.
BANQUO
Hold, take my sword: — there's husbandry in heaven,
Their candles are all out: — take thee that too. —
A heavy summons lies like lead upon me,
And yet I would not sleep: — merciful powers,
Restrain in me the cursed thoughts that nature
Gives way to in repose! — Give me my sword. —

Who's there?
    Enter MACBETH, *and a* SERVANT *with a torch.*
MACBETH
A friend.
BANQUO
What, sir, not yet at rest? The king's a-bed:
He hath been in unusual pleasure, and
Sent forth great largess to your officers:
This diamond he greets your wife withal,
By the name of most kind hostess; and shut up
In measureless content.
MACBETH
       Being unprepared,
Our will became the servant to defect;
Which else should free have wrought.
BANQUO
       All's well. —
I dreamt last night of the three weird sisters:
To you they have show'd some truth.
MACBETH
       I think not of them:
Yet, when we can entreat an hour to serve,
We would spend it in some words upon that business,
If you would grant the time.
BANQUO
       At your kind'st leisure.
MACBETH
If you shall cleave to my consent, — when 'tis,
It shall make honour for you.
BANQUO
       So I lose none
In seeking to augment it, but still keep
My bosom franchis'd, and allegiance clear,
I shall be counsell'd.
MACBETH
       Good repose the while!
BANQUO
Thanks, sir: the like to you!
       [*Exeunt* BANQUO *and* FLEANCE.
MACBETH
Go bid thy mistress, when my drink is ready,
She strike upon the bell. Get thee to bed.
       [*Exit* SERVANT.
Is this a dagger which I see before me,
The handle toward my hand? Come, let me clutch thee: —
   I have thee not, and yet I see thee still.
Art thou not, fatal vision, sensible
To feeling as to sight? or art thou but
A dagger of the mind, a false creation,
Proceeding from the heat-oppressed brain?
I see thee yet, in form as palpable
As this which now I draw.
Thou marshall'st me the way that I was
   going;
And such an instrument I was to use.
Mine eyes are made the fools o'th'other
   senses,
Or else worth all the rest: I see thee still;
And on thy blade and dudgeon gouts of
   blood,
Which was not so before. — There's no
   such thing:
It is the bloody business which informs
Thus to mine eyes. — Now o'er the one
   half-world
Nature seems dead, and wicked dreams abuse
The curtain'd sleep; now witchcraft celebrates
Pale Hecate's offerings; and wither'd murder,
Alarum'd by his sentinel, the wolf,
Whose howl's his watch, thus with his stealthy pace,
With Tarquin's ravishing strides, towards his design
Moves like a ghost. — Thou sure and firm-set earth,
Hear not my steps, which way they walk, for fear
Thy very stones prate of my whereabout,
And take the present horror from the time,
Which now suits with it. — Whiles I threat, he lives:
Words to the heat of deeds too cold breath gives.
       [*A bell rings.*
I go, and it is done; the bell invites me.
Hear it not, Duncan; for it is a knell
That summons thee to heaven or to hell.   [*Exit.*

SCENE II

The same.

Enter LADY MACBETH.

LADY MACBETH
That which hath made them drunk hath made me bold;
What hath quench'd them hath given me fire. — Hark!
  — Peace!

was the owl that shriek'd, the fatal bellman,
Which gives the stern'st good-night. — He is about it:
The doors are open; and the surfeited grooms
Do mock their charge with snores: I have drugg'd their
   possets,
That death and nature do contend about them,
Whether they live or die.

MACBETH [*within*].
                Who's there? what, ho!

LADY MACBETH
Alack, I am afraid they have awak'd,
And 'tis not done: — th'attempt, and not the deed,
Confounds us. — Hark! — I laid their daggers ready;
He could not miss 'em. — Had he not resembled
My father as he slept, I had done't. — My husband!

        Enter MACBETH.

MACBETH
I have done the deed. — Didst thou not hear a noise?

LADY MACBETH
I heard the owl scream and the crickets cry.
Did not you speak?

MACBETH
       When?

LADY MACBETH
         Now.

MACBETH
          As I descended?

LADY MACBETH
Ay.

MACBETH
Hark! —
Who lies i'th'second chamber?

LADY MACBETH
           Donalbain.

MACBETH
This is a sorry sight. [*Looking on his hands.*

LADY MACBETH
A foolish thought, to say a sorry sight.

MACBETH
There's one did laugh in's sleep, and one cried
   'Murder!'
That they did wake each other: I stood and heard them:
But they did say their prayers, and address'd them
Again to sleep.

LADY MACBETH
    There are two lodg'd together.

MACBETH
One cried 'God bless us!' and 'Amen!' the other;
As they had seen me, with these hangman's hands.
Listening their fear, I could not say 'Amen!'
When they did say 'God bless us!'

LADY MACBETH
         Consider it not so deeply.

MACBETH
But wherefore could not I pronounce 'Amen'?
I had most need of blessing, and 'Amen'
Stuck in my throat.

LADY MACBETH
       These deeds must not be thought
After these ways; so, it will make us mad.

MACBETH
Methought I heard a voice cry, 'Sleep no more!
Macbeth does murder sleep,' — the innocent sleep,
Sleep that knits up the ravell'd sleave of care,
The death of each day's life, sore labour's bath,
Balm of hurt minds, great nature's second course,
Chief nourisher in life's feast, —

LADY MACBETH
         What do you mean?

MACBETH
Still it cried 'Sleep no more!' to all the house:
'Glamis hath murder'd sleep, and therefore Cawdor
Shall sleep no more — Macbeth shall sleep no more!'

LADY MACBETH
Who was it that thus cried? Why, worthy thane,
You do unbend your noble strength, to think
So brainsickly of things. — Go get some water,
And wash this filthy witness from your hand. —
Why did you bring these daggers from the place?
They must lie there: go carry them, and smear
The sleepy grooms with blood.

MACBETH
         I'll go no more:
I am afraid to think what I have done;
Look on't again I dare not.

LADY MACBETH
        Infirm of purpose!
Give me the daggers: the sleeping and the dead

Are but as pictures: 'tis the eye of childhood
That fears a painted devil. If he do bleed,
I'll gild the faces of the grooms withal;
For it must seem their guilt. [*Exit. Knock within.*

MACBETH
        Whence is that knocking?
How is't with me, when every noise appals me?
What hands are here? ha! they pluck out mine eyes!
Will all great Neptune's ocean wash this blood
Clean from my hand? No; this my hand will rather
The multitudinous seas incarnadine,
Making the green one red.

        Enter LADY MACBETH.

LADY MACBETH
My hands are of your colour; but I shame
To wear a heart so white. [*Knock.*] I hear a knocking
At the south entry: — retire we to our chamber:
A little water clears us of this deed:
How easy is it, then! Your constancy
Hath left you unattended. — [*Knock.*] Hark! more
   knocking:
Get on your nightgown, lest occasion call us,
And show us to be watchers: — be not lost
So poorly in your thoughts.

MACBETH
To know my deed, 'twere best not know myself. [*Knock.*
Wake Duncan with thy knocking! I would thou couldst!
                    [*Exeunt.*

SCENE III

The same.

Enter a PORTER. *Knocking within.*

PORTER
Here's a knocking indeed! If a man were porter of
hell-gate, he should have old turning the key. —
[*Knock.*] Knock, knock, knock! Who's there, i'th'name
of Belzebub? Here's a farmer that hang'd himself on
th'expectation of plenty: come in time; have napkins
enow about you; here you'll sweat for't. [*Knock.*] Knock,
knock! Who's there, i'th'other devil's name? Faith,
here's an equivocator that could swear in both the
scales against either scale; who committed treason
enough for God's sake, yet could not equivocate to
heaven: O, come in, equivocator. — [*Knock.*] Knock,
knock, knock! Who's there? Faith, here's an English
tailor come hither, for stealing out of a French hose:
come in, tailor; here you may roast your goose. —
[*knock.*] Knock, knock; never at quiet! What are you? —
But this place is too cold for hell. I'll devil-porter it no
further: I had thought to have let in some of all
professions, that go the primrose way to th'everlasting
bonfire. — [*Knock.*] Anon, anon! I pray you, remember
the porter. [*Opens the gate.*

    Enter MACDUFF *and* LENNOX.

MACDUFF
Was it so late, friend, ere you went to bed,
That you do lie so late?

PORTER
Faith, sir, we were carousing till the second cock: and
drink, sir, is a great provoker of three things.

MACDUFF
What three things does drink especially provoke?

PORTER
Marry, sir, nose-painting, sleep, and urine. Lechery,
sir, it provokes, and unprovokes; it provokes the desire,
but it takes away the performance: therefore, much
drink may be said to be an equivocator with lechery: it
makes him, and it mars him; it sets him on, and it takes
him off; it persuades him, and disheartens him; makes
him stand to, and not stand to; in conclusion,
equivocates him in a sleep, and, giving him the lie,
leaves him.

MACDUFF
I believe drink gave thee the lie last night.

PORTER
That it did, sir, i'the very throat on me: but I requited
him for his lie; and, I think, being too strong for him,
though he took up my legs sometime, yet I made a shift
to cast him.

MACDUFF
Is thy master stirring? —
Our knocking has awak'd him; here he comes.

    Enter MACBETH.

LENNOX
Good morrow, noble sir.

MACBETH
       Good morrow, both.

MACDUFF
Is the king stirring, worthy thane?

MACBETH
       Not yet.

MACDUFF
He did command me to call timely on him:
I have almost slipp'd the hour.

MACBETH
       I'll bring you to him.

MACDUFF
I know this is a joyful trouble to you;
But yet 'tis one.

MACBETH
The labour we delight in physics pain.
This is the door.

MACDUFF
       I'll make so bold to call,
For 'tis my limited service. [*Exit.*

LENNOX
Goes the king hence to-day?

MACBETH
       He does: he did appoint so.

LENNOX
The night has been unruly: where we lay,
Our chimneys were blown down; and, as they say,
Lamentings heard i'th'air; strange screams of death;
And prophesying, with accents terrible,
Of dire combustion and confus'd events
New hatch'd to th'woeful time: the obscure bird
Clamour'd the livelong night: some say, the earth
Was feverous and did shake.

MACBETH
       'Twas a rough night.

LENNOX
My young remembrance cannot parallel
A fellow to it.

      Enter MACDUFF.

MACDUFF
O horror, horror, horror! Tongue nor heart
Cannot conceive nor name thee!

      MACBETH *and* LENNOX.

What's the matter?

MACDUFF
Confusion now hath made his masterpiece!
Most sacrilegious murder hath broke ope
The Lord's anointed temple, and stole thence
The life o'th'building!

MACBETH
       What is't you say? the life?

LENNOX
Mean you his majesty?

MACDUFF
Approach the chamber, and destroy your sight
With a new Gorgon: — do not bid me speak;
See, and then speak yourselves.
        [*Exeunt* MACBETH *and* LENNOX.
           Awake, awake! —
Ring the alarum-bell — murder and treason! —
Banquo and Donalbain! Malcolm! awake!
Shake off this downy sleep, death's counterfeit,
And look on death itself! up, up, and see
The great doom's image! Malcolm! Banquo!
As from your graves rise up, and walk like sprites,
To countenance this horror! [*Bell rings.*

      Enter LADY MACBETH.

LADY MACBETH
       What's the business,
That such a hideous trumpet calls to parley
The sleepers of the house? speak, speak!

MACDUFF
       O gentle lady,
'Tis not for you to hear what I can speak:
The repetition, in a woman's ear,
Would murder as it fell.

      Enter BANQUO.
       O Banquo, Banquo,
Our royal master's murder'd!

LADY MACBETH
       Woe, alas!
What, in our house?

BANQUO
       Too cruel any where. —
Dear Duff, I prithee, contradict thyself,
And say it is not so.

     Enter MACBETH, LENNOX, *and* ROSS.

LADY MACBETH Give me the daggers.

MACBETH
Had I but died an hour before this chance,
I had liv'd a blessed time; for, from this instant,
There's nothing serious in mortality:
All is but toys: renown and grace is dead;
The wine of life is drawn, and the mere lees
Is left this vault to brag of.

Enter MALCOLM and DONALBAIN.

DONALBAIN
What is amiss?

MACBETH
                    You are, and do not know't:
The spring, the head, the fountain of your blood
Is stopp'd, — the very source of it is stopp'd.

MACDUFF
Your royal father's murder'd.

MALCOLM
                    O, by whom?

LENNOX
Those of his chamber, as it seem'd, had done't:
Their hands and faces were all badg'd with blood;
So were their daggers, which, unwip'd, we found
Upon their pillows:
They stared, and were distracted; no man's life
Was to be trusted with them.

MACBETH
O, yet I do repent me of my fury,
That I did kill them.

MACDUFF
                    Wherefore did you so?

MACBETH
Who can be wise, amaz'd, temperate and furious,
Loyal and neutral, in a moment? No man:
The expedition of my violent love
Outrun the pauser, reason. Here lay Duncan,
His silver skin lac'd with his golden blood;
And his gash'd stabs look'd like a breach in nature
For ruin's wasteful entrance: there, the murderers,
Steep'd in the colours of their trade, their daggers
Unmannerly breech'd with gore: who could refrain,
That had a heart to love, and in that heart
Courage to make's love known?

LADY MACBETH
                    Help me hence, ho!

MACDUFF
Look to the lady.

MALCOLM [aside to DONALBAIN].
                    Why do we hold our tongues,
That most may claim this argument for ours?

DONALBAIN [aside to MALCOLM].
What should be spoken here, where our fate,
Hid in an auger-hole, may rush, and seize us?
Let's away;
Our tears are not yet brew'd.

MALCOLM [aside to DONALBAIN].
                    Nor our strong sorrow
Upon the foot of motion.

BANQUO
                    Look to the lady: —
                    [LADY MACBETH is carried out.
And when we have our naked frailties hid,
That suffer in exposure, let us meet,
And question this most bloody piece of work,
To know it further. Fears and scruples shake us:
In the great hand of God I stand; and thence
Against the undivulg'd pretence I fight
Of treasonous malice.

MACDUFF
                    And so do I.

ALL
                    So all.

MACBETH
Let's briefly put on manly readiness,
And meet i'th'hall together.

ALL
                    Well contented.
                    [Exeunt all but MALCOLM and DONALBAIN.

MALCOLM
What will you do? Let's not consort with them:
To show an unfelt sorrow is an office
Which the false man does easy. I'll to England.

DONALBAIN
To Ireland I; our separated fortune
Shall keep us both the safer: where we are,
There's daggers in men's smiles: the near in blood,
The nearer bloody.

MALCOLM
                    This murderous shaft that's shot
Hath not yet lighted; and our safest way
Is to avoid the aim. Therefore, to horse;
And let us not be dainty of leave-taking,
But shift away: there's warrant in that theft
Which steals itself, when there's no mercy left.
                    [Exeunt

SCENE IV
Without MACBETH'S castle.

Enter ROSS and an OLD MAN.

OLD MAN
Threescore and ten I can remember well:
Within the volume of which time I have seen
Hours dreadful and things strange; but this sore night
Hath trifled former knowings.

ROSS
                    Ha, good father,
Thou seest, the heavens, as troubled with man's act,
Threatens his bloody stage: by th'clock 'tis day,
And yet dark night strangles the travelling lamp:
Is't night's predominance, or the day's shame,
That darkness does the face of earth entomb,
When living light should kiss it?

OLD MAN
                    'Tis unnatural,
Even like the deed that's done. On Tuesday last,
A falcon, towering in her pride of place,
Was by a mousing owl hawk'd at and kill'd.

ROSS
And Duncan's horses, — a thing most strange and
          certain, —
Beauteous and swift, the minions of their race,
Turn'd wild in nature, broke their stalls, flung out,
Contending 'gainst obedience, as they would make
War with mankind.

OLD MAN
                    'Tis said they eat each other.

ROSS
They did so, — to th'amazement of mine eyes,
That look'd upon't. — Here comes the good Macduff.
                    Enter MACDUFF.
How goes the world, sir, now?

MACDUFF
                    Why, see you not?

ROSS
Is't known who did this more than bloody deed?

MACDUFF
Those that Macbeth hath slain.

ROSS
                    Alas, the day!
What good could they pretend?

MACDUFF
                    They were suborn'd:
Malcolm and Donalbain, the king's two sons,
Are stol'n away and fled; which puts upon them
Suspicion of the deed.

ROSS
                    'Gainst nature still:
Thriftless ambition, that wilt ravin up
Thine own life's means! — Then 'tis most like
The sovereignty will fall upon Macbeth.

MACDUFF
He is already nam'd; and gone to Scone
To be invested.

ROSS
                    Where is Duncan's body?

MACDUFF
Carried to Colme-kill,
The sacred storehouse of his predecessors,
And guardian of their bones.

ROSS
                    Will you to Scone?

MACDUFF
No, cousin, I'll to Fife.

ROSS
                    Well, I will thither.

MACDUFF
Well, may you see things well done there, — adieu, —
Lest our old robes sit easier than our new!

ROSS
Farewell, father.

OLD MAN
God's benison go with you; and with those
That would make good of bad, and friends of foes!
                    [Exeunt

ACT III

SCENE I

Forres. The palace.

Enter BANQUO.

BANQUO
Thou hast it now, — king, Cawdor, Glamis, all,
As the weird women promis'd; and, I fear,
Thou play'dst most foully for't: yet it was said
It should not stand in thy posterity;
But that myself should be the root and father
Of many kings. If there come truth from them, —
As upon thee, Macbeth, their speeches shine, —
Why, by the verities on thee made good,
May they not be my oracles as well,
And set me up in hope? But, hush; no more.
  Sennet sounded. Enter MACBETH, *as king*;
LADY MACBETH, *as queen*; LENNOX, ROSS,
  LORDS, LADIES, *and* ATTENDANTS.

MACBETH
Here's our chief guest.

LADY MACBETH
      If he had been forgotten,
It had been as a gap in our great feast,
And all-thing unbecoming.

MACBETH
To-night we hold a solemn supper, sir,
And I'll request your presence.

BANQUO
      Let your highness
Command upon me; to the which my duties
Are with a most indissoluble tie
For ever knit.

MACBETH
Ride you this afternoon?

BANQUO
      Ay, my good lord.

MACBETH
We should have else desired your good advice —
Which still hath been both grave and prosperous —
In this day's council; but we'll take't to-morrow.
Is't far you ride?

BANQUO
As far, my lord, as will fill up the time
'Twixt this and supper: go not my horse the better,
I must become a borrower of the night
For a dark hour or twain.

MACBETH
      Fail not our feast.

BANQUO
My lord, I will not.

MACBETH
We hear, our bloody cousins are bestow'd
In England and in Ireland; not confessing
Their cruel parricide, filling their hearers
With strange invention: but of that to-morrow;
When therewithal we shall have cause of state
Craving us jointly. Hie you to horse: adieu,
Till you return at night. Goes Fleance with you?

BANQUO
Ay, my good lord: our time does call upon's.

MACBETH
I wish your horses swift and sure of foot;
And so I do commend you to their backs.
Farewell.   [*Exit* BANQUO.
Let every man be master of his time
Till seven at night; to make society
The sweeter welcome, we will keep ourself
Till supper-time alone: while then, God be with you!
  [*Exeunt all but* MACBETH *and an* ATTENDANT.
Sirrah, a word with you: attend those men
Our pleasure?

ATTENDANT
They are, my lord, without the palace-gate.

MACBETH
Bring them before us.   [*Exit* ATTENDANT.
      To be thus is nothing;
But to be safely thus. — Our fears in Banquo
Stick deep; and in his royalty of nature
Reigns that which would be fear'd; 'tis much he dares;
And, to that dauntless temper of his mind,
He hath a wisdom that doth guide his valour
To act in safety. There is none but he
Whose being I do fear: and, under him,
My Genius is rebuk'd; as, it is said,
Mark Antony's was by Cæsar. He chid the sisters,
When first they put the name of king upon me,
And bade them speak to him; then, prophet-like,

They hail'd him father to a line of kings:
Upon my head they plac'd a fruitless crown,
And put a barren sceptre in my gripe,
Thence to be wrench'd with an unlineal hand,
No son of mine succeeding. If't be so,
For Banquo's issue have I fil'd my mind;
For them the gracious Duncan have I murder'd;
Put rancours in the vessel of my peace
Only for them; and mine eternal jewel
Given to the common enemy of man,
To make them kings, the seed of Banquo kings!
Rather than so, come, fate, into the list,
And champion me to th'utterance! — Who's there?
  Enter ATTENDANT, *with two* MURDERERS.
Now go to the door, and stay there till we call.
      [*Exit* ATTENDANT.
Was it not yesterday we spoke together?

FIRST MURDERER
It was, so please your highness.

MACBETH
      Well then, now
Have you consider'd of my speeches? Know
That it was he, in the times past, which held you
So under fortune; which you thought had been
Our innocent self: this I made good to you
In our last conference, past in probation with you,
How you were borne in hand, how cross'd, the
  instruments,
Who wrought with them, and all things else that might
To half a soul and to a notion crazed
Say 'Thus did Banquo.'

FIRST MURDERER
      You made it known to us.

MACBETH
I did so; and went further, which is now
Our point of second meeting. Do you find
Your patience so predominant in your nature,
That you can let this go? Are you so gospell'd,
To pray for this good man and for his issue,
Whose heavy hand hath bow'd you to the grave,
And beggar'd yours for ever?

FIRST MURDERER
      We are men, my liege.

MACBETH
Ay, in the catalogue ye go for men;
As hounds, and greyhounds, mongrels, spaniels, curs,
Shoughs, water-rugs, and demi-wolves, are clept
All by the name of dogs: the valued file
Distinguishes the swift, the slow, the subtle,
The housekeeper, the hunter, every one
According to the gift which bounteous nature
Hath in him clos'd; whereby he does receive
Particular addition, from the bill
That writes them all alike: and so of men.
Now, if you have a station in the file,
Not i'th'worst rank of manhood, say't;
And I will put that business in your bosoms,
Whose execution takes your enemy off;
Grapples you to the heart and love of us,
Who wear our health but sickly in his life,
Which in his death were perfect.

SECOND MURDERER
      I am one, my liege,
Whom the vile blows and buffets of the world
Hath so incens'd, that I am reckless what
I do to spite the world.

FIRST MURDERER
      And I another,
So weary with disasters, tugg'd with fortune,
That I would set my life on any chance,
To mend it, or be rid on't.

MACBETH
      Both of you
Know Banquo was your enemy.

BOTH MURDERERS
      True, my lord.

MACBETH
So is he mine; and in such bloody distance,
That every minute of his being thrusts
Against my near'st of life: and though I could
With barefac'd power sweep him from my sight,
And bid my will avouch it, yet I must not,
For certain friends that are both his and mine,
Whose loves I may not drop, but wail his fall
Who I myself struck down: and thence it is,
That I to your assistance do make love;
Masking the business from the common eye
For sundry weighty reasons.

SECOND MURDERER
      We shall, my lord,

Perform what you command us.

FIRST MURDERER
      Though our lives —

MACBETH
Your spirits shine through you. Within this hour at
  most,
I will advise you where to plant yourselves;
Acquaint you with the perfect spy o'th'time,
The moment on't; for't must be done to-night,
And something from the palace; always thought
That I require a clearness: and with him —
To leave no rubs nor botches in the work —
Fleance his son, that keeps him company,
Whose absence is no less material to me
Than is his father's, must embrace the fate
Of that dark hour. Resolve yourselves apart:
I'll come to you anon.

BOTH MURDERERS
      We are resolv'd, my lord.

MACBETH
I'll call upon you straight: abide within.
      [*Exeunt* MURDERERS.
It is concluded: — Banquo, thy soul's flight,
If it find heaven, must find it out to-night.   [*Exit.*

SCENE II

The palace.

Enter LADY MACBETH *and a* SERVANT.

LADY MACBETH
Is Banquo gone from court?

SERVANT
Ay, madam, but returns again to-night.

LADY MACBETH
Say to the king, I would attend his leisure
For a few words.

SERVANT
      Madam, I will.   [*Exit.*

LADY MACBETH
      Naught's had, all's spent,
Where our desire is got without content:
'Tis safer to be that which we destroy,
Than, by destruction, dwell in doubtful joy.
  Enter MACBETH.
How now, my lord! why do you keep alone,
Of sorriest fancies your companions making;
Using those thoughts which should indeed have died
With them they think on? Things without all remedy
Should be without regard: what's done is done.

MACBETH
We have scotch'd the snake, not kill'd it:
She'll close, and be herself; whilst our poor malice
Remains in danger of her former tooth.
But let the frame of things disjoint, both the worlds
  suffer,
Ere we will eat our meal in fear, and sleep
In the affliction of these terrible dreams
That shake us nightly: better be with the dead,
Whom we, to gain our peace, have sent to peace,
Than on the torture of the mind to lie
In restless ecstasy. Duncan is in his grave;
After life's fitful fever he sleeps well;
Treason has done his worst: nor steel, nor poison,
Malice domestic, foreign levy, nothing,
Can touch him further.

LADY MACBETH
      Come on; gentle my lord,
Sleek o'er your rugged looks; be bright and jovial
Among your guests to-night.

MACBETH
      So shall I, love;
And so, I pray, be you: let your remembrance
Apply to Banquo; present him eminence, both
With eye and tongue: unsafe the while that we
Must lave our honours in these flattering streams;
And make our faces vizards to our hearts,
Disguising what they are.

LADY MACBETH
      You must leave this.

MACBETH
O, full of scorpions is my mind, dear wife!
Thou know'st that Banquo and his Fleance lives.

LADY MACBETH
But in them nature's copy's not eterne.

MACBETH
There's comfort yet; they are assailable;
Then be thou jocund: ere the bat hath flown
His cloister'd flight; ere, to black Hecate's summons,
The shard-borne beetle with his drowsy hums
Hath rung night's yawning peal, there shall be done

MACBETH Here's our chief guest.

A deed of dreadful note.
LADY MACBETH
              What's to be done?
MACBETH
Be innocent of the knowledge, dearest chuck,
Till thou applaud the deed. — Come, seeling night,
Scarf up the tender eye of pitiful day;
And with thy bloody and invisible hand
Cancel and tear to pieces that great bond
Which keeps me pale! — Light thickens; and the crow
Makes wing to th'rooky wood:
Good things of day begin to droop and drowse;
Whiles night's black agents to their preys do rouse. —
Thou marvell'st at my words: but hold thee still;
Things bad begun make strong themselves by ill:
So, prithee, go with me.   *[Exeunt.*

SCENE III

A park, with a gate leading to the palace.

Enter three MURDERERS.

FIRST MURDERER
But who did bid thee join with us?
THIRD MURDERER
              Macbeth.
SECOND MURDERER
He needs not our mistrust; since he delivers
Our offices, and what we have to do,
To the direction just.
FIRST MURDERER
           Then stand with us.
The west yet glimmers with some streaks of day:
Now spurs the lated traveller apace
To gain the timely inn; and near approaches
The subject of our watch.
THIRD MURDERER
            Hark! I hear horses.
BANQUO [*within*].
Give us a light there, ho!
SECOND MURDERER
            Then 'tis he: the rest
That are within the note of expectation
Already are i'th'court.
FIRST MURDERER
           His horses go about.
THIRD MURDERER
Almost a mile: but he does usually,
So all men do, from hence to th'palace-gate
Make it their walk.
SECOND MURDERER
           A light, a light!
THIRD MURDERER
           'Tis he.
FIRST MURDERER
Stand to't.
    Enter BANQUO, *and* FLEANCE *with a torch.*
BANQUO
It will be rain to-night.
FIRST MURDERER
           Let it come down.

               [They assault BANQUO.
BANQUO
O, treachery! — Fly, good Fleance, fly, fly, fly!
Thou mayst revenge. — O slave!
            [Dies. FLEANCE *escapes.*
THIRD MURDERER
Who did strike out the light?
FIRST MURDERER
           Was't not the way?
THIRD MURDERER
There's but one down; the son is fled.
SECOND MURDERER
           We have lost
Best half of our affair.
FIRST MURDERER
Well, let's away, and say how much is done. *[Exeunt.*

SCENE IV

A room of state at the palace.

Banquet prepared. Enter MACBETH,
LADY MACBETH, ROSS, LENNOX,
LORDS, *and* ATTENDANTS.

MACBETH
You know your own degrees, sit down: at first
And last the hearty welcome.
LORDS
           Thanks to your majesty.
MACBETH
Ourself will mingle with society,
And play the humble host.
Our hostess keeps her state; but, in best time,
We will require her welcome.
LADY MACBETH
Pronounce it for me, sir, to all our friends;
For my heart speaks they are welcome.
MACBETH
See, they encounter thee with their hearts' thanks. —
Both sides are even: here I'll sit i'th'midst:
    Enter FIRST MURDERER *to the door.*
Be large in mirth; anon we'll drink a measure
The table round. — There's blood on thy face.
MURDERER
'Tis Banquo's, then.
MACBETH
'Tis better thee without than he within.
Is he dispatch'd?
MURDERER
My lord, his throat is cut; that I did for him.
MACBETH
Thou art the best o'th'cut-throats: yet he's good
That did the like for Fleance: if thou didst it,
Thou art the nonpareil.
MURDERER
           Most royal sir,
Fleance is scaped.
MACBETH
Then comes my fit again: I had else been perfect;
Whole as the marble, founded as the rock;
As broad and general as the casing air:
But now I am cabin'd, cribb'd, confined, bound in

To saucy doubts and fears. But Banquo's safe?
MURDERER
Ay, my good lord: safe in a ditch he bides,
With twenty trenched gashes on his head;
The least a death to nature.
MACBETH
           Thanks for that:
There the grown serpent lies; the worm, that's fled,
Hath nature that in time will venom breed,
No teeth for th'present. — Get thee gone: to-morrow
We'll hear ourselves again.   *[Exit* MURDERER.
LADY MACBETH
           My royal lord,
You do not give the cheer: the feast is sold
That is not often vouch'd, while 'tis a-making,
'Tis given with welcome: to feed were best at home;
From thence the sauce to meat is ceremony;
Meeting were bare without it.
MACBETH
           Sweet remembrancer! —
Now, good digestion wait on appetite,
And health to both!
LENNOX
           May't please your highness sit.

    Enter the GHOST *of* BANQUO, *and sits in*
    MACBETH'S *place.*

MACBETH
Here had we now our country's honour roof'd,
Were the grac'd person of our Banquo present;
Who may I rather challenge for unkindness
Than pity for mischance!
ROSS
           His absence, sir,
Lays blame upon his promise. Please't your highness
To grace us with your royal company.
MACBETH
The table's full.
LENNOX
           Here is a place reserv'd, sir.
MACBETH
Where?
LENNOX
Here, my good lord. What is't that moves your
   highness?
MACBETH
Which of you have done this?
LORDS
           What, my good lord?
MACBETH
Thou canst not say I did it: never shake
Thy gory locks at me.
ROSS
Gentlemen, rise: his highness is not well.
LADY MACBETH
Sit, worthy friends: — my lord is often thus,
And hath been from his youth: pray you, keep seat;
The fit is momentary; upon a thought
He will again be well: if much you note him,
You shall offend him, and extend his passion:
Feed, and regard him not. — Are you a man?
MACBETH
Ay, and a bold one, that dare look on that
Which might appal the devil.
LADY MACBETH
           O proper stuff!
This is the very painting of your fear:
This is the air-drawn dagger which, you said,
Led you to Duncan. O, these flaws and starts,
Impostors to true fear, would well become
A woman's story at a winter's fire,
Authoris'd by her grandam. Shame itself!
Why do you make such faces? When all's done,
You look but on a stool.
MACBETH
Prithee, see there! behold! look! lo! how say you?—
Why, what care I? If thou canst nod, speak too. —
If charnel-houses and our graves must send
Those that we bury back, our monuments
Shall be the maws of kites.   *[GHOST disappears.*
LADY MACBETH
           What, quite unmann'd in folly?
MACBETH
If I stand here, I saw him.
LADY MACBETH
           Fie, for shame!
MACBETH
Blood hath been shed ere now, i'th'olden time,
Ere human statute purg'd the gentle weal;

Ay, and since too, murders have been perform'd
Too terrible for the ear: the time has been,
That, when the brains were out, the man would die,
And there an end; but now they rise again,
With twenty mortal murders on their crowns,
And push us from our stools: this is more strange
Than such a murder is.

LADY MACBETH
                My worthy lord,
Your noble friends do lack you.

MACBETH
                I do forget: —
Do not muse at me, my most worthy friends;
I have a strange infirmity, which is nothing
To those that know me. Come, love and health to all;
Then I'll sit down. — Give me some wine; fill full. —
I drink to th'general joy o' the whole table,
And to our dear friend Banquo, whom we miss;
Would he were here! to all, and him, we thirst,
And all to all.

LORDS
            Our duties, and the pledge.

Enter GHOST.

MACBETH
Avaunt! and quit my sight! let the earth hide thee!
Thy bones are marrowless, thy blood is cold;
Thou hast no speculation in those eyes
Which thou dost glare with!

LADY MACBETH
              Think of this, good peers,
But as a thing of custom: 'tis no other;
Only it spoils the pleasure of the time.

MACBETH
What man dare, I dare:
Approach thou like the rugged Russian bear,
The arm'd rhinoceros, or the Hyrcan tiger;
Take any shape but that, and my firm nerves
Shall never tremble: or be alive again,
And dare me to the desert with thy sword;
If trembling I inhabit then, protest me
The baby of a girl. Hence, horrible shadow!
Unreal mockery, hence!   [GHOST *vanishes.*
         Why, so; — being gone,
I am a man again. — Pray you, sit still.

LADY MACBETH
You have displac'd the mirth, broke the good meeting,
With most admired disorder.

MACBETH
             Can such things be,
And overcome us like a summer's cloud,
Without our special wonder? You make me strange
Even to the disposition that I owe,
When now I think you can behold such sights,
And keep the natural ruby of your cheeks,
When mine is blanch'd with fear.

ROSS
             What sights, my lord?

LADY MACBETH
I pray you, speak not; he grows worse and worse;
Question enrages him: at once, good night: —
Stand not upon the order of your going,
But go at once.

LENNOX
        Good night; and better health
Attend his majesty!

LADY MACBETH
        A kind good night to all!
[*Exeunt all but* MACBETH *and* LADY MACBETH.

MACBETH
It will have blood; they say blood will have blood:
Stones have been known to move, and trees to speak;
Augurs, and understood relations have
By maggot-pies and choughs and rooks brought forth
The secret'st man of blood. — What is the night?

LADY MACBETH
Almost at odds with morning, which is which.

MACBETH
How say'st thou, that Macduff denies his person
At our great bidding?

LADY MACBETH
        Did you send to him, sir?

MACBETH
I hear it by the way; but I will send:
There's not a one of them but in his house
I keep a servant fee'd. I will to-morrow,
And betimes I will, to the weird sisters go:
More shall they speak; for now I am bent to know,
By the worst means, the worst. For mine own good,
All causes shall give way: I am in blood

MACBETH I will advise you where to plant yourselves.

Stepp'd in so far, that, should I wade no more,
Returning were as tedious as go o'er:
Strange things I have in head, that will to hand;
Which must be acted ere they may be scann'd.

LADY MACBETH
You lack the season of all natures, sleep.

MACBETH
Come, we'll to sleep. My strange and self-abuse
Is the initiate fear, that wants hard use: —
We are yet but young in deed.   [*Exeunt.*

SCENE V

A heath.

Thunder. Enter the three WITCHES, *meeting* HECATE.

FIRST WITCH
Why, how now, Hecate! you look angerly.

HECATE
Have I not reason, beldams as you are,
Saucy and overbold? How did you dare
To trade and traffic with Macbeth
In riddles and affairs of death;
And I, the mistress of your charms,
The close contriver of all harms,
Was never call'd to bear my part,
Or show the glory of our art?
And, which is worse, all you have done
Hath been but for a wayward son,
Spiteful and wrathful; who, as others do,
Loves for his own ends, not for you.
But make amends now: get you gone,
And at the pit of Acheron
Meet me i' the morning: thither he
Will come to know his destiny:
Your vessels and your spells provide,
Your charms, and every thing beside.
I am for the air; this night I'll spend
Unto a dismal and a fatal end:
Great business must be wrought ere noon:
Upon the corner of the moon
There hangs a vaporous drop profound;
I'll catch it ere it come to ground:
And that, distill'd by magic sleights,
Shall raise such artificial sprites,
As, by the strength of their illusion,
Shall draw him on to his confusion:
He shall spurn fate, scorn death, and bear
He hopes 'bove wisdom, grace, and fear:

And you all know security
Is mortals' chiefest enemy.
    [*Music and a song within,* 'Come away, come away,' *etc.*
Hark! I am call'd; my little spirit, see,
Sits in a foggy cloud, and stays for me.   [*Exit.*

FIRST WITCH
Come, let's make haste; she'll soon be back again.
                [*Exeunt.*

SCENE VI

Forres. A room in the palace.

Enter LENNOX *and another* LORD.

LENNOX
My former speeches have but hit your thoughts,
Which can interpret further: only, I say,
Things have been strangely borne. The gracious Duncan
Was pitied of Macbeth: — marry, he was dead: —
And the right-valiant Banquo walk'd too late;
Whom, you may say, if't please you, Fleance kill'd,
For Fleance fled: men must not walk too late.
Who cannot want the thought, how monstrous
It was for Malcolm and for Donalbain
To kill their gracious father? damned fact!
How it did grieve Macbeth! did he not straight,
In pious rage, the two delinquents tear,
That were the slaves of drink and thralls of sleep?
Was not that nobly done? Ay, and wisely too;
For 'twould have anger'd any heart alive
To hear the men deny't. So that, I say,
He has borne all things well: and I do think
That, had he Duncan's sons under his key, —
As, an't please heaven, he shall not, — they should find
What 'twere to kill a father; so should Fleance.
But, peace! — for from broad words, and 'cause he fail'd
His presence at the tyrant's feast, I hear,
Macduff lives in disgrace: sir, can you tell
Where he bestows himself?

LORD
             The son of Duncan,
From whom this tyrant holds the due of birth,
Lives in the English court; and is received
Of the most pious Edward with such grace,
That the malevolence of fortune nothing
Takes from his high respect: thither Macduff
Is gone to pray the holy king, upon his aid

MACBETH Thy bones are marrowless, thy blood is cold.

To wake Northumberland and warlike Siward:
That, by the help of these — with Him above
To ratify the work — we may again
Give to our tables meat, sleep to our nights;
Free from our feasts and banquets bloody knives;
Do faithful homage, and receive free honours; —
All which we pine for now: and this report
Hath so exasperate the king, that he
Prepares for some attempt of war.

LENNOX
                Sent he to Macduff?

LORD
He did: and with an absolute 'Sir, not I',
The cloudy messenger turns me his back,
And hums, as who should say, 'You'll rue the time
That clogs me with this answer.'

LENNOX
               And that well might
Advise him to a caution, to hold what distance
His wisdom can provide. Some holy angel
Fly to the court of England, and unfold
His message ere he come; that a swift blessing
May soon return to this our suffering country
Under a hand accurs'd!

LORD
           I'll send my prayers with him.
                       [Exeunt.

ACT IV

SCENE I

A cavern. In the middle, a caldron boiling.

Thunder. Enter the three WITCHES.

FIRST WITCH
Thrice the brinded cat hath mew'd.

SECOND WITCH
Thrice and once the hedge-pig whined.

THIRD WITCH
Harpier cries: — 'tis time, 'tis time.

FIRST WITCH
    Round about the caldron go;
    In the poison'd entrails throw. —
    Toad, that under cold stone
    Days and nights has thirty-one
    Swelter'd venom sleeping got,
    Boil thou first i' the charmed pot.

ALL
    Double, double toil and trouble;
    Fire, burn; and, caldron, bubble.

SECOND WITCH
    Fillet of a fenny snake,
    In the cauldron boil and bake;
    Eye of newt, and toe of frog,
    Wool of bat, and tongue of dog,
    Adder's fork, and blind-worm's sting,
    Lizard's leg, and howlet's wing, —
    For a charm of powerful trouble,
    Like a hell-broth boil and bubble.

ALL
    Double, double toil and trouble;
    Fire, burn; and, caldron, bubble.

THIRD WITCH
    Scale of dragon; tooth of wolf;
    Witches' mummy; maw and gulf
    Of the ravin'd salt-sea shark;
    Root of hemlock digg'd i' the dark;
    Liver of blaspheming Jew;
    Gall of goat; and slips of yew
    Silver'd in the moon's eclipse;
    Nose of Turk, and Tartar's lips;
    Finger of birth-strangled babe
    Ditch-deliver'd by a drab, —
    Make the gruel thick and slab:
    Add thereto a tiger's chaudron,
    For th'ingredients of our caldron.

ALL
    Double, double toil and trouble;
    Fire, burn; and, caldron, bubble.

SECOND WITCH
    Cool it with a baboon's blood,
    Then the charm is firm and good.
                 Enter HECATE.

HECATE
O, well done! I commend your pains;
And every one shall share i' the gains;
    And now about the caldron sing,
    Live elves and fairies in a ring,
    Enchanting all that you put in.
      [Music and a song, 'Black spirits', etc.

                      [Exit HECATE.

SECOND WITCH
By the pricking of my thumbs,
Something wicked this way comes: —
    Open, locks,
    Whoever knocks!
                Enter MACBETH.

MACBETH
How now, you secret, black, and midnight hags!
What is't you do?

ALL
             A deed without a name.

MACBETH
I conjure you, by that which you profess, —
Howe'er you come to know it, — answer me:
Though you untie the winds, and let them fight
Against the churches; though the yesty waves
Confound and swallow navigation up;
Though bladed corn be lodg'd, and trees blown down;
Though castles topple on their warders' heads;
Though palaces and pyramids do slope
Their heads to their foundations; though the treasure
Of nature's germens tumble all together,
Even till destruction sicken, — answer me
To what I ask you.

FIRST WITCH
           Speak.

SECOND WITCH
              Demand.

THIRD WITCH
                  We'll answer.

FIRST WITCH
Say, if th'hadst rather hear it from our mouths,
Or from our masters?

MACBETH
             Call 'em, let me see 'em.

FIRST WITCH
Pour in sow's blood, that hath eaten
Her nine farrow; grease that's sweaten
From the murderer's gibbet throw
Into the flame.

ALL
           Come, high or low;
Thyself and office deftly show!

    Thunder. FIRST APPARITION: *an arm'd head.*

MACBETH
Tell me, thou unknown power, —

FIRST WITCH
               He knows thy thought:
Hear his speech, but say thou naught.

FIRST APPARITION
Macbeth! Macbeth! Macbeth! beware Macduff;
Beware the thane of Fife. — Dismiss me: — enough.
                      [Descends.

MACBETH
Whate'er thou art, for thy good caution, thanks;
Thou hast harp'd my fear aright: — but one word more,

FIRST WITCH
He will not be commanded: here's another,
More potent than the first.
    Thunder. SECOND APPARITION: *a bloody child.*

SECOND APPARITION
Macbeth! Macbeth! Macbeth! —

MACBETH
Had I three ears, I'ld hear thee.

SECOND APPARITION
Be bloody, bold, and resolute; laugh to scorn
The power of man, for none of woman born
Shall harm Macbeth.   *[Descends.*

MACBETH
Then live, Macduff: what need I fear of thee?
But yet I'll make assurance double sure,
And take a bond of fate: thou shalt not live;
That I may tell pale-hearted fear it lies,
And sleep in spite of thunder.

Thunder. THIRD APPARITION: *a child crown'd, with*
a tree in his hand.

What is this,
That rises like the issue of a king,
And wears upon his baby-brow the round
And top of sovereignty?

ALL

Listen, but speak not to't.

THIRD APPARITION

Be lion-mettled, proud; and take no care
Who chafes, who frets, or where conspirers are:
Macbeth shall never vanquish'd be, until
Great Birnam wood to high Dunsinane hill
Shall come against him.   [*Descends.*

MACBETH

That will never be:
Who can impress the forest; bid the tree
Unfix his earth-bound root? Sweet bodements! good!
Rebellion's head, rise never, till the wood
Of Birnam rise, and our high-plac'd Macbeth
Shall live the lease of nature, pay his breath
To time and mortal custom. — Yet my heart
Throbs to know one thing: tell me, — if your art
Can tell so much, — shall Banquo's issue ever
Reign in this kingdom?

ALL

Seek to know no more.

MACBETH

I will be satisfied: deny me this,
And an eternal curse fall on you! Let me know: —
Why sinks that caldron? and what noise is this?
                              [*Hautboys.*

FIRST WITCH

Show!

SECOND WITCH

Show!

THIRD WITCH

Show!

ALL

Show his eyes, and grieve his heart;
Come like shadows, so depart!
A show of eight KINGS, *the last with a glass in his hand;*
BANQUO'S GHOST *following.*

MACBETH

Thou art too like the spirit of Banquo: down!
Thy crown does sear mine eyeballs: — and thy hair,
Thou other gold-bound brow, is like the first: —
A third is like the former. — Filthy hags!
Why do you show me this? — A fourth? — Start, eyes! —
What, will the line stretch out to th'crack of doom? —
Another yet? — A seventh? — I'll see no more: —
And yet the eighth appears, who bears a glass
Which shows me many more; and some I see
That twofold balls and treble sceptres carry:
Horrible sight! — Now, I see 'tis true;
For the blood-bolter'd Banquo smiles upon me,
And points at them for his. —What, is this so?

FIRST WITCH

Ay, sir, all this is so: — but why
Stands Macbeth thus amazedly? —
Come, sisters, cheer we up his sprites,
And show the best of our delights:
I'll charm the air to give a sound,
While you perform your antic round;
That this great king may kindly say
Our duties did his welcome pay.
        [*Music. The* WITCHES *dance, and vanish.*

MACBETH

Where are they? Gone? — Let this pernicious hour
Stand aye accursed in the calendar! —
Come in, without there!

Enter LENNOX.

LENNOX

What's your Grace's will?

MACBETH

Saw you the weird sisters?

LENNOX

No, my lord.

MACBETH

Came they not by you?

LENNOX

No, indeed, my lord.

MACBETH

Infected be the air whereon they ride;
And damn'd all those that trust them! — I did hear
The galloping of horse: who was't came by?

LENNOX

'Tis two or three, my lord, that bring you word
Macduff is fled to England.

HECATE O, well done! I commend your pains.

MACBETH

Fled to England!

LENNOX

Ay, my good lord.

MACBETH

Time, thou anticipatest my dread exploits:
The flighty purpose never is o'ertook
Unless the deed go with it: from this moment
The very firstlings of my heart shall be
The firstlings of my hand. And even now,
To crown my thoughts with acts, be it thought and
    done:
The castle of Macduff I will surprise;
Seize upon Fife; give to the edge o'th'sword
His wife, his babes, and all unfortunate souls
That trace him in his line. No boasting like a fool;
This deed I'll do before this purpose cool:
But no more sights! — Where are these gentlemen?
Come, bring me where they are.   [*Exeunt.*

SCENE II

Fife. A room in MACDUFF'S *castle.*

Enter LADY MACDUFF, *her* SON, *and* ROSS.

LADY MACDUFF

What had he done, to make him fly the land?

ROSS

You must have patience, madam.

LADY MACDUFF

He had none:
His flight was madness: when our actions do not,
Our fears do make us traitors.

ROSS

You know not
Whether it was his wisdom or his fear.

LADY MACDUFF

Wisdom! to leave his wife, to leave his babes,
His mansion, and his titles, in a place
From whence himself does fly? He loves us not;
He wants the natural touch: for the poor wren,
The most diminutive of birds, will fight,
Her young ones in her nest, against the owl.
All is the fear, and nothing is the love;
As little is the wisdom, where the flight
So runs against all reason.

ROSS

My dearest coz,
I pray you, school yourself: but for your husband,
He is noble, wise, judicious, and best knows
The fits o'th'season. I dare not speak much further:
But cruel are the times, when we are traitors,
And do not know ourselves; when we hold rumour
From what we fear, yet know not what we fear,
But float upon a wild and violent sea
Each way and move.—I take my leave of you:
Shall not be long but I'll be here again:
Things at the worst will cease, or else climb upward
To what they were before. — My pretty cousin,
Blessing upon you!

LADY MACDUFF

Father'd he is, and yet he's fatherless.

ROSS

I am so much a fool, should I stay longer,
It would be my disgrace and your discomfort:
I take my leave at once.   [*Exit.*

LADY MACDUFF

Sirrah, your father's dead:
And what will you do now? How will you live?

SON

As birds do, mother.

LADY MACDUFF

What, with worms and flies?

SON

With what I get, I mean; and so do they.

LADY MACDUFF
Poor bird! thou'ldst never fear the net nor lime,
The pitfall nor the gin.
SON
Why should I, mother? Poor birds they are not set for.
My father is not dead, for all your saying.
LADY MACDUFF
Yes, he is dead; how wilt thou do for a father?
SON
Nay, how will you do for a husband?
LADY MACDUFF
Why, I can buy me twenty at any market.
SON
Then you'll buy 'em to sell again.
LADY MACDUFF
Thou speak'st with all thy wit: and yet, i'faith,
With wit enough for thee.
SON
Was my father a traitor, mother?
LADY MACDUFF
Ay, that he was.
SON
What is a traitor?
LADY MACDUFF
Why, one that swears and lies.
SON
And be all traitors that do so?
LADY MACDUFF
Every one that does so is a traitor, and must be hang'd.
SON
And must they all be hang'd that swear and lie?
LADY MACDUFF
Every one.
SON
Who must hang them?
LADY MACDUFF
Why, the honest men.
SON
Then the liars and swearers are fools; for there are liars
and swearers enow to beat the honest men, and hang
up them.
LADY MACDUFF
Now, God help thee, poor monkey! But how wilt thou
do for a father?
SON
If he were dead, you'ld weep for him: if you would not,
it were a good sign that I should quickly have a new
father.
LADY MACDUFF
Poor prattler, how thou talk'st!

Enter a MESSENGER.

MESSENGER
Bless you, fair dame! I am not to you known,
Though in your state of honour I am perfect.
I doubt some danger does approach you nearly:
If you will take a homely man's advice,
Be not found here; hence, with your little ones.
To fright you thus, methinks, I am too savage;
To do worse to you were fell cruelty,
Which is too nigh your person. Heaven preserve you!
I dare abide no longer.   [*Exit.*
LADY MACDUFF
                              Whither should I fly?
I have done no harm. But I remember now
I am in this earthly world; where to do harm
Is often laudable; to do good, sometime
Accounted dangerous folly: why then, alas,
Do I put up that womanly defence,
To say I have done no harm?

Enter MURDERERS.
                              What are these faces?
FIRST MURDERER
Where is your husband?
LADY MACDUFF
I hope, in no place so unsanctified
Where such as thou mayst find him.
FIRST MURDERER
                              He's a traitor!
SON
Thou liest, thou shag-hair'd villain!
FIRST MURDERER
                    What, you egg!   [*Stabbing him.*
Young fry of treachery!
SON
                    He has kill'd me, mother:
Run away, I pray you!   [*Dies.*
    [*Exit* LADY MACDUFF, *crying 'Murder!' and
      pursued by the* MURDERERS.

SCENE III

England. Before the KING'S *palace.*

Enter MALCOLM *and* MACDUFF.

MALCOLM
Let us seek out some desolate shade, and there
Weep our sad bosoms empty.
MACDUFF
                              Let us rather
Hold fast the mortal sword; and, like good men!
Bestride our down-fall'n birthdom: each new morn
New widows howl; new orphans cry; new sorrows
Strike heaven on the face, that it resounds
As if it felt with Scotland, and yell'd out
Like syllable of dolour.
MALCOLM
                              What I believe, I'll wail;
What know, believe; and what I can redress,
As I shall find the time to friend, I will.
What you have spoke, it may be so perchance.
This tyrant, whose sole name blisters our tongues,
Was once thought honest: you have lov'd him well;
He hath not touch'd you yet. I am young; but
    something
You may deserve of him through me, and wisdom
To offer up a weak, poor, innocent lamb
T'appease an angry god.
MACDUFF
I am not treacherous.
MALCOLM
                              But Macbeth is.
A good and virtuous nature may recoil
In an imperial charge. But I shall crave your pardon;
That which you are, my thoughts cannot transpose:
Angels are bright still, though the brightest fell:
Though all things foul would wear the brows of grace,
Yet grace must still look so.
MACDUFF
                              I have lost my hopes.
MALCOLM
Perchance even there where I did find my doubts.
Why in that rawness left you wife and child,
Those precious motives, those strong knots of love,
Without leave-taking? — I pray you,
Let not my jealousies be your dishonours,
But mine own safeties: — you may be rightly just,
Whatever I shall think.
MACDUFF
                    Bleed, bleed, poor country!
Great tyranny, lay thou thy basis sure,
For goodness dare not check thee! wear thou thy
    wrongs,
Thy title is affeer'd! — Fare thee well, lord:
I would not be the villain that thou think'st
For the whole space that's in the tyrant's grasp,
And the rich East to boot.
MALCOLM
                    Be not offended:
I speak not as in absolute fear of you.
I think our country sinks beneath the yoke;
It weeps, it bleeds; and each new day a gash
Is added to her wounds: I think, withal,
There would be hands uplifted in my right;
And here, from gracious England, have I offer
Of goodly thousands: but, for all this
When I shall tread upon the tyrant's head,
Or wear it on my sword, yet my poor country
Shall have more vices than it had before;
More suffer, and more sundry ways than ever,
By him that shall succeed.
MACDUFF
                    What should he be?
MALCOLM
It is myself I mean: in whom I know
All the particulars of vice so grafted,
That, when they shall be open'd, black Macbeth
Will seem as pure as snow; and the poor state
Esteem him as a lamb, being compared
With my confineless harms.
MACDUFF
                    Not in the legions
Of horrid hell can come a devil more damn'd
In evils to top Macbeth.
MALCOLM
                    I grant him bloody,
Luxurious, avaricious, false, deceitful,
Sudden, malicious, smacking of every sin
That has a name: but there's no bottom, none,
In my voluptuousness: your wives, your daughters,
Your matrons, and your maids, could not fill up
The cistern of my lust; and my desire
All continent impediments would o'erbear,
That did oppose my will: better Macbeth
Than such an one to reign.
MACDUFF
                    Boundless intemperance
In nature is a tyranny; it hath been
Th'untimely emptying of the happy throne,
And fall of many kings. But fear not yet
To take upon you what is yours: you may
Convey your pleasures in a spacious plenty,
And yet seem cold, the time you may so hoodwink.
We have willing dames enough; there cannot be
That vulture in you, to devour so many
As will to greatness dedicate themselves,
Finding it so inclined.
MALCOLM
                    With this, there grows,
In my most ill-compos'd affection, such
A stanchless avarice, that, were I king,
I should cut off the nobles for their lands;
Desire his jewels, and this other's house:
And my more-having would be as a sauce
To make me hunger more; that I should forge
Quarrels unjust against the good and loyal,
Destroying them for wealth.
MACDUFF
                    This avarice
Sticks deeper; grows with more pernicious root
Than summer-seeming lust; and it hath been
The sword of our slain kings: yet do not fear;
Scotland hath foisons to fill up your will,
Of your mere own: all these are portable,
With other graces weigh'd.
MALCOLM
But I have none: the king-becoming graces,
As justice, verity, temperance, stableness,
Bounty, perseverance, mercy, lowliness,
Devotion, patience, courage, fortitude,
I have no relish of them; but abound
In the division of each several crime,
Acting it many ways. Nay, had I power, I should
Pour the sweet milk of concord into hell,
Uproar the universal peace, confound
All unity on earth.
MACDUFF
                    O Scotland, Scotland!
MALCOLM
If such a one be fit to govern, speak:
I am as I have spoken.
MACDUFF
                    Fit to govern!
No, not to live. — O nation miserable,
With an untitled tyrant bloody-sceptred,
When shalt thou see thy wholesome days again,
Since that the truest issue of thy throne
By his own interdiction stands accursed,
And does blaspheme his breed? — Thy royal father
Was a most sainted king: the queen that bore thee,
Oftener upon her knees than on her feet,
Died every day she liv'd. Fare thee well!
These evils thou repeat'st upon thyself
Have banish'd me from Scotland. — O my breast,
Thy hope ends here!
MALCOLM
                    Macduff, this noble passion,
Child of integrity, hath from my soul
Wip'd the black scruples, reconcil'd my thoughts
To thy good truth and honour. Devilish Macbeth
By many of these trains hath sought to win me
Into his power; and modest wisdom plucks me
From over-credulous haste: but God above
Deal between thee and me! for even now
I put myself to thy direction, and
Unspeak mine own detraction; here abjure
The taints and blames I laid upon myself,
For strangers to my nature. I am yet
Unknown to woman; never was forsworn;
Scarcely have coveted what was mine own;
At no time broke my faith; would not betray
The devil to his fellow; and delight
No less in truth than life: my first false speaking
Was this upon myself: — what I am truly,
Is thine, and my poor country's, to command: —
Whither, indeed, before thy here-approach,
Old Siward, with ten thousand warlike men,
Already at a point, was setting forth:
Now we'll together; and the chance of goodness
Be like our warranted quarrel! Why are you silent?
MACDUFF
Such welcome and unwelcome things at once

SON Thou liest, thou shag-hair'd villain!

'Tis hard to reconcile.

Enter a DOCTOR.

MALCOLM
Well; more anon. — Comes the king forth, I pray you?
DOCTOR
Ay, sir; there are a crew of wretched souls
That stay his cure: their malady convinces
The great assay of art; but, at his touch,
Such sanctity hath heaven given his hand,
They presently amend.
MALCOLM
        I thank you, doctor.   [*Exit* DOCTOR.
MACDUFF
What's the disease he means?
MALCOLM
               'Tis call'd the evil:
A most miraculous work in this good king;
Which often, since my here-remain in England,
I have seen him do. How he solicits heaven,
Himself best knows: but strangely-visited people,
All swoll'n and ulcerous, pitiful to the eye,
The mere despair of surgery, he cures;
Hanging a golden stamp about their necks,
Put on with holy prayers: and 'tis spoken,
To the succeeding royalty he leaves
The healing benediction. With this strange virtue,
He hath a heavenly gift of prophecy;
And sundry blessings hang about his throne,
That speak him full of grace.
MACDUFF
               See, who comes here?
MALCOLM
My countryman; but yet I know him not.

Enter ROSS

MACDUFF
My ever-gentle cousin, welcome hither.
MALCOLM
I know him now: — good God, betimes remove
The means that makes us strangers!
ROSS
              Sir, amen.
MACDUFF
Stands Scotland where it did?
ROSS
            Alas, poor country, —
Almost afraid to know itself! It cannot
Be call'd our mother, but our grave: where nothing,
But who knows nothing, is once seen to smile;
Where sighs, and groans, and shrieks that rent the air,
Are made, not mark'd; where violent sorrow seems
A modern ecstasy: the dead man's knell
Is there scarce ask'd for who; and good men's lives
Expire before the flowers in their caps,
Dying or e'er they sicken.

MACDUFF
              O, relation
Too nice, and yet too true!
MALCOLM
              What's the newest grief?
ROSS
That of an hour's age doth hiss the speaker;
Each minute teems a new one.
MACDUFF
             How does my wife?
ROSS
Why, well.
MACDUFF
        And all my children?
ROSS
              Well too.
MACDUFF
The tyrant has not batter'd at their peace?
ROSS
No; they were well at peace when I did leave 'em.
MACDUFF
Bet not a niggard of your speech: how goes't?
ROSS
When I came hither to transport the tidings,
Which I have heavily borne, there ran a rumour
Of many worthy fellows that were out;
Which was to my belief witness'd the rather,
For that I saw the tyrant's power a-foot:
Now is the time of help; your eye in Scotland
Would create soldiers, make our women fight,
To doff their dire distresses.
MALCOLM
            Be't their comfort
We are coming thither: gracious England hath
Lent us good Siward and ten thousand men;
An older and a better soldier none
That Christendom gives out.
ROSS
           Would I could answer
This comfort with the like! But I have words
That would be howl'd out in the desert air,
Where hearing should not latch them.
MACDUFF
           What concern they?
The general cause? or is it a fee-grief
Due to some single breast?
ROSS
           No mind that's honest
But in it shares some woe; though the main part
Pertains to you alone.
MACDUFF
           If it be mine,
Keep it not from me, quickly let me have it.

ROSS
Let not your ears despise my tongue for ever,
Which shall possess them with the heaviest sound
That ever yet they heard.
MACDUFF
          Hum! I guess at it.
ROSS
Your castle is surpris'd; your wife and babes
Savagely slaughter'd: to relate the manner,
Were, on the quarry of these murder'd deer,
To add the death of you.
MALCOLM
         Merciful heaven! —
What, man! ne'er pull your hat upon your brows;
Give sorrow words: the grief that does not speak
Whispers the o'er-fraught heart, and bids it break.
MACDUFF
My children too?
ROSS
        Wife, children, servants, all
That could be found.
MACDUFF
        And I must be from thence! —
My wife kill'd too?
ROSS
      I have said.
MALCOLM
          Be comforted:
Let's make us medicines of our great revenge,
To cure this deadly grief.
MACDUFF
He has no children. — All my pretty ones?
Did you say all? — O hell-kite! — All?
What, all my pretty chickens and their dam
At one fell swoop?
MALCOLM
Dispute it like a man.
MACDUFF
          I shall do so;
But I must also feel it as a man:
I cannot but remember such things were,
That were most precious to me. — Did heaven look on,
And would not take their part? Sinful Macduff,
They were all struck for thee! naught that I am,
Not for their own demerits, but for mine,
Fell slaughter on their souls: heaven rest them now!
MALCOLM
Be this the whetstone of your sword: let grief
Convert to anger; blunt not the heart, enrage it.
MACDUFF
O, I could play the woman with mine eyes,
And braggart with my tongue! — But, gentle heavens,
Cut short all intermission; front to front
Bring thou this fiend of Scotland and myself;
Within my sword's length set him; if he scape,
Heaven forgive him too!
MALCOLM
        This tune goes manly.
Come, go we to the king; our power is ready;
Our lack is nothing but our leave: Macbeth
Is ripe for shaking, and the powers above
Put on their instruments. Receive what cheer you may:
The night is long that never finds the day.   [*Exeunt.*

ACT V

SCENE I

Dunsinane. A room in the castle.

Enter a DOCTOR OF PHYSIC *and a*
WAITING-GENTLEWOMAN.

DOCTOR
I have two nights watch'd with you, but can perceive no
truth in your report. When was it she last walk'd?
GENTLEWOMAN
Since his majesty went into the field, I have seen her
rise from her bed, throw her nightgown upon her,
unlock her closet, take forth paper, fold it, write upon't,
read it, afterwards seal it, and again return to bed; yet
all this while in a most fast sleep.
DOCTOR
A great perturbation in nature, — to receive at once the
benefit of sleep, and do the effects of watching! — In
this slumbery agitation, besides her walking and other
actual performances, what, at any time, have you heard
her say?
GENTLEWOMAN
That, sir, which I will not report after her.

MACDUFF What, all my pretty chickens and their dam.

DOCTOR
You may to me; and 'tis most meet you should.

GENTLEWOMAN
Neither to you nor any one; having no witness to
confirm my speech. — Lo you, here she comes!
Enter LADY MACBETH, *with a taper.*
This is her very guise; and, upon my life, fast asleep.
Observe her; stand close.

DOCTOR
How came she by that light?

GENTLEWOMAN
Why, it stood by her: she has light by her continually;
'tis her command.

DOCTOR
You see, her eyes are open.

GENTLEWOMAN
Ay, but their sense are shut.

DOCTOR
What is it she does now? Look, how she rubs her
hands.

GENTLEWOMAN
It is an accustom'd action with her, to seem thus
washing her hands: I have known her continue in this a
quarter of an hour.

LADY MACBETH
Yet here's a spot.

DOCTOR
Hark! she speaks: I will set down what comes from her,
to satisfy my remembrance the more strongly.

LADY MACBETH
Out, damned spot! out, I say! — One, two: why, then
'tis time to do't. — Hell is murky! — Fie, my lord, fie! a
soldier, and afeard? What need we fear who knows it,
when none can call our power to account? — Yet who
would have thought the old man to have had so much
blood in him?

DOCTOR
Do you mark that?

LADY MACBETH
The thane of Fife had a wife; where is she now? —
What, will these hands ne'er be clean? — No more
o'that, my lord, no more o'that: you mar all with this
starting.

DOCTOR
Go to, go to; you have known what you should not.

GENTLEWOMAN
She has spoke what she should not, I am sure of that:
heaven knows what she has known.

LADY MACBETH
Here's the smell of the blood still: all the perfumes of
Arabia will not sweeten this little hand. Oh, oh, oh!

DOCTOR
What a sigh is there! The heart is sorely charged.

GENTLEWOMAN
I would not have such a heart in my bosom for the
dignity of the whole body.

DOCTOR
Well, well, well, —

GENTLEWOMAN
Pray God it be, sir.

DOCTOR
This disease is beyond my practise: yet I have known
those which have walk'd in their sleep who have died
holily in their beds.

LADY MACBETH
Wash your hands, put on your nightgown; look not so
pale. — I tell you yet again, Banquo's buried; he cannot
come out on's grave.

DOCTOR
Even so?

LADY MACBETH
To bed, to bed; there's knocking at the gate: come,
come, come, come, give me your hand: what's done
cannot be undone: to bed, to bed, to bed. [*Exit.*

DOCTOR
Will she now go to bed?

GENTLEWOMAN
Directly.

DOCTOR
Foul whisperings are abroad: unnatural deeds
Do breed unnatural troubles: infected minds
To their deaf pillows will discharge their secrets:
More needs she the divine than the physician: —
God, God forgive us all! — Look after her;
Remove from her the means of all annoyance,
And still keep eyes upon her: — so, good night:
My mind she has mated, and amaz'd my sight:
I think, but dare not speak.

GENTLEWOMAN
Good night, good doctor. [*Exeunt.*

SCENE II

The country near Dunsinane.

Drum and colours. Enter MENTEITH, CAITHNESS,
ANGUS, LENNOX, *and* SOLDIERS.

MENTEITH
The English power is near, led on by Malcolm,
His uncle Siward, and the good Macduff:
Revenges burn in them; for their dear causes
Would to the bleeding and the grim alarm
Excite the mortified man.

ANGUS
Near Birnam wood
Shall we well meet them; that way are they coming.

CAITHNESS
Who knows if Donalbain be with his brother?

LENNOX
For certain, sir, he is not: I have a file
Of all the gentry: there is Siward's son,
And many unrough youths, that even now
Protest their first of manhood.

MENTEITH
What does the tyrant?

CAITHNESS
Great Dunsinane he strongly fortifies:
Some say he's mad; others, that lesser hate him,
Do call it valiant fury: but, for certain,
He cannot buckle his distemper'd cause
Within the belt of rule.

ANGUS
Now does he feel
His secret murders sticking on his hands;
Now minutely revolts upbraid his faith-breach;
Those he commands move only in command,
Nothing in love: now does he feel his title
Hang loose about him, like a giant's robe
Upon a dwarfish thief.

MENTEITH
Who, then, shall blame
His pester'd senses to recoil and start,
When all that is within him does condemn
Itself for being there?

CAITHNESS
Well, march we on,
To give obedience where 'tis truly ow'd:
Meet we the medicine of the sickly weal;
And with him pour we in our country's purge
Each drop of us.

LENNOX
Or so much as it needs,
To dew the sovereign flower, and drown the weeds.
Make we our march towards Birnam.
[*Exeunt, marching.*

SCENE III

Dunsinane. A room in the castle.

Enter MACBETH, DOCTOR, *and* ATTENDANTS.

MACBETH
Bring me no more reports; let them fly all:
Till Birnam wood remove to Dunsinane,
I cannot taint with fear. What's the boy Malcolm?
Was he not born of woman? The spirits that know
All mortal consequences have pronounc'd me thus,
'Fear not, Macbeth; no man that's born of woman
Shall e'er have power upon thee.' — Then fly, false
thanes,
And mingle with the English epicures:
The mind I sway by and the heart I bear
Shall never sag with doubt nor shake with fear.
Enter a SERVANT.
The devil damn thee black, thou cream-fac'd loon!
Where gott'st thou that goose look?

SERVANT
There is ten thousand —

MACBETH
Geese, villain?

SERVANT
Soldiers, sir.

MACBETH
Go prick thy face, and over-red thy fear,
Thou lily-liver'd boy. What soldiers, patch?
Death of thy soul! those linen cheeks of thine
Are counsellors to fear. What soldiers, whey-face?

SERVANT
The English force, so please you.

LADY MACBETH Out, damned spot! out, I say!

MACBETH
Take thy face hence. [*Exit* SERVANT.
Seyton! — I am sick at heart,
When I behold — Seyton, I say! — This push
Will chair me ever, or dis-seat me now.
I have liv'd long enough: my way of life
Is fall'n into the sear, the yellow leaf;
And that which should accompany old age,
As honour, love, obedience, troops of friends,
I must not look to have; but, in their stead,
Curses not loud but deep, mouth-honour, breath,
Which the poor heart would fain deny, and dare not.—
Seyton!

Enter SEYTON.

SEYTON
What is your gracious pleasure?
MACBETH
What news more?
SEYTON
All is confirm'd, my lord, which was reported.
MACBETH
I'll fight, till from my bones my flesh be hack'd.
Give me my armour.
SEYTON
'Tis not needed yet.
MACBETH
I'll put it on. —
Send out more horses, skirr the country round;
Hang those that talk of fear. — Give me mine armour. —
How does your patient, doctor?
DOCTOR
Not so sick, my lord,
As she is troubled with thick-coming fancies,
That keep her from her rest.
MACBETH
Cure her of that:
Canst thou not minister to a mind diseas'd;
Pluck from the memory a rooted sorrow;
Raze out the written troubles of the brain;
And with some sweet oblivious antidote
Cleanse the stuff'd bosom of that perilous stuff
Which weighs upon the heart?
DOCTOR
Therein the patient
Must minister to himself.
MACBETH
Throw physic to the dogs, — I'll none of it. —
Come, put mine armour on; give me my staff: —
Seyton, send out. — Doctor, the thanes fly from me.
Come, sir, dispatch. — If thou couldst, doctor, cast
The water of my land, find her disease,
And purge it to a sound and pristine health,
I would applaud thee to the very echo,
That should applaud again. — Pull't off, I say. —
What rhubarb, senna, or what purgative drug,
Would scour these English hence? Hear'st thou of
them?
DOCTOR
Ay, my good lord; your royal preparation
Makes us hear something.
MACBETH
Bring it after me. —
I will not be afraid of death and bane,
Till Birnam forest come to Dunsinane.
[*Exeunt all but* DOCTOR.
DOCTOR
Were I from Dunsinane away and clear,
Profit again should hardly draw me here. [*Exit.*

SCENE IV

Country near Dunsinane: a wood in view.

Drum and colours. Enter MALCOLM, OLD SIWARD
and YOUNG SIWARD, MACDUFF, MENTEITH,
CAITHNESS, ANGUS, LENNOX, ROSS,
and SOLDIERS, *marching.*

MALCOLM
Cousins, I hope the days are near at hand
That chambers will be safe.
MENTEITH
We doubt it nothing.
SIWARD
What wood is this before us?
MENTEITH
The wood of Birnam.
MALCOLM
Let every soldier hew him down a bough,m
And bear't before him: thereby shall we shadow
The numbers of our host, and make discovery

MACDUFF And now a wood comes toward Dunsinane.

Err in report of us.
SOLDIERS
It shall be done.
SIWARD
We learn no other but the confident tyrant
Keeps still in Dunsinane, and will endure
Our setting down before't.
MALCOLM
'Tis his main hope:
For where there is advantage to be ta'en,
Both more and less have given him the revolt;
And none serve with him but constrained things,
Whose hearts are absent too.
MACDUFF
Let our just censures
Attend the true event, and put we on
Industrious soldiership.
SIWARD
The time approaches
That will with due decision make us know
What we shall say we have, and what we owe.
Thoughts speculative their unsure hopes relate;
But certain issue strokes must arbitrate:
Towards which advance the war. [*Exeunt, marching.*

SCENE V

Dunsinane. Within the castle.

Enter MACBETH, SEYTON, *and* SOLDIERS, *with
drum and colours.*

MACBETH
Hang out our banners on the outward walls;
The cry is still, 'They come': our castle's strength
Will laugh a siege to scorn: here let them lie
Till famine and the ague eat them up:
Were they not forc'd with those that should be ours,
We might have met them dareful, beard to beard,
And beat them backward home. [*A cry within of women.*
What is that noise?
SEYTON
It is the cry of women, my good lord. [*Exit.*
MACBETH
I have almost forgot the taste of fears:
The time has been, my senses would have cool'd
To hear a night-shriek; and my fell of hair
Would at a dismal treatise rouse and stir
As life were in't: I have supp'd full with horrors;
Direness, familiar to my slaughterous thoughts,
Cannot once start me.

Enter SEYTON.
Wherefore was that cry?
SEYTON
The queen, my lord, is dead.
MACBETH
She should have died hereafter;
There would have been a time for such a word. —
To-morrow, and to-morrow, and to-morrow,
Creeps in this petty pace from day to day.
To the last syllable of recorded time;
And all our yesterdays have lighted fools
The way to dusty death. Out, out, brief candle!

Life's but a walking shadow; a poor player,
That struts and frets his hour upon the stage,
And then is heard no more: it is a tale
Told by an idiot, full of sound and fury,
Signifying nothing.
Enter a MESSENGER.
Thou comest to use thy tongue; thy story quickly.
MESSENGER
Gracious my lord,
I should report that which I say I saw,
But know not how to do it.
MACBETH
Well, say, sir.
MESSENGER
As I did stand my watch upon the hill,
I look'd toward Birnam, and anon, methought,
The wood began to move.
MACBETH
Liar and slave!
MESSENGER
Let me endure your wrath, if't be not so:
Within this three mile may you see it coming;
I say, a moving grove.
MACBETH
If thou speak'st false,
Upon the next tree shalt thou hang alive,
Till famine cling thee: if thy speech be sooth,
I care not if thou dost for me as much. —
I pull in resolution; and begin
To doubt th'equivocation of the fiend,
That lies like truth: 'Fear not, till Birnam wood
Do come to Dunsinane'; — and now a wood
Comes toward Dunsinane. — Arm, arm, and out!
If this which he avouches does appear,
There is nor flying hence nor tarrying here.
I 'gin to be a-weary of the sun,
And wish th'estate o'th'world were now undone. —
Ring the alarum-bell! — Blow, wind! come, wrack!
At least we'll die with harness on our back. [*Exeunt.*

SCENE VI

The same. A plain before the castle.

Drum and colours. Enter MALCOLM, OLD SIWARD,
MACDUFF, *etc., and their* ARMY *with boughs.*

MALCOLM
Now near enough; your leafy screens throw down,
And show like those you are. — You, worthy uncle,
Shall, with my cousin, your right-noble son,
Lead our first battle: worthy Macduff and we
Shall take upon's what else remains to do,
According to our order.
SIWARD
Fare you well. —
Do we but find the tyrant's power to-night,
Let us be beaten, if we cannot fight.
MACDUFF
Make all our trumpets speak; give them all breath,
Those clamorous harbingers of blood and death.
[*Exeunt.*

SCENE VII

The same. Another part of the plain.

Alarums. Enter MACBETH.

MACBETH
They have tied me to a stake; I cannot fly,
But, bear-like, I must fight the course. — What's he
That was not born of woman? Such a one
Am I to fear, or none.

Enter YOUNG SIWARD.

YOUNG SIWARD
What is thy name?

MACBETH
          Thou'lt be afraid to hear it.

YOUNG SIWARD
No; though thou call'st thyself a hotter name
Than any is in hell.

MACBETH
        My name's Macbeth.

YOUNG SIWARD
The devil himself could not pronounce a title
More hateful to mine ear.

MACBETH
        No, nor more fearful.

YOUNG SIWARD
Thou liest, abhorred tyrant; with my sword
I'll prove the lie thou speak'st.

[They fight, and YOUNG SIWARD *is slain.*

MACBETH
        Thou wast born of woman. —
But swords I smile at, weapons laugh to scorn,
Brandish'd by man that's of a woman born.   *[Exit.*

Alarums. Enter MACDUFF.

MACDUFF
That way the noise is. — Tyrant, show thy face!
If thou be'st slain and with no stroke of mine,
My wife and children's ghosts will haunt me still.
I cannot strike at wretched kerns, whose arms
Are hir'd to bear their staves: either thou, Macbeth,
Or else my sword, with an unbatter'd edge,
I sheathe again undeeded. There thou shouldst be;
By this great clatter, one of greatest note
Seems bruited: — let me find him, fortune!
And more I beg not.   *[Exit. Alarum.*

Enter MALCOLM *and* OLD SIWARD.

SIWARD
This way, my lord; — the castle's gently render'd:
The tyrant's people on both sides do fight;
The noble thanes do bravely in the war:
The day almost itself professes yours,
And little is to do.

MALCOLM
        We have met with foes
That strike beside us.

SIWARD
        Enter, sir, the castle.   *[Exeunt. Alarum.*

SCENE VIII

The same. Another part of the plain.

Enter MACBETH.

MACBETH
Why should I play the Roman fool, and die
On mine own sword? whiles I see lives, the gashes
Do better upon them.

Enter MACDUFF.

MACDUFF
        Turn, hell-hound, turn!

MACBETH
Of all men else I have avoided thee:
But get thee back; my soul is too much charg'd
With blood of thine already.

MACDUFF
        I have no words, —
My voice is in my sword; thou bloodier villain
Than terms can give thee out!   *[They fight. Alarum.*

MACBETH
        Thou losest labour:
As easy mayst thou the intrenchant air
With thy keen sword impress, as make me bleed:
Let fall thy blade on vulnerable crests;
I bear a charmed life, which must not yield
To one of woman born.

MACDUFF
        Despair thy charm;
And let the angel whom thou still hast served
Tell thee, Macduff was from his mother's womb
Untimely ripp'd.

MACBETH
Accursed be that tongue that tells me so,
For it hath cow'd my better part of man!
And be these juggling fiends no more believed,
That palter with us in a double sense;
That keep the word of promise to our ear,
And break it to our hope! — I'll not fight with thee.

MACDUFF
Then yield thee, coward,
And live to be the show and gaze o'th'time:
We'll have thee, as our rarer monsters are,
Painted on a pole, and underwrit
'Here may you see the tyrant.'

MACBETH
        I will not yield,
To kiss the ground before young Malcolm's feet,
And to be baited with the rabble's curse.
Though Birnam wood be come to Dunsinane,
And thou oppos'd, being of no woman born,
Yet I will try the last: — before my body
I throw my warlike shield: lay on, Macduff;
And damn'd be him that first cries 'Hold, enough!'

[Exeunt, fighting.

Retreat. Flourish. Enter, with drum and colours,
MALCOLM, OLD SIWARD, ROSS,
THANES, *and* SOLDIERS.

MALCOLM
I would the friends we miss were safe arrived.

SIWARD
Some must go off: and yet, by these I see,
So great a day as this is cheaply bought.

MALCOLM
Macduff is missing, and your noble son.

ROSS
Your son, my lord, has paid a soldier's debt:
He only liv'd but till he was a man,
The which no sooner had his prowess confirm'd
In the unshrinking station where he fought,
But like a man he died.

SIWARD
        Then he is dead?

ROSS
Ay, and brought off the field: your cause of sorrow
Must not be measured by his worth, for then
It hath no end.

SIWARD
        Had he his hurts before?

ROSS
Ay, on the front.

SIWARD
        Why then, God's soldier be he!
Had I as many sons as I have hairs,
I would not wish them to a fairer death:
And so, his knell is knoll'd.

MALCOLM
        He's worth more sorrow,
And that I'll spend for him.

SIWARD
        He's worth no more:
They say he parted well, and paid his score:
And so, God be with him! — Here comes newer comfort.

Enter MACDUFF, *with* MACBETH'S *head.*

MACDUFF
Hail, king! for so thou art: behold, where stands
Th'usurper's cursed head: the time is free:
I see thee compass'd with thy kingdom's pearl,
That speak my salutation in their minds;
Whose voices I desire aloud with mine, —
Hail, King of Scotland!

ALL
        Hail, King of Scotland!   *[Flourish.*

MALCOLM
We shall not spend a large expense of time
Before we reckon with your several loves,
And make us even with you. My thanes and kinsmen,
Henceforth be earls, — the first that ever Scotland
In such an honour nam'd. What's more to do,
Which would be planted newly with the time, —
As calling home our exil'd friends abroad,
That fled the snares of watchful tyranny;
Producing forth the cruel ministers
Of this dead butcher, and his fiend-like queen, —
Who, as 'tis thought, by self and violent hands
Took off her life; — this, and what needful else
That calls upon us, by the grace of Grace,
We will perform in measure, time and place:
So, thanks to all at once and to each one,
Whom we invite to see us crown'd at Scone.

[Flourish. Exeunt.

KING LEAR

DRAMATIS PERSONAE

LEAR, *King of Britain.*
KING OF FRANCE.
DUKE OF BURGUNDY.
DUKE OF CORNWALL.
DUKE OF ALBANY.
EARL OF KENT.
EARL OF GLOSTER.
EDGAR, *son to Gloster.*
EDMUND, *bastard son to Gloster.*

CURAN, *a courtier.*
OSWALD, *steward to Goneril.*
OLD MAN, *tenant to Gloster.*
DOCTOR.
FOOL.
AN OFFICER, *employ'd by Edmund.*
GENTLEMAN, *attendant on Cordelia.*
A HERALD.
SERVANTS *to Cornwall.*

GONERIL,
REGAN,   } *daughters to Lear.*
CORDELIA,

KNIGHTS *attending on Lear,* OFFICERS,
  MESSENGERS, SOLDIERS, *and* ATTENDANTS.

SCENE — *Britain.*

ACT I

SCENE I

KING LEAR'S *palace.*

Enter KENT, GLOSTER, *and* EDMUND.

KENT
I thought the king had more affected the Duke of
Albany than Cornwall.

KENT Is not this your son, my lord?

GLOSTER
It did always seem so to us: but now, in the division of
the kingdom, it appears not which of the dukes he
values most; for equalities are so weigh'd, that curiosity
in neither can make choice of either's moiety.

KENT
Is not this your son, my lord?

GLOSTER
His breeding, sir, hath been at my charge: I have so
often blush'd to acknowledge him, that now I am
brazed to't.

KENT
I cannot conceive you.

GLOSTER
Sir, this young fellow's mother could: whereupon she
grew round-womb'd, and had, indeed, sir, a son for her
cradle ere she had a husband for her bed. Do you smell
a fault?

KENT
I cannot wish the fault undone, the issue of it being so
proper.

GLOSTER
But I have a son, sir, by order of law, some year elder
than this, who yet is no dearer in my account: though
this knave came something saucily into the world
before he was sent for, yet was his mother fair; there
was good sport at his making, and the whoreson must
be acknowledged. — Do you know this noble
gentleman, Edmund?

EDMUND
No, my lord.

GLOSTER
My Lord of Kent: remember him hereafter as my
honourable friend.

EDMUND
My services to your lordship.

KENT
I must love you, and sue to know you better.

EDMUND
Sir, I shall study deserving.

GLOSTER
He hath been out nine years, and away he shall again. —
The king is coming.

Sennet. Enter one bearing a coronet, KING LEAR,
CORNWALL, ALBANY, GONERIL, REGAN,
CORDELIA, *and* ATTENDANTS.

KING LEAR
Attend the Lords of France and Burgundy, Gloster.

GLOSTER
I shall, my liege.   [*Exeunt* GLOSTER *and* EDMUND.

KING LEAR
Meantime we shall express our darker purpose.
Give me the map there. Know we have divided
In three our kingdom: and 'tis our fast intent
To shake all cares and business from our age;
Conferring them on younger strengths, while we
Unburthen'd crawl toward death. — Our son of
  Cornwall,
And you, our no less loving son of Albany,
We have this hour a constant will to publish
Our daughters' several dowers, that future strife
May be prevented now. The princes, France and
  Burgundy,
Great rivals in our youngest daughter's love,
Long in our court have made their amorous sojourn,
And here are to be answer'd. Tell me, my daughters, —
Since now we will divest us both of rule,
Interest of territory, cares of state, —
Which of you shall we say doth love us most?
That we our largest bounty may extend
Where nature doth with merit challenge. Goneril,
Our eldest-born, speak first.

GONERIL
Sir, I love you more than words can wield the matter;
Dearer than eyesight, space, and liberty;
Beyond what can be valued, rich or rare;
No less than life, with grace, health, beauty, honour;
As much as child e'er loved, or father found;
A love that makes breath poor, and speech unable;
Beyond all manner of so much I love you.

CORDELIA [*aside*].
What shall Cordelia do? Love, and be silent.

KING LEAR
Of all these bounds, even from this line to this,
With shadowy forests and with champains rich'd,
With plenteous rivers and wide-skirted meads,
We make thee lady: to thine and Albany's issue
Be this perpetual. What says our second daughter,
Our dearest Regan, wife to Cornwall? Speak.

REGAN
I am made of the self metal as my sister,
And prize me at her worth. In my true heart
I find she names my very deed of love;
Only she comes too short, — that I profess
Myself an enemy to all other joys,
Which the most precious square of sense possesses;
And find I am alone felicitate
In your dear highness' love.

CORDELIA [*aside*].
                                   Then poor Cordelia!
And yet not so; since, I am sure, my love's
More richer than my tongue.

KING LEAR
To thee and thine hereditary ever
Remain this ample third of our fair kingdom;
No less in space, validity, and pleasure,
Than that conferr'd on Goneril. — Now, our joy,
Although our last, not least; to whose young love
The vines of France and milk of Burgundy
Strive to be interest; what can you say to draw
A third more opulent than your sisters? Speak.

CORDELIA
Nothing, my lord.

KING LEAR
Nothing!

CORDELIA
Nothing.

KING LEAR
Nothing will come of nothing: speak again.

CORDELIA
Unhappy that I am, I cannot heave
My heart into my mouth: I love your majesty
According to my bond; nor more nor less.

KING LEAR
How, how, Cordelia! mend your speech a little,
Lest it may mar your fortunes.

CORDELIA
                                   Good my lord,
You have begot me, bred me, lov'd me: I
Return those duties back as are right fit,
Obey you, love you, and most honour you.
Why have my sisters husbands, if they say
They love you all? Haply, when I shall wed,
That lord whose hand must take my plight shall carry
Half my love with him, half my care and duty:
Sure, I shall never marry like my sisters,
To love my father all.

KING LEAR
But goes thy heart with this?

CORDELIA
                                   Ay, good my lord.

KING LEAR
So young, and so untender?

CORDELIA
So young, my lord, and true.

KING LEAR
Let it be so, — thy truth, then, be thy dower:
For, by the sacred radiance of the sun,
The mysteries of Hecate, and the night;
By all the operation of the orbs
From whom we do exist, and cease to be;
Here I disclaim all my paternal care,
Propinquity and property of blood,
And as a stranger to my heart and me

Hold thee, from this, for ever. The barbarous Scythian,
Or he that makes his generation messes
To gorge his appetite, shall to my bosom
Be as well neighbour'd, pitied, and reliev'd,
As thou my sometime daughter.

KENT

                         Good my liege, —

KING LEAR

Peace, Kent!
Come not between the dragon and his wrath. —
I lov'd her most, and thought to set my rest
On her kind nursery. — Hence, and avoid my sight! —
So be my grave my peace, as here I give
Her father's heart from her! — Call France; — who
    stirs?
Call Burgundy. — Cornwall and Albany,
With my two daughters' dowers digest this third:
Let pride, which she calls plainness, marry her.
I do invest you jointly in my power,
Pre-eminence, and all the large effects
That troop with majesty. — Ourself, by monthly
    course,
With reservation of an hundred knights,
By you to be sustain'd, shall our abode
Make with you by due turns. Only we still retain
The name, and all the additions to a king;
The sway, revenue, execution of the rest,
Beloved sons, be yours: which to confirm,
This coronet part betwixt you.   *[Giving the crown.*

KENT

                       Royal Lear,
Whom I have ever honour'd as my king,
Lov'd as my father, as my master follow'd,
As my great patron thought on in my prayers, —

KING LEAR

The bow is bent and drawn, make from the shaft.

KENT

Let it fall rather, though the fork invade
The region of my heart: be Kent unmannerly,
When Lear is mad. What wouldst thou do, old man?
Think'st thou that duty shall have dread to speak,
When power to flattery bows? To plainness honour's
    bound,
When majesty falls to folly. Reverse thy doom;
And, in thy best consideration, check
This hideous rashness: answer my life my judgement,
Thy youngest daughter does not love thee least;
Nor are those empty-hearted whose low sound
Reverbs no hollowness.

KING LEAR

                Kent, on thy life, no more.

KENT

My life I never held but as a pawn
To wage against thine enemies; nor fear to lose it,
Thy safety being the motive.

KING LEAR

                     Out of my sight!

KENT

See better, Lear; and let me still remain
The true blank of thine eye.

KING LEAR

Now, by Apollo, —

KENT

                Now, by Apollo, king,
Thou swear'st thy gods in vain.

KING LEAR

                O, vassal! miscreant!
    [Laying his hand on his sword.

ALBANY *and* CORNWALL

Dear sir, forbear.

KENT

Do;
Kill thy physician, and the fee bestow
Upon thy foul disease. Revoke thy doom;
Or, whilst I can vent clamour from my throat,
I'll tell thee thou dost evil.

KING LEAR

                Hear me, recreant!
On thine allegiance, hear me!
Since thou hast sought to make us break our vow,
Which we durst never yet, and with strain'd pride

To come between our sentence and our power,
Which nor our nature nor our place can bear,
Our potency made good, take thy reward.
Five days we do allot thee, for provision
To shield thee from diseases of the world;
And, on the sixth, to turn thy hated back
Upon our kingdom: if, on the tenth day following,
Thy banish'd trunk be found in our dominions,
The moment is thy death. Away! by Jupiter,
This shall not be revok'd.

KENT

Fare thee well, king: sith thus thou wilt appear,
Freedom lives hence, and banishment is here.
[to CORDELIA*]* The gods to their dear shelter take thee,
    maid,
That justly think'st, and hast most rightly said!.
[to REGAN *and* GONERIL*]* And your large speeches
    may your deeds approve,
That good effects may spring from words of love.
Thus Kent, O princes, bids you all adieu;
He'll shape his old course in a country new.   *[Exit.*

    Flourish. Enter GLOSTER, *with* FRANCE,
        BURGUNDY, *and* ATTENDANTS.

GLOSTER

Here's France and Burgundy, my noble lord.

KING LEAR

My Lord of Burgundy.
We first address towards you, who with this king
Hath rivall'd for our daughter, what, in the least,
Will you require in present dower with her,
Or cease your quest of love?

BURGUNDY

                Most royal majesty,
I crave no more than what your highness offer'd,
Nor will you tender less.

KING LEAR

                Right noble Burgundy,
When she was dear to us, we did hold her so;
But now her price is fall'n. Sir, there she stands:
If aught within that little-seeming substance,
Or all of it, with our displeasure pieced,
And nothing more, may fitly like your Grace,
She's there, and she is yours.

BURGUNDY

                I know no answer.

KING LEAR

Will you, with those infirmities she owes,
Unfriended, new-adopted to our hate,
Dower'd with our curse, and stranger'd with our oath,
Take her, or leave her?

BURGUNDY

                Pardon me, royal sir;
Election makes not up on such conditions.

KING LEAR

Then leave her, sir; for, by the power that made me,
I tell you all her wealth. — *[to* FRANCE*]* For you, great
    king,
I would not from your love make such a stray,
To match you where I hate; therefore beseech you
T'avert your liking a more worthier way
Than on a wretch whom nature is asham'd
Almost t'acknowledge hers.

KING OF FRANCE

                This is most strange,
That she, that even but now was your best object,
The argument of your praise, balm of your age,
Most best, most dearest, should in this trice of time
Commit a thing so monstrous, to dismantle
So many folds of favour. Sure, her offence
Must be of such unnatural degree,
That monsters it, or your fore-vouch'd affection
Fall'n into taint: which to believe of her,
Must be a faith that reason without miracle
Should never plant in me.

CORDELIA

             I yet beseech your majesty, —
If for I want that glib and oily art,
To speak and purpose not; since what I well intend,
I'll do't before I speak, — that you make known
It is no vicious blot, murder, or foulness,
No unchaste action, or dishonour'd step,
That hath depriv'd me of your Grace and favour;
But even for want of that for which I am richer, —
A still-soliciting eye, and such a tongue
As I am glad I have not, though not to have it
Hath lost me in your liking.

KING LEAR

                Better thou
Hadst not been born than not t'have pleas'd me better.

KING LEAR Hence, and avoid my sight!

KING OF FRANCE
Is it but this? a tardiness in nature
Which often leaves the history unspoke
That it intends to do? My Lord of Burgundy,
What say you to the lady? Love's not love
When it is mingled with regards that stand
Aloof from the entire point. Will you have her?
She is herself a dowry.

BURGUNDY
                    Royal Lear,
Give but that portion which yourself proposed,
And here I take Cordelia by the hand,
Duchess of Burgundy.

KING LEAR
Nothing: I have sworn; I am firm.

BURGUNDY
I am sorry, then, you have so lost a father
That you must lose a husband.

CORDELIA
                    Peace be with Burgundy!
Since that respects of fortune are his love,
I shall not be his wife.

KING OF FRANCE
Fairest Cordelia, that art most rich, being poor;
Most choice, forsaken; and most lov'd, despis'd!
Thee and thy virtues here I seize upon:
Be it lawful I take up what's cast away.
Gods, gods! 'tis strange that from their cold'st neglect
My love should kindle to inflam'd respect. —
Thy dowerless daughter, king, thrown to my chance,
Is queen of us, of ours, and our fair France:
Not all the dukes of waterish Burgundy
Can buy this unpriz'd precious maid of me. —
Bid them farewell, Cordelia, though unkind:
Thou losest here, a better where to find.

KING LEAR
Thou hast her, France: let her be thine; for we
Have no such daughter, nor shall ever see
That face of hers again: — Therefore be gone
Without our grace, our love, our benison. —
Come, noble Burgundy.

        [*Flourish. Exeunt* LEAR, BURGUNDY, CORNWALL,
            ALBANY, GLOSTER, *and* ATTENDANTS.

KING OF FRANCE
Bid farewell to your sisters.

CORDELIA
The jewels of our father, with wash'd eyes
Cordelia leaves you: I know you what you are;
And, like a sister, am most loth to call
Your faults as they are nam'd. Love well our father:
To your professed bosoms I commit him:
But yet, alas, stood I within his grace,
I would prefer him to a better place.
So, farewell to you both.

REGAN
Prescribe not us our duties.

GONERIL
                    Let your study
Be to content your lord, who hath receiv'd you
At fortune's alms. You have obedience scanted,
And well are worth the want that you have wanted.

CORDELIA
Time shall unfold what pleated cunning hides:
Who cover faults, at last shame them derides.
Well may you prosper!

KING OF FRANCE
                    Come, my fair Cordelia.
        [*Exeunt* FRANCE *and* CORDELIA.

GONERIL
Sister, it is not a little I have to say of what most nearly
appertains to us both. I think our father will hence
to-night.

REGAN
That's most certain, and with you; next month with us.

GONERIL
You see how full of changes his age is; the observation
we have made of it hath not been little: he always loved
our sister most; and with what poor judgement he hath
now cast her off appears too grossly.

REGAN
'Tis the infirmity of his age: yet he hath ever but
slenderly known himself.

GONERIL
The best and soundest of his time hath been but rash;
then must we look to receive from his age, not alone the
imperfections of long-engraffed condition, but
therewithal the unruly waywardness that infirm and
choleric years bring with them.

REGAN
Such unconstant starts are we like to have from him as

this of Kent's banishment.

GONERIL
There is further compliment of leave-taking between
France and him. Pray you, let's hit together: if our
father carry authority with such dispositions as he
bears, this last surrender of his will but offend us.

REGAN
We shall further think on't.

GONERIL
We must do something, and i' the heat.   [*Exeunt.*

SCENE II

The EARL OF GLOSTER'S *castle.*

Enter EDMUND, *with a letter.*

EDMUND
Thou, nature, art my goddess; to thy law
My services are bound. Wherefore should I
Stand in the plague of custom, and permit
The curiosity of nations to deprive me,
For that I am some twelve or fourteen moon-shines
Lag of a brother? Why bastard? wherefore base?
When my dimensions are as well compact,
My mind as generous, and my shape as true,
As honest madam's issue? Why brand they us
With base? with baseness? bastardy? base, base?
Who, in the lusty stealth of nature, take
More composition and fierce quality
Than doth, within a dull, stale, tired bed,
Go to th'creating a whole tribe of fops,
Got 'tween asleep and wake? — Well, then,
Legitimate Edgar, I must have your land:
Our father's love is to the bastard Edmund
As to th'legitimate: fine word, — legitimate!
Well, my legitimate, if this letter speed,
And my invention thrive, Edmund the base
Shall top th'legitimate — I grow; I prosper: —
Now, gods, stand up for bastards!

                Enter GLOSTER.

GLOSTER
Kent banish'd thus! and France in choler parted!
And the king gone to-night! subscrib'd his power!
Confined to exhibition! All this done
Upon the gad! — Edmund, how now! what news?

EDMUND
So please your lordship, none.
                [*Putting up the letter.*

GLOSTER
Why so earnestly seek you to put up that letter?

EDMUND
I know no news, my lord.

GLOSTER
What paper were you reading?

EDMUND
Nothing, my lord.

GLOSTER
No? What needed, then, that terrible dispatch
of it into your pocket? the quality of nothing
hath not such need to hide itself. Let's see:
come, if it be nothing, I shall not need
spectacles.

EDMUND
I beseech you, sir, pardon me: it is a letter from
my brother, that I have not all o'er-read; and
for so much as I have perused, I find it not fit
for your o'er-looking.

GLOSTER
Give me the letter, sir.

EDMUND
I shall offend, either to detain or give it. The
contents, as in part I understand them, are to
blame.

GLOSTER
Let's see, let's see.

EDMUND
I hope, for my brother's justification, he wrote
this but as an essay or taste of my virtue.

GLOSTER [*reads*].
This policy and reverence of age makes the
world bitter to the best of our times; keeps our
fortunes from us till our oldness cannot relish
them. I begin to find an idle and fond bondage
in the oppression of aged tyranny; who sways,
not as it hath power, but as it is suffer'd. Come
to me, that of this I may speak more. If our
father would sleep till I waked him, you
should enjoy half his revenue for ever, and live
the beloved of your brother,
                    EDGAR.

Hum — conspiracy! — 'Sleep till I waked him, you
should enjoy half his revenue'! — My son Edgar! Had he
a hand to write this? a heart and brain to breed it in? —
When came this to you? Who brought it?

EDMUND
It was not brought me, my lord, — there's the cunning
of it; I found it thrown in at the casement of my closet.

GLOSTER
You know the character to be your brother's?

EDMUND
If the matter were good, my lord, I durst swear it were
his; but, in respect of that, I would fain think it were
not.

GLOSTER
It is his.

EDMUND
It is his hand, my lord; but I hope his heart is not in the
contents.

GLOSTER
Has he never before sounded you in this business?

EDMUND
Never, my lord: but I have heard him oft maintain it to
be fit, that, sons at perfect age, and fathers declining,
the father should be as ward to the son, and the son
manage his revenue.

GLOSTER
O villain, villain! — His very opinion in the letter! —
Abhorr'd villain! Unnatural, detested, brutish villain!
worse than brutish! — Go, sirrah, seek him; I'll
apprehend him: — abominable villain! — Where is he?

EDMUND
I do not well know, my lord. If it shall please you to
suspend your indignation against my brother till you
can derive from him better testimony of his intent, you
shall run a certain course; where, if you violently
proceed against him, mistaking his purpose, it would
make a great gap in your own honour, and shake in
pieces the heart of his obedience. I dare pawn down my
life for him, that he hath writ this to feel my affection to
your honour, and to no further pretence of danger.

GLOSTER
Think you so?

EDMUND
If your honour judge it meet, I will place you where you
shall hear us confer of this, and by an auricular

EDMUND Why brand they us with base?
            with baseness? bastardy?

assurance have your satisfaction; and that without any further delay than this very evening.

GLOSTER
He cannot be such a monster. —

EDMUND
Nor is not, sure.

GLOSTER
To his father, that so tenderly and entirely loves him. — Heaven and earth! — Edmund, seek him out; wind me into him, I pray you: frame the business after your own wisdom. I would unstate myself, to be in a due resolution.

EDMUND
I will seek him, sir, presently; convey the business as I shall find means, and acquaint you withal.

GLOSTER
These late eclipses in the sun and moon portend no good to us: though the wisdom of nature can reason it thus and thus, yet nature finds itself scourged by the sequent effects: love cools, friendship falls off, brothers divide: in cities, mutinies; in countries, discord; in palaces, treason; and the bond crack'd 'twixt son and father. This villain of mine comes under the prediction; there's son against father: the king falls from bias of nature; there's father against child. We have seen the best of our time: machinations, hollowness, treachery, and all ruinous disorders, follow us disquietly to our graves. — Find out this villain, Edmund; it shall lose thee nothing; do it carefully. — And the noble and true-hearted Kent banish'd! his offence, honesty! — 'Tis strange. [*Exit.*

EDMUND
This is the excellent foppery of the world, that, when we are sick in fortune, — often the surfeit of our own behaviour, — we make guilty of our disasters the sun, the moon, and the stars: as if we were villains by necessity; fools by heavenly compulsion; knaves, thieves, and treachers, by spherical predominance; drunkards, liars, and adulterers, by an enforced obedience of planetary influence; and all that we are evil in, by a divine thrusting on: an admirable evasion of whoremaster man, to lay his goatish disposition to the charge of a star! My father compounded with my mother under the dragon's tail; and my nativity was under *ursa major*; so that it follows, I am rough and lecherous. — Fut, I should have been that I am, had the maidenliest star in the firmament twinkled on my bastardizing. — Edgar! pat he comes like the catastrophe of the old comedy: my cue is villainous melancholy, with a sigh like Tom o'Bedlam.
Enter EDGAR.
O, these eclipses do portend these divisions! fa, sol, la, mi.

EDGAR
How now, brother Edmund! what serious contemplation are you in?

EDMUND
I am thinking, brother, of a prediction I read this other day, what should follow these eclipses.

EDGAR
Do you busy yourself with that?

EDMUND
I promise you, the effects he writes of succeed unhappily; as of unnaturalness between the child and the parent; death, dearth, dissolutions of ancient amities; divisions in state, menaces and maledictions against king and nobles; needless diffidences, banishment of friends, dissipation of cohorts, nuptial breaches, and I know not what.

EDGAR
How long have you been a sectary astronomical?

EDMUND
Come, come; when saw you my father last?

EDGAR
The night gone by.

EDMUND
Spake you with him?

EDGAR
Ay, two hours together.

EDMUND
Parted you in good terms? Found you no displeasure in him by word or countenance?

EDGAR
None at all.

EDMUND
Bethink yourself wherein you may have offended him: and at my entreaty forbear his presence till some little time hath qualified the heat of his displeasure; which at this instant so rageth in him, that with the mischief of your person it would scarcely allay.

EDGAR
Some villain hath done me wrong.

EDMUND
That's my fear. I pray you, have a continent forbearance till the speed of his rage goes slower; and, as I say, retire with me to my lodging, from whence I will fitly bring you to hear my lord speak: pray you, go; there's my key: — if you do stir abroad, go arm'd.

EDGAR
Arm'd, brother!

EDMUND
Brother, I advise you to the best; I am no honest man if there be any good meaning toward you: I have told you what I have seen and heard; but faintly, nothing like the image and horror of it: pray you, away.

EDGAR
Shall I hear from you anon?

EDMUND
I do serve you in this business.   [*Exit* EDGAR.
A credulous father! and a brother noble,
Whose nature is so far from doing harms,
That he suspects none; on whose foolish honesty
My practises ride easy! — I see the business. —
Let me, if not by birth, have lands by wit:
All with me's meet that I can fashion fit.   [*Exit.*

SCENE III

The DUKE OF ALBANY'S *palace.*

Enter GONERIL *and* OSWALD, *her steward.*

GONERIL
Did my father strike my gentleman for chiding of his fool?

OSWALD
Ay, madam.

GONERIL
By day and night, he wrongs me; every hour
He flashes into one gross crime or other,
That sets us all at odds: I'll not endure it:
His knights grow riotous, and himself upbraids us
On every trifle. — When he returns from hunting,
I will not speak with him; say I am sick: —
If you come slack of former services,
You shall do well; the fault of it I'll answer.
[*Horns within.*

OSWALD
He's coming, madam; I hear him.

GONERIL
Put on what weary negligence you please,
You and your fellows; I'ld have it come to question:
If he distaste it, let him to our sister,
Whose mind and mine, I know, in that are one,
Not to be over-ruled. Idle old man,
That still would manage those authorities
That he hath given away! — Now, by my life,
Old fools are babes again; and must be us'd
With checks as flatteries, when they are seen abus'd.
Remember what I have said.

OSWALD
                                     Very well, madam.

GONERIL
And let his knights have colder looks among you;
What grows of it, no matter; advise your fellows so:
I would breed from hence occasions, and I shall,
That I may speak: — I'll write straight to my sister,
To hold my very course. — Prepare for dinner. [*Exeunt.*

SCENE IV

A hall in the same.

Enter KENT, *disguised.*

KENT
If but as well I other accents borrow,
That can my speech defuse, my good intent
May carry through itself to that full issue
For which I raz'd my likeness. — Now, banish'd Kent,
If thou canst serve where thou dost stand condemn'd,
So may it come, thy master, whom thou lovest,
Shall find thee full of labours.

Horns within. Enter LEAR, KNIGHTS, *and*
ATTENDANTS.

KING LEAR
Let me not stay a jot for dinner; go get it ready.
[*Exit an* ATTENDANT.
How now! what art thou?

KENT
A man, sir.

KING LEAR
What dost thou profess? what wouldst thou with us?

KENT
I do profess to be no less than I seem; to serve him truly that will put me in trust; to love him that is honest; to converse with him that is wise, and says little; to fear judgement; to fight when I cannot choose; and to eat no fish.

KING LEAR
What art thou?

KENT
A very honest-hearted fellow, and as poor as the king.

KING LEAR
If thou be as poor for a subject as he is for a king, thou art poor enough. What wouldst thou?

KENT
Service.

KING LEAR
Who wouldst thou serve?

KENT
You.

KING LEAR
Dost thou know me, fellow?

KENT
No, sir; but you have that in your countenance which I would fain call master.

KING LEAR
What's that?

KENT
Authority.

KING LEAR
What services canst thou do?

KENT
I can keep honest counsel, ride, run, mar a curious tale in telling it, and deliver a plain message bluntly: that which ordinary men are fit for, I am qualified in: and the best of me is diligence.

KING LEAR
How old art thou?

KENT
Not so young, sir, to love a woman for singing, nor so old to dote on her for any thing: I have years on my back forty-eight.

KING LEAR
Follow me; thou shalt serve me: if I like thee no worse after dinner, I will not part from thee yet. — Dinner, ho, dinner! — Where's my knave? my fool? — Go you, and call my fool hither.   [*Exit an* ATTENDANT.
Enter OSWALD.
You, you, sirrah, where's my daughter?

OSWALD
So please you, —   [*Exit.*

KING LEAR
What says the fellow there? Call the clotpoll back. [*Exit a* KNIGHT.] — Where's my fool, ho? — I think the world's asleep.
Enter KNIGHT.
How now! where's that mongrel?

KNIGHT
He says, my lord, your daughter is not well.

KING LEAR
Why came not the slave back to me when I call'd him?

KNIGHT
Sir, he answer'd me in the roundest manner, he would not.

KING LEAR
He would not!

KNIGHT
My lord, I know not what the matter is; but, to my judgement, your highness is not entertain'd with that ceremonious affection as you were wont; there's a great abatement of kindness appears as well in the general dependants as in the duke himself also and your daughter.

KING LEAR
Ha! say'st thou so?

KNIGHT
I beseech you, pardon me, my lord, if I be mistaken; for my duty cannot be silent when I think your highness wrong'd.

KING LEAR
Thou but rememberest me of mine own conception: I have perceived a most faint neglect of late; which I have rather blamed as mine own jealous curiosity than as a very pretence and purpose of unkindness: I will look further into't. — But where's my fool? I have not seen him this two days.

KNIGHT
Since my young lady's going into France, sir, the fool hath much pined away.

KING LEAR
No more of that; I have noted it well. — Go you, and tell

my daughter I would speak with her. [*Exit an* ATTENDANT.] — Go you, call hither my fool.
[*Exit an* ATTENDANT.

Enter OSWALD.

O, you sir, you, come you hither, sir: who am I, sir?

OSWALD
My lady's father.

KING LEAR
'My lady's father!' my lord's knave: you whoreson dog! you slave! you cur!

OSWALD
I am none of these, my lord; I beseech your pardon.

KING LEAR
Do you bandy looks with me, you rascal? [*Striking him.*

OSWALD
I'll not be struck, my lord.

KENT
Nor tripp'd neither, you base football player.
[*Tripping up his heels.*

KING LEAR
I thank thee, fellow; thou servest me, and I'll love thee.

KENT
Come, sir, arise, away! I'll teach you differences: away, away! If you will measure your lubber's length again, tarry: but away! go to; have you wisdom? so.
[*Pushes* OSWALD *out.*

KING LEAR
Now, my friendly knave, I thank thee: there's earnest of thy service. [*Giving* KENT *money.*

Enter FOOL.

FOOL
Let me hire him too: — here's my coxcomb.
[*Offering* KENT *his cap.*

KING LEAR
How now, my pretty knave! how dost thou?

FOOL
Sirrah, you were best take my coxcomb.

KENT
Why, fool?

FOOL
Why, for taking one's part that's out of favour: nay, an thou canst not smile as the wind sits, thou'lt catch cold shortly: there, take my coxcomb: why, this fellow hath banish'd two on's daughters, and did the third a blessing against his will; if thou follow him, thou must needs wear my coxcomb. — How now, nuncle! Would I had two coxcombs and two daughters!

KING LEAR
Why, my boy?

FOOL
If I gave them all my living, I'd keep my coxcombs myself. There's mine; beg another of thy daughters.

KING LEAR
Take heed, sirrah; — the whip.

FOOL
Truth's a dog must to kennel; he must be whipp'd out, when Lady the brach may stand by the fire and stink.

KING LEAR
A pestilent gall to me!

FOOL
Sirrah, I'll teach thee a speech.

KING LEAR
Do.

FOOL
Mark it, nuncle; —
Have more than thou showest,
Speak less than thou knowest,
Lend less than thou owest,
Ride more than thou goest,
Learn more than thou trowest,
Set less than thou throwest;
Leave thy drink and thy whore,
And keep in-a-door,
And thou shalt have more
Than two tens to a score.

KENT
This is nothing, fool.

FOOL
Then 'tis like the breath of an unfee'd lawyer, — you gave me nothing for't. — Can you make no use of nothing, nuncle?

KING LEAR
Why, no, boy; nothing can be made out of nothing.

FOOL [*to* KENT].
Prithee, tell him, so much the rent of his land comes to: he will not believe a fool.

KING LEAR
A bitter fool!

FOOL
Dost thou know the difference, my boy, between a bitter fool and a sweet fool?

KING LEAR
No, lad; teach me.

FOOL
That lord that counsell'd thee
To give away thy land,
Come place him here by me, —
Do thou for him stand:
The sweet and bitter fool
Will presently appear;
The one in motley here,
The other found out there.

KING LEAR
Dost thou call me fool, boy?

FOOL
All thy other titles thou hast given away; that thou wast born with.

KENT
This is not altogether fool, my lord.

FOOL
No, faith, lords and great men will not let me; if I had a monopoly out, they would have part on't: and ladies too, they will not let me have all fool to myself; they'll be snatching. — Give me an egg, nuncle, and I'll give thee two crowns.

KING LEAR
What two crowns shall they be?

FOOL
Why, after I have cut the egg i'th'middle, and eat up the meat, the two crowns of the egg. When thou clovest thy crown i'th'middle, and gavest away both parts, thou borest thy ass on thy back o'er the dirt: thou hadst little wit in thy bald crown, when thou gavest thy golden one away. If I speak like myself in this, let him be whipp'd that first finds it so. [*Singing.*
Fools had ne'er less wit in a year;
For wise men are grown foppish,
And know not how their wits to wear,
Their manners are so apish.

KING LEAR
When were you wont to be so full of songs, sirrah?

FOOL
I have used it, nuncle, ever since thou madest thy daughters thy mothers: for when thou gavest them the rod, and put'st down thine own breeches, [*Singing.*
Then they for sudden joy did weep,
And I for sorrow sung,
That such a king should play bo-peep,
And go the fools among.
Prithee, nuncle, keep a schoolmaster that can teach thy fool to lie: I would fain learn to lie.

KING LEAR
An you lie, sirrah, we'll have you whipp'd.

FOOL
I marvel what kin thou and thy daughters are: they'll have me whipp'd for speaking true, thou'lt have me whipp'd for lying; and sometimes I am whipp'd for holding my peace. I had rather be any kind o'thing than a fool: and yet I would not be thee, nuncle; thou hast pared thy wit o'both sides, and left nothing i'th'middle: — here comes one o'th'parings.

Enter GONERIL.

KING LEAR
How now, daughter! what makes that frontlet on? Methinks you are too much of late i'th'frown.

FOOL
Thou wast a pretty fellow when thou hadst no need to care for her frowning; now thou art an O without a figure: I am better than thou art now; I am a fool, thou art nothing. — [*to* GONERIL] Yes, forsooth, I will hold my tongue; so your face bids me, though you say nothing.
Mum, mum:
He that keeps nor crust nor crum,
Weary of all, shall want some. —
That's a sheal'd peascod. [*Pointing to* LEAR.

GONERIL
Not only, sir, this your all-licens'd fool,
But other of your insolent retinue
Do hourly carp and quarrel; breaking forth

In rank and not-to-be endured riots. Sir,
I had thought, by making this well known unto you,
To have found a safe redress; but now grow fearful,
By what yourself too late have spoke and done,
That you protect this course, and put it on
By your allowance; which if you should, the fault
Would not scape censure, nor the redresses sleep,
Which, in the tender of a wholesome weal,
Might in their working do you that offence,
Which else were shame, that then necessity
Will call discreet proceeding.

FOOL
For, you trow, nuncle,
The hedge-sparrow fed the cuckoo so long,
That it had its head bit off by its young.
So, out went the candle, and we were left darkling.

KING LEAR
Are you our daughter?

GONERIL
Come, sir,
I would you would make use of that good wisdom
Whereof I know you are fraught; and put away
These dispositions, that of late transform you
From what you rightly are.

FOOL
May not an ass know when the cart draws the horse? —
Whoop, Jug! I love thee.

KING LEAR
Doth any here know me? — Why, this is not Lear:
Doth Lear walk thus? speak thus? Where are his eyes?
Either his notion weakens, or his discernings
Are lethargied — Ha! waking? 'tis not so. —
Who is it that can tell me who I am? —

FOOL
Lear's shadow.

KING LEAR
I would learn that; for, by the marks of sovereignty,
Knowledge, and reason, I should be false-persuaded
I had daughters.

FOOL
Which they will make an obedient father.

KING LEAR
Your name, fair gentlewoman?

KENT Nor tripp'd neither, you base football player.

GONERIL
This admiration, sir, is much o'th'savour
Of other your new pranks. I do beseech you
To understand my purposes aright:
As you are old and reverend, should be wise.
Here do you keep a hundred knights and squires;
Men so disorder'd, so debosh'd, and bold,
That this our court, infected with their manners,
Shows like a riotous inn: epicurism and lust
Make it more like a tavern or a brothel
Than a grac'd palace. The shame itself doth speak
For instant remedy: be, then, desired
By her, that else will take the thing she begs,
A little to disquantity your train;
And the remainder, that shall still depend,
To be such men as may besort your age,
Which know themselves and you.

KING LEAR
                              Darkness and devils! —
Saddle my horses; call my train together. —
Degenerate bastard! I'll not trouble thee:
Yet have I left a daughter.

GONERIL
You strike my people; and your disorder'd rabble
Make servants of their betters.

Enter ALBANY.

KING LEAR
Woe, that too late repents: — [*to* ALBANY] O, sir, are
    you come?
Is it your will? Speak, sir. — Prepare my horses. —
Ingratitude, thou marble-hearted fiend,
More hideous when thou show'st thee in a child
Than the sea-monster!

ALBANY
                    Pray, sir, be patient.

KING LEAR [*to* GONERIL].
Detested kite! thou liest:
My train are men of choice and rarest parts,
That all particulars of duty know,
And in the most exact regard support
The worships of their name. — O most small fault,
How ugly didst thou in Cordelia show!
Which, like an engine, wrench'd my frame of nature
From the fix'd place; drew from my heart all love,
And added to the gall. O Lear, Lear, Lear!
Beat at this gate, that let thy folly in,   [*Striking his head.*
And thy dear judgement out! — Go, go, my people.

ALBANY
My lord, I am guiltless, as I am ignorant
Of what hath mov'd you.

KING LEAR
                      It may be so, my lord. —
Hear, nature, hear; dear goddess, hear!
Suspend thy purpose, if thou didst intend
To make this creature fruitful!
Into her womb convey sterility!
Dry up in her the organs of increase;
And from her derogate body never spring
A babe to honour her! If she must teem,
Create her child of spleen; that it may live,
And be a thwart disnatured torment to her!
Let it stamp wrinkles in her brow of youth;
With cadent tears fret channels in her cheeks;
Turn all her mother's pains and benefits
To laughter and contempt, — that she may feel
How sharper than a serpent's tooth it is
To have a thankless child! — Away, away!   [*Exit.*

ALBANY
Now, gods that we adore, whereof comes this?

GONERIL
Never afflict yourself to know the cause;
But let his disposition have that scope
That dotage gives it.

Enter LEAR.

KING LEAR
What, fifty of my followers at a clap!
Within a fortnight!

ALBANY
                  What's the matter, sir?

KING LEAR
I'll tell thee: — [*to* GONERIL] Life and death! I am
    ashamed
That thou hast power to shake my manhood thus;
That these hot tears, which break from me perforce,
Should make thee worth them. — Blasts and fogs upon
    thee!
Th'untented woundings of a father's curse
Pierce every sense about thee! — Old fond eyes,
Beweep this cause again, I'll pluck ye out,

And cast you, with the waters that you lose,
To temper clay. — Yea, is it come to this?
Let it be so: — I have another daughter,
Who, I am sure, is kind and comfortable:
When she shall hear this of thee, with her nails
She'll flay thy wolvish visage. Thou shalt find
That I'll resume the shape which thou dost think
I have cast off for ever; thou shalt, I warrant thee.
        [*Exeunt* LEAR, KENT, *and* ATTENDANTS.

GONERIL
Do you mark that, my lord?

ALBANY
I cannot be so partial, Goneril,
To the great love I bear you, —

GONERIL
Pray you, content. — What, Oswald, ho! —
[*to the* FOOL] You, sir, more knave than fool, after your
    master.

FOOL
Nuncle Lear, nuncle Lear, tarry, and take the fool with
    thee. —
        A fox, when one has caught her,
        And such a daughter,
        Should sure to the slaughter,
        If my cap would buy a halter:
        So the fool follows after.   [*Exit.*

GONERIL
This man hath had good counsel: — a hundred
    knights!
'Tis politic and safe to let him keep
At point a hundred knights: yes, that, on every dream,
Each buzz, each fancy, each complaint, dislike,
He may enguard his dotage with their powers,
And hold our lives in mercy. — Oswald, I say! —

ALBANY
Well, you may fear too far.

GONERIL
                          Safer than trust too far:
Let me still take away the harms I fear,
Not fear still to be taken: I know his heart.
What he hath utter'd I have writ my sister:
If she sustain him and his hundred knights,
When I have show'd th'unfitness, —

Enter OSWALD.
                                  How now, Oswald!
What, have you writ that letter to my sister?

OSWALD
Ay, madam.

GONERIL
Take you some company, and away to horse:
Inform her full of my particular fear;
And thereto add such reasons of your own
As may compact it more. Get you gone;
And hasten your return. [*Exit* OSWALD.] No, no, my
    lord,
This milky gentleness and course of yours,
Though I condemn not, yet, under pardon,
You are much more attask'd for want of wisdom
Than prais'd for harmful mildness.

ALBANY
How far your eyes may pierce I cannot tell:
Striving to better, oft we mar what's well.

GONERIL
Nay, then —

ALBANY
Well, well; the event.   [*Exeunt.*

SCENE V
Court before the same.

Enter LEAR, KENT, *and* FOOL.

KING LEAR
Go you before to Gloster with these letters. Acquaint
my daughter no further with any thing you know than
comes from her demand out of the letter. If your
diligence be not speedy, I shall be there afore you.

KENT
I will not sleep, my lord, till I have deliver'd your letter.
        [*Exit.*

FOOL
If a man's brains were in's heels, were't not in danger
of kibes?

KING LEAR
Ay, boy.

FOOL
Then, I prithee, be merry; thy wit shall ne'er go
slip-shod.

KING LEAR
Ha, ha, ha!

FOOL
Shalt see thy other daughter will use thee kindly; for
though she's as like this as a crab's like an apple, yet I
can tell what I can tell.

KING LEAR
What canst tell, boy?

FOOL
She will taste as like this as a crab does to a crab. Thou
canst tell why one's nose stands i'th'middle on's face?

KING LEAR
No.

FOOL
Why, to keep one's eyes of either side's nose; that what
a man cannot smell out, he may spy into.

KING LEAR
I did her wrong —

FOOL
Canst tell how an oyster makes his shell?

KING LEAR
No.

FOOL
Nor I neither; but I can tell why a snail has a house.

KING LEAR
Why?

FOOL
Why, to put's his head in; not to give it away to his
daughters, and leave his horns without a case.

KING LEAR
I will forget my nature. — So kind a father! — Be my
horses ready?

FOOL
Thy asses are gone about 'em. The reason why the
seven stars are no more than seven is a pretty reason.

KING LEAR
Because they are not eight?

FOOL
Yes, indeed: thou wouldst make a good fool.

KING LEAR
To take't again perforce! — Monster ingratitude!

FOOL
If thou wert my fool, nuncle, I'ld have thee beaten for
being old before thy time.

KING LEAR
How's that?

FOOL
Thou shouldst not have been old till thou hadst been
wise.

KING LEAR
O, let me not be mad, not mad, sweet heaven!
Keep me in temper: I would not be mad!
        Enter GENTLEMAN.
How now! are the horses ready?

GENTLEMAN
Ready, my lord.

KING LEAR
Come, boy.

FOOL
She that's a maid now, and laughs at my departure,
Keep me in temper: I would not be mad!
Shall not be a maid long, unless things be cut shorter.
        [*Exeunt.*

ACT II

SCENE I
A court within the castle of the EARL OF GLOSTER.

Enter EDMUND *and* CURAN, *meeting.*

EDMUND
Save thee, Curan.

CURAN
And you, sir. I have been with your father, and given
him notice that the Duke of Cornwall and Regan his
duchess will be here with him this night.

EDMUND
How comes that?

CURAN
Nay, I know not. — You have heard of the news
abroad, — I mean the whisper'd ones, for they are yet
but ear-kissing arguments?

EDMUND
Not I: pray you, what are they?

CURAN
Have you heard of no likely wars toward 'twixt the
Dukes of Cornwall and Albany?

EDMUND
Not a word.

CURAN
You may do, then, in time. Fare you well, sir.　　　*[Exit.*

EDMUND
The duke be here to-night? The better! best!
This weaves itself perforce into my business.
My father hath set guard to take my brother;
And I have one thing, of a queasy question,
Which I must act: — briefness and fortune, work! —
Brother, a word; — descend: — brother, I say!
　　　　　Enter EDGAR.
My father watches: — O sir, fly this place;
Intelligence is given where you are hid;
You have now the good advantage of the night: —
Have you not spoken 'gainst the Duke of Cornwall?
He's coming hither; now, i'th'night, i'th'haste,
And Regan with him: have you nothing said
Upon his party 'gainst the Duke of Albany?
Advise yourself.

EDGAR
　　　　　I am sure on't, not a word.

EDMUND
I hear my father coming: — pardon me;
In cunning I must draw my sword upon you: —
Draw: seem to defend yourself: now quit you well. —
Yield: — come before my father. — Light, ho, here!
Fly, brother. — Torches, torches! — So, farewell.
　　　　　[Exit EDGAR.
Some blood drawn on me would beget opinion
　　　　　[Wounds his arm.
Of my more fierce endeavour: I have seen drunkards
Do more than this in sport. — Father, father! —
Stop, stop! — No help?
　　Enter GLOSTER, *and* SERVANTS *with torches.*

GLOSTER
　　　　　Now, Edmund, where's the villain?

EDMUND
Here stood he in the dark, his sharp sword out,
Mumbling of wicked charms, conjuring the moon
To stand's auspicious mistress, —

GLOSTER
　　　　　But where is he?

EDMUND
Look, sir, I bleed.

GLOSTER
　　　　　Where is the villain, Edmund?

EDMUND
Fled this way, sir. When by no means he could —

GLOSTER
Pursue him, ho! — Go after. [*Exeunt some* SERVANTS.] —
　　By no means what?

EDMUND
Persuade me to the murder of your lordship;
But that I told him the revenging gods
'Gainst parricides did all their thunders bend;
Spoke with how manifold and strong a bond
The child was bound to th'father; — sir, in fine,
Seeing how loathly opposite I stood
To his unnatural purpose, in fell motion,
With his prepared sword he charges home
My unprovided body, lanc'd mine arm:
But when he saw my best alarum'd spirits,
Bold in the quarrel's right, rous'd to th'encounter,
Or whether gasted by the noise I made,
Full suddenly he fled.

GLOSTER
　　　　　Let him fly far:
Not in this land shall he remain uncaught;
And found — dispatch. The noble duke my master,
My worthy arch and patron, comes to-night:
By his authority I will proclaim it,
That he which finds him shall deserve our thanks,
Bringing the murderous coward to the stake;
He that conceals him, death.

EDMUND
When I dissuaded him from his intent,
And found him pight to do it, with curst speech
I threaten'd to discover him: he replied,
'Thou unpossessing bastard! dost thou think,
If I would stand against thee, would the reposal
Of any trust, virtue, or worth in thee
Make thy words faith'd? No: what I should deny, —
As this I would: ay, though thou didst produce
My very character, — I'ld turn it all
To thy suggestion, plot, and damned practice:
And thou must make a dullard of the world,
If they not thought the profits of my death
Were very pregnant and potential spurs
To make thee seek it.'

EDMUND Have you not spoken 'gainst the Duke of Cornwall?

GLOSTER
　　　　　Strong and fasten'd villain!
Would he deny his letter? — I never got him. —
　　　　　[Tucket within.
Hark, the duke's trumpets! I know not why he comes. —
All ports I'll bar; the villain shall not scape;
The duke must grant me that: besides, his picture
I will send far and near, that all the kingdom
May have due note of him; and of my land,
Loyal and natural boy, I'll work the means
To make thee capable.
　　Enter CORNWALL, REGAN, *and* ATTENDANTS.

CORNWALL.
How now, my noble friend! since I came hither, —
Which I can call but now, — I have heard strange news.

REGAN
If it be true, all vengeance comes too short
Which can pursue th'offender. How dost, my lord?

GLOSTER
O madam, my old heart is crack'd, is crack'd!

REGAN
What, did my father's godson seek your life?
He whom my father named? your Edgar?

GLOSTER
O lady, lady, shame would have it hid!

REGAN
Was he not companion with the riotous knights
That tend upon my father?

GLOSTER
I know not, madam: — 'tis too bad, too bad.

EDMUND
Yes, madam, he was of that consort.

REGAN
No marvel, then, though he were ill affected:
'Tis they have put him on the old man's death,
To have th'expense and waste of his revenues.
I have this present evening from my sister
Been well inform'd of them; and with such cautions,
That if they come to sojourn at my house,
I'll not be there.

CORNWALL
　　　　　Nor I, assure thee, Regan. —
Edmund, I hear that you have shown your father
A child-like office.

EDMUND
　　　　　'Twas my duty, sir.

GLOSTER
He did bewray his practice: and receiv'd
This hurt you see, striving to apprehend him.

CORNWALL
Is he pursued?

GLOSTER
　　　　　Ay, my good lord.

CORNWALL
If he be taken, he shall never more
Be fear'd of doing harm: make your own purpose,
How in my strength you please. — For you, Edmund,
Whose virtue and obedience doth this instant
So much commend itself, you shall be ours:
Natures of such deep trust we shall much need;
You we first seize on.

EDMUND
　　　　　I shall serve you, sir,
Truly, however else.

GLOSTER
　　　　　For him I thank your Grace.

CORNWALL
You know not why we came to visit you, —

REGAN
Thus out of season, threading dark-eyed night:
Occasions, noble Gloster, of some poise,
Wherein we must have use of your advice: —
Our father he hath writ, so hath our sister,
Of differences, which I least thought it fit
To answer from our home; the several messengers
From hence attend dispatch. Our good old friend,
Lay comforts to your bosom; and bestow
Your needful counsel to our business,
Which craves the instant use.

GLOSTER
　　　　　I serve you, madam:
Your Graces are right welcome.　　*[Exeunt.*

SCENE II
Before GLOSTER'S *castle.*

Enter KENT *and* OSWALD, *severally.*

OSWALD
Good dawning to thee, friend: art of this house?

KENT
Ay.

OSWALD
Where may we set our horses?

KENT
I' the mire.

OSWALD
Prithee, if thou lovest me, tell me.

KENT
I love thee not.

OSWALD
Why, then, I care not for thee.

KENT
If I had thee in Lipsbury pinfold, I would make thee
care for me.

OSWALD
Why dost thou use me thus? I know thee not.

KENT
Fellow, I know thee.

OSWALD
Whart dost thou know me for?

KENT
A knave; a rascal; an eater of broken meats; a base,
proud, shallow, beggarly, three-suited,
hundred-pound, filthy, worsted-stocking knave; a
lily-liver'd, action-taking, whoreson, glass-gazing,
superserviceable, finical rogue; one-trunk-inheriting
slave; one that wouldst be a bawd in way of good
service, and art nothing but the composition of a knave,
beggar, coward, pandar, and the son and heir of a
mongrel bitch: one whom I will beat into clamorous
whining, if thou deniest the least syllable of thy
addition.

OSWALD
Why, what a monstrous fellow art thou, thus to rail on
one that is neither known of thee nor knows thee!

KENT
What a brazen-fac'd varlet art thou, to deny thou
knowest me! Is it two days since I tripp'd up thy heels,
and beat thee, before the king? Draw, you rogue: for,
though it be night, yet the moon shines; I'll make a sop
o' the moonshine of you: draw, you whoreson cullionly
barbermonger, draw.　　*[Drawing his sword.*

OSWALD
Away! I have nothing to do with thee.
KENT
Draw, you rascal: you come with letters against the king; and take Vanity the puppet's part against the royalty of her father: draw, you rogue, or I'll so carbonado your shanks: — draw, you rascal; come your ways.
OSWALD
Help, ho! murder! help!
KENT
Strike, you slave; stand, rogue, stand; you neat slave,
    strike.   [*Beating him.*
OSWALD
Help, ho! murder! murder!

    Enter EDMUND, *with his rapier drawn.*

EDMUND
How now! What's the matter?   [*Parts them.*
KENT
With you, goodman boy, an you please: come.
I'll flesh you; come on, young master.

    Enter CORNWALL, REGAN, GLOSTER, *and*
    SERVANTS.

GLOSTER
Weapons! arms! What's the matter here?
CORNWALL
Keep peace, upon your lives;
He dies that strikes again. What is the matter?
REGAN
The messengers from our sister and the king.
CORNWALL
What is your difference? speak.
OSWALD
I am scarce in breath, my lord.
KENT
No marvel, you have so bestirr'd your valour. You cowardly rascal, nature disclaims in thee: a tailor made thee.
CORNWALL
Thou art a strange fellow: a tailor make a man?
KENT
Ay, a tailor, sir: a stone-cutter or painter could not have made him so ill, though they had been but two hours at the trade.
CORNWALL
Speak yet, how grew your quarrel?
OSWALD
This ancient ruffian, sir, whose life I have spared at suit of his grey beard, —
KENT
Thou whoreson zed! thou unnecessary letter! — My lord, if you will give me leave, I will tread this unbolted villain into mortar, and daub the wall of a jakes with him. — 'Spare my grey beard,' you wagtail?
CORNWALL
Peace, sirrah!
You beastly knave, know you no reverence?
KENT
Yes, sir; but anger hath a privilege.
CORNWALL
Why art thou angry?
KENT
That such a slave as this should wear a sword,
Who wears no honesty. Such smiling rogues as these,
Like rats, oft bite the holy cords a-twain
Which are too intrinse t'unloose; smooth every passion
That in the natures of their lords rebel;
Bring oil to fire, snow to their colder moods;
Renege, affirm, and turn their halcyon beaks
With every gale and vary of their masters,
Knowing naught, like dogs, but following. —
A plague upon your epileptic visage!
Smile you my speeches, as I were a fool?
Goose, if I had you upon Sarum plain,
I'ld drive ye cackling home to Camelot.
CORNWALL
What, art thou mad, old fellow?
GLOSTER
How fell you out? say that.
KENT
No contraries hold more antipathy
Than I and such a knave.
CORNWALL
Why dost thou call him a knave? What's his offence?
KENT
His countenance likes me not.

CORNWALL
No more, perchance, does mine, nor his, nor hers.
KENT
Sir, 'tis my occupation to be plain:
I have seen better faces in my time
Than stands on any shoulder that I see
Before me at this instant.
CORNWALL
                This is some fellow,
Who, having been prais'd for bluntness, doth affect
A saucy roughness, and constrains the garb
Quite from his nature: he cannot flatter, he, —
An honest mind and plain, — he must speak truth!
An they will take it, so; if not, he's plain.
These kind of knaves I know, which in this plainness
Harbour more craft and more corrupter ends
Than twenty silly-ducking observants
That stretch their duties nicely.
KENT
Sir, in good sooth, in sincere verity,
Under the allowance of your great aspect,
Whose influence, like the wreath of radiant fire
On flickering Phœbus' front, —
CORNWALL
                What mean'st by this?
KENT
To go out of my dialect, which you discommend so much. I know, sir, I am no flatterer: he that beguiled you in a plain accent was a plain knave; which, for my part, I will not be, though I should win your displeasure to entreat me to't.
CORNWALL
What was the offence you gave him?
OSWALD
I never gave him any:
It pleas'd the king his master very late
To strike at me, upon his misconstruction;
When he, conjunct, and flattering his displeasure,
Tripp'd me behind; being down, insulted, rail'd,
And put upon him such a deal of man,
That worthied him, got praises of the king
For him attempting who was self-subdued;
And, in the fleshment of this dread exploit,
Drew on me here again.
KENT
           None of these rogues and cowards
But Ajax is their fool.
CORNWALL
           Fetch forth the stocks! —
You stubborn ancient knave, you reverend braggart,
We'll teach you —
KENT
           Sir, I am too old to learn:
Call not your stocks for me: I serve the king;
On whose employment I was sent to you:
You shall do small respect, show too bold malice
Against the grace and person of my master,
Stocking his messenger.
CORNWALL
Fetch forth the stocks! — As I have life and honour,
There shall he sit till noon.
REGAN
Till noon! till night, my lord; and all night too.
KENT
Why, madam, if I were your father's dog,
You should not use me so.
REGAN
           Sir, being his knave, I will.
CORNWALL
This is a fellow of the self-same colour
Our sister speaks of. — Come, bring away the stocks!
           [*Stocks brought out.*
GLOSTER
Let me beseech your Grace not to do so:
His fault is much, and the good king his master
Will check him for't: your purpos'd low correction
Is such as basest and contemned'st wretches
For pilferings and most common trespasses
Are punish'd with: the king must take it ill,
That he, so slightly valued in his messenger,
Should have him thus restrain'd.
CORNWALL
           I'll answer that.
REGAN
My sister may receive it much more worse,
To have her gentleman abus'd, assaulted,
For following her affairs. — Put in his legs. —
           [KENT *is put in the stocks.*
Come, my good lord, away.
           [*Exeunt all but* GLOSTER *and* KENT.

GLOSTER
I am sorry for thee, friend; 'tis the duke's pleasure,
Whose disposition, all the world well knows,
Will not be rubb'd nor stopp'd: I'll entreat for thee.
KENT
Pray, do not, sir: I have watch'd, and travell'd hard;
Some time I shall sleep out, the rest I'll whistle.
A good man's fortune may grow out at heels:
Give you good morrow!
GLOSTER
The duke's to blame in this; 'twill be ill taken.   [*Exit.*
KENT
Good king, that must approve the common saw, —
Thou out of heaven's benediction comest
To the warm sun!
Approach, thou beacon to this under globe,
That by thy comfortable beams I may
Peruse this letter! — Nothing almost sees miracles
But misery: — I know 'tis from Cordelia,
Who hath most fortunately been inform'd
Of my obscured course; and shall find time
From this enormous state, seeking to give
Losses their remedies. — All weary and o'erwatch'd,
Take vantage, heavy eyes, not to behold
This shameful lodging.
Fortune, good night: smile once more; turn thy wheel!
           [*Sleeps.*

SCENE III

The open country.

Enter EDGAR.

EDGAR
I heard myself proclaim'd;
And by the happy hollow of a tree
Escap'd the hunt. No port is free; no place,
That guard, and most unusual vigilance,
Does not attend my taking. Whiles I may scape,
I will preserve myself: and am bethought
To take the basest and most poorest shape
That ever penury, in contempt of man,
Brought near to beast: my face I'll grime with filth;
Blanket my loins: elf all my hair in knots;
And with presented nakedness out-face
The winds and persecutions of the sky.
The country gives me proof and precedent
Of Bedlam beggars, who, with roaring voices,
Strike in their numb'd and mortified bare arms
Pins, wooden pricks, nails, sprigs of rosemary;
And with this horrible object, from low farms,
Poor pelting villages, sheep-cotes, and mills,
Sometime with lunatic bans, sometime with prayers,
Enforce their charity. — 'Poor Turlygod! poor Tom!'
That's something yet: — Edgar I nothing am.   [*Exit.*

SCENE IV

Before GLOSTER'S *castle;* KENT *in the stocks.*

Enter LEAR, FOOL, *and* GENTLEMAN.

KING LEAR
'Tis strange that they should so depart from home,
And not send back my messenger.
GENTLEMAN
           As I learn'd,
The night before there was no purpose in them
Of this remove.
KENT
           Hail to thee, noble master!
KING LEAR
Ha!
Makest thou this shame thy pastime?
KENT
           No, my lord.
FOOL
Ha, ha! he wears cruel garters. Horses are tied by the heads, dogs and bears by the neck, monkeys by the loins, and men by the legs: when a man's over-lusty at legs, then he wears wooden nether-stocks.
KING LEAR
What's he that hath so much thy place mistook
To set thee here?
KENT
           It is both he and she, —
Your son and daughter.
KING LEAR
No.
KENT
Yes.
KING LEAR
No, I say.

KENT
I say, yea.
KING LEAR
No, no, they would not.
KENT
Yes, they have.
KING LEAR
By Jupiter, I swear, no.
KENT
By Juno, I swear, ay.
KING LEAR
                    They durst not do't;
They could not, would not do't; 'tis
          worse than murder,
To do upon respect such violent
          outrage:
Resolve me, with all modest haste,
          which way
Thou mightst deserve, or they impose,
          this usage,
Coming from us.
KENT
                    My lord, when at their home
I did commend your highness' letters
          to them,
Ere I was risen from the place that
          show'd
My duty kneeling, came there a
          reeking post,
Stew'd in his haste, half breathless,
          panting forth
From Goneril his mistress salutations;
Deliver'd letters, spite of intermission,
Which presently they read: on whose contents,
They summon'd up their meiny, straight took horse;
Commanded me to follow, and attend
The leisure of their answer; gave me cold looks:
And meeting here the other messenger,
Whose welcome, I perceiv'd, had poison'd mine, —
Being the very fellow which of late
Display'd so saucily against your highness, —
Having more man than wit about me, drew:
He rais'd the house with loud and coward cries.
Your son and daughter found this trespass worth
The shame which here it suffers.
FOOL
Winter's not gone yet, if the wild-geese fly that way.
          Fathers that wear rags
               Do make their children blind;
          But fathers that bear bags
               Shall see their children kind.
          Fortune, that arrant whore,
          Ne'er turns the key to the poor. —
But, for all this, thou shalt have as many dolours for thy
daughters as thou canst tell in a year.
KING LEAR
O, how this mother swells up toward my heart!
Hysterica passio, — down, thou climbing sorrow,
Thy element's below! — Where is this daughter?
KENT
With the earl, sir, here within.
KING LEAR
Stay here.   Follow me not;   [*Exit.*
GENTLEMAN
Made you no more offence but what you speak of?
KENT
None.
How chance the king comes with so small a train?
FOOL
And thou hadst been set i' the stocks for that question,
thou hadst well deserved it.
KENT
Why, fool?
FOOL
We'll set thee to school to an ant, to teach thee there's
no labouring i' the winter. All that follow their noses
are led by their eyes but blind men; and there's not a
nose among twenty but can smell him that's stinking.
Let go thy hold when a great wheel runs down a hill,
lest it break thy neck with following it; but the great one
that goes up the hill, let him draw thee after. When a
wise man gives thee better counsel, give me mine
again: I would have none but knaves follow it, since a
fool gives it.
          That sir which serves and seeks for gain,
               And follows but for form,
          Will pack when it begins to rain,
               And leave thee in the storm,
          But I will tarry; the fool will stay,
               And let the wise man fly:

KENT Some time I shall sleep out, the rest I'll whistle.

          The knave turns fool that runs away:
          The fool no knave, perdy.
KENT
Where learn'd you this, fool?
FOOL
Not i' the stocks, fool.

Enter LEAR *with* GLOSTER.

KING LEAR
Deny to speak with me? They are sick? they are weary?
They have travell'd all the night? Mere fetches;
The images of revolt and flying-off.
Fetch me a better answer.
GLOSTER
                    My dear lord,
You know the fiery quality of the duke;
How unremoveable and fix'd he is
In his own course.
KING LEAR
Vengeance! plague! death! confusion! —
Fiery? what quality? Why, Gloster, Gloster,
I'ld speak with the Duke of Cornwall and his wife.
GLOSTER
Well, my good lord, I have inform'd them so.
KING LEAR
Inform'd them! Dost thou understand me, man?
GLOSTER
Ay, my good lord.
KING LEAR
The king would speak with Cornwall; the dear father
Would with his daughter speak, commands her
          service:
Are they inform'd of this? — My breath and blood! —
Fiery! the fiery duke! — Tell the hot duke that —
No, but not yet: — may be he is not well:
Infirmity doth still neglect all office
Whereto our health is bound; we are not ourselves
When nature, being oppress'd, commands the mind
To suffer with the body; I'll forbear;
And am fall'n out with my more headier will,
To take the indispos'd and sickly fit
For the sound man. — Death on my state! wherefore
                              [*Looking on* KENT.
Should he sit here? This act persuades me
That this remotion of the duke and her
Is practice only. Give me my servant forth.
Go tell the duke and's wife I'ld speak with them,
Now, presently: bid them come forth and hear me,
Or at their chamber-door I'll beat the drum
Till it cry sleep to death.
GLOSTER
I would have all well betwixt you.   [*Exit.*
KING LEAR
O me, my heart, my rising heart! — but, down
FOOL
Cry to it, nuncle, as the cockney did to the eels when
she put 'em i' the paste alive; she knapp'd 'em o' the
coxcombs with a stick, and cried, 'Down, wantons,
down!' 'Twas her brother that, in pure kindness to his
horse, butter'd his hay.

Enter CORNWALL, REGAN, GLOSTER,
          and SERVANTS.

KING LEAR
Good morrow to you both.
CORNWALL
                    Hail to your Grace!
                         [KENT *here set at liberty.*
REGAN
I am glad to see your highness.
KING LEAR
Regan, I think you are; I know what reason
I have to think so: if thou shouldst not be glad,
I would divorce me from thy mother's tomb,
Sepulchring an adultress. — [*to* KENT] O, are you free?
Some other time for that. — Beloved Regan,
Thy sister's naught: O Regan, she hath tied
Sharp-tooth'd unkindness, like a vulture, here, —
                         [*Points to his heart.*
I can scarce speak to thee; thou'lt not believe
Of how deprav'd a quality — O Regan!
REGAN
I pray you, sir, take patience: I have hope
You less know how to value her desert
Than she to scant her duty.
KING LEAR
                    Say, how is that?
REGAN
I cannot think my sister in the least
Would fail her obligation: if, sir, perchance
She have restrain'd the riots of your followers,
'Tis on such ground, and to such wholesome end,
As clears her from all blame.
KING LEAR
My curses on her!
REGAN
                    O, sir, you are old;
Nature in you stands on the very verge
Of her confine: you should be rul'd, and led
By some discretion that discerns your state
Better than you yourself. Therefore, I pray you,
That to our sister you do make return;
Say you have wrong'd her, sir.
KING LEAR
                    Ask her forgiveness?
Do you but mark how this becomes the house:
'Dear daughter, I confess that I am old;   [*Kneeling.*
Age is unnecessary: on my knees I beg
That you'll vouchsafe me raiment, bed, and food.'
REGAN
Good sir, no more; these are unsightly tricks:
Return you to my sister.
KING LEAR [*rising*].
                    Never, Regan:
She hath abated me of half my train;
Look'd black upon me; struck me with her tongue,
Most serpent-like, upon the very heart: —
All the stored vengeances of heaven fall
On her ingrateful top! Strike her young bones,
You taking airs, with lameness!
CORNWALL
                    Fie, sir, fie!
KING LEAR
You nimble lightnings, dart your blinding flames
Into her scornful eyes! Infect her beauty,
You fen-suck'd fogs, drawn by the powerful sun,
To fall and blast her pride!
REGAN
O the blest gods! so will you wish on me,
When the rash mood is on.
KING LEAR
No, Regan, thou shalt never have my curse:
Thy tender-hefted nature shall not give
Thee o'er to harshness: her eyes are fierce; but thine
Do comfort, and not burn. 'Tis not in thee
To grudge my pleasures, to cut off my train,
To bandy hasty words, to scant my sizes,
And, in conclusion, to oppose the bolt
Against my coming in: thou better know'st
The offices of nature, bond of childhood,
Effects of courtesy, dues of gratitude;
Thy half o' the kingdom hast thou not forgot,
Wherein I thee endow'd.
REGAN
                    Good sir, to the purpose.
KING LEAR
Who put my man i' the stocks?   [*Tucket within.*
CORNWALL
                    What trumpet's that?

REGAN
I know't, — my sister's: this approves her letter,
That she would soon be here.
                    Enter OSWALD.
                              Is your lady come?

KING LEAR
This is a slave, whose easy-borrow'd pride
Dwells in the fickle grace of her he follows. —
Out, varlet, from my sight!

CORNWALL
                    What means your Grace?

KING LEAR
Who stock'd my servant? Regan, I have good hope
Thou didst not know on't. — Who comes here? O heavens,
                    Enter GONERIL.
If you do love old men, if your sweet sway
Allow obedience, if yourselves are old,
Make it your cause; send down, and take my part! —
[*to* GONERIL] Art not ashamed to look upon this
    beard? —
O Regan, wilt thou take her by the hand?

GONERIL
Why not by the hand, sir? How have I offended?
All's not offence that indiscretion finds
And dotage terms so.

KING LEAR
                    O sides, you are too tough;
Will you yet hold? — How came my man i' the stocks?

CORNWALL
I set him there, sir: but his own disorders
Deserv'd much less advancement.

KING LEAR
                         You! did you?

REGAN
I pray you, father, being weak, seem so.
If, till the expiration of your month,
You will return and sojourn with my sister,
Dismissing half your train, come then to me:
I am now from home, and out of that provision
Which shall be needful for your entertainment.

KING LEAR
Return to her, and fifty men dismiss'd?
No, rather I abjure all roofs, and choose
To wage against the enmity o' the air;
To be a comrade with the wolf and owl, —
Necessity's sharp pinch! Return with her?
Why, the hot-blooded France, that dowerless took
Our youngest born, I could as well be brought
To knee his throne, and, squire-like, pension beg
To keep base life afoot. — Return with her?
Persuade me rather to be slave and sumpter
To this detested groom.   [*Pointing at* OSWALD.

GONERIL
                    At your choice, sir.

KING LEAR
I prithee, daughter, do not make me mad:
I will not trouble thee, my child; farewell:
We'll no more meet, no more see one another: —
But yet thou art my flesh, my blood, my daughter;
Or rather a disease that's in my flesh,
Which I must needs call mine: thou art a boil,
A plague-sore, an embossed carbuncle,
In my corrupted blood. But I'll not chide thee;
Let shame come when it will, I do not call it:
I do not bid the thunder-bearer shoot,
Nor tell tales of thee to high-judging Jove:
Mend when thou canst; be better at thy leisure:
I can be patient, I can stay with Regan,
I and my hundred knights.

REGAN
                    Not altogether so:
I look'd not for you yet, nor am provided
For your fit welcome. Give ear, sir, to my sister;
For those that mingle reason with your passion
Must be content to think you old, and so —
But she knows what she does.

KING LEAR
                    Is this well spoken?

REGAN
I dare avouch it, sir: what! fifty followers?
Is it not well? What should you need of more?
Yea, or so many, sith that both charge and danger
Speak 'gainst so great a number? How, in one house,
Should many people, under two commands,
Hold amity? 'Tis hard; almost impossible.

GONERIL
Why might not you, my lord, receive attendance
From those that she calls servants or from mine?

REGAN
Why not, my lord? If then they chanc'd to slack you,

We could control them. If you will come to me, —
For now I spy a danger, — I entreat you
To bring but five-and-twenty: to no more
Will I give place or notice.

KING LEAR
I gave you all —

REGAN
                    And in good time you gave it.

KING LEAR
Made you my guardians, my depositaries;
But kept a reservation to be follow'd
With such a number. What, must I come to you
With five-and-twenty, Regan? said you so?

REGAN
And speak't again, my lord; no more with me.

KING LEAR
Those wicked creatures yet do look well-favour'd,
When others are more wicked: not being the worst
Stands in some rank of praise. — [*to* GONERIL] I'll go
    with thee:
Thy fifty yet doth double five-and-twenty,
And thou art twice her love.

GONERIL
                    Hear me, my lord:
What need you five-and-twenty, ten, or five,
To follow in a house where twice so many
Have a command to tend you?

REGAN
                    What need one?

KING LEAR
O, reason not the need: our basest beggars
Are in the poorest thing superfluous:
Allow not nature more than nature needs,
Man's life is cheap as beast's: thou art a lady;
If only to go warm were gorgeous,
Why, nature needs not what thou gorgeous wear'st,
Which scarcely keeps thee warm. — But, for true need, —
You heavens, give me that patience, patience I need!
You see me here, you gods, a poor old man,
As full of grief as age; wretched in both!
If it be you that stir these daughters' hearts
Against their father, fool me not so much
To bear it tamely; touch me with noble anger,
And let not women's weapons, water-drops,
Stain my man's cheeks! — No, you unnatural hags,
I will have such revenges on you both,
That all the world shall — I will do such things, —
What they are, yet I know not; but they shall be
The terrors of the earth. You think I'll weep;

No, I'll not weep: —
I have full cause of weeping; but this heart
Shall break into a hundred thousand flaws,
Or e'er I'll weep. — O fool, I shall go mad!
        [*Exeunt* LEAR, GLOSTER, KENT, *and* FOOL
                    Storm and tempest

CORNWALL
Let us withdraw; 'twill be a storm.

REGAN
This house is little: the old man and his people
Cannot be well bestow'd.

GONERIL
'Tis his own blame; 'hath put himself from rest,
And must needs taste his folly.

REGAN
For his particular, I'll receive him gladly,
But not one follower.

GONERIL
                    So am I purposed.
Where is my Lord of Gloster?

CORNWALL
Follow'd the old man forth: — he is return'd.
                    Enter GLOSTER.

GLOSTER
The king is in high rage.

CORNWALL
                    Whither is he going?

GLOSTER
He calls to horse; but will I know not whither.

CORNWALL
'Tis best to give him way; he leads himself.

GONERIL
My lord, entreat him by no means to stay.

GLOSTER
Alack, the night comes on, and the bleak winds
Do sorely ruffle; for many miles about
There's scarce a bush.

REGAN
                    O, sir, to wilful men
The injuries that they themselves procure
Must be their schoolmasters. Shut up your doors:
He is attended with a desperate train;
And what they may incense him to, being apt
To have his ear abus'd, wisdom bids fear.

CORNWALL
Shut up your doors, my lord; 'tis a wild night:
My Regan counsels well: come out o' the storm.
                              [*Exeunt*

REGAN And speak't again, my lord; no more with me.

ACT III

SCENE I

A heath.

Storm still. Enter KENT *and a* GENTLEMAN, *severally.*

KENT
Who's there, besides foul weather?

GENTLEMAN
One minded like the weather, most unquietly.

KENT
I know you. Where's the king?

GENTLEMAN
Contending with the fretful element;
Bids the wind blow the earth into the sea,
Or swell the curled waters 'bove the main,
That things might change or cease; tears his white hair,
Which the impetuous blasts, with eyeless rage,
Catch in their fury, and make nothing of;
Strives in his little world of man to out-scorn
The to-and-fro-conflicting wind and rain.
This night, wherein the cub-drawn bear would couch,
The lion and the belly-pinched wolf
Keep their fur dry, unbonneted he runs,
And bids what will take all.

KENT
                            But who is with him?

GENTLEMAN
None but the fool; who labours to out-jest
His heart-struck injuries.

KENT
                    Sir, I do know you;
And dare, upon the warrant of my note,
Commend a dear thing to you. There is division,
Although as yet the face of it be cover'd
With mutual cunning, 'twixt Albany and Cornwall;
Who have — as who have not, that their great stars
Thron'd and set high? — servants, who seem no less,
Which are to France the spies and speculations
Intelligent of our state; what hath been seen,
Either in snuffs and packings of the dukes;
Or the hard rein which both of them have borne
Against the old kind king; or something deeper,
Whereof perchance these are but furnishings; —
But, true it is, from France there comes a power
Into this scatter'd kingdom; who already,
Wise in our negligence, have secret feet
In some of our best ports, and are at point
To show their open banner. — Now to you:
If on my credit you dare build so far
To make your speed to Dover, you shall find
Some that will thank you, making just report
Of how unnatural and bemadding sorrow
The king hath cause to plain.
I am a gentleman of blood and breeding;
And, from some knowledge and assurance, offer
This office to you.

GENTLEMAN
I will talk further with you.

KENT
                    No, do not.
For confirmation that I am much more
Than my out-wall, open this purse, and take
What it contains. If you shall see Cordelia, —
As fear not but you shall, — show her this ring;
And she will tell you who your fellow is
That yet you do not know. Fie on this storm!
I will go seek the king.

GENTLEMAN
Give me your hand: have you no more to say?

KENT
Few words, but, to effect, more than all yet, —
That, when we have found the king, — in which your
   pain
That way, I'll this, — he that first lights on him
Holla the other.   [*Exeunt severally.*

SCENE II

Another part of the heath.

Storm still. Enter LEAR *and* FOOL.

KING LEAR
Blow, winds, and crack your cheeks! rage! blow!
You cataracts and hurricanoes, spout
Till you have drench'd our steeples, drown'd the cocks!
You sulphurous and thought-executing fires,
Vaunt-couriers to oak-cleaving thunderbolts,
Singe my white head! And thou, all-shaking thunder,
Strike flat the thick rotundity o' the world!

Crack nature's moulds, all germens spill at once,
That make ingrateful man!

FOOL
O nuncle, court holy-water in a dry house is better than
this rain-water out o' door. Good nuncle, in, and ask
thy daughters' blessing: here's a night pities neither
wise man nor fool.

KING LEAR
Rumble thy bellyful! Spit, fire! spout, rain!
Nor rain, wind, thunder, fire, are my daughters:
I tax not you, you elements, with unkindness;
I never gave you kingdom, call'd you children;
You owe me no subscription: then let fall
Your horrible pleasure; here I stand, your slave,
A poor, infirm, weak, and despis'd old man: —
But yet I call you servile ministers,
That have with two pernicious daughters join'd
Your high-engender'd battles 'gainst a head
So old and white as this! O! O! 'tis foul!

FOOL
He that has a house to put's head in has a good
head-piece.
         The cod-piece that will house
            Before the head has any,
         The head and he shall louse; —
            So beggars marry many.
         The man that makes his toe
            What he his heart should make
         Shall of a corn cry woe,
            And turn his sleep to wake:
for there was never yet fair woman but she made
mouths in a glass.

KING LEAR
No, I will be the pattern of all patience;
I will say nothing.

                    Enter KENT.

KENT
Who's there?

FOOL
Marry, here's grace and a cod-piece; that's a wise man
and a fool.

KENT
Alas, sir, are you here? things that love night
Love not such nights as these; the wrathful skies
Gallow the very wanderers of the dark,
And make them keep their caves: since I was man,
Such sheets of fire, such bursts of horrid thunder,
Such groans of roaring wind and rain, I never
Remember to have heard: man's nature cannot carry
The affliction nor the fear.

KING LEAR
                    Let the great gods,
That keep this dreadful pother o'er our heads,
Find out their enemies now. Tremble, thou wretch,
That hast within thee undivulged crimes,
Unwhipp'd of justice: hide thee, thou bloody hand;
Thou perjur'd, and thou simular of virtue
That art incestuous: caitiff, to pieces shake,
That under covert and convenient seeming
Hast practis'd on man's life: close pent-up guilts,
Rive your concealing continents, and cry
These dreadful summoners grace. — I am a man
More sinn'd against than sinning.

KENT
                    Alack, bare-headed!
Gracious my lord, hard by here is a hovel;
Some friendship will it lend you 'gainst the tempest:
Repose you there; while I to this hard house —
More harder than the stones whereof 'tis raised;
Which even but now, demanding after you,
Denied me to come in, — return, and force
Their scanted courtesy.

KING LEAR
                    My wits begin to turn. —
Come on, my boy: how dost, my boy? art cold?
I am cold myself. — Where is this straw, my fellow?
The art of our necessities is strange,
That can make vile things precious. Come, your hovel. —
Poor fool and knave, I have one part in my heart
That's sorry yet for thee.

FOOL [*singing*].
         He that has and a little tiny wit, —
            With hey, ho, the wind and the rain, —
         Must make content with his fortunes fit,
            Though the rain it raineth every day.

KING LEAR
True, my good boy. — Come, bring us to this hovel.
                    [*Exeunt* LEAR *and* KENT.

FOOL
This is a brave night to cool a courtezan. — I'll speak a

prophecy ere I go:
When priests are more in word than matter;
When brewers mar their malt with water;
When nobles are their tailors' tutors;
No heretics burn'd, but wenches' suitors;
When every case in law is right;
No squire in debt, nor no poor knight;
When slanders do not live in tongues;
Nor cutpurses come not to throngs;
When usurers tell their gold i' the field;
And bawds and whores do churches build; —
Then shall the realm of Albion
Come to great confusion:
Then comes the time, who lives to see't,
That going shall be us'd with feet.
This prophecy Merlin shall make; for I live before his
time.   [*Exit.*

SCENE III

GLOSTER'S castle.

Enter GLOSTER *and* EDMUND.

GLOSTER
Alack, alack, Edmund, I like not this unnatural dealing.
When I desire their leave that I might pity him, they
took from me the use of mine own house; charged me,
on pain of their perpetual displeasure, neither to speak
of him, entreat for him, nor any way sustain him.

EDMUND
Most savage and unnatural!

GLOSTER
Go to; say you nothing. There is division betwixt the
dukes; and a worse matter than that: I have received a
letter this night; — 'tis dangerous to be spoken; — I
have lock'd the letter in my closet: these injuries the
king now bears will be revenged home; there is part of a
power already footed: we must incline to the king. I will
seek him, and privily relieve him: go you, and maintain
talk with the duke, that my charity be not of him
perceived: if he ask for me, I am ill, and gone to bed.
Though I die for it, as no less is threaten'd me, the king
my old master must be relieved. There is some strange
thing toward, Edmund; pray you, be careful.   [*Exit.*

EDMUND
This courtesy, forbid thee, shall the duke
Instantly know; and of that letter too: —
This seems a fair deserving, and must draw me
That which my father loses, — no less than all:
The younger rises when the old doth fall.   [*Exit.*

SCENE IV

The heath. Before a hovel.

Enter LEAR, KENT, *and* FOOL.

KENT
Here is the place, my lord; good my lord, enter:
The tyranny of the open night's too rough
For nature to endure.   [*Storm still.*

KING LEAR
                    Let me alone.

KENT
Good my lord, enter here.

KING LEAR
                    Wilt break my heart?

KENT
I had rather break mine own. Good my lord, enter.

KING LEAR
Thou think'st 'tis much that this contentious storm
Invades us to the skin: so 'tis to thee;
But where the greater malady is fix'd,
The lesser is scarce felt. Thou'ldst shun a bear;
But if thy flight lay toward the roaring sea,
Thou'ldst meet the bear i' the mouth. When the mind's
   free,
The body's delicate: the tempest in my mind
Doth from my senses take all feeling else
Save what beats there. — Filial ingratitude!
Is it not as this mouth should tear this hand
For lifting food to't? — But I will punish home: —
No, I will weep no more. — In such a night
To shut me out! — Pour on; I will endure: —
In such a night as this! O Regan, Goneril! —
Your old kind father, whose frank heart gave all, —
O, that way madness lies; let me shun that;
No more of that.

KENT
                    Good my lord, enter here.

KING LEAR
Prithee, go in thyself: seek thine own ease:
This tempest will not give me leave to ponder

On things would hurt me more. — But I'll go in.
[*to the* FOOL] In, boy; go first. You houseless poverty, —

Nay, get thee in. I'll pray, and then I'll sleep. —
[*FOOL goes in.*
Poor naked wretches, whereso'er you are,
That bide the pelting of this pitiless storm,
How shall your houseless heads and unfed sides,
Your loop'd and window'd raggedness, defend you
From seasons such as these? O, I have ta'en
Too little care of this! Take physic, pomp;
Expose thyself to feel what wretches feel,
That thou mayst shake the superflux to them,
And show the heavens more just.

EDGAR [*within*].
Fathom and half, fathom and half!
Poor Tom! [*The FOOL runs out from the hovel.*

FOOL
Come not in here, nuncle, here's a spirit. Help me,
help me!

KENT
Give me thy hand. — Who's there?

FOOL
A spirit, a spirit: he says his name's poor Tom.

KENT
What art thou that dost grumble there i' the straw?
Come forth.

      Enter EDGAR *disguised as a madman.*

EDGAR
Away! the foul fiend follows me! —
Through the sharp hawthorn blows the cold wind. —
Hum! go to thy cold bed, and warm thee.

KING LEAR
Hast thou given all to thy two daughters?
And art thou come to this?

EDGAR
Who gives any thing to poor Tom? whom the foul fiend
hath led through fire and through flame through ford
and whirlpool, o'er bog and quagmire; that hath laid
knives under his pillow, and halters in his pew; set
ratsbane by his porridge; made him proud of heart, to
ride on a bay trotting-horse over four-inch'd bridges, to
course his own shadow for a traitor. — Bless thy five
wits! — Tom's a-cold, — O, do de, do de, do de. — Bless
thee from whirlwinds, star-blasting, and taking! Do
poor Tom some charity, whom the foul fiend vexes: —
there could I have him now, — and there, — and there
again, and there. [*Storm still.*

KING LEAR
What, have his daughters brought him to this pass? —
Couldst thou save nothing? Didst thou give 'em all?

FOOL
Nay, he reserved a blanket, else we had been all
shamed.

KING LEAR
Now, all the plagues that in the pendulous air
Hang fated o'er men's faults light on thy daughters!

KENT
He hath no daughters, sir.

KING LEAR
Death, traitor! nothing could have subdued nature
To such a lowness but his unkind daughters. —
Is it the fashion, that discarded fathers
Should have thus little mercy on their flesh?
Judicious punishment! 'twas this flesh begot
Those pelican daughters.

EDGAR
    Pillicock sat on Pillicock-hill: —
Halloo, halloo, loo, loo!

FOOL
This cold night will turn us all to fools and madmen.

EDGAR
Take heed o' the foul fiend: obey thy parents; keep thy
word justly; swear not; commit not with man's sworn
spouse; set not thy sweet heart on proud array. Tom's
a-cold.

KING LEAR
What hast thou been?

EDGAR
A servingman, proud in heart and mind; that curl'd my
hair; wore gloves in my cap; served the lust of my
mistress' heart, and did the act of darkness with her;
swore as many oaths as I spake words, and broke them
in the sweet face of heaven: one that slept in the
contriving of lust, and waked to do it: wine loved I
deeply, dice dearly; and in woman out-paramour'd the
Turk: false of heart, light of ear, bloody of hand; hog in
sloth, fox in stealth, wolf in greediness, dog in
madness, lion in prey. Let not the creaking of shoes nor

EDGAR There could I have him now, — and there, — and there again, and there.

the rustling of silks betray thy poor heart to woman:
keep thy foot out of brothels, thy hand out of plackets,
thy pen from lenders' books, and defy the foul fiend. —
    Still through the hawthorn blows the cold wind:
    Says suum, mun, ha, no, nonny.
Dolphin my boy, my boy, sessa! let him trot by.
[*Storm still.*

KING LEAR
Why, thou wert better in thy grave than to answer with
thy uncover'd body this extremity of the skies. — Is
man no more than this? Consider him well. Thou
owest the worm no silk, the beast no hide, the sheep no
wool, the cat no perfume. — Ha! here's three on's are
sophisticated! — Thou art the thing itself:
unaccommodated man is no more but such a poor,
bare, fork'd animal as thou art. — Off, off, you
lendings! — come, unbutton here. [*Tearing off his clothes.*

FOOL
Prithee, nuncle, be contented; 'tis a naughty night to
swim in. — Now a little fire in a wild field were like an
old lecher's heart, — a small spark, all the rest on's
body cold. — Look, here comes a walking fire.

    Enter GLOSTER, *with a torch.*

EDGAR
This is the foul fiend Flibbertigibbet: he begins at
curfew, and walks till the first cock; he gives the web
and the pin, squints the eye, and makes the hare-lip;
mildews the white wheat, and hurts the poor creature
of earth.
    Swithold footed thrice the old;
    He met the night-mare, and her nine-fold;
       Bid her alight,
       And her troth plight,
    And, aroint thee, witch, aroint thee!

KENT
How fares your Grace?

KING LEAR
What's he?

KENT
Who's there? What is't you seek?

GLOSTER
What are you there?
Your names?

EDGAR
Poor Tom; that eats the swimming frog, the toad, the

tadpole, the wall-newt and the water; that in the fury of
his heart, when the foul fiend rages, eats cow-dung for
sallets; swallows the old rat and the ditch-dog; drinks
the green mantle of the standing pool; who is whipp'd
from tithing to tithing, and stock-punish'd, and
imprison'd; who hath had three suits to his back, six
shirts to his body,
    Horse to ride, and weapon to wear;
    But mice, and rats, and such small deer,
    Have been Tom's food for seven long year.
Beware my follower. — Peace, Smulkin; peace, thou
fiend!

GLOSTER
What, hath your Grace no better company?

EDGAR
The prince of darkness is a gentleman: Modo he's
call'd, and Mahu.

GLOSTER
Our flesh and blood, my lord, is grown so vile,
That it doth hate what gets it.

EDGAR
Poor Tom's a-cold.

GLOSTER
Go in with me: my duty cannot suffer
T'obey in all your daughters' hard commands:
Though their injunction be to bar my doors,
And let this tyrannous night take hold upon you,
Yet have I ventur'd to come seek you out,
And bring you where both fire and food is ready.

KING LEAR
First let me talk with this philosopher. —
What is the cause of thunder?

KENT
Good my lord, take his offer; go into the house.

KING LEAR
I'll talk a word with this same learned Theban. —
What is your study?

EDGAR
How to prevent the fiend, and to kill vermin.

KING LEAR
Let me ask you one word in private.

KENT
Importune him once more to go, my lord;
His wits begin t'unsettle.

GLOSTER
          Canst thou blame him?

His daughters seek his death: — ah, that good Kent! —
He said it would be thus, — poor banish'd man! —
Thou say'st the king grows mad; I'll tell thee, friend,
I am almost mad myself: I had a son,
Now outlaw'd from my blood; he sought my life,
But lately, very late: I lov'd him, friend,
No father his son dearer: true to tell thee,   [*Storm still.*
The grief hath craz'd my wits. — What a night's this! —
I do beseech your Grace, —

KING LEAR
                              O, cry you mercy, sir. —
Noble philosopher, your company.

EDGAR
Tom's a-cold.

GLOSTER
In, fellow, there, into the hovel: keep thee warm.

KING LEAR
Come, let's in all.

KENT
                   This way, my lord.

KING LEAR
                              With him;
I will keep still with my philosopher.

KENT
Good my lord, soothe him! let him take the fellow.

GLOSTER
Take him you on.

KENT
Sirrah, come on; go along with us.

KING LEAR
Come, good Athenian.

GLOSTER
No words, no words: hush.

EDGAR
          Child Rowland to the dark tower came;
          His word was still, — Fie, foh, and fum,
          I smell the blood of a British man.   [*Exeunt.*

SCENE V
GLOSTER'S *castle.*

Enter CORNWALL *and* EDMUND.

CORNWALL
I will have my revenge ere I depart his house.

EDMUND
How, my lord, I may be censured, that nature thus
gives way to loyalty, something fears me to think of.

CORNWALL
I now perceive, it was not altogether your brother's evil
disposition made him seek his death; but a provoking
merit, set a-work by a reproveable badness in himself.

EDMUND
How malicious is my fortune, that I must repent to be
just! This is the letter he spoke of, which approves him
an intelligent party to the advantages of France: O
heavens! that this treason were not, or not I the
detector!

CORNWALL
Go with me to the duchess.

EDMUND
If the matter of this paper be certain, you have mighty
business in hand.

CORNWALL
True or false, it hath made thee Earl of Gloster. Seek
out where thy father is, that he may be ready for our
apprehension.

EDMUND [*aside*].
If I find him comforting the king, it will stuff his
suspicion more fully. — I will persevere in my course
of loyalty, though the conflict be sore between that and
my blood.

CORNWALL
I will lay trust upon thee; and thou shalt find a dearer
father in my love.   [*Exeunt.*

SCENE VI
A farmhouse adjoining the castle.

Enter LEAR, KENT, GLOSTER, FOOL, *and* EDGAR.

GLOSTER
Here is better than the open air; take it thankfully. I will
piece out the comfort with what addition I can: I will
not be long from you.

KENT
All the power of his wits have given way to his
impatience: — the gods reward your kindness!
                              [*Exit* GLOSTER.

EDGAR
Frateretto calls me, and tells me Nero is an angler in
the lake of darkness. — Pray, innocent, and beware the
foul fiend.

FOOL
Prithee, nuncle, tell me whether a madman be a
gentleman or a yeoman?

KING LEAR
A king, a king!

FOOL
No, he's a yeoman that has a gentleman to his son; for
he's a mad yeoman that sees his son a gentleman
before him.

KING LEAR
To have a thousand with red burning spits
Come hissing in upon 'em, —

EDGAR
The foul fiend bites my back.

FOOL
He's mad that trusts in the tameness of a wolf, a
horse's health, a boy's love, or a whore's oath.

KING LEAR
It shall be done; I will arraign them straight. —
[*to* EDGAR] Come, sit thou here, most learned
    justicer; —
[*to the* FOOL] Thou, sapient sir, sit here. — Now, you
    she foxes! —

EDGAR
Look, where he stands and glares! — Want'st thou eyes
at trial, madam?
                   Come o'er the bourn, Bessy, to me.

FOOL
          Her boat hath a leak,
          And she must not speak
          Why she dares not come over to thee.

EDGAR
The foul fiend haunts poor Tom in the voice of a
nightingale. Hopdance cries in Tom's belly for two
white herring. Croak not, black angel; I have no food
for thee.

KENT
How do you, sir? Stand you not so amaz'd:
Will you lie down and rest upon the cushions?

KING LEAR
I'll see their trial first. — Bring in the evidence. —
[*to* EDGAR] Thou robed man of justice, take thy place; —
[*to the* FOOL] And thou, his yoke-fellow of equity,
Bench by his side: — [*to* KENT] You are o' the
    commission,
Sit you too.

EDGAR
Let us deal justly.
          Sleepest or wakest thou, jolly shepherd?
               Thy sheep be in the corn;
          And for one blast of thy minikin mouth
               Thy sheep shall take no harm.
Pur! the cat is grey.

KING LEAR
Arraign her first; 'tis Goneril. I here take my oath
before this honourable assembly, she kick'd the poor
king her father.

FOOL
Come hither, mistress. Is your name Goneril?

KING LEAR
She cannot deny it.

FOOL
Cry you mercy, I took you for a joint-stool.

KING LEAR
And here's another, whose warp'd looks proclaim
What store her heart is made on. — Stop her there!
Arms, arms, sword, fire! — Corruption in the place!
False justicer, why hast thou let her scape?

EDGAR
Bless thy five wits!

KENT
O pity! — Sir, where is the patience now
That thou so oft have boasted to retain?

EDGAR [*aside*].
My tears begin to take his part so much,
They'll mar my counterfeiting.

KING LEAR
The little dogs and all,
Tray, Blanch, and Sweetheart, see, they bark at me.

EDGAR
Tom will throw his head at them. — Avaunt, you curs!
          Be thy mouth or black or white,
          Tooth that poisons if it bite;
          Mastiff, greyhound, mongrel grim,
          Hound or spaniel, brach or lym,
          Or bobtail tike or trundle-tail, —
          Tom will make them weep and wail:

For, with throwing thus my head,
          Dogs leap the hatch, and all are fled.
Do de, de, de. Sessa! Come, march to wakes and fairs
and market-towns. — Poor Tom, thy horn is dry.

KING LEAR
Then let them anatomise Regan; see what breeds about
her heart. Is there any cause in nature that makes these
hard hearts? — [*to* EDGAR] You, sir, I entertain for one
of my hundred; only I do not like the fashion of your
garments: you will say they are Persian attire; but let
them be changed.

KENT
Now, my good lord, lie here and rest awhile.

KING LEAR
Make no noise, make no noise; draw the curtains: so,
so, so: we'll go to supper i' the morning. so, so, so.

FOOL
And I'll go to bed at noon.
                   Enter GLOSTER.

GLOSTER
Come hither, friend; where is the king my master?

KENT
Here, sir; but trouble him not, — his wits are gone.

GLOSTER
Good friend, I prithee, take him in thy arms;
I have o'erheard a plot of death upon him:
There is a litter ready; lay him in 't,
And drive towards Dover, friend, where thou shalt
    meet
Both welcome and protection. Take up thy master:
If thou shouldst dally half an hour, his life,
With thine, and all that offer to defend him,
Stand in assured loss: take up, take up;
And follow me, that will to some provision
Give thee quick conduct.

KENT
                   Oppressed nature sleeps: —
This rest might yet have balm'd thy broken sinews,
Which, if convenience will not allow,
Stand in hard cure. — [*to the* FOOL] Come, help to bear
    thy master;
Thou must not stay behind.

GLOSTER
                   Come, come, away.
     [*Exeunt* KENT, GLOSTER, *and the* FOOL, *bearing off*
                                             LEAR.

EDGAR
When we our betters see bearing our woes,
We scarcely think our miseries our foes.
Who alone suffers suffers, most i' the mind,
Leaving free things and happy shows behind:
But then the mind much sufferance doth o'erskip,
When grief hath mates, and bearing fellowship.
How light and portable my pain seems now,
When that which makes me bend makes the king bow,
He childed as I father'd! — Tom, away!
Mark the high noises; and thy self bewray,
When false opinion, whose wrong thoughts defile thee,
In thy just proof, repeals and reconciles thee.
What will hap more to-night, safe scape the king!
Lurk, lurk.   [*Exit.*

SCENE VII
A room in GLOSTER'S *castle.*

Enter CORNWALL, REGAN, GONERIL, EDMUND,
and SERVANTS.

CORNWALL
Post speedily to my lord your husband; show him this
letter: — the army of France is landed. — Seek out the
traitor Gloster.   [*Exeunt some of the* SERVANTS.

REGAN
Hang him instantly.

GONERIL
Pluck out his eyes.

CORNWALL
Leave him to my displeasure. — Edmund, keep you
our sister company: the revenges we are bound to take
upon your traitorous father are not fit for your
beholding. Advise the duke, where you are going, to a
most festinate preparation: we are bound to the like.
Our posts shall be swift and intelligent betwixt us.
Farewell, dear sister: — farewell, my Lord of Gloster.
                   Enter OSWALD.
How now! where's the king?

OSWALD
My Lord of Gloster hath convey'd him hence:
Some five or six and thirty of his knights,
Hot questrists after him, met him at gate;

Who, with some other of the lords dependants,
Are gone with him towards Dover; where they boast
To have well-armed friends.

CORNWALL

              Get horses for your mistress.

GONERIL

Farewell, sweet lord, and sister.

CORNWALL

Edmund, farewell.

        [*Exeunt* GONERIL, EDMUND, *and* OSWALD.
        Go seek the traitor Gloster,
Pinion him like a thief, bring him before us.

        [*Exeunt other* SERVANTS.
Though well we may not pass upon his life
Without the form of justice, yet our power
Shall do a court'sy to our wrath, which men
May blame, but not control. — Who's there? the
    traitor?

    Enter GLOSTER, *brought in by two or three.*

REGAN

Ingrateful fox! 'tis he.

CORNWALL

Bind fast his corky arms.

GLOSTER

What mean your Graces? — Good my friends, consider
You are my guests: do me no foul play, friends.

CORNWALL

Bind him, I say.   [SERVANTS *bind him.*

REGAN

        Hard, hard. — O filthy traitor!

GLOSTER

Unmerciful lady as you are, I'm none.

CORNWALL

To this chair bind him. — Villain, thou shalt find —
        [REGAN *plucks his beard.*

GLOSTER

By the kind gods, 'tis most ignobly done
To pluck me by the beard.

REGAN

So white, and such a traitor!

GLOSTER

        Naughty lady,
These hairs, which thou dost ravish from my chin,
Will quicken, and accuse thee: I am your host:
With robbers' hands my hospitable favours
You should not ruffle thus. What will you do?

CORNWALL

Come, sir, what letters had you late from France?

REGAN

Be simple-answer'd, for we know the truth.

CORNWALL

And what confederacy have you with the traitors
Late footed in the kingdom?

REGAN

To whose hands have you sent the lunatic king?
Speak.

GLOSTER

I have a letter guessingly set down,
Which came from one that's of a neutral heart,
And not from one oppos'd.

CORNWALL

        Cunning.

REGAN

           And false.

CORNWALL

Where hast thou sent the king?

GLOSTER

        To Dover.

REGAN

Wherefore to Dover? Wast thou not charg'd at peril —

CORNWALL

Wherefore to Dover? Let him answer that.

GLOSTER

I am tied to the stake, and I must stand the course.

REGAN

Wherefore to Dover?

GLOSTER

Because I would not see thy cruel nails
Pluck out his poor old eyes; nor thy fierce sister
In his anointed flesh stick boarish fangs.
The sea, with such a storm as his bare head
In hell-black night endured, would have buoy'd up
And quench'd the stelled fires;
Yet, poor old heart, he help the heavens to rain.
If wolves had at thy gate howl'd that dern time,
Thou shouldst have said 'Good porter, turn the key.'
All cruels else subscrib'd: — but I shall see
The winged vengeance overtake such children.

CORNWALL

See't shalt thou never. — Fellows, hold the chair. —
Upon these eyes of thine I'll set my foot.

GLOSTER

He that will think to live till he be old,
Give me some help! — O cruel! — O you gods!

REGAN

One side will mock another; the other too.

CORNWALL

If you see vengeance, —

FIRST SERVANT

        Hold your hand, my lord:
I have serv'd you ever since I was a child;
But better service have I never done you
Than now to bid you hold.

REGAN

        How now, you dog!

FIRST SERVANT

If you did wear a beard upon your chin,
I'ld shake it on this quarrel. What do you mean?

CORNWALL

My villain!   [*Draws.*

FIRST SERVANT

Nay, then, come on, and take the chance of anger.
    [*Draws. They fight.* CORNWALL *is wounded.*

REGAN

Give me thy sword. — A peasant stand up thus!
    [*Takes a sword from another* SERVANT, *and runs at*
                FIRST SERVANT *behind.*

FIRST SERVANT

O, I am slain! — My lord, you have one eye left
To see some mischief on him. — O!   [*Dies.*

CORNWALL

Lest it see more, prevent it. — Out, vile jelly!
Where is thy lustre now?

GLOSTER

All dark and comfortless. — Where's my son Edmund?
Edmund, enkindle all the sparks of nature
To quit this horrid act.

REGAN

        Out, treacherous villain!
Thou call'st on him that hates thee: it was he
That made the overture of thy treasons to us;
Who is too good to pity thee.

GLOSTER

        O my follies!
Then Edgar was abused. —
Kind gods, forgive me that, and prosper him!

REGAN

Go thrust him out at gates, and let him smell
His way to Dover. [*Exit one with* GLOSTER.] How is't,
my lord? how look you?

CORNWALL

I have receiv'd a hurt: — follow me, lady. —
Turn out that eyeless villain; — throw this slave
Upon the dunghill. — Regan, I bleed apace.
Untimely comes this hurt: give me your arm.
        [*Exit* CORNWALL, *led by* REGAN.

SECOND SERVANT

I'll never care what wickedness I do,
If this man come to good.

THIRD SERVANT

        If she live long,
And in the end meet the old course of death,
Women will all turn monsters.

SECOND SERVANT

Let's follow the old earl, and get the Bedlam
To lead him where he would: his roguish madness
Allows itself to any thing.

THIRD SERVANT

Go thou: I'll fetch some flax and whites of eggs
To apply to his bleeding face. Now, heaven help him!
        [*Exeunt severally.*

ACT IV

SCENE I

The heath.

Enter EDGAR.

EDGAR

Yet better thus, and known to be contemn'd,
Than still contemn'd and flatter'd. To be worst,
The lowest and most dejected thing of fortune,
Stands still in esperance, lives not in fear:
The lamentable change is from the best;
The worst returns to laughter. Welcome, then,
Thou unsubstantial air that I embrace!
The wretch that thou hast blown unto the worst
Owes nothing to thy blasts. — But who comes here?
    Enter GLOSTER, *led by an* OLD MAN.
My father, poorly led? — World, world, O world!
But that thy strange mutations make us hate thee,
Life would not yield to age.

OLD MAN

        O, my good lord,
I have been your tenant, and your father's tenant,
These fourscore years.

GLOSTER

Away, get thee away; good friend, be gone:
Thy comforts can do me no good at all;
Thee they may hurt.

OLD MAN

Alack, sir, you cannot see your way.

GLOSTER

I have no way, and therefore want no eyes;
I stumbled when I saw: full oft 'tis seen,
Our means secure us, and our mere defects
Prove our commodities. — O dear son Edgar,
The food of thy abused father's wrath!
Might I but live to see thee in my touch,
I'ld say I had eyes again!

OLD MAN

        How now! Who's there?

EDGAR [*aside*].

O gods! Who is't can say, 'I am at the worst'?
I am worse than e'er I was.

OLD MAN

        'Tis poor mad Tom.

EDGAR [*aside*].

And worse I may be yet: the worst is not
So long as we can say 'This is the worst.'

OLD MAN

Fellow, where goest?

GLOSTER

        Is it a beggar-man?

OLD MAN

Madman and beggar too.

GLOSTER

He has some reason, else he could not beg.
I'the last night's storm I such a fellow saw;
Which made me think a man a worm: my son
Came then into my mind; and yet my mind
Was then scarce friends with him: I have heard more
    since.
As flies to wanton boys, are we to the gods, —
They kill us for their sport.

EDGAR [*aside*].

        How should this be? —
Bad is the trade that must play fool to sorrow,
Angering itself and others. — Bless thee, master!

GLOSTER

Is that the naked fellow?

OLD MAN

        Ay, my lord.

GLOSTER

Then, prithee, get thee gone: if, for my sake,
Thou wilt o'ertake us hence a mile or twain
I'the way toward Dover, do it for ancient love;
And bring some covering for this naked soul,
Which I'll entreat to lead me.

OLD MAN

        Alack, sir, he is mad.

GLOSTER

'Tis the times' plague, when madmen lead the blind.
Do as I bid thee, or rather do thy pleasure;
Above the rest, be gone.

OLD MAN

I'll bring him the best 'parel that I have,
Come on't what will.   [*Exit.*

GLOSTER

Sirrah, naked fellow, —

EDGAR

Poor Tom's a-cold. — [*aside*] I cannot daub it further.

GLOSTER

Come hither, fellow.

EDGAR [*aside*].

And yet I must. Bless thy sweet eyes, they bleed.

GLOSTER

Know'st thou the way to Dover?

EDGAR

Both stile and gate, horse-way and foot-path. Poor Tom
hath been scared out of his good wits: — bless thee,
good man's son, from the foul fiend! — five fiends
have been in poor Tom at once: of lust, as Obidicut;
Hobbididence, prince of dumbness; Mahu, of stealing;

Modo, of murder; and Flibbertigibbet, of mopping and mowing, — who since possesses chambermaids and waiting-women. So, bless thee, master!

GLOSTER
Here, take this purse, thou whom the heavens' plagues
Have humbled to all strokes: that I am wretched
Makes thee the happier: — heavens, deal so still!
Let the superfluous and lust-dieted man,
That slaves your ordinance, that will not see
Because he doth not feel, feel your power quickly;
So distribution should undo excess,
And each man have enough. — Dost thou know
Dover?

EDGAR
Ay, master.

GLOSTER
There is a cliff, whose high and bending head
Looks fearfully in the confined deep:
Bring me but to the very brim of it,
And I'll repair the misery thou dost bear
With something rich about me: from that place
I shall no leading need.

EDGAR
Give me thy arm:
Poor Tom shall lead thee.   [*Exeunt.*

SCENE II

Before the DUKE OF ALBANY'S *palace.*

Enter GONERIL *and* EDMUND.

GONERIL
Welcome, my lord; I marvel our mild husband
Not met us on the way.

Enter OSWALD.
Now, where's your master?

OSWALD
Madam, within; but never man so changed.
I told him of the army that was landed;
He smil'd at it: I told him you were coming;
His answer was, 'The worse': of Gloster's treachery,
And of the loyal service of his son,
When I inform'd him, then he call'd me sot,
And told me I had turn'd the wrong side out: —
What most he should dislike seems pleasant to him;
What like, offensive.

GONERIL [*to* EDMUND].
Then shall you go no further.
It is the cowish terror of his spirit,
That dares not undertake: he'll not feel wrongs,
Which tie him to an answer. Our wishes on the way
May prove effects. Back, Edmund, to my brother;
Hasten his musters and conduct his powers:
I must change arms at home, and give the distaff
Into my husband's hands. This trusty servant
Shall pass between us: ere long you are like to hear,
If you dare venture in your own behalf,
A mistress's command. Wear this; spare speech;
[*Giving a favour.*
Decline your head: this kiss, if it durst speak,
Would stretch thy spirits up into the air: —
Conceive, and fare thee well.

EDMUND
Yours in the ranks of death.

GONERIL
My most dear Gloster!
[*Exit* EDMUND.
O, the difference of man and man! To thee
A woman's services are due: my fool
Usurps my body.

OSWALD
Madam, here comes my lord.   [*Exit.*

Enter ALBANY.

GONERIL
I have been worth the whistle.

ALBANY
O Goneril!
You are not worth the dust which the rude wind
Blows in your face. I fear your disposition:
That nature which contemns its origin
Cannot be border'd certain in itself;
She that herself will sliver and disbranch
From her material sap, perforce must wither,
And come to deadly use.

GONERIL
No more; the text is foolish.

ALBANY
Wisdom and goodness to the vile seem vile:
Filths savour but themselves. What have you done?
Tigers, not daughters, what have you perform'd?

A father, and a gracious aged man,
Whose reverence the head-lugg'd bear would lick,
Most barbarous, most degenerate! have you madded.
Could my good brother suffer you to do it?
A man, a prince, by him so benefited!
If that the heavens do not their visible spirits
Send quickly down to tame these vile offences,
It will come,
Humanity must perforce prey on itself,
Like monsters of the deep.

GONERIL
Milk-liver'd man!
That bear'st a cheek for blows, a head for wrongs;
Who hast not in thy brows an eye discerning
Thine honour from thy suffering; that not know'st
Fools do those villains pity who are punish'd
Ere they have done their mischief. Where's thy drum?
France spreads his banners in our noiseless land;
With plumed helm thy slayer begins threats;
Whiles thou, a moral fool, sitt'st still, and criest
'Alack, why does he so?'

ALBANY
See thyself, devil!
Proper deformity seems not in the fiend
So horrid as in woman.

GONERIL
O vain fool!

ALBANY
Thou changed and self-cover'd thing, for shame,
Be-monster not thy feature. Were't my fitness
To let these hands obey my blood,
They are apt enough to dislocate and tear
Thy flesh and bones: — howe'er thou art a fiend,
A woman's shape doth shield thee.

GONERIL
Marry, your manhood! mew!

Enter a MESSENGER.

ALBANY
What news?

MESSENGER
O, my good lord, the Duke of Cornwall's dead;
Slain by his servant, going to put out
The other eye of Gloster.

ALBANY
Gloster's eyes!

MESSENGER
A servant that he bred, thrill'd with remorse,
Oppos'd against the act, bending his sword
To his great master; who, thereat enraged,
Flew on him, and amongst them fell'd him dead;
But not without that harmful stroke which since
Hath pluck'd him after.

ALBANY
This shows you are above,
You justicers, that these our nether crimes
So speedily can venge! — But, O poor Gloster!
Lost he his other eye?

MESSENGER
Both, both, my lord. —
This letter, madam, craves a speedy answer;
'Tis from your sister.

GONERIL [*aside*].
One way I like this well;
But being widow, and my Gloster with her,
May all the building in my fancy pluck
Upon my hateful life: another way
The news is not so tart. — I'll read, and answer.   [*Exit.*

ALBANY
Where was his son when they did take his eyes?

MESSENGER
Come with my lady hither.

ALBANY
He is not here.

MESSENGER
No, my good lord; I met him back again.

ALBANY
Knows he the wickedness?

MESSENGER
Ay, my good lord; 'twas he inform'd against him;
And quit the house on purpose, that their punishment
Might have the freer course.

ALBANY
Gloster, I live
To thank thee for the love thou show'dst the king,
And to revenge thine eyes. — Come hither, friend;
Tell me what more thou know'st.   [*Exeunt.*

SCENE III

The French camp near Dover.

Enter KENT *and a* GENTLEMAN.

KENT
Why the King of France is so suddenly gone back,
know you the reason?

GENTLEMAN
Something he left imperfect in the state, which since
his coming forth is thought of; which imports to the
kingdom so much fear and danger, that his personal
return was most required and necessary.

KENT
Who hath he left behind him general?

GENTLEMAN
The Marshal of France, Monsieur La Far.

KENT
Did your letters pierce the queen to any demonstration
of grief?

GENTLEMAN
Ay, sir; she took them, read them in my presence;
And now and then an ample tear trill'd down
Her delicate cheek: it seem'd she was a queen
Over her passion; who, most rebel-like,
Sought to be king o'er her.

KENT
O, then it mov'd her.

GENTLEMAN
Not to a rage: patience and sorrow strove
Who should express her goodliest. You have seen
Sunshine and rain at once: her smiles and tears
Were like a better way: those happy smilets
That play'd on her ripe lip seem'd not to know
What guests were in her eyes; which parted thence
As pearls from diamonds dropp'd. — In brief,
Sorrow would be a rarity most beloved,
If all could so become it.

KENT
Made she no verbal question?

GENTLEMAN
Faith, once or twice she heaved the name of 'father'
Pantingly forth, as if it press'd her heart;
Cried 'Sisters! sisters! — Shame of ladies! sisters!
Kent! father! sisters! What, i' the storm? i' the night?
Let pity not be believed!' — There she shook
The holy water from her heavenly eyes,
And clamour moisten'd: then away she started
To deal with grief alone.

KENT
It is the stars,
The stars above us, govern our conditions;
Else one self mate and mate could not beget
Such different issues. You spoke not with her since?

GENTLEMAN
No.

KENT
Was this before the king return'd?

GENTLEMAN
No, since.

KENT
Well, sir, the poor distressed Lear's i' the town;
Who sometime, in his better tune, remembers
What we are come about, and by no means
Will yield to see his daughter.

GENTLEMAN
Why, good sir?

KENT
A sovereign shame so elbows him: his own
unkindness,
That stripp'd her from his benediction, turn'd her
To foreign casualties, gave her dear rights
To his dog-hearted daughters, — these things sting
His mind so venomously that burning shame
Detains him from Cordelia.

GENTLEMAN
Alack, poor gentleman!

KENT
Of Albany's and Cornwall's powers you heard not?

GENTLEMAN
'Tis so, they are a-foot.

KENT
Well, sir, I'll bring you to our master Lear,
And leave you to attend him: some dear cause
Will in concealment wrap me up awhile;
When I am known aright, you shall not grieve
Lending me this acquaintance. I pray you, go
Along with me.   [*Exeunt.*

SCENE IV

The same. A tent.

Enter, with drum and colours, CORDELIA, DOCTOR, *and* SOLDIERS.

CORDELIA
Alack, 'tis he: why, he was met even now
As mad as the vex'd sea; singing aloud;
Crown'd with rank fumiter and furrow-weeds,
With bur-docks, hemlock, nettles, cuckoo-flowers,
Darnel, and all the idle weeds that grow
In our sustaining corn. — A century send forth;
Search every acre in the high-grown field,
And bring him to our eye. [*Exit an* OFFICER.] —
　　What can man's wisdom
In the restoring his bereaved sense?
He that helps him take all my outward worth.

DOCTOR
There is means, madam:
Our foster-nurse of nature is repose,
The which he lacks; that to provoke in him
Are many simples operative, whose power
Will close the eye of anguish.

CORDELIA
　　　　　　　All blest secrets,
All you unpublish'd virtues of the earth,
Spring with my tears! be aidant and remediate
In the good man's distress! — Seek, seek for him;
Lest his ungovern'd rage dissolve the life
That wants the means to lead it.

　　　　Enter a MESSENGER.

MESSENGER
　　　　　　News, madam;
The British powers are marching hitherward.

CORDELIA
'Tis known before; our preparation stands
In expectation of them. — O dear father,
It is thy business that I go about;
Therefore great France
My mourning and important tears hath pitied.
No blown ambition doth our arms incite,
But love, dear love, and our aged father's right:
Soon may I hear and see him! 　　　　[*Exeunt.*

SCENE V

A room in GLOSTER'S *castle.*

Enter REGAN *and* OSWALD.

REGAN
But are my brother's powers set forth?

OSWALD
　　　　　　　　Ay, madam.

REGAN
Himself in person there?

OSWALD
　　　　　　Madam, with much ado:
Your sister is the better soldier.

REGAN
Lord Edmund spake not with your lord at home?

OSWALD
No, madam.

REGAN
What might import my sister's letter to him?

OSWALD
I know not, lady.

REGAN
Faith, he is posted hence on serious matter.
It was great ignorance, Gloster's eyes being out,
To let him live: where he arrives he moves
All hearts against us: Edmund, I think, is gone,
In pity of his misery, to dispatch
His nighted life; moreover, to descry
The strength o'th'enemy.

OSWALD
I must needs after him, madam, with my letter.

REGAN
Our troops set forth to-morrow: stay with us;
The ways are dangerous.

OSWALD
　　　　　　I may not, madam:
My lady charg'd my duty in this business.

REGAN
Why should she write to Edmund? Might not you
Transport her purposes by word? Belike,
Something — I know not what: — I'll love thee much,
Let me unseal the letter.

OSWALD
　　　　　　Madam, I had rather —

DOCTOR Our foster-nurse of nature is repose, the which he lacks.

REGAN
I know your lady does not love her husband;
I am sure of that: and at her late being here
She gave strange œilliades and most speaking looks
To noble Edmund. I know you are of her bosom.

OSWALD
I, madam?

REGAN
I speak in understanding; you are; I know't:
Therefore I do advise you, take this note:
My lord is dead; Edmund and I have talk'd;
And more convenient is he for my hand
Than for your lady's: — you may gather more.
If you do find him, pray you, give him this;
And when your mistress hears thus much from you,
I pray, desire her call her wisdom to her.
So, fare you well.
If you do chance to hear of that blind traitor,
Preferment falls on him that cuts him off.

OSWALD
Would I could meet him, madam! I should show
What party I do follow.

REGAN
　　　　　　Fare thee well. 　　[*Exeunt.*

SCENE VI

The country near Dover.

Enter GLOSTER, *and* EDGAR *dress'd like a peasant.*

GLOSTER
When shall I come to the top of that same hill?

EDGAR
You do climb up it now: look, how we labour.

GLOSTER
Methinks the ground is even.

EDGAR
　　　　　　Horrible steep.
Hark, do you hear the sea?

GLOSTER
　　　　　　No, truly.

EDGAR
Why, then, your other senses grow imperfect
By your eyes' anguish.

GLOSTER
　　　　　　So may it be, indeed:
Methinks thy voice is alter'd; and thou speak'st
In better phrase and matter than thou didst.

EDGAR
Y'are much deceiv'd: in nothing am I changed
But in my garments.

GLOSTER
　　　　　　Methinks y'are better spoken.

EDGAR
Come on, sir; here's the place: — stand still. —How fearful
And dizzy 'tis to cast one's eyes so low!
The crows and choughs that wing the midway air
Show scarce so gross as beetles: half way down
Hangs one that gathers samphire, — dreadful trade!
Methinks he seems no bigger than his head:
The fishermen, that walk upon the beach,
Appear like mice; and yond tall anchoring bark,
Diminish'd to her cock, — her cock, a buoy
Almost too small for sight: the murmuring surge,
That on the unnumber'd idle pebbles chafes,
Cannot be heard so high. — I'll look no more;
Lest my brain turn, and the deficient sight
Topple down headlong.

GLOSTER
　　　　　　Set me where you stand.

EDGAR
Give me your hand: — you are now within a foot
Of the extreme verge: for all beneath the moon
Would I not leap upright.

GLOSTER
               Let go my hand.
Here, friend, 's another purse; in it a jewel
Well worth a poor man's taking: fairies and gods
Prosper it with thee! Go thou further off;
Bid me farewell, and let me hear thee going.

EDGAR
Now fare you well, good sir.

GLOSTER
              With all my heart.

EDGAR [aside].
Why I do trifle thus with his despair
Is done to cure it.

GLOSTER [kneeling].
            O you mighty gods!
This world I do renounce, and, in your sights,
Shake patiently my great affliction off:
If I could bear it longer, and not fall
To quarrel with your great opposeless wills,
My snuff and loathed part of nature should
Burn itself out. If Edgar live, O, bless him! —
Now, fellow, fare thee well.

EDGAR
             Gone, sir: — farewell.
            [GLOSTER *falls forward.*
[aside] And yet I know not how conceit may rob
The treasury of life, when life itself
Yields to the theft: had he been where he thought,
By this had thought been past. — Alive or dead?
Ho you sir! friend! —Hear you, sir! speak!
[aside] Thus might he pass indeed: yet he revives. —
What are you, sir?

GLOSTER
          Away, and let me die.

EDGAR
Hadst thou been aught but gossamer, feathers, air,
So many fathom down precipitating,
Thou'dst shiver'd like an egg: but thou dost breathe;
Hast heavy substance; bleed'st not; speak'st; art sound.
Ten masts at each make not the altitude
Which thou hast perpendicularly fell:
Thy life's a miracle. Speak yet again.

GLOSTER
But have I fall'n, or no?

EDGAR
From the dread summit of this chalky bourn.
Look up a-height; — the shrill-gorg'd lark so far
Cannot be seen or heard: do but look up.

GLOSTER
Alack, I have no eyes. —
Is wretchedness depriv'd that benefit
To end itself by death? 'Twas yet some comfort,
When misery could beguile the tyrant's rage,
And frustrate his proud will.

EDGAR
           Give me your arm:
Up: — so. — How is't? Feel you your legs? You stand.

GLOSTER
Too well, too well.

EDGAR
        This is above all strangeness.
Upon the crown o' the cliff, what thing was that
Which parted from you?

GLOSTER
        A poor unfortunate beggar.

EDGAR
As I stood here below, methought his eyes
Were two full moons; he had a thousand noses,
Horns whelk'd and wav'd like the enridged sea:
It was some fiend; therefore, thou happy father,
Think that the clearest gods, who make them honours
Of men's impossibilities, have preserv'd thee.

GLOSTER
I do remember now: henceforth I'll bear
Affliction till it do cry out itself
'Enough, enough', and die. That thing you speak of,
I took it for a man; often 'twould say
'The fiend, the fiend': he led me to that place.

EDGAR
Bear free and patient thoughts. — But who comes here?
    Enter LEAR, *fantastically dress'd with wild flowers.*
The safer sense will ne'er accommodate
His master thus.

KING LEAR
No, they cannot touch me for coining; I am the king
  himself.

EDGAR [aside].
O thou side-piercing sight!

KING LEAR
Nature's above art in that respect. — There's your
press-money. That fellow handles his bow like a
crow-keeper: draw me a clothier's yard. — Look, look, a
mouse! Peace, peace; — this piece of toasted cheese will
do't. — There's my gauntlet; I'll prove it on a giant. —
Bring up the brown bills. — O, well flown, bird! — i'the
clout, i'the clout: hewgh! — Give the word.

EDGAR
Sweet marjoram.

KING LEAR
Pass.

GLOSTER
I know that voice.

KING LEAR
Ha! Goneril, — with a white beard! — They flatter'd
me like a dog; and told me I had white hairs in my
beard ere the black ones were there. — To say 'ay' and
'no' to every thing that I said! — 'Ay' and 'no' too was
no good divinity. When the rain came to wet me once,
and the wind to make me chatter; when the thunder
would not peace at my bidding; there I found 'em, there
I smelt 'em out. Go to, they are not men o' their words:
they told me I was every thing; 'tis a lie, — I am not
ague-proof.

GLOSTER
The trick of that voice I do well remember:
Is't not the king?

KING LEAR
        Ay, every inch a king:
When I do stare, see how the subject quakes!
I pardon that man's life. — What was thy cause? —
  Adultery?
Thou shalt not die: die for adultery! No:
The wren goes to't, and the small gilded fly
Does lecher in my sight.
Let copulation thrive: for Gloster's bastard son
Was kinder to his father than my daughters
Got 'tween the lawful sheets.
To't, luxury, pell-mell! for I lack soldiers. —
Behold yond simpering dame,
Whose face between her forks presages snow,
That minces virtue, and does shake the head
To hear of pleasure's name, —
The fitchew nor the soiled horse goes to't
With a more riotous appetite.
Down from the waist they are Centaurs,
Though women all above:
But to the girdle do the gods inherit,
Beneath is all the fiends';
There's hell, there's darkness, there's the sulphurous
  pit,
Burning, scalding, stench, consumption; — fie, fie, fie!
pah, pah! Give me an ounce of civet, good apothecary,
to sweeten my imagination: there's money for thee.

GLOSTER
O, let me kiss that hand!

KING LEAR
Let me wipe it first; it smells of mortality.

GLOSTER
O ruin'd piece of nature! This great world
Shall so wear out to nought. — Dost thou know me?

KING LEAR
I remember thine eyes well enough. Dost thou squiny at
me? No, do thy worst, blind Cupid; I'll not love. —Read
thou this challenge; mark but the penning on't.

GLOSTER
Were all the letters suns, I could not see one.

EDGAR [aside].
I would not take this from report; — it is,
And my heart breaks at it.

KING LEAR
Read.

GLOSTER
What, with the case of eyes?

KING LEAR
O, ho, are you there with me? No eyes in your head, nor
no money in your purse? Your eyes are in a heavy case,
your purse in a light; yet you see how this world goes.

GLOSTER
I see it feelingly.

KING LEAR
What, art mad? A man may see how this world goes
with no eyes. Look with thine ears: see how yond
justice rails upon yond simple thief. Hark, in thine ear:

change places; and, handy-dandy, which is the justice,
which is the thief? — Thou hast seen a farmer's dog
bark at a beggar?

GLOSTER
Ay, sir.

KING LEAR
And the creature run from the cur? There thou mightst
behold the great image of authority: a dog's obeyed in
office. —
Thou rascal beadle, hold thy bloody hand!
Why dost thou lash that whore? Strip thine own back;
Thou hotly lusts to use her in that kind
For which thou whippst her. The usurer hangs the
  cozener.
Through tatter'd clothes small vices do appear;
Robes and furr'd gowns hide all. Plate sin with gold,
And the strong lance of justice hurtless breaks;
Arm it in rags, a pigmy's straw does pierce it.
None does offend, none, — I say, none; I'll able 'em:
Take that of me, my friend, who have the power
To seal the accuser's lips. Get thee glass eyes;
And, like a scurvy politician, seem
To see the things thou dost not. — Now, now, now,
  now:
Pull off my boots: — harder, harder: — so.

EDGAR [aside].
O, matter and impertinency mix'd!
Reason in madness!

KING LEAR
If thou wilt weep my fortunes, take my eyes.
I know thee well enough; thy name is Gloster:
Thou must be patient; we came crying hither:
Thou know'st, the first time that we smell the air,
We wawl and cry. — I will preach to thee: mark.

GLOSTER
Alack, alack the day!

KING LEAR
When we are born, we cry that we are come
To this great stage of fools. — This' a good block: —
It were a delicate stratagem to shoe
A troop of horse with felt: I'll put't in proof;
And when I have stol'n upon these sons-in-law,
Then, kill, kill, kill, kill, kill, kill!

    Enter a GENTLEMAN, *with* ATTENDANTS.

GENTLEMAN
O, here he is: lay hand upon him. — Sir,
Your most dear daughter —

KING LEAR
No rescue? What, a prisoner? I am even
The natural fool of fortune. — Use me well;
You shall have ransom. Let me have a surgeon;
I am cut to the brains.

GENTLEMAN
        You shall have any thing.

KING LEAR
No seconds? all myself?
Why, this would make a man a man of salt,
To use his eyes for garden water-pots,
Ay, and laying autumn's dust.

GENTLEMAN
Good sir, —

KING LEAR
I will die bravely, like a smug bridegroom. What!
I will be jovial: come, come; I am a king;
My masters, know you that.

GENTLEMAN
You are a royal one, and we obey you.

KING LEAR
Then there's life in't. Nay, an you get it, you shall get it
by running. Sa, sa, sa, sa.
        [Exit running. ATTENDANTS *follow.*

GENTLEMAN
A sight most pitiful in the meanest wretch,
Past speaking of in a king! — Thou hast one daughter,
Who redeems nature from the general curse
Which twain have brought her to.

EDGAR
Hail, gentle sir.

GENTLEMAN
       Sir, speed you: what's your will?

EDGAR
Do you hear aught, sir, of a battle toward?

GENTLEMAN
Most sure and vulgar: every one hears that,
Which can distinguish sound.

EDGAR
          But, by your favour,
How near's the other army?

KING LEAR I am the king himself.

GENTLEMAN
Near and on speedy foot; the main descry
Stands on the hourly thought.
EDGAR
                I thank you, sir: that's all.
GENTLEMAN
Though that the queen on special cause is here,
Her army is moved on.
EDGAR
            I thank you, sir.
                [Exit GENTLEMAN.
GLOSTER
You ever-gentle gods, take my breath from me;
Let not my worser spirit tempt me again
To die before you please!
EDGAR
           Well pray you, father.
GLOSTER
Now, good sir, what are you?
EDGAR
A most poor man, made tame to fortune's blows;
Who, by the art of known and feeling sorrows,
Am pregnant to good pity. Give me your hand,
I'll lead you to some biding.
GLOSTER
            Hearty thanks:
The bounty and the benison of heaven
To boot, and boot!
        Enter OSWALD.
OSWALD
        A proclaim'd prize! Most happy!
That eyeless head of thine was first fram'd flesh
To raise my fortunes. — Thou old unhappy traitor,
Briefly thyself remember: — the sword is out

That must destroy thee.
GLOSTER
           Now let thy friendly hand
Put strength enough to't.   *[EDGAR interposes.*
OSWALD
          Wherefore, bold peasant,
Darest thou support a publish'd traitor? Hence;
Lest that the infection of his fortune take
Like hold on thee. Let go his arm.
EDGAR
Chill not let go, zir, without vurther 'casion.
OSWALD
Let go, slave, or thou diest!
EDGAR
Good gentleman, go your gait, and let poor volk pass.
An chud ha' bin zwagger'd out of my life, 'twould not
ha' bin zo long as 'tis by a vortnight. Nay, come not near
the old man; keep out, che vor ye, or ise try whether
your costard or my ballow be the harder: chill be plain
with you.
OSWALD
Out, dunghill!
EDGAR
Chill pick your teeth, zir: come; no matter vor your
foins.   *[They fight, and* EDGAR *knocks him down.*
OSWALD
Slave, thou hast slain me: — villain, take my purse:
If ever thou wilt thrive, bury my body;
And give the letters which thou find'st about me
To Edmund Earl of Gloster; seek him out
Upon the English party: — O, untimely death!
Death!   *[Dies.*
EDGAR
I know thee well: a serviceable villain;
As duteous to the vices of thy mistress

As badness would desire.
GLOSTER
                What, is he dead?
EDGAR
Sit you down, father; rest you. —
Let's see his pockets: the letters that he speaks of
May be my friends. — He's dead; I am only sorry
He had no other death's-man. — Let us see: —
Leave, gentle wax; and, manners, blame us not:
To know our enemies' minds, we'ld rip their hearts;
Their papers, is more lawful.
    [Reads] Let our reciprocal vows be remember'd.
You have many opportunities to cut him off: if your will
want not, time and place will be fruitfully offer'd. There
is nothing done, if he return the conqueror: then am I
the prisoner, and his bed my gaol; from the warmth
loath'd whereof deliver me, and supply the place for
your labour.
        Your — wife, so I would say —
           Affectionate servant,
                            GONERIL.

O undistinguish'd space of woman's will!
A plot upon her virtuous husband's life;
And the exchange my brother! — Here, in the sands,
Thee I'll rake up, the post unsanctified
Of murderous lechers: and, in the mature time,
With this ungracious paper strike the sight
Of the death-practis'd duke: for him 'tis well
That of thy death and business I can tell.
GLOSTER
The king is mad: how stiff is my vile sense,
That I stand up, and have ingenious feeling
Of my huge sorrows! Better I were distract:
So should my thoughts be sever'd from my griefs,
And woes, by wrong imaginations, lose
The knowledge of themselves.
EDGAR
           Give me your hand: *[Drum afar off.*
Far off, methinks, I hear the beaten drum:
Come, father, I'll bestow you with a friend.   *[Exeunt.*

SCENE VII

A tent in the French camp.

Enter CORDELIA, KENT, DOCTOR,
and GENTLEMAN.

CORDELIA
O thou good Kent, how shall I live and work,
To match thy goodness? My life will be too short,
And every measure fail me.
KENT
To be acknowledg'd, madam, is o'erpaid.
All my reports go with the modest truth;
Nor more nor clipp'd, but so.
CORDELIA
              Be better suited:
These weeds are memories of those worser hours:
I prithee, put them off.
KENT
            Pardon, dear madam;
Yet to be known shortens my made intent:
My boon I make it, that you know me not
Till time and I think meet.
CORDELIA
Then be't so, my good lord. — *[to the* DOCTOR]
    How does the king?
DOCTOR
Madam, sleeps still.
CORDELIA
O you kind gods,
Cure this great breach in his abused nature!
Th'untun'd and jarring senses, O, wind up
Of this child-changed father!
DOCTOR
           So please your majesty
That we may wake the king: he hath slept long.
CORDELIA
Be govern'd by your knowledge, and proceed
I' the sway of your own will. Is he array'd?
    Enter LEAR *in a chair carried by* SERVANTS.
GENTLEMAN
Ay, madam; in the heaviness of his sleep
We put fresh garments on him.
DOCTOR
Be by, good madam, when we do awake him;
I doubt not of his temperance.
CORDELIA
                Very well.

DOCTOR
Please you, draw near. — Louder the music there!

CORDELIA
O my dear father! Restoration hang
Thy medicine on my lips; and let this kiss
Repair those violent harms that my two sisters
Have in thy reverence made!

KENT
Kind and dear princess!

CORDELIA
Had you not been their father, these white flakes
Had challeng'd pity of them. Was this a face
To be oppos'd against the warring winds?
To stand against the deep dread-bolted thunder?
In the most terrible and nimble stroke
Of quick, cross lightning? to watch — poor perdu! —
With this thin helm? Mine enemy's dog,
Though he had bit me, should have stood that night
Against my fire; and wast thou fain, poor father,
To hovel thee with swine, and rogues forlorn,
In short and musty straw? Alack, alack!
'Tis wonder that thy life and wits at once
Had not concluded all. — He wakes; speak to him.

DOCTOR
Madam, do you; 'tis fittest.

CORDELIA
How does my royal lord? how fares your majesty?

KING LEAR
You do me wrong to take me out o'the grave: —
Thou art a soul in bliss; but I am bound
Upon a wheel of fire, that mine own tears
Do scald like moulten lead.

CORDELIA
Sir, do you know me?

KING LEAR
You are a spirit, I know: when did you die?

CORDELIA
Still, still, far wide!

DOCTOR
He's scarce awake: let him alone awhile.

KING LEAR
Where have I been? Where am I? — Fair daylight? —
I am mightily abus'd. — I should e'en die with pity,
To see another thus. — I know not what to say. —
I will not swear these are my hands: — let's see;
I feel this pin prick. Would I were assured
Of my condition.

CORDELIA
O, look upon me, sir,
And hold your hands in benediction o'er me: —
No, sir, you must not kneel.

KING LEAR
Pray, do not mock me:
I am a very foolish fond old man,
Fourscore and upward, not an hour more nor less;
And, to deal plainly,
I fear I am not in my perfect mind.
Methinks I should know you, and know this man;
Yet I am doubtful: for I am mainly ignorant
What place this is; and all the skill I have
Remembers not these garments; nor I know not
Where I did lodge last night. Do not laugh at me;
For, as I am a man, I think this lady
To be my child Cordelia.

CORDELIA
And so I am, I am.

KING LEAR
Be your tears wet? yes, faith. I pray, weep not:
If you have poison for me, I will drink it.
I know you do not love me; for your sisters
Have, as I do remember, done me wrong:
You have some cause, they have not.

CORDELIA
No cause, no cause.

KING LEAR
Am I in France?

KENT
In your own kingdom, sir.

KING LEAR
Do not abuse me.

DOCTOR
Be comforted, good madam: the great rage,
You see, is kill'd in him: and yet it is danger
To make him even o'er the time he has lost.
Desire him to go in; trouble him no more
Till further settling.

CORDELIA
Will't please your highness walk?

KING LEAR
You must bear with me:
Pray you now, forget and forgive; I am old and
foolish.
[*Exeunt all but* KENT *and* GENTLEMAN.

GENTLEMAN
Holds it true, sir, that the Duke of Cornwall
was so slain?

KENT
Most certain, sir.

GENTLEMAN
Who is conductor of his people?

KENT
As 'tis said, the bastard son of Gloster.

GENTLEMAN
They say Edgar, his banish'd son, is with the
Earl of Kent in Germany.

KENT
Report is changeable. 'Tis time to look about;
the powers of the kingdom approach apace.

GENTLEMAN
The arbitrement is like to be bloody. Fare you
well, sir.
[*Exit.*

KENT
My point and period will be throughly
wrought,
Or well or ill, as this day's battle's fought. [*Exit.*

ACT V

SCENE I

The British camp, near Dover.

Enter, with drum and colours, EDMUND, REGAN,
OFFICERS, SOLDIERS, *and others.*

EDMUND
Know of the duke if his last purpose hold,
Or whether since he is advised by aught
To change the course: he's full of alteration
And self-reproving: — bring his constant pleasure.
[*To an* OFFICER, *who goes out.*

REGAN
Our sister's man is certainly miscarried.

EDMUND
'Tis to be doubted, madam.

REGAN
Now, sweet lord,
You know the goodness I intend upon you:
Tell me, — but truly, — but then speak the truth,
Do you not love my sister?

EDMUND
In honour'd love.

REGAN
But have you never found my brother's way
To the forfended place?

EDMUND
That thought abuses you.

REGAN
I am doubtful that you have been conjunct
And bosom'd with her, as far as we call hers.

EDMUND
No, by mine honour, madam.

REGAN
I never shall endure her: dear my lord,
Be not familiar with her.

EDMUND
Fear me not: —
She and the duke her husband!
Enter, with drum and colours, ALBANY, GONERIL,
and SOLDIERS.

GONERIL [*aside*].
I had rather lose the battle than that sister
Should loosen him and me.

ALBANY
Our very loving sister, well be-met. —
Sir, this I hear, — the king is come to his daughter,
With others whom the rigour of our state
Forc'd to cry out. Where I could not be honest,
I never yet was valiant: for this business,
It toucheth us, as France invades our land,
Not bolds the king, with others, whom, I fear,
Most just and heavy causes make oppose.

EDMUND
Sir, you speak nobly.

CORDELIA *Sir, do you know me?*

REGAN
Why is this reason'd?

GONERIL
Combine together 'gainst the enemy;
For these domestic and particular broils
Are not the question here.

ALBANY
Let's, then, determine
With the ancient of war on our proceedings.

EDMUND
I shall attend you presently at your tent.

REGAN
Sister, you'll go with us?

GONERIL
No.

REGAN
'Tis most convenient; pray you, go with us.

GONERIL [*aside*].
O, ho, I know the riddle. — I will go.
As they are going out, enter EDGAR *disguised.*

EDGAR
If e'er your Grace had speech with man so poor,
Hear me one word.

ALBANY
I'll overtake you. — Speak.
[*Exeunt all but* ALBANY *and* EDGAR.

EDGAR
Before you fight the battle, ope this letter.
If you have victory, let the trumpet sound
For him that brought it: wretched though I seem,
I can produce a champion that will prove
What is avouched there. If you miscarry,
Your business of the world hath so an end,
And machination ceases. Fortune love you!

ALBANY
Stay till I have read the letter.

EDGAR
I was forbid it.
When time shall serve, let but the herald cry,
And I'll appear again.

ALBANY
Why, fare thee well: I will o'erlook thy paper.
[*Exit* EDGAR.
Enter EDMUND.

EDMUND
The enemy's in view; draw up your powers.
Here is the guess of their true strength and forces
By diligent discovery; — but your haste
Is now urg'd on you.

ALBANY
We will greet the time. [*Exit.*

EDMUND
To both these sisters have I sworn my love;
Each jealous of the other, as the stung
Are of the adder. Which of them shall I take?
Both? one? or neither? Neither can be enjoy'd,

REGAN Now, sweet lord, you know the goodness I intend upon you.

If both remain alive: to take the widow
Exasperates, makes mad her sister Goneril;
And hardly shall I carry out my side,
Her husband being alive. Now, then, we'll use
His countenance for the battle; which being done,
Let her who would be rid of him devise
His speedy taking off. As for the mercy
Which he intends to Lear and to Cordelia, —
The battle done, and they within our power,
Shall never see his pardon; for my state
Stands on me to defend, not to debate.   [*Exit.*

SCENE II

A field between the two camps.

Alarum within. Enter, with drum and colours, LEAR,
CORDELIA, *and their* FORCES *over the stage;*
and exeunt.

Enter EDGAR *and* GLOSTER.

EDGAR
Here, father, take the shadow of this tree
For your good host; pray that the right may thrive:
If ever I return to you again,
I'll bring you comfort.

GLOSTER
                  Grace go with you, sir!   [*Exit* EDGAR.

Alarum and retreat within. Enter EDGAR.

EDGAR
Away, old man, — give me thy hand, — away!
King Lear hath lost, he and his daughter ta'en:
Give me thy hand; come on.

GLOSTER
No farther, sir; a man may rot even here.

EDGAR
What, in ill thoughts again? Men must endure
Their going hence, even as their coming hither:
Ripeness is all: — come on.

GLOSTER
                  And that's true too.   [*Exeunt.*

SCENE III

The British camp, near Dover.

Enter, in conquest, with drum and colours,
EDMUND; LEAR *and* CORDELIA *as prisoners,*
OFFICERS, SOLDIERS, *etc.*

EDMUND
Some officers take them away: good guard,
Until their greater pleasures first be known
That are to censure them.

CORDELIA
                  We are not the first
Who, with best meaning, have incurr'd the worst.
For thee, oppressed king, am I cast down;
Myself could else out-frown false fortune's frown. —
Shall we not see these daughters and these sisters?

KING LEAR
No, no, no, no! Come, let's away to prison:
We two alone will sing like birds i' the cage:
When thou dost ask me blessing, I'll kneel down,
And ask of thee forgiveness: so we'll live,
And pray, and sing, and tell old tales, and laugh
At gilded butterflies, and hear poor rogues
Talk of court news; and we'll talk with them too, —
Who loses and who wins; who's in, who's out; —
And take upon's the mystery of things,
As if we were God's spies: and we'll wear out,
In a wall'd prison, packs and sects of great ones,
That ebb and flow by th'moon.

EDMUND
                  Take them away.

KING LEAR
Upon such sacrifices, my Cordelia,
The gods themselves throw incense. Have I caught
  thee?
He that parts us shall bring a brand from heaven,
And fire us hence like foxes. Wipe thine eyes;
The good-years shall devour them, flesh and fell,
Ere they make us weep: we'll see 'em starve first.
Come.   [*Exeunt* LEAR *and* CORDELIA, *guarded.*

EDMUND
Come hither, captain; hark.
Take thou this note [*giving a paper*]; go follow them to

prison:
One step I have advanc'd thee; if thou dost
As this instructs thee, thou dost make thy way
To noble fortunes: know thou this, that men
Are as the time is: to be tender-minded
Does not become a sword: — thy great employment
Will not bear question; either say thou'lt do't,
Or thrive by other means.

OFFICER
                  I'll do't, my lord.

EDMUND
About it; and write happy when thou hast done.
Mark, — I say, instantly; and carry it so
As I have set it down.

OFFICER
I cannot draw a cart, nor eat dried oats;
If it be man's work, I'll do't.   [*Exit.*

Flourish. Enter ALBANY, GONERIL, REGAN,
OFFICERS, *and* ATTENDANTS.

ALBANY
Sir, you have shown to-day your valiant strain,
And fortune led you well: you have the captives
Who were the opposites of this day's strife:
We do require them of you, so to use them
As we shall find their merits and our safety
May equally determine.

EDMUND
                  Sir, I thought it fit
To send the old and miserable king
To some retention and appointed guard;
Whose age has charms in it, whose title more,
To pluck the common bosom on his side,
An turn our impress'd lances in our eyes,
Which do command them. With him I sent the queen;
My reason all the same; and they are ready
To-morrow, or at further space, t'appear
Where you shall hold your session. At this time
We sweat and bleed: the friend hath lost his friend;
And the best quarrels, in the heat, are curs'd
By those that feel their sharpness: —
The question of Cordelia and her father
Requires a fitter place.

ALBANY
                  Sir, by your patience,
I hold you but a subject of this war,
Not as a brother.

REGAN
                  That's as we list to grace him.
Methinks our pleasure might have been demanded,
Ere you had spoke so far. He led our powers;
Bore the commission of my place and person;
The which immediacy may well stand up
And call itself your brother.

GONERIL
                  Not so hot:
In his own grace he doth exalt himself,
More than in your addition.

REGAN
                  In my rights
By me invested, he compeers the best.

GONERIL
That were the most, if he should husband you.

REGAN
Jesters do oft prove prophets.

GONERIL
                  Holla, holla!
That eye that told you so look'd but a-squint.

REGAN
Lady, I am not well; else I should answer
From a full-flowing stomach. — General,
Take thou my soldiers, prisoners, patrimony;
Dispose of them, of me; the walls are thine:
Witness the world that I create thee here
My lord and master.

GONERIL
                  Mean you to enjoy him?

ALBANY
The let-alone lies not in your good will.

EDMUND
Nor in thine, lord.

ALBANY
                  Half-blooded fellow, yes.

REGAN [*to* EDMUND].
Let the drum strike, and prove my title thine.

ALBANY
Stay yet; hear reason. — Edmund, I arrest thee
On capital treason; and, in thy arrest,
This gilded serpent [*pointing to* GONERIL]. — For your
  claim, fair sister,

I bar it in the interest of my wife;
'Tis she is sub-contracted to this lord,
And I, her husband, contradict your banns.
If you will marry, make your loves to me;
My lady is bespoke.

GONERIL
     An interlude!

ALBANY
Thou art arm'd, Gloster: — let the trumpet sound:
If none appear to prove upon thy person
Thy heinous, manifest, and many treasons,
There is my pledge [*throwing down a glove*]; I'll prove it
 on thy heart,
Ere I taste bread, thou art in nothing less
Than I have here proclaim'd thee.

REGAN
      Sick! O, sick!

GONERIL [*aside*].
If not, I'll ne'er trust medicine.

EDMUND
There's my exchange [*throwing down a glove*]: what in
 the world he is
That names me traitor, villain-like he lies:
Call by thy trumpet: he that dares approach,
On him, on you, who not? I will maintain
My truth and honour firmly.

ALBANY
A herald, ho!

EDMUND
   A herald, ho, a herald!

ALBANY
Trust to thy single virtue; for thy soldiers,
All levied in my name, have in my name
Took their discharge.

REGAN
   My sickness grows upon me.

ALBANY
She is not well; convey her to my tent.
       [*Exit* REGAN, *led*.
   Enter a HERALD.
Come hither, herald. — Let the trumpet sound, —
And read out this.

OFFICER
Sound, trumpet!   [*A trumpet sounds*.

HERALD [*reads*].
If any man of quality or degree within the lists of the
army will maintain upon Edmund, supposed Earl of
Gloster, that he is a manifold traitor, let him appear by
the third sound of the trumpet: he is bold in his
defence.

EDMUND
Sound!   [*First trumpet*.

HERALD
Again!   [*Second trumpet*.
Again!   [*Third trumpet*.
    [*Trumpet answers within*.
 Enter EDGAR, *at the third sound, arm'd,*
   a trumpet before him.

ALBANY
Ask him his purposes, why he appears
Upon this call o'the trumpet.

HERALD
     What are you?
Your name, your quality? and why you answer
This present summons?

EDGAR
    Know, my name is lost;
By treason's tooth bare-gnawn and canker-bit:
Yet am I noble as the adversary
I come to cope.

ALBANY
   Which is that adversary?

EDGAR
What's he that speaks for Edmund Earl of Gloster?

EDMUND
Himself: — what say'st thou to him?

EDGAR
     Draw thy sword,
That, if my speech offend a noble heart,
Thy arm may do thee justice: here is mine.
Behold, it is the privilege of mine honours,
My oath, and my profession: I protest, —
Maugre thy strength, youth, place, and eminence,
Despite thy victor sword and fire-new fortune,
Thy valour and thy heart, — thou art a traitor;
False to thy gods, thy brother, and thy father;
Conspirator 'gainst this high-illustrious prince;
And, from th'extremest upward of thy head
To the descent and dust below thy foot,

EDMUND The one the other poison'd for my sake, and after slew herself.

A most toad-spotted traitor. Say thou 'no',
This sword, this arm, and my best spirits are bent,
To prove upon thy heart, whereto I speak,
Thou liest.

EDMUND
   In wisdom I should ask thy name;
But, since thy outside looks so fair and warlike,
And that thy tongue some say of breeding breathes,
What safe and nicely I might well delay
By rule of knighthood, I disdain and spurn:
Back do I toss these treasons to thy head;
With the hell-hated lie o'erwhelm thy heart;
Which, — for they yet glance by, and scarcely bruise, —
This sword of mine shall give them instant way,
Where they shall rest for ever. — Trumpets, speak!
  [*Alarums. They fight.* EDMUND *falls*.

ALBANY
Save him, save him!

GONERIL
    This is practice, Gloster:
By the law of arms thou wast not bound to answer
An unknown opposite; thou art not vanquish'd,
But cozen'd and beguil'd.

ALBANY
    Shut your mouth, dame,
Or with this paper shall I stop it: — Hold, sir;
Thou worse than any name, read thine own evil: —
No tearing, lady; I perceive you know it.
    [*Gives the letter to* EDMUND.

GONERIL
Say, if I do, — the laws are mine, not thine:
Who can arraign me for't?

ALBANY
    Most monstrous!
Know'st thou this paper?

GONERIL
   Ask me not what I know. [*Exit*.

ALBANY
Go after her: she's desperate; govern her.
    [*To an* OFFICER, *who goes out*.

EDMUND
What you have charg'd me with, that have I done;
And more, much more; the time will bring it out:
'Tis past, and so am I. — But what art thou
That hast this fortune on me? If thou'rt noble,
I do forgive thee.

EDGAR
   Let's exchange charity.
I am no less in blood than thou art, Edmund;
If more, the more thou hast wrong'd me.
My name is Edgar, and thy father's son.
The gods are just, and of our pleasant vices
Make instruments to plague us:
The dark and vicious place where thee he got
Cost him his eyes.

EDMUND
   Thou hast spoken right, 'tis true;
The wheel is come full circle; I am here.

ALBANY
Methought thy very gait did prophesy
A royal nobleness: — I must embrace thee:
Let sorrow split my heart, if ever I
Did hate thee or thy father!

EDGAR
    Worthy prince,
I know't.

ALBANY
Where have you hid yourself?
How have you known the miseries of your father?

EDGAR
By nursing them, my lord. — List a brief tale; —
And when 'tis told, O, that my heart would burst! —
The bloody proclamation to escape,
That follow'd me so near, — O, our lives' sweetness!
That we the pain of death would hourly die
Rather than die at once! — taught me to shift
Into a madman's rags; t'assume a semblance
That very dogs disdain'd: and in this habit
Met I my father with his bleeding rings,
Their precious stones new lost: became his guide,
Led him, begg'd for him, sav'd him from despair;
Never — O fault! — reveal'd myself unto him,
Until some half-hour past, when I was arm'd;
Not sure, though hoping, of this good success,
I ask'd his blessing, and from first to last
Told him my pilgrimage; but his flaw'd heart,
Alack, too weak the conflict to support,
'Twixt two extremes of passion, joy and grief,
Burst smilingly.

EDMUND
     This speech of yours hath mov'd me,
And shall perchance do good: but speak you on;
You look as you had something more to say.

ALBANY
If there be more, more woeful, hold it in;
For I am almost ready to dissolve,
Hearing of this.

EDGAR
     This would have seem'd a period
To such as love not sorrow; but another,
To amplify too much, would make much more,
And top extremity.
Whilst I was big in clamour, came there a man,
Who, having seen me in my worst estate,
Shunn'd my abhorr'd society; but then, finding
Who 'twas that so endured, with his strong arms
He fasten'd on my neck, and bellow'd out
As he'ld burst heaven; threw him on my father;
Told the most piteous tale of Lear and him
That ever ear receiv'd: which in recounting
His grief grew puissant, and the strings of life
Began to crack: twice then the trumpets sounded,
And there I left him tranc'd.

ALBANY
     But who was this?

EDGAR
Kent, sir, the banish'd Kent; who in disguise
Follow'd his enemy king, and did him service
Improper for a slave.

   Enter a GENTLEMAN, *with a bloody knife.*

GENTLEMAN
Help, help, O, help!

EDGAR
     What kind of help?

ALBANY
       Speak, man.

EDGAR
What means that bloody knife?

GENTLEMAN
     'Tis hot, it smokes;
It came even from the heart of — O, she's dead!

ALBANY
Who dead? speak, man.

GENTLEMAN
Your lady, sir, your lady: and her sister
By her is poison'd; she hath confessed it.

EDMUND
I was contracted to them both: all three
Now marry in an instant.

EDGAR
     Here comes Kent.

ALBANY
Produce their bodies, be they alive or dead: —
This judgement of the heavens, that makes us tremble,
Touches us not with pity. [*Exit* GENTLEMAN.
    Enter KENT.
    O, is this he?
The time will not allow the compliment
Which very manners urges.

KENT
     I am come
To bid my king and master aye good night:
Is he not here?

ALBANY
    Great thing of us forgot! —
Speak, Edmund, where's the king? and where's
 Cordelia? —
  [*The bodies of* GONERIL *and* REGAN *are brought in.*
See'st thou this object, Kent?

KENT
Alack, why thus?

EDMUND
    Yet Edmund was belov'd:
The one the other poison'd for my sake,
And after slew herself.

ALBANY
Even so. — Cover their faces.

EDMUND
I pant for life: some good I mean to do,
Despite of mine own nature. Quickly send —
Be brief in it — to the castle; for my writ
Is on the life of Lear and on Cordelia: —
Nay, send in time.

ALBANY
    Run, run, O, run!

EDGAR
To who, my lord? — Who hath the office? send

Thy token of reprieve.

EDMUND
Well thought on: take my sword;
Give it the captain.

ALBANY
    Haste thee, for thy life. [*Exit* EDGAR.

EDMUND
He hath commission from thy wife and me
To hang Cordelia in the prison, and
To lay the blame upon her own despair,
That she fordid herself.

ALBANY
The gods defend her! — Bear him hence awhile.
       [EDMUND *is borne off.*

  Enter LEAR, *with* CORDELIA *dead in his arms;*
   EDGAR, OFFICER, *and others.*

KING LEAR
Howl, howl, howl, howl! — O, you are men of stone:
Had I your tongues and eyes, I'ld use them so
That heaven's vault should crack. — She's gone for
 ever! —
I know when one is dead, and when one lives;
She's dead as earth. — Lend me a looking-glass;
If that her breath will mist or stain the stone,
Why, then she lives.

KENT
    Is this the promis'd end?

EDGAR
Or image of that horror?

ALBANY
    Fall, and cease!

KING LEAR
This feather stirs; she lives! if it be so,
It is a chance which does redeem all sorrows
That ever I have felt.

KENT
    O my good master! [*Kneeling.*

KING LEAR
Prithee, away.

EDGAR
    'Tis noble Kent, your friend.

KING LEAR
A plague upon you, murderers, traitors all!
I might have sav'd her; now she's gone for ever! —
Cordelia, Cordelia! stay a little. Ha!
What is't thou say'st? — Her voice was ever soft,
Gentle, and low, — an excellent thing in woman. —
I kill'd the slave that was a-hanging thee.

OFFICER
'Tis true, my lords, he did.

KING LEAR
    Did I not, fellow?
I have seen the day, with my good biting falchion
I would have made them skip: I am old now,
And these same crosses spoil me. — Who are you?
Mine eyes are not o'the best: — I'll tell you straight.

KENT
If fortune brag of two she lov'd and hated,
One of them we behold.

KING LEAR
This is a dull sight. Are you not Kent?

KENT
     The same,
Your servant Kent: — Where is your servant Caius?

KING LEAR
He's a good fellow, I can tell you that;
He'll strike, and quickly too: — he's dead and rotten.

KENT
No, my good lord; I am the very man, —

KING LEAR
I'll see that straight.

KENT
That, from your first of difference and decay,
Have follow'd your sad steps.

KING LEAR
    You are welcome hither.

KENT
Nor no man else: — all's cheerless, dark, and deadly. —
Your eldest daughters have fordone themselves,
And desperately are dead.

KING LEAR
    Ay, so I think.

ALBANY
He knows not what he says; and vain is it
That we present us to him.

EDGAR
    Very bootless.
    Enter an OFFICER.

OFFICER
Edmund is dead, my lord.

ALBANY
    That's but a trifle here.—
You lords and noble friends, know our intent.
What comfort to this great decay may come
Shall be applied: for us, we will resign,
During the life of this old majesty,
To him our absolute power: — [*to* EDGAR *and* KENT]
 you, to your rights;
With boot, and such addition as your honours
Have more than merited. — All friends shall taste
The wages of their virtue, and all foes
The cup of their deservings. — O, see, see!

KING LEAR
And my poor fool is hang'd! No, no, no life!
Why should a dog, a horse, a rat, have life,
And thou no breath at all? Thou'lt come no more,
Never, never, never, never, never! —
Pray you, undo this button: — thank you, sir. —
Do you see this? Look on her, — look, her lips, —
Look there, look there! —   [*Dies.*

EDGAR
    He faints! — My lord, my lord! —

KENT
Break, heart; I prithee, break!

EDGAR
    Look up, my lord.

KENT
Vex not his ghost: O, let him pass! he hates him
That would upon the rack of this tough world
Stretch him out longer.

EDGAR
    He is gone indeed.

KENT
The wonder is, he hath endured so long:
He but usurp'd his life.

ALBANY
Bear them from hence. — Our present business
Is general woe. — [*to* KENT *and* EDGAR] Friends of my
 soul, you twain
Rule in this realm, and the gored state sustain.

KENT
I have a journey, sir, shortly to go;
My master calls me, — I must not say no.

EDGAR
The weight of this sad time we must obey;
Speak what we feel, not what we ought to say.
The oldest hath borne most: we that are young
Shall never see so much, nor live so long.
    [*Exeunt, with a dead march.*

ANTONY AND CLEOPATRA

DRAMATIS PERSONAE

MARK ANTONY,
OCTAVIUS CAESAR, } *triumvirs.*
M. AEMILIUS LEPIDUS,
SEXTUS POMPEIUS.
DOMITIUS ENOBARBUS,
VENTIDIUS,
EROS,
SCARUS, } *friends to Antony.*
DERCETAS,
DEMETRIUS,
PHILO,

MAECENAS,
AGRIPPA, } *friends to Cæsar.*

DOLABELLA,
PROCULEIUS,
THYREUS, } *friends to Cæsar.*
GALLUS,
MENAS,
MENECRATES, } *friends to Pompey.*
VARRIUS,
TAURUS, *lieutenant-general to Cæsar.*
CANIDIUS, *lieutenant-general to Antony.*
SILIUS, *an officer in Ventidius' army.*
EUPHRONIUS, *an ambassador from Antony to Cæsar.*
ALEXAS, MARDIAN, SELEUCUS, *and* DIOMEDES,
    attendants on Cleopatra.

A SOOTHSAYER.
A CLOWN.

CLEOPATRA, *queen of Egypt.*
OCTAVIA, *sister to Cæsar and wife to Antony.*
CHARMIAN, } *attendants on Cleopatra.*
IRAS,
OFFICERS, SOLDIERS, MESSENGERS, *and other*
    ATTENDANTS.

SCENE — *In several parts of the Roman empire.*

ACT I

SCENE I

Alexandria. A room in CLEOPATRA'S *palace.*

Enter DEMETRIUS *and* PHILO.

PHILO
Nay, but this dotage of our general's
O'erflows the measure: those his goodly eyes,
That o'er the files and musters of the war
Have glow'd like plated Mars, now bend, now turn,
The office and devotion of their view
Upon a tawny front: his captain's heart,
Which in the scuffles of great fights hath burst
The buckles on his breast, reneges all temper,
And is become the bellows and the fan
To cool a gipsy's lust. [*Flourish within.*] Look where they
    come:
Take but good note, and you shall see in him
The triple pillar of the world transform'd
Into a strumpet's fool: behold and see.

Enter ANTONY, CLEOPATRA, *her* LADIES, *the*
    TRAIN, *with* EUNUCHS *fanning her.*

CLEOPATRA
If it be love indeed, tell me how much.

ANTONY
There's beggary in the love that can be reckon'd.

CLEOPATRA
I'll set a bourn how far to be beloved.

Then must thou needs find out new heaven, new earth.

Enter an ATTENDANT.

ATTENDANT
News, my good lord, from Rome.

ANTONY
                Grates me: — the sum.

CLEOPATRA
Nay, hear them, Antony:
Fulvia perchance is angry; or, who knows
If the scarce-bearded Cæsar have not sent
His powerful mandate to you, 'Do this, or this;
Take in that kingdom, and enfranchise that;
Perform't, or else we damn thee.'

ANTONY
                How, my love!

CLEOPATRA
Perchance! nay, and most like: —
You must not stay here longer, — your dismission
Is come from Cæsar; therefore hear it, Antony. —
Where's Fulvia's process? Cæsar's I would say? —
    both? —

Call in the messengers. — As I am Egypt's queen,
Thou blushest, Antony; and that blood of thine
Is Cæsar's homager: else so thy cheek pays shame
When shrill-tongu'd Fulvia scolds. — The messengers!

ANTONY
Let Rome in Tiber melt, and the wide arch
Of the ranged empire fall! Here is my space.
Kingdoms are clay: our dungy earth alike
Feeds beast as man: the nobleness of life
Is to do thus; when such a mutual pair   [*Embracing.*
And such a twain can do't, in which I bind,
On pain of punishment, the world to weet
We stand up peerless.

CLEOPATRA
                Excellent falsehood!
Why did he marry Fulvia, and not love her? —
I'll seem the fool I am not; Antony
Will be himself.

ANTONY
                But stirr'd by Cleopatra. —
Now, for the love of Love and her soft hours,
Let's not confound the time with conference harsh:
There's not a minute of our lives should stretch
Without some pleasure now: — what sport to-night?

CLEOPATRA
Hear the ambassadors.

ANTONY
                Fie, wrangling queen!
Whom every thing becomes, — to chide, to laugh,
To weep; whose every passion fully strives
To make itself, in thee, fair and admired!
No messenger but thine; and all alone,
To-night we'll wander through the streets, and note
The qualities of people. Come, my queen;
Last night you did desire it: — speak not to us.
    [*Exeunt* ANTONY *and* CLEOPATRA *with their* TRAIN.

DEMETRIUS
Is Cæsar with Antonius priz'd so slight?

PHILO
Sir, sometimes, when he is not Antony,
He comes too short of that great property
Which still should go with Antony.

DEMETRIUS
                I am full sorry
That he approves the common liar, who
Thus speaks of him at Rome: but I will hope
Of better deeds to-morrow. Rest you happy!   [*Exeunt.*

SCENE II

The same. Another room.

Enter CHARMIAN, IRAS, ALEXAS,
    and a SOOTHSAYER.

CHARMIAN
Lord Alexas, sweet Alexas, most any thing Alexas, almost
most absolute Alexas, where's the soothsayer that you
praised so to the queen? O, that I knew this husband,
which, you say, must charge his horns with garlands!

ALEXAS
Soothsayer, —

SOOTHSAYER
Your will?

CHARMIAN
Is this the man? — Is't you, sir, that know things?

SOOTHSAYER
In nature's infinite book of secrecy
A little I can read.

CLEOPATRA   If it be love indeed, tell me how much.

ALEXAS Vex not his prescience; be attentive.

ALEXAS

      Show him your hand.
Enter ENOBARBUS.

ENOBARBUS
Bring in the banquet quickly; wine enough
Cleopatra's health to drink.

CHARMIAN
Good sir, give me good fortune.

SOOTHSAYER
I make not, but foresee.

CHARMIAN
Pray, then, foresee me one.

SOOTHSAYER
You shall be yet far fairer than you are.

CHARMIAN
He means in flesh.

IRAS
No, you shall paint when you are old.

CHARMIAN
Wrinkles forbid!

ALEXAS
Vex not his prescience; be attentive.

CHARMIAN
Hush!

SOOTHSAYER
You shall be more beloving than beloved.

CHARMIAN
I had rather heat my liver with drinking.

ALEXAS
Nay, hear him.

CHARMIAN
Good now, some excellent fortune! Let me be married
to three kings in a forenoon, and widow them all: let
me have a child at fifty, to whom Herod of Jewry may
do homage: find me to marry me with Octavius Cæsar,
and companion me with my mistress.

SOOTHSAYER
You shall outlive the lady whom you serve.

CHARMIAN
O excellent! I love long life better than figs.

SOOTHSAYER
You have seen and prov'd a fairer former fortune
Than that which is to approach.

CHARMIAN
Then belike my children shall have no names: prithee,
how many boys and wenches must I have?

SOOTHSAYER
If every of your wishes had a womb,
And fertile every wish, a million.

CHARMIAN
Out, fool! I forgive thee for a witch.

ALEXAS
You think none but your sheets are privy to your
wishes.

CHARMIAN
Nay, come, tell Iras hers.

ALEXAS
We'll know all our fortunes.

ENOBARBUS
Mine, and most of our fortunes, to-night, shall be —

drunk to bed.

IRAS
There's a palm presages chastity, if nothing else.

CHARMIAN
E'en as the o'erflowing Nilus presageth famine.

IRAS
Go, you wild bedfellow, you cannot soothsay.

CHARMIAN
Nay, if an oily palm be not a fruitful prognostication, I
cannot scratch mine ear. — Prithee, tell her but a
worky-day fortune.

SOOTHSAYER
Your fortunes are alike.

IRAS
But how, but how? give me particulars.

SOOTHSAYER
I have said.

IRAS
Am I not an inch of fortune better than she?

CHARMIAN
Well, if you were but an inch of fortune better than I,
where would you choose it?

IRAS
Not in my husband's nose.

CHARMIAN
Our worser thoughts heavens mend! — Alexas, —
come, his fortune, his fortune! — O, let him marry a
woman that cannot go, sweet Isis, I beseech thee! and
let her die too, and give him a worse! and let worse
follow worse, till the worst of all follow him laughing to
his grave, fifty-fold a cuckold! Good Isis, hear me this
prayer, though thou deny me a matter of more weight;
good Isis, I beseech thee!

IRAS
Amen. Dear goddess, hear that prayer of the people!
for, as it is a heart-breaking to see a handsome man
loose-wived, so it is a deadly sorrow to behold a foul
knave uncuckolded: therefore, dear Isis, keep
decorum, and fortune him accordingly!

CHARMIAN
Amen.

ALEXAS
Lo, now, if it lay in their hands to make me a cuckold,
they would make themselves whores but they'ld do't!

ENOBARBUS
Hush! here comes Antony.

CHARMIAN
      Not he; the queen.
Enter CLEOPATRA.

CLEOPATRA
Saw you my lord?

ENOBARBUS
      No, lady.

CLEOPATRA
      Was he not here?

CHARMIAN
No, madam.

CLEOPATRA
He was dispos'd to mirth; but on the sudden
A Roman thought hath struck him. — Enobarbus, —

ENOBARBUS
Madam?

CLEOPATRA
Seek him, and bring him hither. — Where's Alexas?

ALEXAS
Here, at your service. — My lord approaches.

CLEOPATRA
We will not look upon him: go with us.   [*Exeunt.*
Enter ANTONY *with a* MESSENGER *and*
ATTENDANTS.

MESSENGER
Fulvia thy wife first came into the field.

ANTONY
Against my brother Lucius?

MESSENGER
Ay:
But soon that war had end, and the time's state
Made friends of them, jointing their force 'gainst
   Cæsar;
Whose better issue in the war from Italy
Upon the first encounter drave them.

ANTONY
      Well, what worst?

MESSENGER
The nature of bad news infects the teller.

ANTONY
When it concerns the fool or coward. — On: —
Things that are past are done with me. — 'Tis thus;
Who tells me true, though in his tale lie death,
I hear him as he flatter'd.

MESSENGER
      Labienus —
This is stiff news — hath, with his Parthian force,
Extended Asia from Euphrates;
His conquering banner shook from Syria
To Lydia and to Ionia;
Whilst —

ANTONY
Antony, thou wouldst say, —

MESSENGER
      O, my lord!

ANTONY
Speak to me home, mince not the general tongue:
Name Cleopatra as she is call'd in Rome;
Rail thou in Fulvia's phrase; and taunt my faults
With such full licence as both truth and malice
Have power to utter. O, then we bring forth weeds
When our quick minds lie still; and our ills told us
Is as our earing. Fare thee well awhile.

MESSENGER
At your noble pleasure.   [*Exit.*

ANTONY
From Sicyon, ho, the news! Speak there!

FIRST ATTENDANT
The man from Sicyon, — is there such an one?

SECOND ATTENDANT
He stays upon your will.

ANTONY
      Let him appear. —
These strong Egyptian fetters I must break,
Or lose myself in dotage.
Enter another MESSENGER.
      What are you?

SECOND MESSENGER
Fulvia thy wife is dead.

ANTONY
      Where died she?

SECOND MESSENGER
In Sicyon:
Her length of sickness, with what else more serious
Importeth thee to know, this bears.   [*Gives a letter.*

ANTONY
      Forbear me.
    [*Exit* SECOND MESSENGER.
There's a great spirit gone! Thus did I desire it:
What our contempts do often hurl from us,
We wish it ours again; the present pleasure,
By revolution lowering, does become
The opposite of itself: she's good, being gone;
The hand could pluck her back that shov'd her on.
I must from this enchanting queen break off:
Ten thousand harms, more than the ills I know,
My idleness doth hatch. — How now, Enobarbus!
Enter ENOBARBUS.

ENOBARBUS
What's your pleasure, sir?

ANTONY
I must with haste from hence.

ENOBARBUS
Why, then, we kill all our women: we see how mortal
an unkindness is to them; if they suffer our departure,
death's the word.

ANTONY
I must be gone.

ENOBARBUS
Under a compelling occasion, let women die; it were
pity to cast them away for nothing; though, between
them and a great cause, they should be esteem'd
nothing. Cleopatra, catching but the least noise of this,
dies instantly; I have seen her die twenty times upon
far poorer moment: I do think there is mettle in death,
which commits some loving act upon her, she hath
such a celerity in dying.

ANTONY
She is cunning past man's thought.

ENOBARBUS
Alack, sir, no; her passions are made of nothing but the
finest part of pure love: we cannot call her winds and
waters sighs and tears; they are greater storms and
tempests than almanacs can report: this cannot be
cunning in her; if it be, she makes a shower of rain as
well as Jove.

ANTONY
Would I had never seen her!

ENOBARBUS
O, sir, you had then left unseen a wonderful piece of
work; which not to have been blest withal would have
discredited your travel.

ANTONY
Fulvia is dead.

ENOBARBUS
Sir?

ANTONY
Fulvia is dead.

ENOBARBUS
Fulvia!

ANTONY
Dead.

ENOBARBUS
Why, sir, give the gods a thankful sacrifice. When it
pleaseth their deities to take the wife of a man from
him, it shows to man the tailors of the earth;
comforting therein, that when old robes are worn out,
there are members to make new. If there were no more
women but Fulvia, then had you indeed a cut, and the
case to be lamented: this grief is crown'd with
consolation; your old smock brings forth a new
petticoat: — and, indeed, the tears live in an onion that
should water this sorrow.

ANTONY
The business she hath broached in the state
Cannot endure my absence.

ENOBARBUS
And the business you have broach'd here cannot be
without you; especially that of Cleopatra's, which
wholly depends on your abode.

ANTONY
No more light answers. Let our officers
Have notice what we purpose. I shall break
The cause of our expedience to the queen,
And get her leave to part. For not alone
The death of Fulvia, with more urgent touches,
Do strongly speak to us; but the letters too
Of many our contriving friends in Rome
Petition us at home: Sextus Pompeius
Hath given the dare to Cæsar, and commands
The empire of the sea: our slippery people —
Whose love is never link'd to the deserver
Till his deserts are past — begin to throw
Pompey the Great, and all his dignities,
Upon his son; who, high in name and power,
Higher than both in blood and life, stands up
For the main soldier: whose quality, going on,
The sides o' the world may danger: much is breeding,
Which, like the courser's hair, hath yet but life,
And not a serpent's poison. Say, our pleasure,
To such whose place is under us, requires
Our quick remove from hence.

ENOBARBUS
I shall do't. [*Exeunt.*

SCENE III

The same. Another room.

Enter CLEOPATRA, CHARMIAN,
IRAS, *and* ALEXAS.

CLEOPATRA
Where is he?

ENOBARBUS And the business you have broach'd here cannot be without you.

CHARMIAN
I did not see him since.

CLEOPATRA
See where he is, who's with him, what he does: —
I did not send you: — if you find him sad,
Say I am dancing; if in mirth, report
That I am sudden sick: quick, and return.
[*Exit* ALEXAS.

CHARMIAN
Madam, methinks, if you did love him dearly,
You do not hold the method to enforce
The like from him.

CLEOPATRA
What should I do I do not?

CHARMIAN
In each thing give him way, cross him in nothing.

CLEOPATRA
Thou teachest like a fool, — the way to lose him.

CHARMIAN
Tempt him not so too far; I wish, forbear:
In time we hate that which we often fear.
But here comes Antony.

CLEOPATRA
I am sick and sullen.

Enter ANTONY.

ANTONY
I am sorry to give breathing to my purpose, —

CLEOPATRA
Help me away, dear Charmian; I shall fall:
It cannot be thus long, the sides of nature
Will not sustain it.

ANTONY
Now, my dearest queen, —

CLEOPATRA
Pray you, stand further from me.

ANTONY
What's the matter?

CLEOPATRA
I know, by that same eye, there's some good news.
What says the married woman? — You may go:
Would she had never given you leave to come!
Let her not say 'tis I that keep you here, —
I have no power upon you; hers you are.

ANTONY
The gods best know, —

CLEOPATRA
O, never was there queen
So mightily betray'd! yet at the first
I saw the treasons planted.

ANTONY
Cleopatra, —

CLEOPATRA
Why should I think you can be mine and true,
Though you in swearing shake the throned gods,
Who have been false to Fulvia? Riotous madness,
To be entangled with those mouth-made vows
Which break themselves in swearing!

ANTONY
Most sweet queen, —

CLEOPATRA
Nay, pray you, seek no colour for your going,
But bid farewell, and go: when you sued staying,
Then was the time for words: no going then; —
Eternity was in our lips and eyes,

Bliss in our brows' bent; none our parts so poor,
But was a race of heaven: they are so still,
Or thou, the greatest soldier of the world,
Art turn'd the greatest liar.

ANTONY
How now, lady!

CLEOPATRA
I would I had thy inches; thou shouldst know
There were a heart in Egypt.

ANTONY
Hear me, queen:
The strong necessity of time commands
Our services awhile; but my full heart
Remains in use with you. Our Italy
Shines o'er with civil swords: Sextus Pompeius
Makes his approaches to the port of Rome:
Equality of two domestic powers
Breed scrupulous faction: the hated, grown to strength,
Are newly grown to love: the condemn'd Pompey,
Rich in his father's honour, creeps apace
Into the hearts of such as have not thrived
Upon the present state, whose numbers threaten;
And quietness, grown sick of rest, would purge
By any desperate change: my more particular,
And that which most with you should safe my going,
Is Fulvia's death.

CLEOPATRA
Though age from folly could not give me freedom
It does from childishness: — can Fulvia die?

ANTONY
She's dead, my queen:
Look here, and, at thy sovereign leisure, read
The garboils she awak'd; at the last, best:
See when and where she died.

CLEOPATRA
O most false love!
Where be the sacred vials thou shouldst fill
With sorrowful water? Now I see, I see,
In Fulvia's death, how mine receiv'd shall be.

ANTONY
Quarrel no more, but be prepared to know
The purposes I bear; which are, or cease,
As you shall give the advice: by the fire
That quickens Nilus' slime, I go from hence
Thy soldier, servant; making peace or war
As thou affect'st.

CLEOPATRA
Cut my lace, Charmian, come; —
But let it be: — I am quickly ill, and well,
So Antony loves.

ANTONY
My precious queen, forbear;
And give true evidence to his love, which stands
An honourable trial.

CLEOPATRA
So Fulvia told me.
I prithee, turn aside, and weep for her;
Then bid adieu to me, and say the tears
Belong to Egypt: good now, play one scene
Of excellent dissembling; and let it look
Like perfect honour.

ANTONY
You'll heat my blood: no more.

CLEOPATRA
You can do better yet; but this is meetly.

ANTONY

Now, by my sword, —

CLEOPATRA

And target. — Still he mends;
But this is not the best: — look, prithee, Charmian,
How this Herculean Roman does become
The carriage of his chafe.

ANTONY

I'll leave you, lady.

CLEOPATRA

Courteous lord, one word.
Sir, you and I must part, — but that's not it:
Sir, you and I have lov'd, — but there's not it;
That you know well: something it is I would, —
O, my oblivion is a very Antony,
And I am all forgotten.

ANTONY

But that your royalty
Holds idleness your subject, I should take you
For idleness itself.

CLEOPATRA

'Tis sweating labour
To bear such idleness so near the heart
As Cleopatra this. But, sir, forgive me;
Since my becomings kill me, when they do not
Eye well to you: your honour calls you hence;
Therefore be deaf to my unpitied folly,
And all the gods go with you! upon your sword
Sit laurel victory! and smooth success
Be strew'd before your feet!

ANTONY

Let us go. Come;
Our separation so abides, and flies,
That thou, residing here, go'st yet with me,
And I, hence fleeting, here remain with thee.
Away! [*Exeunt.*

SCENE IV

Rome. An apartment in CAESAR'S *house.*

Enter OCTAVIUS CAESAR, *reading a letter,*
LEPIDUS, *and their* TRAIN.

CAESAR

You may see, Lepidus, and henceforth know,
[*Giving him a letter.*
It is not Cæsar's natural vice to hate
Our great competitor: from Alexandria
This is the news: — he fishes, drinks, and wastes
The lamps of night in revel; is not more manlike
Than Cleopatra, nor the queen of Ptolemy
More womanly than he; hardly gave audience, or
Vouchsaf'd to think he had partners: you shall find there
A man who is the abstract of all faults
That all men follow.

LEPIDUS

I must not think there are
Evils enow to darken all his goodness:
His faults, in him, seem as the spots of heaven,
More fiery by night's blackness; hereditary,
Rather than purchas'd; what he cannot change,
Than what he chooses.

CAESAR

You are too indulgent. Let us grant, it is not
Amiss to tumble on the bed of Ptolemy;
To give a kingdom for a mirth; to sit
And keep the turn of tippling with a slave;
To reel the streets at noon, and stand the buffet
With knaves that smell of sweat; say this becomes
him, —
As his composure must be rare indeed
Whom these things cannot blemish, — yet must
Antony
No way excuse his soils, when we do bear
So great weight in his lightness. If he fill'd
His vacancy with his voluptuousness,
Full surfeits, and the dryness of his bones,
Call on him for't: but to confound such time,
That drums him from his sport, and speaks as loud
As his own state and ours, — 'tis to be chid
As we rate boys, who, being mature in knowledge,
Pawn their experience to their present pleasure,
And so rebel to judgement.

Enter a MESSENGER.

LEPIDUS

Here's more news.

MESSENGER

Thy biddings have been done; and every hour,
Most noble Cæsar, shalt thou have report
How 'tis abroad. Pompey is strong at sea;

And it appears he is beloved of those
That only have fear'd Cæsar: to the ports
The discontents repair, and men's reports
Give him much wrong'd.

CAESAR

I should have known no less.
It hath been taught us from the primal state,
That he which is was wish'd until he were;
And the ebb'd man, ne'er lov'd till ne'er worth love,
Comes dear'd by being lack'd. This common body
Like to a vagabond flag upon the stream,
Goes to and back, lackeying the varying tide
To rot itself with motion.

MESSENGER

Cæsar, I bring thee word,
Menecrates and Menas, famous pirates,
Make the sea serve them, which they ear and wound
With keels of every kind: many hot inroads
They make in Italy; the borders maritime
Lack blood to think on't, and flush youth revolt:
No vessel can peep forth, but 'tis as soon
Taken as seen; for Pompey's name strikes more
Than could his war resisted.

CAESAR

Antony,
Leave thy lascivious wassails. When thou once
Wast beaten from Modena, where thou slew'st
Hirtius and Pansa, consuls, at thy heel
Did famine follow; whom thou fought'st against,
Though daintily brought up, with patience more
Than savages could suffer: thou didst drink
The stale of horses, and the gilded puddle
Which beasts would cough at: thy palate then did deign
The roughest berry in the rudest hedge;
Yea, like the stag, when snow the pasture sheets,
The barks of trees thou browsed'st; on the Alps
It is reported thou didst eat strange flesh,
Which some did die to look on: and all this —
It wounds thine honour that I speak it now —
Was borne so like a soldier, that thy cheek
So much as lank'd not.

LEPIDUS

It is pity of him.

CAESAR

Let his shames quickly
Drive him to Rome: 'tis time we twain
Did show ourselves i'th'field, and to that end
Assemble we immediate council: Pompey
Thrives in our idleness.

LEPIDUS

To-morrow, Cæsar,
I shall be furnish'd to inform you rightly
Both what by sea and land I can be able
To front this present time.

CAESAR

Till which encounter,
It is my business too. Farewell.

LEPIDUS

Farewell, my lord; what you shall know meantime
Of stirs abroad, I shall beseech you, sir,
To let me be partaker.

CAESAR

Doubt not, sir;
I knew it for my bond. [*Exeunt.*

SCENE V

Alexandria. A room in CLEOPATRA'S *palace.*

Enter CLEOPATRA, CHARMIAN,
IRAS, *and* MARDIAN.

CLEOPATRA

Charmian, —

CHARMIAN

Madam?

CLEOPATRA

Ha, ha! —
Give me to drink mandragora.

CHARMIAN

Why, madam?

CLEOPATRA

That I might sleep out this great gap of time
My Antony is away.

CHARMIAN

You think of him too much.

CLEOPATRA

O, 'tis treason!

CHARMIAN

Madam, I trust, not so.

CLEOPATRA

Thou, eunuch Mardian!

MARDIAN

What's your highness' pleasure?

CLEOPATRA

Not now to hear thee sing; I take no pleasure
In aught an eunuch has: 'tis well for thee,
That, being unseminar'd, thy freer thoughts
May not fly forth of Egypt. Hast thou affections?

MARDIAN

Yes, gracious madam.

CLEOPATRA

Indeed!

MARDIAN

Not in deed, madam; for I can do nothing
But what indeed is honest to be done:
Yet have I fierce affections, and think
What Venus did with Mars.

CLEOPATRA

O Charmian,
Where think'st thou he is now? Stands he, or sits he?
Or does he walk? or is he on his horse?
O happy horse, to bear the weight of Antony!
Do bravely, horse! for wott'st thou whom thou movest?
The demi-Atlas of this earth, the arm
And burgonet of men. — He's speaking now,
Or murmuring, 'Where's my serpent of old Nile?'
For so he calls me: — now I feed myself
With most delicious poison: — think on me,
That am with Phœbus' amorous pinches black,
And wrinkled deep in time? Broad-fronted Cæsar,
When thou wast here above the ground, I was
A morsel for a monarch; and great Pompey
Would stand, and make his eyes grow in my brow;
There would he anchor his aspect, and die
With looking on his life.

Enter ALEXAS.

ALEXAS

Sovereign of Egypt, hail!

CLEOPATRA

How much unlike art thou Mark Antony!
Yet, coming from him, that great medicine hath
With his tinct gilded thee. —
How goes it with my brave Mark Antony?

ALEXAS

Last thing he did, dear queen,
He kiss'd — the last of many doubled kisses —
This orient pearl: — his speech sticks in my heart.

CLEOPATRA

Mine ear must pluck it thence.

ALEXAS

'Good friend,' quoth he,
'Say, the firm Roman to great Egypt sends
This treasure of an oyster; at whose foot,
To mend the petty present, I will piece
Her opulent throne with kingdoms; all the east,
Say thou, shall call her mistress.' So he nodded,
And soberly did mount an arm-gaunt steed,
Who neigh'd so high, that what I would have spoke
Was beastly dumb'd by him.

CLEOPATRA

What, was he sad or merry?

ALEXAS

Like to the time o'the year between the extremes
Of hot and cold, he was nor sad nor merry.

CLEOPATRA

O well-divided disposition! — Note him,
Note him, good Charmian, 'tis the man; but note him:
He was not sad, — for he would shine on those
That make their looks by his; he was not merry, —
Which seem'd to tell them his remembrance lay
In Egypt with his joy; but between both:
O heavenly mingle! — Be'st thou sad or merry,
The violence of either thee becomes,
So does it no man else. — Mett'st thou my posts?

ALEXAS

Ay, madam, twenty several messengers:
Why do you send so thick?

CLEOPATRA

Who's born that day
When I forget to send to Antony,
Shall die a beggar. — Ink and paper, Charmian. —
Welcome, my good Alexas. — Did I, Charmian,
Ever love Cæsar so?

CHARMIAN

O that brave Cæsar!

CLEOPATRA

Be chok'd with such another emphasis!
Say, the brave Antony.

CHARMIAN

The valiant Cæsar!

CLEOPATRA

By Isis, I will give thee bloody teeth,
If thou with Cæsar paragon again
My man of men.

CHARMIAN

           By your most gracious pardon,
I sing but after you.

CLEOPATRA

           My salad days,
When I was green in judgement: — cold in blood,
To say as I said then! — But, come, away;
Get me ink and paper:
He shall have every day a several greeting,
Or I'll unpeople Egypt.   *[Exeunt.*

ACT II

SCENE I

Messina. A room in POMPEY'S *house.*

Enter POMPEY, MENECRATES,
and MENAS, *in warlike manner.*

POMPEY

If the great gods be just, they shall assist
The deeds of justest men.

MENECRATES

           Know, worthy Pompey,
That what they do delay, they not deny.

POMPEY

Whiles we are suitors to their throne, decays
The thing we sue for.

MENECRATES

           We, ignorant of ourselves,
Beg often our own harms, which the wise powers
Deny us for our good; so find we profit
By losing of our prayers.

POMPEY

           I shall do well:
The people love me, and the sea is mine;
My powers are crescent, and my auguring hope
Says it will come to the full. Mark Antony
In Egypt sits at dinner, and will make
No wars without doors: Cæsar gets money where
He loses hearts: Lepidus flatters both,
Of both is flatter'd; but he neither loves,
Nor either cares for him.

MENAS

           Cæsar and Lepidus
Are in the field; a mighty strength they carry.

POMPEY

Where have you this? 'tis false.

MENAS

           From Silvius, sir.

POMPEY

He dreams: I know they are in Rome together,
Looking for Antony. But all the charms of love,
Salt Cleopatra, soften thy wan'd lip!
Let witchcraft join with beauty, lust with both!
Tie up the libertine in a field of feasts,
Keep his brain fuming; Epicurean cooks
Sharpen with cloyless sauce his appetite;
That sleep and feeding may prorogue his honour
Even till a Lethe'd dulness!

Enter VARRIUS.

           How now, Varrius!

VARRIUS

This is most certain that I shall deliver: —
Mark Antony is every hour in Rome
Expected: since he went from Egypt 'tis
A space for further travel.

POMPEY

           I could have given less matter
A better ear. — Menas, I did not think
This amorous surfeiter would have donn'd his helm
For such a petty war: his soldiership
Is twice the other twain: but let us rear
The higher our opinion, that our stirring
Can from the lap of Egypt's widow pluck
The ne'er-lust-wearied Antony.

MENAS

           I cannot hope
Cæsar and Antony shall well greet together:
His wife that's dead did trespasses to Cæsar;
His brother warr'd upon him; although, I think,
Not moved by Antony.

POMPEY

           I know not, Menas,
How lesser enmities may give way to greater.

Were't not that we stand up against
   them all,
'Twere pregnant they should square
   between themselves;
For they have entertained cause enough
To draw their swords: but how the fear of
   us
May cement their divisions, and bind up
The petty difference, we yet not know.
Be't as our gods will have't! It only
   stands
Our lives upon to use our strongest hands.
Come, Menas.   *[Exeunt.*

SCENE II

Rome. A room in the house of LEPIDUS.

Enter ENOBARBUS *and* LEPIDUS.

LEPIDUS

Good Enobarbus, 'tis a worthy deed,
And shall become you well, to entreat
   your captain
To soft and gentle speech.

ENOBARBUS

           I shall entreat him
To answer like himself: if Cæsar move
   him,
Let Antony look over Cæsar's head,
And speak as loud as Mars. By Jupiter,
Were I the wearer of Antonius' beard,
I would not shave't to-day.

LEPIDUS

           'Tis not a time
For private stomaching.

ENOBARBUS

           Every time
Serves for the matter that is then born in't.

LEPIDUS

But small to greater matters must give way.

ENOBARBUS

Not if the small come first.

LEPIDUS

           Your speech is passion:
But, pray you, stir no embers up. Here comes
The noble Antony.

Enter ANTONY *and* VENTIDIUS.

ENOBARBUS

           And yonder, Cæsar.

Enter CAESAR, MAECENAS, *and* AGRIPPA.

ANTONY

If we compose well here, to Parthia:
Hark, Ventidius.

CAESAR

           I do not know,
Mæcenas; ask Agrippa.

LEPIDUS

           Noble friends,
That which combined us was most great, and let not
A leaner action rend us. What's amiss,
May it be gently heard: when we debate
Our trivial difference loud, we do commit
Murder in healing wounds: then, noble partners, —
The rather, for I earnestly beseech, —
Touch you the sourest points with sweetest terms,
Nor curstness grow to the matter.

ANTONY

           'Tis spoken well.
Were we before our armies, and to fight,
I should do thus.   *[Flourish.*

CAESAR

Welcome to Rome.

ANTONY

Thank you.

CAESAR

Sit.

ANTONY

Sit, sir.

CAESAR

Nay, then.

ANTONY

I learn, you take things ill which are not so,
Or being, concern you not.

CAESAR

           I must be laugh'd at,
If, or for nothing or a little, I
Should say myself offended, and with you
Chiefly i' the world; more laugh'd at, that I should
Once name you derogately, when to sound your name

POMPEY Where have you this? 'tis false.

It not concern'd me.

ANTONY

           My being in Egypt, Cæsar,
What was't to you?

CAESAR

No more than my residing here at Rome
Might be to you in Egypt: yet, if you there
Did practise on my state, your being in Egypt
Might be my question.

ANTONY

           How intend you, practised?

CAESAR

You may be pleas'd to catch at mine intent
By what did here befall me. Your wife and brother
Made wars upon me; and their contestation
Was theme for you, you were the word of war.

ANTONY

You do mistake your business; my brother never
Did urge me in his act: I did inquire it;
And have my learning from some true reports,
That drew their swords with you. Did he not rather
Discredit my authority with yours;
And make the wars alike against my stomach,
Having alike your cause? Of this my letters
Before did satisfy you. If you'll patch a quarrel,
As matter whole you have not to make it with,
It must not be with this.

CAESAR

           You praise yourself
By laying defects of judgement to me; but
You patch'd up your excuses.

ANTONY

           Not so, not so;
I know you could not lack, I am certain on't,
Very necessity of this thought, that I,
Your partner in the cause 'gainst which he fought,
Could not with graceful eyes attend those wars
Which fronted mine own peace. As for my wife,
I would you had her spirit in such another:
The third o' the world is yours; which with a snaffle
You may pace easy, but not such a wife.

ENOBARBUS

Would we had all such wives, that the men might go to
   wars with the women!

ANTONY

So much uncurbable, her garboils, Cæsar,
Made out of her impatience, — which not wanted
Shrewdness of policy too, — I grieving grant
Did you too much disquiet: for that you must
But say, I could not help it.

CAESAR

           I wrote to you
When rioting in Alexandria; you
Did pocket up my letters, and with taunts
Did gibe my missive out of audience.

ANTONY

           Sir,
He fell upon me ere admitted: then
Three kings I had newly feasted, and did want
Of what I was i' the morning: but next day
I told him of myself; which was as much
As to have ask'd him pardon. Let this fellow

Before the gods my knee shall bow my prayers
To them for you.

ANTONY
Good night, sir. — My Octavia,
Read not my blemishes in the world's report:
I have not kept my square; but that to come
Shall all be done by the rule. Good night, dear lady.

OCTAVIA
Good night, sir.

CAESAR
Good night. [*Exeunt* CAESAR *and* OCTAVIA.
Enter SOOTHSAYER.

ANTONY
Now, sirrah, — you do wish yourself in Egypt?

SOOTHSAYER
Would I had never come from thence, nor you
thither!

ANTONY
If you can, your reason?

SOOTHSAYER
I see it in my motion, have it not in my tongue: but yet
hie you to Egypt again.

ANTONY
Say to me
Whose fortunes shall rise higher, Cæsar's or mine?

SOOTHSAYER
Cæsar's.
Therefore, O Antony, stay not by his side:
Thy demon, that's thy spirit which keeps thee, is
Noble, courageous, high, unmatchable,
Where Cæsar's is not; but, near him, thy angel
Becomes a fear, as being o'erpower'd: therefore
Make space enough between you.

ANTONY
Speak this no more.

SOOTHSAYER
To none but thee; no more, but when to thee.
If thou dost play with him at any game,
Thou art sure to lose; and, of that natural luck,
He beats thee 'gainst the odds: thy lustre thickens,
When he shines by: I say again, thy spirit
Is all afraid to govern thee near him;
But he away, 'tis noble.

ANTONY
Get thee gone:
Say to Ventidius I would speak with him: —
[*Exit* SOOTHSAYER.
He shall to Parthia. — Be it art or hap,
He hath spoken true: the very dice obey him;
And, in our sports, my better cunning faints
Under his chance: if we draw lots, he speeds;
His cocks do win the battle still of mine,
When it is all to naught; and his quails ever
Beat mine, inhoop'd, at odds. I will to Egypt:
And though I make this marriage for my peace,
I'the east my pleasure lies.
Enter VENTIDIUS.
O, come, Ventidius,
You must to Parthia: your commission's ready;
Follow me, and receiv't. [*Exeunt.*

SCENE IV

The same. A street.

Enter LEPIDUS, MAECENAS, *and* AGRIPPA.

LEPIDUS
Trouble yourselves no further: pray you, hasten
Your generals after.

AGRIPPA
Sir, Mark Antony
Will e'en but kiss Octavia, and we'll follow.

LEPIDUS
Till I shall see you in your soldier's dress,
Which will become you both, farewell.

MAECENAS
We shall,
As I conceive the journey, be at the Mount
Before you, Lepidus.

LEPIDUS
Your way is shorter;
My purposes do draw me much about:
You'll win two days upon me.

MAECENAS *and* **AGRIPPA**
Sir, good success!

LEPIDUS
Farewell. [*Exeunt.*

ANTONY Read not my blemishes in the world's report.

SCENE V

Alexandria. A room in CLEOPATRA'S *palace.*

Enter CLEOPATRA, CHARMIAN,
IRAS, *and* ALEXAS.

CLEOPATRA
Give me some music, — music, moody food
Of us that trade in love.

ATTENDANT
The music, ho!
Enter MARDIAN.

CLEOPATRA
Let it alone; let's to billiards: come, Charmian.

CHARMIAN
My arm is sore; best play with Mardian.

CLEOPATRA
As well a woman with an eunuch play'd
As with a woman. — Come, you'll play with me, sir?

MARDIAN
As well as I can, madam.

CLEOPATRA
And when good will is show'd, though't come too
short,
The actor may plead pardon. I'll none now: —
Give me mine angle, — we'll to the river: there,
My music playing far off, I will betray
Tawny-finn'd fishes; my bended hook shall pierce
Their slimy jaws; and, as I draw them up,
I'll think them every one an Antony,
And say, 'Ah, ha! y' are caught.'

CHARMIAN
'Twas merry when
You wager'd on your angling; when your diver
Did hang a salt-fish on his hook, which he
With fervency drew up.

CLEOPATRA
That time, — O times! —
I laugh'd him out of patience; and that night
I laugh'd him into patience: and next morn,
Ere the ninth hour, I drunk him to his bed;
Then put my tires and mantles on him, whilst
I wore his sword Philippan.
Enter a MESSENGER.
O, from Italy! —
Ram thou thy fruitful tidings in mine ears,
That long time have been barren.

MESSENGER
Madam, madam, —

CLEOPATRA
Antony's dead! — If thou say so, villain,
Thou kill'st thy mistress: but well and free,
If thou so yield him, there is gold, and here
My bluest veins to kiss, — a hand that kings
Have lipp'd, and trembled kissing.

MESSENGER
First, madam, he is well.

CLEOPATRA
Why, there's more gold.
But, sirrah, mark, we use
To say the dead are well: bring it to that,
The gold I give thee will I melt and pour
Down thy ill-uttering throat.

MESSENGER
Good madam, hear me.

CLEOPATRA
Well, go to, I will;
But there's no goodness in thy face: if Antony
Be free and healthful — so tart a favour
To trumpet such good tidings! If not well,

Thou shouldst come like a Fury crown'd with snakes,
Not like a formal man.

MESSENGER
Will't please you hear me?

CLEOPATRA
I have a mind to strike thee ere thou speak'st:
Yet, if thou say Antony lives, is well,
Or friends with Cæsar, or not captive to him,
I'll set thee in a shower of gold, and hail
Rich pearls upon thee.

MESSENGER
Madam, he's well.

CLEOPATRA
Well said.

MESSENGER
And friends with Cæsar.

CLEOPATRA
Th'art an honest man.

MESSENGER
Cæsar and he are greater friends than ever.

CLEOPATRA
Make thee a fortune from me.

MESSENGER
But yet, madam, —

CLEOPATRA
I do not like 'But yet,' it does allay
The good precedence; fie upon 'But yet'!
'But yet' is as a gaoler to bring forth
Some monstrous malefactor. Prithee, friend,
Pour out the pack of matter to mine ear,
The good and bad together: he's friends with Cæsar;
In state of health thou say'st; and thou say'st, free.

MESSENGER
Free, madam! no; I made no such report:
He's bound unto Octavia.

CLEOPATRA
For what good turn?

MESSENGER
For the best turn i' the bed.

CLEOPATRA
I am pale, Charmian.

MESSENGER
Madam, he's married to Octavia.

CLEOPATRA
The most infectious pestilence upon thee!
[*Strikes him down.*

MESSENGER
Good madam, patience.

CLEOPATRA
What say you? — Hence,
[*Strikes him.*
Horrible villain! or I'll spurn thine eyes
Like balls before me; I'll unhair thy head:
[*She hales him up and down.*
Thou shalt be whipp'd with wire, and stew'd in brine,
Smarting in lingering pickle.

MESSENGER
Gracious, madam,
I that do bring the news made not the match.

CLEOPATRA
Say 'tis not so, a province I will give thee,
And make thy fortunes proud: the blow thou hadst
Shall make thy peace for moving me to rage;
And I will boot thee with what gift beside
Thy modesty can beg.

MESSENGER
He's married, madam.

CLEOPATRA
Rogue, thou hast liv'd too long. [*Draws a knife.*

MESSENGER
Nay, then I'll run. —
What mean you, madam? I have made no fault. [*Exit.*

CHARMIAN
Good madam, keep yourself within yourself:
The man is innocent.

CLEOPATRA
Some innocents scape not the thunderbolt. —
Melt Egypt into Nile! and kindly creatures
Turn all to serpents! — Call the slave again: —
Though I am mad, I will not bite him: — call.

CHARMIAN
He is afeard to come.

CLEOPATRA
I will not hurt him.
[*Exit* CHARMIAN.
These hands do lack nobility, that they strike
A meaner than myself; since I myself
Have given myself the cause.

Enter CHARMIAN *and* MESSENGER.

Come hither, sir.
Though it be honest, it is never good
To bring bad news: give to a gracious message
An host of tongues; but let ill tidings tell
Themselves when they be felt.

MESSENGER
                  I have done my duty.

CLEOPATRA
Is he married?
I cannot hate thee worser than I do,
If thou again say 'Yes.'

MESSENGER
              He's married, madam.

CLEOPATRA
The gods confound thee! dost thou hold there still?

MESSENGER
Should I lie, madam?

CLEOPATRA
            O, I would thou didst,
So half my Egypt were submerg'd, and made
A cistern for scaled snakes! Go, get thee hence:
Hadst thou Narcissus in thy face, to me
Thou wouldst appear most ugly. He is married?

MESSENGER
I crave your highness' pardon.

CLEOPATRA
             He is married?

MESSENGER
Take no offence that I would not offend you:
To punish me for what you make me do
Seems much unequal: he's married to Octavia.

CLEOPATRA
O, that his fault should make a knave of thee,
That art not what th'art sure of! — Get thee hence:
The merchandise which thou hast brought from Rome
Are all too dear for me: lie they upon thy hand,
And be undone by 'em.   [*Exit* MESSENGER.

CHARMIAN
        Good your highness, patience.

CLEOPATRA
In praising Antony, I have dispraised Cæsar.

CHARMIAN
Many times, madam.

CLEOPATRA
          I am paid for't now.
Lead me from hence;
I faint: — O Iras, Charmian! — 'tis no matter. —
Go to the fellow, good Alexas; bid him
Report the feature of Octavia, her years,
Her inclination, let him not leave out
The colour of her hair: — bring me word quickly.
                  [*Exit* ALEXAS.
Let him for ever go: — let him not — Charmian,
Though he be painted one way like a Gorgon,
The other way's a Mars. — [*to* MARDIAN] Bid you Alexas
Bring me word how tall she is. — Pity me, Charmian,
But do not speak to me. — Lead me to my chamber.
                       [*Exeunt.*

SCENE VI

Near Misenum.

Flourish. Enter POMPEY *and* MENAS *at one door,
with drum and trumpet: at another,* CAESAR,
ANTONY, LEPIDUS, ENOBARBUS,
MAECENAS, *with* SOLDIERS *marching.*

POMPEY
Your hostages I have, so have you mine;
And we shall talk before we fight.

CAESAR
             Most meet
That first we come to words; and therefore have we
Our written purposes before us sent;
Which, if thou hast consider'd, let us know
If 'twill tie up thy discontented sword,
And carry back to Sicily much tall youth
That else must perish here.

POMPEY
           To you all three,
The senators alone of this great world,
Chief factors for the gods, — I do not know
Wherefore my father should revengers want,
Having a son and friends; since Julius Cæsar,
Who at Philippi the good Brutus ghosted,
There saw you labouring for him. What was't
That mov'd pale Cassius to conspire; and what
Made the all-honour'd, honest Roman, Brutus,
With the arm'd rest, courtiers and beauteous freedom,
To drench the Capitol, but that they would
Have one man but a man? And that is it
Hath made me rig my navy, at whose burden
The anger'd ocean foams; with which I meant
To scourge th'ingratitude that despiteful Rome
Cast on my noble father.

CAESAR
             Take your time.

ANTONY
Thou canst not fear us, Pompey, with thy sails;
We'll speak with thee at sea: at land, thou know'st
How much we do o'er-count thee.

POMPEY
           At land, indeed
Thou dost o'er-count me of my father's house:
But, since the cuckoo builds not for himself,
Remain in't as thou mayst.

LEPIDUS
         Be pleas'd to tell us —
For this is from the present — how you take
The offers we have sent you.

CAESAR
          There's the point.

ANTONY
Which do not be entreated to, but weigh
What it is worth embraced.

CAESAR
         And what may follow,
To try a larger fortune.

POMPEY
        You have made me offer
Of Sicily, Sardinia; and I must
Rid all the sea of pirates; then, to send
Measures of wheat to Rome; this greed upon,
To part with unhack'd edges, and bear back
Our targes undinted.

CAESAR, ANTONY, *and* LEPIDUS.
        That's our offer.

POMPEY
            Know, then,
I came before you here a man prepared
To take this offer: but Mark Antony
Put me to some impatience: — though I lose
The praise of it by telling, you must know,
When Cæsar and your brother were at blows,
Your mother came to Sicily, and did find
Her welcome friendly.

ANTONY
         I have heard it, Pompey;
And am well studied for a liberal thanks
Which I do owe you.

POMPEY
         Let me have your hand:
I did not think, sir, to have met you here.

ANTONY
The beds i' the east are soft; and thanks to you,
That call'd me, timelier than my purpose, hither;
For I have gain'd by't.

CAESAR
         Since I saw you last,
There is a change upon you.

POMPEY
         Well, I know not
What counts harsh fortune casts upon my face;
But in my bosom shall she never come,
To make my heart her vassal.

LEPIDUS
         Well met here.

POMPEY
I hope so, Lepidus. — Thus we are agreed:
I crave our composition may be written,
And seal'd between us.

CAESAR
         That's the next to do.

POMPEY
We'll feast each other ere we part; and let's
Draw lots who shall begin.

ANTONY
         That will I, Pompey.

POMPEY
No, Antony, take the lot: but, first
Or last, your fine Egyptian cookery
Shall have the fame. I have heard that Julius Cæsar
Grew fat with feasting there.

CLEOPATRA   Rogue, thou hast liv'd too long.

ANTONY
         You have heard much.

POMPEY
I have fair meanings, sir.

ANTONY
         And fair words to them.

POMPEY
Then so much have I heard:
And I have heard, Apollodorus carried —

ENOBARBUS
No more of that: — he did so.

POMPEY
         What, I pray you?

ENOBARBUS
A certain queen to Cæsar in a mattress.

POMPEY
I know thee now: how farest thou, soldier?

ENOBARBUS
         Well;
And well am like to do; for I perceive
Four feasts are toward.

POMPEY
        Let me shake thy hand;
I never hated thee: I have seen thee fight,
When I have envied thy behaviour.

ENOBARBUS
         Sir,
I never lov'd you much; but I ha' prais'd ye,
When you have well deserv'd ten times as much
As I have said you did.

POMPEY
        Enjoy thy plainness,
It nothing ill becomes thee. —
Aboard my galley I invite you all:
Will you lead, lords?

CAESAR, ANTONY, *and* LEPIDUS
        Show us the way, sir.

POMPEY
         Come.
   [*Exeunt all but* MENAS *and* ENOBARBUS.

MENAS [*aside*].
Thy father, Pompey, would ne'er have made this treaty. —
You and I have known, sir.

ENOBARBUS
At sea, I think.

MENAS
We have, sir.

ENOBARBUS
You have done well by water.

MENAS
And you by land.

ENOBARBUS
I will praise any man that will praise me; though it
cannot be denied what I have done by land.

MENAS
Nor what I have done by water.

ENOBARBUS
Yes, something you can deny for your own safety: you
have been a great thief by sea.

MENAS
And you by land.

ENOBARBUS
There I deny my land service. But give me your hand,

MENAS: if our eyes had authority, here they might take two thieves kissing.

MENAS
All men's faces are true, whatsoe'er their hands are.

ENOBARBUS
But there is never a fair woman has a true face.

MENAS
No slander; they steal hearts.

ENOBARBUS
We came hither to fight with you.

MENAS
For my part, I am sorry it is turn'd to a drinking. Pompey doth this day laugh away his fortune.

ENOBARBUS
If he do, sure, he cannot weep't back again.

MENAS
Y'have said, sir. We look'd not for Mark Antony here: pray you, is he married to Cleopatra?

ENOBARBUS
Cæsar's sister is called Octavia.

MENAS
True, sir; she was the wife of Caius Marcellus.

ENOBARBUS
But she is now the wife of Marcus Antonius.

MENAS
Pray ye, sir?

ENOBARBUS
'Tis true.

MENAS
Then is Cæsar and he for ever knit together.

ENOBARBUS
If I were bound to divine of this unity, I would not prophesy so.

MENAS
I think the policy of that purpose made more in the marriage than the love of the parties.

ENOBARBUS
I think so too. But you shall find, the band that seems to tie their friendship together will be the very strangler of their amity: Octavia is of a holy, cold, and still conversation.

MENAS
Who would not have his wife so?

ENOBARBUS
Not he that himself is not so; which is Mark Antony. He will to his Egyptian dish again: then shall the sighs of Octavia blow the fire up in Cæsar; and, as I said before, that which is the strength of their amity shall prove the immediate author of their variance. Antony will use his affection where it is: he married but his occasion here.

MENAS
And thus it may be. Come, sir, will you aboard? I have a health for you.

ENOBARBUS
I shall take it, sir: we have used our throats in Egypt.

MENAS
Come, let's away.   [*Exeunt.*

SCENE VII

On board POMPEY'S *galley, off Misenum.*

Music plays. Enter two or three SERVANTS, *with a banquet.*

FIRST SERVANT
Here they'll be, man. Some o' their plants are ill-rooted already; the least wind i' the world will blow them down.

SECOND SERVANT
Lepidus is high-colour'd.

FIRST SERVANT
They have made him drink alms-drink.

SECOND SERVANT
As they pinch one another by the disposition, he cries out 'No more'; reconciles them to his entreaty, and himself to the drink.

FIRST SERVANT
But it raises the greater war between him and his discretion.

SECOND SERVANT
Why, this is to have a name in great men's fellowship: I had as lief have a reed that will do me no service as a partisan I could not heave.

FIRST SERVANT
To be call'd into a huge sphere, and not to be seen to move in't, are the holes where eyes should be, which pitifully disaster the cheeks.

A sennet sounded. Enter CAESAR, ANTONY, LEPIDUS, POMPEY, AGRIPPA, MAECENAS, ENOBARBUS, MENAS, *with other* CAPTAINS.

ANTONY [*to* CAESAR].
Thus do they, sir: they take the flow o' the Nile
By certain scales i' the pyramid; they know,
By the height, the lowness, or the mean, if dearth
Or foison follow: the higher Nilus swells,
The more it promises: as it ebbs, the seedsman
Upon the slime and ooze scatters his grain,
And shortly comes to harvest.

LEPIDUS
Y'have strange serpents there.

ANTONY
Ay, Lepidus.

LEPIDUS
Your serpent of Egypt is bred now of your mud by the operation of your sun: so is your crocodile.

ANTONY
They are so.

POMPEY
Sit, — and some wine! — A health to Lepidus!

LEPIDUS
I am not so well as I should be, but I'll ne'er out.

ENOBARBUS
Not till you have slept; I fear me you'll be in till then.

LEPIDUS
Nay, certainly, I have heard the Ptolemies' pyramises are very goodly things; without contradiction, I have heard that.

MENAS [*aside to* POMPEY].
Pompey, a word.

POMPEY [*aside to* MENAS].
Say in mine ear: what is't?

MENAS [*whispers in his ear*].
Forsake thy seat, I do beseech thee, captain,
And hear me speak a word.

POMPEY [*aside to* MENAS].
                    Forbear me till anon. —
This wine for Lepidus!

LEPIDUS
What manner o'thing is your crocodile?

ANTONY
It is shaped, sir, like itself; and it is as broad as it hath breadth; it is just so high as it is, and moves with its own organs: it lives by that which nourisheth it; and the elements once out of it, it transmigrates.

LEPIDUS
What colour is it of?

ANTONY
Of its own colour too.

LEPIDUS
'Tis a strange serpent.

ANTONY
'Tis so. And the tears of it are wet.

CAESAR
Will this description satisfy him?

ANTONY
With the health that Pompey gives him, else he is a very epicure.

POMPEY [*aside to* MENAS].
Go hang, sir, hang! Tell me of that? away!
Do as I bid you. — Where's this cup I call'd for?

MENAS [*aside to* POMPEY].
If for the sake of merit thou wilt hear me,
Rise from thy stool.

POMPEY [*aside to* MENAS].
I think th'art mad. The matter?
                    [*Rises, and walks aside.*

MENAS
I have ever held my cap off to thy fortunes.

POMPEY
Thou hast served me with much faith. What's else to say? —
Be jolly, lords.

ANTONY
                    These quicksands, Lepidus,
Keep off them, for you sink.

MENAS
Wilt thou be lord of all the world?

POMPEY
                    What say'st thou?

MENAS
Wilt thou be lord of the whole world? That's twice.

POMPEY
How should that be?

MENAS
                    But entertain it,

And though thou think me poor, I am the man
Will give thee all the world.

POMPEY
                    Hast thou drunk well?

MENAS
No, Pompey, I have kept me from the cup.
Thou art, if thou darest be, the earthly Jove:
Whate'er the ocean pales, or sky inclips,
Is thine, if thou wilt ha't.

POMPEY
                    Show me which way.

MENAS
These three world-sharers, these competitors,
Are in thy vessel: let me cut the cable;
And, when we are put off, fall to their throats:
All then is thine.

POMPEY
                    Ah, this thou shouldst have done,
And not have spoke on't! In me 'tis villainy;
In thee't had been good service. Thou must know,
'Tis not my profit that does lead mine honour;
Mine honour, it. Repent that e'er thy tongue
Hath so betray'd thine act: being done unknown,
I should have found it afterwards well done;
But must condemn it now. Desist, and drink.

MENAS [*aside*].
For this,
I'll never follow thy pall'd fortunes more. —
Who seeks, and will not take when once 'tis offer'd,
Shall never find it more.

POMPEY
                    This health to Lepidus!

ANTONY
Bear him ashore. — I'll pledge it for him, Pompey.

ENOBARBUS
Here's to thee, Menas!

MENAS
                    Enobarbus, welcome!

POMPEY
Fill till the cup be hid.

ENOBARBUS
There's a strong fellow, Menas.

                    [*Pointing to the* ATTENDANT *who
                    carries off* LEPIDUS.

MENAS
Why?

ENOBARBUS
A' bears the third part of the world, man; see'st not?

MENAS
The third part, then, is drunk: would it were all,
That it might go on wheels!

ENOBARBUS
Drink thou; increase the reels.

MENAS
Come.

POMPEY
This is not yet an Alexandrian feast.

ANTONY
It ripens towards it. — Strike the vessels, ho! —
Here's to Cæsar!

CAESAR
                    I could well forbear't.
It's monstrous labour, when I wash my brain,
And it grows fouler.

ANTONY
                    Be a child o' the time.

CAESAR
Possess it, I'll make answer:
But I had rather fast from all four days
Than drink so much in one.

ENOBARBUS [*to* ANTONY].
                    Ha, my brave emperor!
Shall we dance now the Egyptian Bacchanals
And celebrate our drink?

POMPEY
                    Let's ha't, good soldier.

ANTONY
Come, let's all take hands,
Till that the conquering wine hath steep'd our sense
In soft and delicate Lethe.

ENOBARBUS
                    All take hands. —
Make battery to our ears with the loud music: —
The while I'll place you: then the boy shall sing;
The holding every man shall bear as loud
As his strong sides can volley.

[*Music plays.* ENOBARBUS *places them hand in hand.*

The Song.
Come, thou monarch of the vine,
Plumpy Bacchus with pink eyne!
In thy fats our cares be drown'd,
With thy grapes our hairs be crown'd:
Cup us till the world go round,
Cup us till the world go round!

CAESAR
What would you more? — Pompey, good night. —
　Good brother,
Let me request you off: our graver business
Frowns at this levity. — Gentle lords, let's part;
You see we have burnt our cheeks: strong Enobarb
Is weaker than the wine; and mine own tongue
Splits what it speaks: the wild disguise hath almost
Antick'd us all. What needs more words? Good night. —
Good Antony, your hand.

POMPEY
　　　　　　　　　I'll try you on the shore.

ANTONY
And shall, sir: give's your hand.

POMPEY
　　　　　　　O Antony,
You have my father's house, — But, what? we are
　friends.
Come, down into the boat.

ENOBARBUS
　　　　　　　Take heed you fall not.
　[*Exeunt all except* ENOBARBUS *and* MENAS.
Menas, I'll not on shore.

MENAS
　　　　　　　No, to my cabin. —
These drums! — these trumpets, flutes! what! —
Let Neptune hear we bid a loud farewell
To these great fellows: sound and be hang'd, sound
　out! 　　　　[*Sound a flourish, with drums.*

ENOBARBUS
Hoo! says a'. — There's my cap.

MENAS
Hoo! — Noble captain, come. 　　　[*Exeunt.*

ACT III

SCENE I

A plain in Syria.

Enter VENTIDIUS *as it were in triumph, with* SILIUS
and other ROMANS, OFFICERS, *and* SOLDIERS; *the
dead body of* PACORUS *borne before him.*

VENTIDIUS
Now, darting Parthia, art thou struck; and now
Pleas'd fortune does of Marcus Crassus' death
Make me revenger. — Bear the king's son's body
Before our army. — Thy Pacorus, Orodes,
Pays this for Marcus Crassus.

SILIUS
　　　　　　　Noble Ventidius,
Whilst yet with Parthian blood thy sword is warm,
The fugitive Parthians follow; spur through Media,
Mesopotamia, and the shelters whither
The routed fly: so thy grand captain Antony
Shall set thee on triumphant chariots, and
Put garlands on thy head.

VENTIDIUS
　　　　　　　O Silius, Silius,
I have done enough: a lower place, note well,
May make too great an act; for learn this, Silius, —
Better to leave undone, than by our deed
Acquire too high a fame when him we serve's away.
Caesar and Antony have ever won
More in their officer than person: Sossius,
One of my place in Syria, his lieutenant,
For quick accumulation of renown,
Which he achiev'd by the minute, lost his favour.
Who does i' the wars more than his captain can
Becomes his captain's captain: and ambition,
The soldier's virtue, rather makes choice of loss
Than gain which darkens him.
I could do more to do Antonius good,
But 'twould offend him; and in his offence
Should my performance perish.

SILIUS
　　　　　　　Thou hast, Ventidius, that
Without the which a soldier, and his sword,
Grants scarce distinction. Thou wilt write to Antony!

VENTIDIUS
I'll humbly signify what in his name,
That magical word of war, we have effected;
How, with his banners and his well-paid ranks,

The ne'er-yet-beaten horse of Parthia
We have jaded out o'the field.

SILIUS
　　　　　　　Where is he now?

VENTIDIUS
He purposeth to Athens: whither, with what haste
The weight we must convey with's will permit,
We shall appear before him. — On, there; pass along!
　　　　　　　　　　　　[*Exeunt.*

SCENE II

Rome. An ante-chamber in CAESAR'S *house.*

Enter AGRIPPA *at one door
and* ENOBARBUS *at another.*

AGRIPPA
What, are the brothers parted?

ENOBARBUS
They have dispatch'd with Pompey; he is gone;
The other three are sealing. Octavia weeps
To part from Rome; Caesar is sad; and Lepidus,
Since Pompey's feast, as Menas says, is troubled
With the green sickness.

AGRIPPA
　　　　　　　'Tis a noble Lepidus.

ENOBARBUS
A very fine one: O, how he loves Caesar!

AGRIPPA
Nay, but how dearly he adores Mark Antony!

ENOBARBUS
Caesar? Why, he's the Jupiter of men.

AGRIPPA
What's Antony? The god of Jupiter.

ENOBARBUS
Spake you of Caesar? How! the nonpareil!

AGRIPPA
O Antony! O thou Arabian bird!

ENOBARBUS
Would you praise Caesar, say 'Caesar', — go no further.

AGRIPPA
Indeed, he plied them both with excellent praises.

ENOBARBUS
But he loves Caesar best; — yet he loves Antony:
Hoo! hearts, tongues, figures, scribes, bards, poets,
　cannot
Think, speak, cast, write, sing, number, — hoo! —
His love to Antony. But as for Caesar,
Kneel down, kneel down, and wonder.

AGRIPPA
　　　　　　　Both he loves.

ENOBARBUS
They are his shards, and he their beetle. [*Trumpets
　within.*] So, —
This is to horse. — Adieu, noble Agrippa.

AGRIPPA
Good fortune, worthy soldier; and farewell.
　Enter CAESAR, ANTONY, LEPIDUS, *and* OCTAVIA.

ANTONY
No further, sir.

CAESAR
You take from me a great part of
　myself;
Use me well in't. — Sister, prove
　such a wife
As my thoughts make thee, and
　as my furthest band
Shall pass on thy approof. —
　Most noble Antony,
Let not the piece of virtue, which
　is set
Betwixt us as the cement of our love
To keep it builded, be the ram to
　batter
The fortress of it; for better
　might we
Have lov'd without this mean, if
　on both parts
This be not cherish'd.

ANTONY
　　　　　　Make me not offended
In your distrust.

CAESAR
　　　　　　I have said.

ANTONY
　　　　　　You shall not find,
Though you be therein curious,
　the least cause
For what you seem to fear: so, the
　gods keep you,

And make the hearts of Romans serve your ends!
We will here part.

CAESAR
Farewell, my dearest sister, fare thee well:
The elements be kind to thee, and make
Thy spirits all of comfort! fare thee well.

OCTAVIA
My noble brother! —

ANTONY
The April's in her eyes: it is love's spring,
And these the showers to bring it on. — Be cheerful.

OCTAVIA
Sir, look well to my husband's house; and —

CAESAR
　　　　　　　What, Octavia?

OCTAVIA
I'll tell you in your ear.

ANTONY
Her tongue will not obey her heart, nor can
Her heart inform her tongue, — the swan's
　down-feather,
That stands upon the swell at full of tide,
And neither way inclines.

ENOBARBUS [*aside to* AGRIPPA].
Will Caesar weep?

AGRIPPA [*aside to* ENOBARBUS].
　　　　　　　He has a cloud in's face.

ENOBARBUS [*aside to* AGRIPPA].
He were the worse for that were he a horse;
So is he being a man.

AGRIPPA [*aside to* ENOBARBUS].
　　　　　　　Why, Enobarbus,
When Antony found Julius Caesar dead,
He cried almost to roaring; and he wept
When at Philippi he found Brutus slain.

ENOBARBUS [*aside to* AGRIPPA].
That year, indeed, he was troubled with a rheum;
What willingly he did confound he wail'd,
Believe't, till I wept too.

CAESAR
　　　　　　　No, sweet Octavia,
You shall hear from me still; the time shall not
Out-go my thinking on you.

ANTONY
　　　　　　　Come, sir, come;
I'll wrestle with you in my strength of love:
Look, here I have you; thus I let you go,
And give you to the gods.

CAESAR
　　　　　　　Adieu; be happy!

LEPIDUS
Let all the number of the stars give light
To thy fair way!

CAESAR
　　　　　　Farewell, farewell! 　[*Kisses* OCTAVIA.

ANTONY
　　　　　　　Farewell!
　　　　　　　[*Trumpets sound. Exeunt.*

VENTIDIUS Bear the king's son's body before our army.

SCENE III

Alexandria. A room in CLEOPATRA'S *palace.*

Enter CLEOPATRA, CHARMIAN,
IRAS, *and* ALEXAS.

CLEOPATRA
Where is the fellow?

ALEXAS
       Half afeard to come.

CLEOPATRA
Go to, go to.
    Enter the MESSENGER *as before.*
    Come hither, sir.

ALEXAS
       Good majesty,
Herod of Jewry dare not look upon you
But when you are well pleas'd.

CLEOPATRA
       That Herod's head
I'll have: but how, when Antony is gone
Through whom I might command it? — Come thou
near.

MESSENGER
Most gracious majesty, —

CLEOPATRA
       Didst thou behold
Octavia?

MESSENGER
Ay, dread queen.

CLEOPATRA
       Where?

MESSENGER
       Madam, in Rome;
I look'd her in the face, and saw her led
Between her brother and Mark Antony.

CLEOPATRA
Is she as tall as me?

MESSENGER
       She is not, madam.

CLEOPATRA
Didst hear her speak? is she shrill-tongued or low?

MESSENGER
Madam, I heard her speak; she is low-voiced.

CLEOPATRA
That's not so good: — he cannot like her long.

CHARMIAN
Like her! O Isis! 'tis impossible.

CLEOPATRA
I think so, Charmian: dull of tongue, and dwarfish! —
What majesty is in her gait? Remember,
If e'er thou look'dst on majesty.

MESSENGER
       She creeps, —
Her motion and her station are as one;
She shows a body rather than a life.
A statue than a breather.

CLEOPATRA
       Is this certain?

MESSENGER
Or I have no observance.

CHARMIAN
       Three in Egypt
Cannot make better note.

CLEOPATRA
       He's very knowing;
I do perceive't: — there's nothing in her yet: —
The fellow has good judgement.

CHARMIAN
       Excellent.

CLEOPATRA
Guess at her years, I prithee.

MESSENGER
       Madam,
She was a widow, —

CLEOPATRA
       Widow! — Charmian, hark.

MESSENGER
And I do think she's thirty.

CLEOPATRA
Bear'st thou her face in mind? is't long or round?

MESSENGER
Round even to faultiness.

CLEOPATRA
For the most part, too, they are foolish that are so. —
Her hair, what colour?

MESSENGER
       Brown, madam: and her forehead
As low as she would wish it.

CLEOPATRA
       There's gold for thee.
Thou must not take my former sharpness ill: —
I will employ thee back again; I find thee
Most fit for business: go make thee ready;
Our letters are prepared.   [*Exit* MESSENGER.

CHARMIAN
       A proper man.

CLEOPATRA
Indeed, he is so: I repent me much
That so I harried him. Why, methinks, by him,
This creature's no such thing.

CHARMIAN
       Nothing, madam.

CLEOPATRA
The man hath seen some majesty, and should know.

CHARMIAN
Hath he seen majesty? Isis else defend,
And serving you so long!

CLEOPATRA
I have one thing more to ask him yet, good Charmian:
But 'tis no matter; thou shalt bring him to me
Where I will write. All may be well enough.

CHARMIAN
I warrant you, madam.   [*Exeunt.*

SCENE IV

Athens. A room in ANTONY'S *house.*

Enter ANTONY *and* OCTAVIA.

ANTONY
Nay, nay, Octavia, not only that, —
That were excusable, that, and thousands more
Of semblable import, — but he hath waged
New wars 'gainst Pompey; made his will, and read it
To public ear:
Spoke scantly of me: when perforce he could not
But pay me terms of honour, cold and sickly
He vented them; most narrow measure lent me:
When the best hint was given him, he not took't,
Or did it from his teeth.

OCTAVIA
       O, my good lord,
Believe not all; or, if you must believe,
Stomach not all. A more unhappy lady,
If this division chance, ne'er stood between,
Praying for both parts:
The good gods will mock me presently,
When I shall pray, 'O, bless my lord and husband!'
Undo that prayer, by crying out as loud,
'O, bless my brother!' Husband win, win brother,
Prays, and destroys the prayer; no midway
'Twixt these extremes at all.

ANTONY
       Gentle Octavia,
Let your best love draw to that point, which seeks
Best to preserve it: if I lose mine honour,
I lose myself: better I were not yours
Than yours so branchless. But, as you requested,
Yourself shall go between's: the mean time, lady,
I'll raise the preparation of a war
Shall stay your brother: make your soonest haste;
So your desires are yours.

OCTAVIA
       Thanks to my lord.
The Jove of power make me most weak, most weak,
Your reconciler! Wars 'twixt you twain would be
As if the world should cleave, and that slain men
Should solder up the rift.

ANTONY
When it appears to you where this begins,
Turn your displeasure that way; for our faults
Can never be so equal, that your love
Can equally move with them. Provide your going
Choose your own company, and command what cost
Your heart has mind to.   [*Exeunt.*

SCENE V

The same. Another room.

Enter ENOBARBUS *and* EROS, *meeting.*

ENOBARBUS
How now, friend Eros!

EROS
There's strange news come, sir.

ENOBARBUS
What, man?

EROS
Cæsar and Lepidus have made wars upon Pompey.

ENOBARBUS
This is old: what is the success?

EROS
Cæsar, having made use of him in the wars 'gainst
Pompey, presently denied him rivality; would not let
him partake in the glory of the action: and not resting
here, accuses him of letters he had formerly wrote to
Pompey; upon his own appeal, seizes him: so the poor
third is up, till death enlarge his confine.

ENOBARBUS
Then, world, thou hast a pair of chaps, no more;
And throw between them all the food thou hast,
They'll grind the one the other. Where's Antony?

EROS
He's walking in the garden — thus; and spurns
The rush that lies before him; cries 'Fool Lepidus!'
And threats the throat of that his officer
That murder'd Pompey.

ENOBARBUS
       Our great navy's rigg'd.

EROS
For Italy and Cæsar. More, Domitius;
My lord desires you presently: my news
I might have told hereafter.

ENOBARBUS
       'Twill be naught:
But let it be. — Bring me to Antony.

EROS
Come, sir.   [*Exeunt.*

SCENE VI

Rome. A room in CAESAR'S *house.*

Enter CAESAR, AGRIPPA, *and* MAECENAS.

CAESAR
Contemning Rome, he has done all this and more
In Alexandria: here's the manner of't: —
I'the market-place, on a tribunal silver'd,
Cleopatra and himself in chairs of gold
Were publicly enthroned; at the feet sat
Cæsarion, whom they call my father's son,
And all the unlawful issue that their lust
Since then hath made between them. Unto her
He gave the stablishment of Egypt; made her
Of lower Syria, Cyprus, Lydia,
Absolute queen.

MAECENAS
       This in the public eye?

CAESAR
I' the common show-place, where they exercise.
His sons he there proclaim'd the kings of kings;
Great Media, Parthia, and Armenia,
He gave to Alexander; to Ptolemy he assign'd
Syria, Cilicia, and Phœnicia: she
In the habiliments of the goddess Isis
That day appear'd; and oft before gave audience,
As 'tis reported, so.

MAECENAS
       Let Rome be thus inform'd.

AGRIPPA
Who, queasy with his insolence
Already, will their good thoughts call from him.

CAESAR
The people know it; and have now received
His accusations.

AGRIPPA
       Who does he accuse?

CAESAR
Cæsar: and that, having in Sicily
Sextus Pompeius spoil'd, we had not rated him
His part o'the isle: then does he say he lent me
Some shipping unrestored: lastly, he frets
That Lepidus of the triumvirate
Should be depos'd; and, being, that we detain
All his revenue.

AGRIPPA
       Sir, this should be answer'd.

CAESAR
'Tis done already, and the messenger gone.
I have told him, Lepidus was grown too cruel;
That he his high authority abused,
And did deserve his change: for what I have conquer'd,
I grant him part; but then, in his Armenia,
And other of his conquer'd kingdoms, I
Demand the like.

MAECENAS
       He'll never yield to that.

CAESAR
Nor must not, then, be yielded to in this.

Enter OCTAVIA *with her* TRAIN.

OCTAVIA
Hail, Cæsar, and my lord! hail, most dear Cæsar!

CAESAR
That ever I should call thee castaway!

OCTAVIA
You have not call'd me so, nor have you cause.

CAESAR
Why have you stol'n upon us thus! You come not
Like Cæsar's sister: the wife of Antony
Should have an army for an usher, and
The neighs of horse to tell of her approach
Long ere she did appear; the trees by the way
Should have borne men; and expectation fainted,
Longing for what it had not; nay, the dust
Should have ascended to the roof of heaven,
Rais'd by your populous troops: but you are come
A market-maid to Rome; and have prevented
The ostentation of our love, which, left unshown,
Is often left unlov'd: we should have met you
By sea and land; supplying every stage
With an augmented greeting.

OCTAVIA
                Good my lord,
To come thus was I not constrain'd, but did it
On my free will. My lord, Mark Antony,
Hearing that you prepar'd for war, acquainted
My grieved ear withal; whereon I begg'd
His pardon for return.

CAESAR
                Which soon he granted,
Being an obstruct 'tween his lust and him.

OCTAVIA
Do not say so, my lord.

CAESAR
                I have eyes upon him,
And his affairs come to me on the wind.
Where is he now?

OCTAVIA
                My lord, in Athens.

CAESAR
No, my most wronged sister; Cleopatra
Hath nodded him to her. He hath given his empire
Up to a whore; who now are levying
The kings o' the earth for war: he hath assembled
Bocchus, the king of Libya; Archelaus,
Of Cappadocia; Philadelphos, king
Of Paphlagonia; the Thracian king, Adallas;
King Malchus of Arabia; King of Pont;
Herod of Jewry: Mithridates, king
Of Comagene; Polemon and Amyntas,
The kings of Mede and Lycaonia,
With a more larger list of sceptres.

OCTAVIA
                Ay me, most wretched,
That have my heart parted betwixt two friends
That do afflict each other!

CAESAR
                Welcome hither:
Your letters did withhold our breaking forth;
Till we perceiv'd, both how you were wrong led
And we in negligent danger. Cheer your heart:
Be you not troubled with the time, which drives
O'er your content these strong necessities;
But let determin'd things to destiny
Hold unbewail'd their way. Welcome to Rome;
Nothing more dear to me. You are abused
Beyond the mark of thought: and the high gods,
To do you justice, make them ministers
Of us and those that love you. Best of comfort;
And ever welcome to us.

AGRIPPA
                Welcome, lady.

MAECENAS
Welcome, dear madam.
Each heart in Rome does love and pity you:
Only th'adulterous Antony, most large
In his abominations, turns you off;
And gives his potent regiment to a trull,
That noises it against us.

OCTAVIA
                Is it so, sir?

CAESAR
Most certain. Sister, welcome: pray you,
Be ever known to patience: my dear'st sister!   [*Exeunt.*

SCENE VII

ANTONY'S *camp, near Actium.*

Enter CLEOPATRA *and* ENOBARBUS.

CLEOPATRA
I will be even with thee, doubt it not.

ENOBARBUS
But why, why, why?

CLEOPATRA
Thou hast forspoke my being in these wars,
And say'st it is not fit.

ENOBARBUS
                Well, is it, is it?

CLEOPATRA
If not denounc'd against us, why should not we
Be there in person?

ENOBARBUS [*aside*].
                Well, I could reply: —
If we should serve with horse and mares together,
The horse were merely lost; the mares would bear
A soldier and his horse.

CLEOPATRA
                What is't you say?

ENOBARBUS
Your presence needs must puzzle Antony;
Take from his heart, take from his brain, from's time,
What should not then be spared. He is already
Traduc'd for levity; and 'tis said in Rome
That Photinus an eunuch and your maids
Manage this war.

CLEOPATRA
                Sink Rome, and their tongues rot
That speak against us! A charge we bear i' the war,
And, as the president of my kingdom, will
Appear there for a man. Speak not against it;
I will not stay behind.

ENOBARBUS
                Nay, I have done.
Here comes the emperor.

Enter ANTONY *and* CANIDIUS.

ANTONY
                Is it not strange, Canidius,
That from Tarentum and Brundusium
He could so quickly cut the Ionian sea,
And take in Toryne? — You have heard on't, sweet?

CLEOPATRA
Celerity is never more admired
Than by the negligent.

ANTONY
                A good rebuke,
Which might have well becom'd the best of men,
To taunt at slackness. — Canidius, we
Will fight with him by sea.

CLEOPATRA
                By sea! what else?

CANIDIUS
Why will my lord do so?

ANTONY
                For that he dares us to't.

ENOBARBUS
So hath my lord dared him to single fight.

CANIDIUS
Ay, and to wage this battle at Pharsalia,
Where Cæsar fought with Pompey: but these offers,
Which serve not for his vantage, he shakes off;
And so should you.

ENOBARBUS
                Your ships are not well mann'd, —
Your mariners are muleters, reapers, people
Ingross'd by swift impress; in Cæsar's fleet
Are those that often have 'gainst Pompey fought:
Their ships are yare; yours, heavy: no disgrace
Shall fall you for refusing him at sea,
Being prepared for land.

ANTONY
                By sea, by sea.

ENOBARBUS
Most worthy sir, you therein throw away
The absolute soldiership you have by land;
Distract your army, which doth most consist
Of war-mark'd footmen; leave unexecuted
Your own renowned knowledge; quite forgo
The way which promises assurance; and
Give up yourself merely to chance and hazard,
From firm security.

ANTONY
                I'll fight at sea.

OCTAVIA O, my good lord, believe not all.

CLEOPATRA
I have sixty sails, Cæsar none better.

ANTONY
Our overplus of shipping will we burn;
And, with the rest full-mann'd, from the head of Actium
Beat the approaching Cæsar. But if we fail,
We then can do't at land.

Enter a MESSENGER.
                Thy business?

MESSENGER
The news is true, my lord; he is descried;
Cæsar has taken Toryne.

ANTONY
Can he be there in person? 'tis impossible;
Strange that power should be. — Canidius,
Our nineteen legions thou shalt hold by land,
And our twelve thousand horse. — We'll to our ship:
Away, my Thetis!

Enter a SOLDIER.
                How now, worthy soldier?

SOLDIER
O noble emperor, do not fight by sea;
Trust not to rotten planks: do you misdoubt
This sword and these my wounds? Let the Egyptians
And the Phœnicians go a-ducking: we
Have us'd to conquer, standing on the earth,
And fighting foot to foot.

ANTONY
                Well, well: — away!
[*Exeunt* ANTONY, CLEOPATRA, *and* ENOBARBUS.

SOLDIER
By Hercules, I think I am i' the right.

CANIDIUS
Soldier, thou art: but his whole action grows
Not in the power on't: so our leader's led,
And we are women's men.

SOLDIER
                You keep by land
The legions and the horse whole, do you not?

CANIDIUS
Marcus Octavius, Marcus Justeius,
Publicola, and Cælius, are for sea:
But we keep whole by land. This speed of Cæsar's
Carries beyond belief.

SOLDIER
                While he was yet in Rome,
His power went out in such distractions as
Beguil'd all spies.

CANIDIUS
                Who's his lieutenant, hear you?

SOLDIER
They say, one Taurus.

CANIDIUS
                Well I know the man.

Enter a MESSENGER.

MESSENGER
The emperor calls Canidius.

CANIDIUS
With news the time's with labour, and throes forth
Each minute some. [*Exeunt.*

SCENE VIII

A plain near Actium.

Enter CAESAR *and* TAURUS, *with his army, marching.*

CAESAR
Taurus, —

TAURUS
My lord?

CAESAR
Strike not by land; keep whole: provoke not battle,
Till we have done at sea. Do not exceed
The prescript of this scroll: our fortune lies
Upon this jump. [*Exeunt.*

SCENE IX

Another part of the plain.

Enter ANTONY *and* ENOBARBUS.

ANTONY
Set we our squadrons on yond side o'the hill,
In eye of Cæsar's battle; from which place
We may the number of the ships behold,
And so proceed accordingly. [*Exeunt.*

SCENE X

Another part of the plain.

CANIDIUS *marcheth with his land army one way over
the stage; and* TAURUS, *the lieutenant of* CAESAR,
*the other way. After their going in, is heard the
noise of a sea-fight.*

Alarum. Enter ENOBARBUS.

ENOBARBUS
Naught, naught, all naught! I can behold no longer:
Th'Antoniad, the Egyptian admiral,
With all their sixty, fly and turn the rudder:
To see't mine eyes are blasted.

Enter SCARUS.

SCARUS
                        Gods and goddesses,
All the whole synod of them!

ENOBARBUS
                        What's thy passion?

SCARUS
The greater cantle of the world is lost
With very ignorance; we have kiss'd away
Kingdoms and provinces.

ENOBARBUS
                        How appears the fight?

SCARUS
On our side like the token'd pestilence,
Where death is sure. Yon ribaudred nag of Egypt, —
Whom leprosy o'ertake! — i' the midst o'the fight,
When vantage like a pair of twins appear'd,
Both as the same, or rather ours the elder, —
The breese upon her, like a cow in June, —
Hoists sails and flies.

ENOBARBUS
That I beheld:
Mine eyes did sicken at the sight, and could not
Endure a further view.

SCARUS
                        She once being looft,
The noble ruin of her magic, Antony,
Claps on his sea-wing, and, like a doting mallard,
Leaving the fight in height, flies after her:
I never saw an action of such shame;
Experience, manhood, honour, ne'er before
Did violate so itself.

ENOBARBUS
                        Alack, alack!

Enter CANIDIUS.

CANIDIUS
Our fortune on the sea is out of breath,
And sinks most lamentably. Had our general
Been what he knew himself, it had gone well:
O, he has given example for our flight
Most grossly, by his own!

ENOBARBUS
                        Ay, are you thereabouts?

Why, then, good night indeed.

CANIDIUS
Toward Peloponnesus are they fled.

SCARUS
'Tis easy to't; and there I will attend
What further comes.

CANIDIUS
                        To Cæsar will I render
My legions and my horse: six kings already
Show me the way of yielding.

ENOBARBUS
                        I'll yet follow
The wounded chance of Antony, though my reason
Sits in the wind against me. [*Exeunt.*

SCENE XI

Alexandria. A room in CLEOPATRA'S *palace.*

Enter ANTONY *with* ATTENDANTS.

ANTONY
Hark! the land bids me tread no more upon't, —
It is asham'd to bear me! — Friends, come hither:
I am so lated in the world, that I
Have lost my way for ever: — I have a ship
Laden with gold; take that, divide it; fly,
And make your peace with Cæsar.

ALL
                        Fly! not we.

ANTONY
I have fled myself; and have instructed cowards
To run and show their shoulders. — Friends, be gone;
I have myself resolv'd upon a course
Which has no need of you; be gone:
My treasure's in the harbour, take it. — O,
I follow'd that I blush to look upon:
My very hairs do mutiny; for the white
Reprove the brown for rashness, and they them
For fear and doting. — Friends, be gone: you shall
Have letters from me to some friends that will
Sweep your way for you. Pray you, look not sad,
Nor make replies of loathness: take the hint
Which my despair proclaims; let that be left
Which leaves itself: to the sea-side straightway:
I will possess you of that ship and treasure.
Leave me, I pray, a little: pray you now: —
Nay, do so; for, indeed, I have lost command,
Therefore I pray you: — I'll see you by and by.
[*Sits down.*

Enter CLEOPATRA *led by* CHARMIAN *and* IRAS;
EROS *following.*

EROS
Nay, gentle madam, to him, — comfort him.

IRAS
Do, most dear queen.

CHARMIAN
Do! why, what else?

CLEOPATRA
Let me sit down. O Juno!

ANTONY
No, no, no, no, no.

EROS
See you here, sir?

ANTONY
O fie, fie, fie!

CHARMIAN
Madam, —

IRAS
Madam, O good empress, —

EROS
Sir, sir, —

ANTONY
Yes, my lord, yes; — he at Philippi kept
His sword e'en like a dancer; while I struck
The lean and wrinkled Cassius; and 'twas I
That the mad Brutus ended: he alone
Dealt on lieutenantry, and no practice had
In the brave squares of war: yet now — No matter.

CLEOPATRA
Ah, stand by.

EROS
The queen, my lord, the queen.

IRAS
Go to him, madam, speak to him:
He is unqualitied with very shame.

CLEOPATRA
Well then, — sustain me: — O!

EROS
Most noble sir, arise; the queen approaches:

Her head's declin'd, and death will seize her, but
Your comfort makes the rescue.

ANTONY
I have offended reputation, —
A most unnoble swerving.

EROS
                        Sir, the queen.

ANTONY
O, whither hast thou led me, Egypt? See,
How I convey my shame out of thine eyes
By looking back what I have left behind
'Stroy'd in dishonour.

CLEOPATRA
                        O my lord, my lord,
Forgive my fearful sails! I little thought
You would have follow'd.

ANTONY
                        Egypt, thou knew'st too well
My heart was to thy rudder tied by the strings,
And thou shouldst tow me after: o'er my spirit
Thy full supremacy thou knew'st, and that
Thy beck might from the bidding of the gods
Command me.

CLEOPATRA
                        O, my pardon!

ANTONY
                        Now I must
To the young man send humble treaties, dodge
And palter in the shifts of lowness; who
With half the bulk o' the world play'd as I pleas'd,
Making and marring fortunes. You did know
How much you were my conqueror; and that
My sword, made weak by my affection, would
Obey it on all cause.

CLEOPATRA
                        Pardon, pardon!

ANTONY
Fall not a tear, I say; one of them rates
All that is won and lost: give me a kiss;
Even this repays me. — We sent our schoolmaster;
Is a'come back? — Love, I am full of lead. —
Some wine, within there, and our viands! — Fortune
knows
We scorn her most when most she offers blows.
[*Exeunt.*

SCENE XII

CAESAR'S *camp in Egypt.*

Enter CAESAR, DOLABELLA, THYREUS, *with others.*

CAESAR
Let him appear that's come from Antony. —
Know you him?

DOLABELLA
                        Cæsar, 'tis his schoolmaster:
An argument that he is pluck'd, when hither
He sends so poor a pinion of his wing,
Which had superfluous kings for messengers
Not many moons gone by.

Enter EUPHRONIUS, *ambassador from* ANTONY.

CAESAR
                        Approach, and speak.

EUPHRONIUS
Such as I am, I come from Antony:
I was of late as petty to his ends
As is the morn-dew on the myrtle-leaf
To his grand sea.

CAESAR
                        Be't so: — declare thine office.

EUPHRONIUS
Lord of his fortunes he salutes thee, and
Requires to live in Egypt; which not granted,
He lessens his requests; and to thee sues
To let him breathe between the heavens and earth,
A private man in Athens: this for him.
Next, Cleopatra does confess thy greatness;
Submits her to thy might; and of thee craves
The circle of the Ptolemies for her heirs,
Now hazarded to thy Grace.

CAESAR
                        For Antony,
I have no ears to his request. The queen
Of audience nor desire shall fail, so she
From Egypt drive her all-disgraced friend,
Or take his life there: this if she perform,
She shall not sue unheard. So to them both.

EUPHRONIUS
Fortune pursue thee!

ANTONY I have offended reputation, — a most unnoble swerving.

CAESAR
          Bring him through the bands.
                    [*Exit* EUPHRONIUS.
[*to* THYREUS] To try thy eloquence, now 'tis time:
   dispatch;
From Antony win Cleopatra: promise,
And in our name, what she requires: add more,
From thine invention, offers: women are not
In their best fortunes strong; but want will perjure
The ne'er-touch'd vestal: try thy cunning, Thyreus;
Make thine own edict for thy pains, which we
Will answer as a law.

THYREUS
          Cæsar, I go.

CAESAR
Observe how Antony becomes his flaw,
And what thou think'st his very action speaks
In every power that moves.

THYREUS
          Cæsar, I shall.   [*Exeunt.*

SCENE XIII

Alexandria. A room in CLEOPATRA'S *palace.*

Enter CLEOPATRA, ENOBARBUS,
CHARMIAN, *and* IRAS.

CLEOPATRA
What shall we do, Enobarbus?

ENOBARBUS
           Think, and die.

CLEOPATRA
Is Antony or we in fault for this?

ENOBARBUS
Antony only, that would make his will
Lord of his reason. What though you fled
From that great face of war, whose several ranges
Frighted each other? why should he follow?
The itch of his affection should not then
Have nick'd his captainship; at such a point,
When half to half the world oppos'd, he being
The mered question: 'twas a shame no less
Than was his loss, to course your flying flags,
And leave his navy gazing.

CLEOPATRA
          Prithee, peace.
Enter ANTONY *with* EUPHRONIUS, *the ambassador.*

ANTONY
Is that his answer?

EUPHRONIUS
Ay, my lord.

ANTONY
The queen shall, then, have courtesy, so she
Will yield us up.

EUPHRONIUS
          He says so.

ANTONY
               Let her know't. —
To the boy Cæsar send this grizzled head,
And he will fill thy wishes to the brim
With principalities.

CLEOPATRA
          That head, my lord?

ANTONY
To him again: tell him he wears the rose
Of youth upon him; from which the world should note
Something particular: his coin, ships, legions,
May be a coward's; whose ministers would prevail
Under the service of a child as soon
As i' the command of Cæsar: I dare him therefore
To lay his gay comparisons apart,
And answer me declined, sword against sword,
Ourselves alone. I'll write it: follow me.

        [*Exeunt* ANTONY *and* EUPHRONIUS.

ENOBARBUS [*aside*].
Yes, like enough, high-battled Cæsar will
Unstate his happiness, and be stag'd to the show,
Against a sworder! I see men's judgements are
A parcel of their fortunes; and things outward
Do draw the inward quality after them,
To suffer all alike. That he should dream,
Knowing all measures, the full Cæsar will
Answer his emptiness! — Cæsar, thou hast subdued
His judgement too.

        Enter an ATTENDANT.

ATTENDANT
         A messenger from Cæsar.

CLEOPATRA
What, no more ceremony? — See, my women! —
Against the blown rose may they stop their nose
That kneel'd unto the buds. — Admit him, sir.
               [*Exit* ATTENDANT.

ENOBARBUS [*aside*].
Mine honesty and I begin to square.
The loyalty well held to fools does make
Our faith mere folly: yet he that can endure
To follow with allegiance a fall'n lord
Does conquer him that did his master conquer,
And earns a place i' the story.

        Enter THYREUS.

CLEOPATRA
          Cæsar's will?

THYREUS
Hear it apart.

CLEOPATRA
         None but friends: say boldly.

THYREUS
So, haply, are they friends to Antony.

ENOBARBUS
He needs as many, sir, as Cæsar has;
Or needs not us. If Cæsar please, our master
Will leap to be his friend: for us, you know
Whose he is we are, and that is Cæsar's.

THYREUS
                  So. —
Thus then, thou most renown'd: Cæsar entreats,
Not to consider in what case thou stand'st,
Further than he is Cæsar.

CLEOPATRA
         Go on: right royal.

THYREUS
He knows that you embrace not Antony
As you did love, but as you fear'd him.

CLEOPATRA
                O!

THYREUS
The scars upon your honour, therefore, he
Does pity, as constrained blemishes,
Not as deserv'd.

CLEOPATRA
         He is a god, and knows
What is most right: mine honour was not yielded,
But conquer'd merely.

ENOBARBUS [*aside*].
           To be sure of that,
I will ask Antony. — Sir, sir, thou art so leaky,
That we must leave thee to thy sinking, for
Thy dearest quit thee.   [*Exit.*

THYREUS
         Shall I say to Cæsar
What you require of him? for he partly begs
To be desired to give. It much would please him,
That of his fortunes you should make a staff
To lean upon: but it would warm his spirits,
To hear from me you had left Antony,
And put yourself under his shroud,
The universal landlord.

CLEOPATRA
         What's your name?

THYREUS
My name is Thyreus.

CLEOPATRA
         Most kind messenger,
Say to great Cæsar this: — in deputation
I kiss his conquering hand: tell him, I am prompt
To lay my crown at's feet, and there to kneel:
Tell him, from his all-obeying breath I hear
The doom of Egypt.

THYREUS
         'Tis your noblest course.
Wisdom and fortune combating together,
If that the former dare but what it can,
No chance may shake it. Give me grace to lay
My duty on your hand.

CLEOPATRA
         Your Cæsar's father oft,
When he hath mus'd of taking kingdoms in,
Bestow'd his lips on that unworthy place,
As it rain'd kisses.

        Enter ANTONY *and* ENOBARBUS.

ANTONY
         Favours, by Jove that thunders! —
What art thou, fellow?

THYREUS
         One that but performs
The bidding of the fullest man, and worthiest
To have command obey'd.

ENOBARBUS [*aside*].
         You will be whipp'd.

ANTONY
Approach, there! — Ah, you kite! — Now, gods and
   devils!
Authority melts from me: of late, when I cried 'Ho!'
Like boys unto a muss, kings would start forth,
And cry 'Your will?' — Have you no ears? I am
Antony yet.

Enter ATTENDANTS.

Take hence this Jack, and whip him.

ENOBARBUS [*aside*].
'Tis better playing with a lion's whelp
Than with an old one dying.

ANTONY
Moon and stars! —
Whip him. — Were't twenty of the greatest tributaries
That do acknowledge Cæsar, should I find them
So saucy with the hand of she here, — what's her
   name,
Since she was Cleopatra? — Whip him, fellows,
Till, like a boy, you see him cringe his face,
And whine aloud for mercy: take him hence.

THYREUS
Mark Antony, —

ANTONY
Tug him away: being whipp'd,
Bring him again: — this Jack of Cæsar's shall
Bear us an errand to him.

[*Exeunt* ATTENDANTS *with* THYREUS.
You were half blasted ere I knew you: — ha!
Have I my pillow left unpress'd in Rome,
Forborne the getting of a lawful race,
And by a gem of women, to be abus'd
By one that looks on feeders?

CLEOPATRA
Good, my lord, —

ANTONY
You have been a boggler ever: —
But when we in our viciousness grow hard, —
O misery on't! — the wise gods seal our eyes;
In our own filth drop our clear judgements; make us
Adore our errors; laugh at's, while we strut
To our confusion.

CLEOPATRA
O, is't come to this?

ANTONY
I found you as a morsel cold upon
Dead Cæsar's trencher; nay, you were a fragment
Of Cneius Pompey's; besides what hotter hours,
Unregister'd in vulgar fame, you have
Luxuriously pick'd out: for, I am sure,
Though you can guess what temperance should be,
You know not what it is.

CLEOPATRA
Wherefore is this?

ANTONY
To let a fellow that will take rewards,
And say 'God quit you!' be familiar with
My playfellow, your hand; this kingly seal
And plighter of high hearts! — O, that I were
Upon the hill of Basan, to outroar
The horned herd! for I have savage cause;
And to proclaim it civilly, were like
A halter'd neck which does the hangman thank
For being yare about him.

Enter ATTENDANTS *with* THYREUS.
Is he whipp'd?

FIRST ATTENDANT
Soundly, my lord.

ANTONY
Cried he? and begg'd a' pardon?

FIRST ATTENDANT
He did ask favour.

ANTONY
If that thy father live, let him repent
Thou wast not made his daughter; and be thou sorry
To follow Cæsar in his triumph, since
Thou hast been whipp'd for following him: henceforth
The white hand of a lady fever thee,
Shake thou to look on't. — Get thee back to Cæsar,
Tell him thy entertainment: look thou say
He makes me angry with him; for he seems
Proud and disdainful, harping on what I am,
Not what he knew I was: he makes me angry;
And at this time most easy 'tis to do't,
When my good stars, that were my former guides
Have empty left their orbs, and shot their fires
Into th'abysm of hell. If he mislike
My speech and what is done, tell him he has
Hipparchus, my enfranched bondman, whom
He may at pleasure whip, or hang, or torture,
As he shall like, to quit me: urge it thou:
Hence with thy stripes, begone! [*Exit* THYREUS.

CLEOPATRA
Have you done yet?

ANTONY
Alack, our terrene moon
Is now eclips'd; and it portends alone

The fall of Antony!

CLEOPATRA
I must stay his time.

ANTONY
To flatter Cæsar, would you mingle eyes
With one that ties his points?

CLEOPATRA
Not know me yet?

ANTONY
Cold-hearted toward me?

CLEOPATRA
Ah, dear, if I be so,
From my cold heart let heaven engender hail,
And poison it in the source; and the first stone
Drop in my neck: as it determines, so
Dissolve my life! The next Cæsarion smite!
Till, by degrees, the memory of my womb,
Together with my brave Egyptians all,
By the discandying of this pelleted storm,
Lie graveless, — till the flies and gnats of Nile
Have buried them for prey!

ANTONY
I am satisfied.
Cæsar sits down in Alexandria; where
I will oppose his fate. Our force by land
Hath nobly held; our sever'd navy too
Have knit again, and fleet, threatening most sealike.
Where hast thou been, my heart? — Dost thou hear, lady?
If from the field I shall return once more
To kiss these lips, I will appear in blood;
I and my sword will earn our chronicle:
There's hope in't yet.

CLEOPATRA
That's my brave lord!

ANTONY
I will be treble-sinew'd, hearted, breathed,
And fight maliciously: for when mine hours
Were nice and lucky, men did ransom lives
Of me for jests; but now I'll set my teeth,
And send to darkness all that stop me. — Come,
Let's have one other gaudy night: call to me
All my sad captains, fill our bowls; once more
Let's mock the midnight bell.

CLEOPATRA
It is my birth-day:
I had thought t'have held it poor; but, since my lord
Is Antony again, I will be Cleopatra.

ANTONY
We will yet do well.

CLEOPATRA
Call all his noble captains to my lord.

ANTONY
Do so, we'll speak to them; and to-night I'll force
The wine peep through their scars. — Come on, my
   queen;
There's sap in't yet. The next time I do fight,
I'll make death love me; for I will contend
Even with his pestilent scythe.

[*Exeunt all but* ENOBARBUS.

ENOBARBUS
Now he'll outstare the lightning. To be furious,
Is to be frighted out of fear; and in that mood
The dove will peck the estridge; and I see still,
A diminution in our captain's brain
Restores his heart: when valour preys on reason,
It eats the sword it fights with. I will seek
Some way to leave him. [*Exit.*

ACT IV

SCENE I

CAESAR'S *camp at Alexandria.*

Enter CAESAR, AGRIPPA, *and* MAECENAS, *with his army;* CAESAR *reading a letter.*

CAESAR
He calls me boy; and chides, as he had power
To beat me out of Egypt; my messenger
He hath whipp'd with rods; dares me to personal
   combat,
Cæsar to Antony: — let the old ruffian know
I have many other ways to die; meantime
Laugh at his challenge.

MAECENAS
Cæsar must think,
When one so great begins to rage, he's hunted
Even to falling. Give him no breath, but now
Make boot of his distraction: — never anger
Made good guard for itself.

CAESAR
Let our best heads
Know, that to-morrow the last of many battles
We mean to fight: — within our files there are,
Of those that serv'd Mark Antony but late,
Enough to fetch him in. See it done:
And feast the army; we have store to do't,
And they have earn'd the waste. Poor Antony!

[*Exeunt.*

SCENE II

Alexandria. A room in CLEOPATRA'S *palace.*

Enter ANTONY, CLEOPATRA, ENOBARBUS,
CHARMIAN, IRAS, ALEXAS, *with others.*

ANTONY
He will not fight with me, Domitius.

ENOBARBUS
No.

ANTONY
Why should he not?

ENOBARBUS
He thinks, being twenty times of better fortune,
He is twenty men to one.

ANTONY
To-morrow, soldier,
By sea and land I'll fight: or I will live,
Or bathe my dying honour in the blood
Shall make it live again. Woo't thou fight well?

ENOBARBUS
I'll strike, and cry 'Take all.'

ANTONY
Well said; come on. —
Call forth my household servants: let's to-night
Be bounteous at our meal.

Enter three or four SERVITORS.
Give me thy hand,
Thou hast been rightly honest; — so hast thou; —
Thou, — and thou, — and thou: — you have serv'd me
   well,
And kings have been your fellows.

CLEOPATRA [*aside to* ENOBARBUS].
What means this?

ENOBARBUS [*aside to* CLEOPATRA].
'Tis one of those odd tricks which sorrow shoots
Out of the mind.

ANTONY
And thou art honest too.
I wish I could be made so many men,
And all of you clapp'd up together in
An Antony, that I might do you service
So good as you have done.

SERVANTS
The gods forbid!

ANTONY
Well, my good fellows, wait on me to-night:
Scant not my cups; and make as much of me
As when mine empire was your fellow too,
And suffer'd my command.

CLEOPATRA [*aside to* ENOBARBUS].
What does he mean?

ENOBARBUS [*aside to* CLEOPATRA].
To make his followers weep.

ANTONY
Tend me to-night;
May be it is the period of your duty:
Haply you shall not see me more; or if,
A mangled shadow: perchance to-morrow
You'll serve another master. I look on you
As one that takes his leave. Mine honest friends,
I turn you not away; but, like a master
Married to your good service, stay till death:
Tend me to-night two hours, I ask no more,
And the gods yield you for't!

ENOBARBUS
What mean you, sir,
To give them this discomfort? Look, they weep;
And I, an ass, am onion-eyed: for shame,
Transform us not to women.

ANTONY
Ho, ho, ho!
Now the witch take me, if I meant it thus!
Grace grow where those drops fall! My hearty friends,
You take me in too dolorous a sense;
For I spake to you for your comfort, — did desire you
To burn this night with torches: know, my hearts,
I hope well of to-morrow; and will lead you
Where rather I'll expect victorious life
Than death and honour. Let's to supper, come,
And drown consideration. [*Exeunt.*

SCENE III

The same. Before CLEOPATRA'S *palace.*

Enter a company of SOLDIERS.

FIRST SOLDIER
Brother, good night: to-morrow is the day.
SECOND SOLDIER
It will determine one way: fare you well.
Heard you of nothing strange about the streets?
FIRST SOLDIER
Nothing. What news?
SECOND SOLDIER
Belike 'tis but a rumour. Good night to you.
FIRST SOLDIER
Well, sir, good night.
                    They meet other SOLDIERS.
SECOND SOLDIER
Soldiers, have careful watch.
THIRD SOLDIER
And you. Good night, good night.
          [*They place themselves in every corner of the stage.*
FOURTH SOLDIER
Here we: and if to-morrow
Our navy thrive, I have an absolute hope
Our landmen will stand up.
THIRD SOLDIER
                    'Tis a brave army,
And full of purpose.
          [*Music of the hautboys as under the stage.*
FOURTH SOLDIER
                    Peace! what noise?
FIRST SOLDIER
                              List, list!
SECOND SOLDIER
Hark!
FIRST SOLDIER
          Music i' the air.
THIRD SOLDIER
                    Under the earth.
FOURTH SOLDIER
It signs well, does it not?
THIRD SOLDIER
                    No.
FIRST SOLDIER
                    Peace, I say!
What should this mean?
SECOND SOLDIER
'Tis the god Hercules, whom Antony lov'd,
Now leaves him.
FIRST SOLDIER
          Walk; let's see if other watchmen
Do hear what we do?   [*They advance to another post.*
SECOND SOLDIER
                    How now, masters!
SOLDIERS [*speaking together*].
                              How now!
How now! do you hear this?
FIRST SOLDIER
                    Ay; is't not strange?
THIRD SOLDIER
Do you hear, masters? do you hear?
FIRST SOLDIER
Follow the noise so far as we have quarter;
Let's see how it will give off.
SOLDIERS
Content. 'Tis strange.   [*Exeunt.*

SCENE IV

The same. A room in CLEOPATRA'S *palace.*

Enter ANTONY *and* CLEOPATRA, CHARMIAN,
IRAS, *and others attending.*

ANTONY
Eros! mine armour, Eros!
CLEOPATRA
                    Sleep a little.
ANTONY
No, my chuck. — Eros, come; mine armour, Eros!
          Enter EROS *with armour.*
Come, good fellow, put mine iron on: —
If fortune be not ours to-day, it is
Because we brave her: — come.
CLEOPATRA
                    Nay, I'll help too.
What's this for?
ANTONY
          Ah, let be, let be! thou art

The armourer of my heart: — false, false; this, this.
CLEOPATRA
Sooth, la, I'll help: thus it must be.
ANTONY
                    Well, well;
We shall thrive now. — Seest thou, my good fellow?
Go put on thy defences.
EROS
                    Briefly, sir.
CLEOPATRA
Is not this buckled well?
ANTONY
                    Rarely, rarely:
He that unbuckles this, till we do please
To daff't for our repose, shall hear a storm. —
Thou fumblest, Eros; and my queen's a squire
More tight at this than thou: dispatch. — O love,
That thou couldst see my wars to-day, and knew'st
The royal occupation! thou shouldst see
A workman in't.
          Enter an arm'd SOLDIER.
          Good morrow to thee; welcome:
Thou look'st like him that knows a warlike charge:
To business that we love we rise betime,
And go to't with delight.
SOLDIER
                    A thousand, sir,
Early though't be, have on their riveted trim,
And at the port expect you.
          [*Shout. Trumpets flourish.*

Enter CAPTAINS *and* SOLDIERS.

CAPTAIN
The morn is fair. — Good morrow, general.
ALL
Good morrow, general.
ANTONY
                    'Tis well blown, lads:
This morning, like the spirit of a youth
That means to be of note, begins betimes. —
So, so; come, give me that: this way; well
    said. —
Fare thee well, dame, whate'er becomes of
    me:
This is a soldier's kiss: rebukable, [*Kisses her.*
And worthy shameful check it were, to stand
On more mechanic compliment; I'll leave
    thee
Now, like a man of steel. — You that will
    fight,
Follow me close; I'll bring you to't. — Adieu.
          [*Exeunt* ANTONY, EROS,
          CAPTAINS, *and* SOLDIERS.
CHARMIAN
Please you, retire to your chamber.
CLEOPATRA
                    Lead me.
He goes forth gallantly. That he and Cæsar
    might
Determine this great war in single fight!
Then, Antony, — but now — Well, on.   [*Exeunt.*

SCENE V

ANTONY'S *camp near Alexandria.*

Trumpets sound. Enter ANTONY *and* EROS; *a*
SOLDIER *meeting them.*

SOLDIER
The gods make this a happy day to Antony!
ANTONY
Would thou and those thy scars had once prevail'd
To make me fight at land!
SOLDIER
                    Hadst thou done so,
The kings that have revolted, and the soldier
That has this morning left thee, would have still
Follow'd thy heels.
ANTONY
          Who's gone this morning?
SOLDIER
                              Who!
One ever near thee: call for Enobarbus,
He shall not hear thee; or from Cæsar's camp
Say 'I am none of thine.'
ANTONY
                    What say'st thou?
SOLDIER
                              Sir,
He is with Cæsar.

EROS
                    Sir, his chests and treasure
He has not with him.
ANTONY
                    Is he gone?
SOLDIER
                              Most certain.
ANTONY
Go, Eros, send his treasure after; do it;
Detain no jot, I charge thee: write to him —
I will subscribe — gentle adieus and greetings;
Say that I wish he never find more cause
To change a master. — O, my fortunes have
Corrupted honest men! — Dispatch. — Enobarbus!
          [*Exeunt.*

SCENE VI

CAESAR'S *camp before Alexandria.*

Flourish. Enter CAESAR *with* AGRIPPA,
ENOBARBUS, *and others.*

CAESAR
Go forth, Agrippa, and begin the fight:
Our will is Antony be took alive;

CAESAR He calls me boy.

Make it so known.
AGRIPPA
Cæsar, I shall.   [*Exit.*
CAESAR
The time of universal peace is near:
Prove this a prosperous day, the three-nook'd world
Shall bear the olive freely.
          Enter a MESSENGER.
MESSENGER
                    Antony
Is come into the field.
CAESAR
                    Go charge Agrippa
Plant those that have revolted in the van,
That Antony may seem to spend his fury
Upon himself.   [*Exeunt all but* ENOBARBUS.
ENOBARBUS
Alexas did revolt; and went to Jewry on
Affairs of Antony; there did persuade
Great Herod to incline himself to Cæsar,
And leave his master Antony: for this pains
Cæsar hath hang'd him. Canidius, and the rest
That fell away, have entertainment, but
No honourable trust. I have done ill;
Of which I do accuse myself so sorely,
That I will joy no more.
          Enter a SOLDIER *of* CAESAR'S.
SOLDIER
                    Enobarbus, Antony
Hath after thee sent all thy treasure, with

His bounty overplus: the messenger
Came on my guard; and at thy tent is now
Unloading of his mules.

ENOBARBUS
                        I give it you.

SOLDIER
Mock not, Enobarbus.
I tell you true: best you safed the bringer
Out of the host; I must attend mine office,
Or would have done't myself. Your emperor
Continues still a Jove.   [*Exit.*

ENOBARBUS
I am alone the villain of the earth,
And feel I am so most. O Antony,
Thou mine of bounty, how wouldst thou have paid
My better service, when my turpitude
Thou dost so crown with gold! This blows my heart:
If swift thought break it not, a swifter mean
Shall outstrike thought: but thought will do't, I feel.
I fight against thee! — No: I will go seek
Some ditch wherein to die; the foul'st best fits
My latter part of life.   [*Exit.*

SCENE VII

Field of battle between the camps.

Alarum. Drums and trumpets.
Enter AGRIPPA and others.

AGRIPPA
Retire, we have engaged ourselves too far:
Cæsar himself has work, and our oppression
Exceeds what we expected.   [*Exeunt.*
    Alarums. Enter ANTONY and SCARUS wounded.

SCARUS
O my brave emperor, this is fought indeed!
Had we done so at first, we had driven them home
With clouts about their heads.

ANTONY
                        Thou bleed'st apace.

SCARUS
I had a wound there that was like a T,
But now 'tis made an H.

ANTONY
                        They do retire.

SCARUS
We'll beat 'em into bench-holes: I have yet
Room for six scotches more.
                Enter EROS.

EROS
They are beaten, sir; and our advantage serves
For a fair victory.

SCARUS
                Let us score their backs,
And snatch 'em up, as we take hares, behind:
'Tis sport to maul a runner.

ANTONY
                        I will reward thee
Once for thy spritely comfort, and tenfold
For thy good valour. Come thee on.

SCARUS
                        I'll halt after.
                                [*Exeunt.*

SCENE VIII

Under the walls of Alexandria.

Alarums. Enter ANTONY again in a march;
SCARUS, with others.

ANTONY
We have beat him to his camp: — run one before,
And let the queen know of our gests. — To-morrow,
Before the sun shall see's, we'll spill the blood
That has to-day escap'd. I thank you all;
For doughty-handed are you, and have fought
Not as you serv'd the cause, but as't had been
Each man's like mine; you have shown all Hectors.
Enter the city, clip your wives, your friends,
Tell them your feats; whilst they with joyful tears
Wash the congealment from your wounds, and kiss
The honour'd gashes whole. — [*To* SCARUS] Give me
    thy hand;
            Enter CLEOPATRA, attended.
To this great fairy I'll commend thy acts,
Make her thanks bless thee. — [*To* CLEOPATRA] O
    thou day o' the world,
Chain mine arm'd neck; leap thou, attire and all,
Through proof of harness to my heart, and there
Ride on the pants triumphing!

CLEOPATRA
                        Lord of lords!
O infinite virtue, comest thou smiling from
The world's great snare uncaught?

ANTONY
                        My nightingale,
We have beat them to their beds. What, girl! though
    grey
Do something mingle with our younger brown, yet
    ha'we
A brain that nourishes our nerves, and can
Get goal for goal of youth. Behold this man;
Commend unto his lips thy favouring hand: —
Kiss it, my warrior: — he hath fought to-day
As if a god, in hate of mankind, had
Destroy'd in such a shape.

CLEOPATRA
                        I'll give thee, friend,
An armour all of gold; it was a king's.

ANTONY
He hath deserv'd it, were it carbuncled
Like holy Phoebus' car. — Give me thy hand: —
Through Alexandria make a jolly march;
Bear our hack'd targets like the men that owe them:
Had our great palace the capacity
To camp this host, we all would sup together,
And drink carouses to the next day's fate,
Which promises royal peril. — Trumpeters,
With brazen din blast you the city's ear;
Make mingle with rattling tabourines;
That heaven and earth may strike their sounds
    together,
Applauding our approach.   [*Exeunt.*

SCENE IX

CAESAR'S *camp.*

SENTINELS *at their post.*

FIRST SOLDIER
If we be not reliev'd within this hour,
We must return to the court-of-guard: the night
Is shiny; and they say we shall embattle
By the second hour i'the morn.

SECOND SOLDIER
                        This last day was
A shrewd one to's.
            Enter ENOBARBUS.
                O, bear me witness, night, —

THIRD SOLDIER
What man is this?

SECOND SOLDIER
                Stand close, and list him.

ENOBARBUS
Be witness to me, O thou blessed moon,
When men revolted shall upon record
Bear hateful memory, poor Enobarbus did
Before thy face repent! —

FIRST SOLDIER
                        Enobarbus!

THIRD SOLDIER
                                Peace!
Hark further.

ENOBARBUS
O sovereign mistress of true melancholy,
The poisonous damp of night dispunge
    upon me,
That life, a very rebel to my will,
May hang no longer on me: throw my heart
Against the flint and hardness of my fault;
Which, being dried with grief, will break to
    powder,
And finish all foul thoughts. O Antony,
Nobler than my revolt is infamous,
Forgive me in thine own particular;
But let the world rank me in register
A master-leaver and a fugitive.
O Antony! O Antony!   [*Dies.*

SECOND SOLDIER
                        Let's speak
To him.

FIRST SOLDIER
Let's hear him, for the things he speaks
May concern Cæsar.

THIRD SOLDIER
                Let's do so. But he sleeps.

FIRST SOLDIER
Swounds rather; for so bad a prayer as his
Was never yet for sleep.

SECOND SOLDIER
                        Go we to him,

THIRD SOLDIER
Awake, sir, awake; speak to us.

SECOND SOLDIER
                        Hear you, sir?

FIRST SOLDIER
The hand of death hath raught him. [*Drums afar off.*]
    Hark! the drums
Demurely wake the sleepers. Let us bear him
To the court-of-guard: he is of note: our hour
Is fully out.

THIRD SOLDIER
Come on, then;
He may recover yet.   [*Exeunt with the body.*

SCENE X

Ground between the two camps.

Enter ANTONY and SCARUS, with their ARMY.

ANTONY
Their preparation is to-day by sea;
We please them not by land.

SCARUS
                        For both, my lord.

ANTONY
I would they'ld fight i' the fire or i' the air;
We'ld fight there too. But this it is; our foot
Upon the hills adjoining to the city —
Where their appointment we may best discover,
And look on their endeavour —
Shall stay with us: order for sea is given;
They have put forth the haven.   [*Exeunt.*

SCENE XI

Another part of the same.

Enter CAESAR, and his Army.

CAESAR
But being charg'd, we will be still by land,
Which, as I take't, we shall; for his best force
Is forth to man his galleys. To the vales,
And hold our best advantage.   [*Exeunt.*

CLEOPATRA Is not this buckled well?

SCENE XII

Another part of the same.

Enter ANTONY *and* SCARUS.

ANTONY
Yet they are not join'd: where yond pine does stand,
I shall discover all: I'll bring thee word
Straight, how 'tis like to go.   [*Exit.*

SCARUS
             Swallows have built
In Cleopatra's sails their nests: the augurers
Say they know not, — they cannot tell; — look grimly,
And dare not speak their knowledge. Antony
Is valiant, and dejected; and, by starts,
His fretted fortunes give him hope, and fear,
Of what he has, and has not.

        [*Alarum afar off, as at a sea-fight.*

        Enter ANTONY.

ANTONY
             All is lost;
This foul Egyptian hath betrayed me:
My fleet hath yielded to the foe; and yonder
They cast their caps up, and carouse together
Like friends long lost. — Triple-turn'd whore! 'tis thou
Has sold me to this novice; and my heart
Makes only wars on thee. — Bid them all fly;
For when I am reveng'd upon my charm,
I have done all: — bid them all fly; begone.

        [*Exit* SCARUS.

O sun, thy uprise shall I see no more:
Fortune and Antony part here; even here
Do we shake hands. — All come to this? — The hearts
That spaniel'd me at heels, to whom I gave
Their wishes, do discandy, melt their sweets
On blossoming Cæsar; and this pine is bark'd,
That overtopp'd them all. Betray'd I am:
O this false soul of Egypt! this grave charm, —
Whose eye beck'd forth my wars, and call'd them
    home;
Whose bosom was my crownet, my chief end, —
Like a right gipsy, hath, at fast and loose,
Beguil'd me to the very heart of loss. —
What, Eros, Eros!

        Enter CLEOPATRA.
        Ah, thou spell! Avaunt!

CLEOPATRA
Why is my lord enrag'd against his love?

ANTONY
Vanish, or I shall give thee thy deserving,
And blemish Cæsar's triumph. Let him take thee,
And hoist thee up to the shouting plebeians:
Follow his chariot, like the greatest spot
Of all thy sex; most monster-like, be shown
For poor'st diminutives, for doits; and let
Patient Octavia plough thy visage up
With her prepared nails.   [*Exit* CLEOPATRA.
        'Tis well th'art gone,
If it be well to live; but better 'twere
Thou fell'st into my fury, for one death
Might have prevented many. — Eros, ho! —
The shirt of Nessus is upon me: — teach me,
Alcides, thou mine ancestor, thy rage:
Let me lodge Lichas on the horns o'the moon;
And with those hands, that grasp'd the heaviest club,
Subdue my worthiest self. The witch shall die:
To the young Roman boy she hath sold me, and I fall
Under this plot; she dies for't. — Eros, ho!   [*Exit.*

SCENE XIII

Alexandria. A room in CLEOPATRA'S *palace.*

Enter CLEOPATRA, CHARMIAN, IRAS, *and*
MARDIAN.

CLEOPATRA
Help me, my women! O, he is more mad
Than Telamon for his shield; the boar of Thessaly
Was never so emboss'd.

CHARMIAN
           To the monument!
There lock yourself, and send him word you are dead.
The soul and body rive not more in parting
Than greatness going off.

CLEOPATRA
           To the monument! —
Mardian, go tell him I have slain myself;
Say, that the last I spoke was 'Antony,'
And word it, prithee, piteously: hence, Mardian,
And bring me how he takes my death. — To the
    monument!   [*Exeunt.*

SCENE XIV

The same. Another room.

Enter ANTONY *and* EROS.

ANTONY
Eros, thou yet behold'st me?

EROS
           Ay, noble lord.

ANTONY
Sometime we see a cloud that's dragonish;
A vapour sometime like a bear or lion,
A tower'd citadel, a pendant rock,
A forked mountain, or blue promontory
With trees upon't, that nod unto the world,
And mock our eyes with air: thou hast seen these signs;
They are black vesper's pageants.

EROS
           Ay, my lord,

ANTONY
That which is now a horse, even with a thought
The rack dislimns, and makes it indistinct
As water is in water.

EROS
           It does, my lord.

ANTONY
My good knave Eros, now thy captain is
Even such a body: here I am Antony;
Yet cannot hold this visible shape, my knave.
I made these wars for Egypt; and the queen, —
Whose heart I thought I had, for she had mine;
Which, whilst it was mine, had annex'd unto't
A million moe, now lost, — she, Eros, has
Pack'd cards with Cæsar, and false-play'd my glory
Unto an enemy's triumph. —
Nay, weep not, gentle Eros; there is left us
Ourselves to end ourselves.

        Enter MARDIAN.
        O, thy vile lady!
She has robb'd me of my sword.

MARDIAN
           No, Antony;
My mistress lov'd thee, and her fortunes mingled
With thine entirely.

ANTONY
        Hence, saucy eunuch; peace!
She hath betray'd me, and shall die the death.

MARDIAN
Death of one person can be paid but once,
And that she has discharg'd: what thou wouldst do
Is done unto thy hand: the last she spake
Was, 'Antony! most noble Antony!'
Then in the midst a tearing groan did break
The name of Antony; it was divided
Between her heart and lips: she render'd life,
Thy name so buried in her.

ANTONY
        Dead, then?

MARDIAN
           Dead.

ANTONY
Unarm, Eros; the long day's task is done,
And we must sleep. — [*to* MARDIAN] That thou
    depart'st hence safe,
Does pay thy labour richly; go.   [*Exit* MARDIAN.
        Off, pluck off: —
The seven-fold shield of Ajax cannot keep
The battery from my heart. O, cleave, my sides!
Heart, once be stronger than thy continent,
Crack thy frail case! — Apace, Eros, apace. —
No more a soldier: — bruised pieces, go;
You have been nobly borne. — From me awhile.

        [*Exit* EROS.

I will o'ertake thee, Cleopatra, and
Weep for my pardon. So it must be, for now
All length is torture: — since the torch is out,
Lie down, and stray no farther, now all labour
Mars what it does; yea, very force entangles
Itself with strength: seal then, and all is done. —
Eros! — I come, my queen. — Eros! — Stay for me:
Where souls do couch on flowers, we'll hand in hand,
And with our sprightly port make the ghosts gaze:
Dido and her Aeneas shall want troops,
And all the haunt be ours. — Come, Eros, Eros!

        Enter EROS.

EROS
What would my lord?

ANTONY
        Since Cleopatra died,
I have liv'd in such dishonour, that the gods
Detest my baseness. I, that with my sword
Quarter'd the world, and o'er green Neptune's back
With ships made cities, condemn myself to lack
The courage of a woman; less noble mind
Than she which by her death our Cæsar tells
'I am conqueror of myself.' Thou art sworn, Eros,
That, when the exigent should come, — which now
Is come indeed, — when I should see behind me
Th'inevitable prosecution of
Disgrace and horror, that, on my command,
Thou then wouldst kill me: do't; the time is come:
Thou strikest not me, 'tis Cæsar thou defeat'st.
Put colour in thy cheek.

EROS
        The gods withhold me!
Shall I do that which all the Parthian darts,
Though enemy, lost aim, and could not?

ANTONY
           Eros,
Wouldst thou be window'd in great Rome, and see
Thy master thus with pleach'd arms, bending down
His corrigible neck, his face subdued
To penetrative shame, whilst the wheel'd seat
Of fortunate Cæsar, drawn before him, branded
His baseness that ensued?

EROS
        I would not see't.

THIRD SOLDIER Awake, sir, awake; speak to us.

ANTONY
Come, then; for with a wound I must be cured.
Draw that thy honest sword, which thou hast worn
Most useful for thy country.

EROS
     O, sir, pardon me!

ANTONY
When I did make thee free, sworest thou not then
To do this when I bade thee? Do it at once;
Or thy precedent services are all
But accidents unpurpos'd. Draw, and come.

EROS
Turn from me, then, that noble countenance,
Wherein the worship of the whole world lies.

ANTONY
Lo thee!   *[Turning from him.*

EROS
My sword is drawn.

ANTONY
    Then let it do at once
The thing why thou hast drawn it.

EROS
      My dear master,
My captain, and my emperor, let me say,
Before I strike this bloody stroke, farewell.

ANTONY
'Tis said, man; — and farewell.

EROS
Farewell, great chief. Shall I strike now?

ANTONY
      Now, Eros.

EROS
Why, there then *[kills himself]*: thus I do escape the
  sorrow
Of Antony's death.   *[Dies.*

ANTONY
    Thrice-nobler than myself!
Thou teachest me, O valiant Eros, what
I should, and thou couldst not. My queen and Eros
Have by their brave instruction got upon me
A nobleness in record: but I will be
A bridegroom in my death, and run into't
As to a lover's bed. Come, then; and, Eros,
Thy master dies thy scholar: to do thus
     [Falling on his sword.
I learnt of thee. How! not dead? not dead? —
The guard, ho! — O, dispatch me!

Enter DERCETAS *and* GUARD.

FIRST GUARD
     What's the noise?

ANTONY
I have done my work ill, friends: O, make an end
Of what I have begun.

SECOND GUARD
    The star is fall'n.

FIRST GUARD
And time is at his period.

ALL
     Alas, and woe!

ANTONY
Let him that loves me strike me dead.

FIRST GUARD
     Not I.

SECOND GUARD
Nor I.

THIRD GUARD
Nor any one.   *[Exeunt* GUARD.

DERCETAS
Thy death and fortunes bid thy followers fly.
This sword but shown to Cæsar, with this tidings,
Shall enter me with him.

Enter DIOMEDES.

DIOMEDES
Where's Antony?

DERCETAS
    There, Diomed, there.

DIOMEDES
      Lives he?
Wilt thou not answer, man?   *[Exit* DERCETAS.

ANTONY
Art thou there, Diomed? Draw thy sword, and give me
Sufficing strokes for death.

DIOMEDES
    Most absolute lord,
My mistress Cleopatra sent me to thee.

ANTONY
When did she send thee?

DIOMEDES
     Now, my lord.

ANTONY
      Where is she?

DIOMEDES
Lock'd in her monument. She had a prophesying fear
Of what hath come to pass: for when she saw —
Which never shall be found — you did suspect
She had dispos'd with Cæsar, and that your rage
Would not be purg'd, she sent you word she was dead;
But, fearing since how it might work, hath sent
Me to proclaim the truth; and I am come,
I dread, too late.

ANTONY
Too late, good Diomed: — call my guard, I prithee.

DIOMEDES
What, ho, the emperor's guard! The guard, what, ho!
Come, your lord calls!

Enter four or five of the GUARD *of* ANTONY.

ANTONY
Bear me, good friends, where Cleopatra bides;
'Tis the last service that I shall command you.

FIRST GUARD
Woe, woe are we, sir, you may not live to wear
All your true followers out.

ALL
    Most heavy day!

ANTONY
Nay, good my fellows, do not please sharp fate
To grace it with your sorrows: bid that welcome
Which comes to punish us, and we punish it
Seeming to bear it lightly. Take me up:
I have led you oft: carry me now, good friends,
And have my thanks for all.
   [Exeunt, bearing ANTONY.

SCENE XV

The same. A monument.

Enter CLEOPATRA *and her* MAIDS *aloft, with*
CHARMIAN *and* IRAS.

CLEOPATRA
O Charmian, I will never go from hence.

CHARMIAN
Be comforted, dear madam.

CLEOPATRA
     No, I will not:
All strange and terrible events are welcome,
But comforts we despise; our size of sorrow
Proportion'd to our cause, must be as great
As that which makes it.

Enter, below, DIOMEDES.
     How now! is he dead?

DIOMEDES
His death's upon him, but not dead.
Look out o' the other side your monument;
His guard have brought him thither.

Enter, below, ANTONY, *borne by the* GUARD.

CLEOPATRA
      O sun,
Burn the great sphere thou mov'st in! — darkling stand
The varying shore o' the world. — O Antony,
Antony, Antony! — Help, Charmian; help, Iras, help;
—
Help, friends below! — let's draw him hither.

ANTONY
      Peace!
Not Cæsar's valour hath o'erthrown Antony,
But Antony's hath triumph'd on itself.

CLEOPATRA
So it should be, that none but Antony
Should conquer Antony; but woe 'tis so!

ANTONY
I am dying, Egypt, dying; only
I here importune death awhile, until
Of many thousand kisses the poor last
I lay upon thy lips.

CLEOPATRA
    I dare not, dear, —
Dear my lord, pardon, — I dare not,
Lest I be taken: not th'imperious show
Of the full-fortun'd Cæsar ever shall
Be brooch'd with me; if knife, drugs, serpents, have
Edge, sting, or operation, I am safe:
Your wife Octavia, with her modest eyes
And still conclusion, shall acquire no honour
Demuring upon me. — But, come, come, Antony, —
Help me, my women, — we must draw thee up; —
Assist, good friends.

ANTONY
    O, quick, or I am gone.

CLEOPATRA
Here's sport indeed! — How heavy weighs my lord!
Our strength is all gone into heaviness;
That makes the weight: had I great Juno's power,
The strong-wing'd Mercury should fetch thee up,
And set thee by Jove's side. Yet come a little, —
Wishers were ever fools, — O, come, come, come;
  [They heave ANTONY *aloft to* CLEOPATRA.
And welcome, welcome! die where thou hast liv'd:
Quicken with kissing: had my lips that power,
Thus would I wear them out.

ALL
     A heavy sight!

ANTONY
I am dying, Egypt, dying:
Give me some wine, and let me speak a little.

CLEOPATRA
No, let me speak; and let me rail so high,
That the false housewife Fortune break her wheel,
Provok'd by my offence.

ANTONY
    One word, sweet queen:
Of Cæsar seek your honour, with your safety. — O!

CLEOPATRA
They do not go together.

ANTONY
    Gentle, hear me:
None about Cæsar trust but Proculeius.

CLEOPATRA
My resolution and my hands I'll trust;
None about Cæsar.

ANTONY
The miserable change now at my end
Lament nor sorrow at; but please your thoughts
In feeding them with those my former fortunes,
Wherein I liv'd, the greatest prince o' the world,
The noblest; and do now not basely die,
Not cowardly put off my helmet to
My countryman, — a Roman by a Roman
Valiantly vanquish'd. Now my spirit is going;
I can no more.

CLEOPATRA
    Noblest of men, woo't die?
Hast thou no care of me? shall I abide
In this dull world, which in thy absence is
No better than a sty? — O, see, my women,
      *[*ANTONY *dies.*
The crown o'the earth doth melt. — My lord!
O, wither'd is the garland of the war,
The soldiers' pole is fall'n: young boys and girls
Are level now with men; the odds is gone,
And there is nothing left remarkable
Beneath the visiting moon.   *[Faints.*

CHARMIAN
    O, quietness, lady!

IRAS
She is dead too, our sovereign.

CHARMIAN
     Lady!

IRAS
      Madam!

CHARMIAN
O madam, madam, madam!

IRAS
    Royal Egypt, Empress!

CHARMIAN
Peace, peace, Iras!

CLEOPATRA
No more, but e'en a woman, and commanded
By such poor passion as the maid that milks
And does the meanest chares. — It were for me
To throw my sceptre at the injurious gods;
To tell them that this world did equal theirs
Till they had stol'n our jewel. All's but naught;
Patience is sottish, and impatience does
Become a dog that's mad; then is it sin
To rush into the secret house of death,
Ere death dare come to us? — How do you, women?
What, what! good cheer! Why, how now, Charmian!
My noble girls! Ah, women, women, look,
Our lamp is spent, it's out! Good sirs, take heart: —
We'll bury him, and then, what's brave, what's noble,
Let's do it after the high Roman fashion,
And make death proud to take us. Come, away:
This case of that huge spirit now is cold:
Ah, women, women! come; we have no friend
But resolution, and the briefest end.
  [Exeunt; those above bearing off ANTONY'S *body.*

ANTONY I have done my work ill, friends.

ACT V

SCENE I

CAESAR'S *camp before Alexandria.*

Enter CAESAR, AGRIPPA,
DOLABELLA, MAECENAS, GALLUS,
PROCULEIUS, *and others.*

CAESAR
Go to him, Dolabella, bid him yield;
Being so frustrate, tell him he mocks
The pauses that he makes.
DOLABELLA
    Cæsar, I shall. [*Exit.*
Enter DERCETAS, *with the sword of* ANTONY.

CAESAR
Wherefore is that? and what art thou that darest
Appear thus to us?
DERCETAS
   I am call'd Dercetas;
Mark Antony I serv'd, who best was worthy
Best to be serv'd: whilst he stood up and spoke,
He was my master; and I wore my life
To spend upon his haters. If thou please
To take me to thee, as I was to him
I'll be to Cæsar; if thou pleasest not,
I yield thee up my life.
CAESAR
    What is't thou say'st?
DERCETAS
I say, O Cæsar, Antony is dead.
CAESAR
The breaking of so great a thing should make
A greater crack: the round world
Should have shook lions into civil streets,
And citizens to their dens. The death of Antony
Is not a single doom; in the name lay
A moiety of the world.
DERCETAS
    He is dead, Cæsar;
Not by a public minister of justice,
Nor by a hired knife; but that self hand,
Which writ his honour in the acts it did,
Hath, with the courage which the heart did lend it,
Splitted the heart. — This is his sword;
I robb'd his wound of it; behold it stain'd
With his most noble blood.
CAESAR
    Look you sad, friends?
The gods rebuke me, but it is tidings
To wash the eyes of kings.
AGRIPPA
    And strange it is
That nature must compel us to lament
Our most persisted deeds.
MAECENAS
    His taints and honours
Wag'd equal with him.

AGRIPPA
    A rarer spirit never
Did steer humanity: but you, gods, will give us
Some faults to make us men. Cæsar is touch'd.
MAECENAS
When such a spacious mirror's set before him,
He needs must see himself.
CAESAR
    O Antony!
I have follow'd thee to this: — but we do lance
Diseases in our bodies: I must perforce
Have shown to thee such a declining day,
Or look on thine; we could not stall together
In the whole world: but yet let me lament,
With tears as sovereign as the blood of hearts,
That thou, my brother, my competitor
In top of all design, my mate in empire,
Friend and companion in the front of war,
The arm of mine own body, and the heart
Where mine his thoughts did kindle, — that our stars,
Unreconciliable, should divide
Our equalness to this. — Hear me, good friends, —
But I will tell you at some meeter season:
   Enter a MESSENGER.
The business of this man looks out of him;
We'll hear him what he says. — Whence are you?
MESSENGER
A poor Egyptian yet. The queen my mistress,
Confin'd in all she has, her monument,
Of thy intents desires instruction,
That she preparedly may frame herself
To the way she's forc'd to.
CAESAR
    Bid her have good heart:
She soon shall know of us, by some of ours,
How honourable and how kindly we
Determine for her; for Cæsar cannot live
To be ungentle.
MESSENGER
    So the gods preserve thee! [*Exit.*
CAESAR
Come hither, Proculeius. Go, and say
We purpose her no shame: give her what comforts
The quality of her passion shall require,
Lest, in her greatness, by some mortal stroke
She do defeat us; for her life in Rome
Would be eternal in our triumph: go,
And with your speediest bring us what she says,
And how you find of her.
PROCULEIUS
    Cæsar, I shall. [*Exit.*
CAESAR
Gallus, go you along. [*Exit* GALLUS.] Where's
 Dolabella,
To second Proculeius?
AGRIPPA, MAECENAS, *etc.*
    Dolabella!
CAESAR
Let him alone, for I remember now
How he's employ'd: he shall in time be ready.
Go with me to my tent; where you shall see
How hardly I was drawn into this war;

How calm and gentle I proceeded still
In all my writings: go with me, and see
What I can show in this. [*Exeunt.*

SCENE II

Alexandria. A room in the monument.

Enter CLEOPATRA, CHARMIAN, *and* IRAS.

CLEOPATRA
My desolation does begin to make
A better life. 'Tis paltry to be Cæsar;
Not being Fortune, he's but Fortune's knave,
A minister of her will: and it is great
To do that thing that ends all other deeds;
Which shackles accidents, and bolts up change;
Which sleeps, and never palates more the dug,
The beggar's nurse and Cæsar's.
 Enter, to the gates of the monument, PROCULEIUS,
  GALLUS, *and* SOLDIERS.

PROCULEIUS
Cæsar sends greeting to the Queen of Egypt;
And bids thee study on what fair demands
Thou mean'st to have him grant thee.
CLEOPATRA
    What's thy name?
PROCULEIUS
My name is Proculeius.
CLEOPATRA
    Antony
Did tell me of you, bade me trust you; but
I do not greatly care to be deceived,
That have no use for trusting. If your master
Would have a queen his beggar, you must tell him,
That majesty, to keep decorum, must
No less beg than a kingdom: if he please
To give me conquer'd Egypt for my son,
He gives me so much of mine own as I
Will kneel to him with thanks.
PROCULEIUS
    Be of good cheer,
Y' are fall'n into a princely hand, fear nothing:
Make your full reference freely to my lord,
Who is so full of grace, that it flows over
On all that need: let me report to him
Your sweet dependency; and you shall find
A conqueror that will pray in aid for kindness,
Where he for grace is kneel'd to.
CLEOPATRA
    Pray you, tell him
I am his fortune's vassal, and I send him
The greatness he has got. I hourly learn
A doctrine of obedience; and would gladly
Look him i' the face.
PROCULEIUS
    This I'll report, dear lady.
Have comfort, for I know your plight is pitied
Of him that caus'd it.
GALLUS
You see how easily she may be surprised:
 [*Here* PROCULEIUS *and two of the* GUARD *ascend*
  the monument by a ladder placed against a window,
  and, having descended, come behind CLEOPATRA.
  Some of the GUARD *unbar and open the gates.*
[*to* PROCULEIUS *and the* GUARD]
Guard her till Cæsar come. [*Exit.*
IRAS
Royal queen!
CHARMIAN
O Cleopatra! thou art taken, queen!
CLEOPATRA
Quick, quick, good hands. [*Drawing a dagger.*
PROCULEIUS
    Hold, worthy lady, hold:
    [*Seizes and disarms her.*
Do not yourself such wrong, who are in this
Reliev'd, but not betray'd.
CLEOPATRA
    What, of death too,
That rids our dogs of languish?
PROCULEIUS
    Cleopatra,
Do not abuse my master's bounty by
Th'undoing of yourself: let the world see
His nobleness well acted, which your death
Will never let come forth.
CLEOPATRA
    Where art thou, death?
Come hither, come! come, come, and take a queen
Worth many babes and beggars!

PROCULEIUS
                    O, temperance, lady!
CLEOPATRA
Sir, I will eat no meat, I'll not drink, sir;
If idle talk will once be necessary,
I'll not sleep neither: this mortal house I'll ruin,
Do Cæsar what he can. Know, sir, that I
Will not wait pinion'd at your master's court;
Nor once be chastis'd with the sober eye
Of dull Octavia. Shall they hoist me up,
And show me to the shouting varletry
Of censuring Rome? Rather a ditch in Egypt
Be gentle grave unto me! rather on Nilus' mud
Lay me stark-naked, and let the water-flies
Blow me into abhorring! rather make
My country's high pyramides my gibbet,
And hang me up in chains!
PROCULEIUS
                    You do extend
These thoughts of horror further than you shall
Find cause in Cæsar.

Enter DOLABELLA.

DOLABELLA
                    Proculeius,
What thou hast done thy master Cæsar knows,
And he hath sent for thee: for the queen,
I'll take her to my guard.
PROCULEIUS
                    So, Dolabella,
It shall content me best: be gentle to her. —
[to CLEOPATRA] To Cæsar I will speak what you shall
    please,
If you'll employ me to him.
CLEOPATRA
                    Say, I would die.
    [*Exeunt* PROCULEIUS *and* SOLDIERS
DOLABELLA
Most noble empress, you have heard of me?
CLEOPATRA
I cannot tell.
DOLABELLA
                    Assuredly you know me.
CLEOPATRA
No matter, sir, what I have heard or known.
You laugh when boys or women tell their dreams;
Is't not your trick?
DOLABELLA
                    I understand not, madam.
CLEOPATRA
I dreamt there was an emperor Antony: —
O, such another sleep, that I might see
But such another man!
DOLABELLA
                    If it might please ye, —
CLEOPATRA
His face was as the heavens; and therein stuck
A sun and moon, which kept their course, and lighted
The little O, the earth.
DOLABELLA
                    Most sovereign creature, —
CLEOPATRA
His legs bestrid the ocean: his rear'd arm
Crested the world; his voice was propertied
As all the tuned spheres, and that to friends;
But when he meant to quail and shake the orb,
He was as rattling thunder. For his bounty,
There was no winter in't; an autumn 'twas
That grew the more by reaping: his delights
Were dolphin-like; they show'd his back above
The element they liv'd in: in his livery
Walk'd crowns and crownets; realms and islands were
As plates dropp'd from his pocket.
DOLABELLA
                    Cleopatra, —
CLEOPATRA
Think you there was, or might be, such a man
As this I dreamt of?
DOLABELLA
                    Gentle madam, no.
CLEOPATRA
You lie, up to the hearing of the gods.
But, if there be, or ever were, one such,
It's past the size of dreaming: nature wants stuff
To vie strange forms with fancy; yet, t'imagine
An Antony, were nature's piece 'gainst fancy,
Condemning shadows quite.
DOLABELLA
                    Hear me, good madam.
Your loss is as yourself, great; and you bear it

As answering to the weight: would I might never
O'ertake pursued success, but I do feel,
By the rebound of yours, a grief that smites
My very heart at root.
CLEOPATRA
                    I thank you, sir.
Know you what Cæsar means to do with me?
DOLABELLA
I am loth to tell you what I would you knew.
CLEOPATRA
Nay, pray you, sir, —
DOLABELLA
                    Though he be honourable, —
CLEOPATRA
He'll lead me, then, in triumph?
DOLABELLA
Madam, he will; I know't.   [*Flourish and shout within,*
                    'Make way there, — Cæsar!'

Enter CAESAR, GALLUS, PROCULEIUS,
MAECENAS, SELEUCUS, *and others of his* TRAIN.

CAESAR
Which is the Queen of Egypt?
DOLABELLA
It is the emperor, madam.   [CLEOPATRA *kneels.*
CAESAR
Arise, you shall not kneel:
I pray you, rise; rise, Egypt.
CLEOPATRA
                    Sir, the gods
Will have it thus; my master and my lord
I must obey.
CAESAR
                    Take to you no hard thoughts:
The record of what injuries you did us,
Though written in our flesh, we shall remember
As things but done by chance.
CLEOPATRA
                    Sole sir o'the world,
I cannot project mine own cause so well
To make it clear; but do confess I have
Been laden with like frailties which before
Have often sham'd our sex.
CAESAR
                    Cleopatra, know,
We will extenuate rather than enforce:
If you apply yourself to our intents, —
Which towards you are most gentle, — you shall find
A benefit in this change; but if you seek
To lay on me a cruelty, by taking
Antony's course, you shall bereave yourself
Of my good purposes, and put your children
To that destruction which I'll guard them from,
If thereon you rely. I'll take my leave.
CLEOPATRA
And may, through all the world: 'tis yours; and we,
Your scutcheons and your signs of conquest, shall
Hang in what place you please. Here, my good lord.
CAESAR
You shall advise me in all for Cleopatra.
CLEOPATRA
This is the brief of money, plate, and jewels,
I am possess'd of: 'tis exactly valued;
Not petty things omitted. — Where's Seleucus?
SELEUCUS
Here, madam.
CLEOPATRA
This is my treasurer: let him speak, my lord,
Upon his peril, that I have reserv'd
To myself nothing. — Speak the truth, Seleucus.
SELEUCUS
Madam,
I had rather seal my lips than, to my peril,
Speak that which is not.
CLEOPATRA
                    What have I kept back?
SELEUCUS
Enough to purchase what you have made known.
CAESAR
Nay, blush not, Cleopatra: I approve
Your wisdom in the deed.
CLEOPATRA
                    See, Cæsar! O, behold,
How pomp is follow'd! mine will now be yours;
And, should we shift estates, yours would be mine.
The ingratitude of this Seleucus does
Even make me wild: — O slave, of no more trust
Than love that's hired! — What, goest thou back? thou
shalt

Go back, I warrant thee; but I'll catch thine eyes,
Though they had wings: slave, soulless villain, dog!
O rarely base!
CAESAR
                    Good queen, let us entreat you.
CLEOPATRA
O Cæsar, what a wounding shame is this, —
That thou, vouchsafing here to visit me,
Doing the honour of thy lordliness
To one so meek, that mine own servant should
Parcel the sum of my disgraces by
Addition of his envy! Say, good Cæsar,
That I some lady trifles have reserv'd,
Immoment toys, things of such dignity
As we greet modern friends withal; and say,
Some nobler token I have kept apart
For Livia and Octavia, to induce
Their mediation; must I be unfolded
With one that I have bred? The gods! it smites me
Beneath the fall I have. — [to SELEUCUS] Prithee, go
    hence;
Or I shall show the cinders of my spirits
Through the ashes of my chance: wert thou a man,
Thou wouldst have mercy on me.
CAESAR
                    Forbear, Seleucus.   [*Exit* SELEUCUS.
CLEOPATRA
Be it known that we, the greatest, are misthought
For things that others do; and, when we fall,
We answer others' merits in our name,
Are therefore to be pitied.
CAESAR
                    Cleopatra,
Not what you have reserv'd, nor what acknowledg'd,
Put we i'the roll of conquest: still be't yours,
Bestow it at your pleasure; and believe,
Cæsar's no merchant, to make prize with you
Of things that merchants sold. Therefore be cheer'd;
Make not your thoughts your prisons: no, dear queen;
For we intend so to dispose you as
Yourself shall give us counsel. Feed, and sleep:
Our care and pity is so much upon you,
That we remain your friend; and so, adieu.
CLEOPATRA
My master, and my lord!
CAESAR
                    Not so. Adieu.
    [*Flourish. Exeunt* CAESAR *and his* TRAIN.
CLEOPATRA
He words me, girls, he words me, that I should not
Be noble to myself: but, hark thee, Charmian.
                    [*Whispers* CHARMIAN.
IRAS
Finish, good lady; the bright day is done,
And we are for the dark.
CLEOPATRA
                    Hie thee again:
I have spoke already, and it is provided;
Go put it to the haste.
CHARMIAN
                    Madam, I will.

Enter DOLABELLA.

DOLABELLA
Where is the queen?
CHARMIAN
                    Behold, sir.   [*Exit.*
CLEOPATRA
                    Dolabella!
DOLABELLA
Madam, as thereto sworn by your command,
Which my love makes religion to obey,
I tell you this: Cæsar through Syria
Intends his journey; and, within three days,
You with your children will he send before:
Make your best use of this: I have perform'd
Your pleasure and my promise.
CLEOPATRA
                    Dolabella,
I shall remain your debtor.
DOLABELLA
                    I your servant.
Adieu, good queen; I must attend on Cæsar.
CLEOPATRA
Farewell, and thanks.   [*Exit* DOLABELLA.
                    Now, Iras, what think'st thou?
Thou, an Egyptian puppet, shalt be shown
In Rome, as well as I: mechanic slaves,
With greasy aprons, rules, and hammers, shall
Uplift us to the view; in their thick breaths,

Rank of gross diet, shall we be enclouded,
And forc'd to drink their vapour.

IRAS
                    The gods forbid!

CLEOPATRA
Nay, 'tis most certain, Iras: — saucy lictors
Will catch at us, like strumpets; and scald rimers
Ballad us out o' tune: the quick comedians
Extemporally will stage us, and present
Our Alexandrian revels; Antony
Shall be brought drunken forth, and I shall see
Some squeaking Cleopatra boy my greatness
I'the posture of a whore.

IRAS
                    O the good gods!

CLEOPATRA
Nay, that's certain.

IRAS
I'll never see't; for I am sure my nails
Are stronger than mine eyes.

CLEOPATRA
                    Why, that's the way
To fool their preparation, and to conquer
Their most absurd intents.
                    Enter CHARMIAN.
                    Now, Charmian! —
Show me, my women, like a queen: — go fetch
My best attires; — I am again for Cydnus,
To meet Mark Antony: — sirrah Iras, go. —
Now, noble Charmian, we'll dispatch indeed;
And, when thou hast done this chare, I'll give thee
    leave
To play till doomsday. — Bring our crown and all.
Wherefore's this noise? [*Exit* IRAS. *A noise within.*

                    Enter a GUARDSMAN.

GUARDSMAN
                    Here is a rural fellow
That will not be denied your highness' presence:
He brings you figs.

CLEOPATRA
Let him come in.   [*Exit* GUARDSMAN.
                    What poor an instrument
May do a noble deed! he brings me liberty.
My resolution's plac'd, and I have nothing
Of woman in me: now from head to foot
I am marble-constant; now the fleeting moon
No planet is of mine.

                    Enter GUARDSMAN, *with* CLOWN *bringing
                    in a basket.*

GUARDSMAN
                    This is the man.

CLEOPATRA
Avoid, and leave him.   [*Exit* GUARDSMAN.
Hast thou the pretty worm of Nilus there,
That kills and pains not?

CLOWN
Truly I have him: but I would not be the party that
should desire you to touch him, for his biting is
immortal; those that do die of it do seldom or never
recover.

CLEOPATRA
Remember'st thou any that have died on't?

CLOWN
Very many, men and women too. I heard of one of
them no longer than yesterday: a very honest woman,
but something given to lie; as a woman should not do,
but in the way of honesty: how she died of the biting of
it, what pain she felt, — truly, she makes a very good
report o'the worm; but he that will believe all that they
say shall never be saved by half that they do: but this is
most fallible, the worm's an odd worm.

CLEOPATRA
Get thee hence; farewell.

CLOWN
I wish you all joy of the worm.   [*Sets down his basket.*

CLEOPATRA
Farewell.

CLOWN
You must think this, look you, that the worm will do his
kind.

CLEOPATRA
Ay, ay; farewell.

CLOWN
Look you, the worm is not to be trusted but in the
keeping of wise people; for, indeed, there is no
goodness in worm.

CLEOPATRA
Take thou no care; it shall be heeded.

CLOWN
Very good. Give it nothing, I pray you, for it is not
worth the feeding.

CLEOPATRA
Will it eat me?

CLOWN
You must not think I am so simple but I know the devil
himself will not eat a woman: I know that a woman is a
dish for the gods, if the devil dress her not. But, truly,
these same whoreson devils do the gods great harm in
their women; for in every ten that they make, the devils
mar five.

CLEOPATRA
Well, get thee gone; farewell.

CLOWN
Yes, forsooth; I wish you joy o' the worm.   [*Exit.*

                    Enter IRAS *with a robe, crown, etc.*

CLEOPATRA
Give me my robe, put on my crown; I have
Immortal longings in me: now no more
The juice of Egypt's grape shall moist this lip: —
Yare, yare, good Iras; quick. — Methinks I hear
Antony call; I see him rouse himself
To praise my noble act; I hear him mock
The luck of Cæsar, which the gods give men
To excuse their after wrath: — husband, I come:
Now to that name my courage prove my title!
I am fire and air; my other elements
I give to baser life. — So, — have you done?
Come then, and take the last warmth of my lips.
Farewell, kind Charmian; — Iras, long farewell.
                    [*Kisses them.* IRAS *falls and dies.*
Have I the aspic in my lips? Dost fall?
If thou and nature can so gently part,
The stroke of death is as a lover's pinch,
Which hurts, and is desired. Dost thou lie still?
If thus thou vanishest, thou tell'st the world
It is not worth leave-taking.

CHARMIAN
Dissolve, thick cloud, and rain; that I may say
The gods themselves do weep!

CLEOPATRA
                    This proves me base:
If she first meet the curled Antony,
He'll make demand of her, and spend that kiss
Which is my heaven to have. — Come, thou mortal
    wretch,   [*To an asp, which she applies to her breast.*
With thy sharp teeth this knot intrinsicate
Of life at once untie: poor venomous fool,
Be angry, and dispatch. O, couldst thou speak,
That I might hear thee call great Cæsar ass
Unpolicied!

CHARMIAN
                    O eastern star!

CLEOPATRA
                    Peace, peace!
Dost thou not see my baby at my breast,
That sucks the nurse asleep?

CHARMIAN
                    O, break! O, break!

CLEOPATRA
As sweet as balm, as soft as air, as gentle, —
O Antony! — Nay, I will take thee too:
                    [*Applying another asp to her arm.*
                    [*Dies.*
What should I stay —

CHARMIAN
In this vile world? — So, fare thee well. —
Now boast thee, death, in thy possession lies
A lass unparallel'd. — Downy windows, close;
And golden Phœbus never be beheld
Of eyes again so royal! — Your crown's awry;
I'll mend it, and then play.

                    Enter the GUARD, *rushing in.*

FIRST GUARD
Where is the queen?

CHARMIAN
                    Speak softly, wake her not.

FIRST GUARD
Cæsar hath sent —

CHARMIAN
                    Too slow a messenger.
                    [*Applies an asp.*
O, come apace, dispatch: I partly feel thee.

FIRST GUARD
Approach, ho! All's not well: Cæsar's beguil'd.

SECOND GUARD
There's Dolabella sent from Cæsar; call him.

FIRST GUARD
What work is here! — Charmian, is this well done?

CHARMIAN
It is well done, and fitting for a princess
Descended of so many royal kings.
Ah, soldier!   [*Dies.*

                    Enter DOLABELLA.

DOLABELLA
How goes it here?

SECOND GUARD
                    All dead.

DOLABELLA
                    Cæsar, thy thoughts
Touch their effects in this: thyself art coming
To see perform'd the dreaded act which thou
So sought'st to hinder.
[*within*, 'A way there, a way for Cæsar!']

                    Enter CAESAR *and all his* TRAIN, *marching.*

DOLABELLA
O sir, you are too sure an augurer;
That you did fear is done.

CAESAR
                    Bravest at the last,
She levell'd at our purposes, and, being royal,
Took her own way. — The manner of their deaths?
I do not see them bleed.

DOLABELLA
                    Who was last with them?

FIRST GUARD
A simple countryman, that brought her figs:
This was his basket.

CAESAR
                    Poison'd, then.

FIRST GUARD
                    O Cæsar,
This Charmian liv'd but now; she stood and spake:
I found her trimming up the diadem
On her dead mistress; tremblingly she stood,
And on the sudden dropp'd.

CAESAR
                    O noble weakness! —
If they had swallow'd poison, 'twould appear
By external swelling: but she looks like sleep,
As she would catch another Antony
In her strong toil of grace.

DOLABELLA
                    Here, on her breast,
There is a vent of blood, and something blown:
The like is on her arm.

FIRST GUARD
This is an aspic's trail: and these fig-leaves
Have slime upon them, such as the aspic leaves
Upon the caves of Nile.

CAESAR
                    Most probable
That so she died; for her physician tells me
She hath pursued conclusions infinite
Of easy ways to die. — Take up her bed;
And bear her women from the monument: —
She shall be buried by her Antony:
No grave upon the earth shall clip in it
A pair so famous. High events as these
Strike those that make them; and their story is
No less in pity than his glory which
Brought them to be lamented. Our army shall
In solemn show attend this funeral;
And then to Rome. — Come, Dolabella, see
High order in this great solemnity.   [*Exeunt.*

CORIOLANUS

DRAMATIS PERSONAE

CAIUS MARCIUS, *afterwards* CAIUS MARCIUS
   CORIOLANUS, *a noble Roman.*
TITUS LARTIUS, } *generals against the Volscians.*
COMINIUS,
MENENIUS AGRIPPA, *friend to Coriolanus.*
SICINIUS VELUTUS, } *tribunes of the people.*
JUNIUS BRUTUS,
YOUNG MARCIUS, *son to Coriolanus.*
A ROMAN HERALD.

TULLUS AUFIDIUS, *general of the Volscians.*
LIEUTENANT *to Aufidius.*
CONSPIRATORS *with Aufidius.*
A CITIZEN OF ANTIUM.
TWO VOLSCIAN GUARDS.
VOLUMNIA, *mother to Coriolanus.*
VIRGILIA, *wife to Coriolanus.*
VALERIA, *friend to Virgilia.*

GENTLEWOMAN *attending on Virgilia.*
ROMAN *and* VOLSCIAN SENATORS, PATRICIANS,
   AEDILES, LICTORS, SOLDIERS, CITIZENS,
   MESSENGERS, SERVANTS *to Aufidius, and other*
   ATTENDANTS.

SCENE — *Partly Rome and its neighbourhood; partly*
   Corioli and its neighbourhood; and partly Antium.

ACT I

SCENE I

Rome. A street.

Enter a company of mutinous CITIZENS, *with staves,*
clubs, and other weapons.

FIRST CITIZEN
Before we proceed any further, hear me speak.
CITIZENS
Speak, speak.
FIRST CITIZEN
You are all resolved rather to die than to famish?
CITIZENS
Resolved, resolved.
FIRST CITIZEN
First, you know Caius Marcius is chief enemy to the
people.
CITIZENS
We know't, we know't.
FIRST CITIZEN
Let us kill him, and we'll have corn at our own price.
Is't a verdict?
CITIZENS
No more talking on't; let it be done: away, away!
SECOND CITIZEN
One word, good citizens.
FIRST CITIZEN
We are accounted poor citizens; the patricians, good.
What authority surfeits on would relieve us: if they would
yield us but the superfluity, while it were wholesome, we
might guess they relieved us humanely; but they think we
are too dear: the leanness that afflicts us, the object of our
misery, is as an inventory to particularise their
abundance; our sufferance is a gain to them. — Let us
revenge this with our pikes, ere we become rakes: for the
gods know I speak this in hunger for bread, not in thirst
for revenge.
SECOND CITIZEN
Would you proceed especially against Caius Marcius?
CITIZENS
Against him first: he's a very dog to the commonalty.
SECOND CITIZEN
Consider you what services he has done for his country?
FIRST CITIZEN
Very well; and could be content to give him good report
for't, but that he pays himself with being proud.
SECOND CITIZEN
Nay, but speak not maliciously.
FIRST CITIZEN
I say unto you, what he hath done famously, he did it to
that end: though soft-conscienced men can be content
to say it was for his country, he did it to please his
mother, and to be partly proud; which he is, even to the
altitude of his virtue.
SECOND CITIZEN
What he cannot help in his nature, you account a vice
in him. You must in no way say he is covetous.
FIRST CITIZEN
If I must not, I need not be barren of accusations; he
hath faults, with surplus, to tire in repetition. [*Shouts
within.*] What shouts are these? The other side o'the city
is risen: why stay we prating here? To the Capitol!
CITIZENS
Come, come.
FIRST CITIZEN
Soft! who comes here?
SECOND CITIZEN
Worthy Menenius Agrippa; one that hath always loved
the people.

FIRST CITIZEN
He's one honest enough: would all the rest
   were so!

   Enter MENENIUS AGRIPPA.

MENENIUS
What work's, my countrymen, in hand?
   where go you
With bats and clubs? the matter? speak, I
   pray you.
FIRST CITIZEN
Our business is not unknown to the senate;
they have had inkling, this fortnight, what we
intend to do, which now we'll show 'em in
deeds. They say poor suitors have strong
breaths: they shall know we have strong
arms too.
MENENIUS
Why, masters, my good friends, mine honest
   neighbours,
Will you undo yourselves?
FIRST CITIZEN
We cannot, sir, we are undone already.
MENENIUS
I tell you, friends, most charitable care
Have the patricians of you. For your wants,
Your suffering in this dearth, you may
   as well
Strike at the heaven with your staves as
   lift them
Against the Roman state; whose course
   will on
The way it takes, cracking ten thousand
   curbs
Of more strong link asunder than can ever
Appear in your impediment: for the dearth,
The gods, not the patricians, make it; and
Your knees to them, not arms, must help.
   Alack,
You are transported by calamity
Thither where more attends you; and you slander
The helms o'th'state, who care for you like fathers,
When you curse them as enemies.
FIRST CITIZEN
Care for us! True, indeed! They ne'er cared for us yet: —
suffer us to famish, and their store-houses cramm'd
with grain; make edicts for usury, to support usurers;
repeal daily any wholesome act establish'd against the
rich; and provide more piercing statutes daily, to chain
up and restrain the poor. If the wars eat us not up, they
will; and there's all the love they bear us.
MENENIUS
Either you must
Confess yourselves wondrous malicious,
Or be accus'd of folly. I shall tell you
A pretty tale: it may be you have heard it;
But, since it serves my purpose, I will venture
To stale't a little more.
FIRST CITIZEN
Well, I'll hear it, sir: yet you must not think to fob-off
our disgrace with a tale: but, an't please you, deliver.
MENENIUS
There was a time when all the body's members
Rebell'd against the belly; thus accus'd it: —
That only like a gulf it did remain
I'the midst o'the body, idle and unactive,
Still cupboarding the viand, never bearing
Like labour with the rest; where th'other instruments
Did see and hear, devise, instruct, walk, feel,
And, mutually participate, did minister
Unto the appetite and affection common
Of the whole body. The belly answer'd, —

MENENIUS Thou rascal, that art worst in blood to run,
   lead'st first to win some vantage.

FIRST CITIZEN
Well, sir, what answer made the belly?
MENENIUS
Sir, I shall tell you. — With a kind of smile,
Which ne'er came from the lungs, but even thus —
For, look you, I may make the belly smile
As well as speak — it tauntingly replied
To the discontented members, the mutinous parts
That envied his receipt; even so most fitly
As you malign our senators for that
They are not such as you.
FIRST CITIZEN
          Your belly's answer? What!
The kingly-crowned head, the vigilant eye,
The counsellor heart, the arm our soldier,
Our steed the leg, the tongue our trumpeter,
With other muniments and petty helps
In this our fabric, if that they —
MENENIUS
          What then? —
'Fore me, this fellow speaks! — what then? what then?
FIRST CITIZEN
Should by the cormorant belly be restrain'd,
Who is the sink o'the body, —
MENENIUS
          Well, what then?
FIRST CITIZEN
The former agents, if they did complain,
What could the belly answer?
MENENIUS
          I will tell you;
If you'll bestow a small — of what you have little —

MENENIUS Hail, noble Marcius!

Patience awhile, you'll hear the belly's answer.

FIRST CITIZEN
Y' are long about it.

MENENIUS
     Note me this, good friend;
Your most grave belly was deliberate,
Not rash like his accusers, and thus answer'd:
'True is it, my incorporate friends,' quoth he,
'That I receive the general food at first,
Which you do live upon; and fit it is,
Because I am the store-house and the shop
Of the whole body: but, if you do remember,
I send it through the rivers of your blood,
Even to the court, the heart, — to the seat o'the brain;
And, through the cranks and offices of man,
The strongest nerves and small inferior veins
From me receive that natural competency
Whereby they live: and though that all at once,
You, my good friends,' — this says the belly, mark me, —

FIRST CITIZEN
Ay, sir; well, well.

MENENIUS
     'Though all at once can not
See what I do deliver out to each,
Yet I can make my audit up, that all
From me do back receive the flour of all,
And leave me but the bran.' — What say you to't?

FIRST CITIZEN
It was an answer: how apply you this?

MENENIUS
The senators of Rome are this good belly,
And you the mutinous members: for examine
Their counsels and their cares; digest things rightly
Touching the weal o'the common; you shall find,
No public benefit which you receive
But it proceeds or comes from them to you,
And no way from yourselves. — What do you think, —
You, the great toe of this assembly?

FIRST CITIZEN
I the great toe! why the great toe?

MENENIUS
For that, being one o'the lowest, basest, poorest,
Of this most wise rebellion, thou go'st foremost:
Thou rascal, that art worst in blood to run,
Lead'st first to win some vantage. —
But make you ready your stiff bats and clubs:
Rome and her rats are at the point of battle;
The one side must have bale.
    Enter CAIUS MARCIUS.
      Hail, noble Marcius!

MARCIUS
Thanks. — What's the matter, you dissentious rogues,
That, rubbing the poor itch of your opinion,
Make yourselves scabs?

FIRST CITIZEN
    We have ever your good word.

MARCIUS
He that will give good words to thee will flatter
Beneath abhorring. What would you have, you curs,

That like nor peace nor war? the one affrights you,
The other makes you proud. He that trusts to you,
Where he should find you lions, finds you hares;
Where foxes, geese: you are no surer, no,
Than is the coal of fire upon the ice,
Or hailstone in the sun. Your virtue is,
To make him worthy whose offence subdues him,
And curse that justice did it. Who deserves greatness
Deserves your hate; and your affections are
A sick man's appetite, who desires most that
Which would increase his evil. He that depends
Upon your favours swims with fins of lead,
And hews down oaks with rushes. Hang ye! Trust ye?
With every minute you do change a mind;
And call him noble that was now your hate,
Him vile that was your garland. What's the matter,
That in these several places of the city
You cry against the noble senate, who,
Under the gods, keep you in awe, which else
Would feed on one another? — What's their seeking?

MENENIUS
For corn at their own rates; whereof, they say,
The city is well stored.

MARCIUS
     Hang 'em! They say!
They'll sit by the fire, and presume to know
What's done i' the Capitol; who's like to rise,
Who thrives, and who declines; side factions, and give
  out
Conjectural marriages; making parties strong,
And feebling such as stand not in their liking
Below their cobbled shoes. They say there's grain
  enough!
Would the nobility lay aside their ruth,
And let me use my sword, I'ld make a quarry
With thousands of these quarter'd slaves, as high
As I could pick my lance.

MENENIUS
Nay, these are almost thoroughly persuaded;
For though abundantly they lack discretion,
Yet are they passing cowardly. But, I beseech you,
What says the other troop?

MARCIUS
    They are dissolved: hang 'em!
They said they were an-hungry: sigh'd forth proverbs,
That hunger broke stone walls, that dogs must eat,
That meat was made for mouths, that the gods sent not
Corn for the rich men only: — with these shreds
They vented their complainings; which being
  answer'd,
And a petition granted them, a strange one —
To break the heart of generosity,
And make bold power look pale — they threw their
  caps
As they would hang them on the horns o'the moon,
Shouting their emulation.

MENENIUS
     What is granted them?

MARCIUS
Five tribunes to defend their vulgar wisdoms,
Of their own choice: one's Junius Brutus,
Sicinius Velutus, and I know not — 'Sdeath!
The rabble should have first unroof'd the city,
Ere so prevail'd with me: it will in time
Win upon power, and throw forth greater themes
For insurrection's arguing.

MENENIUS
     This is strange.

MARCIUS
Go, get you home, you fragments!
   Enter a MESSENGER, *hastily.*

MESSENGER
Where's Caius Marcius?

MARCIUS
     Here: what's the matter?

MESSENGER
The news is, sir, the Volsces are in arms.

MARCIUS
I am glad on't; then we shall ha' means to vent
Our musty superfluity. — See, our best elders.
  Enter COMINIUS, TITUS LARTIUS, *with other*
  SENATORS; JUNIUS BRUTUS, *and* SICINIUS
     VELUTUS.

FIRST SENATOR
Marcius, 'tis true that you have lately told us, —
The Volsces are in arms.

MARCIUS
     They have a leader,
Tullus Aufidius, that will put you to't.
I sin in envying his nobility;

And were I anything but what I am,
I would wish me only he.

COMINIUS
     You have fought together.

MARCIUS
Were half to half the world by the ears, and he
Upon my party, I'ld revolt, to make
Only my wars with him: he is a lion
That I am proud to hunt.

FIRST SENATOR
     Then, worthy Marcius,
Attend upon Cominius to these wars.

COMINIUS
It is your former promise.

MARCIUS
     Sir, it is;
And I am constant. — Titus Lartius, thou
Shalt see me once more strike at Tullus' face.
What, art thou stiff? stand'st out?

LARTIUS
     No, Caius Marcius;
I'll lean upon one crutch, and fight with t'other,
Ere stay behind this business.

MENENIUS
     O, true-bred!

FIRST SENATOR
Your company to the Capitol; where, I know,
Our greatest friends attend us.

LARTIUS [*to* COMINIUS].
     Lead you on. —
[*to* MARCIUS] Follow Cominius: we must follow you;
Right worthy you priority.

COMINIUS
     Noble Marcius!

FIRST SENATOR [*to the* CITIZENS].
Hence to your homes; be gone!

MARCIUS
     Nay, let them follow:
The Volsces have much corn; take these rats thither
To gnaw their garners. — Worshipful mutiners,
Your valour puts well forth: pray, follow.

    [CITIZENS *steal away. Exeunt all*
    but BRUTUS *and* SICINIUS.

SICINIUS
Was ever man so proud as is this Marcius?

BRUTUS
He has no equal.

SICINIUS
When we were chosen tribunes for the people, —

BRUTUS
Mark'd you his lip and eyes?

SICINIUS
     Nay, but his taunts

BRUTUS
Being mov'd, he will not spare to gird the gods.

SICINIUS
Be-mock the modest moon.

BRUTUS
The present wars devour him! He is grown
Too proud to be so valiant.

SICINIUS
     Such a nature,
Tickled with good success, disdains the shadow
Which he treads on at noon: but I do wonder
His insolence can brook to be commanded
Under Cominius.

BRUTUS
     Fame, at the which he aims, —
In whom already he's well grac'd, — can not
Better be held, nor more attain'd, than by
A place below the first: for what miscarries
Shall be the general's fault, though he perform
To the utmost of a man; and giddy censure
Will then cry out of Marcius, 'O, if he
Had borne the business!'

SICINIUS
     Besides, if things go well,
Opinion, that so sticks on Marcius, shall
Of his demerits rob Cominius.

BRUTUS
     Come:
Half all Cominius' honours are to Marcius,
Though Marcius earn'd them not; and all his faults
To Marcius shall be honours, though, indeed,
In aught he merit not.

SICINIUS
     Let's hence, and hear
How the dispatch is made; and in what fashion,

More than his singularity, he goes
Upon his present action.

BRUTUS
               Let's along.   [*Exeunt.*

SCENE II

Corioli. The Senate-house.

Enter TULLUS AUFIDIUS *with* SENATORS *of Corioli.*

FIRST SENATOR
So, your opinion is, Aufidius,
That they of Rome are enter'd in our counsels,
And know how we proceed.

AUFIDIUS
               Is it not yours?
What ever have been thought on in this state,
That could be brought to bodily act ere Rome
Had circumvention? 'Tis not four days gone
Since I heard thence: these are the words: I think
I have the letter here; yes, here it is: [*Reads.*
'They have press'd a power, but it is not known
Whether for east or west: the dearth is great;
The people mutinous: and it is rumour'd,
Cominius, Marcius your old enemy, —
Who is of Rome worse hated than of you, —
And Titus Lartius, a most valiant Roman,
These three lead on this preparation
Whither 'tis bent: most likely 'tis for you:
Consider of it.

FIRST SENATOR
         Our army's in the field:
We never yet made doubt but Rome was ready
To answer us.

AUFIDIUS
         Nor did you think it folly
To keep your great pretences veil'd till when
They needs must show themselves; which in the
     hatching,
It seem'd, appeared to Rome. By the discovery
We shall be shorten'd in our aim; which was,
To take in many towns, ere, almost, Rome
Should know we were afoot.

SECOND SENATOR
         Noble Aufidius,
Take your commission; hie you to your bands:
Let us alone to guard Corioli:
If they set down before's, for the remove
Bring up your army; but, I think, you'll find
Th'have not prepared for us.

AUFIDIUS
         O, doubt not that;
I speak from certainties. Nay, more,
Some parcels of their power are forth already,
And only hitherward. I leave your honours.
If we and Caius Marcius chance to meet,
'Tis sworn between us, we shall ever strike
Till one can do no more.

ALL
         The gods assist you!

AUFIDIUS
And keep your honours safe!

FIRST SENATOR
         Farewell.

SECOND SENATOR
            Farewell.

ALL
Farewell.   [*Exeunt.*

SCENE III

Rome. A room in MARCIUS' *house.*

Enter VOLUMNIA *and* VIRGILIA, *mother and wife to*
MARCIUS: *they set them down on*
two low stools, and sew.

VOLUMNIA
I pray you, daughter, sing; or express yourself in a more
comfortable sort: if my son were my husband, I should
freelier rejoice in that absence wherein he won honour
than in the embracements of his bed where he would
show most love. When yet he was but tender-bodied,
and the only son of my womb; when youth with
comeliness pluck'd all gaze his way; when, for a day of
kings' entreaties, a mother should not sell him an hour
from her beholding; I — considering how honour
would become such a person; that it was no better than
picture-like to hang by the wall, if renown made it not
stir — was pleased to let him seek danger where he was
like to find fame. To a cruel war I sent him: from
whence he return'd, his brows bound with oak. I tell
thee, daughter, I sprang not more in joy at first hearing

he was a man-child than now in first seeing he had
proved himself a man.

VIRGILIA
But had he died in the business, madam, — how then?

VOLUMNIA
Then his good report should have been my son; I
therein would have found issue. Hear me profess
sincerely, had I a dozen sons, each in my love alike, and
none less dear than thine and my good Marcius, I had
rather had eleven die nobly for their country than one
voluptuously surfeit out of action.

Enter a GENTLEWOMAN.

GENTLEWOMAN
Madam, the Lady Valeria is come to visit you.

VIRGILIA
Beseech you, give me leave to retire myself.

VOLUMNIA
Indeed, you shall not.
Methinks I hear hither your husband's drum;
See him pluck Aufidius down by the hair;
As children from a bear, the Volsces shunning him:
Methinks I see him stamp thus, and call thus, —
'Come on, you cowards! you were got in fear,
Though you were born in Rome': his bloody brow
With his mail'd hand then wiping, forth he goes,
Like to a harvest-man, that's task'd to mow
Or all, or lose his hire.

VIRGILIA
His bloody brow! O Jupiter, no blood!

VOLUMNIA
Away, you fool! it more becomes a man
Than gilt his trophy: the breasts of Hecuba,
When she did suckle Hector, look'd not lovelier
Than Hector's forehead when it spit forth blood
At Grecian sword contemning. — Tell Valeria
We are fit to bid her welcome.
             [*Exit* GENTLEWOMAN.

VIRGILIA
Heavens bless my lord from fell Aufidius!

VOLUMNIA
He'll beat Aufidius' head below his knee,
And tread upon his neck.

Enter VALERIA *with* USHER *and a*
GENTLEWOMAN.

VALERIA
My ladies both, good day to you.

VOLUMNIA
Sweet madam.

VIRGILIA
I am glad to see your ladyship.

VALERIA
How do you both? you are manifest house-keepers.
What are you sewing here? A fine spot, in good faith. —
How does your little son?

VIRGILIA
I thank your ladyship; well, good madam.

VOLUMNIA
He had rather see the swords, and
hear a drum, than look upon his
schoolmaster.

VALERIA
O'my word, the father's son: I'll
swear, 'tis a very pretty boy. O'my
troth, I look'd upon him o'
Wednesday half an hour together:
has such a confirm'd countenance.
I saw him run after a gilded
butterfly; and when he caught it, he
let it go again; and after it again;
and over and over he comes, and up
again; catch'd it again: or whether
his fall enraged him, or how 'twas,
he did so set his teeth, and tear it: O,
I warrant, how he mammock'd it!

VOLUMNIA
One on's father's moods.

VALERIA
Indeed, la, 'tis a noble child.

VIRGILIA
A crack, madam.

VALERIA
Come, lay aside your stitchery: I
must have you play the idle huswife
with me this afternoon.

VIRGILIA
No, good madam; I will not out of
doors.

VALERIA
Not out of doors!

VOLUMNIA
She shall, she shall.

VIRGILIA
Indeed, no, by your patience; I'll not over the threshold
till my lord return from the wars.

VALERIA
Fie, you confine yourself most unreasonably: come,
you must go visit the good lady that lies in.

VIRGILIA
I will wish her speedy strength, and visit her with my
prayers; but I cannot go thither.

VOLUMNIA
Why, I pray you?

VIRGILIA
'Tis not to save labour, nor that I want love.

VALERIA
You would be another Penelope: yet, they say, all the
yarn she spun in Ulysses' absence did but fill Ithaca
full of moths. Come; I would your cambric were
sensible as your finger, that you might leave pricking it
for pity. Come, you shall go with us.

VIRGILIA
No, good madam, pardon me; indeed, I will not forth.

VALERIA
In truth, la, go with me; and I'll tell you excellent news
of your husband.

VIRGILIA
O, good madam, there can be none yet.

VALERIA
Verily, I do not jest with you; there came news from
him last night.

VIRGILIA
Indeed, madam?

VALERIA
In earnest, it's true; I heard a senator speak it. Thus it
is: — The Volsces have an army forth; against whom
Cominius the general is gone, with one part of our
Roman power: your lord and Titus Lartius are set down
before their city Corioli; they nothing doubt prevailing,
and to make it brief wars. This is true, on mine honour;
and so, I pray, go with us.

VIRGILIA
Give me excuse, good madam; I will obey you in every
thing hereafter.

VOLUMNIA
Let her alone, lady: as she is now, she will but disease
our better mirth.

VALERIA
In troth, I think she would. — Fare you well, then. —
Come, good sweet lady. — Prithee, Virgilia, turn thy
solemness out o'door, and go along with us.

VIRGILIA
No, at a word, madam; indeed, I must not. I wish you
much mirth.

VALERIA
Well, then, farewell.   [*Exeunt.*

VOLUMNIA Then his good report should have been my son.

SCENE IV

Before Corioli.

Enter MARCIUS, TITUS LARTIUS, *with drum and colours, with* CAPTAINS *and* SOLDIERS, *as before the city Corioli: to them a* MESSENGER.

MARCIUS
Yonder comes news: — a wager they have met.
LARTIUS
My horse to yours, no.
MARCIUS
        'Tis done.
LARTIUS
            Agreed.
MARCIUS
Say, has our general met the enemy?
MESSENGER
They lie in view; but have not spoke as yet.
LARTIUS
So, the good horse is mine.
MARCIUS
            I'll buy him of you.
LARTIUS
No, I'll nor sell nor give him; lend you him I will
For half a hundred years. — Summon the town.
MARCIUS
How far off lie these armies?
MESSENGER
           Within this mile and half.
MARCIUS
Then shall we hear their 'larum, and they ours. —
Now, Mars, I prithee, make us quick in work,
That we with smoking swords may march from hence,
To help our fielded friends! — Come, blow thy blast.

They sound a parley. Enter two SENATORS *with others on the walls of Corioli.*

Tullus Aufidius, is he within your walls?
FIRST SENATOR
No, nor a man that fears you less than he,
That's lesser than a little. [*Drum afar off.*] Hark, our drums
Are bringing forth our youth! We'll break our walls,
Rather than they shall pound us up: our gates,
Which yet seem shut, we have but pinn'd with rushes;
They'll open of themselves. [*Alarum afar off.*] Hark you,
  far off!
There is Aufidius; list, what work he makes
Amongst your cloven army.
MARCIUS
         O, they're at it!
LARTIUS
Their noise be our instruction. — Ladders, ho!

Enter the ARMY *of the* VOLSCES.

MARCIUS
They fear us not, but issue forth their city.
Now put your shields before your hearts, and fight
With hearts more proof than shields. — Advance,
  brave Titus:
They do disdain us much beyond our thoughts,
Which makes me sweat with wrath. — Come on, my
  fellows:
He that retires, I'll take him for a Volsce,
And he shall feel mine edge.

Alarum. The ROMANS *are beat back to their trenches. Enter* MARCIUS, *cursing.*

MARCIUS
All the contagion of the south light on you,
You shames of Rome! you herd of — Boils and plagues
Plaster you o'er; that you may be abhorr'd
Further than seen, and one infect another
Against the wind a mile! You souls of geese,
That bear the shapes of men, how have you run
From slaves that apes would beat! Pluto and hell!
All hurt behind; backs red, and faces pale
With flight and agued fear! Mend, and charge home,
Or, by the fires of heaven, I'll leave the foe,
And make my wars on you: look to't: come on;
If you'll stand fast, we'll beat them to their wives,
As they us to our trenches. Follow's.

Another alarum, and MARCIUS *follows the* VOLSCES *to the gates, and is shut in.*

So, now the gates are ope: — now prove good seconds:
'Tis for the followers fortune widens them,
Not for the fliers: mark me, and do the like.
           [*Enters the gates.*
FIRST SOLDIER
Fool-hardiness; not I.
SECOND SOLDIER
        Nor I.

FIRST SOLDIER
See, they have shut him in.
ALL
        To the pot, I warrant him.
           [*Alarum continues.*

Enter TITUS LARTIUS.

LARTIUS
What is become of Marcius?
ALL
        Slain, sir, doubtless.
FIRST SOLDIER
Following the fliers at the very heels,
With them he enters; who, upon the sudden,
Clapp'd-to their gates: he is himself alone,
To answer all the city.
LARTIUS
        O noble fellow!
Who, sensible, outdares his senseless sword,
And, when it bows, stands up! Thou art left, Marcius:
A carbuncle entire, as big as thou art,
Were not so rich a jewel. Thou wast a soldier
Even to Cato's wish, not fierce and terrible
Only in strokes, but, with thy grim looks and
The thunder-like percussion of thy sounds,
Thou madest thine enemies shake, as if the world
Were feverous and did tremble.

Enter MARCIUS, *bleeding, assaulted by the enemy.*

FIRST SOLDIER
        Look, sir.
LARTIUS
         O, 'tis Marcius!
Let's fetch him off, or make remain alike.
       [*They fight, and all enter the city.*

SCENE V

Within Corioli. A street.

Enter certain ROMANS, *with spoils.*

FIRST ROMAN
This will I carry to Rome.
SECOND ROMAN
And I this.
THIRD ROMAN
A murrain on't! I took this for silver.
       [*Alarum continues still afar off.*

Enter MARCIUS *and* TITUS LARTIUS *with a trumpet.*

MARCIUS
See here these movers that do prize their hours
At a crack'd drachma! Cushions, leaden spoons,
Irons of a doit, doublets that hangmen would
Bury with those that wore them, these base slaves,
Ere yet the fight be done, pack up: — down with
  them! —
And hark, what noise the general makes! — To him!
There is the man of my soul's hate, Aufidius,
Piercing our Romans: then, valiant Titus, take
Convenient numbers to make good the city;
Whilst I, with those that have the spirit, will haste
To help Cominius.
LARTIUS
        Worthy sir, thou bleed'st;
Thy exercise hath been too violent
For a second course of fight.
MARCIUS
         Sir, praise me not;
My work hath yet not warm'd me: fare you well:
The blood I drop is rather physical
Than dangerous to me: to Aufidius thus
I will appear, and fight.
LARTIUS
        Now the fair goddess, Fortune
Fall deep in love with thee; and her great charms
Misguide thy opposers' swords! Bold gentleman,
Prosperity be thy page!
MARCIUS
        Thy friend no less
Than those she placeth highest! So, farewell.
LARTIUS
Thou worthiest Marcius! —   [*Exit* MARCIUS.
Go, sound thy trumpet in the market-place;
Call thither all the officers o'the town,
Where they shall know our mind: away!   [*Exeunt.*

SCENE VI

Near the camp of COMINIUS.

Enter COMINIUS, *as it were in retire, with* SOLDIERS.

COMINIUS
Breathe you, my friends: well fought; we are come off

Like Romans, neither foolish in our stands
Nor cowardly in retire: believe me, sirs,
We shall be charg'd again. Whiles we have struck,
By interims and conveying gusts we have heard
The charges of our friends. — Ye Roman gods,
Lead their successes as we wish our own,
That both our powers, with smiling fronts encountering,
May give you thankful sacrifice!

Enter a MESSENGER.
         Thy news?
MESSENGER
The citizens of Corioli have issued,
And given to Lartius and to Marcius battle:
I saw our party to their trenches driven,
And then I came away.
COMINIUS
        Though thou speak'st truth,
Methinks thou speak'st not well. How long is't since?
MESSENGER
Above an hour, my lord.
COMINIUS
'Tis not a mile; briefly we heard their drums:
How couldst thou in a mile confound an hour,
And bring thy news so late?
MESSENGER
        Spies of the Volsces
Held me in chase, that I was forc'd to wheel
Three or four miles about; else had I, sir,
Half an hour since brought my report.
COMINIUS
        Who's yonder,
That does appear as he were flay'd? O gods!
He has the stamp of Marcius; and I have
Before-time seen him thus.
MARCIUS [*within*].
        Come I too late?
COMINIUS
The shepherd knows not thunder from a tabor,
More than I know the sound of Marcius' tongue
From every meaner man.

Enter MARCIUS.

MARCIUS
        Come I too late?
COMINIUS
Ay, if you come not in the blood of others,
But mantled in your own.
MARCIUS
        O, let me clip ye
In arms as sound as when I woo'd; in heart
As merry as when our nuptial day was done,
And tapers burn'd to bedward!
COMINIUS
        Flower of warriors,
How is't with Titus Lartius?
MARCIUS
As with a man busied about decrees:
Condemning some to death, and some to exile;
Ransoming him or pitying, threatening the other;
Holding Corioli in the name of Rome,
Even like a fawning greyhound in the leash,
To let him slip at will.
COMINIUS
        Where is that slave
Which told me they had beat you to your trenches?
Where is he? call him hither.
MARCIUS
        Let him alone;
He did inform the truth: but for our gentlemen,
The common file — a plague! — tribunes for them! —
The mouse ne'er shunn'd the cat as they did budge
From rascals worse than they.
COMINIUS
        But how prevail'd you?
MARCIUS
Will the time serve to tell? I do not think.
Where is the enemy? are you lords o' the field?
If not, why cease you till you are so?
COMINIUS
        Marcius,
We have at disadvantage fought, and did
Retire, to win our purpose.
MARCIUS
How lies their battle? know you on which side
They have plac'd their men of trust?
COMINIUS
        As I guess, Marcius,
Their bands i' the vaward are the Antiates,
Of their best trust; o'er them Aufidius,
Their very heart of hope.

MARCIUS

I do beseech you,

By all the battles wherein we have fought,
By th'blood we have shed together, by the vows
We have made to endure friends, that you directly
Set me against Aufidius and his Antiates;
And that you not delay the present, but,
Filling the air with swords advanc'd and darts,
We prove this very hour.

COMINIUS

Though I could wish

You were conducted to a gentle bath,
And balms applied to you, yet dare I never
Deny your asking: take your choice of those
That best can aid your action.

MARCIUS

Those are they

That most are willing. — If any such be here —
As it were sin to doubt — that love this painting
Wherein you see me smear'd; if any fear
Lesser his person than an ill report;
If any think brave death outweighs bad life,
And that his country's dearer than himself;
Let him alone, or so many so minded,
Wave thus, to express his disposition,
And follow Marcius.

[They all shout, and wave their swords;
take him up in their arms, and cast up their caps]

O, me alone! make you a sword of me?
If these shows be not outward, which of you
But is four Volsces? none of you but is
Able to bear against the great Aufidius
A shield as hard as his. A certain number,
Though thanks to all, must I select from all: the rest
Shall bear the business in some other fight,
As cause will be obey'd. Please you to march;
And four shall quickly draw out my command,
Which men are best inclin'd.

COMINIUS

March on, my fellows:

Make good this ostentation, and you shall
Divide in all with us. [Exeunt.

SCENE VII

The gates of Corioli.

TITUS LARTIUS, *having set a guard upon Corioli,
going with drum and trumpet toward* COMINIUS *and*
CAIUS MARCIUS, *enters with a* LIEUTENANT, *other*
SOLDIERS, *and a* SCOUT.

LARTIUS

So, let the ports be guarded: keep your duties,
As I have set them down. If I do send, dispatch
Those centuries to our aid; the rest will serve
For a short holding: if we lose the field,
We cannot keep the town.

LIEUTENANT

Fear not our care, sir.

LARTIUS

Hence, and shut your gates upon's. —
Our guider, come; to the Roman camp conduct us.
[Exeunt.

SCENE VIII

*A field of battle between the Roman and the Volscian
camps.*

Alarum as in battle. Enter MARCIUS *and* AUFIDIUS
at several doors.

MARCIUS

I'll fight with none but thee; for I do hate thee
Worse than a promise-breaker.

AUFIDIUS

We hate alike:

Not Afric owns a serpent I abhor
More than thy fame I envy. Fix thy foot.

MARCIUS

Let the first budger die the other's slave,
And the gods doom him after!

AUFIDIUS

If I fly, Marcius,

Halloo me like a hare.

MARCIUS

Within these three hours, Tullus,

Alone I fought in your Corioli walls,
And made what work I pleas'd: 'tis not my blood
Wherein thou seest me mask'd; for thy revenge
Wrench up thy power to the highest.

AUFIDIUS

Wert thou the Hector

That was the whip of your bragg'd progeny,
Thou shouldst not scape me here.

[Here they fight, and certain VOLSCES come
in the aid of AUFIDIUS. MARCIUS fights
till they be driven in breathless.

Officious, and not valiant, — you have sham'd me
In your condemned seconds. [Exeunt.

SCENE IX

The Roman camp.

*Flourish. Alarum. A retreat is sounded. Enter, at one
door,* COMINIUS *with the* ROMANS; *at another door,*
MARCIUS, *with his arm in a scarf.*

COMINIUS

If I should tell thee o'er this thy day's work,
Thou'lt not believe thy deeds: but I'll report it,
Where senators shall mingle tears with smiles;
Where great patricians shall attend, and shrug,
I'the end admire; where ladies shall be frighted,
And, gladly quak'd, hear more; where the dull
tribunes,
That, with the fusty plebeians, hate thine honours,
Shall say, against their hearts, 'We thank the gods
Our Rome hath such a soldier!'
Yet camest thou to a morsel of this feast,
Having fully dined before.

Enter TITUS LARTIUS, with his power, from the
pursuit.

LARTIUS

O general,

Here is the steed, we the caparison:
Hadst thou beheld —

MARCIUS

Pray now, no more: my mother,

Who has a charter to extol her blood,
When she does praise me grieves me. I have done
As you have done, — that's what I can; induced
As you have been, — that's for my country:
He that has but effected his good will
Hath overta'en mine act.

COMINIUS

You shall not be

The grave of your deserving; Rome must know
The value of her own: 'twere a concealment
Worse than a theft, no less than a traducement,
To hide your doings; and to silence that,
Which, to the spire and top of praises vouch'd,
Would seem but modest: therefore, I beseech you —
In sign of what you are, not to reward
What you have done — before our army hear me.

MARCIUS

I have some wounds upon me, and they smart
To hear themselves remember'd.

COMINIUS

Should they not,

Well might they fester 'gainst ingratitude,
And tent themselves with death. Of all the horses, —
Whereof we have ta'en good, and good store, — of all
The treasure in this field achiev'd and city,
We render you the tenth; to be ta'en forth,
Before the common distribution,
At your only choice.

MARCIUS

I thank you, general;

But cannot make my heart consent to take
A bribe to pay my sword: I do refuse it;
And stand upon my common part with those
That have beheld the doing.

[A long flourish. They all cry, 'Marcius! Marcius!'
cast up their caps and lances:
COMINIUS and LARTIUS stand bare.

MARCIUS

May these same instruments, which you profane,
Never sound more! When drums and trumpets shall
I' the field prove flatterers, let courts and cities be
Made all of false-fac'd soothing! When steel grows
Soft as the parasite's silk, let him be made
A coverture for the wars! No more, I say!
For that I have not wash'd my nose that bled,
Or foil'd some debile wretch, — Which, without note,
Here's many else have done, — you shout me forth
In acclamations hyperbolical;
As if I lov'd my little should be dieted
In praises sauc'd with lies.

COMINIUS

Too modest are you;

More cruel to your good report than grateful
To us that give you truly: by your patience,
If 'gainst yourself you be incens'd, we'll put you —

Like one that means his proper harm — in manacles,
Then reason safely with you. Therefore, be it known,
As to us, to all the world, that Caius Marcius
Wears this war's garland: in token of the which,
My noble steed, known to the camp, I give him,
With all his trim belonging; and from this time,
For what he did before Corioli, call him,
With all the applause and clamour of the host,
CAIUS MARCIUS CORIOLANUS. — Bear
The addition nobly ever!
[Flourish. Trumpets sound and drums.

ALL

Caius Marcius Coriolanus!

CORIOLANUS

I will go wash;
And when my face is fair, you shall perceive
Whether I blush or no: howbeit, I thank you: —
I mean to stride your steed; and at all times,
To undercrest your good addition
To the fairness of my power.

COMINIUS

So, to our tent;

Where, ere we do repose us, we will write
To Rome of our success. — You, Titus Lartius,
Must to Corioli back: send us to Rome
The best, with whom we may articulate,
For their own good and ours.

LARTIUS

I shall, my lord.

CORIOLANUS

The gods begin to mock me. I, that now
Refus'd most princely gifts, am bound to beg
Of my lord general.

COMINIUS

Take't; 'tis yours. What is't?

CORIOLANUS

I sometime lay, here in Corioli,
At a poor man's house; he used me kindly: —
He cried to me; I saw him prisoner;
But then Aufidius was within my view,
And wrath o'erwhelm'd my pity: I request you
To give my poor host freedom.

COMINIUS

O, well begg'd!

Were he the butcher of my son, he should
Be free as is the wind. — Deliver him, Titus.

LARTIUS

Marcius, his name?

CORIOLANUS

By Jupiter, forgot: —

I am weary; yea, my memory is tired. —
Have we no wine here?

COMINIUS

Go we to our tent:

The blood upon your visage dries; 'tis time
It should be look'd to: come. [Exeunt.

SCENE X

The camp of the VOLSCES.

*A flourish. Cornets. Enter TULLUS AUFIDIUS bloody,
with two or three SOLDIERS.*

AUFIDIUS

The town is ta'en!

FIRST SOLDIER

'Twill be deliver'd back on good condition.

AUFIDIUS

Condition! —
I would I were a Roman; for I cannot,
Being a Volsce, be that I am. — Condition!
What good condition can a treaty find
I' the part that is at mercy? — Five times, Marcius,
I have fought with thee; so often hast thou beat me;
And wouldst do so, I think, shouldst we encounter
As often as we eat. — By the elements,
If e'er again I meet him beard to beard,
He's mine, or I am his: mine emulation
Hath not that honour in't it had; for where
I thought to crush him in an equal force,
True sword to sword, I'll potch at him some way,
Or wrath or craft may get him.

FIRST SOLDIER

He's the devil

AUFIDIUS

Bolder, though not so subtle. My valour's poison'd
With only suffering stain by him; for him
Shall fly out of itself: nor sleep nor sanctuary,
Being naked, sick, nor fane nor Capitol,
The prayers of priests nor times of sacrifice,
Embarquements all of fury, shall lift up

Their rotten privilege and custom 'gainst
My hate to Marcius: where I find him, were it
At home, upon my brother's guard, even there,
Against the hospitable canon, would I
Wash my fierce hand in's heart. Go you to the city;
Learn how 'tis held; and what they are that must
Be hostages for Rome.

FIRST SOLDIER
     Will not you go?

AUFIDIUS
I am attended at the cypress grove: I pray you —
'Tis south the city mills — bring me word thither
How the world goes, that to the pace of it
I may spur on my journey.

FIRST SOLDIER
     I shall, sir.   [*Exeunt.*

ACT II

SCENE I

Rome. A public place.

Enter MENENIUS, *with the two* TRIBUNES *of the people,* SICINIUS *and* BRUTUS.

MENENIUS
The augurer tells me we shall have news to-night.
BRUTUS
Good or bad?
MENENIUS
Not according to the prayer of the people, for they love not Marcius.
SICINIUS
Nature teaches beasts to know their friends.
MENENIUS
Pray you, who does the wolf love?
SICINIUS
The lamb.
MENENIUS
Ay, to devour him; as the hungry plebeians would the noble Marcius.
BRUTUS
He's a lamb indeed, that baes like a bear.
MENENIUS
He's a bear indeed, that lives like a lamb. You two are old men: tell me one thing that I shall ask you.
BOTH
Well, sir.
MENENIUS
In what enormity is Marcius poor in, that you two have not in abundance?
BRUTUS
He's poor in no one fault, but stored with all.
SICINIUS
Especially in pride.
BRUTUS
And topping all others in boasting.
MENENIUS
This is strange now: do you two know how you are censured here in the city, I mean of us o' the right-hand file? do you?
BOTH
Why, how are we censured?
MENENIUS
Because you talk of pride now, — will you not be angry?

BOTH
Well, well, sir, well.
MENENIUS
Why, 'tis no great matter; for a very little thief of occasion will rob you of a great deal of patience: give your dispositions the reins, and be angry at your pleasures; at least, if you take it as a pleasure to you in being so. You blame Marcius for being proud?
BRUTUS
We do it not alone, sir.
MENENIUS
I know you can do very little alone; for your helps are many, or else your actions would grow wondrous single: your abilities are too infant-like for doing much alone. You talk of pride: — O that you could turn your eyes toward the napes of your necks, and make but an interior survey of your good selves! O that you could!
BRUTUS
What then, sir?
MENENIUS
Why, then you should discover a brace of unmeriting, proud, violent, testy magistrates, alias fools, as any in Rome.
SICINIUS
Menenius, you are known well enough too.
MENENIUS
I am known to be a humorous patrician, and one that loves a cup of hot wine with not a drop of allaying Tiber in't; said to be something imperfect in favouring the first complaint; hasty and tinder-like upon too trivial motion; one that converses more with the buttock of the night than with the forehead of the morning: what I think I utter, and spend my malice in my breath. Meeting two such wealsmen as you are, — I cannot call you Lycurguses, — if the drink you give me touch my palate adversely, I make a crooked face at it. I cannot say your worships have deliver'd the matter well, when I find the ass in compound with the major part of your syllables: and though I must be content to bear with those that say you are reverend grave men, yet they lie deadly that tell you you have good faces. If you see this in the map of my microcosm, follows it that I am known well enough too? what harm can your bisson conspectuities glean out of this character, if I be known well enough too?
BRUTUS
Come, sir, come, we know you well enough.
MENENIUS
You know neither me, yourselves, nor any thing. You are ambitious for poor knaves' caps and legs: you wear out a good wholesome forenoon in hearing a cause between an orange-wife and a fosset-seller; and then rejourn the controversy of three-pence to a second day of audience. When you are hearing a matter between party and party, if you chance to be pinch'd with the colic, you make faces like mummers; set up the bloody flag against all patience; and, in roaring for a chamber-pot, dismiss the controversy bleeding, the more entangled by your hearing: all the peace you make in their cause is, calling both the parties knaves. You are a pair of strange ones.
BRUTUS
Come, come, you are well understood to be a perfecter giber for the table than a necessary bencher in the Capitol.
MENENIUS
Our very priests must become mockers, if they shall

encounter such ridiculous subjects as you are. When you speak best unto the purpose, it is not worth the wagging of your beards; and your beards deserve not so honourable a grave as to stuff a botcher's cushion, or to be entomb'd in an ass's pack-saddle. Yet you must be saying, Marcius is proud; who, in a cheap estimation, is worth all your predecessors since Deucalion; though peradventure some of the best of 'em were hereditary hangmen. God-den to your worships: more of your conversation would infect my brain, being the herdsmen of the beastly plebeians: I will be bold to take my leave of you. [BRUTUS *and* SICINIUS *go aside.*
  Enter VOLUMNIA, VIRGILIA, *and* VALERIA, *with*
     ATTENDANTS.
How now, my as fair as noble ladies, — and the moon, were she earthly, no nobler, — whither do you follow your eyes so fast?
VOLUMNIA
Honourable Menenius, my boy Marcius approaches; for the love of Juno, let's go.
MENENIUS
Ha! Marcius coming home!
VOLUMNIA
Ay, worthy Menenius; and with most prosperous approbation.
MENENIUS
Take my cap, Jupiter, and I thank thee. — Hoo! Marcius coming home!
VIRGILIA and **VALERIA**
Nay, 'tis true.
VOLUMNIA
Look, here's a letter from him: the state hath another, his wife another; and, I think, there's one at home for you.
MENENIUS
I will make my very house reel to-night: — a letter for me!
VIRGILIA
Yes, certain, there's a letter for you; I saw't.
MENENIUS
A letter for me! it gives me an estate of seven years' health; in which time I will make a lip at the physician: the most sovereign prescription in Galen is but empiricutic, and, to this preservative, of no better report than a horse-drench. — Is he not wounded? he was wont to come home wounded.
VIRGILIA
O, no, no, no.
VOLUMNIA
O, he is wounded; I thank the gods for't.
MENENIUS
So do I too, if it be not too much: brings a' victory in his pocket? the wounds become him.
VOLUMNIA
On's brows: Menenius, he comes the third time home with the oaken garland.
MENENIUS
Has he disciplined Aufidius soundly?
VOLUMNIA
Titus Lartius writes, — they fought together, but Aufidius got off.
MENENIUS
And 'twas time for him too, I'll warrant him that: an he had stay'd by him, I would not have been so fidius'd for all the chests in Corioli, and the gold that's in them. Is the senate possess'd of this?
VOLUMNIA
Good ladies, let's go. — Yes, yes, yes; the senate has letters from the general, wherein he gives my son the whole name of the war: he hath in this action out-done his former deeds doubly.
VALERIA
In troth, there's wondrous things spoke of him.
MENENIUS
Wondrous! ay, I warrant you, and not without his true purchasing.
VIRGILIA
The gods grant them true!
VOLUMNIA
True! pow, wow.
MENENIUS
True! I'll be sworn they are true. — Where is he wounded? — [*to the* TRIBUNES] God save your good worships! Marcius is coming home: he has more cause to be proud. — Where is he wounded?
VOLUMNIA
I'the shoulder and i'the left arm: there will be large cicatrices to show the people, when he shall stand for his place. He receiv'd in the repulse of Tarquin seven hurts i'the body.

MENENIUS Why, then you should discover a brace of unmeriting, proud, violent, testy magistrates.

MENENIUS
One i'the neck, and two i'the thigh, — there's nine that
I know.
VOLUMNIA
He had, before this last expedition, twenty-five wounds
upon him.
MENENIUS
Now it's twenty-seven: every gash was an enemy's
grave. [*A shout and flourish.*] Hark! the trumpets.
VOLUMNIA
These are the ushers of Marcius: before him he carries
noise, and behind him he leaves tears:
Death, that dark spirit, in's nervy arm doth lie;
Which, being advanc'd, declines, and then men die.

A sennet. Trumpets sound. Enter COMINIUS *the
general, and* TITUS LARTIUS; *between them,*
CORIOLANUS, *crown'd with an oaken garland; with*
CAPTAINS *and* SOLDIERS, *and a* HERALD.

HERALD
Know, Rome, that all alone Marcius did fight
Within Corioli gates: where he hath won,
With fame, a name to Caius Marcius; these
In honour follows Coriolanus.
Welcome to Rome, renowned Coriolanus!　　[*Flourish.*
ALL
Welcome to Rome, renowned Coriolanus!
CORIOLANUS
No more of this, it does offend my heart;
Pray now, no more.
COMINIUS
　　　　　　　Look, sir, your mother!
CORIOLANUS
　　　　　　　　　　　O,
You have, I know, petition'd all the gods
For my prosperity.　　　　　　[*Kneels.*
VOLUMNIA
　　　　　Nay, my good soldier, up;
My gentle Marcius, worthy Caius, and
By deed-achieving honour newly named, —
What is it? — Coriolanus must I call thee? —
But O, thy wife!
CORIOLANUS
　　　　　My gracious silence, hail!
Wouldst thou have laugh'd had I come coffin'd home,
That weep'st to see me triumph? Ah, my dear,
Such eyes the widows in Corioli wear,
And mothers that lack sons.
MENENIUS
　　　　　　　Now, the gods crown thee!
CORIOLANUS
And live you yet? — [*to* VALERIA] O my sweet lady,
pardon.
VOLUMNIA
I know not where to turn: — O, welcome home; —
And welcome, general; and y'are welcome all.
MENENIUS
A hundred thousand welcomes: — I could weep,
And I could laugh; I am light and heavy: — welcome:
A curse begin at very root on's heart
That is not glad to see thee! — You are three
That Rome should dote on: yet, by the faith of men,
We have some old crab-trees here at home that will not
Be grafted to your relish. Yet welcome, warriors:
We call a nettle but a nettle, and
The faults of fools but folly.
COMINIUS
　　　　　　Ever right.
CORIOLANUS
Menenius ever, ever.
HERALD
Give way there, and go on!
CORIOLANUS [*to* VOLUMNIA *and* VIRGILIA].
Your hand, and yours:
Ere in our own house I do shade my head,
The good patricians must be visited;
From whom I have receiv'd not only greetings,
But with them change of honours.
VOLUMNIA
　　　　　　　　I have liv'd
To see inherited my very wishes,
And the buildings of my fancy: only there
Is one thing wanting, which I doubt not but
Our Rome will cast upon thee.
CORIOLANUS
　　　　　　Know, good mother,
I had rather be their servant in my way
Than sway with them in theirs.
COMINIUS
　　　　　　On, to the Capitol!

*[Flourish. Cornets.
Exeunt in state, as before.*

BRUTUS *and* SICINIUS
come forward.

BRUTUS
All tongues speak of him, and the
　bleared sights
Are spectacled to see him: your
　prattling nurse
Into a rapture lets her baby cry
While she chats him: the kitchen
　malkin pins
Her richest lockram 'bout her reechy
　neck,
Clamb'ring the walls to eye him:
　stalls, bulks, windows,
Are smother'd up, leads fill'd, and
　ridges hors'd
With variable complexions; all
　agreeing
In earnestness to see him: seld-shown
　flamens
Do press among the popular throngs,
　and puff
To win a vulgar station: our veil'd
　dames
Commit the war of white and damask
　in
Their nicely-gawded cheeks to the
　wanton spoil
Of Phœbus' burning kisses: such a
　pother,
As if that whatsoever god who leads him
Were slily crept into his human
　powers,
And gave him graceful posture.
SICINIUS
　　　　　　　On the sudden,
I warrant him consul.
BRUTUS
　　　　　Then our office may,
During his power, go sleep.
SICINIUS
He cannot temperately transport his honours
From where he should begin and end; but will
Lose those he hath won.
BRUTUS
　　　　In that there's comfort.
SICINIUS
　　　　　　　　　Doubt not
The commoners, for whom we stand, but they,
Upon their ancient malice, will forget,
With the least cause, these his new honours; which
That he will give them make I as little question
As he is proud to do't.
BRUTUS
　　　　　I heard him swear,
Were he to stand for consul, never would he
Appear i' the market-place, nor on him put
The napless vesture of humility;
Nor, showing, as the manner is, his wounds
To the people, beg their stinking breaths.
SICINIUS
　　　　　　　'Tis right.
BRUTUS
It was his word: O, he would miss it, rather
Than carry it but by the suit of the gentry to him,
And the desire of the nobles.
SICINIUS
　　　　　　I wish no better
Than have him hold that purpose, and to put it
In execution.
BRUTUS
　　　'Tis most like he will.
SICINIUS
It shall be to him, then, as our good wills,
A sure destruction.
BRUTUS
　　　　So it must fall out
To him or our authorities. For an end,
We must suggest the people in what hatred
He still hath held them; that to's power he would
Have made them mules, silenc'd their pleaders, and
Dispropertied their freedoms; holding them,
In human action and capacity,
Of no more soul nor fitness for the world
Than camels in the war; who have their provand
Only for bearing burdens, and sore blows
For sinking under them.

VOLUMNIA　Nay, my good soldier, up.

SICINIUS
　　　　　This, as you say, suggested
At some time when his soaring insolence
Shall touch the people, — which time shall not want,
If he be put upon't; and that's as easy
As to set dogs on sheep, — will be his fire
To kindle their dry stubble; and their blaze
Shall darken him for ever.

Enter a MESSENGER.

BRUTUS
　　　　　What's the matter?
MESSENGER
You are sent for to the Capitol. 'Tis thought
That Marcius shall be consul:
I have seen the dumb men throng to see him, and
The blind to hear him speak: matrons flung gloves,
Ladies and maids their scarfs and handkerchers,
Upon him as he pass'd: the nobles bended,
As to Jove's statue; and the commons made
A shower and thunder with their caps and shouts:
I never saw the like.
BRUTUS
　　　　Let's to the Capitol;
And carry with us ears and eyes for the time,
But hearts for the event.
SICINIUS
　　　　　Have with you.　　[*Exeunt.*

SCENE II
The same. The Capitol.

Enter two OFFICERS, *to lay cushions, as it were,
in the Capitol.*

FIRST OFFICER
Come, come, they are almost here. How many stand
for consulships?
SECOND OFFICER
Three, they say: but 'tis thought of every one
Coriolanus will carry it.
FIRST OFFICER
That's a brave fellow; but he's vengeance proud, and
loves not the common people.
SECOND OFFICER
Faith, there had been many great men that have
flatter'd the people, who ne'er loved them; and there be
many that they have loved, they know not wherefore: so
that, if they love they know not why, they hate upon no
better a ground: therefore, for Coriolanus neither to
care whether they love or hate him manifests the true
knowledge he has in their disposition; and, out of his
noble carelessness, lets them plainly see't.

FIRST OFFICER
If he did not care whether he had their love or no, he'd
waved indifferently 'twixt doing them neither good nor
harm: but he seeks their hate with greater devotion
than they can render it him; and leaves nothing
undone that may fully discover him their opposite.
Now, to seem to affect the malice and displeasure of
the people is as bad as that which he dislikes, — to
flatter them for their love.

SECOND OFFICER
He hath deserved worthily of his country: and his
ascent is not by such easy degrees as those who, having
been supple and courteous to the people, bonneted,
without any further deed to heave them at all into their
estimation and report: but he hath so planted his
honours in their eyes, and his actions in their hearts,
that for their tongues to be silent, and not confess so
much, were a kind of ingrateful injury; to report
otherwise were a malice, that, giving itself the lie,
would pluck reproof and rebuke from every ear that
heard it.

FIRST OFFICER
No more of him; he's a worthy man: make way, they are
coming.

*A sennet. Enter the PATRICIANS and the TRIBUNES
of the people, LICTORS before them: CORIOLANUS,
MENENIUS, COMINIUS the consul: SICINIUS and
BRUTUS take their places by themselves:
CORIOLANUS stands.*

MENENIUS
Having determin'd of the Volsces, and
To send for Titus Lartius, it remains,
As the main point of this our after-meeting,
To gratify his noble service that
Hath thus stood for his country: therefore, please you,
Most reverend and grave elders, to desire
The present consul, and last general
In our well-found successes, to report
A little of that worthy work perform'd
By Caius Marcius Coriolanus; whom
We meet here, both to thank, and to remember
With honours like himself.

FIRST SENATOR
⠀⠀⠀⠀⠀⠀⠀⠀⠀⠀Speak, good Cominius:
Leave nothing out for length, and make us think
Rather our state's defective for requital
Than we to stretch it out. — *[to the* TRIBUNES]
Masters o'the people,
We do request your kindest ears; and after,
Your loving motion toward the common body,
To yield what passes here.

SICINIUS
⠀⠀⠀⠀⠀⠀⠀⠀⠀⠀We are convented
Upon a pleasing treaty; and have hearts
Inclinable to honour and advance
The theme of our assembly.

BRUTUS
⠀⠀⠀⠀⠀⠀⠀⠀⠀⠀Which the rather
We shall be blest to do, if he remember
A kinder value of the people than
He hath hereto priz'd them at.

MENENIUS
⠀⠀⠀⠀⠀⠀⠀⠀⠀⠀That's off, that's off;
I would you rather had been silent. Please you
To hear Cominius speak?

BRUTUS
⠀⠀⠀⠀⠀⠀⠀⠀⠀⠀Most willingly:
But yet my caution was more pertinent
Than the rebuke you give it.

MENENIUS
⠀⠀⠀⠀⠀⠀⠀⠀⠀⠀He loves your people;
But tie him not to be their bedfellow. —
Worthy Cominius, speak. — [CORIOLANUS *rises, and
offers to go away.*] Nay, keep your place.

FIRST SENATOR
Sit, Coriolanus; never shame to hear
What you have nobly done.

CORIOLANUS
⠀⠀⠀⠀⠀⠀⠀⠀⠀⠀Your honours' pardon:
I had rather have my wounds to heal again
Than hear say how I got them.

BRUTUS
⠀⠀⠀⠀⠀⠀⠀⠀⠀⠀Sir, I hope
My words disbench'd you not.

CORIOLANUS
⠀⠀⠀⠀⠀⠀⠀⠀⠀⠀No, sir: yet oft,
When blows have made me stay, I fled from words.
You sooth'd not, therefore hurt not: but your people,
I love them as they weigh.

MENENIUS
⠀⠀⠀⠀⠀⠀⠀⠀⠀⠀Pray now, sit down.

CORIOLANUS
I had rather have one scratch my head i'the sun,
When the alarum were struck, than idly sit
To hear my nothings monster'd. ⠀⠀⠀⠀⠀⠀[*Exit.*

MENENIUS
⠀⠀⠀⠀⠀⠀⠀⠀⠀⠀Masters of the people,
Your multiplying spawn how can he flatter —
That's thousand to one good one — when you now see
He had rather venture all his limbs for honour
Than one on's ears to hear't? — Proceed, Cominius.

COMINIUS
I shall lack voice: the deeds of Coriolanus
Should not be utter'd feebly. — It is held
That valour is the chiefest virtue, and
Most dignifies the haver: if it be,
The man I speak of cannot in the world
Be singly counterpois'd. At sixteen years,
When Tarquin made a head for Rome, he fought
Beyond the mark of others: our then dictator,
Whom with all praise I point at, saw him fight,
When with his Amazonian chin he drove
The bristled lips before him: be bestrid
An o'er-press'd Roman, and i' the consul's view
Slew three opposers: Tarquin's self he met,
And struck him on his knee: in that day's feats,
When he might act the woman in the scene,
He prov'd best man i' the field, and for his meed
Was brow-bound with the oak. His pupil age
Man-enter'd thus, he waxed like a sea;
And, in the brunt of seventeen battles since,
He lurch'd all swords of the garland. For this last,
Before and in Corioli, let me say,
I cannot speak him home: he stopp'd the fliers;
And by his rare example made the coward
Turn terror into sport: as weeds before
A vessel under sail, so men obey'd,
And fell below his stem: his sword, death's stamp
Where it did mark, it took; from face to foot
He was a thing of blood, whose every motion
Was tim'd with dying cries: alone he enter'd
The mortal gate of the city, which he painted
With shunless destiny; aidless came off,
And with a sudden re-enforcement struck
Corioli like a planet: now all's his:
When, by and by, the din of war gan pierce
His ready sense; then straight his doubled spirit
Re-quicken'd what in flesh was fatigate,
And to the battle came he; where he did
Run reeking o'er the lives of men, as if
'Twere a perpetual spoil: and till we call'd
Both field and city ours, he never stood
To ease his breast with panting.

MENENIUS
⠀⠀⠀⠀⠀⠀⠀⠀⠀⠀Worthy man!

FIRST SENATOR
He cannot but with measure fit the honours
Which we devise him.

COMINIUS
⠀⠀⠀⠀⠀⠀⠀⠀⠀⠀Our spoils he kick'd at;
And look'd upon things precious as they were
The common muck of the world: he covets less
Than misery itself would give; rewards
His deeds with doing them; and is content
To spend the time to end it.

MENENIUS
⠀⠀⠀⠀⠀⠀⠀⠀⠀⠀He's right noble:
Let him be call'd for.

FIRST SENATOR
⠀⠀⠀⠀⠀⠀⠀⠀⠀⠀Call Coriolanus.

OFFICER
He doth appear.

Enter CORIOLANUS.

MENENIUS
The senate, Coriolanus, are well pleas'd
To make thee consul.

CORIOLANUS
⠀⠀⠀⠀⠀⠀⠀⠀⠀⠀I do owe them still
My life and services.

MENENIUS
⠀⠀⠀⠀⠀⠀⠀⠀⠀⠀It then remains
That you do speak to the people.

CORIOLANUS
⠀⠀⠀⠀⠀⠀⠀⠀⠀⠀I do beseech you,
Let me o'erleap that custom, for I cannot
Put on the gown, stand naked, and entreat them,
For my wounds' sake, to give their suffrage: please you
That I may pass this doing.

SICINIUS
⠀⠀⠀⠀⠀⠀⠀⠀⠀⠀Sir, the people
Must have their voices; neither will they bate
One jot of ceremony.

MENENIUS
⠀⠀⠀⠀⠀⠀⠀⠀⠀⠀Put them not to't: —
Pray you, go fit you to the custom; and
Take to you, as your predecessors have,
Your honour with your form.

CORIOLANUS
⠀⠀⠀⠀⠀⠀⠀⠀⠀⠀It is a part
That I shall blush in acting, and might well
Be taken from the people.

BRUTUS [*to* SICINIUS].
⠀⠀⠀⠀⠀⠀⠀⠀⠀⠀Mark you that?

CORIOLANUS
To brag unto them, — thus I did, and thus; —
Show them th'unaching scars which I should hide,
As if I had receiv'd them for the hire
Of their breath only! —

MENENIUS
⠀⠀⠀⠀⠀⠀⠀⠀⠀⠀Do not stand upon't. —
We recommend to you, tribunes of the people,
Our purpose to them; — and to our noble consul
Wish we all joy and honour.

SENATORS
To Coriolanus come all joy and honour!
⠀⠀⠀⠀[*Flourish of cornets. Exeunt all but* BRUTUS *and*
⠀⠀⠀⠀⠀⠀⠀⠀⠀⠀⠀⠀⠀⠀⠀⠀⠀SICINIUS.

BRUTUS
You see how he intends to use the people.

SICINIUS
May they perceive's intent! He will require them,
As if he did contemn what he requested
Should be in them to give.

BRUTUS
⠀⠀⠀⠀⠀⠀⠀⠀⠀⠀Come, we'll inform them
Of our proceedings here: on the market-place
I know they do attend us. ⠀⠀⠀⠀⠀⠀[*Exeunt.*

SCENE III

The same. The Forum.

Enter seven or eight CITIZENS.

FIRST CITIZEN
Once, if he do require our voices, we ought not to deny
him.

SECOND CITIZEN
We may, sir, if we will.

THIRD CITIZEN
We have power in ourselves to do it, but it is a power
that we have no power to do: for if he show us his
wounds, and tell us his deeds, we are to put our
tongues into those wounds, and speak for them; so, if
he tells us his noble deeds, we must also tell him our
noble acceptance of them. Ingratitude is monstrous:
and for the multitude to be ingrateful, were to make a
monster of the multitude; of the which we being
members, should bring ourselves to be monstrous
members.

FIRST CITIZEN
And to make us no better thought of, a little help will
serve; for once we stood up about the corn, he himself
stuck not to call us the many-headed multitude.

THIRD CITIZEN
We have been call'd so of many; not that our heads are
some brown, some black, some abram, some bald, but
that our wits are so diversely colour'd: and truly I think,
if all our wits were to issue out of one skull, they would
fly east, west, north, south; and their consent of one
direct way should be at once to all the points
o'th'compass.

SECOND CITIZEN
Think you so? Which way do you judge my wit would
fly?

THIRD CITIZEN
Nay, your wit will not so soon out as another man's
will, — 'tis strongly wedged up in a block-head; but if it
were at liberty, 'twould, sure, southward.

SECOND CITIZEN
Why that way?

THIRD CITIZEN
To lose itself in a fog; where being three parts melted
away with rotten dews, the fourth would return for
conscience' sake, to help to get thee a wife.

SECOND CITIZEN
You are never without your tricks: — you may, you may.

THIRD CITIZEN
Are you all resolved to give your voices? But that's no

matter, the greater part carries it. I say, if he would incline to the people, there was never a worthier man. — Here he comes, and in the gown of humility: mark his behaviour. We are not to stay all together, but to come by him where he stands, by ones, by twos, and by threes. He's to make his requests by particulars; wherein every one of us has a single honour, in giving him our own voices with our own tongues: therefore follow me, and I'll direct you how you shall go by him.

ALL
Content, content.   [*Exeunt.*
Enter CORIOLANUS, *in a gown of humility,*
with MENENIUS.

MENENIUS
O sir, you are not right: have you not known
The worthiest men have done't?

CORIOLANUS
                    What must I say? —
'I pray, sir' — Plague upon't! I cannot bring
My tongue to such a pace. 'Look, sir, my
    wounds!
I got them in my country's service, when
Some certain of your brethren roar'd, and
    ran
From the noise of our own drums.'

MENENIUS
                    O me, the gods!
You must not speak of that: you must desire
    them
To think upon you.

CORIOLANUS
                    Think upon me! hang 'em!
I would they would forget me, like the
    virtues
Which our divines lose by 'em.

MENENIUS
                    You'll mar all:
I'll leave you: pray you, speak to 'em, I pray
    you,
In wholesome manner.

CORIOLANUS
                    Bid them wash their faces,
And keep their teeth clean. [*Exit* MENENIUS.] —
    So, here comes a brace.
            Enter two of the CITIZENS.
You know the cause, sir, of my standing here.

FIRST CITIZEN
We do, sir; tell us what hath brought you to't.

CORIOLANUS
Mine own desert.

SECOND CITIZEN
Your own desert!

CORIOLANUS
Ay, not mine own desire.

FIRST CITIZEN
How! not your own desire?

CORIOLANUS
No, sir, 'twas never my desire yet to trouble the poor with begging.

FIRST CITIZEN
You must think, if we give you any thing, we hope to gain by you.

CORIOLANUS
Well, then, I pray, your price o'the consulship?

FIRST CITIZEN
The price is, to ask it kindly.

CORIOLANUS
Kindly! Sir, I pray, let me ha't: I have wounds to show you, which shall be yours in private. — Your good voice, sir; what say you?

SECOND CITIZEN
You shall ha't, worthy sir.

CORIOLANUS
A match, sir. — There's in all two worthy voices begg'd. — I have your alms: adieu.

FIRST CITIZEN
But this is something odd.

SECOND CITIZEN
An'twere to give again, — but 'tis no matter.
                    [*Exeunt the two* CITIZENS.
            Enter two other CITIZENS.

CORIOLANUS
Pray you now, if it may stand with the tune of your voices that I may be consul, I have here the customary gown.

CORIOLANUS You know the cause, sir, of my standing here.

THIRD CITIZEN
You have deserved nobly of your country, and you have not deserved nobly.

CORIOLANUS
Your enigma?

THIRD CITIZEN
You have been a scourge to her enemies, you have been a rod to her friends; you have not, indeed, loved the common people.

CORIOLANUS
You should account me the more virtuous, that I have not

been common in my love. I will, sir, flatter my sworn brother, the people, to earn a dearer estimation of them; 'tis a condition they account gentle: and since the wisdom of their choice is rather to have my hat than my heart, I will practise the insinuating nod, and be off to them most counterfeitly; that is, sir, I will counterfeit the bewitchment of some popular man, and give it bountiful to the desirers. Therefore, beseech you I may be consul.

FOURTH CITIZEN
We hope to find you our friend; and therefore give you our voices heartily.

THIRD CITIZEN
You have received many wounds for your country.

CORIOLANUS
I will not seal your knowledge with showing them. I will make much of your voices, and so trouble you no further.

BOTH CITIZENS
The gods give you joy, sir, heartily!   [*Exeunt.*

CORIOLANUS
Most sweet voices! —
Better it is to die, better to starve,
Than crave the hire which first we do deserve.
Why in this woolvish toge should I stand here,
To beg of Hob and Dick, that do appear,
Their needless vouches? Custom calls me to't: —
What custom wills, in all things should we do't,
The dust on antique time would lie unswept,
And mountainous error be too highly heap'd
For truth to o'er-peer. Rather than fool it so,
Let the high office and the honour go
To one that would do thus. — I am half through;
The one part suffer'd, the other will I do. —
Here come moe voices.
            Enter three CITIZENS *more.*
Your voices: for your voices I have fought;
Watch'd for your voices; for your voices bear
Of wounds two dozen odd; battles thrice six
I have seen, and heard of; for your voices have
Done many things, some less, some more: your voices:
Indeed, I would be consul.

FIFTH CITIZEN
He has done nobly, and cannot go without any honest man's voice.

SIXTH CITIZEN
Therefore let him be consul: the gods give him joy, and make him good friend to the people!

All THREE CITIZENS
Amen, amen. — God save thee, noble consul!   [*Exeunt.*

CORIOLANUS
Worthy voices!

THIRD CITIZEN Are you all resolved to give your voices?

Enter MENENIUS, *with* BRUTUS *and* SICINIUS.

MENENIUS
You have stood your limitation; and the tribunes
Endue you with the people's voice: remains
That, in the official marks invested, you
Anon do meet the senate.

CORIOLANUS
       Is this done?

SICINIUS
The custom of request you have discharged:
The people do admit you; and are summon'd
To meet anon, upon your approbation.

CORIOLANUS
Where? at the senate-house?

SICINIUS
      There, Coriolanus.

CORIOLANUS
May I change these garments?

SICINIUS
       You may, sir.

CORIOLANUS
That I'll straight do; and, knowing myself again,
Repair to the senate-house.

MENENIUS
I'll keep you company. — Will you along?

BRUTUS
We stay here for the people.

SICINIUS
      Fare you well.
    [Exeunt CORIOLANUS *and* MENENIUS.
He has it now; and, by his looks, methinks
'Tis warm at's heart.

BRUTUS
     With a proud heart he wore
His humble weeds. — Will you dismiss the people?
    Enter CITIZENS.

SICINIUS
How now, my masters! have you chose this man?

FIRST CITIZEN
He has our voices, sir.

BRUTUS
We pray the gods he may deserve your loves.

SECOND CITIZEN
Amen, sir: — to my poor unworthy notice,
He mock'd us when he begg'd our voices.

THIRD CITIZEN
       Certainly,
He flouted us downright.

FIRST CITIZEN
No, 'tis his kind of speech, — he did not mock us.

SECOND CITIZEN
Not one amongst us, save yourself, but says
He used us scornfully: he should have show'd us
His marks of merit, wounds receiv'd for's country.

SICINIUS
Why, so he did, I am sure.

ALL THE CITIZENS
     No, no; no man saw 'em.

THIRD CITIZEN
He said he had wounds, which he could show
in private;
And with his hat, thus waving it in scorn,
'I would be consul,' says he; 'aged custom
But by your voices will not so permit me;
Your voices therefore': when we granted that,
Here was, 'I thank you for your voices, — thank you, —
Your most sweet voices: — now you have left your voices,
I have no further with you': — was not this mockery?

SICINIUS
Why either were you ignorant to see't,
Or, seeing it, of such childish friendliness
To yield your voices?

BRUTUS
     Could you not have told him,
As you were lesson'd, — when he had no power,
But was a petty servant to the state,
He was your enemy; ever spake against
Your liberties, and the charters that you bear
I' the body of the weal; and now, arriving
A place of potency, and sway o' the state,
If he should still malignantly remain
Fast foe to the plebeii, your voices might
Be curses to yourselves? You should have said,
That as his worthy deeds did claim no less
Than what he stood for, so his gracious nature
Would think upon you for your voices, and
Translate his malice towards you into love,
Standing your friendly lord.

SICINIUS
     Thus to have said,
As you were fore-advis'd, had touch'd his spirit
And tried his inclination; from him pluck'd
Either his gracious promise, which you might,
As cause had call'd you up, have held him to;
Or else it would have gall'd his surly nature,
Which easily endures not article
Tying him to aught; so, putting him to rage,
You should have ta'en th'advantage of his choler,
And pass'd him unelected.

BRUTUS
      Did you perceive
He did solicit you in free contempt,
When he did need your loves; and do you think
That his contempt shall not be bruising to you,
When he hath power to crush? Why, had your bodies
No heart among you? or had you tongues to cry
Against the rectorship of judgement?

SICINIUS
      Have you,
Ere now, denied the asker? and now again,
Of him that did not ask, but mock, bestow
Your sued-for tongues?

THIRD CITIZEN
He's not confirm'd; we may deny him yet.

SECOND CITIZEN
And will deny him;
I'll have five hundred voices of that sound.

FIRST CITIZEN
I twice five hundred, and their friends to piece 'em.

BRUTUS
Get you hence instantly; and tell those friends
They have chose a consul that will from them take
Their liberties; make them of no more voice
Than dogs, that are as often beat for barking
As therefore kept to do so.

SICINIUS
      Let them assemble;
And, on a safer judgement, all revoke
Your ignorant election: enforce his pride,
And his old hate unto you: besides, forget not
With what contempt he wore the humble weed;
How in his suit he scorn'd you; but your loves,
Thinking upon his services, took from you
Th'apprehension of his present portance, which
Most gibingly, ungravely, he did fashion
After the inveterate hate he bears you.

BRUTUS
      Lay
A fault on us, your tribunes; that we labour'd,
No impediment between, but that you must
Cast your election on him.

SICINIUS
      Say you chose him
More after our commandment than as guided
By your own true affections; and that your minds,
Pre-occupied with what you rather must do
Than what you should, made you against the grain
To voice him consul: lay the fault on us.

BRUTUS
Ay, spare us not. Say we read lectures to you,
How youngly he began to serve his country,
How long continued; and what stock he springs of, —
The noble house o'the Marcians; from whence came
That Ancus Marcius, Numa's daughter's son,
Who, after great Hostilius, here was king;
Of the same house Publius and Quintus were,
That our best water brought by conduits hither;
And Censorinus, nobly named so,
Twice being by the people chosen censor,
Was his great ancestor.

SICINIUS
      One thus descended,
That hath beside well in his person wrought
To be set high in place, we did commend
To your remembrances; but you have found,
Scaling his present bearing with his past,
That he's your fixed enemy, and revoke
Your sudden approbation.

BRUTUS
     Say, you ne'er had done't —
Harp on that still — but by our putting on:
And presently, when you have drawn your number,
Repair to the Capitol.

ALL THE CITIZENS
     We will so: almost all
Repent in their election.   *[Exeunt.*

BRUTUS
     Let them go on;

This mutiny were better put in hazard,
Than stay, past doubt, for greater:
If, as his nature is, he fall in rage
With their refusal, both observe and answer
The vantage of his anger.

SICINIUS
      To the Capitol, come:
We will be there before the stream o' the people;
And this shall seem, as partly 'tis, their own,
Which we have goaded onward. *[Exeunt.*

ACT III

SCENE I

Rome. A street.

Cornets. Enter CORIOLANUS, MENENIUS, *all the*
GENTRY, COMINIUS, TITUS LARTIUS,
and other SENATORS.

CORIOLANUS
Tullus Aufidius, then, had made new head?

LARTIUS
He had, my lord; and that it was which caus'd
Our swifter composition.

CORIOLANUS
So, then, the Volsces stand but as at first;
Ready, when time shall prompt them, to make road
Upon's again.

COMINIUS
     They are worn, lord consul, so,
That we shall hardly in our ages see
Their banners wave again.

CORIOLANUS
      Saw you Aufidius?

LARTIUS
On safe-guard he came to me; and did curse
Against the Volsces, for they had so vilely
Yielded the town: he is retired to Antium.

CORIOLANUS
Spoke he of me?

LARTIUS
     He did, my lord.

CORIOLANUS
      How? what?

LARTIUS
How often he had met you, sword to sword;
That of all things upon the earth he hated
Your person most; that he would pawn his fortunes
To hopeless restitution, so he might
Be call'd your vanquisher.

CORIOLANUS
      At Antium lives he?

LARTIUS
At Antium.

CORIOLANUS
I wish I had a cause to seek him there,
To oppose his hatred fully. Welcome home.
    Enter SICINIUS *and* BRUTUS.
Behold, these are the tribunes of the people,
The tongues o'th'common mouth: I do despise them;
For they do prank them in authority,
Against all noble sufferance.

SICINIUS
      Pass no further.

CORIOLANUS
Ha! what is that?

BRUTUS
It will be dangerous to go on: no further.

CORIOLANUS
What makes this change?

MENENIUS
The matter?

COMINIUS
Hath he not pass'd the noble and the common?

BRUTUS
Cominius, no.

CORIOLANUS
Have I had children's voices?

FIRST SENATOR
Tribunes, give way; he shall to the market-place.

BRUTUS
The people are incens'd against him.

SICINIUS
      Stop,
Or all will fall in broil.

CORIOLANUS
     Are these your herd? —

Must these have voices, that can yield them now,
And straight disclaim their tongues? — What are
your offices?
You being their mouths, why rule you not their teeth?
Have you not set them on?

MENENIUS
Be calm, be calm.

CORIOLANUS
It is a purpos'd thing, and grows by plot,
To curb the will of the nobility:
Suffer't, and live with such as cannot rule,
Nor ever will be rul'd.

BRUTUS
Call't not a plot:
The people cry you mock'd them; and of late,
When corn was given them gratis, you repined;
Scandal'd the suppliants for the people, — call'd them
Time-pleasers, flatterers, foes to nobleness.

CORIOLANUS
Why, this was known before.

BRUTUS
Not to them all.

CORIOLANUS
Have you inform'd them sithence?

BRUTUS
How! I inform them!

CORIOLANUS
You are like to do such business.

BRUTUS
Not unlike,
Each way, to better yours.

CORIOLANUS
Why, then, should I be consul? By yond clouds,
Let me deserve so ill as you, and make me
Your fellow tribune.

SICINIUS
You show too much of that
For which the people stir: if you will pass
To where you are bound, you must inquire your way,
Which you are out of, with a gentler spirit;
Or never be so noble as a consul,
Nor yoke with him for tribune.

MENENIUS
Let's be calm.

COMINIUS
The people are abus'd; set on. This paltering
Becomes not Rome; nor has Coriolanus
Deserv'd this so dishonour'd rub, laid falsely
I'the plain way of his merit.

CORIOLANUS
Tell me of corn!
This was my speech, and I will speak't again, —

MENENIUS
Not now, not now.

FIRST SENATOR
Not in this heat, sir, now.

CORIOLANUS
Now, as I live, I will. — My nobler friends,
I crave their pardons: —
For the mutable, rank-scented meiny, let them
Regard me as I do not flatter, and
Therein behold themselves: I say again,
In soothing them, we nourish 'gainst our senate
The cockle of rebellion, insolence, sedition,
Which we ourselves have plough'd for, sow'd,
and scatter'd,
By mingling them with us, the honour'd number;
Who lack not virtue, no, nor power, but that
Which they have given to beggars.

MENENIUS
Well, no more.

FIRST SENATOR
No more words, we beseech you.

CORIOLANUS
How! no more!
As for my country I have shed my blood,
Not fearing outward force, so shall my lungs
Coin words till their decay against those measles,
Which we disdain should tetter us, yet sought
The very way to catch them.

BRUTUS
You speak o' the people,
As if you were a god to punish, not
A man of their infirmity.

SICINIUS
'Twere well
We let the people know't.

MENENIUS
What, what? his choler?

CORIOLANUS
Choler!
Were I as patient as the midnight sleep,
By Jove, 'twould be my mind!

SICINIUS
It is a mind
That shall remain a poison where it is,
Not poison any further.

CORIOLANUS
Shall remain! —
Hear you this Triton of the minnows? mark you
His absolute 'shall'?

COMINIUS
'Twas from the canon.

CORIOLANUS
'Shall'!
O good, but most unwise patricians! why,
You grave, but reckless senators, have you thus
Given Hydra here to choose an officer,
That with his peremptory 'shall', being but
The horn and noise o'th'monster, wants not spirit
To say he'll turn your current in a ditch,
And make your channel his? If he have power,
Then vail your ignorance; if none, awake
Your dangerous lenity. If you are learn'd,
Be not as common fools; if you are not,
Let them have cushions by you. You are plebeians,
If they be senators: and they are no less,
When, both your voices blended, the great'st taste
Most palates theirs. They choose their magistrate;
And such a one as he, who puts his 'shall',
His popular 'shall', against a graver bench
Than ever frown'd in Greece. By Jove himself,
It makes the consuls base! and my soul aches
To know, when two authorities are up,
Neither supreme, how soon confusion
May enter 'twixt the gap of both, and take
The one by th'other.

COMINIUS
Well, — on to the market-place.

CORIOLANUS
Whoever gave that counsel, to give forth
The corn o' the storehouse gratis, as 'twas used
Sometime in Greece, —

MENENIUS
Well, well, no more of that.

CORIOLANUS
Though there the people had more absolute power, —
I say, they nourish'd disobedience, fed
The ruin of the state.

BRUTUS
Why, shall the people give
One, that speaks thus, their voice?

CORIOLANUS
I'll give my reasons,
More worthier than their voices. They know the corn
Was not their recompense, resting well assured
That ne'er did service for't: being press'd to the war,
Even when the navel of the state was touch'd,
They would not thread the gates: — this kind of service
Did not deserve corn gratis: being i'the war,
Their mutinies and revolts, wherein they show'd
Most valour, spoke not for them: th'accusation
Which they have often made against the senate,
All cause unborn, could never be the native
Of our so frank donation. Well, what then?
How shall this bosom multiplied digest
The senate's courtesy? Let deeds express
What's like to be their words: — 'We did request it;
We are the greater poll, and in true fear
They gave us our demands': — thus we debase
The nature of our seats, and make the rabble
Call our cares fears; which will in time
Break ope the locks o' the senate, and bring in
The crows to peck the eagles.

MENENIUS
Come, enough.

BRUTUS
Enough, with over-measure.

CORIOLANUS
No, take more:
What may be sworn by, both divine and human,
Seal what I end withal! — This double worship, —
Where one part does disdain with cause, the other
Insult without all reason; where gentry, title, wisdom,
Cannot conclude but by the yea and no
Of general ignorance, — it must omit
Real necessities, and give way the while
To unstable slightness: purpose so barr'd, it follows,
Nothing is done to purpose. Therefore, beseech you, —
You that will be less fearful than discreet;

That love the fundamental part of state
More than you doubt the change on't; that prefer
A noble life before a long, and wish
To jump a body with a dangerous physic
That's sure of death without it, — at once pluck out
The multitudinous tongue; let them not lick
The sweet which is their poison: your dishonour
Mangles true judgement, and bereaves the state
Of that integrity which should become't;
Not having the power to do the good it would,
For th'ill which doth control't.

BRUTUS
'Has said enough.

SICINIUS
'Has spoken like a traitor, and shall answer
As traitors do.

CORIOLANUS
Thou wretch, despite o'erwhelm thee! —
What should the people do with these bald tribunes?
On whom depending, their obedience fails
To the greater bench: in a rebellion,
When what's not meet, but what must be, was law,
Then were they chosen: in a better hour,
Let what is meet be said it must be meet,
And throw their power i' the dust.

BRUTUS
Manifest treason!

SICINIUS
This a consul? no.

BRUTUS
The aediles, ho!

Enter an AEDILE.
Let him be apprehended.

SICINIUS
Go, call the people [*exit* AEDILE]: — in whose name
myself
Attach thee as a traitorous innovator,
A foe to the public weal: obey, I charge thee,
And follow to thine answer.

CORIOLANUS
Hence, old goat!

SENATORS, *etc.*
We'll surety him.

COMINIUS
Aged sir, hands off.

CORIOLANUS
Hence, rotten thing! or I shall shake thy bones
Out of thy garments.

SICINIUS
Help, ye citizens!

Enter a rabble of CITIZENS, *with the* AEDILES.

MENENIUS
On both sides more respect.

SICINIUS
Here's he that would take from you all your power.

BRUTUS
Seize him, aediles!

CITIZENS
Down with him! down with him!

SENATORS, *etc.*
Weapons, weapons, weapons!
[*They all bustle about* CORIOLANUS.
Tribunes! — Patricians! — Citizens! — What, ho! —
Sicinius! — Brutus! — Coriolanus! — Citizens! —
Peace, peace, peace! — Stay, hold, peace!

MENENIUS
What is about to be? — I am out of breath;
Confusion's near; I cannot speak. — You, tribunes
To the people! — Coriolanus, patience: —
Speak, good Sicinius.

SICINIUS
Hear me, people; peace!

CITIZENS
Let's hear our tribune: peace! — Speak, speak, speak.

SICINIUS
You are at point to lose your liberties:
Marcius would have all from you; Marcius
Whom late you have nam'd for consul.

MENENIUS
Fie, fie, fie!
This is the way to kindle, not to quench.

FIRST SENATOR
To unbuild the city, and to lay all flat.

SICINIUS
What is the city but the people?

CITIZENS
True,
The people are the city.

BRUTUS
By the consent of all, we were establish'd
The people's magistrates.
CITIZENS
          You so remain.
MENENIUS
And so are like to do.
COMINIUS
That is the way to lay the city flat;
To bring the roof to the foundation,
And bury all, which yet distinctly ranges,
In heaps and piles of ruin.
SICINIUS
          This deserves death.
BRUTUS
Or let us stand to our authority,
Or let us lose it. — We do here pronounce,
Upon the part o'the people, in whose power
We were elected theirs, Marcius is worthy
Of present death.
SICINIUS
          Therefore lay hold of him;
Bear him to the rock Tarpeian, and from thence
Into destruction cast him.
BRUTUS
          Aediles, seize him!
CITIZENS
Yield, Marcius, yield!
MENENIUS
          Hear me one word:
Beseech you, tribunes, hear me but a word.
AEDILES
Peace, peace!
MENENIUS
Be that you seem, truly your country's friends,
And temperately proceed to what you would
Thus violently redress.
BRUTUS
          Sir, those cold ways,
That seem like prudent helps, are very poisonous
Where the disease is violent. — Lay hands upon him,
And bear him to the rock.
CORIOLANUS
          No, I'll die here.   [*Drawing his sword.*
There's some among you have beheld me fighting:
Come, try upon yourselves what you have seen me.
MENENIUS
Down with that sword! — Tribunes, withdraw awhile.
BRUTUS
Lay hands upon him.
MENENIUS
          Help Marcius, help,
You that be noble; help him, young and old!
CITIZENS
Down with him! down with him!

[*In this mutiny the* TRIBUNES, *the* AEDILES,
and the PEOPLE *are beat in.*

MENENIUS
Go, get you to your house; be gone, away!
All will be naught else.
SECOND SENATOR
          Get you gone.
COMINIUS
          Stand fast;
We have as many friends as enemies.
MENENIUS
Shall it be put to that?
FIRST SENATOR
          The gods forbid! —
I prithee, noble friend, home to thy house;
Leave us to cure this cause.
MENENIUS
          For 'tis a sore upon us,
You cannot tent yourself: be gone, beseech you.
COMINIUS
Come, sir, along with us.
CORIOLANUS
I would they were barbarians, as they are,
Though in Rome litter'd; not Romans, as they are not,
Though calv'd i'the porch o'the Capitol. —
MENENIUS
          Be gone;
Put not your worthy rage into your tongue;
One time will owe another.
CORIOLANUS
          On fair ground
I could beat forty of them.

CORIOLANUS Hence, rotten thing! or I shall shake thy bones out of thy garments.

MENENIUS
          I could myself
Take up a brace o'the best of them; yea, the two
  tribunes.
COMINIUS
But now 'tis odds beyond arithmetic;
And manhood is call'd foolery, when it stands
Against a falling fabric. — Will you hence,
Before the tag return? whose rage doth rend
Like interrupted waters, and o'erbear
What they are us'd to bear.
MENENIUS
          Pray you, be gone:
I'll try whether my old wit be in request
With those that have but little: this must be patch'd
With cloth of any colour.
COMINIUS
          Nay, come away.
[*Exeunt* CORIOLANUS, COMINIUS, *and others.*
FIRST PATRICIAN
This man has marr'd his *fortune.*
MENENIUS
His nature is too noble for the world:
He would not flatter Neptune for his trident,
Or Jove for's power to thunder. His heart's his mouth:
What his breast forges, that his tongue must vent;
And, being angry, does forget that ever
He heard the name of death. —   [*A noise within.*
Here's goodly work!
SECOND PATRICIAN
          I would they were a-bed!
MENENIUS
I would they were in Tiber! What the vengeance
Could he not speak 'em fair?
  Enter BRUTUS *and* SICINIUS, *with the rabble again.*
SICINIUS
          Where is this viper,
That would depopulate the city, and
Be every man himself?
MENENIUS
          You worthy tribunes, —
SICINIUS
He shall be thrown down the Tarpeian rock
With rigorous hands; he hath resisted law,
And therefore law shall scorn him further trial
Than the severity of the public power,
Which he so sets at naught.
FIRST CITIZEN
          He shall well know
The noble tribunes are the people's mouths,
And we their hands.
CITIZENS
          He shall, sure on't.
MENENIUS
          Sir, sir, —
SICINIUS
Peace!

MENENIUS
Do not cry havoc, where you should but hunt
With modest warrant.
SICINIUS
          Sir, how comes't that you
Have holp to make this rescue?
MENENIUS
          Hear me speak: —
As I do know the consul's worthiness,
So can I name his faults, —
SICINIUS
          Consul! — what consul?
MENENIUS
The consul Coriolanus.
BRUTUS
          He consul!
CITIZENS
No, no, no, no, no.
MENENIUS
If, by the tribunes' leave, and yours, good people,
I may be heard, I'ld crave a word or two;
The which shall turn you to no further harm
Than so much loss of time.
SICINIUS
          Speak briefly, then;
For we are peremptory to dispatch
This viperous traitor: to eject him hence
Were but our danger; and to keep him here
Our certain death: therefore it is decreed
He dies to-night.
MENENIUS
          Now the good gods forbid
That our renowned Rome, whose gratitude
Towards her deserved children is enroll'd
In Jove's own book, like an unnatural dam
Should now eat up her own!
SICINIUS
He's a disease that must be cut away.
MENENIUS
O, he's a limb that has but a disease;
Mortal, to cut it off; to cure it, easy.
What has he done to Rome that's worthy death?
Killing our enemies, the blood he hath lost —
Which, I dare vouch, is more than that he hath,
By many an ounce — he dropp'd it for his country;
And what is left, to lose it by his country,
Were to us all, that do't and suffer it,
A brand to the end o'the world.
SICINIUS
          This is clean kam.
BRUTUS
Merely awry: when he did love his country,
It honour'd him.
MENENIUS
          The service of the foot
Being once gangren'd, is not then respected
For what before it was.

BRUTUS
We'll hear no more. —
Pursue him to his house, and pluck him thence;
Lest his infection, being of catching nature,
Spread further.

MENENIUS
One word more, one word.
This tiger-footed rage, when it shall find
The harm of unscann'd swiftness, will, too late,
Tie leaden pounds to's heels. Proceed by process;
Lest parties — as he is belov'd — break out,
And sack great Rome with Romans.

BRUTUS
If it were so, —

SICINIUS
What do ye talk?
Have we not had a taste of his obedience?
Our ædiles smote? ourselves resisted? Come, —

MENENIUS
Consider this: — he has been bred i'the wars
Since he could draw a sword, and is ill school'd
In bolted language; meal and bran together
He throws without distinction. Give me leave,
I'll go to him, and undertake to bring him
Where he shall answer, by a lawful form, —
In peace, — to his utmost peril.

FIRST SENATOR
Noble tribunes,
It is the humane way: the other course
Will prove too bloody; and the end of it
Unknown to the beginning.

SICINIUS
Noble Menenius,
Be you, then, as the people's officer. —
Masters, lay down your weapons.

BRUTUS
Go not home.

SICINIUS
Meet on the market-place. We'll attend you there:
Where, if you bring not Marcius, we'll proceed
In our first way.

MENENIUS
I'll bring him to you. —
[to the SENATORS] Let me desire your company: he
    must come,
Or what is worst will follow.

FIRST SENATOR
Pray you, let's to him.
[Exeunt.

SCENE II

A room in CORIOLANUS' house

Enter CORIOLANUS and PATRICIANS

CORIOLANUS
Let them pull all about mine ears; present me
Death on the wheel or at wild horses' heels;
Or pile ten hills on the Tarpeian rock,
That the precipitation might down stretch
Below the beam of sight; yet will I still
Be thus to them.

FIRST PATRICIAN
You do the nobler.

CORIOLANUS
I muse my mother
Does not approve me further, who was wont
To call them woollen vassals, things created
To buy and sell with groats; to show bare heads
In congregations, to yawn, be still, and wonder,
When one but of my ordinance stood up
To speak of peace or war.

Enter VOLUMNIA.
I talk of you:
Why did you wish me milder? would you have me
False to my nature? Rather say, I play
The man I am.

VOLUMNIA
O, sir, sir, sir,
I would have had you put your power well on,
Before you had worn it out.

CORIOLANUS
Let go.

VOLUMNIA
You might have been enough the man you are,
With striving less to be so: lesser had been
The thwartings of your disposition, if
You had not show'd them how ye were disposed
Ere they lack'd power to cross you.

CORIOLANUS
Let them hang.

VOLUMNIA
Ay, and burn too.

Enter MENENIUS with the SENATORS.

MENENIUS
Come, come, you have been too rough, something too
    rough;
You must return and mend it.

FIRST SENATOR
There's no remedy;
Unless, by not so doing, our good city
Cleave in the midst, and perish.

VOLUMNIA
Pray, be counsell'd:
I have a heart as little apt as yours,
But yet a brain that leads my use of anger
To better vantage.

MENENIUS
Well said, noble woman!
Before he should thus stoop to the herd, but that
The violent fit o' the time craves it as physic
For the whole state, I would put mine armour on,
Which I can scarcely bear.

CORIOLANUS
What must I do?

MENENIUS
Return to the tribunes.

CORIOLANUS
Well, what then? what then?

MENENIUS
Repent what you have spoke.

CORIOLANUS
For them? — I cannot do it to the gods;
Must I, then, do't to them?

VOLUMNIA
You are too absolute;
Though therein you can never be too noble,
But when extremities speak. I have heard you say,
Honour and policy, like unsever'd friends,
I' the war do grow together: grant that, and tell me,
In peace what each of them by th'other lose,
That they combine not there.

CORIOLANUS
Tush, tush!

MENENIUS
A good demand.

VOLUMNIA
If it be honour in your wars to seem
The same you are not, — which, for your best ends,
You adopt your policy, — how is it less or worse,
That it shall hold companionship in peace
With honour, as in war; since that to both
It stands in like request?

CORIOLANUS
Why force you this?

VOLUMNIA
Because that now it lies you on to speak
To the people; not by your own instruction,
Nor by the matter which your heart prompts you,
But with such words that are but rooted in
Your tongue, though but bastards, and syllables
Of no allowance to your bosom's truth.
Now, this no more dishonours you at all
Than to take in a town with gentle words,
Which else would put you to your fortune, and
The hazard of much blood.
I would dissemble with my nature, where
My fortunes and my friends at stake required
I should do so in honour: I am, in this,
Your wife, your son, these senators, the nobles;
And you will rather show our general louts
How you can frown than spend a fawn upon 'em,
For the inheritance of their loves, and safeguard
Of what that want might ruin.

MENENIUS
Noble lady! —
Come, go with us; speak fair: you may salve so,
Not what is dangerous present, but the loss
Of what is past.

VOLUMNIA
I prithee now, my son,
Go to them, with this bonnet in thy hand;
And thus far having stretch'd it, — here be with them, —
Thy knee bussing the stones, — for in such business
Action is eloquence, and the eyes of th'ignorant
More learned than the ears, — waving thy head,
Which often, thus, correcting thy stout heart,
Now humble as the ripest mulberry

That will not hold the handling, — or say to them,
Thou art their soldier, and, being bred in broils,
Hast not the soft way which, thou dost confess,
Were fit for thee to use, as they to claim,
In asking their good loves; but thou wilt frame
Thyself, forsooth, hereafter theirs, so far
As thou hast power and person.

MENENIUS
This but done,
Even as she speaks it, why, their hearts were yours;
For they have pardons, being ask'd, as free
As words to little purpose.

VOLUMNIA
Prithee now,
Go, and be rul'd: although I know thou hadst rather
Follow thine enemy in a fiery gulf
Than flatter him in a bower. — Here is Cominius.

Enter COMINIUS.

COMINIUS
I have been i' the market-place; and, sir, 'tis fit
You make strong party, or defend yourself
By calmness or by absence: all's in anger.

MENENIUS
Only fair speech.

COMINIUS
I think 'twill serve, if he
Can thereto frame his spirit.

VOLUMNIA
He must, and will. —
Prithee now, say you will, and go about it.

CORIOLANUS
Must I go show them my unbarb'd sconce? must I
With my base tongue give to my noble heart
A lie that it must bear? Well, I will do't:
Yet, were there but this single plot to lose,
This mould of Marcius, they to dust should grind it,
And throw't against the wind. — To the market-place!
You have put me now to such a part, which never
I shall discharge to the life.

COMINIUS
Come, come, we'll prompt you.

VOLUMNIA
I prithee now, sweet son, — as thou hast said
My praises made thee first a soldier, so,
To have my praise for this, perform a part
Thou hast not done before.

CORIOLANUS
Well, I must do't:
Away, my disposition, and possess me
Some harlot's spirit! my throat of war be turn'd,
Which quired with my drum, into a pipe
Small as an eunuch, or the virgin voice
That babies lulls asleep! the smiles of knaves
Tent in my cheeks; and schoolboys' tears take up
The glasses of my sight! a beggar's tongue
Make motion through my lips; and my arm'd knees,
Who bow'd but in my stirrup, bend like his
That hath receiv'd an alms! — I will not do't;
Lest I surcease to honour mine own truth,
And by my body's action teach my mind
A most inherent baseness.

VOLUMNIA
At thy choice, then:
To beg of thee, it is my more dishonour
Than thou of them. Come all to ruin: let
Thy mother rather feel thy pride than fear
Thy dangerous stoutness; for I mock at death
With as big heart as thou. Do as thou list.
Thy valiantness was mine, thou suck'dst it from me;
But owe thy pride thyself.

CORIOLANUS
Pray, be content:
Mother, I am going to the market-place;
Chide me no more. I'll mountebank their loves,
Cog their hearts from them, and come home beloved
Of all the trades in Rome. Look, I am going:
Commend me to my wife. I'll return consul;
Or never trust to what my tongue can do
I' the way of flattery further.

VOLUMNIA
Do your will. [Exit.

COMINIUS
Away! the tribunes do attend you: arm yourself
To answer mildly; for they are prepared
With accusations, as I hear, more strong
Than are upon you yet.

CORIOLANUS
The word is 'mildly': — pray you, let us go:
Let them accuse me by invention, I

Will answer in mine honour.

MENENIUS
                Ay, but mildly.

CORIOLANUS
Well, mildly be it, then, — mildly!   [*Exeunt.*

SCENE III

The same. The Forum.

Enter SICINIUS *and* BRUTUS.

BRUTUS
In this point charge him home, — that he
    affects
Tyrannical power: if he evade us there,
Enforce him with his envy to the people;
And that the spoil got on the Antiates
Was ne'er distributed.
           Enter an AEDILE.
What, will he come?

AEDILE
            He's coming.

BRUTUS
              How accompanied?

AEDILE
With old Menenius, and those senators
That always favour'd him.

SICINIUS
             Have you a catalogue
Of all the voices that we have procured,
Set down by the poll?

AEDILE
            I have; 'tis ready.

SICINIUS
Have you collected them by tribes?

AEDILE
                 I have.

SICINIUS
Assemble presently the people hither:
And when they bear me say, 'It shall be so
I' th'right and strength o'th'commons,' be it either
For death, for fine, or banishment, then let them,
If I say fine, cry 'Fine', — if death, cry 'Death';
Insisting on the old prerogative
And power i'the truth o'the cause.

AEDILE
               I shall inform them.

BRUTUS
And when such time they have begun to cry,
Let them not cease, but with a din confused
Enforce the present execution
Of what we chance to sentence.

AEDILE
              Very well.

SICINIUS
Make them be strong, and ready for this hint,
When we shall hap to give't them.

BRUTUS
            Go about it. —
              [*Exit* AEDILE.
Put him to choler straight: he hath been used
Ever to conquer, and to have his worth
Of contradiction: being once chaf'd, he cannot
Be rein'd again to temperance; then he speaks
What's in his heart; and that is there which looks
With us to break his neck.

SICINIUS
           Well, here he comes.

Enter CORIOLANUS, MENENIUS, COMINIUS, *with*
SENATORS *and* PATRICIANS.

MENENIUS
Calmly, I do beseech you.

CORIOLANUS
Ay, as an ostler, that for the poorest piece
Will bear the knave by the volume. — The honour'd
    gods
Keep Rome in safety, and the chairs of justice
Supplied with worthy men! plant love among's!
Throng our large temples with the shows of peace,
And not our streets with war!

FIRST SENATOR
            Amen, amen.

MENENIUS
A noble wish.
     Enter the AEDILE, *with* CITIZENS.

SICINIUS
Draw near, ye people.

AEDILE
List to your tribunes; audience! peace, I say!

VOLUMNIA You are too absolute; though therein you
        can never be too noble.

CORIOLANUS
First, hear me speak.

BOTH TRIBUNES
           Well, say. — Peace, ho!

CORIOLANUS
Shall I be charg'd no further than this present?
Must all determine here?

SICINIUS
           I do demand
If you submit you to the people's voices,
Allow their officers, and are content
To suffer lawful censure for such faults
As shall be prov'd upon you?

CORIOLANUS
             I am content.

MENENIUS
Lo, citizens, he says he is content:
The warlike service he has done consider; think
Upon the wounds his body bears, which show
Like graves i'the holy churchyard.

CORIOLANUS
         Scratches with briers,
Scars to move laughter only.

MENENIUS
          Consider further,
That when he speaks not like a citizen,
You find him like a soldier: do not take
His rougher accents for malicious sounds,
But, as I say, such as become a soldier,
Rather than envy you.

COMINIUS
          Well, well, no more.

CORIOLANUS
What is the matter,
That being pass'd for consul with full voice,
I am so dishonour'd, that the very hour
You take it off again?

SICINIUS
          Answer to us.

CORIOLANUS
Say, then: 'tis true, I ought so.

SICINIUS
We charge you, that you have contriv'd to take
From Rome all season'd office, and to wind
Yourself into a power tyrannical;
For which you are a traitor to the people.

CORIOLANUS
How! traitor!

MENENIUS
        Nay, temperately; your promise.

CORIOLANUS
The fires i' the lowest hell fold-in the people!
Call me their traitor! — Thou injurious tribune!
Within thine eyes sat twenty thousand deaths,

In thy hands clutch'd as many millions, in
Thy lying tongue both numbers, I would say
'Thou liest'unto thee with a voice as free
As I do pray the gods.

SICINIUS
         Mark you this, people?

CITIZENS
To the rock, to the rock with him!

SICINIUS
Peace!
We need not put new matter to his charge:
What you have seen him do, and heard him speak,
Beating your officers, cursing yourselves,
Opposing laws with strokes, and here defying
Those whose great power must try him; even this,
So criminal, and in such capital kind,
Deserves th'extremest death.

BRUTUS
        But since he hath
Serv'd well for Rome, —

CORIOLANUS
        What do you prate of service?

BRUTUS
I talk of that, that know it.

CORIOLANUS
You?

MENENIUS
Is this the promise that you made your mother?

COMINIUS
Know, I pray you, —

CORIOLANUS
        I'll know no further:
Let them pronounce the steep Tarpeian death,
Vagabond exile, flaying, pent to linger
But with a grain a day, — I would not buy
Their mercy at the price of one fair word;
Nor check my courage for what they can give,
To have't with saying 'Good morrow.'

SICINIUS
         For that he has,
As much as in him lies, from time to time
Envied against the people, seeking means
To pluck away their power; as now at last
Given hostile strokes, and that not in the presence
Of dreaded justice, but on the ministers
That do distribute it; — in the name o'the people,
And in the power of us the tribunes, we,
Even from this instant, banish him our city;
In peril of precipitation
From off the rock Tarpeian, never more
To enter our Rome gates: i'the people's name,
I say it shall be so.

CITIZENS
        It shall be so,
It shall be so; let him away: he's banish'd,
And it shall be so.

COMINIUS
Hear me, my masters and my common friends, —

SICINIUS
He's sentenced; no more hearing.

COMINIUS
         Let me speak:
I have been consul, and can show for Rome
Her enemies' marks upon me. I do love
My country's good with a respect more tender,
More holy, and profound, than mine own life,
My dear wife's estimate, her womb's increase,
And treasure of my loins; then if I would
Speak that, —

SICINIUS
      We know your drift: — speak what?

BRUTUS
There's no more to be said, but he is banish'd,
As enemy to the people and his country:
It shall be so.

CITIZENS
It shall be so, it shall be so.

CORIOLANUS
You common cry of curs! whose breath I hate
As reek o'the rotten fens, whose loves I prize
As the dead carcasses of unburied men
That do corrupt my air, — I banish you;
And here remain with your uncertainty!
Let every feeble rumour shake your hearts!
Your enemies, with nodding of their plumes,
Fan you into despair! Have the power still
To banish your defenders; till at length
Your ignorance, which finds not till it feels,
Making not reservation of yourselves,
Still your own foes, deliver you, as most

Abated captives; to some nation
That won you without blows! Despising,
For you, the city, thus I turn my back:
There is a world elsewhere.
[*Exeunt* CORIOLANUS, COMINIUS, MENENIUS,
SENATORS, *and* PATRICIANS.

AEDILE
The people's enemy is gone, is gone!

CITIZENS
Our enemy is banish'd! he is gone!
Hoo! hoo! [*They all shout and throw up their caps.*

SICINIUS
Go, see him out at gates, and follow him,
As he hath follow'd you, with all despite;
Give him deserv'd vexation. Let a guard
Attend us through the city.

CITIZENS
Come, come, let's see him out at gates; come: —
The gods preserve our noble tribunes! — come.
[*Exeunt.*

ACT IV

SCENE I

Rome. Before a gate of the city.

Enter CORIOLANUS, VOLUMNIA, VIRGILIA,
MENENIUS, COMINIUS, *with the young*
NOBILITY *of Rome.*

CORIOLANUS
Come, leave your tears; a brief farewell: — the beast
With many heads butts me away. — Nay, mother,
Where is your ancient courage? you were used
To say extremity was the trier of spirits;
That common chances common men could bear;
That, when the sea was calm, all boats alike
Show'd mastership in floating; fortune's blows,
When most struck home, being gentle wounded, craves
A noble cunning: you were used to load me
With precepts that would make invincible
The heart that conn'd them.

VIRGILIA
O heavens! O heavens!

CORIOLANUS
Nay! I prithee, woman, —

VOLUMNIA
Now the red pestilence strike all trades in Rome,
And occupations perish!

CORIOLANUS
What, what, what!
I shall be lov'd when I am lack'd. Nay, mother,
Resume that spirit, when you were wont to say,
If you had been the wife of Hercules,
Six of his labours you'ld have done, and sav'd
Your husband so much sweat. — Cominius,
Droop not; adieu. — Farewell, my wife, — my mother:
I'll do well yet. — Thou old and true Menenius,
Thy tears are salter than a younger man's,
And venomous to thine eyes. — My sometime general,
I have seen the stern, and thou hast oft beheld
Heart-hard'ning spectacles; tell these sad women,
'Tis fond to wail inevitable strokes,
As 'tis to laugh at 'em. — My mother, you wot well
My hazards still have been your solace: and
Believe't not lightly, — though I go alone,
Like to a lonely dragon, that his fen
Makes fear'd and talk'd of more than seen, — your son
Will or exceed the common, or be caught
With cautelous baits and practice.

VOLUMNIA
My first son,
Whither wilt thou go? Take good Cominius
With thee awhile: determine on some course,
More than a wild exposure to each chance
That starts i'the way before thee.

CORIOLANUS
O the gods!

COMINIUS
I'll follow thee a month, devise with thee
Where thou shalt rest, that thou mayst hear of us,
And we of thee: so, if the time thrust forth
A cause for thy repeal, we shall not send
O'er the vast world to seek a single man;
And lose advantage, which doth ever cool
I' the absence of the needer.

CORIOLANUS
Fare ye well:
Thou hast years upon thee; and thou art too full

Of the wars' surfeits, to go rove with one
That's yet unbruis'd: bring me but out at gate. —
Come, my sweet wife, my dearest mother, and
My friends of noble touch; when I am forth,
Bid me farewell, and smile. I pray you, come.
While I remain above the ground, you shall
Hear from me still: and never of me aught
But what is like me formerly.

MENENIUS
That's worthily
As any ear can hear. — Come, let's not weep. —
If I could shake off but one seven years
From these old arms and legs, by the good gods,
I'ld with thee every foot.

CORIOLANUS
Give me thy hand: —
Come. [*Exeunt.*

SCENE II

The same. A street near the gate.

Enter the two TRIBUNES, SICINIUS, BRUTUS, *with
the* AEDILE.

SICINIUS
Bid them all home; he's gone, and we'll no further. —
The nobility are vex'd, whom we see have sided
In his behalf.

BRUTUS
Now we have shown our power,
Let us seem humbler after it is done
Than when it was a-doing.

SICINIUS
Bid them home:
Say their great enemy is gone, and they
Stand in their ancient strength.

BRUTUS
Dismiss them home.
[*Exit* AEDILE.
Here comes his mother.

SICINIUS
Let's not meet her.

BRUTUS
Why?

SICINIUS
They say she's mad.

BRUTUS
They have ta'en note of us: keep on your way.
Enter VOLUMNIA, VIRGILIA, *and* MENENIUS.

VOLUMNIA
O, y'are well met: the hoarded plague o'the gods
Requite your love!

MENENIUS
Peace, peace; be not so loud.

VOLUMNIA
If that I could for weeping, you should hear, —
Nay, and you shall hear some. — [*to* BRUTUS]
Will you be gone?

VIRGILIA [*to* SICINIUS].
You shall stay too: I would I had the power
To say so to my husband.

SICINIUS
Are you mankind?

VOLUMNIA
Ay, fool; is that a shame? — Note but this fool. —
Was not a man my father? Hadst thou foxship
To banish him that struck more blows for Rome
Than thou hast spoken words? —

SICINIUS
O blessed heavens!

VOLUMNIA
More noble blows than ever thou wise words;
And for Rome's good. — I'll tell thee what; — yet go: —
Nay, but thou shalt stay too: — I would my son
Were in Arabia, and thy tribe before him,
His good sword in his hand.

SICINIUS
What then?

VIRGILIA
What then!
He'ld make an end of thy posterity.

VOLUMNIA
Bastards and all. —
Good man, the wounds that he does bear for Rome!

MENENIUS
Come, come, peace.

SICINIUS
I would he had continued to his country
As he began, and not unknit himself

The noble knot he made.

BRUTUS
I would he had.

VOLUMNIA
'I would he had!' 'Twas you incens'd the rabble; —
Rats, that can judge as fitly of his worth
As I can of those mysteries which heaven
Will not have earth to know.

BRUTUS
Pray, let us go.

VOLUMNIA
Now, pray, sir, get you gone:
You have done a brave deed. Ere you go, hear this: —
As far as doth the Capitol exceed
The meanest house in Rome, so far my son, —
This lady's husband here, this, do you see, —
Whom you have banish'd, does exceed you all.

BRUTUS
Well, well, we'll leave you.

SICINIUS
Why stay we to be baited
With one that wants her wits?

VOLUMNIA
Take my prayers with you. —
[*Exeunt* TRIBUNES.
I would the gods had nothing else to do
But to confirm my curses! Could I meet 'em
But once a-day, it would unclog my heart
Of what lies heavy to't.

MENENIUS
You have told them home;
And, by my troth, you have cause. You'll sup with me?

VOLUMNIA
Anger's my meat; I sup upon myself,
And so shall starve with feeding. — Come, let's go:
Leave this faint puling, and lament as I do,
In anger, Juno-like. Come, come, come.

MENENIUS
Fie, fie, fie! [*Exeunt.*

SCENE III

A highway between Rome and Antium.

Enter a ROMAN *and a* VOLSCE, *meeting.*

ROMAN
I know you well, sir, and you know me: your name, I
think, is Adrian.

VOLSCE
It is so, sir: truly, I have forgot you.

ROMAN
I am a Roman; and my services are, as you are, against
'em: know you me yet?

VOLSCE
Nicanor? no?

ROMAN
The same, sir.

VOLSCE
You had more beard when I last saw you; but your
favour is well approved by your tongue. What's the
news in Rome? I have a note from the Volscian state, to
find you out there: you have well saved me a day's
journey.

ROMAN
There hath been in Rome strange insurrections; the
people against the senators, patricians, and nobles.

VOLSCE
Hath been! is it ended, then? Our state thinks not so:
they are in a most warlike preparation, and hope to
come upon them in the heat of their division.

ROMAN
The main blaze of it is past, but a small thing would
make it flame again; for the nobles receive so to heart
the banishment of that worthy Coriolanus, that they
are in a ripe aptness to take all power from the people,
and to pluck from them their tribunes for ever. This
lies glowing, I can tell you, and is almost mature for the
violent breaking out.

VOLSCE
Coriolanus banish'd!

ROMAN
Banish'd, sir.

VOLSCE
You will be welcome with this intelligence,
Nicanor.

ROMAN
The day serves well for them now. I have heard it said,
the fittest time to corrupt a man's wife is when she's
fallen out with her husband. Your noble Tullus
Aufidius will appear well in these wars, his great

opposer, Coriolanus, being now in no request of his country.

VOLSCE
He cannot choose. I am most fortunate, thus accidentally to encounter you: you have ended my business, and I will merrily accompany you home.

ROMAN
I shall, between this and supper, tell you most strange things from Rome; all tending to the good of their adversaries. Have you an army ready, say you?

VOLSCE
A most royal one; the centurions and their charges, distinctly billeted, already in the entertainment, and to be on foot at an hour's warning.

ROMAN
I am joyful to hear of their readiness, and am the man, I think, that shall set them in present action. So, sir, heartily well met, and most glad of your company.

VOLSCE
You take my part from me, sir; I have the most cause to be glad of yours.

ROMAN
Well, let us go together.   [*Exeunt.*

SCENE IV

Antium. Before AUFIDIUS' *house.*

Enter CORIOLANUS *in mean apparel, disguised and muffled.*

CORIOLANUS
A goodly city is this Antium. — City,
'Tis I that made thy widows: many an heir
Of these fair edifices 'fore my wars
Have I heard groan and drop: then know me not;
Lest that thy wives with spits, and boys with stones,
In puny battle slay me.
                    Enter a CITIZEN.
                    Save you, sir.

CITIZEN
And you.

CORIOLANUS
                    Direct me, if it be your will,
Where great Aufidius lies: is he in Antium?

CITIZEN
He is, and feasts the nobles of the state
At his house this night.

CORIOLANUS
                    Which is his house, beseech you?

CITIZEN
This, here, before you.

CORIOLANUS
                    Thank you, sir: farewell.
                    [*Exit* CITIZEN.
O world, thy slippery turns! Friends now fast sworn,
Whose double bosoms seem to wear one heart,
Whose hours, whose bed, whose meal, and exercise,
Are still together, who twin, as 'twere, in love
Unseparable, shall within this hour,
On a dissension of a doit, break out
To bitterest enmity: so, fellest foes,
Whose passions and whose plots have broke their sleep
To take the one the other, by some chance,
Some trick not worth an egg, shall grow dear friends
And interjoin their issues. So with me:
My birth-place hate I, and my love's upon
This enemy town. — I'll enter: if he slay me,
He does fair justice; if he give me way,
I'll do his country service.   [*Exit.*

SCENE V

The same. A hall in AUFIDIUS' *house.*

Music plays. Enter a SERVING-MAN

FIRST SERVING-MAN
Wine, wine, wine! — What service is here!
I think our fellows are asleep.   [*Exit.*
                    Enter another SERVING-MAN.

SECOND SERVING-MAN
Where's Cotus? my master calls for him. —
Cotus!   [*Exit.*
                    Enter CORIOLANUS.

CORIOLANUS
A goodly house: the feast smells well; but I
Appear not like a guest.
                    Enter the first SERVING-MAN.

FIRST SERVING-MAN
What would you have, friend? whence are you?
Here's no place for you: pray, go to the door.   [*Exit.*

CORIOLANUS
I have deserv'd no better entertainment
In being Coriolanus.

                    Enter second SERVING-MAN.

SECOND SERVING-MAN
Whence are you, sir? — Has the porter his eyes in his head, that he gives entrance to such companions? — Pray, get you out.

CORIOLANUS
Away!

SECOND SERVING-MAN
'Away!' get you away.

CORIOLANUS
Now th'art troublesome.

SECOND SERVING-MAN
Are you so brave? I'll have you talk'd with anon.

                    Enter a third SERVING-MAN. *The first meets him.*

THIRD SERVING-MAN
What fellow's this?

SECOND SERVING-MAN
A strange one as ever I look'd on: I cannot get him out o'the house: prithee, call my master to him.

THIRD SERVING-MAN
What have you to do here, fellow? Pray you avoid the house.

CORIOLANUS
Let me but stand; I will not hurt your hearth.

THIRD SERVING-MAN
What are you?

CORIOLANUS
A gentleman.

THIRD SERVING-MAN
A marvellous poor one.

CORIOLANUS
True, so I am.

THIRD SERVING-MAN
Pray you, poor gentleman, take up some other station; here's no place for you; pray you, avoid: come.

CORIOLANUS
Follow your function, go, and batten on cold bits.
                    [*Pushes him away from him.*

THIRD SERVING-MAN
What, you will not? — Prithee, tell my master what a strange guest he has here.

SECOND SERVING-MAN
And I shall.   [*Exit.*

THIRD SERVING-MAN
Where dwell'st thou?

CORIOLANUS
Under the canopy.

THIRD SERVING-MAN
Under the canopy!

CORIOLANUS
Ay.

THIRD SERVING-MAN
Where's that?

CORIOLANUS
I' th'city of kites and crows.

THIRD SERVING-MAN
I' th'city of kites and crows! — What an ass it is! — Then thou dwell'st with daws too?

CORIOLANUS
No, I serve not thy master.

THIRD SERVING-MAN
How, sir! do you meddle with my master?

CORIOLANUS
Ay; 'tis an honester service than to meddle with thy mistress: thou pratest, and pratest; serve with thy trencher, hence!   [*Beats him away.*
                    Enter AUFIDIUS *with the second* SERVING-MAN.

AUFIDIUS
Where is this fellow?

SECOND SERVING-MAN
Here, sir: I'ld have beaten him like a dog, but for disturbing the lords within.   [*Retires.*

AUFIDIUS
Whence comest thou? what wouldst thou? thy name?
Why speak'st not? speak, man: what's thy name?

CORIOLANUS
                    If, Tullus,   [*Unmuffling.*
Not yet thou know'st me, and, seeing me, dost not
Think me for the man I am, necessity
Commands me name myself.

AUFIDIUS
                    What is thy name?

CORIOLANUS
A name unmusical to the Volscians' ears,
And harsh in sound to thine.

AUFIDIUS
                    Say, what's thy name?
Thou hast a grim appearance, and thy face
Bears a command in't; though thy tackle's torn,
Thou show'st a noble vessel: what's thy name?

CORIOLANUS
Prepare thy brow to frown: — know'st thou me yet?

AUFIDIUS
I know thee not: — thy name?

CORIOLANUS
My name is Caius Marcius, who hath done
To thee particularly and to all the Volsces
Great hurt and mischief; thereto witness may
My surname, Coriolanus: the painful service,
The extreme dangers, and the drops of blood
Shed for my thankless country, are requited
But with that surname; a good memory,
And witness of the malice and displeasure
Which thou shouldst bear me: only that name remains;
The cruelty and envy of the people,
Permitted by our dastard nobles, who
Have all forsook me, hath devour'd the rest;
And suffer'd me by the voice of slaves to be
Whoop'd out of Rome. Now, this extremity
Hath brought me to thy hearth; not out of hope —
Mistake me not — to save my life: for if
I had fear'd death, of all the men i' the world
I would have 'voided thee; but in mere spite,
To be full quit of those my banishers,
Stand I before thee here. Then if thou hast
A heart of wreak in thee, that wilt revenge
Thine own particular wrongs, and stop those maims
Of shame seen through thy country, speed thee straight,
And make my misery serve thy turn: so use it,
That my revengeful services may prove
As benefits to thee; for I will fight
Against my canker'd country with the spleen
Of all the under fiends. But if so be
Thou darest not this, and that to prove more fortunes
Th'art tired, then, in a word, I also am
Longer to live most weary, and present
My throat to thee and to thy ancient malice;
Which not to cut would show thee but a fool,
Since I have ever follow'd thee with hate,
Drawn tuns of blood out of thy country's breast,
And cannot live but to thy shame, unless
It be to do thee service.

AUFIDIUS
                    O Marcius, Marcius!
Each word thou hast spoke hath weeded from my heart
A root of ancient envy. If Jupiter
Should from yond cloud speak divine things,
And say ''Tis true', I'd not believe them more
Than thee, all noble Marcius. — Let me twine
Mine arms about that body, where against
My grained ash an hundred times hath broke,
And scarr'd the moon with splinters: here I clip
The anvil of my sword; and do contest
As hotly and as nobly with thy love
As ever in ambitious strength I did
Contend against thy valour. Know thou first
I lov'd the maid I married; never man
Sigh'd truer breath; but that I see thee here,
Thou noble thing! more dances my rapt heart
Than when I first my wedded mistress saw
Bestride my threshold. Why, thou Mars! I tell thee
We have a power on foot; and I had purpose
Once more to hew thy target from thy brawn,
Or lose mine arm for't: thou hast beat me out
Twelve several times, and I have nightly since
Dreamt of encounters 'twixt thyself and me;
We have been down together in my sleep,
Unbuckling helms, fisting each other's throat,
And wak'd half dead with nothing. Worthy Marcius,
Had we no quarrel else to Rome, but that
Thou art thence banish'd, we would muster all
From twelve to seventy; and, pouring war
Into the bowels of ungrateful Rome,
Like a bold flood o'er-bear. O, come, go in,
And take our friendly senators by the hands;
Who now are here taking their leaves of me,
Who am prepared against your territories,
Though not for Rome itself.

CORIOLANUS
                    You bless me, gods!

AUFIDIUS
Therefore, most absolute sir, if thou wilt have

THIRD SERVING-MAN Here's no place for you; pray you, avoid: come.

The leading of thine own revenges, take
The one half of my commission; and set down —
As best thou art experienc'd, since thou know'st
Thy country's strength and weakness — thine own ways;
Whether to knock against the gates of Rome,
Or rudely visit them in parts remote,
To fright them, ere destroy. But come in:
Let me commend thee first to those that shall
Say yea to thy desires. A thousand welcomes!
And more a friend than e'er an enemy;
Yet, Marcius, that was much. Your hand: most
welcome!
[*Exeunt* CORIOLANUS *and* AUFIDIUS. —
The two SERVING-MEN *come forward.*

FIRST SERVING-MAN
Here's a strange alteration!

SECOND SERVING-MAN
By my hand, I had thought to have strucken him with a
cudgel; and yet my mind gave me his clothes made a
false report of him.

FIRST SERVING-MAN
What an arm he has! he turn'd me about with his
finger and his thumb as one would set up a top.

SECOND SERVING-MAN
Nay, I knew by his face that there was something in
him: he had, sir, a kind of face, methought, — I cannot
tell how to term it.

FIRST SERVING-MAN
He had so; looking as it were — Would I were hang'd,
but I thought there was more in him than I could think.

SECOND SERVING-MAN
So did I, I'll be sworn: he is simply the rarest man i' the
world.

FIRST SERVING-MAN
I think he is: but a greater soldier than he you wot on.

SECOND SERVING-MAN
Who, my master?

FIRST SERVING-MAN
Nay, it's no matter for that.

SECOND SERVING-MAN
Worth six on him.

FIRST SERVING-MAN
Nay, not so neither: but I take him to be the greater
soldier.

SECOND SERVING-MAN
Faith, look you, one cannot tell how to say that: for the
defence of a town our general is excellent.

FIRST SERVING-MAN
Ay, and for an assault too.
Enter the third SERVING-MAN.

THIRD SERVING-MAN
O slaves, I can tell you news, — news, you rascals!
FIRST *and* SECOND SERVING-MEN.
What, what, what? let's partake.

THIRD SERVING-MAN
I would not be a Roman, of all nations; I had as lief be a

condemn'd man.
FIRST *and* SECOND SERVING-MEN.
Wherefore? wherefore?

THIRD SERVING-MAN
Why, here's he that was wont to thwack our general, —
Caius Marcius.

FIRST SERVING-MAN
Why do you say 'thwack our general'?

THIRD SERVING-MAN
I do not say 'thwack our general'; but he was always
good enough for him.

SECOND SERVING-MAN
Come, we are fellows and friends: he was ever too hard
for him; I have heard him say so himself.

FIRST SERVING-MAN
He was too hard for him directly, to say the troth on't:
before Corioli he scotch'd him and notch'd him like a
carbonado.

SECOND SERVING-MAN
An he had been cannibally given, he might have broil'd
and eaten him too.

FIRST SERVING-MAN
But, more of thy news?

THIRD SERVING-MAN
Why, he is so made on here within as if he were son
and heir to Mars; set at upper end o' the table; no
question ask'd him by any of the senators, but they
stand bald before him: our general himself makes a
mistress of him; sanctifies himself with's hand, and
turns up the white o'the eye to his discourse. But the
bottom of the news is, our general is cut i' the middle,
and but one half of what he was yesterday; for the other
has half, by the entreaty and grant of the whole table.
He'll go, he says, and sowl the porter of Rome gates by
the ears: he will mow all down before him, and leave
his passage poll'd.

SECOND SERVING-MAN
And he's as like to do't as any man I can imagine.

THIRD SERVING-MAN
Do't! he will do't; for, look you, sir, he has as many
friends as enemies: which friends, sir, as it were, durst
not, look you, sir, show themselves, as we term it, his
friends whilst he's in directitude.

FIRST SERVING-MAN
Directitude! what's that?

THIRD SERVING-MAN
But when they shall see, sir, his crest up again, and the
man in blood, they will out of their burrows, like conies
after rain, and revel all with him.

FIRST SERVING-MAN
But when goes this forward?

THIRD SERVING-MAN
To-morrow; to-day; presently; you shall have the drum
struck up this afternoon: 'tis, as it were, a parcel of their
feast, and to be executed ere they wipe their lips.

SECOND SERVING-MAN
Why, then we shall have a stirring world again. This

peace is nothing, but to rust iron, increase tailors, and
breed ballad-makers.

FIRST SERVING-MAN
Let me have war, say I; it exceeds peace as far as day
does night; it's spritely, waking, audible, and full of
vent. Peace is a very apoplexy, lethargy; mull'd, deaf,
sleepy, insensible; a getter of more bastard children
than war's a destroyer of men.

SECOND SERVING-MAN
'Tis so: and as war, in some sort, may be said to be a
ravisher, so it cannot be denied but peace is a great
maker of cuckolds.

FIRST SERVING-MAN
Ay, and it makes men hate one another.

THIRD SERVING-MAN
Reason; because they then less need one another. The
wars for my money. I hope to see Romans as cheap as
Volscians. — They are rising, they are rising.

All THREE
In, in, in, in! [*Exeunt.*

SCENE VI
Rome. A public place.

Enter the two TRIBUNES, SICINIUS, *and* BRUTUS.

SICINIUS
We hear not of him, neither need we fear him;
His remedies are tame i'the present peace
And quietness of the people, which before
Were in wild hurry. Here do we make his friends
Blush that the world goes well; who rather had,
Though they themselves did suffer by't, behold
Dissentious numbers pest'ring streets, than see
Our tradesmen singing in their shops, and going
About their functions friendly.

BRUTUS
We stood to't in good time. — Is this Menenius?

SICINIUS
'Tis he, 'tis he: O, he is grown most kind
Of late. Hail, sir!
Enter MENENIUS.

BRUTUS
Hail, sir!

MENENIUS
Hail to you both!

SICINIUS
Your Coriolanus, sir, is not much miss'd
But with his friends: the commonwealth doth stand;
And so would do, were he more angry at it.

MENENIUS
All's well; and might have been much better, if
He could have temporis'd.

SICINIUS
Where is he, hear you?

MENENIUS
Nay, I hear nothing: his mother and his wife
Hear nothing from him.
Enter three or four CITIZENS.

CITIZENS
The gods preserve you both!

SICINIUS
God-den, our neighbours.

BRUTUS
God-den to you all, god-den to you all.

FIRST CITIZEN
Ourselves, our wives, and children, on our knees,
Are bound to pray for you both.

SICINIUS
Live, and thrive!

BRUTUS
Farewell, kind neighbours: we wish'd Coriolanus
Had lov'd you as we did.

CITIZENS
Now the gods keep you!

BOTH TRIBUNES
Farewell, farewell. [*Exeunt* CITIZENS.

SICINIUS
This is a happier and more comely time
Than when these fellows ran about the streets
Crying confusion.

BRUTUS
Caius Marcius was
A worthy officer i'the war; but insolent,
O'ercome with pride, ambitious past all thinking,
Self-loving, —

SICINIUS
And affecting one sole throne,
Without assistance.

MENENIUS
           I think not so.
SICINIUS
We should by this, to all our lamentation,
If he had gone forth consul, found it so.
BRUTUS
The gods have well prevented it, and Rome
Sits safe and still without him.

           Enter an AEDILE.

AEDILE
           Worthy tribunes,
There is a slave, whom we have put in prison,
Reports the Volsces with two several powers
Are enter'd in the Roman territories,
And with the deepest malice of the war
Destroy what lies before 'em.
MENENIUS
           'Tis Aufidius,
Who, hearing of our Marcius' banishment,
Thrusts forth his horns again into the world;
Which were inshell'd when Marcius stood for Rome,
And durst not once peep out.
SICINIUS
           Come, what talk you
Of Marcius?
BRUTUS
Go see this rumourer whipp'd. — It cannot be
The Volsces dare break with us.
MENENIUS
           Cannot be!
We have record that very well it can;
And three examples of the like hath been
Within my age. But reason with the fellow,
Before you punish him, where he heard this;
Lest you shall chance to whip your information,
And beat the messenger who bids beware
Of what is to be dreaded.
SICINIUS
           Tell not me:
I know this cannot be.
BRUTUS
           Not possible.

           Enter a MESSENGER.

MESSENGER
The nobles in great earnestness are going
All to the senate-house: some news is come
That turns their countenances.
SICINIUS
           'Tis this slave; —
Go whip him 'fore the people's eyes: — his raising;
Nothing but his report.
MESSENGER
           Yes, worthy sir,
The slave's report is seconded; and more,
More fearful, is deliver'd.
SICINIUS
           What more fearful?
MESSENGER
It is spoke freely out of many mouths —
How probable I do not know — that Marcius,
Join'd with Aufidius, leads a power 'gainst Rome,
And vows revenge as spacious as between
The young'st and oldest thing.
SICINIUS
           This is most likely!
BRUTUS
Rais'd only, that the weaker sort may wish
Good Marcius home again.
SICINIUS
           The very trick on't.
MENENIUS
This is unlikely:
He and Aufidius can no more atone
Than violentest contrariety.

           Enter a second MESSENGER.

SECOND MESSENGER
You are sent for to the senate:
A fearful army, led by Caius Marcius
Associated with Aufidius, rages
Upon our territories; and have already
O'erborne their way, consum'd with fire, and took
What lay before them.

           Enter COMINIUS.

COMINIUS
O, you have made good work!
MENENIUS
           What news? what news?

COMINIUS
You have holp to ravish your own daughters, and
To melt the city leads upon your pates;
To see your wives dishonour'd to your noses, —
MENENIUS
What's the news? what's the news?
COMINIUS
Your temples burnt in their cement; and
Your franchises, whereon you stood, confined
Into an auger's bore.
MENENIUS
           Pray now, your news? —
You have made fair work, I fear me. — Pray, your
    news? —
If Marcius should be join'd with Volscians, —
COMINIUS
                  If!
He is their god: he leads them like a thing
Made by some other deity than nature,
That shapes man better; and they follow him,
Against us brats, with no less confidence
Than boys pursuing summer butterflies,
Or butchers killing flies.
MENENIUS
           You have made good work,
You and your apron-men; you that stood so much
Upon the voice of occupation and
The breath of garlic-eaters!
COMINIUS
           He will shake
Your Rome about your ears.
MENENIUS
           As Hercules
Did shake down mellow fruit. — You have made fair
    work!
BRUTUS
But is this true, sir?
COMINIUS
           Ay; and you'll look pale
Before you find it other. All the regions
Do smilingly revolt; and who resist
Are mock'd for valiant ignorance,
And perish constant fools. Who is't can blame him?
Your enemies and his find something in him.
MENENIUS
We are all undone, unless
The noble man have mercy.
COMINIUS
           Who shall ask it?
The tribunes cannot do't for shame; the people
Deserve such pity of him as the wolf
Does of the shepherds: for his best friends, if they
Should say, 'Be good to Rome,' they charg'd him even
As those should do that had deserv'd his hate,
And therein show'd like enemies.
MENENIUS
           'Tis true:
If he were putting to my house the brand
That should consume it, I have not the face
To say, 'Beseech you, cease.' — You have made fair hands,
You and your crafts! you have crafted fair!
COMINIUS
           You have brought
A trembling upon Rome, such as was never
So incapable of help.
BOTH TRIBUNES
           Say not, we brought it.
MENENIUS
How! Was it we? we lov'd him; but, like beasts
And cowardly nobles, gave way unto your clusters,
Who did hoot him out o'the city.
COMINIUS
           But I fear
They'll roar him in again. Tullus Aufidius,
The second name of men, obeys his points
As if he were his officer: — desperation
Is all the policy, strength, and defence,
That Rome can make against them.

           Enter a troop of CITIZENS.

MENENIUS
           Here come the clusters. —
And is Aufidius with him? — You are they
That made the air unwholesome, when you cast
Your stinking greasy caps in hooting at
Coriolanus' exile. Now he's coming;
And not a hair upon a soldier's head
Which will not prove a whip: as many coxcombs
As you threw caps up will he tumble down,
And pay you for your voices. 'Tis no matter;

If he could burn us all into one coal,
We have deserv'd it.
CITIZENS
Faith, we hear fearful news.
FIRST CITIZEN
           For mine own part,
When I said, banish him, I said, 'twas pity.
SECOND CITIZEN
And so did I.
THIRD CITIZEN
And so did I; and, to say the truth, so did very many of
us: that we did, we did for the best; and though we
willingly consented to his banishment, yet it was
against our will.
COMINIUS
Y' are goodly things, you voices!
MENENIUS
           You have made
Good work, you and your cry! — Shall's to the Capitol?
COMINIUS
O, ay, what else?

           [*Exeunt* COMINIUS *and* MENENIUS.

SICINIUS
Go, masters, get you home; be not dismay'd:
These are a side that would be glad to have
This true which they so seem to fear. Go home,
And show no sign of fear.
FIRST CITIZEN
The gods be good to us! — Come, masters, let's home. I
ever said we were i'the wrong when we banish'd him.
SECOND CITIZEN
So did we all. But, come, let's home.

           [*Exeunt* CITIZENS.

BRUTUS
I do not like this news.
SICINIUS
Nor I.
BRUTUS
Let's to the Capitol. — Would half my wealth
Would buy this for a lie!
SICINIUS
           Pray, let us go.   [*Exeunt.*

SCENE VII

A camp, at a small distance from Rome.

Enter AUFIDIUS *and his* LIEUTENANT.

AUFIDIUS
Do they still fly to the Roman?
LIEUTENANT
I do not know what witchcraft's in him, but
Your soldiers use him as the grace 'fore meat,
Their talk at table, and their thanks at end;
And you are darken'd in this action, sir,
Even by your own.
AUFIDIUS
           I cannot help it now,
Unless, by using means, I lame the foot
Of our design. He bears himself more proudlier,
Even to my person, than I thought he would
When first I did embrace him; yet his nature
In that's no changeling; and I must excuse
What cannot be amended.
LIEUTENANT
           Yet I wish, sir, —
I mean for your particular, — you had not
Join'd in commission with him; but either
Had borne the action of yourself, or else
To him had left it solely.
AUFIDIUS
I understand thee well; and be thou sure,
When he shall come to his account, he knows not
What I can urge against him. Although it seems,
And so he thinks, and is no less apparent
To the vulgar eye, that he bears all things fairly,
And shows good husbandry for the Volscian state,
Fights dragon-like, and does achieve as soon
As draw his sword; yet he hath left undone
That which shall break his neck or hazard mine,
Whene'er we come to our account.
LIEUTENANT
Sir, I beseech you, think you he'll carry Rome?
AUFIDIUS
All places yield to him ere he sits down;
And the nobility of Rome are his:
The senators and patricians love him too:
The tribunes are no soldiers; and their people
Will be as rash in the repeal, as hasty
To expel him thence. I think he'll be to Rome

As is the osprey to the fish, who takes it
By sovereignty of nature. First he was
A noble servant to them; but he could not
Carry his honours even: whether 'twas pride,
Which out of daily fortune ever taints
The happy man; whether defect of judgement,
To fail in the disposing of those chances
Which he was lord of; or whether nature,
Not to be other than one thing, not moving
From the casque to the cushion, but commanding
    peace
Even with the same austerity and garb
As he controll'd the war; but one of these —
As he hath spices of them all, not all,
For I dare so far free him — made him fear'd,
So hated, and so banish'd: but he has a merit,
To choke it in the utterance. So our virtues
Lie in the interpretation of the time;
And power, unto itself most commendable,
Hath not a tomb so evident as a chair
T'extol what it hath done.
One fire drives out one fire; one nail, one nail;
Rights by rights falter, strengths by strengths do fail.
Come, let's away. When, Caius, Rome is thine,
Thou'rt poor'st of all; then shortly art thou mine.
                               [*Exeunt.*

ACT V

SCENE I

Rome. A public place.

Enter MENENIUS, COMINIUS, SICINIUS,
BRUTUS, *and others.*

MENENIUS
No, I'll not go: you hear what he hath said
Which was sometime his general; who lov'd him
In a most dear particular. He call'd me father:
But what o'that? Go, you that banish'd him;
A mile before his tent fall down, and knee
The way into his mercy: nay, if he coy'd
To hear Cominius speak, I'll keep at home.
COMINIUS
He would not seem to know me.
MENENIUS
                        Do you hear?
COMINIUS
Yet one time he did call me by my name:
I urg'd our old acquaintance, and the drops
That we have bled together. Coriolanus
He would not answer to: forbade all names;
He was a kind of nothing, titleless,
Till he had forg'd himself a name o'the fire
Of burning Rome.
MENENIUS
              Why, so, — you have made good work!
A pair of tribunes that have rack'd for Rome
To make coals cheap, — a noble memory!
COMINIUS
I minded him how royal 'twas to pardon
When it was least expected: he replied,
It was a bare petition of a state
To one whom they had punish'd.
MENENIUS
                    Very well:
Could he say less?
COMINIUS
I offer'd to awaken his regard
For's private friends: his answer to me was,
He could not stay to pick them in a pile
Of noisome musty chaff: he said 'twas folly,
For one poor grain or two, to leave unburnt,
And still to nose the offence.
MENENIUS
                For one poor grain or two!
I am one of those; his mother, wife, his child,
And this brave fellow too, we are the grains;
You are the musty chaff; and you are smelt
Above the moon: we must be burnt for you.
SICINIUS
Nay, pray, be patient: if you refuse your aid
In this so never-needed help, yet do not
Upbraid's with our distress. But, sure, if you
Would be your country's pleader, your good tongue,
More than the instant army we can make,
Might stop our countryman.
MENENIUS
               No, I'll not meddle.

SICINIUS
Pray you, go to him.
MENENIUS
               What should I do?
BRUTUS
Only make trial what your love can do
For Rome, towards Marcius.
MENENIUS
            Well, and say that Marcius
Return me, as Cominius is return'd,
Unheard; what then?
But as a discontented friend, grief-shot
With his unkindness? say't be so?
SICINIUS
              Yet your good will
Must have that thanks from Rome, after the measure
As you intended well.
MENENIUS
             I'll undertake't:
I think he'll hear me. Yet, to bite his lip
And hum at good Cominius, much unhearts me.
He was not taken well; he had not din'd:
The veins unfill'd, our blood is cold, and then
We pout upon the morning, are unapt
To give or to forgive; but when we have stuff'd
These pipes and these conveyances of our blood
With wine and feeding, we 've suppler souls
Than in our priest-like fasts: therefore I'll watch him
Till he be dieted to my request,
And then I'll set upon him.
BRUTUS
You know the very road into his kindness,
And cannot lose your way.
MENENIUS
             Good faith, I'll prove him,
Speed how it will: you shall ere long have knowledge
Of my success.   [*Exit.*
COMINIUS
          He'll never hear him.
SICINIUS
               Not?
COMINIUS
I tell you, he does sit in gold, his eye
Red as 'twould burn Rome; and his injury
The gaoler to his pity. I kneel'd before him;
'Twas very faintly he said 'Rise'; dismiss'd me
Thus, with his speechless hand: what he would do
He sent in writing after me; what he would not,
Bound with an oath to yield no fresh conditions:
So that all hope is vain,
Unless in's noble mother and his wife;
Who, as I hear, mean to solicit him
For mercy to his country. Therefore let's hence,
And with our fair entreaties haste them on.   [*Exeunt.*

SCENE II

The Volscian camp before Rome.

The SENTINELS *at their stations.*

Enter MENENIUS *to the* WATCH *or* GUARD.

FIRST SENTINEL
Stay: whence are you?
SECOND SENTINEL
            Stand, and go back.
MENENIUS
You guard like men; 'tis well: but, by your leave,
I am an officer of state, and come
To speak with Coriolanus.
FIRST SENTINEL
           From whence?
MENENIUS
               From Rome.
FIRST SENTINEL
You may not pass, you must return: our general
Will no more hear from thence.
SECOND SENTINEL
You'll see your Rome embrac'd with fire, before
You'll speak with Coriolanus.
MENENIUS
           Good my friends,
If you have heard your general talk of Rome,
And of his friends there, it is lots to blanks
My name hath touch'd your ears: it is Menenius.
FIRST SENTINEL
Be it so; go back: the virtue of your name
Is not here passable.
MENENIUS
           I tell thee, fellow,
The general is my lover: I have been

The book of his good acts, whence men have read
His fame unparallel'd, haply amplified;
For I have ever verified my friends —
Of whom he's chief — with all the size that verity
Would without lapsing suffer: nay, sometimes,
Like to a bowl upon a subtle ground,
I have tumbled past the throw; and in his praise
Have almost stamp'd the leasing: therefore, fellow,
I must have leave to pass.
FIRST SENTINEL
Faith, sir, if you had told as many lies in his behalf as
you have utter'd words in your own, you should not
pass here: no, though it were as virtuous to lie as to live
chastely. Therefore, go back.
MENENIUS
Prithee, fellow, remember my name is Menenius,
always factionary on the party of your general.
SECOND SENTINEL
Howsoever you have been his liar, as you say you have,
I am one that, telling true under him, must say you
cannot pass. Therefore, go back.
MENENIUS
Has he din'd, canst thou tell? for I would not speak
with him till after dinner.
FIRST SENTINEL
You are a Roman, are you?
MENENIUS
I am, as thy general is.
FIRST SENTINEL
Then you should hate Rome, as he does. Can you,
when you have push'd out your gates the very defender
of them, and, in a violent popular ignorance, given
your enemy your shield, think to front his revenges
with the easy groans of old women, the virginal palms
of your daughters, or with the palsied intercession of
such a decay'd dotant as you seem to be? Can you think
to blow out the intended fire your city is ready to flame
in with such weak breath as this? No, you are deceived;
therefore, back to Rome, and prepare for your
execution: you are condemn'd, our general has sworn
you out of reprieve and pardon.
MENENIUS
Sirrah, if thy captain knew I were here, he would use
me with estimation.
SECOND SENTINEL
Come, my captain knows you not.
MENENIUS
I mean, thy general.
FIRST SENTINEL
My general cares not for you. Back, I say, go; lest I let
forth your half-pint of blood; — back, — that's the
utmost of your having: — back.
MENENIUS
Nay, but, fellow, fellow, —
         Enter CORIOLANUS *and* AUFIDIUS.
CORIOLANUS
What's the matter?
MENENIUS
Now, you companion, I'll say an errand for you: you
shall know now that I am in estimation; you shall
perceive that a Jack guardant cannot office me from my
son Coriolanus: guess, but by my entertainment with
him, if thou stand'st not i'the state of hanging, or of
some death more long in spectatorship, and crueller in
suffering; behold now presently, and swound for
what's to come upon thee. — [*to* CORIOLANUS] The
glorious gods sit in hourly synod about thy particular
prosperity, and love thee no worse than thy old father
Menenius does! O my son, my son! thou art preparing
fire for us; look thee, here's water to quench it. I was
hardly moved to come to thee; but being assured none
but myself could move thee, I have been blown out of
our gates with sighs; and conjure thee to pardon Rome,
and thy petitionary countrymen. The good gods
assuage thy wrath, and turn the dregs of it upon this
varlet here, — this, who, like a block, hath denied my
access to thee.
CORIOLANUS
Away!
MENENIUS
How! away!
CORIOLANUS
Wife, mother, child, I know not. My affairs
Are servanted to others: though I owe
My revenge properly, my remission lies
In Volscian breasts. That we have been familiar,
Ingrate forgetfulness shall poison, rather
Than pity note how much. Therefore, be gone.
Mine ears against your suits are stronger than

Your gates against my force. Yet, for I lov'd thee,
Take this along; I writ it for thy sake,   [*Gives a letter.*
And would have sent it. Another word, Menenius,
I will not hear thee speak. — This man, Aufidius,
Was my belov'd in Rome: yet thou behold'st!

AUFIDIUS
You keep a constant temper.
                    [*Exeunt* CORIOLANUS *and* AUFIDIUS.

FIRST SENTINEL
Now, sir, is your name Menenius?

SECOND SENTINEL
'Tis a spell, you see, of much power: you know the way
home again.

FIRST SENTINEL
Do you hear how we are shent for keeping your
greatness back?

SECOND SENTINEL
What cause, do you think, I have to swound?

MENENIUS
I neither care for the world nor your general: for such
things as you, I can scarce think there's any, y'are so
slight. He that hath a will to die by himself, fears it not
from another: let your general do his worst. For you, be
that you are, long; and your misery increase with your
age! I say to you, as I was said to, Away!   [*Exit.*

FIRST SENTINEL
A noble fellow, I warrant him.

SECOND SENTINEL
The worthy fellow is our general: he's the rock, the oak
not to be wind-shaken.   [*Exeunt.*

SCENE III

The tent of CORIOLANUS.

Enter CORIOLANUS, AUFIDIUS, *and others.*

CORIOLANUS
We will before the walls of Rome to-morrow
Set down our host. — My partner in this action,
You must report to the Volscian lords, how plainly
I have borne this business.

AUFIDIUS
                    Only their ends
You have respected; stopp'd your ears against
The general suit of Rome; never admitted
A private whisper, no, not with such friends
That thought them sure of you.

CORIOLANUS
                    This last old man,
Whom with a crack'd heart I have sent to Rome,
Lov'd me above the measure of a father;
Nay, godded me, indeed. Their latest refuge
Was to send him; for whose old love I have,
Though I show'd sourly to him, once more offer'd
The first conditions, which they did refuse,
And cannot now accept; to grace him only
That thought he could do more, a very little
I have yielded to: fresh embassies and suits,
Nor from the state nor private friends, hereafter
Will I lend ear to. — Ha! what shout is this?
                    [*Shout within.*
Shall I be tempted to infringe my vow
In the same time 'tis made? I will not.
          Enter, in mourning habits, VIRGILIA,
          VOLUMNIA, *leading* YOUNG MARCIUS,
          VALERIA, *with* ATTENDANTS.
My wife comes foremost; then the honour'd mould
Wherein this trunk was fram'd, and in her hand
The grandchild to her blood. But, out, affection!
All bond and privilege of nature, break!
Let it be virtuous to be obstinate. —
What is that curt'sy worth? or those doves' eyes,
Which can make gods forsworn? — I melt, and am not
Of stronger earth than others. — My mother bows;
As if Olympus to a molehill should
In supplication nod: and my young boy
Hath an aspect of intercession, which
Great nature cries 'Deny not.' — Let the Volsces
Plough Rome, and harrow Italy: I'll never
Be such a gosling to obey instinct; but stand,
As if a man were author of himself,
And knew no other kin.

VIRGILIA
                    My lord and husband!

CORIOLANUS
These eyes are not the same I wore in Rome.

VIRGILIA
The sorrow that delivers us thus changed
Makes you think so.

CORIOLANUS
                    Like a dull actor now,

I have forgot my part, and I am out,
Even to a full disgrace. — Best of my flesh,
Forgive my tyranny; but do not say,
For that, 'Forgive our Romans.' O, a kiss
Long as my exile, sweet as my revenge!
Now, by the jealous queen of heaven, that kiss
I carried from thee, dear; and my true lip
Hath virgin'd it e'er since. — You gods! I prate,
And the most noble mother of the world
Leave unsaluted: sink, my knee, i' the earth;   [*Kneels.*
Of thy deep duty more impression show
Than that of common sons.

VOLUMNIA
                    O, stand up blest!
Whilst, with no softer cushion than the flint,
I kneel before thee; and unproperly
Show duty, as mistaken all this while
Between the child and parent.   [*Kneels.*

CORIOLANUS
                    What is this?
Your knees to me? to your corrected son?
Then let the pebbles on the hungry beach
Fillip the stars; then let the mutinous winds
Strike the proud cedars 'gainst the fiery sun;
Murd'ring impossibility, to make
What cannot be, slight work.

VOLUMNIA
                    Thou art my warrior;
I holp to frame thee. — Do you know this lady?

CORIOLANUS
The noble sister of Publicola,
The moon of Rome; chaste as the icicle,
That's curdied by the frost from purest snow,
And hangs on Dian's temple: — dear Valeria!

VOLUMNIA
This is a poor epitome of yours,
Which by the interpretation of full time
May show like all yourself.

CORIOLANUS
                    The god of soldiers,
With the consent of supreme Jove, inform
Thy thoughts with nobleness; that thou mayst prove
To shame unvulnerable, and stick i' the wars
Like a great sea-mark, standing every flaw,
And saving those that eye thee!

VOLUMNIA
                    Your knee, sirrah.

CORIOLANUS
That's my brave boy!

VOLUMNIA
Even he, your wife, this lady, and myself,
Are suitors to you.

CORIOLANUS
                    I beseech you, peace:
Or, if you'ld ask, remember this before, —
The things I have forsworn to grant may never
Be held by you denials. Do not bid me
Dismiss my soldiers, or capitulate
Again with Rome's mechanics: — tell me not
Wherein I seem unnatural: desire not
T'ally my rages and revenges with
Your colder reasons.

VOLUMNIA
                    O, no more, no more!
You have said you will not grant us any thing:
For we have nothing else to ask, but that
Which you deny already: yet we will ask;
That, if you fail in our request, the blame
May hang upon your hardness: therefore hear us.

CORIOLANUS
Aufidius, and you Volsces, mark; for we'll
Hear naught from Rome in private. — Your request?

VOLUMNIA
Should we be silent and not speak, our raiment
And state of bodies would bewray what life
We have led since thy exile. Think with thyself
How more unfortunate than all living women
Are we come hither: since that thy sight, which should
Make our eyes flow with joy, hearts dance with
     comforts,
Constrains them weep, and shake with fear and
     sorrow;
Making the mother, wife, and child, to see
The son, the husband, and the father, tearing
His country's bowels out. And to poor we
Thine enmity's most capital: thou barr'st us
Our prayers to the gods, which is a comfort
That all but we enjoy; for how can we,
Alas, how can we for our country pray,
Whereto we are bound, — together with thy victory,

Whereto we are bound? alack, or we must lose
The country, our dear nurse, or else thy person,
Our comfort in the country. We must find
An evident calamity, though we had
Our wish, which side should win; for either thou
Must, as a foreign recreant, be led
With manacles through our streets, or else
Triumphantly tread on thy country's ruin,
And bear the palm for having bravely shed
Thy wife and children's blood. For myself, son,
I purpose not to wait on fortune till
These wars determine: if I cannot persuade thee
Rather to show a noble grace to both parts
Than seek the end of one, thou shalt no sooner
March to assault thy country than to tread —
Trust to 't, thou shalt not — on thy mother's womb
That brought thee to this world.

VIRGILIA
                    Ay, and mine,
That brought you forth this boy, to keep your name
Living to time.

YOUNG MARCIUS
                    A' shall not tread on me;
I'll run away till I am bigger, but then I'll fight.

CORIOLANUS
Not of a woman's tenderness to be,
Requires nor child nor woman's face to see.
I have sat too long.   [*Rising.*

VOLUMNIA
                    Nay, go not from us thus.
If it were so that our request did tend
To save the Romans, thereby to destroy
The Volsces whom you serve, you might condemn us,
As poisonous of your honour: no; our suit
Is, that you reconcile them: while the Volsces
May say, 'This mercy we have show'd'; the Romans,
'This we receiv'd'; and each in either side
Give the all-hail to thee, and cry, 'Be blest
For making up this peace!' Thou know'st, great son,
The end of war's uncertain; but this certain,
That, if thou conquer Rome, the benefit
Which thou shalt thereby reap is such a name,
Whose repetition will be dogg'd with curses;
Whose chronicle thus writ, — 'The man was noble,
But with his last attempt he wip'd it out;
Destroy'd his country; and his name remains
To the ensuing age abhorr'd.' Speak to me, son:
Thou hast affected the fine strains of honour,
To imitate the graces of the gods;
To tear with thunder the wide cheeks o'the air,
And yet to charge thy sulphur with a bolt
That should but rive an oak. Why dost not speak?
Think'st thou it honourable for a noble man
Still to remember wrongs? — Daughter, speak you:
He cares not for your weeping. — Speak thou, boy:
Perhaps thy childishness will move him more
Than can our reasons. — There's no man in the world
More bound to's mother; yet here he lets me prate
Like one i'the stocks. — Thou hast never in thy life
Show'd thy dear mother any courtesy;
When she, poor hen, fond of no second brood,
Has cluck'd thee to the wars, and safely home,
Loaden with honour. Say my request's unjust,
And spurn me back; but if it be not so,
Thou art not honest; and the gods will plague thee,
That thou restrain'st from me the duty which
To a mother's part belongs. — He turns away:
Down, ladies; let us shame him with our knees.
To his surname Coriolanus 'longs more pride
Than pity to our prayers. Down: an end;
This is the last: — so we will home to Rome,
And die among our neighbours. — Nay, behold's:
This boy, that cannot tell what he would have,
But kneels and holds up hands for fellowship,
Does reason our petition with more strength
Than thou hast to deny't. — Come, let us go:
This fellow had a Volscian to his mother;
His wife is in Corioli, and this child
Like him by chance. — Yet give us our dispatch:
I am hush'd until our city be a-fire,
And then I'll speak a little.

CORIOLANUS [*holding her by the hand, silent*].
                    O mother, mother!
What have you done? Behold, the heavens do ope,
The gods look down, and this unnatural scene
They laugh at. O my mother, mother! O!
You have won a happy victory to Rome;
But, for your son, believe it, O, believe it,
Most dangerously you have with him prevail'd,
If not most mortal to him. But, let it come. —
Aufidius, though I cannot make true wars,

I'll frame convenient peace. — Now, good Aufidius,
Were you in my stead, would you have heard
A mother less? or granted less, Aufidius?
AUFIDIUS
I was mov'd withal.
CORIOLANUS
    I dare be sworn you were:
And, sir, it is no little thing to make
Mine eyes to sweat compassion. But, good sir,
What peace you'll make, advise me: for my part
I'll not to Rome, I'll back with you; and pray you,
Stand to me in this cause. — O mother! wife!
AUFIDIUS [aside].
I am glad thou hast set thy mercy and thy honour
At difference in thee: out of that I'll work
Myself a former fortune.
    [The LADIES make signs to CORIOLANUS.
CORIOLANUS [to VOLUMNIA, VIRGILIA, etc]
    Ay, by and by;
But we will drink together; and you shall bear
A better witness back than words, which we,
On like conditions, will have counter-seal'd.
Come, enter with us. Ladies, you deserve
To have a temple built you: all the swords
In Italy, and her confederate arms,
Could not have made this peace.   [Exeunt.

SCENE IV

Rome. A public place.

Enter MENENIUS with SICINIUS.

MENENIUS
See you yond coign o' the Capitol, — yond corner-stone?
SICINIUS
Why, what of that?
MENENIUS
If it be possible for you to displace it with your little
finger, there is some hope the ladies of Rome,
especially his mother, may prevail with him. But I say
there is no hope in't: our throats are sentenced, and
stay upon execution.
SICINIUS
Is't possible that so short a time can alter the condition
of a man?
MENENIUS
There is differency between a grub and a butterfly; yet your
butterfly was a grub. This Marcius is grown from man to
dragon: he has wings; he's more than a creeping thing.
SICINIUS
He loved his mother dearly.
MENENIUS
So did he me: and he no more remembers his mother
now than an eight-year-old horse. The tartness of his
face sours ripe grapes: when he walks, he moves like an
engine, and the ground shrinks before his treading: he
is able to pierce a corslet with his eye; talks like a knell,
and his hum is a battery. He sits in his state, as a thing
made for Alexander. What he bids be done, is finish'd
with his bidding. He wants nothing of a god but
eternity, and a heaven to throne in.
SICINIUS
Yes, mercy, if you report him truly.
MENENIUS
I paint him in the character. Mark what mercy his
mother shall bring from him: there is no more mercy
in him than there is milk in a male tiger; that shall our
poor city find: and all this is 'long of you.
SICINIUS
The gods be good unto us!
MENENIUS
No, in such a case the gods will not be good unto us.
When we banish'd him, we respected not them; and,
he returning to break our necks, they respect not us.

Enter a MESSENGER.

MESSENGER
Sir, if you'ld save your life, fly to your house:
The plebeians have got your fellow-tribune,
And hale him up and down; all swearing, if
The Roman ladies bring not comfort home,
They'll give him death by inches.

Enter another MESSENGER.

SICINIUS
    What's the news?
SECOND MESSENGER
Good news, good news; — the ladies have prevail'd,
The Volscians are dislodg'd, and Marcius gone:
A merrier day did never yet greet Rome,
No, not the expulsion of the Tarquins.

SICINIUS
    Friend,
Art thou certain this is true? is it most certain?
SECOND MESSENGER
As certain as I know the sun is fire:
Where have you lurk'd, that you make doubt of it?
Ne'er through an arch so hurried the blown tide
As the recomforted through the gates. Why, hark you!
    [Trumpets, hautboys, drums beat, all together.
The trumpets, sackbuts, psalteries, and fifes,
Tabors, and cymbals, and the shouting Romans,
Make the sun dance. Hark you!   [A shout within.
MENENIUS
    This is good news.
I will go meet the ladies. This Volumnia
Is worth of consuls, senators, patricians,
A city full; of tribunes, such as you,
A sea and land full. You have pray'd well to-day:
This morning for ten thousand of your throats
I'ld not have given a doit. — Hark, how they joy!
    [Sound still with the shouts.
SICINIUS
First, the gods bless you for your tidings; next,
Accept my thankfulness.
SECOND MESSENGER
    Sir, we have all
Great cause to give great thanks.
SICINIUS
    They are near the city?
SECOND MESSENGER
Almost at point to enter.
SICINIUS
    We will meet them,
And help the joy.   [Exeunt.

SCENE V

The same. A street near the gate.

Enter two SENATORS, with LADIES, passing over the
stage; with other LORDS.

FIRST SENATOR
Behold our patroness, the life of Rome!
Call all your tribes together, praise the gods,
And make triumphant fires; strew flowers before
    them:
Unshout the noise that banish'd Marcius,
Repeal him with the welcome of his mother;
Cry, 'Welcome, ladies, welcome!'
ALL
    Welcome, ladies,
Welcome!
    [A flourish with drums and trumpets. Exeunt.

SCENE VI

Corioli. A public place.

Enter AUFIDIUS, with ATTENDANTS.

AUFIDIUS
Go tell the lords o' the city I am here:
Deliver them this paper: having read it,
Bid them repair to the market-place; where I,
Even in theirs and in the commons' ears,
Will vouch the truth of it. Him I accuse
The city ports by this hath enter'd, and
Intends t'appear before the people, hoping
To purge herself with words: dispatch.
    [Exeunt ATTENDANTS.
    Enter three or four CONSPIRATORS
    of AUFIDIUS' faction.
    Most welcome!
FIRST CONSPIRATOR
How is it with our general?
AUFIDIUS
    Even so
As with a man by his own alms empoison'd,
And with his charity slain.
SECOND CONSPIRATOR
    Most noble sir,
If you do hold the same intent wherein
You wish'd us parties, we'll deliver you
Of your great danger.
AUFIDIUS
    Sir, I cannot tell:
We must proceed as we do find the people.
THIRD CONSPIRATOR
The people will remain uncertain whilst
'Twixt you there's difference; but the fall of either
Makes the survivor heir of all.
AUFIDIUS
    I know it;

And my pretext to strike at him admits
A good construction. I rais'd him, and I pawn'd
Mine honour for his truth: who being so heighten'd,
He water'd his new plants with dews of flattery,
Seducing so my friends; and, to this end,
He bow'd his nature, never known before
But to be rough, unswayable, and free.
THIRD CONSPIRATOR
Sir, his stoutness
When he did stand for consul, which he lost
By lack of stooping, —
AUFIDIUS
    That I would have spoke of:
Being banish'd for't, he came unto my hearth;
Presented to my knife his throat: I took him;
Made him joint-servant with me; gave him way
In all his own desires; nay, let him choose
Out of my files, his projects to accomplish,
My best and freshest men; served his designments
In mine own person; holp to reap the fame
Which he did end all his; and took some pride
To do myself this wrong: till, at the last,
I seem'd his follower, not partner; and
He wag'd me with his countenance, as if
I had been mercenary.
FIRST CONSPIRATOR
    So he did, my lord, —
The army marvell'd at it; and, in the last,
When he had carried Rome, and that we look'd
For no less spoil than glory, —
AUFIDIUS
    There was it; —
For which my sinews shall be stretch'd upon him.
At a few drops of women's rheum, which are
As cheap as lies, he sold the blood and labour
Of our great action: therefore shall he die,
And I'll renew me in his fall. — But, hark!
    [Drums and trumpets sound,
    with great shouts of the PEOPLE.
FIRST CONSPIRATOR
Your native town you enter'd like a post,
And had no welcomes home; but he returns,
Splitting the air with noise.
SECOND CONSPIRATOR
    And patient fools,
Whose children he hath slain, their base throats tear
With giving him glory.
THIRD CONSPIRATOR
    Therefore, at your vantage,
Ere he express himself, or move the people
With what he would say, let him feel your sword,
Which we will second. When he lies along,
After your way his tale pronounc'd shall bury
His reasons with his body.
AUFIDIUS
    Say no more:
Here come the lords.
    Enter the LORDS of the city.
LORDS
You are most welcome home.
AUFIDIUS
    I have not deserv'd it.
But, worthy lords, have you with heed perused
What I have written to you?
LORDS
    We have.
FIRST LORD
    And grieve to hear't.
What faults he made before the last, I think
Might have found easy fines: but there to end
Where he was to begin, and give away
The benefit of our levies, answering us
With our own charge, making a treaty where
There was a yielding, — this admits no excuse.
AUFIDIUS
He approaches: you shall hear him.

Enter CORIOLANUS, marching with drum and colours;
the COMMONERS being with him.

CORIOLANUS
Hail, lords! I am return'd your soldier;
No more infected with my country's love
Than when I parted hence, but still subsisting
Under your great command. You are to know,
That prosperously I have attempted, and,
With bloody passage, led your wars even to
The gates of Rome. Our spoils we have brought home
Doth more than counterpoise a full third part
The charges of the action. We have made peace,
With no less honour to the Antiates

ALL THE CONSPIRATORS Kill, kill, kill, kill, kill him!

Will you be put in mind of his blind fortune,
Which was your shame, by this unholy braggart,
'Fore your own eyes and ears?

All THE CONSPIRATORS
                                        Let him die for't!

ALL THE PEOPLE
Tear him to pieces! — Do it presently! — He kill'd
my son! — My daughter! — He kill'd my cousin
Marcus! — He kill'd my father! —

SECOND LORD
Peace, ho! — no outrage: — peace!
The man is noble, and his fame folds-in
This orb o' the earth. His last offences to us
Shall have judicious hearing. — Stand, Aufidius,
And trouble not the peace.

CORIOLANUS
                        O, that I had him,
With six Aufidiuses, or more, his tribe,
To use my lawful sword!

AUFIDIUS
                        Insolent villain!

ALL THE CONSPIRATORS
Kill, kill, kill, kill, kill him!

            [AUFIDIUS *and the* CONSPIRATORS *draw
            and kill* CORIOLANUS, *who falls:*
            AUFIDIUS *stands on him.*

LORDS
Hold, hold, hold, hold!

AUFIDIUS
My noble masters, hear me speak.

FIRST LORD
                                O Tullus, —

SECOND LORD
Thou hast done a deed whereat valour will weep.

THIRD LORD
Tread not upon him. — Masters all, be quiet;
Put up your swords.

AUFIDIUS
My lords, when you shall know — as in this rage,
Provok'd by him, you cannot — the great danger
Which this man's life did owe you, you'll rejoice
That he is thus cut off. Please it your honours
To call me to your senate, I'll deliver
Myself your loyal servant, or endure
Your heaviest censure.

FIRST LORD
                        Bear from hence his body, —
And mourn you for him: — let him be regarded
As the most noble corse that ever herald
Did follow to his urn.

SECOND LORD
                        His own impatience
Takes from Aufidius a great part of blame.
Let's make the best of it.

AUFIDIUS
                        My rage is gone;
And I am struck with sorrow. — Take him up: —
Help, three o'the chiefest soldiers; I'll be one. —
Beat thou the drum, that it speak mournfully:
Trail your steel pikes. — Though in this city he
Hath widow'd and unchilded many a one,
Which to this hour bewail the injury,
Yet he shall have a noble memory. —
Assist.

            [*Exeunt, bearing the body of* MARCIUS.
            A dead march sounded.

Than shame to the Romans: and we here deliver,
Subscribed by the consuls and patricians,
Together with the seal o'the senate, what
We have compounded on.

AUFIDIUS
                        Read it not, noble lords;
But tell the traitor, in the highest degree
He hath abus'd your powers.

CORIOLANUS
Traitor! — how now!

AUFIDIUS
                Ay, traitor, Marcius!

CORIOLANUS
                        Marcius!

AUFIDIUS
Ay, Marcius, Caius Marcius: dost thou think
I'll grace thee with that robbery, thy stol'n name
Coriolanus, in Corioli? —
You lords and heads o' the state, perfidiously
He has betray'd your business, and given up,
For certain drops of salt, your city Rome —
I say, your city — to his wife and mother;
Breaking his oath and resolution, like
A twist of rotten silk; never admitting
Counsel o'the war; but at his nurse's tears
He whin'd and roar'd away your victory;
That pages blush'd at him, and men of heart
Look'd wond'ring each at other.

CORIOLANUS
                        Hear'st thou, Mars?

AUFIDIUS
Name not the god, thou boy of tears!

CORIOLANUS
                                Ha!

AUFIDIUS
No more.

CORIOLANUS
Measureless liar, thou hast made my heart
Too great for what contains it. Boy! O slave! —
Pardon me, lords, 'tis the first time that ever
I was forc'd to scold. Your judgements, my grave lords,
Must give this cur the lie: and his own notion —
Who wears my stripes impress'd upon him; that
Must bear my beating to his grave — shall join
To thrust the lie unto him.

FIRST LORD
Peace, both, and hear me speak.

CORIOLANUS
Cut me to pieces, Volsces; men and lads,
Stain all your edges on me. — Boy! false hound!
If you have writ your annals true, 'tis there,
That, like an eagle in a dove-cote, I
Flutter'd your Volscians in Corioli:
Alone I did it. — Boy!

AUFIDIUS
                Why, noble lords,

TIMON OF ATHENS

DRAMATIS PERSONAE

TIMON, *a noble Athenian.*
LUCIUS, } *two flattering lords.*
LUCULLUS, }
APEMANTUS, *a churlish philosopher.*
SEMPRONIUS, *another flattering lord.*
ALCIBIADES, *an Athenian captain.*
VENTIDIUS, *one of Timon's false friends.*
FLAVIUS, *steward to Timon.*
POET, PAINTER, JEWELLER, *and* MERCHANT.
AN OLD ATHENIAN.

FLAMINIUS, }
LUCILIUS, } *servants to Timon.*
SERVILIUS, }
CAPHIS, }
PHILOTUS, }
TITUS, } *servants to Timon's creditors.*
HORTENSIUS, }
AND OTHERS, }
A PAGE. A FOOL, THREE STRANGERS.

PHRYNIA, } *mistresses to Alcibiades.*
TIMANDRA, }

CUPID *and* AMAZONS *in the mask.*
Other LORDS, SENATORS, OFFICERS, SOLDIERS,
BANDITTI, *and* ATTENDANTS.

SCENE — *Athens and the woods adjoining.*

ACT I

SCENE I

Athens. A hall in TIMON's *house.*

Enter POET, PAINTER, JEWELLER, MERCHANT,
and others, at several doors.

POET
Good day, sir.
PAINTER
I am glad y'are well.
POET
I have not seen you long: how goes the world?
PAINTER
It wears, sir, as it grows.
POET
              Ay, that's well known:
But what particular rarity? what strange,
Which manifold record not matches? See,
Magic of bounty! all these spirits thy power
Hath conjur'd to attend. I know the merchant.
PAINTER
I know them both; the other's a jeweller.
MERCHANT
O, 'tis a worthy lord.
JEWELLER
            Nay, that's most fix'd.
MERCHANT
A most incomparable man; breath'd, as it were
To an untirable and continuate goodness:
He passes.
JEWELLER
I have a jewel here —
MERCHANT
O, pray, let's see't: for the Lord Timon, sir?
JEWELLER
If he will touch the estimate: but, for that —
POET
  'When we for recompense have prais'd the vile,
  It stains the glory in that happy verse
  Which aptly sings the good.'
MERCHANT
            'Tis a good form.
           [*Looking at the jewel.*

JEWELLER
And rich: here is a water, look ye.
PAINTER
You are rapt, sir, in some work, some dedication
To the great lord.
POET
         A thing slipp'd idly from me.
Our poesy is as a gum, which oozes
From whence 'tis nourish'd: the fire i' the flint
Shows not till it be struck; our gentle flame
Provokes itself, and, like the current, flies
Each bound it chafes. — What have you there?
PAINTER
A picture, sir. — When comes your book forth?
POET
Upon the heels of my presentment, sir. —
Let's see your piece.
PAINTER
'Tis a good piece.
POET
So 'tis: this comes off well and excellent.
PAINTER
Indifferent.
POET
        Admirable: how this grace
Speaks his own standing! what a mental power
This eye shoots forth! how big imagination
Moves in this lip! to the dumbness of the gesture
One might interpret.
PAINTER
It is a pretty mocking of the life.
Here is a touch; is't good?
POET
           I will say of it,
It tutors nature: artificial strife
Lives in these touches, livelier than life.
    Enter certain SENATORS, *and pass over.*
PAINTER
How this lord is follow'd!
POET
The senators of Athens: — happy man!
PAINTER
Look, moe!

POET
You see this confluence, this great flood of visitors.
I have, in this rough work, shap'd out a man,
Whom this beneath-world doth embrace and hug
With amplest entertainment: my free drift
Halts not particularly, but moves itself
In a wide sea of wax: no levell'd malice
Infects one comma in the course I hold;
But flies an eagle flight, bold, and forth on,
Leaving no tract behind.
PAINTER
How shall I understand you?
POET
           I will unbolt to you.
You see how all conditions, how all minds —
As well of glib and slippery creatures as
Of grave and austere quality — tender down
Their services to Lord Timon: his large fortune,
Upon his good and gracious nature hanging,
Subdues and properties to his love and tendance
All sorts of hearts; yea, from the glass-fac'd flatterer
To Apemantus, that few things loves better
Than to abhor himself: even he drops down
The knee before him, and returns in peace
Most rich in Timon's nod.
PAINTER
           I saw them speak together.
POET
Sir,
I have upon a high and pleasant hill
Feign'd Fortune to be thron'd: the base o'the mount
Is rank'd with all deserts, all kind of natures,
That labour on the bosom of this sphere
To propagate their states: amongst them all,
Whose eyes are on this sovereign lady fix'd,
One do I personate of Lord Timon's frame,
Whom Fortune with her ivory hand wafts to her:
Whose present grace to present slaves and servants
Translates his rivals.
PAINTER
        'Tis conceiv'd to scope.
This throne, this Fortune, and this hill, methinks,
With one man beckon'd from the rest below,
Bowing his head against the steepy mount
To climb his happiness, would be well express'd
In our condition.

TIMON 'Tis not enough to help the feeble up, but to support him after.

POET
Nay, sir, but hear me on.
All those which were his fellows but of late, —
Some better than his value, — on the moment
Follow his strides, his lobbies fill with tendance,
Rain sacrificial whisperings in his ear,
Make sacred even his stirrup, and through him
Drink the free air.

PAINTER
Ay, marry, what of these?

POET
When Fortune, in her shift and change of mood,
Spurns down her late beloved, all his dependants,
Which labour'd after him to the mountain's top,
Even on their knees and hands, let him slip down,
Not one accompanying his declining foot.

PAINTER
'Tis common:
A thousand moral paintings I can show,
That shall demonstrate these quick blows of Fortune's
More pregnantly than words. Yet you do well
To show Lord Timon that mean eyes have seen
The foot above the head.

Trumpets sound. Enter LORD TIMON, *addressing
himself courteously to every* SUITOR; *a* SERVANT *of*
VENTIDIUS *talking with him;* LUCILIUS *and other*
ATTENDANTS *following.*

TIMON
Imprison'd is he, say you?

VENTIDIUS' SERVANT
Ay, my good lord; five talents is his debt;
His means most short, his creditors most strait:
Your honourable letter he desires
To those have shut him up; which failing
Periods his comfort.

TIMON
Noble Ventidius! — Well;
I am not of that feather to shake off
My friend when he must need me. I do know him
A gentleman that well deserves a help, —
Which he shall have: I'll pay the debt, and free him.

VENTIDIUS' SERVANT
Your lordship ever binds him.

TIMON
Commend me to him: I will send his ransom;

And, being enfranchis'd, bid him come to me: —
'Tis not enough to help the feeble up,
But to support him after. — Fare you well.

VENTIDIUS' SERVANT
All happiness to your honour! [*Exit.*

Enter an OLD ATHENIAN.

OLD ATHENIAN
Lord Timon, hear me speak.

TIMON
Freely, good father.

OLD ATHENIAN
Thou hast a servant named Lucilius.

TIMON
I have so: what of him?

OLD ATHENIAN
Most noble Timon, call the man before thee.

TIMON
Attends he here, or no? — Lucilius!

LUCILIUS [*coming forward*].
Here, at your lordship's service.

OLD ATHENIAN
This fellow here, Lord Timon, this thy creature,
By night frequents my house. I am a man
That from my first have been inclin'd to thrift;
And my estate deserves an heir more rais'd
Than one which holds a trencher.

TIMON
Well; what further?

OLD ATHENIAN
One only daughter have I, no kin else,
On whom I may confer what I have got:
The maid is fair, o'the youngest for a bride,
And I have bred her at my dearest cost
In qualities of the best. This man of thine
Attempts her love: I prithee, noble lord,
Join with me to forbid him her resort;
Myself have spoke in vain.

TIMON
The man is honest.

OLD ATHENIAN
Therefore he will be, Timon:
His honesty rewards him in itself;
It must not bear my daughter.

TIMON
Does she love him?

OLD ATHENIAN
She is young and apt:
Our own precedent passions do instruct us
What levity's in youth.

TIMON [*to* LUCILIUS].
Love you the maid?

LUCILIUS
Ay, my good lord, and she accepts of it.

OLD ATHENIAN
If in her marriage my consent be missing,
I call the gods to witness, I will choose
Mine heir from forth the beggars of the world,
And dispossess her all.

TIMON
How shall she be endow'd,
If she be mated with an equal husband?

OLD ATHENIAN
Three talents on the present; in future, all.

TIMON
This gentleman of mine hath serv'd me long:
To build his fortune I will strain a little,
For 'tis a bond in men. Give him thy daughter:
What you bestow, in him I'll counterpoise;
And make him weigh with her.

OLD ATHENIAN
Most noble lord
Pawn me to this your honour, she is his.

TIMON
My hand to thee; mine honour on my promise.

LUCILIUS
Humbly I thank your lordship: never may
That state or fortune fall into my keeping,
Which is not owed to you!
[*Exeunt* LUCILIUS *and* OLD ATHENIAN.

POET
Vouchsafe my labour, and long live your lordship!

TIMON
I thank you; you shall hear from me anon:
Go not away. — What have you there, my friend?

PAINTER
A piece of painting, which I do beseech
Your lordship to accept.

TIMON
Painting is welcome.
The painting is almost the natural man;
For since dishonour traffics with man's nature,
He is but outside: these pencill'd figures are
Even such as they give out. I like your work;
And you shall find I like it: wait attendance
Till you hear further from me.

PAINTER
The gods preserve ye!

TIMON
Well fare you, gentleman: give me your hand;
We must needs dine together. — Sir, your jewel
Hath suffer'd under praise.

JEWELLER
What, my lord! dispraise?

TIMON
A mere satiety of commendations.
If I should pay you for't as 'tis extoll'd,
It would unclew me quite.

JEWELLER
My lord, 'tis rated
As those which sell would give: but you well know,
Things of like value, differing in the owners,
Are prized by their masters: believe't, dear lord.
You mend the jewel by the wearing it.

TIMON
Well mock'd.

MERCHANT
No, my good lord; he speaks the common tongue,
Which all men speak with him.

TIMON
Look, who comes here:
Will you be chid?

Enter APEMANTUS.

JEWELLER
We'll bear, with your lordship.

MERCHANT
He'll spare none.

TIMON
Good morrow to thee, gentle Apemantus.

APEMANTUS
Till I be gentle, stay thou for thy good morrow;
When thou art Timon's dog, and these knaves honest.

TIMON
Why dost thou call them knaves? thou know'st them not.
APEMANTUS
Are they not Athenians?
TIMON
Yes.
APEMANTUS
Then I repent not.
JEWELLER
You know me, Apemantus?
APEMANTUS
Thou know'st I do; I call'd thee by thy name.
TIMON
Thou art proud, Apemantus.
APEMANTUS
Of nothing so much as that I am not like Timon.
TIMON
Whither art going?
APEMANTUS
To knock out an honest Athenian's brains.
TIMON
That's a deed thou'lt die for.
APEMANTUS
Right, if doing nothing be death by the law.
TIMON
How likest thou this picture, Apemantus?
APEMANTUS
The best, for the innocence.
TIMON
Wrought he not well that painted it?
APEMANTUS
He wrought better that made the painter; and yet
he's but a filthy piece of work.
PAINTER
Y'are a dog.
APEMANTUS
Thy mother's of my generation: what's she, if I be a
dog?
TIMON
Wilt dine with me, Apemantus?
APEMANTUS
No; I eat not lords.
TIMON
An thou shouldst, thou'ldst anger ladies.
APEMANTUS
O, they eat lords; so they come by great bellies.
TIMON
That's a lascivious apprehension.
APEMANTUS
So thou apprehend'st it: take it for thy labour.
TIMON
How dost thou like this jewel, Apemantus?
APEMANTUS
Not so well as plain-dealing, which will not cost a man
a doit.
TIMON
What dost thou think 'tis worth?
APEMANTUS
Not worth my thinking. — How now, poet!
POET
How now, philosopher!
APEMANTUS
Thou liest.
POET
Art not one?
APEMANTUS
Yes.
POET
Then I lie not.
APEMANTUS
Art not a poet?
POET
Yes.
APEMANTUS
Then thou liest: look in thy last work, where thou
hast feign'd him a worthy fellow.
POET
That's not feign'd, — he is so.
APEMANTUS
Yes, he is worthy of thee, and to pay thee for thy
labour: he that loves to be flatter'd is worthy o'the
flatterer. Heavens, that I were a lord!
TIMON
What wouldst thou do, Apemantus?
APEMANTUS
E'en as Apemantus does now, — hate a lord with my
heart.

TIMON
What thyself?
APEMANTUS
Ay.
TIMON
Wherefore?
APEMANTUS
That I had no angry wit to be a lord. — Art not
thou a merchant?
MERCHANT
Ay, Apemantus.
APEMANTUS
Traffic confound thee, if the gods will not!
MERCHANT
If traffic do it, the gods do it.
APEMANTUS
Traffic's thy god; and thy god confound thee!
Trumpet sounds. Enter a MESSENGER.
TIMON
What trumpet's that?
MESSENGER
'Tis Alcibiades, and some twenty horse,
All of companionship.
TIMON
Pray, entertain them; give them guide to us. —
                        [*Exeunt some* ATTENDANTS.
You must needs dine with me: go not you hence
Till I have thank'd you; when dinner's done,
Show me this piece: — I am joyful of your sights.
             Enter ALCIBIADES *with the rest.*
Most welcome, sir!
APEMANTUS
                      So, so, there! —
Aches contract and starve your supple joints! —
That there should be small love 'mongst these sweet
    knaves,
And all this court'sy! The strain of man's bred out
Into baboon and monkey.
ALCIBIADES
Sir, you have sav'd my longing, and I feed
Most hungerly on your sight.
TIMON
                   Right welcome, sir!
Ere we depart, we'll share a bounteous time
In different pleasures. Pray you, let us in.
                    [*Exeunt all but* APEMANTUS.

             Enter two LORDS.

FIRST LORD
What time o'day is't, Apemantus?
APEMANTUS
Time to be honest.
FIRST LORD
That time serves still.
APEMANTUS
The more accursed thou, that still omitt'st it.
SECOND LORD
Thou art going to Lord Timon's feast?
APEMANTUS
Ay, to see meat fill knaves, and wine heat fools.
SECOND LORD
Fare thee well, fare thee well.
APEMANTUS
Thou art a fool to bid me farewell twice.
SECOND LORD
Why, Apemantus?
APEMANTUS
Shouldst have kept one to thyself, for I mean to
give thee none.
FIRST LORD
Hang thyself!
APEMANTUS
No, I will do nothing at thy bidding: make thy
requests to thy friend.
SECOND LORD
Away, unpeaceable dog, or I'll spurn thee hence!
APEMANTUS
I will fly, like a dog, the heels o'the ass.   [*Exit.*
FIRST LORD
He's opposite to humanity. — Come, shall we in,
And taste Lord Timon's bounty? he outgoes
The very heart of kindness!
SECOND LORD
He pours it out; Plutus, the god of gold,
Is but his steward: no meed, but he repays
Sevenfold above itself; no gift to him
But breeds the giver a return exceeding
All use of quittance.

APEMANTUS He that loves to be flatter'd is worthy
                 o'the flatterer.

FIRST LORD
              The noblest mind he carries
That ever govern'd man.
SECOND LORD
                 Long may he live
In fortunes! — Shall we in?
FIRST LORD
                I'll keep you company.
                       [*Exeunt.*

SCENE II

The same. A room of state in TIMON'S *house.*

Hautboys playing loud music. A great banquet served in;
FLAVIUS *and others attending; and then enter*
LORD TIMON, ALCIBIADES, *the* STATES, *the*
Athenian LORDS, VENTIDIUS *which* TIMON
redeem'd from prison. Then comes, dropping after all,
APEMANTUS, *discontentedly, like himself.*

VENTIDIUS
Most honour'd Timon,
It hath pleas'd the gods to remember my father's age,
And call him to long peace.
He is gone happy, and has left me rich:
Then, as in grateful virtue I am bound
To your free heart, I do return those talents,
Doubled with thanks and service, from whose help
I deriv'd liberty.
TIMON
              O, by no means,
Honest Ventidius; you mistake my love:
I gave it freely ever; and there's none
Can truly say he gives, if he receives:
If our betters play at that game, we must not dare
To imitate them; faults that are rich are fair.
VENTIDIUS
A noble spirit!
TIMON
             Nay, my lords, ceremony
Was but devis'd at first
To set a gloss on faint deeds, hollow welcomes,
Recanting goodness, sorry ere 'tis shown;
But where there is true friendship, there needs none.
Pray, sit; more welcome are ye to my fortunes
Than my fortunes to me.   [*They sit.*
FIRST LORD
My lord, we always have confess'd it.
APEMANTUS
Ho, ho, confess'd it! hang'd it, have you not?
TIMON
O, Apemantus, — you are welcome.
APEMANTUS
                      No;
You shall not make me welcome:
I come to have thee thrust me out of doors.
TIMON
Fie, th'art a churl; y'have got a humour there

Does not become a man; 'tis much to blame. —
They say, my lords, *Ira furor brevis est*;
But yond man is ever angry. —
Go, let him have a table by himself;
For he does neither affect company,
Nor is he fit for't, indeed.

APEMANTUS
Let me stay at thine apperil, Timon:
I come to observe; I give thee warning on't.

TIMON
I take no heed of thee; th'art an Athenian, therefore
welcome: I myself would have no power; prithee,
let my meat make thee silent.

APEMANTUS
I scorn thy meat; 'twould choke me, for I should
ne'er flatter thee. — O you gods, what a number of
men eats Timon, and he sees 'em not! It grieves
me to see so many dip their meat in one man's blood;
and all the madness is, he cheers them up too.
I wonder men dare trust themselves with men:
Methinks they should invite them without knives;
Good for their meat, and safer for their lives
There's much example for't; the fellow that sits
next him now, parts bread with him, pledges the
breath of him in a divided draught, is the readiest
man to kill him:'t has been proved. If I were a
huge man, I should fear to drink at meals;
Lest they should spy my windpipe's dangerous notes:
Great men should drink with harness on their throats.

TIMON
My lord, in heart; and let the health go round.

SECOND LORD
Let it flow this way, my good lord.

APEMANTUS
Flow this way! A brave fellow! he keeps his tides well.
Those healths will make thee and thy state look ill,
Timon. Here's that which is too weak to be a sinner,
honest water, which ne'er left man i'the mire:
This and my food are equals; there's no odds:
Feasts are too proud to give thanks to the gods.
         APEMANTUS' grace.
    Immortal gods, I crave no pelf;
    I pray for no man but myself:
    Grant I may never prove so fond,
    To trust man on his oath or bond;
    Or a harlot, for her weeping;
    Or a dog, that seems a-sleeping;
    Or a keeper with my freedom;
    Or my friends, if I should need 'em.
    Amen. So fall to't:
    Rich men sin, and I eat root.   [*Eats and drinks.*
Much good dich thy good heart, Apemantus!

TIMON
Captain Alcibiades, your heart's in the field now.

ALCIBIADES
My heart is ever at your service, my lord.

TIMON
You had rather be at a breakfast of enemies than
a dinner of friends.

ALCIBIADES
So they were bleeding-new, my lord, there's no meat
like 'em: I could wish my best friend at such a feast.

APEMANTUS
Would all those flatterers were thine enemies then,
that then thou mightst kill 'em, and bid me to 'em!

FIRST LORD
Might we but have that happiness, my lord, that you
would once use our hearts, whereby we might express
some part of our zeals, we should think ourselves for
ever perfect.

TIMON
O, no doubt, my good friends, but the gods themselves
have provided that I shall have much help from you:
how had you been my friends else? Why have you that
charitable title from thousands, did not you chiefly
belong to my heart? I have told more of you to myself
than you can with modesty speak in your own behalf;
and thus far I confirm you. O you gods, think I, what
need we have any friends, if we should ne'er have need
of 'em? They were the most needless creatures living,
should we ne'er have use for 'em; and would most
resemble sweet instruments hung up in cases, that
keep their sounds to themselves. Why, I have often
wish'd myself poorer, that I might come nearer to you.
We are born to do benefits: and what better or properer
can we call our own than the riches of our friends? O,
what a precious comfort 'tis, to have so many, like
brothers, commanding one another's fortunes! O joy,
e'en made away ere't can be born! Mine eyes cannot
hold out water, methinks: to forget their faults, I drink
to you.

APEMANTUS
Thou weep'st to make them drink, Timon.

SECOND LORD
Joy had the like conception in our eyes,
And, at that instant, like a babe sprung up.

APEMANTUS
Ho, ho! I laugh to think that babe a bastard.

THIRD LORD
I promise you, my lord, you mov'd me much.

APEMANTUS
Much!   [*Tucket sounded within.*

TIMON
What means that trump?

        Enter a SERVANT.
        How now!

SERVANT
Please you, my lord, there are certain ladies most
desirous of admittance.

TIMON
Ladies! what are their wills?

SERVANT
There comes with them a forerunner, my lord, which
bears that office, to signify their pleasures.

TIMON
I pray, let them be admitted.

        Enter CUPID.

CUPID
Hail to thee, worthy Timon; — and to all
That of his bounties taste! — The five best senses
Acknowledge thee their patron, and come freely
To gratulate thy plenteous bosom:
The ear, taste, touch, and smell, pleas'd from thy table
rise; —
These only now come but to feast thine eyes.

TIMON
They're welcome all; let 'em have kind admittance: —
Music, make their welcome!   [*Exit* CUPID.

FIRST LORD
You see, my lord, how ample y'are beloved.

   Music. Enter CUPID, *with a Masque of* LADIES *as
Amazons with lutes in their hands, dancing and playing.*

APEMANTUS
Hoy-day, what a sweep of vanity comes this way!
They dance! they are mad women.
Like madness is the glory of this life,
As this pomp shows to a little oil and root.
We make ourselves fools, to disport ourselves;
And spend our flatteries, to drink those men,
Upon whose age we void it up agen,
With poisonous spite and envy.
Who lives, that's not depraved or depraves?
Who dies, that bears not one spurn to their graves
Of their friends' gift?
I should fear those that dance before me now
Would one day stamp upon me:'t has been done;
Men shut their doors against a setting sun.

   The LORDS *rise from table, with much adoring of*
TIMON; *and to show their loves, each singles out an*
AMAZON, *and all dance, men with women, a lofty
strain or two to the hautboys, and cease.*

TIMON
You have done our pleasures much grace, fair ladies,
Set a fair fashion on our entertainment,
Which was not half so beautiful and kind;
You have added worth unto't and lustre,
And entertain'd me with mine own device;
I am to thank you for't.

FIRST LADY
My lord, you take us even at the best.

APEMANTUS
Faith, for the worst is filthy, and would not hold
taking, I doubt me.

TIMON
Ladies, there is an idle banquet attends you,
Please you to dispose yourselves.

ALL LADIES
Most thankfully, my lord.
        [*Exeunt* CUPID *and* LADIES.

TIMON
Flavius, —

FLAVIUS
My lord?

TIMON
        The little casket bring me hither.

FLAVIUS
Yes, my lord. — [*aside*] More jewels yet!
There is no crossing him in's humour;
Else I should tell him, — well, i'faith, I should, —
When all's spent, he'ld be cross'd then, an he could.
'Tis pity bounty had not eyes behind,
That man might ne'er be wretched for his mind.   [*Exit.*

FIRST LORD
Where be our men?

SERVANT
Here, my lord, in readiness.

SECOND LORD
Our horses!

    Enter FLAVIUS *with the casket.*

TIMON
O my friends,
I have one word to say to you: — look you, my good
lord,
I must entreat you, honour me so much
As to advance this jewel; accept and wear it,
Kind my lord.

FIRST LORD
I am so far already in your gifts, —

ALL
So are we all.

      Enter a SERVANT.

SERVANT
My lord, there are certain nobles of the senate newly
alighted, and come to visit you.

TIMON
They are fairly welcome.

FLAVIUS
I beseech your honour, vouchsafe me a word; it does
concern you near.

TIMON
Near! why then, another time I'll hear thee: I prithee,
let's be provided to show them entertainment.

FLAVIUS [*aside*].
I scarce know how.

APEMANTUS Hoy-day, what a sweep of vanity comes this way!

Enter a second SERVANT.

SECOND SERVANT
May it please your honour, Lord Lucius,
Out of his free love, hath presented to you
Four milk-white horses, trapp'd in silver.

TIMON
I shall accept them fairly: let the presents
Be worthily entertain'd.
    Enter a third SERVANT.
              How now! what news?

THIRD SERVANT
Please you, my lord, that honourable gentleman, Lord
Lucullus, entreats your company to-morrow to hunt
with him; and has sent your honour two brace of
greyhounds.

TIMON
I'll hunt with him; and let them be received,
Not without fair reward.

FLAVIUS [aside].
            What will this come to?
He commands us to provide, and give great gifts,
And all out of an empty coffer:
Nor will he know his purse; or yield me this,
To show him what a beggar his heart is,
Being of no power to make his wishes good:
His promises fly so beyond his state,
That what he speaks is all in debt; he owes
For every word: he is so kind, that he now
Pays interest for't; his land's put to their books.
Well, would I were gently put out of office,
Before I were forced out!
Happier is he that has no friend to feed
Than such that do e'en enemies exceed.
I bleed inwardly for my lord.   [*Exit.*

TIMON
          You do yourselves
Much wrong, you bate too much of your own merits: —
Here, my lord, a trifle of our love.

SECOND LORD
With more than common thanks I will receive it.

THIRD LORD
O, he's the very soul of bounty!

TIMON
And now I remember, my lord, you gave good words
the other day of a bay courser I rode on: 'tis yours,
because you liked it.

FIRST LORD
O, I beseech you, pardon me, my lord, in that.

TIMON
You may take my word, my lord; I know, no man can
justly praise but what he does affect: I weigh my
friend's affection with mine own; I'll tell you true. —
I'll call to you.

ALL LORDS
O, none so welcome.

TIMON
I take all and your several visitations
So kind to heart, 'tis not enough to give;
Methinks, I could deal kingdoms to my friends,
And ne'er be weary. — Alcibiades,
Thou art a soldier, therefore seldom rich;
It comes in charity to thee: for all thy living
Is 'mongst the dead; and all the lands thou hast
Lie in a pitch'd field.

ALCIBIADES
Ay, defiled land, my lord.

FIRST LORD
We are so virtuously bound —

TIMON
And so am I to you.

SECOND LORD
So infinitely endear'd —

TIMON
All to you. — Lights, more lights!

FIRST LORD
The best of happiness, honour, and fortunes, keep with
you, Lord Timon!

TIMON
Ready for his friends.
      [*Exeunt all but APEMANTUS and TIMON.*

APEMANTUS
What a coil's here!
Serving of becks, and jutting-out of bums!
I doubt whether their legs be worth the sums
That are given for 'em. Friendship's full of dregs:
Methinks, false hearts should never have sound legs.
Thus honest fools lay out their wealth on court'sies.

TIMON
Now, Apemantus, if thou wert not sullen,

I would be good to thee.

APEMANTUS
No, I'll nothing; for if I should be bribed too, there
would be none left to rail upon thee; and then thou
wouldst sin the faster. Thou givest so long, Timon, I
fear me thou wilt give away thyself in paper shortly:
what need these feasts, pomps, and vain-glories?

TIMON
Nay, an you begin to rail on society once, I am sworn
not to give regard to you. Farewell; and come with
better music.   [*Exit.*

APEMANTUS
So; thou wilt not hear me now, —
Thou shalt not then, I'll lock thy heaven from thee. —
O, that men's ears should be
To counsel deaf, but not to flattery!   [*Exit.*

ACT II

SCENE I

Athens. A room in a SENATOR'S house.

Enter a SENATOR, with papers in his hand.

SENATOR
And late, five thousand; — to Varro and to Isidore
He owes nine thousand; — besides my former sum,
Which makes it five-and-twenty. — Still in motion
Of raging waste? It cannot hold; it will not.
If I want gold, steal but a beggar's dog,
And give it Timon, why, the dog coins gold:
If I would sell my horse, and buy twenty more
Better than he, why, give my horse to Timon,
Ask nothing, give it him, it foals me, straight,
And able horses: no porter at his gate;
But rather one that smiles, and still invites
All that pass by. It cannot hold; no reason
Can found his state in safety. — Caphis, ho!
Caphis, I say!

Enter CAPHIS.

CAPHIS
      Here, sir; what is your pleasure?

SENATOR
Get on your cloak, and haste you to Lord Timon;
Importune him for my moneys; be not ceas'd
With slight denial; nor then silenc'd when —
'Commend me to your master' — and the cap
Plays in the right hand, thus: — but tell him, sirrahm
My uses cry to me, I must serve my turn
Out of mine own; his days and times are past,
And my reliances on his fracted dates
Have smit my credit: I love and honour him;
But must not break my back to heal his finger:
Immediate are my needs; and my relief
Must not be toss'd and turn'd to me in words,
But find supply immediate. Get you gone:
Put on a most importunate aspect,
A visage of demand; for, I do fear,
When every feather sticks in his own wing,
Lord Timon will be left a naked gull,
Which flashes now a phœnix. Get you gone.

CAPHIS
I go, sir.

SENATOR
      Take the bonds along with you,
And have the dates in compt.

CAPHIS
          I will, sir.

SENATOR
                Go.   [*Exeunt.*

SCENE II

The same. A hall in TIMON'S house.

Enter FLAVIUS, with many bills in his hand.

FLAVIUS
No care, no stop! so senseless of expense,
That he will neither know how to maintain it
Nor cease his flow of riot: takes no account
How things go from him; nor resumes no care
Of what is to continue: never mind
Was to be so unwise, to be so kind.
What shall be done? he will not hear, till feel:
I must be round with him, now he comes from hunting.
Fie, fie, fie, fie!

*Enter CAPHIS, and the SERVANTS
of ISIDORE and VARRO.*

CAPHIS
Good even, Varro: what, you come for
money?

VARRO'S SERVANT
Is't not your business too?

CAPHIS
It is: — and yours too, Isidore?

ISIDORE'S SERVANT
It is so.

CAPHIS
Would we were all discharged!

VARRO'S SERVANT
I fear it.

CAPHIS
Here comes the lord.

Enter TIMON, ALCIBIADES, and LORDS, etc.

TIMON
So soon as dinner's done, we'll forth again,
My Alcibiades. — With me? what is your will?

CAPHIS
My lord, here is a note of certain dues.

TIMON
Dues! Whence are you?

CAPHIS
          Of Athens here, my lord.

TIMON
Go to my steward.

CAPHIS
Please it your lordship, he hath put me off
To the succession of new days this month:
My master is awak'd by great occasion
To call upon his own; and humbly prays you,
That with your other noble parts you'll suit
In giving him his right.

TIMON
          Mine honest friend,
I prithee, but repair to me next morning.

CAPHIS
Nay, good my lord, —

TIMON
          Contain thyself, good friend.

VARRO'S SERVANT
One Varro's servant, my good lord, —

ISIDORE'S SERVANT
            From Isidore;
He humbly prays your speedy payment, —

CAPHIS
If you did know, my lord, my master's wants, —

VARRO'S SERVANT
'Twas due on forfeiture, my lord, six weeks and past, —

ISIDORE'S SERVANT
Your steward puts me off, my lord; and I am sent
expressly to your lordship.

TIMON
Give me breath. —
I do beseech you, good my lords, keep on;
I'll wait upon you instantly.
        [*Exeunt ALCIBIADES and LORDS.*
        [*to FLAVIUS*] Come hither: pray you,
How goes the world, that I am thus encounter'd
With clamourous demands of date-broke bonds,
And the detention of long-since-due debts,
Against my honour?

FLAVIUS
          Please you, gentlemen,
The time is unagreeable to this business:
Your importunacy cease till after dinner;
That I may make his lordship understand
Wherefore you are not paid.

TIMON
Do so, my friends. See them well entertain'd.   [*Exit.*

FLAVIUS
Pray, draw near. [*Exit.*
Enter APEMANTUS *and* FOOL.

CAPHIS
Stay, stay, here comes the fool with Apemantus: let's
ha' some sport with 'em.

VARRO'S SERVANT
Hang him, he'll abuse us.

ISIDORE'S SERVANT
A plague upon him, dog!

VARRO'S SERVANT
How dost, fool?

APEMANTUS
Dost dialogue with thy shadow?

VARRO'S SERVANT
I speak not to thee.

APEMANTUS
No, 'tis to thyself. — [*to the* FOOL] Come away.

ISIDORE'S SERVANT [*to* VARRO'S SERVANT].
There's the fool hangs on your back already.

APEMANTUS
No, thou stand'st single, th'art not on him yet.

CAPHIS
Where's the fool now?

APEMANTUS
He last ask'd the question. — Poor rogues, and
usurers' men! bawds between gold and want!

ALL SERVANTS
What are we, Apemantus?

APEMANTUS
Asses.

ALL SERVANTS
Why?

APEMANTUS
That you ask me what you are, and do not know
yourselves. — Speak to 'em, fool.

FOOL
How do you, gentlemen?

ALL SERVANTS
Gramercies, good fool: how does your mistress?

FOOL
She's e'en setting on water to scald such chickens as
you are. Would we could see you at Corinth!

APEMANTUS
Good! gramercy.

FOOL
Look you, here comes my mistress' page.
Enter PAGE.

PAGE [*to the* FOOL].
Why, how now, captain! what do you in this wise
company? — How dost thou, Apemantus?

APEMANTUS
Would I had a rod in my mouth, that I might answer
thee profitably.

PAGE
Prithee, Apemantus, read me the superscription of
these letters: I know not which is which.

APEMANTUS
Canst not read?

PAGE
No.

APEMANTUS
There will little learning die, then, that day thou art
hang'd. This is to Lord Timon; this to Alcibiades. Go;
thou wast born a bastard, and thou'lt die a bawd.

PAGE
Thou wast whelp'd a dog, and thou shalt famish, a
dog's death. Answer not, I am gone.

APEMANTUS
E'en so thou outrunn'st grace. [*Exit* PAGE] Fool, I will
go with you to Lord Timon's.

FOOL
Will you leave me there?

APEMANTUS
If Timon stay at home. — You three serve three
usurers?

ALL SERVANTS
Ay; would they served us!

APEMANTUS
So would I, — as good a trick as ever hangman served
thief.

FOOL
Are you three usurers' men?

ALL SERVANTS
Ay, fool.

FOOL
I think no usurer but has a fool to his servant: my
mistress is one, and I am her fool. When men come to
borrow of your masters, they approach sadly, and go
away merry; but they enter my mistress' house merrily,
and go away sadly: the reason of this?

VARRO'S SERVANT
I could render one.

APEMANTUS
Do it, then, that we may account thee a whoremaster
and a knave; which notwithstanding, thou shalt be no
less esteem'd.

VARRO'S SERVANT
What is a whoremaster, fool?

FOOL
A fool in good clothes, and something like thee. 'Tis a
spirit: sometime't appears like a lord; sometime like a
lawyer; sometime like a philosopher, with two stones
more than's artificial one: he is very often like a knight;
and, generally, in all shapes that man goes up and
down in from fourscore to thirteen, this spirit walks in.

VARRO'S SERVANT
Thou art not altogether a fool.

FOOL
Nor thou altogether a wise man: as much foolery as I
have, so much wit thou lack'st.

APEMANTUS
That answer might have become Apemantus.

ALL SERVANTS
Aside, aside; here comes Lord Timon.
Enter TIMON *and* FLAVIUS.

APEMANTUS
Come with me, fool, come.

FOOL
I do not always follow lover, elder brother, and woman;
sometime the philosopher.
[*Exeunt* APEMANTUS *and* FOOL.

FLAVIUS
Pray you, walk near: I'll speak with you anon.
[*Exeunt* SERVANTS.

TIMON
You make me marvel: wherefore ere this time
Had you not fully laid my state before me;
That I might so have rated my expense
As I had leave of means?

FLAVIUS
You would not hear me,
At many leisures I propos'd.

TIMON
Go to:
Perchance some single vantages you took,
When my indisposition put you back;
And that unaptness made your minister,
Thus to excuse yourself.

FLAVIUS
O my good lord,
At many times I brought in my accounts,
Laid them before you; you would throw them off,
And say, you found them in mine honesty.
When, for some trifling present, you have bid me
Return so much, I have shook my head and wept;
Yea, 'gainst the authority of manners, pray'd you
To hold your hand more close: I did endure
Not seldom, nor no slight checks, when I have
Prompted you, in the ebb of your estate,
And your great flow of debts. My dear-lov'd lord,
Though you hear now — too late — yet now's a time,
The greatest of your having lacks a half
To pay your present debts.

TIMON
Let all my land be sold.

FLAVIUS
'Tis all engag'd, some forfeited and gone;
And what remains will hardly stop the mouth
Of present dues: the future comes apace:
What shall defend the interim? and at length
How goes our reckoning?

TIMON
To Lacedæmon did my land extend.

FLAVIUS
O my good lord, the world is but a word:
Were it all yours to give it in a breath,
How quickly were it gone!

TIMON
You tell me true.

FLAVIUS
If you suspect my husbandry or falsehood,
Call me before the exactest auditors,
And set me on the proof. So the gods bless me,
When all our offices have been oppress'd
With riotous feeders; when our vaults have wept
With drunken spilth of wine; when every room
Hath blaz'd with lights and bray'd with minstrelsy;
I have retired me to a wasteful cock,
And set mine eyes at flow.

TIMON
Prithee, no more.

FLAVIUS
Heavens, have I said, the bounty of this lord!
How many prodigal bits have slaves and peasants
This night englutted! Who is not Lord Timon's?
What heart, head, sword, force, means, but is Lord
Timon's?
Great Timon, noble, worthy, royal Timon!
Ah, when the means are gone that buy this praise,
The breath is gone whereof this praise is made:
Feast-won, fast-lost; one cloud of winter showers,
These flies are couch'd.

TIMON
Come, sermon me no further:
No villainous bounty yet hath pass'd my heart;
Unwisely, not ignobly, have I given.
Why dost thou weep? Canst thou the conscience lack,
To think I shall lack friends? Secure thy heart;
If I would broach the vessels of my love,
And try the argument of hearts by borrowing,
Men and men's fortunes could I frankly use
As I can bid thee speak.

FLAVIUS
Assurance bless your thoughts!

TIMON
And, in some sort, these wants of mine are crown'd,
That I account them blessings; for by these

TIMON Come, sermon me no further.

Shall I try friends: you shall perceive how you
Mistake my fortunes; I am wealthy in my friends. —
Within there! Flaminius! Servilius!

Enter FLAMINIUS, SERVILIUS, *and other*
SERVANTS.

SERVANTS
My lord? my lord? —

TIMON
I will dispatch you severally: — [*to* SERVILIUS] you to
Lord Lucius; — [*to* FLAMINIUS] to Lord Lucullus you;
I hunted with his honour to-day; — [*to another*
SERVANT] you to Sempronius: commend me to their
loves; and, I am proud, say, that my occasions have
found time to use 'em toward a supply of money: let the
request be fifty talents.

FLAMINIUS Fly, damned baseness, to him that worships thee!

FLAMINIUS
As you have said, my lord.
[*Exit with* SERVILIUS *and another* SERVANT.
FLAVIUS [*aside*] —
Lord Lucius and Lucullus? hum!
TIMON [*to another* SERVANT].
Go you, sir, to the senators, —
Of whom, even to the state's best health, I have
Deserv'd this hearing; bid 'em send o'the instant
A thousand talents to me. [*Exit* SERVANT.
FLAVIUS
                    I have been bold —
For that I knew it the most general way —
To them to use your signet and your name;
But they do shake their heads, and I am here
No richer in return.
TIMON
                    Is't true? can't be?
FLAVIUS
They answer, in a joint and corporate voice,
That now they are at fall, want treasure, cannot
Do what they would; are sorry — you are honourable —
But yet they could have wish'd — they know not —
Something hath been amiss — a noble nature
May catch a wrench — would all were well — 'tis pity; —
And so, intending other serious matters,
After distasteful looks and these hard fractions,
With certain half-caps and cold-moving nods
They froze me into silence.
TIMON
                    You gods, reward them! —
Prithee, man, look cheerly. These old fellows
Have their ingratitude in them hereditary:
Their blood is cak'd, 'tis cold, it seldom flows;
'Tis lack of kindly warmth they are not kind;
And nature, as it grows again toward earth,
Is fashion'd for the journey, dull and heavy. —
[*to another* SERVANT] Go to Ventidius, — [*to*
    FLAVIUS] Prithee, be not sad,
Thou art true and honest; ingeniously I speak,
No blame belongs to thee: — [*to the same* SERVANT].

Ventidius lately
Buried his father; by whose death he's stepp'd
Into a great estate: when he was poor,
Imprison'd and in scarcity of friends,
I clear'd him with five talents: greet him from me;
Bid him suppose some good necessity
Touches his friend, which craves to be remember'd
With those five talents. [*Exit* SERVANT.
            [*to* FLAVIUS] That had, give't these fellows
To whom 'tis instant due. Ne'er speak, or think,
That Timon's fortunes 'mong his friends can sink.
FLAVIUS
I would I could not think it: that thought is bounty's
    foe:
Being free itself, it thinks all others so. [*Exeunt.*

ACT III

SCENE I

Athens. A room in LUCULLUS' *house.*

FLAMINIUS *waiting to speak with* LUCULLUS *from
his master, enter a* SERVANT *to him.*

SERVANT
I have told my lord of you; he is coming down to you.
FLAMINIUS
I thank you, sir.

Enter LUCULLUS.

SERVANT
Here's my lord.
LUCULLUS [*aside*].
One of Lord Timon's men? a gift, I warrant. Why, this
hits right; I dreamt of a silver basin and ewer to-night.
— Flaminius, honest Flaminius; you are very
respectively welcome, sir. — Fill me some wine. [*Exit*
SERVANT] — And how does that honourable,
complete freehearted gentleman of Athens, thy very
bountiful good lord and master?
FLAMINIUS
His health is well, sir.
LUCULLUS
I am right glad that his health is well, sir: and what hast
thou there under thy cloak, pretty Flaminius?
FLAMINIUS
Faith, nothing but an empty box, sir; which, in my
lord's behalf, I come to entreat your honour to supply;
who, having great and instant occasion to use fifty
talents, hath sent to your lordship to furnish him,
nothing doubting your present assistance therein.
LUCULLUS
La, la, la, la, — 'nothing doubting,' says he? Alas, good
lord! a noble gentleman 'tis, if he would not keep so
good a house. Many a time and often I ha' dined with
him, and told him on't; and come again to supper to
him, of purpose to have him spend less, and yet he

would embrace no counsel, take no warning by my
coming. Every man has his fault, and honesty is his: I
ha' told him on't, but I could ne'er get him from't.

Enter SERVANT, *with wine.*

SERVANT
Please your lordship, here is the wine.
LUCULLUS
Flaminius, I have noted thee always wise. Here's to
thee.
FLAMINIUS
Your lordship speaks your pleasure.
LUCULLUS
I have observed thee always for a towardly prompt
spirit, — give thee thy due, — and one that knows what
belongs to reason; and canst use the time well, if the
time use thee well: good parts in thee. — [*to* SERVANT]
Get you gone, sirrah. [*Exit* SERVANT] — Draw nearer,
honest Flaminius. Thy lord's a bountiful gentleman:
but thou art wise; and thou know'st well enough,
although thou comest to me, that this is no time to lend
money; especially upon bare friendship, without
security. Here's three solidares for thee: good boy,
wink at me, and say thou saw'st me not. Fare thee well.
FLAMINIUS
Is't possible the world should so much differ,
And we alive that liv'd? Fly, damned baseness,
To him that worships thee! [*Throwing the money back.*
LUCULLUS
Ha! now I see thou art a fool, and fit for thy master.
[*Exit.*
FLAMINIUS
May these add to the number that may scald thee!
Let molten coin be thy damnation,
Thou disease of a friend, and not himself!
Has friendship such a faint and milky heart,
It turns in less than two nights? O you gods,
I feel my master's passion! This slave
Unto dishonour has my lord's meat in him:
Why should it thrive, and turn to nutriment,
When he is turn'd to poison?
O, may diseases only work upon't!
And, when he's sick to death, let not that part of nature
Which my lord paid for, be of any power
To expel sickness, but prolong his hour! [*Exit.*

SCENE II

The same. A public place.

Enter LUCIUS, *with three* STRANGERS.

LUCIUS
Who, the Lord Timon? he is my very good friend, and
an honourable gentleman.
FIRST STRANGER
We know him for no less, though we are but strangers
to him. But I can tell you one thing, my lord, and which
I hear from common rumours, — now Lord Timon's
happy hours are done and past, and his estate shrinks
from him.
LUCIUS
Fie, no, do not believe it; he cannot want for money.
SECOND STRANGER
But believe you this, my lord, that, not long ago, one of
his men was with the Lord Lucullus to borrow so many
talents; nay, urg'd extremely for't, and show'd what
necessity belong'd to't, and yet was denied.
LUCIUS
How!
SECOND STRANGER
I tell you, denied, my lord.
LUCIUS
What a strange case was that! now, before the gods, I
am ashamed on't. Denied that honourable man! there
was very little honour show'd in't. For my own part, I
must needs confess, I have received some small
kindnesses from him, as money, plate, jewels, and
such-like trifles, nothing comparing to his; yet, had he
mistook him, and sent to me, I should ne'er have
denied his occasion so many talents.

Enter SERVILIUS.

SERVILIUS
See, by good hap, yonder's my lord; I have sweat to see
his honour. — [*to* LUCIUS] My honour'd lord, —
LUCIUS
Servilius! you are kindly met, sir. Fare thee well:
commend me to thy honourable virtuous lord, my very
exquisite friend.
SERVILIUS
May it please your honour, my lord hath sent —

LUCIUS
Ha! what has he sent? I am so much endear'd to that
lord; he's ever sending: how shall I thank him, think'st
thou? And what has he sent now?

SERVILIUS
'Has only sent his present occasion now, my lord;
requesting your lordship to supply his instant use with
so many talents.

LUCIUS
I know his lordship is but merry with me;
He cannot want fifty-five hundred talents.

SERVILIUS
But in the mean time he wants less, my lord.
If his occasion were not virtuous,
I should not urge it half so faithfully.

LUCIUS
Dost thou speak seriously, Servilius?

SERVILIUS
Upon my soul, 'tis true, sir.

LUCIUS
What a wicked beast was I to disfurnish myself against
such a good time, when I might ha' shown myself
honourable! how unluckily it happen'd, that I should
purchase the day before for a little part, and undo a
great deal of honour! — Servilius, now, before the
gods, I am not able to do, — the more beast, I say: — I
was sending to use Lord Timon myself, these
gentlemen can witness; but I would not, for the wealth
of Athens, I had done't now. Commend me bountifully
to his good lordship; and I hope his honour will
conceive the fairest of me, because I have no power to
be kind: — and tell him this from me, I count it one of
my greatest afflictions, say, that I cannot pleasure such
an honourable gentleman. Good Servilius, will you
befriend me so far, as to use mine own words to him?

SERVILIUS
Yes, sir, I shall.

LUCIUS
I'll look you out a good turn, Servilius.
[*Exit* SERVILIUS.
True, as you said, Timon is shrunk indeed;
And he that's once denied will hardly speed. [*Exit.*

FIRST STRANGER
Do you observe this, Hostilius?

SECOND STRANGER
Ay, too well.

FIRST STRANGER
Why, this
Is the world's soul; and just of the same piece
Is every flatterer's spirit. Who can call him
His friend that dips in the same dish? for, in
My knowing, Timon has been this lord's father,
And kept his credit with his purse;
Supported his estate; nay, Timon's money
Has paid his men their wages: he ne'er drinks,
But Timon's silver treads upon his lip;
And yet — O, see the monstrousness of man
When he looks out in an ungrateful shape! —
He does deny him, in respect of his,
What charitable men afford to beggars.

THIRD STRANGER
Religion groans at it.

FIRST STRANGER
For mine own part,
I never tasted Timon in my life,
Nor came any of his bounties over me,
To mark me for his friend; yet, I protest,
For his right noble mind, illustrious virtue,
And honourable carriage,
Had his necessity made use of me,
I would have put my wealth into donation,
And the best half should have return'd to him,
So much I love his heart; but: I perceive
Men must learn now with pity to dispense;
For policy sits above conscience. [*Exeunt.*

SCENE III

The same. A room in SEMPRONIUS' *house.*

Enter SEMPRONIUS, *and a* SERVANT *of* TIMON'S.

SEMPRONIUS
Must he needs trouble me in't, — hum! — 'bove all
others?
He might have tried Lord Lucius or Lucullus;
And now Ventidius is wealthy too,
Whom he redeem'd from prison: all these
Owe their estates unto him.

SERVANT
My lord,
They have all been touch'd, and found base metal; for

They have all denied him.

SEMPRONIUS
How! have they denied him?
Has Ventidius and Lucullus denied him?
And does he send to me? Three? hum! —
It shows but little love or judgement in him:
Must I be his last refuge! His friends, like physicians,
Thrive, give him over: must I take th'cure upon me?
'Has much disgrac'd me in't; I'm angry at him,
That might have known my place: I see no sense for't,
But his occasions might have woo'd me first;
For, in my conscience, I was the first man
That e'er received gift from him:
And does he think so backwardly of me now,
That I'll requite it last? No:
So it may prove an argument of laughter
To the rest, and 'mongst lords I be thought a fool.
I'd rather than the worth of thrice the sum,
'Had sent to me first, but for my mind's sake;
I'd such a courage to do him good. But now return,
And with their faint reply this answer join:
Who bates mine honour shall not know my coin. [*Exit.*

SERVANT
Excellent! Your lordship's a goodly villain. The devil
knew not what he did when he made man politic, — he
cross'd himself by't: and I cannot think but, in the end,
the villainies of man will set him clear. How fairly this
lord strives to appear foul! takes virtuous copies to be
wicked; like those that, under hot ardent zeal, would set
whole realms on fire:
Of such a nature is his politic love. This was my lord's
best hope; now all are fled, Save the gods only: now his
friends are dead,
Doors, that were ne'er acquainted with their wards
Many a bounteous year, must be employ'd
Now to guard sure their master.
And this is all a liberal course allows; Who cannot keep
his wealth must keep his house.
[*Exit.*

SCENE IV

The same. A hall in TIMON'S *house.*

Enter two SERVANTS *of* VARRO, *and the* SERVANT
of LUCIUS, *meeting* TITUS, HORTENSIUS,
and other SERVANTS *of* TIMON'S *creditors,
waiting his coming out.*

VARRO'S FIRST SERVANT
Well met; good morrow, Titus and Hortensius.

TITUS
The like to you, kind Varro.

HORTENSIUS
Lucius!
What, do we meet together?

LUCIUS' SERVANT
Ay, and I think
One business does command us all; for mine
Is money.

TITUS
So is theirs and ours.

Enter PHILOTUS.

LUCIUS' SERVANT
And Sir Philotus too!

PHILOTUS
Good day at once.

LUCIUS' SERVANT
Welcome, good brother.
What do you think the hour?

PHILOTUS
Labouring for nine.

LUCIUS' SERVANT
So much?

PHILOTUS
Is not my lord seen yet?

LUCIUS' SERVANT
Not yet.

PHILOTUS
I wonder on't; he was wont to shine at seven.

LUCIUS' SERVANT
Ay, but the days are waxed shorter with him:
You must consider that a prodigal course
Is like the sun's;
But not, like his, recoverable. I fear
'Tis deepest winter in Lord Timon's purse;
That is, one may reach deep enough, and yet
Find little.

PHILOTUS
I am of your fear for that.

TITUS
I'll show you how t'observe a strange event.
Your lord sends now for money.

HORTENSIUS
Most true, he does.

TITUS
And he wears jewels now of Timon's gift,
For which I wait for money.

HORTENSIUS
It is against my heart.

LUCIUS' SERVANT
Mark, how strange it shows,
Timon in this should pay more than he owes;
And e'en as if your lord should wear rich jewels,
And send for money for 'em.

HORTENSIUS
I'm weary of this charge, the gods can witness:
I know my lord hath spent of Timon's wealth,
And now ingratitude makes it worse than stealth.

VARRO'S FIRST SERVANT
Yes, mine's three thousand crowns: what's yours?

LUCIUS' SERVANT
Five thousand mine.

VARRO'S FIRST SERVANT
'Tis much deep: and it should seem by the sum
Your master's confidence was above mine,
Else, surely, his had equall'd.

Enter FLAMINIUS.

TITUS
One of Lord Timon's men.

LUCIUS' SERVANT
Flaminius! — Sir, a word: pray, is my lord ready to
come forth?

FLAMINIUS
No, indeed, he is not.

TITUS
We attend his lordship; pray, signify so much.

FLAMINIUS
I need not tell him that; he knows you are too diligent.
[*Exit.*

Enter FLAVIUS *in a cloak, muffled.*

LUCIUS' SERVANT
Ha! is not that his steward muffled so?
He goes away in a cloud: call him, call him.

TITUS
Do you hear, sir?

BOTH VARRO'S SERVANTS
By your leave, sir, —

FLAVIUS
What do ye ask of me, my friends?

TITUS
We wait for certain money here, sir.

FLAVIUS
Ay,
If money were as certain as your waiting,
'Twere sure enough.
Why then preferr'd you not your sums and bills
When your false masters eat of my lord's meat?
Then they could smile, and fawn upon his debts,
And take down the int'rest into their gluttonous maws.
You do yourselves but wrong to stir me up;
Let me pass quietly:
Believe't, my lord and I have made an end;
I have no more to reckon, he to spend.

LUCIUS' SERVANT
Ay, but this answer will not serve.

FLAVIUS
If 'twill not serve, 'tis not so base as you;
For you serve knaves. [*Exit.*

VARRO'S FIRST SERVANT
How! what does his cashier'd worship mutter?

VARRO'S SECOND SERVANT
No matter what; he's poor, and that's revenge enough.
Who can speak broader than he that has no house to
put his head in? such may rail against great buildings.

Enter SERVILIUS.

TITUS
O, here's Servilius; now we shall know some answer.

SERVILIUS
If I might beseech you, gentlemen, to repair some
other hour, I should derive much from't; for, take't of
my soul, my lord leans wondrously to discontent: his
comfortable temper has forsook him; he's much out of
health, and keeps his chamber.

LUCIUS' SERVANT
Many do keep their chambers are not sick:
And, if it be so far beyond his health,

Methinks he should the sooner pay his debts,
And make a clear way to the gods.

SERVILIUS
                  Good gods!

TITUS
We cannot take this for an answer, sir.

FLAMINIUS [within].
Servilius, help! — My lord! my lord!

Enter TIMON, *in a rage;* FLAMINIUS *following.*

TIMON
What, are my doors oppos'd against my passage?
Have I been ever free, and must my house
Be my retentive enemy, my gaol?
The place which I have feasted, does it now,
Like all mankind, show me an iron heart?

LUCIUS' SERVANT
Put in now, Titus.

TITUS
My lord, here is my bill.

LUCIUS' SERVANT
Here's mine.

HORTENSIUS
And mine, my lord.

BOTH VARRO'S SERVANTS
And ours, my lord.

PHILOTUS
All our bills.

TIMON
Knock me down with 'em: cleave me to the girdle.

LUCIUS' SERVANT
Alas, my lord, —

TIMON
Cut my heart in sums.

TITUS
Mine, fifty talents.

TIMON
Tell out my blood.

LUCIUS' SERVANT
Five thousand crowns, my lord.

TIMON
Five thousand drops pays that. — What yours? — and
yours?

VARRO'S FIRST SERVANT
My lord, —

VARRO'S SECOND SERVANT
My lord, —

TIMON
Tear me, take me, and the gods fall upon you!   [*Exit.*

HORTENSIUS
Faith, I perceive our masters may throw their caps at
their money: these debts may well be call'd desperate
ones, for a madman owes 'em.   [*Exeunt.*

Enter TIMON *and* FLAVIUS.

TIMON
They have e'en put my breath from me, the slaves.
Creditors! — devils.

FLAVIUS
My dear lord, —

TIMON
What if it should be so?

FLAVIUS
My lord, —

TIMON
I'll have it so. — My steward!

FLAVIUS
Here, my lord.

TIMON
So fitly? Go, bid all my friends again,
Lucius, Lucullus, and Sempronius; all:
I'll once more feast the rascals.

FLAVIUS
                O my lord,
You only speak from your distracted soul;
There is not so much left to furnish out
A moderate table.

TIMON
            Be it not in thy care; go,
I charge thee, invite them all: let in the tide
Of knaves once more; my cook and I'll provide.
              [*Exeunt.*

SCENE V

The same. The senate-house.

The Senate sitting.

FIRST SENATOR
My lord, you have my voice to it; the fault's

Bloody; 'tis necessary he should die:
Nothing emboldens sin so much as mercy.

SECOND SENATOR
Most true; the law shall bruise him.

Enter ALCIBIADES *attended.*

ALCIBIADES
Honour, health, and compassion to the senate!

FIRST SENATOR
Now, captain?

ALCIBIADES
I am an humble suitor to your virtues;
For pity is the virtue of the law,
And none but tyrants use it cruelly.
It pleases time and fortune to lie heavy
Upon a friend of mine, who, in hot blood,
Hath stepp'd into the law, which is past depth
To those that, without heed, do plunge into't.
He is a man, setting his fault aside.,
Of comely virtues:
Nor did he soil the fact with cowardice,
An honour in him which buys out his fault;
But with a noble fury and fair spirit,
Seeing his reputation touch'd to death,
He did oppose his foe:
And with such sober and unnoted passion
He did behave his anger, ere 'twas spent,
As if he had but prov'd an argument.

FIRST SENATOR
You undergo too strict a paradox,
Striving to make an ugly deed look fair:
Your words have took such pains, as if they labour'd
To bring manslaughter into form, and set
Quarrelling upon the head of valour; which
Indeed is valour misbegot, and came
Into the world when sects and factions
Were newly born:
He's truly valiant that can wisely suffer
The worst that man can breathe; and make his wrongs
His outsides, — to wear them like his raiment,
   carelessly;
And ne'er prefer his injuries to his heart,
To bring it into danger.
If wrongs be evils, and enforce us kill,
What folly 'tis to hazard life for ill!

ALCIBIADES
My lord, —

FIRST SENATOR
You cannot make gross sins look clear:
To revenge is no valour, but to bear.

ALCIBIADES
My lords, then, under favour, pardon me,
If I speak like a captain: —
Why do fond men expose themselves to battle,
And not endure all threats? sleep upon't,
And let the foes quietly cut their throats,
Without repugnancy? If there be
Such valour in the bearing, what make we
Abroad? why, then, women are more valiant
That stay at home, if bearing carry it;
And the ass more captain than the lion; the felon
Loaden with irons wiser than the judge,
If wisdom be in suffering. O my lords,
As you are great, be pitifully good:
Who cannot condemn rashness in cold blood?
To kill, I grant, is sin's extremest gust;
But, in defence, by mercy, 'tis most just.
To be in anger is impiety;
But who is man that is not angry?
Weigh but the crime with this.

SECOND SENATOR
You breathe in vain.

ALCIBIADES
          In vain! his service done
At Lacedæmon and Byzantium
Were a sufficient briber for his life.

FIRST SENATOR
What's that?

ALCIBIADES
        Why, I say, my lords, 'has
done fair service,
And slain in fight many of your enemies:
How full of valour did he bear himself
In the last conflict, and made plenteous
   wounds!

SECOND SENATOR
He has made too much plenty with 'em,
He's a sworn rioter: he has a sin that often
Drowns him, and takes his valour prisoner:
If there were no foes, that were enough
To overcome him: in that beastly fury

He has been known to commit outrages
And cherish factions: 'tis inferr'd to us
His days are foul, and his drink dangerous.

FIRST SENATOR
He dies.

ALCIBIADES
         Hard fate! he might have died in war.
My lords, if not for any parts in him, —
Though his right arm might purchase his own time,
And be in debt to none, — yet, more to move you,
Take my deserts to his, and join 'em both:
And, for I know your reverend ages love
Security, I'll pawn my victories, all
My honours to you, upon his good returns.
If by this crime he owes the law his life,
Why, let the war receive't in valiant gore;
For law is strict, and war is nothing more.

FIRST SENATOR
We are for law, — he dies; urge it no more,
On height of our displeasure: friend or brother,
He forfeits his own blood that spills another.

ALCIBIADES
Must it be so? it must not be. My lords,
I do beseech you, know me.

SECOND SENATOR
How!

ALCIBIADES
Call me to your remembrances.

THIRD SENATOR
                What!

ALCIBIADES
I cannot think but your age has forgot me;
It could not else be I should prove so base
To sue, and be denied such common grace:
My wounds ache at you.

FIRST SENATOR
          Do you dare our anger?
'Tis in few words, but spacious in effect;
We banish thee for ever.

ALCIBIADES
           Banish me!
Banish your dotage; banish usury,
That makes the senate ugly.

FIRST SENATOR
If after two days' shine, Athens contain thee,
Attend our weightier judgement. And, not to swell our
   spirit,
He shall be executed presently.   [*Exeunt* SENATORS.

ALCIBIADES
Now the gods keep you old enough; that you may live
Only in bone, that none may look on you!
I'm worse than mad: I have kept back their foes,
While they have told their money, and let out
Their coin upon large interest; I myself
Rich only in large hurts; — all those for this?
Is this the balsam that the usuring senate
Pours into captains' wounds? Banishment!
It comes not ill; I hate not to be banish'd;
It is a cause worthy my spleen and fury,
That I may strike at Athens. I'll cheer up
My discontented troops, and lay for hearts.
'Tis honour with most lands to be at odds;
Soldiers should brook as little wrongs as gods.   [*Exit.*

ALCIBIADES Banish your dotage; banish usury,
   that makes the senate ugly.

SCENE VI

The same. A magnificent room in TIMON'S house.

Music. Tables set out: SERVANTS attending. Enter, at several doors, divers LORDS, — LUCIUS, LUCULLUS, SEMPRONIUS, — SENATORS, etc., and VENTIDIUS.

FIRST LORD
The good time of day to you, sir.
SECOND LORD
I also wish it to you. I think this honourable lord did but try us this other day.
FIRST LORD
Upon that were my thoughts tiring when we encounter'd: I hope it is not so low with him as he made it seem in the trial of his several friends.
SECOND LORD
It should not be, by the persuasion of his new feasting.
FIRST LORD
I should think so: he hath sent me an earnest inviting, which many my near occasions did urge me to put off; but he hath conjured me beyond them, and I must needs appear.
SECOND LORD
In like manner was I in debt to my importunate business, but he would not hear my excuse. I am sorry, when he sent to borrow of me, that my provision was out.
FIRST LORD
I am sick of that grief too, as I understand how all things go.
SECOND LORD
Every man here's so. What would he have borrow'd of you?
FIRST LORD
A thousand pieces.
SECOND LORD
A thousand pieces!
FIRST LORD
What of you?
SECOND LORD
He sent to me, sir, — Here he comes.

Enter TIMON and ATTENDANTS.

TIMON
With all my heart, gentlemen both: — and how fare you —
FIRST LORD
Ever at the best, hearing well of your lordship.
SECOND LORD
The swallow follows not summer more willing than we your lordship.
TIMON [*aside*].
Nor more willingly leaves winter; such summer-birds are men. — Gentlemen, our dinner will not recompense this long stay: feast your ears with the music awhile, if they will fare so harshly o'the trumpet's sound; we shall to't presently.
FIRST LORD
I hope it remains not unkindly with your lordship, that I return'd you an empty messenger.
TIMON
O, sir, let it not trouble you.
SECOND LORD
My noble lord, —
TIMON
Ah, my good friend, — what cheer?
SECOND LORD
My most honourable lord, I am e'en sick of shame, that, when your lordship this other day sent to me I was so unfortunate a beggar.
TIMON
Think not on't, sir.
SECOND LORD
If you had sent but two hours before, —
TIMON
Let it not cumber your better remembrance. —
Come, bring in all together. [*The banquet brought in.*
SECOND LORD
All cover'd dishes!
FIRST LORD
Royal cheer, I warrant you.
THIRD LORD
Doubt not that, if money and the season can yield it.
FIRST LORD
How do you? What's the news?
THIRD LORD
Alcibiades is banish'd: hear you of it?

FIRST AND SECOND LORDS
Alcibiades banish'd!
THIRD LORD
'Tis so, be sure of it.
FIRST LORD
How! how!
SECOND LORD
I pray you, upon what?
TIMON
My worthy friends, will you draw near?
THIRD LORD
I'll tell you more anon. Here's a noble feast toward.
SECOND LORD
This is the old man still.
THIRD LORD
Will't hold? will't hold?
SECOND LORD
It does: but time will — and so —
THIRD LORD
I do conceive.
TIMON
Each man to his stool, with that spur as he would to the lip of his mistress: your diet shall be in all places alike. Make not a city feast of it, to let the meat cool ere we can agree upon the first place: sit, sit. The gods require our thanks.
You great benefactors, sprinkle our society with thankfulness. For your own gifts, make yourselves praised: but reserve still to give, lest your deities be despised. Lend to each man enough, that one need not lend to another; for, were your godheads to borrow of men, men would forsake the gods. Make the meat be beloved more than the man that gives it. Let no assembly of twenty be without a score of villains: if there sit twelve women at the table, let a dozen of them be — as they are. The rest of your foes, O gods, — the senators of Athens, together with the common tag of people, — what is amiss in them, you gods, make suitable for destruction. For these my present friends — as they are to me nothing, so in nothing bless them, and to nothing are they welcome.
— Uncover, dogs, and lap.
[*The dishes are uncover'd, and seen to be full of warm water.*

SOME SPEAK
What does his lordship mean?
SOME OTHER
I know not.
TIMON
May you a better feast never behold,
You knot of mouth-friends! smoke and lukewarm water
Is your perfection. This is Timon's last:
Who, stuck and spangled with your flattery,
Washes it off, and sprinkles in your faces
[*Throwing the water in their faces.*
Your reeking villainy. Live loathd, and long,
Most smiling, smooth, detested parasites,
Courteous destroyers, affable wolves, meek bears,
You fools of fortune, trencher-friends, time's flies,
Cap and knee slaves, vapours, and minute-jacks!
Of man and beast the infinite malady
Crust you quite o'er! — What, dost thou go?
Soft! take thy physic first, — thou too, — and thou; —
Stay, I will lend thee money, borrow none. —
[*Throws the dishes at them, and drives them out.*
What, all in motion? Henceforth be no feast
Whereat a villain's not a welcome guest.
Burn, house! sink, Athens! henceforth hated be
Of Timon man and all humanity! [*Exit.*

Enter the LORDS, SENATORS, etc.

FIRST LORD
How now, my lords!
SECOND LORD
Know you the quality of Lord Timon's fury?
THIRD LORD
Push! did you see my cap?
FOURTH LORD
I have lost my gown.
FIRST LORD
He's but a mad lord, and naught but humour sways him. He gave me a jewel the other day, and now he has beat it out of my hat: — did you see my jewel?

THIRD LORD
Did you see my cap?
SECOND LORD
Here 'tis.
FOURTH LORD
Here lies my gown.
FIRST LORD
Let's make no stay.
SECOND LORD
Lord Timon's mad.
THIRD LORD
I feel't upon my bones.
FOURTH LORD
One day he gives us diamonds, next day stones. [*Exeunt.*

ACT IV

SCENE I

Without the walls of Athens.

Enter TIMON.

TIMON
Let me look back upon thee. O thou wall,
That girdlest in those wolves, dive in the earth,
And fence not Athens! Matrons, turn incontinent!
Obedience fail in children! slaves and fools,
Pluck the grave wrinkled senate from the bench,
And minister in their steads! to general filths
Convert o'the instant, green virginity, —
Do't in your parents' eyes! bankrupts, hold fast
Rather than render back, out with your knives,
And cut your trusters' throats! bound servants, steal!
Large-handed robbers your grave masters are,
And pill by law: maid, to thy master's bed, —
Thy mistress is o'the brothel! son of sixteen,
Pluck the lin'd crutch from thy old limping sire,
With it beat out his brains! piety, and fear,
Religion to the gods, peace, justice, truth,
Domestic awe, night-rest, and neighbourhood,
Instruction, manners, mysteries, and trades,
Degrees, observances, customs, and laws,
Decline to your confounding contraries,
And let confusion live! — Plagues incident to men,
Your potent and infectious fevers heap
On Athens, ripe for stroke! thou cold sciatica,
Cripple our senators, that their limbs may halt
As lamely as their manners! lust and liberty,
Creep in the minds and marrows of our youth,
That 'gainst the stream of virtue they may strive,
And drown themselves in riot! itches, blains,
Sow all the Athenian bosoms; and their crop
Be general leprosy! breath infect breath;
That their society, as their friendship, may
Be merely poison! Nothing I'll bear from thee
But nakedness, thou detestable town!
Take thou that too, with multiplying bans!

Timon will to the woods; where he shall find
The unkindest beast more kinder than mankind.
The gods confound — hear me, you good gods all —
The Athenians both within and out that wall!
And grant, as Timon grows, his hate may grow
To the whole race of mankind, high and low!
Amen.   [*Exit.*

SCENE II

Athens. A room in TIMON'S *house.*

Enter FLAVIUS, *with two or three* SERVANTS.

FIRST SERVANT
Hear you, master steward, — where's our master?
Are we undone? cast off? nothing remaining?

FLAVIUS
Alack, my fellows, what should I say to you?
Let me be recorded by the righteous gods,
I am as poor as you.

FIRST SERVANT
                          Such a house broke!
So noble a master fall'n! All gone! and not
One friend to take his fortune by the arm,
And go along with him!

SECOND SERVANT
                          As we do turn our backs
From our companion thrown into his grave,
So his familiars from his buried fortunes
Slink all away; leave their false vows with him,
Like empty purses pick'd; and his poor self,
A dedicated beggar to the air,
With his disease of all-shunn'd poverty,
Walks, like contempt, alone. — More of our fellows.

Enter other SERVANTS.

FLAVIUS
All broken implements of a ruin'd house.

THIRD SERVANT
Yet do our hearts wear Timon's livery;
That see I by our faces; we are fellows still,
Serving alike in sorrow: leak'd is our bark;
And we, poor mates, stand on the dying deck,
Hearing the surges threat: we must all part
Into this sea of air.

FLAVIUS
                          Good fellows all,
The latest of my wealth I'll share amongst you.
Wherever we shall meet, for Timon's sake,
Let's yet be fellows; let's shake our heads, and say,
As 'twere a knell unto our master's fortunes,
'We have seen better days.' Let each take some;
                          [*Giving them money.*
Nay, put out all your hands. Not one word more:
Thus part we rich in sorrow, parting poor.
                 [SERVANTS *embrace, and part several ways.*
O, the fierce wretchedness that glory brings us!
Who would not wish to be from wealth exempt,
Since riches point to misery and contempt?
Who'd be so mock'd with glory? or to live
But in a dream of friendship?
To have his pomp, and all what state compounds,
But only painted, like his varnish'd friends?
Poor honest lord, brought low by his own heart,
Undone by goodness! Strange, unusual blood,
When man's worst sin is, he does too much good!
Who, then, dares to be half so kind agen?
For bounty, that makes gods, does still mar men.
My dearest lord, — blest, to be most accurst,
Rich, only to be wretched, — thy great fortunes
Are made thy chief afflictions. Alas, kind lord!
He's flung in rage from this ingrateful seat
Of monstrous friends; nor has he with him to
Supply his life, or that which can command it.
I'll follow and inquire him out:
I'll ever serve his mind with my best will;
Whilst I have gold, I'll be his steward still.   [*Exit.*

SCENE III

The woods. Before TIMON'S *cave.*

Enter TIMON.

TIMON
O blessed breeding sun, draw from the earth
Rotten humidity; below thy sister's orb
Infect the air! Twinn'd brothers of one womb, —
Whose procreation, residence, and birth,
Scarce is dividant, — touch them with several fortunes;
The greater scorns the lesser: not nature,
To whom all sores lay siege, can bear great fortune,
But by contempt of nature.
Raise me this beggar, and deny't that lord;

The senator shall bear contempt hereditary,
The beggar native honour.
It is the pasture lards the rother's sides,
The want that makes him lean. Who dares, who dares,
In purity of manhood stand upright,
And say, 'This man's a flatterer'? if one be,
So are they all; for every grise of fortune
Is smooth'd by that below: the learned pate
Ducks to the golden fool: all is oblique;
There's nothing level in our cursed natures,
But direct villainy. Therefore, be abhorr'd
All feasts, societies, and throngs of men!
His semblable, yea, himself, Timon disdains:
Destruction fang mankind! — Earth, yield me roots!
                          [*Digging.*
Who seeks for better of thee, sauce his palate
With thy most operant poison! — What is here?
Gold? yellow, glittering, precious gold? No, gods,
I am no idle votarist: roots, your clear heavens!
Thus much of this will make black white; foul, fair;
Wrong, right; base, noble; old, young; coward, valiant.
Ha, you gods! why this? what this, you gods? Why, this
Will lug your priests and servants from your sides;
Pluck stout men's pillows from below their heads:
This yellow slave
Will knit and break religions, bless th'accurst;
Make the hoar leprosy ador'd; place thieves,
And give them title, knee, and approbation,
With senators on the bench: this is it
That makes the wappen'd widow wed again;
She, whom the spital-house and ulcerous sores
Would cast the gorge at, this embalms and spices
To th'April day again. Come, damned earth,
Thou common whore of mankind, that putt'st odds
Among the route of nations, I will make thee
Do thy right nature. — [*March within.*] Ha! a drum? —
Th'art quick,
But yet I'll bury thee: thou'lt go, strong thief,
When gouty keepers of thee cannot stand: —
Nay, stay thou out for earnest.   [*Keeping some gold.*
      Enter ALCIBIADES, *with drum and fife, in warlike
           manner;* PHRYNIA *and* TIMANDRA.

ALCIBIADES
                          What art thou there? speak.

TIMON
A beast, as thou art. The canker gnaw thy heart,
For showing me again the eyes of man!

ALCIBIADES
What is thy name? Is man so hateful to thee,
That art thyself a man?

TIMON
I am *misanthropos*, and hate mankind.
For thy part, I do wish thou wert a dog,
That I might love thee something.

ALCIBIADES
                          I know thee well;
But in thy fortunes am unlearn'd and strange.

TIMON
I know thee too; and more than that I know thee,
I not desire to know. Follow thy drum;
With man's blood paint the ground, gules, gules:
Religious canons, civil laws are cruel;
Then what should war be? This fell whore of thine
Hath in her more destruction than thy sword,
For all her cherubim look.

PHRYNIA
                          Thy lips rot off!

TIMON
I will not kiss thee; then the rot returns
To thine own lips again.

ALCIBIADES
How came the noble Timon to this change?

TIMON
As the moon does, by wanting light to give:
But then renew I could not, like the moon;
There were no suns to borrow of.

ALCIBIADES
Noble Timon, what friendship may I do thee?

TIMON
None, but to maintain my opinion.

ALCIBIADES
What is it, Timon?

TIMON
Promise me friendship, but perform none: if thou wilt
not promise, the gods plague thee, for thou art a man! if
thou dost perform, confound thee, for thou art a man!

ALCIBIADES
I have heard in some sort of thy miseries.

TIMON
Thou saw'st them, when I had prosperity.

ALCIBIADES
I see them now; then was a blessed time.

TIMON
As thine is now, held with a brace of harlots.

TIMANDRA
Is this th'Athenian minion, whom the world
Voic'd so regardfully?

TIMON
                          Art thou Timandra?

TIMANDRA
Yes.

TIMON
Be a whore still: they love thee not that use thee;
Give them diseases, leaving with thee their lust.
Make use of thy salt hours: season the slaves
For tubs and baths; bring down rose-cheeked youth to
The tub-fast and the diet.

TIMANDRA
                          Hang thee, monster!

ALCIBIADES
Pardon him, sweet Timandra; for his wits
Are drown'd and lost in his calamities. —
I have but little gold of late, brave Timon,
The want whereof doth daily make revolt
In my penurious band: I have heard, and griev'd,
How cursed Athens, mindless of thy worth,
Forgetting thy great deeds, when neighbour states,
But for thy sword and fortune, trod upon them, —

TIMON
I prithee, beat thy drum, and get thee gone.

ALCIBIADES
I am thy friend, and pity thee, dear Timon.

TIMON
How dost thou pity him whom thou dost trouble?
I had rather be alone.

ALCIBIADES
                          Why, fare thee well:
Here's some gold for thee.

TIMON
                          Keep it, I cannot eat it.

ALCIBIADES
When I have laid proud Athens on a heap, —

TIMON
Warr'st thou 'gainst Athens?

ALCIBIADES
                          Ay, Timon, and have cause.

TIMON
The gods confound them all in thy conquest;
And thee after, when thou hast conquer'd!

ALCIBIADES
                                      Why me,
Timon?

TIMON
That, by killing of villains, thou wast born to conquer
My country.
Put up thy gold: go on, — here's gold, — go on;
Be as a planetary plague, when Jove
Will o'er some high-vic'd city hang his poison
In the sick air: let not thy sword skip one:
Pity not honour'd age for his white beard, —
He is an usurer: strike me the counterfeit matron, —
It is her habit only that is honest,
Herself's a bawd: let not the virgin's cheek
Make soft thy trenchant sword; for those milk-paps,
That through the window-bars bore at men's eyes,
Are not within the leaf of pity writ,
But set them down horrible traitors: spare not the babe,
Whose dimpled smiles from fools exhaust their mercy;
Think it a bastard, whom the oracle
Hath doubtfully pronounc'd thy throat shall cut,
And mince it sans remorse: swear against objects;
Put armour on thine ears and on thine eyes,
Whose proof, nor yells of mothers, maids, nor babes,
Nor sight of priests in holy vestments bleeding,
Shall pierce a jot. There's gold to pay soldiers:
Make large confusion; and, thy fury spent,
Confounded be thyself! Speak not, be gone.

ALCIBIADES
Hast thou gold yet? I'll take the gold thou givest me,
Not all thy counsel.

TIMON
Dost thou, or dost thou not, heaven's curse upon thee!

PHRYNIA *and* TIMANDRA
Give us some gold, good Timon: hast thou more?

TIMON
Enough to make a whore forswear her trade,
And to make whores, a bawd. Hold up, you sluts,
Your aprons mountant: you are not oathable, —
Although, I know, you'll swear, terribly swear,

Into strong shudders and to heavenly agues,
Th'immortal gods that hear you; — spare your oaths,
I'll trust to your conditions: be whores still;
And he whose pious breath seeks to convert you,
Be strong in whore, allure him, burn him up;
Let your close fire predominate his smoke,
And be no turncoats: yet may your pains, six months,
Be quite contrary: and thatch your poor thin roofs
With burdens of the dead; — some that were hang'd,
No matter: — wear them, betray with them: whore still;
Paint till a horse may mire upon your face:
A pox of wrinkles!

PHRYNIA *and* **TIMANDRA**
Well, more gold: — what then? —
Believe't, that we'll do any thing for gold.

TIMON
Consumptions sow
In hollow bones of man; strike their sharp shins,
And mar men's spurring. Crack the lawyer's voice,
That he may never more false title plead,
Nor sound his quillets shrilly: hoar the flamen,
That scolds against the quality of flesh,
And not believes himself: down with the nose,
Down with it flat; take the bridge quite away
Of him that, his particular to foresee,
Smells from the general weal: make curl'd-pate
    ruffians bald;
And let the unscarr'd braggarts of the war
Derive some pain from you: plague all;
That your activity may defeat and quell
The source of all erection. — There's more gold: —
Do you damn others, and let this damn you,
And ditches grave you all!

PHRYNIA *and* **TIMANDRA**
More counsel with more money, bounteous Timon.

TIMON
More whore, more mischief first; I've given you earnest.

ALCIBIADES
Strike up the drum towards Athens! — Farewell,
    Timon:
If I thrive well, I'll visit thee again.

TIMON
If I hope well, I'll never see thee more.

ALCIBIADES
I never did thee harm.

TIMON
Yes, thou spokest well of me.

ALCIBIADES
                        Call'st thou that harm?

TIMON
Men daily find it. Get thee away, and take
Thy beagles with thee.

ALCIBIADES
                    We but offend him. — Strike!
[*Drum beats. Exeunt* ALCIBIADES, PHRYNIA, *and*
                        TIMANDRA.

TIMON
That nature, being sick of man's unkindness,
Should yet be hungry! — Common mother, thou,
                                    [*Digging.*
Whose womb unmeasurable, and infinite breast,
Teems, and feeds all; whose self-same mettle,
Whereof thy proud child, arrogant man, is puff'd,
Engenders the black toad and adder blue,
The gilded newt and eyeless venom'd worm,
With all th'abhorred births below crisp heaven
Whereon Hyperion's quickening fire doth shine;
Yield him, who all thy human sons doth hate,
From forth thy plenteous bosom, one poor root!
Ensear thy fertile and conceptious womb;
Let it no more bring out ingrateful man!
Go great with tigers, dragons, wolves, and bears;
Teem with new monsters, whom thy upward face
Hath to the marbled mansion all above
Never presented! — O, a root, — dear thanks! —
Dry up thy marrows, vines, and plough-torn leas;
Whereof ingrateful man, with liquorish draughts
And morsels unctuous, greases his pure mind,
That from it all consideration slips! —
                Enter APEMANTUS.
More man? plague, plague!

APEMANTUS
I was directed hither: men report
Thou dost affect my manners, and dost use them.

TIMON
'Tis, then, because thou dost not keep a dog,
Whom I would imitate: consumption catch thee!

APEMANTUS
This is in thee a nature but infected;
A poor unmanly melancholy sprung

From change of fortune. Why this spade? this place?
This slave-like habit; and these looks of care?
Thy flatterers yet wear silk, drink wine, lie soft;
Hug their diseased perfumes, and have forgot
That ever Timon was. Shame not these woods.
By putting on the cunning of a carper.
Be thou a flatterer now, and seek to thrive
By that which has undone thee: hinge thy knee,
And let his very breath, whom thou'lt observe,
Blow off thy cap; praise his most vicious strain,
And call it excellent: thou wast told thus;
Thou gavest thine ears like tapsters that bid welcome
To knaves and all approachers: 'tis most just
That thou turn rascal; hadst thou wealth again,
Rascals should have't. Do not assume my likeness.

TIMON
Were I like thee, I'd throw away myself.

APEMANTUS
Thou hast cast away thyself, being like thyself;
A madman so long, now a fool. What, think'st
That the bleak air, thy boisterous chamberlain,
Will put thy shirt on warm? will these moss'd trees,
That have outliv'd the eagle, page thy heels,
And skip when thou point'st out? will the cold brook,
Candied with ice, caudle thy morning taste,
To cure thy o'er-night's surfeit? Call the creatures
Whose naked natures live in all the spite
Of wreakful heaven, whose bare unhoused trunks,
To the conflicting elements expos'd,
Answer mere nature; bid them flatter thee;
O, thou shalt find —

TIMON
                    A fool of thee: depart.

APEMANTUS
I love thee better now than e'er I did.

TIMON
I hate thee worse.

APEMANTUS
                Why?

TIMON
                    Thou flatter'st misery.

APEMANTUS
I flatter not; but say thou art a caitiff.

TIMON
Why dost thou seek me out?

APEMANTUS
                        To vex thee.

TIMON
Always a villain's office or a fool's.
Dost please thyself in't?

APEMANTUS
                        Ay.

TIMON
                    What! a knave too?

APEMANTUS
If thou didst put this sour-cold habit on
To castigate thy pride, 'twere well: but thou
Dost it enforcedly; thou'ldst courtier be again,
Wert thou not beggar. Willing misery
Outlives incertain pomp, is crown'd before:
The one is filling still, never complete;
The other, at high wish: best state, contentless,
Hath a distracted and most wretched being,
Worse than the worst, content.
Thou shouldst desire to die, being miserable.

TIMON
Not by his breath that is more miserable.
Thou art a slave, whom Fortune's tender arm
With favour never clasp'd; but bred a dog.
Hadst thou, like us from our first swath, proceeded
The sweet degrees that this brief world affords
To such as may the passive drugs of it
Freely command, thou wouldst have plung'd thyself
In general riot; melted down thy youth
In different beds of lust; and never learn'd
The icy precepts of respect, but follow'd
The sugar'd game before thee. But myself,
Who had the world as my confectionary;
The mouths, the tongues, the eyes, and hearts of men
At duty, more than I could frame employment;
That numberless upon me stuck, as leaves
Do on the oak, have with one winter's brush
Fell from their boughs, and left me open, bare
For every storm that blows; — I, to bear this,
That never knew but better, is some burden:
Thy nature did commence in sufferance, time
Hath made thee hard in't. Why shouldst thou hate
    men?
They never flatter'd thee: what hast thou given?
If thou wilt curse, — thy father, that poor rag,

Must be thy subject; who, in spite, put stuff
To some she-beggar, and compounded thee
Poor rogue hereditary. Hence, be gone! —
If thou hadst not been born the worst of men,
Thou hadst been a knave and flatterer.

APEMANTUS
                            Art thou proud yet?

TIMON
Ay, that I am not thee.

APEMANTUS
                        I, that I was
No prodigal.

TIMON
            I, that I am one now:
Were all the wealth I have shut up in thee,
I'ld give thee leave to hang it. Get thee gone. —
That the whole life of Athens were in this!
Thus would I eat it.   [*Gnawing a root.*

APEMANTUS
                Here; I'll mend thy feast.
                        [*Offering him something.*

TIMON
First mend my company, take away thyself.

APEMANTUS
So I shall mend mine own, by the lack of thine.

TIMON
'Tis not well mended so, it is but botch'd;
If not, I would it were.

APEMANTUS
What wouldst thou have to Athens?

TIMON
Thee thither in a whirlwind. If thou wilt,
Tell them there I have gold; look, so I have.

APEMANTUS
Here is no use for gold.

TIMON
                    The best and truest;
For here it sleeps, and does no hired harm.

APEMANTUS
Where liest o'nights, Timon?

TIMON
                        Under that's above me.
Where feed'st thou o'days, Apemantus?

APEMANTUS
Where my stomach finds meat; or, rather, where I eat
it.

TIMON
Would poison were obedient, and knew my mind!

APEMANTUS
Where wouldst thou send it?

TIMON
To sauce thy dishes.

APEMANTUS
The middle of humanity thou never knewest, but the
extremity of both ends: when thou wast in thy gilt and
thy perfume they mock'd thee for too much curiosity;
in thy rags thou know'st none, but art despised for the
contrary. There's a medlar for thee; eat it.

TIMON
On what I hate I feed not.

APEMANTUS
Dost hate a medlar?

TIMON
Ay, though it look like thee.

APEMANTUS
An th'hadst hated meddlers sooner, thou shouldst
have loved thyself better now. What man didst thou
ever know unthrift that was beloved after his means?

TIMON
Who, without those means thou talk'st of, didst thou
ever know beloved?

APEMANTUS
Myself.

TIMON
I understand thee; thou hadst some means to keep a
dog.

APEMANTUS
What things in the world canst thou nearest compare
to thy flatterers?

TIMON
Women nearest; but men, men are the things
themselves. What wouldst thou do with the world,
Apemantus, if it lay in thy power?

APEMANTUS
Give it the beasts, to be rid of the men.

TIMON
Wouldst thou have thyself fall in the confusion of men,
and remain a beast with the beasts?

APEMANTUS
Ay, Timon.

TIMON
A beastly ambition, which the gods grant thee t'attain
to! If thou wert the lion, the fox would beguile thee; if
thou wert the lamb, the fox would eat thee: if thou wert
the fox, the lion would suspect thee, when,
peradventure, thou wert accused by the ass: if thou
wert the ass, thy dulness would torment thee, and still
thou livedst but as a breakfast to the wolf: if thou wert
the wolf, thy greediness would afflict thee, and oft thou
shouldst hazard thy life for thy dinner: wert thou the
unicorn, pride and wrath would confound thee, and
make thine own self the conquest of thy fury: wert thou
a bear, thou wouldst be kill'd by the horse: wert thou a
horse, thou wouldst be seized by the leopard: wert thou
a leopard, thou wert german to the lion, and the spots
of thy kindred were jurors on thy life: all thy safety were
remotion, and thy defence absence. What beast couldst
thou be, that were not subject to a beast? and what a
beast art thou already, that seest not thy loss in
transformation!

APEMANTUS
If thou couldst please me with speaking to me, thou
mightst have hit upon it here: the commonwealth of
Athens is become a forest of beasts.

TIMON
How has the ass broke the wall, that thou art out of the city?

APEMANTUS
Yonder comes a poet and a painter: the plague of
company light upon thee! I will fear to catch it, and give
way: when I know not what else to do, I'll see thee again.

TIMON
When there is nothing living but thee, thou shalt be
welcome. I had rather be a beggar's dog than
Apemantus.

APEMANTUS
Thou art the cap of all the fools alive.

TIMON
Would thou wert clean enough to spit upon!

APEMANTUS
A plague on thee, thou art too bad to curse!

TIMON
All villains that do stand by thee are pure.

APEMANTUS
There is no leprosy but what thou speak'st.

TIMON
If I name thee. —
I'll beat thee, but I should infect my hands.

APEMANTUS
I would my tongue could rot them off!

TIMON
Away, thou issue of a mangy dog!
Choler does kill me that thou art alive;
I swound to see thee.

APEMANTUS
Would thou wouldst burst!

TIMON
Away, thou tedious rogue! I am sorry I shall lose a
stone by thee. [*Throws a stone at him.*

APEMANTUS
Beast!

TIMON
Slave!

APEMANTUS
Toad!

TIMON
Rogue, rogue, rogue!
I am sick of this false world; and will love naught
But even the mere necessities upon't.
Then, Timon, presently prepare thy grave;
Lie where the light foam of the sea may beat
Thy grave-stone daily: make thine epitaph,
That death in me at others' lives may laugh.
O thou sweet king-killer, and dear divorce
[*Looking on the gold.*
'Twixt natural son and sire! thou bright defiler
Of Hymen's purest bed! thou valiant Mars!
Thou ever young, fresh, lov'd and delicate wooer,
Whose blush doth thaw the consecrated snow
That lies on Dian's lap! thou visible god,
That solder'st close impossibilities,
And makest them kiss! that speak'st with every tongue,
To every purpose! O thou touch of hearts!
Think, thy slave man rebels; and by thy virtue
Set them into confounding odds, that beasts
May have the world in empire!

APEMANTUS [*coming forward*].
Would 'twere so! —

But not till I am dead. — I'll say thou'st gold:
Thou wilt be throng'd to shortly.

TIMON
Throng'd to!

APEMANTUS
Ay.

TIMON
Thy back, I prithee.

APEMANTUS
Live, and love thy misery!

TIMON
Long live so, and so die! [*Exit* APEMANTUS.] I am
quit. —
More things like men? — Eat, Timon, and abhor
them.

Enter BANDITTI.

FIRST BANDIT
Where should he have this gold? It is some poor
fragment, some slender ort of his remainder:
the mere want of gold, and the falling-from of
his friends, drove him into this melancholy.

SECOND BANDIT
It is noised he hath a mass of treasure.

THIRD BANDIT
Let us make the assay upon him: if he care not
for't, he will supply us easily; if he covetously
reserve it, how shall's get it?

SECOND BANDIT
True; for he bears it not about him, 'tis hid.

FIRST BANDIT
Is not this he?

BANDITTI
Where?

SECOND BANDIT
'Tis his description.

THIRD BANDIT
He; I know him.

BANDITTI
Save thee, Timon.

TIMON
Now, thieves?

BANDITTI
Soldiers, not thieves.

TIMON
Both too; and women's sons.

BANDITTI
We are not thieves, but men that much do want.

TIMON
Your greatest want is, you want much: of meat.
Why should you want? Behold, the earth hath roots;
Within this mile break forth a hundred springs;
The oaks bear mast, the briers scarlet hips;
The bounteous housewife, nature, on each bush
Lays her full mess before you. Want! why want?

FIRST BANDIT
We cannot live on grass, on berries, water,
As beasts and birds and fishes.

TIMON
Nor on the beasts themselves, the birds, and fishes;
You must eat men. Yet thanks I must you con,
That you are thieves profess'd; that you work not
In holier shapes: for there is boundless theft
In limited professions. Rascal thieves,
Here's gold. Go, suck the subtle blood o'the grape,
Till the high fever seethe your blood to froth,
And so scape hanging: trust not the physician;
His antidotes are poison, and he slays
More than you rob: take wealth and lives
together;
Do villainy, do, since you protest to do't,
Like workmen. I'll example you with thievery:
The sun's a thief, and with his great attraction
Robs the vast sea: the moon's an arrant thief,
And her pale fire she snatches from the sun:
The sea's a thief, whose liquid surge resolves
The moon into salt tears: the earth's a thief,
That feeds and breeds by a composture stol'n
From general excrement: each thing's a thief:
The laws, your curb and whip, in their
rough power
Have uncheck'd theft. Love not yourselves:
away,
Rob one another. There's more gold. Cut
throats;
All that you meet are thieves: To Athens go:
Break open shops; nothing can you steal,
but thieves
Do lose it: steal not less for this I give you;
And gold confound you howsoe'er! Amen.

TIMON I had rather be a beggar's dog
than Apemantus.

THIRD BANDIT
'Has almost charm'd me from my profession, by
persuading me to it.

FIRST BANDIT
'Tis in the malice of mankind that he thus advises us;
not to have us thrive in our mystery.

SECOND BANDIT
I'll believe him as an enemy, and give over my trade.

FIRST BANDIT
Let us first see peace in Athens; there is no time so
miserable but a man may be true. [*Exeunt* BANDITTI.

Enter FLAVIUS.

FLAVIUS
O you gods!
Is yond despis'd and ruinous man my lord?
Full of decay and failing?
O monument and wonder of good deeds
Evilly bestow'd!
What an alteration of honour
Has desperate want made!
What viler thing upon the earth than friends
Who can bring noblest minds to basest ends!
How rarely does it meet with this time's guise,
When man was wish'd to love his enemies!
Grant I may ever love, and rather woo
Those that would mischief me than those that do! —
'Has caught me in his eye: I will present
My honest grief unto him; and, as my lord,
Still serve him with my life. — My dearest master!

TIMON
Away! what art thou?

THIRD BANDIT Let us make the assay upon him.

FLAVIUS

         Have you forgot me, sir?

TIMON

Why dost ask that? I have forgot all men;
Then, if thou grant'st th'art man, I have forgot thee.

FLAVIUS

An honest poor servant of yours.

TIMON

Then I know thee not:
I never had honest man about me, I; all
I kept were knaves, to serve in meat to villains.

FLAVIUS

The gods are witness,
Ne'er did poor steward wear a truer grief
For his undone lord than mine eyes for you.

TIMON

What, dost thou weep? — come nearer; — then I love
  thee,
Because thou art a woman, and disclaim'st
Flinty mankind; whose eyes do never give
But thorough lust and laughter. Pity's sleeping:
Strange times, that weep with laughing, not with weeping!

FLAVIUS

I beg of you to know me, good my lord,
T'accept my grief, and, whilst this poor wealth lasts,
To entertain me as your steward still.

TIMON

Had I a steward
So true, so just, and now so comfortable?
It almost turns my dangerous nature mild.
Let me behold thy face. Surely, this man
Was born of woman. —
Forgive my general and exceptless rashness,
You perpetual-sober gods! I do proclaim
One honest man, — mistake me not, — but one;
No more, I pray, — and he's a steward. —
How fain would I have hated all mankind!
And thou redeem'st thyself: but all, save thee,
I fell with curses.
Methinks thou art more honest now than wise;
For, by oppressing and betraying me,
Thou might'st have sooner got another service:
For many so arrive at second masters,
Upon their first lord's neck. But tell me true, —
For I must ever doubt, though ne'er so sure, —
Is not thy kindness subtle-covetous,
A usuring kindness, and, as rich men deal gifts,
Expecting in return twenty for one?

FLAVIUS

No, my most worthy master; in whose breast
Doubt and suspect, alas, are plac'd too late:
You should have fear'd false times when you did feast:
Suspect still comes where an estate is least.
That which I show, heaven knows, is merely love,
Duty and zeal to your unmatched mind,
Care of your food and living; and, believe it,
My most honour'd lord,
For any benefit that points to me,
Either in hope or present, I'ld exchange
For this one wish, — that you had power and wealth
To requite me, by making rich yourself.

TIMON

Look thee, 'tis so! — Thou singly honest man,
Here, take: — the gods, out of my misery,

Have sent thee treasure. Go, live rich and happy,
But thus condition'd: — thou shalt build from men;
Hate all, curse all; show charity to none;
But let the famish'd flesh slide from the bone,
Ere thou relieve the beggar: give to dogs
What thou deny'st to men; let prisons swallow 'em,
Debts wither 'em to nothing: be men like blasted
  woods,
And may diseases lick up their false bloods!
And so, farewell, and thrive.

FLAVIUS

         O, let me stay,
And comfort you, my master.

TIMON

         If thou hatest
Curses, stay not; fly, whilst thou art blest and free:
Ne'er see thou man, and let me ne'er see thee.

           [*Exeunt severally.*

ACT V

SCENE I

The woods. Before TIMON'S *cave.*

Enter POET *and* PAINTER; TIMON *watching them
from his cave.*

PAINTER

As I took note of the place, it cannot be far where he
abides.

POET

What's to be thought of him? does the rumour hold for
true, that he's so full of gold?

PAINTER

Certain: Alcibiades reports it; Phrynia and Timandra
had gold of him: he likewise enrich'd poor straggling
soldiers with great quantity: 'tis said he gave unto his
steward a mighty sum.

POET

Then this breaking of his has been but a try for his
friends.

PAINTER

Nothing else: you shall see him a palm in Athens again,
and flourish with the highest. Therefore 'tis not amiss
we tender our loves to him, in this supposed distress of
his: it will show honestly in us; and is very likely to load
our purposes with what they travail for, if it be a just
true report that goes of his having.

POET

What have you now to present unto him?

PAINTER

Nothing at this time but my visitation: only I will
promise him an excellent piece.

POET

I must serve him so too, — tell him of an intent that's
coming toward him.

PAINTER

Good as the best. Promising is the very air o'the time;
it opens the eyes of expectation: performance is ever
the duller for his act; and, but in the plainer and
simpler kind of people, the deed of saying is quite out
of use. To promise is most courtly and fashionable:
performance is a kind of will or testament which
argues a great sickness in his judgement that makes
it.

         Enter TIMON *from his cave.*

TIMON [*aside*].

Excellent workman! thou canst not paint a man so bad
as is thyself.

POET

I am thinking what I shall say I have provided for him:
it must be a personating of himself; a satire against the
softness of prosperity, with a discovery of the infinite
flatteries that follow youth and opulency.

TIMON [*aside*].

Must thou needs stand for a villain in thine own work?
wilt thou whip thine own faults in other men? Do so, I
have gold for thee.

POET

Nay, let's seek him:
Then do we sin against our own estate,
When we may profit meet, and come too late.

PAINTER

True;
When the day serves, before black-corner'd night,
Find what thou want'st by free and offer'd light.
Come.

TIMON [*aside*].

I'll meet you at the turn. — What a god's gold,
That he is worshipp'd in a baser temple
Than where swine feed!
'Tis thou that rigg'st the bark and plough'st the foam;
Settlest admired reverence in a slave:
To thee be worship! and thy saints for aye
Be crown'd with plagues, that thee alone obey! —
Fit I meet them.   [*Coming forward.*

POET

Hail, worthy Timon!

PAINTER

         Our late noble master!

TIMON

Have I once liv'd to see two honest men?

POET

Sir,
Having often of your open bounty tasted,
Hearing you were retired, your friends fall'n off,
Whose thankless natures — O abhorred spirits! —
Not all the whips of heaven are large enough —
What! to you,
Whose star-like nobleness gave life and influence
To their whole being! — I am rapt, and cannot cover
The monstrous bulk of this ingratitude
With any size of words.

TIMON

Let it go naked, men may see't the better:
You that are honest, by being what you are,
Make them best seen and known.

PAINTER

         He and myself
Have travail'd in the great shower of your gifts,
And sweetly felt it.

TIMON

         Ay, you are honest men.

PAINTER

We are hither come to offer you our service.

TIMON

Most honest men! Why, how shall I requite you?
Can you eat roots, and drink cold water? no.

BOTH

What we can do, we'll do, to do you service.

TIMON

Y'are honest men: y'have heard that I have gold;
I am sure you have: speak truth; y'are honest men.

PAINTER

So it is said, my noble lord: but therefore
Came not my friend nor I.

TIMON

Good honest men! — Thou draw'st a counterfeit
Best in all Athens: th'art, indeed, the best;
Thou counterfeit'st most lively.

PAINTER

         So, so, my lord.

TIMON

E'en so, sir, as I say. — And, for thy fiction,
Why, thy verse swells with stuff so fine and smooth,
That thou art even natural in thine art. —
But, for all this, my honest-natured friends,
I must needs say you have a little fault:
Marry, 'tis not monstrous in you; neither wish I
You take much pains to mend.

BOTH

         Beseech your honour
To make it known to us.

TIMON

         You'll take it ill.

BOTH

Most thankfully, my lord.

TIMON

         Will you, indeed?

BOTH

Doubt it not, worthy lord.

TIMON

There's never a one of you but trusts a knave,
That mightily deceives you.

BOTH

         Do we, my lord?

TIMON

Ay, and you hear him cog, see him dissemble,
Know his gross patchery, love him, feed him,
Keep in your bosom: yet remain assured
That he's a made-up villain.

PAINTER

I know none such, my lord.

POET

         Nor I.

FLAVIUS Lord Timon! Timon! Look out, and speak to friends.

TIMON
Look you, I love you well; I'll give you gold,
Rid me these villains from your companies:
Hang them or stab them, drown them in a draught,
Confound them by some course, and come to me,
I'll give you gold enough.

BOTH
Name them, my lord, let's know them.

TIMON
You that way, and you this, — but two in company:
Each man apart, all single and alone,
Yet an arch-villain keeps him company.
[*to the* PAINTER] If, where thou art, two villains shall
    not be,
Come not near him. — [*to the* POET] If thou wouldst
    not reside
But where one villain is, then him abandon. —
Hence, pack! there's gold, — you came for gold, ye
    slaves:
[*to the* PAINTER] You have work for me, there's
    payment: hence. —
[*to the* POET] You are an alchemist, make gold of that: —
Out, rascal dogs!
    [*Beats and drives them out, and then retires to his cave.*

    Enter FLAVIUS *and two* SENATORS.

FLAVIUS
It is in vain that you would speak with Timon,
For he is set so only to himself,
That nothing but himself, which looks like man,
Is friendly with him.

FIRST SENATOR
                Bring us to his cave:
It is our pact and promise to th'Athenians
To speak with Timon.

SECOND SENATOR
                At all times alike
Men are not still the same: 'twas time and griefs
That fram'd him thus: time, with his fairer hand,
Offering the fortunes of his former days,
The former man may make him. Bring us to him.
And chance it as it may.

FLAVIUS
                Here is his cave. —
Peace and content be here! Lord Timon! Timon!

Look out, and speak to friends: th'Athenians,
By two of their most reverend senate, greet thee:
Speak to them, noble Timon.
                Enter TIMON *out of his cave.*

TIMON
Thou sun, that comfort'st, burn! — Speak, and be
    hang'd:
For each true word, a blister! and each false
Be as cauterizing to the root o'the tongue,
Consuming it with speaking!

FIRST SENATOR
                Worthy Timon, —

TIMON
Of none but such as you, and you of Timon.

FIRST SENATOR
The senators of Athens greet thee, Timon.

TIMON
I thank them; and would send them back the plague,
Could I but catch it for them.

FIRST SENATOR
                O, forget
What we are sorry for ourselves in thee.
The senators with one consent of love
Entreat thee back to Athens; who have thought
On special dignities, which vacant lie
For thy best use and wearing.

SECOND SENATOR
                They confess
Toward thee forgetfulness too general, gross:
Which now the public body, — which doth seldom
Play the recanter, — feeling in itself
A lack of Timon's aid, hath sense withal
Of its own fail, restraining aid to Timon;
And send forth us, to make their sorrow'd render,
Together with a recompense more fruitful
Than their offence can weigh down by the dram;
Ay, even such heaps and sums of love and wealth
As shall to thee blot out what wrongs were theirs,
And write in thee the figures of their love,
Ever to read them thine.

TIMON
                You witch me in it;
Surprise me to the very brink of tears:
Lend me a fool's heart and a woman's eyes,

And I'll beweep these comforts, worthy senators.

FIRST SENATOR
Therefore, so please thee to return with us,
And of our Athens — thine and ours — to take
The captainship, thou shalt be met with thanks,
Allow'd with absolute power, and thy good name
Live with authority: — so soon we shall drive back
Of Alcibiades th'approaches wild;
Who, like a boar too savage, doth root up
His country's peace.

SECOND SENATOR
                And shakes his threat'ning sword
Against the walls of Athens.

FIRST SENATOR
                Therefore, Timon, —

TIMON
Well, sir, I will; therefore, I will, sir; thus: —
If Alcibiades kill my countrymen,
Let Alcibiades know this of Timon,
That Timon cares not. But if he sack fair Athens,
And take our goodly aged men by the beards,
Giving our holy virgins to the stain
Of contumelious, beastly, mad-brain'd war,
Then let him know, and tell him Timon speaks it,
In pity of our aged and our youth
I cannot choose but tell him that I care not,
And let him take't at worst; for their knives care not,
While you have throats to answer: for myself,
There's not a whittle in th'unruly camp
But I do prize it at my love, before
The reverend'st throat in Athens. So I leave you
To the protection of the prosperous gods,
As thieves to keepers.

FLAVIUS
                Stay not, all's in vain.

TIMON
Why, I was writing of my epitaph;
It will be seen to-morrow: my long sickness
Of health and living now begins to mend,
And nothing brings me all things. Go, live still;
Be Alcibiades your plague, you his,
And last so long enough!

FIRST SENATOR
                We speak in vain.

TIMON
But yet I love my country; and am not
One that rejoices in the common wrack,
As common bruit doth put it.

FIRST SENATOR
                That's well spoke.

TIMON
Commend me to my loving countrymen, —

FIRST SENATOR
These words become your lips as they pass through
them.

SECOND SENATOR
And enter in our ears like great triumphers
In their applauding gates.

TIMON
                Commend me to them;
And tell them that, to ease them of their griefs,
Their fears of hostile strokes, their aches, losses,
Their pangs of love, with other incident throes
That nature's fragile vessel doth sustain
In life's uncertain voyage, I will
Some kindness do them, — I'll teach them to prevent
Wild Alcibiades' wrath.

FIRST SENATOR
I like this well: he will return again.

TIMON
I have a tree, which grows here in my close,
That mine own use invites me to cut down,
And shortly must I fell it: tell my friends,
Tell Athens, in the sequence of degree,
From high to low throughout, that whoso please
To stop affliction, let him take his haste,
Come hither, ere my tree hath felt the axe,
And hang himself: — I pray you, do my greeting.

FLAVIUS
Trouble him no further; thus you still shall find him.

TIMON
Come not to me again: but say to Athens,
Timon hath made his everlasting mansion
Upon the beached verge of the salt flood;
Who once a day with his embossed froth
The turbulent surge shall cover: thither come,
And let my grave-stone be your oracle. —
Lips, let sour words go by, and language end:
What is amiss, plague and infection mend!
Graves only be men's works, and death their gain!

Sun, hide thy beams! Timon hath done his reign. [*Exit.*

FIRST SENATOR
His discontents are unremovably
Coupled to nature.

SECOND SENATOR
Our hope in him is dead: let us return,
And strain what other means is left unto us
In our dear peril.

FIRST SENATOR
        It requires swift foot.   [*Exeunt.*

SCENE II

Before the walls of Athens.

Enter two SENATORS *and a* MESSENGER.

FIRST SENATOR
Thou hast painfully discover'd: are his files
As full as thy report?

MESSENGER
      I have spoke the least:
Besides, his expedition promises
Present approach.

SECOND SENATOR
We stand much hazard, if they bring not Timon.

MESSENGER
I met a courier, one mine ancient friend;
Whom, though in general part we were opposed,
Yet our old love had a particular force,
And made us speak like friends: — this man was riding
From Alcibiades to Timon's cave,
With letters of entreaty, which imported
His fellowship i'the cause against your city,
In part for his sake mov'd.

FIRST SENATOR
      Here come our brothers.

Enter SENATORS *from* TIMON.

THIRD SENATOR
No talk of Timon, nothing of him expect.
The enemies' drum is heard, and fearful scouring
Doth choke the air with dust: in, and prepare:
Ours is the fall, I fear; our foes the snare.   [*Exeunt.*

SCENE III

The woods. TIMON'S *cave, and a rude tomb seen.*

Enter a SOLDIER *in the woods, seeking* TIMON.

SOLDIER
By all description this should be the place.
Who's here? speak, ho! — No answer? — What is this?
Timon is dead, who hath outstretch'd his span:
Some beast rear'd this; here does not live a man.
Dead, sure; and this his grave. —
What's on this tomb I cannot read; the character
I'll take with wax:
Our captain hath in every figure skill,
An aged interpreter, though young in days:
Before proud Athens he's set down by this,
Whose fall the mark of his ambition is.   [*Exit.*

SCENE IV

Before the walls of Athens.

Trumpets sound. Enter ALCIBIADES
with his POWERS.

ALCIBIADES
Sound to this coward and lascivious town
Our terrible approach.   [*A parley sounded.*
      The SENATORS *appear upon the walls.*
Till now you have gone on, and fill'd the time
With all licentious measure, making your wills
The scope of justice; till now, myself, and such
As slept within the shadow of your power,
Have wander'd with our travers'd arms, and breath'd
Our sufferance vainly: now the time is flush,
When crouching marrow, in the bearer strong,
Cries, of itself, 'No more': now breathless wrong
Shall sit and pant in your great chairs of ease;
And pursy insolence shall break his wind
With fear and horrid flight.

FIRST SENATOR
        Noble and young,
When thy first griefs were but a mere conceit,
Ere thou hadst power, or we had cause of fear,
We sent to thee; to give thy rages balm,
To wipe out our ingratitude with loves
Above their quantity.

SECOND SENATOR
        So did we woo
Transformed Timon to our city's love
By humble message and by promis'd means:
We were not all unkind, nor all deserve
The common stroke of war.

FIRST SENATOR
        These walls of ours
Were not erected by their hands from whom
You have receiv'd your griefs; nor are they such
That these great towers, trophies, and schools should
    fall
For private faults in them.

SECOND SENATOR
        Nor are they living
Who were the motives that you first went out;
Shame, that they wanted cunning, in excess,
Hath broke their hearts. March, noble lord,
Into our city, with thy banners spread:
By decimation, and a tithed death, —
If thy revenges hunger for that food
Which nature loathes, — take thou the destin'd tenth;
And by the hazard of the spotted die
Let die the spotted.

FIRST SENATOR
        All have not offended;
For those that were, it is not square to take
On those that are, revenges: crimes, like lands,
Are not inherited. Then, dear countryman,
Bring in thy ranks, but leave without thy rage:
Spare thy Athenian cradle, and those kin
Which, in the bluster of thy wrath, must fall
With those that have offended: like a shepherd,
Approach the fold, and cull th'infected forth.
But kill not all together.

SECOND SENATOR
        What thou wilt,
Thou rather shalt enforce it with thy smile
Than hew to't with thy sword.

FIRST SENATOR
        Set but thy foot
Against our rampired gates, and they shall ope;
So thou wilt send thy gentle heart before,
To say thou'lt enter friendly.

SECOND SENATOR
        Throw thy glove,
Or any token of thine honour else,
That thou wilt use the wars as thy redress,
And not as our confusion, all thy powers
Shall make their harbour in our town, till we
Have seal'd thy full desire.

ALCIBIADES
        Then there's my glove;
Descend, and open your uncharged ports:
Those enemies of Timon's, and mine own,
Whom you yourselves shall set out for reproof,
Fall, and no more: and — to atone your fears
With my more noble meaning — not a man
Shall pass his quarter, or offend the stream
Of regular justice in your city's bounds,
But shall be render'd to your public laws
At heaviest answer.

SENATORS
      'Tis most nobly spoken.

ALCIBIADES
Descend, and keep your words.
   [*The* SENATORS *descend, and open the gates.*

Enter a SOLDIER.

SOLDIER
My noble general, Timon is dead;
Entomb'd upon the very hem o' the sea;
And on his gravestone this insculpture, which
With wax I brought away, whose soft impression
Interprets for my poor ignorance.

ALCIBIADES [*reads*].
Here lies a wretched corse, of wretched soul bereft:
Seek not my name: a plague consume you wicked
    caitiffs left!
Here lie I, Timon; who, alive, all living men did hate:
Pass by, and curse thy fill; but pass, and stay not here
    thy gait.
These well express in thee thy latter spirits:
Though thou abhorr'dst in us our human griefs,
Scorn'dst our brain's flow, and those our droplets
    which
From niggard nature fall, yet rich conceit
Taught thee to make vast Neptune weep for aye
On thy low grave, on faults forgiven. Dead
Is noble Timon: of whose memory
Hereafter more. — Bring me into your city,
And I will use the olive with my sword:
Make war breed peace; make peace stint war;
    make each
Prescribe to other, as each other's leech. —
Let our drums strike.   [*Exeunt.*

PERICLES, PRINCE OF TYRE

DRAMATIS PERSONAE

ANTIOCHUS, *King of Antioch.*
PERICLES, *Prince of Tyre.*
HELICANUS, } *two lords of Tyre.*
ESCANES, }
SIMONIDES, *King of Pentapolis.*
CLEON, *governor of Tarsus.*
LYSIMACHUS, *governor of Mytilene.*
CERIMON, *a lord of Ephesus.*
THAILARD, *a lord of Antioch.*
PHILEMON, *servant to Cerimon.*

LEONINE, *servant to Dionyza.*
MARSHAL.
A PANDAR.
BOULT, *his servant.*
THE DAUGHTER OF ANTIOCHUS.
DIONYZA, *wife to Cleon.*
THAISA, *daughter to Simonides.*
MARINA, *daughter to Pericles and Thaisa.*
LYCHORIDA, *nurse to Marina.*
A BAWD.

LORDS, LADIES, KNIGHTS, GENTLEMEN,
  SAILORS, PIRATES, FISHERMEN, *and*
  MESSENGERS.

DIANA.

GOWER, *as* CHORUS.

SCENE — *Dispersedly in various countries.*

ACT I

Enter GOWER.

Before the palace of Antioch.

GOWER

To sing a song that old was sung,
From ashes ancient Gower is come,
Assuming man's infirmities,
To glad your ear and please your eyes.
It hath been sung at festivals,
On ember-eves and holy-ales;
And lords and ladies in their lives
Have read it for restoratives:
The purchase is to make men glorious;
Et bonum quo antiquius, eo melius.
If you, born in these latter times,
When wit's more ripe, accept my rimes,
And that to hear an old man sing
May to your wishes pleasure bring,
I life would wish, and that I might
Waste it for you, like taper-light. —
This Antioch, then, Antiochus the Great
Built up, this city, for his chiefest seat;
The fairest in all Syria, —
I tell you what mine authors say:
This king unto him took a fere,
Who died and left a female heir,
So buxom, blithe, and full of face,
As heaven had lent her all his grace;
With whom the father liking took,
And her to incest did provoke: —
Bad child; worse father! to entice his own
To evil should be done by none:
But custom what they did begin
Was with long use account no sin.
The beauty of this sinful dame
Made many princes thither frame,
To seek her as a bed-fellow,
In marriage-pleasures play-fellow:
Which to prevent he made a law, —
To keep her still, and men in awe, —
That whoso ask'd her for his wife,
His riddle told not, lost his life:
So for her many a wight did die,
As yon grim looks do testify.
What now ensues, to the judgement of your eye
I give, my cause who best can justify.   [*Exit.*

SCENE I

Antioch. A room in the palace.

Enter ANTIOCHUS, PERICLES, *and* FOLLOWERS.

ANTIOCHUS

Young prince of Tyre, you have at large received
The danger of the task you undertake.

PERICLES

I have, Antiochus, and, with a soul
Embolden'd with the glory of her praise,
Think death no hazard in this enterprise.

ANTIOCHUS

Bring in our daughter, clothed like a bride,
For the embracements even of Jove himself;
At whose conception, till Lucina reign'd,
Nature this dowry gave, to glad her presence,
The senate-house of planets all did sit,
To knit in her their best perfections.

Music. Enter ANTIOCHUS' DAUGHTER.

PERICLES

See where she comes, apparell'd like the spring,
Graces her subjects, and her thoughts the king
Of every virtue gives renown to men!

ANTIOCHUS *Before thee stands this fair Hesperides.*

Her face the book of praises, where is read
Nothing but curious pleasures, as from thence
Sorrow were ever raz'd, and testy wrath
Could never be her mild companion.
You gods that made me man, and sway in love,
That have inflam'd desire in my breast
To taste the fruit of yon celestial tree,
Or die in the adventure, be my helps,
As I am son and servant to your will,
To compass such a boundless happiness!

ANTIOCHUS

Prince Pericles, —

PERICLES

That would be son to great Antiochus.

ANTIOCHUS

Before thee stands this fair Hesperides,
With golden fruit, but dangerous to be touch'd;
For death-like dragons here affright thee hard:
Her face, like heaven, enticeth thee to view
Her countless glory, which desert must gain;
And which, without desert, because thine eye
Presumes to reach, all thy whole heap must die.
Yon sometimes famous princes, like thyself,
Drawn by report, adventurous by desire,
Tell thee, with speechless tongues and semblance pale,
That, without covering, save yon field of stars,
Here they stand martyrs, slain in Cupid's wars;
And with dead cheeks advise thee to desist
For going on death's net, whom none resist.

PERICLES

Antiochus, I thank thee, who hath taught
My frail mortality to know itself,
And by those fearful objects to prepare
This body, like to them, to what I must;

For death remember'd should be like a mirror,
Who tells us life's but breath, to trust it error.
I'll make my will, then; and, as sick men do,
Who know the world, see heaven, but, feeling woe,
Gripe not at earthly joys, as erst they did;
So I bequeath a happy peace to you
And all good men, as every prince should do;
My riches to the earth from whence they came; —
But my unspotted fire of love to you.
       [*To the* DAUGHTER *of* ANTIOCHUS.
Thus ready for the way of life or death,
I wait the sharpest blow.

ANTIOCHUS

Scorning advice, — read the conclusion, then:
Which read and not expounded, 'tis decreed,
As these before thee, thou thyself shalt bleed.

DAUGHTER OF ANTIOCHUS

Of all say'd yet, mayst thou prove prosperous!
Of all say'd yet, I wish thee happiness!

PERICLES

Like a bold champion, I assume the lists,
Nor ask advice of any other thought
But faithfulness and courage.   [*Reads the riddle.*
   'I am no viper, yet I feed
    On mother's flesh which did me breed.
   I sought a husband, in which labour
   I found that kindness in a father:
   He's father, son, and husband mild;
   I mother, wife, and yet his child.
   How they may be, and yet in two,
   As you will live, resolve it you.
Sharp physic is the last: but, O you powers
That give heaven countless eyes to view men's acts,
Why cloud they not their sights perpetually,
If this be true, which makes me pale to read it? —Fair
   glass of light, I lov'd you, and could still,
    [*Takes hold of the hand of the* PRINCESS.
Were not this glorious casket stored with ill:
But I must tell you, — now my thoughts revolt;
For he's no man on whom perfections wait
That, knowing sin within, will touch the gate.
You are a fair viol, and your sense the strings;
Who, finger'd to make man his lawful music,
Would draw heaven down, and all the gods, to hearken;
But being play'd upon before your time,
Hell only danceth at so harsh a chime.
Good sooth, I care not for you.

ANTIOCHUS

Prince Pericles, touch not, upon thy life,
For that's an article within our law,
As dangerous as the rest. Your time's expired:
Either expound now, or receive your sentence.

PERICLES

Great king,
Few love to hear the sins they love to act;
'Twould braid yourself too near for me to tell it.
Who has a book of all that monarchs do,
He's more secure to keep it shut than shown:
For vice repeated is like the wandering wind,
Blows dust in others' eyes, to spread itself;
And yet the end of all is bought thus dear,
The breath is gone, and the sore eyes see clear
To stop the air would hurt them. The blind mole casts
Copp'd hills towards heaven, to tell the earth is
   throng'd
By man's oppression; and the poor worm doth die for't.
Kings are earth's gods; in vice their law's their will;
And if Jove stray, who dares say Jove doth ill?
It is enough you know; and it is fit,
What being more known grows worse, to smother it.
All love the womb that their first being bred,
Then give my tongue like leave to love my head.

ANTIOCHUS [*aside*].
Heaven, that I had thy head! he has found the
  meaning:
But I will gloze with him. — Young prince of Tyre,
Though by the tenuor of our strict edict,
Your exposition misinterpreting,
We might proceed to cancel of your days;
Yet hope, succeeding from so fair a tree
As your fair self, doth tune us otherwise:
Forty days longer we do respite you;
If by which time our secret be undone,
This mercy shows we'll joy in such a son:
And until then your entertain shall be,
As doth befit our honour, and your worth.
                    [*Exeunt all but* PERICLES.

PERICLES
How courtesy would seem to cover sin,
When what is done is like an hypocrite,
The which is good in nothing but in sight!
If it be true that I interpret false,
Then were it certain you were not so bad
As with foul incest to abuse your soul;
Where now you're both a father and a son
By your untimely claspings with your child, —
Which pleasure fits a husband, not a father;
And she an eater of her mother's flesh
By the defiling of her parent's bed;
And both like serpents are, who though they feed
On sweetest flowers, yet they poison breed.
Antioch, farewell! for wisdom sees, those men
Blush not in actions blacker than the night,
Will shun no course to keep them from the light.
One sin, I know, another doth provoke;
Murder's as near to lust as flame to smoke:
Poison and treason are the hands of sin,
Ay, and the targets, to put off the shame:
Then, lest my life be cropp'd to keep you clear,
By flight I'll shun the danger which I fear.   [*Exit.*

                Enter ANTIOCHUS.

ANTIOCHUS
He hath found the meaning, for the which we mean
To have his head.
He must not live to trumpet forth my infamy,
Nor tell the world Antiochus doth sin
In such a loathed manner;
And therefore instantly this prince must die;
For by his fall my honour must keep high. —
Who attends us there?

                Enter THALIARD.

THALIARD
                Doth your highness call?
ANTIOCHUS
Thaliard,
You are of our chamber, and our mind partakes
Her private actions to your secrecy:
And for your faithfulness we will advance you.
Thaliard, behold, here's poison, and here's gold;
We hate the prince of Tyre, and thou must kill him:
It fits thee not to ask the reason why,
Because we bid it. Say, is it done?
THALIARD
                My lord,
'Tis done.
ANTIOCHUS
Enough.
                Enter a MESSENGER.
Let your breath cool yourself, telling your haste.
MESSENGER
My lord, prince Pericles is fled.   [*Exit.*
ANTIOCHUS
                As thou
Wilt live, fly after; and, like an arrow shot
From a well-experienc'd archer, hits the mark
His eye doth level at, so thou ne'er return
Unless thou say 'Prince Pericles is dead.'
THALIARD
My lord,
If I can get him within my pistol's length,
I'll make him sure enough: so, farewell to your highness.
ANTIOCHUS
Thaliard, adieu! [*Exit* THALIARD.] Till Pericles be dead
My heart can lend no succour to my head.   [*Exit.*

SCENE II

Tyre. A room in the palace.

Enter PERICLES.

PERICLES [*to* LORDS *without*].
Let none disturb us. — Why should this charge of
thoughts,
The sad companion, dull-eyed melancholy,
Be my so-used a guest as not an hour,
In the day's glorious walk or peaceful night,
The tomb where grief should sleep, can breed me
  quiet?
Here pleasures court mine eyes, and mine eyes shun
  them,
And danger, which I fear'd, is at Antioch,
Whose arm seems far too short to hit me here:
Yet neither pleasure's art can joy my spirits,
Nor yet the other's distance comfort me.
Then it is thus: the passions of the mind,
That have their first conception by mis-dread,
Have after-nourishment and life by care;
And what was first but fear what might be done,
Grows elder now, and cares it be not done.
And so with me: — the great Antiochus —
'Gainst whom I am too little to contend,
Since he's so great can make his will his act —
Will think me speaking, though I swear to silence;
Nor boots it me to say I honour him,
If he suspect I may dishonour him:
And what may make him blush in being known,
He'll stop the course by which it might be known;
With hostile forces he'll o'erspread the land,
And with th'ostent of war will look so huge,
Amazement shall drive courage from the state;
Our men be vanquish'd ere they do resist,
And subjects punish'd that ne'er thought offence:
Which care of them, not pity of myself,
Who am no more but as the tops of trees,
Which fence the roots they grow by and defend them,
Makes both my body pine and soul to languish,
And punish that before that he would punish.

Enter HELICANUS *and other* LORDS.

FIRST LORD
Joy and all comfort in your sacred breast!
SECOND LORD
And keep your mind, till you return to us,
Peaceful and comfortable!
HELICANUS
Peace, peace, and give experience tongue.
They do abuse the king that flatter him:
For flattery is the bellows blows up sin;
The thing the which is flatter'd, but a spark,
To which that blast gives heat and stronger glowing;
Whereas reproof, obedient, and in order,
Fits kings, as they are men, for they may err.
When Signior Sooth here does proclaim a peace,
He flatters you, makes war upon your life.
Prince, pardon me, or strike me, if you please;
I cannot be much lower than my knees.
PERICLES
All leave us else; but let your cares o'erlook
What shipping and what lading's in our haven,
And then return to us. [*Exeunt* LORDS.] Helicanus,
  thou
Hast moved us: what seest thou in our looks?
HELICANUS
An angry brow, dread lord.
PERICLES
If there be such a dart in princes' frowns,
How durst thy tongue move anger to our face?
HELICANUS
How dare the plants look up to heaven, from whence
They have their nourishment?
PERICLES
                Thou know'st I have power
To take thy life from thee.
HELICANUS [*kneeling*].
I have ground the axe myself;
Do you but strike the blow.
PERICLES
                Rise, prithee, rise.
Sit down: thou art no flatterer:
I thank thee for it; and heaven forbid
That kings should let their ears hear their faults chid!
Fit counsellor and servant for a prince,
Who by thy wisdom mak'st a prince thy servant,
What wouldst thou have me do?
HELICANUS
                To bear with patience
Such griefs as you yourself do lay upon yourself.
PERICLES
Thou speak'st like a physician, Helicanus,
That minister'st a potion unto me
That thou wouldst tremble to receive thyself.
Attend me, then: I went to Antioch,
Where, as thou know'st, against the face of death,
I sought the purchase of a glorious beauty,
From whence an issue I might propagate,
Are arms to princes, and bring joys to subjects.
Her face was to mine eye beyond all wonder;
The rest — hark in thine ear — as black as incest:
Which by my knowledge found, the sinful father
Seem'd not to strike, but smooth: but thou know'st
  this,
'Tis time to fear when tyrants seem to kiss.
Which fear so grew in me, I hither fled,
Under the covering of a careful night,
Who seem'd my good protector, and, being here,
Bethought me what was past, what might succeed.
I knew him tyrannous; and tyrants' fears
Decrease not, but grow faster than the years:
And should he doubt it, — as no doubt he doth, —
That I should open to the listening air
How many worthy princes' bloods were shed,
To keep his bed of blackness unlaid ope, —
To lop that doubt, he'll fill this land with arms,
And make pretence of wrong that I have done him;
When all, for mine, if I may call offence,
Must feel war's blow, who spares not innocence:
Which love to all, — of which thyself art one,
Who now reprovest me for't, —
HELICANUS
Alas, sir!
PERICLES
Drew sleep out of mine eyes, blood from my cheeks,
Musings into my mind, with thousand doubts
How I might stop this tempest, ere it came;
And finding little comfort to relieve them,
I thought it princely charity to grieve them.
HELICANUS
Well, my lord, since you have given me leave to speak,
Freely will I speak. Antiochus you fear,
And justly too, I think, you fear the tyrant,
Who either by public war or private treason
Will take away your life.
Therefore, my lord, go travel for a while,
Till that his rage and anger be forgot,
Or till the Destinies do cut his thread of life.
Your rule direct to any; if to me,
Day serves not light more faithful than I'll be.
PERICLES
I do not doubt thy faith;
But should he wrong my liberties in my absence?
HELICANUS
We'll mingle our bloods together in the earth,
From whence we had our being and our birth.
PERICLES
Tyre, I now look from thee, then, and to Tarsus
Intend my travel, where I'll hear from thee;
And by whose letters I'll dispose myself.
The care I had and have of subjects' good
On thee I lay, whose wisdom's strength can bear it.
I'll take thy word for faith, not ask thine oath:
Who shuns not to break one will sure crack both:
But in our orbs we'll live so round and safe,
That time of both this truth shall ne'er convince,
Thou show'dst a subject's shine, I a true prince.
                                    [*Exeunt.*

SCENE III

Tyre. An ante-chamber in the palace.

Enter THALIARD.

THALIARD
So, this is Tyre, and this the court. Here must I kill
King Pericles; and if I do it not, I am sure to be hang'd
at home: 'tis dangerous. — Well, I perceive he was a
wise fellow and had good discretion, that, being bid to
ask what he would of the king, desired he might know
none of his secrets: now do I see he had some reason
for't; for if a king bid a man be a villain, he's bound by
the indenture of his oath to be one. — Hush! here
come the lords of Tyre.

Enter HELICANUS *and* ESCANES, *with other* LORDS.

HELICANUS
You shall not need, my fellow peers of Tyre,
Further to question me of your king's departure:
His seal'd commission, left in trust with me,
Doth speak sufficiently he's gone to travel.
THALIARD [*aside*].
How! the king gone!
HELICANUS
If further yet you will be satisfied,
Why, as it were unlicens'd of your loves,
He would depart, I'll give some light unto you.
Being at Antioch, —

CLEON I'll, then, discourse our woes, felt several years.

THALIARD [aside].
          What from Antioch?
HELICANUS
Royal Antiochus — on what cause I know not —
Took some displeasure at him, — at least he judg'd so;
And doubting lest that he had err'd or sinn'd,
To show his sorrow, he'ld correct himself;
So puts himself unto the shipman's toil,
With whom each minute threatens life or death.
THALIARD [aside].
Well, I perceive I shall not be hang'd now, although I
would; but since he's gone, the king's seas must
please, — he scap'd the land, to perish at the sea. I'll
present myself. — Peace to the lords of Tyre!
HELICANUS
Lord Thaliard from Antiochus is welcome.
THALIARD
From him I come
With message unto princely Pericles;
But since my landing I have understood
Your lord has betook himself to unknown travels,
My message must return from whence it came.
HELICANUS
We have no reason to desire it,
Commended to our master, not to us:
Yet, ere you shall depart, this we desire, —
As friends to Antioch, we may feast in Tyre. [*Exeunt.*

SCENE IV

Tarsus. A room in the GOVERNOR'S *house.*
Enter CLEON, *the Governor of Tarsus, with his wife*
DIONYZA, *and others.*

CLEON
My Dionyza, shall we rest us here,
And by relating tales of others' griefs,
See if 'twill teach us to forget our own?
DIONYZA
That were to blow at fire in hope to quench it;
For who digs hills because they do aspire
Throws down one mountain to cast up a higher.
O my distressed lord, even such our griefs are;
Here they are but felt, and seen with mischief's eyes,
But like to groves, being topp'd, they higher rise.
CLEON
O Dionyza,
Who wanteth food, and will not say he wants it,
Or can conceal his hunger till he famish?
Our tongues and sorrows do sound deep our woes
Into the air; our eyes do weep, till tongues
Fetch breath that may proclaim them louder; that,
If heaven slumber while their creatures want,
They may awake their helps to comfort them.
I'll, then, discourse our woes, felt several years,
And, wanting breath to speak, help me with tears.
DIONYZA
I'll do my best, sir.

CLEON
This Tarsus, o'er which I have the government,
A city on whom Plenty held full hand,
For Riches strew'd herself even in the streets;
Whose towers bore heads so high they kiss'd the
    clouds,
And strangers ne'er beheld but wonder'd at;
Whose men and dames so jetted and adorn'd,
Like one another's glass to trim them by:
Their tables were stored full, to glad the sight,
And not so much to feed on as delight;
All poverty was scorn'd, and pride so great,
The name of help grew odious to repeat.
DIONYZA
O, 'tis too true.
CLEON
But see what heaven can do! By this our change,
These mouths who but of late earth, sea, and air,
Were all too little to content and please,
Although they gave their creatures in abundance,
As houses are defil'd for want of use,
They are now starv'd for want of exercise:
Those palates who, not yet two summers younger,
Must have inventions to delight the taste,
Would now be glad of bread, and beg for it:
Those mothers who, to nousle up their babes,
Thought naught too curious, are ready now
To eat those little darlings whom they lov'd.
So sharp are hunger's teeth, that man and wife
Draw lots who first shall die to lengthen life:
Here stands a lord, and there a lady weeping;
Here many sink, yet those which see them fall
Have scarce strength left to give them burial.
Is not this true?
DIONYZA
Our cheeks and hollow eyes do witness it.
CLEON
O, let those cities that of Plenty's cup
And her prosperities so largely taste,
With their superfluous riots, hear these tears!
The misery of Tarsus may be theirs.
    Enter a LORD.
LORD
Where's the lord governor?
CLEON
Here.
Speak out thy sorrows which thou bring'st in haste,
For comfort is too far for us to expect.
LORD
We have descried, upon our neighbouring shore,
A portly sail of ships make hitherward.
CLEON
I thought as much.
One sorrow never comes but brings an heir,
That may succeed as his inheritor;
And so in ours: some neighbouring nation,

Taking advantage of our misery,
Hath stuff'd these hollow vessels with their power,
To beat us down, the which are down already;
And make a conquest of unhappy me,
Whereas no glory's got to overcome.
LORD
That's the least fear; for, by the semblance
Of their white flags display'd, they bring us peace
And come to us as favourers, not as foes.
CLEON
Thou speak'st like him's untutor'd to repeat:
Who makes the fairest show means most deceit.
But bring they what they will and what they can,
What need we fear?
The ground's the lowest, and we are half-way there.
Go tell their general we attend him here,
To know for what he comes, and whence he comes,
And what he craves.
LORD
I go, my lord. [*Exit.*
CLEON
Welcome is peace, if he on peace consist;
If wars, we are unable to resist.
    Enter PERICLES *with* ATTENDANTS.
PERICLES
Lord Governor, for so we hear you are,
Let not our ships and number of our men
Be, like a beacon fired, t'amaze your eyes.
We have heard your miseries as far as Tyre,
And seen the desolation of your streets:
Nor come we to add sorrow to your tears,
But to relieve them of their heavy load;
And these our ships, you happily may think
Are like the Trojan horse was stuff'd within
With bloody veins, expecting overthrow,
Are stored with corn to make your needy bread,
And give them life whom hunger starv'd half dead.
ALL
The gods of Greece protect you!
And we'll pray for you.
PERICLES
          Arise, I pray you, rise:
We do not look for reverence, but for love,
And harbourage for ourself, our ships, and men.
CLEON
The which when any shall not gratify,
Or pay you with unthankfulness in thought,
Be it our wives, our children, or ourselves,
The curse of heaven and men succeed their evils!
Till when, — the which I hope shall ne'er be seen, —
Your Grace is welcome to our town and us.
PERICLES
Which welcome we'll accept; feast here awhile,
Until our stars that frown lend us a smile. [*Exeunt.*

ACT II

Enter GOWER.

GOWER
Here have you seen a mighty king
His child, I wis, to incest bring;
A better prince, and benign lord,
That will prove awful both in deed and word.
Be quiet, then, as men should be,
Till he hath pass'd necessity.
I'll show you those in troubles reign,
Losing a mite, a mountain gain.
The good in conversation —
To whom I give my benison —
Is still at Tarsus, where each man
Thinks all is writ he spoken can;
And, to remember what he does,
Build his statue to make him glorious:
But tidings to the contrary
Are brought your eyes; what need speak I?
DUMB-SHOW
Enter, at one door, PERICLES, *talking with* CLEON, *all
the* TRAIN *with them. Enter, at another door, a*
GENTLEMAN, *with a letter to* PERICLES; PERICLES
shows the letter to CLEON; *gives the* MESSENGER *a
reward, and knights him. Exit* PERICLES *at one door,
and* CLEON *at another.*

Good Helicane, that stay'd at home,
Not to eat honey like a drone
From others' labours; for though he strive
To killen bad, keep good alive;
And to fulfil his prince' desire,
Sends word of all that haps in Tyre:

How Thaliard came full bent with sin
And hid intent to murder him;
And that in Tarsus was not best
Longer for him to make his rest.
He, doing so, put forth to seas,
Where when men been, there's seldom ease;
For now the wind begins to blow;
Thunder above, and deeps below,
Make such unquiet, that the ship
Should house him safe is wrack'd and split;
And he, good prince, having all lost,
By waves from coast to coast is toss'd:
All perishen of man, of pelf,
Ne aught escapen but himself;
Till fortune, tired with doing bad,
Threw him ashore, to give him glad:
And here he comes. What shall be next,
Pardon old Gower, — this longs the text.   [*Exit.*

SCENE I

Pentapolis. An open place by the sea-side.

Enter PERICLES, *wet.*

PERICLES
Yet cease your ire, you angry stars of heaven!
Wind, rain, and thunder, remember, earthly man
Is but a substance that must yield to you;
And I, as fits my nature, do obey you:
Alas, the sea hath cast me on the rocks,
Wash'd me from shore to shore, and left me breath
Nothing to think on but ensuing death:
Let it suffice the greatness of your powers
To have bereft a prince of all his fortunes;
And having thrown him from your watery grave,
Here to have death in peace is all he'll crave.

Enter three FISHERMEN.

FIRST FISHERMAN
What, ho, Pilch!

SECOND FISHERMAN
Ha, come and bring away the nets!

FIRST FISHERMAN
What, Patch-breech, I say!

THIRD FISHERMAN
What say you, master?

FIRST FISHERMAN
Look how thou stirr'st now! come away, or I'll fetch
thee with a wanion.

THIRD FISHERMAN
Faith, master, I am thinking of the poor men that were
cast away before us even now.

FIRST FISHERMAN
Alas, poor souls, it grieved my heart to hear what pitiful
cries they made to us to help them, when, well-a-day,
we could scarce help ourselves.

THIRD FISHERMAN
Nay, master, said not I as much when I saw the porpus,
how he bounced and tumbled? they say they're
half-fish, half-flesh: a plague on them, they ne'er come
but I look to be wash'd. Master, I marvel how the fishes
live in the sea.

FIRST FISHERMAN
Why, as men do a-land, — the great ones eat up the
little ones: I can compare our rich misers to nothing so

fitly as to a whale; a' plays and tumbles, driving the
poor fry before him, and at last devours them all at a
mouthful: such whales have I heard on o'the land, who
never leave gaping till they've swallow'd the whole
parish, church, steeple, bells, and all.

PERICLES [*aside*].
A pretty moral.

THIRD FISHERMAN
But, master, if I had been the sexton, I would have been
that day in the belfry.

SECOND FISHERMAN
Why, man?

THIRD FISHERMAN
Because he should have swallow'd me too: and when I
had been in his belly, I would have kept such a jangling
of the bells, that he should never have left, till he cast
bells, steeple, church, and parish, up again. But if the
good King Simonides were of my mind, —

PERICLES [*aside*].
Simonides!

THIRD FISHERMAN
We would purge the land of these drones, that rob the
bee of her honey.

PERICLES [*aside*].
How from the finny subject of the sea
These fishers tell the infirmities of men;
And from their watery empire recollect
All that may men approve or men detect! —
Peace be at your labour, honest fishermen.

SECOND FISHERMAN
Honest! good fellow, what's that? If it be a day fits you,
search out of the calendar, and nobody look after it.

PERICLES
May see the sea hath cast upon your coast.

SECOND FISHERMAN
What a drunken knave was the sea to cast thee in our
way!

PERICLES
A man whom both the waters and the wind,
In that vast tennis-court, have made the ball
For them to play upon, entreats you pity him;
He asks of you, that never used to beg.

FIRST FISHERMAN
No, friend, cannot you beg? Here's them in our country
of Greece gets more with begging than we can do with
working.

SECOND FISHERMAN
Canst thou catch any fishes, then?

PERICLES
I never practised it.

SECOND FISHERMAN
Nay, then thou wilt starve, sure; for here's nothing to be
got now-a-days, unless thou canst fish for't.

PERICLES
What I have been I have forgot to know;
But what I am, want teaches me to think on:
A man throng'd up with cold: my veins are chill,
And have no more of life than may suffice
To give my tongue that heat to ask your help;
Which if you shall refuse, when I am dead,
For that I am a man, pray see me buried.

FIRST FISHERMAN
Die quoth-a? Now gods forbid't! I have a gown here;

come, put it on; keep thee warm. Now, afore me, a
handsome fellow! Come, thou shalt go home, and we'll
have flesh for holidays, fish for fasting-days, and
moreo'er puddings and flap-jacks; and thou shalt be
welcome.

PERICLES
I thank you, sir.

SECOND FISHERMAN
Hark you, my friend, — you said you could not beg.

PERICLES
I did but crave.

SECOND FISHERMAN
But crave! Then I'll turn craver too, and so I shall scape
whipping.

PERICLES
Why, are all your beggars whipp'd, then?

SECOND FISHERMAN
O, not all, my friend, not all; for if all your beggars were
whipp'd, I would wish no better office than to be
beadle. — But, master, I'll go draw up the net.

[*Exit with* THIRD FISHERMAN.

PERICLES [*aside*].
How well this honest mirth becomes their labour!

FIRST FISHERMAN
Hark you, sir, — do you know where ye are?

PERICLES
Not well.

FIRST FISHERMAN
Why, I'll tell you: this is call'd Pentapolis, and our king
the good Simonides.

PERICLES
The good Simonides, do you call him?

FIRST FISHERMAN
Ay, sir; and he deserves so to be call'd for his peaceable
reign and good government.

PERICLES
He is a happy king, since he gains from his subjects the
name of good by his government. How far is his court
distant from this shore?

FIRST FISHERMAN
Marry, sir, half a day's journey: and I'll tell you, he hath
a fair daughter, and to-morrow is her birth-day; and
there are princes and knights come from all parts of the
world to just and tourney for her love.

PERICLES
Were my fortunes equal to my desires, I could wish to
make one there.

FIRST FISHERMAN
O, sir, things must be as they may; and what a man
cannot get, he may lawfully deal for — his wife's soul.

Enter SECOND *and* THIRD FISHERMEN, *drawing
up a net.*

SECOND FISHERMAN
Help, master, help! here's a fish hangs in the net, like a
poor man's right in the law; 'twill hardly come out. Ha!
bots on't, 'tis come at last, and 'tis turn'd to a rusty
armour.

PERICLES
An armour, friends! I pray you, let me see it. —
Thanks, fortune, yet, that, after all thy crosses,
Thou givest me somewhat to repair myself;
And though it was mine own, part of my heritage,
Which my dead father did bequeath to me,
With this strict charge, even as he left his life,
'Keep it, my Pericles; it hath been a shield
'Twixt me and death'; — and pointed to this brace;
'For that it sav'd me, keep it; in like necessity —
The which the gods protect thee from! — may defend
thee.'
It kept where I kept, I so dearly lov'd it;
Till the rough seas, that spare not any man,
Took it in rage, though calm'd have given't again:
I thank thee for't; my shipwreck now's no ill,
Since I have here my father's gift in's will.

FIRST FISHERMAN
What mean you, sir?

PERICLES
To beg of you, kind friends, this coat of worth,
For it was sometime target to a king;
I know it by this mark. He lov'd me dearly,
And for his sake I wish the having of it;
And that you'ld guide me to your sovereign's court,
Where with it I may appear a gentleman;
And if that ever my low fortunes better,
I'll pay your bounties; till then rest your debtor.

FIRST FISHERMAN
Why, wilt thou tourney for the lady?

PERICLES
I'll show the virtue I have borne in arms.

THIRD FISHERMAN Master, I marvel how the fishes live in the sea.

PERICLES An armour, friends! I pray you, let me see it.

FIRST FISHERMAN
Why, do'e take it, and the gods give thee good on't!
SECOND FISHERMAN
Ay, but hark you, my friend; 'twas we that made up this
garment through the rough seams of the waters: there
are certain condolements, certain vails. I hope, sir, if
you thrive, you'll remember from whence you had
them.
PERICLES
Believe't, I will.
By your furtherance I am cloth'd in steel;
And, spite of all the rapture of the sea,
This jewel holds his building on my arm:
Unto thy value I will mount myself
Upon a courser, whose delightful steps
Shall make the gazer joy to see him tread. —
Only, my friend, I yet am unprovided
Of a pair of bases.
SECOND FISHERMAN
We'll sure provide: thou shalt have my best gown to
make thee a pair: and I'll bring thee to the court myself.
PERICLES
Then honour be but a goal to my will,
This day I'll rise, or else add ill to ill.   [*Exeunt.*

SCENE II

*The same. A public way or platform leading to the lists. A
pavilion by the side of it for the reception of the* KING,
PRINCESS, LORDS, *etc.*

Enter SIMONIDES, THAISA, LORDS, *and*
ATTENDANTS.

SIMONIDES
Are the knights ready to begin the triumph?
FIRST LORD
They are, my liege;
And stay your coming to present themselves.
SIMONIDES
Return them, we are ready; and our daughter,
In honour of whose birth these triumphs are,
Sits here, like beauty's child, whom nature gat
For men to see, and seeing wonder at.   [*Exit a* LORD.
THAISA
It pleaseth you, my royal father, to express
My commendations great, whose merit's less.
SIMONIDES
It's fit it should be so; for princes are
A model, which heaven makes like to itself:
As jewels lose their glory if neglected,
So princes their renown if not respected.
'Tis now your honour, daughter, to explain
The labour of each knight in his device.
THAISA
Which, to preserve mine honour, I'll perform.

The FIRST KNIGHT *passes by, and his* SQUIRE
presents his shield to the PRINCESS.

SIMONIDES
Who is the first that doth prefer himself?
THAISA
A knight of Sparta, my renowned father;
And the device he bears upon his shield
Is a black Aethiop reaching at the sun;
The word, *Lux tua vita mihi.*

SIMONIDES
He loves you well that holds his life of you.
                    [*The* SECOND KNIGHT *passes.*
Who is the second that presents himself?
THAISA
A prince of Macedon, my royal father;
And the device he bears upon his shield
Is an arm'd knight that's conquer'd by a lady;
The motto thus, in Spanish, *Piu por dulzura que por
fuerza.*   [*The* THIRD KNIGHT *passes.*
SIMONIDES
And what's the third?
THAISA
                    The third of Antioch;
And his device, a wreath of chivalry;
The word, *Me pompæ provexit apex.*
                    [*The* FOURTH KNIGHT *passes.*
SIMONIDES
What is the fourth?
THAISA
A burning torch that's turned upside down;
The word, *Quod me alit, me extinguit.*
SIMONIDES
Which shows that beauty hath his power and will,
Which can as well inflame as it can kill.
                    [*The* FIFTH KNIGHT *passes.*
THAISA
The fifth, an hand environed with clouds,
Holding out gold that's by the touchstone tried;
The motto thus, *Sic spectanda fides.*
                    [*The* SIXTH KNIGHT *passes.*
SIMONIDES
And what's
The sixth and last, the which the knight himself
With such a graceful courtesy deliver'd?
THAISA
He seems to be a stranger; but his present is
A wither'd branch, that's only green at top;
The motto, *In hac spe vivo.*
SIMONIDES
A pretty moral;
From the dejected state wherein he is,
He hopes by you his fortunes yet may
    flourish.
FIRST LORD
He had need mean better than his outward
    show
Can any way speak in his just commend;
For, by his rusty outside, he appears
To have practis'd more the whipstock than
    the lance.
SECOND LORD
He well may be a stranger, for he comes
To an honour'd triumph strangely
    furnished.
THIRD LORD
And on set purpose let his armour rust
Until this day, to scour it in the dust.
SIMONIDES
Opinion's but a fool, that makes us scan
The outward habit by the inward man.
But stay, the knights are coming: we'll
    withdraw
Into the gallery.   [*Exeunt.*
    [*Great shouts, and all cry* 'The mean knight!'

SCENE III

The same. A hall of state; a banquet prepared.

Enter SIMONIDES, THAISA, LADIES, LORDS, *and*
KNIGHTS, *from tilting.*

SIMONIDES
Knights,
To say you're welcome were superfluous.
To place upon the volume of your deeds,
As in a title-page, your worth in arms,
Were more than you expect, or more than's fit,
Since every worth in show commends itself.
Prepare for mirth, for mirth becomes a feast:
You are princes and my guests.
THAISA
But you, my knight and guest;
To whom this wreath of victory I give,
And crown you king of this day's happiness.
PERICLES
'Tis more by fortune, lady, than my merit.
SIMONIDES
Call it by what you will, the day is yours;
And here, I hope, is none that envies it.
In framing an artist, art hath thus decreed,
To make some good, but others to exceed;
And you are her labour'd scholar. — Come, queen
    o'the feast, —
For, daughter, so you are, — here take your place:
Marshal the rest, as they deserve their grace.
KNIGHTS
We are honour'd much by good Simonides.
SIMONIDES
Your presence glads our days: honour we love;
For who hates honour hates the gods above.
MARSHAL
Sir, yonder is your place.
PERICLES
                    Some other is more fit.
FIRST KNIGHT
Contend not, sir; for we are gentlemen
That neither in our hearts nor outward eyes
Envy the great nor do the low despise.
PERICLES
You are right courteous knights.
SIMONIDES
                    Sit, sir, sit. —
By Jove, I wonder, that is king of thoughts,
These cates resist me, he not thought upon.
THAISA [*aside*].
By Juno, that is queen of marriage,
All viands that I eat do seem unsavoury,
Wishing him my meat. — Sure, he's a gallant
    gentleman.
SIMONIDES
He's but a country gentleman;
Has done no more than other knights have done;
Has broken a staff or so; so let it pass.
THAISA [*aside*].
To me he seems like diamond to glass.

SIMONIDES But stay, the knights are coming.

THAISA To whom this wreath of victory I give.

PERICLES [aside].
Yon king's to me like to my father's picture,
Which tells me in that glory once he was;
Had princes sit, like stars, about his throne,
And he the sun, for them to reverence;
None that beheld him, but, like lesser lights,
Did vail their crowns to his supremacy:
Where now his son like a glow-worm in the night,
The which hath fire in darkness, none in light:
Whereby I see that Time's the king of men,
For he's their parent, and he is their grave,
And gives them what he will, not what they crave.

SIMONIDES
What, are you merry, knights?

KNIGHTS
Who can be other in this royal presence?

SIMONIDES
Here, with a cup that's stored unto the brim, —
As you do love, fill to your mistress' lips, —
We drink this health to you.

KNIGHTS
We thank your Grace.

SIMONIDES
Yet pause awhile:
Yon knight doth sit too melancholy,
As if the entertainment in our court
Had not a show might countervail his worth.
Note it not you, Thaisa?

THAISA
What is it
To me, my father?

SIMONIDES
O, attend, my daughter:
Princes, in this, should live like gods above,
Who freely give to every one that comes
To honour them:
And princes not doing so are like to gnats,
Which make a sound, but kill'd are wonder'd at.
Therefore to make his entertain more sweet,
Here, say we drink this standing-bowl of wine to him.

THAISA
Alas, my father, it befits not me
Unto a stranger knight to be so bold:
He may my proffer take for an offence,
Since men take women's gifts for impudence.

SIMONIDES
How!
Do as I bid you, or you'll move me else.

THAISA [aside].
Now, by the gods, he could not please me better.

SIMONIDES
And furthermore tell him, we desire to know of him,
Of whence he is, his name and parentage.

THAISA
The king my father, sir, has drunk to you.

PERICLES
I thank him.

THAISA
Wishing it so much blood unto your life.

PERICLES
I thank both him and you, and pledge him freely.

THAISA
And further he desires to know of you,
Of whence you are, your name and parentage.

PERICLES
A gentleman of Tyre, — my name, Pericles;
My education been in arts and arms; —
Who, looking for adventures in the world,
Was by the rough seas reft of ships and men,
And, after shipwrack, driven upon this shore.

THAISA
He thanks your Grace; names himself Pericles,
A gentleman of Tyre,
Who only by misfortune of the seas
Bereft of ships and men, cast on this shore.

SIMONIDES
Now, by the gods, I pity his misfortune,
And will awake him from his melancholy. —
Come, gentlemen, we sit too long on trifles,
And waste the time, which looks for other revels.
Even in your armours, as you are address'd,
Will very well become a soldier's dance.
I will not have excuse, with saying this
Loud music is too harsh for ladies' heads,
Since they love men in arms as well as beds.
[The KNIGHTS dance.
So, this was well ask'd, 'twas so well perform'd. —
Come, sir;
Here is a lady that wants breathing too:
And I have heard, you knights of Tyre
Are excellent in making ladies trip;
And that their measures are as excellent.

PERICLES
In those that practise them they are, my lord.

SIMONIDES
O, that's as much as you would be denied
Of your fair courtesy.
[The KNIGHTS and LADIES dance.
Unclasp, unclasp:
Thanks, gentlemen, to all; all have done well,
[to PERICLES] But you the best. — Pages and lights, to
conduct
These knights unto their several lodgings! — [to
PERICLES] Yours, sir,
We have given order to be next our own.

PERICLES
I am at your Grace's pleasure.

SIMONIDES
Princes, it is too late to talk of love;
And that's the mark I know you level at:
Therefore each one betake him to his rest;
To-morrow all for speeding do their best. [Exeunt.

SCENE IV

Tyre. A room in the GOVERNOR'S *house.*

Enter HELICANUS *and* ESCANES.

HELICANUS
No, Escanes, know this of me, —
Antiochus from incest liv'd not free:
For which, the most high gods not minding longer
To withhold the vengeance that they had in store,
Due to this heinous capital offence,
Even in the height and pride of all his glory,
When he was seated in a chariot
Of an inestimable value, and his daughter with him,
A fire from heaven came, and shrivell'd up
Their bodies, even to loathing; for they so stunk,
That all those eyes adored them ere their fall
Scorn now their hand should give them burial.

ESCANES
'Twas very strange.

HELICANUS
And yet but justice; for though
This king were great, his greatness was no guard
To bar heaven's shaft, but sin had his reward.

ESCANES
'Tis very true.

Enter two or three LORDS.

FIRST LORD
See, not a man in private conference
Or council has respect with him but he.

SECOND LORD
It shall no longer grieve without reproof.

THIRD LORD
And curs'd be he that will not second it.

FIRST LORD
Follow me, then. — Lord Helicane, a word.

HELICANUS
With me? and welcome: — happy day, my lords.

FIRST LORD
Know that our griefs are risen to the top,
And now at length they overflow their banks.

HELICANUS
Your griefs! for what? wrong not the prince you love.

FIRST LORD
Wrong not yourself, then, noble Helicane;
But if the prince do live, let us salute him,
Or know what ground's made happy by his breath.
If in the world he live, we'll seek him out;
If in his grave he rest, we'll find him there;
And be resolv'd he lives to govern us,
Or dead, give's cause to mourn his funeral,
And leave us to our free election.

SECOND LORD
Whose death's indeed the strongest in our censure:
And knowing this kingdom is without a head, —
Like goodly buildings left without a roof,
Soon fall to ruin, — your noble self,
That best know how to rule and how to reign,
We thus submit unto, our sovereign.

ALL
Live, noble Helicane!

HELICANUS
For honour's cause, forbear your suffrages:
If that you love Prince Pericles, forbear.
Take I your wish, I leap into the seas,
Where's hourly trouble for a minute's ease.
A twelvemonth longer, let me entreat you

To forbear the absence of your king;
If in which time expired, he not return,
I shall with aged patience bear your yoke.
But if I cannot win you to this love,
Go search like nobles, like noble subjects,
And in your search spend your adventurous worth;
Whom if you find, and win unto return,
You shall like diamonds sit about his crown.

FIRST LORD
To wisdom he's a fool that will not yield;
And since Lord Helicane enjoineth us,
We with our travels will endeavour it.

HELICANUS
Then you love us, we you, and we'll clasp hands:
When peers thus knit, a kingdom ever stands. [*Exeunt.*

SCENE V

Pentapolis. A room in the palace.

Enter SIMONIDES, *reading of a letter, at one door: the* KNIGHTS *meet him.*

FIRST KNIGHT
Good morrow to the good Simonides.

SIMONIDES
Knights, from my daughter this I let you know,
That for this twelvemonth she'll not undertake
A married life.
Her reason to herself is only known,
Which yet from her by no means can I get.

SECOND KNIGHT
May we not get access to her, my lord?

SIMONIDES
Faith, by no means; she has so strictly
Tied her to her chamber, that 'tis impossible.
One twelve moons more she'll wear Diana's livery;
This by the eye of Cynthia hath she vow'd,
And on her virgin honour will not break it.

THIRD KNIGHT
Loth to bid farewell, we take our leaves.
[*Exeunt* KNIGHTS.

SIMONIDES
So,
They are well dispatch'd; now to my daughter's letter:
She tells me here, she'll wed the stranger knight,
Or never more to view nor day nor light.
'Tis well, mistress; your choice agrees with mine;
I like that well: — nay, how absolute she's in't,
Not minding whether I dislike or no!
Well, I do commend her choice;
And will no longer have it be delay'd. —
Soft! here he comes: I must dissemble it.

Enter PERICLES.

PERICLES
All fortune to the good Simonides!

SIMONIDES
To you as much, sir! I am beholding to you
For your sweet music this last night: I do
Protest my ears were never better fed
With such delightful pleasing harmony.

PERICLES
It is your Grace's pleasure to commend;
Not my desert.

SIMONIDES
Sir, you are music's master.

PERICLES
The worst of all her scholars, my good lord.

SIMONIDES
Let me ask you one thing:
What do you think of my daughter, sir?

PERICLES
A most virtuous princess.

SIMONIDES
And she is fair too, is she not?

PERICLES
As a fair day in summer, — wondrous fair.

SIMONIDES
Sir, my daughter thinks very well of you;
Ay, so well, that you must be her master,
And she will be your scholar: therefore look to it.

PERICLES
I am unworthy for her schoolmaster.

SIMONIDES
She thinks not so; peruse this writing else.

PERICLES [*aside*].
What's here?
A letter, that she loves the knight of Tyre!
'Tis the king's subtilty to have my life. —
O, seek not to entrap me, gracious lord,
A stranger and distressed gentleman,

That never aim'd so high to love your daughter,
But bent all offices to honour her.

SIMONIDES
Thou hast bewitch'd my daughter, and thou art
A villain.

PERICLES
By the gods, I have not:
Never did thought of mine levy offence;
Nor never did my actions yet commence
A deed might gain her love or your displeasure.

SIMONIDES
Traitor, thou liest.

PERICLES
Traitor!

SIMONIDES
Ay, traitor.

PERICLES
Even in his throat — unless it be the king —
That calls me traitor, I return the lie.

SIMONIDES [*aside*].
Now, by the gods, I do applaud his courage.

PERICLES
My actions are as noble as my thoughts,
That never relish'd of a base descent.
I came unto your court for honour's cause,
And not to be a rebel to her state;
And he that otherwise accounts of me,
This sword shall prove he's honour's enemy.

SIMONIDES
No?
Here comes my daughter, she can witness it.

Enter THAISA.

PERICLES
Then, as you are as virtuous as fair,
Resolve your angry father, if my tongue
Did e'er solicit, or my hand subscribe
To any syllable that made love to you.

THAISA
Why, sir, say if you had,
Who takes offence at that would make me glad?

SIMONIDES
Yea, mistress, are you so peremptory? —
[*aside*] I am glad on't with all my heart. —
I'll tame you; I'll bring you in subjection.
Will you, not having my consent,
Bestow your love and your affections
Upon a stranger? — [*aside*] who, for aught I know,
May be — nor can I think the contrary —
As great in blood as I myself. —
Therefore hear you, mistress; either frame
Your will to mine, — and you, sir, hear you,
Either be rul'd by me, or I will make you —
Man and wife:
Nay, come, your hands and lips must seal it too;
And being join'd, I'll thus your hopes destroy; —
And for a further grief, — God give you joy! —
What, are you both pleas'd?

THAISA
Yes, — if you love me, sir.

PERICLES
Even as my life, or blood that fosters it.

SIMONIDES
What, are you both agreed?

BOTH
Yes, if't please your majesty.

SIMONIDES
It pleaseth me so well, that I will see you wed;
And then with what haste you can get you to bed.
[*Exeunt.*

ACT III

Enter GOWER.

GOWER
Now sleep yslaked hath the rout;
No din but snores the house about,
Made louder by the o'er-fed breast
Of this most pompous marriage-feast.
The cat, with eyne of burning coal,
Now crouches fore the mouse's hole;
And crickets sing at the oven's mouth,
Aye the blither for their drouth.
Hymen hath brought the bride to bed,
Where, by the loss of maidenhead,
A babe is moulded. — Be attent,
And time that is so briefly spent
With your fine fancies quaintly eche:
What's dumb in show I'll plain with speech.

SIMONIDES And she is fair too, is she not?

DUMB-SHOW

Enter PERICLES *and* SIMONIDES, *at one door, with* ATTENDANTS; *a* MESSENGER *meets them, kneels, and gives* PERICLES *a letter:* PERICLES *shows it* SIMONIDES; *the* LORDS *kneel to* PERICLES. *Then enter* THAISA *with child, with* LYCHORIDA, *a nurse: the* KING *shows her the letter; she rejoices: she and* PERICLES *take leave of her father, and depart with* LYCHORIDA *and their* ATTENDANTS. *Then exeunt* SIMONIDES *and the rest.*

By many a dern and painful perch
Of Pericles the careful search,
By the four opposing coigns
Which the world together joins,
Is made with all due diligence
That horse and sail and high expense
Can stead the quest. At last from Tyre —
Fame answering the most strange inquire —
To th'court of King Simonides
Are letters brought, the tenour these: —
Antiochus and his daughter dead;
The man of Tyrus on the head
Of Helicanus would set on
The crown of Tyre, but he will none:
The mutiny he there hastes t'oppress;
Says to 'em, if King Pericles
Come not home in twice six moons,
He, obedient to their dooms,
Will take the crown. The sum of this,
Brought hither to Pentapolis,
Yravished the regions round,
And every one with claps can sound,
'Our heir-apparent is a king!'
Who dreamt, who thought of such a thing?'
Brief, he must hence depart to Tyre:
His queen with child makes her desire —
Which who shall cross? — along to go: —
Omit we all their dole and woe: —
Lychorida, her nurse, she takes,
And so to sea. Their vessel shakes
On Neptune's billow; half the flood
Hath their keel cut: but fortune's mood
Varies again; the grisled north
Disgorges such a tempest forth,
That, as a duck for life that dives,

LYCHORIDA Here's all that is left living of your queen.

So up and down the poor ship drives:
The lady shrieks, and, well-a-near,
Does fall in travail with her fear:
And what ensues in this fell storm
Shall for itself itself perform.
I nill relate, action may
Conveniently the rest convey;
Which might not what by me is told.
In your imagination hold
This stage the ship, upon whose deck
The sea-toss'd Pericles appears to speak.

[*Exit.*

SCENE I

Enter PERICLES, *a-shipboard.*

PERICLES
Thou god of this great vast, rebuke these surges,
Which wash both heaven and hell; and thou, that hast
Upon the winds command, bind them in brass,
Having call'd them from the deep! O, still
Thy deafening, dreadful thunders; gently quench
Thy nimble, sulphurous flashes! — O, how, Lychorida,
How does my queen? — Thou stormest venomously;
Wilt thou spit all thyself? — The seaman's whistle
Is as a whisper in the ears of death,
Unheard. — Lychorida! — Lucina, O
Divinest patroness, and midwife gentle
To those that cry by night, convey thy deity
Aboard our dancing boat; make swift the pangs
Of my queen's travails!
Enter LYCHORIDA, *with an* INFANT.
Now, Lychorida!

LYCHORIDA
Here is a thing too young for such a place,
Who, if it had conceit, would die, as I
Am like to do: take in your arms this piece
Of your dead queen.

PERICLES
How, how, Lychorida!

LYCHORIDA
Patience, good sir; do not assist the storm.
Here's all that is left living of your queen, —
A little daughter: for the sake of it,
Be manly, and take comfort.

PERICLES
O you gods!
Why do you make us love your goodly gifts,
And snatch them straight away? We here below
Recall not what we give, and therein may
Vie honour with you.

LYCHORIDA
Patience, good sir,
Even for this charge.

PERICLES
Now, mild may be thy life!

For a more blustrous birth had never babe:
Quiet and gentle thy conditions! for
Thou art the rudeliest welcome to this world
That ever was prince's child. Happy what follows!
Thou hast as chiding a nativity
As fire, air, water, earth, and heaven can make,
To herald thee from the womb: even at the first
Thy loss is more than can thy portage quit,
With all thou canst find here. — Now, the good gods
Throw their best eyes upon't!

Enter two SAILORS.

FIRST SAILOR
What courage, sir? God save you!

PERICLES
Courage enough: I do not fear the flaw;
It hath done to me the worst. Yet, for the love
Of this poor infant, this fresh-new seafarer,
I would it would be quiet.

FIRST SAILOR
Slack the bolins there! — Thou wilt not, wilt thou?
Blow, and split thyself.

SECOND SAILOR
But sea-room, an the brine and cloudy billow kiss the
moon, I care not.

FIRST SAILOR
Sir, your queen must overboard: the sea works high,
the wind is loud, and will not lie till the ship be clear'd
of the dead.

PERICLES
That's your superstition.

FIRST SAILOR
Pardon us, sir; with us at sea it hath been still observed;
and we are strong in custom.
Therefore briefly yield her; for
she must overboard straight.

PERICLES
As you think meet. — Most
wretched queen!

LYCHORIDA
Here she lies, sir.

PERICLES
A terrible childbed hast thou
had, my dear;
No light, no fire: th'unfriendly
elements
Forgot thee utterly; nor have I
time
To give thee hallow'd to thy
grave, but straight
Must cast thee, scarcely
coffin'd, in the ooze;
Where, for a monument upon
thy bones,
And aye-remaining lamps,

the belching whale
And humming water must o'erwhelm thy corpse,
Lying with simple shells. — O Lychorida,
Bid Nestor bring me spices, ink and paper,
My casket and my jewels; and bid Nicander
Bring me the satin coffer: lay the babe
Upon the pillow: hie thee, whiles I say
A priestly farewell to her: suddenly, woman.
[*Exit* LYCHORIDA.

SECOND SAILOR
Sir, we have a chest beneath the hatches, caulk'd and
bitumed ready.

PERICLES
I thank thee. — Mariner, say what coast is this?

SECOND SAILOR
We are near Tarsus.

PERICLES
Thither, gentle mariner,
Alter thy course for Tyre. When canst thou reach it?

SECOND SAILOR
By break of day, if the wind cease.

PERICLES
O, make for Tarsus! —
There will I visit Cleon, for the babe
Cannot hold out to Tyrus: there I'll leave it
At careful nursing. — Go thy ways, good mariner:
I'll bring the body presently. [*Exeunt.*

SCENE II

Ephesus. A room in CERIMON'S *house.*

Enter CERIMON, *a* SERVANT, *and some* PERSONS
who have been shipwrack'd.

CERIMON
Philemon, ho!

Enter PHILEMON.

PHILEMON
Doth my lord call?

CERIMON
Get fire and meat for these poor men:
'T has been a turbulent and stormy night.

SERVANT
I have been in many; but such a night as this,
Till now, I ne'er endured.

CERIMON
Your master will be dead ere you return;
There's nothing can be minister'd to nature
That can recover him. — [*to* PHILEMON] Give this to
the pothecary,
And tell me how it works. [*Exeunt all but* CERIMON.

Enter two GENTLEMEN.

FIRST GENTLEMAN
Good morrow.

SECOND GENTLEMAN
Good morrow to your lordship.

CERIMON
Gentlemen,
Why do you stir so early?

FIRST GENTLEMAN
Sir,
Our lodgings, standing bleak upon the sea,
Shook as the earth did quake;
The very principals did seem to rend,
And all-to topple: pure surprise and fear
Made me to quit the house.

SECOND GENTLEMAN
That is the cause we trouble you so early;

FIRST SERVANT Sir, even now did the sea toss upon our shore this chest.

CERIMON This queen will live: nature awakes.

'Tis not our husbandry.

CERIMON
                    O, you say well.

FIRST GENTLEMAN
But I much marvel that your lordship, having
Rich tire about you, should at these early hours
Shake off the golden slumber of repose.
'Tis most strange,
Nature should be so conversant with pain,
Being thereto not compell'd.

CERIMON
                    I hold it ever,
Virtue and cunning were endowments greater
Than nobleness and riches: careless heirs
May the two latter darken and expend;
But immortality attends the former,
Making a man a god. 'Tis known, I ever
Have studied physic, through which secret art,
By turning o'er authorities, I have —
Together with my practice — made familiar
To me and to my aid the blest infusions
That dwell in vegetives, in metals, stones;
And I can speak of the disturbances
That nature works, and of her cures; which doth give
     me
A more content in course of true delight
Than to be thirsty after tottering honour,
Or tie my treasure up in silken bags,
To please the fool and death.

SECOND GENTLEMAN
Your honour has through Ephesus pour'd forth
Your charity, and hundreds call themselves
Your creatures, who by you have been restored:
And not your knowledge, your personal pain, but even
Your purse, still open, hath built Lord Cerimon
Such strong renown as time shall never —

Enter two or three SERVANTS *with a chest.*

FIRST SERVANT
So; lift there.

CERIMON
                    What is that?

FIRST SERVANT
                    Sir, even now

Did the sea toss upon our shore this chest:
'Tis of some wrack.

CERIMON
                    Set't down, let's look upon't.

SECOND GENTLEMAN
'Tis like a coffin, sir.

CERIMON
                    Whate'er it be,
'Tis wondrous heavy. Wrench it open straight:
If the sea's stomach be o'ercharg'd with gold,
'Tis a good constraint of fortune it belches upon us.

SECOND GENTLEMAN
'Tis so, my lord.

CERIMON
                    How close 'tis caulk'd and bitumed! —
Did the sea cast it up?

FIRST SERVANT
I never saw so huge a billow, sir,
As toss'd it upon shore.

CERIMON
                    Wrench it open;
Soft! — it smells most sweetly in my sense.

SECOND GENTLEMAN
A delicate odour.

CERIMON
As ever hit my nostril. — So, up with it. —
O you most potent gods! what's here? a corse!

FIRST GENTLEMAN
Most strange!

CERIMON
Shrouded in cloth of state; balm'd and entreasured
with full bags of spices! A passport too! — Apollo,
perfect me in the characters!   [*Reads from a scroll.*
     'Here I give to understand, —
     If e'er this coffin drive a-land, —
     I, King Pericles, have lost
     This queen, worth all our mundane cost.
     Who finds her, give her burying;
     She was the daughter of a king:
     Besides this treasure for a fee,
     The gods requite his charity!
If thou liv'st, Pericles, thou hast a heart
That even cracks for woe! — This chanc'd to-night.

SECOND GENTLEMAN
Most likely, sir.

CERIMON
                    Nay, certainly to-night;
For look how fresh she looks! — They were too rough
That threw her in the sea. — Make a fire within:
Fetch hither all my boxes in my closet. —
                              [*Exit a* SERVANT.
Death may usurp on nature many hours,
And yet the fire of life kindle again
The o'erpress'd spirits. I heard of an Egyptian
That had nine hours lien dead,
Who was by good appliance recovered.
     Enter a SERVANT, *with boxes, napkins, and fire.*
Well said, well said; the fire and cloths. —
The rough and woeful music that we have,
Cause it to sound, beseech you.
The viol once more: — how thou stirr'st, thou block! —
The music there! — I pray you, give her air. —
Gentlemen, this queen will live: nature awakes;
A warmth breathes out of her: she hath not been
Entranc'd above five hours: see how she gins
To blow into life's flower again!

FIRST GENTLEMAN
                    The heavens,
Through you, increase our wonder, and set up
Your fame for ever.

CERIMON
                    She is alive; behold,
Her eyelids, cases to those heavenly jewels
Which Pericles hath lost, begin to part
Their fringes of bright gold; the diamonds
Of a most praised water do appear,
To make the world twice rich. — Live,
And make us weep to hear your fate, fair creature,
Rare as you seem to be!   [*She moves.*

THAISA
                    O dear Diana,
Where am I? Where's my lord? What world is this?

SECOND GENTLEMAN
Is not this strange?

FIRST GENTLEMAN
                    Most rare.

CERIMON
                    Hush, my gentle neighbours!
Lend me your hands; to the next chamber bear her.
Get linen: now this matter must be look'd to,
For her relapse is mortal. Come, come;
And Aesculapius guide us!
                    [*Exeunt, carrying out* THAISA.

SCENE III

Tarsus. A room in the GOVERNOR'S *house.*

Enter PERICLES, CLEON, DIONYZA, *and*
LYCHORIDA *with* MARINA *in her arms.*

PERICLES
Most honour'd Cleon, I must needs be gone;
My twelve months are expired, and Tyrus stands
In a litigious peace. You, and your lady,
Take from my heart all thankfulness! The gods
Make up the rest upon you!

CLEON
Your shafts of fortune, though they hurt you mortally,
Yet glance full wanderingly on us.

DIONYZA
                    O your sweet queen!
That the strict Fates had pleas'd you had brought her
     hither,
To have blest mine eyes with her!

PERICLES
                    We cannot but obey
The powers above us. Could I rage and roar
As doth the sea she lies in, yet the end
Must be as 'tis. My gentle babe Marina, — whom,
For she was born at sea, I have nam'd so, — here
I charge your charity withal, leaving her
The infant of your care; beseeching you
To give her princely training, that she may be
Manner'd as she is born.

CLEON
                    Fear not, my lord, but think
Your grace, that fed my country with your corn, —
For which the people's prayers still fall upon you, —
Must in your child be thought on. If neglection
Should therein make me vile, the common body,
By you reliev'd, would force me to my duty:
But if to that my nature need a spur,
The gods revenge it upon me and mine,
To the end of generation!

PERICLES

> I believe you;
> Your honour and your goodness teach me to't,
> Without your vows. — Till she be married, madam,
> By bright Diana, whom we honour, all
> Unscissar'd shall this hair of mine remain,
> Though I show ill in't. So I take my leave.
> Good madam, make me blessed in your care
> In bringing up my child.

DIONYZA

> I have one myself,
> Who shall not be more dear to my respect
> Than yours, my lord.

PERICLES

> Madam, my thanks and prayers.

CLEON

> We'll bring your Grace e'en to the edge o'th'shore,
> Then give you up to the meek'st Neptune and
> The gentlest winds of heaven.

PERICLES

> I will embrace
> Your offer. Come, dearest madam. — O, no tears,
> Lychorida, no tears:
> Look to your little mistress, on whose grace
> You may depend hereafter. — Come, my lord. [*Exeunt.*

SCENE IV

Ephesus. A room in CERIMON'S *house.*

Enter CERIMON *and* THAISA.

CERIMON

> Madam, this letter, and some certain jewels,
> Lay with you in your coffer: which are
> At your command. Know you the character?

THAISA

> It is my lord's.
> That I was shipp'd at sea, I well remember,
> Even on my eaning time; but whether there
> Deliver'd, by the holy gods,
> I cannot rightly say. But since King Pericles,
> My wedded lord, I ne'er shall see again,
> A vestal livery will I take me to,
> And never more have joy.

CERIMON

> Madam, if this you purpose as ye speak,
> Diana's temple is not distant far,
> Where you may abide till your date expire.
> Moreover, if you please, a niece of mine
> Shall there attend you.

THAISA

> My recompense is thanks, that's all;
> Yet my good will is great, though the gift small. [*Exeunt.*

MARINA To strew thy green with flowers.

ACT IV

Enter GOWER.

GOWER

> Imagine Pericles arriv'd at Tyre,
> Welcom'd and settled to his own desire.
> His woeful queen we leave at Ephesus,
> Unto Diana there's a votaress.
> Now to Marina bend your mind,
> Whom our fast-growing scene must find
> At Tarsus, and by Cleon train'd
> In music, letters; who hath gain'd
> Of education all the grace,
> Which makes her both the heart and place
> Of general wonder. But, alack,
> That monster envy, oft the wrack
> Of earned praise, Marina's life
> Seeks to take off by treason's knife.
> And in this kind hath our Cleon
> One daughter, and a wench full grown,
> Even ripe for marriage-rite; this maid
> Hight Philoten: and it is said
> For certain in our story, she
> Would ever with Marina be:
> Be't when she weav'd the sleided silk
> With fingers long, small, white as milk;
> Or when she would with sharp needle wound
> The cambric, which she made more sound
> By hurting it; or when to the lute
> She sung, and made the night-bird mute,
> That still records with moan; or when
> She would with rich and constant pen
> Vail to her mistress Dian; still
> This Philoten contends in skill
> With absolute Marina: so
> With the dove of Paphos might the crow
> Vie feathers white. Marina gets
> All praises, which are paid as debts,
> And not as given. This so darks
> In Philoten all graceful marks,
> That Cleon's wife, with envy rare,
> A present murderer does prepare
> For good Marina, that her daughter
> Might stand peerless by this slaughter.
> The sooner her vile thoughts to stead,
> Lychorida, our nurse, is dead:
> And cursed Dionyza hath
> The pregnant instrument of wrath
> Press'd for this blow. The unborn event
> I do commend to your content:
> Only I carry winged time
> Post on the lame feet of my rime;
> Which never could I so convey,
> Unless your thoughts went on my way. —
> Dionyza does appear,
> With Leonine, a murderer.

[*Exit.*

SCENE I

Tarsus. An open place near the sea-shore.

Enter DIONYZA *and* LEONINE.

DIONYZA

> Thy oath, remember; thou hast sworn to do't:
> 'Tis but a blow, which never shall be known.
> Thou canst not do a thing in the world so soon,
> To yield thee so much profit. Let not conscience,
> Which is but cold, inflaming love in thy bosom,
> Enslave too nicely; nor let pity, which
> Even women have cast off, melt thee, but be
> A soldier to thy purpose.

LEONINE

> I will do't; but yet she is a goodly creature.

DIONYZA

> The fitter, then, the gods should have her. — Here
> she comes weeping for her only nurse's death. —
> Thou art resolved?

LEONINE

> I am resolved.

Enter MARINA, *with a basket of flowers.*

MARINA

> No, I will rob Tellus of her weed,
> To strew thy green with flowers: the yellows, blues,
> The purple violets, and marigolds,
> Shall, as a carpet, hang upon thy grave,
> While summer-days do last. — Ay me! poor maid,
> Born in a tempest, when my mother died,
> This world to me is like a lasting storm,
> Whirring me from my friends.

DIONYZA

> How now, Marina! why do you keep alone?
> How chance my daughter is not with you? Do not
> Consume your blood with sorrowing: you have
> A nurse of me. Lord, how your favour's chang'd
> With this unprofitable woe! Come,
> Give me your flowers, ere the sea mar it.
> Walk with Leonine; the air is quick there,
> And it pierces and sharpens the stomach. — Come,
> Leonine, take her by the arm, walk with her.

MARINA

> No, I pray you;
> I'll not bereave you of your servant.

DIONYZA

> Come, come;
> I love the king your father, and yourself,
> With more than foreign heart. We every day
> Expect him here: when he shall come, and find
> Our paragon to all reports thus blasted,
> He will repent the breadth of his great voyage;
> Blame both my lord and me, that we have taken
> No care to your best courses. Go, I pray you,
> Walk, and be cheerful once again; reserve
> That excellent complexion, which did steal
> The eyes of young and old. Care not for me;
> I can go home alone.

MARINA

> Well, I will go;
> But yet I have no desire to it.

DIONYZA

> Come, come,
> I know 'tis good for you. —
> Walk half an hour, Leonine, at the least:
> Remember what I have said.

LEONINE

> I warrant you, madam.

DIONYZA

> I'll leave you, my sweet lady, for a while:
> Pray, walk softly, do not heat your blood:
> What! I must have a care of you.

MARINA

> My thanks, sweet madam. —
> [*Exit* DIONYZA.
> Is this wind westerly that blows?

LEONINE

> South-west.

MARINA

> When I was born, the wind was north.

LEONINE

> Was't so?

MARINA

> My father, as nurse said, did never fear,
> But cried 'Good seamen!' to the sailors, galling
> His kingly hands, haling ropes;
> And, clasping to the mast, endured a sea
> That almost burst the deck.

LEONINE

> When was this?

MARINA

> When I was born:
> Never was waves nor wind more violent;
> And from the ladder-tackle washes off
> A canvas-climber. 'Ha!' says one, 'wilt out?'
> And with a dropping industry they skip
> From stem to stern: the boatswain whistles, and
> The master calls, and trebles their confusion.

LEONINE

> Come, say your prayers.

MARINA

> What mean you?

LEONINE

> If you require a little space for prayer,
> I grant it: pray; but be not tedious, for
> The gods are quick of ear, and I am sworn
> To do my work with haste.

MARINA

> Why will you kill me?

LEONINE

> To satisfy my lady.

MARINA

> Why would she have me kill'd?
> Now, as I can remember, by my troth,
> I never did her hurt in all my life:
> I never spake bad word, nor did ill turn
> To any living creature: believe me, la,
> I never kill'd a mouse, nor hurt a fly:
> I trod upon a worm once 'gainst my will,
> But I wept for it. How have I offended,
> Wherein my death might yield her any profit,
> Or my life imply her any danger?

THIRD PIRATE Come, let's have her aboard suddenly.

LEONINE
My commission
Is not to reason of the deed, but do't.
MARINA
You will not do't for all the world, I hope.
You are well-favour'd, and your looks foreshow
You have a gentle heart. I saw you lately,
When you caught hurt in parting two that fought:
Good sooth, it show'd well in you: do so now:
Your lady seeks my life; come you between,
And save poor me, the weaker.
LEONINE
                    I am sworn,
And will dispatch.
            Enter PIRATES.
FIRST PIRATE
Hold, villain!   [LEONINE *runs away.*
SECOND PIRATE
A prize! a prize!
THIRD PIRATE
Half-part, mates, half-part. Come, let's have her aboard
    suddenly.
            [*Exeunt* PIRATES *with* MARINA.
            Enter LEONINE.
LEONINE
These roguing thieves serve the great pirate Valdes;
And they have seized Marina. Let her go:
There's no hope she will return. I'll swear
    she's dead,
And thrown into the sea. — But I'll see further:
Perhaps they will but please themselves upon her,
Not carry her aboard. If she remain,
Whom they have ravish'd must by me be slain.   [*Exit.*

SCENE II

Mytilene. A room in a brothel.

Enter PANDAR, BAWD, *and* BOULT.

PANDAR
Boult, —
BOULT
Sir?
PANDAR
Search the market narrowly; Mytilene is full of
gallants. We lost too much money this mart by being
too wenchless.
BAWD
We were never so much out of creatures. We have but
poor three, and they can do no more than they can do;
and they with continual action are even as good as
rotten.
PANDAR
Therefore let's have fresh ones, whate'er we pay for
them. If there be not a conscience to be used in every
trade, we shall never prosper.
BAWD
Thou sayest true: 'tis not our bringing up of poor
bastards, — as, I think, I have brought up some
eleven, —

BOULT
Ay, to eleven; and brought them down again. —
But shall I search the market?
BAWD
What else, man? The stuff we have, a strong wind will
blow it to pieces, they are so pitifully sodden.
PANDAR
Thou sayest true: they're too unwholesome,
o'conscience. The poor Transylvanian is dead, that lay
with the little baggage.
BOULT
Ay, she quickly poop'd him; she made him roast-meat
for worms. — But I'll go search the market.   [*Exit.*
PANDAR
Three or four thousand chequins were as pretty a
proportion to live quietly, and so give over.
BAWD
Why to give over, I pray you? is it a shame to get when
we are old?
PANDAR
O, our credit comes nòt in like the commodity, nor the
commodity wages not with the danger: therefore, if in
our youths we could pick up some pretty estate, 'twere
not amiss to keep our door hatch'd. Besides, the sore
terms we stand upon with the gods will be strong with
us for giving o'er.
BAWD
Come, other sorts offend as well as we.
PANDAR
As well as we! ay, and better too; we offend worse.
Neither is our profession any trade; it's no calling. —
But here comes Boult.
        Enter BOULT, *with the* PIRATES *and* MARINA.
BOULT [*to* MARINA].
Come your ways. — My masters, you say she's a virgin?
FIRST PIRATE
O, sir, we doubt it not.
BOULT
Master, I have gone through for this piece, you see: if
you like her, so; if not, I have lost my earnest.
BAWD
Boult, has she any qualities?
BOULT
She has a good face, speaks well, and has excellent
good clothes: there's no further necessity of qualities
can make her be refused.
BAWD
What's her price, Boult?
BOULT
I cannot be bated one doit of a thousand pieces.
PANDAR
Well, follow me, my masters, you shall have your
money presently. — Wife, take her in; instruct her
what she has to do, that she may not be raw in her
entertainment.   [*Exeunt* PANDAR *and* PIRATES.
BAWD
Boult, take you the marks of her, — the colour of her
hair, complexion, height, her age, with warrant of her
virginity; and cry, 'He that will give most shall have her
first.' Such a maidenhead were no cheap thing, if men
were as they have been. Get this done as I command you.

BOULT
Performance shall follow.   [*Exit.*
MARINA
Alack that Leonine was so slack, so slow!
He should have struck, not spoke; or that these
    pirates —
Not enough barbarous — had not o'erboard thrown me
For to seek my mother!
BAWD
Why lament you, pretty one?
MARINA
That I am pretty.
BAWD
Come, the gods have done their part in you.
MARINA
I accuse them not.
BAWD
You are light into my hands, where you are like to live.
MARINA
The more my fault
To scape his hands where I was like to die.
BAWD
Ay, and you shall live in pleasure.
MARINA
No.
BAWD
Yes, indeed shall you, and taste gentlemen of all
fashions: you shall fare well; you shall have the
difference of all complexions. What! do you stop your
ears?
MARINA
Are you a woman?
BAWD
What would you have me be, an I be not a woman?
MARINA
An honest woman, or not a woman.
BAWD
Marry, whip thee, gosling: I think I shall have
something to do with you. Come, you're a young
foolish sapling, and must be bow'd as I would have
you.
MARINA
The gods defend me!
BAWD
If it please the gods to defend you by men, then men
must comfort you, men must feed you, men must stir
you up. — Boult's return'd.
            Enter BOULT.
Now, sir, hast thou cried her through the market?
BOULT
I have cried her almost to the number of her hairs; I
have drawn her picture with my voice.
BAWD
And I prithee tell me, how dost thou find the
inclination of the people, especially of the younger
sort?
BOULT
Faith, they listen'd to me as they would have hearken'd
to their father's testament. There was a Spaniard's
mouth so water'd, that he went to bed to her very
description.
BAWD
We shall have him here to-morrow with his best ruff
on.
BOULT
To-night, to-night. But, mistress, do you know the
French knight that cowers i' the hams?
BAWD
Who, Monsieur Veroles?
BOULT
Ay, he: he offer'd to cut a caper at the proclamation; but
he made a groan at it, and swore he would see her
to-morrow.
BAWD
Well, well; as for him, he brought his disease hither:
here he does but repair it. I know he will come in our
shadow, to scatter his crowns in the sun.
BOULT
Well, if we had of every nation a traveller, we should
lodge them with this sign.
BAWD [*to* MARINA].
Pray you, come hither awhile. You have fortunes
coming upon you. Mark me: you must seem to do that
fearfully which you commit willingly, despise profit
where you have most gain. To weep that you live as ye
do makes pity in your lovers: seldom but that pity
begets you a good opinion, and that opinion a mere
profit.

MARINA
I understand you not.

BOULT
O, take her home, mistress, take her home: these blushes of hers must be quench'd with some present practice.

BAWD
Thou sayest true, i'faith, so they must; for your bride goes to that with shame which is her way to go with warrant.

BOULT
Faith, some do, and some do not. But, mistress, if I have bargain'd for the joint, —

BAWD
Thou mayst cut a morsel off the spit.

BOULT
I may so.

BAWD
Who should deny it? — Come, young one, I like the manner of your garments well.

BOULT
Ay, by my faith, they shall not be changed yet.

BAWD
Boult, spend thou that in the town: report what a sojourner we have; you'll lose nothing by custom. When nature flamed this piece, she meant thee a good turn; therefore say what a paragon she is, and thou hast the harvest out of thine own report.

BOULT
I warrant you, mistress, thunder shall not so awake the beds of eels as my giving out her beauty stir up the lewdly-inclined. I'll bring home some to-night.

BAWD
Come your ways; follow me.

MARINA
If fires be hot, knives sharp, or waters deep,
Untied I still my virgin knot will keep.
Diana, aid my purpose!

BAWD
What have we to do with Diana? Pray you, will you go with us? [Exeunt.

SCENE III

Tarsus. A room in the GOVERNOR'S house.

Enter CLEON and DIONYZA.

DIONYZA
Why, are you foolish? Can it be undone?

CLEON
O Dionyza, such a piece of slaughter
The sun and moon ne'er look'd upon!

DIONYZA
                    I think
You'll turn a child again.

CLEON
Were I chief lord of all this spacious world,
I'ld give it to undo the deed. — O lady,
Much less in blood than virtue, yet a princess
To equal any single crown o' the earth
I' the justice of compare! — O villain Leonine!
Whom thou hast poison'd too!
If thou hadst drunk to him, 't had been a kindness
Becoming well thy fact: what canst thou say
When noble Pericles shall demand his child?

DIONYZA
That she is dead. Nurses are not the Fates,
To foster it, nor ever to preserve.
She died at night; I'll say so. Who can cross it?
Unless you play the pious innocent,
And for an honest attribute cry out
'She died by foul play.'

CLEON
                    O, go to. Well, well,
Of all the faults beneath the heavens, the gods
Do like this worst.

DIONYZA
                    Be one of those that think
The petty wrens of Tarsus will fly hence,
And open this to Pericles. I do shame
To think of what a noble strain you are,
And of how coward a spirit.

CLEON
                    To such proceeding
Who ever but his approbation added,
Though not his prime consent, he did not flow
From honourable sources.

DIONYZA
                    Be it so, then:
Yet none does know, but you, how she came dead,
Nor none can know, Leonine being gone.
She did distain my child, and stood between
Her and her fortunes: none would look on her,
But cast their gazes on Marina's face;
Whilst ours was blurted at, and held a malkin,
Not worth the time of day. It pierc'd me thorough;
And though you call my course unnatural,
You not your child well loving, yet I find
It greets me as an enterprise of kindness
Perform'd to our sole daughter.

CLEON
                    Heavens forgive it!

DIONYZA
And as for Pericles,
What should he say? We wept after her hearse,
And yet we mourn: her monument
Is almost finish'd, and her epitaphs
In glittering golden characters express
A general praise to her, and care in us
At whose expense 'tis done.

CLEON
                    Thou art like the harpy,
Which, to betray, dost, with thine angel's face,
Seize with thine eagle's talons.

DIONYZA
You are like one that superstitiously
Doth swear to the gods that winter kills the flies:
But yet I know you'll do as I advise. [Exeunt.

Enter GOWER, before the monument of MARINA at Tarsus.

GOWER
Thus time we waste, and longest leagues make short;
Sail seas in cockles, have and wish but for't;
Making — to take your imagination —
From bourn to bourn, region to region.
By you being pardon'd, we commit no crime
To use one language in each several clime
Where our scenes seem to live. I do beseech you
To learn of me, who stand i'th'gaps to teach you,
The stages of our story. Pericles

Is now again thwarting the wayward seas,
Attended on by many a lord and knight,
To see his daughter, all his life's delight.
Old Helicanus goes along: behind
Is left to govern it, you bear in mind,
Old Escanes, whom Helicanus late
Advanc'd in time to great and high estate.
Well-sailing ships and bounteous winds have brought
This king to Tarsus — think his pilot thought;
So with his steerage shall your thoughts grow on —
To fetch his daughter home, who first is gone.
Like motes and shadows see them move awhile;
Your ears unto your eyes I'll reconcile.

DUMB-SHOW
*Enter PERICLES, at one door, with all his train;
CLEON and DIONYZA at the other. CLEON shows
PERICLES the tomb; whereat PERICLES makes
lamentation, puts on sackcloth, and in a mighty passion
departs. Then exeunt CLEON, DIONYZA, and the rest.*

See how belief may suffer by foul show!
This borrow'd passion stands for true old woe;
And Pericles, in sorrow all devour'd,
With sighs shot through, and biggest tears
    o'ershower'd,
Leaves Tarsus, and again embarks. He swears
Never to wash his face, nor cut his hairs:
He puts on sackcloth, and to sea. He bears
A tempest, which his mortal vessel tears,
And yet he rides it out. Now please you wit
The epitaph is for Marina writ
By wicked Dionyza.

[Reads the inscription on MARINA'S monument.
'The fairest, sweet'st, and best lies here,
Who wither'd in her spring of year.
She was of Tyrus the king's daughter,
On whom foul death hath made this slaughter;
Marina was she call'd; and at her birth,
Thetis, being proud, swallow'd some part o'th'earth:
Therefore the earth, fearing to be o'erflow'd,
Hath Thetis' birth-child on the heavens bestow'd:
Wherefore she does — and swears she'll never stint —
Make raging battery upon shores of flint.'
No visor does become black villainy
So well as soft and tender flattery.
Let Pericles believe his daughter's dead,
And bear his courses to be ordered
By Lady Fortune; while our scene must play
His daughter's woe and heavy well-a-day
In her unholy service. Patience, then,
And think you now are all in Mytilen. [Exit.

SCENE IV

Mytilene. A street before the brothel.

Enter, from the brothel, two GENTLEMEN.

FIRST GENTLEMAN
Did you ever hear the like?

SECOND GENTLEMAN
No, nor never shall do in such a place as this, she being once gone.

FIRST GENTLEMAN
But to have divinity preach'd there! did you ever dream of such a thing?

SECOND GENTLEMAN
No, no. Come, I am for no more bawdy-houses: — shall's go hear the vestals sing?

FIRST GENTLEMAN
I'll do any thing now that is virtuous; but I am out of the road of rutting for ever. [Exeunt.

SCENE V

The same. A room in the brothel.

Enter PANDAR, BAWD, and BOULT.

PANDAR
Well, I had rather than twice the worth of her she had ne'er come here.

BAWD
Fie, fie upon her! she's able to freeze the god Priapus, and undo a whole generation. We must either get her ravish'd, or be rid of her. When she should do for clients her fitment, and do me the kindness of our profession, she has me her quirks, her reasons, her master reasons, her prayers, her knees; that she would make a puritan of the devil, if he should cheapen a kiss of her.

BOULT
Faith, I must ravish her, or she'll disfurnish us of all our cavaliers, and make all our swearers priests.

CLEON The sun and moon ne'er look'd upon!

PANDAR
Now, the pox upon her green-sickness for me!
BAWD
Faith, there's no way to be rid on't but by the way to the pox. — Here comes the Lord Lysimachus disguised.
BOULT
We should have both lord and lown, if the peevish baggage would but give way to customers.

Enter LYSIMACHUS.

LYSIMACHUS
How now! How a dozen of virginities?
BAWD
Now, the gods to-bless your honour!
BOULT
I am glad to see your honour in good health.
LYSIMACHUS
You may so; 'tis the better for you that your resorters stand upon sound legs. How now, wholesome iniquity! Have you that a man may deal withal, and defy the surgeon?
BAWD
We have here one, sir, if she would — but there never came her like in Mytilene.
LYSIMACHUS
If she'd do the deed of darkness, thou wouldst say.
BAWD
Your honour knows what 'tis to say well enough.
LYSIMACHUS
Well, call forth, call forth.
BOULT
For flesh and blood, sir, white and red, you shall see a rose; and she were a rose indeed, if she had but —
LYSIMACHUS
What, prithee?
BOULT
O, sir, I can be modest.
LYSIMACHUS
That dignifies the renown of a bawd, no less than it gives a good report to a member to be chaste.

[Exit BOULT.

BAWD
Here comes that which grows to the stalk, — never pluck'd yet, I can assure you.

Enter BOULT *with* MARINA.

Is she not a fair creature?
LYSIMACHUS
Faith, she would serve after a long voyage at sea. Well, there's for you: — leave us.
BAWD
I beseech your honour, give me leave: a word, and I'll have done presently.
LYSIMACHUS
I beseech you, do.
BAWD *[to* MARINA].
First, I would have you note, this is an honourable man.
MARINA
I desire to find him so, that I may worthily note him.
BAWD
Next, he's the governor of this country, and a man whom I am bound to.
MARINA
If he govern the country, you are bound to him indeed; but how honourable he is in that, I know not.
BAWD
Pray you, without any more virginal fencing, will you use him kindly? He will line your apron with gold.
MARINA
What he will do graciously, I will thankfully receive.
LYSIMACHUS
Ha' you done?
BAWD
My lord, she's not paced yet: you must take some pains to work her to your manage. — Come, we will leave his honour and her together. — Go thy ways.

[Exeunt BAWD, PANDAR, *and* BOULT.

LYSIMACHUS
Now, pretty one, how long have you been at this trade?
MARINA
What trade, sir?
LYSIMACHUS
Why, I cannot name't but I shall offend.
MARINA
I cannot be offended with my trade. Please you to name it.
LYSIMACHUS
How long have you been of this profession?

MARINA
E'er since I can remember.
LYSIMACHUS
Did you go to't so young? Were you a gamester at five or at seven?
MARINA
Earlier too, sir, if now I be one.
LYSIMACHUS
Why, the house you dwell in proclaims you to be a creature of sale.
MARINA
Do you know this house to be a place of such resort, and will come into't? I hear say you are of honourable parts, and are the governor of this place.
LYSIMACHUS
Why, hath your principal made known unto you who I am?
MARINA
Who is my principal?
LYSIMACHUS
Why, your herb-woman; she that sets seeds and roots of shame and iniquity. O, you have heard something of my power, and so stand aloof for more serious wooing. But I protest to thee, pretty one, my authority shall not see thee, or else look friendly upon thee. Come, bring me to some private place: come, come.
MARINA
If you were born to honour, show it now;
If put upon you, make the judgement good
That thought you worthy of it.
LYSIMACHUS
How's this? how's this? — Some more; be sage.
MARINA
For me,
That am a maid, though most ungentle fortune
Have plac'd me in this sty, where, since I came,
Diseases have been sold dearer than physic, —
O, that the gods
Would set me free from this unhallow'd place,
Though they did change me to the meanest bird
That flies i' the purer air!
LYSIMACHUS
I did not think
Thou couldst have spoke so well; ne'er dreamt thou couldst.
Had I brought hither a corrupted mind,
Thy speech had alter'd it. Hold, here's gold for thee:
Persever in that clear way thou goest,
And the gods strengthen thee!
MARINA
The good gods preserve you!
LYSIMACHUS
For me, be you thoughten
That I came with no ill intent; for to me
The very doors and windows savour vilely.
Fare thee well. Thou art a piece of virtue, and
I doubt not but thy training hath been noble. —
Hold, here's more gold for thee. —
A curse upon him, die he like a thief,
That robs thee of thy goodness! If thou dost
Hear from me, it shall be for thy good.

Enter BOULT.

BOULT
I beseech your honour, one piece for me.
LYSIMACHUS
Avaunt, thou damned doorkeeper!
Your house, but for this virgin that doth prop it,
Would sink, and overwhelm you. Away! *[Exit.*
BOULT
How's this? We must take another course with you. If your peevish chastity, which is not worth a breakfast in the cheapest country under the cope, shall undo a whole household, let me be gelded like a spaniel. Come your ways.
MARINA
Whither would you have me?
BOULT
I must have your maidenhead taken off, or the common hangman shall execute it. Come your ways. We'll have no more gentlemen driven away. Come your ways, I say.

Enter BAWD.

BAWD
How now! what's the matter?
BOULT
Worse and worse, mistress; she has here spoken holy words to the Lord Lysimachus.

BAWD
O abominable!
BOULT
She makes our profession as it were to stink afore the face of the gods.
BAWD
Marry, hang her up for ever!
BOULT
The nobleman would have dealt with her like a nobleman, and she sent him away as cold as a snowball; saying his prayers too.
BAWD
Boult, take her away; use her at thy pleasure: crack the glass of her virginity, and make the rest malleable.
BOULT
An if she were a thornier piece of ground than she is, she shall be plough'd.
MARINA
Hark, hark, you gods!
BAWD
She conjures: away with her! Would she had never come within my doors! — Marry, hang you! — She's born to undo us. — Will you not go the way of women-kind? Marry, come up, my dish of chastity with rosemary and bays! *[Exit.*
BOULT
Come, mistress; come your ways with me.
MARINA
Whither wilt thou have me?
BOULT
To take from you the jewel you hold so dear.
MARINA
Prithee, tell me one thing first.
BOULT
Come now, your one thing.
MARINA
What canst thou wish thine enemy to be?
BOULT
Why, I could wish him to be my master, or rather, my mistress.
MARINA
Neither of these are so bad as thou art,
Since they do better thee in their command.
Thou hold'st a place, for which the pained'st fiend
Of hell would not in reputation change:
Thou art the damned doorkeeper to every
Coistrel that comes inquiring for his Tib;
To the choleric fisting of every rogue
Thy ear is liable; thy food is such
As hath been belch'd on by infected lungs.
BOULT
What would you have me do? go to the wars, would you? where a man may serve seven years for the loss of a leg, and have not money enough in the end to buy him a wooden one?
MARINA
Do any thing but this thou doest. Empty
Old receptacles, or common shores, of filth;
Serve by indenture to the common hangman:
Any of these ways are yet better than this;
For what thou professest, a baboon, could he speak,
Would own a name too dear. — O, that the gods
Would safely deliver me from this place! —
Here, here's gold for thee.
If that thy master would gain by me,
Proclaim that I can sing, weave, sew, and dance,
With other virtues, which I'll keep from boast;
And I will undertake all these to teach.
I doubt not but this populous city will
Yield many scholars.
BOULT
But can you teach all this you speak of?
MARINA
Prove that I cannot, take me home again,
And prostitute me to the basest groom
That doth frequent your house.
BOULT
Well, I will see what I can do for thee: if I can place thee, I will.
MARINA
But amongst honest women.
BOULT
Faith, my acquaintance lies little amongst them. But since my master and mistress have bought you, there's no going but by their consent: therefore I will make them acquainted with your purpose, and I doubt not but I shall find them tractable enough. Come, I'll do for thee what I can; come your ways. *[Exeunt.*

ACT V

Enter GOWER.

GOWER
Marina thus the brothel scapes, and chances
Into an honest house, our story says.
She sings like one immortal, and she dances
As goddess-like to her admired lays;
Deep clerks she dumbs; and with her needle composes
Nature's own shape, of bud, bird, branch, or berry,
That even her art sisters the natural roses;
Her inkle, silk, twin with the rubied cherry:
That pupils lacks she none of noble race,
Who pour their bounty on her; and her gain
She gives the cursed bawd. Here we her place;
And to her father turn our thoughts again,
Where we left him, on the sea. We there him lost:
Whence, driven before the winds, he is arrived
Here where his daughter dwells; and on this coast
Suppose him now at anchor. The city strived
God Neptune's annual feast to keep: from whence
Lysimachus our Tyrian ship espies,
His banners sable, trimm'd with rich expense;
And to him in his barge with fervour hies.
In your supposing once more put your sight
Of heavy Pericles; think this his bark:
Where what is done in action, more, if might,
Shall be discover'd; please you, sit, and hark.   [*Exit.*

SCENE I

On board PERICLES' *ship, off Mytilene. A pavilion on deck, with a curtain before it;* PERICLES *within it, reclined on a couch. A barge lying beside the Tyrian vessel.*

Enter two SAILORS, *one belonging to the Tyrian vessel, the other to the barge; to them* HELICANUS.

TYRIAN SAILOR [*to the* SAILOR *of Mytilene*].
Where is Lord Helicanus? he can resolve you. O, here
he is. — Sir, there is a barge put off from Mytilene, and
in it is Lysimachus the governor, who craves to come
aboard. What is your will?
HELICANUS
That he have his. Call up some gentlemen.
TYRIAN SAILOR
Ho, gentlemen! my lord calls.

Enter two or three GENTLEMEN.

FIRST GENTLEMAN
Doth your lordship call?
HELICANUS
Gentlemen, there is some of worth would come
    aboard: I pray ye, greet them fairly.
[*The* GENTLEMEN *and the two* SAILORS *descend, and
                go on board the barge.*

Enter, from thence, LYSIMACHUS *and* LORDS, *with
    the* GENTLEMEN *and the two* SAILORS.

TYRIAN SAILOR
Sir, this is the man that can, in aught you would,
resolve you.
LYSIMACHUS
Hail, reverend sir! the gods preserve you!
HELICANUS
And you, sir, to outlive the age I am,
And die as I would do.
LYSIMACHUS
                    You wish me well.
Being on shore, honouring of Neptune's triumphs,
Seeing this goodly vessel ride before us,
I made to it, to know of whence you are.
HELICANUS
First, what is your place?
LYSIMACHUS
                    I am the governor
Of this place you lie before.
HELICANUS
Sir,
Our vessel is of Tyre, in it the king;
A man who for this three months hath not spoken
To any one, nor taken sustenance
But to prorogue his grief.
LYSIMACHUS
Upon what ground is his distemperature?
HELICANUS
'Twould be too tedious to repeat;
But the main grief springs from the loss
Of a beloved daughter and a wife.

LYSIMACHUS
May we not see him?
HELICANUS
You may;
But bootless is your sight, — he will not speak
To any.
LYSIMACHUS
        Yet let me obtain my wish.
HELICANUS
Behold him. [*Draws the curtains, and discovers
    PERICLES.*] This was a goodly person,
Till the disaster that, one mortal night,
Drove him to this.
LYSIMACHUS
Sir king, all hail! the gods preserve you!
Hail, royal sir!
HELICANUS
It is in vain; he will not speak to you.
FIRST LORD
Sir,
We have a maid in Mytilen, I durst wager,
Would win some words of him.
LYSIMACHUS
                    'Tis well bethought.
She, questionless, with her sweet harmony
And other chosen attractions, would allure,
And make a battery through his deafen'd parts,
Which now are midway stopp'd:
She is all happy as the fairest of all,
And, with her fellow maids, is now upon
The leafy shelter that abuts against
The island's side.
        [*Whispers* FIRST LORD; *who goes off in the
                        barge of* LYSIMACHUS.
HELICANUS
Sure, all's effectless; yet nothing we'll omit
That bears recovery's name. But, since your kindness
We have stretch'd thus far, let us beseech you
That for our gold we may provision have,
Wherein we are not destitute for want,
But weary for the staleness.
LYSIMACHUS
                    O, sir, a courtesy
Which if we should deny, the most just gods
For every graff would send a caterpillar,
And so inflict our province. — Yet once more
Let me entreat to know at large the cause
Of your king's sorrow.
HELICANUS
                    Sit, sir: I will recount it to you: —
But, see, I am prevented.
    Enter, from the barge, FIRST LORD, *with* MARINA
                and a young LADY.
LYSIMACHUS
                    O, here is

PERICLES Like one I lov'd indeed. What were thy friends?

The lady that I sent for. — Welcome, fair one! —
Is't not a goodly presence?
HELICANUS
                    She's a gallant lady.
LYSIMACHUS
She's such a one, that, were I well assured
Came of a gentle kind and noble stock,
I'ld wish no better choice, and think me rarely wed. —
Fair one, all goodness that consists in bounty
Expect even here, where is a kingly patient:
If that thy prosperous and artificial feat
Can draw him but to answer thee in aught,
Thy sacred physic shall receive such pay
As thy desires can wish.
MARINA
                    Sir, I will use
My utmost skill in his recovery,
Provided
That none but I and my companion maid
Be suffer'd to come near him.
LYSIMACHUS
                    Come, let's leave her:
And the gods make her prosperous!   [MARINA *sings.*
LYSIMACHUS
Mark'd he your music?
MARINA
                    No, nor look'd on us.
LYSIMACHUS
See, she will speak to him.
MARINA
Hail, sir! my lord, lend ear.
PERICLES
Hum, ha!
MARINA
I am a maid,
My lord, that ne'er before invited eyes,
But have been gaz'd on like a comet: she speaks,
My lord, that, may be, hath endured a grief
Might equal yours, if both were justly weigh'd.
Though wayward fortune did malign my state,
My derivation was from ancestors
Who stood equivalent with mighty kings:
But time hath rooted out my parentage,
And to the world and awkward casualties
Bound me in servitude. — [*aside*] I will desist;
But there is something glows upon my cheek,
And whispers in mine ear, 'Go not till he speak.'
PERICLES
My fortunes — parentage — good parentage —
To equal mine! — was it not thus? what say you?
MARINA
I said, my lord, if you did know my parentage,
You would not do me violence.
PERICLES
I do think so. — Pray you, turn your eyes upon me.
You are like something that — What country-woman?

Here of these shores?

MARINA
                No, nor of any shores:
Yet I was mortally brought forth, and am
No other than I appear.

PERICLES
I am great with woe, and shall deliver weeping.
My dearest wife was like this maid, and such a one
My daughter might have been: my queen's square
    brows;
Her stature to an inch; as wand-like straight;
As silver-voic'd; her eyes as jewel-like,
And cas'd as richly; in pace another Juno;
Who starves the ears she feeds, and makes them
    hungry,
The more she gives them speech. — Where do you
    live?

MARINA
Where I am but a stranger: from the deck
You may discern the place.

PERICLES
                Where were you bred?
And how achiev'd you these endowments, which
You make more rich to owe?

MARINA
If I should tell my history, it would seem
Like lies disdain'd in the reporting.

PERICLES
                Prithee, speak:
Falseness cannot come from thee; for thou look'st
Modest as Justice, and thou seem'st a palace
For the crown'd Truth to dwell in: I will believe thee,
And make my senses credit thy relation
To points that seem impossible; for thou look'st
Like one I lov'd indeed. What were thy friends?
Didst thou not say, when I did push thee back, —
Which was when I perceiv'd thee, — that thou camest
From good descending?

MARINA
              So indeed I did.

PERICLES
Report thy parentage. I think thou said'st
Thou hadst been toss'd from wrong to injury,
And that thou thought'st thy griefs might equal mine,
If both were open'd.

MARINA
           Some such thing
I said, and said no more but what my thoughts
Did warrant me was likely.

PERICLES
            Tell thy story;
If thine consider'd prove the thousandth part
Of my endurance, thou art a man, and I
Have suffer'd like a girl: yet thou dost look
Like Patience gazing on kings' graves, and smiling
Extremity out of act. What were thy friends?
How lost thou them? Thy name, my most kind virgin?
Recount, I do beseech thee: come, sit by me.

MARINA
My name is Marina.

PERICLES
         O, I am mock'd,
And thou by some incensed god sent hither
To make the world to laugh at me.

MARINA
          Patience, good sir,
Or here I'll cease.

PERICLES
        Nay, I'll be patient,
Thou little know'st how thou dost startle me,
To call thyself Marina.

MARINA
        The name
Was given me by one that had some power, —
My father, and a king.

PERICLES
       How! a king's daughter?
And call'd Marina?

MARINA
        You said you would believe me;
But, not to be a troubler of your peace,
I will end here.

PERICLES
       But are you flesh and blood?
Have you a working pulse? and are no fairy?
Motion! — Well; speak on. Where were you born?
And wherefore call'd Marina?

MARINA
         Call'd Marina
For I was born at sea.

PERICLES
       At sea! what mother?

MARINA
My mother was the daughter of a king;
Who died the minute I was born,
As my good nurse Lychorida hath oft
Deliver'd weeping.

PERICLES
       O, stop there a little! —
[*aside*] This is the rarest dream that e'er dull sleep
Did mock sad fools withal: this cannot be:
My daughter's buried. — Well: — where were you
    bred?
I'll hear you more, to the bottom of your story,
And never interrupt you.

MARINA
You scorn: believe me, 'twere best I did give o'er.

PERICLES
I will believe you by the syllable
Of what you shall deliver. Yet, give me leave: —
How came you in these parts? where were you bred?

MARINA
The king my father did in Tarsus leave me;
Till cruel Cleon, with his wicked wife,
Did seek to murder me: and having woo'd
A villain to attempt it, who having drawn to do't,
A crew of pirates came and rescued me;
Brought me to Mytilene. But, good sir,
Whither will you have me? Why do you weep? It may be
You think me an impostor: no, good faith;
I am the daughter to King Pericles,
If good King Pericles be.

PERICLES
Ho, Helicanus!

HELICANUS
Calls my lord?

PERICLES
Thou art a grave and noble counsellor,
Most wise in general: tell me, if thou canst,
What this maid is, or what is like to be,
That thus hath made me weep?

HELICANUS
         I know not; but
Here is the regent, sir, of Mytilene
Speaks nobly of her.

LYSIMACHUS
        She never would tell
Her parentage; being demanded that,
She would sit still and weep.

PERICLES
O Helicanus, strike me, honour'd sir;
Give me a gash, put me to present pain;
Lest this great sea of joys rushing upon me
O'erbear the shores of my mortality,
And drown me with their sweetness. — O, come
    hither,
Thou that begett'st him that did thee beget;
Thou that wast born at sea, buried at Tarsus,
And found at sea again! — O Helicanus,
Down on thy knees, thank the holy gods as loud
As thunder threatens us: this is Marina. —
What was thy mother's name? tell me but that,
For truth can never be confirm'd enough,
Though doubts did ever sleep.

MARINA
        First, sir, I pray,
What is your title?

PERICLES
I am Pericles of Tyre: but tell me now
My drown'd queen's name, as in the rest you said
Thou hast been godlike perfect:
Be heir of kingdoms, and another life
To Pericles thy father.

MARINA
Is it no more to be your daughter than
To say my mother's name was Thaisa?
Thaisa was my mother, who did end
The minute I began.

PERICLES
Now, blessing on thee! rise; thou art my child. —
Give me fresh garments. — Mine own, Helicanus, —
She is not dead at Tarsus, as she would have been,
By savage Cleon: she shall tell thee all;
When thou shalt kneel, and justify in knowledge
She is thy very princess. — Who is this?

HELICANUS
Sir, 'tis the governor of Mytilene,
Who, hearing of your melancholy state,
Did come to see you.

PERICLES
I embrace you.
Give me my robes. — I am wild in my beholding. —
O heavens bless my girl! — But, hark, what music? —
Tell Helicanus, my Marina, tell him
O'er, point by point, for yet he seems to doubt,
How sure you are my daughter. — But, what music?

HELICANUS
My lord, I hear none.

PERICLES
None!
The music of the spheres! — List, my Marina.

LYSIMACHUS
It is not good to cross him; give him way.

PERICLES
Rarest sounds! Do ye not hear?

LYSIMACHUS
        My lord, I hear.   [*Music.*

PERICLES
Most heavenly music!
It nips me unto listening, and thick slumber
Hangs upon mine eyes: let me rest.   [*Sleeps.*

LYSIMACHUS
A pillow for his head: —
So, leave him all. — Well, my companion friends,
If this but answer to my just belief,
I'll well remember you.
        [*Exeunt all but* PERICLES.
        DIANA *appears.*

DIANA
My temple stands in Ephesus: hie thee thither,
And do upon mine altar sacrifice.
There, when my maiden priests are met together,
Before the people all,
Reveal how thou at sea didst lose thy wife:
To mourn thy crosses, with thy daughter's, call,
And give them repetition to the life.
Or perform my bidding, or thou liv'st in woe;
Do it, and happy; by my silver bow!
Awake, and tell thy dream.   [*Disappears.*

PERICLES
Celestial Dian, goddess argentine,
I will obey thee. — Helicanus!
    Enter HELICANUS, LYSIMACHUS, MARINA, *etc.*

HELICANUS
        Sir?

PERICLES
My purpose was for Tarsus, there to strike
The inhospitable Cleon; but I am
For other service first: toward Ephesus
Turn our blown sails; eftsoons I'll tell thee why. —
[*to* LYSIMACHUS] Shall we refresh us, sir, upon your
    shore,
And give you gold for such provision
As our intents will need?

LYSIMACHUS
Sir,
With all my heart; and, when you come ashore,
I have another suit.

PERICLES
        You shall prevail,
Were it to woo my daughter; for it seems
You have been noble towards her.

LYSIMACHUS
        Sir, lend me your arm.

PERICLES
Come, my Marina.   [*Exeunt.*
    Enter GOWER, *before the temple of* DIANA *at Ephesus.*

GOWER
Now our sands are almost run;
More a little, and then dumb.
This, my last boon, give me, —
For such kindness must relieve me,
That you aptly will suppose
What pageantry, what feats, what shows,
What minstrelsy, and pretty din,
The regent made in Mytilin,
To greet the king. So he thriv'd,
That he is promis'd to be wiv'd
To fair Marina; but in no wise
Till he had done his sacrifice,
As Dian bade: whereto being bound,
The interim, pray you, all confound.
In feather'd briefness sails are fill'd,
And wishes fall out as they're will'd.
At Ephesus, the temple see,
Our king, and all his company.
That he can hither come so soon,
Is by your fancies' thankful doom.   [*Exit.*

SCENE II

The temple of DIANA at Ephesus; THAISA standing near the altar, as high priestess; a number of VIRGINS on each side; CERIMON and other INHABITANTS of Ephesus attending.

Enter PERICLES, with his train; LYSIMACHUS, HELICANUS, MARINA, and a LADY.

PERICLES
Hail, Dian! to perform thy just command,
I here confess myself the king of Tyre;
Who, frighted from my country, did wed
At Pentapolis the fair Thaisa.
At sea in childbed died she, but brought forth
A maid-child call'd Marina; who, O goddess,
Wears yet thy silver livery. She at Tarsus
Was nurs'd with Cleon; who at fourteen years
He sought to murder: but her better stars
Brought her to Mytilene; 'gainst whose shore
Riding, her fortunes brought the maid aboard us,
Where, by her own most clear remembrance, she
Made known herself my daughter.

THAISA
                        Voice and favour! —
You are, you are — O royal Pericles! —   [*Faints.*

PERICLES
What means the nun? she dies! help, gentlemen!

CERIMON
Noble sir,
If you have told Diana's altar true,
This is your wife.

PERICLES
                Reverend appearer, no;
I threw her overboard with these very arms.

CERIMON
Upon this coast, I warrant you.

PERICLES
                        'Tis most certain.

CERIMON
Look to the lady; — O, she's but overjoy'd. —
Early one blustering morn this lady was
Thrown upon this shore. I oped the coffin,
Found there rich jewels; recover'd her, and plac'd her
Here in Diana's temple.

PERICLES
                May we see them?

CERIMON
Great sir, they shall be brought you to my house,
Whither I invite you. — Look, Thaisa is
Recover'd.

THAISA
        O, let me look!

If he be none of mine, my sanctity
Will to my sense bend no licentious ear,
But curb it, spite of seeing. — O, my lord,
Are you not Pericles? Like him you speak,
Like him you are: did you not name a tempest,
A birth, and death?

PERICLES
                The voice of dead Thaisa!

THAISA
That Thaisa am I, supposed dead
And drown'd.

PERICLES
Immortal Dian!

THAISA
                Now I know you better. —
When we with tears parted Pentapolis,
The king my father gave you such a ring.   [*Shows a ring.*

PERICLES
This, this: no more, you gods! your present kindness
Makes my past miseries sport: you shall do well,
That on the touching of her lips I may
Melt, and no more be seen. — O, come, be buried
A second time within these arms.

MARINA
                        My heart
Leaps to be gone into my mother's bosom.
                        [*Kneels to THAISA.*

PERICLES
Look, who kneels here! Flesh of thy flesh, Thaisa;
Thy burden at the sea, and call'd Marina
For she was yielded there.

THAISA
                Blest, and mine own!

HELICANUS
Hail, madam, and my queen!

THAISA
                        I know you not.

PERICLES
You have heard me say, when I did fly from Tyre,
I left behind an ancient substitute:
Can you remember what I call'd the man?
I have nam'd him oft.

THAISA
                'Twas Helicanus, then.

PERICLES
Still confirmation:
Embrace him, dear Thaisa; this is he.
Now do I long to hear how you were found;
How possibly preserv'd; and who to thank,
Besides the gods, for this great miracle.

THAISA
Lord Cerimon, my lord; this is the man,
Through whom the gods have shown their power

that can
From first to last resolve you.

PERICLES
                        Reverend sir,
The gods can have no mortal officer
More like a god than you. Will you deliver
How this dead queen re-lives?

CERIMON
                        I will, my lord.
Beseech you, first go with me to my house,
Where shall be shown you all was found with her;
How she came placed here in the temple;
No needful thing omitted.

PERICLES
Pure Dian, bless thee for thy vision! I
Will offer night-oblations to thee, — Thaisa,
This prince, the fair-betrothed of your daughter,
Shall marry her at Pentapolis. — And now,
This ornament
Makes me look dismal will I clip to form;
And what this fourteen years no razor touch'd,
To grace thy marriage-day, I'll beautify.

THAISA
Lord Cerimon hath letters of good credit, sir,
My father's dead.

PERICLES
Heavens make a star of him! Yet there, my queen,
We'll celebrate their nuptials, and ourselves
Will in that kingdom spend our following days:
Our son and daughter shall in Tyrus reign. —
Lord Cerimon, we do our longing stay
To hear the rest untold: sir, lead's the way.   [*Exeunt.*

Enter GOWER.

GOWER
In Antiochus and his daughter you have heard
Of monstrous lust the due and just reward:
In Pericles, his queen and daughter, seen,
Although assail'd with fortune fierce and keen,
Virtue preserv'd from fell destruction's blast,
Led on by heaven, and crown'd with joy at last:
In Helicanus may you well descry
A figure of truth, of faith, of loyalty:
In reverend Cerimon there well appears
The worth that learned charity aye wears:
For wicked Cleon and his wife, when fame
Had spread their cursed deed, and honour'd name
Of Pericles, to rage the city turn,
That him and his they in his palace burn;
The gods for murder seemed so content
To punish them, — although not done, but meant.
So, on your patience evermore attending,
New joy wait on you! Here our play has ending.   [*Exit.*

CYMBELINE

DRAMATIS PERSONAE

CYMBELINE, *King of Britain.*
CLOTEN, *son to the Queen by a former husband.*
POSTHUMUS LEONATUS, *a gentleman, husband to*
   Imogen.
BELARIUS, *a banish'd lord, disguised under the name of*
   Morgan.
GUIDERIUS, } *sons to Cymbeline, disguised under the*
ARVIRAGUS, } *names of Polydore and Cadwal,*
          } *supposed sons of Belarius.*
PHILARIO, *friend to Posthumus,* }
IACHIMO, *friend to Philario,*   } *Italians.*

A FRENCH GENTLEMAN, *friend to Philario.*
CAIUS LUCIUS, *general of the Roman forces.*
A ROMAN CAPTAIN.
TWO BRITISH CAPTAINS.
PISANIO, *servant to Posthumus.*
CORNELIUS, *a physician.*
TWO LORDS *of Cymbeline's court.*
TWO GENTLEMEN *of the same.*
TWO GAOLERS.

QUEEN, *wife to Cymbeline.*

IMOGEN, *daughter to Cymbeline by a former Queen.*
HELEN, *woman to Imogen.*

LORDS, LADIES, ROMAN SENATORS, TRIBUNES,
  a SOOTHSAYER, *a* DUTCH GENTLEMAN, *a*
  SPANISH GENTLEMAN, MUSICIANS,
  OFFICERS, CAPTAINS, SOLDIERS,
  MESSENGERS, *and* ATTENDANTS.

APPARITIONS.

SCENE — *Sometimes in Britain, sometimes in Italy.*

ACT I

SCENE I

Britain. The garden of CYMBELINE'S *palace.*

Enter two GENTLEMEN.

FIRST GENTLEMAN
You do not meet a man but frowns: our bloods
No more obey the heavens than our courtiers
Still seem as does the king.

SECOND GENTLEMAN
              But what's the matter?

FIRST GENTLEMAN
His daughter, and the heir of's kingdom, whom
He purpos'd to his wife's sole son — a widow
That late he married — hath referr'd herself
Unto a poor but worthy gentleman: she's wedded;
Her husband banish'd; she imprison'd: all
Is outward sorrow; though, I think, the king
Be touch'd at very heart.

SECOND GENTLEMAN
             None but the king?

FIRST GENTLEMAN
He that hath lost her too: so is the queen,
That most desired the match: but not a courtier,
Although they wear their faces to the bent
Of the king's looks, hath a heart that is not
Glad at the thing they scowl at.

SECOND GENTLEMAN
             And why so?

FIRST GENTLEMAN
He that hath miss'd the princess is a thing
Too bad for bad report: and he that hath her —
I mean, that married her, alack, good man!
And therefore banish'd — is a creature such
As, to seek through the regions of the earth
For one his like, there would be something failing
In him that should compare: — I do not think
So fair an outward, and such stuff within,
Endows a man but he.

SECOND GENTLEMAN
             You speak him far.

FIRST GENTLEMAN
I do extend him, sir, within himself;
Crush him together, rather than unfold
His measure duly.

SECOND GENTLEMAN
           What's his name and birth?

FIRST GENTLEMAN
I cannot delve him to the root: his father
Was call'd Sicilius, who did join his honour
Against the Romans with Cassibelan,
But had his titles by Tenantius, whom
He serv'd with glory and admired success, —
So gain'd the sur-addition Leonatus:
And had, besides this gentleman in question,
Two other sons, who, in the wars o'the time,
Died with their swords in hand; for which their father,
Then old and fond of issue, took such sorrow,
That he quit being; and his gentle lady,
Big of this gentleman our theme, deceas'd
As he was born. The king he takes the babe
To his protection; calls him Posthumus Leonatus;
Breeds him, and makes him of his bed-chamber;
Puts to him all the learnings that his time
Could make him the receiver of; which he took,
As we do air, fast as 'twas minister'd;
And in's spring became a harvest, liv'd in court, —
Which rare it is to do — most prais'd, most lov'd;

A sample to the youngest; to the more mature
A glass that feated them; and to the graver
A child that guided dotards; to his mistress,
For whom he now is banish'd, — her own price
Proclaims how she esteem'd him and his virtue:
By her election may be truly read
What kind of man he is.

SECOND GENTLEMAN
           I honour him
Even out of your report. But, pray you, tell me,
Is she sole child to the king?

FIRST GENTLEMAN
           His only child.
He had two sons, — if this be worth your hearing,
Mark it, — the eldest of them at three years old,
I'the swathing-clothes the other, from their nursery
Were stol'n; and to this hour no guess in knowledge
Which way they went.

SECOND GENTLEMAN
           How long is this ago?

FIRST GENTLEMAN
Some twenty years.

SECOND GENTLEMAN
That a king's children should be so convey'd!
So slackly guarded! and the search so slow,
That could not trace them!

FIRST GENTLEMAN
           Howsoe'er 'tis strange,
Or that the negligence may well be laugh'd at,
Yet is it true, sir.

SECOND GENTLEMAN
           I do well believe you.

FIRST GENTLEMAN
We must forbear: here comes the gentleman,
The queen, and princess.   [*Exeunt.*

Enter the QUEEN, POSTHUMUS, *and*
IMOGEN.

QUEEN
No, be assur'd you shall not find me, daughter,
After the slander of most stepmothers,
Evil-eyed unto you: you're my prisoner, but
Your gaoler shall deliver you the keys
That lock up your restraint. — For you,
   Posthumus,
So soon as I can win the offended king,
I will be known your advocate: marry, yet
The fire of rage is in him; and 'twere good
You lean'd unto his sentence with what patience
Your wisdom may inform you.

POSTHUMUS
           Please your highness,
I will from hence to-day.

QUEEN
           You know the peril. —
I'll fetch a turn about the garden, pitying
The pangs of barr'd affections; though the king
Hath charg'd you should not speak together.   [*Exit.*

IMOGEN
           O
Dissembling courtesy! How fine this tyrant
Can tickle where she wounds! — My dearest
   husband,
I something fear my father's wrath; but
   nothing —
Always reserv'd my holy duty — what
His rage can do on me: you must be gone;
And I shall here abide the hourly shot
Of angry eyes; not comforted to live,

But that there is this jewel in the world,
That I may see again.

POSTHUMUS
           My queen! my mistress!
O lady, weep no more, lest I give cause
To be suspected of more tenderness
Than doth become a man! I will remain
The loyal'st husband that did e'er plight troth:
My residence in Rome at one Philario's;
Who to my father was a friend, to me
Known but by letter: thither write, my queen,
And with mine eyes I'll drink the words you send,
Though ink be made of gall.

Enter QUEEN.

QUEEN
           Be brief, I pray you:
If the king come, I shall incur I know not
How much of his displeasure. — [*aside*] Yet I'll move
   him
To walk this way: I never do him wrong,
But he does buy my injuries, to be friends;
Pays dear for my offences.   [*Exit.*

POSTHUMUS
           Should we be taking leave
As long a term as yet we have to live,
The loathness to depart would grow. Adieu!

IMOGEN
Nay, stay a little:
Were you but riding forth to air yourself,

POSTHUMUS I will remain the loyal'st husband that
did e'er plight troth.

Such parting were too petty. Look here, love;
This diamond was my mother's: take it, heart;
But keep it till you woo another wife,
When Imogen is dead.

POSTHUMUS

How, how! another? —
You gentle gods, give me but this I have,
And sear up my embracements from a next
With bonds of death! — Remain, remain thou here
                                                    [*Putting on the ring.*
While sense can keep it on! And, sweetest, fairest,
As I my poor self did exchange for you,
To your so infinite loss; so in our trifles
I still win of you: for my sake wear this;
It is a manacle of love; I'll place it
Upon this fairest prisoner.
                                    [*Putting a bracelet upon her arm.*

IMOGEN

O the gods!
When shall we see again?

POSTHUMUS

Alack, the king!

Enter CYMBELINE *and* LORDS.

CYMBELINE

Thou basest thing, avoid! hence, from my sight!
If after this command thou fraught the court
With thy unworthiness, thou diest: away!
Thou'rt poison to my blood.

POSTHUMUS

The gods protect you!
And bless the good remainders of the court!
I am gone.   [*Exit.*

IMOGEN

There cannot be a pinch in death
More sharp than this is.

CYMBELINE

O disloyal thing,
That shouldst repair my youth, thou heap'st
A year's age on me!

IMOGEN

I beseech you, sir,
Harm not yourself with your vexation:
I am senseless of your wrath; a touch more rare
Subdues all pangs, all fears.

CYMBELINE

Past grace? obedience?

IMOGEN

Past hope, and in despair; that way, past grace.

CYMBELINE

That mightst have had the sole son of my queen!

IMOGEN

O blest, that I might not! I chose an eagle,
And did avoid a puttock.

CYMBELINE

Thou took'st a beggar; wouldst have made my throne
A seat for baseness.

IMOGEN

No; I rather added
A lustre to it.

CYMBELINE

O thou vile one!

IMOGEN

Sir,
It is your fault that I have lov'd Posthumus:
You bred him as my playfellow; and he is
A man worth any woman; overbuys me
Almost the sum he pays.

CYMBELINE

What, art thou mad!

IMOGEN

Almost, sir: heaven restore me! — Would I were
A neat-herd's daughter, and my Leonatus
Our neighbour shepherd's son!

CYMBELINE

Thou foolish thing! —

Enter QUEEN.

They were again together: you have done
Not after our command. Away with her,
And pen her up.

QUEEN

Beseech your patience. — Peace,
Dear lady daughter, peace! — Sweet sovereign,
Leave us to ourselves; and make yourself some comfort
Out of your best advice.

CYMBELINE

Nay, let her languish
A drop of blood a day; and, being aged,

Die of this folly!
                                    [*Exeunt* CYMBELINE *and* LORDS.

QUEEN

Fie! you must give way.
Enter PISANIO.
Here is your servant. — How now, sir! What news?

PISANIO

My lord your son drew on my master.

QUEEN

Ha!
No harm, I trust, is done?

PISANIO

There might have been,
But that my master rather play'd than fought,
And had no help of anger: they were parted
By gentlemen at hand.

QUEEN

I am very glad on't.

IMOGEN

Your son's my father's friend; he takes his part. —
To draw upon an exile! — O brave sir! —
I would they were in Afric both together;
Myself by with a needle, that I might prick
The goer-back. — Why came you from your master?

PISANIO

On his command: he would not suffer me
To bring him to the haven; left these notes
Of what commands I should be subject to,
When't pleas'd you to employ me.

QUEEN

This hath been
Your faithful servant: I dare lay mine honour
He will remain so.

PISANIO

I humbly thank your highness.

QUEEN

Pray, walk awhile.

IMOGEN

About some half-hour hence,
I pray you, speak with me: you shall at least
Go see my lord aboard: for this time leave me.   [*Exeunt.*

SCENE II

The same. A public place.

Enter CLOTEN *and two* LORDS.

FIRST LORD

Sir, I would advise you to shift a shirt; the violence of
action hath made you reek as a sacrifice: where air
comes out, air comes in: there's none abroad so
wholesome as that you vent.

CLOTEN

If my shirt were bloody, then to shift it. — Have I hurt
him?

SECOND LORD [*aside*].

No, faith: not so much as his patience.

FIRST LORD

Hurt him! his body's a passable carcass, if he be not
hurt: it is a thoroughfare for steel, if it be not hurt.

SECOND LORD [*aside*].

His steel was in debt; it went o'the backside the town.

CLOTEN

The villain would not stand me.

SECOND LORD [*aside*].

No; but he fled forward still, toward your face.

FIRST LORD

Stand you! You have land enough of your own; but he
added to your having; gave you some ground.

SECOND LORD [*aside*].

As many inches as you have oceans. — Puppies!

CLOTEN

I would they had not come between us.

SECOND LORD [*aside*].

So would I, till you had measured how long a fool you
were upon the ground.

CLOTEN

And that she should love this fellow, and refuse me!

SECOND LORD [*aside*].

If it be a sin to make a true election, she is damn'd.

FIRST LORD

Sir, as I told you always, her beauty and her brain go
not together: she's a good sign, but I have seen small
reflection of her wit.

SECOND LORD [*aside*].

She shines not upon fools, lest the reflection should
hurt her.

CLOTEN

Come, I'll to my chamber. Would there had been some
hurt done!

SECOND LORD [*aside*].

I wish not so; unless it had been the fall of an ass,
which is no great hurt.

CLOTEN

You'll go with us?

SECOND LORD

I'll attend your lordship.

CLOTEN

Nay, come, let's go together.

SECOND LORD

Well, my lord.   [*Exeunt.*

SCENE III

A room in CYMBELINE'S *palace.*

Enter IMOGEN *and* PISANIO.

IMOGEN

I would thou grew'st unto the shores o'the haven,
And question'dst every sail: if he should write,
And I not have it, 'twere a paper lost,
As offer'd mercy is. What was the last
That he spake to thee?

PISANIO

It was, 'His queen, his queen!'

IMOGEN

Then wav'd his handkerchief?

PISANIO

And kiss'd it, madam.

IMOGEN

Senseless linen! happier therein than I! —
And that was all?

PISANIO

No, madam; for so long
As he could make me with this eye or ear
Distinguish him from others, he did keep
The deck, with glove, or hat, or handkerchief,
Still waving, as the fits and stirs of's mind
Could best express how slow his soul sail'd on,
How swift his ship.

IMOGEN

Thou shouldst have made him
As little as a crow, or less, ere left
To after-eye him.

PISANIO

Madam, so I did.

IMOGEN

I would have broke mine eye-strings; crack'd them, but
To look upon him; till the diminution
Of space had pointed him sharp as my needle;
Nay, follow'd him, till he had melted from
The smallness of a gnat to air; and then
Have turn'd mine eye and wept. — But, good Pisanio,
When shall we hear from him?

PISANIO

Be assured, madam,
With his next vantage.

IMOGEN

I did not take my leave of him, but had
Most pretty things to say: ere I could tell him
How I would think on him, at certain hours,
Such thoughts and such; or I could make him swear
The shes of Italy should not betray
Mine interest and his honour; or have charg'd him,
At the sixth hour of morn, at noon, at midnight,
T'encounter me with orisons, for then
I am in heaven for him; or ere I could
Give him that parting kiss which I had set
Betwixt two charming words, comes in my father,
And, like the tyrannous breathing of the north,
Shakes all our buds from growing.

Enter a LADY.

LADY

The queen, madam,
Desires your highness' company.

IMOGEN

Those things I bid you do, get them dispatch'd. —
I will attend the queen.

PISANIO

Madam, I shall.   [*Exeunt.*

SCENE IV

Rome. PHILARIO'S *house.*

Enter PHILARIO, IACHIMO, *a* FRENCHMAN, *a*
DUTCHMAN, *and a* SPANIARD.

IACHIMO

Believe it, sir, I have seen him in Britain: he was then of
a crescent note; expected to prove so worthy as since he
hath been allow'd the name of: but I could then have
look'd on him without the help of admiration, though

the catalogue of his endowments had been tabled by
his side, and I to peruse him by items.

PHILARIO
You speak of him when he was less furnish'd than now
he is with that which makes him both without and
within.

FRENCHMAN
I have seen him in France: we had very many there
could behold the sun with as firm eyes as he.

IACHIMO
This matter of marrying his king's daughter —
wherein he must be weigh'd rather by her value than
his own — words him, I doubt not, a great deal from
the matter.

FRENCHMAN
And then his banishment, —

IACHIMO
Ay, and the approbation of those that weep this
lamentable divorce under her colours are wonderfully
to extend him; be it but to fortify her judgement, which
else an easy battery might lay flat, for taking a beggar
without less quality. But how comes it he is to sojourn
with you? how creeps acquaintance?

PHILARIO
His father and I were soldiers together; to whom I have
been often bound for no less than my life. — Here
comes the Briton: let him be so entertain'd amongst
you as suits, with gentlemen of your knowing, to a
stranger of his quality.
                    Enter POSTHUMUS.
I beseech you all, be better known to this gentleman;
whom I commend to you as a noble friend of mine:
how worthy he is I will leave to appear hereafter, rather
than story him in his own hearing.

FRENCHMAN
Sir, we have known together in Orleans.

POSTHUMUS
Since when I have been debtor to you for courtesies,
which I will be ever to pay, and yet pay still.

FRENCHMAN
Sir, you o'er-rate my poor kindness: I was glad I did
atone my countryman and you; it had been pity you
should have been put together with so mortal a
purpose as then each bore, upon importance of so
slight and trivial a nature.

POSTHUMUS
By your pardon, sir, I was then a young traveller; rather
shunn'd to go even with what I heard than in my every
action to be guided by others' experiences: but, upon
my mended judgement, — if I offend not to say it is
mended, — my quarrel was not altogether slight.

FRENCHMAN
Faith, yes, to be put to the arbitrement of swords; and
by such two that would, by all likelihood, have
confounded one the other, or have fall'n both.

IACHIMO
Can we, with manners, ask what was the difference?

FRENCHMAN
Safely, I think: 'twas a contention in public, which may,
without contradiction, suffer the report. It was much
like an argument that fell out last night, where each of
us fell in praise of our country mistresses; this
gentleman at that time vouching, and upon warrant of
bloody affirmation, his to be more fair, virtuous, wise,
chaste, constant-qualified, and less attemptable, than
any the rarest of our ladies in France.

IACHIMO
That lady is not now living; or this gentleman's
opinion, by this, worn out.

POSTHUMUS
She holds her virtue still, and I my mind.

IACHIMO
You must not so far prefer her fore ours of Italy.

POSTHUMUS
Being so far provoked as I was in France, I would abate
her nothing; though I profess myself her adorer, not
her friend.

IACHIMO
As fair and as good — a kind of hand-in-hand
comparison — had been something too fair and too
good for any lady in Britany. If she went before others I
have seen, as that diamond of yours outlustres many I
have beheld, I could not but believe she excell'd many:
but I have not seen the most precious diamond that is,
nor you the lady.

POSTHUMUS
I praised her as I rated her: so do I my stone.

IACHIMO
What do you esteem it at?

POSTHUMUS
More than the world enjoys.

IACHIMO
Either your unparagon'd mistress is dead, or she's
outprized by a trifle.

POSTHUMUS
You are mistaken: the one may be sold, or given, or if
there were wealth enough for the purchase, or merit for
the gift: the other is not a thing for sale, and only the
gift of the gods.

IACHIMO
Which the gods have given you?

POSTHUMUS
Which, by their graces, I will keep.

IACHIMO
You may wear her in title yours: but, you know, strange
fowl light upon neighbouring ponds. Your ring may be
stol'n too: so, your brace of unprizable estimations, the
one is but frail, and the other casual; a cunning thief, or
a that-way-accomplish'd courtier, would hazard the
winning both of first and last.

POSTHUMUS
Your Italy contains none so accomplish'd a courtier to
convince the honour of my mistress; if, in the holding
or loss of that, you term her frail. I do nothing doubt
you have store of thieves; notwithstanding, I fear not
my ring.

PHILARIO
Let us leave here, gentlemen.

POSTHUMUS
Sir, with all my heart. This worthy signior, I thank him,
makes no stranger of me; we are familiar at first.

IACHIMO
With five times so much conversation, I should get
ground of your fair mistress; make her go back, even to
the yielding, had I admittance, and opportunity to
friend.

POSTHUMUS
No, no.

IACHIMO
I dare thereupon pawn the moiety of my estate to your
ring; which, in my opinion, o'ervalues it something:
but I make my wager rather against your confidence
than her reputation; and, to bar your offence herein
too, I durst attempt it against any lady in the world.

POSTHUMUS
You are a great deal abused in too bold a persuasion;
and I doubt not you sustain what y'are worthy of by
your attempt.

IACHIMO
What's that?

POSTHUMUS
A repulse: though your attempt, as you call it, deserve
more, — a punishment too.

PHILARIO
Gentlemen, enough of this: it came in too suddenly; let
it die as it was born, and, I pray you, be better
acquainted.

IACHIMO
Would I had put my estate and my neighbour's on the
approbation of what I have spoke!

POSTHUMUS
What lady would you choose to assail?

IACHIMO
Yours; whom in constancy you think stands so safe. I
will lay you ten thousand ducats to your ring, that,
commend me to the court where your lady is, with no
more advantage than the opportunity of a second
conference, and I will bring from thence that honour of
hers which you imagine so reserved.

POSTHUMUS
I will wage against your gold, gold to it: my ring I hold
dear as my finger; 'tis part of it.

IACHIMO
You are afraid, and therein the wiser. If you buy ladies'
flesh at a million a dram, you cannot preserve it from
tainting: but I see you have some religion in you, that
you fear.

POSTHUMUS
This is but a custom in your tongue; you bear a graver
purpose, I hope.

IACHIMO
I am the master of my speeches; and would undergo
what's spoken, I swear.

POSTHUMUS
Will you? — I shall but lend my diamond till your
return: — let there be covenants drawn between's: my
mistress exceeds in goodness the hugeness of your
unworthy thinking: I dare you to this match: here's my
ring.

PHILARIO
I will have it no lay.

IACHIMO
By the gods, it is one. — If I bring you no sufficient
testimony that I have enjoy'd the dearest bodily part of
your mistress, my ten thousand ducats are yours; so is
your diamond too: if I come off, and leave her in such
honour as you have trust in, she your jewel this your
jewel, and my gold are yours; provided I have your
commendation for my more free entertainment.

POSTHUMUS
I embrace these conditions; let us have articles betwixt
us. — Only, thus far you shall answer: if you make your
voyage upon her, and give me directly to understand
you have prevail'd, I am no further your enemy; she is
not worth our debate: if she remain unseduced, — you
not making it appear otherwise, — for your ill opinion,
and the assault you have made to her chastity, you shall
answer me with your sword.

IACHIMO
Your hand, — a covenant: we will have these things set
down by lawful counsel, and straight away for Britain,
lest the bargain should catch cold and starve: I will
fetch my gold, and have our two wagers recorded.

POSTHUMUS
Agreed.   [*Exeunt* POSTHUMUS *and* IACHIMO.

FRENCHMAN
Will this hold, think you?

PHILARIO
Signior Iachimo will not from it. Pray, let us follow 'em.
                                        [*Exeunt.*

SCENE V

Britain. A room in CYMBELINE'S *palace.*

Enter QUEEN, LADIES, *and* CORNELIUS.

QUEEN
Whiles yet the dew's on ground, gather those flowers;
Make haste: who has the note of them?

FIRST LADY
                                    I, madam.

QUEEN
Dispatch. —   [*Exeunt* LADIES.
Now, master doctor, have you brought those drugs?

CORNELIUS
Pleaseth your highness, ay: here they are, madam:
                              [*Presenting a small box.*
But I beseech your Grace, without offence, —
My conscience bids me ask, — wherefor you have
Commanded of me these most poisonous compounds,
Which are the movers of a languishing death;
But, though slow, deadly?

QUEEN
                    I wonder, doctor,
Thou ask'st me such a question. Have I not been
Thy pupil long? Hast thou not learn'd me how

QUEEN Now, master doctor, have you brought those drugs?

IACHIMO The worthy Leonatus is in safety, and greets your highness dearly.

To make perfumes? distil? preserve? yea, so
That our great king himself doth woo me oft
For my confections? Having thus far proceeded,
Unless thou think'st me devilish, — is't not meet
That I did amplify my judgement in
Other conclusions? I will try the forces
Of these thy compounds on such creatures as
We count not worth the hanging, — but none human, —
To try the vigour of them, and apply
Allayments to their act; and by them gather
Their several virtues and effects.

CORNELIUS
              Your highness
Shall from this practise but make hard your heart:
Besides, the seeing these effects will be
Both noisome and infectious.

QUEEN
              O, content thee. —
[aside] Here comes a flattering rascal: upon him
Will I first work: he's for his master,
An enemy to my son. —

Enter PISANIO.
           How now, Pisanio! —
Doctor, your service for this time is ended;
Take your own way.

CORNELIUS [aside].
           I do suspect you, madam;
But you shall do no harm.

QUEEN [to PISANIO].
           Hark thee, a word.

CORNELIUS [aside].
I do not like her. She doth think she has
Strange lingering poisons: I do know her spirit,
And will not trust one of her malice with
A drug of such damn'd nature. Those she has
Will stupefy and dull the sense awhile;
Which first, perchance, she'll prove on cats and dogs,
Then afterward up higher: but there is
No danger in what show of death it makes,
More than the locking-up the spirits a time,
To be more fresh, reviving. She is fool'd
With a most false effect; and I the truer,
So to be false with her.

QUEEN
           No further service, doctor,
Until I send for thee.

CORNELIUS
           I humbly take my leave.   [Exit.

QUEEN
Weeps she still, say'st thou? Dost thou think in time
She will not quench, and let instructions enter
Where folly now possesses? Do thou work:
When thou shalt bring me word she loves my son,
I'll tell thee on the instant thou art then
As great as is thy master; greater, — for
His fortunes all lie speechless, and his name
Is at last gasp: return he cannot, nor
Continue where he is: to shift his being
Is to exchange one misery with another;
And every day that comes comes to decay
A day's work in him. What shalt thou expect,

To be depender on a thing that leans, —
Who cannot be new built, nor has no friends,
     [The QUEEN drops the box: PISANIO takes it up.
So much as but to prop him? — Thou takest up
Thou know'st not what; but take it for thy labour:
It is a thing I made, which hath the king
Five times redeem'd from death: I do not know
What is more cordial. — nay, I prithee, take it;
It is an earnest of a further good
That I mean to thee. Tell thy mistress how
The case stands with her; do't as from thyself.
Think what a chance thou chancest on; but think
Thou hast thy mistress still, — to boot, my son,
Who shall take notice of thee: I'll move the king
To any shape of thy preferment, such
As thou'lt desire; and then myself, I chiefly,
That set thee on to this desert, am bound
To load thy merit richly. Call my women:
Think on my words.   [Exit PISANIO.
          A sly and constant knave;
Not to be shak'd; the agent for his master;
And the remembrancer of her to hold
The hand-fast to her lord. — I have given him that,
Which, if he take, shall quite unpeople her
Of liegers for her sweet; and which she after,
Except she bend her humour, shall be assured
To taste of too.

Enter PISANIO *and* LADIES.
       So, so: — well done, well done:
The violets, cowslips, and the primroses,
Bear to my closet. — Fare thee well, Pisanio;
Think on my words.
          [Exeunt QUEEN and LADIES.

PISANIO
          And shall do:
But when to my good lord I prove untrue,
I'll choke myself: there's all I'll do for you.   [Exit.

SCENE VI

Another room in the palace.

Enter IMOGEN.

IMOGEN
A father cruel, and a step-dame false;
A foolish suitor to a wedded lady,
That hath her husband banish't; — O, that husband!
My supreme crown of grief! and those repeated
Vexations of it! Had I been thief-stol'n,
As my two brothers, happy! but most miserable
Is the desire that's glorious: blest be those,
How mean soe'er, that have their honest wills,
Which seasons comfort. — Who may this be? Fie!

Enter PISANIO *and* IACHIMO.

PISANIO
Madam, a noble gentleman of Rome
Comes from my lord with letters.

IACHIMO
          Change you, madam?
The worthy Leonatus is in safety,
And greets your highness dearly.   [Presents a letter.

IMOGEN
          Thanks, good sir:
You're kindly welcome.

IACHIMO [aside].
All of her that is out of door most rich!
If she be furnish'd with a mind so rare,
She is alone the Arabian bird; and I
Have lost the wager. Boldness be my friend!
Arm me, audacity, from head to foot!
Or, like the Parthian, I shall flying fight;
Rather, directly fly.

IMOGEN [reads].
He is one of the noblest note, to whose kindnesses I am
most infinitely tied. Reflect upon him accordingly, as
you value your trust — LEONATUS.
So far I read aloud:
But even the very middle of my heart
Is warm'd by the rest, and takes it thankfully. —
You are as welcome, worthy sir, as I
Have words to bid you; and shall find it so,
In all that I can do.

IACHIMO
          Thanks, fairest lady. —
What, are men mad? Hath nature given them eyes
To see this vaulted arch, and the rich crop
Of sea and land, which can distinguish 'twixt
The fiery orbs above, and the twinn'd stones
Upon the unnumber'd beach? and can we not
Partition make with spectacles so precious
'Twixt fair and foul?

IMOGEN
          What makes your admiration?

IACHIMO
It cannot be i'the eye; for apes and monkeys,
'Twixt two such shes, would chatter this way, and
Contemn with mows the other: nor i'the judgement;
For idiots, in this case of favour, would
Be wisely definite: nor i the appetite;
Sluttery, to such neat excellence opposed,
Should make desire vomit emptiness,
Not so allured to feed.

IMOGEN
What is the matter, trow?

IACHIMO
          The cloyed will, —
That satiate yet unsatisfied desire, that tub
Both fill'd and running, — ravening first the lamb,
Longs after for the garbage.

IMOGEN
          What, dear sir,
Thus raps you? Are you well?

IACHIMO
Thanks, madam; well. — [to PISANIO] Beseech you,
sir,
Desire my man's abode where I did leave him:
He's strange and peevish.

PISANIO
          I was going, sir,
To give him welcome.   [Exit.

IMOGEN
Continues well my lord? His health, beseech you?

IACHIMO
Well, madam.

IMOGEN
Is he dispos'd to mirth? I hope he is.

IACHIMO
Exceeding pleasant; none a stranger there
So merry and so gamesome: he is call'd
The Briton reveller.

IMOGEN
          When he was here
He did incline to sadness, and oft-times
Not knowing why.

IACHIMO
          I never saw him sad.
There is a Frenchman his companion, one
An eminent monsieur, that, it seems, much loves
A Gallian girl at home; he furnaces
The thick sighs from him; whiles the jolly Briton —
Your lord, I mean — laughs from's free lungs, cries 'O,
Can my sides hold, to think that man — who knows
By history, report, or his own proof,
What woman is, yea, what she cannot choose
But must be — will his free hours languish for
Assured bondage?'

IMOGEN
          Will my lord say so?

IACHIMO
Ay, madam; with his eyes in flood with laughter:
It is a recreation to be by,

And hear him mock the Frenchman. But, heavens
   know,
Some men are much to blame.

IMOGEN
                         Not he, I hope.

IACHIMO
Not he: but yet heaven's bounty towards him might
Be us'd more thankfully. In himself, 'tis much;
In you, which I account his, beyond all talents.
Whilst I am bound to wonder, I am bound
To pity too.

IMOGEN
              What do you pity, sir?

IACHIMO
Two creatures heartily.

IMOGEN
                  Am I one, sir?
You look on me: what wrack discern you in me
Deserves your pity?

IACHIMO
             Lamentable! What,
To hide me from the radiant sun, and solace
I' the dungeon by a snuff?

IMOGEN
               I pray you, sir,
Deliver with more openness your answers
To my demands. Why do you pity me?

IACHIMO
That others do —
I was about to say — enjoy your — But
It is an office of the gods to venge it,
Not mine to speak on't.

IMOGEN
            You do seem to know
Something of me, or what concerns me: pray you —
Since doubting things go ill often hurts more
Than to be sure they do; for certainties
Either are past remedies, or, timely knowing,
The remedy then born — discover to me
What both you spur and stop.

IACHIMO
             Had I this cheek
To bathe my lips upon; this hand, whose touch,
Whose every touch, would force the feeler's soul
To the oath of loyalty; this object, which
Takes prisoner the wild motion of mine eye,
Fixing it only here; — should I — damn'd then —
Slaver with lips as common as the stairs
That mount the Capitol; join gripes with hands
Made hard with hourly falsehood — falsehood, as
With labour; then by-peeping in an eye
Base and illustrous as the smoky light
That's fed with stinking tallow; — it were fit
That all the plagues of hell should at one time
Encounter such revolt.

IMOGEN
            My lord, I fear,
Has forgot Britain.

IACHIMO
           And himself. Not I,
Inclin'd to this intelligence, pronounce
The beggary of his change; but 'tis your Graces
That from my mutest conscience to my tongue
Charms this report out.

IMOGEN
           Let me hear no more.

IACHIMO
O dearest soul, your cause doth strike my heart
With pity, that doth make me sick! A lady
So fair, and fasten'd to an empery
Would make the great'st king double, to be partner'd
With tomboys, hired with that self-exhibition
Which your own coffers yield! with diseas'd ventures
That play with all infirmities for gold
Which rottenness can lend nature! such boil'd stuff
As well might poison poison! Be reveng'd;
Or she that bore you was no queen, and you
Recoil from your great stock.

IMOGEN
              Reveng'd!
How should I be reveng'd? If this be true, —
As I have such a heart that both mine ears
Must not in haste abuse, — if it be true,
How should I be reveng'd?

IACHIMO
            Should he make me
Live, like Diana's priest, betwixt cold sheets,
Whiles he is vaulting variable ramps,
In your despite, upon your purse? Revenge it.
I dedicate myself to your sweet pleasure;

More noble than that runagate to your bed;
And will continue fast to your affection,
Still close as sure.

IMOGEN
           What ho, Pisanio!

IACHIMO
Let me my service tender on your lips.

IMOGEN
Away! — I do condemn mine ears that have
So long attended thee. — If thou wert honourable,
Thou wouldst have told this tale for virtue, not
For such an end thou seek'st, — as base as strange.
Thou wrong'st a gentleman who is as far
From thy report as thou from honour; and
Solicit'st here a lady that disdains
Thee and the devil alike. — What ho, Pisanio! —
The king my father shall be made acquainted
Of thy assault: if he shall think it fit,
A saucy stranger, in his court, to mart
As in a Romish stew, and to expound
His beastly mind to us, — he hath a court
He little cares for and a daughter who
He not respects at all. — What, ho, Pisanio! —

IACHIMO
O happy Leonatus! I may say:
The credit that thy lady hath of thee
Deserves thy trust, and thy most perfect goodness
Her assured credit. — Blessed live you long!
A lady to the worthiest sir that ever
Country call'd his! and you his mistress, only
For the most worthiest fit! Give me your pardon.
I have spoke this, to know if your affiance
Were deeply rooted; and shall make your lord
That which he is, new o'er: and he is one
The truest manner'd; such a holy witch,
That he enchants societies into him;
Half all men's hearts are his.

IMOGEN
           You make amends.

IACHIMO
He sits 'mongst men like a descended god:
He hath a kind of honour sets him off,
More than a mortal seeming. Be not angry,
Most mighty princess, that I have adventur'd
To try your taking of a false report; which hath
Honour'd with confirmation your great judgement
In the election of a sir so rare,
Which you know cannot err: the love I bear him
Made me to fan you thus; but the gods made you,
Unlike all others, chaffless. Pray, your pardon.

IMOGEN
All's well, sir: take my power i'the court for yours.

IACHIMO
My humble thanks. I had almost forgot
T'entreat your Grace but in a small request,
And yet of moment too, for it concerns
Your lord, myself, and other noble friends,
Are partners in the business.

IMOGEN
           Pray, what is't?

IACHIMO
Some dozen Romans of us, and your lord —
The best feather of our wing — have mingled sums
To buy a present for the emperor;
Which I, the factor for the rest, have done
In France: 'tis plate of rare device, and jewels
Of rich and exquisite form; their
    values great;
And I am something curious, being
    strange,
To have them in safe stowage: may it
    please you
To take them in protection?

IMOGEN
           Willingly;
And pawn mine honour for their
    safety: since
My lord hath interest in them, I will
    keep them
In my bedchamber.

IACHIMO
         They are in a trunk,
Attended by my men: I will make bold
To send them to you, only for this
    night;
I must aboard to-morrow.

IMOGEN
           O, no, no.

IACHIMO
Yes, I beseech; or I shall short my word

By lengthening my return. From Gallia
I cross'd the seas on purpose and on promise
To see your Grace.

IMOGEN
         I thank you for your pains:
But not away to-morrow!

IACHIMO
         O, I must, madam:
Therefore I shall beseech you, if you please
To greet your lord with writing, do't to-night:
I have outstood my time; which is material
To the tender of our present.

IMOGEN
           I will write.
Send your trunk to me; it shall safe be kept,
And truly yielded you. You're very welcome.   *[Exeunt.*

ACT II

SCENE I

Britain. Before CYMBELINE'S *palace.*

Enter CLOTEN *and two* LORDS.

CLOTEN
Was there ever man had such luck! when I kiss'd the
jack, upon an up-cast to be hit away! I had a hundred
pound on't: and then a whoreson jackanapes must take
me up for swearing; as if I borrow'd mine oaths of him,
and might not spend them at my pleasure.

FIRST LORD
What got he by that? You have broke his pate with your
bowl.

SECOND LORD [*aside*].
If his wit had been like him that broke it, it would have
run all out.

CLOTEN
When a gentleman is disposed to swear, it is not for any
standers-by to curtail his oaths, ha?

SECOND LORD
No my lord; [*aside*] nor crop the ears of them.

CLOTEN
Whoreson dog! I give him satisfaction? Would he had
been one of my rank!

SECOND LORD [*aside*].
To have smelt like a fool.

CLOTEN
I am not vex'd more at any thing in the earth: a pox on't!
I had rather not be so noble as I am; they dare not fight
with me, because of the queen my mother: every
Jack-slave hath his bellyful of fighting, and I must go
up and down like a cock that nobody can match.

SECOND LORD [*aside*].
You are cock and capon too; and you crow, cock, with
your comb on.

CLOTEN
Sayest thou?

SECOND LORD
It is not fit your lordship should undertake every
companion that you give offence to.

CLOTEN
No, I know that: but it is fit I should commit offence to
my inferiors.

SECOND LORD
Ay, it is fit for your lordship only.

ILOTEN When a gentleman is disposed to swear, it is not for any
standers-by to curtail his oaths, ha?

CLOTEN Come on; tune: if you can penetrate her with your fingering, so; we'll try with tongue too.

CLOTEN
Why, so I say.

FIRST LORD
Did you hear of a stranger that's come to court to-night?

CLOTEN
A stranger, and I not know on't!

SECOND LORD [*aside*].
He's a strange fellow himself, and knows it not.

FIRST LORD
There's an Italian come; and, 'tis thought, one of Leonatus' friends.

CLOTEN
Leonatus! a banish'd rascal; and he's another, whatsoever he be. Who told you of this stranger?

FIRST LORD
One of your lordship's pages.

CLOTEN
Is it fit I went to look upon him? is there no derogation in't?

SECOND LORD
You cannot derogate, my lord.

CLOTEN
Not easily, I think.

SECOND LORD [*aside*].
You are a fool granted; therefore your issues, being foolish, do not derogate.

CLOTEN
Come, I'll go see this Italian: what I have lost to-day at bowls I'll win to-night of him. Come, go.

SECOND LORD
I'll attend your lordship.
     [*Exeunt* CLOTEN *and* FIRST LORD.
That such a crafty devil as is his mother
Should yield the world this ass! a woman that
Bears all down with her brain; and this her son
Cannot take two from twenty, for his heart,
And leave eighteen. Alas, poor princess,
Thou divine Imogen, what thou endurest,
Betwixt a father by thy step-dame govern'd,
A mother hourly coining plots, a wooer
More hateful than the foul expulsion is
Of thy dear husband, than that horrid act
Of the divorce he'ld make! The heavens hold firm
The walls of thy dear honour; keep unshak'd
That temple, thy fair mind; that thou mayst stand,
T'enjoy thy banish'd lord and this great land!   [*Exit.*

SCENE II

IMOGEN'S *bedchamber: a trunk in one corner of it.*

Enter IMOGEN *in her bed, and a* LADY.

IMOGEN
Who's there? my woman Helen?

LADY
           Please you, madam.

IMOGEN
What hour is it?

LADY
         Almost midnight, madam.

IMOGEN
I have read three hours, then: mine eyes are weak:
Fold down the leaf where I have left: to bed:
Take not away the taper, leave it burning;
And if thou canst awake by four o'clock,
I prithee, call me. Sleep hath seiz'd me wholly.
             [*Exit* LADY.
To your protection I commend me, gods!
From fairies, and the tempters of the night,
Guard me, beseech ye!
      [*Sleeps.* IACHIMO *comes from the trunk.*

IACHIMO
The crickets sing, and man's o'er-labour'd sense
Repairs itself by rest. Our Tarquin thus
Did softly press the rushes, ere he waken'd
The chastity he wounded. — Cytherea,
How bravely thou becomest thy bed! fresh lily!
And whiter than the sheets! That I might touch!
But kiss; one kiss! — Rubies unparagon'd,
How dearly they do't! — 'Tis her breathing that
Perfumes the chamber thus: the flame o' the taper
Bows toward her; and would under-peep her lids,
To see the enclosed lights, now canopied
Under these windows, white and azure, laced
With blue of heaven's own tinct. — But my design
To note the chamber: I will write all down: —
Such and such pictures; — there the window; — such
The adornment of her bed; — the arras, figures,
Why, such and such; — and the contents o'the story, —
Ah, but some natural notes about her body,
Above ten thousand meaner movables
Would testify, t'enrich mine inventory: —
O sleep, thou ape of death, lie dull upon her!
And be her sense but as a monument,
Thus in a chapel lying! — Come off, come off; —
            [*Taking off her bracelet.*
As slippery as the Gordian knot was hard! —
'Tis mine; and this will witness outwardly,
As strongly as the conscience does within,
To the madding of her lord. — On her left breast
A mole cinque-spotted, like the crimson drops
I'the bottom of a cowslip: here's a voucher,
Stronger than ever law could make: this secret
Will force him think I have pick'd the lock, and ta'en
The treasure of her honour. No more. To what end?
Why should I write this down, that's riveted,
Screw'd to my memory? — She hath been reading late
The tale of Tereus; here the leaf's turn'd down
Where Philomel gave up. — I have enough:
To the trunk again, and shut the spring of it. —
Swift, swift, you dragons of the night, that dawning
May bare the raven's eye! I lodge in fear;
Though this a heavenly angel, hell is here.
               [*Clock strikes.*
One, two, three, — Time, time!
       [*Goes into the trunk. Scene closes.*

SCENE III

An ante-chamber adjoining IMOGEN'S *apartments.*

Enter CLOTEN *and* LORDS.

FIRST LORD
Your lordship is the most patient man in loss, the most coldest that ever turn'd up ace.

CLOTEN
It would make any man cold to lose.

FIRST LORD
But not every man patient after the noble temper of your lordship. You are most hot and furious when you win.

CLOTEN
Winning will put any man into courage. If I could get this foolish Imogen, I should have gold enough. It's almost morning, is't not?

FIRST LORD
Day, my lord.

CLOTEN
I would this music would come: I am advised to give her music o'mornings; they say it will penetrate. —
             [*Enter* MUSICIANS.
Come on; tune: if you can penetrate her with your fingering, so; we'll try with tongue too: if none will do, let her remain; but I'll never give o'er. First, a very excellent good-conceited thing; after, a wonderful sweet air, with admirable rich words to it, — and then let her consider.

             Song
   Hark, hark! the lark at heaven's gate sings,
     And Phœbus gins arise,
   His steeds to water at those springs
     On chalic'd flowers that lies;
   And winking Mary-buds begin
     To ope their golden eyes:
   With every thing that pretty is,
     My lady sweet, arise;
        Arise, arise!

CLOTEN
So, get you gone. If this penetrate, I will consider your music the better: if it do not, it is a vice in her ears, which horse-hairs and calves'-guts, nor the voice of unpaved eunuch to boot, can never amend.
            [*Exeunt* MUSICIANS.

SECOND LORD
Here comes the king.

CLOTEN
I am glad I was up so late; for that's the reason I was up so early: he cannot choose but take this service I have done fatherly.
       Enter CYMBELINE *and* QUEEN.
Good morrow to your majesty and to my gracious mother.

CYMBELINE
Attend you here the door of our stern daughter?
Will she not forth?

CLOTEN
I have assail'd her with musics; but she vouchsafes no notice.

CYMBELINE
The exile of her minion is too new;
She hath not yet forgot him: some more time
Must wear the print of his remembrance out,
And then she's yours.

QUEEN
         You are most bound to the king,
Who lets go by no vantages that may
Prefer you to his daughter. Frame yourself
To orderly solicits, and be friended
With aptness of the season; make denials
Increase your services; so seem as if
You were inspired to do those duties which
You tender to her; that you in all obey her,
Save when command to your dismission tends,
And therein you are senseless.

CLOTEN
            Senseless! not so.
       Enter a MESSENGER.

MESSENGER
So like you, sir, ambassadors from Rome;
The one is Caius Lucius.

CYMBELINE
         A worthy fellow,
Albeit he comes on angry purpose now;
But that's no fault of his: we must receive him
According to the honour of his sender;
And towards himself, his goodness forespent on us,
We must extend our notice. — Our dear son,

When you have given good morning to your mistress,
Attend the queen and us; we shall have need
T'employ you towards this Roman. — Come, our
   queen.   *[Exeunt all but* CLOTEN.

CLOTEN
If she be up, I'll speak with her; if not,
Let her lie still and dream. — By your leave, ho! —
                      [Knocks.
I know her women are about her: what
If I do line one of their hands? 'Tis gold
Which buys admittance; oft it doth; yea, and makes
Diana's rangers false themselves, yield up
Their deer to the stand o'the stealer; and 'tis gold
Which makes the true man kill'd, and saves the thief;
Nay, sometime hangs both thief and true man: what
Can it not do and undo? I will make
One of her women lawyer to me; for
I yet not understand the case myself. —
By your leave.   *[Knocks.*

        Enter a LADY.

LADY
Who's there that knocks?
CLOTEN
             A gentleman.
LADY
                   No more?
CLOTEN
Yes, and a gentlewoman's son.
LADY
               That's more
Than some, whose tailors are as dear as yours,
Can justly boast of. What's your lordship's pleasure?
CLOTEN
Your lady's person: is she ready?
LADY
                Ay,
To keep her chamber.
CLOTEN
            There is gold for you;
Sell me your good report.
LADY
How! my good name? or to report of you
What I shall think is good? — The princess!

       Enter IMOGEN.

CLOTEN
Good morrow, fairest: sister, your sweet hand.
                  [Exit LADY.
IMOGEN
Good morrow, sir. You lay out too much pains
For purchasing but trouble: the thanks I give
Is telling you that I am poor of thanks,
And scarce can spare them.
CLOTEN
           Still, I swear I love you.
IMOGEN
If you but said so, 'twere as deep with me:
If you swear still, your recompense is still
That I regard it not.
CLOTEN
          This is no answer.
IMOGEN
But that you shall not say, I yield being silent,
I would not speak. I pray you, spare me: faith,
I shall unfold equal discourtesy
To your best kindness: one of your great knowing
Should learn, being taught, forbearance.
CLOTEN
To leave you in your madness, 'twere my sin:
I will not.
IMOGEN
Fools are not mad folks.
CLOTEN
          Do you call me fool?
IMOGEN
As I am mad, I do:
If you'll be patient, I'll no more be mad;
That cures us both. I am much sorry, sir,
You put me to forget a lady's manners,
By being so verbal: and learn now, for all,
That I, which know my heart, do here pronounce,
By the very truth of it, I care not for you;
And am so near the lack of charity, —
To accuse myself, — I hate you; which I had rather
You felt than make't my boast.
CLOTEN
          You sin against
Obedience, which you owe your father. For
The contract you pretend with that base wretch, —

One bred of alms, and foster'd with cold dishes,
With scraps o' the court, — it is no contract, none:
And though it be allow'd in meaner parties —
Yet who than he more mean? — to knit their
   souls —
On whom there is no more dependency
But brats and beggary — in self-figur'd knot;
Yet you are curb'd from that enlargement by
The consequence o'the crown; and must not foil
The precious note of it with a base slave,
A hilding for a livery, a squire's cloth,
A pantler, not so eminent.
IMOGEN
             Profane fellow!
Wert thou the son of Jupiter, and no more
But what thou art besides, thou wert too base
To be his groom: thou wert dignified enough,
Even to the point of envy, if 'twere made
Comparative for your virtues, to be styled
The under-hangman of his kingdom; and
   hated
For being preferr'd so well.
CLOTEN
          The south-fog rot him!
IMOGEN
He never can meet more mischance than
   come
To be but nam'd of thee. His meanest garment,
That ever hath but clipp'd his body, is dearer
In my respect than all the hairs above thee,
Were they all made such men.
        Enter PISANIO.
          How now, Pisanio!
CLOTEN
'His garment'! Now, the devil —
IMOGEN
To Dorothy my woman hie thee presently —
CLOTEN
'His garment'!
IMOGEN
        I am sprited with a fool;
Frighted, and anger'd worse: — go bid my woman
Search for a jewel that too casually
Hath left mine arm: it was thy master's; shrew me,
If I would lose it for a revenue
Of any king's in Europe. I do think
I saw't this morning: confident I am
Last night 'twas on mine arm; I kiss'd it:
I hope it be not gone to tell my lord
That I kiss aught but he.
PISANIO
           'Twill not be lost.
IMOGEN
I hope so: go and search.   *[Exit* PISANIO.
CLOTEN
        You have abus'd me: —
'His meanest garment'!
IMOGEN
         Ay, I said so, sir:
If you will make't an action, call witness to't.
CLOTEN
I will inform your father.
IMOGEN
         Your mother too:
She's my good lady; and will conceive, I hope,
But the worst of me. So, I leave you, sir,
To the worst of discontent.   *[Exit.*
CLOTEN
        I'll be reveng'd: —
'His meanest garment'! — Well.

SCENE IV

Rome. PHILARIO'S *house.*

Enter POSTHUMUS *and* PHILARIO.

POSTHUMUS
Fear it not, sir: I would I were so sure
To win the king, as I am bold her honour
Will remain hers.
PHILARIO
      What means do you make to him?
POSTHUMUS
Not any; but abide the change of time;
Quake in the present winter's state, and wish
That warmer days would come: in these fear'd hopes,
I barely gratify your love; they failing,
I must die much your debtor.
PHILARIO
Your very goodness and your company
O'erpays all I can do. By this, your king

PHILARIO Your very goodness and your company
   o'erpays all I can do.

Hath heard of great Augustus: Caius Lucius
Will do's commission throughly: and I think
He'll grant the tribute, send the arrearages,
Or look upon our Romans, whose remembrance
Is yet fresh in their grief.
POSTHUMUS
          I do believe —
Statist though I am none, nor like to be —
That this will prove a war; and you shall hear
The legions now in Gallia sooner landed
In our not-fearing Britain than have tidings
Of any penny tribute paid. Our countrymen
Are men more order'd than when Julius Cæsar
Smil'd at their lack of skill, but found their courage
Worthy his frowning at: their discipline
Now mingled with their courages will make known
To their approvers they are people such
That mend upon the world.
PHILARIO
          See! Iachimo!

       Enter IACHIMO.

POSTHUMUS
The swiftest harts have posted you by land;
And winds of all the corners kiss'd your sails,
To make your vessel nimble.
PHILARIO
          Welcome, sir.
POSTHUMUS
I hope the briefness of your answer made
The speediness of your return.
IACHIMO
          Your lady
Is one of the fairest that I have look'd upon.
POSTHUMUS
And therewithal the best; or let her beauty
Look through a casement to allure false hearts,
And be false with them.
IACHIMO
         Here are letters for you.
POSTHUMUS
Their tenour good, I trust.
IACHIMO
          'Tis very like.
PHILARIO
Was Caius Lucius in the Britain court
When you were there?
IACHIMO
         He was expected then,
But not approach'd.
POSTHUMUS
         All is well yet. —
Sparkles this stone as it was wont? or is't not
Too dull for your good wearing?
IACHIMO
         If I had lost it,
I should have lost the worth of it in gold.
I'll make a journey twice as far, t'enjoy
A second night of such sweet shortness which
Was mine in Britain; for the ring is won.
POSTHUMUS
The stone's too hard to come by.
IACHIMO
         Not a whit,
Your lady being so easy.

POSTHUMUS
                              Make not, sir,
Your loss your sport: I hope you know that we
Must not continue friends.
IACHIMO
                              Good sir, we must,
If you keep covenant. Had I not brought
The knowledge of your mistress home, I grant
We were to question further: but I now
Profess myself the winner of her honour,
Together with your ring; and not the wronger
Of her or you, having proceeded but
By both your wills.
POSTHUMUS
                              If you can make't apparent
That you have tasted her in bed, my hand
And ring is yours: if not, the foul opinion
You had of her pure honour gains or loses
Your sword or mine, or masterless leaves both
To who shall find them.
IACHIMO
                              Sir, my circumstances,
Being so near the truth as I will make them,
Must first induce you to believe: whose strength
I will confirm with oath; which, I doubt not,
You'll give me leave to spare, when you shall find
You need it not.
POSTHUMUS
                              Proceed.
IACHIMO
                              First, her bedchamber, —
Where, I confess, I slept not; but profess
Had that was well worth watching, — it was hang'd
With tapestry of silk and silver; the story
Proud Cleopatra, when she met her Roman,
And Cydnus swell'd above the banks, or for
The press of boats or pride: a piece of work
So bravely done, so rich, that it did strive
In workmanship and value; which I wonder'd
Could be so rarely and exactly wrought,
Since the true life on't was —
POSTHUMUS
                              This is true;
And this you might have heard of here, by me
Or by some other.
IACHIMO
                              More particulars
Must justify my knowledge.
POSTHUMUS
                              So they must,
Or do your honour injury.
IACHIMO
                              The chimney
Is south the chamber; and the chimney-piece
Chaste Dian bathing: never saw I figures
So lively to report themselves: the cutter
Was as another nature, dumb; outwent her,
Motion and breath left out.
POSTHUMUS
                              This is a thing
Which you might from relation likewise reap,
Being, as it is, much spoke of.
IACHIMO
                              The roof o'the chamber
With golden cherubins is fretted: her andirons —
I had forgot them — were two winking Cupids
Of silver, each on one foot standing, nicely
Depending on their brands.
POSTHUMUS
                              This is her honour! —
Let it be granted you have seen all this, — and praise
Be given to your remembrance, — the description
Of what is in her chamber nothing saves
The wager you have laid.
IACHIMO
                              Then, if you can,
                              [*Pulling out the bracelet.*
Be pale: I beg but leave to air this jewel; see! —
And now 'tis up again; it must be married
To that your diamond; I'll keep them.
POSTHUMUS
                              Jove! —
Once more let me behold it: is it that
Which I left with her?
IACHIMO
                              Sir, — I thank her, — that:
She stripp'd it from her arm; I see her yet;
Her pretty action did outsell her gift,
And yet enrich'd it too: she gave it me, and said
She priz'd it once.

POSTHUMUS
                              May be she pluck'd it off
To send it me.
IACHIMO
                              She writes so to you, doth she?
POSTHUMUS
O, no, no, no! 'tis true. Here, take this too;
                              [*Gives the ring.*
It is a basilisk unto mine eye,
Kills me to look on't. — Let there be no honour
Where there is beauty; truth, where semblance; love,
Where there's another man: the vows of women
Of no more bondage be to where they are made
Than they are to their virtues; which is nothing. —
O, above measure false!
PHILARIO
                              Have patience, sir,
And take your ring again; 'tis not yet won:
It may be probable she lost it; or
Who knows if one of her women, being corrupted,
Hath stol'n it from her?
POSTHUMUS
                              Very true;
And so, I hope, he came by't. — Back my ring:
Render to me some corporal sign about her,
More evident than this; for this was stol'n.
IACHIMO
By Jupiter, I had it from her arm.
POSTHUMUS
Hark you, he swears; by Jupiter he swears.
'Tis true, — nay, keep the ring, — 'tis true: I am sure
She would not lose it: her attendants are
All sworn and honourable: — they induc'd to steal it!
And by a stranger! — No, he hath enjoy'd her:
The cognisance of her incontinency
Is this, — she hath bought the name of whore thus
    dearly. —
There, take thy hire; and all the fiends of hell
Divide themselves between you!
PHILARIO
                              Sir, be patient:
This is not strong enough to be believ'd

Of one persuaded well of —
POSTHUMUS
                              Never talk on't;
She hath been colted by him.
IACHIMO
                              If you seek
For further satisfying, under her breast —
Worthy the pressing — lies a mole, right proud
Of that most delicate lodging: by my life,
I kiss'd it; and it gave me present hunger
To feed again, though full. You do remember
This stain upon her?
POSTHUMUS
                              Ay, and it doth confirm
Another stain, as big as hell can hold,
Were there no more but it.
IACHIMO
                              Will you hear more?
POSTHUMUS
Spare your arithmetic: never count the turns;
Once, and a million!
IACHIMO
                              I'll be sworn —
POSTHUMUS
                              No swearing.
If you will swear you have not done't, you lie;
And I will kill thee, if thou dost deny
Thou'st made me cuckold.
IACHIMO
                              I'll deny nothing.
POSTHUMUS
O, that I had her here, to tear her limb-meal!
I will go there and do't i'the court; before
Her father: — I'll do something —   [*Exit.*
PHILARIO
                              Quite besides
The government of patience! — You have won:
Let's follow him, and pervert the present wrath
He hath against himself.
IACHIMO
                              With all my heart.   [*Exeunt.*

CYMBELINE Now say, what would Augustus Cæsar with us?

SCENE V

Another room in PHILARIO'S house.

Enter POSTHUMUS.

POSTHUMUS
Is there no way for men to be, but women
Must be half-workers? We are all bastards:
And that most venerable man which I
Did call my father, was I know not where
When I was stamp'd; some coiner with his tools
Made me a counterfeit: yet my mother seem'd
The Dian of that time: so doth my wife
The nonpareil of this. — O, vengeance, vengeance!
Me of my lawful pleasure she restrain'd,
And pray'd me oft forbearance; did it with
A pudency so rosy, the sweet view on't
Might well have warm'd old Saturn; that I thought her
As chaste as unsunn'd snow: — O, all the devils! —
This yellow Iachimo, in an hour, — was't not? —
Or less, — at first? — perchance he spoke not, but,
Like a full-acorn'd boar, a German one,
Cried 'O!' and mounted; found no opposition
But what he look'd for should oppose, and she
Should from encounter guard. — Could I find out
The woman's part in me! For there's no motion
That tends to vice in man, but I affirm
It is the woman's part: be it lying, note it,
The woman's; flattering, hers; deceiving, hers;
Lust and rank thoughts, hers, hers; revenges, hers;
Ambitions, covetings, change of prides, disdain,
Nice longing, slanders, mutability,
All faults that may be nam'd, nay, that hell knows,
Why, hers, in part or all; but rather, all;
For even to vice
They are not constant, but are changing still
One vice, but of a minute old, for one
Not half so old as that. I'll write against them,
Detest them, curse them: — yet 'tis greater skill
In a true hate, to pray they have their will:
The very devils cannot plague them better. *[Exit.*

ACT III

SCENE I

Britain. A room of state in CYMBELINE'S palace.

Enter in state CYMBELINE, QUEEN, CLOTEN, and LORDS at one door, and at another CAIUS LUCIUS and ATTENDANTS.

CYMBELINE
Now say, what would Augustus Cæsar with us?

CAIUS LUCIUS
When Julius Cæsar, whose remembrance yet
Lives in men's eyes and will to ears and tongues
Be theme and hearing ever, was in this Britain
And conquer'd it, Cassibelan, thine uncle, —
Famous in Cæsar's praises, no whit less
Than in his feats deserving it, — for him
And his succession granted Rome a tribute,
Yearly three thousand pounds; which by thee lately
Is left untender'd.

QUEEN
                    And, to kill the marvel,
Shall be so ever.

CLOTEN
                    There be many Cæsars,
Ere such another Julius. Britain is
A world by itself; and we will nothing pay
For wearing our own noses.

QUEEN
                    That opportunity,
Which then they had to take from's, to resume
We have again. — Remember, sir, my liege,
The kings your ancestors, together with
The natural bravery of your isle, which stands
As Neptune's park, ribbed and paled in
With rocks unscalable and roaring waters;
With sands that will not bear your enemies' boats,
But suck them up to the topmast. A kind of conquest
Cæsar made here; but made not here his brag
Of 'Came, and saw, and overcame': with shame —
The first that ever touch'd him — he was carried
From off our coast, twice beaten; and his shipping —
Poor ignorant baubles! — on our terrible seas,
Like egg-shells mov'd upon their surges, crack'd
As easily 'gainst our rocks: for joy whereof
The famed Cassibelan, who was once at point —
O giglot Fortune! — to master Cæsar's sword,
Made Lud's-town with rejoicing fires bright,
And Britons strut with courage.

CLOTEN
Come, there's no more tribute to be paid: our kingdom
is stronger than it was at that time; and, as I said, there
is no more such Cæsars: other of them may have
crook'd noses; but to owe such straight arms, none.

CYMBELINE
Son, let your mother end.

CLOTEN
We have yet many among us can gripe as hard as
Cassibelan: I do not say I am one; but I have a hand. —
Why tribute? why should we pay tribute? If Cæsar can
hide the sun from us with a blanket, or put the moon in
his pocket, we will pay him tribute for light; else, sir, no
more tribute, pray you now.

CYMBELINE
You must know,
Till the injurious Romans did extort
This tribute from's, we were free: Cæsar's ambition, —
Which swell'd so much that it did almost stretch
The sides o'the world, — against all colour, here
Did put the yoke upon's; which to shake off
Becomes a warlike people, whom we reckon
Ourselves to be. We do say, then, to Cæsar,
Our ancestor was that Mulmutius which
Ordain'd our laws, — whose use the sword of Cæsar
Hath too much mangled; whose repair and franchise
Shall, by the power we hold, be our good deed,
Though Rome be therefore angry; — Mulmutius made
     our laws,
Who was the first of Britain which did put
His brows within a golden crown, and call'd
Himself a king.

LUCIUS
                    I am sorry, Cymbeline,
That I am to pronounce Augustus Cæsar —
Cæsar, that hath more kings his servants than
Thyself domestic officers — thine enemy:
Receive it from me, then: — war and confusion
In Cæsar's name pronounce I 'gainst thee: look
For fury not to be resisted. — Thus defied,
I thank thee for myself.

CYMBELINE
                    Thou art welcome, Caius.
Thy Cæsar knighted me; my youth I spent
Much under him; of him I gather'd honour;
Which he to seek of me again, perforce,
Behoves me keep at utterance. I am perfect
That the Pannonians and Dalmatians for
Their liberties are now in arms, — a precedent
Which not to read would show the Britons cold:
So Cæsar shall not find them.

LUCIUS
                    Let proof speak.

CLOTEN
His majesty bids you welcome. Make pastime with us a
day or two, or longer: if you seek us afterwards in other
terms, you shall find us in our salt-water girdle: if you
beat us out of it, it is yours; if you fall in the adventure,
our crows shall fare the better for you; and there's an
end.

LUCIUS
So, sir.

CYMBELINE
I know your master's pleasure, and he mine:
All the remain is 'Welcome.' *[Exeunt.*

SCENE II

Another room in the palace.

Enter PISANIO, with a letter.

PISANIO
How! of adultery? Wherefore write you not
What monster's her accuser? Leonatus!
O master! what a strange infection
Is fall'n into thy ear! What false Italian,
As poisonous-tongued as handed, hath prevail'd
On thy too ready hearing? Disloyal! No:
She's punish'd for her truth; and undergoes,
More goddess-like than wife-like, such assaults
As would take in some virtue. O my master!
Thy mind to her is now as low as were
Thy fortunes. How! that I should murder her?
Upon the love, and truth, and vows, which I
Have made to thy command? I, her? her blood?
If it be so to do good service, never
Let me be counted serviceable. How look I,
That I should seem to lack humanity
So much as this fact comes to? *[reading]* 'Do't: the letter
That I have sent her, by her own command

Shall give thee opportunity': — O damn'd paper!
Black as the ink that's on thee! Senseless bauble,
Art thou a feodary for this act, and look'st
So virgin-like without? — Lo, here she comes. —
I am ignorant in what I am commanded.

Enter IMOGEN.

IMOGEN
How now, Pisanio!

PISANIO
Madam, here is a letter from my lord.

IMOGEN
Who? thy lord? that is my lord, — Leonatus?
O, learn'd indeed were that astronomer
That knew the stars as I his characters;
He'ld lay the future open. You good gods,
Let what is here contain'd relish of love,
Of my lord's health, of his content, — yet not
That we two are asunder; let that grieve him:
Some griefs are medicinable; that is one of them,
For it doth physic love; — of his content
All but in that! — Good wax, thy leave: blest be
You bees that make these locks of counsel! Lovers,
And men in dangerous bonds, pray not alike:
Though forfeiters you cast in prison, yet
You clasp young Cupid's tables. — Good news, gods!
                    [Reads.
Justice, and your father's wrath, should he take me in
his dominion, could not be so cruel to me, as you, O the
dearest of creatures, would even renew me with your
eyes. Take notice that I am in Cambria, at
Milford-Haven: what your own love will, out of this,
advise you, follow. So, he wishes you all happiness, that
remains loyal to his vow, and your, increasing in love, —
                    LEONATUS POSTHUMUS.
O, for a horse with wings! Hear'st thou, Pisanio?
He is at Milford-Haven: read, and tell me
How far 'tis thither. If one of mean affairs
May plod it in a week, why may not I
Glide thither in a day? Then, true Pisanio, —
Who long'st, like me, to see thy lord; who long'st, —
O, let me bate, — but not like me; — yet long'st,
But in a fainter kind; — O, not like me;
For mine's beyond beyond, — say, and speak thick, —
Love's counsellor should fill the bores of hearing,
To the smothering of the sense, — how far it is
To this same blessed Milford: and, by the way,
Tell me how Wales was made so happy as
T'inherit such a haven: but, first of all,
How we may steal from hence; and for the gap
That we shall make in time, from our hence-going
And our return, to excuse: — but first, how get hence:
Why should excuse be born or e'er begot?
We'll talk of that hereafter. Prithee, speak,
How many score of miles may we well ride
'Twixt hour and hour?

PISANIO
                    One score 'twixt sun and sun,
Madam,'s enough for you, and too much too.

IMOGEN
Why, one that rode to's execution, man,
Could never go so slow: I have heard of riding wagers,
Where horses have been nimbler than the sands
That run i'the clock's behalf: — but this is foolery: —
Go bid my woman feign a sickness; say
She'll home to her father: and provide me presently
A riding-suit, no costlier than would fit
A franklin's housewife.

PISANIO
                    Madam, you're best consider.

IMOGEN
I see before me, man: nor here, nor here,
Nor what ensues, but have a fog in them,
That I cannot look through. Away, I prithee;
Do as I bid thee: there's no more to say;
Accessible is none but Milford way. *[Exeunt.*

SCENE III

Wales: a mountainous country with a cave.

Enter BELARIUS, GUIDERIUS, and ARVIRAGUS.

BELARIUS
A goodly day not to keep house, with such
Whose roof's as low as ours! Stoop, boys: this gate
Instructs you how t'adore the heavens, and bows you
To morning's holy office: the gates of monarchs
Are arch'd so high, that giants may jet through
And keep their impious turbans on, without
Good morrow to the sun. — Hail, thou fair heaven!
We house i'the rock, yet use thee not so hardly
As prouder livers do.

BELARIUS Hail, thou fair heaven!

GUIDERIUS
      Hail, heaven!

ARVIRAGUS
            Hail, heaven!

BELARIUS
Now for our mountain sport: up to yond hill,
Your legs are young; I'll tread these flats. Consider,
When you above perceive me like a crow,
That it is place which lessens and sets off;
And you may then revolve what tales I have told you
Of courts, of princes, of the tricks in war:
This service is not service, so being done,
But being so allow'd: to apprehend thus,
Draws us a profit from all things we see;
And often, to our comfort, shall we find
The sharded beetle in a safer hold
Than is the full-wing'd eagle. O, this life
Is nobler than attending for a check,
Richer than doing nothing for a bribe,
Prouder than rustling in unpaid-for silk:
Such gain the cap of him that makes 'em fine,
Yet keeps his book uncross'd: no life to ours.

GUIDERIUS
Out of your proof you speak: we, poor unfledg'd,
Have never wing'd from view o'the nest, nor know not
What air's from home. Haply this life is best,
If quiet life be best; sweeter to you
That have a sharper known; well corresponding
With your stiff age: but unto us it is
A cell of ignorance; travelling a-bed;
A prison for a debtor, that not dares
To stride a limit.

ARVIRAGUS
           What should we speak of
When we are old as you? when we shall hear
The rain and wind beat dark December, how,
In this our pinching cave, shall we discourse
The freezing hours away? We have seen nothing:
We are beastly; subtle as the fox for prey;
Like warlike as the wolf for what we eat:
Our valour is to chase what flies; our cage
We make a quire, as doth the prison'd bird,
And sing our bondage freely.

BELARIUS
              How you speak!
Did you but know the city's usuries,
And felt them knowingly: the art o'the court,
As hard to leave as keep; whose top to climb
Is certain falling, or so slippery that
The fear's as bad as falling: the toil o'the war,
A pain that only seems to seek out danger
I'the name of fame and honour; which dies i'the
     search;
And hath as oft a slanderous epitaph
As record of fair act; nay, many times
Doth ill deserve by doing well; what's worse,
Must court'sy at the censure: — O boys, this story
The world may read in me: my body's mark'd
With Roman swords; and my report was once
First with the best of note: Cymbeline lov'd me;
And when a soldier was the theme, my name
Was not far off: then was I as a tree
Whose boughs did bend with fruit: but in one night,
A storm or robbery, call it what you will,
Shook down my mellow hangings, nay, my leaves,
And left me bare to weather.

GUIDERIUS
              Uncertain favour!

BELARIUS
My fault being nothing, — as I have told you oft, —
But that two villains, whose false oaths prevail'd
Before my perfect honour, swore to Cymbeline
I was confederate with the Romans: so,
Follow'd my banishment; and, this twenty years,
This rock and these demesnes have been my world:
Where I have liv'd at honest freedom; paid
More pious debts to heaven than in all
The fore-end of my time. — But, up to the mountains!
This is not hunters' language: — he that strikes
The venison first shall be the lord o'the feast;
To him the other two shall minister;
And we will fear no poison, which attends
In place of greater state. I'll meet you in the valleys.
         [Exeunt GUIDERIUS and ARVIRAGUS.
How hard it is to hide the sparks of nature!
These boys know little they are sons to the king;

Nor Cymbeline dreams that they are alive.
They think they are mine; and, though train'd up thus
    meanly
I'the cave wherein they bow, their thoughts do hit
The roofs of palaces; and nature prompts them,
In simple and low things, to prince it much
Beyond the trick of others. This Polydore, —
The heir of Cymbeline and Britain, who
The king his father call'd Guiderius, — Jove!
When on my three-foot stool I sit, and tell
The warlike feats I have done, his spirits fly out
Into my story: say, 'Thus mine enemy fell,
And thus I set my foot on's neck'; even then
The princely blood flows in his cheek, he sweats,
Strains his young nerves, and puts himself in posture
That acts my words. The younger brother, Cadwal, —
Once Arviragus, — in as like a figure,
Strikes life into my speech, and shows much more
His own conceiving. — Hark, the game is rous'd! —
O Cymbeline! heaven and my conscience knows
Thou didst unjustly banish me: whereon,
At three and two years old, I stole these babes;
Thinking to bar thee of succession, as
Thou reft'st me of my lands. Euriphile,
Thou wast their nurse; they took thee for their mother,
And every day do honour to her grave:
Myself, Belarius, that am Morgan call'd,
They take for natural father. — The game is up.   [Exit.

SCENE IV
Near Milford-Haven.

Enter PISANIO *and* IMOGEN.

IMOGEN
Thou told'st me, when we came from horse, the place
Was near at hand: — ne'er long'd my mother so
To see me first, as I have now: — Pisanio! man!
Where is Posthumus? What is in thy mind,
That makes thee stare thus? Wherefore breaks that
    sigh
From th'inward of thee? One, but painted thus,
Would be interpreted a thing perplex'd
Beyond self-explication: put thyself
Into a haviour of less fear, ere wildness
Vanquish my staider senses. What's the matter?
Why tender'st thou that paper to me, with
A look untender? If't be summer news,
Smile to't before; if winterly, thou need'st
But keep that countenance still. — My husband's
    hand!
That drug-damn'd Italy hath out-crafted him,
And he's at some hard point. — Speak, man: thy
    tongue
May take off some extremity, which to read
Would be even mortal to me.

PISANIO
             Please you, read;
And you shall find me, wretched man, a thing
The most disdain'd of fortune.

IMOGEN [*reads*].
Thy mistress, Pisanio, hath play'd the strumpet in my
bed; the testimonies whereof lie bleeding in me. I
speak not out of weak surmises; but from proof as
strong as my grief, and as certain as I expect my
revenge. That part thou, Pisanio, must act for me, if thy
faith be not tainted with the breach of hers. Let thine
own hands take away her life: I shall give thee
opportunity at Milford-Haven: she hath my letter for
the purpose: where, if thou fear to strike, and to make
me certain it is done, thou art the pandar to her
dishonour, and equally to me disloyal.

PISANIO
What shall I need to draw my sword? the paper
Hath cut her throat already. — No, 'tis slander;
Whose edge is sharper than the sword; whose tongue
Outvenoms all the worms of Nile; whose breath
Rides on the posting winds, and doth belie
All corners of the world: kings, queens, and states,
Maids, matrons, nay, the secrets of the grave
This viperous slander enters. — What cheer, madam?

IMOGEN
False to his bed! What is it to be false?
To lie in watch there, and to think on him?
To weep 'twixt clock and clock? if sleep charge nature,
To break it with a fearful dream of him,
And cry myself awake! that's false to's bed, is it?

PISANIO
Alas, good lady!

IMOGEN
I false! Thy conscience witness: — Iachimo,
Thou didst accuse him of incontinency;

Thou then look'dst like a villain; now, methinks,
Thy favour's good enough. — Some jay of Italy,
Whose mother was her painting, hath betray'd him:
Poor I am stale, a garment out of fashion;
And, for I am richer than to hang by the walls,
I must be ripp'd: — to pieces with me! — O,
Men's vows are women's traitors! All good seeming,
By thy revolt, O husband, shall be thought
Put on for villainy; not born where't grows,
But worn a bait for ladies.

PISANIO
     Good madam, hear me.

IMOGEN
True honest men being heard, like false Aeneas,
Were, in his time, thought false; and Sinon's weeping
Did scandal many a holy tear, took pity
From most true wretchedness: so thou, Posthumus,
Wilt lay the leaven on all proper men;
Goodly and gallant shall be false and perjur'd
From thy great fail. — Come, fellow, be thou honest:
Do thou thy master's bidding: when thou see'st him,
A little witness my obedience: look!
I draw the sword myself: take it, and hit
The innocent mansion of my love, my heart:
Fear not; 'tis empty of all things but grief:
Thy master is not there; who was, indeed,
The riches of it: do his bidding; strike.
Thou mayst be valiant in a better cause;
But now thou seem'st a coward.

PISANIO
     Hence, vile instrument!
Thou shalt not damn my hand.

IMOGEN
     Why, I must die;
And if I do not by thy hand, thou art
No servant of thy master's: 'gainst self-slaughter
There is a prohibition so divine
That cravens my weak hand. Come, here's my heart: —
Something's afore't: soft, soft! we'll no defence; —
Obedient as the scabbard. What is here?
The scriptures of the loyal Leonatus
All turn'd to heresy? Away, away,
Corrupters of my faith! you shall no more
Be stomachers to my heart. Thus may poor fools
Believe false teachers: though those that are betray'd
Do feel the treason sharply, yet the traitor
Stands in worse case of woe.
And thou, Posthumus, thou that didst set up
My disobedience 'gainst the king my father,
And make me put into contempt the suits
Of princely fellows, shalt hereafter find
It is no act of common passage, but
A strain of rareness: and I grieve myself
To think, when thou shalt be disedg'd by her
That now thou tirest on, how thy memory
Will then be pang'd by me. — Prithee, dispatch:
The lamb entreats the butcher: where's thy knife?
Thou art too slow to do thy master's bidding,
When I desire it too.

PISANIO
     O gracious lady,
Since I receiv'd command to do this business,
I have not slept one wink.

IMOGEN
     Do't and to bed then.

PISANIO
I'll wake mine eyeballs out first.

IMOGEN
     Wherefore, then,
Didst undertake it? Why hast thou abused
So many miles with a pretence? this place?
Mine action, and thine own? our horses' labour?
The time inviting thee? the perturb'd court
For my being absent, whereunto I never
Purpose return? Why hast thou gone so far,
To be unbent when thou hast ta'en thy stand,
Th'elected deer before thee?

PISANIO
     But to win time
To lose so bad employment; in the which
I have consider'd of a course. Good lady,
Hear me with patience.

IMOGEN
     Talk thy tongue weary; speak:
I have heard I am a strumpet; and mine ear,
Therein false struck, can take no greater wound,
Nor tent to bottom that. But speak.

PISANIO
     Then, madam,
I thought you would not back again.

IMOGEN
     Most like,
Bringing me here to kill me.

PISANIO
     Not so, neither:
But if I were as wise as honest, then
My purpose would prove well. It cannot be
But that my master is abused:
Some villain, ay, and singular in his art,
Hath done you both this cursed injury.

IMOGEN
Some Roman courtezan.

PISANIO
     No, on my life.
I'll give but notice you are dead, and send him
Some bloody sign of it; for 'tis commanded
I should do so: you shall be miss'd at court,
And that will well confirm it.

IMOGEN
     Why, good fellow,
What shall I do the while? where bide? how live?
Or in my life what comfort, when I am
Dead to my husband?

PISANIO
     If you'll back to the court, —

IMOGEN
No court, no father; nor no more ado
With that harsh, noble, simple nothing, —
That Cloten, whose love-suit hath been to me
As fearful as a siege.

PISANIO
     If not at court,
Then not in Britain must you bide.

IMOGEN
     Where then?
Hath Britain all the sun that shines? Day, night,
Are they not but in Britain? I'the world's volume
Our Britain seems as of it, but not in't;
In a great pool a swan's nest: prithee, think
There's livers out of Britain.

PISANIO
     I am most glad
You think of other place. Th'ambassador,
Lucius the Roman, comes to Milford-Haven
To-morrow: now, if you could wear a mind
Dark as your fortune is, and but disguise
That which, t'appear itself, must not yet be
But by self-danger, you should tread a course
Pretty and full of view; yea, happily, near
The residence of Posthumus, — so nigh at least
That though his actions were not visible, yet
Report should render him hourly to your ear
As truly as he moves.

IMOGEN
     O, for such means!
Though peril to my modesty, not death on't,
I would adventure.

PISANIO
     Well, then, here's the point:
You must forget to be a woman; change
Command into obedience; fear and niceness —
The handmaids of all women, or, more truly,
Woman it pretty self — into a waggish courage;
Ready in gibes, quick-answer'd, saucy, and
As quarrelous as the weasel; nay, you must
Forget that rarest treasure of your cheek,
Exposing it — but, O, the harder heart!
Alack, no remedy! — to the greedy touch
Of common-kissing Titan; and forget
Your laboursome and dainty trims, wherein
You made great Juno angry.

IMOGEN
     Nay, be brief:
I see into thy end, and am almost
A man already.

PISANIO
     First, make yourself but like one.
Fore-thinking this, I have already fit —
'Tis in my cloak-bag — doublet, hat, hose, all
That answer to them: would you, in their serving,
And with what imitation you can borrow
From youth of such a season, fore noble Lucius
Present yourself, desire his service, tell him
Wherein you're happy, — which you'll make him
 know,
If that his head have ear in music, — doubtless
With joy he will embrace you; for he's honourable,
And, doubling that, most holy. Your means abroad,
You have me, rich; and I will never fail
Beginning nor supplyment.

IMOGEN
     Thou art all the comfort
The gods will diet me with. Prithee, away:
There's more to be consider'd; but we'll even
All that good time will give us: this attempt
I am soldier to, and will abide it with
A prince's courage. Away, I prithee.

PISANIO
Well, madam, we must take a short farewell,
Lest, being miss'd, I be suspected of
Your carriage from the court. My noble mistress,
Here is a box; I had it from the queen:
What's in't is precious; if you are sick at sea,
Or stomach-qualm'd at land, a dram of this
Will drive away distemper. To some shade,
And fit you to your manhood: may the gods
Direct you to the best!

IMOGEN
     Amen: I thank thee. [*Exeunt.*

SCENE V

A room in CYMBELINE'S *palace.*

Enter CYMBELINE, QUEEN, CLOTEN,
LUCIUS, *and* LORDS.

CYMBELINE
Thus far; and so, farewell.

LUCIUS
     Thanks, royal sir.
My emperor hath wrote, I must from hence;
And am right sorry that I must report ye
My master's enemy.

CYMBELINE
     Our subjects, sir,
Will not endure his yoke; and for ourself
To show less sovereignty than they, must needs
Appear unkinglike.

LUCIUS
     So, sir, I desire of you
A conduct overland to Milford-Haven. —
Madam, all joy befall your Grace, and you!

CYMBELINE
My lords, you are appointed for that office;
The due of honour in no point omit. —
So, farewell, noble Lucius.

LUCIUS
     Your hand, my lord.

CLOTEN
Receive it friendly; but from this time forth
I wear it as your enemy.

LUCIUS
     Sir, the event
Is yet to name the winner: fare you well.

CYMBELINE
Leave not the worthy Lucius, good my lords,
Till he have cross'd the Severn. — Happiness!
     [*Exeunt* LUCIUS *and* LORDS.

QUEEN
He goes hence frowning: but it honours us
That we have given him cause.

CLOTEN
     'Tis all the better;
Your valiant Britons have their wishes in it.

CYMBELINE
Lucius hath wrote already to the emperor
How it goes here. It fits us therefore ripely
Our chariots and our horsemen be in readiness:
The powers that he already hath in Gallia
Will soon be drawn to head, from whence he moves
His war for Britain.

QUEEN
     'Tis not sleepy business;
But must be look'd to speedily and strongly.

CYMBELINE
Our expectation that it would be thus
Hath made us forward. But, my gentle queen,
Where is our daughter? She hath not appear'd
Before the Roman, nor to us hath tender'd
The duty of the day: she looks us like
A thing more made of malice than of duty:
We have noted it. — Call her before us; for
We have been too slight in sufferance.
     [*Exit an* ATTENDANT.

QUEEN
     Royal sir,
Since the exile of Posthumus, most retired
Hath her life been; the cure whereof, my lord,
'Tis time must do. Beseech your majesty,
Forbear sharp speeches to her: she's a lady
So tender of rebukes, that words are strokes,
And strokes death to her.

Enter ATTENDANT.

CYMBELINE
            Where is she, sir? How
Can her contempt be answer'd?
ATTENDANT
            Please you, sir,
Her chambers are all lock'd; and there's no answer
That will be given to the loud'st noise we make.
QUEEN
My lord, when last I went to visit her,
She pray'd me to excuse her keeping close;
Whereto constrain'd by her infirmity,
She should that duty leave unpaid to you,
Which daily she was bound to proffer: this
She wish'd me to make known; but our great court
Made me to blame in memory.
CYMBELINE
            Her doors lock'd?
Not seen of late? Grant, heavens, that which I fear
Prove false!   [*Exit.*
QUEEN
Son, I say, follow the king.
CLOTEN
That man of hers, Pisanio, her old servant,
I have not seen these two days.
QUEEN
         Go, look after. [*Exit* CLOTEN.
Pisanio, thou that stand'st so for Posthumus! —
He hath a drug of mine; I pray his absence
Proceed by swallowing that; for he believes
It is a thing most precious. But for her,
Where is she gone? Haply, despair hath seiz'd her;
Or, wing'd with fervour of her love, she's flown
To her desired Posthumus: gone she is
To death or to dishonour; and my end
Can make good use of either: she being down,
I have the placing of the British crown.

Enter CLOTEN.

How now, my son!
CLOTEN
       'Tis certain she is fled.
Go in and cheer the king: he rages; none
Dare come about him.
QUEEN [*aside*].
           All the better: may
This night forestall him of the coming day!   [*Exit.*
CLOTEN
I love and hate her: for she's fair and royal,
And that she hath all courtly parts more exquisite
Than lady, ladies, woman; from every one
The best she hath, and she, of all compounded,
Outsells them all, — I love her therefore: but,
Disdaining me, and throwing favours on
The low Posthumus, slanders so her judgement,
That what's else rare is chok'd; and in that point
I will conclude to hate her, nay, indeed,
To be reveng'd upon her. For, when fools
Shall —

Enter PISANIO.

    Who is here? What, are you packing, sirrah?
Come hither: ah, you precious pander! Villain,
Where is thy lady? In a word; or else
Thou art straightway with the fiends.
PISANIO
            O, good my lord! —
CLOTEN
Where is thy lady? or, by Jupiter —
I will not ask again. Close villain,
I'll have this secret from thy heart, or rip
Thy heart to find it. Is she with Posthumus?
From whose so many weights of baseness cannot
A dram of worth be drawn.
PISANIO
          Alas, my lord,
How can she be with him? When was she miss'd?
He is in Rome.
CLOTEN
      Where is she, sir? Come nearer;
No further halting: satisfy me home
What is become of her.
PISANIO
O, my all-worthy lord! —
CLOTEN
         All-worthy villain!
Discover where thy mistress is at once,
At the next word, — no more of 'worthy lord';
Speak, or thy silence on the instant is
Thy condemnation and thy death.

PISANIO
            Then, sir,
This paper is the history of my knowledge
Touching her flight.   [*Presenting a letter.*
CLOTEN
        Let's see't. — I will pursue her
Even to Augustus' throne.
PISANIO [*aside*].
          Or this, or perish.
She's far enough; and what he learns by this
May prove his travel, not her danger.
CLOTEN
            Hum!
PISANIO [*aside*].
I'll write to my lord she's dead. O Imogen,
Safe mayst thou wander, safe return agen!
CLOTEN
Sirrah, is this letter true?
PISANIO
Sir, as I think.
CLOTEN
It is Posthumus' hand; I know't. — Sirrah, if thou
wouldst not be a villain, but do me true service,
undergo those employments wherein I should have
cause to use thee with a serious industry, — that is,
what villainy soe'er I bid thee do, to perform it directly
and truly, — I would think thee an honest man: thou
shouldst neither want my means for thy relief, nor my
voice for thy preferment.
PISANIO
Well, my good lord.
CLOTEN
Wilt thou serve me? — for since patiently and
constantly thou hast stuck to the bare fortune of that
beggar Posthumus, thou canst not, in the course of
gratitude, but be a diligent follower of mine, — wilt
thou serve me?
PISANIO
Sir, I will.
CLOTEN
Give me thy hand; here's my purse. Hast any of thy late
master's garments in thy possession?
PISANIO
I have, my lord, at my lodging, the same suit he wore
when he took leave of my lady and mistress.
CLOTEN
The first service thou dost me, fetch that suit hither: let
it be thy first service; go.
PISANIO
I shall, my lord.   [*Exit.*
CLOTEN
Meet thee at Milford-Haven! — I forgot to ask him one
thing; I'll remember't anon: — even there, thou villain
Posthumus, will I kill thee. — I would these garments
were come. She said upon a time — the bitterness of it
I now belch from my heart — that she held the very
garment of Posthumus in more respect than my noble
and natural person, together with the adornment of my
qualities. With that suit upon my back, will I ravish her:
first kill him, and in her eyes; there shall she see my
valour, which will then be a torment to her contempt.
He on the ground, my speech of insultment ended on
his dead body, and when my lust hath dined, — which,
as I say, to vex her I will execute in the clothes that she
so praised, — to the court I'll knock her back, foot her
home again. She hath despised me rejoicingly, and I'll
be merry in my revenge.
        Enter PISANIO, *with the clothes.*
Be those the garments?
PISANIO
Ay, my noble lord.
CLOTEN
How long is't since she went to Milford-Haven?
PISANIO
She can scarce be there yet.
CLOTEN
Bring this apparel to my chamber; that is the second
thing that I have commanded thee: the third is, that
thou wilt be a voluntary mute to my design. Be but
duteous and true, preferment shall tender itself to thee.
— My revenge is now at Milford: would I had wings to
follow it! — Come, and be true.   [*Exit.*
PISANIO
Thou bidd'st me to my loss: for, true to thee
Were to prove false, which I will never be,
To him that is most true. — To Milford go,
And find not her whom thou pursuest. — Flow, flow,
You heavenly blessings, on her! — This fool's speed
Be cross'd with slowness; labour be his meed!   [*Exit.*

SCENE VI

Wales: before the cave of BELARIUS.

Enter IMOGEN, *in boy's clothes.*

IMOGEN
I see a man's life is a tedious one:
I have tired myself; and for two nights together
Have made the ground my bed. I should be sick,
But that my resolution helps me. — Milford,
When from the mountain-top Pisanio show'd thee,
Thou wast within a ken: O Jove! I think
Foundations fly the wretched; such, I mean,
Where they should be reliev'd. Two beggars told me
I could not miss my way: will poor folks lie,
That have afflictions on them, knowing 'tis
A punishment or trial? Yes; no wonder,
When rich ones scarce tell true: to lapse in fullness
Is sorer than to lie for need; and falsehood
Is worse in kings than beggars. — My dear lord!
Thou art one o' the false ones: now I think on thee
My hunger's gone; but even before, I was
At point to sink for food. — But what is this?
Here is a path to't: 'tis some savage hold:
I were best not call; I dare not call: yet famine,
Ere clean it o'erthrow nature, makes it valiant.
Plenty and peace breeds cowards; hardness ever
Of hardiness is mother. — Ho! who's here?
If any thing that's civil, speak; if savage,
Take or lend. Ho! — No answer? then I'll enter.
Best draw my sword; and if mine enemy
But fear the sword like me, he'll scarcely look on't.
Such a foe, good heavens!   [*Exit into the cave.*

Enter BELARIUS, GUIDERIUS, *and* ARVIRAGUS.

BELARIUS
You, Polydore, have prov'd best woodman, and
Are master of the feast: Cadwal and I
Will play the cook and servant; 'tis our match:
The sweat of industry would dry and die,
But for the end it works to. Come; our stomachs
Will make what's homely savoury: weariness
Can snore upon the flint, when resty sloth
Finds the down-pillow hard. — Now, peace be here,
Poor house, that keep'st thyself!
GUIDERIUS
          I am thoroughly weary.
ARVIRAGUS
I am weak with toil, yet strong in appetite.
GUIDERIUS
There is cold meat i'the cave; we'll browse on that,
Whilst what we have kill'd be cook'd.
BELARIUS
          Stay; come not in.
         [*Looking into the cave.*

IMOGEN Best draw my sword; and if mine enemy but
fear the sword like me, he'll scarcely look on't.

But that it eats our victuals, I should think
Here were a fairy.
GUIDERIUS
    What's the matter, sir?
BELARIUS
By Jupiter, an angel! or, if not,
An earthly paragon! — Behold divineness
No elder than a boy!

Enter IMOGEN.

IMOGEN
Good masters, harm me not:
Before I enter'd here, I call'd; and thought
To have begg'd or bought what I have took: good troth,
I have stol'n naught; nor would not, though I had
  found
Gold strew'd i'the floor. Here's money for my meat:
I would have left it on the board, so soon
As I had made my meal; and parted
With prayers for the provider.
GUIDERIUS
     Money, youth?
ARVIRAGUS
All gold and silver rather turn to dirt!
And 'tis no better reckon'd, but of those
Who worship dirty gods.
IMOGEN
    I see you're angry:
Know, if you kill me for my fault, I should
Have died had I not made it.
BELARIUS
    Whither bound?
IMOGEN
To Milford-Haven.
BELARIUS
What's your name?
IMOGEN
Fidele, sir. I have a kinsman who
Is bound for Italy; he embark'd at Milford;
To whom being going, almost spent with hunger,
I am fall'n in this offence.
BELARIUS
    Prithee, fair youth,
Think us no churls, nor measure our good minds
By this rude place we live in. Well encounter'd!
'Tis almost night: you shall have better cheer
Ere you depart; and thanks to stay and eat it. —
Boys, bid him welcome.
GUIDERIUS
    Were you a woman, youth,
I should woo hard but be your groom: — in honesty,
I bid for you as I do buy.
ARVIRAGUS
    I'll make't my comfort
He is a man: I'll love him as my brother: —
And such a welcome as I'ld give to him
After long absence, such is yours: most welcome!
Be sprightly, for you fall 'mongst friends.
IMOGEN
    'Mongst friends,
If brothers. — [*aside*] Would it had been so, that they
Had been my father's sons! then had my prize
Been less; and so more equal ballasting
To thee, Posthumus.
BELARIUS
    He wrings at some distress.
GUIDERIUS
Would I could free't!
ARVIRAGUS
    Or I; whate'er it be,
What pain it cost, what danger! Gods!
BELARIUS
    Hark, boys. [*Whispering.*
IMOGEN
Great men,
That had a court no bigger than this cave,
That did attend themselves, and had the virtue
Which their own conscience seal'd them, — laying by
That nothing-gift of differing multitudes, —
Could not out-peer these twain. Pardon me, gods!
I'ld change my sex to be companion with them,
Since Leonatus's false.
BELARIUS
    It shall be so.
Boys, we'll go dress our hunt. — Fair youth, come in:
Discourse is heavy, fasting; when we have supp'd,
We'll mannerly demand thee of thy story,
So far as thou wilt speak it.
GUIDERIUS
    Pray, draw near.

ARVIRAGUS
The night to the owl, and morn to the lark, less
welcome.
IMOGEN
Thanks, sir.
ARVIRAGUS
I pray, draw near.   [*Exeunt.*

SCENE VII

Rome. A public place.

Enter two SENATORS *and* TRIBUNES.

FIRST SENATOR
This is the tenour of the emperor's writ, —
That since the common men are now in action
'Gainst the Pannonians and Dalmatians;
And that the legions now in Gallia are
Full weak to undertake our wars against
The fall'n-off Britons; that we do incite
The gentry to this business. He creates
Lucius pre-consul: and to you the tribunes,
For this immediate levy, he commends
His absolute commission. Long live Cæsar!
FIRST TRIBUNE
Is Lucius general of the forces?
SECOND SENATOR
    Ay.
FIRST TRIBUNE
Remaining now in Gallia?
FIRST SENATOR
    With those legions
Which I have spoke of, whereunto your levy
Must be supplyant: the words of your commission
Will tie you to the numbers, and the time
Of their dispatch.
FIRST TRIBUNE
   We will discharge our duty. [*Exeunt.*

ACT IV

SCENE I

Wales: the forest near the cave of BELARIUS.

Enter CLOTEN.

CLOTEN
I am near to the place where they should meet, if
Pisanio have mapp'd it truly. How fit his garments
serve me! Why should his mistress, who was made by
him that made the tailor, not
be fit too? the rather — saving
reverence of the word — for
'tis said a woman's fitness
comes by fits. Therein I must
play the workman. I dare
speak it to myself, — for it is
not vainglory for a man and
his glass to confer; in his own
chamber, I mean, — the lines
of my body are as well drawn
as his; no less young, more
strong, not beneath him in
fortunes, beyond him in the
advantage of the time, above
him in birth, alike conversant
in general services, and more
remarkable in single
oppositions: yet this
imperceiverant thing loves
him in my despite. What
mortality is! Posthumus, thy
head, which now is growing
upon thy shoulders, shall
within this hour be off; thy
mistress enforced; thy
garments cut to pieces before
her face: and all this done,
spurn her home to her father;
who may happily be a little
angry for my so rough usage;
but my mother, having power
of his testiness, shall turn all
into my commendations. My
horse is tied up safe: out,
sword, and to a sore purpose!
Fortune, put them into my
hand! This is the very
description of their
meeting-place; and the fellow
dares not deceive me. [*Exit.*

SCENE II

Before the cave of BELARIUS.

Enter BELARIUS, GUIDERIUS, ARVIRAGUS, *and*
IMOGEN *from the cave.*

BELARIUS [*to* IMOGEN].
You are not well: remain here in the cave;
We'll come to you after hunting.
ARVIRAGUS [*to* IMOGEN].
    Brother, stay here:
Are we not brothers?
IMOGEN
    So man and man should be;
But clay and clay differs in dignity,
Whose dust is both alike. I am very sick.
GUIDERIUS
Go you to hunting; I'll abide with him.
IMOGEN
So sick I am not, — yet I am not well;
But not so citizen a wanton as
To seem to die ere sick: so please you, leave me;
Stick to your journal course: the breach of custom
Is breach of all. I am ill; but your being by me
Cannot amend me; society is no comfort
To one not sociable: I am not very sick,
Since I can reason of it. Pray you, trust me here:
I'll rob none but myself; and let me die,
Stealing so poorly.
GUIDERIUS
    I love thee; I have spoke it:
How much the quantity, the weight as much,
As I do love my father.
BELARIUS
    What? how! how!
ARVIRAGUS
If it be sin to say so, sir, I yoke me
In my good brother's fault: I know not why
I love this youth; and I have heard you say,
Love's reason's without reason: the bier at door,
And a demand who is't shall die, I'd say,
'My father, not this youth.'
BELARIUS [*aside*].
    O noble strain!
O worthiness of nature! breed of greatness!
Cowards father cowards, and base things sire base:
Nature hath meal and bran, contempt and grace.
I'm not their father; yet who this should be,
Doth miracle itself, loved before me. —
'Tis the ninth hour o' the morn.

GUIDERIUS I love thee; I have spoke it: how much the quantity,
the weight as much, as I do love my father.

ARVIRAGUS
                              Brother, farewell.
IMOGEN
I wish ye sport.
ARVIRAGUS
                    You health. — So please you, sir.
IMOGEN [*aside*].
These are kind creatures. Gods, what lies I have heard!
Our courtiers say all's savage but at court:
Experience, O, thou disprovest report!
Th'imperious seas breed monsters; for the dish
Poor tributary rivers as sweet fish.
I am sick still; heart-sick: — Pisanio,
I'll now taste of thy drug.   [*Swallows some.*
GUIDERIUS
                    I could not stir him:
He said he was gentle, but unfortunate;
Dishonestly afflicted, but yet honest.
ARVIRAGUS
Thus did he answer me: yet said, hereafter
I might know more.
BELARIUS
                    To the field, to the field! —
We'll leave you for this time: go in and rest.
ARVIRAGUS
We'll not be long away.
BELARIUS
                    Pray, be not sick,
For you must be our housewife.
IMOGEN
                              Well or ill,
I am bound to you.
BELARIUS
              And shalt be ever.
                    [*Exit* IMOGEN *into the cave.*
This youth, how'er distress'd, appears he hath had
Good ancestors.
ARVIRAGUS
              How angel-like he sings!
GUIDERIUS
But his neat cookery! he cut our roots in characters;
And sauc'd our broths, as Juno had been sick,
And he her dieter.
ARVIRAGUS
                    Nobly he yokes
A smiling with a sigh, — as if the sigh
Was that it was for not being such a smile;
The smile mocking the sigh, that it would fly
From so divine a temple, to commix
With winds that sailors rail at.
GUIDERIUS
                              I do note
That grief and patience, rooted in him both,
Mingle their spurs together.
ARVIRAGUS
                    Grow, patience!
And let the stinking elder, grief, untwine
His perishing root with the increasing vine!
BELARIUS
It is great morning. Come, away! — Who's there?
                    Enter CLOTEN.
CLOTEN
I cannot find those runagates; that villain
Hath mock'd me: — I am faint.
BELARIUS
                    'Those runagates'!
Means he not us? I partly know him; 'tis
Cloten, the son o' the queen. I fear some ambush.
I saw him not these many years, and yet
I know 'tis he. — We are held as outlaws: hence!
GUIDERIUS
He is but one: you and my brother search
What companies are near: pray you, away;
Let me alone with him.
                    [*Exeunt* BELARIUS *and* ARVIRAGUS.
CLOTEN
                    Soft! — What are you
That fly me thus? some villain mountaineers?
I have heard of such. — What slave art thou?
GUIDERIUS
                              A thing
More slavish did I ne'er than answering
A slave without a knock.
CLOTEN
                    Thou art a robber,
A law-breaker, a villain: yield thee thief.
GUIDERIUS
To who? to thee? What art thou? Have not I

An arm as big as thine? a heart as big?
Thy words, I grant, are bigger; for I wear not
My dagger in my mouth. Say what thou art,
Why I should yield to thee?
CLOTEN
                    Thou villain base,
Know'st me not by my clothes?
GUIDERIUS
                    No, nor thy tailor, rascal,
Who is thy grandfather: he made those clothes,
Which, as it seems, make thee.
CLOTEN
                    Thou precious varlet,
My tailor made them not.
GUIDERIUS
                    Hence, then, and thank
The man that gave them thee. Thou art some fool;
I am loath to beat thee.
CLOTEN
                    Thou injurious thief,
Hear but my name, and tremble.
GUIDERIUS
                    What's thy name?
CLOTEN
Cloten, thou villain.
GUIDERIUS
Cloten, thou double villain, be thy name,
I cannot tremble at it: were it Toad, or Adder, Spider,
'Twould move me sooner.
CLOTEN
                    To thy further fear,
Nay, to thy mere confusion, thou shalt know
I am son to the queen.
GUIDERIUS
                    I am sorry for't; not seeming
So worthy as thy birth.
CLOTEN
                    Art not afeard?
GUIDERIUS
Those that I reverence, those I fear, — the wise:
At fools I laugh, not fear them.
CLOTEN
                    Die the death:
When I have slain thee with my proper hand,
I'll follow those that even now fled hence,
And on the gates of Lud's-town set your heads:
Yield, rustic mountaineer.   [*Exeunt, fighting.*
                    Enter BELARIUS *and* ARVIRAGUS.
BELARIUS
No company's abroad?
ARVIRAGUS
None in the world: you did mistake him, sure.
BELARIUS
I cannot tell: — long is it since I saw him,
But time hath nothing blurr'd those lines of favour
Which then he wore; the snatches in his voice,
And burst of speaking, were as his: I am absolute
'Twas very Cloten.
ARVIRAGUS
                    In this place we left them:
I wish my brother make good time with him,
You say he is so fell.
BELARIUS
                    Being scarce made up,
I mean, to man, he had not apprehension
Of roaring terrors; for defect of judgement
Is oft the cause of fear. — But, see, thy brother.
                    Enter GUIDERIUS *with* CLOTEN'S *head.*
GUIDERIUS
This Croten was a fool, an empty purse, —
There was no money in't: not Hercules
Could have knock'd out his brains, for he had none:
Yet I not doing this, the fool had borne
My head as I do his.
BELARIUS
                    What hast thou done?
GUIDERIUS
I am perfect what: cut off one Cloten's head,
Son to the queen, after his own report;
Who call'd me traitor, mountaineer; and swore
With his own single hand he'ld take us in,
Displace our heads where — thank the gods! — they
    grow,
And set them on Lud's-town.
BELARIUS
                    We are all undone.
GUIDERIUS
Why, worthy father, what have we to lose

But that he swore to take our lives? The law
Protects not us: then why should we be tender
To let an arrogant piece of flesh threat us,
Play judge and executioner all himself,
For we do fear the law? What company
Discover you abroad?
BELARIUS
                    No single soul
Can we set eye on; but in all safe reason
He must have some attendants. Though his humour
Was nothing but mutation, — ay, and that
From one bad thing to worse; not frenzy, not
Absolute madness could so far have rav'd,
To bring him here alone: although, perhaps,
It may be heard at court, that such as we
Cave here, hunt here, are outlaws, and in time
May make some stronger head; the which he hearing —
As it is like him — might break out, and swear
He'ld fetch us in; yet is't not probable
To come alone, either he so undertaking,
Or they so suffering: then on good ground we fear,
If we do fear this body hath a tail,
More perilous than the head.
ARVIRAGUS
                    Let ordinance
Come as the gods foresay it: howsoe'er,
My brother hath done well.
BELARIUS
                    I had no mind
To hunt this day: the boy Fidele's sickness
Did make my way long forth.
GUIDERIUS
                    With his own sword,
Which he did wave against my throat, I have ta'en
His head from him: I'll throw't into the creek
Behind our rock; and let it to the sea,
And tell the fishes he's the queen's son, Cloten:
That's all I reck.   [*Exit.*
BELARIUS
                    I fear 'twill be reveng'd:
Would, Polydore, thou hadst not done't! though valour
Becomes thee well enough.
ARVIRAGUS
                    Would I had done't,
So the revenge alone pursued me! — Polydore,
I love thee brotherly; but envy much
Thou hast robb'd me of this deed: I would revenges,
That possible strength might meet, would seek us
    through,
And put us to our answer.
BELARIUS
                    Well, 'tis done: —
We'll hunt no more to-day, nor seek for danger
Where there's no profit. I prithee, to our rock;
You and Fidele play the cooks: I'll stay
Till hasty Polydore return, and bring him
To dinner presently.
ARVIRAGUS
                    Poor sick Fidele!
I'll willingly to him: to gain his colour
I'ld let a parish of such Clotens blood,
And praise myself for charity.   [*Exit.*
BELARIUS
                    O thou goddess,
Thou divine Nature, how thyself thou blazon'st
In these two princely boys! They are as gentle
As zephyrs, blowing below the violet,
Not wagging his sweet head; and yet as rough,
Their royal blood enchaf'd, as the rudest wind,
That by the top doth take the mountain pine,
And make him stoop to the vale. 'Tis wonder
That an invisible instinct should frame them
To royalty unlearn'd; honour untaught;
Civility not seen from other; valour,
That wildly grows in them, but yields a crop
As if it had been sow'd. Yet still it's strange
What Cloten's being here to us portends,
Or what his death will bring us.
                    Enter GUIDERIUS.
GUIDERIUS
                    Where's my brother?
I have sent Cloten's clotpoll down the stream,
In embassy to his mother: his body's hostage
For his return.   [*Solemn music.*
BELARIUS
                    My ingenious instrument!
Hark, Polydore, it sounds! But what occasion
Hath Cadwal now to give it motion? Hark!
GUIDERIUS
Is he at home?

GUIDERIUS I have sent Cloten's clotpoll down the stream, in embassy to his mother.

BELARIUS
         He went hence even now.
GUIDERIUS
What does he mean? since death of my dear'st mother
It did not speak before. All solemn things
Should answer solemn accidents. The matter?
Triumphs for nothing, and lamenting toys,
Is jollity for apes, and grief for boys.
Is Cadwal mad?
BELARIUS
         Look, here he comes,
And brings the dire occasion in his arms
Of what we blame him for!
    Enter ARVIRAGUS, *with* IMOGEN *as dead, bearing*
      her in his arms.
ARVIRAGUS
         The bird is dead
That we have made so much on. I had rather
Have skipp'd from sixteen years of age to sixty,
To have turn'd my leaping-time into a crutch,
Than have seen this.
GUIDERIUS
         O sweetest, fairest lily!
My brother wears thee not the one half so well
As when thou grew'st thyself.
BELARIUS
         O melancholy!
Who ever yet could sound thy bottom? find
The ooze, to show what coast thy sluggish crare
Might easiliest harbour in? — Thou blessed thing!
Jove knows what man thou mightst have made; but I,
Thou diedst, a most rare boy, of melancholy! —
How found you him?
ARVIRAGUS
         Stark, as you see:
Thus smiling, as some fly had tickled slumber,
Not as death's dart, being laugh'd at; his right cheek
Reposing on a cushion.
GUIDERIUS
         Where?
ARVIRAGUS
         O'the floor;
His arms thus leagued: I thought he slept; and put
My clouted brogues from off my feet, whose rudeness
Answer'd my steps too loud.
GUIDERIUS
         Why, he but sleeps:
If he be gone, he'll make his grave a bed;
With female fairies will his tomb be haunted,
And worms will not come to't.
ARVIRAGUS
         With fairest flowers,

Whilst summer lasts, and I live here, Fidele,
I'll sweeten thy sad grave: thou shalt not lack
The flower that's like thy face, pale primrose; nor
The azur'd harebell, like thy veins; no, nor
The leaf of eglantine, whom not to slander,
Out-sweeten'd not thy breath: the ruddock would,
With charitable bill, — O bill, sore-shaming
Those rich-left heirs that let their fathers lie
Without a monument! — bring thee all this;
Yea, and furr'd moss besides, when flowers are none,
To winter-ground thy corse.
GUIDERIUS
         Prithee, have done;
And do not play in wench-like words with that
Which is so serious. Let us bury him,
And not protract with admiration what
Is now due debt. — To the grave!
ARVIRAGUS
         Say, where shall's lay him?
GUIDERIUS
By good Euriphile, our mother.

ARVIRAGUS
         Be't so:
And let us, Polydore, though now our voices
Have got the mannish crack, sing him to the ground,
As once our mother; use like note and words,
Save that Euriphile must be Fidele.
GUIDERIUS
Cadwal,
I cannot sing: I'll weep, and word it with thee;
For notes of sorrow out of tune are worse
Than priests and fanes that lie.
ARVIRAGUS
         We'll speak it, then.
BELARIUS
Great griefs, I see, medicine the less; for Cloten
Is quite forgot. He was a queen's son, boys:
And, though he came our enemy, remember
He was paid for that: though mean and mighty, rotting
Together have one dust, yet reverence —
That angel of the world — doth make distinction
Of place 'tween high and low. Our foe was princely;
And though you took his life as being our foe,
Yet bury him as a prince.
GUIDERIUS
         Pray you, fetch him hither.
Thersites' body is as good as Ajax',
When neither are alive.
ARVIRAGUS
         If you'll go fetch him,
We'll say our song the whilst. — Brother, begin.
              [*Exit* BELARIUS.
GUIDERIUS
Nay, Cadwal, we must lay his head to th'east;
My father hath a reason for't.
ARVIRAGUS
         'Tis true.
GUIDERIUS
Come on, then, and remove him.
ARVIRAGUS
         So. — Begin.
    Song.
GUIDERIUS
    Fear no more the heat o'the sun,
      Nor the furious winter's rages;
    Thou thy worldly task hast done,
      Home art gone, and ta'en thy wages:
    Golden lads and girls all must,
    As chimney-sweepers, come to dust.
ARVIRAGUS
    Fear no more the frown o'the great,
      Thou art past the tyrant's stroke;
    Care no more to clothe and eat;
      To thee the reed is as the oak:
    The sceptre, learning, physic, must
    All follow this, and come to dust.
GUIDERIUS
    Fear no more the lightning-flash,

ARVIRAGUS The bird is dead that we have made so much on.

ARVIRAGUS
Nor th'all-dreaded thunder-stone;
GUIDERIUS
Fear not slander, censure rash;
ARVIRAGUS
Thou hast finish'd joy and moan:
BOTH
All lovers young, all lovers must,
Consign to thee, and come to dust.
GUIDERIUS
No exorciser harm thee!
ARVIRAGUS
Nor no witchcraft charm thee!
GUIDERIUS
Ghost unlaid forbear thee!
ARVIRAGUS
Nothing ill come near thee!
BOTH
Quiet consummation have;
And renowned be thy grave!

Enter BELARIUS *with the body of* CLOTEN.

GUIDERIUS
We have done our obsequies: come, lay him down.
BELARIUS
Here's a few flowers; but 'bout midnight, more:
The herbs that have on them cold dew o'the night
Are strewings fitt'st for graves. — Upon their faces. —
You were as flowers, now wither'd: even so
These herblets shall, which we upon you strow. —
Come on, away: apart upon our knees.
The ground that gave them first has them again:
Their pleasures here are past, so is their pain.

[Exeunt BELARIUS, GUIDERIUS, *and* ARVIRAGUS.

IMOGEN *[awaking]*.
Yes, sir, to Milford-Haven; which is the way? —
I thank you. — By yond bush? — Pray, how far thither?
'Ods pittikins! can it be six mile yet? —
I have gone all night: — faith, I'll lie down and sleep.
But, soft! no bedfellow: — O gods and goddesses!

[Seeing the body of CLOTEN.

These flowers are like the pleasures of the world;
This bloody man, the care on't. — I hope I dream;
For so I thought I was a cave-keeper,
And cook to honest creatures: but 'tis not so;
'Twas but a bolt of nothing, shot at nothing,
Which the brain makes of fumes: our very eyes
Are sometimes like our judgements, blind. Good faith,
I tremble stiff with fear: but if there be
Yet left in heaven as small a drop of pity
As a wren's eye, fear'd gods, a part of it!
The dream's here still: even when I wake, it is
Without me, as within me; not imagin'd, felt.
A headless man! — The garments of Posthumus!
I know the shape of's leg: this is his hand;
His foot Mercurial; his Martial thigh;
The brawns of Hercules: but his Jovial face —
Murder in heaven? — How! — 'Tis gone. — Pisanio,
All curses madded Hecuba gave the Greeks,
And mine to boot, be darted on thee! Thou,
Conspired with that irregulous devil, Cloten,
Hast here cut off my lord. — To write and read
Be henceforth treacherous! — Damn'd Pisanio
Hath with his forged letters, — damn'd Pisanio —
From this most bravest vessel of the world
Struck the main-top! — O Posthumus! alas,
Where is thy head? where's that? Ay me! where's that?
Pisanio might have kill'd thee at the heart,
And left thy head on. — How should this be? Pisanio?
'Tis he and Cloten: malice and lucre in them
Have laid this woe here. O, 'tis pregnant, pregnant!
The drug he gave me, which he said was precious
And cordial to me, have I not found it
Murderous to the senses? That confirms it home:
This is Pisanio's deed and Cloten's: O! —
Give colour to my pale cheek with thy blood,
That we the horrider may seem to those
Which chance to find us: O, my lord, my lord!

[Throws herself on the body.

Enter LUCIUS, CAPTAINS, *and a* SOOTHSAYER.

CAPTAIN
To them the legions garrison'd in Gallia,
After your will, have cross'd the sea; attending
You here at Milford-Haven with your ships:
They are in readiness.
LUCIUS
But what from Rome?
CAPTAIN
The senate hath stirr'd up the confiners
And gentlemen of Italy; most willing spirits,

That promise noble service: and they come
Under the conduct of bold Iachimo,
Sienna's brother.
LUCIUS
When expect you them?
CAPTAIN
With the next benefit o'the wind.
LUCIUS
This forwardness
Makes our hopes fair. Command our present numbers
Be muster'd; bid the captains look to't. — Now, sir,
What have you dream'd of late of this war's purpose?
SOOTHSAYER
Last night the very gods show'd me a vision, —
I fast and pray'd for their intelligence, — thus:
I saw Jove's bird, the Roman eagle, wing'd
From the spongy south to this part of the west,
There vanish'd in the sunbeams: which portends —
Unless my sins abuse my divination —
Success to the Roman host.
LUCIUS
Dream often so,
And never false. — Soft, ho! what trunk is here
Without his top? The ruin speaks that sometime
It was a worthy building. — How! a page!
Or dead, or sleeping on him? But dead, rather;
For nature doth abhor to make his bed
With the defunct, or sleep upon the dead. —
Let's see the boy's face.
CAPTAIN
He's alive, my lord.
LUCIUS
He'll, then, instruct us of this body. — Young one,
Inform us of thy fortunes; for it seems
They crave to be demanded. Who is this
Thou makest thy bloody pillow? Or who was he
That, otherwise than noble nature did,
Hath alter'd that good picture? What's thy interest
In this sad wrack? How came it? Who is it?
What art thou?
IMOGEN
I am nothing; or if not,
Nothing to be were better. This was my master,
A very valiant Briton and a good,
That here by mountaineers lies slain: — alas!
There is no more such masters: I may wander
From east to occident, cry out for service,
Try many, all good, serve truly, never
Find such another master.
LUCIUS
'Lack, good youth!
Thou movest no less with thy complaining than
Thy master in bleeding: say his name, good friend.
IMOGEN
Richard du Champ. — *[aside]* If I do lie, and do
No harm by it, though the gods hear, I hope
They'll pardon it. — Say you, sir?
LUCIUS
Thy name?
IMOGEN
Fidele, sir.
LUCIUS
Thou dost approve thyself the very same:
Thy name well fits thy faith, thy faith thy name.
Wilt take thy chance with me? I will not say
Thou shalt be so well master'd; but, be sure,
No less belov'd. The Roman emperor's letters,
Sent by a consul to me, should not sooner
Than thine own worth prefer thee: go with me.
IMOGEN
I'll follow, sir. But first, an't please the gods,
I'll hide my master from the flies, as deep
As these poor pickaxes can dig: and when
With wild wood-leaves and weeds I ha' strew'd his grave,
And on it said a century of prayers,
Such as I can, twice o'er, I'll weep and sigh;
And leaving so his service, follow you,
So please you entertain me.
LUCIUS
Ay, good youth;
And rather father thee than master thee. —
My friends,
The boy hath taught us manly duties: let us
Find out the prettiest daisied plot we can,
And make him with our pikes and partisans
A grave: come, arm him. — Boy, he is preferr'd
By thee to us; and he shall be interr'd
As soldiers can. Be cheerful; wipe thine eyes:
Some falls are means the happier to arise. *[Exeunt.*

SCENE III

A room in CYMBELINE'S *palace.*

Enter CYMBELINE, LORDS, PISANIO, *and*
ATTENDANTS.

CYMBELINE
Again; and bring me word how 'tis with her.
A fever with the absence of her son;
[Exit an ATTENDANT.
A madness, of which her life's in danger, — Heavens,
How deeply you at once do touch me! Imogen,
The great part of my comfort, gone; my queen
Upon a desperate bed, and in a time
When fearful wars point at me; her son gone,
So needful for this present: it strikes me, past
The hope of comfort. — But for thee, fellow,
Who needs must know of her departure, and
Dost seem so ignorant, we'll enforce it from thee
By a sharp torture.
PISANIO
Sir, my life is yours,
I humbly set it at your will: but, for my mistress,
I nothing know where she remains, why gone,
Nor when she purposes return. Beseech your highness
Hold me your loyal servant.
FIRST LORD
Good my liege,
The day that she was missing he was here:
I dare be bound he's true, and shall perform
All parts of his subjection loyally. For Cloten,
There wants no diligence in seeking him,
And will, no doubt, be found.
CYMBELINE
The time is troublesome. —
[to PISANIO] We'll slip you for a season; but our jealousy
Does yet depend.
FIRST LORD
So please your majesty,
The Roman legions, all from Gallia drawn,
Are landed on your coast; with a supply
Of Roman gentlemen, by the senate sent.
CYMBELINE
Now for the counsel of my son and queen! —
I am amaz'd with matter.
FIRST LORD
Good my liege,
Your preparation can affront no less
Than what you hear of: come more, for more you're ready:
The want is, but to put those powers in motion
That long to move.
CYMBELINE
I thank you. Let's withdraw;
And meet the time as it seeks us. We fear not
What can from Italy annoy us; but
We grieve at chances here. — Away!
[Exeunt all but PISANIO.
PISANIO
I heard no letter from my master since
I wrote him Imogen was slain: 'tis strange:
Nor hear I from my mistress, who did promise
To yield me often tidings; neither know I
What is betid to Cloten; but remain
Perplex'd in all: — the heavens still must work.
Wherein I am false I am honest: not true, to be true:
These present wars shall find I love my country,
Even to the note o' the king, or I'll fall in them.
All other doubts, by time let them be clear'd:
Fortune brings in some boats that are not steer'd. *[Exit.*

SCENE IV

Wales: before the cave of BELARIUS.

Enter BELARIUS, GUIDERIUS, *and* ARVIRAGUS.

GUIDERIUS
The noise is round about us.
BELARIUS
Let us from it.
ARVIRAGUS
What pleasure, sir, find we in life, to lock it
From action and adventure?
GUIDERIUS
Nay, what hope
Have we in hiding us? This way, the Romans
Must or for Britons slay us, or receive us
For barbarous and unnatural revolts
During their use, and slay us after.

BELARIUS

Sons,
We'll higher to the mountains; there secure us.
To the king's party there's no going: newness
Of Cloten's death — we being not known, not muster'd
Among the bands — may drive us to a render
Where we have liv'd; and so extort from's that
Which we have done, whose answer would be death
Drawn on with torture.

GUIDERIUS

This is, sir, a doubt
In such a time nothing becoming you,
Nor satisfying us.

ARVIRAGUS

It is not likely
That when they hear the Roman horses neigh,
Behold their quarter'd fires, have both their eyes
And ears so cloy'd importantly as now,
That they will waste their time upon our note,
To know from whence we are.

BELARIUS

O, I am known
Of many in the army: many years,
Though Cloten then but young, you see, not wore him
From my remembrance. And, besides, the king
Hath not deserv'd my service nor your loves;
Who find in my exile the want of breeding,
The certainty of this hard life; aye hopeless
To have the courtesy your cradle promis'd,
But to be still hot summer's tanlings, and
The shrinking slaves of winter.

GUIDERIUS

Than be so,
Better to cease to be. Pray, sir, to the army:
I and my brother are not known; yourself
So out of thought, and thereto so o'ergrown,
Cannot be question'd.

ARVIRAGUS

By this sun that shines,
I'll thither: what thing is it that I never
Did see man die! scarce ever look'd on blood,
But that of coward hares, hot goats, and venison!
Never bestrid a horse, save one that had
A rider like myself, who ne'er wore rowel
Nor iron on his heel! I am asham'd
To look upon the holy sun, to have
The benefit of his blest beams, remaining
So long a poor unknown.

GUIDERIUS

By heavens, I'll go:
If you will bless me, sir, and give me leave,
I'll take the better care; but if you will not,
The hazard therefore due fall on me by
The hands of Romans!

ARVIRAGUS

So say I, — Amen.

BELARIUS

No reason I, since of your lives you set
So slight a valuation, should reserve
My crack'd one to more care. Have with you, boys!
If in your country wars you chance to die,
That is my bed too, lads, an there I'll lie:
Lead, lead. — [aside] The time seems long; their blood
 thinks scorn,
Till it fly out, and show them princes born. [Exeunt.

ACT V

SCENE I

Britain. The Roman camp.

Enter POSTHUMUS *with a bloody handkerchief.*

POSTHUMUS

Yea, bloody cloth, I'll keep thee; for I wish'd
Thou shouldst be colour'd thus. You married ones,
If each of you should take this course, how many
Must murder wives much better than themselves
For wrying but a little! — O Pisanio!
Every good servant does not all commands:
No bond but to do just ones. — Gods! if you
Should have ta'en vengeance on my faults, I never
Had liv'd to put on this: so had you saved
The noble Imogen to repent; and struck
Me, wretch more worth your vengeance. But, alack,
You snatch some hence for little faults; that's love,
To have them fall no more: you some permit
To second ills with ills, each elder worse,
And make them dread it, to the doers' thrift.
But Imogen is your own: do your best wills,

And make me blest to obey! — I am
 brought hither
Among the Italian gentry, and to fight
Against my lady's kingdom: 'tis enough
That, Britain, I have kill'd thy mistress;
 peace!
I'll give no wound to thee. Therefore,
 good heavens,
Hear patiently my purpose: — I'll
 disrobe me
Of these Italian weeds, and suit myself
As does a Briton peasant: so I'll fight
Against the part I come with; so I'll die
For thee, O Imogen, even for whom my life
Is, every breath, a death: and thus,
 unknown,
Pitied nor hated, to the face of peril
Myself I'll dedicate. Let me make men
 know
More valour in me than my habits show.
Gods, put the strength o'the Leonati in me!
To shame the guise o'the world, I will
 begin
The fashion, — less without and more
within. [Exit.

SCENE II

*A field between the British and
Roman camps.*

Enter LUCIUS, IACHIMO, IMOGEN,
and the ROMAN ARMY *at one door, and
the* BRITON ARMY *at another;*
LEONATUS POSTHUMUS *following, like
a poor soldier. They march over and go out.
Then enter again, in skirmish,* IACHIMO
and POSTHUMUS: *he vanquisheth and
disarmeth* IACHIMO, *and then leaves him.*

IACHIMO

The heaviness and guilt within my bosom
Takes off my manhood: I have belied a lady,
The princess of this country, and the air on't
Revengingly enfeebles me; or could this carl,
A very drudge of nature's, have subdued me
In my profession? Knighthoods and honours, borne
As I wear mine, are titles but of scorn.
If that thy gentry, Britain, go before
This lout as he exceeds our lords, the odds
Is that we scarce are men, and you are gods. [Exit.
The battle continues; the BRITONS *fly;* CYMBELINE *is
taken: then enter, to his rescue,* BELARIUS,
GUIDERIUS, *and* ARVIRAGUS.

BELARIUS

Stand, stand! We have the advantage of the ground;
The lane is guarded: nothing routs us but
The villainy of our fears.

GUIDERIUS and ARVIRAGUS

Stand, stand, and fight!
Enter POSTHUMUS, *and seconds the* BRITONS: *they
rescue* CYMBELINE, *and all exeunt. Then re-enter*
LUCIUS, IACHIMO, *and* IMOGEN.

LUCIUS

Away, boy, from the troops, and save thyself;
For friends kill friends, and the disorder's such
As war were hoodwink'd.

IACHIMO

'Tis their fresh supplies.

LUCIUS

It is a day turn'd strangely: or betimes
Let's re-inforce, or fly. [Exeunt.

SCENE III

Another part of the field.

Enter POSTHUMUS *and a Briton* LORD.

LORD

Camest thou from where they made the stand?

POSTHUMUS

I did:
Though you, it seems, come from the fliers.

LORD

I did.

POSTHUMUS

No blame be to you, sir; for all was lost,
But that the heavens fought: the king himself
Of his wings destitute, the army broken,
And but the backs of Britons seen, all flying
Through a strait lane; the enemy full-hearted,
Lolling the tongue with slaughtering, having work

POSTHUMUS Yea, bloody cloth, I'll keep thee;
 for I wish'd thou shouldst be colour'd thus.

More plentiful than tools to do't, struck down
Some mortally, some slightly touch'd, some falling
Merely through fear; that the strait pass was damm'd
With dead men hurt behind, and cowards living
To die with lengthen'd shame.

LORD

Where was this lane?

POSTHUMUS

Close by the battle, ditch'd, and wall'd with turf;
Which gave advantage to an ancient soldier, —
An honest one, I warrant; who deserved
So long a breeding as his white beard came to,
In doing this for's country: — athwart the lane,
He, with two striplings, — lads more like to run
The country base than to commit such slaughter;
With faces fit for masks, or rather fairer
Than those for preservation cased or shame, —
Made good the passage; cried to those that fled,
'Our Britain's harts die flying, not our men:
To darkness fleet, souls that fly backwards! Stand;
Or we are Romans, and will give you that
Like beasts, which you shun beastly, and may save,
But to look back in frown: stand, stand!' — These three,
Three thousand confident, in act as many, —
For three performers are the file when all
The rest do nothing, — with this word, 'Stand, stand,'
Accommodated by the place, more charming
With their own nobleness, — which could have turn'd
A distaff to a lance, — gilded pale looks,
Part shame, part spirit renew'd; that some, turn'd
 coward
But by example, — O, a sin in war,
Damn'd in the first beginners! — gan to look
The way that they did, and to grin like lions
Upon the pikes o'the hunters. Then began
A stop i'the chaser, a retire; anon
A rout, confusion-thick: forthwith they fly
Chickens, the way which they stoop'd eagles; slaves,
The strides they victors made: and now our cowards, —
Like fragments in hard voyages — became
The life o'the need: having found the back-door open
Of the unguarded hearts, heavens, how they wound!
Some slain before; some dying; some their friends
O'er-borne i'the former wave: ten, chas'd by one,
Are now each one the slaughter-man of twenty:
Those that would die or e're resist are grown
The mortal bugs o'the field.

LORD

This was strange chance, —
A narrow lane, an old man, and two boys!

POSTHUMUS

Nay, do not wonder at it: you are made

Rather to wonder at the things you hear
Than to work any. Will you rime upon't,
And vent it for a mockery? Here is one:
'Two boys, an old man twice a boy, a lane,
Preserv'd the Britons, was the Romans' bane.'

LORD
Nay, be not angry, sir.

POSTHUMUS
        'Lack, to what end?
Who dares not stand his foe, I'll be his friend;
For if he'll do as he is made to do,
I know he'll quickly fly my friendship too.
You have put me into rime.

LORD
        Farewell; you're angry.

POSTHUMUS
Still going?   [Exit LORD.
This is a lord! O noble misery!
To be i' the field, and ask, what news, of me!
To-day how many would have given their honours
To have sav'd their carcasses! took heel to do't,
And yet died too! I, in mine own woe charm'd,
Could not find death where I did hear him groan,
Nor feel him where he struck: being an ugly monster,
'Tis strange he hides him in fresh cups, soft beds,
Sweet words; or hath more ministers than we
That draw his knives i' the war. Well, I will find him:
For being now a favourer to the Briton,
No more a Briton, I have resum'd again
The part I came in: fight I will no more,
But yield me to the veriest hind that shall
Once touch my shoulder. Great the slaughter is
Here made by the Roman; great the answer be
Britons must take: for me, my ransom's death;
On either side I come to spend my breath;
Which neither here I'll keep nor bear agen,
But end it by some means for Imogen.

   Enter two Briton CAPTAINS and SOLDIERS.

FIRST CAPTAIN
Great Jupiter be prais'd! Lucius is taken:
'Tis thought the old man and his sons were angels.

SECOND CAPTAIN
There was a fourth man, in a silly habit,
That gave the affront with them.

FIRST CAPTAIN
        So 'tis reported:
But none of 'em can be found. — Stand! who's there?

POSTHUMUS
A Roman;
Who had not now been drooping here, if seconds
Had answer'd him.

SECOND CAPTAIN
        Lay hands on him; a dog! —
A leg of Rome shall not return to tell
What crows have peck'd them here: — he brags his
   service
As if he were of note: bring him to the king.

   *Enter CYMBELINE, BELARIUS, GUIDERIUS,
ARVIRAGUS, PISANIO, and Roman CAPTIVES. The
CAPTAINS present POSTHUMUS to CYMBELINE,
who delivers him over to a GAOLER: then exeunt omnes.*

SCENE IV

A prison.

   Enter POSTHUMUS and two GAOLERS.

FIRST GAOLER
You shall not now be stol'n, you have locks upon you;
So graze as you find pasture.

SECOND GAOLER
        Ay, or a stomach.
        [Exeunt GAOLERS.

POSTHUMUS
Most welcome, bondage! for thou art a way,
I think, to liberty: yet am I better
Than one that's sick o'the gout; since he had rather
Groan so in perpetuity than be cured
By the sure physician, death; who is the key
T'unbar these locks. My conscience, thou art fetter'd
More than my shanks and wrists: you good gods, give
   me
The penitent instrument to pick that bolt,
Then free for ever! Is't enough I am sorry?
So children temporal fathers do appease;
Gods are more full of mercy. Must I repent?
I cannot do it better than in gyves,
Desired more than constrain'd: to satisfy,
If of my freedom 'tis the main part, take
No stricter render of me than my all.

I know you are more clement than vile men,
Who of their broken debtors take a third,
A sixth, a tenth, letting them thrive again
On their abatement: that's not my desire:
For Imogen's dear life take mine; and though
'Tis not so dear, yet 'tis a life; you coin'd it:
'Tween man and man they weigh not every stamp;
Though light, take pieces for the figure's sake:
You rather mine, being yours: and so, great powers,
If you will take this audit, take this life,
And cancel these cold bonds. — O Imogen!
I'll speak to thee in silence.   [Sleeps.

   *Solemn music. Enter, as in an apparition, SICILIUS
LEONATUS, father to POSTHUMUS, an old man,
attired like a warrior; leading in his hand an ancient
matron, his wife, and mother to POSTHUMUS, with
music before them: then, after other music, follow the two
young LEONATI, brothers to POSTHUMUS, with
wounds as they died in the wars. They circle
POSTHUMUS round, as he lies sleeping.*

SICILIUS
    No more, thou thunder-master, show
      Thy spite on mortal flies:
    With Mars fall out, with Juno chide,
      That thy adulteries
        Rates and revenges.
    Hath my poor boy done aught but well,
      Whose face I never saw?
    I died whilst in the womb he stay'd
      Attending nature's law:
    Whose father then, as men report
      Thou orphans' father art,
    Thou shouldst have been, and shielded him
      From this earth-vexing smart.

MOTHER
    Lucina lent not me her aid,
      But took me in my throes;
    That from me was Posthumus ripp'd,
      Came crying 'mongst his foes,
        A thing of pity!

SICILIUS
    Great nature, like his ancestry,
      Moulded the stuff so fair,
    That he deserv'd the praise o'the world,
      As great Sicilius' heir.

FIRST BROTHER
    When once he was mature for man,
      In Britain where was he
    That could stand up his parallel;
      Or fruitful object be
    In eye of Imogen, that best
      Could deem his dignity?

MOTHER
    With marriage wherefore was he mock'd,
      To be exil'd, and thrown
    From Leonati seat, and cast
      From her his dearest one,
        Sweet Imogen?

SICILIUS
    Why did you suffer Iachimo,
      Slight thing of Italy,
    To taint his nobler heart and brain
      With needless jealousy;
    And to become the geck and scorn
      O'the other's villainy?

SECOND BROTHER
    For this, from stiller seats we came,
      Our parents, and us twain,
    That, striking in our country's cause,
      Fell bravely, and were slain;
    Our fealty and Tenantius' right
      With honour to maintain.

FIRST BROTHER
    Like hardiment Posthumus hath
      To Cymbeline perform'd:
    Then, Jupiter, thou king of gods,
      Why hast thou thus adjourn'd
    The graces for his merits due;
      Being all to dolours turn'd?

SICILIUS
    Thy crystal window ope; look out;
      No longer exercise
    Upon a valiant race thy harsh
      And potent injuries.

MOTHER
    Since, Jupiter, our son is good,
      Take off his miseries.

SICILIUS
    Peep through thy marble mansion; help;
      Or we poor ghosts will cry

    To the shining synod of the rest
      Against thy deity.

BOTH BROTHERS
    Help, Jupiter; or we appeal,
      And from thy justice fly.

   *JUPITER descends in thunder and lightning, sitting
upon an eagle: he throws a thunderbolt. The GHOSTS
fall on their knees.*

JUPITER
    No more, you petty spirits of region low,
      Offend our hearing; hush! How dare you ghosts
    Accuse the thunderer, whose bolt, you know,
      Sky-planted, batters all rebelling coasts?
    Poor shadows of Elysium, hence; and rest
      Upon your never-withering banks of flowers:
    Be not with mortal accidents oppress'd;
      No care of yours it is; you know 'tis ours.
    Whom best I love I cross; to make my gift,
      The more delay'd, delighted. Be content;
    Your low-laid son our godhead will uplift:
      His comforts thrive, his trials well are spent.
    Our Jovial star reign'd at his birth, and in
      Our temple was he married. — Rise, and fade! —
    He shall be lord of lady Imogen,
      And happier much by his affliction made.
    This tablet lay upon his breast; wherein
      Our pleasure his full fortune doth confine:
    And so, away! no further with your din
      Express impatience, lest you stir up mine. —
      Mount, eagle, to my palace crystalline.
                [Ascends.

SICILIUS
He came in thunder; his celestial breath
Was sulphurous to smell: the holy eagle
Stoop'd, as to foot us: his ascension is
More sweet than our blest fields: his royal bird
Prunes the immortal wing, and cloys his beak,
As when his god is pleas'd.

ALL
        Thanks, Jupiter!

SICILIUS
The marble pavement closes, he is enter'd
His radiant roof. — Away! and, to be blest,
Let us with care perform his great behest.
          [The GHOSTS vanish.

POSTHUMUS [waking].
Sleep, thou hast been a grandsire, and begot
A father to me; and thou hast created
A mother and two brothers: but — O scorn! —
Gone! they went hence so soon as they were born:
And so I am awake. — Poor wretches that depend
On greatness' favour dream as I have done;
Wake, and find nothing. — But, alas, I swerve:
Many dream not to find, neither deserve,
And yet are steep'd in favours; so am I,
That have this golden chance, and know not why.
What fairies haunt this ground? A book? O rare one!
Be not, as is our fangled world, a garment
Nobler than that it covers: let thy effects
So follow, to be most unlike our courtiers,
As good as promise.   [Reads.
Whenas a lion's whelp shall, to himself unknown,
without seeking find, and be embraced by a piece of
tender air; and when from a stately cedar shall be
lopp'd branches, which, being dead many years, shall
after revive, be jointed to the old stock, and freshly
grow; then shall Posthumus end his miseries, Britain
be fortunate, and flourish in peace and plenty.
'Tis still a dream; or else such stuff as madmen
Tongue, and brain not: either both, or nothing:
Or senseless speaking, or a speaking such
As sense cannot untie. Be what it is,
The action of my life is like it, which
I'll keep, if but for sympathy.

   Enter FIRST GAOLER.

FIRST GAOLER
Come, sir, are you ready for death?

POSTHUMUS
Over-roasted rather; ready long ago.

FIRST GAOLER
Hanging is the word, sir: if you be ready for that, you
are well cook'd.

POSTHUMUS
So, if I prove a good repast to the spectators, the dish
pays the shot.

FIRST GAOLER
A heavy reckoning for you, sir. But the comfort is, you
shall be call'd to no more payments, fear no more
tavern-bills; which are often the sadness of parting, as

the procuring of mirth: you come in faint for want of meat, depart reeling with too much drink; sorry that you have paid too much, and sorry that you are paid too much; purse and brain both empty, — the brain the heavier for being too light, the purse too light being drawn of heaviness: of this contradiction you shall now be quit. — O, the charity of a penny cord! it sums up thousands in a trice: you have no true debitor and creditor but it; of what's past, is, and to come, the discharge: — your neck, sir, is pen, book, and counters; so the acquittance follows.

POSTHUMUS
I am merrier to die than thou art to live.

FIRST GAOLER
Indeed, sir, he that sleeps feels not the toothache: but a man that were to sleep your sleep, and a hangman to help him to bed, I think he would change places with his officer; for, look you, sir, you know not which way you shall go.

POSTHUMUS
Yes, indeed do I, fellow.

FIRST GAOLER
Your death has eyes in's head, then; I have not seen him so pictured: you must either be directed by some that take upon them to know, or to take upon yourself that which I am sure you do not know; or jump the after-inquiry on your own peril: and how you shall speed in your journey's end, I think you'll never return to tell one.

POSTHUMUS
I tell thee, fellow, there are none want eyes to direct them the way I am going, but such as wink and will not use them.

FIRST GAOLER
What an infinite mock is this, that a man should have the best use of eyes to see the way of blindness! I am sure hanging's the way of winking.

Enter a MESSENGER.

MESSENGER
Knock off his manacles; bring your prisoner to the king.

POSTHUMUS
Thou bring'st good news, — I am call'd to be made free.

FIRST GAOLER
I'll be hang'd, then.

POSTHUMUS
Thou shalt be then freer than a gaoler; no bolts for the dead.

[*Exeunt* POSTHUMUS *and* MESSENGER.

FIRST GAOLER
Unless a man would marry a gallows, and beget young gibbets, I never saw one so prone. Yet, on my conscience, there are verier knaves desire to live, for all he be a Roman: and there be some of them too that die against their wills; so should I, if I were one. I would we were all of one mind, and one mind good; O, there were desolation of gaolers and gallowses! I speak against my present profit; but my wish hath a preferment in't.

[*Exit.*

SCENE V
CYMBELINE'S *tent.*

Enter CYMBELINE, BELARIUS, GUIDERIUS, ARVIRAGUS, PISANIO, LORDS, OFFICERS, *and* ATTENDANTS.

CYMBELINE
Stand by my side, you whom the gods have made
Preservers of my throne. Woe is my heart
That the poor soldier, that so richly fought,
Whose rags sham'd gilded arms, whose naked breast
Stepp'd before targes of proof, cannot be found:
He shall be happy that can find him, if
Our grace can make him so.

BELARIUS
I never saw
Such noble fury in so poor a thing;
Such precious deeds in one that promis'd naught
But beggary and poor looks.

CYMBELINE
No tidings of him?

PISANIO
He hath been search'd among the dead and living,
But no trace of him.

CYMBELINE
To my grief, I am
The heir of his reward; which I will add
To you, the liver, heart, and brain of Britain,

[*To* BELARIUS, GUIDERIUS, *and* ARVIRAGUS.
By whom I grant she lives. 'Tis now the time
To ask of whence you are: — report it.

BELARIUS
Sir,
In Cambria are we born, and gentlemen:
Further to boast were neither true nor modest,
Unless I add we are honest.

CYMBELINE
Bow your knees.
Arise my knights o'the battle; I create you
Companions to our person, and will fit you
With dignities becoming your estates.

Enter CORNELIUS *and* LADIES.
There's business in these faces. — Why so sadly
Greet you our victory? you look like Romans,
And not o'the court of Britain.

CORNELIUS
Hail, great king!
To sour your happiness, I must report
The queen is dead.

CYMBELINE
Who worse than a physician
Would this report become? But I consider
By medicine life may be prolong'd, yet death
Will seize the doctor too. — How ended she?

CORNELIUS
With horror, madly dying, like her life;
Which, being cruel to the world, concluded
Most cruel to herself. What she confess'd
I will report, so please you: these her women
Can trip me, if I err; who with wet cheeks
Were present when she finish'd.

CYMBELINE
Prithee, say.

CORNELIUS
First, she confess'd she never lov'd you; only
Affected greatness got by you, not you:
Married your royalty, was wife to your place;
Abhorr'd your person.

CYMBELINE
She alone knew this;
And, but she spoke it dying, I would not
Believe her lips in opening it. Proceed.

CORNELIUS
Your daughter, whom she bore in hand to love
With such integrity, she did confess
Was as a scorpion to her sight; whose life,
But that her flight prevented it, she had
Ta'en off by poison.

CYMBELINE
O most delicate fiend!
Who is't can read a woman? — Is there more?

CORNELIUS
More, sir, and worse. She did confess she had
For you a mortal mineral; which, being took,
Should by the minute feed on life, and, lingering,
By inches waste you: in which time she purpos'd,
By watching, weeping, tendance, kissing, to
O'ercome you with her show; yes, and in time,
When she had fitted you with her craft, to work
Her son into the adoption of the crown:
But, failing of her end by his strange absence,
Grew shameless-desperate; open'd, in despite
Of heaven and men, her purposes; repented
The evils she hatch'd were not effected; so,
Despairing, died.

CYMBELINE
Heard you all this, her women?

LADIES
We did, so please your highness.

CYMBELINE
Mine eyes
Were not in fault, for she was beautiful;
Mine ears, that heard her flattery; nor my heart,
That thought her like her seeming; it had been vicious
To have mistrusted her: yet, O my daughter!
That it was folly in me, thou mayst say,
And prove it in thy feeling. Heaven mend all!

[*Enter* LUCIUS, IACHIMO, *the* SOOTHSAYER, *and
other Roman* PRISONERS, *guarded;* POSTHUMUS
behind, and IMOGEN.
Thou comest not, Caius, now for tribute; that
The Britons have raz'd out, though with the loss
Of many a bold one; whose kinsmen have made suit
That their good souls may be appeas'd with slaughter
Of you their captives, which ourself have granted:
So think of your estate.

LUCIUS
Consider, sir, the chance of war: the day

Was yours by accident; had it gone with us,
We should not, when the blood was cool, have
threaten'd
Our prisoners with the sword. But since the gods
Will have it thus, that nothing but our lives
May be call'd ransom, let it come: sufficeth
A Roman with a Roman's heart can suffer:
Augustus lives to think on't: and so much
For my peculiar care. This one thing only
I will entreat; my boy, a Briton born,
Let him be ransom'd: never master had
A page so kind, so duteous-diligent,
So tender over his occasions, true,
So feat, so nurse-like: let his virtue join
With my request, which I'll make bold your highness
Cannot deny; he hath done no Briton harm,
Though he have serv'd a Roman: save him, sir,
And spare no blood beside.

CYMBELINE
I have surely seen him:
His favour is familiar to me. —
Boy, thou hast look'd thyself into my grace,
And art mine now. — I know not why, nor wherefore,
To say, 'Live, boy': ne'er thank thy master; live:
And ask of Cymbeline what boon thou wilt,
Fitting my bounty and thy state, I'll give it;
Yea, though thou do demand a prisoner,
The noblest ta'en.

IMOGEN
I humbly thank your highness.

LUCIUS
I do not bid thee beg my life, good lad;
And yet I know thou wilt.

IMOGEN
No, no: alack,
There's other work in hand: I see a thing
Bitter to me as death: your life, good master,
Must shuffle for itself.

LUCIUS
The boy disdains me,
He leaves me, scorns me: briefly die their joys
That place them on the truth of girls and boys. —
Why stands he so perplex'd?

CYMBELINE
What wouldst thou, boy?
I love thee more and more: think more and more
What's best to ask. Know'st him thou look'st on? speak,
Wilt have him live? Is he thy kin? thy friend?

IMOGEN
He is a Roman; no more kin to me
Than I to your highness; who, being born your vassal,
Am something nearer.

CYMBELINE
Wherefore eyest him so?

IMOGEN
I'll tell you, sir, in private, if you please
To give me hearing.

CYMBELINE
Ay, with all my heart,
And lend my best attention. What's thy name?

IMOGEN
Fidele, sir.

CYMBELINE
Thou'rt my good youth, my page;
I'll be thy master: walk with me; speak freely.

[CYMBELINE *and* IMOGEN *converse apart.*

BELARIUS
Is not this boy reviv'd from death?

ARVIRAGUS
One sand another
Not more resembles that sweet rosy lad
Who died, and was Fidele. — What think you?

GUIDERIUS
The same dead thing alive.

BELARIUS
Peace, peace! see further; he eyes us not; forbear;
Creatures may be alike: were't he, I am sure
He would have spoke to us.

GUIDERIUS
But we saw him dead.

BELARIUS
Be silent; let's see further.

PISANIO [*aside*].
It is my mistress:
Since she is living, let the time run on
To good or bad.

[CYMBELINE *and* IMOGEN *come forward.*

CYMBELINE
Come, stand thou by our side;

Make thy demand aloud. — [to IACHIMO] Sir, step
   you forth;
Give answer to this boy, and do it freely;
Or, by our greatness and the grace of it,
Which is our honour, bitter torture shall
Winnow the truth from falsehood. — On, speak to
   him.

IMOGEN
My boon is, that this gentleman may render
Of whom he had this ring.

POSTHUMUS [aside].
                                 What's that to him?

CYMBELINE
That diamond upon your finger, say
How came it yours?

IACHIMO
Thou'lt torture me to leave unspoken that
Which, to be spoke, would torture thee.

CYMBELINE
                                        How! me?

IACHIMO
I am glad to be constrain'd to utter that
Which torments me to conceal. By villainy
I got this ring: 'twas Leonatus' jewel;
Whom thou didst banish; and — which more may
   grieve thee,
As it doth me — a nobler sir ne'er liv'd
'Twixt sky and ground. Wilt thou hear more, my lord?

CYMBELINE
All that belongs to this.

IACHIMO
               That paragon, thy daughter, —
For whom my heart drops blood, and my false spirits
Quail to remember — Give me leave; I faint.

CYMBELINE
My daughter! what of her? Renew thy strength:
I had rather thou shouldst live while nature will
Than die ere I hear more: strive, man, and speak.

IACHIMO
Upon a time, — unhappy was the clock
That struck the hour! — it was in Rome, — accurst
The mansion where! — 'twas at a feast, — O, would
Our viands had been poison'd, or at least
Those which I heav'd to head! — the good Posthumus —
What should I say? he was too good to be
Where ill men were; and was the best of all
Amongst the rarest of good ones — sitting sadly,
Hearing us praise our loves of Italy
For beauty that made barren the swell'd boast
Of him that best could speak; for feature, laming
The shrine of Venus, or straight-pight Minerva,
Postures beyond brief nature; for condition,
A shop of all the qualities that man
Loves woman for; besides, that hook of wiving,
Fairness which strikes the eye, —

CYMBELINE
                              I stand on fire:
Come to the matter.

IACHIMO
                 All too soon I shall,
Unless thou wouldst grieve quickly. — This
   Posthumus,
Most like a noble lord in love, and one
That had a royal lover, took his hint;
And, not dispraising whom we prais'd, — therein
He was as calm as virtue, — he began
His mistress' picture; which by his tongue being made,
And then a mind put in't, either our brags
Were crack'd of kitchen-trulls, or his description
Prov'd us unspeaking sots.

CYMBELINE
                      Nay, nay, to the purpose.

IACHIMO
Your daughter's chastity — there it begins.
He spake of her, as Dian had hot dreams,
And she alone were cold: whereat I, wretch,
Made scruple of his praise; and wager'd with him
Pieces of gold 'gainst this which then he wore
Upon his honour'd finger, to attain
In suit the place of's bed, and win this ring
By hers and mine adultery. He, true knight,
No lesser of her honour confident
Than I did truly find her, stakes this ring;
And would so, had it been a carbuncle
Of Phœbus' wheel; and might so safely, had it
Been all the worth of's car. Away to Britain
Post I in this design: — well may you, sir,
Remember me at court; where I was taught
Of your chaste daughter the wide difference
'Twixt amorous and villainous. Being thus quench'd

Of hope, not longing, mine Italian brain
Gan in your duller Britain operate
Most vilely; for my vantage, excellent:
And, to be brief, my practice so prevail'd,
That I return'd with simular proof enough
To make the noble Leonatus mad,
By wounding his belief in her renown
With tokens thus and thus; averring notes
Of chamber-hanging, pictures, this her bracelet, —
O cunning, how I got it! — nay, some marks
Of secret on her person, that he could not
But think her bond of chastity quite crack'd,
I having ta'en the forfeit. Whereupon —
Methinks, I see him now —

POSTHUMUS [coming forward].
                           Ay, so thou dost,
Italian fiend! — Ay me, most credulous fool,
Egregious murderer, thief, any thing
That's due to all the villains past, in being,
To come! — O, give me cord, or knife, or poison,
Some upright justicer! Thou, king, send out
For torturers ingenious: it is I
That all the abhorred things o' the earth amend
By being worse than they. I am Posthumus,
That kill'd thy daughter: — villain-like, I lie;
That caus'd a lesser villain than myself,
A sacrilegious thief, to do't: — the temple
Of virtue was she; yea, and she herself.
Spit, and throw stones, cast mire upon me, set
The dogs o' the street to bay me: every villain
Be call'd Posthumus Leonatus; and
Be villainy less than 'twas! — O Imogen!
My queen, my life, my wife! O Imogen,
Imogen, Imogen!

IMOGEN
                Peace, my lord; hear hear —

POSTHUMUS
Shall's have a play of this? Thou scornful page,
There lie thy part.   [Striking her: she falls.

PISANIO
                  O, gentlemen, help!
Mine and your mistress! — O, my lord Posthumus!
You ne'er kill'd Imogen till now. — Help, help! —
Mine honour'd lady!

CYMBELINE
                  Does the world go round?

POSTHUMUS
How comes these staggers on me?

PISANIO
                            Wake, my mistress!

CYMBELINE
If this be so, the gods do mean to strike me
To death with mortal joy.

PISANIO
                     How fares my mistress?

IMOGEN
O, get thee from my sight;
Thou gavest me poison: dangerous fellow, hence!
Breathe not where princes are.

CYMBELINE
                           The tune of Imogen!

PISANIO
Lady,
The gods throw stones of sulphur on me, if
That box I gave you was not thought by me
A precious thing; I had it from the queen.

CYMBELINE
New matter still?

IMOGEN
              It poison'd me.

CORNELIUS
                        O gods! —
I left out one thing which the queen confess'd,
Which must approve thee honest: 'If Pisanio
Have,' said she, 'given his mistress that confection
Which I gave him for cordial, she is served
As I would serve a rat.'

CYMBELINE
                     What's this, Cornelius?

CORNELIUS
The queen, sir, very oft importun'd me
To temper poisons for her; still pretending
The satisfaction of her knowledge only
In killing creatures vile, as cats and dogs,
Of no esteem: I, dreading that her purpose
Was of more danger, did compound for her
A certain stuff, which, being ta'en, would cease
The present power of life; but in short time
All offices of nature should again
Do their due functions. — Have you ta'en of it?

IMOGEN
Most like I did, for I was dead.

BELARIUS
                             My boys,
There was our error.

GUIDERIUS
                  This is, sure, Fidele.

IMOGEN
Why did you throw your wedded lady from you?
Think that you are upon a lock; and now
Throw me again.   [Embracing him.

POSTHUMUS
                Hang there like fruit, my soul,
Till the tree die!

CYMBELINE
               How now, my flesh, my child!
What, makest thou me a dullard in this act?
Wilt thou not speak to me?

IMOGEN
                     Your blessing, sir.
                                  [Kneeling.

BELARIUS
Though you did love this youth, I blame ye not;
You had a motive for't.

                    [To GUIDERIUS and ARVIRAGUS.

CYMBELINE
                     My tears that fall
Prove holy water on thee! Imogen,
Thy mother's dead.

IMOGEN
               I am sorry for't, my lord.

CYMBELINE
O, she was naught: and long of her it was
That we meet here so strangely: but her son
Is gone, we know not how nor where.

PISANIO
                                My lord,
Now fear is from me, I'll speak troth. Lord Cloten,
Upon my lady's missing, came to me
With his sword drawn; foam'd at the mouth, and
   swore,
If I discover'd not which way she was gone,
It was my instant death. By accident,
I had a feigned letter of my master's
Then in my pocket; which directed him
To seek her on the mountains near to Milford;
Where, in a frenzy, in my master's garments,
Which he enforc'd from me, away he posts
With unchaste purpose, and with oath to violate
My lady's honour: what became of him
I further know not.

GUIDERIUS
                 Let me end the story:
I slew him there.

CYMBELINE
              Marry, the gods forfend!
I would not thy good deeds should from my lips
Pluck a hard sentence: prithee, valiant youth,
Deny't again.

GUIDERIUS
           I have spoke it, and I did it.

CYMBELINE
He was a prince.

GUIDERIUS
A most incivil one: the wrongs he did me
Were nothing prince-like; for he did provoke me
With language that would make me spurn the sea,
If it could so roar to me: I cut off's head;
And am right glad he is not standing here
To tell this tale of mine.

CYMBELINE
                     I am sorry for thee:
By thine own tongue thou art condemn'd, and must
Endure our law: thou'rt dead.

IMOGEN
                          That headless man
I thought had been my lord.

CYMBELINE
                        Bind the offender,
And take him from our presence.

BELARIUS
                            Stay, sir king:
This man is better than the man he slew,
As well descended as thyself; and hath
More of thee merited than a band of Clotens
Had ever scar for. — [to the GUARD] Let his arms
   alone:
They were not born for bondage.

CYMBELINE Wilt thou undo the worth thou art unpaid for, by tasting of our wrath?

CYMBELINE
       Why, old soldier
Wilt thou undo the worth thou art unpaid for,
By tasting of our wrath? How of descent
As good as we?

ARVIRAGUS
    In that he spake too far.

CYMBELINE
And thou shalt die for't.

BELARIUS
      We will die all three:
But I will prove that two on's are as good
As I have given out him. — My sons, I must,
For mine own part, unfold a dangerous speech,
Though, haply, well for you.

ARVIRAGUS
      Your danger's ours.

GUIDERIUS
And our good his.

BELARIUS
    Have at it, then! —
By leave, — thou hadst, great king, a subject who
Was call'd Belarius.

CYMBELINE
    What of him? he is
A banish'd traitor.

BELARIUS
    He it is that hath
Assum'd this age: indeed, a banish'd man;
I know not how a traitor.

CYMBELINE
    Take him hence:
The whole world shall not save him.

BELARIUS
      Not too hot:
First pay me for the nursing of thy sons;
And let it be confiscate all, so soon
As I have receiv'd it.

CYMBELINE
    Nursing of my sons!

BELARIUS
I am too blunt and saucy: here's my knee:
Ere I arise, I will prefer my sons;
Then spare not the old father. Mighty sir,
These two young gentlemen, that call me father,
And think they are my sons, are none of mine;
They are the issue of your loins, my liege,
And blood of your begetting.

CYMBELINE
    How! my issue!

BELARIUS
So sure as you your father's. I, old Morgan,
Am that Belarius whom you sometime banish'd:
Your pleasure was my mere offence, my punishment
Itself, and all my treason; that I suffer'd

Was all the harm I did. These gentle princes —
For such and so they are — these twenty years
Have I train'd up: those arts they have as I
Could put into them; my breeding was, sir, as
Your highness knows. Their nurse, Euriphile,
Whom for the theft I wedded, stole these children
Upon my banishment: I mov'd her to't;
Having receiv'd the punishment before,
For that which I did then: beaten for loyalty
Excited me to treason: their dear loss,
The more of you 'twas felt, the more it shap'd
Unto my end of stealing them. But, gracious sir,
Here are your sons again; and I must lose
Two of the sweet'st companions in the world.
The benediction of these covering heavens
Fall on their heads like dew! for they are worthy
To inlay heaven with stars.

CYMBELINE
    Thou weep'st, and speak'st.
The service that you three have done is more
Unlike than this thou tell'st. I lost my children:
If these be they, I know not how to wish
A pair of worthier sons.

BELARIUS
    Be pleas'd awhile. —
This gentleman, whom I call Polydore,
Most worthy prince, as yours, is true Guiderius:
This gentleman, my Cadwal, Arviragus,
Your younger princely son: he, sir, was lapp'd
In a most curious mantle, wrought by the hand
Of his queen-mother, which, for more probation,
I can with ease produce.

CYMBELINE
    Guiderius had
Upon his neck a mole, a sanguine star;
It was a mark of wonder.

BELARIUS
    This is he;
Who hath upon him still that natural stamp:
It was wise nature's end in the donation,
To be his evidence now.

CYMBELINE
    O, what, am I
A mother to the birth of three? Ne'er mother
Rejoic'd deliverance more. — Blest pray you be,
That, after this strange starting from your orbs,
You may reign in them now! — O Imogen,
Thou hast lost by this a kingdom.

IMOGEN
    No, my lord;
I have got two worlds by't. — O my gentle brothers,
Have we thus met? O, never say hereafter
But I am truest speaker: you call'd me brother,
When I was but your sister; I you brothers,
When ye were so indeed.

CYMBELINE
    Did you e'er meet?

ARVIRAGUS
Ay, my good lord.

GUIDERIUS
    And at first meeting lov'd;
Continued so, until we thought he died.

CORNELIUS
By the queen's dram she swallow'd.

CYMBELINE
    O rare instinct!
When shall I hear all through? This fierce abridgement
Hath to it circumstantial branches, which
Distinction should be rich in. — Where? how liv'd you?
And when came you to serve our Roman captive?
How parted with your brothers? how first met them?
Why fled you from the court? and whither? These,
And your three motives to the battle, with
I know not how much more, should be demanded;
And all the other by-dependances,
From chance to chance: but nor the time nor place
Will serve our long inter'gatories. See,
Posthumus anchors upon Imogen;
And she, like harmless lightning, throws her eye
On him, her brother, me, her master, hitting
Each object with a joy: the counterchange
Is severally in all. Let's quit this ground,
And smoke the temple with our sacrifices. —
[*to* BELARIUS] Thou art my brother; so we'll hold thee
  ever.

IMOGEN
You are my father too; and did relieve me,
To see this gracious season.

CYMBELINE
    All o'erjoy'd,
Save these in bonds: let them be joyful too,
For they shall taste our comfort.

IMOGEN
    My good master,
I will yet do you service.

LUCIUS
    Happy be you!

CYMBELINE
The forlorn soldier, that so nobly fought,
He would have well becom'd this place, and grac'd
The thankings of a king.

POSTHUMUS
    I am, sir,
The soldier that did company these three
In poor beseeming; 'twas a fitment for
The purpose I then follow'd. — That I was he,
Speak, Iachimo: I had you down, and might
Have made you finish.

IACHIMO
    I am down again: [*Kneeling.*
But now my heavy conscience sinks my knee,
As then your force did. Take that life, beseech you,
Which I so often owe: but your ring first;
And here the bracelet of the truest princess
That ever swore her faith.

POSTHUMUS
    Kneel not to me:
The power that I have on you is to spare you;
The malice towards you to forgive you: live,
And deal with others better.

CYMBELINE
    Nobly doom'd!
We'll learn our freeness of a son-in-law;
Pardon's the word to all.

ARVIRAGUS
    You holp us, sir,
As you did mean indeed to be our brother;
Joy'd are we that you are.

POSTHUMUS
Your servant, princes. — Good my lord of Rome,
Call forth your soothsayer: as I slept, methought
Great Jupiter, upon his eagle back'd,
Appear'd to me, with other spritely shows
Of mine own kindred: when I wak'd, I found
This label on my bosom; whose containing
Is so from sense in hardness, that I can
Make no collection of it: let him show
His skill in the construction.

LUCIUS
    Philarmonus, —

SOOTHSAYER
Here, my good lord.

LUCIUS
    Read, and declare the meaning.

SOOTHSAYER [*reads*].
Whenas a lion's whelp shall, to himself unknown,
without seeking find, and be embraced by a piece of
tender air; and when from a stately cedar shall be
lopp'd branches, which, being dead many years, shall
after revive, be jointed to the old stock, and freshly
grow; then shall Posthumus end his miseries, Britain
be fortunate, and flourish in peace and plenty.
Thou, Leonatus, art the lion's whelp:
The fit and apt construction of thy name,
Being Leo-natus, doth import so much:
[*to* CYMBELINE] The piece of tender air, thy virtuous
    daughter,
Which we call *mollis aer*; and *mollis aer*
We term it *mulier*: [*to* POSTHUMUS] which mulier I
    divine
Is thy most constant wife; who, even now,
Answering the letter of the oracle,
Unknown to you, unsought, were clipp'd about
With this most tender air.

CYMBELINE
                    This hath some seeming.
SOOTHSAYER
The lofty cedar, royal Cymbeline,
Personates thee: and thy lopp'd branches point
Thy two sons forth; who, by Belarius stol'n,
For many years thought dead, are now revived,
To the majestic cedar join'd; whose issue
Promises Britain peace and plenty.
CYMBELINE
                        Well,
My peace we will begin: — and, Caius Lucius,
Although the victor, we submit to Cæsar,
And to the Roman empire; promising
To pay our wonted tribute, from the which
We were dissuaded by our wicked queen;
Whom heavens, in justice, both on her and hers,
Have laid most heavy hand.
SOOTHSAYER
The fingers of the powers above do tune
The harmony of this peace. The vision

Which I made known to Lucius, ere the stroke
Of this yet scarce-cold battle, at this instant
Is full accomplish'd; for the Roman eagle,
From south to west on wing soaring aloft,
Lessen'd herself, and in the beams o'the sun
So vanish'd; which foreshow'd our princely eagle,
Th'imperial Cæsar, should again unite
His favour with the radiant Cymbeline,
Which shines here in the west.
CYMBELINE
                    Laud we the gods;
And let our crooked smokes climb to their nostrils
From our blest altars. Publish we this peace
To all our subjects. Set we forward: let
A Roman and a British ensign wave
Friendly together: so through Lud's-town march:
And in the temple of great Jupiter
Our peace we'll ratify; seal it with feasts. —
Set on there! — Never was a war did cease,
Ere bloody hands were wash'd, with such a peace.
                                        [*Exeunt*.

THE WINTER'S TALE

DRAMATIS PERSONAE

LEONTES, *King of Sicilia.*
MAMILLIUS, *young Prince of Sicilia.*
CAMILLO,
ANTIGONUS, } *four lords of Sicilia.*
CLEOMENES,
DION,
POLIXENES, *King of Bohemia.*
FLORIZEL, *Prince of Bohemia.*
ARCHIDAMUS, *a lord of Bohemia.*

OLD SHEPHERD, *reputed father of Perdita.*
CLOWN, *his son.*
AUTOLYCUS, *a rogue.*
A MARINER.
GAOLER.
HERMIONE, *queen to Leontes.*
PERDITA, *daughter to Leontes and Hermione.*
PAULINA, *wife to Antigonus.*
EMILIA, *a lady attending on Hermione.*

MOPSA,
DORCAS, } *shepherdesses.*

Other LORDS *and* GENTLEMEN, LADIES,
OFFICERS, *and* SERVANTS, SHEPHERDS *and*
SHEPHERDESSES.

TIME, *as* CHORUS.

SCENE — *Sometimes in Sicilia, sometimes in Bohemia.*

CAMILLO Shook hands, as over a vast.

ACT I

SCENE I

Sicilia. Antechamber in LEONTES' *palace.*

Enter CAMILLO *and* ARCHIDAMUS.

ARCHIDAMUS
If you shall chance, Camillo, to visit Bohemia, on the
like occasion whereon my services are now on foot, you
shall see, as I have said, great difference betwixt our
Bohemia and your Sicilia.

CAMILLO
I think, this coming summer, the King of Sicilia means
to pay Bohemia the visitation which he justly owes
him.

ARCHIDAMUS
Wherein our entertainment shall shame us we will be
justified in our loves; for, indeed, —

CAMILLO
Beseech you, —

ARCHIDAMUS
Verily, I speak it in the freedom of my knowledge: we
cannot with such magnificence — in so rare — I know
not what to say. — We will give you sleepy drinks, that
your senses, unintelligent of our insufficience, may,
though they cannot praise us, as little accuse us.

CAMILLO
You pay a great deal too dear for what's given freely.

ARCHIDAMUS
Believe me, I speak as my understanding instructs me,
and as mine honesty puts it to utterance.

CAMILLO
Sicilia cannot show himself over-kind to Bohemia.
They were train'd together in their childhoods; and
there rooted betwixt them such an affection, which
cannot choose but branch now. Since their more
mature dignities and royal necessities made separation
of their society, their encounters, though not personal,
hath been royally attorney'd with interchange of gifts,
letters, loving embassies; that they have seem'd to be
together, though absent; shook hands, as over a vast;
and embraced, as it were, from the ends of opposed

winds. The heavens continue their loves!

ARCHIDAMUS
I think there is not in the world either malice or matter
to alter it. You have an unspeakable comfort of your
young prince Mamillius: it is a gentleman of the
greatest promise that ever came into my note.

CAMILLO
I very well agree with you in the hopes of him: it is a
gallant child; one that, indeed, physics the subject,
makes old hearts fresh: they that went on crutches ere
he was born desire yet their life to see him a man.

ARCHIDAMUS
Would they else be content to die?

CAMILLO
Yes; if there were no other excuse why they should
desire to live.

ARCHIDAMUS
If the king had no son, they would desire to live on
crutches till he had one.   [*Exeunt.*

SCENE II

A room of state in the same.

Enter LEONTES, POLIXENES, HERMIONE,
MAMILLIUS, CAMILLO, *and* ATTENDANTS.

POLIXENES
Nine changes of the watery star hath been
The shepherd's note since we have left our throne
Without a burden: time as long again
Would be fill'd up, my brother, with our thanks;
And yet we should, for perpetuity,
Go hence in debt: and therefore, like a cipher,
Yet standing in rich place, I multiply
With one we-thank-you many thousands more
That go before it.

LEONTES
                    Stay your thanks awhile,
And pay them when you part.

POLIXENES
                    Sir, that's to-morrow.
I am question'd by my fears, of what may chance
Or breed upon our absence: that may blow
No sneaping winds at home, to make us say,

'This is put forth too truly!' Besides, I have stay'd
To tire your royalty.

LEONTES
                    We are tougher, brother,
Than you can put us to't.

POLIXENES
                    No longer stay.

LEONTES
One seven-night longer.

POLIXENES
                    Very sooth, to-morrow.

LEONTES
We'll part the time between's, then: and in that I'll no
gainsaying.

POLIXENES
                    Press me not, beseech you, so.
There is no tongue that moves, none, none i'the world,
So soon as yours, could win me: so it should now,
Were there necessity in your request, although
'Twere needful I denied it. My affairs
Do even drag me homeward: which to hinder,
Were, in your love, a whip to me; my stay,
To you a charge and trouble: to save both,
Farewell, our brother.

LEONTES
                    Tongue-tied, our queen? speak you.

HERMIONE
I had thought, sir, to have held my peace until
You had drawn oaths from him not to stay. You, sir,
Charge him too coldly. Tell him, you are sure
All in Bohemia's well; this satisfaction
The by-gone day proclaim'd: say this to him,
He's beat from his best ward.

LEONTES
                    Well said, Hermione.

HERMIONE
To tell, he longs to see his son, were strong:
But let him say so then, and let him go;
But let him swear so, and he shall not stay,
We'll thwack him hence with distaffs. —
Yet of your royal presence I'll adventure
The borrow of a week. When at Bohemia
You take my lord, I'll give you my commission
To let him there a month behind the gest
Prefix'd for's parting: — yet, good deed, Leontes,
I love thee not a jar o'the clock behind
What lady she her lord. — You'll stay?

POLIXENES
                    No, madam.

HERMIONE
Nay, but you will?

POLIXENES
                    I may not, verily.

HERMIONE
Verily!
You put me off with limber vows; but I,
Though you would seek t'unsphere the stars with
oaths,
Should yet say, 'Sir, no going.' Verily,
You shall not go: a lady's 'verily' is
As potent as a lord's. Will you go yet?
Force me to keep you as a prisoner,
Not like a guest; so you shall pay your fees
When you depart, and save your thanks. How say you?
My prisoner, or my guest? by your dread 'verily,'
One of them you shall be.

POLIXENES
                    Your guest, then, madam:
To be your prisoner should import offending;
Which is for me less easy to commit
Than you to punish.

LEONTES Still virginalling upon his palm?

HERMIONE

Not your gaoler, then,
But your kind hostess. Come, I'll question you
Of my lord's tricks and yours when you were boys:
You were pretty lordings then?

POLIXENES

We were, fair queen,
Two lads that thought there was no more behind
But such a day to-morrow as to-day,
And to be boy eternal.

HERMIONE

Was not my lord the verier wag o'the two?

POLIXENES

We were as twinn'd lambs that did frisk i'the sun
And bleat the one at the other: what we changed
Was innocence for innocence; we knew not
The doctrine of ill-doing, no, nor dream'd
That any did. Had we pursued that life,
And our weak spirits ne'er been higher rear'd
With stronger blood, we should have answer'd heaven
Boldly, 'Not guilty'; the imposition clear'd
Hereditary ours.

HERMIONE

By this we gather
You have tripp'd since.

POLIXENES

O my most sacred lady,
Temptations have since then been born to's; for
In those unfledg'd days was my wife a girl;
Your precious self had then not cross'd the eyes
Of my young playfellow.

HERMIONE

Grace to boot!
Of this make no conclusion, lest you say
Your queen and I are devils: yet, go on;
Th'offences we have made you do, we'll answer;
If you first sinn'd with us, and that with us
You did continue fault, and that you slipp'd not
With any but with us.

LEONTES

Is he won yet?

HERMIONE

He'll stay, my lord.

LEONTES

At my request he would not.
Hermione, my dear'st, thou never spokest
To better purpose.

HERMIONE

Never?

LEONTES

Never, but once.

HERMIONE

What! have I twice said well? when was't before?
I prithee tell me; cram's with praise, and make's
As fat as tame things: one good deed dying tongueless
Slaughters a thousand waiting upon that.
Our praises are our wages: you may ride's
With one soft kiss a thousand furlongs, ere
With spur we heat an acre. But to the goal: —
My last good deed was to entreat his stay:
What was my first? it has an elder sister,
Or I mistake you: O, would her name were Grace!
But once before I spoke to the purpose: when?
Nay, let me have't; I long.

LEONTES

Why, that was when
Three crabbed months had sour'd themselves to death,
Ere I could make thee open thy white hand,
And clap thyself my love: then didst thou utter,
'I am yours for ever.'

HERMIONE

'Tis Grace indeed. —
Why, lo you now, I have spoke to the purpose twice:
The one for ever earn'd a royal husband;
Th'other for some while a friend.

[Giving her hand to POLIXENES.

LEONTES [*aside*].

Too hot, too hot!
To mingle friendship far, is mingling bloods.
I have *tremor cordis* on me, — my heart dances;
But not for joy, — not joy. — This entertainment
May a free face put on; derive a liberty
From heartiness, from bounty's fertile bosom,
And well become the agent;'t may, I grant:
But to be paddling palms and pinching fingers,
As now they are; and making practis'd smiles,
As in a looking-glass; and then to sigh, as 'twere
The mort o'the deer; O, that is entertainment
My bosom likes not, nor my brows! — Mamillius,
Art thou my boy?

MAMILLIUS

Ay, my good lord.

LEONTES

I' fecks!
Why, that's my bawcock. What, hast smutch'd thy
nose? —
They say it is a copy out of mine. Come, captain,
We must be neat; — not neat, but cleanly, captain:
And yet the steer, the heifer, and the calf,
Are all call'd neat. — Still virginalling
Upon his palm? — How now, you wanton calf!
Art thou my calf?

MAMILLIUS

Yes, if you will, my lord.

LEONTES

Thou want'st a rough pash, and the shoots that I have,
To be full like me; — yet they say we are
Almost as like as eggs; women say so,
That will say any thing: but were they false
As o'er-dyed blacks, as wind, as waters, — false
As dice are to be wish'd by one that fixes
No bourn 'twixt his and mine; yet were it true
To say this boy were like me. — Come, sir page,
Look on me with your welkin eye: sweet villain!
Most dear'st! my collop! — Can thy dam? — may't be? —
Affection! thy intention stabs the centre:
Thou dost make possible things not so held,
Communicatest with dreams; — how can this be? —
With what's unreal thou coactive art,
And fellow'st nothing: then 'tis very credent
Thou mayst co-join with something; and thou dost,
And that beyond commission, and I find it, —
And that to the infection of my brains
And hardening of my brows.

POLIXENES

What means Sicilia?

HERMIONE

He something seems unsettled.

POLIXENES

How, my lord!
What cheer? how is't with you, best brother?

HERMIONE

You look
As if you held a brow of much distraction:
Are you moved, my lord?

LEONTES

No, in good earnest. —
How sometimes nature will betray its folly,
Its tenderness, and make itself a pastime
To harder bosoms! — Looking on the lines
Of my boy's face, methoughts I did recoil
Twenty-three years; and saw myself unbreech'd,
In my green velvet coat; my dagger muzzled,
Lest it should bite its master, and so prove,
As ornaments oft do, too dangerous:
How like, methought, I then was to this kernel,
This squash, this gentleman. — Mine honest friend,
Will you take eggs for money?

MAMILLIUS

No, my lord, I'll fight.

LEONTES

You will? why, happy man be's dole? — My brother,
Are you so fond of your young prince as we
Do seem to be of ours?

POLIXENES

If at home, sir,
He's all my exercise, my mirth, my matter:
Now my sworn friend, and then mine enemy;
My parasite, my soldier, statesman, all:
He makes a July's day short as December;
And with his varying childness cures in me
Thoughts that would thick my blood.

LEONTES

So stands this squire
Offic'd with me. We two will walk, my lord,
And leave you to your graver steps. — Hermione,
How thou lovest us, show in our brother's welcome;
Let what is dear in Sicily be cheap:
Next to thyself and my young rover, he's
Apparent to my heart.

HERMIONE

If you would seek us,
We are yours i'the garden: shall's attend you there?

LEONTES

To your own bents dispose you: you'll be found,
Be you beneath the sky. — [*aside*] I am angling now,
Though you perceive me not how I give line.
Go to, go to!
How she holds up the neb, the bill to him!
And arms her with the boldness of a wife
To her allowing husband!

[*Exeunt* POLIXENES, HERMIONE, *and*
ATTENDANTS.
Gone already!
Inch-thick, knee-deep, o'er head and ears a fork'd one!
Go, play, boy, play: thy mother plays, and I
Play too; but so disgraced a part, whose issue
Will hiss me to my grave: contempt and clamour
Will be my knell. — Go, play, boy, play. — There have
been,
Or I am much deceiv'd, cuckolds ere now;
And many a man there is, even at this present,
Now while I speak this, holds his wife by th'arm,
That little thinks she has been sluic'd in's absence,
And his pond fish'd by his next neighbour, by

Sir Smile, his neighbour: nay, there's comfort in't,
Whiles other men have gates, and those gates open'd,
As mine, against their will: should all despair
That have revolted wives, the tenth of mankind
Would hang themselves. Physic for't there's none;
It is a bawdy planet, that will strike
Where 'tis predominant; and 'tis powerful, think it,
From east, west, north, and south: be it concluded,
No barricado for a belly; know't;
It will let in and out the enemy
With bag and baggage: many thousand on's
Have the disease, and feel't not. — How now, boy!

MAMILLIUS
I am like you, they say.

LEONTES
Why, that's some comfort.
What, Camillo there?

CAMILLO
Ay, my good lord.

LEONTES
Go, play, Mamillius; thou'rt an honest man.
[*Exit* MAMILLIUS.
Camillo, this great sir will yet stay longer.

CAMILLO
You had much ado to make his anchor hold:
When you cast out, it still came home.

LEONTES
Didst note it?

CAMILLO
He would not stay at your petitions; made
His business more material.

LEONTES
Didst perceive it? —
[*aside*] They're here with me already; whispering,
    rounding,
'Sicilia is a — so-forth': 'tis far gone,
When I shall gust it last. — How came't, Camillo,
That he did stay?

CAMILLO
At the good queen's entreaty.

LEONTES
At the queen's be't: 'good' should be pertinent;
But, so it is, it is not. Was this taken
By any understanding pate but thine?
For thy conceit is soaking, will draw in
More than the common blocks: — not noted, is't,
But of the finer natures? by some severals
Of head-piece extraordinary? lower messes
Perchance are to this business purblind? say.

CAMILLO
Business, my lord! I think most understand
Bohemia stays here longer.

LEONTES
Ha!

CAMILLO
Stays here longer.

LEONTES
Ay, but why?

CAMILLO
To satisfy your highness, and the entreaties
Of our most gracious mistress.

LEONTES
Satisfy
Th'entreaties of your mistress! — satisfy! —
Let that suffice. I have trusted thee, Camillo,
With all the nearest things to my heart, as well
My chamber-councils; wherein, priest-like, thou
Hast cleans'd my bosom, — I from thee departed
Thy penitent reform'd: but we have been
Deceiv'd in thy integrity, deceiv'd
In that which seems so.

CAMILLO
Be it forbid, my lord!

LEONTES
To bide upon't, — thou art not honest; or,
If thou inclinest that way, thou art a coward,
Which hoxes honesty behind, restraining
From course required; or else thou must be counted
A servant grafted in my serious trust,
And therein negligent; or else a fool
That seest a game play'd home, the rich stake drawn,
And takest it all for jest.

CAMILLO
My gracious lord,
I may be negligent, foolish, and fearful;
In every one of these no man is free,
But that his negligence, his folly, fear,
Among the infinite doings of the world,
Sometime puts forth. In your affairs, my lord,
If ever I were wilful-negligent,

It was my folly; if industriously
I play'd the fool, it was my negligence,
Not weighing well the end; if ever fearful
To do a thing, where I the issue doubted,
Whereof the execution did cry out
Against the non-performance, 'twas a fear
Which oft infects the wisest: these, my lord,
Are such allow'd infirmities that honesty
Is never free of. But, beseech your Grace,
Be plainer with me; let me know my trespass
By its own visage: if I then deny it,
'Tis none of mine.

LEONTES
Ha'not you seen, Camillo, —
But that's past doubt, you have, or your eye-glass
Is thicker than a cuckold's horn, — or heard, —
For, to a vision so apparent, rumour
Cannot be mute, — or thought, — for cogitation
Resides not in that man that does not think, —
My wife is slippery? If thou wilt confess, —
Or else be impudently negative,
To have nor eyes nor ears nor thought, — then say
My wife's a hobby-horse; deserves a name
As rank as any flax-wench that puts-to
Before her troth-plight: say't, and justify't.

CAMILLO
I would not be a stander-by to hear
My sovereign mistress clouded so, without
My present vengeance taken:'shrew my heart,
You never spoke what did become you less
Than this; which to reiterate were sin
As deep as that, though true.

LEONTES
Is whispering nothing?
Is leaning cheek to cheek? is meeting noses?
Kissing with inside lip? stopping the career
Of laughter with a sigh? — a note infallible
Of breaking honesty; — horsing foot on foot?
Skulking in corners? wishing clocks more swift?
Hours, minutes? noon, midnight? and all eyes
Blind with the pin-and-web, but theirs, theirs only,
That would unseen be wicked? is this nothing?
Why, then the world and all that's in't is nothing;
The covering sky is nothing; Bohemia nothing;
My wife is nothing; nor nothing have these nothings,
If this be nothing.

CAMILLO
Good my lord, be cured
Of this diseas'd opinion, and betimes;
For 'tis most dangerous.

LEONTES
Say it be, 'tis true.

CAMILLO
No, no, my lord.

LEONTES
It is; you lie, you lie:
I say thou liest, Camillo, and I hate thee;
Pronounce thee a gross lout, a mindless slave;
Or else a hovering temporiser, that
Canst with thine eyes at once see good and evil,
Inclining to them both; were my wife's liver
Infected as her life, she would not live
The running of one glass.

CAMILLO
Who does infect her?

LEONTES
Why, he that wears her like his medal, hanging
About his neck, Bohemia: who — if I
Had servants true about me, that bare eyes
To see alike mine honour as their profits,
Their own particular thrifts, — they would do that
Which should undo more doing: ay, and thou,
His cupbearer, — whom I from meaner form
Have bench'd, and rear'd to worship; who mayst see
Plainly, as heaven sees earth, and earth sees heaven,
How I am galled, — mightst bespice a cup,
To give mine enemy a lasting wink;
Which draught to me were cordial.

CAMILLO
Sir, my lord,
I could do this, and that with no rash potion,
But with a lingering dram, that should not work
Maliciously like poison: but I cannot
Believe this crack to be in my dread mistress,
So sovereignly being honourable.
I have lov'd thee, —

LEONTES
Make that thy question, and go rot!
Dost think I am so muddy, so unsettled,
To appoint myself in this vexation; sully
The purity and whiteness of my sheets, —

MAMILLIUS I am like you, they say.

Which to preserve is sleep, which being spotted
Is goads, thorns, nettles, tails of wasps;
Give scandal to the blood o'the prince my son, —
Who I do think is mine, and love as mine, —
Without ripe moving to't? Would I do this?
Could man so blench?

CAMILLO
I must believe you, sir:
I do; and will fetch off Bohemia for't;
Provided that, when he's remov'd, your highness
Will take again your queen as yours at first,
Even for your son's sake; and thereby for sealing
The injury of tongues in courts and kingdoms
Known and allied to yours.

LEONTES
Thou dost advise me
Even so as I mine own course have set down:
I'll give no blemish to her honour, none.

CAMILLO
My lord,
Go then; and with a countenance as clear
As friendship wears at feasts, keep with Bohemia
And with your queen. I am his cupbearer:
If from me he have wholesome beverage,
Account me not your servant.

LEONTES
This is all: —
Do't, and thou hast the one half of my heart;
Do't not, thou splitt'st thine own.

CAMILLO
I'll do't, my lord.

LEONTES
I will seem friendly, as thou hast advis'd me. [*Exit.*

CAMILLO
O miserable lady! – But, for me,
What case stand I in? I must be the poisoner
Of good Polixenes: and my ground to do't
Is the obedience to a master; one
Who, in rebellion with himself, will have
All that are his so too. — To do this deed,
Promotion follows: if I could find example
Of thousands that had struck anointed kings,
And flourish'd after, I'ld not do't; but since
Nor brass nor stone nor parchment bears not one,
Let villainy itself forswear't. I must
Forsake the court: to do't, or no, is certain
To me a break-neck. — Happy star reign now!
Here comes Bohemia.

Enter POLIXENES.

POLIXENES
This is strange: methinks
My favour here begins to warp. Not speak? —
Good day, Camillo.

CAMILLO
Hail, most royal sir!

POLIXENES
What is the news i'the court?

CAMILLO
None rare, my lord.

POLIXENES Do you know, and dare not be intelligent to me?

POLIXENES
The king hath on him such a countenance
As he had lost some province, and a region
Lov'd as he loves himself: even now I met him
With customary compliment; when he,
Wafting his eyes to the contrary, and falling
A lip of much contempt, speeds from me; and
So leaves me, to consider what is breeding
That changes thus his manners.

CAMILLO
I dare not know, my lord.

POLIXENES
How! dare not! do not. Do you know, and dare not?
Be intelligent to me: 'tis thereabouts;
For, to yourself, what you do know, you must,
And cannot say you dare not. Good Camillo,
Your chang'd complexions are to me a mirror,
Which shows me mine chang'd too; for I must be
A party in this alteration, finding
Myself thus alter'd with 't.

CAMILLO
                              There is a sickness
Which puts some of us in distemper; but
I cannot name the disease; and it is caught
Of you that yet are well.

POLIXENES
                    How! caught of me!
Make me not sighted like the basilisk:
I have look'd on thousands, who have sped the better
By my regard, but kill'd none so. Camillo, —
As you are certainly a gentleman; thereto
Clerk-like experienc'd, which no less adorns
Our gentry than our parents' noble names,
In whose success we are gentle, — I beseech you,
If you know aught which does behove my knowledge
Thereof to be inform'd, imprison't not
In ignorant concealment.

CAMILLO
                         I may not answer.

POLIXENES
A sickness caught of me, and yet I well!
I must be answer'd. — Dost thou hear, Camillo,
I conjure thee, by all the parts of man
Which honour does acknowledge, — whereof the least
Is not this suit of mine, — that thou declare
What incidency thou dost guess of harm
Is creeping toward me: how far off, how near;
Which way to be prevented, if to be;
If not, how best to bear it.

CAMILLO
                        Sir, I will tell you;
Since I am charg'd in honour, and by him
That I think honourable: therefore mark my counsel,
Which must be even as swiftly follow'd as
I mean to utter it, or both yourself and me
Cry 'lost', and so good night!

POLIXENES
                          On, good Camillo.

CAMILLO
I am appointed him to murder you.

POLIXENES
By whom, Camillo?

CAMILLO
                    By the king.

POLIXENES
                          For what?

CAMILLO
He thinks, nay, with all confidence he swears,
As he had seen't, or been an instrument
To vice you to't, that you have touch'd his queen
Forbiddenly.

POLIXENES
            O, then my best blood turn
To an infected jelly, and my name
Be yok'd with his that did betray the Best!
Turn then my freshest reputation to
A savour that may strike the dullest nostril
Where I arrive, and my approach be shunn'd,
Nay, hated too, worse than the great'st infection
That e'er was heard or read!

CAMILLO
                         Swear his thought over
By each particular star in heaven and
By all their influences, you may as well
Forbid the sea for to obey the moon,
As or by oath remove, or counsel shake
The fabric of his folly, whose foundation
Is pil'd upon his faith, and will continue
The standing of his body.

POLIXENES
                      How should this grow?

CAMILLO
I know not: but I am sure 'tis safer to
Avoid what's grown than question how 'tis born.
If, therefore, you dare trust my honesty,
That lies enclosed in this trunk, which you
Shall bear along impawn'd, — away to-night!
Your followers I will whisper to the business;
And will, by twos and threes, at several posterns,
Clear them o'the city: for myself, I'll put
My fortunes to your service, which are here
By this discovery lost. Be not uncertain;
For, by the honour of my parents, I
Have utter'd truth: which if you seek to prove,
I dare not stand by; nor shall you be safer
Than one condemn'd by the king's own mouth,
    thereon
His execution sworn.

POLIXENES
                    I do believe thee:
I saw his heart in's face. Give me thy
    hand:
Be pilot to me, and thy places shall
Still neighbour mine. My ships are
    ready, and
My people did expect my
    hence-departure
Two days ago. — This jealousy
Is for a precious creature: as she's rare,
Must it be great; and, as his person's
    mighty,
Must it be violent; and as he does
    conceive
He is dishonour'd by a man which ever
Profess'd to him, why, his revenges
    must
In that be made more bitter. Fear
    o'ershades me:
Good expedition be my friend, and
    comfort

The gracious queen, part of his theme, but nothing
Of his ill-ta'en suspicion! Come, Camillo;
I will respect thee as a father, if
Thou bear'st my life off hence: let us avoid.

CAMILLO
It is in mine authority to command
The keys of all the posterns: please your highness
To take the urgent hour: come, sir, away.   [*Exeunt.*

ACT II

SCENE I

Sicilia. LEONTES' *palace.*

Enter HERMIONE, MAMILLIUS, *and* LADIES.

HERMIONE
Take the boy to you: he so troubles me,
'Tis past enduring.

FIRST LADY
                Come, my gracious lord,
Shall I be your playfellow?

MAMILLIUS
                      No, I'll none of you.

FIRST LADY
Why, my sweet lord?

MAMILLIUS
You'll kiss me hard, and speak to me as if
I were a baby still. — I love you better.

SECOND LADY
And why so, my lord?

MAMILLIUS
                  Not for because
Your brows are blacker; yet black brows, they say,
Become some women best, so that there be not
Too much hair there, but in a semicircle,
Or a half-moon made with a pen.

SECOND LADY
                          Who taught ye this?

MAMILLIUS
I learn'd it out of women's faces. — Pray now,
What colour are your eyebrows?

FIRST LADY
                          Blue, my lord.

MAMILLIUS
Nay, that's a mock: I have seen a lady's nose
That has been blue, but not her eyebrows.

FIRST LADY
                                   Hark ye;
The queen your mother rounds apace: we shall
Present our services to a fine new prince
One of these days; and then you'ld wanton with us,
If we would have you.

SECOND LADY
                  She is spread of late
Into a goodly bulk; good time encounter her!

HERMIONE
What wisdom stirs amongst you? Come, sir, now
I am for you again: pray you, sit by us,
And tell's a tale.

MAMILLIUS
              Merry or sad shall't be?

HERMIONE
As merry as you will.

MAMILLIUS
A sad tale's best for winter: I have one

MAMILLIUS A sad tale's best for winter.

Of sprites and goblins.

HERMIONE

Let's have that, good sir.
Come on, sit down: — come on, and do your best
To fright me with your sprites; you're powerful at it.

MAMILLIUS

There was a man, —

HERMIONE

Nay, come, sit down; then on.

MAMILLIUS

Dwelt by a churchyard: — I will tell it softly;
Yond crickets shall not hear it.

HERMIONE

Come on, then,
And give't me in mine ear.

Enter LEONTES, ANTIGONUS, LORDS, *and*
GUARDS.

LEONTES

Was he met there? his train? Camillo with him?

FIRST LORD

Behind the tuft of pines I met them; never
Saw I men scour so on their way: I eyed them
Even to their ships.

LEONTES

How blest am I
In my just censure, in my true opinion! —
Alack, for lesser knowledge! how accurst
In being so blest! — There may be in the cup
A spider steep'd, and one may drink, depart,
And yet partake no venom; for his knowledge
Is not infected: but if one present
Th'abhorr'd ingredient to his eye, make known
How he hath drunk, he cracks his gorge, his sides,
With violent hefts: — I have drunk, and seen the
    spider.
Camillo was his help in this, his pandar: —
There is a plot against my life, my crown;
All's true that is mistrusted: — that false villain,
Whom I employ'd, was pre-employ'd by him:
He has discover'd my design, and I
Remain a pinch'd thing: yea, a very trick
For them to play at will. — How came the posterns
So easily open?

FIRST LORD

By his great authority;
Which often hath no less prevail'd than so,
On your command.

LEONTES

I know't too well. —
Give me the boy: — I am glad you did not nurse him;
Though he does bear some signs of me, yet you
Have too much blood in him.

HERMIONE

What is this? sport?

LEONTES

Bear the boy hence; he shall not come about her;
Away with him! — and let her sport herself
    [*Exit* MAMILLIUS *with some of the* GUARDS.
With that she's big with; — for 'tis Polixenes
Has made thee swell thus.

HERMIONE

But I'd say he had not,
And I'll be sworn you would believe my saying,
Howe'er you lean to the nayward.

LEONTES

You, my lords,
Look on her, mark her well; be but about
To say, 'She is a goodly lady,' and
The justice of your hearts will thereto add,
''Tis pity she's not honest, honourable':
Praise her but for this her without-door form, —
Which, on my faith, deserves high speech, — and
    straight
The shrug, the hum, or ha, — these petty brands
That calumny doth use: — O, I am out,
That mercy does; for calumny will sear
Virtue itself: — these shrugs, these hums and ha's,
When you have said 'she's goodly', come between
Ere you can say 'she's honest': but be't known,
From him that has most cause to grieve it should be,
She's an adultress.

HERMIONE

Should a villain say so,
The most replenish'd villain in the world,
He were as much more villain: you, my lord,
Do but mistake.

LEONTES

You have mistook, my lady,
Polixenes for Leontes: O thou thing!

Which I'll not call a creature of thy place,
Lest barbarism, making me the precedent,
Should a like language use to all degrees,
And mannerly distinguishment leave out
Betwixt the prince and beggar! — I have said
She's an adultress; I have said with whom:
More, she's a traitor; and Camillo is
A feoderary with her; and one that knows,
What she should shame to know herself
But with her most vile principal, that she's
A bed-swerver, even as bad as those
That vulgars give bold'st titles; ay, and privy
To this their late escape.

HERMIONE

No, by my life,
Privy to none of this. How will this grieve you,
When you shall come to clearer knowledge, that
You thus have publish'd me! Gentle my lord,
You scarce can right me throughly then, to say
You did mistake.

LEONTES

No; if I mistake
In those foundations which I build upon,
The centre is not big enough to bear
A schoolboy's top. — Away with her to prison!
He who shall speak for her is afar off guilty
But that he speaks.

HERMIONE

There's some ill planet reigns:
I must be patient till the heavens look
With an aspect more favourable. Good my lords,
I am not prone to weeping, as our sex
Commonly are; the want of which vain dew
Perchance shall dry your pities; but I have
That honourable grief lodg'd here which burns
Worse than tears drown: beseech you all, my lords,
With thoughts so qualified as your charities
Shall best instruct you, measure me; and so
The king's will be perform'd!

LEONTES [*to the* GUARDS].

Shall I be heard?

HERMIONE

Who is't that goes with me? Beseech your highness
My women may be with me; for, you see,
My plight requires it. Do not weep, good fools;
There is no cause: when you shall know your mistress
Has deserv'd prison, then abound in tears
As I come out: this action I now go on
Is for my better grace. Adieu, my lord:
I never wish'd to see you sorry; now
I trust I shall. — My women, come; you have leave.

LEONTES

Go, do our bidding; hence!
    [*Exeunt* HERMIONE *and* LADIES, *with* GUARDS.

FIRST LORD

Beseech your highness, call the queen again.

ANTIGONUS

Be certain what you do, sir, lest your justice
Prove violence; in the which three great ones suffer,
Yourself, your queen, your son.

FIRST LORD

For her, my lord,
I dare my life lay down, and will do't, sir,
Please you t'accept it, that the queen is spotless
I'the eyes of heaven and to you; I mean,
In this which you accuse her.

ANTIGONUS

If it prove
She's otherwise, I'll keep my stables where
I lodge my wife; I'll go in couples with her;
Than when I feel and see her no further trust her;
For every inch of woman in the world,
Ay, every dram of woman's flesh, is false,
If she be.

LEONTES

Hold your peaces.

FIRST LORD

Good my lord, —

ANTIGONUS

It is for you we speak, not for ourselves:
You are abus'd, and by some putter-on,
That will be damn'd for't; would I knew the villain,
I would land-damn him. Be she honour-flaw'd, —
I have three daughters; the eldest is eleven;
The second and the third, nine and some five;
If this prove true, they'll pay for't; by mine honour,
I'll geld 'em all; fourteen they shall not see,
To bring false generations: they are co-heirs;
And I had rather glib myself than they
Should not produce fair issue.

LEONTES

Cease; no more.
You smell this business with a sense as cold
As is a dead man's nose: but I do see't and feel't,
As you feel doing thus; and see withal
The instruments that feel.

ANTIGONUS

If it be so,
We need no grave to bury honesty:
There's not a grain of it the face to sweeten
Of the whole dungy earth.

LEONTES

What! lack I credit?

FIRST LORD

I had rather you did lack than I, my lord,
Upon this ground; and more it would content me
To have her honour true than your suspicion,
Be blam'd for't how you might.

LEONTES

Why, what need we
Commune with you of this, but rather follow
Our forceful instigation? Our prerogative
Calls not your counsels; but our natural goodness
Imparts this: which, if you — or stupefied,
Or seeming so in skill — cannot or will not
Relish a truth, like us, inform yourselves
We need no more of your advice: the matter,
The loss, the gain, the ordering on't, is all
Properly ours.

ANTIGONUS

And I wish, my liege,
You had only in your silent judgement tried it,
Without more overture.

LEONTES

How could that be?
Either thou art most ignorant by age,
Or thou wert born a fool. Camillo's flight,
Added to their familiarity, —
Which was as gross as ever touch'd conjecture,
That lack'd sight only, naught for approbation
But only seeing, all other circumstances
Made up to the deed, — doth push on this proceeding:
Yet, for a greater confirmation, —
For, in an act of this importance 'twere
Most piteous to be wild, — I have dispatch'd in post
To sacred Delphos, to Apollo's temple,
Cleomenes and Dion, whom you know
Of stuff'd sufficiency: now, from the oracle
They will bring all; whose spiritual counsel had,
Shall stop or spur me. Have I done well?

FIRST LORD

Well done, my lord.

LEONTES

Though I am satisfied, and need no more
Than what I know, yet shall the oracle
Give rest to the minds of others; such as he
Whose ignorant credulity will not
Come up to the truth. So have we thought it good
From our free person she should be confined,
Lest that the treachery of the two fled hence
Be left her to perform. Come, follow us;
We are to speak in public; for this business
Will raise us all.

ANTIGONUS [*aside*].

To laughter, as I take it,
If the good truth were known.   [*Exeunt.*

SCENE II

A prison.

Enter PAULINA *and* ATTENDANTS.

PAULINA

The keeper of the prison, — call to him;
Let him have knowledge who I am.
    [*Exit an* ATTENDANT.
Good lady!
No court in Europe is too good for thee;
What dost thou, then, in prison?
    Enter ATTENDANT, *with the* GAOLER.
Now, good sir,
You know me, do you not?

GAOLER

For a worthy lady,
And one who much I honour.

PAULINA

Pray you, then,
Conduct me to the queen.

GAOLER

I may not, madam: to the contrary
I have express commandment.

PAULINA
                Here's ado,
To lock up honesty and honour from
Th'access of gentle visitors! — Is't lawful, pray you,
To see her women? any of them? Emilia?

GAOLER
So please you, madam,
To put apart these your attendants, I
Shall bring Emilia forth.

PAULINA
           I pray now, call her. —
Withdraw yourselves.   [*Exeunt* ATTENDANTS.

GAOLER
         And, madam,
I must be present at your conference.

PAULINA
Well, be't so, prithee.   [*Exit* GAOLER.
Here's such ado to make no stain a stain,
As passes colouring.
      Enter GAOLER, *with* EMILIA.
          Dear gentlewoman,
How fares our gracious lady?

EMILIA
As well as one so great and so forlorn
May hold together: on her frights and griefs, —
Which never tender lady hath borne greater, —
She is something before her time deliver'd.

PAULINA
A boy?

EMILIA
       A daughter; and a goodly babe,
Lusty, and like to live; the queen receives
Much comfort in't; says, 'My poor prisoner,
I am innocent as you.'

PAULINA
         I dare be sworn: —
These dangerous unsafe lunes i'the king, beshrew
   them!
He must be told on't, and he shall: the office
Becomes a woman best; I'll take't upon me:
If I prove honey-mouth'd, let my tongue blister,
And never to my red-look'd anger be
The trumpet any more. — Pray you, Emilia,
Commend my best obedience to the queen:
If she dares trust me with her little babe,
I'll show't the king, and undertake to be
Her advocate to the loud'st. We do not know
How he may soften at the sight o' the child:
The silence often of pure innocence
Persuades, when speaking fails.

EMILIA
         Most worthy madam,
Your honour and your goodness is so evident,
That your free undertaking cannot miss
A thriving issue: there is no lady living
So meet for this great errand. Please your ladyship
To visit the next room, I'll presently
Acquaint the queen of your most noble offer;
Who but to-day hammer'd of this design,
But durst not tempt a minister of honour,
Lest she should be denied.

PAULINA
         Tell her, Emilia,
I'll use that tongue I have: if wit flow from't,
As boldness from my bosom, let't not be doubted
I shall do good.

EMILIA
       Now be you blest for it!
I'll to the queen: please you, come something nearer.

GAOLER
Madam, if't please the queen to send the babe,
I know not what I shall incur to pass it,
Having no warrant.

PAULINA
       You need not fear it, sir:
This child was prisoner to the womb, and is,
By law and process of great nature, thence
Freed and enfranchis'd; not a party to
The anger of the king, nor guilty of,
If any be, the trespass of the queen.

GAOLER
I do believe it.

PAULINA
Do not you fear: upon mine honour, I
Will stand betwixt you and danger.   [*Exeunt.*

SCENE III
LEONTES' *palace.*

Enter LEONTES, ANTIGONUS, LORDS, *and* ATTENDANTS.

LEONTES
Nor night nor day no rest: it is but weakness
To bear the matter thus, — mere weakness. If
The cause were not in being, — part o' the cause,
She, the adultress; for the harlot king
Is quite beyond mine arm, out of the blank
And level of my brain, plot-proof; but she
I can hook to me: — say that she were gone,
Given to the fire, a moiety of my rest
Might come to me again. — Who's there?

FIRST SERVANT [*advancing*].
             My lord?

LEONTES
How does the boy?

FIRST ATTENDANT
        He took good rest to-night;
'Tis hop'd his sickness is discharged.

LEONTES
To see his nobleness!
Conceiving the dishonour of his mother,
He straight declined, drooped, took it deeply,
Fasten'd and fix'd the shame on't in himself,
Threw off his spirit, his appetite, his sleep,
And downright languish'd. – Leave me solely: — go,
See how he fares.   [*Exit* FIRST ATTENDANT.] —
   Fie, fie! no thought of him; —
The very thought of my revenges that way
Recoil upon me: in himself too mighty,
And in his parties, his alliance; let him be,
Until a time may serve: for present vengeance,
Take it on her. Camillo and Polixenes
Laugh at me, make their pastime at my sorrow:
They should not laugh, if I could reach them; nor
Shall she, within my power.

Enter PAULINA, *with a child.*

FIRST LORD
         You must not enter.

PAULINA
Nay, rather, good my lords, be second to me:
Fear you his tyrannous passion more, alas,
Than the queen's life? a gracious innocent soul,
More free than he is jealous.

ANTIGONUS
         That's enough.

SECOND ATTENDANT
Madam, he hath not slept to-night: commanded
None should come at him.

PAULINA
        Not so hot, good sir:
I come to bring him sleep. 'Tis such as you, —
That creep like shadows by him, and do sigh
At each his needless heavings, — such as you
Nourish the cause of his awaking: I
Do come, with words as medicinal as true,
Honest as either, to purge him of that humour
That presses him from sleep.

LEONTES
        What noise there, ho?

PAULINA
No noise, my lord; but needful conference
About some gossips for your highness.

LEONTES
          How! —
Away with that audacious lady! — Antigonus,
I charg'd thee that she should not come about me:
I knew she would.

ANTIGONUS
       I told her so, my lord,
On your displeasure's peril and on mine,
She should not visit you.

LEONTES
       What, canst not rule her?

PAULINA
From all dishonesty he can: in this, —
Unless he take the course that you have done,
Commit me for committing honour, — trust it,
He shall not rule me.

ANTIGONUS
       La you now, you hear:
When she will take the rein, I let her run;
But she'll not stumble.

PAULINA
       Good my liege, I come, —

PAULINA The good queen — hath brought you
      forth a daughter; here 'tis.

And, I beseech you, hear me, who profess
Myself your loyal servant, your physician,
Your most obedient counsellor; yet that dares
Less appear so, in comforting your evils,
Than such as most seem yours: — I say, I come
From your good queen.

LEONTES
         Good queen!

PAULINA
Good queen, my lord, good queen; I say good queen;
And would by combat make her good, so were I
A man, the worst about you.

LEONTES
         Force her hence.

PAULINA
Let him that makes but trifles of his eyes
First hand me: on mine own accord I'll off;
But first I'll do my errand. — The good queen —
For she is good — hath brought you forth a daughter;
Here 'tis; commends it to your blessing.
           [*Laying down the child.*

LEONTES
         Out!
A mankind witch! Hence with her, out o'door, —
A most intelligencing bawd!

PAULINA
        Not so:
I am as ignorant in that as you
In so entitling me; and no less honest
Than you are mad; which is enough, I'll warrant,
As this world goes, to pass for honest.

LEONTES
        Traitors!
Will you not push her out? — Give her the bastard: —
[*to* ANTIGONUS] Thou dotard, thou art woman-tired,
   unroosted
By thy Dame Partlet here: — take up the bastard;
Take't up, I say; give't to thy crone.

PAULINA
        For ever
Unvenerable be thy hands, if thou
Takest up the princess by that forced baseness
Which he has put upon't!

LEONTES
       He dreads his wife.

PAULINA
So I would you did; then 'twere past all doubt
You'ld call your children yours.

LEONTES
       A nest of traitors!

ANTIGONUS
I am none, by this good light.

PAULINA
       Nor I; nor any,

But one, that's here, and that's himself; for he
The sacred honour of himself, his queen's,
His hopeful son's, his babe's, betrays to slander,
Whose sting is sharper than the sword's; and will not —
For, as the case now stands, it is a curse;
He cannot be compell'd to't — once remove
The root of his opinion, which is rotten
As ever oak or stone was sound.

LEONTES
                                        A callet
Of boundless tongue, who late hath beat her husband,
And now baits me! — This brat is none of mine;
It is the issue of Polixenes:
Hence with it, and together with the dam
Commit them to the fire!

PAULINA
                                        It is yours;
And, might we lay the old proverb to your charge,
So like you, 'tis the worse. — Behold, my lords,
Although the print be little, the whole matter
And copy of the father, — eye, nose, lip;
The trick of's frown; his forehead, nay, the valley,
The pretty dimples of his chin and cheek; his smiles;
The very mould and frame of hand, nail, finger: —
And thou, good goddess Nature, which hast made it
So like to him that got it, if thou hast
The ordering of the mind too, 'mongst all colours
No yellow in't, lest she suspect, as he does,
Her children not her husband's!

LEONTES
                                        A gross hag! —
And, losel, thou art worthy to be hang'd,
That wilt not stay her tongue.

ANTIGONUS
                                        Hang all the husbands
That cannot do that feat, you'll leave yourself
Hardly one subject.

LEONTES
                                        Once more, take her hence.

PAULINA
A most unworthy and unnatural lord
Can do no more.

LEONTES
                                        I'll ha' thee burnt.

PAULINA
                                        I care not:
It is an heretic that makes the fire,
Not she which burns in't. I'll not call you tyrant;
But this most cruel usage of your queen —
Not able to produce more accusation
Than your own weak-hing'd fancy — something
        savours
Of tyranny, and will ignoble make you,
Yea, scandalous to the world.

LEONTES
                                        On your allegiance
Out of the chamber with her! Were I a tyrant,
Where were her life? she durst not call me so,
If she did know me one. Away with her!

PAULINA
I pray you do not push me; I'll be gone. —
Look to your babe, my lord; 'tis yours: Jove send her
A better-guiding spirit! — What needs these hands?
You, that are thus so tender o'er his follies,
Will never do him good, not one of you.
So, so: — farewell; we are gone.   [Exit.

LEONTES
Thou, traitor, hast set on thy wife to this. —
My child? away with't! — even thou, that hast
A heart so tender o'er it, take it hence,
And see it instantly consum'd with fire;
Even thou, and none but thou. Take it up straight.
Within this hour bring me word 'tis done,
And by good testimony; or I'll seize thy life,
With what thou else call'st thine. If thou refuse,
And wilt encounter with my wrath, say so;
The bastard-brains with these my proper hands
Shall I dash out. Go, take it to the fire;
For thou sett'st on thy wife.

ANTIGONUS
                                        I did not, sir:
These lords, my noble fellows, if they please,
Can clear me in't.

LORDS
                                        We can: — my royal liege,
He is not guilty of her coming hither.

LEONTES
You're all liars.

FIRST LORD
Beseech your highness, give us better credit:

We have always truly serv'd you; and beseech
So to esteem of us: and on our knees we beg,
As recompense of our dear services
Past and to come, that you do change this purpose,
Which being so horrible, so bloody, must
Lead on to some foul issue: we all kneel.

LEONTES
I am a feather for each wind that blows:
Shall I live on, to see this bastard kneel
And call me father? better burn it now
Than curse it then. But be it; let it live.
It shall not neither. — You, sir, come you hither;
                                        [To ANTIGONUS.
You that have been so tenderly officious
With Lady Margery, your midwife, there,
To save this bastard's life, — for 'tis a bastard,
So sure as this beard's grey, — what will you adventure
To save this brat's life?

ANTIGONUS
                                        Any thing, my lord,
That my ability may undergo,
And nobleness impose: at least, thus much, —
I'll pawn the little blood which I have left
To save the innocent: — any thing possible.

LEONTES
It shall be possible. Swear by this sword
Thou wilt perform my bidding.

ANTIGONUS
                                        I will, my lord.

LEONTES
Mark, and perform it; seest thou? for the fail
Of any point in't shall not only be
Death to thyself, but to thy lewd-tongued wife,
Whom for this time we pardon. We enjoin thee,
As thou art liegeman to us, that thou carry
This female bastard hence; and that thou bear it
To some remote and desert place, quite out
Of our dominions; and that there thou leave it,
Without more mercy, to its own protection
And favour of the climate. As by strange fortune
It came to us, I do in justice charge thee,
On thy soul's peril and thy body's torture,
That thou commend it strangely to some place
Where chance may nurse or end it. Take it up.

ANTIGONUS
I swear to do this, though a present death
Had been more merciful. — Come on, poor babe:
Some powerful spirit instruct the kites and ravens
To be thy nurses! Wolves and bears, they say,
Casting their savageness aside, have done
Like offices of pity. — Sir, be prosperous
In more than this deed does require! —
        and blessing,
Against this cruelty, fight on thy side,
Poor thing, condemn'd to loss!
                                        [Exit with the child.

LEONTES
                                        No, I'll not rear
Another's issue.

                        Enter a SERVANT.

SERVANT
                                        Please your highness, posts
From those you sent to the oracle are
        come
An hour since: Cleomenes and Dion,
Being well arriv'd from Delphos, are both
        landed
Hasting to the court.

FIRST LORD
                                        So please you, sir, their speed
Hath been beyond account.

LEONTES
                                        Twenty-three days
They have been absent: 'tis good speed;
        foretells
The great Apollo suddenly will have
The truth of this appear. Prepare you,
        lords;
Summon a session, that we may
        arraign
Our most disloyal lady; for, as she
        hath
Been publicly accus'd, so shall she
        have
A just and open trial. While she lives,
My heart will be a burden to me. Leave
        me;
And think upon my bidding.   [Exeunt.

ACT III

SCENE I

Sicilia. A street in some town.

Enter CLEOMENES *and* DION.

CLEOMENES
The climate's delicate; the air most sweet;
Fertile the isle; the temple much surpassing
The common praise it bears.

DION
                                        I shall report,
For most it caught me, the celestial habits —
Methinks I so should term them — and the reverence
Of the grave wearers. O, the sacrifice!
How ceremonious, solemn, and unearthly
It was i'the offering!

CLEOMENES
                                        But, of all, the burst
And the ear-deafening voice o'the oracle,
Kin to Jove's thunder, so surpris'd my sense,
That I was nothing.

DION
                                        If the event o'the journey
Prove as successful to the queen, — O, be't so! —
As it has been to us rare, pleasant, speedy,
The time is worth the use on't.

CLEOMENES
                                        Great Apollo
Turn all to the best! These proclamations,
So forcing faults upon Hermione,
I little like.

DION
                                        The violent carriage of it
Will clear or end the business: when the oracle —
Thus by Apollo's great divine seal'd up —
Shall the contents discover, something rare
Even then will rush to knowledge. — Go; fresh horses!
And gracious be the issue!   [Exeunt.

SCENE II

A Court of Justice.

Enter LEONTES, LORDS, *and* OFFICERS.

LEONTES
This sessions — to our great grief, we pronounce —
Even pushes 'gainst our heart; the party tried,
The daughter of a king, our wife, and one

FIRST OFFICER Hermione ... thou art here accused
and arraign'd of high treason.

Of us too much belov'd. Let us be clear'd
Of being tyrannous, since we so openly
Proceed in justice; which shall have due course,
Even to the guilt or the purgation. —
Produce the prisoner.

FIRST OFFICER
It is his highness' pleasure that the queen
Appear in person here in court. Silence!

   HERMIONE *is brought in guarded;* PAULINA *and*
      LADIES *attending.*

LEONTES
Read the indictment.

FIRST OFFICER [*reads*].
Hermione, queen to the worthy Leontes, King of
Sicilia, thou art here accused and arraign'd of high
treason, in committing adultery with Polixenes, king of
Bohemia, and conspiring with Camillo to take away the
life of our sovereign lord the king, thy royal husband:
the pretence whereof being by circumstances partly
laid open, thou, Hermione, contrary to the faith and
allegiance of a true subject, didst counsel and aid them,
for their better safety, to fly away by night.

HERMIONE
Since what I am to say must be but that
Which contradicts my accusation, and
The testimony on my part no other
But what comes from myself, it shall scarce boot me
To say, 'Not guilty': mine integrity
Being counted falsehood, shall, as I express it,
Be so receiv'd. But thus: if powers divine
Behold our human actions, as they do,
I doubt not, then, but innocence shall make
False accusation blush, and tyranny
Tremble at patience. You, my lord, best know,
Who least will seem to do so, my past life
Hath been as continent, as chaste, as true,
As I am now unhappy: which is more
Than history can pattern, though devis'd
And play'd to take spectators; for, behold me, —
A fellow of the royal bed, which owe
A moiety of the throne, a great king's daughter,
The mother to a hopeful prince, — here standing
To prate and talk for life and honour 'fore
Who please to come and hear. For life, I prize it
As I weigh grief, which I would spare: for honour
'Tis a derivative from me to mine,
And only that I stand for. I appeal
To your own conscience, sir, before Polixenes
Came to your court, how I was in your Grace,
How merited to be so; since he came,
With what encounter so uncurrent I
Have strain'd, t'appear thus: if one jot beyond
The bound of honour, or in act or will
That way inclining, harden'd be the hearts
Of all that hear me, and my near'st of kin
Cry 'Fie' upon my grave!

LEONTES
               I ne'er heard yet
That any of these bolder vices wanted
Less impudence to gainsay what they did
Than to perform it first.

HERMIONE
            That's true enough;
Though 'tis a saying, sir, not due to me.

LEONTES
You will not own it.

HERMIONE
           More than mistress of
Which comes to me in name of fault, I must not
At all acknowledge. For Polixenes, —
With whom I am accus'd, — I do confess
I lov'd him, as in honour he required;
With such a kind of love as might become
A lady like me; with a love even such,
So and no other, as yourself commanded:
Which not to have done, I think had been in me
Both disobedience and ingratitude
To you and toward your friend; whose love had spoke,
Even since it could speak, from an infant, freely,
That it was yours. Now, for conspiracy,
I know not how it tastes; though it be dish'd
For me to try how: all I know of it
Is, that Camillo was an honest man;
And why he left your court, the gods themselves,
Wotting no more than I, are ignorant.

LEONTES
You knew of his departure, as you know
What you have underta'en to do in's absence.

HERMIONE
Sir,

HERMIONE I doubt not, then, but innocence shall make false accusation blush.

You speak a language that I understand not:
My life stands in the level of your dreams,
Which I'll lay down.

LEONTES
           Your actions are my dreams;
You had a bastard by Polixenes,
And I but dream'd it: as you were past all shame, —
Those of your fact are so, — so past all truth:
Which to deny concerns more than avails; for as
Thy brat hath been cast out, like to itself,
No father owning it, — which is, indeed,
More criminal in thee than it, — so thou
Shalt feel our justice; in whose easiest passage
Look for no less than death.

HERMIONE
          Sir, spare your threats:
The bug which you would fright me with I seek.
To me can life be no commodity:
The crown and comfort of my life, your favour,
I do give lost; for I do feel it gone,
But know not how it went: my second joy
And first-fruits of my body, from his presence
I am barr'd, like one infectious: my third comfort,
Starr'd most unluckily, is from my breast,
The innocent milk in it most innocent mouth,
Haled out to murder: myself on every post
Proclaim'd a strumpet; with immodest hatred
The child-bed privilege denied, which 'longs
To women of all fashion; lastly, hurried
Here to this place, i' the open air, before
I have got strength of limit. Now, my liege,
Tell me what blessings I have here alive,
That I should fear to die? Therefore, proceed.
But yet hear this; mistake me not: — for life,
I prize it not a straw; but for mine honour,
Which I would free, if I shall be condemn'd
Upon surmises, all proofs sleeping else,
But what your jealousies awake, — I tell you,
'Tis rigour, and not law. — Your honours all,
I do refer me to the oracle:
Apollo be my judge!

FIRST LORD
          This your request
Is altogether just: — therefore, bring forth,
And in Apollo's name, his oracle.

          [*Exeunt certain* OFFICERS.

HERMIONE
The Emperor of Russia was my father:

O, that he were alive, and here beholding
His daughter's trial! that he did but see
The flatness of my misery, — yet with eyes
Of pity, not revenge!

     Enter OFFICERS, *with* CLEOMENES *and* DION.

FIRST OFFICER
You here shall swear upon this sword of justice,
That you, Cleomenes and Dion, have
Been both at Delphos; and from thence have brought
The seal'd-up oracle, by the hand deliver'd
Of great Apollo's priest; and that, since then,
You have not dar'd to break the holy seal,
Nor read the secrets in't.

CLEOMENES *and* DION
          All this we swear.

LEONTES
Break up the seals, and read.

FIRST OFFICER [*reads*].
Hermione is chaste; Polixenes blameless; Camillo a
true subject; Leontes a jealous tyrant; his innocent babe
truly begotten; and the king shall live without an heir, if
that which is lost be not found.

LORDS
Now blessed be the great Apollo!

HERMIONE
            Praised!

LEONTES
Hast thou read truth?

FIRST OFFICER
          Ay, my lord; even so
As it is here set down.

LEONTES
There is no truth at all i' the oracle:
The sessions shall proceed: this is mere falsehood.

      Enter an ATTENDANT *hastily.*

ATTENDANT
My lord the king, the king!

LEONTES
         What is the business?

ATTENDANT
O sir, I shall be hated to report it!
The prince your son, with mere conceit and fear
Of the queen's speed, is gone.

LEONTES
          How! gone!

ATTENDANT

                        Is dead.

LEONTES

Apollo's angry; and the heavens themselves
Do strike at my injustice. [HERMIONE *faints*.]
   How now, there!

PAULINA

This news is mortal to the queen: — look down,
And see what death is doing.

LEONTES

                Take her hence:
Her heart is but o'ercharg'd; she will recover: —
I have too much believ'd mine own suspicion: —
Beseech you, tenderly apply to her
Some remedies for life.

   [*Exeunt* PAULINA *and* LADIES, *with* HERMIONE.
          Apollo, pardon
My great profaneness 'gainst thine oracle!
I'll reconcile me to Polixenes;
New woo my queen; recall the good Camillo,
Whom I proclaim a man of truth, of mercy;
For, being transported by my jealousies
To bloody thoughts and to revenge, I chose
Camillo for the minister, to poison
My friend Polixenes: which had been done,
But that the good mind of Camillo tardied
My swift command, though I with death and with
Reward did threaten and encourage him,
Not doing it and being done: he, most humane,
And fill'd with honour, to my kingly guest
Unclasp'd my practice; quit his fortunes here,
Which you knew great; and to the certain hazard
Of all incertainties himself commended,
No richer than his honour: — how he glisters
Thorough my rust! and how his piety
Does my deeds make the blacker!

           Enter PAULINA.

PAULINA

                Woe, the while!
O, cut my lace, lest my heart, cracking it,
Break too!

FIRST LORD

          What fit is this, good lady?

PAULINA

What studied torments, tyrant, hast for me?
What wheels? racks? fires? what flaying? boiling?
In leads or oils? what old or newer torture
Must I receive, whose every word deserves
To taste of thy most worst? Thy tyranny
Together working with thy jealousies, —
Fancies too weak for boys, too green and idle
For girls of nine, — O, think what they have done,
And then run mad indeed, — stark mad! for all
Thy by-gone fooleries were but spices of it.
That thou betray'dst Polixenes, 'twas nothing, —
That did but show thee, of a fool, inconstant,
And damnable ingrateful, nor was't much,
Thou wouldst have poison'd good Camillo's honour,
To have him kill a king; — poor trespasses,
More monstrous standing by: whereof I reckon
The casting forth to crows thy baby daughter,
To be or none, or little, — though a devil
Would have shed water out of fire ere done't;
Nor is't directly laid to thee, the death
Of the young prince, whose honourable thoughts —
Thoughts high for one so tender — cleft the heart
That could conceive a gross and foolish sire
Blemish'd his gracious dam: this is not, no,
Laid to thy answer: but the last, — O lords,
When I have said, cry 'Woe,' — the queen, the queen,
The sweet'st, dear'st creature's dead; and vengeance for't
Not dropp'd down yet.

FIRST LORD

          The higher powers forbid!

PAULINA

I say she's dead; I'll swear't. If word nor oath
Prevail not, go and see: if you can bring
Tincture or lustre in her lip, her eye,
Heat outwardly or breath within, I'll serve you
As I would do the gods. — But, O thou tyrant!
Do not repent these things; for they are heavier
Than all thy woes can stir: therefore betake thee
To nothing but despair. A thousand knees
Ten thousand years together, naked, fasting,
Upon a barren mountain, and still winter
In storm perpetual, could not move the gods
To look that way thou wert.

LEONTES

             Go on, go on:

Thou canst not speak too much; I have deserved
All tongues to talk their bitterest.

FIRST LORD

              Say no more:
Howe'er the business goes, you have made fault
I' the boldness of your speech.

PAULINA

             I am sorry for't:
All faults I make, when I shall come to know them,
I do repent. Alas! I have show'd too much
The rashness of a woman! he is touch'd
To the noble heart. — What's gone, and what's past help,
Should be past grief: do not receive affliction
At my petition; I beseech you, rather
Let me be punish'd, that have minded you
Of what you should forget. Now, good my liege,
Sir, royal sir, forgive a foolish woman:
The love I bore your queen, — lo, fool again! —
I'll speak of her no more, nor of your children;
I'll not remember you of my own lord,
Who is lost too: take your patience to you,
And I'll say nothing.

LEONTES

          Thou didst speak but well,
When most the truth; which I receive much better
Than to be pitied of thee. Prithee, bring me
To the dead bodies of my queen and son:
One grave shall be for both; upon them shall
The causes of their death appear, unto
Our shame perpetual. Once a day I'll visit
The chapel where they lie; and tears shed there
Shall be my recreation: so long as nature
Will bear up with this exercise, so long
I daily vow to use it. Come, and lead me
To these sorrows.   [*Exeunt*.

SCENE III

Bohemia. A desert country near the sea.

Enter ANTIGONUS *with the child, and a* MARINER.

ANTIGONUS

Thou art perfect, then, our ship hath touch'd upon
The deserts of Bohemia?

MARINER

            Ay, my lord; and fear
We have landed in ill time: the skies look grimly,
And threaten present blusters. In my conscience,
The heavens with that we have in hand are angry,
And frown upon's.

ANTIGONUS

Their sacred wills be done! — Go, get aboard;
Look to thy bark: I'll not be long before
I call upon thee.

MARINER

Make your best haste; and go not
Too far i'the land: 'tis like to be loud weather;
Besides, this place is famous for the creatures
Of prey that keep upon't.

ANTIGONUS

            Go thou away:
I'll follow instantly.

MARINER

           I am glad at heart
To be rid so o'the business.   [*Exit*.

ANTIGONUS

          Come, poor babe: —
I have heard, — but not believ'd, — the spirits o'the dead
May walk again: if such thing be, thy mother
Appear'd to me last night; for ne'er was dream
So like a waking. To me comes a creature,
Sometimes her head on one side, some another;
I never saw a vessel of like sorrow,
So fill'd and so becoming: in pure white robes,
Like very sanctity, she did approach
My cabin where I lay; thrice bow'd before me;
And, gasping to begin some speech, her eyes
Became two spouts: the fury spent, anon
Did this break from her: 'Good Antigonus,
Since fate, against thy better disposition,
Hath made thy person for the thrower-out
Of my poor babe, according to thine oath, —
Places remote enough are in Bohemia, —
There weep, and leave it crying; and, for the babe
Is counted lost for ever, Perdita,
I prithee, call't. For this ungentle business,
Put on thee by my lord, thou ne'er shalt see
Thy wife Paulina more': — and so, with shrieks,
She melted into air. Affrighted much,
I did in time collect myself; and thought

This was so, and no slumber. Dreams are toys:
Yet, for this once, yea, superstitiously,
I will be squared by this. I do believe
Hermione hath suffer'd death; and that
Apollo would, this being indeed the issue
Of King Polixenes, it should here be laid,
Either for life or death, upon the earth
Of its right father. — Blossom, speed thee well!
    [*Laying down the child, with a scroll*.
There lie; and there thy character: there these;
               [*Laying down a bundle*.
Which may, if fortune please, both breed thee, pretty,
And still rest thine. — The storm begins: — poor wretch,
                   [*Thunder*.
That, for thy mother's fault, art thus expos'd
To loss and what may follow! — Weep I cannot,
But my heart bleeds: and most accurst am I
To be by oath enjoin'd to this. — Farewell!
The day frowns more and more: — thou'rt like to have
A lullaby too rough: — I never saw
The heavens so dim by day. — A savage clamour! —
    [*Noise of hunters, dogs, and bears within*.
Well may I get aboard! — This is the chase:
I am gone for ever.   [*Exit, pursued by a bear*.

       Enter an old SHEPHERD.

SHEPHERD

I would there were no age between ten and
three-and-twenty, or that youth would sleep out the
rest; for there is nothing in the between but getting
wenches with child, wronging the ancientry, stealing,
fighting — Hark you now! — Would any but these
boil'd brains of nineteen and two-and-twenty hunt this
weather? They have scared away two of my best sheep,
which I fear the wolf will sooner find than the master:
if any where I have them, 'tis by the sea-side, browzing
of ivy. Good luck, an't be thy will! what have we here?
[*Seeing the child*.] Mercy on's, a barne; a very pretty
barne! A boy or a child, I wonder? A pretty one; a very
pretty one: sure, some scape: though I am not bookish,
yet I can read waiting-gentlewoman in the scape. This
has been some stair-work, some trunk-work, some
behind-door-work: they were warmer that got this than
the poor thing is here. I'll take it up for pity: yet I'll tarry
till my son come; he hallooed but even now. — Whoa,
ho, hoa!

CLOWN [*within*].

Hilloa, loa!

SHEPHERD

What, art so near? If thou'lt see a thing to talk on when
thou art dead and rotten, come hither.

         Enter CLOWN.

What ail'st thou, man?

CLOWN

I have seen two such sights, by sea and by land! — but I
am not to say it is a sea, for it is now the sky: betwixt the
firmament and it you cannot thrust a bodkin's point.

SHEPHERD

Why, boy, how is it?

CLOWN

I would you did but see how it chafes, how it rages, how
it takes up the shore! — but that's not to the point. O,
the most piteous cry of the poor souls! sometimes to
see 'em, and not to see 'em; now the ship boring the
moon with her mainmast, and anon swallow'd with
yest and froth, as you'ld thrust a cork into a hogshead.
And then for the land-service, — to see how the bear
tore out his shoulder-bone; how he cried to me for help,
and said his name was Antigonus, a nobleman: — but
to make an end of the ship, — to see how the sea
flap-dragon'd it: — but, first, how the poor souls roar'd,
and the sea mock'd them; — and how the poor
gentleman roar'd, and the bear mock'd him, both
roaring louder than the sea or weather.

SHEPHERD

Name of mercy, when was this, boy?

CLOWN

Now, now; I have not wink'd since I saw these sights:
the men are not yet cold under water, nor the bear half
dined on the gentleman, — he's at it now.

SHEPHERD

Would I had been by, to have help'd the nobleman!

CLOWN

I would you had been by the ship-side, to have help'd
her: there your charity would have lack'd footing.

SHEPHERD

Heavy matters! heavy matters! but look thee here, boy.
Now bless thyself: thou met'st with things dying, I with
things new-born. Here's a sight for thee; look thee, a
bearing-cloth for a squire's child! look thee here; take
up, take up, boy; open't. So, let's see: it was told me I

should be rich by the fairies; this is some changeling: open't. What's within, boy?

CLOWN
You're a made old man: if the sins of your youth are forgiven you, you're well to live. Gold! all gold!

SHEPHERD
This is fairy gold, boy, and 'twill prove so; up with't, keep it close: home, home, the next way. We are lucky, boy; and to be so still, requires nothing but secrecy. — Let my sheep go: — come, good boy, the next way home.

CLOWN
Go you the next way with your findings. I'll go see if the bear be gone from the gentleman, and how much he hath eaten: they are never curst, but when they are hungry: if there be any of him left, I'll bury it.

SHEPHERD
That's a good deed. If thou mayst discern by that which is left of him what he is, fetch me to the sight of him.

CLOWN
Marry, will I; and you shall help to put him i'the ground.

SHEPHERD
'Tis a lucky day, boy, and we'll do good deeds on't.

[*Exeunt.*

ACT IV

Enter TIME, *the* CHORUS.

TIME
I, — that please some, try all; both joy and terror
Of good and bad; that makes and unfolds error, —
Now take upon me, in the name of Time,
To use my wings. Impute it not a crime
To me or my swift passage, that I slide
O'er sixteen years, and leave the growth untried
Of that wide gap; since it is in my power
To o'erthrow law, and in one self-born hour
To plant and o'erwhelm custom. Let me pass
The same I am, ere ancient'st order was,
Or what is now receiv'd: I witness to
The times that brought them in; so shall I do
To the freshest things now reigning, and make stale
The glistering of this present, as my tale
Now seems to it. Your patience this allowing,
I turn my glass, and give my scene such growing
As you had slept between. Leontes leaving,
The effects of his fond jealousies so grieving
That he shuts up himself, — imagine me,
Gentle spectators, that I now may be
In fair Bohemia; and remember well,
I mention'd a son o'the king's, which Florizel
I now name to you; and with speed so pace
To speak of Perdita, now grown in grace
Equal with wond'ring: what of her ensues,
I list not prophesy; but let Time's news
Be known when 'tis brought forth: — a shepherd's daughter,
And what to her adheres, which follows after,
Is the argument of Time. Of this allow,
If ever you have spent time worse ere now;
If never, yet that Time himself doth say
He wishes earnestly you never may.   [*Exit.*

SCENE I

Bohemia. POLIXENES' *palace.*

Enter POLIXENES *and* CAMILLO.

POLIXENES
I pray thee, good Camillo, be no more importunate: 'tis a sickness denying thee any thing; a death to grant this.

CAMILLO
It is fifteen years since I saw my country: though I have, for the most part, been air'd abroad, I desire to lay my bones there. Besides, the penitent king, my master, hath sent for me; to whose feeling sorrows I might be some allay, or I o'erween to think so, — which is another spur to my departure.

POLIXENES
As thou lovest me, Camillo, wipe not out the rest of thy services by leaving me now: the need I have of thee, thine own goodness hath made; better not to have had thee than thus to want thee: thou, having made me businesses which none without thee can sufficiently manage, must either stay to execute them thyself, or take away with thee the very services thou hast done; which if I have not enough consider'd, — as too much I cannot, — to be more thankful to thee shall be my study; and my profit therein, the heaping friendships. Of that fatal country Sicilia, prithee speak no more; whose very naming punishes me with the remembrance of that penitent, as thou call'st him, and reconciled king, my brother; whose loss of his most precious queen and children are even now to be afresh lamented. Say to me, when saw'st thou the Prince Florizel, my son? Kings are no less unhappy, their issue not being gracious, than they are in losing them when they have approved their virtues.

CAMILLO
Sir, it is three days since I saw the prince. What his happier affairs may be, are to me unknown: but I have missingly noted, he is of late much retired from court, and is less frequent to his princely exercises than formerly he hath appear'd.

POLIXENES
I have consider'd so much, Camillo, and with some care; so far, that I have eyes under my service which look upon his removedness; from whom I have this intelligence: — that he is seldom from the house of a most homely shepherd; a man, they say, that from very nothing, and beyond the imagination of his neighbours, is grown into an unspeakable estate.

CAMILLO
I have heard, sir, of such a man, who hath a daughter of most rare note: the report of her is extended more than can be thought to begin from such a cottage.

POLIXENES
That's likewise part of my intelligence; but I fear the angle that plucks our son thither. Thou shalt accompany us to the place; where we will, not appearing what we are, have some question with the shepherd; from whose simplicity I think it not uneasy to get the cause of my son's resort thither. Prithee, be my present partner in this business, and lay aside the thoughts of Sicilia.

CAMILLO
I willingly obey your command.

POLIXENES
My best Camillo! — We must disguise ourselves.

[*Exeunt.*

SCENE II

A road near the SHEPHERD'S *cottage.*

Enter AUTOLYCUS, *singing.*

When daffodils begin to peer,
  With hey! the doxy over the dale,
Why, then comes in the sweet o' the year;
  For the red blood reigns in the winter's pale.

The white sheet bleaching on the hedge,
  With hey! the sweet birds, O, how they sing!
Doth set my pugging tooth on edge;
  For a quart of ale is a dish for a king.

The lark, that tirra-lirra chants,
  With hey! with hey! the thrush and the jay,
Are summer songs for me and my aunts,
  While we lie tumbling in the hay.

I have served Prince Florizel, and, in my time, wore three-pile; but now I am out of service:

But shall I go mourn for that, my dear?
  The pale moon shines by night:
And when I wander here and there,
  I then do most go right.

If tinkers may have leave to live,
  And bear the sow-skin budget,
Then my account I well may give,
  And in the stocks avouch it.

My traffic is sheets; when the kite builds, look to lesser linen. My father named me Autolycus; who being, as I am, litter'd under Mercury, was likewise a snapper-up of unconsider'd trifles. With die and drab I purchased this caparison; and my revenue is the silly cheat: gallows and knock are too powerful on the highway; beating and hanging are terrors to me; for the life to come, I sleep out the thought of it. — A prize! a prize!

Enter CLOWN.

CLOWN
Let me see: — every 'leven wether tods; every tod yields pound and odd shilling: fifteen hundred shorn, what comes the wool to?

AUTOLYCUS [*aside*].
If the springe hold, the cock's mine.

CLOWN
I cannot do't without counters. — Let me see; what am I to buy for our sheep-shearing feast? Three pound of sugar; five pound of currants; rice — what will this sister of mine do with rice? But my father hath made her mistress of the feast, and she lays it on. She hath made me four-and-twenty nosegays for the shearers, — three-man songmen all, and very good ones; but they are most of them means and bases; but one puritan amongst them, and he sings psalms to hornpipes. I must have saffron, to colour the warden-pies; mace; dates, — none, that's out of my note; nutmegs, seven; a race or two of ginger, — but that I may beg; four pound of prunes, and as many of raisins o'the sun.

AUTOLYCUS
O, that ever I was born!   [*Grovelling on the ground.*

CLOWN
I' the name of me, —

AUTOLYCUS
O, help me, help me! pluck but off these rags; and then, death, death!

CLOWN
Alack, poor soul! thou hast need of more rags to lay on thee, rather than have these off.

AUTOLYCUS
O sir, the loathsomeness of them offends me more than the stripes I have received, which are mighty ones and millions.

CLOWN
Alas, poor man! a million of beating may come to a great master.

AUTOLYCUS
I am robb'd, sir, and beaten; my money and apparel ta'en from me, and these detestable things put upon me.

CLOWN
What, by a horseman or a footman?

POLIXENES Say to me, when saw'st thou the Prince Florizel, my son?

AUTOLYCUS Now I am out of service.

AUTOLYCUS
A footman, sweet sir, a footman.

CLOWN
Indeed, he should be a footman by the garments he has
left with thee: if this be a horseman's coat, it hath seen
very hot service. Lend me thy hand, I'll help thee: come,
lend me thy hand.   [*Helping him up.*

AUTOLYCUS
O, good sir, tenderly, O!

CLOWN
Alas, poor soul!

AUTOLYCUS
O, good sir, softly, good sir! I fear, sir, my shoulder-blade
is out.

CLOWN
How now! canst stand?

AUTOLYCUS
Softly, dear sir [*picks his pocket*]; good sir, softly. You
ha'done me a charitable office.

CLOWN
Dost lack any money? I have a little money for thee.

AUTOLYCUS
No, good sweet sir; no, I beseech you, sir: I have a
kinsman not past three quarters of a mile hence, unto
whom I was going; I shall there have money, or any
thing I want: offer me no money, I pray you, — that
kills my heart.

CLOWN
What manner of fellow was he that robb'd you?

AUTOLYCUS
A fellow, sir, that I have known to go about with
troll-my-dames: I knew him once a servant of the
prince: I cannot tell, good sir, for which of his virtues it
was, but he was certainly whipp'd out of the court.

CLOWN
His vices, you would say; there's no virtue whipp'd out
of the court: they cherish it, to make it stay there; and
yet it will no more but abide.

AUTOLYCUS
Vices, I would say, sir. I know this man well: he hath
been since an ape-bearer; then a process-server, — a
bailiff; then he compass'd a motion of the Prodigal
Son, and married a tinker's wife within a mile where
my land and living lies; and, having flown over many
knavish professions, he settled only in rogue: some call
him Autolycus.

CLOWN
Out upon him! prig, for my life, prig: he haunts wakes,
fairs, and bear-baitings.

AUTOLYCUS
Very true, sir; he, sir, he; that's the rogue that put me
into this apparel.

CLOWN
Not a more cowardly rogue in all Bohemia; if you had

but look'd big and spit at him, he'ld have run.

AUTOLYCUS
I must confess to you, sir, I am no fighter; I am false of
heart that way; and that he knew, I warrant him.

CLOWN
How do you now?

AUTOLYCUS
Sweet sir, much better than I was; I can stand and walk:
I will even take my leave of you, and pace softly towards
my kinsman's.

CLOWN
Shall I bring thee on the way?

AUTOLYCUS
No, good-faced sir: no, sweet sir.

CLOWN
Then fare thee well: I must go buy spices for our
sheep-shearing.

AUTOLYCUS
Prosper you, sweet sir! [*Exit* CLOWN.] Your purse is
not hot enough to purchase your spice. I'll be with you
at your sheep-shearing too: if I make not this cheat
bring out another, and the shearers prove sheep, let me
be unroll'd, and my name put in the book of virtue!
                                                      [*Sings.*

    Jog on, jog on, the footpath way,
        And merrily hent the stile-a:
    A merry heart goes all the day,
        Your sad tires in a mile-a.   [*Exit.*

SCENE III

Before the SHEPHERD'S *cottage.*

Enter FLORIZEL *and* PERDITA.

FLORIZEL
These your unusual weeds to each part of you
Do give a life: no shepherdess; but Flora
Peering in April's front. This your sheep-shearing
Is as a meeting of the petty gods,
And you the queen on't.

PERDITA
                                    Sir, my gracious lord,
To chide at your extremes, it not becomes me, —
O, pardon that I name them! — your high self,
The gracious mark o'the land, you have obscured
With a swain's wearing; and me, poor lowly maid,
Most goddess-like prank'd up: but that our feasts
In every mess have folly, and the feeders
Digest it with a custom, I should blush
To see you so attired; sworn, I think,
To show myself a glass.

FLORIZEL
                                    I bless the time
When my good falcon made her flight across
Thy father's ground.

PERDITA
                                Now Jove afford you cause!
To me the difference forges dread; your greatness
Hath not been used to fear. Even now I tremble
To think your father, by some accident,
Should pass this way, as you did: O, the Fates!
How would he look, to see his work, so noble,
Vilely bound up? What would he say? Or how
Should I, in these my borrow'd flaunts,
    behold
The sternness of his presence?

FLORIZEL
                                        Apprehend
Nothing but jollity. The gods themselves,
Humbling their deities to love, have taken
The shapes of beasts upon them: Jupiter
Became a bull, and bellow'd; the green
    Neptune
A ram, and bleated; and the fire-rob'd god,
Golden Apollo, a poor humble swain,
As I seem now: — their transformations
Were never for a piece of beauty rarer, —
Nor in a way so chaste, since my desires
Run not before mine honour, nor my lusts
Burn hotter than my faith.

PERDITA
                                    O, but, sir,
Your resolution cannot hold, when 'tis
Opposed, as it must be, by the power of the
    king:
One of these two must be necessities.
Which then will speak, — that you must
    change this purpose,
Or I my life.

FLORIZEL
                    Thou dearest Perdita,

With these forc'd thoughts, I prithee, darken not
The mirth o'the feast: or I'll be thine, my fair,
Or not my father's; For I cannot be
Mine own, nor any thing to any, if
I be not thine: to this I am most constant,
Though destiny say no. Be merry, gentle;
Strangle such thoughts as these with any thing
That you behold the while. Your guests are coming:
Lift up your countenance, as it were the day
Of celebration of that nuptial which
We two have sworn shall come.

PERDITA
                                        O Lady Fortune,
Stand you auspicious!

FLORIZEL
                                See, your guests approach:
Address yourself to entertain them sprightly,
And let's be red with mirth.

Enter SHEPHERD, *with* POLIXENES *and* CAMILLO
disguised; CLOWN, MOPSA, DORCAS, *and other*
SHEPHERDS *and* SHEPHERDESSES.

SHEPHERD
Fie, daughter! when my old wife liv'd, upon
This day she was both pantler, butler, cook;
Both dame and servant; welcom'd all; serv'd all;
Would sing her song and dance her turn; now here,
At upper end o'the table, now i'the middle;
On his shoulder, and his; her face o'fire
With labour, and the thing she took to quench it,
She would to each one sip. You are retired,
As if you were a feasted one, and not
The hostess of the meeting: pray you, bid
These unknown friends to's welcome; for it is
A way to make us better friends, more known.
Come, quench your blushes, and present yourself
That which you are, mistress o'the feast: come on,
And bid us welcome to your sheep-shearing,
As your good flock shall prosper.

PERDITA [*to* POLIXENES].
                                        Sir, welcome: —
It is my father's will I should take on me
The hostess-ship o'the day. — [*to* CAMILLO]
    You're welcome, sir. —
Give me those flowers there, Dorcas. — Reverend sirs,
For you there's rosemary and rue; these keep
Seeming and savour all the winter long:
Grace and remembrance be to you both,
And welcome to our shearing!

POLIXENES
                                    Shepherdess, —
A fair one are you, — well you fit our ages
With flowers of winter.

PERDITA
                            Sir, the year growing ancient, —
Not yet on summer's death, nor on the birth
Of trembling winter, — the fairest flowers o'the season
Are our carnations, and streak'd gillyvors,
Which some call nature's bastards: of that kind
Our rustic garden's barren; and I care not
To get slips of them.

POLIXENES
                        Wherefore, gentle maiden,

AUTOLYCUS O, good sir, tenderly, O!

PERDITA For you there's rosemary and rue; ... grace and remembrance be to you both.

Do you neglect them?

PERDITA
                For I have heard it said,
There is an art which, in their piedness, shares
With great creating nature.

POLIXENES
                Say there be;
Yet nature is made better by no mean,
But nature makes that mean: so, over that art
Which you say adds to nature, is an art
That nature makes. You see, sweet maid, we marry
A gentler scion to the wildest stock,
And make conceive a bark of baser kind
By bud of nobler race: this is an art
Which does mend nature, — change it rather; but
The art itself is nature.

PERDITA
                So it is.

POLIXENES
Then make your garden rich in gillyvors,
And do not call them bastards.

PERDITA
                I'll not put
The dibble in earth to set one slip of them;
No more than, were I painted, I would wish
This youth should say, 'twere well, and only therefore
Desire to breed by me. — Here's flowers for you;
Hot lavender, mints, savory, marjoram;
The marigold, that goes to bed wi the sun,
And with him rises weeping: these are flowers
Of middle summer, and, I think, they are given
To men of middle age. Y're very welcome.

CAMILLO
I should leave grazing, were I of your flock,
And only live by gazing.

PERDITA
                Out, alas!
You'd be so lean, that blasts of January
Would blow you through and through. — Now, my
    fair'st friend,
I would I had some flowers o'the spring that might
Become your time of day; — and yours, and yours,
That wear upon your virgin branches yet
Your maidenheads growing: — O Proserpina,
For the flowers now, that, frighted, thou lett'st fall
From Dis's wagon! daffodils,
That come before the swallow dares, and take

The winds of March with beauty; violets dim,
But sweeter than the lids of Juno's eyes
Or Cytherea's breath; pale primroses,
That die unmarried, ere they can behold
Bright Phœbus in his strength, — a malady
Most incident to maids; bold oxlips and
The crown-imperial; lilies of all kinds,
The flower-de-luce being one! O, these I lack,
To make you garlands of; and my sweet friend,
To strew him o'er and o'er!

FLORIZEL
                What, like a corse?

PERDITA
No, like a bank for love to lie and play on;
Not like a corse; or if, — not to be buried,
But quick, and in mine arms. — Come, take your
    flowers:
Methinks I play as I have seen them do
In Whitsun pastorals: sure, this robe of mine
Does change my disposition.

FLORIZEL
                What you do
Still betters what is done. When you speak, sweet,
I'd have you do it ever: when you sing,
I'd have you buy and sell so; so give alms;
Pray so; and, for the ord'ring your affairs,
To sing them too: when you do dance, I wish you
A wave o'the sea, that you might ever do
Nothing but that; move still, still so,
And own no other function: each your doing,
So singular in each particular,
Crowns what you are doing in the present deeds,
That all your acts are queens.

PERDITA
                O Doricles,
Your praises are too large: but that your youth,
And the true blood which peeps fairly through't,
Do plainly give you out an unstain'd shepherd,
With wisdom I might fear, my Doricles,
You woo'd me the false way.

FLORIZEL
                I think you have
As little skill to fear as I have purpose
To put you to't. — But, come; our dance, I pray:
Your hand, my Perdita: so turtles pair,
That never mean to part.

PERDITA
                I'll swear for 'em.

POLIXENES
This is the prettiest low-born lass that ever
Ran on the green-sward: nothing she does or seems
But smacks of something greater than herself,
Too noble for this place.

CAMILLO
                He tells her something
That makes her blood look out: good sooth, she is
The queen of curds and cream.

CLOWN
                Come on, strike up!

DORCAS
Mopsa must be your mistress: marry, garlic,
To mend her kissing with!

MOPSA
                Now, in good time!

CLOWN
Not a word, a word; we stand upon our manners. —
Come, strike up!
    [*Music. Here a dance of Shepherds and Shepherdesses.*

POLIXENES
Pray, good shepherd, what fair swain is this
Which dances with your daughter?

SHEPHERD
They call him Doricles; and boasts himself
To have a worthy feeding: I but have it
Upon his own report, and I believe it;
He looks like sooth. He says he loves my daughter:
I think so too; for never gaz'd the moon
Upon the water, as he'll stand, and read,
As 'twere, my daughter's eyes: and, to be plain,
I think there is not half a kiss to choose
Who loves another best.

POLIXENES
                She dances featly.

SHEPHERD
So she does any thing; though I report it,
That should be silent: if young Doricles
Do light upon her, she shall bring him that
Which he not dreams of.

          Enter a SERVANT.

SERVANT
O master, if you did but hear the pedlar at the door, you
would never dance again after a tabor and pipe; no, the
bagpipe could not move you: he sings several tunes
faster than you'll tell money; he utters them as he had
eaten ballads, and all men's ears grew to his tunes.

CLOWN
He could never come better; he shall come in: I love a
ballad but even too well, if it be doleful matter merrily
set down, or a very pleasant thing indeed and sung
lamentably.

SERVANT
He hath songs for man or woman, of all sizes, — no
milliner can so fit his customers with gloves: he has the
prettiest love-songs for maids; so without bawdry,
which is strange; with such delicate burdens of 'dildos'
and 'fadings', 'jump her and thump her'; and where
some stretch-mouth'd rascal would, as it were, mean
mischief, and break a foul jape into the matter, he
makes the maid to answer, 'Whoop, do me no harm,
good man'; puts him off, slights him, with 'Whoop, do
me no harm, good man.'

POLIXENES
This is a brave fellow.

CLOWN
Believe me, thou talkest of an admirable-conceited
fellow. Has he any unbraided wares?

SERVANT
He hath ribands of all the colours i'the rainbow; points
more than all the lawyers in Bohemia can learnedly
handle, though they come to him by the gross; inkles,
caddisses, cambrics, lawns: why, he sings 'em over, as
they were gods or goddesses; you would think a smock
were a she-angel, he so chants to the sleeve-hand, and
the work about the square on't.

CLOWN
Prithee, bring him in; and let him approach singing.

PERDITA
Forewarn him that he use no scurrilous words in's
tunes.   [*Exit* SERVANT.

CLOWN
You have of these pedlars, that have more in them than
you'd think, sister.

PERDITA
Ay, good brother, or go about to think.

Enter AUTOLYCUS, *singing*.
Lawn as white as driven snow;
Cyprus black as e'er was crow;
Gloves as sweet as damask roses;
Masks for faces and for noses;
Bugle-bracelet, necklace-amber,
Perfume for a lady's chamber;
Golden quoifs and stomachers,
For my lads to give their dears;
Pins and poking-sticks of steel,
What maids lack from head to heel:
Come buy of me, come; come buy, come buy;
Buy lads, or else your lasses cry:
Come buy.

CLOWN
If I were not in love with Mopsa, thou shouldst take no money of me; but being enthrall'd as I am, it will also be the bondage of certain ribands and gloves.

MOPSA
I was promised them against the feast; but they come not too late now.

DORCAS
He hath promised you more than that, or there be liars.

MOPSA
He hath paid you all he promised you; may be, he has paid you more, — which will shame you to give him again.

CLOWN
Is there no manners left among maids? will they wear their plackets where they should bear their faces? Is there not milking-time, when you are going to bed, or kiln-hole, to whistle-off these secrets, but you must be tittle-tattling before all our guests? 'tis well they are whispering. Clamour your tongues, and not a word more.

MOPSA
I have done. Come, you promised me a tawdry-lace and a pair of sweet gloves.

CLOWN
Have I not told thee how I was cozen'd by the way, and lost all my money?

AUTOLYCUS
And, indeed, sir, there are cozeners abroad: therefore it behoves men to be wary.

CLOWN
Fear not thou, man, thou shalt lose nothing here.

AUTOLYCUS
I hope so, sir; for I have about me many parcels of charge.

CLOWN
What hast here? ballads?

MOPSA
Pray now, buy some: I love a ballet in print a-life, for then we are sure they are true.

AUTOLYCUS
Here's one to a very doleful tune. How a usurer's wife was brought to bed of twenty money-bags at a burden, and how she long'd to eat adders' heads and toads carbonadoed.

MOPSA
Is it true, think you?

AUTOLYCUS
Very true; and but a month old.

DORCAS
Bless me from marrying a usurer!

AUTOLYCUS
Here's the midwife's name to't, one Mistress Taleporter, and five or six honest wives that were present. Why should I carry lies abroad?

MOPSA
Pray you now, buy it.

CLOWN
Come on, lay it by: and let's first see more ballads, we'll buy the other things anon.

AUTOLYCUS
Here's another ballad, Of a fish, that appear'd upon the coast on Wednesday the fourscore of April, forty thousand fadom above water, and sung this ballad against the hard hearts of maids: it was thought she was a woman, and was turn'd into a cold fish for she would not exchange flesh with one that loved her: the ballad is very pitiful, and as true.

DORCAS
Is it true too, think you?

AUTOLYCUS
Five justices' hands at it, and witnesses more than my pack will hold.

CLOWN
Lay it by too: another.

AUTOLYCUS This is a passing merry one, and goes to the tune of '*Two maids wooing a man*'.

AUTOLYCUS
This is a merry ballad, but a very pretty one.

MOPSA
Let's have some merry ones.

AUTOLYCUS
Why, this is a passing merry one, and goes to the tune of 'Two maids wooing a man': there's scarce a maid westward but she sings it; 'tis in request, I can tell you.

MOPSA
We can both sing it: if thou'lt bear a part, thou shalt hear; 'tis in three parts.

DORCAS
We had the tune on't a month ago.

AUTOLYCUS
I can bear my part; you must know 'tis my occupation: have at it with you!
Song.

AUTOLYCUS
    Get you hence, for I must go;
    Where, it fits not you to know.

DORCAS
    Whither?

MOPSA
            O, whither?

DORCAS
                Whither?

MOPSA
    It becomes thy oath full well,
    Thou to me thy secrets tell:

DORCAS
    Me too, let me go thither.

MOPSA
    Or thou go'st to the grange or mill:

DORCAS
    If to either, thou dost ill.

AUTOLYCUS
    Neither.

DORCAS
            What, neither?

AUTOLYCUS
                Neither.

DORCAS
    Thou hast sworn my love to be;

MOPSA
    Thou hast sworn it more to me:
    Then, whither go'st? say, whither?

CLOWN
We'll have this song out anon by ourselves: my father and the gentlemen are in sad talk, and we'll not trouble

them. — Come, bring away thy pack after me. — Wenches, I'll buy for you both. — Pedlar, let's have the first choice. — Follow me, girls.
            [*Exit with* DORCAS *and* MOPSA.

AUTOLYCUS
And you shall pay well for 'em. —   [*Singing*.

        Will you buy any tape,
          Or lace for your cape,
    My dainty duck, my dear-a?
        Any silk, any thread,
        Any toys for your head,
    Of the new'st and fin'st, fin'st wear-a?
          Come to the pedlar;
          Money's a meddler;
    That doth utter all men's ware-a.   [*Exit*.

            Enter SERVANT.

SERVANT
Master, there is three carters, three shepherds, three neat-herds, three swine-herds, that have made themselves all men of hair, — they call themselves Saltiers: and they have a dance which the wenches say is a gallimaufry of gambols, because they are not in't; but they themselves are o' the mind, — if it be not too rough for some that know little but bowling, — it will please plentifully.

SHEPHERD
Away! we'll none on't: here has been too much homely foolery already. — I know, sir, we weary you.

POLIXENES
You weary those that refresh us: pray, let's see these four threes of herdsmen.

SERVANT
One three of them, by their own report, sir, hath danced before the king; and not the worst of the three but jumps twelve foot and a half by the squier.

SHEPHERD
Leave your prating: since these good men are pleased, let them come in; but quickly now.

SERVANT
Why, they stay at door, sir.   [*Exit*.
            Here a dance of twelve Satyrs.

POLIXENES
O, father, you'll know more of that hereafter. —
[*to* CAMILLO] Is it not too far gone? 'Tis time to part them.
He's simple and tells much. — How now, fair
  shepherd!
Your heart is full of something that does take

Your mind from feasting. Sooth, when I was young,
And handed love as you do, I was wont
To load my she with knacks: I would have ransack'd
The pedlar's silken treasury, and have pour'd it
To her acceptance; you have let him go,
And nothing marted with him. If your lass
Interpretation should abuse, and call this
Your lack of love or bounty, you were straited
For a reply, at least if you make care
Of happy holding her.

FLORIZEL
                                    Old sir, I know
She prizes not such trifles as these are:
The gifts she looks from me are pack'd and lock'd
Up in my heart; which I have given already,
But not deliver'd. — O, hear me breathe my life
Before this ancient sir, who, it should seem,
Hath sometime lov'd! I take thy hand, — this hand,
As soft as dove's down and as white as it,
Or Ethiopian's tooth, or the fann'd snow that's bolted
By the northern blasts twice o'er.

POLIXENES
                                    What follows this? —
How prettily the young swain seems to wash
The hand was fair before! — I have put you out: —
But to your protestation; let me hear
What you profess.

FLORIZEL
                                    Do, and be witness to't.

POLIXENES
And this my neighbour too?

FLORIZEL
                                    And he, and more
Than he, and men, the earth, the heavens, and all: —
That, were I crown'd the most imperial monarch,
Thereof most worthy; were I the fairest youth
That ever made eye swerve; had force and knowledge
More than was ever man's, — I would not prize them
Without her love; for her employ them all;
Commend them, and condemn them, to her service,
Or to their own perdition.

POLIXENES
                                    Fairly offer'd.

CAMILLO
This shows a sound affection.

SHEPHERD
                                    But, my daughter,
Say you the like to him?

PERDITA
                                    I cannot speak
So well, nothing so well; no, nor mean better:
By the pattern of mine own thoughts I cut out
The purity of his.

SHEPHERD
                                    Take hands, a bargain! —
And, friends unknown, you shall bear witness to't:
I give my daughter to him, and will make
Her portion equal his.

FLORIZEL
                                    O, that must be
I' the virtue of your daughter: one being dead,
I shall have more than you can dream of yet:
Enough then for your wonder. But, come on;
Contract us 'fore these witnesses.

SHEPHERD
                                    Come, your hand; —
And, daughter, yours.

POLIXENES
                                    Soft, swain, awhile, beseech you;
Have you a father?

FLORIZEL
                                    I have: but what of him?

POLIXENES
Knows he of this?

FLORIZEL
                                    He neither does nor shall.

POLIXENES
Methinks a father
Is, at the nuptial of his son, a guest
That best becomes the table. Pray you, once more;
Is not your father grown incapable
Of reasonable affairs? is he not stupid
With age and alt'ring rheums? can he speak? hear?
Know man from man? dispute his own estate?
Lies he not bed-rid? and again does nothing
But what he did being childish?

FLORIZEL
                                    No, good sir;
He has his health, and ampler strength indeed
Than most have of his age.

POLIXENES
                                    By my white beard,
You offer him, if this be so, a wrong
Something unfilial: reason my son
Should choose himself a wife; but as good reason
The father, — all whose joy is nothing else
But fair posterity, — should hold some counsel
In such a business.

FLORIZEL
                                    I yield all this;
But, for some other reasons, my grave sir,
Which 'tis not fit you know, I not acquaint
My father of this business.

POLIXENES
                                    Let him know't.

FLORIZEL
He shall not.

POLIXENES
                                    Prithee, let him.

FLORIZEL
                                    No, he must not.

SHEPHERD
Let him, my son; he shall not need to grieve
At knowing of thy choice.

FLORIZEL
                                    Come, come, he must not. —
Mark our contract.

POLIXENES
                                    Mark your divorce, young sir,
                                    [_Discovering himself._
Whom son I dare not call; thou art too base
To be acknowledg'd: thou a sceptre's heir,
That thus affects a sheep-hook! — Thou old traitor,
I am sorry that, by hanging thee, I can but
Shorten thy life one week. — And thou, fresh piece
Of excellent witchcraft, who, of force, must know
The royal fool thou copest with, —

SHEPHERD
                                    O, my heart!

POLIXENES
I'll have thy beauty scratch'd with briers, and made
More homely than thy state. — For thee, fond boy,
If I may ever know thou dost but sigh
That thou no more shalt see this knack, — as never
I mean thou shalt, — we'll bar thee from succession;
Not hold thee of our blood, no, not our kin,
Far' than Deucalion off: — mark thou my words: —
Follow us to the court. — Thou churl, for this time,
Though full of our displeasure, yet we free thee
From the dead blow of it. — And you, enchantment,
Worthy enough a herdsman; yea, him too
That makes himself, but for our honour therein,
Unworthy thee, — if ever henceforth thou
These rural latches to his entrance open,
Or hoop his body more with thy embraces,
I will devise a death as cruel for thee
As thou art tender to't.   [_Exit._

PERDITA
                                    Even here undone!
I was not much afeard; for once or twice
I was about to speak, and tell him plainly,
The selfsame sun that shines upon his court
Hides not his visage from our cottage, but
Looks on alike. [_to_ FLORIZEL] Will't please you, sir, be
     gone?
I told you what would come of this: beseech you,
Of your own state take care: this dream of mine, —
Being now awake, I'll queen it no inch farther,
But milk my ewes and weep.

CAMILLO
                                    Why, how now, father!
Speak ere thou diest.

SHEPHERD
                                    I cannot speak, nor think,
Nor dare to know that which I know. — [_to_ FLORIZEL]
     O sir,
You have undone a man of fourscore three,
That thought to fill his grave in quiet, — yea,
To die upon the bed my father died,
To lie close by his honest bones! but now
Some hangman must put on my shroud, and lay me
Where no priest shovels-in dust. — [_to_ PERDITA] O
     cursed wretch,
That knew'st this was the prince, and wouldst adventure
To mingle faith with him! — Undone! undone!
If I might die within this hour, I have liv'd
To die when I desire.   [_Exit._

FLORIZEL
                                    Why look you so upon me?
I am but sorry, not afeard; delay'd,

But nothing alter'd: what I was, I am;
More straining on for plucking back; not following
My leash unwillingly.

CAMILLO
                                    Gracious my lord,
You know your father's temper: at this time
He will allow no speech, — which I do guess
You do not purpose to him; — and as hardly
Will he endure your sight as yet, I fear:
Then, till the fury of his highness settle,
Come not before him.

FLORIZEL
                                    I not purpose it.
I think Camillo?

CAMILLO
                                    Even he, my lord.

PERDITA
How often have I told you 'twould be thus!
How often said my dignity would last
But till 'twere known!

FLORIZEL
                                    It cannot fail but by
The violation of my faith; and then
Let nature crush the sides o' the earth together,
And mar the seeds within! — Lift up thy looks: —
From my succession wipe me, father! I
Am heir to my affection.

CAMILLO
                                    Be advised.

FLORIZEL
I am, — and by my fancy: if my reason
Will thereto be obedient, I have reason;
If not, my senses, better pleas'd with madness,
Do bid it welcome.

CAMILLO
                                    This is desperate, sir.

FLORIZEL
So call it: but it does fulfil my vow;
I needs must think it honesty. Camillo,
Not for Bohemia, nor the pomp that may
Be thereat glean'd; for all the sun sees, or
The close earth wombs, or the profound seas hide
In unknown fadoms, will I break my oath
To this my fair beloved: therefore, I pray you,
As you have e'er been my father's honour'd friend,
When he shall miss me, — as, in faith, I mean not
To see him any more, — cast your good counsels
Upon his passion: let myself and fortune
Tug for the time to come. This you may know,
And so deliver, — I am put to sea
With her who here I cannot hold on shore;
And, most opportune to her need, I have
A vessel rides fast by, but not prepared
For this design. What course I mean to hold
Shall nothing benefit your knowledge, nor
Concern me the reporting.

CAMILLO
                                    O my lord,
I would your spirit were easier for advice,
Or stronger for your need!

FLORIZEL
                                    Hark, Perdita. —
                                    [_Taking her aside._
[_to_ CAMILLO] I'll hear you by and by.

CAMILLO
                                    He's irremovable,
Resolv'd for flight. Now were I happy, if
His going I could frame to serve my turn;
Save him from danger, do him love and honour;
Purchase the sight again of dear Sicilia,
And that unhappy king, my master, whom
I so much thirst to see.

FLORIZEL
                                    Now, good Camillo,
I am so fraught with curious business, that
I leave out ceremony.

CAMILLO
                                    Sir, I think
You have heard of my poor services, i'the love
That I have borne your father?

FLORIZEL
                                    Very nobly
Have you deserv'd: it is my father's music
To speak your deeds; not little of his care
To have them recompens'd as thought on.

CAMILLO
                                    Well, my lord,
If you may please to think I love the king,
And, through him, what's nearest to him, which is
Your gracious self, embrace but my direction, —

If your more ponderous and settled project
May suffer alteration, — on mine honour
I'll point you where you shall have such receiving
As shall become your highness; where you may
Enjoy your mistress, — from the whom, I see,
There's no disjunction to be made, but by,
As heavens forefend! your ruin; — marry her;
And — with my best endeavours in your absence —
Your discontenting father strive to qualify,
And bring him up to liking.

FLORIZEL
      How, Camillo,
May this, almost a miracle, be done?
That I may call thee something more than man,
And, after that, trust to thee.

CAMILLO
      Have you thought on
A place whereto you'll go?

FLORIZEL
      Not any yet:
But as the unthought-on accident is guilty
To what we wildly do, so we profess
Ourselves to be the slaves of chance, and flies
Of every wind that blows.

CAMILLO
      Then list to me:
This follows, — if you will not change your purpose,
But undergo this flight, — make for Sicilia;
And there present yourself and your fair princess —
For so I see she must be — 'fore Leontes:
She shall be habited as it becomes
The partner of your bed. Methinks I see
Leontes opening his free arms, and weeping
His welcomes forth; asks thee, the son, forgiveness,
As 'twere i' the father's person; kisses the hands
Of your fresh princess; o'er and o'er divides him
'Twixt his unkindness and his kindness, — the one
He chides to hell, and bids the other grow
Faster than thought or time.

FLORIZEL
      Worthy Camillo,
What colour for my visitation shall I
Hold up before him?

CAMILLO
      Sent by the king your father
To greet him and to give him comforts. Sir,
The manner of your bearing towards him, with
What you, as from your father, shall deliver,
Things known betwixt us three, I'll write you down:
The which shall point you forth at every sitting
What you must say; that he shall not perceive
But that you have your father's bosom there,
And speak his very heart.

FLORIZEL
      I am bound to you:
There is some sap in this.

CAMILLO
      A course more promising
Than a wild dedication of yourselves
To unpath'd waters, undream'd shores, most certain
To miseries enough: no hope to help you;
But, as you shake off one, to take another:
Nothing so certain as your anchors; who
Do their best office, if they can but stay you
Where you'll be loth to be: besides, you know
Prosperity's the very bond of love,
Whose fresh complexion and whose heart together
Affliction alters.

PERDITA
      One of these is true:
I think affliction may subdue the cheek,
But not take in the mind.

CAMILLO
      Yea, say you so?
There shall not, at your father's house, these seven
 years
Be born another such.

FLORIZEL
      My good Camillo,
She's as forward of her breeding as she is
I' the rear o' her birth.

CAMILLO
      I cannot say 'tis pity
She lacks instructions, for she seems a mistress
To most that teach.

PERDITA
      Your pardon, sir, for this;
I'll blush you thanks.

FLORIZEL
      My prettiest Perdita! —

But, O, the thorns we stand upon! — Camillo, —
Preserver of my father, now of me,
The medicine of our house! — how shall we do?
We are not furnish'd like Bohemia's son,
Nor shall appear in Sicilia.

CAMILLO
      My lord,
Fear none of this: I think you know my fortunes
Do all lie there: it shall be so my care
To have you royally appointed as if
The scene you play were mine. For instance, sir,
That you may know you shall not want, — one word.
       [They talk aside.

     Enter AUTOLYCUS.

AUTOLYCUS
Ha, ha! what a fool Honesty is! and Trust, his sworn
brother, a very simple gentleman! I have sold all my
trumpery; not a counterfeit stone, not a riband, glass,
pomander, brooch, table-book, ballad, knife, tape,
glove, shoe-tie, bracelet, horn-ring, to keep my pack
from fasting: they throng who should buy first, as if my
trinkets had been hallow'd, and brought a benediction
to the buyer: by which means I saw whose purse was
best in picture; and what I saw, to my good use I
remember'd. My clown — who wants but something to
be a reasonable man — grew so in love with the
wenches' song, that he would not stir his pettitoes till
he had both tune and words; which so drew the rest of
the herd to me, that all their other senses stuck in ears:
you might have pinch'd a placket, — it was senseless;
'twas nothing to geld a codpiece of a purse; — I would
have filed keys off that hung in chains: no hearing, no
feeling, but my sir's song, and admiring the nothing of
it. So that, in this time of lethargy, I pick'd and cut most
of their festival purses; and had not the old man come
in with a whoobub against his daughter and the king's
son, and scared my choughs from the chaff, I had not
left a purse alive in the whole army.
  [CAMILLO, FLORIZEL, and PERDITA *come forward.*

CAMILLO
Nay, but my letters, by this means being there
So soon as you arrive, shall clear that doubt.

FLORIZEL
And those that you'll procure from King Leontes, —

CAMILLO
Shall satisfy your father.

PERDITA
      Happy be you!
All that you speak shows fair.

CAMILLO
      Who have we here?
       [Seeing AUTOLYCUS.
We'll make an instrument of this; omit
Nothing may give us aid.

AUTOLYCUS [*aside*].
If they have overheard me now, — why, hanging.

CAMILLO
How now, good fellow! why shakest thou so? Fear not,
man; here's no harm intended to thee.

AUTOLYCUS
I am a poor fellow, sir.

CAMILLO
Why, be so still; here's nobody will steal that from thee:
yet, for the outside of thy poverty, we must make an
exchange; therefore discase thee instantly, — thou
must think there's a necessity in't, — and change
garments with this gentleman: though the pennyworth
on his side be the worst, yet hold thee, there's some
boot.
       [Giving money.

AUTOLYCUS
I am a poor fellow, sir. — [*aside*] I know ye well enough.

CAMILLO
Nay, prithee, dispatch: the gentleman is half flay'd
already.

AUTOLYCUS
Are you in earnest, sir? — [*aside*] I smell the trick on't.

FLORIZEL
Dispatch, I prithee.

AUTOLYCUS
Indeed, I have had earnest; but I cannot with conscience
take it.

CAMILLO
Unbuckle, unbuckle. —
  [FLORIZEL and AUTOLYCUS *exchange garments.*
Fortunate mistress, — let my prophecy
Come home to ye! — you must retire yourself
Into some covert: take your sweetheart's hat,
And pluck it o'er your brows; muffle your face;

Dismantle you; and, as you can, disliken
The truth of your own seeming; that you may —
For I do fear eyes over — to shipboard
Get undescried.

PERDITA
      I see the play so lies
That I must bear a part.

CAMILLO
      No remedy. —
Have you done there?

FLORIZEL
      Should I now meet my father,
He would not call me son.

CAMILLO
      Nay, you shall have no hat. —
       [Giving it to PERDITA.
Come, lady, come. — Farewell, my friend.

AUTOLYCUS
      Adieu, sir.

FLORIZEL
O Perdita, what have we twain forgot!
Pray you, a word.   *[They converse apart.*

CAMILLO [*aside*].
What I do next, shall be to tell the king
Of this escape, and whither they are bound;
Wherein, my hope is, I shall so prevail
To force him after: in whose company
I shall review Sicilia, for whose sight
I have a woman's longing.

FLORIZEL
      Fortune speed us! —
Thus we set on, Camillo, to the sea-side.

CAMILLO
The swifter speed the better.
  [Exeunt FLORIZEL, PERDITA, *and* CAMILLO.

AUTOLYCUS
I understand the business, I hear it: to have an open
ear, a quick eye, and a nimble hand, is necessary for a
cut-purse; a good nose is requisite also, to smell out
work for the other senses. I see this is the time that the
unjust man doth thrive. What an exchange had this
been without boot! What a boot is here with this
exchange! Sure, the gods do this year connive at us, and
we may do any thing extempore. The prince himself is
about a piece of iniquity, — stealing away from his
father with his clog at his heels: if I thought it were not
a piece of honesty to acquaint the king withal, I would
do't: I hold it the more knavery to conceal it; and
therein am I constant to my profession.

   Enter CLOWN *and* SHEPHERD.

Aside, aside; — here is more matter for a hot brain:
every lane's end, every shop, church, session, hanging,
yields a careful man work.

CLOWN
See, see; what a man you are now! There is no other
way but to tell the king she's a changeling, and none of
your flesh and blood.

SHEPHERD
Nay, but hear me.

CLOWN
Nay, but hear me.

SHEPHERD
Go to, then.

CLOWN
She being none of your flesh and blood, your flesh
and blood has not offended the king; and so your
flesh and blood is not to be punish'd by him. Show
those things you found about her; those secret
things, all but what she has with her: this being
done, let the law go whistle; I warrant you.

SHEPHERD
I will tell the king all, every word, yea, and his son's
pranks too, — who, I may say, is no honest man neither
to his father nor to me, to go about to make me the
king's brother-in-law.

CLOWN
Indeed, brother-in-law was the furthest off you could
have been to him; and then your blood had been the
dearer by I know not how much an ounce.

AUTOLYCUS [*aside*].
Very wisely, puppies!

SHEPHERD
Well, let us to the king: there is that in this fardel will
make him scratch his beard.

AUTOLYCUS [*aside*].
I know not what impediment this complaint may be to
the flight of my master.

CLOWN
Pray heartily he be at palace.

AUTOLYCUS [*aside*].
Though I am not naturally honest, I am so sometimes by chance: — let me pocket up my pedlar's excrement. [*Takes off his false beard.*] — How now, rustics! whither are you bound?

SHEPHERD
To the palace, an it like your worship.

AUTOLYCUS
Your affairs there? what? with whom? the condition of that fardel, the place of your dwelling, your names, your ages, of what having, breeding, and any thing that is fitting to be known, discover.

CLOWN
We are but plain fellows, sir.

AUTOLYCUS
A lie; you are rough and hairy. Let me have no lying: it becomes none but tradesmen, and they often give us soldiers the lie: but we pay them for it with stamp'd coin, not stabbing steel; therefore they do not give us the lie.

CLOWN
Your worship had like to have given us one, if you had not taken yourself with the manner.

SHEPHERD
Are you a courtier, an't like you, sir?

AUTOLYCUS
Whether it like me or no, I am a courtier. See'st thou not the air of the court in these enfoldings? hath not my gait in it the measure of the court? receives not thy nose court-odour from me? reflect I not on thy baseness court-contempt? Think'st thou, for that I insinuate, or toaze from thee thy business, I am therefore no courtier? I am courtier cap-a-pe; and one that will either push on or pluck back thy business there: whereupon I command thee to open thy affair.

SHEPHERD
My business, sir, is to the king.

AUTOLYCUS
What advocate hast thou to him?

SHEPHERD
I know not, an't like you.

CLOWN [*aside to* SHEPHERD].
Advocate's the court-word for a pheasant: say you have none.

SHEPHERD
None, sir; I have no pheasant, cock nor hen.

AUTOLYCUS
How blest are we that are not simple men!
Yet nature might have made me as these are,
Therefore I will not disdain.

CLOWN [*aside to* SHEPHERD].
This cannot be but a great courtier.

SHEPHERD [*aside to* CLOWN].
His garments are rich, but he wears them not handsomely.

CLOWN [*aside to* SHEPHERD].
He seems to be the more noble in being fantastical: a great man, I'll warrant; I know by the picking on's teeth.

AUTOLYCUS
The fardel there? what's i'the fardel? Wherefore that box?

SHEPHERD
Sir, there lies such secrets in this fardel and box, which none must know but the king; and which he shall know within this hour, if I may come to the speech of him.

AUTOLYCUS
Age, thou hast lost thy labour.

SHEPHERD
Why, sir?

AUTOLYCUS
The king is not at the palace; he is gone aboard a new ship to purge melancholy and air himself: for, if thou be'st capable of things serious, thou must know the king is full of grief.

SHEPHERD
So 'tis said, sir, — about his son, that should have married a shepherd's daughter.

AUTOLYCUS
If that shepherd be not in hand-fast, let him fly: the curses he shall have, the tortures he shall feel, will break the back of man, the heart of monster.

CLOWN
Think you so, sir?

AUTOLYCUS
Not he alone shall suffer what wit can make heavy and vengeance bitter; but those that are germane to him, though removed fifty times, shall all come under the hangman: which though it be great pity, yet it is necessary. An old sheep-whistling rogue, a ram-tender, to offer to have his daughter come into grace! Some say he shall be stoned; but that death is too soft for him, say I: draw our throne into a sheep-cote! all deaths are too few, the sharpest too easy.

CLOWN
Has the old man e'er a son, sir, do you hear, an't like you, sir?

AUTOLYCUS
He has a son, — who shall be flay'd alive; then, 'nointed over with honey, set on the head of a wasps' nest; then stand till he be three quarters and a dram dead; then recover'd again with aqua-vitæ or some other hot infusion; then, raw as he is, and in the hottest day prognostication proclaims, shall he be set against a brick-wall, the sun looking with a southward eye upon him, — where he is to behold him with flies blown to death. But what talk we of these traitorly rascals, whose miseries are to be smiled at, their offences being so capital? Tell me — for you seem to be honest plain men — what you have to the king: being something gently consider'd, I'll bring you where he is aboard, tender your persons to his presence, whisper him in your behalfs; and if it be in man besides the king to effect your suits, here is man shall do it.

CLOWN [*aside to* SHEPHERD].
He seems to be of great authority: close with him; give him gold: and though authority be a stubborn bear, yet he is oft led by the nose with gold: show the inside of your purse to the outside of his hand, and no more ado. Remember, — stoned, and flay'd alive.

SHEPHERD
An't please you, sir, to undertake the business for us, here is that gold I have: I'll make it as much more, and leave this young man in pawn till I bring it you.

AUTOLYCUS
After I have done what I promised?

SHEPHERD
Ay, sir.

AUTOLYCUS
Well, give me the moiety. — Are you a party in this business?

CLOWN
In some sort, sir: but though my case be a pitiful one, I hope I shall not be flay'd out of it.

AUTOLYCUS
O, that's the case of the shepherd's son: — hang him, he'll be made an example.

CLOWN [*aside to* SHEPHERD].
Comfort, good comfort! We must to the king, and show our strange sights: he must know 'tis none of your daughter nor my sister; we are gone else. — Sir, I will give you as much as this old man does, when the business is perform'd; and remain, as he says, your pawn till it be brought you.

AUTOLYCUS
I will trust you. Walk before toward the sea-side; go on the right hand: I will but look upon the hedge, and follow you.

CLOWN [*aside to* SHEPHERD].
We are blest in this man, as I may say, even blest.

SHEPHERD [*aside to* CLOWN].
Let's before, as he bids us: he was provided to do us good.   [*Exeunt* SHEPHERD *and* CLOWN.

AUTOLYCUS
If I had a mind to be honest, I see Fortune would not suffer me: she drops booties in my mouth. I am courted now with a double occasion, — gold, and a means to do the prince my master good; which who knows how that may turn back to my advancement? I will bring these two moles, these blind ones, aboard him: if he think it fit to shore them again, and that the complaint they have to the king concerns him nothing, let him call me rogue for being so far officious; for I am proof against that title, and what shame else belongs to't. To him will I present them: there may be matter in it.   [*Exit.*

AUTOLYCUS The fardel there? what's i'the fardel? Wherefore that box?

ACT V

SCENE I

Sicilia. LEONTES' *palace.*

Enter LEONTES, CLEOMENES, DION, PAULINA, *and others.*

CLEOMENES
Sir, you have done enough, and have perform'd
A saint-like sorrow: no fault could you make,
Which you have not redeem'd; indeed, paid down
More penitence than done trespass: at the last,
Do as the heavens have done, forget your evil;
With them, forgive yourself.

LEONTES
                              Whilst I remember
Her and her virtues, I cannot forget
My blemishes in them; and so still think of
The wrong I did myself: which was so much,
That heirless it hath made my kingdom; and
Destroy'd the sweet'st companion that e'er man
Bred his hopes out of.

PAULINA
                    True, too true, my lord:
If, one by one, you wedded all the world,
Or from the all that are took something good,
To make a perfect woman, she you kill'd
Would be unparallel'd.

LEONTES
                    I think so. Kill'd!
She I kill'd! I did so: but thou strikest me
Sorely, to say I did; it is as bitter
Upon thy tongue as in my thought: now, good now,
Say so but seldom.

CLEOMENES
                    Not at all, good lady:
You might have spoken a thousand things that would
Have done the time more benefit, and grac'd
Your kindness better.

PAULINA
                    You are one of those
Would have him wed again.

DION

If you would not so,
You pity not the state, nor the remembrance
Of his most sovereign name; consider little
What dangers, by his highness' fail of issue,
May drop upon his kingdom, and devour
Incertain lookers-on. What were more holy
Than to rejoice the former queen is well?
What holier than, — for royalty's repair,
For present comfort, and for future good, —
To bless the bed of majesty again
With a sweet fellow to't?

PAULINA

There is none worthy,
Respecting her that's gone. Besides, the gods
Will have fulfill'd their secret purposes;
For has not the divine Apollo said,
Is't not the tenor of his oracle,
That King Leontes shall not have an heir
Till his lost child be found? which that it shall,
Is all as monstrous to our human reason
As my Antigonus to break his grave
And come again to me; who, on my life,
Did perish with the infant. 'Tis your counsel
My lord should to the heavens be contrary,
Oppose against their wills. — [to LEONTES] Care not
    for issue;
The crown will find an heir: great Alexander
Left his to the worthiest; so his successor
Was like to be the best.

LEONTES

Good Paulina,
Who hast the memory of Hermione,
I know, in honour, — O, that ever I
Had squared me to thy counsel! — then, even now,
I might have look'd upon my queen's full eyes;
Have taken treasure from her lips, —

PAULINA

And left them
More rich for what they yielded.

LEONTES

Thou speak'st truth.
No more such wives; therefore, no wife: one worse,
And better used, would make her sainted spirit
Again possess her corpse, and on this stage —
Where we offend her now — appear soul-vex'd,
And begin, 'Why to me?'

PAULINA

Had she such power,
She had just cause.

LEONTES

She had; and would incense me
To murder her I married.

PAULINA

I should so.
Were I the ghost that walk'd, I'ld bid you mark
Her eye, and tell me for what dull part in't
You chose her; then I'ld shriek, that even your ears
Should rift to hear me; and the words that follow'd
Should be, 'Remember mine.'

LEONTES

Stars, stars,
And all eyes else dead coals! — fear thou no wife;
I'll have no wife, Paulina.

PAULINA

Will you swear

CLEOMENES Do as the heavens have done, forget your evil

Never to marry but by my free leave?

LEONTES

Never, Paulina; so be blest my spirit!

PAULINA

Then, good my lords, bear witness to his oath.

CLEOMENES

You tempt him over-much.

PAULINA

Unless another,
As like Hermione as is her picture,
Affront his eye.

CLEOMENES

Good madam, —

PAULINA

I have done.
Yet, if my lord will marry, — if you will, sir,
No remedy, but you will, — give me the office
To choose you a queen: she shall not be so young
As was your former; but she shall be such
As, walk'd your first queen's ghost, it should take joy
To see her in your arms.

LEONTES

My true Paulina,
We shall not marry till thou bidd'st us.

PAULINA

That
Shall be when your first queen's again in breath;
Never till then.

Enter a GENTLEMAN.

GENTLEMAN

One that gives out himself Prince Florizel,
Son of Polixenes, with his princess, — she
The fairest I have yet beheld, — desires access
To your high presence.

LEONTES

What with him? he comes not
Like to his father's greatness: his approach,
So out of circumstance and sudden, tells us
'Tis not a visitation fram'd, but forc'd
By need and accident. What train?

GENTLEMAN

But few,
And those but mean.

LEONTES

His princess, say you, with him?

GENTLEMAN

Ay, the most peerless piece of earth, I think,
That e'er the sun shone bright on.

PAULINA

O Hermione,
As every present time doth boast itself
Above a better gone, so must thy grave
Give way to what's seen now! Sir, you yourself
Have said and writ so; but your writing now
Is colder than that theme, 'She had not been,
Nor was not to be equall'd'; — thus your verse
Flow'd with her beauty once: 'tis shrewdly ebb'd
To say you have seen a better.

GENTLEMAN

Pardon, madam:
The one I have almost forgot, — your pardon;
The other, when she has obtain'd your eye,
Will have your tongue too. This is a creature,
Would she begin a sect, might quench the zeal
Of all professors else; make proselytes
Of who she but bid follow.

PAULINA

How! not women?

GENTLEMAN

Women will love her, that she is a
    woman
More worth than any man; men, that
    she is
The rarest of all women.

LEONTES

Go, Cleomenes;
Yourself, assisted with your
    honour'd friends,
Bring them to our embracement.
            [*Exeunt* CLEOMENES *and others.*
            Still, 'tis strange
He thus should steal upon us.

PAULINA

Had our prince,
Jewel of children, seen this hour, he
    had pair'd
Well with this lord: there was not full
    a month
Between their births.

LEONTES

Prithee, no more; cease; thou know'st
He dies to me again when talk'd of: sure,
When I shall see this gentleman, thy speeches
Will bring me to consider that which may
Unfurnish me of reason. — They are come.
        [*Enter* CLEOMENES *and others, with* FLORIZEL *and*
                            PERDITA.

Your mother was most true to wedlock, prince;
For she did print your royal father off,
Conceiving you: were I but twenty-one,
Your father's image is so hit in you,
His very air, that I should call you brother,
As I did him, and speak of something wildly
By us perform'd before. Most dearly welcome!
And your fair princess-goddess! — O, alas,
I lost a couple, that 'twixt heaven and earth
Might thus have stood, begetting wonder, as
You, gracious couple, do! and then I lost —
All mine own folly — the society,
Amity too, of your brave father, whom,
Though bearing misery, I desire my life
Once more to look on him.

FLORIZEL

By his command
Have I here touch'd Sicilia, and from him
Give you all greetings, that a king, at friend,
Can send his brother; and, but infirmity —
Which waits upon worn times — hath something
    seiz'd
His wish'd ability, he had himself
The lands and waters 'twixt your throne and his
Measur'd to look upon you; whom he loves —
He bade me say so — more than all the sceptres,
And those that bear them, living.

LEONTES

O my brother,
Good gentleman, the wrongs I have done thee stir
Afresh within me; and these thy offices,
So rarely kind, are as interpreters
Of my behindhand slackness! — Welcome hither,
As is the spring to the earth. And hath he too
Expos'd this paragon to the fearful usage —
At least ungentle — of the dreadful Neptune,
To greet a man not worth her pains, much less
The adventure of her person?

FLORIZEL

Good my lord,
She came from Libya.

LEONTES

Where the warlike Smalus,
That noble honour'd lord, is fear'd and lov'd?

FLORIZEL

Most royal sir, from thence; from him, whose daughter
His tears proclaim'd his, parting with her: thence,
A prosperous south-wind friendly, we have cross'd
To execute the charge my father gave me,
For visiting your highness: my best train
I have from your Sicilian shores dismiss'd;
Who for Bohemia bend, to signify
Not only my success in Libya, sir,
But my arrival, and my wife's, in safety
Here where we are.

LEONTES

The blessed gods
Purge all infection from our air whilst you
Do climate here! You have a holy father,
A graceful gentleman: against whose person,
So sacred as it is, I have done sin:
For which the heavens, taking angry note,
Have left me issueless; and your father's blest,
As he from heaven merits it, with you,
Worthy his goodness. What might I have been,
Might I a son and daughter now have look'd on,
Such goodly things as you!

Enter a LORD.

LORD

Most noble sir,
That which I shall report will bear no credit,
Were not the proof so nigh. Please you, great sir,
Bohemia greets you from himself by me;
Desires you to attach his son, who has —
His dignity and duty both cast off —
Fled from his father, from his hopes, and with
A shepherd's daughter.

LEONTES

Where's Bohemia? speak.

LORD

Here in your city; I now came from him:
I speak amazedly; and it becomes

My marvel and my message. To your court
Whiles he was hastening, — in the chase, it seems,
Of this fair couple, — meets he on the way
The father of this seeming lady, and
Her brother, having both their country quitted
With this young prince.

FLORIZEL
                                Camillo has betray'd me;
Whose honour and whose honesty till now
Endured all weathers.

LORD
                        Lay't so to his charge:
He's with the king your father.

LEONTES
                                    Who? Camillo?

LORD
Camillo, sir; I spake with him; who now
Has these poor men in question. Never saw I
Wretches so quake: they kneel, they kiss the earth;
Forswear themselves as often as they speak:
Bohemia stops his ears, and threatens them
With divers deaths in death.

PERDITA
                            O my poor father!
The heaven set spies upon us, will not have
Our contract celebrated.

LEONTES
                        You are married?

FLORIZEL
We are not, sir, nor are we like to be;
The stars, I see, will kiss the valleys first: —
The odds for high and low's alike.

LEONTES
                                    My lord,
Is this the daughter of a king?

FLORIZEL
                            She is,
When once she is my wife.

LEONTES
That 'once', I see by your good father's speed,
Will come on very slowly. I am sorry,
Most sorry, you have broken from his liking,
Where you were tied in duty; and as sorry
Your choice is not so rich in worth as beauty,
That you might well enjoy her.

FLORIZEL
                            Dear, look up:
Though Fortune, visible an enemy,
Should chase us, with my father, power no jot
Hath she to change our loves. — Beseech you, sir,
Remember since you ow'd no more to time
Than I do now: with thought of such affections,
Step forth mine advocate; at your request
My father will grant precious things as trifles.

LEONTES
Would he do so, I'ld beg your precious mistress,
Which he counts but a trifle.

PAULINA
                            Sir, my liege,
Your eye hath too much youth in't: not a month
'Fore your queen died, she was more worth such gazes
Than what you look on now.

LEONTES
                            I thought of her,
Even in these looks I made. — [*to* FLORIZEL] But your
    petition
Is yet unanswer'd. I will to your father:
Your honour not o'erthrown by your desires,
I am friend to them and you: upon which errand
I now go toward him; therefore follow me,
And mark what way I make: come, good my lord.
                                            [*Exeunt.*

SCENE II

Before LEONTES' *palace.*

Enter AUTOLYCUS *and a* GENTLEMAN.

AUTOLYCUS
Beseech you, sir, were you present at this relation?

FIRST GENTLEMAN
I was by at the opening of the fardel, heard the old
shepherd deliver the manner how he found it:
whereupon, after a little amazedness, we were all
commanded out of the chamber; only this, methought I
heard the shepherd say he found the child.

AUTOLYCUS
I would most gladly know the issue of it.

FIRST GENTLEMAN
I make a broken delivery of the business; — but the
changes I perceived in the king and Camillo were very

notes of admiration: they seem'd
almost, with staring on one another, to
tear the cases of their eyes; there was
speech in their dumbness, language in
their very gesture; they look'd as they
had heard of a world ransom'd, or one
destroy'd: a notable passion of wonder
appear'd in them; but the wisest
beholder, that knew no more but seeing,
could not say if the importance were joy
or sorrow, — but in the extremity of the
one, it must needs be. — Here comes a
gentleman that happily knows more.
        Enter another GENTLEMAN.
The news, Rogero?

SECOND GENTLEMAN
Nothing but bonfires: the oracle is
fulfill'd; the king's daughter is found:
such a deal of wonder is broken out
within this hour, that ballad-makers
cannot be able to express it. — Here
comes the Lady Paulina's steward: he
can deliver you more.
        Enter a third GENTLEMAN.
How goes it now, sir? this news, which
is call'd true, is so like an old tale, that
the verity of it is in strong suspicion:
has the king found his heir?

THIRD GENTLEMAN
Most true, if ever truth were pregnant
by circumstance: that which you hear
you'll swear you see, there is such
unity in the proofs. The mantle of
Queen Hermione's; her jewel about
the neck of it; the letters of Antigonus,
found with it, which they know to be his character; the
majesty of the creature, in resemblance of the mother;
the affection of nobleness, which nature shows above
her breeding; and many other evidences, — proclaim
her with all certainty to be the king's daughter. Did you
see the meeting of the two kings?

SECOND GENTLEMAN
No.

THIRD GENTLEMAN
Then have you lost a sight, which was to be seen, cannot
be spoken of. There might you have beheld one joy
crown another, so and in such manner, that it seem'd
sorrow wept to take leave of them, — for their joy waded
in tears. There was casting up of eyes, holding up of
hands, with countenance of such distraction, that they
were to be known by garment, not by favour. Our king,
being ready to leap out of himself for joy of his found
daughter, as if that joy were now become a loss, cries 'O,
thy mother, thy mother!' then asks Bohemia
forgiveness; then embraces his son-in-law; then again
worries he his daughter with clipping her; now he
thanks the old shepherd, which stands by like a
weather-bitten conduit of many kings' reigns. I never
heard of such another encounter, which lames report to
follow it, and undoes description to do it.

SECOND GENTLEMAN
What, pray you, became of Antigonus, that carried
hence the child?

THIRD GENTLEMAN
Like an old tale still, which will have matter to rehearse,
though credit be asleep, and not an ear open. He was
torn to pieces with a bear: this avouches the shepherd's
son; who has not only his innocence, which seems
much, to justify him, but a handkerchief and rings of
his, that Paulina knows.

FIRST GENTLEMAN
What became of his bark and his followers?

THIRD GENTLEMAN
Wrack'd the same instant of their master's death, and
in view of the shepherd: so that all the instruments
which aided to expose the child were even then lost
when it was found. But, O, the noble combat that, 'twixt
joy and sorrow, was fought in Paulina! She had one eye
declined for the loss of her husband, another elevated
that the oracle was fulfill'd: she lifted the princess from
the earth; and so locks her in embracing, as if she
would pin her to her heart, that she might no more be
in danger of losing.

FIRST GENTLEMAN
The dignity of this act was worth the audience of kings
and princes, for by such was it acted.

THIRD GENTLEMAN
One of the prettiest touches of all, and that which
angled for mine eyes — caught the water, though not
the fish — was when, at the relation of the queen's
death, with the manner how she came to't, — bravely

CLOWN Give me thy hand.

confess'd and lamented by the king, — how
attentiveness wounded his daughter; till, from one sign
of dolour to another, she did, with an 'Alas,' I would
fain say, bleed tears; for I am sure my heart wept blood.
Who was most marble there changed colour; some
swounded, all sorrow'd: if all the world could have
seen't, the woe had been universal.

FIRST GENTLEMAN
Are they return'd to the court?

THIRD GENTLEMAN
No: the princess hearing of her mother's statue, which is
in the keeping of Paulina, — a piece many years in
doing, and now newly perform'd by that rare Italian
master, Julio Romano, who, had he himself eternity, and
could put breath into his work, would beguile Nature of
her custom, so perfectly he is her ape: he so near to
Hermione hath done Hermione, that they say one
would speak to her, and stand in hope of answer: —
thither with all greediness of affection are they gone; and
there they intend to sup.

SECOND GENTLEMAN
I thought she had some great matter there in hand; for
she hath privately twice or thrice a day, ever since the
death of Hermione, visited that removed house. Shall
we thither, and with our company piece the rejoicing?

FIRST GENTLEMAN
Who would be thence that has the benefit of access?
every wink of an eye, some new grace will be born: our
absence makes us unthrifty to our knowledge. Let's
along.   [*Exeunt* GENTLEMEN.

AUTOLYCUS
Now, had I not the dash of my former life in me, would
preferment drop on my head. I brought the old man
and his son aboard the prince; told him I heard them
talk of a fardel, and I know not what: but he at that time,
overfond of the shepherd's daughter, — so he then
took her to be, — who began to be much sea-sick, and
himself little better, extremity of weather continuing,
this mystery remain'd undiscover'd. But 'tis all one to
me; for had I been the finder-out of this secret, it would
not have relish'd among my other discredits. — Here
come those I have done good to against my will, and
already appearing in the blossoms of their fortune.

            Enter SHEPHERD *and* CLOWN.

SHEPHERD
Come, boy; I am past mroe children, but thy sons and
daughters will be all gentlemen born.

CLOWN
You are well met, sir. You denied to fight with me this
other day, because I was no gentleman born. See you
these clothes? say you see them not, and think me still
no gentleman born: you were best say these robes are
not gentlemen born: give me the lie, do; and try
whether I am not now a gentleman born.

AUTOLYCUS
I know you are now, sir, a gentleman born.

CLOWN
Ay, and have I been so any time these four hours.

SHEPHERD
And so have I, boy.

CLOWN
So you have: — but I was a gentleman born before my father; for the king's son took me by the hand, and call'd me brother; and then the two kings call'd my father brother; and then the prince my brother and the princess my sister call'd my father father; and so we wept, — and there was the first gentleman-like tears that ever we shed.

SHEPHERD
We may live, son, to shed many more.

CLOWN
Ay; or else 'twere hard luck, being in so preposterous estate as we are.

AUTOLYCUS
I humbly beseech you, sir, to pardon me all the faults I have committed to your worship, and to give me your good report to the prince my master.

SHEPHERD
Prithee, son, do; for we must be gentle, now we are gentlemen.

CLOWN
Thou wilt amend thy life?

AUTOLYCUS
Ay, an it like your good worship.

CLOWN
Give me thy hand: I will swear to the prince thou art as honest a true fellow as any is in Bohemia.

SHEPHERD
You may say it, but not swear it.

CLOWN
Not swear it, now I am a gentleman? Let boors and franklins say it, I'll swear it.

SHEPHERD
How if it be false, son?

CLOWN
If it be ne'er so false, a true gentleman may swear it in the behalf of his friend: — and I'll swear to the prince thou art a tall fellow of thy hands, and that thou wilt not be drunk; but I know thou art no tall fellow of thy hands, and that thou wilt be drunk: but I'll swear it; and I would thou wouldst be a tall fellow of thy hands.

AUTOLYCUS
I will prove so, sir, to my power.

CLOWN
Ay, by any means prove a tall fellow: if I do not wonder how thou darest venture to be drunk, not being a tall fellow, trust me not. — [*Trumpets within.*] Hark! the kings and the princes, our kindred, are going to see the queen's picture. Come, follow us: we'll be thy good masters. [*Exeunt.*

SCENE III

A chapel in PAULINA'S *house.*

Enter LEONTES, POLIXENES, FLORIZEL, PERDITA, CAMILLO, PAULINA, LORDS, *and* ATTENDANTS.

LEONTES
O grave and good Paulina, the great comfort
That I have had of thee!

PAULINA
      What, sovereign sir,
I did not well, I meant well. All my services
You have paid home: but that you have vouchsafed
With your crown'd brother and these your contracted
Heirs of your kingdoms my poor house to visit,
It is a surplus of your Grace, which never
My life may last to answer.

LEONTES
      O, Paulina,
We honour you with trouble: — but we came
To see the statue of our queen: your gallery
Have we pass'd through, not without much content
In many singularities; but we saw not
That which my daughter came to look upon,
The statue of her mother.

PAULINA
      As she liv'd peerless,
So her dead likeness, I do well believe,
Excels whatever yet you look'd upon,
Or hand of man hath done; therefore I keep it
Lonely, apart. But here it is: prepare
To see the life as lively mock'd as ever
Still sleep mock'd death: behold, and say 'tis well.

PAULINA Draws a curtain, and discovers Hermione standing as a statue.

[PAULINA *draws a curtain, and discovers* HERMIONE *standing as a statue.*

I like your silence, — it the more shows off
Your wonder: but yet speak; — first, you, my liege:
Comes it not something near?

LEONTES
      Her natural posture! —
Chide me, dear stone, that I may say indeed
Thou art Hermione; or rather, thou art she
In thy not chiding, for she was as tender
As infancy and grace. — But yet, Paulina,
Hermione was not so much wrinkled, nothing
So aged as this seems.

POLIXENES
      O, not by much.

PAULINA
So much the more our carver's excellence;
Which lets go by some sixteen years, and makes her
As she liv'd now.

LEONTES
      As now she might have done,
So much to my good comfort, as it is
Now piercing to my soul. O, thus she stood,
Even with such life of majesty, — warm life,
As now it coldly stands, — when first I woo'd her!
I am asham'd: does not the stone rebuke me
For being more stone than it? — O royal piece,
There's magic in thy majesty; which has
My evils conjur'd to remembrance, and
From thy admiring daughter took the spirits,
Standing like stone with thee!

PERDITA
      And give me leave,
And do not say 'tis superstition that
I kneel, and then implore her blessing. — Lady,
Dear queen, that ended when I but began,
Give me that hand of yours to kiss.

PAULINA
      O, patience!
The statue is but newly fix'd, the colour's
Not dry.

CAMILLO
My lord, your sorrow was too sore laid on,
Which sixteen winters cannot blow away,
So many summers dry: scarce any joy
Did ever so long live; no sorrow
But kill'd itself much sooner.

POLIXENES
      Dear my brother,
Let him that was the cause of this have power
To take off so much grief from you as he
Will piece up in himself.

PAULINA
      Indeed, my lord,
If I had thought the sight of my poor image
Would thus have wrought you, — for the stone is mine, —
I'ld not have show'd it.

LEONTES
      Do not draw the curtain.

PAULINA
No longer shall you gaze on't, lest your fancy
May think anon it moves.

LEONTES
      Let be, let be. —
Would I were dead, but that, methinks, already —
What was he that did make it? — See, my lord,
Would you not deem it breath'd? and that those veins
Did verily bear blood?

POLIXENES
      Masterly done:
The very life seems warm upon her lip.

LEONTES
The fixture of her eye has motion in't,
As we are mock'd with art.

PAULINA
      I'll draw the curtain:
My lord's almost so far transported, that
He'll think anon it lives.

LEONTES
      O sweet Paulina,
Make me to think so twenty years together!

No settled senses of the world can match
The pleasure of that madness. Let't alone.

PAULINA
I am sorry, sir, I have thus far stirr'd you; but
I could afflict you further.

LEONTES
     Do, Paulina;
For this affliction has a taste as sweet
As any cordial comfort. — Still, methinks,
There is an air comes from her: what fine chisel
Could ever yet cut breath? Let no man mock me,
For I will kiss her.

PAULINA
     Good my lord, forbear:
The ruddiness upon her lip is wet;
You'll mar it, if you kiss it; stain your own
With oily painting. Shall I draw the curtain?

LEONTES
No, not these twenty years.

PERDITA
     So long could I
Stand by, a looker-on.

PAULINA
     Either forbear,
Quit presently the chapel, or resolve you
For more amazement. If you can behold it,
I'll make the statue move indeed, descend
And take you by the hand: but then you'll think, —
Which I protest against, — I am assisted
By wicked powers.

LEONTES
     What you can make her do,
I am content to look on; what to speak,
I am content to hear; for 'tis as easy
To make her speak as move.

PAULINA
     It is required
You do awake your faith. Then all stand still;
Or those that think it is unlawful business
I am about, let them depart.

LEONTES
     Proceed:
No foot shall stir.

PAULINA
     Music, awake her; strike! —   [*Music.*
'Tis time; descend; be stone no more; approach;
Strike all that look upon with marvel. Come;
I'll fill your grave up: stir, nay, come away;
Bequeath to death your numbness, for from him
Dear life redeems you. — You perceive she stirs:

  [HERMIONE *comes down from the pedestal.*

Start not; her actions shall be holy as
You hear my spell is lawful: do not shun her,
Until you see her die again; for then
You kill her double. Nay, present your hand:
When she was young, you woo'd her; now in age
Is she become the suitor.

LEONTES
     O, she's warm!
If this be magic, let it be an art
Lawful as eating.   [*Embracing her.*

POLIXENES
     She embraces him.

CAMILLO
She hangs about his neck:
If she pertain to life, let her speak too.

POLIXENES
Ay, and make't manifest where she has liv'd,
Or how stolen from the dead.

PAULINA
     That she is living,
Were it but told you, should be hooted at
Like an old tale: but it appears she lives,
Though yet she speak not. Mark a little while. —
Please you to interpose, fair madam; kneel,
And pray your mother's blessing. — Turn, good lady;
Our Perdita is found.

  [*Presenting* PERDITA, *who kneels to* HERMIONE.

HERMIONE
     You gods, look down,
And from your sacred vials pour your Graces
Upon my daughter's head! — Tell me, mine own,
Where hast thou been preserv'd? where liv'd? how
  found
Thy father's court? for thou shalt hear that I, —
Knowing by Paulina that the oracle
Gave hope thou wast in being, — have preserv'd
Myself to see the issue.

PAULINA
     There's time enough for that:
Lest they desire, upon this push, to trouble
Your joys with like relation. — Go together,
You precious winners all; your exultation
Partake to every one. I, an old turtle,
Will wing me to some wither'd bough, and there
My mate, that's never to be found again,
Lament till I am lost.

LEONTES
     O, peace, Paulina!
Thou shouldst a husband take by my consent,
As I by thine a wife: this is a match,
And made between's by vows. Thou hast found mine;
But how, is to be question'd; for I saw her,
As I thought, dead; and have, in vain, said many
A prayer upon her grave. I'll not seek far, —
For him, I partly know his mind, — to find thee
An honourable husband. Come, Camillo,
And take her by the hand; whose worth and honesty
Is richly noted; and here justified
By us, a pair of kings. — Let's from this place. —
What! look upon my brother: — both your pardons,
That e'er I put between your holy looks
My ill suspicions. — This your son-in-law,
And son unto the king, whom heavens directing,
Is troth-plight to your daughter. — Good Paulina,
Lead us from hence; where we may leisurely
Each one demand, and answer to his part
Perform'd in this wide gap of time, since first
We were dissever'd; hastily lead away. [*Exeunt.*

THE TEMPEST

DRAMATIS PERSONAE

ALONSO, *King of Naples.*
SEBASTIAN, *his brother.*
PROSPERO, *the right Duke of Milan.*
ANTONIO, *his brother, the usurping Duke of Milan.*
FERDINAND, *son to the King of Naples.*
GONZALO, *an honest old counsellor.*
ADRIAN,
FRANCISCO, } *lords.*
CALIBAN, *a savage and deformed slave.*

TRINCULO, *a jester.*
STEPHANO, *a drunken butler.*
MASTER OF A SHIP, BOATSWAIN, *and*
  MARINERS.
MIRANDA, *daughter to Prospero.*

ARIEL, *an airy spirit.*
IRIS,
CERES, } *presented by spirits.*

JUNO,
NYMPHS, } *presented by spirits.*
REAPERS,

OTHER SPIRITS ATTENDING ON PROSPERO.

SCENE — *A ship at sea; afterwards an island.*

ACT I

SCENE I

A ship at sea: a tempestuous noise of thunder and lightning heard.

Enter a SHIP-MASTER *and a* BOATSWAIN.

SHIP-MASTER
Boatswain!

BOATSWAIN
Here, master: what cheer?

SHIP-MASTER
Good, speak to the mariners: fall to't yarely, or we run ourselves a-ground: bestir, bestir.   [*Exit.*

Enter MARINERS.

BOATSWAIN
Heigh, my hearts! cheerly, cheerly, my hearts! yare, yare! Take in the topsail! Tend to the master's whistle! [*Exeunt* MARINERS.] — Blow, till thou burst thy wind, if room enough!

Enter ALONSO, SEBASTIAN, ANTONIO,
     FERDINAND, GONZALO, *and others.*

ALONSO
Good boatswain, have care. Where's the master? Play the men.

BOATSWAIN
I pray now, keep below.

ANTONIO
Where is the master, boatswain?

BOATSWAIN
Do you not hear him? You mar our labour: keep your cabins: you do assist the storm.

GONZALO
Nay, good, be patient.

BOATSWAIN
When the sea is. Hence! What cares these roarers for the name of king? To cabin: silence! trouble us not.

GONZALO
Good, yet remember whom thou hast aboard.

BOATSWAIN
None that I more love than myself. You are a counsellor; if you can command these elements to silence, and work the peace of the present, we will not hand a rope more; use your authority: if you cannot, give thanks you have lived so long, and make yourself ready in your cabin for the mischance of the hour, if it so hap. — Cheerly, good hearts! — Out of our way, I say.   [*Exit.*

GONZALO
I have great comfort from this fellow: methinks he hath no drowning-mark upon him; his complexion is perfect gallows. Stand fast, good Fate, to his hanging! make the rope of his destiny our cable, for our own doth little advantage! If he be not born to be hang'd, our case is miserable.   [*Exeunt.*

Enter BOATSWAIN.

BOATSWAIN
Down with the topmast! yare; lower, lower! Bring her to try with main-course! [*A cry within.*] A plague upon this howling! they are louder than the weather or our office.
     Enter SEBASTIAN, ANTONIO, *and* GONZALO.
Yet again! what do you here? Shall we give o'er, and drown? Have you a mind to sink?

SEBASTIAN
A pox o'your throat, you bawling, blasphemous, incharitable dog!

BOATSWAIN
Work you, then.

ANTONIO
Hang, cur, hang! you whoreson, insolent noisemaker, we are less afraid to be drown'd than thou art.

GONZALO
I'll warrant him for drowning; though the ship were no stronger than a nutshell, and as leaky as an unstanch'd wench.

BOATSWAIN
Lay her a-hold, a-hold! set her two courses off to sea again: lay her off!

Enter MARINERS *wet.*

MARINERS
All lost! to prayers, to prayers! all lost!

BOATSWAIN
What, must our mouths be cold?

GONZALO
The king and prince at prayers! let's assist them,
For our case is as theirs.

SEBASTIAN
                    I'm out of patience.

ANTONIO
We are merely cheated of our lives by drunkards:
This wide-chapp'd rascal, — would thou mightst lie drowning,
The washing of ten tides!

GONZALO
                    He'll be hang'd yet,
Though every drop of water swear against it,
And gape at widest to glut him.
          [*A confused noise within,* — 'Mercy on us!' —
'We split, we split!' — 'Farewell, my wife and children!' —
'Farewell, brother!' — 'We split, we split, we split!']

ANTONIO
Let's all sink with the king.

SEBASTIAN
                    Let's take leave of him.
          [*Exeunt* ANTONIO *and* SEBASTIAN.

GONZALO
Now would I give a thousand furlongs of sea for an acre of barren ground, — long heath, broom, furze, any thing. The wills above be done! but I would fain die a dry death.   [*Exeunt.*

SCENE II

The island: before PROSPERO'S *cell.*

Enter PROSPERO *and* MIRANDA.

MIRANDA
If by your art, my dearest father, you have
Put the wild waters in this roar, allay them.
The sky, it seems, would pour down stinking pitch,
But that the sea, mounting to the welkin's cheek,
Dashes the fire out. O, I have suffer'd
With those that I saw suffer! a brave vessel,
Who had, no doubt, some noble creature in her,
Dash'd all to pieces. O, the cry did knock
Against my very heart! Poor souls, they perish'd!
Had I been any god of power, I would
Have sunk the sea within the earth, or ere
It should the good ship so have swallow'd, and
The fraughting souls within her.

PROSPERO
                    Be collected;
No more amazement: tell your piteous heart
There's no harm done.

MIRANDA
                    O, woe the day!

PROSPERO
                    No harm.

I have done nothing but in care of thee,
Of thee, my dear one, thee, my daughter, who
Art ignorant of what thou art, naught knowing
Of whence I am, nor that I am more better
Than Prospero, master of a full poor cell,
And thy no greater father.

MIRANDA
                        More to know
Did never meddle with my thoughts.

PROSPERO
                              'Tis time
I should inform thee further. Lend thy hand,
And pluck my magic garment from me. So:
                    [*Lays down his mantle.*
Lie there, my art. Wipe thou thine eyes; have comfort.
The direful spectacle of the wrack, which touch'd
The very virtue of compassion in thee,
I have with such provision in mine art
So safely order'd, that there is no soul —
No, not so much perdition as an hair
Betid to any creature in the vessel
Which thou heard'st cry, which thou saw'st sink. Sit down;
For thou must now know further.

MIRANDA
                      You have often
Begun to tell me what I am; but stopp'd,
And left me to a bootless inquisition,
Concluding, 'Stay, not yet.'

PROSPERO
                      The hour's now come;
The very minute bids thee ope thine ear:
Obey, and be attentive. Canst thou remember
A time before we came unto this cell?
I do not think thou canst, for then thou wast not
Out three years old.

MIRANDA
                    Certainly, sir, I can.

PROSPERO
By what? by any other house or person?
Of any thing the image tell me that
Hath kept with thy remembrance.

MIRANDA
                    'Tis far off,
And rather like a dream than an assurance
That my remembrance warrants. Had I not
Four or five women once that tended me?

PROSPERO
Thou hadst, and more, Miranda. But how is it
That this lives in thy mind? What see'st thou else
In the dark backward and abysm of time?
If thou rememb'rest aught ere thou camest here,
How thou camest here thou mayst.

MIRANDA
                    But that I do not.

PROSPERO
Twelve year since, Miranda, twelve year since,
Thy father was the Duke of Milan, and
A prince of power.

MIRANDA
                Sir, are not you my father?

PROSPERO
Thy mother was a piece of virtue, and
She said thou wast my daughter; and thy father
Was Duke of Milan; thou his only heir,
And princess, no worse issued.

MIRANDA
                  O the heavens!
What foul play had we, that we came from thence?
Or blessed was't we did?

PROSPERO
                Both, both, my girl:
By foul play, as thou say'st, were we heav'd thence;
But blessedly holp hither.

MIRANDA
                O, my heart bleeds
To think o'the teen that I have turn'd you to,
Which is from my remembrance! Please you, further.

PROSPERO
My brother, and thy uncle, call'd Antonio, —
I pray thee, mark me, — that a brother should
Be so perfidious! — he whom, next thyself,
Of all the world I lov'd, and to him put
The manage of my state; as, at that time,
Through all the signiories it was the first,
And Prospero the prime duke, being so reputed
In dignity, and for the liberal arts
Without a parallel: those being all my study,
The government I cast upon my brother,
And to my state grew stranger, being transported

And rapt in secret studies. Thy false uncle —
Dost thou attend me?

MIRANDA
                Sir, most heedfully,

PROSPERO
Being once perfected how to grant suits,
How to deny them, who t'advance, and who
To trash for over-topping, new created
The creatures that were mine, I say, or chang'd 'em,
Or else new-form'd 'em; having both the key
Of officer and office, set all hearts i'the state
To what tune pleas'd his ear; that now he was
The ivy which had hid my princely trunk,
And suck'd my verdure out on't. Thou attend'st not.

MIRANDA
O, good sir, I do.

PROSPERO
              I pray thee, mark me.
I, thus neglecting worldly ends, all dedicate
To closeness, and the bettering of my mind
With that which, but by being so retired,
O'er-priz'd all popular rate, in my false brother
Awak'd an evil nature; and my trust,
Like a good parent, did beget of him
A falsehood, in its contrary as great
As my trust was; which had indeed no limit,
A confidence sans bound. He being thus lorded,
Not only with what my revenue yielded,
But what my power might else exact, like one
Who having into truth, by telling of it,
Made such a sinner of his memory,
To credit his own lie, he did believe
He was indeed the duke; out o'the substitution,
And executing the outward face of royalty,
With all prerogative: — hence his ambition growing, —
Dost thou hear?

MIRANDA
            Your tale, sir, would cure deafness.

PROSPERO
To have no screen between this part he play'd
And him he play'd it for, he needs will be
Absolute Milan. Me, poor man, my library
Was dukedom large enough: of temporal royalties
He thinks me now incapable; confederates —
So dry he was for sway — with the King of Naples
To give him annual tribute, do him homage,
Subject his coronet to his crown, and bend
The dukedom, yet unbow'd, — alas, poor Milan! —
To most ignoble stooping.

MIRANDA
            O the heavens!

PROSPERO
Mark his condition, and the event; then tell me
If this might be a brother.

MIRANDA
            I should sin
To think but nobly of my grandmother:
Good wombs have borne bad sons.

PROSPERO
            Now the condition.
The King of Naples, being an enemy
To me inveterate, hearkens my brother's suit;
Which was, that he, in lieu o' the premises, —
Of homage, and I know not how much tribute, —
Should presently extirpate me and mine
Out of the dukedom, and confer fair Milan,
With all the honours, on my brother: whereon,
A treacherous army levied, one midnight
Fated to the purpose, did Antonio open
The gates of Milan; and, i'the dead of darkness,
The ministers for the purpose hurried thence
Me and thy crying self.

MIRANDA
            Alack, for pity!
I, not rememb'ring how I cried out then,
Will cry it o'er again: it is a hint
That wrings mine eyes to't.

PROSPERO
            Hear a little further,
And then I'll bring thee to the present business
Which now's upon's; without the which this story
Were most impertinent.

MIRANDA
            Wherefore did they not
That hour destroy us?

PROSPERO
            Well demanded, wench:

PROSPERO No more amazement: tell your piteous heart there's no harm done.

My tale provokes that question. Dear, they durst not,
So dear the love my people bore me, nor set
A mark so bloody on the business; but
With colours fairer painted their foul ends.
In few, they hurried us aboard a bark,
Bore us some leagues to sea; where they prepared
A rotten carcass of a butt, not rigg'd,
Nor tackle, sail, nor mast; the very rats
Instinctively had quit it: there they hoist us,
To cry to the sea that roar'd to us; to sigh
To the winds, whose pity, sighing back again,
Did us but loving wrong.

MIRANDA
            Alack, what trouble
Was I then to you!

PROSPERO
            O, a cherubin
Thou wast that did preserve me! Thou didst smile,
Infused with a fortitude from heaven,
When I have deck'd the sea with drops full salt,
Under my burden groan'd; which rais'd in me
An undergoing stomach, to bear up
Against what should ensue.

MIRANDA
            How came we ashore?

PROSPERO
By Providence divine.
Some food we had, and some fresh water, that
A noble Neapolitan, Gonzalo,
Out of his charity (who being then appointed
Master of this design), did give us, with
Rich garments, linens, stuffs, and necessaries,
Which since have steaded much; so, of his gentleness,
Knowing I lov'd my books, he furnish'd me,
From mine own library, with volumes that
I prize above my dukedom.

MIRANDA
            Would I might
But ever see that man!

PROSPERO
            Now I arise:
          [*Resuming his mantle.*
Sit still, and hear the last of our sea-sorrow.
Here in this island we arrived; and here
Have I, thy schoolmaster, made thee more profit
Than other princesses' can, that have more time
For vainer hours, and tutors not so careful.

MIRANDA
Heavens thank you for't! And now, I pray you, sir,
For still 'tis beating in my mind, your reason
For raising this sea-storm?

PROSPERO
            Know thus far forth.

By accident most strange, bountiful Fortune,
Now my dear lady, hath mine enemies
Brought to this shore; and by my prescience
I find my zenith doth depend upon
A most auspicious star, whose influence
If now I court not, but omit, my fortunes
Will ever after droop. Here cease more questions:
Thou art inclin'd to sleep; 'tis a good dulness,
And give it way: I know thou canst not chuse. —
         [MIRANDA *sleeps.*
Come away, servant, come! I am ready now:
Approach, my Ariel; come!

      Enter ARIEL.

ARIEL
All hail, great master! grave sir, hail! I come
To answer thy best pleasure; be't to fly,
To swim, to dive into the fire, to ride
On the curl'd clouds, — to thy strong bidding task
Ariel and all his quality.

PROSPERO
       Hast thou, spirit,
Perform'd to point the tempest that I bade thee?

ARIEL
To every article.
I boarded the king's ship; now on the beak,
Now in the waist, the deck, in every cabin,
I flam'd amazement: sometime I'ld divide,
And burn in many places; on the topmast,
The yards, and bowsprit, would I flame distinctly,
Then meet, and join. Jove's lightnings, the precursors
O'the dreadful thunder-claps, more momentary
And sight-outrunning were not; the fire, and cracks
Of sulphurous roaring, the most mighty Neptune
Seem to besiege, and make his bold waves tremble,
Yea, his dread trident shake.

PROSPERO
      My brave spirit!
Who was so firm, so constant, that this coil
Would not infect his reason?

ARIEL
       Not a soul
But felt a fever of the mad, and play'd
Some tricks of desperation. All but mariners
Plung'd in the foaming brine, and quit the vessel,
Then all a-fire with me: the king's son, Ferdinand,
With hair up-staring, — then like reeds, not hair, —
Was the first man that leapt; cried, 'Hell is empty,
And all the devils are here.'

PROSPERO
      Why, that's my spirit!
But was not this nigh shore?

ARIEL
      Close by, my master.

PROSPERO
But are they, Ariel, safe?

ARIEL
      Not a hair perish'd;
On their sustaining garments not a blemish,
But fresher than before: and, as thou bad'st me,
In troops I have dispers'd them 'bout the isle.
The king's son have I landed by himself;
Whom I left cooling of the air with sighs
In an odd angle of the isle, and sitting,
His arms in this sad knot.

PROSPERO
      Of the king's ship
The mariners, say how thou hast disposed,

PROSPERO Sit still, and hear the last of our sea-sorrow.

And all the rest o'the fleet.
ARIEL
      Safely in harbour
Is the king's ship; in the deep nook, where once
Thou call'dst me up at midnight to fetch dew
From the still-vex'd Bermoothes, there she's hid:
The mariners all under hatches stow'd;
Who, with a charm join'd to their suffer'd labour,
I have left asleep: and for the rest o' the fleet,
Which I dispers'd, they all have met again,
And are upon the Mediterranean flote,
Bound sadly home for Naples;
Supposing that they saw the king's ship wrack'd,
And his great person perish.

PROSPERO
      Ariel, thy charge
Exactly is perform'd; but there's more work.
What is the time o'the day?

ARIEL
      Past the mid season.

PROSPERO
At least two glasses. The time 'twixt six and now
Must by us both be spent most preciously.

ARIEL
Is there more toil? Since thou dost give me pains,
Let me remember thee what thou hast promis'd,
Which is not yet perform'd me.

PROSPERO
      How now? moody?
What is't thou canst demand?

ARIEL
      My liberty.

PROSPERO
Before the time be out? no more!

ARIEL
      I prithee,
Remember I have done thee worthy service;
Told thee no lies, made thee no mistakings, serv'd
Without or grudge or grumblings; thou did promise
To bate me a full year.

PROSPERO
      Dost thou forget
From what a torment I did free thee?

ARIEL
       No.

PROSPERO
Thou dost; and think'st it much to tread the ooze
Of the salt deep,
To run upon the sharp wind of the north,
To do me business in the veins o'the earth
When it is bak'd with frost.

ARIEL
      I do not, sir.

PROSPERO
Thou liest, malignant thing! Hast thou forgot
The foul witch Sycorax, who with age and envy
Was grown into a hoop? hast thou forgot her?

ARIEL
No, sir.

PROSPERO
      Thou hast. Where was she born? speak; tell me.

ARIEL
Sir, in Argier.

PROSPERO
      O, was she so? I must
Once in a month recount what thou hast been,
    Which thou forgett'st. This damn'd
      witch Sycorax,
    For mischiefs manifold, and sorceries
      terrible
    To enter human hearing, from Argier,
    Thou know'st, was banish'd: for one
      thing she did
    They would not take her life. Is not this
      true?

ARIEL
Ay, sir.

PROSPERO
This blue-eyed hag was hither brought
    with child,
And here was left by the sailors. Thou,
    my slave,
As thou report'st thyself, was then her
    servant;
And, for thou wast a spirit too delicate
To act her earthy and abhorr'd
    commands,
Refusing her grand hests, she did
    confine thee,

By help of her more potent ministers,
And in her most unmitigable rage,
Into a cloven pine; within which rift
Imprison'd, thou didst painfully remain
A dozen years; within which space she died,
And left thee there; where thou didst vent thy groans
As fast as mill-wheels strike. Then was this island —
Save for the son that she did litter here,
A freckled whelp hag-born — not honour'd with
A human shape.

ARIEL
      Yes, Caliban, her son.

PROSPERO
Dull thing, I say so; he, that Caliban,
Whom now I keep in service. Thou best know'st
What torment I did find thee in; thy groans
Did make wolves howl, and penetrate the breasts
Of ever-angry bears: it was a torment
To lay upon the damn'd, which Sycorax
Could not again undo: it was mine art,
When I arrived and heard thee, that made gape
The pine, and let thee out.

ARIEL
      I thank thee, master.

PROSPERO
If thou more murmur'st, I will rend an oak,
And peg thee in his knotty entrails, till
Thou'st howl'd away twelve winters.

ARIEL
      Pardon, master:
I will be correspondent to command,
And do my spiriting gently.

PROSPERO
      Do so; and after two days
I will discharge thee.

ARIEL
      That's my noble master!
What shall I do? say what; what shall I do?

PROSPERO
Go make thyself like a nymph o'the sea: be subject
To no sight but thine and mine: invisible
To every eyeball else. Go take this shape,
And hither come in't: go; hence with diligence!
         [*Exit* ARIEL.
Awake, dear heart, awake! thou hast slept well;
Awake!

MIRANDA [*waking*].
    The strangeness of your story put
Heaviness in me.

PROSPERO
      Shake it off. Come on;
We'll visit Caliban my slave, who never
Yields us kind answer.

MIRANDA
      'Tis a villain, sir,
I do not love to look on.

PROSPERO
      But, as 'tis,
We cannot miss him: he does make our fire,
Fetch in our wood; and serves in offices
That profit us. — What, ho! slave! Caliban!
Thou earth, thou! speak.

CALIBAN [*within*].
      There's wood enough within.

PROSPERO
Come forth, I say! there's other business for thee:
Come, thou tortoise, when?
    Enter ARIEL *like a water-nymph.*
Fine apparition! My quaint Ariel,
Hark in thine ear.

ARIEL
      My lord, it shall be done.   [*Exit.*

PROSPERO
Thou poisonous slave, got by the devil himself
Upon thy wicked dam, come forth!
      Enter CALIBAN.

CALIBAN
As wicked dew as e'er my mother brush'd
With raven's feather from unwholesome fen
Drop on you both! a south-west blow on ye,
And blister you all o'er!

PROSPERO
For this, be sure, to-night thou shalt have cramps,
Side-stitches that shall pen thy breath up; urchins
Shall, for that vast of night that they may work,
All exercise on thee; thou shalt be pinch'd
As thick as honeycomb, each pinch more stinging
Than bees that made 'em.

PROSPERO Thou best know'st what torment I did find thee in.

CALIBAN

> I must eat my dinner.
> This island's mine, by Sycorax my mother,
> Which thou tak'st from me. When thou camest first,
> Thou strok'dst me, and made much of me; wouldst
>   give me
> Water with berries in't; and teach me how
> To name the bigger light, and how the less,
> That burn by day and night: and then I lov'd thee,
> And show'd thee all the qualities o'the isle,
> The fresh springs, brine-pits, barren place and fertile:
> Cursed be I that did so! All the charms
> Of Sycorax, toads, beetles, bats, light on you!
> For I am all the subjects that you have,
> Which first was mine own king: and here you sty me
> In this hard rock, whiles you do keep from me
> The rest o' the island.

PROSPERO

> Thou most lying slave,
> Whom stripes may move, not kindness! I have used
>   thee,
> Filth as thou art, with human care, and lodg'd thee
> In mine own cell, till thou didst seek to violate
> The honour of my child.

CALIBAN

> O ho, O ho! would't had been done!
> Thou didst prevent me; I had peopled else
> This isle with Calibans.

PROSPERO

> Abhorred slave,
> Which any print of goodness wilt not take,
> Being capable of all ill! I pitied thee,
> Took pains to make thee speak, taught thee each hour
> One thing or other: when thou didst not, savage,
> Know thine own meaning, but wouldst gabble like
> A thing most brutish, I endow'd thy purposes
> With words that made them known. But thy vile race,
> Though thou didst learn, had that in't which good
>   natures
> Could not abide to be with; therefore wast thou
> Deservedly confin'd into this rock,
> Who hadst deserved more than a prison.

CALIBAN

> You taught me language; and my profit on't
> Is, I know how to curse. The red plague rid you
> For learning me your language!

PROSPERO

> Hag-seed, hence!
> Fetch us in fuel; and be quick, thou'rt best,
> To answer other business. Shrugg'st thou, malice?
> If thou neglect'st, or dost unwillingly
> What I command, I'll rack thee with old cramps,
> Fill all thy bones with aches, make thee roar,
> That beasts shall tremble at thy din.

CALIBAN

> No, 'pray thee. —
> [aside] I must obey: his art is of such power,
> It would control my dam's god, Setebos,
> And make a vassal of him.

PROSPERO

> So, slave; hence!
>   [Exit CALIBAN.

Enter ARIEL, invisible, playing and singing;
FERDINAND following.

ARIEL'S *song.*

> Come unto these yellow sands,
> And then take hands:
>   Court'sied when you have
>   and kiss'd, —
> The wild waves whist, —
>   Foot it featly here and there;
>   And, sweet sprites,
>   the burden bear.
> Hark, hark!
> [*Burden, dispersedly, within.*
>   Bow, wow.]
> The watch-dogs bark:
> [*Burden, dispersedly, within.*
>   Bow, wow.]
> Hark, hark! I hear
> The strain of strutting chanticleer.
> [*Cry:* Cock-a-diddle-dow.]

FERDINAND

> Where should this music be? i' the air
>   or the earth?
> It sounds no more: — and, sure, it
>   waits upon
> Some god o' the island. Sitting on a
>   bank,
> Weeping again the king my father's
>   wrack,
> This music crept by me upon the waters,
> Allaying both their fury and my passion
> With its sweet air: thence I have follow'd it,
> Or it hath drawn me rather: — but 'tis gone.
> No, it begins again.

ARIEL *sings.*

> Full fadom five thy father lies;
>   Of his bones are coral made;
> Those are pearls that were his eyes;
>   Nothing of him that doth fade
> But doth suffer a sea-change
> Into something rich and strange.
> Sea-nymphs hourly ring his knell:
>   [*Burden within.* Ding-dong.]
> Hark! now I hear them, — Ding-dong, bell.

FERDINAND

> The ditty does remember my drown'd father: —
> This is no mortal business, nor no sound
> That the earth owes. — I hear it now above me.

PROSPERO

> The fringed curtains of thine eye advance,
> And say what thou see'st yond.

MIRANDA

> What is't? a spirit?
> Lord, how it looks about! Believe me, sir,
> It carries a brave form: — but 'tis a spirit.

PROSPERO

> No, wench; it eats, and sleeps, and hath such senses
> As we have, such. This gallant which thou see'st
> Was in the wrack; and, but he's something stain'd
> With grief, that's beauty's canker, thou mightst call
>   him
> A goodly person: he hath lost his fellows,
> And strays about to find 'em.

MIRANDA

> I might call him
> A thing divine; for nothing natural
> I ever saw so noble.

PROSPERO [aside].

> It goes on, I see,
> As my soul prompts it. — Spirit, fine spirit!
>   I'll free thee
> Within two days for this.

FERDINAND

> Most sure, the goddess
> On whom these airs attend! — Vouchsafe my
>   prayer
> May know if you remain upon this island;
> And that you will some good instruction give
> How I may bear me here: my prime request,
> Which I do last pronounce, is, O you wonder!
> If you be maid or no?

MIRANDA

> No wonder, sir;
> But certainly a maid.

FERDINAND

> My language! heavens!
> I am the best of them that speak this speech,
> Were I but where 'tis spoken.

PROSPERO

> How! the best!
> What wert thou, if the King of Naples heard thee?

FERDINAND

> A single thing, as I am now, that wonders
> To hear thee speak of Naples. He does hear me;
> And that he does I weep: myself am Naples;
> Who with mine eyes, never since at ebb, beheld
> The king my father wrack'd.

MIRANDA

> Alack! for mercy!

FERDINAND

> Yes, faith, and all his lords; the Duke of Milan
> And his brave son being twain.

PROSPERO [aside].

> The Duke of Milan
> And his more braver daughter could control thee,
> If now 'twere fit to do't. At the first sight
> They have chang'd eyes. Delicate Ariel,
> I'll set thee free for this! — A word, good sir;
> I fear you have done yourself some wrong: a word.

MIRANDA

> Why speaks my father so ungently? This
> Is the third man that e'er I saw; the first
> That e'er I sigh'd for: pity move my father
> To be inclin'd my way!

FERDINAND

> O, if a virgin,
> And your affection not gone forth, I'll make you
> The queen of Naples.

PROSPERO

> Soft, sir! one word more. —
> [aside] They are both in either's powers: but this swift
>   business
> I must uneasy make, lest too light winning
> Make the prize light. — One word more; I charge thee
> That thou attend me: thou dost here usurp
> The name thou owest not; and hast put thyself
> Upon this island as a spy, to win it
> From me, the lord on't.

FERDINAND

> No, as I am a man.

MIRANDA

> There's nothing ill can dwell in such a temple:
> If the ill spirit have so fair a house,
> Good things will strive to dwell with't.

PROSPERO

> Follow me.
> Speak not you for him; he's a traitor. Come;
> I'll manacle thy neck and feet together:
> Sea-water shalt thou drink; thy food shall be
> The fresh-brook muscles, wither'd roots, and husks
> Wherein the acorn cradled. Follow.

FERDINAND

> No;
> I will resist such entertainment till
> Mine enemy has more power.
>   [*Draws, and is charm'd from moving.*

MIRANDA

> O dear father,
> Make not too rash a trial of him, for
> He's gentle, and not fearful.

PROSPERO

> What, I say,
> My foot my tutor? Put thy sword up, traitor;
> Who makest a show, but darest not strike, thy
>   conscience
> Is so possess'd with guilt: come from thy ward;
> For I can here disarm thee with this stick,
> And make thy weapon drop.

PROSPERO What, ho! slave! Caliban! thou earth, thou! speak.

MIRANDA

    Beseech you, father! —

PROSPERO

Hence! hang not on my garments.

MIRANDA

      Sir, have pity;

I'll be his surety.

PROSPERO

    Silence! one word more
Shall make me chide thee, if not hate thee. What,
An advocate for an impostor! hush!
Thou think'st there is no more such shapes as he,
Having seen but him and Caliban: foolish wench!
To the most of men this is a Caliban,
And they to him are angels.

MIRANDA

     My affections
Are, then, most humble; I have no ambition
To see a goodlier man.

PROSPERO

    Come on; obey:
Thy nerves are in their infancy again,
And have no vigour in them.

FERDINAND

     So they are:
My spirits, as in a dream, are all bound up.
My father's loss, the weakness which I feel,
The wrack of all my friends, nor this man's threats
To whom I am subdued, are but light to me,
Might I but through my prison once a day
Behold this maid: all corners else o'the earth
Let liberty make use of; space enough
Have I in such a prison.

PROSPERO [*aside*].

    It works. — Come on. —
       [*To* FERDINAND.
Thou hast done well, fine Ariel! — Follow me. —
       [*To* FERDINAND.
Hark what thou else shalt do me.   [*To* ARIEL.

MIRANDA

    Be of comfort;
My father's of a better nature, sir,
Than he appears by speech: this is unwonted
Which now came from him.

PROSPERO

    Thou shalt be as free
As mountain winds: but then exactly do
All points of my command.

ARIEL

    To the syllable.

PROSPERO

Come, follow. — Speak not for him.   [*Exeunt.*

PROSPERO My brave spirit!

ACT II

SCENE I

Another part of the island.

Enter ALONSO, SEBASTIAN, ANTONIO,
GONZALO, ADRIAN, FRANCISCO, *and others.*

GONZALO

Beseech you, sir, be merry; you have cause,
So have we all, of joy; for our escape
Is much beyond our loss. Our hint of woe
Is common; every day some sailor's wife,
The masters of some merchant, and the merchant,
Have just our theme of woe; but for the miracle,
I mean our preservation, few in millions
Can speak like us: then wisely, good sir, weigh
Our sorrow with our comfort.

ALONSO

     Prithee, peace.

SEBASTIAN

He receives comfort like cold porridge.

ANTONIO

The visitor will not give him o'er so.

SEBASTIAN

Look, he's winding up the watch of his wit; by and by it will strike.

GONZALO

Sir, —

SEBASTIAN

One: tell.

GONZALO

When every grief is entertain'd that's offer'd,
Comes to the entertainer —

SEBASTIAN

A dollar.

GONZALO

Dolour comes to him, indeed; you have spoken truer than you purposed.

SEBASTIAN

You have taken it wiselier than I meant you should.

GONZALO

Therefore, my lord, —

ANTONIO

Fie, what a spendthrift is he of his tongue!

ALONSO

I prithee, spare.

GONZALO

    Well, I have done: but yet, —

SEBASTIAN

He will be talking.

ANTONIO

Which, of he or Adrian, for a good wager, first begins to crow?

SEBASTIAN

The old cock.

ANTONIO

The cockerel.

SEBASTIAN

Done! The wager?

ANTONIO

A laughter.

SEBASTIAN

A match!

ADRIAN

Though this island seem to be desert, —

SEBASTIAN

Ha, ha, ha!

ANTONIO

So: you've paid.

ADRIAN

Uninhabitable, and almost inaccessible, —

SEBASTIAN

Yet, —

ADRIAN

Yet, —

ANTONIO

He could not miss't.

ADRIAN

It must needs be of subtle, tender, and delicate temperance.

ANTONIO

Temperance was a delicate wench.

SEBASTIAN

Ay, and a subtle; as he most learnedly deliver'd.

ADRIAN

The air breathes upon us here most sweetly.

SEBASTIAN

As if it had lungs, and rotten ones.

ANTONIO

Or as 'twere perfumed by a fen.

GONZALO

Here is everything advantageous to life.

ANTONIO

True; save means to live.

SEBASTIAN

Of that there's none, or little.

GONZALO

How lush and lusty the grass looks! how green!

ANTONIO

The ground, indeed, is tawny.

SEBASTIAN

With an eye of green in't.

ANTONIO

He misses not much.

SEBASTIAN

No; he doth but mistake the truth totally.

GONZALO

But the rarity of it is, — which is indeed almost beyond credit, —

SEBASTIAN

As many vouch'd rarities are.

GONZALO

That our garments, being, as they were, drench'd in the sea, hold, notwithstanding, their freshness and glosses, being rather new-dyed than stain'd with salt water.

ANTONIO

If but one of his pockets could speak, would it not say he lies?

SEBASTIAN

Ay, or very falsely pocket up his report.

GONZALO

Methinks our garments are now as fresh as when we put them on first in Afric, at the marriage of the king's fair daughter Claribel to the King of Tunis.

FERDINAND Where should this music be?

SEBASTIAN
'Twas a sweet marriage, and we prosper well in our return.

ADRIAN
Tunis was never graced before with such a paragon to their queen.

GONZALO
Not since widow Dido's time.

ANTONIO
Widow! a pox o'that! How came that widow in? widow Dido!

SEBASTIAN
What if he had said 'widower Aeneas' too? Good Lord, how you take it!

ADRIAN
Widow Dido said you? you make me study of that: she was of Carthage, not of Tunis.

GONZALO
This Tunis, sir, was Carthage.

ADRIAN
Carthage?

GONZALO
I assure you, Carthage.

ANTONIO
His word is more than the miraculous harp.

SEBASTIAN
He hath raised the wall, and houses too.

ANTONIO
What impossible matter will he make easy next?

SEBASTIAN
I think he will carry this island home in his pocket, and give it his son for an apple.

ANTONIO
And, sowing the kernels of it in the sea, bring forth more islands.

GONZALO
Ay.

ANTONIO
Why, in good time.

GONZALO
Sir, we were talking that our garments seem now as fresh as when we were at Tunis at the marriage of your daughter, who is now queen.

ANTONIO
And the rarest that e'er came there.

SEBASTIAN
Bate, I beseech you, widow Dido.

ANTONIO
O, widow Dido: ay, widow Dido.

GONZALO
Is not, sir, my doublet as fresh as the first day I wore it? I mean, in a sort.

ANTONIO
That sort was well fish'd for.

GONZALO
When I wore it at your daughter's marriage?

ALONSO
You cram these words into mine ears against
The stomach of my sense. Would I had never
Married my daughter there! for, coming thence,
My son is lost; and, in my rate, she too,
Who is so far from Italy removed,
I ne'er again shall see her. O thou mine heir
Of Naples and of Milan, what strange fish
Hath made his meal on thee?

FRANCISCO
Sir, he may live:
I saw him beat the surges under him,
And ride upon their backs; he trod the water,
Whose enmity he flung aside, and breasted
The surge most swoll'n that met him; his bold head
'Bove the contentious waves he kept, and oar'd
Himself with his good arms in lusty stroke
To the shore, that o'er his wave-worn basis bow'd,
As stooping to relieve him: I not doubt
He came alive to land.

ALONSO
No, no, he's gone.

SEBASTIAN
Sir, you may thank yourself for this great loss,
That would not bless our Europe with your daughter,
But rather lose her to an African;
Where she, at least, is banish'd from your eye,
Who hath cause to wet the grief on't.

ALONSO
Prithee, peace.

SEBASTIAN
You were kneel'd to, and importun'd otherwise,
By all of us; and the fair soul herself
Weigh'd, between loathness and obedience, at
Which end o'the beam should bow. We have lost your son,
I fear, for ever: Milan and Naples have
More widows in them of this business' making
Than we bring men to comfort them:
The fault's your own.

ALONSO
So is the dear'st o'the loss.

GONZALO
My lord Sebastian,
The truth you speak doth lack some gentleness,
And time to speak it in: you rub the sore,
When you should bring the plaster.

SEBASTIAN
Very well.

ANTONIO
And most chirurgeonly.

GONZALO
It is foul weather in us all, good sir,
When you are cloudy.

SEBASTIAN
Foul weather!

ANTONIO
Very foul.

GONZALO
Had I plantation of this isle, my lord, —

ANTONIO
He'd sow't with nettle-seed.

SEBASTIAN
Or docks, or mallows.

GONZALO
And were the king on't, what would I do?

SEBASTIAN
Scape being drunk for want of wine.

GONZALO
I' the commonwealth I would by contraries
Execute all things; for no kind of traffic
Would I admit; no name of magistrate;
Letters should not be known; riches, poverty,
And use of service, none; contract, succession,
Bourn, bound of land, tilth, vineyard, none;
No use of metal, corn, or wine, or oil;
No occupation; all men idle, all;
And women too, — but innocent and pure;
No sovereignty, —

SEBASTIAN
Yet he would be king on't.

ANTONIO
The latter end of his commonwealth forgets the beginning.

GONZALO
All things in common nature should produce
Without sweat or endeavour: treason, felony,
Sword, pike, knife, gun, or need of any engine,
Would I not have; but nature should bring forth,
Of its own kind, all foison, all abundance,
To feed my innocent people.

SEBASTIAN
No marrying 'mong his subjects?

ANTONIO
None, man; all idle; whores and knaves.

GONZALO
I would with such perfection govern, sir,
T'excel the golden age.

SEBASTIAN
'Save his majesty!

ANTONIO
Long live Gonzalo!

GONZALO
And, — do you mark me, sir? —

ALONSO
Prithee, no more: thou dost talk nothing to me.

GONZALO
I do well believe your highness; and did it to minister occasion to these gentlemen, who are of such sensible and nimble lungs that they always use to laugh at nothing.

ANTONIO
'Twas you we laugh'd at.

GONZALO
Who in this kind of merry fooling am nothing to you: so you may continue, and laugh at nothing still.

ANTONIO
What a blow was there given!

SEBASTIAN
An it had not fallen flat-long.

GONZALO
You are gentlemen of brave mettle; you would lift the moon out of her sphere, if she would continue in it five weeks without changing.

Enter ARIEL, *invisible, playing solemn music.*

SEBASTIAN
We would so, and then go a bat-fowling.

ANTONIO
Nay, good my lord, be not angry.

GONZALO
No, I warrant you; I will not adventure my discretion so weakly. Will you laugh me asleep, for I am very heavy?

ANTONIO
Go sleep, and hear us.

[*All sleep except* ALONSO,
SEBASTIAN, *and* ANTONIO.

ALONSO
What, all so soon asleep! I wish mine eyes
Would, with themselves, shut up my thoughts: I find
They are inclin'd to do so.

SEBASTIAN
Please you, sir,
Do not omit the heavy offer of it:
It seldom visits sorrow; when it doth,
It is a comforter.

ANTONIO
We two, my lord,
Will guard your person while you take your rest,
And watch your safety.

ALONSO
Thank you. — Wondrous heavy.
[ALONSO *sleeps. Exit* ARIEL.

SEBASTIAN
What a strange drowsiness possesses them!

ANTONIO
It is the quality o'the climate.

SEBASTIAN
Why
Doth it not, then, our eyelids sink? I find not
Myself dispos'd to sleep.

ANTONIO
Nor I; my spirits are nimble.
They fell together all, as by consent;
They dropp'd, as by a thunder-stroke. What might,
Worthy Sebastian, O, what might? — No more: —
And yet me thinks I see it in thy face,
What thou shouldst be: the occasion speaks thee; and
My strong imagination sees a crown
Dropping upon thy head.

SEBASTIAN
What, art thou waking?

ANTONIO
Do you not hear me speak?

SEBASTIAN
I do; and surely
It is a sleepy language, and thou speak'st
Out of thy sleep. What is it thou didst say?
This is a strange repose, to be asleep
With eyes wide open; standing, speaking, moving,
And yet so fast asleep.

ANTONIO
Noble Sebastian,
Thou lett'st thy fortune sleep, — die, rather; wink'st
Whiles thou art waking.

SEBASTIAN
Thou dost snore distinctly;
There's meaning in thy snores.

ANTONIO
I am more serious than my custom: you
Must be so too, if heed me; which to do
Trebles thee o'er.

SEBASTIAN
Well, I am standing water.

ANTONIO
I'll teach you how to flow.

SEBASTIAN
Do so: to ebb
Hereditary sloth instructs me.

ANTONIO
O,
If you but knew how you the purpose cherish
Whiles thus you mock it! how, in stripping it,
You more invest it! Ebbing men, indeed,
Most often do so near the bottom run
By their own fear or sloth.

SEBASTIAN
Prithee, say on:
The setting of thine eye and cheek proclaim

A matter from thee; and a birth, indeed,
Which throes thee much to yield.

ANTONIO

Thus, sir:
Although this lord of weak remembrance, this,
Who shall be of as little memory
When he is earth'd, hath here almost persuaded, —
For he's a spirit of persuasion, only
Professes to persuade, — the king his son's alive,
'Tis as impossible that he's undrown'd
As he that sleeps here swims.

SEBASTIAN

I have no hope
That he's undrown'd.

ANTONIO

O, out of that 'no hope'
What great hope have you! no hope, that way, is
Another way so high a hope that even
Ambition cannot pierce a wink beyond,
But doubts discovery there. Will you grant with me
That Ferdinand is drown'd?

SEBASTIAN

He's gone.

ANTONIO

Then, tell me,
Who's the next heir of Naples?

SEBASTIAN

Claribel.

ANTONIO

She that is queen of Tunis; she that dwells
Ten leagues beyond man's life; she that from Naples
Can have no note, unless the sun were post, —
The man-i' the-moon's too slow, — till new-born chins
Be rough and razorable; she that — from whom
We all were sea-swallow'd, though some cast again;
And, by that destiny, to perform an act
Whereof what's past is prologue; what to come,
In yours and my discharge.

SEBASTIAN

What stuff is this! — How say you?
'Tis true, my brother's daughter's queen of Tunis;
So is she heir of Naples; 'twixt which regions
There is some space.

ANTONIO

A space whose every cubit
Seems to cry out, 'How shall that Claribel
Measure us back to Naples? Keep in Tunis,
And let Sebastian wake!' — Say, this were death
That now hath seiz'd them; why, they were no worse
Than now they are. There be that can rule Naples
As well as he that sleeps; lords that can prate
As amply and unnecessarily
As this Gonzalo; I myself could make
A chough of as deep chat. O, that you bore
The mind that I do! what a sleep were this
For your advancement! Do you understand me?

SEBASTIAN

Methinks I do.

ANTONIO

And how does your content
Tender your own good fortune?

SEBASTIAN

I remember
You did supplant your brother Prospero.

ANTONIO

True:
And look how well my garments sit upon me;
Much feater than before: my brother's servants
Were then my fellows; now they are my men.

SEBASTIAN

But, for your conscience, —

ANTONIO

Ay, sir; where lies that? if 'twere a kibe,
'Twould put me to my slipper: but I feel not
This deity in my bosom: twenty consciences,
That stand 'twixt me and Milan, candied be they,
And melt, ere they molest! Here lies your brother,
No better than the earth he lies upon,
If he were that which now he's like, that's dead;
Whom I, with this obedient steel, three inches of it,
Can lay to bed for ever; whiles you, doing thus,
To the perpetual wink for aye might put
This ancient morsel, this Sir Prudence, who
Should not upbraid our course. For all the rest,
They'll take suggestion as a cat laps milk;
They'll tell the clock to any business that
We say befits the hour.

SEBASTIAN

Thy case, dear friend,
Shall be my precedent; as thou gott'st Milan,

I'll come by Naples. Draw thy sword: one stroke
Shall free thee from the tribute which thou pay'st;
And I the king shall love thee.

ANTONIO

Draw together;
And when I rear my hand, do you the like,
To fall it on Gonzalo.

SEBASTIAN

O, but one word.
Enter ARIEL, invisible, with music and song.

ARIEL

My master through his art foresees the danger
That you, his friend, are in; and sends me forth, —
For else his project dies, — to keep them living.
[*Sings in* GONZALO'*s ear.*
While you here do snoring lie,
Open-eyed conspiracy
His time doth take.
If of life you keep a care,
Shake off slumber, and beware:
Awake, awake!

ANTONIO

Then let us both be sudden.

GONZALO [*waking*].

Now, good angels
Preserve the king! Why, how now? ho, awake!
Why are you drawn? wherefore this ghastly looking?

ALONSO [*waking*].

What's the matter?

SEBASTIAN

Whiles we stood here securing your repose,
Even now, we heard a hollow burst of bellowing
Like bulls, or rather lions: did 't not wake you?
It struck mine ear most terribly.

ALONSO

I heard nothing.

ANTONIO

O, 'twas a din to fright a monster's ear,
To make an earthquake! sure, it was the roar
Of a whole herd of lions.

ALONSO

Heard you this, Gonzalo?

GONZALO

Upon mine honour, sir, I heard a humming,
And that a strange one too, which did awake me:
I shak'd you, sir, and cried: as mine eyes open'd,
I saw their weapons drawn: — there was a noise,
That's verily. 'Tis best we stand upon our guard,
Or that we quit this place; let's draw our weapons.

ALONSO

Lead off this ground; and let's make further search
For my poor son.

GONZALO

Heavens keep him from these beasts!
For he is, sure, i' the island.

ALONSO

Lead away.

ARIEL

Prospero my lord shall know what I have done: —
So, king, go safely on to seek thy son. [*Exeunt.*

SCENE II

Another part of the island.

*Enter CALIBAN with a burden of wood. A noise of
thunder heard.*

CALIBAN

All the infections that the sun sucks up
From bogs, fens, flats, on Prosper fall, and make him
By inch-meal a disease! His spirits hear me,
And yet I needs must curse. But they'll nor pinch,
Fright me with urchin-shows, pitch me i' the mire,
Nor lead me, like a firebrand, in the dark
Out of my way, unless he bid 'em: but
For every trifle are they set upon me;
Sometime like apes, that mow and chatter at me
And after bite me; then like hedgehogs, which
Lie tumbling in my barefoot way, and mount
Their pricks at my footfall; sometime am I
All wound with adders, who with cloven tongues
Do hiss me into madness. Lo, now, lo!
Here comes a spirit of his; and to torment me
For bringing wood in slowly. I'll fall flat;
Perchance he will not mind me.

Enter TRINCULO.

TRINCULO

Here's neither bush nor shrub, to bear off any weather
at all, and another storm brewing; I hear it sing i' the

wind: yond same black cloud, yond huge one, looks like
a foul bombard that would shed his liquor. If it should
thunder as it did before, I know not where to hide my
head: yond same cloud cannot choose but fall by
pailfuls. — What have we here? a man or a fish? dead
or alive? A fish: he smells like a fish; a very ancient and
fish-like smell; a kind of, not of the newest, Poor-John.
A strange fish! Were I in England now, as once I was,
and had but this fish painted, not a holiday fool there
but would give a piece of silver: there would this
monster make a man; any strange beast there makes a
man: when they will not give a doit to relieve a lame
beggar, they will lay out ten to see a dead Indian. Legg'd
like a man! and his fins like arms! Warm, o' my troth! I
do now let loose my opinion, hold it no longer, — this
is no fish, but an islander, that hath lately suffer'd by a
thunderbolt. [*Thunder.*] Alas, the storm is come again!
my best way is to creep under his gaberdine; there is no
other shelter hereabout: misery acquaints a man with
strange bedfellows. I will here shroud till the dregs of
the storm be past.
[*Creeps under* CALIBAN'S *gaberdine.*
Enter STEPHANO, *singing; a bottle in his hand.*

STEPHANO

I shall no more to sea, to sea,
Here shall I die ashore, —
This is a very scurvy tune to sing at a man's funeral:
well, here's my comfort. [*Drinks.*
The master, the swabber, the boatswain, and I,
The gunner, and his mate,
Loved Mall, Meg, and Marian, and Margery,
But none of us cared for Kate;
For she had a tongue with a tang,
Would cry to a sailor, Go hang!
She loved not the savour of tar nor of pitch;
Yet a tailor might scratch her where'er she did itch.
Then, to sea, boys, and let her go hang!
This is a scurvy tune too: but here's my comfort.
[*Drinks.*

CALIBAN

Do not torment me: — O!

STEPHANO

What's the matter? Have we devils here? Do you put
tricks upon's with savages and men of Inde? ha! I have
not scaped drowning, to be afeard now of your four
legs; for it hath been said, As proper a man as ever went
on four legs cannot make him give ground; and it shall
be said so again, while Stephano breathes at nostrils.

CALIBAN

The spirit torments me: — O!

STEPHANO

This is some monster of the isle with four legs, who
hath got, as I take it, an ague. Where the devil should he
learn our language? I will give him some relief, if it be
but for that. If I can recover him, and keep him tame,
and get to Naples with him, he's a present for any
emperor that ever trod on neat's-leather.

CALIBAN Perchance he will not mind me.

TRINCULO What have we here? a man or a fish?

CALIBAN
Do not torment me, prithee; I'll bring my wood home faster.
STEPHANO
He's in his fit now, and does not talk after the wisest. He shall taste of my bottle: if he have never drunk wine afore, it will go near to remove his fit. If I can recover him, and keep him tame, I will not take too much for him; he shall pay for him that hath him, and that soundly.
CALIBAN
Thou dost me yet but little hurt; thou wilt anon, I know it by thy trembling: now Prosper works upon thee.
STEPHANO
Come on your ways; open your mouth; here is that which will give language to you, cat: open your mouth; this will shake your shaking, I can tell you, and that soundly: you cannot tell who's your friend: open your chaps again.
TRINCULO
I should know that voice: it should be — but he is drown'd; and these are devils: — O, defend me!
STEPHANO
Four legs and two voices, — a most delicate monster! His forward voice, now, is to speak well of his friend; his backward voice is to utter foul speeches and to detract. If all the wine in my bottle will recover him, I will help his ague. — Come, — Amen! I will pour some in thy other mouth.
TRINCULO
Stephano! —
STEPHANO
Doth thy other mouth call me? — Mercy, mercy! This is a devil, and no monster: I will leave him; I have no long spoon.
TRINCULO
Stephano! — if thou be'st Stephano, touch me, and speak to me; for I am Trinculo, — be not afeard, — thy good friend, Trinculo.
STEPHANO
If thou be'st Trinculo, come forth: I'll pull thee by the lesser legs: if any be Trinculo's legs, these are they. [Draws TRINCULO out by the legs.] — Thou art very Trinculo indeed! How camest thou to be the siege of this moon-calf? can he vent Trinculos?
TRINCULO
I took him to be kill'd with a thunder-stroke. — But art thou not drown'd, Stephano? I hope, now, thou art not drown'd. Is the storm overblown? I hid me under the dead moon-calf's gaberdine for fear of the storm. And art thou living, Stephano? O Stephano, two Neapolitans scaped!
STEPHANO
Prithee, do not turn me about; my stomach is not constant.
CALIBAN [aside].
These be fine things, an if they be not sprites. That's a brave god, and bears celestial liquor: I will kneel to him.
STEPHANO
How didst thou scape? How camest thou hither? swear, by this bottle, how thou camest hither. I escaped upon a butt of sack, which the sailors heaved overboard, by this bottle! which I made of the bark of a tree with mine own hands, since I was cast ashore.

CALIBAN
I'll swear, upon that bottle, to be thy true subject; for the liquor is not earthly.
STEPHANO
Here; swear, then, how thou escapedst.
TRINCULO
Swum ashore, man, like a duck: I can swim like a duck, I'll be sworn.
STEPHANO
Here, kiss the book. Though thou canst swim like a duck, thou art made like a goose.
TRINCULO
O Stephano, hast any more of this?
STEPHANO
The whole butt, man: my cellar is in a rock by the sea-side, where my wine is hid. — How now, moon-calf! how does thine ague?
CALIBAN
Hast thou not dropp'd from heaven?
STEPHANO
Out o'the moon, I do assure thee: I was the man-i'the-moon when time was.
CALIBAN
I have seen thee in her, and I do adore thee: my mistress show'd me thee, and thy dog, and thy bush.
STEPHANO
Come, swear to that; kiss the book: — I will furnish it anon with new contents: — swear.
TRINCULO
By this good light, this is a very shallow monster! — I afeard of him! — a very weak monster: — the man-i'the-moon! — a most poor credulous monster! — Well drawn, monster, in good sooth.
CALIBAN
I'll show thee every fertile inch o'the island; and I will kiss thy foot: I prithee, be my god.
TRINCULO
By this light, a most perfidious and drunken monster! when's god's asleep, he'll rob his bottle.
CALIBAN
I'll kiss thy foot; I'll swear myself thy subject.
STEPHANO
Come on, then; down, and swear.
TRINCULO
I shall laugh myself to death at this puppy-headed monster. A most scurvy monster! I could find in my heart to beat him, —
STEPHANO
Come kiss.
TRINCULO
But that the poor monster's in drink: an abominable monster!
CALIBAN
I'll show thee the best springs; I'll pluck thee berries; I'll fish for thee, and get thee wood enough.
A plague upon the tyrant that I serve!
I'll bear him no more sticks, but follow thee,
Thou wondrous man.
TRINCULO
A most ridiculous monster, to make a wonder of a poor drunkard!
CALIBAN
I prithee, let me bring thee where crabs grow;
And I with my long nails will dig thee pig-nuts;
Show thee a jay's nest, and instruct thee how
To snare the nimble marmoset; I'll bring thee
To clustering filberts, and sometimes I'll get thee
Young scamels from the rock. Wilt thou go with me?
STEPHANO
I prithee now, lead the way, without any more talking. — Trinculo, the king and all our company else being drown'd, we will inherit here. Here, bear my bottle: fellow Trinculo, we'll find him by and by again.
CALIBAN [sings drunkenly].
　　　Farewell, master; farewell, farewell!
TRINCULO
A howling monster; a drunken monster!
CALIBAN
　　　No more dams I'll make for fish;
　　　　　Nor fetch in firing
　　　　　At requiring;
　　　Nor scrape trencher, nor wash dish:
　　　　　'Ban, 'Ban, Ca–Caliban
　　　Has a new master: get a new man.
Freedom, high-day! high-day, freedom! freedom, high-day, freedom!
STEPHANO
O brave monster! lead the way. 　　　　　[Exeunt.

ACT III

SCENE I

Before PROSPERO'S cell.

Enter FERDINAND, bearing a log.

FERDINAND
There be some sports are painful, and their labour
Delight in them sets off: some kinds of baseness
Are nobly undergone; and most poor matters
Point to rich ends. This my mean task
Would be as heavy to me as odious, but
The mistress which I serve quickens what's dead,
And makes my labours pleasures: O, she is
Ten times more gentle than her father's crabb'd;
And he's compos'd of harshness. I must remove
Some thousands of these logs, and pile them up,
Upon a sore injunction: my sweet mistress
Weeps when she sees me work; and says such baseness
Had never like executor. I forget:
But these sweet thoughts do even refresh my labour;
Most busiless, when I do it.

　　　Enter MIRANDA; and PROSPERO behind.

MIRANDA
　　　　　　　Alas, now, pray you,
Work not so hard: I would the lightning had
Burnt up those logs that you are enjoin'd to pile!
Pray, set it down, and rest you: when this burns,
'Twill weep for having wearied you. My father
Is hard at study; pray, now, rest yourself:
He's safe for these three hours.
FERDINAND
　　　　　　　O most dear mistress,
The sun will set before I shall discharge
What I must strive to do.
MIRANDA
　　　　　　　If you'll sit down,
I'll bear your logs the while: pray, give me that;
I'll carry it to the pile.
FERDINAND
　　　　　　　No, precious creature;
I had rather crack my sinews, break my back,
Than you should such dishonour undergo,
While I sit lazy by.
MIRANDA
　　　　　　　It would become me
As well as it does you: and I should do it
With much more ease; for my good will is to it,
And yours it is against.
PROSPERO [aside].
　　　　　　　Poor worm, thou art infected!
This visitation shows it.
MIRANDA
　　　　　　　You look wearily.
FERDINAND
No, noble mistress; 'tis fresh morning with me
When you are by at night. I do beseech you, —
Chiefly that I might set it in my prayers, —
What is your name?
MIRANDA
　　　　　　　Miranda: — O my father,
I've broke your hest to say so!

FERDINAND
                    Admired Miranda!
Indeed the top of admiration; worth
What's dearest to the world! Full many a lady
I have eyed with best regard; and many a time
The harmony of their tongues hath into bondage
Brought my too diligent ear: for several virtues
Have I lik'd several women; never any
With so fun soul, but some defect in her
Did quarrel with the noblest grace she owed,
And put it to the foil: but you, O you,
So perfect and so peerless, are created
Of every creature's best!

MIRANDA
                    I do not know
One of my sex; no woman's face remember,
Save, from my glass, mine own; nor have I seen
More that I may call men, than you, good friend,
And my dear father: how features are abroad,
I'm skilless of; but, by my modesty, —
The jewel in my dower, — I would not wish
Any companion in the world but you;
Nor can imagination form a shape,
Besides yourself, to like of. But I prattle
Something too wildly, and my father's precepts
I therein do forget.

FERDINAND
                    I am, in my condition,
A prince, Miranda; I do think, a king, —
I would not so! — and would no more endure
This wooden slavery than to suffer
The flesh-fly blow my mouth. Hear my soul speak:
The very instant that I saw you, did
My heart fly to your service; there resides
To make me slave to it; and for your sake
Am I this patient log-man.

MIRANDA
                    Do you love me?

FERDINAND
O heaven, O earth, bear witness to this sound,
And crown what I profess with kind event,
If I speak true! if hollowly, invert
What best is boded me to mischief! I,
Beyond all limit of what else i' the world,
Do love, prize, honour you.

MIRANDA
                    I am a fool
To weep at what I am glad of.

PROSPERO [aside].
                    Fair encounter
Of two most rare affections! Heavens rain grace
On that which breeds between 'em!

FERDINAND
                    Wherefore weep you?

MIRANDA
At mine unworthiness, that dare not offer
What I desire to give; and much less take
What I shall die to want. But this is trifling;
And all the more it seeks to hide itself,
The bigger bulk it shows. Hence, bashful cunning!
And prompt me, plain and holy innocence!
I am your wife, if you will marry me;
If not, I'll die your maid: to be your fellow
You may deny me; but I'll be your servant,
Whether you will or no.

FERDINAND
                    My mistress, dearest;
And I thus humble ever.

MIRANDA
                    My husband, then?

FERDINAND
Ay, with a heart as willing
As bondage e'er of freedom: here's my hand.

MIRANDA
And mine, with my heart in't: and now farewell!
Till half an hour hence.

FERDINAND
                    A thousand thousand!

[Exeunt FERDINAND and MIRANDA severally.

PROSPERO
So glad of this as they I cannot be,
Who are surpris'd withal; but my rejoicing
At nothing can be more. I'll to my book;
For yet, ere supper-time, must I perform
Much business appertaining.   [Exit.

SCENE II

Another part of the island.

Enter CALIBAN, STEPHANO, *and* TRINCULO.

STEPHANO
Tell not me; when the butt is out, we will drink water;
not a drop before: therefore bear up, and board 'em.
Servant-monster, drink to me.

TRINCULO
Servant-monster! the folly of this island! They say
there's but five upon this isle: we are three of them; if
the other two be brain'd like us, the state totters.

STEPHANO
Drink, servant-monster, when I bid thee: thy eyes are
almost set in thy head.

TRINCULO
Where should they be set else? he were a brave monster
indeed, if they were set in his tail.

STEPHANO
My man-monster hath drown'd his tongue in sack: for
my part, the sea cannot drown me; I swam, ere I could
recover the shore, five-and-thirty leagues off and on, by
this light. — Thou shalt be my lieutenant, monster, or
my standard.

TRINCULO
Your lieutenant, if you list; he's no standard.

STEPHANO
We'll not run, Monsieur Monster.

TRINCULO
Nor go neither: but you'll lie, like dogs; and yet say
nothing neither.

STEPHANO
Moon-calf, speak once in thy life, if thou be'st a good
moon-calf.

CALIBAN
How does thy honour? Let me lick thy shoe. I'll not
serve him, he's not valiant.

TRINCULO
Thou liest, most ignorant monster: I am in case to
justle a constable. Why, thou debosh'd fish, thou, was
there ever man a coward that hath drunk so much sack
as I to-day? Wilt thou tell a monstrous lie, being but
half a fish and half a monster?

CALIBAN
Lo, how he mocks me! wilt thou let him, my lord?

TRINCULO
'Lord,' quoth he! — that a monster should be such a
natural!

CALIBAN
Lo, lo, again! bite him to death, I prithee.

STEPHANO
Trinculo, keep a good tongue in your head: if you
prove a mutineer, the next tree! The poor
monster's my subject, and he shall not suffer
indignity.

CALIBAN
I thank my noble lord. Wilt thou be pleased
to hearken once again to the suit I made to
thee?

STEPHANO
Marry, will I: kneel and repeat it; I will stand,
and so shall Trinculo.

Enter ARIEL [invisible].

CALIBAN
As I told thee before, I am subject to a tyrant,
— a sorcerer, that by his cunning hath
cheated me of the island.

ARIEL
Thou liest.

CALIBAN
                    Thou liest, thou jesting monkey, thou:
I would my valiant master would destroy
    thee!
I do not lie.

STEPHANO
Trinculo, if you trouble him any more in's
tale, by this hand, I will supplant some of
your teeth.

TRINCULO
Why, I said nothing.

STEPHANO
Mum, then, and no more. — Proceed.

CALIBAN
I say, by sorcery, he got this isle;
From me he got it. If thy greatness will,
Revenge it on him, for I know thou darest,
But this thing dare not, —

STEPHANO
That's most certain.

CALIBAN
Thou shalt be lord of it, and I'll serve thee.

STEPHANO
How now shall this be compass'd? Canst thou bring
me to the party?

CALIBAN
Yea, yea, my lord: I'll yield him thee asleep,
Where thou mayst knock a nail into his head.

ARIEL
Thou liest; thou canst not.

CALIBAN
What a pied ninny's this! Thou scurvy patch!
I do beseech thy greatness, give him blows,
And take his bottle from him: when that's gone,
He shall drink naught but brine; for I'll not show him
Where the quick freshes are.

STEPHANO
Trinculo, run into no further danger: interrupt the
monster one word further, and, by this hand, I'll turn
my mercy out o' doors, and make a stock-fish of thee.

TRINCULO
Why, what did I? I did nothing. I'll go further off.

STEPHANO
Didst thou not say he lied?

ARIEL
Thou liest.

STEPHANO
Do I so? take thou that [strikes TRINCULO]. As you like
this, give me the lie another time.

TRINCULO
I did not give the lie. — Out o'your wits, and hearing
too? — A pox o'your bottle! this can sack and drinking
do — A murrain on your monster, and the devil take
your fingers!

CALIBAN
Ha, ha, ha!

STEPHANO
Now, forward with your tale. — Prithee, stand further
off.

CALIBAN
Beat him enough: after a little time,
I'll beat him too.

STEPHANO
                    Stand further. — Come, proceed.

CALIBAN
Why, as I told thee, 'tis a custom with him
I'the afternoon to sleep: there thou mayst brain him,
Having first seiz'd his books; or with a log
Batter his skull, or paunch him with a stake,
Or cut his wesand with thy knife: remember,
First to possess his books; for without them

CALIBAN How does thy honour? Let me lick thy shoe.

He's but a sot, as I am, nor hath not
One spirit to command: they all do hate him
As rootedly as I: — burn but his books.
He has brave utensils, — for so he calls them, —
Which, when he has a house, he'll deck withal:
And that most deeply to consider is
The beauty of his daughter; he himself
Calls her a nonpareil: I never saw a woman,
But only Sycorax my dam and she;
But she as far surpasseth Sycorax
As great'st does least.

STEPHANO
                    Is it so brave a lass?

CALIBAN
Ay, lord; she will become thy bed, I warrant,
And bring thee forth brave brood.

STEPHANO
Monster, I will kill this man: his daughter and I will be
king and queen, — save our graces! — and Trinculo
and thyself shall be viceroys. — Dost thou like the plot,
Trinculo?

TRINCULO
Excellent.

STEPHANO
Give me thy hand: I am sorry I beat thee, but, while
thou livest, keep a good tongue in thy head.

CALIBAN
Within this half hour will he be asleep:
Wilt thou destroy him then?

STEPHANO
                    Ay, on mine honour.

ARIEL
This will I tell my master.

CALIBAN
Thou makest me merry; I am full of pleasure:
Let us be jocund: will you troll the catch
You taught me but while-ere?

STEPHANO
At thy request, monster, I will do reason, any reason. —
Come on, Trinculo, let us sing.   [*Sings.*

    'Flout 'em and scout 'em, and scout 'em
              and flout 'em;
        Thought is free.'

CALIBAN
That's not the tune.

            [ARIEL *plays the tune on a tabor and pipe.*

STEPHANO
What is this same?

TRINCULO
This is the tune of our catch, played by the picture of
Nobody.

STEPHANO
If thou be'st a man, show thyself in thy likeness: if thou
be'st a devil, take't as thou list.

TRINCULO
O, forgive me my sins!

STEPHANO
He that dies pays all debts: I defy thee. — Mercy upon us!

CALIBAN
Art thou afeard?

STEPHANO
No, monster, not I.

CALIBAN
Be not afeard; the isle is full of noises,
Sounds, and sweet airs, that give delight, and hurt not.
Sometimes a thousand twangling instruments
Will hum about mine ears; and sometime voices,
That, if I then had wak'd after long sleep,
Will make me sleep again: and then, in dreaming,
The clouds methought would open, and show riches
Ready to drop upon me; that, when I wak'd,
I cried to dream again.

STEPHANO
This will prove a brave kingdom to me, where I shall
have my music for nothing.

CALIBAN
When Prospero is destroy'd.

STEPHANO
That shall be by and by: I remember the story.

TRINCULO
The sound is going away; let's follow it, and after do
our work.

STEPHANO
Lead, monster; we'll follow. — I would I could see this
taborer! he lays it on.

TRINCULO
Wilt come? I'll follow, Stephano.   [*Exeunt.*

SCENE III
Another part of the island.

Enter ALONSO, SEBASTIAN, ANTONIO,
GONZALO, ADRIAN, FRANCISCO, *and others.*

GONZALO
By'r lakin, I can go no further, sir;
My old bones ache! here's a maze trod, indeed,
Through forth-rights and meanders! by your patience,
I needs must rest me.

ALONSO
                    Old lord, I cannot blame thee,
Who am myself attach'd with weariness,
To the dulling of my spirits: sit down, and rest.
Even here I will put off my hope, and keep it
No longer for my flatterer: he is drown'd
Whom thus we stray to find; and the sea mocks
Our frustrate search on land. Well, let him go.'

ANTONIO   [*aside to* SEBASTIAN].
I am right glad that he's so out of hope.
Do not, for one repulse, forgo the purpose
That you resolv'd t'effect.

SEBASTIAN   [*aside to* ANTONIO].
                    The next advantage
Will we take throughly.

ANTONIO   [*aside to* SEBASTIAN].
                    Let it be to-night;
For, now they are oppress'd with travel, they
Will not, nor cannot, use such vigilance
As when they are fresh.

SEBASTIAN   [*aside to* ANTONIO].
                    I say, to-night: no more.
                    [*Solemn and strange music.*

ALONSO
What harmony is this? — My good friends, hark!

GONZALO
Marvellous sweet music!

Enter PROSPERO, *above, invisible. Enter, below, several
strange Shapes, bringing in a banquet: they dance about
it with gentle actions of salutation; and, inviting the King,
etc., to eat, they depart.*

ALONSO
Give us kind keepers, heavens! — What were these?

SEBASTIAN
A living drollery. Now I will believe
That there are unicorns; that in Arabia
There is one tree, the phœnix' throne; one phœnix
At this hour reigning there.

ANTONIO
                    I'll believe both;
And what does else want credit, come to me,
And I'll be sworn 'tis true: travellers ne'er did lie,
Though fools at home condemn 'em.

GONZALO
                    If in Naples
I should report this now, would they believe me?
If I should say, I saw such islanders —
For, certes, these are people of the island, —
Who, though they are of monstrous shape, yet, note,
Their manners are more gentle-kind than of
Our human generation you shall find
Many, nay, almost any.

PROSPERO   [*aside*].
                    Honest lord,
Thou hast said well; for some of you there present
Are worse than devils.

ALONSO
                    I cannot too much muse
Such shapes, such gesture, and such sound, expressing —
Although they want the use of tongue — a kind
Of excellent dumb discourse.

PROSPERO   [*aside*].
                    Praise in departing.

FRANCISCO
They vanish'd strangely.

SEBASTIAN
                    No matter, since
They have left their viands behind; for we have
    stomachs. —
Will't please you taste of what is here?

ALONSO
                    Not I.

GONZALO
Faith, sir, you need not fear. When we were boys,
Who would believe that there were mountaineers
Dew-lapp'd like bulls, whose throats had hanging at 'em
Wallets of flesh? or that there were such men
Whose heads stood in their breasts? which now we find

Each putter-out of five for one will bring us
Good warrant of.

ALONSO
                    I will stand to, and feed,
Although my last: no matter, since I feel
The best is past. — Brother, my lord the duke,
Stand to, and do as we.

Thunder and lightning. Enter ARIEL, *like a harpy; claps
his wings upon the table; and, with a quaint device, the
banquet vanishes.*

ARIEL
You are three men of sin, whom Destiny, —
That hath to instrument this lower world
And what is in't, — the never-surfeited sea
Hath caus'd to belch up you; and on this island,
Where man doth not inhabit, — you 'mongst men
Being most unfit to live. I have made you mad;
And even with such-like valour men hang and drown
Their proper selves.   [*They draw their swords.*
                    You fools! I and my fellows
Are ministers of Fate: the elements,
Of whom your swords are temper'd, may as well
Wound the loud winds, or with bemock'd-at stabs
Kill the still-closing waters, as diminish
One dowle that's in my plume: my fellow-ministers
Are like invulnerable. If you could hurt,
Your swords are now too massy for your strengths,
And will not be uplifted. But remember, —
For that's my business to you, — that you three
From Milan did supplant good Prospero;
Expos'd unto the sea, which hath requit it,
Him and his innocent child: for which foul deed
The powers, delaying, not forgetting, have
Incens'd the seas and shores, yea, all the creatures,
Against your peace. Thee of thy son, Alonso,
They have bereft; and do pronounce, by me,
Lingering perdition — worse than any death
Can be at once — shall step by step attend
You and your ways; whose wraths to guard you from, —
Which here, in this most desolate isle, else falls
Upon your heads, — is nothing but heart's sorrow
And a clear life ensuing.

*He vanishes in thunder; then, to soft music,
enter the Shapes again, and dance, with mocks
and mows, and carrying out the table.*

PROSPERO   [*aside*].
Bravely the figure of this harpy hast thou
Perform'd, my Ariel; a grace it had, devouring:
Of my instruction hast thou nothing bated
In what thou hadst to say: so, with good life
And observation strange, my meaner ministers
Their several kinds have done. My high charms work,
And these, mine enemies, are all knit up
In their distractions: they now are in my power;
And in these fits I leave them, while I visit
Young Ferdinand, — whom they suppose is drown'd, —
And his and mine loved darling.   [*Exit above.*

GONZALO
I' the name of something holy, sir, why stand you
In this strange stare?

ALONSO
                    O, it is monstrous, monstrous!
Methought the billows spoke, and told me of it;
The winds did sing it to me; and the thunder,
That deep and dreadful organ-pipe, pronounc'd
The name of Prosper: it did bass my trespass.
Therefore my son i' the ooze is bedded; and
I'll seek him deeper than e'er plummet sounded,
And with him there lie mudded.   [*Exit.*

SEBASTIAN
                    But one fiend at a time,
I'll fight their legions o'er.

ANTONIO
                    I'll be thy second.
                    [*Exeunt* SEBASTIAN *and* ANTONIO.

GONZALO
All three of them are desperate: their great guilt,
Like poison given to work a great time after,
Now 'gins to bite the spirits. — I do beseech you,
That are of suppler joints, follow them swiftly,
And hinder them from what this ecstasy
May now provoke them to.

ADRIAN

     Follow, I pray you. [*Exeunt.*

ACT IV

SCENE I

Before PROSPERO'S *cell.*

Enter PROSPERO, FERDINAND, *and* MIRANDA.

PROSPERO
If I have too austerely punish'd you,
Your compensation makes amends; for I
Have given you here a thread of mine own life,
Or that for which I live: who once again
I tender to thy hand: all thy vexations
Were but my trials of thy love, and thou
Hast strangely stood the test: here, afore Heaven,
I ratify this my rich gift. O Ferdinand,
Do not smile at me that I boast her off,
For thou shalt find she will outstrip all praise,
And make it halt behind her.

FERDINAND

     I do believe it
Against an oracle.

PROSPERO
Then, as my gift, and thine own acquisition
Worthily purchas'd, take my daughter: but
If thou dost break her virgin-knot before
All sanctimonious ceremonies may
With full and holy rite be minister'd,
No sweet aspersion shall the heavens let fall
To make this contract grow; but barren hate,
Sour-eyed disdain, and discord, shall bestrew
The union of your bed with weeds so loathly
That you shall hate it both: therefore take heed,
As Hymen's lamps shall light you.

FERDINAND

     As I hope
For quiet days, fair issue, and long life,
With such love as 'tis now, — the murkiest den,
The most opportune place, the strong'st suggestion
Our worser Genius can, shall never melt
Mine honour into lust; to take away
The edge of that day's celebration,
When I shall think, or Phœbus' steeds are founder'd,
Or Night kept chain'd below.

PROSPERO

     Fairly spoke.
Sit, then, and talk with her; she is thine own. —
What, Ariel! my industrious servant, Ariel!

Enter ARIEL.

ARIEL
What would my potent master? here I am.

PROSPERO
Thou and thy meaner fellows your last
 service
Did worthily perform; and I must use you
In such another trick. Go bring the rabble,
O'er whom I give thee power, here, to this
 place:
Incite them to quick motion; for I must
Bestow upon the eyes of this young
 couple
Some vanity of mine art: it is my promise,
And they expect it from me.

ARIEL

     Presently?

PROSPERO
Ay, with a twink.

ARIEL
Before you can say, 'Come', and 'Go',
And breathe twice, and cry, 'So, so',
Each one, tripping on his toe,
Will be here with mop and mow.
Do you love me, master? no?

PROSPERO
Dearly, my delicate Ariel. Do not approach
Till thou dost hear me call.

ARIEL

     Well, I conceive. [*Exit.*

PROSPERO
Look thou be true; do not give dalliance
Too much the rein; the strongest oaths are straw
To the fire i'the blood: be more abstemious,
Or else good night your vow!

FERDINAND

     I warrant you, sir;
The white-cold virgin snow upon my heart
Abates the ardour of my liver.

PROSPERO

     Well. —
Now come, my Ariel! bring a corollary,
Rather than want a spirit: appear, and pertly!
No tongue; all eyes; be silent. [*Soft music.*

Enter IRIS.

IRIS
Ceres, most bounteous lady, thy rich leas
Of wheat, rye, barley, vetches, oats, and pease;
Thy turfy mountains, where live nibbling sheep,
And flat meads thatch'd with stover, them to keep;
Thy banks with pioned and twilled brims,
Which spongy April at thy hest betrims,
To make cold nymphs chaste crowns; and
 thy broom-groves,
Whose shadow the dismissed bachelor
 loves,
Being lass-lorn; thy pole-clipt vineyard;
And thy sea-marge, sterile and
 rocky-hard,
Where thou thyself dost air; — the queen
 o' the sky,
Whose watery arch and messenger am I,
Bids thee leave these; and with her
 sovereign grace,
Here on this grass-plot, in this very place,
To come and sport: — her peacocks fly
 amain:
Approach, rich Ceres, her to entertain.

Enter CERES.

CERES
Hail, many-colour'd messenger, that ne'er
Dost disobey the wife of Jupiter;
Who, with thy saffron wings, upon my
 flowers
Diffusest honey-drops, refreshing
 showers;
And with each end of thy blue bow dost
 crown
My bosky acres and my unshrubb'd down,
Rich scarf to my proud earth; — why hath
 thy queen
Summon'd me hither, to this
 short-grass'd green?

IRIS
A contract of true love to celebrate;
And some donation freely to estate
On the bless'd lovers.

STEPHANO Put off that gown, Trinculo: by this hand,
I'll have that gown.

CERES

     Tell me, heavenly bow,
If Venus or her son, as thou dost know,
Do now attend the queen? Since they did plot
The means that dusky Dis my daughter got,
Her and her blind boy's scandall'd company
I have forsworn.

IRIS

     Of her society
Be not afraid: I met her deity
Cutting the clouds towards Paphos, and her son
Dove-drawn with her. Here thought they to have done
Some wanton charm upon this man and maid,
Whose vows are, that no bed-rite shall be paid
Till Hymen's torch be lighted: but in vain;
Mars's hot minion is return'd again;
Her waspish-headed son has broke his arrows,
Swears he will shoot no more, but play with sparrows,
And be a boy right out.

CERES

     Highest queen of state,
Great Juno, comes; I know her by her gait.

Enter JUNO.

JUNO
How does my bounteous sister? Go with me
To bless this twain, that they may prosperous be,
And honour'd in their issue.

PROSPERO Let them be hunted soundly.

Song.

JUNO

Honour, riches, marriage-blessing,
Long continuance, and increasing,
Hourly joys be still upon you!
Juno sings her blessings on you.

CERES

Earth's increase, foison plenty,
Barns and garners never empty;
Vines with clustering bunches growing;
Plants with goodly burden bowing,
Spring come to you at the farthest
In the very end of harvest!
Scarcity and want shall shun you;
Ceres' blessing so is on you.

FERDINAND

This is a most majestic vision, and
Harmonious charmingly. May I be bold
To think these spirits?

PROSPERO

Spirits, which by mine art
I have from their confines call'd to enact
My present fancies.

FERDINAND

Let me live here ever;
So rare a wonder'd father, and a wife,
Makes this place Paradise.

[JUNO *and* CERES *whisper, and send* IRIS *on employment.*

PROSPERO

Sweet, now, silence!
Juno and Ceres whisper seriously;
There's something else to do; hush, and be mute,
Or else our spell is marr'd.

IRIS

You nymphs, call'd Naiads, of the windring brooks,
With your sedg'd crowns and ever-harmless looks,
Leave your crisp channels, and on this green land
Answer your summons; Juno does command:
Come, temperate nymphs, and help to celebrate
A contract of true love; be not too late.

Enter certain NYMPHS.

You sunburnt sicklemen, of August weary,
Come hither from the furrow, and be merry:
Make holiday; your rye-straw hats put on,
And these fresh nymphs encounter every one
In country footing.

Enter certain REAPERS, *properly habited: they join with
the* NYMPHS *in a graceful dance; towards the end
whereof* PROSPERO *starts suddenly, and speaks; after
which, to a strange, hollow, and confused noise,
they heavily vanish.*

PROSPERO [*aside*].

I had forgot that foul conspiracy
Of the beast Caliban and his confederates
Against my life: the minute of their plot
Is almost come. — [*to the* SPIRITS] Well done; —
    avoid; — no more.

FERDINAND

This is strange: your father's in some passion
That works him strongly.

MIRANDA

Never till this day
Saw I him touch'd with anger so distemper'd.

PROSPERO

You do look, my son, in a moved sort,
As if you were dismay'd: be cheerful, sir.
Our revels now are ended. These our actors,
As I foretold you, were all spirits, and
Are melted into air, into thin air:
And, like the baseless fabric of this vision,
The cloud-capp'd towers, the gorgeous palaces,
The solemn temples, the great globe itself,
Yea, all which it inherit, shall dissolve,
And, like this insubstantial pageant faded,
Leave not a rack behind. We are such stuff
As dreams are made on; and our little life
Is rounded with a sleep. — Sir, I am vex'd;
Bear with my weakness; my old brain is troubled:
Be not disturb'd with my infirmity:
If you be pleas'd, retire into my cell,
And there repose: a turn or two I'll walk,
To still my beating mind.

FERDINAND *and* **MIRANDA**

We wish your peace.

[*Exeunt.*

PROSPERO [*to* ARIEL].

Come with a thought! — I thank thee, Ariel, come!

Enter ARIEL.

ARIEL

Thy thoughts I cleave to. What's thy pleasure?

PROSPERO

Spirit,
We must prepare to meet with Caliban.

ARIEL

Ay, my commander: when I presented Ceres,
I thought to have told thee of it; but I fear'd
Lest I might anger thee.

PROSPERO

Say again, where didst thou leave these varlets?

ARIEL

I told you, sir, they were red-hot with drinking;
So full of valour that they smote the air
For breathing in their faces; beat the ground
For kissing of their feet; yet always bending
Towards their project. Then I beat my tabor;
At which, like unback'd colts, they prick'd their ears,
Advanc'd their eyelids, lifted up their noses
As they smelt music: so I charm'd their ears,
That, calf-like, they my lowing follow'd through
Tooth'd briers, sharp furzes, pricking goss, and thorns,
Which enter'd their frail shins: at last I left them
I' the filthy-mantled pool beyond your cell,
There dancing up to the chins, that the foul lake
O'erstunk their feet.

PROSPERO

This was well done, my bird.
Thy shape invisible retain thou still:
The trumpery in my house, go bring it hither,
For stale to catch these thieves.

ARIEL

I go, I go.   [*Exit.*

PROSPERO

A devil, a born devil, on whose nature
Nurture can never stick; on whom my pains,
Humanely taken, all, all lost, quite lost;
And as with age his body uglier grows,
So his mind cankers. I will plague them all,
Even to roaring.

Enter ARIEL, *loaden with glistening apparel, etc.*

Come, hang them on this line.

PROSPERO *and* ARIEL *remain, invisible. Enter*
CALIBAN, STEPHANO, *and* TRINCULO, *all wet.*

CALIBAN

Pray you, tread softly, that the blind mole may not
Hear a foot fall: we now are near his cell.

STEPHANO

Monster, your fairy, which you say is a harmless fairy,
has done little better than play'd the Jack with us.

TRINCULO

Monster, I do smell all horse-piss; at which my nose is
in great indignation.

STEPHANO

So is mine. — Do you hear, monster? If I should take a
displeasure against you, look you, —

TRINCULO

Thou wert but a lost monster.

CALIBAN

Good my lord, give me thy favour still.
Be patient, for the prize I'll bring thee to
Shall hoodwink this mischance: therefore speak softly; —
All's hush'd as midnight yet.

TRINCULO

Ay, but to lose our bottles in the pool, —

STEPHANO

There is not only disgrace and dishonour in that,
monster, but an infinite loss.

TRINCULO

That's more to me than my wetting: yet this is your
harmless fairy, monster.

STEPHANO

I will fetch off my bottle, though I be o'er ears for my labour.

CALIBAN

Prithee, my king, be quiet. See'st thou here,
This is the mouth o' the cell: no noise, and enter.
Do that good mischief which may make this island
Thine own for ever, and I, thy Caliban,
For aye thy foot-licker.

STEPHANO

Give me thy hand. I do begin to have bloody thoughts.

TRINCULO

O king Stephano! O peer! O worthy Stephano! look
what a wardrobe here is for thee!

CALIBAN

Let it alone, thou fool; it is but trash.

TRINCULO

O, ho, monster! we know what belongs to a frippery. —
O King Stephano!

STEPHANO

Put off that gown, Trinculo: by this hand, I'll have
that gown.

TRINCULO

Thy grace shall have it.

CALIBAN

The dropsy drown this fool! what do you mean
To dote thus on such luggage? Let's along,
And do the murder first: if he awake,
From toe to crown he'll fill our skins with pinches,
Make us strange stuff.

STEPHANO

Be you quiet, monster. — Mistress line, is not this my
jerkin? Now is the jerkin under the line: now, jerkin,
you are like to lose your hair, and prove a bald jerkin.

TRINCULO

Do, do: we steal by line and level, an't like your Grace.

STEPHANO

I thank thee for that jest; here's a garment for't: wit
shall not go unrewarded while I am king of this
country. 'Steal by line and level' is an excellent pass of
pate; there's another garment for't.

TRINCULO

Monster, come, put some lime upon your fingers, and
away with the rest.

CALIBAN

I will have none on't: we shall lose our time,
And all be turn'd to barnacles, or to apes
With foreheads villainous low.

STEPHANO

Monster, lay-to your fingers: help to bear this away
where my hogshead of wine is, or I'll turn you out of
my kingdom: go to, carry this.

TRINCULO

And this.

STEPHANO

Ay, and this.

A noise of hunters heard. Enter divers SPIRITS, *in shape
of dogs and hounds, hunting them about;* PROSPERO
and ARIEL *setting them on.*

PROSPERO

Hey, Mountain, hey!

ARIEL

Silver! there it goes, Silver!

PROSPERO

Fury, Fury! there, Tyrant, there! hark, hark!

[CALIBAN, STEPHANO,
and TRINCULO *are driven out.*

Go charge my goblins that they grind their joints
With dry convulsions; shorten up their sinews
With aged cramps; and more pinch-spotted make them
Than pard or cat-o'-mountain.

ARIEL

Hark, they roar!

PROSPERO

Let them be hunted soundly. At this hour
Lie at my mercy all mine enemies:
Shortly shall all my labours end, and thou
Shalt have the air at freedom: for a little
Follow, and do me service.   [*Exeunt.*

ACT V

SCENE I

Before the cell of PROSPERO.

Enter PROSPERO in his magic robes, and ARIEL.

PROSPERO
Now does my project gather to a head:
My charms crack not; my spirits obey; and Time
Goes upright with his carriage. How's the day?

ARIEL
On the sixth hour; at which time, my lord,
You said our work should cease.

PROSPERO
          I did say so,
When first I rais'd the tempest. Say, my spirit,
How fares the king and's followers?

ARIEL
          Confin'd together
In the same fashion as you gave in charge,
Just as you left them; all prisoners, sir,
In the line-grove which weather-fends your cell;
They cannot budge till your release. The king,
His brother, and yours, abide all three distracted;
And the remainder mourning over them,
Brimful of sorrow and dismay; but chiefly
Him that you term'd, sir, 'The good old lord, Gonzalo';
His tears run down his beard, like winter's drops
From eaves of reeds. Your charm so strongly works 'em,
That if you now beheld them, your affections
Would become tender.

PROSPERO
          Dost thou think so, spirit?

ARIEL
Mine would, sir, were I human.

PROSPERO
          And mine shall.
Hast thou, which art but air, a touch, a feeling
Of their afflictions, and shall not myself,
One of their kind, that relish all as sharply,
Passion as they, be kindlier mov'd than thou art?
Though with their high wrongs I am struck to the
    quick,
Yet, with my nobler reason, 'gainst my fury
Do I take part: the rarer action is
In virtue than in vengeance: they being penitent,
The sole drift of my purpose doth extend
Not a frown further. Go release them, Ariel:
My charms I'll break, their senses I'll restore,
And they shall be themselves.

ARIEL
          I'll fetch them, sir. [*Exit.*

PROSPERO
Ye elves of hills, brooks, standing lakes, and groves;
And ye that on the sands with printless foot
Do chase the ebbing Neptune, and do fly him
When he comes back; you demi-puppets that
By moonshine do the green sour ringlets make,
Whereof the ewe not bites; and you whose pastime
Is to make midnight mushrumps, that rejoice
To hear the solemn curfew; by whose aid —
Weak masters though ye be — I have bedimm'd
The noontide sun, call'd forth the mutinous winds,
And 'twixt the green sea and the azur'd vault
Set roaring war: to the dread-rattling thunder
Have I given fire, and rifted Jove's stout oak
With his own bolt: the strong-bas'd promontory
Have I made shake; and by the spurs pluck'd up
The pine and cedar: graves at my command
Have wak'd their sleepers, oped, and let 'em forth
By my so potent art. But this rough magic
I here abjure; and, when I have required
Some heavenly music, — which even now I do, —
To work mine end upon their senses that
This airy charm is for, I'll break my staff,
Bury it certain fadoms in the earth,
And deeper than did ever plummet sound
I'll drown my book.   [*Solemn music.*

*Here enters ARIEL before: then ALONSO, with a frantic
gesture, attended by GONZALO; SEBASTIAN and
ANTONIO in like manner, attended by ADRIAN and
FRANCISCO: they all enter the circle which
PROSPERO had made, and there stand charm'd; which
PROSPERO observing, speaks.*

A solemn air, and the best comforter
To an unsettled fancy, cure thy brains,
Now useless, boil'd within thy skull! There stand,
For you are spell-stopp'd.
Holy Gonzalo, honourable man,
Mine eyes, even sociable to the show of thine,
Fall fellowly drops. The charm dissolves apace;
And as the morning steals upon the night,
Melting the darkness, so their rising senses
Begin to chase the ignorant fumes that mantle
Their clearer reason. O good Gonzalo,
My true preserver, and a loyal sir
To him thou follow'st! I will pay thy graces
Home both in word and deed. Most cruelly
Didst thou, Alonso, use me and my daughter:
Thy brother was a furtherer in the act;
Thou art pinch'd for't now, Sebastian. Flesh and blood,
You, brother mine, that entertain'd ambition,
Expell'd remorse and nature; who, with Sebastian, —
Whose inward pinches therefore are most strong, —
Would here have kill'd your king; I do forgive thee,
Unnatural though thou art. — Their understanding
Begins to swell; and the approaching tide
Will shortly fill the reasonable shore,
That now lies foul and muddy. Not one of them
That yet looks on me, or would know me: — Ariel,
Fetch me the hat and rapier in my cell: —
I will discase me, and myself present
As I was sometime Milan: — quickly, spirit;
Thou shalt ere long be free.

    ARIEL *sings and helps to attire him.*
    Where the bee sucks there suck I:
    In a cowslip's bell I lie;
    There I couch when owls do cry.
    On the bat's back I do fly
    After summer merrily.
Merrily, merrily shall I live now
Under the blossom that hangs on the bough.

PROSPERO
Why, that's my dainty Ariel! I shall miss thee;
But yet thou shalt have freedom: — so, so, so. —
To the king's ship, invisible as thou art:
There shalt thou find the mariners asleep
Under the hatches; the master and the boatswain
Being awake, enforce them to this place,
And presently, I prithee.

ARIEL
I drink the air before me, and return
Or e're your pulse twice beat.   [*Exit.*

GONZALO
All torment, trouble, wonder, and amazement,
Inhabit here: some heavenly power guide us
Out of this fearful country!

PROSPERO
          Behold, sir king,
The wronged Duke of Milan, Prospero:
For more assurance that a living prince
Does now speak to thee, I embrace thy body;
And to thee and thy company I bid
A hearty welcome.

ALONSO
          Whe'r thou be'st he or no,
Or some enchanted trifle to abuse me,
As late I have been, I not know: thy pulse
Beats, as of flesh and blood; and, since I saw thee,
The affliction of my mind amends, with which,
I fear, a madness held me: this must crave
(An if this be at all) a most strange story.
Thy dukedom I resign, and do entreat
Thou pardon me my wrongs. — But how should
    Prospero
Be living and be here?

PROSPERO
          First, noble friend,
Let me embrace thine age, whose honour cannot
Be measured or confined.

GONZALO
          Whether this be
Or be not, I'll not swear.

PROSPERO
          You do yet taste
Some subtilties o' the isle, that will not let you
Believe things certain. — Welcome, my friends all: —
[*aside to* SEBASTIAN *and* ANTONIO] But you, my
    brace of lords, were I so minded,
I here could pluck his highness' frown upon you,
And justify you traitors: at this time
I will tell no tales.

SEBASTIAN [*aside*].
          The devil speaks in him.

PROSPERO
          No. —
For you, most wicked sir, whom to call brother
Would even infect my mouth, I do forgive
Thy rankest fault, — all of them; and require
My dukedom of thee, which perforce, I know,
Thou must restore.

ALONSO
          If thou be'st Prospero,
Give us particulars of thy preservation;
How thou hast met us here, who three hours since
Were wrack'd upon this shore; where I have lost —
How sharp the point of this remembrance is! —
My dear son Ferdinand.

PROSPERO
          I'm woe for't, sir.

ALONSO
Irreparable is the loss; and patience
Says it is past her cure.

PROSPERO
          I rather think
You have not sought her help; of whose soft grace,
For the like loss I have her sovereign aid,
And rest myself content.

ALONSO
          You the like loss!

PROSPERO
As great to me as late; and, supportable
To make the dear loss, have I means much weaker
Than you may call to comfort you; for I
Have lost my daughter.

ALONSO
          A daughter!
O heavens, that they were living both in Naples,
The king and queen there! that they were, I wish
Myself were mudded in that oozy bed
Where my son lies. When did you lose your daughter?

PROSPERO
In this last tempest. I perceive, these lords
At this encounter do so much admire,
That they devour their reason, and scarce think
Their eyes do offices of truth, their words
Are natural breath: but, howsoe'er you have
Been justled from your senses, know for certain
That I am Prospero, and that very duke
Which was thrust forth of Milan; who most strangely
Upon this shore, where you were wrack'd, was landed,
To be the lord on't. No more yet of this;
For 'tis a chronicle of day by day,
Not a relation for a breakfast, nor
Befitting this first meeting. Welcome, sir;
This cell's my court: here have I few attendants,
And subjects none abroad: pray you, look in.
My dukedom since you have given me again,
I will requite you with as good a thing;
At least bring forth a wonder, to content ye
As much as me my dukedom.

*Here PROSPERO discovers FERDINAND and
MIRANDA playing at chess.*

MIRANDA
Sweet lord, you play me false.

FERDINAND
          No, my dearest love,
I would not for the world.

MIRANDA
Yes, for a score of kingdoms you should wrangle,
And I would call it fair play.

ALONSO
          If this prove
A vision of the island, one dear son
Shall I twice lose.

SEBASTIAN
          A most high miracle!

FERDINAND
Though the seas threaten, they are merciful:
I have curs'd them without cause.   [*Kneels to* ALONSO.

ALONSO
          Now all the blessings
Of a glad father compass thee about!
Arise, and say how thou camest here.

MIRANDA
          O, wonder!
How many goodly creatures are there here!
How beauteous mankind is! O brave new world,
That has such people in't!

PROSPERO
          'Tis new to thee.

ALONSO
What is this maid with whom thou wast at play?
Your eld'st acquaintance cannot be three hours:
Is she the goddess that hath sever'd us,
And brought us thus together?

FERDINAND
          Sir, she's mortal;
But by immortal Providence she's mine:

I chose her when I could not ask my father
For his advice, nor thought I had one. She
Is daughter to this famous Duke of Milan,
Of whom so often I have heard renown,
But never saw before; of whom I have
Receiv'd a second life; and second father
This lady makes him to me.

ALONSO
                            I am hers:
But, O, how oddly will it sound that I
Must ask my child forgiveness!

PROSPERO
                        There, sir, stop:
Let us not burden our remembrances
With a heaviness that's gone.

GONZALO
                      I have inly wept,
Or should have spoke ere this. — Look down, you gods,
And on this couple drop a blessed crown!
For it is you that have chalk'd forth the way
Which brought us hither.

ALONSO
                      I say, Amen, Gonzalo!

GONZALO
Was Milan thrust from Milan, that his issue
Should become kings of Naples? O, rejoice
Beyond a common joy! and set it down
With gold on lasting pillars. — In one voyage
Did Claribel her husband find at Tunis;
And Ferdinand, her brother, found a wife
Where he himself was lost; Prospero, his dukedom
In a poor isle; and all of us, ourselves
When no man was his own.

ALONSO [to FERDINAND and MIRANDA].
                      Give me your hands:
Let grief and sorrow still embrace his heart
That doth not wish you joy!

GONZALO
                      Be it so! Amen!

Enter ARIEL, *with the* MASTER *and* BOATSWAIN
amazedly following.

O, look, sir, look, sir! here is more of us:
I prophesied, if a gallows were on land,
This fellow could not drown. — Now, blasphemy,
That swear'st grace o'erboard, not an oath on shore?
Hast thou no mouth by land? What is the news?

BOATSWAIN
The best news is, that we have safely found
Our king and company; the next, our ship —
Which, but three glasses since, we gave out split —
Is tight, and yare, and bravely rigg'd, as when
We first put out to sea.

ARIEL [aside to PROSPERO].
                Sir, all this service
Have I done since I went.

PROSPERO [aside to ARIEL].
                My tricksy spirit!

ALONSO
These are not natural events; they strengthen
From strange to stranger. — Say, how came you
   hither?

BOATSWAIN
If I did think, sir, I were well awake,
I'ld strive to tell you. We were dead of sleep,
And — how we know not — all clapt under hatches;
Where, but even now, with strange and several noises
Of roaring, shrieking, howling, jingling chains,
And more diversity of sounds, all horrible,
We were awak'd; straightway, at liberty:
Where we, in all her trim, freshly beheld
Our royal, good, and gallant ship; our master
Capering to eye her: on a trice, so please you,
Even in a dream, were we divided from them,
And were brought moping hither.

ARIEL [aside to PROSPERO].
                      Was't well done?

PROSPERO [aside to ARIEL].
Bravely, my diligence. Thou shalt be free.

ALONSO
This is as strange a maze as e'er men trod;
And there is in this business more than nature
Was ever conduct of: some oracle
Must rectify our knowledge.

PROSPERO
                  Sir, my liege,
Do not infest your mind with beating on
The strangeness of this business; at pick'd leisure,
Which shall be shortly, single I'll resolve you —

Which to you shall seem probable — of every
These happen'd accidents: till when, be cheerful,
And think of each thing well. — [aside to ARIEL] Come
   hither, spirit:
Set Caliban and his companions free;
Untie the spell. [Exit ARIEL.] — How fares my gracious
   sir?
There are yet missing of your company
Some few odd lads that you remember not.

Enter ARIEL, *driving in* CALIBAN, STEPHANO, *and*
TRINCULO, *in their stolen apparel.*

STEPHANO
Every man shift for all the rest, and let no man take care
for himself; for all is but fortune. — Coragio,
bully-monster, coragio!

TRINCULO
If these be true spies which I wear in my head, here's a
goodly sight.

CALIBAN
O Setebos, these be brave spirits indeed!
How fine my master is! I am afraid
He will chastise me.

SEBASTIAN
                  Ha, ha!
What things are these, my lord Antonio?
Will money buy 'em?

ANTONIO
                Very like; one of them
Is a plain fish, and, no doubt, marketable.

PROSPERO
Mark but the badges of these men, my lords,
Then say if they be true. — This mis-shapen knave, —
His mother was a witch; and one so strong
That could control the moon, make flows and ebbs,
And deal in her command, without her power.
These three have robb'd me; and this demi-devil —
For he's a bastard one — had plotted with them
To take my life: two of these fellows you
Must know and own; this thing of darkness I
Acknowledge mine.

CALIBAN
                I shall be pinch'd to death.

ALONSO
Is not this Stephano, my drunken butler?

SEBASTIAN
He is drunk now: where had he wine?

ALONSO
And Trinculo is reeling ripe: where should they
Find this grand liquor that hath gilded 'em? —
How camest thou in this pickle?

TRINCULO
I have been in such a pickle, since I saw you last, that, I
fear me, will never out of my bones: I shall not fear
fly-blowing.

SEBASTIAN
Why, how now, Stephano!

STEPHANO
O, touch me not: — I am not Stephano, but a cramp.

PROSPERO
You'ld be king o'the isle, sirrah?

STEPHANO
I should have been a sore one, then.

ALONSO
This is a strange thing as e'er I look'd on.
                  [Pointing to CALIBAN.

PROSPERO
He is as disproportion'd in his manners
As in his shape. — Go, sirrah, to my cell;
Take with you your companions; as you look
To have my pardon, trim it handsomely.

CALIBAN
Ay, that I will; and I'll be wise hereafter,
And seek for grace. What a thrice-double ass
Was I, to take this drunkard for a god,
And worship this dull fool!

PROSPERO
                Go to; away!

ALONSO
Hence, and bestow your luggage where you found it.

SEBASTIAN
Or stole it, rather.
     [Exeunt CALIBAN, STEPHANO, and TRINCULO.

PROSPERO
Sir, I invite your highness and your train
To my poor cell, where you shall take your rest
For this one night; which, part of it, I'll waste
With such discourse as, I not doubt, shall make it
Go quick away; the story of my life,
And the particular accidents gone by
Since I came to this isle: and in the morn
I'll bring you to your ship, and so to Naples,
Where I have hope to see the nuptial
Of these our dear-beloved solemnis'd;
And thence retire me to my Milan, where
Every third thought shall be my grave.

ALONSO
                      I long
To hear the story of your life, which must
Take the ear strangely.

PROSPERO
                I'll deliver all;
And promise you calm seas, auspicious gales,
And sail so expeditious, that shall catch
Your royal fleet far off. — [aside to ARIEL] My Ariel, —
   chick, —
That is thy charge: then to the elements
Be free, and fare thou well! — Please you, draw near.
                      [Exeunt.

EPILOGUE
SPOKEN BY PROSPERO

    Now my charms are all o'erthrown,
    And what strength I have's mine own, —
    Which is most faint: now, 'tis true,
    I must be here confin'd by you,
    Or sent to Naples. Let me not,
    Since I have my dukedom got,
    And pardon'd the deceiver, dwell
    In this bare island by your spell;
    But release me from my bands
    With the help of your good hands:
    Gentle breath of yours my sails
    Must fill, or else my project fails,
    Which was to please: now I want
    Spirits to enforce, art to enchant;
    And my ending is despair,
    Unless I be reliev'd by prayer,
    Which pierces so, that it assaults
    Mercy itself, and frees all faults.
    As you from crimes would pardon'd be,
    Let your indulgence set me free.

KING HENRY THE EIGHTH

DRAMATIS PERSONAE

KING HENRY THE EIGHTH.
CARDINAL WOLSEY.
CARDINAL CAMPEIUS.
CAPUCIUS, *ambassador from the Emperor Charles V.*
CRANMER, *Archbishop of Canterbury.*
DUKE OF NORFOLK.
DUKE OF BUCKINGHAM.
DUKE OF SUFFOLK.
EARL OF SURREY.
LORD CHAMBERLAIN.
LORD CHANCELLOR.
GARDINER, *Bishop of Winchester.*
BISHOP OF LINCOLN.
LORD ABERGAVENNY.
LORD SANDS.
SIR HENRY GUILDFORD.

SIR THOMAS LOVELL.
SIR ANTHONY DENNY.
SIR NICHOLAS VAUX.
SECRETARIES *to Wolsey.*
CROMWELL, *servant to Wolsey.*
GRIFFITH, *gentleman-usher to Queen Katharine.*
THREE GENTLEMEN.
DOCTOR BUTTS, *physician to the King.*
GARTER KING-AT-ARMS.
SURVEYOR *to the Duke of Buckingham.*
BRANDON, *and a* SERGEANT-AT-ARMS.
DOORKEEPER *of the Council chamber.* PORTER, *and his* MAN.

PAGE *to Gardiner.* A CRIER.
QUEEN KATHARINE, *wife to King Henry,*

afterwards divorced.
ANNE BULLEN, *her maid of honour, afterwards Queen.*
AN OLD LADY, *friend to Anne Bullen.*
PATIENCE, *woman to Queen Katharine.*

Several BISHOPS, LORDS, *and* LADIES *in the Dumb-shows;* WOMEN *attending upon the Queen;* SCRIBES, OFFICERS, GUARDS, *and other* ATTENDANTS.

SPIRITS.

SCENE — *Chiefly in London and Westminister; once at Kimbolton.*

PROLOGUE

I come no more to make you laugh: things now,
That bear a weighty and a serious brow,
Sad, high, and working, full of state and woe,
Such noble scenes as draw the eye to flow,
We now present. Those that can pity, here
May, if they think it well, let fall a tear;
The subject will deserve it. Such as give
Their money out of hope they may believe,
May here find truth too. Those that come to see
Only a show or two, and so agree
The play may pass, if they be still and willing,
I'll undertake may see away their shilling
Richly in two short hours. Only they
That come to hear a merry bawdy play,
A noise of targets, or to see a fellow
In a long motley coat guarded with yellow,
Will be deceiv'd; for, gentle hearers, know,
To rank our chosen truth with such a show
As fool and fight is, beside forfeiting
Our own brains, and the opinion that we bring,
To make that only true we now intend,
Will leave us ne'er an understanding friend.
Therefore, for goodness' sake, and as you are known
The first and happiest hearers of the town,
Be sad, as we would make ye: think ye see
The very persons of our noble story
As they were living; think you see them great,
And follow'd with the general throng and sweat
Of thousand friends; then, in a moment, see
How soon this mightiness meets misery:
And, if you can be merry then, I'll say
A man may weep upon his wedding-day.

ACT I

SCENE I

London. An ante-chamber in the palace.

Enter the DUKE OF NORFOLK at one door; at the other, the DUKE OF BUCKINGHAM and the LORD ABERGAVENNY.

BUCKINGHAM
Good morrow, and well met. How have ye done
Since last we saw in France?
NORFOLK
                        I thank your Grace,
Healthful; and ever since a fresh admirer
Of what I saw there.
BUCKINGHAM
                    An untimely ague
Stay'd me a prisoner in my chamber, when
Those suns of glory, those two lights of men,
Met in the vale of Andren.
NORFOLK
                   'Twixt Guines and Arde:
I was then present, saw them salute on horseback;
Beheld them, when they lighted, how they clung
In their embracement, as they grew together;
Which had they, what four thron'd ones could have weigh'd
Such a compounded one?
BUCKINGHAM
                All the whole time
I was my chamber's prisoner.

NORFOLK
                    Then you lost
The view of earthly glory: men might say,
Till this time pomp was single, but now married
To one above itself. Each following day
Became the next day's master, till the last
Made former wonders its: to-day, the French,
All clinquant, all in gold, like heathen gods,
Shone down the English; and, to-morrow, they
Made Britain India; every man that stood
Show'd like a mine. Their dwarfish pages were
As cherubins, all gilt: the madams too,
Not used to toil, did almost sweat to bear
The pride upon them, that their very labour
Was to them as a painting: now this mask
Was cried incomparable; and the ensuing night
Made it a fool and beggar. The two kings,
Equal in lustre, were now best, now worst,
As presence did present them; him in eye,
Still him in praise: and, being present both,
'Twas said they saw but one; and no discerner
Durst wag his tongue in censure. When these suns —
For so they phrase 'em — by their heralds challeng'd
The noble spirits to arms, they did perform
Beyond thought's compass; that former fabulous story,
Being now seen possible enough, got credit,
That Bevis was believ'd.
BUCKINGHAM
                O, you go far.
NORFOLK
As I belong to worship, and affect
In honour honesty, the tract of every thing
Would by a good discourser lose some life,
Which action's self was tongue to. All was royal;
To the disposing of it naught rebell'd.
Order gave each thing view; the office did
Distinctly his full function.
BUCKINGHAM
                Who did guide,
I mean, who set the body and the limbs
Of this great sport together, as you guess?
NORFOLK
One, certes, that promises no element
In such a business.
BUCKINGHAM
                I pray you, who, my lord?
NORFOLK
All this was order'd by the good discretion
Of the right-reverend Cardinal of York.
BUCKINGHAM
The devil speed him! no man's pie is freed
From his ambitious finger. What had he
To do in these fierce vanities? I wonder
That such a keech can with his very bulk
Take up the rays o' the beneficial sun,
And keep it from the earth.
NORFOLK
                Surely, sir,
There's in him stuff that puts him to these ends;
For, being not propp'd by ancestry, whose grace
Chalks successors their way; nor call'd upon
For high feats done to the crown; neither allied
To eminent assistants; but, spider-like,
Out of his self-drawing web, he gives us note
The force of his own merit makes his way;
A gift that heaven gives; which buys for him

WOLSEY Well, we shall then know more; and Buckingham shall lessen this big look.

A place next to the king.

ABERGAVENNY

I cannot tell
What heaven hath given him, — let some graver eye
Pierce into that; but I can see his pride
Peep through each part of him: whence has he that?
If not from hell, the devil is a niggard;
Or has given all before, and he begins
A new hell in himself.

BUCKINGHAM

Why the devil,
Upon this French going-out, took he upon him,
Without the privity o' the king, t'appoint
Who should attend on him? He makes up the file
Of all the gentry; for the most part such
To whom as great a charge as little honour
He meant to lay upon; and his own letter,
The honourable board of council out,
Must fetch him in the papers.

ABERGAVENNY

I do know
Kinsmen of mine, three at the least, that have
By this so sicken'd their estates, that never
They shall abound as formerly.

BUCKINGHAM

O, many
Have broke their backs with laying manors on 'em
For this great journey. What did this vanity
But minister communication of
A most poor issue?

NORFOLK

Grievingly I think,
The peace between the French and us not values
The cost that did conclude it.

BUCKINGHAM

Every man,
After the hideous storm that follow'd, was
A thing inspired; and, not consulting, broke
Into a general prophecy, — That this tempest,
Dashing the garment of this peace, aboded
The sudden breach on't.

NORFOLK

Which is budded out;
For France hath flaw'd the league, and hath attach'd
Our merchants' goods at Bourdeaux.

ABERGAVENNY

Is it therefore
The ambassador is silenc'd?

NORFOLK

Marry, is't.

ABERGAVENNY

A proper title of a peace; and purchas'd
At a superfluous rate!

BUCKINGHAM

Why, all this business
Our reverend cardinal carried.

NORFOLK

Like it your Grace,
The state takes notice of the private difference
Betwixt you and the cardinal. I advise you, —
And take it from a heart that wishes towards you
Honour and plenteous safety, — that you read
The cardinal's malice and his potency
Together; to consider further, that
What his high hatred would effect wants not
A minister in his power. You know his nature,
That he's revengeful; and I know his sword
Hath a sharp edge: it's long, and, 't may be said,
It reaches far; and where 'twill not extend,
Thither he darts it. Bosom up my counsel,
You'll find it wholesome. — Lo, where comes that rock
That I advise your shunning.

Enter CARDINAL WOLSEY, *the purse borne before him; certain of the* GUARD, *and two* SECRETARIES *with papers. The* CARDINAL *in his passage fixeth his eye on* BUCKINGHAM, *and* BUCKINGHAM *on him, both full of disdain.*

WOLSEY

The Duke of Buckingham's surveyor, ha?
Where's his examination?

FIRST SECRETARY

Here, so please you.

WOLSEY

Is he in person ready?

FIRST SECRETARY

Ay, please your Grace.

WOLSEY

Well, we shall then know more; and Buckingham
Shall lessen this big look.

[Exeunt WOLSEY *and his* TRAIN.

BUCKINGHAM

This butcher's cur is venom-mouth'd, and I
Have not the power to muzzle him; therefore best
Not wake him in his slumber. A beggar's book
Outworths a noble's blood.

NORFOLK

What, are you chaf'd?
Ask God for temperance; that's the appliance only
Which your disease requires.

BUCKINGHAM

I read in's looks
Matter against me; and his eye reviled
Me, as his abject object: at this instant
He bores me with some trick: he's gone to the king;
I'll follow, and outstare him.

NORFOLK

Stay, my lord,
And let your reason with your choler question
What 'tis you go about: to climb steep hills
Requires slow pace at first: anger is like
A full-hot horse, who being allow'd his way,
Self-mettle tires him. Not a man in England
Can advise me like you: be to yourself
As you would to your friend.

BUCKINGHAM

I'll to the king;
And from a mouth of honour quite cry down
This Ipswich fellow's insolence; or proclaim
There's difference in no persons.

NORFOLK

Be advised;
Heat not a furnace for your foe so hot
That it do singe yourself: we may outrun,
By violent swiftness, that which we run at,
And lose by over-running. Know you not,
The fire that mounts the liquor till't run o'er,
In seeming t'augment it wastes it? Be advised:
I say again, there is no English soul
More stronger to direct you than yourself,
If with the sap of reason you would quench,
Or but allay, the fire of passion.

BUCKINGHAM

Sir,
I'm thankful to you; and I'll go along
By your prescription: but this top-proud fellow, —
Whom from the flow of gall I name not, but
From sincere motions, — by intelligence,
And proofs as clear as founts in July, when
We see each grain of gravel, I do know
To be corrupt and treasonous.

NORFOLK

Say not, treasonous.

BUCKINGHAM

To the king I'll say't; and make my vouch as strong
As shore of rock. Attend. This holy fox,
Or wolf, or both, — for he is equal ravenous
As he is subtle, and as prone to mischief
As able to perform't; his mind and place
Infecting one another, yea, reciprocally, —
Only to show his pomp as well in France
As here at home, suggests the king our master
To this last costly treaty, the interview,
That swallow'd so much treasure, and like a glass
Did break i' the rinsing.

NORFOLK

Faith, and so it did.

BUCKINGHAM

Pray, give me favour, sir. This cunning cardinal
The articles o' the combination drew
As himself pleas'd; and they were ratified
As he cried, 'Thus let be': to as much end
As give a crutch to the dead: but our count-cardinal
Has done this, and 'tis well; for worthy Wolsey,
Who cannot err, he did it. Now this follows, —
Which, as I take it, is a kind of puppy
To the old dam, treason, — Charles the emperor,
Under pretence to see the queen his aunt, —
For 'twas indeed his colour, but he came
To whisper Wolsey, — here makes visitation:
His fears were, that the interview betwixt
England and France might, through their amity,
Breed him some prejudice; for from this league
Peep'd harms that menac'd him: he privily
Deals with our cardinal; and, as I trow, —
Which I do well; for, I am sure, the emperor
Paid ere he promis'd; whereby his suit was granted
Ere it was ask'd; — but when the way was made,
And pav'd with gold, the emperor thus desired, —
That he would please to alter the king's course,
And break the foresaid peace. Let the king know —

As soon he shall by me — that thus the cardinal
Does buy and sell his honour as he pleases,
And for his own advantage.

NORFOLK

I am sorry
To hear this of him; and could wish he were
Something mistaken in't.

BUCKINGHAM

No, not a syllable:
I do pronounce him in that very shape
He shall appear in proof.

Enter BRANDON, *a* SERGEANT-AT-ARMS *before him, and two or three of the* GUARD.

BRANDON

Your office, sergeant; execute it.

SERGEANT

Sir,
My lord the Duke of Buckingham and Earl
Of Hereford, Stafford, and Northampton, I
Arrest thee of high treason, in the name
Of our most sovereign king.

BUCKINGHAM

Lo, you, my lord,
The net has fall'n upon me! I shall perish
Under device and practice.

BRANDON

I am sorry
To see you ta'en from liberty, to look on
The business present: 'tis his highness' pleasure
You shall to the Tower.

BUCKINGHAM

It will help me nothing
To plead mine innocence; for that dye is on me
Which makes my whitest part black. The will of heaven
Be done in this and all things! — I obey. —
O my Lord Aberga'ny, fare you well!

BRANDON

Nay, he must bear you company. — [*to*
ABERGAVENNY] The king
Is pleas'd you shall to the Tower, till you know
How he determines further.

ABERGAVENNY

As the duke said,
The will of heaven be done, and the king's pleasure
By me obey'd!

BRANDON

Here is a warrant from
The king t'attach Lord Montacute; and the bodies
Of the duke's confessor, John de la Car,
One Gilbert Peck, his chancellor, —

BUCKINGHAM

So, so;
These are the limbs o' the plot: — no more, I hope.

BRANDON

A monk o' the Chartreux.

BUCKINGHAM

O, Nicholas Hopkins?

BRANDON

He.

BUCKINGHAM

My surveyor is false; the o'er-great cardinal
Hath show'd him gold; my life is spann'd already:
I am the shadow of poor Buckingham,
Whose figure even this instant cloud puts on,
By darkening my clear sun. — My lord, farewell.

[Exeunt.

SCENE II

The same. The council-chamber.

Cornets. Enter KING HENRY, *leaning on the* CARDINAL'S *shoulder; the* NOBLES *and* SIR THOMAS LOVELL: *the* CARDINAL *places himself under the* KING'S *feet on his right side.*

KING HENRY

My life itself, and the best heart of it,
Thanks you for this great care: I stood i'the level
Of a full-charg'd confederacy, and give thanks
To you that chok'd it. Let be call'd before us
That gentleman of Buckingham's: in person
I'll hear him his confessions justify;
And point by point the treasons of his master
He shall again relate.

A noise within, crying 'Room for the Queen!' *Enter* QUEEN KATHARINE, *usher'd by the* DUKES OF NORFOLK *and* SUFFOLK: *she kneels. The* KING *riseth from his state, takes her up, kisses and placeth her by him.*

QUEEN KATHARINE

Nay, we must longer kneel: I am a suitor.

KING HENRY My life itself, and the best heart of it,
thanks you for this great care.

KING HENRY
Arise, and take place by us: — half your suit
Never name to us; you have half our power:
The other moiety, ere you ask, is given;
Repeat your will, and take it.
QUEEN KATHARINE
                              Thank your majesty.
That you would love yourself, and in that love
Not unconsider'd leave your honour, nor
The dignity of your office, is the point
Of my petition.
KING HENRY
                Lady mine, proceed
QUEEN KATHARINE
I am solicited, not by a few,
And those of true condition, that your subjects
Are in great grievance: there have been commissions
Sent down among 'em, which hath flaw'd the heart
Of all their loyalties: wherein, although,
My good lord cardinal, they vent reproaches
Most bitterly on you, as putter-on
Of these exactions, yet the king our master, —
Whose honour heaven shield from soil! — even he
    escapes not
Language unmannerly, yea, such which breaks
The sides of loyalty, and almost appears
In loud rebellion.
NORFOLK
                Not almost appears;
It doth appear; for, upon these taxations,
The clothiers all, not able to maintain
The many to them longing, have put off
The spinsters, carders, fullers, weavers, who,
Unfit for other life, compell'd by hunger
And lack of other means, in desperate manner
Daring the event to the teeth, are all in uproar,
And danger serves among them.
KING HENRY
                        Taxation!
Wherein? and what taxation? — My lord cardinal,
You that are blam'd for it alike with us,
Know you of this taxation?
WOLSEY
                    Please you, sir,
I know but of a single part, in aught
Pertains to the state; and front but in that file
Where others tell steps with me.
QUEEN KATHARINE
                            No, my lord,
You know no more than others: but you frame

Things that are known alike;
    which are not wholesome
To those which would not know
    them, and yet must
Perforce be their acquaintance.
    These exactions,
Whereof my sovereign would
    have note, they are
Most pestilent to the hearing;
    and, to bear 'em,
The back is sacrifice to the load.
    They say
They are devis'd by you; or else
    you suffer
Too hard an exclamation.
KING HENRY
    Still exaction!
The nature of it? in what kind,
    let's know,
Is this exaction?
QUEEN KATHARINE
I am much too venturous
In tempting of your patience;
    but am bolden'd
Under your promis'd pardon.
    The subjects' grief
Comes through commissions,
    which compel from each
The sixth part of his substance,
    to be levied
Without delay; and the pretence
    for this
Is nam'd, your wars in France:
    this makes bold mouths:
Tongues spit their duties out,
    and cold hearts freeze
Allegiance in them; their curses
    now
Live where their prayers did: and
    it's come to pass,
That tractable obedience is a slave
To each incensed will. I would your highness
Would give it quick consideration, for
There is no primer business.
KING HENRY
                        By my life,
This is against our pleasure.
WOLSEY
                        And for me,
I have no further gone in this than by
A single voice; and that not past me but
By learned approbation of the judges. If I am
Traduc'd by ignorant tongues, which neither know
My faculties nor person, yet will be
The chronicles of my doing, — let me say
'Tis but the fate of place, and the rough brake
That virtue must go through. We must not stint
Our necessary actions, in the fear
To cope malicious censurers; which ever,
As ravenous fishes, do a vessel follow
That is new-trimm'd, but benefit no further
Than vainly longing. What we oft do best,
By sick interpreters, once weak ones, is
Not ours, or not allow'd; what worst, as oft,
Hitting a grosser quality, is cried up
For our best action. If we shall stand still,
In fear our motion will be mock'd or carp'd at,
We should take root here where we sit, or sit
State-statues only.
KING HENRY
                    Things done well,
And with a care, exempt themselves from fear;
Things done without example, in their issue
Are to be fear'd. Have you a precedent
Of this commission? I believe, not any.
We must not rend our subjects from our laws,
And stick them in our will. Sixth part of each?
A trembling contribution! Why, we take
From every tree top, bark, and part o' the timber;
And, though we leave it with a root, thus hack'd,
The air will drink the sap. To every county
Where this is question'd send our letters, with
Free pardon to each man that has denied
The force of this commission: pray, look to't;
I put it to your care.
WOLSEY [to the SECRETARY].
A word with you.
Let there be letters writ to every shire,
Of the king's grace and pardon. The grieved commons
Hardly conceive of me; let it be nois'd
That through our intercession this revokement

And pardon comes: I shall anon advise you
Further in the proceeding.   [Exit SECRETARY.
            Enter SURVEYOR.
QUEEN KATHARINE
I am sorry that the Duke of Buckingham
Is run in your displeasure.
KING HENRY
                    It grieves many:
The gentleman is learn'd, and a most rare speaker;
To nature none more bound; his training such,
That he may furnish and instruct great teachers,
And never seek for aid out of himself.
Yet see,
When these so noble benefits shall prove
Not well dispos'd, the mind growing once corrupt,
They turn to vicious forms, ten times more ugly
Than ever they were fair. This man so complete,
Who was enroll'd 'mongst wonders, and when we,
Almost with ravish'd listening, could not find
His hour of speech a minute; he, my lady,
Hath into monstrous habits put the graces
That once were his, and is become as black
As if besmear'd in hell. Sit by us; you shall hear —
This was his gentleman in trust — of him
Things to strike honour sad. Bid him recount
The fore-recited practices; whereof
We cannot feel too little, hear too much.
WOLSEY
Stand forth, and with bold spirit relate what you,
Most like a careful subject, have collected
Out of the Duke of Buckingham.
KING HENRY
                        Speak freely.
SURVEYOR
First, it was usual with him, every day
It would infect his speech, — that if the king
Should without issue die, he'll carry it so
To make the sceptre his: these very words
I've heard him utter to his son-in-law,
Lord Aberga'ny; to whom by oath he menac'd
Revenge upon the cardinal.
WOLSEY
                Please your highness, note
His dangerous conception in this point.
Not friended by his wish, to your high person
His will is most malignant; and it stretches
Beyond you, to your friends.
QUEEN KATHARINE
                        My learn'd lord cardinal,
Deliver all with charity.
KING HENRY
                    Speak on:
How grounded he his title to the crown,
Upon our fail? to this point hast thou heard him
At any time speak aught?
SURVEYOR
                    He was brought to this
By a vain prophecy of Nicholas Henton.
KING HENRY
What was that Henton?
SURVEYOR
                Sir, a Chartreux friar,
His confessor; who fed him every minute
With words of sovereignty.
KING HENRY
                    How know'st thou this?
SURVEYOR
Not long before your highness sped to France,
The duke being at the Rose, within the parish
Saint Lawrence Poultney, did of me demand
What was the speech among the Londoners
Concerning the French journey: I replied,
Men fear'd the French would prove perfidious,
To the king's danger. Presently the duke
Said, 'twas the fear, indeed; and that he doubted
'Twould prove the verity of certain words
Spoke by a holy monk; 'that oft,' says he,
'Hath sent to me, wishing me to permit
John de la Car, my chaplain, a choice hour
To hear from him a matter of some moment':
Whom after, under the confession's seal,
He solemnly had sworn, that what he spoke
My chaplain to no creature living but
To me should utter, with demure confidence
This pausingly ensued, — 'Neither the king nor's
    heirs,
Tell you the duke, shall prosper: bid him strive
To gain the love o'the commonalty: the duke
Shall govern England.'

QUEEN KATHARINE
If I know you well,
You were the duke's surveyor, and lost your office
On the complaint o'the tenants: take good heed
You charge not in your spleen a noble person,
And spoil your nobler soul: I say, take heed;
Yes, heartily beseech you.

KING HENRY
Let him on.
Go forward.

SURVEYOR
On my soul, I'll speak but truth.
I told my lord the duke, by the devil's illusions
The monk might be deceiv'd; and that 'twas dangerous
for him
To ruminate on this so far, until
It forg'd him some design, which, being believ'd,
It was much like to do: he answer'd, 'Tush,
It can do me no damage'; adding further,
That, had the king in his last sickness fail'd,
The cardinal's and Sir Thomas Lovell's heads
Should have gone off.

KING HENRY
Ha! what, so rank? Ah-ha!
There's mischief in this man: — canst thou say
further?

SURVEYOR
I can, my liege.

KING HENRY
Proceed.

SURVEYOR
Being at Greenwich,
After your highness had reprov'd the duke
About Sir William Blomer, —

KING HENRY
I remember
Of such a time: — being my sworn servant,
The duke retain'd him his. — But on; what hence?

SURVEYOR
'If,' quoth he, 'I for this had been committed,
As, to the Tower, I thought, I would have play'd
The part my father meant to act upon
The usurper Richard; who, being at Salisbury,
Made suit to come in's presence; which if granted,
As he made semblance of his duty, would
Have put his knife into him.'

KING HENRY
A giant traitor!

WOLSEY
Now, madam, may his highness live in freedom,
And this man out of prison?

QUEEN KATHARINE
God mend all!

KING HENRY
There's something more would out of thee; what
say'st?

SURVEYOR
After 'the duke his father,' with 'the knife,'
He stretch'd him, and, with one hand on his dagger,
Another spread on's breast, mounting his eyes,
He did discharge a horrible oath; whose tenour
Was, — were he evil used, he would outgo
His father by as much as a performance
Does an irresolute purpose.

KING HENRY
There's his period,
To sheathe his knife in us. He is attach'd;
Call him to present trial: if he may
Find mercy in the law, 'tis his; if none,
Let him not seek't of us: by day and night!
He's traitor to the height.   [*Exeunt.*

SCENE III

An ante-chamber in the palace.

Enter the LORD CHAMBERLAIN *and* LORD SANDS.

LORD CHAMBERLAIN
Is't possible the spells of France should juggle
Men into such strange mysteries?

SANDS
New customs,
Though they be never so ridiculous,
Nay, let 'em be unmanly, yet are follow'd.

LORD CHAMBERLAIN
As far as I see, all the good our English
Have got by the late voyage is but merely
A fit or two o' the face; but they are shrewd ones;
For when they hold 'em, you would swear directly
Their very noses had been counsellors
To Pepin or Clotharius, they keep state so.

SANDS
They have all new legs, and lame ones: one would take
it,
That never saw 'em pace before, the spavin
Or springhalt reign'd among 'em.

LORD CHAMBERLAIN
Death! my lord,
Their clothes are after such a pagan cut too,
That, sure, th'have worn out Christendom.
                    Enter SIR THOMAS LOVELL.
                                        How now!
What news, Sir Thomas Lovell?

LOVELL
Faith, my lord,
I hear of none, but the new proclamation
That's clapp'd upon the court-gate.

LORD CHAMBERLAIN
What is't for?

LOVELL
The reformation of our travell'd gallants,
That fill the court with quarrels, talks, and tailors.

LORD CHAMBERLAIN
I'm glad 'tis there: now I would pray our monsieurs
To think an English courtier may be wise,
And never see the Louvre.

LOVELL
They must either —
For so run the conditions — leave those remnants
Of fool and feather, that they got in France,
With all their honourable points of ignorance
Pertaining thereunto, — as fights and fireworks;
Abusing better men than they can be,
Out of a foreign wisdom, — renouncing clean
The faith they have in tennis, and tall stockings,
Short blister'd breeches, and those types of travel,
And understand again like honest men;
Or pack to their old playfellows: there, I take it,
They may, *cum privilegio,* wear away
The lag end of their lewdness, and be laugh'd at.

SANDS
'Tis time to give 'em physic, their diseases
Are grown so catching.

LORD CHAMBERLAIN
What a loss our ladies
Will have of these trim vanities!

LOVELL
Ay, marry,
There will be woe indeed, lords: the sly whoresons
Have got a speeding trick to lay down ladies;
A French song and a fiddle has no fellow.

SANDS
The devil fiddle 'em! I am glad they are going;
For, sure, there's no converting of 'em: now
An honest country lord, as I am, beaten
A long time out of play, may bring his plain-song,
And have an hour of hearing; and, by'r lady,
Held current music too.

LORD CHAMBERLAIN
Well said, Lord Sands;
Your colt's tooth is not cast yet.

SANDS
No, my lord;
Nor shall not, while I have a stump.

LORD CHAMBERLAIN
Sir Thomas,
Whither were you a-going?

LOVELL
To the cardinal's:
Your lordship is a guest too.

LORD CHAMBERLAIN
O, 'tis true:
This night he makes a supper, and a great one,
To many lords and ladies; there will be
The beauty of this kingdom, I'll assure you.

LOVELL
That churchman bears a bounteous mind indeed,
A hand as fruitful as the land that feeds us;
His dews fall every where.

LORD CHAMBERLAIN
No doubt he's noble;
He had a black mouth that said other of him.

SANDS
He may, my lord, — 'has wherewithal; in him
Sparing would show a worse sin than ill doctrine:
Men of his way should be most liberal;
They are set here for examples.

LORD CHAMBERLAIN
True, they are so;
But few now give so great ones. My barge stays;
Your lordship shall along. — Come, good Sir Thomas,
We shall be late else; which I would not be,
For I was spoke to, with Sir Henry Guildford,
This night to be comptrollers.

SANDS
I'm your lordship's.   [*Exeunt.*

SCENE IV

The presence-chamber in York-Place.

Hautboys. A small table under a state for the
CARDINAL, *a longer table for the guests. Then enter*
ANNE BULLEN *and divers other* LADIES *and*
GENTLEWOMEN, *as guests, at one door; at another
door, enter* SIR HENRY GUILDFORD.

GUILDFORD
Ladies, a general welcome from his Grace
Salutes ye all; this night he dedicates
To fair content and you: none here, he hopes,
In all this noble bevy, has brought with her
One care abroad; he would have all as merry
As, first, good company, good wine, good welcome,
Can make good people —
        Enter LORD CHAMBERLAIN, LORD SANDS, *and*
                SIR THOMAS LOVELL.
                O, my lord, y'are tardy:
The very thought of this fair company
Clapp'd wings to me.

LORD CHAMBERLAIN
You are young, Sir Harry Guildford.

SANDS
Sir Thomas Lovell, had the cardinal
But half my lay thoughts in him, some of these
Should find a running banquet ere they rested,
I think would better please 'em: by my life,
They are a sweet society of fair ones.

LOVELL
O, that your lordship were but now confessor
To one or two of these!

SANDS
I would I were;
They should find easy penance.

LOVELL
Faith, how easy?

SANDS
As easy as a down-bed would afford it.

LORD CHAMBERLAIN
Sweet ladies, will it please you sit? — Sir Harry,
Place you that side; I'll take the charge of this:
His Grace is entering. — Nay, you must not freeze;
Two women plac'd together makes cold weather: —
My Lord Sands, you are one will keep 'em waking;
Pray, sit between these ladies.

SANDS
By my faith,
And thank your lordship. — By your leave, sweet ladies:
If I chance to talk a little wild, forgive me;
I had it from my father.

ANNE BULLEN
Was he mad, sir?

SANDS
O, very mad, exceeding mad, in love too:
But he would bite none; just as I do now, —
He would kiss you twenty with a breath.   [*Kisses her.*

LORD CHAMBERLAIN
Well said, my lord. —
So, now y' are fairly seated. — Gentlemen,
The penance lies on you, if these fair ladies
Pass away frowning.

SANDS
For my little cure,
Let me alone.
        Hautboys. Enter CARDINAL WOLSEY, *attended, and
                takes his state.*

WOLSEY
Y'are welcome, my fair guests: that noble lady,
Or gentleman, that is not freely merry,
Is not my friend: this, to confirm my welcome;
And to you all, good health.   [*Drinks.*

SANDS
Your Grace is noble: —
Let me have such a bowl may hold my thanks,
And save me so much talking.

WOLSEY
My Lord Sands,
I am beholding to you: cheer your neighbours. —
Ladies, you are not merry: — gentlemen,
Whose fault is this?

SANDS
The red wine first must rise

KING HENRY *A health, gentlemen! Let it go round.*

In their fair cheeks, my lord; then we shall have 'em
Talk us to silence.

ANNE BULLEN
     You are a merry gamester,
My Lord Sands.

SANDS
    Yes, if I make my play.
Here's to your ladyship: and pledge it, madam,
For 'tis to such a thing, —

ANNE BULLEN
     You cannot show me.

SANDS
I told your Grace they would talk anon.
    [Drum and trumpet; chambers discharged.

WOLSEY
       What's that?

LORD CHAMBERLAIN
Look out there, some of ye. *[Exit a* SERVANT.

WOLSEY
     What warlike voice,
And to what end, is this? — Nay, ladies, fear not;
By all the laws of war y'are privileged.
    Enter SERVANT.

LORD CHAMBERLAIN
How now! what is't?

SERVANT
     A noble troop of strangers, —
For so they seem: th'have left their barge, and landed;
And hither make, as great ambassadors
From foreign princes.

WOLSEY
     Good Lord Chamberlain,
Go, give 'em welcome; you can speak the French
  tongue;
And, pray, receive 'em nobly, and conduct 'em
Into our presence, where this heaven of beauty
Shall shine at full upon them. — Some attend him.
 [Exit CHAMBERLAIN, attended. All rise, and tables
          removed.
You have now a broken banquet; but we'll mend it.
A good digestion to you all: and once more
I shower a welcome on ye; — welcome all.
 Hautboys. Enter KING *and others, as* MASKERS,
  habited like shepherds, usher'd by the LORD
 CHAMBERLAIN. *They pass directly before the*
  CARDINAL, *and gracefully salute him.*
A noble company! what are their pleasures?

LORD CHAMBERLAIN
Because they speak no English, thus they pray'd
To tell your Grace, — that, having heard by fame
Of this so noble and so fair assembly
This night to meet here, they could do no less,
Out of the great respect they bear to beauty,
But leave their flocks; and, under your fair conduct,
Crave leave to view these ladies, and entreat
An hour of revels with 'em.

WOLSEY
     Say, Lord Chamberlain,
They have done my poor house grace; for which I pay
 'em
A thousand thanks, and pray 'em take their pleasures.
      [They choose LADIES.
    The KING *chooses* ANNE BULLEN.

KING HENRY
The fairest hand I ever touch'd! O beauty,
Till now I never knew thee! *[Music. Dance.*

WOLSEY
My lord, —

LORD CHAMBERLAIN
   Your Grace?

WOLSEY
     Pray, tell 'em thus much from me: —
There should be one amongst 'em, by his person,
More worthy this place than myself; to whom,
If I but knew him, with my love and duty
I would surrender it.

LORD CHAMBERLAIN
     I will, my lord.
      [Whispers the MASKERS.

WOLSEY
What say they?

LORD CHAMBERLAIN
    Such a one, they all confess,
There is indeed; which they would have your Grace
Find out, and he will take it.

WOLSEY
     Let me see, then.
       [Comes from his state.
By all your good leaves, gentlemen; — here I'll make
My royal choice.

KING HENRY
    Ye have found him, cardinal:
        [Unmasking.
You hold a fair assembly; you do well, lord:
You are a churchman, or, I'll tell you, cardinal,

I should judge now unhappily.

WOLSEY
     I am glad
Your Grace is grown so pleasant.

KING HENRY
     My Lord Chamberlain,
Prithee, come hither: what fair lady's that?

LORD CHAMBERLAIN
An't please your Grace, Sir Thomas Bullen's daughter, —
The Viscount Rochford, — one of her highness'
  women.

KING HENRY
By heaven, she is a dainty one. — Sweetheart,
I were unmannerly, to take you out,
And not to kiss you [*kisses her*]. — A health, gentlemen!
Let it go round.

WOLSEY
Sir Thomas Lovell, is the banquet ready
I' the privy chamber?

LOVELL
    Yes, my lord.

WOLSEY
      Your Grace,
I fear, with dancing is a little heated.

KING HENRY
I fear, too much.

WOLSEY
    There's fresher air, my lord,
In the next chamber.

KING HENRY
Lead in your ladies, every one: sweet partner,
I must not yet forsake you: let's be merry:
Good my lord cardinal, I have half a dozen healths
To drink to these fair ladies, and a measure
To lead 'em once again; and then let's dream
Who's best in favour. — Let the music knock it.
      [Exeunt with trumpets.

ACT II

SCENE I

London. A street.

Enter two GENTLEMEN, *at several doors.*

FIRST GENTLEMAN
Whither away so fast?

SECOND GENTLEMAN
    O, — God save ye!
Ev'n to the hall, to hear what shall become
Of the great Duke of Buckingham.

FIRST GENTLEMAN
      I'll save you
That labour, sir. All's now done, but the ceremony
Of bringing back the prisoner.

SECOND GENTLEMAN
     Were you there?

FIRST GENTLEMAN
Yes, indeed, was I.

SECOND GENTLEMAN
    Pray, speak what has happen'd.

FIRST GENTLEMAN
You may guess quickly what.

SECOND GENTLEMAN
     Is he found guilty?

FIRST GENTLEMAN
Yes, truly is he, and condemn'd upon't.

SECOND GENTLEMAN
I am sorry for't.

FIRST GENTLEMAN
    So are a number more.

SECOND GENTLEMAN
But, pray, how pass'd it?

FIRST GENTLEMAN
I'll tell you in a little. The great duke
Came to the bar; where to his accusations
He pleaded still, not guilty, and alleged
Many sharp reasons to defeat the law.
The king's attorney, on the contrary,
Urg'd on the examinations, proofs, confessions
Of divers witnesses; which the duke desired
To have brought, *viva voce*, to his face:
At which appear'd against him his surveyor;
Sir Gilbert Peck his chancellor; and John Car,
Confessor to him; with that devil-monk,
Hopkins, that made this mischief.

SECOND GENTLEMAN
     That was he

That fed him with his prophecies?
FIRST GENTLEMAN
                              The same.
All these accus'd him strongly; which he fain
Would have flung from him, but, indeed, he could not:
And so his peers, upon this evidence,
Have found him guilty of high treason. Much
He spoke, and learnedly, for life; but all
Was either pitied in him or forgotten.
SECOND GENTLEMAN
After all this, how did he bear himself?
FIRST GENTLEMAN
When he was brought again to the bar, to hear
His knell rung out, his judgement, — he was stirr'd
With such an agony, he sweat extremely,
And something spoke in choler, ill, and hasty:
But he fell to himself again, and sweetly
In all the rest show'd a most noble patience.
SECOND GENTLEMAN
I do not think he fears death.
FIRST GENTLEMAN
                    Sure, he does not, —
He never was so womanish; the cause
He may a little grieve at.
SECOND GENTLEMAN
                    Certainly
The cardinal is the end of this.
FIRST GENTLEMAN
                    'Tis likely,
By all conjectures: first, Kildare's attainder,
Then deputy of Ireland; who removed,
Earl Surrey was sent thither, and in haste too,
Lest he should help his father.
SECOND GENTLEMAN
                    That trick of state
Was a deep envious one.
FIRST GENTLEMAN
                    At his return
No doubt he will requite it. This is noted,
And generally, — whoever the king favours,
The cardinal instantly will find employment,
And far enough from court too.
SECOND GENTLEMAN
                    All the commons
Hate him perniciously, and, o' my conscience,
Wish him ten fadom deep: this duke as much
They love and dote on; call him bounteous
    Buckingham,
The mirror of all courtesy, —
FIRST GENTLEMAN
                    Stay there, sir,
And see the noble ruin'd man you speak of.

Enter BUCKINGHAM *from his arraignment; tip-staves before him; the axe with the edge towards him; halberds on each side: accompanied with* SIR THOMAS LOVELL, SIR NICHOLAS VAUX, SIR WILLIAM SANDS, *and common people, etc.*

SECOND GENTLEMAN
Let's stand close, and behold him.
BUCKINGHAM
                    All good people,
You that thus far have come to pity me,
Hear what I say, and then go home and lose me.
I have this day receiv'd a traitor's judgement,
And by that name must die: yet, heaven bear witness,
And if I have a conscience, let it sink me,
Even as the axe falls, if I be not faithful!
The law I bear no malice for my death;
'T has done, upon the premises, but justice:
But those that sought it I could wish more Christians:
Be what they will, I heartily forgive 'em:
Yet let 'em look they glory not in mischief,
Nor build their evils on the graves of great men;
For then my guiltless blood must cry against 'em.
For further life in this world I ne'er hope,
Nor will I sue, although the king have mercies
More than I dare make faults. You few that lov'd me,
And dare be bold to weep for Buckingham,
His noble friends and fellows, whom to leave
Is only bitter to him, only dying,
Go with me, like good angels, to my end;
And, as the long divorce of steel falls on me,
Make of your prayers one sweet sacrifice,
And lift my soul to heaven. — Lead on, o'God's name.
LOVELL
I do beseech your Grace, for charity,
If ever any malice in your heart
Were hid against me, now to forgive me frankly.

BUCKINGHAM
Sir Thomas Lovell, I as free forgive you
As I would be forgiven: I forgive all;
There cannot be those numberless offences
'Gainst me that I cannot take peace with: no black envy
Shall mark my grave. — Commend me to his Grace;
And, if he speak of Buckingham, pray, tell him
You met him half in heaven: my vows and prayers
Yet are the king's; and, till my soul forsake,
Shall cry for blessings on him: may he live
Longer than I have time to tell his years!
Ever belov'd and loving may his rule be!
And when old time shall lead him to his end,
Goodness and he fill up one monument!
LOVELL
To the water-side I must conduct your Grace;
Then give my charge up to Sir Nicholas Vaux,
Who undertakes you to your end.
VAUX
                    Prepare there,
The duke is coming: see the barge be ready;
And fit it with such furniture as suits
The greatness of his person.
BUCKINGHAM
                    Nay, Sir Nicholas,
Let it alone; my state now will but mock me.
When I came hither, I was lord high constable
And Duke of Buckingham; now, poor Edward Bohun:
Yet I am richer than my base accusers,
That never knew what truth meant: I now seal it;
And with that blood will make 'em one day groan for't.
My noble father, Henry of Buckingham,
Who first rais'd head against usurping Richard,
Flying for succour to his servant Banister,
Being distress'd, was by that wretch betray'd,
And without trial fell; God's peace be with him!
Henry the Seventh succeeding, truly pitying
My father's loss, like a most royal prince,
Restored me to my honours, and, out of ruins,
Made my name once more noble. Now his son,
Henry the Eighth, life, honour, name, and all
That made me happy, at one stroke has taken
For ever from the world. I had my trial,
And, must needs say, a noble one; which makes me
A little happier than my wretched father:
Yet thus far we are one in fortunes, — both
Fell by our servants, by those men we lov'd most;
A most unnatural and faithless service!
Heaven has an end in all: yet, you that hear me,
This from a dying man receive as certain: —
Where you are liberal of your loves and counsels
Be sure you be not loose; for those you make friends
And give your hearts to, when they once perceive
The least rub in your fortunes, fall away
Like water from ye, never found again
But where they mean to sink ye. All good people,
Pray for me! I must now forsake ye: the last hour
Of my long weary life is come upon me.
Farewell: and when you would say something that is
    sad,
Speak how I fell. — I have done; and God forgive me!
                    [*Exeunt* BUCKINGHAM *and* TRAIN.
FIRST GENTLEMAN
O, this is full of pity! — Sir, it calls,
I fear, too many curses on their heads
That were the authors.
SECOND GENTLEMAN
                    If the duke be guiltless,
'Tis full of woe: yet I can give you inkling
Of an ensuing evil, if it fall,
Greater than this.
FIRST GENTLEMAN
                    Good angels keep it from us!
What may it be? You do not doubt my faith, sir?
SECOND GENTLEMAN
This secret is so weighty, 'twill require
A strong faith to conceal it.
FIRST GENTLEMAN
                    Let me have it;
I do not talk much.
SECOND GENTLEMAN
                    I am confident;
You shall, sir: did you not of late days hear
A buzzing of a separation
Between the king and Katharine?
FIRST GENTLEMAN
                    Yes, but it held not:
For when the king once heard it, out of anger
He sent command to the lord mayor straight
To stop the rumour, and allay those tongues
That durst disperse it.

SECOND GENTLEMAN
                    But that slander, sir,
Is found a truth now: for it grows again
Fresher than e'er it was; and held for certain
The king will venture at it. Either the cardinal,
Or some about him near, out of malice
To the good queen, possess'd him with a scruple
That will undo her: to confirm this too,
Cardinal Campeius is arriv'd, and lately;
As all think, for this business.
FIRST GENTLEMAN
                    'Tis the cardinal;
And merely to revenge him on the emperor
For not bestowing on him, at his asking,
The archbishopric of Toledo, this is purpos'd.
SECOND GENTLEMAN
I think you have hit the mark: but is't not cruel
That she should feel the smart of this? The cardinal
Will have his will, and she must fall.
FIRST GENTLEMAN
                    'Tis woeful.
We are too open here to argue this;
Let's think in private more.   [*Exeunt.*

SCENE II
An ante-chamber in the palace.

Enter the LORD CHAMBERLAIN, *reading this letter.*

LORD CHAMBERLAIN
'My lord, the horses your lordship sent for, with all the
care I had, I saw well chosen, ridden, and furnish'd.
They were young and handsome, and of the best breed
in the north. When they were ready to set out for
London, a man of my lord cardinal's, by commission
and main power, took 'em from me; with this reason,
— His master would be served before a subject, if not
before the king; which stopp'd our mouths, sir.'
I fear he will indeed: well, let him have them:
He will have all, I think.

Enter to the LORD CHAMBERLAIN *the* DUKES OF NORFOLK *and* SUFFOLK.

NORFOLK
Well met, my lord chamberlain.
LORD CHAMBERLAIN
Good day to you both, your Graces.
SUFFOLK
How is the king employ'd?
LORD CHAMBERLAIN
                    I left him private,
Full of sad thoughts and troubles.
NORFOLK
                    What's the cause?
LORD CHAMBERLAIN
It seems the marriage with his brother's wife
Has crept too near his conscience.
SUFFOLK
                    No, his conscience
Has crept too near another lady.
NORFOLK
                    'Tis so:
This is the cardinal's doing, the king-cardinal:
That blind priest, like the eldest son of fortune,
Turns what he list. The king will know him one day.
SUFFOLK
Pray God he do! he'll never know himself else.
NORFOLK
How holily he works in all his business!
And with what zeal! for, now he has crack'd the league
'Tween us and the emperor, the queen's great nephew,
He dives into the king's soul, and there scatters
Dangers, doubts, wringing of the conscience,
Fears, and despairs, — and all these for his marriage:
And out of all these to restore the king,
He counsels a divorce; a loss of her
That, like a jewel, has hung twenty years
About his neck, yet never lost her lustre;
Of her that loves him with that excellence
That angels love good men with; even of her
That, when the greatest stroke of fortune falls,
Will bless the king: and is not this course pious?
LORD CHAMBERLAIN
Heaven keep me from such counsel! 'Tis most true
These news are everywhere; every tongue speaks 'em,
And every true heart weeps for't: all that dare
Look into these affairs see this main end, —
The French king's sister. Heaven will one day open
The king's eyes, that so long have slept upon
This bold bad man.

SUFFOLK
                    And free us from his slavery.

NORFOLK
We had need pray,
And heartily, for our deliverance;
Or this imperious man will work us all
From princes into pages: all men's honours
Lie like one lump before him, to be fashion'd
Into what pitch he please.

SUFFOLK
                    For me, my lords,
I love him not, nor fear him; there's my creed:
As I am made without him, so I'll stand,
If the king please; his curses and his blessings
Touch me alike, th'are breath I not believe in.
I knew him, and I know him; so I leave him
To him that made him proud, the Pope.

NORFOLK
                              Let's in;
And with some other business put the king
From these sad thoughts, that work too much upon
    him: —
My lord, you'll bear us company?

LORD CHAMBERLAIN
                         Excuse me;
The king has sent me otherwhere: besides,
You'll find a most unfit time to disturb him:
Health to your lordships!

NORFOLK
                Thanks, my good lord chamberlain.
    [*Exit* LORD CHAMBERLAIN; *and the* KING *draws the
                curtain and sits reading pensively.*

SUFFOLK
How sad he looks! sure, he is much afflicted.

KING HENRY
Who's there, ha?

NORFOLK
                Pray God he be not angry.

KING HENRY
Who's there, I say? How dare you thrust yourselves
Into my private meditations?
Who am I, ha?

NORFOLK
A gracious king that pardons all offences
Malice ne'er meant: our breach of duty this way
Is business of estate; in which we come
To know your royal pleasure.

KING HENRY
                    Ye are too bold:
Go to; I'll make ye know your times of business:
Is this an hour for temporal affairs, ha?
    Enter WOLSEY *and* CAMPEIUS, *with a commission.*
Who's there? my good lord cardinal? — O my Wolsey,
The quiet of my wounded conscience;
Thou art a cure fit for a king. — [*to* CAMPEIUS] You're
    welcome,
Most learned reverend sir, into our kingdom:
Use us and it. — [*to* WOLSEY] My good lord, have great
    care
I be not found a talker.

WOLSEY
                    Sir, you cannot.
I would your Grace would give us but an hour
Of private conference.

KING HENRY [*to* NORFOLK *and* SUFFOLK].
                    We are busy; go.

NORFOLK [*aside to* SUFFOLK].
This priest has no pride in him!

SUFFOLK   [*aside to* NORFOLK].
                              Not to speak of:
I would not be so sick though for his place:
But this cannot continue.

NORFOLK [*aside to* SUFFOLK].
                    If it do,
I'll venture one have-at-him.

SUFFOLK [*aside to* NORFOLK].
                    I another.
            [*Exeunt* NORFOLK *and* SUFFOLK.

WOLSEY
Your Grace has given a precedent of wisdom
Above all princes, in committing freely
Your scruple to the voice of Christendom:
Who can be angry now? what envy reach you?
The Spaniard, tied by blood and favour to her,
Must now confess, if they have any goodness,
The trial just and noble. All the clerks,
I mean the learned ones, in Christian kingdoms
Have their free voices: Rome, the nurse of judgement,
Invited by your noble self, hath sent
One general tongue unto us, this good man,

This just and learned priest, Cardinal Campeius, —
Whom once more I present unto your highness.

KING HENRY
And once more in mine arms I bid him welcome,
And thank the holy conclave for their loves:
They have sent me such a man I would have wish'd for.

CAMPEIUS
Your Grace must needs deserve all strangers' loves,
You are so noble. To your highness' hand
I tender my commission; by whose virtue,
The court of Rome commanding, you, my lord
Cardinal of York, are join'd with me their servant
In the unpartial judging of this business.

KING HENRY
Two equal men. The queen shall be acquainted
Forthwith for what you come. Where's Gardiner?

WOLSEY
I know your majesty has always lov'd her
So dear in heart, not to deny her that
A woman of less place might ask by law, —
Scholars allow'd freely to argue for her.

KING HENRY
Ay, and the best she shall have; and my favour
To him that does best: God forbid else. Cardinal,
Prithee, call Gardiner to me, my new secretary:
I find him a fit fellow.   [*Exit* WOLSEY.
        Enter WOLSEY, *with* GARDINER.

WOLSEY [*aside to* GARDINER].
Give me your hand: much joy and favour to you;
You are the king's now.

GARDINER [*aside to* WOLSEY].
                    But to be commanded
For ever by your Grace, whose hand has rais'd me.

KING HENRY
Come hither, Gardiner.   [*Walks and whispers.*

CAMPEIUS
My Lord of York, was not one Doctor Pace
In this man's place before him?

WOLSEY
                    Yes, he was.

CAMPEIUS
Was he not held a learned man?

WOLSEY
                    Yes, surely.

CAMPEIUS
Believe me, there's an ill opinion spread, then,
Even of yourself, lord cardinal.

WOLSEY
                    How! of me?

CAMPEIUS
They will not stick to say you envied him;
And fearing he would rise, he was so virtuous,
Kept him a foreign man still; which so griev'd him,
That he ran mad and died.

WOLSEY
                    Heaven's peace be with him!
That's Christian care enough: for living murmurers
There's places of rebuke. He was a fool;
For he would needs be virtuous: that good fellow,
If I command him, follows my appointment:
I will have none so near else. Learn this, brother,
We live not to be gripp'd by meaner persons.

KING HENRY
Deliver this with modesty to the queen.
                        [*Exit* GARDINER.
The most convenient place that I can think of
For such receipt of learning is Black-Friars;
There ye shall meet about this weighty
    business: —
My Wolsey, see it furnish'd. — O, my lord
Would it not grieve an able man to leave
So sweet a bedfellow? But, conscience,
    conscience, —
O, 'tis a tender place! and I must leave her. [*Exeunt.*

SCENE III

An ante-chamber in the QUEEN'S *apartments.*

Enter ANNE BULLEN *and an old* LADY.

ANNE BULLEN
Not for that neither: here's the pang that
    pinches: —
His highness having liv'd so long with her,
    and she
So good a lady that no tongue could ever
Pronounce dishonour of her, — by my life,
She never knew harm-doing; — O, now, after
So many courses of the sun enthroned,

Still growing in a majesty and pomp, — the which
To leave a thousand-fold more bitter than
'Tis sweet at first t'acquire, — after this process,
To give her the avaunt! it is a pity
Would move a monster.

OLD LADY
                Hearts of most hard temper
Melt and lament for her.

ANNE BULLEN
                O, God's will! much better
She ne'er had known pomp: though't be temporal,
Yet, if that quarrel, fortune, do divorce
It from the bearer, 'tis a sufferance panging
As soul and body's severing.

OLD LADY
                    Alas, poor lady!
She's a stranger now again.

ANNE BULLEN
                    So much the more
Must pity drop upon her. Verily,
I swear, 'tis better to be lowly born,
And range with humble livers in content,
Than to be perk'd up in a glistering grief,
And wear a golden sorrow.

OLD LADY
                    Our content
Is our best having.

ANNE BULLEN
                By my troth and maidenhead,
I would not be a queen.

OLD LADY
                    Beshrew me, I would,
And venture maidenhead for't; and so would you,
For all this spice of your hypocrisy:
You, that have so fair parts of woman on you,
Have too a woman's heart; which ever yet
Affected eminence, wealth, sovereignty;
Which, to say sooth, are blessings; and which gifts —
Saving your mincing — the capacity
Of your soft cheveril conscience would receive,
If you might please to stretch it.

ANNE BULLEN
                        Nay, good troth, —

OLD LADY
Yes, troth, and troth; — you would not be a queen?

ANNE BULLEN
No, not for all the riches under heaven.

OLD LADY
'Tis strange; a three-pence bow'd would hire me,
Old as I am, to queen it: but, I pray you,
What think you of a duchess? have you limbs
To bear that load of title?

ANNE BULLEN
                    No, in truth.

OLD LADY
Then you are weakly made: pluck off a little;
I would not be a young count in your way,
For more than blushing comes to: if your back
Cannot vouchsafe this burd en, 'tis too weak
Ever to get a boy.

OLD LADY Then you are weakly made: pluck off a little.

ANNE BULLEN
How you do talk!
I swear again, I would not be a queen
For all the world.
OLD LADY
In faith, for little England
You'ld venture an emballing: I myself
Would for Carnarvonshire, although there long'd
No more to the crown but that. — Lo, who comes here?

Enter the LORD CHAMBERLAIN.

LORD CHAMBERLAIN
Good morrow, ladies. What were't worth to know
The secret of your conference?
ANNE BULLEN
My good lord,
Not your demand; it values not your asking:
Our mistress' sorrows we were pitying.
LORD CHAMBERLAIN
It was a gentle business, and becoming
The action of good women: there is hope
All will be well.
ANNE BULLEN
Now, I pray God, amen!
LORD CHAMBERLAIN
You bear a gentle mind, and heavenly blessings
Follow such creatures. That you may, fair lady,
Perceive I speak sincerely, and high note's
Ta'en of your many virtues, the king's majesty
Commends his good opinion of you, and
Does purpose honour to you no less flowing
Than Marchioness of Pembroke; to which title
A thousand pound a year, annual support,
Out of his grace he adds.
ANNE BULLEN
I do not know
What kind of my obedience I should tender;
More than my all is nothing: nor my prayers
Are not words duly hallow'd, nor my wishes
More worth than empty vanities; yet prayers and
wishes
Are all I can return. Beseech your lordship,
Vouchsafe to speak my thanks and my obedience,
As from a blushing handmaid, to his highness;
Whose health and royalty I pray for.
LORD CHAMBERLAIN
Lady,
I shall not fail t'approve the fair conceit
The king hath of you. — [*aside*] I have perus'd her well;
Beauty and honour in her are so mingled,
That they have caught the king: and who knows yet
But from this lady may proceed a gem
To lighten all this isle? — I'll to the king,
And say I spoke with you.
ANNE BULLEN
My honour'd lord.
[*Exit* LORD CHAMBERLAIN.

OLD LADY
Why, this it is; see, see!
I have been begging sixteen years in court, —
Am yet a courtier beggarly, — nor could
Come pat betwixt too early and too late
For any suit of pounds; and you, O fate!
A very fresh-fish here, — fie, fie, fie upon
This compell'd fortune! — have your mouth fill'd up
Before you open it.
ANNE BULLEN
This is strange to me.
OLD LADY
How tastes it? is it bitter? forty pence, no.
There was a lady once — 'tis an old story —
That would not be a queen, that would she not,
For all the mud in Egypt: have you heard it?
ANNE BULLEN
Come, you are pleasant.
OLD LADY
With your theme, I could
O'ermount the lark. The Marchioness of Pembroke!
A thousand pounds a year — for pure respect!
No other obligation! By my life,
That promises more thousands: honour's train
Is longer than his foreskirt. By this time
I know your back will bear a duchess: — say,
Are you not stronger than you were?
ANNE BULLEN
Good lady,
Make yourself mirth with your particular fancy,
And leave me out on't. Would I had no being,
If this salute my blood a jot: it faints me,
To think what follows.

The queen is comfortless, and we forgetful
In our long absence: pray, do not deliver
What here y' have heard to her.
OLD LADY
What do you think me?
[*Exeunt.*

SCENE IV

A hall in Black-Friars

Trumpets, sennet, and cornets. Enter two VERGERS, with short silver wands; next them, two SCRIBES, in the habit of doctors; after them, the ARCHBISHOP OF CANTERBURY alone; after him, the BISHOPS OF LINCOLN, ELY, ROCHESTER, and SAINT ASAPH; next them, with some small distance, follows a GENTLEMAN bearing the purse, with the great seal, and a cardinal's hat; then two PRIESTS, bearing each a silver cross; then a GENTLEMAN-USHER bare-headed, accompanied with a SERGEANT-AT-ARMS bearing a silver mace; then two GENTLEMEN bearing two great silver pillars; after them, side by side, the two CARDINALS; two NOBLEMEN with the sword and mace. The KING takes place under the cloth of state; the two CARDINALS sit under him as judges. The QUEEN takes place some distance from the KING. The BISHOPS place themselves on each side the court, in manner of a consistory; below them, the SCRIBES. The LORDS sit next the BISHOPS. The rest of the ATTENDANTS stand in convenient order about the hall.

WOLSEY
Whilst our commission from Rome is read,
Let silence be commanded.
KING HENRY
What's the need?
It hath already publicly been read,
And on all sides the authority allow'd;
You may, then, spare that time.
WOLSEY
Be't so. — Proceed.
SCRIBE
Say, Henry King of England, come into the court.
CRIER
King Henry of England, *etc.*
KING HENRY
Here.
SCRIBE
Say, Katharine Queen of England, come into the court.
CRIER
Katharine Queen of England, *etc.*
[*The QUEEN makes no answer, rises out of her chair, goes about the court, comes to the KING, and kneels at his feet; then speaks.*

QUEEN KATHARINE
Sir, I desire you do me right and justice;
And to bestow your pity on me: for
I am a most poor woman, and a stranger,
Born out of your dominions; having here
No judge indifferent, nor no more
assurance
Of equal friendship and proceeding.
Alas, sir,
In what have I offended you? what cause
Hath my behaviour given to your
displeasure,
That thus you should proceed to put me
off,
And take your good grace from me?
Heaven witness,
I have been to you a true and humble
wife,
At all times to your will conformable;
Ever in fear to kindle your dislike,
Yea, subject to your countenance, —
glad or sorry,
As I saw it inclin'd. When was the hour
I ever contradicted your desire,
Or made it not mine too? Or which of
your friends
Have I not strove to love, although I knew
He were mine enemy? what friend of
mine
That had to him deriv'd your anger, did I
Continue in my liking? nay, gave notice
He was from thence discharg'd? Sir, call
to mind
That I have been your wife, in this
obedience,
Upward of twenty years, and have been
blest

With many children by you: if, in the course
And process of this time, you can report,
And prove it too, against mine honour aught,
My bond to wedlock, or my love and duty,
Against your sacred person, in God's name,
Turn me away; and let the foul'st contempt
Shut door upon me, and so give me up
To the sharp'st kind of justice. Please you, sir,
The king, your father, was reputed for
A prince most prudent, of an excellent
And unmatch'd wit and judgement: Ferdinand,
My father, King of Spain, was reckon'd one
The wisest prince that there had reign'd by many
A year before: it is not to be question'd
That they had gather'd a wise council to them
Of every realm, that did debate this business,
Who deem'd our marriage lawful. Wherefore I humbly
Beseech you, sir, to spare me, till I may
Be by my friends in Spain advis'd; whose counsel
I will implore: if not, i'the name of God,
Your pleasure be fulfill'd!
WOLSEY
You have here, lady, —
And of your choice, — these reverend fathers; men
Of singular integrity and learning,
Yea, the elect o'the land, who are assembled
To plead your cause: it shall be therefore bootless
That longer you defer the court; as well
For your own quiet, as to rectify
What is unsettled in the king.
CAMPEIUS
His Grace
Hath spoken well and justly: therefore, madam,
It's fit this royal session do proceed;
And that, without delay, their arguments
Be now produced and heard.
QUEEN KATHARINE
Lord cardinal, —
To you I speak.
WOLSEY
Your pleasure, madam?
QUEEN KATHARINE
Sir,
I am about to weep; but, thinking that
We are a queen, — or long have dream'd so, — certain
The daughter of a king, my drops of tears
I'll turn to sparks of fire.
WOLSEY
Be patient yet.

QUEEN KATHARINE Lord cardinal, — To you I speak.

QUEEN KATHARINE
I will, when you are humble; nay, before,
Or God will punish me. I do believe,
Induc'd by potent circumstances, that
You are mine enemy; and make my challenge
You shall not be my judge: for it is you
Have blown this coal betwixt my lord and me, —
Which God's dew quench! Therefore I say again,
I utterly abhor, yea, from my soul
Refuse you for my judge; whom, yet once more,
I hold my most malicious foe, and think not
At all a friend to truth.

WOLSEY
               I do profess
You speak not like yourself; who ever yet
Have stood to charity, and display'd the effects
Of disposition gentle, and of wisdom
O'ertopping woman's power. Madam, you do me
   wrong:
I have no spleen against you; nor injustice
For you or any: how far I have proceeded,
Or how far further shall, is warranted
By a commission from the consistory,
Yea, the whole consistory of Rome. You charge me
That I have blown this coal: I do deny it:
The king is present: if it be known to him
That I gainsay my deed, how may he wound,
And worthily, my falsehood! yea, as much
As you have done my truth. But if he know
That I am free of your report, he knows
I am not of your wrong. Therefore in him
It lies to cure me: and the cure is, to
Remove these thoughts from you: the which before
His highness shall speak in, I do beseech
You, gracious madam, to unthink your speaking,
And to say no more.

QUEEN KATHARINE
            My lord, my lord,
I am a simple woman, much too weak
T'oppose your cunning. Y' are meek and
   humble-mouth'd;
You sign your place and calling, in full seeming,
With meekness and humility: but your heart
Is cramm'd with arrogancy, spleen, and pride.
You have, by fortune, and his highness' favours,
Gone slightly o'er low steps, and now are mounted
Where powers are your retainers, and your wards
(Domestics to you); serve your will as't please
Yourself pronounce their office. I must tell you,
You tender more your person's honour than
Your high profession spiritual: that again
I do refuse you for my judge; and here,
Before you all, appeal unto the Pope,
To bring my whole cause 'fore his holiness,
And to be judg'd by him.
        [*She curtsies to the* KING, *and offers to depart.*

CAMPEIUS
           The queen is obstinate,
Stubborn to justice, apt to accuse it, and
Disdainful to be tried by't: 'tis not well.
She's going away.

KING HENRY
Call her again.

CRIER
Katharine Queen of England, come into the court.

GENTLEMAN USHER
Madam, you are call'd back.

QUEEN KATHARINE
What need you note it? pray you, keep your way:
When you are call'd, return. — Now, the Lord help,
They vex me past my patience! — Pray you, pass on:
I will not tarry; no, nor ever more
Upon this business my appearance make
In any of their courts.
        [*Exeunt* QUEEN *and her* ATTENDANTS.

KING HENRY
          Go thy ways, Kate:
That man i'the world who shall report he has
A better wife, let him in naught be trusted,
For speaking false in that: thou art, alone —
If thy rare qualities, sweet gentleness,
Thy meekness saint-like, wife-like government,
Obeying in commanding, and thy parts
Sovereign and pious else, could speak thee out —
The queen of earthly queens — she's noble born;
And, like her true nobility, she has
Carried herself towards me.

WOLSEY
           Most gracious sir,
In humblest manner I require your highness,
That it shall please you to declare, in hearing

Of all these ears, — for where I am robb'd and bound,
There must I be unloos'd; although not there
At once and fully satisfied, — whether ever I
Did broach this business to your highness; or
Laid any scruple in your way, which might
Induce you to the question on't? or ever
Have to you — but with thanks to God for such
A royal lady — spake one the least word that might
Be to the prejudice of her present state,
Or touch of her good person?

KING HENRY
          My lord cardinal,
I do excuse you; yea, upon mine honour,
I free you from't. You are not to be taught
That you have many enemies, that know not
Why they are so, but, like to village-curs,
Bark when their fellows do: by some of these
The queen is put in anger. Y'are excus'd:
But will you be more justified? you ever
Have wish'd the sleeping of this business; never
Desired it to be stirr'd; but oft have hinder'd, oft,
The passages made toward it: — on my honour,
I speak my good lord cardinal to this point,
And thus far clear him. Now, what mov'd me to't,
I will be bold with time and your attention: —
Then mark the inducement. Thus it came; — give heed
to't: —
My conscience first receiv'd a tenderness,
Scruple, and prick, on certain speeches utter'd
By the Bishop of Bayonne, then French ambassador;
Who had been hither sent on the debating
A marriage 'twixt the Duke of Orleans and
Our daughter Mary: i'the progress of this business,
Ere a determinate resolution, he —
I mean the bishop — did require a respite;
Wherein he might the king his lord advertise
Whether our daughter were legitimate,
Respecting this our marriage with the dowager,
Sometimes our brother's wife. This respite shook
The bottom of my conscience, enter'd me,
Yea, with a splitting power, and made to tremble
The region of my breast; which forc'd such way,
That many maz'd considerings did throng,
And press'd in with this caution. First, methought
I stood not in the smile of heaven; who had
Commanded nature, that my lady's womb,
If it conceiv'd a male child by me, should
Do no more offices of life to't than
The grave does to the dead; for her male issue
Or died where they were made, or shortly after
This world had air'd them: hence I took a thought,
This was a judgement on me; that my kingdom,
Well worthy the best heir o' the world, should not
Be gladded in't by me: then follows, that
I weigh'd the danger which my realms stood in
By this my issue's fail; and that gave to me
Many a groaning throe. Thus hulling in
The wild sea of my conscience, I did steer
Toward this remedy, whereupon we are
Now present here together; that's to say,
I meant to rectify my conscience — which
I then did feel full sick, and yet not well —
By all the reverend fathers of the land
And doctors learn'd. First I began in private
With you, my Lord of Lincoln; you remember
How under my oppression I did reek,
When I first mov'd you.

BISHOP OF LINCOLN
        Very well, my liege.

KING HENRY
I have spoke long: be pleas'd yourself to say
How far you satisfied me.

BISHOP OF LINCOLN
         So please your highness,
The question did at first so stagger me, —
Bearing a state of mighty moment in't,
And consequence of dread, — that I committed
The daring'st counsel which I had to doubt;
And did entreat your highness to this course
Which you are running here.

KING HENRY
          I then mov'd you,
My Lord of Canterbury; and got your leave
To make this present summons: — unsolicited
I left no reverend person in this court;
But by particular consent proceeded
Under your hands and seals: therefore, go on;
For no dislike i'the world against the person
Of the good queen, but the sharp thorny points
Of my alleged reasons, drive this forward:
Prove but our marriage lawful, by my life

And kingly dignity, we are contented
To wear our mortal state to come with her,
Katharine our queen, before the primest creature
That's paragon'd o'the world.

CAMPEIUS
         So please you highness,
The queen being absent, 'tis a needful fitness
That we adjourn this court till further day:
Meanwhile must be an earnest motion
Made to the queen, to call back her appeal
She intends unto his holiness.   [*They rise to depart.*

KING HENRY [*aside*].
         I may perceive
These cardinals trifle with me: I abhor
This dilatory sloth and tricks of Rome.
My learn'd and well-beloved servant, Cranmer,
Prithee, return: with thy approach, I know,
My comfort comes along. — Break up the court:
I say, set on.   [*Exeunt in manner as they enter'd.*

ACT III

SCENE I

London. The QUEEN'S *apartments.*

Enter QUEEN *and her* WOMEN *as at work.*

QUEEN KATHARINE
Take thy lute, wench: my soul grows sad with troubles;
Sing, and disperse 'em, if thou canst: leave working.
           Song.
   Orpheus with his lute made trees,
   And the mountain-tops that freeze,
      Bow themselves, when he did sing:
   To his music plants and flowers
   Ever sprung; as sun and showers
      There had made a lasting spring.

   Every thing that heard him play,
   Even the billows of the sea,
      Hung their heads, and then lay by.
   In sweet music is such art,
   Killing care and grief of heart
      Fall asleep, or hearing, die.
      Enter a GENTLEMAN.

QUEEN KATHARINE
How now!

GENTLEMAN
An't please your Grace, the two great cardinals
Wait in the presence.

QUEEN KATHARINE
        Would they speak with me?

GENTLEMAN
They will'd me say so, madam.

QUEEN KATHARINE
         Pray their Graces
To come near. [*Exit* GENTLEMAN.] What can be their
   business
With me, a poor weak woman, fall'n from favour?
I do not like their coming, now I think on't,
They should be good men; their affairs as righteous:
But all hoods make not monks.
      Enter the two CARDINALS, WOLSEY *and*
           CAMPEIUS.

WOLSEY
         Peace to your highness!

QUEEN KATHARINE
Your Graces find me here part of a housewife:
I would be all, against the worst may happen.
What are your pleasures with me, reverend lords?

WOLSEY
May it please you, noble madam, to withdraw
Into your private chamber, we shall give you
The full cause of our coming.

QUEEN KATHARINE
         Speak it here;
There's nothing I have done yet, o'my conscience,
Deserves a corner: would all other women
Could speak this with as free a soul as I do!
My lords, I care not, — so much I am happy
Above a number, — if my actions
Were tried by every tongue, every eye saw 'em,
Envy and base opinion set against 'em,
I know my life so even. If your business
Seek me out, and that way I am wise in,
Out with it boldly: truth loves open dealing.

WOLSEY
Tanta est erga te mentis integritas, regina serenissima, —

QUEEN KATHARINE *Ye have angels' faces, but heaven knows your hearts.*

QUEEN KATHARINE
O, good my lord, no Latin;
I am not such a truant since my coming,
As not to know the language I have liv'd in:
A strange tongue makes my cause more strange,
   suspicious;
Pray, speak in English: here are some will thank you,
If you speak truth, for their poor mistress' sake, —
Believe me, she has had much wrong: lord cardinal,
The willing'st sin I ever yet committed
May be absolv'd in English.

WOLSEY
           Noble lady,
I am sorry my integrity should breed —
And service to his majesty and you —
So deep suspicion, where all faith was meant.
We come not by the way of accusation,
To taint that honour every good tongue blesses,
Nor to betray you any way to sorrow, —
You have too much, good lady; but to know
How you stand minded in the weighty difference
Between the king and you; and to deliver,
Like free and honest men, our just opinions,
And comforts to your cause.

CAMPEIUS
           Most honour'd madam,
My Lord of York, — out of his noble nature,
Zeal and obedience he still bore your Grace, —
Forgetting, like a good man, your late censure
Both of his truth and him, which was too far, —
Offers, as I do, in a sign of peace,
His service and his counsel.

QUEEN KATHARINE [*aside*].
           To betray me.
My lords, I thank you both for your good wills;
Ye speak like honest men, — pray God, ye prove so! —
But how to make ye suddenly an answer,
In such a point of weight, so near mine honour, —
More near my life, I fear, — with my weak wit,
And to such men of gravity and learning,
In truth, I know not. I was set at work
Among my maids; full little, God knows, looking
Either for such men or such business.
For her sake that I have been, — for I feel
The last fit of my greatness, — good your Graces,
Let me have time and counsel for my cause:
Alas, I am a woman, friendless, hopeless!

WOLSEY
Madam, you wrong the king's love with these fears:
Your hopes and friends are infinite.

QUEEN KATHARINE
           In England
But little for my profit: can you think, lords,
That any Englishman dare give me counsel?
Or be a known friend, 'gainst his highness' pleasure, —
Though he be grown so desperate to be honest, —
And live a subject? Nay, forsooth, my friends,
They that must weigh out my afflictions,
They that my trust must grow to, live not here:
They are, as all my other comforts, far hence,
In mine own country, lords.

CAMPEIUS
           I would your Grace
Would leave your griefs, and take my counsel.

QUEEN KATHARINE
           How, sir?

CAMPEIUS
Put your main cause into the king's protection;
He's loving and most gracious: 'twill be much
Both for your honour better and your cause;
For if the trial of the law o'ertake ye,
You'll part away disgrac'd.

WOLSEY
           He tells you rightly.

QUEEN KATHARINE
Ye tell me what ye wish for both, my ruin:
Is this your Christian counsel? out upon ye!
Heaven is above all yet; there sits a judge
That no king can corrupt.

CAMPEIUS
           Your rage mistakes us.

QUEEN KATHARINE
The more shame for ye: holy men I thought ye,
Upon my soul, two reverend cardinal virtues;
But cardinal sins and hollow hearts I fear ye;
Mend 'em, for shame, my lords. Is this your comfort?
The cordial that ye bring a wretched lady, —
A woman lost among ye, laugh'd at, scorn'd?
I will not wish ye half my miseries;
I have more charity: but say, I warn'd ye;
Take heed, for heaven's sake, take heed, lest at once
The burden of my sorrows fall upon ye.

WOLSEY
Madam, this is a mere distraction;
You turn the good we offer into envy.

QUEEN KATHARINE
Ye turn me into nothing: woe upon ye,
And all such false professors! Would you have me —
If you have any justice, any pity,
If ye be any thing but churchmen's habits —
Put my sick cause into his hands that hates me?
Alas, has banish'd me his bed already, —
His love, too long ago! I am old, my lords,
And all the fellowship I hold now with him
Is only my obedience. What can happen
To me above this wretchedness? all your studies
Make me a curse like this.

CAMPEIUS
           Your fears are worse.

QUEEN KATHARINE
Have I liv'd thus long — let me speak myself,
Since virtue finds no friends — a wife, a true one?
A woman — I dare say, without vain-glory —
Never yet branded with suspicion?
Have I with all my full affections
Still met the king? lov'd him next heaven? obey'd him?
Been, out of fondness, superstitious to him?
Almost forgot my prayers to content him?
And am I thus rewarded? 'tis not well, lords.
Bring me a constant woman to her husband,
One that ne'er dream'd a joy beyond his pleasure;
And to that woman, when she has done most,

Yet will I add an honour, — a great patience.

WOLSEY
Madam, you wander from the good we aim at.

QUEEN KATHARINE
My lord, I dare not make myself so guilty,
To give up willingly that noble title
Your master wed me to: nothing but death
Shall e'er divorce my dignities.

WOLSEY
           Pray, hear me.

QUEEN KATHARINE
Would I had never trod this English earth,
Or felt the flatteries that grow upon it!
Ye have angels' faces, but heaven knows your hearts.
What will become of me now, wretched lady!
I am the most unhappy woman living. —
[*to her* WOMEN] Alas, poor wenches, where are now
   your fortunes!
Shipwrack'd upon a kingdom, where no pity,
No friends, no hope; no kindred weep for me;
Almost no grave allow'd me: — like the lily,
That once was mistress of the field and flourish'd,
I'll hang my head and perish.

WOLSEY
           If your Grace
Could but be brought to know our ends are honest,
You'ld feel more comfort. Why should we, good lady,
Upon what cause, wrong you? alas, our places,
The way of our profession is against it:
We are to cure such sorrows, not to sow 'em.
For goodness' sake, consider what you do;
How you may hurt yourself, ay, utterly
Grow from the king's acquaintance, by this carriage.
The hearts of princes kiss obedience,
So much they love it; but to stubborn spirits
They swell, and grow as terrible as storms.
I know you have a gentle, noble temper,
A soul as even as a calm: pray, think us
Those we profess, peace-makers, friends, and servants.

CAMPEIUS
Madam, you'll find it so. You wrong your virtues
With these weak women's fears: a noble spirit,
As yours was put into you, ever casts
Such doubts, as false coin, from it. The king loves you;
Beware you lose it not: for us, if please you
To trust us in your business, we are ready
To use our utmost studies in your service.

QUEEN KATHARINE
Do what ye will, my lords: and, pray, forgive me,
If I have us'd myself unmannerly;
You know I am a woman, lacking wit
To make a seemly answer to such persons.
Pray, do my service to his majesty:
He has my heart yet; and shall have my prayers
While I shall have my life. Come, reverend fathers,
Bestow your counsels on me: she now begs,
That little thought, when she set footing here,
She should have bought her dignities so dear. [*Exeunt.*

SCENE II

Ante-chamber to the KING'S *apartment.*

Enter the DUKE OF NORFOLK, *the* DUKE OF
SUFFOLK, *the* EARL OF SURREY, *and the* LORD
CHAMBERLAIN.

NORFOLK
If you will now unite in your complaints,
And force them with a constancy, the cardinal
Cannot stand under them: if you omit
The offer of this time, I cannot promise
But that you shall sustain more new disgraces,
With these you bear already.

SURREY
           I am joyful
To meet the least occasion that may give me
Remembrance of my father-in-law, the duke,
To be reveng'd on him.

SUFFOLK
           Which of the peers
Have uncontemn'd gone by him, or at least
Strangely neglected? when did he regard
The stamp of nobleness in any person
Out of himself?

LORD CHAMBERLAIN
           My lords, you speak your pleasures:
What he deserves of you and me I know;
What we can do to him, — though now the time
Gives way to us, — I much fear. If you cannot
Bar his access to the king, never attempt
Any thing on him; for he hath a witchcraft

Over the king in's tongue.
NORFOLK
                        O, fear him not;
His spell in that is out: the king hath found
Matter against him that for ever mars
The honey of his language. No, he's settled,
Not to come off, in his displeasure.
SURREY
                                 Sir,
I should be glad to hear such news as this
Once every hour.
NORFOLK
                    Believe it, this is true:
In the divorce his contrary proceedings
Are all unfolded; wherein he appears
As I would wish mine enemy.
SURREY
                          How came
His practices to light?
SUFFOLK
                       Most strangely.
SURREY
                            O, how, how?
SUFFOLK
The cardinal's letters to the Pope miscarried,
And came to the eye o' the king: wherein was read,
How that the cardinal did entreat his holiness
To stay the judgement o' the divorce; for if
It did take place, 'I do,' quoth he, 'perceive
My king is tangled in affection to
A creature of the queen's, Lady Anne Bullen.'
SURREY
Has the king this?
SUFFOLK
                  Believe it.
SURREY
                       Will this work?
LORD CHAMBERLAIN
The king in this perceives him, how he coasts
And hedges his own way. But in this point
All his tricks founder, and he brings his physic
After his patient's death: the king already
Hath married the fair lady.
SURREY
                      Would he had!
SUFFOLK
May you be happy in your wish, my lord!
For, I profess, you have it.
SURREY
                     Now, all my joy
Trace the conjunction!
SUFFOLK
                    My amen to't!
NORFOLK
                        All men's!
SUFFOLK
There's order given for her coronation:
Marry, this is yet but young, and may be left
To some ears unrecounted. — But, my lords,
She is a gallant creature, and complete
In mind and feature: I persuade me, from her
Will fall some blessing to this land, which shall
In it be memoris'd.
SURREY
                  But, will the king
Digest this letter of the cardinal's?
The Lord forbid!
NORFOLK
                   Marry, amen!
SUFFOLK
                     No, no;
There be more wasps that buzz about his nose
Will make this sting the sooner. Cardinal Campeius
Is stol'n away to Rome; hath ta'en no leave;
Has left the cause o'the king unhandled; and
Is posted, as the agent of our cardinal,
To second all his plot. I do assure you
The king cried 'Ha!' at this.
LORD CHAMBERLAIN
               Now, God incense him,
And let him cry 'Ha!' louder!
NORFOLK
                  But, my lord,
When returns Cranmer?
SUFFOLK
He is return'd in his opinions; which
Have satisfied the king for his divorce,
Together with all famous colleges
Almost in Christendom: shortly, I believe,

His second marriage shall be publish'd, and
Her coronation. Katharine no more
Shall be call'd queen, but princess dowager
And widow to Prince Arthur.
NORFOLK
                  This same Cranmer's
A worthy fellow, and hath ta'en much pain
In the king's business.
SUFFOLK
                He has; and we shall see him
For it an archbishop.
NORFOLK
               So I hear.
SUFFOLK
               'Tis so. —
The cardinal!

Enter WOLSEY *and* CROMWELL.

NORFOLK

NORFOLK Observe, observe, he's moody.

         Observe, observe, he's moody.
WOLSEY
The packet, Cromwell.
Gave't you the king?
CROMWELL
            To his own hand, in's bedchamber.
WOLSEY
Look'd he o'the inside of the papers?
CROMWELL
                  Presently
He did unseal them: and the first he view'd,
He did it with a serious mind; a heed
Was in his countenance. You he bade
Attend him here this morning.
WOLSEY
               Is he ready
To come abroad?
CROMWELL
           I think, by this he is.
WOLSEY
Leave me awhile.   [*Exit* CROMWELL.
It shall be to the Duchess of Alençon,
The French king's sister: he shall marry her. —
Anne Bullen! No; I'll no Anne Bullens for him:
There's more in't than fair visage. — Bullen!
No, we'll no Bullens. — Speedily I wish
To hear from Rome. — The Marchioness of Pembroke!
NORFOLK
He's discontented.
SUFFOLK
             May be, he hears the king
Does whet his anger to him.
SURREY
               Sharp enough,
Lord, for thy justice!
WOLSEY
The late queen's gentlewoman, a knight's daughter,
To be her mistress' mistress! the queen's queen! —
This candle burns not clear: 'tis I must snuff it;
Then out it goes. — What though I know her virtuous
And well deserving? yet I know her for
A spleeny Lutheran; and not wholesome to

Our cause, that she should lie i'the bosom of
Our hard-rul'd king. Again there is sprung up
An heretic, an arch one, Cranmer; one
Hath crawl'd into the favour of the king,
And is his oracle.
NORFOLK
               He's vex'd at something.
SURREY
I would 'twere something that would fret the string,
The master-cord on's heart!
SUFFOLK
               The king, the king!
Enter KING, *reading of a schedule, and* LOVELL.

KING HENRY
What piles of wealth hath he accumulated
To his own portion! and what expense by the hour
Seems to flow from him! How, i' the name of thrift,
Does he rake this together? — Now, my lords, —
Saw you the cardinal?
NORFOLK
              My lord, we have
Stood here observing him: some strange commotion
Is in his brain: he bites his lip, and starts;
Stops on a sudden, looks upon the ground,
Then lays his finger on his temple; straight
Springs out into fast gait; then stops again,
Strikes his breast hard; and anon he casts
His eye against the moon: in most strange postures
We have seen him set himself.
KING HENRY
               It may well be;
There is a mutiny in's mind. This morning
Papers of state he sent me to peruse,
As I required: and wot you what I found
There, — on my conscience, put unwittingly?
Forsooth, an inventory, thus importing, —
The several parcels of his plate, his treasure,
Rich stuffs, and ornaments of household; which
I find at such proud rate, that it out-speaks
Possession of a subject.
NORFOLK
             It's heaven's will:
Some spirit put this paper in the packet,
To bless your eye withal.
KING HENRY
             If we did think
His contemplation were above the earth,
And fix'd on spiritual objects, he should still
Dwell in his musings: but I am afraid
His thinkings are below the moon, not worth
His serious considering.

               [KING *takes his seat; whispers* LOVELL,
                    who goes to the CARDINAL.

WOLSEY
               Heaven forgive me! —
Ever God bless your highness!
KING HENRY
               Good my lord,
You are full of heavenly stuff, and bear the inventory
Of your best graces in your mind; the which
You were now running o'er: you have scarce time
To steal from spiritual leisure a brief span
To keep your earthly audit: sure, in that
I deem you an ill husband, and am glad
To have you therein my companion.
WOLSEY
                     Sir,
For holy offices I have a time; a time
To think upon the part of business which
I bear i'the state; and nature does require
Her times of preservation, which perforce
I, her frail son, amongst my brethren mortal,
Must give my tendance to.
KING HENRY
             You have said well.
WOLSEY
And ever may your highness yoke together,
As I will lend you cause, my doing well
With my well saying!
KING HENRY
             'Tis well said again;
And 'tis a kind of good deed to say well:
And yet words are no deeds. My father lov'd you:
He said he did; and with his deed did crown
His word upon you. Since I had my office,
I have kept you next my heart; have not alone
Employ'd you where high profits might come home,
But pared my present havings, to bestow
My bounties upon you.

KING HENRY Read o'er this.

WOLSEY [*aside*].
                    What should this mean?
SURREY [*aside*].
The Lord increase this business!
KING HENRY
                    Have I not made you
The prime man of the state? I pray you, tell me,
If what I now pronounce you have found true:
And, if you may confess it, say withal,
If you are bound to us or no. What say you?
WOLSEY
My sovereign, I confess your royal graces,
Shower'd on me daily, have been more than could
My studied purposes requite; which went
Beyond all man's endeavours: — my endeavours
Have ever come too short of my desires,
Yet fil'd with my abilities: mine own ends
Have been mine so, that evermore they pointed
To the good of your most sacred person and
The profit of the state. For your great graces
Heap'd upon me, poor undeserver, I
Can nothing render but allegiant thanks;
My prayers to heaven for you; my loyalty,
Which ever has and ever shall be growing,
Till death, that winter, kill it.
KING HENRY
                    Fairly answer'd;
A loyal and obedient subject is
Therein illustrated: the honour of it
Does pay the act of it; as, i' the contrary,
The foulness is the punishment. I presume
That, as my hand has open'd bounty to you,
My heart dropp'd love, my power rain'd honour, more
On you than any; so your hand and heart,
Your brain, and every function of your power,
Should, notwithstanding that your bond of duty,
As 'twere in love's particular, be more
To me, your friend, than any.
WOLSEY
                    I do profess
That for your highness' good I ever labour'd
More than mine own; that am, have, and will be, —
Though all the world should crack their duty to you,
And throw it from their soul; though perils did
Abound, as thick as thought could make 'em, and
Appear in forms more horrid, — yet my duty,
As doth a rock against the chiding flood,
Should the approach of this wild river break,
And stand unshaken yours.
KING HENRY
                    'Tis nobly spoken. —
Take notice, lords, he has a loyal breast,
For you have seen him open 't. — Read o'er this;
                    [*Giving him papers.*
And after, this: and then to breakfast with
What appetite you have.

[*Exit* KING, *frowning upon* WOLSEY:
the NOBLES *throng after him,
smiling and whispering.*
WOLSEY
                    What should this mean?
What sudden anger's this? how have I
    reap'd it?
He parted frowning from me, as if ruin
Leap'd from his eyes: so looks the
    chafed lion
Upon the daring huntsman that has
    gall'd him;
Then makes him nothing. I must read
    this paper;
I fear, the story of his anger. — 'Tis so;
This paper has undone me: — 'tis the
    account
Of all that world of wealth I have drawn
    together
For mine own ends; indeed, to gain the
    Popedom,
And fee my friends in Rome. O
    negligence,
Fit for a fool to fall by! what cross devil
Made me put this main secret in the
    packet
I sent the king? — Is there no way to
    cure this?
No new device to beat this from his
    brains?
I know 'twill stir him strongly; yet I
    know
A way, if it take right, in spite of
    fortune,
Will bring me off again. — What's this?
    — 'To the Pope!'
The letter, as I live, with all the business
I writ to's holiness. Nay, then, farewell!
I have touch'd the highest point of all my greatness;
And, from that full meridian of my glory,
I haste now to my setting: I shall fall
Like a bright exhalation in the evening,
And no man see me more.

Enter to WOLSEY *the* DUKES OF NORFOLK *and*
SUFFOLK, *the* EARL OF SURREY, *and*
the LORD CHAMBERLAIN.

NORFOLK
Hear the king's pleasure, cardinal; who commands you
To render up the great seal presently
Into our hands; and to confine yourself
To Asher-house, my Lord of Winchester's,
Till you hear further from his highness.
WOLSEY
                    Stay, —
Where's your commission, lords? words cannot carry
Authority so weighty.
SUFFOLK
                    Who dare cross 'em,
Bearing the king's will from his mouth expressly?
WOLSEY
Till I find more than will or words to do it, —
I mean your malice, — know, officious lords,
I dare and must deny it. Now I feel
Of what coarse metal ye are moulded, — envy:
How eagerly ye follow my disgraces,
As if it fed ye! and how sleek and wanton
Ye appear in every thing may bring my ruin!
Follow your envious courses, men of malice;
You have Christian warrant for 'em, and, no doubt,
In time will find their fit rewards. That seal,
You ask with such a violence, the king —
Mine and your master — with his own hand gave me;
Bade me enjoy it, with the place and honours,
During my life; and, to confirm his goodness,
Tied it by letters-patents: — now, who'll take it?
SURREY
The king, that gave it.
WOLSEY
                    It must be himself, then.
SURREY
Thou art a proud traitor, priest.
WOLSEY
                    Proud lord, thou liest:
Within these forty hours Surrey durst better
Have burnt that tongue than said so.
SURREY
                    Thy ambition,
Thou scarlet sin, robb'd this bewailing land
Of noble Buckingham, my father-in-law:
The heads of all thy brother cardinals —

With thee and all thy best parts bound together —
Weigh'd not a hair of his. Plague of your policy!
You sent me deputy for Ireland;
Far from his succour, from the king, from all
That might have mercy on the fault thou gavest him;
Whilst your great goodness, out of holy pity,
Absolv'd him with an axe.
WOLSEY
                    This, and all else
This talking lord can lay upon my credit,
I answer is most false. The duke by law
Found his deserts: how innocent I was
From any private malice in his end,
His noble jury and foul cause can witness.
If I lov'd many words, lord, I should tell you
You have as little honesty as honour;
That I in the way of loyalty and truth
Toward the king, my ever royal master,
Dare mate a sounder man than Surrey can be,
And all that love his follies.
SURREY
                    By my soul,
Your long coat, priest, protects you; thou shouldst feel
My sword i' the life-blood of thee else. — My lords,
Can ye endure to hear this arrogance?
And from this fellow? If we live thus tamely,
To be thus jaded by a piece of scarlet,
Farewell nobility; let his Grace go forward,
And dare us with his cap like larks.
WOLSEY
                    All goodness
Is poison to thy stomach.
SURREY
                    Yes, that goodness
Of gleaning all the land's wealth into one,
Into your own hands, cardinal, by extortion;
The goodness of your intercepted packets
You writ to the Pope against the king: your goodness,
Since you provoke me, shall be most notorious. —
My Lord of Norfolk, — as you are truly noble,
As you respect the common good, the state
Of our despis'd nobility, our issues,
Whom, if he live, will scarce be gentlemen, —
Produce the grand sum of his sins, the articles
Collected from his life: — I'll startle you
Worse than the scaring bell, when the brown wench
Lay kissing in your arms, lord cardinal.
WOLSEY
How much, methinks, I could despise this man,
But that I'm bound in charity against it!
NORFOLK
Those articles, my lord, are in the king's hand:
But, thus much, they are foul ones.
WOLSEY
                    So much fairer
And spotless shall mine innocence arise,
When the king knows my truth.
SURREY
                    This cannot save you:
I thank my memory, I yet remember
Some of these articles; and out they shall.
Now, if you can blush, and cry guilty, cardinal,
You'll show a little honesty.
WOLSEY
                    Speak on, sir;
I dare your worst objections: if I blush,
It is to see a nobleman want manners.
SURREY
I had rather want those than my head. — Have at you!
First, that, without the king's assent or knowledge,
You wrought to be a legate; by which power
You maim'd the jurisdiction of all bishops.
NORFOLK
Then, that in all you writ to Rome, or else
To foreign princes, *Ego et Rex meus*
Was still inscrib'd; in which you brought the king
To be your servant.
SUFFOLK
                    Then, that, without the knowledge
Either of king or council, when you went
Ambassador to the emperor, you made bold
To carry into Flanders the great seal.
SURREY
Item, you sent a large commission
To Gregory de Cassalis, to conclude,
Without the king's will or the state's allowance,
A league between his highness and Ferrara.
SUFFOLK
That, out of mere ambition, you have caus'd
Your holy hat to be stamp'd on the king's coin.

SURREY
Then, that you have sent innumerable substance —
By what means got, I leave to your own conscience —
To furnish Rome, and to prepare the ways
You have for dignities; to the mere undoing
Of all the kingdom. Many more there are;
Which, since they are of you, and odious,
I will not taint my mouth with.

LORD CHAMBERLAIN
O my lord,
Press not a falling man too far! 'tis virtue:
His faults lie open to the laws; let them,
Not you, correct him. My heart weeps to see him
So little of his great self.

SURREY
I forgive him.

SUFFOLK
Lord cardinal, the king's further pleasure is, —
Because all those things you have done of late,
By your power legatine, within this kingdom,
Fall into the compass of a *præmunire*, —
That therefore such a writ be sued against you;
To forfeit all your goods, lands, tenements,
Chattels, and whatsoever, and to be
Out of the king's protection: — this is my charge.

NORFOLK
And so we'll leave you to your meditations
How to live better. For your stubborn answer
About the giving back the great seal to us,
The king shall know it, and, no doubt, shall thank you.
So fare you well, my little good lord cardinal.

[*Exeunt all but* WOLSEY.

WOLSEY
So farewell to the little good you bear me.
Farewell, a long farewell, to all my greatness!
This is the state of man: to-day he puts forth
The tender leaves of hope; to-morrow blossoms,
And bears his blushing honours thick upon him;
The third day comes a frost, a killing frost,
And — when he thinks, good easy man, full surely
His greatness is a-ripening — nips his root,
And then he falls, as I do. I have ventured,
Like little wanton boys that swim on bladders,
This many summers in a sea of glory,
But far beyond my depth: my high-blown pride
At length broke under me; and now has left me,
Weary and old with service, to the mercy
Of a rude stream, that must for ever hide me.
Vain pomp and glory of this world, I hate ye:
I feel my heart new open'd. O, how wretched
Is that poor man that hangs on princes' favours!
There is, betwixt that smile we would aspire to,
That sweet aspect of princes, and their ruin,
More pangs and fears than wars or women have;
And when he falls, he falls like Lucifer,
Never to hope again.

Enter CROMWELL, *standing amazed.*
Why, how now, Cromwell!

CROMWELL
I have no power to speak, sir.

WOLSEY
What, amaz'd
At my misfortunes? can thy spirit wonder
A great man should decline? Nay, an you weep,
I am fall'n indeed.

CROMWELL
How does your Grace?

WOLSEY
Why, well;
Never so truly happy, my good Cromwell.
I know myself now; and I feel within me
A peace above all earthly dignities,
A still and quiet conscience. The king has cured me,
I humbly thank his Grace; and from these shoulders,
These ruin'd pillars, out of pity, taken
A load would sink a navy, — too much honour:
O, 'tis a burden, Cromwell, 'tis a burden
Too heavy for a man that hopes for heaven!

CROMWELL
I am glad your Grace has made that right use of it.

WOLSEY
I hope I have: I am able now, methinks —
Out of a fortitude of soul I feel —
To endure more miseries and greater far
Than my weak-hearted enemies dare offer. —
What news abroad?

CROMWELL
The heaviest and the worst
Is your displeasure with the king.

WOLSEY
God bless him!

CROMWELL
The next is, that Sir Thomas More is chosen
Lord Chancellor in your place.

WOLSEY
That's somewhat sudden:
But he's a learned man. May he continue
Long in his highness' favour, and do justice
For truth's sake and his conscience; that his
bones,
When he has run his course and sleeps in
blessings,
May have a tomb of orphans' tears wept on 'em!
—
What more?

CROMWELL
That Cranmer is return'd with welcome,
Installed Lord Archbishop of Canterbury.

WOLSEY
That's news indeed.

CROMWELL
Last, that the Lady Anne,
Whom the king hath in secrecy long married,
This day was view'd in open as his queen,
Going to chapel; and the voice is now
Only about her coronation.

WOLSEY
There was the weight that pull'd me down. O
Cromwell,
The king has gone beyond me: all my glories
In that one woman I have lost for ever:
No sun shall ever usher forth mine honours,
Or gild again the noble troops that waited
Upon my smiles. Go, get thee from me, Cromwell;
I am a poor fall'n man, unworthy now
To be thy lord and master: seek the king;
That sun, I pray, may never set! I have told him
What and how true thou art: he will advance thee;
Some little memory of me will stir him —
I know his noble nature — not to let
Thy hopeful service perish too: good Cromwell,
Neglect him not; make use now, and provide
For thine own future safety.

CROMWELL
O my lord,
Must I, then, leave you? must I needs forgo
So good, so noble, and so true a master?
Bear witness, all that have not hearts of iron,
With what a sorrow Cromwell leaves his lord.
The king shall have my service; but my prayers
For ever and for ever shall be yours.

WOLSEY
Cromwell, I did not think to shed a tear
In all my miseries; but thou hast forced me,
Out of thy honest truth, to play the woman.
Let's dry our eyes: and thus far hear me, Cromwell;
And — when I am forgotten, as I shall be,
And sleep in dull cold marble, where no mention
Of me more must be heard of — say, I taught thee,
Say, Wolsey — that once trod the ways of glory,
And sounded all the depths and shoals of honour —
Found thee a way, out of his wrack, to rise in;
A sure and safe one, though thy master miss'd it.
Mark but my fall, and that that ruin'd me.
Cromwell, I charge thee, fling away ambition:
By that sin fell the angels; how can man, then,
The image of his Maker, hope to win by it?
Love thyself last; cherish those hearts that hate thee;
Corruption wins not more than honesty.
Still in thy right hand carry gentle peace,
To silence envious tongues. Be just, and fear not:
Let all the ends thou aim'st at be thy country's,
Thy God's, and truth's: then if thou fall'st, O Cromwell,
Thou fall'st a blessed martyr! Serve the king;
And, — prithee, lead me in:
There take an inventory of all I have,
To the last penny; 'tis the king's: my robe,
And my integrity to heaven, is all
I dare now call mine own. O Cromwell, Cromwell!
Had I but serv'd my God with half the zeal
I serv'd my king, he would not in mine age
Have left me naked to mine enemies.

CROMWELL
Good sir, have patience.

WOLSEY
So I have. Farewell
The hopes of court! my hopes in heaven do dwell.

[*Exeunt.*

WOLSEY Farewell the hopes of court!
my hopes in heaven do dwell.

ACT IV

SCENE I

A street in Westminster.

Enter two GENTLEMEN, *meeting one another.*

FIRST GENTLEMAN
Y'are well met once again.

SECOND GENTLEMAN
So are you.

FIRST GENTLEMAN
You come to take your stand here, and behold
The Lady Anne pass from her coronation?

SECOND GENTLEMAN
'Tis all my business. At our last encounter
The Duke of Buckingham came from his trial.

FIRST GENTLEMAN
'Tis very true: but that time offer'd sorrow;
This, general joy.

SECOND GENTLEMAN
'Tis well: the citizens,
I am sure, have shown at full their royal minds —
As, let 'em have their rights, they are ever forward —
In celebration of this day with shows,
Pageants, and sights of honour.

FIRST GENTLEMAN
Never greater,
Nor, I'll assure you, better taken, sir.

SECOND GENTLEMAN
May I be bold to ask at what that contains,
That paper in your hand?

FIRST GENTLEMAN
Yes; 'tis the list
Of those that claim their offices this day
By custom of the coronation.
The Duke of Suffolk is the first, and claims
To be high-steward; next, the Duke of Norfolk,
He to be earl marshal: you may read the rest.

SECOND GENTLEMAN
I thank you, sir: had I not known those customs,
I should have been beholding to your paper.
But, I beseech you, what's become of Katharine,
The princess dowager? how goes her business?

FIRST GENTLEMAN
That I can tell you too. The Archbishop
Of Canterbury, accompanied with other
Learned and reverend fathers of his order,
Held a late court at Dunstable, six miles off
From Ampthill, where the princess lay; to which
She was often cited by them, but appear'd not:
And, to be short, for not appearance and
The king's late scruple, by the main assent
Of all these learned men she was divorc'd,
And the late marriage made of none effect:
Since which she was remov'd to Kimbolton,
Where she remains now sick.

SECOND GENTLEMAN The trumpets sound: stand close, the queen is coming.

SECOND GENTLEMAN

             Alas, good lady! — [*Trumpets.*
The trumpets sound: stand close, the queen is coming.

THE ORDER OF THE CORONATION

A lively flourish of trumpets. Then enter,

1. *Two* JUDGES.
2. LORD CHANCELLOR, *with the purse and mace before him.*
3. CHORISTERS, *singing.*   [*Music.*
4. MAYOR OF LONDON, *bearing the mace. Then* GARTER, *in his coat of arms, and on his head he wore a gilt copper crown.*
5. MARQUESS DORSET, *bearing a sceptre of gold, on his head a demi-coronal of gold. With him, the* EARL OF SURREY, *bearing the rod of silver with the dove, crown'd with an earl's coronet. Collars of SS.*
6. DUKE OF SUFFOLK, *in his robe of estate, his coronet on his head, bearing a long white wand, as high-steward. With him, the* DUKE OF NORFOLK, *with the rod of marshalship, a coronet on his head. Collars of SS.*
7. *A canopy borne by four of the* CINQUE-PORTS; *under it, the* QUEEN *in her robe, in her hair richly adorn'd with pearl, crown'd. On each side of her, the* BISHOPS OF LONDON *and* WINCHESTER.
8. *The old* DUCHESS OF NORFOLK, *in a coronal of gold, wrought with flowers, bearing the* QUEEN'S *train.*
9. *Certain* LADIES *or* COUNTESSES, *with plain circlets of gold without flowers.*

    [*Exeunt, first passing over the stage in order and state; and then a great flourish of trumpets.*

A royal train, believe me. — These I know: —
Who's that that bears the sceptre?

FIRST GENTLEMAN

             Marquess Dorset:
And that the Earl of Surrey, with the rod.

SECOND GENTLEMAN

A bold brave gentleman. — That should be
The Duke of Suffolk?

FIRST GENTLEMAN

             'Tis the same, — high-steward.

SECOND GENTLEMAN

And that my Lord of Norfolk?

FIRST GENTLEMAN

             Yes.

SECOND GENTLEMAN   [*looking on the* QUEEN].
             Heaven bless thee!
Thou hast the sweetest face I ever look'd on. —
Sir, as I have a soul, she is an angel;
Our king has all the Indies in his arms,
And more and richer, when he strains that lady:
I cannot blame his conscience.

FIRST GENTLEMAN

             They that bear
The cloth of honour over her are four barons
Of the Cinque-ports.

SECOND GENTLEMAN

Those men are happy; and so are all are near her.
I take it, she that carries up the train

Is that old noble lady, Duchess of Norfolk?

FIRST GENTLEMAN

It is; and all the rest are countesses.

SECOND GENTLEMAN

Their coronets say so. These are stars indeed;
And sometimes falling ones.

FIRST GENTLEMAN

             No more of that.
       [*Enter a* THIRD GENTLEMAN.
God save you, sir! where have you been broiling?

THIRD GENTLEMAN

Among the crowd i'the abbey; where a finger
Could not be wedg'd in more: I am stifled
With the mere rankness of their joy.

SECOND GENTLEMAN

             You saw
The ceremony?

THIRD GENTLEMAN

             That I did.

FIRST GENTLEMAN

             How was it?

THIRD GENTLEMAN

Well worth the seeing.

SECOND GENTLEMAN

             Good sir, speak it to us.

THIRD GENTLEMAN

As well as I am able. The rich stream
Of lords and ladies, having brought the queen
To a prepar'd place in the choir, fell off
A distance from her; while her Grace sat down
To rest awhile, some half an hour or so,
In a rich chair of state, opposing freely
The beauty of her person to the people.
Believe me, sir, she is the goodliest woman
That ever lay by man: which when the people
Had the full view of, such a noise arose
As the shrouds make at sea in a stiff tempest,
As loud, and to as many tunes: hats, cloaks, —
Doublets, I think, — flew up; and had their faces
Been loose, this day they had been lost. Such joy
I never saw before. Great-bellied women,
That had not half a week to go, like rams
In the old time of war, would shake the press,
And make 'em reel before 'em. No man living
Could say, 'This is my wife,' there; all were woven
So strangely in one piece.

SECOND GENTLEMAN

             But what follow'd?

THIRD GENTLEMAN

At length her Grace rose, and with modest paces
Came to the altar; where she kneel'd, and, saint-like,
Cast her fair eyes to heaven, and pray'd devoutly:
Then rose again, and bow'd her to the people:
When by the Archbishop of Canterbury
She had all the royal makings of a queen;
As holy oil, Edward Confessor's crown,
The rod, and bird of peace, and all such emblems
Laid nobly on her: which perform'd, the choir,
With all the choicest music of the kingdom,
Together sung *Te Deum*. So she parted,
And with the same full state pac'd back again
To York-place, where the feast is held.

FIRST GENTLEMAN

             Sir,
You must no more call it York-place, that's past;
For, since the cardinal fell, that title's lost:
'Tis now the king's, and call'd Whitehall.

THIRD GENTLEMAN

             I know it;
But 'tis so lately alter'd, that the old name
Is fresh about me.

SECOND GENTLEMAN

             What two reverend bishops
Were those that went on each side of the queen?

THIRD GENTLEMAN

Stokesly and Gardiner; the one of Winchester,
Newly preferr'd from the king's secretary;
The other, London.

SECOND GENTLEMAN

             He of Winchester
Is held no great good lover of the archbishop's,
The virtuous Cranmer.

THIRD GENTLEMAN

             All the land knows that:
However, yet there is no great breach; when it comes,
Cranmer will find a friend will not shrink from him.

SECOND GENTLEMAN

Who may that be, I pray you?

THIRD GENTLEMAN

             Thomas Cromwell;
A man in much esteem with the king, and truly
A worthy friend. The king
Has made him master o' the jewel house,
And one, already, of the privy-council.

SECOND GENTLEMAN

He will deserve more.

THIRD GENTLEMAN

             Yes, without all doubt. —
Come, gentlemen, ye shall go my way, which
Is to the court, and there ye shall be my guests:
Something I can command. As I walk thither,
I'll tell ye more.

BOTH

             You may command us, sir.   [*Exeunt.*

SCENE II

Kimbolton.

Enter KATHARINE, *dowager, sick; led between* GRIFFITH, *her gentleman-usher, and* PATIENCE, *her woman.*

GRIFFITH

How does your Grace?

KATHARINE

             O Griffith, sick to death!
My legs, like loaden branches, bow to the earth,
Willing to leave their burden. Reach a chair: —
So, — now, methinks, I feel a little ease.
Didst thou not tell me, Griffith, as thou led'st me,
That the great child of honour, Cardinal Wolsey,
Was dead?

GRIFFITH

             Yes, madam; but I think your Grace,
Out of the pain you suffer'd, gave no ear to't.

KATHARINE

Prithee, good Griffith, tell me how he died:
If well, he stepp'd before me, happily,
For my example.

GRIFFITH

             Well, the voice goes, madam:
For after the stout Earl Northumberland
Arrested him at York, and brought him forward —
As a man sorely tainted — to his answer,
He fell sick suddenly, and grew so ill
He could not sit his mule.

KATHARINE

             Alas, poor man!

GRIFFITH

At last, with easy roads, he came to Leicester,
Lodg'd in the abbey; where the reverend abbot,
With all his covent, honourably receiv'd him;
To whom he gave these words, — 'O father abbot,
An old man, broken with the storms of state,
Is come to lay his weary bones among ye;
Give him a little earth for charity!'
So went to bed; where eagerly his sickness
Pursued him still: and, three nights after this,
About the hour of eight, — which he himself
Foretold should be his last, — full of repentance,
Continual meditations, tears, and sorrows,
He gave his honours to the world again,
His blessed part to heaven, and slept in peace.

KATHARINE O Griffith, ... reach a chair.

KATHARINE
So may he rest; his faults lie gently on him!
Yet thus far, Griffith, give me leave to speak him,
And yet with charity. He was a man
Of an unbounded stomach, ever ranking
Himself with princes; one that by suggestion
Tith'd all the kingdom: simony was fair-play;
His own opinion was his law: i' the presence
He would say untruths; and be ever double
Both in his words and meaning: he was never,
But where he meant to ruin, pitiful:
His promises were, as he then was, mighty;
But his performance, as he is now, nothing:
Of his body he was ill, and gave
The clergy ill example.

GRIFFITH
                          Noble madam,
Men's evil manners live in brass; their virtues
We write in water. May it please your highness
To hear me speak his good now?

KATHARINE
                          Yes, good Griffith;
I were malicious else.

GRIFFITH
                          This cardinal,
Though from an humble stock, undoubtedly
Was fashion'd to much honour from his cradle.
He was a scholar, and a ripe and good one;
Exceeding wise, fair-spoken, and persuading:
Lofty and sour to them that lov'd him not;
But to those men that sought him sweet as summer.
And though he were unsatisfied in getting, —
Which was a sin, — yet in bestowing, madam,
He was most princely: ever witness for him
Those twins of learning that he rais'd in you,
Ipswich and Oxford! one of which fell with him,
Unwilling to outlive the good that did it;
The other, though unfinish'd, yet so famous,
So excellent in art, and still so rising,
That Christendom shall ever speak his virtue.
His overthrow heap'd happiness upon him;
For then, and not till then, he felt himself,
And found the blessedness of being little:
And, to add greater honours to his age
Than man could give him, he died fearing God.

KATHARINE
After my death I wish no other herald,
No other speaker of my living actions,
To keep mine honour from corruption,
But such an honest chronicler as Griffith.
Whom I most hated living, thou hast made me,
With thy religious truth and modesty,
Now in his ashes honour: peace be with him! —
Patience, be near me still; and set me lower:
I have not long to trouble thee. — Good Griffith,
Cause the musicians play me that sad note
I nam'd my knell, whilst I sit meditating
On that celestial harmony I go to.
                          [Sad and solemn music.

GRIFFITH
She is asleep: good wench, let's sit down quiet,
For fear we wake her: — softly, gentle Patience.

*The vision. Enter, solemnly tripping
one after another, six personages,
clad in white robes, wearing on their
heads garlands of bays, and golden
vizards on their faces; branches of
bays or palm in their hands. They
first congee unto her, then dance;
and, at certain changes, the first two
hold a spare garland over her head;
at which the other four make
reverent curtsies; then the two that
held the garland deliver the same to
the other next two, who observe the
same order in their changes, and
holding the garland over her head:
which done, they deliver the same
garland to the last two, who likewise
observe the same order; at which (as
it were by inspiration) she makes in
her sleep signs of rejoicing, and
holdeth up her hands to heaven: and
so in their dancing they vanish,
carrying the garland with them.
The music continues.*

KATHARINE
Spirits of peace, where are ye? are ye
   all gone,
And leave me here in wretchedness
   behind ye?

GRIFFITH
Madam, we are here.

KATHARINE
                          It is not you I call for:
Saw ye none enter since I slept?

GRIFFITH
                          None, madam.

KATHARINE
No? Saw you not, even now, a blessed troop
Invite me to a banquet; whose bright faces
Cast thousand beams upon me, like the sun?
They promis'd me eternal happiness;
And brought me garlands, Griffith, which I feel
I am not worthy yet to wear: I shall,
Assuredly.

GRIFFITH
I am most joyful, madam, such good dreams
Possess your fancy.

KATHARINE
                          Bid the music leave;
They are harsh and heavy to me.   [*Music ceases.*

PATIENCE [*aside*].
                          Do you note
How much her Grace is alter'd on the sudden?
How long her face is drawn? how pale she looks,
And of an earthy colour? Mark her eyes!

GRIFFITH [*aside*].
She is going, wench: pray, pray.

PATIENCE [*aside*].
                          Heaven comfort her!
          Enter a MESSENGER.

MESSENGER
An't like your Grace, —

KATHARINE
                          You are a saucy fellow:
Deserve we no more reverence?

GRIFFITH
                          You are to blame,
Knowing she will not lose her wonted greatness,
To use so rude behaviour: go to, kneel.

MESSENGER
I humbly do entreat your highness' pardon;
My haste made me unmannerly. There's staying
A gentleman, sent from the king, to see you.

KATHARINE
Admit him entrance, Griffith: but this fellow
Let me ne'er see again.
          [*Exeunt* GRIFFITH *and* MESSENGER.
          Enter GRIFFITH, *with* CAPUCIUS.
                          If my sight fail not,
You should be lord ambassador from the emperor,
My royal nephew, and your name Capucius.

CAPUCIUS
Madam, the same, — your servant.

KATHARINE
                          O my lord,
The times and titles now are alter'd strangely
With me since first you knew me. But, I pray you,
What is your pleasure with me?

CAPUCIUS
                          Noble lady,
First, mine own service to your Grace; the next,
The king's request that I would visit you;
Who grieves much for your weakness, and by me
Sends you his princely commendations,
And heartily entreats you take good comfort.

KATHARINE
O my good lord, that comfort comes too late;
'Tis like a pardon after execution:
That gentle physic, given in time, had cured me;
But now I am past all comforts here, but prayers.
How does his highness?

CAPUCIUS
                          Madam, in good health.

KATHARINE
So may he ever do! and ever flourish,
When I shall dwell with worms, and my poor name
Banish'd the kingdom! — Patience, is that letter,
I caus'd you write, yet sent away?

PATIENCE
                          No, madam.
                     [*Giving it to* KATHARINE.

KATHARINE
Sir, I most humbly pray you to deliver
This to my lord the king; —

CAPUCIUS
                          Most willing, madam.

KATHARINE
In which I have commended to his goodness
The model of our chaste loves, his young daughter, —
The dews of heaven fall thick in blessings on her! —
Beseeching him to give her virtuous breeding; —
She is young, and of a noble modest nature;
I hope she will deserve well; — and a little
To love her for her mother's sake, that lov'd him,
Heaven knows how dearly. My next poor petition
Is, that his noble Grace would have some pity
Upon my wretched women, that so long
Have follow'd both my fortunes faithfully:
Of which there is not one, I dare avow, —
And now I should not lie, — but will deserve,
For virtue and true beauty of the soul,
For honesty and decent carriage,
A right good husband, let him be a noble;
And, sure, those men are happy that shall have 'em.
The last is, for my men; — they are the poorest,
But poverty could never draw 'em from me, —
That they may have their wages duly paid 'em,
And something over to remember me by:
If heaven had pleas'd to have given me longer life
And able means, we had not parted thus.
These are the whole contents: — and, good my lord,
By that you love the dearest in this world,
As you wish Christian peace to souls departed,
Stand these poor people's friend, and urge the king
To do me this last right.

CAPUCIUS
                          By heaven, I will,
Or let me lose the fashion of a man!

KATHARINE
I thank you, honest lord. Remember me
In all humility unto his highness:
Say his long trouble now is passing
Out of this world; tell him, in death I bless'd him,
For so I will. — Mine eyes grow dim. — Farewell,
My lord. — Griffith, farewell. — Nay, Patience,
You must not leave me yet: I must to bed;
Call in more women. — When I'm dead, good wench,
Let me be us'd with honour: strew me over
With maiden flowers, that all the world may know
I was a chaste wife to my grave: embalm me,
Then lay me forth; although unqueen'd, yet like
A queen, and daughter to a king, inter me.
I can no more.   [*Exeunt, leading* KATHARINE.

ACT V

SCENE I

London. A gallery in the palace.

Enter GARDINER, *bishop of Winchester, a* PAGE *with
a torch before him, met by* SIR THOMAS LOVELL.

GARDINER
It's one o'clock, boy, is't not?

BOY
                          It hath struck.

GARDINER
These should be hours for necessities,

GARDINER He's a rank weed, Sir Thomas, and we must root him out.

Not for delights; times to repair our nature
With comforting repose, and not for us
To waste these times. — Good hour of night, Sir
   Thomas!
Whither so late?

LOVELL
                    Came you from the king, my lord?

GARDINER
I did, Sir Thomas; and left him at primero
With the Duke of Suffolk.

LOVELL
                    I must to him too,
Before he go to bed. I'll take my leave.

GARDINER
Not yet, Sir Thomas Lovell. What's the matter?
It seems you are in haste: an if there be
No great offence belongs to't, give your friend
Some touch of your late business: affairs that walk —
As they say spirits do — at midnight have
In them a wilder nature than the business
That seeks dispatch by day.

LOVELL
                    My lord, I love you;
And durst commend a secret to your ear
Much weightier than this work. The queen's in labour,
They say, in great extremity; and fear'd
She'll with the labour end.

GARDINER
                    The fruit she goes with
I pray for heartily, that it may find
Good time, and live: but for the stock, Sir Thomas,
I wish it grubb'd up now.

LOVELL
                    Methinks I could
Cry the amen; and yet my conscience says
She's a good creature, and, sweet lady, does
Deserve our better wishes.

GARDINER
                    But, sir, sir, —
Hear me, Sir Thomas: y'are a gentleman
Of mine own way; I know you wise, religious;
And, let me tell you, it will ne'er be well, —
'Twill not, Sir Thomas Lovell, take't of me, —
Till Cranmer, Cromwell, her two hands, and she,
Sleep in their graves.

LOVELL
                    Now, sir, you speak of two
The most remark'd i'the kingdom. As for Cromwell, —
Beside that of the jewel-house, is made master
O'the rolls, and the king's secretary; further, sir,
Stands in the gap and trade of moe preferments,
With which the time will load him. The archbishop
Is the king's hand and tongue; and who dare speak
One syllable against him?

GARDINER
                    Yes, yes, Sir Thomas,
There are that dare; and I myself have ventured
To speak my mind of him: and, indeed, this day —
Sir, I may tell it you, I think — I have
Incens'd the lords o'the council that he is —

For so I know he is, they know he is —
A most arch heretic, a pestilence
That does infect the land: with which they moved,
Have broken with the king; who hath so far
Given ear to our complaint, — of his great grace
And princely care, foreseeing those fell mischiefs
Our reasons laid before him, — hath commanded
To-morrow morning to the council-board
He be convented. He's a rank weed, Sir Thomas,
And we must root him out. From your affairs
I hinder you too long: good night, Sir Thomas.

LOVELL
Many good nights, my lord: I rest your servant.
                    [Exeunt GARDINER and PAGE.
            Enter KING and SUFFOLK.

KING HENRY
Charles, I will play no more to-night;
My mind's not on't; you are too hard for me.

SUFFOLK
Sir, I did never win of you before.

KING HENRY
But little, Charles;
Nor shall not, when my fancy's on my play. —
Now, Lovell, from the queen what is the news?

LOVELL
I could not personally deliver to her
What you commanded me, but by her woman
I sent your message; who return'd her thanks
In the great'st humbleness, and desired your highness
Most heartily to pray for her.

KING HENRY
                    What say'st thou, ha?
To pray for her? what, is she crying out?

LOVELL
So said her woman; and that her suff'rance made
Almost each pang a death.

KING HENRY
                    Alas, good lady!

SUFFOLK
God safely quit her of her burden, and
With gentle travail, to the gladding of
Your highness with an heir!

KING HENRY
                    'Tis midnight, Charles;
Prithee, to bed; and in thy prayers remember
The estate of my poor queen. Leave me alone;
For I must think of that which company
Would not be friendly to.

SUFFOLK
                    I wish your highness
A quiet night; and my good mistress will
Remember in my prayers.

KING HENRY
                    Charles, good night. [Exit SUFFOLK.
            Enter SIR ANTHONY DENNY.
Well, sir, what follows?

DENNY
Sir, I have brought my lord the archbishop
As you commanded me.

KING HENRY
                    Ha! Canterbury?

DENNY
Ay, my good lord.

KING HENRY
'Tis true: where is he, Denny?

DENNY
He attends your highness' pleasure.

KING HENRY
                    Bring him to us.   [Exit DENNY.

LOVELL [aside].
This is about that which the bishop spake:
I am happily come hither.
            Enter CRANMER and DENNY.

KING HENRY
Avoid the gallery. [LOVELL seems to stay.] Ha! I have
   said. Be gone.
What!   [Exeunt LOVELL and DENNY.

CRANMER [aside].
      I am fearful: — wherefore frowns he thus?
'Tis his aspect of terror. All's not well.

KING HENRY
How now, my lord! you do desire to know
Wherefore I sent for you.

CRANMER [kneeling].
                    It is my duty
T'attend your highness' pleasure.

KING HENRY
                    Pray you, arise,
My good and gracious Lord of Canterbury.
                    [CRANMER rises.
Come, you and I must walk a turn together;
I have news to tell you: come, come, give me your hand.
Ah, my good lord, I grieve at what I speak,
And am right sorry to repeat what follows:
I have, and most unwillingly, of late
Heard many grievous, I do say, my lord,
Grievous complaints of you; which, being consider'd,
Have mov'd us and our council, that you shall
This morning come before us; where, I know,
You cannot with such freedom purge yourself,
But that, till further trial in those charges
Which will require your answer, you must take
Your patience to you, and be well contented
To make your house our Tower: you a brother of us,
It fits we thus proceed, or else no witness
Would come against you.

CRANMER [kneeling].
                    I humbly thank your highness;
And am right glad to catch this good occasion
Most thoroughly to be winnow'd, where my chaff
And corn shall fly asunder: for, I know,
There's none stands under more calumnious tongues
Than I myself, poor man.

KING HENRY
                    Stand up, good Canterbury:
Thy truth and thy integrity is rooted
In us, thy friend: give me thy hand, stand up:
Prithee, let's walk. Now, by my holy-dame,
                    [CRANMER rises.
What manner of man are you! My lord, I look'd
You would have given me your petition, that
I should have ta'en some pains to bring together
Yourself and your accusers: and to have heard you,
Without indurance, further.

CRANMER
                    Most dread liege,
The good I stand on is my truth and honesty:
If they shall fail, I, with mine enemies,
Will triumph o'er my person; which I weigh not,
Being of those virtues vacant. I fear nothing
What can be said against me.

KING HENRY
                    Know you not
How your state stands i'the world, with the whole
   world?
Your enemies are many, and not small; their practices
Must bear the same proportion; and not ever
The justice and the truth o'the question carries
The due o'the verdict with it: at what ease
Might corrupt minds procure knaves as corrupt
To swear against you! such things have been done.
You are potently oppos'd; and with a malice
Of as great size. Ween you of better luck,
I mean, in perjur'd witness, than your Master,
Whose minister you are, whiles here He lived
Upon this naughty earth? Go to, go to;
You take a precipice for no leap of danger,
And woo your own destruction.

KING HENRY Now, by thy looks I guess thy message. Is the queen deliver'd?

CRANMER
God and your majesty
Protect mine innocence, or I fall into
The trap is laid for me!
KING HENRY
Be of good cheer;
They shall no more prevail than we give way to.
Keep comfort to you; and this morning see
You do appear before them. If they shall chance,
In charging you with matters, to commit you,
The best persuasions to the contrary
Fail not to use, and with what vehemency
The occasion shall instruct you: if entreaties
Will render you no remedy, this ring
Deliver them, and your appeal to us
There make before them. — Look, the good man weeps!
He's honest, on mine honour. God's blest mother!
I swear he is true-hearted; and a soul
None better in my kingdom. — Get you gone,
And do as I have bid you. [*Exit* CRANMER.] He has strangled
His language in his tears.
Enter OLD LADY.

GENTLEMAN [*within*].
Come back: what mean you?
OLD LADY
I'll not come back; the tidings that I bring
Will make my boldness manners. — Now, good angels
Fly o'er thy royal head, and shade thy person
Under their blessed wings!
KING HENRY
Now, by thy looks
I guess thy message. Is the queen deliver'd?
Say ay; and of a boy.
OLD LADY
Ay, ay, my liege;
And of a lovely boy: the God of heaven
Both now and ever bless her! — 'tis a girl, —
Promises boys hereafter. Sir, your queen
Desires your visitation, and to be
Acquainted with this stranger: 'tis as like you
As cherry is to cherry.
KING HENRY
Lovell!
Enter LOVELL.

LOVELL
Sir?
KING HENRY
Give her an hundred marks. I'll to the queen. [*Exit.*
OLD LADY
An hundred marks! By this light, I'll ha' more.
An ordinary groom is for such payment.
I will have more, or scold it out of him.
Said I for this, the girl was like to him?
I will have more, or else unsay't; and now,
While it is hot, I'll put it to the issue. [*Exeunt.*

SCENE II

Before the council-chamber.

Enter CRANMER; PURSUIVANTS,
PAGES, *and* FOOTBOYS.

CRANMER
I hope I am not too late; and yet the gentleman,
That was sent to me from the council, pray'd me
To make great haste. — All fast? what means this? —
Ho!
Who waits there? — Sure, you know me?
Enter KEEPER.

KEEPER
Yes, my lord;
But yet I cannot help you.
CRANMER
Why?

KEEPER
Your Grace must wait till you be call'd for.
Enter DOCTOR BUTTS.

CRANMER
So.

BUTTS [*aside*].
This is a piece of malice. I am glad
I came this way so happily: the king
Shall understand it presently. [*Exit.*
CRANMER [*aside*].
'Tis Butts,
The king's physician: as he pass'd along,
How earnestly he cast his eyes upon me!
Pray heaven, he sound not my disgrace! For certain,
This is of purpose laid by some that hate me —
God turn their hearts! I never sought their malice —
To quench mine honour: they would shame to make me
Wait else at door, a fellow-counsellor,
Among boys, grooms, and lackeys. But their pleasures
Must be fulfill'd, and I attend with patience.
Enter the KING *and* BUTTS *at a window above.*

BUTTS
I'll show your Grace the strangest sight —
KING HENRY
What's that, Butts?
BUTTS
I think your highness saw this many a day.
KING HENRY
Body o' me, where is it?
BUTTS
There, my lord:
The high promotion of his Grace of Canterbury;
Who holds his state at door, 'mongst pursuivants,
Pages, and footboys.
KING HENRY
Ha! 'tis he, indeed:
Is this the honour they do one another?
'Tis well there's one above 'em yet. I had thought
They had parted so much honesty among 'em —
At least, good manners — as not thus to suffer
A man of his place, and so near our favour,
To dance attendance on their lordships' pleasures,
And at the door too, like a post with packets.
By holy Mary, Butts, there's knavery:
Let 'em alone, and draw the curtain close;
We shall hear more anon. [*Curtain drawn.*
*A council-table brought in with chairs and stools and placed
under the state. Enter* LORD CHANCELLOR, *places
himself at the upper end of the table on the left hand; a seat
being left void above him, as for* CANTERBURY'S *seat;*

KEEPER Your Grace must wait till you be call'd for.

DUKE OF SUFFOLK, DUKE OF NORFOLK, SURREY, LORD CHAMBERLAIN, GARDINER, seat themselves in order on each side. CROMWELL at lower end, as secretary.

LORD CHANCELLOR
Speak to the business, master secretary:
Why are we met in council?

CROMWELL
                                            Please your honours,
The chief cause concerns his Grace of Canterbury.

GARDINER
Has he had knowledge of it?

CROMWELL
                                            Yes.

NORFOLK
                                            Who waits there?

KEEPER
Without, my noble lords?

GARDINER
                                            Yes.

KEEPER
                                            My lord archbishop;
And has done half an hour, to know your pleasures.

LORD CHANCELLOR
Let him come in.

KEEPER
                        Your Grace may enter now.
                        [*CRANMER approaches the council-table.*

LORD CHANCELLOR
My good lord archbishop, I'm very sorry
To sit here at this present, and behold
That chair stand empty: but we all are men,
In our own natures frail and culpable;
Of our flesh; few are angels: out of which frailty
And want of wisdom, you, that best should teach us,
Have misdemean'd yourself, and not a little,
Toward the king first, then his laws, in filling
The whole realm, by your teaching and your chaplains, —
For so we are inform'd, — with new opinions,
Divers and dangerous; which are heresies,
And, not reform'd, may prove pernicious.

GARDINER
Which reformation must be sudden too,
My noble lords; for those that tame wild horses
Pace 'em not in their hands to make 'em gentle,
But stop their mouths with stubborn bits, and spur
   'em,
Till they obey the manage. If we suffer —
Out of our easiness, and childish pity
To one man's honour — this contagious sickness,
Farewell all physic: and what follows then?
Commotions, uproars, with a general taint
Of the whole state: as, of late days, our neighbours,
The upper Germany, can dearly witness,
Yet freshly pitied in our memories.

CRANMER
My good lords, hitherto, in all the progress
Both of my life and office, I have labour'd,
And with no little study, that my teaching
And the strong course of my authority
Might go one way, and safely; and the end
Was ever, to do well: nor is there living —
I speak it with a single heart, my lords —
A man that more detests, more stirs against,
Both in his private conscience and his place,
Defacers of a public peace, than I do.
Pray heaven, the king may never find a heart
With less allegiance in it! Men that make
Envy and crooked malice nourishment
Dare bite the best. I do beseech your lordships
That, in this case of justice, my accusers,
Be what they will, may stand forth face to face,
And freely urge against me.

SUFFOLK
                                      Nay, my lord,
That cannot be: you are a counsellor,
And, by that virtue, no man dare accuse you.

GARDINER
My lord, because we have business of more moment,
We will be short with you. 'Tis his highness' pleasure,
And our consent, for better trial of you,
From hence you be committed to the Tower;
Where, being but a private man again,
You shall know many dare accuse you boldly,
More than, I fear, you are provided for.

CRANMER
Ah, my good Lord of Winchester, I thank you;
You are always my good friend; if your will pass,
I shall both find your lordship judge and juror,
You are so merciful: I see your end, —

'Tis my undoing: love and meekness, lord,
Become a churchman better than ambition:
Win straying souls with modesty again,
Cast none away. That I shall clear myself,
Lay all the weight ye can upon my patience,
I make as little doubt, as you do conscience
In doing daily wrongs. I could say more,
But reverence to your calling makes me modest.

GARDINER
My lord, my lord, you are a sectary,
That's the plain truth: your painted gloss discovers,
To men that understand you, words and weakness.

CROMWELL
My Lord of Winchester, you are a little,
By your good favour, too sharp; men so noble,
However faulty, yet should find respect
For what they have been: 'tis a cruelty
To load a falling man.

GARDINER
                              Good master secretary,
I cry your honour mercy; you may, worst
Of all this table, say so.

CROMWELL
                              Why, my lord?

GARDINER
Do not I know you for a favourer
Of this new sect? ye are not sound.

CROMWELL
                                            Not sound?

GARDINER
Not sound, I say.

CROMWELL
                        Would you were half so honest!
Men's prayers then would seek you, not their fears.

GARDINER
I shall remember this bold language.

CROMWELL
                                            Do.
Remember your bold life too.

LORD CHANCELLOR
                                      This is too much;
Forbear, for shame, my lords.

GARDINER
                                      I have done.

CROMWELL
                                            And I.

LORD CHANCELLOR
Then thus for you, my lord: — it stands agreed,
I take it, by all voices, that forthwith
You be convey'd to the Tower a prisoner,
There to remain till the king's further pleasure
Be known unto us: — are you all agreed, lords?

ALL
We are.

CRANMER
            Is there no other way of mercy,
But I must needs to the Tower, my lords?

GARDINER
                                            What other
Would you expect? you are strangely troublesome. —
Let some o' the guard be ready there.

Enter GUARD.

CRANMER
                                            For me?
Must I go like a traitor thither?

GARDINER
                                      Receive him,
And see him safe i' the Tower.

CRANMER
                                      Stay, good my lords,
I have a little yet to say. Look there, my lords;
By virtue of that ring I take my cause
Out of the gripes of cruel men, and give it
To a most noble judge, the king my master.

LORD CHANCELLOR
This is the king's ring.

SURREY
                              'Tis no counterfeit.

SUFFOLK
'Tis the right ring, by heaven: I told ye all,
When we first put this dangerous stone a-rolling,
'Twould fall upon ourselves.

NORFOLK
                                      Do you think, my lords,
The king will suffer but the little finger
Of this man to be vex'd?

LORD CHANCELLOR
                                      'Tis now too certain:

How much more is his life in value with him!
Would I were fairly out on't!

CROMWELL
                                      My mind gave me,
In seeking tales and informations
Against this man, — whose honesty the devil
And his disciples only envy at, —
Ye blew the fire that burns ye: now have at ye!

Enter KING, frowning on them; takes his seat.

GARDINER
Dread sovereign, how much are we bound to heaven
In daily thanks, that gave us such a prince;
Not only good and wise, but most religious:
One that, in all obedience, makes the church
The chief aim of his honour; and, to strengthen
That holy duty, out of dear respect,
His royal self in judgement comes to hear
The cause betwixt her and this great offender.

KING HENRY
You were ever good at sudden commendations,
Bishop of Winchester. But know, I come not
To hear such flatteries now, and in my presence;
They are too thin and bare to hide offences.
To me, you cannot reach, you play the spaniel,
And think with wagging of your tongue to win me;
But, whatsoe'er thou takest me for, I'm sure
Thou hast a cruel nature and a bloody. —
[*to* CRANMER] Good man, sit down. Now let me see
   the proudest
He, that dares most, but wag his finger at thee:
By all that's holy, he had better starve
Than but once think this place becomes thee not.

SURREY
May it please your Grace, —

KING HENRY
                                      No, sir, it does not please me.
I had thought I had had men of some understanding
And wisdom of my council; but I find none.
Was it discretion, lords, to let this man,
This good man, — few of you deserve that title, —
This honest man, wait like a lousy footboy
At chamber-door? and one as great as you are?
Why, what a shame was this! Did my commission
Bid ye so far forget yourselves? I gave ye
Power as he was a counsellor to try him,
Not as a groom: there's some of ye, I see,
More out of malice than integrity,
Would try him to the utmost, had ye mean;
Which ye shall never have while I live.

LORD CHANCELLOR
                                      Thus far,
My most dread sovereign, may it like your Grace
To let my tongue excuse all. What was purpos'd
Concerning his imprisonment, was rather —
If there be faith in men — meant for his trial,
And fair purgation to the world, than malice, —
I'm sure, in me.

KING HENRY
                  Well, well, my lords, respect him;
Take him, and use him well, he's worthy of it.
I will say thus much for him, — if a prince
May be beholding to a subject, I
Am, for his love and service, so to him.
Make me no more ado, but all embrace him:
Be friends, for shame, my lords! — My Lord of
   Canterbury,
I have a suit which you must not deny me;
That is, a fair young maid that yet wants baptism,
You must be godfather, and answer for her.

CRANMER
The greatest monarch now alive may glory
In such an honour: how may I deserve it,
That am a poor and humble subject to you?

KING HENRY
Come, come, my lord, you'ld spare your spoons: you
shall have two noble partners with you; the old
Duchess of Norfolk, and Lady Marquess Dorset: will
these please you? —
Once more, my Lord of Winchester, I charge you,
Embrace and love this man.

GARDINER
                                      With a true heart
And brother-love I do it.

CRANMER
                                      And let heaven
Witness, how dear I hold this confirmation.

KING HENRY
Good man, those joyful tears show thy true heart:
The common voice, I see, is verified
Of thee, which says thus, 'Do my Lord of Canterbury

KING HENRY With this kiss take my blessing: God protect thee!

A shrewd turn, and he is your friend for ever.' —
Come, lords, we trifle time away; I long
To have this young one made a Christian.
As I have made ye one, lords, one remain;
So I grow stronger, you more honour gain.   [*Exeunt.*

SCENE III

The palace-yard.

Noise and tumult within. Enter PORTER *and his* MAN.

PORTER
You'll leave your noise anon, ye rascals: do you take the
court for Parish-garden? ye rude slaves, leave your
gaping.
[*within*] Good master porter, I belong to the larder.
PORTER
Belong to the gallows, and be hang'd, ye rogue! is this a
place to roar in? — Fetch me a dozen crab-tree staves,
and strong ones: these are but switches to 'em. — I'll
scratch your heads: you must be seeing christenings!
do you look for ale and cakes here, you rude rascals?
MAN
Pray, sir, be patient: 'tis as much impossible —
Unless we sweep 'em from the door with cannons —
To scatter 'em, as 'tis to make 'em sleep
On May-day morning; which will never be:
We may as well push against Powle's as stir 'em.
PORTER
How got they in, and be hang'd?
MAN
Alas, I know not; how gets the tide in?
As much as one sound cudgel of four foot —
You see the poor remainder — could distribute,
I made no spare, sir.
PORTER
         You did nothing, sir.
MAN
I am not Samson, nor Sir Guy, nor Colbrand,
To mow 'em down before me: but if I spar'd any
That had a head to hit, either young or old,

He or she, cuckold or cuckold-maker,
Let me ne'er hope to see a chine again;
And that I would not for a cow, God save her!
[*within*] Do you hear, master porter?
PORTER
I shall be with you presently, good master puppy.
— Keep the door close, sirrah.
MAN
What would you have me do?
PORTER
What should you do, but knock 'em down by the
dozens? Is this Moorfields to muster in? or have we
some strange Indian with the great tool come to court,
the women so besiege us? Bless me, what a fry of
fornication is at door! On my Christian conscience, this
one christening will beget a thousand; here will be
father, godfather, and all together.
MAN
The spoons will be the bigger, sir. There is a fellow
somewhat near the door, — he should be a brazier by
his face, for, o'my conscience, twenty of the dog-days
now reign in's nose; all that stand about him are under
the line, they need no other penance: that fire-drake did
I hit three times on the head, and three times was his
nose discharg'd against me: he stands there, like a
mortar-piece, to blow us. There was a haberdasher's
wife of small wit near him, that rail'd upon me, till her
pink'd porringer fell off her head, for kindling such a
combustion in the state. I miss'd the meteor once, and
hit that woman, who cried out 'Clubs!' when I might
see from far some forty truncheoners draw to her
succour, which were the hope o'the Strond, where she
was quarter'd. They fell on; I made good my place: at
length they came to the broomstaff to me; I defied 'em
still: when suddenly a file of boys behind 'em, loose
shot, deliver'd such a shower of pebbles, that I was fain
to draw mine honour in, and let 'em win the work: the
devil was amongst 'em, I think, surely.
PORTER
These are the youths that thunder at a playhouse, and

fight for bitten apples; that no audience, but the
Tribulation of Tower-hill, or the Limbs of Limehouse,
their dear brothers, are able to endure. I have some of
'em in *Limbo Patrum*, and there they are like to dance
these three days; besides the running banquet of two
beadles that is to come.
        Enter the LORD CHAMBERLAIN.
LORD CHAMBERLAIN
Mercy o'me, what a multitude are here!
They grow still too: from all parts they are coming,
As if we kept a fair here! Where are these porters,
These lazy knaves? — Y'have made a fine hand,
    fellows:
There's a trim rabble let in: are all these
Your faithful friends o'the suburbs? We shall have
Great store of room, no doubt, left for the ladies,
When they pass back from the christening.
PORTER
            An't please your honour,
We are but men; and what so many may do,
Not being torn a-pieces, we have done:
An army cannot rule 'em.
LORD CHAMBERLAIN
            As I live,
If the king blame me for't, I'll lay ye all
By the heels, and suddenly; and on your heads
Clap round fines for neglect: y'are lazy knaves;
And here ye lie baiting of bombards, when
Ye should do service. Hark! the trumpets sound;
Th'are come already from the christening:
Go, break among the press, and find a way out
To let the troop pass fairly; or I'll find
A Marshalsea shall hold ye play these two months.
PORTER
Make way there for the princess!
MAN
            You great fellow,
Stand close up, or I'll make your head ache!
PORTER
You i'the chamblet,
Get up o'the rail; I'll peck you o'er the pales else!
                  [*Exeunt.*

SCENE IV

The palace.

Enter trumpets, sounding; then two ALDERMEN, LORD
MAYOR, GARTER, CRANMER, DUKE OF
NORFOLK *with his marshal's staff,* DUKE OF
SUFFOLK, *two* NOBLEMEN *bearing great
standing-bowls for the christening-gifts; then four*
NOBLEMEN *bearing a canopy, under which the*
DUCHESS OF NORFOLK, *godmother, bearing the*
CHILD *richly habited in a mantle, etc., train borne by a*
LADY; *then follows the* MARCHIONESS OF DORSET,
the other godmother, and LADIES. *The* TROOP *pass
once about the stage and* GARTER *speaks.*

GARTER
Heaven, from thy endless goodness, send prosperous
life, long, and ever happy, to the high and mighty
princess of England, Elizabeth!
      Flourish. Enter KING *and* GUARD.
CRANMER [*kneeling*].
And to your royal Grace, and the good queen,
My noble partners and myself thus pray; —
All comfort, joy, in this most gracious lady,
Heaven ever laid up to make parents happy,
May hourly fall upon ye!
KING HENRY
           Thank you, good lord Archbishop:
What is her name?
CRANMER
         Elizabeth.
KING HENRY
           Stand up, lord. —
          [*The* KING *kisses the* CHILD.
With this kiss take my blessing: God protect thee!
Into whose hand I give thy life.
CRANMER
          Amen.
KING HENRY
My noble gossips, y'have been too prodigal:
I thank ye heartily; so shall this lady,
When she has so much English.
CRANMER
          Let me speak, sir,
For heaven now bids me; and the words I utter
Let none think flattery, for they'll find 'em truth.
This royal infant — heaven still move about her! —

Though in her cradle, yet now promises
Upon this land a thousand thousand blessings,
Which time shall bring to ripeness: she shall be —
But few now living can behold that goodness —
A pattern to all princes living with her,
And all that shall succeed: Saba was never
More covetous of wisdom and fair virtue
Than this pure soul shall be: all princely graces,
That mould up such a mighty piece as this is,
With all the virtues that attend the good,
Shall still be doubled on her: truth shall nurse her,
Holy and heavenly thoughts still counsel her:
She shall be lov'd and fear'd: her own shall bless her;
Her foes shake like a field of beaten corn,
And hang their heads with sorrow: good grows with
    her:
In her days every man shall eat in safety,
Under his own vine, what he plants; and sing
The merry songs of peace to all his neighbours:
God shall be truly known; and those about her
From her shall read the perfect ways of honour,
And by those claim their greatness, not by blood.
Nor shall this peace sleep with her: but as when
The bird of wonder dies, the maiden phœnix,
Her ashes new create another heir,
As great in admiration as herself;
So shall she leave her blessedness to one,

When heaven shall call her from this cloud of
    darkness,
Who from the sacred ashes of her honour
Shall star-like rise, as great in fame as she was,
And so stand fix'd: peace, plenty, love, truth, terror,
That were the servants to this chosen infant,
Shall then be his, and like a vine grow to him:
Wherever the bright sun of heaven shall shine,
His honour and the greatness of his name
Shall be, and make new nations: he shall flourish,
And, like a mountain cedar, reach his branches
To all the plains about him: — our children's children
Shall see this, and bless heaven.

KING HENRY
                              Thou speakest wonders.

CRANMER
She shall be, to the happiness of England,
An aged princess; many days shall see her,
And yet no day without a deed to crown it.
Would I had known no more! but she must die, —
She must, the saints must have her, — yet a virgin;
A most unspotted lily shall she pass
To the ground, and all the world shall mourn her.

KING HENRY
O lord archbishop,
Thou hast made me now a man! never before
This happy child, did I get any thing:

This oracle of comfort has so pleas'd me,
That when I am in heaven I shall desire
To see what this child does, and praise my Maker. —
I thank ye all. — To you, my good lord mayor,
And your good brethren, I am much beholding;
I have receiv'd much honour by your presence,
And ye shall find me thankful. — Lead the way, lords: —
Ye must all see the queen, and she must thank ye;
She will be sick else. This day, no man think
'Has business at his house; for all shall stay:
This little one shall make it holiday.   [*Exeunt.*

EPILOGUE

'Tis ten to one this play can never please
All that are here: some come to take their ease,
And sleep an act or two; but those, we fear,
W'have frighted with our trumpets; so, 'tis clear,
They'll say 'tis naught: others, to hear the city
Abus'd extremely, and to cry 'That's witty!'
Which we have not done neither: that, I fear,
All the expected good w'are like to hear
For this play at this time, is only in
The merciful construction of good women;
For such a one we show'd 'em: if they smile,
And say 'twill do, I know, within a while
All the best men are ours; for 'tis ill hap,
If they hold when their ladies bid 'em clap.

VENUS AND ADONIS

Vilia miretur vulgus : mihi flavus Apollo
Pocula Castalia plena ministret aqua.

TO THE RIGHT HONOURABLE HENRY WRIOTHESLEY,
EARL OF SOUTHAMPTON, AND BARON OF TITCHFIELD.

RIGHT HONOURABLE,

I know not how I shall offend in dedicating my unpolished lines to your Lordship, nor how the world will censure me for choosing so strong a prop to support so weak a burden: only if your Honour seem but pleased, I account myself highly praised, and vow to take advantage of all idle hours, till I have honour'd you with some graver labour. But if the first heir of my invention prove deform'd, I shall be sorry it had so noble a godfather: and never after ear so barren a land, for fear it yield me still so bad a harvest. I leave it to your honourable survey, and your Honour to your heart's content, which I wish may always answer your own wish, and the world's hopeful expectation.

Your Honour's in all duty,
WILLIAM SHAKESPEARE.

Even as the sun with purple-colour'd face
Had ta'en his last leave of the weeping morn,
Rose-cheek'd Adonis hied him to the chase;
Hunting he loved, but love he laugh'd to scorn:
　Sick-thoughted Venus makes amain unto him,
　And like a bold-fac'd suitor gins to woo him.

'Thrice-fairer than myself,' thus she began,
'The field's chief flower, sweet above compare,
Stain to all nymphs, more lovely than a man,
More white and red than doves or roses are;
　Nature that made thee, with herself at strife,
　Saith that the world hath ending with thy life.

'Vouchsafe, thou wonder, to alight thy steed,
And rein his proud head to the saddle-bow;
If thou wilt deign this favour, for thy meed
A thousand honey secrets shalt thou know:
　Here come and sit, where never serpent hisses;
　And being set, I'll smother thee with kisses;

'And yet not cloy thy lips with loath'd satiety,
But rather famish them amid their plenty,
Making them red and pale with fresh variety;
Ten kisses short as one, one long as twenty:
　A summer's day will seem an hour but short,
　Being wasted in such time-beguiling sport.'

With this she seizeth on his sweating palm,
The precedent of pith and livelihood,
And, trembling in her passion, calls it balm,
Earth's sovereign salve to do a goddess good:
　Being so enrag'd, desire doth lend her force
　Courageously to pluck him from his horse.

Over one arm the lusty courser's rein,
Under her other was the tender boy,
Who blush'd and pouted in a dull disdain,
With leaden appetite, unapt to toy;
　She red and hot as coals of glowing fire,
　He red for shame, but frosty in desire.

The studded bridle on a ragged bough
Nimbly she fastens: — O, how quick is love! —
The steed is stalled up, and even now
To tie the rider she begins to prove:
　Backward she push'd him, as she would be thrust,
　And govern'd him in strength, though not in lust.

So soon was she along as he was down,
Each leaning on their elbows and their hips:
Now doth she stroke his cheek, now doth he frown,
And gins to chide, but soon she stops his lips;
　And kissing speaks, with lustful language broken,
　'If thou wilt chide, thy lips shall never open.'

He burns with bashful shame; she with her tears
Doth quench the maiden burning of his cheeks;
Then with her windy sighs and golden hairs
To fan and blow them dry again she seeks:
　He saith she is immodest, blames her miss;
　What follows more she murders with a kiss.

Even as an empty eagle, sharp by fast,
Tires with her beak on feathers, flesh, and bone,
Shaking her wings, devouring all in haste,
Till either gorge be stuff'd, or prey be gone;
　Even so she kiss'd his brow, his cheek, his chin,
　And where she ends she doth anew begin.

'Alas, poor world, what treasure hast thou lost!'

Forc'd to content, but never to obey,
Panting he lies, and breatheth in her face;
She feedeth on the steam as on a prey,
And calls it heavenly moisture, air of grace;
　Wishing her cheeks were gardens full of flowers,
　So they were dew'd with such distilling showers.

Look how a bird lies tangled in a net,
So fasten'd in her arms Adonis lies;
Pure shame and aw'd resistance made him fret,
Which bred more beauty in his angry eyes:
　Rain added to a river that is rank
　Perforce will force it overflow the bank.

Still she entreats, and prettily entreats,
And to a pretty ear she tunes her tale;
Still is he sullen, still he lours and frets,
'Twixt crimson shame and anger ashy-pale;
　Being red, she loves him best; and being white,
　Her best is better'd with a more delight.

Look how he can, she cannot choose but love;
And by her fair immortal hand she swears,
From his soft bosom never to remove,
Till he take truce with her contending tears,
　Which long have rain'd, making her cheeks all wet;
　And one sweet kiss shall pay this comptless debt.

Upon this promise did he raise his chin,
Like a dive-dapper peering through a wave,
Who, being look'd on, ducks as quickly in;
So offers he to give what she did crave;
　But when her lips were ready for his pay,
　He winks, and turns his lips another way.

Never did passenger in summer's heat
More thirst for drink than she for this good turn.
Her help she sees, but help she cannot get;
She bathes in water, yet her fire must burn:
　'O, pity,' gan she cry, 'flint-hearted boy!
　'Tis but a kiss I beg; why art thou coy?

'I have been woo'd, as I entreat thee now,
Even by the stern and direful god of war,
Whose sinewy neck in battle ne'er did bow,
Who conquers where he comes in every jar;
　Yet hath he been my captive and my slave,
　And begg'd for that which thou unask'd shalt have.

'Over my altars hath he hung his lance,
His batter'd shield, his uncontrolled crest,
And for my sake hath learnt to sport and dance,
To toy, to wanton, dally, smile, and jest;
　Scorning his churlish drum and ensign red,
　Making my arms his field, his tent my bed.

'Thus he that overrul'd I oversway'd,
Leading him prisoner in a red-rose chain:
Strong-temper'd steel his stronger strength obey'd,
Yet was he servile to my coy disdain.
　O, be not proud, nor brag not of thy might,
　For mast'ring her that foil'd the god of fight!

'Touch but my lips with those fair lips of thine, —
Though mine be not so fair, yet are they red, —
The kiss shall be thine own as well as mine: —
What see'st thou in the ground? hold up thy head:
　Look in mine eyeballs, there thy beauty lies;
　Then why not lips on lips, since eyes in eyes?

'Art thou asham'd to kiss? then wink again,
And I will wink; so shall the day seem night;
Love keeps his revels where there are but twain;
Be bold to play, our sport is not in sight:
　These blue-vein'd violets whereon we lean
　Never can blab, nor know not what we mean.

'The tender spring upon thy tempting lip
Shows thee unripe; yet mayst thou well be tasted:
Make use of time, let not advantage slip;
Beauty within itself should not be wasted:
　Fair flowers that are not gather'd in their prime
　Rot and consume themselves in little time.

'Were I hard-favour'd, foul, or wrinkled-old,
Ill-nurtured, crooked, churlish, harsh in voice,
O'erworn, despised, rheumatic, and cold,
Thick-sighted, barren, lean, and lacking juice,
    Then mightst thou pause, for then I were not for thee;
    But having no defects, why dost abhor me?

'Thou canst not see one wrinkle in my brow;
Mine eyes are grey, and bright, and quick in turning;
My beauty as the spring doth yearly grow,
My flesh is soft and plump, my marrow burning;
    My smooth moist hand, were it with thy hand felt,
    Would in thy palm dissolve, or seem to melt.

'Bid me discourse, I will enchant thine ear,
Or, like a fairy, trip upon the green,
Or, like a nymph, with long dishevell'd hair,
Dance on the sands, and yet no footing seen:
    Love is a spirit all compact of fire,
    Not gross to sink, but light, and will aspire.

'Witness this primrose bank whereon I lie;
These forceless flowers like sturdy trees support me;
Two strengthless doves will draw me through the sky,
From morn till night, even where I list to sport me:
    Is love so light, sweet boy, and may it be
    That thou should think it heavy unto thee?

'Is thine own heart to thine own face affected?
Can thy right hand seize love upon thy left?
Then woo thyself, be of thyself rejected,
Steal thine own freedom, and complain on theft.
    Narcissus so himself himself forsook,
    And died to kiss his shadow in the brook.

'Torches are made to light, jewels to wear,
Dainties to taste, fresh beauty for the use,
Herbs for their smell, and sappy plants to bear;
Things growing to themselves are growth's abuse:
    Seeds spring from seeds, and beauty breedeth beauty;
    Thou wast begot; to get it is thy duty.

'Upon the earth's increase why shouldst thou feed,
Unless the earth with thy increase be fed?
By law of nature thou art bound to breed,
That thine may live when thou thyself art dead;
    And so, in spite of death, thou dost survive,
    In that thy likeness still is left alive.'

By this, the love-sick queen began to sweat,
For, where they lay, the shadow had forsook them,
And Titan, tired in the mid-day heat,
With burning eye did hotly overlook them;
    Wishing Adonis had his team to guide
    So he were like him, and by Venus' side.

And now Adonis, with a lazy sprite,
And with a heavy, dark, disliking eye,
His louring brows o'erwhelming his fair sight,
Like misty vapours when they blot the sky, —
    Souring his cheeks, cries, 'Fie, no more of love!
    The sun doth burn my face; I must remove.'

'Ay me,' quoth Venus, 'young, and so unkind?
What bare excuses makest thou to be gone!
I'll sigh celestial breath, whose gentle wind
Shall cool the heat of this descending sun:
    I'll make a shadow for thee of my hairs;
    If they burn too, I'll quench them with my tears.

'The sun that shines from heaven shines but warm,
And, lo, I lie between that sun and thee:
The heat I have from thence doth little harm,
Thine eye darts forth the fire that burneth me;
    And were I not immortal, life were done
    Between this heavenly and earthly sun.

'Art thou obdurate, flinty, hard as steel,
Nay, more than flint, for stone at rain relenteth?
Art thou a woman's son, and canst not feel
What 'tis to love? how want of love tormenteth?
    O, had thy mother borne so hard a mind,
    She had not brought forth thee, but died unkind.

'What am I, that thou shouldst contemn me this?
Or what great danger dwells upon my suit?
What were thy lips the worse for one poor kiss?
Speak, fair; but speak fair words, or else be mute:
    Give me one kiss, I'll give it thee again,
    And one for interest, if thou wilt have twain.

'Fie, lifeless picture, cold and senseless stone,
Well-painted idol, image dull and dead,
Statue contenting but the eye alone,
Thing like a man, but of no woman bred!
    Thou art no man, though of a man's complexion,
    For men will kiss even by their own direction.'

This said, impatience chokes her pleading tongue,
And swelling passion doth provoke a pause;
Red cheeks and fiery eyes blaze forth her wrong;
Being judge in love, she cannot right her cause:
    And now she weeps, and now she fain would speak,
    And now her sobs do her intendments break.

Sometime she shakes her head, and then his hand,
Now gazeth she on him, now on the ground;
Sometime her arms infold him like a band:
She would, he will not in her arms be bound;
    And when from thence he struggles to be gone,
    She locks her lily fingers one in one.

'Fondling,' she saith, 'since I have hemm'd thee here
Within the circuit of this ivory pale,
I'll be a park, and thou shalt be my deer;
Feed where thou wilt, on mountain or in dale:
    Graze on my lips; and if those hills be dry,
    Stray lower, where the pleasant fountains lie.

'Within this limit is relief enough,
Sweet bottom-grass, and high delightful plain,
Round rising hillocks, brakes obscure and rough,
To shelter thee from tempest and from rain:
    Then be my deer, since I am such a park;
    No dog shall rouse thee, though a thousand bark.'

At this Adonis smiles as in disdain,
That in each cheek appears a pretty dimple:
Love made those hollows, if himself were slain,
He might be buried in a tomb so simple;
    Foreknowing well, if there he came to lie,
    Why, there Love liv'd, and there he could not die.

These lovely caves, these round enchanting pits,
Open'd their mouths to swallow Venus' liking.
Being mad before, how doth she now for wits?
Struck dead at first, what needs a second striking?
    Poor queen of love, in thine own law forlorn,
    To love a cheek that smiles at thee in scorn!

Now which way shall she turn? what shall she say?
Her words are done, her woes the more increasing;
The time is spent, her object will away,
And from her twining arms doth urge releasing.
    'Pity,' she cries, 'some favour, some remorse!'
    Away he springs, and hasteth to his horse.

But, lo, from forth a copse that neighbours by,
A breeding jennet, lusty, young, and proud,
Adonis' trampling courser doth espy,
And forth she rushes, snorts, and neighs aloud:
    The strong neck'd steed, being tied unto a tree,
    Breaketh his rein, and to her straight goes he.

Imperiously he leaps, he neighs, he bounds,
And now his woven girths he breaks asunder;
The bearing earth with his hard hoof he wounds,
Whose hollow womb resounds like heaven's thunder;
    The iron bit he crusheth 'tween his teeth,
    Controlling what he was controlled with.

His ears up-prick'd; his braided hanging mane
Upon his compass'd crest now stand on end;
His nostrils drink the air, and forth again,
As from a furnace, vapours doth he send:
    His eye, which scornfully glisters like fire,
    Shows his hot courage and his high desire.

Sometime he trots, as if he told the steps,
With gentle majesty and modest pride;
Anon he rears upright, curvets and leaps,
As who should say, 'Lo, thus my strength is tried;
    And this I do to captivate the eye
    Of the fair breeder that is standing by.'

What recketh he his rider's angry stir,
His flattering 'Holla' or his 'Stand, I say'?
What cares he now for curb or pricking spur?
For rich caparisons or trapping gay?
    He sees his love, and nothing else he sees,
    For nothing else with his proud sight agrees.

Look, when a painter would surpass the life
In limning out a well-proportion'd steed,
His art with nature's workmanship at strife,
As if the dead the living should exceed;
    So did this horse excel a common one
    In shape, in courage, colour, pace, and bone.

Round-hoof'd, short-jointed, fetlocks shag and long,
Broad breast, full eye, small head, and nostril wide,
High crest, short ears, straight legs, and passing strong,
Thin mane, thick tail, broad buttock, tender hide:
    Look, what a horse should have he did not lack,
    Save a proud rider on so proud a back.

Sometime he scuds far off, and there he stares;
Anon he starts at stirring of a feather;
To bid the wind a base he now prepares,
And whe'r he run or fly they know not whether;
    For through his mane and tail the high wind sings,
    Fanning the hairs, who wave like feath'red wings.

He looks upon his love, and neighs unto her;
She answers him, as if she knew his mind:
Being proud, as females are, to see him woo her,
She puts on outward strangeness, seems unkind;
    Spurns at his love, and scorns the heat he feels,
    Beating his kind embracements with her heels.

Then, like a melancholy malcontent,
He vails his tail, that, like a falling plume,
Cool shadow to his melting buttock lent:
He stamps, and bites the poor flies in his fume.
    His love, perceiving how he was enraged,
    Grew kinder, and his fury was assuaged.

His testy master goeth about to take him;
When, lo, the unback'd breeder, full of fear,
Jealous of catching, swiftly doth forsake him,
With her the horse, and left Adonis there:
    As they were mad, unto the wood they hie them,
    Out-stripping crows that strive to over-fly them.

All swoll'n with chafing, down Adonis sits,
Banning his boist'rous and unruly beast:
And now the happy season once more fits,
That love-sick Love by pleading may be blest;
    For lovers say, the heart hath treble wrong
    When it is barr'd the aidance of the tongue.

An oven that is stopp'd, or river stay'd,
Burneth more hotly, swelleth with more rage:
So of concealed sorrow may be said;
Free vent of words love's fire doth assuage;
    But when the heart's attorney once is mute,
    The client breaks, as desperate in his suit.

He sees her coming, and begins to glow,
Even as a dying coal revives with wind,
And with his bonnet hides his angry brow;
Looks on the dull earth with disturbed mind;
    Taking no notice that she is so nigh,
    For all askance he holds her in his eye.

O, what a sight it was, wistly to view
How she came stealing to the wayward boy!
To note the fighting conflict of her hue,
How white and red each other did destroy!
    But now her cheek was pale, and by and by
    It flash'd forth fire, as lightning from the sky.

Now she was just before him as he sat,
And like a lowly lover down she kneels;
With one fair hand she heaveth up his hat,
Her other tender hand his fair cheek feels:
    His tenderer cheek receives her soft hand's print,
    As apt as new-fall'n snow takes any dint.

O, what a war of looks was then between them!
Her eyes petitioners to his eyes suing;
His eyes saw her eyes as they had not seen them;
Her eyes woo'd still, his eyes disdain'd the wooing:
    And all this dumb-play had his acts made plain
    With tears, which, chorus-like, her eyes did rain.

Full gently now she takes him by the hand,
A lily prison'd in a gaol of snow,
Or ivory in an alabaster band;
So white a friend engirts so white a foe:
    This beauteous combat, wilful and unwilling,
    Show'd like two silver doves that sit a-billing.

Once more the engine of her thoughts began:
'O fairest mover on this mortal round,
Would thou wert as I am, and I a man,
My heart all whole as thine, thy heart my wound;
    For one sweet look thy help I would assure thee,
    Though nothing but my body's bane would cure thee.'

'Give me my hand,' saith he; 'why dost thou feel it?'
'Give me my heart,' saith she, 'and thou shalt have it;
O, give it me, lest thy hard heart do steel it,
And being steel'd, soft sighs can never grave it:
    Then love's deep groans I never shall regard,
    Because Adonis' heart hath made mine hard.'

'For shame,' he cries, 'let go, and let me go;
My day's delight is past, my horse is gone,
And 'tis your fault I am bereft him so:
I pray you hence, and leave me here alone;
    For all my mind, my thought, my busy care
    Is how to get my palfrey from the mare.'

Thus she replies: 'Thy palfrey, as he should,
Welcomes the warm approach of sweet desire:
Affection is a coal that must be cool'd;
Else, suffer'd, it will set the heart on fire:
    The sea hath bounds, but deep desire hath none;
    Therefore no marvel though thy horse be gone.

'How like a jade he stood, tied to the tree,
Servilely master'd with a leathern rein!
But when he saw his love, his youth's fair fee,
He held such petty bondage in disdain:
    Throwing the base thong from his bending crest,
    Enfranchising his mouth, his back, his breast.

'Who sees his true-love in her naked bed,
Teaching the sheets a whiter hue than white,
But, when his glutton eye so full hath fed,
His other agents aim at like delight?
    Who is so faint, that dares not be so bold
    To touch the fire, the weather being cold?

'Let me excuse thy courser, gentle boy;
And learn of him, I heartily beseech thee,
To take advantage on presented joy;
Though I were dumb, yet his proceedings teach thee:
    O, learn to love; the lesson is but plain,
    And once made perfect, never lost again.'

'I know not love,' quoth he, 'nor will not know it,
Unless it be a boar, and then I chase it;
'Tis much to borrow, and I will not owe it;
My love to love is love but to disgrace it;
    For I have heard it is a life in death,
    That laughs, and weeps, and all but with a breath.

'Who wears a garment shapeless and unfinish'd?
Who plucks the bud before one leaf put forth?
If springing things be any jot diminish'd,
They wither in their prime, prove nothing worth:
    The colt that's back'd and burden'd being young
    Loseth his pride, and never waxeth strong.

'You hurt my hand with wringing; let us part,
And leave this idle theme, this bootless chat:
Remove your siege from my unyielding heart;
To love's alarms it will not ope the gate:
    Dismiss your vows, your feigned tears, your flatt'ry;
    For where a heart is hard they make no batt'ry.'

'What! canst thou talk?' quoth she, 'hast thou a tongue?
O, would thou hadst not, or I had no hearing!
Thy mermaid's voice hath done me double wrong;
I had my load before, now press'd with bearing:
    Melodious discord, heavenly tune harsh-sounding,
    Ear's deep-sweet music, and heart's deep-sore
        wounding.

'Had I no eyes but ears, my ears would love
That inward beauty and invisible;
Or were I deaf, thy outward parts would move
Each part in me that were but sensible:
    Though neither eyes nor ears, to hear nor see,
    Yet should I be in love by touching thee.

'Say, that the sense of feeling were bereft me,
And that I could not see, nor hear, nor touch,
And nothing but the very smell were left me,
Yet would my love to thee be still as much;
    For from the stillitory of thy face excelling
    Comes breath perfum'd, that breedeth love by
        smelling.

'But, O, what banquet wert thou to the taste,
Being nurse and feeder of the other four!
Would they not wish the feast might ever last,
And bid Suspicion double-lock the door,
    Lest Jealousy, that sour unwelcome guest,
    Should, by his stealing in, disturb the feast?'

Once more the ruby-colour'd portal open'd,
Which to his speech did honey passage yield;
Like a red morn, that ever yet betoken'd
Wrack to the seaman, tempest to the field,
    Sorrow to shepherds, woe unto the birds,
    Gusts and foul flaws to herdmen and to herds.

This ill presage advisedly she marketh:
Even as the wind is hush'd before it raineth,
Or as the wolf doth grin before he barketh,
Or as the berry breaks before it staineth,
    Or like the deadly bullet of a gun,
    His meaning struck her ere his words begun.

And at his look she flatly falleth down,
For looks kill love, and love by looks reviveth:
A smile recures the wounding of a frown;
But blessed bankrout, that by love so thriveth!
    The silly boy, believing she is dead,
    Claps her pale cheek, till clapping makes it red;

And all-amaz'd brake off his late intent,
For sharply he did think to reprehend her,
Which cunning love did wittily prevent:
Fair fall the wit that can so well defend her!
    For on the grass she lies as she were slain,
    Till his breath breatheth life in her again.

He wrings her nose, he strikes her on the cheeks,
He bends her fingers, holds her pulses hard;
He chafes her lips; a thousand ways he seeks
To mend the hurt that his unkindness marr'd:
    He kisses her; and she, by her good will,
    Will never rise, so he will kiss her still.

The night of sorrow now is turn'd to day:
Her two blue windows faintly she up-heaveth,
Like the fair sun, when in his fresh array
He cheers the morn, and all the earth relieveth:
    And as the bright sun glorifies the sky,
    So is her face illumin'd with her eye;

Whose beams upon his hairless face are fix'd,
As if from thence they borrow'd all their shine.
Were never four such lamps together mix'd,
Had not his clouded with his brow's repine;
    But hers, which through the crystal tears gave light,
    Shone like the moon in water seen by night.

'O, where am I?' quoth she; 'in earth or heaven,
Or in the ocean drench'd, or in the fire?
What hour is this? or morn or weary even?
Do I delight to die, or life desire?
    But now I liv'd, and life was death's annoy;
    But now I died, and death was lively joy.

'O, thou didst kill me: kill me once again:
Thy eyes' shrewd tutor, that hard heart of thine,
Hath taught them scornful tricks, and such disdain,
That they have murder'd this poor heart of mine;
    And these mine eyes, true leaders to their queen,
    But for thy piteous lips no more had seen.

'Long may they kiss each other, for this cure!
O, never let their crimson liveries wear!
And as they last, their verdure still endure,
To drive infection from the dangerous year!
    That the star-gazers, having writ on death,
    May say, the plague is banish'd by thy breath.

'Pure lips, sweet seals in my soft lips imprinted,
What bargains may I make, still to be sealing?
To sell myself I can be well contented,
So thou wilt buy, and pay, and use good dealing;
    Which purchase if thou make, for fear of slips
    Set thy seal-manual on my wax-red lips.

'A thousand kisses buys my heart from me;
And pay them at thy leisure, one by one.
What is ten hundred touches unto thee?
Are they not quickly told and quickly gone?
    Say, for non-payment that the debt should double,
    Is twenty hundred kisses such a trouble?'

'Fair queen,' quoth he, 'if any love you owe me,
Measure my strangeness with my unripe years:
Before I know myself, seek not to know me;
No fisher but the ungrown fry forbears:
    The mellow plum doth fall, the green sticks fast,
    Or being early pluck'd is sour to taste.

'Look, the world's comforter, with weary gait,
His day's hot task hath ended in the west;
The owl, night's herald, shrieks, 'tis very late;
The sheep are gone to fold, birds to their nest;
    And coal black clouds that shadow heaven's light
    Do summon us to part and bid good night.

'Now let me say "Good night," and so say you;
If you will say so, you shall have a kiss.'
'Good night,' quoth she; and, ere he says 'Adieu,'
The honey fee of parting tender'd is:
    Her arms do lend his neck a sweet embrace;
    Incorporate then they seem; face grows to face:

Till, breathless, he disjoin'd, and backward drew
The heavenly moisture, that sweet coral mouth,
Whose precious taste her thirsty lips well knew,
Whereon they surfeit, yet complain on drouth:
    He with her plenty press'd, she faint with dearth,
    Their lips together glued, fall to the earth.

Now quick desire hath caught the yielding prey,
And glutton-like she feeds, yet never filleth;
Her lips are conquerors, his lips obey,
Paying what ransom the insulter willeth;
    Whose vulture thought doth pitch the price so high,
    That she will draw his lips' rich treasure dry:

And having felt the sweetness of the spoil,
With blindfold fury she begins to forage;
Her face doth reek and smoke, her blood doth boil,
And careless lust stirs up a desperate courage;
    Planting oblivion, beating reason back,
    Forgetting shame's pure blush and honour's wrack.

Hot, faint, and weary with her hard embracing,
Like a wild bird being tam'd with too much handling,
Or as the fleet-foot roe that's tired with chasing,
Or like the froward infant still'd with dandling,
    He now obeys, and now no more resisteth,
    While she takes all she can, not all she listeth.

What wax so frozen but dissolves with temp'ring,
And yields at last to every light impression?
Things out of hope are compass'd oft with vent'ring,
Chiefly in love, whose leave exceeds commission:
    Affection faints not like a pale-fac'd coward,
    But then woos best when most his choice is froward.

When he did frown, O, had she then gave over,
Such nectar from his lips she had not suck'd.
Foul words and frowns must not repel a lover;
What though the rose have prickles, yet 'tis pluck'd;
    Were beauty under twenty locks kept fast,
    Yet love breaks through and picks them all at last.

For pity now she can no more detain him;
The poor fool prays her that he may depart:
She is resolv'd no longer to restrain him;
Bids him farewell, and look well to her heart,
    The which, by Cupid's bow she doth protest,
    He carries thence incaged in his breast.

'Sweet boy,' she says, 'this night I'll waste in sorrow,
For my sick heart commands mine eyes to watch.
Tell me, Love's master, shall we meet to-morrow?
Say, shall we? shall we? wilt thou make the match?'
    He tells her, no; to-morrow he intends
    To hunt the boar with certain of his friends.

'The boar!' quoth she; whereat a sudden pale,
Like lawn being spread upon the blushing rose,
Usurps her cheek; she trembles at his tale,
And on his neck her yoking arms she throws:
    She sinketh down, still hanging by his neck,
    He on her belly falls, she on her back.

Now is she in the very lists of love,
Her champion mounted for the hot encounter:
All is imaginary she doth prove,
He will not manage her, although he mount her;
    That worse than Tantalus' is her annoy,
    To clip Elysium, and to lack her joy.

Even so poor birds, deceiv'd with painted grapes,
Do surfeit by the eye and pine the maw:
Even so she languisheth in her mishaps
As those poor birds that helpless berries saw.
    The warm effects which she in him finds missing,
    She seeks to kindle with continual kissing.

But all in vain; good queen, it will not be:
She hath assay'd as much as may be prov'd;
Her pleading hath deserved a greater fee;
She's Love, she loves, and yet she is not lov'd.
    'Fie, fie,' he says, 'you crush me; let me go;
    You have no reason to withhold me so.'

'Thou hadst been gone,' quoth she, 'sweet boy, ere this,
But that thou told'st me thou wouldst hunt the boar.
O, be advis'd! thou know'st not what it is
With javelin's point a churlish swine to gore,
    Whose tushes never-sheath'd he whetteth still,
    Like to a mortal butcher bent to kill.

'On his bow-back he hath a battle set
Of bristly pikes, that ever threat his foes;
His eyes, like glow-worms, shine when he doth fret;
His snout digs sepulchres where'er he goes;
    Being mov'd, he strikes whate'er is in his way,
    And whom he strikes his crooked tushes slay.

'His brawny sides, with hairy bristles arm'd,
Are better proof than thy spear's point can enter;
His short thick neck cannot be easily harm'd;
Being ireful, on the lion he will venter:
    The thorny brambles and embracing bushes,
    As fearful of him, part; through whom he rushes.

'Alas, he naught esteems that face of thine,
To which Love's eyes pay tributary gazes;
Nor thy soft hands, sweet lips, and crystal eyne,
Whose full perfection all the world amazes;
    But having thee at vantage, — wondrous dread! —
    Would root these beauties as he roots the mead.

'O, let him keep his loathsome cabin still;
Beauty hath nought to do with such foul fiends:
Come not within his danger by thy will;
They that thrive well take counsel of their friends.
    When thou didst name the boar, not to dissemble,
    I fear'd thy fortune, and my joints did tremble.

'Didst thou not mark my face? was it not white?
Saw'st thou not signs of fear lurk in mine eye?
Grew I not faint? and fell I not downright?
Within my bosom, whereon thou dost lie,
    My boding heart pants, beats, and takes no rest,
    But, like an earthquake, shakes thee on my breast.

'For where Love reigns, disturbing Jealousy
Doth call himself Affection's sentinel;
Gives false alarms, suggesteth mutiny,
And in a peaceful hour doth cry "Kill, kill!"
    Distemp'ring gentle Love in his desire,
    As air and water do abate the fire.

'This sour informer, this bate-breeding spy,
This canker that eats up Love's tender spring,
This carry-tale, dissentious Jealousy,
That sometime true news, sometime false doth bring,
    Knocks at my heart, and whispers in mine ear,
    That if I love thee, I thy death should fear:

'And more than so, presenteth to mine eye
The picture of an angry-chafing boar,
Under whose sharp fangs on his back doth lie
An image like thyself, all stain'd with gore;
    Whose blood upon the fresh flowers being shed
    Doth make them droop with grief and hang the head.

'What should I do, seeing thee so indeed,
That tremble at the imagination?
The thought of it doth make my faint heart bleed,
And fear doth teach it divination:
    I prophesy thy death, my living sorrow,
    If thou encounter with the boar to-morrow.

'But if thou needs wilt hunt, be rul'd by me;
Uncouple at the timorous flying hare,
Or at the fox which lives by subtlety,
Or at the roe which no encounter dare:
    Pursue these fearful creatures o'er the downs,
    And on thy well-breath'd horse keep with thy
        hounds.

'And when thou hast on foot the purblind hare,
Mark the poor wretch, to overshoot his troubles
Now he outruns the wind, and with what care
He cranks and crosses with a thousand doubles:
    The many musets through the which he goes
    Are like a labyrinth to amaze his foes.

'Sometime he runs among a flock of sheep,
To make the cunning hounds mistake their smell,
And sometime where earth-delving conies keep,
To stop the loud pursuers in their yell;
    And sometime sorteth with a herd of deer:
    Danger deviseth shifts; wit waits on fear:

'For there his smell with others being mingled,
The hot scent-snuffing hounds are driven to doubt,
Ceasing their clamorous cry till they have singled
With much ado the cold fault cleanly out;
    Then do they spend their mouths: Echo replies
    As if another chase were in the skies.

'By this, poor Wat, far off upon a hill,
Stands on his hinder legs with list'ning ear,
To hearken if his foes pursue him still:
Anon their loud alarums he doth hear;
    And now his grief may be compared well
    To one sore sick that hears the passing-bell.

'Then shalt thou see the dew-bedabbled wretch
Turn, and return, indenting with the way;
Each envious brier his weary legs doth scratch,
Each shadow makes him stop, each murmur stay;
    For misery is trodden on by many,
    And being low never reliev'd by any.

'Lie quietly, and hear a little more;
Nay, do not struggle, for thou shalt not rise:
To make thee hate the hunting of the boar,
Unlike myself thou hear'st me moralise,
    Applying this to that, and so to so;
    For love can comment upon every woe.

'Where did I leave?' 'No matter where,' quoth he;
'Leave me, and then the story aptly ends:
The night is spent.' 'Why, what of that?' quoth she.
'I am,' quoth he, 'expected of my friends;
    And now 'tis dark, and going I shall fall.'
    'In night,' quoth she, 'desire sees best of all.

'But if thou fall, O, then imagine this,
The earth, in love with thee, thy footing trips,
And all is but to rob thee of a kiss.
Rich preys make true-men thieves; so do thy lips
    Make modest Dian cloudy and forlorn,
    Lest she should steal a kiss, and die forsworn.

'Now of this dark night I perceive the reason:
Cynthia for shame obscures her silver shine,
Till forging Nature be condemn'd of treason,
For stealing moulds from heaven that were divine;
    Wherein she fram'd thee, in high heaven's despite,
    To shame the sun by day, and her by night.

'And therefore hath she brib'd the Destinies
To cross the curious workmanship of Nature,
To mingle beauty with infirmities,
And pure perfection with impure defeature;
    Making it subject to the tyranny
    Of mad mischances and much misery;

'As burning fevers, agues pale and faint,
Life-poisoning pestilence, and frenzies wood,
The marrow-eating sickness, whose attaint
Disorder breeds by heating of the blood:
    Surfeits, imposthumes, grief, and damn'd despair,
    Swear nature's death for framing thee so fair.

'And not the least of all these maladies
But in one minute's fight brings beauty under:
Both favour, savour, hue, and qualities,
Whereat the impartial gazer late did wonder,
    Are on the sudden wasted, thaw'd, and done,
    As mountain snow melts with the midday sun.

'Therefore, despite of fruitless chastity,
Love-lacking vestals, and self-loving nuns,
That on the earth would breed a scarcity
And barren dearth of daughters and of sons,
    Be prodigal: the lamp that burns by night
    Dries up his oil to lend the world his light.

'What is thy body but a swallowing grave,
Seeming to bury that posterity
Which by the rights of time thou needs must have,
If thou destroy them not in dark obscurity?
    If so, the world will hold thee in disdain,
    Sith in thy pride so fair a hope is slain.

'So in thy self thyself art made away;
A mischief worse than civil home-bred strife,
Or theirs whose desperate hands themselves do slay,
Or butcher-sire that reaves his son of life.
    Foul-cank'ring rust the hidden treasure frets,
    But gold that's put to use more gold begets.'

'Nay, then,' quoth Adon, 'you will fall again
Into your idle over-handled theme:
The kiss I gave you is bestow'd in vain,
And all in vain you strive against the stream;
    For, by this black-fac'd night, desire's foul nurse,
    Your treatise makes me like you worse and worse.

'If love have lent you twenty thousand tongues,
And every tongue more moving than your own,
Bewitching like the wanton mermaid's songs,
Yet from mine ear the tempting tune is blown;
    For know, my heart stands armed in mine ear,
    And will not let a false sound enter there;

'Lest the deceiving harmony should run
Into the quiet closure of my breast;
And then my little heart were quite undone,
In his bedchamber to be barr'd of rest.
    No, lady, no; my heart longs not to groan,
    But soundly sleeps, while now it sleeps alone.

'What have you urg'd that I cannot reprove?
The path is smooth that leadeth on to danger:
I hate not love, but your device in love,
That lends embracements unto every stranger.
    You do it for increase: O strange excuse,
    When reason is the bawd to lust's abuse!

'Call it not love, for Love to heaven is fled,
Since sweating Lust on earth usurp'd his name;
Under whose simple semblance he hath fed
Upon fresh beauty, blotting it with blame;
    Which the hot tyrant stains and soon bereaves,
    As caterpillars do the tender leaves.

'Love comforteth like sunshine after rain,
But Lust's effect is tempest after sun;
Love's gentle spring doth always fresh remain,
Lust's winter comes ere summer half be done;
    Love surfeits not, Lust like a glutton dies;
    Love is all truth, Lust full of forged lies.

'More I could tell, but more I dare not say;
The text is old, the orator too green.
Therefore, in sadness, now I will away;
My face is full of shame, my heart of teen:
    Mine ears, that to your wanton talk attended,
    Do burn themselves for having so offended.'

With this, he breaketh from the sweet embrace
Of those fair arms which bound him to her breast,
And homeward through the dark laund runs apace;
Leaves Love upon her back deeply distress'd.
    Look, how a bright star shooteth from the sky,
    So glides he in the night from Venus' eye;

Which after him she darts, as one on shore
Gazing upon a late-embarked friend,
Till the wild waves will have him see no more,
Whose ridges with the meeting clouds contend:
    So did the merciless and pitchy night
    Fold-in the object that did feed her sight.

Whereat amaz'd, as one that unaware
Hath dropp'd a precious jewel in the flood,
Or stonish'd as night-wanderers often are,
Their light blown out in some mistrustful wood;
    Even so confounded in the dark she lay,
    Having lost the fair discovery of her way.

And now she beats her heart, whereat it groans,
That all the neighbour caves, as seeming troubled,
Make verbal repetition of her moans;
Passion on passion deeply is redoubled:
    'Ay me!' she cries, and twenty times, 'Woe, woe!'
    And twenty echoes twenty times cry so.

She, marking them, begins a wailing note,
And sings extemporally a woeful ditty;
How love makes young men thrall, and old men dote;
How love is wise in folly, foolish-witty:
    Her heavy anthem still concludes in woe,
    And still the choir of echoes answer so.

Her song was tedious, and outwore the night,
For lovers' hours are long, though seeming short:
If pleas'd themselves, others, they think, delight
In such-like circumstance, with such-like sport:
    Their copious stories, oftentimes begun,
    End without audience, and are never done.

For who hath she to spend the night withal,
But idle sounds resembling parasits;
Like shrill-tongu'd tapsters answering every call,
Soothing the humour of fantastic wits?
    She says, ''Tis so': they answer all, ''Tis so';
    And would say after her, if she said 'No.'

Lo, here the gentle lark, weary of rest,
From his moist cabinet mounts up on high,
And wakes the morning, from whose silver breast
The sun ariseth in his majesty;
    Who doth the world so gloriously behold,
    That cedar-tops and hills seem burnish'd gold.

Venus salutes him with this fair good-morrow:
'O thou clear god, and patron of all light,
From whom each lamp and shining star doth borrow
The beauteous influence that makes him bright,
    There lives a son, that suck'd an earthly mother,
    May lend thee light, as thou dost lend to other.'

This said, she hasteth to a myrtle grove,
Musing the morning is so much o'erworn,
And yet she hears no tidings of her love:
She hearkens for his hounds and for his horn:
    Anon she hears them chant it lustily,
    And all in haste she coasteth to the cry.

And as she runs, the bushes in the way
Some catch her by the neck, some kiss her face,
Some twined about her thigh to make her stay:
She wildly breaketh from their strict embrace,
    Like a milch doe, whose swelling dugs do ache,
    Hasting to feed her fawn hid in some brake.

By this, she hears the hounds are at a bay:
Whereat she starts, like one that spies an adder
Wreath'd up in fatal folds just in his way,
The fear whereof doth make him shake and shudder;
    Even so the timorous yelping of the hounds
    Appals her senses and her spirit confounds.

For now she knows it is no gentle chase,
But the blunt boar, rough bear, or lion proud,
Because the cry remaineth in one place,
Where fearfully the dogs exclaim aloud:
    Finding their enemy to be so curst,
    They all strain court'sy who shall cope him first.

This dismal cry rings sadly in her ear,
Through which it enters to surprise her heart;
Who, overcome by doubt and bloodless fear,
With cold-pale weakness numbs each feeling part:
    Like soldiers, when their captain once doth yield,
    They basely fly, and dare not stay the field.

Thus stands she in a trembling ecstasy;
Till, cheering up her senses all dismay'd,
She tells them 'tis a causeless fantasy,
And childish error, that they are afraid;
    Bids them leave quaking, bids them fear no more: —
    And with that word she spied the hunted boar;

Whose frothy mouth, bepainted all with red,
Like milk and blood being mingled both together,
A second fear through all her sinews spread,
Which madly hurries her she knows not whither:
    This way she runs, and now she will no further,
    But back retires to rate the boar for murther.

A thousand spleens bear her a thousand ways;
She treads the path that she untreads again;
Her more than haste is mated with delays,
Like the proceedings of a drunken brain,
    Full of respects, yet naught at all respecting;
    In hand with all things, nought at all effecting.

Here kennell'd in a brake she finds a hound,
And asks the weary caitiff for his master;
And there another licking of his wound,
'Gainst venom'd sores the only sovereign plaster;
    And here she meets another sadly scowling,
    To whom she speaks, and he replies with
      howling.

When he hath ceas'd his ill-resounding noise,
Another flap-mouth'd mourner, black and grim,
Against the welkin volleys out his voice;
Another and another answer him,
    Clapping their proud tails to the ground below,
    Shaking their scratch'd ears, bleeding as they go.

Look how the world's poor people are amazed
At apparitions, signs, and prodigies,
Whereon with fearful eyes they long have gazed,
Infusing them with dreadful prophecies;
    So she at these sad signs draws up her breath,
    And, sighing it again, exclaims on Death.

'Hard-favour'd tyrant, ugly, meagre, lean,
Hateful divorce of love.' — Thus chides she Death, —
'Grim-grinning ghost, earth's worm, what dost thou
    mean
To stifle beauty and to steal his breath,
    Who when he liv'd, his breath and beauty set
    Gloss on the rose, smell to the violet?

'If he be dead, — O no, it cannot be,
Seeing his beauty, thou shouldst strike at it; —
O yes, it may; thou hast no eyes to see,
But hatefully at random dost thou hit.
    Thy mark is feeble age; but thy false dart
    Mistakes that aim, and cleaves an infant's heart.

'Hadst thou but bid beware, then he had spoke,
And, hearing him, thy power had lost his power.
The Destinies will curse thee for this stroke;
They bid thee crop a weed, thou pluck'st a flower:
    Love's golden arrow at him should have fled,
    And not Death's ebon dart, to strike him dead.

'Dost thou drink tears, that thou provok'st such weeping?
What may a heavy groan advantage thee?
Why hast thou cast into eternal sleeping
Those eyes that taught all other eyes to see?
    Now Nature cares not for thy mortal vigour,
    Since her best work is ruin'd with thy rigour.'

Here overcome, as one full of despair,
She vail'd her eyelids, who, like sluices, stopp'd
The crystal tide that from her two cheeks fair
In the sweet channel of her bosom dropp'd;
    But through the flood-gates breaks the silver rain,
    And with his strong course opens them again.

O, how her eyes and tears did lend and borrow!
Her eye seen in the tears, tears in her eye;
Both crystals, where they view'd each other's sorrow, —
Sorrow that friendly sighs sought still to dry;
    But like a stormy day, now wind, now rain,
    Sighs dry her cheeks, tears make them wet again.

Variable passions throng her constant woe,
As striving who should best become her grief;
All entertain'd, each passion labours so,
That every present sorrow seemeth chief,
    But none is best: then join they all together,
    Like many clouds consulting for foul weather.

By this, far off she hears some huntsman hollo;
A nurse's song ne'er pleas'd her babe so well:
The dire imagination she did follow
This sound of hope doth labour to expel;
    For now reviving joy bids her rejoice,
    And flatters her it is Adonis' voice.

Whereat her tears began to turn their tide,
Being prison'd in her eye like pearls in glass;
Yet sometimes falls an orient drop beside,
Which her cheek melts, as scorning it should pass,
    To wash the foul face of the sluttish ground,
    Who is but drunken when she seemeth drown'd.

O hard-believing love, how strange it seems
Not to believe, and yet too credulous!
Thy weal and woe are both of them extremes;
Despair and hope makes thee ridiculous:
    The one doth flatter thee in thoughts unlikely,
    In likely thoughts the other kills thee quickly.

Now she unweaves the web that she hath wrought;
Adonis lives, and Death is not to blame;
It was not she that call'd him all to-naught:
Now she adds honours to his hateful name;
    She clepes him king of graves, and grave for kings,
    Imperious supreme of all mortal things.

'No, no,' quoth she, 'sweet Death, I did but jest;
Yet pardon me I felt a kind of fear
Whenas I met the boar, that bloody beast
Which knows no pity, but is still severe:
    Then, gentle shadow, — truth I must confess, —
    I rail'd on thee, fearing my love's decease.

''Tis not my fault: the boar provok'd my tongue;
Be wreak'd on him, invisible commander;
'Tis he, foul creature, that hath done thee wrong;
I did but act, he's author of thy slander:
    Grief hath two tongues; and never woman yet
    Could rule them both without ten women's wit.'

Thus hoping that Adonis is alive,
Her rash suspect she doth extenuate;
And that his beauty may the better thrive,
With Death she humbly doth insinuate;
    Tells him of trophies, statues, tombs, and stories
    His victories, his triumphs, and his glories.

'O Jove,' quoth she, 'how much a fool was I
To be of such a weak and silly mind
To wail his death who lives, and must not die
Till mutual overthrow of mortal kind!
    For he being dead, with him is beauty slain,
    And, beauty dead, black chaos comes again.

'Fie, fie, fond love, thou art so full of fear
As one with treasure laden hemm'd with thieves;
Trifles, unwitnessed with eye or ear,
Thy coward heart with false bethinking grieves.'
    Even at this word she hears a merry horn,
    Whereat she leaps that was but late forlorn.

As falcons to the lure, away she flies;
The grass stoops not, she treads on it so light;
And in her haste unfortunately spies
The foul boar's conquest on her fair delight;
    Which seen, her eyes, as murder'd with the view,
    Like stars asham'd of day, themselves withdrew;

Or as the snail, whose tender horns being hit,
Shrinks backwards in his shelly cave with pain,
And there, all smother'd up, in shade doth sit,
Long after fearing to creep forth again;
    So at his bloody view her eyes are fled
    Into the deep-dark cabins of her head:

Where they resign their office and their light
To the disposing of her troubled brain;
Who bids them still consort with ugly night,
And never wound the heart with looks again;
    Who, like a king perplexed in his throne,
    By their suggestion gives a deadly groan,

Whereat each tributary subject quakes;
As when the wind, imprison'd in the ground,
Struggling for passage, earth's foundation shakes,
Which with cold terror doth men's minds confound,
    This mutiny each part doth so surprise,
    That from their dark beds once more leap her eyes;

And, being open'd, threw unwilling light
Upon the wide wound that the boar had trench'd
In his soft flank; whose wonted lily white
With purple tears, that his wound wept, was drench'd:
    No flower was nigh, no grass, herb, leaf, or weed,
    But stole his blood, and seem'd with him to bleed.

This solemn sympathy poor Venus noteth;
Over one shoulder doth she hang her head;
Dumbly she passions, franticly she doteth;
She thinks he could not die, he is not dead:
    Her voice is stopp'd, her joints forget to bow;
    Her eyes are mad that they have wept till now.

Upon his hurt she looks so steadfastly,
That her sight dazzling makes the wound seem three;
And then she reprehends her mangling eye,
That makes more gashes where no breach should be:
    His face seems twain, each several limb is doubled;
    For oft the eye mistakes, the brain being troubled.

'My tongue cannot express my grief for one,
And yet,' quoth she, 'behold two Adons dead!
My sighs are blown away, my salt tears gone,
Mine eyes are turn'd to fire, my heart to lead:
    Heavy heart's lead, melt at mine eyes' red fire!
    So shall I die by drops of hot desire.

'Alas, poor world, what treasure hast thou lost!
What face remains alive that's worth the viewing?
Whose tongue is music now? what canst thou boast
Of things long since, or any thing ensuing?
    The flowers are sweet, their colours fresh and trim;
    But true-sweet beauty liv'd and died with him.

'Bonnet nor veil henceforth no creature wear!
Nor sun nor wind will ever strive to kiss you:
Having no fair to lose, you need not fear;
The sun doth scorn you, and the wind doth hiss you:
    But when Adonis liv'd, sun and sharp air
    Lurk'd like two thieves, to rob him of his fair:

'And therefore would he put his bonnet on,
Under whose brim the gaudy sun would peep;
The wind would blow it off, and, being gone,
Play with his locks: then would Adonis weep;
    And straight, in pity of his tender years,
    They both would strive who first should dry his tears.

'To see his face the lion walk'd along
Behind some hedge, because he would not fear him;
To recreate himself when he hath sung,
The tiger would be tame, and gently hear him;
    If he had spoke, the wolf would leave his prey,
    And never fright the silly lamb that day.

'When he beheld his shadow in the brook,
The fishes spread on it their golden gills;
When he was by, the birds such pleasure took,
That some would sing, some other in their bills
    Would bring him mulberries and ripe-red cherries;
    He fed them with his sight, they him with berries.

'But this foul, grim, and urchin-snouted boar,
Whose downward eye still looketh for a grave,
Ne'er saw the beauteous livery that he wore;
Witness the entertainment that he gave:
    If he did see his face, why then I know
    He thought to kiss him, and hath kill'd him so.

''Tis true, 'tis true; thus was Adonis slain:
He ran upon the boar with his sharp spear,
Who did not whet his teeth at him again,
But by a kiss thought to persuade him there;
    And nuzzling in his flank, the loving swine
    Sheath'd, unaware, the tusk in his soft groin.

'Had I been tooth'd like him, I must confess,
With kissing him I should have kill'd him first;
But he is dead, and never did he bless
My youth with his; the more am I accurst.'
    With this, she falleth in the place she stood,
    And stains her face with his congealed blood.

She looks upon his lips, and they are pale;
She takes him by the hand, and that is cold;
She whispers in his ears a heavy tale,
As if they heard the woeful words she told;
    She lifts the coffer-lids that close his eyes,
    Where, lo, two lamps, burnt out, in darkness lies;

Two glasses, where herself herself beheld
A thousand times, and now no more reflect;
Their virtue lost, wherein they late excell'd,
And every beauty robb'd of his effect:
    'Wonder of time,' quoth she, 'this is my spite,
    That, thou being dead, the day should yet be light.

'Since thou art dead, lo, here I prophesy
Sorrow on love hereafter shall attend:
It shall be waited on with jealousy,
Find sweet beginning, but unsavoury end;
    Ne'er settled equally, but high or low;
    That all love's pleasure shall not match his woe.

'It shall be fickle, false, and full of fraud;
Bud and be blasted in a breathing-while;
The bottom poison, and the top o'erstraw'd
With sweets that shall the truest sight beguile:
    The strongest body shall it make most weak,
    Strike the wise dumb, and teach the fool to speak.

'It shall be sparing and too full of riot,
Teaching decrepit age to tread the measures;
The staring ruffian shall it keep in quiet,
Pluck down the rich, enrich the poor with treasures;
    It shall be raging-mad and silly-mild,
    Make the young old, the old become a child.

'It shall suspect where is no cause of fear;
It shall not fear where it should most mistrust;
It shall be merciful and too severe,
And most deceiving when it seems most just;
    Perverse it shall be where it shows most toward,
    Put fear to valour, courage to the coward.

'It shall be cause of war and dire events,
And set dissension 'twixt the son and sire;
Subject and servile to all discontents,
As dry combustious matter is to fire:
    Sith in his prime Death doth my love destroy,
    They that love best their loves shall not enjoy.'

By this, the boy that by her side lay kill'd
Was melted like a vapour from her sight;
And in his blood, that on the ground lay spill'd,
A purple flower sprung up, chequer'd with white,
    Resembling well his pale cheeks, and the blood
    Which in round drops upon their whiteness stood.

She bows her head the new-sprung flower to smell,
Comparing it to her Adonis' breath;
And says within her bosom it shall dwell,
Since he himself is reft from her by Death:
    She crops the stalk, and in the breach appears
    Green-dropping sap, which she compares to tears.

'Poor flower,' quoth she, 'this was thy father's guise, —
Sweet issue of a more sweet-smelling sire, —
For every little grief to wet his eyes:
To grow unto himself was his desire,
    And so 'tis thine; but know, it is as good
    To wither in my breast as in his blood.

'Here was thy father's bed, here in my breast;
Thou art the next of blood, and 'tis thy right:
Lo, in this hollow cradle take thy rest,
My throbbing heart shall rock thee day and night:
    There shall not be one minute in an hour
    Wherein I will not kiss my sweet love's flower.'

Thus weary of the world away she hies,
And yokes her silver doves; by whose swift aid
Their mistress, mounted, through the empty skies
In her light chariot quickly is convey'd;
    Holding their course to Paphos, where their queen
    Means to immure herself and not be seen.

LUCRECE

TO THE RIGHT HONOURABLE HENRY WRIOTHESLEY,

EARL OF SOUTHAMPTON, AND BARON OF TITCHFIELD.

The love I dedicate to your Lordship is without end; whereof this pamphlet, without beginning, is but a superfluous moiety. The warrant I have of your honourable disposition, not the worth of my untutor'd lines, makes it assured of acceptance. What I have done is yours; what I have to do is yours; being part in all I have, devoted yours. Were my worth greater, my duty would show greater; meantime, as it is, it is bound to your Lordship, to whom I wish long life, still lengthen'd with all happiness.

Your Lordship's in all duty,
WILLIAM SHAKESPEARE.

THE ARGUMENT

Lucius Tarquinius (for his excessive pride surnamed Superbus), after he had caused his own father-in-law Servius Tullius, to be cruelly murder'd, and, contrary to the Roman laws and customs, not requiring or staying for the people's suffrages, had possess'd himself of the kingdom, went, accompanied with his sons and other noblemen of Rome, to besiege Ardea. During which siege the principal men of the army meeting one evening at the tent of Sextus Tarquinius, the king's son, in their discourses after supper every one commended the virtues of his own wife; among whom Collatinus extoll'd the incomparable chastity of his wife Lucretia. In that pleasant humour they all posted to Rome; and intending, by their secret and sudden arrival, to make trial of that which every one had before avouch'd, only Collatinus finds his wife, though it were late in the night, spinning amongst her maids: the other ladies were all found dancing and revelling, or in several disports. Whereupon the noblemen yielded Collatinus the victory, and his wife the fame. At that time Sextus Tarquinius, being inflamed with Lucrece' beauty, yet smothering his passions for the present, departed with the rest back to the camp; from whence he shortly after privily withdrew himself, and was (according to his estate) royally entertain'd and lodged by Lucrece at Collatium. The same night he treacherously stealeth into her chamber, violently ravish'd her, and early in the morning speedeth away. Lucrece, in this lamentable plight, hastily dispatcheth messengers, one to Rome for her father, another to the camp for Collatine. They came, the one accompanied with Junius Brutus, the other with Publius Valerius; and finding Lucrece attired in mourning habit, demanded the cause of her sorrow. She, first taking an oath of them for her revenge, reveal'd the actor, and whole manner of his dealing, and withal suddenly stabb'd herself. Which done, with one consent they all vow'd to root out the whole hated family of the Tarquins; and bearing the dead body to Rome, Brutus acquainted the people with the doer and manner of the vile deed, with a bitter invective against the tyranny of the king: wherewith the people were so moved, that with one consent and a general acclamation the Tarquins were all exiled, and the state government changed from kings to consuls.

From the besieg'd Ardea all in post,
Borne by the trustless wings of false desire,
Lust-breathed Tarquin leaves the Roman host,
And to Collatium bears the lightless fire
Which, in pale embers hid, lurks to aspire
    And girdle with embracing flames the waist
    Of Collatine's fair love, Lucrece the chaste.

Haply that name of 'chaste' unhap'ly set
This bateless edge on his keen appetite;
When Collatine unwisely did not let
To praise the clear unmatched red and white
Which triumph'd in that sky of his delight,
    Where mortal stars, as bright as heaven's beauties,
    With pure aspects did him peculiar duties.

For he the night before, in Tarquin's tent,
Unlock'd the treasure of his happy state;
What priceless wealth the heavens had him lent
In the possession of his beauteous mate;
Reckoning his fortune at such high-proud rate,
    That kings might be espoused to more fame,
    But king nor peer to such a peerless dame.

O happiness enjoy'd but of a few!
And, if possess'd, as soon decay'd and done
As is the morning's silver-melting dew
Against the golden splendour of the sun!
An expired date, cancell'd ere well begun:
    Honour and beauty, in the owner's arms,
    Are weakly fortress'd from a world of harms.

Beauty itself doth of itself persuade
The eyes of men without an orator;
What needeth, then, apologies be made,
To set forth that which is so singular?
Or why is Collatine the publisher
    Of that rich jewel he should keep unknown
    From thievish ears, because it is his own?

Perchance his boast of Lucrece' sovereignty
Suggested this proud issue of a king;
For by our ears our hearts oft tainted be:
Perchance that envy of so rich a thing,
Braving compare, disdainfully did sting
    His high-pitch'd thoughts, that meaner men should vaunt
    That golden hap which their superiors want.

But some untimely thought did instigate
His all-too-timeless speed, if none of those:
His honour, his affairs, his friends, his state,
Neglected all, with swift intent he goes
To quench the coal which in his liver glows.
    O rash-false heat, wrapp'd in repentant cold,
    Thy hasty spring still blasts, and ne'er grows old!

When at Collatium this false lord arriv'd,
Well was he welcom'd by the Roman dame,
Within whose face Beauty and Virtue striv'd
Which of them both should underprop her fame:
When virtue bragg'd, Beauty would blush for shame;
    When beauty boasted blushes, in despite
    Virtue would stain that o'er with silver white.

But beauty, in that white intituled,
From Venus' doves doth challenge that fair field:
Then Virtue claims from Beauty Beauty's red,
Which Virtue gave the golden age to gild
Their silver cheeks, and call'd it then their shield;
    Teaching them thus to use it in the fight, —
    When shame assail'd, the red should fence the white.

This heraldry in Lucrece' face was seen,
Argued by Beauty's red and Virtue's white:
Of either's colour was the other queen,
Proving from world's minority their right:
Yet their ambition makes them still to fight;
    The sovereignty of either being so great,
    That oft they interchange each other's seat.

This silent war of lilies and of roses,
Which Tarquin view'd in her fair face's field,
In their pure ranks his traitor eye encloses;
Where, lest between them both it should be kill'd,
The coward captive vanquished doth yield
    To those two armies that would let him go,
    Rather than triumph in so false a foe.

Now thinks he that her husband's shallow tongue, —
The niggard prodigal that prais'd her so, —
In that high task hath done her beauty wrong,
Which far exceeds his barren skill to show:
Therefore that praise which Collatine doth owe
    Enchanted Tarquin answers with surmise,
    In silent wonder of still-gazing eyes.

This earthly saint, adored by this devil,
Little suspecteth the false worshipper;
For unstain'd thoughts do seldom dream on evil;
Birds never lim'd no secret bushes fear:
So guiltless she securely gives good cheer
    And reverend welcome to her princely guest,
    Whose inward ill no outward harm express'd:

For that he colour'd with his high estate,
Hiding base sin in plaits of majesty;
That nothing in him seem'd inordinate,
Save sometime too much wonder of his eye,
Which, having all, all could not satisfy,
    But, poorly rich, so wanteth in his store,
    That, cloy'd with much, he pineth still for more.

But she, that never cop'd with stranger eyes,
Could pick no meaning from their parling looks,
Nor read the subtle-shining secrecies
Writ in the glassy margents of such books:
She touch'd no unknown baits, nor fear'd no hooks;
    Nor could she moralise his wanton sight,
    More than his eyes were open'd to the light.

He stories to her ears her husband's fame,
Won in the fields of fruitful Italy;
And decks with praises Collatine's high name,
Made glorious by his manly chivalry
With bruised arms and wreaths of victory:
    Her joy with heav'd-up hand she doth express,
    And, wordless, so greets heaven for his success.

Far from the purpose of his coming thither,
He makes excuses for his being there:
No cloudy show of stormy blustering weather
Doth yet in this fair welkin once appear;
Till sable Night, mother of dread and fear,
    Upon the world dim darkness doth display,
    And in her vaulty prison stows the Day.

For then is Tarquin brought unto his bed,
Intending weariness with heavy sprite;
For, after supper, long he questioned
With modest Lucrece, and wore out the night:
Now leaden slumber with life's strength doth fight,
    And every one to rest themselves betake,
    Save thieves, and cares, and troubled minds, that wake.

As one of which doth Tarquin lie revolving
The sundry dangers of his will's obtaining;
Yet ever to obtain his will resolving,
Though weak-built hopes persuade him to abstaining:
Despair to gain doth traffic oft for gaining;
    And when great treasure is the meed proposed,
    Though death be adjunct, there's no death supposed.

Those that much covet are with gain so fond,
That what they have not, that which they possess,
They scatter and unloose it from their bond,
And so, by hoping more, they have but less;
Or, gaining more, the profit of excess
    Is but to surfeit, and such griefs sustain,
    That they prove bankrout in this poor-rich gain.

The aim of all is but to nurse the life
With honour, wealth, and ease, in waning age;
And in this aim there is such thwarting strife,
That one for all, or all for one we gage;
As life for honour in fell battles' rage;
    Honour for wealth; and oft that wealth doth cost
    The death of all, and all together lost.

So that in vent'ring ill we leave to be
The things we are for that which we expect;
And this ambitious foul infirmity,
In having much, torments us with defect
Of that we have: so then we do neglect
  The thing we have; and, all for want of wit,
  Make something nothing by augmenting it.

Such hazard now must doting Tarquin make,
Pawning his honour to obtain his lust;
And for himself himself he must forsake:
Then where is truth, if there be no self-trust?
When shall he think to find a stranger just,
  When he himself himself confounds, betrays
  To slanderous tongues and wretched hateful
    days?

Now stole upon the time the dead of night,
When heavy sleep had clos'd up mortal eyes:
No comfortable star did lend his light,
No noise but owls' and wolves' death-boding cries;
Now serves the season that they may surprise
  The silly lambs: pure thoughts are dead and still,
  While lust and murder wakes to stain and kill.

And now this lustful lord leap'd from his bed,
Throwing his mantle rudely o'er his arm;
Is madly toss'd between desire and dread;
Th'one sweetly flatters, th'other feareth harm;
But honest fear, bewitch'd with lust's foul charm,
  Doth too-too oft betake him to retire,
  Beaten away by brain-sick rude desire.

Into the chamber wickedly he stalks.

His falchion on a flint he softly smiteth,
That from the cold stone sparks of fire do fly;
Whereat a waxen torch forthwith he lighteth,
Which must be lode-star to his lustful eye;
And to the flame thus speaks advisedly,
  'As from this cold flint I enforc'd this fire,
  So Lucrece must I force to my desire.'

Here pale with fear he doth premeditate
The dangers of his loathsome enterprise,
And in his inward mind he doth debate
What following sorrow may on this arise:
Then looking scornfully, he doth despise
  His naked armour of still-slaughter'd lust,
  And justly thus controls his thoughts unjust:

'Fair torch, burn out thy light, and lend it not
To darken her whose light excelleth thine:
And die, unhallow'd thoughts, before you blot
With your uncleanness that which is divine;
Offer pure incense to so pure a shrine:
  Let fair humanity abhor the deed
  That spots and stains love's modest snow-white
    weed.

'O shame to knighthood and to shining arms!
O foul dishonour to my household's grave!
O impious act, including all foul harms!
A martial man to be soft fancy's slave!
True valour still a true respect should have;
  Then my digression is so vile, so base,
  That it will live engraven in my face.

'Yea, though I die, the scandal will survive,
And be an eye-sore in my golden coat;
Some loathsome dash the herald will contrive,
To cipher me how fondly I did dote;
That my posterity, sham'd with the note,
  Shall curse my bones, and hold it for no sin
  To wish that I their father had not bin.

'What win I, if I gain the thing I seek?
A dream, a breath, a froth of fleeting joy.
Who buys a minute's mirth to wail a week?
Or sells eternity to get a toy?
For one sweet grape who will the vine destroy?
  Or what fond beggar, but to touch the crown,
  Would with the sceptre straight be stricken
    down?

'If Collatinus dream of my intent,
Will he not wake, and in a desperate rage
Post hither, this vile purpose to prevent?
This siege that hath engirt his marriage,
This blur to youth, this sorrow to the sage,
  This dying virtue, this surviving shame,
  Whose crime will bear an ever-during blame?

'O, what excuse can my invention make,
When thou shalt charge me with so black a deed?
Will not my tongue be mute, my frail joints shake,
Mine eyes forgo their light, my false heart bleed?
The guilt being great, the fear doth still exceed;
  And extreme fear can neither fight nor fly,
  But coward-like with trembling terror die.

'Had Collatinus kill'd my son or sire,
Or lain in ambush to betray my life,
Or were he not my dear friend, this desire
Might have excuse to work upon his wife,
As in revenge or quittal of such strife:
  But as he is my kinsman, my dear friend,
  The shame and fault finds no excuse nor end.

'Shameful it is; — ay, if the fact be known:
Hateful it is; — there is no hate in loving:
I'll beg her love; — but she is not her own:
The worst is but denial and reproving:
My will is strong, past reason's weak removing.
  Who fears a sentence or an old man's saw
  Shall by a painted cloth be kept in awe.'

Thus, graceless, holds he disputation
'Tween frozen conscience and hot burning will,
And with good thoughts makes dispensation,
Urging the worser sense for vantage still;
Which in a moment doth confound and kill
  All pure effects, and doth so far proceed,
  That what is vile shows like a virtuous deed.

Quoth he, 'She took me kindly by the hand,
And gaz'd for tidings in my eager eyes,
Fearing some hard news from the warlike band,
Where her beloved Collatinus lies.
O, how her fear did make her colour rise!
  First red as roses that on lawn we lay,
  Then white as lawn, the roses took away.

'And how her hand, in my hand being lock'd,
Forced it to tremble with her loyal fear!
Which struck her sad, and then it faster rock'd,
Until her husband's welfare she did hear;
Whereat she smiled with so sweet a cheer,
  That had Narcissus seen her as she stood,
  Self-love had never drown'd him in the flood.

'Why hunt I, then, for colour or excuses?
All orators are dumb when beauty pleadeth;
Poor wretches have remorse in poor abuses;
Love thrives not in the heart that shadows dreadeth:
Affection is my captain, and he leadeth;
  And when his gaudy banner is display'd,
  The coward fights, and will not be dismay'd.

'Then, childish fear avaunt! debating die!
Respect and reason wait on wrinkled age!
My heart shall never countermand mine eye:
Sad pause and deep regard beseems the sage;
My part is youth, and beats these from the stage:
  Desire my pilot is, beauty my prize;
  Then who fears sinking where such treasure lies?'

As corn o'ergrown by weeds, so heedful fear
Is almost chok'd by unresisted lust.
Away he steals with open listening ear,
Full of foul hope and full of fond mistrust;
Both which, as servitors to the unjust,
  So cross him with their opposite persuasion,
  That now he vows a league, and now invasion.

Within his thought her heavenly image sits,
And in the self-same seat sits Collatine:
That eye which looks on her confounds his wits;
That eye which him beholds, as more divine,
Unto a view so false will not incline;
  But with a pure appeal seeks to the heart,
  Which once corrupted takes the worser part;

And therein heartens up his servile powers,
Who, flatter'd by their leader's jocund show,
Stuff up his lust, as minutes fill up hours;
And as their captain, so their pride doth grow,
Paying more slavish tribute than they owe.
  By reprobate desire thus madly led,
  The Roman lord marcheth to Lucrece' bed.

The locks between her chamber and his will,
Each one by him enforc'd, retires his ward;
But, as they open, they all rate his ill,
Which drives the creeping thief to some regard:
The threshold grates the door to have him heard;
  Night-wandering weasels shriek to see him there;
  They fright him, yet he still pursues his fear.

As each unwilling portal yields him way,
Through little vents and crannies of the place
The wind wars with his torch to make him stay,
And blows the smoke of it into his face,
Extinguishing his conduct in this case;
  But his hot heart, which fond desire doth scorch,
  Puffs forth another wind that fires the torch:

And being lighted, by the light he spies
Lucretia's glove, wherein her needle sticks:
He takes it from the rushes where it lies,
And griping it, the needle his finger pricks;
As who should say, 'This glove to wanton tricks
  Is not inured; return again in haste;
  Thou see'st our mistress' ornaments are chaste.'

But all these poor forbiddings could not stay him;
He in the worst sense consters their denial:
The doors, the wind, the glove, that did delay him,
He takes for accidental things of trial;
Or as those bars which stop the hourly dial,
    Who with a lingering stay his course doth let,
    Till every minute pays the hour his debt.

'So, so,' quoth he, 'these lets attend the time,
Like little frosts that sometime threat the spring,
To add a more rejoicing to the prime,
And give the sneaped birds more cause to sing.
Pain pays the income of each precious thing;
    Huge rocks, high winds, strong pirates, shelves and
        sands,
    The merchant fears, ere rich at home he lands.'

Now is he come unto the chamber-door
That shuts him from the heaven of his thought,
Which with a yielding latch, and with no more,
Hath barr'd him from the blessed thing he sought.
So from himself impiety hath wrought,
    That for his prey to pray he doth begin,
    As if the heavens should countenance his sin.

But in the midst of his unfruitful prayer,
Having solicited th'eternal power
That his foul thoughts might compass his fair fair,
And they would stand auspicious to the hour,
Even there he starts: — quoth he, 'I must deflower:
    The powers to whom I pray abhor this fact,
    How can they, then, assist me in the act?

'Then Love and Fortune be my gods, my guide!
My will is back'd with resolution:
Thoughts are but dreams till their effects be tried;
The blackest sin is clear'd with absolution;
Against love's fire fear's frost hath dissolution.
    The eye of heaven is out, and misty night
    Covers the shame that follows sweet delight.'

This said, his guilty hand pluck'd up the latch,
And with his knee the door he opens wide.
The dove sleeps fast that this night-owl will catch:
Thus treason works ere traitors be espied.
Who sees the lurking serpent steps aside;
    But she, sound sleeping, fearing no such thing,
    Lies at the mercy of his mortal sting.

Into the chamber wickedly he stalks,
And gazeth on her yet-unstained bed.
The curtains being close, about he walks,
Rolling his greedy eyeballs in his head:
By their high treason is his heart misled;
    Which gives the watch-word to his hand full soon
    To draw the cloud that hides the silver moon.

Look, as the fair and fiery-pointed sun,
Rushing from forth a cloud, bereaves our sight;
Even so, the curtain drawn, his eyes begun
To wink, being blinded with a greater light:
Whether it is that she reflects so bright,
    That dazzleth them, or else some shame
        supposed;
    But blind they are, and keep themselves
        enclosed.

O, had they in that darksome prison died!
Then had they seen the period of their ill;
Then Collatine again, by Lucrece' side,
In his clear bed might have reposed still:
But they must ope, this blessed league to kill;
    And holy-thoughted Lucrece to their sight
    Must sell her joy, her life, her world's delight.

Her lily hand her rosy cheek lies under,
Cozening the pillow of a lawful kiss;
Who, therefore angry, seems to part in sunder,
Swelling on either side to want his bliss;
Between whose hills her head entombed is:
    Where, like a virtuous monument, she lies,
    To be admired of lewd unhallow'd eyes.

Without the bed her other fair hand was,
On the green coverlet; whose perfect white
Show'd like an April daisy on the grass,
With pearly sweat, resembling dew of night.
Her eyes, like marigolds, had sheath'd their light,
    And canopied in darkness sweetly lay,
    Till they might open to adorn the day.

Her hair, like golden threads, play'd with her breath;
O modest wantons! wanton modesty!
Showing life's triumph in the map of death,
And death's dim look in life's mortality:
Each in her sleep themselves so beautify,
    As if between them twain there were no strife,
    But that life liv'd in death, and death in life.

Her breasts, like ivory globes circled with blue,
A pair of maiden worlds unconquered,
Save of their lord no bearing yoke they knew,
And him by oath they truly honoured.
These worlds in Tarquin new ambition bred;
    Who, like a foul usurper, went about
    From this fair throne to heave the owner out.

What could he see but mightily he noted?
What did he note but strongly he desired?
What he beheld, on that he firmly doted,
And in his will his wilful eye he tired.
With more than admiration he admired
    Her azure veins, her alabaster skin,
    Her coral lips, her snow-white dimpled chin.

As the grim lion fawneth o'er his prey,
Sharp hunger by the conquest satisfied,
So o'er this sleeping soul doth Tarquin stay,
His rage of lust by gazing qualified;
Slack'd, not suppress'd; for standing by her side,
    His eye, which late this mutiny restrains,
    Unto a greater uproar tempts his veins:

And they, like straggling slaves for pillage
        fighting,
Obdurate vassals fell exploits effecting,
In bloody death and ravishment delighting,
Nor children's tears nor mother's groans respecting,
Swell in their pride, the onset still expecting.
    Anon his beating heart, alarum striking,
    Gives the hot charge, and bids them do their
        liking.

His drumming heart cheers up his burning eye,
His eye commends the leading to his hand;
His hand, as proud of such a dignity,
Smoking with pride, march'd on to make his stand
On her bare breast, the heart of all her land;
    Whose ranks of blue veins, as his hand did scale,
    Left their round turrets destitute and pale.

They, mustering to the quiet cabinet
Where their dear governess and lady lies,
Do tell her she is dreadfully beset,
And fright her with confusion of their cries:
She, much amaz'd, breaks ope her lock'd-up eyes,
    Who, peeping forth this tumult to behold,
    Are by his flaming torch dimm'd and controll'd.

Imagine her as one in dead of night
From forth dull sleep by dreadful fancy waking,
That thinks she hath beheld some ghastly sprite,
Whose grim aspect sets every joint a-shaking;
What terror 'tis! but she, in worser taking,
    From sleep disturbed, heedfully doth view
    The sight which makes supposed terror true.

Wrapp'd and confounded in a thousand fears,
Like to a new-kill'd bird she trembling lies;
She dares not look; yet, winking, there appears
Quick-shifting antics, ugly in her eyes:
Such shadows are the weak brain's forgeries;
    Who, angry that the eyes fly from their lights,
    In darkness daunts them with more dreadful
        sights.

His hand, that yet remains upon her breast, —
Rude ram, to batter such an ivory wall! —
May feel her heart — poor citizen! — distress'd,
Wounding itself to death, rise up and fall,
Beating her bulk, that his hand shakes withal.
    This moves in him more rage, and lesser pity,
    To make the breach, and enter this sweet city.

First, like a trumpet, doth his tongue begin
To sound a parley to his heartless foe;
Who o'er the white sheet peers her whiter chin,
The reason of this rash alarm to know,
Which he by dumb demeanour seeks to show;
    But she with vehement prayers urgeth still
    Under what colour he commits this ill.

Thus he replies: 'The colour in thy face —
That even for anger makes the lily pale,
And the red rose blush at her own disgrace —
Shall plead for me and tell my loving tale:
Under that colour am I come to scale
    Thy never-conquer'd fort: the fault is thine,
    For those thine eyes betray thee unto mine.

'Thus I forestall thee, if thou mean to chide:
Thy beauty hath ensnared thee to this night,
Where thou with patience must my will abide;
My will that marks thee for my earth's delight,
Which I to conquer sought with all my might;
    But as reproof and reason beat it dead,
    By thy bright beauty was it newly bred.

'I see what crosses my attempt will bring;
I know what thorns the growing rose defends;
I think the honey guarded with a sting;
All this beforehand counsel comprehends:
But will is deaf, and hears no heedful friends;
    Only he hath an eye to gaze on beauty,
    And dotes on what he looks, 'gainst law or duty.

'I have debated, even in my soul,
What wrong, what shame, what sorrow I shall
        breed;
But nothing can affection's course control,
Or stop the headlong fury of his speed.
I know repentant tears ensue the deed,
    Reproach, disdain, and deadly enmity;
    Yet strive I to embrace mine infamy.'

This said, he shakes aloft his Roman blade,
Which, like a falcon towering in the skies,
Coucheth the fowl below with his wings' shade,
Whose crooked beak threats if he mount he dies:
So under his insulting falchion lies
    Harmless Lucretia, marking what he tells
    With trembling fear, as fowl hear falcon's bells.

'Lucrece,' quoth he, 'this night I must enjoy thee:
If thou deny, then force must work my way,
For in thy bed I purpose to destroy thee:
That done, some worthless slave of thine I'll slay,
To kill thine honour with thy life's decay;
    And in thy dead arms do I mean to place him,
    Swearing I slew him, seeing thee embrace him.

'So thy surviving husband shall remain
The scornful mark of every open eye;
Thy kinsmen hang their heads at this disdain,
Thy issue blurr'd with nameless bastardy:
And thou, the author of their obloquy,
    Shalt have thy trespass cited up in rimes,
    And sung by children in succeeding times.

'But if thou yield, I rest thy secret friend:
The fault unknown is as a thought unacted;
A little harm done to a great good end
For lawful policy remains enacted.
The poisonous simple sometime is compacted
    In a pure compound; being so applied,
    His venom in effect is purified.

'Then, for thy husband and thy children's sake,
Tender my suit: bequeath not to their lot
The shame that from them no device can take,
The blemish that will never be forgot;
Worse than a slavish wipe or birth-hour's blot:
    For marks descried in men's nativity
    Are nature's faults, not their own infamy.'

Here with a cockatrice' dead-killing eye
He rouseth up himself, and makes a pause;
While she, the picture of pure piety,
Like a white hind under the gripe's sharp claws,
Pleads, in a wilderness where are no laws,
    To the rough beast that knows no gentle right,
    Nor aught obeys but his foul appetite.

But when a black-fac'd cloud the world doth
        threat,
In his dim mist the aspiring mountains hiding,
From earth's dark womb some gentle gust doth get,
Which blows these pitchy vapours from their
        biding,
Hindering their present fall by this dividing;
    So his unhallow'd haste her words delays,
    And moody Pluto winks while Orpheus plays.

Yet, foul night-waking cat, he doth but dally,
While in his hold-fast foot the weak mouse panteth:
Her sad behaviour feeds his vulture folly,
A swallowing gulf that even in plenty wanteth:
His ear her prayers admits, but his heart granteth
    No penetrable entrance to her plaining:
    Tears harden lust, though marble wear with raining.

Her pity-pleading eyes are sadly fixed
In the remorseless wrinkles of his face;
Her modest eloquence with sighs is mixed,
Which to her oratory adds more grace.
She puts the period often from his place;
    And midst the sentence so her accent breaks,
    That twice she doth begin ere once she speaks.

She conjures him by high almighty Jove,
By knighthood, gentry, and sweet friendship's oath,
By her untimely tears, her husband's love,
By holy human law, and common troth,
By heaven and earth, and all the power of both,
    That to his borrow'd bed he make retire,
    And stoop to honour, not to foul desire.

Quoth she, 'Reward not hospitality
With such black payment as thou hast pretended;
Mud not the fountain that gave drink to thee;
Mar not the thing that cannot be amended;
End thy ill aim before thy shoot be ended;
    He is no woodman that doth bend his bow
    To strike a poor unseasonable doe.

'My husband is thy friend, — for his sake spare me;
Thyself art mighty, — for thine own sake leave me;
Myself a weakling, — do not, then, ensnare me;
Thou look'st not like deceit, — do not deceive me.
My sighs, like whirlwinds, labour hence to heave
    thee:
    If ever man were mov'd with woman's moans,
    Be moved with my tears, my sighs, my groans:

'All which together, like a troubled ocean,
Beat at thy rocky and wrack-threatening heart,
To soften it with their continual motion;
For stones dissolv'd to water do convert.
O, if no harder than a stone thou art,
    Melt at my tears, and be compassionate!
    Soft pity enters at an iron gate.

'In Tarquin's likeness I did entertain thee:
Hast thou put on his shape to do him shame?
To all the host of heaven I complain me,
Thou wrong'st his honour, wound'st his princely
    name.
Thou art not what thou seem'st; and if the same,
    Thou seem'st not what thou art, a god, a king;
    For kings like gods should govern every thing.

'How will thy shame be seeded in thine age,
When thus thy vices bud before thy spring!
If in thy hope thou darest do such outrage,
What darest thou not when once thou art a king?
O, be remember'd, no outrageous thing
    From vassal actors can be wip'd away;
    Then kings' misdeeds cannot be hid in clay.

'This deed will make thee only lov'd for fear;
But happy monarchs still are fear'd for love:
With foul offenders thou perforce must bear,
When they in thee the like offences prove,
If but for fear of this, thy will remove;
    For princes are the glass, the school, the book,
    Where subjects' eyes do learn, do read, do look.

'And wilt thou be the school where Lust shall learn?
Must he in thee read lectures of such shame?
Wilt thou be glass wherein it shall discern
Authority for sin, warrant for blame,
To privilege dishonour in thy name?
    Thou back'st reproach against long-living laud,
    And mak'st fair reputation but a bawd.

'Hast thou command? by him that gave it thee,
From a pure heart command thy rebel will:
Draw not thy sword to guard iniquity,
For it was lent thee all that brood to kill.
Thy princely office how canst thou fulfil,
    When, pattern'd by thy fault, foul Sin may say,
    He learnt to sin, and thou didst teach the way?

'Think but how vile a spectacle it were,
To view thy present trespass in another.
Men's faults do seldom to themselves appear;
Their own transgressions partially they smother:
This guilt would seem death-worthy in thy brother.
    O, how are they wrapt in with infamies
    That from their own misdeeds askance their eyes!

'To thee, to thee, my heav'd-up hands appeal,
Not to seducing lust, thy rash relier:
I sue for exil'd majesty's repeal:
Let him return, and flattering thoughts retire:
His true respect will prison false desire,
    And wipe the dim mist from thy doting eyne,
    That thou shalt see thy state, and pity mine.'

'Have done,' quoth he: 'my uncontrolled tide
Turns not, but swells the higher by this let.
Small lights are soon blown out, huge fires abide,
And with the wind in greater fury fret:
The petty streams that pay a daily debt
    To their salt sovereign, with their fresh falls' haste
    Add to his flow, but alter not his taste.'

'Thou art,' quoth she, 'a sea, a sovereign king;
And, lo, there falls into thy boundless flood
Black lust, dishonour, shame, misgoverning,
Who seek to stain the ocean of thy blood.
If all these petty ills shall change thy good,
    Thy sea within a puddle's womb is hearsed,
    And not the puddle in thy sea dispersed.

'So shall these slaves be king, and thou their slave;
Thou nobly base, they basely dignified;
Thou their fair life, and they thy fouler grave:
Thou loathed in their shame, they in thy pride:
The lesser thing should not the greater hide;
    The cedar stoops not to the base shrub's foot,
    But low shrubs wither at the cedar's root.

'So let thy thoughts, low vassals to thy state' —
'No more,' quoth he; 'by heaven, I will not hear
    thee:
Yield to my love; if not, enforced hate,
Instead of love's coy touch, shall rudely tear thee;
That done, despitefully I mean to bear thee
    Unto the base bed of some rascal groom,
    To be thy partner in this shameful doom.'

This said, he sets his foot upon the light,
For light and lust are deadly enemies:
Shame folded up in blind-concealing night,
When most unseen, then most doth tyrannise.
The wolf hath seiz'd his prey, the poor lamb cries;
    Till with her own white fleece her voice controll'd
    Entombs her outcry in her lips' sweet fold:

For with the nightly linen that she wears
He pens her piteous clamours in her head;
Cooling his hot face in the chastest tears
That ever modest eyes with sorrow shed.
O, that prone lust should stain so pure a bed!
    The spots whereof could weeping purify,
    Her tears should drop on them perpetually.

But she hath lost a dearer thing than life,
And he hath won what he would lose again:
This forced league doth force a further strife;
This momentary joy breeds months of pain;
This hot desire converts to cold disdain:
    Pure Chastity is rifled of her store,
    And Lust, the thief, far poorer than before.

Look, as the full-fed hound or gorged hawk,
Unapt for tender smell or speedy flight,
Make slow pursuit, or altogether balk
The prey wherein by nature they delight;
So surfeit-taking Tarquin fares this night:
    His taste delicious, in digestion souring,
    Devours his will, that liv'd by foul devouring.

O, deeper sin than bottomless conceit
Can comprehend in still imagination!
Drunken Desire must vomit his receipt,
Ere he can see his own abomination.
While Lust is in his pride, no exclamation
    Can curb his heat, or rein his rash desire,
    Till, like a jade, Self-will himself doth tire.

And then with lank and lean discolour'd cheek,
With heavy eye, knit brow, and strengthless pace,
Feeble Desire, all recreant, poor, and meek,
Like to a bankrout beggar wails his case:
The flesh being proud, Desire doth fight with Grace,
    For there it revels; and when that decays,
    The guilty rebel for remission prays.

So fares it with this faultful lord of Rome,
Who this accomplishment so hotly chased;
For now against himself he sounds this doom, —
That through the length of times he stands disgraced:
Besides, his soul's fair temple is defaced;
    To whose weak ruins muster troops of cares,
    To ask the spotted princess how she fares.

She says, her subjects with foul insurrection
Have batter'd down her consecrated wall,
And by their mortal fault brought in subjection
Her immortality, and made her thrall
To living death and pain perpetual:
    Which in her prescience she controlled still,
    But her foresight could not forestall their will.

Even in this thought through the dark night he
    stealeth,
A captive victor that hath lost in gain;
Bearing away the wound that nothing healeth,
The scar that will, despite of cure, remain;
Leaving his spoil perplex'd in greater pain.
    She bears the load of lust he left behind,
    And he the burden of a guilty mind.

He like a thievish dog creeps sadly thence;
She like a wearied lamb lies panting there;
He scowls, and hates himself for his offence;
She, desperate, with her nails her flesh doth tear;
He faintly flies, sweating with guilty fear;
    She stays, exclaiming on the direful night;
    He runs, and chides his vanish'd, loath'd delight.

He thence departs a heavy convertite;
She there remains a hopeless castaway;
He in his speed looks for the morning light;
She prays she never may behold the day,
'For day,' quoth she, 'night's scapes doth open lay,
    And my true eyes have never practis'd how
    To cloak offences with a cunning brow.

'They think not but that every eye can see
The same disgrace which they themselves behold;
And therefore would they still in darkness be,
To have their unseen sin remain untold;
For they their guilt with weeping will unfold,
    And grave, like water that doth eat in steel,
    Upon my cheeks what helpless shame I feel.'

Here she exclaims against repose and rest,
And bids her eyes hereafter still be blind.
She wakes her heart by beating on her breast,
And bids it leap from thence, where it may find
Some purer chest to close so pure a mind.
    Frantic with grief thus breathes she forth her spite
    Against the unseen secrecy of night:

'O comfort-killing Night, image of hell!
Dim register and notary of shame!
Black stage for tragedies and murders fell!
Vast sin-concealing chaos! nurse of blame!
Blind muffled bawd! dark harbour for defame!
    Grim cave of death! whisp'ring conspirator
    With close-tongued treason and the ravisher!

'O hateful, vaporous, and foggy Night!
Since thou art guilty of my cureless crime,
Muster thy mists to meet the eastern light,
Make war against proportion'd course of time;
Or if thou wilt permit the sun to climb
    His wonted height, yet ere he go to bed,
    Knit poisonous clouds about his golden head.

'With rotten damps ravish the morning air;
Let their exhal'd unwholesome breaths make sick
The life of purity, the supreme fair,
Ere he arrive his weary noon-tide prick;
And let thy misty vapours march so thick,
    That in their smoky ranks his smother'd light
    May set at noon, and make perpetual night.

'Were Tarquin Night, as he is but Night's child,
The silver-shining queen he would distain;
Her twinkling handmaids too, by him defil'd,
Through Night's black bosom should not peep again:
   So should I have co-partners in my pain;
     And fellowship in woe doth woe assuage,
     As palmers' chat makes short their pilgrimage.

'Where now I have no one to blush with me,
To cross their arms, and hang their heads with mine,
To mask their brows, and hide their infamy;
But I alone, alone must sit and pine,
   Seasoning the earth with showers of silver brine,
     Mingling my talk with tears, my grief with groans,
     Poor wasting monuments of lasting moans.

'O Night, thou furnace of foul-reeking smoke,
Let not the jealous Day behold that face
Which underneath thy black all-hiding cloak
Immodestly lies martyr'd with disgrace!
   Keep still possession of thy gloomy place,
     That all the faults which in thy reign are made
     May likewise be sepulchred in thy shade!

'Make me not object to the tell-tale Day!
The light will show, character'd in my brow,
The story of sweet chastity's decay,
The impious breach of holy wedlock vow:
   Yea, the illiterate, that know not how
     To cipher what is writ in learned books,
     Will quote my loathsome trespass in my looks.

'The nurse, to still her child, will tell my story,
And fright her crying babe with Tarquin's name:
The orator, to deck his oratory,
Will couple my reproach to Tarquin's shame;
   Feast-finding minstrels, tuning my defame,
     Will tie the hearers to attend each line,
     How Tarquin wronged me, I Collatine.

'Let my good name, that senseless reputation,
For Collatine's dear love be kept unspotted:
If that be made a theme for disputation,
The branches of another root are rotted,
   And undeserv'd reproach to him allotted
     That is as clear from this attaint of mine
     As I, ere this, was pure to Collatine.

'O unseen shame! invisible disgrace!
O unfelt sore! crest-wounding, private scar!
Reproach is stamp'd in Collatinus' face,
And Tarquin's eye may read the mot afar,
How he in peace is wounded, not in war.
   Alas, how many bear such shameful blows,
     Which not themselves, but he that gives them
     knows!

'If, Collatine, thine honour lay in me,
From me by strong assault it is bereft.
My honey lost, and I, a drone-like bee,
Have no perfection of my summer left,
But robb'd and ransack'd by injurious theft:
   In thy weak hive a wandering wasp hath crept,
     And suck'd the honey which thy chaste bee
     kept.

'Yet am I guilty of thy honour's wrack, —
Yet for thy honour did I entertain him;
Coming from thee, I could not put him back,
For it had been dishonour to disdain him:
   Besides, of weariness he did complain him,
     And talk'd of virtue: — O unlook'd-for evil,
     When virtue is profan'd in such a devil!

'Why should the worm intrude the maiden bud?
Or hateful cuckoos hatch in sparrows' nests?
Or toads infect fair founts with venom mud?
Or tyrant folly lurk in gentle breasts?
Or kings be breakers of their own behests?
   But no perfection is so absolute,
     That some impurity doth not pollute.

'The aged man that coffers-up his gold
Is plagued with cramps and gouts and painful fits;
And scarce hath eyes his treasure to behold,
And like still-pining Tantalus he sits,
And useless barns the harvest of his wits,
   Having no other pleasure of his gain
     But torment that it cannot cure his pain.

'So then he hath it when he cannot use it,
And leaves it to be master'd by his young;
Who in their pride do presently abuse it:
Their father was too weak, and they too strong,
To hold their cursed-blessed fortune long.
   The sweets we wish for turn to loathed sours
     Even in the moment that we call them ours.

'Unruly blasts wait on the tender spring;
Unwholesome weeds take root with precious flowers;
The adder hisses where the sweet birds sing;
What virtue breeds iniquity devours:
We have no good that we can say is ours,
   But ill-annexed Opportunity
     Or kills his life or else his quality.

'O Opportunity, thy guilt is great!
'Tis thou that execut'st the traitor's treason;
Thou sett'st the wolf where he the lamb may get;
Whoever plots the sin, thou point'st the season;
'Tis thou that spurn'st at right, at law, at reason;
   And in thy shady cell, where none may spy him,
     Sits Sin, to seize the souls that wander by him.

'Thou makest the vestal violate her oath;
Thou blow'st the fire when temperance is thaw'd;
Thou smother'st honesty, thou murder'st troth;
Thou foul abettor! thou notorious bawd!
Thou plantest scandal, and displacest laud:
   Thou ravisher, thou traitor, thou false thief,
     Thy honey turns to gall, thy joy to grief!

'Thy secret pleasure turns to open shame,
Thy private feasting to a public fast,
Thy smoothing titles to a ragged name,
Thy sugar'd tongue to bitter wormwood taste:
Thy violent vanities can never last.
   How comes it, then, vile Opportunity,
     Being so bad, such numbers seek for thee?

'When wilt thou be the humble suppliant's friend,
And bring him where his suit may be obtained?
When wilt thou sort an hour great strifes to end?
Or free that soul which wretchedness hath chained?
Give physic to the sick, ease to the pained?
   The poor, lame, blind, halt, creep, cry out for thee;
     But they ne'er meet with Opportunity.

'The patient dies while the physician sleeps;
The orphan pines while the oppressor feeds;
Justice is feasting while the widow weeps;
Advice is sporting while infection breeds:
Thou grant'st no time for charitable deeds:
   Wrath, envy, treason, rape, and murder's rages,
     Thy heinous hours wait on them as their pages.

'When Truth and Virtue have to do with thee,
A thousand crosses keep them from thy aid:
They buy thy help; but Sin ne'er gives a fee,
He gratis comes; and thou art well appaid
As well to hear as grant what he hath said.
   My Collatine would else have come to me
     When Tarquin did, but he was stay'd by thee.

'Guilty thou art of murder and of theft,
Guilty of perjury and subornation,
Guilty of treason, forgery, and shift,
Guilty of incest, that abomination;
An accessory by thine inclination
   To all sins past, and all that are to come,
     From the creation to the general doom.

'Mis-shapen Time, copesmate of ugly Night,
Swift subtle post, carrier of grisly care,
Eater of youth, false slave to false delight,
Base watch of woes, sin's pack-horse, virtue's
  snare;
Thou nursest all, and murder'st all that are:
   O, hear me, then, injurious, shifting Time!
     Be guilty of my death, since of my crime.

'Why hath thy servant Opportunity
Betray'd the hours thou gavest me to repose,
Cancell'd my fortunes, and enchained me
To endless date of never-ending woes?
Time's office is to fine the hate of foes;
   To eat up errors by opinion bred,
     Not spend the dowry of a lawful bed.

'Time's glory is to calm contending kings,
To unmask falsehood, and bring truth to light,
To stamp the seal of time in aged things,
To wake the morn, and sentinel the night,
To wrong the wronger till he render right,
   To ruinate proud buildings with thy hours,
     And smear with dust their glittering golden towers;

'To fill with worm-holes stately monuments,
To feed oblivion with decay of things,
To blot old books and alter their contents,
To pluck the quills from ancient ravens' wings,
To dry the old oak's sap, and cherish springs,
   To spoil antiquities of hammer'd steel,
     And turn the giddy round of Fortune's wheel;

'To show the beldam daughters of her daughter,
To make the child a man, the man a child,
To slay the tiger that doth live by slaughter,
To tame the unicorn and lion wild,
To mock the subtle in themselves beguil'd,
   To cheer the ploughman with increaseful crops
     And waste huge stones with little water-drops.

'Why work'st thou mischief in thy pilgrimage,
Unless thou couldst return to make amends?
One poor retiring minute in an age
Would purchase thee a thousand thousand friends,
Lending him wit that to bad debtors lends:
   O, this dread night, wouldst thou one hour come
   back,
     I could prevent this storm, and shun thy wrack!

'Thou ceaseless lackey to eternity,
With some mischance cross Tarquin in his flight:
Devise extremes beyond extremity,
To make him curse this cursed crimeful night:
Let ghastly shadows his lewd eyes affright;
   And the dire thought of his committed evil
     Shape every bush a hideous shapeless devil.

'Disturb his hours of rest with restless trances,
Afflict him in his bed with bed-rid groans;
Let there bechance him pitiful mischances,
To make him moan; but pity not his moans:
Stone him with harden'd hearts, harder than stones;
   And let mild women to him lose their mildness,
     Wilder to him than tigers in their wildness.

'Let him have time to tear his curled hair,
Let him have time against himself to rave,
Let him have time of Time's help to despair,
Let him have time to live a loathed slave,
Let him have time a beggar's orts to crave,
   And time to see one that by alms doth live
     Disdain to him disdained scraps to give.

'Let him have time to see his friends his foes,
And merry fools to mock at him resort;
Let him have time to mark how slow time goes
In time of sorrow, and how swift and short
His time of folly and his time of sport;
   And ever let his unrecalling crime
     Have time to wail th'abusing of his time.

'O Time, thou tutor both to good and bad,
Teach me to curse him that thou taught'st this ill!
At his own shadow let the thief run mad,
Himself himself seek every hour to kill!
Such wretched hands such wretched blood should spill;
   For who so base would such an office have
     As slanderous death's-man to so base a slave?

'The baser is he, coming from a king,
To shame his hope with deeds degenerate:
The mightier man, the mightier is the thing
That makes him honour'd, or begets him hate;
For greatest scandal waits on greatest state.
   The moon being clouded presently is miss'd,
     But little stars may hide them when they list.

'The crow may bathe his coal-black wings in mire,
And unperceiv'd fly with the filth away;
But if the like the snow-white swan desire,
The stain upon his silver down will stay.
Poor grooms are sightless night, kings glorious day:
   Gnats are unnoted wheresoe'er they fly,
     But eagles gaz'd upon with every eye.

'Out, idle words, servants to shallow fools!
Unprofitable sounds, weak arbitrators!
Busy yourselves in skill-contending schools;
Debate where leisure serves with dull debaters;
To trembling clients be you mediators:
    For me, I force not argument a straw,
    Since that my case is past the help of law.

'In vain I rail at Opportunity,
At Time, at Tarquin, and uncheerful Night;
In vain I cavil with mine infamy,
In vain I spurn at my confirm'd despite:
This helpless smoke of words doth me no right.
    The remedy indeed to do me good
    Is to let forth my foul defiled blood.

'Poor hand, why quiver'st thou at this decree?
Honour thyself to rid me of this shame;
For if I die, my honour lives in thee;
But if I live, thou livest in my defame:
Since thou couldst not defend thy loyal dame,
    And wast afeard to scratch her wicked foe,
    Kill both thyself and her for yielding so.'

This said, from her betumbled couch she starteth,
To find some desperate instrument of death:
But this no slaughter-house no tool imparteth
To make more vent for passage of her breath;
Which, thronging through her lips, so vanisheth
    As smoke from Aetna, that in air consumes,
    Or that which from discharged cannon fumes.

'In vain,' quoth she, 'I live, and seek in vain
Some happy mean to end a hapless life.
I fear'd by Tarquin's falchion to be slain,
Yet for the self-same purpose seek a knife:
But when I fear'd I was a loyal wife:
    So am I now: — O no, that cannot be;
    Of that true type hath Tarquin rifled me.

'O, that is gone for which I sought to live,
And therefore now I need not fear to die.
To clear this spot by death, at least I give
A badge of fame to slander's livery;
A dying life to living infamy:
    Poor helpless help, the treasure stol'n away,
    To burn the guiltless casket where it lay!

'Well, well, dear Collatine, thou shalt not know
The stained taste of violated troth;
I will not wrong thy true affection so,
To flatter thee with an infringed oath;
This bastard graff shall never come to growth:
    He shall not boast who did thy stock pollute
    That thou art doting father of his fruit.

'Nor shall he smile at thee in secret thought,
Nor laugh with his companions at thy state;
But thou shalt know thy interest was not bought
Basely with gold, but stol'n from forth thy gate.
For me, I am the mistress of my fate,
    And with my trespass never will dispense,
    Till life to death acquit my forc'd offence.

'I will not poison thee with my attaint,
Nor fold my fault in cleanly-coin'd excuses;
My sable ground of sin I will not paint,
To hide the truth of this false night's abuses:
My tongue shall utter all; mine eyes, like sluices,
    As from a mountain-spring that feeds a dale,
    Shall gush pure streams to purge my impure tale.'

By this, lamenting Philomel had ended
The well-tun'd warble of her nightly sorrow,
And solemn night with slow sad gait descended
To ugly hell; when, lo, the blushing morrow
Lends light to all fair eyes that light will borrow:
    But cloudy Lucrece shames herself to see,
    And therefore still in night would cloister'd be.

Revealing day through every cranny spies,
And seems to point her out where she sits weeping;
To whom she sobbing speaks: 'O eye of eyes,
Why pry'st thou through my window? leave thy
    peeping;
Mock with thy tickling beams eyes that are
    sleeping:
    Brand not my forehead with thy piercing light,
    For day hath naught to do what's done by night.'

Thus cavils she with every thing she sees:
True grief is fond and testy as a child,
Who wayward once, his mood with naught agrees:
Old woes, not infant sorrows, bear them mild;
Continuance tames the one; the other wild,
    Like an unpractis'd swimmer plunging still,
    With too much labour drowns for want of skill.

So she, deep-drenched in a sea of care,
Holds disputation with each thing she views,
And to herself all sorrow doth compare;
No object but her passion's strength renews;
And as one shifts, another straight ensues:
    Sometime her grief is dumb, and hath no words;
    Sometime 'tis mad, and too much talk affords.

The little birds that tune their morning's joy
Make her moans mad with their sweet melody:
For mirth doth search the bottom of annoy;
Sad souls are slain in merry company;
Grief best is pleas'd with grief's society:
    True sorrow then is feelingly sufficed
    When with like semblance it is sympathised.

'Tis double death to drown in ken of shore;
He ten times pines that pines beholding food;
To see the salve doth make the wound ache more;
Great grief grieves most at that would do it good;
Deep woes roll forward like a gentle flood,
    Who, being stopp'd, the bounding banks o'erflows;
    Grief dallied with nor law nor limit knows.

'You mocking birds,' quoth she, 'your tunes entomb
Within your hollow swelling feather'd breasts,
And in my hearing be you mute and dumb:
My restless discord loves no stops nor rests;
A woeful hostess brooks not merry guests:
    Relish your nimble notes to pleasing ears;
    Distress likes dumps when time is kept with tears.

'Come, Philomel, that sing'st of ravishment,
Make thy sad grove in my dishevell'd hair:
As the dank earth weeps at thy languishment,
So I at each sad strain will strain a tear,
And with deep groans the diapason bear;
    For burden-wise I'll hum on Tarquin still,
    While thou on Tereus descant'st better skill.

'And whiles against a thorn thou bear'st thy part,
To keep thy sharp woes waking, wretched I,
To imitate thee well, against my heart
Will fix a sharp knife, to affright mine eye;
Who, if it wink, shall thereon fall and die.
    These means, as frets upon an instrument,
    Shall tune our heart-strings to true languishment.

'And for, poor bird, thou sing'st not in the day,
As shaming any eye should thee behold,
Some dark-deep desert, seated from the way,
That knows not parching heat nor freezing cold,
Will we find out; and there we will unfold
    To creatures stern sad tunes, to change their kinds:
    Since men prove beasts, let beasts bear gentle
        minds.'

As the poor frighted deer, that stands at gaze,
Wildly determining which way to fly,
Or one encompass'd with a winding maze,
That cannot tread the way out readily;
So with herself is she in mutiny,
    To live or die, which of the twain were better,
    When life is sham'd, and death reproach's debtor.

'To kill myself,' quoth she, 'alack, what were it,
But with my body my poor soul's pollution?
They that lose half with greater patience bear it
Than they whose whole is swallow'd in confusion.
That mother tries a merciless conclusion
    Who, having two sweet babes, when death takes one,
    Will slay the other, and be nurse to none.

'My body or my soul, which was the dearer,
When the one pure, the other made divine?
Whose love of either to myself was nearer,
When both were kept for heaven and Collatine?
Ay me! the bark pill'd from the lofty pine,
    His leaves will wither, and his sap decay;
    So must my soul, her bark being pill'd away.

'Her house is sack'd, her quiet interrupted,
Her mansion batter'd by the enemy;
Her sacred temple spotted, spoil'd, corrupted,
Grossly engirt with daring infamy:
Then let it not be call'd impiety,
    If in this blemish'd fort I make some hole
    Through which I may convey this troubled soul.

'Yet die I will not till my Collatine
Have heard the cause of my untimely death;
That he may vow, in that sad hour of mine,
Revenge on him that made me stop my breath.
My stained blood to Tarquin I'll bequeath,
    Which by him tainted shall for him be spent,
    And as his due writ in my testament.

'My honour I'll bequeath unto the knife
That wounds my body, so dishonoured.
'Tis honour to deprive dishonour'd life;
The one will live, the other being dead:
So of shame's ashes shall my fame be bred;
    For in my death I murder shameful scorn:
    My shame so dead, mine honour is new-born.

'Dear lord of that dear jewel I have lost,
What legacy shall I bequeath to thee?
My resolution, love, shall be thy boast,
By whose example thou reveng'd mayst be.
How Tarquin must be us'd, read it in me:
    Myself, thy friend, will kill myself, thy foe,
    And, for my sake, serve thou false Tarquin so.

'This brief abridgement of my will I make: —
My soul and body to the skies and ground;
My resolution, husband, do thou take;
Mine honour be the knife's that makes my wound;
My shame be his that did my fame confound;
    And all my fame that lives disbursed be
    To those that live, and think no shame of me.

'Thou, Collatine, shalt oversee this will;
How was I overseen that thou shalt see it!
My blood shall wash the slander of mine ill;
My life's foul deed, my life's fair end shall free it.
Faint not, faint heart, but stoutly say "So be it":
    Yield to my hand; my hand shall conquer thee:
    Thou dead, both die and both shall victors be.'

This plot of death when sadly she had laid,
And wip'd the brinish pearl from her bright eyes,
With untun'd tongue she hoarsely calls her maid,
Whose swift obedience to her mistress hies;
For fleet-wing'd duty with thought's feathers flies.
    Poor Lucrece' cheeks unto her maid seem so
    As winter meads when sun doth melt their snow.

Her mistress she doth give demure good-morrow,
With soft-slow tongue, true mark of modesty,
And sorts a sad look to her lady's sorrow,
For why her face wore sorrow's livery;
But durst not ask of her audaciously
    Why her two suns were cloud-eclipsed so,
    Nor why her fair cheeks overwash'd with woe.

But as the earth doth weep, the sun being set,
Each flower moisten'd like a melting eye,
Even so the maid with swelling drops gan wet
Her circled eyne, enforc'd by sympathy
Of those fair suns set in her mistress' sky,
    Who in a salt-wav'd ocean quench their light,
    Which makes the maid weep like the dewy night.

A pretty while these pretty creatures stand,
Like ivory conduits coral cisterns filling:
One justly weeps; the other takes in hand
No cause, but company, of her drops spilling:
Their gentle sex to weep are often willing;
    Grieving themselves to guess at others' smarts,
    And then they drown their eyes, or break their
        hearts.

For men have marble, women waxen, minds,
And therefore are they form'd as marble will;
The weak oppress'd, the impression of strange kinds
Is form'd in them by force, by fraud, or skill:
Then call them not the authors of their ill,
    No more than wax shall be accounted evil
    Wherein is stamp'd the semblance of a devil.

Their smoothness, like a goodly champaign plain,
Lays open all the little worms that creep;
In men, as in a rough-grown grove, remain
Cave-keeping evils that obscurely sleep:
Through crystal walls each little mote will peep:
    Though men can cover crimes with bold stern looks,
    Poor women's faces are their own faults' books.

No man inveigh against the wither'd flower,
But chide rough winter that the flower hath kill'd:
Not that devour'd, but that which doth devour,
Is worthy blame. O, let it not be hild
Poor women's faults, that they are so fulfill'd
    With men's abuses: those proud lords, to blame,
    Make weak-made women tenants to their shame.

The precedent whereof in Lucrece view,
Assail'd by night with circumstances strong
Of present death, and shame that might ensue
By that her death, to do her husband wrong:
Such danger to resistance did belong,
    That dying fear through all her body spread;
    And who cannot abuse a body dead?

By this, mild patience bid fair Lucrece speak
To the poor counterfeit of her complaining:
'My girl,' quoth she, 'on what occasion break
Those tears from thee, that down thy cheeks are
        raining?
If thou dost weep for grief of my sustaining,
    Know, gentle wench, it small avails my mood:
    If tears could help, mine own would do me good.

'But tell me, girl, when went'— and there she stay'd
Till after a deep groan — 'Tarquin from hence?'
'Madam, ere I was up,' replied the maid,
'The more to blame my sluggard negligence:
Yet with the fault I thus far can dispense, —
    Myself was stirring ere the break of day,
    And ere I rose was Tarquin gone away.

'But, lady, if your maid may be so bold,
She would request to know your heaviness.'
'O, peace!' quoth Lucrece: 'if it should be told,
The repetition cannot make it less,
For more it is than I can well express:
    And that deep torture may be call'd a hell
    When more is felt than one hath power to tell.

'Go, get me hither paper, ink, and pen, —
Yet save that labour, for I have them here.
What should I say? — One of my husband's men
Bid thou be ready, by and by, to bear
A letter to my lord, my love, my dear:
    Bid him with speed prepare to carry it;
    The cause craves haste, and it will soon be writ.'

Her maid is gone, and she prepares to write,
First hovering o'er the paper with her quill:
Conceit and grief an eager combat fight;
What wit sets down is blotted straight with will;
This is too curious-good, this blunt and ill:
    Much like a press of people at a door,
    Throng her inventions, which shall go before.

At last she thus begins: 'Thou worthy lord
Of that unworthy wife that greeteth thee,
Health to thy person! next vouchsafe t'afford —
If ever, love, thy Lucrece thou wilt see —
Some present speed to come and visit me.
    So, I commend me from our house in grief:
    My woes are tedious, though my words are brief.'

Here folds she up the tenour of her woe,
Her certain sorrow writ uncertainly.
By this short schedule Collatine may know
Her grief, but not her grief's true quality:
She dares not thereof make discovery,
    Lest he should hold it her own gross abuse,
    Ere she with blood had stain'd her stain'd excuse.

Besides, the life and feeling of her passion
She hoards, to spend when he is by to hear her;
When sighs and groans and tears may grace the
        fashion
Of her disgrace, the better so to clear her
From that suspicion which the world might bear her.
    To shun this blot, she would not blot the letter
    With words, till action might become them better.

To see sad sights moves more than hear them told;
For then the eye interprets to the ear
The heavy motion that it doth behold,
When every part a part of woe doth bear.
'Tis but a part of sorrow that we hear:
    Deep sounds make lesser noise than shallow
        fords,
    And sorrow ebbs, being blown with wind of words.

Her letter now is seal'd, and on it writ,
'At Ardea to my lord with more than haste.'
The post attends, and she delivers it,
Charging the sour-fac'd groom to hie as fast
As lagging fowls before the northern blast:
    Speed more than speed but dull and slow she
        deems:
    Extremity still urgeth such extremes.

The homely villain court'sies to her low;
And, blushing on her, with a steadfast eye
Receives the scroll without or yea or no,
And forth with bashful innocence doth hie.
But they whose guilt within their bosoms lie
    Imagine every eye beholds their blame;
    For Lucrece thought he blush'd to see her shame:

When, silly groom! God wot, it was defect
Of spirit, life, and bold audacity.
Such harmless creatures have a true respect
To talk in deeds, while others saucily
Promise more speed, but do it leisurely:
    Even so this pattern of the worn-out age
    Pawn'd honest looks, but laid no words to gage.

His kindled duty kindled her mistrust,
That two red fires in both their faces blaz'd;
She thought he blush'd, as knowing Tarquin's lust,
And, blushing with him, wistly on him gaz'd;
Her earnest eye did make him more amazed:
    The more she saw the blood his cheeks replenish,
    The more she thought he spied in her some blemish.

But long she thinks till he return again,
And yet the duteous vassal scarce is gone.
The weary time she cannot entertain,
For now 'tis stale to sigh, to weep, to groan:
So woe hath wearied woe, moan tired moan,
    That she her plaints a little while doth stay,
    Pausing for means to mourn some newer way.

At last she calls to mind where hangs a piece
Of skilful painting, made for Priam's Troy;
Before the which is drawn the power of Greece,
For Helen's rape the city to destroy,
Threatening cloud-kissing Ilion with annoy;
    Which the conceited painter drew so proud,
    As heaven, it seem'd, to kiss the turrets bow'd.

A thousand lamentable objects there,
In scorn of nature, art gave lifeless life:
Many a dry drop seem'd a weeping tear,
Shed for the slaughter'd husband by the wife:
The red blood reek'd, to show the painter's strife;
    And dying eyes gleam'd forth their ashy lights,
    Like dying coals burnt out in tedious nights.

There might you see the labouring pioneer
Begrim'd with sweat, and smeared all with dust;
And from the towers of Troy there would appear
The very eyes of men through loop-holes thrust,
Gazing upon the Greeks with little lust:
    Such sweet observance in this work was had,
    That one might see those far-off eyes look sad.

In great commanders grace and majesty
You might behold, triumphing in their faces;
In youth, quick bearing and dexterity;
And here and there the painter interlaces
Pale cowards, marching on with trembling paces;
    Which heartless peasants did so well resemble
    That one would swear he saw them quake and
        tremble.

In Ajax and Ulysses, O, what art
Of physiognomy might one behold!
The face of either cipher'd either's heart;
Their face their manners most expressly told:
In Ajax' eyes blunt rage and rigour roll'd;
    But the mild glance that sly Ulysses lent
    Show'd deep regard and smiling government.

There pleading might you see grave Nestor stand,
As 'twere encouraging the Greeks to fight;
Making such sober action with his hand,
That it beguil'd attention, charm'd the sight:
In speech, it seem'd, his beard, all silver white,
    Wagg'd up and down, and from his lips did fly
    Thin winding breath, which purl'd up to the sky.

About him were a press of gaping faces,
Which seem'd to swallow up his sound advice;
All jointly listening, but with several graces,
As if some mermaid did their ears entice,
Some high, some low, — the painter was so nice;
    The scalps of many, almost hid behind,
    To jump up higher seem'd, to mock the mind.

Here one man's hand lean'd on another's head,
His nose being shadow'd by his neighbour's ear;
Here one, being throng'd, bears back, all bol'n and red;
Another, smother'd, seems to pelt and swear;
And in their rage such signs of rage they bear,
    As, but for loss of Nestor's golden words,
    It seem'd they would debate with angry swords.

For much imaginary work was there;
Conceit deceitful, so compact, so kind,
That for Achilles' image stood his spear,
Grip'd in an armed hand; himself, behind,
Was left unseen, save to the eye of mind;
    A hand, a foot, a face, a leg, a head,
    Stood for the whole to be imagined.

And from the walls of strong-besieged Troy
When their brave hope, bold Hector, march'd to field,
Stood many Trojan mothers, sharing joy
To see their youthful sons bright weapons wield;
And to their hope they such odd action yield,
    That through their light joy seemed to appear,
    Like bright things stain'd, a kind of heavy fear.

And from the strond of Dardan, where they fought,
To Simois' reedy banks the red blood ran,
Whose waves to imitate the battle sought
With swelling ridges; and their ranks began
To break upon the galled shore, and than
    Retire again, till meeting greater ranks,
    They join, and shoot their foam at Simois' banks.

To this well-painted piece is Lucrece come,
To find a face where all distress is stell'd.
Many she sees where cares have carved some,
But none where all distress and dolour dwell'd,
Till she despairing Hecuba beheld,
    Staring on Priam's wounds with her old eyes,
    Which bleeding under Pyrrhus' proud foot lies.

In her the painter had anatomised
Time's ruin, beauty's wrack, and grim care's reign:
Her cheeks with chops and wrinkles were disguised;
Of what she was no semblance did remain:
Her blue blood chang'd to black in every vein,
    Wanting the spring that those shrunk pipes
        had fed,
    Show'd life imprison'd in a body dead.

On this sad shadow Lucrece spends her eyes,
And shapes her sorrow to the beldam's woes,
Who nothing wants to answer her but cries,
And bitter words to ban her cruel foes:
The painter was no god to lend her those;
    And therefore Lucrece swears he did her wrong,
    To give her so much grief, and not a tongue.

'Poor instrument,' quoth she, 'without a sound,
I'll tune thy woes with my lamenting tongue;
And drop sweet balm in Priam's painted wound,
And rail on Pyrrhus that hath done him wrong;
And with my tears quench Troy that burns
        so long;
    And with my knife scratch out the angry eyes
    Of all the Greeks that are thine enemies.

'Show me the strumpet that began this stir,
That with my nails her beauty I may tear.
Thy heat of lust, fond Paris, did incur
This load of wrath that burning Troy doth bear:
Thy eye kindled the fire that burneth here;
    And here in Troy, for trespass of thine eye,
    The sire, the son, the dame, and daughter die.

'Why should the private pleasure of some one
Become the public plague of many more?
Let sin, alone committed, light alone
Upon his head that hath transgressed so;
Let guiltless souls be freed from guilty woe:
    For one's offence why should so many fall,
    To plague a private sin in general?

'Lo, here weeps Hecuba, here Priam dies,
Here manly Hector faints, here Troilus swounds,
Here friend by friend in bloody channel lies,
And friend to friend gives unadvised wounds,
And one man's lust these many lives confounds:
    Had doting Priam check'd his son's desire,
    Troy had been bright with fame, and not with fire.'

Here feelingly she weeps Troy's painted woes:
For sorrow, like a heavy-hanging bell,
Once set on ringing, with his own weight goes;
Then little strength rings out the doleful knell:
So Lucrece, set a-work, sad tales doth tell
    To pencill'd pensiveness and colour'd sorrow;
    She lends them words, and she their looks doth
        borrow.

She throws her eyes about the painting round,
And who she finds forlorn she doth lament.
At last she sees a wretched image bound,
That piteous looks to Phrygian shepherds lent:
His face, though full of cares, yet show'd content;
    Onward to Troy with the blunt swains he goes,
    So mild that Patience seem'd to scorn his woes.

In him the painter labour'd with his skill
To hide deceit, and give the harmless show
An humble gait, calm looks, eyes wailing still,
A brow unbent, that seem'd to welcome woe;
Cheeks neither red nor pale, but mingled so
    That blushing red no guilty instance gave,
    Nor ashy pale the fear that false hearts have.

But, like a constant and confirmed devil,
He entertain'd a show so seeming just,
And therein so ensconc'd his secret evil,
That jealousy itself could not mistrust
False-creeping craft and perjury should thrust
    Into so bright a day such black-fac'd storms,
    Or blot with hell-born sin such saint-like forms.

The well-skill'd workman this mild image drew
For perjured Sinon, whose enchanting story
The credulous old Priam after slew;
Whose words, like wildfire, burnt the shining glory
Of rich-built Ilion, that the skies were sorry,
    And little stars shot from their fixed places,
    When their glass fell wherein they view'd their faces.

This picture she advisedly perused,
And chid the painter for his wondrous skill,
Saying, some shape in Sinon's was abused;
So fair a form lodg'd not a mind so ill:
And still on him she gaz'd; and gazing still,
    Such signs of truth in his plain face she spied,
    That she concludes the picture was belied.

'It cannot be,' quoth she, 'that so much guile' —
She would have said 'can lurk in such a look';
But Tarquin's shape came in her mind the while,
And from her tongue 'can lurk' from 'cannot' took:
'It cannot be' she in that sense forsook,
    And turn'd it thus, 'It cannot be, I find,
    But such a face should bear a wicked mind:

'For even as subtle Sinon here is painted,
So sober-sad, so weary, and so mild,
As if with grief or travail he had fainted,
To me came Tarquin armed; so beguil'd
With outward honesty, but yet defil'd
    With inward vice: as Priam him did cherish,
    So did I Tarquin; so my Troy did perish.

'Look, look, how listening Priam wets his eyes,
To see those borrow'd tears that Sinon sheeds!
Priam, why art thou old, and yet not wise?
For every tear he falls a Trojan bleeds:
His eye drops fire, no water thence proceeds;
    Those round clear pearls of his, that move
        thy pity,
    Are balls of quenchless fire to burn thy city.

We will revenge the death of this true wife.

'Such devils steal effects from lightless hell;
For Sinon in his fire doth quake with cold,
And in that cold hot-burning fire doth dwell;
These contraries such unity do hold,
Only to flatter fools, and make them bold:
    So Priam's trust false Sinon's tears doth flatter,
    That he finds means to burn his Troy with water.'

Here, all enrag'd, such passion her assails,
That patience is quite beaten from her breast.
She tears the senseless Sinon with her nails,
Comparing him to that unhappy guest
Whose deed hath made herself herself detest:
    At last she smilingly with this gives o'er;
    'Fool, fool!' quoth she, 'his wounds will not be sore.'

Thus ebbs and flows the current of her sorrow,
And time doth weary time with her complaining.
She looks for night, and then she longs for morrow,
And both she thinks too long with her remaining;
Short time seems long in sorrow's sharp sustaining:
    Though woe be heavy, yet it seldom sleeps;
    And they that watch see time how slow it creeps.

Which all this time hath overslipp'd her thought,
That she with painted images hath spent;
Being from the feeling of her own grief brought
By deep surmise of others' detriment;
Losing her woes in shows of discontent.
    It easeth some, though none it ever cured,
    To think their dolour others have endured.

But now the mindful messenger, come back,
Brings home his lord and other company:
Who finds his Lucrece clad in mourning black;
And round about her tear-distained eye
Blue circles stream'd, like rainbows in the sky:
    These water-galls in her dim element
    Foretell new storms to those already spent.

Which when her sad-beholding husband saw,
Amazedly in her sad face he stares:
Her eyes, though sod in tears, look'd red and raw,
Her lively colour kill'd with deadly cares.
He hath no power to ask her how she fares;
    Both stood, like old acquaintance in a trance,
    Met far from home, wondering each other's chance.

At last he takes her by the bloodless hand,
And thus begins: 'What uncouth ill event
Hath thee befall'n, that thou dost trembling stand?
Sweet love, what spite hath thy fair colour spent?
Why art thou thus attired in discontent?
    Unmask, dear dear, this moody heaviness,
    And tell thy grief, that we may give redress.'

Three times with sighs she gives her sorrow fire,
Ere once she can discharge one word of woe:
At length address'd to answer his desire,
She modestly prepares to let them know
Her honour is ta'en prisoner by the foe;
    While Collatine and his consorted lords
    With sad attention long to hear her words.

And now this pale swan in her watery nest
Begins the sad dirge of her certain ending:
'Few words,' quoth she, 'shall fit the trespass best,
Where no excuse can give the fault amending:
In me more woes than words are now depending;
    And my laments would be drawn out too long,
    To tell them all with one poor tired tongue.

'Then be this all the task it hath to say:
Dear husband, in the interest of thy bed
A stranger came, and on that pillow lay
Where thou wast wont to rest thy weary head;
And what wrong else may be imagined
    By foul enforcement might be done to me,
    From that, alas, thy Lucrece is not free.

'For in the dreadful dead of dark midnight,
With shining falchion in my chamber came
A creeping creature, with a flaming light,
And softly cried, "Awake, thou Roman dame,
And entertain my love; else lasting shame
    On thee and thine this night I will inflict,
    If thou my love's desire do contradict.

' "For some hard-favour'd groom of thine," quoth he,
"Unless thou yoke thy liking to my will,
I'll murder straight, and then I'll slaughter thee,
And swear I found you where you did fulfil
The loathsome act of lust, and so did kill
    The lechers in their deed: this act will be
    My fame, and thy perpetual infamy."

'With this, I did begin to start and cry;
And then against my heart he set his sword,
Swearing, unless I took all patiently,
I should not live to speak another word;
So should my shame still rest upon record,
    And never be forgot in mighty Rome
    Th'adulterate death of Lucrece and her groom.

'Mine enemy was strong, my poor self weak,
And far the weaker with so strong a fear:
My bloody judge forbade my tongue to speak;
No rightful plea might plead for justice there:
His scarlet lust came evidence to swear
    That my poor beauty had purloin'd his eyes;
    And when the judge is robb'd, the prisoner dies.

'O, teach me how to make mine own excuse!
Or, at the least, this refuge let me find, —
Though my gross blood be stain'd with this abuse,
Immaculate and spotless is my mind;
That was not forc'd; that never was inclin'd
    To accessary yieldings, but still pure
    Doth in her poison'd closet yet endure.'

Lo, here, the hopeless merchant of this loss,
With head declin'd, and voice damm'd up with woe,
With sad-set eyes, and wretched arms across,
From lips new-waxen pale begins to blow
The grief away that stops his answer so:
    But, wretched as he is, he strives in vain;
    What he breathes out his breath drinks up again.

As through an arch the violent roaring tide
Outruns the eye that doth behold his haste,
Yet in the eddy boundeth in his pride
Back to the strait that forc'd him on so fast;
In rage sent out, recall'd in rage, being past:
    Even so his sighs, his sorrows, make a saw,
    To push grief on, and back the same grief draw.

Which speechless woe of his poor she attendeth,
And his untimely frenzy thus awaketh:
'Dear lord, thy sorrow to my sorrow lendeth
Another power; no flood by raining slaketh.
My woe too sensible thy passion maketh
    More feeling-painful: let it, then, suffice
    To drown one woe, one pair of weeping eyes.

'And for my sake, when I might charm thee so,
For she that was thy Lucrece, — now attend me:
Be suddenly revenged on my foe,
Thine, mine, his own: suppose thou dost defend me
From what is past: the help that thou shalt lend me
    Comes all too late, yet let the traitor die;
    For sparing justice feeds iniquity.

'But ere I name him, you fair lords,' quoth she,
Speaking to those that came with Collatine,
'Shall plight your honourable faiths to me,
With swift pursuit to venge this wrong of mine;
For 'tis a meritorious fair design
    To chase injustice with revengeful arms:
    Knights, by their oaths, should right poor ladies'
        harms.'

At this request, with noble disposition
Each present lord began to promise aid,
As bound in knighthood to her imposition,
Longing to hear the hateful foe bewray'd.
But she, that yet her sad task hath not said,
    The protestation stops. 'O, speak,' quoth she,
    'How may this forced stain be wip'd from me?

'What is the quality of mine offence,
Being constrain'd with dreadful circumstance?
May my pure mind with the foul act dispense,
My low-declined honour to advance?
May any terms acquit me from this chance?
    The poison'd fountain clears itself again;
    And why not I from this compelled stain?'

With this, they all at once began to say,
Her body's stain her mind untainted clears;
While with a joyless smile she turns away
The face, that map which deep impression bears
Of hard misfortune, carv'd in it with tears.
    'No, no,' quoth she, 'no dame, hereafter living,
    By my excuse shall claim excuse's giving.'

Here with a sigh, as if her heart would break,
She throws forth Tarquin's name: 'He, he,' she says,
But more than 'he' her poor tongue could not speak;
Till after many accents and delays,
Untimely breathings, sick and short assays,
    She utters this, 'He, he, fair lords, 'tis he
    That guides this hand to give this wound to me.'

Even here she sheathed in her harmless breast
A harmful knife, that thence her soul unsheathed:
That blow did bail it from the deep unrest
Of that polluted prison where it breath'd:
Her contrite sighs unto the clouds bequeath'd
    Her winged sprite, and through her wounds doth fly
    Life's lasting date from cancell'd destiny.

Stone-still, astonish'd with this deadly deed,
Stood Collatine and all his lordly crew;
Till Lucrece' father, that beholds her bleed,
Himself on her self-slaughter'd body threw;
And from the purple fountain Brutus drew
    The murderous knife, and, as it left the place,
    Her blood, in poor revenge, held it in chase;

And bubbling from her breast, it doth divide
In two slow rivers, that the crimson blood
Circles her body in on every side,
Who, like a late-sack'd island, vastly stood
Bare and unpeopled in this fearful flood.
    Some of her blood still pure and red remain'd
    And some look'd black, and that false Tarquin stain'd.

About the mourning and congealed face
Of that black blood a watery rigol goes,
Which seems to weep upon the tainted place:
And ever since, as pitying Lucrece' woes,
Corrupted blood some watery token shows;
    And blood untainted still doth red abide,
    Blushing at that which is so putrefied.

'Daughter, dear daughter,' old Lucretius cries,
'That life was mine which thou hast here deprived.
If in the child the father's image lies,
Where shall I live now Lucrece is unlived?
Thou wast not to this end from me derived.
    If children pre-decease progenitors,
    We are their offspring, and they none of ours.

'Poor broken glass, I often did behold
In thy sweet semblance my old age new born;
But now that fair fresh mirror, dim and old,
Shows me a bare-bon'd death by time outworn:
O, from thy cheeks my image thou hast torn,
    And shiver'd all the beauty of my glass,
    That I no more can see what once I was.

'O time, cease thou thy course, and last no longer,
If they surcease to be that should survive.
Shall rotten death make conquest of the stronger,
And leave the faltering feeble souls alive?
The old bees die, the young possess their hive:
    Then live, sweet Lucrece, live again, and see
    Thy father die, and not thy father thee.'

By this, starts Collatine as from a dream,
And bids Lucretius give his sorrow place;
And then in key-cold Lucrece' bleeding stream
He falls, and bathes the pale fear in his face,
And counterfeits to die with her a space;
    Till manly shame bids him possess his breath,
    And live to be revenged on her death.

The deep vexation of his inward soul
Hath serv'd a dumb arrest upon his tongue;
Who, mad that sorrow should his use control,
Or keep him from heart-easing words so long,
Begins to talk; but through his lips do throng
    Weak words, so thick come in his poor heart's aid,
    That no man could distinguish what he said.

Yet sometime 'Tarquin' was pronounced plain,
But through his teeth, as if the name he tore.
This windy tempest, till it blow up rain,
Held back his sorrow's tide, to make it more;
At last it rains, and busy winds give o'er:
    The son and father weep with equal strife
    Who should weep most, for daughter or for wife.

The one doth call her his, the other his,
Yet neither may possess the claim they lay.
The father says, 'She's mine.' 'O, mine she is,'
Replies her husband; 'do not take away
My sorrow's interest; let no mourner say
    He weeps for her, for she was only mine,
    And only must be wail'd by Collatine.'

'O,' quoth Lucretius, 'I did give that life
Which she too early and too late hath spill'd.'
'Woe, woe,' quoth Collatine, 'she was my wife,
I ow'd her, and 'tis mine that she hath kill'd.'
'My daughter' and 'my wife' with clamours fill'd
    The dispers'd air, who, holding Lucrece' life,
    Answer'd their cries, 'my daughter' and 'my wife.'

Brutus, who pluck'd the knife from Lucrece' side,
Seeing such emulation in their woe,
Began to clothe his wit in state and pride,
Burying in Lucrece' wound his folly's show.
He with the Romans was esteemed so
    As silly-jeering idiots are with kings,
    For sportive words and uttering foolish things:

But now he throws that shallow habit by,
Wherein deep policy did him disguise;
And arm'd his long-hid wits advisedly,
To check the tears in Collatinus' eyes.
'Thou wronged lord of Rome,' quoth he, 'arise:
    Let my unsounded self, suppos'd a fool,
    Now set thy long-experienc'd wit to school.

'Why, Collatine, is woe the cure for woe?
Do wounds help wounds, or grief help grievous
        deeds?
Is it revenge to give thyself a blow
For his foul act by whom thy fair wife bleeds?
Such childish humour from weak minds proceeds:
    Thy wretched wife mistook the matter so,
    To slay herself, that should have slain her foe.

'Courageous Roman, do not steep thy heart
In such relenting dew of lamentations;
But kneel with me, and help to bear thy part,
To rouse our Roman gods with invocations,
That they will suffer these abominations,
    Since Rome herself in them doth stand disgraced,
    By our strong arms from forth her fair streets chased.

'Now, by the Capitol that we adore,
And by this chaste blood so unjustly stained,
By heaven's fair sun that breeds the fat earth's store,
By all our country rights in Rome maintained,
And by chaste Lucrece' soul that late complained
    Her wrongs to us, and by this bloody knife,
    We will revenge the death of this true wife.'

This said, he struck his hand upon his breast,
And kiss'd the fatal knife, to end his vow;
And to his protestation urg'd the rest,
Who, wondering at him, did his words allow:
Then jointly to the ground their knees they bow;
    And that deep vow, which Brutus made before,
    He doth again repeat, and that they swore.

When they had sworn to this advised doom,
They did conclude to bear dead Lucrece thence,
To show her bleeding body thorough Rome,
And so to publish Tarquin's foul offence:
Which being done with speedy diligence,
    The Romans plausibly did give consent
    To Tarquin's everlasting banishment.

SONNETS

TO THE ONLIE BEGETTER OF THESE INSVING SONNETS MR. W. H. ALL HAPPINESSE AND THAT ETERNITIE PROMISED BY OVR EVER-LIVING POET WISHETH THE WELL-WISHING ADVENTVRER IN SETTING FORTH T. T.

1

From fairest creatures we desire increase,
That thereby beauty's Rose might never die,
But as the riper should by time decease,
His tender heir might bear his memory:
But thou, contracted to thine own bright eyes,
Feed'st thy light's flame with self-substantial fuel,
Making a famine where abundance lies,
Thyself thy foe, to thy sweet self too cruel.
Thou that art now the world's fresh ornament,
And only herald to the gaudy spring,
Within thine own bud buriest thy content,
And, tender churl, mak'st waste in niggarding.
      Pity the world, or else this glutton be,
      To eat the world's due, by the grave and thee.

2

When forty winters shall besiege thy brow,
And dig deep trenches in thy beauty's field,
Thy youth's proud livery, so gaz'd on now,
Will be a totter'd weed, of small worth held:
Then being ask'd where all thy beauty lies,
Where all the treasure of thy lusty days;
To say, within thine own deep-sunken eyes,
Were an all-eating shame and thriftless praise.
How much more praise deserv'd thy beauty's use,
If thou couldst answer, 'This fair child of mine
Shall sum my count, and make my old excuse,'
Proving his beauty by succession thine!
      This were to be new made when thou art old,
      And see thy blood warm when thou feel'st it cold.

Thou that art now the world's fresh ornament.

3

Look in thy glass, and tell the face thou viewest
Now is the time that face should form another;
Whose fresh repair if now thou not renewest,
Thou dost beguile the world, unbless some mother.
For where is she so fair whose unear'd womb
Disdains the tillage of thy husbandry?
Or who is he so fond will be the tomb
Of his self-love, to stop posterity?
Thou art thy mother's glass, and she in thee
Calls back the lovely April of her prime:
So thou through windows of thine age shalt see,
Despite of wrinkles, this thy golden time.
      But if thou live, remember'd not to be,
      Die single, and thine image dies with thee.

4

Unthrifty loveliness, why dost thou spend
Upon thyself thy beauty's legacy?
Nature's bequest gives nothing, but doth lend;
And, being frank, she lends to those are free.
Then, beauteous niggard, why dost thou abuse
The bounteous largess given thee to give?
Profitless usurer, why dost thou use
So great a sum of sums, yet canst not live?
For having traffic with thyself alone,
Thou of thyself thy sweet self dost deceive.
Then how, when nature calls thee to be gone,
What acceptable audit canst thou leave?
      Thy unus'd beauty must be tomb'd with thee,
      Which, used, lives th'executor to be.

5

Those hours, that with gentle work did frame
The lovely gaze where every eye doth dwell,
Will play the tyrants to the very same,
And that unfair which fairly doth excel:
For never-resting time leads summer on
To hideous winter and confounds him there;
Sap check'd with frost, and lusty leaves quite gone,
Beauty o'ersnow'd, and bareness every where:
Then, were not summer's distillation left,
A liquid prisoner pent in walls of glass,
Beauty's effect with beauty were bereft,
Nor it, nor no remembrance what it was:
      But flowers distill'd, though they with winter meet,
      Leese but their show; their substance still lives
      sweet.

6

Then let not winter's ragged hand deface
In thee thy summer, ere thou be distill'd:
Make sweet some vial; treasure thou some place
With beauty's treasure, ere it be self-kill'd.
That use is not forbidden usury,
Which happies those that pay the willing loan;
That's for thyself to breed another thee,
Or ten times happier, be it ten for one;
Ten times thyself were happier than thou art,
If ten of thine ten times refigured thee:
Then what could death do, if thou shouldst depart,
Leaving thee living in posterity?
      Be not self-will'd, for thou art much too fair
      To be death's conquest and make worms thine heir.

7

Lo, in the orient when the gracious light
Lifts up his burning head, each under eye
Doth homage to his new-appearing sight,
Serving with looks his sacred majesty;
And having climb'd the steep-up heavenly hill,
Resembling strong youth in his middle age,
Yet mortal looks adore his beauty still,
Attending on his golden pilgrimage;
But when from highmost pitch, with weary car,
Like feeble age, he reeleth from the day,
The eyes, 'fore duteous, now converted are
From his low tract and look another way:
      So thou, thyself outgoing in thy noon,
      Unlook'd on diest, unless thou get a son.

8

Music to hear, why hear'st thou music sadly?
Sweets with sweets war not, joy delights in joy.
Why lov'st thou that which thou receiv'st not gladly,
Or else receiv'st with pleasure thine annoy?
If the true concord of well-tuned sounds,
By unions married, do offend thine ear,
They do but sweetly chide thee, who confounds
In singleness the parts that thou shouldst bear.
Mark how one string, sweet husband to another,
Strikes each in each by mutual ordering;
Resembling sire and child and happy mother,
Who, all in one, one pleasing note do sing:
      Whose speechless song, being many, seeming one,
      Sings this to thee, 'Thou single wilt prove none.'

9

Is it for fear to wet a widow's eye
That thou consumest thyself in single life?
Ah! if thou issueless shalt hap to die,
The world will wail thee, like a makeless wife;
The world will be thy widow, and still weep
That thou no form of thee hast left behind,
When every private widow well may keep
By children's eyes her husband's shape in mind.
Look, what an unthrift in the world doth spend,
Shifts but his place, for still the world enjoys it;
But beauty's waste hath in the world an end,
And kept unus'd, the user so destroys it.
      No love toward others in that bosom sits
      That on himself such murd'rous shame commits.

10

For shame deny that thou bear'st love to any,
Who for thyself art so unprovident.
Grant, if thou wilt, thou art belov'd of many,
But that thou none lov'st is most evident;
For thou art so possess'd with murd'rous hate,
That 'gainst thyself thou stick'st not to conspire,
Seeking that beauteous roof to ruinate,
Which to repair should be thy chief desire.
O, change thy thought, that I may change my mind!
Shall hate be fairer lodg'd than gentle love?
Be, as thy presence is, gracious and kind,
Or to thyself, at least, kind-hearted prove:
      Make thee another self, for love of me,
      That beauty still may live in thine or thee.

11

As fast as thou shalt wane, so fast thou grow'st
In one of thine, from that which thou departest;
And that fresh blood which youngly thou bestow'st
Thou mayst call thine when thou from youth
      convertest.
Herein lives wisdom, beauty, and increase;
Without this, folly, age, and cold decay:
If all were minded so, the times should cease,
And threescore year would make the world away.
Let those whom Nature hath not made for store,
Harsh, featureless, and rude, barrenly perish:
Look, whom she best endow'd she gave the more;
Which bounteous gift thou shouldst in bounty cherish:
      She carv'd thee for her seal, and meant thereby
      Thou shouldst print more, not let that copy die.

12

When I do count the clock that tells the time,
And see the brave day sunk in hideous night;
When I behold the violet past prime,
And sable curls all silver'd o'er with white;
When lofty trees I see barren of leaves,
Which erst from heat did canopy the herd,
And summer's green, all girded up in sheaves,
Borne on the bier with white and bristly beard;
Then of thy beauty do I question make,
That thou among the wastes of time must go,
Since sweets and beauties do themselves forsake,
And die as fast as they see others grow;
   And nothing 'gainst Time's scythe can make defence
   Save breed, to brave him when he takes thee hence.

13

O that you were yourself! but, love, you are
No longer yours than you yourself here live:
Against this coming end you should prepare,
And your sweet semblance to some other give.
So should that beauty which you hold in lease
Find no determination; then you were
Yourself again, after yourself's decease,
When your sweet issue your sweet form should bear.
Who lets so fair a house fall to decay,
Which husbandry in honour might uphold
Against the stormy gusts of winter's day
And barren rage of death's eternal cold?
   O, none but unthrifts: dear my love, you know
   You had a father; let your son say so.

14

Not from the stars do I my judgement pluck;
And yet methinks I have astronomy,
But not to tell of good or evil luck,
Of plagues, of dearths, or seasons' quality;
Nor can I fortune to brief minutes tell,
Pointing to each his thunder, rain, and wind,
Or say with princes if it shall go well,
By oft predict that I in heaven find:
But from thine eyes my knowledge I derive,
And, constant stars, in them I read such art,
As truth and beauty shall together thrive,
If from thyself to store thou wouldst convert;
   Or else of thee this I prognosticate:
   Thy end is truth's and beauty's doom and date.

15

When I consider every thing that grows
Holds in perfection but a little moment,
That this huge stage presenteth naught but shows
Whereon the stars in secret influence comment;
When I perceive that men as plants increase,
Cheered and check'd even by the self-same sky,
Vaunt in their youthful sap, at height decrease,
And wear their brave state out of memory;
Then the conceit of this inconstant stay
Sets you most rich in youth before my sight,
Where wasteful Time debateth with Decay,
To change your day of youth to sullied night;
   And, all in war with Time, for love of you,
   As he takes from you, I engraft you new.

16

But wherefore do not you a mightier way
Make war upon this bloody tyrant, Time?
And fortify yourself in your decay
With means more blessed than my barren rime?
Now stand you on the top of happy hours;
And many maiden gardens, yet unset,
With virtuous wish would bear you living flowers,
Much liker than your painted counterfeit:
So should the lines of life that life repair,
Which this, Time's pencil, or my pupil pen,
Neither in inward worth nor outward fair,
Can make you live yourself in eyes of men.
   To give away yourself keeps yourself still;
   And you must live, drawn by your own sweet skill.

17

Who will believe my verse in time to come,
If it were fill'd with your most high deserts?
Though yet, heaven knows, it is but as a tomb
Which hides your life, and shows not half your parts.
If I could write the beauty of your eyes,
And in fresh numbers number all your Graces,
The age to come would say, 'This poet lies,
Such heavenly touches ne'er touch'd earthly faces?
So should my papers, yellow'd with their age,
Be scorn'd, like old men of less truth than tongue;
And your true rights be term'd a poet's rage,
And stretched metre of an antique song;
   But were some child of yours alive that time,
   You should live twice, in it and in my rime.

18

Shall I compare thee to a summer's day?
Thou art more lovely and more temperate:
Rough winds do shake the darling buds of May,
And summer's lease hath all too short a date:
Sometime too hot the eye of heaven shines,
And often is his gold complexion dimm'd;
And every fair from fair sometime declines,
By chance, or nature's changing course, untrimm'd;
But thy eternal summer shall not fade,
Nor loose possession of that fair thou ow'st;
Nor shall Death brag thou wander'st in his shade,
When in eternal lines to time thou grow'st:
   So long as men can breathe, or eyes can see,
   So long lives this, and this gives life to thee.

19

Devouring Time, blunt thou the lion's paws,
And make the earth devour her own sweet brood;
Pluck the keen teeth from the fierce tiger's jaws,
And burn the long-liv'd phœnix in her blood;
Make glad and sorry seasons as thou fleets,
And do whate'er thou wilt, swift-footed Time,
To the wide world and all her fading sweets;
But I forbid thee one most heinous crime:
O, carve not with thy hours my love's fair brow,
Nor draw no lines there with thine antique pen;
Him in thy course untainted do allow
For beauty's pattern to succeeding men.
   Yet, do thy worst, old Time: despite thy wrong,
   My love shall in my verse ever live young.

20

A woman's face, with Nature's own hand painted,
Hast thou, the master-mistress of my passion;
A woman's gentle heart, but not acquainted
With shifting change, as is false women's fashion;
An eye more bright than theirs, less false in rolling,
Gilding the object whereupon it gazeth;
A man in hew all *Hews* in his controlling,
Which steals men's eyes, and women's souls amazeth.
And for a woman wert thou first created;
Till Nature, as she wrought thee, fell a-doting,
And by addition me of thee defeated,
By adding one thing to my purpose nothing.
   But since she prick'd thee out for women's pleasure,
   Mine be thy love, and thy love's use their treasure.

21

So is it not with me as with that Muse
Stirr'd by a painted beauty to his verse,
Who heaven itself for ornament doth use,
And every fair with his fair doth rehearse;
Making a couplement of proud compare,
With sun and moon, with earth and sea's rich gems,
With April's first-born flowers, and all things rare
That heaven's air in this huge rondure hems.
O, let me, true in love, but truly write,
And then believe me, my love is as fair
As any mother's child, though not so bright
As those gold candles fix'd in heaven's air:
   Let them say more that like of hearsay well;
   I will not praise that purpose not to sell.

22

My glass shall not persuade me I am old,
So long as youth and thou are of one date;
But when in thee time's furrows I behold,
Then look I death my days should expiate.
For all that beauty that doth cover thee
Is but the seemly raiment of my heart,
Which in thy breast doth live, as thine in me:
How can I, then, be elder than thou art?
O, therefore, love, be of thyself so wary
As I, not for myself, but for thee will;
Bearing thy heart, which I will keep so chary
As tender nurse her babe from faring ill.
   Presume not on thy heart when mine is slain;
   Thou gav'st me thine, not to give back again.

23

As an unperfect actor on the stage,
Who, with his fear is put besides his part,
Or some fierce thing replete with too much rage,
Whose strength's abundance weakens his own heart;
So I, for fear of trust, forget to say
The perfect ceremony of love's rite,
And in mine own love's strength seem to decay,
O'ercharg'd with burden of mine own love's might.
O, let my books be, then, the eloquence
And dumb presagers of my speaking breast;
Who plead for love, and look for recompense,
More than that tongue that more hath more express'd.
   O, learn to read what silent love hath writ:
   To hear with eyes belongs to love's fine wit.

24

Mine eye hath play'd the painter, and hath stell'd
Thy beauty's form in table of my heart;
My body is the frame wherein 'tis held,
And perspective it is best painter's art.
For through the painter must you see his skill,
To find where your true image pictur'd lies;
Which in my bosom's shop is hanging still,
That hath his windows glazed with thine eyes.
Now see what good turns eyes for eyes have done:
Mine eyes have drawn thy shape, and thine for me
Are windows to my breast, where-through the sun
Delights to peep, to gaze therein on thee;
   Yet eyes this cunning want to grace their art,
   They draw but what they see, know not the heart.

25

Let those who are in favour with their stars
Of public honour and proud titles boast,
Whilst I, whom fortune of such triumph bars,
Unlook'd for joy in that I honour most.
Great princes' favourites their fair leaves spread
But as the marigold at the sun's eye;
And in themselves their pride lies buried,
For at a frown they in their glory die.
The painful warrior famoused for fight,
After a thousand victories once foil'd,
Is from the book of honour razed quite,
And all the rest forgot for which he toil'd:
   Then happy I, that love and am beloved
   Where I may not remove nor be removed.

26

Lord of my love, to whom in vassalage
Thy merit hath my duty strongly knit,
To thee I send this written ambassage,
To witness duty, not to show my wit:
Duty so great, which wit so poor as mine
May make seem bare, in wanting words to show it,
But that I hope some good conceit of thine
In thy soul's thought, all naked, will bestow it;
Till whatsoever star that guides my moving,
Points on me graciously with fair aspect,
And puts apparel on my totter'd loving,
To show me worthy of thy sweet respect:
   Then may I dare to boast how I do love thee;
   Till then not show my head where thou mayst prove me.

27

Weary with toil, I haste me to my bed,
The dear repose for limbs with travel tired;
But then begins a journey in my head,
To work my mind, when body's work's expired:
For then my thoughts, from far where I abide,
Intend a zealous pilgrimage to thee,
And keep my drooping eyelids open wide,
Looking on darkness which the blind do see:
Save that my soul's imaginary sight
Presents thy shadow to my sightless view,
Which, like a jewel hung in ghastly night,
Makes black night beauteous, and her old face new.
   Lo, thus, by day my limbs, by night my mind,
   For thee and for myself no quiet find.

28

How can I, then, return in happy plight,
That am debarr'd the benefit of rest?
When day's oppression is not eas'd by night,
But day by night, and night by day, oppress'd?
And each, though enemies to either's reign,
Do in consent shake hands to torture me;

The one by toil, the other to complain
How far I toil, still farther off from thee.
I tell the day, to please him thou art bright,
And dost him grace when clouds do blot the heaven:
So flatter I the swart-complexion'd night,
When sparkling stars twire not thou gild'st the even.
    But day doth daily draw my sorrows longer,
    And night doth nightly make grief's strength seem
      stronger.

29

When, in disgrace with Fortune and men's eyes,
I all alone beweep my outcast state,
And trouble deaf heaven with my bootless cries,
And look upon myself, and curse my fate,
Wishing me like to one more rich in hope,
Featur'd like him, like him with friends possess'd
Desiring this man's art, and that man's scope,
With what I most enjoy contented least;
Yet in these thoughts myself almost despising,
Haply I think on thee, — and then my state,
Like to the lark at break of day arising
From sullen earth, sings hymns at heaven's gate;
    For thy sweet love remember'd such wealth brings,
    That then I scorn to change my state with kings.

30

When to the sessions of sweet silent thought
I summon up remembrance of things past,
I sigh the lack of many a thing I sought,
And with old woes new wail my dear times' waste:
Then can I drown an eye, unus'd to flow,
For precious friends hid in death's dateless night,
And weep afresh love's long-since-cancell'd woe,
And moan the expense of many a vanish'd sight:
Then can I grieve at grievances foregone,
And heavily from woe to woe tell o'er
The sad account of fore-bemoaned moan,
Which I new pay as if not paid before.
    But if the while I think on thee, dear friend,
    All losses are restor'd, and sorrows end.

31

Thy bosom is endeared with all hearts,
Which I by lacking have supposed dead;
And there reigns love, and all love's loving parts,
And all those friends which I thought buried.
How many a holy and obsequious tear
Hath dear religious love stol'n from mine eye,
As interest of the dead, which now appear
But things remov'd, that hidden in thee lie!
Thou art the grave where buried love doth live,
Hung with the trophies of my lovers gone,
Who all their parts of me to thee did give;
That due of many now is thine alone:
    Their images I lov'd I view in thee,
    And thou, all they, hast all the all of me.

32

If thou survive my well-contented day,
When that churl Death my bones with dust shall
    cover,
And shalt by fortune once more re-survey
These poor rude lines of thy deceased lover:
Compare them with the bettering of the time,
And though they be outstripp'd by every pen,
Reserve them for my love, not for their rime,
Exceeded by the height of happier men.
O, then vouchsafe me but this loving thought:
'Had my friend's Muse grown with this growing age,
A dearer birth than this his love had brought,
To march in ranks of better equipage:
    But since he died, and poets better prove,
    Theirs for their style I'll read, his for his love.'

33

Full many a glorious morning have I seen
Flatter the mountain-tops with sovereign eye,
Kissing with golden face the meadows green,
Gilding pale streams with heavenly alchemy;
Anon permit the basest clouds to ride
With ugly rack on his celestial face,
And from the forlorn world his visage hide,
Stealing unseen to west with this disgrace:
Even so my sun one early morn did shine
With all-triumphant splendour on my brow;
But, out, alack! he was but one hour mine,
The region cloud hath mask'd him from me now.

Yet him for this my love no whit disdaineth;
    Suns of the world may stain when heaven's sun
      staineth.

34

Why didst thou promise such a beauteous day,
And make me travel forth without my cloak,
To let base clouds o'ertake me in my way,
Hiding thy bravery in their rotten smoke?
'Tis not enough that through the cloud thou break,
To dry the rain on my storm-beaten face,
For no man well of such a salve can speak
That heals the wound, and cures not the disgrace:
Nor can thy shame give physic to my grief;
Though thou repent, yet I have still the loss:
The offender's sorrow lends but weak relief
To him that bears the strong offence's cross.
    Ah, but those tears are pearl which thy love
      sheeds,
    And they are rich, and ransom all ill deeds.

35

No more be griev'd at that which thou hast done:
Roses have thorns, and silver fountains mud;
Clouds and eclipses stain both moon and sun,
And loathsome canker lives in sweetest bud.
All men make faults, and even I in this,
Authorizing thy trespass with compare,
Myself corrupting, salving thy amiss,
Excusing 'their sins more than thy sins are';
For to thy sensual fault I bring in sense, —
Thy adverse party is thy advocate, —
And 'gainst myself a lawful plea commence:
Such civil war is in my love and hate,
    That I an accessary needs must be
    To that sweet thief which sourly robs from me.

36

Let me confess that we two must be twain,
Although our undivided loves are one:
So shall those blots that do with me remain,
Without thy help, by me be borne alone.
In our two loves there is but one respect,
Though in our lives a separable spite,
Which though it alter not love's sole effect,
Yet doth it steal sweet hours from love's delight.
I may not evermore acknowledge thee,
Lest my bewailed guilt should do thee shame;
Nor thou with public kindness honour me,
Unless thou take that honour from thy name:
    But do not so; I love thee in such sort,
    As, thou being mine, mine is thy good report.

37

As a decrepit father takes delight
To see his active child do deeds of youth,
So I, made lame by Fortune's dearest spite,
Take all my comfort of thy worth and truth;
For whether beauty, birth, or wealth, or wit,
Or any of these all, or all, or more,
Entitled in their parts do crowned sit,
I make my love engrafted to this store:
So then I am not lame, poor, nor despis'd,
Whilst that this shadow doth such substance give,
That I in thy abundance am suffic'd,
And by a part of all thy glory live.
    Look, what is best, that best I wish in thee:
    This wish I have; then ten times happy me!

38

How can my Muse want subject to invent,
While thou dost breathe, that pour'st into my
    verse
Thine own sweet argument, too excellent
For every vulgar paper to rehearse?
O, give thyself the thanks, if aught in me
Worthy perusal stand against thy sight;
For who's so dumb that cannot write to thee,
When thou thyself dost give invention light?
Be thou the tenth Muse, ten times more in worth
Than those old nine which rimers invocate;
And he that calls on thee, let him bring forth
Eternal numbers to outlive long date.
    If my slight Muse do please these curious days,
    The pain be mine, but thine shall be the praise.

39

O, how thy worth with manners may I sing,
When thou art all the better part of me?
What can mine own praise to mine own self bring?
And what is't but mine own when I praise thee?
Even for this let us divided live,
And our dear love lose name of single one,
That by this separation I may give
That due to thee which thou deserv'st alone.
O absence, what a torment wouldst thou prove,
Were it not thy sour leisure gave sweet leave
To entertain the time with thoughts of love,
Which time and thoughts so sweetly doth deceive,
    And that thou teachest how to make one twain,
    By praising him here who doth hence remain!

40

Take all my loves, my love, yea, take them all;
What hast thou then more than thou hadst before?
No love, my love, that thou mayst true love call;
All mine was thine before thou hadst this more.
Then, if for my love thou my love receivest,
I cannot blame thee for my love thou usest;
But yet be blam'd, if thou this self deceivest
By wilful taste of what thyself refusest.
I do forgive thy robbery, gentle thief,
Although thou steal thee all my poverty;
And yet, love knows, it is a greater grief
To bear love's wrong than hate's known injury.
    Lascivious grace, in whom all ill well shows,
    Kill me with spites; yet we must not be foes.

41

Those pretty wrongs that liberty commits,
When I am sometimes absent from thy heart,
Thy beauty and thy years full well befits,
For still temptation follows where thou art.
Gentle thou art, and therefore to be won,
Beauteous thou art, therefore to be assailed;
And when a woman woos, what woman's son
Will sourly leave her till she have prevailed?
Ay me! but yet thou might'st my seat forbear,
And chide thy beauty and thy straying youth,
Who lead thee in their riot even there
Where thou art forc'd to break a twofold truth, —
    Hers, by thy beauty tempting her to thee,
    Thine, by thy beauty being false to me.

42

That thou hast her, it is not all my grief,
And yet it may be said I lov'd her dearly;
That she hath thee, is of my wailing chief,
A loss in love that touches me more nearly.
Loving offenders, thus I will excuse ye:
Thou dost love her, because thou know'st I love her;
And for my sake even so doth she abuse me,
Suff'ring my friend for my sake to approve her.
If I lose thee, my loss is my love's gain,
And losing her, my friend hath found that loss;
Both find each other, and I lose both twain,
And both for my sake lay on me this cross:
    But here's the joy: my friend and I are one;
    Sweet flattery! then she loves but me alone.

43

When most I wink, then do mine eyes best see,
For all the day they view things unrespected;
But when I sleep, in dreams they look on thee,
And, darkly bright, are bright in dark directed.
Then thou, whose shadow shadows doth make bright,
How would thy shadow's form form happy show
To the clear day with thy much clearer light,
When to unseeing eyes thy shade shines so!
How would, I say, mine eyes be blessed made
By looking on thee in the living day,
When in dead night thy fair imperfect shade
Through heavy sleep on sightless eyes doth stay!
    All days are nights to see till I see thee,
    And nights bright days when dreams do show thee me.

44

If the dull substance of my flesh were thought,
Injurious distance should not stop my way;
For then, despite of space, I would be brought,
From limits far remote, where thou dost stay.
No matter then although my foot did stand
Upon the farthest earth remov'd from thee;

For nimble thought can jump both sea and land,
As soon as think the place where he would be.
But, ah, thought kills me, that I am not thought,
To leap large lengths of miles when thou art gone,
But that, so much of earth and water wrought,
I must attend time's leisure with my moan;
   Receiving naught by elements so slow
   But heavy tears, badges of either's woe.

45

The other two, slight air and purging fire,
Are both with thee, wherever I abide;
The first my thought, the other my desire,
These present-absent with swift motion slide.
For when these quicker elements are gone
In tender embassy of love to thee,
My life, being made of four, with two alone
Sinks down to death, oppress'd with melancholy,
Until life's composition be recured
By those swift messengers return'd from thee,
Who even but now come back again, assured
Of thy fair health, recounting it to me:
   This told, I joy; but then no longer glad,
   I send them back again, and straight grow sad.

46

Mine eye and heart are at a mortal war,
How to divide the conquest of thy sight;
Mine eye my heart thy picture's sight would bar,
My heart mine eye the freedom of that right.
My heart doth plead that thou in him dost lie —
A closet never pierc'd with crystal eyes —
But the defendant doth that plea deny,
And says in him thy fair appearance lies.
To cide this title is impanneled
A quest of thoughts, all tenants to the heart;
And by their verdict is determined
The clear eye's moiety and the dear heart's part:
   As thus; mine eye's due is thy outward part,
   And my heart's right thy inward love of heart.

47

Betwixt mine eye and heart a league is took,
And each doth good turns now unto the other:
When that mine eye is famish'd for a look,
Or heart in love with sighs himself doth smother,
With my love's picture then my eye doth feast,
And to the painted banquet bids my heart;
Another time mine eye is my heart's guest,
And in his thoughts of love doth share a part:
So, either by thy picture or my love,
Thyself away art present still with me;
For thou not farther than my thoughts canst move,
And I am still with them, and they with thee;
   Or, if they sleep, thy picture in my sight
   Awakes my heart to heart's and eye's delight.

48

How careful was I, when I took my way,
Each trifle under truest bars to thrust,
That to my use it might unused stay
From hands of falsehood, in sure wards of trust!
But thou, to whom my jewels trifles are,
Most worthy comfort, now my greatest grief,
Thou, best of dearest, and mine only care,
Art left the prey of every vulgar thief.
Thee have I not lock'd up in any chest,
Save where thou art not, though I feel thou art,
Within the gentle closure of my breast,
From whence at pleasure thou mayst come and part;
   And even thence thou wilt be stol'n, I fear,
   For truth proves thievish for a prize so dear.

49

Against that time, if ever that time come,
When I shall see thee frown on my defects,
Whenas thy love hath cast his utmost sum,
Call'd to that audit by advis'd respects;
Against that time when thou shalt strangely pass,
And scarcely greet me with that sun, thine eye,
When love, converted from the thing it was,
Shall reasons find of settled gravity;
Against that time do I ensconce me here
Within the knowledge of mine own desert,
And this my hand against myself uprear,
To guard the lawful reasons on thy part:
   To leave poor me thou hast the strength of laws,
   Since why to love I can allege no cause.

50

How heavy do I journey on the way,
When what I seek, — my weary travel's end —
Doth teach that ease and that repose to say,
'Thus far the miles are measured from thy friend!'
The beast that bears me, tired with my woe,
Plods dully on, to bear that weight in me,
As if by some instinct the wretch did know
His rider lov'd not speed, being made from thee:
The bloody spur cannot provoke him on
That sometimes anger thrusts into his hide;
Which heavily he answers with a groan,
More sharp to me than spurring to his side;
   For that same groan doth put this in my mind;
   My grief lies onward, and my joy behind.

51

Thus can my love excuse the slow offence
Of my dull bearer when from thee I speed:
From where thou art why should I haste me thence?
Till I return, of posting is no need.
O, what excuse will my poor beast then find,
When swift extremity can seem but slow?
Then should I spur, though mounted on the wind,
In winged speed no motion shall I know:
Then can no horse with my desire keep pace;
Therefore desire, of perfect'st love being made,
Shall neigh, no dull flesh in his fiery race;
But love, for love, thus shall excuse my jade, —
   Since from thee going he went wilful-slow,
   Towards thee I'll run, and give him leave to go.

52

So am I as the rich, whose blessed key
Can bring him to his sweet up-locked treasure,
The which he will not every hour survey,
For blunting the fine point of seldom pleasure.
Therefore are feasts so solemn and so rare,
Since, seldom coming, in that long year set,
Like stones of worth they thinly placed are,
Or captain jewels in the carcanet.
So is the time that keeps you, as my chest,
Or as the wardrobe which the robe doth hide,
To make some special instant special blest,
By new unfolding his imprison'd pride.
   Blessed are you, whose worthiness gives scope,
   Being had, to triumph, being lack'd, to hope.

53

What is your substance, whereof are you made,
That millions of strange shadows on you tend?
Since every one hath, every one, one shade,
And you, but one, can every shadow lend.
Describe Adonis, and the counterfeit
Is poorly imitated after you;
On Helen's cheek all art of beauty set,
And you in Grecian tires are painted new:
Speak of the spring, and foison of the year;
The one doth shadow of your beauty show,
The other as your bounty doth appear;
And you in every blessed shape we know.
   In all external grace you have some part,
   But you like none, none you, for constant heart.

54

O, how much more doth beauty beauteous seem
By that sweet ornament which truth doth give!
The rose looks fair, but fairer we it deem
For that sweet odour which doth in it live.
The canker-blooms have full as deep a dye
As the perfumed tincture of the roses,
Hang on such thorns, and play as wantonly
When summer's breath their masked buds discloses:
But, for their virtue only is their show,
They live unwoo'd, and unrespected fade,
Die to themselves. Sweet roses do not so;
Of their sweet deaths are sweetest odours made:
   And so of you, beauteous and lovely youth,
   When that shall vade, my verse distils your truth.

55

Not marble, nor the gilded monuments
Of princes, shall outlive this powerful rime;
But you shall shine more bright in these contents
Than unswept stone, besmear'd with sluttish time.
When wasteful war shall statues overturn,
And broils root out the work of masonry,
Nor Mars his sword nor war's quick fire shall burn
The living record of your memory.
'Gainst death and all-oblivious enmity
Shall you pace forth; your praise shall still find room
Even in the eyes of all posterity
That wears this world out to the ending doom.
   So, till the judgement that yourself arise,
   You live in this, and dwell in lovers' eyes.

56

Sweet love, renew thy force; be it not said
Thy edge should blunter be than appetite,
Which but to-day by feeding is allay'd,
To-morrow sharpen'd in his former might:
So, love, be thou; although to-day thou fill
Thy hungry eyes even till they wink with fullness,
To-morrow see again, and do not kill
The spirit of love with a perpetual dullness.
Let this sad int'rim like the ocean be
Which parts the shore, where two contracted new
Come daily to the banks, that, when they see
Return of love, more blest may be the view;
   Or call it winter, which, being full of care,
   Makes summer's welcome thrice more wish'd, more
    rare.

57

Being your slave, what should I do but tend
Upon the hours and times of your desire?
I have no precious time at all to spend,
Nor services to do, till you require.
Nor dare I chide the world-without-end hour
Whilst I, my sovereign, watch the clock for you,
Nor think the bitterness of absence sour
When you have bid your servant once adieu;
Nor dare I question with my jealous thought
Where you may be, or your affairs suppose,
But, like a sad slave, stay and think of nought
Save, where you are how happy you make those.
   So true a fool is love, that in your Will,
   Though you do any thing, he thinks no ill.

58

That god forbid that made me first your slave,
I should in thought control your times of pleasure,
Or at your hand the account of hours to crave,
Being your vassal, bound to stay your leisure!
O, let me suffer, being at your beck,
The imprison'd absence of your liberty;
And patience, tame to sufferance, bide each check,
Without accusing you of injury.
Be where you list, your charter is so strong,
That you yourself may privilege your time
To what you will; to you it doth belong
Yourself to pardon of self-doing crime.
   I am to wait, though waiting so be hell;
   Not blame your pleasure, be it ill or well.

59

If there be nothing new, but that which is
Hath been before, how are our brains beguil'd,
Which, labouring for invention, bear amiss
The second burden of a former child!
O, that record could with a backward look,
Even of five hundred courses of the sun,
Show me your image in some antique book,
Since mind at first in character was done!
That I might see what the old world could say
To this composed wonder of your frame;
Whether we are mended, or whe'r better they,
Or whether revolution be the same.
   O, sure I am, the wits of former days
   To subjects worse have given admiring praise.

60

Like as the waves make towards the pebbled shore,
So do our minutes hasten to their end;
Each changing place with that which goes before,
In sequent toil all forwards do contend.
Nativity, once in the main of light,
Crawls to maturity, wherewith being crown'd,
Crooked eclipses 'gainst his glory fight,
And Time that gave doth now his gift confound.
Time doth transfix the flourish set on youth,
And delves the parallels in beauty's brow,
Feeds on the rarities of nature's truth,
And nothing stands but for his scythe to mow:
   And yet, to times in hope my verse shall stand,
   Praising thy worth, despite his cruel hand.

61

Is it thy will thy image should keep open
My heavy eyelids to the weary night?
Dost thou desire my slumbers should be broken,
While shadows like to thee do mock my sight?
Is it thy spirit that thou send'st from thee
So far from home into my deeds to pry,
To find out shames and idle hours in me,
The scope and tenour of thy jealousy?
O, no! thy love, though much, is not so great:
It is my love that keeps mine eye awake;
Mine own true love that doth my rest defeat,
To play the watchman ever for thy sake:
    For thee watch I whilst thou dost wake elsewhere,
    From me far off, with others all too near.

62

Sin of self-love possesseth all mine eye,
And all my soul, and all my every part;
And for this sin there is no remedy,
It is so grounded inward in my heart.
Methinks no face so gracious is as mine,
No shape so true, no truth of such account;
And for myself mine own worth do define,
As I all other in all worths surmount.
But when my glass shows me myself indeed,
Beated and chopp'd with tann'd antiquity,
Mine own self-love quite contrary I read;
Self so self-loving were iniquity.
    'Tis thee, myself, that for myself I praise,
    Painting my age with beauty of thy days.

63

Against my love shall be, as I am now,
With Time's injurious hand crush'd and o'erworn;
When hours have drain'd his blood, and fill'd his
    brow
With lines and wrinkles; when his youthful morn
Hath travell'd on to age's steepy night;
And all those beauties whereof now he's king
Are vanishing or vanish'd out of sight,
Stealing away the treasure of his spring;
For such a time do I now fortify
Against confounding age's cruel knife,
That he shall never cut from memory
My sweet love's beauty, though my lover's life:
    His beauty shall in these black lines be seen,
    And they shall live, and he in them still green.

64

When I have seen by Time's fell hand defaced
The rich proud cost of outworn buried age;
When sometime lofty towers I see down-razed,
And brass eternal slave to mortal rage;
When I have seen the hungry ocean gain
Advantage on the kingdom of the shore,
And the firm soil win of the watery main,
Increasing store with loss, and loss with store;
When I have seen such interchange of state,
Or state itself confounded to decay;
Ruin hath taught me thus to ruminate, —
That Time will come and take my love away.
    This thought is as a death, which cannot choose
    But weep to have that which it fears to lose.

65

Since brass, nor stone, nor earth, nor boundless sea,
But sad mortality o'ersways their power,
How with this rage shall beauty hold a plea,
Whose action is no stronger than a flower?
O, how shall summer's honey breath hold out
Against the wrackful siege of battering days,
When rocks impregnable are not so stout,
Nor gates of steel so strong, but Time decays?
O fearful meditation! where, alack,
Shall Time's best jewel from Time's chest lie hid?
Or what strong hand can hold his swift foot back?
Or who his spoil of beauty can forbid?
    O, none, unless this miracle have might,
    That in black ink my love may still shine bright.

66

Tired with all these, for restful death I cry, —
As, to behold Desert a beggar born,
And needy Nothing trimm'd in jollity,
And purest Faith unhappily forsworn,
And gilded Honour shamefully misplac'd,
And maiden Virtue rudely strumpeted,

And right Perfection wrongfully disgrac'd,
And Strength by limping Sway disabled,
And Art made tongue-tied by Authority,
And Folly, doctor-like, controlling Skill,
And simple Truth miscall'd Simplicity,
And captive Good attending captain Ill:
    Tired with all these, from these would I be gone,
    Save that, to die, I leave my love alone.

67

Ah, wherefore with infection should he live,
And with his presence grace impiety,
That sin by him advantage should achieve,
And lace itself with his society?
Why should false painting imitate his cheek,
And steel dead seeing of his living hue?
Why should poor beauty indirectly seek
Roses of shadow, since his rose is true?
Why should he live, now Nature bankrput is,
Beggar'd of blood to blush through lively veins?
For she hath no exchequer now but his,
And, proud of many, lives upon his gains.
    O, him she stores, to show what wealth she had
    In days long since, before these last so bad.

68

Thus in his cheek the map of days outworn,
When beauty liv'd and died as flowers do now,
Before these bastard signs of fair were born,
Or durst inhabit on a living brow;
Before the golden tresses of the dead,
The right of sepulchres, were shorn away,
To live a second life on second head;
Ere beauty's dead fleece made another gay:
In him those holy antique hours are seen,
Without all ornament, itself, and true,
Making no summer of another's green,
Robbing no old to dress his beauty new;
    And him as for a map doth Nature store,
    To show false Art what beauty was of yore.

69

Those parts of thee that the world's eye doth view
Want nothing that the thought of hearts can mend;
All tongues, the voice of souls, give thee that due,
Uttering bare truth, even so as foes commend.
Thy outward thus with outward praise is crown'd;
But those same tongues, that give thee so thine own,
In other accents do this praise confound
By seeing farther than the eye hath shown.
They look into the beauty of thy mind,
And that, in guess, they measure by thy deeds;
Then, churls, their thoughts, although their eyes were kind,
To thy fair flower add the rank smell of weeds:
    But why thy odour matcheth not thy show,
    The soil is this, that thou dost common grow.

70

That thou art blam'd shall not be thy defect,
For slander's mark was ever yet the fair;
The ornament of beauty is suspect,
A crow that flies in heaven's sweetest air.
So thou be good, slander doth but approve
Thy worth the greater, being woo'd of time;
For canker vice the sweetest buds doth love,
And thou present'st a pure unstained prime.
Thou hast pass'd by the ambush of young days,
Either not assail'd, or victor being charg'd;
Yet this thy praise cannot be so thy praise,
To tie up envy evermore enlarg'd:
    If some suspect of ill mask'd not thy show,
    Then thou alone kingdoms of hearts shouldst owe.

71

No longer mourn for me when I am dead
Than you shall hear the surly sullen bell
Give warning to the world that I am fled
From this vile world, with vilest worms to dwell:
Nay, if you read this line, remember not
The hand that writ it; for I love you so,
That I in your sweet thoughts would be forgot,
If thinking on me then should make you woe.
O, if, I say, you look upon this verse
When I perhaps compounded am with clay,
Do not so much as my poor name rehearse;
But let your love even with my life decay;
    Lest the wise world should look into your moan,
    And mock you with me after I am gone.

72

O, lest the world should task you to recite
What merit lived in me, that you should love,
After my death, dear love, forget me quite,
For you in me can nothing worthy prove;
Unless you would devise some virtuous lie,
To do more for me than mine own desert,
And hang more praise upon deceased I
Than niggard truth would willingly impart:
O, lest your true love may seem false in this,
That you for love speak well of me untrue,
My name be buried where my body is,
And live no more to shame nor me nor you.
    For I am sham'd by that which I bring forth,
    And so should you, to love things nothing worth.

73

That time of year thou mayst in me behold
When yellow leaves, or none, or few, do hang
Upon those boughs which shake against the cold,
Bare ruin'd choirs, where late the sweet birds sang.
In me thou see'st the twilight of such day
As after sunset fadeth in the west;
Which by and by black night doth take away,
Death's second self, that seals up all in rest.
In me thou see'st the glowing of such fire,
That on the ashes of his youth doth lie,
As the death-bed whereon it must expire,
Consum'd with that which it was nourish'd by.
    This thou perceiv'st, which makes thy love more
        strong,
    To love that well which thou must leave ere long.

74

But be contented: when that fell arrest
Without all bail shall carry me away,
My life hath in this line some interest,
Which for memorial still with thee shall stay.
When thou reviewest this, thou dost review
The very part was consecrate to thee:
The earth can have but earth, which is his due;
My spirit is thine, the better part of me:
So, then, thou hast but lost the dregs of life,
The prey of worms, my body being dead;
The coward conquest of a wretch's knife,
Too base of thee to be remembered.
    The worth of that is that which it contains,
    And that is this, and this with thee remains.

75

So are you to my thoughts as food to life,
Or as sweet-season'd showers are to the ground;
And for the peace of you I hold such strife
As 'twixt a miser and his wealth is found;
Now proud as an enjoyer, and anon
Doubting the filching age will steal his treasure;
Now counting best to be with you alone,
Then better'd that the world may see my pleasure:
Sometime all full with feasting on your sight,
And by and by clean starved for a look;
Possessing or pursuing no delight,
Save what is had or must from you be took.
    Thus do I pine and surfeit day by day,
    Or gluttoning on all, or all away.

76

Why is my verse so barren of new pride,
So far from variation or quick change?
Why, with the time, do I not glance aside
To new-found methods and to compounds strange?
Why write I still all one, ever the same,
And keep invention in a noted weed,
That every word doth almost tell my name,
Showing their birth, and where they did proceed?
O, know, sweet love, I always write of you,
And you and love are still my argument;
So all my best is dressing old words new,
Spending again what is already spent:
    For as the sun is daily new and old,
    So is my love still telling what is told.

77

Thy glass will show thee how thy beauties wear,
Thy dial how thy precious minutes waste;
The vacant leaves thy mind's imprint will bear,
And of this book this learning mayst thou taste.
The wrinkles which thy glass will truly show,
Of mouthed graves will give thee memory;

Thou by thy dial's shady stealth mayst know
Time's thievish progress to eternity.
Look, what thy memory cannot contain,
Commit to these waste blanks, and thou shalt find
Those children nurs'd, deliver'd from thy brain,
To take a new acquaintance of thy mind.
    These offices, so oft as thou wilt look,
    Shall profit thee, and much enrich thy book.

78

So oft have I invok'd thee for my Muse,
And found such fair assistance in my verse,
As every alien pen hath got my use,
And under thee their poesy disperse.
Thine eyes, that taught the dumb on high to sing,
And heavy ignorance aloft to fly,
Have added feathers to the learned's wing,
And given grace a double majesty.
Yet be most proud of that which I compile,
Whose influence is thine, and born of thee:
In others' works thou dost but mend the style,
And arts with thy sweet graces graced be;
    But thou art all my art, and dost advance
    As high as learning my rude ignorance.

79

Whilst I alone did call upon thy aid,
My verse alone had all thy gentle grace;
But now my gracious numbers are decay'd,
And my sick Muse doth give another place.
I grant, sweet love, thy lovely argument
Deserves the travail of a worthier pen;
Yet what of thee thy poet doth invent
He robs thee of, and pays it thee again.
He lends thee virtue, and he stole that word
From thy behaviour; beauty doth he give,
And found it in thy cheek; he can afford
No praise to thee but what in thee doth live.
    Then thank him not for that which he doth say,
    Since what he owes thee thou thyself dost pay.

80

O, how I faint when I of you do write,
Knowing a better spirit doth use your name,
And in the praise thereof spends all his might,
To make me tongue-tied, speaking of your fame!
But since your worth, wide as the ocean is,
The humble as the proudest sail doth bear,
My saucy bark, inferior far to his,
On your broad main doth wilfully appear.
Your shallowest help will hold me up afloat,
While he upon your soundless deep doth ride;
Or, being wrack'd, I am a worthless boat,
He of tall building and of goodly pride:
    Then if he thrive, and I be cast away,
    The worst was this; my love was my decay.

81

Or I shall live your epitaph to make,
Or you survive when I in earth am rotten;
From hence your memory death cannot take,
Although in me each part will be forgotten.
Your name from hence immortal life shall have,
Though I, once gone, to all the world must die:
The earth can yield me but a common grave,
When you entombed in men's eyes shall lie.
Your monument shall be my gentle verse,
Which eyes not yet created shall o'er-read;
And tongues to be your being shall rehearse,
When all the breathers of this world are dead;
    You still shall live — such virtue hath my pen —
    Where breath most breathes, even in the mouths of
    men.

82

I grant thou wert not married to my Muse,
And therefore mayst without attaint o'erlook
The dedicated words which writers use
Of their fair subject, blessing every book.
Thou art as fair in knowledge as in hue,
Finding thy worth a limit past my praise;
And therefore art enforc'd to seek anew
Some fresher stamp of the time-bettering days.
And do so, love; yet when they have devis'd
What strained touches rhetoric can lend,
Thou truly fair wert truly sympathis'd
In true plain words by thy true-telling friend;
    And their gross painting might be better us'd
    Where cheeks need blood; in thee it is abus'd.

83

I never saw that you did painting need,
And therefore to your fair no painting set;
I found, or thought I found, you did exceed
The barren tender of a poet's debt:
And therefore have I slept in your report,
That you yourself, being extant, well might show
How far a modern quill doth come too short,
Speaking of worth, what worth in you doth grow.
This silence for my sin you did impute,
Which shall be most my glory, being dumb;
For I impair not beauty, being mute,
When others would give life, and bring a tomb.
    There lives more life in one of your fair eyes
    Than both your poets can in praise devise.

84

Who is it that says most? which can say more
Than this rich praise, that you alone are you?
In whose confine immured is the store
Which should example where your equal grew.
Lean penury within that pen doth dwell
That to his subject lends not some small glory,
But he that writes of you, if he can tell
That you are you, so dignifies his story:
Let him but copy what in you is writ,
Not making worse what nature made so clear,
And such a counterpart shall fame his wit,
Making his style admired everywhere.
    You to your beauteous blessings add a curse,
    Being fond on praise, which makes your praises
    worse.

85

My tongue-tied Muse in manners holds her still,
While comments of your praise, richly compil'd,
Reserve their character with golden quill,
And precious phrase by all the Muses fil'd.
I think good thoughts, whilst others write good words,
And, like unletter'd clerk, still cry 'Amen'
To every hymn that able spirit affords
In polish'd form of well-refined pen.
Hearing you prais'd, I say ''Tis so, 'tis true,'
And to the most of praise add something more;
But that is in my thought, whose love to you,
Though words come hindmost, holds his rank before.
    Then others for the breath of words respect,
    Me for my dumb thoughts, speaking in effect.

86

Was it the proud full sail of his great verse,
Bound for the prize of all-too-precious you,
That did my ripe thoughts in my brain inhearse,
Making their tomb the womb wherein they grew?
Was it his spirit, by spirits taught to write
Above a mortal pitch, that struck me dead?
No, neither he, nor his compeers by night
Giving him aid, my verse astonished.
He, nor that affable familiar ghost
Which nightly gulls him with intelligence,
As victors, of my silence cannot boast;
I was not sick of any fear from thence:
    But when your countenance fill'd up his line,
    Then lack'd I matter, that enfeebled mine.

87

Farewell! thou art too dear for my possessing,
And like enough thou know'st thy estimate:
The charter of thy worth gives thee releasing;
My bonds in thee are all determinate.
For how do I hold thee but by thy granting?
And for that riches where is my deserving?
The cause of this fair gift in me is wanting,
And so my patent back again is swerving.
Thyself thou gav'st, thy own worth then not knowing,
Or me, to whom thou gav'st it, else mistaking;
So thy great gift, upon misprision growing,
Comes home again, on better judgement making.
    Thus have I had thee, as a dream doth flatter,
    In sleep a king, but waking no such matter.

88

When thou shalt be dispos'd to set me light,
And place my merit in the eye of scorn,
Upon thy side against myself I'll fight,
And prove thee virtuous, though thou art forsworn.
With mine own weakness being best acquainted,
Upon thy part I can set down a story

Of faults conceal'd, wherein I am attainted:
That thou, in losing me, shalt win much glory:
And I by this will be a gainer too;
For bending all my loving thoughts on thee,
The injuries that to myself I do,
Doing thee vantage, double-vantage me.
    Such is my love, to thee I so belong,
    That for thy right myself will bear all wrong.

89

Say that thou didst forsake me for some fault,
And I will comment upon that offence:
Speak of my lameness, and I straight will halt,
Against thy reasons making no defence.
Thou canst not, love, disgrace me half so ill,
To set a form upon desired change,
As I'll myself disgrace: knowing thy will,
I will acquaintance strangle, and look strange;
Be absent from thy walks; and in my tongue
Thy sweet beloved name no more shall dwell,
Lest I, too much profane, should do it wrong,
And haply of our old acquaintance tell.
    For thee, against myself I'll vow debate,
    For I must ne'er love him whom thou dost hate.

90

Then hate me when thou wilt; if ever, now;
Now, while the world is bent my deeds to cross,
Join with the spite of fortune, make me bow,
And do not drop in for an after-loss:
Ah, do not, when my heart hath scap'd this sorrow,
Come in the rearward of a conquer'd woe;
Give not a windy night a rainy morrow,
To linger out a purpos'd overthrow.
If thou wilt leave me, do not leave me last,
When other petty griefs have done their spite,
But in the onset come: so shall I taste
At first the very worst of fortune's might;
    And other strains of woe, which now seem woe,
    Compar'd with loss of thee will not seem so.

91

Some glory in their birth, some in their skill,
Some in their wealth, some in their bodies' force;
Some in their garments, though new-fangled ill;
Some in their hawks and hounds, some in their horse;
And every humour hath his adjunct pleasure,
Wherein it finds a joy above the rest:
But these particulars are not my measure;
All these I better in one general best.
Thy love is better than high birth to me,
Richer than wealth, prouder than garments' cost,
Of more delight than hawks and horses be;
And having thee, of all men's pride I boast:
    Wretched in this alone, that thou mayst take
    All this away, and me most wretched make.

92

But do thy worst to steal thyself away,
For term of life thou art assured mine;
And life no longer than thy love will stay,
For it depends upon that love of thine.
Then need I not to fear the worst of wrongs,
When in the least of them my life hath end.
I see a better state to me belongs
Than that which on thy humour doth depend:
Thou canst not vex me with inconstant mind,
Since that my life on thy revolt doth lie.
 O, what a happy title do I find,
Happy to have thy love, happy to die!
    But what's so blessed-fair that fears no blot?
    Thou mayst be false, and yet I know it not.

93

So shall I live, supposing thou art true,
Like a deceived husband; so love's face
May still seem love to me, though alter'd new;
Thy looks with me, thy heart in other place:
For there can live no hatred in thine eye,
Therefore in that I cannot know thy change.
In many's looks the false heart's history
Is writ in moods and frowns and wrinkles strange;
But heaven in thy creation did decree
That in thy face sweet love should ever dwell;
Whate'er thy thoughts or thy heart's workings be,
Thy looks should nothing thence but sweetness tell.
    How like Eve's apple doth thy beauty grow,
    If thy sweet virtue answer not thy show!

94

They that have power to hurt and will do none,
That do not do the thing they most do show,
Who, moving others, are themselves as stone,
Unmov'd, cold, and to temptation slow;
They rightly do inherit heaven's graces,
And husband nature's riches from expense;
They are the lords and owners of their faces,
Others but stewards of their excellence.
The summer's flower is to the summer sweet,
Though to itself it only live and die;
But if that flower with base infection meet,
The basest weed outbraves his dignity:
　　For sweetest things turn sourest by their deeds;
　　Lilies that fester smell far worse than weeds.

95

How sweet and lovely dost thou make the shame
Which, like a canker in the fragrant rose,
Doth spot the beauty of thy budding name!
O, in what sweets dost thou thy sins enclose!
That tongue that tells the story of thy days,
Making lascivious comments on thy sport,
Cannot dispraise but in a kind of praise;
Naming thy name blesses an ill report.
O, what a mansion have those vices got
Which for their habitation chose out thee,
Where beauty's veil doth cover every blot,
And all things turn to fair that eyes can see!
　　Take heed, dear heart, of this large privilege;
　　The hardest knife ill-us'd doth lose his edge.

96

Some say, thy fault is youth, some wantonness;
Some say, thy grace is youth and gentle sport;
Both grace and faults are lov'd of more and less:
Thou mak'st faults graces that to thee resort.
As on the finger of a throned queen
The basest jewel will be well esteem'd,
So are those errors that in thee are seen
To truths translated, and for true things deem'd.
How many lambs might the stern wolf betray,
If like a lamb he could his looks translate!
How many gazers mightst thou lead away,
If thou wouldst use the strength of all thy state!
　　But do not so; I love thee in such sort,
　　As thou being mine, mine is thy good report.

97

How like a winter hath my absence been
From thee, the pleasure of the fleeting year!
What freezings have I felt, what dark days seen!
What old December's bareness every where!
And yet this time remov'd was summer's time;
The teeming autumn, big with rich increase,
Bearing the wanton burden of the prime,
Like widow'd wombs after their lords' decease:
Yet this abundant issue seem'd to me
But hope of orphans and unfather'd fruit;
For summer and his pleasures wait on thee,
And, thou away, the very birds are mute;
　　Or, if they sing, 'tis with so dull a cheer,
　　That leaves look pale, dreading the winter's near.

98

From you I have been absent in the spring,
When proud-pied April, dress'd in all his trim,
Hath put a spirit of youth in every thing,
That heavy Saturn laugh'd and leap'd with him.
Yet nor the lays of birds, nor the sweet smell
Of different flowers in odour and in hue,
Could make me any summer's story tell,
Or from their proud lap pluck them where they grew:
Nor did I wonder at the lily's white,
Nor praise the deep vermilion in the rose;
They were but sweet, but figures of delight,
Drawn after you, — you pattern of all those.
　　Yet seem'd it winter still, and, you away,
　　As with your shadow I with these did play.

99

The forward violet thus did I chide:
Sweet thief, whence didst thou steal thy sweet that smells,
If not from my love's breath? The purple pride
Which on thy soft cheek for complexion dwells
In my love's veins thou hast too grossly dyed.
The lily I condemned for thy hand;

And buds of marjoram had stol'n thy hair:
The roses fearfully on thorns did stand,
One blushing shame, another white despair;
A third, nor red nor white, had stol'n of both,
And to his robbery had annex'd thy breath;
But, for his theft, in pride of all his growth
A vengeful canker eat him up to death.
　　More flowers I noted, yet I none could see
　　But sweet or colour it had stol'n from thee.

100

Where art thou, Muse, that thou forgett'st so long
To speak of that which gives thee all thy might?
Spend'st thou thy fury on some worthless song,
Dark'ning thy power to lend base subjects light?
Return, forgetful Muse, and straight redeem
In gentle numbers time so idly spent;
Sing to the ear that doth thy lays esteem,
And gives thy pen both skill and argument.
Rise, resty Muse, my love's sweet face survey,
If Time have any wrinkle graven there;
If any, be a satire to decay,
And make Time's spoils despised everywhere.
　　Give my love fame faster than Time wastes life;
　　So thou prevent'st his scythe and crooked knife.

101

O truant Muse, what shall be thy amends
For thy neglect of truth in beauty dyed?
Both truth and beauty on my love depends;
So dost thou too, and therein dignified.
Make answer, Muse: wilt thou not haply say,
'Truth needs no colour, with his colour fix'd;
Beauty no pencil, beauty's truth to lay;
But best is best, if never intermix'd'?
Because he needs no praise, wilt thou be dumb?
Excuse not silence so: for't lies in thee
To make him much outlive a gilded tomb,
And to be prais'd of ages yet to be.
　　Then do thy office, Muse; I teach thee how
　　To make him seem long hence as he shows now.

102

My love is strengthen'd, though more weak in
　　seeming;
I love not less, though less the show appear:
That love is merchandis'd whose rich esteeming
The owner's tongue doth publish everywhere.
Our love was new, and then but in the spring,
When I was wont to greet it with my lays;
As Philomel in summer's front doth sing,
And stops her pipe in growth of riper days:
Not that the summer is less pleasant now
Than when her mournful hymns did hush the night,
But that wild music burdens every bough,
And sweets grown common lose their dear delight.
　　Therefore, like her, I sometime hold my tongue,
　　Because I would not dull you with my song.

103

Alack, what poverty my Muse brings forth,
That having such a scope to show her pride,
The argument, all bare, is of more worth
Than when it hath my added praise beside!
O, blame me not, if I no more can write!
Look in your glass, and there appears a face
That overgoes my blunt invention quite,
Dulling my lines, and doing me disgrace.
Were it not sinful, then, striving to mend,
To mar the subject that before was well?
For to no other pass my verses tend
Than of your Graces and your gifts to tell;
　　And more, much more, than in my verse can sit,
　　Your own glass shows you when you look in it.

104

To me, fair friend, you never can be old,
For as you were when first your eye I eyed,
Such seems your beauty still. Three winters' cold
Have from the forests shook three summers' pride;
Three beauteous springs to yellow autumn turn'd
In process of the seasons have I seen,
Three April perfumes in three hot Junes burn'd,
Since first I saw you fresh, which yet are green.
Ah, yet doth beauty, like a dial-hand,
Steal from his figure, and no pace perceived;
So your sweet hue, which methinks still doth stand,
Hath motion, and mine eye may be deceived:

For fear of which, hear this, thou age unbred, —
Ere you were born was beauty's summer dead.

105

Let not my love be call'd idolatry,
Nor my beloved as an idol show,
Since all alike my songs and praises be
To one, of one, still such, and ever so.
Kind is my love to-day, to-morrow kind,
Still constant in a wondrous excellence;
Therefore my verse to constancy confin'd,
One thing expressing, leaves out difference.
Fair, kind, and true, is all my argument, —
Fair, kind, and true, varying to other words;
And in this change is my invention spent,
Three themes in one, which wondrous scope
　　affords.
　　Fair, kind, and true, have often liv'd alone,
　　Which three till now never kept seat in one.

106

When in the chronicle of wasted time
I see descriptions of the fairest wights,
And beauty making beautiful old rime
In praise of ladies dead and lovely knights,
Then, in the blazon of sweet beauty's best,
Of hand, of foot, of lip, of eye, of brow,
I see their antique pen would have express'd
Even such a beauty as you master now.
So all their praises are but prophecies
Of this our time, all you prefiguring;
And, for they look'd but with divining eyes,
They had not skill enough your worth to sing:
　　For we, which now behold these present days,
　　Have eyes to wonder, but lack tongues to praise.

107

Not mine own fears, nor the prophetic soul
Of the wide world dreaming on things to come,
Can yet the lease of my true love control,
Suppos'd as forfeit to a confin'd doom.
The mortal moon hath her eclipse endured,
And the sad augurs mock their own presage;
Incertainties now crown themselves assured,
And peace proclaims olives of endless age.
Now with the drops of this most balmy time
My love looks fresh, and Death to me subscribes,
Since, spite of him, I'll live in this poor rime,
While he insults o'er dull and speechless tribes:
　　And thou in this shalt find thy monument,
　　When tyrants' crests and tombs of brass are
　　spent.

108

What's in the brain, that ink may character,
Which hath not figur'd to thee my true spirit?
What's new to speak, what new to register,
That may express my love, or thy dear merit?
Nothing, sweet boy; but yet, like prayers divine,
I must each day say o'er the very same;
Counting no old thing old, thou mine, I thine,
Even as when first I hallow'd thy fair name.
So that eternal love in love's fresh case
Weighs not the dust and injury of age,
Nor gives to necessary wrinkles place,
But makes antiquity for aye his page;
　　Finding the first conceit of love there bred,
　　Where time and outward form would show it
　　dead.

109

O, never say that I was false of heart,
Though absence seem'd my flame to qualify.
As easy might I from myself depart
As from my soul, which in thy breast doth lie:
That is my home of love: if I have rang'd,
Like him that travels I return again,
Just to the time, not with the time exchang'd,
So that myself bring water for my stain.
Never believe, though in my nature reign'd
All frailties that besiege all kinds of blood,
That it could so preposterously be stain'd,
To leave for nothing all thy sum of good;
　　For nothing this wide universe I call,
　　Save thou, my Rose; in it thou art my all.

110

Alas, 'tis true I have gone here and there,
And made myself a motley to the view,
Gor'd mine own thoughts, sold cheap what is most dear,
Made old offences of affections new;
Most true it is that I have look'd on truth
Askance and strangely: but, by all above,
These blenches gave my heart another youth,
And worse essays prov'd thee my best of love.
Now all is done, have what shall have no end:
Mine appetite I never more will grind
On newer proof, to try an older friend,
A god in love, to whom I am confin'd.
    Then give me welcome, next my heaven the best,
    Even to thy pure and most most loving breast.

111

O, for my sake do you with Fortune chide,
The guilty goddess of my harmful deeds,
That did not better for my life provide
Than public means which public manners breeds.
Thence comes it that my name receives a brand;
And almost thence my nature is subdu'd
To what it works in, like the dyer's hand:
Pity me, then, and wish I were renew'd;
Whilst, like a willing patient, I will drink
Potions of eisel 'gainst my strong infection;
No bitterness that I will bitter think,
Nor double penance, to correct correction.
    Pity me, then, dear friend, and I assure ye
    Even that your pity is enough to cure me.

112

Your love and pity doth the impression fill
Which vulgar scandal stamp'd upon my brow;
For what care I who calls me well or ill,
So you o'er-green my bad, my good allow?
You are my all-the-world, and I must strive
To know my shames and praises from your tongue;
None else to me, nor I to none alive,
That my steel'd sense or changes right or wrong.
In so profound abysm I throw all care
Of others' voices, that my adder's sense
To critic and to flatterer stopped are.
Mark how with my neglect I do dispense:
    You are so strongly in my purpose bred,
    That all the world besides methinks are dead.

113

Since I left you, mine eye is in my mind;
And that which governs me to go about
Doth part his function, and is partly blind,
Seems seeing, but effectually is out;
For it no form delivers to the heart
Of bird, of flower, or shape, which it doth latch:
Of his quick objects hath the mind no part,
Nor his own vision holds what it doth catch;
For if it see the rud'st or gentlest sight,
The most sweet favour or deformed'st creature,
The mountain or the sea, the day or night,
The crow or dove, it shapes them to your feature:
    Incapable of more, replete with you,
    My most true mind thus maketh mine untrue.

114

Or whether doth my mind, being crown'd with you,
Drink up the monarch's plague, this flattery?
Or whether shall I say, mine eye saith true,
And that your love taught it this alchemy,
To make of monsters and things indigest
Such cherubins as your sweet self resemble,
Creating every bad a perfect best,
As fast as objects to his beams assemble?
O, 'tis the first; 'tis flatt'ry in my seeing,
And my great mind most kingly drinks it up:
Mine eye well knows what with his gust is greeing,
And to his palate doth prepare the cup:
    If it be poison'd, 'tis the lesser sin
    That mine eye loves it, and doth first begin.

115

Those lines that I before have writ do lie,
Even those that said I could not love you dearer:
Yet then my judgement knew no reason why
My most full flame should afterwards burn clearer.
But reckoning Time, whose million'd accidents
Creep in 'twixt vows, and change decrees of kings,

Tan sacred beauty, blunt the sharp'st intents,
Divert strong minds to the course of alt'ring things;
Alas, why, fearing of Time's tyranny,
Might I not then say, 'Now I love you best,'
When I was certain o'er incertainty,
Crowning the present, doubting of the rest?
    Love is a babe; then might I not say so,
    To give full growth to that which still doth grow.

116

Let me not to the marriage of true minds
Admit impediments. Love is not love
Which alters when it alteration finds,
Or bends with the remover to remove:
O, no! it is an ever-fixed mark,
That looks on tempests, and is never shaken;
It is the star to every wandering bark,
Whose worth's unknown, although his height be taken.
Love's not Time's fool, though rosy lips and cheeks
Within his bending sickle's compass come;
Love alters not with his brief hours and weeks,
But bears it out even to the edge of doom.
    If this be error, and upon me proved,
    I never writ, nor no man ever loved.

117

Accuse me thus: that I have scanted all
Wherein I should your great deserts repay;
Forgot upon your dearest love to call,
Whereto all bonds do tie me day by day;
That I have frequent been with unknown minds,
And given to time your own dear-purchas'd right;
That I have hoisted sail to all the winds
Which should transport me farthest from your sight.
Book both my wilfulness and errors down,
And on just proof surmise accumulate;
Bring me within the level of your frown,
But shoot not at me in your waken'd hate;
    Since my appeal says I did strive to prove
    The constancy and virtue of your love.

118

Like as, to make our appetites more keen,
With eager compounds we our palate urge;
As, to prevent our maladies unseen,
We sicken to shun sickness when we purge;
Even so, being full of your ne'er-cloying sweetness,
To bitter sauces did I frame my feeding;
And, sick of welfare, found a kind of meetness
To be diseas'd, ere that there was true needing.
Thus policy in love, t'anticipate
The ills that were not, grew to faults assured,
And brought to medicine a healthful state,
Which, rank of goodness, would by ill be cured:
    But thence I learn, and find the lesson true,
    Drugs poison him that so fell sick of you.

119

What potions have I drunk of Siren tears,
Distill'd from limbecks foul as hell within,
Applying fears to hopes, and hopes to fears,
Still losing when I saw myself to win!
What wretched errors hath my heart committed,
Whilst it hath thought itself so blessed never!
How have mine eyes out of their spheres been fitted
In the distraction of this madding fever!
O benefit of ill! now I find true
That better is by evil still made better;
And ruin'd love, when it is built anew,
Grows fairer than at first, more strong, far greater.
    So I return rebuk'd to my content,
    And gain by ill thrice more than I have spent.

120

That you were once unkind befriends me now,
And for that sorrow which I then did feel
Needs must I under my transgression bow,
Unless my nerves were brass or hammer'd steel.
For if you were by my unkindness shaken,
As I by yours, y'have pass'd a hell of time;
And I, a tyrant, have no leisure taken
To weigh how once I suffer'd in your crime.
O, that our night of woe might have remember'd
My deepest sense, how hard true sorrow hits,
And soon to you, as you to me then, tender'd
The humble salve which wounded bosoms fits!
    But that, your trespass, now becomes a fee;
    Mine ransoms yours, and yours must ransom me.

121

'Tis better to be vile than vile esteemed,
When not to be receives reproach of being;
And the just pleasure lost, which is so deemed
Not by our feeling, but by others' seeing:
For why should others' false adulterate eyes
Give salutation to my sportive blood?
Or on my frailties why are frailer spies,
Which in their wills count bad what I think good?
No, I am that I am; and they that level
At my abuses reckon up their own:
I may be straight, though they themselves be bevel;
By their rank thoughts my deeds must not be
    shown;
    Unless this general evil they maintain —
    All men are bad, and in their badness reign.

122

Thy gift, thy tables, are within my brain
Full character'd with lasting memory,
Which shall above that idle rank remain,
Beyond all date, even to eternity:
Or, at the least, so long as brain and heart
Have faculty by nature to subsist;
Till each to raz'd oblivion yield his part
Of thee, thy record never can be miss'd.
That poor retention could not so much hold,
Nor need I tallies thy dear love to score;
Therefore to give them from me was I bold,
To trust those tables that receive thee more:
    To keep an adjunct to remember thee
    Were to import forgetfulness in me.

123

No, Time, thou shalt not boast that I do change:
Thy pyramids built up with newer might
To me are nothing novel, nothing strange;
They are but dressings of a former sight.
Our dates are brief, and therefore we admire
What thou dost foist upon us that is old;
And rather make them born to our desire
Than think that we before have heard them told.
Thy registers and thee I both defy,
Not wondering at the present nor the past;
For thy records and what we see doth lie,
Made more or less by thy continual haste.
    This I do vow, and this shall ever be,
    I will be true, despite thy scythe and thee.

124

If my dear love were but the child of state,
It might for Fortune's bastard be unfather'd,
As subject to Time's love or to Time's hate,
Weeds among weeds, or flowers with flowers
    gather'd.
No, it was builded far from accident;
It suffers not in smiling pomp, nor falls
Under the blow of thralled discontent,
Whereto the inviting time our fashion calls:
It fears not policy, that heretic,
Which works on leases of short-number'd hours,
But all alone stands hugely politic,
That it nor grows with heat nor drowns with showers.
    To this I witness call the fools of Time,
    Which die for goodness, who have liv'd for crime.

125

Were't aught to me I bore the canopy,
With my extern the outward honouring,
Or laid great bases for eternity,
Which proves more short than waste or ruining?
Have I not seen dwellers on form and favour
Lose all, and more, by paying too much rent,
For compound sweet forgoing simple savour,
Pitiful thrivers, in their gazing spent?
No, let me be obsequious in thy heart,
And take thou my oblation, poor but free,
Which is not mix'd with seconds, knows no art,
But mutual render, only me for thee.
    Hence, thou suborn'd informer! a true soul
    When most impeach'd stands least in thy control.

126

O thou, my lovely boy, who in thy power
Dost hold Time's fickle glass, his sickle-hour;
Who hast by waning grown, and therein show'st
Thy lovers withering, as thy sweet self grow'st;

If Nature, sovereign mistress over wrack,
As thou goest onwards, still will pluck thee back,
She keeps thee to this purpose, that her skill
May Time disgrace, and wretched minutes kill.
Yet fear her, O thou minion of her pleasure!
She may detain, but not still keep, her treasure:
  Her audit, though delay'd, answer'd must be,
  And her quietus is to render thee.

127

In the old age black was not counted fair,
Or if it were, it bore not beauty's name;
But now is black beauty's successive heir,
And beauty slander'd with a bastard shame:
For since each hand hath put on nature's power,
Fairing the foul with art's false borrow'd face,
Sweet beauty hath no name, no holy bower,
But is profan'd, if not lives in disgrace.
Therefore my mistress' eyes are raven black,
Her eyes so suited, and they mourners seem
At such who, not born fair, no beauty lack,
Slandering creation with a false esteem:
  Yet so they mourn, becoming of their woe,
  That every tongue says beauty should look so.

128

How oft, when thou, my music, music play'st,
Upon that blessed wood whose motion sounds
With thy sweet fingers, when thou gently sway'st
The wiry concord that mine ear confounds,
Do I envy those jacks that nimble leap
To kiss the tender inward of thy hand,
Whilst my poor lips, which should that harvest reap,
At the wood's boldness by thee blushing stand!
To be so tickled, they would change their state
And situation with those dancing chips,
O'er whom thy fingers walk with gentle gait,
Making dead wood more blest than living lips.
  Since saucy jacks so happy are in this,
  Give them thy fingers, me thy lips to kiss.

129

The expense of spirit in a waste of shame
Is lust in action; and till action, lust
Is perjur'd, murd'rous, bloody, full of blame,
Savage, extreme, rude, cruel, not to trust;
Enjoy'd no sooner but despised straight;
Past reason hunted; and no sooner had,
Past reason hated, as a swallow'd bait,
On purpose laid to make the taker mad:
Mad in pursuit, and in possession so;
Had, having, and in quest to have, extreme;
A bliss in proof, and prov'd, a very woe;
Before, a joy propos'd; behind, a dream.
  All this the world well knows; yet none knows well
  To shun the heaven that leads men to this hell.

130

My mistress' eyes are nothing like the sun;
Coral is far more red than her lips' red:
If snow be white, why then her breasts are dun;
If hairs be wires, black wires grow on her head.
I have seen roses damask'd, red and white,
But no such roses see I in her cheeks;
And in some perfumes is there more delight
Than in the breath that from my mistress reeks.
I love to hear her speak, yet well I know
That music hath a far more pleasing sound:
I grant I never saw a goddess go;
My mistress, when she walks, treads on the ground.
  And yet, by heaven, I think my love as rare
  As any she belied with false compare.

131

Thou art as tyrannous, so as thou art,
As those whose beauties proudly make them cruel;
For well thou know'st to my dear doting heart
Thou art the fairest and most precious jewel.
Yet, in good faith, some say that thee behold,
Thy face hath not the power to make love groan.
To say they err I dare not be so bold,
Although I swear it to myself alone.
And, to be sure that is not false I swear,
A thousand groans, but thinking on thy face,
One on another's neck, do witness bear
Thy black is fairest in my judgement's place.
  In nothing art thou black save in thy deeds,
  And thence this slander, as I think, proceeds.

132

Thine eyes I love, and they, as pitying me,
Knowing thy heart torments me with disdain,
Have put on black, and loving mourners be,
Looking with pretty ruth upon my pain.
And truly not the morning sun of heaven
Better becomes the grey cheeks of the east,
Nor that full star that ushers in the even
Doth half that glory to the sober west,
As those two mourning eyes become thy face:
  O, let it, then, as well beseem thy heart
To mourn for me, since mourning doth thee grace,
And suit thy pity like in every part.
    Then will I swear Beauty herself is black,
    And all they foul that thy complexion lack.

133

Beshrew that heart that makes my heart to groan
For that deep wound it gives my friend and me!
Is't not enough to torture me alone,
But slave to slavery my sweet'st friend must be?
Me from myself thy cruel eye hath taken,
And my next self thou harder hast engrossed:
Of him, myself, and thee, I am forsaken;
A torment thrice threefold thus to be crossed.
Prison my heart in thy steel bosom's ward,
But then my friend's heart let my poor heart bail;
Whoe'er keeps me, let my heart be his guard;
Thou canst not then use rigour in my jail:
    And yet thou wilt; for I, being pent in thee,
    Perforce am thine, and all that is in me.

134

So, now I have confess'd that he is thine,
And I myself am mortgag'd to thy will,
Myself I'll forfeit, so that other mine
Thou wilt restore, to be my comfort still:
But thou wilt not, nor he will not be free,
For thou art covetous, and he is kind;
He learn'd but, surety-like, to write for me,
Under that bond that him as fast doth bind.
The statute of thy beauty thou wilt take,
Thou usurer, that putt'st forth all to use,
And sue a friend came debtor for my sake;
So him I lose through my unkind abuse.
    Him have I lost; thou hast both him and me:
    He pays the whole, and yet am I not free.

135

Whoever hath her wish, thou hast thy *Will*,
And *Will* to boot, and *Will* in over-plus;
More than enough am I that vex thee still,
To thy sweet will making addition thus.
Wilt thou, whose will is large and spacious,
Not once vouchsafe to hide my will in thine?
Shall will in others seem right gracious,
And in my will no fair acceptance shine?
The sea, all water, yet receives rain still,
And in abundance addeth to his store;
So thou, being rich in *Will*, add to thy *Will*
One will of mine, to make thy large *Will* more.
    Let no unkind, no fair beseechers kill;
    Think all but one, and me in that one *Will*.

136

If thy soul check thee that I come so near,
Swear to thy blind soul that I was thy *Will*,
And will, thy soul knows, is admitted there;
Thus far for love my love-suit, sweet, fulfil.
Will will fulfil the treasure of thy love,
Ay, fill it full with wills, and my will one.
In things of great receipt with ease we prove
Among a number one is reckon'd none:
Then in the number let me pass untold,
Though in thy store's account I one must be;
For nothing hold me, so it please thee hold
That nothing me, a something, sweet, to thee:
    Make but my name thy love, and love that still,
    And then thou lovest me, for my name is *Will*.

137

Thou blind fool, Love, what dost thou to mine eyes,
That they behold, and see not what they see?
They know what beauty is, see where it lies,
Yet what the best is take the worst to be.
If eyes, corrupt by over-partial looks,
Be anchor'd in the bay where all men ride,

Why of eyes' falsehood hast thou forged hooks,
Whereto the judgement of my heart is tied?
Why should my heart think that a several plot
Which my heart knows the wide world's common
    place?
Or mine eyes seeing this, say this is not,
To put fair truth upon so foul a face?
    In things right-true my heart and eyes have erred,
    And to this false plague are they now transferred.

138

When my love swears that she is made of truth,
I do believe her, though I know she lies,
That she might think me some untutor'd youth,
Unlearned in the world's false subtleties.
Thus vainly thinking that she thinks me young,
Although she knows my days are past the best,
Simply I credit her false-speaking tongue:
On both sides thus is simple truth suppress'd.
But wherefore says she not she is unjust?
And wherefore say not I that I am old?
O, love's best habit is in seeming trust,
And age in love loves not to have years told:
    Therefore I lie with her and she with me,
    And in our faults by lies we flatter'd be.

139

O, call not me to justify the wrong
That thy unkindness lays upon my heart;
Wound me not with thine eye, but with thy tongue;
Use power with power, and slay me not by art.
Tell me thou lov'st elsewhere; but in my sight,
Dear heart, forbear to glance thine eye aside:
What need'st thou wound with cunning, when thy
    might
Is more than my o'erpress'd defence can bide?
Let me excuse thee: ah, my love well knows
Her pretty looks have been mine enemies;
And therefore from my face she turns my foes,
That they elsewhere might dart their injuries:
    Yet do not so; but since I am near slain,
    Kill me outright with looks, and rid my pain.

140

Be wise as thou art cruel; do not press
My tongue-tied patience with too much disdain;
Lest sorrow lend me words, and words express
The manner of my pity-wanting pain.
If I might teach thee wit, better it were,
Though not to love, yet, love, to tell me so;
As testy sick men, when their deaths be near,
No news but health from their physicians know;
For, if I should despair, I should grow mad,
And in my madness might speak ill of thee:
Now this ill-wresting world is grown so bad,
Mad slanderers by mad ears believed be.
    That I may not be so, nor thou belied,
    Bear thine eyes straight, though thy proud heart go
    wide.

141

In faith, I do not love thee with mine eyes,
For they in thee a thousand errors note;
But 'tis my heart that loves what they despise,
Who, in despite of view, is pleas'd to dote;
Nor are mine ears with thy tongue's tune
    delighted;
Nor tender feeling to base touches prone,
Nor taste, nor smell, desire to be invited
To any sensual feast with thee alone:
But my five wits nor my five senses can
Dissuade one foolish heart from serving thee,
Who leaves unsway'd the likeness of a man,
Thy proud heart's slave and vassal wretch to be:
    Only my plague thus far I count my gain,
    That she that makes me sin awards me pain.

142

Love is my sin, and thy dear virtue hate,
Hate of my sin, grounded on sinful loving:
O, but with mine compare thou thine own state,
And thou shalt find it merits not reproving,
Or, if it do, not from those lips of thine,
That have profan'd their scarlet ornaments
And seal'd false bonds of love as oft as mine,
Robb'd others' beds' revenues of their rents.
Be it lawful I love thee, as thou lov'st those
Whom thine eyes woo as mine importune thee:

Root pity in thy heart, that, when it grows,
Thy pity may deserve to pitied be.
    If thou dost seek to have what thou dost hide,
    By self-example mayst thou be denied!

143

Lo, as a careful housewife runs to catch
One of her feather'd creatures broke away,
Sets down her babe, and makes all swift dispatch
In pursuit of the thing she would have stay;
Whilst her neglected child holds her in chase,
Cries to catch her whose busy care is bent
To follow that which flies before her face,
Not prizing her poor infant's discontent:
So runn'st thou after that which flies from thee,
Whilst I thy babe chase thee afar behind;
But if thou catch thy hope, turn back to me,
And play the mother's part, kiss me, be kind:
    So will I pray that thou mayst have thy *Will*,
    If thou turn back, and my loud crying still.

144

Two loves I have of comfort and despair,
Which like two spirits do suggest me still:
The better angel is a man right fair,
The worser spirit a woman colour'd ill.
To win me soon to hell, my female evil
Tempteth my better angel from my side,
And would corrupt my saint to be a devil,
Wooing his purity with her foul pride.
And whether that my angel be turn'd fiend
Suspect I may, yet not directly tell;
But being both from me, both to each friend,
I guess one angel in another's hell:
    Yet this shall I ne'er know, but live in doubt,
    Till my bad angel fire my good one out.

145

Those lips that Love's own hand did make
Breath'd forth the sound that said 'I hate'
To me that languish'd for her sake:
But when she saw my woeful state,
Straight in her heart did mercy come,
Chiding that tongue that ever sweet
Was us'd in giving gentle doom;
And taught it thus anew to greet;
'I hate' she alter'd with an end,
That follow'd it as gentle day
Doth follow night, who like a fiend
From heaven to hell is flown away;
    'I hate' from hate away she threw,
    And sav'd my life, saying — 'Not you.'

146

Poor soul, the centre of my sinful earth —
My sinful earth these rebel powers array —
Why dost thou pine within and suffer dearth,
Painting thy outward walls so costly gay?
Why so large cost, having so short a lease,
Dost thou upon thy fading mansion spend?
Shall worms, inheritors of this excess,
Eat up thy charge? is this thy body's end?
Then, soul, live thou upon thy servant's loss,
And let that pine to aggravate thy store;
Buy terms divine in selling hours of dross;
Within be fed, without be rich no more:
    So shalt thou feed on Death, that feeds on men,
    And Death once dead, there's no more dying then.

147

My love is as a fever, longing still
For that which longer nurseth the disease;
Feeding on that which doth preserve the ill,
The uncertain sickly appetite to please.
My reason, the physician to my love,
Angry that his prescriptions are not kept,
Hath left me, and I desperate now approve
Desire is death, which physic did except.
Past cure I am, now reason is past care,
And frantic-mad with evermore unrest;
My thoughts and my discourse as madmen's are,
At random from the truth vainly express'd;
    For I have sworn thee fair, and thought thee bright,
    Who art as black as hell, as dark as night.

148

O me, what eyes hath Love put in my head,
Which have no correspondence with true sight!
Or, if they have, where is my judgement fled,
That censures falsely what they see aright?
If that be fair whereon my false eyes dote,
What means the world to say it is not so?
If it be not, then love doth well denote
Love's eye is not so true as all men's: no.
How can it? O, how can Love's eye be true,
That is so vex'd with watching and with tears?
No marvel, then, though I mistake my view;
The sun itself sees not till heaven clears.
    O cunning Love! with tears thou keep'st me blind,
    Lest eyes well-seeing thy foul faults should find.

149

Canst thou, O cruel! say I love thee not,
When I, against myself, with thee partake?
Do I not think on thee, when I forgot
Am of myself, all tyrant for thy sake?
Who hateth thee that I do call my friend?
On whom frown'st thou that I do fawn upon?
Nay, if thou lour'st on me, do I not spend
Revenge upon myself with present moan?
What merit do I in myself respect,
That is so proud thy service to despise,
When all my best doth worship thy defect,
Commanded by the motion of thine eyes?
    But, love, hate on, for now I know thy mind;
    Those that can see thou lov'st, and I am blind.

150

O, from what power hast thou this powerful might
With insufficiency my heart to sway?
To make me give the lie to my true sight,
And swear that brightness doth not grace the day?
Whence hast thou this becoming of things ill,
That in the very refuse of thy deeds
There is such strength and warrantise of skill,
That, in my mind, thy worst all best exceeds?
Who taught thee how to make me love thee more,
The more I hear and see just cause of hate?
O, though I love what others do abhor,
With others thou shouldst not abhor my state:
    If thy unworthiness rais'd love in me,
    More worthy I to be belov'd of thee.

151

Love is too young to know what conscience is;
Yet who knows not conscience is born of love?
Then, gentle cheater, urge not my amiss,
Lest guilty of my faults thy sweet self prove:
For, thou betraying me, I do betray
My nobler part to my gross body's treason;
My soul doth tell my body that he may
Triumph in love; flesh stays no farther reason;
But, rising at thy name, doth point out thee
As his triumphant prize. Proud of this pride,
He is contented thy poor drudge to be,
To stand in thy affairs, fall by thy side.
    No want of conscience hold it that I call
    Her 'love' for whose dear love I rise and fall.

152

In loving thee thou know'st I am forsworn,
But thou art twice forsworn, to me love swearing;
In act thy bed-vow broke, and new faith torn
In vowing new hate after new love bearing.
But why of two oaths' breach do I accuse thee,
When I break twenty? I am perjur'd most;
For all my vows are oaths but to misuse thee,
And all my honest faith in thee is lost:
For I have sworn deep oaths of thy deep kindness,
Oaths of thy love, thy truth, thy constancy;
And, to enlighten thee, gave eyes to blindness,
Or made them swear against the thing they see;
    For I have sworn thee fair; more perjur'd I,
    To swear against the truth so foul a lie!

153

Cupid laid by his brand, and fell asleep:
A maid of Dian's this advantage found,
And his love-kindling fire did quickly steep
In a cold valley-fountain of that ground;
Which borrow'd from this holy fire of Love
A dateless lively heat, still to endure,
And grew a seething bath, which yet men prove
Against strange maladies a sovereign cure.
But at my mistress' eye Love's brand new-fired,
The boy for trial needs would touch my breast;
I, sick withal, the help of bath desired,
And thither hied, a sad distemper'd guest,
    But found no cure: the bath for my help lies
    Where Cupid got new fire, — my mistress' eyes.

154

The little Love-god lying once asleep
Laid by his side his heart-inflaming brand,
Whilst many nymphs that vow'd chaste life to keep
Came tripping by; but in her maiden hand
The fairest votary took up that fire
Which many legions of true hearts had warm'd;
And so the general of hot desire
Was sleeping by a virgin hand disarm'd.
This brand she quenched in a cool well by,
Which from Love's fire took heat perpetual,
Growing a bath and healthful remedy
For men diseas'd; but I, my mistress' thrall,
    Came there for cure, and this by that I prove,
    Love's fire heats water, water cools not love.

A LOVER'S COMPLAINT

From off a hill whose concave womb re-worded
A plaintful story from a sistering vale,
My spirits t'attend this double voice accorded,
And down I laid to list the sad-tun'd tale;
Ere long espied a fickle maid full pale,
Tearing of papers, breaking rings a-twain,
Storming her world with sorrow's wind and rain.

Upon her head a platted hive of straw,
Which fortified her visage from the sun,
Whereon the thought might think sometime it saw
The carcass of a beauty spent and done:
Time had not scythed all that youth begun,
Nor youth all quit; but, spite of heaven's fell rage,
Some beauty peep'd through lattice of sear'd age.

Oft did she heave her napkin to her eyne,
Which on it had conceited characters,
Laundering the silken figures in the brine
That season'd woe had pelleted in tears,
And often reading what content it bears;
As often shrieking undistinguish'd woe,
In clamours of all size, both high and low.

Sometimes her levell'd eyes their carriage ride,
As they did battery to the spheres intend;
Sometime diverted their poor balls are tied
To th'orbed earth; sometimes they do extend
Their view right on; anon their gazes lend
To every place at once, and nowhere fix'd,
The mind and sight distractedly commix'd.

Her hair, nor loose nor tied in formal plat,
Proclaim'd in her a careless hand of pride;
For some, untuck'd, descended her sheav'd hat,
Hanging her pale and pined cheek beside;
Some in her threaden fillet still did bide,
And, true to bondage, would not break from thence,
Though slackly braided in loose negligence.

A thousand favours from a maund she drew
Of amber, crystal, and of beaded jet,
Which one by one she in a river threw,
Upon whose weeping margent she was set;
Like usury, applying wet to wet,
Or monarch's hands that let not bounty fall
Where want cries some, but where excess begs all.

Of folded schedules had she many a one,
Which she perus'd, sigh'd, tore, and gave the flood;
Crack'd many a ring of posied gold and bone,
Bidding them find their sepulchres in mud,
Found yet more letters sadly penn'd in blood,
With sleided silk feat and affectedly
Enswath'd, and seal'd to curious secrecy.

These often bath'd she in her fluxive eyes,
And often kiss'd, and often gan to tear;
Cried, 'O false blood, thou register of lies,
What unapproved witness dost thou bear!
Ink would have seem'd more black and damned here!'
This said, in top of rage the lines she rents,
Big discontent so breaking their contents.

A reverend man that graz'd his cattle nigh —
Sometime a blusterer, that the ruffle knew
Of court, of city, and had let go by
The swiftest hours, observed as they flew —
Towards this afflicted fancy fastly drew,
And, privileg'd by age, desires to know
In brief the grounds and motives of her woe.

So slides he down upon his grained bat,
And comely-distant sits he by her side;
When he again desires her, being sat,
Her grievance with his hearing to divide:
If that from him there may be aught applied
Which may her suffering ecstasy assuage,
'Tis promis'd in the charity of age.

'Father,' she says, 'though in me you behold
The injury of many a blasting hour,
Let it not tell your judgement I am old;
Not age, but sorrow, over me hath power:
I might as yet have been a spreading flower,
Fresh to myself, if I had self-applied
Love to myself, and to no love beside.

'But, woe is me! too early I attended
A youthful suit — it was to gain my grace —
Of one by nature's outwards so commended,
That maidens' eyes stuck over all his face:
Love lack'd a dwelling, and made him her place;
And when in his fair parts she did abide,
She was new lodg'd, and newly deified.

'His browny locks did hang in crooked curls;
And every light occasion of the wind
Upon his lips their silken parcels hurls.
What's sweet to do, to do will aptly find:
Each eye that saw him did enchant the mind;
For on his visage was in little drawn
What largeness thinks in Paradise was sawn.

'Small show of man was yet upon his chin;
His phœnix down began but to appear,
Like unshorn velvet, on that termless skin,
Whose bare out-bragg'd the web it seem'd to wear:
Yet show'd his visage by that cost more dear;
And nice affections wavering stood in doubt
If best were as it was, or best without.

'His qualities were beauteous as his form,
For maiden-tongu'd he was, and thereof free;
Yet, if men mov'd him, was he such a storm
As oft 'twixt May and April is to see,
When winds breathe sweet, unruly though they be,
His rudeness so with his authoris'd youth
Did livery falseness in a pride of truth.

'Well could he ride, and often men would say,
"That horse his mettle from his rider takes:
Proud of subjection, noble by the sway,
What rounds, what bounds, what course, what stop he
    makes!"
And controversy hence a question takes,
Whether the horse by him became his deed,
Or he his manage by the well-doing steed.

'But quickly on this side the verdict went:
His real habitude gave life and grace
To appertainings and to ornament,
Accomplish'd in himself, not in his case:
All aids, themselves made fairer by their place,
Came for additions; yet their purpos'd trim
Piec'd not his grace, but were all grac'd by him.

'So on the tip of his subduing tongue
All kind of arguments and question deep,
All replication prompt, and reason strong,
For his advantage still did wake and sleep:
To make the weeper laugh, the laugher weep,
He had the dialect and different skill,
Catching all passions in his craft of will:

'That he did in the general bosom reign
Of young, of old; and sexes both enchanted,
To dwell with him in thoughts, or to remain
In personal duty, following where he haunted:
Consents bewitch'd, ere he desire, have granted;
And dialogu'd for him what he would say,
Ask'd their own wills, and made their wills obey.

'Many there were that did his picture get,
To serve their eyes, and in it put their mind;
Like fools that in th'imagination set
The goodly objects which abroad they find
Of lands and mansions, theirs in thought assign'd;
And labouring in more pleasures to bestow them
Than the true gouty landlord which doth owe them:

'So many have, that never touch'd his hand,
Sweetly suppos'd them mistress of his heart.
My woeful self, that did in freedom stand,
And was my own fee-simple, not in part,
What with his art in youth, and youth in art,
Threw my affections in his charmed power,
Reserv'd the stalk, and gave him all my flower.

A reverend man ... desires to know in brief the grounds and motives of her woe.

'Yet did I not, as some my equals did,
Demand of him, nor being desired yielded;
Finding myself in honour so forbid,
With safest distance I mine honour shielded:
Experience for me many bulwarks builded
Of proofs new-bleeding, which remain'd the foil
Of this false jewel, and his amorous spoil.

'But, ah! who ever shunn'd by precedent
The destin'd ill she must herself assay?
Or forc'd examples, 'gainst her own content,
To put the by-pass'd perils in her way?
Counsel may stop awhile what will not stay;
For when we rage, advice is often seen
By blunting us to make our wits more keen.

'Nor gives it satisfaction to our blood,
That we must curb it upon others' proof;
To be forbid the sweets that seem so good,
For fear of harms that preach in our behoof.
O appetite, from judgement stand aloof!
The one a palate hath that needs will taste,
Though Reason weep, and cry, "It is thy last."

'For further I could say, "This man's untrue,"
And knew the patterns of his foul beguiling;
Heard where his plants in others' orchards
    grew,
Saw how deceits were gilded in his smiling;
Knew vows were ever brokers to defiling;
Thought characters and words merely but art,
And bastards of his foul adulterate heart.

'And long upon these terms I held my city,
Till thus he gan besiege me: "Gentle maid,
Have of my suffering youth some feeling pity,
And be not of my holy vows afraid:
That's to ye sworn to none was ever said;
For feasts of love I have been call'd unto,
Till now did ne'er invite, nor never woo.

' "All my offences that abroad you see
Are errors of the blood, none of the mind;
Love made them not; with acture they may be,
Where neither party is nor true nor kind:
They sought their shame that so their shame did find;
And so much less of shame in me remains,
By how much of me their reproach contains.

' "Among the many that mine eyes have seen,
Not one whose flame my heart so much as warm'd,
Or my affection put to the smallest teen,
Or any of my leisures ever charm'd:
Harm have I done to them, but ne'er was harm'd;
Kept hearts in liveries, but mine own was free,
And reign'd, commanding in his monarchy.

' "Look here, what tributes wounded fancies sent me,
Of paled pearls and rubies red as blood;
Figuring that they their passions likewise lent me
Of grief and blushes, aptly understood
In bloodless white and the encrimson'd mood;
Effects of terror and dear modesty,
Encamp'd in hearts, but fighting outwardly.

' "And, lo, behold these talents of their hair,
With twisted metal amorously impleach'd,
I have receiv'd from many a several fair — ,
Their kind acceptance weepingly beseech'd, —
With the annexions of fair gems enrich'd,
And deep-brain'd sonnets that did amplify
Each stone's dear nature, worth, and quality.

' "The diamond, — why, 'twas beautiful and hard,
Whereto his invis'd properties did tend;
The deep-green emerald, in whose fresh regard
Weak sights their sickly radiance do amend;
The heaven-hued sapphire, and the opal blend
With objects manifold: each several stone,
With wit well blazon'd, smil'd or made some
    moan.

' "Lo, all these trophies of affections hot,
Of pensiv'd and subdued desires the tender,
Nature hath charg'd me that I hoard them not,
But yield them up where I myself must render,
That is, to you, my origin and ender;
For these, of force, must your oblations be,
Since I their altar, you enpatron me.

' "O, then, advance of yours that phraseless hand,
Whose white weighs down the airy scale of praise;
Take all these similes to your own command,
Hallow'd with sighs that burning lungs did raise;
What me your minister, for you obeys,
Works under you; and to your audit comes
Their distract parcels in combined sums.

' "Lo, this device was sent me from a nun,
A sister sanctified, of holiest note;
Which late her noble suit in court did shun,
Whose rarest havings made the blossoms dote;
For she was sought by spirits of richest coat,
But kept cold distance, and did thence remove,
To spend her living in eternal love.

' "But, O my sweet, what labour is't to leave
The thing we have not, mastering what not strives, —
Paling the place which did no form receive,
Playing patient sports in unconstrained gyves?
She that her fame so to herself contrives,
The scars of battle scapeth by the flight,
And makes her absence valiant, not her might.

' "O, pardon me, in that my boast is true:
The accident which brought me to her eye
Upon the moment did her force subdue,
And now she would the caged cloister fly:
Religious love put out Religion's eye:
Not to be tempted, would she be immured,
And now, to tempt all, liberty procured.

' "How mighty, then, you are, O, hear me tell!
The broken bosoms that to me belong
Have emptied all their fountains in my well,
And mine I pour your ocean all among:
I strong o'er them, and you o'er me being strong,
Must for your victory us all congest,
As compound love to physic your cold breast.

' "My parts had power to charm a sacred nun,
Who, disciplin'd, ay, dieted in grace,
Believ'd her eyes when they t'assail begun,
All vows and consecrations giving place:
O most potential love! vow, bond, nor space,
In thee hath neither sting, knot, nor confine,
For thou art all, and all things else are thine.

' "When thou impressest, what are precepts worth
Of stale example? When thou wilt inflame,
How coldly those impediments stand forth
Of wealth, of filial fear, law, kindred, fame!
Love's arms are peace, 'gainst rule, 'gainst sense,
    'gainst shame:
And sweetens, in the suffering pangs it bears,
The aloes of all forces, shocks, and fears.

' "Now all these hearts that do on mine depend,
Feeling it break, with bleeding groans they pine;
And supplicant their sighs to you extend,
To leave the battery that you make 'gainst mine,
Lending soft audience to my sweet design,
And credent soul to that strong-bonded oath
That shall prefer and undertake my troth."

'This said, his watery eyes he did dismount,
Whose sights till then were levell'd on my face;
Each cheek a river running from a fount
With brinish current downward flow'd apace:
O, how the channel to the stream gave grace!
Who glaz'd with crystal gate the glowing roses
That flame through water which their hue encloses.

'O father, what a hell of witchcraft lies
In the small orb of one particular tear!
But with the inundation of the eyes
What rocky heart to water will not wear?
What breast so cold that is not warmed here?
O cleft effect! cold modesty, hot wrath,
Both fire from hence and chill extincture hath.

'For, lo, his passion, but an art of craft,
Even there resolv'd my reason into tears;
There my white stole of chastity I daft,
Shook off my sober guards and civil fears;
Appear to him, as he to me appears,
All melting; though our drops this difference bore,
His poison'd me, and mine did him restore.

'In him a plenitude of subtle matter,
Applied to cautels, all strange forms receives,
Of burning blushes, or of weeping water,
Or swounding paleness; and he takes and leaves,
In either's aptness, as it best deceives,
To blush at speeches rank, to weep at woes,
Or to turn white and swound at tragic shows:

'Gentle maid, have of my suffering youth some feeling pity.'

'That not a heart which in his level came
Could scape the hail of his all-hurting aim,
Showing fair nature is both kind and tame;
And, veil'd in them, did win whom he would maim:
Against the thing he sought he would exclaim;
When he most burnt in heart-wish'd luxury,
He preach'd pure maid, and prais'd cold chastity.

'Thus merely with the garment of a Grace
The naked and concealed fiend he cover'd;
That th'unexperient gave the tempter place,
Which, like a cherubin, above them hover'd.
Who, young and simple, would not be so lover'd?
Ay me! I fell; and yet do question make
What I should do again for such a sake.

'O, that infected moisture of his eye,
O, that false fire which in his cheek so glow'd,
O, that forc'd thunder from his heart did fly,
O, that sad breath his spongy lungs bestow'd,
O, all that borrow'd motion seeming ow'd,
Would yet again betray the fore-betray'd,
And new pervert a reconciled maid!'

THE PASSIONATE PILGRIM

1

When my love swears that she is made of truth,
I do believe her, though I know she lies,
That she might think me some untutor'd youth,
Unskilful in the world's false forgeries.
Thus vainly thinking that she thinks me young,
Although I know my years be past the best,
I smiling credit her false-speaking tongue,
Outfacing faults in love with love's ill rest.
But wherefore says my love that she is young?
And wherefore say not I that I am old?
O, love's best habit is a soothing tongue,
And age, in love, loves not to have years told.
 Therefore I'll lie with love, and love with me,
 Since that our faults in love thus smother'd be.

2

Two loves I have, of comfort and despair,
That like two spirits do suggest me still;
My better angel is a man right fair,
My worser spirit a woman colour'd ill.
To win me soon to hell, my female evil
Tempteth my better angel from my side,
And would corrupt my saint to be a devil,
Wooing his purity with her fair pride.
And whether that my angel be turn'd fiend,
Suspect I may, yet not directly tell:
For being both to me, both to each friend,
I guess one angel in another's hell:
 The truth I shall not know, but live in doubt,
 Till my bad angel fire my good one out.

3

Did not the heavenly rhetoric of thine eye,
'Gainst whom the world could not hold argument,
Persuade my heart to this false perjury?
Vows for thee broke deserve not punishment.
A woman I forswore; but I will prove,
Thou being a goddess, I forswore not thee:
My vow was earthly, thou a heavenly love;
Thy grace being gain'd cures all disgrace in me.
My vow was breath, and breath a vapour is;
Then, thou fair sun, that on this earth dost shine,
Exhale this vapour vow; in thee it is:
If broken, then it is no fault of mine.
 If by me broke, what fool is not so wise
 To break an oath, to win a paradise?

4

Sweet Cytherea, sitting by a brook
With young Adonis, lovely, fresh and green,
Did court the lad with many a lovely look,
Such looks as none could look but beauty's queen.
She told him stories to delight his ear,
She show'd him favours to allure his eye;
To win his heart, she touch'd him here and there;
Touches so soft still conquer chastity.
But whether unripe years did want conceit,
Or he refus'd to take her figur'd proffer,
The tender nibbler would not touch the bait,
But smile and jest at every gentle offer:
 Then fell she on her back, fair queen, and toward:
 He rose and ran away; ah, fool too froward.

5

If love make me forsworn, how shall I swear to love?
O never faith could hold, if not to beauty vow'd:
Though to myself forsworn, to thee I'll constant prove;
Those thoughts, to me like oaks, to thee like osiers bow'd.
Study his bias leaves, and makes his book thine eyes,
Where all those pleasures live that art can comprehend.
If knowledge be the mark, to know thee shall suffice;
Well learned is that tongue that well can thee
 commend:
All ignorant that soul that sees thee without wonder;
Which is to me some praise, that I thy parts admire:
Thine eye Jove's lightning seems, thy voice his
 dreadful thunder,
Which, not to anger bent, is music and sweet fire.
 Celestial as thou art, O do not love that wrong,
 To sing heaven's praise with such an earthly tongue.

6

Scarce had the sun dried up the dewy morn,
And scarce the herd gone to the hedge for shade,
When Cytherea, all in love forlorn,
A longing tarriance for Adonis made
Under an osier growing by a brook,
A brook where Adon used to cool his spleen:
Hot was the day; she hotter that did look
For his approach, that often there had been.
Anon he comes, and throws his mantle by,
And stood stark naked on the brook's green brim:
The sun look'd on the world with glorious eye,
Yet not so wistly as this queen on him:
 He, spying her, bounc'd in, whereas he stood:
 'O Jove,' quoth she, 'why was not I a flood!'

7

Fair is my love, but not so fair as fickle,
Mild as a dove, but neither true nor trusty,
Brighter than glass and yet, as glass is, brittle,
Softer than wax and yet as iron rusty:
 A lily pale, with damask dye to grace her,
 None fairer, nor none falser to deface her.

Her lips to mine how often hath she joined,
Between each kiss her oaths of true love swearing!
How many tales to please me hath she coined,
Dreading my love, the loss whereof still fearing!
 Yet in the midst of all her pure protestings,
 Her faith, her oaths, her tears, and all were jestings.

She burnt with love, as straw with fire flameth;
She burnt out love, as soon as straw out-burneth;
She fram'd the love, and yet she foil'd the framing;
She bade love last, and yet she fell a-turning.
 Was this a lover, or a lecher whether?
 Bad in the best, though excellent in neither.

8

If music and sweet poetry agree,
As they must needs, the sister and the brother,
Then must the love be great 'twixt thee and me,
Because thou lovest the one and I the other.
Dowland to thee is dear, whose heavenly touch
Upon the lute doth ravish human sense;
Spenser to me, whose deep conceit is such
As passing all conceit needs no defence.
Thou lovest to hear the sweet melodious sound
That Phœbus' lute, the queen of music, makes;
And I in deep delight am chiefly drown'd
Whenas himself to singing he betakes.
 One god is god of both, as poets feign;
 One knight loves both, and both in thee remain.

9

Fair was the morn when the fair queen of love,
 * * * * * * * *
Paler for sorrow than her milk-white dove,
For Adon's sake, a youngster proud and wild;
Her stand she takes upon a steep-up hill:
Anon Adonis comes with horn and hounds;
She, silly queen, with more than love's good will,
Forbade the boy he should not pass those grounds:
'Once,' quoth she, 'did I see a fair sweet youth
Here in these brakes deep-wounded with a boar,
Deep in the thigh, a spectacle of ruth!
See, in my thigh,' quoth she, 'here was the sore.'
 She showed hers: he saw more wounds than one,
 And blushing fled, and left her all alone.

O, sweet shepherd, hie thee, for methinks thou stay'st too long.

10

Sweet rose, fair flower, untimely pluck'd, soon vaded,
Pluck'd in the bud and vaded in the spring!
Bright orient pearl, alack, too timely shaded!
Fair creature, kill'd too soon by death's sharp sting!
 Like a green plum that hangs upon a tree,
 And falls through wind before the fall should be.

I weep for thee and yet no cause I have;
For why thou left'st me nothing in thy will:
And yet thou left'st me more than I did crave;
For why I craved nothing of thee still:
 O yes, dear friend, I pardon crave of thee,
 Thy discontent thou didst bequeath to me.

11

Venus, with young Adonis sitting by her
Under a myrtle shade, began to woo him:
She told the youngling how god Mars did try her,
And as he fell to her, so fell she to him.
'Even thus,' quoth she, 'the warlike god embrac'd me,'
And then she clipp'd Adonis in her arms;
'Even thus,' quoth she, 'the warlike god unlac'd me,'
As if the boy should use like loving charms;
'Even thus,' quoth she, 'he seized on my lips,'
And with her lips on his did act the seizure:
And as she fetched breath, away he skips,
And would not take her meaning nor her pleasure.
 Ah, that I had my lady at this bay,
 To kiss and clip me till I run away!

12

Crabbed age and youth cannot live together:
Youth is full of pleasance, age is full of care;
Youth like summer morn, age like winter weather;
Youth like summer brave, age like winter bare.
Youth is full of sport, age's breath is short;
   Youth is nimble, age is lame;
Youth is hot and bold, age is weak and cold;
   Youth is wild, and age is tame.
Age, I do abhor thee; youth, I do adore thee;
   O, my love, my love is young!
Age, I do defy thee: O, sweet shepherd, hie thee,
   For methinks thou stay'st too long.

13

Beauty is but a vain and doubtful good;
A shining gloss that vadeth suddenly;
A flower that dies when first it gins to bud;
A brittle glass that's broken presently:
   A doubtful good, a gloss, a glass, a flower,
   Lost, vaded, broken, dead within an hour.

And as goods lost are seld or never found,
As vaded gloss no rubbing will refresh,
As flowers dead lie wither'd on the ground,
As broken glass no cement can redress,
   So beauty blemish'd once for ever lost,
   In spite of physic, painting, pain and cost.

14

Good night, good rest. Ah, neither be my share:
She bade good night that kept my rest away;
And daft me to a cabin hang'd with care,
To descant on the doubts of my decay.
   'Farewell,' quoth she, 'and come again to-morrow':
   Fare well I could not, for I supp'd with sorrow.

Yet at my parting sweetly did she smile,
In scorn or friendship, nill I conster whether:
'T may be, she joy'd to jest at my exile,
'T may be, again to make me wander thither:
   'Wander', a word for shadows like myself,
   As take the pain, but cannot pluck the pelf.

15

Lord, how mine eyes throw gazes to the east!
My heart doth charge the watch; the morning rise
Doth cite each moving sense from idle rest.
Not daring trust the office of mine eyes,
   While Philomela sits and sings, I sit and mark,
   And wish her lays were tuned like the lark;

For she doth welcome daylight with her ditty,
And drives away dark dismal-dreaming night:
The night so pack'd, I post unto my pretty;
Heart hath his hope and eyes their wished sight;
   Sorrow chang'd to solace and solace mix'd with
      sorrow;
   For why she sigh'd, and bade me come to-morrow.

Were I with her, the night would post too soon;
But now are minutes added to the hours;
To spite me now, each minute seems a moon;
Yet not for me, shine sun to succour flowers!
   Pack night, peep day; good day, of night now borrow:
   Short, night, to-night, and length thyself to-morrow.

SONNETS TO SUNDRY NOTES OF MUSIC

1

It was a lording's daughter, the fairest one of three,
That liked of her master as well as well might be,
Till looking on an Englishman, the fair'st that eye
   could see,
  Her fancy fell a-turning.
Long was the combat doubtful that love with love did
   fight,
To leave the master loveless, or kill the gallant knight:
To put in practice either, alas, it was a spite
  Unto the silly damsel!
But one must be refused; more mickle was the pain
That nothing could be used to turn them both to gain,
For of the two the trusty knight was wounded with
   disdain:
  Alas, she could not help it!
Thus art with arms contending was victor of the day,
Which by a gift of learning did bear the maid away:
Then, lullaby, the learned man hath got the lady gay;
  For now my song is ended.

2

On a day, alack the day!
Love, whose month was ever May,
Spied a blossom passing fair,
Playing in the wanton air:
Through the velvet leaves the wind
All unseen gan passage find;
That the lover, sick to death,
Wish'd himself the heaven's breath.
'Air,' quoth he, 'thy cheeks may blow;
Air, would I might triumph so!
But, alas! my hand hath sworn
Ne'er to pluck thee from thy thorn:
Vow, alack! for youth unmeet:
Youth, so apt to pluck a sweet.
Thou for whom Jove would swear
Juno but an Ethiope were;
And deny himself for Jove,
Turning mortal for thy love.'

3

My flocks feed not,
My ewes breed not,
My rams speed not;
  All is amiss:
Love's denying,
Faith's defying,
Heart's renying,
  Causer of this.
All my merry jigs are quite forgot,
All my lady's love is lost, God wot:
Where her faith was firmly fix'd in love,
There a nay is placed without remove.
  One silly cross
  Wrought all my loss;
O frowning Fortune, cursed, fickle dame!
  For now I see
  Inconstancy
More in women than in men remain.

In black mourn I,
All fears scorn I,
Love hath forlorn me,
  Living in thrall:
Heart is bleeding,
All help needing,
O cruel speeding,
  Fraughted with gall.
My shepherd's pipe can sound no deal:
My wether's bell rings doleful knell;
My curtal dog, that wont to have play'd,
Plays not at all, but seems afraid;
  My sighs so deep
  Procure to weep,
In howling wise, to see my doleful plight.
  How sighs resound
  Through heartless ground,
Like a thousand vanquish'd men in bloody fight!

Clear wells spring not,
Sweet birds sing not,
Green plants bring not
  Forth their dye;

Herds stand weeping,
Flocks all sleeping,
Nymphs back peeping
  Fearfully:
All our pleasure known to us poor swains,
All our merry meetings on the plains,
All our evening sport from us is fled,
All our love is lost, for Love is dead.
  Farewell, sweet lass,
  Thy like ne'er was
For a sweet content, the cause of all my moan:
  Poor Corydon
  Must live alone;
Other help for him I see that there is none.

4

Whenas thine eye hath chose the dame,
And stall'd the deer that thou shouldst strike,
Let reason rule things worthy blame,
As well as fancy partial like:
  Take counsel of some wiser head,
  Neither too young nor yet unwed.

And when thou comest thy tale to tell,
Smooth not thy tongue with filed talk,
Lest she some subtle practice smell, —
A cripple soon can find a halt; —
  But plainly say thou lovest her well,
  And set thy person forth to sell.

What though her frowning brows be bent,
Her cloudy looks will calm ere night:
And then too late she will repent
That thus dissembled her delight;
  And twice desire, ere it be day,
  That which with scorn she put away.

What though she strive to try her strength,
And ban and brawl, and say thee nay,
Her feeble force will yield at length,
When craft hath taught her thus to say:
  'Had women been so strong as men,
  In faith, you had not had it then.'

And to her will frame all thy ways;
Spare not to spend, and chiefly there
Where thy desert may merit praise,
By ringing in thy lady's ear:
  The strongest castle, tower and town,
  The golden bullet beats it down.

Serve always with assured trust,
And in thy suit be humble true;
Unless thy lady prove unjust,
Press never thou to choose anew:
  When time shall serve, be thou not slack
  To proffer, though she put thee back.

The wiles and guiles that women work,
Dissembled with an outward show,
The tricks and toys that in them lurk,
The cock that treads them shall not know.
  Have you not heard it said full oft,
  A woman's nay doth stand for nought?

Think women still to strive with men,
To sin and never for to saint:
There is no heaven, by holy then,
When time with age shall them attaint.
  Were kisses all the joys in bed,
  One woman would another wed.

But, soft! enough — too much, I fear —
Lest that my mistress hear my song:
She will not stick to round me on the ear,
To teach my tongue to be so long:
  Yet will she blush, here be it said,
  To hear her secrets so bewray'd.

5

Live with me, and be my love,
And we will all the pleasures prove
That hills and valleys, dales and fields,
And all the craggy mountains yields.

There will we sit upon the rocks,
And see the shepherds feed their flocks,
By shallow rivers, by whose falls
Melodious birds sing madrigals.

There will I make thee a bed of roses,
With a thousand fragrant posies,
A cap of flowers, and a kirtle
Embroider'd all with leaves of myrtle.

A belt of straw and ivy buds,
With coral clasps and amber studs;
And if these pleasures may thee move,
Then live with me and be my love.

LOVE'S ANSWER

If that the world and love were young,
And truth in every shepherd's tongue,
These pretty pleasures might me move
To live with thee and be thy love.

6

As it fell upon a day
In the merry month of May,
Sitting in a pleasant shade
Which a grove of myrtles made,
Beasts did leap and birds did sing,
Trees did grow and plants did spring;
Every thing did banish moan,
Save the nightingale alone:
She, poor bird, as all forlorn,
Lean'd her breast up-till a thorn,
And there sung the dolefull'st ditty,
That to hear it was great pity:
'Fie, fie, fie,' now would she cry;
'Tereu, Tereu!' by and by;
That to hear her so complain,
Scarce I could from tears refrain;
For her griefs so lively shown
Made me think upon mine own.
Ah, thought I, thou mourn'st in vain!
None takes pity on thy pain:
Senseless trees they cannot hear thee;
Ruthless beasts they will not cheer thee:
King Pandion he is dead;
All thy friends are lapp'd in lead;
All thy fellow birds do sing,
Careless of thy sorrowing.
Even so, poor bird, like thee,
None alive will pity me.
Whilst as fickle Fortune smiled,
Thou and I were both beguiled.

  Every one that flatters thee
Is no friend in misery.
Words are easy, like the wind;
Faithful friends are hard to find:
Every man will be thy friend
Whilst thou hast wherewith to spend;
But if store of crowns be scant,
No man will supply thy want.
If that one be prodigal,
Bountiful they will him call,
And with such-like flattering,
'Pity but he were a king';
If he be addict to vice,
Quickly him they will entice;
If to women he be bent,
They have at commandement:
But if Fortune once do frown,
Then farewell his great renown;
They that fawn'd on him before
Use his company no more.
He that is thy friend indeed,
He will help thee in thy need:
If thou sorrow, he will weep;
If thou wake, he cannot sleep;
Thus of every grief in heart
He with thee doth bear a part.
These are certain signs to know
Faithful friend from flattering foe.

THE PHOENIX AND TURTLE

Let the bird of loudest lay,
On the sole Arabian tree,
Herald sad and trumpet be,
To whose sound chaste wings obey.

But thou shrieking harbinger,
Foul precurrer of the fiend,
Augur of the fever's end,
To this troop come thou not near!

From this session interdict
Every fowl of tyrant wing,
Save the eagle, feather'd king:
Keep the obsequy so strict.

Let the priest in surplice white,
That defunctive music can,
Be the death-divining swan,
Lest the requiem lack his right.

And thou treble-dated crow,
That thy sable gender makest
With the breath thou giv'st and takest,
'Mongst our mourners shalt thou go.

Here the anthem doth commence:
Love and constancy is dead;
Phœnix and the turtle fled
In a mutual flame from hence.

So they lov'd, as love in twain
Had the essence but in one;
Two distincts, division none:
Number there in love was slain.

Hearts remote, yet not asunder;
Distance, and no space was seen
'Twixt the turtle and his queen:
But in them it were a wonder.

So between them love did shine,
That the turtle saw his right
Flaming in the phœnix' sight;
Either was the other's mine.

Property was thus appalled,
That the self was not the same;
Single nature's double name
Neither two nor one was called.

Reason, in itself confounded,
Saw division grow together,
To themselves yet either neither,
Simple were so well compounded;

That it cried, How true a twain
Seemeth this concordant one!
Love hath reason, reason none,
If what parts can so remain.

Whereupon it made this threne
To the phœnix and the dove,
Co-supremes and stars of love,
As chorus to their tragic scene.

THRENOS

Beauty, truth, and rarity,
Grace in all simplicity,
Here enclos'd in cinders lie.

Death is now the phœnix' nest;
And the turtle's loyal breast
To eternity doth rest,

Leaving no posterity:
'Twas not their infirmity,
It was married chastity.

Truth may seem, but cannot be;
Beauty brag, but 'tis not she;
Truth and beauty buried be.

To this urn let those repair
That are either true or fair;
For these dead birds sigh a prayer.

SIR THOMAS MORE

SCENE VI

The Gate of St. Martin's-le-Grand.

Enter LINCOLN, DOLL [*his wife*], CLOWN [BETTS],
GEORGE BETTS, WILLIAMSON, *others,*
and a Sergeant at Arms.

LINCOLN
Peace, hear me. He that will not see a red herring at a
Harry groat, butter at eleven-pence a pound, meal at
nine shillings a bushel, and beef at four nobles a stone,
list to me.
GEO. BETTS
It will come to that pass, if strangers be suffered. Mark him.
LINCOLN
Our country is a great eating country, argo they eat
more in our country than they do in their own.
CLOWN BETTS
By a halfpenny loaf a day. Troy weight.
LINCOLN
They bring in strange roots, which is merely to the
undoing of poor prentices, for what's a sorry parsnip to
a good heart?
WILLIAMSON
Trash, trash; they breed sore eyes, and 'tis enough to
infect the City with the palsy.
LINCOLN
Nay, it has infected it with the palsy, for these bastards
of dung, as you know they grow in dung, have infected
us, and it is our infection will make the City shake,
which partly comes through the eating of parsnips.
CLOWN BETTS
True, and pumpions together.
SERGEANT
What say you to the mercy of the king? Do you refuse it?
LINCOLN
You would have us upon th'hip, would you? No, marry
do we not; we accept of the king's mercy, but we will
show no mercy upon the strangers.
SERGEANT
You are the simplest things that ever stood in such a
question.
LINCOLN
How say you now! Prentices simple! Down with him!
ALL
Prentices simple! Prentices simple!

Enter the LORD MAYOR, SURREY, SHREWSBURY,
[PALMER, CHOLMELEY, MORE.]

MAYOR
Hold! In the king's name, hold!

SURREY
Friends, Masters, Countrymen —
MAYOR
Peace, ho! Peace! I charge you keep the peace.
SHREWSBURY
My Masters, Countrymen —
WILLIAMSON
The noble Earl of Shrewsbury, let's hear him.
GEO. BETTS
We'll hear the Earl of Surrey.
LINCOLN
The Earl of Shrewsbury.
BETTS
We'll hear both.
ALL
Both! Both! Both! Both!
LINCOLN
Peace, I say! Peace! Are you men of wisdom, or what
are you?
SURREY
What you will have them, but not men of wisdom.
ALL
We'll not hear my Lord of Surrey! No, No, No, No, No!
Shrewsbury! Shrewsbury!
MORE
Whilst they are o'er the bank of their obedience,
Thus will they bare down all things.
LINCOLN
Sheriff More speaks! Shall we hear Sheriff More
speak?
DOLL
Let's hear him! A keeps a plentiful shrievalty, and a
made my brother Arthur Watchins Sergeant Safe's
yeoman. Let's hear Sheriff More.
ALL
Sheriff More! More! More! Sheriff More!
MORE
Even by the rule you have among yourselves,
Command still audience.
ALL
Surrey! Surrey!
ALL
More! More!
LINCOLN }
BETTS } Peace! Peace! Silence! Peace!
MORE
You that have voice and credit with the number,
Command them to a stillness.

LINCOLN
A plague on them! They will not hold their peace. The
devil cannot rule them!
MORE
Then what a rough and riotous charge have you,
To lead those that the devil cannot rule.
Good masters, hear me speak.
DOLL
Aye, by the mass will we, More. Thou art a good
housekeeper, and I thank thy good worship for my
brother Arthur Watchins.
ALL
Peace! Peace!
MORE
Look! What you do offend, you cry upon;
That is the peace. Not one of you here present
(Had there such fellows liv'd when you were babes)
That could have topp'd the peace, as now you would.
The peace wherein you have till now grown up
Had been ta'en from you, and the bloody times
Could not have brought you to the state of men.
Alas, poor things! What is it you have got,
Although we grant you get the thing you seek?
BETTS
Marry, the removing of the strangers, which cannot
choose but much advantage the poor handicrafts of the
City.
MORE
Grant them remov'd, and grant that this your noise
Hath chid down all the majesty of England;
Imagine that you see the wretched strangers,
Their babies at their backs, with their poor luggage,
Plodding to th'ports and coasts for transportation,
And that you sit as kings in your desires,
Authority quite silenc'd by your brawl,
And you in ruff of your opinions clothed,
What had you got? I'll tell you. You had taught
How insolence and strong hand should prevail,
How order should be quell'd — and by this pattern
Not one of you should live an aged man;
For other ruffians, as their fancies wrought,
With selfsame hand, self reasons and self right
Would shark on you, and men like ravenous fishes
Would feed on one another.
DOLL
Before God, that's as true as the Gospel!
LINCOLN
Nay, this is a sound fellow, I tell you; let's mark him.

MORE
Let me set up before your thoughts, good friends,
One supposition, which if you will mark,
You shall perceive how horrible a shape
Your innovation bears. First, 'tis a sin
Which oft th'apostle did forwarn us of,
Urging obedience to authority.
And 'twere no error if I told you all,
You were in arms 'gainst God.
ALL
Marry, God forbid that!
MORE
Nay, certainly you are.
For to the king God hath his office lent
Of dread, of justice, power and command;
Hath bid him rule, and will'd you to obey.
And to add ampler majesty to this,
He hath not only lent the king his figure,
His throne and sword, but given him his own name,
Calls him a god on earth. What do you, then,
Rising 'gainst him that God himself installs
But rise 'gainst God? What do you to your souls
In doing this, O desperate as you are?
Wash your foul minds with tears, and those same hands
That you like rebels lift against the peace

Lift up for peace, and your unreverent knees
Make them your feet. To kneel to be forgiven
Is safer wars than ever you can make
Whose discipline is riot. In! In! To your obedience;
Why even your wars
Cannot proceed but by obedience.
What rebel captain,
As mutinies are incident, by his name
Can still the rout? Who will obey a traitor?
Or how can well that proclamation sound
When there is no addition but a rebel
To qualify a rebel? You'll put down strangers,
Kill them, cut their throats, possess their houses,
And lead the majesty of law in liom
To slip him like a hound. Say now the king
(As he is clement, if th'offender mourn)
Should so much come too short of your great trespass
As but to banish you — whither would you go?
What country, by the nature of your error,
Should give you harbour? Go you to France or
  Flanders,
To any German prince, to Spain or Portugal,
Nay, anywhere that not adheres to England,
Why, you must needs be strangers. Would you be
  pleas'd

To find a nation of such barbarous temper
That, breaking out in hideous violence,
Would not afford you an abode on earth,
Whet their detested knives against your throats,
Spurn you like dogs, and like as if that God
Ow'd not nor made not you, nor that the elements
Were not all appropriate to your comforts,
But charter'd unto them what would you think
To be thus us'd? This is the strangers' case,
And this your mountainish inhumanity.
ALL
Faith, a says true. Let's do as we may be done by.
LINCOLN
We'll be ruled by you, Master More, if you'll stand our
  friend to procure our pardon.
MORE
Submit you to these noble gentlemen,
Entreat their mediation to the king,
Give up yourself to form, obey the magistrate,
And there's no doubt, but mercy may be found
If you so seek.

GLOSSARY

References are given only for words having more than one meaning, the first use of each sense being then noted.

Abate, *v.t.* to diminish. M.N.D. III. 2. 432. Deduct, except. L.L.L. v. 2. 539. Cast down. Cor. III. 3. 134. Blunt. R III. v. 5. 35. Deprive. Lear, II. 4. 159.

Abatement, *sb.* diminution Lear, I. 4. 59. Depreciation. Tw.N. I. 1. 13.

Abjects, *sb.* outcasts, servile persons.

Able, *v.t.* to warrant.

Abode, *v.t.* to forebode. 3 H VI. V. 6. 45.

Abode, *sb.* stay, delay. M. of V. II. 6. 77.

Abodements, *sb.* forebodings.

Abram, *adj.* auburn.

Abridgement, *sb.* short entertainment, for pastime.

Abrook, *v.t.* to brook, endure.

Absey book, *sb.* ABC book, or primer.

Absolute, *adj.* resolved. M. for M. III. 1. 5. Positive. Cor. III. 2. 39. Perfect. H V. III. 7. 26. Complete. Tp. I. 2. 109; Lucr. 853.

Aby, *v.t.* to atone for, expiate.

Accite, *v.t.* to cite, summon.

Acknown, *adj.* cognisant.

Acture, *sb.* performance.

Addition, *sb.* title, attribute.

Adoptious, *adj.* given by adoption.

Advice, *sb.* consideration.

Aery, *sb.* eagle's nest or brood. R III. I. 3. 265, 271. Hence generally any brood. Ham. II. 2. 344.

Affectioned, *p.p.* affected.

Affeered, *p.p.* sanctioned, confirmed.

Affiance, *sb.* confidence, trust.

Affined, *p.p.* related. T. & C. I. 3. 25. Bound. Oth. I. 1. 39.

Affront, *v.t.* to confront, meet.

Affy, *v.t.* to betroth. 2 H VI. IV. 1. 80. *v.t.* to trust. T.A. I. 1. 47.

Aglet-baby, *sb.* small figure cut on the tag of a lace (Fr. *aiguillette*). T. of S. I. 2. 78.

Agnize, *v.t.* to acknowledge, confess.

Agood, *adv.* much.

Aim, *sb.* a guess.

Aim, to cry aim, to encourage, an archery term.

Alderliefest, *adj.* most loved of all.

Ale, *sb.* alehouse.

All amort, completely dejected (Fr. *a la mort*).

Allicholy, *sb.* melancholy.

Allow, *v.t.* to approve.

Allowance, *sb.* acknowledgement, approval.

Ames-ace, *sb.* the lowest throw of the dice.

Anchor, *sb.* anchorite, hermit.

Ancient, *sb.* ensign, standard. 1 H IV. IV. 2. 32. Ensign, ensign-bearer. 1 H IV. IV. 2. 24.

Ancientry, *sb.* antiquity, used of old people, W.T. III. 3. 62. Of the gravity which belongs to antiquity, M.A. II. 1. 75.

Angel, *sb.* gold coin, worth about 10s.

Antic, *adj.* fantastic. Ham. I. 5. 172.

Antick, *v.t.* to make a buffoon of. A. & C. II. 7. 126.

Antick, *sb.* buffoon of the old plays.

Appeal, *sb.* impeachment.

Appeal, *v.t.* to impeach.

Apperil, *sb.* peril.

Apple-john, *sb.* a shrivelled winter apple.

Argal, corruption of the Latin *ergo*, therefore.

Argo, corruption of *ergo*, therefore.

Aroint thee, begone, get thee gone.

Articulate, *v.i.* to make articles of peace. Cor. I. 9. 75. *v.t.* to set forth in detail. 1 H IV. V. 1. 72.

Artificial, *adj.* working by art.

Askance, *v.t.* to make look askance or sideways, make to avert.

Aspic, *sb.* asp.

Assured, *p.p.* betrothed.

Atone, *v.t.* to reconcile. R II. I. 1. 202. Agree. As V. 4. 112.

Attorney, *sb.* proxy, agent.

Attorneyed, *p.p.* done by proxy. W T. I. 1. 28. Engaged as an attorney, M. for M. V. 1. 383.

Attribute, *sb.* reputation.

Avail, *sb.* profit.

Avise, *v.t.* to inform. Are you avised? = Do you know?

Awful, *adj.* filled with regard for authority.

Awkward, *adj.* contrary.

Baby, *sb.* a doll.

Baccare, go back, a spurious Latin word.

Back-trick, a caper backwards in dancing.

Baffle, *v.t.* to disgrace (a recreant knight).

Bale, *sb.* evil, mischief.

Ballow, *sb.* cudgel.

Ban, *v.t.* curse. 2 H VI. II. 4. 25. *sb.* a curse. Ham. III. 2. 269.

Band, *sb.* bond.

Bank, *v.t.* sail along the banks of.

Bare, *v.t.* to shave.

Barn, *v.t.* to put in a barn.

Barn, or Barne, *sb.* bairn, child.

Base, *sb.* a rustic game. Bid the base = Challenge to a race. Two G. I. 2. 97.

Bases, *sb.* knee-length skirts worn by mounted knights.

Basilisco-like, Basilisco, a character in the play of *Soliman and Perseda*.

Basilisk, *sb.* a fabulous serpent. H V. V. 2. 17. A large cannon. 1 H IV. II. 3. 57.

Bate, *sb.* strife.

Bate, *v.i.* flutter as a hawk. 1 H IV. IV. 1. 99. Diminish. 1 H IV. III. 3. 2.

Bate, *v.t.* abate. Tp. I. 2. 250. Beat down, weaken. M. of V. III. 3. 32.

Bavin, *adj.* made of bavin or brushwood. 1 H IV. III. 2. 61.

Bawbling, *adj.* trifling, insignificant.

Baw-cock, *sb.* fine fellow (Fr. *beau coq*.) H V. III. 2. 25.

Bay, *sb.* space between the main timbers in a roof.

Beadsman, *sb.* one who is hired to offer prayers for another.

Bearing-cloth, *sb.* the cloth in which a child was carried to be christened.

Bear in hand, to deceive with false hopes.

Beat, *v.i.* to meditate. 2 H IV. II. 1. 20. Throb. Lear, III. 4. 14.

Becoming, *sb.* grace.

Beetle, *sb.* a heavy mallet, 2 H IV. I. 2. 235. Beetle-headed = heavy, stupid. T. of S. IV. 1. 150.

Behave, *v.t.* to control.

Behest, *sb.* command.

Behove, *sb.* behoof.

Be-lee'd, *p.p.* forced to lee of the wind.

Bench, *v.i.* to seat on the bench of justice. Lear, III. 6. 38. *v.t.* to elevate to the bench. W.T. I. 2. 313.

Bench-hole, the hole of a privy.

Bergomask, a rustic dance, named from Bergamo in Italy.

Beshrew, *v.t.* to curse; but not used seriously.

Besort, *v.t.* to fit, suit.

Bestraught, *adj.* distraught.

Beteem, *v.t.* to permit, grant.

Bezonian, *sb.* a base and needy fellow.

Bias, *adj.* curving like the bias side of a bowling bowl.

Biggen, *sb.* a nightcap.

Bilbo, *sb.* a Spanish rapier, named from Bilbao or Bilboa.

Bilboes, *sb.* stocks used for punishment on shipboard.

Birdbolt, *sb.* a blunt-headed arrow used for birds.

Bisson, *adj.* dim-sighted. Cor. II. 1. 65. Bisson rheum = blinding tears. Ham. II. 2. 514.

Blacks, *sb.* black mourning clothes.

Blank, *sb.* the white mark in the centre of a target.

Blank, *v.t.* to blanch, make pale.

Blanks, *sb.* royal charters left blank to be filled in as occasion dictated.

Blench, *sb.* a swerve, inconsistency.

Blistered, *adj.* padded out, puffed.

Block, *sb.* the wood on which hats are made. M.A. I. 1. 71. Hence, the style of hat. Lear, IV. 6. 185.

Blood-boltered, *adj.* clotted with blood.

Blowse, *sb.* a coarse beauty.

Bob, *sb.* smart rap, jest.

Bob, *v.t.* to beat hard, thwack. R III. V. 3. 335. To obtain by fraud, cheat. T. & C. III. 1. 69.

Bodge, *v.i.* to budge.

Bodkin, *sb.* small dagger, stiletto.

Boggle, *v.i.* to swerve, shy, hesitate.

Boggler, *sb.* swerver.

Boln, *adj.* swollen.

Bolt, *v.t.* to sift, refine.

Bolter, *sb.* a sieve.

Bombard, *sb.* a leathern vessel for liquor.

Bona-robas, *sb.* flashily dressed women of easy virtue.

Bonnet, *v.i.* to doff the hat, be courteous.

Boot, *sb.* profit. 1 H VI. IV. 6. 52. That which is given over and above. R III. IV. 4. 65. Booty. 3 H VI. IV. 1. 13.

Boots, *sb.* Give me not the boots = do not inflict on me the torture of the boots, which were employed to wring confessions.

Bosky, *adj.* woody.

Botcher, *sb.* patcher of old clothes.

Bots, *sb.* small worms in horses.

Bottled, *adj.* big-bellied.

Brabble, *sb.* quarrel, brawl.

Brabbler, *sb.* a brawler.

Brach, *sb.* a hound-bitch.

Braid, *adj.* deceitful.

Braid, *v.t.* to upbraid, reproach.

Brain, *v.t.* to conceive in the brain.

Brazed, *p.p.* made like brass, perhaps hardened in the fire.

Breeched, *p.p.* as though wearing breeches. Mac. II. 3. 120.

Breeching, *adj.* liable to be breeched for a flogging.

Breese, *sb.* a gadfly.

Brib'd-buck, *sb.* perhaps a buck distributed in presents.

Brock, *sb.* badger.

Broken, *adj.* of a mouth with some teeth missing.

Broker, *sb.* agent, go-between.

Brownist, a follower of Robert Brown, the founder of the sect of Independents.

Buck, *v.t.* to wash and beat linen.

Buck-basket, *sb.* a basket to take linen to be bucked.

Bucking, *sb.* washing.

Buckle, *v.i.* to encounter hand to hand, cope. 1. H VI. I. 2. 95. To bow. 2 H VI. I. 1. 141.

Budget, *sb.* a leather scrip or bag.

Bug, *sb.* bugbear, a thing causing terror.

Bugle, *sb.* a black bead.

Bully, *sb.* a fine fellow.

Bully-rook, *sb.* a swaggering cheater.

Bung, *sb.* pickpocket.

Burgonet, *sb.* close-fitting Burgundian helmet.

Busky, *adj.* woody.

By-drinkings, *sb.* drinks taken between meals.

Caddis, *sb.* worsted trimming, galloon.

Cade, *sb.* cask, barrel.

Caitiff, *sb.* captive, slave, a wretch. *adj.* R II. I. 2. 53.

Caliver, *sb.* musket.

Callet, *sb.* trull, drab.

Calling, *sb.* appellation.

Calm, *sb.* qualm.

Canaries = quandary.

Canary, *sb.* a lively Spanish dance. *v.i.* to dance canary.

Canker, *sb.* the dog-rose or wild-rose. 1 H IV. I. 3. 176. A worm that destroys blossoms. M.N.D. II. 2.3.

Canstick, *sb.* candlestick.

Cantle, *sb.* piece, slice.

Canton, *sb.* canto.

Canvass, *v.t.* shake as in a sieve, take to task.

Capable, *adj.* sensible. As III. 5. 23. Sensitive, susceptible. Ham. III. 4. 128. Comprehensive. Oth. III. 3. 459. Able to possess. Lear, II. 1. 85.

Capocchia, *sb.* the feminine of capocchio (Ital.), simpleton.

Capriccio, *sb.* caprice, fancy.

Captious, *adj.* either a contraction of capacious or a coined word meaning capable of receiving.

Carack, *sb.* a large merchant ship.

Carbonado, *sb.* meat scotched for boiling. *v.t.* to hack like a carbonado.

Card, *sb.* a cooling card = a sudden and decisive stroke.

Card, *v.t.* to mix (liquids).

Cardecu, *sb.* quarter of a French crown (*quart d'écu*).

Care, *v.i.* to take care.

Careire, career, *sb.* a short gallop at full speed.

Carlot, *sb.* peasant.

Carpet consideration, On, used of those made knights for court services, not for valour in the field.

Carpet-mongers, *sb.* carpet-knights.

Carpets, *sb.* tablecloths.

Case, *v.t.* to strip off the case or skin of an animal. A.W. III. 6. 103. Put on a mask. 1 H IV. II. 2. 55.

Case, *sb.* skin of an animal. Tw.N. V. 1.163. A set, as of musical instruments, which were in fours. H V. III. 2. 4.

Cashiered, *p.p.* discarded; in M.W.W. I. 1. 168 it probably means relieved of his cash.

Cataian, *sb.* a native of Cathay, a Chinaman; a cant word.

Cater-cousins, good friends.

Catlings, *sb.* catgut strings for musical instruments.

Cautel, *sb.* craft, deceit, stratagem.

Cautelous, *adj.* crafty, deceitful.

Ceased, *p.p.* put off.

Censure, *sb.* opinion, judgement.

Certify, *v.t.* to inform, make certain.

Cess, *sb.* reckoning; out of all cess = immoderately.

Cesse = cease.

Champain, *sb.* open country.

Channel, *sb.* gutter.

Chape, *sb.* metal end of a scabbard.

Chapless, *adj.* without jaws.

Charact, *sb.* a special mark or sign of office.

Chare, *sb.* a turn of work.

Charge, *sb.* weight, importance. W.T. IV. 3. 258. Cost, expense. John I. 1. 49.

Chaudron, *sb.* entrails.

Check, *sb.* rebuke, reproof.

Check, *v.t.* to rebuke, chide.

Check, *v.i.* to start on sighting game.

Cherry-pit, *sb.* a childish game consisting of pitching cherry-stones into a small hole.

Cheveril, *sb.* leather of kid skin. R. & J. II. 3. 85. *adj.* Tw.N. III. 1. 12.

Che vor ye = I warn you.

Chewet, *sb.* chough. 1 H IV. V. 1. 29. (Fr. *chouette* or *chutte*). Perhaps with play on other meaning of chewet, *i.e.*, a kind of meat pie.

Childing, *adj.* fruitful.

Chop, *v.t.* to clop, pop.

Chopine, *sb.* shoe with a high sole.

Choppy, *adj.* chapped.

Christendom, *sb.* Christian name.

Chuck, *sb.* chick, term of endearment.

Chuff, *sb.* churl, boor.

Cinque pace, *sb.* a slow stately dance. M.A. II. 1. 72.
  Compare sink-a-pace in Tw.N. I. 3. 126.
Cipher, *v.t.* to decipher.
Circumstance, *sb.* particulars, details. Two G. I. 1. 36.
  Ceremonious phrases. M. of V. I. 1. 154.
Circumstanced, *p.p.* swayed by circumstance.
Citizen, *adj.* town-bred, effeminate.
Cittern, *sb.* guitar.
Clack-dish, *sb.* wooden dish carried by beggars.
Clamour, *v.t.* to silence.
Clapper-claw, *v.t.* to thrash, drub.
Claw, *v.t.* to scratch, flatter.
Clepe, *v.t.* to call.
Cliff, *sb.* clef, the key in music.
Cling, *v.t.* to make shrivel up.
Clinquant, *adj.* glittering with gold or silver lace or
  decorations.
Close, *sb.* cadence in music. R II. II. 1. 12. *adj.* secret. T. of
  S. Ind. I. 127. *v.i.* to come to an agreement, make terms.
  Two G. II. 5. 12.
Closely, *adv.* secretly.
Clout, *sb.* bull's-eye of a target.
Clouted, *adj.* hobnailed (others explain as patched).
Cobloaf, *sb.* a crusty, ill-shapen loaf.
Cockered, *p.p.* pampered.
Cockle, *sb.* the corncockle weed.
Cockney, *sb.* a city-bred person, a foolish wanton.
Cock-shut time, *sb.* twilight.
Codding, *adj.* lascivious.
Codling, *sb.* an unripe apple.
Cog, *v.i.* to cheat. R III I. 3. 48. *v.t.* to get by cheating, filch.
  Cor. III. 2. 133.
Coistrel, *sb.* groom.
Collection, *sb.* inference.
Collied, *p.p.* blackened, darkened.
Colour, *sb.* pretext. Show no colour, or bear no colour =
  allow of no excuse.
Colours, fear no colours = fear no enemy, be afraid of
  nothing.
Colt, *v.t.* to make a fool of, gull.
Combinate, *adj.* betrothed.
Combine, *v.t.* to bind.
Comfect, *sb.* comfit.
Commodity, *sb.* interest, advantage. John, II. 1. 573. Cargo
  of merchandise. Tw.N. III. 1. 46.
Comparative, *adj.* fertile in comparisons. 1 H IV. I. 2. 83.
Comparative, *sb.* a rival in wit. 1 H IV. III. 2. 67.
Compassed, *adj.* arched, round.
Complexion, *sb.* temperament.
Comply, *v.i.* to be ceremonious.
Composition, *sb.* agreement, consistency.
Composture, *sb.* compost.
Composure, *sb.* composition. T. & C. II. 3. 238; A. & C. I. 4.
  22. Compact. T. & C. II. 3. 100.
Compt. *sb.* account, reckoning.
Comptible, *adj.* susceptible, sensitive.
Con, *v.t.* to study, learn; con thanks = give thanks.
Conceptious, *adj.* apt at conceiving.
Conclusion, *sb.* experiment.
Condolement, *sb.* lamentation. Ham. I. 2. 93. Consolation,
  Per. II. 1. 150.
Conduce, *v.i.* perhaps to tend to happen.
Conduct, *sb.* guide, escort.
Confiners, *sb.* border peoples.
Confound, *v.t.* to waste. 1 H IV. I. 3. 100. Destroy. M. of V.
  III. 2. 278.
Congied, *p.p.* taken leave (Fr. *congé*).
Consent, *sb.* agreement, plot.
Consist, *v.i.* to insist.
Consort, *sb.* company, fellowship. Two G. III. 2. 84; IV. 1.
  64. *v.t.* to accompany. C. of E. I. 2. 28.
Conspectuity, *sb.* power of vision.
Constant, *adj.* consistent.
Constantly, *adv.* firmly, surely.
Conster, *v.t.* to construe, interpret.
Constringed, *p.p.* compressed.
Consul, *sb.* senator.
Containing, *sb.* contents.
Contraction, *sb.* the making of the marriage-contract.
Contrive, *v.t.* to wear out, spend. T. of S. I. 2. 273. Conspire.
  J.C. II. 3. 16.
Control, *v.t.* to check, contradict.
Convent, *v.t.* to summon.
Convert, *v.i.* to change.
Convertite, *sb.* a penitent.
Convince, *v.t.* to overcome. Mac. I. 7. 64. Convict. T. & C. II.
  2. 130.
Convive, *v.i.* to banquet together.
Convoy, *sb.* conveyance, escort.
Copatain hat, *sb.* a high-crowned hat.
Cope, *v.t.* to requite. M. of V. IV. 1. 412.
Copesmate, *sb.* a companion.
Copped, *adj.* round-topped.
Copulatives, *sb.* persons desiring to be coupled in marriage.
Copy, *sb.* theme, text. C. of E. V. 1. 62. Tenure. Mac. III. 2.
  37.
Coranto, *sb.* a quick, lively dance.
Corky, *adj.* shrivelled (with age).
Cornet, *sb.* a band of cavalry.

Corollary, *sb.* a supernumerary.
Cosier, *sb.* botcher, cobbler.
Costard, *sb.* an apple, the head (slang).
Cote, *v.t.* to come up with, pass on the way.
Cot-quean, *sb.* a man who busies himself in women's
  affairs.
Couch, *v.t.* to make to cower.
Counter, *adv.* to run or hunt counter is to trace the scent of
  the game backwards.
Counter, *sb.* a metal disk used in reckoning.
Counter-caster, *sb.* one who reckons by casting up counters.
Countermand, *v.t.* to prohibit, keep in check. C. of E. IV. 2.
  37. Contradict. Lucr. 276.
Countervail, *v.t.* to outweigh.
County, *sb.* count. As II. 1. 67.
Couplet, *sb.* a pair.
Courser's hair, a horse's hair laid in water was believed to
  turn into a serpent.
Court holy-water, *sb.* flattery.
Courtship, *sb.* courtly manners.
Convent, *sb.* a convent.
Cox my passion = God's passion.
Coy, *v.t.* to fondle, caress. M.N.D. IV. 1. 2. *v.i.* to disdain.
  Cor. V. 1. 6.
Crack, *v.i.* to boast. *sb.* an urchin.
Crank, *sb.* winding passage. *v.i.* to wind, twist.
Crants, *sb.* garland, chaplet.
Crare, *sb.* a small sailing vessel.
Crisp, *adj.* curled.
Cross, *sb.* a coin (stamped with a cross).
Cross-row, *sb.* alphabet.
Crow-keeper, *sb.* a boy, or scare-crow, to keep crows from
  corn.
Cullion, *sb.* a base fellow.
Cunning, *sb.* knowledge, skill. *adj.* knowing, skilful,
  skilfully wrought.
Curb, *v.i.* to bow, cringe obsequiously.
Curdied, *p.p.* congealed.
Curiosity, *sb.* scrupulous nicety.
Curst, *adj.* bad-tempered.
Curtal, *adj.* having a docked tail. *sb.* a dock-tailed horse.
Customer, *sb.* a loose woman.
Cut, *sb.* a bobtailed horse.
Cuttle, *sb.* a bully.

Daff, *v.t.* to doff. Daff aside = thrust aside slightingly.
Darraign, *v.t.* to arrange, order the ranks for battle.
Dash, *sb.* mark of disgrace.
Daubery, *sb.* false pretence, cheat.
Day-woman, *sb.* dairy-woman.
Debosht, *p.p.* debauched.
Deck, *sb.* pack of cards.
Deem, *sb.* doom; opinion.
Defeat, *v.t.* to disguise. Oth. I. 3. 333. Destroy. Oth. IV. 2. 160.
Defeature, *sb.* disfigurement.
Defend, *v.t.* to forbid.
Defuse, *v.t.* to disorder and make unrecognizable.
Defused, *p.p.* disordered, shapeless.
Demerit, *sb.* desert.
Denier, *sb.* a small French coin.
Dern, *adj.* secret, dismal.
Detect, *v.t.* to discover, disclose.
Determinate, *p.p.* determined upon. Tw.N. II. 1. 10.
  Decided. Oth. IV. 2. 229. Ended. Sonn. LXXXVII. 4. *v.t.*
  bring to an end. R II. I. 3.
Dich, *v.i.* do to, happen to.
Diet, *v.t.* keep strictly, as if by a prescribed regimen.
Diffidence, *sb.* distrust, suspicion.
Digression, *sb.* transgression.
Diminutives, *sb.* the smallest of coins.
Directitude, *sb.* a blunder for some word unknown. Cor. IV.
  5. 205.
Disanimate, *v.t.* to discourage.
Disappointed, *p.p.* unprepared.
Discandy, *v.i.* to thaw, melt.
Discipled, *p.p.* taught.
Disclose, *v.t.* to hatch. *sb.* the breaking of the shell by the
  chick on hatching.
Disme, *sb.* a tenth.
Distain, *v.t.* to stain, pollute.
Dive-dapper, *sb.* dabchick.
Dividant, *adj.* separate, different.
Dotant, *sb.* dotard.
Doubt, *sb.* fear, apprehension.
Dout, *v.t.* to extinguish.
Dowlas, *sb.* coarse linen.
Dowle, *sb.* down, the soft plumage of a feather.
Down-gyved, *adj.* hanging down about the ankle like gyves.
Dribbling, *adj.* weakly shot.
Drugs, *sb.* drudges.
Drumble, *v.i.* to be sluggish or clumsy.
Dry-beat, *v.t.* to cudgel, thrash.
Dry-foot. To draw dry-foot, track by scent.
Dudgeon, *sb.* the handle of a dagger.
Due, *v.t.* to endue.
Dump, *sb.* a sad strain.
Dup, *v.t.* to open.

Ean, *v.i.* to yean, lamb.

Ear, *v.t.* to plough, till.
Eche, *v.t.* to eke out.
Eftest, *adv.* readiest.
Eftsoons, *adv.* immediately.
Egal, *adj.* equal.
Egally, *adv.* equally.
Eisel, *sb.* vinegar.
Elf, *v.t.* to mat hair in a tangle; believed to be the work of elves.
Emballing, *sb.* investiture with the crown and sceptre.
Embarquement, *sb.* hindrance, restraint.
Ember-eyes, *sb.* vigils of Ember days.
Embowelled, *p.p.* emptied, exhausted.
Emmew, *v.t.* perhaps to mew up.
Empiricutic, *adj.* empirical, quackish.
Emulation, *sb.* jealous rivalry.
Enacture, *sb.* enactment, performance.
Encave, *v.t.* to hide, conceal.
Encumbered, *p.p.* folded.
End, *sb.* still an end = continually.
End, *v.t.* to get in the harvest.
Englut, *v.t.* to swallow.
Enlargement, *sb.* liberty, liberation.
Enormous, *adj.* out of the norm, monstrous.
Enseamed, *p.p.* defiled, filthy.
Ensear, *v.t.* to sear up, make dry.
Enshield, *adj.* enshielded, protected.
Entertain, *v.t.* to take into one's service.
Entertainment, *sb.* service.
Entreat, *v.t.* to treat.
Entreatments, *sb.* invitations.
Ephesian, *sb.* boon companion.
Eryngoes, *sb.* roots of the sea-holly, a supposed aphrodisiac.
Escot, *v.t.* to pay for.
Espial, *sb.* a spy.
Even Christian, *sb.* fellow Christian.
Excrement, *sb.* anything that grows out of the body, as hair,
  nails, etc. Used of the beard. M. of V. III. 2. 84. Of the
  hair. C. of E. II. 2. 79. Of the moustache. L.L.L. V. 1. 98.
Exhibition, *sb.* allowance, pension.
Exigent, *sb.* end. 1 H VI. II. 5. 9. Exigency, critical need. J. C.
  V. 1. 19.
Exion, *sb.* blunder for action.
Expiate, *v.t.* to terminate. Sonn. XXII. 4.
Expiate, *p.p.* ended. R III. III. 3. 24.
Exsufflicate, *adj.* inflated, both literally and metaphorically.
Extent, *sb.* seizure. As III. 1. 17. Violent attack. Tw.N. IV. 1.
  51. Condescension, favour. Ham. II. 2. 377. Display.
  T. A. IV. 4. 3.
Extraught, *p.p.* extracted.
Extravagancy, *sb.* vagrancy, aimless wandering about.
Eyas, *sb.* a nestling, a young hawk just taken from the nest.
Eyas-musket, *sb.* the young sparrow-hawk.
Eye, *v.i.* to appear, look to the eye.

Facinerious, *adj.* wicked.
Fadge, *v.i.* to succeed, suit.
Fading, *sb.* the burden of a song.
Fair, *v.t.* to make beautiful.
Fairing, *sb.* a gift.
Faitor, *sb.* evil-doer.
Fangled, *adj.* fond of novelties.
Fap, *adj.* drunk.
Farced, *p.p.* stuffed out.
Fardel, *sb.* a burden, bundle.
Fat, *adj.* cloying. *sb.* vat.
Favour, *sb.* outward appearance, aspect. In pl. = features.
Fear, *v.t.* to frighten. 3 H VI. III. 3. 226. Fear for. M. of V. III.
  5. 3.
Feat, *adj.* neat, dexterous.
Feat, *v.t.* to fashion, form.
Feeder, *sb.* servant.
Fee-farm, *sb.* a tenure without limit of time.
Fellowly, *adj.* companionable, sympathetic.
Feodary, *sb.* confederate.
Fere, *sb.* spouse, consort.
Ferret, *v.t.* to worry.
Festinate, *adj.* swift, speedy.
Fet, *p.p.* fetched.
Fico, *sb.* a fig (Span.).
File, *sb.* list.
File, *v.t.* to defile. Mac. III. 1. 65. Smooth, polish. L.L.L. V. 1.
  II. *v.i.* to walk in file. H VIII. III. 2. 171.
Fill-horse, *sb.* a shaft-horse.
Fills, *sb.* shafts.
Fineless, *adj.* endless, infinite.
Firago, *sb.* virago.
Firk, *v.t.* to beat.
Fitchew, *sb.* pole-cat.
Fitment, *sb.* that which befits.
Flap-dragon, *sb.* snap-dragon, or small burning object,
  lighted and floated in a glass of liquor, to be swallowed
  burning. L.L.L. V. 1. 43. 2 H IV. II. 4. 244. *v.t.* to swallow
  like a flap-dragon. W.T. III. 3. 100.
Flaw, *sb.* gust of wind. Ham. V. 1. 223. Small flake of ice. 2
  H IV. IV. 4. 35. Passionate outburst. M. for M. II. 3. 11. A
  crack. Lear, II. 4. 288. *v.t.* make a flaw in, break. H VIII. I.
  1. 95; I. 2. 21.
Fleer, *sb.* sneer. Oth. IV. 1. 83. *v.i.* to grin; sneer. L.L.L. V. 2.
  109.

Fleshment, *sb.* encouragement given by first success.
Flewed, *p.p.* with large hanging chaps.
Flight, *sb.* a long light arrow.
Flighty, *adj.* swift.
Flirt-gill, *sb.* light wench.
Flote, *sb.* sea.
Flourish, *v.t.* to ornament, gloss over.
Fobbed, *p.p.* cheated, deceived.
Foil, *sb.* defeat. I H VI. III. 3. 11. *v.t.* to defeat, mar. Pass. P. 99
Foin, *v.i.* to thrust (in fencing).
Fopped, *p.p.* cheated, fooled.
Forbod, *p.p.* forbidden.
Fordo, *v.t.* to undo, destroy.
Foreign, *adj.* dwelling abroad.
Fork, *sb.* the forked tongue of a snake. M. for M. III. 1. 16. The barbed head of an arrow. Lear, I. 1. 146. The junction of the legs with the trunk. Lear. IV. 6. 120.
Forked, *p.p.* barbed. As II. 1. 24. Horned as a cuckold. T. & C. I. 2. 164.
Forslow, *v.i.* to delay.
Forspeak, *v.t.* to speak against.
Fosset-seller, *sb.* a seller of taps.
Fox, *sb.* broadsword.
Foxship, *sb.* selfish and ungrateful, cunning.
Fracted, *p.p.* broken.
Frampold, *adj.* turbulent, quarrelsome.
Frank, *v.t.* to pen in a frank or sty. R III. 1. 3. 314. *sb.* a sty. 2 H IV. II. 2. 145. *adj.* liberal. Lear, III. 4. 20.
Franklin, *sb.* a yeoman.
Fraught, *sb.* freight, cargo, load. Tw.N. V. 1. 59. *v.t.* to load, burden. Cym. I. 1. 126. *p.p.* laden. M. of V. II. 8. 30. Stored. Two G. III. 2. 70.
Fraughtage, *sb.* cargo. C. of E. IV. 1. 8.
Fraughting, *part. adj.* constituting the cargo.
Frize, *sb.* a kind of coarse woollen cloth with a nap.
Frontier, *sb.* an outwork in fortification. 1 H IV. II. 3. 56. Used figuratively. 1 H IV. I. 3. 19.
Fruitful, *adj.* bountiful, plentiful.
Frush, *v.t.* to bruise, batter.
Frutify, blunder for certify. M. of V II. 2. 132.
Fubbed off, *p.p.* put off with excuses. 2 H IV. II. 1. 34.
Fullams, *sb.* a kind of false dice.

Gad, *sb.* a pointed instrument. T.A. IV. 1. 104. Upon the gad = on the spur of the moment, hastily. Lear, I. 2. 26.
Gage, *v.t.* to pledge.
Gaingiving, *sb.* misgiving.
Galliard, *sb.* a lively dance.
Gallimaufry, *sb.* medley, tumble.
Gallow, *v.t.* to frighten.
Gallowglass, *sb.* heavy- armed Irish foot-soldier.
Gallows, *sb.* a rogue, one fit to be hung.
Gallows-bird, *sb.* one that merits hanging.
Garboil, *sb.* uproar, commotion.
Gaskins, *sb.* loose breeches.
Gastness, *sb.* ghastliness, terror.
Geck, *sb.* dupe.
Generation, *sb.* offspring.
Generous, *adj.* nobly born.
Gennet, *sb.* a Spanish horse.
Gentry, *sb.* rank by birth. M.W. W. II. 1. 51. Courtesy. Ham. II. 2. 22.
German, *sb.* a near kinsman.
Germen, *sb.* germ, seed.
Gest, *sb.* a period of sojourn; originally the halting place in a royal progress.
Gib, *sb.* an old rom-cat.
Gibbet, *v.t.* to hang, as a barrel when it is slung.
Gig, *sb.* top.
Giglot, *adj.* wanton. 1 H VI. IV. 7. 41. *sb.* M. for M. V. 1. 345.
Gillyvors, *sb.* gillyflowers.
Gimmal-bit, *sb.* a double bit, or one made with double rings.
Gimmer, *sb.* contrivance, mechanical device.
Ging, *sb.* gang, pack.
Gird, *sb.* a scoff, jest. 2 H VI. III. 1. 131. *v.t.* to taunt, gibe at. 2 H IV. I. 2. 6.
Gleek, *sb.* scoff. 1 H VI. IV. 2. 12. *v.i.* to scoff. M.N.D. III. 1. 145.
Glib, *v.t.* to geld.
Gloze, *v.i.* to comment. H V. I. 2. 40. T. & C. II. 2. 165. To use flattery. R I!. II. 1. 10; T.A. IV. 4. 35.
Gnarling, *pr.p.* snarling.
Godden, *sb.* good den, good even.
God'ild, God yield, God reward.
God-jer = good-year.
Good-year, *sb.* a meaningless interjection. M.A. I. 3. 1. Some malific power. Lear, V. 3. 24.
Goss, *sb.* gorse.
Gossip, *sb.* sponsor. Two G. III. 1. 269. *v.t.* to stand sponsor for. A. W. I. 1. 176.
Gorbellied, *adj.* big-bellied.
Graff, *sb.* graft, scion. *v.t.* to graft.
Grain, *sb.* a fast colour. Hence in grain = ingrained.
Gratility, *sb.* gratuity.
Gratulate, *adj.* gratifying.
Greek, *sb.* boon companion.
Grise, *sb.* a step.

Guard, *v.t.* to trim, ornament.
Guardant, *sb.* sentinel, guard.
Guidon, *sb.* standard, banner.
Gules, *adj.* red, in heraldry.
Gust, *sb.* taste. *v.t.* to taste.

Hackney, *sb.* loose woman.
Haggard, *sb.* untrained hawk.
Haggled, *p.p.* hacked, mangled.
Hair, *sb.* texture, nature. 1 H IV. IV. 1. 61. Against the hair = against the grain. R. & J. II. 3. 97.
Handfast, *sb.* betrothal, contract. Cym. I. 5. 78. Custody. W.T. IV. 3. 778.
Handsaw, *sb.* corruption of heronshaw, a heron.
Hardiment, *sb.* daring deed.
Harlot, *adj.* lewd, base.
Hatched, *p.p.* closed with a hatch or half door. Per. IV. 2. 33. Engraved. T. & C. I. 3. 65.
Havoc, to cry havoc = cry no quarter. John, II. 1. 357. *v.t.* cut to pieces, destroy. H V. I. 2. 193.
Hawking, *adj.* hawk-like.
Hay, *sb.* a round dance. L.L.L. V. 1. 147. A term in fencing when a hit is made (Ital. *hai*, you have it). R. & J. II. 4. 27.
Hebenon, *sb.* perhaps the yew (Germ. *Eiben*). Ebony and henbane have been suggested.
Hefts, *sb.* heavings.
Helm, *v.t.* to steer.
Helpless, *adj.* not helping, useless. R III. I. 2. 13; Lucr. 1027. Incurable, Lucr. 756.
Hent, *sb.* grasp, hold. Ham. III. 3. 88. *v.t.* to hold, pass. M. for M. IV. 6. 14.
Hermit, *sb.* beadsman, one bound to pray for another.
Hild = held.
Hilding, *sb.* a good-for-nothing.
Hoar, *adj.* mouldy, R. & J. II. 3. 136. *v.i.* to become mouldy. R. & J. II. 3. 142.
Hoar, *v.t.* to make hoary or white, as with leprosy.
Hobby-horse, *sb.* a principal figure in the old morris dance. L.L.L. III. 1. 30. A light woman. M.A. III. 2. 68.
Hob-nob, have or not have, hit or miss.
Hold in, *v.i.* to keep counsel.
Holding, *sb.* the burden of a song. A. & C. II. 7. 112. Fitness, sense. A.W. IV. 2. 27.
Holy-ales, *sb.* rural festivals.
Honest, *adj.* chaste.
Honesty, *sb.* chastity. M.W.W. II. 2. 234. Decency. Tw.N. II. 3. 85. Generosity, liberality. Tim. III. 1. 30.
Honey-seed, blunder for homicide, 2 H IV. II. 1. 52.
Honey-suckle, blunder for homicidal. 2 H IV. II. 1. 50.
Hoodman, *sb.* the person blinded in the game of hoodman-blind.
Hoodman-blind, *sb.* blind-man's buff.
Hot at hand, not to be held in.
Hot-house, *sb.* bagnio, often in fact a brothel as well.
Hox, *v.t.* to hough, hamstring.
Hoy, *sb.* a small coasting vessel.
Hugger-mugger, In, stealthily and secretly.
Hull, *v.i.* to float.
Hulling, *pr. p.* floating at the mercy of the waves.

Ignomy, *sb.* ignominy.
Imbar, *v.t.* to bar in, make secure. H V. I. 2. 94.
Imboss, *v.t.* to hunt to death.
Imbossed, *p.p.* swollen. As II. 7. 67. Foaming at the mouth. T. of S. Ind. I. 16.
Immanity, *sb.* savageness, ferocity.
Immoment, *adj.* insignificant.
Immures, *sb.* surrounding walls.
Imp, *v.t.* to graft new feathers to a falcon's wing.
Impair, *adj.* unsuitable.
Impale, *v.t.* to encircle.
Impart, *v.t.* to afford, grant. Lucr. 1039; Sonn. LXXII. 8. *v.i.* to behave oneself. Ham. I. 2. 112.
Imperceiverant, *adj.* lacking in perception.
Impeticos, *v.t.* to put in the petticoat or pocket.
Importance, *sb.* importunity. John, II. 1. 7. Import. W.T. V. 2. 19. Question at issue, that which is imported. Cym. I. 5. 40.
Imposition, *sb.* command, injunction. M. of V. I. 2. 106. Penalty. M. for M. I. 2. 186.
Imposthume, *sb.* abscess.
Imprese, *sb.* device with a motto.
Include, *v.t.* to conclude, end.
Incontinent, *adj.* immediate.
Incony, *adj.* dainty, delicate.
Indent, *v.i.* to make terms.
Index, *sb.* introduction (in old books the index came first).
Indifferency, *sb.* impartiality.
Indirectly, *adv.* wrongly, unjustly.
Indurance, *sb.* durance, imprisonment.
Infest, *v.t.* to vex, trouble.
Inherit, *v.t.* to possess. Tp. IV. 1. 154. To cause to possess, put in possession. R II. I. 1. 85. *v.i.* to take possession. Tp. II. 2. 182.
Inheritor, *sb.* possessor.
Injury, *sb.* insult.
Inkhorn mate, *sb.* bookworm.
Inkle, *sb.* coarse tape.
Insisture, *sb.* persistence.

Intenible, *adj.* incapable of holding.
Intention, *sb.* aim, direction.
Intermissive, *adj.* intermitted, interrupted.
Intrinse, *adj.* tightly drawn.
Invised, *adj.* unseen, a doubtful word.
Irregulous, *adj.* lawless.

Jack, *sb.* figure that struck the bell in old clocks. R III. IV. 2. 114. A term of contempt. R III. I. 3. 72. The small bowl aimed at in the game of bowls. Cym. II. 1. 2. The key of a virginal. Sonn. CXXVIII. 5. A drinking vessel. T. of S. IV. 1. 48.
Jade, *v.t.* to play the jade with, run away with. Tw.N. II. 5. 164. Drive like a jade. A. & C. III. 1. 34. Treat with contempt. H VIII. III. 2. 280.
Jakes, *sb.* a privy.
Jar, *sb.* a tick of the clock. W.T. I. 2. 43.
Jar, *v.t.* to tick. R II. V. 5. 51. *v.i.* to guard. 1 H VI. III. 1. 70. *sb.* a quarrel. 1 H VI. I. 1. 44.
Jesses, *sb.* straps attaching the legs of a hawk to the fist.
Jet, *v.i.* to strut. Tw.N. II. 4. 32. Advance threateningly. R III. II. 4. 51.
Journal, *adj.* diurnal, daily.
Jowl, *v.t.* to knock, dash.

Kam, *adj.* crooked, away from the point.
Keech, *sb.* a lump of tallow or fat.
Keel, *v.t.* to cool.
Ken, *sb.* perception, sight. *v.t.*to know.
Kern, *sb.* light-armed foot-soldier of Ireland.
Kibe, *sb.* chilblain on the heel.
Kicky-wicky, *sb.* a pet name.
Killen = to kill.
Kiln-hole, *sb.* the fireplace of an oven or kiln.
Kind, *sb.* nature. M. of V. I. 3. 84. *adj.* natural. Lucr. 1423. *adv.* kindly. Tim. I. 2. 224.
Kindle, *v.t.* to bring forth young. As III. 2. 343. Incite. As I. 1. 179.
Knack, *sb.* a pretty trifle.
Knap, *v.t.* to gnaw, nibble. M. of V. III. 1. 9. Rap. Lear, II. 4. 123.

Laboursome, *adj.* elaborate.
Laced mutton, *sb.* slang for courtesan.
Lade, *v.t.* to empty, drain.
Land-damn. Unrecognizably corrupt word in W.T. II. 1. 143.
Lapsed, *p.p.* caught, surprised. Tw.N. III. 3. 36.
Latch, *v.t.* to catch, lay hold of.
Latten, *sb.* a mixture of copper and tin. M.W.W. I. 1. 153.
Laund, *sb.* glade.
Lavolt, *sb.* a dance in which two persons bound high and whirl round.
Lay for, *v.t.* to strive to win.
Leasing, *sb.* lying, falsehood.
Leave, *sb.* liberty, license.
Leer, *sb.* complexion.
Leese, *v.t.* to lose.
Leet, *sb.* a manor court. T. of S. Ind. II. 87. The time when such is held. Oth. III. 3. 140.
Leiger, *sb.* ambassador.
Length, *sb.* delay.
Let, *v.t.* to hinder. Tw.N. V. 1. 246; Ham. I. 4. 85. Detain. W.T. I. 2. 41. Forbear. Lucr. 10. *p.p.* caused. Ham. IV. 6. 11. *sb.* hindrance. H V. V. 2. 65.
Let-alone, *sb.* hindrance, prohibition.
Level, *sb.* aim, line of fire. R. & J. III. 3. 102. *v.i.* to aim. R III. IV. 4. 202. Be on the same level. Oth. I. 3. 239. *adv.* evenly. Tw.N. II. 4. 32.
Lewd, *adj.* base, vile.
Libbard, *sb.* leopard.
Liberal, *adj.* licentious. Liberal conceit = elaborate design. Ham. V. 2. 152. *adv.* freely, openly. Oth. V. 2. 220.
Lieger, *sb.* ambassador.
Lifter, *sb.* thief.
Light, *p.p.* lighted.
Likelihood, *sb.* sign, indication.
Lime, *v.t.* to put lime into liquor. M.W.W. I. 3. 14. Smear with bird-lime. 2 H VI. I. 3. 86. Catch with bird-lime. Tw.N. III. 4. 75. Cement. 3 H VI. V. 1. 84.
Limit, *sb.* appointed time. R II. I. 3. 151. *v.t.* to appoint. John. V. 2. 123.
Line, *v.t.* to draw, paint. As III. 2. 93. Strengthen, fortify. 1 H IV. II. 3. 85.
Line-grove, *sb.* a grove of lime trees.
Linsey-woolsey, *sb.* gibberish (literally, mixed stuff).
Lipsbury pinfold. Perhaps = between the teeth.
List, *sb.* desire, inclination. Oth. II. 1. 105. Limit, boundary. 1 H IV. IV. 1. 51. Lists for combat. Mac. III. 1. 70.
Lither, *adj.* flexible, gentle.
Livery, *sb.* delivery of a freehold into the possession of the heir.
Lob, *sb.* lubber, lout.
Lockram, *sb.* coarse linen.
Lodge, *v.t.* to lay flat, beat down.
Loggats, *sb.* a game somewhat resembling bowls.
Loof, *v.t.* to luff, bring close to the wind.
Losel, *sb.* a wasteful, worthless fellow.
Lout, *v.t.* to make a lout or fool of.

Lown, *sb.* base fellow.
Luce, *sb.* pike or jack.
Lurch, *v.t.* to win a love set at a game; bear off the prize easily. Cor. II. 2. 102. *v.i.* to skulk. M. W. W. II. 2. 25.
Lym, *sb.* bloodhound; so called from the leam or leash used to hold him.

Maggot-pie, *sb.* magpie.
Main, *sb.* a call at dice. 1 H IV. IV. 1. 47. Mainland. Lear, III. 1. 6. The chief power. Ham. V. 4. 15.
Main-course, *sb.* mainsail.
Main'd, *p.p.* maimed.
Makeless, *adj.* mateless, widowed.
Malkin, *sb.* slattern.
Mallard, *sb.* a wild drake.
Mallecho, *sb.* mischief (Span. *malhecho*).
Malt-horse, *sb.* brewer's horse.
Mammering, *pr.p.* hesitating.
Mammet, *sb.* a doll.
Mammock, *v.t.* to tear in pieces.
Manakin, *sb.* little man.
Mankind, *adj.* masculine, applied to a woman.
Manner, with the = in the act, red-handed.
Mare, *sb.* nightmare. To ride the wild mare = play at see-saw.
Mark, *sb.* thirteen shillings and fourpence.
Mart, *v.i.* to market, traffic. Cym. I. 6. 150. *v.t.* to vend, traffic with. J. C. IV. 3. 11.
Mastic, *sb.* used to stop decayed teeth.
Match, *sb.* compact, bargain. M. of V. III. 1. 40. Set a match = make an appointment. 1 H IV. I. 2. 110.
Mate, *v.t.* to confound, make bewildered. C. of E. III. 2. 54. Match, cope with. H VIII. III. 2. 274.
Material, *adj.* full of matter.
Maugre, *prep.* in spite of.
Maund, *sb.* a basket.
Mazard, *sb.* skull.
Meacock, *adj.* spiritless, pusillanimous.
Mealed, *p.p.* mingled, compounded.
Mean, *sb.* the intermediate part between the tenor and treble.
Meiny, *sb.* attendants, retinue.
Mell, *v.i.* to meddle.
Mered, He being the mered question—the question concerning him alone. A. & C. III. 13. 10.
Mess, *sb.* a set of four. L.L.L. IV. 3. 204. Small quantity. 2 H IV. II. 1. 95. Lower messes = inferiors, as messing at the lower end of the table. W.T. I. 2. 226.
Mete, *v. i.* to mete at = aim at.
Metheglin, *sb.* a kind of mead, made of honey and water.
Micher, *sb.* truant.
Miching, *adj.* sneaking, stealthy.
Mineral, *sb.* a mine.
Minikin, *adj.* small, pretty.
Minion, *sb.* darling, favourite. John, II. 1. 392. Used contemptuously. 2 H VI. I. 3. 82. A pert, saucy person. 2 H VI. I. 3. 136.
Mirable, *adj.* admirable.
Mire, *v.i.* to be bemired, sink as into mire.
Misdread, *sb.* fear of evil.
Misprision, *sb.* mistake. M.N.D. III. 2. 90. Contempt. A.W. II. 3. 153.
Misproud, *adj.* viciously proud.
Miss, *sb.* misdoing.
Missingly, *adv.* regretfully.
Missive, *sb.* messenger.
Misthink, *v.t.* to misjudge.
Mobled, *p.p.* having the face or head muffled.
Modern, *adj.* commonplace, trite.
Module, *sb.* mould, form.
Moldwarp, *sb.* mole.
Mome, *sb.* blockhead, dolt.
Momentany, *adj.* momentary, lasting an instant.
Monster, *v.t.* to make monstrous.
Month's mind, *sb.* intense desire or yearning.
Moralize, *v.t.* to interpret, explain.
Mort, *sb.* trumpet notes blown at the death of the deer.
Mortal, *adj.* deadly.
Mortified, *p.p.* deadened, insensible.
Mot, *sb.* motto, device.
Mother, *sb.* the disease *hysterica passio*.
Motion, *v.t.* to propose, counsel. 1 H VI. I. 3. 63. *sb.* a puppet show. W.T. IV. 3. 96. A puppet. Two G. II. 1. 91. Solicitation, proposal, suit. C. of E. I. 1. 60. Emotion, feeling, impulse. Tw.N. II. 4. 18.
Motive, *sb.* a mover, instrument, member.
Mountant, *adj.* lifted up.
Mow, *sb.* a grimace. *v.i.* to grimace.
Moy, *sb.* probably some coin.
Muleter, *sb.* muleteer.
Mulled, *p.p.* flat, insipid.
Mummy, *sb.* a medical or magical preparation originally made from mummies.
Murdering-piece, *sb.* a cannon loaded with chain-shot.
Murrion, *adj.* infected with the murrain.
Muse, *v.i.* to wonder. John, III. 1. 317. *v.t.* to wonder at. Tp. III. 3. 36.
Muset, *sb.* a gap or opening in a hedge.
Muss, *sb.* scramble.

Mutine, *sb.* mutineer.
Mystery, *sb.* profession. M. for M. IV. 2. 28. Professional skill. A.W. III. 6. 65.

Nayword, *sb.* pass-word, M.W.W. II. 2. 126. A by-word. Tw.N. II. 3. 132.
Neat, *adj.* trim, spruce.
Neb, *sb.* bill or beak.
Neeld, *sb.* needle.
Neeze, *v.i.* to sneeze.
Neif, *sb.* fist.
Next, *adj.* nearest.
Nick, *sb.* out of all nick, beyond all reckoning.
Night-rule, *sb.* revelry.
Nill = will not.
Nine-men's-morris, *sb.* a rustic game.
Note, *sb.* list, catalogue. W.T. IV. 2. 47. Note of expectation = list of expected guests. Mac. III. 3. 10. Stigma, mark of reproach. R II. I. 1. 43. Distinction. Cym. II. 3. 12. knowledge, observation. Lear, III. 1. 18.
Nott-pated, *adj.* crop-headed.
Nousle, *v.t.* to nurse, nourish delicately.
Nowl, *sb.* noddle.
Nuthook, *sb.* slang for catchpole.

Oathable, *adj.* capable of taking an oath.
Object, *sb.* anything presented to the sight; everything that comes in the way.
Obsequious, *adj.* regardful of funeral rites. 3 H VI. II. 5. 118. Funereal, having to do with obsequies. T. A. V. 3. 153.
Observance, *sb.* observation. Oth. III. 3. 151. Homage. 2 H IV. IV. 3. 15. Ceremony. M. of V. II. 2. 194.
Obstacle, *sb.* blunder for obstinate.
Occupation, *sb.* trade (in contemptuous sense). Cor. IV. 1. 14. Voice of occupation = vote of working men. Cor. IV. 6. 98.
Odd, *adj.* unnoticed. Tp. I. 2. 223. At odds. T. & C. IV. 5. 265.
Oeillades, *sb.* amorous glances.
O' ergrown, *p.p.* bearded. Cym. IV. 4. 33. Become too old. M. for M. I. 3. 22.
O'erstrawed, *p.p.* overstrewn.
Office, *v.t.* to office all = do all the domestic service. A. W. III. 2. 128. Keep officiously. Cor. V. 2. 61.
Oneyers, *sb.* unexplained word.
Opposition, *sb.* combat, encounter.
Orb, *sb.* orbit. R. & J. II. 1. 151. Circle. M.N.D. II. 1. 9. A heavenly body. M. of V. V. 1. 60. The earth. Tw.N. III. 1. 39.
Ordinant, *adj.* ordaining, controlling.
Ordinary, *sb.* a public dinner at which each man pays for his own share.
Ort, *sb.* remnant, refuse.
Ouphs, *sb.* elves, goblins.
Outrage, *sb.* outburst of rage.
Overscutch'd, *p.p.* over-whipped, over-switched (perhaps in a wanton sense).
Overture, *sb.* disclosure. W.T. II. 1. 172. Declaration. Tw.N. I. 5. 208.
Owe, *v.t.* to own, possess.

Packing, *sb.* plotting, conspiracy.
Paddock, *sb.* toad. Ham. III. 4. 191. A familiar spirit in the form of a toad. Mac. I. 1. 9.
Pajock, *sb.* term of contempt, by some said to mean peacock.
Pale, *sb.* enclosure, confine.
Palliament, *sb.* robe.
Parcel-bawd, *sb.* half-bawd.
Paritor, *sb.* apparitor, an officer of the Bishops' Court.
Part, *sb.* party, side.
Partake, *v.t.* to make to partake, impart. W.T. V. 3. 132. To share. J.C. II. 1. 305.
Parted, *p.p.* endowed.
Partisan, *sb.* a kind of pike.
Pash, *sb.* a grotesque word for the head. W.T. I. 2. 128. *v.t.* to smite, dash. T. & C. II. 3. 202.
Pass, *v.t.* to pass sentence on. M. for M. II. 1. 19. Care for. 2 H VI. IV. 2. 127. Represent. L.L.L. V. 1. 123. Make a thrust in fencing. Tw.N. III. 1. 44.
Passage, *sb.* passing to and fro. C. of E. III. 1. 99. Departure, death. Ham. III. 3. 86. Passing away. 1 H IV. II. 2. Occurrence. A.W. I. 1. 19. Process, course. R. & J. Prol. 9. Thy passages of life = the actions of thy life. 1 H IV. III. 2. 8. Passages of grossness = gross impositions. Tw.N. III. 2. 70. Motion. Cor. V. 6. 76.
Passant. In heraldry, the position of an animal walking.
Passion, *sb.* passionate poem. M.N.D. V. 1. 306; Sonn. XX. 2.
Passionate, *v.t.* to express with emotion. T.A. III. 2. 6. *adj.* displaying emotion. 2 H VI. I. 1. 104. Sorrowful. John, II. 1. 544.
Passy measures, a corruption of the Italian *passamezzo*, denoting a stately and measured step in dancing.
Patch, *sb.* fool.
Patchery, *sb.* knavery, trickery.
Patronage, *v.t.* to patronize, protect.
Pavin, *sb.* a stately dance of Spanish or Italian origin.

Pawn, *sb.* a pledge.
Peach, *v.t.* to impeach, accuse.
Peat, *sb.* pet, darling.
Pedascule, *sb.* vocative, pedant, schoolmaster.
Peevish, *adj.* childish, silly. 1 H VI. V. 3. 186. Fretful, wayward. M. of V. I. 1. 86.
Peise, *v.t.* to poise, balance. John, II. 1. 575. Retard by making heavy. M. of V. III. 2. 22. Weigh down. R III. V. 3. 106.
Pelt, *v.i.* to let fly with words of opprobrium.
Pelting, *adj.* paltry.
Penitent, *adj.* doing penance.
Periapt, *sb.* amulet.
Period, *sb.* end, conclusion. A. & C. IV. 2. 25. *v.t.* to put an end to. Tim. I. 1. 103.
Perked up, *p.p.* dressed up.
Perspective, *sb.* glasses so fashioned as to create an optical illusion.
Pert, *adj.* lively, brisk.
Pertaunt-like, *adv.* word unexplained and not yet satisfactorily amended. L.L.L. V. 2. 67.
Pervert, *v.t.* to avert, turn aside.
Pettitoes, *sb.* feet; properly pig's feet.
Pheeze, *v.t.* beat, chastise, torment.
Phisnomy, *sb.* physiognomy.
Phraseless, *adj.* indescribable.
Physical, *adj.* salutary, wholesome.
Pia mater, *sb.* membrane that covers the brain; used for the brain itself.
Pick, *v.t.* to pitch, throw.
Picked, *p.p.* refined, precise.
Picking, *adj.* trifling, small.
Piece, *sb.* a vessel of wine.
Pight, *p.p.* pitched.
Piled, *p.p* = peeled, bald, with quibble on 'piled' of velvet.
Pill, *v.t.* to pillage, plunder.
Pin, *sb.* bull's-eye of a target.
Pin-buttock, *sb.* a narrow buttock.
Pioned, *adj.* doubtful word: perhaps covered with marsh-marigold, or simply dug.
Pip, *sb.* a spot on cards. A pip out = intoxicated, with reference to a game called one and thirty.
Pitch, *sb.* the height to which a falcon soars, height.
Placket, *sb.* opening in a petticoat, or a petticoat.
Planched, *adj.* made of planks.
Plantage, *sb.* plants, vegetation.
Plantation, *sb.* colonizing.
Plausive, *adj.* persuasive, pleasing.
Pleached, *adj.* interlaced, folded.
Plurisy, *sb.* superabundance.
Point-devise, *adj.* precise, finical. L.L.L. V. 1. 19. *adv.* Tw.N. II. 5. 162.
Poking-sticks, *sb.* irons for setting out ruffs.
Pole-clipt, *adj.* used of vineyards in which the vines are grown around poles.
Polled, *adj.* clipped, laid bare.
Pomander, *sb.* a ball of perfume.
Poor-John, *sb.* salted and dried hake.
Porpentine, *sb.* porcupine.
Portable, *adj.* supportable, endurable.
Portage, *sb.* port-hole. H V. III. 1. 10. Port-dues. Per. III. 1. 35.
Portance, *sb.* deportment, bearing.
Posse, *v.t.* to curdle.
Posy, *sb.* a motto on a ring.
Potch, *v.i.* to poke, thrust.
Pottle, *sb.* a tankard; strictly a two quart measure.
Pouncet-box, *sb.* a box for perfumes, pierced with holes.
Practice, *sb.* plot.
Practisant, *sb.* accomplice.
Practise, *v.i.* to plot, use stratagems. Two G. IV. 1. 47. *v.t.* to plot. John, IV. 1. 20.
Precedent, *sb.* rough draft. R III. III. 6. 7. Prognostic, indication. V. & A. 26.
Prefer, *v.t.* to promote, advance. Two G. II. 4. 154. Recommend. Cym. II. 3. 50. Present offer. M.N.D. IV. 2. 37.
Pregnant, *adj.* ready-witted, clever. Tw.N. II. 2. 28. Full of meaning. Ham. II. 2. 209. Ready. Ham. III. 2. 66. Plain, evident. M. for M. II. 1. 23.
Prenzie, *adj.* demure.
Pretence, *sb.* project, scheme.
Prick, *sb.* point on a dial. 3 H VI. I. 4. 34. Bull's-eye. L.L.L. IV. 1. 132. Prickle. As III. 2. 113. Skewer. Lear, II. 3. 16.
Pricket, *sb.* a buck of the second year.
Prick-song, *sb.* music sung from notes.
Prig, *sb.* a thief.
Private, *sb.* privacy. Tw.N. III. 4. 90. Private communication. John, IV. 3. 16.
Prize, *sb.* prize-contest. T.A. I. 1. 399. Privilege. 3 H VI. I. 4. 59. Value. Cym. III. 6. 76.
Probal, *adj.* probable, reasonable.
Proditor, *sb.* traitor.
Proface, *int.* much good may it do you!
Propagate, *v.t.* to augment.
Propagation, *sb.* augmentation.
Proper-false, *adj.* handsome and deceitful.
Property, *sb.* a tool or instrument. M.W.W. III. 4. 10. *v.t.* to make a tool of. John, V. 2. 79.

Pugging, *adj.* thievish.
Puisny, *adj.* unskilful, like a tyro.
Pun, *v.t.* to pound.
Punk, *sb.* strumpet.
Purchase, *v.t.* to acquire, get. *sb.* acquisition, booty.
Pursuivant, *sb.* a herald's attendant or messenger.
Pursy, *adj.* short-winded, asthmatic.
Puttock, *sb.* a kite.
Puzzel, *sb.* a filthy drab (Italian *puzzolente*).

Quaintly, *adv.* ingeniously, deliberately.
Qualification, *sb.* appeasement.
Quality, *sb.* profession, calling, especially that of an actor. Two G. IV. 1. 58. Professional skill. Tp. I. 2. 193.
Quarter, *sb.* station. John, V. 5. 20. Keep fair quarter = keep on good terms with, be true to. C. of E. II. 1. 108. In quarter = on good terms. Oth. II. 3. 176.
Quat, *sb.* pimple.
Quatch-buttock, *sb.* a squat or flat buttock.
Quean, *sb.* wench, hussy.
Queasiness, *sb.* nausea, disgust.
Queasy, *adj.* squeamish, fastidious. M.A. II. 1. 368. Disgusted. A. & C. III. 6. 20.
Quell, *sb.* murder.
Quest, *sb.* inquest, jury. R III. I. 4. 177. Search, inquiry, pursuit. M. of V. I. 1. 172. A body of searchers. Oth. I. 2. 46.
Questant, *sb.* aspirant, candidate.
Quicken, *v.t.* to make alive. A.W. II. 1. 76. Refresh, revive. M. of V. II. 7. 52. *v.i.* to become alive, revive. Lear, III. 7. 40.
Quietus, *sb.* settlement of an account.
Quill, *sb.* body. 2 H VI. I. 3. 3.
Quillet, *sb.* quibble.
Quintain, *sb.* a figure set up for tilting at.
Quire, *sb.* company.
Quittance, *v.i.* to requite. 1 H VI. II. 1. 14. *sb.* acquittance. M. W. W. I. 1. 10. Requital. 2 H IV. I. 1. 108.
Quoif, *sb.* cap.
Quoit, *v.t.* to throw.
Quote, *v.t.* to note, examine.

Rabato, *sb.* a kind of ruff.
Rabbit-sucker, *sb.* sucking rabbit.
Race, *sb.* root. W.T. IV. 3. 48. Nature, disposition. M. for M. II. 4. 160. Breed. Mac. II. 4. 15.
Rack, *v.t.* stretch, strain. M. of V. I. 1. 181. Strain to the utmost. Cor. V. 1. 16.
Rack, *sb.* a cloud or mass of clouds. Ham. II. 2. 492. *v.i.* move like vapour. 3 H VI. II. 1. 27.
Rampired, *p.p.* fortified by a rampart.
Ramps, *sb.* wanton wenches.
Ranges, *sb.* ranks.
Rap, *v.t.* to transport.
Rascal, *sb.* a deer out of condition.
Raught, *impf.* & *p.p.* reached.
Rayed, *p.p.* befouled. T. of S. IV. 1. 3. In T. of S. III. 2. 52 it perhaps means arrayed, *i.e.* attacked.
Raze, *sb.* root.
Razed, *p.p.* slashed.
Reave, *v.t.* to bereave.
Rebate, *v.t.* to make dull, blunt.
Recheat, *sb.* a set of notes sounded to call hounds off a false scent.
Rede, *sb.* counsel.
Reechy, *adj.* smoky, grimy.
Refell, *v.t.* to refute.
Refuse, *sb.* rejection, disowning. *v.t.* to reject, disown.
Reguerdon, *v.t.* to reward, guerdon.
Remonstrance, *sb.* demonstration.
Remotion, *sb.* removal.
Renege, *v.t.* to deny.
Renying, *pres. p.* denying.
Replication, *sb.* echo. J.C. I. 1. 50. Reply. Ham. IV. 2. 12.
Rere-mice, *sb.* bats.
Respected, blunder for suspected.
Respective, *adj.* worthy of regard. Two G. IV. 4. 197. Showing regard. John, I. 1. 188. Careful. M. of V. V. 1. 156.
Respectively, *adv.* respectfully.
Rest, *sb.* set up one's rest is to stand upon the cards in one's hand, be fully resolved.
Resty, *adj.* idle, lazy.
Resume, *v.t.* to take.
Reverb, *v.t.* to resound.
Revolt, *sb.* rebel.
Ribaudred, *adj.* ribald, lewd.
Rid, *v.t.* to destroy, do away with.
Riggish, *adj.* wanton.
Rigol, *sb.* a circle.
Rim, *sb.* midriff or abdomen.
Rivage, *sb.* shore.
Rival, *sb.* partner, companion. M.N.D. III. 2. 156. *v.i.* to be a competitor. Lear, I. 1. 191.
Rivality, *sb.* partnership, participation.
Rivelled, *adj.* wrinkled.
Road, *sb.* roadstead, port. Two G. 11. 4. 185. Journey. H VIII. IV. 2. 17. Inroad, incursion. H V. I. 2. 138.
Roisting, *adj.* roistering, blustering.

Romage, *sb.* bustle, turmoil.
Ronyon, *sb.* scurvy wretch.
Rook, *v.i.* to cower, squat.
Ropery, *sb.* roguery.
Rope-tricks, *sb.* knavish tricks.
Roping, *pr.p.* dripping.
Roted, *p.p.* learned by heart.
Rother, *sb.* an ox, or animal of the ox kind.
Round, *v.i.* to whisper. John, II. 1. 566. *v.t.* to surround. M.N.D. IV. 1. 52.
Round, *adj.* straightforward, blunt, plainspoken. C. of E. II. 1. 82.
Rouse, *sb.* deep draught, bumper.
Rout, *sb.* crowd, mob. C. of E. III. 1. 101. Brawl. Oth. II. 3. 210.
Row, *sb.* verse or stanza.
Roynish, *adj.* scurvy; hence coarse, rough.
Rub, *v.i.* to encounter obstacles. L.L.L. IV. 1. 139. Rub on, of a bowl that surmounts the obstacle in its course. T. & C. III. 2. 49. *sb.* impediment, hindrance; from the game of bowls. John, III. 4. 128.
Ruffle, *v.i.* to swagger, bully. T.A. I. 1. 314.
Ruddock, *sb.* the redbreast.
Rudesby, *sb.* a rude fellow.
Rump-fed, *adj.* pampered; perhaps fed on offal, or else fat-rumped.
Running banquet, a hasty refreshment (fig.).
Rush aside, *v.t.* to pass hasitily by, thrust aside.
Rushling, blunder for rustling.

Sad, *adj.* grave, serious. M. of V. II. 2. 195. Gloomy, sullen. R II. V. 5. 70.
Sagittary, *sb.* a centaur. T. & C. V. 5. 14. The official residence in the arsenal at Venice. Oth. I. 1. 160.
Sallet, *sb.* a close-fitting helmet. 2 H VI. IV. 10. 11. A salad. 2 H VI. IV. 10. 8.
Salt, *sb.* salt-cellar. Two G. III. 1. 354. *adj.* lecherous. M. for M. V. 1. 399. Stinging, bitter. T. & C. I. 3. 371.
Salutation, *sb.* give salutation to my blood = make my blood rise.
Salute, *v.t.* to meet. John, II. 1. 590. To affect. H VIII. II. 3. 103.
Sanded, *adj.* sandy-coloured.
Say, *sb.* a kind of silk.
Scald, *adj.* scurvy, scabby. H V. V. 1. 5.
Scale, *v.t.* to put in the scales, weigh.
Scall = scald. M.W.W. III. 1. 115.
Scamble, *v.i.* to scramble.
Scamel, *sb.* perhaps a misprint for seamell, or seamew.
Scantling, *sb.* a scanted or small portion.
Scape, *sb.* freak, escapade.
Sconce, *sb.* a round fort. H VIII. 6. 73. Hence a protection for the head. C. of E. II. 2. 37. Hence the skull. Ham. V. 1. 106. *v.r.* to ensconce, hide. Ham. III. 4. 4.
Scotch, *sb.* notch. *v.t.* to cut, slash.
Scrowl, *v.i.* perhaps for to scrawl.
Scroyles, *sb.* scabs, scrofulous wretches.
Scrubbed, *adj.* undersized.
Scull, *sb.* shoal of fish.
Seal, *sb.* to give seals = confirm, carry out.
Seam, *sb.* grease, lard.
Seconds, *sb.* an inferior kind of flour.
Secure, *adj.* without care, confident.
Security, *sb.* carelessness, want of caution.
Seedness, *sb.* sowing with seed.
Seel, *v.t.* to close up a hawk's eyes.
Self-admission, *sb.* self-approbation.
Semblative, *adj.* resembling, like.
Sequestration, *sb.* separation.
Serpigo, *sb.* tetter or eruption on the skin.
Sessa, *int.* exclamation urging to speed.
Shard-borne, *adj.* borne through the air on shards.
Shards, *sb.* the wing cases of beetles. A. & C. III. 2. 20. Potsherds. Ham. V. 1. 254.
Sharked up, *p.p.* gathered indiscriminately.
Shealed, *p.p.* shelled.
Sheep-biter, *sb.* a malicious, niggardly fellow.
Shent, *p.p.* scolded, rebuked. M.W.W. I. 4. 36.
Shive, *sb.* slice.
Shog, *v.i.* to move, jog.
Shore, *sb.* a sewer.
Shrewd, *adj.* mischievous, bad.
Shrewdly, *adv.* badly.
Shrewdness, *sb.* mischievousness.
Shrieve, *sb.* sheriff.
Shroud, *sb.* shelter, protection.
Siege, *sb.* seat. M. for M. IV. 2. 98. Rank. Ham. IV. 7. 75. Excrement. Tp. II. 2. 111.
Significant, *sb.* sign, token.
Silly, *adj.* harmless, innocent. Two G. IV. 1. 72. Plain, simple. Tw.N. II. 4. 46.
Simular, *adj.* simulated, counterfeited. Cym. V. 5. 20. *sb.* simulator, pretender. Lear, III. 2. 54.
Sitch, *adv.* and *conj.* since.
Skains-mates, *sb.* knavish companions.
Slab, *adj.* slabby, slimy.
Sleeve-hand, *sb.* wristband.
Sleided, *adj.* untwisted.
Slipper, *adj.* slippery.

Slobbery, *adj.* dirty.
Slubber, *v.t.* to slur over, do carelessly.
Smatch, *sb.* smack, taste.
Sneak-cup, *sb.* a fellow who shirks his liquor.
Sneap, *v.t.* to pinch, nip. L.L.L. I. 1. 100. *sb.* snub, reprimand. 2 H IV. II. 1. 125.
Sneck up, contemptuous expression = go and be hanged.
Snuff, *sb.* quarrel. Lear, III. 1. 26. Smouldering wick of a candle. Cym. I. 6. 87. Object of contempt. A.W. I. 2. 60. Take in snuff = take offence at. L.L.L. V. 2. 22.
Sob, *sb.* a rest given to a horse to regain its wind.
Solidare, *sb.* a small coin.
Sonties, *sb.* corruption of saints.
Sooth, *sb.* flattery.
Soothers, *sb.* flatterers.
Sophy, *sb.* the Shah of Persia.
Sore, *sb.* a buck of the fourth year.
Sorel, *sb.* a buck of the third year.
Sort, *sb.* rank. M.A. I. 1. 6. Set, company. R III. V. 3. 316. Manner. M. of V. I. 2. 105. Lot. T. & C. I. 3. 376.
Sort, *v.t.* to pick out. Two G. III. 2. 92. To rank. Ham. II. 2. 270. To arrange, dispose. R III. II. 2. 148. To adapt. 2 H VI. II. 4. 68. *v.i.* to associate. V. & A. 689. To be fitting. T. & C. I. 1. 109. Fall out, happen. M.N.D. III. 2. 352.
Souse, *v.t.* to swoop down on, as a falcon.
Sowl, *v.t.* to lug, drag by the ears.
Span-counter, *sb.* boy's game of throwing a counter so as to strike, or rest within a span of, an opponent's counter.
Speed, *sb.* fortune, success.
Speken = speak.
Sperr, *v.t.* to bar.
Spital, *sb.* hospital.
Spital house, *sb.* hospital.
Spleen, *sb.* quick movement. M.N.D. I. 1. 146. Fit of laughter. L.L.L. III. 1. 76.
Spot, *sb.* pattern in embroidery.
Sprag, *adj.* sprack, quick, lively.
Spring, *sb.* a young shoot.
Springhalt, *sb.* a lameness in horses.
Spurs, *sb.* the side roots of a tree.
Squandering, *adj.* roving, random. As II. 7. 57.
Square, *sb.* the embroidery about the bosom of a smock or shift. W.T. IV. 3. 212. Most precious square of sense = the most sensitive part. Lear, I. 1. 74.
Square, *v.i.* to quarrel.
Squash, *sb.* an unripe peascod.
Squier, *sb.* square, rule.
Squiny, *v.i.* to look asquint.
Staggers, *sb.* giddiness, bewilderment. A.W. II. 3. 164. A disease of horses. T. of S. III. 2. 53.
Stale, *sb.* laughing stock, dupe. 3 H VI. III. 3. 260. Decoy. T. of S. III. 1. 90. Stalking-horse. C. of E. II. 1. 101. Prostitute. M.A. II. 2. 24. Horse-urine. A. & C. I. 4. 62.
Stamp, *v.t.* to mark as genuine, give currency to.
Standing, *sb.* duration, continuance. W.T. I. 2. 430. Attitude. Tim. I. 1. 34.
Standing-tuck, *sb.* a rapier standing on end.
Staniel, *sb.* a hawk, the kestrel.
Stare, *v.i.* to stand on end.
State, *sb.* attitude. L.L.L. IV. 3. 183. A chair of state. 1 H IV. II. 4. 390. Estate, fortune. M. of V. III. 2. 258. States (pl.) = persons of high position. John, II. 1. 395.
Statute-caps, *sb.* woollen caps worn by citizens as decreed by the Act of 1571.
Staves, *sb.* shafts of lances.
Stead, *v.t.* to help.
Stead up, *v.t.* to take the place of.
Stelled, *p.p.* fixed. Lucr. 1444. Sonn. XXIV. 1. Starry. Lear, III. 7. 62.
Stickler-like, *adj.* like a stickler, whose duty it was to separate combatants.
Stigmatic, *adj.* marked by deformity.
Stillitory, *sb.* a still.
Stint, *v.i.* to stop, cease. R. & J. I. 3. 48. *v.t.* to check, stop. T. & C. IV. 5. 93.
Stock, *sb.* a dowry. Two G. III. 1. 305. A stocking. Two G. III. 1. 306; 1 H IV. II. 4. 118. A thrust in fencing. M.W.W. II. 3. 24. *v.t.* to put in the stocks. Lear, II. 2. 333.
Stomach, *sb.* courage. 2 H IV. I. 1. 129. Pride. T. of S. V. 2. 177.
Stomaching, *sb.* resentment.
Stone-bow, *sb.* a cross-bow for shooting stones.
Stoop, *sb.* a drinking vessel.
Stricture, *sb.* strictness.
Stride, *v.t.* to overstep.
Stover, *sb.* cattle fodder.
Stuck, *sb.* a thrust in fencing.
Subject, *sb.* subjects, collectively.
Subscribe, *v.i.* to be surety. A.W. III. 6. 84. Yield, submit. 1 H VI. II. 4. 44. *v.t.* to admit, acknowledge. M.A. V. 2. 58.
Subtle, *adj.* deceptively smooth.
Successantly, *adv.* in succession.
Sufferance, *sb.* suffering. M. for M. II. 2. 167. Patience. M. of V. I. 3. 109. Loss. Oth. II. 1. 23. Death penalty. H V. II. 2. 158.
Suggest, *v.t.* to tempt.
Suit, *sb.* service, attendance. M. for M. IV. 4. 19. Out of suits with fortune = out of fortune's service.
Supervise, *sb.* inspection.

Suppliance, *sb.* pastime.

Sur-addition, *sb.* an added title.

Surmount, *v.i.* to surpass, exceed. 1 H VI. V. 3. 191. *v.t.* to surpass. L.L.L. V. 2. 677.

Sur-reined, *p.p.* overridden.

Suspect, *sb.* suspicion.

Swarth, *adj.* black. T.A. II. 3. 71. *sb.* swath. Tw.N. II. 3. 145.

Swoopstake, *adv.* in one sweep, wholesale.

Tag, *sb.* rabble.

Take, *v.t.* to captivate. W.T. IV. 3. 119. Strike. M.W.W. IV. 4. 32. Take refuge in. C. of E. V. 1. 36. Leap over. John, V. 2. 138. Take in = conquer. A. & C. I. 1. 23. Take out = copy. Oth. III. 3. 296. Take thought = feel grief for. J.C. II. 1. 187. Take up = get on credit. 2 H VI. IV. 7. 125. Reconcile. Tw.N. III. 4. 294. Rebuke. Two G. I. 2. 134.

Tallow-keech, *sb.* a vessel filled with tallow.

Tanling, *sb.* one tanned by the sun. John, IV. 1. 117. Incite. Ham. II. 2. 358.

Tarre, *v.t.* to set on dogs to fight.

Taste, *sb.* trial, proof. *v.t.* to try, prove.

Tawdry-lace, *sb.* a rustic necklace.

Taxation, *sb.* satire, censure. As I. 2. 82. Claim, demand. Tw.N. I. 5. 210.

Teen, *sb.* grief.

Tenable, *adj.* capable of being kept.

Tend, *v.i.* to wait, attend. Ham. I. 3. 83. Be attentive. Tp. I. 1. 6. *v.t.* to tend to, regard. 2 H VI. I. 1. 204. Wait upon. A. & C. II. 2. 212.

Tendance, *sb.* attention. Tim. I. 1. 60. Persons attending. Tim. I. 1. 74.

Tender, *v.t.* to hold dear, regard. R III. I. 1. 44. *sb.* care, regard. 1 H IV. V. 4. 49.

Tender-hefted, *adj.* set in a delicate handle or frame.

Tent, *sb.* probe. T. & C. II. 2. 16. *v.t.* to probe. Ham. II. 2. 608. Cure. Cor. I. 9. 31.

Tercel, *sb.* male goshawk.

Termless, *adj.* not to be described.

Testerned, *p.p.* presented with sixpence.

Testril, *sb.* sixpence.

Tetchy, *adj.* irritable.

Tetter, *sb.* skin erruption. Ham. I. 5. 71. *v.t.* to infect with tetter. Cor. III. 1. 99.

Than = then, Lucr. 1440.

Tharborough, *sb.* third borough, constable.

Thick, *adv.* rapidly, close.

Thirdborough, *sb.* constable.

Thisne, perhaps = in this way. M.N.D. I. 2. 48.

Thoughten, *p.p.* be you thoughten = entertain the thought.

Thrall, *sb.* thraldom, slavery. Pass. P. 266. *adj.* enslaved. V. & A. 837.

Three-man beetle, a rammer operated by three men.

Three-man songmen, three-part glee-singers.

Three-pile, *sb.* the finest kind of velvet.

Three-piled, *adj.* having a thick pile. M. for M. I. 2. 32. Superfine (met.). L.L.L. V. 2. 407.

Tickle, *adj.* unstable. 2 H VI. I. 1. 216. Tickle of the sere, used of lungs readily prompted to laughter; literally hair-triggered. Ham. II. 2. 329.

Ticklish, *adj.* wanton.

Tight, *adj.* swift, deft. A. & C. IV. 4. 15. Water-tight, sound. T. of S. II. 1. 372.

Tightly, *adv.* briskly, smartly.

Time-pleaser, *sb.* time server, one who complies with the times.

Tire, *sb.* headdress. Two G. IV. 4. 187. Furniture. Per II. 2. 21.

Tire, *v.i.* to feed greedily. 3 H VI. I. 1. 269. *v.t.* make to feed greedily. Lucr. 417.

Tisick, *sb.* phthisic, a cough.

Toaze, *v.t.* to draw out, untangle.

Tod, *sb.* Twenty-eight pounds of wool. *v.t.* to yield a tod.

Toged, *adj.* wearing a toga.

Toll, *v.i.* to pay toll. A.W. V. 3. 147. *v.t.* to take toll. John, III. 1. 154.

Touch, *sb.* trait. As V. 4. 27. Dash, spice. R III. IV. 4. 157. Touchstone. R III. IV. 2. 8. Of noble touch = of tried nobility. Cor. IV. 1. 49. Brave touch = fine test of valour. M.N.D. III. 2. 70. Slight hint. H VIII. V. 1. 13. Know no touch = have no skill. R II. I. 3. 165.

Touse, *v.t.* to pull, tear.

Toy, *sb.* trifle, idle fancy, folly.

Tract, *sb.* track, trace. Tim. I. 1. 53. Course. H VIII. I. 1. 40.

Train, *v.t.* to allure, decoy. 1 H VI. I. 3. 25. *sb.* bait, allurement. Mac. IV. 3. 118.

Tranect, *sb.* ferry, a doubtful word.

Translate, *v.t.* to transform.

Trash, *v.t.* lop off branches. Tp. I. 2. 81. Restrain a dog by a trash or strap. Oth. II. 1. 307.

Traverse, *v.i.* to march to the right or left.

Tray-trip, *sb.* a game at dice, which was won by throwing a trey.

Treachors, *sb.* traitors.

Treatise, *sb.* discourse.

Trench, *v.t.* to cut. Two G. III. 2. 7. Divert from its course by digging. H IV. III. 1. 112.

Troll-my-dames, *sb.* the French game of *trou madame*, perhaps akin to bagatelle.

Tropically, *adv.* figuratively.

True-penny, *sb.* an honest fellow. Ham. I. 5. 150.

Try, *sb.* trial, test. Tim. VI. 1. 9. Bring to try = bring a ship as close to the wind as possible.

Tub, *sb.* and tubfast, *sb.* a cure of venereal disease by sweating and fasting.

Tuck, *sb.* rapier.

Tun-dish, *sb.* funnel.

Turk, to turn Turk = to be a renegade. M.A. III. 4. 52. Turk Gregory = Pope Gregory VII. 1 H IV. V. 3. 125.

Twiggen, *adj.* made of twigs or wicker.

Twilled, *adj.* perhaps, covered with sedge or reeds.

Twire, *v.i.* to twinkle.

Umber, *sb.* a brown colour.

Umbered, *p.p.* made brown, darkened.

Umbrage, *sb.* a shadow.

Unaneled, *adj.* not having received extreme unction.

Unbarbed, *adj.* wearing no armour, bare.

Unbated, *adj.* unblunted.

Unbraced, *adj.* unbuttoned.

Uncape, *v.i.* to uncouple, throw off the hounds.

Uncase, *v.i.* to undress.

Unclew, *v.t.* to unwind, undo.

Uncolted, *p.p.* deprived of one's horse. 1 H IV. II. 2. 41.

Uncomprehensive, *adj.* incomprehensible.

Unconfirmed, *adj.* inexperienced.

Undercrest, *v.t.* to wear upon the crest.

Undertaker, *sb.* agent, person responsible to another for something.

Underwrite, *v.t.* to submit to.

Undistinguished, *adj.* not to be seen distinctly, unknowable.

Uneath, *adv.* hardly, with difficulty.

Unfolding, *adj.* unfolding star, the star at whose rising the shepherd lets the sheep out of the fold.

Unhappy, *adj.* mischievous, unlucky.

Unhatched, *p.p.* unhacked. Tw.N. III. 4. 234. Undisclosed. Oth. III. 4. 140.

Unhouseled, *adj.* without having received the sacrament.

Union, *sb.* large pearl.

Unkind, *adj.* unnatural. Lear, I. 1. 261. Childless. V. & A. 204.

Unlived, *p.p.* deprived of life.

Unpaved, *adj.* without stones.

Unpinked, *adj.* not pinked, or pierced with eyelet holes.

Unraked, *adj.* not made up for the night.

Unrecuring, *adj.* incurable.

Unrolled, *p.p.* struck off the roll.

Unseeming, *pr.p.* not seeming.

Unseminared, *p.p.* deprived of seed or virility.

Unset, *adj.* unplanted.

Unshunned, *adj.* inevitable.

Unsifted, *adj.* untried, inexperienced.

Unsquared, *adj.* unsuitable.

Unstate, *v.t.* to deprive of dignity.

Untented, *adj.* incurable.

Unthrift, *sb.* prodigal. *adj.* good for nothing.

Untraded, *adj.* unhackneyed.

Unyoke, *v.t.* to put off the yoke, take ease after labour. Ham. V. 1. 55. *v.t.* to disjoin. John, III. 1. 241.

Up-cast, *sb.* a throw at bowls; perhaps the final throw.

Upshoot, *sb.* decisive shot.

Upspring, *sb.* a bacchanalian dance.

Upstaring, *adj.* standing on end.

Urchin, *sb.* hedgehog. T.A. II. 3. 101. A goblin. M.W.W. IV. 4. 49.

Usance, *sb.* interest.

Use, *sb.* interest. M.A. II. 1. 269. Usage. M. for M. I. 1. 40. In use = in trust. M. of V. IV. 1. 383.

Use, *v.r.* to behave oneself.

Uses, *sb.* manners, usages.

Utis, *sb.* boisterous merriment.

Vade, *v.i.* to fade.

Vail, *v.t.* setting (of the sun). T. & C. V. 8. 7. *v.t.* to lower, let fall. 1 H VI. V. 3. 25. *v.i.* to bow. Per. IV. Prol. 29.

Vails, *sb.* a servant's perquisites.

Vain, for vain = to no purpose.

Vantbrace, *sb.* armour for the forearm.

Vast, *adj.* waste, desolate, boundless.

Vaunt-couriers, *sb.* fore-runners.

Vaward, *sb.* vanguard. 1 H VI. I. 1. 132. The first part. M.N.D. IV. 1. 106.

Vegetives, *sb.* plants.

Velvet-guards, *sb.* velvet linings, used metaphorically of those who wear them. 1 H IV. III. 1. 256.

Veney, or venew, *sb.* a fencing bout, a hit.

Venge, *v.t.* to avenge.

Vent, *sb.* discharge. Full of vent = effervescent like wine.

Via, *interj.* away, on!

Vice, *sb.* the buffoon in old morality plays. R III. III. 1. 82. *v.t.* to screw (met.) W.T. I. 2. 415.

Vinewedst, *adj.* mouldy, musty.

Violent, *v.i.* to act violently, rage.

Virginalling, *pr.p.* playing with the fingers as upon the virginals.

Virtuous, *adj.* efficacious, powerful. Oth. III. 4. 110. Essential. M.N.D. III. 2. 367. Virtuous season = benignant influence. M. for M. II. 2. 168.

Vouch, *sb.* testimony, guarantee. 1 H VI. V. 3. 71. *v.i.* to assert, warrant.

Vizard, *sb.* mask.

Waft, *v.t.* to beckon. C. of E. II. 2. 108. To turn. W.T. I. 2. 371.

Wag, *v.i.* and *v.t.* to move, stir. R III. III. 5. 7. To go one's way. M.A. V. 1. 16.

Wage, *v.t.* to stake, risk. 1 H IV. 4. 20. *v.i.* to contend. Lear, II. 4. 210. Wage equal = be on an equality with. A. & C. v. 1. 31.

Wanion, *sb.* with a wanion = with a vengeance.

Wanton, *sb.* one brought up in luxury, an effeminate person. John, V. 1. 70. *v.i.* to dally, play. W.T. II. 1. 18.

Wappened, *p.p.* of doubtful meaning, perhaps worn out, stale.

Ward, *sb.* guardianship. A.W. I. 1. 5. Defence. L.L.L. III. 1. 131. Guard in fencing. 1 H IV. II. 4. 198. Prison, custody. 2 H VI. V. 1. 112. Lock, bolt. Tim. III. 3. 38. *v.t.* to guard. R III. V. 3. 254.

Warden-pies, *sb.* pies made with the warden, a large baking pear.

Warrantize, *sb.* security, warranty.

Warrener, *sb.* keeper of a warren, gamekeeper.

Watch, *sb.* a watch candle that marked the hours.

Watch, *v.t.* to tame by keeping from sleep.

Waters, *sb.* for all waters = ready for anything.

Wealsmen, *sb.* statesmen.

Web and pin. *sb.* cataract of the eye.

Weeding, *sb.* weeds.

Weet, *v.t.* to know.

Welkin, *sb.* the blue, the sky. Tw.N. II. 3. 61. *adj.* sky-blue. W.T. I. 2. 136.

Whiffler, *sb.* one who cleared the way for a procession, carrying the whiffle or staff of his office.

Whist, *adj.* still, hushed.

Whittle, *sb.* a clasp-knife.

Whoobub, *sb.* hubbub.

Widowhood, *sb.* rights as a widow.

Wilderness, *sb.* wildness.

Wimpled, *p.p.* blindfolded. (A wimple was a wrap or handkerchief for the neck.)

Winchester goose, *sb.* a venereal swelling in the groin, the brothels of Southwark being in the jurisdiction of the Bishop of Winchester.

Window-bars, *sb.* lattice-like embroidery worn by women across the breast.

Windring, *adj.* winding.

Wink, *sb.* a closing of the eyes, sleep. Tp. II. 1. 281. *v.i.* to close the eyes, be blind, be in the dark. C. of E. III. 2. 58.

Winter-ground, *v.t.* to protect a plant from frost by bedding it with straw.

Wipe, *sb.* a brand, mark of shame.

Wise-woman, *sb.* a witch.

Witch, *sb.* used of a man also; wizard.

Woman, *v.t.* woman me = make me show my woman's feelings.

Woman-tired, *adj.* henpecked.

Wondered, *p.p.* performing wonders.

Wood, *adj.* mad.

Woodman, *sb.* forester, hunter. M.W.W. V. 5. 27. In a bad sense, a wencher. M. for M. IV. 4. 163.

Woollen, to lie in the = either to lie in the blankets, or to be buried in flannel, as the law in Shakespeare's time prescribed.

Word, to be at a word = to be as good as one's word.

Word, *v.t.* to represent. Cym. I. 4. 15. To deceive with words. A. & C. V. 2. 191.

World, *sb.* to go to the world = to be married. A woman of the world = a married woman. A world to see = a marvel to behold.

Wrangler, *sb.* an opponent, a tennis term.

Wreak, *sb.* revenge. T.A. IV. 3. 33. *v.t.* to revenge. T.A. IV. 3. 51.

Wreakful, *adj.* revengeful.

Wrest, *sb.* a tuning-key.

Wring, *v.i.* to writhe.

Write, *v.r.* to describe oneself, claim to be. Writ as little beard = claimed as little beard. A.W. II. 3. 62.

Writhled, *adj.* shrivelled up, wrinkled.

Wry, *v.i.* to swerve.

Yare, *adj.* and *adv.* ready, active, nimble.

Yarely, *adv.* readily, briskly.

Yearn, *v.t.* and *v.i.* to grieve.

Yellows, *sb.* jaundice in horses.

Yerk, *v.t.* to lash out at, strike quickly.

Yest, *sb.* froth, foam.

Yesty, *adj.* foamy, frothy.

Younker, *sb.* a stripling, youngster novice.

Yslaked, *p.p.* brought to rest.

Zany, *sb.* a fool, buffoon.

On the occasion of the dedication of Montvale's new library, my wish is that you enjoy these brilliant writings as much as I have.

Sincerely,

Charlotte Vandervalk
N.J. Assemblywoman
3/28/04

My grandfather, **PAT DOYLE,** loved the land more than any man I ever met. His big hands held the plough and his big horses stretched their strength until they were wet with sweat and rain. He braved the weather with fierce determination and was the last to leave the field. Unbuckling his team, he hung their dripping harness on the wall, wiped the wetness from his steaming face and said,

"It's a terrible day,
THANKS BE TO GOD."

This is his plough, as pictured in June, 2002. He last used it in 1954, when he was 80 years old.

Portrait of Patrick Doyle, by Tom Dunn
"It's a terrible day, thanks be to God!"

This book is dedicated

to

Pat Doyle   (1874 – 1959)

and

To anyone anywhere who is having "a terrible day."

iii

It's a Terrible Day, Thanks be to God!

Michael Doyle

Foreword by
Daniel Berrigan, S. J.

The Heart of Camden Housing
Camden, NJ 08104

COPYRIGHT © Copyright 2003 Michael Doyle

Published by The Heart Of Camden Inc.
1742 Ferry Avenue
Camden, NJ 08108

ISBN 0-9717662-0-7

Printed in United States of America
1   2   3   4   5   03   04   05   06   07

Acknowledgements

I would like to thank the many people who helped bring this book to fruition, especially Daniel Berrigan, S.J., Edward Burt, Susan Cedrone, Michael Cook, Don Harle, Fr. Frank McDermott, Rosemarie McBride, Leonard Metz, Dale Mezzacappa, Emma Neal, Carolyn Nicosia, and Francis Taylor.

And Rosetta Creegan Doyle, my mother, who for almost thirty years faithfully wrote letters of life to me that flowed like a stream. Each one, without fail, bearing these four words: *"Thanks be to God!"*

Thanks

Tom Dunn of Belford, NJ for the portrait of Pat Doyle; Johnny O'Reilly of Cavan, Ireland, for the photograph of the plough; Zhongjie Shing of Cherry Hill, NJ for the drawing of Michael Doyle; Pauline O'Reilly of Dublin, Ireland, for the drawing of the plough in the rain.

Special Appreciation

Dear Daniel,

Thank you for consenting to write a Foreword for this book. To me, it is a great honor. You have been my hero since 1965 and the light gets brighter with the years.

The only problem about putting a Daniel Berrigan Foreword on my book is this: it's like putting a golden knob on the makeshift door I made for the barn. "So what!" I say. It will gleam in the sun.

Thank you, Dan, for doing this.

Michael Doyle

Foreword

Dear Michael,

Your letters arrived here, if I count rightly all 145 of them, descending on this stricken city in a fell swoop. You can have no idea – no mercy, in fact!

To what compare the gift? It was like a surfeit of manna falling in the wilderness of '02.

It was like receiving 145 love letters in a single batch.

It was too much, just like God.

How many times, I thought marveling, does Michael have to repeat – across the miles and years, to the peregrines and stay-puts of Sacred Heart family, and to our benighted world as well – 'I love you'?

Will 145 times do?

The letters offer the hint of a better answer, very subtle, subverting, Irish.

Why, it's not matter of numbers at all. It's a matter of the seasons that turn and turn with the whirling globe, the moods that try our human fiber to the utmost – and enable us beyond the utmost. Of the anniversary of events awful or ecstatic, of the newborn children to be lifted up, of deaths and near deaths, of close shaves, of going under, of lives cheated and admirable, broken and mended.

So. 'I love you', that litany and mantra. We learn it by heart in these letters. Learn that we've got to say it, repeat it, write it down plain, mean it. We've got to invoke poems, summon ghosts and ancestors, outrageous metaphors and contrasts, dress the page up for Christmas and Easter, for baptisms and burials, tip the hat to the sweetest cheat of all – memories.

You've got to make of very little (not much more that the clay of the sixth day of the famous First Week), a transfiguration.

Much of little.

Many years have gone down river since you Michael, priest, were sent to a sad city, Camden.

To do what? The letters groan and smile, weep and rejoice, telling of the task. To do whatever is sought, wept for, pled for by those who cross your life. To play Reverend Jack-of-All-Trades, to comfort the sorrowful and shore up the distressed, to set the drug-ridden and discouraged on a better path, to shelter the bare survivors of a wicked system, to bend an ear as the sorely-tried raise their outcry.

As time passed and you stayed on in Camden, it became evident that putting pen to paper, composing and sending off those letters, offered something crucial; what Peter Maurin used to call 'clarification of thought'. Not only your thought, the thinking of those who gathered the manna.

Clarify then! Who is my neighbor? Who is God, what is godly behavior? How are we to live humanly in a viciously inhuman time?

Of course, Michael, such a book as you envision - letters by turn nimble, bracing, audacious, elegant, witty – 'won't sell'.

As you need no reminding, Christianity wasn't meant to.

And the manna in the wilderness, as the Good Book insists, fell for free.

With Sabbath, we're told, came rest. And a !THANK YOU! that shook Mount Sinai.

Michael, thank you.

Daniel

Preface

Camden, New Jersey is the poorest city in the United States, if the children are counted. On a recent visit here, U.S. Senator Jon S. Corzine of New Jersey had this to say: "I have been everywhere in the world and except for Kabul, I have seen nothing like Camden."

Over the past 34 years, I have grown to love this city that was, before I came, strong and greatly admired. The city that supported life with churches and synagogues, restaurants and theatres, the building of ships and the manufacture of everything.

> *Where Campbell stirred his steaming soups*
> *And a million wheels went round and round*
> *Here Whitman sang the whirr in words*
> *And Victor snared the golden sounds.*

Today, it is poor as a plucked chicken. As the organization Camden Churches Organized for People proclaims: this city is on life supports. The purpose of this book is to call Camden to life. It is a cry to the heart of this generous nation, to people of good will everywhere, to do what needs to be done and what surely can be done, to make this city worthy of the thousands of children trying to grow up in it. It can become a beautiful city on the mile-wide Delaware River flowing between it and Philadelphia.

I have worked here for almost thirty-four years and failed…. I like to think, nicely. But my trust in God has not failed, so I often quote my grandfather, Pat Doyle, who proclaimed many a time when things didn't work out well: "It's a terrible day, thanks be to God." I was born in Ireland on his sixtieth birthday, November 3, 1934, and the present I was to him that day can never match the gift he was to me for the next 24 years. The memory of him still strengthens me on any day that's "terrible."

I wrote these monthly letters over the past seventeen years, beginning in 1984, not as the makings of a book, but as lifelines to many people, without whom, Sacred Heart Church's many ministries in Camden would not survive. It was Fr. Frank McDermott (1912-2000), beloved teacher at St. Thomas More High School in Philadelphia, PA and pastor of Assumption Church at 11ᵗʰ and Spring Garden Streets, who, in his eighty-fourth year, made me promise that these letters would be made into a book. "They are a ministry," he said.

I had never thought of them in that way. To me they are the music, sad and glad, of some of the things that happen and have happened around Sacred Heart in Camden and also around the green fields of my childhood. The first one dated November 1984 deals with the murder of Edith Rose Orsini of Emerald Street and the last one, December 2001, presents the young widow, Lynne Beckman Pescherine and the child within her. She came to Sacred Heart to be blessed on the First Sunday of Advent. Her husband, Michael, was on the 89th floor of the South Tower when Flight 175 shattered it. She bravely bore life out of that mangled mountain in Manhattan that had flattened our hope.

Over the intervening years, my stories of death and life, my memories and reflections on this and that, have been going out to people across the United States and a few to Canada, England, Germany, France, Australia and Ireland. They still go out every month.

So, here is a collection of them in prose and poetry! Great literary names are acknowledged like Yeats, Tennyson, Shelley, Wordsworth, Whitman, Goldsmith, Heaney, Colum, Joyce, Angelou, Chesterton, Pasternak, Virgilio, Berrigan, Merton and Kazantzakis, but the unacknowledged poems are my own. I write, I think, with a fairly consistent note of hope in spite of what might be called the melancholy musings of an aging Irishman.

Beyond the musings or maybe in them is the practical plea for the abandoned homes of Camden. Three thousand of them. "Each row house," said Daniel Berrigan in his reflection on Camden," staring blindly out of its sockets." They must be rebuilt for the sake of the children. The Heart of Camden Housing is hope with a hammer in its hand for the recovery of the city. Every penny from the sale of this book will go to help our housing effort. To help people of modest means to own their homes. Hopefully one day, it will be read with happy eyes in beautiful houses that are now ugly eyesores.

Beauty in Camden is not found in the scenes that I see but in the human faces that I observe. In this book, the letter of May 1986, entitled *Do Not Crush* makes the point: "I wish you could see Camden and then see the lovely little children who are trying to grow up here in ugly situations – like so many flowers in fields of old tires and broken bottles. Oh, if I had a wish, it would be that the world of little children would be soft and beautiful as our tender God first intended – before we tore His dreams with our greed and neglect."

There were no books in the home I was raised in, because there was no money to buy them. But there was great conversation around the hearth and something that was said well would be remembered. So, here are one hundred and forty-five letters, each one a chat when you have a moment. They go to you with blessing and gratitude and a hope that you will have the faith my grandfather had to always trust what happens. No matter what happens, may you be able to say as he did, "It's a terrible day, thanks be to God."

Michael Doyle

Camden, New Jersey   May 20, 2002

Contents

1984
Edith's Wings 3

1985
A Little Flutter in the Heart..5
The Time Is Ripe 6
White Heather for the Heart 8

1986
Straight from the Heart..11
Some Thoughts.... 12
Do Not Crush..14
"What Are Those Lumps on the Water?" 16
It's a Long, Long Way to Camden! 16
If Clay Can Smile the Dead Will Rise 19
Your Name in Our Stone Is a Wish in the Heart! 21
Christmas in Camden..23

1987
"In Every Person There is a Story" 23
Clay and Incense...25
New Fire in the Heart 27
The Long Lens of the Years 28
The Graves That Grief Dug in Our Hearts 30

1988
A Glow on the Faces of Those I Love 31
"The House That I Shaped in My Heart" 32
Golden Wonders..34
Our Little Bit of Green 36
We Don't All Fit in a Volkswagen Anymore...37
Hands for Sacred Heart...38
Broken Bits of Hope 39

1989
It's Heart Breaking Sometimes 40
Catherine Mannion Root...42
The Plumber of the Horn Pipes 44
May Is A Good Month 46
Solstice in Lockerbie 47
Goat's Milk in a Jam Jar 49
May the Angels of Thy Light Dwell Within These Walls...51
"Ye'll Have More Tea!" 53

1990

A Candle Burning in a Bitter Wind 54
Hope from the Ashes 56
Keep the Fire on the Hearth 58
Putting Wings on Eager Minds 60
"I Want to Grow Up and Do Good" 61
The Girl on Gelsha Hill 62
Blessed Baskets 63

1991

A Fallen World 64
Others Will be Towed 66
Celebrating the Rebirth of Ourselves 67
The Loss of Moss 69
The Greatness of God in the Weakness We Are 71
Charming Portraits of God 72
Love Makes the Heart Sacred 73

1992

Thanks for a Thousand Baskets! 74
The Irish and Whitman 75
Burning Issues – Burning Bushes 77
"A Big Green Tree of Peace in Our Hearts" 79
Moss on the Shoe 81
"I Hold My Crucifix Against My Heart" 83

1993

Thanks for the Tea 85
Truth On Track 87
Fires, Tempests and Loose Nuts on the Way 89
The Long View 91
A Fire on the Wet Hearth 93
In The Softness of the Thistle Seed 95
Keep the Lamp Alive ! 97
"He Cried All The Way Home" 99
A   Thousand Strangers 101

1994

Your Face in the "Pongers" of the Poor 103
The Valentine of a Lifetime 105
A Kiss of Light Upon the Tears 107
O Mia Bambino Caro 109
Mary Mc Kenna Was Never "Bet" 111
We're All in the Same Boat 113
I   Hear You Calling Me 115
We Remember in November 117
"I Love You" 119

1995

A Window in My World...121

Torn Sails Upon the Sea 123

Roses in the Rain..125

Life in a Chestnut Tree 127

No "Gubban" on the Wind 129

My Eyes Have Seen Salvation..131

The Point...133

Save the Deep Smiles of Their Souls 135

Generosity, of Course, Is the Key 137

Blood and Poinsettias..139

1996

Niederhauser There!..141

I Just Wanted to Make It Fun...143

Dipping into the Tidal Sorrow 145

The Lovely Mine Birds Sing 147

Hooker on the Horse Trough 151

"Keep Love Alive"!...153

Building Houses and Paring Horns 155

What About Ye, Fr. Jimmy!...157

An Angel for Anita Rose 159

1997

"O Lord, Hear My Voice!"...161

"God, We Know You Can Do It!"..163

The Sorrow of the Rain. The Joy of the Sun. 165

A Timepiece for Peacetime..167

"You Have to Have Faith"...169

Milking Her Cows in the Morning 171

Still Coming Up Roses 173

In the Light of Day 175

A Hidden Hope Named Nicholas 177

1998

A Toast to a Tree..179

If Pews Could Talk..181

The Plough and the Stars...183

Easter Findings...185

The Last Two Words 187

Camden's Gift to Me...189

A Message into the Middle Passage of Our Hearts......................191

Singing Her Song after Milking Time 193

"I Still Light the Little Candle for You" 195

A Tom Gaudette Doesn't Die..197

"A Warm Man Full of Fire"...199

A Toast to Thomas Merton 201

1999

Angels from the Ashes 203
Will It Ever Be "Wonderful Here?" 205
It's a Heifer 207
Pugin's Rose 211
The Lord God Planted a Garden in Eden . . . (Gen. 2,8) 213
Fire in Seventeen Syllables 215
"A Little Heart Pumping Away" 217
Life Begins After Forty 218
Life Begins After Forty 219
The Gentle Annies 221
"Feed My Lambs" 223

2000

Camden, 2000 – A New Symphony of Hope 226
A Center of Order in Our Hearts 227
Touched by an Angel 229
The Sound of Music 231
"Welcome, O Life!" 233
"In dreams I was a ship, and sail'd the boundless seas" 235
Our Smiling Treasures 237
Light in the Darkness 239
We Fall to Fly 241
Falling Leaves 243
Ploughing with the Stars 245

2001

God Be with You in 2001 247
No Bridge Over Troubled Waters – Yet 248
Sister Peg Hynes of The Heart of Camden Housing 250
Kevin O'Donnell 252
Tonya's Dream 254
"That They May Be One" 256
I Could Write a Book 258
Are You Going Away With No Word of Farewell 260
Saint Ciaran Has Landed 262
"Tread Softly…" 264
Breaking Water for the Birth of Hope 266
Come, O Come, Emmanuel 268

Edith's Wings

November 1984

Hi:

We have been hurt here in the Heart. The geese are gone and they bore away some of our sunshine. A sad wet wind grieves in the last leaves of Camden.

On October 13, Edith Rose Orsini, 45, faithful member of Sacred Heart Church, was struck on the head as she sat on the steps of her home on Emerald Street, by a man crazed by something ugly and evil and certainly not understandable. She was eating a bowl of soup when he smashed her skull with the metal leg of a kitchen table. She collapsed—the afternoon sun was warm in the red golden leaves of fall and the air was full of the Saturday sounds of children—and she sank like a rose bashed on a stone.

The soup bowl, empty now, was there on the step...where she lay.

Minutes dragged their numb feet until police and ambulance reached the spot. Then sirens swiftly tore the air to Cooper Hospital. There, Edith lingered for seven days in a sort of space capsule of bleak medical entanglement, and then she died.

But during these seven days, her husband Andy waded through all this medical clutter and ministered to his unconscious wife with faith and affection that would stir spring water in a stone. With tender hands, he made countless crosses on her body and never ceased to speak to her and assure her that heaven awaited her, that it was all right to go, murmuring Happy Birthday, Happy Christmas, Happy Anniversary forever.

You'd have to know Andy. He's a trip. Comical, unusual, opinionated and delightful. But when it came to what mattered, he was a star. Unmatchable.

Three days after she died, the neighborhood people gathered on Edith's door step with a large cross and small candles and listened to the words of Lamentations: "The favors of the Lord are not exhausted." They sang strong hymns and saw hope again in an ancient truth that the cross—the deadly weapon that killed Jesus as viciously as the lethal metal that killed Edith—is now the sign of our salvation. It stands tall on the top of our churches and hangs hopefully around our necks.

On the following evening we gathered in the church for the viewing and funeral Mass. The children came first. She loved them. Unskilled in many ways she always tried to care for the children. (She had none of her own.) Every morning she came to our schoolyard to help "the babies" (kindergartners) into their classroom. On the day before she was attacked, she made three attempts to bake a birthday cake for little Darlene Venell of Jasper Street and it flopped three times, but her love did not. A little boy came to Andy at the viewing and handed him a four-inch feather, "It fell on my head," he said, "when I was standing outside the church." And then solemnly, "It must be from Miss Edith's wings."

The Church was full. The night gathered us in with soft light of candles and warm colors of harvest – leaves and pumpkins and the goodness of God. With utmost grace Don and Rosemarie Harle, godparents at her baptism on Easter Sunday four years ago, covered her casket with the white garment of glory. "Blessed are the poor in spirit," the gospel declared, "the reign of God is theirs. Blessed are the lowly, they shall inherit the earth…the single-hearted, they shall see God." O Edith, always there, shyly on the edge of the group, central only at the coffeepot to pour, or suggest another cup, or cleaning up when we were gone. "Your life was hidden with Christ in God." (Col.3, 3)

Of all the adults in our church, Edith Rose was above all the most innocent. When we gathered for her funeral we knew we were tied to ancient times when Christians assembled in catacombs or underground or background and celebrated life, celebrated that Christ is risen, because one, an innocent one, was slain and lifted up. Now we await the blessings of the Spirit. Lambs are slain to save the world. We know that the lamb's blood on our doorstep, on the doorpost of Sacred Heart, will avert evil and ultimately bring life, not death, to Camden. Thank you for sharing the ache of the Heart.

Michael Doyle

The Holy Innocents

I saw the little lambs of April on the hill
Shelter from the final fling of winter wind
Then stretch like bedside mats up on the green
When the sun got through the clouds
That crowd like cold sheep around his face
Black and white above the rain drenched land.
Suddenly a stir of bird or breeze
Or the prick of wakening appetite
And the lambs leap and stoop and seek
Those sure soft spots beneath the woolly bunk
And grab the little lactic nozzles of delight.
Then tails begin to wriggle in a cosmic dance
of life
And tides to tumble on the shore and bees
To fondle petals in the first sweet flowers of
the year
And Eden's early innocence comes back to
mind

Too delicate and fine, like daffodils as yet
Untouched by any icy whip of wind.
But, when the heavy darkness came…a
dream!
I saw the rounded bosom of the hill
Square-sided like a butcher's block
And I heard a baby scream
Red-splattered on the dew-wet green.
But a table linen quickly covered up the
scene
As humans warm in their woolen
sweaters sat
With silver knives and manners curtly
civilized
Then one by one they chewed the tender
chops
And talked of peace and freedom in the
world.

A Little Flutter in the Heart

Valentine's Day, 1985

Hi!

A good HEART this church is, holding all, holding on, for a hundred years. It began October 13, 1885. So, this year, we must eat, drink, dance, and tell stories. Simply, celebrate with our whole HEART. Now let me tell you a February story, a heartbreaking one.

KATIE COFSKY

I met her in the autumn fullness of her mother who came to Mass at the edge of Advent 1981 and asked to be blessed in her holy expectation. Hope was high then but somehow hope never knows what may happen along the way when the path bends in the shadowed woods.

Katie came on December 21, 1981, a crucial time when the long night seems to win against tired winter light. A fragile child, whom mother's milk and tears or prayers couldn't sustain for long. She clung to life like the numbered days of snow in Spring.

On Thursday, February 10th, on the 51st day of her life, Katie was baptized at home in the pure snow that Sister Rosemarie Kolmer gathered from evergreens by the door. It melted in maternal warmth and Katie went under it, down with Christ into a grave of a hundred thousand tears, but then, up on eagle's wings and on to God. She died that afternoon.

On February 13th she was brought to Sacred Heart rectory – a tiny body in a tiny box. Pale, frail, still...a snowflake wake in a warm room. Standing sadly there, were her parents Donald and Marge Cofsky and her small brother Jonathan. We carried her to the Church for the Mass of the Angels and placed her before the altar in the light of the great menorah because her father, who is Jewish, needed to know, as we all did, the comfort of the God of Abraham, and little Katie Cofsky. We read from Genesis, about Noah looking at a sad flooded world without flowers or sunshine and somehow hoping that things would get better. He sent out a dove but it returned and stayed. We thought of little Jonathan. Noah sent out another dove and it came back with a bit of hope in its beak, an olive branch which said that things were looking up, the flood was going down, the tops of trees were showing. Maybe Donald and Marge could hope that one day a child would come to them and soothe away some of their sorrow. Finally Noah sent out the third dove and it never came back. The flood was gone. That dove, the dove that never returned, brought hope to the world. Fly high, dear Katie, up into the bright blue heavens. Fly high above all the troubled waters of the world.

In time, on September 11, 1983, Michael was born to Donald and Marge and to those who could see, there was an olive branch in his tiny hand. I think of little Katie now when winter is losing ground and Spring is coming on, and her dogwood by the church is stirring to life. But it is always the dove I see, going away to bring hope to the world and leaving behind an anxious flutter in the HEART.

Michael Doyle

The Time Is Ripe

August 6, 1985

Hi:

Gradually, almost imperceptibly, the quieting of the passion and pace of the summer begins to take place. The earth slows down in August, like a pregnant woman beginning to feel the weight in her womb. The winds playfully whisper and rustle in the wheat fields of the world.

So I invite you to come to the church of my childhood (not St. Colmcille's where I was baptized and where my parents are buried) but to an oatsfield—an oatsfield in August in Ireland. There in my "church" I often sat alone and listened to the whisper of the wind in the golden ears and I heard the voice of God. There I invite you, where the sound is better than the oratory of the pulpits or the Vatican balconies. It is the temple of the tender touch of God where you feel protected by a playful and good-natured God who will, if we trust, feed the needs of the world, and our own as well.

Maybe later we will go up to Antrim and go to Ballycastle to "the old Lammas fair in Ballycastle" and ask an old woman there, hanging clothes on a line on a windy day: "What does Lammas mean?" And she will stop and tell us, that years ago in the beginning of August, people took the flour from the first wheat and made a loaf for Mass. So loaf-mass became Lammas. I will tell her that we celebrated Lammas at Sacred Heart on the first Sunday of August with a great new loaf, rich and fresh and round and delicious. We broke it and ate it and we felt we were taking the whole cosmos into ourselves. The cosmos at it's best. The Christ. We became what we ate. 'Twas great!

And then we will go back to the oatsfield to look and listen. We will see that all the green has turned to gold in a wonderful transformation. It's August 6th, the Transfiguration, the day when Jesus went up to the top of the holy mountain, and his face shone like the sun, like the oats shining now. The sun! O it's a wonderful thing. It brings out the gold that is always in the green and now it's dazzling. Like Jesus. Like you and me when we get to the top of the mountain, when we ripen, when the cosmos comes into its own, when the sun comes out...on the dark side of you and me.

We must not forget the dark side of the blinding flash of evil that hit the world on August 6th forty years ago. Men rained death on the children. Hiroshima and Nagasaki were evaporated like street maps in a furnace. Those who did such deeds may have switched on mills or turned on threshers but they never listened to God's whisper in an oatsfield.

Our Church in Camden has stalks of rye and oats in the windows on these days of August. Stalks of rye and oats on podium and pulpit and processional cross. Myrlie Misskelly, Eleanor Vine and her children went to a rye field near Batsto and Pleasant Mills, NJ. There they listened, gathered rye, and tried to bring its fullness to our church. Because, says Eleanor "we need an absolute link with what's happening in the earth in each of her seasons." Absolutely, because we are the earth, conscious of herself but not nearly conscious enough!

It was indeed appropriate in this centennial year of our parish that the women and the children went to a field near Pleasant Mills where the first Catholic Church in South Jersey was erected in 1826. Dedicated on August 15th, 1830, it was named St. Mary's of the Assumption. For a while it was a mission of the Immaculate Conception Church in Camden and attended by Father Patrick Byrne who founded our original Sacred Heart. Unfortunately it was destroyed by fire in 1899 but the spot is still holy with the graves of its early parishioners.

We remembered them in the great August feast of the Assumption with prayers and stalks of rye from Pleasant Mills. The women and men wore marigolds (Mary-gold) and we celebrated Mary's Assumption as the lifting of the first precious fruit of a Cosmic Harvest.

August is the month of the feast of ultimate transformation. We become more conscious that the sweet ripening that is happening in the earth is happening in us. Its August, dear friend, and the time is ripe.

Michael Doyle

Ripe

Ripe. The grain droops.
Too tired to hold up its head
My mother in her chair
There, softly drifting, dreaming
Sleepy as oats in August
Puffed and woolly as ears untouched
When the scythe went by
Leaning on flowers, briars
Bent by storms, clinging to a season
That is passing away.
So I plead with the Autumn
In the evening and ask her to linger,
Listen, "the oats is golden in the sun"
And one more song should be sung
One more bell should be rung
Then the weather will be fine
It will be holy gathering time.

September, 1983

White Heather for the Heart

November 12, 1985

Hi!

    This is the first full day of my 12th year in Sacred Heart in Camden and I hope it will be easier than my 11th, which was demanding and difficult and painfully good. There was no time in it for vacation and the healing of my being that I always find in Ireland.

    Today Rose Knebles came here, with a pot of black bog earth from Donegal and a sprig of heather growing in it. Special heather...not just the purple mantle that grows on moor and mountain but white heather from Kindrum Hill. She and Jane McGeever struggled up the steep slope, which was too difficult for them. But not for young Martin McGroarty. Limber as a March hare, he went up over the steep side. "You have to have a head for heights," he said, "to get white heather from the top of Kindrum Hill." It's near Kerrykeel, which every mapmaker knows, is near Letterkenny, County Donegal.

    Anyway the heather came to Camden today on a misty melancholy morning in November when the dead seem near to us and the living near to tears. Cool and damp as Donegal in June.

    Rose and Jane, like several other Sacred Heart people, have gone, in this Centennial year of our parish, to graves and groves and other holy places to bring blessings back for all of us. To Merton in Kentucky and Teilhard de Chardin in Poughkeepsie and St. Patrick up in Down. To Francis in Assisi and others in Italy and France and even my own Mother's grave in Ireland.

    This year will be remembered as a year of celebration and calamity. We have attempted to gather some stories of our own parish people and write a book, which is now in painful labor towards completion. We planned a Centennial Dinner Dance in the Halloran Plaza of Pennsauken, NJ on October 4th, which had to be relocated to the Woodbine Inn at the last moment because the hotel broke its contract. We had a great time at the Woodbine. Six hundred people with good food and drink, music and memories. Plaques were presented to three parishioners honoring them as citizens of our century. They combined, between them, 266 years of faithful life. On Sunday, October the 13th, exactly 100 years since the parish was incorporated, 500 people gathered for a Centennial Mass in our Church. Afterwards the congregation walked to the old Star Theater, now a community hall, led by the cross of Christ and the Camden Catholic School Band. Bringing up the rear was an old white man and a young black woman—John McGuire and Christine DeLarge - trustees of our parish, riding on a horse and wagon - a surrey with a fringe on top. We all ate and drank and shared a festive day.

    On Monday, October 14th, we began the first full day of our second century at Sacred Heart. At 2:05 PM, five minutes after the Third Grade children had left their classroom for a short recess, a whole section of ceiling crashed down on their empty desks. No photo, colored or otherwise, could adequately portray what happened or could have happened. It was the crushing weight of the fallen slabs strewn across the mangled classroom that caused tears and terror in staff and children alike. All could imagine the dead and the dying, a school that would be an unbearable memory, and the flattened spirit of Sacred Heart. Miraculously no one was hurt. Our school was first blessed on December 28th, 1919, on the Feast of the Holy Innocents, the Martyred Babies of long ago. It still survives in their holy protection.

Our school building is closed temporarily and our 221 children have been moved to another parish school that closed some years ago. We will reopen on the eve of Thanksgiving Day to give thanks to God for the lives that were saved and our school that will be greatly renovated. The cause of the accident has not been legally determined but our school and this South Camden neighborhood have been undergoing an enormous assault from heavy equipment digging huge trenches for a sewer pipe eight feet in diameter. Sixty million gallons of raw sewage from Camden County will flow daily into this poor neighborhood to be treated in a facility now under construction. Anyway, the Camden County Sewage Authority has put up a fund to remove and replace all ceilings in Sacred Heart School, install electrical fixtures, repair and paint damaged walls. As in all renovation, one thing leads to another, and now many things need to be done that are not related to the accident. So the effort goes on.

Just like Rose and Jane. They struggled up the mountain for the white heather. When they could go no further, someone helped. Someone went to the top and brought down a special sprig. In the old Irish story of the White Heather, Oscar, dying on the mountain side, sent purple heather to his beloved Malvina. She wept unceasingly and whenever her tears fell on heather, it turned white. But whoever finds it today, finds joy.

May we all be helped by one another and go on with tears and struggle to the top of the mountain. There the light is bright and the heather is white because sorrow turns into joy.

Michael Doyle

Excerpt of Michael Doyle's Closing Statement

The best book you will ever read is the life you have lived. It has stories of death and birth and sickness and pain and striving and worrying and not being sure and anxiety. It has all those things in it. It's full of memories poured in by generations that came before you and things that happened to them and to you. It is a storehouse of good things and you have an imagination. George Bernard Shaw said that "Christ is killed in every generation by those who have no imagination." You have to have imagination to sense the value of life. You have to dream. You have to see things in the mind, not in pure raw logic, but in the imagination, in the difference of you. You will see something of the value of life. Law is so very useful and so very good in helping us to protect life, but it is not life and it is not as good as life. Law is the banks of the river and the water is the life. The stream flows and the banks must widen if the stream gets fuller. The law must make room for life, and not the other way around, ever.

Camden 28 Trial 1973

The New Year

January, 1986

Hi:

Happy New Year! May we all be alive at this time next year. "Mad alive" as the Irish say. Mad enough to begin again where we failed before. Trusting doggedly in that great redemptive paradox—the success of failure.

The New Year began here beautifully during the celebration of Mass, which started at 11 p.m. approximately. The old bronze bell in the tower rang out the midnight hour as the priest (by some divine accident) proclaimed that most generous and good-natured act of God; "This is My Body which is given up for you," in painful and indeed ultimate responsibility. Christ's great effective words they are, lifting, elevating, and consecrating the world—the bits and pieces of our daily grind and the high expansive urge of a new year's point in time.

Such a time calls forth the collective consciousness of millions and fuses their wishes into thrusts of hope. The old day dies and the new morning breaks inexorably into being.

One precious wish, in this cosmic bundle of blessings, was that of my friend Eugenie Kelly. Sitting with a couple of friends in Haddonfield, New Jersey, she lifted a glass in a toast to the best that's yet to be. It was a parting glass. Moments later she stood up partially, said "I have to…" and died. The first phone call of 1986 was the sad news of her death.

Only 45, she hadn't the heart to go on. Now, a beat forever in the holy heart of God.

Not for her, to die in the tired worn moments of an old year but in the first fresh breath of a new day. Happy New Year, dear Eugenie! You step-danced out of old time and into new and took your place with the stars. Your passing went sharply to the very marrow of deep meaning in this New Year's celebration. "This is My Body which is given up for you."

Now the wind is weak in her chestnut hair
Where vigor once was wild as spring
Pain, in time, has carved its truth
Like the yew-tree hearts upon her youth.
But her Celtic grace is always there
When the trees are green or winter bare.
And just as Time was in travail
To press New Year's Day across the line
Her toast was water weak and pale
As others drank their lively wine.
Then, amidst good wishes of eager breath,
Death slipped in and choked our cheer,
For while we stood with empty hearts
Beside our freshly welcomed year.
Her water…. changed to summer wine
Our wine to winter tears.

Michael Doyle

Straight from the Heart

February, 1986

Hi:

Italians and all warm-hearted people may know about the old Roman feast of Lupercalia, which is a festival of the god of fertility and pastoral care in its most earthy and primitive sense. It was held on February 15th when the "Februa," or purification rites took place and a few other things as well. Our February still bears the name of those ancient rites and at its midriff point also retains a flutter of excitement for the heart and all its romantic vagaries. Valentines Day! It bears the name of a third-century bishop who was martyred on February 14th, 270 AD, under the persecution of Claudius II. The good bishop died on the eve of Lupercalia, but his supreme sacrifice of heroic generosity got connected and badly smothered under the stirrings of an easier and more romantic form of love.

If there are any bishops' conferences in heaven, St. Valentine must take a ribbing because he has become more popular on earth than the "big leaguers" like Peter and Paul. Not even Saint Patrick does better, even though he gets longer parades in New York and Savannah and bigger toasts than the blushing bishop of love. There are those who say that the birds begin to mate on Valentine's Day. Cardinals...l shouldn't say it!

Anyway, it doesn't really matter that Valentine may never have mounted a red heart on his mitre. His feast of love that puts red hearts on candy, cards and bumper stickers is as welcome as warm weather in the winter. The time is right. It wouldn't work in November or September or the Fourth of July. However, it is most welcome here in the middle of February when we are all weary of the winter, and hoping that it might be wearing out.

It is time for the sun to get up earlier and nudge the sleeping earth and wake her up. It is time the primal mating call be heard in the silence of the world. It is time to think of the giant glaciers melting and flowing in menstrual streams upon the earth.

So here's to love! To every touch and bond and gesture that ever nourished life from the savage urge of instinct to save the species to the awesome act of martyrs laying down their lives to save the world. Here's to every means of transportation and communication that tries to make this far-flung world into a friendly village meeting!

Happy Valentine to birds and bees and bare winter trees as the lively sap starts to stir inside their limbs. Thanks, old Valentine, Your Excellency, for giving us a name to carry all this "carry on." It is a great name, melodic and romantic as a waltz at a wedding. It is much better than Wolfgang, Casimir, Cupid, or even Fred!

Happy Valentine to you and all the world!

Michael Doyle

Some Thoughts....

Hi!

No amount of religion or philosophy, maturity of age or experience, will ever remove my deep resentment when I drive along the country roads of Ireland where hedges follow hedges with the same mix of briar and bush, the same tone and hue of berry and blossom, and suddenly the green national colors of Ireland change into the harsh red intrusion of England. Suddenly, every mailbox and flag, every telephone kiosk and schoolhouse, glares at me in a rage of red. It cuts into the heart of Irish hospitality and insults the land of the open door.

Seizing part of Ireland as the British did and changing its identity is like kidnapping a child from a family and changing its name. The mother's cry will die only when her child comes home. That cry for unity is the true voice of Ireland – perennial, enduring, unrelenting. Ireland is humble and strong like the grass in the field. She will be there when the feet that walk on her face are buried beneath her. She will be there, whole as she was when her hills were young.

Whole as she was when the high kings reigned in Tara and Patrick was a shepherd boy on the hill of Slane. Or later when he came back with good news for the Gael that humanity was raised up to unthinkable heights of dignity. When death was brought down forever. And then, when Spring was in the air, he lit the Easter fire, which infuriated the king who always lit his pagan fire first, and was told by his druid seers that if he did not put out this intruding fire, it would never be extinguished. It still burns bravely. It might have died under the ashes of the ages in the long nights of national suffering but this blessed spark breaks out undaunted when morning comes.

Five years ago, on the eve of St. Patrick's Day, my friend John McNamee and I went up the hill in Armagh to visit the 112th successor of St. Patrick, Cardinal Tomas O'Fiaich, the primate of all Ireland. His jurisdiction does not acknowledge the division of Ireland but looks at her whole face the way the sun does on a bright and happy morning. But one cannot ignore what that jigsaw cut has done to her. It has scarred her face and ruined her smile for sixty years and more. "The English must get out of Ireland," said the cardinal. Then he poured three shots of whiskey in sparkling Waterford glasses and we drank a silent toast to the best hopes of that blessed shepherd of Slane and this pleasant priest of Armagh who is trying his best to stand in those old shepherd shoes and carry on his dream.

The challenge of that dream still goes out from the hills of Armagh to the shores of South Africa, to the streets of Manila, to the bloody back roads of Central America, to the broken-down houses of Camden and the built-up cells of Long Kesh.

Patrick's sons and daughters in every generation, with great courage, have crossed rivers and mountains and deserts to plant crosses in soil of every sort, rocks and bogs, sand and swamps and snow.

But the Irish have failed too, sometimes, when it comes to crossing the street and reaching across lines of political diversity, religion, difference, or racial variety. They have embraced the blacks in Africa and rejected them in Boston, Massachusetts, or Gloucester City, New Jersey. A man with a name like Ronald Reagan, whose ancestors hail from Ballyporeen (the town of the small potatoes), County Tipperary, is pushing questionable policies in Central America. The people of Ireland know that and consequently their welcome was less than expected when he came to visit them. Great numbers of Irish missionaries in Central America are close to the poor and closer to the truth.

Patrick's dream is in fair shape and the great fire of Slane that he lit so long ago will be lit again this Easter Sunday on the hills and hollows of the world. Not only a flame in bits of sticks and stumps of candles but in the eyes of believing people. Because it is more than the fire from an Irish hill or the spark that was sheltered in an Irish hand. It is a blazing stick from the Burning Bush, the enduring light from a passage grave and the victory of light and life in the Easter Rising of Christ.

Michael Doyle

A Lamp in the Widow's Window
(Excerpt)

They are almost all gone now,
Those children carried to time with her
When this century broke water.
Teens when Pearse plastered proclamations
Of liberty across the granite eyes of England.
And young muscles flexed in rebellion
Until they fell for Ireland.
Their generation was strong as the clout of the wind
When command went out in whispered shouts,
That "the Blacksmith" was about to hurl fire
At some stone bridge or barrack wall.
Then these saw-soldiers cut tall trees and made them fall
Across narrow roads and blocked a British empire.
They saw the stranger's castle stripped and bare
And the Union Jack brought low at last,
As the green and gold went up the pole
On three fields of the four in Ireland.

Do Not Crush

May, 1986

Hi!

Thanks for starting to read this letter. It's not easy to be interested in what I have to say when so many say so much. Sometimes I'm not sure what to say to you but I must keep in touch. If I don't—a lifeline will be broken and a lot of good things at Sacred Heart will die.

I would be delighted to hear from you. Sometimes I wince a little when I think maybe you are bothered by my letters and you say to yourself, "I wish that priest in Camden would stop sending me those letters."

I wish you could see Camden and see the lovely little children who are trying to grow up here in ugly situations—like so many flowers in fields of old tires and broken bottles. Oh, if I had a wish it would be that the world of little children would be soft and beautiful as our tender God first intended—before we tore His dreams with our greed and neglect.

I always say it's not fair that Camden is Camden. It's not fair to the children. The children are innocent—they are the soft green sprouts of Spring that always renew the world.

Sometimes I see men and women hardened by time and all washed out like the hills of Appalachia and I wonder what were their first few years of life like and what happened in the little places where they played. Right here on Broadway, on the blocks above and below Sacred Heart, the prostitutes adorn every corner in all weather. They are like hardy fisherwomen casting their lines in the constant stream of traffic. The windowless walls of gutted houses gape down like skeletons with holes for eyes on a tragic human scene. At 3:15 PM, Anna May carefully guides little children with Sacred Heart uniforms across the street when the light changes. May God's holy angels always get them safely across the street and off it before they harden and crack like the pavements and the prostitutes and the failed plans for urban renewal.

Yesterday, I attended a meeting in the mayor's office as people painfully tried to grapple with the problem of providing shelters for the homeless. Poor Camden! Deliberately, the poorest towns of the state are set up like sitting ducks so that the homeless will descend on them—suburban towns do not have medical and other resources for the poor—so Camden, overburdened already with unbearable problems, will draw the homeless like moths to a light in a dark night...there to hang aimlessly and maybe burn out. Every town should take its fair share of the poor—as my mother used to say, "Many hands make light work." May God help all of us to help the poor and save ourselves. Mother Teresa often says: "Touch the poor and you touch Christ, touch Christ and you will be saved. Touch the poor."

A couple of weeks ago (April 24th) I attended a dinner in Philadelphia at which my friend Joe Balzano was honored as Man of the Year by the Maritime Society. It was in the Union League, heavy in trappings of wealth—big steaks and big chandeliers. Leaving the place, I walked towards my car and saw some trash on the sidewalk for the morning pick-up. What caught my eye was the wig on the pile. That's interesting, I thought. I never saw a wig in the trash before. When I got closer, oh my...there was a head in the matted hair. A man was sleeping on a vent and catching a wisp of steam from the Union League. Half of his body, hips to toes, was in a cardboard box. Long and narrow, for stacks of styrofoam cups, he had pulled it on for the night. Pondering his predicament and wondering about the ways things go wrong and how hard it is to rectify them, I walked on thoughtfully...stopped and looked back. The bottom of the box in large black letters said:

DO NOT CRUSH.

God help us all!

In that excellent little book entitled Selected Haiku by Nick Virgilio, the following poem is included:

On the cardboard box
Holding the frozen wino
Fragile: Do Not Crush

For Father Michael Doyle

When his book was published by Burn & Lake Press of Sherbrooke, Canada, Nick insisted that he wrote the poem for me because I told him the story.

I will end with an excerpt from my lament for Nick Virgilio entitled "On My Last Journey":

The old linden tree trembled in the root-cracked pavement
When his overcoat was carried in the door
That he bravely wore when he went forth...
The shoes too, limp now, in a friend's hand.
"The soles are soiled" someone said aloud...
Of course they are and worn too
With walking near the dismal creeks
Or waiting on the dirty city street
Bent with bags of all he carried.
Standing there, amused, intense, alone.
His wave forever framed in the rear view of our mind.

Michael Doyle

"What Are Those Lumps on the Water?"

August 7, 1986

Hi!

Ten years ago today, Mother Teresa of Calcutta came to Sacred Heart and prayed for Camden. In one sense it seems like yesterday and in another like a hundred years ago.

But a hundred years ago, this church was walls...gradually going up, stone by stone, at the hands of Philip McDonald and his mason-men. But the church they built had no better day in its century of service than that hot afternoon in August, when the Queen of the Poor in her sandals and sari came up our old aisle to the altar.

"We do not welcome you, Mother Teresa," I said that day, "because you are famous, but because God has done wonderful things to you and holy is His name." Then Dana Redd, a third-grade student at our School, gave her a lei of flowers gathered in nearby backyards of Camden. She put it on. But she immediately took it from her shoulders and laid it before the altar. I felt she was placing our broken city in the hands of God.

Then she prayed. The congregation prayed with her. For this "town I love so well," its old and lonely people, its homeless and jobless and hopeless. For its hurt people, zoned out, priced out of better places and concentrated here. Especially the young – God help them – trying to grow up. Frail flowers struggling to survive in heavy traffic.

Anyway, ten years have come and gone. We're here. Last Friday, forty-three Camden children (babies or unborn a decade ago) went to the ocean for a week's vacation in a program sponsored by Sacred Heart. At the sight of the sea, little Jessica Rivera, six years old, asked innocently, "what are those lumps on the water"? But in a short time she was riding those "lumps" and their cool softness was soothing her body and being that can so easily harden here on the bumps of hot tar and cracked concrete that make up the stern surface of Camden.

Over in the school today I put soft joint-compound on some cracks in the walls. This I want to harden so that the place will be ready for 225 children on September 3rd. Only ten of them are Catholics from Sacred Heart Parish. Our parish does not have many Catholic children, but a great care for all "the frail flowers"—Baptist and Methodist, Presbyterian and Pentecostal. "Suffer the little children to come...", not just the little Catholic ones.

So you can see there are a lot of "lumps" in our troubled waters. In our throats too, when we think of the children, the city, and the uncertainty of it all. But with a bit of courage, like little Jessica, we will face our "lumps" and ride them out. Or as Mother Teresa says, our difficulties are merely the "distressing disguise of Christ' walking in the world. Maybe walking on the water and putting all "the lumps" under His feet.

Nice going, Jessica!

Michael Doyle

It's a Long, Long Way to Camden!

September 8, 1986

Hi!

In one sense, today is the wrong day to write to you but in another it is the right one. Right, because it is the feast of the birth of God's mother – a day of great beginnings in this season of fresh September starts. Wrong, perhaps, because it is the day, 27 years ago, that I left Ireland to go to some "far away mission" called Camden on the east coast of North America. A sort of sad day for me where the leaves are wet in the backwoods of my memory. My green passport announced in my native language that my eyes were "gorm" (blue) and my hair was "ordhonn" (auburn). The eyes are blue still!

On that day 27 years ago, a few hours before I left on my long journey, I crashed my car into the back end of a trailer of milk cans. The driver, on his tractor, had decided to stop and chat with a woman in a cabbage plot plucking the green leaves into her flowered apron. She dropped her cabbage when a little green Austin came 'round the bend on a narrow road and crashed. It was the end of the old Austin but not of the young Michael Doyle. He had miles to go.

Later that same day he left home, his cousin Josie Rourke driving him to Cobh, County Cork, to catch the S.S. America to New York. On the way, by a lonely road In Tipperary, in the dark of night, the car stuttered to a stop. Out of gas. Should he have turned back there and then!!

He didn't. Six days later he arrived in New York. The fog was low on the scrapers of the sky. He blessed himself and walked onto a Continent. It was September 14th, the Feast of the Holy Cross. Over the years in one way or another, by design or accident, most of us get our share of its holy splinters.

So on these days each year I do reflect on my week in that great womb of water between the Cobh of Cork and the Pier of New York. A time of my life between two holy feasts of the church—the birth of the Mother of God and the glorious outcome of the Cross where her Son died in shame.

Twenty-seven years! Somewhere among my "vast holdings," there is a photo of myself as a small freckled faced fellow with "the blue eyes and auburn hair" and black suit standing on the deck of the S.S. America in the cool cloudy circle of the sea. Yesterday I saw a most recent print of the same fellow with white hair and black suit in a cemetery in Perth Amboy. Still on his feet, thanks be to God! Now, as pastor of Sacred Heart Church in Camden, he was standing in a white cloud of incense at the grave of William H. Lynch in St. Mary's cemetery in Perth Amboy, NJ.·

So on August 27th, ten people from Sacred Heart went on a Centennial pilgrimage to his grave. To the last resting place of this "heartbroken" man to let him know that the Heart is sacred

---

* Fr. Lynch, the first pastor of Sacred Heart in 1885, left in '88, broken by the enormity of the debt, $35,000 and a Sunday collection of $2.50. He died on Aug. 27, 1921.

still...beating bravely, sometimes fretfully, on a truck-torn corner in Camden. It's a long time and "a long, long way to Tipperary."

Well! Our school opened with 225 children. We are trying to fix five houses and change them from death traps of fire to places of warmth for children. People come to Sacred Heart for candles...not to light them in front of their statues but in front of their children because their electricity has been cut off. Three Camden children died recently in a fire in a house of no electricity.

Sr. Peg Hynes, SSJ, has joined our staff and our struggles to restore abandoned homes. We are on our way, renewed in strength to hold up the heavy cross against the oncoming darkness.

Twenty-seven years ago a man stopped on a very dark road in Tipperary and gave me two gallons of gasoline. I don't remember his name but he still goes on with me in the gratitude of my heart. You too, if you stop and help, when you see us stuck on the road. We will go on together.

It's a long, long way to the Camden we see in our Heart.

Michael Doyle

Along the Whitethorn Lane

Lifetime years away from all I really am,
My body staggers back to where my life began,
But is it me you see, along the whitethorn lane
When you hear my slower step and call my name?
You think you see the freckled film in the fog of long ago
When sticky shutters stuttered open to all they didn't know.
Bright-ready too I seemed as life's young dream unfurled,
But never for the bloody scenes of this unfolding world.
They marred the soft exposure of every eager frame
And yet...it's me, you see along the whitethorn lane
When the tattered picture passes and you call me by my name.

If Clay Can Smile the Dead Will Rise

October, 1986

Hi!

Any practical person would advise me to share my burdens as well as my hopes with you and tell you the needs that need your help. Like the awful burden of keeping a school open for poor children. Yes, I do ask you to sponsor children in our school and I do ask you to help us with housing...to put light and life in the blind sockets that were once the windows of Camden. I want you to share the joy of making Camden smile again in the awesome beauty of her children. In the "terrible beauty" of gaping holes "changed utterly" into wonderful windows of warmth and Christmas candlelight. As Tennyson says "Come my friends, 'tis not too late to seek a newer world."

Father Joe Messina, I am happy to tell you, has come to join me in the streets and the sanctuary and the hope-filled story of Sacred Heart.

So ... I want you to rejoice too in this lovely time of Autumn when the mist puts tears on the golden leaves, but at the same time adds fresh sparkle to their last smiles in the sun. All that is close to this heart of mine that tends, almost always, to be melancholy but not depressed. I am always ready for the bright breaks of fun that come like the light of my youth laughing on the fields when the rain has cleared.

I have to tell you then of "Stevie" (Eugene O'Reilly) who often bent me helplessly over my bicycle with laughter when I met him on my way from school. With dialogue fit for the Abbey Theatre, he recounted the sayings of several hardy characters that walked the wet fields of North Longford where we lived. On stage in parish plays that were produced each Lent when dances were not allowed, he performed with a natural skill and wit that was better than Barry Fitzgerald. Stevie was our mailman, and he rode his bicycle over the roads of Moyne and Colmcille carrying a few letters in his old bag and lots of laughter in his happy heart.

He was a noted player of Gaelic football for over 30 years with the grit and enduring determination of a Pete Rose except that his only pay was pride and joy in the game he played and the aches and pains he carried to his grave

Stevie died in 1972, and later his tombstone in Colmcille churchyard, near my parents' grave, fell and broke in several parts. It made me smile when I saw it.

Stevie! My poem is for you...just a few "bits of laughter" at the thought of you.

Stevie's Stone

Stevie's stone broke, and fell on his grave,
Not by a stroke or foul wind
Harsh as Maeve, but by the joke
That he, each day, from *his lively clay*
Decides to *tell his buried friends,*
So, his stone cracked and split its sides.
Then bones rattled in dry rot wood
And skulls laughed as best they could,
All underground there were minor quakes
With more *fun than their own wakes.*
They all laughed at the joke and a half
That Stevie made with words that strayed
From local clods of every grade.

I looked at the stone as soon as I came
And there was his name, intact on a piece,
Around it, the bits in laughter were laid,
Eugene O'Reilly, and the craic *that he made.*
Then I knew that humor was a name for God,
The only touch that gets *under the sod,*
Because the constant laughter in Stevie's eyes
Said "If clay can smile, the dead will rise."

Human clay surely needs humor around here. As Sr. Marge Sullivan used to say: "Nothing's easy at Sacred Heart." But the bouncing balls of energy that show up every morning at the school of Sacred Heart are sprightly clay indeed. Smiles they are on the face of the earth in spite of all that's trampled down and hardened in the ground.

Michael Doyle

PS "Craic" means "fun" in Irish.

Your Name in Our Stone Is a Wish in the Heart!

November 29, 1986

Hi!

Christmas at Sacred Heart lasts for 40 days. When the merchants are finished with it, we begin to celebrate it, and we do just that from December 25th until February 2nd. Forty Days! So your card will not be late. It's not a bad way to brighten up our world and get through a weary winter in Camden.

Our old church, 1886—1986, with its raveled edges and cracked plaster, deserves to be adorned, this Christmas, with good wishes from everywhere, until its walls are covered with cards of Centennial celebration.

Some weeks ago, November 9th, we solemnly blessed our church. Fr. Joe Messina, new associate at Sacred Heart, walked in procession to its baptismal, communion, and gathering places and also its four corners and sang fervent prayers for their holy continuation. At a later Mass I anointed the same places with the oil of the olive tree to bring strength and soothing comfort to all the stones and timbers that were hewn into a house of God a hundred years ago. Walking with me in the procession was John Lyons who was born in Camden in 1894. He has lived in every decade of Sacred Heart's 100 years. We finished the oiling. John was making his way back to the pew. Suddenly, a gasp from some of the congregation drew all eyes to him. He fell on the hard floor. It wasn't his limbs that gave out (they are almost as old as the church), No! It was the eyes. He didn't see the step and missed it. But, amazingly he was on his feet as fast as he fell. "I never felt a thing," he said. And a few days later he attended our Centennial Dinner Dance at the Woodbine Inn. "Little Fred Astaire" they used to call this old bandleader, 70 years ago, when he played and danced on the fast floors of Camden and Philadelphia.

So, we will not so much remember that he fell but that he got up immediately. God bless you John! You gave us great example. We will pick ourselves up and go on steadily into our second century as a church of generous service in Camden.

Last July 4, 1986, we opened the cornerstone of our church and the lead box within it, both placed there on July 4, 1886. In the box were 11 newspapers, five from Camden, and five from Philadelphia and one from New York, dated July 3rd and 4th, 1886. Also there were five coins: a 50-cent piece, 1829; a dime, 1873; a nickel, 1884; a three-cent piece, 1873; and a half-dime, 1853; and two other items: 50 cents and 25 cents, both in paper money.

We will put your name and good wishes in our cornerstone on March 7, 1987. The hundredth anniversary of the first Mass in Sacred Heart. We will put the old newspapers and money back in the stone plus items from these times.

On July 4, 1987 the following letter will be placed in a sealed lead box in the cornerstone.

LETTER TO THOSE WHO AT SOME FUTURE TIME
MAY OPEN THE CORNERSTONE OF SACRED HEART CHURCH
CAMDEN, NEW JERSEY AND LOOK AT ITS CONTENTS

July 4, 1987

Greetings and blessings from us to you.

We gather here today at Broadway and Ferry in Camden, to look back with awe at the huge throng (7,000 people) that stood with high hopes on this bleak spot 101 years ago.

We stand here now, a little more than one percent of that vast crowd and, with a hundred years of hindsight, we look forward with a more cautious hope at a future we can but poorly attempt to fathom or envision. But this we know: that the God of Abraham, of William H. Lynch (our first pastor), and Christina De Large (our present trustee), is the faithful God of our future. We stand here on this corner of Camden that is torn by trucks and worn by greed and neglect. We stand among houses, many of which are empty, boarded, and blind. We stand on Broadway that has far too many people drinking from bottles in brown paper bags and others selling their drugs or their bodies on the Street.

And yet today our sister city across the river is full of fireworks exploding in gigantic flowers of light to celebrate our Constitution. So, with Bible in hand and Constitution in place, and human nature unchanged in its unlimited potential for good and its persistent tendency to fail, we place our hope in a Creator God who transforms our flaws into beauty and our failure into victory. We have hope that our dear earth will not be destroyed by the ugly nuclear weapons that now infest it. We have hope that the killing diseases of AIDS and cancer will be checked and cured and prevented. We are trying to be a church of justice so that the Holy Bread we break and share on Sunday may be an effective and universal catalyst for the better distribution of the goods of the earth. We are praying that the faith that was nurtured and sustained in this holy church for a hundred years may not fail in us but be handed on in better condition because it was tested in the struggle of these unusual times.

May you who read this live in a world in which it is easier for people to be good and fair and generous. May your work be more creative than ours and your time less pressured. May war and weapons be dusty memorials in the museums of your world. May the peace of Christ envelop the whole earth.

God bless everyone in this world.

Michael Doyle

Christmas in Camden

December, 1986

Hi:

Yesterday, Sacred Heart's bell rang on National Public Radio across the United States.

It recalled for us Christmas 1983, when John McGuire and Joe Balzano gripped a bell-rope in the foyer of our church, pulled it down to earth, and sent out a sound of hope upon the world. It was the new sound of an old bell that had been found in a pile of scrap at Camden Iron & Metal. John Bantivoglio donated it to Sacred Heart. Cast in Philadelphia in 1853, its 350 pounds of bronze ended up – down and out – in this metal morgue of twisted brokenness. Yet, somehow it escaped the claws of the big crane that would have dumped it in the craw of a cargo ship and taken it away to a foreign furnace to be melted down for less worthy purposes. Who knows, it might have ended up as bullets in the chests of young men or women crying for life.

But no, thank God, it was destined to be hoisted up to the tower of Sacred Heart.

> *To hang high above the lowly scrap,*
> *And drop a rope in hope that hands*
> *Old or young would reach and pull.*

They did. It rings every day and yesterday it rang for Christmas from sea to shining sea...a heartbeat sound of hope for a broken world.

Last night a man called from Texas. He had just heard our bell on NPR's "All Things Considered". A widower, he wants us to ring it today for Paul, the deceased husband of a widow he likes in Wisconsin. Sweet sounds of hope that maybe...broken lives can be welded into one.

So, let it ring! Let it ring for you this Christmas too. Let it be a sign of hope that amidst all the broken bits of life, something whole and good survives. Something bright and beautiful in the manger of our lowest moments.

As Tim and Gail Gooney wrote yesterday: "The wise men who followed the star found the Holy Infant in a stable. We followed the star and found the Holy Spirit in Sacred Heart. Thanks be to God."

So ring the bell!

> *Our eager muscles moved the metal,*
> *And the bell that fell arose to tell*
> *This tired town of broken sounds,*
> *Listen Camden! All is well.*

Happy Christmas!

Michael Doyle

"In Every Person There is a Story"

February, 1987

Hi!

I had a *lovely* letter today from my friends Frank and Edna Plageman of Laurel Springs, N.J. Both are ill and up in years. Frank wrote:

I am now on my third cycle of chemotherapy and seem to be responding. Edna is still confined to a wheelchair and walker and has much pain. We are two maturing plants whose seeds of life are still clinging to the mother plant. However we are ready (God's will be done) for the seed to drop into mother earth. As we await with joyful Faith, Hope, and Love for the time of resurrection. We would like to be buried from Sacred Heart when the time comes. Please give all our love to all at Sacred Heart. May God bless everyone. Pax Caritas.

Edna and Frank Plageman

Surely the Plagemans' days "are full of light." Frank came to Mass in September when we celebrated the feast of Holy Cross, and when people held up their crosses against the oncoming darkness, Frank held up a big branch in bloom with blood-red berries clinging in the green. Now the seeds of life are ready to drop into mother earth.

Oh, the stories! Twenty-five years ago Fenne Hess (who died of cancer at 47) and I used to play golf on Mondays in Marlton. We spent half the time in the bushes looking for the balls and rousing rabbits that were never disturbed on Saturdays by good golfers. I never learned how to play golf, but I listened to many great stories that Fenne – a newsman with the *Philadelphia Inquirer* – told me between sliced balls, sand traps, and frightened rabbits. Once, when I asked him how he could make every story interesting he said: "in every person there is a story." Now those words are carved on his gravestone in Calvary Cemetery and deeply engraved on my mind as well. I love stories.

Like Al Konat's! Al saw Sacred Heart Church on *60 Minutes* and came "to check it out." He stayed. Came on Saturdays to work and on Sundays to worship. I asked him to fix a light in the church that had baffled several "experts." On Wednesday, November 17, 1984, Al died while leading an AA Meeting in Cinnaminson. "I really never stopped drinking until I found God," he said, then his head dropped to the table. In the homily-eulogy at his funeral I said that I had "only one thing against Al Konat. He never fixed the light at the back of the church." It was still out. But as soon as I got back from the cemetery that day, Ben Hill, who had tried so often to find the cause of the problem said: "Guess what!" I said: "The light is on." It was. It is. Not only that! Two months later, a stranger arrived one morning at Sacred Heart and said "a friend of mine told me to come here and help if I had any time. I'm an electrician." Who told him? Al Konat! Jack Dershimer helped to rewire the whole church.

Al Konat had sent his message: "I'll enlighten you, Michael Doyle "In every person there's a story."

Michael Doyle

Clay and Incense

Eastertime, 1987

Hi!

Once in a while, something ordinary and casual grabs us with a measure of meaning that is new and deep and astonishing. For me, the other day, it was something sadly penetrating when I glanced at my father's old pipe, still and lifeless on my bedroom windowsill. Dust-laden for a long time and dead-cold for almost twenty years, it suddenly burned a hole in my heart.

I missed my father as if he had died the day before. He died in 1967, a few months before I came to Camden City. I'm glad he didn't ever have to come here. He would have curled up in a tremble and died like a salmon in the sand.

He was fortunate to be able to swim in his own stream and be nourished by the familiar land of his childhood. Hard work, yes! But the old pipe reminded me of his ability to pause and find "a wee bit of comfort" in laying down his spade or shovel and taking out the pipe with its cool, smooth feel in the heel of his hand. Next came the "half-quarter" of tobacco from which he cut a few slivers with his bone-handled penknife and broke them down with his fingers and filled his pipe. Then with his back to the wind, he bent and cracked a "friendly" match, lit his pipe, and put on the lid. It was a ritual. How often I saw him walking through a frosty potato field in the winter—the hands falling off him with the cold—and yet when the peasant incense of his pipe rose up around the eaves of his cap, he was refusing to be pulled down by the wet clay that clung to his heavy hobnail boots!

It is this combination of clay and incense that is the stuff of life. Too much of either is as good as one without the other. No good! We must have a balance between ashes and Easter. Some dirt on our heads and hands in the restoration of the earth...the restoration of ourselves. For us here in Camden, it is the dust of dark, damp, abandoned houses being transformed into homes and the sun coming through new windows of glass with bright light and life.

How can we ever think of Camden and its 20,000 children—one of the worst cities in North America—and not lift a finger, or a hammer, or a collection, or a voice to help it. Our diocese which is called Camden and stretches from here to Cape May celebrates its golden jubilee this year and the condition of this city casts some tarnish on the gold. And yet within the past month three suburban parishes, St. Peter Celestine and St. Mary, both of Cherry Hill, and St. Andrew of Gibbsboro, have each decided to take on some of the dust of Camden and work towards an Easter of urban and human development. They have decided to bring three houses back to life.

The Heart of Camden Housing Corporation needs plumbers, electricians, carpenters, painter's helpers, roofers, and funds to fix up Camden. We need people of faith who deserve to get dirt on their hands and wings on their lives to rebuild a city of God. People of hard work and hope who will not be stopped by dirt or rubble or impossibility, but whose faith and determination will ascend like Easter incense before the face of God.

I cannot light the pipe that died on October11, 1967. But our Sacred Heart community tries to walk in the mud without being bogged down. It tries to light good incense every Sunday that rises and writes strong prayers on the poor air of this battered town. Prayers for you and me to enable us to stand on this side of life and rise on the other side of death.

May the Spirit of God lift you up and bear you on to reach the peak of all you are!

Happy Easter to you!

Michael Doyle

A Lamp in the Widow's Window
(excerpt)

They lived forty years in desert times
Reared their young on scanty store
Wore torn clothes that others wore
And clogged their toes with wooden soles.
They plowed their field when time was lea,
Gathered ripened wisdom in jugs and jars,
One careful eye on earth and plough
And one that looked at stars.
They gave God a chance to have His way
When it made good sense or struck them "odd."
They hay was cut. It was teeming rain,
"Ah! A terrible day, thanks be to God!"
They tamed life's horse, its mane of wind
For the saner gait and the harnessed haul
But once in a while, when the time was right
They kicked up their heels, hob nails and all.

New Fire in the Heart

September 23, 1987

Hi!

Almost thirty years ago, in the summer of 1958, my family moved from the old house where I was born into a new one that we built a few yards away. It was a melancholy journey...leaving the old hearth where five generations of Doyles were warmed by one continuous fire, and coming into new cold concrete where life would begin again. When all the furniture was transferred, my parents carried out their solemn transition with that splendid sense of the sacred that survives almost always in a peasant people. My father placed the last coals of the old hearth in a bucket, my mother took the large picture of the Sacred Heart from the kitchen wall, lifted it high, and they walked together across the farmyard into the new house. The picture was hung, the fire was lit, and life began.

On this first day of Autumn our year is turning on the hinge of the harvest. Bright blossoms and blouses are changing to falling leaves and warmer clothes. It is a beginning time of much more clarity than the feeble new-year feeling of dreary January days. We get a sense of starting again every September. The birth of the Holy Mother, the new start of Rosh Hashanah, and the opening of schools. Plans, programs, and plenty of good will.

Here in Camden the Benjamin Franklin Bridge was recently transformed into a glowing nightly necklace over the Delaware River to celebrate the Constitution. Sacred Heart School opened on September the 9th for its 67th year, with 233 children, a new principal named Shirley Howe, and three new teachers. It opened to the final tapping of Tom Harnick's hammer doing last-minute repairs to the school he graduated from in 1924 and still cherishes after 60 years.

We cannot even begin to imagine a time 60 years down the road. But the children will remember the Sacred Heart of 1987 and the struggle of a Catholic school without many Catholics in a poor neighborhood in Camden. Every child in this broken city deserves a better environment, a better education, and a better break.

God Almighty, help us to help some of them! May our school be blessed! May the bright glow on the Ben Franklin Bridge light a path to a better future for all of us, because "we the people" are waiting a long time. Like Tom Harnick's hammer, may the hum of helping hands be heard anew.

We are determined to begin again with the Heart of Christ as the high model of our lives. We are determined to keep alive the great traditions of our faith. Like my father walking forward with old coals in a bucket, let us together light new fires in our lifetime to warm up the cold weather of the world.

Michael Doyle

The Long Lens of the Years

October, 1987

Hi!

Last week I looked down the lens of my camera at every child in our school. I photographed 230 of them, one by one. It is my hope that you will sponsor one of them, and that a picture of a Camden child (or children) will soon decorate the door of your refrigerator or grace the top of your table. Most important, touch the insides of your heart.

The faces I saw in my camera were full of exquisite beauty. Framed in the harshness of a terrible environment, they announced over and over again that the only beauty in Camden is in the human face.

I wish I could look down the long lens of the years and see how these children turn out. But all that is in the "dark room" of a future we must await. We can only hope for the best.

Recently I wrote a few thoughts about a man who lived across the street from Sacred Heart and died three months ago. Looking at him was like looking through a lens of broken glass. This is what I saw.

I saw him picking beer cans off the street,
A thin hard harvest, famine-hungry for flat aluminum
And other stuff to sell for mean junkyard nickels
And take his daughter to MacDonalds,
If he ever had enough. He didn't.
A memory is all she has of his tired bent intentions.
The white wool of the worn years
Clung 'round his scruffy neck
Like dried out moss on a dying tree.
Too old for this second crop of children
Growing up from his troubled roots.
Three generations struggling in a single spot of space
Colliding in a narrow door of time
There was no place for him except the floor.
And there in desperate heat of this July
He lay down one night and died.
His heart like some old unbalanced clock
Stopped dead and never moved again.
Run over like the cans beneath the pick-up truck,
In early years. Too many stuck within his hand
Before they emptied down his throat
And hit the street or it hit him.
Cigarettes as well and uncertain food
Helping out to do him in. Poor man! Not nice poor
Sweet as Francis with a bird of broken wing.

But the poor – a pain sometimes – bleak and blamed
By all, but the Savior, in the end.
By the children too. They were chanced easily into life
Without a notion of the stakes
And the block of time it takes
To bring them to their prime.
Yet, Jesus spoke of sparrows falling down,
How sure they are of help upon the ground.
But will flattened cans ever open
Into cups of common good,
And reason cease to question why they should?
Still, hope staggers from the gutters to insure
That God has not been able to ignore
The ever blessed bother of the poor

Last week I looked down the lens of my camera at the faces of our children and photographed them one by one. Hours later I saw the pictures developed. So quick! So beautiful! But long will be the wait for the real development. God bless these children! May they not be overcome by their weakness or overrun by the weight of what will happen. May they all come out well in the end.

Michael Doyle

Anita Rose
(excerpt)

For Anita Rose, I must whisper that her ears may never hear
The words I say to others as I ask their fervent prayer.
The day they took her from maternity and out the open door
To start the journey of her life to whatever is in store.
The day they covered her in white and took her out to greet
The sun and moon and stars and all she'll ever meet
In Camden back on Broadway at Chelton west and east
Her mother's in her spot selling "love" upon the street.

The Graves That Grief Dug in Our Hearts

November 16, 1987

Hi!

We sometimes forget to thank God for memory but November is a good time to remember. A nostalgic time of mist on falling leaves and bright light on all our friends in glory. We visit the holy places where we buried the smiles that blessed us, and the graves that grief dug in our hearts where the dead we love are sleeping.

I am aware, as I write, that one year ago today, November 16, 1986, my dear friend Siobhan McKenna died. And as the lids lowered on her great icon eyes, a curtain closed on one of the world's most authentic stage actresses. She loved to listen to stories about Sacred Heart and they certainly continue.

Last Wednesday I completed 13 years on this sacred spot. Is it getting easier? Let me tell you! A few days ago thieves stole $1,875 worth of new Christmas toys that we had procured for poor Camden children. Tomorrow and the days following, more than 750 people will line up in our church and sign up for Christmas baskets. Nearby we are restoring six houses for poor people that soon will have light in the windows and warmth in the walls. In September we provided homes to 16 other families with small mortgages without interest or profit. Renters were changed into owners through our Heart of Camden Housing Corporation. On we go, trying to be encouraged by the few things we do and not crippled by the many we cannot.

A few months before she died, Siobhan asked me to write my story (we all should), and sometime ago I wrote a few words for her (melancholy as usual) that today suits my sad November mood as I remember her and the many who have gone.

Tell Me, Dear Siobhan!

"You must write your story"
She said to me last June.
And she so soon to die
And I so full of fear to hear again
The call to dip my pen in all
The tears I am. "But wetlands"
She said, "need your hands and head.
Cultivate before it's late!
And all your strength is gone."
I will try, Siobhan!
To delve within the deep mix of damp bog I am.
Full of past, bits of soft stuff,
Life smothered, buried, drowned
But enough backbone of hard bog oak
To stand my underground.

Heather-hidden self, wild but no way nearly free.
Bogs are sometimes cut to pieces,
Squeezed and wrung and hung out to dry,
To warm field-stones into hearths,
And bring aching bones to life.
Yet the bog is always wet.
And hears the cries of curlew and wind,
And feels the fret of white-faced birch
Bent and badly broken in the storm.
But even when the August sun is warm,
It merely dries the sagging skin of paths,

And ravelled crags above the cold soft lasting mass
That saves the many stories of the past.
My question! Is the story in the quiet bog?
Like forgotten butter buried in a barrel.
Waiting there for chance to bring it up.
Or is it in the dreams of one
With warm legs beside the hearth,
Gazing in the changing turf I cut
And building worlds with the mind
Before the ashes come and all the dreams are gone?
Tell me, dear Siobhan!

Michael Doyle

A Glow on the Faces of Those I Love

January, 1988

Hi!

Clark DeLeon, the well known columnist for the Philadelphia Inquirer, came with his family to Sacred Heart for Mass on Christmas Eve and wrote warmly about it in his column the following Sunday. "The light was there in the darkness, all right." He said, "It felt good to see it again and to have seen its glow on the faces of those I love."

I have always felt that if clay can smile the dead will rise. But that smile is the smile from within. It is not the view in the lens of NASA with its awesome glance at the globe, or the staggering vistas from the Windows of the World in New York, or Christmas magic in the windows of Wanamaker's in Philadelphia that star in the vast firmament of the human mind. No, it's the light in the eyes that breaks through the darkness of our depression, through the monotony of our effort to have hope in the apparent failure of our dream. There is more divinity in the sweet dimples of the manger-Child at the breast than in the mighty mountains of Everest or the rich river valleys of the world. So once again we climb down from the perch of our own importance and search for the bright child in the manger of our lowest moments. To find anew, as a baby finds her toes, and be delighted. To find again that the child in us, with its tender trust and sprightly hope, is alive and well and has been saved in spite of all the mad monarchs of greed and stupidity that always seek to slaughter our innocence.

It is that birth of beauty within us, that breaks through the crust of our jawbones and the droop of our eyes and floods the world with a billion smiles. Oils it even into gladness. As Clark DeLeon said, "it always feels good to see it again...the glow on the faces of those I love."

So at Sacred Heart "the light was (is) there in the darkness." Smiles spilled into smiles as food and money, toys and baskets, and hundreds of helping hands brought Christmas dinner to 3500 people and toys to 1300 children. Sr. Peg Hynes guided the greatest outpouring of Christmas generosity since the parish began in 1885: 831 big baskets of food were delivered to the homes of this area. My last letter lamented the theft of $1,875.00 worth of toys. We never got them back but we received three times that amount from people who heard they were stolen. "A light in the darkness."

So this is a letter of gratitude. A basketfull, a heartfull, a cup overflowing to you for your good wishes and prayers voiced or not, for the donation of your money, your help, your vehicle, your time to bring a bit of warmth to the smelly "stable" that this neighborhood often is and make a spot where God is born.

Michael Doyle

"The House That I Shaped in My Heart"

Easter, 1988

Hi!

I was 12 in '46 – 1946 that is, and our sow was in labor. "Sick of the piggin,'" my father said, and "aye," he would let me sit up all night by myself and take care of her. So, on my little stool I sat in the sty, with a lamp, an anxious sow, and between the slithering arrivals of little pigs, I tried to draw the holy face of Padraig Pearse. No small feat for a lad with a blunt pencil, messy interruptions, and sticky fingers. Pearse would be proud.

He was one of the most beloved in the long line of men and women who were and are willing to die for the sovereign integrity of my little island on the edge of Europe. A poet-patriot! The British executed him and his brother Willie too in Stonebreakers' Yard in Dublin. It was Easter 1916 and the hope arose that life – richly conscious of national dignity – would rise from the ashes of his failure. It did. Old backs badly bent by years of oppression straightened up and young cowed chests swelled in admiration for the land they lived on and the great stories they were fed on. More than 30 years had passed and his spirit was still permeating the humble scene of a farrowing sow and the mind of the boy who carefully watched her.

It was above all his "aishling," his dream, that was so enchanting and challenging to the young imagination with a pig in the night. A vision that got to its feet as soon as he fell in Stonebreakers' Yard. It was the vision of a fool and Pearse was the first to acknowledge it in his poem, The Fool.

> *And the wise have pitied the fool that hath striven to give a life,*
> *In the world of time and space among the bulks of actual things,*
> *To a dream that was dreamed in the heart and only the heart could hold.*
> *O wise men riddle me this: What if the dream come true?*
> *What if the dream come true? And if millions unborn shall dwell*
> *In the house that I shaped in my heart, the noble house of my thought?*

Twenty years passed before the boy by the sow came to the City of Camden and now he has spent twenty more years scratching the face of his dream in the dust of this terrible town. Waiting, waiting, waiting...at the backside of an old city for the birth of a New Jerusalem. He dreamt that one day suburban churches would come back to the city and transform cold abandoned houses into homes of living warmth. On Saturday, March 12, 1988, Fr. John Killeen with his forty parishioners from St. Mary's in Cherry Hill celebrated Mass in the sparkling living room of 412 Viola Street Camden, NJ. The house had been dead. They brought it back to life.

I was twelve in '46, waiting for pigs to be born and drawing my dream in the dim light of the night. Well, when morning came I had 12 little snouts suckling eagerly on their mother...each with a place of its own. And by-and-by there would be more coming where they came from!

The Birth of a Pig

The paraffin lamp was hanging
on a rusty nail.
The flame flickered in fright on
the wasting wick
Which in better days or worse
was a strip of an old man's hat.
It flickered to a restless
movement of life and things.
There was an urgency in the air
of the night,
In every lick of the light and in
every stir of the straw.

I sat on an old stool,
My back to the wall, quiet in
body and jumpy in spirit.
The sow was making her bed.
"She's sick of the piggin," my
father said.
"She'll do it before morning."
By now everyone was asleep...
Everyone except the sow in the
pain of giving birth,
A lamp struggling to stay alive,
and me.
She shuffled anxiously back and
forth, nosing the straw in every
direction.
Grabbing it in her mouth and
shifting it this way and that.
I was overwhelmed by the gen-
erous forces that stirred in her,
To straighten out the world for
the coming of her young.
It seemed to me, however,
That the best efforts did not bet-
ter her bed,
They made it worse.
Wherever it looked good she
tore right in and dismantled it,
And continued to undo what had
been done.
But results didn't matter.
Far better than the lay of her
bedding

Was the strong surging power of
her motherhood.
Life's endless urgency to make
things better for the future.
The results were not sketched in
straw on a pigsty floor.
They were poured into the great
mystery of life
Where all good urges are born,
and return for preservation.
Finally, after turning and
twisting in countless ways,
She laid her trailing body on a
tangled mat of straw.
I sat near the end to watch the
beginning.
Life, I knew, demanded the rever-
ence of waiting.
Waiting...
This moment had taken its time.
Thirteen years is a good while.
But my father had waited for the
emergence of my timid manhood.
Somehow he knew it was about to
come,
So he left me alone...
Alone with a sow in the night to
attend to the birth of her young.

I watched and waited.
I gazed at the quiet spread of her
body
And wondered where in there did
the little ones lie.
Her bulging teats were full -
Little hills of milk,
Where life could feast on the
peaks and frolic in the valleys
between.
Her body heaved,
Her feet kicked against the straw.
I could see the pain race across
her body like dark clouds in an
Irish sky.
I rubbed my hand along her belly
and talked to her aching heart

She grunted in a hoarse and tender way.
She knew I was there,
And that was all I wanted her to
know.

I searched for signs of life.
They came...
Those strange and messy heralds
of emerging life.
Her pain increased.
The mighty forces of the ages
gathered up inside her,
converged,
And pressed in unison to launch
new life upon the earth.
My heart beat with hers,
And I thought I could see the
little one, coming from afar,
And sailing down her stretching
body.
Yes! Could it be?
Oh my God!
Sliding down the unrelenting
flow
And then slipping through the
slimy sluice of life into my
waiting hands.
A pig!
My first - her first!
Wet in the messy wrappings of
her gift,
But fresh and new as a lamb in
the fields of Eden.
With eager hands I broke the
cord that linked it to an ageless
line of life,
And with trembling hands
I carried it to meet its mother.
And oh my friend, the sound she
made,
Filled my heart with a flood of
tenderness
As she grunted welcome to her
very own.

Michael Doyle

Golden Wonders

May, 1988

Hi!

He thoroughly enjoyed the last day of his life with a spade in his hand. Digging potatoes. By evening, rows of round "golden wonders" stretched out before him like the long path of his years...well-strewn with the rewards of his work. I could never compete with my father with a spade in my hand. So, like Seamus Heaney, I opt for the pen. Heaney, of course, digs deep with a tiny nib. I merely scratch the surface.

Anyway, today, May 20, 1988, I am celebrating the men and women who wrote with spades in the soft sand of this location when they broke ground for Sacred Heart on May 20, 1886. On this day in 1873 Walt Whitman came to Camden and turned some new ground with his extraordinary pen. On this day, 1973, the jury of "The Camden 28" trial wrote "not guilty" in an historic legal verdict. On this day I am writing to you. Important stuff! I want my pen to dig "golden wonders" out of the common clay of our ordinary lives.

I recently realized that if I live (as my grandfather used to say "if God spares me") until June 15th, I will be 20 years in Camden City. 1968. That's when I came. What a terrible year it was! Bobby Kennedy spoke in Camden's Convention Hall on April 1st and said, "The only real purpose in this world is to make some contribution towards making things better. We can do it." He headed for Indiana and was there when Martin Luther King was murdered in Memphis. April 4th. Nine weeks later Kennedy himself was murdered in Los Angeles. June 6th. Those April and June bullets tore a hole in the world. Before the year was out the gathering of Democrats in Chicago turned into an explosion rather than a convention. Richard Nixon was elected. By December Thomas Merton died strangely in Bangkok. Some say he was murdered too.
"Make things better." Camden today is worse than it was in 1968.

But the sun may be coming out. This is Pentecost Time. The old feast of Shavout when God and the people agreed to work together. Pentecost. The Spirit of Christ laden with gifts of great courage, high and clear communication filled the hearts of frightened fishermen, and they broke out of their locked closets of fear and confusion and took on the world. Peter, James, and John...the whole bunch of them. Cripples walked. Camden will get on its feet. "We can do it."

That first Pentecost was the founding Convention of the Christian Churches. Simple people passed resolutions to organize the world. Slowly...they were walking!

On June 4,1988, nineteen churches in the City of Camden will gather in an historic Founding Convention to set the structure and the direction of a church-based community organization in this city. Shoestring clusters of Christians will plait their strings into a rope of hope and move a mountain. With your help "we can do it." We need the push of your prayer and the power of your spirit. We need your hands and your head and your heart.

Camden 1988. We are determined to break ground, break water, break bread, break out in a new day. We invoke the Spirit of Christ, the spirit of Merton and King and Kennedy. The power in Walt Whitman's poems and John Doyle's potatoes.

By evening, rows of "golden wonders" stretched out before him like the long path of his years...well-strewn with the rewards of his work.

My Father

When the wind whipped the last leaves from the chestnut trees
And the gray gap opened in the old whin hedge on the hill
He came, a man, walking on the land
There was mud on his boots and on his patched pants
And under the limestone nails of his hands
Dirt! Oh, no. It was the earth
And to the earth he was related by blood.

The blue in his eyes – all the weathers knew.
The rain traced the years, salt tears in the soft surface of his face.
And cut wrinkled furrows in his fields
Where the water deepened its way to the sea.
A peasant! Ah! More! A priest!
And more reverence there in the shadow of his cap
Then any bright-eyed glance at the Sistine ceiling in the light
With all its artistic sweep and the brush of angel's wing.

I know. I know because I came to him a thousand times
To show him what I had and what I had done
And instantly from the depths of his heart
A joy rose before me like the eager dawning of the day.
God's secret glee when the first spark spoke
And that divine emerging smile made its sweet maiden voyage in the dark
It was a look of the fullest appreciation that he had never used before
For the first time he was calling it forth from the bottom of his being
To bathe my moment in his utterly human blessing.

He was my father.

Michael Doyle

Our Little Bit of Green

July, 1988

Hi!

Last year at this time, I was in Ballycastle, the town of Lammas Fair (I wish I were there now). North of Belfast, it is a beautiful little town on the coast of Antrim. It looks out on Rathlin Island and, beyond that, to the green and purple hills of Scotland. The air is clear and crisp, the pace slow and friendly. A place where wheat would grow and bread would rise. The world seemed civilized.

Today I was thinking of the dwarfed wheat and corn in the fields of North America. Something is wrong. The sun is baking our brains into madness and burning up the soft growth in the land.

Maybe we will realize that after flesh and blood there are no material things more important than land and water. How precious is this generous mother that feeds our bodies *and* builds our bones. Even when death and decay take away our warmth and make us so unacceptable, the earth takes us completely to her. Generously, without any rejection or indignity.

But, our Mother is weakening. Dick Harmon, the great community organizer, says that he fears "the earth has AIDS." Tortured by traffic, raped and abused by greed, the air poisoned by fossil fuels, the soil and water partially contaminated by toxic waste, our dear earth is sick. She hasn't been herself in a long time. She is losing her resistance and immunity to the forces that assail her. There must be a line beyond which she may not recover. Right now the terrible heat feels like a fever that is burning up the face of the earth.

We need a revolution. A turning back to the earth as prodigal sons and daughters who have been wandering and wasting. We need to live with less. We need to recycle more. We need to foster reverence for the good mother that gives us life.

Recently, Sacred Heart procured a vacant lot beside our school and with the help of many friends transformed it into a children's garden. It is our earth-classroom. The children water it daily and its vegetables and flowers are growing splendidly.

Yesterday I saw Barbara Pfeiffer sitting in it with five children engaged in an art project. Young minds blossoming in harmony with bursting buds and flowers. And God was there "walking in the garden in the cool of the day" (Gen. 3). In Camden!

Michael Doyle

We Don't All Fit in a Volkswagen Anymore

August, 1988

Hi!

On August 15, 1954, the Doyle family piled into a small car to take my sister Anna Mae Doyle to a convent in Belturbet, County Cavan, where she joined the Mercy order of Catherine McAuley. We were close. A sad little community making a painful donation of a cherished treasure to God. Anna Mae Doyle was the most light-hearted and good-natured child of John Doyle and Rose Creegan. She would be known later as "the laughing love of God." But we left her in tears at Belturbet. She was 17.

Twenty-one years later, on November 7, 1975, we brought her body back to be buried. It was night. We had followed the hearse in a Volkswagen from the Richmond Hospital in Dublin past the spot north of Navan where a car had hit her two days before. At the foot of Belturbet's main street, crowds of people, old and young, lame and sick, surrounded the hearse and almost carried it to the church. I turned to my grieving mother and said: "when we came here in '54 we could all fit in this Volkswagen. Look at her family now."

One year before she died, I came to Sacred Heart. 1974. She was happy. She promised me she would always pray for this church. "If God needs any asking, I'll be doing it," is the way she phrased it. She has. It has been blessed.

Its family, far and near, has grown immensely. Friends have stood by, in prayer and work, in love and support, and formed in their various ways the ever-widening and converging circles of the Heart. These circles of connection express the never-ending energy in the heart beat of Christ.

The Human Circles of the Heart. These are some of them: The faithful people around the table for daily Eucharist. The wonderful worshipping community of Sunday Mass. The constant volunteers. The employed staff with big jobs and small pay. The school children, their parents, principal and teachers. The people who do maintenance. The people who come to the door for food or furniture. The people who donate food and money. The parishes that provide canned food, toys, and children's clothes. The people who give the money for 750 turkeys and Christmas baskets. The good people who receive them. The people who donate Christmas toys for 1,300 children. Those who receive them. The people who have helped the Heart of Camden buy 31 houses in four years. The workers who bring them from shells of disaster to warm homes of life. The Heart of Camden residents now living in and paying for their own homes. The people who have built neighborhood gardens. All those in community organizing who help this neighborhood and city. The people who sponsor children in our school every year. The many people who send donations and good wishes and remember us in prayer. Those who read Sacred Heart's monthly letters and pray for our work.

Great circles! A powerful concentration! We might say we are moving in big circles now! We don't all fit in a Volkswagen any more.

Michael Doyle

Hands for Sacred Heart

October, 1988

Hi!

I was nine for most of 1944, growing up on a farm where I could give a hand, even a little hand to fix the barn door, or make a box where hens could lay their eggs, or put a wooden bottom in a bucket when tinker's tin was all away at the World War. I hated pulling weeds that always grew again in wet potato fields, or washing dishes that were so quickly back in use. Give me the fixin' job—the one that's done when done, and I would forget to eat. But I never will forget my mother's words when such a task was done. "God bless your hands!" she always said. It was the fullest blessing on my being. Nothing, no, nothing from the mouth of pope or patriarch could match its worth. It lifted up my hands to heaven.

Now the century is twice the age it was in '44 and I am here in Camden where the "fixers" hardly ever win against the "breakers" of house and home and heart. God bless all the hands that help, and sad I am to say that many, recently, who were a part of Sacred Heart, have grown old and stiff. Their tools have fallen to the floor and we have waked them with their cold folded fingers on their chests and rosary beads they couldn't feel. Beloved they were! John McGuire, 87, helping here for nine and fifty years. Gone now, and weeds are back and growing in the flowerpots that miss his care. Margaret Kelly, 93, here since '24, whose finger tips have lived on piano keys and prayer beads since 1910. For the silent movies of another time, for clubs and pubs and parties, for the old of Sacred Heart and our children too, she played her lively tunes. For Harry Reasoner when *60 Minutes* came to Sacred Heart, and finally this June, with tired sinews played her "Four-Leafed Clover," which now at last she's looking over. We will remember! And Tom, too, this September. His gifted hands, with sweat, anointed countless broken things at Sacred Heart and repaired them well. Tom Harnick born here in 1908, but really Austrian in origin. The world was a broken violin. He had to fix it perfectly. God bless his holy hands.

God bless all the hands that help with mops and brooms and organ keys, with wrench and pipe and typewriter, with food, materials, and money, with chalk and chalice and vacuum cleaner, with pen and vase and paint brush, with Bible, bulb, and basket, with hammer, ladder, and lawnmower, with computer, hoe, and coffeepot, with all the tools we use in the transformation of the world.

In our chapel we have a statue of the Sacred Heart, but the hands are missing. But maybe that's the way it should be here. What good are plaster hands? Sacred Heart needs hands of flesh and bone, hands of work and worth, your own. God bless them.

Thanks for giving us a hand!

Michael Doyle

Broken Bits of Hope

November, 1988

Hi!

About one week ago, on Sunday night November 13th, vandals ripped through a layer of lexan in our church and smashed the lower section of a beautiful old stained glass window. In doing so, they violated something sacred that has been penetrated and enlivened by the light of every single day since 1886. A sad sight this shattered treasure on a hard terrazzo floor! So old it was...and yet so freshly new in the sunshine of the morning.

But in the heap of broken glass, there was one, only one, piece intact. In black letters on red, it bore the name of the man whose family donated the window, one hundred years ago. William O'Rourke. The violence did not damage his respected name or efface his honored memory.

So this week my thoughts are very much on stained glass and brokenness, violence, and shattered hopes. We are all in a way like stained glass...dull bits of glass of every hue and color, stained, bonded sometimes by the leaden links of tired relationships, and yet when God's light shines through we glow in beautiful manifestations of goodness that are at once unique, linked, and universal. No wonder we are crushed when stained glass is shattered and lies in a heap of broken bits on the ground.

I see Camden. I see its people oppressed and violated and then cut and caught on the jagged edges of their own brokenness. Out of line of the light. Out of focus. Out of place. Out of it. Precious people badly broken.

So, once again my plea goes out, hoping like a baby's cry to cut through all the cushions of good intentions and get into your heart where your sympathy, compassion, and all the active generosity of your nature are safely stored.

Camden is still Camden. It turns eyes to salted tears, too often. 0 my God, the children! Thousands of them. Sacred Heart is still an artery of modest hope struggling to stay open. It is your heart's help that makes this Holy Artery so Sacred. Don't let anything block your generosity.

We need Thanksgiving and Christmas to remind us all that giving is our normal and natural inclination, because that's the way God made us.

I know that his Holy Name is still intact among all the broken bits of life upon the world. I know too, that you will help us to pick up the pieces of shattered hopes and ideals and raise them up. You will help us put the pieces back together so that the light of God will shine through stained glass and stained lives and make them lovely in the morning.

"I wanna make it shine."

Michael Doyle

It's Heart Breaking Sometimes

January, 1989

Hi!

A recent card from a person who received one of the 818 Christmas baskets expresses her genuine gratitude She writes: Glory to God in the highest and on earth peace, good will to all. Praising and thanking God and the church of Sacred Heart for being there for my family and me this Christmas. Thank you!" Her thanks is for the gift you gave.

A Break in the Roof

Our grand old church was gored by a terrible wind on Wednesday, December 28, 1988 at 4:45 pm. A huge section of roof, 25 by 40 feet (shingle, rafters, and tongue-in-groove sheathing), was ripped off and dropped on Ferry Avenue. But God was with us. The light at Broadway and Ferry turned green. The traffic moved just in time. No one was killed or injured. The downpour of rain that would have ruined the ceilings and canvas paintings stopped miraculously as soon as the church was stricken. No rain fell until temporary rafters and tarpaulin were in place. So our church is wrapped in a huge red bandage awaiting permanent repair. That repair will be complicated, dangerous, and expensive. But we must go on. The light at Broadway and Ferry is green!

A Break in the Heart

Our dear friend and parishioner, Nick Virgilio, one of the world's greatest Haiku poets in the English language, died on Tuesday, January 3rd, in Washington, D.C. Stricken while taping a poetry presentation with Scott Simon for the TV program "Nightwatch," he was taken to George Washington University Hospital where he died at 2:10 PM. A daily visitor to Sacred Heart's kitchen where he made tea, answered phones, washed dishes, and tried out his most recent haiku on me or anyone who was there. Nick was an irrepressible genius who often mined gems of wisdom from the gutters and the dismal dishwaters of the world. We all really loved Nick. I miss him and will continue to miss him "with ever-returning Spring."

His poems in the Japanese form (no more than 17 syllables) are kernels of incredible depth and feeling!

> *On my last journey*
> *alone on the road at dawn:*
> *first sight of the sea.*

But somehow we must ride out our sadness:

> *lily:*
> *out of the water...*
> *out of itself.*

So. A break in the roof. A break in the Heart. But as my father used to say, "God is as good as He ever was." With us always...all the way to the sea!

On My Last Journey
(excerpt)

When the poet died, we crumbled at his side,
But not enough to ease the pain,
Alive too much. Feeling all the stomach bottom strain,
Disengage and sink so low and clutch
Until it bent us all like a stricken stand of birch
Around a gaping brown-black hole in snow.
The eyelids closed on the search-light eyes
And the coffin top slammed shut so fast
Our reaching fingers caught and ripped apart
Blue and black the pain and ache and dent in every heart.
The sack of kittens chilled the lily pond
And flowers froze in twisted scarecrows in the cold.
The autumn wind turned angry in the winter rain
And tore the wreath in shreds upon the door.
The jangled strings of broken violins
Tangled in the bobbin threads and tattered ends,
As jumbled memories whirled in the nightmare of the mind.

We had often seen him coming from the market place at noon
Where he heard the fleshy words
With vowels on the ends, squeezing meanings
With the gestures that tugged ancestral strings
Resurrecting kitchen smells and all the garlic in his genes.
He wore his father's tie and more of him
When he went to Washington and Nightwatch
To launch his word upon the waves.
But now his clothes are coming home
Disembodied bits...items in a plastic bag.

Silent instigators of screen door shadows
Long ago, of marines with cruel news
Double-edged, that cut the flower from the rose,
Slashed the fiddle strings and bow
And killed the flowing laughter on Niagara.
No parents now to see this second set
Of 'effects' coming through their door. Two dead!
"They held each other and the folded flag," he said.
One death enough to tear their smiles in two
And hang them drooping on the edges of their days.

Now, their poet, in that town of Pentagon.
"Spentagon," he yelled. "Repentagon!"
Washington,
There his brother's name was carved in stone,
And he went yesterday to chisel in his own.
And pour out that high voltage breath
That rocked his body like a sail boat in a storm.
His last hot gasps in that town of tired words,
High-strung syllables they were
And "for the record" worthy to be heard.
A searing light amidst the flutter of this mad-moth age.
Silent now, prone on that formica top
Wrapped like a Buddha in a sheet of snow
With strong protruding face and a tag upon your toe.
Dead. It simply read: "N. Virgilio."
But I didn't need a tag to know your name
"Like the lily poem, I know you well," I said.
"By heart I do and I will take you home..."

Michael Doyle

Catherine Mannion Root

February, 1989

Hi!

On August 31, 1988, I rode in Jerry Faladin's car from the flat streets of San Bernardino, California to the cliff-top of Running Springs, up a twisting climbing highway that was built in the '30s by Franklin Roosevelt's W. P. A. It clings to the mountain like a swallow's nest to a rafter. We ascended from 800 feet above sea level to 6,800 feet—that's 6,000 feet—in 30 minutes. The road is called The Rim of the World.

All this might have impressed me at another time. Not that day! I had just been to the edge of glory. I had come to San Bernardino to visit a shrine. I had made my visit before I made my ascent. Consequently my mind on the mountain was down in the valley—my knees on the floor where she blessed me.

I was thankful. Thankful to God, to Jerry Faladin, to all that is. It was Jerry, a deacon at St. Bernardine's in San Bernardino, who called me on July 19th and asked if Sacred Heart had a record of the baptism of Catherine Mannion. We did. She was born on July 21, 1888, and baptized here by our founding pastor, William Lynch, on August 19, 1888, and after a hundred years she is still alive and alert and faithful. Our church was one year old when her godmother, Mary King, carried her into it to be baptized.

I wanted to see that face on which the water fell from the hand of Fr. Lynch a hundred years ago. So I made a two-day trip to California, my only one so far, and was well rewarded.

Catherine Mannion's face was bright with delight when she greeted Jerry and me in her charming little house on Rialto Drive with its stone pillar porch and roses by the door. Here she lives with Genevieve her daughter. Both with walkers because Genevieve, in a recent accident, broke her hip.

"I got a wonderful memory' says Catherine right away. "I remember everything and I have never been sick. God has been very good to me." Except!! "See, when I was a baby I was sick a lot...so the doctor said the only thing to do is move into the country. So I (sic) went out there and got a goat and that's what I was raised on...a nanny goat." Evidently she got well and has had no relapse in a hundred years. "Back home" as she calls Camden, "we lived on Miller Street (off Chelton) and I only went to one church, Sacred Heart" (she and her family moved to California in 1906 when she was 18, and she has been in St. Bernardine's parish for 82 years. There she married Harry Root in 1909 and raised four children.) "I loved my church, Sacred Heart. I went there every Sunday with my daddy and many times in the winter there was snow on the ground. My daddy worked on the railroad, the Reading Railroad. I remember he used to do the writing for the Reading Railroad (gold leaf the sides of the cars). He used to send me up to get his paper, silver paper for the Reading Railroad, and that's what he did."

I showed her a picture of Fr. Lynch who baptized her. "My dear father" she said to him and kissed the picture with a reverence that awed me. She did the same when I handed her the bottle of baptismal water I had brought from the font in Sacred Heart where she had been baptized a hundred years before. The religious rituals of her childhood were nearer to her than her fingertips. She showed me her rosary beads. "I made them," she said. "I made a thousand rosary beads." She did too, until she fell in the garden some years ago.

Her emotions, like those of a little child, would shift suddenly from giggles of delight to tears that were a mixture of delight and sadness. Then her voice would rise in prayer and she would sing lullaby prayers of great sweetness. Half of her was in heaven, I thought. "I want to go home," she said tearfully (to God). "I'm not happy here." But then she was giggling about "back home" in Camden and Sacred Heart. The church of her childhood. "I used to go to vespers in Sacred Heart with my daddy on Sunday evenings." She didn't say anything about the vespers. But "we always stopped for ice cream in the summer, and, and, and (her voice rose to a high pitch of delight) oyster stew in the winter. I liked nice things."

This letter, dear friend, is only a tiny taste of an extraordinary moment. Too short... like my visit to Catherine Mannion Root.

I arose to go. She hugged me with a strength that surprised me. And then...taking some holy water from the bottle I had brought her (I knelt down) she rubbed it into my face, raised her hand, made a cross and blessed me "in the name of the Father and of the Son and of the Holy Ghost." Then she carefully cupped my face in her great old hands that have been holy in this world for more than a hundred years.

It was the blessing of a lifetime!

Michael Doyle

The Passover Woman

She has been struggling in the world
Since Spring was in her morning
The Woman. Veiled. Misunderstood,
With her tides of strength and flow
Her moon-measured blood
A menstrual daub on the door posts
Of her hut with basket weave
Where she wove the fabric of our form
And frightened off the killing angel
With its mean bat bite of death
And built a barricade of flesh
And hid her seeds beneath a steadfast bone.
Then deep within her dark wet cave
She fashioned ancient aqueducts

Sent in streams of precious blood
To feed her secrets there.
And otter-like she dammed the water round
To shield the hiding spot.

But stirrings came in time
The nest itself was too confined
And the future kicked against the barriers
That beginnings carefully had made.
So she rose with mighty labor
Before Moses touched the sea
And broke the water in her body
To make the passage safe for me.

The Plumber of the Horn Pipes

March, 1989

Hi!

It is always painfully poignant when we have to bury the precious temples of creativity that nourish our lives. For two years in a row, on the 7th of January, I was part of the tears and the snow and the funeral of an artist. This year it was Nick Virgilio, one of the greatest Haiku poets in the English language. Last year it was Ed Reavy, widely held as the greatest composer of Irish traditional music since Turlough O'Carolan, the blind Irish harper who died in 1738.

I attended Ed's funeral Mass in St. Dorothy's Church in Drexel Hill, where Mick Moloney and Eugene O'Donnell played Reavy music in the choir loft. A few selections, merely, from the 500 tunes the plumber had composed in his basement when his day's work was done.

He learned his first notes as a child in Pat Clarke's kitchen in Cootehill, not far from Barnagrove, Co. Cavan, where he was born in 1898. At the age of 14 he left his home not far from where "the Shannon River rises" and went to Philadelphia. There he worked as a plumber, composed his music, and played his fiddle for three-quarters of a century.

I was unable to attend the burial service in St. Charles Cemetery in Drexel Hill. Later Mick Moloney described it to me on the telephone: "Seamus Egan," he said, "had planned to play one of Ed's tunes on the uillean pipes. He had just learned it, but the pipes would not work in the cold. It was 10 degrees. So we cut the tips off a pair of gloves and he played the lament on the tin whistle. There wasn't a dry eye at the grave."

My poem tries to save that sacred scene.

The plumber of the hornpipes is dead.
The old diviner with the hazel bow,
Who found the Shannon's source
And made its magic waters flow across the world.
"NO!" she said "he's not dead,
How could Reavy die!"
"And who are you to say?"
"I am the Wind: The Wind
That drove the clouds in herds
Above the Cavan hills and Drexel too
And whispered to the oats in Barnagrove.
I am the breeze that kissed O'Carolan's face
With moisture on my lips
'Til notes danced within his mind
Like flames behind a blind.
I am the breath in Reavy's body—

I used to whistle in his mouth
Merely oxygen upon arrival
But virgin music coming out.
He would hold me in the evenings
And we'd play within his soul.
He tamed me with his reverence
But I always had to go
So I bore him sounds of sweetness—
Some were sad and some were glad—
And he composed half a thousand tunes
About the happy times we had."
"Hush!" I whispered. Did you see his fiddle
On the altar—silent as a stone—
And his body on the grave in Drexel Hill?
It was clamped on the hole in a final salute
Like an old finger frozen on a flute.
Did you see the people in a circle
Standing sadly in the snow,
When the pipes refused to play in the cold
"I was there" she said.
"I am the Breath of the earth.
Every mouth is a wisp of my prayer
Breathing blessings of incense
On the bites of the air
Because life has the edge on the ice.

Listen! my friend to the lad with the whistle
With his fingertips timid and cold.
See the life that he brings to the old man's tune
And the leaks that he brings to the eyes
See Reavy arise from the holes in the tin...
And announce on his grave: "I'm alive!"

Michael Doyle

May Is A Good Month

May, 1989

Hi!

May, I say, is a good month. Lovely here, and in the land of my birth as well. There, the poet wrote, "the whitethorn blossoms are in bloom," and when they are, the hedges of the land from end to end, are bright and white as rows of first communion children in church. Thousands of miles of fresh pink-white innocence.

I was confirmed in the faith of my mothers and fathers on the first day of May, 1944. The world was at war, and Ireland having refused to fight on the side of England which still occupied part of her by force, was ostracized economically. People were poor as church mice in Camden. For my confirmation, my mother bought my first new shirt. I was nine. I can still smell it and remember the fresh new feel of it. Fifteen years later, on the last day of May, I washed my face and my feet in the early morning, put on the alb that my mother made on her old sewing machine, laid down my 132 pounds on a flagstone floor in St. Peter's Seminary in Wexford, and was ordained a priest.

Time has torn the new blue shirt of '44 and worn the white alb of '59. But Spring and May and especially Easter demand our ardent renewal in life and hope and creativity. More assuring than the blossoms, ultimately, is the fact that the fallen leaves of last year nourish their growth. In death and darkness, life and stars are found. There is nothing in the gospels that promotes the formula that life will be easier if we struggle to make it so. Jesus didn't come to make things easy but to put us at ease with its demanding reality and ultimate outcome.

Jesus didn't get much help between the arena of his agony and the place of his execution. Lean it was when Veronica's towel is remembered still. It just got the blood out of His eyes. It was her courage in a mob scene that He rewarded with his face, not the worth of her rag.

Churches, individuals, and institutions of good will must begin to face "the economic apartheid" as Archbishop Rembert Weakland calls the racism and prejudice against the poor that are preventing any solution to our urban death camps. Don't just hang a crucifix on the wall! Come to Camden and walk down a battered block. It is, believe me, the Via Dolorosa — a street of sorrows.

A long way from the fresh face of the boy in the blue shirt and the young lad flat on the flagstones. But it's nourishing to return. May I say, is a good month!

Michael Doyle

Solstice in Lockerbie

June, 1989

Hi!

    As we approach the bright summer solstice in this month of June, people may remember that at solstice time last December, Pan Am Flight 103 exploded over Lockerbie, Scotland. The tragedy stunned the world. After the list of the dead was published, people began to call Sacred Heart because Michael Doyle of NJ. was on it. I couldn't get Lockerbie out of my mind. This poem is my lament for Michael Doyle and all who died and all who cling for life "on this grim planet." (Note: Newgrange is in Ireland. There, at the winter solstice, if the weather is right, the rising sun penetrates a small hole in a huge burial mound, which is 5,000 years old and lights up a passage to a stone chamber of the dead sixty feet inside the hill.)

The low aim for the old hole in the hill
Newgrange!
Out of range of the rays.
Winter light waits vainly
On the rim of the earth.
Eager to enter the womb of the dead.
Reverently!
And fertilize cold ashes into eggs
For the life of the world,
Thwarted.
Smog smothers the holy mound
And wrecks the mating mood.
Cosmic catastrophe!
Rejected rays rage in the heavens
Violence seethes in the skies
The monster of madness leaps from its lair
And tramples the software of the mind
The earth quakes in Armenia
Evil creeps through the crack in the cranium.
Pan bird bursts in the sky
And all falls to the ground
Death above,
Death below,
Death everywhere.
Lockerbie littered with bits of broken bodies
Bloody hail of limbs and luggage
Night falls in burned blankets
 Search lights,
Sensors,
Divers
Poke in the stones for the dead.

Pause!
Pause, humankind and ponder
This tiny try at oblivion!
Enough!
Not enough to scare you
Proud pilgrim on this grim planet.
You still play with fire!
And fire works never really work.
War never wins.
Look!
Look at the earth!
Clay pigeon she is,
Circling,
Loaded
Bombs in her womb
Bombs in her belly
Bombs in her craw
Too full!
Burp!
Throwing up,
Throwing down
Dead duck
Black nothing
Dust endless dust.
Oblivion.
God coughs where the world was... No light!
"Waste and void and darkness covers the face..."
He says nothing this time,
Just pokes in the ash heap
That once was our earth!
He's looking for the black box,
Eons after sun-stop.
Alone
Weeping
Searching
He wants to listen to the tape
Of the human race,
The weapons race
And find out, somehow,
What the hell went wrong.

Michael Doyle

Goat's Milk in a Jam Jar

September, 1989

Hi!

I have to write this letter at home because there is where I am. I have to write it about home because I first left it today...30 years ago, to go to the Camden Diocese. For better or for worse! September 8, 1959.

When the car pulled away from my parents' waving hands I cried for the first mile or so. As we passed Myles Reilly's house, my cousin Josie Rourke (the driver) brought a shivering smile to my wet face with stories about Mattie Lennon whom we both knew. One of them: Mattie out in the field calling his goat every evening. She would come, lie down, and then Mattie would sit on her and milk her into a jam jar. Such local lore strengthened me that day when the theology of vocation or mission didn't mean a thing to a weeping freckled fellow leaving home. Back there my father and mother "wet the floor" (my sister Phyllis Doyle said) with their tears.

The sun woke me up today in the room where both of them were waked, and I went to their grave at noon with flowers from their garden in my hand and white hair on my head to show them what time and tide have done to the face whose shape and lines they knew by heart. The Doyle plot by the parish church of St. Colmcille was carpeted in clover. The sunlight was making diamonds of the raindrops of morning...a million glistened on their grassy grave.

How painful the parting of parents everywhere when the little ships they built with their own ribs and bones and blood are torn from their moorings. "I have been through this so many times"—my father's parting words in 1967, four months before he died. "God be with you—my mother's last fading blessing in 1983...her bright mind slipping inevitably, like dew in the warming day.

No wonder, then, I talked to them today...on this day of good beginnings – the day I went away. The Blessed Mother's day (her birthday) when the child that would be called Mary left the enclosure of her own holy nurturing. A day of starts, new ones fresh as morning. In the church I lit candles, the little ones (once called penny candles—nothing for a penny now) the same sort my father lit every Sunday after Mass. Six, he lit—one for each of his children and one for their parents. Bright stars they were in the world I knew. Early this morning (2 a.m.) as I stood in my doorway I thought I could reach the plough if I stretched. So near it seemed and the north star there determining all direction. The ceiling of the night was a canopy of more stars than I had ever seen. Grateful I was to be awake when my world was asleep in this cathedral of the awesome grandeur of God. Far from Camden where the only star is a street lamp in a tangle of wires under an umbrella of depressing smog. But there too are the stars in the bright eyes of those who smile anyway. I visited my mother's old home yesterday where my great-grandfather, Hugh Creegan, tilled the wet "killing fields" in the famine of 1847 and my grandparents Michael and Mary Creegan raised 13 children in a small house. My other grandfather, Pat Doyle, used to say of big families in small houses (and, many there were) "you couldn't find your own leg in the morning." But my mother and all her eight brothers and four sisters found legs (short ones 'tis true) and raised 73 pairs of legs, 140 of them still walking down the world.

It was good to be in the old house by Lake Bailba in Leitrim with its low-peeked roof and wide walls. There, in her day, my grandmother baked a hundred pounds of flour every week to feed her baker's dozen. There, my grandfather came through the small doorway with armfuls of wool after shearing his sheep in Tully, and she whirred her old spinning wheel into action and made yarn to clothe them. "A terra' for spinnin' was Mary Creegan" says old Matt McKenna, her nephew, who often watched her as a child.

Well, it's late on September 8th and the day is gone and 30 years gone too, since I left home for Camden in 1959. John Kennedy was running for President and John XXIII was announcing a Vatican Council and Mattie Lennon was milking his goat in a jam jar.

I have tried in this letter to tether in a bit of my passing times and milk a little sustenance for my journey before the goat runs off again into the dark bushes on the mountain. I'll be back before you read this letter. Back again to start again to cope with Camden, but thank God, with a few mouthfuls of goat's milk in my jam jar.

Michael Doyle

The Moon in Cloone

The oven cold where she baked her bread
A baker's dozen children feeding
That nursed upon her ample breasts
'Til all their urgent needs were sleeping.

"Ne'er so happy," the mother said,
"When I baked a bag of flour a week."
"Ne'er so sad" when they had to leave
And sorrow flooded the freckled cheeks.

O the throb of life – the hay a rearin'
Turf a cuttin' the sheep a shearin'
Knittin', fiddlin', the fleece a spinnin'
The children dancin' in Drumkeeran.

Feathered fast they left the nest
Eight, one by one, went out the lane
The face was gone at the misty bend
The door was wet with the lonesome rain.

They bade farewell to the land they loved
And faces too they might never see
For many days in gray-green circles
They crossed the wide Atlantic sea.

May the Angels of Thy Light Dwell Within These Walls

October, 1989

Hi!

I have a little black book (and you are in it) because it is full of blessings. It is called *The Priest's New Ritual*. I was new myself when I got it on September 8, 1961, but it is old enough to have its blessings in Latin and to have received its "Imprimatur" from Michael J. Curley, Archbishop of Baltimore, on November 1, 1926. It has been with me on many journeys...in my pocket when I climbed a ladder to exorcise a draftboard in 1971 and when I drove the other day to bless a warehouse (70,000 sq. ft.) on River Road.

Page 275 is a well worn spot where it says: "*Ad introitum ergo nostrum benedicere, et sanctificare digneris hanc domum,*" which translates as: "at our entrance, therefore, deign to bless and to sanctify this house," and continues: "as thou didst deign to bless the house of Abraham, Isaac, and Jacob; and may the Angels of thy light dwell within the walls of this house and may they protect it and those who dwell in it, through Christ Our Lord. Amen." The English words are fairly ancient too but the idea of "Angels within the walls" seems wonderfully good within a house or the city limits or the sides of my T-shirt.

I have been thinking about angels and houses since I went to New York on October 2nd and sat in the Dag Hammarskjöld Auditorium in the United Nations Building and participated in World Habitat Day for North America. Sister Peg Hynes was there too to receive an award from the United Nations Center for Human Settlements (Habitat) for our Heart of Camden Housing. Our little shoestring housing effort in Camden was being honored: "in recognition of a significant contribution to the provision of adequate shelter to the poorest segments of the community." Four other groups were also honored.

The program was introduced by Agwu M. Okali, a Nigerian, the director of the New York office of Habitat. Then we were addressed in French by Antoine Blanca, the Director General for Development and International Economic Cooperation. A message was also read from Dr. Arcot Ramachandran, the Executive Director of the United Nations Center for Human Settlements which is located in Nairobi, Kenya, pointing out that shelter and health go together: "10,000 people," he informed us "die every day from diseases and accidents directly attributed to inadequate shelter." Ms. Polly Bergen charmed everyone with big smiles and perfect diction as she presented the citation to Sr. Peg. Then we were all "wined and dined," shown the great halls of the General Assembly of the United Nations and Security Council and, lest we forget, small displays of melted matter from the ashes of Nagasaki where the citizens and the houses were incinerated in 1945.

On this World Habitat Day, it was easy enough to sense deeply that this planet is our home and that all humans are vulnerable and need adequate shelter upon it. One billion of our brothers and sisters still lack it. It was October 2nd, the feast of Our Guardian Angels in our Catholic tradition. A good day for praying to God that the Angels of Light dwell within the walls of the world. A good day for praying that we might let God share in building the walls so as not to labor in vain. A good day in these times of homelessness and Hugo, crack houses in our cities and earthquakes in San Francisco, China, Armenia, and across the world, to ponder the present prostitution of houses in raw real estate greed which can only bring world-wide devastation. We have to sense again that shelter is a sacred right and that a home is a sacred place where the Angels of Light should be invoked before the gas and electricity are turned on.

I wonder, is there a Guardian Angel for Camden, NJ...maybe one with drooping wing. The drooping wing is surely the half-hearted effort of our faith and prayer to call into action the ever-ready power of God. "Move the stone!" Jesus ordered at the grave of Lazarus. We have to put our hand to Camden (helpless as it seems) before God will bring this corpse of a city to its feet. Pray that "the Angels of Light dwell within these walls" to ensure their renovation and brighten up the dark gutted windows with new life and light.

The "Angels of Light" are beginning to brighten up a bit of Camden. Thousands of "corpses" remain entombed… awaiting hands to "move the stone."

New life in old walls! That's our goal. "May the angels of God's light dwell within these walls! May they always dwell within your own! Amen.

Michael Doyle

Edna

A pound of nails,
Points poking my hand
From a broken bag
I was in Olsen's
And Edna was there.
Hardware everywhere
Cardboard boxes
Buried in dust,
And old stuff…
Waiting like a spinster's hand
For the touch of a handyman.
Buzzers, locks and iron grill
Bars and a barking dog, kill
Welcome, until Edna speaks.
Soft as cotton wool among her nuts
And bolts and metal things.
A petal left on a rusting rock
Dying there among her stock.

"Ye'll Have More Tea!"

November, 1989

Hi!

"Will ya," my father used to say, "is a bad fella." An old saying handed down for generations in the Irish language, it emphasized that making the visitor decide whether to have tea or not was a hindrance to hospitality. The visitor's words were, "Ah, you shouldn't have bothered," as she or he accepted the mug of tea and the piece of homemade bread. "A drop in yer hand," such an offering was always called.

My mother loved to say "Ye'll have more tea!" as she came with her teapot to refill the mug. In September 1983, the last time I saw her, three months before she died, when her mind had faded into deep silence, those four words would come when almost all her words were gone. "Ye'll have more tea!"

One morning as I sat at the kitchen table having breakfast and she sat near the stove she said: "Ye'll have more tea!" Now the teapot – a small one – was within my reach on the stove. But I knew she wanted to pour it and it was a moment of communion before she slipped away again into her holy world. She put her hand on the teapot, tried to lift it, but wasn't able. I didn't say anything. Then she turned, went to the drawer, and came back with a knife. A knife! "Oh," I thought to myself, "my poor mother... her great mind is gone ...all gone." Not so fast! She walked to the teapot on the stove, took the handle in her right hand and with her left put the back of the blade under the spout and with her two hands lifted the teapot and poured the mug of tea. It was the last thing she ever did for me in this world. It will be with me as long as my mind is.... My mother caring to the end and this last bright spot in the dull dark that veiled her final days. Her ingenuity upon which she always relied, intact still, when all else was in tatters. Above all, the faithful generosity of her helping hand.

I recall these stories because I know none that can better set the mood of the coming season of Christmas when we together create "a bright spot in the dull dark" of greed and indifference that trample our days and rob our lives. It is the season of ultimate hospitality. Our eyes and our windows and our hearts will be bright with the lights of worldwide welcome.

In the holy moment of supreme hospitality, the angel Gabriel didn't say, "Will ya," but "Mary, you have found grace with God. You shall conceive in your womb and bring forth a son and you shall name him Jesus. He shall be great and shall be called the Son of the Most High" (Luke 1:30). And Mary, if she were from Connemara would have said, "You shouldn't have bothered. It's too good you are." She did say: "Be it done unto me according to your word!" (Luke 1:38). The alignment of creation with its creator. The grandest acceptance in all the world of God's most awesome invitation.

Michael Doyle

A Candle Burning in a Bitter Wind

February, 1990

Hi!

My great-grandfather, Johnny Doyle, was born in 1841, the only son of Pat Doyle and Catherine Campbell. I am happy that he first saw the light of day on that richly nourishing day of candles and light and enlightenment that is February 2nd. Candlemas Day. It is a wonderful day of profound and magical meaning. Coming 40 days after Christmas Day, it is the midway point between the Winter Solstice and the Spring Equinox. The "hinge of the year," it is called because the curved cosmic door of this northern hemisphere is half closed by the darkness of winter and half opened to the brightness of Spring. The groundhog of Punxsutawney, PA, comes out to check his shadow and sometimes—most times in fact—he doesn't see it. By some shy mystery there is no shadow because there is not enough light.

On February 2nd, we recall the gospel story of Mary and Joseph bringing Jesus to present him in the temple of Jerusalem when he was a child of 40 days. Waiting there were Simeon and Anna, old and weary with the waiting, Adam and Eve, as it were, in the weeds of what went wrong. The whole world waited in a winter of terrible discontent.

Simeon looked at the child and knew that God had come. He took him in his arms and immediately the crust of his chest and this old earth were warmed and opened and flooded with emotion. The sharp brown eyes, deep-set beneath the brows of the years, glistened at the feel and the face of the sacred child. Hope heaved and sighed and soft rain fell on the fields of the world. Simeon looked at the young mother to whom life had come like light in a window and told her that she would be pierced by a shadow that would break her heart.

My great-grandfather was only six years old in 1847 when a fungus accidentally carried to Ireland from the United States killed the potato crop, and the smell of death spread irreparably across the land. A million people died and a million more boarded ships for foreign lands...coffin ships they were, many of them, where starving people died from disease of every kind. A cluster of 12 childbearing Doyle families in my neighborhood before the famine, was cut to four in a few short years. However, little Johnny Doyle survived. Thanks be to God. One tiny candle held out in the cold and biting wind.

He grew. A small man, strong as an ox, who carried his plough on his shoulders, tilled his bogland furrows, and raised three sons, strong as he. He almost lived long enough to see the end of British landlords and some of Ireland free. He died in 1921.

I am writing this on a waiting jet, delayed on the ground in Tampa Airport. Right now, it cannot reverse, which it must, before it can go forward. Nevertheless, my mind has no such problem. It goes back to the Candlemas child of 1841 and the young man in the famine-frightened fields with a donkey and two-wheel cart. The long-eared one refusing often to go backward through the gap. But I am convinced that God always sends new life to get us started when we're stopped, to warm old chests that are cold, and re-seed old fields that are fallow.

Consequently we must fix old houses that are gutted and bring back the Camdens that are lost. God always helps us to renew our tattered dreams. Let us grow old, then, counting Springs...with more trust because we have seen their faithful comings.

Just now (11:20 a.m. February 10, 1990) the plane began to reverse. At 11:23 a.m. it's going forward. At 11:28 it's in the air – 90 minutes late. Johnny Doyle is in his cart and his donkey is on her way

Back along that wholesome line of life that ties you so umbilically to all the folks who bred and fed the branches of your tree, we salute especially the faithful ones who, against all the odds, kept the candle burning in the bitter wind.

I thank you, Johnny Doyle, great-grandfather of my life. I thank you from my seat above the sun-lit clouds. Thirty thousand feet above the donkey cart. But I see you there, going where you're going and getting there...with an everlasting candle in your hand.

Bless me, holy man, as I go by!

Michael Doyle

The Coulter Man
(excerpt)

My grandfather with clay brown boots
Big, whang tied — "Liberty" he always sought
In shoes — strides to the headland
Where the burlapped oats awaits
Mud-daubed corduroys, harrowed flat
By ash made loy and spade
Where left-handed Doyles on hardy knees
Levered centuries of wet rush land
Gallowses stretching from odd-sized buttons
A man of fields and the feel of land
His huge hands broadened by evolving need
To scoop the golden oats and sow the seed.

Hope from the Ashes

March, 1990

Hi!

John Lyons, our oldest parishioner, died on March 15 at 96. Less we are without him. He was an Irishman in Camden because the blood in his veins came from Galway and Mayo. The world walked in green when we waked him; his tie for the last mile, a strip of shamrocks. Four days before he closed them forever, he opened his bright blue eyes in Lourdes Hospital in Camden and said: "Hi Father! How is Sacred Heart?" It is a good question, John! A good question for Lent!

Well, we are here! As Dan Berrigan says: "Don't just do something! Stand there!" We have been standing here on the corner of Broadway and Ferry since 1886...eight or nine years before you got to your feet, John. We have had more than a hundred Lents and more than a hundred Easters. Each one in the Spring of the passing years, called us back to life. Called us back to begin again.

This year on February 28th, Ash Wednesday, we daubed on the ashes again to remind ourselves, lest we forget, that life comes from buried bulbs, bodies, and seeds. On that day, Wilma Carr (55), our neighbor and parishioner, was dying with as much dignity as anyone has amidst the medical machines of an ICU. "I'll be going soon," she said. "Where are you going Wilma?" I asked. "I'm going to the Lord," she said, as casually as if she were going to the store. Probably for a poor woman like Wilma Carr...with less anxiety. Her friend, Gail Gooney, coming from Sacred Heart with ashes, touched her forehead to Wilma's. The daub of death met the pain of death and Wilma's word was: "I love you." It arose from the ashes...valid as Easter in the morning.

Memories of our dead haiku poet, Nick Virgilio – misty still in the year since he died – rise to the mind. His haiku:

> *my palsied mother,*
> *pressing my forehead on hers*
> *this Ash Wednesday.*

Wilma died on March 11th. How is Sacred Heart? That's how it is, John!

Two men from the neighborhood were arrested the other day – Pee Wee and Duck – for deliberately setting fire to two men and a woman while they slept in two abandoned houses on Arlington Street. The men died. The woman was badly burned. Fires continue to make ashes of our hopes. I knew one of the men. "Teabags," they always called him. He did work for me. A great fisherman, always smiling...killed on March 15, his 34th birthday. His name, Preston Frederick Fleming, Jr. It was a name you could see in lights. But it's hard to see the lights with the ashes in your eyes and yet, at the word of Jesus, the blind washed their eyes with mud and saw clearly. But how much mud! The word at the Laundromat here today was the murdered prostitute found on a nearby vacant lot this morning. How is Sacred Heart? It's heartbroken John, sometimes!

Here in the neighborhood, a few yards from the church, is a street of dilapidation called Emerald. A woeful block indeed! Our Heart of Camden Housing is determined to renovate five houses there. Three buildings have been demolished and we are planning to establish a garden where the rubble and the garbage (ashes) were. Maybe we will plant a cross first. It seems to work when Eden (or Emerald) goes to weeds. Part of the garden will grow fruits and flowers for our altar on Sunday. This garden will be an earth-altar-garden proclaiming for Earth Day and all days that our Earth is the great altar of all offerings, demanding the care and reverence that God first intended. One of the buildings we demolished had housed the man who was convicted for killing Edith Rose Orsini on October 13, 1984, as she sat on her stoop at 427 Emerald Street. There is lambs' blood on the doorposts of Emerald Street. We will plant a rose. Another demolished building on that Street was formerly DelBuono's Bakery. Years of decaying garbage have long since wiped away the living smells of baking bread. "Unless the grain of wheat falls to the earth and dies, it remains just a grain of wheat. But if it dies it produces much fruit" (John 12:23). Beneath the brittle oven bricks of DelBuono's, is the earth, ever there, ever ready to grow wheat again. And a vine too for bread and wine and resurrection.

How is Sacred Heart? It is always struggling to live, John. And, as you know better than I, Christ rises from the dead and ultimately all is well. May His Easter blessing of Everlasting Life come upon you, John, and Wilma, Teabags, and Dave, Nick, and Edith, and the poor nameless one in the vacant lot! Come, Holy Easter, with the best of all blessings for everyone!

The Meeting
(excerpt)

Two old men meet again in the evening of their lives,
As death arrives in the rain, stands at a decent distance,
And demands that one, the weaker one come away,
The other, stronger, may stay a little longer…

An old worn hand rests on the other's chest
And bones bind the two in a bond unbreakable,
Strong as the long sinews of the spirit
That clay or decay can in no way diminish.
They talk not of ache or age, of ill fate or finished state

Jobs done, wars won, the way they were, no, none of these,
But their church, time there, in work and prayer,
Their part at Sacred Heart, stored still.
All else they had, gone bad, except this spirit stuff,
This better bread. Enough, to hold them over 'til they're dead.
Cyril, flattened on the bed, said:
"John, I'll soon be gone. But I'm not afraid.
I'm not afraid to die.
Tell them! Tell them, I said good-bye."

Keep the Fire on the Hearth

June, 1990

Hi!

On March 6,1887, at the first Mass celebrated in Sacred Heart Church in Camden, Michael Joseph O'Farrell, the bishop of our diocese which was Trenton then, read the passage from the Bible about Jacob's Ladder (Gen. 28). A great story it is. Jacob, "when the sun had set," picked a stone from the place where he was, fell asleep with his head resting on it, and dreamed of a ladder reaching to heaven with angels on the rungs going up and down. He poured oil on the stone in the morning and consecrated it as a memorial of his meeting with God. Michael Joseph O'Farrell poured oil on a slab of marble in Sacred Heart on March 6th, 1887.

This stuff is on my mind because I just gave a talk in Boston (a keynote address, no less) in that grand old Episcopal Church of the Trinity in Copley Square. I have become "an international expert" on the restoration of sacred buildings which was the subject of the conference called Sacred Trusts 111 in Boston. Three years ago I spoke on the subject in Philadelphia, two years ago in Ottawa, Canada, and this year in Boston, and so I could say the following in my opening remarks: "If it is fitting that I, rather than someone else, should give the keynote address to this distinguished assembly, which will in the next three days, exchange hours upon hours of professional ideas about the stewardship and preservation of sacred properties, it is perhaps because I know almost nothing about these very important things." So much for the expert!! Why then do I get invited? Well, maybe it's the accent or the stories or the combination of both. Anyway, I did ask an important question in Boston which my friend Fr. Thaddeus Sapio had asked of me a couple of weeks ago. "How many Irishmen does it take," he asked, "to change a light bulb?" I, thinking I knew, said, three. One to hold the bulb and two to twist the ladder. "No," he corrected, "it takes four Irishmen to change a light bulb. One to twist in the new bulb and three to talk about the grand old bulb that now is no more." A plan of preservation would do much more to keep the grand old bulb beaming or a grand old church standing.

The heart of my talk was that the best way to keep a hearth going is to keep a fire burning. Indeed there is not much point in restoring an old hearth unless you light a fire on it to warm the people.

When I came to Sacred Heart several years ago (I told the crowd in Boston) my hair was red and the church's dark roof had many leaks. Now the church has a new roof. It's red, and look at me! Anyway, on my very first day at Sacred Heart I entered the church and there was a banner with many words hanging in front of the beautiful old sanctuary lamp. (God protect us from banners of many words.) The first thing I did was to climb a ladder to let the old light shine. So the restoration of a church calls for the restoration of genuine ritual. There must be good signs and symbols and stories in the midst of the stones and the trusses and the timbers. Nothing is so needed in the midst of the monstrous distractions of this age, in which we are blinded by so much visual pollution and battered into submission by the curse of excessive amplification...nothing is so needed as authentic living symbols and rituals that go beneath our proud and fallible intellects and touch the core of our consciousness. (You see I can get carried away when I am let loose in Boston.) But at Sacred Heart we have tried and we are still trying to build a good fire on our aging hearth... good celebration within the sacred old walls of our church.

I noticed at the conference that there wasn't one word among the many workshops about the restoration of tired old pastors. Maybe they just fall asleep like Jacob and dream of ladders. Hopefully not just the ones up to their sagging gutters but all the way to God.

Right now we are putting new gutters on Sacred Heart and digging new drainage lines to keep the terrible downpours off our brownstone walls and foundations. Our church is in great need of plaster and paint and restoration of the beautiful canvas paintings on the ceilings. The poor need beauty as well as bread. I know you will help us. As Solzhenitsyn once said, taking a line from Dostoevsky, "there are three things that will save the world, truth, goodness, and beauty, and if the first two fail, beauty will do it." It contains the other two.

Our "Sacred Hearth" is well worth saving because the fire on it is bright and beautiful.

Michael Doyle

The Beauty of a Rusting Roof
(excerpt)

But I look at many aging sheds
And feel the feel I felt at ten
As autumn brings her paint and brush
I love what rust has done to them.
The mirror use to be my friend
My hair was chestnuts in the fall
But now the winter snow has come
To blanket chestnuts leaves and all.
So I wish my head was like a shed
Silver-gray when it was young
And when the weather had its fun
A lovely rust when the day is done

Putting Wings on Eager Minds

August, 1990

Hi!

I'm just back in Camden after being home in Ireland. I am fortunate, thank God, that I can go back to the farm where I was born. It is never easy to return to Camden, and for many years now, no matter what time my trans-Atlantic flight gets into New York, I do not come into Camden until late at night. I ease in quietly. The change from the soft fields of my childhood to the hard glass-strewn sidewalks of Camden is harsh indeed.

Reality hits quickly enough. But I get strength every time I go home and dip my toes in the stream where my tiny steps began. I went to the bog a few weeks ago and gathered turf (peat) for the kitchen fire, and with my two nieces I mowed the long grass on the graves of my parents in Colmcille churchyard. We brought the grass home to a heifer that is expecting her first calf in the small field by the back door. She whisked it into her mouth with obvious pleasure and I know my father and mother were smiling that the grass of their graves was feeding the future in a young black and white cow. I visited the old Latin School of Moyne where I spent my teenage years. When I started it, it was a rare two-room link to the old revered "Hedge-schools." They were the underground schools maintained by people when, by English law, education was a crime in Ireland.

But life clung in holes dark as wombs
Waiting for a window in the world.
The sun was not allowed to shine
On the dark awful hours of the mind.
But it found a way to steal between the clouds
And shone on the north side of hedges
In valleys where the young wore the moss
From the stones where they sat
And listened to the lark above the meadow
And there a great underground teacher
With his learned head above the clay
Made new worlds with his words
That put wings on eager minds
To sunshine fields far away
From the thatch dripping eaves of the night.

Education was never a crime in this country (except for slaves), but a God-centered public school is illegal so Catholic schools struggle desperately to stay alive, particularly in the inner cities. The costs are mounting despite sacrificial efforts to keep them down.

The sun will find a way to shine on the dark awful hours of the mind. Teachers will be found down in Camden to put wings on eager minds to sunshine fields far away. God always finds a way. As the holy gospel proclaims, "I am the way, the truth and the life."

Michael Doyle

"I Want to Grow Up and Do Good"

October, 1990

Hi!

You have become accustomed to the tone and the texture of these letters over the years. It is a tone of sadness that gives a glimpse in the haze of things at the unfinished fellow that I am. A melancholy boy that gazed at the dying fire on the hearth when sleep had quieted all the others, and found peace in the wet glimmer of leafless trees and half cracked chestnuts carried away on the brown streams of winter. Still unchanged as I turn 56 on the feast of Malachy when two hands of fingers can no longer tell my age as they have done for over half a century. I have to turn to my toes.

I have a great fear of satisfaction. I think it is a deadly disease. Nikos Kazantzakis says in The Saviors of God: "Suddenly, the Cry tears at our entrails once more, like an eagle. The Cry is not outside us. It sits in the center of our hearts, and cries out. God shouts: 'Burn your houses! I am coming! Burn your ideas, smash your thoughts! Whoever has found the solution cannot find me!'"

Sacred Heart parish turned 105 on Saturday, the 13th, and I want to declare again that the sanctuary lamp is lit and the coffee pot is on, but we still seek solutions. It was an impoverished place when it started and it broke the health of its first pastor. But the area thrived on the building of battleships. We lived off the sword and died as Jesus predicted. This year our country will spend more than $290 billion in military expenses while thousands of Camden children live in a "bombed out" city where the housing projects are concentrated for the poor. It's a tragedy. People are being killed in large numbers in our bankrupt cities while the military spends almost a billion dollars a day and uses 200,000 men and women to erect a "desert shield" around the price of a gallon of oil.

Cry! We all should cry. "We must mend," says Camus "what has been torn apart, and make justice imaginable again in a world so obviously unjust." This poor planet is sagging with the weight of its weapons. If I only had the money that goes into one tank, I wouldn't be begging from you for our dear children. Oh, God help us! Just as soon as the cold front began to melt in the Russian snow and we hoped at last that maybe cities and children would be more important than bombs and bullets, our country rushed off and erected a hot front in the sand. To hell with the cities, the children, and a cure for cancer!

So here I am still! Your melancholy beggar-man pleading for the children of Sacred Heart!

Michael Doyle

The Girl on Gelsha Hill

November, 1990

Hi!

In 1925, my mother's brother, Hughie Creegan, the fifth son in a great family of eight boys and five girls, was walking up Gelsha Hill in North Longford to visit his sister, Kate. There, he "met for the first time a lassie walking down the hill with her bike because the tire was flat." Hughie fixed the puncture for Mary Jane Tunney and she rode off. But not too far! They finally parted 56 years later in December of 1981 when Hughie died. They had raised eight children who in turn raised 31 children. I am always amazed at the wonderful little ways that God works. I think the Holy Spirit must be the Holy Organizer of Coincidences, who pulls good out of the chance concurrence of the bits and pieces of lives and events as they whirl in the wild orbit of it all.

Hughie would never have met the girl on Geisha Hill but for a flat tire on her bike. She would have passed him like the wind if she had had air in that tire.

So, I suppose, if Sacred Heart had air in all its wheels and wasn't slowed by flats and blowouts, you and I would not meet so often on either side of pathetic appeals.

Sometimes I think of Sacred Heart as a stool with four legs; one or two of them always a little shorter than the other. But that is a static view. We may wobble but we do move. A better image would be a durable old Model T with bald tires and at least one tire always very low and all tires needing air.

The four wheels upon which we run are 1) The liturgical-sacramental ministry; 2) The school that attempts to give a God-centered education to poor children in Camden; 3) Food for the needy every month and right now people are asking "when do we sign up for the Christmas baskets?" 4) The Heart of Camden, which has renovated 35 houses in five years to sell at cost to needy families without profit or interest. It is working now on 15 houses and has five or six waiting for a church or a corporation or any group to take them on.

If we didn't have this national feast of Thanksgiving, Sacred Heart would have to invent it. But we have one here every Sunday, every day in fact, as we thank God for you and hold your hopes and needs in our hands and hearts in the Holy Eucharist. You are a bright beat in the Heart of Christ.

Thanks, Hughie Creegan, for stopping to lend a hand to the girl with the flat on Gelsha Hill! God blessed you abundantly. It is surely not as charming to stop and help an "old Model T" that's down to the rims on the hard road. But many people give a hand to the Heart, time and time again. You help us...and off we go with air in our tires and the wind in our hair.

"Thanks be to God for the flat," said Hughie Creegan. "If we had no trouble we wouldn't meet you at all."

Michael Doyle

Blessed Baskets

December, 1990

Hi!

"Down by the Salley Gardens" was not only in William Butler Yeat's poem but was also a special spot among the nooks and sheltered coves of my childhood. But my garden had no romance beyond the croak of frogs or the song of birds and no lovers bigger than finches ever met by the branches. Each year my father cut the Spring's new growth of salleys for mending old baskets and making new ones. Creels we called them, and two of them astride a plodding donkey was mass transportation in many parts of Ireland a century ago.

I loved to watch Johnny Brennan of Smear weaving my father's fresh salleys into a strong creel that would carry peat and potatoes for many a day.

I have baskets on my mind because last Tuesday, November 20, John Waterhouse drove from Vineland to Sacred Heart with 800 baskets that we bought in Hammonton, NJ. They too have a fresh, new look about them, white as pine, hooped with stripes of red and green. Christmas baskets! Empty! But we will fill them

Christmas, despite all its excessive commercialism, is the most glorious period of collective generosity on the earth. People seek to make people happy with gifts to them and blessings on them. It is an opportunity when that which we truly are, comes to the surface, for one shining moment. Too soon, it's gone...in the mad traffic and the mean economic methods of the world. Again, we know it is there. It is the time when the face of God appears in the face of the earth. We all add a bit to the crinkle and the sparkle of that Holy Countenance.

On November 27, the sign-up for the Christmas baskets started at Sacred Heart with block-long lines. This year the people, mostly women, walked past our new outdoor statue of the Mother of God, which was donated and blessed on September 8, 1990. From the start, she was entitled "Our Lady of Camden" by Father Leonard Carrieri who created her. To the women of Camden (from whom Leonard drew her face) she looks familiar. She is in stride, walking down the world with a look of quiet determination on her face and a big basket in her hand. The basket is full of food. Beneath her clothes, her body bulges slightly with the Child. Another wonderful basket! The weave of the womb within! Two baskets! Full! And Christmas baskets, they both surely are.

Michael Doyle

Excerpt of Michael Doyle's Closing Statement

Seven of you are women. You know in a woman's way the meaning of life, the rhythms of life, what it takes to bear a child and rear it. You know something that I don't know. You have seen the consequence of war in the last half-century and you are part of an American people. You are free people and you can make a decision and it will hold and it will make a difference.
Camden 28 Trial 1973

A Fallen World

February, 1991

Hi!

On October 14, 1985, at 2:05 PM, five minutes after Sacred Heart's Third-Grade children went outside for an unscheduled break, the heavy metal and concrete ceiling of their classroom fell on their desks with a terrible crash. The children went outside, thanks be to God, because their teacher wanted to reward them because they had been good, and the Fall day was bright and beautiful. The opposite of both situations was easily and often the case. The collapse of the ceiling was caused by heavy equipment (30 tons in weight) used to dig trenches in a nearby street for a pipe that is seven feet in diameter. Through that pipe Camden County now sends down its sewage to be stored and treated in this neighborhood. Sixty million gallons every day. Almost every toilet in Camden County is lined up for us and so every flush of 400,000 people is sent to us. To Camden! To Camden! To Camden! And thus the raw sewage comes here and its odors often permeating our air, our noses, and the places where we must live and breathe. It is sent here (and soon all the trash of the county will be burned here as well) because anything that would lessen real estate values in the county is dumped on the poor in Camden. Not one penny of taxes is paid on the 40 acres of riverfront property on which the county sewage facility is located in the city. The whole thing is unjust, and smacks of a mean indifference that has its roots in greed and racism. The big machine that came in to dig up Viola Street and almost killed our children, wasn't here to help Camden but to create a channel to flush hundreds of thousands of toilets away from better neighborhoods and into our own.

Why am I writing about this? Because the thought of the falling ceiling, that by some miracle of God, did not crush our children to death, fills me with a terrible sadness as I think of the children of the Middle East. One never has the right to endanger the lives and limbs of the innocent children with massive bombings or to crush their nerves with terror in the skies above them. Oh, how evil it all is!

And the big machine that came crashing into our neighborhood to pipe sewage away from better places, reminds me of all the efforts that are being made to liberate oil and money in the Middle East. As some kid's sign said in Glassboro the other day: "How many lives per gallon, George?" Or as old Frank Messina mentioned a short time ago: looking at his son he said to me: "I wouldn't let that man die for all the oil in the world." Better still, I wouldn't let that man kill for all the oil in the world.

Oh, God help us again! Massive power is like meat in the sun. It always goes bad. The colossal damage done to the earth and humankind by the empires of all time is staggering. For example, Ireland still bleeds from the brutal division and oppression of the former English Empire. Iraq is bleeding today from the same British interference that set up Kuwait and cut off Iraq almost completely from the Gulf. Now, with self-righteous arrogance, England, with the US, wants to bomb Iraq to liberate it.

War is such a deadly trap. It is so evil—more barbaric now than ever before in our human existence on the planet. Old men are still eager to send young men to kill and be killed. And when the old men send the young men and women out to the killing fields, the young take the hearts and concerns of their loved ones with them. And so all are caught up in the tragedy.

It seems that our society has been manipulated into believing that killing other young men and women that are forced to war is good. Iraqi mothers and fathers will weep for years to come and North American mothers and fathers will weep the same salty tears. Quick War! The sand will be snow before the hate of this one cools in the Middle East.

Oh, how isolated we all have become in the breakdown of almost all community! Now we hunger for even the shallow unity of a super bowl of football or a super bowl of war in prime time. Now the balls are bombs and the touchdowns are massive explosions.

I had always hoped that TV would show us the blood of war on T-shirts in the living room so that powerful old men could no longer fool us and send our children to die while they don't get a scratch or their children either. But TV now loves its captive audience and is promoting the war for its own profit. There's a lot of money to be made if you get a lot of people interested in anything.

This demon of war-madness will not be cast out by presidential prayers to a universal God or by the yellow ribbons of "our side" at the war game, but by a national fast to open our hearts to the God of Iraq and the God of the United States who is the same God of all the world. We must fast before we pray on this one.

Camden is and will continue to be the casualty of war—the victim of the waste of the weapons makers and users. The body count for murder in the US for 1990 is 23,000.) A lot of body bags. I still have pictures of the scene, the day the falling ceiling bent the metal desks in our Third-Grade classroom. On the floor that day, on its side, was the toppled globe of the world.

"Lord, make us instruments of Your peace!" Not any version we concoct.

Michael Doyle

Original Blessing
(excerpt)

It was the serpent that got between people
And poisoned the hands that reached out
To stiffen in fingers of pointing
And trust into glances of doubt
No more is the earth into icons
But ploughs into bullets instead
The smoke does not rise like incense
The smell is the smell of the dead.

Others Will be Towed

March, 1991

Hi:

Eugene O' Donnell, the famous fiddler from Derry came to Mass at Sacred Heart last Sunday as he often does. You may have heard his music. His renditions of Irish airs create surges of sweetness and sadness that can start sighs in the stars. Well, he arrived on Sunday. No fiddle! Instead, a green and white sign for the churchyard. "Parking for Irish Only. All Others Will Be Towed." Eugene can pluck the funny bones of our feelings as well as tug at the heartstrings of our sorrows. The sign!! Ridiculous! And yet...

I like the sign at this time of the year, when we celebrate St. Patrick and everyone is invited to be Irish and park within the open field of a worldwide feast. Some no doubt may cheapen its meaning with too much loud green nonsense.

But there is inspiration for everyone in the song and story and long struggle of the people to achieve independence for a tiny island the size of Maine. There is a kinship with a friendly people and the waves of laughter that rise above the depths of a long sadness. The rain-drenched fields of Ireland always sparkle when the sun comes out and dries the tears from every leaf. But no sun ever lifts the sadness of the Motherland mourning the loss of her children and the cruel division of her household by foreign intrusion. As Tommy Makem's song says: "Her four green fields. One of them's in bondage," still.

Now, as I, Michael Doyle, celebrate St. Patrick's Day, I must be aware that my first name, which is Hebrew, means "who is like God?" and my last name, "Doyle" (Dubh Gall in Irish), means "black foreigner." Not quite an endearing title when those Scandinavians got it in Wexford 900 years ago. But the black foreigners who came in armor (that's why they were black) in one century were more Irish than the Irish in the next. So, I don't want the flag of Norway planted in my father's field, or the flag of Iraq forced on Philadelphia or the flag of England forced on part of Ireland. So the everlasting word of the Irish to the English is, as it was to all previous invaders: "Be Irish in Ireland or leave!"

We can not blame the English people today for the pride and greed of their past empire that meddled so much in the world and gave us the Kuwaits and Northern Irelands. Invasions make wounds that don't heal and sow seeds of deadly discontent. But England needs to give a date (even if it is 2010) for the departure of its troops and its dominance from Ireland. The two warring factions in the North will in time have to make the best of it. They will have to come together eventually. Paddy Doherty of Derry says: "the marriage cannot be consummated while the third party is in the room." England must prepare to go.

So, on this St. Patrick's Day, I would like to enlarge Eugene's sign over that precious bit of Ireland that is "in bondage." Let it say: Be Irish in Ireland (and English in England)! If you don't want to be Irish in Ireland you should be towed. Carefully always, with the least amount of damage to your car.

Michael Doyle

Celebrating the Rebirth of Ourselves

May, 1991

Hi!

"We will celebrate the baby's first birthday in this house." The woman saying these words was standing in a hip-high carpet of garbage that covered every square inch of the house she was in. That goes for two floors, not to mention the basement, which was beyond what is mentionable. It was a gray brick building in the 400 block of Webster Street in Camden, and once upon a time it was a home with warmth and beauty and the dignity of life. Abandoned and abused, it was put on the auction block with an opening bid of $1,000. Nobody bid against me. Sold in seconds. Now, Sacred Heart owned it. Not lock, stock, and barrel! Just it and its garbage.

The year was the winter of early 1985. Hoa Bui needed a home. The baby in her arms needed a home as well. Thanhan was three months old. I had toyed with the idea of having the "house" cleaned out before I showed it to her. Would she turn and run from the rats, real or imagined, beneath the piles that surrounded her? But she stood her ground with her baby tucked carefully to her chest and said simply: "We will celebrate the baby's first birthday in this house."

We did. Nine months later, on November 30, we celebrated it in a beautiful home. Thanhan waddled around and plopped on a new soft carpet. Kitchen smells of cooking food filled the air. Light was bright in the windows of the house and in the eyes of all who were in it. Thanhan's father was so happy that he could not eat anything. But many others made up for him. They were the Heart of Camden volunteers who worked on it. The house was blessed, room by room, with special prayers for each. It is our custom, in a Heart of Camden house blessing, that those who fixed the kitchen are the ones to sprinkle holy water on it and so on for all the other areas.

After the meal was eaten, a teenage boy picked up his guitar and the Vietnamese people began to sing the songs of their homeland. Far, far away they were from the rice fields of Vietnam. Far from the homes they were reared in and the parents some would never see again. So they sang songs and strung out the lifelines that tied them to all that ever nurtured them. It was a long and treacherous journey they had made to this battered street in Camden, NJ, but food and drink and song and, above all, a house of their own, had bonded them back to all that gave them their start and linked them forward to the life that lay ahead.

This house was the Heart of Camden's first venture on the 400 block of Webster Street, and a blessed one it was. Today we have six houses restored on that block and volunteers from Sacred Heart Church are working every Saturday on number seven. On Sunday, June 2, at 12:30 PM, we will have a celebration at the corner of Webster and Holcaine in which we will celebrate the restoration of eight more houses. All told, 14 homes completed there and two to be finished later. A great advancement since a young mother and baby stood in desolation and invited salvation. "This day, salvation has come to your house" (Luke 19:9).

Sr. Peg Hynes, the Director of the Heart of Camden Housing, says, "After doing 46 houses in six years, we have learned a lot. We learn every day." Our goal is to change renters into owners and achieve stability in our neighborhood. We seek simply to promote human development through urban renewal. We charge no interest and we make no profit. We've had two failures in five years, but we learned from them. We learned that everyone is not capable of home ownership. But, house by house, we build our hope that one day, Camden will be restored.

Above all, the restoration of a home restores the volunteers who restore it. We need churches, institutions, factories, any group to take a house in Camden and bring it back to life. It takes about a year and a half, Saturday by Saturday. Of course, all depends on its condition.

I wish everyone in the U.S. had the joy of helping to bring a house that was dead back to life. All it takes is summed up in what Sr. Peg calls the three M's: money, materials, and muscle (volunteers). Sr. Peg can work with any approach. Oh, it takes faith too and a bit of openness to the cry of a mother and child in Nazareth or Detroit or Webster Street, Camden. That's what it takes! The payoff: we celebrate the rebirth of ourselves in the houses we renovate.

Michael Doyle

The Woman

"You're not born a woman,"
Says de Beauvoir, "you become one."
Well!
Shall the stream always bathe the stone
Swirling for her life around
Soothing corners to be smooth
Letting ancient granite bones
Penetrate her eager flow?
NO!
She will wear the stones to sand
Until they join the cosmic flow
Moving slower than the water
But onward with her to the shore.

The Loss of Moss

July, 1991

Hi!

The air in Sacred Heart Church is not conditioned by any cooling invention. It is conditioned by an atmosphere that is polluted by trucks and trash and the smells of a sewage treatment plant. It was so hot here, that at Mass last Sunday, when the gospel reading had Jesus urging his overly active disciples to take a break and "rest a while", I told the sweating people that I would offer them two choices. One was a homily (sermon), the other was a glass of cold spring water. "Me or the water", I bravely said. But I didn't wait for the answer. Smart! Two small carts loaded with containers of cold water moved up the aisle. We all drank. No sermon that I ever gave got more compliments than the cup of cold water. "By restful waters He leads them to revive their drooping spirits" (Psalm 22). I don't know what we will do if the blistering weather continues. One man jokingly suggested Italian ice for this coming Sunday. They might be asking for gin and tonic by the end of August.

My hope, all these years is, that my letters to you could be tiny bits of refreshment in the ongoing grind of our lives. "But", you say, "often they are not". Right enough! Sad little twists of thought sometimes!

It is a different world we live in than the one of ages past. Our poor antennatic (I made up the word) heads are trampled by a constant traffic jam of tragedies at home and abroad. And to all of it we have to have some approach. We might think of burying our heads but how long can ostriches live under sand? And if we try to deal with too much of it, we are soon burned out like moths on a headlight. So it is good to take a break - to come up for air or come down for a cup of cold water. It is the pause, that regular re-occurring Sabbath that saves our sanity. It is a stop to start again with more vigor than before. Some people drift into semi-comas and just hang there for life- times.

On Saturday, July 27th, we paused here to bless 1632 Ferry Ave. This row house is the 48th in the Heart of Camden's marvelous shoestring effort to rehabilitate abandoned houses around our church. People from St. Margaret's Church in Woodbury Heights, N.J. worked on this house for a long time and overcame many depressing difficulties to bring this "dead one" back to life. But God bless them, they persevered. This week twenty-one Baptist young people from churches around the State are working for the Heart of Camden fixing houses for several senior citizens. In addition, 90 young people in an organization called Evangelical Organization for the Promotion of Education have come to Camden to run nine summer camp programs for children. Several Jesuit volunteers are working in Camden as well. There are so many bits of good going on.

And yet, there is no hint whatever that all these bits of good are anywhere near the "critical mass" impact that would change the destructive way things are and seem to stay. There were eight shootings this weekend in this little town. What will it take for this generous great nation to wake up to its deadly plight? We have more murders, more rapes, more savage assaults, more prisoners and more money than any country in the world. However the vast amount of the slaughter is taking place in the lower economic slice of the population. And the largest slice has not become sufficiently worried yet. Our cities have become desperate concentration camps of poverty and violence and they will tear this nation apart if it does not deal with them. We need a massive change in our basic political and economic philosophy. Our enemy is not on some far away frontier but right in our own neighborhoods. Our war must be a war to stop the sad waste of human potential. If it is more expensive to be in jail than to go to Harvard (and it is) then we all should be locked up in Looneyville.

"Stop," says Jesus "and rest!" The people of this country have been too busy for a hundred years both at work and at play. Our drive for material security has made us too individualistic, too distracted, too easily manipulated by managers of minds and matter and too uncritical of the image makers and the high priests of the media message. There is no wellspring of wisdom coming up out of the ground level of our nation or at the grass roots level where everything nourishing starts.

The poet Seamus Heaney, when asked did he write any poetry during his annual semester at Harvard, replied: "There is no moss on the stones here." When I am dead and buried please put something on my grave that will block a lawn mower because I would rather have knee-high grass and weeds than a flat mat stone to accommodate the little mad lawn mower.

No moss on the stones here
Heaney, where our dead lined bones
Are whipped by the frenzied belts of greed,
Making needs to drive us mad.
When we had enough...more stuff!
When I die, make sure
My gravestone's not run over
When the lawn mower comes to mow!
I want the moss to grow
On the quiet letters of my name.

Michael Doyle

The Greatness of God in the Weakness We Are

August, 1991

Hi:

Jean Ritzke, a woman who lives in Camden, where she has borne many burdens in her effort to help the poor, chided me for my last letter. "You have many fellow warriors," she wrote, "many with the soul, if not the words, of poets. Know yourself as one of many, and one who is the voice of many. Do not be disheartened at the hopelessness of our task. Christ healed one leper at a time; there is much love but also a bit of hubris in your longing to achieve the 'critical mass.' You serve God, let Him decide what the results signify. It is in our weakness that we discover the greatness of God." I underlined the "bit of hubris." Hubris is Greek for pride. There is some pride, she says, in longing that many bits of good will achieve universal good. "Let God decide what the results signify!" You're right, Jean!

I was talking to our new principal, Janet Williams, about our school that will, with the help of God, open on September 4 for its 73rd year. The thought of that, doesn't make me feel much like a warrior. It makes me feel like the beggar I am. I was telling Janet about my first visit to a department store in New York City shortly after I "got off the boat" on September 14, 1959. There was a sale and my cousin Rosaleen Creegan was looking at a winter jacket. "That would be a great jacket for Danny," she said. Then she put it down. "Ah well! He doesn't get paid 'til Thursday." I was dumbfounded. My Irish image of the USA then was one of teeming wealth. That my cousin couldn't buy half the store, never mind a winter jacket, was an eye-opener for this immigrant destined for Camden, NJ. There, he would spend much of his life begging from those who have a little more for those who have, strangely enough, a lot less. Lots of time thanking people, too. The many, like yourself, who give drops of sweat and blood to the Sacred Heart. Like Shirley Howe, our great departing principal, who donated her last year, in its entirety and who will come this year to help when she can.

Dottie Realdine, that splendid lady who has been keeping our books for 20 years, gave us the final word on the cost of operating the school last year: $247,000. This year: $280,000. That's a lot of "winter jackets" in Camden. This place is not getting any better.

Harry Reasoner called about a year ago and asked if I thought 60 Minutes should come back to look at Camden. I said: "It's too soon. Nothing is really changed." I didn't want to tell him that it had gotten worse in the seven years since he was here. Now he's gone too. God rest him! But we still use his poignant words on our sponsorship form: 'People come to Sacred Heart. to this lonely church in a forlorn neighborhood. They bring food for the poor, money for the school and they listen to the priest plead for Camden."

This city is full of beautiful children...flowers they are, precious ones, trying to grow in very heavy traffic. I know you will help. As Jean Ritzke wrote: "It is in our weakness (poverty) that we discover the greatness of God." You have shown that greatness to us often and God bless you for it.

Michael Doyle

Charming Portraits of God

September, 1991

Hi:

Glancing over old letters from my mother, who died in 1983, I came across one that was written on July 5, 1965. Addressed to me at St. Peter Celestine Church, 402 N. Kings Highway, Cherry Hill, NJ, a quarter of a century ago, it seemed like something from another life. It's a long time since I left Kings Highway...I have been on Beggars Low-way for years.

Anyway, my mother wrote as follows: "We heard from Anna Mae (my late sister, Anna Mae Doyle) that you were back at the university and that, I am sure, accounts for the scarcity of time for letter writing." (Mothers do have a way of saying it.) "However, it is good to know you are well and able for the work laid out for you." (A mother's trust.) "It sure seems a long time since I dressed you in a velvet suit and set you off for Pulladoey School and you are cramming into that poor head of yours ever since." I was four and a half years old then and so it was "a long time." In July of 1965, it was 26 years since I started my two-mile walk to school with very short legs and very high hopes. In a black "velvet suit." She doesn't mention the white flat buttons as big as quarters. She made it on her old sewing machine, which was all she brought as a bride. That and her hands for the hard work and her heart with its hope for little boys and girls to bear and clothe and "set off" to school.

Millions of mothers and fathers have memories of those first mornings and the hopes that rode on those starting steps to school. Mothers and fathers are no less eager, this September, that their children get enough education to live worthy and creative lives.

The little boy in the black velvet suit and the big white buttons never knew when he learned to add and subtract, that he would be dealing with deficits in a poor town in rich America. But he learned to multiply too and discovered the meaning of his mother's wise words: "many hands make light work." Many contributions add up to make it easier for everyone..

The beauty of children and the verve and sparkling hope they bring to all of us, are surely one of the most charming portraits of God's work in the world. The diversity of their color and culture only adds to the goodness and universal innocence with which all children begin. Damage to a child through neglect, or poverty, is a loss without limit.

I need your help to get the sponsors. I never knew that I would be involved with school so long. It was 26 years in 1965 when my mother looked back at my first day. It is now 26 more years since she wrote that letter. Fifty two years since her little lad, velvet clad, toddled off on a happy morning. The moths of time have eaten my little velvet suit and the soft innocence it enclosed, but I do declare (regardless of all comments to the contrary) that I still have all my buttons.

Michael Doyle

Love Makes the Heart Sacred

October, 1991

Hi:

Two boys, Luan Vu, 12 and Chuong Vu, 11, left Vietnam with their mother on September 24 and after stopping in Bankok, arrived in Philadelphia, Pa., on September 26, 1991.

There, they were reunited with their father, Vuong, and their mother with her husband. It was seven years since that painful parting, when he said goodbye and escaped with the boat people. After seven days at sea, he reached safety in October, 1984. Little Luan was five and Chuong was four. Eventually, Vuong reached Camden and lived at 707 Morgan Boulevard, a Sacred Heart house. It is now the only occupied house on an abandoned block. There he lived and longed for the day when his family could come to him. Many times I saw him in Sacred Heart Church praying by the candle he had lit at the Sacred Heart shrine. Many times he cried. I knew what he was praying for. The years went by. Letters and pictures of his growing boys lifted his spirits when the mail came. Finally, his prayers were answered. On Sunday, September 29, 1991, he "floated" into Sacred Heart for the 10:30 Mass with his boys and their mother. Sheer indescribable joy emanated from him.

On Monday he took the children to H.B. Wilson School to register them. There was some misunderstanding. Then he took them to Sacred Heart. We accepted them.

On Sunday, October 6, when we celebrated human life from the first fusion of its existence to the full glory of its eternal attainment, I presented Luan and Chuong to the people of Sacred Heart as two smiling children with the right to life. Our school will help them to develop it. I promised that one year hence they will speak to the congregation of Sacred Heart on the first Sunday of October 1992. In English. They will, too.

I thank you for supporting our school in Camden. It is a school with a Heart. A school for Luan Vu and Chuong Vu and every other child who comes to the door from around the battered block or around the distant world.

It takes a lot of love to make a heart and a lot of love to make a Heart Sacred.

Michael Doyle

Clay in the Clouds
(excerpt)
O Holy deep-down Urging One!
You call the clay to be...
Knowing well my embryonic face is hidden
In the damp-dark of every lump of dust.
In every ant hill and ash-heap, I am,
In awesome Everest, or the tiny dunes
That children make from holes beside the sea.

Thanks for a Thousand Baskets!

January, 1992

Hi:

Viola Yocko! You never heard of Viola Yocko? I didn't either. Until Christmas Eve. She lives on Pavonia Street. It's really a block long lane in South Camden, NJ, starting on Kaighn Avenue and going to Liberty. It's not far to Liberty but it's very narrow and potholed. Everything rattles on it. No wider than a stretching handshake. Only three occupied houses on Pavonia. Two on one side and one – a green leaning contraption – on the other. That's Viola Yocko's!

It was our mailman, Levi, who first mentioned Viola Yocko of Pavonia the poorest lady he knows. Levi goes from door to door in South Camden singing psalms. You believe a mailman who is always cheerful, smiling and singing psalms. On a Camden Street in the rain. "Could we spare a basket for this lady?" Indeed we could.

Sacred Heart's Christmas Basket project 1991 had delivered 990 baskets on December 21. A few stragglers had come since then and a few pleas from people who saw more need. Like Levi. So we were on the road on Christmas Eve with the last of the baskets. We came to Pavonia. I knocked on an old wooden weather-beaten screen door and waited. There stood Viola, all 53 inches of her in her thongs. No stockings. Red sweater and dress. Her face and hands blackened with the smoke and soot of her little wood stove. The living room was half filled with sticks that someone had cut for her. The walls darker than her face. I saw the faint outline of a large Sacred Heart picture on the wall. "I have the Blessed Mother, too," she said. I could see the framed face faintly there beneath what time and rain and fire had done.

Time, 74 years of it, had weathered the little woman too and smoke and soot had darkened the hardy face, but nothing dimmed the light in the two blue eyes. Bright as Christmas candles in a dark room they were. Her soul jumpin' through them.

Rosemarie McBride, of Sacred Heart staff, and I brought in the basket and the turkey and laid them on the table. She couldn't contain her delight. "We must pray," she said. She prays with everyone who comes. ("She prays with me too," says Levi, the mailman). So she reached over to Corrine (a friend) and the basket bearers and made a circle of prayer. Each one was asked to pray. She left herself for last. "Jesus," she said, showing the delight of a poor child with a new toy, *"I wasn't dreamin' of anything this Christmas. You died for me. That's enough."* I was awed by it all. The prayers, the scene, the delight, the rich abundance of God's love in the bleak poverty. The reality of Christmas! And it was Viola Yocko who brought it home. There, on the table behind her, a basket of food. By some chance! Some chance, indeed! It was Sacred Heart's 1000th basket for 1991. The wonderful works of God! The blessing of Viola Yocko was pouring out over the whole effort and it would spill over every single person who lent a hand, spread a word or gave a donation. And upon those who were poor enough to receive them. Thanks, Viola!

Michael Doyle

The Irish and Whitman

March, 1992

Hi:

We're in the middle of March. Bits of green are emerging in the gray ground for St. Patrick's Day. Every year some of us here in Sacred Heart and around the Delaware Valley gather in the evening of that happy day in the Walt Whitman Cultural Center in Camden (2nd and Cooper) and celebrate in a simple way with good Irish soda bread, songs, poems and whatever people can do. We always guarantee the bread. That's enough.

March this year is a special one, not only for the Irish (and who isn't in March) on St. Patrick's Day but also for people all over the world because this March is the centennial of Walt Whitman's death. He died on March 26, 1892.

So, the Irish and Whitman! Padraig Pearse, who was only 12 years old when Whitman died in Camden in 1892, was one of the most beloved of all Irish patriots and was my favorite even as a child. Interestingly enough, it was said of him many years after his execution in 1916 that he was deeply influenced by three notable people: Jesus Christ, Francis of Assisi and Walt Whitman.

Pearse probably never knew that Whitman in the early years of his work on New York newspapers was a caustic critic of the Irish. "In 1848," according to Paul Zweig, in his book, *The Making of a Poet* (Basic Books Inc.), "Walt Whitman was twenty nine years old and had not written a single text that we now remember. During the previous three years he had been editor of the *Brooklyn Daily Eagle* and before that had run a series of Democratic electoral campaign sheets across the river in Manhattan. He had acquired something of a reputation as a polemic journalist with a sharp tongue, a radical Democrat who could be uncomfortably shrill in his opinion of immigrant workers especially the Irish." For a time he admired Oliver Cromwell because he was a great enemy of kings and priests. Some years before, in 1842, when he was chief editor of the newspaper Aurora in New York, he attacked Bishop John Hughes of New York as "a hypocritical scoundrel" who had with "bands of filthy wretches," "Catholics and ignorant Irish," promoted a bill in the state legislature to get public money for private schools. (*Walt Whitman, A Life*, by Justin Kaplan, Simon and Schuster, NY). On election day, April 12, 1842, Catholics and Protestants fought in the streets of New York. A no-popery mob attacked St. Patrick's Cathedral and stoned the bishop's residence. Whitman had hoped they'd get "the reverend hypocrite's head." That was Whitman at twenty-three.

But he changed. Thirteen years later, in 1855, he produced his masterpiece *Leaves of Grass*. It was, according to Ralph Waldo Emerson, "the most extraordinary piece of wit and wisdom that America has yet contributed." In it, Whitman celebrated the "mystery of ordinariness." Gone was that sharp biting pen of an inadequate journalist and in its place the poet who set out single-handedly to put America to music...who listened to America singing in all her varying sounds and put great expansive words to the song of her soul.

In 1865 he wrote "Old Ireland." In it we find reverence for the grieving Mother whose children in James Joyce's words had crossed "the bowl of bitter tears" to the United States but, says Whitman, are "new blood, young and strong in another county."

Old Ireland

Far hence amid an isle of wondrous beauty,
Crouching over a grave an ancient sorrowful mother,
Once a queen, now lean and tatter'd seated on the ground,
Her old white hair drooping dishevel'd round her shoulders,
At her feet fallen an unused royal harp,
Long silent, she too long silent, mourning her shrouded hope and heir,
Of all the earth her heart most full of sorrow because most full o f love.
Yet a word ancient mother,
You need crouch there no longer on the cold ground with forehead
        between your knees,
O you need not sit there veil'd in your old white hair so dishevel'd,
For know you the one you mourn is not in that grave,
It was an illusion, the son you love was not really dead,
The Lord is not dead, he is risen again young and strong in another country,
Even while you wept there by your fallen harp by the grave,
What you wept for was translated, pass'd from the grave,
The winds favor'd and the sea sail'd it,
And now with rosy and new blood,
Moves to-day in a new country.

Walt Whitman   1865

Bundles of blessings on you today and everyday! "The Lord is not dead, he is risen again young and strong in another country."

Michael Doyle

Camden's Spring

Camden's Spring is Harleigh's Hill   *In a frozen kiss on their mother's breast.*
Awash with Whitman's daffodils.   *Bright Easter's joy was placed on ice*
I went in Holy Week   *And Jesus Christ was buried twice.*
When winter was, I thought, behind,   *But still...*
To see if April's sudden snow   *No matter what the winter kills*
Had hurt the hope I always find.   *Camden's Spring is Harleigh's Hill*
Alas! the daffodils were laid to rest   *Awash with Whitman's daffodils.*

Burning Issues — Burning Bushes

May, 1992

Hi:

When I saw Marconi in that current Broadway play, *Dancing at Lughnasa*, I was transported back to my home and the teens of my years in the 50's. Marconi's part is very important. Marconi is the radio. The same bulky, battery-powered contraption that first entered my home in 1950. No electricity. The dry battery had to be replaced and the "wet one" had to be recharged. It took days.

That radio changed the hearth scene. It brought the voices and sounds of strangers through old impenetrable walls for the first time and into minds long nurtured by the songs and stories of those they knew.

Today, television! The hearth is now a pictured glass. A new, frightening phenomenon is pounding on human consciousness everywhere in the world at a pace and scope and with an immensity of images that should in time turn all of us into gaping unimaginative copycats. In some respects, it can be an evil, oblong eye that is a curse upon our times, poisoning our spirits with dissatisfaction and manipulating us into becoming addicts of the ultimate drug, "MORE." More of everything.

Its power over the poor, especially the young teenager poor, is deadly, because "the tube" is always there telling them what they could have and their own circumstances screaming what they don't have. Tough strains on the high-voltage emotions of the teen years. Then, the drugs! The moneymakers. Turf. Guns. Blood-splattered sidewalks. And, as always, the innocent often dying in the crossfire. More urban body bags cumulatively than came out of Vietnam.

A few days ago, I was looking back to my childhood years. A poor boy was I in terms of material things. No kid in Camden owns less. But there was no Marconi or Mitsubishi tantalizing me with the sounds and images of what I could have and consequently emphasizing what I didn't have.

On this day in May, 1992, after 24 years in Camden, I spent my first night of deep fear in this city. I feared that the burning rage that we saw in the City of the Angels after the acquittal of the policemen who beat Rodney King would ignite around me. It didn't, thanks be to God. The admirable patience of the many offended people who waited for our system of justice to render a fair verdict was mocked and insulted and all hell broke loose in Los Angeles. It is a terrible tragedy. More than 50 people dead. More urban body bags. God help us all. The looting was awful, too. But materially much less than the looting committed by the Savings and Loan. Would that we were as horrified by that bunch. But we didn't see it with our own eyes. We are creatures of the image.

Oh, if only we had a National Guard with hammers and saws and Marines who did nothing but plumbing! The threat to the future of this nation is not in Iraq, but in the inner core of our deadly cities. What kind of madness in 1992 sanctions a US military budget of $292 billion when the Soviet Union is not a threat and our own urban ghettos are war zones!

Even though we are still in Easter season, we must put on "the ashes of the angels" – "las cenizas de los Angeles" – and repent. "Repent" is to try to put back things the way they should be. We have to stop deliberately making two nations in what's supposed to be a United States. We must try to realize that all of us have decided that it is okay to warehouse our poor to protect our own real estate investments. Such population control, which provides short-term rewards, will ultimately bring terrible disasters on our children. It will turn dreams into ashes for more than the minorities.

Let us begin again to build bridges and, at least, use our inner city churches as legitimate connectors of urban and suburban America. We have built a wall that is higher and harder to bring down than the one the Communists built in Berlin. But we must begin again, no matter what the winter wind has done. We must begin again as May begins with bright blossoms of hope. God does not speak any more from "burning bushes" but is certainly saying something from the burning cities of our nation. They are the burning issues of our time.

Michael Doyle

A Bodhran Broken in a Fallen Hand
(excerpt)

The mind goes back to catch the times
In the wireless thing beneath the thatch
When music spreads from foreign climes
And local songs seemed out of touch.
The coals of old that were raked too long
Would smother soon without a start
But the Clancy brothers came along
And lit a fire on the chilly hearth.

They hit the floor with hobnail boots
With sticks and strings and pipes of air
And blew the fire to a blaze
Till the sparks of it went everywhere.
Across "the bowl of bitter tears"
Where the hearth was now a pictured glass
The one from Beare with whitened eyes
Gave the Clancy lads their starting chance.

"A Big Green Tree of Peace in Our Hearts"

July, 1992

Hi!

"I come from Camden, a fine example of how most people do not care what happens to the environment. I think this attitude is slowly changing. I hope in the future that mother earth will one day again have the beauty that has been stripped from her." So said Cheo Walker, a young man from Camden, as he read his words in the Emerald Street Garden (one block from Sacred Heart Church) on June 26, when the Mayor of Camden came to plant a tree. In the garden that day were young people from around the world. From Camden, too, and other parts of New Jersey. They were gathered in what was called the Heart of Camden Peace Trees Project. About 65 in all, not counting 20 Earth Stewards, Juvenile Services personnel and other volunteers who staffed the project. There, in the newly formed garden, on the site of DelBuono's original bakery, life had begun again. There the world's young people stood in a circle of hope, a yeast in their own way, as Jesus would say, that would penetrate far into the masses of the world and lift life a little and make it more palatable. Ten from Scotland, one from England, four from India, four from Saskatchewan in Canada, five from Costa Rica, five from Sacred Heart, two from Ireland, six from Russia, and about twenty from other parts of New Jersey. They came to Camden, sponsored by the Earth Stewards Network which began its first Peace Trees project in Auroville, India in 1988. It was founded by Danaan Parry and directed to reduce conflict and release the earth and her energies for the good of all.

In Camden, the young people and the staff broke the concrete of old pavements and planted 225 trees along the streets around Sacred Heart. In eighteen days, from June 21 to July 9, the world came to Camden and gave new lungs of life to Walt Whitman's city because it was the centennial of his death. His passing on March 26, 1892, was no match for the vibrancy and ever widening exuberance of his life. So, the cement was broken. Life began again. Life, too, in people; as distance and uncertainty broke down, cultural differences cleared away and the delightful bonding of people timidly emerged. Faces, cautious and defensive at first meetings, were flooded with tears at the partings. Enough almost to water the trees they planted. Certainly the ones in the heart.

Some words now from these young people who worked and played in this damaged part of the planet and blessed it with a healthy bit of beauty:

Vladimar Poliakov, Russia: "I do not like this place because it smells and it's dirty, but I like the people I've met here."
Marta Cartin, Costa Rica: "We come to show how we can create a better world in a peaceful way by planting seeds of hope."
Boyd Sanders, Saskatchewan, Canada: "Trees are the foundation of life, we are building that foundation."
Sean Mallon, Ireland: "Joining nations together to understand each other and trying to work together peacefully, we are saving the environment and beautifying areas of decay."

Candace Longjohn, Saskatchewan, Canada: "With communication, anything can happen. What really amazes me is the support of honest friendship."

Mathew Dennis, England: "Camden County Sewage treatment plant was put in Camden City, resulting in a stench that affects everyone in Camden City. This is not right. I am glad that I can work with people who are trying to improve the environment for generations to come."

Tarmilarasan, India: "We are the young future of the light. This is my second Peace Trees…..When I came here, I put my energy to make beautiful streets in Camden. I did my best what I could. When I finish my heart will be full of joy."

Sindra Jung, Scotland: "Being here has shown me how well off I am compared to some people that I have met."

John Gibson, Sacred Heart, Camden: "I have learned how to plant trees, and the environment necessary for a tree to live."

Kevin Lindsay, Pennsauken, NJ: "I would like to see everyone, including kids, start cleaning up since we are the future. Whatever the world becomes we've made it."

Meabh O'Hare, Ireland: "I've learned the importance of community in places like Camden."

David "Cochise" Lawrence, Camden, NJ: "I have begun a growth of hope in helping a once beautiful city become beautiful again."

Vladislav Golunov, Novosibirsk, Russia: "I found people are basically the same all over the world. I thought America was a rich country and I was surprised to find the need for a soup kitchen. I hope that what we planted will be cared for by the Camden people."

Madhabi, India: "The first day I noticed the aggressive side of the Camden neighborhood but by midway I noticed a change and neighbors came forward to help. Nature is the footprint of divinity."

Donald Sanders, Camden, NJ: "I learned to love people no matter what country they came from."

Ximena Valldeperas, Costa Rica: "I think the people from Camden need to put a little effort to wake up this city."

Roman Ivanov, Moscow, Russia: "The problem is not in what we see, the problem is in ourselves. We need to change attitudes towards the environment we live in. The young people from around the world have got a lot of energy and enthusiasm to revive this dead area and by planting trees together, use our energy for the common good. The concrete we broke is a concrete of our indifference as much as it is cement, water and stone. *We need to plant a big green tree of peace in our hearts.*"

These are some of the thoughts of these international young people, ranging in age from thirteen to early twenties. All written in English; all coming up out of their beings like "a big green tree of peace in our hearts."

I will never forget the sight of a U.S. Army man in uniform standing by the generator that he brought and a young Russian with "body electric" poised on the jackhammer breaking concrete to plant a tree in Camden.

Patti Gibson of Sacred Heart, Camden, says it well: "Our achievement was to make Camden better." Indeed, you did, Patti!

Michael Doyle

Moss on the Shoe

August, 1992

Hi!

The bit of earth where God gave me life calls me every time I'm home to close encounters with it, and these are intimate and interesting and always nourishing to my weary soul and body. Recently, my brother Pat Doyle and I began to dig out an egg tree hedge that was no longer needed. It was older than either one of us. There, leafless in the fall of '34, when I first opened tiny eyes 20 feet to the west of it. There, too, when my father died in '67, 25 years ago.

I never liked an egg tree bush although I liked its name, which it got because its berries, cherry size, are white as morning snow. I didn't like it because my teachers, even in the early grades, cut it for the rods they often used unfairly and caused hurts and tears and smarting memories. Anyway, as we were digging out the egg tree hedge we found a shoe. A man's shoe. One that used to be laced up the instep. Fourteen holes. Seven a side. It was my father's. One of his Sunday shoes. One that got polished every Saturday night. One that he wore on October 10, 1967, a Tuesday, when he suddenly mentioned evening Mass in Colmcille. Pat feels that he was out of tobacco and thought about Mass and a chance to get the fillings for his beloved pipe. Anyway he went to Mass and got his half-quarter in McKeon's shop. He never smoked it. He took off his Sunday shoes and never put them on again. He died the next day.

So now, here is the shoe, 25 years later almost totally covered in the rich green moss that was growing on it. No laces. The tongue, more than any other part, completely green. It was not just the shoe that overwhelmed me, but the green untrodden quietude of the moss. The stillness of it. And there was that damp poignant emptiness that stepped with a granite foot upon my heart.

I have a feeling anyhow about feet and death and shoes and morning laces tied that other hands often open when feet are turning cold.

> *One day was the last one the old man tied them,*
> *He died before it was time to untie them,*
> *When the eyelids of evening came down to their rest,*
> *The hard knot of death was tight on his chest.*

My family will always remember what my father's grandchild, Geraldine Doyle, said when she came into the kitchen from the room where he was waked: "Granda's toes are not moving. He has no tickles atal." Her tender sense of death at two and a half!

None of us remember our first toddling step, but there was a moment when we took it, and it brought delight to every eye that saw it and every eager ear that heard of it. It was our journey's start, that step that stretched all of three inches on this little planet earth that travels 25,000 miles to ride the rim of its orbit. And what will be the total on that imaginary "odometer" hidden on our heels or toes to measure out and record the miles and miles of all our nights and days. (For the Greeks: *hodus* is the word for *way, metron* the word for *measure*.) But green moss on this quiet shoe can send the mind on silent wings to other levels and other ways unmeasurable. To crosses carried or falls taken; to risings wrought, and struggles up uneven hills of hardship. The stretching of the sinews of the soul is part of what it takes. The steps upon the "bloody slopes' of what it costs to cope and reach beyond our reach before we die.

And there is always that "beggar of a corn," as my father put it, that often made him hobble. "The hard excessence of the skin in the toes or other parts of the feet" that Virtues English Dictionary says "is occasioned by the pressure of shoes." My father wouldn't know or use language such as that, but he knew the pressure that makes us struggle on and dare not stop except to rest awhile and then go on. On, until our day is done, our miles are run, our steps are counted from cradle side to graveside and our shoes are laid aside.

It's nice to have a pair of shoes we like to wear (not too many pairs) and see the wear and tear of time and tide when heels, like life, need straightening by hands we've come to know. Don't leave too many shoes behind in clean white-papered boxes! Let those who tidy up the place where we have fallen down, see the shoes we wore and wore well with walking, dancing too. Not to mention the tapping that we did to rhythms in the earth below. Rhyms in the heart that beats with love and sends its lively stir to every heel and toe. Be glad of life at every age it is and even when the tapping seems to stop in those we knew by heart, know that:

> *The dance goes on when feet turn blue,*
> *There is tapping somewhere for each rotting shoe.*
> *And leprechauns constantly hammering and chanting*
> *Preparing all shoes worn our with the dancing:*
> *Sing cobbler, little cobbler, do what you do*
> *Stitch the past to the future in your grandfather's shoe.*

So, my August break in the place where I was born is a good time to pause and gaze upon my father's shoe; motionless, except for the silent stir of growing moss upon the years. It speaks to me of rest before September comes and the clamor of the children looking once again for their school to open and the Sponsors who will keep it open for them.

But for now, I put my fathers shoe beneath a boxwood bush he set where the moss is free to grow. And I...I simply walk away.

Michael Doyle

"I Hold My Crucifix Against My Heart"

October, 1992

Hi:

Today, as I write, is October 13th. A special anniversary day for us here because it was on October 13th that Father William Lynch signed the documents incorporating Sacred Heart parish in Camden, NJ. That was in 1885. He came up from St. Mary's in Gloucester to become the founding pastor of Sacred Heart parish and lived at 1911 Broadway, Camden. Grover Cleveland was President of the United States, Jesse Pratt was Mayor of Camden, and Walt Whitman, bearded bard of ordinary things, often rode up and down Broadway on his horse and buggy. Croft's block-long Worsted Yarn Mills rose behind Father Lynch's house and employed hundreds of people. The mills still stand today. No yarn woven now in the grand old building, but in its shadow, on a half burned block of Arlington, Charlene Abel lives, the bright hazel-eyed student of Sacred Heart whose smiling face adorns our sponsor fliers this year with a plea to all to help our school.

I sat down today, this anniversary day, and listened to Charlene, a fourth-grade student and a member of this parish that Father Lynch began 107 years ago. She spoke easily about our school and how much she likes it. "It's very educative (her word) and has nice people to help you when you have problems. There's nothing to worry about." Recently, I have begun to realize how much our principal, teachers and staff mean to the children in terms of giving them a real sense of being safe. "They protect you," says Charlene. One begins to understand how anxious children here feel on the streets and even in their homes. "Sometimes there are fights on the street. People throwing things, running from police and everything. Yesterday there was a big fight on my street, just because someone said, 'you're eating macaroni and butter.' Three kids said it to four grown-up women. Then the moms and dads got into it, nieces and nephews - pipes, knives, forks and a big blunt steel bat...the blood was everywhere. The police came. They didn't catch the people. I'm not happy on that street. And there's a lot of drugs around my way. They go to the cars and sell. The drugs upset me the most. I see stealing and bad fights. Every Friday on the corner of Jefferson and Broad there's a shoot-out. At night I hear shots. It makes me scared. I go into mom's room and curl up with her."

It was hard to believe that this beautiful little girl has seen so much so soon. She was born on January 19, 1983 - not even a decade on this earth and yet she is trying to cope with daily tragedy around her. "The reason they take drugs...they might be so mad (angry) they think they (drugs) might help them!" She continues: "there's a lot of those women on Broadway, you see them. They try to get men to pick them up. They take men into a house and they get money from them."

But life in spite of everything continues to be resilient in our children. Says Charlene: "I like going to girls' Little League. I made six homeruns. I like to play soccer, kick ball and battle ball. It's good."

I asked her about religion in school. "I learn about Jesus" she said, "and his disciples. We just learned about the good Samaritan and how he helped the man that was robbed. The priest or the Levite didn't help." (I covered my face.) And does religion help you? "Yes," she said. "You receive the Holy Spirit. I have Jesus in my heart and I know he will forgive me for my sins. I learn more and more. Our teacher tries to do her best. Every day she has us get our journals and make an entry in it - how the day was...what happened on the weekend."

And what do you want to be, Charlene? She mused for awhile. "secretary," she said, "or a manager of a hair styling place." (She will never style anyone's hair as well as God styled her own.). "A singer. I'm pretty good. I like to sing songs about Jesus...hymns, like, 'God is Good.' Sometimes I make up my own songs. Last night I was making one up. It was: 'Jesus might just have everything you need.' I was singing it in the bathtub."

No wonder Jesus said: "Let the children come to me and do not hinder them. It is to such as these that the Kingdom of God belongs." Indeed! And just like him who wept over his city and voiced the hopes of his heart, Charlene, using her fingers, ticked off her wishes for Camden: "I wish there was no drugs, no murders, none of those ladies that stand on the corner and Camden would just be clean." Then she says the same thing in another way: "I dream when I go to sleep that all those ladies are out; all the drug dealers, out. Out of the universe! Out of here! They would become clean and Camden becomes clean."

I wonder what Father Lynch of 1885 would say, whose place I take, if he took mine. I think he would be glad he named our church for the Sacred Heart as he listened to Charlene Abel and the pain and hope of her youthful heart. It is surely sacred too and it calls to us to try to save the children and they will save us.

I just wanted you who know her smiling face to know her fears and faith and spread the word for all our children. "I'm afraid," she says, "to play on my street. I stay in and do my homework and watch TV." But in Sacred Heart "there is nothing to worry about. They protect you." And her final wish: "I want to go here 'til 8th grade." For myself and for you and for all who help and will help Sacred Heart, I say to Charlene: "We will keep it open for you, love." And we will try to make Camden a better place for children. It is listed now as the worst in the state.

"I pray," says Charlene, "that people wouldn't fight and there wouldn't be so much violence and that when I walk to school I would be safe." Nine years old. And lest anyone should have any doubt about the power of her prayer, she said: "When I pray, I hold my crucifix against my heart." She holds us all.

Michael Doyle

Thanks for the Tea

February, 1993

Hi:

I went last October to Tampa, Florida, with my friend Joe Pacera, a Senior Vice President at Lourdes Hospital in Camden, NJ, to attend a Leadership Conference on an Emerging Vision for the Health System of the Franciscan Sisters of Allegany. There, in the luxurious lap of the Hyatt Regency West Shore Hotel, I stayed in room 507 and he, a wall away, in 509.

One morning before I got up, a cup of tea arrived for me "courtesy of the man next door". The few lines that follow were scribbled by me then, as Whitman said they should (on stoop, or log, or ferryboat) where and whenever the feel is fresh within the heart.

Joe Pacera died unexpectedly on January 23, 1993.   He was 54.

The knock. The wooden tray for tea.
The small white jug just for me.
Schonwald delpht, double dots and all
The gesture, Joe's, 509, a wall away
In this martin house with holes for four hundred birds and more
Migrating south to see the sway of Canary Island palms.
And feel the heavy heat of Tampa Bay.
Thanks for the tea! Mist and sea. The second sip
That stirred the sleeping memories of bare mornings long ago,
Of colds and coughs and concrete floors
And breath like incense on the rise
From pillows in the half-eight dark of day.
My father, up already, his cap on before his socks
Whang-tied boots, arching over ashes, thongs in hand
Eager there to resurrect the buried coals of yesterday.
And build a better fire for today upon an ancient hearth.
Then the "schall" of spring well water into the deep metalic dark
The chimney starts to breathe upon the morning air
Jackdaws shiver off a little on the frosty thatch
While down below fat finches pick and pause
Amid the salt and pepper stones (This soft sofa hurts my back)
The water bubbles to a boil and sings a morning song
Sends his hand to fetch the old red canister
Silvered by a thousand thumbs
And an ornate spoon half buried there
To measure out the leaves into the warmed pot.
The water rushes madly now through duckneck spout
And spills itself upon the tea, the Ceylonese have sent
To lift the spirit of a famished land.

The pot sits its seconds out beside the hearth
"To draw", to draw the essence out

And change comes, a Cana-change of color, taste and tone
Sugar now, and milk, the "grey cow's" milk he milked the night before
(She always had a drop when winter cows were dry)
And every day he brought the tea to my mother's opening eyes
Steaming hot, rising with her breath before she rose.
His ritual of care since '32 they bonded back in Cloone
And she came to bear the children that she bore.
He lit the fire in her heart and stoked it to the warmth of his own
A heart of happiness renewed in spite of all
The drudgery of damp eaves-dripping days.
Their glow brighter than the stars when frosty nights were new.
Warmer too, I say, than any summer's day.
Thank you, Joe, for the drop of tea in Tampa!
A cup of magic moments full, and running over.
Coals covered by the ashes of more than forty years
Alive now.
I sit and sip the tea of tears and tender times beside the fire.

I did tell Joe how much his cup of tea meant to me, and I told him, too, about my father's faithful ritual every morning. I didn't know then that eyes would soon be wells of water when he went away. But I do know that while I have the time, I should bring that water to a boil and send a cup of tea to you (like the one he sent to me), "courtesy of" Michael Doyle.

Michael Doyle

For Tom O'Rourke

It's hard to think of it
Tom O'Rourke sick to death
As to hear them tell the story long ago
That Jesus Christ the healing one
The hands, the eyes, the words
They healed. The threads he wore
Kissed the woman's hidden wound
And she at once was well.
Then He, Himself, wounded once
And worn down as well
Sick, bloodied on the ground. Oh, No!
And Tom, too, that wholesome man

Happy, healthy, in mind, in memory
In attitude of heart, in the focus of his days
In grace and good humor, in every way
Reaching graciously over bruised reeds
To touch that infected sore he saw
In slum streets and death rows
And all the violent manufacture for the war.
Did his best to cleanse
With the pure cotton wool of himself
(No steel wood to scrape the evil out)
Soaked now like Jesus was
To heal the whole bloody thing.

Truth On Track

March, 1993

Hi:

The month is March as I write but will be April as you read. It has been a memorable month here, where the whole area was clobbered with the snowstorm of the century. Many people died with shovels in their hands and not enough sense to know that their shoveling days were over. God rest them all and comfort those who miss them! I shoveled snow myself, was warned by several people, and being always sensible and obedient, proceeded to shovel for two and a half hours. Oh dear!

Snow is beautiful but it is too hard on hearts and hips. It should stay on the high ground like clouds and mountain sheep. Someday I want to go to Austria where seventy percent of the land rises into magnificent mountains. Their heads, like my own, always capped with snow, holding out in the sun.

Today, my day off, I came over to 30 Street Station in Philadelphia (12 minutes from Sacred Heart). I didn't come to go anywhere or await anybody. I came to sit in a "pew" in this grand cathedral of Comin' and Goin'. (Two tired angels of all our days and years.) I came to write. It's an interesting place, with people resting and rushing, greeting and parting and, of course, phoning, feeding and flushing. Not much silence; the barking voice that says: "may I have your attention please," doesn't wait for my response.

I have trains on my mind since Sunday at St. Malachy's in Philadelphia, where my friend John McNamee is pastor. A gracious place it is, of hospitality and celebration, that is at once elegant and easy and always uplifting. There, Christ Church Choir presented a Requiem in memory of Franz Jagerstatter. Daniel Berrigan, S.J. gave a meditation on him. It was searing as a lazer light, on the courage of that brave Austrian peasant, who stood up to Hitler's might with his lonely concience and backed it with his life. Franziska, the young wife of August 9, 1943, when he was beheaded, had planned to speak at St. Malachy's but illness now at eighty cancelled her trip to the U.S. Hence Berrigan! He talked of Jagerstatter's dream of a train going to hell with so many people on it, clerics and lay. All nice people, polite and reasonable; crowding through the doors. Some pushing. Some helping. All taking the train. Too timid not to. The train of going - along. The train to hell.

On a marble platform beneath the lenten cross was Bob McGovern's great wood sculpture of Jagerstatter, with a bible in one hand and flames by the other, burning the swatstika; the "bent cross" as Dan said, of inestimable evil. Bob had chiseled this one with a severe edge; sharp as pain that cuts to the marrow.

Trains! Chisels! Jagerstatter! Lent! Death! Life!

Austria! It was the Benedictines of Ireland who brought Christianity to Austria. Indeed the original Cathedral of Salzburg was consecrated by St. Virgil, an Irish born bishop, in 774. (If only my friend, Nick Virgilio, great haiku poet, was alive to read this). Anyway, it is only fitting that the Church of Sacred Heart, built by Philip McDonald of Cavan, under the direction of architect Jeremiah O'Rourke of Dublin, should presently be undergoing preservation and restoration under the direction of the noted international artist and paint conservator, Othmar Carli. Othmar is from Austria.

Doesn't this letter feel like a train station? Comin' and Goin'. Anyway, Othmar has brought two of our paintings back to life. There are 19 more to be done. All on canvas. Twelve of them over 60 square feet in size. Up there since 1908. The first one saved by Othmar, is Mary Magdalene Washing the Feet of Jesus. His feet are clean again. Outside; the prostitutes, the trucks and the pollution. Not easy to clean all that up.

But hope hangs on. Last Tuesday Othmar directed the return of a restored angel to the east wall of our church. Surely, a "fallen" angel. She was covered by the fall-out of rain damage for twenty years. I had never seen her face. "Anybody with sense would throw this in the trash" he said. But Michael Doyle (not noted for sense) wanted her to be the symbol of new life in our church and in Camden. Now it's back to life. Miraculous!

Only Othmar could have done it. Even the canvas, threadbare with the damage of the years, since Ferdinand Baraldi painted it in 1908, had to be shored up and strengthened. The lime from the plaster, broken down by polluted rain, had eaten the painting like termites in timber.

When Othmar speaks about the preservation of old churches, synagogues or any sacred place, his eyes fill with tears. He is remembering the day when he, as a six year old boy, was taken out of school with all the children and made to watch the burning of the local synagogue by the Nazis. His life is dedicated especially to the preservation of all that is old and sacred and also to the new and creative beauty that comes forth from his soul. And yet, I think he would be more at home in any of the past nine centuries that he is in this one.

Pray, dear friend of Sacred Heart, that we will find the ways and means to preserve the beauty of the special space that we call Sacred Heart in Camden! Even if we are poor, we still must be dedicated to beauty. Our God is a God of beauty. Who could improve on the design and color of Camden's common weeds?

Behind me, in this station, there is a mighty bronze angel holding up a lifeless body. Beneath, is a large pedestal covered with names "in memory of the men and women of the Pennsylvania Railroad" who died in the Second World War.

May Othmar's "risen" angel be one of hope and life in this "war" torn town of Camden! May we all struggle against the powers of evil and gain strength from a simple Austrian farmer who refused to get on the train of "going along". Franz Jagerstatter. Like Jesus in Jerusalem, he gave his life to keep the whole truth on track.

Christ is Risen! Happy Easter to you!

Michael Doyle

Fires, Tempests and Loose Nuts on the Way

May, 1993

Hi:

My memory today goes back to a warm summer afternoon in 1968 when I drove into Camden City with all that I owned in the back seat of my Chevy Impala. I was 33. I had been assigned to St. Joseph's Church on Federal Street after having been removed from my post as a religion teacher in Holy Spirit High School near Atlantic City. My outspoken opposition to the Vietnam War had landed me in Camden, and I have been here all these years. By June 15, please God, it will be 25 years.

It has not been easy. I should have known in late 1967 and early '68 that some tough terrain lay ahead on the road that would rise before me. "Cry!" says Dag Hammarskjold. "Cry if you will! The path chose you and in the end, you will say 'thank you'." I hope so.

Speaking of "the end," I thought I had met it one Saturday in the fall of '67 as I was driving my old blue Chevy (fins and all) along the Garden State Parkway. I was on my way from Northfield, NJ to Yonkers, NY where I went once a week to help a group called Catholics for Latin America. Somewhere south of New York City, a terrible feeling came over me that I was going to be killed that day. It was so strong that I thought that even the utility poles were laughing at me. I pulled over and stopped the car, got my pen and a piece of paper to write down that I was going to be killed. I thought it would be interesting to people that I had the premonition. But then, I thought, I'm giving in to it, and if I write I am helping it to happen. No, I said to myself, I will not write   I'll pray.

I went on my way, prayed as I went, through a dull dark noontime day (all cars had lights on), crossed over the George Washington Bridge and turned north in the rain on the Henry Hudson Parkway. At the first turnoff opposite Yonkers, the traffic lights were changing as I approached. I hesitated, and then applied the brakes. The car swerved, first to the left, then to the right, then left again into the southbound lanes. I saw two trees come at me ("I'm dead"). Then it swerved back, spun around three times and stopped facing north in the center lane of the southbound side. Then I drove off on the shoulder facing north by the southbound lanes and three cars whizzed by at 60 miles an hour. One in each lane. I sank down on top of the steering wheel and didn't move for 20 minutes.

The following week I left my car at a gas station in Northfield so that I could get two front-wheel tires. I picked it up when the job was done and started home. Suddenly, it seemed that the bottom fell out of my stomach as the car tore into a nearby lawn and stopped at a doorstep. My front wheel had come off. The lug nuts had not been tightened. It was towed away and the station had it repaired with a new fender, etc. Three weeks later I picked it up and started up Tilton Road. I heard a strange noise. At this point, I'm very conscious of all noises. I pulled off the road into another gas station. My other front wheel was about to come off. The nuts on it had also been loose since I got the new tires and had never been tightened. Nuts!

A few weeks passed and I borrowed a friend's station wagon to haul turkeys that I bought for poor people in Atlantic City for Christmas. While I was doing this, my car, parked by my friend's house, was hit by a drunken driver in a pickup truck and totally destroyed. Then I needed more than turkeys myself.

Anyway, I decided to buy a used car from an auto body shop in Pleasantville, NJ. A Pontiac Tempest. It would not be ready for several weeks. I waited. Impatiently. The owner lent me his wife's small Corvair for the weekend. It had all the power of a Singer sewing machine. On Sunday afternoon, I went down to John Quinn's house in Northfield. John, an FBI agent, liked to play pingpong, and I did too. When I reversed out of his driveway on Cedar Bridge Road to return home that evening, it reversed across the road but would not go forward no matter what I tried. And I tried desperately. Car lights appeared on the crest of the hill. I was a sitting duck. I tried again. The lights were still coming. I slid over into the passenger seat and just as I did, the oncoming car crashed into the Corvair and drove the door into the spot I had just moved from. A couple and two children. Nobody really hurt. Thank God! John Quinn came running out. He thought I was dead. The police came. Hours of reports. The auto body shop was called. The wife's wrecked Corvair was towed away.

One week later, my Tempest was ready. Thirteen thousand miles. I loved it. A few days after I got it, as I was returning from Holy Spirit High School, I stopped at a Hess station in Pleasantville. I got gas and pulled out onto Shore Road. I heard a slight thud. I looked in the mirror because I thought a bumper had grazed me. Suddenly horns were blaring. I couldn't see anything. I pulled off the road in case an ambulance was coming. Then, I saw the smoke. I got out of the car and as soon as I did, my beautiful Tempest went up in flames.

I called the auto body people. They towed away my dead Tempest. They felt sorry for me and sold me a Chevy Impala with 3,000 miles on it, for the same money.

A few weeks later, my job as a religion teacher at Holy Spirit ended. Was this a crash course for Camden? I was sent to this city. I arrived in my Chevy Impala. Safely!

So prayer, yours and mine, on all my dark dull days still gets me through fires, tempests and loose nuts in the wheels of time and fortune. For a quarter of a century in Camden. Thanks be to God!

Michael Doyle

My Mind Had Wandered to Sinead

O God help us! Rain! Rain! Rain!
On that half eyed windshield pane
Blinding, blinding all, only one wiper wiping
"No vision…there is no vision" Where? Where?
The fiat on from nowhere. Look! Look out!
Hurtling into the last eager step she took
To shatter shield and bond and bone
To absolutely shatter everything.

The Long View

June, 1993

Hi:

Pat Doyle was often heard to say to his dawdling grandson (me), "You'll be late for your own funeral." I hope so. Anyway, I know I am late with this letter. It's for June. We're in July.

Speaking of funerals, with the death of Dan Mulligan of Rossduff on May 23rd, every one of the two generations of family, friends and neighbors who raised me has had a funeral. Indeed, several of my own generation as well. I have said before (that never stops me) that when I go home to Ireland I recognize more names on the stones in our cemetery than I do on the road. The last time I was there, I was looking at the long hay growing up around the name of my cousin, Father Edward Kiernan, "who died 24th March, 1980, aged 67 years, ministered in Cape Town, South Africa." He was always my connection to that troubled country and he has been on my mind since Sunday, when I went over to Philadelphia to see Nelson Mandela. I didn't see him, but I heard him. Not that that was easy either, with protests booming behind me. July 4th.. The price of democracy.

It was just great to be in Philadelphia when this man of courage was there, the man whom South Africa imprisoned for 27 years in the interest of promoting apartheid: white power, white wealth, white ways in Africa; and black enslavement. Nelson Mandela. He never lost his hope, his nerve, his determination to be free. Above all, I wanted to share a moment with the man who could, when all is said and done (both terrible, as far as he was concerned), still speak the truth, and as the president said on Sunday, "without bitterness." What a splendid example of humanity on planet earth today!

Twenty-seven years! I was reading the Catholic Worker this morning before I got up and I found some words that Dorothy Day wrote back in 1972 on that other great man, Cesar Chavez, who died recently. Struggling bravely for a lifetime, he, like Mandela, still spoke without bitterness. "I don't think most people realize how great Cesar's vision is," she wrote. "He has *the long view*. And in faith, believes that, by non-violent means, a person can attain to a decent life on the good earth."

Recently I found in my room a yellowing picture from *The Philadelphia Inquirer* of Cesar Chavez breaking bread with Robert Kennedy to end a fast on March 10, 1968, three months before Kennedy was murdered in Los Angeles. Chavez did many shorter fasts and one long one that nearly killed him, 36 days, in 1988. Stubborn, persistent, non-violent, he was not, as Sean O'Casey said of James Larkin, "trumpet-tongued for justice." But his deeply spiritual faithfulness was a clarion call to all. "He had the long view."

Trained in community organizing by Saul Alinsky, he never lost the vision that poor people could be organized into a force for good for all humankind. He just kept at it and he died in his sleep on April 23, 1993, weary with two days of testimony on the stand in San Luis, Arizona. He was 66 years old.

Last Sunday, July 4th at Sacred Heart, we celebrated the laying of the cornerstone of our church 107 years ago and tried to renew again the faith that is the real foundation of any church. The persistent hope. The strength for the long haul. The vision. The "long view." We all need to do that.

Camden is worse today than it was 25 years ago when I came to it. 1968. The same year that Bobby Kennedy came and charged us to do something to make things better. Sacred Heart has made a contribution. We have. We still can.

Our 73rd eighth grade has graduated. Last Tuesday evening we blessed our 63rd renovated house, and 15 more are being worked on. Hundreds still lie in abandonment. The long view. On August 7, 1983, the Farm Labor Organizing Committee (FLOC) walking from Ohio arrived in Camden, NJ (600 miles) to demand, after 10 years of effort, that Campbell Soup make a contract with the farm workers in Ohio who picked their tomatoes and cucumbers. When they walked over the Ben Franklin Bridge that Sunday, Cesar Chavez walked with them on the last miles of their journey. Sacred Heart planned a Mass of welcome and gratitude at the Cathedral of the Immaculate Conception in Camden. We had a 55 gallon drum of water in the sanctuary and we washed the tired feet of 80 farm workers with fresh water for each pair. It was my privilege to wash the feet of Cesar Chavez. I was surely cleansed by washing them.

May his spirit be a clean spring water in this world, cooling its anger and soothing its troubled soil poisoned by pesticides. May he wake up the lazy and strengthen the weak and help us all to keep the "long view" and hold out 'til the end.

The grass is long on my cousin's grave, but as Walt Whitman says, it is enduring grass, like the spirit of everyone we admire; there, there still, when all the feet that trampled it are gone.

Michael Doyle

The Pain of the Rain - A Dream
(excerpt)

"I'll ask it to rain," he said.
He was an old man, slight,
His hair well clipped and white.
He had a blackthorn cane.
"The earth can't feel my pain,"
He exclaimed, "Until it's very bad.
Then the fields finally feel it.
It must go through me

Before they pick it up."
I knew he meant it.
He was silent now...
I saw the furrows deepen in his forehead,
And the tremble of an oncoming ache
A light breeze stirred...
His eyes filled with tears.
It began to rain.

A Fire on the Wet Hearth

July, 1993

Hi:

The narrow road, that runs from my birthplace in Longford to Ballinagh in County Cavan, has more twists and bends than sallies in a creel. It must have been traced by some pre-historic eel weaving its way to the water. Indeed, it swings over the Erne River at an angle of 90 degrees and it is to the oxter of that bend by the water, that I want to take you today.

There, in a tiny prefab house, provided by Cavan County Council, (like freeholders here) an old man lives alone. John O'Neill. Over 80 now, his two brothers dead these several years, Johnny Nail (the nickname) has lived in this lovely spot all his life. A railroad man in younger years and then a road worker for the county, where he hid his age or never gave it a thought until he was over 70. A bout of illness took him to the hospital where his age was discovered and he had to retire. His life in the tiny council house is "alright". It keeps the rain off his bed and it's warm in the winter. And Mrs. Scott, from across the road makes a bit of dinner for him every day and brings it over. But life is not the same. Not the same as it was in the old house a few feet away where he lived all his life. In its day, the house was beautiful: thatched, white washed, lace curtained windows, and from the half door you could almost touch the swans sailing by on the Erne or cast a line and a worm in the water.

Time took its toll on Johnny Nail and the fine Irish house he lived in. Rain and wind wore his roof away and farmers stopped sowing oats and the golden straw vanished from the fields. That straw was roofs and all the skilled thatchers died. Johnny's house had more leaks than all the pots and pans he owned. Today it's roofless. Its gables point geometrically to the clouds. Its chimney, tall and naked in the rain.

But in every vacation time, when I drive by, rain or shine, I look for the smoke from that forlorn chimney and the roofless house it stands in. Every day Johnny Nail goes over to the old house and lights the fire on the hearth. The old walls around him, the cloudy sky above him; he stays as long as he can.

Sad. Tender too. With no where near the poignant faithfulness of Johnny Nail, we have tried to keep the fire going on the "hearth" of our church. One that would be warm and welcoming and would create a bit of nourishment and hope. Keep the fire going, no matter what! (That is our motto.) And roofs will come and cover us. Walls will stand and protect us. Windows will glow in the morning and brighten the days of our lives.

The smoke of Johnny Nail's fire rising from his roofless house on a wet and windless evening is a picture of undaunted spirit. Melancholy, perhaps. But surely, life's aging breath in the face of death.

"I was there," She said. "I am the breath of the earth
Every voice is a wisp of my prayer

> *Breathing blessings of incense on the bites of the air*
> *Because life has the edge on the ice."*

It is an edge I see all the time. On December 28, 1989 a twister hit Sacred Heart Church in a downpour of rain and lifted one thousand square feet of roof, shingles and flooring, completely off and dumped it on Ferry Avenue. The traffic light changed at the right moment; cars and trucks moved on and nobody was hit or hurt. Thanks be to God! Then the rain stopped miraculously. In two days a new temporary roof of wood and tarpaulin was erected and twenty-one magnificent canvas paintings on the walls and ceiling of our church never took a drop of rain.

Today, 75 years after Ferdinand Baraldi of Philadelphia created these beautiful paintings, they are covered with the dirt and the damage of the years. Most of them are 60 square feet in size and they depict great scenes from our salvation story.

I have a problem. I don't know how to ask for the money it takes to save them. It's hard enough for me to ask for the children, for food, and the housing. But for paintings !!!

Am I responsible for saving the beauty that people put here in this church 75 years ago; now that all around it, there is so much decay and desolation! Do the poor deserve beauty? Did God ever make anything that is ugly? A daisy or a dandelion! But then they have their own preservation system. Too good, perhaps and too easy to maintain.

It will cost $5,000 to save each painting. Or $100,000 to save them all. Say a prayer that we will find the right way to save them. I often say what somebody else said: "You never see a u-haul after a hearse." So! Maybe I could say: remember Sacred Heart in your will! It may be the will of God. But above all, may His will be a long and good life for you. Maybe you want to donate to the restoration of the paintings in memory of someone you love. The cracks are being mended. The walls are being painted. They haven't been touched since 1938. It will take three years. Maybe you don't think all this is the right thing to do.

Anyway. You can't say I didn't ask you. We have four paintings done. Wills of those who are gone, got us started. The beauty of these four is awesome.

Sometimes I feel sorry for myself, begging, always begging, and I hate to do it. But then I get the chance to tell stories and I love that. My heart fills now to tell you (and my melancholy nature takes some sweet delight in the scene) about old Johnny Nail keeping the fire alive in the rain. The roof is gone. The family is gone. All is gone except the flickering flame in his heart.

But one thing is true. The smoke from his wet naked chimney is a bright sign of hope to me going by in the rain. He would never imagine that I'd write to tell you that I saw it. Not in a thousand years! Johnny Nail would never never dream that his fire could light up some deep dark spot in your heart. Tell me it does!

Michael Doyle

In The Softness of the Thistle Seed

August, 1993

Hi:

Once a year I write from Ireland, and this I'm doing now. For home, continues to be, after all these years, the spot where I was born. Between the hills of North Longford I came at the end of a high-hedged lane. It is a quarter of a mile in length, and still, as it was in the beginning, only horse-wagon wide. Cars meet and one reverses to the nearest gap to get by. Here I squeezed through a narrow "lane" myself on November 3rd. It was my grandfather's 60th birthday. He was born in 1874.

Nearing home this past Monday, on the seventy-mile journey from Dublin Airport, I passed Johnny Nail's place again and the roofless home I mentioned in my last letter, and sure enough, the smoke was rising bravely from his naked chimney. So Johnny is alive. Thank God! Indeed he is alive. Still sending up clear reports of it, in wonderful wisps of blue.

Today I walked the land. The land that made my body and my bones. The hand, too, that holds this pen and the brain that makes it ramble on. And on......I walked here where the cows walk and leave their tracks and more.....along the way. I must. That's how I know who I am, after all these years in Camden.

At Home

It's here in this quiet place
That moss does grow upon my years
And wrens build nests and little ones
When stickiness is gone and feathers free,
Fly.
My words have grown wings
And timid now no more
Are free to fly and swerve and play
And ride upon the morning air
And bring whatever they can bring
To anyone who's out, about, wandering...
And wondering.

I walked in the meadow today that my father mowed every year, swath by swath, with slow back-breaking swings of a scythe. This land is reclaimed from wet wild-heathered bog by two centuries of Doyles and today it is managed by Geraldine Doyle with a sophistication that five generations of Doyle men could hardly dream of.

I walked in its long grass and everywhere I could see the signs of harvest. The first haws are on the whitethorn; fields and trees, weeds and flowers are heavy with seeds and drooping, like elderly people, with the wonderful weight of the future. White fluffs of thistle seeds, borne on the wind, flew over my head on the way to God knows where. Soft as cotton wool they were, or a baby's face and yet in the softness of a thistle seed, there is, as in all life, the hidden possibility of thorns that can hurt and hinder later.

I went past the doorway that I came through on my first full day in the world and great sweeps of yellow flowers are growing across the doorstep because that doorway is not used any more. Big, leafy nasturtiums (the nose twisters) lay claim now to the spot that is worn by almost two centuries of family clogs and shoes. They all walked through that doorway and only a few, four to be exact, are left whose feet have not gone cold.

Here, a century and a half ago, Catherine stood
And smelled the smell of famine on the land.
My mother! Grand, shawl shouldered,
Doubly great to me and Pat, her man,
My grandfather's grandfather, standing by her side
Their little John, asleep inside and unaware
Of all the blackening death that crept upon the green.
But The Famine failed to stop the stars
And John in time did have a son
A Pat, whose son, a John would father me.
And by this half door they stood, all of them
And saw the stars, the stars I see.
They are shining brightly still.
But does it matter anyhow? This spot!
This planet dot! This latitude and longitude
Of my port of entry in the world.
Not much I think, nor indeed where I depart
But how I fared upon the road and sea.
But let me tell you now
Lest our paths chance not again:
On this night I see the stars
And no place else are they so clear
Because I first came out of here.

Thanks, dear friend, if you have read this far and shared the sentimental musings of my wandering mind! I have time. Time to realize that every inch of the land I love is consecrated by the sweat and hardship of those whose dreams and stories live within me. And the blood of many, too, blackened on the green. The sadness of it all!

So, Camden and my failures there are not far below the surface of my melancholy mind. Our school will re-open on September 8th. A great beginning day. We have erected a new access that will make our children safer going out and protect them from anything unsafe coming in. But, above all, the doors wouldn't open without you.

I'm having a good time. So, I send you big bundles of the best blessings from Ireland.

Michael Doyle

Keep the Lamp Alive !

September, 1993

Hi:

A card, that I received from Susan Cedrone, shortly before I left for Ireland on my recent vacation had these kind words: "I always get a sick, sad feeling when you leave for home – perhaps because one time I don't expect you to return – our loss, but your 'peace.'" Well! I returned. Easing back into Camden in the darkness as I have done for 25 years, I looked at it as little as I could, so that the harsh broken edges of hopes and houses and lives would not hurt, right away, the womb-feel softness of my dear green fields.

It's forty years, this September 3rd, since I first put on a black suit (that Pat Shiels remade from one that my uncle Father Pakie Doyle wore before he died in 1951 at age 47 in Immaculate Conception Church in Jacksonville, FL) and cycled into town, to a bus, to a train, to a Seminary. The bike didn't go flat, the bus didn't break down, the train ran and so here I am. Back to work! In Camden, New Jersey. Forty years! Speak of "a sick, sad feeling!" No! Not really!

On that day when I "made" the bus on my bike, hundreds of children were making their way to Sacred Heart School in Camden. Msgr. Edward Lucitt was pastor. Sr. Mary Wytkof was principal for the opening of its 33rd year. Every classroom had a Dominican sister in a black and white habit and wall-to-wall children. Their families packed our church at each of the several masses on Sundays.

Today the Catholic population for the most part is gone. The sisters have gone, many to God and none to replace them. The children have grown, graduated and gone on their way. Thousands of them have turned out well. Some have failed.

But there is no failure in the consistent effort of many people over the years to sustain the school of Sacred Heart. However, the people who kept it going years ago, were for the most part, the people who had children in it.

Today, Sacred Heart Catholic School is still open. Most of its children are Baptist, trying to grow up in the troubled streets of South Camden. But they are our children. Last year, their parents paid ninety-nine thousand dollars in tuition to provide a Christian education for them. And in addition, you, who have no children in our school, provided an additional two hundred thousand dollars to give them that education.

It is a much more difficult job to keep Sacred Heart School open today than it was 40 years ago. The task seems frightening. But God is good. I assure you, we do our very best to keep the costs down. The fact is that it costs seven times as much to educate a child in a Camden public school as it does in Sacred Heart.

Thoughts like these, on this daunting task, convince me right away that I'm back to work. In Camden, New Jersey.

Speaking of tasks! Recently, I did a most pleasant one. The wedding of my niece Rosemarie Doyle and Sean Cusack in Ireland. It took place in the Franciscan Abbey of

Multifarnham Co. Westmeath, "which continues to function as a Catholic Church for more than 700 years." This Abbey, founded in 1270, was suppressed by Henry the Eighth in 1540. It was raided by British troops in 1590, burned down in 1601 by government troops, and burned again in 1604; its priests arrested and imprisoned in 1614 and 1617 and the abbey suppressed again in 1618. It was attacked in 1648 and its worst fate came with Cromwell in 1651, when it was plundered and burned and all the friars driven away. But the survivors always came back and started again. Even though, after Cromwell, they used locations near the ruined abbey for 177 years, they never gave up. Came back and came back. Today the light is on. The Franciscans are ministering. And the centuries old church is completely restored.

There, at a big round stone (the altar), within those old walls, that witnessed centuries of fire and sword, the wedding took place. New life blossomed again with hope and love among old stones bonded there for 700 years. Neither death nor plunder ever broke them completely apart. I thought of Sacred Heart and how we are trying in our own little way to keep the lamp alive in Camden's battered times. We keep doing it. Saving the school for the children and abandoned houses for the people. Both waiting for a window in every sense of the word.

We try. We try again. In wind and pouring rain. We strive to keep the lamp alive.

Michael Doyle

The Hedge School

(excerpt)

They waited too in other dismal times
When fjord folk tore the eggs
From each monastic nest.
Waited while our neighbors crossed the Mearin drain
With Norman names and blades
Some like Henry with worn wives and wicked virtue
Couldn't bear the vesper bell or knell
And the bards and books were banished too
Blocked by barbed wire and broken harps
Then Cromwell came with cruel crowds
And cut the heads off soaring hawks
And little chickens too beneath the tender wing.

"He Cried All The Way Home"

October, 1993

Hi:

I write this time from a splendid spot on the top of "a wee mountain" in the Poconos, PA (2,200 feet above the distant sea), on a crest where Vista Lane meets Sky Drive. Below in the valley, Boulder Lake shelters at the still green feet of Big Boulder Ski Slopes. I am here to spend a day and a half with my brother J.J. Doyle, a great priest from St. Mary's Church in Edgeworthstown, Ireland. He's on a visit to the U.S. His first in ten years.

We came yesterday. The warm sun and the night's frost were painting Fall's golden flames across the Poconos and a hundred types of trees shimmered in their glory; breezes whispered to every lovely leaf in a last dance before they die. To the north, the noonday light dipped the mountain in a lake that's known as Harmony. As Peter said at Tabor long ago: "It is good for us to be here." Mt.17, 7.

In a neighbor's place, a trough of birdseed has competitions going among some of the small creatures that share this mountain with us. Little birds dart in and fly away with a seed or two, because four bluejays constantly frighten them away. I didn't like the bluejays, but then a squirrel came and planked herself (himself) in the trough as solidly as John Kruk on first base. Then the bluejays had to fight every inch of the way. Two chipmonks arrived as well and bulged their jowls to breaking points with the birdseed. I expected them to spit. They didn't.

Today, the warm sun is gone. The fire is burning brightly on the hearth. Outside, a misty wind is whipping some of the splendid leaves from the trees – pen in hand by a wall-wide window, I am – and my melancholy soul is swimming like a trout in a tumbling stream.

> *Oh the lids are frozen shut*
> *On many evening eyes I knew*
> *They lit the lamp and saw my face*
> *And smiled my name when I met them*
> *In the wet leaf lane of long ago.*
> *There by the bend, where I turned my head*
> *To see my mother's waving hand.*

We will leave today and descend to Camden, to levels lower than the stormy sea. I am thinking of my friend John McNamee's great new book *Diary of a City Priest* (Sheed and Ward). The chapter entitled, "Going Away and Coming Back," like the others, breaks the heart, as the harshness and helplessness of his North Philadelphia streets tear apart the softness of his soul.

Anyway, my first job this evening will be to center on holy scripture a CCOP (Camden Churches Organized for People) forum at Sacred Heart for candidates seeking to be mayor of Camden. A new one will be elected on November 2nd, the sixth in my twenty-five years in this city and during that time, conditions have worsened with every passing day.

The candidates' talk was, as always, crime, drugs, jobs, youth, housing and "Camden dumped on." Oh the terrible impossibility of it all! One of the children we had to let go from Sacred Heart last year because he came to school with a gun, was arrested recently for shooting a neighborhood boy. According to Time, 100,000 children carry guns to school every day.

In today's Philadelphia Inquirer Neal Pierce, the well-known writer on urban issues, says that "by every measure, we are the most violent, mayhem and murder-prone nation of the developed world. Today's cresting level of utter hopelessness among inner-city youth – combined with the bath of television, movie and video administered violence that affects the minds of our young people – is translating into stray bullets flying in more communities."

He goes on: "unless our continent-wide wave of senseless violence suddenly abates – and there's little reason to believe it will – violence is posed to become an overarching issue of American politics, state, local and federal."

And sadly he asks: "To what avail?" Not much, I answer. This country's sick love affair with the gun and the NRA's evil stranglehold on the nation's lawmakers adds more every day to the 200 million guns already in the hands of our people and within reach of their children.

One day in late summer, 1903, my grandfather Michael Creegan took down the hunting gun that always rested above his hearth and went down to the lake that bordered his land. His son Michael, 13, went with him and little Jimmy followed. He was only five. They walked in the long grass by the shore looking for wild ducks and when one rose, suddenly, my grandfather fired and the duck fell in the weeds. Michael ran to fetch it and his father (my grandfather), mused at the slim pickings it would make for the two boys with him and his eight other children back at the house. Michael found the dead duck and, "God help us, found its nest too and three little ones in it." Their mother, hanging by her legs, dead in his hand. "Little Jimmy cried all the way home."

Guns leave human gaps in the nests of the nation every day, but more frightening than the murders themselves is the remorseless attitude of most of those who commit them, not to mention the callous indifference of the moneymakers on the guns and the greedy lobbyists behind them. And, God help us, the still unstirred public outcry at it all.

"Little Jimmy" grew to manhood, married Katie Farrelly in '27 and they filled the house with lovely freckled life. In 1953 when the oldest of their sixteen children was twenty-five and the youngest six, their mother died at the age of 51 and the nest where she nurtured each of them was wet with all the tears that lamented her. Jimmy died in 1976, 23 years later, but he never got over the aching loss of Katie. Never once. "He cried all the way home."

O God grant that all the tears of those who grieve may cool the rage of this gun-mad age and rust its killing weapons into dust!

Michael Doyle

A Thousand Strangers

December, 1993

Hi:

Do you believe that Christmas day is only three weeks away? I remember a time when minutes were minutes but now hours are minutes and I have no sense of waiting. Maybe that's the reason why our childhood Christmases are so vivid in our minds. We used to wait. Eagerly.

I "couldn't wait" for that special night when we went to Mass in a hired "motor car." Neither I, nor the families I knew, had even a bicycle, so we had no sense of speed. Twenty-five miles an hour was comparable to a rocket. But we knew no rockets, only the dart of a bird from a branch or the race of a hare from a greyhound. On Christmas night, we were on our way:

> *We were on our way to church, freckled faces to the glass*
> *In a hired motor car to attend midnight Mass*
> *Oh the feelin' of the speedin' like the shooting of a star*
> *And the trees going backward as we stared from the car.*
> *Now our hurried pace of life is driven much too fast*
> *We see nothing racing backwards except the present to the past.*

Our childhood Christmases were magical times when we made moments into memories, and even though we didn't realize it, we stored them safely in our hearts. Mostly glad. Some sad. But all of them good. We all can tell stories of a Christmas time, years ago, and even if we cannot now re-enact the way things were, we can tell the story. And if we do, (like the tale of Bal Shem Tov) "God will come." Each of us has one.

> *I used to know a secret tree*
> *A holly tree where berries hid,*
> *Its prickly branches knew my name*
> *At Christmas time I always came.*
> *Today I walked the fields again*
> *And looked at things with older eyes*
> *No more I saw but saw it more*
> *Than when I dawdled as a boy.*
> *But my holly tree was lying flat*
> *And all the trees beside it lay*
> *The chain-saw smoke was in the air*
> *The white of trunks was on the clay.*
> *And I wondered sadly why bleeding cuts*
> *Are part of all our struggling births*
> *Why easy scenes are puffs of foam*
> *And pain alone the stuff of poems.*

No matter how we try today to soften the hard edges of life in this holy season, we are aware that the real essence of Christmas is demanding stuff. God became weakness. That tested our concern, and we didn't do too well. Homes or inns had no room for the homeless mother when the water broke. The doors were shut. The local monarch did his best to kill her child. Slaughtered many children in his madness. Only the shepherds, unwelcome themselves in most places, with their rags and their smells, came over to greet him. That's why, I suppose, we try to recover and celebrate Christmas with acts of hospitality and welcome ever since. The people in Bethlehem were people like us. We often say too: if only I knew. As Mother Teresa says "Jesus still comes in the distressing disguise of the poor."

The most moving story I ever read – it haunted me for years as a child – was in my grammar (National) school book. It was about a little boy who was playing by his home when a ragged stranger came by and shared in the fun with him. The little boy enjoyed him greatly and was having a wonderful time. Suddenly his father discovered the ragged stranger and yelled at him to get going. The boy begged and cried. But the stranger left and went down the hill towards the river that was wide and flooded. The boy ran after him, stopped, and called for his father. He came. The stranger was "walking on the flooded river and there was a light at his feet."

I don't have to tell you that a thousand "strangers" will come to Sacred Heart this Christmas and ask us for a turkey and a basket of food., They will come as Christ comes in the most "distressing disguises of the poor" and when they leave, we may not see them walking over the Newton Creek with a light at their feet, but most of them walk over "troubled waters" every day that most of us would be too frightened to step on.

Please spread the word! Tell people about the way that Christ comes and how easy it is to miss the blessing! Tell them! Tell them we all need to give something as much as the poor need to get it. Tell them the truth!

Michael Doyle

Bright Open Door
(Excerpt)

But a donkey would be welcome
With the Holy Mother on its back.
She could waddle to the hearth
And shelter from the rain
In that one-windowed hut
By "John the Doctors" lane.

Grass has covered the location
Of Pat Nixon's little place
"Nara" stone upon a stone
It's gone without a trace.
But Brian's beaming face
And the candles on the floor
Are still shining in our minds
Near that bright open door.

Your Face in the "Pongers" of the Poor

January, 1994

Hi:

Happy New Year to you! May God be with you for all your nights and days 'til that new calendar is filled and "filed" and fetched away.

My thanks to you for the Christmas words you wrote yourself and the lovely wishes too. I write with gratitude as well for Camden people, old and young, whose Christmas table had your turkey on it and plates of healthy food you bought for them. All were given with as much respect as possible when receiver has to face the giver and face the fact, too, that their roles will likely never be reversed. It is not easy to honor the poor and we fail often in this demanding task. But, we try. Fourteen hundred (1400) children got toys from Sacred Heart in a program where parents pay a little bit, and for it, they get the dignity of purchase and the dignity of choice for their children. May God multiply the "loaves and fishes" that you placed upon the tables of the poor, and above all, may justice be ladled out soon for those who wait in the long lines.

The winter here has been mild in the old year but turned sharply cold in the new. Most recently, freezing evening rain and bright noonday sun transformed abandoned lots, weeds, trees, eaves and everything into an endless necklace of diamonds glittering in the light. For several days, the most awesome winter beauty in any lifetime.

There was glitter, too, the other day in Jackie Turlington's earrings, big as beer cans, (she bought them "at the 99 Cents Store"), when she came to get five dollars for kerosene. She has lived for several winters without heat, light or water and by some miracle, her smile still gleams like the sparkling ice on those abandoned shells in Camden. I bet she didn't buy the kerosene. But it would be hard not to love Jackie with all her glitter and dance in the bitter cold.

Today's (January 11) New York Times editorializes about the Transit Authority's "crack down on begging" and asks "should government be telling people not to exercise compassion at a time when poverty is at its most visible since the Depression."

One of my earliest memories, going back to when I was slightly over two years old, was of "tinker" women sitting in my mother's kitchen. They had come to beg for a little food and they had holy pictures for sale in a basket that they left down on the floor. My eyes were very near the floor then and they feasted on the pictures. I still can see them...and my mother, too, who always helped those poor women. The tinkers. They lived in canvas and burlap tents by the wet road and their men made tin mugs we called "pongers" and fixed all the leaking buckets in the countryside. Like the swallows, they would come back to the same roadside spots and soon were off again for awhile, leaving behind the useless bits of things they cast away.

The tinkers setting up again in the old spot

Where the rags of other stays bind the briars
Beneath the dripping leaves of early spring
Old shoes, odd ones left together there,
Some moss-greened by time, some left not so long.
The grass grown back except the burnt spot
Lit again. The smell of smoke — whin root and sycamore —
Stirs around the weathered woman, there.
The hair plaited, brown, the shawl plaid,
Hunkered down to bake her bread.
Rain on her hair, drops hiss on the oven lid
But she weathers all for the "weans" she bore
And the wee one rising like the bread
Beneath the warm lid of flesh and bone.
Her man with sheets of tin, hammer taps
Slender anvil of his trade, anchored in a sod
Sits upon a log, scissors out his shining metal
As silver slivers curl up and drop
He bends his glinting tin, rims the lip
Then seams the ends and bottoms too
Rivets blunted tight, to hold the handle on
A ponger made. To our house he came
Two strings of gleaming pongers from his neck
My mother bought a little one for me
And in its shining bottom I saw my face
But the tinker's face was in it first
Yet he seldom saw his own
Beneath the constant coating of the rain.
No man for mirrors, he. I wonder
Did he see himself less or more
Than others saw him. Less I fear
And there wasn't much to spare
When other classes took their bite
Just a bit of curled tin flattened out
Beneath the solemn strata of it all.
And yet he made the mirror of my morning face
Before the many dents and falls
Damaged all his tinker hands had wrought
Or I, the image that it so gladly gave.

Again, I thank you. May our faces be seen in the "pongers" of the poor when we reach out to fill them and God's own image in the empty vessels that we are...worn into brightness by the generosity of our lives!

(P.S. "weans," pronounced "wains," means wee-ones, children.)

Michael Doyle

The Valentine of a Lifetime

February, 1994

Hi:

Maybe it's the weather. This year's February is fierce. Even Valentine's Day in the middle of it, didn't have enough warmth for most people to melt the ice that strangled them. But it did for me.

Poor St. Valentine. There is no saint whose name is more widely known and whose life is less known. But there he is...the darling of every card shop and candy store, every restaurant, jeweler and florist. Not only in Italy where he lived, but all over the world.

Isn't it amusing that the holy man's bones ended up in the crypt of a Dublin Church. Nothing very romantic in that. But it's fun to contrast cool, damp days under dripping Dublin eaves with the flaming passion of the sun on the sands of Palermo. I don't know what that means...

But I do know that in this corner of Camden, the heart is sacred. *Cor ad cor Loquitur.* Valentine was a martyr of a man on a Roman street. He had love enough in his heart to lay down his life for his faith. Tough love, indeed. But any love is better than no love. Even if it's only expression is a heart-shaped balloon on a frosty day in February.

It's half a century since I first heard of Valentine and this is the first year that I ever planned anything for it. I planned a treat for myself. A visit to a young girl named Leah Young. Thirteen, she is, in the sweet blossom of her youth.

Leah has been a student at Sacred Heart since kindergarten. In recent years, her youthful energy began to wane. But she entered 8th grade this past September. Shortly afterwards, she was out of school and into St. Christopher's Hospital in Philadelphia.

It wasn't the first time. One year before, in 1992, after periods when her head drooped on the desk and she struggled up the stairs to her classroom, her mother, Marion, took her to a doctor. Bronchitis, it seemed. The doctor, baffled that she was able to attend school, committed her to the hospital immediately. Leah Young's heart was doomed. Without a transplant she would die. Thus began her wait for a heart. Her wait in the line...the most poignant line in the world, where children wait for hearts from children yet to die. That noble paradox where life is renewed out of the dregs of death.

Leah knew. She came back to school. Struggled on. Never complained. Finished seventh grade. Promoted to eighth. Summer dragged on. No heart. Lots of heart. She returned in September. But not for long. By October, she was back in St. Christopher's, still hoping for a new heart and her mother knowing well that her only child would never leave alive without one. The days wore on. Christmas came and a virus struck. By now she was down to two in the long line. Her condition worsened. The doctors felt that even if they had a heart for her, she couldn't live to receive it. Her mother hardly left her side; her aunt, her great aunt, her grandmother, all wonderful nourishing women around her.

I saw Leah on January 15. She was dying. The doctor gave her two hours to live. I was thinking about her funeral as I left the hospital and the loving mother who would soon be left alone. I thought of Calvary and the great women there who stood their ground, braver and more resourceful than the men who gave up.

The women by Leah's bed didn't give up. Defying the doctor, they sought another opinion. Her diagnosis was faxed to Pittsburgh. Soon the decision was made to move her to Temple Hospital in Philadelphia. She didn't loose her spot on the waiting line and her chance for a heart, if a heart ever came. Leah told her mother: "I saw the angels. I'm going to live." Late on February 4th, somewhere in the United States, a thirteen-year-old girl, whose name she'll never know, died. She gave her heart to Leah Young. Less than five hours after it stopped beating in the one, it began beating in the other. Leah Young is alive and well.

My treat to myself on Valentine's Day, 1994, was to see the girl who was dead; now, so smilingly alive. The girl from Sacred Heart had a new heart of her own. "Happy Valentine's Day," she said into my tape recorder, to our children and staff. "I'll be there soon." Minutes later she was plowing energetically into a hoagie like any teenager in America. It was all so miraculous. The sad face I had seen at the edge of death, beamed now with a sweetness that awed me. The Valentine of a lifetime.

All over our school, the walls have a sign: "Leah has a new heart." And the news of it gives a new heart to us all. Thanks and praises be to God!

It will be a day of days when Leah Young returns to Sacred Heart with her new heart beating and her face smiling and all of us rejoicing. And beneath it all, a tinge of sadness for the mother who mourns somewhere for her thirteen-year-old daughter who died. But her beat goes on in little Leah Young of Sacred Heart.

Michael Doyle

Note: Leah Young died of cancer on May 31, 2002.

The Count-up

Two generations gone! The grand one
That raised the ones that reared me
And those who bore me, gone too
And some who came with me to play
The games and times when years were long
Weeks were months, waited bells, eternity,
Limped off before the game was ended
And did not again come out to play
The hills don't care who walks

Upon the fields with ambitious plans
Or prides enormous progress made
When years of evenings close upon the world
Did someone count the heartbeats of my youth
That seemed to throb unendingly
As tides tug and tease the reeds upon the shore.
And is there, each day, a mighty calculation
The number gone. The number still to go.

A Kiss of Light Upon the Tears

March, 1994

Hi:

It's the day after St. Patrick's Day. I should have written on the day before it. I'm tired. The happy holiday of my homeland was for me a mad-meeting work day, whipping me from one place to another with no time for lunch and two minutes to gobble down one potato before I rushed off to read poetry at the Walt Whitman Center in Camden. From there I went to St. Malachy's rectory in Philadelphia at 11 p.m. to drink a toast to St. Patrick with my friends John McNamee and Daniel Berrigan. Don't ask me what time I got home!

Anyway. It is a good thing that this March letter was written a few weeks ago when I wrote a poem called "A Salute to Eugene O'Donnell." I knew that its "kiss of light upon the tears" would be enough to stir the sad-glad rhythms of the Celtic soul. "So." as John McNamee says (that's what he says). It will do for March.

Eugene O'Donnell of Derry, who has been here in Philadelphia for 37 years and been my friend for more than half of them, is thinking of going back to live in "the town I love so well." Derry. One would hope he was only thinkin' and that "it would go off him." But then I remember the story of the Tipperary man who was warned about the flood in the time of Noah. He looked up at the Galtee mountains and said "It'ill only be a shower."

When Eugene O'Donnell lifts his violin, and plays the slow Irish airs, no one in the world can do it better. The music almost lifts him off the ground. He still stands on his toes but his body and soul leap and stretch out on the strings as the most exquisite sound rises and touches the timbre of the heart with a haunting sweetness.

In 1957, he emigrated to Philadelphia from his beloved Derry, that marvelous city on the Foyle with its heroic history; its name, the oak, sacred to the druids who preceded its holy patron, St. Columba. It is the great gateway city of County Derry and also Donegal, situated on the edge of Inishowen that enchanted land between Lough Swilly and Lough Foyle.

Eugene, bears the famous clan name of O'Donnell, whose great chief Red Hugh with his contemporary Hugh O'Neill are heroic stars in the national memory. They were forced to leave Ireland after the Battle of Kinsale at the beginning of the seventeenth century and from the consequences of that loss, Ireland has suffered since. "But the lively limbs of the clans remained." In Eugene O'Donnell's fiddle, we hear the ache of Ireland's soul, weeping with Deirdre long ago, or The Mother in Pearse's poem in 1916 or Rosalyn Sands in '81.

On November 9, 1977, six years before her death, my mother came to Sacred Heart. It was her birthday and Eugene came. After dinner, he lifted his fiddle, stood before her and played three lovely airs to her. They were her gift on that happy day. I still see her sitting erect on the edge of a green couch listening to his awesome sound. It flooded her soul with the tears of her wet doorstep long ago when eight of her twelve brothers and sisters parted from their weeping parents, to cross the wide-wide Atlantic; some never to come home again. She bore the sweet memory of Eugene and his music into eternity.

My thanks is my poem "A Salute to Eugene O' Donnell."

An acorn fell on the lips of the Foyle
In the dark of a winter's day
It fell in the wisp of a thrush's nest
That the wind had torn away.

The wisp was set in a druid's track
As he walked through Inishowen
The dent of his heel in a flaxen field
'Twas there the seed was sown

The thrush kept watch from a whitethorn bush
'Til a bard came by in May
Sang a lonesome note he heard in his heart
And buried the seed in clay.

The oak grew tall and Colum came
To sing in the shade below
The songs of old that the thrush had heard
And the new that she didn't know.

But the robin said with a modest nod
This bright new sound is good
It's the Lord of life who died and rose
I wear His badge of blood

The son of God and the planet's sun
Go back to the primal night
When a kiss on the mouth of the purest dark
Made a smile of broad day light.

So the birds sang loud on the oak tree top
And mixed the old with the new
And the harpers heard in the fields below
And the children heard them too.

The Chieftains glanced at their native sky
The clouds a cross on the sun

They bade farewell to their holy hills.
And sailed out one by one.

But the lively limbs of the clans remained
And danced to the dawning day
With bodhrans, flutes and violins
They kept their grief at bay.

And the Derry air was a breath of life
On a cold and frosty day
It whistled bright on summer's morn
It choked on famine clay.

It rode the lonesome Foyle to sea
In the boats that went away
It sighed at night in foreign fields
But it rose at dawn to play.

It lifted high the people's "NO"
To heavy hands that held them down
That tried to take their sacred leaf
And crush it with a crown.

But life took wing in the sadness there
When O'Donnell rose with a daring bow.
To play the notes that the thrush had heard
And the songs that the people know.

He stood where bardic feet have stood
And soared his tunes where angels hear
He saved the whispers of the wind
And the kiss of light upon the tears.

He carved his fiddle from bits of time
And stretched his sinews into strings
He built his bow from human ties
His pain and joy made it sing.

Michael Doyle

O Mia Bambino Caro

April, 1994

Hi:

Sacred Heart Church sits, I would say, amid much misery in Camden, NJ and yet the blessings, that come to this little block where Broadway and Ferry, Jasper and Fourth meet on our planet, continue to amaze me daily, after all these years.

Speaking of blessings!! On April 17, 1894, in the French seaport town of Marseilles, Catherina Martin was laboring to give birth to her first child. Twenty-three years before, she had been born herself in Dragoniere near Sampeyre – over the nearby border – high in the Piedmonte mountains of Italy. There she was raised and stayed with her grandparents even after her father, Guiseppe and mother, Sair Maddalena, left to find work in Marseilles. She followed them later and there met and married Bartholomew Genovesi. He too was away from home, born in Capriglia near Pietrasanta in 1863, high in the Tuscany region of Northern Italy. There his parents, Domenico Genovesi and Emilia Battaglia, raised ten children, growing grapes and making wine, tending olive trees, making olive oil and feeding their happy cluster on good food. Bartholomew Genovesi did not pursue the farming life but sought work in the marble quaries for which Pietrasanta is known. But not as well known as nearby Carrara. He moved to Marseilles where he labored to cut and set and polish the hard durable stone of his trade.

But none of his labor on the rough edged marble was ever so severe as the labor of his wife, Catherina, on the soft little body she was bringing forth on April 17, 1894. Soft headed he was, Remo, as he slithered into this world; and time would tell that this little body of flesh and bones would have its own brand of "marble" durability.

Who could have dreamed that exactly 100 years later, Remo Genovesi, would walk up to the altar of Sacred Heart Church in Camden, NJ at 12 noon on April 17, 1994 and, in clear voice, bless the congregation in the name of the Father, the Son and the Holy Spirit. Well, he did. On his hundredth birthday. Water broke again as it did long ago in Marseilles and flooded our faces with tears of joy. Sorrow's cost was in the blessing too. Because on the young mother who bore him, like Mary of Nazareth, the shadow of the cross fell sadly along the long path of her life.

Her second child, a girl, died young of cholera and then her heartbroken husband began pondering life in the USA. He moved his wife and little Remo back to his parents' house in Capriglia and said good-bye. The aching hand that waved fondly to him waved above the baby boy she bore within. Her husband made his way to the marble quarries of the new world and began to work for the Vermont Marble Company in Rutland. He looked forward to the day his family would join him. It was the hopeful year of 1900.

Meanwhile, back in Pietrasanta the boy Remo (and his new brother Narville) ate and slept and grew. He still remembers those tender years as his grandfather took him by the hand to operas and concerts in the squares of Pietrasanta and other Tuscany towns.

Then there was the day that plunged the family and neighbors in Capriglia into a terrible sadness. Word reached the mountain that Remo's father was killed crossing a wide cluster of train tracks on a cold winter's day in Vermont. The year was 1902. Remo was eight years old. Narville was one. Their dead father, far away, was only thirty-nine.

Catherina, grief-stricken and bewildered, readied her little ones and left the security of Capriglia and set sail on the liner *George Washington* from Genoa for the raw hope of new life in Rutland, Vermont.

It was a new world for her and here she would raise her children and live out her life for fifty years. Little Remo, eight years old, entered a three-room school of nine grades and wall-to-wall children whose language he didn't speak. One of them, Agnes McDermott, could recall eighty years later how "sorry she felt for the new boy who seemed so lonely and serious." She remembered, too, the day her father told of the man who was killed on the railroad tracks.

Twenty-three years later, at 7:00am on June 29, 1925, she took the hand of that 'new boy," now lonely no more, and married him in Rutland, VT. They had to catch the train to Albany, to catch the steamer to New York; then off to Atlantic City for a honeymoon and hand-in-hand happily down the world for the next 64 years.

The "lonely" Italian boy had made real progress, learned English quickly, and at age fifteen, went to work to help his mother. At 16, he began cutting stone at Vermont Marble at six cents an hour. For his 60-hour week, he took home $3.60. But as his skills increased, so did his wages; when his honeymoon was over, he had a solid job in the Vermont Marble Company in Philadelphia. His work can still be seen in Philadelphia, Washington and many other cities. It can be seen, too (although he would give much of the credit to Agnes) in the four children they raised: Mary, Robert, Paul and Jean.

Remo Genovesi retired at the age of 68 and now thirty-two years later, he lives by himself in Haddon Heights, NJ, cooks his own breakfast and lunch, goes for walks and lifts weights to keep his "marble" arms strong. His mind is clear. His heart is happy. His conversation is sparkling. He is six years older than this century and in much better shape, a splendid bridge over its "troubled waters." When he raised his voice in blessing over the people of Sacred Heart on his 100th Birthday, he raised it over you as well and all who have shared the century with him.

Then, our gift to him. Our own extraordinary mezzo-soprano, Barbara Dever, soared to soprano, as she sang to him Puccini's O Mio Bambino Caro. Our Church of the Sacred Heart was eight years old when Remo Genovesi was born. He and it, had to wait a hundred years to hear such a sound. O Mio Babbino Caro (Oh My Beloved Daddy). He was back with his grandfather, Dominico Genovesi, listening to opera in Petrasanto long ago and all the tears of the partings were lifted into the noonday sun. The blessing of a lifetime!!

Michael Doyle

Mary Mc Kenna Was Never "Bet"

July, 1994

Hi:

Fifty years ago today, on July 18, 1944, Mary McKenna Creegan died in the Townland of Drumkeeran, near Cloone, County Leitrim. She was my grandmother. She died in her home where she had lived for almost 60 years, ever since Michael Creegan (whose name I bear) took her as a bride of 23 over the few small fields that separated her family's farm from his own. With him she conceived and raised their thirteen children, five daughters and eight sons, between 1886 and 1906.

On today's date, 100 years ago, she was tending to her first six children, all under eight, not to mention hens and chickens, cows and calves, sows and their little ones. Her husband was out on the land but his father, Hugh Creegan, at 79, was still able to help her mind the children. Seven more would follow, the tenth, Rosetta in 1901; the first in the shining century. She would grow up to be my mother. Matthew, John Francis, Patrick, Michael, Mary Ann, Hugh, Kate, Jimmy, Bridget, Rosetta, Peter, Elizabeth, and Terence.

As they grew, she labored strenuously to wash and feed them, hanging her pots of potatoes or porridge on the iron crook that swung like a gate over her hearth fire. Her hands kneaded loaf after loaf of bread every day and churned the milk of her cows into butter to spread upon it. She tattered and carded the fleece from the sheeps' back and her spinning wheel whirred ever so softly...and the little ones slept as she eased out the wool she would knit to clothe them.

"I was never so happy," she said late in life, when all were gone save one, "as when I was baking a bag of flour a week." That was at least 112 pounds of flour that went through her holy hands before it got to the fingers and mouths of her growing children. She was a great woman of prayer and ingenuity, with her stories and her laughter...and the sorrow too that had its place in her heart. "Ah," she said of the children, "when they're feathered, they always have to fly."

Before her twins were born in 1903, her firstborn, Matthew, was on a ship leaving Ireland to cross the "bowl of bitter tears." He landed on Ellis Island, near New York, after many days at sea. It was just the beginning. After Matthew, it was Patrick, then Michael, then Mary Ann, then John Francis, then Hughie, then Kate. The grieving at the partings was sad as a wake for the young. The doorstep was wet with the tears of Mary and Michael as one after another, the first seven children that they raised, waved good-bye from the bend in the lane. On their way, all of them, to the US. Mary and Michael had seen their own brothers go and never return and they fretted as their child moved away: would they ever see the sweet face again. Of the eight who went (Terry left in 1925) to the US, three returned to stay, three they never saw again, and two they saw once.

But all thirteen children grew up to be good people. They married and raised seventy-three children, of which I am one. Fifty-two in Ireland and twenty-one in the United States.

Fortunately Mary Creegan was able to tend to her daughters as they gave birth to her grandchildren.

Today, as I think of her slipping from this world in a birth to a new, I feel grateful that she was there with her hands and her kindly wisdom when I first saw the light of day.

> *Soft-headed then I slithered on to linen sheets*
> *Beneath the dripping roof of thatch*
> *My grandmother there with soothing words*
> *Knowing well herself, the pain and sweat-wet joy of birth*
> *Her own baker's dozen up and out*
> *Five heads of hair she plaited in her time*
> *Eight sons she washed and fed*
> *There now to welcome me and lend a holy hand*
> *She cleaned the wrappings from my face*
> *And found the traces of her own.*

I remember her at later births in our house with her red wrap around petticoat and huge safety pins (I was little and allowed to look), her long black skirt and high-laced boots and the sweet round face of her, under a navy veil on a Sunday.

She raised her own children well and her thirteen lived 1,045 years on this earth and when all their ages are added, they average 80 years for each. Mary set the pace herself, with 82.

At the burial of Peter, the last of her children to die, in 1984, one of his nephews Pakie Joe Creegan paused as he shoveled in the clay on the coffin and said: "God's going to be dealing from this deck from now on." All thirteen gone and now the 73 are next to follow them. But, 68 are still on the lands of the living and one of them is writing to you today.

Last year, over in Katie O'Briens' (a restaurant five miles from Camden) I met Maggie Curran, a cousin from home. She told me what her grandmother said back in '27 when she learned that my grandmother was tending to her daughter Mary Ann who had just given birth to her first child. She was told that the baby was lying on a blanket inside the horse's collar beside the fire. She (using the maiden name) said of my grandmother: "Mary McKenna was never 'bet.'" There was no cradle yet and Mary McKenna Creegan tucked her grandson in a horse's collar by the fire. She was never "bet;" never beaten for a plan.

That statement filled me with delight and confidence. She will always help me to find a way. Find a way to deal with the limitations of Sacred Heart. Find a way to fix houses, get sponsors, keep our school open for our children, so that they will not fly unfeathered and fall to the ground. Put a "horse's collar" of collective care around them to keep them safe from the dangers of the world.

Let it be said, that by the grace of God and the prayers of a golden grandmother: "Sacred Heart was never 'bet.'"

Michael Doyle

We're All in the Same Boat

August, 1994

Greetings from Ireland!

Last Sunday evening, August 21, I attended my primary school reunion in Ireland, the first ever held since classes began on December 1, 1848. Obviously, not everyone was able to be there. But my parish church was packed for the Mass and the banquet room full as well for dining and dancing 'til 3:00 AM. My second grade teacher, Rose Lynch, was there. Well into her eighties now, her mind sharper than my own (is that saying anything!). She said to me: "It's very hard out there where you have been working. I'm going to start praying tomorrow that you come back and get a nice easy place here in Ireland." She taught 2nd and 3rd grade in the school of my childhood for 43 years; leaving only when it closed in 1973.

My school in Pulladoey, County Longford was called St. Colmcille's, named for the great patron saint of my parish, not to mention Derry and Iona and all Ireland itself. He founded a monastic settlement in my rural neighborhood in 550 A.D. It was situated on an island called Inch Mor on nearby Lough Gowna. Only the ruins of the monastery remain with its old cemetery and now my school, one of five small schools in the parish, is abandoned too. For 20 years.

Before the Mass, led by Father J.J. Doyle, we gathered in the school, which is two miles from the church, and we walked through all the rooms. Three. That's all it ever had. In one of them, where I studied mightily in three grades named Low Infants, High Infants and First Class, there is now a big opening in the slates where I could see the beautiful sky, blue and white, going by. It would have been a great window for a dreamer long ago. Just recently, and for this reunion, the poor school was rescued from Mother Nature before she almost completely enveloped it.

In 1939, when I was four-and-a-half years old, I began walking two and one tenth miles up the Cornadrung Road to school with very short legs and big expectations.

We were delighted to welcome the dear daffodils
That Melia had planted and spring always showed,
The lambs and the ewes that leaped on the hill
By the beautiful Cornadrung Road.

Oats on the wind was fine fertile seed
The soil was soft, the sods were harrowed,
The sower had burlap strapped to his thighs
By the beautiful Cornadrung Road.

The chestnuts that fell on road and on lane
Were dropped in the ashes to see them explode
And the wind whipped the leaves from the whitethorn bush

By the beautiful Cornadrung Road

We ran in the rain like goats in a storm,
Had a wonderful time whenever it snowed,
Loved the cool crisp feel and crackle of ice
On the beautiful Cornadrung Road.

So it is somewhat overwhelming to see what time and tide have done to the school and to me and to all those who came back to be together.

St. Colmcille's School is open no more
Abandoned like Inch where the holy monks rowed
The weeds and the briars have padlocked the doors.
No children are walking the Cornadrung Road.

But walking steadily at the Reunion and enjoying it immensely was past pupil Charles Reilly who is 83. Not only that, but "the big girl" who took him by the hand to school the first day; she was there. In fine fettle, too. Rose Sheridan. She started school in 1911.

Katie McGlade couldn't come but she sent her best regards. She's 98. She used to come to our school from the other side of the lake. Her Aunt Margaret (a teacher) rowed the boat across the lake every day. That was in 1901.

Well! Anyway! I have schools on my mind. And, of course Sacred Heart in my own. It too should celebrate. In January, 1995, it will be 75 years old. A school with a heart that never missed a beat for three quarters of a century. It faced depression times and war times, sad times and glad times but it kept going and countless children have been helped to live good and generous lives.

It is our turn now and we're keeping it going. Not really...God is keeping it going, miraculously. As you know, all the families at Sacred Heart pay tuition and you as a sponsor supplement what they do. So once again I ask you to help the children who are trying to grow up in the harshness of Inner City Camden. I wonder will they ever have a School Reunion on this side of heaven. Who knows!

I never thought that I would have a reunion in the first school of my life. I went with my usual uncertainty about these things but I had a wonderful time and the joy I felt was the joy of a child, light and playful...as faces lit faces after more than forty years. It was magic. We're so right because we're trying to give the children a chance at Sacred Heart.

Like Katie McGlade coming to school in 1901. Through waves and rain and winter wind. But she had help. Margaret rowed the boat and brought her safely back and forth. A special sponsor she was. Every day.

We're all in the same boat.

Michael Doyle

I Hear You Calling Me

October 1994

Hi:

"John McCormack (the great Irish tenor) came from Dublin to Camden to record. I will go from Camden to Dublin to record." With these words, Barbara Dever, Sacred Heart's great liturgical singer for the past 18 years, announced that she would go to Dublin on September 22, 1994. There, Barbara, the mezzo-soprano whose magnificent voice is gaining great respect in operatic circles around the world, would star as Amneris in two performances of Verdi's splendid opera, Aida, at The Point Theater in Dublin. Also, on October 2 (the Feast of the Angels) she would sing Amneris for the recording of Aida at Ireland's National Concert Hall. It will be a record that the people of Sacred Heart and many admirers will look forward to hearing and, I dare say, John McCormack, if he were alive, would honor it with his praise.

Ten years ago, and five years before she made her debut in Virginia as Azucena in *Il Trovatore*, Barbara Dever celebrated the centenary of McCormack's birth (June 14, 1884) by singing some of his favorite songs, including *I Hear You Calling Me*, at the Walt Whitman Center in Camden. There, only a few yards from the spot where McCormack himself made hundreds of records at the Victor Talking Machine Company (later RCA), she lifted his songs on the air of Camden as he had done there so splendidly from 1910 when his contract was signed until it ended in 1938.

It was appropriate that she sang his songs in the Walt Whitman Center, a beautiful edifice that cost 200,000 dollars in 1916 and was donated as a children's library to the people of Camden by Eldridge Johnson (1867-1945), the inventor of the mechanism that made Thomas Edison's "Talking Machine" really work, and also made it successful , world wide. This Victor Talking Machine in Camden, NJ and its sister corporation, His Master's Voice in England, made tenors like John McCormack and Enrico Caruso famous. Their high notes made the new machine that captured them a household name everywhere. And indeed, the name Camden, NJ whirled on the records around this earth as it whirled on its axis before the sun of the universe.

The invention was a revolutionary gift to humanity. People had depicted the scenes the human eye could see for a million years, but no one had captured the sounds the ear could hear until Thomas Edison did it 117 years ago. (My grandfather was three years old then). It was December 6, 1877, the feast of St. Nicholas the gift giver, when the first recorded words on the planet were heard on Edison's machine in Menlo Park, New Jersey: "Mary had a little lamb."

But for John McCormack and Barbara Dever, the gift of gifts is not the machine that records the voice and transmits it, but the voice itself and they both have used it magnificently to praise the Supreme Creator who invented it. Their sound and their posture of reverence before the altar of God have lifted many a heart to heaven. My eyes fill with tears when I hear Barbara sing, Panis Angelicus in Sacred Heart (the words of Thomas Aquinas to the music of Cesar Franck) and I recall the story of John McCormack singing the same hymn before a million people at the closing Mass of the Eucharistic Congress in Dublin in 1932. My parents, John Doyle and Rosetta Creegan, were in the Phoenix Park to hear him. They listened together. It was the week before they were wed. Eighteen months later, they, God bless them, gave me, their second child, my very first instant of existence.

Many people who come to Sacred Heart in Holy Week and the great Easter Sundays that follow it, have been moved and elevated by Barbara Dever's splendid singing and so it was of great interest to me to read that it was around the same season that John McCormack came to sing in Camden in years gone by. In her biography, entitled, I Hear You Calling Me, his wife Lily, writes: "For years, every Easter we took the children to Atlantic City for two weeks. John made records for the Victor Company in Camden during the week and he generally gave a concert in Atlantic City on Palm Sunday, rested during Holy Week then back to New York in time for his Easter Sunday Concert. At the end of Easter week I always went with John to Camden to hear the records he had made during the week. He was a perfectionist about his work and would rather do a record over a dozen times than pass it, if he felt it had the slightest flaw!" His perfection paid off, because the royalties from his work in Camden from 1910 to 1938 amounted to more than two and a half billion dollars.

And no song was better known than I Hear You Calling Me, composed by a struggling songwriter named Charles Marshall and sung for the first time by McCormack in Queen's Hall in London in 1908. He recorded it for Victor in Camden in 1910, 1911, 1921 and 1927.

I love the name of that song and it makes my mind leap to our Camden children and the dream in God's heart that calls to each one of them. Indeed, when all is said and done, no record ever made in Camden is more important than the record cut in the tender memories of our children. But oh, the anxieties that rush in to heighten fears of scratch and screech, of takes rejected, of broken records and heaps of scrap in time!

I think of our school and its gallant efforts to tape in the good and erase the bad and enable our children to hear the pure good sounds of themselves.

Here they pray everyday. May they gladly respond to the God of their dreams with: I Hear You Calling Me.

Michael Doyle

In Loving Memory of Jean McCarthy
(Excerpt)
But you could light the lamp behind the oldest eyes
And make them beam upon your dawning face
Aye, and blind the dreamy eyes of lads too young
When morning kissed the color of your golden hair
And tossed the freckles freely here and there
Around the grin and low surprising laugh we loved.
All matched so well the oats in warm August fields
Or sunlit chestnuts floating on a smiling stream.

We Remember in November

November 3, 1994, 2 a.m.

Hi:

I am awake at this wee hour and I am finding it hard to believe that 60 years ago today, my grandfather Pat Doyle got his first glimpse of me…minutes after I was born on his 60th birthday. I was his birthday present, but in no way was I the gift to him that he was to me for the next 24 years. We were both born in the same house, probably in the same room, where his father was born on February 2, 1841, and his grandmother, too, in the early 1800's.

He was a great man. I don't know how many men he met in the 60 years he lived before he saw me, but I have met no better than he, in the sixty years I have lived since I first met him. And with all his heart, he loved me, crying inconsolably when I went to the seminary and weeping when he met me, three months later, coming home on vacation.

He was a farmer and a great ploughman and his face knew all the rains of Ireland and was wet, too, so many times, with the salt-taste tears of his terrible sorrows.

At the beginning of this century, he raised his baby boys when their mother died, lived long enough to bury two of them and he, with nine years left to live…not a day of which was without a quiet tear to love them.

He was a great man to talk, too, telling his stories with the best of wit and language and wisdom. How often I watched him come into the kitchen when terrible rains drove him from the field where he was ploughing. Seventy years in age and fifty in strength. I knew he had to stop his work, undo chains, remove harness, take care of horses, but this man would walk to the hearth, shake the rain from his cap into the fire and say: **"It's a terrible day, thanks be to God."**

Speaking of legs! One day he came in the rain to walk me home from school. With an umbrella. My legs were four-and-a-half years old and the journey was two-and-one-tenth miles. He described my size as "two hands higher than a duck" and when he put down his big boot, I had to take a full step just for the length of his foot. "I thought we'd never see home again," he said. We did, but no later growth on my part could ever follow in his footsteps or match his worthy stride upon the world.

In 1958, when I came home from the seminary with a "Roman collar," Pakie Mulligan, a parishioner from Aughnacliffe, gave me a lift from the local town. When I got out of the car, he looked at me and said, "If you're half as good a priest as your grandfather is a man, you'll be alright." He drove on. The years, too, have gone. Thirty-six of them. And I have to say (to him if he can hear), "I'm still not half as good."

He knew and his father before him knew how many times my grandfather put up our little home and farm as collateral to help others save their own. He lived under foreign landlords and often told me about Michael Davitt and his Land League, to "put an end to rack-renting, eviction and landlord oppression."

His father was 4½ when the Great Hunger struck in 1845 and he himself was 4½ four-and-a-half when the potatoes failed again in 1879. The following year, 10,000 tenant farmers were driven off their land by foreign landlords. No wonder my grandfather loved the few fields we owned and every inch of them was tended and turned over by the strength of his mighty hands. There was always clay on his boots and his patched corduroys, but it wasn't dirt. It was the earth, and to the earth he was related by blood.

I would love to tell him about Camden and Sacred Heart. "A terrible place," I would say, "thanks be to God." I would tell him about our schoolchildren: the little ones "two hands higher than a duck," and the older ones who are many hands higher. How they need to be sheltered not just from the rain and the cold, but from the deadly things that fall upon their lives. I would tell him about you and how you help by sponsoring a child or children in our schools. For $300 each. More than he ever had to his name.

I would tell him about the thousand baskets and the way we try to feed people at Christmas. He would like that...a man, who never in his life had a break from this work of feeding and sheltering human beings and domestic animals, would understand the great work it is to feed the needy. He who planted crops and harvested them for several widows all his life and never expected or received any payments whatever, would know the value and the responsibility of helping God's beloved poor.

Like myself, he wasn't great at asking people to help him. But he gave of himself in a way I can only admire. From on high, I pray that he will give me a hand to plough a furrow in the fields of the future and plant a solid seed of life to come.

Oh he cut his furrows in the fields of time
And he sowed his splendid seeds upon the soil.
It's growing well...growing well, Grandfather.
Battered by some storms but only slightly bent.
Damaged by some draught but never really lost.
There's water wet enough in all the tears you shed.
Enough to give me life when I am dead.

May he and all those you remember, rest in peace!

Michael Doyle

"I Love You"

December, 1994

Hi:

"You have two choices," Frank McDermott said to me years ago, "you can either be efficient or charitable." And Frank, an aging noble priest in Philadelphia, has always made his church a doorway of charity and hospitality for the poor.

Forty years ago, I was recruited for this "mission" in the US by a priest of the Camden diocese who visited my seminary and told us country peasants that "the chancery office in Camden is the most efficient in the world." Not knowing what a chancery office was then (or now!) I was amazed. Five years later, after a long boat ride across the Atlantic, my uncles Patrick and Hughie Creegan with my aunts Peggy and Mary Jane took me into the City of Camden (September 18, 1959) for my appointment at said chancery office. I was still amazed enough that we passed the blessed place several times because I was looking for a basilica. Instead it was a converted row house on Cooper Street. When I entered, five minutes late, having come all the way from a green field in the center of Ireland, the same priest glared at me over his bifocals and said: "You're late for your first appointment." Then I knew what efficiency meant. Oh, God help us ! Hospitality was dead on arrival, there.

My first pastor was indeed kind enough but he hardly ever talked. I was far from home and not at home in any place where I couldn't blather on about fields and ploughs, cows and sows, and friendly faces in the lane (like I do to you).

Earlier this year I wrote a letter to an ailing priest, George Sharkey, a man like Frank with a great mind and wonderful hospitality, to tell him before he died how much he did to make me feel really welcome in North America. I was assigned to his parish in September 1961 and arrived on a Saturday afternoon at his split-level makeshift rectory on Cambridge Road in Cherry Hill and found him hearing confessions in the den. Everywhere there was a pile of this and a pile of that and no discernible relationship between them. But he emerged with sparkling eyes of sheer welcome that could only be outdone by his mother, Annie Flood of Lugganammer, Couny Leitrim, a few fields away from my own mother's birthplace. Oh, she was funny! His laughter would shake him down to his toes as he listened to her. How often she would call on the phone looking for him: "Honey" (a word not used outside the bee hives back in Lugganammer), she would say to me, "Where is will o' the wisp?" Of course, I didn't know.

But I knew I was at home. That first day we talked. I mean I talked. As he listened I could see in his eyes a kindness I knew in my father's face. After a long dinner at Kenny's, he began readying the "stuff" for the mass at two public schools on Sunday. His parish of St. Peter Celestine was only three months old. He made two piles on the floor of tattered vestments and various accoutrements that he must have found in some old church cellar and here they were, mixed in with this and that – everything from a ciborium to the handle bars of a bicycle. And yet there was not in his great heart the slightest disrespect for the least thing in God's creation. At 11pm he said to me: "How do you like your eggs?" Poached, I said, not knowing what to say. He slapped the little bowler hat on the head and out he went. The next morning there was a poacher on the kitchen table. His mother's, I suppose. He went to Camden to fetch it. I had come a long way from the chancery office. Hospitality was now alive and well in my world.

But my world was also full of charming surprises that were often unbelievable. None more incredible than my first floundering attempt to cook a TV dinner in George Sharkey's kitchen. I found the refrigerator easily enough. And the TV dinner. It was the oven that gave me trouble. It was not under the rings. There was no hearth. I saw a thing in the wall with glass and knobs. This may be it. I pulled open the door and two golf balls rolled out into my hands. I peered in and saw some old socks. This couldn't be the oven. I gave up and called the only name I knew in the parish, Doris Matlack. It was the oven. Doris cooked my TV dinner in her kitchen.

I don't know why the two balls were in the oven. Maybe he just felt sorry for anything that was walloped without mercy around a wet green field. He loved golf.

But he loved people and there was always plenty of warmth for them. While I was there, that warmth widened through the work of parishioner Joan Mullin to include a parish called Sacred Heart in Camden, where, back then, some people were poor. That was 1965. And so for almost thirty years, the good people of St. Peter Celestine have reached out to this parish, especially at Christmas.

A few months ago I visited Msgr. Sharkey, in the last stages of the cancer that had plundered his body of all its vitality. Bending over his bed, I greeted him. He opened his eyes, knew me, and with feeble voice said: "I love you." Three words. I will cherish them as long as I live. He didn't have many more words to say in this world, so I want to highlight these three for Christmas, when he will not be around in the way he was.

For Christmas 1992, he came to Sacred Heart. He was sick, limping, and in pain, but he had a load of food to help the poor. Last year he wasn't able to come. It was his last Christmas but he still sent in food for the baskets. Indeed, he always rejoiced in our efforts for a thousand baskets and all the bustling "inefficiency" that happens when great generosity meets deep human need in a magical Christmas moment.

Christmas is always the hospitality and availability of God in human form, welcoming and enticing as a baby in a house without a door. Or indeed the heroic beauty of an old friend opening his eyes on his deathbed to say: "I love you."

I know you will help us to celebrate Christmas in the way we should as an old church, faithful as ever to its sacred name – the Church of the Heart. And this time we salute George Sharkey, who like you, helped Christmas to happen here these many years. He may never have known what he had in those piles of things on the floor but we always knew where we stood when we came to his door.

Michael Doyle

A Window in My World

February, 1995

Hi:

A few days ago (February 22, it was) I went down to the banks of the mile-wide Delaware, a river that links us to distant beginnings more cosmic and primal than the long bloodlines of our lives.

But bloodlines were on my mind as I stood by this awesome artery. I picked this day because my beloved grandfather, Pat Doyle, whose loins gave me life, died on February 22, thirty-six years ago. I came to the river for a ritual.

I came to pour a small portion of blessed water from Russia into the Delaware in Camden, and as I poured, I was very conscious of what Irina Soiko solemnly said when she gave me the water in St. Petersburg. It was not only what she said but the way she said it...with a sincerity of faith that awed me. "One drop of the consecrated water would consecrate the ocean." I was very conscious too of the moment one month ago when I stood at the edge of the Neva River in St. Petersburg with Irina and her friend Gulia Anastas – their breath like incense in a temperature of 15 below – to pour holy water from Camden onto the ice that awaits Spring and thawing and free flow to the Baltic Sea. John Purves of Haddonfield, NJ caught the action in his camera, which may only be a blessed blur because his hands were shaking for fear I would walk on the ice with my bottle to where the ducks were splashing in the freezing water. He is a lawyer and knew the complications of explaining that he lost me in the Neva on our way to church. "Last seen trying to pour water in the river." But all went well and we prayerfully rejoiced that the goodness of a God who had melted the frigid cold war would mingle the holy water from Sacred Heart with the waves of the Neva.

It has become a custom here at Sacred Heart that when we bless water each year in commemoration of the Lord's Baptism, we all take a portion of it to pour into the rivers, streams and oceans of the earth. In the pouring we bless the world.

On January 17, I arrived on Finnair in Helsinki after a night flight across the northern eave of the earth – high over Greenland, Iceland, Norway, Sweden and Finland. A bright star kept pace with my window all the way to the dawn... like a beckoning guide to an amber epiphany. Then a short forty-five minute hop over the Gulf of Finland. The plane eased down into the whiteness of winter. I was in Russia.

The snow was light. Withered weeds poked through, waiting for better weather. That would come in May – snow here to stay from November to April. Around me everybody's breath was obviously much warmer than the air it was meeting.

Thus began my eight days in Russia...a gift from the Camden Iron and Metal Company that shares the neighborhood where I live. Eight momentous days. They were filled with one splendid experience after another in this town named for a man who was named by Jesus himself. St. Peter. It was situated originally on 101 islands where the Neva flows into the sea.

Another Peter, whom History calls "great," founded it in 1703 and laid it out with careful plans as a strategic presence to protect Russia's access to the Baltic, which he wrestled from Sweden that had cut it off for hundreds of years. It has had three names: St. Petersburg until 1914. Petrograd until 1924. Leningrad until 1991 and now St. Petersburg again. Its name is German, its face European. Peter, who traveled and studied in many countries of Europe, brought the best architects, masons and artists from abroad to build his city. He wanted it to be "a window to Europe" for Russia but it certainly was a window to Russia for me.

It is a city of bridges, 365 of them spanning the 65 rivers, channels, streams and canals that cross the city like veins in a body. Bridges are usually up for ships between 2 and 5 a.m. so it mightn't be wise to stay out to the wee hours and be stuck on the wrong island.

St. Nicholas Cathedral is a sacred bridge that spanned time and difficulty since Savva Chevakinsky designed it in 1753. Its doors never closed, the only Russian Orthodox Church in St. Petersburg to stay open through all the worst stages of Communist rule.

Irina Soiko took me to Vespers of the Epiphany in St. Nicholas, where her father, Boris, has been the head priest for many years. It was Wednesday evening, 6 p.m., January 18. (The Orthodox Christmas and subsequent feasts are 13 days after ours). For three hours we stood (no pews) in the crowded church while the alternate chanting of the Vespers by priests and choir never ceased. Icons everywhere, on walls, pillars, in the upper and lower church, at every turn of the stairs where multitudes of thin brown candles burned brightly. The old wooden floors were worn by 200 years of the worshipers walking in every direction, kissing the icons of their choice and lighting new candles that they just bought. The solemn faces in the candlelight burdened with needs only known in the heart. The heavenly chant goes on, the people stand, kneel and continuously bless themselves in the Orthodox way as they watch the vested priests stride to and from the Iconostasis, swinging censers of incense.

The following day, I attended the Divine Liturgy of the Epiphany from 10 am to 1 pm. When I arrived, the elegant baroque cathedral, turquoise and white, was resplendent in the snow and pure morning light. A big hammer, high in the separate soaring bell-tower was rhythmically hitting the bell and calling the people. The chanting of the prayers of the Eucharist was magnificent even though I didn't understand a word. At times Irina would kneel down and kiss the floor in reverence for the sacred action taking place. The lighting of the candles never ceased. At the end there was a solemn blessing of a huge tank of water. It's always done at the Epiphany and people come with gallons and big jugs from their kitchens and as Irina said, "I drink a mouthful of the consecrated water every morning for my purification." That's the water I took home to bless the Delaware.

The Metropolitan (like Cardinal) who learned from me through translations that on that very day, January 19, Sacred Heart School had opened in 1920, seventy-five years ago. He immediately prayed in Russian for blessings on our school in Camden.

Time was when the people of Leningrad (St. Petersburg) and Camden feared missiles of mutual destruction. Now they were exchanging blessings on the children and holy water of mutual consecration.

Michael Doyle

Torn Sails Upon the Sea

March, 1995

Hi:

"I looked at the phone. I looked at it several times." My brother J.J.'s words, two weeks ago. "I know when I pick it up," he thought, "things will change." He picked it up. And they changed. Indeed. They changed for those who know him and for those who love him. The phone was by his hospital bed in St. Vincent's in Dublin. He was alone. Fifty-five years old. Numb. Numb from the news he had just received. Cancer. Cancer in his lungs.

"I felt like I just got a kick of a horse," he said. (Reminiscent of our grandfather's words many years ago in times of terrible trouble.) "I wanted to go out into the middle of a bog where no one could hear me and cry out. Roar as loud as I could."

So, for the month of March I will dip my pen in the sadness that I feel and write to you. My mind is on lungs, the breath of life filling them, the sighs and songs coming from them. "Lung" reminds me of that same Irish word for a sailing ship. Hence my poem!

The shadows of the dark clouds often veiled the familiar face of Crott
I've seen them come and stay all day
Above the meadow green, the golden yield, the purple blossoms of pink potatoes
Just when the morning sun had softly kissed the scene
They wiped away the laugh from every field.
The sun was slow to come and dry the crystal tears
On all the troubled trees and leaves and trembling blades of grass
But we learned how to linger in the valley and be still
With humble hope that looked for help beyond the highest hill
And sure enough the light would come, slanting o'er the lea,
And all the shadows that the clouds could make
Ran and hid beneath the surface of the dark trout lake.
But now, strange fears form in the playground of the mind
And we sigh at night at the constant crying of the wind.
Pondering the news that a nightmare rode so roughly to impart
On hard horse hooves that shattered all the tender mosses of the heart
Shadows on the lungs (sailing ships have the same Gaelic name)
White sails on the boat-ribs of his oaten-fashioned frame
Hoisted in the energy of all his growing years
That swelled with happy songs and the ones he sang with tears
Drawing air for the first mumbled prayers at his mother's holy knee
And writing life with his breath on winter mornings going to school
The boy who whistled for his coupled goats to hustle home for milking
And took note of their reactions to know the weather's feeling
Shadows on the white sails we saw them come and go
And fitful waves always tired as they tumbled to and fro

And we learned not to fear awful fury of the sea.
Because the ship was sailing steadily beyond the middle latitudes
The route was clear, the rock points sharp, but the lighthouse stood to warn
So the ship seemed strong enough to stay the course in any darkening storm
Yet the canvas weakened gradually in the flailing winter gale
And soon enough developed a badly torn sail.
Then frowns formed deeply on searching weathered faces
Not the way the sand smoothes the sand, when the wind wipes the traces.
But no one yet had said the word that all the sailors dread
That makes the captains weep where tears are seldom shed
They know the sails that stand so strong against winter wind and rain
Can be torn badly in the storm when nature goes insane
Like a secret fire burning that even water scarcely quells
And one by one the canvas strands begin to lacerate themselves
Then the tears wet his body like an ardent summer rain
Running rivulets of sorrow down a dark window pane.
Flattened by the blow as if a horse had kicked his head
He struggled for a word and this is what he said
"Give me the middle of a bog to be far away from everyone!
To cry the loudest that I'm able, 'til all my crying's done."
He knew well the frozen quiet of that backward, lonely place
Where winter waits 'til summer to feel its first human face
But he didn't mind the creatures that lived upon the moor
And he didn't mind them listening when his heart would break and roar.
The hare could raise her ears in her simple heather den
And little birds could shudder 'neath a bunch of withered whins,
The water hens upon the river could hurry to the rim
And crows clustered on white birches could stop their cawing then
And his crying could connect to every sigh and plea
In the universal aching of earth and sky and sea
From the pangs of birth, the sting of death, the whirl of galaxies
From the wounded whale upon the shore, to every bleeding little knee
Because Christ is crying in the Garden in a cosmic agony
For a sailing ship with torn sails in the middle of the sea
A broken brother in the bogland calling out to me.

J.J. Doyle is assistant priest at St. Mary's Church, Edgeworthstown, County Longford, Ireland. He is a holy man, with a childlike softness and a delightful goodness about him.

It was on February 28th that he got his heavy news and the phone carried it from one anxious heart to another. February 28th is a special day because my friend Joe Bell, a sea captain himself, died on February 28th, 1973. Before he died, he spoke special words to me, in a troubled time, as a big tear coursed its way down his long face. I remember them and I pass them on to you and to every struggling ship upon the sea. "Ride out the storm!"

Roses in the Rain

April, 1995

Happy Easter!

Recently, I picked up a copy of Boris Pasternak's great novel, *Doctor Zhivago*. The first and last time I read it was in 1967. That's 28 years ago, a number that likes to cycle itself in moons and special phases of life. I remember my encounter well, so moved was I by the story. I put it down, got up and went for a walk. I had to. A cold wet evening hung in heavily on Shore Road, Northfield, NJ, where I lived at the time. After some distance, I stopped and talked with a woman in a funny hat who was planting roses in the rain. She was a teacher, she told me, and a grafter of roses. "This is a new rose," she said. "I need a name." It was long and thin like life sometimes, with few leaves and many thorns. Maybe it would bloom, someday...lovely and soft in the bright month of June. "Call it, Zhivago!" I said. She did.

The word Zhivago means life at its best, as Thomas Merton tells us in one of the two great essays he wrote on the extraordinary symbolism that permeates the famous novel. He and Pasternak were literary correspondents; both confined to their "dachas," with minds traversing every level of the universe and meeting spiritually on the journey. It means "life" as Jesus understood it, when He said: "I came that you may have life and that you may have it more abundantly." Jn.10, 13. While I could cup my hands and drink some refreshing drops from the surface of the story, Merton could lower a bucket into the great depths of the water.

But after 28 years, I still could remember that page 13 had great stuff and I wanted to read it again. It had the words of Nikolai Nikolaievich Vedeniapin. He was a former priest, the brother of Zhivago's mother who had just been buried. Uncle Nikolai, as little Yura Zhivago called him then. They were driving across fields in a two-horse open carriage to Duplyanka one day in the summer of 1903. They were on their way to see Ivan Ivanovich Voskoboinikos, an author of popular textbooks. "It was the Feast of the Virgin of Kazan." Later in the day, Nikolai and Ivan got into a discussion about "new talent in science and literature." It was here that Nikolai, the "former priest," presents his splendid words on life. "How many things in the world deserve our loyalty?" he asks. "Very few indeed. I think one should be loyal to immortality, which is another word for life, a stronger word for it. One must be true to immortality – true to Christ."

" 'Hmm' said Ivan Ivanovich, and he tried to change the subject, but Nikolai persists. "As I was saying, one must be true to Christ...man does not live in a state of nature but in history, and history as we know it now began with Christ, and that Christ's Gospel is its foundation. Now what is history? It is the centuries of systematic explorations of the riddle of death, with a view to over-coming death. That's why people discover mathematical infinity and electromagnetic waves, this why they write symphonies. Now you can't advance in this direction without a certain faith. You can't make such discoveries without spiritual equipment and the basic elements of this equipment are in the gospels. What are they? To begin with, love of one's neighbor, which is the supreme form of vital energy...once it fills the heart, it has to overflow and spend itself. And then the two basic ideals of modern man — without them he is unthinkable — the idea of free personality and the idea of life as sacrifice. Mind you, all this is extraordinarily new. There was no history in this sense among the ancients. They had blood and beastliness and cruelty and pockmarked Caligulas who do not suspect how untalented every enslaver is. They had the boastful dead eternity of bronze monuments and marble columns. It was not until after the coming of Christ that time and man could breathe freely. It was not until after Him that people began to live toward the future. Man does not die in a ditch like a dog — but at home in history, while the work toward the conquest of death is in full swing; he dies sharing in this work."

No wonder Pasternak received so much abuse from Soviet authorities and media when Zhivago was published in 1957. But time would prove that nothing could kill the Russian trust in Easter. The daffodils would rise from the snow. Christ is risen from the dead. Far greater than Christmas time is the joy that permeates Russian society with the celebration of their beloved Paskha — Easter itself. On bright human breath that is often times obvious in April, the heartiest words in the world are shouted one to another across the Slavonic lands on Easter morning: Christoss Voskresse – Christ is Risen. No compliment to humanity is greater than the one that should be given for people's consistent confidence in the victory of life over death. For a million years and more. As Nikolai Nikolaievich said so well: "One should be loyal to immortality."

So, a toast to you and the hope you have in the outcome of death! In spite of the fact that death is so emphatically real. A toast to the life that throbs in your own dear self! Bodies wear out, but you...you are worth keeping forever.

Tears. Yes! Tears cut graves in the heart. The cross follows our feet for the nailing. Faces are often wet with the weeping. Like red roses in the rain. But they will bloom in June.

What great hope hid in the heart of the old Russian woman I saw in the cemetery near Holy Trinity Church in St. Petersburg! She bent and lit her little brown candle in the snow and kissed the granite tomb. It was 15 below. What chance has death! I say. As Zhivago's lovely poem, Holy Week, puts it:

> *All Creatures hear the voice of Spring*
> *In the still of night, believing*
> *That when good weather comes*
> *Death itself shall be destroyed*
> *By the travail of the Resurrection.*

Indeed!

Michael Doyle

Life in a Chestnut Tree

May, 1995

Hi:

It's the middle of May as I write. Later, it will be, as you read. (No one ever makes a brake for little clockwork wheels.) It's Mothers' Day! And all of us who miss a mother, call back the times we know by heart. Welcoming them back to mind. Ah, it was death that froze the face that for so long has shone upon our own…with all the smiles that blessed our coming home. Gone! All gone so quickly. But not like the lilac blossoms that Padraic Colum mourned. "Gone without a word that praised us." We have many words of praise. But, how fast the time runs by! For good moments seem to have only lilac blossom life. As Colum cautions sadly, "You did not know how short the playing time."

Great playing time for me as a child was in the trees. These trees that I miss were horse chestnut trees that grew in a grove a few feet from my old home's half-door. They were my world and how my mother laughed as she listened to the "box" in the branches. I pretended I was a radio hidden in the leaves. Each tree was my friend. I watched their big broad arms break out in buds and welcome the large sheltering leaves every Spring. From the sturdy blossoms that stood like white conical cathedrals in the sun, the great green balls grew with the precious chestnuts within. And, oh, the color of the ripened chestnuts in the little white wombs where they formed. Color, like no other. So lovely, when it shone on a filly trotting down the sunny field.

Up there in my green canopies I had my secret home. Lost, I was. Lost, in the joy I found when I climbed. True enough, as I got older, I never had the inclination or the invitation to ascend to the high branch of any institution or authority, but as a child I was president of every tree within my reach and beyond it. Every roof and chimney, too. My parents' hearts often missed a beat that they were not meant to miss.

Above all, my chestnut trees were festivals of pleasure, going from one exciting presentation to another. Autumn came every year to rust and ripen all my trees. And the chestnuts fell.

> *Oh give me the thud and crack*
> *And bright brown burst of chestnuts.*
> *When the cozy round white wombs*
> *Drop from November trees*
> *And the cage of my chest will heave*
> *And tug on the moorings of long ago.*

Then winter came and all was bare as bones. And in the night, the wind would cry among the trees in the deep dark. They would bend and reach and scratch the sky in their own arbor ache and agony.

Well, there came a year like no other. It washed away the Summer and the Fall. And the wet turf that were meant to make a cooking fire and the only heat we would have for the Winter, never dried in the bog. There was no money for any other fuel. My father had to cut down the trees. All but one…it died later. I think, of loneliness. The loss of my trees left a raw gap in my world. Silly as it seems, I still grieve for my horse chestnut trees, like Citizen Kane for the Rosebud sleigh of his childhood.

Now that I have moved into the aging autumn of my life, and my two brothers are ill, one with congestive heart failure and the other with cancer in his lungs, my thoughts turn to my trees with their large leaves and the rains heavy upon them and that special spot where we played as children.

Today, May 17th, two days before my brother J.J.'s 56th birthday, it's raining in Camden. I hear his weakening voice on the phone from Ireland. Torn sails upon the sea. The doctor's word, unsaid 'til now, "Nothing can be done." Medically, anyway. "How short the playing time."

We were a grove – a sibling chestnut grove of six. One, "little Anna Mae," here for a week and gone – a lilac blossom in the rain. Then, another Anna Mae, who took the name and rose with dancing eyes and chestnut hair to give God a loving face upon the world. A Sister of Mercy, gone at 38, cut down by a cruel car on a wet November night. And now, J.J., a priest with a tender heart and the soul of a saint, weakening as the cancer chews down the noble life within him. And here I am, in this part of the world where all the horse chestnut trees have died. Almost all. Only two, I know of in Camden, growing in a graveyard. They blossom brightly every Spring, but come the Fall, no chestnuts ever come.

But hope is never not the better part of every human heart. A parcel came this Easter time, among all the crazy junk that rides the burdened mule of mail these days. A yard-long cardboard box, triangular and light…from Florida. After days, I opened it. A mesh of roots, no soil, dry as a bone, at the end of a stick. A gift for me, with instructions. How to plant a chestnut tree. I planted it. For weeks it was there like a standing stick in the mud. I checked the other day and, God be praised! The buds are breaking out on my tiny chestnut tree. And no doubt, there's sorrow deep enough around to keep it watered for awhile. It's growing. May it blossom by and by…when the sun has dried the raindrops on the leaves!

Please pray for my dear brother J.J.

Michael Doyle

April 24, 1991

(Excerpt)

And even when the sun breaks through
To coax away the raindrops from the green
And dry the wings of birds and butterflies
It has not yet and I wonder will it ever dry
The leaves that lie upon the silent stones
Beneath the conscious flow of all my days and dreams.

No "Gubban" on the Wind

June, 1995

Hi:

My brother, J.J. Doyle, died at 4:50 pm on Sunday, June 4, 1995. It was Pentecost. The day before, he said his last two words in the world: "That's good!" That was it. All his words were spoken. Just labored breathing then. A pause on Sunday afternoon. A sigh...and he was gone. White awesome silence settled in on us all.

I am writing to you on the Aer Lingus jet, St. Brigid, coming back to Camden after burying him. Silent white bedspread clouds close in on my last glimpse of the green fields where we laid him, near a hedge of wild whitethorn bushes in bloom, and a row of evergreen trees that he and the men of Moydow, County Longford, planted seven years ago.

It feels like seven years since the other plane – the one I came on – was easing in over Dublin. But it was only May 25th. I was conscious that it was the Feast of the Holy Ascension into Heaven and I was descending into Ireland. I was thinking of J.J. – the huge issues, wider than the world, as the mind clings to hope in the face of long dark despair; fears of falling off the edge of our fragile existence into a vast unknown.

By 8:45 a.m. I was pulling out of Connolly Station and heading from Dublin to Longford, where J.J. was waiting. I loved the train ride as fields after fields rolled past my window – all of them hedged by whitethorn bushes in bloom (I hadn't seen them since 1959). As a boy I used to think that the whole country at this time of year was ready for First Holy Communion. Nothing but miles and miles of lovely lace, white and pink, in the sun.

There was a purring noise in J.J's room as I entered (a nebulizer in action) pumping his damaged lungs. The torn sails upon the sea. There was a clear plastic mask over his mouth and nose. He reached up his arms and hugged me. "Ah," he said, "they put a 'gubban' on me." I hadn't heard that old Irish word in many, many years. The canister with homemade holes that was placed on little calves' mouths to keep them from suckling on each other. Poor J.J. was losing his ability to suckle on that great body of air that had nourished his life ever since May 19, 1939, when Rosetta Creegan Doyle brought him forth to breathe upon the world. Aye, and sing his songs too. And, God bless him, to his last conscious breath, he never complained or lost his sense of humor.

The 'gubban' came off and we talked. I told him that I enjoyed seeing the (hawthorn) whitethorn blossoms after so long a time and he with his cancered lungs said:

> *How sweet is Tipperary*
> *In the springtime of the year*
> *When the hawthorn blossoms are in bloom*
> *And the feathered folk assemble*
> *And the air is all a-tremble*
> *With their singing and their winging to and fro.*

And he went on to complete the second verse. I gave him a bound copy of my own timid attempts at poetry that is dedicated to him, which says in part: "To the tenderness of his nature, I dedicate my words and the bit of meaning that lives within them. But I have found no word more noble than the one he bravely makes with his own flesh and blood." He read the dedication slowly; silently forming the words on his lips. Then he looked up with a great smile and said: "No words." And I have none either to adequately tell you all that happened.

No one loved a chat better than J.J. Doyle. Now, talking hurt him. He would get an attack and need the nebulizer and the "gubban" would go on again. So, to keep him from talking I would read my poems and he would fall asleep. It was a tender time between us.

He was at home with those he loved. The doctor came everyday and two nurses. There was someone in the room, twenty-four hours a day, and the Foggy Dew tape by Eugene O' Donnell and James Mac Cafferty played soothingly, night and day. He talked when he could and read his Breviary Prayers 'til his eyes wouldn't focus. June 2nd.

On that Friday, I walked by myself to the graveyard (ten minutes away) in Moydow to look for the place of his rest. It is the sad duty of people every day. One is so highly conscious. I saw everything, heard everything: A calf suckling happily; birds, cows…a pigeon cooing, lambs bleating in the next field – every sight and sound.

Exactly seventy-two hours later, I ritually threw a handful of clay into the most caringly-made grave I had ever seen. Dug by his friend Michael McKeon, the four sides lined to the bottom with fresh green moss interspersed with beautiful flowers. Soft as a wren's nest. But, oh, it wasn't soft at all. The coffin was lowered. As I read the prayers a bee flew down into the grave and drew nectar from a lovely laurel flower to feed the future.

That handful of clay I threw at his burial, brought me back to the eve of Ash Wednesday, February 28th, when he came home from the hospital flattened by the news he had just received: Cancer in both lungs. Not for him this year, a touch of ashes on his forehead and a gentle reminder. No! Ashes on his lungs and the hard hit of death in his heart. Thus began his long lent. He had painful days in Holy Week and worse days to come. People reached to him in prayer and love from the five continents of the world. "It was worth getting cancer," he said to me, "to have all these people praying." Easter Sunday came and the Sundays of Easter that follow. I was there for the sixth one, May 28th.

On that day we concelebrated Mass at the kitchen table. His first day in a wheelchair. *"Sinn a bfuil,"* he said at the end. The old Irish phrase for: That's it. That's all that is. It was his last Mass. One week later, he died. Oh, a good and gentle man! The priest with the childlike heart. It was Pentecost. The fullness of Easter. My precious time with him was aligned with the original great novena – the nine days of prayer between Ascension Thursday and Pentecost Sunday. Nine days when the first disciples gathered with the Holy Mother and locked themselves in because of overwhelming fear. Then came the "Mighty Wind" of the Spirit! Their hearts swelled with life and courage. J.J. too, trapped in his torn sails, and abiding fears as well. Ever since Ash Wednesday. Come Holy Spirit! "Behold I make all things new." Rv.21,6. The Holy Wind came. The sailing ship sighed and filled and moved away. Ah, J.J.!

Michael Doyle

My Eyes Have Seen Salvation

July, 1995

Hi!

In 1908, Maurice E. Bric, the pastor of Sacred Heart, Camden, from 1888 to 1913, commissioned Ferdinand Baraldi of Philadelphia to create a score of oil paintings on canvas for the church. By the end of that year, 17 large depictions of Old and New Testament scenes (12 of them almost 60 square feet in area) adorned the ceilings and walls of this church, which, at the time, was nearing the celebration of the parish Silver Jubilee in 1910.

For more than 80 years now, these paintings have glanced down on one congregation after another and held on to their locations amidst the grime and the dirt of all the years. They weathered the blackening smoke of the coal-stove era, and the choking exhaust of today's trucks going by. Not to mention the polluted rain that seeped in, the whitening lime that washed on, and the darkening incense that rose up. And of course, the carbon content of the countless candles that were lighted. Along the way the plaster cracked and the paint peeled and the once beautiful church aged with a frayed face of neglect and damage.

So, when Don Harle began to paint the church on November 30, 1992, more than 50 years had passed since the hairs of a brush had touched it the last time. He has been working steadily for two and a half years; working alone against the dirt and the damage, cleaning the surfaces, knitting the cracks, graining the beams, restoring the stencils, and painting the wails, the woodwork, and the ceiling. And when, after some years, he lays down his brush, it will (not the same one) have touched every square inch of the interior surface of the church and he will have touched all the floor too, sweeping up after his work.

Don is doing this because Othmar Carli, an Austrian artist from York, PA, who is director of the project, and who is bringing the canvas paintings back to life, has, since he started, taught Don most of the skills he uses. The meeting of these two men, the fusion of their talents, is the miracle of Sacred Heart's restoration.

"Father Bric," the contract of 1908 states, "selected the contents of the paintings." Among the large ones, he chose Melchizedek, the king of Salem, at the door of his tent; Mary and Joseph being married by a rabbi; the Birth of Jesus; the Presentation in the Temple; the Holy Family; the Baptism of Jesus by John the Baptist; the Multipliation of the Loaves and Fishes; Mary Magdalene washing Jesus' feet; Peter being given the keys; the Prodigal Son; the Raising of Lazarus from the Dead; Mary the Mother of Sorrows; the Resurrection-Ascension; and the Assumption of Mary into Heaven.

My favorite among all these is the Presentation in the Temple. I love its celebration on February 2, Candlemas Day (Luke 2:22), forty days after Christmas Day, Groundhog Day in Punxsutawny, PA. The hinge of the year, the halfway point between the winter solstice and the spring equinox. In this story, as often in our own, it was not the event that was most exciting but some of the people who were present. Mary and Joseph met old Simeon and Anna...and soon the new baby's body was warming each of them. And instantly their hearts leaped into the boundless joy of a dream long dreamed, totally fulfilled. Adam and Eve got back their original smile...old faces beamed again on the outside of Eden.

Several years ago, my brother J.J. and I went to our parish of Colmcille in County Longford to look up in the baptismal books the name of our great-grandfather, John Doyle. To our surprise, we found four babies called John Doyle, born between 1834 and the famine of 1845. Any one of them could have been our great-grandfather. However, one of them was born on February 2, 1841. Candlemas Day. The Feast of the Presentation. That's the one we wanted. His father was Pat Doyle; his mother, Catherine Campbell. A year later we found from another source that the baby of February 2, 1841 was indeed our great-grandfather. A famine child! But he survived, thanks be to God. The candle held out in all the bite of the bitter wind.

J.J. found strength in the Candlemas boy of 1841. I, too.

One year before he died, J.J. wrote an article called "The Winding Road," in which he describes how miserable his first day at school was. Other days were not much better. "I felt like running home and forgetting about school. I could not. I had to stand my ground. My grandfather, Pat Doyle, told me that my great-grandfather Johnny Doyle (born 1841) went to a hedge school...near Paddy of the Hills. He had a big hill to climb to learn all these great things. I was Johnny Doyle too and I must follow in his big footsteps."

So when I mentioned to J.J. a few days before he died that I wanted to pay for the saving of the Presentation painting in memory of Johnny Doyle and all the Doyles who have come and gone since, he was delighted. "We all must contribute something to it," he said. We will. What I didn't say to him was that I wanted this painting in the memory of the two Johnny Doyles, himself and his great-grandfather and all in between.

After J.J.'s funeral on June 6th, 1995, I came back to his room and the empty bed where he died. There, I lifted his breviary from the windowsill where he had placed it on Friday. I opened it at random and read:

Nunc dimittis.

Simeon's words: "Now you can dismiss your servant, according to your word, in peace, because my eyes have seen salvation." The words of the Presentation in the Temple. The Gospel of Candlemas. I took that as J. J. Doyle's word to me: "I got to the top of the hill with my great grandfather." Indeed he did. As old Simeon said: "My eyes have seen salvation." Lk. 2.

Michael Doyle

The Point

August 1995

Hi:

As I take pen in hand on this 22nd day to write my August letter to you, I can't help remembering that on this day, 24 years ago, I went to prison for tryng to stop the Vietnam War. My cry was for Camden, then, as now. The money that could build my city up was used to bomb many villages down. The graphic images of that war are vivid still – the napalm raging in thatch and timber and, O my God, in the flesh of children.

I had seen, as is often seen in the urban ghetto, the little bodies of burned children and I had stood in shock by the collective grave that covered them. It had been my sad duty, as I told the jury that acquitted me, to enter the Camden County morgue on a terrible day and identify the bodies of six little lifeless lambs – I knew their chatter and their play.....now so still – and their dear father lost too in the fire that killed them. The McCanns of East Camden; 45 S. 28th Street, a few yards from St. Joseph's where I worked at the time. April 22, 1970 – that dark and fatal night. Joseph, 9. Kathryn, 7. James, 4. Diana, 3. Lisa, 2. And Nancy, 1. Their father, Joseph, 46. He had pushed their mother out a second story window in a desperate act to save her. He never knew that she fell on a slab of concrete and was paralyzed from the waist down and she didn't know for three weeks that her whole family had perished. On another terrible day I went into Cooper Hospital with her dear father to tell her.

And it is still true today that there is more money for making weapons of war and storing them safely, than there is for building good homes for the poor and saving children in them. How many inches of black print come out of our damaged cities every year, describing the charred bodies of our children, dead in inadequate houses. Faulty wiring is blamed, faulty heating, but seldom the faulty decisions of powerful people far too far away to hear the children cry.

No one, it seems, heard the cries of 13-year-old Shaline Sequinot stabbed to death a few weeks ago near Camden's Pyne Poynt School where she did so well as a student. Her lovely young body lay in the long weeds over a horrid weekend of heat so harsh...only dental records would positively identify poor Shaline's body by Monday. Her red blood baked black on the green leaves that touched her. There at the Point she was, where the Cooper meets the Delaware, where the pines grew long ago, where William Cooper came down the river from Burlington in 1677 to start a life at what he called Pyne Poynt. He came down the Delaware and soon his Cooper name would wipe away the one the Lenni Lenape (Native Americans there for a thousand years) gave the smaller river that flowed into it.

The point of their meeting is still called Pyne Poynt or simply The Point. From that point Camden eventually grew. The pines are gone and indeed most of the beauty of an earlier time. (But it could be recovered.) When it was incorporated, it had only 1100 people. It only grew in the 20th century, in wealth and power and population (120,000 at peak, 87,000 now). Today it is poor as a plucked chicken with all the problems and bankruptcy of inner city, U.S.A.

Now, in the place where the rivers meet in Camden, the city's old shut-down dump remains – 50 acres that is a mountainous "bomb" of God knows what. There too on the other side of the Cooper is Pyne Poynt School – a prison-looking building with chain-link fence and barbed wire and screaming graffiti.

There Shaline was brutally murdered in the soft spring of her years. Her young body left to the indignities of the night and the scorching defacement of the sun. This town, old, broken and dangerous, throbs with the heartbeat of 20,000 children. God help us all!

I walked one night with many people in North Camden to the awful spot in the weeds. And there Fr. Rick Malloy tried gallantly to comfort the children. I found no comfort. Just a gnawing uneasy feeling about them all and the cruel casualty that Camden is and continues to be. My mind went to the recently restored painting of the Mother of Sorrows in Sacred Heart...a strong woman with a large lap and a young mother draped in agony across it; behind her a dead child sprawled on some steps amidst a splatter of strewn roses. I had a hard time with that painting. Before restoration it had a faded cross behind the mother's chair. Now the cross is clear and strong and some comfort comes. Some glimmer of meaning. Some cleft of hope.

Maybe it's my Irish background. Or maybe it's the fact that I stepped off the boat and walked into America for the first time on September 14, 1959, the Feast of the Holy Cross. I don't really like churches with spires that are merely a soaring point. I like the Cross on top.

I think it's the point.

Michael Doyle

Nothing Bends
(Excerpt)

Loneliness roamed the distant hills
Seeking a nest to warm its cold
But no nest was found in all the world
That was warm the way a womb enfolds
No, this angular box is on the floor
It's flat and hard and out of place
With metal handles to lift and lower
For the whale of the earth to swallow it whole.

Save the Deep Smiles of Their Souls

October, 1995

Hi!

It's autumn when we look for fruits upon the ridge of time.

> *My father's time from whose loins leapt*
> *The blossom of my eager growth*
> *The hips and hands that transubstantiated clay*
> *To blood and bone to build my chance*
> *To walk upon pleasant unplowed fields*
> *He weakening now. The Aran banners dug*
> *Enough to feed the future when he's gone.*

God picked that autumn evening for my father's passing, after a day of joyful work. It was the old fruitful feast of the Maternity of Mary.

> *His tired feet eased out this final time,*
> *The weighted "brogs" aside for another day, please God!*
> *Prayers. Friendly words. Bed. Five minutes. He was dead.*

Twenty-eight years of good times and terrible times have flowed past most of us... bearing many a leaf and broken branch onward to the sea. Sturdy stumps and roots too, from which our chance and genes have leaped. A long time!

> *Since his toes went cold that Wednesday*
> *In potato-picking time when October was eleven*
> *In the Fall of sixty-seven.*

I have written before of finding his shoe, hidden in the eggtree hedge:

> *His empty shoe. Unlaced,*
> *Green almost all the way with moss, moist*
> *In all the sad departed years since he walked away.*

I am keenly aware in this loveliest time of the year that the harvest is here. And will be for me, too, one of these days or nights, and oh, even still, the slim pickings the Harvester will find. Not so, my father, on that last day of his life when he dug out his rows of perfect potatoes.

> *Rows of Aran banners, long, laid out*
> *White, clean, even, not one nicked or cut in two*
> *So keen his eye for where to dip his spade*
> *And lever out on that old left knee*
> *The happy harvest of all his laboring years.*

It is very easy, on this day of tribal memory, to let my mind wander back to the dripping eaves of autumn long ago, the misty evenings of lamps lit and freckled ferns along the narrow lane. It goes to potatoes, to silent shoes and moss, to withered stalks and spades, to falling leaves, to fields and family, and to the poet, Seamus Heaney.

Yeats picked "silver apples of the moon and golden apples of the sun," but Seamus Heaney, a poorer man, oldest of nine, picked potatoes, "fingers dead in the cold." And wet clay weighing him down in the small fields outside Bellaghy, County Derry. There he watched his father digging, and he, not as good a man with a spade, would dig with a pen. And dig, he did, till the poems came tumbling out. We have watched the blossoms bloom and last week he won the Nobel Prize for Literature, the golden potato, as it were … for all the deep mind-delving dips of his spade. The Nobel Committee cited him for "works of lyrical beauty and ethical depth, which exalt everyday miracles and the living past." Indeed he has exalted the simple ordinary things – "the music of what happens" in face and field, in snout-shaped water pump and lane, clothes drying on the line or a frog spawning in the spring.

His poetry seems to have become more difficult since he began to hold "the Chair of Poetry at Oxford" (it's high-backed) or "the Boylston Professorship of Rhetoric and Oratory at Harvard." Lofty levels, "spirit levels", for a potato-picker from Bellaghy!

Modern traffic is heavy at times and it's hard to conceive anything in heavy traffic. Jesus declares "the wayside" to be the first casualty of the sower's seed. Too hard from the trampling for anything to take root. Noisy media mindlessness pounds through closed doors, cracks, and cranium, making the monastery of the mind into a mall of madness. Seamus Heaney seeks a "refinement of feelings" with his poems, or what Padraic Colum's drover whispered, "I could quiet your herds with my words, with my words."

Sacred Heart's phone rang today (my father hardly ever heard a phone ring) with the word that a 14-year-old boy shot and killed himself. Oh, guns, guns, guns, and the havoc of it all!

There are some heartrending cries in " the music of what happens."Seamus Heaney, it was the death of your four-year old brother, knocked down and killed, that tore the first poem from your heart. But God's songmaker continues to say: "Lift up your heart!" Lift the fallen, too!

Michael Doyle

Excerpt of Michael Doyle's Closing Statement

What do you do when a child is on fire in a war that was a mistake and you can't extinguish the flame – the napalm flame with water or anything else? What are you to do about that? What do you do with an old man whose bones are splintered by anti-personnel weapons in a war that was a mistake? It's a terrible burden on us little people. We have no answer to that. There is no answer in the law for a child on fire in a war that was a mistake.

Camden 28 Trial 1973

Generosity, of Course, Is the Key

November, 1995

Hi!

The hearth in the old home I was born in, with its blue-breath smoke and welcoming fire, was the focus of daily life in the kitchen of my childhood. It was the spot where all our food was cooked, all our heat was located, and all our chatting was centered. Very exciting it was for me to learn in later life (my high school was called The Latin School) that in the Latin language the word focus means "the hearth."

Could that be the reason why, a few years ago, when I was asked to speak at a conference in Philadelphia on the preservation of churches and sacred places, that I said the following: "If you want to save a hearth, then you build a fire! It's all I know." Believe it or not, the following year I was called to speak at a similar conference in Ottawa, and the year after that, it was the keynote address in Holy Trinity Church in Copley Square in Boston. And last year I journeyed to New Bedford, Massachusetts to proclaim my thesis: "The Fire saves the Hearth. It's all I know, still."

I am amused sometimes when I read the misspelled name of our beloved Sacred Heart that the junk mail monster, after he eats our trees, throws up upon our world. We are called the Sacred Heat, the Scared Heart (we are scared sometimes), and once in awhile the Sacred Hearth. That's the one I like. It's a heartwarming word.

I like it because many people try, and have for these many years tried, to create a warm fire of generosity and hospitality here. This is a good time of year to acknowledge them. November is the time to remember...to salute all who came here or helped here for the past 123 years. They all have laid some of themselves on the "hearth" that is sacred still. They built and continue to build a fire to warm the world.

And in the line-up of the living and the dead, no one stands out more nobly than John McGuire, who helped out here for 59 years and who gave to the Sacred Heart his own.

John was conceived, "when this century broke water." He was born in its ninth month and lived for 87 of its years. He tended to Sacred Heart with the faithfulness and devotion of a mother to a baby. By the time he died on November 24, 1987, he had accumulated a bucket full of keys with the means and the constant patience to open anything that was ever hinged at Sacred Heart. (We put them all in his casket when we buried him.) Some people were not long in bed when John was up each morning and out, picking up the beer bottles that they had carelessly discarded in the street. He opened the church doors at 6 a.m. "in case there's a trucker who wants to come in and light a candle." And, of course, the only trucker who ever came in was the one who came to lighten his load of candles by delivering them. But oh, the stars that came to light in the eyes of the angels as John tended to countless little tasks in the dark of the day before the sun rose in the morning.

He readied the church on a Sunday before anyone came and tidied it up when everyone went home. We miss him, still.

Where's John

The hymn sheets lay like leaves
In a grove of flattened pews,
Storm strewn on a Sunday afternoon.
Baby chewed or crushed by crude – fists
That insist on paper sounds to drown
The song, or aeroplaned around
Like swallows near the ground.
Where has care gone, faithful John?
Not there – always there – to come behind
And find what carelessness has done.
Bend the tired hinges of his hips
And collect the scattered bits that
Broke away and lay like litter on the grass,
Right there where we tidied up our world
At the Sunday morning Mass.

John's actions, hidden as they were, spoke loudly as the wind in the chimney, but his words were soft as smoke and seldom spoken. Memorable as any words I ever heard were the ones he said to me one day sitting in his living room across the street from this building he tended so faithfully. "That church is my heart." Or the winter's morning when rain and fierce frost had blended to ice up every eave and wire and keyhole. "I got the church door open," said John with a bright eye and a small smile. "How, John?" The keyhole was solid ice." His answer awed me. "I just kept breathing on it," John said quietly. Keys and ice-packed keyholes, an old man's breath in the cold of the morning melting an opening in the gates of heaven. "That church is my heart."

On November 24, the anniversary of his death, we will install a stained glass window at the entrance to our church hall to honor John McGuire. Made by the great stained-glass artist Paul Skelly as a gift to John, who, says Paul, "helped me many a time and would never take anything." It depicts a golden key unlocking a heart-shaped church. And the words, "That church is my heart. Generosity, of course, is the key. And every setting sun will brighten his memory till the dawn of the day.

Blood and Poinsettias

December, 1995

Hi:

This evening the melting ice hangs like tears from the branches of a hawthorn tree on Ferry Avenue. Silver beads of sorrow for Richard Barbour. It was planted in his memory by his friends Katie Hartman and Steve Dunbar on their wedding day, May 26, 1991. One month before, Richard, who was preparing to be their bestman, was murdered at a MAC Machine in Philadelphia. His remorseless young killer 17 said: "he shouldn't have hesitated." Tonight the haws are as red as blood in the last bits of snow.

Everything changed on that fatal night, April 28, and all that came back to mind on Sunday (December 10) when we baptized little Riley Richard Dunbar, a few feet from the tree, and for a moment the water clung like tears to his little head before it fell back into the font. We are indeed baptized into the death of Christ. The baby bears the name of his parents' murdered friend but tears eased into smiles as his father raised him high above his head to the triple shout of the people: Christ is Risen. Indeed, He is risen.

But more weeping would follow. Enough to baptize him again...or even immerse him, I think, in a tub of tears. Somehow, by God's design, his baptism that recalled a terrible memory, took place during the Mass on December 10th, when we gathered in Sacred Heart with parents and relatives to remember Camden's 58 murdered people during the past eleven months.

I called their names in the silent church. One by one. And, one by one, the mother, or the father, or the relative, or a chosen person from our congregation came forward to light a candle for the dead and stand in a horseshoe formation that stretched across the front and down three quarter ways on the side aisles of Sacred Heart. Fifty-eight candles. Fifty-eight people standing. Fifty-eight people murdered in this bloody city since January 1. The population is only eighty-seven thousand. O my God! Realization of the magnitude of the slaughter pounded like a hammer in our hearts. We prayed. Barbara Dever lifted us in song on Eagle's Wings. Spontaneously, the fifty-eight candles were hoisted in the air forming two great arms around the world in an embrace of light. Tears, tears, tears...glistening in the candle glow. Light leaped out of a terrible darkness. The courage of a mother facing the fact of a murdered child and her faith in God holding still. On her face "a terrible beauty is born", as William Butler Yeats would say. It's Christmas in Camden!

Those fifty-eight candles were held aloft in honor of the dead, in hope for the future, in a cry to God to have mercy on us because God alone knows where we all fit into the tragedy that lets the Camdens of this world go to hell.

CBS-TV was here to film a segment for the program Sunday Morning. So the candles will be beamed across the nation this Sunday (December 24) as a cry to America. They are piercing distress signals in a big ocean of darkness. They are flaming tongues of fire yelling to the world: we have a Bosnia in our own backyard. They are the cries of mothers: the death of my child is as important in God's eyes as any death in Bosnia, or Belfast; any death in the ranks of the military or the halls of Congress.

I said to Elliot Bernstein who came here twelve years ago to do a piece for *60 Minutes* and who came again last week to do a Camden Christmas at Sacred Heart: "You cannot look at Christmas in Camden this year without looking at the heart breaking list of the murdered."

So, our Camden Christmas has tears falling, songs rising, a mother beaming at her baptized son, a mother mourning her murdered one, a dark abandoned house being gutted, a young expectant mother moving into a gleaming one, just completed by the Heart of Camden Housing. It has toys for 1700 children, and 1,004 families requesting a Christmas basket. All that!

Camden! Oh Camden! Blood and poinsettias.

And, yet, there is always that stir of undying hope in the manger of our lowest moments.

May God of the poor always have a home in your heart!

Camden's Heartbreaking List

1.	1/1/95	Hanh Ngo	20.	3/27/95	Juan Ponce	39.	8/21/95	Armando Rivera
2.	1/1/95	Thanh Le	21.	4/6/95	Ceyton Brown	40.	8/23/95	Rosalee Watson
3.	1/1/95	Nghia Nhuyen	22.	4/15/95	Robert Jordan	41.	8/25/95	Conception Gomez
4.	1/16/95	Darnell Fisher	23.	4/24/95	Jose Orta	42.	8/27/95	Marcero Harper
5.	1/17/95	Reginald Johnson	24.	4/29/95	Toran Dorsey	43.	8/28/95	Carlos Hernandez
6.	1/18/95	Kirby Brunch, Jr	25.	4/30/95	Patrick Pollard	44.	8/30/95	Ernest Alford
7.	1/18/95	Mark Winston	26.	5/16/95	Jose Quintana	45.	9/5/95	Bruce Riley, Jr
8.	1/19/95	Jesus Rivera	27.	5/17/95	Nathaniel Redd, Sr.	46.	10/12/95	Kier Thomas
9.	1/19/95	Miguel Sanchez	28.	5/21/95	Rashan Finney	47.	10/12/95	Henry Wynn
10.	1/22/95	ChristineWilliams	29.	6/1/95	Loreli Truluck	48.	10/19/95	Bernadette Moses
11.	1/22/95	Leon Mitchell	30.	6/9/95	Rasheen Jones	49.	10/22/95	Clarence Jones
12.	1/22/95	BarringtonBeresford	31.	6/17/95	Andrew Alexander	50.	11/3/95	Brett Neal
13.	1/28/95	Rodney Turner	32.	6/30/95	Winston Morgan	51.	11/11/95	Robin Stephens
14.	1/28/95	MargaretWilson	33.	7/14/95	Percival Smith	52.	11/13/95	John Garrett
15.	2/9/95	Ainsley Hawthorne	34.	7/19/95	Jose Vega	53.	11/15/95	Milton Elam
16.	2/16/95	Luis Reyes	35.	8/7/95	Shaline Sequinot	54.	11/18/95	Anthony Wiley
17.	2/23/95	Maurice Potter	36.	8/8/95	Paul Collier	55.	11/27/95	Edwin Posada
18.	3/19/95	Lynwal Williams	37.	8/9/95	Ronald Greene	56.	11/27/95	MarieAdel Raminez
19.	3/27/95	Edwin Ponce	38.	8/12/95	Juan Diaz	57.	11/29/95	Gerold Wallace
						58.		Unknown

Niederhauser There!

January, 1996

Hi!

"Niederhauser, here!" The voice on Sacred Heart's phone was deeper than usual and laden with tones of importance. "I'm at Broadway and Market," he said, "I'll be there in 15 minutes...to see Michael Doyle." Five minutes later "Niederhauser, here!" The same tone. "I'm at Broadway and Mickle. I'll be there in 11 minutes." He was walking. And there was yet another call. "Niederhauser, here!" He was nearer. Somewhere on Broadway. And after all that — would you believe, he didn't come at all.

But he came, unannounced, many times after that. David Peter Niederhauser. With his ardent causes, his funny caps, his chest of buttons, his knee length scarf, his homeless blanket slung around the slender shoulders. Sixty-three, he was, with the old madness of a prophet in his eyes and sometimes the wild wine of the street in his veins.

"Can I have nine seconds of your time?" he'd say. I knew how long David's seconds were. They had the same chance of containment as a fire in a paper factory. And yet, I feel badly now that I often avoided his causes and his chatter and the flattening intensity of it all. I feel badly. ..now that he's dead.

David was down and out, with white hair to his waist, when he was stabbed in the hallway of a vacant apartment building at 311 Cooper Street in the dark early hours of December 23. He was pronounced dead in Cooper Hospital at 6:06 a.m. A homeless man but always refusing welfare. Alone too, but always needing people. There had to be buried somewhere deeply beneath the high levels of his consciousness, a tender memory of a home in Williamstown, MA, long ago.There his little baby body was warm and loved on his very first Christmas in this world. 1932. But ah, dear God, on this Christmas day, his broken body was cold and untended in the freezer drawer of the Camden County morgue. But then there was nothing cold about the fiery spirit that was there no longer. He was one of the last of the 60 victims on Camden's streets of slaughter in 1995.

We gathered again on Friday, January 5, at Epiphany Lutheran Church at 7th and Market Streets to remember David. One candle burned in front of a small wooden box, no bigger than his boot, where all his ashes were laid. We preached and we prayed, told stories and cried. We sang "We Shall Overcome." Someday! Sometime! No one dared say soon. Epiphany time in Epiphany Church when we recall that the wise saw a star. God knows we felt a desperate need for a star...any flickering sign of hope for Camden's broken heart and bloodshot eyes.

We listened to Luke: "The Angel said to them, 'You have nothing to fear. I come to proclaim good news to you – tidings of great joy to be shared by the whole people. This day in David's city a savior has been born to you, the Messiah and Lord.'" We've had a terrible year, with unending sorrow in "David's city." We surely need a savior.

Poor David had tried to be one in his tattered uneasy lifetime. The son of highly educated parents (his mother a graduate of Columbia, his father had a doctorate from Princeton and shared an office with Albert Einstein), David himself held a Master's degree in humanities from the University of Michigan and was, according to Rev. Robert Wilson of Jersey City, "a brilliant social activist in Detroit and Buffalo." He burned with zeal to establish a compassionate society. Even in the last years when his mind was astray, his ideals were not. "We need," he proclaimed, "a greed-free coalition." He wanted a water that would lift all the boats, the poor little craft as well as the great tall ships. And when he failed to lift the poor he became poor himself. Rev. Wilson knew David, his wife, and their four sons well (two of whom wept in the front pew), before his burning ideals tore his mind and severed his family. Paying tribute to the zeal that consumed him, Rev. Wilson said: "David suffered from Messianic burnout." He had in his heart the same urgent sense of organizing the powerless that motivated great leaders like Martin Luther King, Jr., Saul Alinsky, Tom Gaudette and Maggie Kuhn, all of whom he knew.

And then David died in a doorway. In the way. There. In the pathway of evil. His poor tired body, taking the blows, the stabs six times, the sins of us all. And may we take from him the challenge to do our best to build a greed-free society.

In the final words of the service, Rev. Margaret Hertz-Lane pleaded with great big tears in her eyes, "Let his death not be forgotten." And those same words, the biggest headlines poor David ever drew, graced the Courier Post the next day.

David's funeral was good for us. We sensed somehow that hope was rising from the ashes of this silly little man, with his cry for change. "Niederhauser, here," he said. And "not all there," was often said. But we all know now that in that haven where the homeless find a home, the door opened wide at the very first knock, because "Niederhauser, here" was heard and heeded there, where God had prepared a place for him.

And Niederhauser there, will make a better New Year for Camden. I know it.

"Cockle Seed'
(Dedicated to David Niederhauser)

Out of the trees, traipsing the sand
In search of land for herd's milk
And the sweet savings of banker bees.
With these they could go on,
And risk seeds in turned sods
Wait for woman gods to shoot
Stalks through earth's eager pores
And build belief in sowers' seeds
That rich relief was only weather away
From feeding all their human needs.

But a weed grew on human need
A cockle-seed in the golden corn
And few indeed, escaped its thorn.
It pricked so many in the gut
About the time their cord was cut,
That they bit their mothers' breasts to blood
And lived by grabbing all they could.
And will not now be satisfied
Until all their ugly greeds collide
And all the earth has died.

I Just Wanted to Make It Fun

February 1996

Hi:

There are four letter words and there are four letter words. Did you ever hear of "Eral?" An unfair question. Eral is a left over bit from a bigger word. You are thinking this doesn't make much sense. It doesn't. So we'll leave it...hanging.

Today I write with a blackened thumb, blackened with our all-day service of putting dark crosses of ashes on warm faces at Sacred Heart. It's hard for me to avoid the somber note of mortality as I put daubs of dirt on devout frowning foreheads. But I also know that there is nothing sad about putting a bit of dirt on the buried bulb of a daffodil.

And, I would say, that Sacred Heart in Camden is a lively center that is energized by the ever-vibrant heartbeat of Christ at the core of all the good things that happen. Now, the Sunday before Ash Wednesday is always celebrated here as Carnival Sunday, when we try to recover the original meaning of those old Catholic words carnevale, which means "good-bye meat," and Mardi Gras, which means "Fat Tuesday." Both are connected to Lent when people abstained from meat for most of the 40 days before Easter. In times gone by, as Ash Wednesday neared, people had a party to get rid of all the meat products, and so invented Mardi Gras. The meat was gobbled up before it spoiled (no refrigeration). It was Carnival time, good-bye to meat until Easter comes.

Thus it was that on February 18, 1996, we had our Carnival celebration at Sacred Heart with pink flowers and bright saucy colors in balloons, streamers, clothes, and clowns. People circled in a dance down the wall-aisles at the beginning and the end of Mass. To "The Lord of the Dance," they danced. To the God of life, their hearts leaped; in the fun of the feeling that God invented play, they danced against the heavy clay from which their dancing feet are made. They danced against the icy grip of death.

Because the dance goes on when feet turn blue
There's tapping somewhere for each rotting shoe.

After coffee and Elgin Diner pancakes (pancakes were big on "Fat Tuesday" for mopping up the gravies and the greases), everybody went home with a lighter step.

Now, the next morning, even though it wasn't early, I saw the winter sun in my window rising over the 1700 block of Fillmore Street. That battered block was on my mind. There, a few days before when night had fallen on that lightless house, 1738, without heat or water, Jackie Turlington closed the bright brown eyes that had lit her way down the troubled years of her life. Forty-five in all. As the sun rose I knew that her weary body would be carried into Sacred Heart at 9 a.m. and I would lead her funeral service at 10:00.

Dear, dear Jackie! With all her addictions and destitution, she was one playful smile on the broken face of this neighborhood, the likes of which will not be seen again. The church with its carnival tones and saucy decor was just right for Jackie. How often she said to me: "I love you," and meant it, too, even after I yelled at her or would not give her the money to feed her addictions. "A dime is worth more than ten cents," she would say, and she always told people that I was her friend. But I failed. I failed to find a way to keep her warm in the winter. No matter what was done, she always went back to the desolate houses on Fillmore Street and the addictions that consumed her. But she was a great lady beneath it all. I always felt she was a star in a fog with fewer and fewer clearances for the shining sweetness of her soul. Oh, I wish Sacred Heart had a Catholic Worker House of Hospitality where the Jackies and all Les Miserables that I know could sit and eat a bowl of hot soup in the winter. A bit of care and dignity for those whose twisted dreams are killing them.

We took Jackie's body down to The Land of Canaan in Glassboro, N.J. It was a great scene. The white hearse. The line of cars, the headlights, the orange FUNERAL stickers. All eased into the graveyard, with its yellow dirt road and pure bridal bedspread of snow. A lone man with a shovel would fill the grave where we placed her.

It seemed just right that after the prayers I pulled a poem by Maya Angelou from my pocket and read "Still I Rise." Some of it:

> *You may write me down in history*
> *With your bitter, twisted lies,*
> *You may trod me in the very din*
> *But still, like dust, I'll rise.*
>
> *You may shoot me with your words,*
> *You may cut me with your eyes,*
> *You may kill me with your hatefulness,*
> *But still like air, I rise.*
>
> *Leaving behind nights of terror and fear*
> *I rise*
> *Into a daybreak that's wondrously clear*
> *I rise*
> *Bringing the gifts that my ancestors gave,*
> *I am the dream and the hope of the slave.*
> *I rise*
> *I rise*
> *I rise.*

It was Maya to Jackie, woman to woman: Rise! At the end of it all, Jackie would rise in her splendid smile and her style and all the good humor of her heart. So, I took the orange sticker with its word FUNERAL from the windshield and tore "ERAL" off. I just wanted to make it "FUN." For Jackie coming home.

Michael Doyle

Dipping into the Tidal Sorrow

March, 1996

Hi!

Just about the time I could form the three "syllabler" in a tiny mouth, I learned how to spell it. Potato. My grandfather Pat Doyle taught me and often called upon me to perform my baby feat in front of his old friends, (Pebbie's) Charlie Reilly and (Big John's) Tommy Reilly-both of Rossduff-and others who came for the great chats that circled the hearth of my childhood. It was a big word. It stood for more than the mind could manage, and its meaning had been mashed into the collective memory with a sledge-like pounding that was indelible.

While my grandfather often asked me to spell the correct English word for the special spud, that was not the word he used for the Aran Banners he planted or the Golden Wonders he dug. Our daily word was the Irish one, praeta, and its place in the sad story of our race has no equal. You don't have to dig far into the fields of our national literature before you find the Heaneys and the Kavanaghs and others turning up the potato with the spade-like blade of their pens. Some have dipped into the tidal sorrow that followed the failure of the potato, the terrible famine of 1845 and the four years that followed. In the next half-century, starvation, disease, and immigration cut the population of almost nine million in half in a destruction on a scale unequaled in the world.

Now in the mid-90s of the twentieth century, we are trying to look back through the sad silence that hangs like a mist over the past 150 years. It was all too much. There is silent grass over thousands of shallow unmarked graves, or huge holes where many lie together, across the land of Ireland. The dead was too heavy for the worsening weakness of the living. We have our accounts of the hinged-bottom coffin that loaded, transported, and dumped the dead. The animals that ate the untended bodies. And worst of all, when death tore families apart in the middle of the Atlantic on the "coffin" ships that bore them toward the USA, what unfathomable sorrow when the dead child or parent was tossed into the terror of the sea. What anger, what remorse, what lessons for today when we think of the greed and abuse of power that led to this calamity and paralyzed real, adequate measures to deal with it! England had abolished the Irish parliament in 1801 and by bribery forced the hated Union on the people. Ireland was ruled from London. That government was responsible. Its help was too little, too late, and cut off too soon.

Back in the 1840's, my great-great-grandfather Pat Doyle and my great-great-grandmother Catherine Campbell tilled the small bog-based farm I was born on. They had to pay rent to some landlord in England because the British presumed to own the land of Ireland. Sub-letting to pay the rent was very common. The coming of the potato, which provided staple food, the availability of turf for the fire for heat and cooking, the little sod-houses that people could easily erect...all this gave rise to a great increase in marriages. The population exploded.

My great-great-grandmother Catherine gave birth to a son on February 2, 1841, and she called him John. Later that year, a census of Ireland was taken and the population was listed at 8,175,124. And, no way, in rural Ireland, were all the people counted. It would be fair to say the population was nearer to nine million. In the previous 60 years it had increased by more than 172 percent. It was a desperately poor population. Any little money it had went to England for rent.

British landowners in Ireland shipped grain to the English market all through the famine. And that market was allowed to follow its course – no interference by government – regardless of how many got slaughtered. Do we not hear a lot today about allowing "the market" to have its way...regardless?

My great-grandfather John Doyle was four-and-a-half years old when the fungus (same say carried from the USA) brought the black death on the green stalks and the pink-white blossoms of the potato fields. Growth was cut at the clay, and the potatoes below, small as cherries, could not get any bigger. Fear tore the nerves of the people as if some horrible curse had ridden in over the land in the breath of a hot wet wind.

The potato had been such a blessing. It became the lifeline of the teeming population of Ireland. Developed by the Incas in the valleys of the Andes, it first reached Europe through the Spaniards and then through the English. It was a wonder crop and it was as much at home in Ireland as the heather in the bog. In bogland and grassland, in mountainland and wetland it grew gloriously. It's as hardy as a human being and loves the cool air of the high ground and the land of the northern hemisphere. (Russia produces 25 percent of the potatoes of the world.) But in 1845, 1846, 1847, and 1848, it had no resistance to, and there was no prevention for, the fungus that flattened it. In time a solution was found.

The famine child of 1841 had a son Pat Doyle who taught me to spell potato and Pat had a son John who was my father. These men sprayed the potato stalks with a blue liquid that prevented blight, and no two men loved the land they worked on more than they. I still recall my first day with these two men when I worked in the field. I was nine.

> *I was there, with men who knew the men who turned the famine sod.*
> *And I felt the primal ancient bonding of blood and earth and God.*

It is a great bonding. I am, as millions are, tied to a tragedy that changed the face of this nation and left its mark on the soul of the Irish people. Exile is my lot and the lot of the many who first saw the light of day on that little island on the edge of Europe.

A sad reflection, I suppose. But on this St. Patrick's Day it takes only five hours to fly from New York to Dublin. My sister Philomena Doyle visited me this week with her husband Johnny O'Reilly. She was born in the same house where our great-grandfather was born in 1841. They enjoyed their visit but had this to say about Camden: "It still looks a sad place. The scale of decay is difficult to believe—whole streets falling apart and full of rubbish, but still a few families hanging in there against the odds. A terrible place for young people."

A famine scene of sorts...in the midst of plenty. I wonder what they'll say in 150 years? May God hold you in the hollow of his hand!

Michael Doyle

The Lovely Mine Birds Sing

April, 1996

Hi:

I had never heard of the "mine birds," but recently I did, and since then, the picture of their poignant perch in the dark, haunts my mind. Sr. Mary Scullion mentioned them when she came to Sacred Heart on March 22 to speak in our Lenten Series on the state of the U.S. economy. Sr. Mary has devoted her life to promoting the dignity and humanity of the homeless people of Philadelphia and to providing work and homes for them. She spoke movingly about the prophetic role of the homeless in North America today. "The miners" she said "used to take canaries into the coal mines with them for protection....When the small birds fell, the miners knew it was time to get out. Death had arrived. Deadly gases that would kill everybody.

So, the increasing number of prone forms of homeless men on city grates or homeless women in dingy doorways, are songbirds stilled—not by gases from below, but by greed and power from above. They are warning signs to all of us.

Today I have mines on my mind. I have, because I want to tell you about a miner named John Harvilla, of Freeland, Pennsylvania, and I want to tell you for Easter.

Freeland, in the coal regions of Northern Pennsylvania, was so called because the town's area was free from coal mining operations. John worked instead at Jedda and Upper Lehigh and other surrounding places. There he was, the timber man.....when the shaft was dug, he was there with his timbers to prop up the weight of the world and prevent it from burying his friends forever.

John was a boy in the mines with the vigor of youth and brawn when this century was a baby. He worked his lifetime as the timberman of the mines, a person of trust to his fellow workers below and faith and devotion to his God above.

His daughter Julia Harvilla who was buried from this church on April 28, 1984, often recalled her bursting joy as a child on Easter morning when her father returned with the breads he had taken to church for the blessing. Only then could the children eat. She recalled too the wonderful greetings on his lips for everyone he met: Kristos Voskres! Christ is Risen!

So, in this holy season of life, let us pause with my little poem and acknowledge the miner's happy Easter in Freeland—his hard and heroic life too, in the dark depths of the earth, and above all, the early shouts of his hope to his neighbors on Easter morning. Thanks, John, for giving meaning to this great day for all of us.

The Timberman

The timberman stepped from the depths of the mine
And shook the coal dust from his hair
Now opens his door at the break of the day
When Easter is fresh in the air.

His body is scrubbed of the black of the earth
His shirt is white as the snow
His loaves are set to be taken to church
And he is preparing to go.

To go to the church in the bright morning air
While the children are still in their beds
No one can eat from table or trough
Till the blessings are poured on the breads.

Now the man from the mine is on his way home
When all of the prayers are said
The smiles of his children upon his return
Would coax anyone back from the dead.

The timberman knows the dark of the tomb
And Khristos Voskres he can say
Because Easter is real in his body and bones
As he strides on top of the clay.

His greetings have power unknown to the priest
Who never was down in the hole
Or washed Easter Eve the coal from his chest
And rinsed all the sins from his soul.

O hail to the timberman under the ground
Who gives Easter its chance every day
As he props up the weight of the grave with his hands
So his brothers can rise from the clay.

Hail, I say, to the Spirit of God who calls life into the cold dust of all those who were once so warmly with us. Christ is Risen!

Life has the edge—no matter how dark the shaft, how deep the hole, how deadly the gas, and even if the timbers crack and give; ultimately...ultimately, my dear friend, the lovely mine birds sing.

Michael Doyle

Ah Well!

June, 1996

Hi!

"God is there," says Edwina Gateley, "when nothing is there." Nothing in the head, in the heart, in the hope that we ought to have. God will surely be present in this letter. Present I mean, as I put my pen to paper because there's nothing in my mind. No thoughts, no words, no "nothing" worthy of your eyes or your interest.

I recently returned to Camden after a week in Ireland where I went for the first anniversary of my brother's death and to purchase a headstone for his grave. Returning to Camden always has an unsettling and "dewombing" effect on my being. I need time.

For a year now I dreaded my next arrival in Dublin because the arms that so eagerly reached out to welcome me were under the brown earth where we laid them. But my sister Phyllis was there with her sweet warmth, her husband Johnny O'Reilly, and a wonderful welcome from both of them. Then into Dublin's Fair City in the not so early morning and yet on this Whit Monday (a national holiday) almost everyone was still asleep. O'Connell Street was a country lane. They took me up to Bewley's on Grafton Street (there since 1840) where their four children (28 to 20) arrived one by one, for breakfast. 'Twas great!

My next stop was J.J.'s grave, 70 miles north-westward in County Longford. It was as brown as when I left it a year ago and then I remembered the rabbits eating grass when I first came to look for a spot. They nibble off every blade and blossom that attempt to grow there. I really don't like the association of rabbits and Easter but they surely do announce life around the granite stillness of a graveyard. There was a small bottle of water on the grave, holy water there for the ritual of pouring in an act of blessing. Before I left, the sky began to do its own watering. A frequent blessing in that part of the world.

Speaking of watering, when I got home I filled a glass of water and proposed a toast. Ever since I was in St. Petersburg, I cherish the great value of a toast and the wonderful Russian custom of long formal toasts around the dinner table. Good words and VODKA! Eulogies in the literal sense and you don't have to drop dead to get them. Anyway, my drink was water. It was new. Our uisge (ish-gah, Irish word for water) used to come from our own spring well on the farm but for many years now, it was piped from Lough Gowna. Over usage by others on the pipe left us often with only a trickle and so we recently dug a well that is 260 feet below the field in front of the house. This was my first taste of the water that comes up through 220 feet of solid rock to slake my thirst. That called for a toast to the living water in a rock and also to all the hearts we love...some, many now, still as stone beneath the brown level of the ground.

And a nod to the old well that was...

Our daily honored shrine, humble yet sublime
Like cows at milking time, sadly now no more.

I carried water from the well to a terracotta crock.
My hands could always tell from little dents and swell
Whenever I would fill it
For the pots and the kettles and the little porridge skillet.
The pathway worn in our field by a century of shoes
Is long ago gone, through deadly lack of use.

But the mind, thanks be to God, can make paths of its own, take us walking along them, to lower white enamel buckets into the depths of ordinary things. Ah, well!

On Thursday, June 6th, I went with my cousin Johnny Creegan down into Leitrim, a county that lies like a long lean woman with her head on the edge of the sea and her toes in center of Ireland. We drove for a while along the great artery of Ireland, the Shannon, where our ancestor rowed against the flow from Limerick to Leitrim in 1701 to found his branch of the Creegan tree and give both of us the life that courses in our veins. On the bleak side of Arigna, Sliabh-an-Iarainn (the Iron Mountain), we gazed down at the silver spread of water where the Shannon long ago broke banks and filled the valley with Lough Allen. Wild mountain land on the way with hardly a house or bush, where the sheep and the lambs with the curlew and the ceannbawn (bog cotton) are as content as could be on the moor and the mountain. On we went—Balinamore, Drumshanbo, Drumkeeran! I wanted to reach Glencar. Dúiche Yeats, the sign said: Yeats' country, Glencar Waterfall, Co. Leitrim. And there it was—a bright bridal veil fashioned from "the wandering water" and falling, falling over the moss-green breast of the hill. This place was part of the fairies' enticement sang Yeats, in The Stolen Child.

Then over the few miles to Drumcliff in Sligo, where William Butler Yeats is buried and the discovery that the church, is St. Columba's, and so long before such names as Church of Ireland existed, a poet-prince, Colmcille, founded a monastery here in the shadow of Ben Bulben. All this took me home again to where five generations of Doyles are buried in ground named for the same holy saint in Longford. St. Colmcille. This great saint was born in Donegal in 531 when Christianity was a hundred years old in Ireland. His world was not unfamiliar with old druids and oak grove temples and eyelids lowered in worship before the great circle of the sun.

Today I am on another mission. The great saint would surely smile at me, "a Colmcille man" wandering through local graveyards to find the perfect model of a Celtic cross to mark the grave of my brother. I found it, with its limestone circle for the sun in ancient Ireland, and the eternal light too emanating from the cross of the Christian world. Kevin O'Connor of Cavan will carve it all in a stone for my dear brother J.J.

So! A Busy Week! Jet stream and blood stream. The Shannon—the man rowing against river. Water falling from the heights and surging from the depths. A cold stone cross with a circle of fire. Raindrops and tear drops. A glass of water. A toast to life!
Ah, well!

Michael Doyle

Hooker on the Horse Trough

July, 1996

Hi!

In December 1995, when Charlie Gonzalez, SJ, left the hallowed halls of Georgetown University where he was a professor of theology for many years, and came to the desolate streets of South Camden to develop a ministry to the Latino people whose numbers are growing around Sacred Heart, he was following in the footsteps of heroic Jesuits who were the first priests to consecrate bread and wine on the kitchen tables of South Jersey 250 years ago. Father Theodore Schneider, SJ, who was assigned from Baltimore, MD, to be assistant pastor of St. Joseph's in Willings Alley, the first Catholic Church in Philadelphia, crossed the Delaware and baptized John Martin Alter in October 1743 during Mass in the home of Maurice Lorent near a glassblowing factory in Salem County, NJ. It was the first recorded Catholic Baptism in South Jersey. Fr. Charlie has baptized several Latino children since he came to Sacred Heart eight months ago. Indeed the urban terrain of Camden in 1996 is hardly less daunting than the perilous trails of South Jersey for the pioneering Jesuits of the mid-eighteenth century.

Charlie is also following in the footsteps of Patrick Byrne, another Georgetown man (he took courses there after coming from Ireland as a young man after the Famine) who was ordained in 1860 in St. Mary's in Baltimore for the diocese of Newark which included all of New Jersey. He came to Camden in 1863 and built the Immaculate Conception Church at Broadway and Market.

At that time Camden extended southward to Kaighn Avenue, but in 1871 its boundaries were enlarged to include all lands south to the Newton Creek. The Woodbury Pike, now known as Broadway, went through it, an area of scattered housing and farmlands. Fr. Byrne established a mission church here and called it Sacred Heart in 1871, two years before Walt Whitman came to Camden. By next year, 1997, that will be 125 years ago. We will celebrate it. In 1886 the new church of Sacred Heart was built at Broadway and Ferry, about half way between Kaighn Avenue and Newton Creek.

Well, time has changed the territory...many times. The country road Woodbury Pike/Broadway changed into a channel of heavy industry and commerce that was the pride of South Jersey and time changed that channel into a hardened artery that is lined with abandoned buildings. No longer the stores, the theatres, the beautifully constructed mills. Only the churches hold on to life and hope. This section of Broadway, Sacred Heart's section, is noted today for the commerce of the body. Along every corner wholesale prostitution, bodies for sale all hours of the day and night for less than lunch. Poor drug-damaged women enslaved, owned, and abused. Surely a great sorrow for a church whose fountain-source and inspiration is the Heart. The Sacred Heart of all hearts.

Indeed, we have many ministries to the poor of Camden: a school, a housing program, a medical clinic, a food program, a thrift store for children's clothing, a family resource center, a friendly ministry of God's grace and goodness to many. But we fail. We do not yet have a vehicle that serves in any organized way, the homeless, the drug damaged, the women for sale on the streets.

Edwina Gateley came to Camden recently and spoke urgently to us on her work with prostitutes in Chicago, and we were awed by the powerful faith and courage that inspired her to reach out to the inner person that is so often encrusted in the hardened pretense of the prostitute.

Edwina's energy and spirit gave new meaning and challenge to the work of restoration that is still going on in our church. Our *first* painting three and a half years ago was Mary Magdalen (60 square feet) now cleaned and restored to the ceiling of Sacred Heart, her long red hair draped on the feet of Jesus to dry them. Jesus had reached her crusted soul, and like the rock that Moses struck, her eyes flooded like a fountain that will never dry up again. We have many Marys waiting for the love that would break their hearts—break them open to the goodness of God.

People here are praying and pondering. A soup kitchen? A house of hospitality? A healing spot. A meeting place where the very poor, the hardened poor could be honored. Some deep well where a woman comes for water...and maybe a word with Someone.

The history of Camden states that "public drinking fountains were put into service on May 1st, 1904." They have long since dried up. There is one without water in a little park by Sacred Heart. Several years ago, we moved it from 4th and Newton Streets to protect it. Like Camden itself, it was hit by a truck. It has a granite trough on one side for the horses, a sea shell shape on the other for humans, and two low troughs for cats and dogs. Carved biblical words announce to the humans that "The fear of the Lord is a Fountain of Life." Indeed it is.

This year, like all years, we celebrated the Feast of Corpus Christi with Benediction in the park. We put a lid on the horse trough and it became the altar for the monstrance. We celebrated the Body of Christ and the penetration of all creation with the Spirit of God. Every bit of creation, every damaged particle, every body that is holy or hardened, that is loved, or abused or prostituted. Charlie Gonzalez lifted the monstrance, turned north, south, east, west and blessed the world. When he stepped back, there beneath the cloth of the altar, was a word scrawled on the great belly of the fountain. One word: HOOKER. It was a call to make the fountain flow, to strike the rock. A call to help Mary to weep, to know love, to see her beautiful face in the water.

Why else! Why else was Hooker on the horse trough!

Michael Doyle

"Keep Love Alive"!

August, 1996

Hi!

Join me, if you will, in this letter, and we will visit a wonderful woman and recall the day she came here to pray. Join me because I know you know her!

She was 18, a young Albanian student, when she entered the convent of the Sisters of Loreto in Ireland in 1928. She was 66 when she came to Camden and walked up the aisle of Sacred Heart Church on a hot August afternoon in 1976. The seventh. It was a Saturday. By then, this geography teacher from St. Mary's High School in Calcutta was a permanent mark on the map of the earth and a permanent hope in the heart of humanity. Agnes, the schoolgirl of Skopje, Albania, was Mother Teresa of Calcutta. Her white sari, bordered in blue, familiar to millions; the white sandaled feet had walked the world.

She came to Sacred Heart in 1976 because Michael Doyle, testing the edges of his hope that she would respond to "a nobody," asked her to come. Come to "a very poor city and pray for the women of Camden!"

Well, she came. She came, to a packed church that awaited her, and all who were here that day can recall her holy presence. Those who are still on the lands of the living and those who are gone before us in spirit. The moment was immortal.

So, twenty years later, August 7, 1996, we gathered (a much smaller number) to tell the stories and pray the prayers again that we prayed with Mother Teresa of Calcutta in Sacred Heart twenty years ago. We recalled how she challenged us to try "to keep love alive," and always "see Christ in the distressing disguise of the poor." We remembered how we prayed—especially for the children of Camden, "that their tender souls may be saved from the evils that surround them." They are frail flowers, we told her, trying to grow up in heavy traffic. Everyone remembered the poignant moment when Dana Redd, a third-grade student at Sacred Heart School, gave Mother Teresa a lei of flowers gathered in the gardens of Camden. By this time I had mentioned that Dana's parents died very tragically one month before. Mother Teresa blessed the child and embraced her tenderly in her sorrow. Dana was only eight years old.

But, last week, she was our speaker at our Mother Teresa anniversary. Now she is a strikingly beautiful woman of 28. Our own Sacred Heart student—returning to address us. No frail flower anymore, but a splendid young person of strength, education, and bright moral worth. A star. Still a Camden resident, she works as an aide to Freeholder Riletta Cream and she spoke of her efforts to serve people, to help children, to give back, to create that "village" that is needed to raise a child. She spoke movingly of her gratitude to Sacred Heart for its care and attention in her sorrow, for her schooling, and also the enormous consolation it was for her and her grandparents, Bernard & Hazel Peoples, that she was chosen to represent our church in the presentation of the flowers to Mother Teresa of Calcutta twenty years ago.

The lei of flowers intact still, was part of a display of pictures and memorabilia of the great visit. The flowers withered brown. The passing of twenty years takes many people and changes many things—shapes, colors, views, sights and sounds.

But there is no taking away from Mother Teresa's message of love and service, no taking away from Sacred Heart School's influence on Dana Redd and her message of love and service. I wish all those who helped our school twenty years ago could see Dana now and hear her proclaim her faith, her confidence, and her genuine love.

It is good for all of us to meet her, if only in a letter. Good, because now we must start again to help to keep Sacred Heart School open for all the Danas of today—252 trying to grow up in Camden. Frail flowers, every one of them. Trying to grow up in heavy traffic. But we will try to keep them together in a living lei that holds against the bruises and abuses of our times.

So! One more time I go forth, pen in hand, to test the edges of my hope that God can use "a nobody" like me to ask you to help our children in Camden.

Help us to "keep love alive" in our school of Sacred Heart!

The Passover

One day at Summer's end
I watched my aging mother
Walking toward the bend
Of a wooded path
And as she slowly went
She bent and plucked
A bunch of wild flowers
From a brown dried-out sod
To place upon her kitchen altar
To the Sacred Heart of God.
The path was dark in part
The early evening light

Was being shut out
For about a hundred feet
By trees whose leaves
Always block the sun
Until the Autumn wind
Comes to take them off
Cleanly, one by one.
She walked on calmly
To where the shadows ended
And the path of light began
Then stepped over bravely into brightness
With the flowers in her hand.

Building Houses and Paring Horns

October, 1996

Hi!

My niece, Geraldine Doyle, is a highly respected farmer who drives her big tractor through small fields and narrow roads in Rossduff, County Longford. Her dog Dusty always perches happily behind her. At the moment she is having a house built on the Doyle farm which she owns, the same land that was owned by her great-great-great-grandmother Catherine Campbell Doyle in 1840. The house is a broad building with three good-sized bedrooms and space in the attic for more if needed and even though it is rising with the gray square look of hard concrete blocks, it is nevertheless taking shape in the clear urge of nesting time. Geraldine will marry Michael Dobson in August.

It is one small field away from the house where Catherine conceived her first child in May of 1840 and there she struggled to save that little boy in the deadly years of the famine. Had she failed I would never have life or the opportunity to say: Thank you, Mother Catherine! Great and grand you are, indeed. I salute her and the six generations that have thus far come from her. Especially the first three and some of the fourth that have gone before us. But her old house is still standing where she left it. It had no bathroom in her time, nor in mine, and there I was raised from the mid-thirties to the early fifties.

Of course, Geraldine's house will have all the amenities of a modern home. Not only that, it will also have an office with its own separate entrance. An office!! I wish my grandfather were alive to see what has happened to farming since he unbuckled his horses in the late autumn of his life. Geraldine's office will have a computer on which she will record her cows' times and her calves' births; everything from milk quotas to heifers' numbers and Vet visits. Etcetera. It is the first office ever built in the townland of Rossduff since the creation of the world.

The view from Geraldine's kitchen window is magnificent...splendid scenes in shades of green, with all their whin-whitethorn hedges, their quilted shapes and beauty, as far as the eye can see.

A couple of months ago I stood in that bay window, glassless yet, with a video camera in my hand and filmed the familiar fields of my childhood. It was my first venture with a video (you see how advanced I am). Anyway, I am now able for the first time to bring the fields of my early life to Camden and here they seem even greener than they are. This masterpiece has noises that it shouldn't have and accidental footage (literally) of the ground at my feet.

Now, ironically enough, in a few days' time, the people of Ireland will see on Irish Television the stark, desolate landscape of Camden, NJ, where this native son has lived for the past 28 years. On Wednesday, October 23rd, at 10:35 p.m., a TV program called *Stateside* will be seen in Ireland. It will include a segment on Sacred Heart and I think it will contrast "the green-green grass of home" with some of the lightless, abandoned houses of this city

The Irish people will see a rainbow of beautiful children in our school—Latino, African-American, Vietnamese, and white – who struggle to grow up in these tough neighborhoods of Camden. The contrasts in the film have often pounded through my mind over the years. I have thought about the poverty of my own childhood and compared it to that of the children of Camden. Any child in this city today has better clothes and more of them than I had. There were no toys in my home or books and no money to buy them. My Christmas stocking each year had an orange and a pencil. My parents had hardly any money at all. But they had work, wageless work, on the small farm that grew the crops that fed us. They had faith, and dignity, and stability. The land bonded them to God and to one another. And the daily hardship of their lives had meaning in the stories of the sufferings of Christ that they loved. Oh, it all made sense to them. And, as in Geraldine's window, their eyes had beauty to see every day in the views that were all around them.

So I think to myself that there are different kinds of poverty. The Camden one is deadly. The lack of meaningful work will ultimately poison the heart. The absence of beauty for the eyes of Camden's children is a crime in a country that is about to spend more than $44 billion on 20 batwing B2 bombers for dropping nuclear bombs. What "Edens" that could make across this nation! For the children.

And God never intended that an inner-city wasteland would be the empty lot of the children. Beauty is always the right of the innocent eyes.

We need help. For some reason or other, the casualties of war are counted, the casualties of economic injustice don't count. One person killed by a bomb in Belfast is world news; thousands of murders annually in the inner cities of this nation are not world news. A political death is deemed important, an economic death is not. And yet it is the economic pressure that brings on the deaths. In the economic calamity of 1932, there were 31 murders in Camden. In prosperous years, very few.

So! Serious changes are needed before it's too late. If one were to stand on Geraldine's land and look down the lens of long ago, one would see the majestic red deer of Ireland striding across the valley with its ever-growing antlers in the wind. In time the horns of that species reached a twelve-foot span. But the red deer is extinct. Its weapons became too wide for the way.

So, let's get into building homes and paring horns and all will be so much better.

Michael Doyle

What About Ye, Fr. Jimmy!

November, 1996

Hi!

There was Derry and Doherty on the cheque...two great names associated indissolubly, in good times and in bad, in sickness and in health; wedded as it were long before the tides of the last thousand years began to toss themselves daily on the green edges of the Foyle. It was a cheque with feel, the feel of goodness about it. This cheque had the warmth of an oak leaf in an autumn sun. It was a cheque from Ireland, and it came from one of my quiet heroes there, Fr. Jimmy Doherty of Derry. A thing of spirit, holier than a holy card, bearing within it 300 dollars to sponsor a child in Sacred Heart School, but Glory be to God, worth far more than that, in meaning to and blessing upon our school, our mission, our struggling children in Camden.

Fr. Jimmy came to Sacred Heart in August 1990, with his friend, Brian Brady, a priest too from Derry, and they met our children, worshipped in our church and chatted in our kitchen. We ate in the rectory chapel, and there he sat in the blue armchair we carried down from the second floor. Fr. Jimmy has multiple sclerosis.

In March of 1980, in that severe month of ploughing and harrowing for the planting, Lent time, too, Jimmy got the word. A hard medical word. Indeed that's what the Greek word sclerosis means: hardening. Hard for Jimmy. Hard for his family. He is one of nine. But no hardening of tissues had any lessening effect on the arteries of his generosity or on the sinews of his noble spirit. In fact the opposite is true.

I visited Jimmy two months ago in his home in Derry. Pax Vobis, he calls it and Pax Vobis he is. More incapacitated now than when he was here six years ago, he is confined to a wheelchair. His words slower, his energy lesser. His good humor undiminished. For 29 years he has ministered to the people. At first, as a bright, young, handsome man with a heart full of fun and a head full of questions, he rode out on the white horse of his intellect to conquer every question on sight, including the ultimate one: who is God. "Rushing around doing good things," he wrote in 1985, "I lost my own sense of goodness. I became so involved in doing, that I forgot who I was. We were up to our eyes in the troubles—bombings, shootings, rioting, sectarian battles, and I became almost totally discouraged." He decided to listen more and talk less "being present more than questioning." He found peace until... "there's always," he says "an <u>until</u> with God—he kicked the feet from under me again." The MS hit. And for this, God bless him, he had only one question: "Why, God, did you give me this gift?" And he meant *gift*. The man of a thousand questions had moved from inquiry to contemplation. As Mary, the holy virgin did long ago. She moved from "How can this be?" to "My soul magnifies the Lord." Fr. Jimmy moved from the mystery of suffering to "the mystery that is suffering" and he says, "[it] leads me directly to the mystery who is God."

Fr. Jimmy, more than anyone I know, has become the wounded healer. By printed and spoken word and above all, by his word made flesh (made suffering flesh), he has been a light and inspiration to many people across the world.

In a tiny red book called Pray a Little, he composed heartfelt prayers for each of six sets of 14 Stations of the Cross—the stations of the Northern Ireland Cross. "Jesus Christ" he says "walked with us and is still walking with us through the rubble, the destruction, the blood and the cross. He has been there before and he calls us to come through it with hope—hope in a transformation."

I wish he could come back and write from the rich deposit of his wounded heart, the Stations of the Camden Cross. Healing words of hope for the "Camden condition" of our own lives and times.

"We need," I say. Sometimes I think need needs to take a rest. It doesn't. But then genuine need is a burning bush that is not consumed and God is always in it.

Fr. Jimmy wrote to me last August. ("Using one finger." Time was when he could fly with all ten on the computer.) He began his letter with these words: "What about ye, Michael!" In this letter I say "What about ye, Jimmy!" You fill many an empty basket, many an empty life, with the richness and fullness of your wounded self. "Give my love" he wrote "to my many friends in Sacred Heart!" I will indeed, Fr. Jimmy. I will, indeed. Love like that makes the Heart more sacred.

Michael Doyle

(On August 8th 2002, Fr. Jimmy's noble soul lifted to God.)

John McNamee

The path chose him, bright eyed dreamer
     that he is
With his rope and pail and the well of words
     within him
He had it in him, the makings....
The stretched sinews of wet Tyrone land,
The crystal faith that mined black bread in
     Pennsylvania
So the hounding call had to flatten him forty
     years ago
Oil his softer hands and bind his wounded
     center in a sacred bandage.
But he arose, and bit by bit, he shed the tight
     ecclesial clothes
To make his honest way back to urban mines
To bodies flat as clay upon the city grates
To bend a knee, to lend a hand, to lift a
broken heart.
There he buys his altar bread upon the street
At markets open-aired and rough
Where wheat is battered by abuse
And grapes are trampled by indifference
Then raises truthful toast to God every
     Sunday in St. Malachy's.
And all the while the mine bird sings within
     his solemn soul
A song as sad as exiles leaving in the lashing
     rain
And yet when the sun breaks out upon his
     burdened brow
Oh God, the laughing-after shower scenes,
     I see,
On every field and wall, on every face he
loves.

An Angel for Anita Rose

December, 1996

Hi!

"My soul magnifies the Lord" sang Barbara Dever on December 1st, the First Sunday of Advent. For eighteen years and long before she became an opera star, she has sung this song of praise in Sacred Heart for expecting mothers and their babes within.

Eleven, this year. Hidden life bulging in their bodies; candles burning in their hands. The tenderness of it all. The mystery. The tears with all their quiet meanings in older eyes that watched. The hope. The sharp cost of life. "We bless you and the child within you." That was our prayer, leaning out over the edge of the road...around the bend of what is yet to be. Eleven hidden little heartbeats in the Sacred Heart of the universe.

The scene was holy. But beyond the stones, beyond the strong red doors, out there.... Broadway. The tear of tires on the tar. The grind of brakes. The boarded shops and houses. The polluting trucks. The prostitutes. We cannot forget where we are. Broadway and Ferry. Between Camden County's big pink trash burner and the eighty-million-gallons-a-day sewage plant.

But then Jesus died outside the walls. On Broadway. We must go there too.

One day last August I set out to visit one of Sacred Heart's most revered parishioners, Rose Pritchard. I crossed Broadway at Chelton. As I did, a young women of the streets beckoned. A bright smile under a great shock of light brown hair. I drove on.

Where the air is often putrid smell
For wings and lungs and clothes-on-line
Where houses, almost all, abandoned, droop
And day is always night where windows were.
There, in crow black cloth from head to toe
She stands and beckons men to stop.
No more the smiles that early whispers coaxed

The first that ever eager eyes beheld
Now drug-induced are forced to smother pain
Her love for sale for the cruel cost of lunch.
But, ah, worst of all, on the humpbacked bridge
Her body big with growing life to come
The two for sale for the paltry price of one.

Rose Pritchard wasn't home. I looked in her flower garden and then out to the big block-long park that she reclaimed from a Camden junk yard with her own hands. As I drove away, a sign on a boarded house caught my eye. "Genesis," it said. My mind went to Edwina Gateley and her work with prostitutes in Chicago at the Genesis House, where starts are made. So, unlike the Wise who followed their Star, I went back the way I came. The pregnant prostitute was still there. I gave her two dollars for cold drinks. "I know where Sacred Heart is at. The one with the cross. I'm a Catholic. Thank you, Father!"

O God almighty and Mary mild,   *What Bethlehem of broken dream,*
What savage world surrounds this child,   *What Nazareth of dirt and death,*
What Eden this of smell and sewer,   *What the hell has happened here!*

Questions circling questions like a mad dog for its tail. And no answers. Not much room in the inn of human understanding for a young suburban woman bulging with child on Broadway. For sale on the street. Catholic, educated, a college degree, bright, nice. Crippled by coke. No natal care. No hope. No nothing.

Later when I saw her on the street at night, I would return with milk and cookies. Band-aid blessings for sure. I made an appointment at the Osborn Clinic at Our Lady of Lourdes Hospital. Went to find her at the abandoned house she lives in. She was gone. "Hiding," her friend (a prostitute, too), said. "She's scared."

On August 22, I visited the grave of a dear friend, Anita Ricci, who died tragically in August, 1986. Returned to hear that my pregnant friend came to see me. Upset. I found her on Broadway and took her to Osborn. Less than twelve hours later, in the early hours of a warm morning, a child is born. Cesarean section. A girl. On the Feast of St. Rose of Lima. Her mother, knowing she could not care for her, never saw or touched her.

But the nameless little shock of crow black hair
Sent out her primal cry on waves of August air,
A wondering cry of why and what and where,
Silent ache the only answer in anyone who cares.

The child was named, by request, Anita Rose. For the great woman of Lima, for my deceased friend, and indeed for Rose Pritchard.

Recently, I had a letter from the Department of Youth and Family Services asking my help to find the mother of "the baby girl, A.K.A. Anita Rose" and take her to sign "surrender papers." I did. She did. Anita Rose is "doing well," almost four months old. Of course, there are still uncertainties. Adoption is proceeding. May the Christ who was born in an "abandoned spot" in Bethlehem be there for this most innocent child!

Her mother "loves a cheese steak." We had one at Weber's on the way back to her "abandoned house" (no light, no water). Then I went to see Rose Pritchard. She was making wings for angels that she was preparing for our Christmas Fair. Angels droop without them. There were so many angels on the kitchen table that I couldn't find the sugar.

So, dear friend, promise me! Promise me you'll make an angel in your mind for Anita Rose! And, maybe, a wing and a prayer for her poor mother.
"God bless us everyone!"

Michael Doyle

"O Lord, Hear My Voice!"

February, 1997

Hi!

The clocks have begun to tick, the tongues to talk; we are moving inexorably to the end of the 20th century. On April 5th there will be only a thousand days till the bells begin to ring at the great midnight moment of December 31, 1999. A thousand days of life!

Looking back to the last Camden count-down a hundred years ago, this town (in 1897) geared up with massive manufacturing energy as big waves of workers found jobs on the banks of the Delaware, and Camden became the best little industrial town in North America.

Incorporated as a city of 1100 on February 13, 1828, Camden, one mile from Philadelphia, grew from a village into a thriving town of almost 75,000 as the century ended.

It had had its uncertain start in 1764. The marking out of land into lots in 1764 was the first major invasion of the previous Native American way. To former generations, land was like the sea…it belonged to all. Now the Europeans were coming with their ways and their measurements and their fences. William Cooper, the first of that name, came in 1680 and settled at the Point (Pyne Point) where the smaller river (now called Cooper) flowed into the Delaware. In time the name Cooper would encircle this area like a hoop on a barrel. The location was excellent with the mile wide Delaware, between it and Philadelphia, the largest city on this continent at that time.

The name Camden was chosen to honor Charles Pratt, the Earl of Camden and Lord Chief Justice of England, a good friend of the colonists in their struggle for independence.

The little village of Camden didn't "take off" until it got a ride on a railroad. The lines that linked Camden to Perth Amboy, NJ, in 1834 and thence to New York set Camden as a central manufacturing location with easy ferry access to Philadelphia and rail to ferry links for New York.

So, Camden, NJ! With its 85,000 people today (125,000 in 1950) it is still by far the largest of the many Camdens in the United States and indeed the most desperately troubled.

There are at least 15 other Camdens in this nation with populations (1990) ranging from 14,300 in Camden, Ouachita County, Arkansas, to the smallest, Camden, Ray County, Missouri, with 238 people. Camden, Wilcox County, Alabama, population 2406. Camden, Kent County, Delaware, 960. Camden up in Schuyler County, Illinois, 345. Carrol County, Indiana, has a Camden with 618 people. Knox County, Maine, promotes a Camden with 4,022. Michigan has one in Hillsdale County with 1984 Camdenites. The Empire State has one in Oneida County, population 2552. North Carolina has a Camden County, and a Camden city of 350 people. One in Preble County, Ohio, population 2210. Next in size after Arkansas, South Carolina has a Camden of 6,696 people in Kershaw County. Tennessee has 3,643 people in Camden, Benton County, and big Texas has a little Camden of 300 people in Polk County. Finally, northwest of Jackson, Mississippi, there is a Camden of 500 people in Madison County. All told, the fifteen other Camdens have a population of 34,254, less than half the number that struggles here in Camden, NJ.

The people of my Camden hardly have heard of many of the other Camdens of the country, but I'm sure that many of them have heard of Camden, NJ. Particularly the oldest people. They heard of the Victor Talking Machine, the Victrola, or their mother had an old gramophone and the records were made in Camden, NJ. It was the recording capital of the world. They saw the logo of Nipper the dog listening to His Master's Voice.

A hundred years ago (1894) Eldridge Reeves Johnson, a machine shop operator in Camden, NJ, invented a new spring motor for a hand-powered gramophone and perfected his own version of the disc talking machine. His business grew from his first building on Front Street (1899) to 34 buildings in 1927 with floor space of 57 acres, one of the largest industries in the United States as spinning Victor records were heard around the globe. The ending years of the last century were wonderfully creative times in Camden, NJ.

I went the other day to Market Street, my old Minolta in tow, to photograph the famous RCA Victor building in its dilapidated condition and the Victor word above the door. I focused in on the stained glass Nipper window in the tower top, the dog, the fifteen poignant letters by his paws, His Master's Voice. But alas, the three words the world knew were down to two: His Master's...the Voice was gone. And the voice was everything—the sound of human song in matter that astounded all the world a hundred years ago. Gone. Mute. Silent as the Victor letters in the granite grooves. His Master's——-blank. A sign of our abandonment.

My letter: a plea to God that His voice be heard among the ruins. A plea to the Camden people of the nation to voice a prayer for this Camden, this casualty of the "progress" that passed us by. A plea that we get a voice where power is and resources are to rebuild our broken city. A plea! A plea! A Thousand Days of Prayer and action that a new miracle of creativity and restoration begins.

"O Lord, hear my voice and let my cry come to thee!"

Michael Doyle

O River, Ever Mother
(Excerpt)

Railroads linked to ferries
As water weds the land.
1834 Conception. Camden

Liner berth, sudden birth.
Victor talks, the first impression.
War booms. Ten million tombs.
Twenty-nine. Deep depression.

"God, We Know You Can Do It!"

April, 1997

Hi!

Many years ago I was asked to say the opening prayer at an expensive political dinner in Camden County. A well-heeled crowd had gathered...not a worn sole in the bunch. Each person there was hoping for some political or economic advantage. The MC looked at the program booklet and announced me and my prayer. All heads bowed in unison. Many eyes closed solemnly. For some reason or other, all this was amusing to me so I began by saying: "I'm not sure that God attends political dinners." Some eyelids lifted. Some soles shifted. "But," I continued, "In case the good Lord is here, let us pray." We prayed. I was never again invited to a political dinner. Maybe God felt bad. Maybe God has to show up at all of them and it is too much. Maybe I was too flip.

But I cannot help feeling, whenever power sits down to eat, be it political, economic or military, that religion has the same importance as a candle on the table. It's nice. Adds a little lustre to the scene. But, in all honesty, the dead steer or salmon or chicken is the reality. You can't blame "the Reverend" for feeling a bit used, whether it's a big name with big platitudes at inaugural solemnities or little nobodies like myself mumbling something piously in Camden County.

All this leads me to ponder the place of prayer in "the real world." Is it a lit candle on the table of reality or is it connected to the core of any lasting goodness in all reality. Is it a side issue or a central factor? Central, I would say. If God is light, prayer is not an ornamental extra on the lamp; it is the switch. At hand for everyone. It triggers the piston power of effective and lasting transformation. Its use invites the sun to warm the world, the moon to tug the tides, and the stars to make a night we love. It is the heart's leap to God, our connection to the beloved dead who are gone before us, to the uncertain future coming toward us. It is the truth-seeker in the sorting of all things, the sense-maker amidst the choices and confusions of our lives. It is the lifeline that dangles within reach above the dark oblivion. At its deepest level it is the music that we hear in our hearts when the breath of God infuses the flute that is all creation.

Somehow God's hands are tied in our own. Prayer unties them like the limbs of Lazarus bound in the tomb. To do what needs to be done. I never think of Lazarus without thinking of Camden, the stone that seems too big, or the muscles that seem too weak, too tired, too busy, too indifferent to move it.

Camden sits here on the Delaware River with a seven-fathom waterway to the world, three hours by road to Washington, DC, less that two to New York, forty-five minutes to Trenton, NJ, ten minutes to Independence Hall, Philadelphia, and 000,000,000 seconds to God. All these secular centers of power or wealth or both are connected to Camden by phone, fax and computer, by rail and road, by satellite hook-up and wires strung-up, by paper, paper, paper pushing and rushing back and forth, responding and corresponding...and yet we are a sinking city, daily becoming poorer in the wealthiest nation in the world. Because we are weak and poor we have become at the hands of Camden County the victim of environmental injustice that is racist and barbaric.

This city is bankrupt but we are a city of small churches and big hopes. We will never go "hope-rupt." We still have our super swift connection to God. This letter is a plea to pray. To pray for Camden. To test again the place of prayer in the real world. To state that the real world is not real without it.

As this century winds down with less than 1000 days to go (975 from May 1st) I put before you a request to pray for Camden every day. I am inspired by two neighborhood women, Sarah Byers and Anita Thomas of whom I might say quoting Oliver Goldsmith's *Deserted Village* (with a very slight alteration):

> *Truth from their lips prevailed with double sway*
> *And fools, who came to scoff, remained to pray.*

Several years ago, when a house next door to Sarah burned down in an area of many abandoned houses, she and Anita began to pray for their neighborhood. At first, they decided they would do it each day "at house cleaning time." Then they would do it anytime but they prayed every day. They also met twice a week and walked their block (Jackson Street, 4th to Broadway) and prayed. "God, we know you can do it!" they pleaded. And God did. Eighteen eyesores all around them were transformed into beautiful homes by The Heart of Camden Housing Corporation. It was the prayers of Sarah and Anita that put the hammers in the hands. Houses on every side of Sarah's home were renovated, forcing her landlord to renovate hers. It was miraculous. "Hebrews 11:1 was our inspiration," they said. "Faith is the realization of what is hoped for and evidence of things not seen." Anita and Sarah had the faith. They held on to "the evidence of things not seen." As time went on, the miracle happened in front of their eyes. In front of ours, too. Thanks be to God!

A Prayer For Camden

> *Almighty God, we praise you for all you have done.*
> *Help us with all that you want us to do!*
> *Come, Holy Creator, rebuild the City of Camden*
> *So that we do not labor in vain without you.*
> *Come, Holy Savior, heal all that is broken*
> *In our lives and in our streets.*
> *Come, Holy Spirit, inspire us with energy and*
> *Willingness to rebuild Camden City*
> *To your honor and glory.*

Amen.

Michael Doyle

The Sorrow of the Rain. The Joy of the Sun.

Hi:

"I hope I can see you from wherever I am going. I want you to talk to me and draw upon my strength."

Pamela Markgraf, 52 years old, dying with cancer in her home at Lake Orion, Michigan, spoke these tender words to her daughter, Leigh, her only child, on March 6, 1997. She knew she might not live until May 3rd, when Leigh would wed Tim Kelly in St. Mary's Church in Williamston, MI. Her daughter "meant more to her," she said on March 10, "than the world." At Leigh's birth, Pamela had said "I never knew I could love this way." April came. "I don't want to leave you," she whispered as both women wept in their embrace. They had walked together over rough roads and smooth. Leigh's parents divorced when she was quite young. Mid-April came, the 15th. "I love you," said Leigh to her mother, who by now, "was not or didn't seem with it." But, nevertheless, she responded weakly, "I love you." Leigh began to cry. Pamela reached up and touched her face. "Don't cry," she said. Three days later, she was dead.

Her daughter shared these sacred moments with me when I went to Michigan three weeks ago. Hard as it was, Leigh and Tim had decided to proceed with their plans and there they were, a young wonderfully handsome couple, when I landed in Lansing on May 1st. This would be the sixth time I participated in a Kelly wedding, and Jack and Jan still have two more sons and a daughter. And, at the moment, there's no talk of the seminary by the two boys, or indeed by Kristina, either.

It is all of 18 years since I made my first trip to the Wolverine State shortly after Jack Kelly became the head of the Horticulture Department at Michigan State. I came to baptize Kristina, their youngest, on November 19, 1979. My letter for the following month had this to say: "Kristina's eight brothers and sisters from 19 to 9 took part in the preparations. Marci, the oldest, made a stole; Andrea, the baptismal garment; Danny, a cross; and Kurt, the decorations. Sean typed some of Barbara Dever's songs and Claudia typed Sam Mackintosh's great creed. Not to be outdone, "Tim and Michael fetched the water, which of course was taken from the great spring-fed pond in front of the Kelly home. Water from the edge was 'not clear enough,' so they boarded a canoe, paddled to the center, lowered a beige bucket and filled a big black pot. Launched into the deep, as it were, to get the best water." Kristina's baptism 18 years ago was a most memorable gathering.

Now, time, marriage and work have scattered the Kellys from Corvallis in Oregon to Hampden in Maine. But by May 2nd, the clan had convened and the home by the pond was packed with children, parents, grandparents, several cats that lived in the garage, a brown dog, an eight-foot Burmese albino snake that coiled in a big glass box near my bedroom door, a lizard-like creature from Australia, and a chirping canary near the dining room table. The youngest member of the crowd, Sophie Marie Kelly, only 15 days old, in from Vermont, met the multitude for the first time. Born on April 17, the day before Pamela Markgraf died, she would be baptized on the day before Pamela's daughter Leigh would be wed. Kristina Kelly, the baptismal baby of 18 years ago, would be Sophie's godmother.

So, before the wedding rehearsal on Friday, we had another Kelly baptism. Water! We needed water again. Would you believe that Michael, the boy in the canoe 18 years ago, dressed in a wetsuit, flappers on the feet and all (temperature 48 degrees on land), dove into the depths of the pond and brought up the cold spring water for his little niece's baptism. An hour later, in the happy view of several levels of Kelly eyes, et al., Sophie Marie went under it, gallantly. And Tim and Leigh, on the eve of their wedding, held the Easter candle to light the baby's baptismal candle, held it also to light their own journey in the world and to wish eternal light to her mother gone before them.

Saturday came quickly. My sixth Kelly wedding (you'd think I'd get the hang of it) was indeed the most demanding. Leigh and I had agreed that her mother must be part of it. Not only in the lone white rose and candle on the altar, but in word and feeling, too. The beautiful bride came up the aisle on her father's arm, her face flooded with tears beneath her full hanging veil. No veiling her awesome sorrow now.

But God is good. I could point to Michael Kelly, the best man, in his well-fitted tuxedo and recall his wet outfit of yesterday as he brought up the spring water from the dark depths of the pond. Nothing less would be good enough. We must, I said, go down into the deep dark sorrow of this moment. We must speak the mother's name, her life, the stretch of the horses she rode, the reach of her heart to the children at risk in Chippewa Valley schools, her death, her hope to see her daughter on this day. Her aching plea: "Talk to me." Her precious promise: "Draw upon my strength!" Leigh Markgraf wept quietly. And we must, I said, bring up from that wet depth, the spring water, the living water of her mother's hope and blessing on Leigh and Tim as long as they live. The blessing came and will come. Leigh raised her chin and smiled and rose and made her vow to Tim and he to her. And, thanks be to God, on that damp dark day in Michigan, the sun came out and blessed the late afternoon with a bridal brightness.

The reception was held at Michigan State University in the greenhouse of The Plant and Soil Sciences Building. A great place, indeed. There and everywhere the soil needs the sorrow of the rain and the joy of the sun, and then life, ah, sweet life, begins…and grows and blooms.

"Don't cry!" she said.

Michael Doyle

A Timepiece for Peacetime

June, 1997

Hi!

Hearses on their way to Sacred Heart Church in Camden often share these streets with trucks of scrap on their way to Camden Iron and Metal. But it can be said that neither set of vehicles is on a dead end journey to oblivion. Both bear their burdens toward certain possibilities of transformation. One surely much more extraordinary than the other. But the drivers hear the same funeral bell in the brownstone tower of Sacred Heart: three hundred and fifty pounds of bronze swing and bong—the bell itself rescued from a scrap pile in Camden and donated to the church by John Bantivoglio in 1983.

Few, I fear, would agree with me that there is more mystery (not necessarily beauty) and sources of theological fascination in the hills of scrap in Camden, than in many of the hills and hollows of the world. Someone somewhere must have written a book called *Meditations on a Scrap Pile*. Out of print now, I suppose, and dumped in a waste paper bin at the back of nowhere: the mind plays where it will.

Right now my mind takes wing over the northern sea to the outskirts of St. Petersburg where Victor Nikolai Tisenko, a professor at the State Technical University of St. Petersburg (the M.I.T. of Russia) picked mushrooms in the cold. The mind leaps easily from this to the years, only recently gone, when thoughts of cold wars and mushroom clouds often triggered terror on both sides of an impenetrable wall. But these mushrooms were being picked for a meal, a meal that Victor and Tatyana cooked for a happy group of Russian and American people in their home. A group eager to eat good food and drink good vodka and lift their cups from the table in countless toasts to the friendship they share and the hope they have for a new cooperative venture in technology. At the table in St. Petersburg on that January evening in 1995 were John Bantivoglio of Camden Iron and Metal and the vice president of Rustec, Jim MacFarlane, also Dr. Alexander (Sacha) Elkind, John Purves and Clive Anderson, all employed by that company, Dr. Vladimir Kolosov, Executive Director of the Engineering Association of Russia. Irina Soiko was there too and she brought, beyond the grace of God, an elegant interpretation of languages. Also there, for no reason at all, Michael Doyle.

And no one enjoyed the time more than he. The walk from the hotel to the Tisenko home in the beautiful snow-clad St. Petersburg. The house itself (now two apartments) sits by the Moika Canal (the washing canal), one of the many canals constructed for Peter the Great as the veins of his Venice of the North. Here in this house Grigori Rasputin used to visit a friend. History tells us that Rasputin manipulated his way into the lives of Czar Nicholas II and the Czarina and brought great trouble to Russia before he was murdered in 1916. Preserved within the house by an elderly woman in the second apartment is the note: "I was here. I didn't catch you. Grigori." One senses chills colder than the climate. Beside this house is also the magnificent Church of the Blood, built on the bloody spot where Alexander II was assassinated in 1881. Another visit to the Tisenko house in times past, and one of sweet blessing, was that of

Alexander Pushkin, Russia's greatest poet, who also died in this neighborhood in 1837 after his tragic duel.

But regardless of history's harsh realities (I could point to far more bloody murder spots in a stone's throw circle around Sacred Heart), our dinner of four hours and far more courses was exquisite and delightful.

There was much to celebrate. John Bantivoglio, with the eye of a scrapyard genius observing the gates of heaven, figured that after Perestroika, Russia with all its arsenal of weapons might be a gold mine of scrap. So, three years before, he sent his son John and Jim MacFarlane to Russia. Victor Tisenko was their contact and interpreter. The scrap enterprise didn't materialize but John bravely underwrote a project involving Russian technology whereby a new method was found to automatically sort scrap metal. For example, the many metals of a car, after it is ground into giblets. Thus was born Rustec which is based in Camden. Dr. Elkind, formerly of Drexel University, a Russian scientist with doctorates from Russia and the US, was hired to head a research team of Russians and Americans to develop the technology. All their effort, all their hope and meaning was toasted again and again around the table in St. Petersburg. Big cohesive machines of war had divided people from people, but little bits of scrap had unified them. From a box of bits of metal sent from Camden to Russia a new bond was forged.

Engineers, physicists, and scientists from Victor's State Technical University in St. Petersburg where so many inventors of awesome weaponry—tanks, planes, nuclear bombs—were educated and graduated and members too of the top secret Central Institute for Materials, also in St. Petersburg, all came together to turn their heads and their hands to cleaning and recycling very complicated waste materials. One of the most inspiring transformations from weaponry scrap that came out of that Institute is a beautiful replica of the famous French-made clock that was given as a gift to Nicholas II, the last Czar of Russia and which is on view to all in the Hermitage Museum. This replica clock is made from the casings of Soviet artillery shells ground into dust for the new creation. The swords into ploughs at last. It's time. It's time. *It's time.*

This year, in Holy Week, the Rustec Team of Americans and Russians with friends and supporters gathered in Camden to witness the metal sorting machine and other inventions in action and to celebrate the astounding effort thus far. At lunch in Camden's Harbor League, which completed the program, Victor Tisenko gave me one of the clocks made from artillery shells. He gave it for Sacred Heart Church. And on the evening of that same day, Victor, raised as he was in the communistic non-religious Soviet Union, came to the Seder at Sacred Heart. At it, the clock was presented to the people. Victor wept. No words for the depth of the feelings that he never experienced before. "They will be with me as long as I live," he said.

So the clock made from the weapons of Russia will tell us the time to ring the bell lifted from the scrapyards of Camden and both will call us to build a world from the bits and pieces, into peace and real justice for all.

Michael Doyle

"You Have to Have Faith"

July, 1997

Hi!

A priest called the rectory today asking for me. Polite and most proper, was he; the "M" word and all.

"Not here," said Clare, "he's burying a dog."

"*His* dog?"

"Oh, no, not Nipper! A down the street."

All true enough.

I awoke this morning realizing that July is 21, that I must write a letter to you and there aren't the makings of half a thought in my head. Ah, well! Maybe like Mr. Micawber in the pinch he was always in, I'll proceed "in case anything turned up."

So far among the this and the that of today (and it's only 12:45 pm), I set up an appointment at the Osborn Clinic for an unwed mother nineteen years of age, thirteen in appearance. I attended to the needs of a dead dog. And I had lunch with a prostitute enslaved to cocaine. Three views of life. Its uneasy start. Its desperate struggle. Its pathetic end.

This day began before I slept...a day to recall the awesome lunar adventure 28 years ago. People over forty remember that mighty cosmic journey and destination. All eyes were on the monstrance of the moon, July 21, 1969. Human feet making their first soled imprint on the lunar landscape. But this morning at 1AM, that same moon was in my window round as a shilling and shining like silver. A circle of white fire in the distant dark. As Shelley said:

> *The orbéd maiden with white fire laden*
> *What mortals call the moon.*

Ever since that day 28 years ago (I had just completed my first year in this city), we are aware that some clumsy familiarity has invaded her majestic privacy but her face before dawn today was bright as an angel's eyes. Brighter than the shy young mother's smile (she, invaded too)...some clouds there to shadow her tender hope. But she will smile deeply by and by. The mystery of her precious stirrings ("kicking" she said) far more awesome than any weightless astronautical jumps in the moon dust.

But getting back to earth....a dead dog at a doorstep will do it every time. A German Shepherd. A woman inside unable to move it. No answer at any of the services and "important people coming at 9 am." So she called the rectory. It was a first for me. But it brought back special memories of the Buddhist monks who came to Sacred Heart in 1982 after walking from Los Angeles. They were on their way to the Special Session on Disarmament at the U.N. in New York. For every step of their journey they chanted a prayer for peace, urging it into all things. Along the way to make twenty miles a day, they never lost their stride, but on seeing a dead bird or flattened carcass on the roadway, one of them, took two sticks, lifted the remains, carried it to the side, dug a hole, and buried it. Then ran forward to catch up with the march. They had a profound sense of the sacredness of all life. Mother Earth is always ready to take back to herself the bodies of all her creatures no matter how lifeless, decayed and unwanted. So I dug a hole in a weedy unused lot and buried the dog.

The whole episode reminded me of the story Sr. Margaret Sikora told me about the nuns' dog that died at her sister's convent in the Bronx. Too much tar there and concrete for easy burial, so the ingenious nuns put their old German shepherd in a suitcase (a big one) and two of them lugged the thing to the subway. At the station a courteous man helped the women in the brown Franciscan habits to lift the load onto the train. They were on their way to the convent in Yonkers, New York where there was land enough to bury a dead dog. All going well so far. However, at their stop a big surprise awaited them. The suitcase was gone. The courteous man had stolen it. Theirs' wasn't the only surprise of the day.

Strange twists in the streets and stories of these old towns. "What will happen to you when you get old?" I asked the woman of the streets over BLT sandwiches in the kitchen. "I dunno" she said, "you just have to have faith." Indeed you do. "Where did you sleep last night?" I said. "In a car. Beth and me." Their abandoned house was recently boarded up. Now an abandoned car. Beth on Broadway too, for years, totally addicted. "All the women are," she said. The car is in an alley between Broadway and Fillmore. "Near the gas station." That's abandoned too. It's last owner murdered there three years ago.

So. A car going nowhere. Its occupants asleep at the steering wheel of their lives. Their economy far from Greenspan's smile or frown. Their safety, far from "our national interests". That protection by the U.S. military, costs more than half a million a minute.

But as Sheri said, "you have to have faith." I wasn't impressed, but next morning the Mass celebrated the Feast of Mary Magdalene who slept in a few uncertain places herself. The opening prayer had these words addressed to God: "Your Son first entrusted to Mary Magdalene the joyful news of his resurrection."

And it got as far as us. Thanks be to God!

Rain On the Pane

(Excerpt)

I am not alive, not dead either
Slumped somewhere in between
Hanging in, hanging on
Too inactive to be depressed
Without a dream
Without a hope
Wishing for a cosmic coma
Wherein I could rest
And wait for dreams and words and morning
In the silent solstice of the world.

Milking Her Cows in the Morning

September, 1997

Hi!

Greetings from Ireland! Greetings from the spot I was born in! There I awoke recently to the hum of a tractor going by. Who could be on it? Herself? No! Not today! August 29th? The day she had chosen? I looked out the window. It was herself. Geraldine Doyle, the oldest and most bonded to the land of all my eight nieces, was driving her tractor out the half mile lane from our farm to the main road. (The lane no wider than the tractor she drove; the main road a super highway of 15 feet). Anyway, Geraldine had just milked her 23 Friesian cows and was hauling 162 gallons of milk (four milkings) to a large mobile tank that waited at the roadway. I rushed out and headed up the lane to meet her returning. Soon she came on her old Massey Ferguson (it's 31 years old), a gleaming smile on her face and dried cow manure on her Wellingtons. She was getting married at one o'clock.

And sure enough at 1 pm Geraldine Mary Doyle walked up the aisle at Sacred Heart Church in Arva, County Cavan, on the arms of her father and mother. Indeed she did. Up all the way to the altar, her lovely wedding dress trailing behind her, and as William Butler Yeats put it: "She had the walk of a queen."

There in the presence of her family, friends, and neighbors, and God too, happily among them, she married Michael Dobson, a farmer like herself. They both wept unabashedly so great was their joy, their friendship so beautiful.

They had listened well to the Word of God which they had chosen so carefully. From Sirach: "There is nothing so delightful as faithful friends." St. Paul in Chapter Twelve advised the Romans and consequently the trusting couple: "Have a profound respect for each other. Do not give up if trials come. Treat everyone with equal kindness. Make real friends with the poor. Make hospitality your special care. Do all you can to live in peace with everyone." And finally, the best advice of all from Luke: "Do not judge and you will not be judged. Forgive and you will be forgiven." They exchanged icons as a sign of mutual sharing of all they are and possess. The three Mulligan sisters and their mother lifted the level of everything with music and song ever so reverently: City of God, A Iosa Mhílís, Ar nathair (the Our Father), Shalom, and the Canticle of Isaiah, and finally as Geraldine and Michael with sweet smiles and high hopes set forth on the first aisle of their world, they strode to the sounds of Sing to the Mountain.

They ate at 5 pm in Longford and danced till 1 am in the morning. Then 300 hands made the longest human arch I ever saw, and the couple (omitting all the usual garter gymnastics) walked under the arch to be kissed and blessed and sent on their way. It was great. The bonded hands above them seemed to stretch over the journey ahead of them......a tender reassurance that God will be their shelter in the cold wet wind, a strength against any bitter storms that might assail them.

I remember how they cried two years ago when my brother Fr. J.J. Doyle blessed them and their engagement rings with the last labored breaths of his life. He died a few days later. His absence at their wedding was a poignant presence for all of us.

Over the past year Geraldine has been as busy as birds in the spring guiding the construction of her new house on the Doyle farm. The site on high ground overlooks the old one I was born in and the newer one she was raised in and indeed the whole valley that the souls of the Doyles have been nourished on.....since 1840.

The last move on our farm was in 1958 when we moved from the old pre-famine house to the one Geraldine's parents live in today. That move was recounted in one of my letters, describing my father filling a bucket with the coals of the last fire and my mother taking down the Sacred Heart picture and walking together the thirty feet that separated the old door from the new. The Sacred Heart was placed on the wall, the coals in the stove, and life began.

In that house the next generation of five daughters (Geraldine included) were conceived and reared. Last week when the newly married couple returned to sleep for the first time in their new house on the hill, Geraldine's father Pat carried the coals from their stove in a bucket and Margaret her mother carried a beautiful old crucifix that belonged to the bride's great grandmother. The smoke as they walked up the lane (125 yards) rose in clouds around their heads in the wind. The crucifix was placed on the mantle of the new house, the coals were placed in the grate, and life leaped to its feet once again.

Geraldine knows well the genes of goodness that have preceded her as we urge God's blessing on the fortunes of history that will follow her. She knows the crucifix is a good one made holy by the hardship of her great grandmother who revered it. And if ever she needs strong sinews in her soul she knows where to look for the strengthening. Her great grandmother Margaret Gray, who was born in 1855, married James Reilly in 1879 and in the next eighteen years gave birth to eleven children. Two died, and when the youngest was born, her husband (driven by the drink) left for Liverpool and never returned. So the cross in memory of her heroic effort went up the hill in her granddaughter's hand to a place of honor in her great granddaughter's new house. There it reminds us all of the valiant woman with her nine who wiped the tears from her eyes, found food somehow to feed them, and bits of space in a very small house to bed them.

In honor of her and her great granddaughter's marriage to Michael Dobson, the Doyles of Rossduff will sponsor a child at Sacred Heart in gratitude to God and in hope that all the children of Sacred Heart will be cared for.

By the time you read this letter I'll be back, please God, at Broadway and Ferry to see our sparkling, spruced-up school and all its happy children. I will rejoice in the sponsorships coming in to help them. I am very confident that they will come. They will come in many ways and from many places.....even from a woman on the day of her wedding milking her cows in the morning.

Michael Doyle

Still Coming Up Roses

October, 1997

Hi,

My intention for October was to write about Mother Teresa of Calcutta. But circumstances changed my mind.

"You were at Rose's," someone said to me on Wednesday. October 1st it was. "The smell's in your sweater." Not the smell of roses, even though this day, the feast of Therese of Lisieux is surely associated with the scent of the world's favorite flower. Didn't the young saint say she "would spend her heaven doing good on earth, sending down showers of roses." But the odor in my wool was the bitter smoke smell of Rose Pritchard's badly burnt house. Not a square inch of its surface, walls or ceiling, no square inch of anything in it, without its coat of oily awful blackness. A fire at 4 pm on September 24th changed her delightful old house in the section of South Camden called Sweet Potato Hill, into a windowless coal mine of cinders and dark clinging dust. It was baked too thick on the mirror to write "God help us." I tried but I couldn't write God on the glass.

Today I knew Rose (staying with her sister) would come back with her weakened eyes to sift through the ashes of all that happened. Here she, the daughter of Lithuanian immigrants, was born in 1916, in this house which her father Peter Paul Balunas had built before he married her mother Veronica Margaret Priceta. Here she has lived all of her 80 years and eleven months. From here she went to school at Sacred Heart in the 1920s, and in all those years since, we haven't educated a more valiant student than the Rose of Sweet Potato Hill. From this house she followed the footsteps of her mother as she tended to St. George's Lithuanian Church at 9th and Chelton and scrubbed the old wooden floor, stretched the white altar linen freshly washed and ironed, and set in their vases the beautiful wild flowers that they planted.

Since St. George's closed down in July of 1973, Rose has turned her kitchen into a center of endless creative endeavors for Sacred Heart. Here (alone, since her husband died a quarter of a century ago), she constructs her angels and epiphany gift-bearers to be sold at our Christmas Fair. Here she annually boils and decorates 40 dozen Easter eggs for the people of Sacred Heart. Here she bakes her great cakes to be sold at its fair. Here she provides and cooks the food for our annual parish picnics. It's endless. And all the while, this big "mite" comes from a widow with a very small mite of Social Security.

As I waited for Rose by her now boarded (bandaged) house, I thought to myself: St. Therese's day is a good one on which to write my October letter about the death of Mother Teresa. But on second thoughts, my tiny tribute is hardly necessary in the vast acreage of print and pictures that has spread over the world at the news of her passing. Maybe, the way to honor Mother Teresa in Camden is to write about Rose Pritchard. After all the great woman of Calcutta came to Sacred Heart in 1976 to pray for the women of Camden and surely Rose Pritchard is one of the best of them. But not nearly the neediest – her house undoubtedly badly burned from the fire, but unlike many in this town who are badly enflamed or burnt out by drugs and other deadly substances, Rose's own soul and center, the dwelling place of her own fine spirit, is still strong and good. "I will use the stove in the cafeteria [of Sacred Heart] to bake the cakes for the Fair" she said as all her own useless kitchen equipment was hauled off in a dump truck. Her mind on Sacred Heart and its needs, no thought to her own. Mother Teresa would hardly do better. I watched her pick through the damaged things in her living room, trying to save what she could. Lifting up a small piece of blackened lace, "It belonged to my mother," she said. "I'll save it to make an angel." To her niece who wanted to throw something out: "If you throw everything old out, you'll have to throw me out too." And then to me: "we'll need that if we have another picnic." How could her mind be on parish picnics in the midst of her own dismal situation. I watched her walk through the ugly skeleton of her beloved kitchen, her face quietly determined, the solid steps sure as ever, as she said, "We'll make it."

Sacred Heart people have stepped in to bring her house back to life. She didn't ask. But we want to assure her that we are her insurance. So, from now, for the time it takes, it will be Saturday by Saturday at 9th and Chelton. Many hands will make light work as they always do.

With her own two hands, several years ago, Rose Pritchard herself transformed a block-long piece of city property into a park, planted trees and flowers, and has mowed it and tended to it for thirty years. No pay, no committee, just her own endless generosity for the common good. She has kept it beautiful for the neighbors and indeed for Sacred Heart's annual picnics.

Rose, who makes angels out of what others throw away, and makes a green garden-park of trees and flowers out of an abandoned junk yard, has this October faced into a tougher challenge when her world, her life-long space, the cherished kitchen of her pots and pans, her chats and tea pots, was destroyed. She grieves. But her hope holds on like a root in a rock. This rose, God bless her, didn't wilt when the wind was at its worst. She stood her ground. Like Mother Teresa herself, she is a woman of down-to-earth tenacity and hardy faith.

Wouldn't it be great if our students of the nineties, whom we are sponsoring and educating at Sacred Heart today, would be able to come out of the fire of life's difficulties as solid and strong as the student of the twenties, Rose Genevieve Balunas. Holding their own in the storms. Building gardens of beauty out of the junkyards of the world. Weaving angels' wings out of the battered and the worn bits of human experience. Very simply, no matter how the weather worsens, through fire and water (and firemen's axes), no matter what happens, still coming up Roses.

My intention for October was to write about Mother Teresa of Calcutta. So I wrote about Rose Pritchard of Camden. And I have no doubt that the holy women of Lisieux and Calcutta will spend some of their heaven tending to the Rose of Sweet Potato Hill.

Michael Doyle

In the Light of Day

November, 1997

Hi,

November is a melancholy month. The lovely leaves let go their grip and fall. The mind reaches to recall the bright smiles we knew before the eyelids closed, and faces too, gone beneath the cloth, the coffin lid, the cruel clay that covered them. We gaze more longingly at photographs we love, falling leaves we caught before the sun went down.

A church is most surely a mother with many memories and Sacred Heart has its stack of pictures, some old as our church's bleak beginnings 125 years ago, and some as fresh as Nicholas dripping drops of baptismal water last Sunday afternoon. But among them all, for this month's letter I will mention two. One is of Mother Teresa smiling in Sacred Heart Church on August 7, 1976, with a loaf of bread in her hands while her friend Eileen Egan looks on approvingly from the side. The other is of Sr. Peter Claver of Philadelphia beaming before our altar in 1988 with the icon of her friend Dorothy Day in her hands. Four notable women. I know there are mountain peaks in the world called the Three Sisters, but these Four Sisters are…one can only think of Himalayan altitudes. And the central gravitational point is surely Dorothy Day.

On November 8 we celebrate the 100th anniversary of her birth on Pineapple Street in Brooklyn. She died on November 29, 1980, on East 3rd Street in Manhattan. She was 83. Four years before, she gave an address to 800 women at the Eucharistic Congress in Philadelphia on August 6, 1976, where "in loving disagreement" with the official mind of the Congress, she who measured everything by the Gospel of Jesus, chided us for not asking God to forgive us for dropping an atomic bomb on the civilian people of Hiroshima. Dorothy's talk in Philadelphia was her last public address to the world. Her weakened condition weakened more. But she lived long enough to receive birthday greetings from a pope, Paul VI in Rome, delivered by a cardinal, Terence Cooke in New York.

I went to her 80th birthday Mass in St. Joseph's Church in New York (Dorothy too ill to be there) when Frank Sheed, 80 himself, came over from London to give the homily. Among many things, he said that when Dorothy opened her houses in 1933 to feed, clothe, and house the poor [today there are about 120 houses], "she didn't call them Houses of Charity because that is the coldest word in the English language. She didn't call them Houses of Love, that has to be the sloppiest. No, she called them Houses of Hospitality. Now there's a word that has not been damaged yet."

Our God, thanks be to God, is a God of hospitality, welcoming to the table, the sinners, the unwanted, even me. No exclusionary zoning or racial lines or glass ceilings in heaven. The limitless hospitality of God and the immeasurable dignity of every human person was Dorothy's Gospel. It is the Gospel of Christ. She had no tolerance for the killing of any of God's children. And she had an unbreakable loyalty to the workers of the world, especially those near the bottom of the scale.

After a searching start in her early years, she turned to God, became a Catholic, and never wavered in her struggle. Two men helped her greatly, Peter Maurin from 1932 with his radical

Christian philosophy, and Fr. John Hugo with his retreats from 1940. She chose poverty like a Francis of Assisi and lived her life serving poor down-and-outs with all her mind and strength. She put her paper *The Catholic Worker* on the street on May Day 1933 at a penny a copy—it is still on the street at a penny a copy. And with that, she communicated with humanity. In 1965, it was airmailed to every bishop in the world during the last session of the Vatican Council when war and peace were being discussed. Six times a year, it comes faithfully, and this last issue, November-December 1997, has articles for Dorothy's 100th birthday by Eileen Egan and Sr. Peter Claver. Eileen is a great woman of God herself. She is a writer and a tireless worker in relief and development programs for refugees and victims of war. She is a founder of Pax Christi USA and an associate editor of *The Catholic Worker*. Eileen accompanied Dorothy (her friend since 1943) to Australia, to India to meet Mother Teresa, to the Vatican Council where Dorothy did a ten-day fast urging the bishops to teach words of true peacemaking. When they voted on the peace section of the "The Church in the Modern World" they condemned indiscriminate warfare, supported conscientious objection, linked arms expenditures to the unmet needs of the poor and pointed to Gospel nonviolence as a possible position for Catholics. Eileen accompanied Dorothy to Rome again in 1967 to the Congress of the Laity where Dorothy and an astronaut were the two North Americans chosen to receive communion from Pope Paul VI. And finally she came with Dorothy to Philadelphia in 1976 and on August 7 Eileen brought Mother Teresa to Sacred Heart.

Sr. Peter Claver, an extraordinary Trinitarian Sister, who herself was born in 1899, and who after "retirement" began teaching in Holmesburg Prison in Philadelphia when she was 80, is a friend and spiritual companion of Dorothy Day's since 1933. I say "is" because I'm sure she still is. It was she who brought Dorothy to Fr. Hugo in 1940. In her article in the current *Catholic Worker*, she says Dorothy "was driven by love." The love of God and the love of all people. "The weapons" of her struggle to change things "were spiritual ones. Prayer, fasting, almsgiving, daily Mass, and a hour before the Blessed Sacrament. God released the Holy Spirit in her soul."

The more I think of these four great women, the smaller I feel before them. Two living. Two dead. All very alive. Three of them came to Sacred Heart in Camden and surely brought the blessing of the fourth. I heard Dorothy Day speak once, and she was introduced by a priest as the greatest Catholic of the century in this country. Many people all over the world revere her and some try to walk in her light. As one might say, in the light of Day.

May the prayers and powers of this holy foursome help to transform this town and make it better for the people who live in it. We need housing, jobs, better education, and food on the table. And above all, we need a renewal of spirit.

Once again I turn to you as we set our hearts to fill a thousand baskets for Christmas. Help us to make Sacred Heart a place that a thousand families can turn to. Let it become, this Christmastime at least, a House of Hospitality.

Michael Doyle

A Hidden Hope Named Nicholas

December, 1997

Hi,

His beautiful mother Stephanie Balzano Fischette handed me her naked baby and I lowered him reverently and horizontally into the waters of the fish-shaped font in front of me. "Nicholas Michael," I said, "I baptize you in the name of the Father and of the Son and of the Holy Spirit." It was a sacred rite, old in a way as the first man or woman who ever lowered a lithe body into a river, and felt its flow and the shiver of primal liberation. Old as Noah and his story of naval rescue long ago. Harkening back to the freedom march of Moses and his people bravely into the sea and out safely on the other side. Or Jesus himself going under in the Jordan for alignment and cosmic transformation. And above all, his going down in bloody death only to rise three days later when he got the better of it.

Nicholas Michael was definitely at home in the water that his grand-uncle Joe Balzano, a man of rivers and depths himself, fetched solemnly from the stove to baptize him. It was warm as the womb that this dear child left much too soon last May after only 27 weeks in the making. He weighed in on May 29th at the whopping avoirdupois of one pound and thirteen ounces. Then to the dismay of his worried weight watchers he dropped to one pound and eight ounces. That's only 24 little ounces of humanity on the big broad highway of the world. For this little handful of flesh it was a very traumatic and frightening world indeed, with its needles and tubes and all sorts of machines. Suddenly he was out of the soft womb and into a thicket of strange medical equipment. He was a full nine weeks old before his father Michael got his first clear look at his face. Bystanders, his parents were, watching his heroic struggle for life. Through glass they often glanced at him and gave him their love, their energy, their prayers, and ours. They waited with desperate hope.

Their story of waiting is surely linked to the world's wait for the child-savior of Bethlehem. Michael and Stephanie waited through ten years of marriage. Little Joseph came in 1988. I led the heartbreaking prayers by his tiny grave in Calvary Cemetery. The years went by....no little sound at all in the silence of their sorrow.

One year ago their dog Halley, the companion of their ten long years, and a friendly presence in their continuous ache for life, died. For Stephanie it was a last straw. She had no heart to celebrate Christmas. But with Michael's encouragement she finally did.

She didn't know then that there was a hidden hope beneath the surface of her sorrow. In the quiet of her body new life had imperceptibly begun. A hidden joy. A baby....on the way. Thanks be to God! The best of gifts. A Christmas child within. She would call him Nicholas. So like Anna of old and Mary of Nazareth, Stephanie would sing the great mothering song: "My soul magnifies the Lord and my spirit rejoices in God my savior. He who is mighty has done great things for me and holy is his name" (Luke 2).

Now, as Christmas comes again with all its festive color and sound, its joyous bonding of family and friends across the earth, its happy homecomings, there are still countless people on this planet who are burdened with illness or age and the separations that often go with them. Then there are those who are flattened by tragedy and overwhelming grief. Many people do not have the heart to celebrate in the awful unfairness of the world.

But as little Nicholas tells us, the real hope of Christmas is always a hidden hope. It's a seed in the ashes of reality that is indestructible.   It rises from beneath the sorrow, the helplessness, the long dark despair. Christmas is the birth of the life-giver in this valley of death, a hope that endures no matter what.

Camden is a tough test of hope most of the time. Side by side with the names of the saints which we chanted at Mass on Sunday, November 23rd, we called out to God the names of the 36 persons murdered in this city during the past year: 5 women, 30 men, and one child. The most recent and indeed the most awful murder of all took place on Monday, November 17. Paula Macklin, a widow, 45 years old and a Kindergarten teacher, who lived on the south side of this parish, was found by her son Michael on the kitchen floor. The killing knife still stuck in the dear body that bore him.

So, for sure, many people have to dig deeply to find that seed of hope that doesn't drown in the depths of their sorrow. And they do, God bless them. They do. We don't have to look far to realize that the cradle and the cross are made from the same tree and without them the lights and the gifts and the festive seasons are as good as green grass on a landfill.

Right now, baby Nicholas, you are a sight for the sore sorrowing eyes of the world. A breath of heroic life in the struggle of it all. The hope we need to go on. Thanks be to God again!

I will always remember your father as he held you aloft at the end of your baptism, full stretch up like *Kunte Kinte*, all ten pounds of you, as we proclaimed loudly and clearly "Christ is risen." God is greater than the worst that can happen. So from baby Nicholas Michael, from the hope that he is, from the core of his awesome struggle to live (he was *eight* ounces lighter than Kelsey Ann, the smallest of the McCaughey septuplets and four weeks less in his mother's womb), I say Happy Christmas. And for myself too, Happy Christmas to you!

Michael Doyle

See The Flame

I look at the hearth many times
* Maybe it will inspire a worthy poem*
But failure after failure are crinkled in my hand
With pure paper sounds the little child has known.
Then the yellow ball is made and deftly thrown
Lands upon the fire…perfect aim!
As the child with astonishment proclaims
"Is that your poem?"
"Yes", I solemnly say, "See the flame!"

A Toast to a Tree

January, 1998

Hi!

Sacred Heart Church was packed with people on Christmas Eve. No light except one solitary candle. Outside the night was raw and wet and dark. Twenty-four hours before, Dawn McCary's half-naked body was dumped at 3rd and Viola, a few hundred yards from the church. Twenty-four years old. Strangled. Murder victim number 43 in Camden's bloody line-up for 1997.

A woman stepped up to the shrine altar and lit the center candle of the menorah, and then one by one, all the candles. All through the lighting, Barbara Dever sang "O Come, O Come, Emmanuel." We did our best to sing along with her. The light increased gradually. Then almost simultaneously the huge Christmas tree and the crib exploded in wondrous brightness. Twenty-five hundred clear little bulbs turned a 23-foot spruce tree into a wide silver-blue pyramid of stars.

I watched the transformation of darkness from the choir loft where I had been waiting before Mass in a clutter of paint cans and brushes, the raw materials of the church's ongoing restoration. As I watched, I knew we were celebrating the struggling hope of Camden's weary resurrection and our own ultimate transformation into better beings; worth keeping forever, maybe. I marveled at the great tree that had just been transfigured into light – an exaggerated exposition perhaps of our resistance to the present darkness that sometimes seems to strangle our lives and hopes. What bright expectations prompted the happy McCary parents 24 years ago to name their baby girl, Dawn!

This tree, I thought, is a tree with a story. The sweep of it with its multitudes of stars is, in a way, a little galaxy of gratitude celebrating the hundreds of people who help Sacred Heart's mission with prayer and blessing; with donations of time, materials, and money. Eighteen hundred children got toys here this Christmas and one thousand and eighty Christmas baskets were packed and delivered through your generosity. Thanks be to you again and again! Thanks be to God!

Maybe we should have two trees. One for all those who blessed us by giving; the other for all those who blessed us by receiving. It is in the hammock that hangs between them that God is born.

Anyway, our tree, which grew in their lawn, was a gift from the Kellys of Collingswood, New Jersey. Its thousands of blue-green needles point to many special people and incidents of life in the 28 years of its growth. Names rise to mind for acknowledgment but none more beloved than Eugenie Kelly who loved this tree and nurtured it to health in its early illnesses. Remembering too how the wind cried in the limbs, that cold New Year's Eve when she, the young mother of three, raised her glass of water at 12:01 a.m., her three companions their wine, to toast the coming time: 1986. The glasses down, she died. The tree down now. Her name, the crying wind, the season that we're in, recalls Eugene, Eugene O'Donnell and his violin who has these many years, composed an annual "Lament for the Dying Tree." The dying Christmas tree of Sacred Heart, as it nears its season's end. Let me toast the two of them, Eugenie and Eugene! Artists both, of authentic beauty, of noble note, of Celtic dance and story, all the sweet epiphany of ancient Ireland's soul.

And I toast the tree. In its shadow the Kelly girls grew. The blue tree began with them and grew far above them. Its roots dug in to hold its ground, too much, 'tis said, till the sidewalk cracked and rose. Now the Kelly house for sale. The tree must go. Sad news for the Kelly three, their father, too. The axe is always hard on trees and bonds or any cherished thing we possess or possesses us.

It was first base for all outdoor Kelly games – " a painful one" Denise would add. The clearest marker for any traveler to 222 Burwood Avenue. "Birds nesting there" Fiona said when she stood beneath with life nestling in her womb as well. "The tree was the sentinel for my whole life" says Monique, 26, "sure as the sun it welcomed me in the morning and waited for me in the evening." It was a waiting post for: "my first day at school, mother's first heart attack (I was 5), the school bus, my first date, prom, graduation, sister's wedding, part of all the pictures and the memories of my life. Now it is wonderful to be able to share something with Sacred Heart that has been a constant part of our lives." There, in sorrow and in joy. 'Tis time to call Eugene. Maybe issue a command: "Up on your toes, my friend! Dip your bow in the tears of times gone by. Let the strings sing out the sorrows and the joys of the way we were." Eugenie Kelly! Come to mind, I bid you! Let the sun, the bent beam of winter glint again upon your auburn hair! Take my hand in your two small hands and make me feel as you always did, much better than I am. Then I'll face the future bravely. Treasures! Treasures surely, these two in years of Christmas scenes at Sacred Heart. Eugenie often here to celebrate the Kings-a-coming. Her face its own Epiphany. Eugene, fiddle chinned in church to play at Celtic Spring with Mick Moloney, Seamus Egan, and Jimmy Keane, and then craft each year in the evening interlude his sweet "Lament for the Dying Tree."

And so again, Eugene. At home now. Far too far away beyond the mist and sea to glimpse this Christmas tree. But pluck, I say, a sound from the Derry air and make a tune to lament this dying Kelly tree. And we will shear the sturdy branches off and build a fire and dream a dream before the ashes come. And we'll shape a bit into a cross to sense the meaning of our lives. And some ashes too we'll carry to Eugenie's grave and a little also to the place where Dawn went down in the dark of night. So when all is said and done, and no matter what is said and done, there is a happy ending to the story. Because angels on the wing have been heard at night to sing that ashes have a future in the dawning of the Day.

Michael Doyle

If Pews Could Talk

February, 1998

Hi,

If pews could talk, they could tell a tale of trees and times gone by, when the wind assailed them or the rain delighted them. Or maybe deadly days of chainsaw smoke and gash when their shapely elegance was flattened – the mill they all went through, the chisel's edge that cut them, the mortise knit that bound them, the rough spots sanded smooth – all this happened before they took their place in a brownstone church in Camden. Row by row, the trees are pews, plain and simple now, so far away from sway and sky, the earth, the air, the water; the sun that gave them life. And yet it was here at Sacred Heart that these pews found their greatest stories. Here the people have been coming for one hundred years and more to sit and stand and kneel. Here they pray and sing. Here they weep at times. Here God shows up to see them.

On Sunday last at our 8:30 Mass, the front two pews were filled with people and their special stories. The first with dear Sen Tran, white-veiled in mourning for her beloved husband Nguyen Van Hai. Grieving with her in the pew, her five daughters (one is still in Vietnam) and her three sons. Hai died in Camden on Friday evening, February 13th, at the age of 78. Behind them, John Donnelly, the father, with his four daughters and two sons (one not present), grieving for their delightful mother Betty. She died in Camden and was buried on February 13th. Seventy-four years old. Present also was Betty's sister, Mary.

At the 10:30 Mass, the same two pews were filled again. The Wisely brothers, William and Mark, with babies for baptism. Abigail, in her mother Tina's arms, Mark in Lauriel's. The babies going under the water, in ritual sign of life's struggle through death into resurrection. The water in the font was calm, but all that will change, we know.

At the funerals of Betty and Hai in Sacred Heart, their baptisms were remembered, one in Philadelphia in 1923; one in Vietnam in 1920. Betty, the second oldest of the five children of Harry Griffin (a plumber) and Esther Hogan, was raised in Torresdale, Philadelphia. Hai, the second youngest of five children of Nguyen Van Chiem (a farmer) and Nguyen Thi Tuy, was raised in Phat Diem in northern Vietnam. Betty was six when the Great Depression flattened human hope and eleven when her father died, leaving a young widow with five children under twelve. The Griffin household knew hunger, and dinner was sometimes bread and apple butter, and never without laughter. In time Betty and John Donnelly filled their plates with food and their home with the seven children she bore. And she lived her life with selfless generosity, patient discipline, and good humor.

Hai was three in Phat Diem when Betty was born. He had begun to talk and walk and grow up on a farm that grew rice and vegetables. His life was school and farm work and peaceful time in Phat Diem Church. As a young man he saw the gathering storms that permeated Vietnam after World War II. The Japanese, the Chinese, the French, the English, were involved in his country. And the U.S., too, from the 1950s onward, as weapons providers. Ho Chi Minh. The siege and fall of Dien Bien Phu. 1954. The demarcation line at the 17th Parallel. Hai and his three sisters went south in 1954 and there he met and married a young woman he had distantly known in his hometown church. (His older brother, following tradition, did not leave home because their parents were buried nearby.) Hai had become a photographer and with his wife, eventually, raised nine children.

1968. The Vietnam War. The Tet Offensive. Hai's family lived near a South Vietnamese military camp. A target. Splinter bombs exploded nearby. Hai built a sandbagged shelter three feet high in which the anxious family sought safety. On one occasion he rigged up a board on his bicycle, placed four little children on it, and raced to the church, three other children and their mother racing alongside. The church had a basement and the family lived there for two weeks as the bombs continued to fall.

In 1975, Saigon fell. Phu Nhuam, where Hai's family lived, was near an airport and crowds of people descended there to escape the country, including the Nguyen family. Except Hai. He felt obligated to his sisters not to leave them. So he tore up his U.S. photographer's pass that would have given him preference. The family didn't escape. But his second-oldest daughter, Oahn, set her mind on it. Over six years, 1977-1983, she tried 23 times. On many occasions she paid out the gold for the boat ride, but no boat appeared. Finally, with her husband and three-month-old baby, who was given "something" to prevent crying, the family got on a small boat at night. It was very dangerous. They made their way sixty miles to Vung Tau, near Saigon. There they got on a fishing boat where they spent 54 hours in the Indian Ocean before being rescued. They made their way to Singapore and in 1984 arrived in Camden. Six weeks after Oahn escaped, her sister Lien, with her husband and son, made the same dangerous journey. Both escapes caused wrenching anxiety in the family. In 1993 Hai himself, with his wife, three daughters and two sons, came to Camden. The journey was no longer dangerous, but he still did not want to leave (he had one sister living in Vietnam) and only did so because his oldest married daughter, forced to stay behind, would be with his sister. (At the time, only parents already in the U.S. could sponsor married daughters to emigrate.)

Hai died hoping against hope that he would live till May 7th (five years here) when he would pursue citizenship and be able to bring his oldest daughter from Vietnam and see her again. He mentioned this sadly on the day he died.

After partially telling these stories at the 10:30 Mass, I asked the young parents: "Do you still want your babies baptized?" "Absolutely" said Lauriel. Later I saw her standing bravely with her baby on one arm and a lighted candle held aloft in the other hand, singing the *Our Father*. "Thy will be done on earth as it is in heaven." And two little children set off on their journey to God with the strengthening blessing of Betty and Hai. God be with them, all four of them!

So if pews could talk or dear people like Hai and Betty, they would say that it's not the growing trees or the young limbs of children that are important at the end of the day. Nor is it the axe that fells or the death that kills. No, it is the ending that God has written to the story. A happy ending that is a New Beginning. To it each and every one is invited.

Michael Doyle

The Plough and the Stars

March, 1998

Hi,

Recently, my sister Phyllis Doyle and her husband Johnny O'Reilly, visiting me from Ireland, suggested delightfully that they would take me out to dinner. Where, was a question for them, and they left the answer to me. "The Plough and the Stars," I said. "I have never been there." Ten minutes of driving took us from Sacred Heart in Camden to a spot near 2nd and Chestnut in Philadelphia. There was a fire burning and a warm welcome from the owners, Marion Ryder, Jerome Donovan, and Austin McGrath. Austin's from County Tyrone. Above all, the food was great. Not only that, but when the bill came, it didn't come. Our dinners were on the house.

And I hadn't even told Austin that my mother's people came from Tyrone. A long time ago, however. They went down to the Battle of Kinsale (County Cork) in 1601 with their chieftain, Hugh O'Neill, and there they joined a Spanish contingent against the British. The Irish were defeated and the north of Ireland lost its strength that day and was soon taken over by British settlers, who, to this very day, fly the British flag over that part of Ireland. Unionists they call themselves. They want to live on the Island of Ireland and be part of the larger Island of Britain. Thus the problem.

The defeated Creegans did not return to Tyrone but settled in the southern county of Limerick. Over one hundred years later, a Creegan came up from there to Leitrim and from him, six generations later, came my mother. But for the Battle of Kinsale you would have been spared my stories, and because of it and many other things, I am able to tell how well we were treated in "The Plough and the Stars."

It's March and I can get away with it. Memories flood back to me of other great evenings in Philadelphia and none better than dining with my friend Siobhan McKenna (God rest her) after her great performance as Bessie Burgess in Sean O'Casey's "The Plough and the Stars." She loved that play and I love the name of it. I think it would be hard to say more with five words than "the plough and the stars." They always trigger in my mind a depth of meaning and a joy of spirit, and yet the poetic brightness of them can fill my eyes with tears. They form such an inspiring image of reality. On a broad swath of cloth, the plough and the stars was the labor flag of Ireland as poor working people struggled for justice a long century ago.

I will always regret that this image did not become the national flag of Ireland when we won back 26 counties of our island in 1922. Instead we hoisted the "green, white and orange" hoping generously that it would signify some unity between the native Irish people and the more "recent" settlers (more than 300 years) who always want to keep England in Ireland. They, under the leadership of the Dutchman William of Orange, defeated the Catholics at the Battle of the Boyne and they celebrate that victory over their neighbors with lots of orange pageantry every twelfth of July. Orange is nice but you don't want too much of it. A field of green with a touch of orange is surely better than a field of orange grass with a wisp of green. Anyway our tricolor flag of unity is illegal in six counties of the small island of Ireland. And the straight lines of the green and orange with the white between them remind me anyway of division.

Ah! The Plough and the Stars! It will always be in my heart the flag of Ireland calling us to look above and beyond the stupid boundaries that God never intended. One does not have to think too deeply to realize that the hammer and sickle would be inadequate for the Russian people. Both of these tools bend the body to the earth, but the plough and the stars call us not only to work in the earth but also to lift up our mind in admiration to the heavens.

The greatest ploughman I ever knew was my grandfather Pat Doyle who every year in February took the coulter of his plough (the sod cutter) to Farrel McKeon's forge, and there

> *with his anvil on a tree stump,*
> *his fire and his bellows,*
> *he hammered out the blunted blade*
> *until the reddened passion of its edge*
> *could open up a furrow*
> *in the darkened earth below*
> *for seeds to have a groove in which to grow.*
> *But my grandfather wanted me to know*
> *that the creator made them grow*
> *so the priest blessed the simple salt*
> *a pinch for every field*
> *to put the taste of God's abundance*
> *on the holy watched-for yield.*

The coulter-man I called him. His plough the cutting edge of all the hope he had and the rain on his face the sadness of his heart. In the course of his 84 years he buried two wives, two of his three children, and the only two brothers he had. He wept as no man I ever knew wept in this world.

> *The rains filled his furrow with their sorrow*
> *all his life, his eyes the overflow*
> *from head to toe a human font of tears.*

And yet this noble ploughman with his tidal sorrow never ever failed to look up at the stars of heaven with the powerful reverence of an Abraham. "It's a terrible day, thanks be to God," his words for the marvelous motto of his whole life.

So on this St. Patrick's Day I salute my grandfather who bore the name of the great saint as well as anyone. He showed me with the heroic effort of his life the bright beautiful wisdom of The Plough and the Stars.

Michael Doyle

Easter Findings

April 1, 1998

Hi:

Many years ago Felix Doyle and Pat were two bachelor brothers living on the farm next to the one I was reared on. Far out relatives of my own, I'm sure, but dead before I was born to know them. They left no children; no one knows their resting place in the churchyard, but some endearing stories do remain to remind us of them. None more charming than one that could be entitled: "The Ass Knows" or "The Ass's Nose Knows."

Anyway, I would like to say that every ass was a useful and respected animal in the world of my childhood, even though G.K. Chesterton before he praises the creature, says,

> *The tattered outlaw of the earth*
> *Of ancient crooked will;*
> *Starve, scourge, deride me: I am dumb,*
> *I keep my secret still.*

And even though a small scar beneath my right eye reminds me of an ass's kick in the face when I toddled too near before I was five. Older boys had frightened the hoofed mammal out of its wits. In its unassuming ways, it is always the friend of the unassuming, bearing in every age the tattered burdens of the poor. Surefooted in the bogland, the survivor in the wasteland. Its humble gait never denotes power, like the battle-bred horses of the Romans, or the fancy prance at the royal gates of Windsor. No four-footed asses there. No bicycles with the limousines. Yet the modest little wheels sometimes gleam in the sun. The ass carried the day and the Author of all days on that one great moment in Jerusalem. Chesterton catches it:

> *Fools! For I also had my hour*
> *One far fierce hour and sweet:*
> *There was a shout about my ears*
> *And palms before my feet*

No Oscar that day for the high-strung steeds of Caesar.

I made my entry into Jerusalem in a taxi on a Sunday in July 1995. I had come to hear Barbara Dever of Sacred Heart sing Verdi's *Requiem*. She had been chosen by Zubin Mehta to do it – a magnificent moment in her career that she attributed to my brother, Father J.J. Doyle, who had died one month before. "J.J. got this for me," she said at the news, "I'll sing the *Requiem* for him in Jerusalem." She did, and I was there, and she poured her whole heart into it together with the hundred-member Israeli Philharmonic, a hundred-member choir from Prague, three other singers, and Mehta conducting. The event ended with a "wee hour" toast to all that happened that day. By some extraordinary convergence of things, on that same day there was a month's-mind Mass for J.J. Doyle in the parish where he ministered, an annual Mass in the parish cemetery where he's buried, and the *Requiem* in Jerusalem, each unconnected in scheduling, each united in a proclamation that all is well. It was a great day.

I arrived in Jerusalem at 10:45 a.m. In my comfortable taxi I was aware that Jesus entered Jerusalem triumphantly and was hailed as a king, only to be killed before the week was out. He rode in on an ass – a proud moment for the creature, that "one fierce hour and sweet." No horses, no chariot, no line of limousines, no Pope-mobile, even. God on an ass. I came with my luggage, the baggage of my life. A tourist trying to be a pilgrim. Observing, but hoping to be changed.

I looked across from the Notre Dame of Jerusalem, where I stayed, and I saw the Mount of Olives, that lookout (Mt. Scopus) of the Romans. I was surprised at the height and dimension of it and delighted to see for the first time the contour of land unchanged since Jesus made his way with sore feet among the stones. Then I entered the Old City through New Gate at the Christian quarter. I saw streets named St. Francis and Ave Maria and through their narrow width (two people at arm's length could stretch from wall to wall) I came to the Holy Sepulchre, the most special spot in Christendom. Churches clutter and cling to it, as someone said, like barnacles on a boat. Latin, Greek, Orthodox, Armenian, Syrian, Coptic, Ethiopian, watch each other warily. All to say, it's holy ground. Its twenty-foot high, weather-beaten doors have been guarded by the same Moslem family for generations. On this day, a boy not more than eleven years old was the guard.. I went to the tomb by bending low, lit a candle and prayed for the many people in my heart. Old candles there, censors, icons, all helping to say, "Holy, holy, holy."

This tomb is the womb of all Christian hope. It is empty. How many holes in the punctured surface of the planet contain the remains of human bodies and bones. But, thanks be to God, the empty tomb of Jesus announces hope at the core of the impossible and the farthest far-fetched dream of the heart. Christ is Risen and the God who once breathed life into nostrils of dust will call each one by name from the nameless nowheres of the world.

The joy of Easter! Maybe thoughts like these can crease the face of the earth into a fearful frown. Easter has to be lighthearted as the breaking of day. Lightheaded, maybe.

I almost forgot Felix Doyle and Pat and their ass that opened gates, burrowed into their clay-covered heaps to eat their potatoes. To thwart her, Felix and Pat decided, brilliantly, to bury their potatoes in the potato field. But they didn't mark the spot and after a night of rain, they couldn't find their buried treasures.

> *So they had to go and get the ass*
> *With its fettered feet in sour grass.*
> *Then she put her nostrils to the ground*
> *And the missing spuds were quickly found.*
> *Now if I could only find that ass*
> *And let it graze the graveyard grass*
> *I know she'd lie where she found it best*
> *Where Pat and Felix are laid to rest.*

So I wish you a Happy Easter because God will surely find your last resting place and lift you up to glory.

Michael Doyle

The Last Two Words

May, 1998

Hi!

There's an Aran sweater in my closet (too worn to be worn now) that my mother, Rosetta Doyle, knitted for me in the spring of 1973 as she sat in a federal courtroom in Camden, NJ. She had come from Ireland in her 72nd year to visit a grieving friend and also to be present at most of the fifteen-week trial of the "Camden 28." With 16 men and women (11 had been severed), I was legally represented and also a *pro se* defendant, defending myself against the seven counts of which I was charged for illegal protest against the Vietnam War.

Serious stuff! FBI director J. Edgar Hoover and Attorney General John Mitchell had announced on August 22nd, 1971, in a joint news conference in Washington, DC, that if convicted on all counts, we could get 47 years in prison. The trial started on February 5th. Winter's grip was everywhere. Cold and tight as the government's hold on our lives. The trial labored on. As the days got longer, tempers sometimes got shorter, anxieties higher, and all the while, words, words, words, never ending…utterly interminable. But with good humor and real respect for us, Judge Clarkson Fisher (God rest him) guided this trial with the largest *pro se* defense in American history.

Over this long haul, the jury members did their best to listen as the defendants transformed the courtroom into a college course on the whole issue of war and peace. They, the jury members, were silent but in some instances bodies spoke in their own unmistakable language. Anna Bertino, a juror, told me following the trial that she watched my mother knitting the sweater day by day. "Her needles moved faster," she said, "when things heated up and then eased back to their quiet pace again." I noticed that the juror beside Anna often slept during the trial. A smart move. But Anna woke him up if things were going good for us and let him sleep if they were not. That was body language enough to assure me that Anna Bertino, God bless her, would not convict us.

Finally, on May 17, the jury got the case. It was a Thursday afternoon. A long weekend crawled by. Waiting. No verdict. Good news or bad news! Anybody's guess.

On Sunday, when, as a visiting priest, I had just finished the 10:30 Mass at St. Anne's in Westville, NJ, two Franciscan sisters said, "The verdict's in…it's on the radio." I decided to have a big breakfast. No verdict could be announced until I arrived, as all defendants had to be present. I knew that if the process were slowed down, many supporters would have time to come to Camden. An acquittal would make history. People would be there. We might be found guilty, and still people would be there to stand with us.

I was the last defendant to arrive, and a great crowd had gathered on the street. Everybody was waiting for the word. Only the jurors had it. And all had to wait for it – the Justice Department and the defendants, the supporters and the detractors, the judges and the jailers. The power was in the hands of the people for once in their lives.

In my closing statement I had said to the jury that I was not happy that John Barry, as prosecutor, had the last word in the trial. "But," I said to the jury, "he doesn't have the last word, you have the last word. And on second thought, you have the last two words."

I entered the courtroom. It was full. "Where were you?" the question on everybody's mind. My mother was there with Rita Bell and many dear friends. Her hands were still. No needles. No wool. I sat down. A courtroom friend during our long trial came over and whispered in my ear, "They all went to Mass at Our Lady of Good Counsel in Moorestown." Then she was gone. "They all" was the jury. I leaned back my head and said to myself, "We're acquitted." It was a simple deduction. There are only four Catholics on the jury. Anna Bertino is the staunchest. She will not convict me. If the other eleven went to Sunday Mass with Anna Bertino, they must be agreeing with her. *We're acquitted.*

The judge came in. Then the jury, one by one, and took their places. Clarkson Fisher spoke the question that was burning holes in our minds. (It resonated with the one I was asked when I first took the stand: "Did you do it?" "Yes, I did," I answered under oath.) The foreman stood up. He pronounced the verdict on all counts for all defendants. It was not the last word. It was the last two words: *"Not guilty."* The courtroom exploded in joy and spilled out onto Fourth and Market Streets. May 20, 1973. Twenty-five years ago.

We ended that happy day with Mass at St. George's Catholic Church in Camden, followed by a party downstairs. The place was packed. Friends, supporters…even some of the courtroom marshals came to celebrate with us. In the midst of all this, my bishop, George Guilfoyle, RIP, called and congratulated me. "Come and see me tomorrow," he said. "Now you can get back to your priestly duties." I went to see him the next day. "You don't look too happy," he said. "I'm not," I said. "Why not?" "Because of what you said last night. Let me tell you something. I was about my priestly duty all through this action and trial." He apologized. He was far more kind and supportive than I expected. Shortly afterwards, he appointed me to St. Joan of Arc parish in Camden and in November, 1974, as pastor of Sacred Heart, where my "priestly duty" has taken many a twist and turn since.

But no twist more interesting or turn more enjoyable than the (almost) four-month trial of the "Camden 28." I was focused on the issue that still haunts me. How could a country spend so much on the weapons of war and let a Camden continue to be a place of destruction for many of its children? I had shown slides in the courtroom of war-ravaged Vietnam interspersed with slides of dilapidated buildings in Camden. Camden is a casualty of a war economy, I said then, and it still is. Why is so much of our taxes used to make weapons we do not need, and not to rebuild our inner cities with good houses that we do?

Twenty-five years have passed since May 20, 1973.

On May 29, 1998, I will raise a glass and salute my sisters and brothers of the "Camden 28," the issues they raised, the supporters they had, the lawyers who advised them, the judge who honored them, the jury that acquitted them, and the dear Irish mother who knitted an Aran sweater for one of them in a federal courtroom. And, I dare say, whose prayer before God knits the best shield of protection in all the world.

Michael Doyle

Camden's Gift to Me

June, 1998

Hi:

There was a great crowd of people in the Harbour League when she entered. A great mix of humanity, old and young, rich and poor, of many creeds and races, had gathered on the sixth floor of this elegant Camden club. June 15, 1998. Exactly thirty years had passed since I drove my Chevy into Camden on June 15, 1968. And now, after this sizable slice of my lifetime, I was still on my feet and they were on theirs to honor me. But no collective word or act would match the entry of Annie Fletcher McMurtrie. My heart leapt at the sight of her. Her presence an unsurpassable gift. She kissed me and said, "I love you." She was 105 years old last January.

It was hard to believe the eyes and seeing is believing. She had insisted on coming to celebrate my moment. All the way from South Philadelphia, back to the town she was born in. January 10, 1893. My thirty years are a wisp in the wind compared to the heroic journey of her life and the continual irrepressible song in her heart. Before she left, she stood in the center of the crowd, raised her arms and proclaimed, "God bless everyone."

Annie first opened her eyes about two blocks from Mickle Street, where Walt Whitman lived most of the last 19 years of his life and she was in utero faintly throbbing, when Walt's heart stopped on March 26, 1892. Like myself, he was happy he was here. "I will never regret," he said one time, "that I was left over in Camden. It has brought me blessed returns." And to me, the same…blessed returns. That's why I wanted to celebrate on June 15 and not on any day near it. Friends made sure that I could. These friends generously celebrated what they thought I had done for Camden; I wanted to celebrate what Camden had done for me. And they, God bless them, gave me the chance to do it.

I celebrated the fact that Camden had defined me, brought me close to the real issues of the second half of this century and given me a yardstick by which I could measure the successes and failures of this powerful nation. I came to realize that Camden was a casualty of progress, the best visual aid in America as to what went wrong.

Camden was once a powerful city. When Annie Fletcher was born in 1893, it was poised for massive expansion in industry and manufacture. The Victor Talking Machine was invented here and soon the best singing voices of the day were brought to the households of the world from Camden, New Jersey. (Nipper the dog included). New York Shipyard was launched in South Camden and became the biggest in the nation, employing thousands of workers. But it thrived on war (37,000 workers in World War II). It lived by the sword and died by the sword. And, of course, the profits of the shareholders who didn't work were often more important than the livelihoods of the workers who did. I saw Camden go through massive dislocation because of fears and racism and real estate exploitation.

I have watched Camden get poorer. Sadly enough, it is worse today than it was in 1968. The killing drug scene. The tragic murder rate. I watched the waste of the war economy and the unconscionable neglect of urban centers like Camden. Massive expenditures on national security while urban citizens are not secure. No attempt to count the urban body bags because those in them don't count. Plenty of money to walk safely in space but not much for the Camdens of this world to make a safe space to walk. Camden has shown me these things.

My eyes have been opened in Camden and my soul has been strengthened. I celebrate that. I celebrate the heroic struggle of the people with their churches and community organizations. I salute those who have generously shared in Sacred Heart's efforts to help. The school, Heart of Camden Housing, the food sharing, the medical clinic.

I haven't seen God in a burning bush, but I hear Him speak from the burning issues of the day, and they are all in Camden. And now, Annie's blessing gives me hope.

So, I celebrate. By the grace of God, I am not paralyzed by all that I cannot do into not being able to do the bit I can do. At least, not for long. Looking at the big picture I most surely failed. But I want to qualify that on my gravestone:

Give me an old lump of stone
Unhewn and weather beaten
To stand upon the place I lie
Big enough to sit upon
And small enough for tired feet
To touch the ground.
There small children's jumps
Will be safe on summer afternoons.
Cut my name on the north side
Where the sun seldom stops to shine
Cut it deep where rain can run
And drops can hide and tiny mosses
Grow to green the letter levels there.
Cut '34, my birth, I'm told
And the partner year it waits to meet
And side by side they'll stay in stone
'Til time and tide will wear them down
Below the best that eyes can do.
And there three words of measurement

To sum my days of sun and cloud
And dreams of dark and dreary nights
And sleepy spots by warm walls
And times when all the weight of things
Paralyzed the strength I had
To do the bit I came to do.
So, artist, with your chisel sharp
Have a glass of winter wine
And cut the letter "he" for me
And then a sip, and then a cut
'Til "failed" is carved in perfectly
And please, my friend, no dismal dot
To stop at that and say no more
One word more for goodness sake
To make a plea to passing wind
Tis all I ask when I am gone
One kindly word to qualify, "he failed"
Give me, "nicely."

Michael Doyle

A Message into the Middle Passage of Our Hearts

July, 1998

Hi!

The path where the pavement used to be is rain-raveled now and worn. Weeds, thigh-high and more, rise amid broken bits of concrete. Here the marchers walked on Broadway in Camden. Friday, July 3, 1998. They were on their way to Africa by way of Brazil, to walk all the way that is land and sail all the way that is sea. Suddenly, one of them edged quickly to the side and touched the graffiti on a dilapidated wall. A Buddhist monk! Just as quickly she slipped back into pace with the sixty men and women who were walking with her, African, Asian, European, and American. Her shaved head drew all attention to her luminous eyes. Her garments, like those of the other ten or twelve marching monks, were saffron on white. Easy on the eyes as the rising of the sun. The pace never slackened as she moved. Missing not a beat on her slender drum and its rhythmic, bone-soothing sound. Everyone walking in harmony with the drumbeat of the many and the continuous chant of all. *Na Mu Myo Ren Ge Kyo*——that haunting mantra of the Nipponzan Myohoji Buddhist Order that urges peace to all the earth and especially to the spot where the footsteps fall as the chant goes on.

It was a great blessing to walk even a short way with them. I was in step with the holy Interfaith Pilgrimage of the Middle Passage that began in Massachusetts on May 30. It is "an interfaith, intercultural group seeking racial reconciliation," as they pray their way for more than a thousand miles down the east coast of the United States, then through the Caribbean to Brazil and over the ocean to Africa. Then southward: their destination Cape Town, by June of 1999. They are retracing the routes of the slave traders linking Africa and the United States. The Middle Passage refers to the route by which the slaves were transported to the ports of the Caribbean, Brazil, and North America.

On land and water, it is a way of sorrow. A *via dolorosa*. Not fourteen stations of the cross where Catholics ponder sites of sorrow as Jesus is led to execution, but millions of places on the planet where the inhumanity of humans to humans defies all human understanding. More than forty million African people were torn from their motherland, chained in the stinking holds of the slave ships, and sold on the auction blocks of the Americas. Originally, all this took place to boost the profits in the sugar economy. Twenty percent of the slaves were sold in North America, and eighty percent in the rest of the hemisphere. Only the heart of God is big enough to hold the sorrow of the story. The lash, the rope, the rape, the chains, the "no way out"; death the only way to be free at last.

So, men and women are walking the walk and sailing the sea and waking the dead and grieving the grief that still lingers in the places where atrocious deeds were done. Unknown latitudes, too, where dead slaves sank into the deep terror of the sea. Live ones, also, when provisions were low and a long way to go. These pilgrims will pray the way, day by day, where the trade routes ran. With heartfelt contrition, they will wipe some of the sadness from the face of the earth.

There is a silence in these places of sorrow that is crying for a voice to speak, to acknowledge, to reconcile, to heal, to be laid to rest. The pilgrims lend themselves to that cry and call us to rid ourselves of the racism that still lingers in our hearts. It was good that the pilgrims came to Camden, which is, in a sense, a casualty of continuing racism. They came and prayed their way through it. They came with faith and strength and were met with welcome and hospitality. At Lourdes Hospital with food and acknowledgement. At Macedonia Church to remember a safe house for slaves in the underground railroad. At Pyne Poynt, by the Delaware River, where slaves were unloaded to avoid a commercial tax in Philadelphia. At Friends' Meeting House to acknowledge the Quakers who befriended the slaves. At Sacred Heart, where the pilgrims were welcomed with words and prayer, bells and incense, not to mention food for lunch.

As the pilgrims left Sacred Heart, they circled in prayer to venerate the church and then with the beat of the drums, the chant of the mantra, the hoist of the flags, they walked in the weeds along South Broadway and over the Ben Franklin Bridge to Philadelphia. On from there to Baltimore, Washington, Richmond, Norfolk, Raleigh, Durham, Winston-Salem, Charlotte, Columbia, St. Helena Island, Charleston, Atlanta, Birmingham, Montgomery, Mobile, Biloxi, and they will reach New Orleans by November 3rd.

Later in November they set sail to Cuba, Jamaica, Haiti, Dominican Republic, Puerto Rico, Virgin Islands, Barbados, Trinidad, and Tobago.

By December they will reach Bahia, Brazil, and on January 1st, 1999, they hope to reach Dakar in Africa. There they will be joined by a parallel march from Europe and they will walk through sixteen countries before they reach Cape Town by May 31, 1999.

"God be with you," we prayed as the marchers made their way down the aisle of Sacred Heart and onward to Africa. We will go with them in spirit, our school children will go with them too. Indeed most of our children bear in their bodies the life of those who were torn from the African motherland by the cruel hand of slavery. These children are still tasting the effects of racial injustice.

But we hope this pilgrimage of reconciliation will make things better. That, just as the Buddhist woman touched the scrawl on a dilapidated wall in Camden to heal it, people will be touched and renewed as the message of the pilgrims makes its way through the Middle Passage of our hearts.

Michael Doyle

Singing Her Song after Milking Time

August, 1998

Hi:

"This is a sacred place," I said, "this church in the center of the graveyard where many of those we loved are buried. In honor of them, in honor of everyone here, and everyone ever associated with this Church of St. Colmcille in County Longford, I now ask Barbara Dever to open up her awesome voice and sing." The eager applause quieted and the golden voice of one of the world's greatest mezzo sopranos launched into the Latin masterpiece *Panis Angelicus*. The latter, in the lovely words of Thomas Aquinas, took my mind with the waves of the sound, out the open doors to the nearby stones and Celtic crosses and the silence of the earth beneath them. Birds paused and cows turned heads because no such sound had ever been heard on the hill. My mind went immediately to the spot near the side door where green grass grows on the dust of Doyles long gone, bodies that bore me or bore life to me over a span of 150 years. "*O res mirabile*," Barbara proclaimed again in glorious tones. O most wonderful reality! Amen! Amen from breeze and bird and grazing cow, from a church of living listeners, from the sacred silence of the dead.

It was better than a good dream when I realized I wasn't dreaming. Barbara Dever (Breuer her name when I first met her), a young student from Camden City, caught my attention as a 13-year-old freshman in my class in Camden Catholic High School. Not her voice, but her goodness and her sense of responsibility. And she began to sing at the Masses I led in McGuire Project in this city in 1969, almost 30 years ago. At Sacred Heart, Barbara has been leading liturgical song for over 20 years. When her two children were quite young she went back to college to develop her voice, and entered opera. Now she's a world star, noted particularly for her great performances of the demanding mezzo roles in Giuseppe Verdi's operas. On hearing her for the first time, in a practice for a performance with himself, Luciano Pavarotti, the great tenor, said, "At last, a Verdi mezzo." Last March Placido Domingo, who had not sung in his beloved Mexico City for 13 years gave one performance of *Samson and Delilah*, and he chose Barbara Dever to be his Delilah. It was the high moment of her career.

But now she was in Colmcille. The country church of my childhood, where my baptism and confirmation and the funerals of my family took place, where my first Mass was offered. Singing. Doing it out of the goodness of her heart. And the people were awed because she would bother. They worked hard to prepare, choosing the time with an eye on the cows: before or after milking time. They went for "after"—cows and cow milkers much more content. She had sung in many time zones across the world, from the Metropolitan Opera in New York to the Arena in Verona; in cities like Jerusalem, Palermo, Vancouver, Buenos Aires, Florence, Tel Aviv, Dublin, Miami, Washington, and many more, but nowhere after milking time. And yet singing at milking time was my favorite memory of singing as a child. I crept to the byre to listen to my father's song as the first strains of milk made music on the tin bottom of a tinker's gallon.

As I listened now, it was the sounds of strings as Barbara strapped on her guitar and sang her own religious compositions: "Table of Jesus" and "Song of the Heart." Then, with accompanist Martin Cahill, she completed the first half with rousing spirituals: "Ride on, King Jesus," "He's Got the Whole World in His Hands." She had the whole congregation in her heart.

After intermission, Barbara was back with beautiful songs of Ireland, the ones that the great tenor John MacCormack had made famous with recordings by RCA Victor in Camden, N.J., many years ago. As they listened to Barbara and her daughter Shauna, the people thought they had died and gone to heaven—"Mother Machree," "Down by the Sally Gardens," "The Rose of Tralee," "She Moved through the Fair," "Believe Me, If All Those Endearing Young Charms," "My Lagan Love," and "I Hear You Calling Me." A short pause and then the operatic selections: "Habanera," from Carmen, "O Mio Babino Caro" from Gianni Schicchi, and "Mon Coeur" from *Samson and Delilah*. All were ecstatic and tried to say it in a thundering standing ovation. "This evening will be talked about for 50 years!" was voiced by many. Everyone "honored" that someone so great would come to Colmcille. A star in the fields. To her encores of "Danny Boy" and "The Irish Blessing" the only true response was tears and there were plenty of them. Then tea and talk, autographs, and "Thanks be to God."

It was too much. "Coming Home" we called her concert. The girl with a Camden childhood had come home to the church of my childhood. Home to the common core of joyous gratitude for life, for God's gifts, for the fulfillment of everyone. For the blessing of a singularly magnificent voice, the hard work that developed it, the first teacher, Sr. Mary Joseph, who encouraged it in a Camden classroom.

Near and dear to me and to you is the hope that the latent talent in the Camden children of Sacred Heart might be fostered too and not lost forever. Who knows what possibilities lie behind a little face poring over a page in our school. Barbara Dever's "Coming Home" concert in Colmcille was surely a great tribute to talent encouraged in a Camden classroom, fostered and later perfected…a call that calls children to come home to the best that is in them and to us to help them.

Michael Doyle

No Sound in the World Enchanted Me More
(excerpt)

I was standing below a hole in the wall
Reaching as near as my size would allow
Listening in awe to my father inside
Singing a song while milking a cow
And the hole that vented the cool evening air
Was a crack in the loft where the angels adore
'Twas the first time I heard my father in song
No sound in the world enchanted me more.

"I Still Light the Little Candle for You"

September, 1998

Hi:

I have loved a pen in my hand since I first made my mark with a burnt stick on a stone. Primitive, perhaps. Human enough, nonetheless. Not so, my father. The spade was his pen and he used one well; till quitting time on the day he died. Yet during the last seven years of his life when I first came to New Jersey, he took in hand the tiny unfamiliar tool and wrote his annual letter to me. At Christmas. One page. No small task for him. I have them all in a cherished album. His news was of children and cows. A neighbor "gone up the road." God rest her! Towards the end of the letter—the part I always looked for—"I still light the little candle for you." That he did. Lit six penny candles after Mass in Arva, one for each of his five children and one for my mother and himself. Women usually did this little ritual. Men seldom. He did it every Sunday.

I went into the church called Sacred Heart in Arva, County Cavan. On September 2nd. I found the same candle stand he used and lit my candles. Ten pence each now. I lit one for the children of Sacred Heart and prayed for them as he prayed for me. God save them! You alone know what lies ahead for each one of them. Tiny lights these candles are against the darkness of all the evil that exists…but then all the darkness in the world cannot extinguish the smallest candle ever made.

Tiny lamps were big lights in the pre-electric rural world I grew up in. And lamp light in a distant window was great consolation against the vivid imagination of a twelve-year-old Michael Doyle cautiously walking home through pitch dark fields in the dead of night. I grew up with bonfires on hills in May and June lit to the lingering traces of times when people were tuned to pre-christian gods of crops and cattle or the solstice dawning of the day.

I read recently that Michael Collins speaking at the village of Ballinalee in my native North Longford mentioned our highest hill (Cairnhill) "where the beacon fires were lighted when the French landed in Killala." That was in 1798 when the Irish, inspired by the American Revolution of '76 and the French Revolution of '89, rose in rebellion against the colonizing might of the British Empire. The Irish with help from France that was too little and too late were finally crushed by the British in the nearby village of Ballinamuck. It was my grandmother's village and her grandfather had vivid stories of that terrible day of slaughter. September 8th, 1798. Thomas Flanagan's novel, now in film, tells the story in *The Year of the French*.

For the first week of this September the people gathered in Ballinamuck for a c entenary remembrance. It was a week of prayer and song, dance and story and a reenactment of the battle (not a good idea) on Saturday, September 5th, and the opening of a Peace Garden. In the garden, there is a granite monument which has a dove on top with an olive branch. On the front, wheat growing up through broken swords and pikes. I went there on September 1st and listened to a competition of story tellers (that's a battle I like). At the end of it, I was asked to sing. Refusing with the plea that "these people should not be afflicted so," I, thinking of my grandmother, got up and recited a poem that I wrote for the remembrance: "A Lament for Ballinamuck."

Afterwards Liam Clancy and Robbie O'Connell came to sing and play till three o'clock in the morning. Pausing, of course, to cool their pipes with a hearty taste of Arthur Guiness. Both had performed in separate concerts for the Heart of Camden Housing, and they sang a song at Ballinamuck in honor of Sacred Heart and praised the work in Camden. Small world! A lovely link on a happy evening.

Speaking of links! The British Army of 1798 that lined up against the small combined forces of French and Irish were 30,000; 15,000 under General Gerard Lake in Ballinamuck, and 15,000 in nearby support under Viceroy Cornwallis. The French and Irish together, less than 2,000. The French immediately surrendered and were given safe passage back to France. The Irish got no such chance—500 were slaughtered in a bog. And hundreds taken prisoner were hanged in the small towns of Longford and Leitrim by command of Cornwallis and Lake. Both were English commanders in the American Revolutionary war. Both surrendered at Yorktown, Virginia, in 1781. Both were given the freedom to go home by George Washington, and thus they made their way to Ballinamuck to slaughter prisoners there. One can only lament:

> *Now the eyes of dawn are opening, and weeping makes them red*
> *And a clinging mist has veiled the pallor in the faces of the dead.*
> *The little birds of Ballinamuck have flown in fear away.*
> *The robin's breast is dripping wet where she touched the reddened clay*
> *And no note or song of morning rose to greet the starting day*
> *"Mo bhron, mo bhron, 's trocaire De"[1] was all anyone could say.*

Mounds in Ballinamuck and local towns rise over the places where the young bodies were heaped and covered, and parents never knew where they lay.

> *How many wide-eyed youths since the Rising back in May*
> *Were heaped in holes together with no blessing on the clay,*
> *Or desecrated on the field in the madness of the fray.*
> *"Mo bhron, mo bhron, 's trocaire De" was all anyone could say.*

This letter has wandered far (like children do) from the tiny candle light with which it began. But that little light has the reach of the heart, the plea of the soul to God, the prayer of my father to save the children on the twisting road that lies before them when those different drummers pound their sound upon the world.

Michael Doyle

---

[1] Irish: "My sorrow, my sorrow, o mercy of God."

A Tom Gaudette Doesn't Die

October, 1998

Hi:

An "ill wind" laden with unbearable odors still blows in over our beloved Sacred Heart area from the massive county sewage plant nearby. Yet it was this stink that stirred people to life and gave birth to community organizing in Camden, NJ, 18 years ago.

And thus it was that a small book entitled *Reveille for Radicals* got to Sacred Heart. In it was the trumpet call of Saul Alinsky (1909-1972) announcing that the only way to make genuine democracy work, indeed the only way to live, is to organize people and empower them to run and continue to try to run their own lives and communities. "The pursuit of happiness is never ending," he said, because "the happiness lies in the pursuit."

His own pursuit began in streets of poverty and crime where Sarah and Benjamin Alinsky, Jewish immigrants from Russia, brought up their only son in what he termed a "slum within a slum" in Chicago. He studied criminology at the University of Chicago, investigating the Capone gang in the streets and inmate life in Joliet State Prison. He realized early that poverty breeds crime, that prisons make it worse and the only solution is to organize the poor and the weak to fight for their rights and establish their dignity. It is all about power. He began in Back of Yards, a West Side slum in Chicago, learned as he went along, and started the magnificent movement of Community Organizing in this country and far beyond. His Industrial Areas Foundation is still flourishing.

People like Kathleen O'Toole, who saw our start at community organizing in 1980, came to share it. Then Steve Honeyman, who guided the birth of Camden Churches Organized for People, which today includes 18 churches and tackles housing, crime and education with the able direction of Joe Fleming. Several nationally known community organizers came to Camden: Dick Harmon, Jose Carrasco, Scott Reed, Msgr. Jack Egan, Cesar Chavez, and the great Tom Gaudette.

My mind was on all these links as the jet eased in over Midway Airport. Chicago was Tom Gaudette to me. He was dead below. Kathleen O'Toole met me with welcome and the Gaudette home was bright as Christmas, a light in every window and smiling light on every Gaudette face I saw.

The next day, September 23, 1998, as Tom's wife Kay, their daughter and six sons, partners, and children took their places at his funeral in Christ the King Church.

Msgr. Jack Egan, a priest for 55 years, led the Mass. He had asked Alinsky to hire Tom in 1961, and Tom with Kay's blessing began to work for him. He was 38, with a business degree from Boston College, a good job and six children, and he went into community organizing at half the salary he was making, and God bless him, dedicated his life totally to it. Like Alinsky he became a great community organizer in Chicago, training many who are doing the work today, and later guided many organizers across the country.

"Tom Gaudette was an angry man in the finest sense," said Egan. "He hated to see people get pushed around and spent most of his life trying his level best to correct the ills brought on by prejudice, discrimination, and poverty."

After Communion there were three short eulogies. Fr. John Baumann, SJ, co-founder and director of PICO, spoke with genuine gratitude to Tom who first introduced him into community organizing and continued to be a fatherly friend to him.

Then Tom's son John with wonderful ease regaled us with comments about his father and brought the first smiles of the day to every face, especially those of his family.

Now it was my own turn and a great honor it was to have one.

"One could be haunted," I said, "for saying the wrong thing at this funeral. Indeed for saying anything at Tom Gaudette's funeral. For presuming that Tom Gaudette would ever have a funeral. A Tom Gaudette doesn't die."

Then I mentioned Seamus Heaney's poem *From the Republic of Conscience*. "In honor of Tom I am not going to read it. Go to the library! Find it and read it for him."

I went on. "Word from Heaven this morning is that Tom Gaudette has arrived and things got interesting right away. He almost got into an argument with Jesus. Listen:

Says Tom, "I waited my whole life to challenge your overuse of the word sheep. That's right, sheep. Like: Feed my lambs, feed my sheep. Or my sheep follow me, etc. It's not good organizing."

"Wait a minute, Tom!" says Jesus. "What should I have said, 'Feed my cubs? Feed my lions!' People were not familiar with lions. You start where people are. More than anyone, you know that. Tom, look at the people I organized and had others organize. Peter, Paul – no pushovers. Look at the names of your children: Mary, Tom, Francis, Paul, Daniel, James, John. My people. Look at what my people did. Some sheep, Tom!!"

"By the way," says Tom, "where's Alinsky?"

"He was here. He'll be back. Eternal rest was too much for him."

"But where is he?"

Jesus smiled.

"Don't tell me!"

"Yes," says Jesus, "he's organizing down below."

"'Noooo,' says Tom, his lips protruding. "How is he doing at it?'

"Well," says Jesus, "he got a batch up here but then some of the folks who were here left when they saw who was coming in."

"O God," says Tom, "this is great. This is Heaven!!!"

That's Tom Gaudette! He knew that all ill winds, indeed the worst winds in the world, can be changed into a breath of fresh air.

Michael Doyle

"A Warm Man Full of Fire"

November 11, 1998

Hi:

In November 1982 my friend Daniel Berrigan, SJ, wrote an article on this city entitled "A Showcase of Sorrow." It was published in *U.S. Catholic* and it had this to say about Sacred Heart. "It's a matter of not giving up, not folding, not going under. Keeping a school going, a liturgy going, a community going. An only hope. Saying to others—teachers, lawyers, doctors—come, lend a hand. Sitting down with the mayor, sitting down with the poor. You put an extra leaf in the table. And somehow there's enough (though barely). Enough eucharist, enough soup, enough shelter (enough? barely). Bare bones. Survival. Also, you live at the bottom. Where people are forced to live, you choose to live." Berrigan put a question mark after these words on Camden, "But this city?" It was not a question. It was a cry. A *cri de coeur.* A cry of the heart. "Take one rutted, gutted boarded-up building, a row house staring blindly out of its sockets—at what? Another row house, gutted, rutted, boarded up—. Everything 'former'; you should have seen us once; why, we made everything, from pens to battleships." Too many battleships were made and not enough lifeboats for those going under and now the pens are describing the city as a "Showcase of Sorrow."

It's November again. Sixteen years have passed since Dan penned his poignant picture of Walt Whitman's city. And in spite of magnificent work against great obstacles by non-profit housing groups like the Heart of Camden, St. Joseph's Carpenter Society and other efforts, there are still 3,000 abandoned "rutted, gutted boarded-up buildings" in this city.

Of all the structures still being used, 46% do not pay taxes. According to a city official, the total property tax income received for 1997 was twenty million dollars. The budget was over a hundred million. And 55% of all of it went for the police force and fire department. We had plenty of fires and 44 murders among our 85,000 inhabitants. We were over eighty million dollars short for city expenses and hadn't a penny for a pencil in our school system. Public education cost an extra 225 million. The State pays most of the three hundred million dollars that is our annual deficit, the County some of it, but then because we are debtors on our knees, we are forced to accept all the local "unwantables" in real estate, USA. Every ugly industry in a national pattern of environmental and racial injustice. Something to ponder: It costs roughly the same amount to keep a prisoner in Camden's state prison as it does to keep a student in Princeton.

Our "Showcase of Sorrow" is in reality a cruel consequence of success. The country's priorities are far from the notion of urban transformation. You could hardly blame us if, while we salute the recent space mission of John Glenn and the six "unknowns", we still think that the glow in the deep brown eyes of a Camden child is far more important than the sight of any galaxy in the universe.

The Christmas story readying itself for yet another telling will show us a star bending its rays and bowing its luster before the holy child's face in a food trough.

And then there is the weapons industry. Dan Berrigan relates to that. He knows that the Camden child could teach the proud missile makers great lessons. "Take my hand" the little Camden child says, "and walk with me. Walk my streets to school. Will your bombs save me? If you want to defend me, come and live on my block. Maybe you are afraid "

Dan has always connected the waste on the weapons of massive destruction with the neglect of poor children. He has written brilliantly and spoken eloquently in prose and poetry and is always able to mix the marrow nicking edge of his words with the softer musings of his mischievous nature. Playing all the while and deadly serious all the time. That's Dan.

I went to Fordham University on October 16, with my friends John McNamee of Philadelphia and Bob and Aileen McGovern of Narberth, PA, when Dan was presented with the Campion Medal of the Editorial Board of the Catholic Book Club. Dan has written more than 40 books. "They [the presenters] just got here before the undertaker," Berrigan whispered as I greeted him. Funny as ever. The proclamation for the occasion has this to say: "Daniel J. Berrigan, SJ, priest and prophet has awakened our society to the injustices that spring from the madness of nuclear proliferation as well as poverty and racism. Who can forget his dramatic protests against the war in Vietnam and the silent days and months he spent in jail writing, organizing Bible-study groups, and praying? His activities, not matter what form they take, emerge from a deep belief that all human life is sacred." If Seamus Heaney's pen is his spade, Berrigan's ballpoint is a blade that cuts to the quick of hypocrisy and opens an astonishing clarity of gospel responsibility.

Dan accepted the medal with only a word or two, the gist of which was the promise "to continue as an unrepentent felon." It was a happy evening. Besides McNamee and the McGoverns, some other "old" friends as well, Jerome and Carol Berrigan, Tom Gumbleton (auxiliary bishop of Detroit), James Carroll, Paul Mayer, Pat O'Brien—poet-priest from Mayo—all agreeing that Berrigan is still what Thomas Merton said he was: "A warm man full of fire, the right kind, and a real Jesuit."

Thank God, Dan Berrigan, the "man full of fire", continues to be the bright light that he always was. He is with us. And the poor are too. God's favorite people. With us for our salvation. I with a weaker pen have tried to tell you that they are. Twenty-four years ago today, I came to Sacred Heart. I came to tell you.

The Mass For The Acquittal Of The Camden 28
(Excerpt)

Grapes plucked from the vine and bruised in the doubt
Pressed in the pain of the long legal route.
But now, Gathered People, the flat bread is rising
Laughing and crackling and ready for breaking.
The wine is just waiting to drive us all wild
With outbursts of joy at the freedom unfurled,
In the breaking and entry of God in the world.

Michael Doyle

A Toast to Thomas Merton

December, 1998

Hi:

The word Kentucky has many meanings in the Native American language in which it is formed. The one I like is The Land of Tomorrow. There was a day that I spent in that blue grass land with Fr. John McNamee and part of it I must admit, we spent at a bar in the airport of Louisville. There we poured one shot of Kentucky bourbon, raised our glasses in a toast to Thomas Merton and talked endlessly as if there was no tomorrow.

We had flown to Louisville and motored to the Trappist monastery of Our Lady of Gethsemani on December 10, 1988, 47 years exactly after Thomas Merton had entered that monastery on December 10, 1941, and 20 years after he died, on December 10, 1968.

I had asked John to accompany me on this pilgrimage to Gethsemani because I wanted to place Merton's icon on his grave, the original one for Holy Thomas that Robert Lentz had created and Sacred Heart parish had commissioned in 1986 to celebrate its 100th Anniversary. There is a tradition that an icon should be placed on the grave of the one whose face luminously emanates from it. No tradition yet for bourbon on the side, although John and I had a slug of Jameson in the cemetery where we laid Dorothy Day's icon by her tombstone one cold wet day on Staten Island. Merton himself would have had a beer and Dorothy probably a fresh cup of coffee. But both of them, who became the two greatest U.S. Catholics of this century, could in younger and wilder days down their share of what the Irish call *uisce beatha* (literally, water of life).

Now the years have slid down the throat of time (gulped) since that good day in Gethsemani with John and Trappists Br. Patrick Hart and Fr. Matt Kelty, dear friends of Merton, and several others in memorable hospitality. So this December 10, 1998, is the 30th year since the most famous monk in the world was killed by a faulty fan in Bangkok. 1968. That year. Martin Luther King, Jr., on April 4th. Robert Kennedy, June 7th. Thomas Merton, on December 10th. A time of tears. Important for me too: I came to Camden.

I met Merton on the printed page in the early '50s when I read *The Seven Storey Mountain*, his best-selling autobiographical reflection, published in 1948. And in the next 20 years, what could only be described as a tidal wave of words poured from his pen, bearing life-giving seeds from his silence to be sown across the world. Nothing like it (almost 50 books) was ever seen in monastic life before and likely never will again. It was like an explosion of fire from the silent surface of the sea – a "beautiful noise" from the monastic quiet. The one, who had chosen to be tongue-tied for God, spoke in volumes to the multitudes. His interests ranged from the Desert Fathers of old to the Harlem mothers of his day. God is everywhere and Merton's mind was with God. He got around and hardly ever left the monastery. His only long trip in 27 years as a monk brought him to his death.

Bringing him to his birth in Prades, France, on January 31, 1915, was a convergence of lives. His father, Owen Merton of Welsh, English, and Scottish ancestry, came from Christchurch, New Zealand. His mother, Ruth Jenkins, with a Quaker background, was born in the U.S. They met in Paris and started life in Prades, in the Pyrenees, where his artist father went to paint. There "in the shadow of some French mountains on the borders of Spain," he wrote in the opening lines of *The Seven Storey Mountain*, "I came into the world."

The First World War was raging and many things were uncertain. Merton's young life became a burdened experience of uprootedness and sadness. When he was about a year old, the family crossed the Atlantic, a dangerous voyage in wartime, and set up life in Flushing, Long Island, and later in Douglaston, New York, where his maternal grandparents lived. He was only six, and his brother John Paul was three, when their mother died of cancer. At seven his father took him to Bermuda for three years, and then to France where he went to school. Five years later, in 1928, his father took him to England and an English public school, but on January 18, 1931, a few days before Tom's 16th birthday, his father died in London. In 1933 this bright young student visited Rome, his grandparents in New York, then returned to England and entered Cambridge University. The following year he suddenly left Cambridge for the U.S. (Mysterious reasons. Rumored that he wasn't able to face responsibility for a young woman's pregnancy) and entered Columbia University. On November 16, 1938, he was received into the Catholic Church in Corpus Christi Church in New York City. Gained an M.A. in 1939 and failed to gain acceptance into the Franciscan Order ("I had had a rather wild life," he wrote) but did secure a teaching position at the Franciscan College of St. Bonaventure. In 1941 he spent Holy Week at Gethsemani and later that year he entered the Monastery.

Thomas Merton left the world on December 10, 1941, but in many ways the world continued to knock on the door of his heart and mind. More sorrow came. In 1943, his young brother John Paul was killed in the war. But the more his soul was purified by prayer and self-sacrifice, and deepened by contemplation, the more he embraced the world with compassion – more than any cloistered monk before him. Like a mother's reach to a wayward child. He met God not only in the burning bush of his heart's desire but also in the burning issues of his day. People looked to him in admiration, from the Dalai Lama to Eldridge Cleever, who said in *Soul on Ice* that no white person wrote so feelingly of Harlem as Thomas Merton. He was above all a man of peace. "It's my intention," he wrote, "to make my entire life a rejection of, a protest against, the crimes and injustice of war and political tyranny." On February 24, 1965, a madman came to Gethsemani to kill him because of his teachings. Other monks saved their famous brother.

Three years later he was killed in Bangkok at the age of 53. A great man. He wrote in early years of *The Seven Storey Mountain*, but Merton himself will always be a mountain of many storeys. Writing of him in this letter is like sending a few pebbles to my friends. But maybe you have visited the mountain and have seen for yourself.

His journey is done. We go on, stumbling. John and I missed our plane out of Louisville (my fault). We came home to Philadelphia via Atlanta (like the Magi). But we got back. To do our bit. As you do yours and gain, we hope, our place in The Land of Tomorrow.

Angels from the Ashes

January, 1999

Hi:

Strangely enough, I am aware that my mind in this first letter of the New Year 1999 is not focused on the future as it should, but still lingers on the last month of the year that is gone. The gladness and deep sadness of it. Not ready yet to get a grip on the fact that the final run is on for the finish line. The year 2000 will soon burst upon our consciousness with fierce intensity.

I'm still in December, needing in the mad pace of things to savor Christmastime more—its demanding preparation and wonderful celebration at Sacred Heart. Your donations of food and prayer and money and time and gifts. Generosity and gratitude met once again in Camden, and God was born in the meeting.

On the cosmic level, light leaped to its agile feet as the increasing darkness crept in to kill it. Over in Ireland the first rays of the rising sun on December 21 shone through a hole in a hill at Newgrange, County Meath, and lit up a 60-foot passage to the oldest room in the world where it beamed on stone basins for the ashes of the dead. It has been doing this for 5,000 years, but only at that solstice time and only if the dark clouds clear.

I was glad to hear that they cleared this year and so the ancient tomb was touched by the sunlight on the shortest day of the year. The light kissed the darkness and woke it up at the deep dark core of death.

Here at Sacred Heart the clouds didn't clear as easily. Two of our most wonderful women died in December. Both up in years, both strong and good. Time, relentless as ever, stole the last sweet light from their eyes, which had so often blessed our own. Rose Pritchard, whom you met in my letter of October 1997 (when her house burned), and Dorothy Harrington, who lived in the same south section of Camden as Rose, 8th and 9th Streets near the railroad, in Sweet Potato Hill.

I went twice to New St. Mary's Cemetery, to the old apple orchard in Bellmawr, NJ, that has become a field of stones without branch or blossom. The first time I went, the winter sun was slanting low across them as a young boy walked slowly with a big cross in his hands. Behind him, his father (Rose's nephew) carried her ashes in a small off-white box. The rest of us followed. We stopped and the box was laid over a hole in the earth that was hardly big enough to hold a lilac or rose or any little bush for the planting. The awesome diminishment of death. Rose's ashes lighter than any dozen of the 500 eggs she decorated for our Easters these many years. Lighter than any of the countless cakes she made for us; weighing in light as her angels and kings of lace and *papier mâché* for all our Christmases. Her friend Sr. Rosemarie Kolmer placed three soft open roses on the box, and the holy water falling from a sprig of evergreen clung to the petals like tears on a young face. Wisps of incense whipped by the wind enveloped the box from a clay pot in front of it. All the while I mumbled on with the prayers. At some point a slight thud broke in—the pot cracked under the leaping incense. The vessel of clay could no longer hold her spirit. Ashes to Easter on a cold winter's day in a graveyard. Rose had lifted into glory.

Five days later, with her Irish rosary beads in her hands, with which she had blessed her body repeatedly in the last hours, Dorothy Harrington died. She was 87. Her life was hard work and prayer, fortitude and the birthing of 11 children between 1931 and 1950, nine of whom she raised to adulthood. Another valiant woman of the many I miss in the pews of Sacred Heart. When I told Dorothy's story and some of the hardships that burdened it, a friend said, "Angela's Ashes." I was quick to say, "I don't like that book." Oh, I marvel at the brilliance of the writing but I lament the exaggeration and unfairness that were deemed necessary to market an Irish mother.

But back to Dorothy and a bit of her story about fire and water and the ashes of an outhouse when she brought forth life upon the world. The birth of her 11th child whom she would call Peter Paul to celebrate her survival by "robbing Peter to pay Paul." April 11, it was, 1950. Dorothy went into labor pain in her home in South Camden. Her husband was in no pain. Dorothy had married the iceman in 1930, and when the iceman cometh, he sometimes bringeth more than the ice. (But Joe was a good man most of the time.) At this time Dorothy was sweating. There was no gas in the cylinder and no firewood for the pot-bellied stoves. Outside, her second son Frank (age 17) grabbed bricks and made a fireplace for his mother's two galvanized wash basins. Then he chopped down the outhouse and built a fire to heat water for his laboring mother. A neighbor woman came. Peter Paul came. All were washed in the warm water. The outhouse was in ashes. The father was sleeping. The baby was breathing. His mother was feeding and God was smiling upon the world. That's why it's hard right now for me to look forward without looking backward at these two valiant women of Sacred Heart.

Finally, as we enter 1999, I ask Rose and Dorothy who have entered eternal light, to bless you with the hope that always sustained them—to see gains lift out of losses and angels arise from the ashes of the earth.

Michael Doyle

A Half Ploughed Field

I love to feast my eyes upon
The rare beauty of a half-ploughed field
Bare breasted land with a grass skirt on
Eager for the wetness in the soft dew of night
Half hoping for a seed from the shadow of the sky
And the first kiss of light as dawn comes by.

Will It Ever Be "Wonderful Here?"

February, 1999

Hi:

In January 1983 Harry Reasoner and CBS' *60 Minutes* came to Sacred Heart and produced a segment that aired on March 20 entitled "Michael Doyle's Camden." It criticized the powerful forces that placed all Camden County's 'unwantables,' things that depress real estate values and profit, among the poor people of Camden. For example, 46 sewer plants were shut down in Camden County and now all that sewage with its horrific odors flows into Camden City. We have the garbage incinerator, plus prisons, *et cetera, et cetera*. It was not a pleasant picture that beamed to the nation in 1983, but it was a true one.

Most of the blame for conditions inside the city was placed on raw power and indifference outside it. After the broadcast, many local movers and shakers reacted angrily. Today most of the very vocal ones have long since left the city and some who represented the corporate sector have not only left but their industries have left, too. The piece itself was criticized as being too subjective. Maybe it was. It did, however, win an Emmy.

Among the many pictures of Camden that flashed across the screen, from the happy ceremony of Mamie Eisenhower "christening" the *Savannah* (the first nuclear-powered cargo and passenger ship in the world) at the nearby shipyard in July, 1959 before 15,000 people, to the heartbreaking scenes of urban desolation that scarred the face of Camden in 1983, were these words: "For Ash Wednesday, Harry Reasoner," I said, "For Ash Wednesday I would like to get this dirt that they say is Camden and just put that on the foreheads of this society and say: THINK! Why is this place the way it is?"

The years have gone by. Many faces of the elderly that *60 Minutes* filmed at Mass in Sacred Heart are gone today and so are the factories of Campbell Soup and R.C.A. that Harry Reasoner described as "going strong."

Now it's Ash Wednesday 1999, the last one before the bells ring for the heart-pounding realization of 2000 A.D. On February 17, with only 318 days to go before the cosmic silence shatters, we gathered at Sacred Heart and put ashes on our foreheads. Not for us the clean easy ashes of last year's burned palm! NO! We went out and brought back some of the ashes of a burned-out building. Plenty of them nearby; more than 3,000 abandoned homes pockmark the face of this once-thriving city, many of them incinerated shells. Looking over a list of some of the fires that blackened these skies across many years is like calling ghosts from the embers of the way we were. In 1856 the ferryboat *New Jersey* burned while crossing the Delaware and fifty people died. The Miller-Rittenhouse licorice factory on Jefferson Street burned in 1902. The shipping department of Victor Talking Machine in 1904. Mickle Street Armory in 1906 (three firemen died). The Y.M.C.A. in 1932. The huge Hollingshead Factory in 1940 (10 people died). The Linden Baptist church in 1953. Camden Catholic High School in 1960. In the riots of 1971, Broadway went up in flames. Over the past 30 years numerous fires have consumed homes and blocks and businesses, killing scores of people, many of them children. The saddest duty of my life was entering a morgue in 1971 to identify Joe McCann and his five little children. All killed by fire in their home. Fire is a frequent cruel killer in urban poverty.

The dust of the palm is hardly enough for an Ash Wednesday in Camden. It does call us to repent our broken promises, but the ashes of Camden, in a deep and organic way, portray the broken promise of the nation of which we are all a part. As I often say, Camden is the best visual aid in America for what has gone wrong and is still going wrong. The victim of the progress. The sorrow in the success. The starvation in the surplus.

Many of those who came to Sacred Heart for ashes care about Camden. It's not easy to care enough. The *60 Minutes* piece proclaimed that if "Jesus cried over Jerusalem, he would scream over Camden." But wearing the ashes of its ruins in faith is a cry for its transformation, for our transformation, for resurrection of life from death. A little African-American girl came into Sacred Heart Church today for the first time…..walking in front of her mother. She paused, looked around at the newly renovated church, and lifted up her little six-year-old arms. Then, loudly and in sheer delight, said "Oh, it's wonderful here."

Each November we remember the dead in a special way at Mass in Sacred Heart and on the last Sunday of that month of memories, light a candle for each one who fell in the annual slaughter of our city. The name, the age, the weapon…39 from November '97 to November '98 murdered in this town of 85,000 people. Blood on whose hands! I'm not sure. But ashes on our heads is good. It is a start. A realization. A cry to God to change our hearts. To change the national direction. I wish I could put some Camden ashes on the forehead of our current President. On July 17, 1992, 15 hours after he was nominated in New York, William Jefferson Clinton made his first stop on his journey to the White House. It was in Camden. Chances are, he's never thought of it since. (Did I read that he likes Walt Whitman's *Leaves of Grass*?) Yet, in the past seven years, perhaps 250 citizens have been murdered in this little urban concentration of poverty. Strange words these are in times of economic success and national surplus. Political questions and disagreements are now arising as to what to do with it. The military will certainly get more. It has too much. Drug enforcement will get more. It will get nowhere. Social Security will be strengthened and it should.

But the Camdens of this nation! The urban and rural wastelands of poverty where so many citizens are killed. What of them! Thank God our young people are not dying on frontiers or front lines far away. But they are dying on the back alleys of urban America.

I am writing this in church with a rough, blackened thumb from daubing ashes on foreheads, black and white and brown, calling to you to focus your faith on the ashes of Camden as we move on towards this great millennium of time. Pray that America will come to the front lines of our cities to protect our children, not with guns, but with hammers and saws and jobs and tools of transformation.

O God, grant that someday the ashes will be washed from the face of our city, that it will be rebuilt and renewed, that little Camden children will look at it as God always willed they would, raise their little arms in sheer delight and say, "It's wonderful here."

Michael Doyle

It's a Heifer

March, 1999

Hi:

Sacred Heart's computer does not say "You've Got Mail." However, it does post the message clearly that mail has arrived. Then comes the date, the time, the title. It's the title that often amuses me. Like my last one: "It's a Heifer." I knew right away that it was not a diocesan document. (Why does bull come to mind?) How many parishes in the world ever get an e-mail entitled, "It's a Heifer"? Somehow, "It's a Ewe," might have been more pastoral. The message was from Ireland. News from the farm I was born on … a cow calved. She had a female calf. A heifer. Both well. All is well. The female's arrival is good news because milk is still profitable there whereas a male's beef is not – because of the collapse of the Russian market. Chances are you didn't know that. Now you do. Anyway it's "the music of what happens," which in ancient Ireland was the best music in the world.

And computers are, on a personal level, sharing that music around the globe. Isn't it wonderful to have the technology that can connect delightedly and inexpensively the "music" of a cow calving in Ireland to a priest contemplating in Camden.

Contemplating Spring! "Nothing is so beautiful as Spring," wrote Gerard Manley Hopkins. Everyone should have memorable spots of meetings with Spring … romantic or nostalgic places of contact with her. Places where something happened. Love blossomed, sorrow maybe, joy … and forever changed the scene. I love to see the chestnut trees come back to life in Camden's Evergreen Cemetery. (Am I Irish, or what?) Also there, is the corner where the babies' graves lie beneath the leaves. I love to see the infancy of grass in every crack and opening. I will always remember dear Josephine Lagocki of Camden's Sweet Potato Hill who had her first heart attack "raking leaves off the crocus" in her garden. And there was my friend Nick Virgilio, the haiku poet. Gone too. He puts it inimitably,

> *my spring love affair*
> *the old upright Remington*
> *wears a new ribbon.*

Indeed, the music of Spring calls creation to do that cosmic dance. From the roaring plunge of the breaking glacier to the melting eave on the nearest flower patch. Waking hibernations and migration preparations. The huge hormonal energy of the earth. The heifer calf gulping her first breath and the eight-ton baby blue whale suckling on her mother – a substantial cow more than a hundred feet long. (I'm a long way out to sea now.)

Back to the land. I want to go back to Spring there and place my smaller stride in my grandfather's footsteps and walk with him, smell the Spring with him, engage it intimately as he did in the earth that he loved. Spring for us began on February 1ˢᵗ. Celtic Spring. Now, the feast of St. Brigid, the matron of land and cows and big blessings upon them. Believe it or not, I was many years in this country before I realized that Spring began on March 21ˢᵗ. For me it was Feb. 1ˢᵗ. *Imbolg* time in the Celtic calendar, which in the words of Michael Drumm, "was a festival of springtime celebrating the start of tilling, the birth of lambs and the return of fishermen to the sea." It was the time for my grandfather to go to Farrel McKeon's forge. A place of fire and smoke, of talk and smells, an old thatched temple of rustic rites for Spring. Mad hot shoes, newly forged, burned into horse and donkey hooves. Farrel would shear the shaggy winter hair off the horses and:

> *Clean slate grey skin appears*
> *Straight-edged along the belly side*
> *Ready for the stretch of link on link*
> *The tension of the tow*
> *When earth in some ancient foreplay*
> *Resists the penetration of the plough*
> *And yet oozes eager invitation to the Spring.*

Spring is a call to us to sharpen our wits and shear off the shaggy clutter that encumbers us. A call to find our cutting edge in the fire of the spirit. To go for it … go for genuine involvement in something wholesome for the good of others. Make a start. Begin again as the earth begins again in the great rhythm of life.

The sadness of autumn's falling leaves always reminds me that many will never see the great greening of the earth again (St. Patrick's Day, too). None of us can be sure. So every time we see it, we should rejoice. Thanks be to God!

We should rejoice in every sign of life we see in daily bread and breath … even an announcement of a cow's new calf (with all her software in place) on Gateway EV 700.

Happy Spring! Happy Easter! May we all pass over into life that will never cease…Spring without end. Amen.

Michael Doyle

The Sweetness of Love

I saw a shy brown heifer one morning
Bending over and licking her young
Replacing the cut cord that tied them
With the long red touch of her tongue
Tasting herself in the wetness
Nature's grease when the going was good
And meeting the stir that was in her
After pressing as hard as she could
Feeling two little nozzles of breathing
Kissing the breath in her own
Urging blood and energy flowing
To muscles and sinews and bones
The mystery of instinct's directions
Insists that the twosome should meet

The rub and shove of the licking
Brings the wee one up on its feet
The hind legs are limp underneath him
Like the last of the top in a spin
And suddenly up on the front ones
He sways like a swing in the wind
But slowly unsteadily onward
As if he was staggering by
Then his head slides into the hollow
Where her udder hangs under her thigh
And his mouth opens up to the milking
That heaven alone could have sent
The sweetness of love comes upon him
And he drinks to his heart's content.

Ferdinand Baraldi

April, 1999

Hi:

Too much hot air can cause trouble when it meets the cold. For this reason, the Capitol building in Washington, DC, has had its share of storms. Inside and outside. On October 18, 1990, a huge thunderstorm walloped the great dome and the subsequent downpour overflowed the gutters, ran down the paintings and created puddles in the Rotunda. That got attention. A million dollars right away to investigate the cause and fix the leaks. Puddles in the Rotunda are tidal. It was discovered that the mighty cast-iron dome of the Capitol, up there since 1863, is cracked. You knew it! Corrosion in two hundred places. Thirty million dollars is the present estimate for ongoing repair. The paintings of the great Constantino Brumidi and Filippo Costaggino, who took over from him, were damaged. Nothing small about all this. But lest you think that lightweights have no clout in Washington, DC, it was also discovered that the flooding gutters that woke up the Congress were clogged completely with "twigs, feathers and bird droppings."

One phase of the restoration is the removal of twelve coats of lead-based paint. In that terrible job the nameless workers who will remove the layers will meet the nameless workers who applied them. But interest in this enormous task will bring many names to the surface for our knowledge and appreciation. One is Ferdinand Paul Baraldi, who painted many churches in Pennsylvania, New Jersey, New York, Massachusetts, and Maryland. His name is well-known to me because in 1908 he painted Sacred Heart Church in Camden and adorned its ceilings and walls with seventeen beautiful canvas paintings. For that I thank God and I also thank Ellen O'Leary.

Baraldi was born in Modena, near Bologna, Italy, around 1866 and came to the U.S. with an Italian contractor to work as a skilled young painter on the Capitol building. When the job was done he returned to his port-of-entry, Baltimore, to await the ship that would take him to Italy. In church one day he graciously offered to repair a statue of Mary of Nazareth that was badly damaged by rainwater. The pastor quickly found a roofer who, with Ferdinand, fixed the leak and then the young artist turned his attention to the statue. All went well with plaster and paint until he got to the hands. They were beyond repair. Out for a cup of coffee, he noticed the hands of the waitress who served him. Lovely. Would she? She would. She gave him her hands to model the Virgin's, and she gave him her hand to hold for the rest of his life. She married him. Three sons and a daughter, she gave him, too, and the joy of all his years. Her name was Ellen O'Leary from County Cork.

On that memorable day in Baltimore, Ferdinand and Ellen were both in the same boat. They were waiting for ships to take them back to their respective native lands. But they met and the broken hands of a statue made their unbroken bond for all their days. Instead of two separate ways on the sea going home, it was one way for them. On the train to Philadelphia for a home of their own. There they raised Paul, Albina, Lawrence Ferdinand, and Henry at 1344 Boston Avenue, near the great church of Our Lady of Mercy to which they belonged.

The children were in their teens, two nearing the end of them, when their father came over to Camden, NJ to paint a 21-year-old church called Sacred Heart. The year was 1908. He contracted with the pastor, Maurice Bric, to paint seventeen large canvas paintings (fifteen of them over sixty square feet) and glue them to the ceilings and walls of Sacred Heart. In addition he painted the whole church in a decorative and beautiful manner. All for $2900. Beauty was important to the people of this church even though they were fairly poor in 1908. Somehow they knew what Dostoevski knew so well, that "beauty will save the world."

Now, thanks be to God, the beauty that Ferdinand Baraldi brought to Sacred Heart ninety years ago, long damaged by dirt and rainwater, is being restored by Othmar Carli and Don Harle. And on April 1, 1999, four Baraldis and spouses (the oldest grandson in his 87th year) came to Camden to gaze in admiration at the paintings that their grandfather made in 1908. They knew that they themselves didn't exist because he worked on the Capitol or helped to fix a leak on a church roof in Baltimore, but because he had tried to fix the broken hands of Holy Mary. That was the moment. Into it stepped Ellen O'Leary. From it came the lives that came and will come. One of them, Henry Baraldi, was eight months old when Ferdinand died on May 2, 1921, and was waked where he had lived, at 1344 Boston Avenue in Philadelphia.

So, I suppose, it is the job of every generation to peel the grime off time and reveal the beauty beneath. Especially the beauty of stories which saves the lives of the people they enshrine. But no painting has ever renewed itself. It is vulnerable to all the accidents that can sometimes converge into a catastrophe, like thunder and rain colliding with bird droppings in a government gutter and the massive renovation it engendered.

So, today I salute Ferdinand Baraldi who reached up to paint biblical scenes on the ceilings of Sacred Heart and many other ceilings as well. I also salute him because he reached out to Ellen O'Leary and they created living "portraits" to admire them and be nourished by their meaning for many generations to come.

Michael Doyle

Flying By...
(Excerpt)

What is the purpose of these two windows
Inches 'neath this snowy cap?
That years have weathered upon my brow
Except to see and save a bit
As bees the nectar of the weeds
That will wither 'ere the winter comes
And store against the night
When petals close
And doors
And clouded eyes.
I see.
Ah yes! I see
A flower in the morning light
Growing in a crack upon the broken wall
I wonder! That's all.

Pugin's Rose

May, 1999

Hi:

There are thirty thousand people in the United States who bear the name Doyle. It is an eye-opener of a word that means "black foreigner." Some say it's a Norse name, others the name given to the black armored Danes who invaded eastern Ireland in the tenth century. A great county on the southeast coast is full of these Viking Doyles, as I discovered when I spent six years in St. Peter's Seminary run by the Diocese of Ferns, in the seaport town of Wexford.

Forty years ago, this May 31st, I was ordained a priest with fourteen other young fellows who had weathered the six years with me in Wexford. Space was limited that day in St. Peter's Chapel, an interesting edifice completed in 1840 and designed by the famous English architect Augustus Welby Pugin, who was the leader of the Gothic revival in England. (After St. Peter's he designed the Houses of Parliament in London.) Anyway, I was allowed to invite only sixteen people to the ordination. They stood with me on May 31, 1959, two parents, two sisters, two brothers, two first cousins, four aunts and four priests. Only three, a brother and a sister and a cousin are standing today.

> *The scythe above has swung its swath*
> *Roadway wide through those I love.*

Time, and surely forty years of it, would freeze shut the many eyes and smiles that blessed me. But they were all there to greet me when I came home "to say" my first Mass the next day in St. Colmcille's, County Longford, the church of my childhood. Some of them said the rosary in the pews that day, and whatever the young redheaded priest was doing at the altar was no distraction to them. But their tested faith was far more powerful than mine, then or now. I remember my next-field neighbor, Pakie Mulligan, a man I always admired, a farmer my father's age, climbing over a hedge of briars and whitethorn bushes, to kneel down in the wet lane, cap in hand, for my blessing. I wasn't fit to clean the clay from his heavy shoes. Thanks be to God I knew it. I knew it then. He and the many who knew me from the cradle, ordained me just as much as the Bishop's words in Wexford. They wept for me when I went away and I for them when I came back and saw their names chiseled in the churchyard.

Forty years have closed more than the eyes of people I knew, and "the doorways they darkened." They have closed down many seminaries in Ireland and recently Brendan Comiskey, that wonderfully gifted Bishop of Ferns, closed down St. Peter's after more than 150 years of use. I got the word in a letter from the last president, Father Oliver Doyle (that name again). The trains that carried so many black-clad lads to Wexford every year, are heading now for other destinations. But, as my mother always said, "God never closed a door without opening another one" … hopefully a better one. And as Bishop Comiskey claims, "There's nothing unusual about periods of pain in the church. They are periods of hope."

On http://indigo.ie/~ferns/index.html, his web site for his Diocese of Ferns in Wexford, the theme is "From Memory to Mission." Look back for wisdom and get strength to go forward. But alas for the time being, as far as St. Peter's is concerned, it is "from mission to memory." The chapel there will be dedicated to the memory of the many teachers and students who prayed in it and the seminarians who were ordained in it. A letter to me yesterday had a request for memorial money to save the chapel's historic window. Pugin's rose. The sun has beamed through it on bright days and barely eked through on wet ones. The rain often on it … streams of it, for 159 years.

> *Black ankle edged soutanes*
> *Covered up the clabar of our lives*
> *And we hardly saw that rose window*
> *In the early eyelid shelter of our prayer*
> *Up there in the gable wall waiting for the sun to wake it*
> *Glass stained until the light changed the panes into glory*
> *Water into wine every day it didn't rain.*
> *There under the sunflower wheel*
> *We went flat on flags one day*
> *For vows and oils and bandaged hands for Christ*
> *But arose to break the bread of battered wheat*
> *And lift a glass of sweat and blood*
> *To toast the God who made the world.*
> *So now we're told as we get old*
> *That the seminary is closed*
> *That Pugin's rose is wilting in the cold*
> *And with it we are weather beaten too*
> *Since we arose and unbound*
> *Went out to stand our ground*
> *In all the winter wind and rain.*
> *Some panes intact, some cracked, some bent*
> *Some badly broken in the storms*
> *But all radiate in a way from the outer edges*
> *Of lofty levels, or the cow tracks where we went*
> *And even from the grave where*
> *The tired pieces came apart for now*
> *We will all come back*
> *We will come with gifts of light and shadow too*
> *With stains for seminary glass*
> *With sweat and blood for glue*
> *We will come*
> *That our lives and times be as good as new*
> *When the sun has dried the rain*
> *When the rose has bloomed again.*

Thanks be to God! Forty years! Thanks and praises be to God!

Michael Doyle

The Lord God Planted a Garden in Eden . . . (Gen. 2,8)

June, 1999

Hi:

Today is Monday. In one sense it is a sun-day. It is the great solstice of the summer of 1999. I'm on Ferry Avenue, making my way to 2nd Street. I pass Camden County's "nasal-cidal" sewage plant on the left, a scrapyard on the right, a pickle factory on the left, and I'm blocked by trucks at the cocoa-bean warehouse. So I turn off to the right and then to the left and make my way. All the while I am reciting a verse or two from the "Song of the Open Road."

Afoot and lighthearted I take to the open road,
Hearty, free, the world before me leading wherever I choose.

I had Walt Whitman on my mind because I was on my way to a new garden being built in Camden. And he was, too. The Children's Garden beside the Aquarium. Just a few minutes' walk from Walt's old home on Mickle Street. And this garden, which will open on July 2, is even in its unfinished state, magnificent. Along it, on the west side, is the mile-wide flow of the Delaware. Beyond, the Philadelphia skyline smiling in the sun. To the east, the bankrupt broken city of Camden, with its cracks, its rust, and its struggling hope.

Two hundred and thirty five years ago, before this town existed, Jacob Cooper of Philadelphia advertised the sale of land here (40 acres in 167 lots) and made his pitch with the slogan, "soil fitted for gardening." There has been too much heavy trampling of the soil since then. Many years later, John James Audubon made a lengthy visit to Camden and sketched the birds along its winding dirt lanes and in its three beautiful public gardens. As time went on, expanding industry with all its indifference rolled over the gardens, and Camden lost them all. And, of course, time took the industry, too, and more.

But gardens have a home in the heart. We learned early that "the Lord God planted a garden in Eden, to the East, and put there the human being He had formed." *Genesis 2:8*. He didn't put Adam in a wasteland. And when the Savior of the world faced into the cruel cost of saving humanity, "He went forth from his disciples beyond the torrent of Cedron, where there was a garden." *John 18:2*. And there, "his sweat became as drops of blood running down upon the ground." *Luke 22:44*. Furthermore, "in the place where he was crucified, there was a garden, and in the garden a new tomb in which no one had been laid. There, they laid Jesus." *(John 20:41)* At the crack of dawn on the following Sunday, Mary of Magdala found an empty tomb and seeing Jesus, thought "he was the gardener." *John 20:15*. Until he said, "Mary." That was the great moment when life got the better of death on a Sunday morning in a garden.

Oh, gardens! They nurture the body and the spirit. They are places of life and death and cradles always of continuous civilization. Each does it in its own way from the private postage-stamp plot by a rowhouse in Camden to the 700-acre Garden of the Gods in Colorado to Nebuchadnezzar's Hanging Gardens of Babylon between the great bronze gate of Ishtar and the Euphrates River in Iraq. A wonder of the world in the fifth century B.C.

With gladness I entered the Children's Garden in Camden. Walt Whitman (John Giannotti's statue of him) had arrived on a flatbed truck from Rutgers University. Ever since John created it, the statue, with suit, boots, open shirt, hat, and a large butterfly on his hand, had no genuine home. For a while, he was in City Hall. It was no place for Walt with a butterfly on his hand. Nor, indeed, was Rutgers, where students often have butterflies on the edges of their alimentary canals. So the butterfly area in Michael Devlin's Children's Garden is a great spot for Walt to stand.

It was raining mildly as I got there – a good blessing on a garden. Walt by this time was strapped to a chain and hanging from a towering crane. Twisting ever so slightly, as a nearby carousel was being installed. Meanwhile, workmen were drilling holes in a circular concrete base, three for each of Walt's feet. "We used concrete," explained architect Tim Kearney, "because we felt that he wouldn't like a grand pedestal of granite." True enough, Whitman was all into celebrating the ordinary. But I doubt he will like the triple bolts in his soles, not with the *Song of the Open Road* in his heart. Tim and Michael showed the garden to me, with its plants and flowers, its ginkgo trees by the rocks with fastened fossils and metal dinosaurs, its fountains and small waterfalls, its bushes and Celtic stone circle, its shaped bushes to sit in and on, its educational center and cozy story-telling haven, etc. etc. Not to mention that somebody is presently raising caterpillars for the garden to be monarchs of all they survey in Whitman's little lepidopterous section.

And then, there are the ladybugs. They're coming, too. On July 2, children will release 144,000 ladybugs in the Children's Garden. So, insects beware. This is L. B. day in Camden. Here, for sure, the mind will make worlds and sprout wings to visit them. For the Greeks the symbol of the soul was a butterfly-winged girl called Psyche. And ginkgo trees swing us back over millions of years into the nearly impenetrable mists of long ago. Here young imaginations will sing the *Song of the Open Road*.

In this city I often ache at the thought that the beauty of Eden is always God's intention for the window-eyes of the children. Not the ugliness of gutted shells where homes should be. Listen to Whitman:

> *There was a child went forth every day;*
> *And the first object he looked upon, that object he became.*

Let this garden be a call to America's conscience to create a policy of urban transformation. Camden's twenty thousand children can insist, "I'm not just a caterpillar crawling on the cabbage and falling through the holes I have made. Give me a chance! Give me beauty! Because I can fly. I can fly. I can fly."

Michael Doyle

Fire in Seventeen Syllables

July, 1999

Hi:

Nick Virgilio's tombstone, 300 yards from Walt Whitman's in Camden's Harleigh Cemetery, is a slender granite podium with his most famous haiku poem carved upon it.

lily:
out of the water…
out of itself

Readings of haiku poems, those little gems of 17 syllables or less (a form developed over the centuries in Japan), are done from this podium on Nick's birthday, June 28, every year since he died 10 years ago. This year, would you believe it, three of mine were read there. You thought I wouldn't be able to yell "fire" in 17 syllables.

In 1984, I began this series of monthly musings and I have continued for 15 years. So sometimes, I repeat myself, not really myself, but a story that is worth repeating.

In November, 1970, I organized youth Masses on Sunday evenings at St. Joseph's Church in East Camden. For one of them, which focused on peace in the midst of the Vietnam War, I went to the *Courier Post* and got the names and towns of 300 people from South Jersey who had been killed in Vietnam. There were 30 from the city of Camden. All the names were typed on index cards and were given to the young people as they entered the church. After the gospel, I began reading the 300 names and as each name was called, a boy or girl stood up until all 300 were standing, standing for those who had fallen. The young people kept their index cards and hopefully remembered. The name on my card was Lawrence J. Virgilio. Time passed. My own life moved into wonderful and turbulent times of protest against the meaningless slaughter in Vietnam. But wherever I went, the card of Lawrence J. Virgilio went with me.

One day in July, 1974, when I was assistant pastor at St. Joan of Arc in Camden, I was called to the rectory office to meet an elderly couple requesting that a Mass be offered for their son. "We want it for his anniversary," she said, and began to cry. "It's seven years," he said. "Mom will never get over it." He looked at her. "My son was killed in Vietnam," she said. "That war…" Her voice trailed off and her face flooded with tears. After a moment I asked, "What was his name?" They both said it: "Lawrence J. Virgilio."

I asked them to wait. I went to my room and returned with my card. Lawrence J. Virgilio. And my story. Then we all cried.

On May 16, 1976, I wrote a letter about this meeting that was published in the *Catholic Star Herald* by the editor, Msgr. Sal Adamo. Nick Virgilio, Larry's brother, read it and called me. I had heard of him – a haiku poet in Camden – but didn't know anything about haiku. We became instant friends. He often came to Sacred Heart rectory and I heard haiku poetry six days a week whether I liked it or not. I generally did, and I certainly liked Nick. He showed off his latest haiku with the enthusiasm of a child with a new toy. He mined beauty from the miseries of life with a minimum of words that unfailingly touched our deepest emotions. A poor man wearing, as he always said, "dead men's clothes." But his index fingers hit the old Remington by the washing machine in the basement and cranked out some of the best haiku in the English language. And, indeed, the most poignant, elegaic poems for his brother Larry. I often listened to his public readings at the Walt Whitman Cultural Arts Center where, between the poems, he talked non-stop ...his early years as a radio announcer created in him a terrible fear of silent gaps whenever he was "on." Once, after reading a grieving haiku for Larry, he said, "When my brother was killed in Vietnam, the hawk died in me." He, much older than Larry, had served with the U.S. Navy. This poem in his book, *Selected Haiku,* is written in memory of his brother.

> *deep in rank grass*
> *through a bullet-riddled helmet:*
> *an unknown flower*

Nick not only grieved for his brother, who was killed on July 24, 1967, but also for his mother and father. He always felt that the Vietnam War killed them, too. Two marines came with the news. The parents were out. Two hours later, the parents returned. All the while, the soldiers waited in a car, and Nick waited inside.

> *telegram in hand,*   *the autumn wind*
> *the shadow of the marine*   *has torn the telegram and more*
> *darkens our screen door*   *from mother's hand*
>
> *on the darkened wall*   *flag-covered coffin:*
> *of my dead brother's bedroom:*   *the shadow of the bugler*
> *the dates and how tall*   *slips into the grave*
>
> *my gold star mother*   *Viet Nam monument*
> *and father hold each other*   *darkened by the autumn rain*
> *and the folded flag*   *my dead brother's name*

His father died in 1979, and his mother, her health wrecked by the loss of her son, lingered until November, 1988.

Less than two months later, on January 3, 1989, Nick died at the taping of an interview for CBS *Nightwatch* in Washington. I went with Frank Falco to a morgue in the Capital to bring his body home. The dead silence of the long journey with this man of constant energy and high voltage words overwhelmed me.

We buried him in New St. Mary's, Bellmawr, NJ on January 7, 1989. But on his birthday, we buried him again, in Harleigh. June 28, 1989. The podium on his grave, with the pond in front of it, is a place of great inspiration in Camden. I think of Nick in his "dead men's clothes," catching moments casual as caterpillars and painting wings on them with words until they fly and delight us. We could do worse than to walk with a keen eye in this dead man's shoes and sing a song to every little interesting thing that happens.

Michael Doyle

"A Little Heart Pumping Away"

August, 1999

Hi:

You met Geraldine Doyle Dobson before, the niece who farms the land I was born on …the bride on her tractor delivering the milk of her cows on the day she was wed. A recent e-mail from her fields had this to say: "Well I had my first check-up in the hospital yesterday (July 9th) and it was great. I had a scan done and saw the baby clearly; a head and a body with a little heart pumping away …ribs and organs, etc. But the cutest thing was a little hand coming up and it looked for all the world like it waved to us. You could see the fingers and then, turning over, it disappeared from the screen. It was pretty amazing. I am due on the 23rd of November. That makes me very happy as that is Granda Reilly's birthday." She entitled her message: "Waving from the Womb."

Well, Geraldine, we are waving, too. Waving welcomes to this little one and to all the wee ones on their way, waving or not waving, in every womb in the world. Our ardent wish is this: that there be enough nourishment to build these bodies of bones and brains; prayers, too, constant prayers, to build sturdy spirits to face the winds of times unknown and make it through.

As the poet, William Butler Yeats, would pray in *A Prayer for My Daughter,*

> *She can, though every face should scowl*
> *And every windy quarter howl*
> *Or every bellows burst, be happy still.*

There is a statue of Carrera marble in New Orleans that has weathered every wind since 1884. Sculptured by Alexander Doyle, it may be the first statue to honor a woman in the United States. A woman who, among many things, "built her business up to 40 cows" (more than Geraldine), Margaret Gaffney Haughery (1813-1882). She, in an unbelievable way, withstood the storms that assailed her, withstood them heroically, did good works beyond the telling and by the grace of God was "happy still."

Five miles from Geraldine's farm, Margaret Gaffney was born in a small house in Tully, near Carrigallen, County Leitrim. Her first movements were felt by her mother in 1813; her "wave" unseen in the water, so long ago. She was only five when poverty forced her parents to take three children with them and to leave three behind them, as they set sail across the ocean to Baltimore, Maryland. Their hopes to unite the family as soon as they could were dashed to pieces, when, four years later, they and a daughter were swept away by a fever. Little Margaret was an orphan at nine and soon parted from her brother whom she never saw again – not to mention the three other siblings in Ireland. A kindly neighbor (Mrs. Richards) took her in and loved her as her own.

In 1834 Margaret Gaffney was 21 and she married Charles Haughery in Baltimore, a man of fragile health who also had emigrated from Ireland. The following year the couple moved to New Orleans because of his weak lungs. But that year two horrendous epidemics of yellow fever and cholera killed 10,000 people. A baby was on the way. Charles' health did not improve and after the birth of Frances, his doctor suggested an ocean journey, so he went back to Ireland where he died shortly afterwards. At the time cholera took hundreds of babies in New Orleans and it wasn't long before baby Frances was gone to God as well.

Margaret was twenty-five. Alone. Alone again. She grieved to her heart's breaking point but somehow in her sorrow she saw beyond herself. She saw that there was no place for destitute widows and no place for orphaned children. So Margaret made room in her womb and in her heart before there was any place in New Orleans.

She got a job as a laundress at the elegant St. Charles Hotel and saved her pennies. Next was a dairy job. Those who were up early enough could see Margaret every morning in her calico dress, her shawl, her drawstring bonnet pushing a milk cart door to door in the predawn mist of New Orleans.

Eventually she met Sister Frances Regis Barrett of the Sisters of Charity and they were of one mind and heart in regards to the orphans of New Orleans. They would do something. Margaret went to work for a bakery, started a fund, saved what she could and raised money. Within a year she and Sr. Regis opened St. Theresa's Orphanage Asylum on Camp Street. It housed 160 girls. But much more was needed. Then Margaret, with her savings and a loan, bought a failing bakery and turned it into a success. It was called Margaret's Steam & Mechanical Bakery. It sold "Margaret's Bread." In fact, New Orleans called her "The Bread Woman."

Then she bought a dairy and ran it successfully, too. Her profit went to build more orphanages. She and Sr. Regis (together for 45 years) built three orphanages and a chapel and she continued to help them. When she died in 1882, her will gave everything to the orphanages of New Orleans. In her lifetime she earned and gave half a million dollars. Her aging statue is a plump apple-cheeked woman in a calico dress and shawl with her left arm around a little girl. It has a one word inscription: "Margaret" – the greatest word in New Orleans. "No one," said her obituary, "has been borne to the tomb more generally respected or greatly loved." It concluded, "Long shall we seek her likeness – long in vain."

In this story we also salute her unknown neighbor, Mrs. Richards, who took the little nine-year-old orphan into her home and into her heart. It was an investment in a child and oh, what dividends it paid in the countless saved children of New Orleans.

And so I come again to ask you to save children by sponsoring them in Sacred Heart School. They need your help and they get it every year. They are not waving from the womb but from the classroom, which is a womb in a way, to nourish our children and give them a birth into a better life. May holy Margaret of New Orleans bless the work!

And may God bless what Geraldine saw on a happy day, "a little heart pumping away." A little heart that's sacred, too.

Michael Doyle

Life Begins After Forty

Hi:

Recently, Rose Lynch, 90 now, who taught me in second grade, kissed me in Ireland and told me she prays for me every day. I told her about Sacred Heart School so that she might pray for it, too.

Today is September 3, 1999. Evening is easing in over my very first view of this earth and will, no matter what I do, steal the soft scene of the familiar fields I love and from which I was made. The fields I left, forty-six years ago today, to enter St. Peter's Seminary in Wexford. 1953. I was 18, nearer in truth to the word without the "een" than with that tacked to it. I moved away slowly against the hill of the lane – my suitcase on my bicycle – on my way to the bus. My father and mother and grandfather cried as if I was leaving home forever. I didn't think so. But they knew that from then on, I would only come home to visit. And their generations had seen cruel emigration take many away and the dear faces were never seen again once they disappeared at the bend of the lane.

On my back, for the first time, was a second-hand black clerical suit, altered to fit me by Pat Sheils of Smear, who made clothes in his cottage for three generations of Doyles. The suit belonged to my uncle, Father Patrick Doyle, who died two years before in Immaculate Conception Rectory in Jacksonville, Fla. Felled by a stroke at the age of 47 and 23 years of ministry. I will never be big enough to wear his clothes, even though I am longer at Sacred Heart than he had altogether in several parishes in Florida. No wonder my grandfather cried so much when I left, he was crying for him, too. Due to the Depression and World War II, he only saw him twice between 1927 and 1951, when he died.

In my suitcase, on my bike, was a black second-hand soutane (cassock) that would cover five feet of this body. It would be my extraordinary everyday outfit from then on – neck to ankles, it fronted more buttons than seven concertinas. Well worn, it was. It belonged to my cousin, Father Phil McGee, and my neighbor Rose Anne Mulligan cut it down to size and turned it inside-out to fit me. (Even then, I was trying to keep the best side out.) And sure enough, it covered up the "clabar" on this boy of little belongings and made him look respectable, even important. And he wasn't. To many people in Ireland, the name Phil McGee is revered enormously, and when he died suddenly in 1975 at the age of 47, too, the grief of the people in my native county was inconsolable. If I was turned inside-out half a dozen times, I would never be worthy to wear his clothes. But they were on me.

I don't know why I am giving you this first-hand account of my second-hand beginnings. I once gave my black suit to a poor alcoholic man after he died in Camden. It looked great on him in his casket and was a sobering sight for me, too. He might remember me at the throne of God.

From here on, I am rewriting this letter. It's only right for it to be second-hand. Writing on the plane. I will land in New York's Kennedy Airport later this afternoon. Forty years ago today, I landed in New York the first time. A bewildered, auburn-haired boy on September 14, 1959. Forty years ago I didn't know what I was getting into. Now, I do. I'm getting into Camden. The injustice of what has been done to it. The immensity of the brokenness of it, the little bits of hope rising from the cracks in it. The Heart of Camden Housing and others trying to fix it. The Sacred Heart School and others trying to lift it. A great place for the focus of imagination and faith and the core generosity of the American people.

Forty years! "I failed nicely," as I always say, but I will try again and try again.

At reunions in Ireland this September, I met eight of the 18 that I started with 46 years ago. Fifteen were ordained. Seven have died – four priests and three who left the seminary. All good people. Of the 11 alive, one is twice a widower and maybe will save the rest of us. Ten still in black outfits (sometimes); two in Florida; one in Lancaster; England; two in Wexford, Ireland; one in Wales; one in Longford, Ireland; one in Pitman, NJ; one in Fermanagh, Ireland, and one in Camden. We prayed for those who are gone and drank a toast to whatever time we have and the work we still will do. Parting, we went our separate ways.

This plane is nearing Newfoundland – a good name for that meditative space in the mind after 40 years on a desert road. There is a sense of new time in an old world as the millennial moment eases toward us. A fresh start to see old situations in a new way. To use old things with new purposes. That was a way of life in the world I grew up in. Once when I was visiting my grandmother's land, fifty years after she died, I came to a gap with a gate between two big ash trees. It was near the home where she raised her thirteen children. The gate was second-hand, one half made from the metal gate-like crook that held her pots over the hearth fire. The other half was the side of a wrought-iron bed. Years ago, when her children were small, there was a wooden gate there where they looked through the bars at the world beyond them.

Two Ash Trees
(excerpt)

The rains of the years never ceased
'Til the wooden gate was worn down
They lashed as well on the graveyard grass
Where her body rests beneath the ground.
Half a century since she died,
I came, a grandchild glad because
The ash trees there where they always were
A sacred gate where the old one was.
The gate-like crook from her warm hearth
Where she hung her oven to bake her bread

Was half the gate on the ash tree gap
The other half a wrought-iron bed.
I came to look where my mother looked
A child attuned to ploughs and stars
My heart a mix of joy and tears
At the worlds I saw beyond these bars.
The bed was forged in burning coals
It singed her limbs with great desire
And she conceived her children here
In a holy oven above the fire.

Forty years ago today I sailed into New York Harbor after five days on the water. Today I flew into Kennedy Airport after seven hours in the air. Back to Camden! I come back asking God for a new vision on old realities because he said, "I will make all things new."

Michael Doyle

The Gentle Annies

October 16, 1999

Hi:

I cannot write down October, 1999 without acknowledging the fact that my grandfather, Pat Doyle, eloped with his gentle Annie in October of 1899. On that happy autumn day, the leaves were turning to the shining chestnut color of her hair. The golden oats was flailed on his barn floor and ready for the mill. The hay was thatched in the haggart to be safe from the winter wind and the rain. The turf (peat) was ricked and ready to warm the hearth of the household. The potatoes dug and heaped under coverings of rushes and clay. Enough. Enough surely to sustain life till the harvest comes again. The peasant mantra of many moments in his day was "Thanks be to God!" Especially his holy harvest days were filled with constant gratitude.

Pat Doyle was nearing 25 in '99. His father, six years old in 1847, was a child of the famine (The Great Hunger) when Ireland lost one-third of its population – the greatest human casualty from hunger to any country in the known history of the world. People after this famine, feared the coming of children and did not want the young to marry. They wanted them to wait. Consequently, Pat Doyle had to elope with Annie Kiernan. They were married in St. Columcille Church, County Longford, on October 16, 1899. One hundred years ago today. God bless them.

There is no story more important for any of us than those moments, tender and unknown, when couples, millions of them, covenanted down the centuries to bear and rear the children who would carry life in sacred vessels onward ever onward to that eager awesome moment when you or I began. It would take some time to say thank you to each and every couple in the relay of the human race down to us. Without any one of them, we would never be. They kept the flame alive in spite of all the storms that assailed it.

Annie and Pat were married for eleven weeks when the church bells rang with all the hope of New Year's Day 1900. And in the infant years of this century, Annie bore three sons into the world, John, James, and Pat. But all that joy was changed, suddenly, when Annie Doyle was stricken with a heart attack and died on March 13, 1906 leaving the three little lads under five to their heart-broken father. He cried:

For Annie, his golden bride from Smear
Dead when this century was six and left
The three she bore within it, to his care.

The three boys grew up and 25 years later, all of them went by car to St. Mary's Church in the little town of Cloone, County Leitrim, and there John married Rosetta Creegan. His brother, James, was the best man. His brother, Pat, said the Mass and blessed the ring he placed upon her finger. The three brothers who lost their mother before they were five and never had a sister, brought the bride back. She was my mother.

That happy marriage was 35 years old when my father died in 1967 and his two sons led the Mass for him by the bed where he was waked... our altar an old wooden bureau that we learned later belonged to his mother. Annie Kiernan Doyle brought it with her when she came as a bride in 1899.

I have Annie on my mind. It is because my most revered friend in all the world died on October 2, 1999. Annie Fletcher McMurtrie. She was 106 years old when her great soul lifted to God on the holy Feast of the Guardian Angels. Annie Fletcher, who appeared in my letter of September, 1996, was born in Camden on January 10, 1893 and grew up in Philadelphia. She was nearing her seventh birthday when Pat Doyle eloped with his own Annie in October of 1899 and their three little boys were eight and under when Annie Fletcher eloped over the Delaware River to Camden with her teamster boy, Charlie McMurtrie. It was December 20, 1909. She was 16. Two children came quickly, John in 1911 and Susan in 1912. Four would follow 16 years later in the late twenties and early thirties. The youngest in the womb when the father died in 1934. Annie was widowed for 65 years.

> *Yet she had the lonesome winter nights*
> *When widows are young and windows cry*
> *But sunrise tenderly touched the pane.*
> *Her morning eyes were bright and dry.*

She nurtured her children with a joyous spirit and unconditional love. And over the years her children's children came and their children's children, too. A hundred and six in all came from this little temple of God that almost touched three centuries. There was a child for every year that she lived. She sang when she worked and it made the work easier. And what a worker she was, doing the laundry in the basement when she was a hundred years old. She sang to her sorrows and many she had. She sang to her children's rising for the day and to their slipping into sleep for the night. She sang *Happy Birthday* over the phone to her vast tribe and attended all their celebrations. She sang daily to the birds of the morning in praise of God. Her favorite, *The Mockingbird Song*. She sang to her son, John, on his 82nd birthday and later when he was dying, she somehow found strength to hold him – a very heavy man – in her arms, speaking to him with words of awesome tenderness.

And she told me that she holds Sacred Heart Church and Camden in her dear heart. I know she prayed for both every day. Annie walked into this Church on May 31, 1999…the doors of which first opened in 1887, six years before she was born a few blocks away. Her words, constantly spoken: "Tell them I love them with all my heart."

Not long before she died, she laid her hand on her granddaughter's body to bless the two babies growing within. Due in December, she indicated that she wouldn't be here to meet them but added, "I will walk behind them all their lives."

At her funeral, which I led in Our Lady of Mt. Carmel Church in South Philadelphia, a lone mockingbird flew around the Church during the entire Mass.

So, whether with an old bedroom bureau at a wake or a mockingbird at a funeral, these gentle Annies have a way of letting us know that all is well. They will walk behind us, lest we fall, all the days of our lives.

Michael Doyle

"Feed My Lambs"

November, 1999

Hi:

The holy Church of Sacred Heart stands on the corner of Broadway and Ferry Avenue, halfway between south Camden's two sets of exits for Route 676 and all the trucks that use them. With the trucks come the prostitutes with Wawa hours and the combination is certainly a deadly menace to our little children walking to and from school every day. Lambs in the midst of big 24 wheeler wolves on the road and hard-drug addicted women on the sidewalk.

Coming up Broadway in the first post-midnight moments of November 11, 1999 (the 25th anniversary of my coming to Sacred Heart), I pass a woman I know waiting to sell herself on the street. And I am very aware that her ultrasound scan was in my hand the day before. An echo back from the depths…an echo of life from the troubled womb in her body. The traducer had sent in the sound waves at the Osborn Clinic of Our Lady of Lourdes Hospital, Camden, and, lo and behold, unlike the dark dead silence of the seas where the planes plunged, the echoes came back announcing life. Oh, the awesome mystery of it all! Lowering the high frequency waves into the amniotic fluid (from amnos, the Greek word for lambs at yeaning time), the eager echo comes back from the deep mess below, a boy, doing well, due for birthing (yeaning in the language of the lambs) on December 27. On the holy feast of John, the beloved disciple whose only message was: *Love one another*.

And how, we ask in the wear and tear of trucks upon the tar, can any flower grow! There, where time is money. And love, too, and bodies craving for substances that wreck them. This mother's "home" an abandoned house on Chelton Avenue; no water, light or heat. No food or cup or can opener. And yet, she's nice. And a baby 40 days away. A Christmas child, innocent as an angel is. And when this little one (not her first) will be born, his mother will shut down her instincts once again. Fear will not permit a touch, a sight, or sound. The cord will be swiftly cut – the mother cut adrift again. Not free, the prisoner of drugs that strangle her. The victim of some unknown wound within.

But God sleeps in the storms, and waits the waking cry for help.

Love does not die when all else does – even in the cruel Calvaries of our time. "L" is always caught in the middle of that harsher word, violence. It is the first letter of love.

The God who stirs the amniotic fluid with a miracle of life takes His soundings of our ragged world with ultrasounds that no created ear or instrument could ever hear, and finds the buried good below and brings it up to birth. For us to see and love and serve. To feed and educate and nourish.

And so, somehow, this November letter gets around from the battered basket of a womb in Camden to a basket of food for Christmas. A thousand baskets and more. You will help. I know you will. God bless you. You always do … for the holy Lamb at yeaning time.

Michael Doyle

An Eternal Now

January, 2000

Hi:

"We observed his star at its rising and have come," (Matthew 2,2). Thus the three royal visitors announced where they got the idea to come to Jerusalem. We all get our stars in one way or another to beckon us onward to hope and salvation. Some stars flicker in unlikely places like the polluted Newton Creek in Camden, where the late, great haiku poet Nick Virgilio gazed one night and wrote this:

> *down from the stone bridge,*
> *alone in the darkness:*
> *the star in the creek*

I can only marvel at the wild goodness of God when people see twinkles in the autumn evening of my own life and, wonder of wonders, sometimes benefit from the sighting. Like the woman who came on Christmas Eve. Burdened she was by a mother near death's door, a husband out of work, and three children needing a better Christmas. Other ragged elements, too. It was easy to listen with sympathy and attention. Easy to share the wisdom of some stories and to give her turkeys and plenty of food. She felt better, thanks be to God.

Since she was not from Camden and not Catholic, I asked her why she came to Sacred Heart. "Well," she said, "the other day I put the newspaper (the *Courier-Post)* under the dog (untrained), and when I looked down, I saw your face. I lifted the paper, read the story, and here I am." Imagine that for a star in the creek! No matter what mess we're in, God can bend down and lift us up and save us. That's Christmas! With that story to tell, I preached to 500 people at Sacred Heart's last Christmas Eve Mass of 1999.

Barbara Dever, home from doing *Aida* in Vienna and *The Messiah* in Mexico, sang *Come, O Come Emmanuel* and we all joined her on the refrain, "Rejoice, Rejoice!" Nine times we sang as the big menorah was lit above the crib. And rejoice we did at the ever-deepening realization that God will save us from eternal darkness.

Our church in South Camden has had 127 Christmases in two centuries and this last one December 25, 1999 is number 128. Then the days eased quickly towards their endings and towards the end of the twentieth century. The millennial moment. (Maybe not mathematically, but certainly emotionally and psychologically.)

We have been looking forward in prayer. On the same day that Paris started its countdown (April 5, 1997) with huge electronic numbers in light, we started our countdown with a thousand days of the *Prayer for Camden*. And on New Year's Eve after Mass at 10 PM, we walked in procession to the nearby Delaware River, the great mother of the city of Philadelphia on one side and Camden on the other. A mile wide flow of 300 miles building a highway to the ends of the earth. No better image of the great mystery of time in all the world.

So we stood by the flow. Barbara Dever led us in the song she had composed for this awesome millennial realization.

In the river of time we stand
To heal the past and bless the future
In the river of time we stand.

With two minutes left in the 20th century, we moved into the familiar words of the great 13th century theologian. Thomas Aquinas' masterpiece, *Tantum Ergo*, rose above the waters. And the monstrance of Eucharistic benediction rose in blessing as the clocks of Eastern Standard Time struck the wondrous millennial moment.

A wood fire burned strongly in the metal circle of a truck wheel rim by the river. It was a bright pause in the miles and miles of an old wheel's time on the road. People warmed their hands and toasted time with sips of champagne or danced in the sand to the sounds of *Golden Slippers*. And before they left, they prayerfully poured blessed water into the river. It was their own spirit into the flow of time.

And all the while the river flowed and the time passed, but we had in a way stopped the flow to sense that there is an *eternal now* too good to pass away.

Hello, 2000! May your every moment in it be blessed abundantly.

Michael Doyle

The Millers of Rossduff
(excerpt)

The mill and wheel are gone today.
Not a stone upon a stone.
The water prattles to itself in a senile sort of way.
The Millers gone to rest as well
Without a stone to bear their name...
But their millstone discs made music once
On a cosmic gramophone
Flowed down the streams of consciousness
To seas and shores unknown.
In quiet spots I hear the hum
- When my soul steals time alone –
Of fire, wheels and water
Changing oats to flesh and bones.

Camden, 2000 – A New Symphony of Hope

February, 2000

Hi:

In a place called California where the surface sometimes cracks from pressures down below, Grace Annabelle Giacchino was born two weeks ago on February 14th. Love's fond word emerged in flesh and form on Valentine's Day, 2000. Frail. All 72 urgent ounces of her suddenly out on her own. Pulled from her moorings as Caesar was (they say) into a great wide unknown. Then air, lungs, gulps; her first sound a cry. In it, nevertheless, joy and hope.

Her mother, Jamie, "on pretty strict bed-rest" since August. Hospitalized for three weeks. No easy journey this, from the deep mysterious silence of conception to that first cry, a conscious astonishment always. Primal as the roar of a glacier breaking water in the Spring.

Over the long, uneasy ceiling-gazing months of Jamie's pregnancy, a certain anxiety weighed in on the whole Giacchino family. Surely on Michael, for his wife and this child.

But in a way, it was a good time for this creative man, this creator of music, to do the task that he alone laid upon himself. To compose a symphony of hope for Camden, NJ. To sing to this city flat on its back and pull to the surface the life that waits to be born.

One year ago, Michael Giacchino, Jr. who writes music for Dreamworks, TV drama, and some Spielberg movies, had the urge to write a piece on Camden after attending Mass at Sacred Heart. Thus came the dream to write a symphony for Camden, to sing to its start, to sing to its growth, to sing to its sorrow, to sing to its hope rising from its ashes.

He did it. Twenty-three minutes of music for *Camden 2000*. It opens with a cry of despair from the gaping window-wide mouths of Camden's 4000 abandoned buildings. Like an old forlorn mother rambling in memories, the music takes us back to beginnings: the river, the struggle to grow but alas the profit driven forces that built it would ultimately doom it.

In the second movement, one hears the shift of the shuttles and the hum of the wheels as the music celebrates one of the greatest little towns of industrial work in the world. Everything made here: Campbell's soups, Victor's records, everything from battle ships to toilet seats. The music in this movement ends with the sad sounds of "oh what happened."

In the final movement, there is a call for a new path, a new inspiration, a new commitment of resources, a new way. It calls Camden to life. Life that lives not just on market forces but on the development of human spirit that survives all forces.

By the great Mother River of our ailing city, a cry will rise from the belly of Camden like the first cry of hope that Grace Annabelle called forth in California on Valentine's Day 2000. It's the cry of every child born in this city. A cry of life. A call to act. A new hope upon the world.

Michael Doyle

A Center of Order in Our Hearts

March, 2000

Hi:

If I had it together, you would be reading this letter on St. Patrick's Day. But I haven't it together. So you may be reading these March musings on April Fools' Day and you will be thinking of me.

Today I am thinking of Fr. Frank McDermott. There's a man who has it together. But then he was born on St. Patrick's Day. March 17, 1912. On Green Street (would you believe it) in Philadelphia. Before that, he shared tight quarters in his mother's womb with his twin brother Joseph. For nine cozy months in the *City of Brotherly Love*. To this day he feels that twins are touching, hands-on people. They like physical presence. "St. Thomas, the disciple, a twin," he says, "had to have his hands on Jesus' wounds before he would believe a thing about the resurrection."

I don't know whether Frank and his twin brother made any little kicks towards entry into this world in the days that preceded St. Patrick's Day, 1912. But the sight of him on March 15, 2000, eighty-eight years later, entering Sacred Heart Church on the cedar handicap access with his aluminum walker, was a wonderful treat for me. "This church," he said, "is worth walking to from Philadelphia. There's a great sense of love here – a great sense of holiness. It makes you want to pray." He's a great church himself, with a beholder's eye for beauty and an ever ready heart to praise it.

Over lunch in the Train Station Restaurant in Gloucester with his friend Frank McGinty, he regaled us with his stories, his wisdom and his joyous spirit. His days as a teacher at "Tommy More". The Philadelphia high school that wouldn't die. Closed now for twenty-five years, this school like its patron, Saint Thomas More, (hanged and beheaded in the tower of London because he basically would not give moral approval to the machinations of Henry VIII) could not be kept down. Its alumni and their families keep it alive in cheerful and honorable memory.

"At our last alumni meeting," says Frank McDermott, "it was brought up that the only information on an unidentified man, in the Philadelphia morgue since January, was a card inscribed *'St. Thomas More High School'*." There are some things we never let go. Especially good memories.

Frank charmed us with his story of "punishing" his young student at "Tommy More" who had a detention for some infraction. "Come with me young man," he said after classes and took him to a room in the school that had a piano. "Sit down young man and I am going to play an hour of Mozart."

"Couldn't it be something popular?" pleaded the student.

"Mozart," said Frank, "is popular music!" It's beauty Frank hoped would touch his student at the depth of his being where his own beauty waited to emerge.

"Music is ordered sounds," says Frank. "Good music helps to create a center in us, a center of order in the heart. When I was twelve my mother took me to hear John McCormack in New York. I will never forget it."

McCormack, the greatest Irish singer of all time (1884-1945), created a joy among Irish immigrants in the United States that no one else could ever emulate. His concerts in the great cities (as many as seventy-four a year even while he was singing opera) ranged from beautiful arias to American Folk and the splendid songs of his homeland. He touched people deeply and created centers of inspiration in the hearts of all that heard him. And they heard him not only on the stages of three continents but also on eight hundred and sixteen recordings that he made. Most of them in Camden, New Jersey, with the Victor label on them.

It was in spring that he came every year to this city which was then a renowned recording center of the sound of music. Enrico Caruso came too. He and McCormack were men of friendship and mutual respect. As late as 1961 the *Philadelphia Inquirer* published a Hatlo cartoon that began with *"Enrico Caruso and John McCormack chance to meet on a corner in old New York."* The first drawings have Caruso rushing over to say: "Hello, John! How's the world's greatest tenor?" Response from McCormack: "Hello, Enrico…you tell me – how is the world's greatest tenor?" The cartoon continues with a traffic jam of horses and trams and many people trying to answer the question: "Who is the greatest?" Each one was the greatest depending on the accent of the speaker.

In any case it was a win-win situation for Camden's recording industry in those glory days when the century was young.

But Frank McDermott, the boy from Green Street, who lost his twin brother in the epidemic flu of 1917 when he was 5, who lost his mother when he was 15, who heard John McCormack sing in New York in 1924, who lived through the terrible Depression, two World Wars and countless lesser ones… I salute this great priest walking cheerfully in Camden at the edge of his eighty-eighth birthday. He can still touch the very center of my being with hope and high spirit and the wisdom of his wonderful words.

Listening to him reassured me, as no one had, that the new symphony *Camden 2000* which I wrote about in my last letter will help to create a "center of order" at the core of all that is going wrong here. We have made a symphony of our struggles and we will sing to our emerging hope. On May 13th. And make a recording on our hearts too in Camden, New Jersey.

After lunch, Fr. Frank taking a deep breath on a spring-like day in this millennial year said, " I feel refreshed. I wish I were 40 years younger." Now that's the spirit – the words of the twin child of St. Patrick's Day 1912 with his hands-on sense of the physical, and deep inspiration as well. He calls us to lay our hands on the wounds of Camden and trust in its total transformation. God bless you, Frank!

Touched by an Angel

April, 2000

Hi:

Recently, the *New York Times* had a story which opened with these words: "Camden, N.J., March 30 - The ills of this desperate city deepened today with the indictment of its mayor, Milton Milan, on 19 charges of corruption, ranging from laundering drug money and taking bribes from organized crime leaders, to stealing his own computer, collecting the insurance and then selling it to a naïve office volunteer for three times its worth."

Thus March 2000 ended in Camden, which the *Times* has proclaimed as "the poorest city in New Jersey and one of the poorest in the nation." And April opened. (Some say that's the meaning of the word.) It often opens to the Passover- Easter time of uneven weather in these latitudes but improves as time goes on. One is reminded of Pasternak's words : "the travail of the Resurrection."

"Travail" is a good word. It is a word of faith in a way, conveying perfectly the demanding aches and upheavals of birthing preliminaries, central pain and untidy aftermaths. But out of it, life is launched and on we go, thanks be to God. Camden, I want to think, is in travail and not in the disintegration of a terminal calamity. Easter, after all, is our annual announcement that there is hope for ashes.

I wish that the problem of Camden was only the indictment of the mayor. In all honesty, Camden is an indictment of all levels of government, federal, state, county, and city, not to mention a society that waits for the god of profit to save the children. We are a long way from genuine solutions. In the meantime, we must do our bit and trust in the Great Multiplier of short supply and the Healer of bits and pieces. We have to live in the meantime. Find meaning even in the most mean and miserable of times.

"Your life has meaning," said Fr. Eugene Walsh. It has meaning no matter what. He was often heard to say: "Jesus Christ told us two things. Your life has meaning and you'll live forever. If you get a better deal, take it."

A few days ago, I went to see a young woman, 35 years old, who more than anyone I know, gives daily pain-filled witness to Eugene Walsh's words. Her name, so dear to many people at Sacred Heart, is Mary Beth Thomas. Back again in Jefferson Hospital in Philadelphia where she has had more than seventy surgical procedures over a twenty-year period ever since the day this exceedingly bright, energetic, fifteen year old sprained her ankle running up the stairs at Haddonfield High. She was stricken with Reflex Sympathetic Distrophy, a progressive disease affecting her immune system and much more. She had meningitis three times, septic bacterial infections in her blood eight times sending her temperature to 105 degrees. She hit that burning point again only a few days ago.

It had cooled down when I saw her, cheerful as ever, on the third floor of Jefferson, thankful that she had a window to see the outside world even if it was only an old brick wall.

She always wants a window and makes one with her mind if the walls don't have one. At home in Haddonfield, she has one for her garden with the woods beyond, the birds and the twenty wild dogwoods in the Spring. Her God is "a good God." She is always very grateful for her religion and unbreakable faith. How does she cope ? "Life " she says, " is a beautiful gift." She knows her life has meaning and her pain is redemptive. She gives her daily pain that unborn babies may live. That they may have life and have it more abundantly…those at risk from disease, addiction, and especially abortion. A labor pain of prayer.

She went on excitedly to tell me about her newly found hobby of making angels when she's able. Spools for feet and ribbons and long hair fastened to the head with hot glue. "Don't leave any bald spots, Mary Beth." I said. Bald angels could disturb people who like very thin Italian spaghetti. (I made it up.)

I told her about meeting a man earlier in the day in Camden who said after a short conversation, "Are you an angel?" Mary Beth laughed. I said, "It's my accent." Not many Irish accents in Camden and Roma Downey is from Ireland, the star of *Touched by an Angel*. She is from Derry and her name is short for Rose Mary. Mary Beth likes to watch her in the TV program on Sunday evenings. Like myself, Roma is no angel but if she met Mary Beth she would know she met one. Oh, yes! The cheerful acceptance of suffering, the powerful prayers, the miracle of her enduring beautiful mind, her love of God and his holy mother, her good humor… her twenty years of pain since she was fifteen. Enough to convince anyone.

Her mother Audrey says, "by the grace of God, she turned negative into positive."

As we enter Holy Week and the travail of a bad Friday turning into a good one, we look with reverence at Mary Beth Thomas. She exemplifies the core energy, efficacy, and example we need for the mission of Sacred Heart to the City of Camden. "The ills of this desperate city," says *The Times,* "deepened today." And so did the pain and power of Mary Beth. With God's help we will turn negative into positive, ashes to Easter, and death into life!

Michael Doyle

Eight Zero Zero
(Excerpt)

Her coffin, canvas covered, dry now, her body
Reeled ashore from the bottom of the sea
Where searcher's lights and grope scraped
The bottom of every heart that loved her
Dripping in the tidal sorrow that washed
The smile from intercontinental eyes world wide.
No lifting wings we saw but a dead bird's dive
The flying womb a millstone tumbling tomb
Flight eight zero zero……down
Hope's unanchored now. Nothing holds. Zero, zero…
Oh what baptismal faith we needed
In that Long Island Sound, that unfathomable silence
To lift the water weighted dead
From the darkest depths of night.

The Sound of Music

May, 2000

Hi:

There was no music in the home I was raised in...no gramaphone, no radio, no musical instrument. The birds, of course, sang in the summer bushes of the morning and my father, John Doyle, sang to the cows he was milking in the evening. I mentioned before, that I often crept to the hole in the wall by the cow's head to listen to the sweet songs he sang.

There were other pleasing sounds in my world as well: the patter of rain on the rusting roof above my bed, the clink, clink, clink of Farrel McKeon's hammer on the old anvil in his forge, as our mare waited for new horse shoes and I waited with her for the happy ride home.

My father's song went silent in potato picking time of 1967, the eleventh of October it was. On the day before he died, unknown to him or to me, a baby's first sound was heard in his birth and this first cry, welcome in the world, was not exactly the sound of music. The baby's name, Michael Giacchino, Jr. In that same year of 1967, seven months before Michael was born in Riverside, NJ, (born by the river) and ten miles from there in Camden Catholic High School, a young sophomore starred as Mother Abbess in *The Sound of Music*. Her name today is Barbara Dever and the sound of her song has encircled the world. Two weeks ago and 33 years later, this mezzo-soprano filled the South Jersey Performing Arts Center in Camden with Mother Abbess' song, *Climb Every Mountain*. It was her encore to cap a night filled with the sound of music and song. The world premiere of the symphony, *Camden 2000*, was performed by the Haddonfield Symphony in a magnificent Concert of Hope in Camden. This 25-minute work had been recently composed by the baby of October 10, 1967, Michael Giacchino. I had asked my father, dead so long in one sense, that peasant-performer of milk-made music and song, to bless the evening. And blessed it was. Even the rain came torrentially to sound its sounds on the metal roof of the E-Centre. With thunder and lightning, God joined the orchestra for its initial musical cry of desperation for Camden's condition.

The symphony in three movements under the baton of Dan Hege took the audience of 1500 people through the story of Camden. The first movement, *Born to the River,* laments its present tragedy, and takes us back to its birth by the Delaware River. The second movement, *Made in Camden,* celebrates its astonishing rise in noisy factories and magnificent manufacture and then its gradual decline into scenes of rusting wheels and gaping holes where the windows were. The third movement named *Illumination* called our attention to the hope of a bright new path. One hundred voices of the Abundant Harvest Choir with Barbara Dever in the midst of them chanted "Fiat Lux" above the woods and the strings. These words, the first command of Creation in the chaos, "Let there be light." And, sure enough, there was light. Before each movement, Michael Doyle narrated the lines, "the poetic introduction" that Michael Giacchino, the young composer of the symphony, asked him to write:

The woman wails by the broken wall
With urban pain upon her heart
The darkness spreads its fearful veil
And turmoil rips her peace apart.

Then Campbell stirred his steaming soups
And a million wheels went round and round
As Whitman sang the whirr in words
And Victor snared the golden sounds.

O Camden, Camden, do not despair
When hope is shattered by death and doubt
Your mother is still within your reach
Her milk will heal your blistered mouth.

Let's make our sorrow into song
And put our ardent wills in tune
A symphony of hearts and hands
To restore a broken City soon.

The trees were hewn for humankind
The ore unearthed and smelted down
The birds were dazed by the constant hum
And the shifting shuttles of a factory town.

O Camden, Camden, rise up and live!
Your river-mother is always young
She'll give you birth as she did before
And break her water in the shining sun.

It was a great evening. The sounds of Camden were celebrated: the raw and the rough, the clang of broken bits in the scrap yard morgues of the City, the cry of the victim, the shouts of success, the crushing blows of demolition, the vibrant hammers of restoration. There, too, the silence of sorrow and the urge of a dreaming heart, all harmonized and lifted up in a symphony hope for Camden. The sound of music lifted our souls anew. Memories took us to the sweeping grandeur of the alpine vistas of Austria but here we lifted the awful scenes of a broken city struggling for rebirth. (There was an anvil from Camden in the percussion section of the orchestra and a hammer as well pounding out the sounds of transformation for every bent and broken bit in the fire.)

People wept. People rejoiced, rainbow-like, after a long and dreadful downpour. A millennium concert of hope was envisioned and a millennium concert of hope was realized. It was an evening of powerful inspiration calling everyone to do something to transform this City which will help to transform everyone who does something. It was a concert of practical outcome as well. The flutes became the handles of hammers, the bows the stretch of the saws to rebuild our city. A concert of inspiration and perspiration. Linking the success of the past with the pain of the present and the hope of the future. Thanks be to God! Thanks to the hard workers and happy listeners. Thanks to the Camden people who came when their city was honored. Thanks to many people, the proceeds of every ticket went to The Heart of Camden Housing for its work of urban rehabilitation.

Thanks to my dear father milking his cow who first showed me the way to lift the monotony of a dreary day into song and to the young genius, Michael Giacchino, Jr. who lifted the sad story of Camden into glorious music, to Dan Hege for pulling all the sounds into symphony and to Barbara Dever who called us again to *Climb Every Mountain* that confronts us and every obstacle in Camden. Thanks to all of them for stirring the heart of the universe with the sound of music.

Michael Doyle

"Welcome, O Life!"

June 16, 2000

Hi:

I just came back from the *Plough and the Stars*, that fine restaurant near 2ⁿᵈ and Chestnut in Philadelphia. I was invited to come at 7:30 AM to eat breakfast and listen to snatches of James Joyce's *Ulysses*. Bloomsday, it is. June 16ᵗʰ. That day was special to Joyce (1882-1941) because he and his beloved Nora Barnacle took their first stroll on Dublin's Sandymount Strand on June 16ᵗʰ, and later he chose it to be a day in the life of Leopold Bloom in *Ulysses*, a difficult book that was initially banned everywhere and now in this year 2000 is proclaimed as "the book of the century."

His picture on this special morning menu adorned four delectable choices. I picked "Crepes/Irish Pancakes. Crepes filled with strawberries, pineapple, orange and raspberries with a caramelized Irish Mist orange sauce" and good coffee. Joyce, whose life was often burdened with poverty could be dangerous if let loose with words like "caramelized Irish Mist orange sauce." He could make it explode. Nevertheless it was a tasty breakfast which I enjoyed greatly and Joyce would probably enjoy it, too. It seemed continental and he was a continental man.

He had exiled himself from all that had nourished him, his family (he was one of fifteen children, ten survived), his church, his Ireland, and then out on his own completely, he would turn in on himself and fish for a new way in the stream of his own consciousness. Not for him an encounter with old wisdom, theology, or literature. As he wrote: "April 26…Welcome, O Life! I go to encounter for the millionth time, the reality of experience and to forge in the smithy of my soul the uncreated conscience of my race." He began *Ulysses* in Trieste in 1914, worked on it for five years in Zurich and completed it in 1922.

After the "caramelized" whatever in the *Plough and the Stars* and the magnificent gibberish of James Joyce, I headed back to Camden at 9:15 AM. It was a Doyle Day in a way because I began work in Camden City for the first time on June 16, 1968. Thirty-two years ago. So today I go forth to "encounter for the millionth time, the reality of experience" in this tough town.

Back in 1968, Camden was ravelling. The country seemed to be coming apart, too. On April 1ˢᵗ, Bobby Kennedy spoke at Camden's Convention Hall, a powerful building that was torn down to build a Veterans Hospital that was never built. Three days later, Martin Luther King was murdered in Memphis. Sixty-six days later, Bobby Kennedy was murdered in Los Angeles. In Camden, he said: "The only real purpose in this world is to make some contribution toward making things better. We can do it." That same year the Democratic Convention exploded in Chicago and Thomas Merton was electrocuted in Bangkok. And God knows what else happened.

In those past thirty-two years, the country has become more prosperous and Camden has become less. But there are many people here, in many organizations, who are making "a contribution toward making things better." But, nevertheless, Camden is bankrupt with a capital B. Its taxes provide only one-fifth of the city budget and it has no city revenue for its

19,000 school children. The State is about to take it over with as much power over it as new legislation will allow. Camden is a city left behind. A car on the great train of American progress that was unhitched and the train seems to have no way of turning back and linking it up again.

So, the turning around of Camden will be the turning around of this nation. The turning around of this nation's conscience. It will be beyond solutions through corporate profit-making for a long time to come. Its deficit for city and school budgets is 325 million. But regardless of deficits, Camden must be changed into a place worthy of its children. We need a national and state urban agenda to save cities like Camden, New Jersey.

With that in mind, Camden Churches Organized for People and the Concerned Black Clergy organization filled St. Joseph's Church in East Camden on June 13th with 1200 people to call upon the State of New Jersey to adopt "a bold and creative plan" of recovery for this City.

The people prayed fervently that anyone in the State who would rise to rule our lives must bend to embrace our struggles and our vision for a new city for the children. And before 1200 witnesses, Ms. Jane Kenny, head of the Department of Community Affairs, and Speaker of the Assembly, Jack Collins, gave strong "Amens" to this vision and the where with all to accomplish it with the cooperation of the people. Wise observers warn that "they can promise you anything now that the Governor's second term is winding down." But we have been praying and working and God is not winding down. Ms. Kenny, quoting Robert Frost, said the State would take "the road less traveled." The other road went nowhere. It will make "all the difference."

They were still reading *Ulysses* when I left the *Plough and the Stars* and crossed the Ben Franklin Bridge to begin my 33rd year of work in Camden. Failing nicely I always say in case anyone wants to say badly. I came back to a housing meeting to focus again on the rebuilding of our neighborhood by The Heart of Camden.

For this city to turn around, the country has to turn away from blaming the poor. We who work with the people of Camden have been privileged and blessed and maybe each of us should say "Welcome, O Life! I go to encounter for the millionth time the reality of experience and to forge in the smithy of my soul the uncreated conscience" of my country.

Michael Doyle

The Night of the Big Wind
(Excerpt)

Did it rain on Bloomsday that year of '41
When the cruel Janus winds blew the lighthouse down?
That bright spark of Candlesmas that took in '82
And was there any star awake that dreary night
When Colum's cabin light went out as well?
We blew upon our hands in the dark of night
And cried," how short the playing time."

"In dreams I was a ship, and sail'd the boundless seas"

Walt Whitman

July, 2000

Hi:

Conor Scott is three, he says, and he is telling the truth. I baptized him when he was about five months old and he says he remembers it. Now that's stretching things. Conor loves to play in the shallow end of his parents' pool and that may be the water he is "remembering." He also loves to wrestle energetically on the floor with his father or his godfather…an amazing feat seeing that in his early days he weighed in with all the intimidating tonnage of three pounds and four ounces. He loves to wrestle with "big" words as well and when his little sailboat sank in the pool recently, he was delighted to hear his mother say that "it capsized." Some Sundays later when the priest in church was about to immerse a baby in the baptismal font, our man Conor piped up with this query: "Is he going to capsize the baby?"

In this town of Camden where hope often capsizes in the best of weather, it is good to feel the buoyancy of little children on any day. These words literally are wind in our sails.

No wonder, then, that many hearts were buoyed on Camden's waterfront by the sight of the tall ships sailing up the Delaware River on June 23rd. OpSail 2000, the event was named. I sat with friends on the river's edge in our little sliver of a park in South Camden, between a scrap yard and sewage plant and had the best view in the world. A crack of beauty it was, like a flower in a broken pavement.

Flowing past me, the great mile-wide waterway, its dark depth 46 feet below, its beginnings 200 miles north, its destination, the Atlantic Ocean, ninety miles south. It is the great Delaware, the longest, deepest fresh waterway in America, taking its name from an Englishman, the Captain General of the colony of Virginia, Lord De la Ware (an aristocratic somersault from his true name Thomas West) who tried to sail up its waters in 1610. Henry Hudson tried and failed, too, but had more success on the great river of New York State that bears his name. Cornelius Jacobson Mey sailed up the Delaware and sailed back to its mouth where Cape May recalls his efforts. The river, whose original name was Chickohocki, mothered many towns along its banks and none more important than the two that bridge to each other across it, Camden and Philadelphia. Our skyline above the sailing ships was, of course, Philadelphia, the national shrine of North America.

The hours went by faster than the river. No questions, no analysis needed. Emotions moved with the mighty Delaware and miles of flowing veins resonated with a river older than the first flow in human veins. And the same air that bulged the sails like a bagpipe, heaved in the chests of the onlookers with life and energy and maybe the makings of a song. On the way up the river these sailing ships were coming from afar….out of the dim mists of long before long ago. As far back as 6000 BC, humans were harnessing the wind to push vessels over the waters. But they could only sail where the wind went and nowhere when she wasn't with them. Thousands of years passed before the science of sailing against the wind was developed. The Phoenicians were the early masters of the art. And the world has been the better for it. Indeed, many have moved forward so well and have reached new levels of development that were only achieved because there were so many forces against them.

The tall ships arrived bearing their colors and national identities. Four to anchor in Camden, the rest in Philadelphia. They sailed elegantly into view underneath the Walt Whitman Bridge. Between their comings, I read from Whitman's *Specimen Days*. Tugs moved seriously about their business, seagulls about theirs, and a duck with five little ones in tow bending on the waves like little lumps on a string. Whitman would have loved it. He felt at home on the Delaware during his 19 years in Camden. "Then the Camden Ferry," he says. "What exhilaration, change, people, business, by day. What soothing, silent, wondrous hours, at night, crossing on the boat, most of all to myself - pacing the deck, alone, forward and aft. What communion with the waters, the air, the exquisite *chiaroscuro* – the sky and stars, that speak no word, nothing to the intellect, yet so eloquent, so communicative to the soul."

Whitman, who set out to put the whole rough-hewn North American experience into a song of itself, always celebrated the ordinary because it was extraordinary….he would surely approve of our perch by the river between a sewage plant and a scrap yard. "What communion with the waters…so eloquent, so communicative to the soul."

It was here that we stood by the river six months ago at twelve midnight as January 2000 began. Time is the flow of the water, so much has passed, and so much more has to come. There is something great about seeing a tall ship much like the Great Spirit sailing against the flow of time and tide, clarifying for us that God is not confined to the present. With God's help, water is never irrevocably over the dam and that's that. We are neither paralyzed by a past we cannot change or a future we cannot know. The Spirit of God can sail against time and tide…against the flow of everything that ever flowed and bring a new beauty to it.

It was good to be there when the tall ships came. To be there as the river flowed in front of me, Camden people watched beside me, and Whitman's vibrant words came out of me. Because Camden has three treasures that cannot be taken from it: its people, its river, and Walt Whitman. And Camden right now has to sail against the tide. Its residential taxes should be reduced to encourage new people to come and encourage long timers to stay. It needs a revolution in the opposite direction of revolutions – a temporary one. Radical surgery. It needs to hand over authority and responsibility for its transformation to the State that is rich in human and financial resources. The car has to be put in the shop until it gets a new engine and a total overhaul. Then there will be a vehicle to steer and somewhere to go. It will be hard for people to sail against the winds of prevailing political wisdom.

But life out of death is the core truth of Camden people's faith. We have to go down completely in order to rise completely or even adequately. To paraphrase little Conor's words: "This baby may have to be capsized!"

Michael Doyle

Our Smiling Treasures

August 10, 2000
(Lughnasa)

Hi:

Camden was a young city of 20 years when its largest cemetery, Evergreen, was incorporated in 1848. It was never ever-green but it is often over grown; its metal fence is mostly bent and broken and its ownership is bankrupt. Both the living and the dead are in sore financial straits in this town.

In recent years I have watched the children make their way to and from the new Riletta Cream School. They walked, God help them, on Ferry Avenue's dirt path (pavement) that runs along that broken fence. A chatter of hope, nonetheless, among the tombstones and rusting endings of things. At the intersection of Ferry and Mt. Ephraim Avenues, they pass a heartbreaking corner, twenty four hundred square feet of baby plots with tiny metal markers that often rest underneath a brown blanket of fallen leaves. It is a harvest, surely, of infant mortality rates that are way too high. *Time Magazine* in an article on this City eight years ago, speaks of "the far corner of Camden's Evergreen Cemetery…buried babies…a thicket of tin markers" and the devastating truth that "twenty babies out of every thousand born here never reach their first birthday. More than triple the national average." And those who do reach school age should not be "left behind" any longer in a town that is too unfit for their tender growing years. Often I would see the Cream School kids at risk on the street in the rain, because they could not walk on the muddy path by the graveyard. One of my millennial year dreams was to create a safe path for these children and it has been accomplished, easily I would say, by a request to County Freeholders Riletta Cream and Laurelle Cummings. So, this September, the children will walk on a new concrete pathway that is three and half feet wide and about 1,272 feet long. Safe. At least from the rage of the road and its killing consequences. I look forward to seeing them on this new path in September. They will, at times, dart in and out of the gaps in the broken graveyard fence – a sign maybe that life is not constrained by the stillness of the stones.

I remember an old song (am I that old) that played with the plea "Don't fence me in." The current promise of "no child will be left behind" does not answer the question "behind what?" It certainly does not mean behind the apartheid fence that separates a poor urban child from a better environment outside the city. After living in Camden for thirty-two years, I often claim that the fundamental school problem of our inner cities is a real estate problem. Too many poor people in one congested area and no break in the fence to share affordable housing and better educational opportunities in "Evergreen" USA. No national policy of urban transformation either and the children have only one chance to grow up.

Camden has 19,000 children in public school and one thousand in Catholic school. Sacred Heart teaches about two hundred and thirty of them and without you, it would teach none of them. Your prayers and donations keep our doors open and our lights on. Years ago there were eleven catholic schools in this city. Today there are four parish grammar schools and one new Christian Brothers School with three grades. So, the ongoing struggle to save and promote these schools for the children is a very worthy one. These 20,000 children have to live in Camden, most of their teachers, however, do not. They have the means to live elsewhere, and the right of course to do it.

As I write, all is quiet in the halls of Sacred Heart School. The only sounds are the near inaudible touches of paintbrushes on the walls and wet mops on the floors, all soft in our annual summer silence. But we are less than a month away from the "beautiful noise" of children arriving. Nothing, on wet days or dry, brightens up this old planet that we share or this old city in the mornings like the sounds of children arriving for school. They have cheered up Jasper and Fourth Streets since January 20, 1920 – the day Sacred Heart's doors first opened for class.

Standing among hundreds of children that day was Catherine Larkin of 6th Street and today, August 10, 2000, eighty years later, she sent over a pound cake for Michael Doyle because she heard "it's the only cake he likes." Like herself, it was light and right and ready to share. Catherine was nine when the Sacred Heart School began and thirteen when she graduated in 1924. And over the years this revered graduate has walked down the paths of this world with grace and dignity and the light of God at her feet. She still drives her car safely and makes pound cake perfectly.

So today I salute every one of the thousands of children who attended Sacred Heart School over the past 80 years. But especially I ask you to pray for "our children 2000." They will come from the uneasy streets of Camden. Like 4th and Emerald last night where the air was filled with the sounds of war, gun shots, the whack of baseball bats and the curses of the drug dealers. It is in these scenes that our dear Sacred Heart children are left behind. They are dear to God, too, and we together will try to save them.

Listening this morning to the story of today's (August 10th) saint, the third century martyr Lawrence, I thought of the children of Camden. Before he was burned alive, he was ordered by the Roman Prefect to hand over the most valuable treasures of the church. Lawrence presented the poor children of Rome. So to you I present our smiling treasures and ask you to be a sponsor. The new path by the broken graveyard fence is a good image of the path I want you to build beneath the children's feet. A path of light and learning to lift them up and lead them on and bring them through the fences that for now tend to keep them far behind.

Michael Doyle

Solid Ties

I look along the lines today
To where the railroad tracks are one
Then I walk spread-eagled toward the spot
But they move before I come.

So I walk again and look again
But no union shows between them
They keep their distance all the time
Yet there's solid ties beneath them.

Light in the Darkness

September 8, 2000

Hi:

There are cobwebs on the small red door in Ireland where I first walked into this world. Pink oxalis flowers in a big terracotta colored pot sit in the way. The house is entered elsewhere now and used for farmyard storage. But like any childhood place, it is the storage well of my memories where I annually come and dip to get them. Here I am on September 8, 2000, at home in County Longford, and from here I left for Camden 41 years ago today. In this old house I was conceived and borne to birth, my father too, my grandfather, my great-grandfather, my great-great-grandmother around 1810. Beyond that, it is all too misty for the eyes.

From here they were borne at the end of their days by horse and horseless wagon to the holy ground of St. Columcille in a place called Augnacliffe, the Field of the Stone. Called so, because in Mulligan's field near the churchyard, is a dolmen of four big stones holding a massive top stone of 20 tons. It has been standing there for 3000 years marking the spot where someone "of importance" (isn't everyone?) is laid to rest. "If Stones could speak." People come to marvel at it and Mulligan's fresian cows graze around it and at times scratch their hind quarters against the low levels of it. Low levels indeed.

When my father died on October 11, 1967, I had the privilege of placing the first stone, a tombstone, on our little plot of 54 square feet that is there near the Dolmen and has been holding the dust of the Doyles since 1834. It's a small stone, plane as he would want it, with celtic interlacing carvings in the corners. "Anything will do me" – the generous other-centered way that he was. But nevertheless, when his stone was finished I beheld in the granite: "October 11, 1967" – the date of his death. Carved perfectly. I had to contact my illustrious monument maker to say: "My father wouldn't care, but you have to get that second 'b' out of Octobber." He did. "If stones could speak."

No stones in Ireland can speak more than the ancient memorial arrangement of them in the Bend of the Boyne. Ah stones! I cannot help the fact that large stones enchant me and take me far from the tar and trucks of Camden. Indeed, strengthen me annually to come back to it. Their silence. Their story. Their strength to withstand the weather, whatever way it is.

The River Boyne melanders through County Meath and in one of its great loups, Neolithic peoples built extraordinary passage graves more that 5000 years ago. And no better have been found in the world. The big ones there, older than the pyramids of Egypt, with mounds an acre in size, are Newgrange, Knowth and Dowth. There are 37 smaller ones nearby and more than 200 known at this point in the rest of Ireland.

I often go to Newgrange where I walk about 60 feet on a very narrow ascending path between 43 standing stones into a cruciform chamber in the center of the hill. On the floor are three large stone basins for the ashes of the dead. There is an opening above the rock lintel of the entrance that is 40 inches wide and ten inches high but its purpose was not initially understood when excavations were done in the early sixties. By 1969, the great passage grave was restored, but what did it mean? Noting that Stonehenge in England was focused on the Summer Solstice, Professor M. J. Kelly who had for years studied and restored Newgrange, entered the passage grave on the morning of December 21, 1969 and watched for sunrise on the shortest day of the year. The Winter Solstice. That day, fortunately, no rain, no clouds. At 8:54 AM, the sun edged above the horizon about three miles away. Four minutes later, a ray of light shone through the 10 inch opening above the entrance to the tomb, and lit up the chamber 60 feet inside the hill. Lit up the stone basins where the ashes of the dead had been placed. On the day of least light, the god of those ancient peoples 5,200 years ago, touched the ashes of their dead, and most certainly, the hope of their lives. It did it for 17 minutes on five days near the Solstice and then it was gone until the following year. "If stones could speak." The waiting list to see this annual phenomenon stretches for years and a wet cloudy morning can wipe out the chance of ever personally seeing it.

But, I was thinking, no rain or cloud can wipe out your chance of seeing new understandings light up the eyes of a child. A greater miracle in the long run. An opening into worlds not known. Children learning to spell October correctly.

I have a photograph waiting to be the doorway to a new website for Sacred Heart's many ministries. A picture of a sunrise on Easter morning in Camden coming through an ugly alley, a "passage grave" of abandoned houses, to light up the Church of Sacred Heart. Like Newgrange, a radiant beam of hope.

I began this letter to you with a spider's website on an old closed doorway in Ireland and I will end it with a promise of a Sacred Heart website to the world. It will be, as with all we try to do, a light of life on the old ashes of Camden.

Michael Doyle

The Hedge School
(excerpt)

The setting sun on Dunbeggan hill
Threw the great stone's shadow prostrate
On the spot where royal bones are dust.
Still the stone stood its ground
Through nights without an end
And waited for the morning
Long before the holy women wondered
Who could move the stone.

We Fall to Fly

October, 2000

Hi:

Above a door that is always very welcoming to me in Ireland, the sign *Edelweiss* is cut in wood. It is the home of my sister, Philomena Doyle, and her husband of 33 years, Johnny O'Reilly. They built it around the time that *The Sound of Music* was urging the western world "follow every rainbow until you find your dream." So they named their dream (a home of their own) Edelweiss, the favorite flower, "small and white, clean and bright," everywhere in Austria. There in the shelter of one of Cavan's many rounded hills, it nestles comfortably. There they raised their four children who by now are up and out and on their own.

This year they had two visitors from Africa that built a nest in their low-roofed garage behind the house. A pair of swallows. They built it with mud and binding strips of dry hay, rounded it with their breasts, and lined it softly for the four little ones they hatched within it.

The coming of the swallows in late spring is a joy to everyone. They usually return by some divine navigational instinct to the place where they lived before, right to the same barn rafter or garage door after journeying over all of Africa, the Mediterranean Sea and Western Europe. Feeding on the wing, they bring the summer on their little blue-black backs to Ireland. They were the weather forecasters of my childhood days, flying low for the coming rain and high for a bright tomorrow. I remember my disappointment when I came to the "terrible" climactic conclusion that it was the low atmospheric pressure that pushed the insects down and the swallows followed. I was much happier in the childlike wonder that these angelic swallows knew it would rain tomorrow and flew low to tell me.

On September 8th this year, I arrived at *Edelweiss*. My spirits were low and the swallows were low as well. No one was home for a time, and that was good because I wanted to be alone. At 5 PM I lit a candle and set it down on a little stone in the living room. My mind was on another room in Hahnemann Hospital in Philadelphia. Not exactly a living room. There, after prayer by Fr. John McNamee and Frank McGinty, the medical life supports were removed from Frank McDermott, 88, a priest beloved to me and to many others as well. I wrote of him before (March 2000). "Pray," he said to me on the phone before I left for Ireland. "Pray that I will be worthy to meet God my Father." Indeed he is. "It will be great," he continued, "to remember the good times in this world." There will be stories for his twin brother, Joseph, who died when they were five. Stories for him about his days as a teacher of English at "Tommy More" (St. Thomas More High School in Philadelphia). All about the twin spires of his beloved Assumption Church at 11th and Spring Garden, ever pointing to heaven for both of them. How he grieved when archdiocesan officials closed it. He, the great pastor, there for 31years. The neighborhood, black and poor and Baptist, he nevertheless thought they wouldn't close it, because St. Katherine Drexel was baptized inside it. But they did, and hauled the baptismal font away.

I went outside to see the young swallows that recently had grown to nest-bursting proportions. Well! They had all been coaxed that very day to fall into their first flight in the world. It was the day we celebrate the birth of Mary of Nazareth.

> *On this day when the sacred tether severed*
> *To release the shining morning star*
> *I go from these wet and heavy fields*
> *That McDermott men ploughed before they rowed away*
> *I go in mind across the same lonesome sea*
> *To tremble now as life's artificial cords are cut*
> *This last high noon in Philadelphia.*
> *Now, Father Frank, you'll have to fly away*
> *Death the ultimate free fall, 'til confidence unfurls*
> *Those sinewed wings you made, you made so well*
> *With ever active service to the bother of the world.*
>
> *Yesterday I watched the swallows busy on the wing*
> *Searching high and low to find the flying food*
> *And feed their hungry mouthed brood*
> *But not for long will this intensive care go on*
> *The nest is weakening from the bulging growth within.*
> *The life supports will soon be cut of constant food supply*
> *As nature's course is coaxing the fearful birds to fly*
> *And Father Frank, you must let go today*
> *For your soul's nest is naught but broken clay*
> *A cosmic crack has shattered hall and windowpane*
> *Where every laugh and word and protest were proclaimed*
> *And the truth beneath the rubbish was always clearly named.*
>
> *O God of falling swallows will you take his tired hand*
> *On this new ecstatic flight over Ireland.*

Fr. Frank McDermott lived for 21 hours after all the cords were cut and then … out and up and on his way. His body was buried in Holy Cross Cemetery in Yeadon, PA. on September 13, 2000. May he rest in peace.

Frank honored me by liking these monthly letters that I send and made me promise that I would have them published. I didn't tell him that I tried and was not successful. Maybe now this revered English teacher at "Tommy More" and LaSalle College will find a way where ways are always found.

I began to write this letter when the life supports were severed in Philadelphia and the candle that I lit slowly burned down to a stone in Ireland. It was my tie to what was happening in Hahnemann. Night eased in on *Edelweiss*. The swallows settled down to sleep. The light lingered and went out. The stone was warm for a while. Then it was cold.

Michael Doyle

Falling Leaves

November 8, 2000

Hi:

There is a calendar in the Heart where memory highlights certain days with stars of joy and hope and tinges others with shadows of grief and pain. The latter for me, November 8th. Twenty-five years ago today I watched alone as two men shoveled wet clay until the grave was filled for my sister Anna Mae Doyle. A Sister of Mercy she was, and my closest friend in the world as well. Only thirty-eight years old when she was killed by an automobile three days before. If I was near enough I would go today to that little convent cemetery (three thousand miles away) where the Erne River on its way to the sea mourns past it every day.

Instead I went to Harleigh Cemetery in Camden where I often go and annually in autumn for its seasonal feasts of multicolored gifts. I went for Anna Mae. Her lovely auburn hair in every autumn leaf and tree. Her laughing eyes gone 'til some summer day … some distant summer day.

But I also went for Tom. The flowers fresh upon his grave. There since Saturday, November 4th, when we bore him to his rest as leaves and tears fell … these, the only silence amidst the graveyard chimes, the murmured prayers and the football game that roared beyond the fence in Parkside. That mix would fare well in the words of Walt Whitman – the solemn tonnage of his massive burial stones nearby; not to mention what Tom's friend, Nick Virgilio, could do with a lonesome haiku. He here, too. His slender tombstone shadowed in the pond as a heron bends breast-wards above her ghostly whiteness in the water.

Tom Gough, a dear friend for twenty years, whose career as a psychologist began before words like healing, hospital and hospitality were replaced by market, managed care and medical industry. He was let go some time ago by a Philadelphia institution after twenty-three years of service. A healer who sought out Henri Nouwen in person to guide him in his life of unsurpassed compassion. Severed. Without severance recompense or respect. He sank into a depression that overwhelmed him. On November 1st, the Feast of All Saints, Tom, unable to face the reality of taking a new job that awaited him and unable to face the reality of not taking it, instead took his life, whatever little was left of it. One is reminded of Nikos Kazantzakis in his great book *Report to Greco* where it is declared that when the old boatman Charon comes to ferry him across the Styx, there will be hardly anything left to carry. Nothing there for death to drool on.

Each of us at Sacred Heart who knew Tom had some donation of his tenderness in our inside pockets, some touch of his ever present affirmation and reverence. Several years ago he and Judy moved from Haddonfield to Goshen, New Jersey, and since then we only saw them on special occasions. A loss indeed. His last visit five days before he died weighs in on the mind now with unforgettable poignancy. October 27th. I knew that the sun rose unnoticed in these latitudes on that damp and dreary morning. I knew because on the last days of October, Sacred Heart's morning prayer group meets at 7:40 AM inside the open doors of the church. The rising sun on those days and at that time pours through the doorway and lights up the center aisle and floods the altar. On October 27th, there was no bright sun to welcome. A cold edge instead. We left the doors open nevertheless. Then the surprise! Tom Gough walked in. He had come, burdened, hoping somehow there would be prayers. His arrival brought brighter smiles than the sun.

"Tom, you are better than several suns," I said. He stayed, prayed, attended Mass, had a cup of coffee and talked to me for over an hour. Troubled. His good-byes a plea for prayers. Tender hearted as ever. I think now, too late I think, that his devastated mind was (as Greek mythology has it) on appointments with that old boatman and the other side of the river. God rest his soul!

As his casket was carried through our church doorway to Harleigh Cemetery on November 4th, the sun was there to light the three stained glass words above it with awesome clarity: *Go in Peace!* Oh, it's the light, the perpetual light that changes stained glass into glory.

So, November! Melancholy always. More so this year. Tom told me when he came that he and Judy had read my last letter the night before. "We cried together," he said. Lifelines cut. Judy will cry for this one, too. God help her!

God help her and the six they raised so well and all who grieve so painfully as they try to find their way through the coming seasons, the tender times remembered, the years that lie ahead. This letter like many I write, is a heartfelt response to "the music of what happens."

Last December on that Solstice day, December 21, Tom Gough wrote his millennium prayer on a piece of paper for Sacred Heart Church. On the back of it, *The Second Coming* by W.B. Yeats and that ominous line, "Things fall apart; the centre cannot hold."

"Lamb of God, have mercy on us," Tom prayed, "Keep us close to your Sacred Heart. Allow our broken hearts to beat always with love and compassion for all living things." On the day of least light he wrote it. That's the day it begins to increase. "Come Jesus," he continued, "Lamb of God, have mercy on us. Allow us to wake up in time – to save Camden and all the world."

It's a holy prayer. God grant its humble plea to heal times past and bless the times to come. Tom Gough and Anna Mae Doyle met in my mind as the leaves were falling in Harleigh. She, killed as she walked in the rain at night … by a car with only one windshield wiper working. He, killed on another kind of night by blind forces that ran over him. In some small way the falling leaves helped to soften the jagged edges of tragedy. God is with them when they bud to life and when they ease away and even when the storm tears them from the trees. As my grandfather often said: "It's a terrible day, thanks be to God." We are Thanksgiving People and no matter what, we always say: "Thanks be to God!"

Michael Doyle

Ploughing with the Stars

December, 2000

Hi:

I had never met Paddy o' the hill. I heard him. The sound of his shouts had shaken my little four-year-old frame even though there was a valley in Rossduff between our fields and his house on the hill. In the valley the river murmured over the stones to Lough Gowna and turned the old water wheel for McNaboe's mill on the way. Sometimes, after big rains which often came, the river rose, out of control, and tore angrily onward leaving its brown swirling force frothing on the bushes. That frightened me. But not as much as Paddy o' the hill. He roared. And the sound leaped across the hedges and landed between my toes. He roared at his long-eared ass in the oats field. Trespassing. At his cows breaking into the unmowed meadow. He roared at life and its mad rush to go wrong. And he walloped his errant animals with a litany of adjectives that left little birds fluttering anxiously in the bushes and big dogs barking at the wind.

Life (I pushed it) went downhill for me one day near the half-door when I annoyed my little sister terribly. My mother came out exasperated and said, "Go away to Paddy o' the hill's." Then she turned back into the kitchen and I turned my face toward my doom. I crossed into the next farmer's field, which had a "forest" of ferns two feet taller than my head. I headed north in the right direction for Paddy o' the hill's. I was leaving home. Going away. Alone. I knew the river was down below. There was no "kesh," as we called it, no bridge.

Maybe it was my guardian angel, who wasn't mad at me, who nudged me to turn right. So I did. Crossed the ditch into Mulligan's field and headed east. Two fields farther on, I came upon a man ploughing with two horses. He stopped his team and waited. When I came as far as him, I put my little boot on the low middle part of the plough and said, "Tie that." No "please" or "hello" or anything. After all, I was on a long journey to God-knows-where, and I couldn't tie my shoelaces. Dan Mulligan let go the handles of the plough and the reins of the horses and tied my shoe. I will never forget him. In the last years of his life I always sent a few dollars at Christmas to thank him.

My adventure had brought me into a scene of wonderful work. It was "a conspiracy," I know now, in the most literal and sacred sense of the word. The earth, the plough, the horses, the man … in an interaction of enormous consequence. An opus Dei. I hadn't read much (I remember I could spell potato). I hadn't read James Burke's *Connections,* which was published in 1978 forty years later. It states, "This simple implement (the scratch-plough by the Nile in 4000 BC) may arguably be called the most fundamental invention in the history of humanity, and the invention that brought civilization into being, because it was the instrument of surplus." Before that, people were no better than the birds, every single one picking. Every one in the hunt for food. Seeking game with an arrow or poking with a stick to sow a seed in the soil. The plough brought extra food so now people could take time and hollow out the stick and make a flute to play or draw wild animals on a rock with a chip of flint or a burned branch. Civilization was launched. The wooden ploughs got bigger and it took more oxen to pull them. People had to share oxen and so began to live closer together in permanent clusters. The primitive village. The horse took over the plough in the 9th century and agriculture expanded enormously. Another boost was horseshoes in the 11th century which made ploughing far more flexible. They were nailed painlessly to the hooves of the horses and unlike my shoes, never needed to be tied.

Now that mine were tied, I walked to the Mulligan farmhouse and informed everyone there that I had left home. No one voiced any surprise, but I was given a piece of bread. Next the rattle of a cart was heard in the lane and there was my father returning from the town. I ran to him and climbed up on the cart and rode home with him. As we neared the house, I saw my dear mother bending under a barbed-wire fence in a field and, I didn't know then, she was heavy with child. Coming back burdened after searching for me in fields of ferns and an open well below them. I had long since ceased to be bodily within her, but God help her, the labor pain of raising me had obviously not ceased at all.

More than 60 years have come and gone since that eventful day in my life. I return to it in these December musings, as Christmas 2000 nears and people try to celebrate it with great efforts at communication and expressions of good will and generosity. But at the root of it all is the celebration that an all-powerful God came down to earth. Not a bad direction for any of us, especially if we have an inflated notion of power, political, corporate, ecclesiastical or financial. So Christmas, 2000 announces an old wisdom of looking at things in a new way – a new and beautiful balance in our sense of reality. Our God, we can declare, is very down-to-earth.

My story takes me back to the ploughman Dan Mulligan, who tied my shoes. He was one of the many farming people I knew in my childhood. One of many people who with my parents helped to raise me. They were people of faith and fields and the earth's holy yield that fed their families.

They ploughed their fields when time was lea
Gathered ripened wisdom in jugs and jars
One careful eye on earth and plough
And one that looked at stars.

They had their plough in the earth and their stars in the sky. Some of those stars formed a plough in the heavens to till the endless stretches of their imagination. That their God could come down and be a baby in a furrow was no bother for them to believe. I salute them and all who stop what they are doing, bend to the needs of the children and tie up the loose ends that might trip them. I salute those who reach out to help anyone who is lost and needs to find a way to come home. Above all, I salute the woman, weighty with child, bending under the barbed wire barriers of the world in her onward effort to give new life to us all. Now, that's Christmas.

May the goodness that you are, grow into its fullness!

Michael Doyle

God Be with You in 2001

January, 2001

Hi:

The year 1885, like any period before it or after it, was a time when many things happened. I just know of three among the uncountable number that occurred. 1) Michael Creegan married Mary McKenna and from their union thirteen children were born and raised. 2) Friedrich Nietzsche, whose ideas and writings on several subjects are deeply and rightly appreciated, completed his famous book, *Also Sprach Zarathustra*, in which he proclaimed that "God is dead." 3) Sacred Heart parish was established in South Camden, New Jersey. Now, one hundred and fifteen years later Nietzsche is dead. Dead for a hundred years and Sacred Heart is still proclaiming that God is alive. Mary and Michael's thirteen have raised seventy-three and the seventy-three have raised two hundred and thirty-eight. The number now … God alone knows.

Let it be said that the son of Rosetta (tenth of the thirteen) doth by this letter proclaim that God is very much alive. Even in Camden. I dare say especially in Camden. After a week of celebration of Christian unity in this poor city, the fervor of the peoples' faith in God expressed in word, in song and in dance was awesome. The celebrations of Liturgy in Sacred Heart over the Advent and Christmas times in seasonal and funeral masses left no doubt that Nietzsche was wrong. The influence of God on human thought, on elevation of spirit, on hope and behavior is powerful still. This church that started when he announced the futility of such a start continues to celebrate the sure presence of God in this world. "God almighty!" is all I can say when I see the meeting of need and generosity in the Christmas projects of Sacred Heart. And the spirit of God soars on the twin wings of generosity and gratitude. It was Christmas in Camden.

Camden was no paradise in 1885. A cyclone walloped it that year. It was terribly polluted. This milltown had changed to an industrial city. The heavy influx of immigrants created great tensions. The ashes of every home were thrown in the streets and the garbage as well. That was the scene when Sacred Heart started.

In 1896, a composer in Germany named Richard Strauss who greatly admired Nietzshe, created a piece of music named *Also Sprach Zarathustra*, which he based on Nietzshe's book of the same name. But over seventy years would pass before his composition became well known as the theme music of Stanley Kubrick's famous movie, *2001: A Space Odyssey*. That was back in 1968, the year I made my own uneasy odyssey into Camden City. And some years later a liturgist named Sam Mackintosh suggested *Also Sprach Zarathustra* as the opening music for the fire that broke the darkness of our Easter vigil at Sacred Heart. Thus the music (based on Nietzshe's book of 1885 that declared God is dead) that delighted millions in the movie houses of the world began to pound the walls of this church which was established in 1885 to proclaim Christ is risen. Indeed He is Risen. Alive and well.

Stanley Kubrick died in 2000. He didn't make it to 2001. Neither did my mother, who was born in 1901. Her last words to me as I left her in 1983 three months before she died are my words to you in 2001: "God be with you."

Michael Doyle

No Bridge Over Troubled Waters — Yet

February, 2001

Hi:

The Irish sing a song with some uneasy reference to their nearby neighbors: "Thank God we're surrounded by 'wather'." Once upon a time the territory of Camden, NJ was an island. Whether the Native American people, the Armewamex, here for a thousand years before the Europeans came, had any such songs, I don't know. Anyway, they were surrounded by water. They were inclosed on the west and north by the mighty Delaware River; on the east by the Cooper; on the south by the Newton Creek. Swamps and water channels near today's Route 130 linked the Cooper to the Newton. The Native Americans didn't last long once the Europeans came. Far too soon they were gone and with them the lovely names of the lands and waterways they inhabited. Replaced by new ones that are British and Dutch and awfully dull. The first fords of the Armewamex beyond their island were formed from floating dugout trees that were their early crude canoes. It was the way to get across.

The other shore, or the other bank, has always called out its challenge to human beings to cross to it. Thus, bridges. The stone axe of the Neolithic woodsman felled a tree to cross a stream. It was the first bridge. 1500 BC. Flat stones in icy lands and ropes of fibrous stems and vines in warm ones made primitive bridges. Humanity was determined to cross to the other side. Always on the move. From this side to that side, from near side to far side. From womb to tomb and beyond.

But bridges over rivers, streams and deep ravines have always been easier to build than bridges over the chasms of difference that are contained in cultures and color, in economics and politics and religion. And yet, it was wars and economic plunder that drove the building of material bridges with unstoppable determination. Both, especially the former, have killed or endangered the human bonds that tie people together.

Fifty years ago I pored over Greek and Latin accounts of war and plunder in times before Christ was born. Many a night in poor light I plowed through Latin stories of Caesar's Gallic Wars, learning how the Romans built bridges in 55 BC to expand their power. Or the Greek stories of Cyrus and the bridges he built for the Persian conquest of Babylon in 537 BC. In fact, bridge-builders were an essential corps of their armies. They were essential to conquest and commerce across the world.

The first known Roman bridge was the Pons Sublicius (Bridge of Piles) over the Tiber (621 BC). At that time, women were thrown into the river to appease the rage of the river gods and the chief priest responsible for building the bridge was called the Pontifex Maximus (supreme bridge-builder), a title taken over later by the emperors. It is now the title of the Pope, the Supreme Pontiff, whose mission is not accomplished in stone or ropes of steel, but in mediation to God and efforts at links of love around the world. The one enduring bridge is always love, as Paul proclaims to the Corinthians.

Rust and rot, the wear and tear of time, will take all bridges down. I have noticed over the years how the salt of the winter storms eats the paint and more off the Ben Franklin Bridge across the Delaware into Camden. It was one of the longest suspension bridges in the world at its opening in 1926. Thirteen years ago, on April 5, 1987, the papers carried a frightening story of the collapse of a New York Thruway bridge into the raging Scholarie Creek eighty feet below. The flood tore away the foundation of the pillars that supported it. Ten people died in the desperate drop of three cars and a tractor trailer. I remember speaking to Anne McDonald at the time, whose father the stone mason Philip McDonald, built Sacred Heart Church one hundred years before. He was also a builder of many stone bridges in the Camden-Philadelphia area. "Papa's bridges are not falling," she said proudly. It was a statement that a Pope would wish for. The Pontifex Maximus. "Papa's bridges are still standing."

Speaking of standing bridges, some years ago Frances Rapp showed me her wedding ring when I visited her on Viola Street in Camden. She was elderly and ill with cancer, her body getting smaller by the day. She showed me the ring on her finger because she had wrapped black thread around it to keep it from falling off. The ring was loosing her finger, but her finger was not loosing the ring. She made sure that her bridge would hold against all the odds of her lifetime. In spite of wars and abuses, broken treaties and promises, her covenant held. "A bridge over troubled waters". Neither weakened or broken by age or illness or even death itself. She had the courage to build it and the goodness to sustain it.

Recently, an Associated Press story in the Camden Courier-Post headlined these words (February 20, 2001): "Thirty-seven percent of NJ bridges are 'deficient'." The top headline in the same paper declared, "Highland students work to bridge the racial divide." It was a February front page in Black History Month that unintentionally linked the bridges on all the levels of their meaning.

Today Camden is a good bit bigger in area than the island of long ago. But there are ten bridges crossing water to get through it and out of it. The narrow neck between the Cooper River and the Newton Creek is no longer water. But some people, especially those living near Route 130, where massive flooding occurs, might still claim that Camden is an island. Recently, the state of New Jersey offered help to move these residents out and relocate them. In the course of public meetings to deal with this situation, a request was made to build a bridge across Route 130. It would be a walkway for children to safely cross. It would be a link from the little village of Woodlynne on the edge of Camden into Collingswood, N.J. But the Collingswood municipal government vehemently refused such a bridge because, as the Courier reported, "unsavory elements" would cross over. From Camden! Not from Collingswood.

So. Bridges! They're hard to build, sometimes…especially over the deep creeks of racism and the economic chasms of our country. How hard it is to build them over the troubled waters of the world. Ah, Love!

Sister Peg Hynes of The Heart of Camden Housing

March 17, 2001

Hi:

Today is a good day to start a letter about a great person. It's St. Patrick's Day, and sure enough, the faith and tradition that inspire her life were borne from the woods and clearings where that great man preached and prayed more than 15 centuries ago. In those days, wavelengths were nothing more than the mind's play on the immeasurable roll of the sea. Patrick had only the range of his own voice, hoarse in the damp air of ancient Ireland. But his word was heard, from the glens of Antrim in the north to the Macgillcuddy Reeks in the south, from Tara to Connemarra and the wild rock gardens of the western world.

It was here in the stone fenced fields near Gort that Nellie Burke and Tom Hynes grew up a century ago. The evening sun of their young years went down daily behind the curve of the sea in Galway Bay. Toward that setting sun they sailed, both of them, in separate ships and reached morning in America. Mere acquaintances in Galway, they bonded in Philadelphia with vows to God and one another at the altar of St. Columba at 24th and Lehigh, June 5, 1929. From there they sailed on together. It would not be plain sailing for them or for many others in 1929 – when the bottom fell out of the nation's sure ship of success.

Tom was a motorman on Trolley 33 (among others) for P.T.C. (now SEPTA). Thirty-three was a lucky number because in the Depression year of 1933, Nellie Burke brought forth the second of her five children. Margaret Mary, her parents named her in the baptismal book, but "Peggy" they called her at cradle, table and everywhere else. Her home on W. Harold Street had many Irish neighbors in a place called Swampoodle in North Philadelphia. Nearby the Phillies baseball team made their home in Shibe Park (Connie Mack Stadium). There, too, "The Whiz Kids" (Richie Ashburn was one of them) played their baseball and the Hynes girls loved them. The family struggled to make ends meet but the Hynes door had easy hinges from its openings to those in need. There was faith and friendship, hearty laughter and fun as well.

At St. Columba's, Peg attended eight grades of schooling and received the first four sacraments of her childhood. It was the center of her life. Then to high school, an opportunity not available to her parents back in Galway. Tom Hynes was three when Mary Michon and Father Philip R. McDevitt (the first Bishop McDevitt) established a center for the education of Catholic girls in 1901. Later named after Mary's brother, John W. Hallahan, it was there for Peg when she came in 1947 – the first Catholic High School for girls in the U.S. It has graduated more than 37,000 of them in the past 100 years. None any better than Peg Hynes. A star among the stars of its century of educated women is Peg Hynes of Swampoodle. Along the young years of her life, her diligent studies, the basketball court, the softball field, the home where she helped, took up most of her time. When she strode out the door of Hallahan High fifty years ago, this Distinguished Honor Student, this All-Catholic Basketball Player, this President of the Athletic Association, took in tow, together with her high school diploma, the Scholar/Athlete Award in the Class of '51. Not only a bright star of books and hoops and first base in softball, she was a great young woman of genuine goodness.

After graduating, she worked at Ford and Kendig on Broad Street, played basketball and softball in several leagues and danced the boards of the Irish Center. But soon God's piper called her away to a hill of chestnut trees where the Sisters of St. Joseph received her into their order. She earned a BA from Chestnut Hill College and an MA from the Jesuits at Boston College. Now she devoted herself to other women's children in the classrooms at St. Stephen's in Philadelphia, Epiphany in Plymouth Meeting, and St. John's in Hillsdale, NJ. A big change from the lithe athletic young woman on the floors and fields of Philadelphia into the nun's long black habit with all but the front of her face encased in a white veil; even the light-hearted name, Peg Hynes, hidden in the formal Sister Francis de Sales. But she was happy and good at what she did. Education, thirty years in it, as teacher and then principal at St. Athanasius, Christ the King, Norwood-Fontbonne Academy (all in Philadelphia) and Holy Trinity in Washington, D.C. before she made a turn in the road in 1986.

Two days have passed since I started this letter. And today is March 19th, the Feast of St. Joseph, that generous conscientious provider in whose example Peg Hynes has modeled her life. She came to Sacred Heart fourteen years ago (the long black habit gone, and the Salesian name as well) to take on the leadership of the Heart of Camden Housing that had been established by this church two years before. Surely, it is the most difficult housing assignment in America. Camden is America's poorest city when one measures by children. No longer getting a school and staff ready for the children to come to...now Sister Peg would strive to see that there would be a good house for them to go home to. In her heart she heard the cry expressed so well in Padraic Colum's poem, *An Old Woman of the Roads,*

I am praying to God on high
For a little house, a house of my own
Out of the winds and rains way.

For fourteen years she has worked at it, begging, praying to get abandoned houses rebuilt and owned by people who have no other place to live. No place but this neighborhood wedged between Camden County's huge sewer plant and trash burner and countless other industrial enemies of human lungs and lives. She battles on for her neighborhood housing. This past year she battled breast cancer as well. Here in South Camden the hoops are higher and more jagged. The floorboards are broken. The softball isn't soft and the pitch of things is underhanded in terrible ways. It's a night game without lights but she is a star.

Now she has come to another turn in the road. She will do fundraising and public relations and the massive inspiration of others to her cause. This is a salute to all she has done, a hand of help to all she wants to do. May God help her to accomplish it.

One week before we honor her, Sister Peg Hynes will be among the first inductees into the Hallahan Hall of Fame. Not for the baskets she hit in the big gyms of Philadelphia but "the three pointers" of heroic generosity that she has hit so often, especially in Camden.

P.S. (January 2003) Sister Peg Hynes was killed on December 21st, 2002 when the car in which she was a passenger was struck head-on by a 2002 Lincoln driven by a man allegedly on crack cocaine, who was steering the vehicle with his knees. A cruel clash between good and evil. She died as Jesus died, giving all in one final flood of blood in a broken aorta. All she had in her heart.

Michael Doyle

Kevin O'Donnell

April, 2001

Hi:

The first full moon of Spring has once again loomed large above the red-roofed tower of Sacred Heart. It is my favorite moon…the one that Jesus saw on his last nights. The moon of Moses and Aaron. The moon of liberation. A white magic mark on the dark calendar of the sky. Reminding us to celebrate. Passover and Easter have come around again.

Easter is a great time. Christians celebrate the resurrection of Christ from the darkness of death and consequently there is hope for every spec of human dust.

There is nothing more emphatic than death. The force of its brutal clarity leaves us shaken in the stillness. We cling to that last faint pulse of the lives we love – the last fond feel of warmth growing cold.

Five weeks ago, I drove down Sunset Road in Burlington County, NJ shortly before eight in the morning. I had death on my mind. I was on my way to the bedside of Kevin O'Donnell. He could probably die before noon. Anthony Drive by his house had two lines of cars. Family and friends clustered inside, bent by the weight of what was happening. Doctors and staff would arrive at nine. Kevin had decided on December 26th that by mid-February he would have his life supports removed from all that was left of his lithe young body that had so often careened down the slopes of Big Boulder with the wind in his hair and skis on his feet. There was that day in '94 when he fell on the slopes. Not injured. No. Much worse than that. He couldn't get up. Subsequent testing revealed the dreaded ALS (Amyotrophic Lateral Sclerosis). It killed Lou Gehrig at 38. It would take Kevin at 36. In the last few months there was nothing left but hearing and seeing. He could not eat or drink, speak or breathe. The eyelids were the only muscle he could move and the lips ever so slightly forming uncertain letters with which his family made words one by one. His mind perfect within.

> *Every limb, every muscle and sinew*
> *Not an impulse was left to entice*
> *His mind entombed and still shining*
> *Like a Christmas light frozen in ice.*

Not an adequate image. Kevin's light was buried in warmth…it soon would lose to the cold. But never the warmth of his goodness and generosity. He had good humor and great patience. He never complained. Instead used every ounce of his energy for the good of others.

Kevin O'Donnell knew he had a lot to live for. Most specifically his wife Jodi DiMarco and their daughter Alina O'Donnell.

Jodi and Kevin met ten years ago when she invited him to the home-warming of her carriage house apartment in Mt. Holly, NJ. He came "armed" with two men and a woman. The two handsome faces met with 13 steps in the stairs between them. She turned his head. The glance eternal. O'Donnell and Di Marco. The O's on the ends fused into one ring to hold them. They were married on January 25, 1992. Winter it was, but to the young pair, it was snow on the hills and the swish of skis on the slopes. But a wind unseen cried in the mountains and tears froze in cold beads on the branches.

The tears now were warm in the O'Donnell living room. At 8:30 a.m., I decided to pray. I went to find Jodi to tell her that I did not expect her at the prayers. Kevin, of course, prone upon his bed in his special room. I found her in the kitchen. "Ah," she said, "I'm going in to cuddle." It would be the last time.

We prayed. Kevin wanted me. Inside, he opened his icon eyes and I read the prayers for the dying and those tender scripture passages that are there at the end of it all. He closed his eyes and peace enveloped his face. Jodi tucked beside him. God tucked between them.

How else could they have achieved such heroic levels of life. "This is my body which is given for you." The care by family and friends that sustained him, 24 hours a day, was extraordinary. Well nigh miraculous is the fact that Kevin continued in his job at Commerce Bank, there and home, until June of 2000. Commerce adjusted with admirable cooperation. But Jodi made it all work by twining her strength to him with an overwhelming generosity.

And Kevin turned his suffering into service as he counseled others and campaigned for Medicare changes to give immediate benefits to ALS patients. Sen. Torricelli, who co-sponsored the bill, announced: "Were it not for Kevin, the bill would not have become law."

God bless the mother that bore him and the labor pain of his long illness, and God bless the hand that severed the cord that tied him to her on October 20, 1964. Now the doctors were readying him for a severing of inestimable sorrow. His beloved brother, Jimmy, read his lip letters that called for me again. This time, the eyes didn't open. I just stood there making crosses of blessing on his forehead for 20 minutes.

> *The gift that he asked for at Christmas*
> *A decision in sadness made known*
> *A break from the metal that bound him*
> *He would live or he'd die on his own.*

He died at 1:10 p.m., Feb. 21. His last words: "Turn my head. I want to see my wife."

In this Easter time, I want to celebrate the many resurrections of heroic fortitude in the life and times of Kevin O'Donnell, his wife Jodi, and all his family. Laboriously, letter by letter formed the words of his wishes: Mass of Resurrection in Sacred Heart at which his mother would speak and Jodi, too. (Both did with dignity.) And after the cemetery, a good dinner for all at The Touch of Class and a good time too. Many other wishes as well.

Kevin, you are surely an Easter man. Eternal peace and freedom to you.

> *On the day that the fetters were severed*
> *He rose from that landing of old*
> *It was just thirteen steps up to heaven*
> *He was there before he was cold.*

Michael Doyle

Tonya's Dream

May, 2001

Hi!

A priest, who has spent most of his life in South Jersey shore parishes, was once quoted in *The Philadelphia Inquirer* as saying about me: "It's hard to get Michael off his cross."

But actually it is hard to get away from crosses down here. The cross of awfully polluted air in this neighborhood, the broken sidewalks, the broken lives, the ugly scenes that wail for beautification, the dilapidated houses that must be restored for the children.

Speaking of crosses! On a wet April morning three weeks ago, a group of people from Sacred Heart followed our large Christmas tree cross, which some of them by turns, carried through the streets of South Camden. It was light, surprisingly too light for the bloody Way of the Cross we were on. This is the Via Dolorosa (the Path of Sorrows) in our Sacred Heart neighborhood.   The day was Friday the thirteenth, Good Friday 2001.   We walked and stopped, prayed and walked. In a radius of a couple of blocks, we circled the church with its own twelve-foot gold colored cross on the top of the tower. It was a perfect point of reference.

On the ground, blood marked the spots where we stopped. At our first station, Ferry and Jackson, a man was murdered. At 4th and Webster, a woman. At Broadway near Carl Miller Blvd., (Van Hook) a man and a woman. Nearby at the liquor store, a policeman. At the northwest corner of Broadway and Ferry, four murders. At the southeast corner, one murder. (Between them, Sacred Heart Church). At Ferry and Sixth, we stopped at one of Camden's 150 open air drug markets. Then down Sixth to Viola where Kevin Walls was shot a few months ago. Where his mother bent beside her bleeding son and tried to say the 23rd Psalm in his ear. *Though I walk in the valley of death, I fear no evil.* There's plenty of fear at 6th and Viola.   There now the most pathetic of urban shrines. His name scrawled on an abandoned wall. Dozens of beer bottles arranged for the glint and glow of a burnt out candle. A teddy bear soiled and wet on an abandoned step. Soft wishes in a hard hearted-place.

> *Kevin, that tender word: "sweetly conceived".*
> *With love! The Lord only knows!*
> *But a mother's love with a farfetched psalm*
> *Breastfeeds him now as his hot blood flows.*

Then to Broadway and Viola - cowled youths with drugs for sale. A man in a pick-up truck removes his hat. On to Arlington Street, the worst in America. Ruined by the radon of the lamp makers long ago. Bad light. Children here, citizens of the land "that holds these truths to be ...".   Three murders here. I have a proud picture of "Tea Bags" with an eel he caught in the Cooper. He died in a fire set to kill him. West on Jefferson, a mother and daughter carrying the cross to 3rd and Viola. The abandoned backyard area where the young body of Dawn McCary was dumped. Two women said the prayers at the foot of the cross. weary and we were only meditating ... praying to God Almighty to bring some hope to this cruel desolation. We had two more stops. On to Emerald Street past Sacred Heart's vegetable garden where Del Buono's Bakery used to be, we come to 427. A Vietnamese mother and son, the bearers of the cross. There opposite their home, we remembered Edith Rose Orsini, the childless gentle shepherdess of the little children of Sacred Heart. Battered to death by a crazed addict as she sat eating soup on her stoop. A sunny Autumn afternoon in October. His weapon the broken leg of a kitchen table. Round the corner to Emerald and Broadway to the last station and the most recent murder in the neighborhood. Clara Braxton stabbed in front of her door by her estranged husband. Then, we entered the Church. We needed to go in. We needed "the restful waters" of Barbara Wall's psalm. We were only looking. How much consolation she needs! Oh what poverty and pain!

I have often walked the Via Dolorosa of Sacred Heart, but somehow this year it devastated me. Maybe the fresh blood on two spots so near...I just had to write about it...the weight lifts in the words. It's easy to be angry with a country that is more interested in spy planes along the borders of China than bloodshed on the sidewalks of Camden, New Jersey.

And, oh, some wonderful people live in the scenes I described. People of dignity and beauty and faith in the God of love undeterred. Especially mothers who stand beneath the cross of urban crucifixions ... weeping for the way it is and still dreaming of basic opportunities that they so assuredly deserve.

One of them is a young woman, an aide in our third grade, a young mother who lives on the Via Dolorosa. Tonya McCoy also works at night and leads morning prayer in a neighborhood house before she goes to school. Tonya was chosen to express her own dreams for Camden at Bishop DiMarzio's Palm Sunday celebration by the Delaware.

"My dream for Camden," she said, "is a neighborhood where everybody gets along. A city where I could walk around and feel safe, where I could walk on streets that were all paved, with flowers growing, and trees planted and different art structures. A city that could provide training for its residents to be able to work with dignity. A city where my child could walk around and not have to worry about being robbed or attacked. A city where my child could go to the movies. (Not one movie house in a city of 85,000 people.) A city where the streets are clean, no litter or drug dealers hanging on corners. A city where no houses are abandoned, no homeless people sleeping in the park. A neighborhood that when you walked around on a nice day, people would know one another, and be sitting outside on their steps or porches, children playing in their yards or in front of their houses. A city where I can be proud to say I was born and raised here. A city that you don't just hear all the negative things about it. A city where people are not afraid to come to and visit. A city with beautiful houses and parks. A city where children could come to and have a nice day just walking around."

Tonya's dream is a cry for resurrection in the urban desolation she lives in. God Almighty, she has a right to "a city where I could walk around and feel safe, a city where children could come and have a nice day just walking around."

Thanks for "walking around" with me on the Via Dolorosa. May your journey in the mind be a stir in the heart to do what you can for the resurrection of Camden. The Heart of Camden Housing is one of the great hopes we have on the Via Dolorosa. It needs your help.

Michael Doyle

"That They May Be One"

June, 2001

Hi:

He was a man of patents, 350 of them, and poems, too. To name his most famous invention, he brought forth the Greek word for power, *dynamis*, to call his creation, dynamite. It had good uses and bad, magnifying the destructive power of war in his time. But his name is known for his last will and testament, which annually provides prizes in money and medals for excellence in five areas of human endeavor: physics, medicine, chemistry, literature, and for, "the person who shall have done the most or the best work for fraternity between nations, for abolition or reduction of standing armies and for holding and promotion of peace congresses." It was the influence of Austrian countess and peace advocate Bertha von Suttner that moved Alfred Nobel away from the sticks of dynamite to the olive branch of peace.

In 2001, another Austrian, Othmar Carli, painted eight faces of peace on the wall of Sacred Heart Church. Four had won the Nobel Peace Prize; all were worthy of it. Five were men who were murdered for working for peace and justice; three, women who died in their beds, worn to death in their efforts for the same.

In Othmar's 77-square-foot painting is above the Baptismal Font. The baptisms beneath it are the ritual acts of going down with Christ into death, death to sin, death to injustice, domination, and violence in order to rise to a new life of justice and love and peace. As the Russians pray at Easter: "We must forgive all things for the sake of the resurrection."

Othmar's peacemakers span 140 years, a time of explosives, from Nobel's dynamite of 1866 to the atomic bombs of 1945 to the killing tools of 1991's Gulf War. These faces, with their cultures, philosophies and religious faith, present us with a wonderful sweep of the world. Four are Catholic, one Jewish, one Muslim, one Baptist and one Hindu. The Far East, the Middle East, North America-Europe, and Latin America are mapped in honored human features, with the words of Jesus and all true religious leaders: "That they may be one."

Katherine Drexel (1858-1955), born in Philadelphia. Her father left $14 million to his three daughters when he died in 1885. Katherine, deeply religious, founded the Sisters of the Most Blessed Sacrament in 1891 and used her wealth to provide schools, churches and service to Native Americans and African Americans. She was canonized on Oct. 3, 2000.

Mohandas Gandhi (1869-1948) was born in Por Bandar, India, educated there and in England, where he became a lawyer. He worked initially in South Africa where he took up the cause of oppressed Indians and later, at home, took up the cause of justice and freedom for the Indian people. With prayer, fasting, non-violent action, and organizing, he overthrew the British Empire in India. His life is the greatest example of non-violent power in the world. He was assassinated on Jan. 30, 1948 on his way to evening prayer.

Dorothy Day (1897-1980) was born in Brooklyn, NY. After her young years of hard living, she found God, became a Catholic, and was transformed by a sense of God's unlimited love in the face of her baby Tamara. The father left them, but she rose to a call to found the Catholic Worker in 1932 with Peter Maurin. Its purpose to this day is non-violent works of justice and peace and service of the poor. At her death she was recognized as the greatest U.S. Catholic of the twentieth century.

Mother Teresa (1910-1997) Agnes Gonxha Bojaxhiu, born in Skopje, Albania, joined the Sisters of Loretta in 1928 and trained in Dublin, Ireland and Darjeeling, India. After teaching in India for several years, she founded the Missionaries of Charity in Calcutta in 1950. Her mission was to "the poorest of the poor", especially those dying in the streets of Calcutta. She became an example to the world. On August 7, 1976, she came to Sacred Heart and prayed for the women of Camden. In 1979 she won the Nobel Prize for Peace.

Oscar Romero (1917-1980) was born in Cuidad Barrios in El Salvador. At twelve, he began working as a carpenter but soon aspired to the priesthood and was ordained in Rome in 1942. An able administrator and good preacher, he became a bishop in 1970 and later, archbishop of San Salvador. He spoke out against the horrendous injustice under which his people lived. "I am bound as pastor," he said, "to give my life for those whom I love, and that is all Salvadorans, even those who [will] to kill me." In 1978 he gave documents describing injustices in El Salvador to the pope. Less than a year later he was murdered as he said Mass.

Anwar Sadat (1918-1981), one of 13 children, was raised in Mit Abul Kom, north of Cairo when Egypt was a British colony. As the years went on, Gandhi became one of his heroes. He trained as a soldier and became a friend of the future leader Gamel Nasser, who naturalized the Suez Canal in 1956. After Nasser's sudden death in 1970, Sadat moved into power and expelled the Soviets. But he is most famous for his "sacred mission" to Jerusalem and the Camp David Accords of 1978, an action for which he risked his life and received the Nobel Peace Prize. On Oct. 6, 1981, he was assassinated.

Yitzhak Rabin (1922-1995) was born in Jerusalem. He planned to be a farmer but became a soldier and helped Israel to defeat Egypt in the Six Day War of 1967. Later he became the leader of the Labor Party and prime minister. As the Israeli / Palestinian conflict continued, Rabin worked for peace. In 1994, when an agreement was reached in which the Palestinians took control of Gaza and Jericho, he won the Nobel Peace Prize. A second phase was signed in September 1995. Rabin continued to strive for peace. On November 6, 1995, just after declaring, "It is possible to make peace, peace opens the door to a better economy and society, peace is not just a prayer," he was murdered.

Martin Luther King Jr. (1929-1968), born in Atlanta, Georgia, was a brilliant young student, who skipped 6th and 12th grades and entered Morehouse College at fifteen. He earned a PhD in 1955, having become a minister in 1948, the year his hero Gandhi was assassinated. Like the Mahatma, he took up the civil rights struggle of black Americans and became their greatest leader in non-violent agitation for justice. In 1964 he became the youngest recipient of the Nobel Peace Prize and an inspiration to the world. Arrested more than 20 times, assaulted four times, he was murdered on April 4, 1968 at the age of 39.

Sacred Heart's painted wall is for all. It is a call to justice and peace. A place to pray, a place to ponder the noblest work in the world.

Michael Doyle

I Could Write a Book

July, 2001

Hi:

One hot night, three weeks ago I walked from the front door of Sacred Heart Church down Ferry Avenue to the front door of the rectory. In that short distance, one of the women of the street (there are many) stopped me with a question I never heard in the seminary: "Your place or mine!" I answered with my own: "What is your place like?" She answered: "I have no electricity in the house, only candles."

Is it any wonder that I write letters! Around here there are poems and stories in every sorrowing face and pothole. This letter is about my letters.

I have always loved that aspect of the Russian tradition, which proclaims that "it is the responsibility of the living to keep the dead alive." But I have found, too, that the dead can keep an idea alive in my heart better than the living. That must be Irish.

When I was in secondary school fifty years ago, my weekend assignments usually included an essay in the Irish language and an essay in the English. Irish was my favorite subject and at the end of my secondary schooling, it was my best grade. But I also liked writing my English essay. On one of them, Fr. Peter Bohan wrote, "V.G." and said, "Someday, you will write a book." I told my mother. Thirty years later, she said to me out of the blue (with her memory beginning to fade), "Remember when Fr. Bohan said to you that one day you will write a book?" I said, "yes," and she didn't say any more. Not long afterwards, she died. 1983. I still haven't produced the book, but I have been writing.

Fourteen years after her death, another English teacher at the long-closed but ever unending high school of St. Thomas More in Philadelphia, Fr. Frank McDermott, made me promise that I would publish my monthly letters in a book. He was 85 at the time. "They are a ministry," he said. I had never thought of such an idea and it was a great encouragement to me. "These letters are a unique history of life in an inner city parish and you have to publish them." Fr. McDermott died on September 9, 2000. Speaking to him was like speaking to my grandfather because they both displayed that clarity of thought and energy of action, not to mention good use of language and a solid hope about life in general.

So, to Fr. Frank McDermott I say, and to the late Fr. Peter Bohan I say, and to my dear mother Rosetta Creegan Doyle I say: "I have tried to publish these letters in a book. But I have failed. Nicely." The reason: Jeremy Langford, editor-in-chief of Sheed & Ward, summed it up best. He wrote, "I am sorry to report that after much deliberation we have decided to decline on publishing your book. As I said in my e-mail to you, books like this, wonderful as yours is, are very difficult to sell. We all like the book, but fear that we would be unable to sell it well enough to adequately cover the costs involved in producing it. Yours in Christ, Jeremy Langford."

Michael Farrell, writer and former editor of the *National Catholic Reporter,* had this to say. "I read much of the letters. The material – no surprise – is very good. I think it would make an excellent book, a book that would sell (it's easy enough to make a book, selling it is another matter). Highlights and strengths that occur to me: history of a parish where Christianity is gritty and authentic, where essential values are fought for and sometimes won under conditions Jesus Christ was up to fighting for (and only sometimes win); the emphasis on hope is good; also the emphasis on community; the stories are very beguiling, and so is the poetry; also the way you leap from great names like your old buddy Whitman to other great names such as the old postman (Stevie). The strong Irish strain will also be popular." Robert Ellsberg, the editor of Orbis Press, said that he "wanted the ideas to be developed more." But then I wouldn't be writing a letter to you like I'm doing now. A little bit of a thing to go with your tea or your coffee or a beer in the basement.

So......the doors closed one after another. Now, my mother always claimed that when one door closes or all doors close, God will open another. And she's right. The phone rang one day – it was Leonard Metz of TPC Graphics. I didn't know him but he was on my mailing list...like you. Imagine this! He knew Fr. Frank McDermott. "He was my English teacher in 'Tommy More' high school." Then I knew that the dead are not dead. Or idle, either. He will produce my book. A hardcover collection of most of the letters from 1985 to 2001. The plan is to sell the books, make a profit, and every penny goes to help the Heart of Camden, to fix abandoned houses in this dilapidated area of our city. Initially I plan to print 3,000 copies. The Heart of Camden is the publisher. However, I need about 20,000 dollars to do it. I'll put that problem in the hands of the three who are gone, Fr. Frank, Fr. Peter and my mother Rosetta. They will help me to find it.

Speaking of money! The woman of the street asked me for two dollars to go to the local square-holed wall down on Broadway to get some Chinese food. "Do you have any children?" I asked. "Four," she said, "one died." She began to cry. All the while, her labored voice, husky with asthma as the trucks rolled by. I gave her three dollars and she headed down towards that trash-strewn hole-in-the-wall where hard people hang. Did she buy the food? I don't know.

Someday, I hope that she, like the weeping woman who washed the Lord's feet, will find peace and eternal light in God's place. Brighter by far than the dying candles in her darkness or indeed all the glowing wattage of the world. O God help us all!

I could write a book.

I want to write a verse
Not because Nicholas said I should
Or my mother prayed I would
As her hearse went up the road.
No! What moves me is the cry
That haunts my heart of clay
And bids it break and say
Who I am, before I die.

March 3, 1984

Michael Doyle

Are You Going Away With No Word of Farewell

August 2001

Hi:

Neil Diamond is on the road again (as John Denver would say) with his new release *"Three Chord Opera."* Recently he was on TV with a call-in show of people's favorites. He didn't sing mine: "That Was The Last Thing On My Mind.*"* It almost always brings me to tears, tears I understand. Not the idle, incomprehensible sorrows that soak the heart in Tennyson's poem:

> *Tears, idle tears, I know not what they mean*
> *Tears from the depth of some divine despair*
> *Rise in the heart and gather to the eyes*
> *In looking at the happy autumn-fields*
> *And thinking of the days that are no more.*

Autumn-fields indeed, fallen leaves, despair, "divine despair," her wet face on the road … going away. The smile I knew and the sheen of her chestnut hair. On November 5, 1975, a sorrow came over me from nowhere, "from the depth of some divine despair" that overwhelmed me. My chest was being crushed as in a vise. I asked to hear the record that Neil Diamond sings. "That sad song." I was in the home of my friend Rita Bell in Cherry Hill, N.J. and she asked, "What's the name of it?" I didn't know. Titles were called to me. "That's it," I said, "That Was The Last Thing On My Mind." It was played.

> *Are you going away with no word of farewell,*
> *Shall there be not a trace left behind.*

My chest eased a little. That night I didn't sleep well. At 6 a.m. the phone rang. My brother-in-law, Johnny O'Reilly phoned from Ireland: "Anna Mae was hit by a car… yesterday…6 p.m…she is not expected to live." Four hours later she died. My dear sister. Thirty-eight. A Mercy nun. Delightful. A great nurse working in Ireland. My best friend in all the world. And she didn't go away with no word of farewell. At the hour the doctors in Dublin decided that nothing could be done, she sent the sadness, the premonition, the need for Neil Diamond's song. But why that song? I didn't know at the time.

A year after her death, in listening to an unlabeled tape to hear what was on it, I heard the voice of Anna Mae reciting a poem followed by my other sister, Phyllis, and a friend Paddy Smith, singing "That Was The Last Thing On My Mind." Anna Mae and I had listened to it together in May of 1972. *"The days that are no more."*

This day, not yet "no more," is August 6th , a day that has come around a hundred ninety-one times since the poet Tennyson was born on it in 1809 and 56 times since The Bomb was dropped on this day in 1945. "Some divine despair" there, too, as the children of God lost their innocence in a new and terrible way. And worse bombs are right now stockpiled around the world. More than enough to wipe out all life.

And yet in spite of Tennyson's "divine despair" and the terrible incineration of 1945, this day (August 6th), is the holy Christian feast of the Transfiguration. The preview on the mountain of the awesome beauty of human transformation.

No one in the modern world has held up the great possibility of human transformation from degradation better than Mother Teresa of Calcutta, whose name is on my mind today because tomorrow we celebrate the 25th anniversary of her visit to Sacred Heart in 1976.

Well, we celebrated it in a magnificent way. August 7, 2001 began at Sacred Heart with word that a local young woman who was evicted last week was taken to the hospital to have a baby and another older woman, drug afflicted, was taken into the same hospital after being savagely beaten by local drug dealers. Twenty-five years ago I asked Mother Teresa to come to Sacred Heart and pray for all the women of Camden. She came and prayed. Obviously her prayers are still needed. Actually in the celebration, we used the very same program of prayers and songs that we used on August 7, 1976. The very same singer, too, Barbara Dever. And the same eight-year-old Sacred Heart student Dana Redd, who presented a lei of flowers to Mother Teresa 25 years ago, was present as a strikingly beautiful and articulate young woman who wove a lei of words into a wonderful message for us. The lei that she gave to Mother Teresa was on a table in the church, withered and dried out but intact still. Nothing withered about the lovely Dana Redd and the clear, fresh life in her words.

This Sacred Heart student is now a newly elected member of Camden City Council. She prays daily for guidance. She talked about our school and church which she loves. How both had formed her and honored her. How she had been "chosen to be Mother Mary in the Christmas play". How she had been chosen to present a lei of flowers gathered from neighborhood gardens to Mother Teresa of Calcutta. "I was here with my grandparents," she said, "awed by everything." I went up to Mother Teresa and I remember how small she was. She embraced me and blessed me." Dana then mentioned her parents. I had never heard her speak of the tragedy before. "My parents," she said, "had died only 3 weeks before Mother Teresa came. Murder/suicide. They went on vacation. They never came back. I was always expecting them to come back." *Are You Going Away With No Word of Farewell?*

I had told Mother Teresa the story before she met Dana. You could hear a pin drop. "What I learned from Mother Teresa's life is that we must be people of faith in God and service to one another and to those in need. Service, that's the message I got from Mother Teresa. That's the message I give to you tonight."

My Mind Had Wandered To Sineád
(Excerpt)

Below, a celtic cross with its metal fáinne forged
Within the reddening sun and hissing rain
To soothe the cosmic passion and the pain
And mark the holy rupture where she rests.
There for the prayer of any pilgrim coming near
And the silence of a cry in the seabed of a tear.

Saint Ciaran Has Landed

September, 2001

Hi:

I wrote my September letter in Ireland before all this happened. Before September 11, 2001. O, God Almighty, have mercy on us. That day exploded in the core of our human consciousness and blew out the center of our hearts. Initially, I think, it knocked the bottom out of the deepest wellspring of our peace. Silence was the only good word we had.

The only one I had anyway. People who know me know that I am not great at the bedside of tragedy. I am nothing but a silent lump of sorrow. So no letter yet. I had plenty of time because my return flight was canceled for six days. Now I am on an Aer Lingus jet. September 20th. Coming back at last. I will try to write from here.

Come to think of it, my August letter was focused somewhat on this sad September. "Are you going away with no word of farewell?" Far from the bright morning faces of dear people that Tuesday, leaving to catch planes or work on them, rushing to arrive at fire halls or police stations, the World Trade Towers in New York or the Pentagon offices in Virginia…far from their minds was any tragic thought of never coming home again. My August letter also had "Tears from the depth of some divine despair…" (Tennyson) and other lines like these "God coughs where the world was…poking in the ash heap that once was our world, looking for the black box, weeping, weeping, weeping…."

Maybe this is a good place to write my September letter. On Flight EI 105. Seat 35A. A window on the world. The plane's name is Saint Ciarán. I am more conscious of this flight today than any other in my 39 years of flying. I couldn't take my eyes off a baby, nine months or so, smiling delightfully at me as I waited in line this morning. The softness which is always so endearing in an infant face, seemed more soft and fragile now. The mind-bending vision of United Airlines Flight 175 crashing into the South Tower at the speed of 450 miles an hour will never leave our minds. Matter into matter, high human achievement into high human achievement, the oil of the earth exploding in fire that evaporated everything and everyone in its reach and the haunting realization branded on our memories, that men who share this earth with us, deliberately planned and piloted soft innocent flesh into the consuming inferno they created. They turned a marvelous flying womb of life and human connection into a monstrous bomb of death and destruction. Those twin towers have stood there like a gigantic number eleven (11) on Manhattan and they were turned into zero, into a twenty-storey mangled mountain of rubble, entombing the bits and the bodies of more than 3,000 innocent women and men. .

How fragile is this vessel of clay that is the sacred container of the life we live! How evil it is to crush it for any reason. Today I listened again to the video of airborne safety. It has always seemed so helpless to me. Surely more so, now. I blessed myself…that would be my safety, that and Saint Ciarán. I was no way at ease this time going away from the spot I was born in. I know there's a hole in America's heart and hope and my flight will be into it. And no doubt a buckle in this nation's towering pride, no matter what is said or done. The tidal tears and all the hoses of the New York Fire Department are still not able to quench the smoldering pile or indeed the rage that will blaze for a long time. Nor indeed ease the terror at the first air strike that rained death on the American mainland. My sympathy, my deepest sympathy to you. Your world has changed terribly since I left on this vacation. Mine, too.

And, O my God, we now hear the shattering words of war. That it will be long. Wars are long. In fact, they never end. They are always somewhere smoldering like volcanoes. They are never blessed. "Infinite Justice" is reserved for very High Authority.

So, we have been praying to that High Authority and so have you. The churches in Ireland had bigger congregations of prayer last Friday than they had at Easter. Deep down it is hard to trust that any mortal or group of mortals knows what is the right thing to do. We turn to you, O God, that "Thy will be done on earth as it is in heaven." There is no restoration of the broken human ties of September 11th, no consolation or salvation in the stock exchange, the media or all the military might of the world. We are humbled before God into genuine cries for help.

I just had dinner at 37,000 feet somewhere that I am leaving at eight miles a minute. I had wine from Australia, spring water from Tyrone, and a cup of tea full to the brim and still as a photo. And a Jacob's biscuit. All so civilized…far from the monstrous madness of terrorism. But it isn't far away anymore. It comes quickly. It will be very hard to stop it. Only prayer and fasting, I think, will cast out a demon like this. It is a twisted diabolical direction, far beyond the range of any weapon or warlike word. It is God who turns a tragedy like this into an impulse for the transformation of the world.

Indeed, nothing is far away now. We are learning more about Afghanistan. Its terrain. Its famine. Its children. Its harboring of Osama Bin Laden. Its soil infested by 10 million landmines left by the Russians. We are learning that death is no stranger there…from disease, malnutrition, and the land mines that kill 20 to 25 people every day. People there have been under war for 23 years. How do we separate the innocent from the guilty with our weapons of mass destruction. Wars never end.

God help America and bless it with wisdom to do what's right. Help us not to leave landmines of hate along the highways of history.

It would surely add to the success of the terrorists of September 11, 2001 if the US slaughtered far more innocent people than they did. O God help us all. Bring good out of bad. It is always your holy will. Into Your Hands, we place the children of the world. (Just now two little ones, 3 and 4, walked by in the aisle of this plane as if all this was normal.) God bless them and the struggling ones in Camden, too. Their world was hard enough. It will be harder now.

This plane is easing into the edge of Kennedy Airport. There are rain drops running down my window. It's very cloudy. There's a lonesome mourning sky over New York.

Saint Ciarán has landed.

Michael Doyle

"Tread Softly...."

October, 2001

Hi:

Pauline Marie O'Reilly is my niece and she came into this world to live in the same year I came into Camden City to work. In the ending times of the sixties it was; a decade, which seemed too short for all that happened. Her birth in 1968 and her continuing emergence as a woman of engaging beauty and maturity – she is a commercial artist and a registered practitioner of homeopathy – have been a source of comfort against all the shattering events of 1968.

Recently I purchased a book and while one should not judge a book by its cover, I have to say that I was enticed to buy it, not only by the great poems within it, but also because Pauline did the art on the cover. *Popular Irish Poetry* it is called, selected by Louis Bell. Her design is an oblong painting of cloths pieced together in mostly several hues of blue and a taste of orange and other colors. Framing the work is a border of words – four lines of the eight in *He Wishes for the Cloths of Heaven* by William Butler Yeats:

> *Had I the Heavens' embroidered cloths*
> *Enwrought with golden and silver light*
> *The blue and the dim and the dark cloths*
> *Of night and light and the half-light.*

Not for Yeats the brilliant beauty of the rising sun astonishing the stones on Knocknarea or the fullness of the golden apple sinking in the sea beyond the Rosses. No! It's the later weave he wants "the blue and the dim and the dark cloths of night...". A more obvious modesty that veils a deeper mystery. One should not so much be enthused by the clothed slender alignment on the fashion runway with her highly skilled pretense, as with what is behind the veils of a lesser glow. Behind the veils of age or ache or a youthful face that's plain. As the Little Prince says: "It is only with the heart that one sees rightly."

Sometimes we have to ascend to see. Climb a mountain or even 87 steps in a walk-up apartment, on 84th Street in New York's West Side. There one receives a wondrous welcome from Pauline O'Reilly's grandaunt, Helen O'Reilly. Grand indeed! On March 13, 2001, she celebrated her birthday with what she wanted most. Mass in her apartment. Helen was born in Colcrum near Ballycastle, County Antrim (where the Auld Lammas Fair is still celebrated) on March 13, 1901. On the anniversary of that day, a hundred years later, Sacred Heart's world-renowned opera singer, Barbara Dever, climbed the 87 steps, took a deep breath and sang *Danny Boy* to Helen O'Reilly as she sat in her favorite chair with closed eyes and awesome reverence on her beautiful unwrinkled face.

One would never expect, glancing at her now, that there are such wings on her mind, that her memory is so perfect, and her life is of such inestimable value on this earth. No monk or monastery has a more faithfully scheduled day, every day of the week.

Helen O'Reilly ascended the six flights of steps as a bride in June of 1927. The last time she walked up was the weekend of her hundredth birthday. She has been walking up to the same apartment for 74 years. Alone as a widow for 23 years, she has filled her days since she retired with several scheduled times of daily prayer, conversations on the phone, a little TV and visits that her mind makes to the living and the dead that she knows. Going back to her mother who died when she was four and to all those gone before her that she loves, Helen spends some time with each of them. "I remember my mother," she says, "standing at the fence with a yellow shawl on her shoulders. I was digging in moss with a spoon and I looked up." She also visits the living, relatives and friends, and goes in her mind to Canada where she lived once and to Ireland to homes and familiar places every day. "I pray for them all," she says "and tell them I will love them for all eternity."

Suddenly, from her soul came the words: "I'm afraid another big war will break out." Helen said this on August 24th just 17 days before the tragedies of September 11th. One thing for sure, Helen does her best with her prayers and good life to hold back the tide of evil. Then she went on to talk about chocolate chip cookies and even mentioned Alan Greenspan and the lowering of the interest rate. She was a bride of two years in 1929.

Wouldn't the teacher who taught her reading, writing, and 'rithmatic in the primary school of Drumadone, County Antrim long ago, be amazed to know that little Helen is still alert and learning almost a hundred years afterwards! Talking Federal Reserve and Alan Green Whatshisname. Teachers don't dare hope for such an outcome. But much more than math and percentages, someone or several *someones*, fostered in her heart the dream of life lived well, a discipline that is now a flowing ritual for the elevation and perfection of time, a reverence for all that is good and wholesome, a dream of everlasting life. O how great, how immeasurably great is every generous investment of time and treasure in a child.

Inside the cover of the book that Pauline O'Reilly adorned, is the Yeats poem of reverence in relationship that inspired her art. Would that every child in Sacred Heart School was inspired by this poem and also by the values of Helen O'Reilly and her hundred years of life. But it is 87 steps to the threshold of her goodness. We must help our children to seek their dreams…one step at a time.

> *Had I the Heavens' embroidered cloths*
> *Enwrought with golden and silver light*
> *The blue and the dim and the dark cloths*
> *Of night and light and the half light.*
> *I would spread the clothes under your feet:*
> *But I, being poor, have only my dreams;*
> *I have spread my dreams under your feet;*
> *Tread softly because you tread on my dreams.*
> *William Butler Yeats*

O God, we cry to you now to soften the terrible trample that is bruising the dreams of us all.

Michael Doyle

Breaking Water for the Birth of Hope

November, 2001

Hi:

Once upon a youthful freckled time, I climbed and crawled with my sister, Anna Mae, and a crowd of pilgrims to the top of St. Patrick's Mountain in Mayo. It took five hours on a wet dark night in July of 1953. At the summit, we went to Mass where Patrick had fasted and prayed more than 1500 years ago. There, he talked with God. There, promises were made and a deal was cut, as it were, in rock. (Not on loose leaf anyway.) It was something like Moses on Sinai, with God's severe signature in stone. There was talk of snakes, too, not rattlers in Ireland but maybe the silent kind that could sneak up on you and steal your soul.

Meeting God on high ground is common in many religions. It expresses a sense of ascent to the dizzy heights of divinity. Up there in Mayo, the rain cleared and the sun rose for us and we careened down the mountain in the morning with windows on the world of green fields below, Clew Bay and the blue waves of the Atlantic beyond. A new sense of wings and wonder. The shoes we wore we never wore again. They were cut from our feet by the stones.

On October 5th last year, I was invited by Theresa Silk to lead a prayer at the podium in the Windows on the World Restaurant, floor 107, in one of the cloud-touching Trade Towers of New York. I remember saying to the great assembly of people, there to support *Futures and Options for Kids*, that these high levels in the clouds are good places to pray to God. But not as good as Mayo if you come up in the elevator.

This year I was invited back on October 4th to that same awesome restaurant but Alas! Alas!… The place where I stood was not standing anymore. This man-made mountain was crushed back into the earth from which it had arisen. Time receded. One backward into Zero. Weight that soared against the grip of gravity was now weight without wings, falling, falling into oblivion. A gaping open sore in the side of our national stature. The woeful wound in Manhattan has swallowed 3,000 people and is wounding the workers on the site everyday. More than eight thousand injuries since September 11, 2001. For a while, men and women were struggling there without masks in all the dangers, the dust, and death's cruel casualties …breathing everything. Even the dust of smiles that are dead, ride on the breath of the living. "Come, Holy Spirit and renew the face of the earth."

Camden, which has more scrap hauled into it than any town of its size in the world, where the brokeness of our age is heaved into colossal hills of entanglement, is a good place to meditate on the jagged hole in Ground Zero, Manhattan. John Bantivoglio, who heads the largest scrap yard in Camden, says that the horrendous heap of two million tons of brokeness in New York should be hauled to one place and there a holy hill – a park – of sadness and remembrance should be created. Because the dust of the dead is in the dust of it all and the blood of the victims has blessed this heart-breaking heap of matter. On it we could pray and God would be there with every name alive in His heart. And Tennyson's poem would be an apt inscription:

Oh yet we trust that somehow good
Will be the final goal of ill,
To pangs of nature, sins of will,
Defects of doubt, and taints of blood;

That nothing walks with aimless feet;
That not one life shall be destroyed,
Or cast as rubbish to the void,
When God hath made the pile complete.

So this year with weight on our hearts and war in our world, we turn to thoughts of Christmas 2001. We are aware that the newly born Babe was wrapped in swaddling clothes and laid in an earth made manger. Simply a hole in the ground where animals bent to feed. No high rise of pride there. We can do no better than bend to the children to feed them and educate them. We will do what we should. That is their God-given right on planet Earth today. We will pray too that the day will come soon when the children of Afghanistan know that God loves them because nothing but food is falling from the skies. Last year Sacred Heart, with your cooperation and generosity, gave out 1130 Christmas Baskets. As always we will go for a thousand baskets and hope for the best.

Christmas 2001. Let us celebrate hope in a tragic time. Hope. It is the essential ministry of our faith. We proclaim, no matter what, that "Life has the edge." Above all, we have to create new windows on the world. Ones that never shatter. Never splinter our view. Windows with a vision that is a million miles high on the indestructible elevation of God's Holy Spirit.

On November 21, 2001 down by the river in Camden, the Delaware River Port Authority will break ground for the construction of a Fishing Pier, a wide brick walkway and extensive beautification. It is the only sliver of access to the water that we have in this forsaken and burdened neighborhood. This window on the river will be built between a massive sewage plant and a huge scrap heap. But the mother river is there. God is with us there. We will break water for the birth of hope against all the odds of waste and smell, fear and terror, and every heap of brokeness in the world. A new height for us. A new view. A dream coming true. Our shoes are worn with walking on the rough stones of our time.

Thanks be to God.

Michael Doyle

Come, O Come, Emmanuel

December, 2001

Hi:

Trenton brown stones, quarried in Lambertville, NJ, floated down the Delaware River to Camden on big open barges in May of 1886. Then they were hauled by horses from the riverbank to Broadway and Ferry and built into walls three feet thick by Philip McDonald and his six half-brothers. It was a nine-month miracle of masonry that is Sacred Heart Church today.

Time and rust have long since silenced the sounds of hammers and chisels and relegated to the dust the eager hands that held them. But inside the bonded stones other sounds arose. The hum of prayer, the swell of bell and organ bellows, and for the past twenty-five years the powerful voice of Barbara Dever. With us now only when the world doesn't need her. In Tokyo this month. In New Orleans last month. The city of the golden sounds, with an airport called after Louis Armstrong and a theatre, where she sang Fricka in Wagner's *Die Walküre*, named after Mahalia Jackson.

New Orleans conjures high voltage excitement in most minds today with its Mardi Gras, its jazz, its Preservation Hall, the French Quarter in the curve of the Mississippi River. A shape that suggested the lunar title, Crescent City. (No wonder the rocket that launched the first man to the moon was built near the big bend in the Mississippi.)

Yet, I have a particularly poignant feeling whenever I think of New Orleans, Louisiana. The thousands of young immigrants, especially the Irish after the Famine of 1847, who went there in search of work and the thousands who died there of yellow fever. All unaware that death rode on the wings of wicked little mosquitoes from the low lying swamps of the Mississippi. In 1853, more than eleven thousand people died of yellow fever in New Orleans.

And one of the young men who died there in the 1850's was born in County Cavan, Ireland. He was the father of Philip McDonald. Philip built Sacred Heart. His father emigrated there in 1857 leaving his wife and their year old son in Ireland. One year later, he died in New Orleans and then his young wife left this baby with grandparents to come to the United States. Probably looking for her husband. Then, the Civil War. She couldn't get back and settled in Philadelphia, married a horse farm owner, named John Beatty, from Germantown (Philadelphia) and had six sons. Meanwhile her first born, Philip McDonald is growing up in Ireland. He was twelve before he was able to come to the United States to the home of his mother, her husband, and six brothers, none of whom he knew. Unhappy in school, he dropped out and became an apprentice to a stonemason and learned how to lay stone. Then he taught the trade to his six half brothers. In 1886, the seven brothers built Sacred Heart Church in nine months.

Sad as it is, had his father not died in New Orleans, none of this would have happened. Somehow sorrow moistens the telling of every true story and no good story is ever true without it. There were tears in the drops of water that Bishop Michael O'Farrell poured into the wine at the first Mass in the new Church of Sacred Heart on March 7, 1887. And there were tears, too, in the water that was poured into the chalice last Sunday (December 2) in Sacred Heart when Lynn Beckman Pescherine and ten other young expectant mothers were blessed at the first Advent Mass of 2001. Her baby is due in March 2002. That is vaguely reminiscent of Sacred Heart's completion in March 1887, nine months after ground was broken in May of 1886.

A few years ago, Lynn Beckman left the famous city of New Orleans where she was born and settled in New York City. There she met a very handsome, young man from New Jersey named Michael Pescherine. He worked for K.B.W., a company that handles bonds. She, with Hilton Hotels. Their friendship grew and they sealed it for good on September 4, 1999. Their Wedding Day. This year, the summer wind had happy whispers of little life. "Tidings of great joy" for their second wedding anniversary. Exactly one week later......September 11th. Michael was on the 89th floor of the South Tower when Flight 175 shattered it. It collapsed in rubble at 10 AM. Into your hands, O Lord, we commend your spirit, Michael, your life, and the silent dreams that slept in your soul.

So, with big tears and great courage, his wife, the girl from New Orleans, walked to the altar of Sacred Heart bearing their child in her body and hope in her heart that she will bring their love to birth when the Spring begins to break through the fallen leaves.

The young man who went to her city 144 years ago, didn't live to see his son grow up but his son surely grew and built the Church of Sacred Heart in Camden, a place for her when she came for blessing on herself and the baby boy within her.

God bless her. She is bearing the precious gift of life out of a very heavy mountain of rubble in Manhattan that had flattened all our hope. Come, O Come Emmanuel!

Michael Doyle

A Tribute to Philip McDonald
(Built Sacred Heart Church in 1886)

He took a heap of broken stones

Cold, ill shaped and odd,

And wove them all, big and small

Into a sacred womb of God.

Index

People

Abel, Charlene, 83, 84
Adamo, Msgr. Sal, 215
Alinsky, Saul, 91, 142, 197, 198
Alter, John Martin, 151
Anastas, Gulia, 121
Anderson, Clive, 167
Aquinas, St. Thomas, 115, 193, 225
Balunas, Peter Paul, 173
Balunas, Rose Genevieve, 174
Balzano, Joseph, 14, 23, 177
Bantivoglio, John, 23, 167, 168, 266
Baraldi, Ferdinand, 88, 94, 131, 209, 210
Barbour, Richard, 100, 139
Battaglia, Emilia, 109
Bell, Joe, 124
Bell, Rita, 188, 260
Bergen, Polly, 51
Bernstein, Elliott, 140
Berrigan, Daniel, 56, 87, 107, 199, 200
Berrigan, Jerome and Carol, 200
Brady, Brian, 157
Brennan, Johnny, 63
Bric, Fr. Maurice, 131, 210
Bui, Hoa, 67
Burke, Nellie, 250
Byers, Sarah, 164
Byrne, Fr. Patrick, 7, 151
Campbell, Catherine (great-great-grandmother), 54, 132, 145, 155
Camus, Albert, 61
Carli, Othmar, 88, 131, 210, 256
Carr, Wilma, 56
Carrasco, Jose, 197
Carrieri, Fr. Leonard, 63
Carroll, James, 200
Cartin, Marta, 79
Caruso, Enrico, 115, 228
Chardin, Teilhard de, 8
Chavez, Cesar, 91, 92, 197
Clancy Brothers, 78
Clancy, Liam, 196
Clarke, Pat, 44

Claver, Sr. Peter, 175, 176
Cleveland, Grover, 83
Cofsky, Donald and Marge, 5
Cofsky, Michael, 5
Colum, Padraic, 127, 136, 251
Cooke, Terence Cardinal, 175
Cooper, Jacob, 213
Cooper, William, 133, 161
Cosfky, Katie, 5
Creegan, Bridget, 111
Creegan, Elizabeth, 111
Creegan, Hugh, 62, 111, 119
Creegan, Hugh (grandfather), 111
Creegan, Hugh (great-grandfather), 49
Creegan, Jimmy, 111
Creegan, John Francis, 111
Creegan, Johnny, 150
Creegan, Kate, 111
Creegan, Mary, 247
Creegan, Mary (grandmother, 111
Creegan, Mary (grandmother), 49, 50, 111, 112
Creegan, Mary Ann, 111
Creegan, Mary Jane, 119
Creegan, Matthew, 111
Creegan, Michael, 247
Creegan, Michael (grandfather), 49, 100
Creegan, Michael (uncle), 111
Creegan, Patrick, 111, 119
Creegan, Peggy, 119
Creegan, Peter, 111
Creegan, Rosaleen, 71
Creegan, Rosetta, 37, 111, 115, 129, 187, 221, 247, 258, 259
Creegan, Terence, 111
Cromwell, Oliver, 75
Curley, Archbishop Michael, 51
Curran, Maggie, 112
Cusack, Sean, 97
Day, Dorothy, 91, 175, 176, 201, 256
DeLarge, Christina, 8
DeLeon, Clark, 31
Dennis, Mathew, 80

Dershimer, Jack, 24
Dever, Barbara, 110, 115, 116, 139, 159, 165, 179, 185, 193, 194, 224, 231, 232, 261, 264, 268
Dobson, Michael, 155, 171, 172
Doherty, Fr. Jimmy, 157
Doherty, Paddy, 66
Domingo, Placido, 193
Dostoevsky, Fyodor, 59
Downey, Roma, 230
Doyle, Anna Mae, 37, 72, 128, 243, 244, 260, 266
Doyle, Annie (grandmother), 221
Doyle, Annie Kiernan, 222
Doyle, Annie McKiernan (grandmother), 221
Doyle, Fr. Pakie, 97
Doyle, Fr. Pakie (uncle), 221
Doyle, Geraldine, 81, 95, 155, 171, 217
Doyle, J.J., 99, 113, 124, 129, 130, 132, 149, 150, 172, 185
Doyle, James (uncle), 221
Doyle, John (father), 37, 221
Doyle, Johnny (great-grandfather), 54
Doyle, Michael, 15, 17, 24, 47, 66, 86, 88, 141, 153, 167, 195, 205, 231, 238
Doyle, Pat (brother), 81
Doyle, Pat (grandfather), 49, 91, 117, 121, 132, 145, 146, 184, 221, 222
Doyle, Pat (great-great-grandfather), 54, 132, 145
Doyle, Philomena, 241
Doyle, Philomena (Phyllis O'Reilly), 146
Doyle, Philomena (Phyllis O'Reilly), 49
Doyle, Rosemarie, 97
Dunbar, Richard Riley, 139
Dunbar, Steve, 139
Edison, Thomas, 115
Egan, Msgr. Jack, 197
Egan, Seamus, 44, 180
Einstein, Albert, 142
Elkind, Dr. Alexander, 167
F, Catherine, 43
Faladin, Jerry, 42
Farrelly, Katie, 100
Fischette, Nicholas Michael, 177
Fischette, Stephanie Balzano, 177
Fitzgerald, Barry, 19

Fleming, Joe, 197
Fleming, Preston Jr., 56
Flood, Annie, 119
Francis of Assisi, 75, 176
Franck, Cesar, 115
Gateley, Edwina, 149, 152, 159
Gaudette, Tom, 142, 197, 198
Genovesi, Bartholomew, 109
Genovesi, Domenico, 109
Genovesi, Remo, 109, 110
Gibson, John, 80
Gibson, Patti, 80
Goldsmith, Oliver, 164
Golunov, Vladislav, 80
Gonzalez, Fr. Charlie, 151, 152
Gooney, Tim and Gale, 23
Grey, Margaret, 172
Gumbleton, Bishop Thomas, 200
Hammarskjold, Dag, 89
Harle, Don, 131, 210
Harmon, Dick, 36, 197
Harnick, Tom, 27, 38
Hartman, Katie, 139
Harvilla, John, 147
Harvilla, Julia, 147
Heaney, Seamus, 34, 70, 136, 198, 200
Hertz-Lane, Rev. Margaret, 142
Hess, Fenne, 24
Hill, Ben, 24
Honeyman, Steve, 197
Howe, Shirley, 27, 71
Hughes, Bishop John, 75
Hugo, Fr. John, 176
Hynes, Sr. Peg, 18, 31, 51, 67, 250, 251
Hynes, Tom, 250
Ivanov, Roman, 80
Jagerstatter, Franz, 87, 88
John XXIII, Pope, 50
Johnson, Eldridge, 115, 162
Joyce, James, 76, 233
Jung, Sindra, 80
Kaplan, Justin, 75
Kazantzakis, Nikos, 61, 243
Keane, Jimmy, 180
Kelly, Claudia, 165
Kelly, Eugenie, 10, 179, 180
Kelly, Jack, 165

Kelly, Kristina, 165
Kelly, Margaret, 38
Kelly, Michael, 165
Kelly, Sean, 165
Kelly, Tim, 165
Kennedy, President John F., 50
Kennedy, Sen. Robert, 34, 91, 92, 201, 233
Kiernan, Fr. Edward, 91
Killeen, Fr. John, 32
King, Dr. Martin Luther, 34, 142, 201, 233, 257
King, Mary, 42
King, Rodney, 77
Kinte, Kunte, 178
Kolmer, Sr. Rosemarie, 5, 203
Kolosov, Dr. Vladimir, 167
Konat, Al, 24
Kruk, John, 99
Kuhn, Maggie, 142
Larkin, James, 91
Lawrence, David "Cochise", 80
Lennon, Mattie, 49, 50
Lindsay, Kevin, 80
Longjohn, Candace, 80
Lorent, Maurice, 151
Lucitt, Msgr. Edward, 97
Lynch, Fr. William, 17, 22, 42, 83
Lynch, Rose, 113, 219
Lyons, John, 21, 56
Mac Cafferty, James, 130
MacDonald, Anne, 249
MacFarlane, Jim, 167, 168
Mackintosh, Sam, 165, 247
Macklin, Michael, 178
Macklin, Paula, 178
Maddalena, Giuseppe and Sair, 109
Madhabi, 80
Makem, Tommy, 66
Mallon, Sean, 79
Malloy, Fr. Rick, 134
Mandela, Nelson, 91
Mannion, Catherine, 42
Markgraf, Leigh, 166
Marshall, Charles, 116
Martin, Catherina, 109
Matlack, Doris, 120
Maurin, Peter, 175, 256

May, Anna, 14
Mayer, Paul, 200
McAuley, Catherine, 37
McBride, Rosemarie, 74
McCann, Diana, 133
McCann, James, 133
McCann, Joseph Jr., 133
McCann, Joseph Sr., 133
McCann, Kathryn, 133
McCann, Lisa, 133
McCann, Nancy, 133
McCary, Dawn, 179
McCaughey, Kelsey Ann, 178
McCormack, John, 115, 228
McCormack, Lily, 116
McDermott, Fr. Frank, 119, 227, 228, 241, 242, 258, 259
McDonald, Philip, 16, 88, 249, 268, 269
McGovern, Aileen, 200
McGovern, Bob, 87, 200
McGroarty, Martin, 8
McGuire, John, 8, 23, 38, 137, 138
McKenna, Siobhan, 30, 183
McKeon, Farrel, 207
McKeon, Michael, 130
McMurtrie, Annie Fletcher, 222
McMurtrie, Charlie, 222
McMurtrie, John, 222
McNamee, Fr. John, 12, 87, 99, 107, 200, 201, 241
Merton, Thomas, 8, 34, 125, 200, 201, 202, 233
Messina, Fr. Joe, 19, 21
Messina, Frank, 64
Misskelly, Myrlie, 6
Moloney, Mick, 44, 180
Mulligan, Dan, 91, 245, 246
Mulligan, Pakie, 117, 211
Mullin, Joan, 120
Neal Pierce, 100
Nicholas II, Czar, 167, 168
Niederhauser, David Peter, 141, 142
Nietzsche, Fredrich, 247
Nixon, President Richard, 34
O'Brien, Pat, 200
O'Carolan, Turlough, 44
O'Casey, Sean, 91, 183
O'Connell, Robbie, 196

O'Donnell, Eugene, 44, 66, 107, 108, 130, 180
O'Farrell, Bishop Michael, 58, 268
O'Fiaich, Cardinal Tomas, 12
O'Hare, Meabh, 80
Okali, Agwu M., 51
O'Neill, Hugh, 107
O'Neill, John (Johnny Nail), 93
O'Reilly, Eugene (Stevie), 19, 20
O'Reilly, Johnny, 149, 183, 241, 260
O'Rourke, Jeremiah, 88
O'Rourke, Tom, 86
O'Rourke, William, 39
Orsini, Andy, 3
Orsini, Edith Rose, 3, 57, 255
Pacera, Joe, 85
Pamela Markgraf, 165
Pasternak, Boris, 125, 126, 229
Paul VI, Pope, 175, 176
Pearse, Padraig, 32, 75
Peoples, Bernard and Hazel, 153
Pfeiffer, Barbara, 36
Plageman, Edna and Frank, 24
Pratt, Charles, 161
Pratt, Jesse, 83
Priceta, Veronica Margaret, 173
Pritchard, Rose, 159, 160, 173, 174, 203
Purves, John, 121, 167
Pushkin, Alexander, 168
Quinn, John, 90
Ramachandran, Dr. Arcot, 51
Rasputin, Grigori, 167
Reagan, President Ronald, 13
Realdine, Dottie, 71
Reasoner, Harry, 38, 71, 205
Reavy, Ed, 44
Redd, Dana, 16, 153, 154, 261
Reed, Scott, 197
Reilly, (Big John's) Tommy, 145
Reilly, Charlie, 145
Reilly, James, 172
Reilly, Myles, 49
Ricci, Anita, 160
Ritzke, Jean, 71
Rivera, Jessica, 16
Roosevelt, President Franklin D., 42
Rose, Pete, 19
Rourke, Josie, 17, 49

Sanders, Boyd, 79
Sanders, Donald, 80
Sands, Rosalyn, 107
Sapio, Fr. Thaddeus, 58
Schneider, Fr. Theodore SJ, 151
Scott, Conor, 235
Scullion, Sr. Mary, 147
Sequinot, Shaline, 133, 140
Sharkey, Msgr. George, 119, 120
Sheed, Frank, 175
Shiels, Pat, 97
Sikora, Sr. Margaret, 170
Simon, Scott, 40
Skelly, Paul, 138
Soiko, Boris, 122
Soiko, Irina, 121, 122, 167
Solzhenitsyn, Alexander, 59
Sullivan, Sr. Marge, 20
Tarmilarasan, 80
Teresa, Mother, 14, 16, 102, 153, 154, 173, 174, 175, 176, 257, 261
Thomas, Anita, 164
Thomas, Mary Beth, 229, 230
Tisenko, Victor Nikolai, 167, 168
Tunney, Mary Jane, 62
Turlington, Jackie, 103, 143
Vaddleperas, Ximena, 80
Venell, Darlene, 3
Verdi, Guiseppe, 115, 185, 193
Vine, Eleanor, 6
Virgilio, Lawrence J., 215
Virgilio, Nick, 15, 40, 44, 56, 87, 207, 215, 224, 243
Vladimar Poliakov, 79
Vu, Chuong, 73
Vu, Luan, 73
Walsh, Fr. Eugene, 229
Waterhouse, John, 63
Weakland, Archbishop Rembert, 46
Whitman, Walt, 34, 35, 75, 83, 92, 151, 189, 206, 213, 214, 215, 235, 236, 243
Wilson, Rev. Robert, 142
Wytkof, Sr. Mary, 97
Yeats, William Butler, 136, 139, 150, 171, 217, 244, 264, 265
Yocko, Viola, 74
Young, Leah, 105, 106
Zweig, Paul, 75

Poems by Michael Doyle

A Bodhran Broke in Fallen Hand, 78
A Half Ploughed Field, 204
A Lamp in the Widow's Window (excerpt), 13, 26, 222, 246
A Nose for Potatoes (excerpt), 186
A Salute of Eugene O'Donnell, 108
Ah Well (excerpt), 149
Alone Along the Lane (excerpt), 99
Along the Whitethorn Lane, 18
Anita Rose (excerpt), 29, 159
April 24, 1991 (excer[t), 128
At Home, 95
Camden 2000, 232
Camden's Spring, 76
Clay in the Clouds (excerpt), 73, 112, 127
Cockle Seed, 142
Edna, 52
Eight Zero Zero (excerpt), 230
Flying By (excerpt), 210
For Father Frank McDermott, 242
For Tom O'Rourke, 86
Give Me "Nicely" ", 190
I Want to Write a Verse, 259
In Loving Memory of Jean McCarthy (excerpt), 116
John McNamee, 158
Kevin Wahls, 254
Lament for Ballinamuck (excerpt), 196
Listen Camden! All Is Well (excerpt), 23
Moss on the Shoe (excerpt), 135
My Father, 35
My Mind Had Wandered to Sinead (excerpt), 90, 261
No Moss, 70
No Sound in the World Enchanted Me More (excerpt), 194
Nothing Bends (excerpt), 134
O River, Ever Mother (excerpt), 162
On My Last Journey (excerpt), 15, 41
Original Blessing (excerpt), 65

Picking Beer Cans Off the Street, 28
Port of Entry (excerpt), 96
Pugin's Rose, 212
Rain on the Pane (excerpt), 170
Ripe, 7
See the Flame, 178
Solid Ties, 238
Solstice '88, 47
Stevie's Stone, 20
Tell Me, Dear Siobhan, 30
Thanks for the Tea, 85
The Tinkers, 103
The Beauty of a Rusting Roof (excerpt), 59
The Birth of a Pig, 33
The Bright Open Door (excerpt), 101
The Cornadrung Road (excerpt), 113
The Coulter Man (excerpt), 55, 118, 184, 208, 221
The Hedge School (excerpt), 60, 98, 240
The Holy Innocents, 4
The Little Cobbler (excerpt), 82
The Mass for the Acquittal of the 'Camden 28', 200
The Meeting (excerpt), 57
The Millers of Rossduff (excerpt), 225
The Moon in Cloone (excerpt), 50
The Pain of the Rain - A Dream (excerpt), 92
The Passover, 154
The Passover Woman, 43
The Plumber of the Hornpipes, 44
The Stuff of Poems (excerpt), 101
The Timberman, 148
The Tinkers, 103
The Woman, 68
Thirteen Steps (excerpt), 252, 253
Torn Sails Upon the Sea, 123
Two Ash Trees (excerpt), 220
Where's John, 138
Wine Into Water, 10

Sister Peg Hynes S.S.J.
(1933 – 2002)

She was born in Philadelphia on June 7, 1933, the second of the five daughters of Nellie Burke and Tom Hynes, emigrants from Gort, County Galway. She received her first four sacraments and her grammer school education at St. Columbia's at 24th and Lehigh. Then on to Hallahan High, a star student all the way in books and basketball, swimming and softball. At 21, she entered the Sisters of St. Joseph in Chestnut Hill, received degrees from Chestnut Hill College and Boston College and became a first class teacher and principal in several Catholic schools.

In 1986, after 30 years in education, she became the director of The Heart of Camden Housing in South Camden, New Jersey and spent the next sixteen years trying to provide home ownership for poor people. Her work in housing and social service made her in the eyes of many the mother of the poor . . . "the heart" of Camden. She strove, as the poet proclaimed *"to give a life . . . to a dream, a dream, that was dreamed in the heart and only the heart could hold."*

It wasn't easy. But she could say . . .

What if the dream come true?
And if millions unborn shall dwell
In the house that I shaped in my heart,
The noble house of my thought?
                    Pardraig Pearse

She died on the darkest day, December 21, 2002.
Now that "noble house" has the light on.

The Church of the Sacred Heart, Camden, NJ

The little wooden building established in Camden in 1871 at 8ᵗʰ and Van Hook St. (now Carl Miller Boulevard) is the first church in the state of New Jersey to be called Sacred Heart. At first a mission, it became a parish in 1885 and one year later a new church was built at Broadway and Ferry. The mortgage was $35,000; the Sunday collection was $2.50 and the first pastor, William Lynch had a nervous breakdown. South Camden was poor then, but, with the coming of the New York Shipyard at the turn of the century, the area developed. However, the success of the shipyard was based on wars. That was unfortunate, because Jesus had a fairly serious warning for those who live by the sword.

One hundred years later, this South Camden area is very poor again. Sacred Heart's ministry, which is based on good Eucharistic liturgy as its core, is expressed in various efforts on behalf of the poor. A Catholic grammar school with 240 children, most of them Baptist. A Housing Program. Food Programs of cooked meals and shared groceries. Clothing for children at the thrift store, *Clothes from the Heart.* Neighborhood help at the Family Resource Center in after-school care. Medical help from volunteer doctors and nurses. Community Organizing to empower people.

The struggle of Sacred Heart today is to always affirm life after death and to proclaim that there could be life before death as well.

Welcome to Sacred Heart! Here we try to be at least as friendly as an Irish Pub.

Sacred Heart Church, Broadway & Ferry, Camden, NJ 08104
Telephone: (856) 966-6700   Fax: (856) 756-0102 E-mail: shcamden@bellatlantic.net

The Heart of Camden Housing Corporation

The Heart of Camden Housing effort is the most difficult housing assignment in North America. It is an attempt to create home ownership and stability in the poorest section of the poorest city in this country. Started by Michael Doyle in 1984, it was initially directed by Sister Marge Sullivan and a Board of Directors. In 1986, Sister Peg Hynes took over the task and led The Heart of Camden with extraordinary generosity for the next 14 years. Her work continues in fundraising for this utterly important work. Today, the Executive Director is Chris Auth who took over in 2001.

Its mission is to create affordable homes for private ownership. It is an uphill battle. The worth of renovated houses here continues to be a little more than one third of the cost of the renovation.

The Heart of Camden needs and deserves our support to enable it to create homes that people of modest means can own, beauty they can see, and social services they can obtain.

P.S. That was the dream of Sister Peg Hynes, the beloved director of "The Heart" for fourteen years. Sister Peg died tragically on December 21ˢᵗ, 2002. The driver of the car that killed her was allegedly crazed on crack cocaine. God rest her. She was "the heart" of Camden. May her dream come true.

The Heart of Camden, 1742 Ferry Avenue, Camden NJ 08014
Telephone: (856) 966-1212

Publishing Donors

Amerman, Craig
Atkinson, James J. III & Mary A.
Bailey, Charles
Beckmeyer, Karen E.
Brann, Henry & Betsi Bell
Broderick, Edna F.
Callaghan, John W. Sr. & Marie T.
Campbell, Sylvia L.
Campling, Maryann
Caracciolo, Angelo J. & Kathryn F.
Casey, Sarah A.
Cavicchio, Joseph A. Jr. & Theresa
Cedrone, Susan
Chagnon, Lucille T.
Corrigan, Gregory M. Jr.
Coughlin, Dennis J. & Kathleen R.
Creegan, Patrick J. & Patreece Williams
Daley, Michael J. & Mary-Elizabeth Dunn
D'Anastasio, John
Doyle, John E. & Elisa Dearhouse
Emanuele, Marianna
Feloney, Joan K.
Finn-Cusick, Ann Marie
Flynn, Mary D.
Franciscan Sisters of the Atonement
Giacchino, Michael & Josephine
Gilsenan, John S.
Gooney, Timothy & Gail
Griffith, Linda L.
Gumbaz, Ron
Guretse, Albert F. & Lois E.
Harrington, Francis J. & Jacqueline R.
Hartman, Katie Herrick, Paul G. & Berna S.
Holm, Ronald O. & Kay L.
Hyland, Richard S. & Anne M.
Jennings, Jean
Jordan, Robert
Kazlacunas, Matilda - R.I.P.
Kelly, Donald C. & Christine Kuehn
King, Margaret M. Kolmer, Rosemarie

Lafferty, Eleanor M.
Lafferty, Jim - RIP
Lafferty, Joseph J.
Larmer, Lynda A.
Lucas, Mary A.
McCarthy, Dorothy E. - R.I.P.
McClain, John F. Jr. & Judith I.
McCloskey, Anita
McDonnell, Rose G.
McKiernan, Eoin John
McLaverty, Nancy Dooley
Meehan, Rev. Joseph J.
Melockoff, Michael J. & Evelyn R.
Michael, Elvera Moss, Frank V. & Patricia A.
Motsek, Michael & Theresa R.
Neal, Emma
Nevins, Susan E.
Nowlan, Philip F. & Annette K.
O'Brien, Francis & Mary Claire
O'Donnell, Renee
Pandorf, Richard J. & Mary Lou
Pierce, J. Peter & Karen K.
Reilly, Charles E. & Kathleen V.
Rumley, C. J.
Ryan, Robert J. & Ann L.
Sannelli, Robert J. & Lillian A.
Sawyer, Barbara M. & Robert R.
Schilsky, Margaret Lyndon
Schmincke, James C. & Helen M.
Scott, Geraldine Whitaker
Sellani, Roseann
Sheerin, Kathryn A.
Simandle, Jerome & Jane Darton
Stokes, Patricia S.
Toner, Michael P.
Tremblay, Kathryn K.
Tucker, William H.
Virgilio, Anthony
Zelis, Mark T. & Rebecca A.

Michael Doyle was born on November 3, 1934 on a farm in Rossduff, County Longford, Ireland, educated at St. Peter's Seminary in Wexford and ordained a priest in 1959. Recruited by the Diocese of Camden, NJ, he taught high school and served many urban and suburban parishes before being appointed pastor in 1974 of Sacred Heart Church in Camden, one of the poorest parishes in the poorest city in America. A committed pacifist, he was arrested and acquitted for raiding a draft board during the Vietnam War as part of the Camden 28. At Sacred Heart, he founded the Heart of Camden, which renovates abandoned houses and sells them to low-income families, and a free medical clinic for the many people who lack health benefits. He also helped establish Camden Churches Organized for People, a faith-based effort in community organizing. In 1983 Harry Reasoner interviewed him for an Emmy-winning segment of *60 Minutes* entitled "Michael Doyle's Camden." He was subsequently featured in 1995 on *CBS Sunday Morning*. He is quoted extensively in local and national publications on the plight of Camden and cities like it in America.

Credits

"Old Ireland" on p. 74 and the excerpt from "Song of the Open Road" on p. 213 is taken from *Leaves of Grass* by Walt Whitman, Bantam Books, Bantam Classic Edition, New York, 1983.

The excerpt from Percy Bysshe Shelley's "The Cloud" on p.167 is taken from Representative Poetry On-line, Editor, I. Lancashire; Publisher, Web Development Group, Inf. Tech. Services, Univ. of Toronto Lib. Originally published in *Prometheus Unbound* (1820).

The excerpt from Alfred Lord Tennyson's "The Princess: A Medley: Tears, Idle Tears" on pages 258 and 265 is taken from Representative Poetry On-line: Editor, I. Lancashire; Publisher, Web Development Group, Inf. Tech. Services, Univ. of Toronto Lib. Originally published in *The Princess: A Medley* (London: E. Moxen, 1847).

The excerpt from G.K. Chesterton's "The Donkey" on p.183 is taken from Modern British Poetry, ed. By Louis Untermeyer, New York: Harcourt, Brace and Howe, 1920; Bartleby.com, 1999.

The excerpt from Padraic Colum's "An Old Woman of the Roads" on p. 249 is taken from Modern British Poetry, ed. By Louis Untermeyer, New York: Harcourt, Brace and Howe, 1920; Bartleby.com, 1999.

The quote on p. 59 is from *The Saviors of God; spiritual exercises* by Nikos Kazantzakis. Translated, with an introduction by Kimon Friar. New York: Simon and Shuster (1960).

The excerpt from Maya Angelou's "And Still I Rise" on p. 142 is taken from *And Still I Rise*, New York: Random House, 1978.

The quote on p. 123 is from *Doctor Zhivago* by Boris Pasternak, translated from the Russian by Max Hayward and Manya Harari. London: Collins and Harvill Press, 1958.

The excerpts from William Butler's Yeats poetry on pp. 215 ("A Prayer for My Daughter") and 262-3 ("He Wishes for the Cloths of Heaven") are taken from Yeats: Collected Poems.